USEFUL SUBJECT INDEX TERM

Administration
- Agents
- Financial operations
  - Accounting
  - Funding
  - Payroll
  - Taxes
- Legal aspects
  - Censorship
  - Contracts
  - Copyright
  - Liabilities
  - Regulations
- Personnel
  - Labor relations
  - Unions
- Planning/operation
  - Producing
- Public relations
  - Advertising
  - Community relations
  - Marketing

Audience
- Audience composition
- Audience-performer relationship
- Audience reactions/comments

Basic theatrical documents
- Choreographies
- Film treatments
- Librettos
- Miscellaneous texts
- Playtexts
- Promptbooks
- Scores

Design/technology
- Costuming
- Equipment
- Lighting
- Make-up
- Masks
- Projections
- Properties
- Puppets
- Scenery
- Sound
- Special effects
- Technicians/crews
- Wigs

Institutions
- Institutions, associations
- Institutions, producing
- Institutions, research
- Institutions, service
- Institutions, social
- Institutions, special
- Institutions, training

Performance/production
- Acting
- Acrobatics
- Aerialists
- Aquatics
- Animal acts
- Choreography
- Clowning
- Dancing
- Directing
- Equestrian acts
- Equilibrists
- Instrumentalists
- Juggling
- Magic
- Martial arts
- Puppeteers
- Singing
- Staging

Performance spaces
- Amphitheatres/arenas
- Fairgrounds
- Found spaces
- Halls
- Religious structures
- Show boats
- Theatres
  - Auditorium
  - Foyer
  - Orchestra pit
  - Stage,
    - Adjustable
    - Apron
    - Arena
    - Proscenium
  - Support areas

Plays/librettos/scripts
- Adaptations
- Characters/roles
- Dramatic structure
- Editions
- Language
- Plot/subject/theme

Reference materials
- Bibliographies
- Catalogues
- Collected Materials
- Databanks
- Descriptions of resources
- Dictionaries
- Directories
- Discographies
- Encyclopedias
- Glossaries
- Guides
- Iconographies
- Indexes
- Lists
- Videographies
- Yearbooks

Relation to other fields
- Anthropology
- Economics
- Education
- Ethics
- Literature
- Figurative arts
- Philosophy
- Politics
- Psychology
- Religion
- Sociology

Research/historiography
- Methodology
- Research tools

Theory/criticism
- Aesthetics
- Deconstruction
- Dialectics
- Feminist criticism
- New historicism
- Phenomenology
- Reader response
- Reception
- Semiotics

Training
- Apprenticeship
- Teaching methods
  - Training aids

Other frequent subjects
- AIDS
- Alternative theatre
- Amateur theatre
- Archives/libraries
- Avant-garde theatre
- Awards
- Black theatre
- Broadway theatre
- Burlesque
- Casting
- Children's theatre
- Community theatre
- Computers
- Conferences
- Creative drama
- Educational theatre
- Elizabethan theatre
- Experimental theatre
- Farce
- Feminist theatre
- Festivals
- Folklore
- Fundraising
- Gay/Lesbian theatre
- Gender studies
- Health/safety
- Hispanic theatre
- Improvisation
- Indigenous theatre
- Jacobean theatre
- Jewish theatre
- Liturgical drama
- Management, stage
- Medieval theatre
- Metadrama
- Minstrelsy
- Monodrama
- Movement
- Multiculturalism
- Music hall
- Mystery plays
- Mythology
- Neoclassicism
- Off Broadway theatre
- Off-off Broadway theatre
- Open-air theatre
- Parody
- Passion plays
- Performance spaces
- Playhouses
- Playwriting
- Political theatre
- Popular entertainment
- Press
- Radio drama
- Regional theatre
- Religious theatre
- Renaissance theatre
- Restoration theatre
- Ritual-ceremony
- Satire
- Story-telling
- Street theatre
- Summer theatre
- Touring companies
- Transvestism
- Vaudeville
- Voice
- Women in theatre
- Workshops
- Yiddish theatre

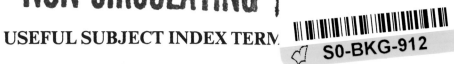

INTERNATIONAL BIBLIOGRAPHY OF THEATRE: 1998

International Bibliography of Theatre: 1998

Published by the Theatre Research Data Center, Brooklyn College, City University of New York, NY 11210 USA.

This publication was made possible in part with in-kind support and services provided by Brooklyn College and the University Computing & Information Services of the City University of New York.

The paper used in this book complies with the Permanent Paper Standard issued by the National Information Standards Organization (Z39.48-1984).

THE THEATRE RESEARCH DATA CENTER

Rosabel Wang, Director

The Theatre Research Data Center at Brooklyn College houses, publishes and distributes the International Bibliography of Theatre. Inquiries about the bibliographies and the databank are welcome. Telephone (718) 951-5998; FAX (718) 951-4606; E-Mail RXWBC@CUNYVM.CUNY.EDU.

INTERNATIONAL BIBLIOGRAPHY OF THEATRE: 1998

Benito Ortolani, Editor

Catherine Hilton, Executive Editor   Margaret Loftus Ranald, Associate Editor

Rosabel Wang, Systems Analyst

Rose Bonczek, Managing Editor   Helen Huff, Online Editor

Mickey Ryan, Research Editor

The International Bibliography of Theatre project is sponsored by:
the American Society for Theatre Research
the Theatre Library Association
The International Association of Libraries and Museums of the Performing Arts
in cooperation with
The International Federation for Theatre Research.

Theatre Research Data Center
New York 2001

QUICK ACCESS GUIDE

GENERAL

The Classed Entries are equivalent to library shelf arrangements.
The Indexes are equivalent to a library card catalogue.

SEARCH METHODS

By subject:

Look in the alphabetically arranged Subject Index for the relevant term(s), topic(s) or name(s): e.g., Feminist criticism; *Macbeth*; Shakespeare, William; Gay theatre; etc.
Check the number at the end of each relevant précis.
Using that number, search the Classed Entries section to find full information.

By country:

Look in the Geographical-Chronological Index for the country related to the *content* of interest.
Note: Countries are arranged in alphabetical order and then subdivided chronologically.
Find the number at the end of each relevant précis.
Using that number, search the Classed Entries section to find full information.

By periods:

Determine the country of interest.
Look in the Geographical-Chronological Index, paying special attention to the chronological subdivisions.
Find the number at the end of each relevant précis.
Using that number, search the Classed Entries section to find full information.

By authors of listed books or articles:

Look in the alphabetically arranged Document Authors Index for the relevant names.
Using the number at the end of each Author Index entry, search the Classed Entries section to find full information.

SUGGESTIONS

Search a variety of possible subject headings.
Search the **most specific subject heading** first, e.g., if interested in acting in Ibsen plays, begin with Ibsen, Henrik, rather than the more generic Acting or Plays/librettos/scripts.
When dealing with large clusters of references under a single subject heading, note that items are listed in **alphabetical order of content geography** (Afghanistan to Zimbabwe). Under each country items are ordered alphabetically by author, following the same numerical sequence as that of the Classed Entries.

TABLE OF CONTENTS

TAXONOMY .... Front Cover
QUICK ACCESS GUIDE iv
ACKNOWLEDGMENTS vi
A GUIDE FOR USERS 1
CLASSED ENTRIES 9
- Theatre in General 9
- Dance 52
- Dance-drama 73
- Drama 75
- Media 202
- Mime 212
- Mixed Entertainment 213
- Music-drama 223
- Puppetry 249

SUBJECT INDEX 253
GEOGRAPHICAL–CHRONOLOGICAL INDEX 669
DOCUMENT AUTHORS INDEX 753
FINDING LIST: PERIODICAL TITLES WITH ACRONYMS 773
LIST OF PERIODICALS IN ACRONYM ORDER 781
ABBREVIATIONS .... Back Cover

ACKNOWLEDGMENTS

We are grateful to the many institutions and individuals who have helped us make this volume possible:

Brooklyn College: President Christoph Kimmich, Professor Benito Ortolani;

President Bruce McConachie, ASTR;

President Claudia Balk, SIBMAS;

President Josette Féral and the University Commission of FIRT;

Hedvig Belitska-Scholtz, National Széchényi Library, Budapest;

Magnus Blomkvist, Drottningholms Teatermuseum;

Ole Bøgh, University of Copenhagen, Denmark;

Temple Hauptfleisch, University of Stellenbosch:

Danuta Kuźnicka, Polska Akademia Nauk, Warsaw;

Tamara Il. Lapteva, Russian State Library, Moscow;

Lindsay Newman, University of Lancaster Library:

Louis Rachow, International Theatre Institute, New York;

Michael Ribaudo and Pat Reber, CUNY/Computing & Information Services, New York;

Willem Rodenhuis, Universiteit van Amsterdam;

Francka Slivnik, National Theatre and Film Museum, Ljubljana;

Jarmila Svobodová, Theatre Institute, Prague;

Alessandro Tinterri, Museo Biblioteca dell'Attore di Genova;

Sirkka Tukiainen, Central Library of Theatre and Dance, Helsinki;

And we thank our field bibliographers whose contributions have made this work a reality:

Maria Olga Bieńka	Polska Akademia Nauk, Warsaw
Magnus Blomkvist	Drottningholms Teatermuseum
Rose Bonczek	Brooklyn College, City Univ. of New York
Magdolna Both	National Széchényi Library, Budapest
Johan Callens	Free University of Brussels
Michael Chiasson	Resource Centre for the Arts Theatre Company St. John's, NF
Sarah Corner-Walker	University of Copenhagen, Denmark
Clifford O. Davidson	Western Michigan Univ., Kalamazoo, MI
Jayne Fenwick-White	Glyndebourne Festival Opera, Lewes
Ramona Floyd	Sandbox Theatre Productions, New York, NY
Steven H. Gale	Kentucky State University, Frankfort, KY
Carol Goodger-Hill	University of Guelph, ON
James Hatch	Hatch-Billops Collection, New York, NY
Catherine Hilton	University of Massachusetts, Amherst
Jane Hogan	TCI, Theatre Crafts International, New York, NY
Claire Hudson	Theatre Museum,London
Helen Huff	Graduate Center, City Univ. of New York
Valentina Jakushkina	State Library of Russia, Moscow
Grzegorz Janikowski	Polska Akademia Nauk, Warsaw
Aila Kettunen	Central Library of Theatre and Dance, Helsinki
Jarosław Komorowski	Polska Akademia Nauk, Warsaw
Joanna Krakowska-Narożniak	Polska Akademia Nauk, Warsaw
William L. Maiman	TCI, Theatre Crafts International, New York, NY
Margaret Majewska	Polish Centre of the International Theatre Institute, Warsaw;
Michaela Mertová	Theatre Institut, Prague
Alenka Mihalič-Klemenčič	University of Maribor Library, Slovenia
Clair Myers	Elon College, Elon, NC
Lindsay Newman	University of Lancaster, UK
Danila Parodi	Museo Biblioteca dell'Attore di Genova
Michael Patterson	De Montfort University, UK
Miroslava Přikrylová	Theatre Institut, Prague
Margaret Loftus Ranald	Queens College, City Univ. of New York
Willem Rodenhuis	Universiteit van Amsterdam
Mickey Ryan	Synergy Ensemble Theatre Company, Islip, NY
James Shaw	Shakespeare Institute, University of Birmingham, UK
Francka Slivnik	National Theatre and Film Museum, Ljubljana
Heike Stange	Freie Universität Berlin
Juan Villegas	GESTOS Revista de Teoria y Practica del Teatro Hispanico, Univ. of Cal.-Irvine
David Whiteley	Université du Québec à Montréal
Ralf Zünder	Universität Hamburg/Hamburger Theatersammlung

A GUIDE FOR USERS

SCOPE OF THE BIBLIOGRAPHY

Materials Included

The ***International Bibliography of Theatre: 1998*** lists theatre books, book articles, dissertations, journal articles and miscellaneous other theatre documents published during 1998. It also includes items from prior years received too late for inclusion in earlier volumes. Published works (with the exceptions noted below) are included without restrictions on the internal organization, format, or purpose of those works. Materials selected for the Bibliography deal with any aspect of theatre significant to research, without historical, cultural or geographical limitations. Entries are drawn from theatre histories, essays, studies, surveys, conference papers and proceedings, catalogues of theatrical holdings of any type, portfolios, handbooks and guides, dictionaries, bibliographies, and other reference works, records and production documents.

Materials Excluded

Reprints of previously published works are usually excluded unless they are major documents which have been unavailable for some time. In general only references to newly published works are included, though significantly revised editions of previously published works are treated as new works. Purely literary scholarship is generally excluded, since it is already listed in established bibliographical instruments. An exception is made for material published in journals completely indexed by *IBT.* Studies in theatre literature, textual studies, and dissertations are represented only when they contain significant components that examine or have relevance to theatrical performance.

Playtexts are excluded unless they are published with extensive or especially noteworthy introductory material, or when the text is the first translation or adaptation of a classic from an especially rare language into a major language. Book reviews and reviews of performances are not included, except for those reviews of sufficient scope to constitute a review article, or clusters of reviews published under one title.

Language

There is no restriction on language in which theatre documents appear, but English is the primary vehicle for compiling and abstracting the materials. The Subject Index gives primary importance to titles in their original languages, transliterated into the Roman Alphabet where necessary. Original language titles also appear in Classed Entries that refer to plays in translation and in the précis of Subject Index items.

CLASSED ENTRIES

Content

The **Classed Entries** section contains one entry for each document analyzed and provides the user with complete information on all material indexed in this volume. It is the only place where publication citations may be found and where detailed abstracts are furnished. Users are advised to familiarize themselves with the elements and structure of the Taxonomy to simplify the process of locating items indexed in the **classed entries** section.

Organization

Entries follow the order provided in Columns I, II and III of the Taxonomy.

Column I classifies theatre into nine categories beginning with Theatre in General and thereafter listed alphabetically from "Dance" to "Puppetry." Column II divides most of the nine Column I categories into a number of subsidiary components. Column III headings relate any of the previously selected Column I and Column II categories to specific elements of the theatre. A list of Useful Subject Index Terms is also given (see frontpapers). These terms are also sub-components of the Column III headings.

Examples:

> Items classified under "Theatre in General" appear in the Classed Entries before those classified under "Dance" in Column I, etc.
>
> Items classified under the Column II heading of "Musical theatre" appear before those classified under the Column II heading of "Opera," etc.

Items further classified under the Column III heading of "Administration" appear before those classified under "Design/technology," etc.

Every group of entries under any of the divisions of the **Classed Entries** is printed in alphabetical order according to its content geography: e.g., a cluster of items concerned with plays related to Spain, classified under "Drama" (Column I) and "Plays/librettos/scripts" (Column III) would be printed together after items concerned with plays related to South Africa and before those related to Sweden. Within these country clusters, each group of entries is arranged alphabetically by author.

Relation to Subject Index
When in doubt concerning the appropriate Taxonomy category for a **Classed Entry** search, the user should refer to the **Subject Index** for direction. The **Subject Index** provides several points of access for each entry in the **Classed Entries** section. In most cases it is advisable to use the **Subject Index** as the first and main way to locate the information contained in the **Classed Entries.**

TAXONOMY TERMS

The following descriptions have been established to clarify the terminology used in classifying entries according to the Taxonomy. They are used for clarification only, as a searching tool for users of the Bibliography. In cases where clarification has been deemed unnecessary (as in the case of "Ballet", "*Kabuki*", "Film", etc.) no further description appears below. Throughout the Classed Entries, the term "General" distinguishes miscellaneous items that cannot be more specifically classified by the remaining terms in the Column II category. Sufficient subject headings enable users to locate items regardless of their taxonomical classification.

THEATRE IN GENERAL: Only for items which cannot be properly classified by categories "Dance" through "Puppetry," or for items related to more than one theatrical category.

DANCE: Only for items published in theatre journals that are indexed by *IBT*, or for dance items with relevance to theatre.

DANCE-DRAMA: Items related to dramatic genres where dance is the dominant artistic element. Used primarily for specific forms of non-Western theatre, e.g., *Kathakali, Nō.*

DRAMA: Items related to playtexts and performances where the spoken word is traditionally considered the dominant element. (i.e., all Western dramatic literature and all spoken drama everywhere). An article on acting as a discipline will also fall into this category, as well as books about directing, unless these endeavors are more closely related to musical theatre forms or other genres.

MEDIA: Only for media related-items published in theatre journals completely indexed by *IBT*, or for media items with relevance to theatre.

MIME: Items related to performances where mime is the dominant element. This category comprises all forms of mime from every epoch and/or country.

PANTOMIME: Both Roman Pantomime and the performance form epitomized in modern times by Étienne Decroux and Marcel Marceau. English pantomime is indexed under "Mixed Entertainment."

MIXED ENTERTAINMENT: Items related either 1) to performances consisting of a variety of performance elements among which none is considered dominant, or 2) to performances where the element of spectacle and the function of broad audience appeal are dominant. Because of the great variety of terminology in different circumstances, times, and countries for similar types of spectacle, such items as café-concert, quadrille réaliste, one-person shows, night club acts, pleasure gardens, tavern concerts, night cellars, saloons, Spezialitätentheater, storytelling, divertissement, rivistina, etc., are classified under "General", "Variety acts", or "Cabaret", etc. depending on time period, circumstances, and/or country.

Variety acts: Items related to variety entertainment of mostly unconnected "numbers", including some forms of vaudeville, revue, petite revue, intimate revue, burlesque, etc.

PUPPETRY: Items related to all kinds of puppets, marionettes and mechanically operated figures.

N.B.: Notice that entries related to individuals are classified according to the Column III category describing the individual's primary field of activity: e.g., a manager under "Administration," a set designer under "Design/technology," an actor under "Performance/production," a playwright under "Plays/librettos/scripts," a teacher under "Training," etc.

CITATION FORMS

Basic bibliographical information

Each citation includes the standard bibliographical information: author(s), title, publisher, pages, and notes, preface, appendices, etc., when present. Journal titles are usually given in the form of an acronym, whose corresponding title may be found in the **List of Periodicals**. Pertinent publication information is also provided in this list.

Translation of original language

When the play title is not in English, a translation in parentheses follows the original title. Established English translations of play titles or names of institutions are used when they exist. Names of institutions, companies, buildings, etc., unless an English version is in common use, are as a rule left untranslated. Geographical names are given in standard English form as defined by *Webster's Geographical Dictionary* (3rd ed. 1997).

Time and place

An indication of the time and place to which a document pertains is included wherever appropriate and possible. The geographical information refers usually to a country, sometimes to a larger region such as Europe or English-speaking countries. The geographical designation is relative to the time of the content: Russia is used before 1917, USSR to 1991; East and West Germany 1945-1990; Roman Empire until its official demise, Italy thereafter. When appropriate, precise dates related to the content of the item are given. Otherwise the decade or century is indicated.

Abstract

Unless the content of a document is made sufficiently clear by the title, the classed entry provides a brief abstract. Titles of plays not in English are given in English translation in the abstract, except for most operas and titles that are widely known in their original language. If the original title does not appear in the document title, it is provided in the abstract.

Spelling

English form is used for transliterated personal names. In the **Subject Index** each English spelling refers the users to the international or transliterated spelling under which all relevant entries are listed.

Varia

Affiliation with a movement and influence by or on individuals or groups is indicated only when the document itself suggests such information.

When a document belongs to more than one Column I category of the Taxonomy, the other applicable Column I categories are cross-referenced in the **Subject Index**.

Document treatment

"Document treatment" indicates the type of scholarly approach used in the writing of the document. The following terms are used in the present bibliography:

- **Bibliographical studies** treat as their primary subject bibliographic material.
- **Biographical studies** are articles on part of the subject's life.
- **Biographies** are book-length treatments of entire lives.
- **Critical studies** present an evaluation resulting from the application of criteria.
- **Empirical research** identifies studies that incorporate as part of their design an experiment or series of experiments.
- **Historical studies** designate accounts of individual events, groups, movements, institutions, etc., whose primary purpose is to provide a historical record or evaluation.
- **Histories-general** cover the whole spectrum of theatre–or most of it–over a period of time and typically appear in one or several volumes.
- **Histories-specific** cover a particular genre, field, or component of theatre over a period of time and usually are published as a book.
- **Histories-sources** designate source materials that provide an internal evaluation or account of the treated subject: e.g. interviews with theatre professionals.
- **Histories-reconstruction** attempt to reconstruct some aspect of the theatre.
- **Instructional materials** include textbooks, manuals, guides or any other publication to be used in teaching.
- **Reviews of performances** examine one or several performances in the format of review articles, or clusters of several reviews published under one title.

Technical studies examine theatre from the point of view of the applied sciences or discuss particular theatrical techniques.
Textual studies examine the texts themselves for origins, accuracy, and publication data.

Example with diagram

Here follows an example (in this case a book article) of a **Classed Entries** item with explanation of its elements:

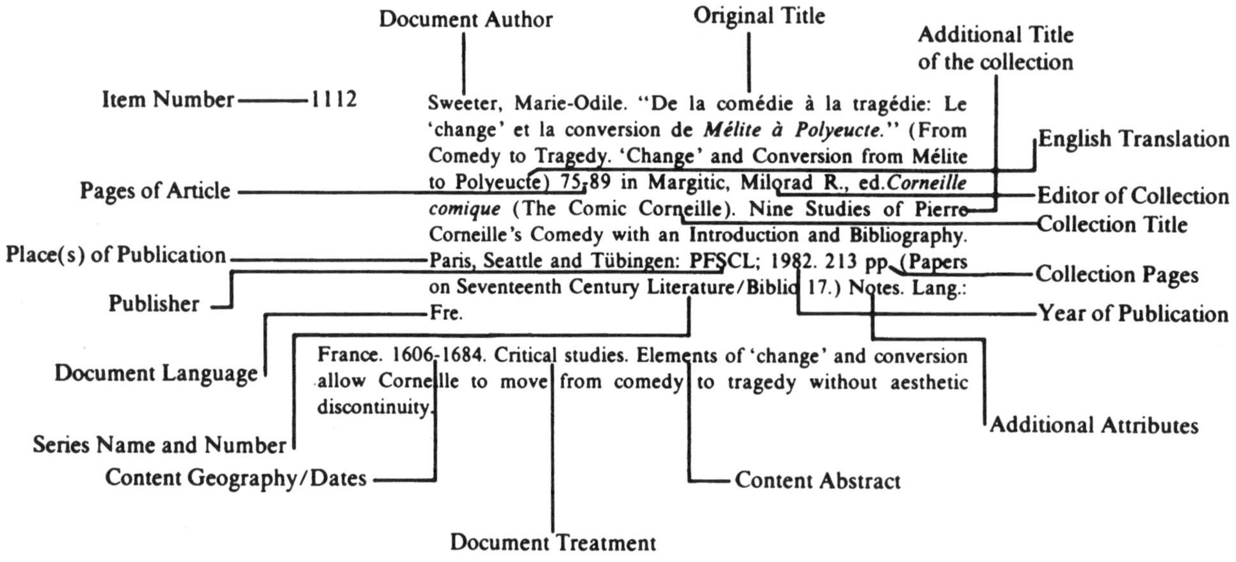

SUBJECT INDEX

Function

The Subject Index is a primary means of access to the major aspects of documents referenced by the **Classed Entries**.

Content

Each **Subject Index** item contains

(a) subject headings, e.g., names of persons, names of institutions, forms and genres of theatre, elements of the theatre arts, titles of plays.
(b) column III category indicating primary focus of the entry
(c) short abstracts describing the items of the **Classed Entries** related to the subject heading
(d) content country, city, time and language of document
(e) the number of the **Classed Entry** from which each Subject Index item was generated.

Standards

Names of persons, including titles of address, are listed alphabetically by last names according to the standard established in *Anglo-American Cataloguing Rules* (Library of Congress, 2nd edition, 1978).

All names and terms originating in non-Roman alphabets, including Russian, Greek, Chinese and Japanese have been transliterated and are listed by the transliterated forms.

Geographical names are spelled according to *Webster's Geographical Dictionary* (3rd ed. 1997).

"SEE" references direct users from common English spellings or titles to names or terms indexed in a less familiar manner.

Example:

Chekhov, Anton
SEE
Čechov, Anton Pavlovič

Individuals are listed in the Subject Index when:

(a) they are the primary or secondary focus of the document;
(b) the document addresses aspects of their lives and/or work in a primary or supporting manner;
(c) they are the author of the document, but only when their life and/or work is also the document's primary focus;
(d) their lives have influenced, or have been influenced by, the primary subject of the document or the writing of it, as evidenced by explicit statement in the document.

This Subject Index is particularly useful when a listed individual is the subject of numerous citations. In such cases a search should not be limited only to the main subject heading (e.g., Shakespeare). A more relevant one (e.g., *Hamlet*) could bring more specific results.

"SEE" References

Institutions, groups, and social or theatrical movements appear as subject headings, following the above criteria. Names of theatre companies, theatre buildings, etc. are given in their original languages or transliterated. "See" references are provided for the generally used or literally translated English terms;

Example: "Moscow Art Theatre" directs users to the company's original title:

Moscow Art Theatre
SEE
Moskovskij Chudožestvennyj Akademičeskij Teat'r

No commonly used English term exists for "Comédie-Française," it therefore appears only under its title of origin. The same is true for *commedia dell'arte*, Burgtheater and other such terms.

Play titles appear in their original languages, with "SEE" references next to their English translations. Subject headings for plays in a third language may be provided if the translation in that language is of unusual importance.

Widely known opera titles are not translated.

Similar subject headings

Subject headings such as "Politics" and "Political theatre" are neither synonymous nor mutually exclusive. They aim to differentiate between a phenomenon and a theatrical genre. Likewise, such terms as "Feminism" refer to social and cultural movements and are not intended to be synonymous with "Women in theatre." The term "Ethnic theatre" is used to classify any type of theatrical literature or performance where the ethnicity of those concerned is of primary importance. Because of the number of items, and for reasons of accessibility, "African-American theatre," "Native American theatre" and the theatre of certain other ethnic groups are given separate subject headings.

Groups/movements, periods, etc.

Generic subject headings such as "Victorian theatre," "Expressionism," etc., are only complementary to other more specific groupings and do not list all items in the bibliography related to that period or generic subject: e.g., the subject heading "Elizabethan theatre" does not list a duplicate of all items related to Shakespeare, which are to be found under "Shakespeare," but lists materials explicitly related to the actual physical conditions or style of presentation typical of the Elizabethan theatre. For a complete search according to periods, use the **Geographical-Chronological Index**, searching by country and by the years related to the period.

Subdivision of Subject Headings

Each subject heading is subdivided into Column III categories that identify the primary focus of the cited entry. These subcategories are intended to facilitate the user when searching under such broad terms as "African-American theatre" or "*King Lear.*" The subcategory helps to identify the relevant cluster of entries. Thus, for instance, when the user is interested only in African-American theatre companies, the subheading "Institutions" groups all the relevant items together. Similarly, the subheading "Performance/production" groups together all the items dealing with production aspects of *King Lear*. It is, however, important to remember that these subheadings (i.e. Column III categories) are not subcategories of the subject heading itself, but of the main subject matter treated in the entry.

Printing order

Short abstracts under each subject heading are listed according to Column III categories. These categories are organized alphabetically. Short abstracts within each cluster, on the other hand, are arranged sequentially according to the item number they refer to in the Classed Entries. This enables the frequent user to recognize immediately the location and classification of the entry. If the user cannot find one specific subject heading, a related term may suffice, e.g., for Church dramas, see Religion. In some cases, a "SEE" reference is provided.

Example with diagram

Here follows an example of a **Subject Index** entry with explanation of its elements:

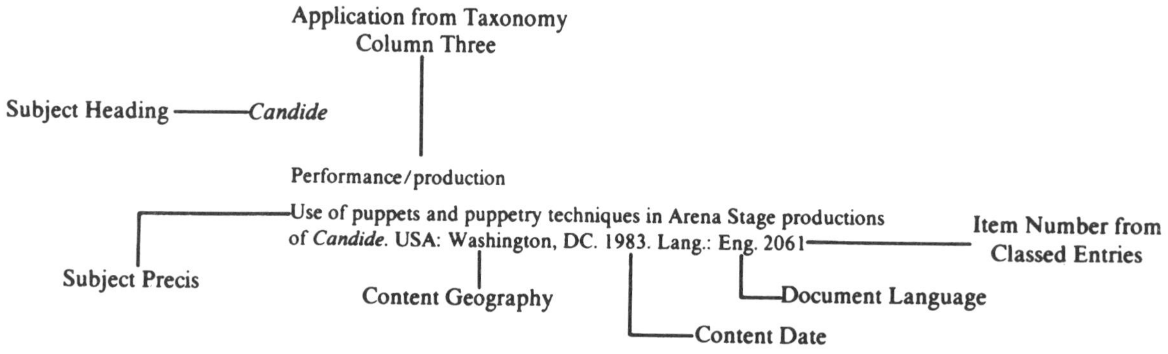

GEOGRAPHICAL-CHRONOLOGICAL INDEX

Organization

The **Geographical-Chronological Index** is arranged alphabetically by the country relevant to the subject or topic treated. The references under each country are then subdivided by date. References to articles with contents of the same date are then listed according to their category in the Taxonomy's Column III. The last item in each Geographical-Chronological Index listing is the number of the Classed Entry from which the listing was generated.

Example: For material on Drama in Italy between World Wars I and II, look under Italy, 1918-1939. In the example below, entries 2734, 2227 and 891 match this description.

Italy — cont'd

1907-1984. **Theory/criticism.**
Cruelty and sacredness in contemporary theatre poetics. Germany. France. Lang.: Ita. 2734

1914. **Plays/librettos/scripts.**
Comparative study of *Francesca da Rimini* by Riccardo Zandonai and *Tristan und Isolde* by Richard Wagner. Lang.: Eng. 3441

1920-1936. **Plays/librettos/scripts.**
Introductory analysis of twenty-one of Pirandello's plays Lang.: Eng. 2227

1923-1936. **Institutions.**
History of Teatro degli Indipendenti. Rome. Lang.; Ita. 891

1940-1984. **Performance/production.**
Italian tenor Giuseppe Giacomini speaks of his career and art. New York, NY. Lang.; Eng. 3324

Dates

Dates reflect the content period covered by the item, not the publication year. However, the publication year is used for theoretical writings and for assessments of old traditions, problems, etc. When precise dates cannot be established, the decade (e.g., 1970-1979) or the century (e.g., 1800-1899) is given.

Biographies and histories

In the case of biographies of people who are still alive, the year of birth of the subject and the year of publication of the biography are given. The same criterion is followed for histories of institutions such as theatres or companies which are still in existence. The founding date of such institutions and the date of publication of the entry are given—unless the entry explicitly covers only a specific period of the history of the institution.

Undatable content

No dates are given when the content is either theoretical or not meaningfully definable in time. Entries without date(s) print first.

DOCUMENT AUTHORS INDEX

The term "Document Author" means the author of the article or book cited in the **Classed Entries**. The author of the topic under discussion, e.g., Molière in an article about one of his plays, is *not* found in the **Document Authors Index**. (See Subject Index).

The **Document Authors Index** lists these authors alphabetically and in the Roman alphabet. The numbers given after each name direct the researcher to the full citations in the Classed Entries section.

N.B.: Users are urged to familiarize themselves with the Taxonomy and the indexes provided. The four-way access to research sources possible through consultation of the Classed Entries section, the Subject Index, the Geographical-Chronological Index and the Document Authors Index is intended to be sufficient to locate even the most highly specialized material.

CLASSED ENTRIES

THEATRE IN GENERAL

Administration

1 Radbourne, Jennifer. "The Role of Government in Marketing the Arts." *JAML.* 1998 Spr; 28(1): 67-82. Notes. Biblio. Tables. Lang.: Eng.

1996. Empirical research. ■The role of government in aiding arts organizations in finding new audiences and markets.

2 Fotheringham, Richard. "Boundary Riders and Claim Jumpers: The Australian Theatre Industry." 20-37 in Kelly, Veronica, ed. *Our Australian Theatre in the 1990s.* (Australian Playwrights 7.) Notes. Index. Biblio. Illus.: Photo. 2. Lang.: Eng.

Australia. 1990-1998. Historical studies. ■Economic forces behind the current Australian theatre industry, specifically government funding and support for the arts.

3 Hartog, Joh. "The Computerized Gaze and the Performing Arts." *ADS.* 1998 Apr.; 32: 109-130. Notes. Tables. Lang.: Eng.

Australia: Adelaide. 1991-1998. Historical studies. ■Mission and description of the database developed by the Adelaide Festival Centre Trust to store data relating to events presented by the Trust. It is used to gauge economic aspects and cultural impact of the events.

4 Mulcahy, Kevin V. "Cultural Patronage in Comparative Perspective: Public Support for the Arts in France, Germany, Norway, and Canada." *JAML.* 1998 Win; 28(4): 247-263. Notes. Tables. Lang.: Eng.

Canada. France. Germany. Norway. 1905-1998. Historical studies. ■Compares the cultural policy of Canada, France, Germany, and Norway.

5 Mulvad, Ninette. "Fremme fodbalderne." (On Your Toes.) *TE.* 1998 Apr.; 88: 12-15. Illus.: Photo. Photo. B&W. 2. Lang.: Dan.

Denmark: Aalborg. 1993-1998. Histories-sources. ■Interview with Malene Schwartz, manager of Aalborg Teater, about the importance of nurturing the new talents in the company.

6 Blankemeyer, Silke. "Theater lässt sich nicht wie Schokoriegel vermarkten." (Theatre Is Not Marketed Like a Chocolate Bar.) *DB.* 1998; 5: 40-42. Illus.: Photo. B&W. 5. Lang.: Ger.

Germany. 1994-1998. Histories-sources. ■Blankemeyer, manager of the office for public relations and marketing of four theatres in North Rhine-Westphalia (Westfälisches Landestheater Castrop-Rauxel, Rheinisches Landestheater Neuss, Burghofbühne Wesel, and Landestheater Detmold) describes her work, which takes into consideration the different artistic images of each theatre.

7 Günter, Bernd. "Soll das Theater sich zu Markte tragen?" (Shall Theatre Risk its Hide?)*DB.* 1998; 5: 14-20. Illus.: Photo. B&W. 5. Lang.: Ger.

Germany. 1998. Critical studies. ■Discusses ideas to implement advertising, sponsorship, and marketing in an effective and efficient form to improve the audience-theatre relationship in the light of budget cuts, economic problems, and decreasing spectators.

8 Hagedorn, Volker. "Fremder, halte inne..." (Stranger, Stop.) *DB.* 1998; 6: 29-31. Illus.: Photo. B&W. 5. Lang.: Ger.

Germany: Braunschweig. 1997-1998. Historical studies. ■Portrait of theatre-manager Wolfgang Gropper at Staatstheater Braunschweig and the specific difficulties between theatre and audience in this town.

9 Heym, Anne. "'Heute geht es uns gut...'." ('Today We Are Doing Well...'.) *DB.* 1998; 5: 26-29. Illus.: Photo. B&W. 5. Lang.: Ger.

Germany: Cottbus. 1992-1998. Histories-sources. ■Manager of public relations and marketing department describes the specific conditions at Staatstheater Cottbus and possibilities to win new spectators by regional press work, days of 'open door'.

10 Hinkel, Roland. "Tourismus und Theater—eine Beziehung mit Zukunft." (Tourism and Theatre—a Relationship With a Future.) *DB.* 1998; 5: 38-39. Illus.: Photo. B&W. 3. Lang.: Ger.

Germany. 1993-1998. Histories-sources. ■Hinkel, theatre-manager of the theatres in the North Harz Mountains, discusses cooperation with tourist organizations (guest performances, open-air theatres, improvement of advertising and marketing in cooperation with hotels).

11 Merschmeier, Michael; Wille, Franz. "Über Hamburg, das Zählen von Kaffeebohnen & die Kunst des Fortwurstelns." (On Hamburg, Bean-Counting and the Art of Muddling-Through.) *THeute.* 1998; 8/9: 4-11. Illus.: Photo. B&W. 8. Lang.: Ger.

Germany: Hamburg. 1993-2000. Histories-sources. ■Conversation with theatre-manager Frank Baumbauer at Deutsches Schauspielhaus Hamburg about concepts, public and labor relations, cultural policy, and budget cuts in Hamburg.

12 Stobernack, Michael. "Der Alptraum: Leere Theaterränge." (The Nightmare: Empty Seats.) *DB.* 1998; 5: 34-37. Illus.: Photo. B&W. 3. Lang.: Ger.

Germany. 1998. Histories-sources. ■Describes a questionnaire for a qualitative analysis of the public to improve the economy of theatres.

13 Wieck, Thomas. "Schuldig!" (Guilty!)*TZ.* 1998; 5: 14-17. Lang.: Ger.

Germany. 1989-1998. Critical studies. ■Analyzing the system of municipal and state theatre in Germany. Describes the possibility of change in East Germany since 1989, to create a politico-cultural alternative to that system.

14 Zünder, Ralf. "Im Namen der Umverteilung." (In the Name of Redistribution.) *BGs.* 1998; 6-7: 24-25. Illus.: Photo. B&W. 2. Lang.: Ger.

Germany: Berlin. 1998. Historical studies. ■Response to Peter Stolzenberg's opinion on off-theatres in *BGs* (1998) 3, 9-10. Includes an interview with Winfried Radeke and Ilka Seifert from Neuköllner Oper, one of the houses discussed by Stolzenburg.

15 Róna, Katalin; Koncz, Zsuzsa, photo. "Karosszék a magasban: Beszélgetés Léner Péterrel." (The Director's Chair:

THEATRE IN GENERAL: —Administration

Interview with Péter Léner.) *Sz.* 1998; 31(5): 36-38. Illus.: Photo. B&W. 5. Lang.: Hun.

Hungary: Budapest. 1960-1998. Histories-sources. ■Managing director of the József Attila Theatre talks about the way he now conceives his professional task and about the challenges of a so-called suburban theatre and its public.

16 Ruszt, József; Kiss, Csaba; Spiró, György. "Bunkóság vagy szuverenitás? A szerzői jog és a színházi rendezők." (The Problems of Sovereignty: Authors' Rights and Theatre Directors.) *Sz.* 1998; 31(8): 30-39. Illus.: F. B&W. 10. Lang.: Hun.

Hungary. 1990-1998. Histories-sources. ■Round-table on the topic of authors' rights organized by the periodical *Színház.* The discussion revolved around the freedom of theatres to treat texts according to their own needs and aims and the right of the author to demand absolute fidelity to what is written.

17 Boorsma, Miranda. *Marketing van theater en andere kunsten.* (Marketing of Theatre and Other Arts.) Amsterdam: Boekmanstichting; 1998. 150 pp. Pref. Tables. Biblio. Illus.: Photo. B&W. 13. Lang.: Dut.

Netherlands. 1990-1995. Histories-specific. ■Several marketing strategies are applied to the performing arts.

18 Hagoort, Giep. *Strategische dialoog in de kunstensector. Interactieve strategievorming in een kunstorganisatie.* (Strategic Dialogue in the Arts. Interactive Strategy-Building in an Arts Organization.) Delft: Eburon; 1998. 206 pp. Pref. Index. Notes. Tables. Biblio. Illus.: Graphs. Plan. 38. Lang.: Dut.

Netherlands. 1998. Critical studies. ■Examines different methods of organization building in the arts.

19 Parandovskij, Ja. "Žizn'." (Life.) *Mecenat i mir.* 1998; 6-7: 7-19. Lang.: Rus.

Poland. 1998. Histories-sources. ■Excerpts from 'The Alchemy of Words' by a Polish writer and scholar on the history of patronage.

20 Reiss, Alvin H. "Romanian Arts Groups Face New Funding." *FundM.* 1998 Oct.; 29(8): 29-31. Illus.: Photo. B&W. 2. Lang.: Eng.

Romania. 1989-1998. Historical studies. ■Changing face of of arts funding in Romania since the fall of Ceausescu. Traditionally government-funded, arts groups now receive private and corporate support.

21 Hallin, Ulrika. "På spaning efter den nya teaterpubliken." (Looking For the New Audiences.) *Tningen.* 1998; 21(1): 11-14. Illus.: Photo. B&W. Lang.: Swe.

Sweden: Stockholm. 1995-1998. Critical studies. ■The efforts of the theatre organization Brytpunkt, independent theatre groups, and Stockholms Stadsteatern's Backstage to attract new young audiences to the theatre.

22 Most, Henrik. "Højt belagt teater i Stockholm." (Exciting Theatre in Stockholm.) *TE.* 1998 Apr.; 88: 35-38. Illus.: Photo. B&W. 2. Lang.: Dan.

Sweden: Stockholm. 1998. Critical studies. ■Stockholm is cultural capital of Europe 1998. The cultural year began New Year's Eve with Staffan Valdemar Holm's production of Carl Orff's *Carmina Burana.*

23 Fleming, Brent Leonard. *Theatre Management Procedures: An Operations Manual for the Cultural Center Theatres in Taiwan, the Republic of China.* Lubbock, TX: Texas Tech Univ; 1987. 322 pp. Biblio. Notes. [Ph.D. Dissertation, Univ. Microfilms Order No. 8713596.] Lang.: Eng.

Taiwan. 1985-1987. Instructional materials. ■The development of the manual was sponsored by the Fulbright Foundation as a response to the challenge of combining current Taiwanese arts management practices with Western management techniques.

24 Norris, James. "Trying Hard." *PlPl.* Feb 1998; 519: 10-11. Illus.: Photo. B&W. 1. Lang.: Eng.

UK-England: London. 1996-1998. Histories-sources. ■John Tusa, Managing Director of Barbican Centre, on his past two years there and on the state of performing arts financing around London.

25 Norris, James. "Something For Everyone." *PlPl.* May 1998; 522: 10-11. Lang.: Eng.

UK-England: London. 1998. Histories-sources. ■Interview with artistic director Graham Sheffield on attempts of his Barbican Centre to attract a wide audience with programming in diverse performing and media arts.

26 Ramsden, Timothy. "Summer In The Cities." *PlPl.* 1998 Sep.; 526: 24. Lang.: Eng.

UK-England: London. 1998. Historical studies. ■Recent trend in London theatres of producing shows during the summer.

27 Waites, Aline. "Just a Second." *PlPl.* June 1998; 523: 10. Lang.: Eng.

UK-England: London. 1998. Critical studies. ■Explains and critiques practice of giving magazine critics tickets for second nights rather than premieres.

28 Archer, Stephen M. "*E pluribus unum*: Bernhardt's 1905-1906 Farewell Tour." 159-174 in Engle, Ron, ed.; Miller, Tice L., ed. *The American Stage: Social and Economic Issues from the Colonial Period to the Present.* Cambridge: Cambridge UP; 1993. 320 pp. Pref. Notes. Index. Illus.: Photo. 1. Lang.: Eng.

USA. 1905-1906. Historical studies. ■The tension between the Theatrical Syndicate and the Shubert Organization over the large sums of money generated by Bernhardt's U.S. tour.

29 Brizzell, Cindy. "ARTNOW: A (Stumbling) Movement Towards Arts Advocacy." *TDR.* 1998 Spr; 42(1): 122-158. Notes. Biblio. Illus.: Photo. B&W. 2. Lang.: Eng.

USA: Washington, DC. 1997. Historical studies. ■Detailed account of ARTNOW arts advocacy demonstration. Includes the program of events for the day.

30 Brock, David Carl. *The Town Dramatic: A Demographic, Anecdotal, and Personality Evaluation of Participants in a Rural Community Theatre.* Commerce, TX: East Texas State Univ; 1987. 226 pp. Biblio. Notes. [M.A. Thesis, Univ. Microfilms Order No. 1331591.] Lang.: Eng.

USA. 1986. Empirical research. ■Delineates various aspects of personnel participating in community theatre productions, using survey, demographic data, profiles, and data on plays and areas of participation.

31 Carlson, Marvin. "The Development of the American Theatre Program." 101-114 in Engle, Ron, ed.; Miller, Tice L., ed. *The American Stage: Social and Economic Issues from the Colonial Period to the Present.* Cambridge: Cambridge UP; 1993. 320 pp. Pref. Notes. Index. Lang.: Eng.

USA. 1875-1899. Historical studies. ■The playbill as an important record of changing social and economic forces operative in the theatre.

32 Copp, Karen Hadley. *The State of the Corporate-Arts Relationship as Viewed Through the Perspective of the Non-profit Theatre.* Columbus, OH: Ohio State Univ; 1988. 259 pp. Biblio. Notes. [Ph.D. Dissertation, Univ. Microfilms Order No. AAC 8820275.] Lang.: Eng.

USA. 1980-1988. Histories-specific. ■The decline in corporate funding for the arts. Examines modern history of the corporate-arts relationship.

33 Davis, Peter A. "Puritan Mercantilism and the Politics of Anti-Theatrical Legislation in Colonial America." 18-29 in Engle, Ron, ed.; Miller, Tice L., ed. *The American Stage: Social and Economic Issues from the Colonial Period to the Present.* Cambridge: Cambridge UP; 1993. 320 pp. Pref. Notes. Index. Lang.: Eng.

USA. 1770-1830. Historical studies. ■Argues that business interests and anti-British sentiment were more important than religious reasons for the anti-theatrical legislation.

34 Goldberg, Phyllis. "Gabrielle Kurlander, Actress and Entrepreneur, Brings Performance into the Philanthropy Marketplace." *FundM.* 1998 Feb.; 28(12): 14-18. Illus.: Photo. Color. 3. Lang.: Eng.

USA: New York, NY. 1998. Biographical studies. ■Kurlander, president of the Community Literacy Research Project, uses performance as a strategy to generate funding.

35 Herron, Donna G.; Hubbard, Tamara S.; Kirner, Amy E.; Newcomb, Lynn; Reiser-Memmer, Michelle; Robertson, Michael E., II; Smith, Matthew W.; Tullio, Leslie A.; Young, Jennifer S. "The Effect of Gender on the Career Advancement of Arts Managers." *JAML.* 1998 Spr; 28(1): 27-40. Notes. Tables. Lang.: Eng.

THEATRE IN GENERAL: —Administration

USA. 1996. Empirical research. ■Results of a study conducted by the students of the Masters of Arts Management Program at Carnegie Mellon University to assess whether gender was a consideration in the advancement of arts administrators.

36 Hodsoll, Frank. "Measuring Success and Failure in Government and the Arts." *JAML.* 1998 Fall; 28(3): 230-239. Notes. Lang.: Eng.

USA. 1998. Critical studies. ■Proposes alternate methods of measuring success and failure for use by government and arts agencies to better gauge overall performance by cultural institutions.

37 Infante, Andrea Elizabeth. *Cultural Connections: The Influence of Target Marketing on the Sales Success of Eight International Performance Events at the Carpenter Performing Arts Center During the 1996-1997 and 1997-1998 Seasons.* Long Beach, CA: California State Univ; 1998. 76 pp. Notes. Biblio. [M.A. Thesis, Univ. Microfilms Order No. AAC 1390933.] Lang.: Eng.

USA: Long Beach, CA. 1996-1998. Empirical research. ■Analysis of marketing strategies and their effect on ticket sales.

38 Jackson, Maria-Rosario. "Arts and Culture Indicators in Community Building: Project Update." *JAML.* 1998 Fall; 28(3): 201-205. Notes. Lang.: Eng.

USA. 1996-1998. Empirical research. ■Update on a project undertaken to develop arts and culture-related neighborhood indicators. The project focuses on arts presence in inner-city areas and the use of existing data collection practices within mainstream and community-based arts organizations.

39 Kaple, Deborah; Rivkin-Fish, Ziggy; Louch, Hugh; Morris, Lori; DiMaggio, Paul. "Comparing Sample Frames for Research on Arts Organizations: Results of a Study in Three Metropolitan Areas." *JAML.* 1998 Spr; 28(1): 41-66. Notes. Tables. Lang.: Eng.

USA. 1997. Empirical research. ■Study focused on finding a reliable sample frame for collecting data generalizable to the population of area surrounding the cultural organization to help arts groups in development, policy, and advocacy efforts.

40 Karas, Sandra. "Tax Law Changes May Help in 1998." *EN.* 1998 Jan/Feb.; 83(1): 1. Lang.: Eng.

USA. 1998. Historical studies. ■Report on changes in income tax regulations for the year.

41 King, Kevin H. "New Attitudes and Technologies Make Now the Right Time to Create a 'Virtual' Association." *FundM.* 1998 June; 29(4): 22-23. Lang.: Eng.

USA. 1998. Critical studies. ■Strongly advises an organization to incorporate the World Wide Web into its fundraising tool kit in order to expand its base of possible donors.

42 Langley, Stephen. "Multiculturalism Versus Technoculturalism: Its Challenge to American Theatre and the Functions of Arts Management." 278-289 in Engle, Ron, ed.; Miller, Tice L., ed. *The American Stage: Social and Economic Issues from the Colonial Period to the Present.* Cambridge: Cambridge UP; 1993. 320 pp. Pref. Notes. Index. Lang.: Eng.

USA. 1990-1993. Historical studies. ■Speculates on how an ethnically diverse and highly technological population will affect the theatre of the twenty-first century.

43 Magnuson, Landis Kelly. *Circle Stock Repertoire Theatre in America, 1907-1957.* Urbana-Champaign, IL: Univ. of Illinois; 1988. 316 pp. Biblio. Notes. [Ph.D. Dissertation, Univ. Microfilms Order No. AAC 8815384.] Lang.: Eng.

USA. 1907-1957. Historical studies. ■Examines the widely used, but virtually unreported, method of circle stock touring practiced by American repertory theatre companies in the first half of this century, from its introduction by theatre impresario Al Trahern to financial motivations, performance aspects, and management.

44 Marra, Kim. "A Lesbian Marriage of Cultural Consequence: Elisabeth Marbury and Elsie de Wolfe, 1886-1933." 104-128 in Schanke, Robert A., ed.; Marra, Kim, ed. *Passing Performances: Queer Readings of Leading Players in American Theatre History.* Ann Arbor, MI: Univ of Michigan P; 1998. 338 pp. (Triangulations: Lesbian/Gay/Queer Theatre/Drama/Performance.) Notes. Index. Illus.: Photo. 1. Lang.: Eng.

USA. 1886-1933. Historical studies. ■Examines the personal and professional lives of theatrical agent Elisabeth Marbury and interior designer Elsie de Wolfe. Argues that their lesbianism strongly supported their lives and careers.

45 Martin, Dan J.; Rich, J. Dennis. "Assessing the Role of Formal Education in Arts Administration Training." *JAML.* 1998 Spr; 28(1): 4-26. Notes. Append. Tables. Lang.: Eng.

USA. 1998. Empirical research. ■The effect of formal training on arts administrators.

46 Martin, Deborah Gail. *Texas Tech University Theatre Season Subscription Campaign: A Marketing Analysis and Plan.* Lubbock, TX: Texas Tech Univ; 1998. 127 pp. Notes. Biblio. [Ph.D. Dissertation, Univ. Microfilms Order No. AAC 9826462.] Lang.: Eng.

USA: Lubbock, TX. 1997-1998. Empirical research. ■Examines the results of formal marketing research conducted at the Texas Tech University Department of Theatre and Dance, specifically addressing the audience profiles of the Mainstage season subscribers.

47 Moore, Dick. "Meet the Staff: Carol Waaser Continues as Eastern Director." *EN.* 1998 Oct/Nov.; 83(3): 6. Illus.: Photo. 1. Lang.: Eng.

USA: New York, NY. 1998. Historical studies. ■Profile of Carol Waaser, director of Equity's Eastern Region.

48 Moore, Dick. "The 83." *EN.* 1998 Sep.; 83(7): 8. Illus.: Photo. 1. Lang.: Eng.

USA: Chicago, IL. 1998. Historical studies. ■Short biographical sketch of Equity Council member Tom Joyce, representing the Central Region.

49 Moore, Dick. "Atlanta, Georgia: 'The Big Peach'." *EN.* 1998 July/Aug.; 83(6): 5. Lang.: Eng.

USA: Atlanta, GA. 1998. Historical studies. ■Report on current theatre and Equity business in the Atlanta area.

50 Moore, Dick. "Regional Report: Central Texas, What a Hot Spot." *EN.* 1998 Sep.; 83(7): 5. Lang.: Eng.

USA: Austin, TX, San Antonio, TX. 1998. Historical studies. ■Reports on the state of Equity activity in the Central Texas Liaison area.

51 Moore, Dick. "Eisenberg Reports on Finances, Merger and Organizing Efforts." *EN.* 1998 Jan/Feb.; 83(1): 1. Lang.: Eng.

USA. 1998. Historical studies. ■Report by Equity Director Alan Eisenberg at the Eastern Regional membership meeting. Topics discussed were finances, merger efforts and organizing efforts.

52 Moore, Dick. "BC/EFA Holiday Appeal Sets New Record." *EN.* 1998 Jan/Feb.; 83(1): 1, 3. Illus.: Photo. B&W. 9. Lang.: Eng.

USA: New York, NY. 1998. Historical studies. ■Reports on the 10th Anniversary of Broadway Cares/Equity Fights AIDS.

53 Moore, Dick. "Council Affirms Support for the Broadway Initiative." *EN.* 1998 Jan/Feb.; 83(1): 1. Lang.: Eng.

USA. 1998. Historical studies. ■Reports on the Actors' Equity Council affirming its support of the Broadway Initiative, a zoning proposal that allows a theatre owner to transfer the theatre's air rights to private developers.

54 Moore, Dick. "Equity, Canadian Equity Clarify Reciprocal Agreement." *EN.* 1998 Jan/Feb.; 83(1): 1. Lang.: Eng.

USA. Canada. 1998. Historical studies. ■Report on negotiations between Canadian and American Actors' Equity on compensation issues between the two unions.

55 Moore, Dick. "Eisenberg Goes on the Road." *EN.* 1998 Jan/Feb.; 83(1): 2. Lang.: Eng.

USA. 1998. Historical studies. ■Reports on Executive Director Alan Eisenberg's trips around the country to check on union issues.

56 Moore, Dick. "Jack Goldstein Leaves Equity: Named Executive Director of Theatre Development Fund." *EN.* 1998 Jan/Feb.; 83(1): 2. Illus.: Photo. B&W. 1. Lang.: Eng.

USA: New York, NY. 1998. Historical studies. ■Report on Jack Goldstein, special assistant to the President, and his new position as Executive Director of the Theatre Development Fund.

THEATRE IN GENERAL: —Administration

57 Moore, Dick. "Equity's Bonding Policy and How It Works." *EN.* 1998 Jan/Feb.; 83(1): 2. Lang.: Eng.
USA. 1998. Historical studies. ■Report on changes in Actors' Equity theatre bonding policy.

58 Moore, Dick. "Credit Union Offers New 1998 IRAs." *EN.* 1998 Jan/Feb.; 83(1): 2. Lang.: Eng.
USA. 1998. Historical studies. ■Reports of changes to IRAs as part of the Taxpayer Relief Act and the benefits to performers.

59 Moore, Dick. "Clinton Names New NEA Chair." *EN.* 1998 Jan/Feb.; 83(1): 2. Lang.: Eng.
USA. 1998. Historical studies. ■Reports on the nomination of William J. Ivey to head the National Endowment for the Arts.

60 Moore, Dick. "Salary Increases Highlight New Off-Broadway Contract." *EN.* 1998 Jan/Feb.; 83(1): 4. Lang.: Eng.
USA. 1998. Historical studies. ■Reports on Equity's new four-year agreement with the League of Off Broadway Theatres and Producers.

61 Moore, Dick. "Robeson Centennial Gets Underway." *EN.* 1998 Jan/Feb.; 83(1): 7. Lang.: Eng.
USA. 1898-1998. Historical studies. ■Reports on the preparations by the Paul Robeson Foundation for the centennial of American actor Paul Robeson.

62 Moore, Dick. "East West Players in L.A. Moves from 99-Seat Plan to Contract." *EN.* 1998 Mar.; 83(2): 1. Lang.: Eng.
USA: Los Angeles, CA. 1998. Historical studies. ■Reports on the signing of a new Equity contract for the East West Players.

63 Moore, Dick. "Council Approves New Agreement for New Orleans." *EN.* 1998 Mar.; 83(2): 1-2. Lang.: Eng.
USA: New Orleans, LA. 1998. Historical studies. ■Reports on new agreement establishing terms and conditions for Equity members working in New Orleans.

64 Moore, Dick. "Business Theatre Contract Approved: Salaries Go Up 3 Percent." *EN.* 1998 Mar.; 83(2): 2. Lang.: Eng.
USA: New York, NY. 1998. Historical studies. ■Reports on the terms and conditions of a new Business Theatre Contract which includes a three percent salary increase.

65 Moore, Dick. "Now's the Time to Make Changes in Health Insurance Coverage." *EN.* 1998 Apr.; 83(3): 1. Lang.: Eng.
USA: New York, NY. 1998. Historical studies. ■Reports on the 'open enrollment period' for changing health insurance coverage.

66 Moore, Dick. "New Three-Year Agreement with Second City in Central Region." *EN.* 1998 Mar.; 83(2): 2. Lang.: Eng.
USA: Chicago, IL, Detroit, MI. 1998. Historical studies. ■Report on improvements in salary, changes in stage manager work rules, disability leave, pay-out for vacations and sick days plus an increase in per diem in the new three-year agreement covering actors and stage managers at Second City companies in Chicago and Detroit.

67 Moore, Dick. "Supreme Court Rules Against Credit Unions." *EN.* 1998 Apr.; 83(3): 1. Lang.: Eng.
USA: New York, NY. 1998. Historical studies. ■Reports on the latest Supreme Court ruling against credit unions and its repercussions on the Actors Federal Credit Union.

68 Moore, Dick. "Dames Draw Dollars for Women's Health." *EN.* 1998 Apr.; 83(3): 8. Lang.: Eng.
USA: New York, NY. 1998. Historical studies. ■Reports on the annual benefit for the Actors' Fund of America's Phyllis Newman Women's Health Initiative, performed at the Shubert Theatre in conjunction with Actors' Equity.

69 Moore, Dick. "Jekyll and Hyde Clubs Sign with Equity." *EN.* 1998 May; 83(4): 1, 9. Lang.: Eng.
USA: New York, NY. 1998. Historical studies. ■Reports on the signing of Eerie Entertainment's Jekyll and Hyde themed restaurants to Equity contracts.

70 Moore, Dick. "House Passes Credit Union Bill: Fight Moves to the Senate." *EN.* 1998 May; 83(4): 1. Lang.: Eng.
USA: New York, NY. 1998. Historical studies. ■Reports on the passage of the Credit Union Bill by the House of Representatives, protecting the right of Americans to join a credit union.

71 Moore, Dick. "For the Record." *EN.* 1998 May; 83(4): 1, 9. Lang.: Eng.
USA: New York, NY. 1998. Historical studies. ■Reports on votes by Equity Council on recent issues.

72 Moore, Dick. "Easter Bonnet Competition in New York Raises $1,793,136." *EN.* 1998 May; 83(4): 3. Illus.: Photo. 3. Lang.: Eng.
USA: New York, NY. 1998. Historical studies. ■Account of the 12th Annual Easter Bonnet Competition to raise funds for Broadway Cares/ Equity Fights AIDS.

73 Moore, Dick. "Broadway Initiative Brings Theatre Community Together at City Planning Hearing." *EN.* 1998 June; 83(5): 1, 7. Lang.: Eng.
USA: New York, NY. 1998. Historical studies. ■Reports on the current debate on the Theatre District rezoning proposal. Theatre professionals support the initiative, community activists do not.

74 Moore, Dick. "The Tony Awards." *EN.* 1998 June; 83(5): 1, 7. Lang.: Eng.
USA: New York, NY. 1950-1998. Historical studies. ■Recounts the history of the Tony Awards.

75 Moore, Dick. "Spotlight on the Actor." *EN.* 1998 June; 83(5): 3. Illus.: Photo. 3. Lang.: Eng.
USA: New York, NY. 1998. Histories-sources. ■Interviews with actors (Cary Barker, Mary Sheehan and Patricia Dell) on the state of the union.

76 Moore, Dick. "Broadway Bares for Broadway Cares." *EN.* 1998 June; 83(5): 2. Illus.: Photo. 2. Lang.: Eng.
USA: New York, NY. 1998. Historical studies. ■Reports on the Broadway Bares benefit for Broadway Cares/Equity Fights AIDS. Conceived, directed and choreographed by Jerry Mitchell.

77 Moore, Dick. "Is Anybody There? Does Anybody Care? Yes, Indeed!" *EN.* 1998 June; 83(5): 3. Lang.: Eng.
USA: New York, NY. 1998. Historical studies. ■Reports on follow-up efforts to report on rules and regulations, Workers' Compensation, risk and injury and other issues to union population in current Broadway shows.

78 Moore, Dick. "Three... Two... One... LAUNCH!" *EN.* 1998 July/Aug.; 83(6): 1, 6. Illus.: Photo. 1. Lang.: Eng.
USA: New York, NY. 1998. Historical studies. ■Reports on the recent launch of the Equity website. Article recounts history and development of the idea as well as funding matters.

79 Moore, Dick. "New Dinner Theatre Contracts in Place in All Regions." *EN.* 1998 July/Aug.; 83(6): 1. Lang.: Eng.
USA: New York, NY. 1998. Historical studies. ■Report of recent negotiations with Equity dinner theatres across the country.

80 Moore, Dick. "John Holly Set for Second Term as Western Director." *EN.* 1998 July/Aug.; 83(6): 2. Illus.: Photo. 1. Lang.: Eng.
USA: New York, NY. 1998. Historical studies. ■Profile of John Holly, Equity's Western Regional Director/Assistant Executive Director, and his three-year contract for the position.

81 Moore, Dick. "P&H Trustees Report: Benefits Increase for Current, Future Pensioners, Health Fund Also Shows Substantial Improvements." *EN.* 1998 July/Aug.; 83(6): 3, 6. Lang.: Eng.
USA: New York, NY. 1998. Historical studies. ■Annual report on Equity-League Pension and Health Fund concentrating on the assets of the pension fund, the improvements to the fund, and improvements to the health fund.

82 Moore, Dick. "The 83." *EN.* 1998 July/Aug.; 83(6): 3. Illus.: Photo. 3. Lang.: Eng.
USA: New York, NY. 1998. Historical studies. ■Profiles of two Equity council members, Linda Cameron and Bob Knapp.

83 Moore, Dick. "President Clinton Signs Credit Union Bill." *EN.* 1998 July/Aug.; 83(6): 6. Lang.: Eng.
USA: New York, NY. 1998. Historical studies. ■Report on the recent signing by President Clinton of the Credit Union Membership Access Act and its impact on the Actors Federal Credit Union, sponsored by Equity.

84 Moore, Dick. "Behind the Scenes." *EN.* 1998 July/Aug.; 83(6): 7. Lang.: Eng.

THEATRE IN GENERAL: —Administration

USA: New York, NY. 1998. Historical studies. ■A look at the work of the Equity Stage Manager.

85 Moore, Dick. "Stage Reading Guidelines Are Revised for Eastern Region." *EN*. 1998 July/Aug.; 83(6): 8. Lang.: Eng.

USA: New York, NY. 1998. Historical studies. ■On the creation of Stage Reading Guidelines to protect Equity members in professional stage readings.

86 Moore, Dick. "Equity's Bonding Policy—And How it Works." *EN*. 1998 July/Aug.; 83(6): 8. Lang.: Eng.

USA: New York, NY. 1998. Historical studies. ■Reports on changes in Equity's bonding policy, especially bonds for seasonal theatres.

87 Moore, Dick. "Five Lodge Complaint Against Equity Councillor and 1998 Annual Election." *EN*. 1998 Sep.; 83(7): 1. Lang.: Eng.

USA: New York, NY. 1998. Historical studies. ■Reports of five complaints by Equity members against a Councillor and the 1998 election claiming that procedures had been violated.

88 Moore, Dick. "Organizing Non-Union Tours Remains High Equity Priority." *EN*. 1998 Sep.; 83(7): 1, 6. Lang.: Eng.

USA: New York, NY. 1998. Historical studies. ■Reports on the on-going debate about the pros and cons of organizing non-union tours of theatrical productions.

89 Moore, Dick. "City Council Approves Sale of Theatre Air Rights." *EN*. 1998 Sep.; 83(7): 1, 2. Lang.: Eng.

USA: New York, NY. 1998. Historical studies. ■Reports on the recent approval by the New York City Council to allow twenty-five Broadway theatres to sell their unused air rights to developers. Equity had supported this position.

90 Moore, Dick. "Show Buzz." *EN*. 1998 Sep.; 83(7): 3. Lang.: Eng.

USA: New York, NY. 1998. Historical studies. ■Current news on the theatre and Equity business.

91 Moore, Dick. "Why Is There a Three-Month Waiting Period Before Health Benefits Become Effective?" *EN*. 1998 Sep.; 83(7): 7. Lang.: Eng.

USA: New York, NY. 1998. Historical studies. ■Report on the reasons for the waiting periods required by the Equity-League Pension and Health Trust Funds.

92 Moore, Dick. "Meet the Staff: Kathryn Lamkey Oversees Growth of Equity, Theatre in Central Region." *EN*. 1998 Sep.; 83 (7): 8. Illus.: Photo. 1. Lang.: Eng.

USA: Chicago, IL. 1998. Historical studies. ■Profile of Kathryn Lamkey, Director of the Central Regional Office of Equity.

93 Moore, Dick. "Actor Breaks Leg—It's Not Good Luck." *EN*. 1998 Sep.; 83(7): 8. Lang.: Eng.

USA: New York, NY. 1998. Historical studies. ■Reports on the experience of Equity performer Bryan Hull, who broke his leg while working. Recounts Hull's experience with Equity management in securing sick pay and worker's compensation.

94 Moore, Dick. "1999 National Council Election Gets Underway: 15 Seats Are Open." *EN*. 1998 Dec.; 83(9): 1, 2. Lang.: Eng.

USA: New York, NY. 1998. Historical studies. ■Reports on the upcoming Equity National Council elections. Article describes the nominating process and how to run for the council.

95 Moore, Dick. "Palm View Housing Complex Opens in West Hollywood: Actors' Fund Residence Offers Low-Cost Housing for People with AIDS." *EN*. 1998 Dec.; 83(9): 1, 2. Illus.: Photo. 1. Lang.: Eng.

USA: Hollywood, CA. 1998. Historical studies. ■Reports on the opening of the Palm View residence to house entertainment professionals and others with AIDS. The residence received funds from Equity's Broadway Cares/Equity Fights AIDS and the Actors' Fund.

96 Moore, Dick. "The Headset's Open: A Look at the Work of the Stage Manager." *EN*. 1998 Dec.; 83(9): 2. Lang.: Eng.

USA: New York, NY. 1998. Historical studies. ■Report on specific challenges and working conditions of stage managers.

97 Moore, Dick. "1998: Equity's Year in Review." *EN*. 1998 Dec.; 83(9): 3. Lang.: Eng.

USA: New York, NY. 1998. Historical studies. ■Short calendar of Equity's accomplishments during the year.

98 Moore, Dick. "New CAT Contract in Place Through 2002." *EN*. 1998 Dec.; 83(9): 3. Lang.: Eng.

USA: Chicago, IL. 1998. Historical studies. ■Reports on the approval of a new four-year Chicago Area Theatre (CAT) contract agreement featuring increased salaries, improved working conditions, free housing, and better sick leave and vacation rules.

99 Moore, Dick. "Meet the Staff: Guy Pace, Equity's Own Production Stage Manager." *EN*. 1998 Dec.; 83(9): 6. Illus.: Photo. 1. Lang.: Eng.

USA: New York, NY. 1998. Historical studies. ■Profile of Equity administrator Guy Pace, Assistant Executive Director of National Administration and Finance.

100 Moore, Dick. "The 83." *EN*. 1998 Dec.; 83(9): 12. Illus.: Photo. 1. Lang.: Eng.

USA: New York, NY. 1998. Historical studies. ■Short biographical essay on Equity Council member Patrick Quinn, First Vice-President.

101 Moore, Dick. "Breast Cancer Screening." *EN*. 1998 Sep.; 83(7): 8. Lang.: Eng.

USA: New York, NY. 1998. Historical studies. ■Reports on the breast cancer screening program in New York's Shubert Alley, sponsored by Equity and the Shubert Organization. Article examines history of the program, and how to become involved and receive a screening.

102 Moore, Dick. "SAG, AFTRA Boards Approve Merger Plan: Council Approves Concept." *EN*. 1998 Oct/Nov.; 83(8): 1, 2. Lang.: Eng.

USA: New York, NY. 1998. Historical studies. ■Reports on an approved merger plan by the Screen Actors Guild and the American Federation of Television and Radio Artists.

103 Moore, Dick. "Casting Info Goes Up On Website." *EN*. 1998 Oct/Nov.; 83(8): 1. Lang.: Eng.

USA: New York, NY. 1998. Historical studies. ■Reports on Equity's development of a casting web site. The site includes casting for the theatre, membership and contract information.

104 Moore, Dick. "Robeson Awards Goes to Leonard dePaur." *EN*. 1998 Oct/Nov.; 83(8): 1, 3. Illus.: Photo. 1. Lang.: Eng.

USA: New York, NY. 1910-1998. Historical studies. ■Reports on the presentation of the Paul Robeson Award to Leonard dePaur, musical conductor and arranger.

105 Moore, Dick. "Medical Coverage Ends for Dependents Who Are 19." *EN*. 1998 Oct/Nov.; 83(8): 1. Lang.: Eng.

USA: New York, NY. 1998. Historical studies. ■Reports on the loss of medical coverage for Equity dependents over the age of nineteen.

106 Moore, Dick. "Council Determines Chargeable Offenses." *EN*. 1998 Oct/Nov.; 83(8): 2. Lang.: Eng.

USA: New York, NY. 1998. Historical studies. ■Reports on Equity Council's debate over chargeable offenses for Equity member behavior when not working under an Equity contract.

107 Moore, Dick. "Helen Hunt Helps Holiday Basket Project." *EN*. 1998 Oct/Nov.; 83(8): 2. Illus.: Photo. 1. Lang.: Eng.

USA: New York, NY. 1986-1998. Historical studies. ■Reports on actress Helen Hunt and her support of Equity's annual Stephen J. Falat Basket Project, which delivers holiday baskets to people living with AIDS.

108 Moore, Dick. "Council Approves Two New Pacts: Cabaret, SPT Contracts Extended." *EN*. 1998 Oct/Nov.; 83(8): 3. Lang.: Eng.

USA: New York, NY. 1998. Historical studies. ■Reports on recent Equity debate and approval of two contracts, the Cabaret and the Small Professional Theatre contracts.

109 Moore, Dick. "Broadway Flea Market, Auction Top Half-Million Mark." *EN*. 1998 Oct/Nov.; 83(8): 4. Illus.: Photo. 2. Lang.: Eng.

USA: New York, NY. 1998. Historical studies. ■Reports on the 12th Annual Broadway Flea Market and Grand Auction, which raised funds for Broadway Cares/Equity Fights AIDS.

110 Moore, Dick. "New (or returning) Member Orientation in L.A. Hits an All-Time High." *EN*. 1998 Oct/Nov.; 83(8): 4. Lang.: Eng.

THEATRE IN GENERAL: —Administration

USA: Los Angeles, CA. 1998. Historical studies. ■Reports on the record-breaking membership of the Los Angeles Equity local.

111 Moore, Dick. "Do You Need an Agent? Seminar in New York Explores the Question." *EN.* 1998 Oct/Nov.; 83(8): 5. Lang.: Eng.

USA: New York, NY. 1998. Historical studies. ■Reports on an Equity seminar on finding the right agency. Several agencies participated and over one hundred members attended.

112 Moore, Dick. "Deputy Meetings Are Bustin' Out All Over." *EN.* 1998 Oct/Nov.; 83(3): 6. Illus.: Photo. 1. Lang.: Eng.

USA. 1998. Historical studies. ■Reports on Equity deputy meetings all over the country including New York, Orlando, and San Francisco.

113 Moore, Dick. "Council Is a Family Affair." *EN.* 1998 Oct/Nov.; 83(3): 7. Illus.: Photo. 1. Lang.: Eng.

USA: New York, NY. 1998. Histories-sources. ■Interview profiles a father-daughter team on the Equity council, R. Kim Jordan and her father S. Marc Jordan.

114 Moore, Dick. "Equity Holds Seminar for Young Performers and Parents in New York." *EN.* 1998 Jan/Feb.; 83(1): 5. Illus.: Photo. B&W. 1. Lang.: Eng.

USA: New York, NY. 1998. Historical studies. ■Reports on a seminar for young performers and their families offered by Equity's Young Performers Committee.

115 Pace, Guy. "1998 Annual Membership, Employment and Finance Survey." *EN.* 1998 Dec.; 83(9): 6-11. Tables. Illus.: Graphs. Chart. 12. Lang.: Eng.

USA: New York, NY. 1998. Historical studies. ■Annual compilation/survey of Equity employment and membership statistical data. Includes short history of Equity's employment data, its methodology, and notes to financial statements.

116 Plum, Jay. "Cheryl Crawford: One Not So Naked Individual." 239-261 in Schanke, Robert A., ed.; Marra, Kim, ed. *Passing Performances: Queer Readings of Leading Players in American Theatre History.* Ann Arbor, MI: Univ of Michigan P; 1998. 338 pp. (Triangulations: Lesbian/Gay/Queer Theatre/Drama/Performance.) Notes. Index. Illus.: Photo. 1. Lang.: Eng.

USA. 1902-1986. Biographical studies. ■The impact of gender and sexuality on theatre producer Cheryl Crawford.

117 Ray, Douglass. "Recruiting Celebrities to Tell Your Story." *FundM.* 1998 Jan.; 28(11): 12-16. Illus.: Photo. Color. 1. Lang.: Eng.

USA. 1998. Histories-sources. ■Strategies for courting a celebrity to be spokesperson for a charitable organization. Includes remarks of actor Cliff Robertson, spokesperson for TechnoServe, an organization dedicated to improving technological development.

118 Reis, George R. "1999 Non-Profit Software Guide." *FundM.* 1998 Oct.; 29(8): 17-26. Illus.: Photo. B&W. 1. Lang.: Eng.

USA. 1998. Instructional materials. ■1999 guide to available software for use by non-profit organizations.

119 Reiss, Alvin H. "In-Kind Giving Is Kind to Arts Organizations." *FundM.* 1998 Jan.; 28(11): 22-23. Illus.: Photo. B&W. 1. Lang.: Eng.

USA. 1998. Critical studies. ■Increasing importance of organizations, such as Materials for the Arts, that collect reusable goods from businesses and individuals to distribute among needy not-for-profit arts companies.

120 Reiss, Alvin H. "Arts Incubators Help Local Groups to Grow and Develop Their Potential." *FundM.* 1998 Feb.; 28(12): 20-22. Illus.: Photo. B&W. 3. Lang.: Eng.

USA: Chicago, IL. 1986-1998. Historical studies. ■Profile of Art's Bridge, organization that nurtures fledgling arts groups through the early stages of development by offering a stable financial operations model until the group is able to conduct its own accounting.

121 Reiss, Alvin H. "Survival Philosophy Dangerous to the Health of the Arts." *FundM.* 1998 Mar.; 29(1): 40, 42. Lang.: Eng.

USA. 1998. Critical studies. ■Argues that when arts institutions keep their doors open at all costs, rather than just closing, it leads too often to compromising the artistic mission of a group.

122 Reiss, Alvin H. "Special Event Focuses on Mission While Also Raising Substantial Funds." *FundM.* 1998 May; 29(3): 34-35. Lang.: Eng.

USA. 1998. Critical studies. ■Suggestions for institutions holding large fundraising events such as dinners, openings, etc. Advises that the organization emphasize its cultural mission.

123 Reiss, Alvin H. "Wilmington Uses the Arts to Help Revitalize Riverfront." *FundM.* 1998 Sep.; 29(7): 32-33. Illus.: Photo. B&W. 2. Lang.: Eng.

USA: Wilmington, DE. 1998. Historical studies. ■Report on the revitalization of the Wilmington riverfront, stressing that the First USA Riverfront Arts Center was a key element in obtaining support for the project.

124 Reiss, Alvin H. "Workplace Giving a Growing Source of Arts Support." *FundM.* 1998 Dec.; 29(10): 24-25. Illus.: Photo. B&W. 1. Lang.: Eng.

USA. 1998. Critical studies. ■Report on the relatively new practice for the arts of soliciting funds from individuals in their workplace environments.

125 Reiss, Alvin H. "Big League Cities Need the Arts as Well as Sports." *FundM.* 1998 Nov.; 29(9): 36-37. Illus.: Photo. B&W. 1. Lang.: Eng.

USA. 1989-1998. Critical studies. ■A call for cities with major league sports franchises not to forget the importance of the arts to their prestige. Argues that the spending of public money to erect new sports facilities results in reduced spending for the arts.

126 Rentschler, Ruth. "Museum and Performing Arts Marketing: A Climate of Change." *JAML.* 1998 Spr; 28(1): 83-96. Notes. Biblio. Tables. Lang.: Eng.

USA. 1977-1997. Empirical research. ■Changes in marketing strategies of museums and performing arts groups over a twenty-year period.

127 Richard, Jean-Paul. "Think Pink! Working Under the Chorus Contract: The History of the Chorus Contract." *EN.* 1998 Sep.; 83(7): 7. Illus.: Photo. 1. Lang.: Eng.

USA: New York, NY. 1913. Historical studies. ■Historical examination of the creation of Actors' Equity, with emphasis on abusive theatrical conditions affecting chorus actors.

128 Rieck, Dean. "Powerful Fund-Raising Letters—A to Z." *FundM.* 1998 Apr.; 29(2): 25-28. Lang.: Eng.

USA. 1998. Historical studies. ■Key concepts for the writing of letters to solicit funds from donors. Concepts are listed alphabetically, in dictionary form. Part II appears in *FundM*, 1998 May, 29:3, pp 30-33. Part III in *FundM*, 1998 June, 29:4, pp 28-31.

129 Roberts, Vera Mowry. "'Lady-Managers' in Nineteenth-Century American Theatre." 30-46 in Engle, Ron, ed.; Miller, Tice L., ed. *The American Stage: Social and Economic Issues from the Colonial Period to the Present.* Cambridge: Cambridge UP; 1993. 320 pp. Pref. Notes. Index. Lang.: Eng.

USA. 1800-1900. Historical studies. ■The success of women theatre managers in nineteenth-century American theatre.

130 Rux, Paul. "Funding Information Systems." *FundM.* 1998 Apr.; 29(2): 30-31. Lang.: Eng.

USA. 1998. Critical studies. ■The importance of constant updating and upgrading an organization's fundraising data base.

131 Scharine, Richard. "*Kaleidoscope of the American Dream.*" *JADT.* 1998 Spr; 10(2): 40-58. Notes. Lang.: Eng.

USA: Lawrence, KS. Europe. 1964-1969. Historical studies. ■The cancellation of the Kansas University Theatre Department's government-funded cultural exchange program with Eastern European theatre schools. Focuses on censorship and governmental reaction against one production, *Kaleidoscope of the American Dream.*

132 Schechner, Richard. "Artwhen?" *TDR.* 1998 Spr; 42(1): 5-7. Notes. Lang.: Eng.

USA: Washington, DC. 1997. Historical studies. ■Essay on the failure of the ARTNOW demonstration April 19, 1997, to generate grassroots support for the arts.

THEATRE IN GENERAL: —Administration

133 Seay, Donald Walter. *Sponsored Project Funding: The Development of the Center for the Advancement of Professional Theatre Training and Applied Research at Texas Tech University.* Lubbock, TX: Texas Tech Univ; 1987. 266 pp. Biblio. Notes. [Ph.D. Dissertation, Univ. Microfilms Order No. 8724452.] Lang.: Eng.
USA. 1985-1987. Critical studies. ▪Develops a funding model for small-to moderate-sized theatre arts programs at state-supported institutions of higher education, using the basic steps of non-solicited, sponsored-project fundraising in the public and private sectors.

134 Stepanian, Laurie Anne. *Harry Davis, Theatrical Entrepreneur, Pittsburgh, Pennsylvania, 1893-1927.* Columbia, MO: Univ. of Missouri; 1988. 362 pp. Notes. Biblio. [Ph.D. Dissertation, Univ. Microfilms Order No. 8915342.] Lang.: Eng.
USA: Pittsburgh, PA. 1893-1927. Histories-specific. ▪Focuses on Davis's management style and the transformation of popular and legitimate amusements during his time, including the introduction of early film.

135 Stephenson, Nan Louise. *The Charleston Theatre Management of Charles H. Gilfert, 1817 to 1822.* Lincoln, NB: Univ. of Nebraska; 1988. 896 pp. Notes. Biblio. [Ph.D. Dissertation, Univ. Microfilms Order No. 8904514.] Lang.: Eng.
USA: Charleston, SC. 1817-1822. Histories-specific. ▪Focuses on Gilfert's business methods, especially at the Charleston Theatre, and argues that his management helped to develop the modern American theatre.

136 Stevens, Louise K. "Impacts, Measurements, and Arts Policy: Starting the Change Process." *JAML.* 1998 Fall; 28(3): 225-228. Lang.: Eng.
USA. 1998. Critical studies. ▪The future of impact studies and outcome analysis with regard to cultural policy.

137 Stevenson, David R. "Public Viewing of Descriptive Information about Nonprofit Arts Organizations." *JAML.* 1998 Fall; 28 (3): 211-219. Biblio. Tables. Lang.: Eng.
USA. 1998. Critical studies. ▪Focuses on IRS Form 990, filed by not-for-profit organizations: the information on this form may soon be available to the public over the internet and on CD-ROM. Discusses the impact on cultural groups.

138 Thompson, Eric C. "Contingent Valuation in Arts Impact Studies." *JAML.* 1998 Fall; 28(3): 206-210. Notes. Lang.: Eng.
USA. 1998. Critical studies. ▪Impact analysis as a useful method for determining how the arts affect communities in US cities and states.

139 Vey, Shauna A. *Protecting Childhood: The Campaign to Bar Children from Performing Professionally in New York City, 1874-1919.* New York, NY: City Univ. of New York; 1998. 210 pp. Notes. Biblio. [Ph.D. Dissertation, Univ. Microfilms Order No. AAC 9908375.] Lang.: Eng.
USA: New York, NY. 1874-1919. Historical studies. ▪Examines the work of the Society for the Prevention of Cruelty to Children (SPCC), led by Elbridge T. Gerry, laws prohibiting the exhibition of children in a number of performance venues, and the position of Actors' Equity Association toward stage children.

140 Wilson, Karen Peterson. *A Study of the Managerial Techniques Practiced by Directors of the Theatre at LORT A, B, C, and D Theatres in 1987-88.* Minneapolis, MN: Univ. of Minnesota; 1988. 128 pp. Notes. Biblio. [Ph.D. Dissertation, Univ. Microfilms Order No. 8909480.] Lang.: Eng.
USA. 1987-1988. Histories-specific. ▪Management practices of members of the League of Resident Theatres, including current practices of theatre directors as managers. Argues that management techniques should be integrated into the training of theatre directors.

141 Wyszomirski, Margaret Jane. "Comparing Cultural Policies in the United States and Japan: Preliminary Observations." *JAML.* 1998 Win; 28(4): 265-281. Notes. Tables. Lang.: Eng.
USA. Japan. 1949-1998. Historical studies. ▪Comparison of the cultural policies of the United States and Japan.

142 Wyszomirski, Margaret Jane. "Beyond Economic Impact." *JAML.* 1998 Fall; 28(3): 187-188. Lang.: Eng.
USA. 1998. Critical studies. ▪Introduction to the focus of *JAML* 28:3, articles representing the most current thinking regarding performance, policy evaluation, and impact analyses.

143 Wyszomirski, Margaret Jane. "The Arts and Performance Review, Policy Assessment, and Program Evaluation: Focusing on the Ends of the Policy Cycle." *JAML.* 1998 Fall; 28(3): 191-199. Notes. Lang.: Eng.
USA. 1998. Critical studies. ▪Contextualizes the current interest in outcome analysis of cultural activities and organizations. Calls for better and more regular assessment.

144 Zinno, Sally. "National Arts Stabilization Evaluation Research Project." *JAML.* 1998 Fall; 28(3): 220-224. Tables. Lang.: Eng.
USA. 1998. Critical studies. ▪Description of National Arts Stabilization, a nonprofit arts management group that helps organizations build a strong foundation on which creativity and innovation can flourish.

145 Auerbach, Leslie Ann. *Censorship and East European and Soviet Theatre and Film, 1963-1980: The Censor's Game.* Stony Brook, NY: State Univ. of New York; 1988. 332 pp. Notes. Biblio. [Ph.D. Dissertation, Univ. Microfilms Order No. AAC 8900197.] Lang.: Eng.
USSR. Europe. 1963-1980. Histories-specific. ▪The composition of the censors' ranks and the role of the artist, as well as techniques of resistance and eluding censorship.

Audience

146 Bennett, Susan. *The Role of the Theatre Audience: A Theory of Production and Reception.* Hamilton, ON: McMaster Univ; 1988. Notes. Biblio. [Ph.D. Dissertation, Univ. Microfilms Order No. not available.] Lang.: Eng.
Canada. 1988. Critical studies. ▪Uses Brecht's dramatic theory and practice, and theories of reading, including semiotics, historical and psychoanalytic analysis, film theory, ideological critique and other approaches to reception.

147 Davis, Jim; Emeljanow, Victor. "New Views of Cheap Theatres: Reconstructing the Nineteenth-Century Theatre Audience." *ThS.* 1998 Nov.; 39(2): 53-72. Notes. Lang.: Eng.
England: London. 1835-1861. Critical studies. ▪Audience composition and reception at selected London theatres, including the Surrey. Argues that a full description can only be attempted by studying demographic information such as census reports, police reports, and patterns of urban transportation.

148 Koski, Pirkko. "Katsojan yllätyksellinen rooli." (The Audience: Unreliable Necessity of the Theatre.) *Teat.* 1998; 53(7): 4-6. Illus.: Photo. Color. B&W. 2. Lang.: Fin.
Finland. 1998. Critical studies. ▪Discusses audience fickleness and the drawback that presents when using an audience to gauge the merit of theatrical work.

149 Mäkinen, Eija. "Seitsemän silmäparia." (Seven Pairs of Eyes.) *Teat.* 1998; 53(7): 8-11. Illus.: Photo. Color. B&W. 7. Lang.: Fin.
Finland. 1998. Histories-sources. ▪Surveys seven people who attend theatrical performances to get an idea of the different reasons audience members have for going to the theatre.

150 Rainio, Elina. "Katsojan paikka ja asema esitysten estetiikassa." (The Audience: Its Place and Position.) *TeatterT.* 1998; 1: 32-34. Lang.: Fin.
Finland. 1998. Critical studies. ▪The role of the audience in live performance. Argues it is the audience's responsibility to question, influence, and even take action in performance.

151 Jankowiak, Günter. "Von den Gründen, Theater für Kinder zu machen." (On Reasons to Make Theatre for Children.) *G&GBKM.* 1998; 128: 6-11. Illus.: Photo. B&W. 2. Lang.: Ger.
Germany: Hannover. 1998. Historical studies. ▪The opening speech of 'Spurensuche' (Looking for tracks), the 4th workshop of the free children's theatre scene: how an independent children's theatre-maker can influence children.

THEATRE IN GENERAL: —Audience

152 Roth, Wilhelm. "Lust, Frust–Popcornschlacht." (Pleasure, Frustration–Popcorn Battle.) *DB.* 1998; 9: 38-42. Illus.: Photo. B&W. 3. Lang.: Ger.
Germany. 1998. Critical studies. ▪Analyzes the relationship between theatres and student audiences with respect to Schauspiel Leipzig, Deutsches Theater and Maxim Gorki Theater of Berlin, Thalia Theater (Hamburg), Staatstheater Schwerin and Frankfurter Schauspielhaus (Frankfurt am Main) and the role of theatre pedagogues.

153 Siebenhaar, Klaus. "Der Zuschauer–das bekannte Wesen." (The Spectator–the Well-Known Being.) *dRAMATURg.* 1998; 1: 27-32. Lang.: Ger.
Germany: Berlin. 1993-1998. Critical studies. ▪Suggestions on how to interpret data from research on audiences to develop marketing concepts with clear purpose.

154 Franses, Philip Hans; Gras, Henk. "Theatre-going in Rotterdam, 1802-1853: A Statistical Analysis of Ticket Sales." *ThS.* 1998 Nov.; 39(2): 73-97. Notes. Lang.: Eng.
Netherlands: Rotterdam. 1802-1853. Critical studies. ▪Examines patterns of theatre-going in Rotterdam at an unnamed theatre built by a group of businessmen of the city's thriving merchant class, based on the group's archives. Includes statistical analysis.

155 Heteren, Lucia van. *Theater, kritiek, jury en publieu. De totstandkoming van het kwaliteitsoordeel bij theater.* (Theatre, Critics, Judging and Audience. The Creation of a Quality Judgment in Theatre.) Groningen: Passage Vitgeverij; 1998. 224 pp. Index. Tables. Biblio. Pref. Illus.: Diagram. B&W. 5. Lang.: Dut.
Netherlands. 1987-1996. Empirical research. ▪Examines the results of a ten-year study on audience responses at theatre festivals in the Netherlands.

156 Davis, Tracy C.; McConachie, Bruce. "Introductory Essay." *ThS.* 1998 Nov.; 39(2): 1-6. Notes. Lang.: Eng.
North America. Europe. 1795-1997. Critical studies. ▪Introductory essay to a volume on the role and function of the spectator in performance. Argues that spectating has the potential of powerful, politicized, and highly nuanced forms of exchange between those 'doing' the performance and those 'seeing' the performance.

157 Bank, Rosemarie K. "Hustlers in the House: The Bowery Theatre as a Mode of Historical Information." 47-64 in Engle, Ron, ed.; Miller, Tice L., ed. *The American Stage: Social and Economic Issues from the Colonial Period to the Present.* Cambridge: Cambridge UP; 1993. 320 pp. Pref. Notes. Index. Lang.: Eng.
USA. 1830-1860. Historical studies. ▪How the American theatre responded to gender-based social issues such as women in the audience, many of whom were prostitutes. Includes analysis of how theatre historians frame and discuss these issues.

158 Chansky, Dorothy. "*Theatre Arts Monthly* and the Construction of the Modern American Theatre Audience." *JADT.* 1998 Win ; 10(1): 51-75. Notes. Lang.: Eng.
USA. 1916-1940. Historical studies. ▪Examines the role of *Theatre Arts Monthly* in American audience construction. Focuses on the journal's role in broadening and educating audiences for non-commercial and commercial theatre.

159 Chansky, Dorothy. "The 47 Workshop and the 48 States: George Pierce Baker and the American Theatre Audience." *THSt.* 1998; 53: 135-146. Notes. Lang.: Eng.
USA: Cambridge, MA. 1918-1924. Historical studies. ▪Examines the nature of 'audience construction,' where theatre practitioners create attitudes, beliefs, and behaviors concerning theatregoing in the minds and bodies of actual or potential spectators. Focuses George Pierce Baker's 47 Workshop, his innovative process of handpicking audiences, and one 47 Workshop production, Lydia Garrison's *The Trap.*

160 Kubler, John Albert. *A Reassessment of the Aesthetics of Audience Response and Audience-Performer Interaction in the Theatrical Event: The Transpersonal Paradigm.* Urbana-Champaign, IL: Univ. of Illinois; 1987. 345 pp. Notes. Biblio. [Ph.D. Dissertation, Univ. Microfilms Order No. AAC 8721682.] Lang.: Eng.
USA. 1970-1981. Empirical research. ▪Analysis of information from such disparate fields as aesthetics, literary theory, neurophysiology, sports psychology, communicology, social psychology, quantum physics, parapsychology, and transpersonal psychology.

161 Rainer, Cosima. "Das Phänomen der kreischenden Mädchen." (The Phenomenon of Screeching Girls.) *MuK.* 1998; 40 (2-4): 9-28. Notes. Illus.: Photo. B&W. 2. Lang.: Ger.
USA. UK-England. 1950-1970. Critical studies. ▪Focuses on the teen girl audience since 1950 and uses women's studies, theatre research and Anglo-American press and film documents as tools to illustrate the importance of this audience to all forms of entertainment.

162 Wolf, Stacy. "Civilizing and Selling Spectators: Audiences at the Madison Civic Center." *ThS.* 1998 Nov.; 39(2): 7-24. Notes. Illus.: Photo. B&W. 3. Lang.: Eng.
USA: Madison, WI. 1993-1997. Critical studies. ▪Audience reliance on and resistance to the structuring of expectations at the Madison, Wisconsin, Civic Center.

Basic theatrical documents

163 Filatov, L.; Bykov, L.,. *Stichi. Pesni. Parodii. Skazki. P'esy. Kinopovesti.* (Poems, Songs, Parodies, Fairy Tales, Plays, Movie Scenarios.) Ekaterinburg: U-Faktorija; 1998. 544 pp. Lang.: Rus.
Russia: Moscow. 1998. ▪Writings by film actor Leonid Filatov, including plays and film scenarios.

164 Vysockij, V.S.; Dobrochotov, A.A. *Izbrannoe.* (Selections.) St. Petersburg: Diamant; 1998. 512 pp. Lang.: Rus.
Russia: Moscow. 1960-1970. ▪Actor Vladimir Vysockij's poems and songs written between 1960-1970.

Design/technology

165 Kotovič, T.V. "Dialogičeskij krest: (Prostranstvo—vremja teatra)." (Dialectical Cross: (Space—Theatrical Time).) 129-142 in *Bachtinskie čtenija, III.* Vitebsk: 1998. Lang.: Rus.
1998. Critical studies. ▪Directions in present-day scenic design.

166 Penny, Simon. "'The Time Has Come, the Walrus said' ..." *PM.* 1988; 56/57: 15-19. Biblio. Illus.: Photo. B&W. 4. Lang.: Eng.
1913-1988. Historical studies. ▪Developments in technology and its application by artists since the early twentieth century.

167 Thelestam, Sunniva. "Frispel–en härlig kväll." (An Opening Pass–a Wonderful Night.) *ProScen.* 1998; 22(5): 23-24 . Illus.: Photo. Color. Lang.: Swe.
1998. Historical studies. ▪Report from a project of staging a costume exhibition made by nine designers and directors in cooperation.

168 Triebold, Wilhelm. "Theater soll wie ein Unfall sein." (Theatre Should Be Like an Accident.) *TZ.* 1998; 5: 24-27. Illus.: Photo. B&W. 5. Lang.: Ger.
Austria: Graz. Germany: Stuttgart. 1979-1998. Biographical studies. ▪A portrait of set designer Martin Zehetgruber, his working methods and his cooperation with director Martin Kušej at Staatstheater Stuttgart.

169 "1998 Lighting Equipment & Accessories Directory." *LD&A.* 1998 Mar.; 28(3): 47-134. Lang.: Eng.
Canada. USA. 1998. Technical studies. ▪Directory of manufacturers and distributors of lighting equipment and accessories in the USA and Canada.

170 Napoleon, Davi. "Mara Blumenfeld." *TCI.* 1998 Oct.; 32(9): 52-53. Illus.: Photo. Color. 3. Lang.: Eng.
Canada. 1992-1998. Biographical studies. ▪Career of costume designer Blumenthal.

171 Carlsson, Lars-Åke. "Teknikermöte på Cuba." (A Meeting of Technicians in Cuba.) *ProScen.* 1998; 22(2): 20-21 . Illus.: Photo. Color. Lang.: Swe.
Cuba: Havana. 1998. Historical studies. ▪Report from the meeting of Asociación Cubana de Ingenieros y Técnicos de los Artes Escénicas (ACITAE).

172 Bílková, Marie. "Costume Designs of the Youngest Generation/Le costume par la jeune génération." *CzechT.* 1998

THEATRE IN GENERAL: —Design/technology

June; 14: 45-50. Illus.: Dwg. Sketches. B&W. 15. Lang.: Eng, Fre.
Czech Republic. 1990-1998. Historcal studies. ▪Costume designs of Kateřina Štefková and Zuzana Štefunková.

173 Unruh, Delbert. "Jan Dušek: Making Connections." *TD&T.* 1998 Win; 34(5): 9-15. Notes. Illus.: Design. Photo. Color. B&W. 16. Lang.: Eng.
Czech Republic: Prague. 1970-1998. Biographical studies. ▪Profile of Dušek, one of the founders of the 'Action Design' movement among Czech set designers, which led to the scenographic revolution in his country during the 1970s.

174 Johnson, David. "Johansen Resigns as Head of Martin." *TCI.* 1998 Mar.; 32(3): 14-15. Lang.: Eng.
Denmark: Copenhagen. 1998. Historical studies. ▪Report on the resignation of founder and managing director of the lighting equipment company the Martin Group.

175 Thelestam, Sunniva. "Eldor Rentor—En levande legend." (Eldor Rentor—A Living Legend.) *ProScen.* 1998; 22(1): 23-26. Illus.: Photo. B&W. Color. Lang.: Swe, Eng, Ger.
Estonia: Tallin. 1925-1998. Biographical studies. ▪Profile of the designer Eldor Rentor, with reference to his works for Estonia Teater.

176 Burkhardt, Peter. "Neue Medien—Der zweite Schritt." (New Media—Second Part.) *BtR.* 1998; 2: 28-31. Notes. Illus.: Graphs. 2. Lang.: Ger.
Europe. 1998. Technical studies. ▪Part 2 of the series on the application of new media. Describes practical aspects of how to get access to the internet and criteria for selecting the right provider.

177 Custer, Marianne; Winkelsesser, Karin, transl. "Kostümbild: Im Osten, Westen und Weiten Westen." (Costumes: In the East, West and Far West.) *BtR.* 1998; 5: 8-12. Illus.: Design. 6. Lang.: Ger.
Europe. USA. 1945-1998. Historical studies. ▪Costume designer and professor in Tennessee, Custer, who is working on a book project concerning costumes in Europe, compares theatre concepts, the training and work of costume designers in eastern Europe and USA.

178 Hummig, Wolfgang. "Pyrotechnik als künstlerisches Ausdrucksmittel." (Pyrotechnics as a Creative Artistic Element.) *BtR.* 1998; 4: 8-13. Illus.: Photo. Color. 9. Lang.: Ger.
Europe. 1200 B.C.-1998 A.D. Historical studies. ▪Traces the history of pyrotechnics for 3000 years in Europe. Describes the modern using of fire effects and the corresponding professional training for their realization.

179 Helavuori, Hanna-Leena. "Maija Pekkanen, näkymättómyyden mestari." (Maija Pekkanen: Mistress of Disguise.) *Teat.* 1998; 53(3): 36-39. Illus.: Photo. Color. B&W. 3. Lang.: Fin.
Finland. 1998. Histories-sources. ▪Interview with costume designer Pekkanen on what she deems to be the responsibilities of a designer.

180 Lahtinen, Outi. "Matkalla lavastustaiteilijaksi." (On the Way to Becoming a Stage Designer.) *Teat.* 1998; 53(6): 38-41. Illus.: Photo. Color. B&W. 5. Lang.: Fin.
Finland. 1998. Critical studies. ▪Critique of teaching methods used to train set designers that focus too much on detail without giving the student a feel for the totality of the undertaking.

181 Arenhill, Jan. "Seminarium om teatersäkerhet." (A Seminar on Theatre Safety.) *ProScen.* 1998; 22(2): 10-13. B&W. Lang.: Swe.
France: Paris. 1998. Historical studies. ▪A report from the ACTSAFE conference organized by the Centre d'Information Professionnelle aux Techniques du Spectacle, Theatre Technicians Training Services, and Deutsche Theatertechnische Gesellschaft, where all sorts of risks of the daily work at theatres were scrutinized, with reference to the training of technicians.

182 Lecat, Jean-Guy; Vinter, Marie, transl. "Det levende rum." (The Living Space.) *TE.* 1998 July; 89: 7-11. Illus.: Photo. B&W. 3. Lang.: Dan.
France. Denmark. 1975-1998. Histories-sources. ▪Set designer Jean-Guy Lecat writes about his cooperation with Peter Brook and the importance of finding a theatrical space that takes into consideration both the actors and intimacy with the audience.

183 Winkelsesser, Karin. "Hält die Verbindung zwischen 'Kunst und Kommerz'." (Keep Connection Between 'Art and Commerce'.) *BtR.* 1998; 2: 67-68. Illus.: Photo. Color. 1. Lang.: Ger.
France: Paris. 1998. Historical studies. ▪Impressions from the 13th Salon de Théâtre at Paris and the part of set and costume design and training institutions.

184 "Firmen stellen sich vor." (Companies Present Themselves.) *BtR.* 1998; 3: 60-89. Lang.: Ger.
Germany. 1998. Technical studies. ▪Companies related to stage equipment present their products and activities.

185 Ebeling, Robert; Winkelsesser, Karin. "Ein zu wenig beachtetes szenisches Element: das Kostüm." (A Scenic Element Given Too Little Attention: Costume.) *BtR.* 1998; 5: 13-17. Illus.: Design. Photo. Color. 4. Lang.: Ger.
Germany. 1995-1998. Histories-sources. ▪Set and costume designer Robert Ebeling depicts his typical work day as freelance artist in a fictive short drama. Also includes an interview with him about the subject of costumes.

186 Gardner, Carl. "The European Market." *LD&A.* 1998 Oct.; 28(10): 49-51. Illus.: Photo. Color. B&W. 14. Lang.: Eng.
Germany: Hannover. 1998. Historical studies. ▪Survey of the 1998 World Light Fair which focuses on new equipment and trends.

187 Grosser, Helmut. "Walther Unruh—Werk und Wirkung." (Walther Unruh—His Work and Influence.) *BtR.* 1998; 3: 48-59. Illus.: Photo. B&W. Color. 6. Lang.: Ger.
Germany. 1898-1998. Biographical studies. ▪Lecture commemorating the 100th anniversary of the birth of Walther Unruh, architect and innovator in stage technology. Uses Unruh's career as a framework for a discussion of twentieth-century German theatre technology and its exponents.

188 Keller, Max. "Faszination Licht." (Fascination Light.) *BtR.* 1998; 1: 8-16. Append. Illus.: Photo. B&W. Color. 42. Lang.: Ger.
Germany: Munich. 1997. Histories-sources. ▪Lighting designer at Münchner Kammerspiele describes lighting concepts, various kinds of lighting and their implementation in theatre, concepts of technical implementations (sources of light, the use of industry lighting, color and filter, light and space).

189 Mäcken, Walter. "Ausbildungsberufe 2000." (Qualified Jobs 2000.) *BtR.* 1998; 3: 16-36. Append. Illus.: Photo. B&W. Color. 6. Lang.: Ger.
Germany. Austria. 1998. Histories-sources. ▪Account of how to become a professional theatrical technician and engineer: the educational and real-world requirements. Also remarks on other theatrical support disciplines, particularly costuming.

190 Mihan, Jörg. "Vom Bühnenbild zur ästhetischen Gesamtverantwortung." (From Set Design to Complete Aesthetic Responsibility.) *TZ.* 1998; 6: 16-19. Illus.: Photo. B&W. 6. Lang.: Ger.
Germany. 1953. Biographical studies. ▪Portrait of the scenographer Klaus Noack from his education in set and costume design, his works at Berliner Ensemble, and his direction at Volkstheater Rostock and Freie Kammerspielen Magdeburg.

191 Molloy, Jacqueline. "Another Iceberg Heard From." *TCI.* 1998 July; 32(7): 11. Illus.: Dwg. Color. 1. Lang.: Eng.
Germany: Münster, Leipzig. Australia: Perth. 1998. Technical studies. ▪Scenic elements designed by Robert Schiller, in which is constructed a faux Titanic, for the German group of street performers Theater Titanick's performance of their collaborative show *Titanic* in a public park during the Festival of Perth.

192 Winkelsesser, Karin. "Licht-Einstellungen." (Light-Views.) *BtR.* 1998; 1: 26-30. Illus.: Photo. B&W. 3. Lang.: Ger.
Germany. 1998. Histories-sources. ▪Interviews with technical director Uwe Arsand at Berliner Ensemble, director and actress Katja Paryla at Nationaltheater Weimar, director and set designer Michael Simon at Schaubühne Berlin, and the critic Michael Merschmeier on the meaning of lighting in theatre today.

193 Bőgel, József. "Album Bárdy Margit színpadi tervezőművészetéről." (An Album on the Art of Costume

THEATRE IN GENERAL: —Design/technology

Designer Margit Bárdy.) *SFo.* 1997/1998; 24/25(3-4, 1-2): 66-68. Illus.: Photo. B&W. 2. Lang.: Hun.
Hungary. Germany: Munich. 1929-1997. Technical studies. ■A biographical introduction to an album about the activity of costume designer Margit Bárdy living in Germany after 1956.

194 Boschán, Daisy, et al., ed. *Díszletek és jelmezek.* (Set and Costume Designs.) Budapest: Do-Int Stúdió; 1998. 77 pp. Pref. Append. Illus.: Design. Photo. B&W. Color. Lang.: Hun.
Hungary. 1957-1991. Histories-sources. ■An album of the works by set and costume designer Péter Makai (1932-1991).

195 Kiss, Krisztina. "Bolyongás a térben." (Wandering in Space.) *Ellenfény.* 1998; 3(4): 58-59. Illus.: Photo. B&W. 4. Lang.: Hun.
Hungary: Budapest. 1998. Critical studies. ■A brief survey of designers' exhibition at the Art Hall, Budapest, June 19-August 16, 1998.

196 Kovács, Dezső. "Elvarázsolt kastély, avagy tervezők labirintusában." (The Miracle Castle, or in the Maze of Designers.) *Sz.* 1998; 31(12): 45-48. Illus.: Photo. B&W. 7. Lang.: Hun.
Hungary: Budapest. 1998. Critical studies. ■A report on 'Spectacle,' an exhibition of environments and sets by Hungarian designers at Budapest's Art Hall.

197 Szegő, György, ed. *Látvány: Magyar művészet a színház és a film között.* (Spectacle: Hungarian Art Between the Theatre and Film.) Budapest: Műcsarnok; 1998. 76 pp. Illus.: Photo. Design. Dwg. B&W. Color. 97. Lang.: Hun.
Hungary: Budapest. 1998. Histories-sources. ■The catalogue of an exhibition arranged at the Art Hall in Budapest, June 19-August 16.

198 Moen, Debi. "Sci-Fi Supermarket." *LD&A.* 1998 Mar.; 28(3): 34-38. Illus.: Photo. Color. 5. Lang.: Eng.
Ireland. 1997. Technical studies. ■Willie Williams' futuristic designs that fuse elements of video and lighting for rock band U2's world tour in 1997.

199 Bucci, Moreno. *Il teatro di Galileo Chini.* (The Theatre of Galileo Chini.) Florence: Maschietto & Musolino; 1998. 111 pp. Biblio. Illus.: Dwg. Sketches. Photo. Print. B&W. Lang.: Ita.
Italy. 1908-1956. Histories-sources. ■Catalogue of an exhibition of the scenographies for theatre and opera of Galileo Chini.

200 Clark, Mike. "Ado Cantin." *TCI.* 1998 Feb.; 32(2): 30. Illus.: Photo. Color. 2. Lang.: Eng.
Italy: Verona. 1967-1998. Technical studies. ■Profile of set designer/builder Ado Cantin.

201 Clark, Mike. "Light Years." *LDim.* 1998 Jan-Feb.; 22(1): 46-49, 81-83. Illus.: Photo. Color. 9. Lang.: Eng.
Italy. 1946-1998. Critical studies. ■Examines the theatre lighting design work and career of Guido Baroni and his daughter Lucilla Baroni.

202 De Chirico, Giorgio. *Memorie della mia vita.* (Memories of My Life.) Milan: Bompiani; 1998. 304 pp. Pref. Biblio. Illus.: Photo. Dwg. Sketches. B&W. 24. Lang.: Ita.
Italy. 1888-1978. Histories-sources. ■A new edition of the 1962 autobiography of Italian painter and scenographer Giorgio De Chirico.

203 Greenwald, Helen M. "Realism on the Stage: Belasco, Puccini, and the California Sunset." 279-296 in Radice, Mark A., ed. *Opera in Context: Essays on Historical Staging from the Late Renaissance to the Time of Puccini.* Portland, OR: Amadeus P; 1998. 410 pp. Notes. Index. Tables. Biblio. Lang.: Eng.
Italy. USA. 1890-1910. Historical studies. ■The effect of stage lighting on the development of realism and naturalism in theatre and opera. Considers the use of lighting as a narrative and artistic element in the original productions of David Belasco's *Girl of the Golden West* (1905) and Puccini's opera *La Fanciulla del West* (1910).

204 Vescovo, Marisa; Levi, Paolo. *E. Guglielminetti. Pittura e scultura.* (E. Guglielminetti: Painting and Sculpture.) Rome: Elede; 1998. 203 pp. Illus.: Dwg. Sketches. Pntg. 9. [Two vols.] Lang.: Ita.
Italy. 1961-1997. Biographical studies. ■The paintings and sculptures by the Italian painter and scenographer Eugenio Guglielminetti.

205 Kleinas, Levas. "Lietuvos Operos ir baleto Teatro—ny utrustning lyser upp framtiden." (The Lithuanian Opera and Ballet Theatre—New Lighting Equipment Lights Up the Future.) *ProScen.* 1998, vo 22(1): 42-45, 77. Illus.: Photo. Color. Lang.: Swe, Eng, Ger.
Lithuania: Vilnius. 1974-1998. Technical studies. ■A presentation of the lighting equipment at Lietuvos Valstybinis Operos ir Baleto Teatro, modernized thanks to a bilateral Italian-Lithuanian Fund, with reference to a Lithuanian text machine.

206 Kull, Gustaf. "Utbildning och teknik möts i Amsterdam." (Education and Technique Meet at Amsterdam.) *ProScen.* 1998; 22(4): 32-33. Illus.: Photo. B&W. Lang.: Swe.
Netherlands: Amsterdam. 1998. Historical studies. ■Report from the meeting of OISTAT and Verenigung voor Podiumtechnologie about education of technicians, with reference to Amsterdam's Theaterschool.

207 Lemmerman, Hans, ed.; Lonink, Miranda, ed. *Sprekende theaterbeelden. Zestien hedendaagse theatervormgevers.* (Speaking Theatre Images: Sixteen Contemporary Theatre Designers.) Arnhem: De Zwaluw; 1998. 179 pp. Illus.: Graphs. Photo. B&W. Color. 140. Lang.: Dut.
Netherlands. 1990-1998. Historical studies. ■An overview of the work of younger designers working for the Dutch theatre.

208 Vries, Lyckle de. *Gerard de Lairesse. An Artist Between Stage and Studio.* Amsterdam: Amsterdam UP; 1998. 220 pp. Index. Notes. Biblio. Pref. Illus.: Photo. Plan. Dwg. B&W. Color. 68. Lang.: Eng.
Netherlands. 1640-1711. Biographies. ■Examines the seventeenth-century painter Gerard de Lairesse, who frequently designed and painted stage productions.

209 "The 1998 Progress Report." *LD&A.* 1998 Nov.; 28(11): 41-60. Illus.: Photo. Color. B&W. 117. Lang.: Eng.
North America. 1998. Technical studies. ■The Illumination Engineering Society of North America's report on the best of equipment, literature, accessories, and design in the world of architectural and theatrical lighting design and application.

210 Bierke, Astrid. "En siste medling fra NoTT98." (A Last Report From NoTT98.) *ProScen.* 1998; 22(3): 12-13. Illus.: Photo. B&W. Lang.: Nor.
Norway: Oslo. 1998. Historical studies. ■Survey of NoTT98 at Oslo.

211 Jacobsson, Rigg-Olle. "Personflygning på Oslo Nye Teater." (Flying Person at Oslo Nye Teater.) *ProScen.* 1998; 22(4) : 6-10. Illus.: Photo. B&W. Lang.: Swe.
Norway: Oslo. 1998. Technical studies. ■A report from the seminar about flying on stage, with references to the technical aspects, harnesses, and safety.

212 Guderian-Czaplińska, Ewa. "Tadeusz Orłowicz." *PaT.* 1998; 47(1-2): 225-259. Notes. Illus.: Photo. Poster. B&W. 12. Lang.: Pol.
Poland: Cracow. Germany: Neubrandenburg. UK-England: London. 1907-1976. Biographical studies. ■The life and work of Polish scenographer Tadeusz Orłowicz in Poland, in Polish POW-theatres in Germany, and in post-World War II London.

213 Batasova, M. "Otpusti, pečal', otpusti..." (Let Go, Sadness, Let Go...)*Russkaja provincija.* 1998; 2: 63-64. Lang.: Rus.
Russia: Tver'. 1998. Biographical studies. ■Profile of scene designer N. Panova.

214 Cunningham, Rebecca. "The Russian Women Artist/Designers of the Avant-Garde." *TD&T.* 1998 Spr; 34(2): 38-51. Biblio. Gloss. Illus.: Photo. Design. Color. B&W. 13. Lang.: Eng.
Russia. USSR. 1880-1949. Historical studies. ■History of female theatrical designers of the Russian avant-garde movement such as Natalija Gončarova, Ljubov Popova, Aleksandra Ekster, Sonia Delaunay, and Varvara Stepanova.

215 Kumankov, Jėvgenij. *Vospominanija. Grafika. Živopis'. Teatr. Kino.* (Recollections. Graphics, Art, Theatre, Cinema.) Moscow: Galart; 1998. 156 pp. Lang.: Rus.
Russia. 1998. Histories-sources. ■Scene designer Jėvgenij Kumankov on his life and art.

THEATRE IN GENERAL: —Design/technology

216 Sel'vinskaja, T. "Propavšij sjužet." (The Lost Episode.) *Avtograf.* 1998; 3: 42-45. Lang.: Rus.
Russia. 1998. Histories-sources. ■Author, artist, and scenographer Tatjana Sel'vinskaja on her work.

217 Strutinskaja, E.I. *Iskanija chudožnikov teatra: Petersburg—Petrograd—Leningrad, 1910-1920-e gg.* (Scene Designers of Theatres: Petersburg—Petrograd—Leningrad, 1910-1920s.) Moscow: 1998. 246 pp. Lang.: Rus.
Russia: St. Petersburg. 1910-1929. Historical studies. ■Two decades of St. Petersburg scene design.

218 Gabršek-Prosenc, Meta. *Maks Kavčič 1909-1973—med sliko in sceno.* (Maks Kavčič 1909-1973—Between Painting and Scenery.) Maribor: The Art Gallery; 1998. 223 pp. Index. Biblio. Illus.: Photo. B&W. Color. 24. Lang.: Slo.
Slovenia. 1945-1972. Histories-specific. ■A survey of the life and work of the Slovene painter Maks Kavčič, who worked as a scenographer in the theatres of Ljubljana and Maribor. Includes a complete list of his scenographic works.

219 Hočevar, Meta. *Prostori igre.* (Performance Spaces.) Ljubljana: Mestno gledališče ljubljansko; 1998. 97 pp. (Knjižnica Mestnega gledališča ljubljanskega 127.) Index. Illus.: Dwg. B&W. 7. Lang.: Slo.
Slovenia. 1997. Instructional materials. ■Director, set designer, and architect Hočevar describes the basic characteristics and functions of stage spaces within a production as well as props, such as doors, chairs, water, and clothing.

220 Jacobsson, Rigg-Olle. "Ur Riggarens låda." (From the Box of the Rigger.) *ProScen.* 1998; 22(5): 46. Illus.: Photo. B&W. Lang.: Swe.
Sweden: Stockholm. 1998. Technical studies. ■Important information about the wires of the truss, how to lock them properly and how to control the thimbles.

221 Johansson, Ove. "AVAB i ny tappning." (AVAB in a New Version.) *ProScen.* 1998; 22(5): 18. Illus.: Photo. Color. Lang.: Swe.
Sweden: Stockholm. 1998. Technical studies. ■Profile of the lighting equipment company AVAB Scandinavia AB after its restructuring.

222 Kristoffersson, Birgitta. "På språng med Lennart Mörk." (On the Way With Lennart Mörk.) *Dramat.* 1998; 6 (2): 14-17. Illus.: Photo. Color. Lang.: Swe.
Sweden: Stockholm. France: Paris. 1958-1998. Histories-sources. ■Interview with the set designer Lennart Mörk about his career and cooperation with directors like Alf Sjöberg and Ingmar Bergman, with reference to his scenography for Wagner's *Tristan und Isolde* produced by Stein Winge at Opéra Bastille.

223 Nielsen, Ulf. "Möte kring ett ljusbord." (A Meeting Around a Lighting Control.) *ProScen.* 1998; 22(5): 16-17. Illus.: Photo. B&W. Lang.: Swe.
Sweden: Stockholm. 1998. Historical studies. ■Report from a meeting of light operators about the VLC light controls at Dansens Hus.

224 Sandström, Ulf. "Från grundläggande *Ljusteknik* till *Stage Lighting Controls.*" (From the Fundamental *Ljusteknik* To *Stage Lighting Controls.*) *ProScen.* 1998; 22(5): 20-22. Illus.: Photo. B&W. Color. Lang.: Swe.
Sweden. USA. 1992-1997. Critical studies. ■The author's view of the development of lighting since the advent of computer use, with reference to his books *Ljusteknik* and *Stage Lighting Controls* (Oxford & Boston: Focal Press, 1997).

225 Svenstam, Åke. "Från hantverk till ingenjörskonst." (From Handicraft To Engineering.) *ProScen.* 1998; 22(2): 24-26. Illus.: Photo. B&W. Lang.: Swe.
Sweden: Malmö. 1998. Technical studies. ■Examines new academic education of stage hands and technicians for the theatre at Malmö Högskola.

226 Thorell, Bernt. "Frisse lämnar ett stort tomrum efter sig." (Frisse Leaves a Great Blank Behind Him.) *ProScen.* 1998 ; 22(2): 7-9. Illus.: Photo. B&W. Lang.: Swe.
Sweden: Solna. 1920-1998. Biographical studies. ■Obituary of the man who oversaw technical rehabilitation of the restored Södra Teatern to a real theatre and as an one-time editor of the journal *ProScen*: Karl-Gunnar Frisell, alias Frisse.

227 Thorell, Bernt. "Nott en Sttf-produkt." (NoTT A Product of STTF.) *ProScen.* 1998; 22(3): 7-10. Illus.: Photo. B&W. Lang.: Swe.
Sweden: Stockholm, Gothenburg. 1983-1998. Historical studies. ■Short history of the combined conference and fair Nordisk TeaterTeknik (NoTT) and the ideas behind the concept.

228 Abdel-Latif, Mahmoud Hammam. *Rhythmic Space and Rhythmic Movement: The Adolphe Appia/Jaques-Dalcroze Collaboration.* Columbus, OH: Ohio State Univ; 1988. 178 pp. Biblio. Notes. [Ph.D. Dissertation, Univ. Microfilms Order No. AAC 8907181.] Lang.: Eng.
Switzerland. 1906-1915. Histories-specific. ■The influence of composer and music educator Émile Jaques-Dalcroze 'eurhythmics' rhythm movement on designer/theorist Adolphe Appia's 'rhythmic space' in stage settings.

229 Barbour, David; Lampert-Gréaux, Ellen. "PLASA's 21st Anniversary." *LDim.* 1998 Oct.; 22(10): 122-159. Lang.: Eng.
UK-England: London. 1998. Historical studies. ■Review of exhibits for the Professional Lighting and Sound Associations show in September.

230 Barbour, David; Lampert-Gréaux, Ellen; McHugh, Catherine. "PLASA." *TCI.* 1998 Nov.; 32(10): 68-83. Lang.: Eng.
UK-England: London. 1998. Historical studies. ■Report on the Professional Lighting and Sound Associations trade show held in London.

231 Emeljanow, Victor. "Erasing the Spectator: Observations on Nineteenth Century Lighting." *THSt.* 1998; 53: 107-116. Notes. Lang.: Eng.
UK-England. 1820-1906. Historical studies. ■The impact of lighting on the relationship between the stage and its spectators in the auditorium.

232 Howard, Pamela. "Ralph Koltai: Landscapes of the Theatre." *TD&T.* 1998 Spr; 34(2): 22-26. Illus.: Photo. Color. 12. Lang.: Eng.
UK-England. 1944-1998. Historical studies. ■Profile of set designer Koltai.

233 Lampert-Gréaux, Ellen. "AC Lighting." *TCI.* 1998 Aug/Sep.; 32(8): 40. Illus.: Photo. Color. 2. Lang.: Eng.
UK-England. 1998. Technical studies. ■Profile of the lighting technology manufacterer AC Lighting Ltd., specializing in design and manufacture of lighting consoles.

234 Maiman, William L. "Behind the Scenes." *TCI.* 1998 Aug/Sep.; 32(8): 40-41. Illus.: Photo. Color. 1. Lang.: Eng.
UK-England. USA. 1998. Technical studies. ■Report on the North American warehouse of theatrical lighting equipment owned and operated by AC Lighting Ltd.

235 Moles, Steve. "The Live! Show." *TCI.* 1998 May; 32(5): 19-20. Lang.: Eng.
UK-England: London. 1998. Technical studies. ■Report on the equipment fair showcasing theatrical lighting and sound gear.

236 Nobling, Torsten. "Mycket att se på årets Plasa." (A Lot to See At the PLASA This Year.) *ProScen.* 1998; 22(5): 39-43. Illus.: Photo. B&W. Lang.: Swe.
UK-England: London. 1998. ■Report from the twenty-first PLASA Light & Sound Show.

237 Vincent, Renée. "The Influences of Isadora Duncan on the Designs of Edward Gordon Craig." *TD&T.* 1998 Win; 34(1): 37-48. Biblio. Illus.: Design. Color. B&W. 11. Lang.: Eng.
UK-England. 1904-1905. Technical studies. ■Examines the influence of dancer Isadora Duncan's friendship on the designs of Craig.

238 "The 1997 TCI Sound Products of the Year." *TCI.* 1998 Feb.; 32(2): 32-33. Illus.: Photo. Color. 6. Lang.: Eng.
USA. 1997. Technical studies. ■A rating of the best new theatrical sound equipment available in 1997.

239 "The 1997 TCI Lighting Products of the Year." *TCI.* 1998 Mar.; 32(3): 30-31. Lang.: Eng.
USA. 1997. Technical studies. ■A rating of the best new theatrical lighting products available in 1997.

THEATRE IN GENERAL: —Design/technology

240 "LDI98: The Workshops." *TCI.* 1998 Oct.; 32(9): 36-42. Lang.: Eng.
USA: Las Vegas, NV. 1998. Historical studies. ■Calendar of workshops and seminars scheduled for the LDI98 conference.

241 "Buyers Guide 1998." *TCI.* 1998 Dec.; 32(11): 19-203. Index. Lang.: Eng.
USA. 1998. Instructional materials. ■A guide to manufacturers and equipment for lighting, scenic, sound, costuming, projections, make-up, and special effects equipment. Contains a directory of website addresses for technical equipment manufacturers and servers.

242 "Industry Resources Special Issue." *TCI.* 1998 June; 32(6): 1-220. Illus.: Photo. Color. 2. Lang.: Eng.
USA. 1998. Instructional materials. ■Entire issue devoted to an Industry Resources guide for equipment and services.

243 "Special Report: The 1997 TCI Awards." *TCI.* 1998 Jan.; 32(1): 22-23. Illus.: Photo. B&W. 4. Lang.: Eng.
USA. 1998. Technical studies. ■On the 1998 Theatre Crafts International Awards given to theatre architect Hugh Hardy, lighting designer Lewis Lee, director/designer Julie Taymor, and composer/sound designer David Van Tieghem.

244 "Exhibiting in Phoenix." *LDim.* 1998 Oct.; 22(10): 118-121. Lang.: Eng.
USA: Phoenix, AZ. 1998. Historical studies. ■List of exhibitors and booth numbers for the 1998 LDI convention.

245 "1998 IESNA Software Survey." *LD&A.* 1998 Oct.; 28(10): 53-62. Lang.: Eng.
USA. 1998. Technical studies. ■Survey of manufacturers of computer software to assist in lighting design.

246 "Lighting Dimensions 1998-99 Buyers Guide." *LDim.* 1998 Aug.; 22(7): 1-268. Illus.: Photo. Color. 450. Lang.: Eng.
USA. 1998. ■Entire issue devoted to buyers guide for lighting equipment and services for the industry.

247 "Lighting Dimensions 1998 Industry Resources Guide." *LDim.* 1998 Dec.; 22(11): 1-272. Illus.: Photo. Color. 46. Lang.: Eng.
USA. 1998. ■Entire issue devoted to 1998 Industry Resources Guide.

248 "Back to School: Brush Up Old Skills or Learn New Ones at LDI Workshops." *LDim.* 1998 Oct.; 22(9): 102-110. Lang.: Eng.
USA: Phoenix, AZ. 1998. Historical studies. ■Details upcoming workshops at the 98 LDI expo—from hands-on tutorials to panel discussions.

249 "USITT Lighting Design Commission: Portfolio Guidelines for Designers." *TD&T.* 1998 Win; 34(1): 59-66. Tables. Illus.: Photo. Lighting. Color. B&W. 7. Lang.: Eng.
USA. 1998. Instructional materials. ■United States Institute for Theatre Technology's guidelines for professional portfolio building for the lighting designer.

250 "1998-1999 USITT Membership Directory." *TD&T.* 1998; 34(4): 1-192. Lang.: Eng.
USA. 1998-1999. ■Membership directory for the United States Institute for Theatre Technology (USITT).

251 "USITT Design Exhibition 1998." *TD&T.* 1998 Sum; 34(3): 37-52. Illus.: Design. Dwg. Photo. Sketches. Color. B&W. 45. Lang.: Eng.
USA: Long Beach, CA. 1998. Historical studies. ■Report on the 1998 United States Institute for Theatre Technology's 1998 exposition in Long Beach, CA, with emphasis on young designers, including costumers Nic Ularu, Linda Pisano, Cameron Lee Roberts, Nancy Hills, Christine P. Duffield, Laura Crow, Alexandra Bonds, D. Bartlett Blair, set designers Tony Andrea, Troy Hourie, John Iacovelli, Grace Williams, and light designer R. Lee Kennedy.

252 "My Old School." *TCI.* 1998 Oct.; 32(9): 68-74. Illus.: Photo. Dwg. Color. 6. Lang.: Eng.
USA. 1998. Histories-sources. ■Professional theatrical designers of all disciplines share information about their schools and the training they received there. Includes a list of universities in the United States offering degrees in professional theatrical design and technology. Participants are: Campbell Baird, Susan Benson, Gabriel Berry, Marie Anne Chiment, Jeff Croiter, David Gallo, Jon Gottlieb, David Grill, Willa Kim, James Kronzer, Scott Lehrer, Peter Maradudin, Neil Patel, Carrie Robbins, Tom Ruzika, Narelle Sissons, Sal Tagliarino, David Woolard.

253 Arthur, Thomas H. "The Heritage of Paul Reinhardt." *TD&T.* 1998 Sum; 34(3): 68-71. Illus.: Dwg. Photo. Color. B&W. 12. Lang.: Eng.
USA. 1998. Biographical studies. ■Life and career of the veteran costumer.

254 Barbour, David. "Broadway Lighting Master Classes." *TCI.* 1998 Mar.; 32(3): 19-21 ia. Illus.: Photo. Color. 7. Lang.: Eng.
USA: New York, NY. 1997. Historical studies. ■Report on the conference for lighting designers, held December 11-14, 1997, in New York.

255 Barbour, David. "David Gallo." *TCI.* 1998 Apr.; 32(4): 30-33. Illus.: Photo. B&W. Color. 18. Lang.: Eng.
USA. 1988-1998. Biographical studies. ■Career of set designer Gallo.

256 Barbour, David. "ESTA Unveils Code of Conduct." *TCI.* 1998 July; 32(7): 14-15, 17. Lang.: Eng.
USA. 1998. Historical studies. ■Report on the Entertainment Services and Technology Association's new code of ethical practices regarding protocols of professional entertainment technology businesses. It was issued as a guideline, and not law.

257 Barbour, David. "In Memoriam: Francis P. De Verna." *TCI.* 1998 Aug/Sep.; 32(8): 24-25. Lang.: Eng.
USA. 1928-1998. Biographical studies. ■Obituary and tribute to the stagehand, lighting expert, and founder of the Four Star Lighting Company.

258 Barbour, David. "The Unexpected Kevin Adams." *LDim.* 1998 Nov.; 22(10): 96-101, 165-167. Illus.: Photo. B&W. 13. Lang.: Eng.
USA. 1979-1998. Historical studies. ■Lighting designer Kevin Adams and his career on Broadway, Off Broadway, and in regional theatre.

259 Bell, Deborah. "Job Hunting? Make That Interview Count!" *SoTh.* 1998 Spr; 39(2): 20-23. Illus.: Photo. 3. Lang.: Eng.
USA. 1998. Instructional materials. ■Job hunting tips for costumers and other theatrical occupations at the 1998 SETC Convention.

260 Bell, Deborah. "From MacBird! to Peter Pan: Costume Designer Jeanne Button Shares Insights." *SoTh.* 1998 Sum; 39(3): 26-27. Illus.: Photo. B&W. 2. Lang.: Eng.
USA. 1965-1998. Historical studies. ■Costume designer Jeanne Button discusses her career in Broadway and Off Broadway theatre.

261 Bergen, Jim van. "Chicago Blues." *TCI.* 1998 Feb.; 32(2): 52-53. Illus.: Photo. Color. 2. Lang.: Eng.
USA: Chicago, IL. 1996-1997. Histories-sources. ■Sound designer for the the Chicago version of the Blue Man Group's *Tubes* at the Briar Street Theatre, discusses the difference in design from the New York show at the Astor Place Theatre.

262 Bloom, Thomas Alan. *Kenneth Macgowan and the Aesthetic Paradigm for the New Stagecraft in America.* Ann Arbor, MI: Univ. of Michigan; 1987. 175 pp. Notes. Biblio. [Ph.D. Dissertation, Univ. Microfilms Order No. AAC 8712074.] Lang.: Eng.
USA. 1912-1940. Critical studies. ■Analysis of critic Kenneth Macgowan's writings on the European 'new stagecraft' in America.

263 Blythe, Keith. "A Pneumatically Tripped, Circular Curtain." *TechB.* 1998 Oct.: 1-2. Illus.: Plan. Diagram. B&W. 4. [TB 1311.] Lang.: Eng.
USA. 1998. Technical studies. ■Plans for rigging a pneumatically activated curtain on a circular track on a tight budget.

264 Boepple, Leanne. "In Memoriam: Samuel Resnick." *TCI.* 1998 May; 32(5): 16. Lang.: Eng.
USA. 1918-1998. Biographical studies. ■Obituary for the co-founder of Barbizon, a worldwide distributor of electrical and video equipment for the entertainment industry.

265 Boepple, Leanne. "In Memoriam: James Tilton." *TCI.* 1998 July; 32(7): 13. Lang.: Eng.
USA. 1938-1998. Biographical studies. ■Obituary for the set and lighting designer.

THEATRE IN GENERAL: —Design/technology

266 Broh, Michael. "Simple and Inexpensive Stained Glass." *TechB.* 1998 Oct.: 1-2. Illus.: Photo. B&W. 3. [TB 1312.] Lang.: Eng.
USA. 1998. Technical studies. ■Inexpensively creating the look of stained glass using vinyl, weather stripping, and three different painting techniques.

267 Busch, April. "Shop-Made Naugahyde." *TechB.* 1998 Jan.: 1-2. Illus.: Photo. B&W. 1. [TB 1304.] Lang.: Eng.
USA. 1998. Technical studies. ■Process to treat muslin to look like Naugahyde furniture upholstery.

268 Cavnar, Matt. "Easy Listening." *TCI.* 1998 Aug/Sep.; 32(8): 22-23. Illus.: Photo. Color. 1. Lang.: Eng.
USA: New Haven, CT. 1998. Technical studies. ■Appraisal of the new sound system installed at John Lyman center for the Performing Arts on the campus of Southern Connecticut State University.

269 Duggan, Robert. "Flipping Trap Unit." *TechB.* 1998 Jan.: 1-3. Illus.: Plan. B&W. 3. [TB 1305.] Lang.: Eng.
USA. 1998. Technical studies. ■Plans, construction, and operation of cheap and easy to build double-faced trap unit.

270 Duggan, Robert. "Tube Steel Perimeter Framing for Flats." *TechB.* 1998 Apr.: 1-2. Illus.: Plan. B&W. 3. [TB 1310.] Lang.: Eng.
USA. 1998. Technical studies. ■Description and plans for building large flats with frames constructed with tubular steel.

271 Elia, Susan. "Of Mice and Muppets." *Dm.* 1998 Dec.; 72(12): 62-65. Illus.: Photo. B&W. Color. 6. Lang.: Eng.
USA. 1935-1998. Biographical studies. ■Costumer Kermit Love, whose career has spanned six decades in the areas of film, dance, theatre, and television.

272 Ellis, Morris Ray. *A Catalog: The Robert L.B. Tobin Collection: Scene Designs: Sixteenth Through Nineteenth Centuries.* Lubbock, TX: Texas Tech Univ; 1987. 259 pp. Biblio. Notes. [Ph.D. Dissertation, Univ. Microfilms Order No. 8806001.] Lang.: Eng.
USA. Europe. 1500-1900. Historical studies. ■Details of project collecting available data, photographing, and cataloging all the original renderings and lithographs of scene designs from the sixteenth through the nineteenth centuries held in the Robert L. B. Tobin Collection.

273 Forbes, Jeff. "Rosco's Horizon." *TCI.* 1998 Feb.; 32(2): 51. Illus.: Photo. Design. Color. 2. Lang.: Eng.
USA. 1998. Technical studies. ■Review of the Rosco/Entertainment Technology Inc.'s new Rosco Horizon lighting software.

274 French, Liz. "Changing Times." *TCI.* 1998 Aug/Sep.; 32(8): 16-18. Illus.: Photo. Color. 1. Lang.: Eng.
USA: New York, NY. 1998. Technical studies. ■Appraisal of the sound system at the historic Mark Hellinger Theatre, now converted into a house of worship dedicated to the conversion of youth street gangs to Christianity.

275 French, Liz. "In Memoriam: Gary Whittington." *TCI.* 1998 Nov.; 32(10): 21. Lang.: Eng.
USA. 1952-1998. Technical studies. ■Obituary for lighting expert and sales manager for the equipment company High End Systems.

276 Gee, Elwyn; Bornhofen, Patricia; Israel, Chip; Winters, Jay; Schwab, Norm; Moen, Debi; Kaye, Ed. "Viva Las Vegas!" *LD&A.* 1998 May; 28(5): 30-72. Illus.: Photo. Color. 33. Lang.: Eng.
USA: Las Vegas, NV. 1998. Technical studies. ■Survey of light designs and equipment, both theatrical and architectural, used for the stages, themed entertainments, hotels, and casinos in Las Vegas.

277 Grauch, Arlene Evangelista. *A Comparison of Four Stage and Motion Picture Productions: Costumes Designed by Irene Sharaff.* Ann Arbor, MI: Univ. of Michigan; 1988. 266 pp. Notes. Biblio. [Ph.D. Dissertation, Univ. Microfilms Order No. 8907042.] Lang.: Eng.
USA. 1933-1976. Histories-specific. ■Comparative study of the methods and techniques used by costume designer Irene Sharaff in four Broadway productions: *The King and I, West Side Story, Flower Drum Song,* and *Funny Girl.*

278 Gregory, Paul; Burtner, Dave; Leslie, Russell; Ranieri, David; Speirs, Jonathan; English, Cheryl. "Lightfair International Seminar Preview." *LD&A.* 1998 Apr.; 28(4): 52-63. Illus.: Photo. Color. 4. Lang.: Eng.
USA: Las Vegas, NV. 1998. Technical studies. ■Preview of the 1998 Lightfair seminar in Las Vegas.

279 Hartmann, David. "Nearly 100 Compete in Design." *SoTh.* 1998 Sum; 39(3): 32. Illus.: Photo. B&W. 1. Lang.: Eng.
USA. 1998. Historical studies. ■Winners of the 1998 Kennedy Center/American College Theatre Festival design competitions.

280 Hill, Ann. "Phenomenon of the Opera." *LD&A.* 1998 Apr.; 28(4): 26-30. Illus.: Photo. Color. 4. Lang.: Eng.
USA: San Francisco, CA. 1998. Technical studies. ■Description of the new stage lighting system installed at the War Memorial Opera House.

281 Hogan, Jane. "Michael Gottlieb." *TCI.* 1998 Feb.; 32(2): 28. Illus.: Photo. B&W. 1. Lang.: Eng.
USA: New York, NY. 1998. Technical studies. ■Profile of lighting designer Michael Gottlieb.

282 Hogan, Jane. "Michael Brown." *TCI.* 1998 Apr.; 32(4): 21-22. Illus.: Photo. B&W. 1. Lang.: Eng.
USA. 1998. Biographical studies. ■Profile of lighting designer Michael Brown.

283 Immerwahr, Michael. "Improved Scene Shop Tuffets." *TechB.* 1998 Apr.: 1. Illus.: Plan. B&W. 1. [TB 1301a.] Lang.: Eng.
USA. 1998. Technical studies. ■Recommendation to build four-wheel tuffets for use in the scene-shop, as opposed to three-wheeled design offered in *TechB* 1301, 1997 Oct.

284 Johnson, David. "In Memoriam: Robert Mackintosh." *TCI.* 1998 Apr.; 32(4): 12. Lang.: Eng.
USA. 1926-1998. Biographical studies. ■Obituary for the costume designer for theatre, television, and nightclubs.

285 Johnson, David. "Sound Like an Egyptian." *TCI.* 1998 Feb.; 32(2): 13-15. Illus.: Photo. Color. 1. Lang.: Eng.
USA: Las Vegas, NV. 1998. Technical studies. ■Michael Cusick's (Specialized Audio-Visual Inc.) newly installed sound and video systems in the Luxor Hotel and Casino's twelve-hundred seat performance space.

286 Johnson, David. "Eastern Acoustic Works." *TCI.* 1998 Mar.; 32(3): 26-28 ia. Illus.: Photo. Color. 4. Lang.: Eng.
USA: Whitinsville, MA. 1996-1998. Historical studies. ■Report on the flourishing state of the sound system manufacturer in the aftermath of the fire which destroyed its manufacturing plant.

287 Johnson, David. "Sounding Off." *TCI.* 1998 Aug/Sep.; 32(8): 52-62. Illus.: Photo. Color. 14. Lang.: Eng.
USA. 1998. Histories-sources. ■Panel discussion among seven sound designers, Tony Meola, Brian Ronan, Guy Sherman, Jim van Bergen, John Gromada, Johnna Doty, and Dan Moses Schreier, regarding technology, environment, audience reaction, and unions.

288 Johnson, David. "NSCA." *TCI.* 1998 Aug/Sep.; 32(8): 63-68. Lang.: Eng.
USA: Las Vegas, NV. 1998. Historical studies. ■Report on the National Systems Contractors Association's NSCA 98 trade show for sound products and technolgy at the Las Vegas Convention Center.

289 Johnson, David. "AES 98." *TCI.* 1998 Dec.; 32(11): 9-18. Lang.: Eng.
USA: San Francisco, CA. 1998. Historical studies. ■Report on the Audio Engineering Society's tradeshow held in San Francisco, CA.

290 Johnson, David, ed. "The Design Challenges of Houses of Worship." *TCI.* 1998 July; 32(7): a1-a28. Illus.: Photo. Dwg. Color. 18. Lang.: Eng.
USA: Long Beach, CA. 1998. Critical studies. ■Special supplement to *TCI* 32:7, concerning the design problems faced by architects and lighting, sound, and support designers in planning houses of religious worship, and adapting existing houses to the needs of theatre and other public exhibitions.

291 Jones, Ellen E. "Imero Fiorentino: Distinguished Lighting Designer 1997." *TD&T.* 1998 Spr; 34(2): 8-13. Illus.: Photo. Color. B&W. 10. Lang.: Eng.

THEATRE IN GENERAL: —Design/technology

USA. 1998. Technical studies. ■Profile of the lighting designer on his being honored by USITT as its most distinguished designer for 1997.

292 Keller, Ron. "Sicangco Charms SETC." *SoTh.* 1998 Sum; 39(3): 25. Lang.: Eng.

USA: Birmingham, AL. 1998. Historical studies. ■Scenic and costume designer Eduardo Sicangco judges the SETC Design Competition.

293 Lampert-Gréaux, Ellen; Johnson, David; Boepple, Leanne; McHugh, Catherine. "That's Entertainment, Too!" *TCI.* 1998 May; 32(5): 33-41. Illus.: Photo. Color. 30. Lang.: Eng.

USA. 1998. Technical studies. ■Report on the explosion of entertainment technology being used in venues not often associated with the industry, such as corporate events, weddings, parties, and booth exhibits at trade shows.

294 Lampert-Gréaux, Ellen. "Updating with Ethernet: The Herberger Theatre Center Gets a Boost for the 90s." *LDim.* 1998 Oct.; 22(9): 42-44. Illus.: Photo. Lighting. B&W. 3. Lang.: Eng.

USA: Phoenix, AZ. 1998. Historical studies. ■Reports on ethernet computer connections for the Herberger Theatre Center. The connections link lighting between two theatres and were designed by Peter Rogers of Strand Lighting.

295 Lee, Cheng Heng. "Collapsible Change Booths Reduction." *TechB.* 1998 Apr.: 1-2. Tables. Illus.: Plan. B&W. 4. [TB 1309.] Lang.: Eng.

USA. 1998. Technical studies. ■Plans and material needed for the construction of collapsible change booths to be used for privacy when actors need to make quick changes.

296 Lile, Jim. "A Flying Rig for Low-Ceiling Theatres." *TechB.* 1998 Apr.: 1-2. Illus.: Plan. Diagram. B&W. 2. [TB 1307.] Lang.: Eng.

USA. 1998. Technical studies. ■Plans for building a fly-system for proscenium theatres with low ceilings.

297 MacQueen, Brian. "Two-Scene Sound Control." *TechB.* 1998 Oct.: 1-3. Illus.: Diagram. B&W. 2. [TB 1314.] Lang.: Eng.

USA. 1998. Technical studies. ■Plans and equipment used for building a two-scene sound controller that allows for playing two beds of sound to be played at one time and smoothly cross-fade when one set of sounds becomes more prominent than the other.

298 Mahfouz, Nazih Habib. *Toward an Aesthetic of Scenography Through Art and Movement-Space-Time.* Evanston, IL: Northwestern Univ; 1987. 248 pp. Biblio. Notes. [Ph.D. Dissertation, Univ. Microfilms Order No. AAC 8729018.] Lang.: Eng.

USA. 1987. Critical studies. ■Ontological approach to the aesthetics of scenography.

299 Maiman, William L. "Bride of Widgets We Love." *TCI.* 1998 Apr.; 32(4): 46-47. Illus.: Photo. B&W. 12. Lang.: Eng.

USA. 1998. Technical studies. ■Report on new and useful gadgets for the discerning technician.

300 Maiman, William L. "Beyond Vaudeville." *TCI.* 1998 Feb.; 32(2): 11-12. Illus.: Photo. Color. 1. Lang.: Eng.

USA: Muskegon, MI. 1998. Technical studies. ■Description of the updated sound system installed in the Frauenthal Theatre.

301 Maiman, William L. "In Memoriam: Glen Cunningham." *TCI.* 1998 Apr.; 32(4): 12. Lang.: Eng.

USA. 1956-1998. Biographical studies. ■Obituary for the lighting designer, who also was a lighting instrument designer.

302 Maiman, William L. "USITT." *TCI.* 1998 July; 32(7): 49-50. Lang.: Eng.

USA: Long Beach, CA. 1998. Historical studies. ■Report on the thirty-eighth annual Conference and Stage Expo of USITT.

303 Maiman, William L. "What to Look for on the Show Floor." *TCI.* 1998 Oct.; 32(9): 86-91. Lang.: Eng.

USA: Las Vegas, NV. 1998. Historical studies. ■Preview of the LDI98 tradeshow being held at the Las Vegas Hilton.

304 Maiman, William L. "Datatron Show Control System with Trax 3.6." *TCI.* 1998 Oct.; 32(9): 80-81. Illus.: Photo. Color. 2. Lang.: Eng.

USA. 1998. Technical studies. ■Appraisal of the Datatron control system for video projections, laser effects, and graphics.

305 Maiman, William L. "Phoenix Rising: A Preview of New Equipment Scheduled for LDI 98." *LDim.* 1998 Oct.; 22(9): 88-101. Illus.: Photo. B&W. 4. Lang.: Eng.

USA: Phoenix, AZ. 1998. Historical studies. ■Details theatrical lighting, sound, lasers, and other specialty equipment, as well as exhibitors of these products at the 98 LDI convention in Phoenix, AZ.

306 Marking, Martha A. "Technical: Polymer Clays Can Be Manipulated to Create Innovative, Inexpensive Theatrical Jewelry." *SoTh.* 1998 Win; 39(1): 30-32. Illus.: Photo. 5. Lang.: Eng.

USA. 1998. Technical studies. ■On the creation of theatrical jewelry from polymer clays. When combined with macrame, beads and other materials, period jewelry can be created at a reasonable cost.

307 Maurer, Katherine. "Jackpot!" *LD&A.* 1998 Jan.; 28(1): 32-34. Illus.: Photo. Color. 5. Lang.: Eng.

USA: Uncasville, CT. 1998. Technical studies. ■Lighting design for the Mohegan Sun Casino, which incorporates both traditional architectural and theatrical techniques.

308 McHugh, Catherine. "Sound & Vision." *TCI.* 1998 Feb.; 32(2): 42-50. Illus.: Photo. Sketches. Design. B&W. Color. 11. Lang.: Eng.

USA. 1996-1997. Technical studies. ■Stage, lighting, and sound design for The Rolling Stones North American concert tour with a sidebar listing designers, crews, and equipment involved.

309 McHugh, Catherine. "In Memoriam: Julian Winter." *TCI.* 1998 Oct.; 32(9): 28. Lang.: Eng.

USA. 1971-1998. Biographical studies. ■Obituary for the lighting technician who primarily worked as tour techie for rock concerts for the production company Light & Sound Design.

310 McHugh, Catherine. "Having It All." *LDim.* 1998 Oct.; 22(9): 46-56. Illus.: Photo. B&W. 7. Lang.: Eng.

USA. 1998. Historical studies. ■Lighting designer John Osborne talks about his design career, highlighting his beginnings in California and his theatre, film, and concert career as well as his growing career as a conference lighting designer.

311 Moeck, Martin. "Teacher's Pet Project." *LD&A.* 1998 Apr.; 28(4): 48-51. Illus.: Photo. Color. 5. Lang.: Eng.

USA: Lawrence, KS. 1998. Technical studies. ■Students at the University of Kansas discover photorealistic computer graphics as an effective design tool. Describes the ins and outs of the cutting-edge technology.

312 Moen, Debi. "Designs on Designers." *LD&A.* 1998 Feb.; 28(2): 38-41. Illus.: Photo. Color. 10. Lang.: Eng.

USA: New York, NY. 1995. Technical studies. ■Jan Kroeze's difficulties designing lights for the 1995 Council of Fashion Designers of America's Awards gala in 1995 at Lincoln Center.

313 Murphy, Mike. "Design: Students Collaborate to Recreate Art on Stage." *SoTh.* 1998 Spr; 39(2): 28-32. Illus.: Photo. 4. Lang.: Eng.

USA: Huntington, WV. 1996-1997. Historical studies. ■Lighting, set, and costume design students at Marshall University combine forces to recreate full scale paintings in a controlled environment. The experience was so successful that it is now part of the university's regular theatre training program.

314 Napoleon, Davi. "Daniel Ostling." *TCI.* 1998 Feb.; 32(2): 28-29. Illus.: Photo. B&W. Color. 2. Lang.: Eng.

USA: Chicago, IL. 1998. Technical studies. ■Profile of set designer Daniel Ostling.

315 Napoleon, Davi. "Catherine Zuber." *TCI.* 1998 Aug/Sep.; 32(8): 44-47. Illus.: Photo. Dwg. Design. B&W. Color. 27. Lang.: Eng.

USA. 1998. Biographical studies. ■Profile of costume designer Catherine Zuber.

316 Nelson, Brad. "Learning to Light." *LDim.* 1998 Oct.; 22(10): 112-116. Illus.: Photo. B&W. 3. Lang.: Eng.

USA: Las Vegas, NV. 1997. Histories-sources. ■A former LDI intern reflects on his college experience learning lighting design and his experiences as an intern at the 1997 conference.

THEATRE IN GENERAL: —Design/technology

317 Quigley, Patrick. "Making It in Nashville." *LD&A.* 1998 Jan.; 28(1): 38-40. Illus.: Photo. Color. 7. Lang.: Eng.
USA: Nashville, TN. 1998. Technical studies. ■Designer Quigley discusses the flexible lighting design he incorporated into the new Nashville Arena, which is adaptable to both sporting events and musical performances.

318 Rand, Herbert Carleton, II. *The Effect of the Absorptivity of Adjacent Walls on Loudspeaker Directivity.* Tallahassee, FL: Florida State Univ; 1987. 383 pp. Notes. Biblio. [Ph.D. Dissertation, Univ. Microfilms Order No. AAC 8802567.] Lang.: Eng.
USA. 1987. Empirical research. ■Loudspeaker directivity in theatre sound systems.

319 Rettig, Shane. "Inexpensive Digital Noise Reduction." *TechB.* 1998 Apr.: 1-2. Illus.: Diagram. B&W. 2. [TB 1308.] Lang.: Eng.
USA. 1998. Technical studies. ■Recommends the budget-conscious sound designer use the noise reduction software, 'SoundHack' available over the internet as an inexpensive alternative to expensive retail software.

320 Rubin, Judith. "Are You Experienced?" *TCI.* 1998 Apr.; 32(4): 34-38, 56-58. Illus.: Photo. Color. 13. Lang.: Eng.
USA: Las Vegas, NV. 1998. Technical studies. ■Report on the seventy-million dollar 'Star Trek: The Experience' attraction at the Las Vegas Hilton. Describes the sound, lighting, and scenic elements that attempt to give the visitor a feel for the outer-space atmosphere of the popular television series and its spinoffs, particularly *Star Trek: The Next Generation.*

321 Ryan, Jim. "Nylon Rollers Revisited." *TechB.* 1998 Jan.: 1-2. Illus.: Plan. B&W. 1. [TB 1303.] Lang.: Eng.
USA. 1998. Technical studies. ■Plans and construction for use of nylon rollers for a turntable. Variation of plans that appeared previously in *TechB* 1137, 1996 Apr.

322 Salzer, Beeb. "Dipping a Toe in the Ocean of Creativity." *TD&T.* 1998 Win; 34(1): 27-36. Notes. Illus.: Photo. Dwg. Sketches. Color. B&W. 5. Lang.: Eng.
USA. 1998. Critical studies. ■Light and set designer Salzer shares thoughts about creativity and beauty in the world of theatrical design. Designers Ming Cho Lee, Ralph Funicello, Peter Maradudin, Robert Israel, James Moody, Patricia Zipprodt, Tony Walton, George Tsypin, and Douglas W. Schmidt add their thoughts on the same subject.

323 Sammler, Ben, ed.; Harvey, Don, ed. "Index." *TechB.* 1998 Apr.: 1-6. [TB 1227-1310.] Lang.: Eng.
USA. 1998. Technical studies. ■Index for *TechB* volumes 11-17 categorized by subject: costumes, lighting, lighting effects, painting, props, rigging, safety, scenery, sound.

324 Schraft, Robin John. *An Investigation of Computer-Aided Theatrical Scenic and Lighting Design.* New York, NY: New York Univ; 1987. 243 pp. Biblio. Notes. [Ph.D. Dissertation, Univ. Microfilms Order No. AAC 8803603.] Lang.: Eng.
USA. 1980-1987. Technical studies. ■Investigates the application of computer-aided drafting and design (CADD) to theatrical scenic and lighting design. Also compares this technique with more traditional methods.

325 Schreiber, Loren. "The Basics of Stage Automation." *TD&T.* 1998 Sum; 34(3): 61-66. Biblio. Illus.: Diagram. Photo. Color. B&W. 3. Lang.: Eng.
USA. 1998. Technical studies. ■The ins and outs of stage automation, with an emphasis on how it has revolutionized set design.

326 Simmons, Pat. "Musser Discusses Career in Lighting Design." *SoTh.* 1998 Sum; 39(3): 6-8. Lang.: Eng.
USA. 1965-1998. Histories-sources. ■Tharon Musser, the recipient of SETC's Distinguished Career Award, shares her thoughts on the lighting designer's role in theatre.

327 Staicer, Judy. "Journey East." *TD&T.* 1998 Spr; 34(2): 14-21. Illus.: Photo. Color. B&W. 13. Lang.: Eng.
USA. China, People's Republic of. 1998. Historical studies. ■Report on a visit of theatre designers and technicians from the United States to China.

328 Stancavage, Sharon. "Meeting of Minds." *LDim.* 1998 Oct.; 22(10): 70-78. Illus.: Photo. B&W. 3. Lang.: Eng.
USA: Tualatin, OR. 1996-1998. Historical studies. ■Examines the merger of two companies—NSI and its 1996 acquisition of Colortran—that service the lighting equipment needs of the music retail market.

329 Thomas, Richard K. "Sound Score Playback Options: Part One." *TD&T.* 1998 Sum; 34(3): 53-59. Notes. Tables. Illus.: Photo. B&W. 9. Lang.: Eng.
USA. 1998. Technical studies. ■Overall rating of Sound Score playback equipment, and the versatility it allows for the sound designer. Continued in *TD&T* 34:5, pp 42-55.

330 Walton, Tony; Boepple, Leanne. "Tony Walton on Pete Feller." *TCI.* 1998 July; 32(7): 16. Illus.: Photo. B&W. 1. Lang.: Eng.
USA. 1920-1998. Biographical studies. ■Set and costume designer reminisces on his experience with the late stage technician Pete Feller. Includes a sidebar obituary for the longtime stage carpenter.

331 Wholsen, Barbara J. "A 4-Sided Steel-Marking Guide." *TechB.* 1998 Oct.: 1. Illus.: Diagram. B&W. 2. [TB 1313.] Lang.: Eng.
USA. 1998. Technical studies. ■Recommends making a four-sided marking tool out of two angle irons and using it to not only speed the construction process, but add uniformity to measurements even when marks are made by several different technicians.

332 Zink, Geoff. "A Low-Voltage Cue-Light System." *TechB.* 1998 Jan.: 1-3. Illus.: Photo. Diagram. Plan. B&W. 4. [TB 1306.] Lang.: Eng.
USA. 1998. Technical studies. ■Description and plans of easy to build cue-light system adaptable to all sorts of cue light control and placement needs.

Institutions

333 Darvay Nagy, Adrienne. "Az ITI születésnapja: The World of Theatre 1994-1996." (The Birthday of ITI: The World of Theatre 1994-1996.) *Sz.* 1998; 31(3): 47-48. Lang.: Hun.
1994-1996. Historical studies. ■The 50th anniversary of the International Theatre Institute (ITI) highlighting its recent publication about world theatre.

334 Klett, Renate. "Bei den Antipoden." (At the Antipodes.) *THeute.* 1998; 5: 31-33. Illus.: Photo. B&W. 2. Lang.: Ger.
Australia: Perth, Adelaide. 1998. Historical studies. ■Impressions from the theatre festivals held in Perth and Adelaide.

335 Abaulin, D. "Služitel' muz." (Servant of the Muse.) *Persona.* 1998; 2: 9-11. Lang.: Rus.
Austria: Vienna. 1998. Biographical studies. ■Profile of O. Černikov, director of a Vienna-based foundation dedicated to the development of the Bolšoj Theatre in Moscow.

336 Loney, Glenn. "The Stone Age Is Over: Peter Stein Stages His Last Salzburg Shows." *WES.* 1998 Spr; 10(2): 65-76. Lang.: Eng.
Austria: Salzburg. 1997. Historical studies. ■Report on the 1998 Salzburg Festival, with emphasis on the departing director Stein's last three stagings: the Alban Berg opera *Wozzeck*, and two plays, Grillparzer's *Libussa* and Ferdinand Raimund's *Der Alpenkönig und Der Menschenfiend.*

337 Massoutre, Guylaine. "Bonheurs au fil du temps." (Pleasures in the Course of Time.) *JCT.* 1998; 89: 40-45. Notes. Illus.: Photo. B&W. 6. Lang.: Fre.
Canada: Montreal, PQ. 1998. Historical studies. ■Account of fifth Coups de théâtre festival of children's theatre. Includes details of forum 'Autour de l'enfant-spectateur (About the Child Spectator)'.

338 Mendenhall, Marie. "Smillie Shines the Spotlight on Saskatchewan Playwrights." *PAC.* 1998; 32(1): 20. Illus.: Photo. B&W. Lang.: Eng.
Canada: Regina, SK. 1998. Historical studies. ■The new artistic director of the Globe Theatre, Ruth Smillie, plans to showcase Saskatchewan playwrights.

339 Paventi, Eza. "On n'a pas tous les jours vingt ans." (It Isn't Every Day You're Twenty Years Old.) *JCT.* 1998; 87: 50-53 . Illus.: Photo. B&W. 6. Lang.: Fre.

THEATRE IN GENERAL: —Institutions

Canada: Montreal, PQ. 1979-1997. Historical studies. ▪Celebrating twenty years of the Ligue National d'Improvisation and its hockey-style improv matches. The value of improvisation for actors.

340 Philips, Magda. "The Secret Life of the NAC." *PAC.* 1998; 31(3): 27-29. Lang.: Eng.

Canada: Ottawa, ON. 1997-1998. Historical studies. ▪Reports on summer backstage tours of the National Arts Centre, which promote education about the arts and attract audiences to performances.

341 Scoll, Shelley. "Unversity of Toronto's Graduate Centre for Study of Drama." *TRC.* 1998 Fall; 19(2): 202-206. Notes. Lang.: Eng.

Canada: Toronto, ON. 1989-1997. Historical studies. ▪Financial and employment conditions of students in University of Toronto's Graduate Centre for Study of Drama, over the period 1989-1997.

342 Vigeant, Louise. "Critiques en visite." (Visiting Critics.) *JCT.* 1998; 88: 172-175. Illus.: Photo. B&W. 2. Lang.: Fre.

Canada: Quebec, PQ. 1998. Historical studies. ▪Describes 1998 workshop of Association internationale des critiques de théâtre (AICT), held for the first time at Quebec, and organized by Association québécoise des critiques de théâtre.

343 Wickham, Philip. "Les AAs, tout sauf anonymes: Les Acteurs Associés." (AA, Anything but Anonymous: Acteurs Associés.) *JCT.* 1998; 88: 176-178. Illus.: Photo. B&W. 2. Lang.: Fre.

Canada. 1995-1998. Historical studies. ▪Quebec's Acteurs Associés offers alternative to agencies, uniting actors willing to manage their own careers with casting agents.

344 Lajos, Sándor. "Színházi capriccio: Divadlo'97 Plzeň." (Theatre Capriccio: Divadlo'97 Plzeň.) *Sz.* 1998; 31(5): 39-43. Illus.: Photo. B&W. 4. Lang.: Hun.

Czech Republic: Pilsen. 1997. Reviews of performances. ▪A brief account of the Czech theatre as experienced at the 1997 Pilsen festival.

345 Nobling, Torsten. "Givande resa till teaterns Estland." (Travel to Estonia.) *ProScen.* 1998; 22(1): 15-22. Illus.: Photo. B&W. Color. Lang.: Swe, Eng, Ger.

Estonia: Tallin, Tartu. 1997. Historical studies. ▪Report from a journey to Estonia, with presentations of Rahvusooper 'Estonia' (Estonia Teater), Tallinna Linnateater, Vene Draamateater and Vanemuine.

346 Fouquet, Ludovic. "Lettre de France." (Letter from France.) *JCT.* 1998; 86: 153-157. Illus.: Photo. B&W. 2. Lang.: Fre.

France: Paris. 1997. Historical studies. ▪Japanese and German plays make an impression at Paris' 1997 Festival d'Automne.

347 Brandt, Ellen. "Grips fährt carrousel." (Grips Has a Ride on Carrousel.) *DB.* 1998; 9: 46-49. Illus.: Photo. B&W. 4. Lang.: Ger.

Germany: Berlin. 1998. Historical studies. ▪Portraits of GRIPS and Carrousel, two children's and young people's theatres in Berlin, their traditions and programs.

348 Dössel, Christine. "Vorhof zum Paradies?" (Anteroom of Paradise?) *THeute.* 1998; 6: 26-35. Illus.: Photo. B&W. 10. Lang.: Ger.

Germany: Munich. 1998. Critical studies. ▪Describes the training at Otto-Falckenberg-Schule and Bayerische Theaterakademie/Hochschule für Musik, including addresses and application procedures.

349 Jahnke, Manfred. "Power...und Magie." (Power...and Magic.) *DB.* 1998; 9: 43-45. Illus.: Photo. B&W. 3. Lang.: Ger.

Germany: Dresden, Stuttgart. 1998. Historical studies. ▪Impressions from the 9th Bundestreffen Jugendclubs an den Theatern (Meeting of young people's theatre clubs) organized by Staatsschauspiel and Theater Junge Generation, and from the 1st International and 7th Baden-Württembergischen Kinder- und Jugendtheatertreffen (Children's and young people's meeting) in Stuttgart. Discusses the meaning of theatre played by children and theatre for children as audience.

350 Krumbholz, Martin. "Hätten Sie's gewusst?" (Would You Have Known?) *THeute.* 1998; 12: 34-40. Illus.: Photo. B&W. 6. Lang.: Ger.

Germany: Frankfurt/Main. 1998. Critical studies. ▪Describes the training at Hochschule für Musik und Darstellende Kunst, courses of studies in acting and directing, including address and application procedures.

351 Laages, Michael. "So fremd im eigenen Land." (A Stranger in One's Own Land.) *DB.* 1998; 9: 53-55. Illus.: Photo. B&W. 4. Lang.: Ger.

Germany: Braunschweig, Hannover. 1998. Historical studies. ▪Impressions from Theaterformen in Braunschweig and Hannover, the program of this avant-garde festival and the difficulty to reach a high standard.

352 Törner, Oliver. "Neugierige und lustvolle Begegnung." (A Curious and Delightful Meeting.) *G&GBKM.* 1998; 128: 1-6. Illus.: Photo. B&W. 2. Lang.: Ger.

Germany: Hannover. 1998. Historical studies. ▪Impressions from 'Spurensuche' (Looking for tracks), the 4th workshop of the free children's theatre scene.

353 Zerull, Ludwig. "Auf Nebenwegen ins Ziel." (By a Roundabout Route to the Goal.) *THeute.* 1998; 10: 42-45. Illus.: Photo. B&W. 4. Lang.: Ger.

Germany: Braunschweig, Hannover. 1998. Historical studies. ▪Impressions from Theaterformen festival in Hannover and Braunschweig, its concept and program.

354 Zünder, Ralf. "Sie wollen zueinander nicht kommen." (They Don't Want to Come Together.) *BGs.* 1998; 4: 9-11. Illus.: Photo. B&W. 6. Lang.: Ger.

Germany: Weimar, Erfurt. 1998. Historical studies. ▪Describes the threatened merger of Deutsches Nationaltheater Weimar and Theater Erfurt and countermeasures, includes an interview with Dietrich Taube, theatre-manager in Erfurt.

355 "A színikritikusok díja 1997/1998." (Theatre Critics' Awards 1997/1998.) *Sz.* 1998; 31(10): 2-14. Illus.: Photo. B&W. 13. Lang.: Hun.

Hungary. 1997-1998. Historical studies. ▪Results of the annual critics' poll as well as the individual votes and short statements of the twenty-one participants.

356 Alpár, Ágnes. *Régi idők színjátszói: A Kisfaludy Színház Ó-Budán 1897.* (Actors of Bygone Days: The Kisfaludy Theatre in Óbuda 1897.) Budapest: Óbudai Múzeum; 1997. 78 pp. (Helytörténeti füzetek.) Append. Illus.: Photo. Poster. B&W. Lang.: Hun.

Hungary: Budapest. 1892-1946. Historical studies. ▪Evoking the memory of the Óbudai Kisfaludy Színház on the occasion of celebrating the 100th anniversary of the foundation of theatre in Óbuda (in the 3rd district of Budapest) with the help of photographs, journals, playbills and posters.

357 Bőgel, József. "A Határon Túli Magyar Színházak 9. Fesztiválja." (9th Festival of Hungarian Theatres of Neighboring Countries.) *SFo.* 1997/1998; 24/25(3-4, 1-2): 6-8. Lang.: Hun.

Hungary: Kisvárda. 1998. Historical studies. ▪An account of the annual meeting of the Hungarian-speaking theatres operating in Hungary's neighboring countries.

358 Csáki, Judit; Koncz, Zsuzsa, photo.; Korniss, Péter, photo. "Színház a városházán." (Theatre at the City Hall.) *Sz.* 1998; 31(4): 2-22. Illus.: Photo. B&W. 21. Lang.: Hun.

Hungary: Budapest. 1994-1998. Critical studies. ▪The chronicle of the change-over at the New Theatre (Új Színház): dismissal of the manager, director Gábor Székely, and the competition for the managerial post. Includes documentation.

359 Fuchs, Lívia; Molnár, Kata, photo. "Közös kockázat: Beszélgetés Szabó Györggyel." (Shared Risk: Interview with György Szabó.) *Ellenfény.* 1998; 3(4): 5-7. Illus.: Photo. B&W. 4. Lang.: Hun.

Hungary: Budapest. 1998. Histories-sources. ▪A talk with the director of the recently opened Trafó, the house of contemporary art, on its programs.

360 Kondorosi, Zoltán. "Ellenszínházak: Beszélgetés Nánay Istvánnal." (Counter-Theatres: Interview with István Nánay.) *Ellenfény.* 1998; 3(1): 2-3. Illus.: Photo. B&W. 2. Lang.: Hun.

THEATRE IN GENERAL: —Institutions

Hungary. 1960-1990. Histories-sources. ■A talk about theatre workshops, their role and importance.

361 Lőkös, Ildikó. "'Miért nem akar mindenki színházat csinálni?': Töredékek a szegedi Egyetemi Színpadról." ('Why Doesn't Everybody Want to Do Theatre?': Fragments of History of the University Stage in Szeged.) *Ellenfény*. 1998; 3(1): 20-23. Illus.: Photo. B&W. 4. Lang.: Hun.

Hungary: Szeged. 1960-1998. Historical studies. ■Notes on the Szeged-based Egyetemi Színpad led by István Paál.

362 Perényi, Balázs; Molnár, Kata, photo. "A körülmények ihlető forrása: Beszélgetés Regős Jánossal." (The Inspiring Spring of Circumstances: Interview with János Regős.) *Ellenfény*. 1998; 3(4): 2-4. Illus.: Photo. B&W. 2. Lang.: Hun.

Hungary: Budapest. 1979-1998. Histories-sources. ■Conversation with the director of Szkéné Theatre, a haven of alternative theatre from the 1970s.

363 Sándor, Erzsi. "Évadok és mércék: A 18. Országos Színházi Találkozó elé." (Seasons and Measures: A Preliminary Talk before the 18th National Theatre Festival.) *Sz.* 1998; 31(6): 3-8. Illus.: Photo. B&W. 6. Lang.: Hun.

Hungary. 1996-1997. Histories-sources. ■A series of interviews with the members of the jury responsible for selecting the festival program: critic Katalin Szűcs, actor György Kézdy and actor-director Lajos Balázsovits, managing director of Játékszín (The Stage).

364 Szabó, István. "Nemzeti Színház 1978-1982." (National Theatre 1978-1982.) *Sz.* 1998; 31(1): 12-13. Illus.: Photo. B&W. 2. Lang.: Hun.

Hungary: Budapest. 1978-1982. Historical studies. ■Chronicle of the period when a highly interesting and much discussed experiment of artistic renewal was attempted at the theatre. Includes list of premieres.

365 Szebeni, Zsuzsa. "Erdélyi jubileumok - Nagyvárad, Sepsiszentgyörgy." (Jubilees in Transylvania—Nagyvárad, Sepsiszentgyörgy.) *Vilag*. 1998 Win; 12: 144-145. Lang.: Hun.

Hungary. Romania. 1798-1998. Historical studies. ■The program of the celebration of Hungarian-language dramatic art in two Transylvanian towns (since 1918 part of Romania): Nagyvárad/Oradea and Sepsiszentgyörgy/Sfântu-Gheorghe.

366 Masi, Alessandro. *Il palazzo del Burcardo. Testimonianze di un restauro.* (The Burcardo Palace: Testimonies of a Repair.) Rome: SIAE; 1998. 171 pp. Illus.: Plan. Maps. Photo. Print. B&W. Color. Lang.: Ita.

Italy: Rome. 1998. Historical studies. ■The restoration of the Burcardo Palace in Rome office of the Italian Society for Authors and Editors and of a library and a theatrical museum.

367 Schneider, Wolfgang. "Nehmt die Kinder ernst!" (Be Serious About Children!) *DB*. 1998; 9: 16-19. Illus.: Photo. B&W. 2. Lang.: Ger.

Italy: Bologna. Sweden: Stockholm. Germany. 1998. Historical studies. ■Argues that children's and young people's theatres are generally of poor quality with the exception of such companies as La Barraca of Bologna and Unga Klara of Stockholm. Makes nineteen political and cultural demands for children's theatre in Germany.

368 Berlin, Zeke. *Takarazuka: A History and Descriptive Analysis of the All-Female Japanese Performance Company.* New York, NY: New York Univ; 1988. 257 pp. Notes. Biblio. [Ph.D. Dissertation, Univ. Microfilms Order No. 8910554.] Lang.: Eng.

Japan. 1914-1988. Histories-specific. ■On the unusual performance style of the highly popular Takarazuka Revue Company. Focuses on production elements, training, history, casting, fans, etc.

369 Söderberg, Olle. "Den lettiska teatervärlden i förvandling." (The Latvian Theatre World in Transformation.) *ProScen.* 1998; 22(1): 60-66. Illus.: Photo. B&W. Color. Lang.: Swe, Eng, Ger.

Latvia: Riga. 1997. Historical studies. ■Report on a visit to Riga with references to Jaunais Rigas Teatris, Latvijas Nacionalais Teatris, Latvijas Nacionala Opera, Studijteatris and Latvijas Valsio Lellu Teatris.

370 Söderberg, Olle. "En positiv vind i Litauen." (A Positive Wind In Lithuania.) *ProScen.* 1998; 22(1): 69-75. Illus.: Photo. B&W. Color. Lang.: Swe, Eng, Ger.

Lithuania: Vilnius. 1993-1998. Critical studies. ■Report on the theatres of today in Vilnius, with references to Lietuvos Valstybinis Operos ir Baleto Teatro with its own shops, Lietuvos Nacionalinis Teatras and Jaunimo Teatras.

371 Callaghan, David. "Paradise Revisited: The Current State of The Living Theatre." *JDTC.* 1998 Spr; 12(2): 115-128. Notes. Illus.: Photo. 2. Lang.: Eng.

North America. 1991-1997. Critical studies. ■Examines the current state of the Living Theatre and its artistic director Judith Malina and compares it to its heyday of the 1960s.

372 Hernik-Spalińska, Jagoda. *Wileńskie Środy Literackie /1927 - 1939/.* (The Literary Wednesdays at Vilna, 1927-1939.) Warsaw: Instytut Badań Literackich; 1998. 338 pp. Index. Illus.: Photo. B&W. 24. Lang.: Pol.

Poland: Vilna. 1927-1939. Historical studies. ■Chronicle of regular weekly meetings of artists and intellectuals in multiethnic Vilna organized by the local branch of the Professional Association of Polish Writers as a forum for the exchange of ideas and opinions about theatre, literature, and politics.

373 Király, Nina. "Kontakt'98." *Vilag.* 1998 Spr; 12: 133-138. Lang.: Hun.

Poland: Toruń. 1998. Historical studies. ■Account of this year's program of the international festival.

374 Konarska-Pabiniak, Barbara. *Płocka Melpomena. Teatr zawodowy i amatorski 1808-1975.* (Płock's Melpomene: Professional and Nonprofessional Theatre, 1808-1975.) Płock: Wojewódzka Biblioteka Publiczna; 1998. 429 pp. Pref. Index. Biblio. Illus.: Plan. Photo. B&W. 69. Lang.: Pol.

Poland: Płock. 1808-1975. Historical studies. ■Polish provincial theatre in the region of Mazovia, where professional companies worked from 1808 to 1939 and nonprofessional companies from 1823 to 1975. A list of theatre companies is included.

375 Tyszka, Juliusz. "The Orange Alternative: Street Happenings as Social Performance in Poland Under Martial Law." *NTQ.* 1998 Nov.; 14(4): 311-323. Notes. Biblio. Illus.: Photo. B&W. 3. [Issue 56.] Lang.: Eng.

Poland: Wroclaw. 1981-1988. Historical studies. ■History of the Orange Alternative (Pomaranczowa Alternatywa), created by the surrealist Waldemar Fydrych, nicknamed 'Major', which through published manifestos and theatrical street happenings confronted the communist regime.

376 Barba, Eugenio. "ISTA in Portugal." *NTQ.* 1998 May; 14(2): 182. [Issue 54.] Lang.: Eng.

Portugal: Lisbon. Denmark: Holstebro. 1998. Historical studies. ■Announces the eleventh session of the International School of Theatre Anthropology, in Lisbon, which will concentrate on research into the fundamental principles that generate the 'presence' or the 'scenic life' of the performer.

377 Bérczes, László; Koncz, Zsuzsa, photo. "Fesztivál Bukarestben." (Festival in Bucharest.) *Sz.* 1998; 31 (4): 45-48. Illus.: Photo. B&W. 3. Lang.: Hun.

Romania: Bucharest. 1998. Reviews of performances. ■Summing up the events and tendencies observed at Bucharest's National Theatre Festival.

378 Darvay Nagy, Adrienne. *Bohócruhában: Kolozsvári és szatmárnémeti magyar színjátszás 1965-1989.* (In Harlequin Coat: Hungarian Theatre at Kolozsvár/Cluj and Szatmárnémeti/Satu Mare 1965-1989.) Marosvásárhely: Mentor; 1998. 251 pp. Biblio. Notes. Lang.: Hun.

Romania: Cluj-Napoca, Satu Mare. Hungary. 1965-1989. Critical studies. ■A collection of essays on recent Hungarian dramatic art in Transylvania.

379 Kiss, László. *A Sepsiszentgyörgyi Magyar Színház története, 1948-1992—Istoria Teatrului Maghiar din Sfântu Gheorghe, 1948-1992.* (History of the Hungarian Theatre of Sepsiszentgyörgy, 1948-1992.) Bucharest: Facultatea de Limbi şi Literaturi Străine Secţia Hungarologie; 1997. 80, 133 fol. Append. Biblio. Lang.: Hun.

THEATRE IN GENERAL: —Institutions

Romania: Sfântu-Gheorghe. 1948-1992. Historical studies. ■Dissertation on the history of a post-war Hungarian-language theatre operating in Sepsiszentgyörgy/Sfântu-Gheorghe, Romania.

380 *Dekada vachtangovskoj školy.* (The Decade of the Vachtangov School.) Moscow: RIK Rusanova; 1998. 128 pp. Lang.: Rus.

Russia: Moscow. 1990-1998. Historical studies. ■Conference of scholars and artists at the Vachtangov School on the goal of late twentieth-century European culture. Reports, performances, and commentaries.

381 Čečetin, A.I. *Istorija teatralizovannych predstavlenij: Progr. dlja studentov fak.'Kul'turovedenie' (Spec. 'Režissura teatraliz. predstavlenij').* (History of Theatrical Shows: Program for the Students of the Faculty of Culture.) Moscow: 1998. 15 pp. Lang.: Rus.

Russia. 1998. Instructional materials. ■Description of theatre history program.

382 Šul'pin, A. "Kanikuly na Teatral'noj ulice." (The Holidays on Teatral'noj Street.) *NTE.* 1998; 4: 44-46. Lang.: Rus.

Russia: Kaluga. 1998. Historical studies. ■Annual festival of theatre where children are the performers.

383 Szebeni, Zsuzsa. "Színházi fesztivál Nyitrán (Divadelná Nitra'98)." (Theatre Festival in Nitra.) *Vilag.* 1998 Win; 12: 148-151. Lang.: Hun.

Slovakia: Nitra. 1998. Historical studies. ■An account of the events and programs of this year's festival.

384 Van Daele, Koen, ed. *Mesto žensk.* (City of Women.) Ljubljana: Open Society Institute–Slovenia; 1998. 31 pp. Illus.: Photo. B&W. 2. [International Festival of Contemporary Arts, Ljubljana, October 10-21, 1998.] Lang.: Slo.

Slovenia: Ljubljana. 1998. Histories-specific. ■Program of the International Festival of Contemporary Arts—City of Women, reflecting several feminist performance events.

385 Bain, Keith. "Make Believe: Standard Bank National Arts Festival Grahamstown, 2-12 July 1998." *SATJ.* 1998 May/Sep.; 12 (1/2): 138-164. Notes. Biblio. Illus.: Photo. B&W. 3. Lang.: Eng.

South Africa, Republic of: Grahamstown. 1998. Historical studies. ■Report on the annual theatre festival.

386 Harryson, Lotta. "Effekt eller hantverk?" (Effects Or Trade?)*Danst.* 1998; 8(6): 41. Illus.: Photo. Color. Lang.: Swe.

Sweden: Stockholm. 1998. Historical studies. ■Report from a seminar on mime, illusionism, *commedia dell'arte* and jesters in the dance and the theatre, arranged by the magazine *Visslingar och Rop (Whistles and Cries).*

387 Exinger, Peter. "Die Narretei eines Idealisten ist schillernd, böse, grossartig." (The Idealist's Folly Is Enigmatic, Bad, Great.) *MuK.* 1998; 40(2-4): 169-187. Notes. Illus.: Photo. B&W. 1. Lang.: Ger.

Switzerland: Zurich. 1926-1938. Biographical studies. ■Describes the directorship of Ferdinand Rieser at Schauspielhaus Zurich, his program, ensemble and his political affiliations.

388 Dungate, Rod. "Just His Metier." *PlPl.* June 1998; 523: 24-25. Lang.: Eng.

UK-England: Bradford. 1996-1998. Histories-sources. ■Duncan Sones, Chief Executive of Metier, UK's only national training organization, on his work creating national standards for arts training and artists.

389 "On Stage at SETC: People and Events at the 1998 SETC Convention." *SoTh.* 1998 Sum; 39(3): 4-5. Illus.: Photo. B&W. 7. Lang.: Eng.

USA: Birmingham, AL. 1998. Historical studies. ■Photographic essay on the 1998 Southeastern Theatre Conference Convention, held in Birmingham, AL.

390 "Children's Theatre Camps Drive TAXI's Success." *SoTh.* 1998 Fall; 39(4): 28-31. Illus.: Photo. B&W. 5. Lang.: Eng.

USA: Louisville, KY. 1992-1998. Historical studies. ■Profile of TAXI Children's Theatre, founded by Trudy Wheeler: operating structure, type of season, attendance, financial support, theatre areas, educational outreach, multicultural practices, and its future.

391 Ayers, Stephen Michael. *The Selection Process of the National Endowment for the Arts' Theatre Program: An Historical-Critical Study.* Boulder, CO: Univ. of Colorado; 1988. 231 pp. Biblio. Notes. [Ph.D. Dissertation, Univ. Microfilms Order No. AAC 8902875.] Lang.: Eng.

USA. 1965-1988. Histories-specific. ■The formation of the National Endowment for the Arts (NEA) and its Theatre Program: development, methods of operation, selection process and overall effectiveness.

392 Belitska-Scholtz, Hedvig. "Az OISTAT-Kongresszus, Pittsburgh (USA): 1997. március 16-18." (The OISTAT Congress, Pittsburgh (USA): March 16-18, 1997.) *SFo.* 1997/1998; 24/25(3-4, 1-2): 13. Lang.: Hun.

USA: Pittsburgh, PA. 1997. Histories-sources. ■A report on the program and events of the annual conference and stage expo by the co-president of the Hungarian Centre of OISTAT.

393 Blain, Lynda Carol. *The Shakespeare Festival of Dallas: An Internship Report.* Lubbock, TX: Texas Tech Univ; 1988. 266 pp. Biblio. Notes. [Ph.D. Dissertation, Univ. Microfilms Order No. AAC 8908500.] Lang.: Eng.

USA: Dallas, TX. 1972-1988. Histories-sources. ■Report on the management of the festival focusing on its organizational structure, financial and management practices, and challenges to the leadership.

394 Bloom, Arthur W. "Science and Sensation, Entertainment and Enlightenment: John Mix and the Columbian Museum and Gardens." *PAR.* 1998; 21: 33-49. Notes. Lang.: Eng.

USA: New Haven, CT. 1796-1820. Historical studies. ■History of John Mix and his New Haven Assembly Hall and Columbian Museum and Gardens where he presented theatre, concerts, lectures, variety acts during a time when New Haven law forbade such entertainments.

395 Bottoms, Stephen J. "The Tangled Flora of Goat Island: Rhizome, Repetition, Reality." *TJ.* 1998 Dec.; 50(4): 421-446. Notes. Illus.: Photo. B&W. 4. Lang.: Eng.

USA: Chicago, IL. 1987-1998. Critical studies. ■The complex strategies of performativity that Goat Island brings to their postmodern work. Focuses on the actors' constructions of performance roles and the nature of spectatorship inherent in their recent work *How Dear to Me the Hour When Daylight Dies.*

396 Burbank, Carol Elizabeth. *Ladies Against Women: Theatre Activism, Parody, and the Public Construction of Citizenship in United States Feminism's Second Wave.* Evanston, IL: Northwestern Univ; 1998. 370 pp. Notes. Biblio. [Ph.D. Dissertation, Univ. Microfilms Order No. AAC 9832560.] Lang.: Eng.

USA: Berkeley, CA. 1979-1993. Histories-specific. ■The development, techniques, and influence of the Berkeley, CA people's theatre troupe Ladies Against Women (LAW), which grew out of the agit-prop, antinuclear activist collective the Plutonium Players. Uses archives, personal interviews, participant observation, and semiotic and dramaturgical analysis of performance documentation to focus on feminist satire.

397 Campbell, Mary Schmidt. "A New Mission for the NEA." *TDR.* 1998 Win; 42(4): 5-9. Notes. Lang.: Eng.

USA. 1998. Critical studies. ■Former New York City Cultural Affairs Commissioner proposes changes in the mission of the NEA in order to strengthen its position as an advocate for the arts.

398 Chach, Maryann. "Reminiscences." *PasShow.* 1997 Fall/Win, 1998 Spr/Sum; 20/21(2/1): 7-9. Illus.: Photo. B&W. 1. Lang.: Eng.

USA: New York, NY. 1987-1998. Histories-sources. ■Current Shubert archivist on working at the archive.

399 Cummings, Scott T. "Get Budged!" *AmTh.* 1998 Dec.; 15(10): 68-70. Illus.: Photo. B&W. 1. Lang.: Eng.

USA: Cambridge, MA. 1998. Histories-sources. ■Playwright Anna Deavere Smith, a founder of the Institute on the Arts and Civic Dialogue at Harvard University, discusses its mission to promote civic discussion through the arts.

400 Duclow, Geraldine. "Philadelphia's Early Pleasure Gardens." *PAR.* 1998; 21: 1-17. Notes. Illus.: Pntg. B&W. 4. Lang.: Eng.

THEATRE IN GENERAL: —Institutions

USA: Philadelphia, PA. 1723-1840. Historical studies. ■History of Philadelphia's public pleasure gardens, where entertainments from concerts to theatrical events were offered.

401 Fletcher, Reagan. "Reminiscences." *PasShow.* 1997 Fall/Win, 1998 Spr/Sum; 20/21(2/1): 9-10. Illus.: Photo. B&W. 1. Lang.: Eng.

USA: New York, NY. 1984-1998. Histories-sources. ■Assistant Shubert archivist on working at the archive.

402 Fortner, Michael; Halbach, Denise; Lee, Teresa; Slusser, Dean. "Overview: The 1998 SETC Convention." *SoTh.* 1998 Sum; 39 (3): 9-13. Illus.: Photo. B&W. 8. Lang.: Eng.

USA: Birmingham, AL. 1998. Historical studies. ■Introductory essay to a special section on the Southeastern Theatre Conference Convention.

403 Frick, John W. "'Fireworks, Bonfires, Balloons and More': New York's Palace Garden." *PAR.* 1998; 21: 19-32. Notes. Illus.: Pntg. B&W. 1. Lang.: Eng.

USA: New York, NY. 1858-1863. Historical studies. ■History of the popular entertainment venue, with emphasis on a changing urban landscape and the public desire for a more 'modern' form of entertainment.

404 Gordy, Douglas W. "Joseph Cino and the First Off Off Broadway Theatre." 303-323 in Schanke, Robert A., ed.; Marra, Kim, ed. *Passing Performances: Queer Readings of Leading Players in American Theatre History.* Ann Arbor, MI: Univ of Michigan P; 1998. 338 pp. (Triangulations: Lesbian/Gay/Queer Theatre/Drama/Performance.) Notes. Index. Illus.: Photo. 1. Lang.: Eng.

USA: New York, NY. 1931-1967. Biographical studies. ■Examines the impact of sexuality on the life and career of theatre producer Joseph Cino, founder of the Off-off Broadway Caffe Cino.

405 Haarbauer, Martha; Haarbauer, Ward. "SETC '98 Preview: 'New' Birmingham Welcomes Convention Goers with Arts and Theatre Events, Varied Cuisine." *SoTh.* 1998 Spr; 39(2): 10-14. Illus.: Photo. 4. Lang.: Eng.

USA: Birmingham, AL. 1998. Historical studies. ■Inside look at performance venues, as well as room and board information, for the host city for the 1998 SETC Convention.

406 Houser, Patricia G. *Virginia Museum Theatre: A Case Study.* Washington, DC: American Univ; 1987. 89 pp. Notes. Biblio. [M.A. Thesis.] Lang.: Eng.

USA: Richmond, VA. 1955-1987. Historical studies. ■History and current administration of the Virginia Museum Theatre, from its beginnings as a community theatre to its current status as a professional institution.

407 Hurley, Erin. "On Interdisciplinarity." *TRC.* 1998 Fall; 19(2): 196-198. Notes. Lang.: Eng.

USA. 1998. Critical studies. ■Increasing importance of interdisciplinarity in post-secondary theatre studies departments, and its importance for graduate student programs.

408 Klautsch, Richard Joseph. *An Historical Analysis of the Clarence B. Hilberry Repertory Theatre, Detroit, Michigan, 1963-1973.* Detroit, MI: Wayne State Univ; 1988. 378 pp. Biblio. Notes. [Ph.D. Dissertation, Univ. Microfilms Order No. AAC 8903235.] Lang.: Eng.

USA: Detroit, MI. 1963-1973. Histories-specific. ■Chronological history of the Clarence B. Hilberry Repertory Theatre's performance training program with emphasis on how a training program could become a theatrical presence in a major metropolitan area without the benefit of being a fully professional enterprise.

409 Kueppers, Brigitte. "Reminiscences." *PasShow.* 1997 Fall/Win, 1998 Spr/Sum; 20/21(2/1): 4-6. Illus.: Photo. B&W. 1. Lang.: Eng.

USA: New York, NY. 1976-1987. Histories-sources. ■Reminiscences of former Shubert archivist on her experiences working for the archive in its infancy.

410 Lasky, Roberta Lynne. *The New Playwrights Theatre, 1927-1929.* Davis, CA: Univ. of California; 1988. 288 pp. Notes. Biblio. [Ph.D. Dissertation, Univ. Microfilms Order No. AAC 8903725.] Lang.: Eng.

USA: New York, NY. 1927-1929. Histories-specific. ■Founded by John Howard Lawson, Michael Gold, Em Jo Basshe, Francis Edwards Faragoh, and John Dos Passos, and supported by Otto Kahn, New Playwrights Theatre Company was the first professional troupe in the United States to label itself a left-wing theatre, while attempting to draw working-class audience support.

411 Lawrence, Happy James. *The State-Wide Tours of the Florida Federal Theatre Project, October, 1937-June, 1939: A Description and Evaluation of Two Seasons on the Road for the 'People's Popular Theatre'.* Tallahassee, FL: Florida State Univ; 1988. 473 pp. Biblio. Notes. [Ph.D. Dissertation, Univ. Microfilms Order No. AAC 8906224.] Lang.: Eng.

USA. 1937-1939. Histories-specific. ■Includes complete descriptions of all company productions and personnel.

412 Lee, Chester. "Golden Touch: Birmingham Children's Theatre Celebrates 50 Years of Enlightening, Entertaining." *SoTh.* 1998 Spr; 39(2): 16-19. Illus.: Photo. 3. Lang.: Eng.

USA: Birmingham, AL. 1947-1998. Historical studies. ■History of the Birmingham Children's Theatre, founded by Dorothy Schwartz, from its beginnings as a shoestring operation to a respected organization with a budget of more than $1 million which brings theatre into the lives of one in every four Alabama schoolchildren.

413 LoMonaco, Marti. "Honoring a True Revolutionary." *PasShow.* 1997 Fall/Win, 1998 Spr/Sum; 20/21(2/1): 41. Lang.: Eng.

USA: New York, NY. 1976-1998. Historical studies. ■Celebration of the director and founder of the Shubert archive, Brooks McNamara.

414 Lopez, A. Grace. *Communicating Through Design: A Study of the Graphic Evolution of Arena Stage.* Washington, DC: American Univ; 1988. 220 pp. Notes. Biblio. [M.A. Thesis, Univ. Microfilms Order No. AAC 1336279.] Lang.: Eng.

USA: Washington, DC. 1950-1987. Histories-specific. ■The history of the Arena Stage graphic design in relationship to its theatrical evolution. Argues that this visual communication has functioned as a tool for promoting theatre.

415 McNamara, Brooks. "Reminiscences." *PasShow.* 1997 Fall/Win, 1998 Spr/Sum; 20/21(2/1): 3-4. Illus.: Photo. B&W. 1. Lang.: Eng.

USA: New York, NY. 1976-1998. Histories-sources. ■Director of the Shubert archive relates his role in the organization of the archive as a resource for students and scholars.

416 Moore, Dick. "Regional Report: Cleveland: Renaissance City." *EN.* 1998 Oct/Nov.; 83(3): 5. Illus.: Photo. 1. Lang.: Eng.

USA: Cleveland, OH. 1998. Historical studies. ■Reports on theatrical activity in Cleveland including the newly restored Allen Theatre, part of the Playhouse Square entertainment complex which includes three other theatres, the Ohio, the State, and the Palace.

417 Napoleon, Davida S. *The Chelsea Theater Center: A History.* New York, NY: New York Univ; 1988. 391 pp. Biblio. Notes. [Ph.D. Dissertation, Univ. Microfilms Order No. AAC 8910594.] Lang.: Eng.

USA: New York, NY. 1965-1988. Histories-specific. ■The organization and history of the Chelsea Theatre Center and its productions through the years.

418 Norman, Stanley Sain. *A Systems Analysis of the Southwest Theatre Association: An Internship.* Lubbock, TX: Texas Tech Univ; 1988. 228 pp. Biblio. Notes. [Ph.D. Dissertation, Univ. Microfilms Order No. AAC 8900955.] Lang.: Eng.

USA. 1988. Histories-specific. ■Report on the management operations of the Southwest Theatre Association. Argues that the use of policy and procedure manuals for arts managers all over the country would make for more efficient management, as well as providing infrastructure for achieving the goals and objectives of the organization.

419 Nunns, Stephen. "An Indispensible Library on the Move." *AmTh.* 1998 July/Aug.; 15(6): 55. Illus.: Photo. B&W. 1. Lang.: Eng.

USA: New York, NY. 1998. Historical studies. ■Report on the move of the New York Public Library for the Performing Arts to temporary facilities while the permanent base undergoes a two-year renovation.

420 Nunns, Stephen. "Ivey's In, but NEA's Prospects Remain Uncertain." *AmTh.* 1998 July/Aug.; 15(6): 56-57. Illus.: Photo. B&W. 1. Lang.: Eng.

THEATRE IN GENERAL: —Institutions

USA: Washington, DC. 1998. Historical studies. ■Report on the new nominee for the chairmanship of the NEA, William J. Ivey.

421 O'Quinn, Jim. "The Ties That Bind." *AmTh.* 1998 Dec.; 15(10): 57-59. Illus.: Photo. B&W. 5. Lang.: Eng.

USA: Tarrytown, NY. 1998. Historical studies. ■Report on a symposium held April 17-19, 1998 in Tarrytown, NY, concerning the relationship between the theatre artist and the theatrical institution.

422 Reiss, Alvin H. "The NEA in the Year 2000: The Final Solution." *FundM.* 1998 Apr.; 29(2): 34-35. Lang.: Eng.

USA: Washington, DC. 1997-2000. Critical studies. ■Whimsical essay on the status of the National Endowment for the Arts in the year 2000, starting with the political flaps surrounding the institution in 1997.

423 Reiss, Alvin H. "Arts Groups Find New Support to Help Woo New Audiences." *FundM.* 1998 June; 29(4): 34-35. Lang.: Eng.

USA: San Francisco, CA, New York, NY. 1998. Critical studies. ■The partnership between arts groups and corporate entities such as Chase Manhattan Bank and the San Francisco Opera, with emphasis on the commission of an opera based on the non-fiction book *Dead Man Walking*, music to be composed by Jake Heggie with libretto by Terrence McNally.

424 Reiss, Alvin H. "A Tale of Two Centers: How Performing Arts Halls in Washington and Newark Are Achieving Success." *FundM.* 1998 July; 29(5): 28-29. Illus.: Photo. B&W. 1. Lang.: Eng.

USA: Washington, DC, Newark, NJ. 1971-1998. Historical studies. ■Financial and artistic success of the John F. Kennedy Center for the Performing Arts and New Jersey Performing Arts Center.

425 Schoenfeld, Gerald. "Reminiscences." *PasShow.* 1997 Fall/Win, 1998 Spr/Sum; 20/21(2/1): 2-3. Illus.: Photo. B&W. 1. Lang.: Eng.

USA: New York, NY. 1949-1998. Histories-sources. ■Chairman of both the Shubert Foundation and Shubert Organization shares his feelings about the Shubert archive and its future as its newsletter, *The Passing Show*, celebrates twenty years of publication.

426 Swartz, Mark. "Reminiscences." *PasShow.* 1997 Fall/Win, 1998 Spr/Sum; 20/21(2/1): 10-12. Illus.: Photo. B&W. 1. Lang.: Eng.

USA: New York, NY. 1988-1998. Histories-sources. ■Assistant Shubert archivist, Swartz, reminisces about working at the archive.

427 Tenney, John. "In the Trenches: The Syndicate-Shubert Theatrical War." *PasShow.* 1998 Fall/Win; 21(2): 1-18. Notes. Illus.: Photo. Poster. Handbill. 14. Lang.: Eng.

USA: New York, NY. 1976-1998. Historical studies. ■History of the battle waged between the Shubert brothers and the theatrical producing body Klaw & Erlanger (the 'Syndicate'). The Shuberts were attempting to break up the Syndicate's stranglehold on booking of theatrical attractions in the Nation's theatres.

428 Witham, Barry B. "The Economic Structure of the Federal Theatre Project." 200-214 in Engle, Ron, ed.; Miller, Tice L., ed. *The American Stage: Social and Economic Issues from the Colonial Period to the Present.* Cambridge: Cambridge UP; 1993. 320 pp. Pref. Notes. Index. Illus.: Photo. 1. Lang.: Eng.

USA. 1935-1939. Historical studies. ■The complex system of economic welfare in relation to the Federal Theatre Project.

429 Yates, Thomas Alfred. *The Covenant Players—Inheritors of and Contributors to the Ancient and Ongoing Dialogue Between Theatre and the Church.* Claremont, CA: School of Theology at Claremont; 1988. 127 pp. Biblio. Notes. [Ph.D. Dissertation, Univ. Microfilms Order No. AAC 8816084.] Lang.: Eng.

USA: Camarillo, CA. 1988. Historical studies. ■History of the Covenant Players, the largest producer of Christian drama in the world.

430 Zvonchenko, Walter. *A Historical Study of the Relation of Theatre and Broadcasting to Land Use in Midtown Manhattan in the Years 1925 through 1928.* New York, NY: City Univ. of New York; 1987. 528 pp. Notes. Biblio. [Ph.D. Dissertation, Univ. Microfilms Order No. AAC 8801780.] Lang.: Eng.

USA: New York, NY. 1925-1928. Historical studies. ■Examines specific factors such as transportation facilities, nontheatrical real estate firms and financial organizations.

431 Ciszkewycz, Ihor. *Transformation—A Discovered Form: Berezil Theater, 1922-1934.* Carbondale, IL: Southern Illinois Univ; 1988. 344 pp. Biblio. Notes. [Ph.D. Dissertation, Univ. Microfilms Order No. AAC 8903682.] Lang.: Eng.

USSR. 1922-1934. Histories-specific. ■Examines the Teat'r Berezil of Les' Kurbas, focusing on his development of visual movement and his concentration on nationalistic themes.

432 Krasiński, Edward. "Z dziejów teatrów żołnierskich. Od Buzułuku do Londynu 1941-1948." (From the History of Soldier's Theatres: From Buzuluk to London, 1941-1948.) *PaT.* 1998; 47(1-2): 1-54. Notes. Illus.: Handbill. Photo. Poster. B&W. 23. Lang.: Pol.

USSR: Buzuluk. UK-England: London. 1941-1948. Historical studies. ■Describes and analyzes the origins and various activities of the primary Polish soldier's theatres in London during World War II and their post-war vicissitudes.

Performance spaces

433 Krexner, Alice. "Das Redoutensaaltheater." (The 'Redoutensaal' Theatre.) *MuK.* 1998; 40(1): 69-113. Notes. Lang.: Ger.

Austria: Vienna. 1918-1992. Historical studies. ■Describes the architectural and administrative history of Redoutentheater from its last days as a court theatre and its new beginning as a state theatre.

434 Court, Paul. "Historical Theatres of Toronto." *TD&T.* 1998 Win; 34(5): 30-33. Illus.: Photo. Color. 4. Lang.: Eng.

Canada: Toronto, ON. 1998. Historical studies. ■Profile of the Pantages, Elgin, Winter Garden, and Royal Alexandra theatres.

435 Howell-Meri, Mark A. "Davies' Bear-Baiting Ring, 1663: The Hope Restored." *TN.* 1998; 52(1): 2-7. Notes. Lang.: Eng.

England: London. 1647-1682. Historical studies. ■Drawings by Wenceslaus Hollar and diary entries by Samuel Pepys indicate that the bear-baiting theatre, opened by Thomas Davies, may have been a restoration of the Hope Theatre.

436 Edström, Per Simon. "En flytande friluftsteater." (A Floating Open-Air Theatre.) *ProScen.* 1998; 22(4): 20-23. Illus.: Dwg. Color. Lang.: Swe.

Europe. 1998. Technical studies. ■Discusses the prospect of developing a flexible open-air theatre on the water.

437 Mortensen, Bo. "Teaterrummets akustik." (The Acoustics of the Performance Space.) *TE.* 1998 July; 89: 18-23. Illus.: Dwg. B&W. 7. Lang.: Dan.

Europe. 340 B.C.-1998 A.D. Historical studies. ■A short history of theatre architecture from ancient Greece to modern European theatre buildings. Acoustics have often been a secondary concern for the builders of theatres, who have favored tradition instead.

438 Tyszka, Juliusz. *Teatr w miejscach nieteatralnych.* (Theatre in Untheatrical Spaces.) Poznan: Wydawnictwo Fundacji Humaniora; 1998. 294 pp. Notes. Pref. Tables. Biblio. Append. Illus.: Photo. Sketches. B&W. 23. Lang.: Pol.

Europe. North America. Asia. 1918-1998. Critical studies. ■Collection of essays on modern worldwide forms of experimental theatre.

439 Haarer, Klaus. "Vom Werdegang eines Velodroms." (On the Development of a Velodrome.) *BtR.* 1998; 5: 14-16. Illus.: Dwg. BW. Color. 4. Lang.: Ger.

Germany: Regensburg. 1898-1998. Historical studies. ■One-hundred year history of the velodrome and its redevelopment as an alternative performing venue for the Städtische Bühnen Regensburg.

440 Linzer, Martin. "Zwischen Tugend und Bedrängung." (Between Virtue and Oppression.) *TZ.* 1998; 5: 4-6. Illus.: Photo. B&W. 2. Lang.: Ger.

Germany: Cottbus. 1908-1998. Histories-sources. ■Interview with director Christoph Schroth about traditions on occasion of the 90th anniversary of the theatre building in Cottbus.

THEATRE IN GENERAL: —Performance spaces

441 Mazanec, Brigitta. "Theater mit Tiefenwirkung." (Theatre With Deep Action.) *DB.* 1998; 12: 23-25. Illus.: Photo. B&W. 4. Lang.: Ger.

Germany: Franfurt. 1978-1998. Historical studies. ▪Portrait of the venue Mousonturm in Frankfurt, a retrospective and future concepts under the management of Dieter Buroch.

442 Phipps, A.M. *South-West German* Naturtheater*: An Investigation into Expressions of Cultural Identity.* Sheffield: Unpublished PhD, Univ. of Sheffield; 1995. Notes. Biblio. [Abstract in *Aslib Index to Theses* 46-6283.] Lang.: Eng.

Germany. 1700-1994. Histories-specific. ▪The history of open-air theatre in Germany in the context of changing attitudes to nature. Examines the constituent elements of space, performer, play, and audience, and assesses the open-air theatre as an important vehicle of cultural identity.

443 Risum, Janne. "Angsten for det tomme rum." (Fear of the Empty Space.) *TE.* 1998 July; 89: 4-6. Illus.: Photo. Dwg. B&W. 2. Lang.: Dan.

Germany. France. UK-England. 1898-1998. Historical studies. ▪During the last 100 years the theatre has left the traditional theatre buildings and conquered new spaces. Max Reinhardt and Vsevolod Mejerchol'd were pioneers in this development.

444 Sonntag-Kunst, Helga. "Disney's *Die Schöne und das Biest* im Si-Centrum Stuttgart." (Disney's *Beauty and the Beast* in SI-Centrum Stuttgart.) *BtR.* 1998; 2: 8-16. Illus.: Photo. Plan. Color. 16. Lang.: Ger.

Germany: Stuttgart. 1997. Technical studies. ▪Describes the venue built specifically for the Disney production: the planning and construction of the technical systems, the set and lighting scheme and sound installations concerning the first performance of *Beauty and the Beast* at Stuttgart.

445 Lennartz, Knut. "Sophokles in Epidauros." (Sophocles in Epidauros.) *DB.* 1998; 11: 40-41. Illus.: Photo. B&W. 3. Lang.: Ger.

Greece: Epidauros. 1938-1998. Historical studies. ▪Describes the Epidauros amphitheatre with respect to Sophocles' *Electra* directed by Michael Marmarinos and played by his company Eros.

446 Bán, Ferenc, illus. "A győztes pályamű." (The Winning Project.) *Sz.* 1998; 31(1): 9-11. Illus.: Design. B&W. 3. Lang.: Hun.

Hungary: Budapest. 1998. Technical studies. ▪The official evaluation of the jury in the competition to design Hugary's new National Theatre. The winner was Ferenc Bán.

447 Gajdó, Tamás; Szegő, György; Korniss, Péter, photo. *Színházkutatás.* (Investigation of a Theatre.) Budapest: Thália Színház; 1998. 236 pp. Pref. Illus.: Photo. B&W. Lang.: Hun.

Hungary: Budapest. 1913-1996. Historical studies. ▪The history of the site of the present-day Thália Színház, recently reconstructed, which has housed theatrical ventures since 1913.

448 Ham, Roderick; Grosser, Helmut; Szegő, György, et al. "Nemzeti Színház tervpályázat." (The National Theatre Project Competition.) *SFo.* 1997/1998; 24/25(3-4, /1-2): 15-22. Illus.: Design. B&W. 9. Lang.: Hun.

Hungary: Budapest. 1996-1997. Technical studies. ▪Evaluation for the 1996/97 competition of the architectural design of the new National Theatre by three members of the jury and the technical description of the winning project by architect Ferenc Bán.

449 Nánay, István; Bán, Ferenc, illus. "A jövő század színháza: Beszélgetés Ölveczky Miklóssal." (The Theatre of the Future: An Interview with Miklós Ölveczky.) *Sz.* 1998; 31(1): 5-8. Illus.: Design. B&W. 2. Lang.: Hun.

Hungary. Norway. 1998. Histories-sources. ▪A talk with the Hungarian-born architect living in Norway about the ideal architectural conditions for construction of Hungary's new National Theatre. Olveczy served on the jury to choose the new design.

450 Szilvási, Zsuzsa. "175 éves a Miskolci Nemzeti Színház." (175th Anniversary of the Miskolc National Theatre.) *SFo.* 1997/1998; 24/25(3-4, 1-2): 27-31. Illus.: Photo. B&W. 7. Lang.: Hun.

Hungary: Miskolc. 1823-1998. Technical studies. ▪The total renovation of the local National Theatre in Miskolc, a city in Eastern Hungary.

451 Boepple, Leanne. "The Royal Treatment." *TCI.* 1998 Oct.; 32(9): 62-63. Illus.: Photo. Color. 6. Lang.: Eng.

Italy. 1998. Critical studies. ▪Report on the 768-seat Broadway-style Princess Theatre, on board the Mediterranean and Caribbean cruise ship the *Grand Princess*, on the eve of its maiden cruise.

452 D'Amico, Alessandro; Verdone, Mario; Zanella, Andrea. *Il Teatro Valle.* (The Valle Theatre.) Rome: Palombi; 1998. 275 pp. Biblio. Illus.: Photo. B&W. Color. 8. Lang.: Ita.

Italy: Rome. 1726-1997. Histories-specific. ▪An illustrated history of the Valle Theatre in Rome.

453 Fiedler, Manfred. "200 Jahre Teatro Comunale in Ferrara." (200 Years of Teatro Comunale in Ferrara.) *BtR.* 1998; 4: 18-21. Notes. Illus.: Photo. Graphs. Color. 10. Lang.: Ger.

Italy: Ferrara. 1798-1998. Histories-sources. ▪History of the Teatro Comunale, the construction and latest renovation that combined the old structure and machinery with modern technology for all kinds of performances.

454 Kvaløy, Pål. "Sceneteknikk ved Trøndelag Teater." (Stage Techniques At Trøndelag Teater.) *ProScen.* 1998 ; 22(3): 24-26. Illus.: Photo. B&W. Lang.: Nor.

Norway: Trondheim. 1997. Technical studies. ▪Description of the technology being used for the stage of the Trøndelag Teater.

455 Nobling, Torsten. "Tröndelag Teater i Trondheim." (The Trøndelag Teater at Trondheim.) *ProScen.* 1998; 22(3): 16-19. Illus.: Photo. Plan. B&W. Lang.: Swe.

Norway: Trondheim. 1994. Critical studies. ▪Looks at the new theatre building which is built around the old Trøndelag theatre building from 1816.

456 Olsen, Trygve. "Teatret i Prinsensgate." (The Theatre at Prinsensgate.) *ProScen.* 1998; 22(3): 20-23. Illus.: Photo. Plan. B&W. Lang.: Nor.

Norway: Trondheim. 1997. Critical studies. ▪Another look at the new theatre building Trøndelag Teater.

457 Thomason, Phillip Brian. *The Coliseo de la Cruz: Madrid's First Enclosed Municipal Playhouse (1737-1859).* Lexington, KY: Univ. of Kentucky; 1987. 364 pp. Notes. Biblio. [Ph.D. Dissertation, Univ. Microfilms Order No. AAC 8806563.] Lang.: Eng.

Spain: Madrid. 1737-1859. Historical studies. ▪History of the Coliseo de la Cruz, constructed on the site of the city's first permanent public theatre—the Corral de la Cruz, continuing a theatrical tradition that began in 1579.

458 Edström, Per Simon. "Den tyske maskinmästaren Reuss betydelse för kulissmaskineriet på Drottningholms Slottsteater." (The Influence of the German Engineer Reuss on the Stage Machinery of Drottningholms Slottsteater.) *ProScen.* 1998; 22(5): 14-15. Illus.: Dwg. B&W. Lang.: Swe.

Sweden: Stockholm. 1755-1766. Histories-sources. ▪Builder Georg Fröman's diary from a journey to Dresden and Vienna, with references to his studies of stage machinery and meeting with engineer Christian Gottlob Reuss for a future machinery at Drottningholms Slottsteater.

459 Winkelsesser, Karin. "...länger Atem bringt neue Kraft." (Longer-Range Planning Brings New Strength.) *BtR.* 1998; 5: 8-13. Illus.: Photo. Plan. Color. 5. Lang.: Ger.

Switzerland: Geneva. 1984-1998. Historical studies. ▪Reports from the eventful fourteen year planning and preparation of Grand Théâtre de Genève. Describes the fly system, the most modern technical level.

460 Allis, Peter. "Ghosties and Ghoulies and Things." *PlPl.* Jan 1998; 518: 9. Illus.: Dwg. 1. Lang.: Eng.

UK-England: London. 1918-1998. Historical studies. ▪Anecdotes of visits to old theatres and variety houses around London, and ghost stories of the Margate Theatre Royal and efforts to keep it open.

461 Howley, Michael P. "Shakespeare: Globe Theatre Opens, Fulfilling Dreams." *SoTh.* 1998 Spr; 39(2): 24-27. Illus.: Photo. 3. Lang.: Eng.

UK-England: London. 1997. Historical studies. ▪Reports on the recently completed restoration of Shakespeare's Globe Theatre and provides information on opportunities for people who live in the Southeast to become involved in the project.

THEATRE IN GENERAL: —Performance spaces

462 Loney, Glenn. "Edinburgh's Traverse Theatre—First Stop on the 1998 Festival Fringe." *WES.* 1998 Fall; 10(3): 83-88. Illus.: Photo. B&W. 3. Lang.: Eng.

UK-Scotland: Edinburgh. 1998. Critical studies. ■Discusses the theatre's advantages as a venue for multiple productions of fringe theatrical fare. It has two stages, and plays host to what is often the best the festival has to offer.

463 Carroll, John F. *Oscar Hammerstein I, 1895-1915: His Creation and Development of New York's Times Square Theatre District.* New York, NY: City Univ. of New York; 1998. 190 pp. Notes. Biblio. [Ph.D. Dissertation, Univ. Microfilms Order No. AAC 9908300.] Lang.: Eng.

USA. 1895-1915. Histories-specific. ■Examines the role of independent theatre entrepreneur Oscar Hammerstein I in the creation and development of New York City's new theatre district, Times Square. Argues that Hammerstein's influence on New York's cultural landscape led to the city's recognition as the nation's center for legitimate theatre productions and for the era's most popular performing art, vaudeville.

464 Condee, William Faricy. *The Interaction of Theatre Space and Performance in Contemporary New York Playhouses.* New York, NY: Columbia Univ; 1987. 690 pp. Notes. Biblio. [Ph.D. Dissertation, Univ. Microfilms Order No. AAC 8723998.] Lang.: Eng.

USA: New York, NY. 1925-1985. Historical studies. ■The theatres studied are: Vivian Beaumont Theatre, Circle in the Square-Uptown, Public Theater, Circle Rep, Roundabout, Second Stage, CSC Rep, Juilliard Drama Theatre, Wooster Group and Squat Theatre.

465 French, Larry; Rogers, Peter. "Bringing the Lights Back on in the San Francisco War Memorial Opera House." *TD&T.* 1998 Spr; 34(2): 53-55. Illus.: Photo. Color. 2. Lang.: Eng.

USA: San Francisco, CA. 1998. Historical studies. ■Report on the new stage light system at the venerable opera house.

466 Henke, James Scott. *From Public House to Opera House: A History of Theatrical Structures in Lancaster, Pennsylvania.* Ann Arbor, MI: Univ. of Michigan; 1987. 137 pp. Biblio. Notes. [Ph.D. Dissertation, Univ. Microfilms Order No. AAC 8720276.] Lang.: Eng.

USA: Lancaster, PA. 1800-1960. Critical studies. ■Traces the creation of theatrical structures and producing organizations in Lancaster to fill in gaps in information concerning theatrical production outside of major population centers and to demonstrate that theatrical production in these outlying areas followed the trend of the larger cities on a smaller scale.

467 Lampert-Gréaux, Ellen. "Cultural Cachet." *TCI.* 1998 Feb.; 32(2): 38-41. Illus.: Photo. Maps. Design. Color. 7. Lang.: Eng.

USA: Newark, NJ. 1988-1998. Technical studies. ■Description of the New Jersey Performing Arts Center with an emphasis of its impact upon the city of Newark. Contains a sidebar listing officials, architects, contractors, and advisors involved in its construction.

468 Lampert-Gréaux, Ellen. "Times Square Story: The Ford Center for the Performing Arts." *TCI.* 1998 July; 32(7): 32-35. Illus.: Photo. Design. Color. 10. Lang.: Eng.

USA: New York, NY. 1998. Technical studies. ■Architectectural critique of the newly built theatre, with an emphasis on its proscenium, auditorium, foyer, and technical set-up.

469 Lampert-Gréaux, Ellen. "A Flowering Arden." *TCI.* 1998 Nov.; 32(10): 10-12. Illus.: Photo. B&W. 1. Lang.: Eng.

USA: Philadelphia, PA. 1998. Critical studies. ■Report on the renovation of the F. Otto Haas Theatre, performance venue for the Arden Theatre Company.

470 Matheson, Katy. "Niblo's Garden and its 'Concert-Saloon', 1828-1846." *PAR.* 1998; 21: 53-105. Notes. Illus.: Photo. B&W. 3. Lang.: Eng.

USA: New York, NY. 1828-1846. Historical studies. ■History of Niblo's Garden, from its opening as a summer retreat in New York City to its development into a year-round venue for theatrical and other entertainments.

471 Oseland, James. "Dinner Theatre, U.S.A." *AmTh.* 1998 Apr.; 15(4): 22-26. Illus.: Photo. B&W. 9. Lang.: Eng.

USA. 1998. Critical studies. ■Report on the state of America's dinner theatres as venues of stage entertainment.

472 Pollack, Steve. "Floors for the Performing Arts: A Primer for Theatre Professionals." *TD&T.* 1998 Win; 34(5): 16-20. Illus.: Plan. Photo. Color. B&W. 3. Lang.: Eng.

USA. 1970-1998. Technical studies. ■Advice for best materials and finishes to use when installing flooring for a stage or rehearsal hall.

473 Ruzika, Donna. "Southern California Theatre." *TD&T.* 1998 Win; 34(1): 8-11. Illus.: Photo. Color. 6. Lang.: Eng.

USA. 1998. Critical studies. ■Survey of Shrine Auditorium, Alex Theatre, Pasadena Civic Auditorium, Hollywood Pantages, and the open-air John Anson Ford Amphitheatre and Greek Theatre.

474 Stasio, Marilyn. "Miracle on Tremont Street." *AmTh.* 1998 Nov.; 15(9): 40-45. Illus.: Photo. B&W. 2. Lang.: Eng.

USA: Boston, MA, Chicago, IL. 1988-1998. Historical studies. ■History behind the renovation of the Emerson Majestic Theatre, which also involved a concerted effort to involve the community in its revival. Includes a sidebar about a similar community effort to save the Rialto Theatre in Chicago, IL.

475 Weathersby, William, Jr. "Stagestruck in Seattle." *TCI.* 1998 Apr.; 32(4): 27-29. Illus.: Photo. Plan. B&W. Color. 9. Lang.: Eng.

USA: Seattle, WA. 1998. Historical studies. ■Report on two new theatres, the Leo Kreielsheimer Theatre which is the new venue added to the Seattle Repertory Theatre, as well as the renovation of Eagles Auditorium, new home of A Contemporary Theatre.

476 Weathersby, William, Jr. "Times Square Story: The New Amsterdam Theatre." *TCI.* 1998 July; 32(7): 27-31. Illus.: Photo. Plan. Color. 10. Lang.: Eng.

USA: New York, NY. 1998. Technical studies. ■Architectectural critique of the newly restored theatre, with an emphasis on its auditorium, foyer, and technical set-up.

477 Weathersby, William, Jr. "Texas Tradition." *TCI.* 1998 Aug/Sep.; 32(8): 48-51. Illus.: Photo. Color. 6. Lang.: Eng.

USA: Ft. Worth, TX. 1998. Critical studies. ■Report on the architectural aspects of the new Bass Performance Hall.

478 Weathersby, William, Jr. "Architecture: San Francisco War Memorial Opera." *TCI.* 1998 Jan.; 32(1): 30-33. Illus.: Photo. Color. 11. Lang.: Eng.

USA: San Francisco, CA. 1997. Technical studies. ■Examines the extensive architectural and technical renovation of the War Memorial Opera House.

479 Weathersby, William, Jr.; Lampert-Gréaux, Ellen. "Times Square Story: The New Times Square." *TCI.* 1998 July; 32(7): 36-37, 42. Illus.: Photo. Dwg. Color. 8. Lang.: Eng.

USA: New York, NY. 1998. Critical studies. ■Report on the revitalization and architectural face-lift being given to Broadway and 42nd Street, and its impact on the theatre district.

Performance/production

480 Levin, M. *I prišel na stadion prazdnik: Učeb. posobie po režissure sport.-teatraliz. prazdnikov.* (And the Holiday Moved to the Stadium: A Guide to Directing Sports and Theatrical Shows.) Moscow: 1998. 12 pp. Lang.: Rus.

Instructional materials. ■Guide to the fine points of directing sport shows and theatrical productions.

481 Ley, Graham. "Performance and Performatives." *JDTC.* 1998 Fall; 13(1): 5-18. Notes. Lang.: Eng.

1998. Critical studies. ■The actor in the European tradition of conventional theatre from the viewpoint of speech-act theory.

482 Moore, Dick. "Show Buzz." *EN.* 1998 Oct/Nov.; 83(8): 3. Lang.: Eng.

1998. Historical studies. ■Recent news on the international theatre scene.

483 Omodele, Oluremi. *Traditional and Contemporary African Drama: A Historical Perspective.* Los Angeles, CA: Univ. of California; 1988. 722 pp. Notes. Biblio. [Ph.D. Dissertation, Univ. Microfilms Order No. AAC 8907579.] Lang.: Eng.

Africa. 1850-1987. Histories-specific. ■Traditional African ritual performance (funerals, weddings, etc.) as a source for contemporary African theatre.

THEATRE IN GENERAL: —Performance/production

484 Stejnberg Gusman, D. "Iniciatičeskij teatr." (The Beginning of Theatre.) *Novyj Akropol'.* 1998; 1(2): 51-60. Lang.: Rus.
Ancient Greece. Roman Empire. India. Egypt. Historical studies. ■History of the development of theatre in Greece, Rome, India, and Egypt.

485 Brown, John Russell. "Theatrical Pillage in Asia: Redirecting the Intercultural Traffic." *NTQ.* 1998 Feb.; 14(1): 9-19. Notes. [Issue 53.] Lang.: Eng.
Asia. North America. Europe. 1976-1997. Historical studies. ■Investigates practical issues of multicultural theatre, notably how far different kinds of theatre depend on being site-specific, in terms not only of the performers, but also of the audiences and their responses.

486 Gilbert, Helen. "Reconciliation? Aboriginality and Australian Theatre in the 1990s." 71-88 in Kelly, Veronica, ed. *Our Australian Theatre in the 1990s.* (Australian Playwrights 7.) Notes. Index. Biblio. Illus.: Photo. 2. Lang.: Eng.
Australia. 1990-1998. Historical studies. ■The current growth of Aboriginal theatre and the presence of Aborigines in the Australian theatre as playwrights, designers, actors, and directors. Groups such as Kooris in Theatre, Ilbijeri, Kooemba Jdarra, and Yirra Yaakin Youth Theatre.

487 Kimber, Robert James. *Performance Space as Sacred Space in Aranda* Corroboree*—An Interpretation of the Organization and Use of Space as a Dramatic Element in the Performance of Selected Aboriginal Rituals in Central Australia.* Boulder, CO: Univ. of Colorado; 1988. 317 pp. Biblio. Notes. [Ph.D. Dissertation, Univ. Microfilms Order No. AAC 8912200.] Lang.: Eng.
Australia. 800 B.C.-1988 A.D. Histories-specific. ■Examines Aboriginal Australian *corroboree*, a form of communal theatre practice originating in ritual and ceremony, with respect to its use of performing space. Uses the theoretical writings of Richard Schechner and Victor Turner to examines its roots in history.

488 Lo, Jacqueline. "Dis/orientations: Contemporary Asian-Australian Theatre." 53-70 in Kelly, Veronica, ed. *Our Australian Theatre in the 1990s.* (Australian Playwrights 7.) Notes. Index. Biblio. Illus.: Photo. 3. Lang.: Eng.
Australia. 1990-1998. Historical studies. ■The current state of Asian-Australian theatre, especially in light of the region's increasing reliance on Asian economic markets. Considers Belvoir Street Theatre's annual Asian Theatre Festival, Jill Shearer's *Shimada*, and Peter Copeman's *Sinakulo.*

489 Milne, Geoffrey. "Theatre in Education: Dead or Alive?" 152-167 in Kelly, Veronica, ed. *Our Australian Theatre in the 1990s.* (Australian Playwrights 7.) Notes. Index. Biblio. Illus.: Photo. 1. Lang.: Eng.
Australia. 1990-1998. Historical studies. ■Examines the current crisis and challenges facing theatre for young people in Australia, seen through the 'professional theatre in education' companies that perform in schools.

490 Mitchell, Tony. "Maintaining Cultural Integrity: Teresa Crea, Doppio Teatro, Italo-Australian Theatre and Critical Multiculturalism." 132-151 in Kelly, Veronica, ed. *Our Australian Theatre in the 1990s.* (Australian Playwrights 7.) Notes. Index. Biblio. Illus.: Photo. 4. Lang.: Eng.
Australia. 1990-1998. Historical studies. ■Italo-Australian theatre in light of multiculturalism. Argues that a 'cultural integrity' can still be attained amid multiculturalism, and specifically examines the Doppio Teatro, founded by Teresa Crea and Christopher Bell.

491 Roberts, Rhoda. "A Passion for Ideas: Black Stage." *ADS.* 1998 Apr.; 32: 3-20. [The Rex Cramphorn lecture for 1997, delivered at Belvoir Street Theatre, Sydney, on Sunday, 23 November 1997.] Lang.: Eng.
Australia: Sydney. 1997. Histories-sources. ■Artistic director of the Festival of Dreaming international arts extravaganza lectures on the place of the Aboriginal arts on the Australian stage.

492 Tait, Peta. "Performing Sexed Bodies in Physical Theatre." 213-228 in Kelly, Veronica, ed. *Our Australian Theatre in the 1990s.* (Australian Playwrights 7.) Notes. Index. Biblio. Illus.: Photo. 3. Lang.: Eng.
Australia. 1990-1998. Historical studies. ■Recent developments in Australian 'physical theatre,' which combines highly physical circus acts, performed in social spaces, with a theoretical and performative emphasis on gendered, or 'sexed' bodies.

493 "Creating a Living Space, or How to Transmit Performative Knowledge." *MimeJ.* 1998; 19: 98-109. Notes. Illus.: Photo. B&W. 4. Lang.: Eng.
Austria: Vienna. Switzerland: Zurich. 1996-1998. Historical studies. ■Report on 'The Speaking Body' museum installation at the Austrian Theatre Museum in Vienna and the Museum for Design in Zurich. Theatre Anthropology Seminars were held at these exhibitions.

494 Götz, Eszter. "Kelet és Nyugat testbeszéde: Parate Labor, Theatermuseum, Bécs, 1998 március/július." (Body Language Between East and West: Parate Labor, Theatermuseum, Vienna, March-July 1998.) *Vilag.* 1998 Spr; 12: 124-127. Lang.: Hun.
Austria: Vienna. 1989-1998. Historical studies. ■Report on the films and lectures of a workshop of theatre anthropology held in Vienna.

495 Kuftinec, Sonja. "Playing with the Borders: Dramaturging Ethnicity in Bosnia." *JDTC.* 1998 Fall; 13(1): 143-155. Notes. Lang.: Eng.
Bosnia. 1996-1998. Critical studies. ■The nature of ethnicity in community-based dramaturgy, based on the author's experiences in Bosnia working with youth theatres.

496 Heritage, Paul. "The Promise of Performance: True Love/Real Love." 154-176 in Boon, Richard, ed.; Plastow, Jane, ed. *Theatre Matters: Performance and Culture on the World Stage.* Cambridge: Cambridge UP; 1998. 203 pp. (Cambridge Studies in Modern Theatre.) Notes. Index. Pref. Lang.: Eng.
Brazil. 1980-1995. Historical studies. ■The role of theatre in Brazil in creating cultural identity, with attention to Augusto Boal's Theatre of the Oppressed and to the more 'pragmatic' theatre practiced in rural areas and shanty towns.

497 Rosa, Marco Camarotti. "Animation, Affirmation, Anarchy: Folk Performance in Brazil." *NTQ.* 1998 May; 14(2): 159-181. Notes. Biblio. Illus.: Photo. B&W. 13. [Issue 54.] Lang.: Eng.
Brazil. 1972-1997. Historical studies. ■Examines the characteristics and dramatic structure of four forms of folk theatre still performed in Northeast Brazil: the *Bumba-meu-boi, Chegança, Pastoril,* and the *Mamulengo.*

498 Bose, Rana. "Theatre Notes on a Bright October Morning in Montreal." *CTR.* Spr 1998; 94: 59-60. Illus.: Photo. B&W. 3. Lang.: Eng.
Canada: Montreal, PQ. 1959-1998. Histories-sources. ■Playwright Rana Bose's memories of influential performances in Calcutta, St. Louis and Montreal.

499 de Blois, Marco. "Tout nu *or not* tout nu: Nudité au théâtre et au cinéma." (To Be Naked Or Not To Be Naked: Nudity in Theatre and Cinema.) *JCT.* 1998; 88: 114-117. Notes. Illus.: Photo. B&W. 3. Lang.: Fre.
Canada: Montreal, PQ. 1995-1997. Critical studies. ■Differing uses of nudity in theatre and film owing to actors' physical presence or absence before the audience.

500 De Gruchy Cook, Patricia Margaret Anne. *National Cultures and Popular Theatre: Four Collective Companies in Quebec and Newfoundland.* Canada: Carleton Univ; 1987. Notes. Biblio. [M.A. Thesis.] Lang.: Eng.
Canada. 1970-1985. Critical studies. ■Alternative theatre in the provinces of Newfoundland and Quebec as a venue for indigenous culture and a vehicle for social criticism. The works of Le Grand Cirque Ordinaire and Le Théâtre Euh! in Quebec, and of the Mummers' Troupe and Codco in Newfoundland are examined.

501 Healey, Michael. "Process, or How to Spend the Grant Money." *CTR.* Winter 1998; 97: 5-7. Notes. Illus.: Photo. B&W. 1. Lang.: Eng.
Canada. 1998. Critical studies. ■Actor/playwright Michael Healy postulates that theatre exists to transmit an essential and ineffable 'small elegant thing' to an audience, and that all theatrical techniques serve only to create the context in which this transmission can take place.

THEATRE IN GENERAL: —Performance/production

502 Lévesque, Solange. "Un rêve d'enfance: Entretien avec Andrée Lachapelle." (A Dream of Childhood: Interview with Andrée Lachapelle.) *JCT.* 1998; 89: 141-156. Illus.: Photo. B&W. 16. Lang.: Fre.
Canada: Montreal, PQ. 1950-1998. Histories-sources. ■Actress Andrée Lachapelle on her career in theatre, film, television and radio.

503 Paventi, Eza. "De l'imagination et de l'invention." (Imagination and Inventiveness.) *JCT.* 1998; 89: 54-56. Illus.: Photo. B&W. 3. Lang.: Fre.
Canada: Montreal, PQ. 1998. Critical studies. ■Need for imagination and inventiveness in children's theatre illustrated by three shows at Montreal's 1998 Coups de théâtre children's theatre festival: Lyle Victor Albert's *Scraping the Surface* by Theatre Terrific (Vancouver), Ronnie Burkett's *Old Friends* by the Theatre of Marionnettes (Calgary) and Manitoba Theatre for Young People (Winnipeg) and Peter Rinderknecht's *Monsieur l'inventeur (Mister Inventor)* Theateragentur, Switzerland.

504 Perkins, Don. "From Megaworlds to Mini-Magic: Catalyst Theatre's Process for Small-Scale Spectacle." *CTR.* Win 1998; 97: 12-17. Biblio. Notes. Illus.: Photo. B&W. 8. Lang.: Eng.
Canada: Edmonton, AB. 1986-1998. Historical studies. ■'Controlled collaborative' process behind Edmonton's experimental Catalyst Theatre and their spectacles *Abundance* (96/97 season) and *Songs for Sinners* (97/98 season).

505 Rewa, Natalie. *Garrison and Amateur Theatricals in Quebec City and Kingston During the British Regime.* Toronto, ON: Univ. of Toronto; 1988. Biblio. Notes. [Ph.D. Dissertation.] Lang.: Eng.
Canada: Quebec, PQ, Kingston, ON. 1763-1867. Histories-specific. ■The public involvement of British army garrisons in local theatrical activity and the relationship between political imperial policy and cultural colonial development.

506 Russo, Peggy Anne. *The Great Stage of Fools: The Stratford Festival's 'King Lear'.* Ann Arbor, MI: Univ. of Michigan; 1988. 215 pp. Biblio. Notes. [Ph.D. Dissertation, Univ. Microfilms Order No. AAC 8812978.] Lang.: Eng.
Canada: Stratford, ON. 1964. Critical studies. ■Analysis of the Stratford Festival Theatre production, directed by Michael Langham, designed by Leslie Hurry, and starring John Colicos.

507 Tracie, Rachel Elisabeth. *Deaf Theatre in Canada: Signposts to an Other Land.* Edmonton, AB: Univ. of Alberta; 1998. 117 pp. Notes. Biblio. [M.A. Thesis, Univ. Microfilms Order No. AAC MQ28912.] Lang.: Eng.
Canada. 1965-1998. Histories-sources. ■The development and subsequent failure of the Canadian Theatre of the Deaf. Includes analysis of Deaf language and culture, styles of Deaf theatre and comparison with the National Theatre of the Deaf in the United States.

508 Vaze, Bageshree. "South Asian." *CTR.* 1998 Spr; 94: 10-13. Notes. Illus.: Photo. B&W. 3. Lang.: Eng.
Canada: Toronto, ON. 1997. Histories-sources. ■Opportunities for professional South Asian actors in Toronto's mainstream theatre, film and television industries, based on interviews with several actors.

509 Wickham, Philip. "Des formes à la recherche d'elles-mêmes." (Forms in Search of Themselves.) *JCT.* 1998; 88: 27-30. Illus.: Photo. B&W. 3. Lang.: Fre.
Canada: Quebec, PQ. 1998. Critical studies. ■Derision as means of breaking with convention in three 1998 productions: *Les Enrobantes (The Wrappers)*, Théâtre Populus Mordicus, *Thanatos* (Théâtre des Moutons Noirs), and *Showtime* (Forced Entertainment).

510 Del Campo, Carmen Alicia. *Theatricality, National Identity and Historic Memory: Rituals of Mourning, Purification and Reconciliation in Post-Dictatorship Chile.* Irvine, CA: Univ. of California; 1998. 335 pp. Biblio. Notes. [Ph.D. Dissertation, Univ. Microfilms Order No. AAC 9816394.] Lang.: Spa.
Chile. 1990-1998. Critical studies. ■Explores theatrical constructions of national identity and history in theatre, ritual and public ceremonies focusing on the public political funeral of Salvador Allende, the Canto Libre (a theatrical event devoted to the symbolic cleansing of the Chile Stadium) and the anonymous popular play, *El desquite (Getting Even).*

511 Chen, Zidu. *Bridging the Cultural Gap: An Analysis of the Chinese Production of Howard Burman's 'Article XXIV'.* Long Beach, CA: California State Univ; 1998. 174 pp. Notes. Biblio. [M.A. Thesis, Univ. Microfilms Order No. AAC 1390927.] Lang.: Eng.
China, People's Republic of: Shanghai. 1995. Histories-sources. ■The author's role as translator and mediator in the process of bridging cultural differences while producing Burman's *Article XXIV* in the People's Republic of China. The play was produced by the Shanghai Theatre Academy in its Experimental Theatre.

512 Lane, Jill. "Blackface Nationalism, Cuba 1840-1868." *TJ.* 1998 Mar.; 50(1): 21-38. Notes. Lang.: Eng.
Cuba: Havana. 1840-1868. Critical studies. ■How blackface stereotypes of the *teatro bufo*, theatre created for Cuban-born whites, enabled the dramatization of anti-colonial sentiment as well as anxieties about racial difference inscripted on bodies as well as in speech.

513 Leon, Barbara A. *The Construction of Afro-Cuban Identity in Cuban Scenic Arts Since 1959.* Irvine, CA: Univ. of California; 1998. 257 pp. Biblio. Notes. [Ph.D. Dissertation, Univ. Microfilms Order No. AAC 9832298.] Lang.: Spa.
Cuba. 1959-1996. Histories-specific. ■Examines Afro-Cuban elements in theatre and popular arts as part of a multicultural national identity constructed by colonial and republican cultural discourses.

514 Rottensten, Rikke. "Ingenuen der blev voksen." (The Ingénue Who Became an Adult.) *TE.* 1998 Apr.; 88: 6-9. Illus.: Photo. Photo. B&W. 2. Lang.: Dan.
Denmark. 1982-1998. Histories-sources. ■Interview with actress Tammi Øst who recently left Det Kongelige Teater (The Royal Theatre) in order to seek new challenges at other theatres in Copenhagen.

515 Jacobs, Alfred Voris, Jr. *The London Theater Season of 1609-1610.* Berkeley, CA: Univ. of California; 1987. 531 pp. Notes. Biblio. [Ph.D. Dissertation, Univ. Microfilms Order No. AAC 8813925.] Lang.: Eng.
England: London. 1609-1610. Historical studies. ■Examination of all Jacobean professional and non-professional theatrical activity in London and its environs in a single year. Analyzes themes, elements of plot and characterization, stylistic techniques, and staging devices.

516 Kobialka, Michal Andrzej. *'Regularis Concordia' and Theatre and Drama of the Early Middle Ages.* New York, NY: City Univ. of New York; 1987. 232 pp. Notes. Biblio. [Ph.D. Dissertation, Univ. Microfilms Order No. AAC 8708295.] Lang.: Eng.
England. 1150-1228. Historical studies. ■Reexamines existing evidence concerning the origin of medieval theatre and drama and analyzes the *Regularis Concordia*, a tenth-century monastic consuetudinary in which the *Quem quaeritis* is located.

517 Marsden, Jean. "Charlotte Charke and the Cibbers: Private Life as Public Spectacle." 65-82 in Baruth, Philip E., ed. *Introducing Charlotte Charke: Actress, Author, Enigma.* Urbana/Chicago, IL: Univ. of Illinois P; 1998. 250 pp. Index. Biblio. Notes. Lang.: Eng.
England. 1713-1760. Historical studies. ■How actor/manager Colley Cibber, his son Theophilus, and his daughter Charlotte Charke presented their private life as public spectacle in their writings, leading to attacks on the family and probably affecting Charke's historical legacy.

518 Taub, Lora Elisabeth. *Enterprising Drama: The Rise of Commercial Theatre in Early Modern London.* San Diego, CA: Univ. of California; 1998. 381 pp. Notes. Biblio. [Ph.D. Dissertation, Univ. Microfilms Order No. AAC 9835408.] Lang.: Eng.
England: London. 1550-1680. Critical studies. ■Traces the early history of the relationship between capital and culture in early modern England, documenting the role of theatre in the transition from feudalism to capitalism. Argues that communication and culture were at the heart of capitalist development from its inception.

519 Eström, Per Simon. "Estländska gäster i Sverige." (Estonian Guests In Sweden.) *ProScen.* 1998; 22(1): 46-51. Lang.: Swe, Eng, Ger.
Estonia. Sweden. 1939-1945. Historical studies. ■Index of the Estonian artists that fled to Sweden during the war, and what became of them.

THEATRE IN GENERAL: —Performance/production

520 Alschitz, Jurij. *La grammatica dell'attore. Il training.* (The Actor's Grammar: Training.) Milan: Ubulibri; 1998. 179 pp. (I manuali ubulibri.) Illus.: Photo. Sketches. Print. B&W. Lang.: Ita.

Europe. 1998. Instructional materials. ■A handbook of training with 150 exercises for actors.

521 Breznik, Maja. "Rojstvo evropskega gledališča iz nesporazuma z antiko." (The Birth of European Theatre Through the Misunderstanding of Antiquity.) 203-213 in Cindrič, Alojz, ed. *Čarnijev zbornik (1931-1996).* A Festschrift for Ludvik Čarni. Ljubljana: Faculty of Arts, Department of Sociology; 1998. 504 pp. (Studies in Humanities and Social Sciences.) Lang.: Slo.

Europe. 1400-1600. Histories-specific. ■Examines important texts at the time of the nascent stage of European theatre, including Vitruvius's *De Architectura*, relied upon for their practical knowledge of theatre. Emphasis on the understanding of the Greek pyramidal scenic pieces called *periaktoi.*

522 Engelander, Rudy. *Shifting Gears: Reflections and Reports on the Contemporary Performing Arts.* Amsterdam: Theater Instituut Nederland; 1998. 104 pp. Pref. Index. Notes. Biblio. Illus.: Photo. B&W. 9. Lang.: Eng.

Europe. 1990-1998. Historical studies. ■An account of the International European Theatre Meeting (IETM) held in Rotterdam, 26-29 March 1998.

523 Levanen, Leo Johannes. *Elaytyminen ja etaannyttaminen teatterikasvatuksessa: Elaytymisen ja etaannyttamisen suhde ja rooli sosialistiseen realismiin pohjautuvan teatteritaiteellisen viestinnan ja vaikuttamisen perusteissa.* (Empathy and Distancing in Theatre Education: The Role and Interrelationship of Empathy and Distancing in Theatrical Communication and Influence, Based on Socialist Realism.) Tampere, Finland: Tampereen Teknillinen Korkeakoulu; 1998. 292 pp. Notes. Biblio. [Ed.D. Dissertation.] Lang.: Fin.

Europe. 1998. Critical studies. ■Argues that the tension between empathy and distancing is revealed as the actor functions on stage as both interpreter and character.

524 Pfeiffer, Gabriele. "Keine Worte für interkulturelles Theater." (No Words for Intercultural Theatre.) *MuK.* 1998; 40 (2-4): 41-50. Notes. Lang.: Ger.

Europe. 1930-1998. Critical studies. ■The different approaches of directors Michele Sambin, Peter Brook, Eugenio Barba, and Antonin Artaud to an intercultural theatre, the correlation between interculturalism, textuality and performance and the balance between theatre of the same and of the difference.

525 Sörenson, Elisabeth. "Varför finns det inte längre några divor?" (Why Are There No Longer Any Divas?) *Dramat.* 1998; 6(3): 11-12. Illus.: Photo. B&W. Lang.: Swe.

Europe. USA. 1890-1998. Critical studies. ■Essay about the phenomenon of the diva, with references to Sarah Bernhardt, Tora Teje, Marlene Dietrich, and Maria Callas.

526 Vanden Heuvel, Michael John. *Performing Drama/ Dramatizing Performance: The Interface Between Experimental Theatre and Postmodern Drama, 1960-Present.* Madison, WI: Univ. of Wisconsin; 1988. 452 pp. Notes. Biblio. [Ph.D. Dissertation, Univ. Microfilms Order No. AAC 8901196.] Lang.: Eng.

Europe. USA. 1960-1987. Histories-specific. ■Postmodern experimental performance from early experimental theatre to current theatre, both mainstream and avant-garde. Considers groups and individuals ranging from Jerzy Grotowski, Richard Schechner, and the Performance Group to Robert Wilson, Richard Foreman, Samuel Beckett, Sam Shepard and the Wooster Group.

527 Allen-Barbour, Kristin. "Tableaux Vivants: Presenting the Past on the French Restoration Stage." *JDTC.* 1998 Spr; 12(2): 89-108. Notes. Lang.: Eng.

France. 1810-1820. Critical studies. ■Argues that the semiotic 'doubleness' in theatrical costumes of the Bourbon era reveals tensions between the historical past and present that is inherent within plays of the period, as well as their staging.

528 Angiolillo, Mary Carmel. *Theatrical Objects as a Sign System: An Object-Text of Jarry's* Ubu Roi *as Staged by Antoine Vitez.* Evanston, IL: Northwestern Univ; 1988. 513 pp. Biblio. Notes. [Ph.D. Dissertation, Univ. Microfilms Order No. AAC 8811445.] Lang.: Eng.

France: Paris. 1985. Critical studies. ■Semiotic examination of the theatrical object, in itself and as a sign system, in Jarry's *Ubu Roi*, staged by Antoine Vitez.

529 Epstein, Lisa Jo. "Flexing Images, Changing Visions: The Twin Poles of Contemporary French Political Theatre." 54-76 in Colleran, Jeanne, ed.; Spencer, Jenny S., ed. *Staging Resistance: Essays on Political Theatre.* Ann Arbor, MI: Univ of Michigan P; 1998. 312 pp. (Theater: Theory/Text/ Performance.) Notes. Index. Illus.: Photo. 3. Lang.: Eng.

France. 1990-1996. Historical studies. ■The work of Augusto Boal's CTO (Parisian Center for the Theatre of the Oppressed) and Ariane Mnouchkine's Théâtre du Soleil as prime examples of French political theatre.

530 Fischer-Lichte, Erika. "Das theatralische Opfer: Zum Funktionswandel von Theater im 20. Jahrhundert." (The Theatrical Sacrifice: Towards Functional Change of Theatre in the 20th Century.) *FMT.* 1998; 13(1): 42-57. Notes. Lang.: Ger.

France. Germany. 1900-1998. Historical studies. ■The presentation and performance of sacrifice on stage with respect to *Vesna svjaščennaja (The Rite of Spring)* by Igor F. Stravinskij, choreographed by Vaclav Nižinskij at Théâtre des Champs-Elysées, *Oidípous Týrannos (Oedipus the King)* by Sophocles directed by Max Reinhardt at Grosses Schauspielhaus, and compared with contemporary performance artists Hermann Nitsch and Marina Abramovič. Describes the social context and the effects on the audience.

531 Free, Rebecca. *The Grande Coquette in French Theatre, 1885-1925.* Bloomington, IN: Indiana Univ; 1998. 227 pp. Biblio. Notes. [Ph.D. Dissertation, Univ. Microfilms Order No. 9834597.] Lang.: Eng.

France: Paris. 1885-1925. Histories-specific. ■Examines the grande coquette character in Parisian theatre as a symbol of femininity and theatricality. Author argues that this archetype reveals the authenticity and artifice in the performance of feminine identity, on and off the stage. Focuses on actresses Suzanne Despres and Cécile Sorel, and plays of Molière and Dumas *fils.*

532 Gould, Evlyn. "Penciled in Paris: Le Festival de Nos Vacances Parisiennes." *PerAJ.* 1998 Jan.; 20(58): 48-54. Illus.: Photo. B&W. 2. Lang.: Eng.

France: Paris. 1997. Historical studies. ■Report on the 1997 Parisian cultural festival celebrating all forms of performing and visual arts.

533 Johnston, Carolyn Jane. *The Politics of Pantomime: Working-Class Theatre in Paris, 1800-1862.* Irvine, CA: Univ. of California; 1998. 332 pp. Notes. Biblio. [Ph.D. Dissertation, Univ. Microfilms Order No. AAC 9821445.] Lang.: Eng.

France: Paris. 1800-1862. Histories-specific. ■History of three working-class theatres, the Théâtre des Funambules, the Théâtre de Madame Saqui and the Théâtre du Petit Lazary: how they interacted with government officials and used pantomimes that stood outside of the literary culture to battle government censorship.

534 Kulesza, Monika. "Markiza de Sévigné o teatrze." (The Marquise de Sévigné on Theatre.) *PaT.* 1998; 47 (3-4): 365-382. Notes. Illus.: Pntg. Dwg. B&W. 5. Lang.: Pol.

France: Paris. 1671-1694. Historical studies. ■Examines the letters of the Madame de Sévigné for evidence about Parisian theatre in the late seventeenth century.

535 van Erven, Eugene. "Some Thoughts on Uprooting Asian Grassroots Theatre." 98-120 in Colleran, Jeanne, ed.; Spencer, Jenny S., ed. *Staging Resistance: Essays on Political Theatre.* Ann Arbor, MI: Univ of Michigan P; 1998. 312 pp. (Theater: Theory/Text/Performance.) Notes. Index. Illus.: Photo. 3. Lang.: Eng.

France. Philippines. 1988-1990. Historical studies. ■Examines the Cry of Asia! Tour, an Asian-Pacific grassroots cultural caravan that toured Europe. Considers practical issues of this type of cultural exchange, rang-

THEATRE IN GENERAL: —Performance/production

ing from financial matters to interpersonal communication, collaboration, and audience expectations.

536 Kuhns, David Frederick. *The Synthetic Actor: A Theoretical Approach to German Expressionist Performance, 1916-1921.* Pittsburgh, PA: Univ. of Pittsburgh; 1988. 303 pp. Biblio. Notes. [Ph.D. Dissertation, Univ. Microfilms Order No. AAC 8911277.] Lang.: Eng.

Germany. 1916-1921. Critical studies. ■Develops a theory of the nature of Expressionist acting by defining the distinguishing surface features of the various modes and underlying assumptions of the nature of 'expression' in acting.

537 Schneider, Wolfgang. "Fünfhundert Jahre Kinder- und Jugendtheater." (Five Hundred Years of Children's and Young People's Theatre.) *Fundevogel.* 1998; 128: 16-33. Lang.: Ger.

Germany. 1579-1998. Bibliographical studies. ■Review of the latest published literature on children's and young people's theatre which changes, completes and corrects the results that Melchior Schedler published in *Kindertheater. Geschichte, Modelle, Projekte* (1972), the first history of children's theatre.

538 Shafer, Yvonne. "Berlin Productions During the Holidays." *WES.* 1998 Spr; 10(2): 47-58. Illus.: Photo. B&W. 12. Lang.: Eng.

Germany: Berlin. 1997-1998. Historical studies. ■Survey of the Berlin theatre, opera, and ballet seasons from December, 1997 through January, 1998.

539 Stumpfe, Mario. "Live Art." *TZ.* 1998; 2: 48-50. Notes. Illus.: Photo. B&W. 1. Lang.: Ger.

UK-England, Sheffield. Germany: Berlin. 1984-1998. Historical studies. ■Influence of the group Forced Entertainment on the live art scene and the Live Art Festival last autumn in Berlin.

540 Galántai, Csaba. "Márkus László emlékezete." (Commemorating László Márkus.) *OperaL.* 1998; 7(4): 28-29. Lang.: Hun.

Hungary. 1881-1948. Biographical studies. ■Profile of the one-time director of the Budapest Opera House on the fiftieth anniversary of his death. He was a jounalist, critic, aesthetician, playwright, costumer and stage designer, stage director and theatre manager. Also covers his association with the Thália Society, Magyar Színház, and National Theatre.

541 Srampickal, Jacob; Boon, Richard. "Popular Theatre for the Building of Social Awareness: The Indian Experience." 135-153 in Boon, Richard, ed.; Plastow, Jane, ed. *Theatre Matters: Performance and Culture on the World Stage.* Cambridge: Cambridge UP; 1998. 203 pp. (Cambridge Studies in Modern Theatre.) Notes. Index. Pref. Lang.: Eng.

India. 1975-1995. Historical studies. ■The use of Indian popular theatre as a vehicle for social protest and awareness, especially through the use of Social Action Groups in rural areas.

542 *Totò partenopeo e parte napoletano. Il teatro, la poesia, la musica.* (Totò Parthenopean and Neapolitan: Theatre, Poetry and Music.) Venice: Marsilio; 1998. 141 pp. Pref. Biblio. Notes. Illus.: Photo. Sketches. Print. B&W. 67. Lang.: Ita.

Italy: Naples. 1898-1998. Histories-sources. ■Catalogue of an exhibition held in Rome on the centenary of the Italian actor Totò (Antonio De Curtis).

543 Bassano, Serena. *Con quella faccia un pò cosí. Battute, bozzetti e autocaricature di Gilberto Govi.* (With a Face Like That: Witty Remarks, Sketches and Caricatures of Gilberto Govi.) Genoa: Feguagiskia Studios; 1998. 63 pp. Illus.: Dwg. Sketches. 8. Lang.: Ita.

Italy: Genoa. 1885-1966. Histories-sources. ■Collection of sketches and caricatures of the Italian dialect actor Gilberto Govi, many by the actor himself.

544 Bene, Carmelo; Grezzi, Enrico. *Discorso su due piedi (il calcio).* (A Small Talk on Two Feet: Football.) Milan: Bompiani; 1998. 121 pp. (Passaggi Bompiani.) Lang.: Ita.

Italy. 1998. Histories-sources. ■A half serious conversation between actor and director Carmelo Bene and journalist Enrico Ghezzi.

545 Berezin, Mabel. *Public Spectacles and Private Enterprises: Theater and Politics in Italy Under Fascism, 1919-1940.* Cambridge, MA: Harvard Univ; 1987. 284 pp. Notes. Biblio. [Ph.D. Dissertation, Univ. Microfilms Order No. AAC 8806064.] Lang.: Eng.

Italy. 1919-1940. Historical studies. ■Argues that Fascism as political movement borrowed its ideology and rhetoric from the theatrical movement, Futurism, and that members of the Italian theatrical community used the Fascist regime to enhance their professional status and lost control of the theatre. Also examines the regime's use of theatrical subsidies and Fascism's appropriation of Socialist people's theatre.

546 Caprara, Valerio. *Spettabile pubblico. Carosello Napoletano di Ettore Giannini.* (Dear Audience: Neapolitan Carousel by Ettore Giannini.) Naples: Guida; 1998. 211 pp. Notes. Illus.: Photo. Print. Color. B&W. Lang.: Ita.

Italy. 1950. Histories-specific. ■Ettore Giannini's film and stage work *Carosello Napoletano (Neapolitan Carousel).*

547 De Monticelli, Roberto. *Le mille notti del critico. Trentacinque anni di teatro vissuti e raccontati da uno spettatore di professione.* (The Critic's Thousand Nights: Thirty-Five Years of Theatre Lived and Reported by a Professional Spectator.) Rome: Bulzoni; 1998. 2976 pp. Notes. Index. [Two volumes.] Lang.: Ita.

Italy. 1974-1987. Reviews of performances. ■Collection of reviews written by De Monticelli for *Corriere della Sera.*

548 Del Cielo, Barbara, ed .; Schenone, Francesca, ed. *La piazza del popolo. La rappresentazione del conflitto sociale nella cultura di base del secondo dopoguerra.* (The People's Square: The Representation of the Social Conflict in the Popular Culture of the Post-World War II Period.) Rocca Grimalda: Edizioni del Laboratorio; 1998. 88 pp. Biblio. Illus.: Photo. Print. B&W. 11. Lang.: Ita.

Italy. 1945-1958. Historical studies. ■Collection of essays on the Teatro di massa (Mass Theatre), which dealt with social and political problems.

549 Di Bernardi, Vito. "La marionetta, la maschera, l'attore. Alcune considerazioni su Angelo Musco." (Puppet, Mask and Actor: Some Considerations about Angelo Musco.) *IlCast.* 1998; 11(31): 5-26. Notes. Lang.: Ita.

Italy. 1872-1937. Biographical studies. ■A reconstruction of the acting of Angelo Musco through the comparison of the reviews of his time and the sequence of his theatre films. Pirandello wrote his first successful plays for this great Sicilian actor.

550 Kiec, Izolda. "'Parada' o Paradzie. Z dziejów teatru i prasy Armii Polskiej na Wschodzie 1942-1947." ('Parada' about Parada: From the History of Theatre and Press of the Polish Army in the East, 1942-1947.) *PaT.* 1998; 47(1-2): 187-193. Notes. Illus.: Photo. B&W. 1. Lang.: Pol.

Italy: Rome. Egypt: Cairo. 1942-1947. Historical studies. ■Examines the theatrical activities by Polish soldiers, in Egypt and Italy during World War II and their coverage in the magazine *Parada.*

551 Marinelli, Donald. *Origins of Futurist Theatricality: The Early Life and Career of F.T. Marinetti.* Pittsburgh, PA: Univ. of Pittsburgh; 1987. 408 pp. Biblio. Notes. [Ph.D. Dissertation, Univ. Microfilms Order No. AAC 8719257.] Lang.: Eng.

Italy. 1876-1909. Historical studies. ■Argues that the early life and career of F.T. Marinetti, leader of the Futurist movement, is itself the model for the Futurist aesthetic.

552 Scarlini, Luca, ed. *Anna Proclemer. Vita e teatro.* (Anna Proclemer. Life and Theatre.) Firenze: Edizioni Polistampa; 1998. 75 pp. Illus.: Photo. B&W. 12. [Firenze, Centro di Promozione Teatro della Pergola 20 February - 22 March 1998.] Lang.: Ita.

Italy. 1923-1998. Histories-sources. ■Catalogue of a small exhibition of letters, photographs, and playbills of the Italian actress Anna Proclemer.

553 Scott, Virginia. "*La virtu et la volupté*: Models for the Actress in Early Modern Italy and France." *ThR.* 1998 Sum ; 23(2): 152-158. Notes. Lang.: Eng.

Italy. France. 1550-1750. Historical studies. ■Contrasts the French courtesan-actress, trained in music, dance, and conversation, such as Marie

THEATRE IN GENERAL: —Performance/production

Champmeslé and Armande Béjart, and the Italian model of 'virtue' such as Isabella Andreini.

554 Valentini, Valentina. "Avanguardia, tradizione e scrittura scenica. Rifondare il teatro/alimentare l'utopia." (Vanguard, Tradition, and Scenic Writing. Re-founding Theatre/Feeding Utopia.) *BiT.* 1998; 48: 11-31. Notes. Lang.: Ita.

Italy. 1960-1985. Critical studies. ■The dynamics and contradictions of the history of the avant-garde, said to have focused on the need to undermine what was specific in theatre and dissolve it in the name of an immediate reflex of political intervention.

555 Goto, Yukihiro. *Suzuki Tadashi: Innovator of Contemporary Japanese Theatre.* Honolulu, HI: Univ. of Hawaii; 1988. 354 pp. Biblio. Notes. [Ph.D. Dissertation, Univ. Microfilms Order No. AAC 8902854.] Lang.: Eng.

Japan. 1939-1984. Histories-specific. ■Examines the career, theory, and practice of the Japanese stage director and acting/movement teacher Tadashi Suzuki and his company the Suzuki Company of Toga (formerly Waseda Little Theatre).

556 Ståhle, Anna Greta. "Ömsa skinn inför öppen ridå." (Cast One's Skin In the Full Glare of Publicity.) *Danst.* 1998; 8(1): 20-21. Illus.: Photo. B&W. Lang.: Swe.

Japan. Russia. Denmark. 1752-1998. Historical studies. ■Essay about changing costumes on stage, with references to *Dojoji*, August Bournonville's *Napoli* and the Russian circus artists Igor and Svetlana Sudarčikov.

557 Haeong, Shik Kim. "Koreanisches Madang-Theater: Seine Konzeption und seine ästhetischen Merkmale anhand dreier Beispiele." (Korean *Madang* Theatre: Its Conception and its Aesthetic Characteristics with Three Examples.) *FMT.* 1998; 13(1): 58-84. Notes. Lang.: Ger.

Korea. 1976-1998. Historical studies. ■The historical and political context of *madang* or *minjung* theatre, a political theatre incorporating elements of theatre and dance. Includes analysis of Kim Chong Ku's *Doesipuri* and *Sori-Kut Ahgu.*

558 Bergmane, Astra. "Har teatern en framtid i Lettland?" (Does Theatre Have a Future In Latvia?)*ProScen.* 1998; 22(1): 32-33. Lang.: Swe, Eng, Ger.

Latvia. 1918-1998. Histories-sources. ■Letter from Latvia about the role of theatre throughout Latvian history, with emphasis on present hard times.

559 Krogerus, Anna. "Suzukia Liettuassa." (Suzuki in Lithuania.) *TeatterT.* 1998; 1: 26-29. Lang.: Fin.

Lithuania. 1998. Historical studies. ■Report on Japanese acting teacher and theorist Tadashi Suzuki's visit to Lithuania and the state of theatre education there.

560 Underiner, Tamara L. "Incidents of Theatre in Chiapas, Tabasco, and Yucatán: Cultural Enactments in Mayan Mexico." *TJ.* 1998 Oct.; 50(3): 349-369. Notes. Illus.: Photo. B&W. 4. Lang.: Eng.

Mexico. 1975-1998. Critical studies. ■Indigenous negotiations of the cultural and political legacy of the Spanish conquest and the power of local patriarchy, as reflected in local indigenous theatre.

561 Al-Sheddi, B. *The Roots of Arabic Theatre.* Durham: Unpublished PhD, Univ. of Durham; 1997. Notes. Biblio. [Abstract in *Aslib Index to Theses* 47-2823.] Lang.: Eng.

Middle East. 225-1995. Histories-specific. ■Demonstrates that the various forms of performance, music, and oral traditions have reflected the artistic, intellectual, and popular taste of the different peoples of the region. Argues that modern Arab dramatists failed in their attempts to produce perfect imitations of European dramatic forms.

562 Blokdijk, Tom. *Het theaterfestival 1998: Essays over acteerstijlen.* (The Theaterfestival 1998: Essays on Acting Styles.) Amsterdam: Stichting Het theaterfestival; 1998. 149 pp. Pref. Index. Biblio. Lang.: Dut.

Netherlands: Amsterdam. 1998. Critical studies. ■An account of a symposium on acting held during the Theaterfestival in September, 1998, in Amsterdam.

563 Kolk, Mieke. *'Wie zou ik zijn alsik zijn kon': vrouw en theater 1975-1998.* ('Who Would I Be If I Could': Women and Theatre, 1975-1998.) Amsterdam: Theater Instituut Nederland; 1998. 247 pp. Pref. Biblio. Index. Illus.: Photo. B&W. 14. Lang.: Dut.

Netherlands. 1975-1998. Historical studies. ■An overview of the role of women in Dutch theatre production between 1975 and 1998.

564 Licher, Edmund; Underdelinden, Sjaak. *Het gevoel heeft verstand geuregen. Brecht in Nederland.* (The Emotions Got Brains: Brecht in the Netherlands.) Amsterdam/Rotterdam: Tin/Aristos; 1998. 245 pp. Pref. Notes. Tables. Illus.: Photo. B&W. 23. Lang.: Dut.

Netherlands. 1940-1998. Critical studies. ■A history of the reception of Brecht's work in the Netherlands.

565 Utz, James Edward, Jr. *Towards a 'Situationist' Theatre: Embracing the Impossible in Dutch Performance.* Eugene, OR: Univ. of Oregon; 1998. 239 pp. Notes. Biblio. [Ph.D. Dissertation, Univ. Microfilms Order No. AAC 9841382.] Lang.: Eng.

Netherlands. 1990-1997. Critical studies. ■The relationship between the theatrical medium and situationist theory in the current theatre milieu of in the Netherlands.

566 Wippoo, Pim; Citroen, Liesbeth. *Podiumangst.* (Stage Fright.) Amsterdam: Boom; 1998. 161 pp. Pref. Illus.: Graphs. Dwg. 8. Lang.: Dut.

Netherlands. 1998. Instructional materials. ■An analysis of stage fright and how to handle it when confronted with it as an actor/singer/performer.

567 Armstrong, Gordon. "Civil War and Civil Discord: Theatrical Representation of the Common Will and the Single Heart in the Terrible Century." *ThR.* 1998 Spr; 23(1): 1-6. Notes. Lang.: Eng.

North America. Europe. Africa. 1975-1998. Historical studies. ■Introductory essay to volume of articles on the nature of twentieth-century civil war and civil discord in theatrical representations and the conditions of performance.

568 Austin, Gayle. "Feminism and Dramaturgy: Musings on Multiple Meanings." *JDTC.* 1998 Fall; 13(1): 121-124. Notes. Lang.: Eng.

North America. 1998. Critical studies. ■The current state of feminist theory and practice in contemporary dramaturgy.

569 Fiske, Jeffrey Thomas. *The Parallel Phenomena of Societal Expansion and Dramatic Response to Ages of Self-Discovery.* Columbus, OH: Ohio State Univ; 1988. 253 pp. Biblio. Notes. [Ph.D. Dissertation, Univ. Microfilms Order No. AAC 8812245.] Lang.: Eng.

North America. Europe. Asia. 500 B.C.-1980 A.D. Historical studies. ■The expansion of world theatre during periods of exploration and territorial acquisition, with respect to societal perspectives and social change. Examines sociological theories of discovery to explain innovations in theatre during eight 'great ages' from the Greeks to twentieth-century America.

570 Haedicke, Susan Chandler. "Dramaturgy in Community-Based Theatre." *JDTC.* 1998 Fall; 13(1): 125-132. Notes. Lang.: Eng.

North America. Asia. South America. 1990-1998. Critical studies. ■The state of dramaturgy in community-based theatres.

571 Neely, Kent. "PRAXIS: An Editorial Statement." *JDTC.* 1998 Spr; 12(2): 109-110. Notes. Lang.: Eng.

North America. 1997-1998. Critical studies. ■Introductory essay to articles about integrating theory into production.

572 Proehl, Geoff. "Rehearsing Dramaturgy: 'Time Is Passing'." *JDTC.* 1998 Fall; 13(1): 103-112. Notes. Lang.: Eng.

North America. 1998. Critical studies. ■Theoretical aspects of dramaturgy including the use of time in rehearsal and the need of the dramaturg to enter fully into that world, not stand outside and give directions.

573 Koloski, Laurie S. *Painting Krakow Red: Politics and Culture in Poland, 1945-1950.* Stanford, CA: Stanford Univ; 1998. 423 pp. Notes. Biblio. [Ph.D. Dissertation, Univ. Microfilms Order No. AAC 9901539.] Lang.: Eng.

Poland. 1945-1950. Histories-specific. ■Theatre in postwar Krakow as a reflection of cultural agendas and an interaction between social and political claims. Author focuses on the socialist politician Boleslaw Drobner and his use of theatre as a metaphor for local autonomy and Mieczyslaw Kotlarczyk's Teatr Rapsodyczny and its agenda of moral and national renewal through Romantic drama.

574 Krasiński, Edward. "Związki i współpraca artystów teatru polskiego i żydowskiego w okresie międzywojennym." (Connections and Collaboration of Polish and Jewish Theatre Artists During the Interwar Period.) 302-311 in Kuligowska-Korzeniewska, Anna, ed.; Leyko, Małgorzata. *Teatr żydowski w Polsce.* Lodz: Wydawnictwo Uniwersytetu Łódz; 1998. 457 pp. Lang.: Pol.
Poland: Warsaw. 1923-1937. Critical studies. ■Examines collaboration between individuals and theatre groups of differing ethnicities, their mutual influence on staging, directing, stage design, exchange of theatre texts, and pedagogy.

575 Osiński, Zbigniew. "Pierwsze laboratorium teatralne Grotowskiego." (The First Theatrical Laboratory of Grotowski's Student Scientific Circle, 1951-1959.) *DialogW.* 1998 Jan.; 1: 116-132. Illus.: Photo. B&W. 1. Lang.: Pol.
Poland: Cracow. 1951-1959. Historical studies. ■The work of Jerzy Grotowski in the Scientific Circle of the Theatre Academy in Cracow while he was studying there and working as a senior assistant, including his research on Stanislavskij and his first attempts at directing.

576 Romanowski, Andrzej. "Dzieje Teatru Polskiego w Wilnie 1905-1915." (The History of Polish Theatre in Vilna, 1905-1915.) *PaT.* 1998; 47(3-4): 451-517. Notes. Illus.: Handbill. Photo. B&W. 21. Lang.: Pol.
Poland: Vilna. 1905-1915. Historical studies. ■Examines theatrical activity in Vilna at the beginning of the twentieth century.

577 Steinlauf, Michael Charles. *Polish-Jewish Theater: The Case of Mark Arnshteyn, A Study of the Interplay Among Yiddish, Polish and Polish-Language Jewish Culture in the Modern Period.* Waltham, MA: Brandeis Univ; 1988. 398 pp. Biblio. Notes. [Ph.D. Dissertation, Univ. Microfilms Order No. AAC 8811132.] Lang.: Eng.
Poland. 1850-1950. Historical studies. ■Examines Polish-Jewish cultural relations as reflected in the Yiddish and Polish theatre: repertoire, performers, performing style, performance sites, audiences and criticism.

578 Kuraś, Marzena. "Teatr Żołnierza Polskiego w Comisani." (Theatre of the Polish Soldier in Comisani.) *PaT.* 1998; 47(1-2): 55-80. Notes. Append. Illus.: Photo. Poster. B&W. 16. Lang.: Pol.
Romania: Comisani. 1939-1940. Historical studies. ■Describes the origin and activity of the Polish soldier's theatre troupe in an internment camp.

579 Arkad'ev, L. "Kak v skazke..." (Like in a Fairy Tale...) *Lehaim.* 1998; 3: 14-16. Lang.: Rus.
Russia. 1998. Biographical studies. ■Profile of actor Arkadij Rajkin.

580 Konecny, Mark Clarence. *The Aesthetics of Performance in Experimental Russian Culture of the 1910s.* Los Angeles, CA: Univ. of Southern California; 1998. 461 pp. Notes. Biblio. [Ph.D. Dissertation, Univ. Microfilms Order No. AAC 9902830.] Lang.: Eng.
Russia. 1910-1915. Critical studies. ■Focuses on the relationship between theatre and the poetic text, the mixing of high and low genres in Russian Modernism, cabaret, theatre and the Futurist aesthetic.

581 Mel'nikova, S.I., ed. "K istorii nemeckogo teatra v Rossii: Doklad Aleksandru I 1806 g." (History of German Theatre in Russia: 1806 Report for Alexander I.) *Istoričeskij archiv.* 1998; 1: 159-165. Lang.: Rus.
Russia. 1806. Historical studies. ■Report on German theatre in Russia prepared for Czar Alexander I.

582 Okunevskaja, T.K. *Tat'janin den'.* (Tatjana's Day.) Moscow: Vagrius; 1998. 448 pp. Lang.: Rus.
Russia. 1998. Histories-sources. ■Memoirs of stage and screen actress Tatjana Okunevskaja.

583 Rajkin, A.I.; Uvarova, E.D., ed. *Vospominanija.* (Recollections.) Moscow: Firma 'Izd-vo AST'; 1998. 480 pp. Lang.: Rus.
Russia. 1998. Histories-sources. ■Actor Arkadij Rajkin on his life and career.

584 Ranevskaja, Faina G.; Zacharov, I.V., ed. *Slučai. Šutki. Aforizmy.* (Listen! Jokes and Aphorisms.) Moscow: Zacharov; 1998. 110 pp. Lang.: Rus.
Russia. 1896-1984. Histories-sources. ■Collection of anecdotes by, and about, singer/actress Ranevskaja.

585 Schanke, Robert A. "Alla Nazimova: 'The Witch of Makeup'." 129-150 in Schanke, Robert A., ed.; Marra, Kim, ed. *Passing Performances: Queer Readings of Leading Players in American Theatre History.* Ann Arbor, MI: Univ of Michigan P; 1998. 338 pp. (Triangulations: Lesbian/Gay/Queer Theatre/Drama/Performance.) Notes. Index. Illus.: Photo. 1. Lang.: Eng.
Russia. USA. 1878-1945. Biographical studies. ■The life and career of actress/director Alla Nazimova.

586 Vesnik, E. "Poznat' drug druga nevozmožno! No ljubit' možno beskonečno." (To Really Get To Know each Other Is Impossible! But It Is Possible To Love One Another Forever.) *Al'jans.* 1998; July: 30-34. Lang.: Rus.
Russia: Moscow. 1998. Histories-sources. ■Interview with stage and film actor Jévgenij Vesnik.

587 Vul'f, V. *Teatral'nyj dožd': Zametki i ėsse.* (Theatrical Rain: Notes and Essays.) Moscow: Znanie; 1998. 192 pp. (Mir iskusstv.) Lang.: Rus.
Russia. 1995-1999. Historical studies. ■Fate of contemporary actors, including those who have faded into theatre and ballet history.

588 Žučkov, V. "Dva veka teatral'nogo volšebstva." (Two Centuries of Theatrical Magic.) *Nižnij Novgorod.* 1998; 2: 164-171. Lang.: Rus.
Russia: Nižnij Novgorod. Historical studies. ■Theatrical history of Nižnij Novgorod.

589 Plesch, Véronique. "*Ludus Sabaudiae*: Observations on Late Medieval Theatre in the Duchy of Savoy." *EDAM.* 1998 Fall; 21(1): 1-20. Notes. Append. Illus.: Pntg. B&W. 1. Lang.: Eng.
Savoy. 1400-1600. Historical studies. ■Includes an appendix with a non-comprehensive chronology of performances.

590 Ahačič, Draga. *Gledališče besede.* (Language Theatre.) Ljubljana: Cankarjeva založba; 1998. 406 pp. Index. Biblio. Illus.: Photo. B&W. 4. Lang.: Slo.
Slovenia. 1997. Critical studies. ■Analysis of theatre as a linguistic phenomenon by a Slovene actress, writer, and director.

591 Bibič, Polde. *Soigralci.* (My Fellow Actors.) Ljubljana: Mladinska knjiga; 1998. 248 pp. Illus.: Photo. B&W. 5. Lang.: Slo.
Slovenia. 1945-1997. Histories-sources. ■A collection of portraits of fellow actors by Slovene actor Polde Bibič.

592 Šav, Vlado. "Ritualno gledališče—od svetega v profano in nazaj." (The Ritual Theatre—from Sacred to Profane and Back Again.) *Dialogi.* 1998; 906(1-2): 11-20. Lang.: Slo.
Slovenia. 1960-1998. Critical studies. ■Examines the characteristics of ritual theatre—spiritualism, aestheticism, and psychology—and its development.

593 Stavbar, Vlasta. *Kulturno dogajanje v Mariboru v letih 1914-1918.* (Cultural Events in Maribor in the Years 1914-1918.) Maribor: Obzorja; 1998. 214 pp. Pref. Index. Append. Illus.: Photo. B&W. 28. Lang.: Slo.
Slovenia: Maribor. 1914-1918. Histories-general. ■Examines the cultural life in Maribor during the First World War. Describes the theatrical events of the period as performed by the two national communities—the German and the Slovene—with a complete repertoire list of performances season by season from 1914 to 1918.

594 Vevar, Rok. "Gledališče na začetku nekega konca." (Theatre at the Beginning of Some End.) *Dialogi.* 1998; 906(1-2): 75-83. Lang.: Slo.
Slovenia. 1994-1997. Critical studies. ■Analyzes Slovene performance and concludes that it shows the influence of foreign stage experiences and of permanent contacts with European creators.

THEATRE IN GENERAL: —Performance/production

595 Vevar, Štefan. *Slovenska gledališka pot.* (The Story of Slovene Theatre.) Ljubljana: DZS; 1998. 115 pp. Pref. Index. Biblio. Illus.: Photo. B&W. 120. Lang.: Slo.

Slovenia. 1867-1997. Histories-general. ▪A condensed overview of Slovene theatre history, including opera, ballet, and puppetry.

596 Zupan, Jože. "Oživljanje spominov." (The Memoir Revival.) 8-28 in *Srečavanja (Meetings).* Ljubljana: Karantanija; 1998. 356 pp. Illus.: Dwg. B&W. 1. Lang.: Slo.

Slovenia. 1960-1997. Histories-sources. ▪Interview with the well-known Slovene actress Milena Zupančič about her life and work.

597 Ekberg, Emil. "Grahamstown–Sydafrikas största kulturfestival." (Grahamstown–The Biggest Cultural Festival of South Africa.) *Tningen.* 1998; 21(5): 46-47. Illus.: Photo. Color. Lang.: Swe.

South Africa, Republic of: Grahamstown. 1998. Historical studies. ▪Report from the Grahamstown National Arts Festival.

598 Feldman, Sharon. "Scenes from the Contemporary Barcelona Stage: La Fura dels Baus's Aspiration to the Authentic." *TJ.* 1998 Dec.; 50(4): 447-472. Notes. Illus.: Photo. B&W. 3. Lang.: Eng.

Spain: Barcelona. 1983-1998. Critical studies. ▪Examines the nature of truth and authenticity in the work of La Fura dels Baus, an alternative theatre company, with emphasis on *M.T.M.*

599 Johnson, Anita Louise. *Spanish Theater Since Franco: From Dictatorship to Democracy.* Madison, WI: Univ. of Wisconsin; 1988. 244 pp. Notes. Biblio. [Ph.D. Dissertation, Univ. Microfilms Order No. AAC 8826049.] Lang.: Eng.

Spain. 1975-1985. Histories-specific. ▪Argues that there has been little experimentation in the democratic period and that the theatre is adhering to traditional patterns. Only in the last few years has a gradual process of theatrical renovation been noted.

600 Brise, Eva. "Skådeplats." (Scene of Actions.) *Tningen.* 1998; 21(1): 15-17. Illus.: Photo. B&W. Lang.: Swe.

Sweden: Stockholm. 1997. Historical studies. ▪Report from a week-long workshop arranged by Teaterkollektivet Rex, where artists, playwrights, one film-maker, and one musician were invited to a joint space free to create what they want, but in communication with each other.

601 Haglund, Birgitta. "Att komma åt helt andra berättelser." (To Reach Quite Other Tales.) *Tningen.* 1998; 21(4): 19-22. Illus.: Photo. B&W. Lang.: Swe.

Sweden. 1983-1998. Histories-sources. ▪Interview with Bengt Andersson, the artistic director of Teater Tre, about his background as a mime and ideas about the total theatre, with reference to his ballet for three excavators *Tu man hand (In Private)* a combination of mime, dance, text and theatre.

602 Rislund, Staffan; Forsberg, Sofia, photo. "Teater som tilltugg." (Theatre As Snacks.) *Tningen.* 1998; 21(1): 41-44. Illus.: Photo. Color. Lang.: Swe.

Sweden: Mariefred. 1993-1998. Historical studies. ▪Report on interactive theatre where you take a week-end at an old inn by the Gripsholm Castle, and take part in a whodunit where you as guest have the possibility to step in.

603 Moore, Dick. "Betty Buckley Headlines World AIDS Fundraiser." *EN.* 1998 Sep.; 83(7): 3. Illus.: Photo. 1. Lang.: Eng.

Switzerland: Geneva. 1998. Historical studies. ▪Reports on actress Betty Buckley's concert performance, sponsored by pharmaceutical company Glaxo Wellcome, at the 12th Annual World AIDS Conference in Geneva. This was also sponsored by Equity's Broadway Cares/Equity Fights AIDS.

604 Kasule, Samuel. "Popular Performance and the Construction of Social Reality in Post-Amin Uganda." *JPC.* 1998 Fall; 31(2) : 39-58. Notes. Biblio. Lang.: Eng.

Uganda. 1979-1998. Historical studies. ▪The various forms of popular entertainment that have developed since the fall of Idi Amin. Discusses theatre, radio drama, traveling musicians, singing groups, and particularly the *Kadongo Kamu* theatrical form that took shape during the 1980s.

605 Cade, Francis. "Around Town." *PlPl.* Feb 1998; 519: 28. Lang.: Eng.

UK-England: London. 1994-1998. Historical studies. ▪New venues and new productions in London, including Onion Shed and their pantomime *Dream Catching* (written and directed by Fergus Dick, 1997) and Jermyn Street Theatre with Neil Marcus, Artistic Director.

606 Chamberlain, Frank. "Creative Forms in Ipswich." *NTQ.* 1998 May; 14(2): 182-185. Notes. [Issue 54.] Lang.: Eng.

UK-England: Ipswich. 1998. Historical studies. ▪Report on the Creative Surges Seminar held in Ipswich under the auspices of the Research Society for Process Orientated Psychology. The seminar was led by Arlene and Jean-Claude Audergon, and includes descriptions of various exercises demonstrated that allow the actor greater freedom to explore the boundaries between the self and the character.

607 Di Gaetani, John Louis. "London and Paris 1998." *WES.* 1998 Spr; 10(2): 81-86. Illus.: Photo. B&W. 2. Lang.: Eng.

UK-England: London. France: Paris. 1998. Historical studies. ▪Impressions accrued during the month of January 1998, bouncing between London and Paris, of the theatre and opera being offered on those respective stages.

608 Draper, Ellen Piper Myer. *Melodrama: The Thought of Fiction.* Austin, TX: Univ. of Texas; 1987. 203 pp. Notes. Biblio. [Ph.D. Dissertation, Univ. Microfilms Order No. AAC 8806317.] Lang.: Eng.

UK-England. USA. 1830-1970. Critical studies. ▪Investigates the concept of excess in nineteenth-century melodrama and in Hollywood film melodramas of the twentieth century. Argues that conflicts between expressiveness and conventionality are at the heart of both.

609 Edwards, Barry. "Presence and Tele-Presence: One Map of Non-Linear Performance Process." *SATJ.* 1998 May/Sep.; 12(1/2): 165-171. Notes. Biblio. Lang.: Eng.

UK-England: London. 1997-1998. Histories-sources. ▪Director/creator's account of developing an untitled, theatrical movement piece, with the OPTIK theatre group, using computers.

610 Kalemba-Kasprzak, Elżbieta. "Teatr Drugiej Emigracji." (Theatre of the Second Emigration.) 23-88 in Kalemba-Kasprzak, Elżbieta, ed.; Ratajczak, Dobrochna, ed. *Dramat i teatr emigracyjny po roku 1939.* Wroclaw: Wiedza o kulturze; 1998. 348 pp. Lang.: Pol.

UK-England: London. 1939-1998. Historical studies. ▪Describes the Polish theatres accompanying Polish soldiers in London.

611 Mieszkowska, Anna. "Czołówka Teatralna Wojska Polskiego nr 1. Lwowska Fala 1939-1946." (The Theatrical Spearhead of the Polish Army No. 1: The Lvovian Wave, 1939-1946.) *PaT.* 1998; 47(1-2): 81-137. Notes. Append. Illus.: Handbill. Photo. Poster. B&W. 23. Lang.: Pol.

UK-England. France. Romania. 1939-1946. Historical studies. ▪Describes the origin of theatrical activities for Polish soldiers in England, France, and Romania during World War II.

612 Morrow, Lee Alan. "Elsie Janis: 'A Comfortable Goofiness'." 151-172 in Schanke, Robert A., ed.; Marra, Kim, ed. *Passing Performances: Queer Readings of Leading Players in American Theatre History.* Ann Arbor, MI: Univ of Michigan P; 1998. 338 pp. (Triangulations: Lesbian/Gay/Queer Theatre/Drama/Performance.) Notes. Index. Illus.: Photo. 2. Lang.: Eng.

UK-England. 1889-1956. Biographical studies. ▪The impact of a gay sensibility on the life and career of vaudeville entertainer, director, writer, producer, and film actor Elsie Janis.

613 Richards, Jeffrey H. "The Politics of Seduction: Theatre, Sexuality, and National Virtue in the Novels of Hannah Foster." 238-257 in Pollock, Della, ed. *Exceptional Spaces: Essays in Performance and History.* Chapel Hill, NC/London: Univ of North Carolina P; 1998. 394 pp. Index. Notes. Lang.: Eng.

UK-England. 1759-1840. Critical studies. ▪Examines the presence of the theatre in the novels of Hannah Foster. Specifically, how the novels treated the sexual/gender identities negotiated and staged in the theatre.

614 Verma, Jatinder. "'Binglishing' the Stage: A Generation of Asian Theatre in England." 126-134 in Boon, Richard, ed.; Plastow, Jane, ed. *Theatre Matters: Performance and Culture on the World Stage.* Cambridge: Cambridge UP; 1998.

THEATRE IN GENERAL: —Performance/production

203 pp. (Cambridge Studies in Modern Theatre.) Index. Pref. Lang.: Eng.

UK-England. 1965-1995. Historical studies. ▪The negotiation and sensibility of Indian theatre in England. Argues that theatre is a tool for cultural identity and social coherence, as well as integration. Focuses on the work of Tara Arts, the longest established Indian theatre company in England.

615 Hrycak, Alexandra Martha. *From the Iron Fist to the Invisible Hand: Writers, Artists and the Nation in Ukraine.* Chicago, IL: Univ. of Chicago; 1998. 485 pp. Notes. Biblio. [Ph.D. Dissertation, Univ. Microfilms Order No. AAC 9841530.] Lang.: Eng.

Ukraine: Lviv, Kiev, Kharkiv. 1990-1995. Historical studies. ▪Investigates Ukrainian theatre as an institutional site for the specific mechanisms by which Ukrainians became nationally conscious. Analyzes results of ethnographic fieldwork in five different Ukrainian theatre companies in Lviv, Kiev, and Kharkiv and argues that theatre is a crucial forum for development of national identity.

616 Allcott, A.M. *1922: Nomadic Ethics and Novelesque Aesthetics.* Buffalo, NY: State Univ. of New York; 1998. 250 pp. Biblio. Notes. [Ph.D. Dissertation, Univ. Microfilms Order No. AAC 9833577.] Lang.: Eng.

USA. 1985-1995. Critical studies. ▪Examines performativity in postmodern 'queer' works including a dance-theatre spectacle *Chairs for Jacob* based on an essay by Virginia Woolf, *K*, a play by Greg Allen, and a dance theatre performance piece, *The Porno Boy Speaks*, by the author.

617 Auletta, Robert; Beachum, Richard; Brizzell, Cindy; Brown, Kenneth; Channer, Lisa; Copelin, David; de Haan, Christopher; Fornes, Maria Irene; Gurantz, Maya; McGurl, Mimi; Moore, Honor; Owens, Rochelle; Price, Jonathan; Robinson, Brian W.; Rogoff, Gordon; Rugg, Rebecca Ann; Sills, Paul; Wardle, Irving; Weinstein, Arnold; Yankowitz, Susan; Munk, Erika, ed. "Anniversary Issue—1968-1998." *ThM.* 1998; 28(3): 6-91. Illus.: Photo. B&W. 19. Lang.: Eng.

USA. 1968-1998. Histories-sources. ▪Past contributors to *Theatre Magazine* share their feelings about the state of theatre and society at the time of the periodical's initial issue, and the changes that have taken place since. Includes poems, excerpts from performances at Yale by Joseph Chaikin's Open Theatre piece *1969 Terminal 1996*, Julian Beck, Judith Malina, and their Living Theatre's *Paradise Now*, and ruminations on politics, censorship, and the future of theatre.

618 Balme, Christopher. "Staging the Pacific: Framing Authenticity in Performances for Tourists at the Polynesian Cultural Center." *TJ.* 1998 Mar.; 50(1): 53-70. Notes. Illus.: Photo. B&W. 5. Lang.: Eng.

USA: Laie, HI. 1963-1997. Critical studies. ▪Argues that 'native' performers at the Polynesian Cultural Center play with tourists' expectations of an authentic 'Other' and so represent themselves as agents of their own staged territory, rather than as foreign objects of the tourist gaze.

619 Barnes-McLain, Noreen. "Bohemian on Horseback: Adah Isaacs Menken." 63-79 in Schanke, Robert A., ed.; Marra, Kim, ed. *Passing Performances: Queer Readings of Leading Players in American Theatre History.* Ann Arbor, MI: Univ of Michigan P; 1998. 338 pp. (Triangulations: Lesbian/Gay/Queer Theatre/Drama/Performance.) Notes. Index. Illus.: Photo. 1. Lang.: Eng.

USA. 1835-1869. Historical studies. ▪Queer historiographic approach to actress Adah Isaacs Menken with reference to her cross-dressing, intimate relations with women, and 'blurred sexuality' both on and off stage.

620 Becker, Becky K. "Review of *Too Much Light Makes the Baby Go Blind*, by the Neo-Futurists." *JDTC.* 1998 Spr; 12(2): 111-114. Notes. Lang.: Eng.

USA: Chicago, IL. 1997. Critical studies. ▪Theory and performance in the Neo-Futurists's production of *Too Much Light Makes the Baby Go Blind.*

621 Bershatsky, Charles. *A Psychoanalytic Study of the Actor.* Union for Experimenting Colleges and Universities; 1988. 197 pp. Notes. Biblio. [Ph.D. Dissertation, Univ. Microfilms Order No. AAC 8912165.] Lang.: Eng.

USA. 1988. Empirical research. ▪Proposes that the actor is a special category of psychoanalytic patient whose narcissism has contradictory features. Uses interviews with actors, a case study of an actor in psychoanalysis, and a detailed description of actors in a time-limited group consisting solely of performers.

622 Bishop, Cynthia Ann. *The Deconstructed Actor: Towards a Postmodern Acting Theory.* Boulder, CO: Univ. of Colorado; 1988. 231 pp. Biblio. Notes. [Ph.D. Dissertation, Univ. Microfilms Order No. AAC 8902879.] Lang.: Eng.

USA. 1988. Critical studies. ▪Examines some of the parameters and definitions of postmodernism and postmodern theatre and isolates the limitations of the structures of modern thought to postmodern theory and criticism in the theatre. Applies deconstructive criticism to performance theory and acting.

623 Bloomquist, Jane McCarthy. *Directing and Designing for Physically Disabled Actors in Educational Theater.* New York, NY: New York Univ; 1988. 319 pp. Biblio. Notes. [Ph.D. Dissertation, Univ. Microfilms Order No. AAC 8811447.] Lang.: Eng.

USA. 1988. Histories-specific. ▪Examines directorial and design considerations necessary to integrate actors with physical disabilities into a theatre production. Presents a history of the disabled in the US, accessibility considerations, and a history of the involvement of disabled individuals in theatre.

624 Bowman, Michael S. "Performing Southern History for the Tourist Gaze: Antebellum Home Tour Guide Performances." 142-158 in Pollock, Della, ed. *Exceptional Spaces: Essays in Performance and History.* Chapel Hill, NC/London: Univ of North Carolina P; 1998. 394 pp. Index. Notes. Lang.: Eng.

USA. 1985-1997. Critical studies. ▪Examines the semiotics of tourism, especially through the phenomenon of antebellum home tours.

625 Bradshaw, Charles Randall. *Acting Analysis of Character Development in Plays by Coward, Mamet, Miller, Molière, Pinter, Shakespeare, and Simon, and Songs by Rogers and Sondheim.* Long Beach, CA: Univ. of California; 1987. 34 pp. Notes. Biblio. [M.F.A. Thesis, Univ. Microfilms Order No. 1330580.] Lang.: Eng.

USA. 1987. Histories-sources. ▪The author's final project for the Master of Fine Arts degree in Acting, which was presented in the Directing Lab at California State University, Long Beach, on March 14, 1987.

626 Cady, Pamela. *Acting Analysis of Character Development in Plays by Noël Coward, Allan Miller, Arthur Miller, Harold Pinter, William Shakespeare, Neil Simon, and William Wycherly, and Songs by Fred Ebb and Bob Fosse and Walter Marks.* Long Beach, CA: Univ. of California; 1987. 30 pp. Notes. Biblio. [M.F.A. Thesis, Univ. Microfilms Order No. 1330581.] Lang.: Eng.

USA. 1987. Histories-sources. ▪The development of the author's M.F.A. Final Project, performed at California State University, Long Beach.

627 Capo, Kay Ellen. "Performing History in the Light of History." 343-386 in Pollock, Della, ed. *Exceptional Spaces: Essays in Performance and History.* Chapel Hill, NC/London: Univ of North Carolina P; 1998. 394 pp. Index. Notes. Lang.: Eng.

USA. 1983-1997. Histories-sources. ▪Recounts author's production of *Thoughts in the Margin*, based on the transcripts of a dissident trial smuggled out of Soviet Lithuania in the 1980s.

628 Casciero, Thomas. *Laban Movement Studies and Actor Training: An Experiential and Theoretical Course for Training Actors in Physical Awareness and Expressivity.* Cincinnati, OH: Union Institute; 1998. 311 pp. Notes. Biblio. [Ph.D. Dissertation, Univ. Microfilms Order No. AAC 9834137.] Lang.: Eng.

USA. 1997-1998. Empirical research. ▪The application of Laban Movement Studies to the training of actors. Includes the study of vocal training methods for actors and singers and the result of master classes, workshops, and undergraduate courses for actors and singers to refine teaching methodologies.

629 Condee, William F. "'Rise and Fall of the Mustache': Opera House and Culture in Late Nineteenth- and Early Twentieth-

Century Appalachia." *JADT.* 1998 Fall; 10(3): 12-20. Notes. Lang.: Eng.
USA. 1875-1925. Historical studies. ■The phenomenon of the opera house theatre, a performance locale that used the word opera to avoid antitheatrical sentiment. Argues that its broad range of performance and non-performance events created a point of intersection for all members of the community.

630 Crisson, James Edward. *Impact Averaging and Social Facilitation: The Effects of a Heterogeneous Audience on Anxiety and Task Performance.* Greensboro, NC: Univ. of North Carolina; 1988. 66 pp. Notes. Biblio. [Ph.D. Dissertation, Univ. Microfilms Order No. AAC 8907835.] Lang.: Eng.
USA. 1987. Empirical research. ■Examines whether heterogeneous audiences make a performer more or less anxious or apprehensive.

631 De Shields, André. "Equity Celebrates African American Heritage Month 1998: A Celebration of Paul Robeson." *EN.* 1998 May; 83(4): 4. Illus.: Photo. 10. Lang.: Eng.
USA. 1998. Historical studies. ■Relates the life and history of Paul Robeson in light of contemporary celebrations of Black Heritage Month.

632 Doyle, Dennis Michael. *A Prolegomenon Toward the Establishment of Ethical Guidelines for the Social Context Performance.* Carbondale, IL: Southern Illinois Univ; 1988. 193 pp. Notes. Biblio. [Ph.D. Dissertation, Univ. Microfilms Order No. AAC 8922381.] Lang.: Eng.
USA. 1987. Histories-specific. ■Investigation of the social context performance according to the dictates of performance studies. Examines the ethical challenges confronting a performance practitioner when involved in a social context performance intent upon changing certain social conditions.

633 Evans, Tracy Ann. *A Participation Production of Brian Way's The Mirrorman.* Long Beach, CA: Univ. of California; 1987. 104 pp. Notes. Biblio. [M.F.A. Thesis, Univ. Microfilms Order No. 1330719.] Lang.: Eng.
USA. 1987. Histories-sources. ■The author's selection, training, and direction of four actors to present a participation play to three elementary-school audiences. Includes development of an approach to participation theatre in the pre-production period through rehearsals and performances.

634 Ferris, Lesley. "Kit and Guth: A Lavender Marriage on Broadway." 197-220 in Schanke, Robert A., ed.; Marra, Kim, ed. *Passing Performances: Queer Readings of Leading Players in American Theatre History.* Ann Arbor, MI: Univ of Michigan P; 1998. 338 pp. (Triangulations: Lesbian/Gay/Queer Theatre/Drama/Performance.) Notes. Index. Illus.: Photo. 1. Lang.: Eng.
USA. 1893-1974. Biographical studies. ■Argues that the marriage of theatre artists Katharine Cornell and Guthrie McClintic was one of 'convenience'.

635 Glenzer, Allison. "Irene Ryan Competition." *SoTh.* 1998 Sum; 39(3): 30. Illus.: Photo. B&W. 1. Lang.: Eng.
USA. 1998. Historical studies. ■The process of auditioning for an Irene Ryan Scholarship.

636 Graham, Duncan W. *Deriving Analytical Vocal Techniques from Performances of Robin Williams.* San Jose, CA: San Jose State Univ; 1998. 93 pp. Notes. Biblio. [M.A. Thesis, Univ. Microfilms Order No. AAC 1391523.] Lang.: Eng.
USA. 1988-1997. Empirical research. ■Addresses the lack of a systematic analysis for vocal performance in actor training. Develops a model to systematically analyze vocal performance and applies it to a representative sample of performances of Robin Williams.

637 Gurkweitz, Dmitri Eugene. *Dmitri E. Gurkweitz's Acting Analysis of Character Development in Plays by Coward, Kirkwood, Pinter, Molière, Tourneur, and Williams, and Screenplays by Bertolucci and Arcalli.* Long Beach, CA: California State Univ; 1988. 39 pp. Notes. Biblio. [M.F.A. Thesis, Univ. Microfilms Order No. AAC 1333830.] Lang.: Eng.
USA: Long Beach, CA. 1988. Histories-sources. ■Analysis of the development and outcome of the M.F.A. Final Acting Project, presented in the Theatre Arts Department Directing Laboratory.

638 Haenni, Sabine. *The Immigrant Scene: The Commercialization of Ethnicity and the Production of Publics in Fiction, Theatre, and the Cinema, 1890-1915.* Chicago, IL: Univ. of Chicago; 1998. 342 pp. Notes. Biblio. [Ph.D. Dissertation, Univ. Microfilms Order No. AAC 9832145.] Lang.: Eng.
USA: New York, NY. 1890-1915. Histories-specific. ■How theatre and cinema mediated between immigrant culture and mainstream commercial culture. Focuses on German and Italian ethnicities.

639 Halperin, Ellen Irene. *Acting and Psychotherapy: Applications of Kinetic and Imaging Techniques to Actor Training, an Empirical Study.* Eugene, OR: Univ. of Oregon; 1988. 305 pp. Biblio. Notes. [Ph.D. Dissertation, Univ. Microfilms Order No. AAC 8825743.] Lang.: Eng.
USA. 1988. Empirical studies. ■Examines the effects of kinetic and imaging techniques on performance and actor training, the history of psychotherapy-derived techniques in actor training, and how to improve criteria for evaluation.

640 Harbeck, James Christopher. *'Containment Is the Enemy': An Ideography of Richard Schechner.* Medford, MA: Tufts Univ; 1998. 274 pp. Notes. Biblio. [Ph.D. Dissertation, Univ. Microfilms Order No. AAC 9828875.] Lang.: Eng.
USA. 1965-1997. Critical studies. ■Argues that the most important element of performer/theatre artist Richard Schechner's ideology is unconstrained creation for each individual.

641 Heidger, John Michael. *Family Ties: A Biography of the Fields on the Frontier Stage.* Columbia, MO: Univ. of Missouri; 1988. 458 pp. Notes. Biblio. [Ph.D. Dissertation, Univ. Microfilms Order No. 8904432.] Lang.: Eng.
USA. 1830-1860. Histories-specific. ■The careers of frontier actors Joseph M. Field, Matthew Field, and Eliza Riddle Field.

642 Hendrick, Pamela R. "Two Opposite Animas? : Voice, Text, and Gender on Stage." *TTop.* 1998 Sep.; 8(2): 113-126. Notes. Biblio. Lang.: Eng.
USA. 1997-1998. Critical studies. ■Examines masculine and feminine constructs that may unconsciously govern actors' vocal and movement approaches to male and female characters onstage. Uses the work and theory of sociolinguistics to argue that analyzing how gender operates linguistically can strengthen students' social awareness, enhance their script interpretation skills, and increase their acting range.

643 Highsaw, Carol Anne. *A Theatre of Action: The Living Newspapers of the Federal Theatre Project.* Princeton, NJ: Princeton Univ; 1988. 434 pp. Biblio. Notes. [Ph.D. Dissertation, Univ. Microfilms Order No. AAC 8901017.] Lang.: Eng.
USA: New York, NY. 1935-1939. Histories-specific. ■A production history of the New York City branch and an analysis of the relation between their form and ideology. Some pieces included are *Triple-A Plowed Under, 1935, Injunction Granted, Power,* and *One-Third of a Nation.*

644 Jackson, Shannon. "Performance at Hull-House: Museum, Microfiche, and Historiography." 261-293 in Pollock, Della, ed. *Exceptional Spaces: Essays in Performance and History.* Chapel Hill, NC/London: Univ of North Carolina P; 1998. 394 pp. Index. Notes. Lang.: Eng.
USA: Chicago, IL. 1890-1997. Critical studies. ■Examines performance at and represented by Hull-House's Labor Museum, with respect to both a performative understanding of historical documents and to the actual performances of the period.

645 Jones, Chris. "The Alternate Route." *AmTh.* 1998 Oct.; 15(8): 80-83. Illus.: Photo. B&W. 2. Lang.: Eng.
USA: New York, NY. 1994-1998. Critical studies. ■Examines the recent surge of entertainment extravaganzas such as *Riverdance* and the Native American themed *Spirit Dance* and solo comedy shows like Rob Becker's *Defending the Caveman,* making their way to Broadway at the expense of more traditional shows.

646 Klein, Stacy A. *Eugenio Barba, Master Craftsman and the Odin Teatret's 'Oxyrhyncus Evangeliet'.* Medford, MA: Tufts Univ; 1988. 331 pp. Biblio. Notes. [Ph.D. Dissertation, Univ. Microfilms Order No. AAC 8816110.] Lang.: Eng.

THEATRE IN GENERAL: —Performance/production

USA. 1988. Critical studies. ■Eugenio Barba and his work at Odin Teatret: theatrical orientations, work on transcultural performance, and his latest performance piece, *Oxyrhyncus Evangeliet.*

647 Lamont, Rosette C. "Cords of Blood." *PerAJ.* 1998 Sep.; 20(3): 62-65. Lang.: Eng.

USA. 1997. Critical studies. ■Report on performance artist/puppeteer/choreographer Hanne Tierney's solo adaptation of Lorca's *Blood Wedding (Bodas de sangre).*

648 Larabee, Ann E. *First-Wave Feminist Theatre, 1890-1930.* Binghamton, NY: State Univ. of New York; 1988. 236 pp. Biblio. Notes. [Ph.D. Dissertation, Univ. Microfilms Order No. AAC 8819910.] Lang.: Eng.

USA. 1890-1930. Critical studies. ■Analyzes plays, rituals, suffrage pageants, the anti-lynching crusade of the NAACP, and the festivals of the Neighborhood Playhouse for new definitions of gender. Women dramatists covered include Djuna Barnes, Susan Glaspell, Edna St. Vincent Millay, Marita Bonner, and Angelina Weld Grimké.

649 Madison, D. Soyini. "That Was My Occupation: Oral Narrative, Performance, and Black Feminist Thought." 319-342 in Pollock, Della, ed. *Exceptional Spaces: Essays in Performance and History.* Chapel Hill, NC/London: Univ of North Carolina P; 1998. 394 pp. Index. Notes. Lang.: Eng.

USA. 1988-1997. Critical studies. ■Examines race and gender in the expression, experience, and performance of oral life history narratives.

650 Marshall, Brenda K. Devore. *A Semiotic Phenomenology of Directing.* Carbondale, IL: Southern Illinois Univ; 1988. 204 pp. Biblio. Notes. [Ph.D. Dissertation, Univ. Microfilms Order No. AAC 8909345.] Lang.: Eng.

USA. 1988. Critical studies. ■Uses semiotics to focus on the role of human communication within the theatrical rite of passage from preperforming to performing. Applies her theory to a student production of *Brecht on Brecht* by George Tabori at Southern Illinois University's Department of Theatre.

651 Maschio, Geraldine. "Effeminacy or Art? The Performativity of Julian Eltinge." *JADT.* 1998 Win; 10(1): 28-38. Notes. Lang.: Eng.

USA. 1890-1930. Historical studies. ■Female impersonation in American theatre. Focuses on Julian Eltinge, one of the premier female impersonators, and analyzes how the female stereotype was constructed.

652 McConachie, Bruce. "Approaching the 'Structure of Feeling' in Grassroots Theatre." *TTop.* 1998 Mar.; 8(1): 33-54. Notes. Biblio. Illus.: Photo. B&W. 2. Lang.: Eng.

USA. 1996-1997. Critical studies. ■The impact of particular images in a community-based student-created community theatre piece, *Walk Together Children.*

653 McDermott, Douglas. "The Theatre and Its Audience: Changing Modes of Social Organization in the American Theatre." 6-17 in Engle, Ron, ed.; Miller, Tice L., ed. *The American Stage: Social and Economic Issues from the Colonial Period to the Present.* Pref. Notes. Index. Lang.: Eng.

USA. 1770-1830. Historical studies. ■Early American theatre, its correlation with other social institutions, and its reflection of the desired level and kind of social control.

654 McNamara, Brooks. "Defining Popular Culture." *THSt.* 1998; 53: 3-12. Notes. Lang.: Eng.

USA. 1990-1997. Historical studies. ■Introductory essay to an issue on popular culture and entertainment and performance in the United States.

655 Merschmeier, Michael. "Im Reich des Löwenkönigs." (In the Empire of Lion King.) *THeute.* 1998; 4: 20-29. Illus.: Handbill. Photo. B&W. 13. Lang.: Ger.

USA: New York, NY. 1998. Critical studies. ■Impressions from Broadway, off and off-off Broadway theatre, about musicals, new plays and politics.

656 Moore, Dick. "Young Performers' Seminar Set for April 4 in New York." *EN.* 1998 Apr.; 83(3): 7. Lang.: Eng.

USA: New York, NY. 1998. Historical studies. ■Announces the Equity Young Performers' Committee Seminar Series which includes support systems for the young performer, careers behind the scenes, a networking session for parents and a clown workshop.

657 Moore, Dick. "Young Performers' Seminar Set, Children and Parents Invited." *EN.* 1998 Oct/Nov.; 83(8): 4. Lang.: Eng.

USA: New York, NY. 1998. Historical studies. ■Reports on the free seminar for young performers and their families, sponsored by Equity's Young Performers' Committee.

658 Moore, Dick. "Show Buzz." *EN.* 1998 July/Aug.; 83(6): 3. Lang.: Eng.

USA: New York, NY. 1998. Historical studies. ■Current news about the theatre and its people.

659 Moore, Dick. "Future of Black Theatre Discussed at Dartmouth Conference." *EN.* 1998 Apr.; 83(3): 1, 7. Lang.: Eng.

USA: Hanover, NH. 1998. Historical studies. ■Reports on a national conference on Black theatre convened by playwright August Wilson.

660 Moore, Dick. "The Celebration Concluded on Monday, February 23 with Cafe Afrocentric in the Club at La Mama." *EN.* 1998 May; 83(4): 5. Illus.: Photo. 14. Lang.: Eng.

USA: New York, NY. 1998. Historical studies. ■Photo essay on Black women celebrating Black History Month by creating poetic homages to Paul Robeson.

661 Moore, Dick. "Show Buzz." *EN.* 1998 Dec.; 83(9): 3. Lang.: Eng.

USA: New York, NY. 1998. Historical studies. ■Short news takes on current theatre events.

662 Newhouse, John William. *An Examination of Closed Circuit Television Integrated Into Avant-Garde Theatre Performance.* New York, NY: New York Univ; 1988. 289 pp. Biblio. Notes. [Ph.D. Dissertation, Univ. Microfilms Order No. AAC 8825255.] Lang.: Eng.

USA: New York, NY. 1978-1986. Critical studies. ■Criteria for the evaluation of video integrated into theatrical performance, with reference to the work of Squat Theatre, the Wooster Group, and Mabou Mines.

663 Oliver, Michael. "Street Theatre Epiphanies: Maryat Lee and the Making of *Dope!.*" *JADT.* 1998 Spr; 10(2): 26-39. Notes. Lang.: Eng.

USA: New York, NY. 1949-1951. Historical studies. ■The work of theatre artist Maryat Lee, focusing on her community work in East Harlem in the 1950s. Specifically analyzes *Dope!*, Lee's multiracial, collaborative, community-created and performed piece, generally considered the first example of urban street theatre.

664 Parnes, Uzi. *Pop Performance, Four Seminal Influences: The Work of Jack Smith, Tom Murrin—The Alien Comic, Ethyl Eichelberger, and the Split Britches Company.* New York, NY: New York Univ; 1988. 628 pp. Biblio. Notes. [Ph.D. Dissertation, Univ. Microfilms Order No. AAC 8825045.] Lang.: Eng.

USA: New York, NY. 1980-1988. Critical studies. ■Examines pop performance, a style of theatre that is a cross between non-narrative performance art and a resurging vaudevillian aesthetic.

665 Postlewait, Thomas. "Sojourning in Never Never Land: The Idea of Hollywood in Recent Theatre Autobiographies." 235-251 in Engle, Ron, ed.; Miller, Tice L., ed. *The American Stage: Social and Economic Issues from the Colonial Period to the Present.* Cambridge: Cambridge UP; 1993. 320 pp. Pref. Notes. Index. Lang.: Eng.

USA. 1950-1990. Historical studies. ■The myth of Hollywood, and its progressive ideals, in the autobiographies of Tennessee Williams, Arthur Miller, Lillian Hellman, Lee Strasberg, Harold Clurman, Cheryl Crawford, John Houseman, Robert Lewis, and Elia Kazan.

666 Pressler, Terra Daugirda. *Transformative Comedy: An Emerging Genre.* Eugene, OR: Univ. of Oregon; 1988. 240 pp. Biblio. Notes. [Ph.D. Dissertation, Univ. Microfilms Order No. AAC 8903835.] Lang.: Eng.

USA. 1975-1988. Critical studies. ■Comic-theory and feminist analysis of transformative comedy, performed typically in monologue form, using characters who are socially disenfranchised, as practiced by Lily Tomlin and Jane Wagner, Whoopi Goldberg, Ntozake Shange, Richard Pryor, and Jane Martin.

667 Riggs, Mike. "Paradox Now." *JADT.* 1998 Fall; 10(3): 21-31. Notes. Lang.: Eng.

THEATRE IN GENERAL: —Performance/production

USA. 1951-1968. Historical studies. ■Examines the creation and production history of the performance piece *Paradise Now* by The Living Theatre, conceived and directed by Julian Beck and Judith Malina.

668 Rix, Roxane. "Learning Alba Emoting." *TTop.* 1998 Mar.; 8(1): 55-72. Notes. Lang.: Eng.

USA. 1995-1998. Critical studies. ■Examines pedagogical issues arising from the Alba Emoting system, involves generating emotion through physical reproduction of scientifically measured patterns of breath, facial expression, and muscle tone.

669 Roach, Joseph R. "Slave Spectacles and Tragic Octoroons: A Cultural Genealogy of Antebellum Performance." 49-76 in Pollock, Della, ed. *Exceptional Spaces: Essays in Performance and History.* Chapel Hill, NC/London: Univ of North Carolina P; 1998. 394 pp. Index. Notes. Lang.: Eng.

USA. 1800-1860. Critical studies. ■The performance of race, gender, and the economics of pleasure and power in nineteenth-century melodramatic plays, including Boucicault's *The Octoroon*, as well as in depictions of slave auctions in paintings.

670 Savant, Anthony Louis. *Acting Analysis of Character Development in Plays by Coward, Mamet, Miller, Molière, Pinter, Shakespeare, and Simon, and Songs by Cohan and Sondheim.* Long Beach, CA: Univ. of California; 1987. 36 pp. Notes. Biblio. [M.F.A. Thesis, Univ. Microfilms Order No. 1330653.] Lang.: Eng.

USA. 1987. Critical studies. ■The development of the author's M.F.A. Final Project in acting, performed at California State University, Long Beach.

671 Schlosberg, Eve Harriett. *Acting Analysis of Character Development in Plays by Congreve, Coward, Miller, Pinter, Shakespeare, and Simon, and Songs by Ebb, Fosse, and Marks.* Long Beach, CA: Univ. of California; 1987. 46 pp. Notes. Biblio. [M.F.A. Thesis, Univ. Microfilms Order No. 1330654.] Lang.: Eng.

USA. 1987. Critical studies. ■Describes a Final Project for the M.F.A. in acting, performed at California State University.

672 Sears, Linda Roseanne. *Women and Improvisation: Transgression, Transformation, and Transcendence.* Denton, TX: Univ. of North Texas; 1998. 144 pp. Notes. Biblio. [M.A. Thesis, Univ. Microfilms Order No. AAC 1390745.] Lang.: Eng.

USA. 1970-1997. Histories-specific. ■Feminist analysis of women's use of improvisation in discovering, creating, and articulating various identities.

673 Squires, Richard. "The Meaning of Ecstasy." *PM.* 1990; 61: 51-59. Illus.: Photo. B&W. 4. Lang.: Eng.

USA. Germany. 1969-1990. Histories-sources. ■Performer relates his out-of-body experience while performing a medicine man's dance, and how that led him to examine the concept of ecstasy, and to seek its antecedents in Greek tragedy.

674 Strand, Ginger. "'My Noble Spartacus': Edwin Forrest and Masculinity on the Nineteenth-Century Stage." 19-40 in Schanke, Robert A., ed.; Marra, Kim, ed. *Passing Performances: Queer Readings of Leading Players in American Theatre History.* Ann Arbor, MI: Univ of Michigan P; 1998. 338 pp. (Triangulations: Lesbian/Gay/Queer Theatre/Drama/Performance.) Notes. Index. Illus.: Dwg. 1. Lang.: Eng.

USA. 1806-1872. Historical studies. ■The impact of homosexual desire in the life of actor Edwin Forrest and his role in the construction of masculinity in the early U.S. republic.

675 Sullivan, Claudia Norene. *Movement Training for the Actor: A Twentieth-Century Comparison and Analysis.* Boulder, CO: Univ. of Colorado; 1987. 213 pp. Notes. Biblio. [Ph.D. Dissertation, Univ. Microfilms Order No. AAC 8723509.] Lang.: Eng.

USA. 1910-1985. Historical studies. ■The importance, use, and training of the actor's body, with emphasis on the twentieth-century training approaches of Stanislavskij, Mejerchol'd, and Grotowski, as well as the movement theories of Moshe Feldenkrais, F.M. Alexander, and Rudolf Laban.

676 Tichy, Charles Allen. *The First Seventy Years of Legitimate Theatre in Omaha, Nebraska.* New York, NY: New York Univ; 1988. 337 pp. Biblio. Notes. [Ph.D. Dissertation, Univ. Microfilms Order No. AAC 8910646.] Lang.: Eng.

USA: Omaha, NB. 1857-1927. Histories-specific. ■Traces the development of legitimate theatre in Omaha from the first recorded performance to the construction of the last grand opera house.

677 Upor, László. "Színház az egész város: Egy évad New Yorkban, 1." (All the Town Is a Stage: A Season in New York, Part 1.) *Sz.* 1998; 31(9): 41-48. Illus.: Photo. B&W. 6. Lang.: Hun.

USA: New York, NY. 1997-1998. Critical studies. ■Hungarian dramaturg and translator on his extended visit to New York. Includes artistic, architectural, financial, and organizational aspects of New York theatrical life. Continued in *Sz* 1998 31:10, pp. 34-43 ('Színházi várostértép') and *Sz* 1998 31:11, pp. 19-27 ('Új Műveket, de rögtön!') devoted to new American playwriting.

678 Valette, Colette L. *The Relationship Between Creativity and Ego Identity of Actors and Actresses.* San Diego, CA: United States International Univ; 1988. 140 pp. Biblio. Notes. [Ph.D. Dissertation, Univ. Microfilms Order No. AAC 8909927.] Lang.: Eng.

USA. 1984-1987. Empirical research. ■Correlational study of eighty-four college theatre students who intended to pursue an acting career.

679 Vowells, John J. *Engaging Experience: Acting's Role in Creative Homily Preparation.* St. Louis, MO: Aquinas Institute; 1998. 160 pp. Notes. Biblio. [Ph.D. Dissertation, Univ. Microfilms Order No. AAC 9821073.] Lang.: Eng.

USA. 1997. Instructional materials. ■A handbook for creative preaching preparation that uses the skills of acting role preparation.

680 Walen, Denise A. "'Such a Romeo as We Had Never Ventured to Hope For': Charlotte Cushman." 41-62 in Schanke, Robert A., ed.; Marra, Kim, ed. *Passing Performances: Queer Readings of Leading Players in American Theatre History.* Ann Arbor, MI: Univ of Michigan P; 1998. 338 pp. (Triangulations: Lesbian/Gay/Queer Theatre/Drama/Performance.) Notes. Index. Illus.: Dwg. 1. Lang.: Eng.

USA. 1816-1876. Biographical studies. ■Same-sex desire and gender aspects in the life and career of actress Charlotte Cushman.

681 Wallace, Lillian Utermohlen. *The Connection of Theatrical Art to Social Issues Through the Dynamics of Performance.* Minneapolis, MN: Walden Univ; 1998. 316 pp. Notes. Biblio. [Ph.D. Dissertation, Univ. Microfilms Order No. AAC 9840073.] Lang.: Eng.

USA. 1965-1997. Empirical research. ■Documentation of the creation and development of a socially relevant performance on the subject of racial intolerance presented to a university audience. Includes discussion of audience reaction.

682 Westfahl, Lynne Lundquist. *The Professional Theatre of San Francisco in the 1850s.* Fullerton, CA: California State Univ; 1988. 150 pp. Notes. Biblio. [M.A. Thesis, Univ. Microfilms Order No. AAC 1335350.] Lang.: Eng.

USA: San Francisco, CA. 1850-1860. Histories-specific. ■Examines the growth of theatrical activity in San Francisco during the 1850s. Focuses on the supporting actors, the plays performed, the theatre buildings, the audiences, and the newspaper critics.

683 White, Robert Allwyn. *I Can't Hear You, Give Me More: The Development of an Introductory Course in Directing.* Cincinnati, OH: Union Institute; 1998. 209 pp. Notes. Biblio. [Ph.D. Dissertation, Univ. Microfilms Order No. AAC 9822006.] Lang.: Eng.

USA: Brevard, NC. 1997-1998. Empirical research. ■Includes an essay discussing the history of the director, a survey of the author's work in the field of directing, and a proposal and description of the approval process for a new course in directing to be taught at Brevard College.

684 Wolfe, Donald. "Freedman Embraces the 'Real' in Live Theatre." *SoTh.* 1998 Sum; 39(3): 14-18. Illus.: Photo. B&W. 1. Lang.: Eng.

THEATRE IN GENERAL: —Performance/production

USA: Birmingham, AL. 1998. Historical studies. ▪Director Gerald Freedman celebrates the beauty of 'real' theatre vs. 'reel' theatre in the SETC convention address.

685 Woods, Alan. "Consuming the Past: Commercial American Theatre in the Reagan Era." 252-266 in Engle, Ron, ed.; Miller, Tice L., ed. *The American Stage: Social and Economic Issues from the Colonial Period to the Present.* Cambridge: Cambridge UP; 1993. 320 pp. Pref. Notes. Index. Lang.: Eng.

USA. 1980-1990. Historical studies. ▪Argues that theatre during the Reagan administration was characterized by sentimentality, ersatz nostalgia, and meaningless spectacle.

686 Zakaryan, James Warren. *Acting Analysis of Character Development in Plays by Congreve, Mamet, Pinter, Shakespeare, Shepard, Wilde, Williams, and a Song by Hamlisch.* Long Beach, CA: Univ. of California; 1987. 39 pp. Notes. Biblio. [M.F.A. Thesis, Univ. Microfilms Order No. 1330679.] Lang.: Eng.

USA. 1987. Critical studies. ▪Process of development of an M.F.A. Final Project in acting, presented in the Laboratory Theatre at California State University.

687 Ukpokodu, I. Peter. "Theatre Rebels of Zimbabwe and Kenya." *ThR.* 1998 Spr; 23(1): 38-43. Notes. Lang.: Eng.

Zimbabwe. Kenya. 1990-1998. Historical studies. ▪The arts in a nation in a state of sociopolitical chaos: focuses on 'rebellious theatrical practices' such as the indigenous Kamiriithu theatre of Kenya, represented by the work of playwright Ngugi wa Thiong'o, and the Zambuko/Izibuko theatre of Zimbabwe.

Plays/librettos/scripts

688 Vaïs, Michel. "Le conte en question: Les Entrées libres de *Jeu.*" (The Story Under Scrutiny: *Jeu*'s Free Admission Series.) *JCT.* 1998; 87: 8-22. Notes. Illus.: Photo. Poster. B&W. 10. Lang.: Fre.

Canada: Montreal, PQ. 1998. Histories-sources. ▪Public forum united story-tellers Oro Anahory and Marc Laberge, and playwrights Yvan Bienvenue and Joël da Silva with critics Lynda Burgoyne and Michel Vaïs to discuss their use of story-telling, its nature and its popularity.

689 *Kazan' v žizni A.M. Gor'kogo i F.I. Šaljapina.* (Kazan in the Life of Gorkij and Šaljapin.) Kazan': 1998. 36 pp. Lang.: Rus.

Tatarstan: Kazan. 1868-1938. Critical studies. ▪Reflections of the city of Kazan on the work of playwright Gorkij and opera singer Šaljapin.

690 Callaghan, David Scott. *Representing the Vietnamese: Race, Culture, and the Vietnam War in American Film and Drama.* New York, NY: City Univ. of New York; 1998. 348 pp. Notes. Biblio. [Ph.D. Dissertation, Univ. Microfilms Order No. AAC 9830689.] Lang.: Eng.

USA. 1965-1993. Critical studies. ▪Examines the ways in which the Vietnamese were represented in cinematic and theatrical recreations of the Vietnam War. Analyzes how the images and themes of such works either reinterpret, reinvent, or reinforce earlier depictions of race and culture as established within the film and stage combat genre.

691 Deans, Jill R. *'Divide the Living Child in Two': Adoption and the Rhetoric of Legitimacy in Twentieth-Century American Literature.* Amherst, MA: Univ. of Massachusetts; 1998. 307 pp. Notes. Biblio. [Ph.D. Dissertation, Univ. Microfilms Order No. AAC 9841859.] Lang.: Eng.

USA. 1960-1997. Critical studies. ▪Argues that adoption narratives reveal the process through which individuals are recognized within the public discourse of family and community. Plays by Edward Albee and John Guare, and recent films are analyzed.

692 Brun, Fritz Constantin. *The Man in the Kremlin: The Image of Ivan the Terrible in Historical Drama.* Stanford, CA: Stanford Univ; 1987. 472 pp. Notes. Biblio. [Ph.D. Dissertation, Univ. Microfilms Order No. AAC 8722968.] Lang.: Eng.

USSR. 1800-1965. Historical studies. ▪The character of Russian Czar Ivan 'the Terrible' in Russian opera, ballet, literature, figurative arts, theatre, and film.

Reference materials

693 Aljanskij, Ju.A. *Azbuka teatra.* (The Alphabet of Theatre.) Moscow: Sovremennik; 1998. 238 pp. (Pod sen'ju družnych muz.) Lang.: Rus.

Histories-general. ▪Covering the history of world theatre, playwrights, directors, actors, performance styles, design conventions, and terminology.

694 Pavis, Patrice; Bosisio, Paolo, ed. *Dizionario del teatro.* (Theatre Dictionary.) Bologna: Zanichelli; 1998. 591 pp. Pref. Gloss. Lang.: Ita.

▪Italian translation of *Dictionnaire du théâtre* (Paris: Editions sociales, 1980).

695 Stapper, Lion; Altena, Peter; Uyen, Michel. *Miti e personaggi della modernità. Dizionario di storia, letteratura, arte, musica e cinema.* (Myths and Characters of Modernity: A Dictionary of History, Literature, Art, Music and Cinema.) Milan: Bruno Mondadori; 1998. 432 pp. Lang.: Ita.

▪Italian translation of *Van Abilard tot Zoroaster* (Nijmegen: Sun, 1994).

696 *Medieval English Theatre.* "Cumulative Index: Volumes 1-20." *MET.* 1998; 20: 127-138. Lang.: Eng.

England. 1979-1998. ▪Alphabetical indexes to articles and reports of productions published in the first twenty volumes of MET.

697 Brown, John Russell, ed.; Savarese, Nicole, ed. *Storia del teatro.* (History of Theatre.) Bologna: Il Mulino; 1998. 668 pp. (Le vie della civiltà.) Biblio. Pref. Index. Illus.: Photo. B&W. 54. Lang.: Ita.

Europe. North America. Asia. Africa. 500 B.C.-1995 A.D. Histories-general. ▪Italian translation of *The Oxford Illustrated History of Theatre* Oxford UP (1995).

698 Molnár, Klára, comp., ed.; Szebeni, Zsuzsa, comp.; Csalló, Erzsébet, biblio. *Évkönyv az 1995/1996. évadra.* (Yearbook of the 1995/1996 Season.) Budapest: Országos Színháztörténeti Múzeum és Intézet; 1998. 186 pp. Biblio. Index. Lang.: Hun.

Hungary. 1995-1996. ▪The annual contains all relevant information concerning the activity of Hungarian professional theatres at home and abroad in the 1995/1996 season with three indexes. A separate chapter is devoted to open-air performances, to permanent professional Hungarian groups beyond our frontiers, to guest performances of Hungarian professional companies abroad and foreign theatres in Hungary. Remarkable theatrical events as festivals, awards, obituaries are also listed. The yearbook is also a practical guide to institutions attached to the theatre. A bibliography of playtexts, books on theatre and theatre reviews published in Hungary is also included.

699 *Il Patalogo ventuno. Annuario dello spettacolo. Teatro.* (The Patalogo 21. 1998 Entertainment Yearbook. Theatre.) Milan: Ubulibri; 1998. 256 pp. Index. Illus.: Photo. B&W. 5. Lang.: Ita.

Italy. 1998. ▪Yearbook of the Italian theatre, festivals, and season with brief critical notations.

700 Ente Teatrale Italiano. *Il teatro per ragazzi. Catalogo delle produzioni 1998/1999.* (Theatre for Youth, Children and Teenagers. Catalogue of 1998-1999 Productions.) Rome: ETI; 1998. 494 pp. (Documenti di teatro 28.) Lang.: Ita.

Italy. 1998-1999. ▪Catalogue of 1998-1999 Italian theatre production for teenagers and children.

701 *Il mondo di Giacomo Casanova. Un veneziano in Europa 1725-1798.* (The World of Giacomo Casanova: A Venetian in Europe, 1725-1798.) Venice: Marsilio; 1998. 267 pp. Illus.: Dwg. Sketches. Pntg. 4. Lang.: Ita.

Italy: Venice. 1725-1798. Biographical studies. ▪Catalogue of an exhibition held in Venice at the Settecento Museum from September 1998 to January 1999 on the life and times of the Venetian dramatist and memoroirist Giacomo Casanova.

702 Cappa, Felice, ed.; Gelli, Piero, ed. *Dizionario dello spettacolo del '900.* (Twentieth Century Entertainment Dictionary.) Milan: Baldini & Castoldi; 1998. 1315 pp. (Le Boe 24.) Lang.: Ita.

Italy. 1900-1998. ▪A dictionary of actors, directors, genres, companies, focused primarily but not exclusively on Italian performing arts.

THEATRE IN GENERAL: —Reference materials

703 Lazzi, Giovanna, ed. *Carte di scena.* (Stage Documents.) Florence: Edizioni Polistampa Firenze; 1998. 130 pp. Pref. Index. Tables. Biblio. 20. [Firenze, Biblioteca Riccardiana 21th December 1998 - 20th March 1999.] Lang.: Ita.
Italy. 1998-1999. ■Catalogue of an exhibition of the manuscripts belonging to the Riccardi Library.

704 Vanni, Simona. "*Le Cronache d'attualità* di Bragaglia. (Indice degli articoli riguardanti lo spettacolo)." (Bragaglia's *Chronicles*: Index of Articles on Performing Arts.) *Ariel.* 1998; 13(3): 129-174. Notes. Append. Illus.: Sketches. 11. Lang.: Ita.
Italy: Rome. 1916-1922. ■Chronology of the articles about theatre and cinema, dance, variety, and music in Anton Giulio Bragaglia's review of the arts.

705 Ortolani, Benito; D'Orazi, Maria Pia, transl. *Il teatro giapponese. Dal rituale sciamanico alla scena contemporanea.* (The Japanese Theatre: From Shamanistic Ritual to Contemporary Pluralism.) Rome: Bulzoni; 1998. 421 pp. (Biblioteca Teatrale 88.) Pref. Gloss. Biblio. Index. Notes. Illus.: Photo. Sketches. Dwg. Print. B&W. 79. Lang.: Ita.
Japan. 350 B.C.-1998 A.D. Histories-specific. ■History of Japanese theatre and drama.

706 Tuganov, R.U. *Bibliografij Kabardino-Balkarii Karačaevo-Čerkesi Adyge drevnejšich vremen po 1917 god: Vyp. 3, t. 2: Kul'tura.* (Bibliography of Kabardino-Balkaria, Karachayevo-Cherkess, and Adygei from Ancient Times to 1917: 3rd Ed. Volume 2: Culture.) Nal'čik: Él'-Fa; 1998. 360 pp. Lang.: Rus.
Karachaevo-Cherkess. Historical studies. ■Bibliography of cultural activities of the region before the Russian Revolution.

707 Kuvakin, A.G., ed. *Znamenatel'nye daty'99: Kalendar' dlja rabotnikov b - k i ljubitelej knigi, nauki, slovesnosti.* (Holidays 1999: Calendar for Workers in Publishing, Sciences, Philosophy.) Moscow: Libereja-Bibinform; 1998. 600 pp. Lang.: Rus.
Russia. 1999. ■Yearbook of events in the arts and sciences in Russia.

708 Vevar, Štefan, ed.; Kocijančič, Katarina, bibliog. *Slovenski gledališki letopsis 1996/1997.* (Slovene Theatre Annual 1996/1997.) Ljubljana: SGFM; 1998. 232 pp. (Tenth expanded edition of the Repertoire of Slovene Theatres 1867/1967.) Pref. Index. [10th Edition.] Lang.: Slo.
Slovenia. 1996-1997. ■A list of drama, opera, ballet, and puppet performances in Slovene professional and amateur theatres, and festivals, during the 1996/1997 season. Also includes a list of performers, awards given to theatre people, detailed and summarized statistics and a bibliography of books, serials, and articles published within this time period.

709 McNamara, Brooks, ed. "A Look Back at *The Passing Show*: An Index to Volumes I-XX." *PasShow.* 1997 Fall/Win, 1998 Spr/Sum; 20/21(2/1): 13-39. Lang.: Eng.
USA: New York, NY. 1976-1998. ■Complete index of the twenty volumes of the Shubert archive newsletter.

710 Wilmeth, Don B. "Popular Entertainment: A New Checklist of Representative Books Published Primarily in the United States Since 1990." *THSt.* 1998; 53: 147-161. Lang.: Eng.
USA. 1990-1997. ■List of recently published books on popular entertainment.

Relation to other fields

711 Hüttler, Michael. "Aspekte des Rituals und seine Beziehung zum Theater." (Aspects of Ritual and its Relationship to Theatre.) *MuK.* 1998; 40(2-4): 85-97. Notes. Lang.: Ger.
1998. Critical studies. ■Describes differences of ritual and theatre from the beginning of man's first need to communicate to today's multimedia driven society.

712 Murav'ëva, I.N. *Merežkovskij i teatr na rubeže 19 i 20 vekov: Avtoref. dis na soisk. ... kand. iskusstvovedenija.* (Merežkovskij and Theatre in the Late 19th and Early 20th Century.) Moscow: 1998. 26 pp. [Dissertation Abstract.] Lang.: Rus.
1890-1909. Critical studies. ■Novelist Dmitri S. Merežkovskij and theatre.

713 Nikitin, V.N. *Psichologija telesnogo soznanija.* (Psychology of Corporeal Knowledge.) Moscow: Aletejja; 1998. 488 pp. Lang.: Rus.
1998. Critical studies. ■Author, psychologist, teacher and actor V.N. Nikitin on his new approach to plastic-cognitive therapy.

714 Schely-Newman, Esther. "Competence and Ideology in Performance: Language Games, Identity and Israeli Bureaucracy in Personal Narrative." *TextPQ.* 1998 Apr.; 18(2): 96-113. Notes. Biblio. Illus.: Photo. B&W. 1. Lang.: Eng.
Israel. 1950-1989. Critical studies. ■Describes an encounter with Israeli bureaucracy in order to examine the function of language code switching as a key discourse strategy.

715 Mayer, Verena. "Arm an Mitteln, reich an Kultur." (Poor in Means, Rich in Culture.) *MuK.* 1998; 40(2-4): 51-66. Notes. Lang.: Ger.
Austria. 1945-1998. Critical studies. ■Analysis of postwar Austrian cultural and theatrical identity as the nation still struggles with its Nazi past and the yearning for its former cultural glory.

716 Harvie, Jennifer. "The Efficacy of Current Graduate Theatre and Drama Training, and Suggestions for Change." *TRC.* 1998 Fall; 19(2): 193-195. Notes. Biblio. Lang.: Eng.
Canada. USA. UK-England. 1998. Critical studies. ■Current state of Ph.D. programs in theatre and drama in Canada, UK and USA, and suggestions for their improvement.

717 Linds, Warren. "Theatre of the Oppressed: Developing a Pedagogy of Solidarity?" *TRC.* 1998 Fall; 19(2): 177-192. Notes. Biblio. Lang.: Eng.
Canada. 1991-1998. Critical studies. ■Critique of Augusto Boal's Theatre of the Oppressed as adapted to dealing with racism in high schools.

718 Rickerd, Julie Rekai. "Yabu Pushelberg." *TCI.* 1998 Oct.; 32(9): 48-51. Illus.: Photo. Dwg. Color. 5. Lang.: Eng.
Canada: Toronto, ON. 1998. Critical studies. ■Profile of the design firm, which specializes in interior design for theatres, restaurants, and themed stores.

719 Kubiak, Anthony. "Scene One/Warning Signs: Puritanism and the Early American Theatres of Cruelty." *JDTC.* 1998 Spr; 12 (2): 15-34. Notes. Lang.: Eng.
Colonial America. 1620-1750. Critical studies. ■Theoretical exploration of the theatricalization of early American Puritan culture. Reassesses 'performative' cultural texts such as diaries and letters to examine the anti-theatrical bias among the early settlers.

720 Mallett, Mark Edmund. *The Transformation of Ritual Performance Traditions in Early American Political Culture.* Urbana-Champaign, IL: Univ. of Illinois; 1998. 309 pp. Biblio. Notes. [Ph.D. Dissertation, Univ. Microfilms Order No. 9904533.] Lang.: Eng.
Colonial America. 1650-1800. Histories-specific. ■How changes in secular ritual forms in early American political culture were connected to the election of civic officials.

721 Herman, Josef. "Od Theatergraphu k socialistickému realismu aneb od experimentu k srozumitelnosti." (From Theatergraph To Socialist Realism—From Experiment to Intelligibility.) *DivR.* 1998 Mar.; 9(1): 24-30. Notes. Lang.: Cze.
Czech Republic. 1925-1950. Histories-specific. ■Changes in the Czech avant-garde theatre from the thirties and the forties with the advent of Socialist Realism and all the political and ideological alterations that came with the change.

722 Karner, Doris. "Jüdische Identitäten in der Prager Theaterszene zwischen 1910 und 1939." (Jewish Identities in the Prague Theatre Scene between 1910 and 1939.) *MuK.* 1998; 40(2-4): 113-124. Notes. Lang.: Ger.
Czechoslovakia: Prague. 1910-1939. Historical studies. ■The reflection in German and Czech language theatres of Jewish culture in the context of antisemitism.

723 Langkilde, Nicole Maria; Davidsen, Mette Hvid. "Kvalitetsvurdering—lad os dog tale om det..." (Evaluation

of Quality—Let Us Talk About It.) *TE.* 1998 Feb.; 87: 17-20. Illus.: Photo. B&W. 1. Lang.: Dan.

Denmark. 1997-1998. Critical studies. ■The difficulties of evaluating the quality of theatre performances in the context of cultural policy and funding.

724 Langsted, Jørn. "Beton—ligusterhaeks—og kvalitetspolitik." (Politics of Concrete, Privet Hedges and Quality.) *TE.* 1998 Feb.; 87: 9-13. Illus.: Photo. Dwg. B&W. 2. Lang.: Dan.

Denmark. 1990-1998. Historical studies. ■Argues that financial support of theatres has stagnated compared to other art forms and that theatre has lost its significance in cultural politics as well as in everyday life.

725 Mulvad, Ninette. "Århus vurderer kvaliteten." (Århus Evaluates Quality.) *TE.* 1998 Feb.; 87: 24-26. Illus.: Photo. Photo. B&W. 2. Lang.: Dan.

Denmark: Århus. 1993-1998. Historical studies. ■How local authorities in Århus evaluate and secure the quality of theatre produced in their jurisdiction.

726 Levine, Laura Ellen. *Men in Women's Clothing: Anti-Theatricality and Effeminization From 1579 TO 1642.* Baltimore, MD: Johns Hopkins Univ; 1987. 320 pp. Notes. Biblio. [Ph.D. Dissertation, Univ. Microfilms Order No. AAC 8807444.]

England. 1579-1642. Historical studies. ■Gender-studies approach to anti-theatrical prejudice with emphasis on transvestism and the fear of the demasculinization of society.

727 Mallory, Anne Boyd. *Acting Out: Theatre, Revolution, and the English Novel, 1790-1848.* Ithaca, NY: Cornell Univ; 1998. 194 pp. Notes. Biblio. [Ph.D. Dissertation, Univ. Microfilms Order No. AAC 9839933.] Lang.: Eng.

England. 1790-1848. Critical studies. ■The association of theatre with revolution in the English novel. Considers not only theatre itself, but theatricalization in the novel and in the larger society and argues that the new genre used theatricalization to examine society.

728 Newham, Paul. "The Voice and the Shadow." *PM.* 1990; 60: 37-47. Notes. Illus.: Photo. B&W. 3. Lang.: Eng.

Europe. 1989. Critical studies. ■Investigates the under-realized potential of the human voice in the light of some psychological considerations deriving from C.G. Jung and James Hillman. Considers the voice as a medium for expression divorced from extraneous narrative structure and draws attention to the research of Alfred Wolfsohn and his pupil Roy Hart, which paralleled developments in psychology.

729 Noller, Joachim. "Maschine und Metaphysik." (Machine and Metaphysics.) *Tanzd.* 1998; 43(4): 16-21. Notes. Illus.: Photo. B&W. 5. Lang.: Ger.

Europe. 1913-1930. Critical studies. ■Phenomenon, functions and symbolism of modern fictional characters as viewed through the lens of Mejerchol'd's biomechanics and Oskar Schlemmer's puppets.

730 Watt, Ian. *Miti dell'individualismo moderno: Faust, don Chisciotte, don Giovanni, Robinson Crusoe.* (Myths of Modern Individualism: Faust, Don Quixote, Don Juan, Robinson Crusoe.) Rome: Donzelli; 1998. 255 pp. Pref. Index. Notes. Append. Lang.: Ita.

Europe. 1587-1998. Critical studies. ■Literary influences of fictional characters. Translation of *Myths of Modern Individualism* (Cambridge/New York, NY, 1996).

731 West, William N. "The Idea of a Theatre: Humanist Ideology and the Imaginary Stage in Early Modern Europe." *RenD.* 1997; 28: 245-287. Notes. Biblio. Illus.: Dwg. Sketches. B&W. 8. Lang.: Eng.

Europe. 1549-1629. Critical studies. ■Discusses the humanist ideologies that led to the burgeoning of theatre in Renaissance Europe.

732 Siltala, Juha. "Heroin chic ja silpova narsismi." (Heroin Chic and Dismembering Narcissism.) *Teat.* 1998; 53(1): 12-15. Illus.: Photo. Color. B&W. 3. Lang.: Fin.

Finland. 1990-1998. Historical studies. ■Examines the 'culture of decadence' pervasive in the 1990s and its reflection in literature, theatre, and film.

733 Beckett, Samuel; Ackerley, C.J., ed. "Demented Particulars: The Annotated *Murphy.*" *JBeckS.* 1997/98 Aut/Spr; 7(1&2): xxvi, 1-255. Notes. Biblio. Lang.: Eng.

France. Ireland. 1935. Critical studies. ■Annotated study of Beckett's novel with an introduction by the editor regarding the work's background.

734 Béhague, Emmanuel. "Rechtsruck." (Swing to the Right.) *TZ.* 1998; 5/Theater in Frankreich: 31-33. Lang.: Ger.

France. 1995-1998. Historical studies. ■Growing strenghth of the right-wing 'Front National', mainly in the south of France and its increasing influence on cultural policy since the regional election in 1998. Includes an interview with Claude Fall, cultural minister, about countermeasures.

735 Maslan, Susan Amy. *Representation and Theatricality in French Revolutionary Theatre and Politics.* Baltimore, MD: Johns Hopkins Univ; 1998. 252 pp. Notes. Biblio. [Ph.D. Dissertation, Univ. Microfilms Order No. AAC 9821161.] Lang.: Eng.

France. 1780-1800. Histories-specific. ■The French revolutionary theatre's radical attempt to refigure theatrical representation and its conflict with the liberal Revolution's establishment of political representation.

736 Murray, Elizabeth. *Nowhere to Hide But Together: A Narrative Case Study of Three Classroom Teachers, a Drama Specialist, and their Supporters Negotiating Toward an Artistic Vision of Teaching through Drama in an Urban Elementary School.* Columbus, OH: Ohio State Univ; 1998. 230 pp. Notes. Biblio. [Ph.D. Dissertation, Univ. Microfilms Order No. AAC 9900879.] Lang.: Eng.

France. 1997. Empirical research. ■How the drama specialist coordinates with other educators to negotiate and interpret artistic approaches to teaching and learning.

737 Bergel, Ralph. "Für den Tag und für die Ewigkeit..." (For a Day and for Eternity...)*DB.* 1998; 5: 46-47. Illus.: Photo. B&W. 3. Lang.: Ger.

Germany: Nordhausen. 1998. Histories-sources. ■Photographer Bergel reflects on the tasks of theatre photography with respect to documentation and stylization, realism and alienation.

738 Burckhardt, Barbara; Wille, Franz. "Menschen im Sandwich." (Persons in Sandwich.) *THeute.* 1998; 8/9: 20-25. Illus.: Photo. B&W. 6. Lang.: Ger.

Germany: Bochum, Cologne. 1991-1998. Histories-sources. ■Conversation with Ute Canaris and Kathinka Dittrich, formerly political cultural heads of departments in Bochum and Köln, about government and budget cuts in their cities.

739 Daiber, Hans. "Intendant geht betteln..." (The Theatre-Manager Goes Begging...)*DB.* 1998; 5: 52-53. Illus.: Photo. B&W. 2. Lang.: Ger.

Germany. 1945-1949. Historical studies. ■Describes the different orders and effects of monetary reform on theatres in East and West Germany.

740 Finger, Evelyn. "Deutsche Passion?" (German Passion?)*TZ.* 1998; 4: 8-9. Illus.: Photo. B&W. 2. Lang.: Ger.

Germany: Eisleben. 1998. Historical studies. ■Effect on cultural policy of the recent electoral gains by the nationalist movement in the region, and its meaning for arts and theatre groups such as Landesbühne Sachsen-Anhalt, Theaterjugendclub, and Kulturamt.

741 Herzinger, Richard. "Das Elend des Zeitalters und des Poeten Hang zum Bizarren." (The Misery of Age and the Poet's Tendency Towards the Bizarre.) *THeute.* 1998; 7: 34-39. Illus.: Pntg. Handbill. 6. Lang.: Ger.

Germany: Berlin. 1810-1811. Historical studies. ■Describes the context of contemporary history and history of ideas in the Romantic period that influenced Heinrich von Kleist's *Berliner Abendblätter* on occasion of a new edition of this periodical by Roland Reuss and Peter Staengle.

742 Merschmeier, Michael. "Aufbruch oder Abbruch?" (Departure or Demolition?)*THeute.* 1998; 6: 6-8. Illus.: Photo. B&W. 3. Lang.: Ger.

Germany: Berlin. 1989-1998. Critical studies. ■Political-cultural effects on Berlin theatres for the last ten years.

743 Merschmeier, Michael; Wille, Franz. "Der neue 'Zeit'-Tango." (The New 'Time'-Tango.) *THeute.* 1998; 1: 32-36. Illus.: Photo. B&W. 3. Lang.: Ger.

Germany: Hamburg. 1996-1998. Histories-sources. ■Conversation with Sigrid Löffler, manager of the feature section of *Die Zeit*, about concepts of a modern feature section and changes in the world of media.

THEATRE IN GENERAL: —Relation to other fields

744 Roth, Wilhelm. "Zeit des Umbruchs." (Time of Change.) *DB.* 1998; 11: 12-14. Illus.: Photo. B&W. 6. Lang.: Ger.
Germany: Frankfurt. 1997-1999. Historical studies. ▪Reports on political and cultural perspectives of various theatres in Franfurt, including Oper, Städtische Bühnen und TAT/Depot.

745 Teschke, Holger. "Terror im Zentrum." (Terror in the Center.) *TZ.* 1998; 1: 57-59. Lang.: Ger.
Germany. 1928-1998. Critical studies. ▪Political , cultural, and social climate in Germany over the last seventy years, and the rise and fall of the political theatre of playwrights like Bertolt Brecht.

746 Vogt, Matthias Theodor. "Was soll ein Bundeskulturminister tun?" (What Shall a Bundeskulturminister Do?)*BGs.* 1998; 6-7: 15-21. Notes. Lang.: Ger.
Germany. 1998. Critical studies. ▪The debate over whether Germany needs a national cultural minister.

747 Wille, Franz. "Für ein Theater auf der Höhe der Widersprüche." (For a Theatre at the Height of Contradictions.) *dRAMATURg.* 1998; 1: 2-5. Illus.: Photo. B&W. 1. Lang.: Ger.
Germany: Berlin. 1998. Critical studies. ▪Discusses the contemporary aim and object of theatre, the relationship between theatre and society and the possibilities of theatre with reference to Frank Castorf's Volksbühne Berlin.

748 Zünder, Ralf. "Das besonders besondere Werturteil." (The Specially Special Value Judgement.) *BGs.* 1998; 3: 9-10. Illus.: Photo. B&W. 4. Lang.: Ger.
Germany: Berlin. 1998. Historical studies. ▪Review of a report by Peter Stolzenberg, a former theatre manager in Heidelberg on quality of private and fringe theatres in Berlin.

749 Zünder, Ralf. "5 Fragen." (5 Questions.) *BGs.* 1998; 8-9: 18-21. Illus.: Photo. B&W. 5. Lang.: Ger.
Germany. 1998. Histories-sources. ▪An inquiry with political and cultural speakers of the parties of Bundestag about theatres, budget cuts and culture in general on occasion of the election in 1998.

750 Levitas, J.B.A. *Irish Theatre and Cultural Nationalism 1890-1914.* Oxford: Unpublished Ph.D., Univ. of Oxford; 1997. Notes. Biblio. [Absract in *Aslib Index to Theses*, 47-10570.] Lang.: Eng.
Ireland. UK-Ireland. 1890-1914. Historical studies. ▪Two aspects of nationalism in Irish theatre: the development of a national theatre as manifest in various organizations, and the history of nationalist movements.

751 Ault, C. Thomas. "Leone Battista Alberti on Theatre Architecture." *TD&T.* 1998 Win; 34(1): 50-58. Notes. Illus.: Dwg. B&W. Architec. Grd.Plan. 5. Lang.: Eng.
Italy. 1440-1470. Historical studies. ▪Architect Alberti's ideas and theories regarding the building of theatres.

752 Tinterri, Alessandro, ed. *Pasquale De Antonis un fotografo a teatro da Visconti a Strehler da Gassman a Mastroianni.* (Pasquale De Antonis: A Photographer at the Theatre from Visconti to Strehler, From Gassman to Mastroianni.) Rome: De Luca; 1998. 114 pp. Lang.: Ita.
Italy. 1908-1998. Histories-sources. ▪Catalogue of an exhibition held in Genoa, Rome, and Teramo in April-May 1998, on the Italian theatre photographer. De Antonis' theatre photos now belong to the Civico Museo Biblioteca dell'Attore in Genoa.

753 Janssens, Lidwine. *Drama is de kunst. Handboek voor dramadocenten.* (The Art Is Drama. Handbook for Teachers of Drama.) Amsterdam: IT&FB—Vitgeverij; 1998. 330 pp. Pref. Biblio. Illus.: Graphs. 15. Lang.: Dut.
Netherlands. 1990-1998. Instructional materials. ▪Practical suggestions on building a curriculum for drama in secondary educational institutions.

754 Lutterbie, John. "The Politics of Dramaturgy." *JDTC.* 1998 Fall; 13(1): 113-120. Notes. Illus.: Dwg. 1. Lang.: Eng.
North America. 1990-1998. Critical studies. ▪Argues that the effect of social and cultural politics on dramaturgy must be recognized.

755 Duany, Jorge. "On Borders and Boundaries: Contemporary Thinking on Cultural Identity." *Gestos.* 1998 Apr.; 13(25): 15-33 . Notes. Biblio. Illus.: Photo. B&W. 1. Lang.: Eng.
Puerto Rico. 1998. Critical studies. ▪Puerto Rico's national identity as commonwealth of the USA or sovereign nation. Includes discussion of how the nationalist debate about cultural identity is constituted and transformed through theatre and the visual arts.

756 Baranova, T.V. "Teatral'naja žizn' v Rossii i UŠA 20-ch godov XX veka v social'no-političeskom: i kul'turnom aspekte." (Theatrical Life in Russia and the USA during the 1920s: Socio-political and Cultural Aspect.) 72-77 in *Platonovskie čtenija.* Samara: 1998. Lang.: Rus.
Russia. USA. 1920-1929. Critical studies. ▪Comparison of politics, society, and culture in 1920s Russia and United States.

757 Eremeeva, A.N. *'Pod rokot graždanskich bur'...': Chudož. žizn' Rossii v 1917-1920 gg.* (Artistic Life in Russia, 1917-1920.) St. Petersburg: Nestor; 1998. 360 pp. Lang.: Rus.
Russia. 1917-1920. Historical studies. ▪Description of the cultural atmosphere at the height of the Revolution.

758 Filatov, L.A.; Gaft, V.O. *Žizn'—teat'r: Sb. stichotvorenij.* (Life—A Theatre: Collection of Poems.) Moscow: ÈKSMO-Press; 1998. 464 pp. Lang.: Rus.
Russia: Moscow. 1998. Critical studies. ▪Poetry by stage and film actors, Leonid Filatov and Valentin Gaft.

759 Kolobov, O.A. *Intellektual'naja èlita Nižegorodskoj oblasti. 1918-1998: Nauč.-sprav. izd.* (The Intellectual Elite of the Nizhegorod Oblast, 1918-1998: Scholarly Edition.) Nižni Novgorod: 1998. 356 pp. Lang.: Rus.
Russia: Nizhegorod. 1918-1998. Historical studies. ▪Intellectual history of the Nižni Novgorod district after the Russian Revolution. Includes discussion of theatre.

760 Mariengof, A.B. *Bessmertnaja trilogija.* (Eternal Trilogy.) Moscow: Vagrius; 1998. 509 pp. Lang.: Rus.
Russia. 1897-1962. Histories-sources. ▪Memoirs of A.B. Mariengof: poet, journalist and playwright. Includes discussion about Russian cultural leaders and theatre.

761 Sal'tina, M. "Kak naučit' ptic letat'?" (How Can We Teach Birds To Fly?)*Kazan'.* 1998; 9-10: 108-110. Lang.: Rus.
Russia: Moscow. Critical studies. ▪Teacher of linguistics at the Russian National Humanitarian University describes her method of having students perform plays in foreign languages as a way for facilitating a student's grasp of those languages.

762 Žukova, I. "ITC predstavljaet." (ITC Presents.) *Filatelija.* 1998; 7: 1-2. Lang.: Rus.
Russia: Moscow. 1998. Historical studies. ▪Postage stamps marking the 125th birthday of Antonina V. Neždanova (1873-1950), and the centennial of Moscow Art Theatre (1898-1998).

763 Podmakovič, Dagmar; Satanikovič, Juliana. "Theater im Spiegel der Politik." (Theatre as Mirrored by Politics.) *DB.* 1998; 4: 41-43. Illus.: Photo. B&W. 2. Lang.: Ger.
Slovakia. 1989-1998. Historical studies. ▪Reviews the influence of the political, cultural and economic changes on theatre, both program and aesthetics, since the change in former Socialist countries.

764 "Laughing When It Hurts." *Econ.* 1998 Oct 3; 349(8088): 96-97. Illus.: Photo. B&W. 1. Lang.: Eng.
South Africa, Republic of. 1995-1998. Critical studies. ▪Discusses themes and subjects chosen by South African novelists and playwrights in the crime-ridden, post-apartheid country. Points to the work of novelist Antjie Krog, Russell Thompson's film *The Sexy Girls*, and Aubrey Sekhabi and Mpumelelo Grootboom's play *Not with My Gun* as examples.

765 Maree, Cathy. "Resistance and Remembrance: Theatre During and After Dictatorship and Apartheid." *SATJ.* 1998 May/Sep.; 12(1/2): 11-33. Notes. Biblio. Lang.: Eng.
South Africa, Republic of. Spain. Chile. 1939-1994. Historical studies. ▪Surveys how playwrights succeeded in writing a contestatory theatre during the dictatorships of Spain, Argentina, Chile, and during the apartheid era in South Africa and if/how they have continued or adapted their work in the context of the new democracies.

766 Eagleton, Julie. "Stockholm, Cultural Capital '98." *PlPl.* Feb 1998; 519: 34. Lang.: Eng.

THEATRE IN GENERAL: —Relation to other fields

Sweden: Stockholm. 1998. Historical studies. ■Stockholm's cultural facilities considered in light of its being named Cultural Capital of Europe for 1998.

767 Chang, Ivy I-Chu. *Remapping Memories and Public Space: The Theatre of Action in Taiwan's Opposition Movement and Social Movements (1986-1997).* New York, NY: New York Univ.; 1998. 417 pp. Notes. Biblio. [Ph.D. Dissertation, Univ. Microfilms Order No. AAC 9907140.] Lang.: Eng.

Taiwan. 1986-1997. Histories-specific. ■How social activists and theatre artists employed theatrical techniques and ritualistic elements to develop performative tactics.

768 Davis, Tracy C. "Filthy-Nay-Pestilential: Sanitation and Victorian Theatres." 161-186 in Pollock, Della, ed. *Exceptional Spaces: Essays in Performance and History.* Chapel Hill, NC/London: Univ of North Carolina P; 1998. 394 pp. Index. Notes. Append. Tables. Lang.: Eng.

UK-England. 1790-1890. Critical studies. ■Correlations among social and cultural performances of sex, gender, class, and nationality, including, among other topics, sanitary reform in nineteenth-century theatre.

769 Raab, Michael. "Eiskalte Dusche." (An Icy Shower.) *DB.* 1998; 11: 32-35. Illus.: Dwg. Photo. B&W. 3. Lang.: Ger.

UK-England. 1997-1998. Historical studies. ■Reports on the current state of culture policy in England and hopes of changes disappointed by Tony Blair's government.

770 Severin, Laura. "Becoming and Unbecoming: Stevie Smith as Performer." *TextPQ.* 1998 Jan.; 18(1): 22-36. Notes. Biblio. Illus.: Sketches. B&W. 3. Lang.: Eng.

UK-England. 1961-1970. Critical studies. ■Critique of poet Stevie Smith's performance style when reading her work in the 1960s.

771 White, G. *The Drama of Everyday Life: Situationist Theory in the Theatre of the Counter-Culture.* Sussex: Unpublished PhD, Univ. of Sussex; 1996. Notes. Biblio. [Abstract in *Aslib Index to Theses* 46-12116.] Lang.: Eng.

UK-England. 1960-1969. Histories-specific. ■Relationship between the theory of the Situationist International and those experimental movements which characterized the British 'counter-culture' period. Assesses the critical legacy of Situationism in the present.

772 Braid, Donald. "'Did it happen or did it not?': Dream Stories, Worldview, and Narrative Knowing." *TextPQ.* 1998 Oct.; 18 (4): 319-343. Notes. Biblio. Lang.: Eng.

UK-Scotland. 1985-1998. Historical studies. ■How narrative discourse works as a way of knowing and communicating ideas about the world. Uses as a model a group of story-tellers called the Travelling People of Scotland.

773 "Culture Wars." *Econ.* 1998 Sep 12; 348(8085): 97-99. Illus.: Photo. B&W. 3. Lang.: Eng.

USA. Europe. 1998. Critical studies. ■Disputes European fears of American cultural hegemony, arguing that only in cinema does the American aesthetic rule. Also warns against cultural protectionism.

774 Anderson, Mary Gresham. *Perceptions About the Use of Selected Theatre Rehearsal Technique Activities: Resources for Socially Emotionally-Disturbed Adolescents.* Kent, OH: Kent State Univ; 1988. 235 pp. Biblio. Notes. [Ph.D. Dissertation, Univ. Microfilms Order No. AAC 8919770.] Lang.: Eng.

USA. 1985-1987. Empirical research. ■The perceptions of theatre specialists regarding the potential use of specific theatre rehearsal technique activities as an educative communication experience for adolescents labelled socially emotionally disturbed (SED) in public secondary schools.

775 Arthurs, Alberta; Hodsoll, Frank. "The Importance of the Arts Sector: How It Relates to the Public Purpose." *JAML.* 1998 Sum; 28(2): 102-108. Notes. Lang.: Eng.

USA. 1997-1998. Critical studies. ■Builds upon the findings of the ninety-second American Assembly convened 1997, Harriman, NY, on the arts as a sector in American life: the importance of considering the arts as a sector and to consider the relationship between that sector and the public purpose.

776 Backstrom, Ellen Lees. *The Effects of Creative Dramatics on Student Behaviors and Attitudes in Literature and Language Arts.* Los Angeles, CA: Univ. of California; 1988. 204 pp. Biblio. Notes. [Ph.D. Dissertation, Univ. Microfilms Order No. AAC 8903648.] Lang.: Eng.

USA. 1980-1987. Empirical research. ■Uses qualitative and quantitative methods to establish the effect of creative dramatics on behavior of grade school children and their attitudes to literature curricula.

777 Bank, Rosemarie. "Brook Farm and the Performance of Heterotopia." *NETJ.* 1998; 9: 1-22. Notes. Biblio. Lang.: Eng.

USA: West Roxbury, MA. 1841-1847. Historical studies. ■The use of role playing in the transcendentalist community Brook Farm. Argues that, as both a real and an ideal community, Brook Farm is an example of what Foucault calls a heterotopia.

778 Browning, Nadine. *Meeting Halfway: Drama Therapy as a Means of Making Connection with a Woman Suffering from Psychosis.* San Francisco, CA: California Institute of Integral Studies; 1998. 101 pp. Notes. Biblio. [M.A. Thesis, Univ. Microfilms Order No. AAC 1390246.] Lang.: Eng.

USA. 1998. Empirical studies. ■Case study of drama therapy applied to establish meaningful connections with patients diagnosed with schizophrenia. Argues that the fictional, 'delusional' nature of drama therapy can penetrate the psychotic state.

779 Carlyon, David. "Theatre Is Action: Teaching a Task-Oriented Intro Class." *TTop.* 1998 Mar.; 8(1): 1-12. Biblio. Lang.: Eng.

USA. 1996-1998. Critical studies. ■An approach to engaging students in large Introduction to Theatre courses, said to support current educational research connecting active student participation to effective learning.

780 Chartrand, Harry Hillman. "Art and the Public Purpose: The Economics of It All." *JAML.* 1998 Sum; 28(2): 109-113. Lang.: Eng.

USA. 1997. Critical studies. ■Criticism of the ninety-second American Assembly's unclear definition of the arts sector and its lack of inclusiveness.

781 Cherbo, Joni Maya. "Introduction: The Arts Sector." *JAML.* 1998 Sum; 28(2): 99-101. Lang.: Eng.

USA. 1998. Critical studies. ■Introduction to the focus of *JAML* 28:2 redefining our conceptualization of the arts sector and illustrating relationships between commercial and not-for-profit arts.

782 Colby, Robert William. *On the Nature of Dramatic Intelligence: A Study of Development Differences in the Process of Characterization by Adolescents.* Cambridge, MA: Harvard Univ; 1988. 312 pp. Biblio. Notes. [Ph.D. Dissertation, Univ. Microfilms Order No. AAC 8811789.] Lang.: Eng.

USA. 1988. Empirical research. ■Examines thirty-one students from the Emerson College Youtheatre to evaluate differences in their enactive abilities.

783 Coleman, Wendy; Wolf, Stacy. "Rehearsing for Revolution: Practice, Theory, Race, and Pedagogy (When Failure Works)." *TTop.* 1998 Mar.; 8(1): 13-32. Notes. Biblio. Lang.: Eng.

USA. 1996-1997. Histories-sources. ■Examines the apparent 'failure' of the authors' co-taught course on African American performance and the meanings of race.

784 Cristiano, Michael. *De-Rolement from Personae Among Performing Artists: Implications of Personality Type and Role Type.* Miami, FL: Miami Institute of Psychology of the Caribbean Center for Advanced Studies; 1998. 153 pp. Notes. Biblio. [Ph.D. Dissertation, Univ. Microfilms Order No. AAC 9905890.] Lang.: Eng.

USA. 1998. Empirical studies. ■The influence of personality type and role type on the process of exiting a role.

785 Cyphert, Dale. "Pleasure, Pedagogy and Oppression in the Heartland." *TextPQ.* 1998 Jan.; 18(1): 37-49. Notes. Biblio. Illus.: Photo. B&W. 3. Lang.: Eng.

USA. 1998. Critical studies. ■Popular culture of the working class of western Iowa. Analyzes the performativity of conversation and storytelling around the communal picnic table.

THEATRE IN GENERAL: —Relation to other fields

786 Cyr, Douglas Philip. *Spirit in Motion: Developing a Spiritual Practice in Drama Therapy.* San Francisco, CA: California Institute of Integral Studies; 1998. 100 pp. Notes. Biblio. [M.A. Thesis, Univ. Microfilms Order No. AAC 1391559.] Lang.: Eng.

USA. 1998. Histories-sources. ■The theoretical and experiential process of developing a spiritual practice within the field of drama therapy. Explores the nature of the self from a variety of psychological perspectives, and introduces the concept of an ontologically and phenomenologically-experienced sense of 'inner spaciousness'.

787 Denman, Stan C. *Theatre and Hegemony in the Churches of Christ: A Case Study Using Abilene Christian University Theatre.* Pittsburgh, PA: Univ. of Pittsburgh; 1998. 271 pp. Notes. Biblio. [Ph.D. Dissertation, Univ. Microfilms Order No. AAC 9837594.] Lang.: Eng.

USA: Abilene, TX. 1995-1998. Histories-specific. ■Examines the role of theatre within the conservative Protestant evangelical subculture of the American South.

788 Doherty, Mary Louise. *A Ritual Analysis of Encounter Groups and Experimental Theatre in the Sixties.* Chicago, IL: Univ. of Chicago; 1987. Notes. Biblio. [Ph.D. Dissertation, Univ. Microfilms Order No. AAC T-30279.] Lang.: Eng.

USA. 1960-1970. Historical studies. ■Examines experimental theatre from a theoretical perspective. Uses anthropological theories of ritual and performance to examine groups such as the Performance Group and the 'happenings' of Allan Kaprow.

789 Edwards, Emily D. "Firewalking: A Contemporary Ritual and Transformation." *TDR.* 1998 Sum; 42(2): 98-114. Notes. Biblio. Illus.: Photo. B&W. 8. Lang.: Eng.

USA. 1998. Critical studies. ■Examines reasons for renewed interest in the ancient ritual of firewalking as a means to active transformation of the spiritual self.

790 Ellis, Kathi E.B. "AATP: University Takes Pioneering Role with Program Designed to Attract African-Americans." *SoTh.* 1998 Win; 39(1): 16-21. Illus.: Photo. 5. Lang.: Eng.

USA: Louisville, KY. 1998. Historical studies. ■In what may be the only program of its kind in the region, the University of Louisville has instituted an African-American Theatre Program along with a minor degree in African-American theatre.

791 Fuoss, Kirk. "Performance as Contestation: An Agonistic Perspective on the Insurgent Assembly." 98-117 in Pollock, Della, ed. *Exceptional Spaces: Essays in Performance and History.* Chapel Hill, NC/London: Univ of North Carolina P; 1998. 394 pp. Index. Notes. Lang.: Eng.

USA: Trenton, NJ. 1936. Critical studies. ■The effectiveness of staged claims on public space, particularly in the form of parodic interventions into official discourse, with particular reference to the Worker's Alliance of America's seizure of the New Jersey State Assembly.

792 Gagnon, Pauline D. "Acting Integrative: Interdisciplinarity and Theatre Pedagogy." *TTop.* 1998 Sep.; 8(2): 189-204. Notes. Biblio. Lang.: Eng.

USA. 1994-1998. Critical studies. ■The challenges for theatre educators of creating interdisciplinary courses.

793 Galligan, Ann M.; Alper, Neil O. "Characteristics of Performing Artists: A Baseline Profile of Sectoral Crossovers." *JAML.* 1998 Sum; 28(2): 155-177. Notes. Biblio. Tables. Lang.: Eng.

USA. 1998. Empirical research. ■Study model set forth to gauge a performing artist's employment categories, and how often an artist moves from one sector to another.

794 Gargano, Cara. "Complex Theatre: Science and Myth in Three Contemporary Performances." *NTQ.* 1998 May; 14(2): 151-158. Notes. Biblio. Illus.: Photo. B&W. 2. [Issue 54.] Lang.: Eng.

USA: New York, NY. 1995-1996. Critical studies. ■Changing social worldview from one based in Newtonian science to one which embraces tenets of quantum sciences. Cites Jonathan Larson's *Rent*, Louise Smith's *Interfacing Joan*, and Richard Foreman's *The Universe (i.e., How It Works)* as theatre pieces which assume the quantum universe and create a holistic mythology that hints at the ritual origin of theatre and moves from a postmodern to a pre-millennial stance.

795 Garrick, David A. "Constructing 'Cathartic Moments' in Theatrical Drama: An Ancient Theory of Drama Meets the New Psychotherapy." *NETJ.* 1998; 9: 99-125. Notes. Biblio. Lang.: Eng.

USA. 1998. Critical studies. ■Argues that new ideas of psychotherapeutic catharsis can be applied to live theatre, concluding that an identifiable 'cathartic moment' can be experienced by dramatic characters directly, and by audiences vicariously.

796 Gilliam, Jobie. *Salvation Army Theatricalities.* Long Beach, CA: California State Univ; 1988. 232 pp. Notes. Biblio. [M.A. Thesis, Univ. Microfilms Order No. AAC 1337311.] Lang.: Eng.

USA. 1865-1950. Histories-specific. ■Examines the use and effectiveness of theatricality in the Salvation Army, specifically elements of musical theatre, open-air pageants, music and dance, oratory, illusion and symbolism, ritual and spectacle.

797 Haynes, Wendy Lynne. *The Theatre as Container for Personal Narrative and the Psychotherapeutic Process.* Palo Alto, CA: Pacific Graduate Institute; 1998. 152 pp. Notes. Biblio. [Ph.D. Dissertation, Univ. Microfilms Order No. AAC 9839600.] Lang.: Eng.

USA. 1998. Empirical studies. ■Explores the therapeutic value of the Soul Stories workshop in which participants tell a personal story using dance, painting, voice, drama, and images, and then craft their story into a dramatic performance which is performed for a small, public community audience.

798 Hiltunen, Sirkku M. Sky. *Therapeutic* Noh *Theatre with Persons with Mental Retardation: A Theatre of Higher Consciousness.* Cincinnati, OH: The Union Institute; 1998. 206 pp. Notes. Biblio. [Ph.D. Dissertation, Univ. Microfilms Order No. AAC 9840864.] Lang.: Eng.

USA. 1998. Empirical studies. ■The development and of a theoretical framework for therapeutic *nō* theatre. Describes using an original story in the form of a simplified classic *nō* story, directing, producing, publicly performing, and videotaping the play with persons with mental retardation.

799 Jones, Jennifer. "Rebels of Their Sex: Nance O'Neil and Lizzie Borden." 83-103 in Schanke, Robert A., ed.; Marra, Kim, ed. *Passing Performances: Queer Readings of Leading Players in American Theatre History.* Ann Arbor, MI: Univ of Michigan P; 1998. 338 pp. (Triangulations: Lesbian/Gay/Queer Theatre/Drama/Performance.) Notes. Index. Illus.: Dwg. 2. Lang.: Eng.

USA. 1874-1965. Historical studies. ■Implications of the rumors of lesbianism surrounding the friendship of Lizzie Borden with actress Nance O'Neil.

800 Kahn, Madeleine. "Teaching Charlotte Charke: Feminism, Pedagogy, and the Construction of the Self." 162-179 in Baruth, Philip E., ed. *Introducing Charlotte Charke: Actress, Author, Enigma.* Urbana/Chicago, IL: Univ. of Illinois P; 1998. 250 pp. Index. Biblio. Notes. Lang.: Eng.

USA. 1998. Historical studies. ■Feminism and the author's students' responses to the serialized autobiography of actress Charlotte Cibber Charke, *A Narrative of the Life of Mrs. Charlotte Charke* (1755).

801 Klein, Jeanne Marie. *Fifth-Grade Children's Processing of Explicit and Implied Features of Live Theatre as a Function of Verbal and Visual Recall.* Lawrence, KS: Univ. of Kansas; 1987. 209 pp. Notes. Biblio. [Ph.D. Dissertation, Univ. Microfilms Order No. AAC 8813419.] Lang.: Eng.

USA. 1985. Empirical research. ■Compares children's cognitive processing of theatre with what is known in television research. Describes thirty-two fifth-graders' dramatic literacy and their apprehension of explicit and implied features of a live theatre production by testing their verbal and visual recall.

802 Knapp, Margaret M. "Narrative Strategies in Selected Studies of American Theatre Economics." 267-277 in Engle, Ron, ed.; Miller, Tice L., ed. *The American Stage: Social and Economic Issues from the Colonial Period to the Present.*

THEATRE IN GENERAL: —Relation to other fields

Cambridge: Cambridge UP; 1993. 320 pp. Pref. Notes. Index. Lang.: Eng.
USA. 1960-1995. Historical studies. ■Analyzes the assumptions, methodologies, and rhetorical strategies used in the study of American theatre economics.

803 Kubiak, Anthony. "Splitting the Difference: Performance and Its Double in American Culture." *TDR.* 1998 Win; 42(4): 91-114. Notes. Biblio. Lang.: Eng.
USA. 1998. Critical studies. ■Comparison of theatrical performance and multiple personality disorder. Emphasizes theories of identity.

804 Loyd, Melissa. *A Path to Forgiveness through Self-Revelatory Experience.* San Francisco, CA: California Institute of Integral Studies; 1998. 65 pp. Notes. Biblio. [M.A. Thesis, Univ. Microfilms Order No. AAC 1390248.] Lang.: Eng.
USA. 1998. Empirical studies. ■The use of drama therapy to discover how forgiveness operates psychologically. Includes results of a written survey and a performance video to argue that theatrical ritual, drama therapy and audience interaction can enhance therapy.

805 Pankratz, David B. "Conclusion: Implementing a Cross-Sectoral Action Agenda." *JAML.* 1998 Sum; 28(2): 178-183. Notes. Lang.: Eng.
USA. 1998. Critical studies. ■Final thoughts on the ninety-second Ammerican Assembly focused on the arts and the public purpose, and a plan for the future.

806 Peters, Monnie; Cherbo, Joni Maya. "The Missing Sector: The Unincorporated Arts." *JAML.* 1998 Sum; 28(2): 115-128. Notes. Biblio. Tables. Lang.: Eng.
USA. 1998. Critical studies. ■Attempts to locate and define the unincorporated arts, which include the community, avocational, traditional, or folk arts.

807 Rossi, Roberto. "Times Square and Potsdamer Platz: Packaging Development as Tourism." *TDR.* 1998 Spr; 42(1): 43-48. Illus.: Photo. B&W. 3. Lang.: Eng.
USA: New York, NY. Germany: Berlin. 1998. Critical studies. ■Economic factors involved in revitalizing these two historic districts.

808 Schor, Alison Linda. *An Integration of Drama Therapy and Buddhism: Finding a Middle Way.* San Francisco, CA: California Institute of Integral Studies; 1998. 76 pp. Notes. Biblio. [M.A. Thesis, Univ. Microfilms Order No. AAC 1391557.] Lang.: Eng.
USA. 1998. Empirical studies. ■Case studies illustrating the theoretical and clinical integration of Buddhism with drama therapy.

809 Sellers-Young, Barbara. "Somatic Processes: Convergence of Theory and Practice." *TTop.* 1998 Sep.; 8(2): 173-188. Notes. Biblio. Lang.: Eng.
USA: Davis, CA. 1990-1997. Histories-sources. ■The author's use of non-Western dance forms as a cross-cultural approach to the teaching of theatre arts.

810 Shattuck, Charles H. "*Quicksilver* Revisited: A Portrait of the American Stage in the 1930s." 190-199 in Engle, Ron, ed.; Miller, Tice L., ed. *The American Stage: Social and Economic Issues from the Colonial Period to the Present.* Cambridge: Cambridge UP; 1993. 320 pp. Pref. Notes. Index. Lang.: Eng.
USA. 1930-1940. Historical studies. ■Analysis of Fitzroy Davis's theatre novel *Quicksilver* (New York, NY: Harcourt, Brace, 1942), based in part on the life of actress Katharine Cornell.

811 Shields, Shirlee Hurst. *History of the General Activities Committee of the Church of Jesus Christ of Latter-Day Saints.* Salt Lake City, UT: Brigham Young Univ; 1987. 161 pp. Notes. Biblio. [Ph.D. Dissertation, Univ. Microfilms Order No. 8712624.] Lang.: Eng.
USA. 1977-1986. Historical studies. ■Analysis of the activities of the committee, which included communications, dance, drama, and recreational music.

812 Sussman, Mark. "New York's Facelift." *TDR.* 1998 Spr; 42(1): 34-42. Notes. Biblio. Illus.: Photo. B&W. 6. Lang.: Eng.
USA: New York, NY. 1998. Critical studies. ■How Times Square's changing facade is altering the theatrical, residential, and commercial communities in the area. Looks at the architecture of the area (both new and old), as well as the legal and political issues involved.

813 Taylor, Jujuan Carolyn. *Black Theatre in Detroit: Exposure/Training Opportunities for Public High School Students.* East Lansing, MI: Michigan State Univ; 1988. 148 pp. Biblio. Notes. [Ph.D. Dissertation, Univ. Microfilms Order No. AAC 8824899.] Lang.: Eng.
USA: Detroit, MI. 1984-1987. Empirical research. ■Evaluation of the state of Black theatre in Detroit and examination of the opportunities currently available to Black high school students for exposure and training in Theatre arts and Black theatre.

814 Voss, Joan M. *A Study of Teaching and Learning from the Perspective of Drama.* New York, NY: Fordham Univ; 1998. 223 pp. Notes. Biblio. [Ed.D. Dissertation, Univ. Microfilms Order No. AAC 9841113.] Lang.: Eng.
USA. 1997. Empirical research. ■The impact of drama on many aspects of classroom life. Focuses on the teaching/learning process and argues that teachers and students act as coaches, directors, critics, writers, and actors in facilitating student learning.

815 Stites, Richard. "Trial as Theatre in the Russian Revolution." *ThR.* 1998 Spr; 23(1): 7-13. Notes. Lang.: Eng.
USSR. 1916-1935. Historical studies. ■Examines the phenomenon of the theatricalization of court trials in post-revolutionary Russian theatre, politics, and culture.

Research/historiography

816 McAuley, Guy. "Towards an Ethnography of Rehearsal." *NTQ.* 1998 Feb.; 14(1): 75-85. Notes. Biblio. [Issue 53.] Lang.: Eng.
1985-1995. Historical studies. ■Description of the postmodern shift in the rehearsal process, with a proposal of an ethnographic model for the analysis of rehearsals.

817 Kelly, Veronica. "Old Patterns, New Energies." 1-19 in Kelly, Veronica, ed. *Our Australian Theatre in the 1990s.* Atlanta, GA/Amsterdam: Rodopi P; 1998. 285 pp. (Australian Playwrights 7.) Notes. Index. Biblio. Illus.: Photo. 2. Lang.: Eng.
Australia. 1990-1997. Historical studies. ■Introductory overview article on recent developments in Australian theatre historiography.

818 Cutler, Anna. "Abstract Body Language: Documenting Women's Bodies in Theatre." *NTQ.* 1998 May; 14(2): 111-118. Notes. Biblio. [Issue 54.] Lang.: Eng.
Europe. 1984-1997. Critical studies. ■Discusses alternative models of documentation of performance, as opposed to traditional forms said to exclude women from records of performances.

819 Melrose, Susan. "My Body, Your Body, Her-His Body: Is/Does Some-Body (Live) There." *NTQ.* 1998 May; 14(2): 119-124. Biblio. [Issue 54.] Lang.: Eng.
Europe. 1984-1997. Critical studies. ■Argues that the primacy of the word in the documentation obscures the existence of effective forms of performance documentation that serve the interests of performers rather than academics.

820 Kotte, Andreas. "Theatralität: Ein Begriff sucht seinen Gegenstand." (Theatricality: A Term in Search of Object.) *FMT.* 1998; 13(2): 117-133. Lang.: Ger.
Germany. 1900-1998. Critical studies. ■Criticizes the overly broad use of the term 'theatricality' in German theatre research.

821 Röttger, Kati. "Geschlechterdifferenz und Theatralität: Erste überlegungen zu einerüberfälligen Verbindung." (Gender Differences and Theatricality: First Reflections on an Overdue Connection.) *FMT.* 1998; 13(2): 134-147. Lang.: Ger.
Germany. France. USA. 1959-1998. Critical studies. ■Discusses the term 'theatricality' and its correspondences to gender studies. Analyzes concepts by Richard Schechner, Erving Goffman, Joachim Fiebach, Helmar Schramm, Judith Butler and Luce Irigaray to develop a perspective of theatre studies.

THEATRE IN GENERAL: —Research/historiography

822 Michalik, Jan. "Od dokumentacji do interpretacji dziejów jednego teatru." (From Documentation to Interpretation of the History of One Theatre.) 25-34 in Kuźnicka, Danuta, ed.; Samsonowicz, Hanna, ed. *Od dokumentacji do interpretacji, od interpretacji do teorii.* Warsaw: Instytut Sztuki Polskiej Akademii Nauk; 1998. 109 pp. Notes. Lang.: Pol.
Poland. 1865-1998. Critical studies. ▪Argues that theatre historians are too interested in great indivduals and best productions and consequently give an inadequate picture of of the theatre of an era. Suggests that the theatre historian should put as much emphasis on the day to day life of the ordinary actors, companies, and productions of an era.

823 Chitrik, A.A. "Sankt-Peterburgskaja gosudarstvennaja teatral'naja biblioteka i eë nemeckoe sobranie." (St. Petersburg's National Theatre Library and Its German Collection.) 205-210 in *Nemcy v Rossii.* St. Petersburg: Dmitrij Bulanin; 1998. Lang.: Rus.
Russia: St. Petersburg. 1998. Historical studies. ▪Description of the German holdings of the National Theatre Library.

824 Guderian-Czaplińska, Ewa. "Stan badań nad dramatem i teatrem emigracyjnym po roku 1939." (State of Research on Drama and Theatre in Exile After 1939.) 9-23 in Kalemba-Kasprzak, Elżbieta, ed.; Ratajczak, Dobrochna, ed. *Dramat i teatr emigracyjny po roku 1939.* Wroclaw: Wiedza o kulturze; 1998. 348 pp. (Dramat w teatrze. Teatr w dramacie 15.) Lang.: Pol.
UK-England: London. 1939-1998. Histories-sources. ▪Presents the main private and public archives of Polish theatre organized in London, which after World War II became a capital of Polish political emigration. The editions of the materials from these archives are also described.

825 Jackson, Mac D.P. "Editing, Attribution Studies, and 'Literature Online': A New Resource for Research in Renaissance Drama." *RORD.* 1998; 37: 1-15. Notes. Lang.: Eng.
UK-England. 1998. Critical studies. ▪Recommendation of the Chadwych-Healey electronic database 'Literature Online' for use by editors and researchers of authorial attribution.

826 Pillay, Kriben. "The Emperor's New Clothes: An Exercise in Virtual Reality." *SATJ.* 1998 May/Sep.; 12(1/2): 185-190. Notes. Lang.: Eng.
UK-England: Bristol. 1998. Historical studies. ▪Report on the Colston Symposium focusing on new approaches to theatre studies and performance analysis.

827 Brockett, Oscar G. "Introduction: American Theatre History Scholarship." 1-5 in Engle, Ron, ed.; Miller, Tice L., ed. *The American Stage: Social and Economic Issues from the Colonial Period to the Present.* Cambridge: Cambridge UP; 1993. 320 pp. Pref. Notes. Index. Lang.: Eng.
USA. 1780-1995. Historical studies. ▪Brief overview of the field of American theatre historiography with respect to the subject of the volume, social and economic issues and their impact on American theatre.

828 Hill, Philip G. "Doctoral Dissertations in Progress, 1998." *TJ.* 1998 May; 50(2): 227-232. Lang.: Eng.
USA. 1998. Bibliographical studies. ▪List of current doctoral dissertations in progress.

829 Wilmeth, Don B. "Checklist of Selected Books on American Theatre, 1960-1990." 290-308 in Engle, Ron, ed.; Miller, Tice L., ed. *The American Stage: Social and Economic Issues from the Colonial Period to the Present.* Cambridge: Cambridge UP; 1993. 320 pp. Pref. Notes. Index. Lang.: Eng.
USA. 1960-1990. Bibliographical studies. ▪A bibliographical checklist of important books on American theatre.

Theory/criticism

830 Fortier, Mark. "Thinking Process." *CTR.* Win 1998; 97: 8-11. Biblio. Lang.: Eng.
1998. Critical studies. ▪Importance to theatre of philosophies regarding politics of process and relationship of process to product, by such cultural theorists as Jacques Derrida and Julia Kristeva.

831 Neely, Kent. "Praxis: An Editorial Statement." *JDTC.* 1998 Fall; 13(1): 157-160. Notes. Lang.: Eng.
1998. Critical studies. ▪Introductory essay on the current state of theory and practice around the world, as seen in realized performance. Essays focus on the role of the media in mediating performance.

832 Rozik, Eli. "The Performance Text as a Macro Speech Act." *SATJ.* 1998 May/Sep.; 12(1/2): 73-89. Notes. Biblio. Lang.: Eng.
1998. Critical studies. ▪Argues that the inclusion of the pragmatic function and structure of dramatic discourse and its rhetorical aims is an essential complement to a semiotic approach in elucidating the nature of theatrical performance.

833 Burgoyne, Lynda. "Du sang! Du sang!" (Blood! Blood!) *JCT.* 1998; 89: 50-53. Notes. Illus.: Photo. B&W. 4. Lang.: Fre.
Canada: Montreal, PQ. 1998. Critical studies. ▪Examples of children's theatre appealing to contemporary children's aesthetics at the Coups de théâtre children's theatre festival.

834 Saint-Jacques, Diane. "Mise en action et mise en fiction: Le processus de production en improvisation." (Activation and Fictionalization: The Production Process of Improvisation.) *TRC.* 1998 Fall; 19(2): 125-139. Notes. Biblio. Lang.: Fre.
Canada: Montreal, PQ. 1998. Critical studies. ▪Activation and fictionalization as tools for analysis of improvisation, derived from observation of improvisations by Montreal drama teachers.

835 Vaïs, Michel. "L'I de l'impureté." (The 'I' of Impurity.) *JCT.* 1998; 88: 161-167. Illus.: Photo. Poster. B&W. 4. Lang.: Fre.
Canada: Quebec, PQ. 1998. Histories-sources. ▪Main points from public forum held in Quebec, PQ, entitled 'L'impureté, ou la fin du 'théâtre-théâtre (Impurity, or the End of 'Theatre-theatre')' with director Normand Daneau, author Eugène Durif, actress Marie Gignac, critic Marie-Christine Lesage and director Michel Nadeau, on the limits of what theatre can be.

836 Brecht, Bertolt; Fodor, Géza, intro.; Szántó, Judit, transl. "Elidegenítés a kínai színházban." (Alienation Effect in Chinese Theatre.) *Sz.* 1998; 31(2): 13-17. Illus.: Photo. B&W. 4. Lang.: Hun.
China. 1910-1950. Critical studies. ▪The first Hungarian translation of Brecht's *Verfremdungseffekte in der chinesischen Schauspielkunst* with critical commentary by Fodor, part of a series on twentieth-century theatre.

837 Quinn, Michael Lowell. *The Semiotic Stage: Prague School Theater Theory.* Stanford, CA: Stanford Univ; 1987. 170 pp. Biblio. Notes. [Ph.D. Dissertation, Univ. Microfilms Order No. 8801007.] Lang.: Eng.
Czechoslovakia. 1925-1930. Critical studies. ▪The early history of the semiotic study of theatre and the Prague Linguistic Circle.

838 Damm, Anja. "Et vindpust henover traetoppe." (A Puff of Wind Over the Treetops.) *TE.* 1998 Apr.; 88: 16-17. Illus.: Photo. B&W. 1. Lang.: Dan.
Denmark. Sweden. UK-England. 1847-1987. Critical studies. ▪Essay on the nature of talent, including the opinions of Stanislavskij, Peter Brook, Søren Kierkegaard, and Ingmar Bergman.

839 Kubiak, Anthony James. *Phobos and Performance: The Stages of Terror.* Milwaukee, WI: Univ. of Wisconsin; 1988. 274 pp. Biblio. Notes. [Ph.D. Dissertation, Univ. Microfilms Order No. AAC 8819375.] Lang.: Eng.
Europe. North America. 500 B.C.-1988 A.D. Critical studies. ▪Examines the concept of 'terror' in the early development of theatre and its manifestations in contemporary theatre. Argues that the history of performance becomes a history of the ways in which terror is objectified as ideology/law and deployed as a means of sociopolitical conditioning.

840 Rainio, Elina. "Magia Woltti." *TeatterT.* 1998; 2: 42-45. Lang.: Fin.
Finland. 1998. Critical studies. ▪Examination of society's fundamental need for theatre, its need to produce theatre, and its place among the arts.

841 Böhnisch, Siemke; Fodor, Géza, intro. "Valószerűség a színházban: A hitelesség elméletéhez." (Reality in the Theatre: Toward a Theory of Authenticity.) *Sz.* 1998; 31(5): 46-48. Lang.: Hun.

THEATRE IN GENERAL: —Theory/criticism

Germany. 1992. Critical studies. ▪Publishing and introducing Böhnisch's theoretical work: the text was originally a lecture at the 1992 Congress of the German Society for Theatre Research.

842 Klotz, Volker; Szántó, Judit, transl.; Fodor, Géza, intro. "Az önmagát eláruló színház, 1. rész." (Theatre Betraying Itself, Part 1.) *Sz.* 1998; 31(11): 44-48. Lang.: Hun.

Germany. 1995. Critical studies. ▪Hungarian translation and commentary on Klotz's article, first published in *Opernwelt* in 1995. Continued in *Sz* 1998 31:12, pp. 26-30.

843 Schirmer, Lothar. "'Der Herr hat heut Kritik'. Theodor Fontane und das Theater seiner Zeit." ('The Gentleman Is Doing a Critique Today': Theodor Fontane and the Theatre in His Time.) *SGT.* 1998; 75: 101-136. Notes. Append. Illus.: Photo. Design. Dwg. Pntg. B&W. Color. Grd.Plan. 42. Lang.: Ger.

Germany: Berlin. 1870-1890. Biographical studies. ▪Novelist Fontane's work as a theatre critic, and how his experiences influenced his novels.

844 Margitházi, Beja. "Kritikus kritizál: Tarján Tamás: Zivatar a publikumnak." (The Critic Criticizes: Tamás Tarján: Thunderstorm to the Public.) *Sz.* 1998; 31(5): 45. Illus.: Photo. B&W. 1. Lang.: Hun.

Hungary. 1993-1996. Critical studies. ▪Notes on the volume of critic Tamás Tarján's collected reviews.

845 Upor, László; Ikládi, László, photo.; Koncz, Zsuzsa, photo.; Györffy, Anna, photo. "Nyelv és gesztus." (Language and Gesture.) *Sz.* 1998; 31(8): 21-25. Illus.: Photo. B&W. 4. Lang.: Hun.

Hungary. 1997. Critical studies. ▪Edited version of a lecture to an international conference held at Hull, England, in September, 1997.

846 Pilkington, Lionel. "Irish Theatre Historiography and Political Resistance." 13-30 in Colleran, Jeanne, ed.; Spencer, Jenny S., ed. *Staging Resistance: Essays on Political Theatre.* Ann Arbor, MI: Univ of Michigan P; 1998. 312 pp. (Theater: Theory/Text/Performance.) Notes. Index. Lang.: Eng.

Ireland. 1897-1996. Historical studies. ▪How the 'radical' Irish literary theatre of W.B. Yeats and the Abbey Theatre has been read as politically progressive despite attempts by its founders to smooth over class conflicts and social differences.

847 Attisani, Antonio. "Beppe in discesa nel tempo." (Beppe Slides in Time.) *BiT.* 1998; 48: 91-110. Lang.: Ita.

Italy. 1985. Histories-sources. ▪Transcription of a video debate between the author and critic Giuseppe Bartolucci dealing with the politics of theatre and the relations between tradition and the avant-garde.

848 Mango, Achille. "Un passo divide il teatro dalla realtà." (One Step Divides Theatre From Reality.) *BiT.* 1998; 48: 111-121. Notes. Lang.: Ita.

Italy. 1998. Critical studies. ▪Argues that theatre must transform technological potential into theatrical material capable of disarticulating the clichés of representation.

849 Mango, Lorenzo. "Il contemporaneo è il moderno di domani." (The Contemporary Is the Modern of Tomorrow.) *BiT.* 1998; 48: 55-89. Lang.: Ita.

Italy. 1960-1995. Critical studies. ▪The adaptation of critical discourse to theatrical changes since the 1960s, as reflected in the work of critic Giuseppe Bartolucci.

850 Ruffini, Franco. "Tra Barthes e Barba." (Between Barthes and Barba.) *BiT.* 1998; 48: 129-136. Notes. Biblio. Lang.: Ita.

Italy. 1982-1998. Critical studies. ▪An approach to Giuseppe Bartolucci's critical methodology.

851 Freeman, John. "The Location and Theory of Looking." *JDTC.* 1998 Spr; 12(2): 129-142. Notes. Lang.: Eng.

North America. 1998. Critical studies. ▪Examines the relationship of performance to different aesthetic theories. Author argues that the theatre must keep a perspective on itself as a location and a theory of looking.

852 Smith, Iris; Still, James. "Letters in Response to JDTC's 'A Feminist Dialogue. . .', Fall 1997." *JDTC.* 1998 Spr; 12(2) : 5-14. Notes. Lang.: Eng.

North America. 1997-1998. Histories-sources. ▪Two respondents to 'A Feminist Dialogue on Theatre for Young Audiences Through Suzan Zeder's plays,' *JDTC* 1997 Spr, 11(2), 115-139, on using feminist theories to explore children's theatre. One letter, from a man, argues for the inclusion of men in the discussion and paradigms, as well as in plays. The other, from a woman, articulates further feminist theories that should be explored.

853 Sullivan, Sharon L. "Notes from JDTC." *JDTC.* 1998 Spr; 12(2): 3. Lang.: Eng.

North America. 1997-1998. Critical studies. ▪Introductory essay on an ongoing discussion about feminist theory and practice and children's theatre, first articulated in the Spring 1997 issue of *JDTC.*

854 Gáspár, Ildikó. "Jan és Jane: Két Jan Kott-kötet." (Jan and Jane: On Two Books by Jan Kott.) *Sz.* 1998; 31(11): 43. Illus.: Photo. B&W. 1. Lang.: Hun.

Poland. 1997-1998. Critical studies. ▪Reviews of recent publications in Hungarian of works by theatre historian and theoretician Jan Kott.

855 Kuźnicka, Danuta. "Kilka uwag o tearalnej myśli Romana Ingardena z perspektywy dzisiejszej." (Several Remarks from Today's Perspective on Roman Ingarden's Thoughts on Theatre.) 67-72 in Kuźnicka, Danuta, ed.; Samsonowicz, Hanna, ed. *Od dokumentacji do interpretacji, od interpretacji do teorii.* Warsaw: Instytut Sztuki Polskiej Akademii Nauk; 1998. 109 pp. Notes. Lang.: Pol.

Poland. 1998. Critical studies. ▪The reciprocal influence of phenomenologist Roman Ingarden and the theatre.

856 Sinko, Grzegorz. "Dzieło czy proces? Literatura-scena-krytyka." (Work of Art or Process? Literature-Stage-Criticism.) 57-66 in Kuźnicka, Danuta, ed.; Samsonowicz, Hanna, ed. *Od dokumentacji do interpretacji, od interpretacji do teorii.* Warsaw: Instytut Sztuki Polskiej Akademii Nauk; 1998. 109 pp. Lang.: Pol.

Poland. 1998. Critical studies. ▪Theatre and reception theory: discusses the work of theorists Wolfgang Iser, Jacques Derrida, Julia Kristeva, Roland Barthes, and Umberto Eco.

857 Inkret, Andrej. *Melanholičan razmerja.* (Melancholic Relations.) Ljubljana: Slovenska matica; 1998. 410 pp. Notes. Index. Lang.: Slo.

Slovenia. 1992-1995. Histories-sources. ▪Excerpts from the diary of a Slovene critic who gives his thoughts on selected theatrical performances and personalities in Slovene theatre.

858 Kermauner, Taras. *Slovenska dramatika—modeli.* (Slovene Drama—Models.) Ljubljana: Faculty of Arts, Slavic Department; 1998. 239 pp. Notes. Biblio. Lang.: Slo.

Slovenia. 1997. Critical studies. ▪An approach to Slovene theatre through new methodology, including abstract synthesis and empirical analysis of individual plays.

859 Saag, Kristjan. "Sidorepliker." (Asides.) *Tningen.* 1998; 21(1): 19. Lang.: Swe.

Sweden. 1998. Critical studies. ▪Collection of aphorisms pertaining to theatre criticism.

860 Anderson, David James. *Theatre Criticism: A Minor Art with a Major Problem.* Columbus, OH: Ohio State Univ; 1988. 104 pp. Biblio. Notes. [Ph.D. Dissertation, Univ. Microfilms Order No. AAC 8824453.] Lang.: Eng.

USA. 1988. Critical studies. ▪Argues that there is no consensus on what theatre criticism is or by what standards it can be evaluated, and attempts to provide a set of criteria for evaluation.

861 Andrews, Rusalyn Herma. *Deaf Theatre Performance: An Aristotelean Approach.* Carbondale, IL: Southern Illinois Univ; 1988. 310 pp. Biblio. Notes. [Ph.D. Dissertation, Univ. Microfilms Order No. AAC 8922372.] Lang.: Eng.

USA. 1988. Critical studies. ▪Analysis of Deaf theatre performance using a lexicon developed by 'translating' Aristotle's critical theories of drama from a style which incorporates aural language and its cultural assumptions to a style which incorporates a visually based language and cultural assumptions.

862 Bordelon, Suzanne. *Gertrude Buck's Democratic Theory of Discourse and Pedagogy: A Cultural History.* Eugene, OR: Univ. of Oregon; 1998. 217 pp. Notes. Biblio. [Ph.D. Disser-

THEATRE IN GENERAL: —Theory/criticism

tation, Univ. Microfilms Order No. AAC 9900285.] Lang.: Eng.

USA. 1890-1920. Histories-specific. ▪The effects of sociologist Gertrude Buck's democratic theories of discourse and pedagogy on the Little theatre movement.

863 Bristol, Michael D. "Sir George Greenwood's Marginalia in the Folger Copy of Mark Twain's *Is Shakespeare Dead?*." *SQ.* 1998 Win; 49(4): 411-416. Notes. Illus.: Photo. B&W. 1. Lang.: Eng.

USA. 1909. Critical studies. ▪Analysis of marginalia in the Folger Library copy of Twain's *Is Shakespeare Dead?*, which was owned by Sir George Greenwood, whose work inspired Twain but was used without Greenwood's permission.

864 Charney, Mark; Slattery, Bryan. "Beyond the Boos: Critics Taught to Earn Respect." *SoTh.* 1998 Fall; 39(4): 24-27. Illus.: Photo. B&W. 1. Lang.: Eng.

USA: Birmingham, AL. 1998. Historical studies. ▪The nature of criticism as taught to students and examined at the 1998 SETC convention.

865 Fiebach, Joachim. "Theaterstudien als Cultural Studies." (Theatre Studies as Cultural Studies.) 183-204 in Fiebach, Joachim, ed.; Mühl-Benninghaus, Wolfgang, ed. *Keine Hoffnung Keine Verzweiflung. Versuche um Theaterkunst und Theatralität.* Berlin: Vistas Verlag GmbH; 1998. 248 pp. (Berliner Theaterwissenschaft 4.) Notes. Lang.: Ger.

USA. UK-England. France. 1957-1998. Historical studies. ▪Reviews cultural studies developed by Richard Johnson, Richard Hoggart, David Morley, and American and French ethnic anthropology developed by Natalie Davis, Milton Singer, and Victor Turner, with respect to theatre research and performance activities as socio-cultural and political communication.

866 Friedman, Michael Brian. *Advice to the Players: Acting Theory in America, 1923 to 1973.* Bloomington, IN: Indiana Univ; 1987. 229 pp. Notes. Biblio. [Ph.D. Dissertation, Univ. Microfilms Order No. AAC 8717796.] Lang.: Eng.

USA. 1923-1973. Critical studies. ▪Surveys modern American ideas on acting, with some European concepts added. Considers realist, anti-realist, symbolist, and activist theories.

867 Halstead, John S. *Autonomous Theater: Theory into Practice.* Salt Lake City, UT: Univ. of Utah; 1987. 210 pp. Biblio. Notes. [Ph.D. Dissertation, Univ. Microfilms Order No. 8803570.] Lang.: Eng.

USA. 1967-1979. Historical studies. ▪Examines the theoretical structure of autonomous theatre, a performance genre that challenged the dominant position of scripted and produced drama. Argues that the form presages performance theory, and gave birth to the environmental theatre, formalism, and self-reflexivity of theatre artists Richard Schechner, Michael Kirby, and Richard Foreman.

868 Kramer, Richard E. "The Power of the Reviewer: Myth or Fact?" *THSt.* 1998; 53: 13-38. Notes. Lang.: Eng.

USA. 1975-1997. Historical studies. ▪Examines contemporary criticism in US theatre and popular entertainment, focusing on the fraught relationship between reviewer and producer, and how audiences interpret 'bad' reviews.

869 Lee, Josephine. "Between Immigration and Hyphenation: The Problems of Theorizing Asian American Theatre." *JDTC.* 1998 Fall; 13(1): 45-70. Notes. Illus.: Photo. B&W. 3. Lang.: Eng.

USA: Minneapolis, MN. 1994-1995. Critical studies. ▪Analysis of cultural constructs behind the terminology used to describe Asian-American performance. Focuses on three productions: Theatre Mu's *River of Dreams*, *Musika!*, a revue staged by a Filipino-American community group, and Ping Chong's *Undesirable Elements* at the Illusion Theatre.

870 Reinelt, Janelle. "Notes for a Radical Democratic Theater: Productive Crises and the Challenge of Indeterminacy." 283-300 in Colleran, Jeanne, ed.; Spencer, Jenny S., ed. *Staging Resistance: Essays on Political Theatre.* Ann Arbor, MI: Univ of Michigan P; 1998. 312 pp. (Theater: Theory/Text/Performance.) Notes. Index. Lang.: Eng.

USA. 1985-1997. Critical studies. ▪The role of activist theatre in Western democracy.

871 Bogatirjov, Pjotr; Fodor, Géza, intro. "Az öltözet mint jel." (The Costume as Sign.) *Sz.* 1998; 31(7): 45-48 . Illus.: Design. B&W. 5. Lang.: Hun.

USSR. 1893-1971. Critical studies. ▪Translation and commentary on Bogatyrëv's essay.

Training

872 Loffree, Carrie. "Intellectual Stimulation versus 'Marketability': Getting the Most (out of) Graduate School Experiences." *TRC.* 1998 Fall; 19(2): 199-201. Biblio. Lang.: Eng.

Canada. 1998. Critical studies. ▪Proposes diversification of activities for students in graduate theatre programs as a method of harmonizing intellectual excellence with marketability.

873 Angelilli, Marco. "'A Play Is Play': il gioco come strumento di ricerca nel lavoro di Jean-Paul Denizon." ('A Play Is Play': Play as a Research Tool in the Work of Jean- Paul Denizon.) *BiT.* 1998; 45/47: 121-174. Notes. Lang.: Ita.

France. 1980-1998. Critical studies. ▪The work of trainer Jean-Paul Denizon, a French actor-director who for several years has been leading a theatrical workshop on Peter Brook's approach.

874 D'Orazi, Maria Pia. "Il teatro delle emozioni." (The Theatre of Emotions.) *BiT.* 1998; 45/47: 175-197. Notes. Lang.: Ita.

Italy: Rome. 1994-1996. Histories-sources. ▪The author's two-year experience of a workshop held by Ferruccio di Cori on 'Spontaneous Theatre' at the Teatro Ateneo of the University 'La Sapienza' in Rome. The workshop uses improvisation as a first means to find out and control emotions.

875 Mireckaja, N.V.; Mireckaja, E.V. *Uroki antičnoj kul'tury: Učeb. posobie dlja uč-sja obščeobrazovat. škol.* (Lessons of Ancient Culture: An Educational Manual for Students.) Obninsk: Titul; 1998. 336 pp. Lang.: Rus.

Italy: Rome. 1998. Instructional materials. ▪Guide to theatrical training.

876 Pfaff, Walter. "Knowledge Is a Matter of Doing." *MimeJ.* 1998; 19: 76-97. Notes. Biblio. Illus.: Photo. B&W. 14. Lang.: Eng.

Poland. Germany. 1998. Histories-sources. ▪The author, a director and teacher, on his mission to deliver the message of Jerzy Grotowski.

877 Saraeva, L.M. "Formirovanie osnov režissersko-dramatičeskogo masterstva buduščich pedagogov." (Formation of a Level of Mastery for Future Directors and Teachers.) 49-53 in *Pedagogičeskie issledovanija.* Kurgan: 1998. Lang.: Rus.

Russia. 1998. Instructional materials. ▪Outline of standards.

878 Hussey, Michael; Eidsvik, Charles. "Interdisciplinary Instruction by Design." *TD&T.* 1998 Win; 34(5): 22-29. Illus.: Photo. Color. 9. Lang.: Eng.

USA: Athens, GA. 1988-1998. Technical studies. ▪Describes method of teaching developed at the University of Georgia using computer animation techniques to aid in the training of its students of scenography.

879 Knox, Dianna Lynn Welch. *The Role of Improvisational Theatre Training in Building Resilience from Member Participants' Perspectives: A Qualitative Study.* Vermillion, SD: Univ. of South Dakota; 1998. 197 pp. Notes. Biblio. [Ed.D. Dissertation, Univ. Microfilms Order No. AAC 9902691.] Lang.: Eng.

USA. 1996-1998. Empirical research. ▪Argues that improvisational training contains objectives designed to facilitate the development of healthy and productive young people by encouraging them to make decisions that reduce or eliminate high-risk behaviors.

880 Rotté, Joanna. "Feldenkrais Revisited: Tension, Talent, and the Legacy of Childhood." *NTQ.* 1998 Nov.; 14(4): 351-356. [Issue 56.] Lang.: Eng.

USA. 1905-1985. Histories-sources. ▪Interview describes how Moshe Feldenkrais developed his influential philosophy and physiology of movement from a background of engineering, eschewing psychoanalytical approaches to remedying poor posture opting for self-correction through the use of the capacity of one's own body and brain.

DANCE

General

Administration

881 Hellström Sveningson, Lis. "Ställ danskonsten i fokus!" (Put the Art of Dance In Focus!) *Danst.* 1998; 8(6): 15, 25-40. Illus.: Photo. B&W. Color. Lang.: Swe.
Sweden. 1998. Historical studies. ▪Report from Dansbiennal 98 at Dansens Hus and Riksteatern, where the dance establishment met the government, more words about the regional situation of the dance and want of funds, than the art itself.

882 Olsson, Irène. "Att passera nålsögat." (To Pass the Eye of a Needle.) *Danst.* 1998; 8(5): 12-14. Lang.: Swe.
Sweden. 1990-1998. Historical studies. ▪Survey of how auditions are managed by the schools and theatres in Sweden.

883 Westman, Nany. "Får alla lov att vara med?" (May Everybody Take Part?) *Danst.* 1998; 8(1): 10. Lang.: Swe.
Sweden. 1998. Historical studies. ▪Presentation of the new art funding program of the Swedish government called Dans i hela landet (Dance Throughout the Land).

884 Fisher, Mark. "Dance under New Labour." *DTJ.* 1998; 14(1): 19. Lang.: Eng.
UK-England. 1998. Histories-sources. ▪British Arts Minister on the state of dance in his country. Touches on funding, training, and the place of British dance on the world stage.

885 Leask, Josephine. "Chisenhale Dance Space: Loss and Gain?" *DTJ.* 1998; 14(3): 24-25. Lang.: Eng.
UK-England: London. 1998. Historical studies. ▪Strategies used by the Chisenhale Dance Space to mount a 'survival campaign' after it lost its funding from the London Arts Board.

886 Young, Henry. "The National Endowment: Preparing for the Future." *Dm.* 1998 Jan.; 72(1): 50-52. Lang.: Eng.
USA. 1998. Critical studies. ▪Offers strategies for dance companies to find new sources of funding in the event of the NEA's possible demise.

Basic theatrical documents

887 Kuo, Yu-Chun. *Ring: Concerto for Dance and Music.* San Diego, CA: Univ. of California; 1988. 76 pp. Notes. Biblio. [Ph.D. Dissertation, Univ. Microfilms Order No. AAC 8908010.] Lang.: Eng.
USA. 1988. ▪Original concerto for dance and music, including dance notation.

Design/technology

888 Hansen, Sophie. "Real-Time Events." *DTJ.* 1998; 14(3): 13-15. Notes. Illus.: Photo. B&W. 1. Lang.: Eng.
1998. Technical studies. ▪Discusses the theoretical versus the practical when applying new stage technology to the needs of a dance production.

889 Ståhle, Anna Greta. "Byta kostym på en trumvirvel." (Change the Costume On a Drum-roll.) *Danst.* 1998; 8(2): 14-15. Illus.: Photo. B&W. Lang.: Swe.
Russia. Sweden. Japan. 1840-1998. Historical studies. ▪Rapid changes of costumes on stage, in Čajkovskij's *Swan Lake*, Cullberg's *Månrenen (The Moondeer)* and Japanese *kabuki.*

Institutions

890 Johansson, Kerstin. "Kuopio–hetast norr om Havanna." (Kuopio–The Hottest Thing North of Havana.) *Danst.* 1998; 8(4): 4-5 . Illus.: Photo. B&W. Color. Lang.: Swe.
Finland: Kuopio. 1998. Historical studies. ▪Report from the festival with mostly guest performances from companies from Latin America.

891 Johansson, Pernilla. "Unga spirande koreografer möts i Paris." (Young Budding Choregraphers Are Meeting In Paris.) *Danst.* 1998; 8(4): 8. Illus.: Photo. B&W. Lang.: Swe.
France: Bagnolet. 1998. Historical studies. ▪Report from the Concours de Bagnolet dance festival.

892 Sieben, Irene; Urbán, Mária, transl. "Ösztön és emberi gép: Pályakép Nagy Józsefről." (Instinct and Human Machine: Portrait of Josef Nadj.) *Ellenfény.* 1998; 3(3): 30-32. Illus.: Photo. B&W. 3. Lang.: Hun.
France. 1990-1998. Histories-sources. ▪Conversation with the dancer-choreographer and director of Centre Chorégraphique National d'Orléans, Josef Nadj, on his life and career.

893 Cody, Gabrielle. "Woman, Man, Dog, Tree: Two Decades of Intimate and Monumental Bodies in Pina Bausch's Tanztheater." *TDR.* 1998 Sum; 42(2): 115-131. Lang.: Eng.
Germany: Wuppertal. 1977-1998. Historical studies. ▪Profile and analysis of the work of the choreographer and her company.

894 Kaán, Zsuzsa; Kanyó, Béla, photo. "'Az értéket értékként kell lezelni!': évadkezdő beszélgetés Dózsa Imrével, a Magyar Táncművészeti Főiskola új főigazgatójával." ('Valuables Must Be Regarded Acording to Their Value': A Year-Opening Interview with Imre Dózsa, General Director of the Hungarian Dance Academy.) *Tanc.* 1998; 29(4): 10-11. Illus.: Photo. B&W. 1. Lang.: Hun.
Hungary. 1998. Histories-sources. ▪Changes in structure and new tendencies in training at the dance school as seen by the director.

895 Lőrinc, Katalin. "Táncfesztivál Veszprémben és Győrött." (Dance Festivals in Veszprém and Győr.) *Tanc.* 1998; 29(3): 24-25. Lang.: Hun.
Hungary: Győr, Veszprém. 1998. Reviews of performances. ▪Survey of the events of the two contemporary dance festivals.

896 Pór, Anna; Kanyó, Béla, photo.; Kádár, Kata, photo. "Visszatekintő töprengések az Interbalettről és a Tavaszi Fesztiválról." (Retrospective Musings about Interballet and the Spring Festival.) *Tanc.* 1998; 29(3): 19-21. Illus.: Photo. B&W. 3. Lang.: Hun.
Hungary: Budapest. 1998. Critical studies. ▪Summary notes on the program of two Budapest festivals with participants from home and abroad.

897 Réfi, Zsuzsanna. "'Ahol mindenki szereti a táncot'." ('Where Everybody Likes Dancing'.) *ZZT.* 1998; 5(4): 4-5. Illus.: Photo. B&W. 1. Lang.: Hun.
Hungary: Budapest. 1998. Histories-sources. ▪Interview with the newly appointed managing director of the Academy of Dance, Imre Dózsa, former solo dancer of the Budapest Opera House, on the problems of training, changes in method, financial operations, cooperation with similar foreign training schools and other future plans.

898 Berggren, Klara. "Skoltimmar att längta till." (Lessons To Be Longed For.) *Danst.* 1998; 8(2): 16-18. Illus.: Photo. B&W. Lang.: Swe.
Sweden: Solna. 1990-1998. Historical studies. ▪The performing arts curriculum of Skytteholmsgymnasiet, where the program includes various kinds of dance in addition to the standard courses.

899 Bohlin, Peter. "Samverkan för dans i hela landet." (Co-operation of Dance Throughout the Land.) *Entré.* 1998; 25 (2): 42. Illus.: Photo. B&W. Lang.: Swe.
Sweden. 1974-1998. Historical studies. ▪Examines the Dans i hela landet (Dance Throughout the Land) project funded by Dansens Hus, Riksteatern, and Statens Kulturråd, with Cecilia Björklund Dahlgren as an overall curator.

900 Hellström Sveningson, Lis. "Lia Schubert–en skapare av dansskolor." (Lia Schubert–a Creator of Dance Schools.) *Danst.* 1998; 8(6): 50-51. Illus.: Photo. B&W. Lang.: Swe.
Sweden: Stockholm, Gothenburg. 1935-1998. Histories-sources. ▪Interview with Lia Schubert about her life before retirement as pedagogue and director of Balettakademien in Stockholm and Gothenburg, with references to the Swedish dancers of today.

901 Wrange, Ann-Marie. "En livskraftig akademi." (A Vital Academy.) *Danst.* 1998; 8(2): 10-12. Illus.: Photo. B&W. Lang.: Swe.
Sweden: Stockholm. 1957-1998. Histories-sources. ▪History of Balettakademien, with an interview with the artistic director Lillemor Lundberg, who began as a pupil in 1957.

902 Wrange, Ann-Marie. "Dansbiennal 98." *Danst.* 1998; 8(6): 25-40. Illus.: Photo. Color. Lang.: Swe.
Sweden: Stockholm. 1998. Historical studies. ▪Report on the seminars about the situation of dance of all genres in Sweden, the attitude of the government and the program called Dans i hela landet (Dance Through-

DANCE: General—Institutions

out the Land), with a discussion among Mats Ek, Jens Östberg and Bodil Persson.

903 Zacharias, Gun. "Dansutbildning utan utklassning." (Dance Education Without Outclassing.) *Danst.* 1998; 8(4): 17. Illus.: Dwg. B&W. Lang.: Swe.

Sweden. 1998. Critical studies. ■Appeal for a more generous and varied education of dancers, with reference to the new offerings of Danshögskolan.

904 Gibson, Rachel. "C.I.A. Investigations." *DTJ.* 1998; 14(4): 30-33. Illus.: Photo. B&W. 2. Lang.: Eng.

UK-Scotland: Glasgow. 1996-1998. Histories-sources. ■Interview with choreographer Gary Lambert, dancer Shelley Baker, visual artist Eloise Robinson, and lighting designer Lee Curran about their work with the dance group Creative Independent Artists.

905 Hutera, Donald. "ART performs ART equals ART." *DTJ.* 1998; 14(4): 22-25. Notes. Illus.: Photo. B&W. 3. Lang.: Eng.

USA: Minneapolis, MN. 1998. Historical studies. ■Report on the exhibition of dance mounted at the museum at the Walker Arts Center which includes photos, drawings, and video and film footage.

906 Jacobson, Daniel. "Peeling Our Eyes." *BR.* 1998 Sum; 26(2): 68-80. Illus.: Photo. B&W. 7. Lang.: Eng.

USA: New York, NY. 1998. Historical studies. ■Report on the 1998 Altogether Different dance festival held in New York.

907 Lomax, Sandra. "Houston's High School for the Arts." *Dm.* 1998 Aug.; 72(8): 70-71. Illus.: Photo. Color. 2. Lang.: Eng.

USA: Houston, TX. 1998. Critical studies. ■Looks at the dance program offered by the Houston High School for the Performing and Visual Arts.

908 Spiegel, Jan Ellen. "Where the Dance Boom Continues." *Dm.* 1998 Feb.; 72(2): 64-69. Illus.: Photo. B&W. 5. Lang.: Eng.

USA. 1963-1998. Historical studies. ■Examines the reasons for the growing strength of regional dance companies in the United States.

Performance spaces

909 Ochaim, Brygida. "Tanz-Architekturen." (Dance Architectures.) *Tanzd.* 1998; 43(4): 22-24. Notes. Illus.: Photo. B&W. 2. Lang.: Ger.

Europe. 1895-1937. Historical studies. ■Variety of performance spaces used by dancers Loie Fuller, La Goulue, Charlotte Bara and Akarova, such as the Moulin Rouge.

910 Ayers, Robert. "Building Connections: Spaces for Dance." *DTJ.* 1998; 14(3): 16-19. Notes. Illus.: Photo. B&W. 2. Lang.: Eng.

UK-Scotland: Glasgow. 1998. Historical studies. ■Report on a one-day conference/roundtable discussion on the need for viable performance space for dance.

Performance/production

911 Gerasimova, I.A. "Vol'nost' v kanone i nevolie v improvizacii: (Dve formy tanca)." (Freedom in Dogma and Lack of Freedom in Improvisation: Two Forms of Dance.) *Polignozis.* 1998; 3: 136-148. Lang.: Rus.

Historical studies. ■About the art of dance, history of the form.

912 Körtvélyes, Géza. "A zene és a tánc találkozása a színpadon - jegyzetek egy témáról." (Music and Dance on the Stage—Notes on a Theme.) *ZZT.* 1998; 5(4): 23-25. Lang.: Hun.

1700-1970. Historical studies. ■The development of theatre dance art from the beginnings up to the present time.

913 Smith, Bryan. "A Dancing Consciousness." 72-80 in Carter, Alexandra, ed. *Routledge Dance Studies Reader.* London/New York, NY: Routledge; 1998. 316 pp. Index. Notes. Biblio. Lang.: Eng.

Australia. USA. 1983-1995. Histories-sources. ■Interview with dancer/choreographer Rebecca Hilton on her career, especially her training, process, and the role of improvisation in her work.

914 Lőrinc, Katalin. "Posztmodern társulatok a bécsi táncheteken." (Post-Modern Ensembles During the Summer Dance Evenings in Vienna.) *Tanc.* 1998; 29(4): 33. Illus.: Photo. B&W. 1. Lang.: Hun.

Austria: Vienna. 1998. Reviews of performances. ■A brief survey of Im Puls Tanz '98: 28 companies during six weeks with 51 evenings of dance performances.

915 Di Bernardi, Vito. "Ram Gopal: la danza classica indiana e il balletto occidentale." (Ram Gopal: Indian Classical Dance and Western Ballet.) *BiT.* 1998; 45/47: 323-348. Notes. Lang.: Ita.

Europe. India. 1930-1960. Biographical studies. ■Examines the work of Ram Gopal, one of the greatest Indian classical dancers, inspired by Diaghilev, Anna Pavlova, and Nijinsky.

916 Ahonen, Piia. "Ongelmallinen proggis." (Problematic Production.) *Tanssi.* 1998; 19(4): 24-26. Illus.: Photo. B&W. 1. Lang.: Fin.

Finland. 1998. Historical studies. ■Focuses on the working relationship between dancer and choreographer.

917 Laakkonen, Johanna. "Ensimmäiset tanssitilastot freelancereista todistavat ponnistelujen määrän." (First Dance Statistics Prove the Value of Freelance Dancers.) *Tanssi.* 1998; 19(2): 4. Illus.: Photo. B&W. 1. Lang.: Fin.

Finland. 1998. Empirical studies. ■Using recently compiled statistics regarding dance performance, concludes that most dance pieces are created by unaffiliated dancers and choreographers.

918 Pakkanen, Päivi. "Lasten käsityksiä tanssitaiteesta." (Children on Dance.) *Tanssi.* 1998; 19(3): 22-25. Illus.: Photo. B&W. 2. Lang.: Fin.

Finland. 1998. Histories-sources. ■Children express their views and experiences in the world of dance.

919 Parviainen, Jaana. "Urheilun, viihteen ja taiteen sulatusuuni." (The Melting Pot of Sport, Entertainment and Art.) *Tanssi.* 1998; 19(3): 18-21. Illus.: Photo. B&W. 3. Lang.: Fin.

Finland. 1998. Histories-sources. ■Interview with ice dancing couple Susanna Rahkamo and Petri Kokko about how athletics and art are fused in their particular discipline.

920 Routti, Laura. "Koreologi vangitsee liikkeen paperille." (The Choreologue Captures the Movement on Paper.) *Tanssi.* 1998 ; 19(3): 28. Illus.: Photo. B&W. 1. Lang.: Fin.

Finland. 1998. Histories-sources. ■Interview with Päivi Eskelinen, the first Benesh method choreologue, or notator of choreography, in Finland.

921 Tawast, Minna. "Televisiossa ei nykyään turhaan tanssita." (They Are Not Dancing on Television for Nothing.) *Tanssi.* 1998; 19(4): 10. Illus.: Photo. B&W. 2. Lang.: Fin.

Finland. 1998. Historical studies. ■The place of dance production on Finnish television.

922 Bennahum, Ninotchka Devorah. *Antonia Merce, La Argentina, 1888-1936: The Art of Sublime Dance in 1920s Paris.* New York, NY: New York Univ; 1998. 350 pp. Notes. Biblio. [Ph.D. Dissertation, Univ. Microfilms Order No. AAC 9907134.] Lang.: Eng.

France. Spain. 1888-1936. Histories-specific. ■Career and life of Spanish dancer Antonia Merce, known as La Argentina, with emphasis on her work with other modernist artists of the 1920s in Paris including Vicente Escudero and Georges Wague.

923 Leask, Josephine. "Between the Earth and the Sky." *DTJ.* 1998; 14(4): 34-37. Notes. Illus.: Photo. B&W. 2. Lang.: Eng.

France: Paris. Benin. 1990-1998. Biographical studies. ■Profile of Paris-based Benin-born choreographer Koffi Koko.

924 Várszegi, Tibor. "Adalékok A véletlen világtörténetéhez." (A Contribution to Coincidence.) *Ellenfény.* 1998; 3(3): 33-44. Illus.: Photo. B&W. 8. Lang.: Hun.

France. 1987-1998. Critical studies. ■Study on Josef Nadj, his company Théâtre du Signe, and their work.

925 Arndt, Roman. "Georg Groke." *Tanzd.* 1998; 42(3): 34-35. Illus.: Photo. B&W. 4. Lang.: Ger.

Germany. Poland. 1904-1972. Biographical studies. ■Career of dancer George Groke who emigrated to Poland in 1933 and returned to his homeland in 1939.

926 Kaán, Zsuzsa; McNicholas, Steve, photo. "STOMP - avagy az ezredvég zenebohócai: Az év showja a Deutsches Theater-

ben." (STOMP, or End-of-Millennium Music Clown: The Show of the Year at Deutsches Theater.) *Tanc.* 1998; 29(3): 32-33. Illus.: Photo. B&W. Color. 3. Lang.: Hun.
Germany: Munich. 1992-1998. Reviews of performances. ■Report on a guest performance by movement group Stomp.

927 Kaposi, Edit. "C.J. v. Feldtenstein: Útmutató a koreográfiai művészet szerént való tánchoz (Braunschweig, 1767, 1772, 1775)." (C.J. von Feldtenstein: Guide to Dance According to the Art of Choreography.) *Tanc.* 1998; 29 (5): 6-7. Notes. Lang.: Hun.
Germany: Braunschweig. 1767-1775. Critical studies. ■Introducing a three-volume book by a dance master from the eighteenth-century, originally published by Schröderchen Buchhandlung in Braunschweig, 1767. Its new edition in 1984 with preface and index was published by dance historian Kurt Petermann, leader of the Leipzig Tanzarchiv, in the series of Documenta Choreologica.

928 Manning, Susan. "Dances of Death: Germany Before Hitler." 259-268 in Carter, Alexandra, ed. *Routledge Dance Studies Reader.* London/New York, NY: Routledge; 1998. 316 pp. Index. Notes. Biblio. Lang.: Eng.
Germany. 1930-1932. Historical studies. ■Gender and politics in German dance, with emphasis on Mary Wigman's *Totenmal (Call of the Dead)* and Kurt Jooss's *Der Grüne Tisch (The Green Table).*

929 Peter, Frank-Manuel. "'Als Tänzer das, was Mary Wigman als Tänzerin bedeutet'." (He Had, as a Male Dancer, the Same Impact as Mary Wigman Had as a Female Dancer.) *Tanzd.* 1998; 43(4): 25-27. Notes. Illus.: Dwg. Photo. B&W. 7. Lang.: Ger.
Germany. 1898-1975. Biographical studies. ■Portrait of dancer, actor, director and choreographer Wolfgang Martin Schede who also worked as photographer, artist and author, on occasion of his 100th birthday.

930 Schneider, Katja. "Hamlet und der Mann mit der Stofffrolle." (Hamlet and the Man with the Roll of Material.) *Tanzd.* 1998 ; 43(4): 32-37. Notes. Illus.: Photo. B&W. 5. Lang.: Ger.
Germany: Bremen, Weimar. 1996-1997. Critical studies. ■Analyzes and compares dance versions of William Shakespeare's *Hamlet*: *Hamlet szenen (Scenes of Hamlet)* adapted and choreographed by Susanne Linke at Bremer Theater and *Hamlet I, II, III* adapted and choreographed by Joachim Schlömer at Deutsches Nationaltheater Weimar.

931 Schneider, Katja. "'Eine homogene jüdische Kultur gibt es nicht'." ('There Is No Homogeneous Jewish Culture'.) *Tanzd.* 1998; 42(3): 36-37. Illus.: Photo. B&W. 3. Lang.: Ger.
Germany: Munich. 1998. Histories-sources. ■Interview with Jewish Museum curator Cornelia Albrecht about the wide diversity of Jewish choreographers.

932 Servos, Norbert. "Pina Bausch: Dance and Emancipation." 36-45 in Carter, Alexandra, ed. *Routledge Dance Studies Reader.* London/New York, NY: Routledge; 1998. 316 pp. Index. Notes. Biblio. Lang.: Eng.
Germany: Wuppertal. 1973-1997. Historical studies. ■Examines the career of choreographer/dancer Pina Bausch and her long assocation with Tanztheater Wuppertal.

933 Servos, Norbert. "Schreibtische der Angst." (Desks of Fear.) *THeute.* 1998; 3: 30-32. Illus.: Photo. B&W. 2. Lang.: Ger.
Germany: Berlin. 1998. Critical studies. ■Analyzes dance performances from Berlin: Johann Kresnigk's choreography *Hotel Lux* at Volksbühne Berlin and Jo Fabian's *Die Krähe (The Crow)* and the political themes.

934 Stöckemann, Patricia. "'Ich hatte keinen Pass, keine Staatsangehörigkeit, nicht'." ('I Had No Passport, No Nationality, Nothing'.) *Tanzd.* 1998; 42(3): 14-18. Pref. Illus.: Photo. B&W. 7. Lang.: Ger.
Germany. 1936-1998. Histories-sources. ■Interview with choreographer Renate Schottelius about her emigration from Nazi Germany to Argentina in 1936 and its consequences for her life and work.

935 Dienes, Gedeon; Lisztes, Edina, photo. "'Az orkesztika az én mozdulatfilozófiám!': Beszélgetés Tatai Mária mozdulatépítéssel." ('Orchestics Is My Movement Philosophy': Interview with Movement Artist Mária Tatai.) *Tanc.* 1998; 29(1): 10-11. Illus.: Photo. B&W. 3. Lang.: Hun.
Hungary. 1981-1998. Histories-sources. ■Tatai describes the work of her Orchestics dance theatre.

936 Dorogi, Katalin. "Megkésett pillanatképek Hajós Kláráról." (Late Snapshots of Klára Hajós.) *Tanc.* 1998; 29(4): 12-13. Illus.: Photo. B&W. 2. Lang.: Hun.
Hungary. 1911-1998. Histories-sources. ■Life and career of the dancer, who taught eurythmics for decades.

937 Falvay, Károly; Eifert, János, photo. "*Raszputyin*: A Közép-Európa Táncszínház új műsora." (*Rasputin*: A New Program by the Central European Dance Theatre.) *Tanc.* 1998; 29(2): 16. Illus.: Photo. B&W. 2. Lang.: Hun.
Hungary: Budapest. 1998. Critical studies. ■Analysis of the new production of the ensemble written and directed by Miklós Köllő.

938 Fuchs, Lívia. "Változatok a test színházára: Kerekasztal-beszélgetés táncos-koreográfusokkal." (Variations on the Theatre of the Body: Round Table Discussion with Dancer-Choreographers.) *Ellenfény.* 1998; 3(5): 2-6. Illus.: Photo. B&W. 6. Lang.: Hun.
Hungary. 1998. Histories-sources. ■The edited version of a discussion with Yvette Bozsik, leader of Yvette Bozsik Társulat, Tamás Juronics, artistic director of the Szeged Contemporary Ballet, and László Rókás, leader of Sofa Trio about the theatre based on dance and movement.

939 Gelencsér, Ágnes. "A modern tánc panorámája: Kétféle tendencia, kétféle minőség." (Panorama of Modern Dance: Two Ways of Tendencies, Two Kinds of Value.) *ZZT.* 1998; 5(1): 35-36. Lang.: Hun.
Hungary: Budapest. 1992-1994. Reviews of performances. ■A comparative analysis of two ensembles who gave guest performances in Hungary at the annual Spring Festivals: the Flemish dance theatre Rosas in 1992 and the Portuguese Ballet Gulbenkian in 1994.

940 Halász, Tamás; Koncz, Zsuzsa, photo. "Apropó Faun." (On 'Faun'.) *Ellenfény.* 1998; 3(1): 64-65. Illus.: Photo. B&W. 3. Lang.: Hun.
Hungary: Budapest. 1997. Critical studies. ■Yvette Bozsik's new choreography for Debussy's *L'après-midi d'un faune.*

941 Kaán, Zsuzsa. "A Sankai Juku a Tháliában." (Sankai Juku at the Thália Theatre.) *Tanc.* 1998; 29(4): 28. Illus.: Photo. B&W. 1. Lang.: Hun.
Hungary: Budapest. 1998. Reviews of performances. ■Notes on the guest performance of the *butō* dance company.

942 Kaán, Zsuzsa. "*Egy faun délelőttje*: Cie, 2 in 1 & Árvai-módra." (*The Morning of a Faun*: Cie, 2 in 1 & Árvai-Manner.) *Tanc.* 1998; 29(5): 18. Lang.: Hun.
Hungary: Budapest. 1998. Reviews of performances. ■Notes on a so-called 'visual dance' alternative production by the Cie, 2 in 1 company using videofilm and other elements of vision at the MU Theatre.

943 Kaposi, Edit. "Mátyás király és a tánc: Gondolatok Hunyadi Mátyás királlyá választásának 540. évfordulóján." (King Mátyás and Dance: Thoughts on the 540th Anniversary of the Coronation of Mátyás Hunyadi.) *Tanc.* 1998; 29(5): 26-27. Notes. Illus.: Photo. MP. B&W. 3. Lang.: Hun.
Hungary. 1413-1485. Historical studies. ■The dance culture at the Renaissance court of the great King Mátyás in Hungary.

944 Königer, Miklós. "Felejtés ellen. Putti Lya-emlékkiállítás a Goethe Intézetben." (Against Oblivion. Lya Putti Commemorative Exhibition at the Goethe Institute.) *Tanc.* 1998; 29(4): 6. Illus.: Photo. B&W. 1. Lang.: Hun.
Hungary. Germany. 1898-1931. Historical studies. ■On an exhibit of Dr. Johann Zeilinger's private collection on the life and career of Hungarian-born star of silent film. The young Lya de Putti had been a dancer at small revue theatres and later she became a film actress in Berlin and then continued her career in America.

945 Lőrinc, Katalin; Papp, Dezső, photo. "*Kabaré*: Bozsik Yvette új produkciója a Kamrában." (*Cabaret*: New Production by Yvette Bozsik at Kamra.) *Tanc.* 1998; 29(6): 22-23. Illus.: Photo. B&W. 3. Lang.: Hun.

DANCE: General—Performance/production

Hungary: Budapest. 1998. Reviews of performances. ■Premiere of Bozsik's new composition at the Kamra (The Chamber) of the Katona József Theatre.

946 Lőrinc, Katalin. "Szeged, Pécs és Győr táncosai az Interbaletten." (Dancers of Szeged, Pécs and Győr at the Interbalett'98.) *ZZT.* 1998; 5(3): 11-14. Illus.: Photo. B&W. 3. Lang.: Hun.

Hungary. 1998. Reviews of performances. ■Three contemporary Hungarian dance companies on the program of the annual festival of dance art, Interbalett '98.

947 Lőrinc, Katalin; Molnár, Kata, photo. "*X.Y.Z.*: Mándy Ildikó új darabja a Trafóban." (*X.Y.Z.*: Ildikó Mándy's New Piece at Trafó.) *Tanc.* 1998; 29(5): 19. Illus.: Photo. B&W. 1. Lang.: Hun.

Hungary: Budapest. 1998. Reviews of performances. ■Account of an alternative one-act 'film-dance-theatre' performance at the House of Contemporary Arts (Trafó).

948 Lőrinc, Katalin; Dusa, Gábor, photo. "*Csillagőrlő*: Az Artus Tánegyüttes bemutatója." (*Starmill*: Premiere by the Artus Dance Ensemble.) *Tanc.* 1998; 29(6): 17. Illus.: Photo. B&W. 1. Lang.: Hun.

Hungary: Budapest. 1998. Reviews of performances. ■New production by the Artus Company as the second part of the *Noe Trilogy*, choreographed by Goda Gábor.

949 Réfi, Zsuzsanna. "'Csak a nézők emlékeiben él': Péntek Kata az akkor és ott művészetéről." ('The Performance Is Alive Only in the Memory of the Audience': Kata Péntek on the Art of 'Then and There'.) *ZZT.* 1998; 5(2): 18-19. Illus.: Photo. B&W. 1. Lang.: Hun.

Hungary. 1987-1998. Biographical studies. ■Snapshot of a young talented dancer.

950 Várnai, Dóra; Molnár, Kata, photo. "Halottak tánca: Butoh ünnep a Szkénében." (Dance of the Dead: *Butō* Festival at the Szkene.) *Ellenfény.* 1998; 3(1): 74-75. Illus.: Photo. B&W. 3. Lang.: Hun.

Hungary: Budapest. 1997. Historical studies. ■The program of the *butō* festival held at the Szkéné Theatre in Budapest.

951 Vazsó, Vera. "Produkálni kell! Beszélgetés Fuchs Líviával." (Production Is a Must! Interview with Lívia Fuchs.) *Ellenfény.* 1998; 3(1): 5-6. Illus.: Photo. B&W. 2. Lang.: Hun.

Hungary: Budapest. 1960-1990. Histories-sources. ■Dance historian, critic, and leading teacher at the Ballet Academy on the importance of workshops in dance.

952 Varley, Julia; Korish, David, transl.; Avila, Roxana, transl. "Sanjukta Panigrahi: Dancer for the Gods." *NTQ.* 1998 Aug. ; 14(3): 249-273. Biblio. Illus.: Photo. B&W. 8. [Issue 55.] Lang.: Eng.

India. 1944-1997. Histories-sources. ■Career of the dancer/choreographer and co-founder of the International School of Theatre Anthropology. Includes the subject's own detailed descriptions of her life and work.

953 Nestvogel, Claudius. "Von Leonardo da Vinci ins 21. Jahrhundert." (From Leonardo da Vinci Into the 21st Century.) *Tanzd.* 1998; 43(4): 13-16. Notes. Illus.: Photo. B&W. 3. Lang.: Ger.

Israel: Jerusalem. 1978-1998. Critical studies. ■Portrait of dancer, choreographer, teacher Amos Hetz and his experiments of movement studies based on the Eshkol-Wachmann notation.

954 Suhr, Moon Ja Minn. *A History of Korean Dance.* Denton, TX: Texas Woman's Univ; 1988. 353 pp. Biblio. Notes. [Ph.D. Dissertation, Univ. Microfilms Order No. AAC 8827492.] Lang.: Eng.

Korea. 1600-1985. Histories-specific. ■Examines the historical, political, social, and cultural background of Korean dance in relation to theatre, costume, and music. Includes discussion of court, religious, folk, mask, and Western influenced modern dance forms, as well as the government's involvement in dance preservation.

955 "Dansen måste använda en större del av ålderstrappan." (The Dance Has To Use a Larger Part of the Age Pyramid.) *Entré.* 1998; 25(3/4): 66-68. Illus.: Photo. B&W. Lang.: Swe.

Netherlands: The Hague. Sweden. 1998. Critical studies. ■An appeal for the possibility to lengthen the careers of dancers, with reference to Nederlands Dans Theater III which employs dancers over the age of forty.

956 Kozel, Susan. "Spacemaking: Experiences of a Virtual Body." 81-88 in Carter, Alexandra, ed. *Routledge Dance Studies Reader.* London/New York, NY: Routledge; 1998. 316 pp. Index. Notes. Biblio. Lang.: Eng.

Netherlands: Amsterdam. 1997. Histories-sources. ■Author's experiences performing in Paul Sermon's *Telematic Dreaming*, in a warehouse, using virtual reality, and reflections on the relationship between the fleshly body and the 'cyber-body'.

957 Leeuwen, Ger van; Wildeman, Maartje. *Dansfotografie in Nederland.* (Dance Photography in the Netherlands.) Amsterdam: ITFB; 1998. 150 pp. Pref. Index. Notes. Biblio. Illus.: Photo. B&W. Color. 100. Lang.: Dut.

Netherlands. 1917-1998. Histories-specific. ■A pictorial history of dance in the Netherlands.

958 Kiepels, Caroline. "Dans för social rättvisa." (Dance For Social Justice.) *Danst.* 1998; 8(1): 8. Illus.: Photo. Color. Lang.: Swe.

Nicaragua. 1979-1998. Histories-sources. ■Interview with the dancer and choreographer Gloria Bacon about the state of dance in Nicaragua.

959 Werner, Frank. "Unruly Bodies." *DTJ.* 1998; 14(3): 20-23. Notes. Illus.: Photo. B&W. 3. Lang.: Eng.

Portugal. 1998. Historical studies. ■Issues of politics and stagnant culture that fire the creativity of Portuguese dancers and choreographers such as João Fiadiero, Francisco Camacho, and Vera Mantero.

960 Portnova, T. "Choreograf, chudožnik i skul'ptor." (Choreographer, Artist and Sculptor.) *DetLit.* 1998; 4: 96-100. Lang.: Rus.

Russia. 1892-1970. Histories-sources. ■Interview with choreographer Kasjan Golejzovskij.

961 Suric, E. "N.S. Poznjakov i E.V. Javorskij: Rabota v oblasti teorii i praktiki tanca (v GAHN, 1920 - 30-e gg)." (N.S. Poznjakov and E.V. Javorskij: Their Work in the Area of the Theory and Practice of Dance.) *Iskusstvoznanie.* 1998; 1: 318-328. Lang.: Rus.

Russia: Moscow. 1920-1939. Critical studies. ■The work of the two choreographers and dance theorists.

962 Da Costa Holton, Kimberly. "Like Blood in Your Mouth: Topographies of Flamenco Voice and Pedagogy in Diaspora." *TextPQ.* 1998 Oct.; 18(4): 300-318. Notes. Biblio. Illus.: Photo. B&W. 1. Lang.: Eng.

Spain. USA. 1901-1998. Historical studies. ■Changes in the flamenco form after years of mixing with different forms world wide. Focus on a small group of Andalusian musicians residing in Chicago, IL.

963 Ångström, Anna. "Dans handlar om rörelsemusikalitet." (Dance Is About the Musicality of Movement.) *Danst.* 1998; 8(3): 6-9. Illus.: Photo. B&W. Lang.: Swe.

Sweden. Africa. Asia. 1908. Histories-sources. ■Interview with Birgit Åkesson about her life, her search for pure dance, her researches in Africa and Asia, as well as her works.

964 Croner, Claes. "Salsafeber." (Salsa Fever.) *Danst.* 1998; 8(6): 48-49. Illus.: Photo. Color. Lang.: Swe.

Sweden. 1970-1998. Critical studies. ■Account of the new popular fad of salsa dancing in Sweden.

965 Hessel, Tina. "Dansmedicin: smärtor och stelhet i nacken." (Dance Medicine: Pains and Stiffness In the Back of the Head.) *Danst.* 1998; 8(4): 14-15. Illus.: Dwg. B&W. Lang.: Swe.

Sweden. 1998. Critical studies. ■Common pains suffered by dancers, their grounding in the spine and back of the head, and how to cure them.

966 Lynge, Claus. "Salto! Växthus, Dance-Greenhouse." (Salto! Dance-Greenhouse.) *Danst.* 1998; 8(6): 13. Illus.: Photo. B&W. Lang.: Swe.

DANCE: General—Performance/production

Sweden: Malmö. Denmark: Copenhagen. 1997. Historical studies. ■Report on the festival of children's dance that is a co-operation between Dansstationen and Danscenen.

967 MacLennan, Karin. "Farah—arabisk folkdansare som skapar nya former." (Farah—an Arabic Folk-dancer Who Creates New Forms.) *Danst.* 1998; 8(6): 16. Illus.: Photo. B&W. Lang.: Swe.

Sweden: Gothenburg. Iraq. 1983-1998. Histories-sources. ■Interview with Farah Al-Bayaty about her background in Iraq, her moving to Sweden and how the Arabic dance has returned her connection to her roots, with reference to the group Zanobia.

968 Wrange, Ann-Marie. "Dansare som blivit doktorer." (Dancers Who Have Turned Doctors.) *Danst.* 1998; 8(4): 12-13: ia. Illus.: Photo. B&W. Lang.: Swe.

Sweden: Stockholm. 1974. Histories-sources. ■Interviews with two dancers, Johan Kakko and Isabel Gustafsson, about their dancing careers and how they changed to a new profession as psychiatrist and general practitioner.

969 Dodds, Sherril. "Carry on Screening." *DTJ.* 1998; 14(2): 12-14. Notes. Illus.: Photo. B&W. 4. Lang.: Eng.

UK-England: London. 1997. Historical studies. ■Report on the 1997 Dance Screen Festival for dance filmmakers.

970 Forrai, Éva. "*A hipochonder madár.*" (The Hypochondriacal Bird.) *Tanc.* 1998; 29(5): 32. Illus.: Photo. B&W. 1. Lang.: Hun.

UK-England: London. 1998. Reviews of performances. ■The performance at the London Dance Umbrella Festival by Javier De Frutos, winner of last year's South Bank Show Award for Dance.

971 Goulden, Jan. "Multimedia Possibilities for Live and Lesbian Performances." *NTQ.* 1998 Aug.; 14(3): 234-248. Notes. Biblio. Illus.: Photo. B&W. 1. [Issue 55.] Lang.: Eng.

UK-England. USA. 1996. Histories-sources. ■Exploration of the possibilities of CD-ROM for use in interactive performance sparked by Lois Weaver's lesbian-themed *Faith and Dancing*, intercut with an interview with Weaver regarding the nature and potential of multimedia in dance.

972 Jeyasingh, Shobana. "Imaginary Homelands: Creating a New Dance Language." 46-52 in Carter, Alexandra, ed. *Routledge Dance Studies Reader.* London/New York, NY: Routledge; 1998. 316 pp. Index. Notes. Biblio. Lang.: Eng.

UK-England. 1991-1994. Histories-sources. ■Choreographer Shobana Jeyasingh on fluctuating boundaries and the search for national identity in her work.

973 Leask, Josephine. "Jonzi D." *DTJ.* 1998; 14(1): 46-47. Notes. Illus.: Photo. B&W. 1. Lang.: Eng.

UK-England: London. 1998. Biographical studies. ■Profile of the London-based urban hip-hop choreographer.

974 Rubidge, Sarah. "Defining Digital Dance." *DTJ.* 1998; 14(4): 41-45. Notes. Illus.: Photo. B&W. 3. Lang.: Eng.

UK-England. 1998. Histories-sources. ■An explanation of 'digital dance' by a choreographer who uses high technology in her work.

975 "Jerome Robbins 1919-1998." *AmTh.* 1998 Oct.; 15(8): 79. Illus.: Photo. B&W. 1. Lang.: Eng.

USA. 1919-1998. Biographical studies. ■Obituary for choreographer/director Robbins.

976 Adler, Reba Ann. *The Dance Direction of Seymour Felix on Broadway and in Hollywood from 1918 through 1953.* New York, NY: New York Univ; 1987. 410 pp. Biblio. Notes. [Ph.D. Dissertation, Univ. Microfilms Order No. AAC 8801510.] Lang.: Eng.

USA. 1918-1953. Historical studies. ■The professional career of dance director Seymour Felix, one of the most popular dance directors of his day, both on Broadway and in Hollywood.

977 Bucher, John Joseph. *Expression and Narrative Within the Dance* Night and Day. Salem, OR: Univ. of Oregon; 1988. 132 pp. Biblio. Notes. [M.A. Thesis, Univ. Microfilms Order No. AAC 1335743.] Lang.: Eng.

USA: Hollywood, CA. 1934. Historical studies. ■Examines symbols and romantic narrative in the dance sequence *Night and Day* choreographed by David Gould and performed by Fred Astaire and Ginger Rogers in the film *The Gay Divorcee* directed by Mark Sandrich.

978 Buckland, Theresa. "Dance and Music Video: Some Preliminary Observations." 278-287 in Carter, Alexandra, ed. *Routledge Dance Studies Reader.* London/New York, NY: Routledge; 1998. 316 pp. Index. Notes. Biblio. Lang.: Eng.

USA. 1987-1997. Historical studies. ■Dance in the entertainment context of music videos by Kate Bush and Michael Jackson, and the relationship between this genre and wider popular culture, especially in terms of gender and the star persona.

979 Butcher, Rosemary. "What's Past Is Prologue: New York Revisited." *DTJ.* 1998; 14(4): 17-21. Notes. Illus.: Photo. B&W. 9. Lang.: Eng.

USA: New York, NY. 1969-1998. Histories-sources. ■Choreographer Butcher shares her thoughts and recollections upon returning to New York after a twenty-five year absence.

980 Croce, Arlene. "Oh, That Pineapple Rag!" 108-112 in Carter, Alexandra, ed. *Routledge Dance Studies Reader.* London/New York, NY: Routledge; 1998. 316 pp. Index. Notes. Biblio. Lang.: Eng.

USA: New York, NY. 1981. Critical studies. ■Croce's original criticism of Twyla Tharp's *The Catherine Wheel* at the Winter Garden Theatre (music by David Byrne).

981 Daly, Ann. "Dancing: A Letter from New York City." *TDR.* 1998 Spr; 42(1): 15-23. Biblio. Illus.: Photo. B&W. 4. Lang.: Eng.

USA: New York, NY. 1996-1997. Critical studies. ■The receding place of dance in American culture. Points to the lackluster New York 1996-97 season as proof of artistic stagnation.

982 Dyer, Richard; Mueller, John. "Two Analyses of 'Dancing in the Dark' (*The Band Wagon*, 1953)." 288-293 in Carter, Alexandra, ed. *Routledge Dance Studies Reader.* London/New York, NY: Routledge; 1998. 316 pp. Index. Notes. Biblio. Lang.: Eng.

USA. 1953. Historical studies. ■Examines choreography of dance in films, specifically the 'Dancing in the Dark' sequence from the musical *The Band Wagon*, directed by Vincente Minnelli, which featured Fred Astaire and Cyd Charisse (music by Arthur Schwartz and Howard Dietz, choreography by Astaire).

983 Horosko, Marian. "Danny & Betty Never Stop." *Dm.* 1998 Sep.; 72(9): 78-80. Illus.: Photo. B&W. 7. Lang.: Eng.

USA. 1959-1998. Biographical studies. ■Profile of husband and wife tap dancers Danny Hoctor and Betty Byrd.

984 Katz, Genevieve. "Life in the Fast Lane." *Dm.* 1998 Nov.; 72(11): 74-77. Lang.: Eng.

USA. 1998. Critical studies. ■Description of the computer software program called *Life Forms* developed to aid choreographers with their ideas when no dancers are available.

985 Malnig, Julie M. *Exhibition Ballroom Dance and Popular Entertainment.* New York, NY: New York Univ; 1987. 365 pp. Biblio. Notes. [Ph.D. Dissertation, Univ. Microfilms Order No. AAC 8722767.] Lang.: Eng.

USA. 1910-1925. Historical studies. ■The influence of exhibition ballroom dance teams on cabaret, vaudeville, and musical theatre in transforming contemporary social dances into theatrical presentations.

986 Malone, Jacqui. "'Keep to the Rhythm and You'll Keep to Life': Meaning and Style in African-American Vernacular Dance." 230-235 in Carter, Alexandra, ed. *Routledge Dance Studies Reader.* London/New York, NY: Routledge; 1998. 316 pp. Index. Notes. Biblio. Lang.: Eng.

USA. 1960-1997. Historical studies. ■Artistic expression in both form and content in African-American dance, with emphasis on rhythm, control, improvisation, angularity, asymmetry, and dynamism.

987 McDonagh, Don; Caras, Steven, photo. "Mia Michaels: Blonde Ambition." *Dm.* 1998 Aug.; 72(8): 58-59. Illus.: Photo. Color. 1. Lang.: Eng.

USA. 1998. Biographical studies. ■Profile of jazz dancer, teacher, and choreographer Michaels.

DANCE: General—Performance/production

988 Patrick, K.C. "Jazz Man." *Dm.* 1998 Aug.; 72(8): 52-57. Illus.: Photo. Color. B&W. 7. Lang.: Eng.
USA: Chicago, IL. 1962-1998. Biographical studies. ▪Profile of jazz dancer/choreographer Gus Giordano and his company Gus Giordano Jazz Dance Chicago.

989 Rainer, Yvonne. "'No' to Spectacle ..." 35 in Carter, Alexandra, ed. *Routledge Dance Studies Reader.* London/New York, NY: Routledge; 1998. 316 pp. Lang.: Eng.
USA. 1965. Historical studies. ▪Reprint of a one-page statement by dancer Yvonne Rainer that originally appeared in the *Tulane Drama Review* 10:2 (1965), p. 178.

990 Reiter, Susan; Kluetmeier, Heinz, photo. "Discover *Stars on Ice.*" *Dm.* 1998 Mar.; 72(3): 86-90. Illus.: Photo. Color. 3. Lang.: Eng.
USA. 1998. Historical studies. ▪Profile of the current touring ice show, which features the talents of many former Olympic figure skating performers.

991 Sulcas, Roslyn. "Bodies of Knowledge." *Dm.* 1998 May; 72(5): 58-61. Illus.: Photo. Color. B&W. 6. Lang.: Eng.
USA. 1998. Critical studies. ▪The increasing tendency for dancers to continue in their careers beyond their fortieth year, said to be a result of better health and changing social perceptions.

992 Zarhina, Regina. "Artistry on Ice." *Dm.* 1998 Feb.; 72(2): 74-77. Illus.: Photo. Color. 5. Lang.: Eng.
USA. 1992-1998. Biographical studies. ▪Profile of touring ice dancers Renee Roca and Gorsha Sur.

Plays/librettos/scripts

993 Canepa, Alessandro. *Adame Miroir di Jean Genet. Il sogno di un'estetica danzata.* (*Adame Miroir* by Jean Genet. The Dream of a Danced Aesthetic.) Genoa: Erga; 1998. 1998 pp. Notes. Lang.: Ita.
France. 1949. Critical studies. ▪An analysis of *Adame Miroir*, the only work for dance written by Jean Genet.

Reference materials

994 Neubauer, Henrik. *Ples skozi stoletja.* (Dance Through the Centuries.) Ljubljana: Forma 7; 1998. 114 pp. Pref. Index. Biblio. Illus.: Photo. B&W. 26. Lang.: Slo.
2000 B.C.-1990 A.D. Histories-general. ▪Popular history of dance and ballet around the world.

995 Otrin, Iko. *Razvoj plesa in baleta.* (Development of Dance and Ballet.) Ljubljana: Debora; 1998. 237 pp. Illus.: Photo. Color. B&W. 15. Lang.: Slo.
2000 B.C.-1990 A.D. Histories-general. ▪A history of dance and ballet from the very beginnings to the present time. Includes a special emphasis on stage dance in general, the American musical, and Slovene dance performance.

Relation to other fields

996 Fraleigh, Sondra. "A Vulnerable Glance: Seeing Dance Through Phenomenology." 135-143 in Carter, Alexandra, ed. *Routledge Dance Studies Reader.* London/New York, NY: Routledge; 1998. 316 pp. Index. Notes. Biblio. Lang.: Eng.
1997. Critical studies. ▪On the nature of phenomenology in dance.

997 "Emigranten und ihre Zufluchtorte." (Emigrants and their Places of Refuge.) *Tanzd.* 1998; 42(3): 19-27. Illus.: Photo. Maps. B&W. 28. Lang.: Ger.
Europe. North America. South America. 1933-1945. Histories-sources. ▪Directory of emigrant and refugee dancers.

998 Aza. "Ät ordentligt!" (Eat Properly!)*Danst.* 1998; 8(1): 18-19. Illus.: Dwg. B&W. Lang.: Swe.
Sweden. 1998. Critical studies. ▪An appeal for dancers to eat properly and be aware of the menace of anorexia or bulimia.

999 Brown, Carol. "Unpacking the Body." *DTJ.* 1998; 14(4): 12-16. Notes. Illus.: Photo. B&W. 2. Lang.: Eng.
UK-England. USA. 1998. Critical studies. ▪Examines the cultural stereotype of the dancer's body.

1000 Mitchell, Jack, photo. "Jack Mitchell: An Autobiography in Photographs." *Dm.* 1998 Sep.; 72(9): 60-63. Illus.: Photo. B&W. 11. Lang.: Eng.
USA. 1960-1995. Historical studies. ▪Gallery of photos of many of dancing's icons taken by the photographer, and culled from his *Icons & Idols: A Photographer's Chronicle of the Arts, 1960-1995* (New York, NY: Amphoto Art, 1998).

Research/historiography

1001 Layson, June. "Dance History Source Materials." 144-153 in Carter, Alexandra, ed. *Routledge Dance Studies Reader.* London/New York, NY: Routledge; 1998. 316 pp. Index. Notes. Biblio. Lang.: Eng.
Europe. North America. 1997. Critical studies. ▪Examines the nature of working with original source materials for the dance historian: types and categories, specific problems, and evaluation.

1002 Linden, Mirjam van der. "Dans wetenschap in Nederland. Een beetje humstmest lian geen liwaad." (Dance Science in the Netherlands: A Little Fertilizer Does Not Hurt.) *Tmaker.* 1998; 2(5): 32-35. Illus.: Photo. B&W. 2. Lang.: Dut.
Netherlands. 1990-1998. Historical studies. ▪Reports on a symposium held in April 1990 on the history of dance in the Netherlands. Symposium also addressed new directions in historical and methodological research.

1003 Desmond, Jane C. "Embodying Difference: Issues in Dance and Cultural Studies." 154-162 in Carter, Alexandra, ed. *Routledge Dance Studies Reader.* London/New York, NY: Routledge; 1998. 316 pp. Index. Notes. Biblio. Lang.: Eng.
North America. Europe. 1998. Critical studies. ▪Argues for kinesthetic semiotics and culturally-based dance/movement research in order to further understanding of how social identities are signalled, formed, and negotiated through bodily movement.

1004 Mason, Francis. "A Conversation with Ann Hutchinson Guest." *BR.* 1998 Win; 26(4): 55-62. Lang.: Eng.
USA. 1998. Histories-sources. ▪Interview with dance historian Guest regarding the history of dance notation.

Theory/criticism

1005 Redfern, Betty. "What Is Art?" 125-134 in Carter, Alexandra, ed. *Routledge Dance Studies Reader.* London/New York, NY: Routledge; 1998. 316 pp. Index. Notes. Biblio. Lang.: Eng.
1997. Critical studies. ▪On the nature of dance as an art form.

1006 Polhemus, Ted. "Dance, Gender and Culture." 171-179 in Carter, Alexandra, ed. *Routledge Dance Studies Reader.* London/New York, NY: Routledge; 1998. 316 pp. Index. Notes. Biblio. Lang.: Eng.
Europe. North America. 1998. Critical studies. ▪Argues that gender and culture must be included in all dance criticism and analysis.

1007 Preston-Dunlop, Valerie; Geary, Angela. "Symbolism and the European Dance Revolution." *DTJ.* 1998; 14(3): 40-45. Notes. Illus.: Photo. B&W. 2. Lang.: Eng.
Europe. 1895-1939. Historical studies. ▪Discusses the strong influence of Symbolism on dance in Europe in the early decades of the twentieth century.

1008 Vesterinen, Minna. "Antiikin tanssin tutkija etsii aerobicin ydintä." (A Scholar of Antique Dance in Search of the Aerobic Essence.) *Tanssi.* 1998; 19(2): 12-14. Illus.: Photo. B&W. 2. Lang.: Fin.
Finland. 1998. Critical studies. ▪Searches for a connection between aerobics and dance, and wonders how far a researcher must stretch to make the connection.

1009 Adshead, Janet. "An Introduction to Dance Analysis." 163-170 in Carter, Alexandra, ed. *Routledge Dance Studies Reader.* London/New York, NY: Routledge; 1998. 316 pp. Index. Notes. Biblio. Lang.: Eng.
North America. Europe. 1998. Critical studies. ▪On the nature of, uses, and challenges for dance analysis and criticism.

1010 Foster, Susan Leigh. "Choreographing History." 180-191 in Carter, Alexandra, ed. *Routledge Dance Studies Reader.*

DANCE: General—Theory/criticism

London/New York, NY: Routledge; 1998. 316 pp. Index. Notes. Biblio. Lang.: Eng.
North America. Europe. 1998. Critical studies. ■'Theoretical manifesto' on the nature of the body, or 'body theorics'.

1011 Grau, Andrée. "Myths of Origin." 197-202 in Carter, Alexandra, ed. *Routledge Dance Studies Reader.* London/New York, NY: Routledge; 1998. 316 pp. Index. Notes. Biblio. Lang.: Eng.
North America. Europe. 1998. Critical studies. ■Examines the earliest beginnings of dance as an art form. Argues that many previous ideas about the origins of dance are myths, and provides some new 'speculations'.

1012 Koritz, Amy E. *Gendering Bodies, Performing Art: Theatrical Dancing and the Performance Aesthetics of Wilde, Shaw and Yeats.* Chapel Hill, NC: Univ. of North Carolina; 1988. 169 pp. Biblio. Notes. [Ph.D. Dissertation, Univ. Microfilms Order No. AAC 8914442.] Lang.: Eng.
UK-England. Ireland. 1890-1950. Critical studies. ■Feminist analysis of the theatrical nature of dance, ranging from Oscar Wilde's *Salome* to George Bernard Shaw's critical writings on acting and dancing, and W.B. Yeats's performance aesthetics and plays for dancers.

1013 Copeland, Roger. "Between Description and Deconstruction." 98-107 in Carter, Alexandra, ed. *Routledge Dance Studies Reader.* London/New York, NY: Routledge; 1998. 316 pp. Index. Notes. Biblio. Lang.: Eng.
USA. Europe. 1997. Critical studies. ■Examines the nature of dance criticism.

1014 Siegel, Marcia B. "Bridging the Critical Distance." 91-97 in Carter, Alexandra, ed. *Routledge Dance Studies Reader.* London/New York, NY: Routledge; 1998. 316 pp. Index. Notes. Biblio. Lang.: Eng.
USA. Europe. 1990. Histories-sources. ■Examines what it is like to be a dance critic.

Training

1015 Sieben, Irene. "Die Anatomie des organischen Lernens." (The Anatomy of Organic Training.) *Tanzd.* 1998; 43(4): 4-7. Lang.: Ger.
Europe. 1900-1998. Historical studies. ■Analysis of the different dancing styles and teaching methods that have developed since the beginning of the twentieth century.

1016 Harri, Minna. "Mirja-Liisa Herhi haluaa kasvattaa itsenäisiä tanssijoita." (Mirja-Liisa Herhi: Educating Independent Dancers.) *Tanssi.* 1998; 19(1): 24-25. Illus.: Photo. B&W. 3. Lang.: Fin.
Finland. 1998. Histories-sources. ■Interview with Herhi regarding her theories about teaching children dance.

1017 Kaiku, Jan-Peter. "Keho on kaikki." (The Body Is All.) *TeatterT.* 1998; 2: 24-27. Lang.: Fin.
Finland. 1998. Historical studies. ■Report on dance teacher Anzu Furukawa's methods while teaching a course for the dance department at Theatre Academy in Finland.

1018 Höglund, Christina. "I begynnelsen var rytm." (In the Beginning Was the Rhythm.) *Danst.* 1998; 8(3): 4-5. Illus.: Photo. B&W. Color. Lang.: Swe.
Sweden: Stockholm. 1966-1998. Histories-sources. ■Interview with Maria Llerena from Cuba, who after a career as dancer and singer now is training small children to react to, create and enjoy rhythm.

1019 Höglund, Christina. "Barnen har blivit annorlunda i sina kroppar." (Children Have Different Bodies.) *Danst.* 1998; 8 (3): 18-19. Illus.: Photo. Color. Lang.: Swe.
Sweden: Stockholm. 1945-1998. Histories-sources. ■Interview with the dance teacher Yvonne Jahn-Olsson about her way to teach dancers, especially children, and how children's bodies have changed during the last 30 years.

1020 Olsson, Irène. "Att tända en gnista hos barnen." (To Light a Spark In the Children.) *Danst.* 1998; 8(3): 22-23. Illus.: Photo. B&W. Lang.: Swe.
Sweden: Stockholm. 1946. Historical studies. ■Profile of Britt-Marie Berggren's dancing school for children.

1021 Schubert, Lia. "Det började i Malmö." (It Started at Malmö.) *Danst.* 1998; 8(6): 52-53. Illus.: Photo. B&W. Lang.: Swe.
Sweden: Malmö, Stockholm, Gothenburg. 1950-1998. Histories-sources. ■Memoirs of Lisa Schubert's life as teacher in Sweden, with references to Cullbergbaletten, Balettakademien, and her colleagues.

1022 Douglas, Paul. "Freeing the Energy." *DTJ.* 1998; 14(1): 25-26. Illus.: Photo. B&W. 1. Lang.: Eng.
UK-England. 1998. Histories-sources. ■Choreographer Douglas recommends introducing the martial arts, particularly aikido, into the regimen of dancers as an avenue of freeing the body and mind from old and entrenched forms of movement.

1023 Horvat, Mojca; Lampič, Miha; Marčac Mirčeta, Mimi; Zagorc, Meta. *Jazz ples.* (Jazz Dance.) Ljubljana: Slovenian Dance Association; 1998. 100 pp. Pref. Biblio. Illus.: Photo. B&W. 45. Lang.: Slo.
USA. Slovenia. 1900-1997. Instructional materials. ■An illustrated handbook of jazz dance written by prominent Slovenian modern jazz dancers and trainers. Includes a description of jazz dance, its historical development, the technical bases, and teaching methods.

1024 Kennedy, Anja. "Gespeicherte Bewegungsmuster durchbrechen." (To Break Through Saved Models of Movement.) *Tanzd.* 1998; 43(4): 8-9. Illus.: Photo. B&W. 2. Lang.: Ger.
USA. 1925-1981. Critical studies. ■Describes Irmgard Bartenieff's development of corrective physical training called the 'Bartenieff fundamentals' based on both her own experiences as dancer and dance therapist and on Rudolf von Laban's work.

1025 Perlman, Doris. "An Unsentimental Journey." *Dm.* 1998 June; 72(6): 60-63. Illus.: Photo. B&W. 9. Lang.: Eng.
USA: Becket, MA. 1950. Histories-sources. ■An alumna of the pioneering summer dance school and festival, Jacob's Pillow, relates her experiences.

Ballet

Administration

1026 Kaán, Zsuzsa; Flügel, J., photo. "Ivan Liška, a Bayerische Staatsballett új igazgatója." (Ivan Liška, the New Ballet Director of Bayerische Staatsballett.) *Tanc.* 1998; 29(3): 31. Illus.: Photo. B&W. 2. Lang.: Hun.
Germany: Munich. 1998. Histories-sources. ■Interview with the new director on his view and future plans.

1027 Salisburgy, Wilma. "Two Companies in Transition." *Dm.* 1998 Dec.; 72(12): 70-73. Illus.: Photo. B&W. Color. 5. Lang.: Eng.
USA: Cleveland, OH, Akron, OH. 1998. Historical studies. ■Financial woes of two Ohio ballet companies teetering on the brink: Cleveland San Jose Ballet and the Ohio Ballet. Focuses on their strategies to cope and continue producing classical dance.

Audience

1028 Garafola, Lynn. "Diaghilev's Cultivated Audience." 214-222 in Carter, Alexandra, ed. *Routledge Dance Studies Reader.* London/New York, NY: Routledge; 1998. 316 pp. Index. Notes. Biblio. Lang.: Eng.
France: Paris. 1906-1914. Historical studies. ■Argues that Diaghilev systematically developed an audience that would be receptive to his future wirk with the Ballets Russes.

Design/technology

1029 Prestenskaja, Ju.L.; Sinel'nikova, T.A.; Chitrik, A.A., ed. *Russkie sezony Sergeja Djagileva: Katalog vystavki.* (Russian Seasons of Sergei Diaghilev: Exhibition Catalog.) St. Petersburg: Giperion; 1998. 40 pp. Lang.: Rus.
Russia: St. Petersburg. 1998. Historical studies. ■Includes costume sketches, letters, photographs and other documents pertaining to the work of the choreographer.

1030 Daniels, Don; Mason, Francis. "A Conversation with Rick Fisher." *BR.* 1998 Win; 26(4): 23-31. Illus.: Photo. B&W. 2. Lang.: Eng.

DANCE: Ballet—Design/technology

UK-England. 1998. Histories-sources. ▪Interview with designer Fisher about his career and his approach to lighting Matthew Bourne's *Swan Lake (Lebedinojė osero).*

1031 Lampert-Gréaux, Ellen. "Reinvented Classics." *TCI.* 1998 Nov.; 32(10): 44-47. Illus.: Photo. Color. 10. Lang.: Eng.

UK-England: London. 1998. Technical studies. ▪Collaboration of choreographer Matthew Bourne, set and costume designer Lez Brotherston, and lighting designer Rick Fisher on Bourne's productions of Čajkovskij's *Swan Lake (Lebedinojė osero)* and Prokofjév's *Cinderella (Zoluška). Swan Lake* was performed at both the Sadler's Wells and Piccadilly, while *Cinderella* was performed at the Royal National Theatre.

1032 Slingerland, Amy L. "Poetic Partnering." *TCI.* 1998 May; 32(5): 62. Illus.: Photo. Design. Color. 4. Lang.: Eng.

USA: San Francisco, CA. 1998. Technical studies. ▪Sandra Woodall's costume designs for the Michael Smuin-choreographed ballet *Cyrano de Bergerac* for the Smuin Ballets.

1033 Slingerland, Amy L. "Enchanted Forest." *TCI.* 1998 July; 32(7): 22-23. Illus.: Photo. Sketches. Dwg. Color. 11. Lang.: Eng.

USA: Houston, TX. 1998. Technical studies. ▪Michael Hagen's sets and Barbara Matera's costumes for the Houston Ballet's version of Čajkovskij's *The Snow Maiden (Sneguročka),* choreographed by Desmond Healey.

1034 Slingerland, Amy L. "Bold Steps." *LDim.* 1998 Mar.; 22(2): 44-47, 79, 81. Illus.: Photo. Lighting. Color. 9. Lang.: Eng.

USA: Cleveland, OH. 1997. Critical studies. ▪Examines the work of lighting designer Marilyn Lowey in the fall season of the Cleveland San Jose Ballet.

1035 Slingerland, Amy L. "Ice Castles: *The Snow Maiden* Dances Through an Enchanted Forest of Light." *LDim.* 1998 July; 22 (6): 60-65, 99. Illus.: Photo. Color. 10. Lang.: Eng.

USA: Houston, TX. 1998. Technical studies. ▪Examines the work of lighting designer Duane Schuler on the Houston Ballet's *The Snow Maiden (Sneguročka),* directed by Ben Stevenson with score arranged by John Lanchbery.

Institutions

1036 Johansson, Kerstin. "Alicia Alonso, en kubansk legend." (Alicia Alonso, a Legend of Cuba.) *Danst.* 1998; 8(6): 42-44. Illus.: Photo. Color. Lang.: Swe.

Cuba: Havana. 1948-1998. Histories-sources. ▪Interview with Alicia Alonso about her career, ballet dancing and Ballet Nacional de Cuba.

1037 Kendall, Elizabeth; Hakli, Kari, photo. "A New Start for the Finnish Ballet." *Dm.* 1998 Aug.; 72(8): 60-63. Illus.: Photo. Color. 6. Lang.: Eng.

Finland: Helsinki. 1992-1998. Historical studies. ▪Changes in the artistic goals in the Finnish National Ballet, Suomen Kansallisballet, since the installation of Jorma Uotinen as artistic director.

1038 Kaán, Zsuzsa; Gesquière, Jean-Charles, photo. "A 8. Párizsi Nemzetközi Táncverseny." (The 8th International Dance Competition in Paris.) *Tanc.* 1998; 29(5): 33. Illus.: Photo. B&W. 3. Lang.: Hun.

France: Paris. 1998. Reviews of performances. ▪An account of the program of the competition of ballet dancers.

1039 Hüster, Wiebke. "Aufbruch zu neuen Ufern." (Emergence to New Banks.) *DB.* 1998; 6: 37-39. Illus.: Photo. B&W. 3. Lang.: Ger.

Germany: Freiburg. 1984-1998. Historical studies. ▪Portrait of Amanda Miller, her ballet company Pretty Ugly, and its first season at Theater Freiburg.

1040 Königer, Miklós. "Tükröződések: Kiállítás a Berlini Georg Kolbe múzeumban." (Reflections: Georg Kolbe Exhibition in Berlin.) *Tanc.* 1998; 29(1): 34. Illus.: Photo. B&W. 7. Lang.: Hun.

Germany: Berlin. 1910-1914. Historical studies. ▪Unique display of various relics of the guest performances of Diaghilev's Ballets Russes in Germany and the impact of their style on German art.

1041 Gelencsér, Ágnes. "Világsztárok és híres balettegyüttesek vendégjátékai." (Guest Performances of World Stars and Famous Ballet Ensembles in Hungary.) *ZZT.* 1998; 5(4): 35-36. Lang.: Hun.

Hungary. 1980-1986. Historical studies. ▪Performances of the Stuttgart and Hamburg ballets.

1042 Gelencsér, Ágnes. "A Rambert Dance Company Budapesten." (The Rambert Dance Company in Budapest.) *Tanc.* 1998; 29 (1): 18. Illus.: Photo. B&W. 6. Lang.: Hun.

Hungary: Budapest. 1998. Reviews of performances. ▪Guest performance of Marie Rambert's ensemble at Budapest Comedy Theatre.

1043 Róna, Katalin. "Gyöngyhalász mentalitással." (With the Mentality of a Pearl-Diver.) *ZZT.* 1998; 5(1): 36-38. Illus.: Photo. Dwg. B&W. 3. Lang.: Hun.

Hungary: Pécs. 1975-1998. Histories-sources. ▪Interview with Dóra Uhrik, director of Pécs, where dance has been taught for twenty-three years thanks to the efforts of choreographer Imre Eck, founding director of Pécs Ballet.

1044 Szabó, Viktória; Kanyó, Béla, photo. "A III. Nemzetközi Rudolf Nurejev Balettverseny Budapesten." (Third International Rudolf Nureyev Ballet Competition.) *Tanc.* 1998; 29(2): 22-23. Illus.: Photo. B&W. 12. Lang.: Hun.

Hungary: Budapest. 1998. Historical studies. ▪Brief summary of the events and participants of the competition.

1045 Vazsó, Vera. "Szárnysuhintások: Beszélgetés Uhrik Dórával." (Swishing of Wings: Interview with Dóra Uhrik.) *Ellenfény.* 1998; 3(2): 58-59. Illus.: Photo. B&W. 2. Lang.: Hun.

Hungary: Pécs. 1978-1998. Histories-sources. ▪A talk with the former solo dancer of Pécs Ballet, dance teacher, and director of the Pécs Art School.

1046 Gordeeva, A. "Baletnyj sezon (1997-98) v Bol'šom: est' povod dlja optimizma." (The 1997-98 Ballet Season at the Bolšoj: There Is Reason To Be Optimistic.) *Sem'ja i škola.* 1998; 3: 55-57. Lang.: Rus.

Russia: Moscow. 1997-1998. Critical studies. ▪Appraisal of the 1997-98 Bolšoj season.

1047 Ostlere, Hilary. "The Sun, the Moon ... and the Star." *Dm.* 1998 Mar.; 72(3): 80-84. Illus.: Photo. Color. 8. Lang.: Eng.

South Korea: Seoul. 1998. Historical studies. ▪Profile of the Universal Ballet Company of Seoul and its artistic director Bruce Steivel, as it embarks on its first United States tour. Contains sidebar profile of ballerina and general director of the company, Julia H. Moon, focusing on her double responsibility within the company.

1048 Abrahamson, Moa; Garafola, Lynn; Bäcker, Mats, photo. "Stockholm Wonder: The Royal Swedish Ballet Celebrates 225 Years." *Dm.* 1998 May; 72(5): 52-59. Illus.: Photo. Color. 14. Lang.: Eng.

Sweden: Stockholm. 1773-1998. Historical studies. ▪Photos of Kungliga Teaterns Balett's anniversary celebration. Includes sidebar focused on its male principal dancers Hans Nilsson, Jan-Erik Wikström, Brendan Collins, Göran Svalberg, and Anders Nordström.

1049 Hellström Sveningson, Lis. "Konflikt på Svenska Balettskolan." (A Conflict At the Swedish Ballet School.) *Danst.* 1998; 8(2): 6-7. Lang.: Swe.

Sweden: Stockholm. 1984. Historical studies. ▪Report on the criticism from parents of the students at the school about the severe discipline and the dismissal of less gifted pupils, with comments by the artistic director Kerstin Lidström and by Christian Lundahl of the Swedish Board of Education.

1050 Hunt, Marilyn; Bäcker, Mats, photo. "Magic in the Down-to-Earth." *Dm.* 1998 Oct.; 72(10): 62-65. Illus.: Photo. Color. 5. Lang.: Eng.

Sweden: Stockholm. 1998. Historical studies. ▪Report on the season offered by the Royal Swedish Ballet for its 225th anniversary.

1051 Reynolds, Nancy. "Aboard the Royal Swedish Ballet Jubilee Express." *BR.* 1998 Win; 26(4): 33-43. Illus.: Photo. B&W. 9. Lang.: Eng.

Sweden: Stockholm. 1998. Historical studies. ▪Report on the ten-day dance festival held to celebrate the Royal Swedish Ballet's 225th anniversary.

DANCE: Ballet—Institutions

1052 Risán, Anton. "Stort tack till Svenska Balettskolan." (Many Thanks To Svenska Balettskolan.) *Danst.* 1998; 8(4): 16. Lang.: Swe.
Sweden: Stockholm. 1996. Histories-sources. ■A former student gives his praise to Svenska Balettskolan in reaction to recent critical voices against the blind discipline the school demands.

1053 Veldhuis, Jenny J.; Kálmán, Tamás, transl.; Bäcker, Mats, photo. "225 éves a Királyi Svéd Balett." (The Royal Swedish Ballet at 225.) *Tanc.* 1998; 29(4): 34-35. Illus.: Photo. B&W. 2. Lang.: Hun.
Sweden: Stockholm. 1773-1998. Historical studies. ■Profile of the Kungliga Teaterns Balett, celebrating the 225th anniversary of its foundation with a festival in June.

1054 Hézső, István. "'Krízisfelhők' a Londoni Royal Operaház felett." ('Clouds of Crisis' over the Royal Ballet of London.) *Tanc.* 1998; 29(5): 31. Illus.: Photo. B&W. 1. Lang.: Hun.
UK-England: London. 1998. Critical studies. ■Survey of the artistic program and the financial operations at the recently reconstructed Covent Garden.

1055 Lukács, András. "Magyar növendékek külföldön: Komplex képzés az Elmhurst Ballet Schoolban." (Hungarian Students Abroad: Overall Training at Elmhurst Ballet School.) *Tanc.* 1998; 29(2): 34. Illus.: Photo. B&W. 1. Lang.: Hun.
UK-England: Camberley. 1997-1998. Histories-sources. ■An account of the teaching method at the Elmhurst School as seen by a Hungarian student.

1056 Diamond, Pamela Hurley; Casey, Kevin, photo. "California Dreaming Comes True." *Dm.* 1998 May; 72(5): 50-53. Illus.: Photo. Color. 4. Lang.: Eng.
USA: Santa Ana, CA. 1983-1998. Historical studies. ■Profile of the Saint Joseph Ballet, which recruits many of its dancers from the inner city.

1057 Gladstone, Valerie. "Ballet Master in Chief." *Dm.* 1998 Nov.; 72(11): 56-59. Illus.: Photo. B&W. Color. 4. Lang.: Eng.
USA: New York, NY. 1983-1998. Biographical studies. ■Looks at the New York City Ballet's artistic director Peter Martins, as the institution heads into its fiftieth year.

1058 Gottschild, Brenda Nixon; Kolnik, Paul, photo. "Pennsylvania Ballet: Achieving a Balance." *Dm.* 1998 Feb.; 72(2): 58-62. Illus.: Photo. B&W. 8. Lang.: Eng.
USA: Philadelphia, PA. 1970-1998. Historical studies. ■Profile of the Pennsylvania Ballet, formerly a financially troubled institution, now on its firmest ground in years.

1059 Lobenthal, Joel. "Ballet Culture and the Individual Talent." *BR.* 1998 Fall; 26(3): 19-25. Illus.: Photo. B&W. 6. Lang.: Eng.
USA: New York, NY. 1998. Critical studies. ■Viewing the new season at American Ballet Theatre through diminishing government support. Dancers such as Ethan Stiefel and Susan Jaffe must travel to achieve their goals.

1060 Wood, Jane Philbin; Walczak, Barbara. "Looking Back." *Dm.* 1998 Nov.; 72(11): 60-65. Illus.: Photo. B&W. 9. Lang.: Eng.
USA: New York, NY. 1947-1948. Histories-sources. ■Recollections of the founding of the New York City Ballet by a dancer (Walczak) and a former gofer, now an agent (Wood).

1061 Zalán, Magda; Sohl, Marty, photo.; Greenhouse, Richard N., photo.; Kolnik, Paul, photo. "Egy öreg hölgy látogatása, avagy 60. évadjába lépett az ABT." (A Visit by an Old Lady: The ABT Has Started its 60th Season.) *Tanc.* 1998; 29(5): 34-35. Illus.: Photo. B&W. 3. Lang.: Hun.
USA: New York, NY. 1998. Historical studies. ■Brief survey of American Ballet Theatre, which became a significant institution under the leadership of Lucia Chase, Oliver Smith, Mikhail Baryshnikov, and Kevin McKenzie between 1980 and 1998.

1062 Zuck, Barbara; Gotschall, Jeff, photo. "A Renaissance in Ohio." *Dm.* 1998 Jan.; 72(1): 54-58. Illus.: Photo. B&W. 5. Lang.: Eng.
USA: Columbus, OH. 1978-1998. Historical studies. ■Profile of the resurgent BalletMet, under the leadership of artistic director and choreographer David Nixon.

Performance/production

1063 Kaán, Zsuzsa; Zeininger, Axel, photo. "Balettestek a Wiener Staatsoperben, 1. rész: Cranko- Prokofjév: *Rómeó és Júlia.*" (Ballet Evenings in Wiener Staatsoper, Part 1: Cranko-Prokofjév: *Romeo and Juliet.*) *Tanc.* 1998; 29(3): 29. Illus.: Photo. B&W. 1. Lang.: Hun.
Austria: Vienna. 1998. Reviews of performances. ■A production of John Cranko's 1962 choreography for *Romeo i Džuljetta* by Prokofjév.

1064 Kaán, Zsuzsa. "Balettestek Bécsben, 2. rész: A Nurejev-féle *Hattyúk tava* a Staatsoperben." (Ballet Evenings in Vienna, Part 2: *Swan Lake* by Nureyev in Staatsoper.) *Tanc.* 1998; 29(4): 32. Illus.: Photo. B&W. 2. Lang.: Hun.
Austria: Vienna. 1998. Reviews of performances. ■The revival of *Swan Lake (Lebedinojė osero)*, choreography by Rudolf Nureyev and music by Čajkovskij at Staatsoper, where it premiered in 1962.

1065 Hézső, István; De Backer, Paul, photo. "A Flamand Királyi Balett vendégjátéka Amszterdamban." (Guest Performance of the Flemish Royal Ballet in Amsterdam.) *Tanc.* 1998; 29(6): 25. Illus.: Photo. B&W. 1. Lang.: Hun.
Belgium: Antwerp. Netherlands: Amsterdam. 1998. Reviews of performances. ■The premieres of Danny Rosseel's choreographies *Seen within a Square* (music by J.S. Bach) and Carl Orff's *Carmina Burana*, by Koninklijk Ballet van Vlaanderen.

1066 Jálics, Kinga. "'A megpróbáltatás a sors bizalma': Beszélgetés Metzger Mártával." ('Ordeals Are the Trust of Fate': An Interview with Márta Metzger.) *OperaL.* 1998; 7(3): 37-39. Illus.: Photo. B&W. 1. Lang.: Hun.
Budapest. 1968-1998. Histories-sources. ■Interview with the dancer, who has been a member of the Hungarian State Opera ballet ensemble for thirty years and is now ballet mistress for the Opera house and Operetta Theatre.

1067 Citron, Paula. "On the Threshold of a Stellar Career." *Dm.* 1998 Oct.; 72(10): 58-61. Illus.: Photo. Color. 4. Lang.: Eng.
Canada: Toronto, ON. 1998. Biographical studies. ■Profile of National Ballet of Canada's promising young ballerina Greta Hodgkinson.

1068 Gyarmati, Zsófia. "Egy újabb *Giselle*: Világpremier Helsinkiben." (Another *Giselle*: World Premiere in Helsinki.) *Tanc.* 1998; 29(6): 24. Illus.: Photo. B&W. 1. Lang.: Hun.
Finland: Helsinki. 1998. Reviews of performances. ■Adam's classical ballet with Sylvie Guillem's new choreography presented by the Finnish National Ballet on October 16, 1998.

1069 Bindig, Susan Frances. *Dancing in Harlequin's World.* New York, NY: New York Univ; 1998. 345 pp. Notes. Biblio. [Ph.D. Dissertation, Univ. Microfilms Order No. AAC 9819748.] Lang.: Eng.
France. 1550-1965. Histories-specific. ■The use of *commedia dell'arte* characters, especially Harlequin, in Western ballet. Draws on iconography, film, live performances, and descriptions of the actions, gestures, postures, movement qualities, and movement sequences that seem to define the character, to chart how Harlequin's movement has evolved and changed.

1070 Burt, Ramsay. "Nijinsky: Modernism and Heterodox Representations of Masculinity." 250-258 in Carter, Alexandra, ed. *Routledge Dance Studies Reader.* London/New York, NY: Routledge; 1998. 316 pp. Index. Notes. Biblio. Lang.: Eng.
France: Paris. 1908-1915. Historical sources. ■Cultural meanings of masculinity inscribed in the body of the male dancer, with emphasis on Nižinsky and the Ballets Russes.

1071 Hézső, István. "'Terpszikhoré jegye alatt': Marie Taglioni, a balettromantika királynője, 1. rész." ('Under Terpsichore's Sign': Marie Taglioni, Queen of Romantic Ballet, Part 1.) *Tanc.* 1998; 29(1): 35-36. Illus.: Photo. B&W. 2. Lang.: Hun.
France. 1804-1836. Historical studies. ■A brief account of life and career of one of the famous ballerina of the 19th century. Continued in *Tanc* 1998 29:2, pp. 34-36 ('A balerina arcképe') and 29:3, pp. 35-36 ('Az aranykor árnyai').

DANCE: Ballet—Performance/production

1072 Jowitt, Deborah. "In Pursuit of the Sylph: Ballet in the Romantic Period." 203-213 in Carter, Alexandra, ed. *Routledge Dance Studies Reader*. London/New York, NY: Routledge; 1998. 316 pp. Index. Notes. Biblio. Lang.: Eng.
France. 1830-1875. Historical studies. ▪Examines French Romantic ballet in light of political and social changes, as well as changes in ballet technique. Focuses on dancer Marie Taglioni and her family.

1073 Kastal'skij, S. "Ispoved' bludnogo syna." (Confession of the Prodigal Son.) *Ogonek*. 1998; 47: 44-47. Lang.: Rus.
France: Lyon. 1998. Histories-sources. ▪K. Kastal'skaja, member of the ballet troupe with the Lyon Opera, on her life in ballet.

1074 Martinuzzi, Paola. "La matrice coreografica nel lavoro teatrale di Robert Wilson." (The Choreographic Matrix in the Work of Robert Wilson.) *BiT*. 1998; 45/47: 107-119. Notes. Lang.: Ita.
France: Paris. 1988. Critical studies. ▪Analysis of *Le Martyre de Saint Sébastien*, a dance work by Robert Wilson based on a drama by Gabriele D'Annunzio and on the music of Claude Debussy.

1075 Párczen, Zsófia; Csillag, Pál, photo. "Magyar növendékek külföldön: élet a párizsi Jeune Balletban." (Hungarian Students Abroad: Life with the Jeune Ballet in Paris.) *Tanc*. 1998; 29(1): 33. Illus.: Photo. B&W. 1. Lang.: Hun.
France: Paris. 1996-1998. Histories-sources. ▪Young ballet dancer describes her training abroad at the Jeune Ballet de France.

1076 Rock, Judith. *Terpsichore at Louis le Grand: Baroque Dance on a Jesuit Stage in Paris*. Berkeley, CA: Graduate Theological Union; 1988. 559 pp. Biblio. Notes. [Ph.D. Dissertation, Univ. Microfilms Order No. AAC 8816901.] Lang.: Eng.
France: Paris. 1660-1761. Histories-specific. ▪Baroque ballets produced in the Jesuit College of Clermont/Louis le Grand, with emphasis on the meeting of baroque style and classical aesthetic, dance technique and production process, relationship to audience and to the Jesuits' educational goals, the ballets as the feminine element of the Jesuit theatre, and the problems and possibilities of restaging them.

1077 Sedov, Ja. "Edinstvennaja zvezda pop-baleta." (The One and Only Star of Pop Ballets.) *Itogi*. 1998; 14: 69-72. Lang.: Rus.
France. 1927-1998. Biographical studies. ▪The French ballet director and choreographer, Maurice Béjart.

1078 Smith, Marian Elizabeth. *Music for the Ballet-Pantomime at the Paris Opera, 1825-1850*. New Haven, CT: Yale Univ; 1988. 414 pp. Notes. Biblio. [Ph.D. Dissertation, Univ. Microfilms Order No. AAC 9009472.] Lang.: Eng.
France. 1825-1850. Histories-specific. ▪Examines the ballet-pantomime music composed at the Paris Opera based on manuscript scores, journals, letters, memoirs, biographies, pamphlets, libretti, payroll records, contracts and other archival sources. Argues that this form is very different from later ballet music forms.

1079 Taras, John. "Balanchine's Bizet." *BR*. 1998 Spr; 26(1): 75-81. Illus.: Photo. B&W. 5. Lang.: Eng.
France: Paris. 1947-1948. Historical studies. ▪Background of Balanchine's choreography for Bizet's *Symphony in C*.

1080 Zakrževskaja, N.I.; Kljavina, T.A.; Storožuk, A.G. *Rudol'f Nureev: Al'bom*. (Rudolf Nureyev: The Album.) St. Petersburg: Ivan Fedorov; 1998. 320 pp. Lang.: Rus.
France. 1938-1993. Biographical studies. ▪Remembrance of the late dancer.

1081 Nugent, Ann. "Eyeing Forsythe." *DTJ*. 1998; 14(3): 26-30. Notes. Illus.: Photo. B&W. 1. Lang.: Eng.
Germany: Frankfurt. 1973-1998. Historical studies. ▪Profile of choreographer William Forsythe and his work at the Ballett Frankfurt as they prepare for their first British season.

1082 Shearer, Sybil. "Mahler, Bernstein, and Neumeier." *Dm*. 1998 July; 72(7): 44-49. Illus.: Photo. Color. 9. Lang.: Eng.
Germany: Hamburg. USA: New York, NY. 1998. Biographical studies. ▪Profile of choreographer John Neumeier of the Hamburg Ballet as he brings it to the Lincoln Center Festival '98 with pieces based on the music of Mahler and Bernstein.

1083 Viola, György. "Bayreuth 1998." *Tanc*. 1998; 29(4): 34. Illus.: Photo. B&W. 1. Lang.: Hun.
Germany: Bayreuth. Hungary. 1998. Reviews of performances. ▪Iván Markó has been the choreographer and ballet director for the 14th season at Bayreuth. This year his ensemble, the Hungarian Festival Ballet, also participated in two productions: *Parsifal* and *Die Meistersinger von Nürnberg*. The stage director of these performances was Wolfgang Wagner.

1084 Wilkins, Darrell. "William Forsythe: An American Iconoclast in Europe." *BR*. 1998 Sum; 26(2): 21-29. Illus.: Photo. B&W. 3. Lang.: Eng.
Germany: Frankfurt. 1949-1998. Biographical studies. ▪Career of American choreographer Forsythe, who is artistic director of Ballett Frankfurt.

1085 Gelencsér, Ágnes. "Világsztárok és híres balettegyüttesek vendégjátékai." (Guest Performances of World Stars and Famous Ballet Ensembles in Hungary.) *ZZT*. 1998; 5(2): 29-31. Lang.: Hun.
Hungary: Budapest. 1975-1978. Reviews of performances. ▪Survey of the series of guest performances by eminent international ballet soloists in Hungary in the 1970s, including Maurice Béjart, Donn Jorge, Daniel Lommel, Michael Denard, and Maina Gielgud.

1086 Gelencsér, Ágnes. "Világsztárok és híres balettegyüttesek vendégjátékai." (Guest Performances of World Stars and Famous Ballet Ensembles in Hungary.) *ZZT*. 1998; 5(3): 36-37. Lang.: Hun.
Hungary. 1975-1978. Reviews of performances. ▪Outstanding dancers of Bolšoj and Kirov ballets as guests (both dancers and ballet masters) in Hungary in the 1970s.

1087 Gelencsér, Ágnes; Kanyó, Béla, photo. "*A rosszul őrzött lány* - új főszereplőkkel." (*La Fille mal Gardée* with New Dancers in the Main Roles.) *Tanc*. 1998; 29(1): 17. Illus.: Photo. B&W. 2. Lang.: Hun.
Hungary: Budapest. 1997. Reviews of performances. ▪Frederick Ashton's choreography for Ferdinand Herold's music, with new dancers at Erkel Színház.

1088 Gelencsér, Ágnes; Kanyó, Béla, photo.; Papp, Dezső, photo. "Néhány szó egy ragyogó Mandarin-előadásról." (Some Comments on the Brilliant Mandarin Performance.) *Tanc*. 1998; 29(2): 18-19. Illus.: Photo. B&W. Color. 3. Lang.: Hun.
Hungary: Budapest. 1998. Reviews of performances. ▪Production of *A csodálatos mandarin (The Miraculous Mandarin)*,one of Bartók's three stage works at the Budapest Opera House with Gyula Harangozó's choreography.

1089 Gelencsér, Ágnes; Schiller, Beatriz, photo. "A Limón Dance Company Amerikából—másodszor." (Limón Dance Company from America—for the Second Time.) *Tanc*. 1998; 29(2): 28-29. Illus.: Photo. B&W. 2. Lang.: Hun.
Hungary: Budapest. 1998. Reviews of performances. ▪Guest performance of the ballet ensemble celebrating its 50 anniversary recently.

1090 Gelencsér, Ágnes; Papp, Dezső, photo. "Érzékenység és tudatosság: Rendhagyó portrévázlat Pártay Lilláról, az *Anna Karenina* 50. előadása után." (Sensitivity and Consciousness: Irregular Portrait of Lilla Pártay after the 50th Performance of *Anna Karenina*.) *Tanc*. 1998; 29(3): 14. Illus.: Photo. B&W. 1. Lang.: Hun.
Hungary. 1991-1998. Reviews of performances. ▪Notes on the ballet adaptation of *Anna Karenina* choreographed by Lilla Pártay.

1091 Gelencsér, Ágnes; Kanyó, Béla, photo. "Balettvizsga, Van Manen-bemutatókkal: A Magyar Táncművészeti Főiskola előadása az Operaházban." (Graduation Concert with van Manen: Choreographies Performance of the Hungarian Dance Academy at the Opera.) *Tanc*. 1998; 29(4): 14-16. Illus.: Photo. B&W. 11. Lang.: Hun.
Hungary: Budapest. 1998. Reviews of performances. ▪An account of the gala concert presented by the students of the Dance Academy, which included the Hungarian premieres of Hans van Manen's *Five Tangos* and *Sarcasm*.

1092 Gelencsér, Ágnes; Kanyó, Béla, photo. "*Anyegin*: A Bajor Állami Balett az Operaházban." (*Onegin*: The Bavarian

State Ballet at the Opera.) *Tanc.* 1998; 29(4): 26-27. Illus.: Photo. B&W. 5. Lang.: Hun.
Hungary: Budapest. 1998. Reviews of performances. ■Guest performance at Budapest Opera House of Bayerische Staatsballett offering Čajkovskij's *Eugene Onegin* choreographed by John Cranko.

1093 Gelencsér, Ágnes; Papp, Dezső, photo. "Kirov-ballerina a *Don Quijote*-ban." (Kirov-Ballerina in Petipa-Minkus: *Don Quixote.*) *Tanc.* 1998; 2(5): 10. Illus.: Photo. B&W. 1. Lang.: Hun.
Hungary: Budapest. 1998. Reviews of performances. ■The classic ballet at the Budapest Opera House with a guest performance of Irma Nioradze as Kitri.

1094 Gelencsér, Ágnes; Papp, Dezső, photo. "Új szereplők a *Giselle*-ben." (New Cast in *Giselle.*) *Tanc.* 1998; 29(5): 11. Illus.: Photo. B&W. 2. Lang.: Hun.
Hungary: Budapest. 1998. Reviews of performances. ■The importance of the renewal of repertory pieces with new dancers from time to time.

1095 Gelencsér, Ágnes; Kanyó, Béla, photo. "Cohen- és North-balettek Győrött: A Győri Balett bemutatója Budapesten." (Ballets by Cohen and North in Győr: the Premiere of Győr Ballet in Budapest.) *Tanc.* 1998; 29 (5): 16. Illus.: Photo. B&W. 2. Lang.: Hun.
Hungary: Budapest. 1998. Reviews of performances. ■Introducing the new productions by the Győr Ballet in Budapest: Robert Cohen's choreography to Vivaldi's *Stabat Mater* and Robert North's *Trojan Games.*

1096 Jálics, Kinga; Papp, Dezső, photo. "'A teljes kiegyensúlyozottságra törekszem': Találkozás Hágai Katalinnal." ('I Strive for Total Balance': Meeting Katalin Hágai.) *OperaL.* 1998; 7(5): 19-22. Illus.: Photo. B&W. 4. Lang.: Hun.
Hungary. 1961-1998. Histories-sources. ■Interview with the Budapest Opera House dancer who appeared in the ballet *The Taming of the Shrew (A Makrancos Kata)*, written and choreographed by László Seregi on the basis of the play by Shakespeare.

1097 Jálics, Kinga; Diner, Tamás, photo. "*Menyegző - A Kékszakállú két arca*: A Magyar Fesztivál Balett bemutatója." (*Wedding - Bluebeard's Two Faces*: Premiere by the Hungarian Festival Ballet.) *Tanc.* 1998 ; 29(2): 24. Illus.: Photo. B&W. 1. Lang.: Hun.
Hungary: Budapest. 1998. Critical studies. ■Analysis of the productions presented by Iván Markó's ensemble.

1098 Jálics, Kinga; Papp, Dezső, photo. "A bizalom stációi: Találkozás Bodor Johannával." (Stages of Confidence: Meeting Johanna Bodor.) *Tanc.* 1998; 29(6): 10-11. Illus.: Photo. B&W. 2. Lang.: Hun.
Hungary. 1984-1998. Histories-sources. ■Conversation with the young ballet dancer on her career and near future plans.

1099 Kaán, Zsuzsa; Kanyó, Béla, photo. "Világsztárok az Operában: A hatodik." (World Stars at the Opera: The 6th.) *Tanc.* 1998; 29(4): 22-23. Illus.: Photo. Color. 8. Lang.: Hun.
Hungary: Budapest. 1998. Reviews of performances. ■An account of the successful gala performance with dancers from home and abroad.

1100 Kaán, Zsuzsa; Papp, Dezső, photo.; Kanyó, Béla, photo. "Seregi, a mágus: Köszöntő a koreográfus negyvenéves operaházi tagsága alkalmából." (Seregi, the Magician: Greeting on Occasion of the 40th Anniversary of the Choreographer's Membership in the Hungarian Opera House.) *Tanc.* 1998; 29(3): 10-13. Illus.: Photo. Color. B&W. 10. Lang.: Hun.
Hungary: Budapest. 1949-1998. Biographical studies. ■Portrait of choreographer László Seregi, and description of a celebration performance of his works by the ballet ensemble of the Budapest Opera House.

1101 Kaán, Zsuzsa; Díner, Tamás, photo. "'Mindig József akartam lenni!': Beszélgetés Markó Ivánnal a Magyar Fesztivál Balett tavaszi premierjéről." ('I Have Always Wanted to Be Joseph!': Interview with Iván Markó about the Spring Premiere of the Hungarian Festival Ballet.) *Tanc.* 1998; 29(6): 12-13. Illus.: Photo. B&W. Color. 7. Lang.: Hun.
Hungary: Budapest. 1998. Histories-sources. ■Preliminary conversation with Iván Markó's on his new ballet *József és testvérei (Joseph and His Brothers).*

1102 Kaán, Zsuzsa; Papp, Dezső, photo. "*Après moi, Tor*: A Szegedi Kortárs Balett bemutatója." (*Après moi, Tor*: New One-Act Pieces on the Repertoire of the Szeged Contemporary Ballet.) *Tanc.* 1998; 29(6): 14-15. Illus.: Photo. B&W. Color. 3. Lang.: Hun.
Hungary: Szeged. 1998. Reviews of performances. ■An account of Uri Ivgi's *Après moi* and Tamás Juronics' *Tor*, music by Ry Cooder, presented by the Szeged Ballet.

1103 Körtvélyes, Géza; Papp, Dezső, photo. "*A fából faragott királyfi* legújabb változata az Operaházban." (The Latest Version of *The Wooden Prince* at the Opera House.) *Tanc.* 1998; 29(2): 20-21. Illus.: Photo. B&W. Color. 2. Lang.: Hun.
Hungary: Budapest. 1998. Reviews of performances. ■The revival of Béla Bartók's ballet choreographed and directed by László Seregi.

1104 Körtvélyes, Géza. "Aktuális-e ma Harangozó?" (Is Gyula Harangozó Still Up-To-Date?)*Tanc.* 1998; 29(5): 20. Illus.: Photo. B&W. 1. Lang.: Hun.
Hungary. 1908-1998. Critical studies. ■Thoughts on the legacy of choreographer Gyula Harangozó (1908-1974) who founded the national ballet. The Hungarian Opera House celebrated the ninetieth anniversary of his birth with a performance of his significant one-act ballets.

1105 Kútszegi, Csaba; Kanyó, Béla, photo. "Balanchine-est." (Balanchine-Evening.) *OperaL.* 1998; 7(1): 9-12. Illus.: Photo. Color. 8. Lang.: Hun.
Hungary: Budapest. 1997. Reviews of performances. ■Three one-act ballets by Balanchine presented at the Hungarian State Opera House: Čajkovskij's *Serenade*, Bizet's *Symphony in C*, and Rieti's *La sonnambula* after Bellini.

1106 Lőrinc, Katalin. "Ritka, rangos vendég: A Rambert Dance Company Magyarországon." (A Rare and Dignified Guest: The Rambert Dance Company in Hungary.) *ZZT.* 1998; 5(2): 6-7. Lang.: Hun.
Hungary: Budapest. 1998. Reviews of performances. ■Five-evening guest performance of the London ballet ensemble in Budapest.

1107 Lőrinc, Katalin; Kanyó, Béla, photo.; Mezey, Béla, photo. "Kossuth-díjas: Hágai Katalin: 'Nekem ezen a pályán csak a táncolás való!'." (Katalin Hágai, Kossuth Prize-Winning Artist: 'It Is Only Dance that I Can Relate to'.) *Tanc.* 1998; 29(2): 10-11. Illus.: Photo. B&W. 2. Lang.: Hun.
Hungary. 1998. Histories-sources. ■Interview with the soloist of the ballet ensemble of Budapest Opera House on the occasion of her recent award.

1108 Lőrinc, Katalin; Ilovszky, Béla, photo. "Krámer *Dekameron*ja Veszprémben." (György Krámer's *Decameron* in Veszprém.) *Tanc.* 1998; 29(5): 17. Illus.: Photo. B&W. 1. Lang.: Hun.
Hungary: Veszprém. 1998. Reviews of performances. ■The ballet adaptation of Boccaccio's famous literary work by dramaturg Győző Dúró and choreographer György Krámer presented by the Veszprém Dance Workshop at the Petőfi Theatre.

1109 Mátai, Györgyi; Pitei, Bebe, photo. "Az Oleg Danovski Balettszínház Budapesten." (Oleg Danovski Ballet Theatre in Budapest.) *Tanc.* 1998; 29(2): 32. Illus.: Photo. B&W. 1. Lang.: Hun.
Hungary: Budapest. 1998. Reviews of performances. ■Guest performance of the only independent ballet ensemble in Romania (Constanza) led by Ana Gabriela Danovski after the death of Oleg Danovski (1996).

1110 Mátai, Györgyi; Papp, Dezső, photo. "*Meztelen rózsa*: Szakály György táncmonológja a Tivoli Színházban." (*Naked Rose*: Dance Monologue by György Szakály at the Tivoli Theatre.) *Tanc.* 1998; 29(6): 16 . Illus.: Photo. B&W. 3. Lang.: Hun.
Hungary: Budapest. 1998. Reviews of performances. ■Lilla Pártay's ballet on the life of the legendary ballet dancer Vaclav Nižinskij, performed by György Szakály with a monologue by László Gábor and music by István Martha.

DANCE: Ballet—Performance/production

1111 Mátai, Györgyi; Kanyó, Béla, photo. "Rockbalett a templomtéren." (Rock Ballet on the Church-Square.) *Tanc.* 1998; 29(4): 18-19. Illus.: Photo. B&W. 5. Lang.: Hun.
Hungary: Budapest. 1998. Reviews of performances. ■Antal Fodor's ballet *A Próba (The Rehearsal)*, to music of J.S. Bach and Gábor Presser, at the open-air stage, Ferencvárosi unnepi Játékok.

1112 Rajk, András; Tóth, László, photo. "'Most egy nagy ,hétfő' az életem!': Találkozás a hatvanéves Orosz Adéllal." ('My Present Life Is One Big Monday': Meeting the 60-Year-Old Adél Orosz.) *Tanc.* 1998; 29 (2): 12-13. Illus.: Photo. B&W. 3. Lang.: Hun.
Hungary. 1954-1998. Histories-sources. ■Interview with the retired prima ballerina of the Budapest Opera House, who was one of the leading dancers of the 60s and 70s.

1113 Réfi, Zsuzsanna. "Fiatal sztárportrék: A beugrások mestre, Nagyszentpéteri Miklós." (Portraits of Young Stars: The Master of Replacing: Miklós Nagyszentpéteri.) *ZZT.* 1998; 5(2): 22-24. Illus.: Photo. B&W. 1. Lang.: Hun.
Hungary. 1989-1998. Histories-sources. ■Career of the young dancer who has won awards for his leading roles.

1114 Róna, Katalin. "Szumrák Vera múltról és jelenről, balettről és öltöztetésről." (Vera Szumrák on Past and Present, Ballet and Dressing.) *ZZT.* 1998; 5(1): 26-29. Illus.: Photo. B&W. 4. Lang.: Hun.
Hungary. 1950-1998. Histories-sources. ■A talk on life and career with the retired solo dancer of the Hungarian State Opera House.

1115 Szász, Anna. "A varázslat nem múlik el: Gyerekekkel a karácsonyi *Diótörő*-előadáson." (Magic Will Never Cease: With Young Audience at the Hungarian State Opera's *Nutcracker* Performance at Christmas.) *Tanc.* 1998; 29(6): 33. Illus.: Design. B&W. 1. Lang.: Hun.
Hungary: Budapest. 1998. Reviews of performances. ■*Ščelkunčik*, Čajkovskij's classic ballet (Vasilij Vajnonen's choreography from 1934) at the Budapest Opera House, a traditional performance in the permanent repertoire, presented during the Christmas season for children.

1116 Vazsó, Vera. "Érintkezések." (Touches.) *Ellenfény.* 1998; 3(3): 46-51. Illus.: Photo. B&W. 5. Lang.: Hun.
Hungary: Budapest. 1998. Histories-sources. ■Round table conversation with critics Lívia Fuchs, Márta Péter and Eszter Szúdy about the dance evening entitled *Mokka* performed by the ballet company of the Budapest Opera House.

1117 Wulff, Helena. "Dans på laddad mark." (Dance On Charged Ground.) *Danst.* 1998; 8(1): 3-6. Illus.: Photo. B&W. Lang.: Swe.
Israel. 1997. Critical studies. ■Report about the contemporary dance in Israel, with reference to the choreographers Ohad Naharin and Rina Schenfeld.

1118 Kaán, Zsuzsa. "Amedeo Amodio *Diótörő*-je Rómában." (Amedeo Amodio's *The Nutcracker* in Rome.) *Tanc.* 1998; 29(6): 30-31. Illus.: Photo. B&W. Color. 4. Lang.: Hun.
Italy: Rome. 1998. Reviews of performances. ■*Lo Schiaccianoci* a new choreography and staging of Čajkovskij's classic ballet at the Sala Milloss, by ballet director Amedeo Amodio, combining elements of *commedia dell'arte*, pantomime, *laterna magica*, and puppet play.

1119 Acocella, Joan. "The Soloist." *NewY.* 1998 19 Jan.: 45-56. Illus.: Dwg. Photo. B&W. 6. Lang.: Eng.
Latvia. USA. 1948-1997. Biographical studies. ■Ballet soloist Mikhail Baryshnikov: his life, career, and recent return to Riga to perform.

1120 Bowen, Christopher. "Enigma Variations." *DTJ.* 1998; 14(3): 4-7. Notes. Illus.: Photo. B&W. 2. Lang.: Eng.
Netherlands. 1951-1998. Critical studies. ■Examination of the ballets of Hans van Manen. *Feetgericht (Partywards)*, *Grosse Fuge*, and *Adagio Hammerklavier* are cited as examples.

1121 Kaán, Zsuzsa; Van Meer, Deen, photo. "Árnyak és fények a Het National Ballet repertoárján: Gyorsfénykép az 50. Holland Fesztiválról, 3. rész." (Light and Shade in the Repertoire of Het National Ballet: A Snapshot of the 50th Holland Festival, Part 3.) *Tanc.* 1998; 29(1): 28-29. Illus.: Photo. B&W. 2. Lang.: Hun.
Netherlands: Amsterdam. 1997. Reviews of performances. ■Survey of the four one-act dance compositions by the National Ballet of the Netherlands presented at the jubilee Holland Festival.

1122 Uitman, Hans. "Das Undine-Thema auf der Amsterdamer Ballettbühne." (The Undine Subject on Amsterdam Ballet Stage.) *MuK.* 1998; 40(1): 39-47. Notes. Illus.: Dwg. 2. Lang.: Ger.
Netherlands: Amsterdam. 1849. Critical studies. ■Analysis of the ballet *Berthalda en Hildebrand of de Waternimf (Berthalda and Hildebrand, or the Water-Nymph)*, adapted from Friedrich de la Motte Fouqué's *Undine* and choreographed by Andries Voitus van Hamme at Stadsschouwburg.

1123 Nasierowski, Tadeusz. *Gdy w mięśniach rodzi się obłukled.* (When Madness Bears on the Muscles.) Warsaw: Wydawnictwo Psychologii I Kultury 'Eneteia'; 1998. 172 pp. Pref. Notes. Biblio. Illus.: Photo. Dwg. Sketches. B&W. 32. Lang.: Pol.
Poland. Russia. France. 1881-1953. Biographical studies. ■The artistic life of Polish born dancer and choreographer Vaclav Nižinskij: his attitude to classical dance and ballet, his artistic career, and his battle with mental illness.

1124 Pudełek, Janina. "Polski Balet Reprezentacyjny 1937-1939." (The Polish National Ballet, 1937-1939.) *PaT.* 1998; 47 (3-4): 518-564. Notes. Append. Illus.: Handbill. Photo. Design. B&W. Color. 43. Lang.: Pol.
Poland. France. USA. 1937-1939. Historical studies. ■Activities of the Polish National Ballet during its European and American tour.

1125 "Galina Ulanova." *Econ.* 1998 Apr 4; 347(8062): 94. Illus.: Photo. B&W. 1. Lang.: Eng.
Russia. 1910-1998. Biographical studies. ■Obituary for the legendary prima ballerina for the Bolšoj Ballet.

1126 Alovert, Nina. "Fantasies of a Dreamer." *Dm.* 1998 Apr.; 72(4): 62-66. Illus.: Photo. Color. B&W. 6. Lang.: Eng.
Russia: St. Petersburg. 1972-1998. Biographical studies. ■Profile of choreographer and artistic director of the St. Petersburg Ballet Theatre, Boris Ejfman.

1127 Alovert, Nina. "Galina Ulanova (1910-1998)." *BR.* 1998 Sum; 26(2): 63-67. Illus.: Photo. B&W. 7. Lang.: Eng.
Russia. 1910-1998. Biographical studies. ■Obituary for the Russian ballerina.

1128 Boglačev, S. "Ditja, raba i žertva ljubvi." (Child, Slave, and Victim of Love.) *Novyj žurnal.* 1998; 2: 166-184. Lang.: Rus.
Russia. Biographical studies. ■Artistic and personal relationship between ballerina Marie Surovščikova and husband/ballet director, Marius Petipa.

1129 Calobanova, V. "Svoboda—mera čeloveka." (Freedom—The Measure of a Person.) *Neva.* 1998; 12: 194-198. Lang.: Rus.
Russia: St. Petersburg. Historical studies. ■Leningrad ballet dancers who emmigrated from Russia: Natalija Makarova, Rudolf Nureyev, Mikhail Baryshnikov, et al.

1130 Černobrivkina, T. "Moment očarovanija." (Moment of Magnetism.) *Persona.* 1998; 4: 26-28. Lang.: Rus.
Russia: Moscow. 1998. Histories-sources. ■Ballet soloist T. Černobrivkina of the Stanislavskij/Nemirovič-Dančenko Theatre on her art.

1131 Dajnjak, A.A. *Maja Pliseckaja.* Minsk: Literatura; 1998. 224 pp. (Žizn' zamečat. ljudej.) Lang.: Rus.
Russia. 1925-1994. Biographical studies. ■Biography of ballerina Maja Pliseckaja.

1132 Djagileva, E.V. *Semejnaja zapis' o Djagilevych.* (The Family's Recordings About Diaghilev.) St.Petersburg: Dmitrij Bulanin; 1998. 288 pp. Lang.: Rus.
Russia. 1872-1929. Histories-sources. ■Reminiscences of the stepmother of Sergei Diaghilev.

1133 Fullington, Doug. "*Raymonda* at 100." *BR.* 1998 Win; 26(4): 77-88. Notes. Lang.: Eng.
Russia. 1898-1998. Historical studies. ■History of the ballet created by Marius Petipa and composer Aleksand'r Glazunov.

DANCE: Ballet—Performance/production

1134 Gaevskij, V. "Velikaja illjuzija: Vosp. o 'Bachčisarajskom fontane'." (The Great Illusion: Recollections About the *Bachčisarian Fountain.*) *Naše nasledie.* 1998; 46: 148-155. Lang.: Rus.
Russia: St. Petersburg. 1934. Historical studies. ▪An account of Boris Asafjev's ballet, *Bahčisarajskij fontan*, performed at the Mariinskij Theatre, directed by R. Zacharov.

1135 Gerdt, O. "Bol'šoj teatr pomirilsja s Mariinkoj. A Baryšnikov—net." (Bolšoj Theatre Made Up With the Mariinskij, But Not Baryshnikov.) *Ogonek.* 1998; 4: 47-49. Lang.: Rus.
Russia: Moscow, St. Petersburg. 1998. Historical studies. ▪Reciprocal tours of the Bolšoj and Mariinskij ballet corps, with comments about Mikhail Baryshnikov.

1136 Kolesova, N. *Natalija Ledovskaja.* Moscow: 1998. 8 pp. Lang.: Rus.
Russia: Moscow. 1998. Biographical studies. ▪Natalija Ledovskaja: Ballet soloist of the Moscow Stanislavskij Nemirovič-Dančenko Music Theatre.

1137 Körtvélyes, Géza; Kanyó, Béla, photo. "A Kreml Ballett - Oroszországból." (Kremlevskij Balet from Russia.) *Tanc.* 1998; 29(2): 27. Illus.: Photo. B&W. 1. Lang.: Hun.
Russia. Hungary: Budapest. 1998. Reviews of performances. ▪Notes on the guest performance of the Russian ballet ensemble at the Interbalett.

1138 Krapivina, E. "'Kukly' i šarži." (Dolls and Czars.) *Neva.* 1998; 2: 212-213. Lang.: Rus.
Russia: Leningrad. 1940. Biographical studies. ▪Graphics designer I. Igin, and his book *Czars*, about ballet dancers Konstantin Sergejėv and Natalija Dudinskaja.

1139 Lobenthal, Joel. "Alla Osipenko." *BR.* 1998 Spr; 26(1): 11-35. Illus.: Photo. B&W. 22. Lang.: Eng.
Russia. 1932-1998. Biographical studies. ▪Life and career of the former Kirov prima ballerina.

1140 Majniece, V. "Carstvennaja zatvornica hrustal'nogo dvorca." (Royal Prisoner in a Crystal Palace.) *MoskZ.* 1998; Oct-Nov: 34-37. Lang.: Rus.
Russia: St. Petersburg. 1998. Histories-sources. ▪Profile of Mariinskij ballerina, Uljana Lopatkina.

1141 Modestov, V. "Bol'šoj balet Jurija Grigoroviča." (The Bolšoj Ballet of Jurij Grigorovič.) *MoskZ.* 1998; Sep-Oct. Lang.: Rus.
Russia: Moscow. 1998. Histories-sources. ▪Profile of ballet director, Jurij Grigorovič.

1142 Nikolaevič, S. "Ninino sčast'e." (Nina's Happiness.) *Domovoj.* 1998; 10: 36-38, 40. Lang.: Rus.
Russia. 1998. Biographical studies. ▪Profile of ballerina Nina Ananiašvili: her involvement with *Sny o Japonii (Dreams of Japan)*, choreographed by A. Rotmanskij.

1143 Novikova, L. "Rodion da Majja." (Rodion and Maja.) *MoskZ.* 1998; Apr: 36-40. Lang.: Rus.
Russia: Moscow. 1998. Biographical studies. ▪Artistic and family profile of ballerina Maja Pliseckaja and her husband, composer Rodion Ščedrin.

1144 Nureyev, Rudolf; Gaevskij, V., ed.; Blend, A., ed. *Avtobiografija.* (Autobiography.) Moscow: Agraf; 1998. 240 pp. (Volšebnaja flejta.) Lang.: Rus.
Russia. Histories-sources. ▪Autobiography of ballet dancer and choreographer Rudolf Nureyev.

1145 Pliseckaja, M. *Ja, Maja Pliseckaja...* (I, Maja Pliseckaja...) Moscow: Novosti; 1998. 496 pp. Lang.: Rus.
Russia. 1998. Histories-sources. ▪Autobiography of ballerina Maja Pliseckaja.

1146 Popovič, I. "Ul'jana Lopatkina: 'Tarakanov ja ne bojus'!'." (Uljana Lopatkina: 'I Am Not Afraid of Roaches!'.) *Ogonek.* 1998; 50: 56-59. Lang.: Rus.
Russia: St. Petersburg. Histories-sources. ▪Ballet soloist with the Mariinskij Theatre on her life and career.

1147 Vasil'ev, V. "Zdes' vse sobiraetsja voedino: Bol'šoj razgovor o Bol'šom." (Here Everybody Comes Together: Important Discussion about Major Aspects.) *Persona.* 1998; 2: 2-11. Lang.: Rus.
Russia: Moscow. 1998. Histories-sources. ▪Ballet master and choreographer Vladimir Vasiljėv discusses the Bolšoj.

1148 Vasil'eva, M. "Baleriny." (The Ballet Dancers.) *Rossija.* 1998; June: 90-93. Lang.: Rus.
Russia: St. Petersburg. 1998. ▪Ballet dancers Uljana Lopatkina and Diana Višneva.

1149 Zarhina, Regina. "Russian Invasion: The Third Wave." *Dm.* 1998 Jan.; 72(1): 76-81. Illus.: Photo. B&W. 10. Lang.: Eng.
Russia. 1901-1998. Historical studies. ▪Influence of Russian dancers and choreographers on world ballet in the twentieth century, and their continued impact as dance faces a new millennium.

1150 Archer, Kenneth; Hodson, Millicent. "Seven Days from the *Dervisher* Diary." *DTJ.* 1998; 14(2): 34-43. Notes. Illus.: Photo. Dwg. B&W. 11. Lang.: Eng.
Sweden: Stockholm. 1997. Histories-sources. ▪Journal kept by choreographer Hodson and scenic consultant Archer while reconstructing Jean Börlin's ballet *Dervisher* for the Royal Swedish Ballet.

1151 Olsson, Irène. "Anneli dansar vidare." (Anneli Dances On.) *Danst.* 1998; 8(2): 3-5. Illus.: Photo. B&W. Color. Lang.: Swe.
Sweden: Stockholm. 1963. Histories-sources. ▪Interview with the ballerina Anneli Alhanko about her career and plans after retiring from Kungliga Baletten.

1152 Olsson, Irène. "En dansare i Formel 1 klass." (A Dancer of the First Class.) *Danst.* 1998; 8(4): 22-25. Illus.: Photo. Color. Lang.: Swe.
Sweden: Stockholm. 1975-1998. Histories-sources. ▪Interview with Göran Svalberg about his career, guest engagements with Maurice Béjart and Deutsche Oper in Berlin.

1153 Sörenson, Margareta. "Kulturhuvudstaden bryter in i danslivet." (The City of Culture Breaks into the Dance World.) *Danst.* 1998; 8(1): 7. Illus.: Photo. B&W. Lang.: Swe.
Sweden: Stockholm. 1998. Historical studies. ▪Presentation of the dance events for this year, with reference to the critical voices heard from the artists.

1154 Vukolov, N. "Avtograf na paschal'nom jajce." (An Autograph.) *EchoP.* 1998; 24: 41-43. Lang.: Rus.
Sweden: Stockholm. 1998. 1984. Historical studies. ▪Discusses Swedish ballet, and the history of the monument to ballerina Galina Ulanova in Stockholm.

1155 "Looking in Vain." *Econ.* 1998 Apr 4; 347(8062): 91-92. Illus.: Photo. B&W. 1. Lang.: Eng.
UK-England. 1998. Critical studies. ▪Laments the lack of new ballets that have the staying power to become part of a troupe's regular repertoire.

1156 Bramley, Ian. "Return of the Narrative." *DTJ.* 1998; 14(4): 26-29. Illus.: Photo. B&W. 3. Lang.: Eng.
UK-England. 1998. Critical studies. ▪Discusses the strong narrative sense in the work of choreographers Matthew Bourne and Mark Murphy.

1157 Driver, Senta. "The Way Ahead." *BR.* 1998 Sum; 26(2): 31-33. Illus.: Photo. B&W. 2. Lang.: Eng.
UK-England: London. 1996-1997. Critical studies. ▪Analysis of Matthew Bourne's choreographies for *Swan Lake (Lebedinojė osero)* and *Cinderella (Zoluška).*

1158 Farjeon, Annabel. "Choreographers: Dancing for de Valois and Ashton." 23-28 in Carter, Alexandra, ed. *Routledge Dance Studies Reader.* London/New York, NY: Routledge; 1998. 316 pp. Index. Notes. Biblio. Lang.: Eng.
UK-England: London. 1930-1940. Histories-sources. ▪Choreographer Annabel Farjeon recalls her years dancing with Ninette de Valois and Frederick Ashton at the Sadler's Wells Ballet Company.

1159 Fleming, Bruce. "Something for Everyone to Dislike." *BR.* 1998 Fall; 26(3): 75-79. Lang.: Eng.
UK-England. 1998. Critical studies. ▪Analysis of Matthew Bourne's gender-confused choreography for *Swan Lake (Lebedinojė osero).*

DANCE: Ballet—Performance/production

1160 Horwitz, Dawn Lille. "A Conversation with Matthew Bourne." *BR.* 1998 Sum; 26(2): 34-42. Illus.: Photo. B&W. 3. Lang.: Eng.
UK-England. 1998. Histories-sources. ■Interview with choreographer Bourne about his career and his artistic goals.

1161 Levene, Louise. "*Cinderella* Makes Progress." *DTJ.* 1998; 14(1): 3-5. Notes. Illus.: Photo. B&W. 3. Lang.: Eng.
UK-England: London. 1998. Critical studies. ■Critique of Matthew Bourne's latest work, Prokofjev's *Cinderella (Zoluška)* at the Piccadilly Theatre.

1162 Newman, Barbara. "Dancers Talking About Performance." 57-65 in Carter, Alexandra, ed. *Routledge Dance Studies Reader.* London/New York, NY: Routledge; 1998. 316 pp. Index. Notes. Biblio. Lang.: Eng.
UK-England. USA. Cuba. 1942-1989. Histories-sources. ■Interviews with dancers: Nora Kaye on her experiences performing as a dancer in Anthony Tudor's *Pillar of Fire* and other roles, Alicia Alonso as Giselle at the Ballet Nacional de Cuba, Tanaquil LeClercq in Balanchine's *The Four Temperaments*, and Peter Martins in Balanchine's *Apollo.*

1163 Rókás, László; Molnár, Kata, photo. "Kérdések egy gentlemanhez: Beszélgetés Christopher Bruce-szal." (Questions to a Gentleman: Interview with Christopher Bruce.) *Ellenfény.* 1998; 3(2): 70-71. Illus.: Photo. B&W. 1. Lang.: Hun.
UK-England: London. 1998. Histories-sources. ■Conversation with the choreographer and artistic director of Rambert Dance Company on the occasion of guest performances in Hungary.

1164 Šakirzjanov, M. "Čarodej tanca." (The Dance Magician.) *Idel'.* 1998; 1: 46-48. Lang.: Rus.
UK-England: London. 1998. Biographical studies. ■The ballet dancer and producer from Tatarstan working in the UK, Irek Muchamedov.

1165 "Remembering Alexandra Danilova." *BR.* 1998 Spr; 26(1): 37-55. Illus.: Photo. B&W. 10. Lang.: Eng.
USA: New York, NY. 1997. Historical studies. ■Text of tributes offered in memory of the late ballerina at the Dance Collection/New York Public Library for the Performing Arts, by those who worked with her, including Irina Baranova, Emily Coleman, Baird Hastings, Barbara Horgan, Robert Lindgren, Sonja Lindgren, Betty Low, Alicia Markova, Bruce Marks, Francis Mason, Seno Osato, Jerome Robbins, Donald Saddler, and Naomi Spector.

1166 Balanchine, George; Mason, Francis. "Four Lost Robbins Ballets." *BR.* 1998 Fall; 26(3): 33-38. Lang.: Eng.
USA: New York, NY. 1949-1952. Historical studies. ■Synopses of four lost Jerome Robbins choreographies contained in the 1953 book *Balanchine's Complete Stories of the Great Ballets: The Guests, The Age of Anxiety, The Pied Piper*, and *Ballade.*

1167 Barnes, Clive. "Jerome Robbins (1918-1998): An Appreciation." *Dm.* 1998 Oct.; 72(10): 54-56. Illus.: Photo. B&W. Color. 2. Lang.: Eng.
USA. 1918-1998. Biographical studies. ■Obituary for the choreographer who had major influence upon the development of dance in both ballet and musical theatre.

1168 Ben-Itzak, Paul; Schatz, Howard, photo. "The Triumph of a Patient Mind." *Dm.* 1998 Jan.; 72(1): 70-74. Illus.: Photo. B&W. 5. Lang.: Eng.
USA: Seattle, WA. 1984-1998. Biographical studies. ■Profile of Pacific Northwest Ballet's prima ballerina, Ariana Lallone.

1169 Chrustaleva, O. "Neogovorennaja territorija Michaila Baryšnikova." (The Hidden Territory of Mikhail Baryshnikov.) *Domovoj.* 1998; 1: 22-33. Lang.: Rus.
USA. 1998. Biographical studies. ■Profile of the ballet dancer and director, living in the United States.

1170 Daniels, Don. "Sex, Murder, and *Agon.*" *BR.* 1998 Fall; 26(3): 26-32. Illus.: Photo. Sketches. B&W. 6. Lang.: Eng.
USA: New York, NY. 1998. Critical studies. ■Highlights of the fall New York City Center performances of the San Francisco Ballet including Balanchine's *Agon* and Robbins' *The Cage.*

1171 Fernandez, Kristina. "Jerome Robbins." *BR.* 1998 Sum; 26(2): 19-20. Lang.: Eng.
USA. 1998. Histories-sources. ■Ballerina Fernandez shares her thoughts on working with choreographer Jerome Robbins as he approaches eighty.

1172 Fullington, Doug. "Alexandra Danilova on *Raymonda.*" *BR.* 1998 Win; 26(4): 73-76. Illus.: Photo. B&W. 4. Lang.: Eng.
USA: New York, NY. 1946. Histories-sources. ■Interview with Danilova regarding Balanchine's 1946 production of the Glazunov ballet at City Center.

1173 Garafola, Lynn. "Nichol Hlinka: Still Beautiful and Going Strong." *Dm.* 1998 Feb.; 72(2): 82-87. Illus.: Photo. Color. 6. Lang.: Eng.
USA: New York, NY. 1975-1998. Biographical studies. ■Profile of the New York City Ballet principal dancer.

1174 Gastineau, Janine; Schatz, Howard, photo. "Standing Tall." *Dm.* 1998 Sep.; 72(9): 64-68. Illus.: Photo. Color. 2. Lang.: Eng.
USA: Denver, CO. 1991-1998. Biographical studies. ■Profile of Colorado Ballet's principal dancer Koichi Kubo.

1175 Gladstone, Valerie. "Active in Seattle." *Dm.* 1998 Feb.; 72(2): 70-73. Illus.: Photo. Color. 2. Lang.: Eng.
USA: Seattle, WA. 1994-1998. Biographical studies. ■Profile of Pacific Northwest Ballet's principal dancer Manard Stewart.

1176 Green, Harris. "West Meets East at ABT." *Dm.* 1998 Oct.; 72(10): 70-72. Illus.: Photo. B&W. Color. 3. Lang.: Eng.
USA: New York, NY. 1981-1998. Biographical studies. ■Profile of Chinese-born soloist for American Ballet Theatre, Yan Chen.

1177 Green, Harris; Costas, photo. "New Generation of New York City Ballet Men." *Dm.* 1998 Nov.; 72(11): 70-73. Illus.: Photo. Color. 5. Lang.: Eng.
USA: New York, NY. 1998. Biographical studies. ■Spotlight on five new male dancers at the New York City Ballet: Benjamin Millepied, Christopher Wheeldon, Sébastien Marcovici, Edward Liang, and James Fayette.

1178 Gregg, Jess. "Eaten Alive." *Dm.* 1998 Jan.; 72(1): 60-64. Illus.: Photo. B&W. 5. Lang.: Eng.
USA: New York, NY. 1961-1998. Histories-sources. ■Playwright and show doctor Gregg describes his relationship with choreographer Agnes De Mille.

1179 Hering, Doris. "'Because It Is a Masterpiece'." *BR.* 1998 Spr; 26(1): 83-87. Illus.: Photo. B&W. 3. Lang.: Eng.
USA. 1960-1998. Historical studies. ■Background on Balanchine's choreography for *Themes and Variations*, music by Čajkovskij.

1180 Horwitz, Dawn Lille. "Elena Kunikova and Les Ballets Trockadero." *BR.* 1998 Fall; 26(3): 69-74. Illus.: Photo. B&W. 5. Lang.: Eng.
USA: New York, NY. 1997. Histories-sources. ■Interview with dancer/choreographer Kunikova regarding her work with the all-male Les Ballets Trockadero de Monte Carlo.

1181 Hunt, Marilyn; Kolnik, Paul, photo. "Refined Zest." *Dm.* 1998 Nov.; 72(11): 66-69. Illus.: Photo. B&W. Color. 6. Lang.: Eng.
USA: New York, NY. 1987-1998. Biographical studies. ■Career of dancer Albert Evans, only the second African-American principal in New York City Ballet's history.

1182 Jordan, Stephanie. "Louis Martinez and Michael Somes on Margot Fonteyn." *BR.* 1998 Win; 26(4): 94-98. Lang.: Eng.
USA. Panama. 1946-1998. Histories-sources. ■Contains two separate interviews relating to Fonteyn—the first with family friend Martinez regarding her life in Panama with her politician husband, the second with choreographer Somes regarding their collaborations. Both touch on her on-stage chemistry with dancer Rudolf Nureyev.

1183 Karz, Zippora; Schatz, Howard, photo. "Dancing Through Diabetes." *Dm.* 1998 Sep.; 72(9): 74-77. Illus.: Photo. Color. 2. Lang.: Eng.
USA: New York, NY. 1983-1998. Histories-sources. ■New York City Ballet soloist Karz shares what it feels to dance while suffering with diabetes.

DANCE: Ballet—Performance/production

1184 Kokich, Kim. "A Conversation with Julie Kent." *BR.* 1998 Win; 26(4): 45-54. Illus.: Photo. B&W. 10. Lang.: Eng.
USA. 1998. Histories-sources. ■Interview with dancer Kent regarding her career and influences.

1185 LeClerq, Tanaquil; Whitaker, Rick. "Jerome Robbins." *BR.* 1998 Sum; 26(2): 13-18. Illus.: Photo. B&W. 6. Lang.: Eng.
USA. 1940-1998. Histories-sources. ■Ballerina LeClerq reminisces about working with choreographer Jerome Robbins on the advent of his eightieth birthday.

1186 Lesschaeve, Jacqueline. "Torse: There Are No Fixed Points in Space." 29-34 in Carter, Alexandra, ed. *Routledge Dance Studies Reader.* London/New York, NY: Routledge; 1998. 316 pp. Index. Notes. Biblio. Lang.: Eng.
USA. 1960-1998. Histories-sources. ■Interview with dancer/choreographer Merce Cunningham on his career and work, especially his ballet *Torse*, music by Maryanne Amacher.

1187 Lőrinc, Katalin; Mezey, Béla, photo. "John Taras?: 'Balanchine-t tartom a legnagyobb koreográfusnak'." (John Taras?: 'I Consider Balanchine to Be the Greatest Choreographer'.) *Tanc.* 1998; 29(1): 12. Illus.: Photo. B&W. 1. Lang.: Hun.
USA: New York, NY. 1919-1998. Histories-sources. ■A conversation with the 78-year-old dancer, ballet-master and choreographer John Taras, one of George Balanchine's colleagues and friends, on the occasion of the premiere of the Balanchine Evening at the Budapest Opera House.

1188 Mason, Francis. "*Jewels.*" *BR.* 1998 Sum; 26(2): 81-95. Illus.: Photo. B&W. 6. Lang.: Eng.
USA: New York, NY. 1967. Histories-sources. ■Panel discussion headed by Francis Mason focusing on Balanchine's ballet *Jewels.* Dancers from the original cast, Edward Villella, Suki Schorer, and Conrad Ludlow, plus Merrill Ashley, a dancer closely identified with Balanchine's work, were on the panel.

1189 Ostlere, Hilary; Schatz, Howard, photo. "Baryshnikov Light and Dark." *Dm.* 1998 May; 72(5): 44. Illus.: Photo. Color. 7. Lang.: Eng.
USA. USSR. 1966-1998. Biographical studies. ■Career of dancer/choreographer Baryshnikov, with particular attention paid to his present status in the dance world and his future plans.

1190 Putnam, Margaret. "Houston Liftoff." *Dm.* 1998 Mar.; 72(3): 92-95. Illus.: Photo. Color. B&W. 4. Lang.: Eng.
USA: Houston, TX. UK-England: London. 1993-1998. Biographical studies. ■Profile of principal dancer Carlos Acosta and his work with both the Royal Ballet and the Houston Ballet.

1191 Sims, Caitlin. "In His Element." *Dm.* 1998 Oct.; 72(10): 74-77. Illus.: Photo. Color. 4. Lang.: Eng.
USA: San Francisco, CA. 1998. Biographical studies. ■Profile of San Francisco Ballet's principal dancer Christopher Stowell.

1192 Vereecke, Father Robert, S.J. "A Dancer's Christmas." *Dm.* 1998 Dec.; 72(12): 74-76. Illus.: Photo. B&W. Color. 3. Lang.: Eng.
USA: Boston, MA. 1980-1998. Histories-sources. ■Jesuit priest's account of his creation of the religious ballet *A Dancer's Christmas*, which is performed every Christmas in Boston.

1193 Willis, Margaret. "Nina Ananiashvili: Houston's Snow Maiden." *Dm.* 1998 Mar.; 72(3): 68-74. Illus.: Photo. Color. 4. Lang.: Eng.
USA: Houston, TX. 1986-1998. Biographical studies. ■Profile of the ballerina who was cast in the lead of Houston Ballet's choreographer Ben Stevenson's original piece *Snow Maiden*, adapted from Čajkovskij's *Sneguročka* and based on Russian folklore.

1194 Zalán, Magda; Friedmann, Gary, photo. "A tánc szíve - a szív tánca: Az 50 éves Barisnyikov születésnapi ajándéka - nekünk." (The Heart of Dance - The Dance of Heart: A 'Birthday' Gift of the 50-Year-Old Baryshnikov, for Us.) *Tanc.* 1998; 29(3): 30. Illus.: Photo. B&W. 1. Lang.: Hun.
USA: Washington, DC. 1990-1998. Reviews of performances. ■A jubilee program by Baryshnikov and his ensemble, the White Oak Dance Project at the Warner Theatre, Washington, including Baryshnikov's solo part, *HeartBeat:mb* (music by Samuel Barber).

1195 Zalán, Magda; Feeley, Bruce R., photo.; Greenfield, Lois, photo. "A fény táncosai: A Parsons Dance Company a Kennedy Centerben." (Dancers of Light: The Parsons Dance Company at the Kennedy Center.) *Tanc.* 1998; 29(5): 36. Illus.: Photo. B&W. 2. Lang.: Hun.
USA: Washington, DC. 1998. Reviews of performances. ■Notes on the outstanding production of the eleven year-old jazz ballet ensemble gaining great success at the Kennedy Center: Parsons' choreography: *Fill the Woods with Light*, music by Phil Woods.

1196 Alovert, Nina. "Baryshnikov, from Classicist to Modernist." *BR.* 1998 Win; 26(4): 87-93. Illus.: Photo. B&W. 6. Lang.: Eng.
USSR. USA. 1969-1998. Biographical studies. ■Career of dancer/choreographer Baryshnikov and the influences of his native and adopted countries.

Relation to other fields

1197 Krymov, V. "Orden baletomanov: Kšesinskaja." (Organization of Ballet Fans: Kšesinskaja.) *Mosk.* 1998; 5: 197-203 . Lang.: Rus.
Russia. Historical studies. ■Excerpts from Krymov's book *Portraits of Unusual Men*, describing the first wave of emigration and its effect on the Russian dance world.

1198 Mason, Francis. "A Conversation with Martha Swope." *BR.* 1998 Fall; 26(3): 39-61. Illus.: Photo. B&W. 16. Lang.: Eng.
USA: New York, NY. 1950-1998. Histories-sources. ■Interview with ballerina turned photographer regarding her experiences in both disciplines.

Theory/criticism

1199 Daugenti, Carl. *Neoclassical Theatre Dance and the Theoretical Work of Gasparo Angiolini, 1761-1765.* Los Angeles, CA: Univ. of California; 1998. 270 pp. Notes. Biblio. [Ph.D. Dissertation, Univ. Microfilms Order No. AAC 9905489.] Lang.: Eng.
Italy. 1761-1765. Critical studies. ■Translations of three theoretical dissertations by dancer/ballet composer Gasparo Angiolini. Includes commentary on historiographic, aesthetic and dramaturgical contexts and the challenges of contemporary dance reconstruction.

1200 Jordan, Stephanie; Thomas, Helen. "Dance and Gender: Formalism and Semiotics Reconsidered." 241-249 in Carter, Alexandra, ed. *Routledge Dance Studies Reader.* London/New York, NY: Routledge; 1998. 316 pp. Index. Notes. Biblio. Lang.: Eng.
USA. Europe. 1946-1982. Critical studies. ■Formalism, structuralism, semiotics, and gender in Siobhan Davies's *Duets* and Balanchine's *The Four Temperaments.* Argues that by using differing analytical strategies, possibilities are opened up for multiple readings.

1201 Macaulay, Alastair. "Spring: Ashton's *Symphonic Variations* in America." 113-118 in Carter, Alexandra, ed. *Routledge Dance Studies Reader.* London/New York, NY: Routledge; 1998. 316 pp. Index. Notes. Biblio. Lang.: Eng.
USA: New York, NY. 1992. Histories-sources. ■Author compares his own critical reviews of Balanchine's *Themes and Variations* at the American Ballet Theatre and Frederick Ashton's *Symphonic Variations.*

Training

1202 Valukin, M.E. *Ličnost' pedagoga choreografii v obučenii klassičeskomu tancu.* (The Identity of the Choreography Teacher in the Teachings of Classical Dance.) Moscow: 1998. 88 pp. Lang.: Rus.
1998. Critical studies. ■The place of the teacher in the world of classical dance.

1203 Harri, Minna. "Aarne Mäntylä koulutta lapsia jotka ovat tästä maailmasta." (Aarne Mäntylä: Teaching Children in the Real World.) *Tanssi.* 1998; 19(1): 21-23. Illus.: Photo. B&W. 5. Lang.: Fin.
Finland. 1998. Histories-sources. ■Interview with Mäntylä, teacher of both modern and classical dance, regarding to his approach to training children.

DANCE: Ballet—Training

1204 Sutinen, Virve. "Kiristääkö balettitossu nykylapsen jalassa." (Are the Children's Ballet Shoes on Too Tight Today?) *Tanssi.* 1998; 19(1): 17-20. Illus.: Photo. B&W. 2. Lang.: Fin.
Finland. 1998. Historical studies. ▪Analysis of classical dance training, with a eye toward how the teaching methods can be changed to appeal more to children.

1205 Handel, Edit. "Demonstráció: A Párizsi Opera balettiskolájának koncertje a Garnier Palotában." (Demonstration: First Appearance of the Ballet School of the Paris Opera at Palais Garnier.) *Tanc.* 1998; 29(6): 27. Illus.: Photo. B&W. 1. Lang.: Hun.
France: Paris. 1998. Reviews of performances. ▪The gala concert of the renowned ballet school at the Opéra de Paris.

1206 Lőrinc, Katalin. "'Remélem a növendékeim szerettek táncolni'." ('I Hope My Students Loved to Dance'.) *ZZT.* 1998; 5(2): 33-34. Illus.: Photo. B&W. 1. Lang.: Hun.
Hungary. 1954-1998. Histories-sources. ▪A talk with Jacqueline Menyhárt, one-time soloist of the Budapest Opera House who now teaches at the Ballet Institute.

1207 Mátai, Györgyi; Kanyó, Béla, photo. "'A legnagyobb vágyam maradt beteljesületlenül': Beszélgetés Koren Tamás balettmesterrel." ('My Greatest Desire Is Unfulfilled': Interview with Ballet Master Tamás Koren.) *Tanc.* 198; 29(2): 14-15. Illus.: Photo. B&W. 3. Lang.: Hun.
Hungary. 1959-1998. Histories-sources. ▪Conversation with the dancer, ballet master and pedagogue on his life and career.

1208 Pliseckaja, M. "'Ničego ne ostaetsja, krome legendy...'." (Nothing Remains Except for the Legend...)*NV.* 1998; 2-3: 55. Lang.: Rus.
Russia: Moscow. 1998. Histories-sources. ▪Ballerina Maja Pliseckaja and her present work in dance training.

1209 Neubauer, Henrik; Pliberšek, Marjan, illustr. *Klasični balet I.* (Classical Ballet I.) Ljubljana: Forma 7; 1998. 46 pp. Illus.: Photo. B&W. 3. Lang.: Slo.
Slovenia. 1998. Instructional materials. ▪A methodological manual for ballet trainers of children. Text is set out on a week-by-week basis to provide a one-year training program.

1210 Sörenson, Margareta. "Dansen, tiden–och en eld." (Dance, Time–and a Fire.) *Danst.* 1998; 8(3): 10. Illus.: Dwg. Photo. B&W. Lang.: Swe.
Sweden: Stockholm. 1998. Critical studies. ▪Comparison of the dance training of the classical tradition and the rich variety of techniques advocated today.

1211 Wrange, Ann-Marie. "Träning genom visualisering." (Training Through Visualization.) *Danst.* 1998; 8(2): 20-21. Illus.: Dwg. B&W. Lang.: Swe.
Sweden: Stockholm. 1998. Historical studies. ▪Description of the relaxation and deep breathing techniques of Tina Hessel.

1212 Anderson, Jack. "Pauline Koner, An American Original." *Dm.* 1998 Jan.; 72(1): 82-84. Illus.: Photo. B&W. 4. Lang.: Eng.
USA: New York, NY. 1920-1998. Biographical studies. ▪Profile of dance teacher Koner.

1213 Gitelman, Claudia. "Louise Kloepper (1910-1996)." *BR.* 1998 Spr; 26(1): 89-94. Illus.: Photo. B&W. 1. Lang.: Eng.
USA. 1910-1996. Biographical studies. ▪Tribute to the late ballet teacher, who honed her craft under the tutelage of influential teacher Mary Wigman.

1214 Kai, Una. "Balanchine's Way." *BR.* 1998 Win; 26(4): 13-21. Illus.: Photo. B&W. 2. Lang.: Eng.
USA. 1947-1998. Histories-sources. ▪Former ballet mistress of Balanchine describes the finer points of his method of training.

1215 Kennedy, Paul; Junion, David, photo. "Waltraud Karkar." *Dm.* 1998 Sep.; 72(9): 88-89. Illus.: Photo. Color. 2. Lang.: Eng.
USA: Wausau, WI. 1998. Biographical studies. ▪Profile of the Central Wisconsin School of Ballet teacher Karkar.

1216 Olsson, Irène. "David Howard–träning för avspända dansare." (David Howard–A Training For Relaxed Dancers.) *Danst.* 1998; 8(2): 13. Illus.: Photo. B&W. Lang.: Swe.
USA. 1966-1998. Histories-sources. ▪Interview with David Howard about his background as dancer and a teacher for thirty years. Critically reappraises classical ballet schools and their methods.

1217 Sarver, Susan. "Harvey Hysell: The Quiet Hero of Classical Ballet." *Dm.* 1998 Apr.; 72(4): 84-86. Illus.: Photo. Color. 2. Lang.: Eng.
USA: New Orleans, LA. 1969-1998. Biographical studies. ▪Profile of classical ballet teacher Hysell, and his New Orleans based school.

Ethnic dance

Design/technology

1218 Johnson, David. "Many Rivers to Cross." *TCI.* 1998 Aug/Sep.; 32(8): 37-39. Illus.: Photo. Color. 4. Lang.: Eng.
Ireland. 1998. Technical studies. ▪Equipment and design employed by audio man Mick O'Gorman for three separate world tours of the dance extravaganza *Riverdance.*

Institutions

1219 Truppel, Mariann; Kádár, Kata, photo.; Korniss, Péter, photo. "A táncvihar éve: A Honvéd Táncszínház ezredvégi kalandozásai." (The Year of Dance Storm: Adventures of the Honvéd Dance Theatre at the End of the Millenium.) *fo.* 1998; 29(6): 28-29. Illus.: Photo. B&W. 3. Lang.: Hun.
Hungary. 1998. Critical studies. ▪Summarizing the ensemble's performances, directed by choreographer Ferenc Novák, at home and abroad in 1998.

1220 Vadasi, Tibor; Korniss, Péter, photo. "Ötvenéves az Erkel Néptáncegyüttes." (Fifty Years of the Erkel Folk Dance Ensemble.) *Tanc.* 1998; 29(6): 18-19. Illus.: Photo. B&W. 2. Lang.: Hun.
Hungary. 1948-1998. Historical studies. ▪Successes of the dance group led by artistic director Tibor Galambos. The ensemble has celebrated its 50th anniversary with a gala performance at the National Theatre.

1221 Carlberg Kriig, Anne. "Lek på blodigt allvar." (Play in Dead Earnest.) *Danst.* 1998; 8(5): 28-29. Illus.: Photo. Color. Lang.: Swe.
Norway: Kongsberg. 1923-1998. Historical studies. ▪Report from Kongsberg Kappleiken, a festival of Norwegian folk-music and folk-dance.

1222 Artamonova, L. "Voskresenskie venzelja." (Voskresensk Festival.) *Vstreča.* 1998; 6: 18-20. Lang.: Rus.
Russia: Voskresensk. 1998. Historical studies. ▪Third Festival Competition of Folk Dance in Voskresensk.

Performance/production

1223 Pičugin, P.A. "Poézija argentinskogo tango." (The Poetry of Argentinian Tango.) *Latinskaja Amerika.* 1998; 12: 65-80. Lang.: Rus.
Argentina. Critical studies. ▪Influence of the tango in world dance.

1224 Albert, Mária; Korniss, Péter, photo. "Koppenhágában a Honvéd Táncszínház." (The Honvéd Dance Theatre in Copenhagen.) *Tanc.* 1998; 29(5): 30. Illus.: Photo. B&W. 1. Lang.: Hun.
Denmark: Copenhagen. 1998. Reviews of performances. ▪Guest performance of the Honvéd folk dance ensemble in Denmark.

1225 Harris, Max. "Sweet Moll and Malinche: Maid Marian Goes to Mexico." 101-110 in Potter, Lois, ed. *Playing Robin Hood: The Legend as Performance in Five Centuries.* Newark, DE: Univ of Delaware P; 1998. 254 pp. Index. Notes. Biblio. Pref. Illus.: Photo. 2. Lang.: Eng.
England. Mexico. 1500-1900. Critical studies. ▪Political reading of the link between the Maid Marian of the English Morris dance and the Malinche figure in Mexican folkdance, in both of which male dancers are disguised as women.

1226 Åberg, Tommy. "Steg att tampas med." (Steps To Tussle With.) *Danst.* 1998; 8(5): 27-28. Illus.: Photo. B&W. Color. Lang.: Swe.

DANCE: Ethnic dance—Performance/production

Greece: Sitia. 1998. Historical studies. ■The difficulty of mastering the intricacies of traditional Cretan dance.

1227 Kaán, Zsuzsa; Kanyó, Béla, photo. "*Napmadarak*: A Fáklya Horvát Táncegyüttes új bemutatója." (*Sunbirds*: Premiere by the Fáklya Croatian Dance Ensemble.) *Tanc.* 1998; 29(6): 20-21. Illus.: Photo. B&W. 4. Lang.: Hun.

Hungary. 1998. Reviews of performances. ■Antal Kricskovics' choreographies presented by the Fáklya ethnic folkdance group under the title *Napmadarak (Sunbirds)*.

1228 Körtvélyes, Géza. "Korszerű tendenciák a magyar táncművészetben: Néptáncművészet és mozgalom (1970-77) 1. rész." (Modern Tendencies in Hungarian Dance Art: Folk Dance: Art and Movement (1970-77) Part 1.) *ZZT.* 1998; 5(1): 30-32. Lang.: Hun.

Hungary. 1970-1977. Historical studies. ■Survey of folk dance training in the 1970s. Continued in *ZZT* 1998 5:2, pp. 9-13, and 5:3, pp. 26-30, with a discussion of choreographers and their ensembles.

1229 Pór, Anna. "Emlékest Molnár István tiszteletére." (Commemorative Evening in Honor of István Molnár.) *Tanc.* 1998; 29(5): 12-13. Illus.: Photo. B&W. 2. Lang.: Hun.

Hungary: Budapest. 1930-1998. Biographical studies. ■The commemoration of István Molnár, folk dancer and choreographer, with a folk dance program.

1230 Barba, Eugenio. "In Memory: Sanjukta Panigrahi: 1944-1997." *TDR.* 1998 Sum; 42(2): 5-8. Illus.: Photo. B&W. 3. Lang.: Eng.

India. 1944-1997. Biographical studies. ■Obituary for the dancer, who specialized in the Indian dance styles of *Bharata natyam* and *Odissi.*

1231 Krasil'nikova, T.; Bukin, A. "Iskat' svoe prizvanie i sledovat' emu." (Look for Your Path in Life and Follow It.) *Novyj Akropol'.* 1998; 1(2): 73-76. Lang.: Rus.

Russia: Moscow. 1998. Biographical studies. ■Profile of indigenous dance choreographer Igor Moisejév.

1232 Levočkina, N.A. "Tradicionnaja narodnaja choreografija sibirskich tatar: predvarit. rezul'taty issledovanija." (Traditional National Siberian Tatar Choreography: Preliminary Research Results.) 133-139 in *Istoričeskij ežegodnik.* Omsk: 1998. Lang.: Rus.

Russia. 1998. Critical studies. ■Examines the folk dance style native to the Tatars of Siberia.

1233 Moisejév, Igor. *Ja vspominaju: Gastrol' dlinoju v žizn'.* (I Remember: Performances of a Lifetime.) Moscow: Soglasie; 1998. 224 pp. Lang.: Rus.

Russia: Moscow. 1926-1998. 1920-1940. Histories-sources. ■Recollections of Igor Moisejév: choreographer, creator and director of the national dance emsemble.

1234 Jyrkkä, Hannele. "Nykyflamencon naiset, miehet ja suosio." (Men, Women and the Popularity of Modern Flamenco.) *Tanssi.* 1998; 19(4): 27-29. Illus.: Photo. B&W. 2. Lang.: Fin.

Spain. Finland. 1998. Historical studies. ■Examines the recent surge in popularity of flamenco dancing in Finland.

1235 Wrange, Ann-Marie. "Gabriela Gutarra—dansar sig in i andra kulturer." (Gabriela Gutarra—Dances Herself Into Other Cultures.) *Danst.* 1998; 8(6): 4-7. Illus.: Photo. B&W. Color. Lang.: Swe.

Spain: Seville. 1980-1998. Histories-sources. ■Interview with Gabriela Gutarra about her career as flamenco dancer, with reference to the flamenco culture in general.

1236 MacLennan, Karin. "Eva, en ren flamencodansare." (Eva, a Pure Flamenco Dancer.) *Danst.* 1998; 8(6): 17. Illus.: Photo. B&W. Lang.: Swe.

Sweden: Gothenburg. Spain. 1990-1998. Histories-sources. ■Interview with Eva Milich about her background in classical ballet and rebirth in the flamenco, with a comparison between the original and the Swedish flamenco.

1237 Wrange, Ann-Marie. "Flamenco, en glöd som sprider sig." (Flamenco, a Spreading Glow.) *Danst.* 1998; 8(6): 8-12. Illus.: Photo. B&W. Color. Lang.: Swe.

Sweden. Spain. 1970. Histories-sources. ■Interview with Janni Berggren about her career as flamenco dancer and teacher, with reference to the situation in Sweden and the recent developments of flamenco.

1238 Forrai, Éva. "London etnikai lázban." (Ethnic Fever in London.) *Tanc.* 1999; 29(1): 32. Illus.: Photo. B&W. 1. Lang.: Hun.

UK-England: London. 1997. Reviews of performances. ■An account of two successful performances in London: a flamenco production by the dance ensemble of choreographer Joaquím Cortez and the guest performance of Ballets Africains of Guinea.

1239 Gladstone, Valerie. "Keeper of Flamenco." *Dm.* 1998 Sep.; 72(9): 70-73. Illus.: Photo. B&W. Color. 4. Lang.: Eng.

USA: New York, NY. 1998. Biographical studies. ■Profile of flamenco dancer and choreographer Carlota Santana, founder of Flamenco Vivo Carlota Santana, with a look at her choreography *Federico*, based on the life of García Lorca.

1240 Magill, Gordon L. "Guiding Light of Daystar." *Dm.* 1998 Aug.; 72(8): 64-68. Illus.: Photo. Color. 5. Lang.: Eng.

USA: Santa Fe, NM. 1966-1998. Biographical studies. ■Profile of choreographer/dancer Rosalie Jones, founder and artistic director of the Native American dance company Daystar.

1241 Zalán, Magda. "A mexikói szarvastánctól a kínai modern balettig: Poszt-népi és neo-etnikus táncegyüttesek Washingtonban, 2. rész." (From the Mexican Stag-Dance to Chinese Modern Ballet: Post-Folkloric and Neo-Ethnic Dance Ensembles, Part 2.) *Tanc.* 1998; 29(1): 30-31. Illus.: Photo. B&W. 3. Lang.: Hun.

USA: Washington, DC. 1997. Reviews of performances. ■Notes on the guest performances of the Ballet Folklórico de Mexico and the Guangdong Dance Company with a brief history of the ensembles.

1242 Bogdanov, G. "Pravda i lož' o narodnom tance." (Truth and Lies About Folk Dance.) *NTE.* 1998; 3: 13-16. Lang.: Rus.

USSR. 1930-1939. Historical studies. ■Folk dancing in the Soviet Union during the 1930s.

Reference materials

1243 Ramovš, Mirko. *Polka je ukazana.* (The Polka Is Ordered.) Ljubljana: Kres; 1998. 269 pp. Pref. Index. Illus.: Design. 2. Lang.: Slo.

Slovenia. 1997. ■The fifth book in a collection of Slovene folk dance. Text describes couple and group dances and features a choreographic description, musical score, and a diagram of each dance.

Training

1244 Ståhle, Anna Greta. "Flamencons svenska moder." (The Swedish Mother of Flamenco.) *Danst.* 1998; 8(6): 18-21. Illus.: Photo. B&W. Color. Lang.: Swe.

Sweden: Stockholm. Spain. 1944-1997. Historical studies. ■Profile of Barbro Thiel-Cramér and her teaching in Sweden of Spanish dancing, with reference to her earlier studies in Spain.

1245 Vail, June. "Orientalisk dans för fria kvinnor i väst." (Oriental Dance For Free Women of The Western World.) *Danst.* 1998; 8(5): 30-31. Illus.: Photo. B&W. Lang.: Swe.

Sweden. 1995. Critical studies. ■The attitude of Swedes toward female dance of North Africa, Arabia, India, and China, with reference to how this attitude changes after practice and to the importance of communication through dance.

Modern dance

Audience

1246 Dunning, Jennifer. "Aliens in New York." *DTJ.* 1998; 14(3): 31-35. Illus.: Photo. B&W. 2. Lang.: Eng.

USA: New York, NY. 1997-1998. Critical studies. ■New York dance critic reports on audience response to visiting British dance companies.

Design/technology

1247 Hüster, Wiebke. "Im Strudel des Daseins." (In the Whirl of Existence.) *DB.* 1998; 12: 20-22. Illus.: Dwg. Photo. B&W. 4. Lang.: Ger.

DANCE: Modern dance—Design/technology

Germany. 1991-1998. Biographical studies. ■A portrait of set and costume designer Frank Leimbach and his collaboration with choreographers Pina Bausch, Susanne Linke and Joachim Schlömer.

1248 Lampert-Gréaux, Ellen. "Geography Lessons." *TCI.* 1998 Feb.; 32(2): 12-13. Illus.: Photo. Color. 1. Lang.: Eng.
USA: New York, NY. 1998. Technical studies. ■Overall design concept for Ralph Lemon's dance piece *Geography* performed at BAM's Majestic Theatre. Lighting by Stan Pressner, costumes by Liz Prince, and visual artist Nari Ward's 'installation' set design.

Institutions

1249 Kolesnikova, E.D. "Bravo, Korpo!" *Latinskaja Amerika.* 1998; 4: 105-106. Lang.: Rus.
Brazil: Belo Horizonte. 1998. Historical studies. ■The contemporary ballet group, Grupo Corpo.

1250 Kevin, Jonna. "Martha Graham goes Havanna." *Danst.* 1998; 8(4): 6-7. Illus.: Photo. B&W. Lang.: Swe.
Cuba: Havana. 1959-1998. Historical studies. ■Report on the state of modern dance in Cuba, with special references to Danza Contemporánea de Cuba, Narciso Medina and Danza Nacional.

1251 Klemsdal, Ole. "En plats där man kan upptäcka världen." (A Place Where You Can Discover the World.) *Danst.* 1998; 8(3): 20-21. Illus.: Photo. B&W. Color. Lang.: Swe.
Norway: Bergen. 1990-1998. Historical studies. ■Profile of the dance company Nye Carte Blanche and its resident choreographer Ina Christel Johannessen, with an interview with the artistic director Karen Foss.

1252 Sedov, Ja. "Naivnost' so vzlomom." (Naivete with the Break In.) *Itogi.* 1998; 40: 60-61. Lang.: Rus.
Russia. 1998. Historical studies. ■Modern dance festival 'The Car's Coming Toward You', held in Moscow and Yekaterinburg, with Russian and British participants.

1253 Wrange, Ann-Marie. "Dokumentär dansteater om tro, hopp & kärlek." (Documentary Dance Theatre About Faith, Hope & Love.) *Danst.* 1998; 8(5): 10-11. Illus.: Photo. B&W. Lang.: Swe.
Sweden: Gothenburg. 1998. Historical studies. ■Report from Göteborgs Dans- och Teaterfestival, with references to *Enter Achilles* with DV8 Physical Theatre and *Sabotage Baby* with Batsheva Dance Company.

1254 Harpe, Bill. "News at Ten." *DTJ.* 1998; 14(3): 36-39. Illus.: Photo. B&W. 5. Lang.: Eng.
UK-England: London. 1988-1998. Historical studies. ■Looks back at the ten years of existence of the Motionhouse Dance Theatre, founded by Louise Richards and Kevin Finnan.

1255 McDonagh, Don. "Ailey Celebrates its Fortieth: Reflections of Alvin." *Dm.* 1998 Dec.; 72(12): 56-61. Illus.: Photo. B&W. Color. 9. Lang.: Eng.
USA: New York, NY. 1958-1998. Historical studies. ■Looks at the Alvin Ailey American Dance Theatre, and its founder and namesake, as it celebrates its fortieth anniversary.

1256 Topaz, Muriel. "A New Company That Makes the Past Come Alive." *Dm.* 1998 July; 72(7): 56-59. Illus.: Photo. Color. B&W. 4. Lang.: Eng.
USA: Los Angeles, CA. 1994-1998. Historical studies. ■Profile of the American Repertory Dance Company which is dedicated to preserving and performing the legacy of past modern dance pioneers.

Performance spaces

1257 Bjerre, Ole. "Transform, det specifikke steds forestilling." (Transform, the Site Specific Performance.) *TE.* 1998 July; 89: 24-27. Illus.: Photo. B&W. 3. Lang.: Dan.
Denmark. 1970-1998. Historical studies. ■The movement of modern dance from the 'black box' stage to new spaces, and the creation of dance pieces in harmony with those spaces.

Performance/production

1258 Burt, Ramsay. "Re-Presentations of Re-Presentations: Reconstruction, Restaging and Originality." *DTJ.* 1998; 14(2): 30-33. Notes. Illus.: Photo. B&W. 2. Lang.: Eng.
1998. Critical studies. ■Argues that originality and innovation can be released in the performance of reconstructed choreographies.

1259 Carter, Alexandra. "The Case for Preservation." *DTJ.* 1998; 14(2): 26-29. Notes. Illus.: Photo. B&W. 1. Lang.: Eng.
1998. Critical studies. ■Argues the historical and artistic value of reconstructing and preserving the choreographies of past masters.

1260 Feliciana, Rita; Sorgeloos, Herman, photo. "A Love-Hate Affair with Dance." *Dm.* 1998 Mar.; 72(3): 96-98. Illus.: Photo. Color. B&W. 4. Lang.: Eng.
Belgium: Brussels. 1981-1998. Biographical studies. ■Profile of dancer/choreographer Anne Teresa De Keersmaeker and her company Rosas.

1261 Russ, Claire. "Choreographers in Conversation: Alain Platel." *DTJ.* 1998; 14(1): 27-30. Illus.: Photo. B&W. 2. Lang.: Eng.
Belgium: Ghent. 1984-1998. Histories-sources. ■Interview with Platel regarding his work with his company, Ballets Contemporains de la Belgique.

1262 Algra, Jacqueline. "Galina Borissova. De Robin Rood van de Bulgaarse dans." (Galina Borissova: The Robin Hood of Bulgarian Dance.) *Tmaker.* 1998; 2(2): 39-42. Illus.: Photo. B&W. 2. Lang.: Dut.
Bulgaria. 1998. Historical studies. ■Galina Borissova, Bulgarian winner of the 1990 Grominger Choreography Festival, is introduced to the Dutch world of dance.

1263 Massoutre, Guylaine. "Corps de femmes par elles-mêmes: Hiver-printemps 1998 en danse." (Women's Bodies By Themselves: Winter-Spring 1998 in Dance.) *JCT.* 1998; 89: 128-136. Illus.: Photo. B&W. 9. Lang.: Fre.
Canada: Montreal, PQ. 1998. Historical studies. ■Women's choreographies and solo dances in 1998 Winter-Spring season in Montreal.

1264 Massoutre, Guylaine. "Montréal cosmopolite: L'automne 1997 en danse." (Cosmopolitan Montreal: Fall 1997 in Dance.) *JCT.* 1998; 87: 128-138. Notes. Illus.: Photo. B&W. 8. Lang.: Fre.
Canada: Montreal, PQ. 1997. Historical studies. ■Montreal's Festival international de nouvelle danse, bringing companies from Portugal, Spain and all over the globe, testifies to the cosmopolitan nature of Montreal's modern dance culture.

1265 Réblová, Kateřina; Med, Milan, illus. "Zpráva o stavu české tvorby v roce 1998." (A Report on the Condition of Czech Dance Production in 1998.) *Tanecni.* 1998 Oct.; 35(2): 2-4. Illus.: Photo. Dwg. B&W. 4. Lang.: Cze.
Czech Republic. 1998. Critical studies. ■The contemporary trends in the Czech dance production, and the direction young choreographers are taking their newest works.

1266 Vangeli, Nina. "The Renaissance of Modern Dance in Prague/La renaissance de la danse moderne à Prague." *CzechT.* 1998 June; 14: 51-55. Illus.: Photo. B&W. 7. Lang.: Eng, Fre.
Czech Republic: Prague. 1997. Critical studies. ■Profiles of three young dancer/choreographers: Monika Rebcová, Petr Tyc and Petr Zuska, their latest dance performances.

1267 Møller, Søren Friis. "Talenter i ny dansk dans." (Talent in New Danish Dance.) *TE.* 1998 Apr.; 88: 30-31. Illus.: Pntg. 1. Lang.: Dan.
Denmark. 1998. Critical studies. ■Modern dance in Denmark has better prospects than ever before due to better financial aid, a new dance school and more media coverage. The next step is to get the productions abroad so that the choreographers can get a chance to see their work develop over more than the average twelve performances that is customary in Denmark.

1268 Fleischer, Mary Rita. *Collaborative Projects of Symbolist Playwrights and Early Modern Dancers.* New York, NY: City Univ. of New York; 1998. 376 pp. Notes. Biblio. [Ph.D. Dissertation, Univ. Microfilms Order No. AAC 9820531.] Lang.: Eng.
Europe. USA. 1916-1934. Historical studies. ■Examines the collaborative nature of projects between symbolist playwrights and eary modern dancers as playwrights incorporated dance into their work in a wide range of contexts. Projects discussed include W.B. Yeats's work with dancer Michio Ito on *At the Hawk's Well* and with Ninette de Valois on *Fighting the Waves* and *The King of the Great Clock Tower*, Gabriele

DANCE: Modern dance—Performance/production

D'Annunzio's projects with Ida Rubinstein, primarily *Le Martyre de Saint Sébastien* with music by Claude Debussy and choreography by Michel Fokine, and *La Pisanelle, ou la mort parfumée*, directed by V. E. Meyer'chold and choreographed by Fokine, Hugo von Hofmannsthal's pantomimes for Grete Wiesenthal, *Amor und Psyche*, *Das fremde Mädchen* and *Die Biene*, and Paul Claudel's collaboration with Jean Börlin and the Ballets Suédois on *L'Homme et son désir* with music by Darius Milhaud.

1269 Hughes, David. "Dance Away the Frontiers: New Dance Work by Four European Women." *PM.* 1989; 58: 66-75. Illus.: Photo. B&W. 4. Lang.: Eng.
Europe. 1989. Critical studies. ■Works choreographed and danced by Angelike Oei, Lea Anderson, Brigitte Farges, and Maria Oliver Antonio show how the physical vocabulary of the dance evolves from the bodies and personalities of the dancers.

1270 Servos, Norbert. "Nullpunkt Tanz." (Ground Zero Dance.) *DB.* 1998; 12: 36-40. Illus.: Photo. B&W. 2. Lang.: Ger.
Europe. 1970-1998. Critical studies. ■Increasing trend toward nudity in dance theatre of the younger generation after the influence of Pina Bausch and Johann Kresnigk.

1271 Simonsen, Majbrit. "To mand frem for en enke." (Two Men in Front of a Widow.) *TE.* 1998 Feb.; 87: 34-39. Illus.: Photo. B&W. 9. Lang.: Dan.
Europe. 1960-1998. Critical studies. ■Men's increasing role in the modern dance world.

1272 Theissen, Hermann. "Tanz-Sprache im Koreodrama." (Koreodrama's Dance-Speech.) *DB.* 1998; 12: 28-31. Illus.: Photo. B&W. 2. Lang.: Ger.
Europe. 1978-1998. Biograhical studies. ■Portrait of choreographer and director Nada Kokotovic and the development of Koreodrama.

1273 Toiminen, Marjaana. "Todellisuus äänten tuolla puolen." (Reality Beyond the Voices.) *Tanssi.* 1998; 19(2): 20-21 . Illus.: Photo. B&W. 3. Lang.: Fin.
Finland. 1998. Histories-sources. ■Interview with Deaf dancer Juho Saarinen about his approach to his craft.

1274 Vuori, Suna. "Ostetaan vähän käytetty sukupuoli." (Wanted: A Slightly Used Gender.) *Tanssi.* 1998; 19(2): 37 . Illus.: Photo. B&W. 3. Lang.: Fin.
Finland. 1998. Critical studies. ■Representation of sexuality and gender in modern dance.

1275 Massoutre, Guylaine. "Improviser et chorégraphier avec des enfants: Entretien avec Jacques Fargearel de la Compagnie du Sillage." (Improvising and Choreographing With Children: Interview With Jacques Fargearel of Compagnie du Sillage.) *JCT.* 1998; 89: 46-49. Notes. Illus.: Photo. B&W. 3. Lang.: Fre.
France. 1998. Histories-sources. ■Choreographer Jacques Fargearel on working with children.

1276 Russ, Claire. "Pas de Deux." *DTJ.* 1998; 14(4): 8-11. Notes. Illus.: Photo. B&W. 3. Lang.: Eng.
France. UK-England. 1994-1998. Histories-sources. ■Choreographer Russ relates her ongoing give and take with French choreographer Anne-Marie Pascoli.

1277 Bartlett, Neil. "What Moves: Pina Bausch." *DTJ.* 1998; 14(4): 4-7. Illus.: Photo. B&W. 2. Lang.: Eng.
Germany: Wuppertal. 1982-1998. Histories-sources. ■Critic discusses his own personal response to the work of Bausch and her Tanztheater.

1278 Biró, Yvette. "Heartbreaking Fragments, Magnificent Whole: Pina Bausch's New Minimyths." *PerAJ.* 1998 May; 20(2): 68-72. Lang.: Eng.
Germany: Wuppertal. 1997. Critical studies. ■Analysis of Bausch's latest piece *Nur du (Only You)* for her Tanztheater.

1279 Blankemeyer, Silke; Servos, Norbert. "Tanztheater im Umbruch." (Dance Theatre in Change.) *DB.* 1998; 12: 14-19. Illus.: Photo. B&W. 8. Lang.: Ger.
Germany: Wuppertal. 1973-1998. Histories-sources. ■Portrait of Pina Bausch's dance theatre and an interview with her about concepts, working methods and choreography on occasion of the 25th anniversary of her company.

1280 Brandstetter, Gabrielle. "Defigurative Choreography: From Marcel Duchamp to William Forsythe." *TDR.* 1998 Win; 42(4): 37-55. Notes. Biblio. Illus.: Photo. B&W. 4. Lang.: Eng.
Germany. France. 1915-1998. Histories-sources. ■Comparison of painter Duchamp's work 'The Large Glass' with choreographies by William Forsythe of Ballett Frankfurt, particularly *Alien/A(c)tion* and *Self Meant to Govern.*

1281 Hartung, Bernd, photo. "Herzlichen Glückwunsch!" (Hearty Congratulations!) *Tanzd.* 1998; 43(4): 28-31. Pref. Illus.: Photo. B&W. 6. Lang.: Ger.
Germany: Wuppertal. 1973-1998. Biographical studies. ■Portrait of choreographer/director Pina Bausch in photographs during a festival celebrating 25 years of dance theatre in Wuppertal.

1282 Henne, Claudia. "Souvenirs, Souvenirs." (Memories, Memories.) *THeute.* 1998; 5: 24-25. Illus.: Photo. B&W. 1. Lang.: Ger.
Germany: Wuppertal. 1998. Critical studies. ■Analysis of Pina Bausch's dance work *Masuca Fogo*, and how it relates to her aesthetic approach.

1283 Schneider, Katja. "ACHTUNG: Ortswechsel." (Attention: Changing Places.) *Tanzd.* 1998; 40(1): 10-11. Illus.: Photo. B&W. 3. Lang.: Ger.
Germany. France. 1970-1998. Biographical studies. ■Portrait of dancer and exhibition curator Brygida Ochaim focusing on her dance work in film working with French filmmaker Claude Chabrol in the movie *The Swindle (Rien ne va plus)* and her mission to reconstruct the work of choreographer Loie Fuller.

1284 Servos, Norbert. "Laban Meets Ballet." *Tanzd.* 1998; 40(1): 4-9. Illus.: Photo. B&W. 3. Lang.: Ger.
Germany: Frankfurt. 1984-1998. Historical studies. ■The dance principle of William Forsythe, director of Ballet Frankfurt since 1984, and how he combines the tenets of Rudolf von Laban with his own to create a new form of movement.

1285 Servos, Norbert. "Alles pulsiert und kracht." (Everything Pulsates and Crashes.) *DB.* 1998; 12: 26-27. Illus.: Photo. B&W. 2. Lang.: Ger.
Germany: Berlin. 1998. Histories-sources. ■Interview with choreographer Sasha Waltz about her self-image as dance maker and her working methods and concepts.

1286 Sieben, Irene. "Der Traum, auf dem Wasser zu tanzen." (The Dream of Dancing on the Water.) *Tanzd.* 1998; 40(1): 12-13. Illus.: Photo. B&W. 3. Lang.: Ger.
Germany: Berlin. 1994-1998. Biographical studies. ■Portrait of dancer Anna Huber, her concepts of contemporary dancing since she moved away from traditional modes of performance to work on the fringes.

1287 Sieben, Irene. "Die überwindung der Ordnung." (The Overcoming of Order.) *Tanzd.* 1998; 42(3): 10-12. Illus.: Photo. B&W. 3. Lang.: Ger.
Germany. USA. 1936-1998. Biographical studies. ■Portrait of dancer, choreographer and teacher Hellmut Gottschild and his analytic choreographies influenced by Mary Wigman.

1288 Stöckemann, Patricia. "'Ernst ist das Leben, heiter die Kunst'." (Life Is Serious, Art Is Funny.) *Tanzd.* 1998; 41 (2): 17-19. Illus.: Photo. B&W. 5. Lang.: Ger.
Germany: Hannover. 1966-1998. Biographical studies. ■Portrait of dancer/choreographer Ralf Jaroschinski and his philosophy of dance.

1289 Veroli, Patricia. "'Aus Furcht vor den Nazis verbrannte ich alles'." ('I Burnt Everything for Fear of Nazis'.) *Tanzd.* 1998; 42(3): 30-33. Pref. Illus.: Photo. B&W. 4. Lang.: Ger.
Germany. 1911-1998. Biographical studies. ■Interview with the dancer, choreographer, pedagogue and researcher Lilian Karina about leaving her native country to escape Nazism.

1290 Wigman, Mary. "Komposition." (Composition.) *Tanzd.* 1998; 42(3): 6-9. Pref. Illus.: Photo. B&W. 4. Lang.: Ger.
Germany: Dresden. 1925. Histories-sources. ■Mary Wigman's own summary of her work and aesthetic essentials, an early document of modern dance published on the twenty-fifth anniversary of her death.

1291 Lőrinc, Katalin. "Fekete Hedvig szabadságról, független táncoslétről, képzettségről és másról." (Hedvig Fekete on

DANCE: Modern dance—Performance/production

Freedom, Independent Status of a Dancer, Training and Other Things.) *ZZT.* 1998; 5(1): 22-24. Illus.: Photo. B&W. 5. Lang.: Hun.

Hungary: Budapest. 1998. Histories-sources. ▪Interview with dancer and choreographer Hedvig Fekete at the contemporary solo dance festival at MU Színház dedicated to the late choreographer Zoltán Imre where she presented her solo piece *Szemrebbenés (Twinkling)* to music of Vivaldi.

1292 Lőrinc, Katalin. "Egy pécsi nyári este az Anna-udvarban." (A Summer Evening in Anna-Courtyard in Pécs.) *Tanc.* 1998; 29(4): 17. Illus.: Photo. B&W. 1. Lang.: Hun.

Hungary: Pécs. 1998. Reviews of performances. ▪Dance performances choreographed by Gábor Hajzer and Tímea Papp in the Anna Utcai Nyári Játékok.

1293 Lőrinc, Katalin; Papp, Dezső, photo. "*Nevess remegve (Emlék)*: A Trafó nyitó műsora." (*Laugh Tremble—Memory*: Opening Program of Trafó.) *Tanc.* 1998; 29(5): 14. Illus.: Photo. B&W. 1. Lang.: Hun.

Hungary: Budapest. 1998. Reviews of performances. ▪A new venture in Budapest's cultural life called Trafó (House of Contemporary Arts) was opened recently with production of Yvette Bozsik's dance company.

1294 Lőrinc, Katalin; Papp, Dezső, photo. "Vénuszok, imádkozó sáskák és... Stefan Zweig: A Budapest Táncszínház új bemutatója." (Venuses, Mantises and... Stefan Zweig: On the New Program of the Budapest Dance Theatre.) *Tanc.* 1998; 29(5): 15. Illus.: Photo. B&W. 1. Lang.: Hun.

Hungary: Budapest. 1998. Reviews of performances. ▪The first premiere of the Budapest Dance Theatre as a professional ensemble at the Thália Theatre, with *Apollók és Vénuszok (Apollos and Venuses)* choreographed by Attila Egerházi.

1295 Vadasi, Tibor. "*Utolsó kontrasztok*: Orsovszky István új műsora Zalaegerszegen." (*Last Contrasts*: István Orsovszky's New Program at Zalaegerszeg.) *Tanc.* 1998; 29(3): 18. Lang.: Hun.

Hungary: Zalaegerszeg. 1998. Reviews of performances. ▪Account of the final part of the series of Orsovszky's choreographies under the title *Kontrasztok (Contrasts).*

1296 Arndt, Roman. "Ruth Abramowitsch-Sorel." *Tanzd.* 1998; 42(3): 28-29. Notes. Illus.: Photo. B&W. 2. Lang.: Ger.

Poland. 1907-1974. Biographical studies. ▪Portrait of dancer, choreographer, and pedagogue Ruth Abramowitsch-Sorel and her emigration to Poland.

1297 Golikova, N. *Istorija ljubvi: A. Dunkan, S. Esenin.* (Story of Love: Isadora Duncan and Sergej Esenin.) Moscow: Zacharov-Ast; 1998. 144 pp. Lang.: Rus.

Russia. 1919-1925. Biographical studies. ▪Profile of the relationship between poet Esenin and dancer Duncan.

1298 Majniece, V. "Edinstvennyj v Rossii: sovremennyj baletnyj teatr B. Ejfmana." (The Only One in Russia: The Contemporary Ballet Theatre of Ejfman.) *MoskZ.* 1998; July-Aug: 38-41. Lang.: Rus.

Russia: St. Petersburg. 1998. ▪Profile of Boris Ejfman's Contemporary Ballet Theatre.

1299 Engdahl, Horace. "Vilande, ändå i rörelse." (Resting, Although In Movement.) *Danst.* 1998; 8(1): 14-17. Illus.: Photo. B&W. Color. Lang.: Swe.

Sweden: Stockholm. 1984-1998. Biographical studies. ▪Portrait of the dancer Anja Birnbaum, with reference to her dancing in the works of Margaretha Åsberg.

1300 Gunne, Nina. "Landskapet i kroppen." (The Landscape of the Body.) *Danst.* 1998; 8(5): 32-35. Illus.: Photo. . Lang.: Swe.

Sweden. Japan. 1990-1998. Histories-sources. ▪Interview with Susanna Åkerlund about her career as *butō* dancer and the history of *butō.*

1301 Högberg, Helena; Harryson, Lotta; Szyber, Bogdan; Lepage, Robert; Newson, Lloyd; Wrange, Ann-Marie. "En skön Pina." (A Wonderful Pina.) *Danst.* 1998; 8(5): 22-26. Illus.: Photo. Color. Lang.: Swe.

Sweden: Stockholm. 1998. Histories-sources. ▪Various opinions regarding Pina Bausch's guest performances in Stockholm, with references to *Café Müller* and *Der Fensterputzer.*

1302 Näslund, Erik; Kieser, Klaus, transl. "'Eine Bewegung muss motiviert sein'." ('A Movement Must Be Motivated'.) *Tanzd.* 1998; 41(2): 20-25. Illus.: Photo. B&W. 9. Lang.: Ger.

Sweden: Stockholm. 1908-1998. Biographical studies. ▪Portrait of dancer/choreographer Birgit Cullberg on occasion of her 90th birthday including a résumé of her work.

1303 Peter, Frank-Manuel. "Die Entdeckung der Langsamkeit." (The Discovery of the Slowness.) *Tanzd.* 1998; 40(1): 14-23. Notes. Illus.: Photo. B&W. 13. Lang.: Ger.

Sweden: Stockholm. 1908-1998. Biographical studies. ▪Portrait of dancer Birgit Åkesson on the occasion of her 90th birthday, includes a résumé of her career.

1304 Sörenson, Margareta. "ET har landat—i en lada." (E.T. Has Landed—On a Farm.) *Danst.* 1998; 8(4): 18-19. Illus.: Photo. B&W. Lang.: Swe.

Sweden: Husby. 1998. Historical studies. ▪Report on choreographer Wayne McGregor's work with Swedish dance students for a joint show in London this summer.

1305 Sörenson, Margareta. "Ana Laguna och Cullbergtraditionen." (Ana Laguna and the Cullberg Tradition.) *Danst.* 1998; 8 (6): 22-24. Illus.: Photo. Color. Lang.: Swe.

Sweden: Stockholm. 1974-1998. Critical studies. ▪Dancer Ana Laguna and how she has adopted the genuine style of Cullbergbaletten, with references to Mats Ek and Birgit Cullberg.

1306 Wrange, Ann-Marie. "Jennie—i egen snurrklass." (Jennie—In a Spinning Class of Her Own.) *Danst.* 1998; 8(3): 14-17. Illus.: Photo. B&W. Color. Lang.: Swe.

Sweden: Stockholm. 1995-1998. Histories-sources. ▪Interview with Jennie Widegren about her studies in USA, and work with Modern Jazz Dans Ensemble and her own company Bounce.

1307 Carter, Gary. "The Complexity of Simplicity." *DTJ.* 1998; 14(1): 8-11. Notes. Illus.: Photo. B&W. 1. Lang.: Eng.

UK-England: London. 1989-1998. Biographical studies. ▪Profile of the career of dancer/choreographer Rosemary Lee. Touches on her work in the medium of film, particularly her direction of her own filmed choreography *Greenman*, performed by dancer Simon Whitehead.

1308 Daniels, Don; Whitaker, Rick. "A Conversation with Keely Garfield." *BR.* 1998 Spr; 26(1): 57-73. Illus.: Photo. B&W. 9. Lang.: Eng.

UK-England. 1998. Histories-sources. ▪Interview with dancer/choreographer about her artistic goals and the influence of Merce Cunningham.

1309 Dodds, Sherril. "A Spanner in the Works." *DTJ.* 1998; 14(1): 12-14. Illus.: Photo. B&W. 1. Lang.: Eng.

UK-England. 1989-1998. Biographical studies. ▪Profile of performer/choreographer Wendy Houstoun.

1310 Hansen, Sophie. "Lean, Mean and Not Entirely Clean." *DTJ.* 1998; 14(1): 6-8. Illus.: Photo. B&W. 5. Lang.: Eng.

UK-England: London. 1997. Historical studies. ▪Report on the Dance Umbrella '97 festival held in London. Continued in *DTJ* (1998) 14:2, pp 15-17, entitled 'High Society'.

1311 Hodson, Millicent; Archer, Kenneth; Wrange, Ann-Marie, transl. "Att återuppväcka avantgardet." (To Revive the Avant-Garde.) *Danst.* 1998; 8(4): 26-31. Illus.: Photo. B&W. Color. Lang.: Swe.

UK-England: London. Sweden: Stockholm. 1920-1998. Histories-sources. ▪Excerpts from a diary about the efforts to reconstruct Jean Börlin's *Dervisher* (1920) for performance for the 225th anniversary of the Royal Swedish Ballet.

1312 Mackrell, Judith. "Michael Clark in Focus." *DTJ.* 1998; 14(3): 8-12. Lang.: Eng.

UK-England. 1995-1998. Histories-sources. ▪Interview with dancer/choreographer on his return to the dance world after a three year absence.

1313 Nyhn, Jaqueline. "Enter Achilles i männens värld." (Enter Achilles In the World of Men.) *Danst.* 1998; 8(5): 5-9 . Illus.: Photo. B&W. Lang.: Swe.

DANCE: Modern dance—Performance/production

UK-England: London. 1995-1998. Histories-sources. ▪Interview with Lloyd Newson, artistic director of DV8 Physical Theatre, about the background and the different versions of *Enter Achilles.*

1314 Spångberg, Mårten. "Aerowaves—dansplats för mångfald." (Aerowaves—a Dance Place For the Many-Faceted.) *Danst.* 1998; 8(6): 54. Lang.: Swe.

UK-England: London. Belgium: Brussels. 1998. Historical studies. ▪Report from one seminar for auditions of new choreographers for the international part of Resolution Festival.

1315 Watson, Keith. "Men Behaving Sadly." *DTJ.* 1998; 14(2): 4-6. Illus.: Photo. B&W. 1. Lang.: Eng.

UK-England: London. 1998. Critical studies. ▪Analysis of choreographer Lea Anderson's dark work *The Featherstonehaughs Draw on the Sketchbooks of Egon Schiele*, a piece she created for the male half of her company Featherstonehaughs (the female unit is known as the Cholmondeleys).

1316 "Everything Feels a Bit Like Dancing." *DTJ.* 1998; 14(2): 7-11. Notes. Illus.: Photo. B&W. 2. Lang.: Eng.

USA. 1990-1998. Histories-sources. ▪Interview with choreographer Bill T. Jones about his work, living with AIDS, and the controversy among critics surrounding his piece *Still/Here.*

1317 Acocella, Joan. "Mark Morris: The Body and What It Means." 269-277 in Carter, Alexandra, ed. *Routledge Dance Studies Reader.* London/New York, NY: Routledge; 1998. 316 pp. Index. Notes. Biblio. Lang.: Eng.

USA. 1980-1997. Historical studies. ▪Analysis of formal movement as well as circumstances of production in Mark Morris's choreography.

1318 Bordwell, Marilyn. "Dancing with Death: Performativity and 'Undiscussible' Bodies in *Still/Here.*" *TextPQ.* 1998 Oct.; 18(4): 369-379. Notes. Biblio. Lang.: Eng.

USA. 1994. Critical studies. ▪Defense of Bill T. Jones' dance piece against the negative criticism it received after its premiere tour through the United States.

1319 Cocuzza, Ginnine. *The Theatre of Angna Enters, American Dance-Mime.* New York, NY: New York Univ; 1987. 512 pp. Biblio. Notes. [Ph.D. Dissertation, Univ. Microfilms Order No. AAC 8712740.] Lang.: Eng.

USA. 1905-1923. Historical studies. ▪The career of concert dancer, mime, and solo performer Angna Enters, compared here to American modern dancers such as Martha Graham, Doris Humphrey, and Charles Weidman.

1320 Cooper, Susan. "Remembering Bill Cratty." *DTJ.* 1998; 14(4): 38-40. Lang.: Eng.

USA. 1974-1998. Biographical studies. ▪Tribute to the late choreographer.

1321 Dempster, Elizabeth. "Women Writing the Body: Let's Watch a Little How She Dances." 223-229 in Carter, Alexandra, ed. *Routledge Dance Studies Reader.* London/New York, NY: Routledge; 1998. 316 pp. Index. Notes. Biblio. Lang.: Eng.

USA. Europe. 1900-1930. Historical studies. ▪The early history of modern dance as a female-centered movement, with emphasis on Isadora Duncan, Loie Fuller, Maud Allen, Ruth St. Denis, Martha Graham, and Yvonne Rainer.

1322 Diamond, Emma. "Beyond Chance." *DTJ.* 1998; 14(1): 43-45. Illus.: Photo. B&W. 2. Lang.: Eng.

USA. 1988-1998. Histories-sources. ▪Choreographer Diamond acknowledges the debt she owes to Merce Cunningham in the development of her own work.

1323 Graham, Martha. "I Am a Dancer." 66-71 in Carter, Alexandra, ed. *Routledge Dance Studies Reader.* Index. Notes. Biblio. Lang.: Eng.

USA. 1930. Histories-sources. ▪Dancer/choreographer Martha Graham's 'personal manifesto' on what it is like to be a dancer and devote one's life to dance.

1324 King, Kenneth. "Dancing (the) Legend: The Art of Frances Alenikoff." *PerAJ.* 1998 May; 20(2): 28-37. Illus.: Photo. B&W. 2. Lang.: Eng.

USA: New York, NY. 1960-1998. Biographical studies. ▪Profile of the avant-garde, septuagenarian, solo dance performer: her aesthetic aims and what she still hopes to achieve.

1325 Kourlas, Gia. "A Verb, Not a Noun." *Dm.* 1998 Apr.; 72(4): 72-75. Illus.: Photo. Color. 5. Lang.: Eng.

USA: New York, NY. 1964-1998. Biographical studies. ▪Career of choreographer Meredith Monk.

1326 Kuhn, Laura. "Cunningham & Cage." *BR.* 1998 Fall; 26(1): 81-98. Illus.: Photo. B&W. 1. Lang.: Eng.

USA. 1944-1998. Histories-sources. ▪Interview with choreographer Merce Cunningham regarding his long-time collaboration with composer John Cage.

1327 Maxim, Nanette; Brazil, Tom, photo. "Dancing for Mark." *Dm.* 1998 June; 72(6): 64-67. Illus.: Photo. Color. 2. Lang.: Eng.

USA: New York, NY. 1980-1998. Biographical studies. ▪Profile of two long-time members of the Mark Morris Dance Group, Tina Fehlandt and Ruth Davidson.

1328 Meisner, Nadine. "Conquering Hero?" *DTJ.* 1998; 14(1): 15-18. Notes. Illus.: Photo. B&W. 3. Lang.: Eng.

USA: New York, NY. 1988-1998. Critical studies. ▪Re-examination of the work of choreographer Twyla Tharp. Characterizes her output of the past decade, including her work with the Royal Ballet and her new dance company Tharp!, as disappointing.

1329 Naude, Alice; Schatz, Howard, photo. "The Challenge of a Higher Plateau." *Dm.* 1998 Apr.; 72(4): 68-71. Illus.: Photo. Color. 3. Lang.: Eng.

USA: New York, NY. 1998. Biographical studies. ▪Profile of choreographer/dancer David Parsons on the eve of his inaugural season as head of his own troupe, the Parsons Dance Company, to be based at Manhattan's City Center.

1330 Ostlere, Hilary; Schatz, Howard, photo. "Fine & Dandy." *Dm.* 1998 Apr.; 72(4): 76-80. Illus.: Photo. Color. 3. Lang.: Eng.

USA: New York, NY. 1980-1998. Biographical studies. ▪Profile of postmodernist choreographer Mark Dendy.

1331 Ostlere, Hilary; Caravaglia, Tom, photo. "Life's an Archive." *Dm.* 1998 Oct.; 72(10): 66-68. Illus.: Photo. Color. 3. Lang.: Eng.

USA: Athens, OH. 1950-1998. Historical studies. ▪Spotlight on dancer/choreographer Murray Louis's efforts to archive his oeuvre, and that of his mentor and partner Alwin Nikolais, which is to be housed in the Vernon Alden Library of the University of Ohio.

1332 Snape, Libby. "Javier de Frutos Exposed." *DTJ.* 1998; 14(2): 18-21. Lang.: Eng.

USA. 1990-1998. Histories-sources. ▪Interview with the choreographer regarding his training and his idiosyncratic movement style.

1333 West, Martha Ullman. "A Conduit to the Future." *Dm.* 1998 May; 72(5): 54-57. Illus.: Photo. Color. 2. Lang.: Eng.

USA: Portland, OR. 1995-1998. Biographical studies. ▪Profile of two influential members of the Portland modern dance community: the founder of the company Conduit, Mary Oslund, and company member and dancer/choreographer Gregg Bielemeier.

1334 Witchel, Leigh. "Neil Greenberg's Trilogy: A Survivor's Tale." *BR.* 1998 Fall; 26(3): 62-68. Illus.: Photo. B&W. 1. Lang.: Eng.

USA. 1994-1998. Critical studies. ▪Analysis of Greenberg's three related choreographies: *Not-About-AIDS-Dance*, *The Disco Project*, and *Part Three.*

1335 Witchel, Leigh. "Paul Taylor's American Paradise." *BR.* 1998 Win; 26(4): 63-71. Illus.: Photo. B&W. 3. Lang.: Eng.

USA. 1977-1998. Biographical studies. ▪Profile of the work and career of choreographer Taylor.

1336 Zalán, Magda; Brazil, Tom, photo. "Kiáltó csendek mozdulatlan mozdulatai: Eiko & Koma a Kennedy Center műsorán." (Motionless Movements of Crying Silences: Eiko & Koma on the Program of Kennedy Center.) *Tanc.* 1998; 29(4): 36. Illus.: Photo. B&W. 1. Lang.: Hun.

DANCE: Modern dance—Performance/production

USA: Washington, DC. 1998. Reviews of performances. ■Notes on two productions, *Pulse* and *Wind* at the Kennedy Center by the New York City-based Japanese dance couple.

Relation to other fields

1337 Manning, Susan. "Coding the Message." *DTJ.* 1998; 14(1): 34-37. Notes. Illus.: Photo. B&W. 1. Lang.: Eng.

USA. 1933-1998. Historical studies. ■Traces the overlap between American modern dance and gay culture. Focuses on choreographers Ted Shawn, Merce Cunningham, and Alvin Ailey as touchstones.

1338 Wittmann, Gabriele. "Tanze dein Bild." (Dance Your Image.) *Tanzd.* 1998; 43(4): 10-12. Illus.: Photo. B&W. 8. Lang.: Ger.

USA: Kentfield, CA. 1978-1998. Biographical studies. ■A portrait of dancer, teacher, and healing facilitator Anna Halprin and her work developing a discipline of dance for therapy, creative expression, and healing at the Tamalpa Institute in California founded by herself and Daria Halprin in 1978.

Theory/criticism

1339 Brownell, Catherine. "A Late Developer: The Language of Dance Criticism." *PM.* 1990; 60: 49-55. Illus.: Photo. B&W. 2. Lang.: Eng.

UK-England: London. 1989. Critical studies. ■Stresses the inadequacy of dance criticism: using the reviews of Merce Cunningham's dance company at Sadler's Wells Theatre, finds the criticism obsessed with narratives, techniques, and kinesthetics to the exclusion of a work's visual, aural, formal, and theatrical components. Also states that presentation of dance on video and television adds a new dimension to its analysis.

1340 Copeland, Roger. "Fatal Abstraction: Merce Cunningham, Formalism and Identity Politics." *DTJ.* 1998; 14(1): 38-42. Notes. Illus.: Photo. B&W. 2. Lang.: Eng.

USA. 1998. Critical studies. ■Argues that Cunningham's formalism reveals more about the complexities of human experience than art that is blatantly political.

Training

1341 Blaskó, Borbála; Papp, Dezső, photo. "Magyar növendékek külföldön: Hol nevelkednek Pina Bausch 'Szegfűi'?" (Hungarian Students Abroad: Where Do Pina Bausch's 'Carnations' Grow?) *Tanc.* 1998; 29(1): 33. Illus.: Photo. B&W. 1. Lang.: Hun.

Germany: Essen. 1996-1998. Histories-sources. ■An account of the teaching method at the Folkwang Hochschule under the direction of Pina Bausch.

1342 Adler-Friess, Aanya. *Elizabeth Waters and Her Tradition: A Study in the Teaching of Contemporary Dance.* Albuquerque, NM: Univ. of New Mexico; 1988. 157 pp. Notes. Biblio. [M.A. Thesis, Univ. Microfilms Order No. 1334139.] Lang.: Eng.

USA. 1920-1950. Histories-specific. ■Examines the teaching methods and philosophy of modern dance teacher Elizabeth Waters, the developer of the dance program of the University of New Mexico.

1343 Nugent, Ann. "Surfing with Steve Paxton." *DTJ.* 1998; 14(1): 20-23. Notes. Illus.: Photo. B&W. 1. Lang.: Eng.

USA. 1973-1998. Histories-sources. ■Interview conducted through e-mail with the founder of 'contact improvisation' about its development and its aim of freeing the body to all its possibilities.

DANCE-DRAMA

General

Basic theatrical documents

1344 Alexandrowicz, Conrad. "*The Wines of Tuscany.*" *CTR.* Win 1998; 97: 66-76. Illus.: Photo. B&W. 2. Lang.: Eng.

Canada: Vancouver, BC. 1996. ■Text of Conrad Alexandrowicz's one-act dance-theatre duet for male performers.

1345 Frasca, Richard A., transl. "*The Dice Game and the Disrobing (Pakaṭai Tuyil)*: A *Terukkūttu* Performance." *ATJ.* 1998 Spr; 15(1): 1-44. Notes. Biblio. Illus.: Photo. Diagram. B&W. 8. Lang.: Eng.

India. 1998. ■Translation of a traditional Indian *terukkūttu* drama piece. Includes an introduction by the translator with a history and description of the performance style.

Performance/production

1346 Tian, Min. "The Reinvention of Shakespeare in Traditional Asian Theatrical Forms." *NTQ.* 1998 Aug.; 14(3): 274-284. Notes. Biblio. [Issue 55.] Lang.: Eng.

China, People's Republic of. India. Japan. 1981-1997. Critical studies. ■Reinvigoration of the works of Shakespeare through the use of traditional forms of Asian theatre, dance, and music.

1347 Jhaveri, Angana. *The Raslila Performance Tradition of Manipur in Northeast India.* East Lansing, MI: Michigan State Univ; 1987. 261 pp. Biblio. Notes. [Ph.D. Dissertation, Univ. Microfilms Order No. AAC 8714337.] Lang.: Eng.

India. 1779-1985. Historical studies. ■Study of the Indian temple performance genre, *raslila.* Documents the performance elements in the context of the tradition and analyzes its inherent principles to derive their value and meaning.

1348 O'Shea, Janet. "'Traditional' Indian Dance and the Making of Interpretive Communities." *ATJ.* 1998 Spr; 15(1): 45-63. Notes. Biblio. Lang.: Eng.

India. 1930-1990. Historical studies. ■Differences between the main styles of South India's *bharata natyam* dance form and the rivalry among their practitioners.

1349 Subhra, Madžumdar. "Malavika Sarukkaj: Novoe izmerenie bharatnat'jama." (Malavika Sarukkai: New Measure of *Bharata natyam.*) *Indija.* 1998; May: 42-44, 3-ja s. obl.. Lang.: Rus.

India. 1998. Biographical studies. ■Profile of Indian performer of classical dance style *bharata natyam.*

1350 Asai, Susan Miyo. *Music and Drama in* Nomai *of Northern Japan.* Los Angeles, CA: Univ. of California; 1988. 376 pp. Notes. Biblio. [Ph.D. Dissertation, Univ. Microfilms Order No. AAC 8822291.] Lang.: Eng.

Japan. 1650-1985. Histories-specific. ■Examines the *nomai*, a dance drama that was introduced to the northern area of Japan by itinerant priests known as *yamabushi* as a means of evangelizing to provincial audiences and is still performed today.

1351 Morley, Carolyn Anne. *The World of the* Kyōgen *Stage: An Analysis of Performance.* New York, NY: Columbia Univ; 1987. 304 pp. Notes. Biblio. [Ph.D. Dissertation, Univ. Microfilms Order No. AAC 8809393.] Lang.: Eng.

Japan. 1400-1700. Historical studies. ■A study of *kyōgen*, the classical comic drama of Japan. Analyzes performance text with the aim of clarifying the relationship between the actor and the audience.

1352 Kim, Deukshin. *Hahoe Pyolsin-Kut: The Oldest Extant Korean Mask-Dance Theatre.* New York, NY: City Univ. of New York; 1987. 290 pp. Notes. Biblio. [Ph.D. Dissertation, Univ. Microfilms Order No. AAC 8801726.] Lang.: Eng.

Korea. 1150-1928. Historical studies. ■Analyzes historical background, general setting relating to village ritual, masks, performers, stage, costumes, properties, music, dance, and dramatic values.

1353 Earnest, Steve. "*Les Enfants Terribles*: A Dance-Opera Spectacle Based on the Story by Jean Cocteau. Adapted by Philip Glass and Susan Marshall. Presented by the Arts Festival of Atlanta. Robert Ferst Center for the Performing Arts, Georgia Institute of Technology, Atlanta, Georgia. 11 September 1997." *JDTC.* 1998 Fall; 13(1): 187-189. Notes. Illus.: Photo. B&W. 1. Lang.: Eng.

North America. 1997. Critical studies. ■Examines the theory behind the choreography and movement style in Philip Glass and Susan Marshall's dance-opera *Les Enfants Terribles*, an adaptation of Jean Cocteau's play of the same name, directed by Glass and Marshall.

1354 Pauka, Kirstin. "The Daughters Take Over?: Female Performers in *Randai* Theatre." *TDR.* 1998 Spr; 42(1): 113-121. Notes. Biblio. Illus.: Photo. B&W. 5. Lang.: Eng.

DANCE-DRAMA: General—Performance/production

Sumatra. 1980-1998. Critical studies. ■Describes the recent influx of female performers into the once all-male Sumatran *randai* dance-drama genre.

1355 Hulton-Baker, Robert. *Tibetan Buddhist Drama.* New York, NY: New York Univ; 1987. 151 pp. Biblio. Notes. [Ph.D. Dissertation, Univ. Microfilms Order No. AAC 8712490.] Lang.: Eng.

Tibet. 1500-1984. Historical studies. ■Detailed analysis of the major characteristics of Tibetan Buddhist drama as seen in the texts of three representative plays, *Drimeh Kundan, Nangsa Ohbum* and *Songtsan Gampo.*

Plays/librettos/scripts

1356 Alexandrowicz, Conrad. "Making *The Wines of Tuscany.*" *CTR.* Win 1998; 97: 62-65. Illus.: Photo. B&W. 2. Lang.: Eng.

Canada: Vancouver, BC. 1992-1996. Histories-sources. ■Writer-director Conrad Alexandrowicz on creating script and choreography of his dance-theatre duet, *The Wines of Tuscany.*

1357 Massoutre, Guylaine. "Images de soi dans l'espace collectif: À propos de la trilogie de Gilles Maheu." (Images of Self in Collective Space: On the Trillogy by Gilles Maheu.) *JCT.* 1998; 87: 24-26. Notes. Illus.: Photo. B&W. 3. Lang.: Fre.

Canada: Montreal, PQ. 1994-1998. Critical studies. ■Attempts to decode visual theatre of Gilles Maheu's trilogy *La Forêt (The Forest), Les Âmes mortes (The Dead Souls)* and *L'Hiver/Winterland* produced by Carbone 14 in 1994, 1996 and 1998.

Relation to other fields

1358 Plowright, Poh Sim. "The Art of Manora: An Ancient Tale of Feminine Power Preserved in South-East Asian Theatre." *NTQ.* 1998 Nov.; 14(4): 373-394. Notes. Biblio. Illus.: Photo. B&W. 5. [Issue 56.] Lang.: Eng.

Ireland. Thailand. Malaysia. Historical studies. ■Relevance of the 'bird-woman' folktale to the communal life of Southeast Asian villagers, showing how each performance serves as a shamanic and healing ritual. Also points to the influence of the tale upon W.B. Yeats' *At the Hawk's Well,* in which a birdwoman guards a miraculous well of water against male intrusion.

Training

1359 Scharbau, Puk. "Det japanske rum." (The Japanese Space.) *TE.* 1998 July; 89: 28-33. Illus.: Photo. B&W. 6. Lang.: Dan.

Japan. Denmark: Copenhagen. 1960-1998. Historical studies. ■Tadashi Suzuki's method of teaching actors and director Anne-Lise Gabold's application of them in her production of Euripides' *The Bacchae (Bákchai)* at the Kanonhallen.

Kabuki

Basic theatrical documents

1360 Harue, Tsutsumi; Bowers, Faubion, transl.; Griffith, David W., transl.; Mariko, Hori, transl. "*Kanadehon Hamlet*: A Play by Tsutsumi Harue." *ATJ.* 1998 Fall; 15(2): 181-229. Notes. Biblio. Illus.: Photo. Dwg. B&W. 7. Lang.: Eng.

Japan. 1997. ■Translation of Harue's *kabuki*-style adaptation of Shakespeare's play with an introduction by the playwright.

1361 Mokuami, Kawatake; Bach, Faith, transl. "*Takatoki*: A *Kabuki* Drama." *ATJ.* 1998 Fall; 15(2): 155-180. Notes. Biblio. Illus.: Photo. Dwg. B&W. 3. Lang.: Eng.

Japan. 1884-1998. ■Translation of Mokuami's *kabuki* drama with an introduction by the translator giving background on the performance style and the play.

Performance/production

1362 Bowers, Faubion. "Tamasaburō in *Elizabeth.*" *ATJ.* 1998 Fall; 15(2): 270-274. Lang.: Eng.

Japan: Tokyo. 1993-1995. Historical studies. ■Report on the success of legendary *onnagata* Bandō Tamasaburō V in playing the title role in Francisco Ors' *Elizabeth* directed by Nuria Espert at the Sezon Gekijo in Tokyo.

1363 Mezur, Katherine Marie. *The Kabuki Onnagata: A Feminist Analysis of the Onnagata Fiction of Female-Likeness.* Honolulu, HI: Univ. of Hawaii; 1998. 346 pp. Biblio. Notes. [Ph.D. Dissertation, Univ. Microfilms Order No. 9829569.] Lang.: Eng.

Japan. 1600-1900. Critical studies. ■Feminist analysis of the gender acts, techniques, and aesthetics that constitute the *onnagata* gender roles of *kabuki.* Argues that these models set a corporeal style that real women emulated in their daily lives.

1364 Secor, James Leo. *Kabuki and Morals: The* Onnagata *Heroine as Ethical Example in the Late Eighteenth Century.* Lawrence, KS: Univ. of Kansas; 1987. 140 pp. Notes. Biblio. [Ph.D. Dissertation, Univ. Microfilms Order No. AAC 8813447.] Lang.: Eng.

Japan. 1770-1800. Critical studies. ■Explores the relationship between *kabuki* and society of the late eighteenth century. Focuses on *kabuki* scripts, social change, the death of Chikamatsu Monzaemon, and the growing importance of the *onnagata* female character.

1365 Vigeant, Louise. "La métamorphose d'une *onnagata.*" (The Metamorphosis of an *Onnagata.*) *JCT.* 1998; 86: 162-164. Notes. Illus.: Photo. B&W. 3. Lang.: Fre.

Japan. 1603-1998. Historical studies. ■History of transformation of *kabuku* dance into *kabuki* and contemporary practice of men portraying women in *kabuki* as demonstrated by *onnagata* dancer Kataoka Kōjiro.

Plays/librettos/scripts

1366 Yoshiko, Uéno. "Robin Hood in Japan." 136-158 in Potter, Lois, ed. *Playing Robin Hood: The Legend as Performance in Five Centuries.* Newark, DE: Univ of Delaware P; 1998. 254 pp. Index. Notes. Biblio. Pref. Illus.: Dwg. 3. Lang.: Eng.

England. 1800-1940. Critical studies. ■The bandit hero of nineteenth-century *kabuki* theatre and the ways in which the Robin Hood legend has been transmitted and transformed in Japan since its introduction at the beginning of the twentieth century.

Theory/criticism

1367 Brandon, James R. "*Kabuki*: Changes and Prospects: An International Symposium." *ATJ.* 1998 Fall; 15(2): 253-269. Lang.: Eng.

Japan: Tokyo. 1996. Historical studies. ■Report on a conference held in Tokyo in 1996 on the state of *kabuki* and its future.

Kathak

Performance/production

1368 Parameswaran, Uma. "A Fine Balance between Authenticity and Experimentation." *CTR.* 1998 Spr; 94: 42-44. Illus.: Photo. B&W. 3. Lang.: Eng.

Canada: Toronto, ON. 1970-1998. Histories-sources. ■Interview with Toronto-based dancer and choreographer Runa Singha explains her use of story-telling elements of Indian *kathak* dance, which she uses for her cycle of choreographies retelling Bible stories.

1369 Subhra, Madžumdar. "Kumudini Lakhija: Pridavaja novyj smysl kathaku." (Kumudini Lakhiya: Giving New Meaning to *Kathak.*) *Indija.* 1998; May: 39-41. Lang.: Rus.

India. 1998. Biographical studies. ■Profile of Lakhiya Kumudini master of Indian dance style *kathak.*

Kathakali

Performance/production

1370 Pitkow, Marlene Beth. *Representations of the Feminine in Kathakali: Dance-Drama of Kerala State, South India.* New York, NY: New York Univ.; 1998. 386 pp. Notes. Biblio. [Ph.D. Dissertation, Univ. Microfilms Order No. AAC 9907189.] Lang.: Eng.

India. 1700-1995. Critical studies. ■Examines how a male community of patrons, composers and artists represent the female characters in *kathakali* and regard actors who specialize in these roles. Focuses on how feminine representation by males articulates the ambiguities with which women, both divine and human, are treated both in history and in contemporary life.

DANCE-DRAMA

Nō

Audience

1371 Groemer, Gerald. "*Nō* at the Crossroads: Commoner Performance During the Edo Period." *ATJ*. 1998 Spr; 15(1): 117-141. Notes. Biblio. Illus.: Dwg. B&W. 2. Lang.: Eng.

Japan. 1603-1868. Historical studies. ▪Refutes the belief that performance of *nō* was exclusively the property of the samurai class, demonstrating that the style was popular among the common folk.

1372 Groemer, Gerald. "Elite Culture for Common Audiences: *Machiiri Nō* and *Kanjin Nō* in the City of Edo." *ATJ*. 1998 Fall; 15(2): 230-252. Notes. Biblio. Tables. Illus.: Photo. Dwg. B&W. Color. 15. Lang.: Eng.

Japan: Edo. 1603-1868. Historical studies. ▪Popularity of the *kanjin nō* and *mariichi nō* styles with common audiences in the city Edo.

Performance/production

1373 Rath, Eric Clemence. *Actors of Influence: Discourse and Institutional Growth in the History of* Noh *Theatre*. Ann Arbor, MI: Univ. of Michigan; 1998. 352 pp. Notes. Biblio. [Ph.D. Dissertation, Univ. Microfilms Order No. AAC 9825329.] Lang.: Eng.

Japan. 1500-1998. Histories-specific. ▪Argues that the *nō* theatre tradition, as constructed by its practitioners disguises the arbitrariness of power relations in politics and the marketplace.

Relation to other fields

1374 Gardner, Richard Alvin. *The Art of Nō: A Reconsideration of the Relation of Religion and Art*. Chicago, IL: Univ. of Chicago; 1988. Biblio. Notes. [Ph.D. Dissertation, Univ. Microfilms Order No. AAC T-30470.] Lang.: Eng.

Japan. 1300-1988. Critical studies. ▪On the critical nature of the relationship between religion and art as reflected in the *nō* theatre of Japan.

DRAMA

Administration

1375 Larrue, Jean-Marc. "Le théâtre au Québec entre 1930 et 1950: les années charnières." (Theatre in Quebec Between 1930 and 1950: The Transition Years.) *AnT*. 1998 Spr; 23: 19-37. Notes. Biblio. Lang.: Fre.

Canada: Montreal, PQ, Quebec, PQ. 1880-1950. Historical studies. ▪State of theatrical production in Quebec prior to 1930, and developments and difficulties of the twenty years following.

1376 Porubjak, Martin. "Identitätsspiele." (Plays of Identity.) *TZ*. 1998; 6: 38-41. Illus.: Photo. B&W. 6. Lang.: Ger.

Czechoslovakia. Czech Republic. Slovakia. 1881-1998. Historical studies. ▪Describes the relationship between the theatres in the Czech Republic and Slovakia, especially the mutual cooperation and support between directors and actors from both countries.

1377 Olsen, Jakob Steen. "På stjernetaepper lyseblå." (Stars.) *TE*. 1998 Apr.; 88: 18-20. Illus.: Photo. B&W. 6. Lang.: Dan.

Denmark. 1930-1997. Historical studies. ▪In the thirties stars like Liva Weel and Bodil Ipsen were essential for the survival of a theatre because they attracted an audience. In the sixties group theatre became the ideal and still today there are very few true stars in Danish theatre.

1378 Gáspár, Máté. "A színház: vállalat és művészet: Interjú Jean-Pierre Miquellel, a Comédie Française igazgatójával." (The Theatre Is Business and Art. An Interview with Jean-Pierre Miquel, Managing Director of the Comédie-Française.) *Sz*. 1998; 31(7): 43-44. Illus.: Photo. B&W. 1. Lang.: Hun.

France. 1998. Histories-sources. ▪Miquel's managerial experiences at the Comédie-Française.

1379 Burckhardt, Barbara; Wille, Franz. "Die Jäger des verlorenen Schatzes." (The Hunters of Lost Treasure.) *THeute*. 1998; 6: 22-25. Illus.: Photo. B&W. 4. Lang.: Ger.

Germany: Bonn. 1998. Histories-sources. ▪Conversation with Tankred Dorst and Hannah Hurtzig, artistic managers of Biennale festival, about European drama and Biennale 1998 at Bonn.

1380 Dorfmüller, Ingo. "Überleben in Pforzheim." (To Survive in Pforzheim.) *DB*. 1998; 6: 45-47. Illus.: Photo. B&W. 4. Lang.: Ger.

Germany: Pforzheim. 1997-1998. Historical studies. ▪Portrait of Ernö Weil, theatre-manager at Theater Pforzheim and the beginning at this house, the future program and ideas of theatre work for audience.

1381 Engelhardt, Barbara. "'Erbsenzählerei'." ('Counting Peas'.) *TZ*. 1998; 1: 6-9. Illus.: Photo. B&W. 1. Lang.: Ger.

Germany: Bruchsal, Esslingen, Tübingen. 1998. Histories-sources. ▪Interviews with Heidemarie Rohweder of Württembergische Landesbühne Esslingen, Peter Dolder of Badische Landbühne Bruchsal and Knut Weber of Landestheater Württemberg-Hohenzollern about the changing cultural landscape in view of years of budget cuts at their theatres.

1382 Frings, Hans-Peter. "Die Stühle." (The Chairs.) *TZ*. 1998; 6: 13-15. Lang.: Ger.

Germany: Magdeburg. 1990-1998. Histories-sources. ▪As dramaturg at Freie Kammerspielen Magdeburg, Frings describes the resonsibilities of a dramaturg at the border between production and perception, business and director, theatre and audience to establish theatre as a continuous place of artistic communication.

1383 Hanke, Dirk Olaf. "Spielräume." (Play Room.) *TZ*. 1998; 5: 28-31. Lang.: Ger.

Germany: Konstanz. 1998. Histories-sources. ▪Dramaturg at Stadttheater Konstanz, describes the new responsibilities of a dramaturg as being a combination of play presenter, go-between, social therapist, and a marketing and development manager.

1384 Krug, Hartmut. "Im Wellental." (In the Valley of Waves.) *DB*. 1998; 6: 48-51. Illus.: Photo. B&W. 3. Lang.: Ger.

Germany: Greifswald, Straslund. 1997-1998. Historical studies. ▪Portrait of Rüdiger Bloch, the theatre-manager of the theatres of West Pomerania in Greifswald and Stralsund, about increasing numbers of audience in the last season.

1385 Linzer, Martin; Tiedemann, Kathrin; Rieger, Maren; Hirche, Knut; Kohse, Petra; Engelhardt, Barbara. "Auf der Suche nach Zeitgenossenschaft." (In Search of a Contemporary Form.) *TZ*. 1998; 4: 16-27. Illus.: Photo. B&W. 8. Lang.: Ger.

Germany. 1998. Histories-sources. ▪Interviews with Sven Schlöttke from Theaterhaus Jena, directors Crescentia Dünsser, Otto Kukla and Knut Hirche from Kammertheater Neubrandenburg, documentary filmmaker/director Thomas Heise and the choreographer Sasha Waltz about ideas, concepts and qualities of a modern theatre. Continued in *TZ* (1998) 5, 18-22, with interviews with directors Matthias Merkle, Michael Talke, and Erich Sedler, and in *TZ* (1998) 6, 24-29, interviewing theatre directors Michael Thalheimer and Ute Rauwald, and film and theatre director Christina Paulhofer.

1386 Merschmeier, Michael; Wille, Franz. "'Ich muss es einfach versuchen'." ('I Must Simply Try It'.) *THeute*. 1998; 5: 26-30 . Illus.: Photo. B&W. 2. Lang.: Ger.

Germany: Berlin. 1996-1998. Histories-sources. ▪Interview with Thomas Ostermeier, artistic director-designate at Schaubühne, formerly director of Deutsches Theater, Baracke.

1387 Gompes, Loes. "Het lichte levensgevoel van jonge toneelmakers verslag van de werkgroep-kassies." (The Lightness of Being: Young Theatremakers' Account of the Kassies Working Group.) *Tmaker*. 1998; 2(2): 12-16. Illus.: Photo. B&W. 3. Lang.: Dut.

Netherlands. 1998. Historical studies. ▪Report on a symposium held on the position of young theatre professionals in the Netherlands.

1388 Lewin, Jan. "Det är viktigt att stå på sig." (It's Important To Stand To It.) *Entré*. 1998: vo 25: is 2: 2-8. Illus.: Photo. B&W. Lang.: Swe.

Sweden: Stockholm. 1970-1998. Histories-sources. ▪Interview with the director of the Svenska Teaterförbundet, Tomas Bolme, about the increasing difficulties for the Swedish theatres in keeping permanent

DRAMA: —Administration

staffs of actors, and the union's need to keep its position among the actors, with reference to plans for a pool of unemployed actors.

1389 Zern, Leif. "Svensk teaterpolitik i et paradigmeskifte." (Swedish Theatre Policy in the Midst of a Paradigm Shift.) *TE*. 1998 Feb.; 87: 21-23. Illus.: Photo. B&W. 1. Lang.: Dan.
Sweden. 1974-1997. Historical studies. ■Argues that the liquidation of Göteborgs Stadsteater has nothing to do with bad economy but in fact indicates an ideological change, in which the state will no longer protect the theatre, which leads to conflict between different interest groups.

1390 Burckhardt, Barbara; Merschmeier, Michael; Wille, Franz. "Auf der Suche nach dem Trojanischen Pferd." (On Looking for the Trojan Horse.) *THeute*. 1998; Yb: 24-38. Illus.: Photo. B&W. 10. Lang.: Ger.
Switzerland: Zurich. Germany: Hannover, Berlin. 1998. Histories-sources. ■Conversation with theatre-managers Volker Hesse of Neumarkt Theater, Ulrich Khuon of Niedersächsische Staatstheater Hannover, Thomas Ostermeier of Baracke of Deutsches Theater, and Frank Castorf of Volksbühne about the future of subsidized theatres.

1391 Feller, Elisabeth. "Apokalypse flau." (Insipid Apocalypse.) *DB*. 1998; 10: 27-29. Illus.: Photo. B&W. 2. Lang.: Ger.
Switzerland: Basel. 1996-1998. Critical studies. ■Impressions of the concepts of Theater Basel under the directorship of Stefan Bachmann. Looks at William Shakespeare's *Troilus and Cressida* directed by Stefan Bachmann, Friedrich Hebbel's *Maria Magdalene* directed by Andreas Kriegenburg, and Giuseppe Verdi's *Otello* directed by Frank Castorf.

1392 Murphy, Hugh Mack, Jr. *The Company of Four at the Lyric, Hammersmith: A Paradigm for the Emergent National Theatre Concept*. Columbus, OH: Ohio State Univ; 1988. 229 pp. Biblio. Notes. [Ph.D. Dissertation, Univ. Microfilms Order No. AAC 8820327.] Lang.: Eng.
UK-England: London. 1945-1956. Histories-specific. ■Examines 'The Company of Four'—Hugh Morgan Griffiths Beaumont, Tyrone Guthrie, Norman Higgins and Rudolf Bing—which produced sixty-nine plays at the Lyric Theatre, Hammersmith.

1393 Norris, James. "A Brash Storekeeper." *PlPl*. 1998 Nov.; 528: 12-13. Lang.: Eng.
UK-England: London. Canada: Toronto, ON. 1982-1998. Histories-sources. ■Producer Ed Mirvish on owning London's Old Vic, and on producing theatre in Toronto versus London.

1394 Raab, Michael. "Ein Leben für die Autoren." (A Life for Playwrights.) *DB*. 1998; 8: 45-47. Illus.: Photo. B&W. 3. Lang.: Ger.
UK-England: London. 1908-1991. Biographical studies. ■Portrait of the theatre-agent Margaret Ramsey who managed playwrights as Alan Ayckbourn, Robert Bolt, Edward Bond, David Hare, Joe Orton and others for thirty years.

1395 "Tom Dent: Free Southern Theatre and Beyond." *BlackM*. 1998 Oct/Nov.; 13(2): 11. Illus.: Photo. B&W. 1. Lang.: Eng.
USA: New Orleans, LA. 1998. Biographical studies. ■Obituary for the one-time board chairman of the Free Southern Theatre.

1396 Caldwell, Carolyn E. *Cheryl Crawford: Her Contributions to the Development of Twentieth-Century American Theatre*. Ann Arbor, MI: Univ. of Michigan; 1987. 209 pp. Notes. Biblio. [Ph.D. Dissertation, Univ. Microfilms Order No. AAC 8801291.] Lang.: Eng.
USA. 1930-1965. Historical studies. ■Producer Cheryl Crawford's contributions to the American stage including her work at the Theatre Guild, her co-founding of the Group Theatre, co-creation of the American Repertory Theatre, and co-founding of the Actors' Studio.

1397 Dineen, Jennifer L. "Sue Frost, Vicki Nolan, Laura Penn: Top Girls." *AmTh*. 1998 Sep.; 15(7): 64-65. Illus.: Photo. B&W. 3. Lang.: Eng.
USA: New Haven, CT, Seattle, WA, East Haddam, CT. 1998. Histories-sources. ■Interview with three top women theatre managers on what it takes to excel at their profession: Sue Frost of the Goodspeed Opera House, Vicki Nolan of Yale Repertory Theatre, and Laura Penn of the Intiman Theatre.

1398 Melton, Christine. "Experiencing the Production Process." *BlackM*. 1998 May/June; 13(1): 9. Illus.: Photo. B&W. 1. Lang.: Eng.
USA: New York, NY. 1997. Histories-sources. ■Playwright's account of the process of getting her play *Still Life Goes On* produced. The play was directed by Count Stovall.

1399 Thomas, Veona. "Standing in the Gap: A Profile of Carrie Jackson." *BlackM*. 1998 Jan/Feb.; 12(6): 7-8. Illus.: Photo. B&W. 1. Lang.: Eng.
USA: New York, NY. 1998. Histories-sources. ■Interview with the new executive director of AUDELCO which is dedicated to generating new audiences for African-American theatre and dance both within and without the African-American community.

Audience

1400 Horner, Olga. "'Us Must Make Lies': Witness, Evidence, and Proof in the York *Resurrection*." *MET*. 1998; 20: 24-76. Notes. Append. Illus.: Photo. B&W. 10. Lang.: Eng.
England: York. 1275-1541. Critical studies. ■The theme of the Resurrection in the *York Cycle* plays from the point of view of the legal assumptions of the fifteenth-century York audience. Explores how and why such audiences might have reacted to certain aspects of the play, which would not be recognized as important by present-day spectators.

1401 Theaterwerkstatt Pilkentafel. "Wie mache ich ein internationales Erfolgsstück?" (How Do I Create an Internationally Successful Play?)*G&GBKM*. 1998; 129: 15-19. Illus.: Photo. B&W. 1. Lang.: Ger.
Germany: Flensburg. 1998. Histories-sources. ■Children's theatre group describes the complexity and quality of cultural exchange from experiences as a touring company.

1402 Blackadder, Neil. "Dr. Kasten, the Freie Bühne, and Audience Resistance to Naturalism." *NTQ*. 1998 Nov.; 14(4): 357-365. Notes. [Issue 56.] Lang.: Eng.
Germany: Berlin. 1889-1890. Historical studies. ■Response of one spectator, a Doctor Isidor Kasten, to the premiere of Gerhart Hauptmann's *Vor Sonnenaufgang (Before Sunrise)*, and how, paradoxically, it illustrates that increased boldness by theatre artists actually led to a more reactionary audience.

1403 Dierks, Lynn. "Arnolt Bronnen's *Vatermord* and the German Youth of 1922." *ThS*. 1998 Nov.; 39(2): 25-38. Notes. Lang.: Eng.
Germany: Frankfurt. 1922. Critical studies. ■Argues that 'spectatorial' presence and response to the premiere of Bronnen's *Der Vatermord (Parricide)* reveals clues to German cultural behavior and practice in Germany leading to the rise of Fascism and Hitler. Also considers Carl Zuckmayer's later play, *Der fröhliche Weinberg (The Happy Vineyard)*.

1404 Trotter, Mary. "Which Fiddler Calls the Tune? The *Playboy* Riots and the Politics of Nationalist Theatre Spectatorship." *ThS*. 1998 Nov.; 39(2): 39-52. Notes. Lang.: Eng.
Ireland: Dublin. 1907. Critical studies. ■The nationalist response to the premiere of John Millington Synge's *The Playboy of the Western World* by the Irish National Theatre Society at the Abbey Theatre. Argues that different tactics for political and cultural resistance were 'performed' during the riots.

1405 Magnusson, Anna. "Kan teatern förändra världen?" (Is It Possible For Theatre To Change The World?)*Dramat*. 1998; 6(2): 40-42. Illus.: Photo. Color. Lang.: Swe.
Sweden: Stockholm. 1998. Histories-sources. ■Interviews with a psychotherapist, an employer, and a young girl, after having seen playwright/director Lars Norén's *Personkrets 3:1* at Kungliga Dramatiska Teatern.

Basic theatrical documents

1406 Costi, Angela. "*Panayiota*." *ADS*. 1998 Apr.; 32: 77-108. Lang.: Eng.
Australia. 1997. ■Text of Costi's play in seventeen scenes.

1407 Bernhard, Thomas; Bou, d'Eugeni, transl. *A la meta*. (To the Goal.) Barcelona: Institut del Teatre de la Disputació de Barcelona; 1994. 167 pp. (Biblioteca Teatral 87.) Biblio. Lang.: Cat.
Austria. 1981. ■Catalan translation of *Am Ziel*.

1408 Schnitzler, Arthur; Formosa, Feliu, transl. *Anatol* i *La megalomania d'Anatol*. (Anatol and The Megolomania of Anatol.) Barcelona: Institut del Teatre de la Diputació de

DRAMA: —Basic theatrical documents

Barcelona; 1998. 144 pp. (Collecció de Teatre Clàssic Universal 51.) Biblio. Lang.: Cat.

Austria. 1889. ■Catalan translation of *Anatol* and *Anatols Grössenwahn* by Schnitzler with an introduction by Adan Kovacsics.

1409 Bose, Rana. "*Five or Six Characters in Search of Toronto.*" *CTR.* Spr 1998; 94: 63-74. Lang.: Eng.

Canada: Toronto, ON. 1993. ■Complete playtext.

1410 Healey, Michael. "*Kicked.*" *CTR.* Win 1998; 97: 77-83. Illus.: Photo. B&W. 1. Lang.: Eng.

Canada: Toronto, ON. 1993. ■Text of one-man show written and performed by Michael Healey.

1411 James, Sheila. "Excerpt from *a canadian monsoon.*" *CTR.* Spr 1998; 94: 51-54. Lang.: Eng.

Canada: Toronto, ON. 1993-1996. ■Excerpt from Toronto playwright Sheila James' *a canadian monsoon.*

1412 Varma, Rahul; Vlachos, Helen; George, Ian Lloyd. "Excerpt from *Job Stealer.*" *CTR.* 1998 Spr; 94: 28-31. Illus.: Photo. B&W. 3. Lang.: Eng.

Canada: Montreal, PQ. 1998. ■Passage about racism from play *Job Stealer* by Rahul Varma, Helen Vlachos and Ian Lloyd George, first produced by Teesri Duniya in Montreal.

1413 Radrigán, Juan. "*El príncipe desolado.*" (The Desolate Prince.) *Gestos.* 1998 Nov.; 13(26): 132-159. Lang.: Spa.

Chile. 1998. ■Text of Radrigán's play.

1414 Yan, Haiping, ed. *Theater and Society: An Anthology of Contemporary Chinese Drama.* Armonk, NY/London: M.E. Sharpe; 1998. 328 pp. (Asia and the Pacific.) Biblio. Lang.: Eng.

China, People's Republic of. 1979-1986. ■Critical anthology of contemporary Chinese drama including *Che zhan (The Bus Stop)* by Gao Xingjian, *Wm (We)* by Wang Peigong and Wang Gui, *Pan Jinlian: Yige nuren de chenlun shi (Pan Jinlian: The History of a Fallen Woman)* by Wei Minglun, and *Sangshuping jishi (Sangshuping Chronicles)* by Chen Zidu.

1415 Šnajder, Slobodan; Gaida, Maria Nicoletta, transl. "*Snake Skin.*" *PerAJ.* 1998 Sep.; 20(3): 79-113. Lang.: Eng.

Croatia. 1998. ■English translation of *Zmijin svlak*, with an introductory note by the playwright.

1416 Abu-Swailem, Abder-Rahim Elayan Moh'd. *Two Plays by Tawfiq Al-Hakim in Translation, with a Critical Introduction.* Urbana-Champaign, IL: Univ. of Illinois; 1987. 281 pp. Notes. Biblio. [Ph.D. Dissertation, Univ. Microfilms Order No. AAC 8721571.] Lang.: Eng.

Egypt. 1930-1945. ■Translations into English of *Ahl Al-kahf (The People of the Cave)* and *Pygmalion.* Includes a summary of Al-Hakim's career.

1417 Hamid, Mohamed Abubakr. *Two Plays by the Islamic Dramatist, Ali Ahmad Bakathir Translated Into English with Critical Commentary.* Urbana-Champaign, IL: Univ. of Illinois; 1988. 363 pp. Biblio. Notes. [Ph.D. Dissertation, Univ. Microfilms Order No. AAC 8908697.] Lang.: Eng.

Egypt. 1908-1969. Critical studies. ■Translation and critical study of two plays by Ali Ahmad Bakathir, *The Secret of Shahrazad* and *Harut and Marut.*

1418 McQuillen, Connie H. *Robert Burton's* Philosophaster*: A Critical Edition with English Translation.* Pullman, WA: Washington State Univ; 1987. 523 pp. Notes. Biblio. [Ph.D. Dissertation, Univ. Microfilms Order No. AAC 8724310.] Lang.: Eng.

England. 1606-1618. ■Critical edition of Burton's Latin academic play. Includes comparison of the extant manuscripts and an original English translation.

1419 Shakespeare, William; Regnault, François, transl. "*Peine d'amour perdue.*" (Love's Labour's Lost.) *AST.* 1998 Nov 15; 1038: 2-59. Illus.: Photo. B&W. 14. Lang.: Fre.

England. France. 1594-1998. ■French translation of Shakespeare's play, adapted and directed by Emmanuel Demarcy-Mota for Compagnie Théâtre des Millefontaines. Includes an introduction by the director, an essay and notes on the translation by the translator, profiles of the actors and production team, and notice of an adaptation for young audiences to be performed in the future.

1420 Shakespeare, William; de Sagarra, Josep M., transl. *Mesura per mesura.* (Measure for Measure.) Barcelona: Institut del Teatre de la Diputació de Barcelona; 1998. 148 pp. (Collecció de Teatre Clàssic Universal 27.) Biblio. Lang.: Cat.

England. 1604. ■Catalan translation of Shakespeare's play.

1421 Shakespeare, William; de Sagarra, Josep M., transl. *Romeo i Julieta.* (Romeo and Juliet.) Barcelona: Institut del Teatre de la Diputació de Barcelona; 1994. 166 pp. (Collecció de Teatre Clàssic Universal 1.) Biblio. Lang.: Cat.

England. 1591. ■Catalan translation of Shakespeare's play.

1422 Shakespeare, William; de Sagarra, Josep M., transl. *El somni d'una nit d'estiu.* (A Midsummer Night's Dream.) Barcelona: Institut del Teatre de la Diputació de Barcelona; 1994. 122 pp. (Collecció de Teatre Clàssic Universal 3.) Biblio. Lang.: Cat.

England. 1595. ■Catalan translation of Shakespeare's play.

1423 "*Les Exclusés ou Le Cabaret de la p'tite misère.*" (The Excluded, or The Poverty Cabaret.) *AST.* 1998 Dec 1; 1039: 2-40. Illus.: Photo. B&W. 16. Lang.: Fre.

France. 1998. ■Dialogue, music, and poetry by several authors as adapted and staged by Isabelle Starkier. Includes an essay by the director, brief biographies of the writers and actors, and a profile of the director and her company Star Théâtre.

1424 d'Anna, Claude; Bonin, Laure. "*Pour la galerie.*" (For the Gallery.) *AST.* 1998 Oct 1; 1035: 2-37. Illus.: Photo. Dwg. B&W. 19. Lang.: Fre.

France. 1998. ■Text of the play as directed by Stephan Meldegg in a coproduction of Théâtre de l'Oeuvre and Théâtre La Bruyère. Includes profiles of the playwrights, directors, Théâtre La Bruyère, actors, and production team.

1425 Gerbaulet, Françoise. "*Le Roi Hâtif.*" (King Hasty.) *AST.* 1998 1 Mar.; 1025: 2-36. Illus.: Photo. B&W. 20. Lang.: Fre.

France. 1993-1998. ■Text of Gerbaulet's play for children, which was originally performed as a radio play in 1993, as produced by Théâtre du Renard, directed by Gérard Rauber. Includes profiles of the author, director, actors, and theatre company.

1426 Guitry, Sacha. "*Jean III ou L'Irrésistible Vocation du fils Mondoucet.*" (John III or the Irresistible Vocation of Young Mondoucet.) *AST.* 1998 1 Jan.; 1021: 3-44. Illus.: Photo. B&W. 21. Lang.: Fre.

France. 1912-1998. ■Text of Guitry's play as revived by director Francis Perrin at Théâtre Montansier. Includes profiles of the author, director, and actors, bibliography and a note on the writing of the play, and excerpts from press reviews.

1427 Haïm, Victor. "*Le Vampire suce toujours deux fois.*" (The Vampire Always Sucks Twice.) *AST.* 1998 Oct 15; 1036: 2-36 . Illus.: Photo. B&W. 18. Lang.: Fre.

France. 1998. ■Text of the play as directed by José Valverde for the Théâtre des Auteurs Vivants. Includes profiles of the playwright and actors, an essay by the director, and reproductions of two manuscript pages with sketches.

1428 Koltès, Bernard-Marie; Belbel, Sergi, transl. *La nit just abans dels boscos.* (The Dark Just Before the Forests.) Barcelona: Institut del Teatre de la Disputació de Barcelona; 1993. 63 pp. (Biblioteca Teatral 81.) Biblio. Lang.: Cat.

France. 1977. ■Catalan translation of *La Nuit juste avant les forêts.*

1429 Lainé, Pascal. "*Capitaine Bringuier.*" *AST.* 1998 July 15; 1034: 3-39. Illus.: Photo. B&W. 22. Lang.: Fre.

France. 1998. ■Text of Lainé's play as produced by the Compagnie Pierre Santini at the Avignon OFF festival. Santini was also director and one of the two actors. Includes profiles of the actors and playwright.

1430 Levoyer, Gérard. "*Mendiants d'amour.*" (Beggars of Love.) *AST.* 1998 15 May; 1030: 2-22. Illus.: Photo. B&W. 14. Lang.: Fre.

France. 1998. ■Text of Levoyer's play as directed by Bernard Bolzer for Théâtre du Ricochet. Includes profiles of the author, director, actors, and theatre company.

1431 Levoyer, Gérard. "*L'Ascenseur.*" (The Elevator.) *AST.* 1998 15 May; 1030: 23-37. Illus.: Photo. B&W. 4. Lang.: Fre.

DRAMA: —Basic theatrical documents

France. 1984-1987. ■Text of Levoyer's play as directed by Yann Le Bonnieck for Théâtre de Dix-Heures. The production appeared at the Avignon festival in 1984 and 1987. Includes excerpts from press reviews.

1432 Marivaux, Pierre Carlet de Chamblain de; Teixidor, Jordi, transl. *El joc de l'amor i de l'atzar.* (The Play of Love and Chance.) Barcelona: Institut del Teatre de la Diputació de Barcelona; 1993. 79 pp. (Collecció de Teatre Clàssic Universal 37.) Biblio. Lang.: Cat.

France. 1730. ■Catalan translation of *Le Jeu de l'amour et du hasard* with an introduction by the translator.

1433 Molière (Poquelin, Jean-Baptiste); Vidal, Josep M., transl. *Les dones sàvies.* (The Learned Ladies.) Barcelona: Institut del Teatre de la Diputació de Barcelona; 1994. 111 pp. (Collecció de Teatre Clàssic Universal 40.) Lang.: Cat.

France. 1672. ■Catalan translation of *Les Femmes savantes* with an introduction on his style of comedy by Emili Teixidor.

1434 Sauvil, Pierre. "*Soleil pour deux.*" (Sun for Two.) *AST.* 1998 Dec 15; 1040: 2-40. Illus.: Photo. B&W. 5. Lang.: Fre.

France. 1998. ■Text of Sauvil's play as directed by Christian Bugeau, Théâtre Montparnasse. Includes profiles of and notes by the playwright and director.

1435 Shart, Raffy. "*Ma femme s'appelle Maurice.*" (My Wife's Name Is Maurice.) *AST.* 1998 Nov 1; 1037: 2-47. Illus.: Photo. B&W. 24. Lang.: Fre.

France. 1998. ■Text of the play as directed by Jean-Luc Moreau at Théâtre du Gymnase. Includes a brief biography and interview with the playwright, profiles of the director, actors, and production team, and excerpts from press reviews.

1436 Visdei, Anca. "*La Médée de Saint-Médard.*" (The Medea of Saint-Medard.) *AST.* 1998 July 1; 1033: 2-33. Illus.: Photo. B&W. 16. Lang.: Fre.

France. 1998. ■Text of Visdei's play as directed by Jacques Échantillon for Comédie de Saint-Étienne. Includes profiles of author, director, and actors, and excerpts from press reviews.

1437 Brecht, Bertolt; Formosa, Clara, transl.; Negre, Isabel, transl.; Formosa, Feliu, transl.; Monton, Ramon, transl.; Fontcuberta, Joan, transl.; Serrallonga, Carme, transl. *Bertolt Brecht: Teatre Complet I.* (Bertolt Brecht: Complete Plays I.) Barcelona: Institut del Teatre de la Disputació de Barcelona; 1999. 720 pp. (Clàssics 5.) Biblio. Pref. Lang.: Cat.

Germany. 1919-1954. ■Catalan translations of *Die Bibel (The Bible), Baal, Trommeln in der Nacht (Drums in the Night), Die Hochzeit (Wedding), Leben Eduards des Zweiten von England (Edward the Second),* with Lion Feuchtwanger, *Mann ist Mann (A Man's a Man), Die Dreigroschenoper (The Threepenny Opera), Aufstieg und Fall der Stadt Mahagonny (Rise and Fall of the City of Mahagonny), Lux in Tenebris, Im Dickicht der Städte (In the Jungle of Cities), Prärie (Prairie), Der Fischzug (The Catch), Er treibt einen Teufel aus (He Exorcizes a Devil),* and *Der Bettler, oder Der tote Hund (The Beggar, or the Dead Dog).*

1438 Aristophanes; Carandell, Christían, transl. *Lisístrata.* (Lysistrata.) Barcelona: Institut del Teatre de la Diputació de Barcelona; 1993. 91 pp. (Collecció de Teatre Clàssic Universal 32.) Lang.: Cat.

Greece. 435 B.C. ■Catalan translation of Aristophanes' comedy with an introduction by the translator.

1439 Scala, Alexander. "A Smock Alley Prompt Book for *Tyrannick Love.*" *TN.* 1998; 52(2): 65-90. Notes. Lang.: Eng.

Ireland: Dublin. 1669-1684. Textual studies. ■Detailed analysis of the promptbook for the Smock Alley Theatre's production of John Dryden's play. Conjectures are offered for the date of the production, identification of the actors, and the staging.

1440 Fo, Dario; Roth, Frans, transl. *Dagboeu van Eva en Andere Teksten voor vrouwen.* (Eve's Diary and Other Texts for Women.) Amsterdam/Leuven: ITFB/Kritak; 1997. 199 pp. Pref. Lang.: Dut.

Italy. 1998. ■Dutch translation of Fo's monologues for women.

1441 Fo, Dario; Kravos, Bogomila, transl. *Burkaški misterij.* (Mistero Buffo.) Radovljica: Didakta; 1998. 114 pp. Pref. Biblio. Lang.: Slo.

Italy. Slovenia. 1969-1997. Histories-sources. ■Slovene translation of Nobel prizewinner Dario Fo's *Mistero Buffo.* Includes an essay on Dario Fo and his political theatre and a bibliography of his work.

1442 Goldoni, Carlo; Desclot, Miquel, transl. *El ventall.* (The Fan.) Barcelona: Institut del Teatre de la Diputació de Barcelona; 1993. 123 pp. (Collecció de Teatre Clàssic Universal 35.) Biblio. Lang.: Cat.

Italy. 1765. ■Catalan translation of *Il Ventaglio* with a chronology of the playwright's life.

1443 Goldoni, Carlo; Melendres, Jaume, transl. *Els enamorats.* (The Lovers.) Barcelona: Institut del Teatre de la Diputació de Barcelona; 1993. 95 pp. (Collecció de Teatre Clàssic Universal 36.) Biblio. Lang.: Cat.

Italy. 1765. ■Catalan translation of *Gl' Innamorati* with an introduction about character conflicts in Goldoni's plays, and a list of all his plays.

1444 Goldoni, Carlo; Puértolas, Pere, transl. *El Café.* (The Coffee Shop.) Barcelona: Institut del Teatre de la Diputació de Barcelona; 1993. 125 pp. (Collecció de Teatre Clàssic Universal 38.) Notes. Biblio. Lang.: Cat.

Italy. 1750. ■Catalan translation of *La Bottega del caffè* with an introduction by Goldoni himself.

1445 Pirandello, Luigi; Barbina, Alfredo, ed. "Un epilogo in versi." (An Epilogue in Verse.) *Ariel.* 1998; 13(1-2): 9-41. Lang.: Ita.

Italy. 1884-1887. ■The text of an untitled, unfinished, and prviously unpublished play in verse by Luigi Pirandello. Includes an introduction by the editor.

1446 Ždanko, O. *Dramaturgi—laureaty Nobelevskoj premii: Hose Ečegaraj-i- Ejsagirre. Gerhart Gauptman. Hasinto Benavente-i-Martines. Judžin O'Nil. Sémjuél' Bekket. Vole Šojinka. Dario Fo.* (The Playwrights—Winners of the Nobel Prize: José Echegaray, Gerhart Hauptmann, Jacinto Benavente, Eugene O'Neill, Samuel Beckett, Wole Soyinka, Dario Fo.) Moscow: Panorama; 1998. 464 pp. (B - ka 'Laureaty Nobel. premii'.) Lang.: Rus.

Italy. 1848-1998. ■Texts of plays by Nobel laureates: José Echegaray (1848-1927), Gerhart Hauptmann (1862-1946), Jacinto Benavente (1866-1954), Eugene O'Neill (1888-1953), Samuel Beckett (1906-1990), Dario Fo (1926-), and Wole Soyinka (1934-). Includes articles about the playwrights.

1447 Berman, Sabina; Versényi, Adam, transl. "*The Mustache.*" *PerAJ.* 1998 May; 20(2): 111-118. Lang.: Eng.

Mexico. 1992. ■English translation of Berman's play.

1448 Gombrowicz, Witold; Kuharski, Allen, transl.; Bukowski, Dariusz, transl. "*History.*" *PerAJ.* 1998 Jan.; 20(58): 99-117. Notes. Lang.: Eng.

Poland. 1998. ■English translation of *Historia.*

1449 Čechov, Anton Pavlovič; Casas, Joan, transl.; Avrova, Nina, transl.; Formasa, Felio, transl. *Anton Txèkhov: Teatre Complet.* (Anton Čechov: Complete Plays.) Barcelona: Institut del Teatre de la Disputació de Barcelona; 1998. 455 pp, 519 pp. (Clàssics 3, 4.) Biblio. Pref. [2 vols.] Lang.: Cat.

Russia. 1884-1904. ■Catalan translations of the plays of Čechov.

1450 Gogol, Nikolaj; Mejerchol'd, Vsevolod; Chambers, David, transl.; Križanskaja, Daria, transl. "*Revizor.*" *ThM.* 1998 ; 28(2): 61-78. Notes. Biblio. Illus.: Photo. Sketches. B&W. 11. Lang.: Eng.

Russia. USSR. 1838-1926. ■Translation of the fourth episode of Mejerchol'd's adaptation of Gogol's *The Inspector General (Revizor).*

1451 Švarc, E.L. *Proza. Stichotvorenija. Dramaturgija.* (Prose, Poetry, Plays.) Moscow: Olimp; 1998. 640 pp. (Škola klassiki.) Lang.: Rus.

Russia. 1998. ■Anthology of literary works, with commentary and annotations, to be used for educational purposes.

1452 Vysockij, V.S.; Žil'cov, S., ed. *Proza. Dramaturgija. Dnevniki. Pis'ma.* (Prose, Drama, Diaries, Letters.) Tula: Tulica; 1998. 660 pp. (Sobr. soč..) Lang.: Rus.

Russia: Moscow. 1998. ■Collected writings of Vladimir Vysockij, including his plays.

DRAMA: —Basic theatrical documents

1453 Vysockij, V.S. *Ja ne ljublju...: Pesni, stichotvorenija.* (I Don't Like...: Songs, Poems.) Moscow: ÈKSMO-Press; 1998. 480 pp. (The Poetry House.) Lang.: Rus.
Russia: Moscow. 1938-1980. ▪Works of singer/actor Vladimir Vysockij.

1454 Car, Evgen. *Poredušov Janoš.* Murska Sobota: Pomurska založba; 1998. 87 pp. Illus.: Photo. B&W. 35. Lang.: Slo.
Slovenia. 1968-1998. ▪The complete text of a monologue *Poredušov Janoš*, by the Slovene actor Evgen Car. Text includes a photographic appendix of Car's stage work.

1455 Filipčič, Emil. "*Suženj akcije (Kralj Peter Šesti).*" (A Slave of Action (King Peter the Sixth).) *Dialogi.* 1998; 904(11-12): 79-110. Lang.: Slo.
Slovenia. 1997. ▪Text of *Suženj akcije—Kralj Peter Šesti (A Slave of Action—King Peter the Sixth)* by Emil Filipčič.

1456 Flisar, Evald. "*Sončne pege.*" (Sunspots.) *Sodobnost.* 1998; 1006(11-12): 928-987. Lang.: Slo.
Slovenia. 1997. ▪Text of *Sončne pege (Sunspots)* by Evald Flisar.

1457 Mikeln, Miloš. *Miklavžev večer.* (St. Nicholas' Eve.) Ljubljana: Knjižna zadruga; 1998. 93 pp. Lang.: Slo.
Slovenia. 1997. ▪Full text of *Miklavžev večer (St. Nicholas' Eve)* by Miloš Mikeln.

1458 Möderndorfer, Vinko; Lukan, Blaž, ed. *Vaja zbora.* (Choir Practice.) Ljubljana: Tespis; 1998. 295 pp. Notes. Lang.: Slo.
Slovenia. 1997. ▪Full texts of three comedies: *Vaja zbora (Choir Practice), Mama je umria dvakrat (Mama Died Twice)*, and *Transvestitska svatba (Transvestite Wedding)*, all by Vinko Möderndorfer.

1459 Mrak, Ivan; Schmidt, Goran, ed. *Izbrano delo.* (Selected Works.) Ljubljana: Mladinska knjiga; 1998. 304 pp. (Knjižnica Kondor 283.) Notes. Index. Biblio. Illus.: Photo. B&W. 3. Lang.: Slo.
Slovenia. 1930-1975. ▪A selection of prose, drama, and diary entries by Mrak, with an introduction by the editor. Plays include *Emigrantska tragedija (An Émigré Tragedy), Marija Tudor (Mary Tudor)*, and *Herodus Magnus.* Book also includes an extensive bibliography with notes on individual performances of the plays.

1460 Ravnjak, Vili. *Feniksov let.* (The Flight of the Phoenix.) Maribor: Vili Ravnjak; 1998. 308 pp. Lang.: Slo.
Slovenia. 1991-1997. ▪Full playtexts of four plays and two screen plays by literary adaptor Vili Ravnjak: *Potovanje v Rim (A Journey to Rome), Aneks (Annex), Tugomer, ali tisti, ki meri žalost (Tugomer, or the One Who Measures Sadness), Vonj črnih vrtnic (The Fragrance of Black Roses), Feniksov let (The Flight of the Phoenix)*, and *Giordano Bruno.*

1461 Rozman, Branko; Poniž, Denis, ed. *Obsodili so Kristusa.* (They Condemned Christ.) Celje: Mohorjeva družba; 1998. 139 pp. (Zbirka Žerjavi 2.) Pref. Notes. Lang.: Slo.
Slovenia. 1990-1997. ▪Three plays by Slovene emigrant writer and dramatist, Branko Rozman: *Obsodili so Kristusa (They Condemned Christ), Človek, ki je umoril Boga (The Man Who Killed God)*, and *Roka za steno (The Hand Behind the Wall).* Also includes a chronology of Rozman's life and work.

1462 Saksida, Igor, ed. *Ime mi je igra.* (The Play Is My Name.) Maribor: Obzorja; 1998. 355 pp. Index. Pref. Lang.: Slo.
Slovenia. 1800-1988. ▪Twelve complete playtexts of Slovene youth drama.

1463 Alberola, Carles. "*Mandíbula afilada.*" (Sharp Chin.) *Gestos.* 1998 Apr.; 13(25): 164-202. Illus.: Photo. Poster. B&W. 3. Lang.: Eng.
Spain. 1997. ▪Text of Alberola's play with an introduction on the playwright's sense of comedy.

1464 Casona, Alejandro; Camp, André, transl. "*Trois diamants, plus une femme.*" (Three Diamonds and One Woman.) *AST.* 1998 15 Apr.; 1028: 2-48. Illus.: Photo. B&W. 26. Lang.: Fre.
Spain. France. 1959-1998. ▪French translation of *Tres diamantes y una mujer* as directed by Pierre Richy for L'Atelier Théâtre des Compagnons. Includes profiles of the author, director, actors, and scenographer.

1465 Egea, Octavi. *Davant l'Empire.* (Inside the Empire.) Barcelona: Institut del Teatre de la Disputació de Barcelona; 1999. 65 pp. (Biblioteca Teatral 97.) Biblio. Lang.: Cat.
Spain-Catalonia. 1999. ▪Text of Egea's play.

1466 Muñoz Pujol, Josep M. *Seducció/Dificultat pel domini de la casa.* (Seduction/Difficulties of Running the House.) Barcelona: Institut del Teatre de la Disputació de Barcelona; 1995. 201 pp. (Biblioteca Teatral 86.) Biblio. Lang.: Cat.
Spain-Catalonia. 1995. ▪Text of two plays by Muñoz Pujol.

1467 Sarrias Fornés, Mercè. *Àfrica 30.* Barcelona: Institut del Teatre de la Disputació de Barcelona; 1997. 74 pp. (Biblioteca Teatral 96.) Biblio. Lang.: Cat.
Spain-Catalonia. 1997. ▪Text of Sarrias' play.

1468 Teixidor, Jordi. *Magnus.* Barcelona: Institut del Teatre de la Disputació de Barcelona; 1994. 88 pp. (Biblioteca Teatral 82.) Biblio. Lang.: Cat.
Spain-Catalonia. 1994. ▪Text of Teixidor's play.

1469 Bezencon, Hélène. "*Arrête de rêver, l'Etrangère.*" (Stop Dreaming, Stranger.) *Mimos.* 1998; 1: I-XXII. Illus.: Photo. B&W. 1. Lang.: Fre.
Switzerland. 1998. ▪Text of a piece on the author Annemarie Schwarzenbach, 1929-1942.

1470 Svetina, Ivo, ed., transl. *Trije tibetanski misteriji.* (Three Tibetan Mysteries.) Ljubljana: Mladinska knjiga; 1998. 334 pp. (Knjižnica Kondor 284.) Notes. Biblio. Lang.: Slo.
Tibet. 1400-1990. ▪Three anonymous characteristic works from the Tibetan dramatic tradition: *Chrimekundan, Jroazanmo* and *Nansal.* Includes history of Tibetan theatre and its relationship to the Buddhist verse tradition.

1471 Ayckbourn, Alan; Lauzier, Gérard, transl. "*1 Table pour 6.*" (Time of My Life.) *AST.* 1998 1 Feb.; 1023: 2-59. Illus.: Photo. B&W. 24. Lang.: Fre.
UK-England. France. 1993-1998. ▪French translation of *Time of My Life* as directed by Alain Sachs at Théâtre du Palais-Royal. Includes profiles of the author, translator, director, actors, and design team.

1472 Barrie, Tom, adapt. "*Example: The Case of Craig and Bentley.*" *PI.* 1998 Oct.; 14(1): 32-45. Lang.: Eng.
UK-England. 1998. ▪Text of a play devised by Belgrade Theatre TIE and adapted and directed by Barrie.

1473 Cooney, Ray; Blanc, Michel, adapt.; Jugnot, Gérard, adapt.; Vaughan, Stewart, transl. "*Espèces menacées.*" (Funny Money.) *AST.* 1998 15 Feb.; 1024: 2-59. Illus.: Photo. B&W. 13. Lang.: Fre.
UK-England. France. 1995-1997. ▪French translation of *Funny Money* as directed by Eric Civanyan for Théâtre de la Michodière. Includes profiles of the author, adaptors, director, and actors, as well as excerpts from press reviews.

1474 Dowie, John. "*Jesus, My Boy.*" *PI.* 1998 Dec.; 14(3): 38-48. Illus.: Photo. B&W. 1. Lang.: Eng.
UK-England. 1998. ▪Text of Dowie's monologue as performed by Tom Conti.

1475 Elton, Ben; Guedj, Attica, transl.; Meldegg, Stephan, transl. "*Popcorn.*" *AST.* 1998 15 Jan.; 1022: 2-47. Illus.: Photo. B&W. 22. Lang.: Fre.
UK-England. France. 1996-1998. ▪French translation of Elton's play as presented by Théâtre La Bruyère, directed by Stephan Meldegg. Includes profiles of author, director, actors, and design team.

1476 Lewis, David. "*Sperm Wars.*" *PI.* 1998 Nov.; 14(2): 30-45. Lang.: Eng.
UK-England. 1998. ▪Text of Lewis' play as directed by Sam Walters at the Orange Tree, Richmond.

1477 Pinter, Harold. "First Draft, *The Homecoming.*" *PintR.* 1998: 1-30. Illus.: Graphs. B&W. 1. Lang.: Eng.
UK-England. 1964. ▪Typescript of the first draft of Pinter's play with holographic corrections.

1478 Shaw, George Bernard; Melendres, Jaume, transl. *L'home i les armes.* (Arms and the Man.) Barcelona: Institut del Teatre de la Diputació de Barcelona; 1998. 121 pp. (Col·lecció de Teatre Clàssic Universal 52.) Lang.: Cat.
UK-England. 1894. ▪Catalan translation of Shaw's play with a translated preface by the playwright.

DRAMA: —Basic theatrical documents

1479 Wilde, Oscar; Melendres, Jaume, transl. *La importancia de ser Frank.* (The Importance of Being Earnest.) Barcelona: Institut del Teatre de la Diputació de Barcelona; 1998. 71 pp. (Collecció de Teatre Clàssic Universal 53.) Lang.: Cat.
UK-England. 1895. ■Catalan translation of Oscar Wilde's comedy with an introduction by the translator.

1480 Alexander, Elizabeth. "*Diva Studies.*" *Callaloo.* 1996 Spr; 19(2): 475-492. Illus.: Photo. B&W. 1. Lang.: Eng.
USA. 1996. ■Excerpt from Alexander's verse play.

1481 Aronin, Marc J. *A Readers' Theatre Program: 'Like Father, Like Son'.* Garden City, NY: Adelphi Univ; 1987. 92 pp. Notes. Biblio. [M.A. Thesis, Univ. Microfilms Order No. AAC 1330479.] Lang.: Eng.
USA. 1987. ■Text of an original play.

1482 Bradley, Eddie Paul, Jr. *Negritude: Three Plays for the African-American Theatre.* Carbondale, IL: Southern Illinois Univ; 1998. 321 pp. Biblio. Notes. [Ph.D. Dissertation, Univ. Microfilms Order No. 9902716.] Lang.: Eng.
USA. 1998. ■Three original plays based on historical incidents: *Ray & Sons, An Evening with Ira Aldridge,* and *Autumn's Song.* Also includes an analysis of the dramatic form of African-American theatre since the Harlem Renaissance.

1483 Criswell, Sheryle. "... *Where Late the Sweet Birds Sang.*" *SoTh.* 1998 Fall; 39(4): 11-22. Lang.: Eng.
USA. 1998. ■Text of ... *Where Late the Sweet Birds Sang* by Sheryle Criswell.

1484 Evarts, William Johnson. *The Ballad of Sam Bass.* Denton, TX: Univ. of North Texas; 1988. 122 pp. Biblio. Notes. [M.A. Thesis, Univ. Microfilms Order No. AAC 1334907.] Lang.: Eng.
USA. 1988. ■Text of original play.

1485 Green, Mark R. "*The Metropolitan* (formerly *The Ten Minute Play*)." *Callaloo.* 1998 Win; 21(1): 165-174. Lang.: Eng.
USA. 1995. ■Complete text of Green's play.

1486 Greenberg, Richard. "*Three Days of Rain.*" *AmTh.* 1998 Mar.; 15(3): 19-37. Illus.: Photo. B&W. 5. Lang.: Eng.
USA. 1998. ■Text of Greenberg's play with an introductory interview with the playwright.

1487 Hoch, Danny. "*Jails, Hospitals & Hip-Hop.*" *AmTh.* 1998 July/Aug.; 15(6): 29-44. Illus.: Photo. B&W. 9. Lang.: Eng.
USA. 1998. ■Text of Hoch's play with an introductory interview with the playwright.

1488 Horovitz, Israel. "*Lebensraum (Espace Vital).*" *AST.* 1998 June 1-15; 1031/1032: 2-46. Illus.: Photo. B&W. 15. Lang.: Fre.
USA. France. 1996-1997. ■French translation of *Lebensraum* as adapted and presented by Compagnie Hercub' at the Avignon festival in 1997. Includes an essay by the playwright, profiles of Compagnie Hercub', the production team and actors, and excerpts from press reviews.

1489 Horovitz, Israel. "*Les Sept Familles.*" (The Primary English Class.) *AST.* 1998 June 1-15; 1031/1032: 47-92. Illus.: Photo. B&W. 10. Lang.: Fre.
USA. France. 1996. ■French translation and adaptation of *The Primary English Class* as directed by Michel Burstin at the Avignon festival with Compagnie Hercub' in 1996. Includes profiles of the actors and production team, excerpts from press reviews.

1490 Jackson, Shannon. "*White Noises.*" *TDR.* 1998 Spr; 42(1): 56-65. Illus.: Photo. B&W. 1. Lang.: Eng.
USA. 1998. ■Text of Jackson's solo piece.

1491 Kalinoski, Richard; Loayza, Daniel, transl. "*Une Bête sur la lune.*" (Beast on the Moon.) *AST.* 1998 1 May; 1029: 2-43. MA. Illus.: Photo. B&W. 12. Lang.: Fre.
USA. France. 1995-1997. ■French translation of *Beast on the Moon* as coproduced by La MC 93 Bobigny and Théâtre Vidy, directed by Irina Brook. Includes profiles of the author, translator, director, and actors, excerpts from press reviews, and an essay on the genocide of Armenians (the subject of the play).

1492 Karp, Jack Martin. *Medicine Men.* Washington, DC: American Univ; 1998. 100 pp. Notes. Biblio. [M.F.A. Thesis, Univ. Microfilms Order No. AAC 1388994.] Lang.: Eng.
USA. 1998. ■Text of *Medicine Men* by Jack Martin Karp, written in fulfillment of an M.F.A. degree.

1493 Kristy-Brooks, Kathleen. *Dreams: A Dramatico.* Boulder, CO: Univ. of Colorado; 1988. 121 pp. Notes. Biblio. [Ph.D. Dissertation, Univ. Microfilms Order No. AAC 8912232.] Lang.: Eng.
USA. 1988. ■Text of original play.

1494 Leight, Warren. "*Side Man.*" *AmTh.* 1998 Dec.; 15(10): 29-47. Illus.: Photo. B&W. 6. Lang.: Eng.
USA. 1998. ■Text of Leight's play with an introductory interview with the playwright.

1495 Lunde, Robert Charles. *The Country Mouse and the City Mouse.* Denton, TX: Univ. of North Texas; 1987. 66 pp. Biblio. Notes. [M.A. Thesis, Univ. Microfilms Order No. 1330280.] Lang.: Eng.
USA. 1986. ■Text of original play.

1496 Mee, Charles L. *History Plays.* Baltimore, MD/London: Johns Hopkins Univ P; 1998. 329 pp. (PAJ Books.) Lang.: Eng.
USA. 1986-1995. ■Collection of plays by Charles L. Mee: *Vienna: Lusthaus, Orestes, The War to End War, The Investigation of the Murder in El Salvador, The Trojan Women a Love Story* and *Time to Burn.*

1497 Meyer, Marlane. "*The Chemistry of Change.*" *AmTh.* 1998 Sep.; 15(7): 35-55. Illus.: Dwg. B&W. 3. Lang.: Eng.
USA. 1998. ■Text of Meyer's play, with an introductory interview with the playwright.

1498 Miller, Susan; Manuel, Alexis, transl. "*Mon sein gauche.*" (My Left Breast.) *AST.* 1998 Dec 1; 1039: 41-58. Illus.: Photo. B&W. 7. Lang.: Fre.
USA. France. 1994-1998. ■Text of Miller's monodrama as adapted by Alexis Manuel and the performer, Michèle Simonnet, and directed by Philippe Noël. Includes profiles of all personnel.

1499 Morton, Carlos. *Three Plays on the Latin Experience in America.* Austin, TX: Univ. of Texas; 1987. 228 pp. Biblio. Notes. [Ph.D. Dissertation, Univ. Microfilms Order No. 8717489.] Lang.: Eng.
USA. 1986. ■Three plays dealing with various aspects of the Latin experience in America—*Johnny Tenorio, Malinche,* and *Hernan Cortez.*

1500 O'Hara, Robert. "*Insurrection: Holding History.*" *AmTh.* 1998 Feb.; 15(2): 25-49. Illus.: Photo. B&W. 6. Lang.: Eng.
USA. 1998. ■Text of O'Hara's play. Includes introductory interview with the playwright.

1501 Parks, Suzan-Lori. "*Venus.*" *Callaloo.* 1996 Spr; 19(2): 301-308. Lang.: Eng.
USA. 1995. ■Complete text of Parks' play.

1502 Purdy, James. "*Heatstroke.*" *PerAJ.* 1998 May; 20(2): 76-81. Lang.: Eng.
USA. 1989. ■Text of Purdy's one-act play.

1503 Ritter, Scott R. *A Day at Musemeci's.* DeKalb, IL: Northern Illinois Univ; 1987. 206 pp. [Ph.D. Dissertation, Univ. Microfilms Order No. AAC 8729551.] Lang.: Eng.
USA. 1987. ■Text of an original play.

1504 Robertson, Beverly J. *GBS: Fighting to Live Again.* Dominguez Hills, CA: California State Univ; 1998. 90 pp. Notes. Biblio. [M.A. Thesis, Univ. Microfilms Order No. AAC 1389348.] Lang.: Eng.
USA. 1997. ■Playtext of original play, *GBS: Fighting to Live Again* by Beverly J. Robertson in fulfillment of an M.A. degree.

1505 Robertson, Lanie; Spinneweber, Rémy, transl. "*Alfred aime O'Keeffe.*" (Alfred Stieglitz Loves O'Keeffe.) *AST.* 1998 15 Mar.; 1026: 2-44. Illus.: Photo. B&W. 24. Lang.: Fre.
USA. France. 1987-1997. ■French translation of *Alfred Stieglitz Loves O'Keeffe* as directed by Georges Werler for Théâtre des 2 Rives. Includes profiles of the author, adaptor/translator, director, actors, notes on the scenography, historical characters, and the Parisian venue, Théâtre Silvia Monfort, as well as excerpts from press reviews.

DRAMA: —Basic theatrical documents

1506 Rose, Chris Edwin. *WWW.chat, Elevator, and Selected Fiction.* Long Beach, CA: California State Univ; 1998. 143 pp. Notes. Biblio. [M.F.A. Thesis, Univ. Microfilms Order No. AAC 1390961.] Lang.: Eng.
USA. 1998. ■Includes texts of two original plays.

1507 Rowe, Catherine Louise. *Contemporary Issues for High School Students.* Dominguez Hills, CA: California State Univ; 1998. 34 pp. Notes. Biblio. [M.A. Thesis, Univ. Microfilms Order No. AAC 1389334.] Lang.: Eng.
USA. 1997. ■Untitled playtext for teenagers that focuses on conflict resolution in fulfillment of an M.A. degree.

1508 Sandberg, Leslie Jean. *The Sisterhood of Dark Sanctuary.* Denton, TX: Univ. of North Texas; 1987. 47 pp. Biblio. Notes. [M.A. Thesis, Univ. Microfilms Order No. 1330289.] Lang.: Eng.
USA. 1986. ■Text of original play.

1509 Scheffer, Will. "*Falling Man* and Other Monologues." *PerAJ.* 1998 May; 20(2): 99-110. Lang.: Eng.
USA. 1997. ■Text of *Falling Man, Alien Boy* and *Tennessee and Me.*

1510 Speisman, Barbara Waddell. *'Zora', 'Color Struck and Weary Blues' and 'Tea with Zora and Marjorie': Three Plays About the Life of Zora Neale Hurston.* Tallahassee, FL: Florida State Univ; 1988. 160 pp. Biblio. Notes. [Ph.D. Dissertation, Univ. Microfilms Order No. AAC 8814435.] Lang.: Eng.
USA. 1988. ■Texts of three original plays.

1511 Taylor, Dominick A. "*Sound Check.*" *Callaloo.* 1998 Win; 21(1): 111-118. Lang.: Eng.
USA. 1994. ■Complete text of Taylor's play.

1512 Tucker, Sharon Gayle. *S.T.C.: A Play in Three Acts.* Memphis, TN: Memphis State Univ; 1988. 105 pp. Biblio. Notes. [M.A. Thesis, Univ. Microfilms Order No. AAC 1334707.] Lang.: Eng.
USA. 1988. ■Text of original play.

Design/technology

1513 Molloy, Jacqueline. "Australia Onstage: Illuminating National Heritage with the Black Swan Theatre Company." *LDim.* 1998 Nov.; 22(10): 90-95. Illus.: Photo. B&W. 14. Lang.: Eng.
Australia: Fremantle. 1998. Historical studies. ■Examines the Black Swan Theatre Company (artistic director Andrew Ross), concentrating on the work of lighting designer Mark Howett on *Cloudstreet* (adapted from novel of same name by Tim Winton), directed by Neil Armfield, staged in a vacant boatshed.

1514 Lesage, Marie-Christine. "Une esthétique du recyclage: Isabelle Larivière, costumière." (An Aesthetic of Recycling: Isabelle Larivière, Costume Designer.) *JCT.* 1998; 86: 122-127. Notes. Illus.: Photo. Sketches. B&W. 9. Lang.: Fre.
Canada: Quebec, PQ. 1994-1995. Biographical studies. ■Costume designer Isabelle Larivière's technique of creating original costumes out of existing clothing, applied to three productions at Théâtre Trident: Johnson's *Volpone* directed by Serge Denoncourt in 1994, Brecht's *Le Cercle de craie caucasien (The Caucasian Chalk Circle)* directed by Denoncourt in 1995, and Shakespeare's *Le songe d'une nuit d'été (A Midsummer Night's Dream)*, directed by Robert Lepage in 1995.

1515 Lesage, Marie-Christine. "Matière vivante: Jean Hazel, scènographe." (Living Matter: Jean Hazel, Set Designer.) *JCT.* 1998; 86: 128-133. Illus.: Photo. B&W. 3. Lang.: Fre.
Canada: Quebec, PQ. 1985-1998. Biographical studies. ■Scenery as sculptural metaphor for the text in set designer Jean Hazel's collaborations with director Gilles Champagne of Théâtre Blanc.

1516 Rickerd, Julie Rekai. "Robert Lepage." *TCI.* 1998 July; 32(7): 19. Illus.: Photo. B&W. Color. 2. Lang.: Eng.
Canada: Quebec, PQ. 1998. Technical studies. ■Director Robert Lepage's set design for his new work *Geometry of Miracles*, about architect Frank Lloyd Wright, performed by his group Ex Machina at a renovated fire station called La Caserne.

1517 Burian, Jarka M. "Svoboda's Scenography for *Faust*: Evolution in the Use of Mirrors." *TD&T.* 1998 Win; 34(5): 34-41. Notes. Biblio. Illus.: Design. Photo. Color. B&W. 10. Lang.: Eng.
Czech Republic: Prague. 1997. Technical studies. ■Josef Svoboda's use of mirrors in his set design for a production of Goethe's *Faust* directed by Václav Hudeček at the Národní Divadlo.

1518 Velemanová, Věra. "Znovusetkání s Liborem Fárou I." (Meeting Libor Fára Anew.) *DivR.* 1998 Sep.; 9(3): 36-54. Notes. Illus.: Photo. Dwg. B&W. 8. Lang.: Cze.
Czech Republic: Prague. 1950-1981. Historical studies. ■The work of scene designer Libor Fára, focuses on his set for Jarry's *Ubu Roi (King Ubu)* directed by Jan Grossman in the Theatre Na zábradlí. Continued in *DivR* 1998 Dec (9:4), 22-23, with discussion of Fára's design for Čechov's *Višnëvyj sad (The Cherry Orchard)*, directed by Jan Kačer at Činoherní klub, 1969.

1519 Thelestam, Sunniva; Rolin, Christina. "En professionell skräddargesäll." (A Professional Tailor Journeyman.) *ProScen.* 1998; 22(5): 33-36. Illus.: Photo. B&W. Color. Lang.: Swe.
Finland: Helsinki. Sweden: Stockholm. 1996-1998. Histories-sources. ■Report from a tailor with five years' experience at Suomen Kansallisteatteri, who went to Stockholms Stadsteatern to learn more about designing and tailoring for costume plays.

1520 Barbour, Kristin Allen. *The Past Present: History and Historical Costumes at the Comédie-Française, 1815-1830.* Kent, OH: Kent State Univ; 1998. 235 pp. Biblio. Notes. [Ph.D. Dissertation, Univ. Microfilms Order No. 9901393.] Lang.: Eng.
France: Paris. 1815-1830. Histories-specific. ■Examines the way history was represented through costume at the Comédie-Française during the Bourbon Restoration. Uses the theories of Michel Foucault to examine large cultural frameworks.

1521 Petzold, Hans-Jörg. "...nur geträumt?" (Only a Dream?) *BtR.* 1998; 4: 14-17. Illus.: Photo. Color. 7. Lang.: Ger.
Germany: Bayreuth. 1997-1998. Historical studies. ■Adaptation by designer Jens Hübner of Giuseppe and Carlo Galli-Bibiena's baroque scenery created for William Shakespeare's *A Midsummer Night's Dream.* On occasion of the 250th anniversary of the baroque opera house Markgräfliches Opernhaus that performance was reconstructed and also the scenery executed by students.

1522 Shafer, Yvonne. "Brecht and Neher, Together Again." *TCI.* 1998 May; 32(5): 17-18. Illus.: Photo. Color. 1. Lang.: Eng.
Germany: Berlin. 1998. Technical studies. ■Report on an exhibition of Caspar Neher's set designs for the plays of Bertolt Brecht at the City Museum of Berlin.

1523 Berezkin, V. "Mesto dejstvija." (A Place To Set Up.) *TeatZ.* 1998; 5-6: 30-34, 45-48. Lang.: Rus.
Russia. 1998. ■Transformation of scene designs into stage sets for the plays of Aleksand'r Ostrovskij. Includes work of Vladimir Dmitriev, Vladimir Šestakov, David Borovskij, Mart Kitaev, and Anatolij Vasiljev.

1524 Johnson, David. "Seating Arrangements." *TCI.* 1998 July; 32(7): 20. Illus.: Photo. Color. 1. Lang.: Eng.
UK-England: London. 1998. Technical studies. ■Paul Anderson's lights, Paul Arditti's sound, and the set design by the Brothers Quay for the Théâtre de Complicité production of Ionesco's *The Chairs (Les Chaises)* at the Royal Court Theatre, directed by Simon McBurney.

1525 Karam, Edward. "Spanish Tatters." *TCI.* 1998 Feb.; 32(2): 15-16. Illus.: Photo. Color. 1. Lang.: Eng.
UK-England: London. 1998. Technical studies. ■Tom Piper's set and costume designs for the RSC production of Kyd's *The Spanish Tragedy* directed by Michael Boyd at The Pit.

1526 Karam, Edward. "All About Realism." *TCI.* 1998 July; 32(7): 8-9. Illus.: Photo. Color. 1. Lang.: Eng.
UK-England: London. 1998. Technical studies. ■Richard Hoover's set design for the Royal National Theatre's production of Tennessee Williams' *Not About Nightingales* at the Cottesloe Theatre under the direction of Trevor Nunn, coproduced by Alley Theatre.

1527 Lampert-Gréaux, Ellen. "Jason Barnes." *TCI.* 1998 Mar.; 32(3): 29. Lang.: Eng.
UK-England: London. 1973-1998. Technical studies. ■Twenty-five year career of the production manager of the National Theatre.

DRAMA: —Design/technology

1528 Wilmore, David. "The Substage Equipment at Her Majesty's Theatre, London." *TN.* 1998; 52(1): 28-45. Notes. Illus.: Design. Print. B&W. 3. Lang.: Eng.
UK-England: London. 1887-1986. Historical studies. ■Description of the original stage machinery at Her Majesty's Theatre, as designed by John White for Herbert Beerbohm Tree. Sections of the original equipment were used in the 1986 production of *The Phantom of the Opera* directed by Harold Prince.

1529 Balsamico, Karen K. *A Record of the Development of the Design Concept and the Design for Scenery for Ondine.* Long Beach, CA: Univ. of California; 1987. 67 pp. Notes. Biblio. [M.F.A. Thesis, Univ. Microfilms Order No. 1332808.] Lang.: Eng.
USA. 1987. Histories-sources. ■Describes the evolution of the author's design concept and scenic design for Jean Giraudoux's *Ondine.*

1530 Barbour, David. "Brian MacDevitt." *TCI.* 1998 Mar.; 32(3): 22-25. Illus.: Photo. Color. 3. Lang.: Eng.
USA: New York, NY. 1997. Technical studies. ■Critique of MacDevitt's lighting designs for three Broadway shows that opened in 1997: *Side Show* by Henry Krieger and Bill Russell and directed by Robert Longbottom at the Richard Rodgers Theatre, Neil Simon's *Proposals* at the Broadhurst directed by Joe Mantello, and Wendy Kesselman's *The Diary of Anne Frank* directed by James Lapine at the Music Box.

1531 Barbour, David. "James Noone: A Set Designer Builds Impressive Body of Work." *TCI.* 1998 Feb.; 32(2): 34-37. Illus.: Photo. Sketches. Design. B&W. Color. 11. Lang.: Eng.
USA: New York, NY. 1986-1998. Technical studies. ■Career of Noone, one of the scene designers at Playwrights Horizons.

1532 Barbour, David. "Damned Yankees." *TCI.* 1998 Mar.; 32(3): 6-7. Illus.: Photo. Color. 2. Lang.: Eng.
USA: New york, NY. 1998. Technical studies. ■E. David Cosier's scenic design for the Signature Theatre's production of two one-act plays by Arthur Miller: *The Last Yankee* and *I Can't Remember Anything* both directed by Joseph Chaikin.

1533 Barbour, David. "Christmas Evil." *TCI.* 1998 Mar.; 32(3): 10-12. Illus.: Photo. Color. 1. Lang.: Eng.
USA: New York, NY. 1998. Technical studies. ■Designer P.K. Wish's costumes for CSC Repertory's production of Aleksand'r Vvedenskij's *Christmas with the Ivanovs (Elka u Ivanovych)* directed by Karin Coonrod.

1534 Barbour, David. "Sin City." *TCI.* 1998 Apr.; 32(4): 7-9. Illus.: Photo. Photo. Color. 1. Lang.: Eng.
USA: New York, NY. 1998. Technical studies. ■Howell Binkley's lighting design for John Logan's drama *Never the Sinner* at the John Houseman Theatre directed by Ethan McSweeney.

1535 Barbour, David. "Private Lives." *TCI.* 1998 Apr.; 32(4): 6-7. Illus.: Photo. Photo. Color. 1. Lang.: Eng.
USA: New York, NY. 1998. Technical studies. ■Allen Moyer's set design for Richard Dresser's *Gun Shy*, directed by Gloria Muzio at Playwrights Horizons.

1536 Barbour, David. "Jungle Life." *TCI.* 1998 May; 32(5): 6. Illus.: Photo. Color. 1. Lang.: Eng.
USA: New York, NY. 1998. Technical studies. ■Santo Loquasto's set designs for Sam Shepard's *Eyes for Consuela*, directed by Shepard, and Jon Robin Baitz's *Mizlansky/Zilinsky*, directed by Joe Mantello, both at The Manhattan Theatre Club.

1537 Barbour, David. "Fools for L'Amour." *TCI.* 1998 May; 32(5): 8-9. Illus.: Photo. Color. 1. Lang.: Eng.
USA: New York, NY. 1998. Technical studies. ■Bill Kellard's costumes for the Roundabout Theatre production of Feydeau's *A Flea in Her Ear (La Puce à l'Oreille)*, directed by Bill Irwin.

1538 Barbour, David. "Junior High School Confidential." *TCI.* 1998 May; 32(5): 13-14. Illus.: Photo. Color. 1. Lang.: Eng.
USA: New York, NY. 1998. Technical studies. ■Derek McLane's set designs for two Off-Broadway plays: the New Group's production of *Hazelwood Junior High* by Rob Urbinati, staged by Scott Elliott at a local school auditorium, and Nicky Silver's *The Maiden's Prayer* at the Vineyard Theatre directed by Evan Yionoulis.

1539 Barbour, David. "The Bard Off Broadway." *TCI.* 1998 May; 32(5): 26-28. Illus.: Photo. Color. 5. Lang.: Eng.
USA: New York, NY. 1998. Technical studies. ■Scenic and lighting design elements in three plays by Shakespeare produced at Off-Broadway venues: Neil Patel's sets and Don Holder's lighting for *Richard II* and *Richard III*, directed by Ron Daniels for Theatre for a New Audience at St. Clements Theatre and Riccardo Hernandez's sets and Scott Zielinski's lights for *Macbeth* at the Martinson Hall, a venue of the Public Theatre, directed by George C. Wolfe.

1540 Barbour, David. "Golden Globe-Trotting." *TCI.* 1998 July; 32(7): 6-7. Illus.: Photo. Color. 1. Lang.: Eng.
USA: New York, NY. 1996-1998. Technical studies. ■David Lander's light design, undertaken as a result of the terminal illness of the original designer Richard Nelson, for David Henry Hwang's *Golden Child*, directed by James Lapine at the Public Theatre, and the subsequent world tour.

1541 Barbour, David. "Dens of Iniquity." *TCI.* 1998 Aug/Sep.; 32(8): 7-9. Illus.: Photo. Color. 1. Lang.: Eng.
USA: New York, NY. 1998. Technical studies. ■Francis O'Connor's bleak set designs for *The Beauty Queen of Leenane* by Martin McDonagh at the Walter Kerr and The Signature Theatre's production of Arthur Miller's *Mr. Peter's Connections*, both directed by Garry Hynes.

1542 Barbour, David. "The Powers That Be." *TCI.* 1998 Aug/Sep.; 32(8): 18-19. Illus.: Photo. B&W. 1. Lang.: Eng.
USA: New York, NY. 1998. Technical studies. ■Three complete sets designed by Michael McGarty for three one-acts by and starring Elaine May and Alan Arkin under the title *Power Plays* at the Promenade Theatre directed by Arkin.

1543 Barbour, David. "A Shakespeare Summer at OSF." *TCI.* 1998 Oct.; 32(9): 15-19. Illus.: Photo. Dwg. Color. 6. Lang.: Eng.
USA: Ashland, OR. 1998. Technical studies. ■Costume designs for three Shakespeare plays being performed at the Oregon Shakespeare Festival: David Zinn's designs for *Henry IV, Part One*, directed by Michael Donald Edwards, Deborah M. Dryden's costumes for *Cymbeline*, directed by James Edmondson, and Charles Berliner's designs for *The Comedy of Errors*, directed by Kenneth Albers.

1544 Barbour, David. "A Rosy Glow." *TCI.* 1998 Oct.; 32(9): 24-26. Illus.: Photo. Color. 1. Lang.: Eng.
USA: New York, NY. 1998. Technical studies. ■Chris Dallos' lighting design for Donald Margulies' *Collected Stories* at the Lucille Lortel Theatre under the direction of William Carden.

1545 Barbour, David. "Kenneth Posner's Winning Season." *LDim.* 1998 July; 22(6): 64-67, 92-96. Illus.: Photo. Color. 8. Lang.: Eng.
USA. 1998. Technical studies. ■Examines the career of lighting designer Kenneth Posner and his current Broadway and Off Broadway work including *The Last Night of Ballyhoo* by Alfred Uhry and the Off Broadway production of Tina Howe's *Pride's Crossing*, directed by Jack O'Brien.

1546 Barbour, David. "Islands of Light." *LDim.* 1998 Oct.; 22(9): 58-61. Illus.: Photo. B&W. 5. Lang.: Eng.
USA: New York, NY. 1998. Historical studies. ■Lighting designer Natasha Katz and her work on Shakespeare's *Twelfth Night*, directed by Nicholas Hytner at Lincoln Center's Vivian Beaumont Theatre.

1547 Barhour, David. "You Can't Go Home Again." *TCI.* 1998 Feb.; 32(2): 10-11. Illus.: Photo. Color. 1. Lang.: Eng.
USA: New York, NY. 1998. Technical studies. ■John Ambrosone's lighting design for David Mamet's *The Old Neighborhood* directed by Scott Zigler at the Booth Theatre.

1548 Colwin, Thomas Leonard. *Magic, Trick-Work, and Illusion in the Vampire Plays.* Lubbock, TX: Texas Tech Univ; 1987. 122 pp. Biblio. Notes. [Ph.D. Dissertation, Univ. Microfilms Order No. 8724427.] Lang.: Eng.
USA. 1820-1977. Critical studies. ■Argues that theatre technicians used the theory and methods of conjuring to create magical stage effects in *The Vampire* by Dumas *(père)*, *Dracula* by Hamilton Deane and John L. Balderston, *Count Dracula* by Ted Tiller, and *The Passion of Dracula* by Bob Hall and David Richmond.

DRAMA: —Design/technology

1549 Hartigan, Patti. "Catherine Zuber: Clowning Around." *AmTh.* 1998 Sep.; 15(7): 74. Illus.: Photo. B&W. 1. Lang.: Eng.

USA. 1998. Biographical studies. ▪Profile of costume designer Catherine Zuber.

1550 Hogan, Jane. "Karen TenEyck: A Surreal Eye." *AmTh.* 1998 Sep.; 15(7): 70-71. Illus.: Photo. B&W. 2. Lang.: Eng.

USA. 1998. Biographical studies. ▪Profile of theatrical scene designer TenEyck.

1551 Hogan, Jane. "On the Horizon." *TCI.* 1998 Apr.; 32(4): 11-12. Illus.: Photo. Photo. Color. 1. Lang.: Eng.

USA: New York, NY. 1998. Technical studies. ▪Meganne George's set design for the Chain Lightning Theatre's production of O'Neill's *Beyond the Horizon* with emphasis on budgetary constraints of Off-Off Broadway theatre. Production was directed by David Travis at the Connelly Theatre.

1552 Hogan, Jane. "To Rule and Die in LA." *TCI.* 1998 Oct.; 32(9): 7-8. Illus.: Photo. Color. 1. Lang.: Eng.

USA: Los Angeles, CA. 1998. Technical studies. ▪Set designer Karen TenEyck's projections for the Shakespeare Festival/LA's production of *Julius Caesar*, performed on the steps of Los Angeles City Hall directed by Andrew Tsao.

1553 Johnson, David. "Noise in the Attic." *TCI.* 1998 Mar.; 32(3): 5. Illus.: Photo. Color. 1. Lang.: Eng.

USA: New York, NY. 1998. Technical studies. ▪Dan Moses Schreier's sound design for Wendy Kesselman's *The Diary of Anne Frank* at the Music Box Theatre under the direction of James Lapine.

1554 Lampert-Gréaux, Ellen. "Hugh Vanstone." *TCI.* 1998 July; 32(7): 24-26. Illus.: Photo. Color. 9. Lang.: Eng.

USA: New York, NY. 1998. Technical studies. ▪Profile of British lighting designer Vanstone on occasion of his New York debut plotting lights for the Broadway production of Yasmina Reza's *'Art'* directed by Matthew Warchus at the Royale, and two RSC productions at BAM, Shakespeare's *Cymbeline* directed by Adrian Noble, and *Hamlet* directed by Warchus.

1555 Lampert-Gréaux, Ellen. "Psychic Spirits." *TCI.* 1998 Aug/Sep.; 32(8): 6-7. Illus.: Photo. Color. 1. Lang.: Eng.

USA: Philadelphia, PA. 1998. Technical studies. ▪Abstract design concept for Blanka Zizka's production of Amy Freed's *The Psychic Life of Savages* at the Wilma. Sets and costumes by Anne C. Patterson, lights and special effects by Russell H. Champa, and sound by Eileen Teague.

1556 Lampert-Gréaux, Ellen; Johnson, David; Barbour, David. "Delirious Illyria." *TCI.* 1998 Oct.; 32(9): 64-67, 76-79. Illus.: Photo. Design. Dwg. B&W. Color. 11. Lang.: Eng.

USA: New York, NY. 1998. Tecnical studies. ▪Eastern influence and the predominance of water in the overall design concept for Nicholas Hytner's production of Shakespeare's *Twelfth Night* at the Lincoln Center Theatre. Sets designed by Bob Crowley, lighting by Natasha Katz, sound by Scott Stauffer, and costumes by Catherine Zuber. Contains a list of the staff and crew involved in the show.

1557 Napoleon, Davi. "War is Hal." *TCI.* 1998 Mar.; 32(3): 5-6. Illus.: Photo. Color. 1. Lang.: Eng.

USA: Ann Arbor, MI. 1998. Technical studies. ▪Nephelie Andonyadis's set design for John Neville-Andrews' production of Shakespeare's *Henry V* at the University of Michigan.

1558 Napoleon, Davi. "Grilling for Gold." *TCI.* 1998 May; 32(5): 5-6. Illus.: Photo. Color. 1. Lang.: Eng.

USA: Chicago, IL. 1998. Technical studies. ▪Derek McLane's backyard set design, and Kenneth Posner's light plot for Eric Bogosian's play *Griller* at the Goodman Theatre directed by Robert Falls.

1559 Napoleon, Davi. "Bring on the Shrews." *TCI.* 1998 May; 32(5): 11-13. Illus.: Photo. Color. 1. Lang.: Eng.

USA: Cambridge, MA. 1998. Technical studies. ▪Use of color in Michael Chybowski's light design and Christine Jones' sets for the Andrei Serban-directed production of Shakespeare's *The Taming of the Shrew* at the American Repertory Theatre.

1560 Napoleon, Davi. "Second City Comedy." *TCI.* 1998 Aug/Sep.; 32(8): 21-22. Illus.: Photo. Color. 1. Lang.: Eng.

USA: Chicago, IL. 1998. Technical studies. ▪Dex Edwards' scenic design for the Shakespeare Repertory Company's production of Shakespeare's *The Comedy of Errors* directed by David Bell.

1561 Nayberg, Yevgenia. *The Scenographic Space of the Historical Play.* Long Beach, CA: California State Univ; 1998. 49 pp. Notes. Biblio. [M.F.A. Thesis, Univ. Microfilms Order No. AAC 1390951.] Lang.: Eng.

USA: Long Beach, CA. 1997. Histories-sources. ▪On the author's creation of the set design for the world premiere of Robert Cohen's *The Prince*, staged at the California State University, in partial fulfillment of the requirements for the degree of M.F.A.

1562 Reaney, Mark. "Virtual Reality Sprouts Wings." *TD&T.* 1998 Spr; 34(2): 27-32. Notes. Illus.: Photo. Diagram. Plan. Color. B&W. 6. Lang.: Eng.

USA: Lawrence, KS. 1997. Technical studies. ▪Use of virtual reality technology to design sets. Audiences at performances of Arthur Kopit's *Wings* at the University of Kansas were given virtual reality helmets to see sets that were projected within the helmets as the actors performed on a mostly bare stage.

1563 Reid, William Nicholas. *A Record of the Design and Execution of Scenery for A Midsummer Night's Dream.* Long Beach, CA: Univ. of California; 1987. 53 pp. Notes. Biblio. [M.F.A. Thesis, Univ. Microfilms Order No. 1330717.] Lang.: Eng.

USA. 1987. Histories-sources. ▪The development of the design and execution of the stage setting for Shakespeare's *A Midsummer Night's Dream* produced at California State University, Long Beach, as the author's final project for the M.F.A. in Design program.

1564 Taylor, Edward Wallace. *Design for Ibsen's* Hedda Gabler*: A Discussion of the Light and Set Design and the Implementation of the Designs.* Louisville, KY: Univ. of Louisville; 1988. 113 pp. Notes. Biblio. [M.F.A. Thesis, Univ. Microfilms Order No. AAC 1334123.] Lang.: Eng.

USA: Louisville, KY. 1988. Histories-specific. ▪M.F.A. design thesis on the lighting and set design for Henrik Ibsen's *Hedda Gabler* at the University of Louisville.

1565 Williamson, Kim. "Drawing, Rendering and Painting: The Historical Method." *TD&T.* 1998 Sum; 34(3): 15-17. Illus.: Photo. Color. 7. Lang.: Eng.

USA. 1900-1998. Technical studies. ▪Discusses the pros and cons of early twentieth-century stage painting techniques for the scenic designers of today.

Institutions

1566 "Where and When." *AmTh.* 1998 May/June; 15(5): 27-37. Illus.: Photo. B&W. 12. Lang.: Eng.

1998. ▪Directory of 1998 theatre festivals being held throughout the world.

1567 Burvill, Tom. "Sidetrack Performance Group and the Post-Modern Turn." 182-194 in Kelly, Veronica, ed. *Our Australian Theatre in the 1990s.* (Australian Playwrights 7.) Notes. Index. Biblio. Illus.: Photo. 2. Lang.: Eng.

Australia: Sydney. 1990-1998. Historical studies. ▪Explores the cultural and political shift that resulted in Sidetrack Theatre Company's changing its name to Sidetrack Performance Group, and changing its aesthetic as well.

1568 Richards, Alison. "Melbourne Women's Circus: Theatre, Feminism, Community." 195-212 in Kelly, Veronica, ed. *Our Australian Theatre in the 1990s.* (Australian Playwrights 7.) Notes. Index. Biblio. Illus.: Photo. 3. Lang.: Eng.

Australia: Melbourne. 1990-1998. Historical studies. ▪Examines the Women's Circus, a feminist community theatre project and the cultural, organizational, and funding base of the group.

1569 Kékesi Kun, Árpád; Walz, Ruth, photo. "A harmadik légtér? Salzburger Festspiele 1997." (The Third Space? Salzburger Festspiele 1997.) *Ellenfény.* 1998; 3(1): 69-73. Illus.: Photo. B&W. 6. Lang.: Hun.

Austria: Salzburg. 1997. Historical studies. ▪Surveying the program of this year's Salzburg Festival.

DRAMA: —Institutions

1570 Koltai, Tamás. "A valóság pólusai: Salzburgi klasszikusok." (The Poles of Reality: Classics at Salzburg.) *Sz.* 1998; 31(11): 7-10. Illus.: Photo. B&W. 2. Lang.: Hun.
Austria: Salzburg. 1998. Reviews of performances. ▪Two Salzburg Festival productions: Shakespeare's *Troilus and Cressida* directed by Stefan Bachmann and Büchner's *Danton's Death (Danton's Tod)* directed by Robert Wilson.

1571 Lennartz, Knut. "In Salzburg und anderswo." (In Salzburg and Elsewhere.) *DB.* 1998; 10: 15-19. Illus.: Photo. B&W. 3. Lang.: Ger.
Austria: Salzburg. 1998. Reviews of performances. ▪Impressions from Salzburger Festspiele under the directorship of Ivan Nagel. Reviews Georg Büchner's *Dantons Tod (Danton's Death)* directed by Robert Wilson, *Geometry of Miracles* written and directed by Robert Lepage, and William Shakespeare's *Troilus and Cressida* directed by Stefan Bachmann.

1572 Merschmeier, Michael; Wille, Franz. "Der ewige Anfänger." (The Eternal Beginner.) *THeute.* 1998; 7: 12-17. Illus.: Photo. B&W. 6. Lang.: Ger.
Austria: Salzburg. 1998. Histories-sources. ▪An interview with Ivan Nagel, drama-manager of Salzburger Festspiele, about Elfriede Jelinek and the program of summer and international festivals.

1573 Wille, Franz. "Bewegung am Laufsteg." (Movement at the Catwalk.) *THeute.* 1998; 10: 6-11. Illus.: Photo. B&W. 6. Lang.: Ger.
Austria: Salzburg. 1998. Reviews of performances. ▪Reports from *Reise durch Jelineks Kopf (Journey through Jelinek's Head)* based on readings, performances, a film program and a fashion show, Georg Büchner's *Dantons Tod (Danton's Death)* directed by Robert Wilson and Elfriede Jelinek's *er nicht als er (he not as himself)* directed by Jossi Wieler during Ivan Nagel's management of Salzburger Festspiele.

1574 Orechanova, G. "Dvenadcat' ščedrych večerov: O gastroljach v Minske MChATa im. M. Gor'kogo." (Twelve Generous Evenings: About the Tour in Minsk of the Moscow Art Theatre.) *Vstreča.* 1998; 2: 4-6. Lang.: Rus.
Belorussia: Minsk. 1998. Historical studies. ▪Account of the Belorussian tour of the Moscow Art Theatre.

1575 Rojtman, Ju. "Druz'ja, sjabry, druz." *TeatZ.* 1998; 5-6: 57-62. Lang.: Rus.
Belorussia: Gomel'. 1998. Historical studies. ▪Slavic Theatre Meeting, an international theatre festival held in Gomel, May 14-17.

1576 Bell, Karen. "Join Us for Lunch." *PAC.* 1998; 31(3): 34-35. Illus.: Photo. B&W. 3. Lang.: Eng.
Canada: Calgary, AB. 1975-1998. Historical studies. ▪Lunchbox Theatre's development program for new plays, Stage One, and its history of transferring productions.

1577 Binning, Sadhu. "Vancouver Sath: South Asian Canadian Theatre in Vancouver." *CTR.* 1998 Spr; 94: 14-17. Lang.: Eng.
Canada: Vancouver, BC. 1972-1989. Histories-sources. ▪Playwright Sadhu Binning discusses history of Punjabi theatre in Vancouver and evolution of Vancouver Sath, a politically-oriented Punjabi theatre collective he co-founded.

1578 Doré, Marc. "Pour une pédagogie en mouvement: Conservatoire d'art dramatique de Québec." (For a Pedagogy In Motion: Conservatioire d'Art Dramatique de Québec.) *JCT.* 1998; 86: 114-116. Illus.: Photo. B&W. 2. Lang.: Fre.
Canada: Quebec, PQ. 1998. Histories-sources. ▪Marc Doré, instructor at the Conservatoire d'art dramatique de Québec, explains his school's method of training as impregnation, expression, and production.

1579 Douglas, James B. "More Canadian Capers." *PlPl.* Jan 1998; 518: 36-37. Illus.: Photo. B&W. 1. Lang.: Eng.
Canada: Niagara-on-the-Lake, ON. 1997. Historical studies. ▪Profile of the 1997 Shaw Festival with comments on many of its productions.

1580 Douglas, James B. "Stratford Festival." *PlPl.* 1998 Nov.; 528: 28-29. Lang.: Eng.
Canada: Stratford, ON. 1998. Historical studies. ▪1998 Stratford Festival and review of several of its productions.

1581 Filewod, Alan. "The Mummers' Troupe, The Canada Council and the Production of Theatre History." *TRC.* 1998 Spr; 19(1): 3-34. Notes. Biblio. Lang.: Eng.
Canada: St. John's, NF. 1972-1982. Historical studies. ▪Crises of ideology, personality, and management in Newfoundland's social-activist Mummers' Troupe in its dealings with national funding agency, Canada Council.

1582 Garebian, Keith. "The Menopausal and Suburban: The 1997 Stratford and Shaw Festivals." *JCNREC.* 1998; 33(1): 154-162. Lang.: Eng.
Canada: Stratford, ON, Niagara-on-the-Lake, ON. 1997. Critical studies. ▪Examines the 1997 seasons at the Stratford and Shaw Festivals.

1583 Gilbert, Reid. "Victoria's Belfry: 'The gentlest ... deepest, darkest play in town?'." *CTR.* 1998 Sum; 95: 79-82. Notes. Illus.: Photo. B&W. 3. Lang.: Eng.
Canada: Victoria, BC. 1974-1998. Historical studies. ▪History of Belfry Theatre Company and its commitment to producing challenging Canadian-themed works.

1584 Groome, Margaret Estelle. *Canada's Stratford Festival, 1953-1967: Hegemony, Commodity, Institution.* Montreal, PQ: McGill Univ; 1988. Notes. Biblio. [Ph.D. Dissertation.] Lang.: Eng.
Canada: Stratford, ON. 1953-1967. Histories-specific. ▪Analyzes the ideology of 'statements of institutional discourse' or information which circulated through various printed documents, including commentaries on the Festival and its work and the Festival's public relations material.

1585 Jubinville, Yves. "La traversée du désert: Lecture discursive des *Cahiers des Compagnons* (1944-1947)." (Crossing the Desert: Discursive Reading of the *Cahiers des Compagnons* 1944-1947.) *AnT.* Spr 1998; 23: 90-106. Notes. Biblio. Lang.: Fre.
Canada: Montreal, PQ. 1944-1947. Critical studies. ▪Analysis of bimonthly bulletin of Émile Legault's theatre company, Les Compagnons du Saint-Laurent. Index providing list of articles in each issue.

1586 Knowles, Richard Paul. "Alternative Pedagogies, Cultural Studies and the Teaching of Drama and Theatre." *TRC.* 1998 Fall ; 19(2): 158-176. Notes. Biblio. Lang.: Eng.
Canada: Guelph, ON. 1998. Critical studies. ▪Report of Pedagogues Working Group, Centre for Cultural Studies/Centre d'etudes sur la culture, University of Guelph. Proposes application of principles of alternative pedagogy and cultural studies to postsecondary intruction of theatre in the context of a Southern Ontario university such as University of Guelph.

1587 Lafon, Dominique. "Le 'solitaire' de Québec: Robert Lepage." (The 'Lone Wolf' from Quebec: Robert Lepage.) *JCT.* 1998; 86: 77-82. Notes. Illus.: Photo. B&W. 3. Lang.: Fre.
Canada: Quebec, PQ. 1998. Historical studies. ▪Director Robert Lepage's motivations for basing his experimental theatre company, Ex Machina, in Montreal, PQ.

1588 Lavoie, Pierre. "Partie remise." (New Bets.) *JCT.* 1998; 88: 23-26. Notes. Illus.: Photo. B&W. 3. Lang.: Fre.
Canada: Quebec, PQ. 1998. Historical studies. ▪Overview of productions at fourth Carrefour international de théâtre, with particular attention to the two Shakespeare productions: *La Tempête (The Tempest,* Théâtre du Trident, directed by Robert Lepage) and *Hamlet* (Lithuanian International Theatre Festival, directed by Eimuntas Nekrošius).

1589 Mercier, Martin. "Influences extérieures, influences mutuelles: Portrait du théâtre de création à Québéc." (External Influences, Mutual Influences: Portrait of Contemporary Devised Theatre in Quebec.) *JCT.* 1998; 86: 106-113. Notes. Illus.: Photo. B&W. 4. Lang.: Fre.
Canada: Quebec, PQ. 1989-1998. Historical studies. ▪Artistic orientation and operating conditions of four companies specializing in original creations, all based in Quebec: Théâtre les Enfants Terribles, Théâtre du Paradox, Théâtre Sortie de Secours and Théâtre des Moutons Noirs.

1590 Ruprecht, Alvina. "Jacques Crête and the Atelier de recherche théâtrale l'Eskabel: 'À Rebours' on the Quebec Stage." *TRC.* 1998 Fall vo 19(1): 63-85. Notes. Biblio. Illus.: Photo. B&W. 4. Lang.: Eng.

DRAMA: —Institutions

Canada: Montreal, PQ. 1971-1989. Historical studies. ■History of director Jacques Crête's Montreal-based avant-garde theatre company, Atelier de recherche théâtrale l'Eskabel, and its experimentation with ritual theatre and sexual identity.

1591 Vaïs, Michel. "Pauvre théâtre québécois!" (Poor Québécois Theatre!) *JCT.* 1998; 88: 10-13. Notes. Illus.: Photo. B&W. 3. Lang.: Fre.

Canada: Quebec, PQ. 1998. Critical studies. ■Expresses dissatisfaction with selection of Québécois productions at the fourth Carrefour international de théâtre.

1592 Varma, Rahul. "Contributing to Canadian Theatre." *CTR.* 1998 Spr; 94: 25-27. Illus.: Photo. B&W. 4. Lang.: Eng.

Canada: Montreal, PQ. 1981-1998. Histories-sources. ■Artistic director and playwright Rahul Varma on his Montreal theatre company, Teesri Duniya, and its efforts to break down stereotypes and create multicultural theatre.

1593 Wassenberg, Anya. "On the Scaffold." *PAC.* 1998; 32(1): 18-19. Illus.: Photo. B&W. 2. Lang.: Eng.

Canada: Hamilton, ON. 1995-1998. Historical studies. ■Examines the work of the Scaffold Theatre Project, led by artistic director Greg Bride, a street theatre company dedicated to bridging the gap between student and professional theatre.

1594 *Gos. ordena 'Znak Početa' russkij dramatičeskij teatr Čuvašskoj Respubliki, 1922-1997.* (The Nationally Awarded 'Sign of Honor': Russian Drama Theatre of the Chuvash Republic, 1922-1997.) Ufa: 1998. 32 pp. Lang.: Rus.

Chuvashia: Ufa. 1922-1997. Historical studies. ■Profile of the Russian theatre in Ufa.

1595 Makeev, M.; Trušin, E. "Na vysote 2600 metrov blistala Taganka." (At the Height of 2600 Meters, the Beauty of Taganka Was Seen.) *EchoP.* 1998; 18: 43-44. Lang.: Rus.

Colombia: Bogotá. 1998. Historical studies. ■Participation of the Taganka Theatre at an international theatre festival.

1596 Roth, Thomas. "Im Sturm der neuen Welt." (In the Storm of the New World.) *TZ.* 1998; 2: 60-63. Illus.: Photo. B&W. 4. Lang.: Ger.

Cuba: Havana. 1986-1998. Historical studies. ■Profile of Teatro Buendía, founded by Flora Lauten, their approach, and their production of Shakespeare's *The Tempest.*

1597 Malpede, Karen. "Idioms and Identities in Cairo." *NTQ.* 1998 Feb.; 14(4): 86-89. [Issue 53.] Lang.: Eng.

Egypt: Cairo. 1997. Historical studies. ■Report on the ninth Cairo International Festival for Experimental Theatre and Symposium on Women's International Theatre.

1598 Aaron, Melissa Diehl. *Global Economics: An Institutional Economic History of the Chamberlain's/King's Men and their Texts, 1599-1642.* Madison, WI: Univ. of Wisconsin; 1998. 436 pp. Notes. Biblio. [Ph.D. Dissertation, Univ. Microfilms Order No. AAC 9836810.] Lang.: Eng.

England. 1599-1642. Histories-specific. ■Shakespeare's plays as the property of the early modern era's most successful theatrical company.

1599 Bly, Mary. "License Taken: Borrowed Prurience and the First Whitefriars Company." *MRDE.* 1998; 10: 149-178. Notes. Lang.: Eng.

England: London. 1607-1608. Historical studies. ■Brief and troubled history of the first Whitefriars, a company that survived barely a year, leaving behind it many lawsuits and jail terms for debt.

1600 Tuuling, Mari; Läänesaar, Monika. "Den estländska teaterns senaste årtionde—en tillbakablick." (A Glimpse Into the Past Decade of Estonian Theatre.) *ProScen.* 1998; 22(1): 34-39. Illus.: Photo. B&W. Color. Lang.: Swe, Eng, Ger.

Estonia. 1985-1998. Historical studies. ■Survey of the theatre and the actors during the last decade under the USSR and the freedom of today.

1601 Kennedy, Dennis. "Shakespeare and Cultural Tourism." *TJ.* 1998 May; 50(2): 175-188. Notes. Lang.: Eng.

Europe. USA. 1950-1997. Critical studies. ■Examines the post-war emergence of Shakespeare festivals and compares it to the contemporary 'Disneyfication' of Shakespearean production.

1602 Valenti, Cristina, ed. *Living with The Living. Il Living Theatre in Europa (1964-1983). Julian Beck pittore.* (Living with The Living: The Living Theatre in Europe, 1964-1983. Julian Beck as a Painter.) Riccione: Comune di Riccione; 1998. 158 pp. Illus.: Photo. Pntg. B&W. 7. Lang.: Ita.

Europe. USA. 1964-1983. Historical studies. ■Profile of the Living Theatre in Europe from 1964 to 1983. Also includes the activities of Julian Beck, leader of the company, as a painter.

1603 Kaiku, Jan-Peter. "The Swedish Institute of Acting—A Small Training Unit with Traditions and New Projects/L'Institut Suédois d'Art Dramatique—Une petite unité de formation qui a des traditions et un nouveau projet." *FT.* 1998; 52: 34-39. Illus.: Photo. Color. B&W. 5. Lang.: Eng, Fre.

Finland: Helsinki. 1908-1998. Historical studies. ■Profile of the Swedish Institute of Acting at the Finnish Theatre Academy.

1604 Koli, Raija. "Less than a Theatre/Moins qu'un théâtre." *FT.* 1998; 52: 28-33. Illus.: Photo. Color. B&W. 9. Lang.: Eng, Fre.

Finland: Helsinki. 1990-1998. Critical studies. ■The proliferation of Swedish-language theatre groups in Helsinki, including Viirus, Unga Teatern, Klockrike, Teater Mars, Flipp Teatern, Monologteatern, Stjärnfall, and Sirius Teatern.

1605 Määttänen, Markus. "Hyviä veljiä ja rakkaita vihollisia." (Good Brothers and Dear Enemies.) *Teat.* 1998; 53(5): 36-39. Illus.: Photo. Color. 3. Lang.: Fin.

Finland: Tampere. 1998. Historical studies. ■Competition and collaboration between two resident theatre companies in the town of Tampere: Tampereen Teatteri and Tampereen Työväen Teatteri.

1606 Zilliacus, Jutta. "A Ripple On the Pond/Bien sûr la surface de l'éstang s'est ridée." *FT.* 1998; 52: 10-13. Illus.: Photo. Color. B&W. 3. Lang.: Eng, Fre.

Finland: Helsinki. 1919-1998. Historical studies. ■Profile of the Swedish-language theatre company Svenska Teatern, now headed by Lars Svedberg.

1607 Conley, Francine Heather. *La Création d'un espace: The Politics of Space in the Early Works of the Théâtre du Soleil.* Madison, WI: Univ. of Wisconsin; 1998. 258 pp. Notes. Biblio. [Ph.D. Dissertation, Univ. Microfilms Order No. AAC 9829131.] Lang.: Eng.

France: Paris. 1970-1995. Critical studies. ■The ideological implications of theatrical space in three of Théâtre du Soleil's early theatrical productions—*1789, L'Âge D'or, Mephisto*—and Ariane Mnouchkine's film, *Molière ou la vie d'un honnête homme.*

1608 DeCock, Jean. "52nd Avignon: Many (Happy) Returns." *WES.* 1998 Fall; 10(3): 47-54. Illus.: Photo. B&W. 5. Lang.: Eng.

France: Avignon. 1998. Historical studies. ■Survey of the fifty-second annual Avignon Festival.

1609 Engelhardt, Barbara. "Ein Vorstadtkrokodil." (A Suburban Crocodile.) *TZ.* 1998; 5/Theater in Frankreich: 18-22. Pref. Illus.: Photo. B&W. 5. Lang.: Ger.

France: Paris. 1988-1998. Histories-sources. ■Interview with playwright, director, and film-maker Xavier Durringer about the company La Lézarde, founded in 1988, and his methods of writing. Includes a short portrait and an extract from *Chroniques des jours entiers, des nuits entières (Whole Days, Whole Nights).*

1610 Epstein, Lisa Jo. *Identity in the Making: Ariane Mnouchkine and the Théâtre du Soleil.* Austin, TX: Univ. of Texas; 1998. 320 pp. Notes. Biblio. [Ph.D. Dissertation, Univ. Microfilms Order No. AAC 9837952.] Lang.: Eng.

France: Paris. 1964-1997. Histories-specific. ■Developments and changes in Théâtre du Soleil's rehearsal techniques, as well as artistic director Ariane Mnouchkine's role in the company. Includes a case study of the company's creation of Molière's *Tartuffe.*

1611 Fuchs, Elinor. "Apocalypse Avignon." *AmTh.* 1998 Oct.; 15(8): 90-91. Illus.: Photo. B&W. 1. Lang.: Eng.

France: Avignon. 1998. Historical studies. ■Report on the Festival d'Avignon theatre celebration.

DRAMA: —Institutions

1612 Hammerstein, Dorothee. "Ruhe für Gérard Philippe." (Silence for Gérard Philippe.) *THeute.* 1998; 10: 30-37. Illus.: Photo. B&W. 7. Lang.: Ger.
France: Avignon. 1998. Historical studies. ▪Impressions from theatre festival in Avignon. Reviews *Surfeurs (Surfers)* written and directed by Xavier Durringer, Véronique Olmi's *Chaos debout (Chaos Standing)* directed by Jacques Lassalle, performances of different Shakespeare plays and Pierre Corneille's *Le Cid* directed by Declan Donnellan.

1613 Schulman, Peter. "Jean-Pierre Miquel: On the State of Today's Comédie-Française." *WES.* 1998 Fall; 10(3): 43-45. Lang.: Eng.
France: Paris. 1993-1998. Histories-sources. ▪Interview with the artistic director of the institution in regards to the changes he's made in the scope of its theatrical goals since he took over in 1993.

1614 Tackels, Bruno. "Sprachbilder im Schattenriss." (Language Images in the Silhouette.) *TZ.* 1998; 5/Theater in Frankreich: 34-37. Illus.: Photo. B&W. 4. Lang.: Ger.
France: Le Mans. 1980-1998. Historical studies. ▪Portrait of Théâtre du Radeau from its beginning under the direction of François Tanguy to this day. Describes the mission and working methods of the company.

1615 Trencsényi, Katalin. "Tour d'Avignon: Fesztiválképek." (Tour d'Avignon: Pictures of a Festival.) *Sz.* 1998; 31(11): 11-15. Illus.: Photo. B&W. 3. Lang.: Hun.
France: Avignon. 1998. Reviews of performances. ▪Some events of this year's Avignon Festival, notably Shakespeare's *King John* directed by Laurent Pelly, *Hamlet* directed by Eimuntas Nekrošius and Ostrovskij's *Groza (The Storm)* directed by Genrietta Janovskaja.

1616 Vasil'čikova, L. "Moj parižskij teat'r." (My Parisian Theatre.) *Naše nasledie.* 1998; 46: 137-147. Lang.: Rus.
France: Paris. 1930-1939. Histories-sources. ▪Director L.L. Vasil'čikova's on her Parisian amateur theatre group.

1617 Wetzel, Johannes. "'Ein Theater für alle'." ('A Theatre for All'.) *TZ.* 1998; 5/Theater in Frankreich: 38-40. Illus.: Photo. B&W. 4. Lang.: Ger.
France: Paris. 1998. Historical studies. ▪Théâtre Gérard-Philippe under the directorship of Stanislas Nordey in a suburb of Paris and his concept of a 'theatre for all'.

1618 Balme, Christopher. "Mediating the Body at Spielart '97: Munich's Festival of Experimental Theatre." *WES.* 1998 Spr; 10 (2): 41-46. Illus.: Photo. B&W. 4. Lang.: Eng.
Germany: Munich. 1997. Historical studies. ▪Report on the Spielart '97 experimental theatre festival.

1619 Balme, Christopher. "Italian Experimental Theatre at Spielart '97 in Munich." *WES.* 1998 Win; 10(1): 77-81. Illus.: Photo. B&W. 3. Lang.: Eng.
Germany: Munich. Italy. 1997. Historical studies. ▪Report on the contributions of experimental Italian theatre companies to the Spielart '97 festival. Focuses on the group Giardini Pensili's collaborative piece *Metrodora*, and Societas Raffaello Sanzio's production of Romeo Castellucci's *Giulio Cesare*, which he created and directed.

1620 Berger, Jürgen. "Blessuren in der Schwabenseele." (Wounds in the Swabian Soul.) *THeute.* 1998; 12: 19-21. Illus.: Photo. B&W. 2. Lang.: Ger.
Germany: Stuttgart. 1998. Historical studies. ▪Describes the start of the theatre season at Staatstheater Stuttgart with performances of Friedrich Schiller's *Die Räuber (The Robbers)* directed by Wilfried Minks and Joe Orton's *Loot* directed by Martina Wrobel.

1621 Brandenburg, Detlef. "Soviel Neuanfang muss sein..." (So Much New Start Has to Be...)*DB.* 1998; 10: 22-26. Illus.: Photo. B&W. 4. Lang.: Ger.
Germany: Bielefeld. 1998. Histories-sources. ▪Interview with the theatre-manager Regula Gerber about the future program of Theater Bielefeld including three departments. Reviews Čajkovskij's *Eugene Onegin* directed by Gregor Horres and Thomas Bernhard's *Vor dem Ruhestand (Eve of Retirement)* directed by Hermann Schein.

1622 Burckhardt, Barbara. "Kalte Technik, heisse Herzen." (Cold Technology, Hot Hearts.) *THeute.* 1998; 3: 34-42. Illus.: Photo. B&W. 9. Lang.: Ger.
Germany: Berlin. 1998. Historical studies. ▪Training at Hochschule der Künste and Ernst-Busch-Schule, both in Berlin, including addresses and application procedures.

1623 Burckhardt, Barbara. "Back to Normal." *THeute.* 1998; 10: 52-56. Illus.: Photo. B&W. 5. Lang.: Ger.
Germany: Berlin. 1998. Historical studies. ▪Impressions from the festival The Next Generation during Berliner Festwochen, with emphasis on modern English-language plays, including Richard Dresser's *Below the Belt*, Mark Ravenhill's *Handbag* and Enda Walsh's *Disco Pigs.*

1624 Cousin, Geraldine. "From Travelling with Footsbarn to 'Wandertheater' with Ton und Kirschen." *NTQ.* 1998 Nov.; 14(4): 299-310. Illus.: Photo. B&W. 9. [Issue 56.] Lang.: Eng.
Germany: Glindow. 1992-1997. Historical studies. ▪Profile of Margarethe Biereye and David Johnston, who left the Footsbarn Travelling Theatre to form their own touring company Ton und Kirschen.

1625 Detje, Robin. "Komödie mit beschränkter Haftung." (Limited Comedy.) *TZ.* 1998; 2: 6-7. Illus.: Photo. B&W. 1. Lang.: Ger.
Germany: Berlin. 1991-1998. Historical studies. ▪Folly and failure of the subsequent directorships of Berliner Ensemble since Manfred Wekwerth's resignation in 1991.

1626 Deuter, Ulrich. "München ist Derrick." (Munich Is Derrick.) *TZ.* 1998; 1: 22-27. Illus.: Photo. B&W. 6. Lang.: Ger.
Germany: Munich. 1997. Historical studies. ▪Survey of Munich theatres, including the Marstall and Residenztheater venues of Bayerisches Staatsschauspiel, Kammerspiele, and the independent theatres Teamtheater Tankstelle, Neues Theater, TamS and Theater 44.

1627 Deuter, Ulrich. "Bittere Hoffnung, schnelle Gewalt." (Bitter Hope, Fast Violence.) *TZ.* 1998; 5: 10-13. Illus.: Photo. B&W. 9. Lang.: Ger.
Germany: Bonn. 1998. Historical studies. ▪Report on the 4th Bonner Biennale, a festival that presents contemporary plays from Europe, including workshops, discussions and readings.

1628 Dietschreit, Frank. "Es ist noch nicht alles aufgegessen." (It Is Not Yet All Eaten.) *TZ.* 1998; 3: 48-50. Illus.: Photo. B&W. 4. Lang.: Ger.
Germany: Berlin. 1950-1998. Historical studies. ▪Portrait of the Carrousel Theater, its origins as Theater der Freundschaft in East Germany, its history as a children's and young people theatre and new perspectives regarding audience and program under the directorship of Manuel Schöbel.

1629 Disch, Matthias. "Theater und Gedenkstätte." (Theatre and Memorial.) *SuT.* 1998; 160: 8-12. Notes. Illus.: Photo. B&W. 3. Lang.: Ger.
Germany: Nordhausen. 1995-1998. Histories-sources. ▪Artistic director of the Theater Jugend Club describes the correlation between acting and experiential memory work and looking for places, such as the former concentration camp Mittelbau-Dora, to put this work into action.

1630 Enge, Herbert. "'Wir lassen Orte sprechen'." ('We Let Places Speak'.) *SuT.* 1998; 160: 20-24. Illus.: Photo. B&W. 4. Lang.: Ger.
Germany: Hamburg. 1988-1998. Histories-sources. ▪Interview with Herbert Enge, director of the company Thalia Treffpunkt, about its history and experiments using acting as a tool to get closer to the crimes of the Holocaust.

1631 Engelhardt, Barbara. "Familientheater mit Anschluss." (Family Theatre with Connection.) *TZ.* 1998; 2: 36-39. Illus.: Photo. B&W. 3. Lang.: Ger.
Germany: Dresden. 1997-1998. Historical studies. ▪Profile of Theater Dresden under the directorship of Dieter Kunze, an institution that experiments with new ideas, including puppetry and film, to reach the youth audience.

1632 Engelhardt, Barbara. "Pfeifen im Wald." (Whistle in the Woods.) *TZ.* 1998; 6: 4-7. Illus.: Dwg. Photo. B&W. 5. Lang.: Ger.
Germany: Stuttgart. 1993-1998. Histories-sources. ▪Interview with Friedrich Schirmer, who has been managing director at Staatstheater Stuttgart, Schauspiel, for five years, and Michael Propfe, the chief dramaturg, about theatre concepts and cultural policy.

DRAMA: —Institutions

1633 Fiebach, Joachim. "Mögliche Optionen." (Possible Options.) *TZ.* 1998; 1: 40-41. Illus.: Photo. B&W. 1. Lang.: Ger.

Germany: Berlin. 1997. Historical studies. ■Notations on the future of Schaubühne with the resignation of its artistic director Andrea Breth.

1634 Gampert, Christian. "Stadttheater oder Vagantenbühne?" (Municipal Theatre or Touring Troupe?)*TZ.* 1998; 1: 10-12. Illus.: Photo. B&W. 3. Lang.: Ger.

Germany: Tübingen. 1996-1997. Historical studies. ■Portrait of Landestheater Württemberg-Hohenzollern and the consequences for repertory companies as they face more budget cuts.

1635 Grund, Stefan. "Höllentanz auf Stelzen." (Hellish Dance on Stilts.) *TZ.* 1998; 6: 44-46. Illus.: Photo. B&W. 4. Lang.: Ger.

Germany: Hamburg. 1998. Reviews of performances. ■Impressions from the summer theatre festival at Kampnagel (Hamburg) with the focal point on Israeli theatre on occasion of 50th anniversary of the state of Israel.

1636 Hagedorn, Volker. "Rätselhaftes Göttingen." (Baffling Göttingen.) *DB.* 1998; 4: 44-45. Illus.: Photo. B&W. 2. Lang.: Ger.

Germany: Göttingen. 1996-1998. Historical studies. ■Portrait of Junges Theater under the directorship of Rolf Johannsmeier, its program and philosophy in relationship to the city.

1637 Heine, Beate. "Die Baracke bebt." (The Baracke Shakes.) *DB.* 1998; 4: 27-29. Illus.: Photo. B&W. 3. Lang.: Ger.

Germany: Berlin. 1996-1998. Historical studies. ■Portrait of Deutsches Theater, Baracke, managed by director Thomas Ostermeier and dramaturg Jens Hillje, their concepts and mission of performing new dramas mainly from Anglo-Saxon countries.

1638 Irmer, Thomas. "Im dritten Jahr des Aufbruch." (In the Third Year of the Beginning.) *TZ.* 1998; 6: 8-11. Illus.: Photo. B&W. 2. Lang.: Ger.

Germany: Leipzig. 1996-1998. Historical studies. ■Profile of Schauspiel Leipzig under the directionship of Wolfgang Engel. Describes *Simple Storys*, a novel by Ingo Schulze, adapted by Anna Langhoff and directed by Lukas Langhoff.

1639 Jahnke, Manfred. "Von Theatern umzingelt." (Surrounded by Theatres.) *TZ.* 1998; 1: 13-15. Illus.: Photo. B&W. 3. Lang.: Ger.

Germany: Esslingen. 1996-1997. Historical studies. ■Portrait of Württembergische Landesbühne Esslingen. Describes the performances of Edward Albee's *Three Tall Women* directed by Barbara Neureiter, William Shakespeare's *Hamlet* directed by Hermann Schmidt Rahmer and Lothar Trolle's *Papa Mama* directed by Karin Koller.

1640 Jahnke, Manfred. "Emotion durch Form." (Emotion through Form.) *TZ.* 1998; 5: 36-40. Illus.: Photo. B&W. 4. Lang.: Ger.

Germany: Munich. 1993-1998. Historical studies. ■Portrait of the children's theatre Schauburg after rebuilding under the direction of George Podt.

1641 Jahnke, Manfred. "Schöne Aussichten in Stuttgart." (Beautiful Views in Stuttgart.) *Fundevogel.* 1998; 128: 5-15. Illus.: Photo. B&W. 2. Lang.: Ger.

Germany: Stuttgart. 1998. Historical studies. ■Report on the 7th Baden-Württembergische Kinder- und Jugentheatertreffen and the 1st Internationales Kinder- und Jugendtheaterfestival.

1642 Jahnke, Manfred. "Mythologie und Entertainement an der deutsch-dänischen Grenze." (Mythology and Entertainment at the German-Danish Border.) *G&GBKM.* 1998; 129: 5-11. Illus.: Photo. B&W. 2. Lang.: Ger.

Germany. Denmark. 1998. Historical studies. ■Impressions from the German-Danish children's theatre festival that took place on both sides of the German-Danish border.

1643 Khuon, Ulrich. "Das Spiel des Schreibens und seine Anstöe." (The Play of Writing and its Impetus.) 9-16 in Gross, Jens; Khuon, Ulrich. *Dea Loher und das Schauspiel Hannover.* Hannover: Niedersächsische Staatstheater Hannover GmbH; 1998. 256 pp. (prinz 8.) Lang.: Ger.

Germany: Hannover. 1992-1998. Historical studies. ■Close cooperation between Staatsschauspiel Hannover and young authors with reference to the theatre's productions of playwright Dea Loher's works such as *Leviathan* directed by Antje Lenkeit, *Fremdes Haus (Stranger's House)*, *Adam Geist* and *Olgas Raum (Olga's Room)*, all three directed by Andreas Kriegenburg, and *Tätowierung (Tattoo)* directed by Olivier Balagna.

1644 Kohse, Petra. "Stachel im Fleisch." (A Thorn in the Flesh.) *TZ.* 1998; 1: 36-38. Illus.: Photo. B&W. 6. Lang.: Ger.

Germany: Dresden. 1993-1998. Historical studies. ■A portrait of TiF (Theater in der Fabrik), its independent development under the directorship of Volker Metzler, and its relationship with Staatsschauspiel Dresden under the directorship of Dieter Görne.

1645 Krug, Hartmut. "Das Theater lebt!" (Theatre Lives!)*DB.* 1998; 11: 48-49. Illus.: Photo. B&W. 3. Lang.: Ger.

Germany: Cottbus. 1908-1998. Historical studies. ■Portrait and history of Staatstheater Cottbus on occasion of its 90th birthday. Describes the anniversary performance of Gotthold Ephraim Lessing's *Minna von Barnhelm* directed by Christoph Schroth.

1646 Krusche, Friedemann. "Brückenschlag ins Niemandsland." (A Link into No Man's Land.) *THeute.* 1998; 10: 48-51. Illus.: Photo. B&W. 3. Lang.: Ger.

Germany: Frankfurt/Oder. 1998. Historical studies. ■Report on the theatre festival in Frankfurt/Oder entitled 'From The Other Side to Here'.

1647 Lennartz, Knut. "Europa in Bonn." *DB.* 1998; 8: 40-44. Illus.: Photo. B&W. 5. Lang.: Ger.

Germany: Bonn. 1998. Historical studies. ■Impressions from the 4th Bonner Biennale, a European theatre festival that supports European contemporary drama.

1648 Lennartz, Knut. "Der Weg nach oben." (The Way Up.) *DB.* 1998; 1: 30-34. Illus.: Photo. B&W. 3. Lang.: Ger.

Germany: Berlin. 1972-1998. Historical studies. ■The course in drama direction at Ernst-Busch-Schule for twenty five years. Reports from Robert Schuster's and Tom Kühnel's first successes at Bat and Maxim Gorki Theater (Berlin) and their first engagement at Frankfurter Schauspielhaus with the direction of Ibsen's *Peer Gynt.*

1649 Lennartz, Knut. "Aller Anfang..." (The First Step...)*DB.* 1998; 6: 24-28. Illus.: Photo. B&W. 4. Lang.: Ger.

Germany: Karlsruhe. 1997-1998. Histories-sources. ■Interview with the theatre-manager Pavel Fieber of Badisches Staatstheater Karlsruhe on his first season there. Resumes successes and flops. Describes the program for the following season and the relationship between theatre and press.

1650 Linzer, Martin. "In der sächsischen Schmuddelecke." (In the Saxon Mess Corner.) *TZ.* 1998; 2: 22-29. Illus.: Photo. B&W. 11. Lang.: Ger.

Germany: Zittau, Bautzen, Görlitz. 1997-1998. Historical studies. ■Divergent and complementary missions of the Gerhart Hauptmann Theater in Zittau, Theater Görlitz, and Deutsch Sorbisches Volkstheater of Bautzen in regard to their poltical views and the cooperation between the institutions.

1651 Lysell, Roland. "Kroppen och rummet—avantgardet i tysk teater." (The Body and the Room—the Avant-garde of the German Theatre.) *Entré.* 1998; 25(3/4): 85-87. Illus.: Photo. B&W. Lang.: Swe.

Germany: Berlin. 1998. Historical studies. ■Report from Theatertreffen in Berlin, with references to Einar Schleef's production of Oscar Wilde's *Salome*, Elfriede Jelinek's *Sportstück*, and Thomas Ostermeier's version of Mark Ravenhill's *Shopping and Fucking.*

1652 Peiseler, Christian. "Der Kopf ist rund, die Bühne eckig." (The Head Is Round, the Stage Angular.) *THeute.* 1998; 2: 50-51. Illus.: Photo. B&W. 2. Lang.: Ger.

Germany. 1998. Historical studies. ■Impressions from Impulse, a festival of free companies from Austria, Germany and Switzerland, in North Rhine-Westphalia.

1653 Pietzsch, Ingeborg. "Legende und Wirklichkeit." (Legend and Reality.) *TZ.* 1998; 4: 60-62. Illus.: Photo. B&W. 2. Lang.: Ger.

Germany: Marburg. 1997-1998. Historical studies. ■Portrait of Nordhessisches Landestheater Marburg, its personnel structure, audience and venues. Describes *The Band* by Peter Dehler and Manuel Schöbel

DRAMA: —Institutions

directed by Ekkehard Dennewitz, *Frank and Stein* by Ken Campbell directed by Frank Damerius.

1654 Preusser, Gerhard. "Jeder ist ein Frankenstein." (Everybody Is a Frankenstein.) *THeute.* 1998; 11: 39-41. Illus.: Photo. B&W. 3. Lang.: Ger.

Germany: Dusseldorf. 1998. Historical studies. ■Describes the start of the season at Düsseldorfer Schauspielhaus including *Frankenstein* after a motif by Mary Shelley by Thirza Bruncken and director Kazuko Watanabe's adaptation of *Effi Briest* after Theodor Fontane's novel.

1655 Preusser, Gerhard. "Geduld der Begriffe, Ungeduld der Bilder." (Patience of Concepts, Impatience of Pictures.) *THeute.* 1998; 12: 16-18. Illus.: Photo. B&W. 2. Lang.: Ger.

Germany: Bochum. 1998. Historical studies. ■Describes the start of the theatre season at Schauspielhaus Bochum with performances of Labiche's *L'Affaire de la rue de Lourcine* directed by Jürgen Kruse and Harold Pinter's *Ashes to Ashes* directed by Dimiter Gotscheff.

1656 Schalk, Axel. "Das Lehrstück vom Einverständnis." (The Didactic Play of Agreement.) *TZ.* 1998; 2: 8-10. Illus.: Photo. B&W. 1. Lang.: Ger.

Germany: Berlin. 1992-1998. Historical studies. ■Inability of artistic directors Peter Sauerbaum and Stephan Suschke to realistically plan a repertory for the troubled Berliner Ensemble.

1657 Schmidt, Dagmar. "Geschichten erzählen, die von den Rätseln des Lebens handeln." (To Tell Stories about the Mysteries of Life.) *dRAMATURg.* 1998; 1: 19-23. Illus.: Photo. B&W. 2. Lang.: Ger.

Germany: Munich. 1998. Histories-sources. ■Dramaturg Schmidt describes the change in children and young people's theatre and the complex relationship of actors and audience based on her experiences at the children's theatre Schauburg.

1658 Schulze-Reimpell, Werner. "Regiestudium in Hamburg." (Study of Direction in Hamburg.) *DB.* 1998; 1: 27-29. Illus.: Photo. B&W. 3. Lang.: Ger.

Germany: Hamburg. 1988-1998. Historical studies. ■Describes the Institut für Theater, Musiktheater und Film founded by Universität und Musikhochschule, and the course of practice-oriented drama direction conducted by Manfred Brauneck and Christof Nel.

1659 Stammen, Silvia. "Vernetzung ist Trumpf." (Networking Is In.) *DB.* 1998; 1: 16-21. Illus.: Photo. B&W. 5. Lang.: Ger.

Germany: Munich. 1985-1998. Historical studies. ■Describes the training in different courses at Bayerische Theaterakademie and the practice at Prinzregententheater, including a review of Wilfried Hiller's *Peter Pan* directed by August Everding at Prinzregententheater and an interview with the critic C. Bernd Sucher about cultural criticism, a new course of studies.

1660 Stammen, Silvia. "Who's That Girl?" *DB.* 1998; 4: 36-37. Illus.: Photo. B&W. 2. Lang.: Ger.

Germany: Munich. 1993-1998. Historical studies. ■Portrait of Marstall, a venue of Bayerisches Staatsschauspiel, under the directorship of Elisabeth Schweeger. Describes the debut performance of Martin Crimp's *Attempts on Her Life* directed by Gerhard Willert.

1661 Stephan, Erika. "Ohne Reiseführer im Dschungel von 'Leipzig East'." (Without a Guide in the Jungle of 'Leipzig East'.) *DB.* 1998; 4: 30-33. Illus.: Photo. B&W. 4. Lang.: Ger.

Germany: Leipzig. 1998. Historical studies. ■The performance of contemporary drama at Schauspiel Leipzig. Includes a review of Ralph Oehme's *Die spanische Lunte (The Spanish Fuse)* directed by Matthias Brenner.

1662 Strein, Jürgen. "Kleine Schritte." (Little Steps.) *TZ.* 1998; 1: 16-17. Illus.: Photo. B&W. 1. Lang.: Ger.

Germany: Bruchsal. 1993-1998. Historical studies. ■Struggle of Badische Landesbühne Bruchsal against decreasing audience attendance and the strategy of overcoming the crisis by presenting a solid repertory.

1663 Stumm, Reinhardt. "Wer nicht dabei war, ist selber schuld!" (The One Who Was Not There Is to Blame!)*THeute.* 1998; 8/9: 26-37. Illus.: Photo. B&W. 9. Lang.: Ger.

Germany: Bonn. 1998. Historical studies. ■Impressions from Biennale festival 1998, where modern European plays were invited, including performances and conversations. Discusses the festival from a political point of view.

1664 Tait, Peta. "Unstable Performance Elements." *NTQ.* 1998 Feb.; 14(1): 89-90. [Issue 53.] Lang.: Eng.

Germany: Munich. 1997. Historical studies. ■Report on the Tenth International Festival of Physical Theatre, the highlight of which was the aerialist inspired *Villa, Villa* by the group De La Guarda under the direction of Diqui James and Pichon Baldinu.

1665 Triebold, Wilhelm. "Aus drei mach 2?" (To Make 2 out of 3?)*DB.* 1998; 12: 45-47. Illus.: Photo. B&W. 3. Lang.: Ger.

Germany: Esslingen, Tübingen. 1998. Historical studies. ■Portrait of Württembergisches Landestheater Esslingen under the direction of Peter Dolder and Landestheater Tübingen under the direction of Knut Weber and their measures against threatened closures and mergers.

1666 Wille, Franz. "Die Theatermacher." (The Theatre-Makers.) *THeute.* 1998; 2: 43-46. Illus.: Photo. B&W. 3. Lang.: Ger.

Germany: Munich. 1997-1998. Critical studies. ■Aesthetic perspectives of the ensemble at Münchner Kammerspiele and their staging of Anton Pavlovic Cechov's *Čajka (The Seagull)* directed by Jens-Daniel Herzog and Thomas Bernhard's *Der Schein trügt (Appearances Are Deceiving)* directed by Dieter Dorn.

1667 Gounaridou, Kiki. "The Sixth Festival of the Theatres of Europe, Thessaloniki." *WES.* 1998 Fall; 10(3): 41-42. Lang.: Eng.

Greece: Thessaloniki. 1997. Historical studies. ■Report on the festival for the Union of the Theatres of Europe, Fall, 1997.

1668 Bóta, Gábor. *Arcok a Szkénéből.* (Faces from the Szkéné.) Budapest: Országos Színháztörténeti Múzeum és Intézet; 1998. 82 pp. (Skenotheke 4.) Append. Illus.: Photo. B&W. 66. Lang.: Hun.

Hungary: Budapest. 1963-1995. Historical studies. ■The thirty-year history of an amateur theatre and alternative workshop operating at the Budapest Technical University in the series of recollections by directors and actors. A survey of the program is also included by a collection of data.

1669 Darvay Nagy, Adrienne. *Színek Kisvárdán.* (Scenes at Kisvárda.) Kisvárda: Informa Lap- és Könyvkiadó Kft.; 1998. 223 pp. Append. Illus.: Photo. B&W. 149. Lang.: Hun.

Hungary: Kisvárda. 1989-1998. Historical studies. ■A richly illustrated book on the ten-year history of the annual festival of Hungarian theatres operating in neighboring countries and abroad with the program, participants, and companies winning various awards.

1670 Galasso, Sabrina, ed.; Valentini, Valentina, ed. *Squat Theatre 1969-1981.* Soveria Mannelli (Catanzaro): Rubbettino; 1998. 196 pp. (Il colibri.) Pref. Biblio. Lang.: Ita.

Hungary. USA: New York, NY. 1969-1981. Historical studies. ■Profile of the Hungarian theatre company that emigrated to the United States in the 1970s after political repression in their country. The group became very important in the underground theatre of New York City.

1671 Perényi, Balázs. "'Létezés'." ('Existence'.) *Ellenfény.* 1998; 3(1): 29-33. Illus.: Photo. B&W. 4. Lang.: Hun.

Hungary: Budapest. 1971-1997. 1971-1997. Historical studies. ■History of the eminent actor-director Tamás Fodor's company called Studio K.

1672 Székely, Gábor; Sziládi, János; Zsámbéki, Gábor. "Tervezet." (The Project.) *Sz.* 1998; 31(1) : 14-25. Illus.: Photo. B&W. 9. Lang.: Hun.

Hungary: Budapest. 1979-1982. Histories-sources. ■Collection of documents regarding plans for the National Theatre experiment in artistic renewal. Includes text of proposals written in 1979 and 1981, as well as commentary on the proposals and an evaluation of the results by the Theatre Department of the Ministry of Culture.

1673 Kaynar, Gad. "National Theatre as Colonized Theatre: The Paradox of HaBima." *TJ.* 1998 Mar.; 50(1): 1-20. Notes. Illus.: Photo. B&W. 5. Lang.: Eng.

Israel. 1920-1998. Critical studies. ■Analysis of HaBimah, the Israeli National Theatre, with emphasis on its early beginnings, the cultural experience of Russian theatre and Zionist ideals. Argues that its authority as a Hebrew institution should not obscure its ambivalence as a colonizing force.

1674 Cipollone, Pierpaola. "Il Giardino di Macbeth: un laboratorio di teatro condotto da Carlo Quartucci con gli studenti dell'Università di Roma 'La Sapienza'." (Macbeth's Gar-

den: A Theatre Workshop Conducted by Carlo Quartucci with Students of the University 'La Sapienza' of Rome.) *BiT.* 1998; 45/47: 209-255. Notes. Lang.: Ita.
Italy: Rome. 1991-1992. Critical studies. ■Quartucci's workshop on Shakespeare's *Macbeth,* which was intended both to carry out research on performing and to turn a group of students into a theatre community.

1675 Hurley, Erin. "Theatre in Italy on the World Wide Web." *WES.* 1998 Win; 10(1): 75-76. Lang.: Eng.
Italy. 1998. Critical studies. ■Small guide to internet addresses for Italian theatrical sites and related organizations.

1676 Blomquist, Kurt. "Möte på Latvijas Dailes Teatris." (Meeting at Latvijas Dailes Teatris.) *ProScen.* 1998; 22(1): 28-30. Illus.: Photo. B&W. Color. Lang.: Swe, Eng, Ger.
Latvia: Riga. 1997. Historical studies. ■Profile of Latvijas Dailes Teatris.

1677 Söderberg, Olle. "Spännande besök mellan Valmeira dramateater och Dalateatern." (An Exciting Exchange Between Valmeira Drama Theater and Dala Theater.) *ProScen.* 1998; 22(1): 52-55. Lang.: Swe, Eng, Ger.
Lithuania: Valmeira. Sweden: Falun. 1996. Historical studies. ■Some notes about the exchange between the Swedish and Lithuanian theatres with reference to the conditions of Lithuania today.

1678 Bots, Pieter. "De groeipijnen van de trust. Op zoek naar een nieuw collectief." (The Growing Pains of the Trust: Seeking a New Collective.) *Tmaker.* 1998; 2(1): 36-40. Illus.: Photo. B&W. 3. Lang.: Dut.
Netherlands: Amsterdam. 1995-1998. Historical studies. ■Presents the history of De Trust, a young company, now that the troupe is targeting a new approach and repertoire.

1679 Rowell, Charles H. "Interview with Felix de Rooy and Norman de Palm." *Callaloo.* 1998 Sum; 21(3): 568-571. Lang.: Eng.
Netherlands: Amsterdam. Netherlands Antilles. 1988. Histories-sources. ■Interview with the founders of the Dutch multicultural theatre company, Cosmic Illusions, about the influence of their native Curaçao on their theatrical vision.

1680 Blumenthal, Eileen. "Arctic Heat." *AmTh.* 1998 Nov.; 15(9): 54-57. Illus.: Photo. B&W. 1. Lang.: Eng.
Norway: Stamsund. 1998. Critical studies. ■Relationship between the company Teater NOR and its home community of Stamsund.

1681 Muinzer, Louis. "The 1998 Ibsen Festival in Oslo." *WES.* 1998 Fall; 10(3): 27-34. Illus.: Photo. B&W. 4. Lang.: Eng.
Norway: Oslo. 1998. Historical studies. ■Report on the 1998 festival dedicated to the work of Ibsen.

1682 Muinzer, Louis. "The Ibsen Stage Festival." *INC.* 1998; 18: 15-17. Illus.: Photo. B&W. 3. Lang.: Eng.
Norway: Oslo. 1998. Historical studies. ■Survey of the 1998 Ibsen Festival.

1683 Muinzer, Louis. "The 1998 Ibsen Festival." *PlPl.* 1998 Nov.; 528: 25. Lang.: Eng.
Norway: Oslo. 1998. Historical studies. ■Multiple perspectives on Ibsen's *Brand* and *Peer Gynt* at Norwegian National Theatre's 1998 Ibsen Festival, with review of many of the productions.

1684 Allain, Paul. "Drama in the Tatras: Teatr St I Witkiewicza." *PM.* 1990(60): 8-13. Illus.: Photo. B&W. 4. Lang.: Eng.
Poland: Zakopane. 1989. Critical studies. ■Profile of the theatre company with comments on performances of Marlowe's *Doctor Faustus* and Witkiewicz' *Beelzebub's Sonata (Sonata Belzebuba).*

1685 Flaszen, Ludwik. "Kilka kluczy do laboratotiów, studiów i instytutów." (A Few Keys to Laboratories, Studios and Institutes.) *DialogW.* 1998 July; 7: 108-117. Illus.: Photo. B&W. 2. Lang.: Pol.
Poland: Cracow, Wrocław, Warsaw. 1930-1998. Historical studies. ■Polish laboratories and institutes devoted to theatrical education in the twentieth century, especially experimental theatre, including Grotowski and Kantor's approaches in the light of Stanislavskij, Osterwa, and Artaud.

1686 Hannowa, Anna. "Wileńskie lata Jakuba Rotbauma." (Jakub Rotbaum at Vilna.) 331-349 in Kozłowska, Mirosława, ed. *Wilno teatralne.* Warsaw: Ogólnopolski Klub Miłośników Litwy; 1998. 478 pp. Lang.: Pol.
Poland: Vilna. 1929-1938. Historical studies. ■New repertory and *mise en scène* of the Jewish theatre group, Trupa Wileńska, under the artistic leadership of Jakub Rotbaum.

1687 Kornas, Tadeusz. "Göttliche Fragen am Ende der Welt." (Divine Questions at the End of the World.) 138-151 in Pochhammer, Sabine, ed. *Utopie: Spiritualität? Spiritualité: une utopie?/Utopia: Spirituality? Spirituality: A Utopia?.* Berlin: Theaterschrift c/o Künstlerhaus Bethanien; 1998. 173 pp. (Theaterschrift 13.) Illus.: Photo. B&W. 2. Lang.: Ger, Fre, Dut, Eng.
Poland: Gardzienice. 1978-1998. Histories-sources. ■Interview with Włodzimierz Staniewski, founder and artistic director of the Gardzienice Theatre Association, regarding the twenty-year history of the institution.

1688 Kubikowski, Tomasz; Stajewski, Marcin. *Ateneum 1928-1998.* (Ateneum Theatre, 1928-1998.) Warszawa: Teatr Ateneum im. Stefana Jaracza; Illus.: Handbill. Photo. Poster. Dwg. Design. B&W. Color. 345. Lang.: Pol.
Poland: Warsaw. 1928-1998. Histories-specific. ■Pictorial history of the Ateneum Theatre in Warsaw, as seen in repertory and documentary photographs.

1689 Leżeńska, Katarzyna. "Habima w Polsce." (HaBimah in Poland.) 181-195 in Kuligowska-Korzeniewska, Anna, ed.; Leyko, Małgorzata, ed. *Teatr żydowski w Polsce.* Lodz: Wydawnictwo Uniwersytetu Łódzkiego; 1998. pp. Lang.: Pol.
Poland. 1926-1938. Historical studies. ■The significance of three visits by the Hebrew theatre company HaBimah to the Polish Jewish community. Audience and press reactions reflected the present state of Jewish culture and the political situation of Jews in Poland.

1690 Linert, Andrzej. *Teatr Śląski im. Stanisława Wyspiańskiego w Katowicach 1949-1992.* (Stanisław Wyspiański's Silesian Theatre in Katowice, 1949-1992.) Katowice: Instytut Górnośląski; 1998. 395 pp. Pref. Index. Illus.: Photo. B&W. 299. Lang.: Pol.
Poland: Katowice. 1949-1992. Historical studies. ■Describes the repertory, staging, and acting at Stanisław Wyspiański's Silesian Theatre (Teatr Śląski). Also examines deliberations on the theatre's artistic profile proposed by its directors, and includes biographical information on the actors that worked there.

1691 Ślusarska, Magdalena. "Wilno teatralne w czasach Stanisława Augusta Poniatowskiego." (Theatre in Vilna During Stanisław August Poniatowski's Reign.) 17-38 in Kozłowska, Mirosława, ed. *Wilno teatralne.* Warsaw: Ogólnopolski Klub Miłośników Litway; 1998. 478 pp. Lang.: Pol.
Poland: Vilna. 1732-1798. Historical studies. ■Examines the theatrical activities of nonprofessional theatres performing in Vilna, from the first Jesuit school theatres up to the great public ceremonies during the time of Stanisław August Poniatowski.

1692 Wysiński, Kazimierz Andrzej. *Związek Artystów Scen Polskich 1950-1998.* (Polish Theatre Association, 1950-1998: A Brief History.) Warsaw: Związek Artystów Scen Polskich; 1998. 199 pp. Notes. Pref. Index. Append. Illus.: Photo. Dwg. B&W. 49. Lang.: Pol.
Poland: Warsaw. 1918-1998. Historical studies. ■Examines the activity of the Polish Theatre Association through the papers of its presidents, Leon Schiller, Gustaw Holoubek, and Andrzej Szczepkowski. Also includes a list of the association's members.

1693 Kántor, Lajos; Kötő, József. *Magyar színház Erdélyben 1919-1992.* (Hungarian Theatre in Transylvania 1919-1992.) Bucharest: Integral; 1998. 206 pp. Append. Illus.: Photo. B&W. 43. Lang.: Hun, Rom.
Romania. Hungary. 1919-1992. Histories-specific. ■A comprehensive study in the history of Hungarian theatre life in Romania with rich collection of data on the operation of professional theatrical companies in chronological order arranged by place.

1694 "100-letie Moskovskogo Chudožestvennogo akademičeskogo teatra." (Centennial of the Moscow Art

DRAMA: —Institutions

Theatre.) *Vestnik archivista.* 1998; 6(48): 143-160. Lang.: Rus.
Russia: Moscow. 1898-1998. Historical studies. ▪Celebration of the institution on its 100th anniversary.

1695 *Omskij akademičeskij teat'r dramy. 125-j sezon: Pis'ma iz teatra, N 15, okt. 1998 g.* (Omsk Drama Theatre. 125th Season. Letters from the Theatre: October 1998.) Omsk: 1998. 96 pp. Lang.: Rus.
Russia: Omsk. 1998. Historical studies. ▪Profile of the Omsk Drama Theatre.

1696 Aleksandrov, S. "Piramida Mel'pomeny: Budni i prazdniki Pskov. akad. teatra dramy im. A.S. Puškina." (The Pyramid of Melpomene: The Weekdays and the Holidays of the Pskov Pushkin Theatre.) *Vstreča.* 1998; 3: 36-37. Lang.: Rus.
Russia: Pskov. Historical studies. ▪Profile of the Pskov Pushkin Theatre.

1697 Bérczes, László. "Don Juannal a zárdában." (At the Nunnery with Don Juan.) *Sz.* 1998; 31(9): 35-37. Illus.: Photo. B&W. 2. Lang.: Hun.
Russia: Moscow. 1998. Historical studies. ▪A report on a visit to Anatolij Vasiljėv's own theatre in Moscow, the Škola Dramatičėskogo Iskusstva.

1698 Bogatyreva, M. "Delo o nasledstve: 26 ili 27 okt. ispolnjaetsja 100 let MChATu." (It Has Something To Do with Heritage: October 26 or 27 Will Mark the Centennial of MAT.) *NV.* 1998; 41: 40-43. Lang.: Rus.
Russia: Moscow. 1998. Historical studies. ▪The two theatres (the Čechov and the Gor'kij) of the Moscow Art Theatre and their artistic directors, Oleg Jėfremov and Tatjana Doronina.

1699 Čečetin, A. *Scenarnoe masterstvo: Progr. dlja studentov fak. 'Kul'turovedenie' (spec. 'Režissura teatraliz. predstavlenij').* (The Art of Playwriting: A Program for Students of the Faculty of Culture.) Moscow: 1998. 14 pp. Lang.: Rus.
Russia: Moscow. 1998. Instructional materials. ▪Description of the playwriting and production program.

1700 Dubrovskij, V. "Moskovskij akademičėskij teat'r im. Vl. Majakovskogo v god svoego 75-letija." (Moscow's Majakovskij Theatre in the Year of Its Seventy-Fifth Anniversary.) 654-658 in *God planety.* Moscow: Respublika; 1998. Lang.: Rus.
Russia: Moscow. 1923-1998. Historical studies. ▪Profile of the Majakovskij Theatre on its 75th anniversary.

1701 Dürr, Carola. "Wo bitte liegt Minusinsk?" (Where Is Minusinsk, Please?)*THeute.* 1998; 5: 33-35. Illus.: Photo. B&W. 2. Lang.: Ger.
Russia: Minusinsk. 1998. Historical studies. ▪Impressions from the international Russian festival and award of 'The Golden Mask' in Minusinsk. Reviews Eugene O'Neill's *A Moon for the Misbegotten* directed by Klim, and Ostrovskij's *Groza (The Storm)* directed by Genrietta Janovskaja.

1702 Fadeeva, I.N. *Vsem, kto ljubit teat'r.* (To All Who Love the Theatre.) Kaliningrad: Jantarn. skaz; 1998. 174 pp. Lang.: Rus.
Russia: Kaliningrad. 1947-1997. Historical studies. ▪History of the Kaliningrad Theatre.

1703 Goder, D. "Konec sjužeta: Énciklopedija MChATa, vypuščennaja k 100-letiju teatra, vpervye bez umolčanij i lži rasskazyvaet o ego žizni." (The End of an Episode: *The Encyclopedia of MAT*, Published to Mark the Theatre's Centennial, Tells about Life as It Is without Half-Truths or Lies.) *Itogi.* 1998; 42: 58-60. Lang.: Rus.
Russia: Moscow. 1898-1998. Historical studies. ▪Describes reference book covering the one hundred years of the Moscow Art Theatre.

1704 Golubovskij, A. "Sto let 'raboty so zritelem'." (One Hundred Years of Working with the Audience.) *Itogi.* 1998; 42: 60-62. Lang.: Rus.
Russia: Moscow. 1898-1998. Historical studies. ▪One hundred years of the Moscow Art Theatre.

1705 Henry, B.J. *Theatrical Parody at the Krivoe zerkalo: Russian teatr miniatyur, 1908-1931.* Oxford: Unpublished PhD, Univ. of Oxford; 1996. Notes. Biblio. [Abstract in *Aslib Index to Theses* 47-5467.] Lang.: Eng.
Russia: St. Petersburg. 1908-1931. Historical studies. ▪History of the presentation of theatrical parodies presented by Krivoje zerkalo, headed by director Nikolaj Jėvrejnov, drawn largely from reviews, advertisements, published and unpublished memoirs, programs, and photographs. Lists the company's several hundred plays and analyzes selected parodies.

1706 Ignatjuk, O. "Teat'r ljudej." (Theatre of People.) *Mosk.* 1998; 12: 157-160. Lang.: Rus.
Russia: Omsk. 1998. Historical studies. ▪Profile of the Omsk Dramatic Theatre, 'Galerka'.

1707 Kuz'mina, S. *Omskij akademičeskij teatr dramy: Pis'ma iz teatra.* (Omsk's Dramatic Theatre: Letters from the Theatre.) Omsk: 1998. 64 pp. Lang.: Rus.
Russia: Omsk. 1998. Historical studies. ▪Profile of Omsk's Dramatic Theatre.

1708 Litvinceva, G. "Palitra radosti: Zametki s obl. festivalja ėstradn. iskusstva v Saratove." (Pitcher of Happiness: Notes from the Stage Festival in Saratov.) *NTE.* 1998; 4: 42-43. Lang.: Rus.
Russia: Saratov. 1998. Historical studies. ▪Account of the Saratov stage festival.

1709 Medvedeva, I. "Dom Ostrovskogo." (The House of Ostrovskij.) *MoskZ.* 1998; July-Aug: 80-81. Lang.: Rus.
Russia: Moscow. 1998. Historical studies. ▪Account of 'Ostrovskij in the House of Ostrovskij', third theatre festival marking the 175th birthday of the Malyj Theatre.

1710 Orechanova, G. "V dialoge s vekom: K 100-letiju MChATa." (In Dialogue with a Century: Centennial of MAT.) *Mosk.* 1998; 10: 158-170. Lang.: Rus.
Russia: Moscow. 1898-1998. Historical studies. ▪Centennial celebration of the Moscow Art Theatre.

1711 Prozorova, N., ed. *Akademičėskij TJuZ Kiseleva, Saratov.* (The Kiselev Youth Theatre, Saratov.) Saratov: 1998. 64 pp. Lang.: Rus.
Russia: Saratov. 1998. Historical studies. ▪Profile of the Kiselev Theatre.

1712 Serazetdinov, B. "Vivat, 'Grotesk'." (Long Live 'Grotesk'.) *Jugra.* 1998; 11: 37. Lang.: Rus.
Russia: Surgut. 1998. Historical studies. ▪Use of satire in the work of Teat'r Grotesk, a student theatre group at the National University.

1713 Shteir, Rachel. "Sisters, Samovars and Second Acts." *AmTh.* 1998 Apr.; 15(4): 27-30. Illus.: Photo. B&W. 3. Lang.: Eng.
Russia: Moscow. 1901-1998. Historical studies. ▪History of performances of Čechov's *Three Sisters (Tri sestry)* by the Moscow Art Theatre.

1714 Solov'eva, I. *Vetvi i korni.* (Branches and Roots.) Moscow: 1998. 160 pp. Lang.: Rus.
Russia: Moscow. 1898-1998. Historical studies. ▪History of Moscow Art Theatre, on the occasion of its centennial.

1715 Stachov, D. "Ešče tot podval." (And The Basement, Too.) *Ogonek.* 1998; 20: 28-33. Lang.: Rus.
Russia: Moscow. 1998. Historical studies. ▪Profile of Oleg Tabakov's Studio Theatre.

1716 Teljakovskij, V.A.; Svetaeva, M.G., ed.; Šichman, S.Ja., ed. *Dnevniki direktora Imperatorskich teatrov. 1898-1901.* (Diaries of the Director of Imperial Theatres, 1898-1901.) Moscow: Artist. Režisser. Teatr; 1998. 748 pp. Lang.: Rus.
Russia: St. Petersburg. 1898-1901. Histories-sources. ▪Diaries of V.A. Teljakovskij: unique reflections on Russian theatrical developments at the turn of the century.

1717 Zajcev, M.S. "Gavrila Solodovnikov i ego teat'r." (Gavrila Solodovnikov and His Theatre.) *MoskZ.* 1998; 11: 55-58. Lang.: Rus.
Russia: Moscow. 1890-1899. Historical studies. ▪Profile of Gavrila Solodovnikov and his Teat'r na Dmitrovke.

1718 Moravec, Dušan. *Desetletje na prepihu.* (A Decade on a Current of Air.) Ljubljana: SGFM; 1998. 139 pp. (Documents of Slovene Theatre and Film Museum 70-71.) Pref. Illus.: Photo. B&W. 15. Lang.: Slo.
Slovenia: Ljubljana. 1951-1961. Histories-specific. ▪A chronology of performances at the Ljubljana Municipal Theatre (Mestno gledališče

ljubljansko) in its first decade, based on handwritten materials by the author, who was the literary manager at the time. It describes the difficulties the theatre faced as a result of managing boards, all of whom interfered with the theatre's repertoire or artistic policy.

1719 Peršak, Tone. *Teoretično samoutemeljevanje slovenskega nacionalnega gledališča.* (Theoretical Self-Affirmation of the Slovene National Theatre.) Ljubljana: SGFM; 1998. 58 pp. (Documents of National Theatre and Film Museum 68.) Lang.: Slo.

Slovenia. Germany. 1789-1867. Histories-specific. ■Explores the Slovene self-image evident in its historical creation of a national theatre. Argues that while G.E. Lessing's theories of autonomous theatre was one model for Slovene theatre pioneers, the importance of the 'art of speech' served as another equally important aesthetic model.

1720 Pusič, Barbara. *Med prevratništvom in apologijo—nacionalna gledališča skozi čas.* (Between Revolution and Apology—National Theatres through the Ages.) Ljubljana: SGFM; 1998. 113 pp. (Documents of National Theatre and Film Museum 69.) Lang.: Slo.

Slovenia. Germany. 1750-1910. Histories-specific. ■The historical process that resulted in the creation of national theatres all over Europe, with emphasis on the Slovene national theatre. Attributes the late development of the Slovene theatre to German cultural and political domination and to the scatteredness of the Slovene theatrical tradition, which was dependent on religious and conservative social classes.

1721 O'Quinn, Jim. "Say It in Catalan." *AmTh.* 1998 Jan.; 15(1): 65-68. Illus.: Dwg. B&W. 2. Lang.: Eng.

Spain-Catalonia: Barcelona. 1997. Historical studies. ■Report on the Grec '97, the annual theatre, music, and dance festival in Barcelona.

1722 Aronsson, Gunnar Martin. "Fassbinder, Herzog och jag." (Fassbinder, Herzog and Me.) *Entré.* 1998; 25(3/4): 72-77. Illus.: Photo. B&W. Lang.: Swe.

Sweden: Stockholm. Germany: Munich. 1968-1998. Histories-sources. ■Personal recollection of the Action-Theater, later called Antitheater with Rainer Werner Fassbinder, which together with his and Werner Herzog's films inspired the Swedish group TeaterX2.

1723 Brovik, Ingela. "Den nya konsten skapas i de fula städerna." (The New Art Is Created In the Ugly Cities.) *Entré.* 1998; 25(3/4): 69-71. Illus.: Photo. B&W. Lang.: Swe.

Sweden: Malmö. 1995-1998. Histories-sources. ■The new investment in culture at the former industrial city Malmö, with interviews with the marketing director Magnus Thure Nilsson at Malmö Dramatiska Teater and the director Staffan Valdemar Holm.

1724 Carlson, Harry G. "Strindberg and O'Neill at the Stockholm Cultural Year Festival: Revisionism and Eroticism." *WES.* 1998 Fall; 10(3): 5-12. Illus.: Photo. B&W. 8. Lang.: Eng.

Sweden: Stockholm. 1998. Historical studies. ■Report on the 1998 theatre festival in Stockholm with emphasis on O'Neill's *Long Day's Journey Into Night*, directed by Thorsten Flinck for Dramaten, Strindberg's *Master Olof (Mäster Olof)*, directed by Mattias Lafolie, *Erik XIV*, directed by Ekaterina Elanskaja for Teat'r Sfera, and *Playing with Fire (Leka med elden)*, produced by Teatro Nacional Chileno, and directed by Staffan Valdemar Holm.

1725 Haglund, Birgitta. "Vi övar oss för att bli teaterchefer." (We Are Practicing Being Theatre Managers.) *Tningen.* 1998; 21(2): 15-17. Illus.: Photo. B&W. Lang.: Swe.

Sweden: Stockholm. 1997-1998. Historical studies. ■Profile of Kvinnliga Dramatiska Teatern (The Female Dramatic Theatre), an independent group of feminist actresses and playwrights, including interviews with Karin Stigsdotter, Bente Danielsson, Sophie Tolstoy Regen and Ann Charlotte Franzén.

1726 Hermansson, Kristina. "Nyskriven svensk dramatik för en ung publik." (New Swedish Plays Written For a Young Audience.) *Tningen.* 1998; 21(5): 7-10. Illus.: Photo. B&W. Color. Lang.: Swe.

Sweden: Borås. 1994-1998. Histories-sources. ■Interview with the artistic manager of Älvsborgsteatern, Ronnie Hallgren, about the theatre for young people and the fruitful cooperation with young Swedish authors, with reference to *Född skyldig (Born Guilty)* based on interviews and produced by Eva Molin.

1727 Hoogland, Rikard. "Teater 23." *Tningen.* 1998; 21(5): 14-15. Illus.: Photo. B&W. Lang.: Swe.

Sweden: Malmö. 1959-1998. Historical studies. ■Report from Teater 23 with its plays for children, with reference to the artistic manager Harald Leander.

1728 Hoogland, Rikard. "Svensk Symbolistisk Teater." (Swedish Symbolist Theatre.) *Tningen.* 1998; 21(5): 13-14. Illus.: Dwg. B&W. Lang.: Swe.

Sweden: Malmö. 1997. Historical studies. ■Profile of the Svensk Symbolisk Teater and its first production of Gustaf Fröding's *En Ghasel (A Gazelle)*, with an interview with the artistic manager Christian Jonsson.

1729 Janzon, Leif. "Vi som älskade varandra så mycket." (We All Loved Each Other So Much.) *Entré.* 1998; 25(3/4): 78-80. Illus.: Photo. B&W. Lang.: Swe.

Sweden. 1960-1969. Historical studies. ■A short survey of the theatre in Sweden since the sixties.

1730 Lahger, Håkan. "Ingrid Dahlberg med dörren öppen." (Ingrid Dahlberg With Her Door Open.) *Dramat.* 1998; 6(2) : 22-25. Illus.: Photo. B&W. Color. Lang.: Swe.

Sweden: Stockholm. 1996-1998. Histories-sources. ■Interview with Ingrid Dahlberg, after her first year as manager of Kungliga Dramatiska Teatern, with reference to the conception of a national theatre.

1731 Lewin, Jan. "När vackra ord blir handling." (When Beautiful Words Turn To Action.) *Entré.* 1998; 25(2): 43. Illus.: Photo. B&W. Lang.: Swe.

Sweden: Borås. 1995-1998. Historical studies. ■Älvsborgsteatern, under its director Ronnie Hallgren, converted from a dance ensemble to tour around the country, with only new Swedish creations aiming at an audience of children and young people.

1732 Lindvag, Anita Lydia. *Elsa Olenius och vår teater.* (Elsa Olenius and Vår Teater.) Lund: Lunds Universitet; 1988. 286 pp. Biblio. Notes. [Ph.D. Dissertation, available from Raben & Sjogren, Box 45022, 104 30 Stockholm, Sweden.] Lang.: Swe.

Sweden: Stockholm. 1942-1980. Historical studies. ■Examines the children's theatre, Vår Teater, founded by Elsa Olenius, and its use of storytelling and dramatization of children's literature.

1733 Rislund, Staffan. "Alternativ till tråkig teater." (The Alternative to a Dull Theatre.) *Entré.* 1998; 25(2): 9-12. Illus.: Photo. B&W. Lang.: Swe.

Sweden: Stockholm. 1989-1998. Historical studies. ■Presentation of improvisations by Stockholms Improvisationsteater (SIT) where you never have a dull moment, inspired by Keith Johnstone's book *Impro* about theatre sport and improvisation.

1734 Wallström, Catharina. "Teatern måste bli mer teatral!" (The Theatre Must Be More Theatrical!) *Tningen.* 1998; 21 (4): 15-18. Illus.: Photo. B&W. Lang.: Swe.

Sweden: Gothenburg. 1992-1998. Histories-sources. ■Interview with the producer Rolf Sossna about his background and way to the group En Annan Teater, with a direct appeal to the audience, using old theatrical techniques, with references to their productions of *Tusen och en natt* and Strindberg's *Ett Drömspel.*

1735 "Jugendtheaterclubs." (Young People's Theatre Clubs.) *Tatr.* 1998; 39: 3-5. Illus.: Photo. B&W. 5. Lang.: Ger, Fre.

Switzerland. 1998. Historical studies. ■Portrait of different theatre groups for young people: Jugendclub Mo, Junges Theater Frauenfeld, Junges Theater Basel, Zanck & Zucker.

1736 Niquille, Marie-Claire. "Harte Arbeit und saftige Früchte." (Hard Work and Juicy Fruit.) *Tatr.* 1998; 39: 8-9. Illus.: Photo. B&W. 3. Lang.: Ger.

Switzerland: Basel. 1998. Historical studies. ■Report on the children's theatre festival Spilplätz, the first meeting of Jugendclubs (young people's clubs) from Swiss theatres.

1737 Stumm, Reinhardt. "Boys Back in Town." *THeute.* 1998; 11: 34-38. Illus.: Photo. B&W. 4. Lang.: Ger.

Switzerland: Basel. 1998. Critical studies. ■Stefan Bachmann's start as theatre-manager of drama in Basel, the financial situation at the institution and newly introduced concepts. Describes Friedrich Hebbel's *Maria Magdalene* directed by Andreas Kriegenburg.

DRAMA: —Institutions

1738 Munk, Erika. "Report from Istanbul: The Meeting of East and West." *ThM.* 1998; 28(2): 91-95. Lang.: Eng.
Turkey: Istanbul. Turkey: Istanbul. 1998. Historical studies. ■Report on the 1998 Istanbul Theatre Festival.

1739 Callens, Johan. "Forced Entertainment: Tijdig Tegentijds." (Forced Entertainment: Timely Countermeasures.) *Documenta.* 1996; 16(3): 201-214. Lang.: Dut.
UK-England: Sheffield. 1996. Historical studies. ■Profile of the Forced Entertainment Theatre Cooperative.

1740 Gilbey, Liz. "Reshaping the Rep." *PI.* 1998 Nov.; 14(2): 12-13. Illus.: Photo. B&W. 3. Lang.: Eng.
UK-England: Birmingham. 1998. Histories-sources. ■Interview with Bill Alexander, artistic director of Birmingham Repertory Theatre.

1741 Muinzer, Louis. "Shakespeare's Globe Reborn." *WES.* 1998 Spr; 10(2): 87-94. Illus.: Photo. B&W. 2. Lang.: Eng.
UK-England: London. 1997-1998. Historical studies. ■Account of the inaugural season of Shakespeare's Globe Theatre with reference to three of the four plays produced there: Shakespeare's *Henry V*, directed by Richard Olivier, *The Winter's Tale*, directed by David Freeman, and Beaumont and Fletcher's *The Maid's Tragedy*, directed by Lucy Bailey.

1742 Paran, Janice. "Caro Newling: Industrial Light and Magic." *AmTh.* 1998 Sep.; 15(7): 63. Illus.: Photo. B&W. 1. Lang.: Eng.
UK-England: London. 1998. Biographical studies. ■Profile of Newling, the executive producer of the Donmar Warehouse theatre.

1743 Ramsden, Timothy. "Edinburgh International Festival." *PlPl.* 1998 Nov.; 528: 23, 29. Lang.: Eng.
UK-England: London. 1998. Critical studies. ■Theatre selections at the 1998 Edinburgh Festival and Edinburgh Fringe Festival.

1744 Ramsden, Timothy. "Spotlight on Watermill Theatre, Newbury." *PlPl.* 1998 Oct.; 527: 24. Lang.: Eng.
UK-England: Newbury. 1998. Historical studies. ■Increased funding keeping Watermill Theatre afloat, allowing innovative productions to continue. Reviews their 1998 production of Kander and Ebb's *Cabaret*, directed by John Doyle.

1745 Robson, Christopher. "Shaftesbury Avenue By the Sea." *PlPl.* June 1998; 523: 31. Lang.: Eng.
UK-England: Chichester. 1998. Histories-sources. ■Andrew Welch, new Festival Director at Chichester, on his programming choices and the effort to recapture Chichester Festival's dwindling audiences.

1746 Smythe, Eva. "Beginners Please!" *PlPl.* June 1998; 523: 28. Lang.: Eng.
UK-England: London. 1998. Critical studies. ■Critique of London theatre schools' practice of producing showcases as means of presenting graduating students to agents and casting directors.

1747 Waites, Aline. "Life Goes On." *PlPl.* Jan 1998; 518: 14. Lang.: Eng.
UK-England: London. 1970-1998. Histories-sources. ■Dan Crawford, proprietor of King's Head pub and theatre, on its founding and history.

1748 Waites, Aline. "Fringe Update." *PlPl.* Mar 1998; 520: 13. Lang.: Eng.
UK-England: London. 1998. Historical studies. ■Funding status of London's fringe theatres: King's Head, Gate and Greenwich Theatre.

1749 Williams, David Alan. *Joint Stock and the Staging of Dialogism: Collaboration, Gender, and Race in Plays and Practice.* Davis, CA: Univ. of California; 1998. 329 pp. Notes. Biblio. [Ph.D. Dissertation, Univ. Microfilms Order No. AAC 9900115.] Lang.: Eng.
UK-England: London. 1974-1989. Histories-specific. ■Draws on Mikhail Bakhtin's theory of dialogism to analyze the theatrical method used by the Joint Stock Theatre Group, which includes exploratory research and interviews, improvisation, writing styles, and rehearsal style. Joint Stock's use of collective action, collaboration and the role of gender and ethnicity in the company is also examined.

1750 "As Good As It Gets." *Econ.* 1998 Aug 29; 348(8083): 74-75. Illus.: Photo. B&W. 1. Lang.: Eng.
UK-Scotland: Edinburgh. 1998. Historical studies. ■Report on the 1998 Edinburgh Fringe Festival.

1751 Goder, D. "Igrajuščie i pojuščie pod doždem." (Playful People and Singing in the Rain.) *Itogi.* 1998 ; 41: 72-75. Lang.: Rus.
UK-Scotland: Edinburgh. 1998. Historical studies. ■Report on the Edinburgh Festival.

1752 Marshalsay, K.A. *The Scottish National Players: in the nature of an experiment 1913-1934.* Glasgow: Unpublished PhD, Univ. of Glasgow; 1991. Notes. Biblio. [Abstract in *Aslib Index to Theses* 47-171.] Lang.: Eng.
UK-Scotland. 1913-1934. Histories-specific. ■Historical account of the Scottish National Players, from the first proposals to the disbanding of the Scottish National Theatre Society. Focuses on its aim to produce plays highlighting Scottish life and character and to engender the audience taste for good drama as well as the establishment of a national theatre.

1753 "Annual Report 1997-98." *AmTh.* 1998 Dec.; 15(10): 87-96. Illus.: Photo. B&W. 14. Lang.: Eng.
USA. 1997-1998. Historical studies. ■Annual report on the activities, projects and grants allocated by the Theatre Communications Group. Includes a list of constituent theatres.

1754 "Theatre Facts 1997." *AmTh.* 1998 Nov.; 15(9): Supp 1-11. Tables. Lang.: Eng.
USA. 1997. Historical studies. ■Report on the practices and performances in the American nonprofit theatre based on Theatre Communications Group's annual fiscal survey.

1755 "Fall 1998 Meeting Celebrates Centennial of *When We Dead Awaken.*" *INC.* 1998; 18: 4-7. Illus.: Photo. B&W. 1. Lang.: Eng.
USA: New York, NY. 1998. Historical studies. ■Report on meeting held by the Ibsen Society of America to note the upcoming centennial of Ibsen's publication of *När vi døde vågner (When We Dead Awaken).*

1756 Allen, Howard. "A Desert Romance." *AmTh.* 1998 Apr.; 15(4): 42-43. Illus.: Photo. B&W. 1. Lang.: Eng.
USA: Tempe, AZ, Tucson, AZ, Phoenix, AZ. 1995-1998. Historical studies. ■The efforts of Tempe's youth theatre Childsplay and the conventional Tuscon and Phoenix based Arizona Theatre Company to join forces in order to reach a broader audience.

1757 Backalenick, Irene. *A History of the Jewish Repertory Theater.* New York, NY: City Univ. of New York; 1987. 309 pp. Notes. Biblio. [Ph.D. Dissertation, Univ. Microfilms Order No. AAC 8708272.] Lang.: Eng.
USA: New York, NY. 1974-1984. Historical studies. ■Chronicles the first ten-year period of the Jewish Repertory Theatre (JRT) in New York City and examines Ran Avni's role as its co-founder and artistic director.

1758 Blackadder, Neil. "A Decade in Helms Country." *AmTh.* 1998 Mar.; 15(3): 44-46. Illus.: Photo. B&W. 2. Lang.: Eng.
USA: Durham, NC. 1989-1998. Historical studies. ■Profile of the theatre company Manbites Dog, and their strategies for continuing to present topical and controversial theatre in the heart of anti-intellectual senator Jesse Helms' home state.

1759 Cantara, Jamie Smith. "Vicky Boone: Frontera Spirit." *AmTh.* 1998 Sep.; 15(7): 66-67. Illus.: Photo. B&W. 1. Lang.: Eng.
USA: Austin, TX. 1998. Biographical studies. ■Profile of Boone, artistic director of Frontera Theatre.

1760 Coggan, Catherine. "Authentic to the Underwear." *AmTh.* 1998 Apr.; 15(4): 44. Illus.: Photo. B&W. 1. Lang.: Eng.
USA: Madrid, NM. 1982-1998. Historical studies. ■Profile of the Engine House Theatre, which specializes in mounting late nineteenth and early twentieth-century melodramas.

1761 Friedman, Martin Edward. *Federal Theatre Project Shakespearean Productions: A Study of Presentational and Organizational Techniques.* Ann Arbor, MI: Univ. of Michigan; 1987. 308 pp. Notes. Biblio. [Ph.D. Dissertation, Univ. Microfilms Order No. AAC 8712115.] Lang.: Eng.
USA. 1935-1939. Historical studies. ■Examines the fifty-four documented productions of Shakespeare's plays by the Federal Theatre Project, with emphasis on regional significance of the productions, and the social issues addressed in the context of the American Depression.

DRAMA: —Institutions

1762 Gagnon, Pauline D. *The Development and Achievement of La MaMa Under the Artistic Direction of Ellen Stewart.* Ann Arbor, MI: Univ. of Michigan; 1987. 262 pp. Biblio. Notes. [Ph.D. Dissertation, Univ. Microfilms Order No. AAC 8712116.] Lang.: Eng.

USA: New York, NY. 1961-1985. Historical studies. ▪The history of the La MaMa Theatre in relation to the theatrical maturation of its founder, Ellen Stewart. Focuses on the institution's importance in contemporary American theatre, its influence, and its development.

1763 Giles, Freda Scott. "Black Theatre: National Festival Showcases Talent of African-American Performers, Writers, Production Groups." *SoTh.* 1998 Win; 39(1): 10-14. Illus.: Photo. 3. Lang.: Eng.

USA: Winston-Salem, NC. 1997. Historical studies. ▪Reports on the annual National Black Theatre Festival, which included a wide variety of provocative performances, speeches and seminars.

1764 Gluck, David. "Dangerous Minds at Play." *AmTh.* 1998 Mar.; 15(3): 47-49. Illus.: Photo. B&W. 1. Lang.: Eng.

USA: Richmond, CA. 1958-1998. Historical studies. ▪Role of the East Bay Center for the Performing Arts in the ressuscitation of a distressed Northern California community.

1765 Griffith, Isela Angelica. *An Unfinished Sculpture: The Revolutionary Work of Judith Malina in America, 1968-1969.* Bronxville, NY: Sarah Lawrence College; 1998. 69 pp. Notes. Biblio. [M.A. Thesis, Univ. Microfilms Order No. AAC 1390595.] Lang.: Eng.

USA. 1968-1969. Histories-specific. ▪Argues that Malina, actress, activist, and founding member of the Living Theatre company, was unable to create an active, mixed-media theatre in the heightened political climate of the late 1960s.

1766 Gussow, Mel. "First Things First." *AmTh.* 1998 Jan.; 15(1): 27. Illus.: Dwg. B&W. 1. Lang.: Eng.

USA: New York, NY. 1997. Histories-sources. ▪Interview with one of the founders of the Actors Studio, Robert Lewis.

1767 Hirsch, Foster. "Arthur Penn's Open Door." *AmTh.* 1998 Jan.; 15(1): 24-26, 28-29. Illus.: Dwg. B&W. 11. Lang.: Eng.

USA: New York, NY. 1997. Biographical studies. ▪Profile of the president of the Actors Studio, Arthur Penn, as the drama school enters its fiftieth year. Includes sidebar comments by actors David Margulies, Sally Kirkland, Julie Harris, Beatrice Roth, Kim Hunter, and playwrights Israel Horovitz and Romulus Linney about the influence of the institution on their work.

1768 Kazacoff, George. *Dangerous Theatre: The Federal Theatre Project as a Forum for New Plays.* New York, NY: New York Univ; 1987. 369 pp. Biblio. Notes. [Ph.D. Dissertation, Univ. Microfilms Order No. AAC 8712756.] Lang.: Eng.

USA. 1935-1939. Historical studies. ▪Examines the activities of the various organizations of the Federal Theatre Project involved with fostering the writing and production of new plays.

1769 Kenney, Janet Rose. *The Free Southern Theater: The Relationship Between Mission and Management.* Eugene, OR: Univ. of Oregon; 1987. 270 pp. Biblio. Notes. [Ph.D. Dissertation, Univ. Microfilms Order No. AAC 8808688.] Lang.: Eng.

USA: New Orleans, LA. 1963-1980. Historical studies. ▪Analyzes the history of the theatre from the perspective of the relationship between the missions it chose and the management that attempted to implement those missions.

1770 Key, Nancy Martin. *A Narrative History of Lake Charles Little Theatre, Lake Charles, Louisiana, 1927-1982.* New York, NY: New York Univ; 1987. 290 pp. Biblio. Notes. [Ph.D. Dissertation, Univ. Microfilms Order No. AAC 8720126.] Lang.: Eng.

USA: Lake Charles, LA. 1927-1982. Historical studies. ▪The activities of the theatre, founded by Rosa Hart, including the goals of the directors, classes, workshops, and non-production activities.

1771 Lechuga, Myriam. *The Saving of the Folger Shakespeare Theatre.* Washington, DC: American Univ; 1987. 114 pp. Notes. Biblio. [M.A. Thesis, Univ. Microfilms Order No. 1331647.] Lang.: Eng.

USA: Washington, DC. 1985-1987. Historical studies. ▪Documents the successful efforts of private and community groups to restructure the theatre.

1772 Matschulatt, Kay. "The House that Monte Built." *AmTh.* 1998 Oct.; 15(8): 84-85. Illus.: Photo. B&W. 1. Lang.: Eng.

USA: Madison, NJ. 1996-1998. Historical studies. ▪New Jersey Shakespeare Festival's artistic director Bonnie Monte, the driving force behind the construction of its new home, the F.M. Kirby Theatre.

1773 Miles, Shanda. "Summit II—Atlanta, Georgia." *BlackM.* 1998 Oct/Nov.; 13(2): 20-21, 23. Lang.: Eng.

USA: Atlanta, GA. 1998. Historical studies. ▪Report on the followup to the National Black Theatre Summit in New Hampshire conducted by the African Grove Institute for the Arts in Atlanta.

1774 Moore, Dick. "Women's Project Celebrates 20 Years: Sponsors Conference Focusing on Creativity and Future of Women in Theatre." *EN.* 1998 Mar.; 83(2): 3. Lang.: Eng.

USA: New York, NY. 1978-1998. Historical studies. ▪Reports on the 20th anniversary of the Women's Project and Productions, founded and still directed by Julia Miles. Includes a short history of the institution and a report on its conference, 'Women in Theatre: Mapping the Sources of Power'.

1775 Moore, Dick. "Chicago's Shakespeare Rep Gets New Home, New Name." *EN.* 1998 Oct/Nov.; 83(3): 5. Illus.: Photo. 1. Lang.: Eng.

USA: Chicago, IL. 1998. Historical studies. ▪The Chicago Shakespeare Theatre, formerly known as the Shakespeare Repertory Theatre, and its new home.

1776 Nouryeh, Andrea Janet. *The Mercury Theatre: A History.* New York, NY: New York Univ; 1987. 384 pp. Biblio. Notes. [Ph.D. Dissertation, Univ. Microfilms Order No. AAC 8801558.] Lang.: Eng.

USA: New York, NY. 1937-1942. Historical studies. ▪Examines the Mercury Theatre, headed by John Houseman as producer and president, Orson Welles as director and vice president, and Augusta Weissberger as secretary and administrative head. Focuses on its direct descendence from the Federal Theatre Project, its internal conflicts, economic problems, critical failures, and shifts to radio and film.

1777 Reiss, Alvin H. "Continuity Breeds Success at Top Regional Theatre." *FundM.* 1998 Aug.; 29(6): 26-27. Illus.: Photo. B&W. 2. Lang.: Eng.

USA: Ashland, OR. 1952-1998. Biographical studies. ▪Profile of executive director emeritus of the Oregon Shakespeare Festival, William Patton, and his forty-seven-year association with the company.

1778 Rifkind, Bryna Beth. *The Palo Alto Children's Theatre, 1932-1997.* New York, NY: New York Univ; 1998. 528 pp. Notes. Biblio. [Ph.D. Dissertation, Univ. Microfilms Order No. AAC 9832763.] Lang.: Eng.

USA: Palo Alto, CA. 1932-1997. Histories-specific. ▪History of the Palo Alto Children's Theatre, the oldest theatre in the US to maintain its original format of theatre by and for children, founded by Hazel Glaister Robertson. Focuses on the theatre's artistic, social and educational programs.

1779 Ryen, Dag. "Humana: 1998 Festival Examines Contemporary Themes." *SoTh.* 1998 Sum; 39(3): 6-8. Illus.: Photo. B&W. 2. Lang.: Eng.

USA: Louisville, KY. 1998. Historical studies. ▪Examines the productions included in the 1998 Humana Festival of New American Plays, presented at the Actors Theatre of Louisville.

1780 Shafer, Yvonne. "The Chain Lightning Theatre." *EOR.* 1998 Spr/Fall; 22(1/2): 174-184. Lang.: Eng.

USA: New York, NY. 1991-1998. Histories-sources. ▪Interview with the founders of the theatre company, Kricker James and Claire Higgins, regarding their production of O'Neill's *The Great God Brown*, directed by James.

1781 Siegal, Nina. "Carey Perloff, Heather Kitchen and Melissa Smith: ACT's Three Sisters." *AmTh.* 1998 Sep.; 15(7): 73-74. Illus.: Photo. B&W. 1. Lang.: Eng.

USA: San Francisco, CA. 1992-1998. Historical studies. ▪Looks at the changes for women at American Conservatory Theatre with the installation of Carey Perloff as artistic director, Heather Kitchen as managing director, and Melissa Smith as conservatory director.

1782 Stovall, Count. "African Grove Institute Strategizes the Future: Summit I—Dartmouth College, New Hampshire." *BlackM.* 1998 Oct/Nov.; 13(2): 7-8, 20. Illus.: Photo. B&W. 1. Lang.: Eng.

USA: Dartmouth, NH. 1998. Historical studies. ■Report on the National Black Theatre Summit 'On Golden Pond.' Event was headed by August Wilson.

1783 Tanitch, Robert. "The Oregon Trail." *PlPl.* 1998 Nov.; 528: 26. Illus.: Photo. B&W. Color. 2. Lang.: Eng.

USA: Ashland, OR. 1998. Historical studies. ■Plays of Ashland's 1998 Oregon Shakespeare Festival. Also announces 1999 season.

1784 Tanitch, Robert. "Alabama Bound." *PlPl.* 1998 Sep.; 527: 28-29. Illus.: Photo. B&W. 1. Lang.: Eng.

USA: Montgomery, AL. 1972-1998. Historical studies. ■Brief history of Montgomery's Alabama Shakespeare Festival and capsule review of the plays in its 1998 season.

1785 Thomas, Melody Ann. *Jeannette Clift George: Founder, Artistic Director and Playwright-in-Residence of the A.D. Players, Houston's Christian Theatre Company.* Boulder, CO: Univ. of Colorado; 1998. 852 pp. Biblio. Notes. [Ph.D. Dissertation, Univ. Microfilms Order No. 9827785.] Lang.: Eng.

USA: Houston, TX. 1967-1997. Histories-specific. ■Examines the contributions of Jeannette Clift George, matriarch of the American Christian Theatre Movement and founder, artistic director and playwright-in-residence of America's longest-running resident Christian theatre company, the A.D. Players of Houston, Texas.

1786 Thompson, Garland Lee. "On the National Black Theatre Summit: An Open E-mail." *BlackM.* 1998 May/June; 13(1): 14. Lang.: Eng.

USA: Dartmouth, NH. 1998. Critical studies. ■Playwright Thompson offers support to August Wilson's efforts to coordinate and produce the conference held at Dartmouth.

1787 Toomer, Jeanette. "National Black Theatre Festival Unites Generations of Artists." *BlackM.* 1998 Jan/Feb.; 12(6): 9, 14-15. Illus.: Photo. B&W. 2. Lang.: Eng.

USA: Winston-Salem, NC. 1997. Historical studies. ■Report on the fifth biennial festival of African-American theatre.

1788 Totland, Steven Bradley. *Telling the Truth: Performing Non-Fiction Texts at Lifeline Theatre.* Evanston, IL: Northwestern Univ; 1998. 282 pp. Notes. Biblio. [Ph.D. Dissertation, Univ. Microfilms Order No. AAC 9832701.] Lang.: Eng.

USA: Chicago, IL. 1996-1998. Histories-specific. ■The development of a governing aesthetic in three productions based on a non-fiction text at Chicago's Lifeline Theatre: *Fanshen, Talking AIDS to Death,* and *The Road to Graceland.*

1789 Vogel, Paula. "Molly Smith: Intuition and Intellect." *AmTh.* 1998 Sep.; 15(7): 78. Illus.: Photo. B&W. 1. Lang.: Eng.

USA: Washington, DC. 1998. Biographical studies. ■Profile of director Smith as she prepares to take over as artistic director of Arena Stage.

1790 Watermeier, Daniel J. "The American Repertory Theatre (1946-47) and the Repertory Ideal, A Case Study." 215-234 in Engle, Ron, ed.; Miller, Tice L., ed. *The American Stage: Social and Economic Issues from the Colonial Period to the Present.* Cambridge: Cambridge UP; 1993. 320 pp. Pref. Notes. Index. Illus.: Photo. 2. Lang.: Eng.

USA: New York, NY. 1946-1947. Historical studies. ■Examines the economic failure of the American Repertory Theatre.

1791 Wegner, Pamela Sydney. *The Women's Project of the American Place Theatre, 1978-1979.* Minneapolis, MN: Univ. of Minnesota; 1987. 327 pp. Biblio. Notes. [Ph.D. Dissertation, Univ. Microfilms Order No. AAC 8805729.] Lang.: Eng.

USA: New York, NY. 1978-1979. Historical studies. ■Examines the project, which was a response to the absence of women playwrights in the mainstream of American theatre. Led by director Julia Miles, it consisted of the work of twenty new women playwrights. Three plays were ultimately selected to be presented to the public as part of a festival of women's theatre.

1792 Williams, Albert. "Charles Newell: Bold Ambition." *AmTh.* 1998 Oct.; 15(8): 74-76. Illus.: Photo. B&W. 2. Lang.: Eng.

USA: Chicago, IL. 1998. Biographical studies. ■Profile of Newell, the artistic director of Chicago's Court Theatre.

1793 Williams, Ian. "Problem Plays—Big Problems." *PlPl.* June 1998; 523: 29. Illus.: Photo. B&W. 1. Lang.: Eng.

USA: Louisville, KY. 1998. Critical studies. ■Depressing content and form in plays of 22nd Annual Humana Festival of New American Plays.

Performance spaces

1794 "Neptune's New 'Rigging'." *PAC.* 1998; 31(4): 13. Illus.: Photo. B&W. 2. Lang.: Eng.

Canada: Halifax, NS. 1963-1998. Historical studies. ■Reports on the return of the Neptune to its renovated building, which is now known as the Theatre School. The building now has a new wardrobe department, two new rehearsal halls, and a refurbished mainstage.

1795 Gilbert, Bernard. "Plateaux." (Stages.) *JCT.* 1998; 86: 59-63. Illus.: Photo. B&W. 4. Lang.: Fre.

Canada: Quebec, PQ. 1992-1998. Historical studies. ■Changing landscape of performance spaces and their use in Quebec.

1796 Lévesque, Solange. "La Dame Blanche." (The Dame Blanche.) *JCT.* 1998; 86: 169-170. Lang.: Fre.

Canada: Quebec, PQ. 1982-1998. Historical studies. ■Creation and uses to date of the Dame Blanche theatre (originally Théâtre Paul-Hébert) as a summer theatre space. Proposal to make it a base of a Molière summer festival.

1797 McNerney, Sheila. "A Vehicle for Discovery: Theatre SKAM's Volaré Venue." *CTR.* Sum 1998(95): 83-88. Notes. Biblio. Lang.: Eng.

Canada: Victoria, BC. 1996. Historical studies. ■Effect on audience perceptions of Theatre SKAM's staging of Norm Foster's *Louis and Dave* inside a Plymouth Volaré at the Victoria Fringe Festival. Directed by performers Amiel Gladstone, Gordon Gammie, and Matthew Payne.

1798 Berry, Herbert. "Folgers MS V.b.275 and the Death of Shakespearean Playhouses." *MRDE.* 1998; 10: 262-293. Notes. Lang.: Eng.

England: London. 1650. Critical studies. ■The manuscript, held at the Folger Library, was intended to correct updates of John Stow's 'Survey of London' (1618) and 'Annales of England' (1632) and contains evidence of theatre closings and other theatrical matters of the early seventeenth century. Examines the document for inaccuracies regarding the respective closings of the Hope, Fortune, Globe, Salisbury Court, Phoenix, and Blackfriars theatres.

1799 Dillon, Janette. "John Rastell's Stage." *MET.* 1996; 18: 15-45. Notes. Biblio. Lang.: Eng.

England: London. 1524-1530. Historical studies. ■Given the scant evidence, speculates as to the size and location, the economics, audience, players, and nature of the theatricals staged at the theatre built by a printer interested in educating the wider populace, John Rastell.

1800 Garlick, Görel. "George Saunders and the Birmingham New Street Theatre: A Conjectural Reconstruction." *TN.* 1998; 52 (3): 130-141. Notes. Illus.: Design. Maps. B&W. Architec. 6. Lang.: Eng.

England: Birmingham. 1772-1902. Historical studies. ■A conjectural reconstruction of the New Street Theatre, which was destroyed by fire in 1793, is put forth, based on limited written accounts and pictorial evidence.

1801 Hodges, C. Walter. "Van Buchel's Swan." *SQ.* 1988 Win; 39(4): 489-494. Notes. Illus.: Dwg. B&W. Architec. 4. Lang.: Eng.

England: London. 1596. Historical studies. ■Examines the sketch of the Swan Theatre by the Dutch scholar Arend van Buchel of Leyden, which he copied from a sketch sent to him from London by Johannes de Witt. Looks for possible clues to Elizabethan theatre performance practices.

1802 Clark, Mike. "Italy Opens Piccolo in Honor of Strehler." *TCI.* 1998 Oct.; 32(9): 26-27. Illus.: Photo. Color. 1. Lang.: Eng.

Italy: Milan. 1998. Historical studies. ■Report on the opening of the Nuovo Piccolo, the new theatre for Piccolo Teatro. It was delayed after the death of Piccolo artistic director Giorgio Strehler, and finally opened in his honor.

1803 Edström, Per Simon. "En dram i Drammen." (A Drama at Drammen.) *ProScen.* 1998; 22(4): 12. Illus.: Photo. B&W. Lang.: Swe.

Norway: Drammen. 1993-1998. Historical studies. ■Critical survey of the rebuilding of Drammens Teater after a fire.

1804 Nielsen, Ulf. "*Kristina från Duvemåla* på Cirkus i Stockholm." (*Kristina från Duvemåla* at Cirkus in Stockkholm.) *ProScen.* 1998; 22(3): 29-33. Illus.: Photo. Lighting. B&W. Lang.: Swe.

Sweden: Stockholm. 1995. Technical studies. ■Report on how the stage of the Cirkus, an arena-style auditorium, was rebuilt to become the biggest stage of Stockholm, to be able to produce Benny Andersson's play *Kristina från Duvemåla* in Lars Rudolfsson's production, with reference to the lighting plot.

1805 Cerasano, S.P. "Raising a Playhouse from the Dust." *SQ.* 1989 Win; 40(4): 483-490. Notes. Biblio. Lang.: Eng.

UK-England: London. 1988-1989. Historical studies. ■Companion essay to Richard C. Kohler's report on the excavation of Philip Henslowe's Rose Theatre (*SQ*, 40:4, pp 475-482).

1806 Egan, Gabriel. "'Geometrical' Hinges and the *Frons Scenae* of the Globe." *TN.* 1998; 52(2): 62-64. Notes. Lang.: Eng.

UK-England: London. 1599-1998. Historical studies. ■Discussion of the stage doors at the new Bankside Shakespeare's Globe Theatre with reference to the staging methods of the original Globe.

1807 Kohler, Richard C. "Excavating Henslowe's Rose." *SQ.* 1989 Win; 40(4): 475-482. Notes. Biblio. Illus.: Photo. Grd. Plan. 3. Lang.: Eng.

UK-England: London. 1988-1989. Historical studies. ■Report on the ongoing excavations of the recently discovered foundation of the Rose Theatre, built by Philip Henslowe.

1808 Macdonald, Robert. "Not Marble nor Gilded Monuments." *ShN.* 1998 Spr; 48(1): 9-10. Lang.: Eng.

UK-England: London. 1989-1997. Historical studies. ■Discusses the fate of the discovered remains of the Globe Theatre, discovered in 1989 and subsequently built over during construction for the renewal of the Bankside section of London.

1809 Orgel, Stephen. "What's the Globe Good For?" *SQ.* 1998 Sum; 49(2): 191-194. Illus.: Photo. B&W. 2. Lang.: Eng.

UK-England: London. 1997. Critical studies. ■Critique of the new Shakespeare's Globe Theatre as a medium for a modern theatre audience to view plays.

1810 Schulz-Reimpell, Werner. "In Shakespeares Schatten." (In Shakespeare's Shadow.) *DB.* 1998; 11: 38-39. Illus.: Photo. B&W. 2. Lang.: Ger.

UK-England: London. 1998. Historical studies. ■Describes the relationship between Shakespeare's Globe Theatre and the traditional staging of *The Merchant of Venice* directed by Richard Olivier, with Norbert Kentrup playing Shylock.

Performance/production

1811 Aronov, L.M. *Opyt postanovki massovogo teatralizovannogo predstavlenija na materiale klassičeskoj dramaturgii.* (The Experience of Widespread Public Productions of Plays Based on Materials Written by Classical Writers.) Moscow: 1998. 17 pp. Lang.: Rus.

1998. Critical studies. ■Effect on the public audience of the availibility of stage adaptations of literary classics.

1812 Grojsman, A.G. *Ličnost'. Tvorčestvo. Reguljacija sostojanij: Rukovodstvo po teatr. i parateatr. psichologii.* (Identity, Art, Regulation of the State of Being: Psychology of Theatre.) Moscow: Magistr; 1998. 434 pp. Lang.: Rus.

1998. Critical studies. ■The use of psychotherapy methods to optimize the work of actors.

1813 Schabert, Ina. "Männertheater." (Men's Theatre.) *SJW.* 1998; 134: 11-28. Notes. Lang.: Ger.

1600-1998. Critical studies. ■Analyzes Shakespeare's women's roles, and discusses the differences in approach when being played by men or women.

1814 Spindler, Fredrika. "Algerisk teater–en motståndsrörelse." (The Theatre of Algeria–a Resistance Movement.) *Dramat.* 1998; 6(2): 26-29. Illus.: Photo. B&W. Lang.: Swe.

Algeria. 1962-1998. Historical studies. ■Survey of the Algerian theatre today, with references to the directors and authors Abdelkader Alloula, Ziani Chérif and Slimane Benaïssa.

1815 Burvill, Tom. "Playing the Fault Lines: Two Political Theater Interventions in the Australian Bicentenary Year 1988." 229-246 in Colleran, Jeanne, ed.; Spencer, Jenny S., ed. *Staging Resistance: Essays on Political Theatre.* Ann Arbor, MI: Univ of Michigan P; 1998. 312 pp. (Theater: Theory/Text/Performance.) Notes. Index. Illus.: Photo. 3. Lang.: Eng.

Australia: Darwin, Sydney. 1988. Historical studies. ■Explores the Darwin Theatre Group's production of *Death at Balibo* and Sidetrack Performance Group's *Whispers in the Heart.*

1816 Fensham, Rachel. "On Not Performing Madness." *TTop.* 1998 Sep.; 8(2): 149-172. Notes. Biblio. Illus.: Photo. B&W. 3. Lang.: Eng.

Australia. 1994. Histories-sources. ■The author's experience as director of a documentary-based performance project, *The Worst Woman in the World*, about women incarcerated in nineteenth-century asylums for the insane. Includes a discussion on the use of melodrama.

1817 Pippen, Judy. "Ranged Between Heaven and Hades: Actors' Bodies in Cross-Cultural Theatre Forms." *ADS.* 1998 Apr.; 32: 23-34. Notes. Illus.: Photo. B&W. 2. Lang.: Eng.

Australia: Brisbane. 1992-1998. Historical studies. ■Experience of Frank Productions, headed by Jacqui Carroll and John Nobbs, and Zen Zen Zo, headed by Simon Woods, in training their actors in styles from Asia, such as the methods of Tadashi Suzuki, and the dance style of *butō.*

1818 Brandenburg, Detlef. "Elfies Marathon-Mann." *DB.* 1998; 3: 10-14. Illus.: Photo. B&W. 4. Lang.: Ger.

Austria: Vienna. 1998. Critical studies. ■Analyzes Elfriede Jelinek's *Sportstück (Sport Play)* directed by Einar Schleef at Burgtheater.

1819 Fritsch, Sibylle. "Neue Rolle für den Star." (A New Role for the Star.) *DB.* 1998; 4: 10-14. Illus.: Photo. B&W. 3. Lang.: Ger.

Austria: Vienna. 1960-1998. Biographical studies. ■Portrait of the actor Helmuth Lohner who is also administrative director of Theater in der Josefstadt for this season, and his new tasks as director.

1820 Kralicek, Wolfgang. "Etikettenschwindel." (Juggling With Names.) *THeute.* 1998; 8/9: 56-58. Illus.: Photo. B&W. 2. Lang.: Ger.

Austria: Vienna. 1998. Reviews of performances. ■Premieres of new plays: George O'Darkney's *Die Blinden von Kilcrobally (The Blind Men of Kilcrobally)* directed by Uwe-Eric Laufenberg at Akademietheater and Franzobel's *Bibapoh* adapted by Michael Kreihsl and directed by Philip Tiedemann at Burgtheater.

1821 Merschmeier, Michael. "Play It Again, George." *THeute.* 1998; 3: 12-13. Illus.: Photo. B&W. 1. Lang.: Ger.

Austria: Vienna. 1998. Critical studies. ■Describes the acting of Gert Voss and Ignaz Kirchner as Hamm and Clov in Samuel Beckett's *Fin de partie (Endgame)* directed by George Tabori at Akademietheater.

1822 Merschmeier, Michael. "Out of Bondy." *THeute.* 1998; 6: 14-15. Illus.: Photo. B&W. 1. Lang.: Ger.

Austria: Vienna. 1998. Critical studies. ■Analyzes Ödön von Horváth's *Figaro lässt sich scheiden (Figaro Gets Divorced)* directed by Luc Bondy at Theater in der Josefstadt and its current meaning.

1823 Merschmeier, Michael. "Das Doppelspiel von Herr und Knecht." (Double Game of Lord and Servant.) *THeute.* 1998; Yb: 46-55 . Illus.: Photo. B&W. 5. Lang.: Ger.

Austria: Vienna. 1988-1998. Historical studies. ■Portrait of Gert Voss and Ignaz Kirchner, the actors of the year, chosen by critics of *Theater Heute*, playing Hamm and Clov in *Fin de partie (Endgame)* by Samuel Beckett directed by George Tabori at Akademietheater. Includes a conversation with Tabori, Voss and Kirchner.

1824 Müry, Andres. "Geometrie der Globalisierung." (Geometry of Globalization.) *THeute.* 1998; 10: 14-15. Illus.: Photo. B&W. 1. Lang.: Ger.

Austria: Salzburg. 1998. Critical studies. ■Analyzes Robert Lepage's *Geometry of Miracles* performed at Salzburger Festspiele.

DRAMA: —Performance/production

1825 Pulvirenti, Grazia. "La fortuna del teatro di Luigi Pirandello nel mosaico culturale austriaco." (The Fortune of Luigi Pirandello's Theatre in the Austrian Cultural Mosaic.) *Ariel.* 1998; 13(1-2): 65-73. Notes. Lang.: Ita.
Austria. 1924-1989. Historical studies. ■Stagings of Pirandello's plays by Austrian and Italian directors, from Max Reinhardt to Giorgio Strehler.

1826 Jakubcová, Alena. "Jednou probudíš cit kouzlem něžně rozechvělých strun ... (Co víme o hudbě v pražských inscenacích druhé poloviny 18. století)." (One Day, All Feeling Is Awakened By Enchanting, Soft Vibrations of Strings: The Use of Music on the Prague Stage in the Eighteenth Century.) *DivR.* 1998 June; 9(2): 33-39. Notes. Lang.: Cze.
Austrian Empire: Prague. 1750-1800. Historical studies. ■Study of musical components in productions of Prague German speaking community.

1827 Strel'cova, E. "Prervannyj polet pastucha Abdrachmana." (The Interrupted Flight of a Shepherd, Abdrachman.) *Respublika Baškortostan.* 1998; 1: 112-113. Lang.: Rus.
Bashkir: Ufa. 1998. Critical studies. ■Performance of *Bibinur, ah, Bibinur!*, directed by Rifkat Israfilov, Bashkir Academic Theatre.

1828 Callens, Johan. "Ter plaatse fietsen: Wilson regisseert Stein." (Running in Place: Wilson Directs Stein.) *De Vlaamse Gids.* 1993 May/June; 77(3): 13-18. Lang.: Fle.
Belgium: Antwerp. 1992. Critical studies. ■Analysis of Robert Wilson's production of Gertrude Stein's *Doctor Faustus Lights the Lights* at deSingel in Antwerp.

1829 D'Ambrosio, Carla. "Il paese di Nod: scrittura scenica e lavoro d'attore di César Brie." (The Land of Nod: Scenic Writing and Acting Work of César Brie.) *BiT.* 1998; 45/47: 257-322. Notes. Lang.: Ita.
Bolivia. 1970-1985. Critical studies. ■The relevance of Brie's diaries to the performance of his *La pista del cabeceo (The Land of Nod).*

1830 Liszka, Tamás. "Színház a bombatölcsérben: Beszélgetés Aleš Kurttal." (Theatre in the Bomb-Crater: Interview with Aleš Kurt.) *Sz.* 1998; 31(11): 17-18. Illus.: Photo. B&W. 1. Lang.: Hun.
Bosnia: Sarajevo. 1998. Histories-sources. ■A talk with the Bosnian director on his life and work in pre-war and post-war Yugoslavia, with reference to *Stop Machine* and the Sarajevski Ratni Teater.

1831 Kuftinec, Sonja. "Walking Through A Ghost Town: Cultural Hauntologie in Mostar, Bosnia-Herzegovina or Mostar: A Performance Review." *TextPQ.* 1998 Jan.; 18(1): 81-95. Notes. Biblio. Illus.: Photo. B&W. 3. Lang.: Eng.
Bosnia-Herzegovina: Mostar. 1997. Histories-sources. ■Dramaturg relates her experiences developing a piece using the experiences of the residents of Mostar in collaboration with American directors Scot McElvany and Goeff Sobelle for performance by the Crane Made Theater: *Letters, or Where Does the Postman Go When All the Street Names Are Changed.*

1832 Atzpodien, Uta. "Und sie dreht sich doch?" (And Does the Earth Turn Nevertheless?)*TZ.* 1998; 3: 52-54. Illus.: Photo. B&W. 2. Lang.: Ger.
Brazil: São Paulo. 1998. Reviews of performances. ■Reviews *Leben des Galilei (The Life of Galileo)* directed by Cibele Forjaz and *Ensaio sobre o Latão* which is an adaptation from Bertolt Brecht's *Messingkauf (The Messingkauf Dialogues)* directed by Sergio Carvalho and performed by Companhia do Latão. Analyzes these different interpretations between the use of typical Brazilian traditions and a debate of Brecht's theory.

1833 Schechner, Richard; Chatterjee, Sudipto. "Augusto Boal: City Councillor: Legislative Theatre and the Chamber in the Streets." *TDR.* 1998 Win; 42(4): 75-90. Illus.: Photo. B&W. 6. Lang.: Eng.
Brazil: Rio de Janeiro. 1992-1996. Histories-sources. ■Interview with the director behind the ideas of the 'theatre of the oppressed' regarding his stint as a member of Rio's city council and its effect on his theatrical work. Includes a letter written by Boal to one of the interviewers on the same subject.

1834 "Le théâtre n'est pas un art de rhétorique, c'est un art de l'action: Entretien avec Gérard Poirier." (The Theatre is Not an Art of Rhetoric, It Is an Art of Action: Interview with Gérard Poirier.) *JCT.* 1998; 87: 100-123. Illus.: Photo. B&W. 11. Lang.: Fre.
Canada: Montreal, PQ. 1942-1998. Histories- sources. ■Actor Gérard Poirier on his career in theatre and film.

1835 Beaufort, Philippe. "Lettre à Jack Robitaille: Fragments." (Letter to Jack Robitaille: Fragments.) *JCT.* 1998; 86: 117-121. Illus.: Photo. B&W. 3. Lang.: Fre.
Canada: Quebec, PQ. 1998. Histories-sources. ■Open letter explores opinions previously expressed by actor Jack Robitaille on acting, his career and theatre in Quebec.

1836 Belzil, Patricia. "Deux Elvis pour deux solitudes." (Two Elvises for Two Solitudes.) *JCT.* 1998; 86: 31-34. Illus.: Photo. B&W. 3. Lang.: Fre.
Canada: Montreal, PQ. 1997. Critical studies. ■Differences between Montreal's Anglophone and Francophone cultures revealed in two 1997 productions of Steve Martin's *Picasso at the Lapin Agile*: one in English at Centaur Theatre directed by Miles Potter and one in French at Théâtre Juste Pour Rire, directed by Denise Filiatrault.

1837 Bulmer, Alex. "Voice and Process: Instinct versus Skill." *CTR.* Win 1998; 97: 36-40. Illus.: Photo. B&W. 2. Lang.: Eng.
Canada: Toronto, ON. UK-England: London. 1986-1998. Histories-sources. ■Voice teacher Alex Bulmer on her training under JoJo Rideout and at London's Central School of Speach and Drama, followed by discussion with fellow voice teacher Kate Lynch.

1838 Cadieux, Anne-Marie. "Narcissismes." (Narcissisms.) *JCT.* 1998; 88: 78-80. Illus.: Photo. B&W. 2. Lang.: Fre.
Canada: Montreal, PQ. 1998. Histories-sources. ■Actress Anne-Marie Cadieux contrasts her experience working in theatre and working in film.

1839 Coulbois, Jean-Claude. "Filmer le théâtre vivant." (Filming Live Theatre.) *JCT.* 1998; 88: 81-86. Notes. Illus.: Photo. B&W. 3. Lang.: Fre.
Canada: Montreal, PQ. 1996-1998. Histories-sources. ■Film-maker Jean-Claude Coulbois on his approach to documenting the creation of theatrical productions.

1840 Daniels, Kelly Dawn. *Creating the Ensemble: A Student Collaboration on Caryl Churchill's 'Cloud Nine'.* Calgary, AB: Univ. of Calgary; 1998. 155 pp. Notes. Biblio. [M.F.A. Thesis, Univ. Microfilms Order No. AAC MQ 31315.] Lang.: Eng.
Canada. 1997. Histories-sources. ■The reinvention of a performance text by a student ensemble in a revival of *Cloud Nine* at the University of Calgary. Analyzes the nature of the ensemble from the director's perspective, the playwright's history, the making of the production, including casting, rehearsals, design, and music.

1841 David, Gilbert. "Shakespeare au Québec: théâtrographie des productions francophones (1945-1998)." (Shakespeare in Quebec: Theatrography of Francophone Productions, 1945-1998.) *AnT.* Spr 1998; 24: 117-138. Notes. Biblio. Index. Lang.: Fre.
Canada: Montreal, PQ, Quebec, PQ. 1945-1998. Histories-sources. ■Chronological list of dates, locations and production information for each of 47 productions of Shakespeare in French translation in Quebec.

1842 David, Gilbert. "Scapin: un archétype au sein de deux institutions." (Scapin: An Archetype Within Two Institutions.) *JCT.* 1998; 89: 8-16. Notes. Illus.: Photo. B&W. 3. Lang.: Fre.
Canada: Montreal, PQ. France: Paris. 1998. Critical studies. ■Social context of two 1998 productions of Molière's *Les Fourberies de Scapin (The Tricks of Scapin)*, one produced by the Comédie-Française and remounted at the Richelieu, directed by Jean-Louis Benoit, the other at Montreal's Théâtre Denise Pelletier, directed by Joseph Saint-Gelais.

1843 Douglas, James B. "Absolutely Shaw." *PlPl.* 1998/99 Dec/Jan.; 529: 36-37. Illus.: Photo. B&W. 1. Lang.: Eng.
Canada: Niagara-on-the-Lake, ON. 1998. Historical studies. ■1998 Shaw Festival with reviews of numerous festival productions.

1844 Gaines, Robert D. "William Hutt: Thirty-Five Years with *King Lear.*" *THSt.* 1998; 53: 39-60. Notes. Illus.: Photo. B&W. 4. Lang.: Eng.

DRAMA: —Performance/production

Canada: Stratford, ON. 1962-1996. Histories-sources. ■Extended interview with Canadian actor William Hutt on his career, but especially on the role of *King Lear* which he first played twenty-five years ago, and his current work in the same play at the Stratford Festival, directed by Richard Monette.

1845 Gibson, K. Jane. "Seeing Double: The Map-Making Process of Robert Lepage." *CTR.* Win 1998; 97: 18-23. Append. Illus.: Photo. B&W. 11. Lang.: Eng.

Canada: Toronto, ON. 1992. Histories-sources. ■Robert Lepage's examination of his creative process and use of technology, and his rehearsal process for his University of Toronto production of Shakespeare's *Macbeth* (1992).

1846 Godin, Jean Cléo. "L'Équipe (1942-1948) de Pierre Dagenais." (Pierre Dagenais' Équipe 1942-1948.) *AnT.* Spr 1998; 23: 74-89. Notes. Biblio. Lang.: Fre.

Canada: Montreal, PQ. 1933-1990. Biographical studies. ■Career of actor/director/writer Pierre Dagenais and history of his theatre troupe, the Équipe (Montreal, PQ).

1847 Guay, Marie-Ginette. "La tragédie de l'infiniment banal: *Concert à la carte.*" (The Tragedy of the Infinitely Trivial: *Request Concert.*) *JCT.* 1998; 86: 139-141. Illus.: Photo. B&W. 3. Lang.: Fre.

Canada: Quebec, PQ. 1995-1997. Histories-sources. ■Actress Marie-Ginette Guay's experience performing the textless solo show *Request Concert (Wunschkonzert)* by Franz Xaver Kroetz, at the Théâtre Périscope in 1995, and again in 1997 directed by Gilles Champagne.

1848 Hawkins, John A. "The Apex and the Base of the Pyramid: The Context for Postwar Postsecondary Educational Theatre in Canada." *TRC.* 1998 Fall; 19(2): 140-157. Notes. Biblio. Lang.: Eng.

Canada: Edmonton, AB. 1919-1998. Critical studes. ■Identifies problematic nature of professional/popular dichotomy in Canadian theatre and its legacy in postsecondary training options such as BA and BFA programs of University of Alberta.

1849 Hennessey, James Todd. *John Ford's 'Tis Pity She's a Whore.* Calgary, AB: Univ. of Calgary; 1998. 118 pp. Notes. Biblio. [M.F.A. Thesis, Univ. Microfilms Order No. AAC MQ31316.] Lang.: Eng.

Canada. 1997. Histories-sources. ■Relates the directorial process involved in the development of John Ford's *'Tis Pity She's a Whore* for performance at the University of Calgary in fulfillment of the requirements for an M.F.A. Directing degree.

1850 Johnston, Denis William. *The Rise of Toronto's Alternative Theatres, 1968-1975.* Toronto, ON: Univ. of Toronto; 1987. Biblio. Notes. [Ph.D. Dissertation, Univ. Microfilms Order No. not available.] Lang.: Eng.

Canada: Toronto, ON. 1968-1975. Historical studies. ■Identifies and discusses three stages in the development of alternative theatre in Toronto: radical (1968-70), nationalist (1970-72), and mainstream (1972-75).

1851 Kemp, Gerard. "Mervyn Blake, Actor Extraordinaire." *PlPl.* Feb 1998; 519: 34. Lang.: Eng.

Canada: Stratford, ON. 1933-1998. Biographical studies. ■Actor Mervyn 'Butch' Blake's career as an actor, in particular his forty-one consecutive seasons at Stratford Festival.

1852 Knowles, Richard Paul. "'The Real of It Would Be Awful': Representing the Real Ophelia in Canada." *ThS.* 1998 May; 39(1) : 21-40. Notes. Illus.: Photo. B&W. 1. Lang.: Eng.

Canada. 1980-1997. Critical studies. ■The representation of the character of Ophelia in Shakespeare's *Hamlet* in Canadian popular culture and performance and the question of who controls women's passage into representation.

1853 Laliberté, Hélène. "Acteur avant tout: Entretien avec Jacques Leblanc." (Above All an Actor: Interview with Jacques Leblanc.) *JCT.* 1998; 86: 83-91. Notes. Illus.: Photo. B&W. 3. Lang.: Fre.

Canada: Quebec, PQ. 1980-1998. Histories-sources. ■Actor Jacques Leblanc on his training and professional experience.

1854 Lévesque, Solange. "Devenir le personage: Entretien avec Paul Hébert." (Becoming the Character: Interview with Paul Hébert.) *JCT.* 1998; 86: 64-76. Notes. Illus.: Photo. B&W. 11. Lang.: Fre.

Canada: Quebec, PQ. 1952-1998. Biographical studies. ■Actor/director Paul Hébert on his career, and on acting and directing.

1855 Lieblein, Leanore; Ladouceur, Louise, transl. "D'une époque ou de tous les temps? Le 'printemps Shakespeare' de 1988." (From One Epoch or For All Times? The 'Spring of Shakespeare' of 1988.) *AnT.* Spr 1998; 24: 100-113. Notes. Biblio. Lang.: Fre.

Canada: Montreal, PQ. 1988. Historical studies. ■Commonalities and diversity of readings among artists and spectators in three Shakespeare productions: *La tempête (The Tempest*, Théâtre Expérimental des Femmes, translated by Michel Garneau and directed by Alice Ronfard), *Songe d'une nuit d'été (A Midsummer Night's Dream*, Théâtre du Nouveau Monde, translated by Michèle Allen and directed by Robert Lepage) and *Le cycle des rois (The Kings Cycle)*, Théâtre Omnibus, François-Victor Hugo translation of four of Shakespeare's history plays into a trilogy, directed by Jean Asselin).

1856 McQuaid, Sean. "*1837: The Farmer's Revolt.*" *ArtsAtl.* 1998; 16(1): 53-54. Illus.: Photo. B&W. 1. Lang.: Eng.

Canada: Charlottetown, PE. 1998. Critical studies. ■The use of multimedia in the production of *1837: The Farmer's Revolt* by Rick Salutin and directed by Bruce Barton at the Carrefour Theatre, a community theatre.

1857 Nadeau, Michel. "D'*Un sofa dans le jardin* à *Ecce Homo*: de l'auteur collectif à l'auteur du collectif." (From *A Sofa In the Garden* to *Ecce Homo*: From Collective Author to Author of the Collective.) *JCT.* 1998; 86: 92-94. Illus.: Photo. B&W. 3. Lang.: Fre.

Canada: Quebec, PQ. 1990-1998. Histories-sources. ■Michel Nadeau, artistic director of Théâtre Niveau Parking describes various methods his company has used to integrate playwriting into the production process.

1858 Nunns, Stephen. "William Hutt: Canada's Secret Weapon." *AmTh.* 1998 Nov.; 15(9): 46-49. Illus.: Photo. B&W. 1. Lang.: Eng.

Canada: Stratford, ON. USA. 1953-1998. Biographical studies. ■Profile of long-time member of the Stratford Festival's acting company, William Hutt.

1859 O'Flaherty, Margo Regan. *'The Learned Ladies': Passion in High Style.* Calgary, AB: Univ. of Calgary; 1998. 111 pp. Notes. Biblio. [M.F.A. Thesis, Univ. Microfilms Order No. AAC MQ31318.] Lang.: Eng.

Canada: Calgary, AB. 1997. Histories-sources. ■Relates the directing approach to a University production of Molière's *The Learned Ladies (Les Femmes savantes)*. Thesis also includes a detailed historical analysis of the play and its history.

1860 Paventi, Eza. "Éloge de l'authenticité: Entretien avec Dominic Champagne." (Praise of Authenticity: Interview with Dominic Champagne.) *JCT.* 1998; 89: 84-91. Illus.: Photo. Pntg. Dwg. B&W. 7. Lang.: Fre.

Canada: Montreal, PQ. 1998. Histories-sources. ■Director Dominic Champagne on creating *Don Quichotte*, an adaptation of Cervantes' *Don Quixote* with playwright Wadji Mouawad for Théâtre du Nouveau Monde.

1861 Paventi, Eza. "En toute simplicité, S.V.P." (In All Simplicity, If You Please.) *JCT.* 1998; 88: 20-22. Illus.: Photo. B&W. 2. Lang.: Fre.

Canada: Montreal, PQ, Quebec, PQ, Toronto, ON. 1998. Critical studies. ■Argues importance of text and acting over special effects, contrasting two simply mounted productions: *Possible Worlds* by John Mighton, Theatre Passe Muraille, and Wadji Mouawad's *Willy Protagoras enfermé dans les toilettes (Willy Protagoras Holed Up in the Toilets)*, Théâtre Ô Parleur, with two highly visual shows (Michel Nadeau's *Ecce Homo*, Théâtre Niveau Parking and *Thanatos*, Théâtre des Moutons Noirs).

1862 Purkhardt, Brigitte. "Bernard-Marie Koltès et la face cachée du désespoir." (Bernard-Marie Koltès and the Hidden Face of Despair.) *JCT.* 1998; 87: 71-98. Notes. Illus.: Photo. B&W. 14. Lang.: Fre.

Canada: Montreal, PQ. 1991-1997. Critical studies. ■Themes in the staging of four plays by Bernard-Marie Koltès: *Dans la solitude des champs de coton (In the Solitude of Cotton Fields*, Espace GO, 1991, directed by Alice Ronfard), *Roberto Zucco* (Nouvelle Compagnie Théâtrale, 1993, directed by Denis Marleau), *Quai ouest (Key West*, Espace GO, 1997, Alice Ronfard, director) and *Combat de nègre et de chiens (Struggle of the Dogs and the Black*, Théâtre du Nouveau Monde, directed by Brigitte Haentjens).

1863 Rowe, Paul. "Faces in the Rock." *ArtsAtl.* 1998; 15(4): 66. Illus.: Photo. B&W. 1. Lang.: Eng.

Canada: St. John's, NF. 1998. Critical studies. ■Examines Fred Hawksley's *Faces in the Rock*, staged by the Beothuk Street Players.

1864 Roy, Irène. "Vivre le théâtre avec passion: Entretien avec Denise Gagnon." (Living Theatre Passionately: Interview with Denise Gagnon.) *JCT.* 1998; 86: 50-58. Illus.: Photo. B&W. 7. Lang.: Fre.

Canada: Quebec, PQ. 1958-1998. Histories-sources. ■Denise Gagnon's experiences as a professional actress in Quebec.

1865 Sperdakos, Paula. "Acting in Canada in 1965: Frances Hyland, Kate Reid, Martha Henry and John Hirsch's *The Cherry Orchard* at Stratford." *TRC.* 1998 Spr; 19(1): 35-62. Notes. Biblio. Lang.: Eng.

Canada: Stratford, ON. 1965. Biographical studies. ■Director John Hirsch's staging of Anton Čechov's *Višnëvyj sad (The Cherry Orchard)* at the Stratford Festival, 1965, as unique point of intersection in careers of Canadian actresses Frances Hyland, Kate Reid and Martha Henry.

1866 Stevenson, Melanie. "À qui appartient Shakespeare? Les tiraillements au sujet du *Hamlet, prince du Québec* de Robert Gurik." (Who Owns Shakespeare? Friction Over *Hamlet, Prince of Quebec* by Robert Gurik.) *AnT.* Spr 1998; 24: 69-84. Notes. Biblio. Lang.: Fre.

Canada: Montreal, PQ, London, ON. 1968. Critical studies. ■Compares adaptation, staging and critical reception of Shakespeare's *Hamlet* by Robert Gurik as *Hamlet, prince du Québec (Hamlet, Prince of Quebec)* at Bateau-théâtre de l'Escale, directed by Roland Laroche with its subsequent retranslation into English as *Hamlet, Prince of Quebec* by Marc Gélinas, London Little Theatre, also directed by Roland Laroche.

1867 Vaïs, Michel; Belzil, Patricia. "Trancher dans le sexe." (Divided by Sex.) *JCT.* 1998; 88: 34-38. Notes. Illus.: Photo. B&W. 3. Lang.: Fre.

Canada: Montreal, PQ. 1998. Histories-sources. ■Male and female perspectives on *Masculin/Féminin (Male/Female)*, written and directed by Michel Laprise, produced by Théâtre Pluriel in 1998, which was presented to audiences segregated by sex.

1868 Vingoe, Mary. "In Pursuit of Process: Reflections." *CTR.* Win 1998; 97: 31-35. Illus.: Photo. B&W. 6. Lang.: Eng.

Canada: Dartmouth, NS. 1980-1998. Histories-sources. ■Mary Vingoe, Artistic Director of Eastern Front Theatre, on her process of directing shows in a three-week rehearsal time-frame.

1869 Walton, Glenn. "The Life of Galileo." *ArtsAtl.* 1998; 15(4): 64-65. Illus.: Photo. B&W. 1. Lang.: Eng.

Canada: Halifax, NS. 1998. Critical studies. ■Reports on the deconstructivist production of Bertolt Brecht's *Leben des Galilei (The Life of Galileo)* by the Irondale Ensemble, staged at the Old Bicycle Shop Cafe. Author analyzes the ensemble's adaptation of the original text.

1870 Wickham, Philip. "La musique, l'écuyère au service du chevaleresque théâtre: Rencontre avec Pierre Benoît, compositeur." (Music, Rider in the Service of Chivalric Theatre: Encounter With Pierre Benoît, Composer.) *JCT.* 1998 ; 89: 101-106. Illus.: Photo. Dwg. B&W. 5. Lang.: Fre.

Canada: Montreal, PQ. 1995-1998. Biographical studies. ■Composer Pierre Benoît's collaborations with director Dominic Champagne and his musical contribution to *Don Quichotte*, an adaptation of Cervantes' *Don Quixote*, by Wadji Mouawad, directed by Champagne at Théâtre du Nouveau Monde.

1871 Wickham, Philip. "Grammaire du corps: Rencontre avec Serge Ouaknine." (Grammar of the Body: Encounter with Serge Ouaknine.) *JCT.* 1998; 89: 170-174. Notes. Illus.: Dwg. Pntg. B&W. 5. Lang.: Fre.

Canada: Montreal, PQ. 1968-1998. Biographical studies. ■Painter/director Serge Ouaknine's use of drawing to document and to aid in creative process in theatre, and his concept of a 'grammar of the body' to create corporeal symbols through actors' movement.

1872 Shen, Grant. "Acting in the Private Theatre of the Ming Dynasty." *ATJ.* 1998 Spr; 15(1): 64-86. Notes. Biblio. Gloss. Lang.: Eng.

China. 1368-1644. Historical studies. ■Examines the singing, dancing, and role playing of private actors and the functions of troupe owners in managing their companies during the Ming Dynasty.

1873 Brockbank, J. Philip. "Shakespeare Renaissance in China." *SQ.* 1988 Sum; 39(2): 195-211. Notes. Illus.: Photo. B&W. 8. Lang.: Eng.

China, People's Republic of: Beijing, Shanghai. 1986. Historical studies. ■Report on the Shakespeare Festival of China, simultaneously held in Beijing and Shanghai.

1874 Chen, Wendi. "G.B. Shaw's Plays on The Chinese Stage: The 1991 Production of *Major Barbara.*" *CLS.* 1998; 35(1): 25-48. Notes. Lang.: Eng.

China, People's Republic of: Beijing. 1991. Critical studies. ■Analysis of the production of *Major Barbara* directed by Ying Ruocheng at the Beijing People's Arts Theatre, the first Shaw play to be mounted in China in eighty years.

1875 Vagapova, N. "Stanovlenie nacional'noj režissury v slovenskom i chorvatskom teatre XIX-XX vv." (Establishment of a National Standard for the Art of Directing in the Slovene and Croatian Theatres of the 19th and 20th Centuries.) 217-233 in *Evropejskoe iskusstvo XIX - XX vekov.* Moscow: 1998. Lang.: Rus.

Croatia. Slovenia. 1800-1998. Historical studies. ■Development of the role of the director on the Croatian and Slovene stage.

1876 "At the End of the 1990s/La fin des années 90." *CzechT.* 1998 June; 14: 2-6. Illus.: Photo. B&W. 7. Lang.: Eng, Fre.

Czech Republic. 1989-1998. Critical studies. ■Development of Czech theatres after the year 1989.

1877 Huslarová, Iva. "Dramatizace (o potížích s národní literární klasikou)." (Dramatization: The Problems of Staging National Literary Classics.) *Svet.* 1998; 9(5): 49-59. Notes. Illus.: Photo. B&W. 3. Lang.: Cze.

Czech Republic: Prague, Brno. 1990-1998. Critical studies. ■Stagings of *Rok na vsi (A Year in the Village)* by Alois and Vilém Mrštík, adapted and directed by Miroslav Krobot at the National Theatre (Prague), and adapted by Břetislav Rychík and directed by Zbyněk Srba at the National Theatre (Brno). *Babička (Grandmother)* by Božena Němcová, adapted by Petr Oslzlý and Ivo Krobot, and directed by Krobot at Divadlo Husa na Provázku (Theatre Goose on a String, Brno). *Romance pro křídlovku (Romance for Flugelhorn)* by František Hrubín, adapted by Ivo Krobot and Josef Kovalčuk, and directed by Krobot at the National Theatre (Prague). *Bloudění (Wandering)* by Jaroslav Durych, adapted by Petr Štindl, Josef Kovalčuk and Jan Antonín Pitínský, and directed by Pitínský at the National Theatre (Prague).

1878 Král, Karel; Tichý, Zdeněk Aleš, ed. "Syn pokračovatel." (Bonding Son.) *Svet.* 1998; 9(5): 17-22. Illus.: Photo. B&W. 2. Lang.: Cze.

Czech Republic. 1973-1998. Histories-sources. ■Interview with director Jakub Krofta regarding his work and philosophy.

1879 Král, Karel; Tichý, Zdeněk Aleš, ed. "Otec zakladatel." (Founding Father.) *Svet.* 1998; 9(5): 9-16. Illus.: Photo. B&W. 2. Lang.: Cze.

Czech Republic: Hradec. 1990-1998. Histories-sources. ■Interview with director Josef Krofta regarding the development of Divadlo Drak in Hradec Králové from 1990.

1880 Morávek, Vladimír; Reslová, Marie, ed. "O outsiderech, naději a řevu absolutna." (About Outsiders, Hope and the Roar of the Absolute.) *DiN.* 1998 Sep 29; 7(16): 6-7. Notes. Illus.: Photo. B&W. 5. Lang.: Cze.

Czech Republic: Hradec. 1985-1998. Histories-sources. ■Interview with director Vladimír Morávek about his performances in the Klicpera Theatre in Hradec Králové.

1881 Patočková, Jana. "Faust As a Theatre of the World/Faust comme théâtre du monde." *CzechT.* 1998 June; 14: 18-26. Illus.: Photo. B&W. 9. Lang.: Eng, Fre.

DRAMA: —Performance/production

Czech Republic: Prague. 1997. Critical studies. ■Analysis of Goethe's *Faust* directed by Otomar Krejča in the National Theatre in Prague.

1882 Pecha, Jiří; Hulec, Vladimír, ed. "Mým královstvím je divadlo." (Theatre Is My Kingdom.) *DiN.* 1998 Nov 24; 7(20): 6-7. Notes. Illus.: Photo. B&W. 4. Lang.: Cze.

Czech Republic. 1967-1998. Histories-sources. ■Interview with actor Jiří Pecha.

1883 Reslová, Marie. "The Silence of Jan Nebeský/Le silence de Jan Nebeský." *CzechT.* 1998 June; 14: 4-17. Illus.: Photo. B&W. 19. Lang.: Eng, Fre.

Czech Republic. 1982-1997. Critical studies. ■Performance style of actor Jan Nebeský.

1884 Škorpil, Jakub. "Vizita nekonečného světa." (Inspection of an Endless World.) *Svet.* 1998; 9(4): 58-62. Illus.: Photo. B&W. 2. Lang.: Cze.

Czech Republic: Prague. 1987-1998. Historical studies. ■Profile of actor/director Jaroslav Dušek and the improvisational style of Divadlo Vizita.

1885 Stehlíková, Eva. "Poučení? (Nad patnácti českými inscenacemi Euripidovy Médei)." (Is There a Lesson to Be Learned?)*DivR.* 1998 Dec.; 9(4): 11-21. Notes. Lang.: Cze.

Czech Republic. 1921-1998. Critical studies. ■Analysis of the fifteen productions of Euripides' *Medea* on Czech stages since 1921.

1886 Baumrin, Seth. "My Grandfather Konstantin Sergeivich: Interview with Eugenio Barba." *MimeJ.* 1998; 19: 28-51. Notes. Illus.: Photo. B&W. 6. Lang.: Eng.

Denmark: Holstebro. 1997. Histories-sources. ■Interview with Barba regarding his acting and directing influences, including Stanislavskij, Grotowski, Mejerchol'd, and Vachtangov.

1887 Bjarke, Kim. "Om den moderne skuespiller og processens poesi." (About the Modern Actor and the Poetry of the Process.) *TE.* 1998 Apr.; 88: 4-5. Illus.: Photo. B&W. 1. Lang.: Dan.

Denmark. 1998. Histories-sources. ■Bjarke, a director, considers the director's preliminary work to be an important condition for the development of good acting by creating an atmosphere of security for the actor.

1888 Cook, Jonathan Paul. "Vildfremmedes intimitet." (The Intimacy Between Strangers.) *TE.* 1998 Apr.; 88: 21-23. Illus.: Photo. B&W. 2. Lang.: Dan.

Denmark. 1997-1998. Histories-sources. ■Cook, director at Brutahlia Teatret, writes about how to develop a group talent and the importance of actors working toward the same goal and sharing a creative language.

1889 Damm, Anja. "Man må ikke vaere fornaermet på et rum." (You Should Not Be Offended By a Playing Area.) *TE.* 1998 July; 89: 12-17. Illus.: Photo. B&W. 3. Lang.: Dan.

Denmark. 1970-1998. Histories-sources. ■Interview with actress Ghita Nørby about how actors adapt to different playing conditions in the various playing areas around the country.

1890 Allison, C. *The Cornish Mediaeval Mystery Play Cycle as Performance Art and in History.* Exeter: Unpublished PhD, Univ. of Exeter; 1997. Notes. Biblio. [Absract in *Aslib Index to Theses*, 47-10561.] Lang.: Eng.

England. 1375-1400. Historical studies. ■Analyzes the Cornish *Ordinalia*, with particular emphasis on its staging. Reference is made to its social, historical, and mythological context, and comparisons are drawn with Eastern Christian traditions.

1891 Baruth, Philip E. "Who Is Charlotte Charke?" 9-62 in Baruth, Philip E., ed. *Introducing Charlotte Charke: Actress, Author, Enigma.* Urbana/Chicago, IL: Univ. of Illinois P; 1998. 250 pp. Index. Biblio. Notes. Lang.: Eng.

England. 1713-1760. Historical studies. ■Overview and introduction to the life and career of actress/writer Charlotte Cibber Charke, daughter of Colley Cibber. Examines the institutions that shaped her, the people she worked with, and the personal, cultural, and political events that influenced her.

1892 Bernstein, Seymour. "A *Hamlet* Performance Problem: 'He Whips His Rapier Out, And ...'." *ShN.* 1998 Spr; 48(1): 17, 26. Notes. Lang.: Eng.

England. 1600-1601. Critical studies. ■Focuses on a performance question: when does Hamlet obtain the rapier with which he kills Polonius in Shakespeare's play?.

1893 Breight, Curtis Charles. *Reality and Representation: Symbolic Performance and Political Power in England in the Early 1590s.* New Haven, CT: Yale Univ; 1988. 367 pp. Notes. Biblio. [Ph.D. Dissertation, Univ. Microfilms Order No. AAC 9008987.] Lang.: Eng.

England. 1590-1595. Critical studies. ■Performance as a potent political weapon, with specific reference to Shakespeare's *Titus Andronicus.*

1894 Cerasano, S.P. "Edward Alleyn's 'Retirement' 1597-1600." *MRDE.* 1998; 10: 98-112. Notes. Lang.: Eng.

England: London. 1597-1600. Histories-reconstruction. ■Examines the period when actor Alleyn left the Lord Admiral's Men, and pieces together, with survivng records and documents, his activities while retired.

1895 Cholij, Irena. "'A Thousand Twangling Instruments': Music and *The Tempest* on the Eighteenth-Century London Stage." *ShS.* 1998; 51: 79-94. Notes. Lang.: Eng.

England: London. 1701-1800. Critical studies. ■Charts the production history of *The Tempest* during the 1700s, focusing specifically on the musical requirements and amendments.

1896 Folkenflik, Robert. "Charlotte Charke: Images and Afterimages." 137-161 in Baruth, Philip E., ed. *Introducing Charlotte Charke: Actress, Author, Enigma.* Urbana/Chicago, IL: Univ. of Illinois P; 1998. 250 pp. Index. Biblio. Notes. Illus.: Dwg. Sketches. 9. Lang.: Eng.

England. 1713-1760. Historical studies. ■Examines images traditionally associated with Charlotte Cibber Charke and determines that most of them do not represent her.

1897 Klepac, Richard L. "The Macklin-Garrick Riots." *TN.* 1998; 52(1): 8-17. Notes. Lang.: Eng.

England: London. 1743-1777. Historical studies. ■The feud between David Garrick and Charles Macklin led to theatre riots in December 1743. Minor disturbances continued in the following year and the feud lasted for the rest of the actors' lives.

1898 Levitt, John. "London Actors in the 1740's-1760's—the Evidence of Robert Baker." *TN.* 1998; 52(2): 111-114 aa no. Lang.: Eng.

England: London. 1740-1779. Historical studies. ■Observations on the styles and manners of actors, including David Garrick, in the preface of Robert Baker's book *Remarks upon the English Language* (1779).

1899 Muse, Amy M. "Nicholas Rowe's *The Tragedy of Jane Shore* Gives Actresses a Hamlet of Their Own." *Restor.* 1998 Win; 13 (2): 43-59. Notes. Lang.: Eng.

England. 1714. Critical studies. ■Critique of the performability of the character of Jane Shore, asserting that it is a role, for actresses, on a par with Hamlet.

1900 Neighbarger, Randy Lyn. *Music for London Shakespeare Productions, 1660-1830.* Ann Arbor, MI: Univ. of Michigan; 1988. 358 pp. Notes. Biblio. [Ph.D. Dissertation, Univ. Microfilms Order No. AAC 8907115.] Lang.: Eng.

England: London. 1660-1830. Histories-specific. ■Argues that theatre managers used contemporary music for Shakespearean productions and altered Shakespeare's texts to fit the music.

1901 Nussbaum, Felicity A. "Afterword: Charlotte Charke's 'Variety of Wretchedness'." 227-243 in Baruth, Philip E., ed. *Introducing Charlotte Charke: Actress, Author, Enigma.* Urbana/Chicago, Il: Univ. of Illinois P; 1998. 250 pp. Index. Biblio. Notes. Lang.: Eng.

England. 1713-1760. Historical studies. ■Examines contemporary resurgence of interest in Charlotte Cibber Charke as well as reasons why she has been ignored by theatre historians.

1902 Remnant, Mary. "Musical Instruments in Early English Drama: Tudor Plays." *EDAM.* 1998 Fall; 21(1): 21-27. Notes. Illus.: Dwg. B&W. 2. Lang.: Eng.

England. 1497-1569. Historical studies. ■Use of musical instruments in *Fulgens and Lucrece* by Henry Medwall, *The Interlude of the Four Elements* by John Rastell, *The Play of the Wether* by John Heywood, *Wyt and Science* by John Redford, *King Johan* by John Bale, *Ralph Royster*

DRAMA: —Performance/production

Doyster by Nicholas Udall, *Gammer Gurton's Needle* by Mr S., Master of Arts, Sackville and Norton's *Gorboduc*, and Thomas Preston's *Cambyses.*

1903 Shawe-Taylor, Desmond. "Eighteenth-Century Performances of Shakespeare Recorded in the Theatrical Portraits at the Garrick Club." *ShS.* 1998; 51: 107-123. Notes. Illus.: Pntg. Dwg. B&W. 13. Lang.: Eng.

England: London. 1702-1814. Historical studies. ■Examines how Shakespeare was interpreted, acted, and produced in the eighteenth century through the evidence provided by the theatrical portrait collection held by the Garrick Club.

1904 Smith, Sidonie. "The Transgressive Daughter and the Masquerade of Self-Representation." 83-106 in Baruth, Philip E., ed. *Introducing Charlotte Charke: Actress, Author, Enigma.* Urbana/Chicago, IL: Univ. of Illinois P; 1998. 250 pp. Index. Notes. Lang.: Eng.

England. 1713-1760. Historical studies. ■Feminist analysis of Charlotte Cibber Charke's life and career, with emphasis on transgressive and subversive acts both in the theatre and in private life.

1905 Stern, T. *A History of Rehearsal in the British Professional Theatre from the Sixteenth to the Eighteenth Century.* Cambridge: Unpublished Ph.D., Univ. of Cambridge; 1997. Notes. Biblio. [Abstract in *Aslib Index to Theses* 47-2840.] Lang.: Eng.

England. 1500-1700. Historcal studies. ■Explores the nature and changing content of rehearsal in English theatre, and considers the way it affects the creation and revision of texts, concluding that full-play-revision was the province of the manager, or prompter, and individual line revision that of the actor.

1906 Straub, Kristina. "The Guilty Pleasures of Female Theatrical Cross-Dressing and the Autobiography of Charlotte Charke." 107-133 in Baruth, Philip E., ed. *Introducing Charlotte Charke: Actress, Author, Enigma.* Urbana/Chicago, IL: Univ. of Illinois P; 1998. 250 pp. Index. Biblio. Notes. Lang.: Eng.

England. 1713-1760. Historical studies. ■The significance of cross-dressing in Charlotte Cibber Charke's life and acting career.

1907 Thomas, Philip V. "Itinerant and Roguish Entertainers in Elizabethan and Stuart Norwich." *TN.* 1998; 52(3): 118-129. Notes. Lang.: Eng.

England: Norwich. 1530-1624. Historical studies. ■Strict regulations controlling unlicensed strolling players and nonprofessional troupes of actors and entertainers and the venue provided by the town of Norwich for such unregulated fare.

1908 Turley, Hans. "'A Masculine Turn of Mind': Charlotte Charke and the Periodical Press." 180-199 in Baruth, Philip E., ed. *Introducing Charlotte Charke: Actress, Author, Enigma.* Urbana/Chicago, IL: Univ. of Illinois P; 1998. 250 pp. Index. Biblio. Notes. Lang.: Eng.

England. 1713-1760. Historical studies. ■The reception by the mainstream press of actress Charlotte Cibber Charke's autobiographical serial memoir, *A Narrative of the Life of Mrs. Charlotte Charke* (1755). Argues that she was associated with the blurring of gender and sexual boundaries, which constituted a threat to the dominant culture.

1909 Vaughan, Virginia Mason. "Race Mattered: *Othello* in Late Eighteenth-Century England." *ShS.* 1998; 51: 57-66. Notes. Illus.: Pntg. Dwg. B&W. 3. Lang.: Eng.

England. 1777-1800. Historical studies. ■Eighteenth-century attitudes toward race as reflected in the casting and performance practices of the role of Othello in Shakespeare's tragedy.

1910 Rischbieter, Henning, comp. "Brecht-Chronik." (Brecht-Chronicle.) *THeute.* 1998; 2: 11-33. Pref. Illus.: Photo. B&W. 21. Lang.: Ger.

Europe. 1961-1997. Histories-sources. ■Compilation of seventeen critics' views of productions of the work of Bertolt Brecht as reported in *Theater heute* over the last thirty-five years to illustrate different staging approaches.

1911 Wilcock, M.S. *Shakespeare and the Director.* Dublin: Unpublished PhD, University College; 1996. Notes. Biblio. [Absract in *Aslib Index to Theses*, 46-12117.] Lang.: Eng.

Europe. 1878-1995. Historical studies. ■Traces the rise of the modern Shakespearean director from William Poel and Georg II, Duke of Saxe-Meiningen, through Craig, Copeau, Brecht, Peter Stein, and Ariane Mnouchkine.

1912 Worthen, W.B. "Shakespeare and Postmodern Production: An Introduction." *ThS.* 1998 May; 39(1): 1-6. Notes. Lang.: Eng.

Europe. North America. 1950-1998. Critical studies. ■Introductory essay on contemporary performances of Shakespeare as sites of complex cultural interactions and theoretical work.

1913 Ahlfors, Bengt. "Theatre in Finland-Swedish/Le Théâtre en Suédois de Finlande." *FT.* 1998; 52: 4-9. Illus.: Photo. Color. B&W. 9. Lang.: Eng, Fre.

Finland: Turku, Vaasa. 1998. Critical studies. ■Playwright Bengt Ahlfors shares his views on the present state of the bilingual Swedish-Finnish theatre in Finland. Includes sidebar profiles of Åbo Svenska Teater headed by Arn-Henrik Blomqvist, and the Wasa Teater headed by Thomas Backlund.

1914 Hotinen, Juha-Pekka. "Dramaturgi, mitä dramaturgi tekee." (What Does a Dramaturg Do?)*TeatterT.* 1998; 2: 46-51. Lang.: Fin.

Finland. 1998. Critical studies. ■Examination of the role of a dramaturg in the development of a script and the mounting of a production.

1915 Jansson, Tomas. "Finland and Swedish Theatre: On the Border Between Finnish and Swedish Theatre/Le théâtre Suédois de Finlande à la Frontière du Finnois et du Suédois de Suède." *FT.* 1998; 52: 20-25. Illus.: Photo. Color. B&W. 9. Lang.: Eng, Fre.

Finland. 1998. Critical studies. ■Survey of the varied nature of theatre offerings throughout Finland, pointing to the remoteness of Finnish cities and towns from one another as a reason it is difficult to pin down a specific national sensibility in its theatre. The Swedish-language theatre seems to have a more focused viewpoint. Contains sidebar profile of Lilla Teatern headed by Tove Granqvist.

1916 Mäkinen, Eija. "Pyhän polte." (Burning the Sacred.) *Teat.* 1998; 53(5): 4-7. Illus.: Photo. Color. B&W. 3. Lang.: Fin.

Finland. 1998. Histories-sources. ■Interview with theatre director Esa Leskinen regarding his approach to his craft.

1917 Niemi, Irmeli. "Becoming Prospero: The Theatrical Career of Lasse Pöysti/Comment devient-on Prospero? Carrière théâtrale de Lasse Pöysti." *FT.* 1998; 52: 14-19. Illus.: Photo. Color. B&W. 3. Lang.: Eng, Fre.

Finland. 1944-1998. Biographical studies. ■Career of stage actor Pöysti.

1918 Ollikainen, Anneli. "Ihanteena itsellinen näyttelijä." (The Independent Actor as Ideal.) *TeatterT.* 1998; 2: 28-39. Illus.: Photo. B&W. 3. Lang.: Fin.

Finland. 1998. Histories-sources. ■Interview with acting teacher Kari Väänänen regarding his acting philosophy and his teching methods.

1919 Ruuskanen, Annukka. "Ei Pidä etsiä vaan löytää." (You Must Not Only Search, You Also Must Find.) *Teat.* 1998; 53(8): 4-8. Illus.: Photo. B&W. 4. Lang.: Eng.

Finland. 1998. Histories-sources. ■Interview with Finnish theatre director Kristian Smeds about his craft and philosophy.

1920 Vuori, Suna. "Tearapia tuki teatteriin." (Therapy Comes to Theatre.) *Teat.* 1998; 53(8): 36-38. Illus.: Dwg. Color. 2. Lang.: Fin.

Finland. 1998. Critical studies. ■Psychotherapy and its influence on theatre and production practices in Finland.

1921 Alonge, Roberto. "Pirandello sulle scene di Parigi." (Pirandello on the Stages of Paris.) *IlCast.* 1998; 11(31): 127-131 . Illus.: Photo. B&W. 1. Lang.: Ita.

France: Paris. 1925-1998. Reviews of performances. ■Reviews of the staging of *Six Characters in Search of an Author (Sei personaggi in cerca d'autore)* by Luigi Pirandello, directed by Jorge Lavelli at the Théâtre Eldorado in Paris.

1922 Boldt-Irons, Leslie Anne. "In Search of a Forgotten Culture: Artaud, Mexico and the Balance of Matter and Spirit." *RomanRev.* 1998 Jan.; 89(1): 123-138. Notes. Lang.: Eng.

DRAMA: —Performance/production

France. Mexico. 1936-1937. Biographical studies. ■Antonin Artaud's journey to Mexico in an attempt to escape Europe's stultifying culture and find in the 'new world' a simpler and more ancient one.

1923 Bouet, Jeanne. "L'art de la déclamation classique." (The Art of Classical Declamation.) *AnT.* Spr 1998; 24: 141-154. Biblio. Notes. Lang.: Fre.

France. 1657-1749. Historical studies. ■Attempts to reconstruct manner of declaiming text in classic French tradition, based on research of historic documents.

1924 Carlson, Marvin. "Report from Paris." *WES.* 1998 Fall; 10(3): 55-62. Illus.: Photo. B&W. 6. Lang.: Eng.

France: Paris. 1998. Historical studies. ■Survey of the Parisian theatre scene, 1998.

1925 Chaudhuri, Una. "Working Out (of) Place: Peter Brook's *Mahabharata* and the Problematics of Intercultural Performance." 77-97 in Colleran, Jeanne, ed.; Spencer, Jenny S., ed. *Staging Resistance: Essays on Political Theatre.* Ann Arbor, MI: Univ of Michigan P; 1998. 312 pp. (Theater: Theory/Text/Performance.) Notes. Index. Lang.: Eng.

France. 1988-1992. Critical studies. ■Examines the interculturalism of Peter Brook's *Mahabharata,* specifically the problems inherent in taking a complex cultural work out of its context.

1926 Cody, Gabrielle. "Report from France: Robert Wilson, Peter Greenaway, and Ariane Mnouchkine." *ThM.* 1998; 28(3): 92-97. Illus.: Photo. B&W. 3. Lang.: Eng.

France: Paris. 1997-1998. Reviews of performances. ■Robert Wilson's production of an adaptation of Marguerite Duras' *La Maladie de la Mort (The Malady of Death)* at Théâtre Bobigny, Peter Greenaway's *One Hundred Objects to Represent the World* at Théâtre Bobigny, and Théâtre du Soleil's production *Et soudain, des nuits d'éveil (And Suddenly, Sleepless Nights)* by Hélène Cixous, directed by Ariane Mnouchkine.

1927 Engelhardt, Barbara. "Theaterbiotop im Kulturschutzgebiet." (A Theatre Biotope in the Cultural Preserve.) *TZ.* 1998; 5/Theater in Frankreich: 26-30. Illus.: Photo. B&W. 8. Lang.: Ger.

France: Avignon. 1998. Historical studies. ■Report on the Festival d'Avignon under the management of Bernard Faivre D'Arcier.

1928 Féral, Josette; Carlson, Marvin, transl. "A Theatre without a Sense of Urgency: The 1996-97 Paris Season." *WES.* 1998 Spr; 10(2): 95-106. Illus.: Photo. B&W. 2. Lang.: Eng.

France: Paris. 1996-1997. Historical studies. ■Report on the lackluster 1996-97 Parisian theatre season.

1929 Féral, Josette. "Un théâtre sans urgence: Une saison à Paris (1996-1997)." (A Theatre Without Urgency: A Season in Paris (1996-1997).) *JCT.* 1998; 86: 35-47. Notes. Illus.: Photo. B&W. 5. Lang.: Fre.

France: Paris. 1996-1997. Historical studies. ■Overview of '96-'97 theatre season in Paris. Concludes that Parisian theatre is institutional, taking itself for granted.

1930 Forgách, András. "Brook bézsben (és Párizsban)." (Brook in Beige, and Paris.) *Sz.* 1998; 31(10): 44-46. Illus.: Photo. B&W. 2. Lang.: Hun.

France: Paris. 1998. Reviews of performances. ■Account of Peter Brook's recent production, *I Am a Phenomenon (Je suis un phénomène)* at the Bouffes du Nord.

1931 Fouquet, Ludovic. "Lettre de France: Festival d'Automne à Paris." (Letter From France: Paris' Festival d'Automne.) *JCT.* 1998; 89: 158-162. Notes. Illus.: Photo. Dwg. B&W. 3. Lang.: Fre.

France: Paris. 1998. Historical studies. ■Overview of plays presented at Paris' 1998 Festival d'Automne, with special attention to *La Ferme du Garet (The Garet Farm),* adapted from book by Raymond Depardon and directed by Marc Feld.

1932 Gasparro, Rosalba. "Pirandello sulla scena francese." (Pirandello on the French Stage.) *Ariel.* 1998; 13(1-2): 75-137. Notes. Lang.: Ita.

France. 1950-1981. Historical studies. ■Brief reconstruction of the stagings of Pirandello's plays with some abstracts from the critics of the period.

1933 Hammerstein, Dorothee. "Das Glück macht, was es will." (Luck Does What It Wants.) *THeute.* 1998; 3: 25-29. Illus.: Photo. B&W. 6. Lang.: Ger.

France: Paris. 1997-1998. Critical studies. ■Impressions from the current theatre season in Paris concerning Heinrich von Kleist's *Penthesilea* directed by Julie Brochen at Théâtre de la Bastille, Bertolt Brecht's *Im Dickicht der Städte (In the Jungle of Cities)* directed by Stéphane Braunschweig and Charles Reznikoff's *Holocauste* directed by Claude Régy, both at Théâtre de la Colline.

1934 Hammerstein, Dorothee. "Der Mann, der nicht vergessen konnte." (The Man Who Could Not Forget.) *THeute.* 1998; 5: 14-16. Illus.: Photo. B&W. 2. Lang.: Ger.

France: Paris. 1998. Critical studies. ■Analysis of Peter Brook's production at Théâtre aux Bouffes du Nord, *Je suis un phénomène (I Am a Phenomenon),* based on Aleksand'r Luria's description (in *The Mind of a Mnemonist*) of an individual with total recall.

1935 Hammerstein, Dorothee. "Goethe, Schiller, Brecht und Müller schenken Frankreich manchen Knüller." (Goethe, Schiller, Brecht and Müller Give France Some Sensations.) *THeute.* 1998; 7: 22-29. Illus.: Photo. B&W. 5. Lang.: Ger.

France. 1998. Reviews of performances. ■Goethe's *Faust* adapted and directed by Jean-François Peyret in Bobigny, Friedrich Schiller's *Die Räuber (The Robbers)* adapted and directed by Dominique Pithoiset at Théâtre de la Ville (Dijon), Bertolt Brecht's *Trommeln in der Nacht (Drums in the Night)* and *Die Kleinbürgerhochzeit (A Respectable Wedding)* directed by Georges Lavaudant at Théâtre de l'Odéon, and Heiner Müller's *Germania III* directed by Jean-Louis Martinelli in Strasbourg.

1936 Kalb, Jonathan. *Beckett in Performance.* New Haven, CT: Yale Univ; 1987. Notes. Biblio. [D.F.A. Dissertation.] Lang.: Eng.

France. 1950-1980. Histories-sources. ■Dramaturg's assessment of the plays of Samuel Beckett, based on the author's personal production experience and interviews with actors and directors.

1937 Lamont, Rosette C. "Letter from Paris (Winter 1997-98)." *WES.* 1998 Spr; 10(2): 5-14. Illus.: Photo. B&W. 4. Lang.: Eng.

France: Paris. 1997-1998. Historical studies. ■Survey of the winter season on the Parisian stage, with particular attention paid to *Check-up,* adapted from several texts by Edward Bond and directed by Carlo Brandt at La Colline, Hélène Cixous' *Et soudain, des nuits d'éveil (And Suddenly, Sleepless Nights),* directed by Ariane Mnouchkine for Théâtre du Soleil, bilingual company Dear Conjunction Theatre's version of Pinter's *The Hothouse,* directed by Les Clack.

1938 Lecure, Bruce. "Seventeenth Century: Actors Should Master the Movements of Molière to Perform Accurate Period Plays." *SoTh.* 1998 Win; 39(1): 4-7. Illus.: Photo. 7. Lang.: Eng.

France. 1622-1673. Historical studies. ■Acting primer on accurate movement for actors in the plays of Molière. Includes a list of resources for seventeenth-century movement.

1939 Lesage, Marie-Christine. "Du ludique au poétique." (From Playfulness to Poetry.) *JCT.* 1998; 88: 14-19. Illus.: Photo. B&W. 4. Lang.: Fre.

France. 1998. Historical studies. ■Contrast between the textless, dance-circus hybrid *Le Cri du caméléon (The Call of the Chameleon)* by Anomalie-Cirque Compagnie, directed by Josef Nadj, and three verbally-oriented French theatre productions: Jean-Luc Lagarce's *J'étais dans ma maison et j'attendais que la pluie vienne (I Was in My House and I Was Waiting for the Rain to Come)* by Théâtre Ouvert, directed by Stanislas Nordey, Antonio Tabucchi's *Pereira prétend (Pereira Claims)* by Théâtre de la Commune, directed by Didier Bezace, and Eugène Durif's *Quel est ce sexe qu'ont les anges? (What Is This Sex that Angels Have?)* by Compagnie Envers du Décor.

1940 Moranti, Sandra, ed. *Un'attrice e il suo tempo. Lettere di Adrienne Le Couvreur 1720-1730.* (An Actress and Her Times: Letters by Adrienne Lecouvreur 1720-1730.) Palermo: Sellerio; 1998. 194 pp. (La nuova diagonale 26.) Lang.: Ita.

France. 1720-1730. Histories-sources. ■A collection of letters on the theme of friendship, written by the French actress Adrienne Lecouvreur.

DRAMA: —Performance/production

1941 Peel, William Thomas. *The Directorial Art of Jacques Copeau at the Vieux Colombier.* Toronto, ON: Univ. of Toronto; 1987. Biblio. Notes. [Ph.D. Dissertation.] Lang.: Eng.
France. 1913-1920. Historical studies. ■Examines the nature and genesis of the theatrical aesthetic of Jacques Copeau, the founding director of the Théâtre du Vieux Colombier. Reconstructs a number of significant productions at the Vieux Colombier in an attempt to examine the director's style: Thomas Heywood's *A Woman Killed with Kindness*, Molière's *Les Fourberies de Scapin*, Shakespeare's *Twelfth Night*, and *Le Paquebot Tenacity* by Charles Vildrac.

1942 Shevtsova, Maria. "Lucinda Childs and Robert Wilson: *La Maladie de la Mort.*" *WES.* 1998 Spr; 10(2): 15-16. Lang.: Eng.
France: Paris. 1997. Critical studies. ■Short account of the performances by Childs and Michel Piccoli in Wilson's stage version of Marguerite Duras' novel at Théâtre Bobigny.

1943 Shevtsova, Maria. "Interview with Lucinda Childs." *WES.* 1998 Spr; 10(2): 17-24. Illus.: Photo. B&W. 1. Lang.: Eng.
France: Paris. 1976-1997. Histories-sources. ■Interview with the actress regarding working with director Robert Wilson in the past, and on the present production of his adaptation of Marguerite Duras' *La maladie de la Mort* at Théâtre Bobigny with co-star Michel Piccoli.

1944 Spindler, Fredrika. "Fanny Ardant." *Dramat.* 1998; 6(3): 78-79. Illus.: Photo. Color. Lang.: Swe.
France: Paris. 1990-1998. Histories-sources. ■Interview with the actress Fanny Ardant about being an actor and the difference being in front of an audience on stage and in front of a film camera.

1945 Taylor, Lib. "Sound Tracks: The Soundscapes of *India Song.*" *ThR.* 1998 Fall; 23(3): 205-214. Notes. Illus.: Photo. B&W. 3. Lang.: Eng.
France. UK-Wales: Mold. 1973-1993. Critical studies. ■Analysis of Marguerite Duras's *India Song*, with respect to the function of the auditory text as a critical commentary on what is seen on stage or screen. Considers the playtext, the film, directed by Duras, and a production directed by Annie Castledine and Anabel Arden at Theatr Clwyd.

1946 Thoss, Michael M. "Im Dickicht von Paris." (In the Jungle of Paris.) *TZ.* 1998; 2: 15-16. Illus.: Photo. B&W. Lang.: Ger.
France. 1997-1998. Reviews of performances. ■Reviews of two French productions of *Im Dickicht der Städte (In the Jungle of Cities)* directed by Hubert Colas and Philippe Duclos at La Métaphore (Lille) and Stéphane Braunschweig's version at Théâtre de la Colline (Paris) on occasion of Brecht's 100th birthday.

1947 Krotov, V.; Romanuško, M. "Znakomstvo s gruzinskim akterom teatra i kino Kikabidze." (Meeting with Georgian Theatre and Film Actor Kikabidze.) *DružNar.* 1998; 6: 176-187. Lang.: Rus.
Georgia. 1998. Histories-sources. ■Interview with actor Vachtang Kikabidze regarding his life and career.

1948 "Brecht heute—eine Umfrage." (Brecht Today—a Poll.) *DB.* 1998; 2: 38-43. Illus.: Photo. B&W. 10. Lang.: Ger.
Germany. 1998. Histories-sources. ■Statements of directors Sven-Eric Bechtolf, Konstanze Lauterbach, B.K. Tragelehn, Manfred Wekwerth, Peter Schroth, Bernarda Horres, Leander Haussmann, Peter Kupke, Ulf Reiher and Herbert Olschok about the meaning of Brecht today, how to learn from his plays and directions.

1949 "Bernhard Minetti 1905-1998." *THeute.* 1998; 11: 12-33. Illus.: Photo. B&W. 25. Lang.: Ger.
Germany. 1905-1998. Biographical studies. ■Compilation of Bernhard Minetti's important roles through photographs, his own reflections on his work, and statements of critics.

1950 Amzoll, Stefan. "Modelle der *Massnahme.*" (Models of *The Measures Taken.*) *TZ.* 1998; 4: 55-57. Illus.: Photo. B&W. 1. Lang.: Ger.
Germany: Berlin, Wuppertal. 1995-1998. Reviews of performances. ■Compares three different interpretations of *Die Massnahme (The Measures Taken)* by Bertolt Brecht and Hanns Eisler: directed by Klaus Emmerich at Berliner Ensemble, by Tom Kühnel and Robert Schuster at Bat and Holk Freytag's production at Schillertheater.

1951 Bai, Ronnie. "Dances with Mei Lanfang: Brecht and the Alienation Effect." *CompD.* 1998 Fall; 32(3): 389-433. Notes. Lang.: Eng.
Germany. China. 1935. Historical studies. ■The influence of the acting techniques of Mei Lanfang upon Brecht's theories of a theatre of alienation.

1952 Barzantny, Tamara. "Erwin Piscators Bilder des Ersten Weltkriegs—*Die Abenteuer des braven Soldaten Schweijk* zum Beispiel." (Erwin Piscator's Images of the First World War: *The Good Soldier Schweik.*) *FMT.* 1998; 13(2): 148-164. Lang.: Ger.
Germany: Berlin. 1928. Biographical studies. ■Director Erwin Piscator's personal interest in *Osudy dobręho vojąka Švejka za světovę vąlky (The Good Soldier Schweik)* by Jaroslav Hašek and the development of *Schwejk im zweiten Weltkrieg (Schweik in the Second World War)* by Bertolt Brecht with Felix Gasbarra and Lotte Lenya.

1953 Benecke, Patricia. "'Wir wollen eine geniale Idee nur noch mal überprüfen'." ('We Only Want to Review a Brilliant Idea Again'.) *THeute.* 1998; Yb: 128-135. Illus.: Photo. B&W. 7. Lang.: Ger.
Germany: Hamburg. 1998. Historical studies. ■Reports from the rehearsals of Joseph Kesselring's *Arsenic and Old Lace* and the working methods of director Christoph Marthaler at Deutsches Schauspielhaus Hamburg.

1954 Bobkova, Hana. "Waar halen ze de types vandaan?" (Where Do They Get the Types?) *Tmaker.* 1998; 2(6): 16-19. Illus.: Photo. B&W. 2. Lang.: Dut.
Germany. Netherlands. 1998. Critical studies. ■Peter Zadek's production of Čechov's *Višnëvyj sad (The Cherry Orchard)* at the Holland Festival, and audience reaction.

1955 Brandenburg, Detlef. "Zwischen Casino und Freddy Quinn." (Between Casino and Freddy Quinn.) *DB.* 1998; 6: 32-36. Illus.: Photo. B&W. 4. Lang.: Ger.
Germany: Wiesbaden. 1997-1998. Historical studies. ■Portrait of Daniel Karasek, drama director at Hessisches Staatstheater Wiesbaden.

1956 Burckhardt, Barbara. "Aus den Tiefen der Ursuppe." (From the Depths of Primordial Soup.) *THeute.* 1998; 5: 22-23. Illus.: Photo. B&W. 1. Lang.: Ger.
Germany: Hamburg. 1998. Critical studies. ■Describes Joseph Kesselring's *Arsenic and Old Lace* directed by Christoph Marthaler at Deutsches Schauspielhaus Hamburg with respect to Marthaler's specific aesthetic approach.

1957 Burckhardt, Barbara. "Es rappelt im Karton, es quietscht das Styropor." (Something Is Rattling in the Box, the Polystyrene Is Sqeaking.) *THeute.* 1998; 7: 50-54. Illus.: Photo. B&W. 4. Lang.: Ger.
Germany: Berlin, Hamburg. 1998. Critical studies. ■Compares two current performances of Bertolt Brecht's *Der Kaukasische Kreidekreis (The Caucasian Chalk Circle)* describing the direction and concept of Stefan Bachmann at Deutsches Schauspielhaus Hamburg and Thomas Langhoff at Deutsches Theater Berlin.

1958 Burckhardt, Barbara. "Aufbruch aus der Bruchbude?" (Emergence from the Hovel?) *THeute.* 1998; 12: 10-15. Illus.: Photo. B&W. 5. Lang.: Ger.
Germany: Berlin. 1998. Critical studies. ■How political changes are reflected in theatre in Berlin. Focuses on productions such as Čechov's *Diadia Vania (Uncle Vanya)* directed by Andrea Breth at Schaubühne, Patrick Marber's *Closer* directed by Uwe Eric Laufenberg at Maxim Gorki Theater, and Enda Walsh's *Disco Pigs* directed by Thomas Ostermeier at Deutsches Theater, Baracke.

1959 Burckhardt, Barbara. "Der Bassist als erste Geige." (The Bass Player as First Violin.) *THeute.* 1998; Yb: 96-102. Illus.: Photo. B&W. 4. Lang.: Ger.
Germany: Berlin. 1997-1998. Historical studies. ■Portrait of Thomas Ostermeier, young director of the year, and Baracke, a venue of Deutsches Theater, theatre of the year chosen by critics of *Theater Heute.*

1960 Carlson, Marla. "Impassive Bodies: Hrotsvit Stages Martyrdom." *TJ.* 1998 Dec.; 50(4): 473-488. Notes. Lang.: Eng.
Germany. 900-1050. Critical studies. ■The configuration of martyrdom in the work of medieval playwright Hrotsvitha.

DRAMA: —Performance/production

1961 Carp, Stefanie. "Muss das Theater sich in die Wirklichkeit auflösen oder sich radikal als Kunstort behaupten?" (Must Theatre Dissolve into Reality or Insist Radically on a Place of Art?)*dRAMATURg*. 1998; 1: 6-11. Illus.: Photo. B&W. 2. Lang.: Ger.
Germany: Hamburg. 1998. Histories-sources. ▪Dramaturg Carp, of Deutsches Schauspielhaus, discusses the contemporary meaning and special quality of theatre with respect to Christoph Schlingensief's mission, a project with homeless persons.

1962 Clemens, Claus. "William Sh. als Nullrisiko." (William Sh. as No Risk.) *SJW*. 1998; 134: 190-197. Illus.: Photo. B&W. 2. Lang.: Ger.
Germany: Cologne, Bochum, Düsseldorf. 1996-1997. Reviews of performances. ▪Performances of Shakespeare's work on the Rhine and the Ruhr: *The Taming of the Shrew* directed by Leander Haussmann at Schauspielhaus Bochum, *A Midsummer Night's Dream* at Schauspielhaus Köln. Compares *As You Like It* translated by Heiner Müller and directed by Dimiter Gotscheff at Schauspielhaus Bochum with Nicolai Sykosch's production of it at Schauspiel Düsseldorf.

1963 Detje, Robin. "Der Komiker im Heldenfach." (The Comic Actor in a Heroic Role.) *THeute*. 1998; Yb: 61-63. Illus.: Photo. B&W. 3. Lang.: Ger.
Germany: Berlin. 1985-1997. Historical studies. ▪Portrait of Matthias Matschke, young actor of the year chosen by critics of *Theater Heute*, and his work at Volksbühne.

1964 Deuter, Ulrich. "Et in Colonia ego." *TZ*. 1998; 2: 30-35. Illus.: Photo. B&W. 8. Lang.: Ger.
Germany: Cologne. 1985-1997. Historical studies. ▪Report on the state of theatre in Cologne, with emphasis on Städtische Bühnen under the directorship of Günter Krämer, Theater am Bauturm, and the companies involved in the free theatre scene Healing Theatre, Studio 7 and c.t.201.

1965 Dieckmann, Friedrich. "Das Mysterienspiel als Volkskomödie." (The Mysteries as Folk Comedy.) *TZ*. 1998; 3: 26-31. Illus.: Photo. B&W. 2. Lang.: Ger.
Germany: Berlin. 1998. Critical studies. ▪Analyzes Bertolt Brecht's *Der Kaukasische Kreidekreis (The Caucasian Chalk Circle)* directed by Thomas Langhoff at Deutsches Theater (Berlin), and his departure from the music of Paul Dessau and the scenery of Karl Appen in the 1953 production.

1966 Dössel, Christine. "Natali mit 'i'—und der Seelig-macher." (Natali with 'i'—and the Seelig-Maker.) *THeute*. 1998; Yb : 56-60. Illus.: Photo. B&W. 3. Lang.: Ger.
Germany: Munich. 1991-1998. Historical studies. ▪Portrait of Natali Seelig, actress of the year chosen by critics of *Theater Heute*, and her work with director Andreas Kriegenburg at Residenztheater.

1967 Ewerbeck, Niels. "Die Sprache des Tuns." (The Language of Doing.) 50-77 in Pochhammer, Sabine, ed. *Utopie: Spiritualität? Spiritualité: une utopie?/Utopia: Spirituality? Spirituality: A Utopia?*. Berlin: Theaterschrift c/o Künstlerhaus Bethanien; 1998. 173 pp. (Theaterschrift 13.) Illus.: Photo. B&W. 3. Lang.: Ger, Fre, Dut, Eng.
Germany: Berlin. 1998. Histories-sources. ▪An interview with Jochen Gerz about his first theatre project *Die Berliner Ermittlung (The Berlin Investigation)* based on Peter Weiss's *Die Ermittlung (The Investigation)*, which was brought to stage by himself and Esther Shalev-Gerz at Berliner Ensemble.

1968 Flimm, Jürgen. "Langsam, langsam, wir haben keine Zeit." (Slowly, Slowly, We Have No Time.) *THeute*. 1998; 1: 6-8. Illus.: Photo. B&W. 7. Lang.: Ger.
Germany: Berlin. 1997. Historical studies. ▪Tribute to Anna Viebrock and Christoph Marthaler who received the Kortner-award 1997 at Volksbühne (Berlin).

1969 Franke, Eckhard. "Fit for Fun im Wertestrudel." (Fit For Fun in the Whirl of Values.) *THeute*. 1998; 1: 15-17. Illus.: Photo. B&W. 4. Lang.: Ger.
Germany: Frankfurt. 1997-1998. Critical studies. ▪Compares the specific vision of young directors concerning Botho Strauss' *Ithaka (Ithaca)* directed by Christian Stückl and Henrik Ibsen's *Peer Gynt* directed by Tom Kühnel and Robert Schuster at Schauspielhaus Frankfurt.

1970 Gross, Robert F. "*Fuhrmann Henschel* and the Ruins of Realism." *TJ*. 1998 Oct.; 50(3): 319-334. Notes. Lang.: Eng.
Germany. 1899-1933. Critical studies. ▪How dramatic realism 'undoes' itself. Uses Gerhart Hauptmann's *Fuhrmann Henschel (Drayman Henschel)* to raise questions about the conventional account of realism and its delegitimation by more recent avant-garde theatre practitioners.

1971 Grundmann, Ute. "Reif für den Zirkus." (Ripe for the Circus.) *DB*. 1998; 1: 43-44. Illus.: Photo. B&W. 2. Lang.: Ger.
Germany: Dresden, Bonn. 1997-1998. Critical studies. ▪Analyzes Tankred Dorst's *Was sollen wir tun (What Shall We Do)*, a play about Lev Tolstoj, directed by Tobias Wellemeyer at Staatsschauspiel (Dresden). Includes a criticism of the same play directed by Antoine Uitdehaag at Schauspielhaus Bonn.

1972 Grundmann, Ute. "Gewalt ist geil, oder nicht?" (Violence Is Cool, Isn't It?)*DB*. 1998; 4: 34-35. Illus.: Photo. B&W. 2. Lang.: Ger.
Germany: Dresden, Hamburg, Stendal. 1998. Critical studies. ▪Compares the productions of Anthony Burgess' *A Clockwork Orange* directed by Karin Beier at Deutsches Schauspielhaus Hamburg, adapted by Marcus Lobbes under the title *A Clockwork Orange 2004* at Theater der Altmark (Stendal), and adapted and directed by András Fricsay Kali Son at Staatsschauspiel Dresden.

1973 Grundmann, Ute. "Die Frau vom Meer." (The Lady from the Sea.) *DB*. 1998; 10: 48-50. Illus.: Photo. B&W. 4. Lang.: Ger.
Germany: Dresden. 1993-1998. Historical studies. ▪Portrait of actress Christine Hoppe, her roles and her working methods at Staatsschauspiel Dresden for five years.

1974 Hamburger, Maik. "Auch im Osten kommt der Richard dicke." (Also in the East Richard Comes Strongly.) *SJW*. 1998; 134: 183-189. Illus.: Photo. B&W. 2. Lang.: Ger.
Germany: Rostock, Leipzig, Berlin, Dessau. 1996-1997. Reviews of performances. ▪The performance of Shakespeare in the former East Germany: *Macbeth* adapted by Heiner Müller and directed by Christina Emig-Könning at Volkstheater Rostock, *Cleopatra. Ein Spiel zwischen Liebe und Macht (Cleopatra. A Play between Love and Power)*, a combination of *Antony and Cleopatra* and Bernard Shaw's *Caesar and Cleopatra* directed by Mirca Erceg at Anhaltinisches Theater Dessau and performances of *Richard III* directed by Wolfgang Engel at Schauspielhaus Leipzig and by Martin Kušej at Volksbühne Berlin.

1975 Hecht, Werner. "Brecht und die Regie." (Brecht and Direction.) *DB*. 1998; 2: 24-27. Notes. Illus.: Photo. B&W. 3. Lang.: Ger.
Germany: Berlin. 1947-1956. Critical studies. ▪Analyzes Bertolt Brecht's production of his own play *Mutter Courage und ihre Kinder (Mother Courage and Her Children)* at Berliner Ensemble. Brecht developed his model for theatrical performance, influencing directors of subsequent stagings of his work.

1976 Höfele, Andreas. "Looking for Richard?" *SJW*. 1998; 134: 178-183. Illus.: Photo. B&W. 2. Lang.: Ger.
Germany: Munich. 1996-1997. Reviews of performances. ▪Two productions of Shakespeare's *Richard III*: directed by Matthias Hartmann at Residenztheater and by Peter Zadek at Münchner Kammerspiele. Compares the different acting styles of Jan-Gregor Kemp and Paulus Manker as Richard.

1977 Hoogland, Rikard. "Nya svar på gamla frågor." (New Answers For Old Questions.) *Tningen*. 1998; 21(3): 44-47. Illus.: Photo. B&W. Lang.: Swe.
Germany: Hamburg, Berlin. 1997. ▪Present day stagings of Brecht's plays in Germany, with references to Stefan Bachmann's production of *Der Kaukasische Kreidekreis (The Caucasian Chalk Circle)* at Schauspielhaus, Frank Castorf's production of *Herr Puntila und sein Knecht Matti (Herr Puntila and His Man Matti)* and Thomas Ostermeier's *Mann ist Mann (A Man's a Man)* at Deutsches Theater, Baracke.

1978 Hütter, Martina; Manthei, Fred; Schwanitz, Dietrich; Weidle, Roland. "'Full of sound and fury...'." *SJW*. 1998; 134: 198-205. Illus.: Photo. B&W. 2. Lang.: Ger.
Germany: Hamburg. 1996-1997. Reviews of performances. ▪Productions of Shakespeare's work in northern Germany: *Twelfth Night* directed by Karin Beier at Deutsches Schauspielhaus Hamburg,

DRAMA: —Performance/production

Romeo and Juliet directed by Sven-Eric Bechtolf at Thalia Theater Hamburg.

1979 Johansen, Karsten. "Jeg hader et kraftløst og energiløst teater." (I Hate a Powerless and Energy-less Theatre.) *TE.* 1998 July; 89: 34-38. Illus.: Photo. B&W. 3. Lang.: Dan.

Germany. 1997-1998. Biographical studies. ■A presentation of the young German director Thomas Ostermeier who was elected young director of the year by *Theater Heute* in 1997. Ostermeier creates very noisy and energetic performances because he dislikes weak theatre.

1980 Kahle, Ulrike. "Natürlich in der Kunst." (Natural in Art.) *THeute.* 1998; 4: 34-41. Illus.: Photo. B&W. 8. Lang.: Ger.

Germany. 1944-1998. Biographical studies. ■Portrait of actress Ilse Ritter, about acting and the important directors who worked with her including Hans Neuenfels, Claus Peymann, Peter Zadek.

1981 Kranz, Dieter. "Entdeckungsreise mit Brecht." (Voyage of Discovery With Brecht.) *DB.* 1998; 2: 28-30. Illus.: Photo. B&W. 4. Lang.: Ger.

Germany: Berlin. 1947-1998. Histories-sources. ■Interview with director Benno Besson who followed Bertolt Brecht to Berlin in 1947, their relationship, Besson's development as director influenced by Brecht and his working methods.

1982 Krumbholz, Martin. "Aschenputtels Metamorphose." (Cinderella's Metamorphosis.) *THeute.* 1998; 8/9: 44-47. Illus.: Photo. B&W. 5. Lang.: Ger.

Germany. 1990-1998. Biographical studies. ■Portrait of the actress Stephanie Eidt and her working methods.

1983 Krusche, Friedemann. "Für das Gesetz und wider." (For Law and Against.) *THeute.* 1998; 4: 50-51. Illus.: Photo. B&W. 2. Lang.: Ger.

Germany: Hannover. 1998. Critical studies. ■Analyzes productions of new plays: Peter Handke's *Zurüstungen für die Unsterblichkeit (Preparations for Immortality)* directed by Hartmut Wickert and Katharina Gericke's *Maienschlager (A May Pop-Song)* directed by Erich Sidler both at Niedersächsische Staatstheater Hannover.

1984 Krusche, Friedemann. "Die wirkliche Tragik ist anderswo." (The Real Tragic Is Elsewhere.) *THeute.* 1998; 6: 45-46. Illus.: Photo. B&W. 2. Lang.: Ger.

Germany. 1998. Reviews of performances. ■Review of Russian dramas focusing on the effects of perestroika: Ljudmila Rasumovskaja's *The Life of Jurij Kuročkina and His Neighbors (Žitije Jurij Kuročkin i ego bližnich)*, known as *Wohnhaft (Resident)* in German, directed by Irmgard Lange at Staatsschauspiel Dresden and Ljudmila Petruševskaja's *Tri devuški v golubom (Three Girls in Blue)* directed by Konstanze Lauterbach at Schauspiel Leipzig.

1985 Laages, Michael. "Das Neueste vom Augenblick." (The Latest of the Moment.) *DB.* 1998; 1: 10-13. Illus.: Photo. B&W. 5. Lang.: Ger.

Germany. 1992-1998. Historical studies. ■A portrait of the actor Herbert Fritsch who has worked at Volksbühne Berlin, Deutsches Schauspielhaus Hamburg and Theater am Turm (Frankfurt/Main), among other places.

1986 Laages, Michael; Brandt, Ellen. "Alt und neu und immergrün." (Old and New and Evergreen.) *DB.* 1998; 2: 10-14. Illus.: Photo. B&W. 3. Lang.: Ger.

Germany. 1998. Reviews of performances. ■Productions of Brecht's plays: *Leben des Galilei (The Life of Galileo)* directed by B.K. Tragelehn at Berliner Ensemble, *Im Dickicht der Städte (In the Jungle of Cities)* directed by Johanna Schall at Deutsches Theater (Berlin), and *Hans Im Glück (Lucky Dog)* directed by Christian Schlüter at Thalia Theater Hamburg on occasion of Brecht's 100th anniversary. Includes an interview with director Johanna Schall.

1987 Langhoff, Anna. "'Der Gummimensch kommt in Sicht'." ('The Rubber Man Comes into View'.) *TZ.* 1998; 3: 36-39. Illus.: Photo. B&W. 2. Lang.: Ger.

Germany: Berlin. 1945-1998. Histories-sources. ■Interview with director Matthias Langhoff about Bertolt Brecht, his importance to the theatre, and history of Berliner Ensemble.

1988 Lau, Mariam. "Er nervt—und alle lieben ihn." (He Gets on Your Nerves—and Everyone Loves Him.) *THeute.* 1998; 5: 4-11. Illus.: Photo. B&W. 7. Lang.: Ger.

Germany. 1993-1998. Critical studies. ■Portrait of director, presenter and leading man Christoph Schlingensief, his works at Volksbühne and other theatres as well as on television with respect to his different form of 'camp'.

1989 Lennartz, Knut. "Die Ochsentour." (The Hard Way.) *DB.* 1998; 1: 40-41. Illus.: Photo. B&W. 3. Lang.: Ger.

Germany: Dortmund. 1984-1998. Biographical studies. ■Portrait of director Angela Brodauf, and her productions of Daniel Call's *Wetterleuchten (Sheet Lightning)*, Michael Frayn's *Here* and Manfred Karge's *Die Eroberung des Südpols (The Conquest of the South Pole)* at Studiobühne.

1990 Lennartz, Knut. "Brecht, Ui, Schall..." *DB.* 1998; 2: 18-23. Illus.: Photo. B&W. 5. Lang.: Ger.

Germany: Berlin. 1959-1998. Histories-sources. ■Interview with the actor Ekkehard Schall about Berliner Ensemble, about acting and working methods, Bertolt Brecht and future projects.

1991 Lennartz, Knut. "Verregnete Bilanz." (A Blance Spoiled by Rain.) *DB.* 1998; 9: 50-52. Illus.: Photo. B&W. 4. Lang.: Ger.

Germany: Bad Hersfeld. 1998. Reviews of performances. ■Impressions from Bad Hersfelder Festspiele under the directorship of Ingo Waszerka. Reviews William Shakespeare's *Richard III* directed by Jérôme Savary, Friedrich Schiller's *Fiesco* directed by David Levin, and Einar Schleef's *Die Party (The Party)* directed by Dieter Klass.

1992 Lennartz, Knut. "A bitter Fool." *DB.* 1998; 11: 10-11. Illus.: Photo. B&W. 3. Lang.: Ger.

Germany. 1905-1998. Biographical studies. ■Tribute to the actor Bernhard Minetti on occasion of his death.

1993 Lennartz, Knut. "Auf Kleists Spuren." (On Kleist's Tracks.) *DB.* 1998; 12: 41-43. Illus.: Photo. B&W. 3. Lang.: Ger.

Germany: Frankfurt/Oder. 1998. Historical studies. ■Impressions from the 8th Kleist Festtage festival in Frankfurt/Oder. Reviews Heinrich von Kleist's *Die Hochzeit von Haiti (The Marriage of Haiti)* adapted and directed by Manfred Weber and Marius von Mayenburg's *Feuergesicht (Fire Face)* directed by Roland May.

1994 Linder, Jutta. "Pirandello sulla scena di lingua tedesca." (Pirandello on German Language Stages.) *Ariel.* 1998; 13(1-2) : 139-156. Notes. Lang.: Ita.

Germany. Austria. 1924-1986. Historical studies. ■The fortune of Pirandello's works in the countries of Germany and Austria from the 1920s to the 1980s. Includes a chronology of the first-nights from 1967 to 1986.

1995 Linzer, Martin. "Suche nach dem Wahrhaftigen." (Looking for What's Truthful.) *TZ.* 1998; 3: 40-42. Illus.: Photo. B&W. 3. Lang.: Ger.

Germany: Cottbus. 1985-1998. Historical studies. ■Portrait of the actor Oliver Bässler and his special approach to acting at Staatstheater Cottbus under the directorship of Christoph Schroth.

1996 Löffler, Sigrid. "Ereiferungs-Arien samt Vergrausungs-Methode." (Arias of Getting Excited Together With the Method of Getting Cruel.) *THeute.* 1998; 2: 47-49. Illus.: Photo. B&W. 2. Lang.: Ger.

Germany. 1997-1998. Critical studies. ■Compares adaptations and performances of Thomas Bernhard's *Alte Meister (Old Masters).* Adapted by Stefanie Carp and directed by Christof Nel at Deutsches Schauspielhaus Hamburg and adapted by Hans Nadolny and directed by Friedo Solter at Deutsches Theater, Kammerspiele.

1997 Lysell, Roland. "Omöjlig utopi, upplysningssaga eller kitsch?" (Impossible Utopia, a Tale of Enlightment or Kitsch?) *Tningen.* 1998; 21(2): 35-39. Illus.: Photo. B&W. Lang.: Swe.

Germany: Berlin. 1998. Critical studies. ■Report from Klaus Michael Grüber's production of Goethe's *Iphigenia in Tauris* at Schaubühne am Lehniner Platz.

1998 Mälhammar, Åsa. "Jag behöver ett klart och noggrant språk för att säga det jag vill." (I Need a Clear and Accurate Language to Be Able to Say What I Want.) *Tningen.* 1998; 21(5): 37-42. Illus.: Photo. B&W. Color. Lang.: Swe.

Germany: Berlin. 1996-1998. Critical studies. ■Director Thomas Ostermeier and his stagings at Deutsches Theater, Baracke in Berlin, with extracts from an interview.

DRAMA: —Performance/production

1999 Masuch, Bettina. "Den Kitsch zuende träumen." (To Dream Kitsch to an End.) *TZ.* 1998; 2: 51-53. Illus.: Photo. B&W. 3. Lang.: Ger.

Germany. 1998. Histories-sources. ■Interview with director Stefan Pucher about working methods, philosophy, and the current cultural aesthetic.

2000 Merck, Nikolaus. "Sehn-Sucht." (Desire.) *TZ.* 1998; 1: 32-35. Illus.: Photo. B&W. 3. Lang.: Ger.

Germany: Rostock. 1995-1997. Biographical studies. ■Portrait of director Christina Emig-Könning, her work at Volkstheater Rostock and her concept of an utopian theatre.

2001 Merck, Nikolaus. "Der rasende Armin." (The Raging Armin.) *TZ.* 1998; 2: 42-45. Illus.: Photo. B&W. 4. Lang.: Ger.

Germany: Nordhausen. 1970-1998. Biographical studies. ■Profile of director Armin Petras, and his approach to contemporary theatre, with a look at two of his productions: *Dantons Tod (Danton's Death)* by Georg Büchner and *Equus* by Peter Shaffer both at Stadttheater in Nordhausen.

2002 Merck, Nikolaus. "Willkommen zurück im Politischen." (Welcome Back to Politics.) *TZ.* 1998; 3: 4-7. Illus.: Photo. B&W. 3. Lang.: Ger.

Germany: Berlin. 1998. Critical studies. ■Analyzes the political past and context in the performance of Jean-Paul Sartre's *Les Mains Sales (Dirty Hands)* directed by Frank Castorf at Volksbühne.

2003 Merschmeier, Michael. "Die Kulissen der Realität." (In the Wings of Reality.) *THeute.* 1998; 11: 42-47. Illus.: Photo. B&W. 3. Lang.: Ger.

Germany: Hamburg, Hannover. Austria: Vienna. 1998. Critical studies. ■Compares different productions of Ödön von Horváth's *Geschichten aus dem Wienerwald (Tales from the Vienna Woods)* directed by Michael Gruner at Volkstheater Vienna, by Martin Kušej at Thalia Theater Hamburg, and by Wolf-Dietrich Sprenger at Niedersächsische Staatstheater Hannover.

2004 Merschmeier, Michael; Wille, Franz. "Wenn der Künstler mit dem Kanzler." (When the Artist with the Chancellor.) *THeute.* 1998; 11: 64-65. Illus.: Photo. B&W. 1. Lang.: Ger.

Germany. 1998. Histories-sources. ■Interview with director and theatre-manager Jürgen Flimm about theatre, politics and culture.

2005 Merschmeier, Michael. "Die Göttlichen." (The Divines.) *THeute.* 1998; 12: 46-51. Illus.: Photo. B&W. 2. Lang.: Ger.

Germany: Berlin, Essen. 1998. Critical studies. ■Compares the performances of Terrence McNally's *The Lisbon Traviata* directed by Fred Berndt at Renaissance Theater (Berlin) and by Jürgen Bosse at Schauspiel Essen.

2006 Meyer-Arlt, Ronald. "Das ätherische in Gummistiefeln." (The Ethereal in Rubber Boots.) *THeute.* 1998; 7: 55-58. Illus.: Photo. B&W. 4. Lang.: Ger.

Germany: Hannover. 1991-1998. Biographical studies. ■Portrait of actress Maike Bollow, her work at Niedersächsische Staatstheater, Schauspiel, and her working methods.

2007 Mumford, M. *Showing the Gestus: A Study of Acting in Brecht's Theatre.* Bristol: Unpublished PhD, Univ. of Bristol; 1997. Notes. Biblio. [Abstract in *Aslib Index to Theses*, 47-8034.] Lang.: Eng.

Germany. 1922-1956. Critical studies. ■Deconstructionist analysis of gestic acting as a series of contradictions, which can be expressed through binary oppositions: public/private, inscription/agency, demonstration/experience, stasis/flux, and populist-materialist/avant-garde. Such acting may serve as both a reactionary and progressive apparatus for societal transformation.

2008 Neubert-Herwig, Christa. "Langhoff, Heinz, Besson und andere." (Langhoff, Heinz, Besson and Others.) *TZ.* 1998; 5: 32-35 . Illus.: Photo. B&W. 7. Lang.: Ger.

Germany: Berlin. 1962-1998. Histories-sources. ■Interview with actor Klaus Piontek, who died in 1998, on his work at Deutsches Theater since 1962.

2009 Preusser, Gerhard. "Kirmes, Kino und Panoptikum." (Fair, Movies and Collection of Curios.) *THeute.* 1998; 7: 44-47. Illus.: Photo. B&W. 3. Lang.: Ger.

Germany: Bochum. 1998. Critical studies. ■The influence on Schauspielhaus Bochum by directors Dimiter Gotscheff, Leander Haussmann and Jürgen Kruse. Reviews Heinrich von Kleist's *Der zerbrochene Krug (The Broken Jug)* directed by Dimiter Gotscheff, Bertolt Brecht's *Die Dreigroschenoper (The Three Penny Opera)* directed by Leander Haussmann and Johann Wolfgang von Goethe's *Urfaust* directed by Jürgen Kruse.

2010 Raddatz, Frank. "'Dem Publikum einen Moment Zeit stehlen'." ('To Steal from the Audience a Moment of Time'.) *TZ.* 1998; 3: 22-23. Illus.: Photo. B&W. 2. Lang.: Ger.

Germany. 1992-1998. Histories-sources. ■Interview with director Andreas Kriegenburg about concepts of theatre and its effects.

2011 Reinhard, Sabine. "Der Dschungel ist eine Rennbahn." (The Jungle Is a Race Track.) *TZ.* 1998; 3: 43-45. Illus.: Photo. B&W. 4. Lang.: Ger.

Germany: Leipzig. 1997-1998. Reviews of performances. ■Impressions from the last season at Schauspiel Leipzig. Reviews *endAusscheid* choreographed by Irina Pauls, Heiner and Irene Müller's *Weiberkomödie (Women's Comedy)* directed by Thomas Bischoff, Daniel Call's *Ehepaar Schiller (The Schillers)*, directed by Wolfgang Engel and Martin Crimp's *Attempts on Her Life* directed by Armin Petras.

2012 Rice, Annabelle; Berglund, Kia; Riise, Michael; Cederberg, Jörgen. "Berliner luft!" (Berlin Air!)*ProScen.* 1998; 22 (5): 10-12. Illus.: Photo. B&W. Lang.: Swe.

Germany: Berlin. 1998. Histories-sources. ■Four Swedish directors give their impressions from a trip to Berlin, with references to Die Distel, Volksbühne, and Berliner Ensemble.

2013 Rischbieter, Henning. "Mörderische Liebesnächte." (Murderous Love Nights.) *THeute.* 1998; 6: 16-19. Illus.: Photo. B&W. 3. Lang.: Ger.

Germany: Munich, Bonn. 1998. Critical studies. ■Describes and compares two productions by Peter Wittenberg: Arthur Schnitzler's *Ruf des Lebens (Call of Life)* at Schauspiel Bonn and Martin McDonagh's *The Beauty Queen of Leenane* at Münchner Kammerspiele.

2014 Robins, Daina Ilze. *Claus Peymann: West German Director.* Medford, MA: Tufts Univ; 1988. 525 pp. Biblio. Notes. [Ph.D. Dissertation, Univ. Microfilms Order No. AAC 8816115.] Lang.: Eng.

Germany. 1960-1984. Historical studies. ■Examines Claus Peymann's career as a director and administrator in the German-speaking theatre, focusing on his work with new playwrights and his interpretations of classical texts.

2015 Rühle, Günther. "Der König ist tot." (The King Is Dead.) *THeute.* 1998; 11: 4-11. Illus.: Photo. B&W. 4. Lang.: Ger.

Germany. 1905-1998. Biographical studies. ■An obituary for actor Bernhard Minetti, his important roles and his ways of working.

2016 Schlueter, June. "English Actors in Kassel, Germany during Shakespeare's Time." *MRDE.* 1998; 10: 238-261. Notes. Append. Lang.: Eng.

Germany: Kassel. 1592-1620. Historical studies. ■Activities in the German town of Kassel of English actors including Robert Browne, George Webster, Edward Monings, and Philip Kingsman. Contains an appendix with the will of Browne's son, also named Robert.

2017 Schreiber, Ulrich. "Ausflüge für William." (Excursions for William.) *THeute.* 1998; 11: 55-58. Illus.: Photo. B&W. 2. Lang.: Ger.

Germany: Wuppertal, Cologne, Oberhausen. 1998. Reviews of performances. ■German productions of Shakespeare: *Hamlet* directed by Klaus Weise at Theater Oberhausen, *Love's Labour's Lost* directed by Frank-Patrick Steckel at Schauspiel Köln and *A Midsummer Night's Dream* directed by Holk Freytag at Schauspiel Wuppertal.

2018 Selling, Jan. "I Berlin råder ett speciellt klimat." (A Special Climate Reigns in Berlin.) *Tningen.* 1998; 21(5): 44.45. Illus.: Photo. Color. Lang.: Swe.

Germany: Berlin. 1998. Histories-sources. ■Interview with Bernd Wilms, artistic director of Maxim Gorki Theater about the production of Fassbinder's *Der Müll, die Stadt und der Tod (Garbage, the City and Death).*

2019 Shevtsova, Maria. "*La Maladie de la Mort.*" *DTJ.* 1998; 14(1): 31-33. Notes. Illus.: Photo. B&W. 1. Lang.: Eng.

DRAMA: —Performance/production

Germany. 1992-1997. Historical studies. ■Collaboration of choreographer Lucinda Childs and director Robert Wilson, in Wilson's stage adaptation of Marguerite Duras' work.

2020 Skasa, Michael. "Sein Kopf—ein überfüllter Tanzsaal." (His Head—an Overcrowded Dance Hall.) *THeute.* 1998; 6: 20-21. Illus.: Photo. B&W. 1. Lang.: Ger.

Germany: Munich. 1998. Critical stduies. ■Analyzes Georg Büchner's *Leonce und Lena (Leonce and Lena)* directed by Andreas Kriegenburg at Residenztheater Munich.

2021 Skasa, Michael. "Deutlich unsichtbare Gluten." (Clearly Invisible Heat.) *THeute.* 1998; 12: 32-33. Illus.: Photo. B&W. 1. Lang.: Ger.

Germany: Munich. 1998. Critical studies. ■Analyzes Federico García Lorca's *Doña Rosita la Soltera (Doña Rosita the Spinster)* directed by Roberto Ciulli at Residenztheater.

2022 Stillmark, Alexander. "Heinar Kipphardt's *Brother Eichmann.*" 254-266 in Schumacher, Claude, ed. *Staging the Holocaust: The Shoah in Drama and Performance.* Cambridge: Cambridge UP; 1998. 355 pp. (Cambridge Studies in Modern Theatre.) Index. Notes. Biblio. Illus.: Photo. 3. Lang.: Eng.

Germany: Berlin. 1984-1992. Histories-sources. ■The author's experience directing Kipphardt's Holocaust drama *Bruder Eichmann (Borther Eichmann).* Focuses on political implications of dramatizing the Nazi Eichmann in front of German audiences.

2023 Stoiber, Rainer M. "'Eine gewisse Verfassung des Geistes'." ('A Certain State of Mind.) *MuK.* 1998; 40(2-4): 139-155. Notes. Lang.: Ger.

Germany. 1727-1767. Critical studies. ■Questions how realistically an actor should play a death scene, the central discussion in Lessing's *Hamburgische Dramaturgie.*

2024 Stumpfe, Mario. "Grenzen sprengen?" (Breaking Borders?) *TZ.* 1998; 4: 40-41. Illus.: Photo. B&W. 10. Lang.: Ger.

Germany: Berlin. 1998. Critical studies. ■Impressions from the theatre workshop 'reich & berühmt (rich & famous)' at Podewil (Berlin). Describes the multimedia concepts of *Genetik Woyzeck (Genetics Woyzeck)* by Harriet Maria Böge and Peter Meining and *Sprechen-Schweigen (Speak-Be Silent)* by Ivan Stanev and Jeanette Spassova.

2025 Tiedemann, Kathrin. "Ich bin kein Mörder, ich bin ein Dieb." (I Am No Murderer, I Am a Thief.) *TZ.* 1998; 1: 44-47. Illus.: Photo. B&W. 6. Lang.: Ger.

Germany: Berlin. 1997. Historical studies. ■Analysis of the production *Die Räuber (The Robbers)* by Friedrich Schiller, directed by Roland Brus and played by prisoners of detention center Berlin-Tegel.

2026 Toben, Ingo. "Die Gewalt des übergangs." (The Violence of Change.) *TZ.* 1998; 5: 46-48. Illus.: Photo. B&W. 1. Lang.: Ger.

Germany: Düsseldorf. 1998. Critical studies. ■Style of Einar Schleef and the future of tragedy focusing on his adaptation and direction of Oscar Wilde's *Salomé* at Düsseldorfer Schauspielhaus.

2027 Walser, Theresia. "Das untaugliche Kind." (The Unsuitable Child.) *THeute.* 1998; 12: 4-9. Illus.: Photo. B&W. 6. Lang.: Ger.

Germany. Switzerland. 1997. Histories-sources. ■Actress and playwright describes German and Swiss children's reactions to the performance of Christmas tales.

2028 Wieck, Thomas. "Querbrecht oder Pappas Theater." (Brecht's Potpourri, or Daddy's Theatre.) *TZ.* 1998; 2: 11-14. Illus.: Photo. B&W. 5. Lang.: Ger.

Germany. 1997-1998. Reviews of performances. ■Reviews productions of Brecht's work over the last season: *Leben des Galilei (The Life of Galileo)* directed by Peter Eschberg at Frankfurter Schauspielhaus, *Der gute Mensch von Sezuan (The Good Person of Szechwan)* directed by Jens Pesel at Theater Krefeld/Mönchengladbach, *Die heilige Johanna der Schlachthöfe (Saint Joan of the Stockyards)* directed by Pierre-Walter Politz at Theater Erfurt and *Der kaukasische Kreidekreis (The Caucasian Chalk Circle)* directed by Alejandro Quintana at Staatstheater Cottbus in honor of the Brecht Centennial.

2029 Wille, Franz. "Modell Münchhausen oder ein fester Griff ins Offene." (The Münchhausen Model or Firmly into the Open.) *THeute.* 1998; Yb: 70-81. Illus.: Photo. B&W. 9. Lang.: Ger.

Germany. 1998. Historical studies. ■Shifting trends of the relationship of society and theatre, society and individualism, with respect to different concepts of directors Frank Castorf, Peter Stein, and Einar Schleef.

2030 Wille, Franz. "Gespenster der Gegenwart." (Ghosts of the Present.) *THeute.* 1998; 3: 4-11. Illus.: Photo. B&W. 5. Lang.: Ger.

Germany: Darmstadt. Austria: Vienna. 1998. Reviews of performances. ■Describes the first performances of new plays concerning the Nazi theme: Elfriede Jelinek's *Sportstück (Sport Play)* directed by Einar Schleef at Burgtheater (Vienna), Felix Mitterer's *In der Löwengrube (In the Lions' Den)* directed by Rudolf Jusits at Volkstheater (Vienna) and Werner Fritsch's *Wondreber Totentanz (Wondreb Dance of Death)* directed by Thomas Krupa at Staatstheater Darmstadt.

2031 Wille, Franz. "Der Traum der Vernunft gebiert Lügen." (The Rational Dream Gives Birth to Lies.) *THeute.* 1998; 4: 6-8. Illus.: Photo. B&W. 1. Lang.: Ger.

Germany: Berlin. 1998. Critical studies. ■Analyzes Johann Wolfgang von Goethe's *Iphigenia auf Tauris* directed by Klaus Michael Grüber at Schaubühne (Berlin).

2032 Wille, Franz. "Ungeheuer, theatralisch." (Monsters, Theatrical.) *THeute.* 1998; 5: 18-21. Illus.: Photo. B&W. 3. Lang.: Ger.

Germany. 1998. Reviews of performances. ■Reviews William Shakespeare's *Titus Andronicus* directed by Tom Kühnel and Robert Schuster at Schauspielhaus Frankfurt/Main, Bertolt Brecht's *Herr Puntila und sein Knecht Matti (Herr Puntila and His Man Matti)* directed by Franz Xaver Kroetz at Münchner Kammerspiele and Albert Camus's *Caligula* directed by Stephan Kimmig at Staatstheater Stuttgart.

2033 Wille, Franz. "Shakespeare gegen Müllers Hoffnung—Ein Spiel auf Zeit." (Shakespeare versus Müller's Hope—A Game of Time.) *THeute.* 1998; 11: 50-53. Illus.: Photo. B&W. 2. Lang.: Ger.

Germany: Leipzig, Hamburg, Berlin. 1998. Reviews of performances. ■German productions of Shakespeare: *Measure for Measure* directed by Karin Beier at Deutsches Schauspielhaus Hamburg, *Othello* directed by Alexander Lang at Deutsches Theater Berlin and *King Lear* directed by Wolfgang Engel at Schauspiel Leipzig.

2034 Wirsing, Sibylle. "Schwitzkästen, Laufsteg und Kühlschrank." (Headlocks, Catwalk and Refrigerator.) *THeute.* 1998; 3: 15-16. Illus.: Photo. B&W. 2. Lang.: Ger.

Germany: Hamburg. 1998. Critical studies. ■Analyzes the productions of Rainald Goetz's *Krieg (War)* directed by Anselm Weber and Lothar Trolle's *Hermes in der Stadt (Hermes in Town)* directed by Dimiter Gotscheff at Deutsches Schauspielhaus Hamburg.

2035 "Christoph Schroth: 'In Search of the Utopian Vision'." 141-150 in Guntner, J. Lawrence, ed.; McLean, Andrew M., ed. *Redefining Shakespeare: Literary Theory and Theater Practice in the German Democratic Republic.* Newark, DE: Univ of Delaware P; 1998. 293 pp. Index. Notes. Pref. Biblio. Illus.: Photo. 2. Lang.: Eng.

Germany, East. 1970-1990. Histories-sources. ■Interview with director Christoph Schroth on his work in the context of socialist drama, and the role Shakespeare played in it.

2036 "Adolf Dresen: 'The Last Remains of the Public Sphere'." 151-162 in Guntner, J. Lawrence, ed.; McLean, Andrew M., ed. *Redefining Shakespeare: Literary Theory and Theater Practice in the German Democratic Republic.* Newark, DE: Univ of Delaware P; 1998. 293 pp. Index. Notes. Pref. Biblio. Illus.: Photo. 1. Lang.: Eng.

Germany, East. 1965-1985. Histories-sources. ■Interview with director Adolf Dresen on his interpretation of *Hamlet* and on working on Shakespeare in the GDR.

2037 "Alexander Lang: 'Theatre Is a Living Process: Asserting Individuality'." 163-171 in Guntner, J. Lawrence, ed.; McLean, Andrew M., ed. *Redefining Shakespeare: Literary Theory and Theater Practice in the German Democratic Republic.* Newark, DE: Univ of Delaware P; 1998. 293 pp. Index. Notes. Pref. Biblio. Illus.: Photo. 1. Lang.: Eng.

DRAMA: —Performance/production

Germany, East. 1970-1990. Histories-sources. ▪Interview with director Alexander Lang on directing Shakespeare in the GDR, his work with Benno Besson, and the politics involved.

2038 "Thomas Langhoff: 'Growing Up with Shakespeare: Furthering the Tradition'." 172-182 in Guntner, J. Lawrence, ed.; McLean, Andrew M., ed. *Redefining Shakespeare: Literary Theory and Theater Practice in the German Democratic Republic.* Newark, DE: Univ of Delaware P; 1998. 293 pp. Index. Notes. Pref. Biblio. Illus.: Photo. 1. Lang.: Eng.

Germany, East. 1970-1990. Histories-sources. ▪Interview with director Thomas Langhoff on his love of Shakespeare and his history directing Shakespeare in the GDR, especially *A Midsummer Night's Dream* and *The Merchant of Venice.*

2039 "Heiner Müller: 'Like Sleeping with Shakespeare' A Conversation with Heiner Müller and Christa and B.K. Tragelehn." 183-195 in Guntner, J. Lawrence, ed.; McLean, Andrew M., ed. *Redefining Shakespeare: Literary Theory and Theater Practice in the German Democratic Republic.* Newark, DE: Univ of Delaware P; 1998. 293 pp. Index. Notes. Pref. Biblio. Illus.: Photo. 2. Lang.: Eng.

Germany, East. 1965-1990. Histories-sources. ▪Interview with playwright Heiner Müller, producer and critic B.K. Tragelehn, and Christa Tragelehn on their interest in Shakespeare, Müller's adaptations of Shakespeare, including *Macbeth*, and his own work *Hamletmaschine*, and the effect of these plays on German audiences.

2040 "B.K. Tragelehn." 196-207 in Guntner, J. Lawrence, ed.; McLean, Andrew M., ed. *Redefining Shakespeare: Literary Theory and Theater Practice in the German Democratic Republic.* Newark, DE: Univ of Delaware P; 1998. 293 pp. Index. Notes. Pref. Biblio. Lang.: Eng.

Germany, East. 1950-1990. Histories-sources. ▪Interview with critic and producer B.K. Tragelehn on his involvement with Shakespeare in the GDR, including aspects of politics, audience reactions, and socialism.

2041 "Frank Castorf: 'Shakespeare and the Marx Brothers'." 208-214 in Guntner, J. Lawrence, ed.; McLean, Andrew M., ed. *Redefining Shakespeare: Literary Theory and Theater Practice in the German Democratic Republic.* Newark, DE: Univ of Delaware P; 1998. 293 pp. Index. Notes. Pref. Biblio. Lang.: Eng.

Germany, East. 1980-1990. Histories-sources. ▪Interview with director/producer Frank Castorf on his work on Shakespeare productions in the GDR, including the political reception of his 'surreal' productions of *Hamlet* and *Othello.*

2042 "Alexander Weigel: 'Theatre Was Always Taken Seriously'." 215-225 in Guntner, J. Lawrence, ed.; McLean, Andrew M., ed. *Redefining Shakespeare: Literary Theory and Theater Practice in the German Democratic Republic.* Newark, DE: Univ of Delaware P; 1998. 293 pp. Index. Notes. Pref. Biblio. Illus.: Photo. 1. Lang.: Eng.

Germany, East. 1970-1990. Histories-sources. ▪Interview with director Alexander Weigel regarding his direction of Shakespeare in a socialist country, censorship, critical debate, and translation challenges.

2043 "Manfred Wekwerth and Robert Weimann: 'Brecht and Beyond'." 226-242 in Guntner, J. Lawrence, ed.; McLean, Andrew M., ed. *Redefining Shakespeare: Literary Theory and Theater Practice in the German Democratic Republic.* Newark, DE: Univ of Delaware P; 1998. 293 pp. Index. Notes. Pref. Biblio. Illus.: Photo. 2. Lang.: Eng.

Germany, East. 1945-1990. Histories-sources. ▪Interview with directors and critics Manfred Wekwerth and Robert Weimann on working with Brecht on Shakespeare, Brecht's influence on their work, their influence on each other, and problems of translation.

2044 "Eva Walch: 'Gender Makes No Difference'." 243-247 in Guntner, J. Lawrence, ed.; McLean, Andrew M., ed. *Redefining Shakespeare: Literary Theory and Theater Practice in the German Democratic Republic.* Newark, DE: Univ of Delaware P; 1998. 293 pp. Index. Notes. Pref. Biblio. Lang.: Eng.

Germany, East. 1982-1990. Histories-sources. ▪Dramaturg Eva Walch on the challenges of being a woman in the GDR theatre, how gender affects Shakespeare production, gender stereotypes in Brecht and Shakespeare, and censorship.

2045 "Johanna Schall: 'The Audiences Now Smell Different'." 248-252 in Guntner, J. Lawrence, ed.; McLean, Andrew M., ed. *Redefining Shakespeare: Literary Theory and Theater Practice in the German Democratic Republic.* Newark, DE: Univ of Delaware P; 1998. 293 pp. Index. Notes. Pref. Biblio. Lang.: Eng.

Germany, East. 1980-1995. Histories-sources. ▪Actor/director Johanna Schall on her love of Shakespeare, her beginnings as a director, working with other women, and changes in theatres and audiences since reunification.

2046 "Katja Paryla: 'Titania à la Marilyn Monroe'." 253-256 in Guntner, J. Lawrence, ed.; McLean, Andrew M., ed. *Redefining Shakespeare: Literary Theory and Theater Practice in the German Democratic Republic.* Newark, DE: Univ of Delaware P; 1998. 293 pp. Index. Notes. Pref. Biblio. Lang.: Eng.

Germany, East. 1975-1995. Histories-sources. ▪Director/actor Katja Paryla on her career, her choices of Shakespeare to direct, and changes in GDR theatre since the fall of the wall.

2047 "Ursula Karusseit: 'Politically Minded People'." 257-264 in Guntner, J. Lawrence, ed.; McLean, Andrew M., ed. *Redefining Shakespeare: Literary Theory and Theater Practice in the German Democratic Republic.* Newark, DE: Univ of Delaware P; 1998. 293 pp. Index. Notes. Pref. Biblio. Lang.: Eng.

Germany, East. 1977-1995. Histories-sources. ▪Director/actor Ursula Karusseit on her career, problems of being a woman in the theatre, the longevity of Shakespeare in German theatre, female stereotypes, and politics in Germany.

2048 Guntner, J. Lawrence. "Introduction: Shakespeare in East Germany: Between Appropriation and Deconstruction." 29-60 in Guntner, J. Lawrence, ed.; McLean, Andrew M., ed. *Redefining Shakespeare: Literary Theory and Theater Practice in the German Democratic Republic.* Newark, DE: Univ of Delaware P; 1998. 293 pp. Index. Notes. Pref. Biblio. Illus.: Photo. 11. Lang.: Eng.

Germany, East. 1945-1990. Historical studies. ▪The appropriation of Shakespeare by the German Democratic Republic, a socialist society, through critical theory, literary history, and theatre practice. Emphasis on the relationship between Shakespeare and GDR politics and cultural policy.

2049 Klotz, Günther. "Shakespeare Contemporized: GDR Shakespeare Adaptations from Bertolt Brecht to Heiner Müller." 84-97 in Guntner, J. Lawrence, ed.; McLean, Andrew M., ed. *Redefining Shakespeare: Literary Theory and Theater Practice in the German Democratic Republic.* Newark, DE: Univ of Delaware P; 1998. 293 pp. Index. Notes. Pref. Biblio. Illus.: Photo. 2. Lang.: Eng.

Germany, East. 1945-1990. Historical studies. ▪Shakespeare adaptations in the GDR, especially in productions of Brecht and Müller, with emphasis on how politics and personal expression were negotiated through the adaptation.

2050 Kuckhoff, Armin-Gerd. "National History and Theatre Performance: Shakespeare on the East German Stage, 1945-1990." 61-72 in Guntner, J. Lawrence, ed.; McLean, Andrew M., ed. *Redefining Shakespeare: Literary Theory and Theater Practice in the German Democratic Republic.* Newark, DE: Univ of Delaware P; 1998. 293 pp. Index. Notes. Pref. Biblio. Lang.: Eng.

Germany, East. 1945-1990. Historical studies. ▪The construction of national identity through the production of Shakespeare on the stages of the GDR.

2051 Naumann, Anna. "Dramatic Text and Body Language: GDR Theatre in Existential Crisis." 111-119 in Guntner, J. Lawrence, ed.; McLean, Andrew M., ed. *Redefining Shakespeare: Literary Theory and Theater Practice in the German Democratic Republic.* Newark, DE: Univ of Delaware P; 1998. 293 pp. Index. Notes. Pref. Biblio. Illus.: Photo. 2. Lang.: Eng.

DRAMA: —Performance/production

Germany, East. 1976-1980. Historical studies. ▪The GDR's 'existential crisis' reflected in three Shakespeare productions: Benno Besson's *Hamlet*, featuring Heidi Kipp as Ophelia, at the Volksbühne, Alexander Lang's *A Midsummer Night's Dream*, featuring Monika Lennartz as Titania, at the Deutsches Theater and Thomas Langhoff's *Midsummer*, featuring Katja Paryla as Titania, at the Maxim Gorki Theater. Focuses on the portrayal of women and the relationship between the plays' dramatic language and the non-verbal language used by the actresses.

2052 Sorge, Thomas. "The Sixties: Hamlet's Utopia Come True?" 98-110 in Guntner, J. Lawrence, ed.; McLean, Andrew M., ed. *Redefining Shakespeare: Literary Theory and Theater Practice in the German Democratic Republic.* Newark, DE: Univ of Delaware P; 1998. 293 pp. Index. Notes. Pref. Biblio. Lang.: Eng.

Germany, East. 1960-1970. Historical studies. ▪The political and social climate of theatre in the GDR during what the author calls the 'socialist classical period,' in which many Shakespeare works were produced, including productions of *Hamlet* by Adolf Dresen and Hans-Dieter Mäde.

2053 Weimann, Robert. "Shakespeare Redefined: A Personal Retrospect." 120-140 in Guntner, J. Lawrence, ed.; McLean, Andrew M., ed. *Redefining Shakespeare: Literary Theory and Theater Practice in the German Democratic Republic.* Newark, DE: Univ of Delaware P; 1998. 293 pp. Index. Notes. Pref. Biblio. Lang.: Eng.

Germany, East. 1945-1995. Histories-sources. ▪Theatre director/critic looks back over forty-five years of Shakespeare production in the GDR.

2054 Proiou, Alkistis; Armati, Angela. "Luigi Pirandello sulla scena greca." (Luigi Pirandello on the Greek Stage.) *Ariel.* 1998; 13(1-2): 177-206. Notes. Lang.: Ita.

Greece. 1914-1995. Historical studies. ▪The staging of Pirandello's plays in Greece, the audience and the critics.

2055 "Pályamozaik." (A Career in Pictures.) *Sz.* 1998; 31(9): 5-14. Illus.: Photo. B&W. 19. Lang.: Hun.

Hungary. 1948-1998. Reviews of performances. ▪Collection of reviews and related photos of noteworthy performances of actor Miklós Gábor.

2056 Balogh, A. Fruzsina; Kovács, Zita, photo. "Ez ilyen egyszerű: Beszélgetés Alföldi Róberttel." (This Is Such A Simple Thing: Interview with Róbert Alföldi.) *Sz.* 1998; 31(7): 27-30. Illus.: Photo. B&W. 4. Lang.: Hun.

Hungary: Budapest. 1998. Histories-sources. ▪A talk with the young actor, who directed Shakespeare's *The Merchant of Venice* at the Tivoli Theatre.

2057 Bán, Zoltán András; Koncz, Zsuzsa, photo. "Kutyakomédia: Kárpáti Péter: *Díszelőadás.*" (Dogs' Comedy: Péter Kárpáti: *Gala Performance.*) *Sz.* 1998; 31(1): 36-39. Illus.: Photo. B&W. 3. Lang.: Hun.

Hungary: Budapest. 1998. Reviews of performances. ▪Péter Kárpáti's play directed by Balázs Simon at the new theatre of Budapest, the Ark.

2058 Bán, Zoltán András; Koncz, Zsuzsa, photo. "Az idő szintjei: Stoppardról még egyszer." (The Levels of Time: Once Again on Stoppard.) *Sz.* 1998; 31(5): 12-14. Illus.: Photo. B&W. 1. Lang.: Hun.

Hungary: Budapest. 1998. Reviews of performances. ▪An oppositional essay on Tom Stoppard's play produced at the Katona József Theatre under the direction of Tamás Ascher.

2059 Bérczes, László; Koncz, Zsuzsa, photo. "A norma teljesítve: Beszélgetés Holl Istvánnal." (Work Completed: Interview with István Holl.) *Sz.* 1998; 31(10): 29-33. Illus.: Photo. B&W. 5. Lang.: Hun.

Hungary. 1960-1998. Histories-sources. ▪Interview with veteran actor Holl regarding his long career.

2060 Bérczes, László; Koncz, Zsuzsa, photo. "Példány és ceruza: Beszélgetés Mohácsi Jánossal." (Copy and Pencil: Interview with János Mohácsi.) *Sz.* 1998; 31(1): 44-48. Illus.: Photo. B&W. 4. Lang.: Hun.

Hungary. 1998. Histories-sources. ▪An edited version of an interview in the series of talks with interesting theatre personalities at the Club Osiris: theatre critic László Bérczes invited János Mohácsi, brilliant and controversial director of the Kaposvár theatre.

2061 Bérczes, László; Szűcs, Zoltán, photo. "Akár a vízfolyás: Színészek Vasziljevről." (As Water Flows: Actors on Vasiljév.) *Sz.* 1998; 31(9): 26-29. Illus.: Photo. B&W. 3. Lang.: Hun.

Hungary: Szolnok. 1998. Histories-sources. ▪A talk with some actors about guest director Anatolij Vasiljév's method and the impact of his production of Ostrovskij: *Bez viny vinovatjė (Guilty Though Innocent)* at the Szigligeti Theatre, Szolnok, on the audience.

2062 Bérczes, László; Koncz, Zsuzsa, photo. "Most már—most még: Beszélgetés Lázár Katival." (Still Now: Interview with Kati Lázár.) *Sz.* 1998; 31(12): 2-7. Illus.: Photo. B&W. 6. Lang.: Hun.

Hungary. 1998. Histories-sources. ▪A talk with the actress of the Csiky Gergely Theatre.

2063 Bíró, Béla. "Molière: *Dom Juan.*" *Sz.* 1998; 31(5): 26-29. Illus.: Photo. B&W. 3. Lang.: Hun.

Hungary. Romania: Sfântu-Gheorghe. 1998. Reviews of performance. ▪Molière's *Dom Juan* directed by Olga Barabás at the Tamási Áron Theatre in Sepsiszentgyörgy/Sfântu-Gheorghe, Romania.

2064 Bódis, Mária. "Egy leányszív vallomásai: Markovits Ilka naplója (1859-1862)." (Confessions of a Young Lady: Ilka Markovits' Diary, 1859-1862.) *Sz.* 1998; 31(8): 44-48. Illus.: Photo. B&W. 5. Lang.: Hun.

Hungary. 1839-1915. Histories-sources. ▪Excerpts from the diary of Ilka Markovits, a practically forgotten 19th-century actress and singer.

2065 Bodó, A. Ottó. "Fakszimile tragédia: *Az ember tragédiája* Kolozsváron." (Facsimile Tragedy: Imre Madách: *The Tragedy of Man* at Kolozsvár/Cluj.) *Sz.* 1998; 31(4): 30-31. Illus.: Photo. B&W. 1. Lang.: Hun.

Hungary. Romania: Cluj-Napoca. 1997. Reviews of performances. ▪Madách's classic play at the Kolozsvári Állami Magyar Színház (Hungarian Theatre of Kolozsvár/Cluj-Napoca, Romania) directed by Imre Csiszár as a guest.

2066 Csáki, Judit; Szűcs, Zoltán, photo. "A negyedik felvonás: Shakespeare: *A velencei kalmár.*" (The Fourth Act: Shakespeare's *The Merchant of Venice.*) *Sz.* 1998; 31(1): 28-30. Illus.: Photo. B&W. 1. Lang.: Hun.

Hungary: Szolnok. 1997. Reviews of performances. ▪Shakespeare's play directed by György Schwajda at Szolnok's Szigligeti Theatre.

2067 Csáki, Judit; Simara, László, photo. "Spiró György: *Kvartett.*" (György Spiró: *Quartet.*) *Sz.* 1998; 31(3): 38-39. Illus.: Photo. B&W. 1. Lang.: Hun.

Hungary: Pécs. 1997. Reviews of performances. ▪György Spiró's play directed by János Vincze at Third Theatre (Harmadik Színház) of Pécs.

2068 Csáki, Judit; Koncz, Zsuzsa, photo. "Miller: *A salemi boszorkányok.*" (Arthur Miller: *The Crucible.*) *Sz.* 1998; 31(5): 17-18. Illus.: Photo. B&W. 2. Lang.: Hun.

Hungary: Budapest. 1998. Reviews of performances. ▪Miller's play directed by actor Péter Rudolf at the Comedy Theatre.

2069 Csáki, Judit; Máthé, András, photo. "Egy regény darabja: Ács János: *A mennyei híd.*" (Part of A Novel: János Ács: *The Heavenly Bridge.*) *Sz.* 1998; 31(7): 33-34. Illus.: Photo. B&W. 2. Lang.: Hun.

Hungary: Debrecen. 1998. Reviews of performances. ▪Director János Ács' play (based on Thornton Wilder's novel *The Bridge of San Luis Rey*) at the Csokonai Theatre, Debrecen directed by Gábor Czeizel.

2070 Cserje, Zsuzsa. "Kortársunk, Ruszt." (Ruszt, Our Contemporary.) *Ellenfény.* 1998; 3(1): 12-16. Illus.: Photo. B&W. 4. Lang.: Hun.

Hungary: Budapest. Hungary: Kecskemét. 1973-1997. Critical studies. ▪A comparative analysis of József Ruszt's two stagings of Shakespeare's *Richard III*: at Kecskemét's Katona József Theatre, 1973, and at Budapest Chamber Theatre, 1997.

2071 Dömötör, Adrienne; Koncz, Zsuzsa, photo. "Beleszerettem a világba: Beszélgetés Szervét Tiborral." (I Am in Love with the World: Interview with Tibor Szervét.) *Sz.* 1998; 31(8): 40-43. Illus.: Photo. B&W. 6. Lang.: Hun.

Hungary. 1988-1998. Histories-sources. ▪Interview with the actor, recently engaged by Budapest's Radnóti Theatre, where his performance

DRAMA: —Performance/production

of Astrov in Čechov's *Uncle Vanya* earned him last year the critics' prize for best acting.

2072 Dömötör, Adrienne; Koncz, Zsuzsa, photo. "Megtalálnak a szerepek: Beszélgetés Gazsó Györggyel." (Meeting the Roles: An Interview with György Gazsó.) *Sz.* 1998; 31(11): 40-42. Illus.: Photo. B&W. 3. Lang.: Hun.
Hungary. 1980-1998. Histories-sources. ■A talk with actor György Gazsó on his career and recent roles.

2073 Forgách, András; Koncz, Zsuzsa, photo. "Bálint András: *INRI.*" (András Bálint: *INRI.*) *Sz.* 1998; 31(3): 40-41. Illus.: Photo. B&W. 2. Lang.: Hun.
Hungary: Budapest. 1997. Reviews of performances. ■A one-man play based on some biblical texts at the Radnóti Miklós Theatre compiled and performed by András Bálint.

2074 Forgách, András; Koncz, Zsuzsa, photo. "Három szín: Miroslav Krleža: *Agónia.*" (Three Acts: Miroslav Krleža: *Agony.*) *Sz.* 1998; 31(5): 13-16. Illus.: Photo. B&W. 3. Lang.: Hun.
Hungary: Budapest. 1998. Reviews of performances. ■Krleža's play directed by Péter Valló at the Katona József Theatre.

2075 Forgács, Miklós. "Násztánc és hangzavar: Csehov tréfái Kassán." (Wedding Dance and Cacophony: Čechov's Comedies at Kosiče.) *Sz.* 1998; 31(6): 25-26. Illus.: Photo. B&W. 2. Lang.: Hun.
Hungary. Slovakia: Košice. 1998. Reviews of performances. ■Čechov's one-act plays—*Medved (The Bear), Predloženijè (The Proposal), Jubilej (Jubilee), Svadba (The Wedding)* —at the Hungarian-speaking Thália Theatre of Kassa/Košice directed by István Verebes as a guest.

2076 Gábor, Miklós. "Juci: Egy öreg hölgy látogatása." (Juci: The Visit of an Old Lady.) *Sz.* 1998; 31(9): 15-19. Illus.: Dwg. B&W. 5. Lang.: Hun.
Hungary. 1971. Histories-sources. ■Excerpt from a novel in press, written and illustrated by the late actor Miklós Gábor.

2077 Gajdó, Tamás. "Párhuzamos életrajzok: Két színművész emléke." (Parallel Biographies: Memory of Two Actors.) *Sz.* 1998; 31(5): 44. Illus.: Photo. B&W. 2. Lang.: Hun.
Hungary. 1998. Critical studies. ■Introducing two biographical works: the autobiography of actor Ádám Szirtes (*Életünk, életem!* Kijárat Kiadó, 1997) and the volume by Gábor Szigethy devoted to Éva Ruttkai, the 'Fairy Queen' of Hungarian stages (*Tündérkirálynő: Töredékek Ruttkai Éváról.* Helikon, 1997).

2078 Gáspár, Máté. "Békés Pál: *Pincejáték.*" (Pál Békés: *Cellar Play.*) *Sz.* 1998; 31(1): 39-41. Illus.: Photo. B&W. 2. Lang.: Hun.
Hungary: Budapest. 1997. Reviews of performances. ■The contemporary playwright's play produced by the Pinceszínház (Cellar Theatre) directed by Zoltán Ternyák.

2079 Gáspár, Máté; Szilágyi, Lenke, photo. "Gombrowicz: *Yvonne, burgundi hercegnő.*" (Witold Gombrowicz: *Yvonne, Princess of Burgundia.*) *Sz.* 1998; 31(3): 35-38. Illus.: Photo. B&W. 3. Lang.: Hun.
Hungary: Budapest. 1997. Reviews of performances. ■Gombrowicz's *Iwona, Księzniczka Burgundia* directed by Gábor Zsámbéki at the Katona József Theatre.

2080 Gáspár, Máté. "Egy beállítás képei: Három Csehov-egyfelvonásos." (Pictures of a Setting: Three One-Act Plays by Čechov.) *Sz.* 1998; 31(6): 21-23. Illus.: Photo. B&W. 2. Lang.: Hun.
Hungary: Dunaújváros. 1998. Reviews of performances. ■Three one-act comedies by Čechov—*Jubilej (Jubilee), Medved (The Bear), Predloženijè (The Proposal)*—directed by Péter Valló at the Bartók Chamber Theatre, Dunaújváros.

2081 Gáspár, Máté; Isza, Ferenc, photo. "És megtestesül az ige: Az értelmi fogyatékosok színháza." (Incarnation: The Theatre of Developmentally Disabled People.) *Sz.* 1998; 31(10): 46-48. Illus.: Photo. B&W. 2. Lang.: Hun.
Hungary: Budapest. 1983-1998. Reviews of performances. ■An account of the Budapest visit of the Belgian Théâtre du Plantin, a company for developmentally disabled actors: *Body* at the Szkéné theatre written and directed by Vincent Logeot.

2082 Joób, Sándor; Szabó, Péter, photo. "Színpadon: az elmélet: Csehov: *Apátlanul.*" (Theory on the Stage: Čechov: *Fatherless.*) *Sz.* 1998; 31(3): 32-35. Illus.: Photo. B&W. 3. Lang.: Hun.
Hungary: Budapest. 1997. Reviews of performances. ■A new version of the author's *Platonov* at the Castle Theatre adapted and directed by Erzsébet Gaál.

2083 Joób, Sándor; Koncz, Zsuzsa, photo. "Magyar vircsaft: Örkény: *Kulcskeresők.*" (Hunky Business: István Örkény: *Searching for the Key.*) *Sz.* 1998; 31(4): 35-37. Illus.: Photo. B&W. 2. Lang.: Hun.
Hungary: Budapest. 1998. Reviews of performances. ■István Örkény's play at the Katona József Theatre directed by Gábor Máté.

2084 Joób, Sándor; Strassburger, Alexandra, photo. "Beszédes képek: Brecht: *A vágóhidak Szent Johannája.*" (Communicative Pictures: Brecht: *Saint Joan of the Stockyards.*) *Sz.* 1998; 31(6): 42-44. Illus.: Photo. B&W. 1. Lang.: Hun.
Hungary: Miskolc. 1998. Reviews of performances. ■*Die Heilige Johanna der Schlachthöfe* at The Hall of Miskolc National Theatre directed by Sándor Zsótér as a guest.

2085 Karsai, György; Erdély, Mátyás, photo.; Koncz, Zsuzsa, photo. "S. Á. kettős érettségije." (Double Final Examination of A.S.)*Sz.* 1998; 31(4): 37-40. Illus.: Photo. B&W. 4. Lang.: Hun.
Hungary: Budapest. 1998. Reviews of performance. ■Two productions directed by Árpád Schilling: his own *Kicsi (The Little One)* and an adaptation of *Lidská tragikomedie (Human Tragicomedy)* by Ladislav Klíma at Katona József Színház, Kamra, as *Alolrol az ibolyat (Pushing up Daisies).*

2086 Kékesi Kun, Árpád; Veréb, Simon, photo. "Háborús játékok: Shakespeare: *Sok hűhó semmiért.*" (War Games: Shakespeare: *Much Ado About Nothing.*) *Sz.* 1998; 31(1): 26-28. Illus.: Photo. B&W. 2. Lang.: Hun.
Hungary: Szeged. 1997. Reviews of performances. ■Shakespeare's play directed by Péter Telihay at the Chamber Theatre of Szeged National Theatre.

2087 Kékesi Kun, Árpád; Koncz, Zsuzsa, photo. "A retorika színháza, a színház retorikája: Thomas Bernhard: *Ritter, Dene, Voss.*" (Theatre of Rethoric, Rhetoric of Theatre: Thomas Bernhard: *Ritter, Dene, Voss.*) *Sz.* 1998; 31 (4): 24-27. Illus.: Photo. B&W. 3. Lang.: Hun.
Hungary: Budapest. 1997. Reviews of performances. ■Bernhard's play at the Bárka Színház (Ark Theatre) directed by László Bagossy.

2088 Kiss, Gabriella; Koncz, Zsuzsa. "Posztnaturalizmus. Hauptmann: *Henschel fuvaros.*" (Postnaturalism. Gerhart Hauptmann: *Drayman Henschel.*) *Sz.* 1998; 31(1): 41-43. Illus.: Photo. B&W. 2. Lang.: Hun.
Hungary: Budapest. 1997. Reviews of performances. ■Hauptmann's *Fuhrmann Henschel* directed by Sándor Zsótér at the Chamber of the Katona József Theatre.

2089 Koltai, Tamás; Németh, Juli, photo.; Ikládi, László, photo. "August és Selma: Két Enquist-dráma." (August and Selma: Two Dramas by Per Olov Enquist.) *Sz.* 1998; 31(5): 19-21. Illus.: Photo. B&W. 3. Lang.: Hun.
Hungary: Budapest. 1998. Reviews of performances. ■Two plays by Enquist in Budapest: *Tribadernas natt (The Night of the Tribades)*, about Strindberg, directed by István Kolos at the Madách Theatre and *The Image Makers (Bildmakarna)*, about Selma Lagerlöf, produced by the Thalia Company at the Merlin Theatre.

2090 Koltai, Tamás; Majoros, Tamás, photo. "Madách: *Az ember tragédiája.*" (Imre Madách: *The Tragedy of Man.*) *Sz.* 1998; 31(4): 27-30. Illus.: Photo. B&W. 3. Lang.: Hun.
Hungary: Eger. 1998. Reviews of performances. ■One of the Hungarian classic plays directed by Sándor Beke at the Gárdonyi Géza Theatre, Eger.

2091 Koltai, Tamás. "Molière: *A mizantróp.*" (Molière: *The Misanthrope.*) *Sz.* 1998; 31(6): 41-42. Lang.: Hun.
Hungary: Budapest. 1998. Reviews of performances. ■*Le Misanthrope* performed by Kleiszter Ugrócsoport at the Thália Stúdió directed by Andor Lukáts.

DRAMA: —Performance/production

2092 Koltai, Tamás; Simara, László, photo. "Az átrium hölgye: Goldoni: *Mirandolina.*" (The Lady of the Atrium: Carlo Goldoni: *Mirandolina.*) *Sz.* 1998; 31(7): 37-39. Illus.: Photo. B&W. 2. Lang.: Hun.
Hungary: Kaposvár. 1998. Reviews of performances. ■Goldoni's *La Locandiera (The Mistress of the Inn)* at the Csiky Gergely Theatre, Kaposvár directed by László Keszég.

2093 Koltai, Tamás. "Jó éjt, királyfi." (Good Night, Sweet Prince.) *Sz.* 1998; 31(9): 1. Lang.: Hun.
Hungary. 1919-1998. Critical studies. ■Editor Tamás Koltai says farewell to actor Miklós Gábor (1919-1998), one of Hungary's most memorable Hamlets.

2094 Kovács, Dezső; Koncz, Zsuzsa, photo. "Molnár Ferenc: *Az üvegcipő.*" (Ferenc Molnár: *The Glass Slipper.*) *Sz.* 1998; 31(2): 37-39. Illus.: Photo. B&W. 2. Lang.: Hun.
Hungary: Budapest. 1997. Reviews of performances. ■Ferenc Molnár's play directed by János Ács at the New Theatre (Új Színház).

2095 Kovács, Dezső; Simara, László, photo. "Bulgakov: *Rettegett Iván Vasziljevics.*" (Michajl Bulgakov: *Ivan the Terrible.*) *Sz.* 1998; 31(5): 2-4. Illus.: Photo. B&W. 2. Lang.: Hun.
Hungary: Kaposvár. 1998. Reviews of performances. ■Bulgakov's *Ivan Vasiljèvič* directed by János Mohácsi at the Csiky Gergely Theatre, Kaposvár.

2096 Kovács, Dezső; Szűcs, Zoltán, photo. "Illúziók és a valóság: Osztrovszkij: *Ártatlan bűnösök.*" (Illusion and Reality: Ostrovskij: *Guilty Though Innocent.*) *Sz.* 1998; 31(9): 20-22. Illus.: Photo. B&W. 2. Lang.: Hun.
Hungary: Szolnok. 1998. Reviews of performances. ■A major event of the theatrical season: Vasiljèv's production of Ostovskij's *Guilty Though Innocent (Bez viny vinovatjè)* at Sziglegeti Theatre, Szolnok.

2097 Kovács, Dezső; Koncz, Zsuzsa, photo.; Benda, Iván, photo. "Bárka-nyitány." (The Ark Has Been Launched.) *Ellenfény.* 1998; 3(2): 14-17. Illus.: Photo. B&W. 3. Lang.: Hun.
Hungary: Budapest. 1997. Reviews of performances. ■Three performances of the new theatrical venture, Bárka Színház: Kárpáti's *Díszelőadás (Gala Performance)* directed by Balázs Simon, Thomas Bernhard's *Ritter, Dene, Voss* directed by László Bagossy and Csaba Kiss' *Shakespeare-királydrámák (Kings and Queens)* directed by the playwright at the Attic Theatre of Győr National Theatre.

2098 Kozma, András; Szűcs, Zoltán, photo. "Túl ártatlanságon, bűnösségen: Egy előadás szimbolikája." (Beyond Innocence, Guilty: The Symbology of a Performance.) *Sz.* 1998; 31(9): 22-26. Illus.: Photo. B&W. 3. Lang.: Hun.
Hungary: Szolnok. 1998. Reviews of performance. ■Symbolism in the production of Ostrovskij's *Bez viny vinovatjè (Guilty Though Innocent)* at the Szigligeti Theatre, Szolnok, directed by Anatolij Vasiljèv.

2099 Lajos, Sándor; Koncz, Zsuzsa, photo. "Lorca és 'Borca': García Lorca: Don Cristobal és Donna Rosita." (Lorca and 'Borca': Federico García Lorca: *The Tragicomedy of Don Cristobal and Dona Rosita.*) *Sz.* 1998; 31(5): 21-24. Illus.: Photo. B&W. 3. Lang.: Hun.
Hungary: Budapest. 1998. Reviews of performances. ■García Lorca's *Doña Rosita la Soltera (Doña Rosita the Spinster)* directed by Gergő Kaszás at the Bárka Színház (The Ark).

2100 Lajos, Sándor; Benda, Iván, photo. "A legrövidebb parancsolat: Dosztojevszkij: *Bűn és bűnhődés.*" (The Shortest Commandment: Dostoèvskij: *Crime and Punishment.*) *Sz.* 1998; 31(6): 27-30. Illus.: Photo. B&W. 3. Lang.: Hun.
Hungary: Győr. 1998. Reviews of performances. ■Dezső Kapás stage adaptation of Dostoèvskij's novel *Prestuplenijè i nakazanijè* based on the version by Ljubimov and Karjakin, directed by Géza Tordy at the Győr National Theatre.

2101 Liszka, Tamás; Benda, Iván. "Tört ütemek. *Shakespeare királydrámák.*" (Broken Rhythm. Csaba Kiss: *Kings and Queens.*) *Sz.* 1998; 31(1): 35-36. Illus.: Photo. B&W. 1. Lang.: Hun.
Hungary: Győr. 1997. Reviews of performances. ■A condensed adaptation of Shakespeare's chronicle plays by Csaba Kiss as a production of Győr Attic Theatre at Budapest's new venue, the Ark (Bárka Színház).

2102 Liszka, Tamás; Koncz, Zsuzsa, photo. "Alföldi Róbert: *A Phaedra-story.*" (Róbert Alföldi: *The Phaedra Story.*) *Sz.* 1998; 31(3): 30-32. Illus.: Photo. B&W. 2. Lang.: Hun.
Hungary: Budapest. 1997. Reviews of performances. ■A creative compilation of different versions of the story of Phaedra and Hipplolytus by actor Róbert Alföldi who directed the play at Pest Theatre.

2103 Liszka, Tamás; Fábry, Péter, photo. "Ötödik K. und K.: Lajos Sándor: *Szűrővizsgálat.*" (The Fifth K & K.: Sándor Lajos: *Screen Test.*) *Sz.* 1998; 31(5): 24-25. Illus.: Photo. B&W. 1. Lang.: Hun.
Hungary: Budapest. 1998. Reviews of performances. ■Sándor Lajos' play directed by Tamás Fodor presented by Studio K theatre workshop.

2104 Liszka, Tamás; Görffy, Anna, photo. "Ahol mindent szabad: Három Csehov-egyfelvonásos." (Where Everything Is Allowed: Three One-Act Plays by Čechov.) *Sz.* 1998; 31(6): 23-24. Illus.: Photo. B&W. 1. Lang.: Hun.
Hungary. Ukraine: Beregovo. 1997. Reviews of performances. ■Čechov's *Medved (The Bear), Predloženijè (The Proposal)* and *O vrede tabaka (On the Harmfulness of Tobacco)* produced by the Illyés Gyula National Theatre, Beregszász/Beregovo at a Budapest guest performance in April, 1997 directed by Attila Vidnyánszky.

2105 Liszka, Tamás; Ilovszky, Béla, photo. "Szigethy András: *Kegyelem.*" (András Szigethy: *Mercy.*) *Sz.* 1998; 31(6): 37-38. Illus.: Photo. B&W. 1. Lang.: Hun.
Hungary: Veszprém. 1998. Reviews of performances. ■András Szigethy's play directed by László Vándorfi at the Latinovits Zoltán Stage, Veszprém.

2106 Liszka, Tamás; Benda, Iván, photo. "Észrevételek: Forgách Péter: *Kaspar.*" (Notes: Péter Forgách: *Kaspar.*) *Sz.* 1998; 31(7): 41-42. Illus.: Photo. B&W. 1. Lang.: Hun.
Hungary: Győr. 1998. Reviews of performances. ■Péter Forgách's play at the Attic Stage of Győr National Theatre directed by the playwright.

2107 Márfi, Attila. *Thália papjai Pécsett: A pécsi színjátszás a 18. században és a reformkorban.* (The Priests of Thalia at Pécs: Dramatic Art at Pécs in the 18th Century and the Age of Reform.) Pécs: Pro Pannonia Kiadói Alapítvány; 1998. 156 pp. (Pannónia könyvek.) Append. Illus.: Maps. Photo. Poster. B&W. 43. Lang.: Hun.
Hungary: Pécs. 1667-1848. Histories-specific. ■A comprehensive study of theatre history in the ancient city of Pécs, a two-thousand-year old episcopal and university center.

2108 Marik, Noémi; Strassburger, Alexandra, photo. "Gogol-bemutató." (Gogol Premiere.) *Sz.* 1998; 31(5): 29-30. Illus.: Photo. B&W. 1. Lang.: Hun.
Hungary: Miskolc. 1998. Reviews of performances. ■Gogol's farce *Revizor (The Inspector General)* directed by Árpád Jutocsa Hegyi at the Miskolc National Theatre.

2109 Mészáros, Tamás. "Hétköznapi fasizmus: Mélyvíz-beszélgetés." (Everyday Fascism: A Round-table Discussion.) *Sz.* 1998; 31(7): 24-26. Illus.: Photo. B&W. 3. Lang.: Hun.
Hungary. 1986-1997. Histories-sources. ■Transcript of a televised discussion of the performance of Shakespeare's *The Merchant of Venice* directed by Róbert Alföldi at the Tivoli. The discussion, led by critic Tamás Mészáros, included the director, philosopher Ágnes Heller, professor of English literature István Géher, and three actors who have played Shylock: Miklós Gábor, Dezső Garas, and Zoltán Rátóti, who appears in Alföldi's production.

2110 Müller, Péter, P.; Simara, László, photo. "Genius Laci: Parti Nagy Lajos: *Ibusár.*" (Genius Laci: Lajos Parti Nagy: *Ibusár.*) *Sz.* 1998; 31(6): 33-36. Illus.: Photo. B&W. 3. Lang.: Hun.
Hungary: Kecskemét, Pécs. 1998. Reviews of performances. ■Lajos Parti Nagy's play directed by László Bagossy at the Katona József Theatre and directed by János Mikuli at the Janus University Stage of Pécs.

2111 Nagy, András; Kovács, Zita, photo. "A velencei bróker: Bemutató a Tivoli Színházban." (The Merchant Riddle: Premiere at the Tivoli Theatre.) *Sz.* 1998; 31(7): 14-19. Illus.: Photo. B&W. 7. Lang.: Hun.

DRAMA: —Performance/production

Hungary: Budapest. 1998. Reviews of performance. ■Shakespeare's *The Merchant of Venice* at Budapest's youngest theatrical venue, Tivoli Theatre (managed by the Budapest Chamber Theatre), directed by actor-director Róbert Alföldi.

2112 Nánay, István; Benda, Iván, photo. "Beszélgetés Kiss Csabával." (Interview with Csaba Kiss.) *Sz.* 1998; 31(3): 27-29. Illus.: Photo. B&W. 3. Lang.: Hun.

Hungary. 1990-1998. Histories-sources. ■A conversation with director Csaba Kiss, considered a representative personality of new directorial tendencies.

2113 Nánay, István; Kassai, Róbert, photo. "Kettő plusz egy: Karnyónék." (Two Plus One: Productions of Mrs. Karnyó by Mihály Csokonai Vitéz.) *Sz.* 1998; 31(6): 30-33. Illus.: Photo. B&W. 3. Lang.: Hun.

Hungary: Budapest. 1998. Reviews of performances. ■Mihály Csokonai Vitéz's *Karnyóné és a két szeleburdiak (Mrs. Karnyó and the Two Feather-Brains)* directed by Iván Hargitai at the Új Színház (New Theatre) and by Hunor Bucz at the Térszínház (Space Theatre).

2114 Perényi, Balázs. "Rutinlázadás: Bornemisza Péter: *Magyar Elektra* - Arvisura, Várszínház." (Routine Uprising: Péter Bornemisza: *Magyar Elektra*—Arvisura, Várszínház.) *Ellenfény.* 1998; 3(5): 42-46. Illus.: Photo. B&W. 5. Lang.: Hun.

Hungary: Budapest. 1988-1998. Critical studies. ■Analysis of two productions of Péter Bornemisza's play directed by István Somogyi at various theatres in 1988 and 1998.

2115 Polgár, Géza. "Műhely-aforizmák: Beszélgetés Ruszt Józseffel." (Workshop Aphorisms: Interview with József Ruszt.) *Ellenfény.* 1998; 3(1): 8-11. Illus.: Photo. B&W. 3. Lang.: Hun.

Hungary. 1963-1997. Histories-sources. ■Spotlight on József Ruszt, founder of the Universitas workshop and the Independent Stage, now artistic director of Budapest Chamber Theatre.

2116 Radics, Viktória; Csutkai, Csaba, photo. "Shakespeare: *Hamlet.*" *Sz.* 1998; 31(2): 30-34. Illus.: Photo. B&W. 3. Lang.: Hun.

Hungary: Nyíregyháza. 1997. Reviews of performances. ■István Verebes' production of his own adaptation at the Móricz Zsigmond Theatre in Nyíregyháza.

2117 Radics, Viktória; Simara, László, photo. "Játék híján a szín: Deák Ferenc: *Fojtás.*" (Instead of a Play: Ferenc Deák: *Tamping.*) *Sz.* 1998; 31(5): 4-7. Illus.: Photo. B&W. 3. Lang.: Hun.

Hungary: Kaposvár. 1998. Reviews of performances. ■Ferenc Deák's play directed by László Babarczy at the Csiky Gergely Theatre, Kaposvár.

2118 Radics, Viktória; Benda, Iván, photo.; Csutkai, Csaba, photo. "Szép Ernő: *Vőlegény.*" (Ernő Szép: *The Fiancé.*) *Sz.* 1998; 31(7): 35-37. Illus.: Photo. B&W. 35-37. Lang.: Hun.

Hungary: Nyíregyháza. Hungary: Győr. 1998. Reviews of performances. ■Two productions of Ernő Szép's play: at the Móricz Zsigmond Theatre, Nyíregyháza directed by Péter Cseke as a guest and at the Győr National Theatre directed by István Illés.

2119 Róna, Katalin. "Új fejezet, régi célok: Beszélgetés Blaskó Péterrel." (A New Chapter, Old Goals: Interview with Péter Blaskó.) *Sz.* 1998; 31(2): 19-22. Illus.: Photo. B&W. 6. Lang.: Hun.

Hungary. 1970-1998. Histories-sources. ■Péter Blaskó until recently was a leading actor of the Katona József Theatre but left to launch a freelance career. He speaks about his decision and outlines his plans for the future.

2120 Ruszt, József; Koncz, Zsuzsa, photo.; Ilovszky, Béla, photo. "Utolsó séta Gábor Miklóssal: Három pont egy megválaszolatlan kérdés végére." (The Last Walk with Miklós Gábor: Three Points after an Unanswered Question.) *Sz.* 1998; 31(9): 2-4. Illus.: Photo. B&W. Lang.: Hun.

Hungary. 1919-1998. Histories-sources. ■Director József Ruszt, a close friend and intimate collaborator, recalls a last meeting with the recently deceased actor.

2121 Sándor, L. István; Koncz, Zsuzsa, photo.; Veréb, Simon, photo. "Árnyalakok: *III. Richárd*-előadások." (Shadows: Performances of *Richard III* by Shakespeare.) *Sz.* 1998; 31(1): 30-35. Illus.: Photo. B&W. 5. Lang.: Hun.

Hungary: Budapest, Zsámbék, Szeged. 1997. Reviews of performances. ■A comparative analysis of three stagings of Shakespeare's play: at Budapesti Kamaraszínház directed by József Ruszt, and in two outdoor performances directed by Bertalan Bagó at Zsámbéki Nyári Színház and by Sándor Zsótér at Szegedi Szabadtéri Játékole.

2122 Sándor, L. István; Máthé, András, photo. "Csak irodalom? Darvasi László: *Bolond Helga.*" (Only Literature? László Darvasi: *Foolish Helga.*) *Sz.* 1998; 31(2): 39-41. Illus.: Photo. B&W. 2. Lang.: Hun.

Hungary: Debrecen. 1997. Reviews of performances. ■László Darvasi's play directed by Gábor Czeizel at the Horváth Árpád Studio Theatre of Csokonai Theatre in Debrecen.

2123 Sándor, L. István; Simara, László, photo. "Régi és új színház? Arthur Miller: *Az ügynök halála.*" (Old and New Theatre? Arthur Miller: *Death of a Salesman.*) *Sz.* 1998; 31(4): 31-34. Illus.: Photo. B&W. 2. Lang.: Hun.

Hungary: Pécs, Szeged. 1998. Reviews of performances. ■A comparative analysis of two productions of Miller's play: at the Pécs National Theatre directed by Tamás Balikó and at the Szeged National Theatre directed by Sándor Zsótér.

2124 Sándor, L. István; Csutkai, Csaba, photo. "Csődjelentések: Csehov: *Ványa bácsi.*" (Prove a Fiasco: Čechov: *Uncle Vanya.*) *Sz.* 1998; 31(6): 15-17. Illus.: Photo. B&W. 3. Lang.: Hun.

Hungary: Nyíregyháza. 1998. Reviews of performances. ■Čechov's *Diadia Vania* at the Móricz Zsigmond Theatre, Nyíregyháza directed by film director János Szász.

2125 Sándor, L. István; Korniss, Péter, photo.; Szűcs, Zoltán, photo. "A színésznő világa: Törőcsik Mari Krucsinyina-alakítása." (The World of an Actress: Mari Törőcsik as Kručinina.) *Sz.* 1998 ; 31(9): 30-35. Illus.: Photo. B&W. 5. Lang.: Hun.

Hungary: Szolnok. 1997. Reviews of performances. ■Detailed examination of Mari Törőcsik's acting and personality in her role in Ostrovskij's *Bez viny vinovatjė (Guilty Though Innocent)* at the Szigligeti Theatre, Szolnok, under the direction of Anatolij Vasiljév as a guest.

2126 Sándor, L. István; Koncz, Zsuzsa, photo.; Veréb, Simon, photo. "Határok és hatások: Zsámbéki Szombatok Nyári Színház." (Borders and Interaction: Zsámbék Summer Theatre.) *Sz.* 1998; 31(11) : 30-36. Illus.: Photo. B&W. 6. Lang.: Hun.

Hungary: Zsámbék. 1998. Reviews of performances. ■Profile of some festival events, including different performances of Molière's *Dom Juan*, with the participation of Romanian, Ukrainian and Transylvania-based Hungarian companies, and the already traditional Romanian-Hungarian co-production directed by Beatrice Bleont who this time selected Shakespeare's *A Midsummer Night's Dream.*

2127 Sándor, L. István. "Posztszovjet káosz: Faragó Béla-Mohácsi István- Mohácsi János: *Krétakör.*" (Post-Soviet Chaos: Béla Faragó-István Mohácsi-János Mohácsi: *The Chalk Circle.*) *Sz.* 1998; 31(12): 23-25. Illus.: Photo. B&W. 2. Lang.: Hun.

Hungary: Nyíregyháza. 1998. Reviews of production. ■A new version of Bertolt Brecht's *Der Kaukasische Kreidekreis*, freely adapted by director János Mohácsi at the Móricz Zsigmond Theatre, Nyíregyháza.

2128 Sándor, L. István. "Jogfolytonosság?: Beszélgetés Székely Gáborral és Novák Eszterrel." (The Continuity of Right? Interview with Gábor Székely and Eszter Novák.) *Ellenfény.* 1998; 3(2): 22-27. Illus.: Photo. B&W. 5. Lang.: Hun.

Hungary: Budapest. 1998. Histories-sources. ■Conversation with Székely, former director of Katona József Theatre and New Theatre (Új Színház, 1994-1997), and with his directing student Eszter Novák, about what the generations can learn from each other, and about how politics can alter their wills.

2129 Sándor, L. István. "Halálzóna: Beszélgetés Szász Jánossal és Schilling Árpáddal." (Death-zone: Interview with János Szász and Árpád Schilling.) *Ellenfény.* 1998; 3(4): 32-38 . Illus.: Photo. B&W. 9. Lang.: Hun.

DRAMA: —Performance/production

Hungary. 1998. Histories-sources. ■Interview with the two directors, both of whom directed Bertolt Brecht's *Baal* during the summer season.

2130 Sándor, L. István. "Mítosz, geometria, álom: Beszélgetés Telihay Péterrel." (Myth, Geometry, Dream: Conversation with Péter Telihay.) *Ellenfény.* 1998; 3(5): 47-51. Illus.: Photo. B&W. 4. Lang.: Hun.

Hungary. 1993-1998. Reviews of performances. ■Edited version of a talk with the young director on his stagings at the Veszprém University organized by the Faculty of Theatre Research.

2131 Schuller, Gabriella; Máthé, András, photo. "Függönyök: *A kivétel és a szabály.*" (Curtains: *The Exception and the Rule.*) *Sz.* 1998; 31(12): 21-23. Illus.: Photo. B&W. 1. Lang.: Hun.

Hungary: Debrecen. 1998. Reviews of performances. ■Brecht's three one-act plays *Die Ausnahme un die Regel (The Exception and the Rule), Bettler, oder der tote Hund (Beggar, or the Dead Dog)*, and *Lux in Tenebris* at the Horváth Árpád Studio Theatre of Csokonai Theatre, Debrecen, directed by József Jámbor.

2132 Sebestyén, Rita; Koncz, Zsuzsa, photo. "A kar megközelítése-a megközelítés kara: Euripidész: *Iphigeneia Auliszban*-Radnóti Színház." (Approaching the Chorus–The Approaching Chorus: Euripides: *Iphigenia in Aulis*–Radnóti Theatre.) *Ellenfény.* 1998; 3(5): 36-39. Illus.: Photo. B&W. 3. Lang.: Hun.

Hungary: Budapest. 1998. Critical studies. ■Essay on the production of Euripides' play directed by Péter Valló at the Radnóti Theatre.

2133 Sediánszky, Nóra; Koncz, Zsuzsa, photo. "A mágikus kert: Tom Stoppard: *Árkádia.*" (The Magic Garden: Tom Stoppard: *Arcadia.*) *Sz.* 1998; 31(6): 9-12. Illus.: Photo. B&W. 3. Lang.: Hun.

Hungary: Budapest. 1998. Reviews of performances. ■Tom Stoppard's play directed by Tamás Ascher at the Katona József Theatre.

2134 Stuber, Andrea; Walter, Péter, photo. "Csehov-közelben: Turgenyev: *Egy hónap falun.*" (Approaching Čechov: Turgenjév: *A Month in the Country.*) *Sz.* 1998; 31(7): 40-41. Illus.: Photo. B&W. 1. Lang.: Hun.

Hungary: Kecskemét. 1998. Reviews of performances. ■Turgenjév's *A Month in the Country (Mesjac v derevne)* play at the Katona József Theatre, Kecskemét, directed by Zoltán Lendvai.

2135 Stuber, Andrea; Ilovszky, Béla, photo.; Veréb, Simon, photo. "Fél tucat Prozorova: Csehov: *Három nővér.*" (A Half-Dozen Prozorova: Čechov: *Three Sisters.*) *Sz.* 1998; 31(6): 18-21. Illus.: Photo. B&W. 3. Lang.: Hun.

Hungary: Veszprém, Szeged. 1998. Reviews of performances. ■Two productions of *Tri sestry* at the Petőfi Theatre, Veszprém, directed by Árpád Árkosi and at the Chamber Theatre of Szeged National Theatre directed by Péter Telihay.

2136 Szántó, Judit; Szabó, Péter, photo. "Kosztolányi-Tasnádi: *Édes Anna.*" (Dezső Kosztolányi-István Tasnádi: *Anna Édes.*) *Sz.* 1998; 31(2): 34-36. Illus.: Photo. B&W. 2. Lang.: Hun.

Hungary: Budapest. 1997. Reviews of performances. ■The stage adaptation of Dezső Kosztolányi's novel directed by András Léner at the Madách Chamber Theatre.

2137 Szántó, Judit; Koncz, Zsuzsa, photo. "Calderón: *VIII. Henrik.*" (Calderón: *Henry VIII.*) *Sz.* 1998; 31 (3): 41-44. Illus.: Photo. B&W. 2. Lang.: Hun.

Hungary: Budapest. 1997. Reviews of performances. ■Hungarian production of Calderón's *La cisma de Inglaterra (The Schism of England)* directed by Péter Telihay at the Radnóti Miklós Színház.

2138 Szántó, Judit; Koncz, Zsuzsa, photo. "A lélektan ártalmairól: Leszkov-Kiss: *Kisvárosi Lady Macbeth.*" (The Harmfulness of Psychology: Leskov-Kiss: *Lady Macbeth of the Provinces.*) *Sz.* 1998; 31(5): 10-13. Illus.: Photo. B&W. 4. Lang.: Hun.

Hungary: Budapest. 1998. Reviews of performances. ■Nikolaj Leskov's novel *Ledi Makbet Mtsenskogo Uezda (Lady Macbeth of the Mtsensk District)* adapted and directed by Csaba Kiss for the stage of the Chamber of the Katona József Theatre.

2139 Szántó, Judit; Ilovszky, Béla, photo. "Colombina piros-zöld kockákban: *A Fedák-ügy.*" (Colombina in Red and Green Costume: The *Fedák Case.*) *Sz.* 1998; 31(6): 39-41. Illus.: Photo. B&W. 2. Lang.: Hun.

Hungary: Budapest. 1998. Reviews of performances. ■A compilation concerned with the adventurous and controversial life of actress Sári Fedák (1879-1955) adapted for the stage and directed by actress Denise Radó at the Underground Stage of József Attila Theatre.

2140 Szigethy, Gábor. "Mezei Mária vályogvára." (The Adobe Castle of Mária Mezei.) *Sz.* 1998; 31(4): 41-42. Illus.: Photo. B&W. 2. Lang.: Hun.

Hungary. 1945-1983. Biographical studies. ■Remembering the actress Mária Mezei (1909-1983) by the expert on her legacy.

2141 Tordai, Zádor; Csutkai, Csaba, photo. "Két szék közt a padlón, avagy laudatio Gaál Erzsébet emlékére." (Between Two Chairs on the Ground, or Laudatio in Memory of Erzsébet Gaál.) *Sz.* 1998; 31(11): 28-29. Illus.: Photo. B&W. 1. Lang.: Hun.

Hungary. 1951-1998. Biographical studies. ■A commemorative article on the unusual career and untimely death of actress and director Erzsébet Gaál (1951-1998).

2142 Török, Tamara; Ilovszky, Béla, photo.; Koncz, Zsuzsa, photo. "Látlelet a szín-házról: Három Molière-előadás." (Report on the Theatre: Three Molière Productions.) *Sz.* 1998; 31(11): 36-38. Illus.: Photo. B&W. 3. Lang.: Hun.

Hungary: Szentendre, Kapolcs, Kőszeg. 1998. Reviews of performances. ■Three performances of Molière's plays at various summer theatres: *Georges Dandin* at the Szentendre Theatre directed by Iván Hargitai, *Le Médecin malgré lui* at the Valley of Arts'98 in Kapolcs directed by Imre Csiszár and *Le Malade imaginaire* at the Kőszeg Castle Theatre directed by Béla Merő.

2143 Upor, László; Koncz, Zsuzsa, photo. "Paál István (1942-1998)." (István Paál, 1942-1998.) *Sz.* 1998; 31(4): 23. Illus.: Photo. B&W. 1. Lang.: Hun.

Hungary: Szolnok. 1942-1998. Biographical studies. ■Obituary for the director of the Szigligeti Theatre, who recently committed suicide.

2144 Urbán, Balázs; Koncz, Zsuzsa, photo. "Zátonyok nélkül: Tasnádi István: *Titanic vízirevü.*" (Without Shelves: István Tasnádi: *The Titanic Water Show.*) *Sz.* 1998; 31(7): 31-33. Illus.: Photo. B&W. 3. Lang.: Hun.

Hungary: Budapest. 1998. Reviews of performances. ■István Tasnádi's play at Bárka Szinhaz (The Ark) 'created by the company'.

2145 Urbán, Balázs; Koncz, Zsuzsa, photo. "Megváltatlanul: Jeles András: *Szenvedéstörténet.*" (Without Redemption: András Jeles: *Passion Play.*) *Sz.* 1998; 31(10): 15-16. Illus.: Photo. B&W. 2. Lang.: Hun.

Hungary: Budapest. 1998. Reviews of performances. ■Film director András Jeles' play at the Chamber stage of Katona József Theatre directed by Gábor Máté.

2146 Varga, Judit; Znamenák, István, photo. "Apátlan nemzedékek: Beszélgetés Ascher Tamással." (Fatherless Generations: Interview with Tamás Ascher.) *Ellenfény.* 1998; 3(2): 2-3. Illus.: Photo. B&W. 2. Lang.: Hun.

Hungary. 1960-1990. Histories-sources. ■A conversation with the director on training new generation of directors at the Academy of Drama and Film.

2147 Zala, Szilárd Zoltán; Farkas, Virág. "Das ewig Weibliche: Gaál Erzsi pályaképe helyett - merő szubjektivitás." (Das ewig Weibliche: A Subjective Portrait of Erzsébet Gaál.) *Ellenfény.* 1998; 3(4): 8-13. Illus.: Photo. B&W. 5. Lang.: Hun.

Hungary. 1951-1998. Biographical studies. ■Life and career of one of the significant personalities of alternative theatre workshops, actor-director Erzsébet Gaál.

2148 Zala, Szilárd Zoltán; Katkó, Tamás, photo. "Rendszerváltás kávészünetben: Bornemisza Péter: *Magyar Electra*-Arvisura, Várszínház." (Changing the Regime in a Coffee Break: Péter Bornemisza: *Magyar Elektra*–Arvisura, Várszínház.) *Ellenfény.* 1998; 3(5): 41-42. Illus.: Photo. B&W. 2. Lang.: Hun.

Hungary: Budapest. 1988-1998. Critical studies. ■Two stagings of Bornemisza's play directed by István Somogyi at different theatres: an alternative production by Arvisura Theatre in 1988 and at the Castle Theatre in 1998.

2149 Zappe, László; Simara, László, photo. "Alkohol, elmebaj, kultúra: Két kaposvári bemutató." (Alcohol, Insanity, Culture: Two Premieres at Kaposvár.) *Sz.* 1998; 31(5): 7-9. Illus.: Photo. B&W. 2. Lang.: Hun.

Hungary: Kaposvár. 1998. Reviews of performances. ▪On the first nights of two productions at the Csiky Gergely Theatre, Kaposvár: Nikolaj Koljada's *Murlin Murlo* directed by Radoslav Milenković and Viktor Jerofejév's *Walpurgis Night (Valpurzina noc)* directed by László Keszég.

2150 Zappe, László; Máthé, András, photo. "Balett és emberiség: Hubay: *Hová lett a rózsa lelke?.*" (Ballet and Mankind: Miklós Hubay: *What Has Become of the Spirit of the Rose?.*) *Sz.* 1998; 31(6): 36-37. Illus.: Photo. B&W. 1. Lang.: Hun.

Hungary: Debrecen. 1998. Reviews of performances. ▪Miklós Hubay's play on Nižinskij directed by György Lengyel at the Chamber Theatre of Kölcsey Cultural Centre, Debrecen.

2151 Chatterjee, Sudipto. "In Memory: Śombhu Mitra." *TDR.* 1998 Spr; 42(1): 8-11. Illus.: Photo. B&W. 1. Lang.: Eng.

India. 1914-1997. Biographical studies. ▪Obituary for the actor and director.

2152 Alsenad, Abedalmutalab Abood. *Professional Production of Shakespeare in Iraq: An Exploration of Cultural Adaptation.* Boulder, CO: Univ. of Colorado; 1988. 206 pp. Biblio. Notes. [Ph.D. Dissertation, Univ. Microfilms Order No. AAC 8819636.] Lang.: Eng.

Iraq. 1880-1988. Histories-specific. ▪How Shakespeare's plays have been produced and adapted to Iraqi cultural values.

2153 Cave, Richard Allen. "Staging *The King's Threshold.*" *YA.* 1998; 13: 158-175. Notes. Illus.: Design. B&W. 1. Lang.: Eng.

Ireland: Dublin. UK-England: London. 1903. Historical studies. ▪Based on a recently discovered stage design by Yeats for his play, examines the background of the play, Yeats's many revisions, and the critical response to its opening in both London and Dublin.

2154 Shaughnessy, Edward L. "O'Neill in Ireland: An Update." *EOR.* 1998 Spr/Fall; 22(1/2): 137-156. Biblio. Append. Illus.: Photo. B&W. 2. Lang.: Eng.

Ireland: Dublin. UK-Ireland: Belfast. 1989-1998. Historical studies. ▪Discusses six productions of O'Neill's work in Dublin and Belfast in the last ten years: *Hughie* directed by Judy Friel for the Abbey, *The Iceman Cometh* in 1990 directed by Roland Jacquerello at the Lyric, and in 1992 directed by Robert Falls at the Abbey, *A Moon for the Misbegotten* directed by Simon Magill for a DubbelJoint Productions tour, *Long Day's Journey Into Night* directed by Karel Reisz at the Gate, and *Anna Christie* directed by Liam Halligan at the Focus. Contains appendix with cast lists, directors, and designers.

2155 Schneider, Wolfgang. "Zwischen dem jährlichen 'Basket of Culture' und dem alltäglichen 'Showbusiness'." (Between the Yearly 'Basket of Culture' and the Daily 'Showbusiness'.) *G&GBKM.* 1998; 127: 10-14. Illus.: Photo. B&W. 1. Lang.: Ger.

Israel. 1993-1998. Critical studies. ▪Notations on the contemporary Israeli children's theatre and its producing conditions. Ten critical questions from an outside standpoint as viewer of about fifty performances.

2156 "But Who Plays the Typewriter." *Econ.* 1998 Nov 7; 349(8093): 91. Illus.: Photo. B&W. 1. Lang.: Eng.

Italy: Calabria. 1998. Critical studies. ▪Report on the performance by Laura Curano, in a small piazza in Calabria, of her solo piece *Olivetti*, written with Gabriele Vacis, based on the life of typewriter manufacturer Camillo Olivetti.

2157 Alonge, Roberto. "Lavia: il sottotesto di *Non si sa come.*" (Lavia: The Subtext in *How Is Unknown.*) *IlCast.* 1998; 11 (33): 103-113. Notes. Illus.: Photo. B&W. 4. Lang.: Ita.

Italy: Turin. 1982-1988. Critical studies. ▪Gabriele Lavia's production of *Na si sa come (How Is Unknown)* by Pirandello for the Teatro Stabile di Torino: analysis and comparison with Lavia's earlier production.

2158 Baffi, Giulio. "An Overview of Neapolitan Theatre." *WES.* 1998 Win; 10(1): 39-42. Illus.: Photo. B&W. 3. Lang.: Eng.

Italy: Naples. 1998. Historical studies. ▪Survey of the burgeoning and varied Naples theatre scene.

2159 Baiardo, Enrico; De Lucis, Fulvio. *Shakespeare e il rap. I 'Sonnetti' secondo Liberovici and Sanguineti.* (Shakespeare and Rap. The *Sonnets* According to Liberovici and Sanguineti.) Genoa: De Ferrari; 1998. 136 pp. Illus.: Photo. B&W. 3. Lang.: Ita.

Italy: Genoa. 1997. Critical studies. ▪Analysis of the staging of *Sonetto. Un travestimento shakespeariano (Sonnet: A Shakespearean Travesty)* by the Italian poet and dramatist Edoardo Sanguineti. The production was directed by Andrea Liberovici at the Teatro Carlo Felice-Sala Eugenio Montale in Genoa.

2160 Carlson, Marvin. "Report from Northern Italy." *WES.* 1998 Win; 10(1): 9-22. Illus.: Photo. B&W. 8. Lang.: Eng.

Italy. 1997-1998. Historical studies. ▪Survey of the rich theatrical activity in the Northern Italian provinces of Lombardy, Emilia-Romagna, Tuscany, Liguria, Piedmont, Venetia, and Friuli-Venezia Giulia.

2161 Carlson, Marvin. "Report from Milan." *WES.* 1998 Win; 10(1): 83-92. Illus.: Photo. B&W. 7. Lang.: Eng.

Italy: Milan. 1997-1998. Historical studies. ▪Survey of the Milanese theatre scene, refering to Giorgio Strehler's Piccolo, larger and smaller venues such as Teatros Manzoni, Carcano, Nuovo, Llitta, San Babila, and Filodrammatici. Mentions, also, co-operative theatres like Teatro dell'Elfo and di Portaromana run by the company Teatridithalia, and 'off' theatres like Teatro Instabile.

2162 Castri, Massimo. "Dai *Taccuini.*" (From *The Notebooks.*) *IlCast.* 1998; 11(32): 69-100. Lang.: Ita.

Italy: Prato. 1996. Histories-sources. ▪The notebooks of the Italian director Massimo Castri with respect to the staging of Goldoni's *Trilogia della villeggiatura (Holiday Trilogy)* at the Teatro Massimo.

2163 Dasgupta, Gautam. "Italian Notes: Strehler, Fo, and the Venice Biennale." *PerAJ.* 1998 Jan.; 20(58): 26-37. Illus.: Photo. B&W. 8. Lang.: Eng.

Italy: Venice. 1947-1998. Historical studies. ▪As Venice hosts the Italian Biennale dedicated to its cultural history, the late director of the Teatro Piccolo and Dario Fo, Nobel Prize-winning playwright, are celebrated for their contributions to the continued prominence of Italy in the world's cultural sphere.

2164 De Curtis, Liliana, ed.; Amorosi, Matilde, ed. *Totò, veniamo a voi con questa mia ...* (Totò, We Come to You with This Letter of Mine.) Venice/Rome: Marsilio/RAI-ERI; 1998. 202 pp. (Gli specchi dello spettacolo.) Pref. Gloss. Lang.: Ita.

Italy: Naples. 1967-1997. Biographical studies. ▪A collection of the messages, appeals, and requests for favors written, sent, or placed on the tomb of actor Totò by his fans.

2165 Di Nocera, Antonella. "Harold Pinter: Two Italian Productions." *WES.* 1998 Win; 10(1): 23-28. Illus.: Photo. B&W. 3. Lang.: Eng.

Italy. 1997. Critical studies. ▪Analysis of two productions of plays by Harold Pinter: *The Hothouse* at Teatro Quirino, directed by Carlo Cecchi and *The Lover*, directed by André Ruth Shammah for Teatro Stabile di Torino at the Benevento Citti Spettacolo Festival.

2166 Di Nocera, Antonella. "Mario Martone: A Neapolitan Director Theatre as a Necessary." *WES.* 1998 Win; 10(1): 43-48. Illus.: Photo. B&W. 3. Lang.: Eng.

Italy: Naples. 1977-1997. Histories-sources. ▪Interview with the director about his theories, theatre in Naples, and his work with the companies Falso Movimento and Teatri Uniti.

2167 Dotto, Giancarlo. *Vita di Carmelo Bene.* (The Life of Carmelo Bene.) Milan: Bompiani; 1998. 422 pp. Illus.: Photo. B&W. 12. Lang.: Ita.

Italy. 1937-1998. Histories-sources. ▪Interview with director Carmelo Bene in which he talks about his life, his passions, and his work.

2168 Finter, Helga. "Primo Levi's Stage Version of *Se questo è un uomo.*" 229-253 in Schumacher, Claude, ed. *Staging the Holocaust: The Shoah in Drama and Performance.* Cambridge: Cambridge UP; 1998. 355 pp. (Cambridge Studies in Modern Theatre.) Index. Notes. Biblio. Illus.: Photo. 4. Lang.: Eng.

DRAMA: —Performance/production

Italy: Turin. 1963-1966. Historical studies. ■Analysis of Gianfranco De Bosio's staging of *Se questo è un uomo (If This Is a Man)*, a Holocaust drama by Primo Levi, for Teatro Stabile di Torino at Teatro Carignano. Focuses on the tension between literary text and the realized production.

2169 Galasso, Sabrina. *Il teatro di Remondi e Caporossi.* (The Theatre of Remondi and Caporossi.) Rome: Bulzoni; 1998. 490 pp. (Biblioteca Teatrale, 98.) Illus.: Photo. Dwg. B&W. 12. Lang.: Ita.

Italy. 1970-1995. Critical studies. ■A study of the dramatic works and performances of authors, directors, and actors Claudio Remondi and Riccardo Caporossi.

2170 Garboli, Cesare. *Un pò prima del piombo.* (Just Before Press Time.) Milan: Sansoni; 1998. 384 pp. (Saggi Sansoni.) Pref. Lang.: Ita.

Italy. 1972-1977. Reviews of performances. ■A collection of reviews of performances by the Italian critic and scholar Cesare Garboli, previously published in the Italian paper *Corriere della Sera* and in the magazine *Il mondo.*

2171 Heed, Sven Åke. "För en mänskligare teater." (For a More Human Theatre.) *Tningen.* 1998; 21(3): 48-51. Illus.: Photo. B&W. Lang.: Swe.

Italy: Milan. 1956-1998. ■Giorgio Strehler's productions of plays by Brecht, with references to *Die Dreigroschenoper (The Three Penny Opera)* and *Leben des Galilei (The Life of Galileo).*

2172 Kolin, Philip. "From Coitus to Craziness: The Italian Premiere of *A Streetcar Named Desire.*" *JADT.* 1998 Spr; 10(2): 74-92. Notes. Lang.: Eng.

Italy: Rome. 1949. Historical studies. ■Audience and critical reaction to the Italian premiere of Tennessee Williams' *A Streetcar Named Desire*, directed by Luchino Visconti, staged by the Rina Morelli-Paolo Stoppa Company at the Eliseo Theatre, and starring Rina Morelli as Blanche and Vittorio Gassman as Stanley.

2173 Mazzocchi, Federica, ed.; Bentoglio, Alberto, ed. *Giorgio Strehler e il suo teatro.* (Giorgio Strehler and His Theatre.) Rome: Bulzoni; 1998. 529 pp. Notes. Pref. Biblio. Lang.: Ita.

Italy. 1936-1996. Critical studies. ■A collection of essays on the Italian director Giorgio Strehler, published as proceedings of a meeting held at Gargnano (Brescia) April 22-26, 1996.

2174 Ovadia, Moni. *Speriamo che tenga. Viaggio di un saltimbanco sospeso tra cielo e terra.* (Let's Hope It Holds: A Journey of an Acrobat Hanging from Sky and Land.) Milan: Mondadori; 1998. 207 pp. (Ingrandimenti.) Lang.: Ita.

Italy. Bulgaria. 1946-1998. Histories-sources. ■The autobiography of the Yiddish actor Moni Ovadia, born in Bulgaria but living and working in Italy.

2175 Pederson, Nadine. "Molière for the Twentieth Century." *WES.* 1998 Win; 10(1): 61-62. Illus.: Photo. B&W. 1. Lang.: Eng.

Italy: Rome. 1997. Critical studies. ■Analysis of A.Artist.Associati's production of *The Learned Ladies (Les Femmes savantes)*, directed by Toni Bertorelli at Teatro Ghione. Argues that another production, Alfiero Alfieri's company's production of Giggi Spaducci's *L'Ora der fregnone c'è pe 'tutti (The Hour of the Idiot Comes to Everyone)*, a play in Roman dialect, is more in line with the spirit of Molière.

2176 Pizzo, Antonio. "Expressing Silence: The Theatre of Remondi and Caporossi." *WES.* 1998 Win; 10(1): 99-102. Illus.: Photo. B&W. 1. Lang.: Eng.

Italy. 1971-1998. Critical studies. ■Analysis of the techniques and philosophy of the actor/clown team of Claudio Remondi and Riccardo Caporossi, and their reliance on objects rather than words to express themselves. Includes examples from their piece *Romitori (Hermits).*

2177 Puppa, Paolo. "Giacinta Pezzana tra scena e pagina." (Giacinta Pezzana Between Page and Stage.) *Ariel.* 1998; 13(3): 41-54. Notes. Lang.: Ita.

Italy. 1841-1919. Biographical studies. ■Life and career of a famous Italian actress of the nineteenth century.

2178 Quazzolo, Paolo. "Pirandello a Trieste." (Pirandello in Trieste.) *Ariel.* 1998; 13(1-2): 353-364. Notes. Illus.: Handbill. 3. Lang.: Ita.

Italy: Trieste. 1926. Historical studies. ■The tour by Pirandello's company Il Teatro d'Arte in Trieste from November 20 to December 3, 1926.

2179 Ragni, Biancamaria. "*Elettra* di Euripide per la regia di Massimo Castri: lavoro teatrale e attivazione dell'immaginario dell'attore." (*Electra* by Euripides under the Direction of Massimo Castri: Theatre Work and Activation of the Actor's Imagination.) *BiT.* 1998; 45/47: 83-106. Notes. Lang.: Ita.

Italy: Spoleto. 1993. Critical studies. ■Follows the rehearsals for *Electra* by Euripides, directed by Massimo Castri at Teatro Stabile dell'Umbria, which opened on December 10, 1993, in Spoleto. The production is said to have been praised by both critics and audiences for its re-invention of the scenic space of Italian theatre, and for the unusual acting of the performers.

2180 Rettig, Claes von. "En seklets teaterman." (Theatre Man of the Century.) *Entré.* 198; 25(1): 36-37. Illus.: Photo. B&W. Lang.: Swe.

Italy. 1940-1998. Historical studies. ■Review of the ideas and productions of Giorgio Strehler, with reference to Piccolo Teatro and Théâtre de l'Europe.

2181 Rühle, Günther. "Die Wirklichkeit der Symbole." (The Reality of Symbols.) *THeute.* 1998; 2: 34-41. Illus.: Photo. B&W. 9. Lang.: Ger.

Italy: Milan. 1921-1997. Biographical studies. ■Portrait of actor and director Giorgio Strehler, the founder of Piccolo Teatro, who died in 1997.

2182 Sessi, Carla Castiglione; Carlson, Marvin, transl. "Where Is the Italian Theatre Headed?" *WES.* 1998 Win; 10(1): 73-74. Lang.: Eng.

Italy. 1998. Critical studies. ■Discusses the overall state of the theatre in Italy and strategies for breaking it out of its sterility.

2183 Sfyris, Panagiotis. "Luca Ronconi/Eugene O'Neill: An American Tragedy." *WES.* 1998 Win; 10(1): 63-66. Illus.: Photo. B&W. 3. Lang.: Eng.

Italy: Rome. 1996-1997. Critical studies. ■Analysis of Ronconi's staging of O'Neill's *Mourning Becomes Electra* at the Teatro di Roma.

2184 Strehler, Giorgio. "Goldoni: per un teatro nazional popolare." (Goldoni: Toward a National Popular Theatre.) *IlCast.* 1998; 11(32): 9-14. Lang.: Ita.

Italy. 1997. Staging. ■Transcript of text read by director Giorgio Strehler on the occasion of his being awarded an honorary degree by the University of Turin.

2185 Tóka, Ágnes. "Budapesti interjú Giorgio Strehlerrel." (Interview with Giorgio Strehler in Budapest.) *Vilag.* 1998 Sum; 12: 25-28. Lang.: Hun.

Italy: Milan. 1993. Histories-sources. ■A talk with the director on the occasion of the 2nd Festival of Union of Theatres of Europe held in Budapest.

2186 Török, Tamara. "Álomszínház." (Dream Theatre.) *Sz.* 1998; 31(8): 2-8. Illus.: Photo. B&W. 7. Lang.: Hun.

Italy: Milan. 1947-1998. Critical studies. ■Account of author's visit to Milan's Piccolo Teatro after the death of its founder and leader, Giorgio Strehler, and his conversations with some of the actors as well as co-director Carlo Battistoni.

2187 Vianello, Daniele; Carlson, Marvin, transl. "Rome: Among Institutional Theatres and Places of Experimentation." *WES.* 1998 Win; 10(1): 49-54. Lang.: Eng.

Italy: Rome. 1994-1998. Critical studies. ■Comparison of the theatres in Rome producing traditional theatrical fare, represented by the government Teatros Quirino and Valle, and the private Teatro Eliseo, with the venues presenting more experimental pieces, such as Centro Teatro Ateneo, the Colosseo, and Teatro Vascello.

2188 Vianello, Daniele; Carlson, Marvin, transl. "Luca Ronconi: The Karamazovs from Page to Stage." *WES.* 1998 Win; 10(1): 55-58. Lang.: Eng.

Italy: Rome. 1997. Critical studies. ■Analysis of Ronconi's adaptation of Dostojévskij's novel *Bratja Karamazov (The Brothers Karamazov)* presented at Teatro Argentina under his own direction.

2189 Wehle, Philippa. "Romeo Castellucci's 'Theatre of Cruelty': *Orestea (Una commedia organica?)* by the Societas Raffaello

DRAMA: —Performance/production

Sanzio." *WES.* 1998 Win; 10(1): 93-96. Illus.: Photo. B&W. 2. Lang.: Eng.
Italy: Cesena. 1997. Reviews of performances. ■Review of Castellucci's free-form adaptation and direction of Aeschylus' *Oresteia* for his company.

2190 Zampelli, Michael Angelo. *Incarnating the Word: Giovan Battista Andreini, Religious Antitheatricalism, and the Redemption of a Profession.* Medford, MA: Tufts Univ; 1998. 396 pp. Notes. Biblio. [Ph.D. Dissertation, Univ. Microfilms Order No. AAC 9906998.] Lang.: Eng.
Italy. 1576-1654. Critical studies. ■The nature of religion and Christian identity in the works and performance career of Giambattista Andreini, including *Adamo*, *La Maddalena*, and *La Maddalena lasciva e penitente.*

2191 Allain, Paul. "Suzuki Training." *TDR.* 1998 Spr; 42(1): 66-89. Notes. Biblio. Illus.: Photo. B&W. 21. Lang.: Eng.
Japan. 1998. Critical studies. ■Detailed description of Tadashi Suzuki's method of actor training.

2192 de Stains, Ian. "Letter From Tokyo." *PlPl.* Mar 1998; 520: 30. Lang.: Eng.
Japan: Tokyo. 1994-1998. Historical studies. ■Theatrical component of Japan's UK98 Festival, including development of *The Chrysanthemum and the Rose* by Elizabeth Handover and Keiko Katsura, directed by Masako Miyazaki, based on Mary Fraser's *A Diplomatist's Wife in Japan*, produced by Tokyo Actors Repertory Company.

2193 Grišeleva, L.D.; Čegodar', N.I. *Japonskaja kul'tura Novogo vremeni.* (Japanese Culture of the New Age.) Moscow: Vost. lit.; 1998. 240 pp. (Kul'tura narodov Vostoka.) Lang.: Rus.
Japan. 1998. Histories-specific. ■Survey of Japanese theatre.

2194 Sorokin, V.F. "Iz istorii rossijsko-kitajskich teatral'nych svjazej (perv. pol. XX v.)." (On the History of the Russian-Japanese Theatrical Relationship During the First Half of the Twentieth Century.) 354 - 352 in *Vostokovedenie i mirovaja kul'tura.* Moscow: 1998. (Pamjatniki ist. mysli.) Lang.: Rus.
Japan. Russia. 1900-1950. Historical studies. ■History of the theatrical relationship between Japan and Russia in the first fifty years of the twentieth century.

2195 Welch, Patricia Marie. *Discourse Strategies and the Humor of 'Rakugo'.* Ann Arbor, MI: Univ. of Michigan; 1998. 440 pp. Biblio. Notes. [Ph.D. Dissertation, Univ. Microfilms Order No. AAC 9840671.] Lang.: Eng.
Japan. 1600-1980. Critical studies. ■Focuses on the popular art form *rakugo*'s working-class roots, oral narrative form, and comic attitudes, and analyzes its role in negotiating social anxieties.

2196 Odenthal, Johannes. "Spirituelle Traditionen im koreaniscchen Theater." (Spiritual Traditions in Korean Theatre.) 98-109 in Pochhammer, Sabine, ed. *Utopie: Spiritualität? Spiritualité: une utopie?/Utopia: Spirituality? Spirituality: A Utopia?.* Berlin: Theaterschrift c/o Künstlerhaus Bethanien; 1998. 173 pp. (Theaterschrift 13.) Illus.: Photo. B&W. 2. Lang.: Ger, Fre, Dut, Eng.
Korea. Germany: Berlin. 1980-1998. Historical studies. ■Report on a symposium held in Berlin on the continuation/rediscovery of traditional Korean dramatic forms. Contains remarks from Korean director Lee Youn Taek.

2197 Morozov, A. *Persony.* (People.) Kazan': Tat. kn. izd-vo; 1998. 398 pp. Lang.: Rus.
Latvia. 1998. Biographical studies. ■Articles about stage and film actors, including Sergej Jurskij.

2198 Drewniak, Łukasz. "Eimuntas Nekrošius: udręka, sanktuarium." (Eimuntas Nekrošius: Torment, Sanctuary.) *DialogW.* 1998 Aug.; 8: 102-120. Illus.: Photo. B&W. 12. Lang.: Pol.
Lithuania. 1952-1998. Biographical studies. ■Artistic profile of Lithuanian director Eimuntas Nekrošius. Analyzes his individual works of the classics as well as his work presented in festivals.

2199 Oseland, James. "Mexican Spitfire." *AmTh.* 1998 Dec.; 15(10): 71-74. Illus.: Photo. B&W. 1. Lang.: Eng.
Mexico: Mexico City. 1998. Historical studies. ■Report on the state of the theatre in Mexico City.

2200 Alkema, Hanny. *Vertel ... Vertel!: 15 jaar theatergroep delta.* (Tell me ... Tell me!: 15 Years of Theatre Group Delta.) Amsterdam: ITFB; 1998. 104 pp. Pref. Illus.: Photo. B&W. 12. Lang.: Dut.
Netherlands: Amsterdam. 1983-1998. Histories-reconstruction. ■Examines the output of the Delta Theatre Company founded by Nels Lekatompessy and Anis de Jong in the Netherlands.

2201 Callens, Johan. "'When I Read the Book': Sam Shepard's *Action.*" 33-49 in Michel, Pierre, ed.; Phillips, Diana, ed.; Lee, Eric, ed. *Belgian Essays on Language and Literature.* Liège: Belgian Association of Anglicists in Higher Education; 1991. 162 pp. Lang.: Dut.
Netherlands: Rotterdam. 1988. Critical studies. ■Apocalyptic postmodernism in Shepard's play as seen in the production by the company De Zaak, under the direction of Peter de Baan.

2202 Haas, Anna de. *De wetten van het treurspel. Over ernstig toneel in Nederland, 1700-1772.* (The Laws of Tragedy: On Serious Drama in the Netherlands, 1700-1772.) Hilversum: Verloren; 1998. 350 pp. Index. Notes. Biblio. Illus.: Photo. Graphs. Dwg. B&W. 15. Lang.: Dut.
Netherlands. 1700-1772. Histories-specific. ■Examines the eighteenth-century Dutch theatre, its organization and objectives.

2203 Panken, Ton. *Een geschiedenis van het jeugdtheater.* (A History of the Theatre for Youth.) Amsterdam: Boom; 1998. 240 pp. Index. Notes. Biblio. Pref. Illus.: Photo. Graphs. Dwg. B&W. 32. Lang.: Dut.
Netherlands. 1800-1995. Histories-specific. ■Examines the development of children's and youth theatre in the Netherlands, including its artistic and pedagogical objectives.

2204 Paridon, Egbert van. *Liever geen bloemen: terugblik van een theaterman.* (No Flowers, Please: A Retrospective of a Theatre Man.) Amsterdam: Theater Instituut Nederland; 1990. 235 pp. Index. Notes. Biblio. Illus.: Photo. B&W. 20. Lang.: Dut.
Netherlands. 1920-1990. Histories-sources. ■Egbert van Paridon reflects on his career in the theatre, his work as a director and actor, and his role in the development of the theatre in the Netherlands.

2205 Retallack, John. "De splendid isolation van het Nederlands toneel." (The Splendid Isolation of Dutch Theatre.) *Tmaker.* 1998; 2(9/10): 36-40. Illus.: Photo. B&W. 4. Lang.: Dut.
Netherlands. 1990-1998. Historical studies. ■Reports on the contemporary Dutch theatre, stressing its identity struggles and audience rates.

2206 Thielemans, Johan. "Digitale Tovenaars." (Digital Magicians.) *Tmaker.* 1998; 2(9/10): 22-26. Illus.: Photo. B&W. 2. Lang.: Dut.
Netherlands. USA. 1970-1998. Historical studies. ■The impact of new technology on the theatre. Overview of experimental use of television in the theatrical space, as practiced by the Wooster Group, Nam June Paik and Guy Cassiers, artistic director of the RO-Theater.

2207 Johnson, Jennifer Anne. *Reinventing the Bard: The Evolution of the Contemporary Shakespearean Director.* Long Beach, CA: California State Univ; 1998. 47 pp. Notes. Biblio. [M.A. Thesis, Univ. Microfilms Order No. AAC 1391639.] Lang.: Eng.
North America. Europe. 1967-1998. Histories-specific. ■Traces the evolution of the Shakespearean director's role in contemporary theatre. Argues that directors must find innovative and meaningful interpretations which speak to today's audiences. Study begins with the work of Peter Brook, including his production of *A Midsummer Night's Dream*, and continues to current American and European directors.

2208 Lorincz, Chester Joseph. *Vocal Technique: Speakers of 'Henry V'.* Calgary, AB: Univ. of Calgary; 1998. 132 pp. Notes. Biblio. [M.F.A. Thesis, Univ. Microfilms Order No. AAC MQ31317.] Lang.: Eng.
North America. UK-England. 1998. Critical studies. ■Comparison of the speaking styles of selected actors delivering text from Shakespeare's *Henry V* including John Gielgud, Laurence Olivier, Ian Holm, Christopher Plummer, William Shatner, Derek Jacobi, and Richard Burton.

DRAMA: —Performance/production

2209 Ramírez, Elizabeth. "Chicanas/Latinas in Performance on the American Stage." *JDTC.* 1998 Fall; 13(1): 133-141. Notes. Lang.: Eng.
North America. 1993-1998. Critical studies. ■The current state of plays from Chicana and Latina female playwrights.

2210 Carlson, Marvin. "Interview with Stein Winge." *WES.* 1998 Fall; 10(3): 35-38. Illus.: Photo. B&W. 1. Lang.: Eng.
Norway: Oslo. 1988-1998. Histories-sources. ■Interview with the former director of the Norwegian National Theatre on the Ibsen Festival he established in Oslo ten years ago, and on directing Ibsen's plays.

2211 Hansell, Sven. "Ett medvetet arbete för att göra Ibsen samtida." (A Deliberate Labor Doing Ibsen Contemporary.) *Tningen.* 1998; 21(4): 47-51. Illus.: Photo. B&W. Lang.: Swe.
Norway: Oslo. 1998. Historical studies. ■Report from the Ibsen festival, with references to Stein Winge's production of Ibsen's *Brand* at Nationaltheatret, Terje Maerli's production of *Rosmersholm*, Ole Anders Tandberg's production of *Lille Eyolf (Little Eyolf)* at Torshovteatret and Eimuntas Nekrošius' *Hamlet* from Lithuania.

2212 Bułat, Mirosława. "Teatry jidyszowe w Wilnie i ich występy gościnne w Krakowie w latach 1918-1933." (Yiddish Theatres at Vilna and their Tours at Cracow, 1918-1933.) 349-371 in Kozłowska, Mirosława, ed. *Wilno teatralne.* Warsaw: Ogólnopolski Klub Miłośników Litwy; 1998. 478 pp. Lang.: Pol.
Poland: Vilna, Cracow. 1918-1939. Historical studies. ■General picture of Yiddish theatre activity at Vilna and its influence on other Jewish cultural centers, including Cracow. Focuses on the Wilner Trupe, directed by Mordechaj Maza, two operetta ensembles, and the company of the Chasza family.

2213 Chojka, Joanna. "Jak wam się podoba albo klucze do Shakespeare'a." (As You Like It or the Keys to Shakespeare.) *DialogW.* 1998 June; 6: 78-92. Illus.: Photo. B&W. 9. Lang.: Pol.
Poland. 1990-1998. Critical studies. ■Examines attempts by contemporary Polish productions of Shakespeare to discover a contemporary meaning and resonance. Productions examined include Krzysztof Nazar's *Hamlet*, Krzysztof Warlikowski's productions of *The Winter's Tale* and *The Taming of the Shrew*, and Piotr Cieślak's *As You Like It.*

2214 Chojka, Joanna. "Techno katharsis?" (Technological Catharsis?)*DialogW.* 1998 Oct.; 10: 133-142. Illus.: Photo. B&W. 5. Lang.: Pol.
Poland: Szczecin. 1989-1998. Biographical studies. ■Examines the work of director Anna Augustynowicz, artistic manager of the Współczesny Theatre in Szczecin. Author focuses on the socio-ethical aspect of her approach.

2215 Ciechowicz, Jan, ed. *Pół wieku 'Teatru Wybrzeże'.* (A Half Century of the 'Wybrzeże' Theatre Przedstawienia, 1946-1996.) Gdansk: Wydawnictwo Uniwersytetu Gdańskiego; 1998. 440 pp. Pref. Index. Illus.: Photo. B&W. 130. Lang.: Pol.
Poland: Gdańsk, Warsaw, Cracow. 1952-1997. Historical studies. ■The most important stagings in the history of the 'Wybrzeże' theatre, including performances directed by Andrzej Wajda, Konrad Swinarski, and Stanisław Hebanowski.

2216 Duniec, Krystyna. "Czyste sumienie Jana Kreczmara." (Clear Conscience of Jan Kreczmar.) *DialogW.* 1998 Sep.; 9: 120-130. Illus.: Photo. B&W. 1. Lang.: Pol.
Poland: Warsaw, Lvov. 1939-1945. Biographical studies. ■The artistic career and life of actor Jan Kreczmar, long-time rector of the Warsaw Theatre Academy. Focuses on his life in Poland during World War II.

2217 Findlay, J.M. "Process and Chaos." *PM.* 1988; 54: 13-16. Notes. Illus.: Photo. B&W. 4. Lang.: Eng.
Poland: Cracow. 1987. Histories-sources. ■Observations on the directorial approach of Tadeusz Kantor, with an interview of Kantor regarding his process.

2218 Goźliński, Paweł. "Szpunt w czarnej dziurze." (In the Black Hole.) *DialogW.* 1998 Aug.; 8: 92-101. Illus.: Photo. B&W. 3. Lang.: Pol.
Poland: Warsaw. 1998. Reviews of performances. ■Review of Jerzy Grzegorzewski's production of Witold Gombrowicz's *The Marriage (Ślub)* at the National Theatre in Warsaw.

2219 Gruszczyński, Piotr. "Młodsi zdolniejsi." (The Younger and More Gifted.) *DialogW.* 1998 Mar.; 3: 86-94. Illus.: Photo. B&W. 6. Lang.: Pol.
Poland. 1989-1998. Critical studies. ■Examines a new generation of Polish stage directors and their work, including Piotr Cieplak, Anna Augustynowicz, Zbigniew Brzoza, Adam Sroka, Grzegorz Jarzyna, and Krzysztof Warlikowski.

2220 Majchrowski, Zbigniew. *Cela Konrada. Powracając do Mickiewicza.* (Konrad's Cell: Returning to Mickiewicz.) Gdansk: Wydawnictwo słowo/obraz/terytoria; Index. Illus.: Photo. B&W. 120. Lang.: Pol.
Poland. 1901-1995. Critical studies. ■Examines different ways of performing the 'great improvisation,' one of the most important scenes of *Forefathers' Eve (Dziady)* by Adam Mickiewicz (1832). Productions examined include those of Wyspiański (1901) and Grzegorzewski (1995).

2221 Osiński, Zbigniew. *Jerzy Grotowski.* Gdansk: Wydawnictwo Słowo/Obraz Terytoria; 1998. 411 pp. Index. Notes. Append. Biblio. Filmography. Illus.: Photo. Graphs. Dwg. Sketches. Poster. B&W. 379. Lang.: Pol.
Poland. 1960-1975. Critical studies. ■Artistic and ritual practice in the work of Jerzy Grotowski and its gnostic and anthropological roots. Also compares Grotowski's laboratory productions with Tadeusz Kantor's work.

2222 Osiński, Zbigniew. "Hebrajskie Studium Dramatyczne w Wilnie 1927-1933." (The Hebrew Dramatic Studio in Vilna, 1927-1933.) 206-229 in Kuligowska-Korzeniewska, Anna, ed.; Leyko, Małgorzata, ed. *Teatr żydowski w Polsce.* Lodz: Wydawnictwo Uniwersytetu Łódzkiego; 1998. 457 pp. Lang.: Pol.
Poland: Vilna. 1927-1933. Critical studies. ■Theatrical activity in the Hebrew Dramatic Studio, based on the work of HaBimah and Polish forms.

2223 Osterloff, Barbara. "Aleksander Zelwerowicz w Wilnie 1929-1931." (Aleksander Zelwerowicz in Vilna, 1929-1931.) 159-196 in Kozłowska, Mirosława, ed. *Wilno teatralne.* Warsaw: Ogólnopolski Klub Miłośników Litwy; 1998. 478 pp. Index. Illus.: Photo. B&W. 16. Lang.: Pol.
Poland: Vilna. 1929-1931. Biographical studies. ■Examines the life of actor/director Aleksander Zelwerowicz, especially his work in Vilna in the comic roles of Aleksander Fredro's plays.

2224 Puukko, Martti. "Teatterin on muututtava." (The Theatre Must Change.) *Teat.* 1998; 53(3): 33-35. Illus.: Photo. Color. 1. Lang.: Fin.
Poland. 1960-1998. Histories-sources. ■Interview with director Andrzej Wajda about the changing face of Polish theatre, and the importance of director/theorists Jerzy Grotowski and Tadeusz Kantor to the country's artistic legacy.

2225 Schlewitt, Carena. "Panzerkreuzer Potemkin und andere Geschichten." (Battleship Potemkin and Other Stories.) *TZ.* 1998; 4: 42-45. Illus.: Photo. B&W. 3. Lang.: Ger.
Poland: Cracow. 1998. Historical studies. ■Impressions from the international festival of alternative theatre in Cracow under the directorship of Krzysztof Lipski, its program and history. Reviews performances of the invited Polish groups Scena Plastyczna KUL (Lublin), Akademia Ruchu (Warsaw), Radykalna Frakcja Mazut (Znin), Studium Teatralne (Warsaw) and Komuna Otwock.

2226 Schwerin von Krosigk, Barbara. "Die Kunst als Vehikel." (Art as Vehicle.) 110-125 in Pochhammer, Sabine, ed. *Utopie: Spiritualität? Spiritualité: une utopie?/Utopia: Spirituality? Spirituality: A Utopia?.* Berlin, Ger: Theaterschrift c/o Künstlerhaus Bethanien; 1998. 173 pp. (Theaterschrift 13.) Illus.: Photo. B&W. 1. Lang.: Ger, Fre, Dut, Eng.
Poland. 1958-1998. Historical studies. ■The work of Polish theatre reformer Jerzy Grotowski, his exploration of the spiritual dimension, and his development towards a radical form of theatre practice occupying the borderland between theatre and mystical exercise.

DRAMA: —Performance/production

2227 Hollingsworth, Anthony Lee. *Recitation and the Stage: The Performance of Senecan Tragedy.* Providence, RI: Brown Univ; 1998. 110 pp. Notes. Biblio. [Ph.D. Dissertation, Univ. Microfilms Order No. AAC 9830454.] Lang.: Eng.
Roman Empire. 4 B.C.-150 A.D. Critical studies. ■Analysis of recitational drama and staged drama, focusing on the plausibility of the performance/staging of Seneca's plays during the time period.

2228 Margitházi, Beja. "Fül a hangnak: Szatmárnémeti előadások." (An Ear for Voices: Performances at Szatmárnémeti/Satu Mare, Romania.) *Sz.* 1998; 31(6): 45-48. Illus.: Photo. B&W. 2. Lang.: Hun.
Romania: Satu Mare. 1998. Reviews of performances. ■Brecht's *Der Kaukasische Kreidekreis (The Caucasian Chalk Circle)* directed by Miklós Tóth and Shakespeare's *King Lear* directed by Miklós Parászka.

2229 Metz, Katalin. *Forgószélben: Harag György, a rendező-mágus.* (In the Whirlwind: Director György Harag the Magician.) Budapest: Országos Színháztörténeti Múzeum és Intézet; 1998. 67 pp. (Skenotheke 3.) Illus.: Photo. B&W. 56. Lang.: Hun.
Romania. Hungary. 1925-1985. Biographical studies. ■Harag's life and career directing Hungarian-language theatre both in Hungary and in Romania.

2230 *Mejerchol'd: K istorii tvorč. metoda.* (Mejerchol'd: Dedicated to the History of the Creative Method.) St. Petersburg: Kul'tInformPress; 1998. 247 pp. Lang.: Rus.
Russia. 1900-1940. Historical studies. ■Discusses the work of the iconoclastic director.

2231 "Iz bezdny." (Out of the Bottomless Pit.) *Sem'ja i škola.* 1998; 3: 70-71. Lang.: Rus.
Russia: St. Petersburg. 1785-1917. Historical studies. ■Account of an exhibition in 1908, put together by theatre journalist, Ju. D. Beljaev: portraits, designs and personal articles of Russian actors of the nineteenth and late eighteenth centuries.

2232 "Poka ja ešče ispytyvaju vostorg ot teatra." (I'm Still Enjoying the Theatre.) *Al'jans.* 1998; 6: 32-35. Lang.: Rus.
Russia: Moscow. 1998. Histories-sources. ■Interview with Armen Džigarchanjan, stage and film actor who founded his own theatre.

2233 Arifdžanov, R. "Kovarstvo i ljubov'." (Backstabbing and Love.) *Persona.* 1998; 2: 22-27. Lang.: Rus.
Russia: Moscow. 1998. Biographical studies. ■Profile of Leonid Truškin, director of the Čechov Theatre.

2234 Aroseva, Olga; Maksimova, V.A. *Bez grima.* (Without Makeup.) Moscow: 1998. 382 pp. Lang.: Rus.
Russia: Moscow. 1998. Histories-sources. ■Recollections of stage and film actresses Olga Aroseva and V.A. Maksimova.

2235 Bajbekov, A. "Mesto pod solncem." (A Place in the Sun.) *Neva.* 1998; 5: 203-205. Lang.: Rus.
Russia: St. Petersburg. 1998. Biographical studies. ■Profile of stage and film actor Vladislav Stržel'čik.

2236 Bashynzhagian, Natella. "Przestrzeń Grotowskiego." (Grotowski's Space.) *DialogW.* 1998 Jan.; 1: 133-144. Illus.: Dwg. Poster. B&W. 4. Lang.: Pol.
Russia. 1913-1998. Historical studies. ■Jerzy Grotowski's reception and interpretation in Russia, the influence of Stanislavskij and Gurdjiev, and the Russian cultural background.

2237 Bednjakova, M. "Samuraj, obezumevšij ot ljubvi." (*The Samurai, Who Lost His Mind Because He Fell Deeply in Love.*) *Znakom'tes' Japonija.* 1998; 7: 32. Lang.: Rus.
Russia: Moscow. 1998. Historical studies. ■Performance by the Tokyo Seinen-za theatre group, at the third international Čechov festival at the Moscow Art Theatre.

2238 Belokopytov, A.A. *MChAT v moej žizni: Vospominanija (aktrisy).* (Moscow Art Theatre in My Life: Recollections of An Actress.) Moscow: Izd-vo Mosk. Chudož. teat'r; 1998. 240 pp. Lang.: Rus.
Russia: Moscow. 1998. Histories-sources. ■Interview with actress G. Kalinovskaja on her work with the Moscow Art Theatre.

2239 Besidžev, M. *Akterskaja sem'ja.* (Actor's Family.) Majkop: Adyg. resp. kn. izd-vo; 1998. 80 pp. Lang.: Rus.
Russia: Majkop. 1998. Biographical studies. ■Profile of actors with the N. Žané/M. Ajtekova Drama Theatre.

2240 Bezeljanskij, Ju. *Vera, Nadežda, Ljubov': Žen. portrety.* (Faith, Hope, Love: Portraits of Women.) Moscow: Raduga; 1998. 480 pp. Lang.: Rus.
Russia. 1800-1998. Biographical studies. ■Iconic Russian actresses and ballerinas of the nineteenth and twentieth centuries: Marija Savina, Vera Komissarževskaja, M. Andreeva, and Mathilde Kšesinskaja.

2241 Burkov, G. *Chronika serdca.* (Chronicle of the Heart.) Moscow: Vagrius; 1998. 318 pp. Lang.: Rus.
Russia. 1933-1990. Histories-sources. ■Theatre and film actor Georgij Burkov on his career.

2242 Bystrickaja, É. "Ljubit' - vopreki vsemu." (To Love Against All Odds.) *Bereginja.* 1998; 3: 4-8. Lang.: Rus.
Russia: Moscow. 1998. Histories-sources. ■Stage and film actress Elina Bystrickaja on her life and career.

2243 Čechova, O.; Vul'f, V., ed. *Moi časy idut inače.* (My Clock Ticks Differently.) Moscow: Vagrius; 1998. 270 pp. Lang.: Rus.
Russia. 1917-1980. Histories-sources. ■Recollections of actress Ol'ga Čechova.

2244 Cholodova, G. "Inoplanetjanin Viktjuk." (E.T. Equals Viktjuk.) *Lica.* 1998; 6: 30-34. Lang.: Rus.
Russia: Moscow. 1998. Histories-sources. ■Interview with director Roman Viktjuk.

2245 D'jakonov, V. "Zolotoj vek saratovskoj sceny." (Golden Age of Saratov's Stage.) *Pamjatniki Otečestva.* 1998; 39(1-2) : 167-172. Lang.: Rus.
Russia: Saratov. Historical studies. ■History of theatrical life.

2246 D'jakonov, V. "Prodannye aktery: Saratov. krepostnye na imperat. scene." (Saratov's Serf Actors on the Imperial Stages.) *Volga.* 1998; 2-3: 138-148. Lang.: Rus.
Russia: St. Petersburg. 1805. Historical studies. ■Lives of the seventy-four serf actors purchased by the crown from A.E. Stolypin, for the newly opened imperial theatre of Czar Alexander I.

2247 Dal', O.; Galadževa, N., ed.; Dal', E., ed. *Dnevniki. Pis'ma. Vospominanija.* (Diaries, Letters, Recollections.) Moscow: 1998. 454 pp. Lang.: Rus.
Russia: Moscow. 1998. Histories-sources. ■Reminiscences of Oleg Dal', author/actor of theatre and film.

2248 Danilova, L.S.; Ismagulova, T.D. *Nikolaj Konstantinovič Simonov: Akter, chudožnik, čelovek.* (Nikolaj Konstantinovič Simonov: Actor, Artist, Person.) St. Petersburg: 1998. 184 pp. Lang.: Rus.
Russia: St. Petersburg. 1998. Biographical studies. ■Profile of the actor.

2249 Demidova, A. "Žizn' na obočine." (Life on the Edge.) *MoskZ.* 1998; Sep-Oct: 44-48. Lang.: Rus.
Russia. 1998. Histories-sources. ■Stage and film actress Alla S. Demidova, on her life and career.

2250 Di Giulio, Maria. "Il teatro di Luigi Pirandello nelle scene russo." (Pirandello's Theatre on Russian Stages.) *Ariel.* 1998; 13(1-2): 207-232. Notes. Lang.: Ita.
Russia. 1905-1989. Historical studies. ■The fortune of Pirandello's theatre in the Soviet culture. Includes a bibliography of Russian essays and books on Pirandello together with a collection of reviews of Russian stagings of Pirandello's works.

2251 Dmitrieva, A.; Konaev, S. "Režisser na vsju žizn'." (A Director for Life.) *TeatZ.* 1998; 4: 14-16. Lang.: Rus.
Russia: Moscow. 1998. Biographical studies. ■Recollections about the director, Anatolij Efros.

2252 Doronina, T. "Dnevnik aktrisy, teatra i kino." (Diary of the Theatre and Film Actress.) *NasSovr.* 1998; 4: 173-184. Lang.: Rus.
Russia: Moscow. 1998. Histories-sources. ■Diary of actress Tatjana Doronina of the Moscow Art Theatre.

2253 Doronina, T. "Nikogda ne bylo tak bol'no, tak oskorbitel'no, kak sejčas ..." (Never So Painful and Degrading As Now.) *Junost'.* 1998; 10: 4-5. Lang.: Rus.

DRAMA: —Performance/production

Russia: Moscow. Histories-sources. ▪Actress Tatjana Doronina: her art, and her work as a director.

2254 Doronina, T. "'Odno iz predloženij bylo igrat' p'januju mamu dočki-narkomanki...'." (One of the Offers Was To Play the Drunken Mother of a Drug Addicted Daughter.) *Vitrina čitajuščej Rossii.* 1998; 11-12: 71-73. Lang.: Rus.

Russia. 1998. Histories-sources. ▪Stage and film actress, Tatjana Doronina on her work.

2255 Doronina, T.V.; Ben'jaš, R., ed. *Dnevnik aktrisy.* (Diary of an Actress.) Moscow: Vagrius; 1998. 316 pp. (Moj dvadcatyj vek.) Lang.: Rus.

Russia: Moscow. 1998. Histories-sources. ▪Recollections of actress Tatjana Doronina of the Moscow Art Theatre.

2256 Drobyševa, N.; Drobyševa, E. "Interv'ju, kotorogo ne bylo." (The Interview That Never Happened.) *TeatZ.* 1998; 4 : 6-9. Lang.: Rus.

Russia: Moscow. 1998. Histories-sources. ▪The Drobyševas, mother and daughter actresses, about the art of an actor and various particulars of their profession.

2257 Durov, L. *Grešnye zapiski.* (Sinful Notes.) Moscow: Algoritm; 1998. 388 pp. (O vremeni i o sebe.) Lang.: Rus.

Russia: Moscow. 1998. Histories-sources. ▪Recollections of stage and film actor Lev Durov.

2258 Elagin, Ju. *Vsevolod Mejerchol'd: Temnyj genij.* (Vsevolod Mejerchol'd: The Dark Genius.) Moscow: Vagrius; 1998. 366 pp. (Biografii.) Lang.: Rus.

Russia. 1874-1940. Biographical studies. ▪Biography of Mejerchol'd.

2259 Epifanova, S. "Gvozdickij." *TeatZ.* 1998; 4: 10-13. Lang.: Rus.

Russia: Moscow. 1998. Biographical studies. ▪The fate of an actor with the Moscow Art Theatre. Artistic portrait of Viktor Gvozdickij.

2260 Féral, Josette. "Le théâtre comme lieu de tous les possibles: Entretien avec Lev Dodine." (Theatre as Location of All Possibilities: Interview With Lev Dodin.) *JCT.* 1998; 87: 150-155. Illus.: Photo. B&W. 2. Lang.: Fre.

Russia. 1997. Histories-sources. ▪Russian director Lev Dodin on influence of Stanislavskij and Mejerchol'd on his direction of actors.

2261 Foht, N. "Poslednjaja kartina Federiko: Ispan. misterija ot Margarity." (Federico's Last Film: Spanish Mystery According to Margarita.) *Persona.* 1998; 4: 10-15. Lang.: Rus.

Russia. Spain. 1998. Histories-sources. ▪Stage and film actress Margarita Terechova, and her impression of Spain.

2262 Fradkina, E. "Muzyka v Izmajlovskom sadu." (Music in the Garden of Izmajlov.) *Neva.* 1998; 11: 216-218. Lang.: Rus.

Russia: St. Petersburg. 1998. Critical studies. ▪Profile of director E. Padve and his work in theatre for young audiences.

2263 Furmanov, R. *Iz žizni sumassedšego antreprenera: Teatr. roman.* (From the Life of a Crazy Impresario: A Theatrical Novel.) St. Petersburg: Beloe i černoe; 1998. 500 pp. Lang.: Rus.

Russia. 1950-1998. Biographical studies. ▪Includes profiles of renowned Russian theatre artists of the second half of the twentieth century.

2264 Gejzer, M. *Michoėls: Žizn' i smert'.* (Michoėls: Life and Death.) Moscow: Žurn. Agenstvo; 1998. 384 pp. Lang.: Rus.

Russia: Moscow. 1998. Biographical studies. ▪Profile of Solomon Michoėls, the murdered actor, director, and manager of Moscow Jewish Theatre.

2265 Ginkas, K. "Patologija artista: (Glavy iz nenapisannoj knigi)." (Pathology of an Artist: Chapters from the Book Not Yet Written.) *TeatZ.* 1998; 4: 2-5. Lang.: Rus.

Russia. 1998. Histories-sources. ▪Director Kama Ginkas on his life and work in children's theatre.

2266 Goder, D. "Dva s polovinoj časa voždelenija: R. Viktjuk postavil 'Salomeju' O. Uajl'da." (Two and a Half Hours of Sexual Tension: Viktjuk's Staging of *Salomé.*) *Itogi.* 1998; 38: 58-59. Lang.: Rus.

Russia: Moscow. 1998. Critical studies. ▪Analysis of Roman Viktjuk's staging of Oscar Wilde's play at Mossovet.

2267 Goder, D. "Von iz Moskvy! Sjuda ja bol'še ne ezdok: O prem'ere 'Gore ot uma' v postanovke O. Men'šikova v teatre im. Mossoveta." (Get Out of Moscow! I Will Never Come Here Again: Premiere of *Wit Works Woe* Directed by O. Menšikov, at the Mossovet Theatre.) *Itogi.* 1998; 37: 56-58. Lang.: Rus.

Russia: Moscow. 1998. Critical studies. ▪Analysis of Oleg Menšikov's production of Aleksand'r Gribojėdov's play.

2268 Goder, D. "Spasibo za popytku." (Thanks for a Good Try.) *Itogi.* 1998; 41: 56-58. Lang.: Rus.

Russia: Moscow. 1998. Critical studies. ▪Two stagings of Shakespeare's *Hamlet*, at the Soviet Army Theatre directed by Robert Sturua, and at the Satirikon directed by Peter Stein.

2269 Goder, D. "Inostrancy v russkom Disnejlende." (Foreigners in the Russian Disneyland.) *Itogi.* 1998; 22: 67-69. Lang.: Rus.

Russia: Moscow. 1998. Critical studies. ▪Productions directed by Declan Donnellan, Tadashi Suzuki, and Robert Wilson.

2270 Goder, D. "Starym taganskim sposobom: Ju. Ljubimov postavil roman Solženicyna 'V kruge pervom'." (Using the Old Taganskij Method: Jurij Ljubimov Directed *The First Circle*, a Play Based on a Novel by Solženicin.) *Itogi.* 1998; 50: 68-69. Lang.: Rus.

Russia: Moscow. 1998. Critical studies. ▪Ljubimov's production of *V kruge pervom (The First Circle)*, adapted from the novel of Aleksand'r Solženicin.

2271 Golubovskij, B.G. *Bol'šie malen'kie teatry.* (The Big Small Theatre.) Moscow: Izd-vo Sabašnikovych; 1998. 464 pp. (Zapisi prošlogo.) Lang.: Rus.

Russia. 1998. Histories-sources. ▪Recollections of producer and director, Boris Golubovskij.

2272 Gončarov, A.A.; Mišarin, A. "Glavnyj talant." (The Main Talent.) *NovRos.* 1998; 1: 52-60. Lang.: Rus.

Russia: Moscow. 1998. Histories-sources. ▪Interview with Andrej Gončarov, author and artistic director of Majakovskij Theatre.

2273 Grečucha, Ž. "Bravo, Tolja!" *Persona.* 1998; 2: 16-21. Lang.: Rus.

Russia: Moscow. 1998. Biographical studies. ▪Recollections about theatre director, Anatolij Efros.

2274 Griščenko, N. "Džul'etta s akkordeonom: Nac. teatr i virtual. real'nost'." (Juliet with Accordion: The Theatre and Virual Reality.) *MolGvar.* 1998; 2: 249-253. Lang.: Rus.

Russia: Belgorod. 1998. Critical studies. ▪Production of Shakespeare's *Romeo and Juliet* presented by Oblastnoj Dramatičėskij Teat'r directed by Michajl Mokejėv.

2275 Groševa, N. "Pjat' večerov s Juriem Nazarovym." (Five Evenings with Jurij Nazarov.) *Nižnij Novgorod.* 1998; 9: 188-191. Lang.: Rus.

Russia. 1998. Biographical studies. ▪Profile of stage and film actor Jurij Nazarov.

2276 Ignatjuk, O. "Blok na scene." (Blok on Stage.) *Mosk.* 1998; 5: 162-163. Lang.: Rus.

Russia: Moscow. 1998. Critical studies. ▪Premiere of *Pesn' sud'by (The Song of Fate)*, adapted from the play by Aleksand'r Blok, directed by Mikle Mizjukov, at the Historical-ethnographic Theatre.

2277 Iljušin, A.; Konovalova, T. "Ne zrelišče, a vyssaja pravda žizni." (Not Mere Spectacle, But the Highest Truth About Life.) *Otk.* 1998; 1: 48-51. Lang.: Rus.

Russia. 1998. Biographical studies. ▪Profile of actor E. Mjazinoj.

2278 Ivanova, S. "Vtoroe voploščenie Esenina." (Second Reincarnation of Esenin.) *Lica.* 1998; 6: 4-9. Lang.: Rus.

Russia: Moscow. 1998. Critical studies. ▪The character of the poet Sergej Esenin, created by actor Sergej Bezrukov, and the Tabakov Theatre Studio.

2279 Jėvrejenov, Nikolaj; Tanjuk, L., ed. *V škole ostroumija: Vosp. o teatre 'Krivoe zerkalo'.* (In the School of Wit: Recollections of the Theatre 'Mirror of Illusion'.) Moscow: Iskusstvo; 1998. 366 pp. Lang.: Rus.

DRAMA: —Performance/production

Russia. 1879-1953. Histories-sources. ■Reminiscences of theatre director, playwright, and theoretician Nikolaj Jėvrejnov about his work with Teat'r Krivoe Zerkalo.

2280 Kalinovskaja, G. "Žizn', prekrasnej kotoroj ne byvaet." (Life Doesn't Get Better Than This.) *NasSovr.* 1998; 10: 204-213. Lang.: Rus.

Russia: Moscow. 1998. Histories-sources. ■Recollections of a Moscow Art Theatre actress.

2281 Kim, Ju. "O Petre Fomenko." (About Pëtr Fomenko.) *TeatZ.* 1998; 4: 31-33. Lang.: Rus.

Russia: Moscow. 1998. Histories-sources. ■Artistic portrait of the director, seen through the eyes of a friend.

2282 Király, Nina, ed.; Koncz, Zsuzsa, photo. *Anatolij Vasziljev: Színházi fúga: Elméleti írásai, próbajegyzetei és értekezések a művészetéről.* (Anatolij Vasiljėv: Theatrical Fugue: His Theoretical Writings, Rehearsal Notes and Essays on His Art.) Budapest: Országos Színháztörténeti Múzeum és Intézet; 1998. 348 pp. Append. Biblio. Index. Illus.: Photo. B&W. 32. Lang.: Hun.

Russia. 1942-1998. Histories-sources. ■Anatolij Vasiljėv's art as reflected in his writings and interviews compiled with the literature on his Hungarian stagings.

2283 Klimontovič, N. "Byli." (They Were.) *Rovesnik.* 1998; 37: 42-47. Lang.: Rus.

Russia: Moscow. 1998. Biographical studies. ■Profile of stage and film actress, E. Majorova, and her husband, scene designer S. Šerstjuk.

2284 Klimova, K. "Cep' volšebnych sovpadenij." (Chain of Magical Incidents.) *Persona.* 1998; 2: 58-61. Lang.: Rus.

Russia: Moscow. 1998. Critical studies. ■Student performances in the State University's theatre.

2285 Koljazin, V. *Tairov, Mejerchol'd i Germanija. Piskator, Brecht i Rossija: Očerki istorii rus.-nem. chudož. svjazej.* (Tairov, Mejerchol'd and Germany. Piscator, Brecht and Russia: Notes on the History of Russian-German Relationship.) Moscow: GITIS; 1998. 264 pp. Lang.: Rus.

Russia. Germany. 1920-1949. Historical studies. ■The relationship and acceptance of Russian theatrical practice in Germany, and German theatrical practice in Russia.

2286 Kolobrodov, I.A. "Byt' znamenitym, no krasivo. Vot ėto podnimaet vvys'." (To Be Famous, but in a Nice Way. This Is What Uplifts You.) *Bereginja.* 1998; 3: 26-28. Lang.: Rus.

Russia: Moscow. 1998. Biographical studies. ■Profile of stage and film actor Anatolij Ktorov.

2287 Konjuškov, E. "Sceny rossijskoj ukrašenie." (The Stages of Russian Decoration.) *Pravoslavnaja beseda.* 1998; 3: 16-20. Lang.: Rus.

Russia: St. Petersburg. 1998. Biographical studies. ■Soul-searching of theatre and film actor, Oleg Borisov.

2288 Kovrov, M. "Ėto nam s neba upalo: K 100-letiju Mosk. Chudož. teatra im. M. Gor'kogo." (This Fell to Us from the Sky: The Centennial of the Moscow Art Theatre.) *NasSovr.* 1998; 8: 255-275. Lang.: Rus.

Russia: Moscow. 1898-1998. Historical studies. ■One hundred years of Čechov plays presented by the Moscow Art Theatre.

2289 Kravcov, A. "Mir lovil ego, no..." (The Whole World Pursued Him, But...)*Smena.* 1998; 3: 104-115. Lang.: Rus.

Russia: St. Petersburg. 1998. Biographical studies. ■Profile of theatre and film actor Nikolaj K. Simonov of the Puškin Theatre.

2290 Krošin, G. "Teatr odnogo Armena." (The Theatre of Armen.) *Lica.* 1998; Sent.: 4-8. Lang.: Rus.

Russia: Moscow. 1998. Biographical studies. ■Profile of stage and film actor Armen B. Džigarchanjan.

2291 Krylov, A.E.; V.F., Ščerbakova. *Mir Vysockogo: Issled. i materialy. T. 2.* (The World of Vysockij: Research and Materials.) Moscow: 1998. 672 pp. Lang.: Rus.

Russia: Moscow. 1938-1980. Biographical studies. ■Collection of information pertaining to Tagankė Theatre actor Vladimir Vysockij.

2292 Ktorov, A. *Artist i devočka: (Vospominanija ob A.P. Ktorove).* (The Actor and the Girl: Recollections of A.P. Ktorov.) St. Petersburg: Politechnika; 1998. 80 pp. Lang.: Rus.

Russia: Moscow. 1998. Histories-sources. ■Moscow Art Theatre actor A.P. Ktorov on life and a career in the theatre.

2293 Levašov, V. *Ubijstvo Michoėlsa.* (The Murder of Michoėls.) Moscow: Olimp; 1998. 480 pp. (Rus. tajny.) Lang.: Rus.

Russia: Moscow. 1948. Biographical studies. ■An account of the murder of Solomon Michoėls, actor and artistic director of Moscow Jewish Theatre.

2294 Makarova, I.V. *Blagodarenie.* (Gratitude.) Moscow: Ros. archiv; 1998. 160 pp. Lang.: Rus.

Russia: Moscow. 1998. Histories-sources. ■Memoirs of stage and film actress, I.V. Makarova.

2295 Makoveckij, S. "Kto skazal, čto Gamlet ne možet byt' ryžim?" (Who Said Hamlet Cannot Be a Redhead?)*NV.* 1998 ; 45: 40-41. Lang.: Rus.

Russia: Moscow. 1998. Histories-sources. ■Stage and film actor Sergej Makoveckij on his life and career.

2296 Mejerchol'd, Vsevolod; Zingerman, B.I. ed.; Fel'dman, O.M., ed. *Nasledie: T. 1: Avtobiogr. materialy.* (The Inheritance, Volume 1: Autobiographical Material.) Moscow: O.G.I.; 1998. 744 pp. Lang.: Rus.

Russia. 1891-1903. Histories-sources. ■Autobiographical writings by director V.E. Mejerchol'd.

2297 Montee, David Duane. *The Neglected Chekhov: Platonov and The Wood Demon.* Lawrence, KS: Univ. of Kansas; 1987. 352 pp. Notes. Biblio. [Ph.D. Dissertation, Univ. Microfilms Order No. AAC 8813432.] Lang.: Eng.

Russia. 1878-1889. Critical studies. ■Examines two early four-act plays by Anton Čechov, *Platonov* and *Lešji (The Wood Demon).* Includes practical aids in staging them.

2298 Morozov, A. "Veličie i prostota aktrisy: Bravo, Pavlina! Bravo!" (The Great and the Ordinary of an Actress: Bravo, Pavlina! Bravo!)*Avtograf.* 1998; 3: 46-48. Lang.: Rus.

Russia. 1998. Biographical studies. ■Profile of actress Pavlina Konopčuk.

2299 Mozgovoj, V. "Farida Muminova, vnučka i babuška." (Farida Muminova, Granddaughter and Grandmother.) *Avtograf.* 1998; 3: 55-56. Lang.: Rus.

Russia: Magnitogorsk. 1998. Biographical studies. ■Profile of stage and film actress Farida Muminova.

2300 Noskov, A.I. "Ščepkiny v Samare." (Ščepkin in Samara.) 90-96 in *Minuvšee prochodit predo mnoj.* Samara: Samar. Dom pečati; 1998. Lang.: Rus.

Russia: Samara. 1788-1863. Biographical studies. ■Life and art of serf actor Michajl Ščepkin during his Samara period.

2301 Novikova, L. "Inna Čurikova v teatral'nom podnebes'e." (Inna Čurikova in the Theatrical Firmament.) *MoskZ.* 1998 ; May/June: 68-72. Lang.: Rus.

Russia: Moscow. 1998. Biographical studies. ■Profile of Lenkom's stage and film actress, Inna Čurikova.

2302 Orechanova, G.A. *Tat'jana Doronina: 'Ja—russkaja aktrisa...'.* (Tatjana Doronina: 'I Am a Russian Actress...'.) Moscow: Rus. mir; 1998. 144 pp. Lang.: Rus.

Russia: Moscow. 1998. Biographical studies. ■Profile of Tatjana Doronina.

2303 Osipova, L. "V Čičikovskoj krugoverti." (*In Čičikov's Chaos.*) *Sem'ja i škola.* 1998; 9-10: 54-55. Lang.: Rus.

Russia: Moscow. 1998. Critical studies. ■Analysis of *V Čičikovskoj krugoverti (In Čičikov's Chaos)*, based on Gogol's *Dead Souls*, written and directed by by Pëtr Fomenko, at his Workshop.

2304 Ovčinnikova, S.; Ovčinnikov, I. "'...Iz Mocarta nam čto-nibud'." (Play Something by Mozart.) *MoskZ.* 1998; Oct-Nov: 44-47. Lang.: Rus.

Russia: Moscow. Russia. 1998. Biographical studies. ■Profile of stage and film actor, Oleg Menšikov.

2305 Patlakh, Irina Fjellner. "En verklig teaterhändelse." (A Real Theatrical Event.) *Tningen.* 1998; 21(2): 40-43. Illus.: Photo. B&W. Color. Lang.: Swe.

DRAMA: —Performance/production

Russia: Moscow, St. Petersburg. 1998. Historical studies. ■A report from the Russian Golden Mask Festival and the directors Sergej Pëtr Ženovač, Pëtr Fomenko, Valerij Fokin and Vladimir Klimenko.

2306 Patlakh, Irina Fjellner. "Moskva teaterns Mecka?" (Moscow the Mecca of Theatre?)*Tningen.* 1998; 21(4): 53-61. Illus.: Photo. B&W. Color. Lang.: Swe.

Russia: Moscow. 1998. Historical studies. ■Report form the International Čechov Festival of Moscow, with references to Christoph Marthaler's production of Čechov's *Tri sestry (Three Sisters)* at Moskovskij Chudožestvénnyj Akademičéskij Teat'r, three different productions of Čechov's *Platonov* by Jerzy Jarocki, Lev Dodin and Jévgenij Marčelli, Robert Wilson's production of *Persefone* and Ariane Mnouchkine's *Et soudain, des nuits d'éveil (And Suddenly, Sleepless Nights).*

2307 Perevozčikov, V. *Pravda smertnogo časa: Vladimir Vysockij, god 1980-j.* (The Truth of the Last Hour Before Death: Vladimir Vysockij, 1980.) M.: Sampo; 1998. 272 pp. Lang.: Rus.

Russia: Moscow. 1980. Biographical studies. ■The last months of actor Vladimir Vysockij.

2308 Pojurovskij, B.M.,. *Andrej Mironov: Sb. vospominanij.* (Andrej Mironov: Memoirs.) Moscow: Centrpoligraf; 1998. 352 pp. Lang.: Rus.

Russia: Moscow. 1998. Biographical studies. ■Biography of actor Andrej Mironov.

2309 Ptuškina, N. "Pessimističeskie zapiski optimista." (Pessimistic Diaries of an Optimist.) *TeatZ.* 1998; 5-6: 39-42. Lang.: Rus.

Russia. 1998. Histories-sources. ■Playwright Nadežda Ptuškina on the problems associated with a play going into production.

2310 Raskova, L. "Gennadij Pečnikov. 50 let na scene." (Gennadij Pečnikov: Fifty Years on Stage.) *DetLit.* 1998; 3: 119-120. Lang.: Rus.

Russia: Moscow. 1998. Biographical studies. ■Profile of actor Gennadij Pečnikov of the Central Children's Theatre.

2311 Raulo, Hanna. "Mitä Siperia opettaa." (What Does Siberia Teach?)*Teat.* 1998; 53(8): 40-43. Illus.: Dwg. Color. 6. Lang.: Fin.

Russia. 1998. Historical studies. ■Report on the flavor of Siberian culture, particularly the theatre.

2312 Rogačevskij, M.L. *Tragedija tragika: Lenid Leonidov.* (The Tragedy of Tragedians: Lenid Leonidov.) Moscow: Iskusstvo; 1998. 390 pp. Lang.: Rus.

Russia: Moscow. 1873-1941. Biographical studies. ■Biography of Moscow Art Theatre actor Lenid M. Leonidov.

2313 Rudnik, N. "Recenzija." (A Review.) *Znamia.* 1998; 7: 237-239. Lang.: Rus.

Russia: Moscow. 1998. Historical studies. ■International conference concerning Vladimir Vysockij and Russian culture during the 1960s, held at the National Center of Culture, in the Vysockij Museum.

2314 Šah-Azizova, T. "Ostrovskij, ego zriteli i geroi." (Ostrovskij, His Audience and Heroes.) *TeatZ.* 1998; 5-6: 2-7. Lang.: Rus.

Russia. 1998. Reviews of performances. ■Reviews of Aleksand'r Ostrovskij's plays being performed in honor of Ostrovskij's 175th birthday.

2315 Sal'nikov, G.I.; D'jakonov, V., ed. "Iz zapisok provincial'nogo aktera." (From the Notes of a Provincial Actor.) *Volga.* 1998; 11-12: 160-172. Lang.: Rus.

Russia: Saratov. 1998. Histories-sources. ■Actor G.I. Sal'nikov on his career and his present work with the Academic Drama Theatre.

2316 Šaparova, O. "Mark Zacharov i 'Lenkom'." (Mark Zacharov and Lenkom.) *Smena.* 1998; 4: 56-67. Lang.: Rus.

Russia: Moscow. Historical studies. ■The work of director Mark Zacharov at the Lenin Comsomol Theatre.

2317 Savčenko, B. *Kumiry rossijskoj éstrady.* (Idols of the Russian Stage.) Moscow: Panorama; 1998. 432 pp. Lang.: Rus.

Russia. 1998. Biographical studies. ■Profiles of actors.

2318 Savvina, I.S. "Kogda ja verju—mne interesno." (When I Believe—I Am Interested.) *Persona.* 1998; 2: 56-57. Lang.: Rus.

Russia: Moscow. 1998. Histories-sources. ■Stage and film actress on her art.

2319 Ščeglov, A. *Ranevskaja: Fragmenty žizni.* (Ranevskaja: Fragments of a Life.) Moscow: Zacharov; 1998. 302 pp. Lang.: Rus.

Russia. 1896-1984. Biographical studies. ■Biography of singer and actress Faina Ranevskaja.

2320 Ščeglov, D. *Faina Ranevskaja: Monolog.* Smolensk: Rusič; 1998. 444 pp. (Ženščina-mif.) Lang.: Rus.

Russia. 1896-1984. Biographical studies. ■Profile of stage and film actress Faina Ranevskaja.

2321 Schuller, Gabriella; Koncz, Zsuzsa, photo. "Rendezői színház helyett: Anatolij Vasziljev: Színházi fúga." (Instead of the Director's Theatre: Anatolij Vasiljév: Theatrical Fugue.) *Sz.* 1998; 31(9): 38-40. Illus.: Photo. B&W. 3. Lang.: Hun.

Russia: Moscow. 1998. Critical studies. ■Introducing a recent Hungarian edition of the Russian director's selected writings *Színházi fúga* (Budapest: OSZMI, 1997).

2322 Šestakova, N. *Pervyj teat'r Stanislavskogo.* (The Early Theatre of Stanislavskij.) Moscow: Iskusstvo; 1998. 192 pp. Lang.: Rus.

Russia: Moscow. 1877-1888. Histories-reconstruction. ■Detailed reconstruction of plays originally performed by the Alekseev Group and directed by Stanislavskij.

2323 Smoktunovskij, I.M.; Kim, A., ed. *Byt'!* (To Exist!)Moscow: Algoritm; 1998. 336 pp. (O vremeni i o sebe.) Lang.: Rus.

Russia: Moscow. 1998. Histories-sources. ■Stage and film actor Innokentij Smoktunovskij on his life and work.

2324 Sokolova, I. "Recenzija." (Reviews of Productions.) *LO.* 1998; 3: 101-103. Lang.: Rus.

Russia: Moscow. Reviews of performances. ■Reviews of productions of the 1998 Moscow theatre season.

2325 Sokur, G.; Denisenko, G. "Sergej Rudzinskij." *Omskaja muza.* 1998; 1: 27-29. Lang.: Rus.

Russia: Omsk. 1998. Biographical studies. ■Reminiscences about Sergej Rudzinskij, the director of Omsk's National Dramatic Fifth Theatre.

2326 Solomin, Ju. "Okazat'sja sozvučnym vremeni." (Current and in Touch with Time.) *Persona.* 1998; 2: 34-43. Lang.: Rus.

Russia: Moscow. 1998. Histories-sources. ■Director Jurij Solomin, about himself and the Malyj Theatre.

2327 Stanislavskij, Konstantin Sergejévič; Solov'eva, I.N., ed. *Sobranie sočinenij. V 9 t.: T. 8: Pis'ma, 1906-1917.* (Collected Writings, Volume 8: Letters, 1906-1917.) Moscow: Iskusstvo; 1998. 592 pp. Lang.: Rus.

Russia. 1906-1917. Histories-sources. ■Collection of letters by the acting teacher and director Konstantin Stanislavskij.

2328 Stanislavskij, Konstantin Sergejévič; Raskina, Raissa, ed. "Stanislavskij: dodici lettere." (Stanislavskij: Twelve Letters.) *BiT.* 1998; 45/47: 349-368. Notes. Illus.: Photo. B&W. 3. Lang.: Ita.

Russia. 1919-1938. Histories-sources. ■Twelve letters of Stanislavskij describe his life full of problems for his and his family's subsistence.

2329 Starikova, L.M. "Dokumental'nye utočnenija k istorii teatra v Rossii petrovskogo vremeni." (Documented Explanations Dedicated to the History of Theatre in Russia During the Time of Peter the Great.) 179-190 in *Pamjatniki kul'tury.* Moscow: Nauka; 1998. Lang.: Rus.

Russia. 1689-1725. Historical studies. ■Descriptions of performances of the time.

2330 Stepanenko, E. "Ivan Kalita russkogo teatra." (The Ivan Kalita of Russian Theatre.) *Rus'.* 1998; 1: 82-86. Lang.: Rus.

Russia. 1851-1899. Biographical studies. ■Profile of Russian dramatic actor and director, Pavel Medvedev.

2331 Stepnov, V. "Medali dlja spektaklja." (Medals for the Play.) *Otčij dom.* 1998; 1: 52-53. Lang.: Rus.

DRAMA: —Performance/production

Russia: Volgograd. ▪Performance of *Boi imeli mestnoe značenie (The Battles Had Localized)*, based on a work by Viačeslav Kondratjėv. Directed by K. Dubinin, Volgograd Dramatic Theatre.

2332 Timofeev, P.T. *Choper: Istorija, byt, kul'tura.* (Choper: Its History, Everyday Life, Culture.) Kaliningrad: Jantarn. skaz; 1998. 222 pp. Lang.: Rus.

Russia. Historical studies. ▪History of theatrical performances put on by the Cossacks of the Choper Valley.

2333 Titarenko, V. *Proščaj, Vysockij: Dokument. chronika pochoron (ijul' 1980 g.).* (Good-bye, Vysockij: A Document Chronicling the Burial in July 1980.) Moscow: 1998. 90 pp. Lang.: Rus.

Russia: Moscow. 1980. Historical studies. ▪Account of the funeral of the playwright/actor Vladimir Vysokij.

2334 Vertinskaja, M. "Umenie žit'—umenie proščat'." (To Be Able To Live, To Be Able To Forgive.) *MoskZ.* 1998; Oct-Nov: 64-67. Lang.: Rus.

Russia: Moscow. 1998. Biographical studies. ▪Stage and film actress M. Vertinskaja, of the Vachtangov Theatre, comments on her father, singer Aleksand'r Vertinskij, and family life.

2335 Veselovskij, S. "Mefistofel' krasoty." (Mephistophelian Beauty.) *Znamya.* 1998; 11: 236-237. Lang.: Rus.

Russia: Moscow. 1998. ▪Analysis of *Priznanija avantjurista Feliksa Krulja (Confessions of Felix Krul, Confidence Man)*, based on Thomas Mann's *Behenntrisse des Hochstapler Felix Krull.* Directed by Andrej Žitinkin at Tabakov's Theatre Studio.

2336 Vesnik, E. *Darju, čto pomnju.* (I Give What I Remember.) Moscow: Vagrius; 1998. 382 pp. Lang.: Rus.

Russia: Moscow. 1998. Histories-sources. ▪Memoirs of the theatre and film actor.

2337 Vinokur, V. *Artist—ėto navsegda.* (The Artist—That Is Forever.) Moscow: 1998. 292 pp. Lang.: Rus.

Russia. 1998. Histories-sources. ▪Actor Vladimir Vinokur on his life and his art.

2338 Vislov, A. "Andrej Žitinkin v kostre teatral'nych ambicij." (Andrej Žitinkin in the Heat of Theatrical Ambitions.) *Al'jans.* 1998; Aug: 24-28. Lang.: Rus.

Russia: Moscow. 1998. Biographical studies. ▪Profile of director Andrej Žitinkin.

2339 Zajcev, S.N. "'V buduščee my smotrim s optimizmom...'." (We Look to the Future with a Lot of Optimism.) *Bibliografija.* 1998; 1: 60-62. Lang.: Rus.

Russia: Moscow. 1998. Histories-sources. ▪The chief editor of the journal *Vagant*, dedicated to the art of Vladimir Vysockij, speaks on the actor and also the future of the journal.

2340 Zlobina, A. "Duši prekrasnye poryvy." (Great Gusts of the Soul.) *Znamia.* 1998; 9, pp 236-238. Lang.: Rus.

Russia: Moscow. 1998. Critical studies. ▪Performance of *V Čičikovskoj krugoverti (In Čičikov's Chaos)*, based on Gogol's *Dead Souls (Mërtvyjė dušy)*, directed by Pëtr Fomenko, at Fomenko Theatre.

2341 Zvezdova, V. "Javlenie Sergeja Bezrukova." (The Appearance of Sergej Bezrukov.) *Nižnij Novgorod.* 1998; 9: 192-194. Lang.: Rus.

Russia: Moscow. Biographical studies. ▪Profile of Sergej Bezrukov: stage, film and television actor with Oleg Tabakov's Studio Theatre.

2342 Gerold, László. "Vágóhídon: Szilágyi Andor: *Pepe.*" (Slaughter-House: Andor Szilágyi: *Pepe.*) *Sz.* 1998; 31(11): 16-17. Illus.: Photo. B&W. 1. Lang.: Hun.

Serbia: Novi Sad. 1998. Reviews of performances. ▪Andor Szilágyi's *Pepe, avagy az angyalok lázadása (Pepe, or the Revolt of Angels)* at Serbia's National Theatre, directed by László Babarczy as a guest.

2343 Worman, Dee A. *Drama, Genre and Pragmatics: A Study of the Krio Theatre.* Waltham, MA: Brandeis Univ; 1998. 290 pp. Notes. Biblio. [Ph.D. Dissertation, Univ. Microfilms Order No. AAC 9819645.] Lang.: Eng.

Sierra Leone: Freetown. 1960-1998. Critical studies. ▪Language pluralism in the playscripts of the Krio theatre of Sierra Leone, with emphasis on *If You Yams White* by Michael Yaarimeh Bangura and the switching of English and Krio languages in the play and performance.

2344 Berry, Cicely; Arko, Andrej, transl. *Igralee in glas.* (The Actor and Voice.) Ljubljana: Pravljično gledališče; 1998. 148 pp. (Šola retorike.) Pref. Biblio. Illus.: Photo. Dwg. B&W. 15. Lang.: Slo.

Slovenia. UK-England. 1973-1993. Instructional materials. ▪Slovene translation and adaptation of Berry's work on vocal training for the actor.

2345 Faganel, Jože. "Oton Župančič—začetnik gledališkega lektorstva." (Oton Župančič—The Founder of Theatrical Language Revision.) *Sodobnost.* 1998; 1006(6-7): 544-547. Lang.: Slo.

Slovenia. 1912-1927. Critical studies. ▪Analyzes the particularly Slovene theatrical profession of *lektor*, or stage consultant, a dramaturg concerned mainly with speech. Argues that playwright Oton Župančič created the idea and practiced it in his work.

2346 Lukan, Blaž. *Dramaturške figure.* (Dramaturgic Figures.) Ljubljana: Maska; 1998. 191 pp. Pref. Index. Lang.: Slo.

Slovenia. 1980-1997. Critical studies. ▪Collection of critical reviews by Blaž Lukan, treating theatre as a living or figurative phenomenon.

2347 Mihurko Poniž, Katja. "Zur Rezeption der osterreichischen Dramatik in Slowenian." (The Reception of Austrian Theatre in Slovenia.) 269-292 in Brandtner, Andreas, ed.; Michler, Werner, ed. *Zur Geschichte der osterreichisch-slowenischen Literaturbeziehungen.* Vienna: Turia & Kant; 1998. 415 pp. Append. Lang.: Ger.

Slovenia. Austria. 1867-1997. Histories-sources. ▪Examines the reception of Austrian drama in Slovene theatres, and shows that a large number of Austrian plays were performed. From 1867 to 1945, it was mostly comedies and burlesques. After World War II, the number of Austrian plays decreased because of the growing interest in other world authors.

2348 Podbevšek, Katja. "Lektoriranje govorjenega (gledališkega)." (The Revision of Spoken (Theatre) Texts.) *Jezik in slovstvo.* 1998; 43(3): 79-88. Lang.: Slo.

Slovenia. 1995-1997. Critical studies. ▪Examines the profession of the *lektor*, or stage language consultant. The fundamental requirements of this work are distinguishing between written and spoken language codes, knowing how to convert written texts into speech, and being familiar with the medium in which a particular text will be realized. A stage language consultant also supervises the register or dialect, pronunciation, sentence phonetics, and non-verbal communication in a theatrical performance.

2349 Bailey, Brett. "Performing So the Spirit May Speak." *SATJ.* 1998 May/Sep.; 12(1/2): 191-202. Biblio. Illus.: Photo. B&W. 3. Lang.: Eng.

South Africa, Republic of. 1997-1998. Histories-sources. ▪The influence of African ritual and ceremony in the author's work as a director, particularly his own pieces iMumbo Jumbo and *Ipi Zombi?* in which he included tribal *sangomas* (witch doctors) in the casts.

2350 Bain, Keith; Hauptfleisch, Gaerin, photo. "Brecht 2001: A Photo Essay." *SATJ.* 1998 May/Sep.; 12(1/2): 212-227. Illus.: Photo. B&W. 18. Lang.: Eng.

South Africa, Republic of: Capetown. 1998. Historical studies. ▪Photographic account of a production of Brecht's first play *Baal*, directed by Chris Vorster at the HB Thom Theatre.

2351 Blumberg, Marcia. "Re-Staging Resistance, Re-Viewing Women: 1990s Productions of Fugard's *Hello and Goodbye* and *Boesman and Lena.*" 123-145 in Colleran, Jeanne, ed.; Spencer, Jenny S., ed. *Staging Resistance: Essays on Political Theatre.* Ann Arbor, MI: Univ of Michigan P; 1998. 312 pp. (Theater: Theory/Text/Performance.) Notes. Index. Illus.: Photo. 1. Lang.: Eng.

South Africa, Republic of. 1993-1994. Critical studies. ▪Gender and politics in performances at the Market Theatre, with emphasis on the male appropriation of the female voice, and the dehistoricizing of the plays' political moments.

2352 Du Toit, Petrus Jacobus. *Amateur Theatre in South Africa.* Pretoria: Univ. of Pretoria; 1987. Biblio. Notes. [Ph.D. Dissertation.] Lang.: Afr.

DRAMA: —Performance/production

South Africa, Republic of. 1861-1982. Historical studies. ■Psychological and philosophical consideration of amateur theatre in the English- and Afrikaans-speaking communities.

2353 Gray, Stephen. "Notes on South Africa and Australian Theatre." *SATJ.* 1998 May/Sep.; 12(1/2): 172-177. Biblio. Lang.: Eng.

South Africa, Republic of. Australia. 1910-1998. Historical studies. ■Essay on Australian theatre in South Africa.

2354 McMurtry, Mervyn. "'Greeks bearing gifts': Athol Fugard's *Orestes* Project and the Politics of Experience." *MD.* 1998 Spr; 41(1): 105-118. Notes. Illus.: Sketches. B&W. 2. Lang.: Eng.

South Africa, Republic of: Cape Town. 1978. Historical studies. ■Fugard's production at Space Theatre of *Orestes,* based on Aeschylus' *Oresteia,* and its subsequent influence upon Fugard's later plays.

2355 Pearce, Brian Michael. "The Director and the South African Theatre." *SATJ.* 1998 May/Sep.; 12(1/2): 203-207. Notes. Lang.: Eng.

South Africa, Republic of. 1998. Critical studies. ■Essay on the lack of research and critical debate with regard to directors in South Africa.

2356 Pillay, Kriben. "Finding an Identity: South African Indian Theatre in Spain." *SATJ.* 1998 May/Sep.; 12(1/2): 178-184. Lang.: Eng.

South Africa, Republic of. 1900-1998. Historical studies. ■Discusses the place of Indian theatre in South Africa, where European and Black cultural traditions are stronger. Essay is in response to a conference in Salamanca in which the focus was on South Africa.

2357 Daniels, Mary Blythe. *Re-visioning Gender on the Seventeenth-Century Spanish Stage: A Study of Actresses and Autoras.* Lexington, KY: Univ. of Kentucky; 1998. 184 pp. Notes. Biblio. [Ph.D. Dissertation, Univ. Microfilms Order No. AAC 9907686.] Lang.: Eng.

Spain. 1600-1700. Histories-specific. ■Feminist analysis of the lives and work of actresses and *autoras* (female heads of acting companies). Focuses on the socio-economic aspects of women in the theatre and the gender ideology behind denunciations of women in seventeenth-century Spanish theatre.

2358 Espinosa Carbonel, Joaquín. "La fortuna scenica di Pirandello in Spagna." (Pirandello's Scenic Fortune in Spain.) *Ariel.* 1998; 13(1-2): 157-166. Notes. Lang.: Ita.

Spain. 1961-1986. Historical studies. ■A brief description of the stagings of Pirandello's plays in Spain.

2359 Gregor, Graham Keith. "Spanish 'Shakespeare-manía': *Twelfth Night* in Madrid, 1996-1997." *SQ.* 1998 Win; 49(4): 421-431. Notes. Illus.: Photo. B&W. 2. Lang.: Eng.

Spain: Madrid. 1996-1997. Historical studies. ■Comparison of two productions of Shakespeare's play at the Madrid Theatre Festival: Gerardo Vera's production at Teatro de la Abadía, and Adrían Daumas' at Ensayo 100.

2360 Leonard, Candyce; Buedel, Barbara. "The Censorship of Social and Personal Violence in *Lista Negra* by Yolanda Pallín." *WES.* 1998 Fall; 10(3): 95-98. Illus.: Photo. B&W. 1. Lang.: Eng.

Spain. 1998. Critical studies. ■Analysis of the premiere production of Pallín's play directed, in environmental fashion, by Eduardo Vasco.

2361 Membrez, Nancy Jane Hartley. *The 'Teatro por horas': History, Dynamics and Comprehensive Bibliography of a Madrid Industry, 1867-1922.* Santa Barbara, CA: Univ. of California; 1987. 1650 pp. Notes. Biblio. [Ph.D. Dissertation, Univ. Microfilms Order No. 8719630.] Lang.: Eng.

Spain. 1867-1922. Historical studies. ■Traces the reemergence of the popular theatre form *teatro por horas* and its content, and shows how the introduction of the cinema and the foreign operetta, coupled with increasing government taxation and regulation, displaced the genre, ultimately precipitating a total theatre crisis by the early 1920s.

2362 Siljunas, V. Ju. "Ispanskij teat'r." (Spanish Theatre.) *Vestnik Rossijskogo gumanitarnogo naučnogo fonda.* 1998; 3: 190-197. Lang.: Rus.

Spain. 1998. Historical studies. ■Overview of the Spanish theatre.

2363 Zatlin, Phyllis. "Max Aub's *San Juan* Finally Reaches Its Destination." *WES.* 1998 Fall; 10(3): 99-100. Illus.: Photo. B&W. 1. Lang.: Eng.

Spain: Madrid. 1998. Critical studies. ■Analysis of Juan Carlos Pérez de la Fuente's production of Aub's play at María Guerrero National Theatre.

2364 Silverstein, Marc. "'Talking bout Some Kind of Atrocity': *Ashes to Ashes* in Barcelona." *PintR.* 1998: 74-85. Notes. Biblio. Lang.: Eng.

Spain-Catalonia: Barcelona. 1996. Critical studies. ■The performance of Pinter's latest play under the playwright's own direction at the Pinter festival in Barcelona.

2365 "Det gyllene O'Neillpriset." (The Golden O'Neill Prize.) *Dramat.* 1998; 6(3): 19-24. Illus.: Photo. B&W. Lang.: Swe.

Sweden: Stockholm. 1956-1998. Historical studies. ■Survey of all the Swedish actors that have been awarded the O'Neill Prize.

2366 "26 x 2." *Dramat.* 1998; 6(3): 39-65. Illus.: Photo. B&W. Color. Lang.: Swe.

Sweden: Stockholm. 1998. Historical studies. ■Twenty-six photographers have photographed their choice of an actor from Kungliga Dramatiska Teatern.

2367 Amble, Lolo. "Den ständige sonen." (The Eternal Son.) *Dramat.* 1998; 6(2): 34-36. Illus.: Photo. B&W. Color. Lang.: Swe.

Sweden: Stockholm. 1998. Histories-sources. ■Interview with Dan Ekborg, who plays James in O'Neill's *Long Day's Journey Into Night* staged by Thorsten Flinck at Kungliga Dramatiska Teatern, with reference to his own background as a son of the late actor Lars Ekborg.

2368 Busk, Yvonne. "För de allra små." (For the Youngest.) *Tningen.* 1998; 21(5): 10-11. Illus.: Photo. B&W. Lang.: Swe.

Sweden: Stockholm. 1998. Historical studies. ■Report from a conference about theatre for young people 2-4 years old, with references to the artistic manager Lena Fridell and the composer Lars-Erik Brossner from En Trappa Ned in Gothenburg.

2369 Claesson, Christina; Ring, Lars; Lundin, Bo; Englund, Claes; Huss, Pia; Saag, Kristjan; Björkstén, Ingmar. "Min favoritroll." (My Favorite Part.) *Entré.* 1998; 25(3/4): 2-17. Illus.: Photo. B&W. Lang.: Swe.

Sweden. 1950. Critical studies. ■Seven critics choose an unforgettable character they have seen or an actor's interpretation, with references to Winnie in Beckett's *Happy Days,* Knappstöparen in Ibsen's *Peer Gynt,* Gunilla Berg's Léonida in Labiche's *La Cagnotte,* Claes Gill's Enrico in Pirandello's *Enrico IV,* Jane Friedman's Linda Loman in Thorsten Flinck's staging of Miller's *Death of a Salesman* at Grupp 98 and Rolf Nordström's Willy Loman in Wiveka Warenfalk's staging at Borås Stadsteater, and Gunn Wållgren's Donna Anna in Shaw's *Man and Superman.*

2370 Ewbank, Inga-Stina. "The Intimate Theatre: Shakespeare Teaches Strindberg Theatrical Modernism." *TJ.* 1998 May; 50(2): 165-174. Notes. Lang.: Eng.

Sweden. 1907-1910. Critical studies. ■Argues that Strindberg's commitment to Shakespeare's plays during his Intimate Theatre days shaped his understanding of the potentialities of theatre and theatrical space.

2371 Fransson, Emma. "Jag känner mig så fruktansvärt bortskämd." (I Feel So Terribly Spoiled.) *Tningen.* 1998 ; 21(1): 4-6. Illus.: Photo. Color. Lang.: Swe.

Sweden: Stockholm. 1988-1998. Histories-sources. ■Interview with the actress Anna Pettersson about her part in Lars Norén's production of his own *Personkrets 3:1 (Circle 3:1),* with reference to her career and women's roles.

2372 Fransson, Emma. "Lite mer mod och galenskap." (Some More Courage and Madness.) *Tningen.* 1998; 21(2): 4-6. Illus.: Photo. B&W. Lang.: Swe.

Sweden: Stockholm. 1994-1998. Histories-sources. ■Interview with the young actress Anna Takanen about her career and her step to directing with Suzanne Osten as mentor, with reference to Osten's *Flickan, Mamman och Soporna (The Girl, the Mommy and the Garbage)* at Klarateatern.

DRAMA: —Performance/production

2373 Freeberg, Debra L. "Strindberg in Malmö, Sweden." *WES*. 1998 Fall; 10(3): 13-20. Illus.: Photo. B&W. 3. Lang.: Eng.
Sweden: Malmö. 1998. Historical studies. ■Report on the Malmö theatre scene, with particular attention paid to Dramatiska Teater's production of Strindberg's *Ett Drömspel (A Dream Play)* directed by Keve Hjelm.

2374 Freeberg, Debra L. "Astrid Lindgren in Stockholm." *WES*. 1998 Fall; 10(3): 21-26. Illus.: Photo. B&W. 3. Lang.: Eng.
Sweden: Stockholm. 1998. Critical studies. ■Discusses two adaptations of Lindgren's children's stories, to honor her ninetieth birthday, by Dramaten: *Allrakärasta syster (My Dearest Sister)*, adapted and directed by Marie Feldtmann and *Mio, Min Mio (Mio, My Mio)*, adapted by Kristina Lugn and directed by Hans Klinga.

2375 Hägglund, Kent. "Min favoritroll." (My Favorite Part.) *Entré*. 1998; 25(2): 30-31. Illus.: Photo. B&W. Lang.: Swe.
Sweden. 1978-1998. Histories-sources. ■Actor Hägglund's choice of Bottom from Shakespeare's *A Midsummer Night's Dream* as the richest part with the most generous possibilities for a good actor.

2376 Helander, Karin. "Barnteaterkrönika." (A Chronicle of Children's Theatre.) *Tningen*. 1998; 21(4): 37-39. Illus.: Photo. B&W. Lang.: Swe.
Sweden. 1998. Historical studies. ■Overview of theatre performances for children during the year.

2377 Hoogland, Rikard. "Just nu är jag Sveriges mest priviligierade regissör." (Right Now I'm the Most Privileged Director of Sweden.) *Tningen*. 1998; 21(5): 3-6. Illus.: Photo. B&W. Color. Lang.: Swe.
Sweden: Malmö. 1997-1998. Histories-sources. ■Interview with director Anders Paulin about his stagings at Malmö Dramatiska Teater, with references to his production of Franz Xaver Kroetz' *Der Drang* and Cristina Gottfridsson's *Cyrano*.

2378 Johansson, Ola. "Fenomenet *Dr. Kokos kärlekslaboratorium*." (The Phenomen of *Dr. Koko's Laboratory of Love*.) *Tningen*. 1998; 21(4): 7-11. Illus.: Photo. B&W. Color. Lang.: Swe.
Sweden: Stockholm. 1998. ■Analysis of *Dr. Kokos kärlekslaboratorium* at Backstage of Stockholms Stadsteater, with references to the producer Maria Blom, performance art, and Lars Norén's *Personkrets 3:1 (Circle 3:1)*.

2379 Josephson, Erland. "Skådespelaren." (The Actor.) *Dramat*. 1998; 6(3): 17. Illus.: Photo. Color. Lang.: Swe.
Sweden. 1945-1998. Histories- sources. ■Actor Erland Josephson writes about the paradox of acting: its being both a science and a game.

2380 Lagercrantz, Ylva. "Vad spelar skådespelerskan för roll?" (What Does the Actress Matter?)*Dramat*. 1998; 6(3): 73-76. Illus.: Photo. B&W. Color. Lang.: Swe.
Sweden: Stockholm. 1945-1998. Histories-sources. ■Interviews with Lena Endre, Marie Göranzon, and Anita Björk, three generations of actresses, about female roles, and what to do to change the dominance of male roles.

2381 Lahger, Håkan. "En guru i stan." (A Guru On the Town.) *Dramat*. 1998; 6(3): 28-29. Illus.: Photo. Color. Lang.: Swe.
Sweden: Stockholm. 1998. Histories-sources. ■Interviews with actors Lil Terselius and Björn Granath about the rehearsal process for Robert Lepage's production of Rojas' *La Celestina* at Kungliga Dramatiska Teatern.

2382 Lahger, Håkan. "Förortsunge i finsalong." (A Young Suburban In the Select Salons.) *Dramat*. 1998; 6(3): 31-32. Illus.: Photo. Color. Lang.: Swe.
Sweden: Stockholm. 1984-1998. Histories-sources. ■Interview with the actor Stefan Larsson about his background in the poor suburbs, his career as an actor and as director of Patrick Marber's *Closer*, and Lars Norén's *Rumäner (Romanians)*.

2383 Lahger, Håkan. "I huvudrollen: Börje Ahlstedt/Krister Henriksson." (Starring: Börje Ahlstedt and Krister Henriksson.) *Dramat*. 1998; 6(3): 68-72. Illus.: Photo. Color. Lang.: Swe.
Sweden: Stockholm. 1962-1998. Histories-sources. ■Interviews with the actors Börje Ahlstedt and Krister Henriksson about their careers and their views on acting.

2384 Magnusson, Anna. "Från repetition till premiär." (From Rehearsals to Opening Night.) *Dramat*. 1998; 6(3): 81-84. Illus.: Photo. Color. Lang.: Swe.
Sweden: Stockholm. 1998. Historical studies. ■Follows actress Gerthi Kulle from the first rehearsal to opening night stage in Thorsten Flinck's production of Brecht's *Der Gute Mensch von Sezuan* at Kungliga Dramatiska Teatern.

2385 Olzon, Janna. "Folklig teater." (Popular Theatre.) *Tningen*. 1998; 21(2): 45-47. Illus.: Photo. Color. Lang.: Swe.
Sweden: Stockholm. 1973-1998. Histories-sources. ■Director Kent Ekberg speaks about his background, his work with the community theatre Enskedespelen, and his aim to let ordinary people or unemployed people be involved in productions like *Die Dreigroschenoper* at Årsta Teater.

2386 Oppered, Inger Marie. "*Mio, Min Mio* framför och bakom scen." (*Mio, My Mio* In Front of The House and Backstage.) *Dramat*. 1998; 6: is 2: 53-55. Illus.: Photo. B&W. Color. Lang.: Swe.
Sweden: Stockholm. 1997. Historical studies. ■Report on the performances of Astrid Lindgren's *Mio, Min Mio* staged by Hans Klinga at Kungliga Dramatiska Teatern.

2387 Persson, Sven Hugo. "Är det fint att vara skådespelare?" (Is It Good To Be an Actor?)*Dramat*. 1998; 6(3): 9. Lang.: Swe.
Sweden. 1800-1998. Critical studies. ■Essay about the changing attitudes towards the actor, both as a professional and as individual.

2388 Rönnberg, Ingergerd. "Regissören som tänker med kroppen." (The Director Who Thinks With Her Body.) *Dramat*. 1998; 6(2): 48-50. Illus.: Photo. B&W. Color. Lang.: Swe.
Sweden: Stockholm. 1996-1998. Histories-sources. ■Interview with director Marie Feldtmann about the art of theatre for children, with reference to her production *Allrakäraste syster (My Dearest Sister)* by Astrid Lindgren and *Ängel och den blå hästen (Angel and the Blue Horse)* by Ulf Stark at Kungliga Dramatiska Teatern.

2389 Schneider, Wolfgang. "Culture, Creativity and Children." *G&GBKM*. 1998; 127: 1-6. Lang.: Ger.
Sweden: Stockholm. 1998. Critical studies. ■Impressions from a visit to Stockholm with its remarkable fondness of children. Describes the children's theatre scene especially Suzanne Osten's *Flickan, Mamman och Soporna (The Girl, the Mommy and the Garbage)* adapted by Erik Uddenberg and directed by Suzanne Osten at Unga Klara.

2390 Sörenson, Elisabeth. "Jan-Olof Strandberg." *Dramat*. 1998; 6(2): 10-13. Illus.: Photo. B&W. Lang.: Swe.
Sweden: Stockholm, Gothenburg, Uppsala. 1948-1998. Histories-sources. ■Interview with the actor Jan-Olof Strandberg, retiring from Kungliga Dramatiska Teatern after fifty years, with reference to all his roles and his view of the new generation of actors.

2391 Stenberg, Roger, photo. "'...det måste bli ett djävla liv'." ('It Had To Be a Damned Row'.) *Dramat*. 1998; 6(2: pp 30-33). Illus.: Photo. B&W. Lang.: Swe.
Sweden: Stockholm. 1998. Historical studies. ■Photographic record of the rehearsals of O'Neill's *Long Day's Journey Into Night*, directed by Thorsten Flinck at Kungliga Dramatisk Teatern.

2392 Stolt, Bengt. "Medieval Religious Drama in Sweden: The Physical Evidence." *EDAM*. 1998 Spr; 20(2): 55-70. Notes. Illus.: Photo. B&W. 6. Lang.: Eng.
Sweden. 1140-1500. Historical studies. ■Evidence in religious artifacts of medieval performance of religious drama in Sweden.

2393 Szalczer, Eszter. "Fresh Approaches to Modern Classics in Stockholm: *Peer Gynt* and *The Father*." *WES*. 1998 Spr; 10 (2): 77-80. Illus.: Photo. B&W. 3. Lang.: Eng.
Sweden: Stockholm. 1997. Critical studies. ■Analysis of fresh twists put to productions of Ibsen's *Peer Gynt*, directed by Ole Anders Tandberg at Riksteater, and Strindberg's *The Father (Fadren)* at the venue Målarsalen and directed by Staffan Valdemar Holm.

2394 Tanitch, Robert. "Weekend in Stockholm." *PlPl*. 1998 Oct.; 527: 26. Illus.: Photo. B&W. Color. 2. Lang.: Eng.
Sweden: Stockholm. 1766-1998. Historical studies. ■Stockholm's year as Cultural Capital of Europe, with history of Drottningholms Slottsteater, and reviews of two Stockholm productions: Gluck's *Don Juan* (Slottste-

ater, choreographed by Regina Beck-Friis) and a re-staging of Pina Bausch's *Café Müller.*

2395 Thuresson, Anders. "Meursault–den Kristus vi förtjänar?" (Meursault–The Christ We Deserve?)*Entré.* 1998; 25 (3/4): 61-65. Illus.: Photo. B&W. Lang.: Swe.

Sweden: Gothenburg. 1998. ■Examines Teater UNO's staging of Albert Camus' *L'Étranger (The Stranger).*

2396 Vogel, Viveka. "Fars–en allvarlig historia." (Farce–A Serious Matter.) *Dramat.* 1998; 6(1): 82-85. Illus.: Photo. Color. B&W. Lang.: Swe.

Sweden: Stockholm. 1998. Histories-sources. ■Actors involved in the new production of Feydeau's *Puce à l'Oreille* staged by Terje Maerli at Kungliga Dramatiska Teatern speak about acting farces, with reference to the earlier production by Mimi Pollack and the actor Ingvar Kjellson.

2397 Wahlin, Claes. "Recept för teater." (A Recipe For Theatre.) *Dramat.* 1998; 6(1): 78-80. Illus.: Photo. B&W. Lang.: Swe.

Sweden: Stockholm. Canada: Montreal, PQ. 1997. Histories-sources. ■Interview with Robert Lepage on his ideas about theatre, his works with Ex Machina and his staging at Kungliga Dramatiska Teatern of Rojas' *Celestina.*

2398 Jauslin, Christian. "Shakespeare-Aufführungen auf den deutschsprachigen Bühnen der Schweiz." (Shakespeare Performances on German Speaking Stages in Switzerland.) *SJW.* 1998; 134: 207-212. Illus.: Dwg. Photo. B&W. 2. Lang.: Ger.

Switzerland: Basel, Zurich. 1996-1997. Reviews of performances. ■*Richard III* directed by Peter Löscher at Stadttheater Basel and *Hamlet* directed by Uwe Eric Laufenberg at Schauspielhaus Zurich.

2399 Merschmeier, Michael. "Sport statt Mord." (Sport Instead of Murder.) *THeute.* 1998; 10: 12-14. Illus.: Photo. B&W. 1. Lang.: Ger.

Switzerland: Basle. 1998. Critical studies. ■Analyzes William Shakespeare's *Troilus and Cressida* directed by Stefan Bachmann at Theater Basel.

2400 Neubert-Herwig, Christa. "Benno Bessons Gänge in die Tiefe." (Benno Besson's Descent Into the Depths.) *TZ.* 1998; 3: 33-35. Illus.: Photo. B&W. 1. Lang.: Ger.

Switzerland: Zurich. 1998. Historical studies. ■Decribes Bertolt Brecht's *Die heilige Johanna der Schlachthöfe (Saint Joan of the Stockyards)* directed by Benno Besson at Schauspielhaus Zürich, with emphasis on the work of Katharina Thalbach as Johanna.

2401 Wille, Franz. "Illusionen von Glück und Theater." (Illusions of Luck and Theatre.) *THeute.* 1998; 11: 76-79. Illus.: Photo. B&W. 4. Lang.: Ger.

Switzerland: Zurich. 1998. Critical studies. ■Analyzes Theresia Walser's *King Kongs Töchter (King Kong's Daughters)* directed by Volker Hesse at Theater Neumarkt.

2402 Wille, Franz. "Spiel mir das Lied vom Tod." (Play the Song of Death for Me.) *THeute.* 1998; 7: 48-49. Illus.: Photo. B&W. 1. Lang.: Ger.

Switzerland: Zurich. 1998. Critical studies. ■Urs Widmer's adaptation of the story *Die schwarze Spinne (The Black Spider)* by Jeremias Gotthel, directed by Volker Hesse at Theater Neumarkt.

2403 Wille, Franz. "Unter Geiern." (Among Vultures.) *THeute.* 1998; 12: 28-32. Illus.: Photo. B&W. 2. Lang.: Ger.

Switzerland: Basel. Austria: Vienna. 1998. Reviews of performances. ■Reviews Wolfgang Bauer's *Magic Afternoon* directed by Stefan Bachmann at Theater Basel and *Bernhard-Dramolette (Bernhard's Small Dramas)* by Thomas Bernhard directed by Philip Tiedemann at Burgtheater (Vienna).

2404 Kumysnikov, H. "Lik stradajuščej duši: Čem oplačen triumf na scene G. Isangulovoj." (The Triumph of the Suffering Soul: The Triumph and Reward of G. Isangulova.) *Kazan'.* 1998; 2: 99-102. Lang.: Rus.

Tatarstan: Kazan. 1998. Biographical studies. ■Profile of actress Isangulova of Tatar Dramatic Theatre.

2405 Kumysnikov, H. "Cvetok iz buketa pervoj tatarskoj aktrisy." (A Flower from the Bouquet of the First Tatar Actress.) *Kazan'.* 1998; 3: 79-81. Lang.: Rus.

Tatarstan. 1998. Biographical studies. ■Profile of actress S. Gizzatulina-Volžskaja.

2406 Pozdnjakova, A.P. *Uganda: Spravočnik.* (Uganda: Information Book.) Moscow: Izdat. firma 'Vost. lit.'; 1998. 224 pp. Lang.: Rus.

Uganda. 1998. Historical studies. ■Overview of Ugandan culture including theatre.

2407 "Reviews of Productions." *LTR.* 1998; 18(9): 570-579, 591. Lang.: Eng.

UK. 1998. ■*Talk of the City* by Stephen Poliakoff, dir by Poliakoff for the RSC at the Swan: rev by Billington, Brown, Butler, Clapp, Coveney, de Jongh, Edwardes, Gore-Langton, Gross, Hagerty, Kingston, Macaulay, Nathan, Peter, Spencer, P. Taylor, Treadwell, Woddis. *Measure for Measure* by William Shakespeare, dir by Michael Boyd for the RSC at the Royal Shakespeare: rev by Billington, Clapp, Coveney, de Jongh, Gore-Langton, Gross, Hagerty, Kingston, Macaulay, Nathan, Peter, Spencer, Stratton, P. Taylor, Treadwell, Woddis. *Thirteenth Night* by Howard Brenton, dir by Sarah Wooley at the Arches: rev by MacDermot, McMillan, Wainwright, Wilson.

2408 "Reviews of Productions." *LTR.* 1998; 18(10): 629-633. Lang.: Eng.

UK-England: London. ■*The Bowler Hat* by Marcel Marceau, dir by Marceau at the Old Vic: rev by Abdulla, Buscovic, Butler, Christopher, Coveney, Curtis, Foss, Gross, Hagerty, Murray, Peter, Spencer. *Maggie* by Claude Harz, dir by Penny Cherns and *Delaney* by Harz, dir by Ranald Graham at the Rosemary Branch: rev by Hamp. *Franziska* by Frank Wedekind, adapt by Eleanor Brown, transl by Philip Ward, dir by Georgina van Welie at the Gate: rev by Curtis, Gardner, Hanks, Kingston, Marlowe, Marmion.

2409 "Reviews of Productions." *LTR.* 1998; 18(10): 634-639. Lang.: Eng.

UK-England: London. 1998. ■*Kindertotenlieder (Songs on the Death of Children)* 5 poems by Friedrich Rückert set to music by Gustav Mahler, dir by Robert Lepage at Lyric Hammersmith: rev by Billington, Christiansen, Church, Driver, Edwardes, Kimberley, R. Jones, Maddocks, Murray, Nightingale, Tumelty. *Monsters of Grace* by Philip Glass and Robert Wilson, lyrics by Jalaluddin Rumi, dir by Wilson at the Barbican: rev by Christiansen, Church, Clements, Conrad, Marowitz, Pettitt, Sutcliffe, Tanner. *The Aspern Papers* by Jonathan Holloway from Henry James' story, dir by Holloway at the Watermans: rev by Kingston.

2410 "Reviews of Productions." *LTR.* 1998; 18(10): 640-649. Lang.: Eng.

UK-England: London. 1998. ■*Nabokov's Gloves* by Peter Moffat, dir by Ian Brown at the Hampstead: rev by Benedict, Billington, Butler, Coveney, Gore-Langton, Gross, Hemming, Kingston, Marmion, Morley, Nathan, Peter, N. Smith, Spencer, Stratton, Woddis. *Sweet Charity* book by Neil Simon, music by Cy Coleman, lyrics by Dorothy Fields, dir by Carol Metcalfe at Victoria Palace: rev by Abdulla, Benedict, Brown, Butler, Coveney, Curtis, Foss, Gore-Langton, Gross, Hagerty, Kellaway, Nathan, Nightingale, Peter, Shuttleworth, Spencer, Sweeting. *The Great Gatsby* by F. Scott Fitzgerald, adapt by Phil Smith, dir by Greg Banks at the New End: rev by Christopher, Morley, R.L. Parry.

2411 "Reviews of Productions." *LTR.* 1998; 18(10): 650-652. Lang.: Eng.

UK-England: London. 1998. ■*Europeans Only* by Pieter-Dirk Uys, dir by Uys at the Tricycle: rev by Buscovic, Games, *Independent*, R.L. Parry, *Time Out*. *The Hypochondriac (Le Malade imaginaire)* by Molière, transl by Alex Batterbee and Lesley McCall, dir by John Horwood at Canal Cafe: rev by R.L. Parry. *The Breakfast Soldiers* by Katie Hims, dir by Nadia Molinari at the Finborough: rev by Cavendish, McPherson. *The Dark House* by Dominic Francis, dir by Suzanne Bell at the Finborough: rev by McPherson, North.

2412 "Reviews of Productions." *LTR.* 1998; 18(10): 653. Lang.: Eng.

UK-England: London. 1998. ■*Trainspotting* by Harry Gibson from Irvine Welsh's novel, dir by Robert Pepper at the Man in the Moon: rev by Dark. *Kingdom on Earth* by Richard Marsh at Upstairs at the Landor: rev by McPherson. *The Sexual Life of a Camel* by Harry Gibson, dir by Simon Dunmore at the Man in the Moon: rev by Logan.

DRAMA: —Performance/production

2413 "Reviews of Productions." *LTR*. 1998; 18(12/13): 750-760. Lang.: Eng.
UK-England: London. 1998. ■*Much Ado About Nothing* by William Shakespeare, dir by Declan Donnellan at the Playhouse: rev by Benedict, Brown, Butler, Cavendish, de Jongh, Gross, Hagerty, Logan, Macaulay, Marlowe, Nathan, Nightingale, Peter, Spencer, Usher, Woddis. *The Orchestra (L'Orchestre)* by Jean Anouilh, transl by Jeremy Sams, dir by Kristine Landon-Smith at Southwark Playhouse: rev by Abdulla, McPherson. *As I Lay Dying* adapt by Edward Kemp from William Faulkner, dir by Tim Supple at the Young Vic: rev by Billington, Butler, Curtis, Edwardes, Gross, Hewison, Kingston, Logan, Macaulay, McPherson, Spencer, Usher.

2414 "Reviews of Productions." *LTR*. 1998; 18(12/13): 760-767. Lang.: Eng.
UK-England: London. 1998. ■*The National Theatre* by David Edgar and *Final Call* by Peter Simmonds, dir by Mervyn Millar at the Finborough: rev by Logan, R.L. Parry. *Brassed Off* adapt by Paul Allen from Mark Herman's film, dir by Deborah Paige at the Olivier: rev by Brown, Butler, de Jongh, Gardner, Hagerty, Marmion, Maume, Nathan, Nightingale, Peter, Shuttleworth, Sierz, N. Smith, Usher, Woddis. *Gas Station Angel* by Ed Thomas, dir by Thomas at the Royal Court: rev by Billington, Cavendish, Curtis, Grant, Gross, Hemming, Marlowe, Nightingale, Peter, Spencer, Usher, Woddis.

2415 "Reviews of Productions." *LTR*. 1998; 18(12/13): 768-777. Lang.: Eng.
UK-England: London. 1998. ■*The Comedy of Errors* and *Henry V* by William Shakespeare, both dir by Edward Hall at the Pleasance: rev by Macaulay. *Elton John's Glasses* by David Farr, dir by Terry Johnson at the Queen's: rev by Billington, Brown, Butler, Clapp, de Jongh, Edwardes, Gore-Langton, Gross, Hagerty, Lister, Morley, Nathan, Nightingale, Sierz, N. Smith, Spencer, Usher, Woddis. *A Dangerous Woman* by Paul Webb, dir by John Brenner at the New End: rev by Abdulla, Christopher, Darvell, Hagerty, Morley, Nathan, Peter.

2416 "Reviews of Productions." *LTR*. 1998; 18(12/13): 777-779. Lang.: Eng.
UK-England: London. 1998. ■*Rum and Vodka* by Conor McPherson, dir by Phil Tinline at Canal Cafe: rev by Cavendish. *Disco Pigs* by Enda Walsh, dir by Pat Kiernan at the Arts: rev by Christopher, Curtis, Marlowe, Shuttleworth. *Stone and Ashes (Cendres de cailloux)* by Daniel Danis, transl by Linda Gaboriau, dir by Philip Graham at the White Bear: rev by Godfrey-Faussett, McPherson.

2417 "Reviews of Productions." *LTR*. 1998; 18(10): 654-659. Lang.: Eng.
UK-England: London, Stratford, Derby. 1998. ■*Steinberg's Day of Atonement* by Anthony Melinkoff, dir by Neil McPherson at Pentameters: rev by Nathan. *The Lost and Moated Land* by Theatre-rites, dir by Penny Bernard at Young Vic Studio: rev by Gardner. *Bad Weather* by Robert Holman, dir by Steven Pimlott for the RSC at The Other Place: rev by Bassett, Billington, Butler, Curtis, Macaulay, Nightingale, Peter, Stratton, Treadwell, Woddis. *The Cherry Orchard (Višněvyj sad)* by Anton Čechov, dir Rimas Tuminas at the Derby Playhouse: rev by Cavendish, *Financial Times*, Gardner, Kingston.

2418 "Reviews of Productions." *LTR*. 1998; 18(12/13): 780-786. Lang.: Eng.
UK-England: London. 1998. ■*Outside on the Street (Draussen vor der Tur)* by Wolfgang Borchert, transl by Tom Fisher, dir by Gordon Anderson at the Gate: rev by Billington, Christopher, Clapp, Curtis, Dark, Gross, Hemming, Logan, Peter. *Life's a Gatecrash* by Terry Hughes, dir by Rosemary Bianchi at the Grace: rev by Costa. *Troilus and Cressida* by William Shakespeare, dir by Alan Strachan at the Open Air: rev by Billington, Clapp, de Jongh, Gore-Langton, Gross, Hagerty, Harris, Hemming, Kingston, Logan, Nathan, Peter, Spencer, Usher. *Saving Winnie* by Jack Milner, dir by Gavin McLaggan at the Finborough: rev by Abdulla.

2419 "Reviews of Productions." *LTR*. 1998; 18(12/13): 789-794. Lang.: Eng.
UK-England: London. 1998. ■*The Unexpected Man (L'homme du hasard)* by Yasmina Reza, transl by Christopher Hampton, dir by Matthew Warchus for the RSC at the Duchess: rev by Bassett, Butler, Gore-Langton, Kingston, Lister, Macaulay, N. Smith, Stratton. *The Second Cosmic Hair Gallery* by Deborah Catesby, dir by Marc Wootton at the Orange Tree Room: rev by Hamp, McPherson. *The Basset Table* by Susannah Centlivre, dir by Polly Irvin at the Tricycle: rev by Butler, Cavendish, Curtis, Foss, Gardner, Gross, Macaulay, Marmion, Nathan, Usher.

2420 "Reviews of Productions." *LTR*. 1998; 18(12/13): 795-801. Lang.: Eng.
UK-England: London. 1998. ■*The Bone Room* by Judith Adams, dir by Janet Gordon and Mark Stuart Currie at the Young Vic Studio: rev by Godfrey-Faussett, Kingston, Woddis. *The Lost Vegas Series* by Julie Jensen, dir by Dawn Lintern at Riverside 3: rev by Cavendish, Curtis, Hemming, Hewison, Nightingale, R.L. Parry. *The Well-Stone (Izutsu)* by Motokiyo Zeami, transl by Richard Grofton and Akemi Hori, and *The Dreaming of the Bones* by W.B. Yeats, both dir by Hori at The Place: rev by Kingston. *Animal Crackers* by George S. Kaufman and Morrie Ryskind, music and lyrics by Bert Kalmar and Harry Ruby, additional songs by Chris Jordan, dir by Emil Wolk and Gregory Hersov at Barbican Outdoors: rev by Billington, Cavendish, Christopher, Coveney, Curtis, Darvell, Hagerty, Hewison, Macaulay, Nathan, Saddler, Spencer, Woddis. *Die Fledermaus* by Johann Strauss, dir by Tony Britten at the Drill Hall: rev by Darvell.

2421 "Reviews of Productions." *LTR*. 1998; 18(12/13): 802-806. Lang.: Eng.
UK-England: London. 1998. ■*The Gift* by Angela de Castro, dir by Josef Houben at The Pit: rev by Curtis, Foss, Gardner, Gilbert, Godfrey-Faussett, Hewison, Judah, Woddis. *Valentines* book and lyrics by Myles Stinton, David Culling, and Martin Hintson, music by Chris Warner, dir by Stinton at the Bird's Nest: rev by Abdulla. *Lifegame* by Keith Johnstone, dir Phelim McDermott and Lee Simpson at Lyric Hammersmith: rev by Bassett, Cavendish, Curtis, Hewison, Judah, O'Farrell, Shuttleworth. *Johnny Song* by Jim Kenworth, dir by James Martin Charlton and *It's Better with a Band* by Brian McCloskey, dir by Celia Bannerman at Croydon Warehouse: rev by Marmion, McPherson.

2422 "Reviews of Productions." *LTR*. 1998; 18(12/13): 807-816. Lang.: Eng.
UK-England: London. 1998. ■*The Old Neighborhood* by David Mamet, dir by Patrick Marber at the Royal Court Downstairs: rev by Benedict, Billington, Brown, Butler, Clapp, de Jongh, Edwardes, Gore-Langton, Gross, Hagerty, Macaulay, Morley, Nathan, Nightingale, Peter, N. Smith, Spencer, Usher, Woddis. *Derby Day* by Brian Thompson, dir by James A. Baker at the Man in the Moon: rev by Edwardes, Hewison, McPherson. *Ashes to Ashes* by Harold Pinter, dir by Titus Muizelaar and *Buff* by Gerardjan Rijnders, dir by Rijnders for Toneelgroep at Riverside 2: rev by Cooper, Edwardes, Fisher, Gardner, McMillan, Saddler, Shuttleworth. *Hedda Gabler* by Henrik Ibsen, dir by Harry Meacher at Pentameters: rev by Godfrey-Faussett, Marlowe.

2423 "Reviews of Productions." *LTR*. 1998; 18(12/13): 817-827. Lang.: Eng.
UK-England: London. 1998. ■*How I Learned to Drive* by Paula Vogel, dir by John Crowley at Donmar Warehouse: rev by Benedict, Billington, Brown, Butler, Clapp, de Jongh, Gore-Langton, Gross, Hagerty, Kingston, Macaulay, Marlowe, Morley, Nathan, Peter, Spencer, Stratton, Usher, Woddis. *Demons and Dybbuks* by Isaac Bashevis Singer, dir by Mike Alfreds at the Richmond: rev by Kingston. *The Prime of Miss Jean Brodie* new stage version of Muriel Spark's novel by Jay Presson Allen, dir by Phyllida Lloyd for the Royal National at the Lyttelton: rev by Benedict, Brown, Butler, Clapp, de Jongh, Edwardes, Gore-Langton, Gross, Hagerty, Hassell, Morley, Nathan, Nightingale, Peter, Usher, Woddis.

2424 "Reviews of Productions." *LTR*. 1998; 18(12/13): 828-835. Lang.: Eng.
UK-England: London. 1998. ■*The Possessed (Besy)* by Dostojėvskij, adapt by Lev Dodin, dir by Dodin for the Malyj Dramatic Theatre at the Barbican: rev by Butler, Cavendish, Clapp, Curtis, Gore-Langton, Macaulay, Nightingale, Spencer. *The Glass Menagerie* by Tennessee Williams, dir by Brian Blessed at BAC Main: rev by Bassett, Cavendish, Gardner, Hewison, Marlowe, Marmion, Shuttleworth. *The Changeling* by Thomas Middleton and William Rowley, dir by Tassos Stevens at BAC: rev by Christopher, Curtis, Edwardes, Hemming, Marlowe.

2425 "Reviews of Productions." *LTR*. 1998; 18(12/13): 836-843. Lang.: Eng.

DRAMA: —Performance/production

UK-England: London. 1998. ■*Whistle Down the Wind* by Andrew Lloyd Webber, Jim Steinman, Patricia Knop, and Gale Edwards from the novel by Mary Hayley Bell and screenplay by Keith Waterhouse and Willis Hall, dir by Edwards at the Aldwych: rev by Benedict, Billington, Brown, Butler, Clapp, Coveney, Curtis, de Jongh, Edwardes, Gore-Langton, Gross, Hagerty, Hewison, Macaulay, Morley, Nathan, Nightingale, N. Smith, Spencer, Woddis. *The Dyke and the Porn Star* by Bayla Travis, dir by Barcy Cogdale at the Drill Hall: rev by Costa.

2426 "Reviews of Productions." *LTR*. 1998; 18(12/13): 846-851, 857-858, 861-864. Lang.: Eng.

UK-England: London, Scarborough. 1998. ■*Digging for Ladies* by Jyll Bradley, dir by Emma Bernard at St. John's Lodge, Regent's Park: rev by Abdulla, Bayley, Foss. *Comic Potential* by Alan Ayckbourn, dir by Ayckbourn at the Stephen Joseph: rev by Billington, Brown, Gore-Langton, Nightingale, Peter, Shuttleworth, Spencer, Usher. *Hey, Mr. Producer* by Julia McKenzie and Cameron Mackintosh, dir by McKenzie and Bob Avian at the Lyceum: rev by Morley, Nightingale, Spencer. *Blue Jam* by Chris Morris, dir by Morris, *Oedipus the King (Oidípous Týrannos)* by Sophocles, transl by Peter Oswald, dir by Tom Morris, *The Tragic Life and Triumphant Death of Julia Pastrano, Ugliest Woman in the World* by Shaun Prendergast, dir by Andrea Brooks all at BAC 2: rev by Bassett, Butler, Christopher, Curtis, Edwardes, Gardner, Higgins, Marlowe, Shuttleworth, D. Wilson.

2427 "Reviews of Productions." *LTR*. 1998; 18(12/13): 844-846. Lang.: Eng.

UK-England: London. 1998. ■*Fragmenting Red* by Tony Craze, *The Cows Are Mad* by Jon Tompkins, *Know Your Rights* by Judy Upton, *Election Night in the Yard* by Roddy McDevitt, *The Head Invents, the Heart Discovers* by Peter Barnes, *Cry If I Want To* by Aidan Healey, *The (Bogus) People's Poem* by Kay Adshead, *The Big Idea* by Helen Kelly, *On the Couch with Enoch* by Tanika Gupta, *The Mandelson Files* by Paul Sirett, *Thanks Mum* by David Eldridge, *Slow Drift* by Rebecca Prichard, *Made in England* by Parv Bancil, *Les Evénements* by James Macdonald, *Stick Stack Stock* by Dona Daley, and *The Ballad of Bony Lairt* by Ronald Fraser-Munro, dir by Deborah Bruce, Lisa Goldman, Lisa Giglio, James Kerr, Bernadette Moran, and Nathan Osgood at BAC: rev by Billington, Curtis, Dark, Edwardes, Godfrey-Faussett, Kingston, Logan, Marlowe, McPherson, Woddis.

2428 "Reviews of Productions." *LTR*. 1998; 18(4): 196-203. Lang.: Eng.

UK-England: London. 1998. ■*Think No Evil of Us: My Life with Kenneth Williams* by David Benson, dir by Benson at the Vaudeville: rev by Abdulla, Curtis, Foss, Spencer. *The Weir* by Conor McPherson, dir by Ian Rickson at the Royal Court Downstairs: rev by Billington, Brown, Clapp, Coveney, de Jongh, Edwardes, Gore-Langton, Gross, Hagerty, Hemming, Morley, Nathan, Nightingale, Peter, N. Smith, Spencer, P. Taylor, Woddis. *Human Being* by Nigel Charnock, dir by Charnock at the Arts: rev by Benedict, I. Brown, Cavendish, Christopher, Foss, Sacks, Sierz.

2429 "Reviews of Productions." *LTR*. 1998; 18(5): 262-266. Lang.: Eng.

UK-England: London. 1998. ■*Club Tropicana* musical revue dir by Santiago Alfonso at the Royal Albert Hall: rev by I. Brown, Coveney, Dromgoole, Macaulay. *Easter (Påsk)* by August Strindberg, transl by Philip Eccles, dir by Robert Tomlinson at the Etcetera: rev by Costa. *Urban Trauma* by Alan Davies, dir by Davies at the Duchess: rev by Bassett, Buckley, Hagerty, Hawkins, Judah, Rampton, S. Taylor, Turpin, R. Williams.

2430 "Reviews of Productions." *LTR*. 1998; 18(4): 203-205. Lang.: Eng.

UK-England: London. 1998. ■*Sexual Perversity in Chicago* by David Mamet, dir by Paul Arendt at Canal Cafe: rev by Pearse. *A Catalogue of Modern City Life (Issey Ogata no Toshiseikatsuno)* by Issey Ogata, dir by Yuzo Morita at the Lyric: rev by Buckley, Judah, R.L. Parry, Shuttleworth, Turpin. *Accidental Death of an Anarchist (Morte accidentale di un anarchico)* by Dario Fo at BAC 2: rev by McPherson.

2431 "Reviews of Productions." *LTR*. 1998; 18(4): 226-235. Lang.: Eng.

UK-England: Stratford. 1998. ■*The Two Gentlemen of Verona* by Shakespeare, dir by Edward Hall for the RSC at the Swan: rev by Bassett, Coveney, de Jongh, Kingston, Logan, Macaulay, Peter, P. Taylor. *The Tempest* by Shakespeare, dir by Adrian Noble for the RSC at the Royal Shakespeare: rev by Billington, G. Brown, Butler, Clapp, Coveney, de Jongh, Edwardes, Gore-Langton, Gross, Hagerty, Macaulay, Nightingale, Peter, Spencer, P. Taylor, Treadwell.

2432 "Reviews of Productions." *LTR*. 1998; 18(4): 206-210. Lang.: Eng.

UK-England: London. 1998. ■*I Am Yours* by Judith Thompson, dir by Nancy Meckler at the Royal Court Upstairs: rev by Benedict, Curtis, Gardner, Hemming, Hewison, Kingston, Logan, Marlowe, Morley, Woddis. *Inspiration*, Gospel performance by Queen Esther Marrow and the Harlem Gospel Singers, musical dir by David A. Tobin at Hackney Empire: rev by Bell, Davis, de Lisle. *10,000 Broken Mirrors* by Tenebris Light, dir by Struan Leslie at the Oval House: rev by Logan. *The Duchess of Malfi* by John Webster, dir by Katherine Bailey Chubb at the Tristan Bates: rev by Godfrey-Faussett.

2433 "Reviews of Productions." *LTR*. 1998; 18(4): 216-225. Lang.: Eng.

UK-England: Leeds, Manchester. 1998. ■*An Experiment with an Air-pump* by Shelagh Stephenson, dir by Matthew Lloyd at Upper Campfield Market: rev by Bassett, Billington, Christopher, Clapp, Peter, Wainwright. *Home Truths* by David Lodge, dir by Anthony Clark at Birmingham Rep: rev by Barber, Clapp, Coveney, Gardner, Nightingale, Peter, Spencer, P. Taylor. *You'll Have Had Your Hole* by Irvine Welsh, dir by Ian Brown at the Courtyard: rev by Billington, Bruce, Clapp, Curtis, Gore-Langton, Hagerty, Nightingale, Peter, Spencer, P. Taylor.

2434 "Reviews of Productions." *LTR*. 1998; 18(6): 358-365. Lang.: Eng.

UK-England: London. 1998. ■*Apocalyptica* by Philip Ridley, dir by Matthew Lloyd at the Hampstead: rev by Bassett, Billington, Clapp, de Jongh, Gore-Langton, Gross, Marlowe, Nightingale, P. Taylor, Woddis. *Timeless* by David Greig, music by Nick Powell, dir by Graham Eatough at Donmar Warehouse: rev by Bruce, Butler, Coveney, Curtis, Farrell, Hemming, Nightingale, P. Taylor. *Sleeping Around* by Hilary Fannin, Mark Ravenhill, Stephen Greenhorn, and Abi Morgan, dir by Vicky Featherstone at Donmar Warehouse: rev by Billington, de Jongh, Kingston, Spencer, Woddis. *Michaelangelo's Slave* by Atar Hadari, dir by Knight Mantell at Wimbledon Studio: rev by Dowden.

2435 "Reviews of Productions." *LTR*. 1998; 18(5): 247-261. Lang.: Eng.

UK-England: London. 1998. ■*Camino Real* by Tennessee Williams, dir by Steven Pimlott for the RSC at the Young Vic: rev by Curtis, Edwardes, Foss, Kingston, Morley, Murray. *Not About Nightingales* by Williams, dir by Trevor Nunn for the Royal National at the Cottesloe: rev by Billington, Brown, Butler, Clapp, Coveney, de Jongh, Edwardes, Foss, Gore-Langton, Gross, Hagerty, Macaulay, Morley, Nathan, Nightingale, Peter, Spencer, P. Taylor, Woddis. *Girls Night Out* by Dave Simpson, dir by Carole Todd at Victoria Palace: rev by Abdulla, Billington, Brown, Butler, Clapp, Coveney, Gore-Langton, Hagerty, Herron, McPherson, Nathan, Nightingale, Spencer, P. Taylor.

2436 "Reviews of Productions." *LTR*. 1998; 18(5): 276-279. Lang.: Eng.

UK-England: London. 1998. ■*Yee-Haw!* by Richard Free and Peter Shrubshall, dir by Greg Harris at the Rosemary Branch: rev by Austin, Benedict. *The Barbers of Surreal* conceived by Forkbeard Fantasy, words by Tim Britton, dir by John Tellet at the Lyric Studio: rev by Benedict, Christopher, Stratton. *The Hansel and Gretel Machine* by David Glass, dir by Glass at the Purcell Room: rev by Brown, Cooper, Gilbert, O'Connor Morse.

2437 "Reviews of Productions." *LTR*. 1998; 18(5): 279-280. Lang.: Eng.

UK-England: London. 1998. ■*Silly Cow* by Ben Elton, dir by Stephen Christopher at the Grace: rev by McPherson. *The Normal Heart* by Larry Kramer, dir by Richard Bridge at the Man in the Moon: rev by Costa. *The Bloody Chamber* adapt by Angela Carter and Keith Lodwick from Carter's short story, dir by Ben Harrison at the London Dungeon: rev by Costa, Davé, Gardner.

2438 "Reviews of Productions." *LTR*. 1998; 18(1/2): 5-9. Lang.: Eng.

UK-England: London. 1998. ■*Things We Do for Love* by Alan Ayckbourn, dir by Ayckbourn at the Gielgud: rev by Billington, Brown, But-

DRAMA: —Performance/production

ler, Clapp, Coveney, de Jongh, Gore-Langton, Gross, Hagerty, Macaulay, Morley, Nathan, Nightingale, Peter, Sierz, N. Smith, Spencer, Stratton, P. Taylor, Woddis. *The Swell* by Daniel Jamieson, dir by Nikki Sved at the Warehouse, Croydon: rev by Christopher, Godfrey-Faussett, McPherson, Saddler. *Epitaph for the Whales (Kujirano Bōyo)* by Yoji Sakate, transl by Mark Sparrow, dir by Kazuyoshi Kushida at the Gate: rev by Christopher, Curtis, Logan, Marlowe, Peter.

2439 "Reviews of Productions." *LTR*. 1998; 18(5): 281-282. Lang.: Eng.

UK-England: London. 1998. ■*The Amber Room* by Michael Black, dir by Ken McClymont at the Old Red Lion: rev by Dark, Hagerty, Logan, Nathan. *Room* by Scott Hamilton, dir by Michael Ruta at the White Bear: rev by Abdulla. *Sabina!* by Chris Dolan, dir by Leslie Finlay at the Pleasance: rev by Christopher, Godfrey-Faussett, Schamus, Woddis.

2440 "Reviews of Productions." *LTR*. 1998; 18(5): 288-292. Lang.: Eng.

UK-England: London. 1998. ■*The Dead Monkey* by Nick Darke, dir by Brennan Street at the New End: rev by Curtis, Gore-Langton, Hagerty, Kingston, Marmion, Nathan, R.L. Parry, Peter, Woddis. *Dust* by Maureen Chadwick, dir by Maggie Norris at BAC Main: rev by Christopher, Logan, Marlowe, Peter. *English Journeys* by Steve Waters, dir by Gemma Bodinetz at the Hampstead: rev by Bassett, Curtis, Davé, Edwardes, Kingston, Woddis.

2441 "Reviews of Productions." *LTR*. 1998; 18(6): 319-322. Lang.: Eng.

UK-England: London. 1998. ■*The Surgeon of Honor (El médico de su honra)* by Calderón, transl by Gwynne Edwards, dir by Judith Roberts at Southwark Playhouse: rev by Butler, Edwardes, Kingston, R.L. Parry, P. Taylor. *Antigone* by Sophocles, transl by Edwards, dir by Phillip Hoffman at the Riverside: rev by Godfrey-Faussett, Macaulay, Nathan, Schamus. *The Frogs (Ranae)* by Aristophanes, transl by David Barrett, dir by June Abbott at the Courtyard: rev by Abdulla, Foss.

2442 "Reviews of Productions." *LTR*. 1998; 18(5): 292-299. Lang.: Eng.

UK-England: London. 1998. ■*The Fire Raisers (Biedermann und die Brandstifter)* by Max Frisch, transl Michael Bullock, dir by Paul Burbridge at the Bridewell: rev by Dark, Marmion. *Krapp's Last Tape* by Samuel Beckett, dir by Edward Petherbridge and David Hunt for the RSC at The Pit: rev by Billington, Brown, Curtis, Macaulay, R.L. Parry, Peter, Wardle. *Waiting for Godot (En attendant Godot)* by Beckett, dir by Peter Hall at the Piccadilly: rev by Butler, Clapp, Coveney, Darvell, de Jongh, Gore-Langton, Hagerty, Morley, Murray, Nathan, Nightingale, Peter, Spencer, Stratton, P. Taylor, Wardle, Woddis. *Releasing Myra?* by Ross Wehner, dir by Peter Mimmack at the Hen & Chickens: rev by Marmion.

2443 "Reviews of Productions." *LTR*. 1998; 18(5): 283-287. Lang.: Eng.

UK-England: London. 1998. ■*In a Little World of Our Own* by Gary Mitchell, dir by Robert Delamere at Donmar Warehouse: rev by Benedict, Billington, Butler, Clapp, Curtis, de Jongh, Nightingale, Spencer. *Tell Me* by Matthew Dunster, dir by Richard Gregory at Donmar Warehouse: rev by Butler, Clapp, de Jongh, Gardner, Gore-Langton, Hemming, Nightingale, Spencer, Wardle, Woddis. *The Unblest* by Ruth Gow, dir by Gow at the King's Head: rev by Buscovic.

2444 "Reviews of Productions." *LTR*. 1998; 18(6): 322-333. Lang.: Eng.

UK-England: London. 1998. ■*A Cage Without Bars* by Chris Humphreys, dir by Philip Grout at the Finborough: rev by Cavendish, McPherson. *The Judas Kiss* by David Hare, dir by Richard Eyre at the Playhouse: rev by Billington, Brown, Butler, Clapp, Coveney, de Jongh, Edwardes, Gore-Langton, Gross, Hagerty, Lister, Macaulay, Morley, Nathan, Nightingale, Norman, Peter, Sierz, N. Smith, Spencer, P. Taylor, Woddis. *The Winter's Tale* by Shakespeare, dir by Spencer Hinton at the Prince: rev by Costa.

2445 "Reviews of Productions." *LTR*. 1998; 18(6): 334-340, 388. Lang.: Eng.

UK-England: London. 1998. ■*Deep Space* by Alex Johnston, dir by Jimmy Fay at the Bush: rev by Bassett, Foss, Gardner, Hagerty, Marmion, Peter, Shuttleworth, Sierz, P. Taylor, Woddis. *Dead on the Ground* by Shôn Dale-Jones, dir by Jonathan Stone at the Pleasance: rev by Schamus, Stratton. *Brief Lives* by Patrick Garland, dir by Garland at the Duchess: rev by Benedict, Coveney, Edwardes, Foss, Gore-Langton, Gross, Hagerty, Macaulay, Marmion, Morley, Nathan, Peter, Spencer, Woddis.

2446 "Reviews of Productions." *LTR*. 1998; 18(6): 356-357. Lang.: Eng.

UK-England: London. 1998. ■*Guards! Guards!* adapt from Terry Pratchett's novel by Geoffrey Cush, dir by Peter Benedict at Hackney Empire: rev by Christopher. *Nine Lives, Ten Tales* by Lil Warren, dir by Elli Papaconstanou at BAC 2: rev by Judah, Logan, R. Williams. *The Girlz* by Judy Upton, dir by George Ormond at the Orange Tree Room: rev by Godfrey-Faussett, Kingston, McPherson.

2447 "Reviews of Productions." *LTR*. 1998; 18(6): 341-347, 388. Lang.: Eng.

UK-England: London. 1998. ■*Kat and the Kings* musical by David Kramer and Taliep Petersen, dir by Kramer at the Vaudeville: rev by Benedict, Brown, Butler, Christopher, de Jongh, Edwardes, Gross, Hagerty, Hawkins, Morley, N. Smith, Spencer, Warren. *Saucy Jack and the Space Vixens* by Charlotte Mann, music by Robin Forrest and Jonathan Croose, lyrics by Mann and Michael Fidler, dir by Keith Strachan at the Queen's: rev by Billington, Coveney, Curtis, Godfrey-Faussett, Hagerty, Ives, Nathan, Nightingale, Shuttleworth, Spencer, Warren, Wright. *Beyond Ecstasy* by John Osborne Hughes, dir by Hughes at the Brix: rev by Logan, Sierz, R. Williams.

2448 "Reviews of Productions." *LTR*. 1998; 18(6): 348-356, 388. Lang.: Eng.

UK-England: London. 1998. ■*After the Orgy* conceived by Volcano Theatre, dir by Paul Davies and Fern Smith at the QEH: rev by Billington, Judah, P. Taylor. *Klub, Flesh,* and *Zero* dir and conceived by Frantic Assembly, with text by Spencer Hazel, at BAC Main: rev by Clapp, Judah, McPherson. *The London Cuckolds* by Edward Ravenscroft, adapt and dir by Terry Johnson for the Royal National at the Lyttleton: rev by Benedict, Billington, Butler, Clapp, Coveney, de Jongh, Edwardes, Gross, Hagerty, Macaulay, Marlowe, Morley, Nathan, Nightingale, Peter, Spencer, P. Taylor, Woddis.

2449 "Reviews of Productions." *LTR*. 1998; 18(7): 433-435. Lang.: Eng.

UK-England: London. 1998. ■*Blavatsky's Tower* by Moira Buffini, dir by Buffini at the Lion and Unicorn: rev by Cavendish, Curtis, Marlowe. *Candida* by George Bernard Shaw, dir by David Evans Rees at the New End: rev by Christopher, Curtis, Dowden, Nathan, North. *Balls* by Peter Dawson, dir by Richard Tate at the Old Red Lion: rev by Abdulla.

2450 "Reviews of Productions." *LTR*. 1998; 18(7): 399-405. Lang.: Eng.

UK-England: London. 1998. ■*The Misanthrope (Le Misanthrope)* by Molière, transl by Ranjit Bolt, dir by Peter Hall at the Piccadilly: rev by Billington, Butler, Clapp, Coveney, de Jongh, Eyres, Foss, Gross, Logan, Macaulay, Nathan, Nightingale, Pearce, Peter, Spencer, P. Taylor. *Two* by Jim Cartwright, dir by Jenny Sealey at the Oval House: rev by Abdulla. *The Criminals (Los delincuentes)* by José Triana, transl by Adrian Mitchell, dir by Ian Brown at the Lyric Studio: rev by Curtis, Marmion, Nightingale, R.L. Parry, Peter, P. Taylor, Woddis.

2451 "Reviews of Productions." *LTR*. 1998; 18(7): 405-412. Lang.: Eng.

UK-England: London. 1998. ■*Stiffs* by Jonathan Ashley, dir by Philip Ives at the Hen & Chickens: rev by Costa. *The Measles (Ospice)* by Ivan Vidić, transl by Boris Bosković, dir by Vidić at the Gate: rev by Curtis, Gardner, Hanks, Kingston, Logan, Marlowe. *Give Me Your Answer, Do!* by Brian Friel, dir by Robin Lefevre at the Hampstead: rev by Billington, Butler, Clapp, Coveney, de Jongh, Gross, Macaulay, Nathan, Nightingale, Peter, N. Smith, Spencer, Stratton, P. Taylor, Woddis.

2452 "Reviews of Productions." *LTR*. 1998; 18(7): 415-422. Lang.: Eng.

UK-England: London. 1998. ■*Table Number 7* and *Harlequinade* by Terence Rattigan, dir by Colin Ellwood at the King's Head: rev by Bassett, Christopher, Coveney, de Jongh, Foss, Godfrey-Faussett, Gross, Hemming, Marmion. *Cloud Nine* by Caryl Churchill, dir by Janet Gill at the White Bear: rev by McPherson. *Closer* by Patrick Marber, dir by Marber at the Lyric: rev by Billington, Butler, Chunn, Clapp, Coveney,

DRAMA: —Performance/production

de Jongh, Edwardes, Gore-Langton, Gross, Macaulay, Marlowe, Nathan, Nightingale, Norman, Peter, Spencer.

2453 "Reviews of Productions." *LTR.* 1998; 18(7): 423-432. Lang.: Eng.
UK-England: London. 1998. ▪*Uncle Vanya (Diadia Vania)* by Anton Čechov, transl by David Lan, dir by Katie Mitchell for the RSC at the Young Vic: rev by Billington, Brown, Butler, Clapp, Coveney, de Jongh, Eyres, Gore-Langton, Gross, Macaulay, Nathan, Nightingale, Peter, N. Smith, Spencer, Stratton, P. Taylor. *The Tango Room* by Louise Warren, dir by Josette Bushell-Mingo at the Loughborough Hotel: rev by Gardner, Logan. *The Dance of Death (Dödsdansen)* by August Strindberg, transl by Carlo Gébler, dir by Nicholas Kent at the Tricycle: rev by Albasini, Basset, Coveney, Curtis, Gardner, Kingston, Logan, Nathan, Peter, P. Taylor, Woddis.

2454 "Reviews of Productions." *LTR.* 1998; 18(7): 441-445. Lang.: Eng.
UK-England: London. 1998. ▪*Marisol* by José Rivera, dir by Patrick Kealey at Southwark Playhouse: rev by Christopher, Curtis, Godfrey-Faussett. *The Bullet* by Joe Penhall, dir by Dominic Cooke at Donmar Warehouse: rev by Benedict, Cavendish, Coveney, de Jongh, Gore-Langton, Gross, Macaulay, Nightingale, Peter, Rubnikovicz, Spencer, P. Taylor. *A Very Important Postman* by Joanna Neary and Brian Mitchell, dir by Louise Cope at the Etcetera: rev by Costa. *Weekenders* by Nathan Goodwin, dir by Goodwin at the Etcetera: rev by Dark.

2455 "Reviews of Productions." *LTR.* 1998; 18(9): 569. Lang.: Eng.
UK-England: London. 1998. ▪*Definitions of Intimacy* adapt and dir from Schnitzler's *La Ronde (Reigen)* by Robin Pritchard at the Prince: rev by Costa. *The Stringless Marionette* by Nicholas McInerny, dir by Marc Wootton at the Orange Tree Room: rev by Kingston. *The Revenger's Tragedy* by Thomas Middleton and Cyril Tourneur, dir by Sam Shammas at the Riverside: rev by Marlowe.

2456 "Reviews of Productions." *LTR.* 1998; 18(7): 449-457. Lang.: Eng.
UK-England. 1998. ▪*Oh, What a Lovely War!* by Charles Chilton and Joan Littlewood, dir by Fiona Laird for the Royal National at the Campbell Park: rev by Benedict, Billington, Coveney, Curtis, Edwardes, Gore-Langton, Nightingale, Peter, Rubnikovicz, Spencer, P. Taylor, Woddis. *Blast from the Past* by Ben Elton, dir by Jude Kelly at the West Yorkshire Playhouse: rev by Benedict, Billington, de Jongh, Gore-Langton, Gross, Macaulay, Nightingale, Peter, Rubnikovicz, Spencer, P. Taylor.

2457 "Reviews of Productions." *LTR.* 1998; 18(8): 475-476. Lang.: Eng.
UK-England: London. 1998. ▪*And the Snake Sheds Its Skin* by David Freeman, music by Habib Faye, dir by Freeman at the Drill Hall: rev by Clements, Milnes, Sutcliffe. *Choirboys* by Declan Croghan, dir by Izzy Mant at the Finborough: rev by Marlowe. *The Sabre's Edge* by William G. Lawrence, dir by John Cording at Baron's Court: rev by North.

2458 "Reviews of Productions." *LTR.* 1998; 18(7): 436-440. Lang.: Eng.
UK-England: London. 1998. ▪*The Cúchulain Cycle: At the Hawk's Well, The Green Helmet, On Baile's Strand, The Only Jealousy of Emer* and *The Death of Cúchulain* by William Butler Yeats, dir by Michael Scott at the Riverside: rev by Foss, Kingston, Logan. *A Woman's Comedy* by Beth Herst, dir by Georgia Bance at Wimbledon Studio: rev by McPherson, Nightingale. *Been So Long* by Che Walker, dir by Roxana Silbert at the Royal Court Upstairs: rev by Bassett, Benedict, Coveney, Curtis, Gardner, Hemming, Kingston, Logan, Marlowe, Peter, Rubnikovicz, Woddis.

2459 "Reviews of Productions." *LTR.* 1998; 18(8): 477-487. Lang.: Eng.
UK-England: London. 1998. ▪*Silas Marner* by Geoffrey Beevers from George Eliot's novel, dir by Beevers at the Orange Tree: rev by Curtis, Kingston, Marmion, McPherson, Shuttleworth. *Seepage* by James Wren, dir by Catriona Murray at the Etcetera: rev by Godfrey-Faussett, Marlowe. *The Iceman Cometh* by Eugene O'Neill, dir by Howard Davies at the Almeida: rev by Benedict, Billington, Brown, Clapp, Coveney, de Jongh, Edwardes, Gross, Hagerty, Hemming, Morley, Nightingale, Pearce, Peter, N. Smith, Spencer, P. Taylor.

2460 "Reviews of Productions." *LTR.* 1998; 18(9): 554-555. Lang.: Eng.
UK-England: London. 1998. ▪*Smoke* by Darren Raper, music by Raper and Nick Murray Brown, dir by Nick Pilton at the Union: rev by Costa. *Cold Draft on Tap* by Peggy Riley, dir by Katie Hall at the Old Red Lion: rev by Godfrey-Faussett, Marlowe. *Sitting in Limbo* by Dawn Penso and Judy Hepburn, dir by Anton Phillips at the Tricycle: rev by Curtis, Logan, Woddis.

2461 "Reviews of Productions." *LTR.* 1998; 18(8): 488-497. Lang.: Eng.
UK-England: London. 1998. ▪*The Unexpected Man (L'Homme du hasard)* by Yasmina Reza, transl by Christopher Hampton, dir by Matthew Warchus for the RSC at The Pit: rev by Benedict, Billington, Brown, Clapp, Coveney, de Jongh, Gross, Hagerty, Hassell, Hemming, Logan, Nightingale, Pearce, Peter, Spencer, P. Taylor, Woddis. *Oh, What a Lovely War!* by Charles Chilton and Joan Littlewood, dir Fiona Laird for the Royal National at the Bernie Spain Gardens: rev by Brown, Foss. *Our Lady of Sligo* by Sebastian Barry, dir by Max Stafford-Clark at the Cottesloe: rev by Benedict, Brown, Clapp, Coveney, Edwardes, Foss, Gross, Hagerty, Kenny, Macaulay, Morley, Nightingale, Peter, P. Taylor.

2462 "Reviews of Productions." *LTR.* 1998; 18(8): 498-507. Lang.: Eng.
UK-England: London. 1998. ▪*The Caracal (De Caracal)* by Judith Herzberg, transl by Rina Vergano, dir by Astrid Hilne, and *Dossier: Ronald Akkerman* by Suzanne van Lohuizen, transl by Saskia A. Bosch, dir by Lucy Pittman-Wallace at the Gate: rev by Cavendish, Christopher, Curtis, Gardner, R.L. Parry. *Serious Money* by Caryl Churchill, dir by Patricia Doyle at the Man in the Moon: rev by Costa, Dark. *New Edna—The Spectacle* by Barry Humphries, music and lyrics by Humphries and Kit Hesketh-Harvey, dir by Alan Strachan at Theatre Royal, Haymarket: rev by Benedict, Buckley, Cavendish, Conrad, Coveney, Daoust, de Jongh, Foss, Gore-Langton, Gross, Hagerty, Kingston, Morley, Nathan, Peter, Shuttleworth, Spencer, P. Taylor, Wareham, Woddis.

2463 "Reviews of Productions." *LTR.* 1998; 18(8): 507-514. Lang.: Eng.
UK-England: London. 1998. ▪*Justice Luck* by Ian Bailey, dir by Alison Edgar, *The B3 Team* by Andrew McCaldon, dir by Nicolette Kay, *The Last Post* by Stephen Plaice, dir by Edgar, *Still Life* by David Read, dir by Toby Wilshire, *Ophelia Speaks* by Dilys Eaton, dir by Helena Uren, *Food* by Grant Watson, dir by Uren, *An American Hero Entertains* by Robert Cohen, dir by Maria Pattinson, *Signing* by Eamon McDonnell, dir by Ruth Fielding all at the Lyric Studio: rev by Marmion. *Perfumes de Tango* conceived and dir by Miguel Angel Zotto and Milena Plebs at the Peacock: rev by Dark, Dougill, Sacks. *The Real Inspector Hound* by Tom Stoppard and *Black Comedy* by Peter Shaffer dir by Greg Doran at the Comedy: rev by Benedict, Billington, Brown, Clapp, Coveney, Curtis, de Jongh, Edwardes, Gore-Langton, Gross, Hagerty, Kingston, Macaulay, Morley, Nathan, Peter, Spencer, P. Taylor.

2464 "Reviews of Productions." *LTR.* 1998; 18(8): 515-516. Lang.: Eng.
UK-England: London. 1998. ▪*The Daughter of the Poet* by Svein Einarsson, dir by Einarsson at the Pleasance: rev by Christopher, Godfrey-Faussett, Marlowe. *Crystal Clear* by Phil Young, dir by Brian Croucher at the Grace: rev by Godfrey-Faussett. *The Soul of the Rice Fields* conceived and performed by the Vietnamese Water Puppet Theatre at the Riverside: rev by Judah. *Glass* by Trevor B. Maynard, dir by Lynne Gagliano at the White Bear: rev by McPherson.

2465 "Reviews of Productions." *LTR.* 1998; 18(9): 535-541. Lang.: Eng.
UK-England: London. 1998. ▪*Shockheaded Peter* a junk opera conceived and created by Julian Blench, Anthony Cairns, Graeme Gilmour, Tamzin Griffin, and Jo Peacock, music by Adrian Hughes, Martyn Jacques, dir by Phelim McDermott and Julian Crouch at the Lyric Hammersmith: rev by Benedict, Butler, Coveney, Curtis, Edwardes, Gardner, Gore-Langton, Gross, Judah, Macaulay, Nathan, R.L. Parry, Spencer. *A Question of Mercy* by David Rabe, dir by Doug Hughes at the Bush: rev by Butler, de Jongh, Gardner, Gross, Kingston, Logan, Macaulay, Marlowe, Morley, Peter, Spencer, P. Taylor, Woddis. *Three Short Breaths* by Lucy Catherine, dir by Robin Dashwood at Croydon Warehouse: rev by Foss, Godfrey-Fausset.

DRAMA: —Performance/production

2466 "Reviews of Productions." *LTR.* 1998; 18(9): 542-554. Lang.: Eng.
UK-England: London. 1998. ■*Othello* by William Shakespeare, dir by Sam Mendes and *Enemy of the People (En Folkefiende)* by Henrik Ibsen, dir by Trevor Nunn for the Royal National respectively at the Lyttleton and Olivier: rev by Macaulay. *Lebensraum* by Israel Horovitz, dir by Michael Fry at the King's Head: rev by Christopher, Curtis, Hassell, Logan, Peter, Shuttleworth. *Show Boat* music by Jerome Kern, book and lyrics by Oscar Hammerstein II, dir by Harold Prince at the Prince Edward: rev by Billington, Brown, Butler, Clapp, Coveney, de Jongh, Edwardes, Gore-Langton, Gross, Hagerty, Kennedy, Macaulay, Morley, Nathan, Peter, N. Smith, Spencer, P. Taylor.

2467 "Reviews of Productions." *LTR.* 1998; 18(9): 556-568. Lang.: Eng.
UK-England: London. 1998. ■*Saturday Night Fever* adapt for stage by Nan Knighton, in collaboration with Arlene Phillips, Paul Nicholas, and Robert Stigwood, from Norman Wexler's screenplay based on a story by Nik Cohn, dir by Phillips at the London Palladium: rev by Billington, Brown, Butler, Clapp, Coveney, de Jongh, Gore-Langton, Gross, Hagerty, Landesman, Lister, Logan, Macaulay, Morley, Nathan, Nightingale, N. Smith, Spencer, P. Taylor. *Across the Bridge* by Anna Cropper and Dahlia Friedland, dir by Tom Sheperd at the New End: rev by R.L. Parry. *Cleansed* by Sarah Kane, dir by James Macdonald at the Royal Court Downstairs: rev by Benedict, Billington, Butler, Clapp, Coveney, de Jongh, Edwardes, Gore-Langton, Gross, Hagerty, Macaulay, Marlowe, Morley, Nathan, Nightingale, Peter, Sierz, Spencer.

2468 "Reviews of Productions." *LTR.* 1998; 18(14): 885-892. Lang.: Eng.
UK-England: London. 1998. ■*Herakles* by Euripides, transl by Kenneth McLeish, dir by Nick Philippou at the Gate: rev by Cavendish, Gardner, Hanks, Kingston, Macaulay, Marlowe, Marmion. *Have the Men Had Enough* by Julia Munrow from Margaret Forster's novel, dir by Munrow at the Old Red Lion: rev by Abdulla, Foss, Wardle. *Sugar Sugar* by Simon Bent, dir by Paul Miller at the Bush: rev by Billington, Cavendish, Clapp, Coveney, Gross, Hagerty, Hewison, Logan, Marmion, Nightingale, N. Smith, Spencer, Woddis.

2469 "Reviews of Productions." *LTR.* 1998; 18(14): 892-895. Lang.: Eng.
UK-England: London. 1998. ■*Immaterial Time* by Gari Jones, dir by Jones at the White Bear: rev by McPherson. *What You Get and What You Expect (Ce qui arrive et ce qu'on attend)* by Jean-Marie Besset, transl by Jeremy Sams, dir by Thierry Harcourt at Lyric Hammersmith: rev by Benedict, Billington, Butler, Clapp, Foss, Hewison, Kingston, Marmion, Morley, Nathan, Woddis. *The Footballer's Wife* by Sam Tilley, dir by Debbie Combe at the Riverside 3: rev by Hewison, Kingston.

2470 "Reviews of Productions." *LTR.* 1998; 18(14): 896-902. Lang.: Eng.
UK-England: London. 1998. ■*After Darwin* by Timberlake Wertenbaker, dir by Lindsay Posner at the Hampstead: rev by Billington, Butler, Cavendish, Clapp, Coveney, Gross, Hewison, Macaulay, Marlowe, Marmion, Morley, Nathan, Spencer, Stratton, Woddis. *Eyam* music by Andrew Peggie, book and lyrics by Stephen Clark, dir by Clive Paget at the Bridewell: rev by Abdulla, Cavendish, Clapp, Foss, Gardner, Thorncroft. *The Curse of Tittikhamon* by Michael Armstrong, songs by Danny Becker and Max Early, dir by Allen Stone: rev by Cavendish, North.

2471 "Reviews of Productions." *LTR.* 1998; 18(15): 959-962. Lang.: Eng.
UK-England: London. 1998. ■*2.5 Minute Ride* by Lisa Kron, dir by Kron at The Pit: rev by Hewison, Logan, McPherson, Nathan, Nightingale, P. Taylor, Thorncroft, Woddis. *Dead Meat* by James Hyland, dir by Sharon Crisp at the Etcetera: rev by Abdulla, Sierz. *Pidgin Macbeth* by William Shakespeare, adapt by Ken Campbell, dir by Campbell and Toby Sedgwick at the Cottesloe: rev by Kingston, Shuttleworth, N. Smith.

2472 "Reviews of Productions." *LTR.* 1998; 18(14): 903-911. Lang.: Eng.
UK-England: London. 1998. ■*Richard III* by William Shakespeare, dir by John Mowat at the Lyric Studio: rev by Hanks, Kingston, Logan, Marmion, McPherson. *Strange Cargo* by Mike Shepherd, dir by Shepherd and John Lee at National Theatre Open Air: rev by Nightingale, Saddler. *Doctor Doolittle* musical by Leslie Bricusse, dir by Steven Pimlott at Labatt's Apollo: rev by Bell, Benedict, Billington, Brown, Butler, Clapp, Coveney, Gore-Langton, Gross, Hagerty, Hassell, Hewison, Logan, Macaulay, S. Moore, Nightingale, Spencer, Woddis.

2473 "Reviews of Productions." *LTR.* 1998; 18(14): 923-927. Lang.: Eng.
UK-England: London. 1998. ■*Manes* by Pera Tatiñá, dir by Tatiñá for La Fura dels Baus at Three Mills Island: rev by Butler, Clapp, Gardner, Horan, Judah, Marmion, Palmer, Stratton. *The Whiteheaded Boy* by Lenox Robinson, dir by Gerard Stembridge at the Greenwich: rev by Gardner, Shuttleworth. *Jamaica House* by Paul Sirett, dir by Kerry Michael at Wickham House E1: rev by Costa, Gardner.

2474 "Reviews of Productions." *LTR.* 1998; 18(14): 911-919. Lang.: Eng.
UK-England: London. 1998. ■*Oklahoma!* by Rodgers and Hammerstein, dir by Trevor Nunn for the Royal National at the Olivier: rev by Benedict, Billington, Brown, Butler, Cavendish, Clapp, Coveney, de Jongh, Foss, Gore-Langton, Gross, Hagerty, Hewison, Lister, Macaulay, Morley, Nathan, Nightingale, Spencer, Woddis. *The Confidential Clerk* by T.S. Eliot, dir by Matthew Hiscock at the Prince: rev by Costa. *The Venetian Twins (I due gemelli Veneziani)* by Carlo Goldoni, adapt and dir by Keith Myers at Southwark Playhouse: rev by Curtis, Dowden, North.

2475 "Reviews of Productions." *LTR.* 1998; 18(14): 927-929. Lang.: Eng.
UK-England: London. 1998. ■*Black Books* by Dylan Moran, dir by Lissa Evans, *Members Only* by Amanda Swift, dir by Jeremy Raison, *Off the Road* by Dan Gooch, dir by Roxana Silbert, *Sisters* by Angie le Mar, dir by Treva Etienne, *All Talk* by Paul McKenzie, dir by Paulette Randall, *Ice Station H.I.P.P.O.* by Adrian Bailey and Jamie Facer, dir by Silbert, *Lara Come Home* by Jeremy Front, dir by Raison, *Moonstompers* by Seamus Hilley, dir by Matthew Francis, and *Arrivederci Barnsley* by Tim Fountain, dir by Gemma Bodinetz all at the Riverside: rev by McPherson, Woddis.

2476 "Reviews of Productions." *LTR.* 1998; 18(15): 949-956. Lang.: Eng.
UK-England: London. 1998. ■*The Man Who Came to Dinner* by Moss Hart and George S. Kaufman, dir by James Burrows for Steppenwolf at the Barbican: rev by Benedict, Billington, Butler, Clapp, Coveney, de Jongh, Hagerty, Macaulay, Marmion, Morley, Nathan, Nightingale, N. Smith, Spencer, Woddis. *The Web* and *The Movie Man* by Eugene O'Neill, dir by Neil Sheffield and Nick Cawdron at Pentameters: rev by Hanks. *Closer Than Ever* musical by Richard Maltby, Jr., and David Shire, dir by Matthew White at the Jermyn Street: rev by Abdulla, Billington, Coveney, Curtis, Darvell, Gross, Hagerty, Hewison, Nathan, Nightingale, Thorncroft. *Judas Worm* by Justin Chubb, dir by Dominic Knutton at the Finborough: rev by Costa.

2477 "Reviews of Productions." *LTR.* 1998; 18(15): 963-968. Lang.: Eng.
UK-England: London. 1998. ■*Otra Tempestad (Another Tempest)* by Racquel Carrió, dir by Flora Lauten at Shakespeare's Globe: rev by Curtis, Kingston, Shuttleworth, Spencer, P. Taylor. *Alice* by Noël Grieg, from Lewis Carroll, dir by Geoff Bullen and Jenny Sealey at the Drill Hall: rev by Kingston. *Room at the Top* by Andrew Taylor, from John Braine's novel, dir by Roy Marsden at the King's Head: rev by Cavendish, Coveney, de Jongh, Foss, Godfrey-Faussett, Gross, Hagerty, Hewison, Nathan, Nightingale. *Funeral Games* by Joe Orton, dir by Kim Bailey at the Man in the Moon: rev by Marlowe.

2478 "Reviews of Productions." *LTR.* 1998; 18(15): 969-971. Lang.: Eng.
UK-England: London. 1998. ■*Ubu Kunst* by Alfred Jarry, transl and adapt by Luis Alberto Soto, with additional text by Gary Stevens, dir by Dan Jemmett at Young Vic Studio: rev by Costa, Foss, Gardner, Judah. *Foxhole* by D.A. Wallis, dir by Ed Woodall at Old Red Lion: rev by Cavendish, Curtis, Edwardes, Gross, Hewison, Nightingale. *Litter* by Alan Fentiman, dir by Suzanne Bell at White Bear: rev by Abdulla, McPherson.

2479 "Reviews of Productions." *LTR.* 1998; 18(16): 997-1005. Lang.: Eng.

DRAMA: —Performance/production

UK-England: London. 1998. ■*No Way to Treat a Lady* musical by Douglas J. Cohen, dir by Neil Marcus at the Arts: rev by Brown, Clapp, Coveney, Darvell, de Jongh, Edwardes, Gross, Hagerty, Hemming, Morley, Nathan, Nightingale, Peter, Russell, P. Taylor, Walsh. *My Mother Was an Alien—Is That Why I'm Gay?* by Nigel Fairs, dir by Fairs at Finborough: rev by Abdulla, McPherson. *May Day New* by Fouad Zloof and Eva Lyn, dir by Hugh Beardsmore-Billings at New End: rev by Cavendish, Christopher, Hemming, Nathan, Sierz.

2480 "Reviews of Productions." *LTR*. 1998; 18(15): 972-985. Lang.: Eng.

UK-England: London. 1998. ■*Closet Land* by Radha Bharadwaj, dir by Michael Cowley at Grace: rev by Christopher. *The Song of Deborah* by Deborah Freeman, dir by Terry John Bates at Cockpit: rev by Carlowe, Marmion. *Gentlemen Prefer Blondes* music by Jule Styne, lyrics by Leo Robin, book by Anita Loos and Joseph Fields, dir by Ian Talbot at Open Air: rev by Bassett, Billington, Brown, Butter, Clapp, Coveney, Darvell, de Jongh, Godfrey-Faussett, Gore-Langton, Gross, Hagerty, Hewison, Nathan, Nightingale, Russell, Shuttleworth, P. Taylor. *Blood Brothers* by Willy Russell, dir by Bob Tomson at the Phoenix: rev by Bassett, Brown, Coveney, Gross, Hagerty, Logan, Marlowe, Morley, Nightingale, Russell, P. Taylor.

2481 "Reviews of Productions." *LTR*. 1998; 18(16): 1005-1007. Lang.: Eng.

UK-England: London. 1998. ■*The Trembling Game* by Robert Hamilton, dir by Trevor Rawlins at Etcetera: rev by Foss, North. *The Clowness (Die Clownin)* by Gerlind Reinshagen, dir by Sabine Bauer at the Gate: rev by Bassett, Christopher, Logan, Marlowe, Peter. *The Country Wife* by William Wycherley, dir by Michael Cabot at Upstairs at the Gatehouse: rev by Godfrey-Faussett, P. Taylor.

2482 "Reviews of Productions." *LTR*. 1998; 18(16): 1008-1014. Lang.: Eng.

UK-England: London. 1998. ■*Happy Savages* by Ryan Craig dir by David Evans Rees at Lyric Studio: rev by Billington, Godfrey-Faussett, Macaulay, McPherson, Nathan, Nightingale, Peter, P. Taylor. *Loot* by Joe Orton, dir by David Frindley at Vaudeville: rev by Butler, Christopher, Coveney, de Jongh, Gross, Hanks, Logan, Marlowe, Morley, Nathan, Peter, P. Taylor. *Oh, What a Lovely War!* by Joan Littlewood and Charles Chilton, dir by Fiona Laird for the Royal National at the Round House: rev by Curtis, Darvell, Kingston, Macaulay, Morley.

2483 "Reviews of Productions." *LTR*. 1998; 18(16): 1047-1049. Lang.: Eng.

UK-England: London. 1998. ■*Juicy Bits* by Kay Adshead, dir by Sarah Davey at Lyric Hammersmith: rev by Christopher, Curtis, Foss, Godfrey-Faussett, Sierz. *The Best of Times: The Showtunes of Jerry Herman*, conceived by Paul Gilger, dir by Bill Starr at the Bridewell: rev by Abdulla, Darvell, Hagerty, Morley. *There's a J in Majorca* by Jane Hannah, dir by Hannah at Canal Cafe: rev by Costa. *Sea Urchins* by Aodhan Madden, dir by Joel Froomkin at the Grace: rev by Christopher, Freedman, Marmion.

2484 "Reviews of Productions." *LTR*. 1998; 18(18): 1125-1128. Lang.: Eng.

UK-England: London. 1998. ■*Hamlet* by Shakespeare, transl by Kazuko Matsuoka, dir by Yukio Ninagawa at the Barbican: rev by Billington, Butler, de Jongh, Macaulay, Nightingale, Spencer, P. Taylor, Woddis. *Biloxi Blues* by Neil Simon, dir by Edward Wilson at Arts: rev by Benedict, Costa. *Dancing at Lughnasa* by Brian Friel, dir by Wilson at Arts: rev by Christopher.

2485 "Reviews of Productions." *LTR*. 1998; 18(16): 1050-1055. Lang.: Eng.

UK-England. 1998. ■*Twelfth Night* by Shakespeare, dir by Gregory Thompson at Lincoln's Inn: rev by Godfrey-Faussett, Woddis. *Fando and Lis* by Fernando Arrabal, transl by Barbara Wright, dir by Thomas Baker at Courtyard: rev by Costa, Foss. *Chimes at Midnight* adapt from Shakespeare's histories by Orson Welles, dir by Patrick Garland at Chichester Festival: rev by Billington, Butler, Coveney, Gilbert, Gross, Hagerty, Kingston, Morley, Nathan, Peter, Spencer, P. Taylor, Thorncroft.

2486 "Reviews of Productions." *LTR*. 1998; 18(17): 1073-1079. Lang.: Eng.

UK-England: London. 1998. ■*The Honest Whore* by Thomas Dekker and Thomas Middleton, dir by Jack Shepherd at Shakespeare's Globe: rev by Costa, Coveney, Curtis, Gross, Hemming, Kellaway, Kingston, Marlowe, Nathan, Spencer. *A Mad World, My Masters* by Middleton, dir by Sue Lefton at Shakespeare's Globe: rev by Butler, Coveney, de Jongh, Godfrey-Faussett, Gross, Hemming, Kellaway, Kingston, Marlowe, Nathan. *The Power of Love* by Sebastian Michael, dir by Michael Cabot at Southwark Playhouse: rev by North.

2487 "Reviews of Productions." *LTR*. 1998; 18(17): 1080-1082. Lang.: Eng.

UK-England: London. 1998. ■*The African Company Presents Richard III* by Carlyle Brown, dir by Courtney Helper at Riverside: rev by Christopher, Curtis, Marmion, Nathan, R.L. Parry. *The Trial* by Anthony Booth, dir by Richard Gallagher at Man in the Moon: rev by Freedman, North. *Les Mots d'Amour* songs of Edith Piaf performed by Caroline Nin, dir by Julia Lara at King's Head: rev by Abdulla, Christopher, Foss, Gross, Nathan.

2488 "Reviews of Productions." *LTR*. 1998; 18(17): 1086-1097. Lang.: Eng.

UK-England: London. 1998. ■*Life Is a Dream (La vida es sueño)* by Pedro Calderón de la Barca, transl by John Clifford, dir by Calixto Bieito at the Royal Lyceum: rev by Billington, Clapp, Coveney, de Jongh, Fisher, Gross, Macaulay, McMillan, Nightingale, Peter, Spencer, P. Taylor. *The Robbers (Die Räuber)* by Friedrich Schiller, transl by Robert David MacDonald, adapt and dir by Philip Prowse at King's Head: rev by Bruce, Butler, Clapp, Coveney, de Jongh, Gross, Macaulay, McMillan, Nightingale, Peter, Spencer, P. Taylor. *Die Änlichen (Lookalikes)* by Botho Strauss, dir by Peter Stein at King's Head: rev by Billington, Clapp, Cooper, Curtis, Fisher, Higgins, Kingston, Macaulay, McMillan, Peter, Spencer.

2489 "Reviews of Productions." *LTR*. 1998; 18(17): 1107-1117. Lang.: Eng.

UK-England. 1998. ■*Tarry Flynn* adapt by Conall Morrison from Patrick Kavanaugh's novel, dir by Morrison for the Abbey Theatre at the Lyttelton: rev by Billington, Curtis, Gilbert, Hanks, Kellaway, Kingston, Logan, McPherson, Morley, Woddis. *Every Day Life in the Sixties* by Camden McDonald, dir by McDonald at the Lion and Unicorn: rev by Freedman. *Gloomy Sunday (Szomorú vasárnap)* by Péter Müller, transl by Andrew Merkle, dir by Stephen Wisker at Jermyn Street: rev by C. Davis, Foss, Hagerty, Marmion, Morley, Nathan. *Song of Singapore* book by Allan Katz, music and lyrics by Erik Frandsen, Michael Garin, Robert Hipkens, and Paula Lockheart, dir by Roger Redfarn at the Minerva, Chichester: rev by Curtis, Gilbert, Gross, Hagerty, Kingston, Morley, O'Connor Morse, Nathan, Spencer, P. Taylor, Thorncroft.

2490 "Reviews of Productions." *LTR*. 1998; 18(18): 1131-1134. Lang.: Eng.

UK-England: London. 1998. ■*Oedipus the King (Oidípous Týrannos)* by Sophocles, transl by Don Taylor, dir by William Kerley at Bloomsbury: rev by Cavendish, Freedman, Logan, North. *A Wife Without a Smile* by Arthur Wing Pinero, dir by Dominic Hill at Orange Tree: rev by Billington, Curtis, Foss, Logan, Macaulay, Nightingale, Peter. *The Girls' Consent (El sí de las niñas)* by Leandro Fernández de Moratín, transl by Sarah Lawson, dir by Kate Bannister and *The Pilgrim (Frei Luís de Sousa)* by Almeida Garrett, transl by Nicholas Round, dir by Bruce Jamieson at the Prince: rev by Billington, North.

2491 "Reviews of Productions." *LTR*. 1998; 18(18): 1135-1145. Lang.: Eng.

UK-England: London. 1998. ■*The Play About the Baby* by Edward Albee, dir by Howard Davies at the Almeida: rev by Billington, Brown, Butler, Clapp, de Jongh, Edwardes, Gilbert, Gross, Hagerty, Hewison, Macaulay, Marlowe, Morley, Nathan, Nightingale, Spencer, P. Taylor, Usher, Woddis. *Blood and Iron* by Richard Carter, dir by Simon Dunmore at the Tristan Bates: rev by Dowden, Logan. *Full Gallop* by Mark Hampton and Mary Louise Wilson, dir by Nicholas Martin at the Hampstead: rev by Benedict, Butler, Clapp, Curtis, Edwardes, Gardner, Gross, Macaulay, Marlowe, Morley, Nathan, Nightingale, Usher, Woddis. *The Odd Couple* by Neil Simon, dir by Joel Froomkin and *The Cemetery Club* by Ivan Menchell, dir by Lisa Giglio both at the Grace: rev by Cavendish, Costa.

2492 "Reviews of Productions." *LTR*. 1998; 18(18): 1146-1149. Lang.: Eng.

DRAMA: —Performance/production

UK-England: London. 1998. ▪*The Lady Boys of Bangkok*, Thai Drag singers dir by Gorsem Sarigakham at the Queen's: rev by Billington, Brennan, Darvell, de Jongh, Dromgoole, Hagerty, Kingston, Marmion, Nathan, Thorncroft. *Personals* book and lyrics by David Crane, Seth Friedman, Marta Kauffman, music by William K. Dresken, Joel Phillip Friedman, Seth Friedman, Alan Menken, Stephen Schwartz, Michael Skloff, dir by Dion McHugh at the New End: rev by Abdulla, Cavendish, Freedman, Nathan, *Times*. *Choirboys* by Declan Croghan, dir by Izzy Mant at the Old Red Lion: rev by Foss, Nightingale, Stratton.

2493 "Reviews of Productions." *LTR*. 1998; 18(18): 1150-1154, 1180. Lang.: Eng.

UK-England: London. 1998. ▪*Crime and Punishment* adapt by Rodney Ackland from Dostojévskij's novel, dir by Phil Willmott at the Finborough: rev by Cavendish, Christopher, Costa, McPherson. *Top Dogs* by Urs Widmer dir by Patricia Benecke at the Truman Building El: rev by Freedman, Stratton. *Crave* by Sarah Kane, dir by Vicky Featherstone at the Royal Court Upstairs: rev by Billington, Brown, Cavendish, Clapp, Coveney, de Jongh, Fisher, Kingston, Macaulay, Marlowe, Nightingale, Peter, Sierz, Stratton, P. Taylor, Wardle.

2494 "Reviews of Productions." *LTR*. 1998; 18(18): 1163-1170. Lang.: Eng.

UK-England: London. 1998. ▪*Groovy Times* by Jonathan Kaufman, dir by Kaufman at the Tabard: rev by Costa, Usher. *Phèdre* by Jean Racine, new version by Ted Hughes, dir by Jonathan Kent at the Albery: rev by Billington, Brown, Butler, Clapp, de Jongh, Edwardes, Gore-Langton, Hagerty, Macaulay, Morley, Nathan, Nightingale, Peter, Sierz, Spencer, P. Taylor, Usher, Wardle, Woddis. *Wasted* by Geraint Cardy, dir by Caroline Fisher at the Etcetera: rev by Cavendish, Freedman.

2495 "Reviews of Productions." *LTR*. 1998; 18(18): 1155-1163. Lang.: Eng.

UK-England: London. 1998. ▪*Via Dolorosa* by David Hare, dir by Stephen Daldry at Royal Court Downstairs: rev by Billington, Black, Brown, Butler, Clapp, de Jongh, Gore-Langton, Hagerty, Morley, Nathan, Nightingale, Peter, N. Smith, Spencer, Stratton, P. Taylor, Usher, Wardle, Woddis. *Miss Julie (Fröken Julie)* by August Strindberg, dir by Jonathan Lovett at the Man in the Moon: rev by McPherson. *Love Upon the Throne* by Patrick Barlow, with additional material by Martin Duncan and John Ramm, dir by Duncan at the Bush: rev by Billington, Brown, Butler, Clapp, Coveney, Edwardes, Fisher, Gore-Langton, Kingston, Marlowe, Morley, Nightingale, Peter, Rubnikowicz, Shuttleworth, Spencer.

2496 "Reviews of Productions." *LTR*. 1998; 18(11): 681-687. Lang.: Eng.

UK-England: London. 1998. ▪*Measure for Measure* by William Shakespeare, dir by Stéphane Braunschweig at the Barbican: rev by Kingston, Marmion, Murray. *Twelfth Night* by Shakespeare, dir by Tim Supple at the Young Vic: rev by Billington, Butler, Cavendish, Darvell, de Jongh, Gross, Macauley, Nightingale, Peter, Spencer. *As You Like It* by Shakespeare, dir by Lucy Bailey at Shakespeare's Globe: rev by Butler, Cavendish, Curtis, Darvell, Hagerty, Kellaway, Nathan, Stratton, Usher, Woddis.

2497 "Reviews of Productions." *LTR*. 1998; 18(18): 1171-1177. Lang.: Eng.

UK-England. 1998. ▪*Cool Heat Urban Beat* conceived and dir by Jeremy Alliger at the Peacock: rev by Bishop, Brennan, Cartwright, Craine, Crisp, Constanti, Dougill, Dromgoole, Foss, Hagerty. *Saul* by Brian Mitchell, based on a work by Vittorio Alfieri, dir by Richard Gofton at Southwark Playhouse: rev by Buscovic, Cavendish, McPherson. *Dead Funny* by Terry Johnson, dir by Caroline Quentin at the Palace (Watford): rev by Curtis, Foss, Gardner, Spencer.

2498 "Reviews of Productions." *LTR*. 1998; 18(11): 687-696. Lang.: Eng.

UK-England: London. 1998. ▪*The Merchant of Venice* by William Shakespeare, dir by Richard Olivier at Shakespeare's Globe: rev by Billington, Clapp, de Jongh, Gross, Kingston, Macaulay, Marmion, Nathan, Peter, N. Smith, Spencer, Usher, Woddis. *A Midsummer Night's Dream* by Shakespeare, dir by Rachel Kavanaugh at the Open Air: rev by Costa, Coveney, Foss, Hemming, Nightingale, Peter. *Bitter Sauce* by Eric Bogosian, *Hydraulics Phat Like Mean*, by Ntozake Shange, *Terminating, or Lass Meine Schmertzen Nicht Verloren Sein, or Ambivalence* by Tony Kushner, *140* by Marsha Norman, *Painting You* by William Finn, *Waiting for Philip Glass* by Wendy Wasserstein, and *The General of Hot Desire*, by John Guare, all dir by Mark Lamos at the Pit: rev by Benedict, Butler, Curtis, Gross, Hewison, Morley, Murray, Nightingale, Spencer, Stratton, Woddis.

2499 "Reviews of Productions." *LTR*. 1998; 18(11): 697-700. Lang.: Eng.

UK-England: London. 1998. ▪*The Betrayal of Nora Blake* musical by John Meyer, dir by Nicholas Grace at the Jermyn Street: rev by Davis, Foss, Godfrey-Faussett, Gross, Hagerty, Morley. *The Shoemaker's Wondrous Wife (La zapatera prodigiosa)* and *How Don Perlimplin Adored Belisa (Amor de don Perlimplín con Belisa en su jardín)* by Federico García Lorca, dir by Andrew Pratt at BAC Main: rev by Cavendish, Logan, R.L. Parry, Shuttleworth. *Pork Bellies* by Molly Fogarty, dir by Rosamunde Hutt at Croydon Warehouse: rev by Foss, Kingston, Stratton.

2500 "Reviews of Productions." *LTR*. 1998; 18(11): 700-705. Lang.: Eng.

UK-England: London. 1998. ▪*Take Away* by Stephen Clark, dir by Stephen Knight at the Lyric Studio: rev by Cavendish, Edwardes, Kingston, McPherson. *Seven Sacraments* a dramatic oratorio by Nicholas Bloomfield, text by Neil Bartlett, dir by Nicholas Kok at the Southwark Cathedral: rev by Christiansen, J. Gilbert, Logan, Morrison. *The Rink* music by John Kander, lyrics by Fred Ebb, book by Terrence McNally, dir by John Gardyne at the Orange Tree: rev by Benedict, Billington, Butler, Cavendish, Hagerty, Morley, N. Smith, Spencer.

2501 "Reviews of Productions." *LTR*. 1998; 18(11): 705-713. Lang.: Eng.

UK-England: London. 1998. ▪*Pippin*, musical by Stephen Schwartz, book by Roger O. Hirson, dir by Mitch Sebastian at the Bridewell: rev by Christopher, Costa, Curtis, Darvell, Hemming. *Copenhagen* by Michael Frayn, dir by Michael Blakemore for the Royal National at the Cottesloe: rev by Benedict, Brown, Butter, Coveney, de Jongh, Edwardes, Gore-Langton, Gross, Hassell, Kellaway, Macaulay, Morley, Nathan, Nightingale, Peter, Sierz, Spencer. *Attar's Conference of the Birds* conceived by Khayaal Theatre Company from the writings of Faridu'd-Din Attar, dir by Lugman Ali at the Tabernacle: rev by Abdulla, Judah.

2502 "Reviews of Productions." *LTR*. 1998; 18(11): 714-719. Lang.: Eng.

UK-England: London. 1998. ▪*Love You, Too* by Doug Lucie, dir by Mike Bradwell at the Bush: rev by Billington, Butler, Cavendish, Clapp, de Jongh, Edwardes, Gross, Kingston, Marlowe, Peter, Thorncroft, Usher, Woddis. *Ooh Ah Showah Khan* by Clifford Oliver, dir by Carole Pluckrose at the Watermans and Pleasance: rev by Christopher. *Billy Liar* by Keith Waterhouse and Willis Hall, dir by Alex Walker at the King's Head: rev by Christopher, Curtis, Foss, Hagerty, Marmion, Usher, Wright. *Talk About the Passion* by Graham Farrow, dir by Pippa Dowse at the Bird's Nest: rev by Godfrey-Faussett.

2503 "Reviews of Productions." *LTR*. 1998; 18(19): 1191-1199. Lang.: Eng.

UK-England: London. 1998. ▪*Peony Pavilion (Mudan ting)* by Tang Xianzu, transl by Cyril Burch, music by Tan Dun, dir by Peter Sellars at the Barbican: rev by Clements, Gilbert, Kimberley, Lively, Logan, Macaulay, Maddocks, Reed, Spencer, Sutcliffe, P. Taylor, Usher, Woddis. *Jinx* by Matt Parker, dir by Piers Clifton at the Orange Tree Room: rev by Godfrey-Faussett. *Handbag* by Mark Ravenhill, dir by Nick Philippou at the Lyric Studio: rev by Billington, Clapp, Gross, Kingston, Lubbock, Macaulay, Marlowe, Marmion, Peter, Sierz, Stratton, P. Taylor, Woddis. *Skin Tight* by Gary Henderson, dir by Cathy Downes at the New End: rev by Cooper, Sierz.

2504 "Reviews of Productions." *LTR*. 1998; 18(11): 720-729. Lang.: Eng.

UK-England. 1998. ▪*The Doctor's Dilemma* by G.B. Shaw, dir by Michael Grandage at the Almeida: rev by Billington, Butler, Clapp, de Jongh, Edwardes, Gross, Macaulay, Nightingale, Peter, Spencer, Usher, Woddis. *Ursula: Fear of the Estuary* by Howard Barker, dir by Barker at the Riverside 2: rev by Gardner, Hewison, Kingston. *Snakes and Ladders* by Julian Maynard Smith and Susannah Hart, dir by Maynard Smith at the Fire Station: rev by Shuttleworth. *Saturday, Sunday... and Monday (Sabato, domenica, lunedì)* by Eduardo De Filippo, transl by Jeremy Sams, dir by Jude Kelly at the Chichester Festival: rev by Benedict, Billington, Brown, Coveney, de Jongh, Gross, Hagerty, Kellaway, Macaulay, Nathan, Nightingale, Peter, Spencer, Woddis.

2505 "Reviews of Productions." *LTR.* 1998; 18(19): 1200-1210. Lang.: Eng.

UK-England: London. 1998. ■*Sperm Wars* by David Lewis, dir by Sam Walters at the Orange Tree: rev by Billington, Cavendish, Curtis, Monahan, Nightingale, Schamus, Shuttleworth, Sierz. *Alarms and Excursions* by Michael Frayn, dir by Michael Blakemore at the Gielgud: rev by Brown, Clapp, Coveney, Curtis, Edwardes, Gardner, Gore-Langton, Gross, Hanks, Hagerty, Marlowe, Morley, Nathan, Nightingale, Peter, Spencer. *The Love of a Good Man* by Howard Barker, dir by Sid Golder at the Onion Shed SW9: rev by Costa.

2506 "Reviews of Productions." *LTR.* 1998; 18(19): 1211-1216. Lang.: Eng.

UK-England: London. 1998. ■*Anna Karenina* by Helen Edmundson, from Tolstoj's novel, dir by Nancy Meckler at Lyric Hammersmith: rev by Bassett, Cavendish, Christopher, Edwardes, Macaulay, Marmion, Montgomery, R.L. Parry. *The Hold* by Peter Simmonds, *Lost in Space* by Diana Flint, *Babysitters* by Andy Gough, *The Changing of the Guard* by Sophia Kingshill, *Sneer* by Chris Lee, *31 Days* by Gill Foreman, *The Redeemer* by Declan Croghan, all dir by Mervyn Millar at the Finborough: rev by Godfrey-Faussett, Schamus. *Miss Evers' Boys* by David Feldshuh, dir by Martin L. Platt at The Pit: rev by Billington, Costa, Curtis, Foss, Nathan, Nightingale, Peter, Shuttleworth, Spencer, P. Taylor, Woddis.

2507 "Reviews of Productions." *LTR.* 1998; 18(19): 1217-1222. Lang.: Eng.

UK-England: London. 1998. ■*Our Country's Good* by Timberlake Wertenbaker, dir by Max Stafford-Clark at the Young Vic: rev by Benedict, Billington, Clapp, Coveney, Curtis, Hanks, Logan, Lubbock, Nathan, Nightingale, Peter, N. Smith, Woddis. *The Lights Twinkle Sometimes* by Paul Prescott, dir by Mark Craven at the Jermyn Street: rev by Shabi. *The Contrast* by Royall Tyler, dir by Melanie Wynyard at the Cochrane: rev by Cavendish, Christopher, Foss, Logan. *The Master and Margarita (Master i Margarita)* by Bulgakov, adapt. by Xavier Leret, dir by Leret at Croydon Warehouse: rev by Brennan, Kingston, Logan, Shabi.

2508 "Reviews of Productions." *LTR.* 1998; 18(19): 1223-1230. Lang.: Eng.

UK-England: London. 1998. ■*Cleo, Camping, Emmanuelle and Dick* by Terry Johnson, dir by Johnson for the Royal National at the Lyttleton: rev by Billington, Brown, Butler, Cavendish, Clapp, Coveney, de Jongh, Edwardes, Gore-Langton, Gross, Peter, Spencer, Woddis. *It's Jackie* by Jackie Clune, dir by Clune at the Drill Hall: rev by Abdulla, Darvell. *Lee Evans*, solo show at the Apollo: rev by Bassett, Bell, Coveney, Daoust, Davis, Hagerty, Rampton, Wright.

2509 "Reviews of Productions." *LTR.* 1998; 18(19): 1231-1242. Lang.: Eng.

UK-England: London. 1998. ■*The Blue Room* by David Hare, dir by Sam Mendes at Donmar Warehouse: rev by Benedict, Billington, Brown, Butler, Clapp, Coveney, de Jongh, Edwardes, Gore-Langton, Gross, Hagerty, Hemming, Morley, Nathan, Nightingale, Peter, N. Smith, Spencer, Tookey, Watson, Woddis. *Une Tempête (A Tempest)* by Aimé Césaire, transl by Philip Crispin, dir by Mick Gordon at the Gate: rev by Billington, Christopher, Marlowe, Marmion, P. Taylor. *Starstruck* by Roy Williams, dir by Indhu Rubasingham at the Tricycle: rev by Bassett, Cavendish, Clapp, Gardner, Gross, Marmion, Morley, Nathan, Nightingale, Shabi, Woddis.

2510 "Reviews of Productions." *LTR.* 1998; 18(19): 1242, 1252-1258. Lang.: Eng.

UK-England. 1998. ■*Under the Influence* conceived and dir by Kate Champion at the Riverside: rev by Cavendish, Dromgoole, McPherson, Nathan. *Katherine Howard* by William Nicholson, dir by Robin Lefevre at the Chichester Festival: rev by Bassett, Brown, Coveney, Curtis, Gardner, Gore-Langton, Gross, Hewison, Macaulay, Nathan, Nightingale. *The Glass Menagerie* by Tennessee Williams, dir by Jacob Murray at the Minerva: rev by Bassett, Christopher, Gardner, Peter, Thorncroft.

2511 "Reviews of Productions." *LTR.* 1998; 18(20): 1275-1277. Lang.: Eng.

UK-England: London. 1998. ■*Play* by Beckett, dir by Joe Harmston and *The Ritual* by Duma Ndlovu, dir by Ndlovu at the Riverside: rev by Christopher, Marmion, McPherson, Stratton. *A Thousand Days* by Sara Clifford, dir by Lucy Pittman-Wallace at the Old Red Lion: rev by Cavendish, Curtis, Godfrey-Faussett, Shabi. *Hymn to Love* by Steve Trafford, Annie Castledine, and Elizabeth Mansfield, dir by Castledine at the Drill Hall: rev by Billington, Darvell, Morley, Shuttleworth.

2512 "Reviews of Productions." *LTR.* 1998; 18(19): 1271-1274. Lang.: Eng.

UK-England: London. 1998. ■*(OR)* created by Shiro Takatani, Toru Koyamada, and Takayuki Fujimoto for Dumb Type at the Barbican: rev by Dromgoole, Gilbert, Meisner. *The Last Flapper* by William Luce, from the writings of Zelda Fitzgerald, dir by Derek Hewitson at the Man in the Moon: rev by McPherson, Morley, North. *Party* by David Dillon, dir by Andrew Neil at the Arts: rev by Christopher, Costa, de Jongh, Foss, Hemming. *The Killing Floor* adapt from Euripides, Aeschylus, Sophocles, and Seneca by Douglas Pye, Matthew Jay Lewis, John White, and Gareth Corke, dir by Corke at the Bridewell: rev by North, R.L. Parry.

2513 "Reviews of Productions." *LTR.* 1998; 18(20): 1278-1290. Lang.: Eng.

UK-England: London. 1998. ■*Steve Coogan: The Man Who Thinks He's It* by Coogan, Henry Normal, Peter Baynham, Armando Ianucci, Julia Davis, and Simon Pegg, dir by Geoff Posner and David Tyler at the Lyceum: rev by Bassett, Bell, Coveney, Davis, Dessau, Gross, Hagerty, Hawkins, Macaulay, Marlowe, Rampton, S. Raylor. *Mum* by Ronnie Barker, dir by Dan Crawford at the King's Head: rev by Billington, Butler, Coveney, Curtis, Foss, Hagerty, Hemming, Kellaway, Marmion, Morley, Nathan, Nightingale, Peter, Spencer, P. Taylor, Woddis. *The Dead Monkey* by Nick Darke, dir by Brennan Street at Whitehall: rev by Benedict, Christopher, Darvell, de Jongh, Gardner, Gore-Langton, Hewison, Kellaway, Stratton, Thorncroft.

2514 "Reviews of Productions." *LTR.* 1998; 18(20): 1290-1301. Lang.: Eng.

UK-England: London. 1998. ■*Summer (L'été)* by Romain Weingarten, transl by Sean McSweeney, dir by McSweeney at Canal Cafe: rev by Gibbs. *Annie* book by Thomas Meehan, music by Charles Strouse, lyrics by Martin Charnin, dir by Charnin at Victoria Palace: rev by Benedict, Brown, Coveney, Darvell, de Jongh, Gardner, Gore-Langton, Gross, Hagerty, Logan, Morley, Nathan, Nightingale, Peter, Spencer, Woddis. *Haroun and the Sea of Stories* adapt by Tim Supple and David Tushingham from the book by Salman Rushdie, dir by Supple for the Royal National at the Cottesloe: rev by Billington, Brown, Butler, de Jongh, Edwardes, Gross, Kellaway, Macaulay, Morley, Nathan, Nightingale, Peter, Spencer, P. Taylor, Woddis.

2515 "Reviews of Productions." *LTR.* 1998; 18(19): 1301-1306. Lang.: Eng.

UK-England: London. 1998. ■*Trickster's Payback* by Martin Glynn, music and lyrics by Felix Cross, dir by Josette Bushell-Mingo at Croydon Warehouse: rev by McPherson, Stratton. *Thieves Like Us* by Biyi Bandele, dir by Mehmet Ergen at Southwark Playhouse: rev by Cavendish, Christopher, Curtis, Gardner. *Yard* by Kaite O'Reilly, dir by Julie-Anne Robinson at the Bush: rev by Bassett, Butler, Coveney, Godfrey-Faussett, Hewison, Kingston, R.L. Parry, P. Taylor. *A Huey P Newton Story* written and dir by Roger Guenveur Smith at The Pit: rev by Cartwright, Curtis, Foss, Hewison, Kingston, Morley, Stratton, Woddis.

2516 "Reviews of Productions." *LTR.* 1998; 18(20): 1307-1315. Lang.: Eng.

UK-England: London. 1998. ■*City of Angels* music by Cy Coleman, lyrics by David Zippel, book by Larry Gelbart, dir by Eileen Gourlay at Upstairs at the Landor: rev by Costa, Marlowe. *West Side Story* book by Arthur Laurents, music by Leonard Bernstein, lyrics by Sondheim, Jerome Robbins, dir and choreography reproduced by Alan Johnson at the Prince Edward: rev by Billington, Brown, Butler, Clapp, Coveney, de Jongh, Edwardes, Gore-Langton, Gross, Hagerty, Hewison, Macaulay, Marlowe, Morley, Nathan, Nightingale, Russell, Spencer, P. Taylor. *The Malcontent* by John Marston, dir by Dominic Druce at Pentameters: rev by Godfrey-Faussett. *A Minute of Silence* by Harris W. Freedman, dir by Freedman at Upstairs at the Gatehouse: rev by Buscovic, Cavendish.

2517 "Reviews of Productions." *LTR.* 1998; 18(20): 1315-1317. Lang.: Eng.

DRAMA: —Performance/production

UK-England: London. 1998. ▪*What? So What?, Suffer Little Children,* and *According to Mark* by Chris Savage King and Caroline Burns Cook, dir by James Martin Charlton at the Etcetera: rev by Godfrey-Faussett. *The Killer Soprano*, Rosemary Ashe in cabaret, dir by Kenny Oldfield at the Grace: rev by Christopher, Darvell. *Conversations with My Agent* by Gary Parker, dir by Gordon Anderson at the Pleasance: *L'Innocente (The Innocent One)* adapt by Claudio Macor from Gabriele D'Annunzio's novel, dir by Macor at the Baron's Court: rev by Cavendish, Costa.

2518 "Reviews of Productions." *LTR.* 1998; 18(21): 1341-1351. Lang.: Eng.
UK-England: London. 1998. ▪*Filumena Marturano* by Eduardo De Filippo, transl by Timberlake Wertenbaker, dir by Peter Hall at the Piccadilly: rev by Brown, Clapp, Coveney, de Jongh, Edwardes, Gore-Langton, Gross, Hagerty, Macaulay, Marlowe, Morley, Nathan, Peter, Spencer, P. Taylor, Walsh, Woddis. *Pidgin Macbeth* by William Shakespeare, adapt by Ken Cambell, dir by Ken and Daisy Campbell at the Piccadilly: rev by Coveney, Curtis, Edwardes, Gardner, Hemming, Spencer, Woddis. *Jasper Carrott in Concert* comic solo by Carrott at Theatre Royal, Haymarket: rev by Games, Hemming, Spencer.

2519 "Reviews of Productions." *LTR.* 1998; 18(24): 1617-1622. Lang.: Eng.
UK-England: Stratford. 1998. ▪*The Lion, the Witch, and the Wardrobe* by C.S. Lewis, adapt by Adrian Mitchell, dir by Adrian Noble for the RSC at the Royal Shakespeare: rev by Billington, Brown, Butler, Clapp, Coveney, Curtis, Gore-Langton, Gross, Hagerty, Kingston, Macaulay, Nathan, Peter, Spencer, P. Taylor, Woddis.

2520 "Reviews of Productions." *LTR.* 1998; 18(21): 1351-1358. Lang.: Eng.
UK-England: London. 1998. ▪*Stripped* by Greg Day, dir by Tony Craven at Riverside 3: rev by Coveney, Darvell, Godfrey-Faussett. *Oresteia* by Aeschylus, adapt by Silviu Purcarete, dir by Purcarete at the Barbican: rev by Billington, Coveney, Kingston, Peter, Spencer, P.Taylor. *The Weir* by Conor McPherson, dir by Ian Rickson at the Royal Court Downstairs: rev by Bassett, Butler, Case, Gross, Hanks. *What Lesbians Do ... On Stage* by Clare Summerskill, dir by Summerskill at the Oval House: rev by Hendry.

2521 "Reviews of Productions." *LTR.* 1998; 18(22): 1438-1441. Lang.: Eng.
UK-England: London. 1998. ▪*Saving Charlotte* by Judi Herman, dir by Jacqui Somerville at the Bridewell: rev by Bassett, Foss, Morley, Nathan, Nightingale, Shuttleworth, Stratton. *The Resurrectionists* by Dominic McHale, dir by Lawrence Till at Croydon Warehouse: rev by Charles, Christopher, Curtis, North. *Picasso: Art Is a Crime* by Kieron Barry, dir by Alison Forth at the Riverside: rev by Abdulla, Freedman.

2522 "Reviews of Productions." *LTR.* 1998; 18(21): 1359-1364. Lang.: Eng.
UK-England: London. 1998. ▪*Herr Puntila and His Man Matti (Herr Puntila und sein Knecht Matti)* by Bertolt Brecht, adapt by Lee Hall, dir by Kathryn Hunter at the Almeida: rev by Billington, Brown, Butler, Clapp, Coveney, de Jongh, Edwardes, Gore-Langton, Gross, Kingston, Macaulay, Marmion, Nightingale, Peter, Shuttleworth, Spencer, P. Taylor. *Her Alabaster Skin* by Nick Green, dir by Emily Barber at the Etcetera: rev by Cavendish, Costa, Marmion, McPherson. *Bye Bye Blackbird* by Willard Simms and *Playing Burton* by Mark Jenkins, both dir by Guy Masterson at the New End: rev by Edwardes, Freedman.

2523 "Reviews of Productions." *LTR.* 1998; 18(21): 1365-1377. Lang.: Eng.
UK-England: London. 1998. ▪*An Experiment with an Airpump* by Shelagh Stephenson, dir by Matthew Lloyd at the Hampstead: rev by Butler, Christopher, Coveney, Curtis, Hagerty, Logan, Marlowe, Morley, Nathan, P. Taylor, Thorncroft, Woddis. *Antony and Cleopatra* and *As You Like It* by William Shakespeare, both dir by Michael Bogdanov at Hackney Empire: rev by Billington, Cavendish, Gibbs, Gross, Hemming, Kingston, Shuttleworth, Spencer. *Antony and Cleopatra* by Shakespeare, dir by Sean Mathias for the Royal National at the Olivier: rev by Billington, Brown, Butler, Clapp, Coveney, de Jongh, Edwardes, Gore-Langton, Hagerty, Marlowe, Morley, Murray, Nathan, Nightingale, Peter, Spencer, P. Taylor, Woddis.

2524 "Reviews of Productions." *LTR.* 1998; 18(145): 879-884. Lang.: Eng.
UK-England: London. 1998. ▪*Monsieur Lovestar and the Man Next Door (Monsieur Lovestar et son voisin de palier)* by Eduardo Manet, transl by David Zaine Mairowitz, dir by Hans-Peter Kellner at the White Bear: rev by Hewison, Kingston, Logan, McPherson. *Shakespeare's Villains* by Steven Berkoff, dir by Berkoff at Theatre Royal, Haymarket: rev by Benedict, Billington, Butler, Coveney, Curtis, Edwardes, Kingston, Macaulay, Morley, Nathan, N. Smith, Spencer, Wardle, Woddis, M. Wright. *Back to Methuselah* by George Bernard Shaw, dir by Richard Malter at the Union: rev by Hemming, Logan, McPherson. *Forbidden Dance* by Seta White and Emma Darwall-Smith, dir by White, Darwall-Smith, and Julia Munrow at the Man in the Moon: rev by R.L. Parry.

2525 "Reviews of Productions." *LTR.* 1998; 18(21): 1377-1379. Lang.: Eng.
UK-England: London. 1998. ▪*Fame* book by José Fernandez, lyrics by Jacques Levy, music by Steve Margoshes, conceived by David de Silva, dir by Runar Borge at the Prince of Wales: rev by Abdulla, Curtis. *Love! Valour! Compassion!* by Terrence McNally, dir by Stephen Henry at the Tristan Bates: rev by Godfrey-Faussett, Morley, Thorncroft. *Exodus* by Neil Biswas and Tara Arts, dir by Jatinder Verma at BAC Grand Hall: rev by Butler, Edwardes, Hewison, Judah, McPherson.

2526 "Reviews of Productions." *LTR.* 1998; 18(21): 1380-1386. Lang.: Eng.
UK-England: London. 1998. ▪*Real Classy Affair* by Nick Grosso, dir by James Macdonald at the Royal Court Upstairs: rev by Billington, Butler, Clapp, Coveney, de Jongh, Edwardes, Gore-Langton, Gross, Hanks, Kingston, Marlowe, Peter, Spencer, P. Taylor. *Boogie Nights* by Jon Conway, Shane Richie, and Terry Morrison, dir by Conway at the Savoy: rev by Bassett, Benedict, Christopher, Coveney, Curtis, Gardner, Hagerty, Hanks, Logan, McPherson. *Psycho-Babble On!* by Richard Doyle, dir by Doyle at the Man in the Moon: rev by Sierz.

2527 "Reviews of Productions." *LTR.* 1998; 18(21): 1406-1414. Lang.: Eng.
UK-England. 1998. ▪Reviews of two concurrent London theatre festivals: The Black theatre-themed 'Zebra Crossing 2' presented by the Talawa Theatre (rev by Logan, Shabi, Stratton) and the British Festival of Visual Theatre (rev by Clapp, Fisher, Gardner, Judah, Loup Nolan, Wilson).

2528 "Reviews of Productions." *LTR.* 1998; 18(21): 1387-1393. Lang.: Eng.
UK-England: London. 1998. ▪*Amadeus* by Peter Shaffer, dir by Peter Hall at the Old Vic: rev by Benedict, Billington, Brown, Butler, Cavendish, Clapp, Coveney, de Jongh, Gore-Langton, Hagerty, Morley, Murray, Nathan, Nightingale, Peter, N. Smith, Spencer, Woddis. *Example: The Case of Craig and Bentley* by Tom Barrie, dir by Barrie at the Finborough: rev by Christopher, Foss, North. *The Gary Oldman Fanclub* by Jonathan Stratford, dir by Barrie Keefe at the Man in the Moon: rev by Gibbs, Logan. *The Immigrant Song* by Mick Martin, dir by Rhys Thomas at the Albany: rev by Gibbs, North.

2529 "Reviews of Productions." *LTR.* 1998; 18(21): 1394-1399. Lang.: Eng.
UK-England: Stratford. 1998. ▪*The School for Scandal* by Richard Brinsley Sheridan, dir by Declan Donnellan for the RSC at the Royal Shakespeare: rev by Billington, Brown, Carnegy, Clapp, Coveney, de Jongh, Edwardes, Gore-Langton, Gross, Hanks, Kingston, Peter, Spencer, P. Taylor.

2530 "Reviews of Productions." *LTR.* 1998; 18(22): 1423-1433. Lang.: Eng.
UK-England: London. 1998. ▪*Jackie: An American Life* by Gip Hoppe, dir by Hoppe at the Queen's: rev by Benedict, Billington, Brown, Coveney, Curtis, Darvell, Hagerty, Hemming, Marmion, Morley, Nathan, Nightingale, Peter, Spencer. *Volunteers* by Brian Friel, dir by Mick Gordon at the Gate: rev by Billington, Butler, Cavendish, Clapp, Foss, Kingston, Marmion, Peter, Shuttleworth. *The House Among the Stars (La Maison suspendue)* by Michel Tremblay, transl by John van Burek, dir by Dominic Hill at the Orange Tree: rev by Curtis, Godfrey-Faussett, Hemming, Kingston, McPherson, Woddis. *Babe XXX* by Nell Dunn, dir by Ricardo Pinto at the Two Way Mirror: rev by Logan.

DRAMA: —Performance/production

2531 "Reviews of Productions." *LTR.* 1998; 18(22): 1434-1437. Lang.: Eng.
UK-England: London. 1998. Reviews of performances. ■*A Family Outing* by Ursula Martinez, dir by Martinez at the Drill Hall: rev by Belcher, Benedict, Brown, Cavendish, Clapp, Edwardes, Foss, Gore-Langton, O'Farrell, Spencer. *The School for Scandal* by Richard Brinsley Sheridan, dir by Declan Donnellan for the RSC at the Barbican: rev by Hagerty, Marlowe, Nathan, Sierz. *Simply Barbra—The Wedding Tour* by Steven Brinberg, dir by Nathan Martin at the Jermyn Street: rev by Davis, Donnelly. *David Copperfield* adapt from Charles Dickens' novel by Harry Meacher, dir by Meacher at Upstairs at the Gatehouse: rev by North.

2532 "Reviews of Productions." *LTR.* 1998; 18(22): 1442-1447. Lang.: Eng.
UK-England: London. 1998. ■*Ugly Rumours* by Tariq Ali and Howard Brenton, dir by Christopher Morahan at the Tricycle: Benedict, Billington, Butler, Clapp, Coveney, Curtis, Edwardes, Gore-Langton, Gross, Hagerty, Macaulay, McMillan, Nightingale, Peter, Raven, Shabi, Sierz, Spencer, Woddis. *Made in England* by Parv Bancil, dir by Lisa Goldman at the Etcetera: rev by Stratton. *Accidental Death of an Anarchist (Morte accidentale di un anarchico)* by Dario Fo, dir by Johnny Brunel at BAC 1: rev by Cavendish, R.L. Parry.

2533 "Reviews of Productions." *LTR.* 1998; 18(22): 1448-1453. Lang.: Eng.
UK-England: London. 1998. ■*Ennio Marchetto* solo performance by Marchetto, dir by Sosthen Hennekam at Lyric Hammersmith: rev by Abdulla, Games, Gibbs, Gross, Judah, Rampton. *Small Domestic Acts* by Joan Lipkin, dir by Rob Hay at Jackson's Lane: rev by Woddis. *The Invention of Love* by Tom Stoppard, dir by Richard Eyre for the Royal National at Theatre Royal, Haymarket: rev by Billington, Coveney, de Jongh, Foss, Macaulay, Morley, Nightingale, Peter, Russell, Stratton, P. Taylor.

2534 "Reviews of Productions." *LTR.* 1998; 18(22): 1454-1461. Lang.: Eng.
UK-England: London. 1998. ■*Stranded* adapt by Katarzyna Deszcz from Ugo Betti's play *Crime on Goat Island (Delitto all'isola delle capre)*, dir by Grainne Byrne at the Young Vic: rev by Cavendish, Charles, Clapp, Curtis, Hemming, Judah, Marmion, Woddis. *Britannicus* by Jean Racine, transl by Robert David MacDonald, dir by Jonathan Kent at the Albery: rev by Billington, Brown, Butler, Clapp, Coveney, de Jongh, Gore-Langton, Gross, Hagerty, Logan, Macaulay, Marlowe, Morley, Nightingale, Peter, Spencer, P. Taylor, Woddis. *My Life in Art* by Andrew Cowie, dir by Candice Joyce at the Etcetera: rev by Abdulla.

2535 "Reviews of Productions." *LTR.* 1998; 18(25/26): 1669-1670. Lang.: Eng.
UK-England: London. 1998. ■*Fascinations from the Crowd* by John Keates, dir by Keates at the Oval House: rev by Charles, North. *Toothless* by Kazuko Hiko, dir by Tim Hope at BAC: rev by Charles, Judah, Logan. *Mary and the Shaman* music by Warren Wills, book and lyrics by Christina Jones, dir by C.M. Jones at BAC: rev by Charles, Judah, North.

2536 "Reviews of Productions." *LTR.* 1998; 18(22): 1462-1472. Lang.: Eng.
UK-England: Stratford, Birmingham. 1998. ■*Richard III* by William Shakespeare, dir by Elijah Moshinsky for the RSC at the Royal Shakespeare: rev by Billington, Brown, Butler, Carnegy, Clapp, Coveney, Curtis, Edwardes, Gilbert, Gross, Hagerty, Hanks, Nightingale, Peter, Russell, Spencer, P. Taylor. *Three Sisters (Tri sestry)* by Anton Čechov, transl by Mike Poulton, dir by Bill Bryden at Birmingham Rep: rev by Brown, Butler, Coveney, Gardner, Gore-Langton, Kingston, Peter, Shuttleworth, Spencer, P. Taylor.

2537 "Reviews of Productions." *LTR.* 1998; 18(23): 1515-1520. Lang.: Eng.
UK-England: London. 1998. ■*Ecstasy* by Mike Leigh, dir by Patrick Davey at the Arts: rev by Charles, Kingston, Macaulay, North, Peter. *Softcops* by Caryl Churchill, dir by Catriona Craig at the Finborough: rev by Logan, McPherson. *Shang-a-Lang* by Catherine Johnson, dir by Mike Bradwell at the Bush: rev by Cavendish, Clapp, de Jongh, Foss, Gardner, Hagerty, Hanks, Kingston, Nathan, Peter, Sierz, Spencer, P. Taylor, Woddis.

2538 "Reviews of Productions." *LTR.* 1998; 18(23): 1495-1500. Lang.: Eng.
UK-England: London. 1998. ■*Troilus and Cressida* by William Shakespeare, dir by Michael Boyd for the RSC at The Pit: rev by Billington, Butler, Edwardes, Freedman, Macaulay, Nathan, Nightingale, Peter, Spencer, P. Taylor, Woddis. *Lips Together, Teeth Apart* by Terrence McNally, dir by Auriol Smith at the Orange Tree: rev by Billington, Cavendish, Curtis, Hemming, Kingston, Marlowe. *The Whisper of a Leaf Falling* by Philippe Cherbonnier, dir by Cherbonnier at Jackson's Lane: rev by Godfrey-Faussett.

2539 "Reviews of Productions." *LTR.* 1998; 18(23): 1501-1506. Lang.: Eng.
UK-England: London. 1998. ■*Crimes of the Heart* by Beth Henley, dir by David Gilmore at the King's Head: rev by Coveney, Curtis, Edwardes, Gibbs, Kingston, Morley, Shuttleworth. *Once Is Never Enough* by Lisa Bluthal, dir by Phil Seren at Canal Cafe: rev by Buscovic. *Much Ado About Everything* solo performance by Jackie Mason at the Playhouse: rev by Bassett, Coveney, Davis, Dessau, Freedman, Gross, Hemming, Jones, Landesman, Nathan, Russell, S. Taylor.

2540 "Reviews of Productions." *LTR.* 1998; 18(23): 1509-1514. Lang.: Eng.
UK-England: London. 1998. ■*Love Upon the Throne* by Patrick Barlow, Martin Duncan, and John Ramm, dir by Duncan at the Comedy: rev by Curtis, Foss, Gore-Langton, Macaulay, Nathan, Nightingale, Spencer, P. Taylor. *Rung/You Are Here* devised, directed, and performed by Quarter Too Theatre Company at the Old Red Lion: rev by Cavendish. *Guiding Star* by Jonathan Harvey, dir by Gemma Bodinetz for the Royal National at the Cottesloe: rev by Brown, Coveney, de Jongh, Gross, Kingston, Marlowe, Nathan, Sierz, Stratton, Woddis.

2541 "Reviews of Productions." *LTR.* 1998; 18(23): 1520-1523. Lang.: Eng.
UK-England: London. 1998. ■*Fourteen Songs, Two Weddings and a Funeral* by Sudha Bhuchara and Kristine Landon-Smith, dir by Landon-Smith at the Lyric Studio: rev by Clapp, Logan, McPherson, Nightingale, Peter, Woddis. *Half Moon* by Jack Shepherd, dir by Shepherd at Southwark Playhouse: rev by Cavendish, Christopher, Curtis, Freedman, Logan. *Tess of the D'Urbervilles* by Michael Fry from Thomas Hardy's novel, dir by Fry and Abigail Anderson at the New End: rev by Charles, North.

2542 "Reviews of Productions." *LTR.* 1998; 18(23): 1545-1550. Lang.: Eng.
UK-England: London. 1998. ■*One Woman: Festival of Theatre and Music* at BAC: rev by Costa, Freedman, Judah. *The Seagull (Čajka)* by Anton Čechov, transl by Tom Stoppard, dir by Jude Kelly at the Courtyard: Billington, Brown, Butler, Cavendish, Clapp, Gore-Langton, Gross, Macaulay, McMillan, Nightingale, Peter, Spencer.

2543 "Reviews of Productions." *LTR.* 1998; 18(23): 1524-1532. Lang.: Eng.
UK-England: London. 1998. ■*Into the Woods* by Stephen Sondheim, book by James Lapine, dir by John Crowley at Donmar Warehouse: rev by Benedict, Billington, Butler, Clapp, Coveney, de Jongh, Edwardes, Gore-Langton, Hagerty, Macaulay, Marlowe, Nathan, Nightingale, Peter, Spencer, Wardle. *Sonny De Ree's Life Flashes Before His Eyes* by Bill Bozzone, dir by Emma Gregory at the Orange Tree Room: rev by Edwardes. *The Storm (Groza)* by Aleksand'r Ostrovskij, transl by Frank McGuinness, dir by Hettie Macdonald at the Almeida: rev by Billington, Butler, Clapp, de Jongh, Edwardes, Foss, Nathan, Nightingale, Peter, Spencer, Stratton, P. Taylor, Thorncroft, Wardle, Woddis.

2544 "Reviews of Productions." *LTR.* 1998; 18(23): 1533-1544. Lang.: Eng.
UK-England: London. 1998. ■*Little Malcolm and His Struggle Against the Eunuchs* by David Halliwell, dir by Denis Lawson at the Hampstead: rev by Billington, Brown, Butler, Clapp, Coveney, de Jongh, Edwardes, Gore-Langton, Hagerty, Marlowe, Murray, Nathan, Nightingale, Peter, Spencer, P. Taylor, Wardle, Woddis. *Stomp* created and dir by Luke Cresswell and Steve McNicholas at the Round House: rev by Bishop, I. Brown, Crisp, Curtis, Freedman, Judah, Levene, Ryles, Wright. *The Best of Times* conceived by Paul Gilger, music and lyrics by Jerry Herman, dir by Bill Starr at the Vaudeville: rev by Coveney, Curtis, Davis, Foss, Gross, Kingston, Logan, Murray, P. Taylor.

DRAMA: —Performance/production

2545 "Reviews of Productions." *LTR*. 1998; 18(24): 1573-1582. Lang.: Eng.
UK-England: London. 1998. ■*Kafka's Dick* by Alan Bennett, dir by Peter Hall at the Piccadilly: rev by Billington, Brown, Butler, Case, Coveney, de Jongh, Gore-Langton, Hagerty, Kellaway, Macaulay, Marlowe, Nathan, Nightingale, Peter, Sierz, Spencer, P. Taylor, Wardle, Woddis. *Being Sellars* by Carl Caufield, dir by Jonathan Biggins at the Man in the Moon: rev by Gibbs, North. *Suppliants* adapt by James Kerr from Aeschylus' *Hikétides (Suppliant Women)*, dir by Kerr at the Gate: rev by Charles, Curtis, Gardner, Logan, Macaulay, Peter. *Giant Steps* by Othniel Smith, dir by Jeff Teare at the Oval House: rev by North.

2546 "Reviews of Productions." *LTR*. 1998; 18(24): 1583-1592. Lang.: Eng.
UK-England: London. 1998. ■*Betrayal* by Harold Pinter, dir by Trevor Nunn for the Royal National at the Lyttelton: rev by Billington, Brown, Butler, Coveney, de Jongh, Edwardes, Gore-Langton, Gross, Hagerty, Kellaway, Macaulay, Marlowe, Nathan, Nightingale, Peter, Sierz, Spencer, P. Taylor, Woddis. *The Perfect Words* by Chris Vance, dir by Kitt O'Neill at the Finborough: rev by Gibbs, North. *Love Bites* comedy solo by Jeff Green at the Apollo: rev by Bassett, Coveney, Daoust, Freedman, Games, Hagerty, T. Jones, Judah, S. Taylor. *All Over Lovely* by Claire Dowie, dir by Colin Watkeys at the Drill Hall: rev by Christopher.

2547 "Reviews of Productions." *LTR*. 1998; 18(24): 1595-1601. Lang.: Eng.
UK-England: London. 1998. ■*Molloy* by Samuel Beckett, dir by Judy Hegarty at the Riverside: rev by Cavendish, Foss, Gardner, R. Jones, Kingston. *Deathwatch (Haute Surveillance)* by Jean Genet, dir by P.A. Neufeldt at the Old Red Lion: rev by Logan, McPherson. *Salomé* by Oscar Wilde, dir by Mick Gordon at the Riverside: rev by Billington, Butler, Coveney, Curtis, Edwardes, Gross, Hagerty, Kellaway, Macaulay, Nathan, Nightingale, Peter, N. Smith, Spencer, P. Taylor, Woddis.

2548 "Reviews of Productions." *LTR*. 1998; 18(24): 1601-1604. Lang.: Eng.
UK-England: London. 1998. ■*Eurydice* by Jean Anouilh, transl by Peter Meyer, dir by Simon Godwin at BAC 1: rev by Abdulla, Gibbs, Kingston. *In Close Relation* devised and dir by Ruth Ben-Tovim and Peader Kirk at the Young Vic: rev by Charles, Curtis, Gardner, Stratton. *The Snow Palace* by Pam Gems, dir by Janet Suzman at the Tricycle: rev by Christopher, de Jongh, Edwardes, Nathan, Peter, P. Taylor, Woddis.

2549 "Reviews of Productions." *LTR*. 1998; 18(24): 1605-1611. Lang.: Eng.
UK-England: London. 1998. ■*Killing Rasputin* by Stephen Clark and Kit Hesketh-Harvey, music by James McConnel, lyrics by Hesketh-Harvey, dir by Ian Brown at the Bridewell: rev by Butler, Cavendish, Foss, Gardner, Gross, Kingston, Logan, Nathan, Spencer. *Yesterday Once More* by Murray Woodfield, dir by Woodfield at the Man in the Moon: rev by Cavendish, Christopher, McPherson. *B22* by Ranjit Khutan, dir by Annabelle Comyn, *About the Boy* by Ed Hime, dir by Rufus Norris, *The Crutch* by Ruwanthie de Chikera, dir by Indhu Rubasingham, *Four* by Christopher Shinn, dir by Richard Wilson, *In the Family* by Sara Barr, dir by Steve Gilroy, *Trade* by Richard Oberg, dir by Janette Smith, *When Brains Don't Count* by Alice Wood, dir by Ian Rickson, *Bluebird* by Simon Stephens, *The Shining* by Leomi Walker, dir by Dawn Walton, *Daughters* by Jackson Ssekiryangko, all at the Royal Court Upstairs: rev by Benedict, Billington, Cavendish, Christopher, Curtis, Gardner, Sierz, Stratton, Woddis.

2550 "Reviews of Productions." *LTR*. 1998; 18(24): 1611-1614. Lang.: Eng.
UK-England: London. 1998. ■*Drag King* by Sarah-Louise Young, dir by Sophie Prideaux at the Etcetera: rev by Charles. *Silent Night* by Steven Berkoff, dir by Nik Wood-Jones at Canal Cafe: rev by Godfrey-Faussett. *Blood Ugly* by Peter Rose, dir by Gari Jones at the White Bear: rev by Logan. *Belle Fontaine* by Nicholas McInerny, dir by Jonathan Lloyd, *Snatch* by Peter Rose, dir by Polly Teale, *Be My Baby* by Amanda Whittinton, dir by Abigail Morris, *The Backroom* by Adrian Pagan, dir by Lloyd, and *Angels and Saints* by Jessica Townsend, dir by Teale at the Pleasance: rev by Billington, Gardner, Kingston, Nightingale, Woddis. *Charlotte's Web* by E.B. White, adapt by Joseph Robinette, music and lyrics by Charles Strouse, dir by Roman Stefanski at the Polka: rev by Haydon.

2551 "Reviews of Productions." *LTR*. 1998; 18(25/26): 1645-1654. Lang.: Eng.
UK-England: London. 1998. ■*The Merchant of Venice* by William Shakespeare, dir by Gregory Doran for the RSC at the Barbican: rev by Butler, de Jongh, Kingston, Marlowe, Murray, Stratton. *Riders to the Sea* and *The Shadow of the Glen* by John Millington Synge and *Purgatory* by William Butler Yeats, all dir by John Crowley for the RSC at The Pit: rev by Curtis, Gardner, Hemming, Kingston, Sierz, N. Smith, Stratton, Woddis. *The Two Gentlemen of Verona* by Shakespeare, dir by Edward Hall for the RSC at The Pit: rev by Costa, Gardner, Gross, Hemming, Marmion, Nathan, Nightingale, Spencer, Woddis.

2552 "Reviews of Productions." *LTR*. 1998; 18(25/26): 1654-1662. Lang.: Eng.
UK-England: London. 1998. ■*Court in the Act (Vous n'avez rien à déclarer?)* by Maurice Hennequin and Pierre Veber, transl by Robert Cogo-Fawcett and Braham Murray, dir by Sam Walters at the Orange Tree: rev by Billington, Cavendish, Curtis, Gross, Kingston, Nathan, P. Taylor. *Jesus, My Boy* by John Dowie, dir by Tom Kinninmont at the Apollo: rev by Billington, Brown, Butler, Clapp, Coveney, de Jongh, Foss, Gross, Hagerty, Logan, Murray, Nathan, Nightingale, Peter, Spencer, P. Taylor. *The Legendary Golem* book and lyrics by Sylvia Freedman, music by Cathy Shostak, dir by Brennan Street at the New End: rev by Cairns, Cliff, Curtis, Freedman, Gardner, Marmion, Nathan, P. Taylor.

2553 "Reviews of Productions." *LTR*. 1998; 18(25/26): 1663-1669. Lang.: Eng.
UK-England: London. 1998. ■*The Demon Headmaster* music by Eric Angus and Cathy Shostak, lyrics by Ian Halsted and Paul James, book by James, dir by Matthew White at the Pleasance: rev by Cavendish, Gibbs, Kingston. *The Wolf Road* by Nick McCarty, dir by Penny Cherns at the Gate: rev by Godfrey-Faussett, Gross, Judah, Marmion. *The Pirates of Penzance* by Gilbert and Sullivan, dir by Stuart Maunder at the Queen's: rev by Allison, Ashley, Christainsen, Gillard, Gross, Macaulay, Nathan, Pappenheim, Seckerson, Sutcliffe. *Late Nite Cathechism* by Vicki Quare and Maripat Donavan, dir by Patrick Trettenero at the Jermyn Street: rev by Abdulla, Curtis, Freedman.

2554 "Reviews of Productions." *LTR*. 1998; 18(25/26): 1671-1677. Lang.: Eng.
UK-England: London. 1998. ■*The King and I* by Rodgers and Hammerstein, dir by Phil Willmott and Tom Barrie at BAC Main: rev by Christopher, Clapp, Costa, Curtis, Darvell, Gardner, Gross, Pearman, Shuttleworth, P. Taylor. *Duck Barton—Special Agent* by Phil Willmott, dir by Ted Craig at Croydon Warehouse: rev by Gross, Hagerty, Kingston, Marmion, McPherson. *Id* by Ann Cleary and Ian McCurrach, dir by Cleary and McCurrach at the Young Vic Studio: rev by Cavendish, Costa, Judah. *If I Were Lifted Up from Earth* by William Tyndale, dir by Gregory Thompson at Lincoln's Inn: rev by Cavendish.

2555 "Reviews of Productions." *LTR*. 1998; 18(25/26): 1678-1686. Lang.: Eng.
UK-England: London. 1998. ■*Peter Pan* by J.M. Barrie, adapt by John Caird and Trevor Nunn, dir by Fiona Laird for the Royal National at the Olivier: rev by Cavendish, Coveney, Darvell, Edwardes, Gore-Langton, Hagerty, Kingston, Macaulay, Nathan, Peter, Spencer, Woddis. *Arabian Nights* adapt by Dominic Cooke, dir by Cooke at the Young Vic: rev by Billington, Cavendish, Clapp, Coveney, Edwardes, Gore-Langton, Gross, Hagerty, Hassell, Hewison, Judah, Macaulay, Nathan, Spencer, P. Taylor. *Forever Plaid* by Stuart Ross, dir by Shauna Kanter at Upstairs at the Gatehouse: rev by Abdulla. *The Adventures of Robyn Hood* by Nona Shepphard, dir by Shepphard at the Drill Hall: rev by Abdulla, Curtis, Woddis.

2556 "Reviews of Productions." *LTR*. 1998; 18(25/26): 1687-1692. Lang.: Eng.
UK-England: London. 1998. ■*Cinderella* by Angela Carter, adapt and dir by Julian Crouch, Phelim McDermott, Lee Simpson, and Neil Bartlett at Lyric Hammersmith: rev by Billington, Brown, Butler, Clapp, Curtis, Gross, Hagerty, Haydon, Hewison, Kingston, Logan, Marlowe, Nathan, Shuttleworth, Spencer, P. Taylor, Woddis. *The Ugly Duckling* by Neil Duffield from the story by Hans Christian Andersen, dir by David Farmer at the Lyric Studio: rev by Connors. *Quatre Mains* written and dir by Andrew Dawson and Josef Houben at the Lyric Studio: rev by Costa, Coveney, Curtis. *The Animals of Farthing Wood* by Keith

Dewhurst, music by Russell Churney, dir by Roxana Silbert at the Pleasance: rev by Haydon, Spencer.

2557 "Reviews of Productions." *LTR.* 1998; 18(25/26): 1693-1699. Lang.: Eng.
UK-England: London. 1998. ■*The Snowman* by Howard Blake, Howard North, and Bill Alexander, music and lyrics by Blake, from Raymond Briggs' story, dir by Alexander at the Peacock: rev by Bayley, de Jongh, Hagerty, Marlowe, Nightingale, Pearman, Shields, Spencer. *Whittington Junior, and His Sensation Cat* by Robert Reece, adapt by Geoffrey Brawn, music and lyrics by Maurice Browning, dir by Brawn at the Players: rev by Curtis, Darvell. *Red Riding Hood and the Wolf* by Jonathan Petherbridge, dir by Petherbridge at the Albany: rev by Hewison. *Cinderella* by David Cregan and Brian Protheroe, dir by Kerry Michael at Theatre Royal, Stratford East: rev by Curtis, Darvell, Godfrey-Faussett, P. Taylor.

2558 "Reviews of Productions." *LTR.* 1998; 18(25/26): 1699-1708. Lang.: Eng.
UK-England. 1998. ■*Dick Whittington* by Susie McKenna, dir by McKenna at Hackney Empire: rev by Darvell, Logan, Nightingale. *A Month in the Country (Mesjac v derevne)* by Brian Friel after Turgenjėv, dir by Michael Boyd for the RSC at the Swan: rev by Billington, Butler, Clapp, Coveney, de Jongh, Edwardes, Gore-Langton, Gross, Kingston, Peter, Spencer, P. Taylor, Thorncroft. *Hindle Wakes* by Stanley Houghton, dir by Helena Kaut-Howson at the Royal Exchange: rev by Bassett, Billington, Brown, Cavendish, Clapp, Coveney, Gore-Langton, Gross, Hagerty, Hulme, Nightingale, Peter, Shuttleworth, P. Taylor.

2559 "Reviews of Productions." *LTR.* 1998; 18(25/26): 1708-1716. Lang.: Eng.
UK-England: Leeds, Manchester. 1998. ■*So Special* by Kevin Hood, dir by Matthew Lloyd at the Royal Exchange Studio: rev by Branigan, Clapp, Hagerty, Nathan, Peter. *Martin Guerre* musical by Alain Boublil, Claude-Michel Schönberg, and Stephen Clark, dir by Conall Morrison at the Quarry: rev by Billington, Brown, Cavendish, Christopher, Coveney, Hagerty, Peter, Shuttleworth, Spencer, P. Taylor. *Present Laughter* by Noël Coward, dir by Malcolm Sutherland at the Courtyard: Billington, Brown, Clapp, Coveney, Gore-Langton, Macaulay, Nightingale, Peter, Spencer, P. Taylor.

2560 "Reviews of Productions." *LTR.* 1998; 18(10): 603-609. Lang.: Eng.
UK-England: London. 1998. ■*Yard Gal* by Rebecca Prichard, dir by Gemma Bodinetz at the Royal Court Upstairs: rev by Benedict, Billington, Coveney, Macaulay, Marlowe, Nightingale, Peter, Spencer. *Talking Beans* by Peter Summers, dir by Summers at the Grace: rev by Costa, McPherson. *Hymn to Love* by Steve Trafford, dir by Annie Castledine at the Drill Hall: rev by Bassett, Benedict, Christopher, Logan. *Love, Lust, and Sawdust* by Graeme Messer, dir by Steven Wrentmore at Hen & Chickens: rev by Abdulla, Foss.

2561 "Reviews of Productions." *LTR.* 1998; 18(10): 610-622. Lang.: Eng.
UK-England: London. 1998. ■*Rent* by Jonathan Larson, dir by Michael Greif at the Shaftesbury: rev by Benedict, Billington, Brown, Butler, Clapp, Coveney, de Jongh, Edwardes, Gore-Langton, Gross, Hagerty, Macaulay, Morley, Nathan, Nightingale, Peter, Sierz, N. Smith, Spencer. *The Interview* by Robert Hamilton, dir by Simon Geal at the Etcetera: rev by Godfrey-Faussett. *3 by Harold Pinter: A Kind of Alaska* dir by Karel Reisz, *The Collection* and *The Lover* dir by Joe Harmston at Donmar Warehouse: rev by Billington, Brown, Butler, Clapp, Coveney, Curtis, de Jongh, Edwardes, Gore-Langton, Gross, Hagerty, Macaulay, Morley, Nathan, Nightingale, Peter, N. Smith, Spencer.

2562 "Reviews of Productions." *LTR.* 1998; 18(10): 622-628. Lang.: Eng.
UK-England: London. 1998. ■*Iphigenia* by Che Walker after Euripides, dir by Benjamin May at Southwark Playhouse: rev by de Jongh, *Time Out*. *Major Barbara* by George Bernard Shaw, dir by Peter Hall at the Piccadilly: rev by Billington, Brown, Butler, Cavendish, Clapp, Coveney, Curtis, de Jongh, Godfrey-Faussett, Gore-Langton, Hagerty, Hassell, Macaulay, Morley, Nightingale, Peter, Spencer. *Goodnight Desdemona, Good Morning Juliet* by Anne-Marie MacDonald, dir by Michael Cowie at the Bridewell: rev by R.L. Parry.

2563 "When Shall We Three Meet Again?" *Econ.* 1998 Jan 10; 346(8050): 73-74. Illus.: Photo. B&W. 1. Lang.: Eng.
UK-England: London. 1998. Critical studies. ■Reflections on the future of repertory companies in Britain and the difficulties of keeping a troupe together. Simon McBurney of Théâtre de Complicité and Adrian Noble of the Royal Shakespeare Company share their views.

2564 "Reviews of Productions." *LTR.* 1998; 18(1/2): 10-20. Lang.: Eng.
UK-England: London. 1998. ■*Alegria* by Cirque du Soleil, dir by Franco Dragone at the Royal Albert Hall: rev by Brown, Clapp, Gardner, Gore-Langton, Gross, Hagerty, Levene, Nathan, Nightingale, Sacks, N. Smith, Spencer, Wright. *The Bound Man* by Andrew Prichard from a story by Ilsa Aichinger, dir by Tassos Stevens at BAC 2: rev by Abdulla, McPherson. *Do You Come Here Often?* by The Right Size (Hamish McColl, Sean Foley, Josef Houben), dir by Houben at the Vaudeville: rev by Butler, Clapp, Coveney, Curtis, Dessau, Gardner, Gross, Hagerty, Hemming, Hewison, McPherson, Morley, Nathan, Nightingale, Spencer, Stratton.

2565 "Reviews of Productions." *LTR.* 1998; 18(1/2): 5-9. Lang.: Eng.
UK-England: London. 1998. ■*Klaxons, Trumpets and Raspberries (Clacson, trombette e pernacchi)* by Dario Fo, transl. by Jonathan Dryden Taylor, dir by Robert Thorogood at the Gate: rev by Billington, Butler, Clapp, Curtis, Gore-Langton, Gross, Hagerty, Logan, Macaulay, Marlowe, Nathan, Nightingale, Peter. *Stalking Realness* devised by Desperate Optimists, dir by Joe Lawlor and Christine Molloy at the Young Vic: rev by Butler, Marlowe, Stratton. *Then What?* and *Squash* by Andrew Payne, dir by Bill Pryde at the Old Red Lion: rev by de Jongh, Dowden, Edwardes, Kingston.

2566 "Reviews of Productions." *LTR.* 1998; 18(1/2): 27-30. Lang.: Eng.
UK-England: London. 1998. ■*Private Lines* by Trevor Suthers, dir by Alex Scrivenor at the White Bear: rev by Cavendish. *The Importance of Being Earnest* by Oscar Wilde, dir by Xavier Leret at the Oval House: rev by Adams, North. *Martin and John* adapt. by Sean O'Neil from Dale Peck's novel *Fucking Martin*, dir by Eileen Vorbach at the Bush: rev by de Jongh, Edwardes, Gardner, Kingston, Macaulay, R.L. Parry, Sierz, Spencer, P. Taylor. *Tales of the Lost Formicans* by Constance Congdon, dir by Spencer Hinton at the Finborough: rev by Marmion.

2567 "Reviews of Productions." *LTR.* 1998; 18(1/2): 31-41. Lang.: Eng.
UK-England: London. 1998. ■*The Day I Stood Still* by Kevin Elyot, dir by Ian Rickson at the Cottesloe: rev by Billington, Brown, Clapp, Coveney, de Jongh, Foss, Gore-Langton, Gross, Hagerty, Hanks, Hewison, Macaulay, Morley, Nathan, Nightingale, Sierz, Spencer, Stratton, P.Taylor. *Journey's End* by R.C. Sherriff, dir by David Evans Rees at the King's Head: rev by Brown, Butler, Coveney, de Jongh, Edwardes, Foss, Gardner, Gross, Hagerty, Hemming, Morley, Nathan, Nightingale, Spencer. *The Snow Queen* musical adapt. of the story by Hans Christian Andersen, book and lyrics by Adrian Mitchell, music by Richard Peaslee, dir by Patricia Birch at the Unicorn: rev by Brown Coveney, Hagerty.

2568 "Reviews of Productions." *LTR.* 1998; 18(1/2): 20-26. Lang.: Eng.
UK-England: London. 1998. ■*Meat on the Bone* by Kit Hesketh-Harvey and Richard Sisson, dir by Ian Brown at the Vaudeville: rev by Abdulla, Billington, Dessau, Gross, Hagerty, McPherson, Morley, Nightingale, Rampton, Spencer. *It, Wit, Don't Give a Shit Girls* by Dillie Keane, Adele Anderson, and Issy van Randwyck, dir by Nina Burns at the Lyric: rev by Dessau. *Like a Dancer* by Barbara Hartridge, dir by John Adams at the New End: rev by Benedict, Billington, Costa, Curtis, Foss, Kingston, Nathan. *See-Saw* by Trish Leo, dir by Karl Hibbert at BAC: rev by Logan.

2569 "Reviews of Productions." *LTR.* 1998; 18(1/2): 42-51. Lang.: Eng.
UK-England: London. 1998. ■*Never Land* by Phyllis Nagy, dir by Steven Pimlott at the Royal Court Upstairs: rev by Billington, Brown, Butler, Clapp, Coveney, de Jongh, Foss, Gore-Langton, Gross, Hanks, Morley, Nathan, Peter, Sierz, Spencer. *Bad Faith* by David Lewis, dir by George Ormond at the Orange Tree Room: rev by Kingston, McPherson. *Amy's View* by David Hare, dir by Richard Eyre for the Royal National at the Aldwych: rev by Billington, Brown, de Jongh, Edwardes, Gore-

Langton, Gross, Hagerty, Hassell, Macaulay, Nathan, Nightingale, Spencer, P. Taylor.

2570 "Reviews of Productions." *LTR*. 1998; 18(1/2): 51-53. Lang.: Eng.

UK-England: London. 1998. ■*Fossil Woman* by Louise Warren, dir by Helena Uren at the Lyric Studio: rev by Kingston, N. Smith, Stratton. *Legacy* by Shauna Kanter, dir by Kanter at the Cockpit: rev by Abdulla, Christopher, Curtis, Hagerty, Marlowe, Nathan. *Brendan's Visit* by Dennis Kelly, dir by Robin Chalmers at the Canal Cafe: rev by Foss, Godfrey- Faussett.

2571 "Reviews of Productions." *LTR*. 1998; 18(1/2): 54-57. Lang.: Eng.

UK-England: London. 1998. ■*Cymbeline* by Shakespeare, dir by Adrian Noble for the RSC at the Barbican: rev by Billington, Clapp, Coveney, de Jongh, Hassell, Macaulay, Nightingale, Spencer, Stratton. *Shopping and Fucking* by Mark Ravenhill, dir by Max Stafford-Clark at the Queen's: rev by Darvell. *Whoredom* by Heather Robson, dir by Adam Curtis at the Clink: rev by Foss, Stratton.

2572 "Reviews of Productions." *LTR*. 1998; 18(1/2): 58-63. Lang.: Eng.

UK-England: London. 1998. ■*Pleasure* by Tim Etchells, dir by Etchells at the ICA: rev by Clapp, Christopher, Curtis, Gardner, Hewison, Judah, Tushingham, Woddis. *Fragments from a Language of Love* from the sonnets of Shakespeare, adapt. and dir by Andrea Brooks at BAC1: rev by Godfrey-Faussett, R.L. Parry. *Iced* by Ray Shell, dir by Felix Cross at the Tricycle: rev by Bassett, Cavendish, de Jongh, Gardner, Gore-Langton, Gross, Hewison, Macaulay, Nightingale, R.L. Parry, Sierz.

2573 "Reviews of Productions." *LTR*. 1998; 18(1/2): 64-71. Lang.: Eng.

UK-England: London. 1998. ■*The Mysteries* inspired by the medieval mystery plays, with additional text by Edward Kemp, dir by Katie Mitchell for the RSC at The Pit: rev by Billington, Clapp, Coveney, Edwardes, Foss, Gore-Langton, Gross, Hanks, Hagerty, Kingston, Macaulay, Nathan, Vallely. *Prince on a White Bike* by Charles Thomas, dir by Mehmet Ergen at Southwark Playhouse: rev by Billington, Cavendish, R. Williams. *Shooting Stars/The Fast Show* by Vic Reeves, Bob Mortimer, and Paul Whitehouse, dir by Ulrike Jonsson at Labatt's Apollo: rev by Buckley, Dessau, Games, Pietrasik, Spencer, S. Taylor, Wareham.

2574 "Reviews of Productions." *LTR*. 1998; 18(1/2): 72-78. Lang.: Eng.

UK-England: London. 1998. ■*Terms of Abuse* by Jessica Townsend, dir by Julie-Anne Robinson at the Hampstead: rev by Benedict, Billington, Butler, Coveney, Curtis, Edwardes, Gore-Langton, Hagerty, Hewison, Kellaway, Macaulay, Marlowe, Morley, Nathan, Nightingale, Spencer. *Pulling Together* by Bob Hescott, dir by Thomas East at the Grace: rev by Marmion, Pearce. *The Woolgatherer* by William Mastrosimone, dir by Sarah Esdaile at BAC: rev by Cavendish, Curtis, Kingston, McPherson.

2575 "Reviews of Productions." *LTR*. 1998; 18(3): 111-115. Lang.: Eng.

UK-England: London. 1998. ■*Fairytaleheart* by Philip Ridley, dir by Ridley at the Hampstead: rev by Butler, Coveney, Curtis, Gardner, Gross, Hagerty, Hemming, Kellaway, Nightingale, R.L. Parry, Spencer, Stratton. *Sin Dykes* by Valerie Mason-John, dir by Dean Hill at the Oval House: rev by Costa. *Darkness Visible* by John Hyatt, dir by Michael Poulton at the Man in the Moon: rev by Costa.

2576 "Reviews of Productions." *LTR*. 1998; 18(1/2): 78-80. Lang.: Eng.

UK-England: London. 1998. ■*Pervy Verse* by Tom Payne, dir by David Cottis, *Still Life* by Danusia Iwaszko, dir by Mehmet Ergen, and *Perpetual Motion* by Iwaszko, dir by Mary Saunders at the Etcetera: rev by Costa. *Mario Benzedrine's Pop-Up Apocalypse* by Boyd Clark, dir by Jack James at the Etcetera: rev by Logan. *Don't Laugh It's My Life* adapt by Told by an Idiot from Molière's *Tartuffe*, dir by John Wright at BAC: rev by Benedict, Butler, Edwardes, Gardner, Gore-Langton, Kingston.

2577 "Reviews of Productions." *LTR*. 1998; 18(3): 116-119. Lang.: Eng.

UK-England: London. 1998. ■*Reader (Leyador)* by Ariel Dorfman, dir by Rob Curry at the Oval House: rev by Curtis, Kingston, Logan, R.L. Parry. *Chaucer in the Sky with Diamonds* by Lawrence Audini from Chaucer's *Canterbury Tales*, dir by Audini at the Riverside: rev by Marmion, McPherson. *Miss Roach's War* adapt by Richard Kane from Patrick Hamilton's novel *Slaves of Solitude*, dir by Jenny Lee at the Warehouse, Croydon: rev by Billington, Clapp, Gross, Logan, McPherson, Nightingale.

2578 "Reviews of Productions." *LTR*. 1998; 18(3): 176-179. Lang.: Eng.

UK-England: London. 1998. ■*Personal Matters* by John Donnelly, dir by Tony Singh at BAC1: rev by Costa, Dowden. *Featuring Loretta* by George F. Walker, dir by Robin Lefevre at the Hampstead: rev by Billington, de Jongh, Logan, Marlowe, Nightingale, Woddis. *Happy Days* by Samuel Beckett, dir by Caroline Smith at BAC Main: rev by Cavendish, Christopher, Murray, P. Taylor.

2579 "Reviews of Productions." *LTR*. 1998; 18(3): 124-127. Lang.: Eng.

UK-England: London. 1998. ■*Dracula* by James Gill from Bram Stoker's novel, dir by Gill at the Hackney Empire: rev by Christopher, Costa, Coveney, Hewison. *Richard III* by Shakespeare, dir by Guy Retallack at the Pleasance: rev by Billington, Coveney, Curtis, Godfrey-Faussett, Gross, Hagerty, Macaulay, P. Taylor. *Don the Burp* by Ray Dobbins and *Shadowboxing* by James Gaddes at the Hen & Chickens: rev by Darvell.

2580 "Reviews of Productions." *LTR*. 1998; 18(1/2): 83-85, 95-97. Lang.: Eng.

UK-England: London. 1998. ■London International Mime Festival 1998 at the Pleasance, ICA, BAC, Albany, Circus Space, Queen Elizabeth Hall, Purcell Room, Royal Festival Hall, Spitz: rev by Billington, I. Brown, Cavendish, Christopher, Dessau, Gardner, Judah, Logan, Shuttleworth. *Junk* by John Retallack from the novel by Melvin Burgess, dir by Retallack at the Oxford Playhouse: rev by Bassett, G. Brown, Butler, Curtis, Gross, Kingston, P. Taylor.

2581 "Reviews of Productions." *LTR*. 1998; 18(3): 119-123. Lang.: Eng.

UK-England: London. 1998. ■*Sixteen* and *A Bit of Rough* by Gilly Fraser, dir by Caroline Noh and Linda Dobell at the Rosemary Branch: rev by Costa. *Easy Access (for the boys)* by Claire Dowie, dir by Dowie at the Drill Hall: rev by de Jongh, Edwardes, Foss, Gardner, Hewison, Kingston, Sierz, P. Taylor. *Blue Window* by Craig Lucas, dir by Joe Harmston at the Old Red Lion: rev by Butler, Costa, Foss, Kingston, Morley. *Barabbas* by Michel de Ghelderode, dir by Eric Standidge at Chelsea Centre: rev by Edwardes.

2582 "Reviews of Productions." *LTR*. 1998; 18(3): 128-133. Lang.: Eng.

UK-England: London. 1998. ■*Lakeboat* by David Mamet, dir by Aaron Mullen at the Lyric Studio: rev by Billington, Butler, Cavendish, Clapp, Foss, Hagerty, Hewison, Morley, Nathan, Nightingale, Spencer, P. Taylor. *Death by Heroine* by Mehrdad Seyf, dir by Seyf at the Riverside: rev by Godfrey-Faussett, R.L. Parry. *Leatherface (Ledergeschicht)* by Helmut Krausser, transl by Anthony Meech, dir by Hans-Peter Kellner and *The Child (Barnet)* by Jon Fosse, transl by Louis Muinzer, dir by Ramin Gray at the Gate: rev by Billington, Cavendish, Marlowe, Peter.

2583 "Reviews of Productions." *LTR*. 1998; 18(3): 133-138. Lang.: Eng.

UK-England: London. 1998. ■*Phaedra (Phèdre)* by Jean Racine, transl by Peter Oswald, dir by Tim Carroll at BAC2: rev by Christopher, Logan, R. Williams. *Romeo and Juliet* by Shakespeare, dir by Rupert Goold at the Greenwich: rev by Bassett, Coveney, de Jongh, Hagerty, Hewison, Macaulay, Stratton. *Sabina!* by Snoo Wilson, dir by Andy Wilson at the Bush: rev by Billington, Butler, Clapp, Coveney, de Jongh, Hagerty, Hewison, Marlowe, Morley, Nathan, Sierz, Stratton, Woddis.

2584 "Reviews of Productions." *LTR*. 1998; 18(3): 139-146. Lang.: Eng.

UK-England: London. 1998. ■*Vagabondage* by Marc Von Henning, dir by Von Henning at the Young Vic Studio: rev by Benedict, Curtis, Edwardes. *Cause Célèbre* by Terence Rattigan, dir by Neil Bartlett at Lyric Hammersmith: rev by Benedict, Billington, G. Brown, Butler, Clapp, Coveney, de Jongh, Edwardes, Foss, Gore-Langton, Gross, Hagerty, Macaulay, Morley, Nathan, Nightingale, Peter, Spencer, P.

Taylor. *The Golem* by Peter Wolf, with additional scenes by Bonnie Greer and Chiman Rahimi, dir Sue Lefton at the Bridewell: rev by Marmion, R. Williams.

2585 "Reviews of Productions." *LTR.* 1998; 18(3): 147-149. Lang.: Eng.
UK-England: London. 1998. ▪*Macbeth* by Shakespeare, dir by Sam Walters at the Orange Tree: rev by Butler, Coveney, Kingston, Marlowe, Marmion, Morley. *Adventures in a Yorkshire Landscape* by Mick Martin, dir by Christopher Masters at the Wimbledon Studio: rev by McPherson. *An Empty Plate in the Café du Grand* by Michael Hollinger, dir by Clive Perrot at the New End: rev by Abdulla. *The Wretched Splendour* by Rebecca Wilby, dir by Ninon Jerome at the Grace: rev by Billington.

2586 "Reviews of Productions." *LTR.* 1998; 18(4): 167-176. Lang.: Eng.
UK-England: London. 1998. ▪*Flight (Bèg)* by Michajl Bulgakov, transl by Ron Hutchinson, dir by Howard Davies for the Royal National at the Olivier: rev by Benedict, Billington, G. Brown, Butler, Clapp, Coveney, de Jongh, Edwardes, Gross, Hagerty, Hassell, Morley, Nathan, Nightingale, Peter, Sierz, Spencer, P. Taylor. *Shadowlands* by William Nicholson, dir by Roger Redfarn at Pentameters: rev by Abdulla. *In Five Years Time (Así que Pasen Cinco Años)* by García Lorca, transl by Marta Momblant, Ribas Chapman and Harry Chapman, dir by Ribas Chapman at Southwark Playhouse: rev by Curtis, Gardner, Godfrey-Faussett, Kingston.

2587 "Reviews of Productions." *LTR.* 1998; 18(3): 179-186. Lang.: Eng.
UK-England: London. 1998. ▪*Everyman* anonymous, dir by Kathryn Hunter and Marcello Magni for the RSC at The Pit: rev by Butler, Curtis, Edwardes, Gross, Murray, Nightingale, Woddis. *Of Blessed Memory* by Gregory Rattner, dir by Gordon Greenberg at the King's Head: rev by Billington, de Jongh, Hagerty, Kingston, Marlowe, Marmion, Nathan, Spencer, Woddis. *King Henry VIII* by Shakespeare, dir by Gregory Doran for the RSC at the Young Vic: rev by Curtis, Foss, gross, Hemming, Kingston, Logan, Morley.

2588 "Reviews of Productions." *LTR.* 1998; 18(3): 186-195. Lang.: Eng.
UK-England: London. 1998. ▪*Skin Deep* by Susan Earl and Dianne Glynn, dir by Janice Phayre at the Finborough: rev by Edwardes, McPherson. *Much Ado About Nothing* by Shakespeare, dir by Michael Boyd for the RSC at the Barbican: rev by de Jongh, Kingston, Morley, Shuttleworth, N. Smith, Stratton. *Naked (Vestire gli ignudi)* by Luigi Pirandello, adapt by Nicholas Wright from a literal translation by Gaynor MacFarlane, dir by Jonathan Kent at the Almeida: rev by Benedict, Billington, G. Brown, Butler, Clapp, Coveney, de Jongh, Gore-Langton, Hagerty, Macaulay, Morley, Nathan, Nightingale, N. Smith, Spencer, Stratton, P. Taylor.

2589 "Different Avenues." *PlPl.* June 1998; 523: 12-13. Illus.: Photo. B&W. 1. Lang.: Eng.
UK-England. USA. India. 1950-1998. Histories-sources. ▪Actor/writer Saeed Jaffrey on his acting career in the USA, the UK and India.

2590 Barranger, Milly S. "Webster Without Tears: A Daughter's Journey." 221-238 in Schanke, Robert A., ed.; Marra, Kim, ed. *Passing Performances: Queer Readings of Leading Players in American Theatre History.* Ann Arbor, MI: Univ of Michigan P; 1998. 338 pp. (Triangulations: Lesbian/Gay/Queer Theatre/Drama/Performance.) Notes. Index. Illus.: Photo. 1. Lang.: Eng.
UK-England. USA. 1905-1972. Biographical studies. ▪The impact of gender and sexuality in the life of theatre director and actor Margaret Webster.

2591 Benecke, Patricia. "Fixer, Monster und andere Traumgestalten." (Fixers, Monsters and Different Figures of Dreams.) *THeute.* 1998; 7: 29-32. Illus.: Photo. B&W. 2. Lang.: Ger.
UK-England: London. 1998. Reviews of performances. ▪Sarah Kane's *Cleansed* directed by James Macdonald at Theatre Downstairs, Philip Glass and Robert Wilson's *Monsters of Grace* directed by Wilson at Barbican Theatre and Gustav Mahler's *Kindertotenlieder (Songs on the Death of Children)* directed by Robert Lepage at Lyric Hammersmith Theatre.

2592 Brenna, Dwayne. "George Dibdin Pitt: Actor and Playwright." *TN.* 1998; 52(1): 24-37. Notes. Lang.: Eng.
UK-England: London. 1806-1808. Historical studies. ▪Life and career of George Dibdin Pitt, a minor actor who also wrote many popular domestic melodramas.

2593 Brown, Susan. "Queen Elizabeth in *Richard III.*" 101-113 in Smallwood, Robert, ed. *Players of Shakespeare 4: Further Essays on Shakespearian Performance by Players with the Royal Shakespeare Company.* Cambridge: Cambridge UP; 1998. 212 pp. Pref. Illus.: Photo. 2. Lang.: Eng.
UK-England: London, Stratford. 1995-1996. Histories-sources. ▪The author's experience playing Queen Elizabeth in Steven Pimlott's production of Shakespeare's *Richard III* at the RSC.

2594 Campbell, Julie. "Interview with Katie Mitchell." *JBeckS.* 1998 Sum; 8(1): 127-140. Illus.: Photo. B&W. 2. Lang.: Eng.
UK-England. 1998. Histories-sources. ▪Interview with actress and director Mitchell on her approach to the plays of Samuel Beckett.

2595 Charles, Peter. "Daniel Massey ... an appreciation." *PlPl.* May 1998; 522: 16. Lang.: Eng.
UK-England: London. 1968-1998. Biographical studies. ▪Life and career of actor Daniel Massey.

2596 Charles, Peter. "Betty Marsden—A Glorious Talent." *PlPl.* Sept 1998; 526: 10. Lang.: Eng.
UK-England: London. 1930-1998. Biographical studies. ▪Remembers career of actress Betty Marsden in a variety of media and genres, from first performance in 1930 to her death in 1998.

2597 Charles, Peter. "The Inimitable Miss Hickson." *PlPl.* 1998/99 Dec/Jan.; 528: 30. Lang.: Eng.
UK-England: London. 1927-1998. Biographical studies. ▪Career on stage and screen of actress Joan Hickson.

2598 Charles, Peter. "An International Actor." *PlPl.* 1998/99 Dec/Jan.; 529: 30-31. Lang.: Eng.
UK-England: London. 1930-1998. Biographical studies. ▪Career on stage and screen of actor Marius Goring.

2599 Charles, Peter. "The Perfect Gentleman—A Tribute to Michael Denison." *PlPl.* 1998 Sep.; 526: 11. Lang.: Eng.
UK-England: London. 1936-1998. Biographical studies. ▪Reviews stage career of actor Michael Denison from training in 1930s to his death in 1998.

2600 Clarke, Sue. "Oh, Vanity Fair!" *PlPl.* Mar 1998; 520: 22-23. Illus.: Photo. B&W. 1. Lang.: Eng.
UK-England: Leeds. 1997. Histories-sources. ▪A cast member's account of Michael Birch's approach to directing West Yorkshire Playhouse's 1997 production of *Vanity Fair* (William Makepeace Thackeray, adaptation by David Nobbs).

2601 Cordner, Michael. "Repeopling the Globe: The Opening Season at Shakespeare's Globe, London 1997." *ShS.* 1998; 51: 205-217. Notes. Lang.: Eng.
UK-England: London. 1997. Reviews of performances. ▪The inaugural season at Shakespeare's Globe: Shakespeare's *The Winter's Tale* directed by David Freeman, and *Henry V* directed by Richard Olivier, Middleton's *A Chaste Maid in Cheapside* directed by Malcolm McKay, and Beaumont and Fletcher's *The Maid's Tragedy* directed by Lucy Bailey.

2602 Dessen, Alan C. "Globe Matters." *SQ.* 1998 Sum; 49(2): 195-203. Illus.: Photo. B&W. 5. Lang.: Eng.
UK-England: London. 1997. Reviews of performances. ▪The official opening season of Shakespeare's Globe Theatre: Shakespeare's *Henry V* and *The Winter's Tale*, directed by Richard Olivier and David Freeman respectively, Thomas Middleton's *A Chaste Maid in Cheapside*, directed by Malcolm McKay, and Beaumont and Fletcher's *The Maid's Tragedy* directed by Lucy Bailey.

2603 Di Gaetani, John Louis. "London and Edinburgh—Summer 1998." *WES.* 1998 Fall; 10(3): 89-94. Illus.: Photo. B&W. 4. Lang.: Eng.
UK-England: London. UK-Scotland: Edinburgh. 1998. Historical studies. ▪Report on the London summer theatre scene and the 1998 Edinburgh Festival.

DRAMA: —Performance/production

2604 Ehrnrooth, Albert. "Upprörande fängelseskildring." (An Outrageous Account of a Jail.) *Tningen.* 1998; 21(2): 34. Illus.: Photo. B&W. Lang.: Swe.

UK-England: London. 1998. Critical studies. ■A look at Tennessee Williams' *Not About Nightingales*, with references to Trevor Nunn's production at National Theatre in London.

2605 Gardner, Viv. "No Flirting with Philistinism: Shakespearean Production at Miss Hornimann's Gaiety Theatre." *NTQ.* 1998 Aug.; 14(3): 220-233. Notes. Biblio. Illus.: Photo. B&W. 7. [Issue 55.] Lang.: Eng.

UK-England: Manchester. 1908-1915. Historical studies. ■Ambivalent attitude of tradition-bound Gaiety Theatre owner Annie Hornimann towards experimental Shakespearean productions presented at her theatre, such as Lewis Casson's *Julius Caesar* and William Poel's *Measure for Measure.*

2606 Glover, Julian. "Friar Lawrence in *Romeo and Juliet.*" 165-176 in Smallwood, Robert, ed. *Players of Shakespeare 4: Further Essays on Shakespearian Performance by Players with the Royal Shakespeare Company.* Cambridge: Cambridge UP; 1998. 212 pp. Pref. Illus.: Photo. 2. Lang.: Eng.

UK-England: London, Stratford. 1995-1996. Histories-sources. ■The author's experience playing Friar Lawrence in Adrian Noble's production of Shakespeare's *Romeo and Juliet* at the RSC.

2607 Goodman, Lizbeth; Coe, Tony; Williams, Huw. "The Multimedia Bard: Plugged and Unplugged." *NTQ.* 1998 Feb.; 14(1): 20-42. Illus.: Photo. B&W. 15. [Issue 53.] Lang.: Eng.

UK-England. 1995-1997. Histories-sources. ■Conversation with actress Fiona Shaw regarding the use of mutimedia in creating and preserving live theatre. Cites examples from Shaw's version of *King Lear* and Cheek by Jowl's all-male *As You Like It* directed by Declan Donnellan at the Albery Theatre.

2608 Goodman, Lizbeth. "Overlapping Dialogue in Overlapping Media: Behind the Scenes of *Top Girls.*" 69-101 in Rabillard, Sheila, ed. *Essays on Caryl Churchill: Contemporary Representations.* Winnipeg, MB/Buffalo, NY: Blizzard; 1998. 224 pp. Biblio. Notes. Illus.: Photo. 5. Lang.: Eng.

UK-England. 1982-1991. Critical studies. ■Using interviews with playwright Caryl Churchill, director Max Stafford-Clark, and actors such as Fiona Shaw, analyzes the original production of *Top Girls* in 1982 and a video production, also directed by Stafford-Clark and featuring Shaw, for the BBC/Open University in 1991.

2609 Gordon, Robert. "3 by Pinter." *PintR.* 1998: 147-151. Lang.: Eng.

UK-England: London. 1998. Critical studies. ■Analysis of the production of three Pinter plays at Donmar Warehouse: *The Lover* and *The Collection* directed by Joe Harmston and *A Kind of Alaska* directed by Karel Reisz.

2610 Greenfield, Peter. "Census of Medieval Drama Productions." *RORD.* 1998; 37: 113-135. Lang.: Eng.

UK-England. 1997. Historical studies. ■Census of productions of medieval plays held in Great Britain in 1997.

2611 Greif, Karen. "A Star Is Born: Feste on the Modern Stage." *SQ.* 1988 Spr; 39(1): 61-78. Notes. Lang.: Eng.

UK-England. 1773-1988. Historical studies. ■Theatrical metamorphosis of the character Feste in theatrical productions of Shakespeare's *Twelfth Night* from the Romantic era to the present.

2612 Hakola, Liisa. *In One Person Many People: The Image of the King in Three RSC Productions of William Shakespeare's King Richard II.* Helsinki: Helsingin Yliopisto; 1988. 198 pp. Biblio. Notes. [Ph.D. Dissertation.] Lang.: Eng.

UK-England. 1973-1984. Critical studies. ■The image of the king in Shakespeare's play, based both on the text and on the physical circumstances of production. Three RSC productions are discussed, directed by John Barton, Terry Hands, and Barry Kyle.

2613 Happé, Peter. "*Damon and Pythias* by Richard Edwards at Shakespeare's Globe." *MET.* 1996; 18: 161-163. Lang.: Eng.

UK-England: London. 1996. Reviews of performances. ■Review of Richard Edwards' *Damon and Pythias*, performed with an all-female cast at Shakespeare's Globe under the direction of Gaynor Macfarlane.

2614 Hunter, Robin. "Harold French Without Tears." *PlPl.* Feb 1998; 519: 30. Lang.: Eng.

UK-England: London. 1900-1998. Biographical studies. ■Actor-director Harold French's life and career on the stage on the occasion of his death.

2615 Jackson, Russell. "Johanna Schopenhauer's Journal: A German View of the London Theatre Scene, 1803-1805." *TN.* 1998; 52 (3): 142-160. Notes. Lang.: Eng.

UK-England: London. Germany. 1803-1805. Histories-sources. ■Brief biographical account of Johanna Schopenhauer, the philosopher's mother, and selected translations from her journal relating to theatres, audiences, and performers at the Drury Lane, Covent Garden, Haymarket, Italian Opera House, and Sadler's Wells.

2616 Jacobi, Derek. "Macbeth." 193-210 in Smallwood, Robert, ed. *Players of Shakespeare 4: Further Essays on Shakespearian Performance by Players with the Royal Shakespeare Company.* Cambridge: Cambridge UP; 1998. 212 pp. Pref. Illus.: Photo. 2. Lang.: Eng.

UK-England: London, Stratford. 1993-1994. Histories-sources. ■The author's experience playing the title role in Shakespeare's *Macbeth* at the RSC, directed by Adrian Noble.

2617 Jesson, Paul. "Henry VIII." 114-131 in Smallwood, Robert, ed. *Players of Shakespeare 4: Further Essays on Shakespearian Performance by Players with the Royal Shakespeare Company.* Cambridge: Cambridge UP; 1998. 212 pp. Pref. Illus.: Photo. 3. Lang.: Eng.

UK-England: London, Stratford. 1996-1997. Histories-sources. ■The author's experience playing Henry VIII in Shakespeare's play at the RSC, directed by Gregory Doran.

2618 Knowles, Richard Paul. "From Dream to Machine: Peter Brook, Robert Lepage, and the Contemporary Shakespearean Director as (Post)Modernist." *TJ.* 1998 May; 50(2): 189-206. Notes. Lang.: Eng.

UK-England. Canada. 1966-1996. Critical studies. ■The 'postmodernist' directing of Robert Lepage's productions of *A Midsummer Night's Dream* and *Elsinore.* Examines continuities between Peter Brook's seminal *Midsummer Night's Dream* and Lepage's and suggests that contemporary practices of Shakespearean directing are very similar to earlier modernist productions.

2619 Lapotaire, Jane. "Queen Katherine in *Henry VIII.*" 132-151 in Smallwood, Robert, ed. *Players of Shakespeare 4: Further Essays on Shakespearian Performance by Players with the Royal Shakespeare Company.* Cambridge: Cambridge UP; 1998. 212 pp. Pref. Illus.: Photo. 2. Lang.: Eng.

UK-England: London, Stratford. 1996-1997. Histories-sources. ■The author's experience playing Queen Katherine in Shakespeare's *Henry VIII* at the RSC, directed by Gregory Doran.

2620 Luscombe, Christopher. "Launcelot Gobbo in *The Merchant of Venice* and Moth in *Love's Labours Lost.*" 18-29 in Smallwood, Robert, ed. *Players of Shakespeare 4: Further Essays on Shakespearian Performance by Players with the Royal Shakespeare Company.* Cambridge: Cambridge Univ P; 1998. 212 pp. Pref. Illus.: Photo. 2. Lang.: Eng.

UK-England: London, Stratford. 1993-1994. Histories-sources. ■The author's experience playing Launcelot Gobbo in Shakespeare's *The Merchant of Venice*, directed by David Thacker, and Moth in Ian Judge's production of *Love's Labour's Lost* at the RSC.

2621 Mahon, John W. "Richard Olivier Directs *The Merchant of Venice.*" *ShN.* 1998 Sum; 48(2): 43. Illus.: Photo. B&W. 1. Lang.: Eng.

UK-England: London. 1998. Historical studies. ■Note on Richard Olivier as he takes on the direction of *The Merchant of Venice* at Shakespeare's Globe.

2622 Marlow, Jane. "Steady Eddie." *PlPl.* Feb 1998; 519: 35. Lang.: Eng.

UK-England: London. 1990-1998. Histories-sources. ■Interview with Eddie Marsan on recent developments in his acting career.

2623 McCabe, Richard. "Autolycus in *The Winter's Tale.*" 60-70 in Smallwood, Robert, ed. *Players of Shakespeare 4: Further Essays on Shakespearian Performance by Players with the*

DRAMA: —Performance/production

Royal Shakespeare Company. Cambridge: Cambridge UP; 1998. 212 pp. Pref. Illus.: Photo. 2. Lang.: Eng.
UK-England: London, Stratford. 1992-1993. Histories-sources. ■The author's experience playing Autolycus in Shakespeare's *The Winter's Tale*, directed by Adrian Noble at the RSC.

2624 Mohamed, M.M.S. *Charles Marowitz: The Semiotics of Collage and Dramatic Classics.* Canterbury: Unpublished PhD, Univ. of Kent; 1997. Notes. Biblio. [Absract in *Aslib Index to Theses*, 47-10574.] Lang.: Eng.
UK-England. USA. 1962-1979. Critical studies. ■Influence of the collage technique of the figurative arts on the approach of director Marowitz to both Shakespearean and non-Shakespearean classic drama.

2625 Nettles, John. "Brutus in *Julius Caesar.*" 177-192 in Smallwood, Robert, ed. *Players of Shakespeare 4: Further Essays on Shakespearian Performance by Players with the Royal Shakespeare Company.* Cambridge: Cambridge UP; 1998. 212 pp. Pref. Illus.: Photo. 2. Lang.: Eng.
UK-England: London, Stratford. 1995. Histories-sources. ■The author's experience playing Brutus in Peter Hall's production of Shakespeare's *Julius Caesar* at the RSC.

2626 Normington, Kate. "Little Acts of Faith: Katie Mitchell's *The Mysteries.*" *NTQ.* 1998 May; 14(2): 99-110. Notes. Biblio. Illus.: Photo. B&W. 4. [Issue 54.] Lang.: Eng.
UK-England: London. 1996-1998. Historical studies. ■Assesses the relevance of the staging of mystery plays by the Royal Shakespeare Company to modern society, especially considering the problems of updating the text, the acting style, and attitudes toward gender representation.

2627 Norseng, Mary Kay. "Ibsen, McKellen, Nunn: The Stockmann Coup?" *WES.* 1998 Fall; 10(3): 79-82. Illus.: Photo. B&W. 2. Lang.: Eng.
UK-England: London. 1998. Critical studies. ■Analysis of Trevor Nunn's staging of Ibsen's *An Enemy of the People (En Folkefiende)* for the Royal National Theatre at the Olivier, and starring Ian McKellen.

2628 Nyberg, Lennart Jan. *The Shakespearean Ideal: Shakespeare Production and the Modern Theatre in Britain.* Uppsala: Uppsalas Universitet; 1988. 144 pp. Biblio. Notes. [Ph.D. Dissertation.] Lang.: Eng.
UK-England. 1960-1980. Histories-specific. ■Argues that the nature of Shakespearean production in England changed because of shifting theatre aesthetics as new dramatists emerged and the theatre was influenced by the work of modern theatre practitioners such as Brecht, Samuel Beckett and Jean Genet.

2629 Roberts, Peter. "Solo Work." *PI.* 1998 Dec.; 14(3): 10-11. Illus.: Photo. B&W. 2. Lang.: Eng.
UK-England. 1998. Biographical studies. ■Profile of actor Tom Conti, performing in the monologue *Jesus, My Boy* by John Dowie at the Apollo.

2630 Roberts, Philip. "The Letters of George Devine to Michel Saint-Denis, 1939-1945." *TN.* 1998; 52(3): 161-171. Notes. Lang.: Eng.
UK-England: London. 1939-1945. Histories-sources. ■Examination of the correspodence between Devine and Saint-Denis during World War II regarding their London Theatre Studio, the formation of the Actor's Company, and Devine's work as a producer at the Old Vic under Tyrone Guthrie.

2631 Robson, Christopher. "Leslie Howard (1893-1943)—The Enigmatic Englishman." *PlPl.* June 1998; 523: 14. Illus.: Photo. B&W. 1. Lang.: Eng.
UK-England: London. USA: New York, NY. 1893-1943. Biographical studies. ■Life and career on stage and on screen of actor Leslie Howard.

2632 Robson, Christopher. "Charles Laughton (1899-1962)—The Supreme Character Actor." *PlPl.* Aug 1998; 525: 20. Illus.: Photo. B&W. 1. Lang.: Eng.
UK-England: London. USA: Hollywood, CA. 1899-1962. Biographical studies. ■Life and career on stage and screen of actor Charles Laughton.

2633 Robson, Christopher. "Robert Donat (1905-1958)—Prince of Players." *PlPl.* 1998 Oct.; 527: 14. Illus.: Photo. B&W. 1. Lang.: Eng.
UK-England: London. 1905-1958. Biographical studies. ■Stage and screen career of actor Robert Donat.

2634 Saag, Kristjan. "Står Shakespeare i vägen?" (Is Shakespeare Standing In the Way?)*Tningen.* 1998; 21(2): 31-33. Illus.: Photo. B&W. Lang.: Swe.
UK-England: London, Stratford. 1998. Critical studies. ■Report on theatre in Great Britain in March and April with references to Michael Boyd's production of Shakespeare's *Much Ado About Nothing* at Royal Shakespeare Company, Patrick Marber's production of his own *Closer* at the Lyric and *Sleeping Around*, a collective play by Mark Ravenhill, Hilary Fannin, Abi Morgan and Stephen Greenhorn at Paines Plough Theatre Company.

2635 Schafer, Elizabeth. "Census of Renaissance Drama Productions." *RORD.* 1998; 37: 63-75. Lang.: Eng.
UK-England. 1997. Historical studies. ■Census of productions of Renaissance plays and staged readings held in Great Britain in 1997.

2636 Shaughnessy, Robert. "The Last Post: *Henry V*, War Culture and the Postmodern Shakespeare." *ThS.* 1998 May; 39(1): 41-61. Notes. Illus.: Photo. B&W. 2. Lang.: Eng.
UK-England. 1970-1994. Critical studies. ■Examines postmodern staging and design practice in England, with emphasis on Matthew Warchus's 1994 staging of Shakespeare's *Henry V* to reveal the postmodern relationship between text and performance, and the verbal and visual order of performance.

2637 Siberry, Michael. "Petruchio in *The Taming of the Shrew.*" 45-59 in Smallwood, Robert, ed. *Players of Shakespeare 4: Further Essays on Shakespearian Performance by Players with the Royal Shakespeare Company.* Cambridge: Cambridge UP; 1998. 212 pp. Pref. Illus.: Photo. 2. Lang.: Eng.
UK-England: London, Stratford. 1995-1996. Histories-sources. ■The author's experience playing Petruchio in Shakespeare's *The Taming of the Shrew* at the RSC, directed by Gale Edwards.

2638 Smallwood, Robert. "Introduction." 1-17 in Smallwood, Robert, ed. *Players of Shakespeare 4: Further Essays on Shakespearian Performance by Players with the Royal Shakespeare Company.* Cambridge: Cambridge UP; 1998. 212 pp. Pref. Illus.: Photo. 4. Lang.: Eng.
UK-England: London, Stratford. 1992-1997. Histories-sources. ■Introductory essay to a collection by Royal Shakespeare Company actors about their performances as Shakespearean characters.

2639 Speaight, George. "New Light on *Mother Goose.*" *TN.* 1998; 52(1): 18-23. Notes. Illus.: Dwg. Print. B&W. 4. Lang.: Eng.
UK-England: London. 1806-1808. Historical studies. ■Evidence of a performance of Thomas Dibdin's *Harlequin and Mother Goose*, staged at Covent Garden with actor Joey Grimaldi, in a children's table game called 'Mother Goose and her golden eggs'. Includes illustrations from the game.

2640 Tennant, David. "Touchstone in *As You Like It.*" 30-44 in Smallwood, Robert, ed. *Players of Shakespeare 4: Further Essays on Shakespearian Performance by Players with the Royal Shakespeare Company.* Cambridge: Cambridge UP; 1998. 212 pp. Pref. Illus.: Photo. 2. Lang.: Eng.
UK-England: London, Stratford. 1996-1997. Histories-sources. ■The author's experience playing Touchstone in Steven Pimlott's production of Shakespeare's *As You Like It* at the RSC.

2641 Teschke, Holger; Monro, Mia, transl. "En av de sju historierna." (One of the Seven Histories.) *Tningen.* 1998; 21(3): 9-11. Illus.: Photo. B&W. Lang.: Swe.
UK-England: London. 1997. Histories-sources. ■Interview with director Simon McBurney about his production of Brecht's *Der Kaukasische Kreidekreis (The Caucasian Chalk Circle)* at the National Theatre.

2642 Troughton, David. "Richard III." 71-100 in Smallwood, Robert, ed. *Players of Shakespeare 4: Further Essays on Shakespearian Performance by Players with the Royal Shakespeare Company.* Cambridge: Cambridge UP; 1998. 212 pp. Pref. Illus.: Photo. 2. Lang.: Eng.
UK-England: London, Stratford. 1995-1996. Histories-sources. ■The author's experience playing Richard III in Shakespeare's play at the RSC, directed by Steven Pimlott.

2643 Voss, Philip. "Menenius in *Coriolanus.*" 152-164 in Smallwood, Robert, ed. *Players of Shakespeare 4: Further Essays on Shakespearian Performance by Players with the Royal*

DRAMA: —Performance/production

Shakespeare Company. Cambridge: Cambridge UP; 1998. 212 pp. Pref. Illus.: Photo. 2. Lang.: Eng.
UK-England: London, Stratford. 1994. Histories-sources. ▪The author's experience playing Menenius in Shakespeare's *Coriolanus*, directed by David Thacker at the RSC's Swan Theatre.

2644 Waites, Aline. "You Can Always Look At The Set!" *PlPl.* Apr 1998; 521: 10-11. Illus.: Photo. B&W. 1. Lang.: Eng.
UK-England: London. 1950-1998. Histories-sources. ▪Actor Michael Williams on his career and on performing in one-man show *Brief Lives*, written and directed by Patrick Garland for the company Theatre of Comedy.

2645 Waites, Aline. "Casting For Godot." *PlPl.* May 1998; 522: 27. Lang.: Eng.
UK-England. 1998. Critical studies. ▪Speculates on possible castings of Samuel Beckett's *Waiting for Godot.*

2646 Waites, Aline. "George Grizzard–Actor." *PlPl.* Aug 1998; 525: 14-15. Illus.: Photo. B&W. . Lang.: Eng.
UK-England: London. USA: New York, NY. 1954-1998. Histories-sources. ▪Actor George Grizzard on his career and his impression of English actors.

2647 Wall, Clare-Marie. *Script, Performance, Perception: The Textual Interplay of Coriolanus.* Boulder, CO: Univ. of Colorado; 1987. 313 pp. Notes. Biblio. [Ph.D. Dissertation, Univ. Microfilms Order No. AAC 8716314.] Lang.: Eng.
UK-England. 1985. Critical studies. ▪Explores Shakespeare's *Coriolanus* as a series of collaborative events, created during the interplay between playwright, theatre team, and audience members using Peter Hall's National Theatre production of the play as an example.

2648 Zern, Leif. "Skådespelarna mellan text & yta." (The Actors Between Text & Surface.) *Dramat.* 1998; 6(3): 15-16. Lang.: Swe.
UK-England. Sweden. 1950-1998. Critical studies. ▪Essay about the different types of actors, and what they have contributed to directors, with references to Laurence Olivier, John Gielgud, Louis Jouvet, and Ulf Palme.

2649 "Edinburgh Festival: Fringe." *LTR.* 1998; 18(16): 1015-1046. Lang.: Eng.
UK-Scotland: Edinburgh. 1998. ▪Supplement to *LTR* 18:16 containing schedules, awards, critical round-ups, and reviews of the Edinburgh Festival Fringe.

2650 "Reviews of Productions." *LTR.* 1998; 18(17): 1097-1104. Lang.: Eng.
UK-Scotland: Edinburgh. 1998. ▪*La Pantera Imperial* by J.S. Bach and Carles Santos, dir by Santos and Josep Vila i Casañas at King's Theatre: rev by Johnson, McMillan, Morrison. *More Stately Mansions* by Eugene O'Neill, adapt by Karl Ragnar Gierow, dir by Ivo van Hove at Royal Lyceum: rev by Clapp, Cooper, Curtis, Fisher, Macaulay, McMillan, Peter, Spencer. *Phèdre* by Jean Racine, dir by Luc Bondy at the King's Theatre: rev by Billington, Cooper, McMillan, Spencer. *Caligula* by Albert Camus, transl by Leonard Nolens, dir by van Hove at Edinburgh Playhouse: rev by Bruce, Cooper, McMillan, Peter, Spencer, P. Taylor.

2651 Bottoms, Stephen J. "Building on the Abyss: Susan Glaspell's *The Verge* in Production." *TTop.* 1998 Sep.; 8(2): 127-148 . Notes. Biblio. Illus.: Photo. B&W. 3. Lang.: Eng.
UK-Scotland: Glasgow. 1996. Histories-sources. ▪The author's experience in directing Susan Glaspell's expressionistic and experimental play *The Verge* in conjunction with the international Glaspell conference. Focuses on the feminist premises on which the production was based.

2652 Norris, James. "A Man of Humility." *PlPl.* Jan 1998; 518: 6-8. Illus.: Photo. B&W. 1. Lang.: Eng.
UK-Scotland: Edinburgh. UK-England: London. 1945-1998. Histories-sources. ▪Actor Ian Richardson on acting technique and on his career.

2653 Weiss, Alfred. "The Edinburgh Festival, 1987." *SQ.* 1988 Spr; 39(1): 79-89. Lang.: Eng.
UK-Scotland: Edinburgh. 1997. Historical studies. ▪Shakespearean influence on the 1987 Edinburgh Festival.

2654 "Season Preview 1998-99." *AmTh.* 1998 Oct.; 15(8): 27-61. Illus.: Photo. Dwg. B&W. 10. Lang.: Eng.
USA. 1998-1999. Histories-sources. ▪Comprehensive list of productions, dates and directors at Theatre Communications Guild constituent theatres across the United States.

2655 "Joseph Maher 1934-1998, Warren Kliewer 1932-1998, E.G. Marshall 1912-1998." *AmTh.* 1998 Oct.; 15(8): 79. Illus.: Photo. B&W. 1. Lang.: Eng.
USA. 1912-1998. Biographical studies. ▪Obituaries for actors Maher and Marshall, and director/playwright/actor Kliewer.

2656 Abel, Sam. "Staging Heterosexuality: Alfred Lunt and Lynn Fontanne's Design for Living." 175-196 in Schanke, Robert A., ed.; Marra, Kim, ed. *Passing Performances: Queer Readings of Leading Players in American Theatre History.* Ann Arbor, MI: Univ of Michigan P; 1998. 338 pp. (Triangulations: Lesbian/Gay/Queer Theatre/Drama/Performance.) Notes. Index. Illus.: Dwg. Photo. 2. Lang.: Eng.
USA. 1887-1983. Biographical studies. ▪'Idealized heterosexuality' in the professional careers and personal lives of theatre couple Alfred Lunt and Lynn Fontanne.

2657 Acker, Barbara Frances. *Perceptual Study of the Effects of Short-Term Vocal Training on the Stageworthy Quality of the Voice.* Detroit, MI: Wayne State Univ; 1987. 49 pp. Notes. Biblio. [Ph.D. Dissertation, Univ. Microfilms Order No. AAC 8714527.] Lang.: Eng.
USA. 1986-1987. Empirical research. ▪Study of the importance of voice training for the actor. Reports on a research project on the perception of the stageworthy quality of the voice.

2658 Applebaum, Susan Rae. "*The Little Princess* Onstage in 1903: Its Historical Significance." *THSt.* 1998; 53: 71-88. Notes. Illus.: Photo. B&W. 4. Lang.: Eng.
USA. 1903. Historical studies. ▪The impact of Frances Hodgson Burnett's *The Little Princess* on popular culture and theatre. Argues that this 'forgotten' production can shed light on transitional forces in theatre at the turn of the century.

2659 Austin, John Lewis. *An Actor's Approach to Performing the Role of Malvolio in Shakespeare's Twelfth Night.* Louisville, KY: Univ. of Louisville; 1987. 88 pp. Notes. Biblio. [M.F.A. Thesis, Univ. Microfilms Order No. 1332981.] Lang.: Eng.
USA. 1987. Historical studies. ▪Interpretation, rehearsal, and performance of Malvolio in Shakespeare's *Twelfth Night*, performed at the Belknap Theatre in fulfillment of requirements for an M.F.A. in Acting.

2660 Bates, Mark. "Acting Music, Scoring Texts." *ThM.* 1998; 28(2): 81-85. Illus.: Diagram. B&W. 1. Lang.: Eng.
USA: New Haven, CT. 1998. Histories-sources. ▪Interview with composer Paul Schmidt on the challenges of scoring music for the reconstruction of Mejerchol'd's staging of Gogol's *The Inspector General (Revizor)*, co-produced by the Yale Drama Department and the St. Petersburg Academy of Theatre Arts, directed by David Chambers.

2661 Bates, Mark. "Directing a National Consciousness." *ThM.* 1998; 28(2): 87-90. Notes. Biblio. Illus.: Photo. B&W. 1. Lang.: Eng.
USA: Cambridge, MA. 1980-1981. Histories-sources. ▪Interview with director Peter Sellars on his production of *The Inspector General (Revizor)* at the American Repertory Theatre, and Mejerchol'd's influence upon it.

2662 Bergmann, Ursula A. *Ursula Bergmann's Acting Analysis of Character Development in Plays by Coward, Pinter, Molière, Shakespeare, Williams, Topor, and McNally.* Long Beach, CA: California State Univ; 1988. 43 pp. Notes. Biblio. [M. F.A. Thesis, Univ. Microfilms Order No. AAC 1333798.] Lang.: Eng.
USA: Long Beach, CA. 1988. Histories-sources. ▪Acting analysis in fulfillment of the M.F.A. in acting, presented at the Directing Laboratory Theatre at California State University.

2663 Bernard, Lauren S. *Studies in French Cultural and Intellectual History.* Houston, TX: Rice Univ; 1998. 112 pp. Notes. Biblio. [M.A. Thesis, Univ. Microfilms Order No. AAC 1389066.] Lang.: Eng.
USA. 1650-1950. Histories-specific. ▪Considers various aspects of French intellectual history, including the work of Molière. Also includes discussion of race and difference and the writings of Taine and Le Bon.

DRAMA: —Performance/production

2664 Boutorabi, Afsaneh. *Acting Analysis of Character Development in Plays by Durang, Molière, Pinter, Shakespeare, Shaw, Shepard, and Williams.* Long Beach, CA: Univ. of California; 1987. 31 pp. Notes. Biblio. [M.F.A. Thesis, Univ. Microfilms Order No. 1330579.] Lang.: Eng.
USA. 1987. Histories-sources. ■Account of the creative process used in the development of the author's MFA Final Project, performed on 14 March 1987.

2665 Braibish Scott, Laura Christine. *Maids, Whores and African Dancers.* Louisville, KY: Univ. of Louisville; 1998. 76 pp. Biblio. Notes. [M.F.A. Thesis, Univ. Microfilms Order No. 1390400.] Lang.: Eng.
USA. 1997. Histories-sources. ■On the author's portrayal of Alma in Tennessee Williams' *Summer and Smoke* in fulfillment of requirements for an M.F.A. in Acting.

2666 Brailow, David G. "Authority and Interpretation: *Hamlet* at Shakespeare Repertory Theatre." *ET.* 1998; 16(2): 187-207. Notes. Biblio. Illus.: Photo. B&W. 2. Lang.: Eng.
USA: Chicago, IL. 1996. Critical studies. ■Analysis of rehearsals, previews, and performances of *Hamlet* at the Shakespeare Repertory Theatre, directed by Barbara Gaines. Argues that meaning is often imparted when interpretation is least controlled, or when one can observe behind the scenes.

2667 Callens, Johan. "FinISHed Story: Elizabeth LeCompte's Intercultural Take on Time and Work." 143-158 in Huber, Werner, ed.; Middeke, Martin, ed. *Anthropological Perspectives: Contemporary Drama in English 5.* Trier: Wissenschaftlicher Verlag; 1996. 212 pp. Lang.: Eng.
USA: New York, NY. 1990-1996. Critical studies. ■Multicultural analysis of LeCompte's direction of the Wooster Group's collaborative piece *Fish Story.*

2668 Chambers, David. "Reconstructing *Revizor.*" *ThM.* 1998; 28(2): 56-60. Illus.: Photo. Design. B&W. 2. Lang.: Eng.
USA: New Haven, CT. 1997. Histories-sources. ■Background on the Yale Drama Department's reconstruction of Mejerchol'd's 1926 staging of Gogol's *The Inspector General (Revizor).* Project was directed by Chambers, as a co-production with the St. Petersburg Academy of Theatre Arts.

2669 Cheng, Kipp. "Someone Lovely This Way Comes." *AmTh.* 1998 July/Aug.; 15(6): 26-27. Illus.: Photo. B&W. 2. Lang.: Eng.
USA. 1993-1998. Biographical studies. ■Profile of three-time Tony Award winning actress Audra McDonald.

2670 Coen, Stephanie. "Michael Mayer." *AmTh.* 1998 Mar.; 15(3): 38-40. Illus.: Photo. B&W. 2. Lang.: Eng.
USA. 1998. Biographical studies. ■Profile of director Michael Mayer.

2671 Coleman, Stephen DuBois. "Arthur French: Drifting Along On a Wave." *BlackM.* 1998 Jan/Feb.; 12(6): 5-6, 15-16. Illus.: Photo. B&W. 2. Lang.: Eng.
USA: New York, NY. 1962-1998. Biographical studies. ■Profile of the veteran actor and original member of the Negro Ensemble Company.

2672 Connors, Thomas. "The Final Frontier?" *AmTh.* 1998 Mar.; 15(3): 42-43. Illus.: Photo. B&W. 1. Lang.: Eng.
USA: Chicago, IL. 1998. Reviews of performances. ■Steppenwolf Theatre's production of Tina Landau's *Space* directed by Landau.

2673 Cunningham, Frank R. "A Newly Discovered Fourth Production of O'Neill's *Lazarus Laughed.*" *EOR.* 1998 Spr/Fall; 22(1/2) : 114-122. Notes. Biblio. Append. Lang.: Eng.
USA: Detroit, MI. 1963. Historical studies. ■Documentation of a previously unknown fourth production of the play, formerly believed to have been produced only three times, at Mercy College in Detroit. Includes appendix containing program information.

2674 Daniels, Rebecca. "Gender, Creativity & Power." *AmTh.* 1998 Sep.; 15(7): 30-31, 80-81. Illus.: Dwg. B&W. 1. Lang.: Eng.
USA. 1996. Histories-sources. ■Directors JoAnne Akalaitis, Roberta Levitow, Timothy Near, Liz Diamond, Zelda Fichandler, Tisa Chang, and Sharon Ott share their views on whether directing is different for men and women. Excerpted from Rebecca Daniels's *Women Stage Directors Speak* (Jefferson, NC: McFarland, 1996).

2675 Dorff, Linda. "Chamber Music." *AmTh.* 1998 Oct.; 15(8): 22-25. Illus.: Photo. B&W. 3. Lang.: Eng.
USA. 1966-1981. Histories-sources. ■Actresses Elizabeth Ashley and Zoe Caldwell, and directors Gregory Mosher and Eve Adamson reflect on working on the later plays of Tennessee Williams.

2676 Drukman, Steven. "Peter Riegert: Speaking of Mamet." *AmTh.* 1998 Jan.; 15(1): 52-53. Illus.: Dwg. B&W. 1. Lang.: Eng.
USA: New York, NY. 1998. Histories-sources. ■Interview with the actor concerning working in the plays of David Mamet.

2677 Drukman, Steven. "Entering the Postmodern Studio: Viewpoint Theory." *AmTh.* 1998 Jan.; 15(1): 30-34. Illus.: Dwg. B&W. 3. Lang.: Eng.
USA. 1998. Critical studies. ■The influence of 'viewpoint theory' of actor training, introduced by dancer-choreographer Mary Overlie in the 1970s as an alternative to method training. Includes sidebar comments on the theory by playwrights, actors, directors and administrators such as Anne Bogart, Robert Moss, Lisa Peterson, Michael Malone, Kevin Kuhlke, Fritz Ertl, Stephan Müller, and Moisés Kaufman.

2678 Edwards, Paul A. *'Putting on the Greeks': Euripidean Tragedy and the Twentieth-Century American Theatre.* Boulder, CO: Univ. of Colorado; 1987. 262 pp. Notes. Biblio. [Ph.D. Dissertation, Univ. Microfilms Order No. AAC 8808270.] Lang.: Eng.
USA. 1915-1969. Historical studies. ■The revival of interest in Euripides and Greek drama, with emphasis on production in the context of their aesthetic and socio-political backgrounds: the 1915 Chicago Little Theatre production of *The Trojan Women*, the 1947 production of Robinson Jeffers' *Medea*, and the 1968 production by the Performance Group of *Dionysus in 69*, based on *The Bákchai* by Euripides.

2679 Farrell, John Edward. *Acting Analysis of Character Development in Plays by Congreve, Mamet, Pinter, Shakespeare, Shepard, Wilde, and Williams.* Long Beach, CA: Univ. of California; 1987. 31 pp. Notes. Biblio. [M.F.A. Thesis, Univ. Microfilms Order No. 1330595.] Lang.: Eng.
USA. 1987. Histories-sources. ■Describes the preparation and performance of the author's Master of Fine Arts Final Project presented in the Director's Laboratory Theatre at California State University, Long Beach.

2680 Finney, James Reed. *Aspects and Correlates of Directors' Nonverbal Behavior in the Rehearsal Process.* Evanston, IL: Northwestern Univ; 1987. 227 pp. Biblio. Notes. [Ph.D. Dissertation, Univ. Microfilms Order No. AAC 8728982.] Lang.: Eng.
USA. 1987. Empirical research. ■Uses interviews with directors and actors to amass statistical data analyzing kinetics, touch, and other nonverbal styles.

2681 Foreman, Richard. "Program Notes on *Pearls for Pigs.*" *TDR.* 1998 Sum; 42(2): 157-159. Notes. Illus.: Photo. B&W. 1. Lang.: Eng.
USA: Hartford, CT. 1997. Histories-sources. ■A note from the director regarding his approach to staging his own play which premiered at Hartford Stage in 1997.

2682 Galvez, Florante P. "The Alternative Black Theatre: A View for the Future." *BlackM.* 1998 May/June; 13(1): 7-8. Illus.: Photo. B&W. 2. Lang.: Eng.
USA. 1998. Critical studies. ■The burgeoning African-American alternative theatre scene and the willingness of Black audiences to support it.

2683 Gelb, Barbara. "Tribute to José Quintero." *EOR.* 1998 Spr/Fall; 22(1/2): 4-5. Lang.: Eng.
USA. 1924-1998. Biographical studies. ■Tribute to the late director who staged many landmark productions of plays by Eugene O'Neill.

2684 Gingrich-Philbrook, Craig. "Autobigraphical Performance and Carnivorous Knowledge: Rae C. Wright's *Animal Instincts.*" *TextPQ.* 1998 Jan.; 18(1): 63-79. Notes. Biblio. Lang.: Eng.
USA: New York, NY. 1997. Critical studies. ■Analysis of Wright's solo piece performed at Dixon's Place, with an emphasis on the audience-performer dynamic.

DRAMA: —Performance/production

2685 Gold, Sylviane. "The Possession of Julie Taymor." *AmTh.* 1998 Sep.; 15(7): 23-25. Illus.: Photo. B&W. 8. Lang.: Eng.
USA. 1980-1998. Biographical studies. ▪Career of director/costumer/mask-maker Julie Taymor.

2686 Gourley, Matthew J. *Biagio Buonaccorsi as Counter-Machiavellianism to Machiavelli in 'The Prince'.* Long Beach, CA: California State Univ; 1998. 61 pp. Notes. Biblio. [M.F.A. Thesis, Univ. Microfilms Order No. AAC 1390119.] Lang.: Eng.
USA. 1997. Histories-sources. ▪On the creation and performance of the character of Biagio Buonaccorsi in the California Repertory Company's production of Robert Cohen's *The Prince*, directed by Ashley Carr at California State University, Long Beach, in fulfillment of requirements for the M.F.A. degree in Acting.

2687 Greene, Alexis. "Frances Sternhagen: A Question of Age." *AmTh.* 1998 Sep.; 15(7): 69-70. Illus.: Photo. B&W. 1. Lang.: Eng.
USA. 1998. Histories-sources. ▪Actress Sternhagen shares her views on playing age for the stage, something she has been doing since she was much younger.

2688 Halperin-Royer, Ellen. "Robert Wilson and the Actor: Performing in *Danton's Death.*" *TTop.* 1998 Mar.; 8(1): 73-92. Notes. Biblio. Illus.: Photo. B&W. 2. Lang.: Eng.
USA: Houston, TX. 1997. Critical studies. ▪Investigates changing actor attitudes toward Robert Wilson's directorial abilities during the process of rehearsing *Danton's Death (Dantons Tod)* at Houston's Alley Theatre. Author observed rehearsals and specifically examined the type of acting technique required.

2689 Hamilton, Lonnée. "Ruby Dee: The Power of Words." *AmTh.* 1998 Sep.; 15(7): 67. Illus.: Photo. B&W. 1. Lang.: Eng.
USA. 1998. Biographical studies. ▪Career of actress Ruby Dee.

2690 Hammett, Charlotte Kaye. *'Crimes of My Heart': My Growth as an Actor with Babe Botrelle, A Description of One Actor's Method.* Louisville, KY: Univ. of Louisville; 1987. 87 pp. Notes. Biblio. [M.F.A. Thesis, Univ. Microfilms Order No. 1330858.] Lang.: Eng.
USA. 1987. Historical studies. ▪Interpretation, rehearsal, and performance of Babe Botrelle in Beth Henley's *Crimes of the Heart*, performed at the Belknap Theatre in fulfillment of requirements for an M.F.A. in acting.

2691 Harbin, Billy J. "Monty Woolley: The Public and Private Man from Saratoga Springs." 262-279 in Schanke, Robert A., ed.; Marra, Kim, ed. *Passing Performances: Queer Readings of Leading Players in American Theatre History.* Ann Arbor, MI: Univ of Michigan P; 1998. 338 pp. (Triangulations: Lesbian/Gay/Queer Theatre/Drama/Performance.) Notes. Index. Illus.: Photo. 1. Lang.: Eng.
USA. 1888-1963. Historical studies. ▪The career of gay actor Monty Woolley.

2692 Heil, LeighAnn. "The Use of Renaissance Dance in Shakespearean Productions: A Director's Guide." *ERev.* 1998 Aut; 6(2): 31-42. Biblio. Lang.: Eng.
USA. 1998. Critical studies. ▪Advice to directors for the use of Renaissance dance when mounting a Shakespearean play.

2693 Houchin, John H. "Eugene O'Neill's 'Woman Play' in Boston." *EOR.* 1998 Spr/Fall; 22(1/2): 48-62. Notes. Lang.: Eng.
USA: Boston, MA. 1929. Historical studies. ▪Account of the cultural battle waged between Boston's mayor and the Theatre Guild over presenting *Strange Interlude* in that city.

2694 Houppert, Karen. "Ruth Maleczech: Her Life in Art." *AmTh.* 1998 Sep.; 15(7): 72-73, 86-87. Illus.: Photo. B&W. 1. Lang.: Eng.
USA: New York, NY. 1970-1998. Biographical studies. ▪Life and career of Maleczech, co-founder of Mabou Mines.

2695 Hulbert, Dan. "Phylicia Rashad." *AmTh.* 1998 July/Aug.; 15(6): 50-51. Illus.: Photo. B&W. 1. Lang.: Eng.
USA: Atlanta, GA. 1998. Histories-sources. ▪Interview with the stage, screen, and television actress as she prepares to take on the role of Euripides' *Medea* in the Alliance Theatre production directed by Kenny Leon.

2696 Ireland, Patricia L. *Blarney Streets: The Staging of Ireland and Irish-America by the Chicago Manuscript Company.* Carbondale, IL: Southern Illinois Univ; 1998. 252 pp. Notes. Biblio. [Ph.D. Dissertation, Univ. Microfilms Order No. AAC 9902723.] Lang.: Eng.
USA. 1875-1915. Critical studies. ▪Examines the Irish and Irish-American characters and stereotypes in professional, traveling and amateur acting companies in the Midwest, including the work of playwright/actors Dion Boucicault, Edmund Falconer, Charles Morton, John H. Wilson, and Sam Ryan.

2697 Jack, George Francis, Jr. *The Elder Son: One Actor's Approach to the Role of Jamie in Eugene O'Neill's* Long Day's Journey Into Night. Louisville, KY: Univ. of Louisville; 1987. 162 pp. Notes. Biblio. [M.F.A. Thesis, Univ. Microfilms Order No. 1330859.] Lang.: Eng.
USA. 1987. Historical studies. ▪Interpretation, rehearsal, and performance of the role of Jamie in Eugene O'Neill's *Long Day's Journey Into Night*, performed at the Belknap Theatre in fulfillment of the thesis project requirement for the M.F.A. in Acting.

2698 Kapelke, Randy. "Preventing Censorship: The Audience's Role in *Sapho* (1900) and *Mrs. Warren's Profession* (1905)." *THSt.* 1998; 53: 117-134. Notes. Illus.: Photo. B&W. 1. Lang.: Eng.
USA. 1900-1905. Historical studies. ▪The failed attempt to force government to censor two American productions, Olga Nethersole's production of Clyde Fitch's *Sapho* and Arnold Daly's production of George Bernard Shaw's *Mrs. Warren's Profession*, both of which were acquitted in court.

2699 Kapelke, Randy B. *Artistic Victories: How the Legitimate Theatre Overcame New York City's Efforts to Impose Censorship on* Sapho *in 1900,* Mrs. Warren's Profession *in 1905 and Other Productions to 1927.* Medford, MA: Tufts Univ; 1998. 373 pp. Notes. Biblio. [Ph.D. Dissertation, Univ. Microfilms Order No. AAC 9828877.] Lang.: Eng.
USA: New York, NY. 1900-1927. Historical studies. ▪The failed attempt by New York City's government to enforce censorship, with emphasis on Olga Nethersole's production of Clyde Fitch's *Sapho* and Arnold Daly's production of George Bernard Shaw's *Mrs. Warren's Profession.*

2700 Kaye, Nick. "Bouncing Back the Impulse: An Interview with Richard Foreman." *PM.* 1990; 61: 31-41. Illus.: Photo. B&W. 6. Lang.: Eng.
USA: New York, NY. 1975-1990. Histories-sources. ▪Interview with Foreman regarding his past philosophy and future plans, which include the creation of a theatre in which the audience listens rather than watches. Reference is made to his production of *Lava.*

2701 Kegl, Rosemary. "'(W)rapping Togas over Elizabethan Garb': Tabloid Shakespeare at the 1934 Chicago World's Fair." *RenD.* 1998; 21: 73-97. Notes. Biblio. Lang.: Eng.
USA: Chicago, IL. 1934. Historical studies. ▪Describes the forty-minute productions of plays by Shakespeare, Shaw, and Marlowe that were presented at a reconstructed Globe Theatre, under the direction of Thomas Wood Stevens, at the 'Merrie England' attraction for the 1934 World's Fair.

2702 Kobayashi, Kaori. "Touring Companies in the Empire: The Miln Company's Productions in Japan." *ADS.* 1998 Apr.; 32: 47-62 . Notes. Illus.: Sketches. B&W. 1. Lang.: Eng.
USA: Chicago, IL. Japan: Yokohama. 1882. Historical studies. ▪History of English-born George Crichton Miln's touring Shakespearean company with emphasis on their work at the Gaiety Theatre in Yokohama, Japan.

2703 Kyzer, Stanley Winford. *'The Diary of Anne Frank': Analysis for Production.* Reno, NV: Univ. of Nevada; 1987. 90 pp. Biblio. Notes. [M.A. Thesis, Univ. Microfilms Order No. AAC 1332205.] Lang.: Eng.
USA. 1955. Histories-sources. ▪Producing *The Diary of Anne Frank* as part of a summer repertory season at the University of Nevada, in fulfillment of requirements for an M.F.A. degree in directing.

DRAMA: —Performance/production

2704 Lahr, John. "Speaking Shakespeare." *NewY.* 1998 7 Sep.: 78-84. Illus.: Photo. B&W. 1. Lang.: Eng.
USA: New York, NY. 1998. Historical studies. ■Description of an actors' workshop on Shakespearean performance by director and playwright John Barton of the Royal Shakespeare Company.

2705 Landro, Vincent. "The Mythologizing of American Regional Theatre." *JADT.* 1998 Win; 10(1): 76-101. Notes. Lang.: Eng.
USA. 1940-1960. Historical studies. ■The early evolution of nonprofit regional theatre, including Nina Vance's Alley Theatre, Margo Jones' Margo Jones Theatre, Zelda Fichandler's Arena Stage, and Herbert Blau and Jules Irving's Actors' Workshop. Emphasizes their multifaceted nature and contrasts this approach with traditional historical critiques of the early theatres.

2706 Marowitz, Charles. "Otherness: The Director and the Discovery of the Actor." *NTQ.* 1998; 14(53): 3-8. [First published in *The Other Way* by Charles Marowitz (NY: Applause, 1998).] Lang.: Eng.
USA. UK-England. 1958-1998. Histories-sources. ■Director and playwright Marowitz charts his discovery of the interrelationship of the actor and director, and his realization of the actor's ultimate autonomy and higher calling.

2707 Martenson, Ed. "Garland Wright 1946-1998." *AmTh.* 1998 Oct.; 15(8): 78. Illus.: Photo. B&W. 1. Lang.: Eng.
USA. 1946-1998. Biographical studies. ■Obituary for director Wright, who was also the longest serving artistic director of the Guthrie Theatre.

2708 Masson, Linda Joyce Krasnow. *Lynne Meadow, Director.* New York, NY: New York Univ; 1987. 310 pp. Biblio. Notes. [Ph.D. Dissertation, Univ. Microfilms Order No. AAC 8801555.] Lang.: Eng.
USA: New York, NY. 1972-1985. Historical studies. ■Examines the professional career of Lynne Meadow, artistic director of the Manhattan Theatre Club. Focuses on Meadow's directing work on three productions—*Ashes* by David Rudkin, *Sally and Marsha* by Sybille Pearson, and Čechov's *Three Sisters (Tri sestry).*

2709 Maupin, Elizabeth. "Mary Hausch." *AmTh.* 1998 Apr.; 15(4): 35-37. Illus.: Photo. B&W. 2. Lang.: Eng.
USA: Gainesville, FL. 1973-1998. Biographical studies. ■Profile of director and co-founder of the Hippodrome State Theatre, Mary Hausch.

2710 McCully, Susan Beth. *How Queer: Race, Gender and the Politics of Production in Contemporary Gay, Lesbian and Queer Theatre.* Madison, WI: Univ. of Wisconsin; 1998. 246 pp. Notes. Biblio. [Ph.D. Dissertation, Univ. Microfilms Order No. AAC 9813119.] Lang.: Eng.
USA. 1970-1997. Critical studies. ■Contemporary queer politics and gay and lesbian theatre. Focuses on the modes of production of six texts at economically diverse performance venues: Chay Yew's *A Language of Their Own*, Gail Burton's *Muses*, Kate Kasten and Sandra de Helen's *Clue in the Old Birdbath*, Elinor Hakim's *A Lesbian Play for Lucy*, Christi Stewart-Brown's *Morticians in Love* and Tony Kushner's *Angels in America.*

2711 McKinley, Jesse. "Who Is Peer Gynt and Why Do We Care?" *AmTh.* 1998 May/June; 15(5): 38-40. Illus.: Photo. B&W. 3. Lang.: Eng.
USA: Providence, RI, New York, NY, Washington, DC, Nacogdoches, TX. 1998. Critical studies. ■Four productions of Ibsen's *Peer Gynt*: David Henry Hwang's adaptation mounted by Trinity Rep directed by Michael Kahn, National Theatre of the Deaf's pared down version staged in Nacogdoches, directed by Will Rhys and Robby Barnett, the Shakespeare Theatre's elaborate production, also directed by Kahn, and Romulus Linney's updated Americanized version *Gint* at Theatre for the New City.

2712 Mejia, Davis. *Julien Cornell: A Moral Pacifist for the Defense.* Long Beach, CA: California State Univ; 1998. 52 pp. Notes. Biblio. [M.F.A. Thesis, Univ. Microfilms Order No. AAC 1390944.] Lang.: Eng.
USA: Long Beach, CA. 1997. Histories-sources. ■On the author's creation and performance of the role of Julien Davis Cornell in *The Trial of Ezra Pound*, directed by Davis Wheeler at California State University, completed as partial fulfillment of the M.F.A. degree in Acting.

2713 Monaghan, Constance. "Mambo Combo." *AmTh.* 1998 Mar.; 15(3): 10-14. Illus.: Photo. B&W. 5. Lang.: Eng.
USA: Berkeley, CA. 1984-1998. Critical studies. ■Profile of the comic troupe Culture Clash as they prepare to to produce their version of Aristophanes' *The Birds (Ornithes)* for the South Coast Repertory. Also includes a sidebar review of the production by Irene Oppenheim.

2714 Monaghan, Constance. "The Duchess of Hollywood." *AmTh.* 1998 Nov.; 15(9): 36-37. Illus.: Photo. B&W. 1. Lang.: Eng.
USA: Los Angeles, CA. 1998. Reviews of performances. ■The Theatre of NOTE's production of Webster's *The Duchess of Malfi* directed by Denise Gillman.

2715 Monk, Charlene Faye. *Passion Plays in the United States: The Contemporary Outdoor Tradition.* Baton Rouge, LA: Louisiana State A&M; 1998. 246 pp. Biblio. Notes. [Ph.D. Dissertation, Univ. Microfilms Order No. 9836892.] Lang.: Eng.
USA. 1920-1995. Histories-specific. ■Traces the development of outdoor passion plays in the US, comparing their content and approach with the continental medieval tradition and analyzing how effectively the current American plays are modifying their presentations to meet the expectations of today's modern society. Analyzes the *Black Hills Passion Play* in North Dakota, the *Great Passion Play* in Eureka Springs, AR, the *Living Word* in Cambridge, OH, *Jesus of Nazareth* in Puyallup, WA, the *Louisiana Passion Play* in Ruston, LA, *The Witness* in Hot Springs, AR, *Worthy Is the Lamb* in Swansboro, NC, and *The Promise* in Glen Rose, TX.

2716 Moore, Dick. "Helen Carey, Max Wright Win Classic Theatre Awards." *EN.* 1998 Jan/Feb.; 83(1): 5. Illus.: Photo. B&W. 1. Lang.: Eng.
USA. 1998. Historical studies. ■Reports on performers Helen Carey and Max Wright winning the Joe A. Callaway Award for their work in Boucicault's *London Assurance* and Čechov's *Ivanov*, respectively.

2717 Moore, Dick. "Friday at the Meeting with Eli." *EN.* 1998 Jan/Feb.; 83(1): 7. Illus.: Photo. B&W. 1. Lang.: Eng.
USA. 1998. Histories-sources. ■Reports on actor Eli Wallach's speech at the Eastern Regional meeting of Actors' Equity, as he spoke on his career as a performer in the theatre.

2718 Moore, Dick. "The Two Elizabeths, or How a Mature, Female Equity Member Found Rewarding Work in Her Chosen Career." *EN.* 1998 Mar.; 83(2): 3. Lang.: Eng.
USA: New York, NY. 1998. Historical studies. ■Reports on Equity member Elizabeth Perry and her creation of a one-woman show, *Sun Flower*, based on the suffragist and early feminist Elizabeth Cady Stanton.

2719 Moore, Dick. "Julyana Soelistyo, Sam Trammell Win Annual Derwent Awards." *EN.* 1998 June; 83(5): 3. Illus.: Photo. 2. Lang.: Eng.
USA: New York, NY. 1998. Historical studies. ■Reports on the Derwent Awards for the most promising female and male performers of the year in New York theatre. This year's awards went to Julyana Soelistyo for her performance in David Henry Hwang's *Golden Child* and Sam Trammell in Eugene O'Neill's *Ah, Wilderness!.*

2720 Moore, Dick. "'I Don't Know What I'm Doing': Robert Prosky Talks About Being an Actor." *EN.* 1998 Sep.; 83(7): 3. Illus.: Photo. 1. Lang.: Eng.
USA: Washington, DC. 1998. Histories-sources. ■Excerpt from a speech by actor Robert Prosky on his receipt of a tribute at the Helen Hayes Awards.

2721 Moore, Frederick Timothy. *Enhancing the Sermon: The Effect of Willow Creek's Homiletical Drama in Free Church Worship.* Princeton, NJ: Princeton Theological Seminary; 1998. 217 pp. Notes. Biblio. [Ph.D. Dissertation, Univ. Microfilms Order No. AAC 9903496.] Lang.: Eng.
USA: Chicago, IL. 1997. Historical studies. ■The use of homiletical drama—a brief one-act play in which a contemporary issue is raised in order to enhance a sermon preached on that issue—as a regular part of Christian worship in the free church tradition. Focuses on the theological and liturgical impact, meaning, and significance of homiletical dramas

and the origin of homiletical drama as it emerged in the Willow Creek Community Church.

2722 Morales, Ed. "New World Order." *AmTh.* 1998 May/June; 15(5): 42-44. Illus.: Photo. B&W. 1. Lang.: Eng.
USA: Hartford, CT. 1998. Reviews of performances. ■Review of Calderón's *La Vida es sueño (Life Is a Dream)*, adapted and directed by José Rivera for the Hartford Stage Company.

2723 Nesbitt, Caroline. "A Farewell to Art." *AmTh.* 1998 Feb.; 15(2): 20-21, 70. Illus.: Dwg. B&W. 4. Lang.: Eng.
USA: New York, NY. 1998. Histories-sources. ■Actress Nesbitt's essay on her experiences when she finally gave up on a career in the theatre.

2724 Novick, Julius. "The Actor's Insecurity." *AmTh.* 1998 Apr.; 15(4): 20-21. Illus.: Dwg. B&W. 1. Lang.: Eng.
USA. 1959-1998. Critical studies. ■Psychology of identity that fuels the insecurity of actors.

2725 O'Brien, Jack. "Ellis Rabb: 1930-1997." *AmTh.* 1998 Mar.; 15(3): 41. Illus.: Photo. B&W. 2. Lang.: Eng.
USA. 1930-1997. Biographical studies. ■Obituaries for actor/director Ellis Rabb, director Giorgio Strehler (1921-1997), and playwright/director David Mark Cohen (1953-1998).

2726 O'Quinn, Jim. "Springtime for Tennessee." *AmTh.* 1998 July/Aug.; 15(6): 54. Illus.: Photo. B&W. 1. Lang.: Eng.
USA: New Orleans, LA. 1998. Historical studies. ■Report on the Tennessee Williams/New Orleans Literary Festival held in honor of the playwright in the city for which he had the greatest affection.

2727 Oseland, James. "The Raw and the Cooked." *AmTh.* 1998 July/Aug.; 15(6): 48. Illus.: Photo. B&W. 1. Lang.: Eng.
USA: Louisville, KY. 1998. Reviews of performances. ■Review of two plays presented at the Actors' Theatre of Louisville: Naomi Wallace's *The Trestle at Pope Lick Creek* directed by Adrian Hall and *Dinner with Friends* by Donald Margulies.

2728 Pacelli, Martha. *Resistant Histories: Contemporary American Documentary Theatre and the Politics of Representation.* Chicago, IL: Univ. of Illinois; 1998. 323 pp. Notes. Biblio. [Ph.D. Dissertation, Univ. Microfilms Order No. AAC 9829712.] Lang.: Eng.
USA. 1966-1993. Critical studies. ■Works examined include Martin Duberman's *In White America*, Eve Merriman, Paula Wagner and Jack Hofsiss's *Out of Our Father's House*, Eric Bentley's *Are You Now Or Have You Ever Been*, Arthur Kopit's *Indians*, Mabou Mines's *Dead End Kids*, Joan Schenkar's *Signs of Life*, Susan Sontag's *Alice in Bed*, and Anna Deavere Smith's *Fires in the Mirror.*

2729 Paran, Janice. "Music in the Lower Depths." *AmTh.* 1998 May/June; 15(5): 45-47. Illus.: Photo. B&W. 1. Lang.: Eng.
USA: Houston, TX. 1998. Reviews of performances. ■Review of Tennessee Williams' early play *Not About Nightingales*, directed by Trevor Nunn at the Alley Theatre.

2730 Patterson Nahas, Heather Ann. *Carefully Balanced at the Top.* Louisville, KY: Univ. of Louisville; 1998. 48 pp. Biblio. Notes. [M.F.A. Thesis, Univ. Microfilms Order No. 1391754.] Lang.: Eng.
USA. 1997. Histories-sources. ■On the author's portrayal of Marlene in Caryl Churchill's *Top Girls* in fulfillment of requirements for an M.F.A. in Acting.

2731 Pendleton, Thomas A. "Tony Randall and the Greatest Actor Who Ever Lived." *ShN.* 1998 Fall; 48(3): 58, 64. Lang.: Eng.
USA. Italy. 1856-1915. Histories-sources. ■Actor Tony Randall discusses his enthusiasm for the Italian actor Tomasso Salvini, who made his career playing in Shakespeare's *Othello.*

2732 Robson, Christopher. "John Barrymore (1882-1942) The Great Profile." *PlPl.* Apr 1998; 521: 15. Illus.: Photo. B&W. 1. Lang.: Eng.
USA: New York, NY. 1882-1942. Biographical studies. ■Theatre and film work of actor John Barrymore.

2733 Robson, Christopher. "Paul Muni (1895-1967)—Painstaking Professional and Perfectionist." *PlPl.* July 1998; 524: 12. Illus.: Photo. B&W. 1. Lang.: Eng.
USA: New York, NY. 1895-1998. Biographical studies. ■Life and career on stage and screen of actor Paul Muni.

2734 Robson, Christopher. "Marie Dressler (1869-1934)—Filmdom's Grande Dame." *PlPl.* 1998 Sep.; 526: 13. Lang.: Eng.
USA: New York, NY. 1869-1934. Biographical studies. ■Career of stage and screen actress Marie Dressler.

2735 Rosten, Bevya. *The Fractured Stage: Gertrude Stein's Influence on American Avant-Garde Directing As Seen in Four Productions of 'Dr. Faustus Lights the Lights'.* New York, NY: City Univ. of New York; 1998. 191 pp. Notes. Biblio. [Ph.D. Dissertation, Univ. Microfilms Order No. AAC 9820576.] Lang.: Eng.
USA. 1940-1995. Historical studies. ■Comparison of productions of Stein's play by four female directors to assess Stein's influence on their work, especially with respect to the use of stage space.

2736 Rosten, Bevya. "The Gesture of Illogic." *AmTh.* 1998 Feb.; 15(2): 16-19. Illus.: Photo. B&W. 4. Lang.: Eng.
USA: New York, NY. 1979-1998. Histories-sources. ■Interview with actress Kate Valk regarding her work with the Wooster Group and their current production *House/Lights*, the group's adaptation of Gertrude Stein's opera text *Doctor Faustus Lights the Lights.*

2737 Saivetz, Deborah. "An Event in Space: The Integration of Acting and Design in the Theatre of JoAnne Akalaitis." *TDR.* 1998 Sum; 42(2): 132-156. Notes. Biblio. Illus.: Photo. B&W. 7. Lang.: Eng.
USA. 1982-1998. Critical studies. ■Examines the director's style which integrates acting, text, and design forming an imagistic and sculptural feel to her work.

2738 Salerno, Patricia Joan. *'Deirdre': A Director's Implementation in Performance of William Butler Yeats's Dramatic Theory.* Louisville, KY: Univ. of Louisville; 1988. 78 pp. Notes. Biblio. [M.F.A. Thesis, Univ. Microfilms Order No. AAC 1334117.] Lang.: Eng.
USA: Louisville, KY. 1988. Histories-sources. ■M.F.A. directing thesis project of William Butler Yeats's one-act play *Deirdre* performed at the University of Louisville's Arena Theatre.

2739 Salmanova, E.M. "Tairov predstavljaet 'Veršiny sčast'ja' Džona Dos Passosa." (Tairov presents *Fortune Heights* by John Dos Passos.) *RLit.* 1998; 1: 129-136. Lang.: Rus.
USA. 1930-1935. Historical studies. ■History of the production, directed by Aleksand'r Tairov, at Kamernyj Teat'r.

2740 Schiffman, Jean. "Lori Holt." *AmTh.* 1998 Apr.; 15(4): 38-39. Illus.: Photo. B&W. 1. Lang.: Eng.
USA: San Francisco, CA. 1978-1998. Biographical studies. ■Profile of Bay Area actress Lori Holt.

2741 Shelton, Lewis E. "David Belasco and the Scientific Perspective." *JADT.* 1998 Win; 10(1): 1-27. Notes. Lang.: Eng.
USA. 1882-1931. Historical studies. ■Analyzes director David Belasco's scientific perspective as it affected his work in the areas of settings, lighting, and acting and his aesthetic of theatre.

2742 Sherin, Edwin. "Roger L. Stevens: 1910-1998." *AmTh.* 1998 Apr.; 15(4): 40. Illus.: Photo. B&W. 1. Lang.: Eng.
USA. Canada. 1910-1998. Biographical studies. ■Obituaries for theatrical producer Stevens, director Kenneth Frankel (1942-1998), Canadian actor Donald Davis (1929-1998), and critic Edith Oliver (1914-1998).

2743 Shull, Thomas Allen. *Acting Analysis of Character Development in Plays by Allen, Molière, Pinter, Shakespeare, Shaw, Shepard, Wagner, and Williams.* Long Beach, CA: Univ. of California; 1987. 45 pp. Notes. Biblio. [M.F.A. Thesis, Univ. Microfilms Order No. 1330657.] Lang.: Eng.
USA. 1987. Critical studies. ■Describes a Final Project for the M.F.A. in acting, performed at California State University.

2744 Stasio, Marilyn. "Jane Alexander: She Stoops to Conquer." *AmTh.* 1998 Sep.; 15(7): 59, 82-83. Illus.: Dwg. B&W. 1. Lang.: Eng.
USA. 1998. Biographical studies. ■Alexander's return to the acting profession after serving as chairman of the NEA.

DRAMA: —Performance/production

2745 Stasio, Marilyn. "Uta Hagen: In Praise of Common Sense." *AmTh.* 1998 Sep.; 15(7): 75. Illus.: Photo. B&W. 1. Lang.: Eng.

USA. 1998. Biographical studies. ■Profile of actress/teacher Uta Hagen, the godmother of contemporary acting.

2746 Swearingen, Darryl Duane. *Acting Analysis of Character Development in Plays by Coward, McLurie, Miller, Molière, Pinter, Rabe, and Shakespeare.* Long Beach, CA: Univ. of California; 1987. 32 pp. Notes. Biblio. [M.F.A. Thesis, Univ. Microfilms Order No. 1330664.] Lang.: Eng.

USA. 1987. Critical studies. ■Process of development of an M.F.A. Final Project in acting, presented in the Laboratory Theatre at California State University.

2747 Templeton, Joan; Shafer, Yvonne; Gordy, Douglas W.; Pronko, Leonard. "Ibsen on Stage." *INC.* 1998; 18: 8-15. Illus.: Photo. B&W. 3. Lang.: Eng.

USA: New York, NY. Norway: Oslo. 1998. Critical studies. ■Analysis of various productions of plays by Ibsen: Romulus Linney's adaptation and direction of *Peer Gynt*, called *Gint*, at Theatre for the New City, and also presented at the Ibsen Festival in Oslo. *A Doll's House (Et Dukkehjem)* at Century Center for the Performing Arts directed by Lee Gundersheimer, Cocteau Repertory's *Hedda Gabler* directed by Eve Adamson, and *The Wild Duck (Vildanden)* presented by Bulldog Theatre Company and directed by Elizabeth Margid.

2748 Tooks, Kim. "Leverne Summers: To Act Is to Do." *BlackM.* 1998 Oct/Nov.; 13(2): 11. Illus.: Photo. B&W. 1. Lang.: Eng.

USA: New York, NY. 1998. Biographical studies. ■Obituary for the actor, killed while saving a little boy from a speeding car.

2749 Tooks, Kim. "Theresa Merritt: Dazzling Star of Stage, Screen, and TV." *BlackM.* 1998 Oct/Nov.; 13(2): 11. Illus.: Photo. B&W. 1. Lang.: Eng.

USA: New York, NY. 1998. Biographical studies. ■Obituary for the actress and singer.

2750 Turner, Beth. "Paul Robeson: The Consummate Actor/Activist." *BlackM.* 1998 Oct/Nov.; 13(2): 5-6, 18-19. Biblio. Lang.: Eng.

USA. 1898-1959. Biographical studies. ■Profile of the legendary actor, singer, athlete, orator, and political activist.

2751 Vallillo, Stephen M. *George M. Cohan, Director.* New York, NY: New York Univ; 1987. 387 pp. Biblio. Notes. [Ph.D. Dissertation, Univ. Microfilms Order No. AAC 8712787.] Lang.: Eng.

USA. 1900-1950. Historical studies. ■Examines the Broadway directing career of actor/singer/dancer George M. Cohan.

2752 Wainscott, Ronald. "Notable American Stage Productions." 96-115 in Manheim, Michael, ed. *The Cambridge Companion to Eugene O'Neill.* Cambridge/New York, NY: Cambridge UP; 1998. 256 pp. (Cambridge Companions to Literature.) Index. Biblio. Illus.: Photo. 2. Lang.: Eng.

USA. 1916-1996. Historical studies. ■Examines several of Eugene O'Neill's plays in best-known professional performances, from the Washington Square Players's 1916 production of *In the Zone*, to the Roundabout Theatre Company's 1993 production of *Anna Christie*, directed by David Leveaux, starring Natasha Richardson, and Al Pacino's 1996 version of *Hughie*, with Pacino directing and acting as Hughie at the Circle in the Square.

2753 Watson-Wright, Susan. *Mrs. Sculley:* Warrior, *Bedlam, and Contradictory Forces in the Age of Reason.* Long Beach, CA: California State Univ; 1998. 54 pp. Notes. Biblio. [M.F.A. Thesis, Univ. Microfilms Order No. AAC 1390140.] Lang.: Eng.

USA: Long Beach, CA. 1997. Histories-sources. ■On the author's creation and performance of the character of Mrs. Sculley in Shirley Gee's *Warrior*, produced at California State University in partial fulfillment of the M.F.A. degree in Acting.

2754 Werner, Jessica. "Tsai Chin: No Stranger to Change." *AmTh.* 1998 Apr.; 15(4): 17, 51-52. Illus.: Photo. B&W. 1. Lang.: Eng.

USA. 1959-1998. Biographical studies. ■Career of Chinese-born actress Tsai Chin, who is in David Henry Hwang's *Golden Child* at the American Conservatory Theatre directed by James Lapine.

2755 Williams, Carolyn. "Boucicault Revived." *PerAJ.* 1998 May; 20(2): 49-53. Illus.: Photo. B&W. 1. Lang.: Eng.

USA. 1997. te Critical studies. ■Review and analysis of Dion Boucicault's play *London Assurance*, directed by Joe Dowling for the Roundabout Theatre Company.

2756 Williams, Philip Middleton. *'A Comfortable House': The Collaboration of Lanford Wilson and Marshall W. Mason on* Fifth of July, Talley's Folly, *and* Talley and Son. Boulder, CO: Univ. of Colorado; 1988. 308 pp. Biblio. Notes. [Ph.D. Dissertation, Univ. Microfilms Order No. AAC 8912231.] Lang.: Eng.

USA: New York, NY. 1978-1986. Histories-specific. ■The nature of the collaborative effort of playwright Lanford Wilson and director Marshall W. Mason on three productions at the Circle Repertory Company.

2757 Wolf, Stacy. "Mary Martin: Washin' That Man Right Outta Her Hair." 283-302 in Schanke, Robert A., ed.; Marra, Kim, ed. *Passing Performances: Queer Readings of Leading Players in American Theatre History.* Ann Arbor, MI: Univ of Michigan P; 1998. 338 pp. (Triangulations: Lesbian/Gay/Queer Theatre/Drama/Performance.) Notes. Index. Illus.: Photo. 1. Lang.: Eng.

USA. 1913-1990. Biographical studies. ■Argues that reading actress/singer Mary Martin as a lesbian illuminates her personal and professional interests, desires, preoccupations, and practices.

2758 Zapp, Peter. *Buddy the Dog at the Heart of 'Warrior'.* Long Beach, CA: California State Univ; 1998. 60 pp. Notes. Biblio. [M.F.A. Thesis, Univ. Microfilms Order No. AAC 1390295.] Lang.: Eng.

USA: Long Beach, CA. 1997. Histories-sources. ■On the author's creation of the role of Billy Cuttle in Shirley Gee's *Warrior*, performed at California State University in partial fulfillment of the requirements for the M.F.A. degree in Acting.

2759 Zimmerman, Mark. "Some Sort of Awakening." *PerAJ.* 1998 May; 20(2): 40-48. Illus.: Photo. B&W. 2. Lang.: Eng.

USA: New York, NY. 1997-1998. te Critical studies. ■Reviews and analyses of four plays presented on the New York stage in the 1997-98 season: *Cablegs* by Steve Bodow, dir by Bodow and John Collins at P.S. 122, *House/Lights* by Gertrude Stein, adapted from *Doctor Faustus Lights the Lights*, dir by Elizabeth LeCompte for the Wooster Group, *Gross Indecency*, written and directed by Moisés Kaufman at the Minetta Lane, and *Shopping and Fucking* by Mark Ravenhill, dir by Max Stafford-Clark and Gemma Bodinetz at the New York Theatre Workshop.

2760 Zinman, Toby. "Beam Me Up, Patrick Stewart." *AmTh.* 1998 Feb.; 15(2): 12-15, 68-70. Illus.: Photo. B&W. 5. Lang.: Eng.

USA: Washington, DC. 1998. Histories-sources. ■Interview with actor Patrick Stewart on his popularity with American audiences due to his role as Captain Picard on *Star Trek: The Next Generation*, and also as he prepares to take on the role of *Othello* for the controversial race-reversed production by the Shakespeare Theatre directed by Jude Kelly.

2761 Zoldessy, Brian. *Acting Analysis of Character Development in Plays by Coward, McLurie, Miller, Molière, Pinter, Rabe, and Shakespeare.* Long Beach, CA: Univ. of California; 1987. 44 pp. Notes. Biblio. [M.F.A. Thesis, Univ. Microfilms Order No. 1330681.] Lang.: Eng.

USA. 1987. Critical studies. ■Describes the creative process used in developing the characters for the Master of Fine Arts Final Acting Project, presented in the Directing Laboratory Theatre at California State University.

2762 Chambers, David. "The Master of Praxis." *ThM.* 1998; 28(2): 50-55. Illus.: Photo. B&W. 5. Lang.: Eng.

USSR. 1926-1939. Historical studies. ■Development of the character of Khlezstakov in Mejerchol'd's staging of Gogol's *Inspector General (Revizor)*, from its opening in 1926 through his many restagings up until his incarceration in 1939. Questions political meaning of the character through its development.

DRAMA: —Performance/production

2763 Clark, Katerina. "Meyerhold's Appropriation of Gogol for 1926 in the Soviet Union." *ThM.* 1998; 28(2): 27-33. Lang.: Eng.
USSR: Moscow. 1926. Historical studies. ■Analysis of Mejerchol'd's 1926 production of Gogol's *The Inspector General (Revizor).* Contains background on Soviet cultural policy of Anatolij Lunačarskij and revolutionary theatre aesthetics.

2764 Clurman, Harold. "An Excerpt from Harold Clurman's Unpublished Diary." *ThM.* 1998; 28(2): 79-80. Lang.: Eng.
USSR: Moscow. 1935. Histories-sources. ■Director Clurman's notes on viewing Mejerchol'd's staging of *The Inspector General (Revizor).*

2765 de Haan, Christopher. "Remembering Between the Lines." *ThM.* 1998; 28(2): 11-18. Illus.: Photo. B&W. 1. Lang.: Eng.
USSR. 1920-1931. Histories-sources. ■Interview with director/historian Mel Gordon on the influence of actor/director/theorist V.E. Mejerchol'd.

2766 Makaryk, Irena. "Shakespeare Right and Wrong." *TJ.* 1998 May; 50(2): 153-164. Notes. Lang.: Eng.
USSR. 1924. Critical studies. ■The modernist style, radical agenda, and furious moral critique of Les' Kurbas' production of Shakespeare's *Macbeth.*

2767 Mejerchol'd, Vsevolod. "Petition." *ThM.* 1998; 28(2): 46-49. Notes. Biblio. Illus.: Photo. B&W. 1. Lang.: Eng.
USSR: Moscow. 1940. Histories-sources. ■Letter sent from prison by Mejerchol'd to Commissar Molotov denying that he was a counter-revolutionary Trotskyite.

2768 Pesochinsky, Nikolai. "Meyerhold and the 'Marxist Critique'." *ThM.* 1998; 28(2): 35-45. Illus.: Photo. Color. B&W. 5. Lang.: Eng.
USSR. 1890-1931. Biographical studies. ■Examines the personal, political, and professional relationship between the Soviet Union's cultural minister Lunačarskij and avant-garde director V.E. Mejerchol'd.

2769 Weinstein, Katherine. "Towards a Theatre of Creative Imagination: Alexander Tairov's O'Neill Productions." *EOR.* 1998 Spr/Fall; 22(1/2): 157-170. Biblio. Lang.: Eng.
USSR. 1926-1929. Historical studies. ■Questions whether Tairov distorted O'Neill's plays for political reasons in his productions in the Soviet Union. Productions cited are *The Hairy Ape, All God's Chillun Got Wings,* and *Desire Under the Elms.*

Plays/librettos/scripts

2770 Brown, John Russell. "Shakespeare's International Currency." *ShS.* 1998; 51: 193-203. Notes. Lang.: Eng.
1998. Critical studies. ■Essay on the current theatre's fixation on staging the works of Shakespeare. Discusses his international appeal, and the lack of another playwright with such a universal voice.

2771 Cisarž, Ja. *Velikie pisateli—dramaturgi.* (The Great Writers—Dramatists.) Moscow: Askon; 1998. 64 pp. (Velikie ljudi.) Lang.: Rus.
Instructional materials. ■Survey of major dramatists.

2772 Woodyard, George. "Making America or Making Revolution: The Theatre of Ricardo Halac in Argentina." 177-198 in Boon, Richard, ed.; Plastow, Jane, ed. *Theatre Matters: Performance and Culture on the World Stage.* Cambridge: Cambridge UP; 1998. 203 pp. (Cambridge Studies in Modern Theatre.) Notes. Index. Pref. Biblio. Lang.: Eng.
Argentina. 1955-1991. Historical studies. ■Examines the theatrical life and career of playwright Ricardo Halac, in relation to major periods of social and political upheaval.

2773 Devlin-Glass, Frances. "Every Man Who Is Not Petruchio Doth Wish He Was: Postfeminist Anxiety and Resistance in *Dead White Males.*" *ADS.* 1998 Apr.; 32: 35-45. Notes. Lang.: Eng.
Australia. 1995. Critical studies. ■Anti-feminism in David Williamson's play, with emphasis on his feminist characters' interpretations of Shakespeare.

2774 Makeham, Paul. "Community Stories: 'Aftershocks' and Verbatim Theatre." 168-181 in Kelly, Veronica, ed. *Our Australian Theatre in the 1990s.* (Australian Playwrights 7.) Notes. Index. Biblio. Illus.: Photo. 3. Lang.: Eng.
Australia: Newcastle, NSW. 1990-1998. Historical studies. ■Examines the documentary play *Aftershocks,* created by community cultural development workers in Newcastle, New South Wales, after an earthquake damaged their city.

2775 Parr, Bruce. "From Gay and Lesbian to Queer Theatre." 89-103 in Kelly, Veronica, ed. *Our Australian Theatre in the 1990s.* (Australian Playwrights 7.) Notes. Index. Biblio. Illus.: Photo. 2. Lang.: Eng.
Australia. 1990-1998. Historical studies. ■The current state of gay and lesbian theatre in Australia and its evolution to queer. Elucidates some of the theoretical issues surrounding the change and some current writers and theatre venues.

2776 Perkins, Elizabeth. "Plays About the Vietnam War: The Agon of the Young." 38-52 in Kelly, Veronica, ed. *Our Australian Theatre in the 1990s.* (Australian Playwrights 7.) Notes. Index. Biblio. Illus.: Photo. 1. Lang.: Eng.
Australia. 1990-1998. Historical studies. ■Analysis of Alan Hopgood's *Private Yuk Objects,* Louis Nowra's *Così* and the Darwin Theatre Group's *Dust Off Vietnam.*

2777 Thomson, Helen. "Dymphna Cusack's Plays." *ADS.* 1998 Apr.; 32: 63-76. Notes. Lang.: Eng.
Australia. 1927-1959. Critical studies. ■Analysis of Cusack's work including *Shallow Cups, Red Sky at Morning,* and *The Golden Girls.*

2778 Thomson, Helen. "Recent Australian Women's Writing for the Stage." 104-116 in Kelly, Veronica, ed. *Our Australian Theatre in the 1990s.* (Australian Playwrights 7.) Notes. Index. Biblio. Illus.: Photo. 2. Lang.: Eng.
Australia. 1972-1998. Historical studies. ■Female plays and playwrights and female-centered theatres in Australia, including the Melbourne Women's Theatre Group and Playworks, a national organization committed to nurturing new women writers for the stage.

2779 Eberhart, Christine. *Zeitkritik in dramen des wiener Expressionismus.* (Social Criticism in Viennese Expressionistic Drama.) Graz: Karl-Franzens Universität Graz; 1987. 207 pp. Notes. Biblio. [Ph.D. Dissertation.] Lang.: Ger.
Austria: Vienna. 1907-1922. Critical studies. ■Analysis of the reflection of social issues in Viennese Expressionist drama, including Kokoschka's *Mörder, Hoffnung der Frauen (Murderer, Hope of Women),* Bronnen's *Der Vatermord (Parricide),* Csokor's *Der grosse Kampf (The Great Struggle), Die rote Strasse (The Red Road),* and *Die Ballade von der Stadt (The Ballad of the City),* and Kaltneker's *Das Bergwerk (The Mine).*

2780 Jelinek, Elfriede. "In einem leeren Haus." (In an Empty House.) *THeute.* 1998; Yb: 85-86. Illus.: Photo. B&W. 2. Lang.: Ger.
Austria: Vienna. 1997. Histories-sources. ■Statement by playwright Jelinek observing the relationship between author and play during a rehearsal. Jelinek was chosen by critics of *Theater Heute* as playwright of the year.

2781 Jonigk, Thomas. "Corporate Identity." *TZ.* 1998; 6: 30-32. Illus.: Photo. B&W. 1. Lang.: Ger.
Austria: Vienna. 1998. Histories-sources. ■Jonigk, a playwright who also works as dramaturg and director at Schauspielhaus, discusses modern texts, developments of a contemporary theatre that leaves behind a repertory based on specific educations and generations, and aesthetic taboos.

2782 Kiebuzinska, Christine. "Elfriede Jelinek's *Nora* Project: Or What Happens When Nora Meets the Capitalists." *MD.* 1998 Spr; 41(1): 134-145. Notes. Lang.: Eng.
Austria. 1979. Critical studies. ■Analysis of Jelinek's adaptation of Ibsen's *A Doll's House (Et Dukkehjem), What Happened After Nora Left Her Husband, or, Pillars of Society (Was geschah, nachdem Nora ihren Mann verlassen hatte, oder, stützen der Gesellschaften).*

2783 Kraus, Karl. "La Conférence. Extrait (1905)." (The Conference: Excerpt.) *ASO.* 1998 Jan/Feb.; 181/182: 170-171. Illus.: Photo. B&W. 2. Lang.: Fre.
Austria: Vienna. 1905. Histories-sources. ■Kraus's account of a private performance, sponsored by him, of Frank Wedekind's *Die Büchse der Pandora (Pandora's Box)* at the Trianon Theater, in which both Kraus and Wedekind played parts.

DRAMA: —Plays/librettos/scripts

2784 Malkin, Jeanette R. "Thomas Bernhard, Jews, *Heldenplatz*." 281-297 in Schumacher, Claude, ed. *Staging the Holocaust: The Shoah in Drama and Performance.* Cambridge: Cambridge UP; 1998. 355 pp. (Cambridge Studies in Modern Theatre.) Index. Notes. Biblio. Illus.: Photo. 1. Lang.: Eng.
Austria. 1988. Critical studies. ▪Themes of memory and non-forgiveness in Thomas Bernhard's Holocaust drama, *Heldenplatz (Heroes' Square)*, originally produced at the Burgtheater, and the ensuing controversy.

2785 Massoth, Anja. "Carl Zuckmayer's dramatisches Werk." (Carl Zuckmayer's Dramatic Work.) *MuK.* 1998; 40(2-4): 99-112. Notes. Lang.: Ger.
Austria: Vienna. 1925-1938. Critical studies. ▪Analysis of the work of Carl Zuckmayer focusing mainly on *Der Schelm von Bergen (The Wag from Bergen)* first performed at Burgtheater (Vienna) in 1934 under the direction of Hermann Röbbeling.

2786 Maurer-Haas, Andrea. *Women Role Models in Plays of Austrian Women Dramatists from the French Revolution to the First World War.* Storrs, CT: Univ. of Connecticut; 1998. 309 pp. Notes. Biblio. [Ph.D. Dissertation, Univ. Microfilms Order No. AAC 9906555.] Lang.: Ger.
Austria. 1776-1914. Histories-specific. ▪Examines female roles in the works of Austrian women dramatists. Compares the changing historical place of women with the fictional depictions and provides a cultural critique on how female dramatists construct characters and reflect social conditions.

2787 Torky, Karin. "Die bösen Mütter." (The Bad Mothers.) *MuK.* 1998; 40(2-4): 125-138. Notes. Lang.: Ger.
Austria. Germany. 1890-1910. Critical studies. ▪Iconic view of motherhood in Frank Wedekind's *Lulu*, Franz Grillparzer's *Libussa* and Hugo von Hofmannsthal's *Elektra.*

2788 Wille, Franz. "Kannibalen und andere Menschenfreunde." (Cannibals and Other Philanthropists.) *THeute.* 1998; 8/9: 12-17. Illus.: Photo. B&W. 3. Lang.: Ger.
Austria: Vienna. 1998. Critical studies. ▪Analyzes the adaptation *Krähwinkelfreiheit (Freedom of Krähwinkel)* assembled by Frank Castorf and his dramaturg Thomas Martin after Johann Nestroy's *Freiheit in Krähwinkel (Freedom in Krähwinkel)*, Elisabeth Spira's *Alltagsgeschichten (Daily Stories)* and Senada Marjanovic's *Herzschmerzen (Heartaches)* all directed by Frank Castorf at Burgtheater (Vienna).

2789 Callens, Johan. "Vijf maal Shakespeare: melodrama, romantiek of bittere ernst." (Five Times Shakespeare: Melodrama, Romanticism or Bitter Earnest.) *Etcetera.* 1983(1): 2-5. Lang.: Dut.
Belgium. Netherlands. 1980-1983. Reviews of performances. ▪Analysis of five Shakespearean productions: *The Tempest* at Koninklijke Vlaamse Schouwburg, directed by Zdenek Kraus. *Pericles* at the Globe in Eindhoven, *Romeo and Juliet* at De Witte Kraai, directed by Sam Bogaerts. *The Merchant of Venice* at RO-Theater, directed by Frans Marijnen. *Richard III* at Malpertuis, directed by Jo Gevers.

2790 Cartwright, John. "From the Old Law to the New: The Brussels *Eerste Bliscap van Maria.*" *MET.* 1998; 20: 118-126. Notes. [Paper presented at SITM Triennial Colloquium, University of Odense, August 1997.] Lang.: Eng.
Belgium: Brussels. 1440-1560. Critical studies. ▪The Seven Joys of Mary were presented annually in the Grande Place, Brussels, in a sequence of seven plays, one each year, of which only the first and last survive. The first, *De Eerste Bliscap van Maria (The First Joy of Mary)*, which is the subject of this article and is ostensibly a miracle or saint's play, sets the scene for the whole cycle.

2791 Vasina, E.N. "Dramaturg, novator, psicholog..." (Playwright, Innovator, Psychologist.) *Latinskaja Amerika.* 1998; 2: 103-109. Lang.: Rus.
Brazil. 1912. Critical studies. ▪Brazilian playwright Nelson Rodrigues and his play *Sete cabras (Seven Goats).*

2792 Ahmad, Shafiuddin. *Performing the Other: Rhetoric, Genre and George Ryga's Drama.* Toronto, ON: York Univ; 1988. Biblio. Notes. [Ph.D. Dissertation.] Lang.: Eng.
Canada. 1967-1985. Critical studies. ▪Language and rhetoric in Ryga's *The Ecstasy of Rita Joe, Grass and Wild Strawberries*, and *Captives of the Faceless Drummer.*

2793 Beddows, Joël. "Pour une poétique du texte de Shakespeare: les formes métriques utilisées par Antonine Maillet et Jean-Louis Roux." (Toward a Poetics of the Shakespearian Text: Metric Forms Employed by Antonine Maillet and Jean-Louis Roux.) *AnT.* Spr 1998; 24: 35-51. Biblio. Notes. Lang.: Fre.
Canada: Montreal, PQ. 1988-1993. Historical studies. ▪Compares metric forms of English and French monologues in Maillet's translations of *Richard III* and *Twelfth Night* and Roux's translations of *Hamlet* and *King Lear.*

2794 Bell, Karen. "Carol Shields: all these years later still digging." *PAC.* 1998; 31(3): 4-6. Illus.: Photo. B&W. 2. Lang.: Eng.
Canada: Winnipeg, MB. 1972-1998. Biographical studies. ▪Recounts the career of novelist/playwright Carol Shields, including her recent work on a radio play, *Thirteen Hands.*

2795 Bergeron, Serge. "L'adaptation de *Mistero Buffo* de Dario Fo par Michel Tremblay: Un agent de mutation culturelle." (The Adaptation of Dario Fo's *Mistero Buffo* by Michel Tremblay: An Agent of Cultural Mutation.) *AnT.* Spr 1998; 23: 146-159. Biblio. Lang.: Fre.
Canada: Montreal, PQ. 1969-1973. Critical studies. ▪Michel Tremblay's adaptation of Dario Fo's *Mistero Buffo, La Résurrection de Lazare (The Resurrection of Lazarus)*, transfers the text from an Italian cultural context to a Québécois cultural context.

2796 Borello, Christine; Lapointe-Cloutier, Marie-Michèle. "Ma rencontre avec trois hommes remarquables: Philippe Soldevila." (My Encounter With Three Remarkable Men: Philippe Soldevila.) *JCT.* 1998; 86: 95-98. Notes. Illus.: Photo. B&W. 2. Lang.: Fre.
Canada: Quebec, PQ. 1995. Histories-sources. ▪Director, actor, and playwright Philippe Soldevila discusses creation of *Le miel est plus doux que le sang (Honey Is Milder Than Blood)*, which he co-wrote with Simone Chartrand.

2797 Brousseau, Elaine. "Personalizing the Political in *The Noam Chomsky Lectures.*" 247-264 in Colleran, Jeanne, ed.; Spencer, Jenny S., ed. *Staging Resistance: Essays on Political Theatre.* Ann Arbor, MI: Univ of Michigan P; 1998. 312 pp. (Theater: Theory/Text/Performance.) Notes. Index. Illus.: Photo. 1. Lang.: Eng.
Canada: Toronto, ON. 1990-1991. Critical studies. ▪Political commentary in *The Noam Chomsky Lectures* by Daniel Brooks and Guillermo Verdecchia, produces at Theatre Passe Muraille.

2798 Craig, Alexander. "Beyond the Norm." *PAC.* 1998; 31(4): 26-27. Illus.: Photo. B&W. 4. Lang.: Eng.
Canada. 1980-1998. Biographical studies. ▪On the future career plans of playwright Norm Foster, one of the most produced playwrights in Canada.

2799 Day, Moira Jean. *Elizabeth Sterling Haynes and the Development of the Alberta Theatre.* Toronto, ON: Univ. of Toronto; 1987. Biblio. Notes. [Ph.D. Dissertation.] Lang.: Eng.
Canada. 1916-1957. Biographical studies. ▪The dramatic career of theatre artist Elizabeth Sterling Haynes from the beginnings of the amateur era to the beginnings of the new professional theatre in Canada.

2800 Dobson, Teresa. "'High-Engender'd Battles': Gender and Power in *Queen Lear.*" *NTQ.* 1998 May; 14(2): 139-145. Notes. Biblio. Illus.: Photo. B&W. 2. [Issue 54.] Lang.: Eng.
Canada: Edmonton, AB. 1995-1997. Critical studies. ▪Analysis of Beau Coleman's *Queen Lear*, an adaptation of the Heath scene in Shakespeare's *King Lear*, which reveals a woman who, having found success in a male-dominated world, comes to confront the nature of that power in the process of relinquishing it.

2801 Ganapathy-Dore, Geetha. "Protest Theatre in France and Canada." *CTR.* 1998 Spr; 94: 18-22. Notes. Illus.: Photo. B&W. 2. Lang.: Eng.
Canada. France. 1980-1998. Historical studies. ▪Treatment of political subject matter in plays of protest theatre in France with comparison to similar Canadian plays.

DRAMA: —Plays/librettos/scripts

2802 Garebian, Keith. "*Frontier & Camp: The Indian Medicine Shows, Plague of the Gorgeous and Other Tales.*" *BooksC.* 1998; 27(3): 35-37. Illus.: Photo. B&W. 1. Lang.: Eng.

Canada. 1996. Critical studies. ▪Review of two collections of plays with gay themes. *Plague of the Gorgeous and Other Tales* (Montreal: Scirocco, 1996) includes *Plague of the Gorgeous* by Gordon Armstrong, *Sex Is My Religion* by Colin Thomas, *Reverse Transcriptease* by Stuart Blackley and Kevin Gregs, *Crowns and Anchors* by Lisa Lowe, and *Remembering Shanghai* by Peter Eliot Weiss. *Frontier & Camp: The Indian Medicine Shows* (Toronto: Exile, 1995) includes *The Moon* and *Dead Indians* by Daniel David Moses.

2803 Godin, Diane. "Un parcours exemplaire." (An Exemplary Journey.) *JCT.* 1998; 89: 92-96. Notes. Illus.: Photo. Dwg. Pntg. B&W. 4. Lang.: Fre.

Canada: Montreal, PQ. 1998. Historical studies. ▪Bridging the temporal gap between Cervantes' *Don Quixote* and the contemporary Québécois public of Wadji Mouawad's adaptation for Théâtre du Nouveau Monde, directed by Dominic Champagne.

2804 Godin, Diane. "Le dragon, l'ogre et le génie." (The Dragon, the Ogre and the Genius.) *JCT.* 1998; 87: 159-164. Notes. Illus.: Photo. B&W. 4. Lang.: Fre.

Canada: Montreal, PQ. 1995-1998. Historical studies. ▪Themes and images in three works by Larry Tremblay: *Ogre*, *The Dragonfly of Chicoutimi* and *Le Génie de la rue Drolet (The Genius of Drolet Street).*

2805 Grace, Sherrill. "Going North on Judith Thompson's *Sled.*" *ET.* 1998; 16(2): 153-164. Notes. Biblio. Lang.: Eng.

Canada. 1997-1998. Critical studies. ▪The idea of 'the North' as presented in Thompson's play *Sled*, and the play's place in the cultural context of 'the North'.

2806 Griffiths, Linda. "Process?" *CTR.* Win 1998; 97: 57-61. Illus.: Photo. B&W. 7. Lang.: Eng.

Canada: Saskatoon, SK. 1970-1998. Histories-sources. ▪Playwright/actress Linda Griffiths on various creative processes behind plays she wrote or collaborated on.

2807 Hellot, Marie-Christiane. "Don Quichotte et Sancho Pança: Le rêveur et son ombre." (Don Quixote and Sancho Panza: The Dreamer and His Shadow.) *JCT.* 1998; 89: 76-83. Notes. Illus.: Photo. Dwg. Pntg. B&W. 5. Lang.: Fre.

Canada: Montreal, PQ. 1998. Critical studies. ▪Functions and meanings of Don Quixote and Sancho Panza in *Don Quichotte*, Wadji Mouawad's adaptation of Cervantes' *Don Quixote*, produced by Théâtre du Nouveau Monde, directed by Dominic Champagne.

2808 Innes, Christopher. "Dreams of Violence: Moving Beyond Colonialism in Canadian and Caribbean Drama." 76-96 in Boon, Richard, ed.; Plastow, Jane, ed. *Theatre Matters: Performance and Culture on the World Stage.* Cambridge: Cambridge UP; 1998. 203 pp. (Cambridge Studies in Modern Theatre.) Notes. Index. Pref. Lang.: Eng.

Canada. Saint Lucia. 1980-1995. Historical studies. ▪The role of theatre in creating a new nationalist culture in parts of both the Caribbean and Canada, with emphasis on plays such as Derek Walcott's *Dream on Monkey Mountain* and Tomson Highway's *Dry Lips Oughta Move to Kapuskasing.*

2809 James, Sheila. "South Asian Women: Creating Theatre of Resilience and Resistance." *CTR.* 1998 Spr; 94: 45-50. Illus.: Photo. B&W. 3. Lang.: Eng.

Canada: Toronto, ON. 1990-1998. Histories-sources. ▪Interview with playwright/director Sheila James on creating theatre with a South Asian perspective, such as her plays *a canadian monsoon* and *All Whispers/No Words.*

2810 Knutson, Susan. "From Marichette to Rosealba and La Sagouine." *CanL.* 1998; 157: 36-53. Notes. Biblio. Lang.: Eng.

Canada. 1870-1998. Critical studies. ▪Explores the impact of the oral tradition and of women on Acadian theatre with reference to plays by Antonine Maillet and Émilie LeBlanc.

2811 Kugler, D.D. "Learning to Hate the Bingo Scenario." *CTR.* Win 1998; 97: 48-51. Biblio. Illus.: Photo. B&W. 1. Lang.: Eng.

Canada. 1998. Critical studies. ▪Ownership, recognition and compensation for playwrights and collaborators in the play development process.

2812 Lafon, Dominique. "Des coulisses de l'histoire aux coulisses du théâtre: la dramaturgie québécoise et la Crise d'Octobre." (From the Wings of History to the Wings of the Theatre: Quebecois Drama and the October Crisis.) *ThR.* 1998 Spr; 23(1): 24-37. Notes. Lang.: Fre, Eng.

Canada. 1970-1990. Historical studies. ▪Examines the October crisis of 1970 as reflected in contemporary plays honoring the event's 20th anniversary. Specifically examines how the plays attempt to come to terms with the violence and terrorism of the past. Plays include *Règlements de compte avec la mémoire (Settling Scores with Memory)*, written by René-Daniel Dubois, and *L'Exécution de Pierre Laporte, les dessous de l'opération (Laporte's Execution: The Hidden Story)* by Pierre Vallières.

2813 Lafon, Dominique. "Shakespeare à l'Arsenal ou Comment une filiale rompt avec la société mère." (Shakespeare at the Arsenal or How a Subsidiary Breaks With the Parent Company.) *AnT.* Spr 1998; 24: 85-99. Notes. Biblio. Lang.: Fre.

Canada. 1981. Critical studies. ▪Director/playwright Jean-Pierre Ronfard's *Vie et mort du Roi Boiteux (Life and Death of the Lame King)*, inspired by Shakespeare's *Richard III*, as development in Québécois tradition of adaptation. Expression of contemporary ideology through family relations.

2814 Lazaridès, Alexandre. "Le temple et la bibliothèque." (The Temple and the Library.) *JCT.* 1998; 87: 54-57. Illus.: Photo. B&W. 2. Lang.: Fre.

Canada: Montreal, PQ. 1998. Critical studies. ▪Collage as a technique to lend immediacy to Greek myths in *L'Histoire des Atrides (The House of Atreus)*, collage of texts by Aeschylus directed by Jean-Pierre Ronfard and produced by AbsoluTheatre, 1998, and *Les Grecs (The Greeks)*, collage of classic texts by Luce Pelletier, Théâtre de l'Opsis, 1998.

2815 Leroux, Élizabeth. "Don Quichotte ou la grande fête triste." (Don Quixote or the Great Sad Feast.) *JCT.* 1998; 89: 107-110. Illus.: Photo. B&W. 2. Lang.: Fre.

Canada: Montreal, PQ. 1998. Critical studies. ▪Contradiction between beautiful form and cynical content in Dominic Champagne's staging of Cervantes' *Don Quixote*, adapted as *Don Quichotte* by Wadji Mouawad for Théâtre du Nouveau Monde.

2816 Lesage, Marie-Christine. *Modalités Analogiques et Structures imagées du langage dramatique actuel: étude du* Syndrome de Cézanne *de Normand Canac-Marquis et de* Celle-Lá *de Daniel Danis.* (Analogical Modalities and Imaged Structures of Current Dramatic Language: A Study of *The Cezanne Syndrome* by Normand Canac-Marquis and *That One* by Daniel Danis.) Quebec, PQ: Université Laval; 1998. 368 pp. Biblio. Notes. [Ph.D. Dissertation, Univ. Microfilms Order No. AAC NQ26074.] Lang.: Fre.

Canada. 1980-1990. Critical studies. ▪Analysis of Quebecois drama in the center of the cinematic, pictorial, and photographic forms that influenced it, with emphasis on the plays by Danis and Canac-Marquis.

2817 McQuaid, Sean. "*Rough Waters.*" *ArtsAtl.* 1998; 16(1): 54-55. Lang.: Eng.

Canada: Charlottetown, PE. 1990-1998. Critical studies. ▪Examines the play *Rough Waters*, by Melissa Mullen, produced at the Theatre PEI. It is focused on maritime and family issues.

2818 Miller, Edith Hoisington. "Man of Many Talents." *PAC.* 1998; 31(4): 16-17. Lang.: Eng.

Canada. 1972-1998. Biographical studies. ▪Examines the life and career of playwright/actor/director Charles Follini.

2819 Mittal, Bina. "Exploring the Immigrant Experience through Theatre: Uma Parameswaran's *Rootless but Green Are the Boulevard Trees.*" *CTR.* 1998 Spr; 94: 32-35. Notes. Lang.: Eng.

Canada: Winnipeg, MB. 1985. Critical studies. ▪Process of acculturation as explored in Uma Parameswaran's play *Rootless but Green Are the Boulevard Trees.*

2820 Parameswaran, Uma. "I Believe in Zapping the Audience." *CTR.* Spr 1998; 94: 55-58. Illus.: Photo. B&W. 5. Lang.: Eng.

Canada: Montreal, PQ. India: Calcutta. 1950-1998. Histories-sources. ▪Interview with playwright Rana Bose on his childhood exposure to the-

DRAMA: —Plays/librettos/scripts

atre in Calcutta, and student experiences with guerrilla theatre, leading to his practice of writing theatre of protest in Montreal.

2821 Peerbaye, Soraya. "A Subtle Politic." *CTR*. 1998 Spr; 94: 5-9. Notes. Illus.: Photo. B&W. 4. Lang.: Eng.
Canada: Toronto, ON, Montreal, PQ. India. 1984-1998. Historical studies. ■Political community theatre voicing concerns of its public in India and Canada, with reference to two scripts by South Asian immigrants: *The DMO* (collective creation by Toronto's Friday Night Theatre Group, set in dramatic form by Krisanthra Sri Bhaggiyadatta) and *Counter Offence* by Montreal-based playwright Rahul Varma.

2822 Proulx, Isabelle. *Création Théâtrale, Inhumain et postmodernité.* (Theatrical Creation, the Inhuman, and Postmodernism.) Ottawa: Univ. of Ottawa; 1998. 113 pp. Biblio. Notes. [M.A. Thesis, Univ. Microfilms Order No. AAC MQ28455.] Lang.: Fre.
Canada. 1998. Histories-sources. ■The creation of an original play in the context of the theatre of cruelty and theories of Lyotard and Adorno.

2823 Raymond, Yves; David, Gilbert. "Autour de *La cathédrale...* (1949) de Jean Despréz: Une création à l'ombre de *Tit-Coq.*" (Of *The Cathedral...* (1949) by Jean Despréz: A Creation in the Shadow of *Tit-Coq.*) *AnT.* Spr 1998; 23: 109-130. Notes. Biblio. Illus.: Photo. Poster. B&W. 9. Lang.: Fre.
Canada: Montreal, PQ. 1949. Historical studies. ■Details of text and staging of *La Cathédrale... (The Cathedral...)* by Despréz, pseudonym of Laurette Laroque, at the Monument National and its critical reception in the press. Incldes extract of play.

2824 Riendeau, Pascal. "Normand Chaurette face à Shakespeare ou Traduisez *Comme il vous plaira....*" (Normand Chaurette Facing Shakespeare or Translating *As You Like It....*) *AnT.* Spr 1998; 24: 17-24. Notes. Biblio. Lang.: Fre.
Canada: Montreal, PQ. 1989-1994. Critical studies. ■Two translations of Shakespeare's *As You Like It*, both by Normand Chaurette, with emphasis on the problematic nature of creating contemporary translations of Shakespeare.

2825 Rowe, Paul. "Maid of Avalon." *ArtsAtl.* 1998; 15(4): 65-66. Illus.: Photo. B&W. 1. Lang.: Eng.
Canada: St. John's, NF. 1950-1998. Critical studies. ■The loose adaptation, by Beni Malone and Chuck Herriott of Wonderbolt Circus, of Brecht's *Der Gute Mensch von Sezuan (The Good Person of Szechwan)* as *Maid of Avalon*, set in a post-apocalyptic Newfoundland. The production was directed by Greg Malone at Resource Center for the Arts.

2826 Sears, Djanet; Smith, Alison Sealy. "The Nike Method." *CTR.* Win 1998; 97: 24-30. Illus.: Photo. B&W. 4. Lang.: Eng.
Canada: Toronto, ON. 1998. Histories-sources. ■Playwright/director Djanet Sears discusses creating all-Black theatre and the creative process for *Harlem Duet* with one of her actors, Alison Sealy Smith.

2827 Shantz, Valerie. *Yvette Nolan: Playwright in Context.* Edmonton, AB: Univ. of Alberta; 1998. 109 pp. Notes. Biblio. [M.A. Thesis, Univ. Microfilms Order No. AAC MQ28909.] Lang.: Eng.
Canada. 1997-1998. Histories-sources. ■Author's experience as a dramaturg working with Canadian playwright Yvette Nolan on her play *Annie Mae's Movement.*

2828 Thomas, Alan. "Introduction." *MD.* 1998 Spr; 41(1): 1-6. Notes. Lang.: Eng.
Canada. 1998. Critical studies. ■Introduction to the focus of *Modern Drama* 41:1, translations of plays.

2829 Van Dyke, Margaret. *Theatrical Re/enactments of Mennonite Identity in the Plays of Veralyn Warkentin and Vern Thiessen.* Edmonton, AB: Univ. of Alberta; 1998. 124 pp. Notes. Biblio. [M.A. Thesis, Univ. Microfilms Order No. AAC MQ28913.] Lang.: Eng.
Canada. 1890-1997. Critical studies. ■Survey of Mennonite drama, with specific analysis of Warkentin's *Chastity Belts* and *Mary and Martha*, which frame the conflict between religious submission and artistic freedom in terms of the community's treatment of women, and Thiessen's *The Courier* and *The Resurrection of John Frum*, which delineate the different social environments in Mennonite life.

2830 Vigeant, Louise. "Don Quichotte de mes rêves." (Don Quixote of My Dreams.) *JCT.* 1998; 89: 97-100. Notes. Illus.: Photo. B&W. 4. Lang.: Fre.
Canada: Montreal, PQ. 1998. Critical studies. ■Dreams and faith in utopia in Wadji Mouawad's adaptation of Cervantes' *Don Quixote* for Théâtre du Nouveau Monde directed by Dominic Champagne.

2831 Vigeant, Louise. "La banalité dans le désordre: Entretien avec Michel Vinaver." (Banality in Disorder: Interview with Michel Vinaver.) *JCT.* 1998; 87: 165-172. Notes. Illus.: Photo. B&W. 3. Lang.: Fre.
Canada: Quebec, PQ. 1969-1998. Histories-sources. ■Playwright Michel Vinaver on his play *La Demande d'emploi (The Interview)* on the occasion of its being staged by Théâtre Niveau Parking (1998, directed by Lorraine Côté).

2832 Wagner, Vit. "*Anne.*" *ArtsAtl.* 1998; 16(1): 55. Illus.: Photo. B&W. 1. Lang.: Eng.
Canada: Toronto, ON. 1911-1998. Critical studies. ■Reports on Paul Ledoux's adaptation, entitled *Anne*, of the popular children's story, *Anne of Green Gables* by Lucy Maud Montgomery, featuring actress Jennie Raymond at the Young People's Theatre.

2833 Wagner, Vit. "*Fathers and Sons.*" *ArtsAtl.* 1998; 16(3): 60-61. Illus.: Photo. B&W. 1. Lang.: Eng.
Canada: Toronto, ON. 1998. Critical studies. ■Reports on the play, *Fathers and Sons* by Don Hannah, produced at the Tarragon Theatre.

2834 Wagner, Vit. "*Monster.*" *ArtsAtl.* 1998; 16(1): 55-56. Illus.: Photo. B&W. 1. Lang.: Eng.
Canada: Toronto, ON. 1998. Critical studies. ■Analyzes the nature of evil in Daniel MacIvor's *Monster*, directed by Daniel Brooks at the Da Da Kamera Canadian Stage Theatre.

2835 Wagner, Vit. "*Camera, Woman.*" *ArtsAtl.* 1998; 16(3): 60. Illus.: Photo. B&W. 1. Lang.: Eng.
Canada: Toronto, ON. 1998. Critical studies. ■Examines the play *Camera, Woman*, by R.M. Vaughan, produced at the Buddies in Bad Times Theatre. The play examines artistic license and creative control through the eyes of a lesbian filmmaker in the 1940s.

2836 Walton, Glenn. "*Corker.*" *ArtsAtl.* 1998; 16(1): 52-53. Illus.: Photo. B&W. 1. Lang.: Eng.
Canada: Halifax, NS. 1994-1998. Critical studies. ■Examines the play *Corker*, written by Wendy Lill and directed by Mary Vingoe at the Neptune Theatre. The play deals with current political issues in a maritime setting.

2837 Young, David. "The Way to *Inexpressible Island.*" *CTR.* Win 1998; 97: 52-56. Illus.: Photo. B&W. 4. [Excerpt from talk to a Creative Arts Seminar, 'Document and Fiction', Glendon College, Toronto, ON, January 1997.] Lang.: Eng.
Canada: Toronto, ON. 1990-1997. Histories-sources. ■Toronto playwright David Young on researching and writing his play *Inexpressible Island.*

2838 Alarcón, Justo; Camilo, Juan. "Juan Radrigán: *El Príncipe Desolado.*" *Gestos.* 1998 Nov.; 13(26): 127-131. Illus.: Photo. B&W. 1. Lang.: Spa.
Chile. 1998. Histories-sources. ■Interview with Radrigán regarding his play.

2839 Gilmore, Elsa M. "Marco Antonio de la Parra's *El padre muerto*: Ekphasis and History." *Gestos.* 1998 Nov.; 13(26): 99-108. Notes. Biblio. Lang.: Eng.
Chile. 1993. Critical studies. ■Analysis of de la Parra's use of preexisting visual images, not necessarily great art work, in his play.

2840 Llamas, Regina Sofia. *Comic Roles and Performance in the Play 'Zhang Xie Zhuangyuan' with a Complete Translation.* Cambridge, MA: Harvard Univ; 1998. 419 pp. Biblio. Notes. [Ph.D. Dissertation, Univ. Microfilms Order No. AAC 9832298.] Lang.: Eng.
China. 960-1127. Histories-specific. ■Examines the function of the three main comic roles (*mo, jing*, and *chou*) in the early Song comic play, *Zhang Xie Zhuangyuan (Top Graduate Zhang Xie)*, as well as some aspects of their performance.

2841 Myhre, Karin Elizabeth. *The Appearances of Ghosts in Northern Dramas.* Berkeley, CA: Univ. of California; 1998.

DRAMA: —Plays/librettos/scripts

315 pp. Notes. Biblio. [Ph.D. Dissertation, Univ. Microfilms Order No. AAC 9902173.] Lang.: Eng.
China. 1260-1368. Histories-specific. ■Investigates the shifting characterizations of demons and ghosts in a variety of different cultural fields through centuries of traditional Chinese culture, as reflected in Yuan dramatic texts.

2842 Conceison, Claire. "The Occidental Other on the Chinese Stage: Cultural Cross-Examination in Guo Shixing's *Bird Men.*" *ATJ.* 1998 Spr; 15(1): 87-101. Notes. Biblio. Gloss. Illus.: Photo. B&W. Color. 9. Lang.: Eng.
China, People's Republic of. 1991. Critical studies. ■Analysis of cultural and political themes in *Niaoren*, particularly the Chinese view of foreign intervention in Chinese life.

2843 Fei, Faye C. "Dramatizing the West in Chinese Spoken Drama." *ATJ.* 1998 Spr; 15(1): 102-116. Notes. Biblio. Gloss. Illus.: Photo. B&W. 3. Lang.: Eng.
China, People's Republic of. 1949-1976. Critical studies. ■Using Foucault's theory of the 'disappearing author', argues that Chinese playwrights do not place individualistic stamps on their work, particularly noticeable in plays dealing with China's relations with foreign powers 1949-1976. Investigates anti-imperialist *huaja* drama of that era.

2844 Kuoshu, Harry H. "Will Godot Come by Bus or Through a Trace? Discussion of a Chinese Absurdist Play." *MD.* 1998 Fall; 41 (3): 461-473. Notes. Lang.: Eng.
China, People's Republic of. 1983. Critical studies. ■Influence of Beckett's *En attendant Godot (Waiting for Godot)* upon Gao Xingjian's *Che zhan (The Bus Stop).*

2845 Sun, William H. "Underground Realism in China." *NTQ.* 1998 Aug.; 14(3): 285-287. [Issue 55.] Lang.: Eng.
China, People's Republic of: Shanghai. 1993-1996. Historical studies. ■Examines modern Chinese theatre's move away from the official socialist realism to a more personal and intimate drama, dubbed 'underground realism' by one of its pioneers, the playwright Zhang Xian.

2846 Shen, Virginia Shiang-Lan. *El nuevo teatro de Colombia: La ideología y la dramaturgía en Enrique Buenaventura, Carlos José Reyes and Jairo Anibal Niño.* (New Colombian Theatre: The Ideology and Dramaturgy of Enrique Buenaventura, Carlos José Reyes, and Jairo Anibal Nino.) Tempe, AZ: Arizona State Univ; 1988. 241 pp. Biblio. Notes. [Ph.D. Dissertation, Univ. Microfilms Order No. AAC 8815637.] Lang.: Spa.
Colombia. 1950-1985. Critical studies. ■Analysis of works by Buenaventura, Reyes, and Niño as representative of Colombian New Theatre, which takes an ideological stance through its satiric challenge to official representatives of lived social realities. Also studies significant theatre groups and directors.

2847 Ulchur Collazos, Leobardo Ivan. *'Los papeles del infierno' de Enrique Buenaventura: Entre la Imagen y la Ideología de la Violencia.* (Enrique Buenaventura's *Leaflets from Hell*: From the Image to the Ideology of Violence.) Austin, TX: Univ of Texas; 1987. 250 pp. Notes. Biblio. [Ph.D. Dissertation, Univ. Microfilms Order No. AAC 8728656.] Lang.: Spa.
Colombia. 1970-1985. Critical studies. ■Politics and violence in the six 'sketches' included in *Los papeles del infierno (Leaflets from Hell)*: *La maestra (The School Teacher)*, *La tortura (The Torture)*, *La autopsia (The Autopsy)*, *La audiencia (The Hearing)*, *La requisa (The Search)*, and *La orgía (The Orgy).*

2848 Panovski, Naum. "Landscape for the New Millenium, Slobodan Šnajder: Croatian Playwright." *PerAJ.* 1998 Sep.; 20(3): 76-78. Illus.: Photo. B&W. 1. Lang.: Eng.
Croatia. 1982-1998. Biographical studies. ■Profile of the playwright, and the influence of the breakup of the Balkan states on his work.

2849 Kovalenko, G.V. "Nacional'nyj teat'r (Čechii) i idejno-chudožestvennye iskanija dvuch vekov." (Czech National Theatre and Ideological Artistic Discoveries of Two Centuries.) 122-129 in *Evropejskoe iskusstvo XIX - XX vekov.* Moscow: 1998. Lang.: Rus.
Czech Republic. 1800-1999. Historical studies. ■History of drama in Czech.

2850 Král, Karel. "Hry o hrách." (Plays About Plays.) *Svet.* 1998; 9(2): 62-65. Lang.: Cze.
Czech Republic. 1990-1997. Critical studies. ■Directions being taken by Czech contemporary playwrights, including Jiří Pokorný, Jan Flemr, Viliam Klimáček, Rostislav Křivánek, Tomáš Horváth, Blanka Kubešová, Josef Beran, Silvester Lavrík, and Roman Sikora.

2851 Reslová, Marie. "The Rhythmic Exorcisms of J.A.P./Les incantations rythmiques de J.A.P." *CzechT.* 1998 June; 14: 32-38. Illus.: Photo. B&W. 9. Lang.: Eng, Fre.
Czech Republic. 1995-1997. Biographical studies. ■Portrait of playwright/director J.A. Pitínský, pen name of Zdeněk Petrželka.

2852 Beck, Dennis Charles. *The Czech Authorial Studio Theatres, 1968-1989: Twenty Years of Rehearsing the Revolution.* Austin, TX: Univ. of Texas; 1998. 607 pp. Notes. Biblio. [Ph.D. Dissertation, Univ. Microfilms Order No. AAC 9837900.] Lang.: Eng.
Czechoslovakia. 1968-1989. Histories-specific. ■Argues that Czech theatres that created their own compositions, thus circumventing censorship, not only created a dramaturgy with the power to resist official ideology and limitations but also influenced historical events.

2853 Lagerlöf, Malin. "Störst av alla meningslösa ting är kärleken." (Love Is the Greatest of All the Meaningless Things.) *Tningen.* 1998; 21(1): 7-10: ia. Illus.: Photo. B&W. Color. Lang.: Swe.
Denmark: Copenhagen. 1989-1998. Histories-sources. ■Interview with the Danish playwright Peter Asmussen about his playwriting, with references to his play *Stranden* and his co-operation with filmmaker Lars von Trier.

2854 Olsen, Jakob Steen. "Teatrenes talentspejdere." (The Theatres' Talent Scouts.) *TE.* 1998 Apr.; 88: 24-29. Illus.: Photo. B&W. 3. Lang.: Dan.
Denmark. 1998. Critical studies. ■A round table discussion with four dramaturgs, Benedikte Hammershøye Nielsen, Janicke Branth, Nicole Maria Langkilde, and Kitte Wagner, about how to recognize new talented playwrights.

2855 Sjögren, Henrik. "Kaj Munk—Nordens Shakespeare." (Kaj Munk—the Shakespeare of the North.) *Entré.* 1998; 25(2): 32-39. Illus.: Photo. B&W. Lang.: Swe.
Denmark. 1898-1944. Critical studies. ■The work of priest/playwright Kaj Munk, and the fate of his plays today.

2856 "Tajna Šekspira razgadana? Da zdravstvuet tajna!" (The Secret of Shakespeare Solved? Viva the Secret!) *Znanie sila.* 1998; 2: 136-139. Lang.: Rus.
England. 1590-1616. Critical studies. ■Critique of book written by I. Galilov, *The Play of William Shakespeare, or the Secret of the Great Phoenix*, dealing with the identity of the English playwright.

2857 Alexander, Catherine M.S. "*The Dear Witches*: Horace Walpole's *Macbeth.*" *RevES.* 1998 May; 49(194): 131-144. Notes. Lang.: Eng.
England. 1743. Critical studies. ■Walpole's personal and political motivation (to attack those responsible for his father's political downfall) and his sources for his creation of his extended parody of the witches' scenes from Shakespeare's play.

2858 Anzi, Anna. *Shakespeare e le arti figurative.* (Shakespeare and Figurative Arts.) Rome: Bulzoni; 1998. 82 pp. Biblio. Lang.: Ita.
England. 1589-1613. Critical studies. ■The influence of figurative arts in the works of William Shakespeare.

2859 Astington, John H. "*Macbeth* and the Rowe Illustrations." *SQ.* 1998 Spr; 49(1): 83-86. Notes. Illus.: Dwg. B&W. 2. Lang.: Eng.
England. 1709-1714. Historical studies. ■Argues that the frontispiece illustrations on separate editions of Nicholas Rowe's *Complete Works of William Shakespeare*, relating the 'show of kings' scene, *Macbeth* (IV.i, 4-18), do not in fact reflect the staging practices of the scene during that time.

2860 Bacon, Delia; Baker, Elliott, ed. "*The Philosophy of the Plays of Shakespeare Unfolded: King Lear.*" *ERev.* 1998 Spr; 6 (1): 45-66. Lang.: Eng.

DRAMA: —Plays/librettos/scripts

England. 1605. Critical studies. ■Reprint of Bacon's analysis of *King Lear* (1857), in which she argues that the author of such a number of masterpieces could not have been motivated by monetary gain but a deliberate desideratum for mankind.

2861 Balašov, N.I. "Slovo v zaščitu avtorstva Šekspira." (A Word in Defense of the Work of Shakespeare.) *Akademičeskie tetradi.* 1998; 5: 3-142. Lang.: Rus.

England. 1564-1616. Critical studies. ■Special issue consisting of Balašova's unpublished book on Shakespeare and Shakespeare studies, with reference to Galilov's *The Play of William Shakespeare, or the Secret of the Great Phoenix.*

2862 Barbour, Kathryn. "Flout 'em and Scout 'em and Scout 'em and Flout 'em: Prospero's Power and Punishment in *The Tempest.*" 159-172 in Kendall, Gillian Murray, ed. *Shakespearean Power and Punishment.* Madison, NJ/London: Fairleigh Dickinson UP; 1998. 219 pp. Index. Notes. Illus.: Pntg. 1. Lang.: Eng.

England. 1611. Critical studies. ■Analysis of Shakespeare's *The Tempest* as an experiment in political control and punishment.

2863 Barfoot, C.C. "*Troilus and Cressida*: 'Praise us as we are tasted'." *SQ.* 1988 Spr; 39(1): 45-57. Notes. Lang.: Eng.

England. 1601-1602. Critical studies. ■Shakespeare's use of the language of the marketplace as a metaphor of treachery in *Troilus and Cressida.*

2864 Barkman, Iris G. *Not Fit for Much: Mothers and Widows in the Comedies of Etherege, Wycherley, and Congreve.* Albuquerque, NM: Univ. of New Mexico; 1998. 223 pp. Notes. Biblio. [Ph.D. Dissertation, Univ. Microfilms Order No. AAC 9839200.] Lang.: Eng.

England. 1642-1729. Critical studies. ■Positive and negative portrayals of motherhood in Restoration drama.

2865 Barnaby, Andrew; Wry, Joan. "Authorized Versions: *Measure for Measure* and the Politics of Biblical Translation." *RenQ.* 1998 Win; 51(4): 1225-1254. Notes. Biblio. Lang.: Eng.

England. 1604. Critical studies. ■Shakespeare's play as a reflection on King James' announced plans to print a new translation of the Bible. Argues that the play's staged conflict between ethical ideal and social practice is a cautionary tale on the dangers of using religious rhetoric in secular political contexts.

2866 Bartolovich, Crystal. "Putting *Tamburlaine* on a (Cognitive) Map." *RenD.* 1998; 21: 29-72. Notes. Biblio. Lang.: Eng.

England. 1587-1588. Critical studies. ■Gauges the merits of Marlowe's play, in both its own period and the present day.

2867 Beach, Vincent Woodrow, Jr. *George Chapman's* Bussy D'Ambois *(c. 1604) and Jacobean Social Attitudes.* New York, NY: City Univ. of New York; 1988. 224 pp. Biblio. Notes. [Ph.D. Dissertation, Univ. Microfilms Order No. AAC 8821067.] Lang.: Eng.

England. 1604. Critical studies. ■The use of historical allusion as a vehicle for heroic tragedy in George Chapman's *Bussy D'Ambois.*

2868 Berek, Peter. "The Jew as Renaissance Man." *RenQ.* 1998 Spr; 51(1): 128-162. Notes. Biblio. Lang.: Eng.

England. 1590-1600. Critical studies. ■The creation of the stereotyped Jew, both comic and frightening, in Marlowe's *The Jew of Malta* and Shakespeare's *The Merchant of Venice*, and its relationship to societal anxiety regarding ostensibly converted Jews.

2869 Berg, James Emmanuel. *Shakespeare and the Staging of 'Feudalism'.* New York, NY: Columbia Univ; 1998. 340 pp. Notes. Biblio. [Ph.D. Dissertation, Univ. Microfilms Order No. AAC 9838881.] Lang.: Eng.

England. 1590-1613. Critical studies. ■Elements of social, economic and political thought in the plays of Shakespeare, with attention to the construction of the feudal world in the chronicle plays.

2870 Berger, Harry, Jr. "The Prince's Dog: Falstaff and the Perils of Speech-Prefixity." *SQ.* 1998 Spr; 49(1): 40-73. Notes. Illus.: Diagram. B&W. 1. Lang.: Eng.

England. 1596-1597. Critical studies. ■Re-examines the relationship between Prince Hal and Falstaff in both parts of *Henry IV* by applying the theory of speech-prefixity.

2871 Bevington, David. "Lyly's *Endymion* and *Midas*: The Catholic Question in England." *CompD.* 1998 Spr; 32(1): 26-46. Notes. Lang.: Eng.

England. 1587-1590. Critical studies. ■The reflection of contemporary religious and social issues in John Lyly's *Endymion* and *Midas.*

2872 Bilby, Monika. *Heroick Vertue: Changing Ideas of Feminine Greatness in the Heroic Drama of the Late Seventeenth Century.* College Park, MD: Univ. of Maryland; 1988. 363 pp. Biblio. Notes. [Ph.D. Dissertation, Univ. Microfilms Order No. AAC 8912265.] Lang.: Eng.

England. 1660-1710. Critical studies. ■Examines Restoration heroic plays for their dramatizations of women's political life.

2873 Bishop, John. "'The Ordinary Course of Nature': Authority in the Restoration *Tempest.*" *Restor.* 1998 Sum; 13(1): 54-69 . Notes. Biblio. Lang.: Eng.

England. 1674. Critical studies. ■Analysis of *The Enchanted island*, Dryden and Davenant's adaptation of Shakespeare's *The Tempest*, with emphasis on the place of authority in a static universe.

2874 Bishop, Thomas Geoffrey. *The Uses of Recognition from Aristotle to Shakespeare: 'A Notable Passion of Wonder'.* New Haven, CT: Yale Univ; 1988. 336 pp. Notes. Biblio. [Ph.D. Dissertation, Univ. Microfilms Order No. AAC 9008986.] Lang.: Eng.

England. 1400-1612. Critical studies. ■Applies Aristotle's treatment of wonder and recognition to selected plays from the medieval English cycles plays and the Elizabethan romantic plays, including Shakespeare's *Pericles.*

2875 Blim, John Miles. *Shakespeare's Montage: Scenic Transitions and the Theatrical Experience.* Evanston, IL: Northwestern Univ; 1987. 208 pp. Notes. Biblio. [Ph.D. Dissertation, Univ. Microfilms Order No. AAC 8728961.] Lang.: Eng.

England. 1590-1613. Critical studies. ■Examines the function of the transitions between scenes in Shakespeare's plays and their part in determining the experience of the audience in the course of performance.

2876 Boling, Ronald Jackson. *The Performance of Madness in 'King Lear'.* Gainesville, FL: Univ. of Florida; 1988. 259 pp. Notes. Biblio. [Ph.D. Dissertation, Univ. Microfilms Order No. AAC 8912035.] Lang.: Eng.

England. 1605-1606. Critical studies. ■Argues that the mad scenes in Shakespeare's *King Lear* are dramatic opportunities for spectacle, creating continual interpretive crises for the characters onstage as well as for the audience.

2877 Borg, Dominica Mary. *The Essential Experience in Shakespeare's Comedies: A New Hermeneutic Synthesis.* New Haven, MA: Yale Univ; 1998. 267 pp. Notes. Biblio. [Ph.D. Dissertation, Univ. Microfilms Order No. AAC 9830383.] Lang.: Eng.

England. 1590-1608. Critical studies. ■Analysis of *Much Ado About Nothing, Twelfth Night* and *Measure for Measure* distinguishing Shakespeare's own contribution from the additions of later interpreters.

2878 Bott, Robin Luana. *'The Makers of Manners': Politeness, Power, and the Instability of Social Relationships in Renaissance Drama.* Boulder, CO: Univ. of Colorado; 1998. 164 pp. Notes. Biblio. [Ph.D. Dissertation, Univ. Microfilms Order No. AAC 9827690.] Lang.: Eng.

England. 1500-1600. Critical studies. ■Examines moments in which codes of politeness are defined and represented in selected plays of Renaissance England using modern language theories.

2879 Bowers, Rick. "'The Luck of Caesar': Winning and Losing in *Antony and Cleopatra.*" *EnSt.* 1998 Nov.; 79(6): 522-535. Notes. Lang.: Eng.

England. 1607. Critical studies. ■Game theory analysis of Shakespeare's play, touching upon audience response, and also the realist materialist nature of the piece.

2880 Breier, René. "The Longleaf Manuscript: Tamora's Great Belly." *ELN.* 1998 Mar.; 35(3): 20-22. Notes. Lang.: Eng.

England. 1590-1594. Critical studies. ■Argues that an illustration of Queen Tamora accompanying the Longleaf Manuscript of Shakespeare's *Titus Andronicus*, depicts a woman, not a male actor, in costume, because of the pregnant swell of her abdomen.

2881 Brooks, Douglas Alan. *From Playhouse to Printing House: Dramas of Authorship in Early Modern England.* New York, NY: Columbia Univ; 1998. 319 pp. Notes. Biblio. [Ph.D. Dissertation, Univ. Microfilms Order No. AAC 9838887.] Lang.: Eng.

England. 1590-1650. Critical studies. ■The profession of playwriting for the early modern London stage. Analyzes general conditions of writing and publishing, as well as individual playwrights and specific plays including the works of Shakespeare, Jonson, Beaumont and Fletcher, and Thomas Heywood.

2882 Brown, Eric C. "'Many a Civil Monster': Shakespeare's Idea of the Centaur." *ShS.* 1998; 51: 175-191. Notes. Lang.: Eng.

England. 1590-1613. Critical studies. ■Images of the mythological centaur appearing in the writing of Shakespeare.

2883 Brown, Eric C. *The Control of Time in Renaissance England: Marlowe, Shakespeare, Jonson, and Donne.* Baton Rouge, LA: Louisiana State A&M; 1998. 262 pp. Notes. Biblio. [Ph.D. Dissertation, Univ. Microfilms Order No. AAC 9836856.] Lang.: Eng.

England. 1590-1620. Critical studies. ■Time as a controllable instrument in Shakespeare's *The Merchant of Venice*, Jonson's *The Alchemist* and masque *Time Vindicated.*

2884 Brown, Pamela Allen. *Better a Shrew than a Sheep: Jest and Gender in Early Modern Popular Culture.* New York, NY: Columbia Univ; 1998. 364 pp. Notes. Biblio. [Ph.D. Dissertation, Univ. Microfilms Order No. AAC 9838888.] Lang.: Eng.

England. 1590-1630. Critical studies. ■Examines jests, merry books, and plays, and their portrayals of non-elite women using wit, skepticism, and collective action against their tormenters in works such as Shakespeare's *The Merry Wives of Windsor, Othello, The Taming of the Shrew, The Winter's Tale* and *A Midsummer Night's Dream*, Ben Jonson's *The Alchemist*, Elizabeth Cary's *Tragedy of Mariam*, Dekker, Chettle, and Haughton's *The Pleasant Comodie of Patient Grissill* and John Fletcher's *The Woman's Prize.*

2885 Brown, Richard Danson. "'A Talkitive Wench (Whose Words a World Hath Delighted In)': Mistress Shore and Elizabethan Complaint." *RevES.* 1998 Nov.; 49(196): 395-415. Notes. Lang.: Eng.

England. 1540-1594. Critical studies. ■Influence of Thomas More's *History of King Richard III* on the depiction of Jane Shore in the anonymous *True Tragedy of Richard III* and Thomas Heywood's *Edward IV.*

2886 Burroughs, Catherine Beauregard. *The Characterization of the Feminine in the Drama of the English Romantic Poets.* Atlanta, GA: Emory Univ; 1988. 235 pp. Biblio. Notes. [Ph.D. Dissertation, Univ. Microfilms Order No. AAC 8816933.] Lang.: Eng.

England. 1794-1840. Critical studies. ■The feminine ideal of the Romantic heroine in Keats's *Otho the Great*, Coleridge's *The Fall of Robespierre*, Wordsworth's *The Borderers*, and Shelley's *The Cenci.*

2887 Canfield, J. Douglas. "Prostitution as Class Prophylactic in George Lillo's Adaptation of Shakespeare's *Pericles* as *Marina.*" *Restor.* 1998 Win; 13(2): 35-42. Biblio. Notes. Lang.: Eng.

England. 1738. Critical studies. ■Lillo's defense of prostitution in his adaptation of Shakespeare's play.

2888 Cartwright, Kent. "The Confusions of *Gallathea*: John Lyly as a Popular Dramatist." *CompD.* 1998 Sum; 32(2): 207-239. Notes. Lang.: Eng.

England. 1584. Critical studies. ■Analysis of Lyly's court comedy as a popular drama.

2889 Caudill, Helen Sue. *Plague as a Force in Jacobean Tragedy.* Pittsburgh, PA: Univ. of Pittsburgh; 1988. 231 pp. Notes. Biblio. [Ph.D. Dissertation, Univ. Microfilms Order No. AAC 8816989.] Lang.: Eng.

England. 1618-1642. Critical studies. ■Plague imagery in the tragedies of John Webster, Cyril Tourneur, William Shakespeare, George Chapman, Francis Beaumont, and John Fletcher as a signpost of anxieties over the corruption of government and the transition from a religious to a scientific worldview.

2890 Chandler, David. "Lady Macbeth's 'Milke' and 'Gall': A Christian Idea?" *ELN.* 1998 Mar.; 35(3): 25-27. Notes. Pref. Lang.: Eng.

England. 1606. Critical studies. ■Idea of Christianity in Lady Macbeth's description of her husband (I:v, 15-18) in Shakespeare's *Macbeth.*

2891 Chaney, Joseph. "Turning to Me: Genres of Cross-Dressing in Charke's *Narrative* and Shakespeare's *The Merchant of Venice.*" 200-226 in Baruth, Philip E., ed. *Introducing Charlotte Charke: Actress, Author, Enigma.* Urbana/Chicago, IL: Univ. of Illinois P; 1998. 250 pp. Index. Biblio. Notes. Lang.: Eng.

England. 1713-1760. Critical studies. ■Examines connections between Charlotte Cibber Charke's *Narrative* and Shakespeare's *The Merchant of Venice*, especially in light of genre and gender analysis.

2892 Charnes, Linda. "'So Unsecret to Ourselves': Notorious Identity and the Material Subject in Shakespeare's *Troilus and Cressida.*" *SQ.* 1989 Win; 40(4): 413-440. Notes. Biblio. Lang.: Eng.

England. 1601-1602. Critical studies. ■Tension between the public and private perception of self in Shakespeare's play.

2893 Clark, Danielle. "'This domestic kingdome or Monarchy': Cary's *The Tragedy of Mariam* and the Resistance to Patriarchal Government." *MRDE.* 1998; 10: 179-200. Notes. Lang.: Eng.

England. 1613. Critical studies. ■Analysis of Elizabeth Cary's play with emphasis on the obligations of marriage within patriarchal government, the role of women in the public sphere as guarantors of male supremacy, and the grounds for female resistance.

2894 Collier, Susanne. "Cutting to the Heart of the Matter: Stabbing the Woman in *Philaster* and *Cymbeline.*" 39-58 in Kendall, Gillian Murray, ed. *Shakespearean Power and Punishment.* Madison, NJ/London: Fairleigh Dickinson UP; 1998. 219 pp. Index. Notes. Illus.: Dwg. Pntg. 2. Lang.: Eng.

England. 1609-1610. Critical studies. ■Argues that the murders of Imogen in Shakespeare's *Cymbeline* and Arethusa in Beaumont and Fletcher's *Philaster* represent ritual sacrifice in which power invested in royal women is transferred to male figures.

2895 Connolly, Jon Jerome. *The Sword and the Pen: Militarism, Masculinity, and Writing in Early Modern England.* Santa Barbara, CA: Univ. of California; 1998. 199 pp. Notes. Biblio. [Ph.D. Dissertation, Univ. Microfilms Order No. AAC 9840764.] Lang.: Eng.

England. 1590-1650. Critical studies. ■Examines representations of masculinity during a period in which the introduction of firearms was revolutionizing the practice of war in England. Draws on the work of military historians to explore various ways English writers tried to imagine a heroic masculinity in a time of military turmoil in the work of Philip Sidney, William Shakespeare, and John Milton.

2896 Cornell, Christine. "*Measure for Measure*'s Angelo: A Scarecrow for the Birds of Prey." *ELN.* 1998 Mar.; 35(3): 22-25. Notes. Lang.: Eng.

England. 1604. Critical studies. ■Meaning of Angelo's 'We must not make a scarecrow of the law' speech (II:i) of Shakespeare's play *Measure for Measure.*

2897 Corum, Richard. *Understanding* Hamlet*: A Student Casebook to Issues, Sources, and Historical Documents.* Westport, CT/London: Greenwood; 1998. 271 pp. (Literature in Context.) Index. Biblio. Illus.: Dwg. Pntg. Sketches. 15. Lang.: Eng.

England. 1532-1608. Instructional materials. ■Collection of document excerpts to help students understand William Shakespeare's *Hamlet.* Includes historical documents that set the cultural context of the period with respect to on theatre and tragedy, melancholy and suicide, the presence of the Ghost, revenge crimes, gender issues, and marriage.

2898 Cox, Catherine S. "'An excellent thing in woman': Virgo and Viragos in *King Lear.*" *MP.* 1998 Nov.; 96(2): 143-157. Notes. Lang.: Eng.

DRAMA: —Plays/librettos/scripts

England. 1605-1606. Critical studies. ■Examines the ambiguous gender constructions of Lear's three daughters in relation to traditional theological and literary ideas of order.

2899 Cox, John D. "Stage Devils in English Reformation Plays." *CompD.* 1998 Spr; 32(1): 85-116. Notes. Illus.: Dwg. B&W. 3. Lang.: Eng.

England. 1530-1583. Historical studies. ■Representations of Satan in plays of the English Reformation.

2900 Crane, Mary Thomas. "Male Pregnancy and Cognitive Permeability in *Measure for Measure.*" *SQ.* 1998 Fall; 49(3): 269-292 . Notes. Lang.: Eng.

England. 1604. Critical studies. ■The cognitive mechanisms through which the human body and embodied brain both originate, and succumb to, linguistic expressions of power in Shakespeare's play.

2901 da Vinci Nichols, Nina. "Who Is Bertram Rossillion?" *ShN.* 1998 Fall; 48(3): 67-68. Notes. Lang.: Eng.

England. 1602-1603. Critical studies. ■Offers Gilbert Talbot, 7th Earl of Shrewsbury, as the model for the character of 'Young' Bertram in Shakespeare's *All's Well That Ends Well.*

2902 Davenport, Edwin. "The Representation of Robin Hood in Elizabethan Drama: *George a Greene* and *Edward I.*" 45-62 in Potter, Lois, ed. *Playing Robin Hood: The Legend as Performance in Five Centuries.* Newark, DE: Univ of Delaware P; 1998. 254 pp. Index. Notes. Biblio. Pref. Lang.: Eng.

England. 1588-1601. Critical studies. ■How Elizabethan professional theatre developed community dramas about Robin Hood in the direction of the history play, with emphasis on George Peele's *Edward I* and the anonymous *George a Greene, the Pinner of Wakefield.*

2903 De Fino, Dean. "Iago Dilated: Delivering Time in *Othello.*" *ERev.* 1998 Aut; 6(2): 44-54. Notes. Lang.: Eng.

England. 1604. Critical studies. ■Results of patience and delay in Shakespeare's tragedy.

2904 De, Esha Niyogi. *The Purpose of Playing: Theater and Ritual in the Revesby Folk Play, 'Summer's Last Will and Testament', and 'Hamlet'.* West Lafayette, IN: Purdue Univ; 1988. 299 pp. Notes. Biblio. [Ph.D. Dissertation, Univ. Microfilms Order No. AAC 8825523.] Lang.: Eng.

England. 1600-1779. Critical studies. ■Examines 'recoveries of ritual' within plots that initially seem only to confirm a nonritualistic theatre, such as Shakespeare's *Hamlet*, the folk play recorded at Revesby in 1779, and Thomas Nashe's *Summer's Last Will and Testament.*

2905 Desai, R.W. "England, the Indian Boy, and the Spice Trade in *A Midsummer Night's Dream.*" *ShN.* 1998 Spr; 48(1): 3-4, 26. Notes. Lang.: Eng.

England. 1594-1595. Critical studies. ■Analysis of Shakespeare's play from the standpoint of the relationship between east and west (India and England), represented by the character of the stolen boy. Concludes in *ShN* 1998 Sum (48:2, pp 39-40, 42).

2906 Detmer, Anne Elizabeth. *Effacing Heroes: A Study of Browning and the Renaissance Dramatists.* Medford, MA: Tufts Univ; 1998. 236 pp. Notes. Biblio. [Ph.D. Dissertation, Univ. Microfilms Order No. AAC 9819712.] Lang.: Eng.

England. 1590-1889. Critical studies. ■The influence of plays by John Webster, Thomas Middleton, and of William Shakespeare on the poetry of Robert Browning. Focuses on Browning's deconstruction of the traditional male hero's abuse of women based on the subversive use of conventional Jacobean forms.

2907 Dharwadker, Aparna. "The Comedy of Dispossession." *StPh.* 1998 Fall; 95(4): 411-434. Notes. Lang.: Eng.

England. 1661-1663. Critical studies. ■The tension between topical imperatives and aesthetic norms in three Restoration anti-Puritan comedies: Abraham Cowley's *Cutter of Coleman Street*, Robert Howard's *The Committee*, and *The Cheats* by John Wilson.

2908 Diehl, Huston. "'Infinite Space': Representation and Reformation in *Measure for Measure.*" *SQ.* 1998 Win; 49(4): 393-410. Notes. Lang.: Eng.

England. 1604. Critical studies. ■Considers Shakespeare's play as the playwright's experimentation with a Protestant aesthetic of the stage.

2909 Dodd, William. "Destined Livery? Character and Person in Shakespeare." *ShS.* 1998; 51: 147-158. Notes. Lang.: Eng.

England. 1604. Critical studies. ■Using *Measure for Measure* as a template, explores two related aspects of character in Shakespearean drama: 'effect' of verbal interaction and the problem of the character's agency.

2910 Doloff, Steven. "Iachimo's Wager and Hans Carvel's Ring in Shakespeare's *Cymbeline.*" *ShN.* 1998 Fall; 48(3): 67. Notes. Lang.: Eng.

England. 1609-1610. Critical studies. ■Traces sources for the 'wager' scene in Shakespeare's play. Offers two possibilities, Bocaccio's *Decameron* and the anonymous English prose story 'Frederyke of Jennen'.

2911 Dutton, Richard. "Shakespeare and Lancaster." *SQ.* 1998 Spr; 49(1): 1-21. Notes. Lang.: Eng.

England. 1590-1599. Critical studies. ■Examines Shakespeare's English history plays for the meaning of the Lancaster family name to the nation and the playwright personally. Also touches on whether or not Shakespeare was a Roman Catholic and argues that the second tetralogy can be construed as plays of succession dealing with Queen Elizabeth I's lack of an heir.

2912 Duvall, Matthew Evan. *Representing Theft and Other Crimes Against Property in Renaissance Dramas on Henry V and in Fielding's 'Amelia'.* New Orleans, LA: Tulane Univ; 1998. 203 pp. Notes. Biblio. [Ph.D. Dissertation, Univ. Microfilms Order No. AAC 9906372.] Lang.: Eng.

England. 1590-1745. Critical studies. ■Focuses on various textual mechanisms in the works that operate to erase contradictions in the construction of property and their representation of exchange.

2913 Eaton, Sara. "'Content with Art'?: Seeing the Emblematic Woman in *The Second Maiden's Tragedy* and *The Winter's Tale.*" 59-88 in Kendall, Gillian Murray, ed. *Shakespearean Power and Punishment.* Madison, NJ/London: Fairleigh Dickinson UP; 1998. 219 pp. Index. Notes. Illus.: Dwg. Sketches. 4. Lang.: Eng.

England. 1604-1625. Critical studies. ■Examines how the 'emblem' tradition reveals and frames the power of women in Shakespeare's *The Winter's Tale* and Thomas Middleton's *The Second Maiden's Tragedy*, especially in the characters of Hermione and the Lady's Ghost.

2914 Epp, Garrett P.J. "'Into a Womannys Lyckenes': Bale's Personification of Idolatry." *MET.* 1996; 18: 63-73. Notes. [Response to Alan Stewart's 'Ydolatricall Sodometrye', *MET* 1993, 15:3-20.] Lang.: Eng.

England. 1536-1546. Critical studies. ■The characters of Sodomy and Idolatry in John Bale's *A Comedy Concernynge Thre Lawes, of Nature, Moses, and Christ*, who are seen only together. Sodomy is represented as a male homosexual, whereas Idolatry signifies a worldly and effeminate desire. It is argued that Bale intended his audience be offended by the concept of homosexuality.

2915 Erne, Lukas. "Biography and Mythography: Rereading Chettle's Alleged Apology to Shakespeare." *EnSt.* 1998 Sep.; 79(5): 430-440. Notes. Lang.: Eng.

England: London. 1592-1607. Historical studies. ■Argues that it is unlikely that the apology to playwrights in the preface to Henry Chettle's *Kind-Harts Dreame* was directed to Shakespeare.

2916 Fenn, Robert Denzel. *William Percy's* Faery Pastorall*: An Old Spelling Edition.* Vancouver, BC: Univ. of British Columbia; 1998. 302 pp. Biblio. Notes. [Ph.D. Dissertation, Univ. Microfilms Order No. AAC NQ27140.] Lang.: Eng.

England. 1603-1646. Textual studies. ■Analysis of an edition of William Percy's *Faery Pastorall*, located in the Huntington Library, focusing on stage directions, descriptions of staging and properties that Percy expected to be at his disposal when mounting the play in court.

2917 Feola, Maryann. "A Poniard's Point of Satire in Marlowe's *The Massacre at Paris.*" *ELN.* 1998 June; 35(4): 6-12. Notes. Lang.: Eng.

England. 1593. Critical studies. ■Elements of satire in Christopher Marlowe's play *The Massacre at Paris.*

2918 Flores, Stephan Paul. *Recognition and Repression: Ideology and Dramatic Success on the London Stage, 1660-1680.* Ann Arbor, MI: Univ. of Michigan; 1988. 153 pp. Biblio. Notes. [Ph.D. Dissertation, Univ. Microfilms Order No. AAC 8821571.] Lang.: Eng.

DRAMA: —Plays/librettos/scripts

England: London. 1660-1680. Critical studies. ▪The of use recognition and repression in Restoration plays including John Dryden's comedies and Nathaniel Lee's tragedies to shape playgoers' relations to ideology.

2919 Floyd-Wilson, Mary. "Temperature, Temperance, and Racial Difference in Ben Jonson's *The Masque of Blackness.*" *ELR.* 1998 Spr; 28(2): 183-209. Notes. Pref. Lang.: Eng.

England. 1605. Critical studies. ▪Analysis of racial temperament and complexion in Jonson's masque using sixteenth- and seventeenth-century climate theory.

2920 Forest-Hill, Lynn. "Lucian's Satire of the Philosophers in Heywood's *Play of the Wether.*" *MET.* 1996; 18: 142-160. Notes. Biblio. Lang.: Eng.

England. 1533. Historical studies. ▪John Heywood's use of Lucian's satire of philosophers from the dialogue *Icaromenippus* in his play to bolster his vehemently anti-clerical viewpoint.

2921 Gatti, Hilary. *Il teatro della coscienza. Giordano Bruno e Amleto.* (The Theatre of Conscience: Giordano Bruno and Hamlet.*) Rome: Bulzoni; 1998. 66 pp. (Piccola Biblioteca Shakespeariana 17.) Lang.: Ita.*

England. 1600-1601. Critical studies. ▪The possible influence of the writings of Giordano Bruno on Shakepeare's *Hamlet.*

2922 Gau, Tracey Marianne. *The Re-presentation of Historical Women in English Renaissance Drama.* Fort Worth, TX: Texas Christian Univ; 1998. 231 pp. Notes. Biblio. [Ph.D. Dissertation, Univ. Microfilms Order No. AAC 9905139.] Lang.: Eng.

England. 1580-1615. Critical studies. ▪Examines the treatment of historical female characters in the works of William Shakespeare, Christopher Marlowe, John Webster, Thomas Dekker and Thomas Middleton. Argues that the playwrights used contemporary discourses to fashion characters and promote social commentary in performance.

2923 George, David. "Cum Notis Variorum: The Proverb in Shakespeare." *ShN.* 1998 Fall; 48(3): 65. Notes. Lang.: Eng.

England. 1568-1613. Critical studies. ▪Shakespeare's use of proverbs in his work, and the probable influence of Roger Aschan's *The Scholemaster*, which heavily uses proverbs.

2924 Godina, Rosemarie. *Common-Sense Editing of a Crux and Female's 'Unruly' Speech.* London, ON: Univ. of Western Ontario; 1998. 107 pp. Notes. Biblio. [Master's Thesis, Univ. Microfilms Order No. AAC MQ30792.] Lang.: Eng.

England. 1590-1593. Critical studies. ▪Argues that the 'unruly' speech of Ariana in Shakespeare's *The Comedy of Errors* is subversive and reveals contradictions inherent in patriarchal attempts to construct language and gender.

2925 Goldberg, Jonathan. "Hamlet's Hand." *SQ.* 1988 Fall; 39(3): 307-327. Notes. Illus.: Dwg. B&W. 8. Lang.: Eng.

England. 1600-1601. Critical studies. ▪Importance of handwriting as reflective of one's character, and its role in Shakespeare's *Hamlet.*

2926 Green, Katherine S. "David Garrick and the Marriage 'Habitus': *The Clandestine Marriage* Revisited." *Restor.* 1998 Win; 13(2): 17-34. Notes. Biblio. Lang.: Eng.

England. 1766. Critical studies. ▪Analysis of Garrick's play as a response to a law issued regarding the curtailing of secret marriage.

2927 Griffin, Eric John. *The Temper of Spain: The Forging of Anti-Hispanic Sentiment in Early Modern England, 1492-1604.* Iowa City, IA: Univ. of Iowa; 1998. 406 pp. Notes. Biblio. [Ph.D. Dissertation, Univ. Microfilms Order No. AAC 9834462.] Lang.: Eng.

England. 1492-1604. Critical studies. ▪Historical implications of the treatment of Spain by early modern England as reflected in its plays and the shifts in Anglo-Iberian cultural relations during the course of the 16th century. Plays examined include Kyd's *The Spanish Tragedy*, Shakespeare's *Othello.*

2928 Grinnell, Richard W. "Naming and Social Disintegration in *The Witch of Edmonton.*" *ET.* 1998; 16(2): 209-223. Notes. Biblio. Lang.: Eng.

England. 1621. Critical studies. ▪Demonology as a vehicle for expressing destabilizing economic and social forces in *The Witch of Edmonton* by John Ford, Thomas Dekker, and William Rowley.

2929 Grubb, Shirley Carr. *Women, Rhetoric, and Power: The Women of Shakespeare's* Richard III *as Collective Antagonist.* Boulder, CO: Univ. of Colorado; 1987. 213 pp. Notes. Biblio. [Ph.D. Dissertation, Univ. Microfilms Order No. AAC 8716258.] Lang.: Eng.

England. 1592-1593. Historical studies. ▪Reassesses the role of the women in Shakespeare's *Richard III*, arguing that the play is a rhetorical document which explores resistance to tyranny and the rule of women.

2930 Guess, Ann H. *'An Echo of the Public Voice': Caricature and Satire in the Plays of Samuel Foote.* Houston, TX: Univ. of Houston; 1998. 269 pp. Notes. Biblio. [Ph.D. Dissertation, Univ. Microfilms Order No. AAC 9839330.] Lang.: Eng.

England. 1775-1800. Critical studies. ▪Argues that the use of topical satire points to Foote's concern for the changing fabric of English society and for the difficulty of curbing the growing materialism of the late eighteenth century.

2931 Haber, Judith. "'My Body Bestow upon My Women': The Space of the Feminine in *The Duchess of Malfi.*" *RenD.* 1997; 28: 133-159. Notes. Biblio. Lang.: Eng.

England. 1613. Critical studies. ▪Subversion of the erotics of patriarchy and conventional tragedy and the threat of pregnancy to the dominant male order in Webster's play.

2932 Hale, John K. "The Name 'Shylock'." *ShN.* 1998 Win; 48(4): 95. Lang.: Eng.

England. 1596. Critical studies. ▪Examines the name 'Shylock,' from Shakespeare's *The Merchant of Venice* for its origin and meaning.

2933 Happé, Peter. "Devils in the *York Cycle*: Language and Dramatic Technique." *RORD.* 1998; 37: 79-98. Notes. Lang.: Eng.

England: York. 1400-1500. Critical studies. ▪Examines the language used by the devils in the *York Cycle* to determine whether or not special features were ascribed to those characters.

2934 Hassal, R. Chris, Jr. "Painted Women: Annunciation Motifs in *Hamlet.*" *CompD.* 1998 Spr; 32(1): 47-84. Notes. Illus.: Pntg. Dwg. B&W. 6. Lang.: Eng.

England. 1600-1601. Critical studies. ▪Shakespeare's use of motifs that reflect the Annunciation to express Hamlet's anger and confusion regarding Ophelia and Gertrude.

2935 Head, Hayden Maxwell. *Envy, Emulation, and Scapegoating in Shakespeare's Second Tetralogy: A Girardian Reading of* Richard II *through* Henry V. Dallas, TX: Univ. of Dallas; 1998. 250 pp. Notes. Biblio. Lang.: Eng.

England. 1590-1599. Critical studies. ▪Examines Shakespeare's *Richard II, 1 Henry IV, 2 Henry IV*, and *Henry V* in light of René Girard's theories of mediated desire, reciprocal violence, and scapegoating.

2936 Hirschfeld, Heather Anne. *Joint Enterprises: Collaborative Drama and the Institutionalization of the English Renaissance Theatre.* Durham, NC: Duke Univ; 1998. 264 pp. Notes. Biblio. [Ph.D. Dissertation, Univ. Microfilms Order No. AAC 9829061.] Lang.: Eng.

England. 1598-1642. Critical studies. ▪Examines collaborative writing as it developed in connection with the gradual institutionalization of the theatre. Suggests various motives for and implications of joint work.

2937 Hopkins, Lisa. "Marlowe, Chapman, Ford and Nero." *ELN.* 1997 Sep.; 35(1): 5-10. Notes. Lang.: Eng.

England. 1587-1631. Critical studies. ▪Influences of Christopher Marlowe's *Tamburlaine*, George Chapman's *The Widow's Tears*, and Roman historian Suetonius on the plot of John Ford's *'Tis Pity She's a Whore.*

2938 Hopkins, Lisa. "John Ford and the Historians." *RORD.* 1998; 37: 17-31. Notes. Lang.: Eng.

England. 1634. Critical studies. ▪How Ford's personal history and those of his circle, as well as England's broad past, informed his play *Perkin Warbeck.*

2939 Hunt, John. "A Thing of Nothing: The Catastrophic Body in *Hamlet.*" *SQ.* 1988 Spr; 39(1): 27-44. Notes. Lang.: Eng.

England. 1600-1601. Critical studies. ▪Analysis of the play's corporeal imagery suggesting that Hamlet cannot act on the Ghost's command until he learns to accept physicality as the image of mentality.

DRAMA: —Plays/librettos/scripts

2940 Hunt, Maurice. "The Hybrid Reformations of Shakespeare's Second Henriad." *CompD.* 1998 Spr; 32(1): 176-206. Notes. Lang.: Eng.

England. 1596-1599. Critical studies. ▪Analysis of the Catholic and Protestant traits possessed by the characters in *Henry IV, Parts I & II* and *Henry V.*

2941 Johnston, Alexandra F. "The Robin Hood of the Records." 27-44 in Potter, Lois, ed. *Playing Robin Hood: The Legend as Performance in Five Centuries.* Newark, DE: Univ of Delaware P; 1998. 254 pp. Index. Notes. Biblio. Pref. Lang.: Eng.

England. 1425-1600. Critical studies. ▪Kinds of activity associated with the name of Robin Hood in early English drama.

2942 Johnston, Alexandra F. "The Emerging Pattern of the Easter Play in England." *MET.* 1998; 20: 3-23. Notes. [Paper presented at SITM Triennial Colloquium, University of Odense, August 1997.] Lang.: Eng.

England. 1180-1557. Historical studies. ▪Considers vernacular plays from the *York, Chester, N-Town,* and *Towneley Cycles,* together with five texts that can be regarded as part of the tradition.

2943 Jones, Ann Rosalind. "Revenge Comedy: Writing, Law, and the Punishing Heroine in *Twelfth Night, The Merry Wives of Windsor,* and *Swetnam, the Woman-Hater, Arraigned by Women.*" 23-38 in Kendall, Gillian Murray, ed. *Shakespearean Power and Punishment.* Madison, NJ/London: Fairleigh Dickinson UP; 1998. 219 pp. Index. Notes. Lang.: Eng.

England. 1597-1616. Critical studies. ▪How women characters accrue and negotiate power through movement in the public sphere, with reference to Maria and Viola in *Twelfth Night,* Mistresses Page and Ford in *The Merry Wives of Windsor,* and the undoing of gender stereotypes in the anonymous *Swetnam.*

2944 Kendall, G.M. "Overkill in Shakespeare." 173-196 in Kendall, Gillian Murray, ed. *Shakespearean Power and Punishment.* Madison, NJ/London: Fairleigh Dickinson UP; 1998. 219 pp. Index. Notes. Lang.: Eng.

England. 1604-1611. Critical studies. ▪Scenes of bodily excess through punishment in Shakespeare's *Measure for Measure, Macbeth* and *The Winter's Tale.* Argues that these efforts to punish ultimately fail to establish and maintain political and social power.

2945 Kénnel, P. "Šekspir: Glavy iz knigi." (Shakespeare: Chapters from the Book.) *Vsemirnaja literatura.* 1998; 10: 136-150. Lang.: Rus.

England. 1589-1613. Critical studies. ▪Discussion of Shakespeare's plays.

2946 Kermode, Lloyd Edward. *Alien Stages: Immigration, Reformation, and Representations of Englishness in Elizabethan Moral and Comic Drama.* Houston, TX: Rice Univ; 1998. 291 pp. Notes. Biblio. [Ph.D. Dissertation, Univ. Microfilms Order No. AAC 9827408.] Lang.: Eng.

England. 1560-1613. Critical studies. ▪The representation of foreigners in sixteenth-century English drama as a reflection of an increased awareness of 'national' identity and ideas of the alien 'other'.

2947 Kerwin, William. "'Physicians are like Kings': Medical Politics and *The Duchess of Malfi.*" *ELR.* 1998 Win; 28(1): 95-117. Notes. Pref. Lang.: Eng.

England. 1613. Critical studies. ▪Medical authority and unstable Jacobean authority as reflected in John Webster's play, *The Duchess of Malfi.*

2948 Kezar, Dennis. "*Julius Caesar* and the Properties of Shakespeare's Globe." *ELR.* 1998 Win; 28(1): 18-46. Notes. Pref. Lang.: Eng.

England. 1599. Critical studies. ▪Violence, antitheatricality, and audience response in regard to Shakespeare's *Julius Caesar.*

2949 Kim, Jin-A. *An Extended Notion of Recognition: A Study of Hamlet, The Three Sisters, and Footfalls.* Ann Arbor, MI: Univ. of Michigan; 1988. 189 pp. Biblio. Notes. [Ph.D. Dissertation, Univ. Microfilms Order No. AAC 8907072.] Lang.: Eng.

England. France. Russia. 1596-1980. Critical studies. ▪An alternative to the traditional interpretation of recongnition in Shakespeare's *Hamlet,* Čechov's *Tri sestry (Three Sisters),* and Beckett's *Footfalls.*

2950 King, Pamela M. "Calender and Text: Christ's Ministry in the York Plays and the Liturgy." *MediumAE.* 1998; 67(1): 30-59. Notes. Tables. Lang.: Eng.

England: York. 1401-1499. Historical studies. ▪Matches the order of the *York Cycle* plays with equivalent readings in the liturgy and in the narrative of the life of Christ.

2951 Kinney, Clare R. "Feigning Female Faining: Spenser, Lodge, Shakespeare, and Rosalind." *MP.* 1998 Feb.; 95(3): 291-315. Notes. Lang.: Eng.

England. 1579-1600. Critical studies. ▪Resemblances and differences of a character named Rosalind in a cycle of eclogues by Edmund Spenser, a prose romance, *Rosalynde,* by Thomas Lodge, and Shakespeare's *As You Like It.*

2952 Kirsch, Arthur. "The Emotional Landscape of *King Lear.*" *SQ.* 1988 Sum; 39(2): 154-170. Notes. Lang.: Eng.

England. 1605-1606. Critical studies. ▪Resonance of physical and emotional feeling in Shakespeare's tragedy.

2953 Kliman, Bernice W. "Rowe 1709 *Macbeth* Illustration Again." *ShN.* 1998 Fall; 48(3): 59-60. Notes. Lang.: Eng.

England. 1709. Critical studies. ▪Defense of the assertion that Hecate is present in Rowe's illustration of the 'Show of Kings' scene in Shakespeare's play. Argues that the illustration may give a hint of how it was staged in post-Restoration productions.

2954 Knight, Stephen. "'Quite Another Man': The Restoration Robin Hood." 167-181 in Potter, Lois, ed. *Playing Robin Hood: The Legend as Performance in Five Centuries.* Newark, DE: Univ of Delaware P; 1998. 254 pp. Index. Notes. Biblio. Pref. Illus.: Dwg. 2. Lang.: Eng.

England. 1660-1730. Critical studies. ▪The transition to the Robin Hood of the Restoration, especially the anonymous *Robin Hood and His Crew of Souldiers* and the anonymous ballad opera, *Robin Hood.*

2955 Kurtz, Martha Anne. *'Present Laughter': Comedy in the Elizabethan History Play.* Toronto, ON: Univ. of Toronto; 1988. 390 pp. Biblio. Notes. [Ph.D. Dissertation, Univ. Microfilms Order No. AAC NN59896.] Lang.: Eng.

England. 1590-1618. Critical studies. ▪Argues that comic scenes and characters in history plays reveal that political attitudes among playwrights and their audiences were more complex and heterogeneous than is usually assumed. Plays considered include Marlowe's *Edward II,* Dekker's *The Shoemaker's Holiday,* and Shakespeare's *Henry VI* plays, *King John, Richard II* and *Henry V.*

2956 Lander, Jesse Macliesh. *Print, Polemic, and Popular Forms: Religion and Community in Early Modern England.* New York, NY: Columbia Univ; 1998. 222 pp. Notes. Biblio. [Ph.D. Dissertation, Univ. Microfilms Order No. AAC 9838965.] Lang.: Eng.

England. 1590-1620. Critical studies. ▪Explores the reciprocal relationship between religious controversy and an emerging print culture. Focuses on the way the writing, printing, and distribution of a number of popular literary forms, including plays, helped shape new visions of community.

2957 Leggatt, Alexander. "Substitution in *Measure for Measure.*" *SQ.* 1988 Fall; 39(3): 342-359. Notes. Lang.: Eng.

England. 1604. Critical studies. ▪Shakespeare's use of the theme of substitution.

2958 Lehmann, Courtney. *What 'Ish' an Auteur? Reconceptualizing Shakespearean Authorship from the Bard to Branagh.* Bloomington, IN: Indiana Univ; 1998. 245 pp. Notes. Biblio. [Ph.D. Dissertation, Univ. Microfilms Order No. AAC 9834607.] Lang.: Eng.

England. 1590-1998. Critical studies. ▪Analysis of authorial practice and the conceptualization of the author in the plays of Shakespeare and their film adaptations by Kenneth Branagh.

2959 Lester, Richard. "Shakespeare's Name." *ERev.* 1998 Aut; 6(2): 4-14. Notes. Lang.: Eng.

England. 1564-1623. Textual studies. ▪Statistical analysis of variant spellings of Shakespeare's name in public documents, folio editions,

DRAMA: —Plays/librettos/scripts

commercial transactions, monuments, and peripheral mentions in epistolary and critical work of the time.

2960 Levin, Richard. "One and One-Half Unrecorded references to *Macbeth* in 1676-1678." *SQ.* 1998 Win; 49(4): 416-420. Notes. Tables. Illus.: Photo. B&W. 1. Lang.: Eng.

England. 1676-1678. Historical studies. ■Points out one definite and one possible allusion to Shakespeare in two short verse pieces.

2961 Levin, Richard A. "The Dark Color of a Cardinal's Discontentment: The Politcal Plot of *Women Beware Women.*" *MRDE.* 1998; 10: 201-217. Notes. Lang.: Eng.

England. 1613-1621. Critical studies. ■Analysis of the oft-misunderstood character of the Cardinal in Middleton's play.

2962 Little, Arthur L., Jr. "Absolute Bodies, Absolute Laws: Staging Punishment in *Measure for Measure.*" 113-129 in Kendall, Gillian Murray, ed. *Shakespearean Power and Punishment.* Madison, NJ/London: Fairleigh Dickinson UP; 1998. 219 pp. Index. Notes. Lang.: Eng.

England. 1604. Critical studies. ■Uses Bakhtin's theory of the body to examines the Duke's attempts to gain psychological power and control of the citizens of Vienna in Shakespeare's *Measure for Measure.*

2963 Litvinova, M. "Portrety Šekspira razgadany." (The Portraits of Shakespeare Resolved.) *Novaja junost'.* 1998; 1-2: 184-194. Lang.: Rus.

England. 1623-1640. Historical studies. ■Portraits of William Shakespeare published during 1623-1640.

2964 Longstaffe, Stephen. "Jack Cade and the Lacies." *SQ.* 1998 Sum; 49(2): 187-190. Notes. Lang.: Eng.

England. 1590-1592. Critical studies. ■Explores reasons why pretender to the throne, Jack Cade, claims descendance from the extinct English noble Lacy family in Shakespeare's *Henry VI, Part Two.*

2965 Macdonald, Ronald R. "The Unheimlich Maneuver: Antithetical Ways of Power in Shakespeare." 197-209 in Kendall, Gillian Murray, ed. *Shakespearean Power and Punishment.* Madison, NJ/London: Fairleigh Dickinson UP; 1998. 219 pp. Index. Notes. Lang.: Eng.

England. 1600-1611. Critical studies. ■Compares the tasks of a political leader seeking control over his subjects with those of a playwright seeking control over his text, with reference to Shakespeare's *The Tempest* and *Hamlet.*

2966 Mack, Michael. *The Analogy of God and Man in Sidney and Shakespeare.* New York, NY: Columbia Univ; 1998. 310 pp. Notes. Biblio. [Ph.D. Dissertation, Univ. Microfilms Order No. AAC 9820200.] Lang.: Eng.

England. 1610-1625. Critical studies. ■Focuses on the poetry of Philip Sidney and Shakespeare's *The Tempest.*

2967 Mackenzie, Clayton G. "Renaissance Emblems of Death and Shakespeare's *King John.*" *EnSt.* 1998 Sep.; 79(5): 425-429. Notes. Lang.: Eng.

England. 1596-1599. Critical studies. ■Influence of painter Hans Holbein's emblematic representations of death (death sowing the seeds of life) on Shakespeare's history play.

2968 Marciano, Lisa Caughlin. *Love's Labour's Lost', 'Twelfth Night', 'The Winter's Tale', and 'The Tempest': The Awareness of Death as a Catalyst to Wisdom in Shakespeare's Comedies.* Dallas, TX: Univ. of Dallas; 1998. 202 pp. Notes. Biblio. [Ph.D. Dissertation, Univ. Microfilms Order No. AAC 9835960.] Lang.: Eng.

England. 1598-1613. Critical studies. ■Regeneration in Shakespeare's *Love's Labour's Lost, Twelfth Night, The Winter's Tale,* and *The Tempest.*

2969 Marsden, Jean I. "Daddy's Girls: Shakespearian Daughters and Eighteenth-Century Ideology." *ShS.* 1998; 51: 17-26. Notes. Lang.: Eng.

England. 1701-1800. Critical studies. ■The role of the obedient daughter as a marker of nationalist ideology in eighteenth-century adaptations of Shakespeare plays such as Garrick's *King Lear,* Richard Cumberland's *Timon of Athens,* and Lillo's version of *Pericles, Marina.*

2970 Marshall, Cynthia. "The Doubled Jaques and Constructions of Negation in *As You Like It.*" *SQ.* 1998 Win; 49(4): 375-392 . Notes. Lang.: Eng.

England. 1599-1600. Critical studies. ■Themes of substitution as affecting the two Jaques characters in Shakespeare's play.

2971 Massai, Sonia. "From *Pericles* to *Marina*: 'While Women are to be Had for Money, Love, or Importunity'." *ShS.* 1998; 51: 67-77. Notes. Lang.: Eng.

England. 1738. Critical studies. ■Examination of Lillo's adaptation of Shakespeare's play for its challenge to cultural assumptions of gender, sexual deviance, property, and propriety.

2972 Massey, Dawn. "*Veritas filia Temporis*: Apocalyptic Polemics in the Drama of the English Reformation." *CompD.* 1998 Spr ; 32(1): 146-175. Notes. Illus.: Dwg. B&W. 2. Lang.: Eng.

England. 1535-1607. Historical studies. ■The Protestant conviction that their religious belief would be vindicated on the Day of Reckoning as represented in such plays as John Puckering's *Horestes,* Dekker's *The Whore of Babylon,* and Thomas Kirchmayer's *Pammachius.*

2973 Maynard, Stephen. "Feasting on Eyre: Community, Consumption, and Communion in *The Shoemaker's Holiday.*" *CompD.* 1998 Fall; 32(3): 327-346. Notes. Lang.: Eng.

England. 1600. Critical studies. ■Compares Thomas Dekker's play with the potlatch ceremony of the Native Americans of the Pacific Northwest Coast.

2974 McAdam, Ian. "Masculinity and Magic in *Friar Bacon and Friar Bungay.*" *RORD.* 1998; 37: 33-61. Notes. Lang.: Eng.

England. 1594. Critical studies. ■The will to power and love in the context of magic and male sexual anxiety in Robert Greene's play.

2975 McCandless, David. "'I'll Pray to Increase Your Bondage': Power and Punishment in *Measure for Measure.*" 89-112 in Kendall, Gillian Murray, ed. *Shakespearean Power and Punishment.* Madison, NJ/London: Fairleigh Dickinson UP; 1998. 219 pp. Index. Notes. Lang.: Eng.

England. 1604. Critical studies. ■The 'psyches' of the characters in Shakespeare's *Measure for Measure* and their desire to punish as a means of embodying power.

2976 McCluskey, Peter Matthew. *'The Stranger's Case': Representations of Flemish Immigrants in English Renaissance Drama, 1515-1635.* Fayetteville, AR: Univ. of Arkansas; 1998. 430 pp. Biblio. Notes. [Ph.D. Dissertation, Univ. Microfilms Order No. AAC 9838325.] Lang.: Eng.

England. 1515-1635. Histories-specific. ■Argues that Elizabethan playwrights developed strategies that addressed the Flemish alien problem indirectly. Plays examined include Thomas Dekker's *The Shoemaker's Holiday* and Henry Glapthorne's *The Hollander.*

2977 McEachern, Claire. "Fathering Herself: A Source Study of Shakespeare's Feminism." *SQ.* 1988 Fall; 39(3): 269-290. Notes. Lang.: Eng.

England. 1590-1616. Critical studies. ■Search for Shakespeare's understanding of women through a search of his sources in their cultural context.

2978 McGrail, Mary Ann. *Shakespeare's Dramas of Tyranny:* Macbeth, Richard III, The Winter's Tale, *and* The Tempest. Cambridge, MA: Harvard Univ; 1988. 330 pp. Biblio. Notes. [Ph.D. Dissertation, Univ. Microfilms Order No. AAC 8908993.] Lang.: Eng.

England. 1595-1612. Critical studies. ■Examines the nature of tyranny and its political implications in Shakespeare's *Macbeth, Richard III, The Winter's Tale,* and *The Tempest.*

2979 McNeill, Fiona. "Gynocentric London Spaces: (Re)Locating Masterless Women in Early Stuart Drama." *RenD.* 1997; 28: 195-244. Notes. Biblio. Illus.: Maps. Dwg. Diagram. B&W. 5. Lang.: Eng.

England. 1604-1608. Critical studies. ■Treatment of the single woman and the challenge to established patriarchy in Middleton and Dekker's *The Roaring Girl* and Nathan Fields' *Amends for Ladies.*

2980 McQuade, Paula. *Casuistry and Tragedy: Cases of Conscience and Dramatizations of Subjectivity in Early Modern England.* Chicago, IL: Univ. of Chicago; 1998. 199 pp. Notes. Biblio. [Ph.D. Dissertation, Univ. Microfilms Order No. AAC 9841554.] Lang.: Eng.

DRAMA: —Plays/librettos/scripts

England. 1600-1671. Critical studies. ■Proposes and traces connections between representations of subjectivity in English tragedy and sixteenth- and seventeenth-century theological discourse which addressed questions of conscience. Works examined include Shakespeare's *Macbeth*, Beaumont and Fletcher's *The Maid's Tragedy*, and Thomas Heywood's *A Woman Killed with Kindness.*

2981 Mikics, David. "Poetry and Politics in *A Midsummer Night's Dream.*" *Raritan.* 1998 Fall; 18(2): 99-119. Lang.: Eng.

England. 1594-1595. Critical studies. ■Analysis of Shakespeare's play with respect to the way in which art can do what politics can not. Recommends that critics shift emphasis back to the poetry in the play rather than obsessing on the politics.

2982 Mills, David. "Anglo-Dutch Theatres: Problems and Possibilities." *MET.* 1996; 18: 85-98. Notes. Biblio. Lang.: Eng.

England. Netherlands. 1495-1525. Historical studies. ■Comparison of the English *Everyman* with its Dutch counterpart *Elckerlijck*, with attention to their printing history, the theatres in which they were performed, and their cultural significance.

2983 Mills, David. "Kissing Cousins: The Four Daughters of God and the Visitation in the N.Town *Mary Play.*" *MET.* 1996; 18: 99-141. Notes. Biblio. Illus.: Photo. B&W. 6. Lang.: Eng.

England. 1120-1501. Historical studies. ■Link between the Four Virtues of Psalm 84:11 and the Visitation, and the relationship between Elizabeth and Mary in the *N-town Mary Play.*

2984 Morrissey, Lee. "Sexuality and Consumer Culture in Eighteenth-Century England: 'Mutual Love from Pole to Pole' in *The London Merchant.*" *Restor.* 1998 Sum; 13(1): 25-40. Notes. Lang.: Eng.

England. 1731. Critical studies. ■Tensions between sexual orientation, moral outlook, and social psychology in Lillo's play.

2985 Munro, Ian Andrew. *Crowded Spaces: Population and Urban Meaning in Early Modern London.* Cambridge, MA: Harvard Univ; 1998. 199 pp. Notes. Biblio. [Ph.D. Dissertation, Univ. Microfilms Order No. AAC 9832449.] Lang.: Eng.

England. 1590-1630. Critical studies. ■The urban crowd in early modern drama, especially in the works of Shakespeare, as the visible manifestation of an increasingly incomprehensible city.

2986 Neill, Michael. "'This Gentle Gentlemen': Social Change and the Language of Status in *Arden of Faversham.*" *MRDE.* 1998 ; 10: 73-97. Notes. Lang.: Eng.

England. 1592. Critical studies. ■Use of language as indicative of social rank and sexuality in the anonymously written play.

2987 Neill, Michael. "'Mulattos', 'Blacks', and 'Indian Moors': *Othello* and Early Modern Constructions of Human Difference." *SQ.* 1998 Win; 49(4): 361-374. Notes. Lang.: Eng.

England. 1604-1998. Critical studies. ■Shakespeare's play and racial ambiguity, colonialism, and late twentieth-century criticism surrounding it.

2988 Neill, Michael. "'Material Flames': The Space of Mercantile Fantasy in John Fletcher's *The Island Princess.*" *RenD.* 1997; 28: 99-131. Notes. Lang.: Eng.

England. 1621. Critical studies. ■Mercantile expansion versus a closed economy as reflected in Fletcher's geographic fantasy play.

2989 Nelson, Alan, H. "George Buc, William Shakespeare, and the Folger *George a Greene.*" *SQ.* 1998 Spr; 49(1): 74-83. Notes. Illus.: Photo. B&W. 3. Lang.: Eng.

England. 1593-1599. Textual studies. ■Analysis of comments written by George Buc, Master of the Revels, on a quarto of the anonymous *George a Greene*, apparently misattributed to Robert Greene. Suggests that Shakespeare provided information on details of some performances.

2990 Noling, Kim H. "Grubbing Up the Stock: Dramatizing Queens in *Henry VIII.*" *SQ.* 1988 Fall; 39(3): 291-306. Notes. Lang.: Eng.

England. 1612-1613. Critical studies. ■Henry's obsession with begetting a male heir and Shakespeare's validation of the king's will through his portrayal of Queens Katherine and Anne in his play.

2991 Norton, James. "Restoration Theories of Confessional Theatre: Rymer, Collier, Congreve." *Restor.* 1998 Sum; 13(1): 41-53 . Notes. Lang.: Eng.

England. 1690-1700. Critical studies. ■Popularity of the confessional style of theatre in England of the 1690s, exemplified by the plays of William Congreve. Also examines two contemporary treatises on the confessional theatre by critics Thomas Rymer and Jeremy Collier.

2992 O'Dair, Sharon Kay. *The Social Self of the Hero in Shakespearean Tragedy.* Berkeley, CA: Univ. of California; 1988. 333 pp. Biblio. Notes. [Ph.D. Dissertation, Univ. Microfilms Order No. AAC 8916819.] Lang.: Eng.

England. 1590-1612. Critical studies. ■The self and its relationship to society in *Hamlet*, *Othello*, *King Lear*, and *Macbeth.*

2993 Pacheco, Anita. "'A mere cupboard of glasses': Female Sexuality and Male Honor in *A Fair Quarrel.*" *ELR.* 1998 Aut; 28 (3): 441-463. Notes. Pref. Lang.: Eng.

England. 1615-1617. Critical studies. ■Tensions and correlations between male and female honor in Thomas Middleton and William Rowley's play.

2994 Perrello, Tony. "Anglo-Saxon Elements of the Gloucester Sub-Plot in *King Lear.*" *ELN.* 1997 Sep.; 35(1): 10-16. Notes. Lang.: Eng.

England. 1605-1606. Critical studies. ■The contentious royal succession after the unexpected death of King Edgar in 975 and Shakespeare's depiction of the Gloucester family in *King Lear.*

2995 Pirnie, Karen Worley. *'As She Saith': Tracing Whoredom in Seventeenth Century London from Bridewell to Southwark.* Tuscaloosa, AL: Univ. of Alabama; 1998. 159 pp. Biblio. Notes. [Ph.D. Dissertation, Univ. Microfilms Order No. AAC 9833668.] Lang.: Eng.

England: London. 1600-1610. Histories-specific. ■Investigates possible causes and meanings of the sudden proliferation of references to prostitution in early seventeenth-century plays, aiming to compare stage situations with the material conditions of prostitution in London outside the theatres.

2996 Pitcher, John. "Samuel Daniel and the Authorities." *MRDE.* 1998; 10: 113-148. Notes. Tables. Illus.: Photo. B&W. 3. Lang.: Eng.

England. 1605. Textual studies. ■Analysis of a copy of the 1605 edition of Daniel's controversial *The Tragedy of Philotas* (in the Folger Library). Focuses on marginal notes by lawyer Anthony Benn with reference to whether or not the play was censored.

2997 Poole, Kristen Elizabeth. "Garbled Martyrdom in Christopher Marlowe's *The Massacre at Paris.*" *CompD.* 1998 Spr; 32(1): 1-25. Notes. Illus.: Dwg. B&W. 1. Lang.: Eng.

England. 1593. Critical studies. ■Analysis of Marlowe's Protestant propaganda play.

2998 Potter, Lois. "The Apotheosis of Maid Marian: Tennyson's *The Foresters* and the Nineteenth-Century Theatre." 182-204 in Potter, Lois, ed. *Playing Robin Hood: The Legend as Performance in Five Centuries.* Newark, DE: Univ of Delaware P; 1998. 254 pp. Index. Notes. Biblio. Pref. Illus.: Photo. Dwg. 4. Lang.: Eng.

England. USA. 1700-1910. Critical studies. ■Tennyson's Robin Hood play *The Foresters* and its relation to earlier and later examples of the genre. The play was produced by Augustin Daly in New York City in 1892 and starred Ada Rehan as Robin Hood.

2999 Powell, Susana. *MediEvil Aspects of Seduction, Corruption and Destruction in Shakespeare's Demonic Women.* New York, NY: City Univ. of New York; 1988. 249 pp. Biblio. Notes. [Ph.D. Dissertation, Univ. Microfilms Order No. AAC 8821115.] Lang.: Eng.

England. 1590-1613. Critical studies. ■Renaissance antifeminism as reflected in female characters who seduce, corrupt and destroy men in Shakespeare's *Othello*, *Julius Caesar*, *Hamlet*, *Titus Andronicus*, *Macbeth*, *King Lear*, *Antony and Cleopatra*, and *Henry IV.*

3000 Price-Hendricks, Margo Jennett. *The Roaring Girls: A Study of Seventeenth-Century Feminism and the Development of Feminist Drama.* Riverside, CA: Univ. of California; 1987. 235 pp. Notes. Biblio. [Ph.D. Dissertation, Univ. Microfilms Order No. 8729413.] Lang.: Eng.

England. 1600-1700. Historical studies. ■The relationship between dramatic representations of women and ideologies based upon gender differences in seventeenth-century city comedy, including the work of Thomas Middleton and Aphra Behn.

3001 Pujante, A. Luis. "*Double Falsehood* and the Verbal Parallels with Shelton's *Don Quixote*." *ShS*. 1998; 51: 95-105. Notes. Lang.: Eng.

England. Spain. 1610-1727. Textual studies. ■Examines parallels between Thomas Shelton's first English translation of Cervantes' novel and Lewis Theobald's play *The Double Falsehood*, which Theobald claimed to be an adaptation of Shakespeare, to determine if the play may be what is left of Shakespeare and Fletcher's lost *Cardenio*.

3002 Raber, Karen L. "'Our wits joined as in matrimony': Margaret Cavendish's Playes and the Drama of Authority." *ELR*. 1998 Aut; 28(3): 464-493. Notes. Pref. Lang.: Eng.

England. 1645-1662. Critical studies. ■Effects of marriage and exile upon playwright Margaret Cavendish. Reconsiders her place among Restoration playwrights.

3003 Ramondetta, Joseph Thomas. *The Scholarly Malcontent on the Elizabethan Jacobean Stage*. Amherst, MA: Univ. of Massachusetts; 1987. 271 pp. Notes. Biblio. [Ph.D. Disseration, Univ. Microfilms Order No. AAC 8710497.] Lang.: Eng.

England. 1590-1642. Critical studies. ■Character of the malcontent scholar in the plays of Elizabethan and Jacobean England, including Shakespeare's *Hamlet*, Chapman's *A Humorous Day's Mirth*, and Massinger's *A Very Woman*.

3004 Ratcliffe, Stephen. "What Doesn't Happen in *Hamlet*: The Ghost's Speech." *MLS*. 1998 Fall; 28(3/4): 125-150. Notes. Lang.: Eng.

England. 1600-1601. Critical studies. ■Analysis of the Ghost's speech in Shakespeare's play (I.5, 59-73) for what it presents to the world of the play, and what it fails to represent to that same world.

3005 Rauen, Margarida Gandara. *Shakespeare's Endings and Effects: A Study of Final Scenes in Quarto and Folio Versions of* The Merry Wives of Windsor, Henry V, *and* Hamlet. East Lansing, MI: Michigan State Univ; 1988. 177 pp. Biblio. Notes. [Ph.D. Dissertation, Univ. Microfilms Order No. AAC 8814898.] Lang.: Eng.

England. 1597-1601. Textual studies. ■Examines differences in the final scenes of Shakespeare's *The Merry Wives of Windsor*, *Henry V* and *Hamlet*, which exist in quarto and folio versions.

3006 Ray, Sid. "'Rape, I fear, was root thy annoy': The Politics of Consent in *Titus Andronicus*." *SQ*. 1998 Spr; 49(1): 22-39. Notes. Lang.: Eng.

England. 1590-1594. Critical studies. ■The right of a woman to consent to marriage as reflective of the ancient right of the social body to consent to the ruling power of a monarch in Shakespeare's play.

3007 Reed, Melissa Ann. *Recurring Images of Symbolic Action in Shakespeare's* Tragedy of Romeo and Juliet*: Initiating the Bard*. Minneapolis, MN: Univ. of Minnesota; 1988. 439 pp. Notes. Biblio. [Ph.D. Dissertation, Univ. Microfilms Order No. 8823562.] Lang.: Eng.

England. 1595-1596. Critical studies. ■The concept of symbolic action in Shakespeare's *Romeo and Juliet*.

3008 Reid, Robert L. "Epiphanal Encounters in Shakespearean Dramaturgy." *CompD*. 1998-99 Win; 32(4): 518-540. Notes. Lang.: Eng.

England. 1590-1613. Critical studies. ■The role of epiphany in the plays of Shakespeare.

3009 Rice, Raymond Joseph. *Politics of Gender in John Marston's Plays*. Storrs, CT: Univ. of Connecticut; 1998. 385 pp. Notes. Biblio. [Ph.D. Dissertation, Univ. Microfilms Order No. AAC 9906717.] Lang.: Eng.

England. 1599-1634. Critical studies. ■The gendered subject in *Antonio and Mellida, Antonio's Revenge, What You Will, The Malcontent, The Fawn, Eastward Ho* and *The Insatiate Countess*.

3010 Ridden, Geoffrey M. "*King Lear* Act III Folk Tale and Tragedy." *RevES*. 1998 Aug.; 49(195): 329-330. Notes. Lang.: Eng.

England. 1605-1606. Critical studies. ■Influence of folklore on Act III of Shakespeare's tragedy.

3011 Ryan, Patrick. "Marlowe's *Edward II* and the Medieval Passion Play." *CompD*. 1998-99 Win; 32(4): 465-495. Notes. Lang.: Eng.

England. 1590-1592. Critical studies. ■Comparison of Marlowe's play to medieval passion plays.

3012 Sabbadini, Silvano. *Il tempo, le rovine e le maschere. Due saggi sui problem plays*. (Time, Ruins, and Masks: Two Essays on the Problem Plays.) Rome: Bulzoni; 1998. 96 pp. (Piccola Biblioteca Shakespeariana 16.) Lang.: Ita.

England. 1601-1604. Critical studies. ■Analysis of *Troilus and Cressida* and *Measure for Measure* by William Shakespeare.

3013 Schiel, Katherine West. "Early Georgian Politics and Shakespeare: The Black Act and Charles Johnson's *Love in a Forest*." *ShS*. 1998; 51: 45-56. Notes. Lang.: Eng.

England. 1723. Historical studies. ■Political context of Johnson's adaptation of Shakespeare's *As You Like It* regarding a law to curtail the activities of a group of rebels who prowled the King's forests in blackface.

3014 Schoch, Richard W. "*Tamburlaine* and the Control of Performative Playing." *ET*. 1998; 17(1): 3-14. Notes. Biblio. Lang.: Eng.

England. 1590-1998. Critical studies. ■Unity of language and action in Marlowe's *Tamburlaine the Great*.

3015 Schwarz, Kathryn. "Fearful Simile: Stealing the Breech in Shakespeare's Chronicle Plays." *SQ*. 1998 Sum; 49(2): 140-167. Notes. Lang.: Eng.

England. 1590-1593. Critical studies. ■The threat to sovereign male authority and the subversion of historical enterprise as embodied in the female characters in Shakespeare's *Henry VI* and *Richard III*.

3016 Shapiro, Michael. "Cross-Dressing in Elizabethan Robin Hood Plays." 77-90 in Potter, Lois, ed. *Playing Robin Hood: The Legend as Performance in Five Centuries*. Newark, DE: Univ of Delaware P; 1998. 254 pp. Index. Notes. Biblio. Pref. Lang.: Eng.

England. 1589-1598. Critical studies. ■Cross-dressing as a Robin Hood disguise in the anonymous *Look About You* and several other plays.

3017 Sheen, J.E. *The Institution of Early Modern Theatre: Gender and the Circulation of Meaning in the Shakespearean Text*. London: Unpublished PhD, Birkbeck College, Univ. of London; 1996. Notes. Biblio. [Abstract in *Aslib Index to Theses* 47-5475.] Lang.: Eng.

England. 1600-1616. Critical studies. ■Argues that Shakespeare can be most fully understood when addressed not in literary terms, but on the basis of the institutional self-interest with which his work seeks to create an audience not for individual plays but for the 'theatre'.

3018 Singman, Jeffrey L. "Munday's Unruly Earl." 63-76 in Potter, Lois, ed. *Playing Robin Hood: The Legend as Performance in Five Centuries*. Newark, DE: Univ of Delaware P; 1998. 254 pp. Index. Notes. Biblio. Pref. Lang.: Eng.

England. 1598-1599. Critical studies. ■Robin Hood in Anthony Munday's *Downfall of Robert Earl of Huntingdon*.

3019 Skura, Meredith. "The Reproduction of Mothering in *Mariam, Queen of Jewry*: A Defense of 'Biographical' Criticism." *Tulsa SWL*. 1997 Spr; 16(1): 27-56. Notes. Lang.: Eng.

England. 1602-1612. Critical studies. ■Feminist analysis of Elizabeth Cary's *The Tragedy of Mariam*, with emphasis on what can be learned from it regarding the life of a woman in early modern patriarchy.

3020 Slights, Camille Wells. "Notaries, Sponges, and Looking-Glasses: Conscience in Early Modern England." *ELR*. 1998 Spr; 28 (2): 231-246. Notes. Pref. Lang.: Eng.

England. 1590-1620. Critical studies. ■Concepts of conscience in early modern literature: references to the poems and sermons of John Donne and plays of Shakespeare, such as *Hamlet* and *Richard III*.

3021 Slights, Jessica; Holmes, Michael Morgan. "Isabella's Order: Religious Acts and Personal Desires." *StPh*. 1998 Sum; 95 (3): 263-292. Notes. Lang.: Eng.

England. 1604. Critical studies. ■Isabella's desire to take the nun's vow as a subversion of early modern gender norms and religious prejudice in Shakespeare's *Measure for Measure*.

DRAMA: —Plays/librettos/scripts

3022 Smith, A.H. "Thomas Creede, *Henry V* Q1, and *The Famous Victories of Henrie the Fifth.*" *RevES.* 1998 Feb.; 49(193): 60-64. Notes. Lang.: Eng.
England. 1599-1600. Textual studies. ▪Comparison of the anonymous *Henrie the Fifth* with the first quarto edition of Shakespeare's play printed by Creede. Argues that the earlier play was mixed in by the printing, resulting in the corrupt quarto.

3023 Smith, Ian. "Barbarian Errors: Performing Race in Early Modern England." *SQ.* 1998 Sum; 49(2): 168-186. Notes. Lang.: Eng.
England. 1604. Critical studies. ▪Racial displacement and imperial desires in the language used by Iago and Othello in Shakespeare's tragedy.

3024 Smith, Molly Easo. *The Darker World Within: Evil in the Tragedies of Shakespeare and His Successors.* Auburn, AL: Auburn Univ; 1988. 296 pp. Biblio. Notes. [Ph.D. Dissertation, Univ. Microfilms Order No. AAC 8925661.] Lang.: Eng.
England. 1620-1642. Critical studies. ▪The preoccupation with madness, violence, revenge, adultery, and incest in early Stuart drama as related to the contemporary socio-political environment.

3025 Smith, Peter J. "M.O.A.I. 'What should that alphabetical position portend?' An Answer to the Metamorphic Malvolio." *RenQ.* 1998 Win; 51(4): 1199-1224. Notes. Biblio. Lang.: Eng.
England. 1600-1601. Textual studies. ▪Attempts to answer Malvolio's riddle, which occurs in Shakespeare's *Twelfth Night*, II.5, and surveys alternative solutions proposed by critics, editors, and actors.

3026 Sofer, Andrew. "The Skull on the Renaissance Stage: Imagination and the Erotic Life of Props." *ELR.* 1998 Win; 28(1): 47-74. Notes. Pref. Illus.: Dwg. B&W. 1. Lang.: Eng.
England. 1606. Critical studies. ▪Symbolism of the skull in Shakespeare's *Hamlet*, Cyril Tourneur's *The Revenger's Tragedy*, and Thomas Dekker's *The Honest Whore, Part I.*

3027 Sokol, B.J. "Prejudice and Law in *The Merchant of Venice.*" *ShS.* 1998; 51: 159-173. Notes. Lang.: Eng.
England. 1596. Critical studies. ▪Analysis of Shakespeare's play using Elizabethan standards of decency and fairness and the prejudicial laws of the realm.

3028 Sternglantz, Ruth Esther. *Degraded Morality: A Study of the Fifteenth-Century Play 'Mankind'.* New York, NY: New York Univ; 1998. 292 pp. Biblio. Notes. [Ph.D. Dissertation, Univ. Microfilms Order No. AAC 9819802.] Lang.: Eng.
England. 1464-1470. Critical studies. ▪Argues that contemporary readings of the play's morality are misleading and that a new critical interpretation is called for.

3029 Sullivan, Garrett A., Jr. "Space, Measurement, and Stalking Tamburlaine." *RenD.* 1997; 28: 3-27. Notes. Biblio. Lang.: Eng.
England. 1587-1588. Critical studies. ▪Measurement of land as a way of understanding sociospatial transformations in Elizabethan England in Marlowe's play.

3030 Summers, Ellen Louise. *The Ends of 'All's Well That Ends Well'.* Chapel Hill, NC: Univ. of North Carolina; 1988. 122 pp. Notes. Biblio. [Ph.D. Dissertation, Univ. Microfilms Order No. AAC 8823480.] Lang.: Eng.
England. 1602-1603. Critical studies. ▪The 'problem' of the happy ending of Shakespeare's comedy, with emphasis on how closure is constructed.

3031 Szilagyi, Stephen. "The Sexual Politics of Behn's *The Rover.*" *StPh.* 1998 Fall; 95(4): 435-455. Notes. Lang.: Eng.
England. 1677. Critical studies. ▪Changing sexual roles and the absent patriarchy in Aphra Behn's play.

3032 Taddei, Mirian Hunter. *Youth and the Sensitive Soul from Jack Jugeler* to *I Henry IV.* Tempe, AZ: Arizona State Univ; 1988. 306 pp. Biblio. Notes. [Ph.D. Dissertation, Univ. Microfilms Order No. AAC 8815641.] Lang.: Eng.
England. 1596-1597. Critical studies. ▪Examines the psychological nature of the 'troubler' personality in the characterizations of Falstaff and Hal in Shakespeare's *Henry IV, Part One.*

3033 Tanner, Martha Alison. *The Genealogy of the Chester Expositor.* New Orleans, LA: Tulane Univ; 1998. 223 pp. Biblio. Notes. [Ph.D. Dissertation, Univ. Microfilms Order No. AAC 9906404.] Lang.: Eng.
England. 1400-1500. Critical studies. ▪Argues that the Expositor character in the *Chester Cycle* medieval mystery plays served as chorus, preacher, and narrator and thus sheds light on the ways in which medieval audiences interpreted dramatic performances.

3034 Thomas, Sidney. "On the Dating of Shakespeare's Early Plays." *SQ.* 1988 Sum; 39(2): 187-194. Notes. Lang.: Eng.
England. 1586-1593. Textual studies. ▪Defends E.K. Chambers' formulations for the dating of Shakespeare's early plays.

3035 Tipton, Alzada J. "'The meanest man ... shall be permitted freely to accuse': The Commoners in *Woodstock.*" *CompD.* 1998 Spr; 32(1): 117-145. Notes. Lang.: Eng.
England. 1592. Critical studies. ▪The dramatic importance of the Commoners in the anonymous play *Woodstock.*

3036 Turner, Henry S. "*King Lear* Without: The Heath." *RenD.* 1998; 21: 161-193. Notes. Biblio. Lang.: Eng.
England. 1605-1606. Critical studies. ▪The vagueness of locale, particularly the 'heath' scene in Shakespeare's tragedy.

3037 Tyler, Mary Kathleen. *Touchstones.* Dominguez Hills, CA: California State Univ; 1998. 65 pp. Notes. Biblio. [M.A. Thesis, Univ. Microfilms Order No. AAC 1387541.] Lang.: Eng.
England. 1590-1613. Critical studies. ▪Examines selected characters in Shakespeare's plays as they interact with the heroes' tragic conflicts, including Virgilia in *Coriolanus*, Banquo in *Macbeth*, Mercutio in *Romeo and Juliet*, and Horatio in *Hamlet.*

3038 Vaughan, Alden T. "Shakespeare's Indian: The Americanization of Caliban." *SQ.* 1988 Sum; 39(2): 137-153. Notes. Lang.: Eng.
England. 1611. Critical studies. ▪Examines Shakespeare's *The Tempest* as an allegory of Colonial America, specifically as it applies to the character of Caliban.

3039 Volodarskaja, L. "Prošloe i buduščee: fantastika i istorija." (Past and Future: Fantasy and History.) *Octiabr.* 1998; 7: 182-184. Lang.: Rus.
England. 1589-1616. Critical studies. ▪Fantasy and history in the plays of Shakespeare.

3040 Walsh, Marcus. "Eighteenth-Century Editing, 'Appropriation', and Interpretation." *ShS.* 1998; 51: 125-139. Notes. Lang.: Eng.
England. 1701-1800. Critical studies. ▪Appraisal of eighteenth-century editing and interpretation of Shakespeare in the broader literary sense, as opposed to singularly theatrical.

3041 Watson, Robert N. "The State of Life and the Power of Death: *Measure for Measure.*" 130-158 in Kendall, Gillian Murray, ed. *Shakespearean Power and Punishment.* Madison, NJ/London: Fairleigh Dickinson UP; 1998. 219 pp. Index. Notes. Lang.: Eng.
England. 1604. Critical studies. ▪Opposition to the power of the state to control procreation and death in Shakespeare's *Measure for Measure.*

3042 Weimann, Robert. "Bifold Authority in Shakespeare's Theatre." *SQ.* 1988 Win; 39(4): 401-417. Notes. Lang.: Eng.
England. 1501-1600. Critical studies. ▪Issues of authority in sixteenth-century England and their reflection in the theatre of Shakespeare.

3043 Werstine, Paul. "The Textual Mystery of Hamlet." *SQ.* 1988 Spr; 39(1): 1-26. Notes. Lang.: Eng.
England. 1600-1623. Textual studies. ▪Debate as to whether Shakespeare revised his plays. Compares the second quarto version of *Hamlet* with the first folio variant of the play.

3044 Wilkes, G.A. "The Chorus Sacerdotum in Fulke Greville's *Mustapha.*" *RevES.* 1998 Aug.; 49(195): 326-328. Notes. Lang.: Eng.
England. 1609-1633. Textual studies. ▪Note on the placement of the chorus which begins 'Oh wearisome Condition of Humanity' in Greville's play.

DRAMA: —Plays/librettos/scripts

3045 Wolf, Richard B. "Goldsmith's Honeywood and the Limits of Character Incoherence." *Restor.* 1998 Win; 13(2): 1-16. Notes. Lang.: Eng.
England. 1767-1768. Critical studies. ■Analysis of the problems of performing the Honeywood character in Goldsmith's play *The Good Natur'd Man.*

3046 Yanosky, Sabrina Klein. *A Theatrical-Critical Approach to* Hamlet*'s Women for Actors and Critics.* Berkeley, CA: Univ. of California; 1987. 274 pp. Notes. Biblio. [Ph.D. Dissertation, Univ. Microfilms Order No. 8726413.] Lang.: Eng.
England. 1600-1601. Critical studies. ■Attempt to bring the separate vocabularies of scholar and performer together in the search for character in Shakespeare's texts, focusing on the two women in *Hamlet.*

3047 Zupančič, Mirko. *Shakespearov dramski imperij.* (Shakespeare's Dramatic Empire.) Ljubljana: Društvo 2000; 1998. 163 pp. Pref. Lang.: Slo.
England. 1590-1613. Critical studies. ■Argues that Shakespeare's plays reflect the eternal nature of all human beings, not just the Elizabethans.

3048 Plastow, Jane; Tsehaye, Solomon. "Making Theatre for a Change: Two Plays of the Eritrean Liberation Struggle." 36-54 in Boon, Richard, ed.; Plastow, Jane, ed. *Theatre Matters: Performance and Culture on the World Stage.* Cambridge: Cambridge UP; 1998. 203 pp. (Cambridge Studies in Modern Theatre.) Notes. Index. Pref. Lang.: Eng.
Eritrea. 1980-1984. Historical studies. ■The use of theatre as a 'cultural weapon' in the Ethiopian-Eritrean war, with emphasis on *Eti Kal'a Quinat (The Other War)* by Alemseged Tesfai and *Kemsie Ntezechrewn Nehru (If It Had Been Like This)* by Afewerki Abraha.

3049 "The Irresistible Rise of Bertolt Brecht." *Econ.* 1998 Oct 17; 349(8090): 99-100. Lang.: Eng.
Europe. 1998. Critical studies. ■Report on the current interest in staging the plays of Brecht in celebration of his centenary year.

3050 Borgstrom, Henrik Carl. *Performing Madness: The Representation of Insanity in Nineteenth and Twentieth Century Theatre, from Jean-Martin Charcot to Marguerite Duras.* Madison, WI: Univ. of Wisconsin; 1998. 269 pp. Biblio. Notes. [Ph.D. Dissertation, Univ. Microfilms Order No. AAC 9829129.] Lang.: Eng.
Europe. 1880-1970. Critical studies. ■The cultural constructs and aesthetics of madness. Analyzes the iconography of madness in nineteenth-century acting guides and their performance codes, and the staging of madness in the avant-garde theatre including the experimental works of Antonin Artaud, Samuel Beckett, Jean Genet, and Marguerite Duras.

3051 Cartwright, John. "The 'Morality Play': Dead End or Main Street?" *MET.* 1996; 18: 3-14. Notes. Lang.: Eng.
Europe. Africa. 1400-1998. Critical studies. ■Argues that post-medieval morality plays are plays of ideas and a form of drama that responds to perpetually changing social conditions. Argument is supported by extending the traditional geographic, and chronologic, boundaries of the genre.

3052 Chirico, Miriam Madeleine. *Speaking with the Dead: O'Neill, Eliot, Sartre and Mythic Revisionary Drama.* Atlanta, GA: Emory Univ; 1998. 257 pp. Biblio. Notes. [Ph.D. Dissertation, Univ. Microfilms Order No. AAC 9830138.] Lang.: Eng.
Europe. USA. 1914-1943. Critical studies. ■Revisions of the Orestes myth in O'Neill's *Mourning Becomes Electra*, T.S. Eliot's *The Family Reunion* and Sartre's *Les Mouches.*

3053 Cosgrove, James Daniel. *The Rebel in Modern Drama.* New York, NY: St. John's Univ; 1988. 279 pp. Biblio. Notes. [Ph.D. Dissertation, Univ. Microfilms Order No. AAC 8900578.] Lang.: Eng.
Europe. 1950-1988. Critical studies. ■The character of the rebel in Eugène Ionesco's *Rhinoceros*, Jean Anouilh's *Antigone*, T.S. Eliot's *Murder in the Cathedral, Saint Joan* by George Bernard Shaw, *Luther* by John Osborne, *Leben des Galilei (The Life of Galileo)* by Bertolt Brecht, and *En Folkefiende (An Enemy of the People)* by Henrik Ibsen.

3054 Goldfarb, Alvin. "Select Bibliography of Holocaust Plays, 1933-1997." 298-349 in Schumacher, Claude, ed. *Staging the Holocaust: The Shoah in Drama and Performance.* Cambridge: Cambridge UP; 1998. 355 pp. (Cambridge Studies in Modern Theatre.) Index. Notes. Biblio. Lang.: Eng.
Europe. North America. 1933-1997. Bibliographical studies. ■Bibliography of Holocaust plays produced worldwide since 1933.

3055 Malkin, Jeanette Rosenzweig. *Verbal Violence in Modern Drama: A Study of Language as Aggression.* New York, NY: New York Univ; 1988. 427 pp. Biblio. Notes. [Ph.D. Dissertation, Univ. Microfilms Order No. AAC 8812642.] Lang.: Eng.
Europe. USA. 1960-1985. Critical studies. ■Aggressive language in Peter Handke's *Kaspar*, Edward Albee's *Who's Afraid of Virginia Woolf?*, and plays of Eugène Ionesco, Harold Pinter, Václav Havel, Franz Xaver Kroetz, Edward Bond, and David Mamet.

3056 McManus, Donald Cameron. *Sans Blaague! Clown as Protagonist in Twentieth-Century Theatre.* Ann Arbor, MI: Univ. of Michigan; 1998. 312 pp. Biblio. Notes. [Ph.D. Dissertation, Univ. Microfilms Order No. 9825302.] Lang.: Eng.
Europe. 1915-1995. Critical studies. ■The use of the clown as a serious character in the work of V.E. Mejerchol'd, Bertolt Brecht, Samuel Beckett, Giorgio Strehler and Dario Fo.

3057 Meyerfeld, Max. "Avant-propos à la traduction d'Une tragédie florentine (1907)." (Foreword to the Translation of *A Florentine Tragedy*, 1907.) *ASO.* 1998 Sep/Oct.; 186: 36-39. Illus.: Dwg. B&W. 3. Lang.: Fre.
Europe. 1895-1907. Histories-sources. ■French translation of Meyerfeld's preface to his German translation of Oscar Wilde's play, which was to become the libretto for the opera *Eine florentinische Tragödie* by Alexander Zemlinsky.

3058 Mize, Roberta Rae. *The Open Wound. A Study of the Devouring Woman in Four Tragedies:* Phaedra *by Jean Racine,* Penthesilea *by Heinrich von Kleist,* Hedda Gabler *by Henrik Ibsen, and* Not I *by Samuel Beckett.* Santa Barbara, CA: Univ. of California; 1998. 185 pp. Notes. Biblio. [Ph.D. Dissertation, Univ. Microfilms Order No. AAC 9840790.] Lang.: Eng.
Europe. 1760-1992. Critical studies. ■How the playwrights use and develop the archetype of the devouring woman.

3059 Nelson, T.G.A. "Doing Things with Words: Another Look at Marriage Rites and Spousals in Renaissance Drama and Fiction." *StPh.* 1998 Fall; 95(4): 351-373. Notes. Lang.: Eng.
Europe. 1563-1753. Critical studies. ■The influence of the law and language of marriage on the work of Shakespeare, Cervantes, Webster, and Goldsmith.

3060 Pottie, Lisa M., ed.; Cameron, Rebecca, ed.; Costello, Charles, ed. "Modern Drama Studies: An Annual Bibliography." *MD.* 1998 Sum; 41(2): 181-302. Lang.: Eng.
Europe. North America. 1899-1998. Bibliographical studies. ■Annual bibliography recording scholarship, criticism, and commentary on dramatic literature and, to a lesser extent, theatre history. Includes articles and books pertaining to playwrights and influential theatre figures other than performers who lived past the year 1899.

3061 Ramanathan, Geetha. *Gender and Madness in Five Modern Plays.* Urbana-Champaign, IL: Univ. of Illinois; 1988. 189 pp. Biblio. Notes. [Ph.D. Dissertation, Univ. Microfilms Order No. AAC 8823230.] Lang.: Eng.
Europe. 1880-1969. Critical studies. ■Considers Georg Büchner's *Woyzeck*, August Strindberg's *Fadren (The Father)*, Luigi Pirandello's *Enrico IV (Henry IV)*, Bertolt Brecht's *Der Gute Mensch von Sezuan (The Good Person of Szechwan)* and Peter Barnes' *The Ruling Class.*

3062 Rogowski, Christian Uwe. *Implied Dramaturgy: Robert Musil and the Crisis of Modern Drama.* Cambridge, MA: Harvard Univ; 1988. 399 pp. Notes. Biblio. [Ph.D. Dissertation, Univ. Microfilms Order No. AAC 8901634.] Lang.: Eng.
Europe. 1880-1930. Critical studies. ■The 'crisis of modern drama' and assumptions about dramatic text/reader and performance spectator interactions in the work of Čechov, Hauptmann, Ibsen, Pirandello and, most specifically, Robert Musil's two full-length plays, *Die Schwärmer*

DRAMA: —Plays/librettos/scripts

(The Enthusiast) and *Vinzenz und die Freundin bedeutender Manner (Vincent and the Lady Friend of Important Men).*

3063 Schumacher, Ernst. "Medea–Frau im Elend." (Medea–Woman in Misery.) *MuK.* 1998; 40(1): 7-38. Notes. Lang.: Ger.

Europe. 450 B.C.-1998 A.D. Historical studies. ■Fascination of European playwrights with the mythical character of Medea throughout ages, such as Seneca, Pierre Corneille, Friedrich Maximilian Klinger, Franz Grillparzer, Hans Henny Jahnn, Matthias Braun and Heiner Müller.

3064 Skloot, Robert. "Holocaust Theatre and the Problem of Justice." 10-26 in Schumacher, Claude, ed. *Staging the Holocaust: The Shoah in Drama and Performance.* Cambridge: Cambridge UP; 1998. 355 pp. (Cambridge Studies in Modern Theatre.) Index. Notes. Biblio. Lang.: Eng.

Europe. 1940-1997. Historical studies. ■Argues that Holocaust drama should leave the 'irreparable and opaque' as its legacy.

3065 Straznicky, Marta. "Recent Studies in Closet Drama." *ELR.* 1998 Win; 28(1): 142-160. Notes. Pref. Lang.: Eng.

Europe. North America. 1998. Historical studies. ■Topical review of recent studies with a bibliography pertaining to research on the subject of closet drama.

3066 Szántó, Judit, transl. "Shylock ringlispílje: Korok, országok, álláspontok." (Shylock's Carousel: Ages, Countries, Interpretations.) *Sz.* 1998; 31(7): 2-13. Illus.: Photo. Design. B&W. 14. Lang.: Hun.

Europe. North America. 1788-1996. Critical studies. ■Summary of two centuries' thought on Shakespeare's *The Merchant of Venice.*

3067 Wille, Franz. "'Nicht viel übriggeblieben vom streunenden Zeitgenossen'." ('Not Much Left of a Wandering Contemporary'.) *THeute.* 1998; 7: 4-11. Illus.: Photo. B&W. 5. Lang.: Ger.

Europe. 1971-1998. Critical studies. ■Analyzes Botho Strauss' changes of themes and writing concerning his plays *Jeffers Akt I & II (Jeffer's Act I and II)* directed by Edith Clever and produced by Schaubühne at Hebbel-Theater and *Die ähnlichen (Lookalikes)* directed by Peter Stein at Theater in der Josefstadt.

3068 Zern, Leif. "Brecht–100 eller död?" (Brecht–100 Or Dead?)*Dramat.* 1998: vo 6(2): 38-39. Lang.: Swe.

Europe. 1898-1998. Critical studies. ■Essay on Bertolt Brecht's influence on his time and his relevance for theatre in the nineties.

3069 Jansson, Tomas. "The Hunt for Play/La chasse aux pièces." *FT.* 1998; 52: 26-27. Illus.: Photo. B&W. 1. Lang.: Eng, Fre.

Finland. 1998. Critical studies. ■Laments the lack of strong Swedish-language drama in Finland. Points to the strength of its writers in the genre of revue, such as Bengt Ahlfors and Johan Bargum, and sees hope in the promise of playwrights Tove Granqvist and Joakim Groth.

3070 Nyytäjä, Outi. "Kuka tappoi naurun." (Who Killed the Laughter.) *Teat.* 1998; 53(8): 9-12. Illus.: Photo. Color. B&W. 4. Lang.: Fin.

Finland. 1950-1998. Historcal studies. ■Analysis of the development of Finnish theatre and film comedies and farces.

3071 Anthony, Elizabeth Mazza. *Storytelling in the Theatre of Marguerite Duras and Marie Redonnet: A Poetics of Relating.* Chapel Hill, NC: Univ. of North Carolina; 1998. 213 pp. Notes. Biblio. [Ph.D. Dissertation, Univ. Microfilms Order No. AAC 9840875.] Lang.: Eng.

France. 1977-1992. Critical studies. ■Analysis of *L'Éden cinéma* and *Savannah Bay* by Marguerite Duras and *Mobie-Diq (Moby Dick)* and *Seaside* by Marie Redonnet. Argues that the stories and memories of characters reveal a preoccupation with ancestors and images of the past.

3072 Beach, Cecilia. "*À Table*: The Power of Food in French Women's Theatre." *ThR.* 1998 Fall; 23(3): 233-241. Notes. Lang.: Eng.

France. 1970-1989. Critical studies. ■Feminist analysis of the way alienation is dramatized in plays that deal with the social and psychological significance of food, with attention to the plays of Chantal Chawaf and Denise Chalem.

3073 Boiron, Chantal. "Dem Dichter ein Theater: Olivier Py." (A Theatre for the Author: Olivier Py.) *TZ.* 1998; 5/Theater in Frankreich: 41-43. Illus.: Photo. B&W. 5. Lang.: Ger.

France: Orléans. 1966-1998. Biographical studies. ■Portrait of the actor, playwright and director Olivier Py, his philosophy and working methods since he took over the Centre Dramatique d'Orléans this year.

3074 Boudreault, Eric. *Espace et Intéraction dans* Phèdre *de Racine: pour une relecture de l'oeuvre à la lumière des travaux d'Erving Goffman.* (Space and Interaction in Racine's *Phèdre*: Toward a Rereading in the Light of Work of Erving Goffman.) Quebec, PQ: Université Laval; 1998. 161 pp. Notes. Biblio. [M.A. Thesis, Univ. Microfilms Order No. AAC MQ26169.] Lang.: Fre.

France. 1667. Critical studies. ■Sociological analysis of Racine's *Phèdre* from the point of view of the interactions of characters.

3075 Bradby, David; Noonan, Mary. "Introduction." *ThR.* 1998 Fall; 23(3): 197-199. Notes. Lang.: Eng.

France. 1998. Critical studies. ■Introductory essay to an issue on the relationship between feminist theory and practice on the French stage.

3076 Brault, Pascale-Anne. "Bernard-Marie Koltès: Théâtre et Vérité." (Bernard-Marie Koltès: Theatre and Truth.) *RomN.* 1997 Fall; 38(1): 103-110. Notes. Biblio. Lang.: Fre.

France. 1835-1837. Critical studies. ■Koltès' ideas of tragedy as embodied in his *Roberto Zucco.*

3077 Bryden, Mary. "*Pour Finir Encore*: A Manuscript Study." *JBeckS.* 1998 Sum; 8(1): 1-14. Notes. Lang.: Eng.

France. Ireland. 1957-1976. Critical studies. ■Dryden and Johnson's theories of translation and their influence on Beckett's self-translated work such as *Endgame (Fin de partie)*, *Not I (Pas moi)*, and his prose piece *For to End Yet Again.*

3078 Christopher, Tracy Elizabeth. *Molière's dévots de la Médecine: Doctors and Faux Dévots Viewed Through the Lens of Pierre Bourdieu's Oracle Effect.* New York, NY: New York Univ.; 1998. 309 pp. Notes. Biblio. [Ph.D. Dissertation, Univ. Microfilms Order No. AAC 9831697.] Lang.: Eng.

France. 1660-1722. Critical studies. ■Analysis of Molière's medical plays as attempts to recast the role of the doctor as the 'oracular deceiver.' Plays discussed are *L'Amour médecin (Doctor Love)*, *Le Médecin malgré lui (The Doctor in Spite of Himself)*, *Monsieur de Pourceaugnac*, and *Le Malade imaginaire (The Imaginary Invalid).*

3079 Consoli, Virginia. *Ionesco: tra drammaturgia e critica.* (Ionesco: Between Dramaturgy and Criticism.) Empoli (Fi): Ibiskos; 1998. 102 pp. Lang.: Ita.

France. 1912-1994. Critical studies. ■The theatre of Eugène Ionesco.

3080 Craik, Kevin Jay. *A Practical Study and Production of Eugène Ionesco's* Exit the King. Reno, NV: Univ. of Nevada; 1987. 87 pp. Biblio. Notes. [M.A. Thesis, Univ. Microfilms Order No. AAC 1330748.] Lang.: Eng.

France. 1962. Critical studies. ■Examines the philosophy and beliefs of playwright Eugène Ionesco as reflected in his play *Le Roi se meurt (Exit the King).*

3081 Creed, Victoria Schanck. *Dramatic Efficiency: Statistical Study of Racine's Theater.* Philadelphia, PA: Univ. of Pennsylvania; 1988. 332 pp. Biblio. Notes. [Ph.D. Dissertation, Univ. Microfilms Order No. AAC 8908320.] Lang.: Eng.

France. 1664-1691. Critical studies. ■Argues that the 'pieds' or syllables of Alexandrine verse in the plays of Jean Racine describe the dramatic efficiency of characters and demonstrate how they use their speech and presence dramatically.

3082 Déprats, Jean-Michel. "La traduction au carrefour des durées." (Translation at the Crossroads of Time.) *AnT.* Spr 1998; 24: 52-68. Notes. Biblio. Lang.: Fre.

France. 1974-1998. Critical studies. ■Translation of classic playtexts as a rapport between past and present, with particular attention to French translations of Shakespeare.

3083 Dobson, Julia. "The Scene of Writing: The Representation of Poetic Identity in Cixous's Recent Theatre." *ThR.* 1998 Fall ; 23(3): 255-260. Notes. Lang.: Eng.

France. 1988-1994. Critical studies. ■Analysis of *L'Histoire (qu'on ne connaîtra Jamais)*, *La Ville parjure*, and *Voile noir voile blanche* by Hélène Cixous. Focus on the theme of the poet's struggle to communicate a vision and the representation of poetic identity.

DRAMA: —Plays/librettos/scripts

3084 Dowd, Garin V. "Nomadology: Reading the Beckettian Baroque." *JBeckS.* 1998 Sum; 8(1): 15-49. Notes. Lang.: Eng.

France. Ireland. 1935-1993. Critical studies. ■Beckett's interest in conceptual impasses in the philosophy of the Age of Reason, and the effect it had on his work.

3085 Duffy, Brian. "The Prisoners in the Cave and Worm in the Pit: Plato and Beckett on Authority and Truth." *JBeckS.* 1998 Sum; 8(1): 51-71. Notes. Lang.: Eng.

France. Ireland. 1953-1986. Critical studies. ■The abuse of power in Beckett's novel *L'Innommable (The Unnameable)* with reference to Plato's allegory of the cave. Also touches on *What Where* and *Ohio Impromptu.*

3086 Engelhardt, Barbara. "Das Magma des Alltäglichen." (The Magma of the Ordinary.) *TZ.* 1998; 5/Theater in Frankreich: 13-14. Illus.: Photo. B&W. 1. Lang.: Ger.

France. 1958-1998. Histories-sources. ■Interview with the playwright Michel Vinaver, his working methods and his preferred subjects, family and work.

3087 Essif, Les. "The Concentrated (Empty) Image: Behind the Fragmented Story in Beckett's Late Plays." *ET.* 1998; 17(1): 15-32. Notes. Biblio. Lang.: Eng.

France. Ireland. 1953-1981. Critical studies. ■Using Artaud's idea of the void, considers how emptiness creates meaning in Beckett's *En attendant Godot (Waiting for Godot)* and *Rockaby.*

3088 Flenga, Vassiliki. "Passages: L'Impromptu de l'Alma ou Le Caméléon du berger d'Eugène Ionesco." (Passages: Ionesco's *Improvisation of the Shepherd's Chameleon.*) *ET.* 1998; 16(2): 177-185. Notes. Biblio. Lang.: Fre.

France. 1970. Critical studies. ■Examines the presence of the author in Ionesco's play.

3089 Freeman, Sandra. "Bisexuality in Cixous's *Le Nom d'Oedipe.*" *ThR.* 1998 Fall; 23(3): 242-248. Notes. Lang.: Eng.

France. 1978. Critical studies. ■Examines the theme of the body's joy in sexual pleasure in Hélène Cixous's *Le Nom d'Oedipe (The Name of Oedipus).* Argues that Cixous succeeds in inventing a powerful language of the body that gives voice to bisexual love.

3090 Freeman, Sara. "'Each in our own, open-ended way, we are multitudinous'—*Les Nombres,* by Andrée Chedid." *ThR.* 1998 Fall; 23(3): 249-254. Notes. Lang.: Eng.

France. 1965. Critical studies. ■Argues that the narrative structures and fragmented characterization techniques in Andrée Chedid's *Les Nombres (The Numbers)* allow Chedid to develop her vision of a utopian, decentered female identity.

3091 House, Jane E. *Themes of Anomie in French Theatre Since 1968.* New York, NY: City Univ. of New York; 1988. 217 pp. Biblio. Notes. [Ph.D. Dissertation, Univ. Microfilms Order No. AAC 8821090.] Lang.: Eng.

France. 1968-1988. Critical studies. ■Examines the cultural chaos, or 'anomie,' created by the May 1968 civil protest and its effects on the theatre.

3092 Ireland, John. "History, Utopia and the Concentration Camp in Gatti's Early Plays." 184-202 in Schumacher, Claude, ed. *Staging the Holocaust: The Shoah in Drama and Performance.* Cambridge: Cambridge UP; 1998. 355 pp. (Cambridge Studies in Modern Theatre.) Index. Notes. Biblio. Illus.: Photo. 4. Lang.: Eng.

France. 1961-1970. Critical studies. ■Armand Gatti's protrayal of the Holocaust in early plays such as *L'Enfant-rat (The Rat Child)* and others.

3093 Ireland, John. "Freedom as Passion: Sartre's Mystery Plays." *TJ.* 1998 Oct.; 50(3): 335-348. Notes. Lang.: Eng.

France. 1940-1945. Critical studies. ■Examines the antitheatrical prejudice in Jean-Paul Sartre's *Bariona* as well as his use of the traditions of the mystery play, while repudiating the religious dimension of the form.

3094 Johnson, Mary Greenwood. *Verbal and Non-Verbal Communication in the Theatre of Marguerite Duras: A Thematic and Semiotic Study.* Madison, WI: Univ. of Wisconsin; 1987. 241 pp. Notes. Biblio. [Ph.D. Dissertation, Univ. Microfilms Order No. AAC 8712419.] Lang.: Eng.

France. 1914-1985. Critical studies. ■Studies both verbal communication as it functions within Marguerite Duras's dramatic texts and the signifiers (silence, music) that communicate additional meanings to the spectator during performance.

3095 Kennedy, Stephen Mark. *The Poetics of Desire in 'The Marriage of Figaro'.* Chapel Hill, NC: Univ. of North Carolina; 1998. 250 pp. Notes. Biblio. [Ph.D. Dissertation, Univ. Microfilms Order No. AAC 9902484.] Lang.: Eng.

France. 1784. Critical studies. ■The nature of eroticism and desire in Beaumarchais' *Le mariage de Figaro (The Marriage of Figaro).*

3096 Kintzler, Catherine. "La Sémiramis de Voltaire et ses fantômes." (Voltaire's *Sémiramis* and Its Phantoms.) *ASO.* 1998 May/June; 184: 72-79. Notes. Illus.: Dwg. B&W. 4. Lang.: Fre.

France. 1748. Historical studies. ■Analysis of Voltaire's play, the source of Rossini's opera *Semiramide,* and a brief comparison with a play of the same name by Crébillon (1717).

3097 Knowles, Dorothy. "Armand Gatti and the Silence of the 1059 Days of Auschwitz." 203-215 in Schumacher, Claude, ed. *Staging the Holocaust: The Shoah in Drama and Performance.* Cambridge: Cambridge UP; 1998. 355 pp. (Cambridge Studies in Modern Theatre.) Index. Notes. Biblio. Illus.: Photo. 3. Lang.: Eng.

France. 1989-1993. Critical studies. ■Playwright Armand Gatti's experiences in a concentration camp as reflected in his marathon environmental theatre pieces *Le Chant* and *Adam quoi.*

3098 Kreis-Schinck, Annette. "Sprache als Abbild, Sprache als Spiel: Zur Instanz des sprechenden Subjects bei Beckett und Stoppard." (Language as Copy, Language as Play: Toward the Meaning of the Speaking Subject in Beckett and Stoppard.) *FMT.* 1998; 13(2): 195-206. Lang.: Ger.

France. Ireland. UK-England. 1945-1998. Critical studies. ■Analyzes the reduction of linguistic communication as absurdist theatre in Beckett's *Not I* and the linguistic profusion of post-absurdist theatre in Stoppard's *Indian Ink.*

3099 Lepine, Jacques Andre. *Idols in the Night: The Ritualization of Violence and Passion in Jean Racine's* Athalie. Stanford, CA: Stanford Univ; 1987. 196 pp. Biblio. Notes. [Ph.D. Dissertation, Univ. Microfilms Order No. 8800971.] Lang.: Eng.

France. 1691. Critical studies. ■Argues that the sacrificial schema underlying Racine's final play is the structure of the dramatic action, connecting this biblical drama to the ritual origins of tragedy.

3100 Lewis, Valerie Hannagan. "Warriors and Runaways: Monique Wittig's *Le Voyage sans fin.*" *ThR.* 1998 Fall; 23(3): 200-204 . Notes. Lang.: Eng.

France. 1985. Critical studies. ■The nature of women's physical presence in Monique Wittig's *Le Voyage sans fin (The Constant Journey).*

3101 Martin, Mary Kathryn. *Form and Narrative: The Theatrical Media of Marguerite Duras.* Berkeley, CA: Univ. of California; 1987. 241 pp. Notes. Biblio. [Ph.D. Dissertation, Univ. Microfilms Order No. 8726292.] Lang.: Eng.

France. 1914-1986. Critical studies. ■On the use of narrative and form as theatrical media in the plays of Marguerite Duras. Works examined include *Le Square, India Song* and *L'Eden cinéma.*

3102 McCready, Susan. "Performing Stability: The Problem of Proof in Alfred de Musset's *Un Caprice* and *La Quenouille de Barbérine.*" *RomN.* 1997 Fall; 38(1): 87-95. Notes. Biblio. Lang.: Eng.

France. 1835-1837. Critical studies. ■Determination and valuation of fidelity in Musset's two plays.

3103 Minogue, Valerie. "'N'est-on pas tous pareils?' Nathalie Sarraute and the Question of Gender." *ThR.* 1998 Fall; 23(3): 267-274. Notes. Lang.: Eng.

France. 1967-1995. Critical studies. ■Examines the nature of feminist questioning of language and authority in the plays of Nathalie Sarraute.

3104 Miyasaki, June. *The Mirror Shattered: Myth, Language, and Historical (Re)Inscription in Recent French-Language Theatre.* Madison, WI: Univ. of Wisconsin; 1998. 262 pp. Biblio. Notes. [Ph.D. Dissertation, Univ. Microfilms Order No. AAC 9839359.] Lang.: Eng.

DRAMA: —Plays/librettos/scripts

France. Martinique. Guadeloupe. 1960-1990. Critical studies. ■Elements of postcolonialism, ethnicity, and feminism in Jean Genet's *Les Paravents (The Screens)*, Hélène Cixous's *Norodom Sihanouk*, Simone Schwarz-Bart's *Ton beau capitaine (Your Handsome Captain)* and Ina Césaire's *Mémoires d'isles (Island Memories)*.

3105 Moraly, Yehuda. "Liliane Atlan's *Un opéra pour Terezin*." 169-183 in Schumacher, Claude, ed. *Staging the Holocaust: The Shoah in Drama and Performance*. Cambridge: Cambridge UP; 1998. 355 pp. (Cambridge Studies in Modern Theatre.) Index. Notes. Biblio. Illus.: Photo. 3. Lang.: Eng.
France. 1986. Critical studies. ■Jewish ritual in *Un opéra pour Terezin* by Liliane Atlan.

3106 Noonan, Mary. "The Spatialization of Loss in the Theatre of Marguerite Duras." *ThR*. 1998 Fall; 23(3): 215-224. Notes. Lang.: Eng.
France. 1970-1982. Critical studies. ■Focuses on Duras's spatialization of pre-verbal memory in relation to narrative representation in *India Song*, *L'Éden cinéma*, *Agatha*, and *Savannah Bay*.

3107 Phillips, John. "The Repressed Feminine: Nathalie Sarraute's *Elle est là*." *ThR*. 1998 Fall; 23(3): 275-282. Notes. Lang.: Eng.
France. 1967-1982. Critical studies. ■Analyzes the metaphorical substructures of language in Nathalie Sarraute's *Elle est là (It Is There)*. Author reads the negative images of women projected in the play as an unconscious expression of ambivalence toward the feminine-maternal.

3108 Pocknell, Brian. "Jean-Claude Grumberg's Holocaust Plays: Presenting the Jewish Experience." *MD*. 1998 Fall; 41(3): 399-410. Notes. Lang.: Eng.
France. 1974-1991. Critical studies. ■Grumberg's treatment of the Jewish experience in his three holocaust-themed plays: *Dreyfus*, *L'Atelier*, and *Zone libre*.

3109 Ratsaby, Michele. *Olympe de Gouges et le théâtre de la Révolution Française*. (Olympe de Gouges and the Theatre of the French Revolution.) New York, NY: City Univ. of New York; 1998. 306 pp. Biblio. Notes. [Ph.D. Dissertation, Univ. Microfilms Order No. AAC 9830757.] Lang.: Fre.
France. 1789-1795. Critical studies. ■Examines revolutionary plays written and presented on the French stage, focusing on the theatre's links to French political and social life, and on the life and works of Olympe de Gouges, a female political writer and playwright.

3110 Redfern, Walter. "A Funny-bone to Pick with Beckett." *JBeckS*. 1998 Sum; 8(1): 101-117. Notes. Lang.: Eng.
France. Ireland. 1953-1986. Critical studies. ■The purpose of humor in the work of Samuel Beckett.

3111 Renaud, Lissa Tyler. *Kandinsky: Dramatist, Dramaturg, and Demiurge of the Theatre*. Berkeley, CA: Univ. of California; 1987. 356 pp. Notes. Biblio. [Ph.D. Dissertation, Univ. Microfilms Order No. 8814032.] Lang.: Eng.
France. 1908-1944. Critical studies. ■Painter Wassily Kandinsky's theatre criticism and plays in relation to pivotal figures from classical to contemporary drama.

3112 Rubidge, Bradley. "The Code of Reciprocation in Corneille's Heroic Drama." *RomanRev*. 1998 Jan.; 89(1): 55-76. Notes. Biblio. Lang.: Eng.
France. 1643-1652. Critical studies. ■Function of generosity and gratitude in Corneille's drama, including *Don Sanche*, *Héraclius*, *Pertharite*, and *Suréna*.

3113 Savarino, Ida. *Antonin Artaud. Nel vortice dell'elettrochoc*. (Antonin Artaud: In the Whirl of Electroshock.) Tivoli (Rome): Sensibili alle foglie; 1998. 117 pp. (Collana Ospiti 6.) Biblio. Lang.: Ita.
France. 1896-1948. Biographical studies. ■The history of the nine years of seclusion of the French author Antonin Artaud in a mental hospital.

3114 Scherer, Colette. "Voltaire tragédien." (Voltaire the Tragedian.) *ASO*. 1998 May/June; 184: 80-83. Illus.: Dwg. B&W. 4. Lang.: Fre.
France. 1746-1748. Historical studies. ■The circumstances of the writing and first performances of Voltaire's *Sémiramis*, source of Rossini's opera *Semiramide*.

3115 Schumacher, Claude. "Charlotte Delbo: Theatre as a Means of Survival." 216-228 in Schumacher, Claude, ed. *Staging the Holocaust: The Shoah in Drama and Performance*. Cambridge: Cambridge UP; 1998. 355 pp. (Cambridge Studies in Modern Theatre.) Index. Notes. Biblio. Illus.: Photo. 1. Lang.: Eng.
France. 1913-1985. Critical studies. ■Examines the work of playwright Charlotte Delbo, a Holocaust survivor, in *Les Hommes (The Men)* and *La Sentence (The Sentence)*.

3116 Seita, Mario. "Le fonti antiche del *Caligula* di Camus." (The Ancient Sources of Camus' *Caligula*.) *IlCast*. 1998; 11 (31): 55-85. Notes. Lang.: Ita.
France. 1937-1958. Critical studies. ■The sources of Albert Camus's play, with emphasis on Suetonius.

3117 Spreng, Eberhard. "Sehr sakral und sehr politisch." (Highly Sacred and Highly Political.) 126-137 in Pochhammer, Sabine, ed. *Utopie: Spiritualität? Spiritualité: une utopie?/ Utopia: Spirituality? Spirituality: a Utopia?*. Berlin: Theaterschrift c/o Künstlerhaus Bethanien; 1998. 173 pp. (Theaterschrift 13.) Illus.: Photo. B&W. 3. Lang.: Ger, Fre, Dut, Eng.
France. 1988-1998. Histories-sources. ■Interview with writer, actor, and director Olivier Py about contemporary meanings of Catholic spirituality and his play *Le Visage d'Orphée (The Face of Orpheus)*.

3118 Taszman, Maurice. "Der Pakt mit dem Teufel." (The Pact with the Devil.) *TZ*. 1998; 5: 15-17. Illus.: Photo. B&W. 3. Lang.: Ger.
France. Switzerland: La Chaux-de-Fonds. 1960-1998. Historical studies. ■Describes Michel Vinaver's *Par-dessus bord (Overboard)*, language, characters, and structure. Reviews a production directed by Roger Planchon and Charles Joris at Théâtre Populaire Romand in 1983. Includes an extract from the play.

3119 Terneuil, Alexandre. "Violence et révolte des femmes dans le théâtre de Marguerite Yourcenar, Nathalie Sarraute et Marguerite Duras." *ThR*. 1998 Fall; 23(3): 261-266. Notes. Lang.: Fre.
France. 1975-1995. Critical studies. ■Analyzes the plays of three female dramatists, Marguerite Duras, Nathalie Sarraute, and Marguerite Yourcenar, in order to show how each relates to structures of male oppression. Includes introduction in English.

3120 Thomas, Jacqueline. "*Happy Days*: Beckett's Rescript of *Lady Chatterley's Lover*." *MD*. 1998 Win; 41(4): 623-634. Notes. Lang.: Eng.
France. Ireland. UK-England. 1961. Critical studies. ■Argues that Lawrence's novel was used by Beckett as a major source for his play.

3121 Van Der Merwe, Quintus. *Reality as Experienced by the Drama Characters in Selected Dramas of Hugo Claus*. Johannesburg: Univ. of South Africa; 1988. Biblio. Notes. [M.A. Thesis.] Lang.: Eng.
France. 1950-1988. Critical studies. ■Argues that the nature of conflict in the plays of Hugo Claus manifests itself in the realistic events, dialogue, interaction of characters, language patterns, sound effects, décor and stage direction.

3122 Verschuer, Leopold von. "Freier Fall und Tanz in der Sprache." (Free Fall and Dance in Language.) *TZ*. 1998; 5/Theater in Frankreich: 8-11. Illus.: Dwg. Photo. B&W. 5. Lang.: Ger.
France. Germany. 1947-1998. Histories-sources. ■The author's experiences translating plays of Valère Novarina particularly working with the language in *Pour Louis de Funès (For Louis de Funès)*.

3123 "Brecht und die Enkel." (Brecht and the Grandchildren.) *DB*. 1998; 2: 34-37. Illus.: Photo. B&W. 4. Lang.: Ger.
Germany. 1998. Histories-sources. ■Statements of playwrights Daniel Call, Albert Ostermaier, Kerstin Specht, and Dea Loher about the meaning of Brecht today.

3124 "'Viele verwechseln uns mit einem Bordell'." ('Many Confuse Us With a Brothel'.) *DB*. 1998; 11: 24-26. Illus.: Photo. B&W. 3. Lang.: Ger.
Germany: Berlin. 1996-1998. Histories-sources. ■Interview with director and theatre-manager Thomas Ostermeier of Deutsches Theater,

DRAMA: —Plays/librettos/scripts

Baracke, about English language plays and the themes dealing with special experiences of reality.

3125 Amzoll, Stefan. "'Es geht um eine ganze Welt'." ('It Is about a Whole World'.) *TZ.* 1998; 4: 50-54. Illus.: Photo. B&W. 1. Lang.: Ger.

Germany: Berlin. 1929-1998. Histories-sources. ▪Interview with the musicologist Gerd Rienäcker about *Die Massnahme (The Measures Taken)* written by Bertolt Brecht and Hanns Eisler.

3126 Balagna, Olivier; Alfred Strasser, transl. "Orpheus' Blick." (Orpheus's Look.) (prinz 8.) Lang.: Ger.

Germany. 1995-1998. Histories-sources. ▪The director who has been working with Dea Loher's plays since 1995 describes her special kind of language, with respect to production of *Tätowierung (Tattoo)* at Staatsschauspiel Hannover.

3127 Bernhardt, Rüdiger. "Im Streit um das Drama. Hans Francks Kampf gegen Gerhart Hauptmann." (In Conflict over Drama: Hans Franck's Fight Against Gerhart Hauptmann.) *MuK.* 1998; 40(1): 49-68. Notes. Lang.: Ger.

Germany. 1910-1948. Biographical studies. ▪Relationship between writers Hans Franck and Gerhart Hauptmann. Analyzes the motives for Franck's antipathy towards Hauptmann's work.

3128 Blumer, Arnold. "BB's 100th Anniversary." *SATJ.* 1998 May/Sep.; 12(1/2): 208-211. Lang.: Eng.

Germany. 1998. Critical studies. ▪Note on the relevance of Bertolt Brecht in his centennial year.

3129 Burckhardt, Barbara. "Knarren, Clowns und Karadzič." (Shooters, Clowns and Karadzič.) *THeute.* 1998; 4: 15-17. Illus.: Photo. B&W. 2. Lang.: Ger.

Germany: Berlin. 1998. Critical studies. ▪Analyzes Jean-Paul Sartre's *Les Mains Sales (Dirty Hands)* directed by Frank Castorf at Volksbühne Berlin in context of the civil war in Yugoslavia.

3130 Burckhardt, Barbara. "Geisterbahnfahrten durch eine unverstandene Welt." (Journeys With Ghost Train Through a Misunderstood World.) *THeute.* 1998; 4: 47-49. Illus.: Photo. B&W. 3. Lang.: Ger.

Germany: Hannover. 1998. Critical studies. ▪Analyzes the first and the latest play written by Dea Loher: *Olgas Raum (Olga's Room)* and *Adam Geist*, both directed by Andreas Kriegenburg at Niedersächsische Staatstheater Hannover.

3131 Burckhardt, Barbara. "Lieber tot sein oder besoffen." (Better to Be Dead, or Drunk.) *THeute.* 1998; 5: 53-56. Illus.: Photo. B&W. 2. Lang.: Ger.

Germany. 1972-1998. Critical studies. ▪Analyzes the family pieces of playwright Marius von Mayenburg *Haarmann, Fräulein Danzer (Miss Danzer), Monsterdämmerung (Monster Twilight)* and *Feuergesicht (Fire Face).*

3132 Burckhardt, Barbara. "Sieben Tode im Konjunktiv." (Seven Deaths in the Subjunctive.) *THeute.* 1998; 8/9: 65-66. Illus.: Photo. B&W. 3. Lang.: Ger.

Germany: Dresden. 1998. Critical studies. ▪Analyzes Sergi Belbel's *Morir (A Moment Before Dying)* first directed by Hasko Weber and performed with students from Felix Mendelssohn Bartholdy College for Music and Theatre at Staatsschauspiel Dresden.

3133 Carlsson, Hasse. "Regeln och undantaget." (The Exception and the Rule.) *Tningen.* 1998; 21(3): 16-17. Illus.: Photo. B&W. Lang.: Swe.

Germany. 1938. Critical studies. ▪Examination of Brecht's play *Die Ausnahme und die Regel (The Exception and the Rule).*

3134 Case, Sue-Ellen; Monro, Mia, transl. "Den som röker blir kallblodig." (He Who Smokes Turns Cold-Blooded.) *Tningen.* 1998; 21(3): 38-43. Illus.: Photo. B&W. Lang.: Swe.

Germany. 1930-1997. Critical studies. ▪Essay about the different meanings of the cigar in Brecht's and Heiner Müller's appearance and in the plays by Brecht.

3135 Dresen, Adolf. "Die zweite Schwierigkeit." (The Second Difficulty.) *TZ.* 1998; 1: 52-54. Lang.: Ger.

Germany. 1934-1998. Critical studies. ▪Analysis of an article written by Bertolt Brecht, *Fünf Schwierigkeiten beim Schreiben der Wahrheit (Five Difficulties Writing the Truth)*, with reference to the relevance of Brecht in a reunified Germany.

3136 Fangauf, Henning. "Grenzgänger." (Border Crosser.) *DB.* 1998; 9: 28-29. Illus.: Photo. B&W. 2. Lang.: Ger.

Germany: Hannover. 1993-1998. Critical studies. ▪Portrait of playwright Hans Zimmer and the pieces *Gestrandet vor Guadeloupe (Stranded in Guadeloupe)* and *Irrläufer. Nach Paris (Stray Letter: To Paris).*

3137 Feinberg, Anat. "George Tabori's Mourning Work in *Jubiläum.*" 267-280 in Schumacher, Claude, ed. *Staging the Holocaust: The Shoah in Drama and Performance.* Cambridge: Cambridge UP; 1998. 355 pp. (Cambridge Studies in Modern Theatre.) Index. Notes. Biblio. Illus.: Photo. 2. Lang.: Eng.

Germany. 1983. Critical studies. ▪Themes of irony and resentment in George Tabori's Holocaust drama, *Jubiläum.*

3138 Gjestvang, Ingrid Leiser. *The Language of Power: Gender Relations and Communication in Dramatic Texts.* Madison, WI: Univ. of Wisconsin; 1998. 277 pp. Biblio. Notes. [Ph.D. Dissertation, Univ. Microfilms Order No. AAC 9829157.] Lang.: Ger.

Germany. 1776-1989. Critical studies. ▪Feminist analysis of dramatic texts including J.M.R. Lenz's *Soldaten*, Gerhart Hauptmann's *Einsame Menschen*, Elsa Bernstein's *Wir Drei* and Marlene Streeruwitz's *Waikiki Beach.*

3139 Grange, William. "Hitler's 'Whiff of Champagne': Curt Goetz and Celebrity in Third Reich." *TA.* 1998; 51: 15-26. Notes. Illus.: Photo. Dwg. B&W. 5. Lang.: Eng.

Germany. 1933-1944. Biographical studies. ▪Success of actor and playwright Goetz during Hitler's reign, with an emphasis on Nazi attitudes toward the theatre.

3140 Grigor'ev, A. "On nazyval sebja dramodelom." (He Called Himself Drama Maker.) *EchoP.* 1998; 6: 41-43. Lang.: Rus.

Germany. 1898-1956. Biographical studies. ▪Profile of German playwright Bertolt Brecht in celebration of his 100th birthday.

3141 Heine, Beate. "Auf den Spuren der Wörter." (On the Track of Words.) *DB.* 1998; 5: 50-51. Illus.: Photo. B&W. 2. Lang.: Ger.

Germany: Kaiserslautern. 1992-1998. Historical studies. ▪Portrait of the playwright Volker Lüdecke concerning his new piece *Darja*, given the Else-Lasker-Schüler award, on occasion of his first performance directed by Miriam Goldschmidt at Pfalztheater Kaiserslautern.

3142 Henderson, Stephen; Bentley, Eric; Merschmeier, Michael. "The Persistence of Brecht." *AmTh.* 1998 May/June; 15(5): 12-17, 54-59. Illus.: Photo. Dwg. B&W. 8. Lang.: Eng.

Germany. USA. 1898-1998. Historical studies. ▪Expresses three points of view as to the reputation, place, and relevance of Bertolt Brecht in the theatre of the late twentieth century on the centennial of his birth.

3143 Justen, Wolfgang Heinrich. *Interpretationen zu späten dramen Georg Kaisers: Das spiel mit literarischen und mythologischen figuren in den schauspielen* Rosamunde Floris *und* Alain und Elise. (Interpretations of Late Plays of Georg Kaiser: The play of Literary and Mythological Figures in *Rosamunde Floris* and *Alain and Elise.*) Houston, TX: Rice Univ; 1987. 500 pp. Biblio. Notes. [Ph.D. Dissertation, Univ. Microfilms Order No. 8718733.] Lang.: Ger.

Germany. 1914-1940. Critical studies. ▪The loss of paradise and mythological structures and symbols in the two plays.

3144 Knopf, Jan. "Stückeschreiben als Produktion." (Playwriting as Production.) *DB.* 1998; 2: 15-17. Illus.: Photo. B&W. 3. Lang.: Ger.

Germany. 1998. Histories-sources. ▪The editor of a new edition of Brecht's works, *Grosse kommentierte Berliner und Frankfurter Ausgabe*, describes the main benefit of this edition which historicizes Brecht's working methods of writing.

3145 Kohse, Petra. "Schleuderprogramm." (Spin Program.) *TZ.* 1998; 4: 28-31. Illus.: Photo. B&W. 4. Lang.: Ger.

Germany: Hannover. 1998. Histories-sources. ▪Speech on May 10 during the 4th Autorentage Hannover. Discusses the correlation between plays and performances, playwrights and directors in general.

DRAMA: —Plays/librettos/scripts

3146 Koltai, Gábor. "*Baal*-vázlat." (A Draft on *Baal.*) *Sz.* 1998; 31(12): 8-10. Illus.: Photo. B&W. 1. Lang.: Hun.
Germany. 1918-1922. Critical studies. ▪An essay on the the aesthetic pecularities of Brecht's early play.

3147 Korb, Richard Alan. *Victimization and Self-Persecution: Homosexuality on the German Stage: 1920s and 1970s.* Pittsburgh, PA: Univ. of Pittsburgh; 1988. 217 pp. Notes. Biblio. [Ph.D. Dissertation, Univ. Microfilms Order No. AAC 8818602.] Lang.: Eng.
Germany. 1920-1980. Histories-specific. ▪Examines German theatre from a gay perspective from the time of 'survival' in the 1920s to the time of 'coming out' in the 1970s. Discusses Carl Sternheim's *Oskar Wilde: Sein Drama*, Ferdinand Bruckner's *Krankheit der Jugend* and *Die Verbrecher*, Rainer Werner Fassbinder's *Die bitteren Tränen der Petra von Kant*, Hans Eppendorfer's *Der Ledermann spricht mit Hubert Fichte*, and Alexander Ziegler's *Samstagabend: Eine Liebesgeschichte.*

3148 Krusche, Friedemann. "Das Scheitern der Komödianten." (The Actors' Failure.) *THeute.* 1998; 1: 21-23. Illus.: Photo. B&W. 2. Lang.: Ger.
Germany. 1997-1998. Critical studies. ▪Analyzes family conflict in Tankred Dorst's *Was sollen wir tun (What Shall We Do)* directed by Tobias Wellemeyer and William Shakespeare's *Hamlet* adapted by Heiner Müller as *Die Hamletmaschine (Hamletmachine)* and directed by Hasko Weber at Staatsschauspiel Dresden.

3149 Långbacka, Ralf. "Brecht 100 år—och sedan?" (Brecht 100 Years—and More?)*Entré.* 1998; 25(1): 2-21. Illus.: Photo. B&W. Lang.: Swe.
Germany. 1898-1998. Critical studies. ▪Reevaluation of Brecht's ideas and plays, their prospects for survival, and whether they can be considered real classics.

3150 Lennartz, Knut. "Klopfzeichen eines Scheintoten?" (Signs of Knocking from a Dead Man?)*DB.* 1998; 3: 15-19. Illus.: Photo. B&W. 5. Lang.: Ger.
Germany. 1998. Reviews of performances. ▪The meaning of the plays of Bertolt Brecht today, with respect to performances of *Der Ozeanflug* directed by Robert Wilson at Berliner Ensemble, *Herr Puntila und sein Knecht Matti (Herr Puntila and His Man Matti)* directed by Peter Kupke at Theater Augsburg, *Der gute Mensch von Sezuan (The Good Person of Szechwan)* directed by Jens Pesel at Theater Krefeld, and *Trommeln in der Nacht (Drums in the Night)* directed by Peter Schroth at Badisches Staatstheater Karlsruhe.

3151 Lennartz, Knut. "Stücke der Zeit." (Contemporary Plays.) *DB.* 1998; 4: 20-22. Illus.: Photo. Color. 3. Lang.: Ger.
Germany: Hannover, Munich. 1990-1998. Historical studies. ▪The ongoing cooperation of playwright Dea Loher and director Andreas Kriegenburg, with respect to *Olgas Raum (Olga's Room)* and *Adam Geist* at Schauspielhaus Hannover and *Blaubart—Hoffnung der Frauen (Bluebeard—Hope of Women)* at Bayerisches Staatsschauspiel.

3152 Ludwig, Volker. "Direkt reagieren-auf Probleme und Sehnsüchte der Kinder." (To React Directly to Children's Problems and Desires.) *dRAMATURg.* 1998; 1: 24-26. Illus.: Photo. B&W. 1. Lang.: Ger.
Germany: Berlin. 1966-1998. Histories-sources. ▪Director and playwright Ludwig describes the continuous perspective of GRIPS, based on the traditional emancipatory children and young people's theatre as it has been developed by his house.

3153 Merschmeier, Michael. "Die Ballade vom reichen BB und vom armen BB." (The Ballad of Rich BB and Poor BB.) *THeute.* 1998; 2: 6-10. Illus.: Photo. B&W. 9. Lang.: Ger.
Germany: Berlin. 1898-1998. Historical studies. ▪Analyzes the contemporary perception of Bertolt Brecht's dramas, copyright problems, the biography written by John Fuegi and the current situation at Berliner Ensemble on occasion of Brecht's 100th birthday.

3154 Nagel, Ivan. "Lügnerin und Wahr-sagerin." (Liar and Soothsayer.) *THeute.* 1998; 11: 60-63. Illus.: Photo. B&W. 2. Lang.: Ger.
Germany. 1998. Histories-sources. ▪Text of Nagel's speech made on presentation of the Büchner-award for playwriting given to Elfriede Jelinek on October 17, 1998.

3155 Nyytäjä, Outi. "Voiko näin huono ihminen olla hyvä kirjailija." (Can Such a Bad Person Be a Good Writer.) *Teat.* 1998; 53(2): 28-29. Illus.: Dwg. Color. 3. Lang.: Fin.
Germany. 1898-1956. Critical studies. ▪Analyzing the work of playwright Bertolt Brecht with a late twentieth-century eye.

3156 Paulin, Roger. "Luise Gottsched und Dorothea Tieck. Vom Schicksal zweier übersetzerinnen." (Luise Gottsched and Dorothea Tieck: On the Fate of Two Translators.) *SJW.* 1998; 134: 108-122. Notes. Lang.: Ger.
Germany. 1739-1833. Biographical studies. ▪Similarities in the lives and careers of two neglected female translators of Shakespeare's work: Luise Gottsched and Dorothea Tieck.

3157 Pfister, Eva. "Narren und Spieler leben gefährlich." (Fools and Actors Live Dangerously.) *DB.* 1998; 4: 38-39. Illus.: Photo. B&W. 2. Lang.: Ger.
Germany: Düsseldorf. 1998. Historical studies. ▪The meaning of the fool in Michael Roes's *Madschun al-Malik. Der Narr des König (Madschun al-Malik, the King's Fool)*, a performance directed and designed by Kazuko Watanabe at Düsseldorfer Schauspielhaus.

3158 Pierce, Nancy Jean Frankian. *Woman's Place in German Turn-of-the-Century Drama: The Function of Female Figures in Selected Plays by Gerhart Hauptmann, Frank Wedekind, Ricarda Huch and Elsa Bernstein.* Irvine, CA: Univ. of California; 1988. 299 pp. Notes. Biblio. [Ph.D. Dissertation, Univ. Microfilms Order No. AAC 8820218.] Lang.: Eng.
Germany. 1890-1910. Critical studies. ▪The function and formal significance of the female figures in plays by both female and male authors.

3159 Popescu-Judetz, Eugenia E. *The Language-Silence Connection in German Expressionist Drama.* Pittsburgh, PA: Univ. of Pittsburgh; 1988. 337 pp. Biblio. Notes. [Ph.D. Dissertation, Univ. Microfilms Order No. AAC 9018773.] Lang.: Eng.
Germany. 1913-1923. Critical studies. ▪Investigates the semiotic function of silence in relationship to language in German Expressionist dramatic texts. Works examined include the plays of Oskar Kokoschka, Wassily Kandinsky, August Stramm, and Georg Kaiser.

3160 Rossi, Doc. "*Hamlet* and *The Life of Galileo.*" *CompD.* 1998-99 Win; 32(4): 496-517. Notes. Lang.: Eng.
Germany. 1600-1932. Critical studies. ▪Argues that Brecht's *Life of Galileo (Leben des Galilei)* is actually his second adaptation of Shakespeare's *Hamlet*, his radio adaptation of Shakespeare's play being the first.

3161 Schmidt, Kekke. "Erbschuld und Freiheitstraum—*Fremdes Haus.*" (Inherited Debt and the Dream of Freedom: *Stranger's House.*) 127-131 in Gross, Jens; Khuon, Ulrich. *Dea Loher und das Schauspiel Hannover.* Hannover: Niedersächsische Staatstheater Hannover GmbH; 1998. 256 pp. (prinz 8.) Lang.: Ger.
Germany. 1998. Critical studies. ▪Analyzes the dramatic structure of Dea Loher's *Fremdes Haus (Stranger's House).*

3162 Schulz, Genia. "Randlagen." (Marginal Situation.) 194-211 in Gross, Jens; Khuon, Ulrich. *Dea Loher und das Schauspiel Hannover.* Hannover: Niedersächsische Staatstheater Hannover GmbH; 1998. 256 pp. (Prinz 8.) Lang.: Ger.
Germany. 1991-1998. Textual studies. ▪Analysis of margin notations made by playwright Dea Loher to her works *Olgas Raum (Olga's Room), Tätowierung (Tattoo), Leviathan, Fremdes Haus (Stranger's House)* and *Adam Geist.*

3163 Strenger, Elisabeth Maria. *The 'Everyman' Morality Plays of Reformation Germany.* New Haven, CT: Yale Univ; 1988. 216 pp. Notes. Biblio. [Ph.D. Dissertation, Univ. Microfilms Order No. AAC 8917738.] Lang.: Eng.
Germany. 1550-1584. Histories-specific. ▪Traces the development of the German morality play and its allegorical didactic methods in the polemic dramas of the Reformation period. Includes discussion of Friedrich Dedekind's *Der christliche Ritter* and Johannes Stricker's *De dudesche Schlomer.*

3164 Tiedtke, Marion. "Du sollst Deiner Sehnsucht nicht nachgeben..." (You Should Not Give Way To Your Desire...)146-150 in Gross, Jens; Khuon, Ulrich. *Dea Loher und das*

DRAMA: —Plays/librettos/scripts

Schauspiel Hannover. Hannover: Niedersächsische Staatstheater Hannover GmbH; 1998. 256 pp. (Prinz 8.) Lang.: Ger.

Germany: Munich. 1998. Historical studies. ■Describes the development of the project *Blaubart—Hoffnung der Frauen (Bluebeard—Hope of Women)* at Bayerisches Staatsschauspiel, the plans of director Andreas Kriegenburg and how Dea Loher created the play based on their ideas.

3165 Tjäder, Per Arne. "Att bygga om en man." (To Rebuild a Man.) *Tningen.* 1998; 21(3): 12-15. Illus.: Photo. B&W. Lang.: Swe.

Germany. 1926. Critical studies. ■Examination of Brecht's play *Mann ist Mann (A Man's a Man).*

3166 Tseng, Tin-Yu. *'Emilia Galotti' and Its Aesthetic Response: A Case Study for the Reader-Response Criticism.* Los Angeles, CA: Univ. of Southern California; 1998. 234 pp. Notes. Biblio. [Ph.D. Dissertation, Univ. Microfilms Order No. AAC 9902878.] Lang.: Eng.

Germany. 1772. Critical studies. ■Examines the problem of literary interpretation in dramatic texts. Uses Lessing's *Emilia Galotti* as a reader-response model to examine the subjective creativity of the author and the relationship of the author and the reader.

3167 Volz, Sabrina Rose. *Women and Sacrifice in Eighteenth-Century German Drama: Lessing's* Emilia Galotti, *Goethe's* Stella, *and Schiller's* Raeuber. University Park, PA: Pennsylvania State Univ; 1998. 248 pp. Notes. Biblio. [Ph.D. Dissertation, Univ. Microfilms Order No. AAC 9836785.] Lang.: Eng.

Germany. 1772-1781. Critical studies. ■The theme of female sacrifice in the three plays.

3168 Walker, John. "City Jungles and Expressionist Reifications from Brecht to Hammett." *Twentieth CL.* 1998 Spr; 44(1): 119-133. Biblio. Lang.: Eng.

Germany. USA. 1923-1926. Critical studies. ■The use of the city, with its 'urban jungle' mythos, as an expressionistic backdrop for Brecht's play *In the Jungle of Cities (Im Dickicht der Städte)* and Dashiell Hammett's novel *Red Harvest.*

3169 Wedekind, Frank. "Préface à 'La Boîte de Pandore': Extrait (1906)." (Preface to *Pandora's Box*: Excerpt.) *ASO.* 1998 Jan/Feb.; 181/182: 182-183. Illus.: Dwg. Photo. B&W. 2. Lang.: Fre.

Germany. 1906. Histories-sources. ■French translation of a section of Wedekind's preface to *Die Büchse der Pandora.*

3170 Wieck, Thomas. "Brecht, später." (Brecht, Later.) *TZ.* 1998; 1: 54-57. Notes. Lang.: Ger.

Germany. 1989-1998. Historical studies. ■Describes the diminishing importance of Brecht in a reunified Germany. Argues that as capitalism increases its hold in the former East Germany, Brecht's relevance may become more influential in the unsubsidized theatre sector.

3171 Wild, Christopher Joachim. *Repraesentatio Immaculata zur Theatralisierung des Jungfräulichen Körpers im Deutschen Drama des 17. und 18. Jahrhunderts.* (*Representatio Immaculata* in the Theatricalization of the Virginal Body in Seventeenth- and Eighteenth-Century German Drama.) Baltimore, MD: Johns Hopkins Univ; 1998. 302 pp. Notes. Biblio. [Ph.D. Dissertation, Univ. Microfilms Order No. AAC 9833004.] Lang.: Ger.

Germany. 1600-1800. Critical studies. ■Traces the historical semiotic shift in German theatre by examining *Catharina von Georgien* by Andreas Gryphius, *Agrippina*, *Epicharis*, and *Ibrahim Sultan* by Daniel Casper von Lohenstein, *Emilia Galotti* by Gotthold Ephraim Lessing, and Friedrich Schiller's *Die Jungfräu von Orleans (The Maid of Orleans).*

3172 Willard, Penelope D. *'Gefühl und Erkenntnis': Ernst Toller's Revisions of His Dramas.* Albany, NY: State Univ. of New York; 1988. 384 pp. Notes. Biblio. [Ph.D. Dissertation, Univ. Microfilms Order No. AAC 8907430.] Lang.: Eng.

Germany. 1920-1939. Textual studies. ■Examines different versions of Ernst Toller's dramas including *Die Wandlung, Masse-Mensch, Die Maschinenstürmer, Hinkemann, Hoppla, wir leben!, Feuer aus den Kesseln, Die blinde Göttin, Nie Wieder Friede!,* and *Pastor Hall.*

3173 Wille, Franz. "'Ich kenne nicht besonders viele glückliche Menschen'." ('I Don't Particularly Know Many Happy People'.) *THeute.* 1998; 2: 61-65. Illus.: Photo. B&W. 4. Lang.: Ger.

Germany. 1964-1998. Histories-sources. ■Interview with playwright Dea Loher about biography, writing and performances of her plays on occasion of her latest play *Adam Geist.*

3174 Wille, Franz. "Sie kann auch anders." (She'd Better Watch It.) *THeute.* 1998; 4: 52-54. Illus.: Photo. B&W. 2. Lang.: Ger.

Germany: Stuttgart. 1998. Critical studies. ■Analyzes Kerstin Specht's latest play *Die Froschkönigin (The Frog Princess)* and the first performance directed by Markus Trabusch at Staatstheater Stuttgart, Schauspiel.

3175 Wille, Franz. "Die Freiheit, nein zu sagen." (The Freedom to Say No.) *THeute.* 1998; 10: 1-2. Illus.: Photo. B&W. 2. Lang.: Ger.

Germany: Berlin. 1976-1998. Historical studies. ■Describes the history of Rainer Werner Fassbinder's *Der Müll, die Stadt und der Tod (Garbage, the City and Death)* and the perception that it is an antisemitic play on occasion of plans to perform it at Maxim Gorki Theater.

3176 Wright, Stephen K. "Was There a Twelfth-Century Play at St. Emmeran?" *MET.* 1996; 18: 74-84. Notes. Biblio. Lang.: Eng.

Germany: Regensburg. 1184-1189. Historical studies. ■A descriptive list in Latin of dramatis personae from a lost play, compiled by the Benedictine Hugo von Lerchenfeld, is identified as stemming from a Creed play, in which apostles and other sacred figures present an exposition of the twelve articles of faith.

3177 Hamburger, Maik. "From Goethe to *Gestus*: Shakespeare into German." 73-83 in Guntner, J. Lawrence, ed.; McLean, Andrew M., ed. *Redefining Shakespeare: Literary Theory and Theater Practice in the German Democratic Republic.* Newark, DE: Univ of Delaware P; 1998. 293 pp. Index. Notes. Pref. Biblio. Lang.: Eng.

Germany, East. 1945-1990. Historical studies. ■Examines challenges of translating Shakespeare's works into German, through the intermediary lens of Bertolt Brecht's *gestus.*

3178 Walther, Ingeborg Christina. *The Theater of Franz Xaver Kroetz.* Ann Arbor, MI: Univ. of Michigan; 1987. 387 pp. Notes. Biblio. [Ph.D. Dissertation, Univ. Microfilms Order No. AAC 8801439.] Lang.: Eng.

Germany, West. 1970-1980. Critical studies. ■Explores the ways in which the theatre of Franz Xaver Kroetz seeks to bridge the modern chasm between language and social reality, between theatre and politics.

3179 Allan, Arlene Leslie. *Signs of His Presence: Hermes in the Theatre of Dionysos.* Kingston, ON: Queen's Univ; 1998. 128 pp. Biblio. Notes. [M.A. Thesis, Univ. Microfilms Order No. AAC MQ31178.] Lang.: Eng.

Greece. 600-411 B.C. Critical studies. ■Explores the relationship of Hermes to Dionysos and to the Greek theatre in which the latter was honored by reading the ancient playtexts in relation to their performance space.

3180 Callens, Johan. "Koining Oidipous, een queeste." (King Oedipus, a Quest.) 3-35 in van Berlaer-Hellemans, Dina; Van Kerkhoven, Marianne; Van den Dries, Luk. *Het teater zoekt ... zoek het teater. Aspekten van het eigentijdse teater in Vlaanderen 2.* Brussels: Vrije Universiteiet of Brussels; 1986. 392 pp. (Studiereeks van de Vrije Universiteiet 25.) Lang.: Dut.

Greece. 420 B.C. Critical studies. ■Analysis of Sophocles' *Oidípous Týrannos (Oedipus the King).*

3181 Clark, Amy C. *Euripides in a Comic Mirror: The 'Tragodoumenai'.* Chapel Hill, NC: Univ. of North Carolina; 1998. 296 pp. Biblio. Notes. [Ph.D. Dissertation, Univ. Microfilms Order No. AAC 9902450.] Lang.: Eng.

Greece. 438-411 B.C. Critical studies. ■The playwright Euripides and his female characters as represented in Aristophanes' *Thesmophoriazusae.*

3182 Del Corno, Dario. *I narcisi di Colono. Drammaturgia del mito nella tragedia greca.* (The Narcissi of Colonus: Drama-

turgy of Myth in the Greek Tragedy.) Milan: Raffaello Cortina; 1998. 185 pp. (Scienza e idee.) Notes. Lang.: Ita.
Greece. 490-406 B.C. Critical studies. ▪The models and dramaturgical technique of Greek tragedy.

3183 Iversen, Paul Andrew. *Menander and the Subversion of Tragedy.* Columbus, OH: Ohio State Univ; 1998. 269 pp. Biblio. Notes. [Ph.D. Dissertation, Univ. Microfilms Order No. AAC 9834005.] Lang.: Eng.
Greece. 342-291 B.C. Critical studies. ▪Examines the local context of Menander's comedy. Argues that Menander struggled to subvert the traditions of tragedy and tragic role playing that preceded him.

3184 Natanblut, Erez. *Mythmaking in the Electra Plays.* Kingston, ON: Queen's Univ; 1998. 115 pp. Biblio. Notes. [M.A. Thesis, Univ. Microfilms Order No. AAC MQ28242.] Lang.: Eng.
Greece. 438-411 B.C. Critical studies. ▪Examines the myth of Orestes and Electra in three extant plays that deal with them as main characters: Aeschylus' *Choephoroi*, Euripides' *Electra* and Sophocles' *Electra*. Argues that a close examination of these plays reveals that details of the myth vary from playwright to playwright.

3185 Zelenak, Michael. "Civic Discourse and Civil Discord in Greek Tragedy." *ThR.* 1998 Spr; 23(1): 69-78. Notes. Lang.: Eng.
Greece. 475-400 B.C. Historical studies. ▪The reflection in Greek tragedy of civic discourse and popular unrest in Athenian democracy and the role of theatre in resolving tensions. Focuses on the plays of Aeschylus, Sophocles, and Euripides.

3186 McKay, Melissa Lynn. *Maryse Condé et le Théâtre Antillais.* (Maryse Condé and Caribbean Theatre.) Athens, GA: Univ. of Georgia; 1998. 251 pp. Biblio. Notes. [Ph.D. Dissertation, Univ. Microfilms Order No. AAC 9836972.] Lang.: Eng.
Guadeloupe. 1965-1996. Critical studies. ▪Analysis of plays by Condé.

3187 Ács, János; Eörsi, István; Gothár, Péter, et al. "Színház és/vagy irodalom: Új Shakespeare- fordításokról." (Theatre and/or Literature: On New Shakespeare Translations.) *Sz.* 1998; 31(8): 15-20. Illus.: Photo. B&W. 5. Lang.: Hun.
Hungary. 1990-1998. Histories-sources. ▪Transcript of a discussion on the problem of translating foreign plays into Hungarian, by the Dramaturgs' Guild with the participation of some leading translators and directors, mostly concerned with the present trend of having a new text for almost all important Shakespeare productions.

3188 Forgách, András; Kovács, Zita, photo.; Ilovszky, Béla, photo. "A velencei dealer: Egy új Shakespeare-fordítás." (The Venice Dealer: A New Translation of Shakespeare's *The Merchant of Venice.*) *Sz.* 1998; 31(7): 20-23. Illus.: Photo. B&W. 3. Lang.: Hun.
Hungary: Budapest. 1998. Critical studies. ▪Analysis of the new translation by Imre Szabó Stein for the production of the Tivoli Theatre under the direction of Róbert Alföldi.

3189 Forgách, András. "Ordítás." (Cry.) *Sz.* 1998; 31(8): 25-28. Illus.: Photo. B&W. 3. Lang.: Hun.
Hungary. 1990-1998. Critical studies. ▪A contribution to the discussion on the newly translated plays of the 1990s by a writer, translator and director.

3190 Kúnos, László; Ilovszky, Béla, photo.; Ikládi, László, photo. "Két úr szolgája." (The Servant of Two Masters.) *Sz.* 1998; 31(8): 28-29. Illus.: Photo. B&W. 2. Lang.: Hun.
Hungary. 1990-1998. Critical studies. ▪An essay on the problems of translations.

3191 Chatterjee, Sudipto. *The Colonial Stage(d): Hybridity, Woman, and the Nation in Nineteenth Century Bengali Theatre.* New York, NY: New York Univ; 1998. 358 pp. Notes. Biblio. [Ph.D. Dissertation, Univ. Microfilms Order No. AAC 9907141.] Lang.: Eng.
India: Calcutta. 1795-1900. Histories-specific. ▪The development of Western-style Bengali theatre in the nineteenth century, as it moved away from its origins as an imitation of English colonial theatres in Calcutta.

3192 Chaudhary, Sheela Devi. *Imagi(ned) Nations: The Politics and Ethics of Representation in Colonial and Postcolonial Narratives of India.* Austin, TX: Univ. of Texas; 1998. 331 pp. Biblio. Notes. [Ph.D. Dissertation, Univ. Microfilms Order No. AAC 9837919.] Lang.: Eng.
India. 1900-1985. Critical studies. ▪Analysis of dramatic texts from Manipuri regional theatre with respect to the discourse of representation, and the construction of self/other categories in colonial and nationalistic writing. Also considers the absence of gender identity.

3193 Dharwadker, Aparna. "Diaspora, Nation, and the Failure of Home: Two Contemporary Indian Plays." *TJ.* 1998 Mar.; 50(1): 71-94. Notes. Illus.: Photo. B&W. 2. Lang.: Eng.
India. 1978-1985. Critical studies. ▪The relationship between diaspora and home in Mahesh Elkunchwar's *Wada Chirebandi (Old Stone Mansion)*, written in Marathi and Cyrus Mistry's *Doongaji House*, written in English.

3194 "Philip Glass." 191-194 in Bryden, Mary, ed. *Samuel Beckett and Music.* Oxford: Clarendon; 1998. 267 pp. Index. Notes. Biblio. Lang.: Eng.
Ireland. France. USA. 1965-1995. Histories-sources. ▪Interview with composer Philip Glass on the influence of playwright Samuel Beckett on his work.

3195 "Luciano Berio." 189-190 in Bryden, Mary, ed. *Samuel Beckett and Music.* Oxford: Clarendon; 1998. 267 pp. Index. Notes. Biblio. Lang.: Eng.
Ireland. France. Italy. 1965-1985. Histories-sources. ▪Interview with composer Luciano Berio on the influence of playwright Samuel Beckett in his work.

3196 Beckett, Walter. "Music in the Works of Samuel Beckett." 181-182 in Bryden, Mary, ed. *Samuel Beckett and Music.* Oxford: Clarendon; 1998. 267 pp. Index. Notes. Biblio. Lang.: Eng.
Ireland. 1912-1945. Histories-sources. ▪Interview with the author, a cousin of playwright Samuel Beckett, reflecting on his childhood and adult relationship with the playwright, and the importance of music in Beckett's early life.

3197 Boltwood, Scott. "'Swapping Stories About Apollo and Cuchulainn': Brian Friel and the De-Gaelicizing of Ireland." *MD.* 1998 Win; 41(4): 573-583. Notes. Lang.: Eng.
Ireland. 1980. Critical studies. ▪Analysis of Friel's play *Translations*, with an emphasis on whether he mourns the passing of Gaelic Ireland's culture and language.

3198 Bryden, Mary. "Beckett and the Sound of Silence." 21-46 in Bryden, Mary, ed. *Samuel Beckett and Music.* Oxford: Clarendon; 1998. 267 pp. Index. Notes. Biblio. Illus.: Photo. 1. Lang.: Eng.
Ireland. France. 1945-1990. Critical studies. ▪The musicality of playwright Samuel Beckett,with specific reference to listening, composing, and conducting.

3199 Callens, Johan. "Samuel Beckett, 1906-1989." *Etcetera.* 1990; 29: 14-15. Lang.: Dut.
Ireland. France. 1906-1989. Biographical studies. ▪Obituary for the absurdist playwright.

3200 Cascetta, Annamaria. "Immagini dell'esistenza. Winnie: il femminile, la speranza, l'illusione." (Images of Existence. Winnie: the Feminine, Hope and Illusion.) *IlCast.* 1998; 11(31): 27-46. Notes. Lang.: Ita.
Ireland. France. 1960-1963. Critical studies. ▪An analysis of Winnie, one of the characters in *Happy Days* by Samuel Beckett.

3201 Daiken, Melanie. "Working with Beckett Texts." 249-256 in Bryden, Mary, ed. *Samuel Beckett and Music.* Oxford: Clarendon; 1998. 267 pp. Index. Notes. Biblio. Illus.: Sketches. 2. Lang.: Eng.
Ireland. France. 1945-1995. Histories-sources. ▪Author recalls her compositions based on playwright Samuel Beckett's poetry.

3202 Devlin, Joseph. "J.M. Synge's *The Playboy of the Western World* and the Culture of Western Ireland under Late Colonial Rule." *MD.* 1998 Fall; 41(3): 371-385. Notes. Lang.: Eng.
Ireland. 1907. Critical studies. ▪Analysis of Synge's play as a reworking of the folktale 'The Brave Little Tailor,' reflecting his sympathy for the disappearing peasant culture of Western Ireland.

DRAMA: —Plays/librettos/scripts

3203 Eaves, Gregory N. "The Anti-Theatre and its Double." *YA*. 1998; 13: 34-61. Notes. Lang.: Eng.
Ireland. 1916-1918. Critical studies. ▪Re-examination of Yeats' play *The Only Jealousy of Emer*, with emphasis on its anti-realist aesthetics, and as an example of his newly formed anti-theatrical poetics regarding drama.

3204 Grindea, Miron. "Beckett's Involvement with Music." 183-185 in Bryden, Mary, ed. *Samuel Beckett and Music*. Oxford: Clarendon; 1998. 267 pp. Index. Notes. Biblio. Lang.: Eng.
Ireland. France. 1955-1995. Histories-sources. ▪The author, a long-time friend of playwright Samuel Beckett, reflects on the playwright's life-long passion for music.

3205 Gussow, Mel. *Conversazioni con (e su) Beckett*. (Conversations with (and about) Beckett.) Milan: Ubulibri; 1998. 176 pp. (La collanina 18.) Lang.: Ita.
Ireland. France. 1998. Histories-sources. ▪Italian translation of *Conversations with and about Beckett* (London: Nick Heine, 1998).

3206 Murphy, Deirdre Ann. *'Who's the Bloody Baritone?': Brendan Behan's Dramatic Use of Song*. Edmonton: Univ. of Alberta; 1998. 134 pp. Notes. Biblio. [M.A. Thesis, Univ. Microfilms Order No. AAC MQ28969.] Lang.: Eng.
Ireland. 1954-1958. Critical studies. ▪How Brendan Behan integrated song and music interludes in his plays *The Quare Fellow* and *The Hostage*.

3207 O'Toole, Fintan. "Shadows Over Ireland." *AmTh*. 1998 July/Aug.; 15(6): 16-19. Illus.: Photo. B&W. 4. Lang.: Eng.
Ireland. 1998. Critical studies. ▪Irish theatre and the cocky, cosmopolitan traditionalism of the new breed of Irish playwrights such as Conor McPherson, Martin McDonagh, Frank McGuinness, Marina Carr, and Sebastian Barry.

3208 Pilling, John. "*Proust* and Schopenhauer: Music and Shadows." 173-178 in Bryden, Mary, ed. *Samuel Beckett and Music*. Oxford: Clarendon; 1998. 267 pp. Index. Notes. Biblio. Lang.: Eng.
Ireland. France. 1931. Critical studies. ▪Samuel Beckett's treatment of music and of Schopenhauer in his early novel *Proust*.

3209 Renner, Pamela. "Haunts of the Very Irish." *AmTh*. 1998 July/Aug.; 15(6): 20-21, 62-63. Illus.: Photo. B&W. 1. Lang.: Eng.
Ireland. 1998. Biographical studies. ▪Profile of the author of *The Weir*, Conor McPherson.

3210 Renton, Andrew. "Texts for Performance/Performing Texts: Samuel Beckett's Anxiety of Self-Regeneration." *PM*. 1990(60): 14-29. Notes. Illus.: Photo. B&W. 8. Lang.: Eng.
Ireland. France. 1950-1989. Critical studies. ▪Breaks down the text of Beckett's later plays *Not I, Stirring Still, Lessness, What Where*, and *That Time* to gauge the playwright's development.

3211 Saag, Kristjan. "Låt Godot vara utan ursprung!" (Let Godot Be Without Any Origin!)*Entré*. 1998; 25(1): 39. Lang.: Swe.
Ireland. France. 1953-1998. Critical studies. ▪Appeal to let Godot and other characters be as they are, and not try to create their genealogies, such as relating Beckett's Godot with Balzac's Godot in *Mercadet*.

3212 Sullivan, Esther Beth. "What Is 'Left to a Woman of the House' When the Irish Situation Is Staged?" 213-226 in Colleran, Jeanne, ed.; Spencer, Jenny S., ed. *Staging Resistance: Essays on Political Theatre*. Ann Arbor, MI: Univ of Michigan P; 1998. 312 pp. (Theater: Theory/Text/Performance.) Notes. Index. Lang.: Eng.
Ireland: Dublin. UK-Ireland: Belfast. 1993-1996. Historical studies. ▪The response to recent Irish history in recent Irish theatre, with reference to plays by Anne Devlin, *Did You Hear the One about the Irishman* and *The Belle of Belfast City* by Christina Reid, Charabanc Theatre Company, and the Abbey's production of *The Gift of the Gorgon* by Peter Shaffer.

3213 Sung, Hae-Kyung. "The Poetics of Purgatory: A Consideration of Yeats's Use of *Nō* Form." *CLS*. 1998; 35(2): 107-115 . Notes. Lang.: Eng.
Ireland. 1914-1939. Critical studies. ▪Influence of Japanese *nō* technique on the writing style of William Butler Yeats.

3214 Teevan, Colin. "Northern Ireland: Our Troy? Recent Versions of Greek Tragedies by Irish Writers." *MD*. 1998 Spr; 41(1): 77-89. Notes. Lang.: Eng.
Ireland. UK-Ireland. 1984-1998. Critical studies. ▪Discusses the merits of various adaptations and translations of Greek tragedy by Irish writers. Plays cited are Tom Paulin's *The Riot Act*, based on Sophocles' *Antigone*, and *Seize the Fire*, based on Aeschylus' *Prometheus Desmotes (Prometheus Bound)*, Brendan Kennelly's translations of *Antigone, Medea*, and *Troádes (The Trojan Women)*, and Seamus Heaney's *The Cure at Troy*, based on Sophocles' *Philoctetes*.

3215 White, Harry. "'Something Is Taking its Course': Dramatic Exactitude and the Paradigm of Serialism in Samuel Beckett." 159-171 in Bryden, Mary, ed. *Samuel Beckett and Music*. Oxford: Clarendon; 1998. 267 pp. Index. Notes. Biblio. Lang.: Eng.
Ireland. France. 1945-1995. Critical studies. ▪Uses the notion of serialism in modern music to analyze the works of Samuel Beckett.

3216 Wolf, Matt. "Martin McDonagh on a Tear." *AmTh*. 1998 Jan.; 15(1): 48-50. Illus.: Dwg. B&W. 2. Lang.: Eng.
Ireland. 1998. Critical studies. ▪Profile of the Irish playwright as his plays *The Beauty Queen of Leenane* and *The Cripple of Inishmaan* make their mark in New York City.

3217 Laor, Dan. "Theatrical Interpretation of the Shoah: Image and Counter-Image." 94-110 in Schumacher, Claude, ed. *Staging the Holocaust: The Shoah in Drama and Performance*. Cambridge: Cambridge UP; 1998. 355 pp. (Cambridge Studies in Modern Theatre.) Index. Notes. Biblio. Illus.: Photo. 2. Lang.: Eng.
Israel. 1944-1995. Historical studies. ▪Changing attitudes toward the Holocaust, as reflected in public discourse and in the treatment of two major historical figures, Hannah Szenes and Israel Kasztner.

3218 Rokem, Freddie. "On the Fantastic in Holocaust Performances." 40-52 in Schumacher, Claude, ed. *Staging the Holocaust: The Shoah in Drama and Performance*. Cambridge: Cambridge UP; 1998. 355 pp. (Cambridge Studies in Modern Theatre.) Index. Notes. Biblio. Lang.: Eng.
Israel. 1980-1995. Historical studies. ▪Explores the limits of representability which contemporary Israeli performers try to extend in order to elicit emotional and intellectual responses. Uses Danny Horowitz's *Uncle Artur* as an example.

3219 "Lettere intorno a *Non si sa come*." (Letters Around *How Is Unknown*.) *IlCast*. 1998; 11(33): 94-99. Notes. Lang.: Ita.
Italy. Austria: Vienna. 1934. Critical studies. ▪Analysis of correspondence among playwright Luigi Pirandello, actor Alexandër Moissiu, and Volkstheater superintendent Rolf Jahn regarding a production of Pirandello's *Non si sa come (How Is Unknown)*.

3220 Acerboni, Giovanni. "Cletto Arrighi e il Teatro Milanese (1869-1876)." (Cletto Arrighi and the Milanese Theatre, 1869-1876.) (Le fonti dello spettacolo teatrale 4.) Notes. Biblio. Index. Append. Lang.: Ita.
Italy: Milan. 1869-1876. Critical studies. ▪The dramas of Cletto Arrighi in the context of Milanese theatrical life.

3221 Alonge, Roberto. "Ritratto di Giacinta." (Portrait of Giacinta.) *IlCast*. 1998; 11(32): 51-68. Notes. Lang.: Ita.
Italy: Venice. 1761. Critical studies. ▪Analysis of the character Giacinta in Goldoni's *Trilogia della villeggiatura (Holiday Trilogy)* as representative of moral disorder in the decaying bourgeoisie.

3222 Artioli, Umberto. "Metafora marina e flusso pneumatico nel carteggio tra Pirandello e la Abba." (Marine Metaphor and Pneumatic Flow in the Correspondence Between Pirandello and Abba.) *IlCast*. 1998; 11(33): 13-31. Notes. Lang.: Ita.
Italy. 1925-1936. Critical studies. ▪Examines the correspondence between playwright Luigi Pirandello and actress Marta Abba in the context of the themes and figures of late Pirandellian artistic production.

3223 Barbina, Alfredo. "Editori di Pirandello." (Pirandello's Publishers.) *Ariel*. 1998; 13(1-2): 257-352. Notes. Lang.: Ita.
Italy. 1888-1936. Historical studies. ▪The difficult relationship between Luigi Pirandello and his publishers until his death.

3224 Barbina, Alfredo. *Elegie ad Amaranta. Ricerche e documenti su Rosso di San Secondo*. (Elegies to Amaranta: Research

DRAMA: —Plays/librettos/scripts

and Documents on Rosso di San Secondo.) Rome: Bulzoni; 1998. 187 pp. (La fenice dei teatri 8.) Biblio. Illus.: Photo. Sketches. B&W. 7. Lang.: Ita.
Italy. 1908-1956. Critical studies. ■A study of the dramatic works of Pier Maria Rosso di San Secondo with a complete critical bibliography of his works from 1908 to 1987.

3225 Barbina, Alfredo. *L'ombra e lo specchio. Pirandello e l'arte del tradurre.* (Mirror and Shadow: Pirandello and the Art of Translation.) Rome: Bulzoni; 1998. 288 pp. (Pubblicazioni dell'Istituto di Studi Pirandelliani 9.) Notes. Lang.: Ita.
Italy. 1886-1936. Critical studies. ■The activity of Luigi Pirandello as a translator.

3226 Bartalini, Paola. *Il teatro di Enrico Bassano fra poesia e impegno civile.* (The Theatre of Enrico Bassano Between Poetry and Civil Obligation.) Genova: Erga; 1998. 145 pp. Notes. Biblio. Illus.: Photo. B&W. 5. Lang.: Ita.
Italy. 1899-1979. Critical studies. ■The plays of the Italian journalist, writer, and theatre critic, Enrico Bassano.

3227 Bazzocchi, Marco Antonio. *Pier Paolo Pasolini.* Milan: Bruno Mondadori; 1998. 233 pp. (Biblioteca degli scrittori.) Index. Biblio. Lang.: Ita.
Italy. 1922-1975. Biographical studies. ■Writer, playwright, director Pier Paolo Pasolini.

3228 Bertolone, Paola. "Appunti per un'interpretazione dei copioni teatrali di Eleonora Duse." (Notes for An Interpretation of the Theatrical Scripts of Eleonora Duse.) *BiT.* 1998; 45/47: 11-34. Notes. Lang.: Ita.
Italy. 1858-1924. Critical studies. ■Analyzes some theatrical scripts of the Italian actress Eleonora Duse, belonging to the Fondazione Cini in Venice.

3229 Bini, Daniela. "Epistolario a teatro. Scrittura dell'assenza e sublimazione dell'erotismo." (Theatre Letters: The Writing of Absence and Sublimated Eroticism.) *IlCast.* 1998; 11(33): 32-46. Notes. Lang.: Ita.
Italy. 1925-1936. Critical studies. ■The relationship between the letters of playwright Luigi Pirandello to actress Marta Abba and the creation of his characters. Argues that Pirandello created a fictional Marta character who replies to questions unanswered in the letters.

3230 Budor, Dominique. "Pirandello, 'Lettere a Marta Abba': intenzionalità e fruizione della lettera." (Pirandello, 'Letters to Marta Abba': Intentionality and Fruition of the Letter.) *IlCast.* 1998; 11(33): 47-55. Notes. Lang.: Ita.
Italy. 1925-1936. Biographical studies. ■The letter as a privileged area of expression that allows for playwright Luigi Pirandello's outbursts of sentiment for the Italian actress Marta Abba.

3231 Chotjewitz-Häfner, Renate. "Das Theater um Dario Fo." (The Theatre about Dario Fo.) *DB.* 1998; 4: 15-19. Illus.: Photo. B&W. 3. Lang.: Ger.
Italy. 1997-1998. Critical studies. ■Portrait of playwright, director and actor Dario Fo, his aesthetic philosophy and form of political theatre reflected in his new play *Il diavolo con le zinne (The Devil with Breasts).* Describes his increasing reputation in Italy after winning the Nobel Prize for literature in 1997.

3232 D'Amico, Alessandro. "Per un primo bilancio." (Toward a Preliminary Assessment.) *IlCast.* 1998; 11(33): 56-60. Lang.: Ita.
Italy. Critical studies. ■Argues that the letters between playwright Luigi Pirandello and actress Marta Alba shed new light on their relationship and demonstrate that Abba did not take advantage of the older man's love.

3233 D'Amico, Sivio; Livio, Gigi, ed. "Resoconto di una cena alla Taverna del Quirinale." (A Report on a Dinner at the 'Taverna del Quirinale'.) *IlCast.* 1998; 11(33): 89-93. Lang.: Ita.
Italy: Rome. 1933. Histories-sources. ■Critic and theatre historian Silvio D'Amico's account of a dinner at which playwright Luigi Pirandello and actress Marta Abba were present.

3234 D'Annunzio, Gabriele; Andreoli, Annamaria, ed. *La nemica. Il debutto teatrale e altri scritti inediti (1888-1892).* (The Enemy. The Theatrical Debut and Other Unpublished Writings, 1888-1892.) Milan: Mondadori; 1998. 244 pp. Notes. Lang.: Ita.
Italy. 1888-1892. Histories-sources. ■A collection of previously unpublished preparatory writings by Gabriele D'Annunzio for his plays and novels.

3235 da Vinci Nichols, Nina. "Pirandello, the Sacred, and the Death of Tragedy." *CompD.* 1998 Sum; 32(2): 240-251. Notes. Lang.: Eng.
Italy. 1936. Critical studies. ■Pirandello's unfinished play *I giganti della montagna (The Mountain Giants)* and his belief in the superiority of imagination over reason.

3236 Decroisette, Françoise. "Le villeggiature prima delle villeggiature." (Holidays Before the *Holiday Trilogy.*) *IlCast.* 1998; 11(32): 35-50. Notes. Lang.: Ita.
Italy. 1751-1761. Critical studies. ■The variety of settings in Goldoni's *Trilogia della villegiatura.*

3237 Doroni, Stefano. *Dall'androne medievale al tinello borghese. Il teatro di Giuseppe Giacosa.* (From the Medieval Hall to the Bourgeois Breakfast Room: Giuseppe Giacosa's Theatre.) Rome: Bulzoni; 1998. 230 pp. (Biblioteca di cultura, 551.) Notes. Biblio. Index. Lang.: Ita.
Italy. 1847-1906. Critical studies. ■Analysis of the dramatic works of Giuseppe Giacosa.

3238 Farrell, Joseph. "Variations on a Theme: Respecting Dario Fo." *MD.* 1998 Spr; 41(1): 19-29. Notes. Lang.: Eng.
Italy. 1978-1998. Critical studies. ■The difficulty of respecting authorial intent when translating Fo's plays. Fo has been known to object to certain published translations, particularly his more political pieces.

3239 Giani, Roberta. "Malaparte e la scena: i suoi scritti teatrali. Con una appendice di lettere inedite di Guido Salvini." (Malaparte and the Stage: His Theatrical Writings.) *Ariel.* 1998; 13(3): 55-113. Notes. [With an appendix of unpublished letters by Guido Salvini.] Lang.: Ita.
Italy. 1905-1956. Historical studies. ■The dramas of the Italian writer Curzio Malaparte and his relationship and collaboration with Guido Salvini.

3240 Giannetti, Laura. *Discourses of Play in Italian Renaissance Comedy.* Storrs, CT: Univ. of Connecticut; 1998. 232 pp. Biblio. Notes. [Ph.D. Dissertation, Univ. Microfilms Order No. AAC 9831876.] Lang.: Ita.
Italy. 1500-1700. Critical studies. ■The imporatance of the ludic dimension in *Cassaria* by Ludovico Ariosto, *La Calandria* by Bernardo Dovizi da Bibbiena, the anonymous *Venexiana* and Girolamo Bargagli's *La Pellegrina.*

3241 Goldoni, Carlo; Casas, Joan, transl. *Memòries.* (Memoirs.) Barcelona: Institut del Teatre de la Disputació de Barcelona; 1999. 747 pp. (Escrits Teòrics 4.) Pref. Notes. Biblio. Lang.: Cat.
Italy. 1707-1793. Histories-sources. ■Memoirs of playwright Goldoni translated into Catalan, with an introduction by the translator.

3242 Holden, Joan. "Fo's Nobel." *ThM.* 1998; 28(2): 7-9. Illus.: Photo. B&W. 1. Lang.: Eng.
Italy. 1998. Critical studies. ■Note on the shock registered among right and left wing political figures over the Nobel Prize for literature being awarded to satirical playwright and performer Dario Fo.

3243 Jenkins, Ron. "The Nobel Jester." *AmTh.* 1998 Feb.; 15(2): 22-24. Illus.: Dwg. Photo. B&W. 5. Lang.: Eng.
Italy. 1998. Biographical studies. ■Profile of Nobel Prize winning playwright Dario Fo, with a sidebar excerpt from his monolgue *Johan Padan.*

3244 Langston, Ann Lizbeth. *Gender and the Comic in the Works of Alessandro Piccolomini.* Riverside, CA: Univ. of California; 1998. 172 pp. Biblio. Notes. [Ph.D. Dissertation, Univ. Microfilms Order No. AAC 9906952.] Lang.: Eng.
Italy. 1508-1578. Critical studies. ■Analysis of the works of the Italian Renaissance playwright, including *Amor Costante (Faithful Love), Alessandro,* and *Dialogo de la Bella Creanza de le Donne, o Raffaella (Dialogue on the Fine Manners of Women, or Raffaella).*

3245 Lauretta, Enzo. "Nota in margine." (A Note in the Margin.) *IlCast.* 1998; 11(33): 61-63. Lang.: Ita.

DRAMA: —Plays/librettos/scripts

Italy. 1925-1936. Critical studies. ■Argues that an analysis of the letters of Luigi Pirandello and Marta Abba is fundamental to re-thinking the Pirandellian biography, as well as Pirandello's conception of actors.

3246 Lazzarini-Dossin, Muriel. *Pirandello e il teatro contemporaneo: La dimostrazione di un errore.* (Pirandello and Contemporary Theatre: The Demonstration of an Error.) Rome: Bulzoni; 1998. 94 pp. Pref. Biblio. Lang.: Ita.

Italy. France. 1998. Critical studies. ■Analysis of the influence of Pirandello's theatre on the French theatre.

3247 Lepschy, Anna Laura, ed. *Pirandello Studies: Journal of the Society for Pirandello Studies, 17.* Canterbury: Univ. of Kent; 1997. 89 pp. Notes. Biblio. Illus.: Photo. B&W. 2. [Formerly *Yearbook of the Society for Pirandello Studies.*] Lang.: Eng.

Italy. 1589-1926. Critical studies. ■Yearbook dedicated to the study of Pirandello which contains material on his letter writing, his plays *The Grafting (L'innesto)* and *Right You Are, If You Think You Are (Così è (se vi pare))*, and the role of the inamorata from *commedia dell'arte* onwards.

3248 Lo Russo, Rosaria. "La primadonna e la dea." (The Primadonna and the Goddess.) *IlCast.* 1998; 11(33): 64-86. Notes. Lang.: Ita.

Italy: Rome. 1925-1927. Critical studies. ■Examines actress Marta Abba's role as the leading actress of the Teatro d'Arte, directed by playwright Luigi Pirandello, and also her role as the 'privileged' interlocutor of Pirandello's dramaturgy from 1925 to 1927.

3249 Manetta, Marco. *Luigi Pirandello.* Milan: Bruno Mondadori; 1998. 304 pp. (Biblioteca degli scrittori.) Index. Biblio. Lang.: Ita.

Italy. 1867-1936. Biographical studies. ■The life and work of playwright Luigi Pirandello.

3250 Manzoni, Giacomo; Redfern, Walter, transl. "Towards a *Parole da Beckett.*" 213-232 in Bryden, Mary, ed. *Samuel Beckett and Music.* Oxford: Clarendon; 1998. 267 pp. Index. Notes. Biblio. Tables. Illus.: Sketches. 2. Lang.: Eng.

Italy. 1970-1971. Histories-sources. ■Composer Giacomo Manzoni and his work *Parole da Beckett (Words by Beckett).*

3251 Melchiori, Angiolina. *Emblems of Renaissance Theatre: A Study of Aretino's Comedies.* New Haven, CT: Yale Univ; 1988. 190 pp. Notes. Biblio. [Ph.D. Dissertation, Univ. Microfilms Order No. AAC 9009461.] Lang.: Eng.

Italy. 1534-1556. Critical studies. ■Focuses on the court as a stage, the power of imagination and the constant attempt to limit it, and the importance of verbal action in *La Cortigiana, La Talanta, Lo Ipocrito, Il Marescalco* and *Il Filosofo* by Pietro Aretino.

3252 Morelli, Giovanni. *Paradosso del farmacista. Il Metastasio nella morsa del tranquillante.* (The Druggist's Paradox: Metastasio in the Grip of Tranquilizers.) Venice: Marsilio; 1998. 297 pp. (Presente storico 8.) Lang.: Ita.

Italy. 1698-1782. Biographical studies. ■The life and works of poet and playwright Pietro Metastasio.

3253 Moretti, Mario; Downward, Lisa, transl. "Italian Drama from the Post World War II Period to Today." *WES.* 1998 Win; 10 (1): 5-8. Illus.: Photo. B&W. 1. Lang.: Eng.

Italy. 1945-1998. Historical studies. ■Development and influences of Italian playwrights over the last fifty-three years.

3254 Moscati, Italo, ed. *Il cattivo Eduardo. Un artista troppo amato e troppo odiato.* (Naughty Eduardo: An Artist Too Much Loved and Too Much Hated.) Venice: Marsilio; 1998. 222 pp. (Ricerche.) Biblio. Append. Illus.: Photo. B&W. 30. Lang.: Ita.

Italy. 1900-1984. Biographical studies. ■A collection of essays on playwright, actor, and director Eduardo De Filippo written by Italian critics, actors, and actresses who worked with him.

3255 Ortolani, Benito. "L'epistolario Pirandello-Abba: lo stato dell'arte." (The Letters Between Pirandello and Abba: The State of the Art.) *IlCast.* 1998; 11(33): 6-12. Lang.: Ita.

Italy. 1925-1936. Biographical studies. ■Analysis of the letters of Luigi Pirandello and Marta Abba with respect to the playwright's attempt to impose the 'theatre of art' on the Italian theatre society of the twenties and thirties, and on his passionate love for Abba.

3256 Owens, Melody Sue. *The Montecassino Passion Play: Theatre in a Monastic Community.* Berkeley, CA: Univ. of California; 1987. 311 pp. Notes. Biblio. [Ph.D. Dissertation, Univ. Microfilms Order No. 8726324.] Lang.: Eng.

Italy. 1100-1200. Critical studies. ■Compares the Montecassino Passion, the earliest known Latin Passion play, with Latin and vernacular passion plays and religious dramas in an attempt to define those qualities that make it particularly stageworthy: its structure, language, dramatic roles, and *mise-en-scène.*

3257 Patapan, Haig. "All's Fair in Love and War: Machiavelli's *Clizia.*" *HPT.* 1998 Win; 19(4): 531-551. Notes. Lang.: Eng.

Italy. 1525. Critical studies. ■Analysis of Machiavelli's comedy as a cautionary tale to instruct future princes about the pitfalls of love.

3258 Pieri, Marzia. "'Grandi intrecci' e 'grandi passioni': dittici e trilogie in Goldoni." (Great Intrigue and Great Passions: Diptychs and Trilogies in Goldoni.) *IlCast.* 1998; 11(32): 15-34. Notes. Lang.: Ita.

Italy: Venice. 1707-1793. Critical studies. ■A study of Goldoni's serial comedies, from *Momolo* to *Zelinda and Lindoro (Zelinda e Lindoro).*

3259 Providenti, Elio. "Lo zio canonico." (The Clerical Uncle.) *Ariel.* 1998; 13(1-2): 249-256. Notes. Lang.: Ita.

Italy. 1784-1863. Biographical studies. ■An essay on Luigi Pirandello's great-uncle, Innocenzo Ricci Gramitto, a priest.

3260 Sfyris, Panagiotis. *Italian Realist Drama, 1860-1918.* New York, NY: City Univ. of New York; 1998. 821 pp. Notes. Biblio. [Ph.D. Dissertation, Univ. Microfilms Order No. AAC 9820578.] Lang.: Eng.

Italy. 1860-1918. Histories-specific. ■The aesthetics and the sociology of the drama that developed in Italy during the first fifty years of its existence as a unified independent European nation. Playwrights whose works are examined include Paolo Giacometti, Teobaldo Ciconi, Paolo Ferrari, Achille Torelli, Giovanni Verga, Giuseppe Giacosa, Gerolamo Rovetta, Marco Praga, E.A. Butti, Roberto Bracco, Sabatino Lopez and Dario Niccodemi.

3261 Sommaiolo, Paolo; D'Aponte, Mimi Gisolfi, transl. "The New Neapolitan Dramaturgy of the 1980s." *WES.* 1998 Win; 10(1): 33-38. Illus.: Photo. B&W. 2. Lang.: Eng.

Italy: Naples. 1980-1989. Historical studies. ■Emergence of young playwrights from the experimental scene of the 1960s and 70s into preeminence during the 1980s. Playwrights focused on are Annibale Ruccello, Manlio Santanelli, and Enzo Moscato.

3262 Taffon, Giorgio. "Ripensare Testori e il suo teatro." (Rethinking Testori and His Theatre.) *Ariel.* 1998; 13(3): 115-128 . Notes. Illus.: Photo. PR. 2. Lang.: Ita.

Italy. 1923-1997. Critical studies. ■Theatrical writings of the Italian writer Giovanni Testori and the stagings of his dramas.

3263 Trebbi, Fernando. *Le porte dell'ombra: sul teatro di D'Annunzio.* (The Doors of Shadow: On D'Annunzio's Theatre.) Rome: Bulzoni; 1998. 260 pp. (Biblioteca Teatrale 99.) Lang.: Ita.

Italy. 1863-1938. Critical studies. ■A study on the theatre of Gabriele D'Annunzio.

3264 Watson, William Van. *Pier Paolo Pasolini and the Theatre of the Word.* Austin, TX: Univ. of Texas; 1987. 395 pp. Biblio. Notes. [Ph.D. Dissertation, Univ. Microfilms Order No. 8806433.] Lang.: Eng.

Italy. 1960-1970. Critical studies. ■Examines the theories and production practices of playwright/film director/theorist Pier Paolo Pasolini as reflected in his 'theatrical manifesto' and plays of the 1960s. Plays include *Calderon, Affabulazione, Pilade,* and *Orgy.*

3265 Wing, Joylynn W.D. *Techniques of Opposition in the Work of Dario Fo.* Stanford, CA: Stanford Univ; 1988. 194 pp. Biblio. Notes. [Ph.D. Dissertation, Univ. Microfilms Order No. AAC 8826266.] Lang.: Eng.

Italy. 1950-1988. Critical studies. ■How Fo's writing and staging techniques undermine his representations of authority.

DRAMA: —Plays/librettos/scripts

3266 Ndigirigi, Josphat Gichingiri. *Ngugi wa Thiong'o's Drama and the Kamiriithu Popular Theatre Experiment.* Los Angeles, CA: Univ. of California; 1998. 328 pp. Notes. Biblio. [Ph.D. Dissertation, Univ. Microfilms Order No. AAC 9823554.] Lang.: Eng.

Kenya: Kamiriithu. 1979-1992. Critical studies. ▪Examines the plays of Ngugi wa Thiong'o in the context of the aesthetic and social dimensions of the Kamiriithu theatre project (plays written for the local community in the village of Kamiriithu). Analyzes *The Trial of Dedan Kimathi, Ngaahika Ndeenda*, and *Maitu Njugira.*

3267 Berg, Eliana Goulart. *The Discourse of Cruelty and the Absurd and the Representation of Difference in the Theatre of Women Playwrights in Latin America.* Madison, WI: Univ. of Wisconsin; 1998. 337 pp. Biblio. Notes. [Ph.D. Dissertation, Univ. Microfilms Order No. AAC 9824587.] Lang.: Eng.

Latin America. 1960-1980. Critical studies. ▪Examines the juncture between Latin American women's dramaturgy and feminism through the theoretical perspective of absurd and cruel drama, with respect to *Fala baixo senão eu grito (Speak Softly, Or I'll Scream)*, *Jorginho, o Machao (Jorginho, the Stud)* and *Roda cor de roda* by Leilah Assunção, *Prova de fogo (Trial by Fire)*, *A flor da pele (Skin Deep)*, *Caminho de volta (Return Trip)* and *O grande amor de nossas vidas (The Great Love of Our Lives)* by Consuelo de Castro, *Los siameses (The Siamese Twins)*, *El campo (The Camp)*, *Decir sí (To Say Yes)* and *El despojamiento (The Plundering)* by Griselda Gambaro, and *Andarse por las ramas (Beating Around the Bush)*, *La señora en su balcón (The Lady on the Balcony)*, *Los perros (The Dogs)*, and *El árbol (The Tree)* by Mexican playwright Elena Garro.

3268 Sassine, Antoun S. *Le voyage dans le théâtre de Georges Schéhadé.* (The Journey in Plays of Georges Schéhadé.) Detroit, MI: Wayne State Univ; 1988. 165 pp. Biblio. Notes. [Ph.D. Dissertation, Univ. Microfilms Order No. AAC 8910376.] Lang.: Fre.

Lebanon. 1940-1989. Critical studies. ▪The concept of the journey in plays of Georges Schéhadé, including discussion of the effects of journeys on plot, the major traveling characters, and their symbolic aspects.

3269 Hawkes, Sophie. *The Drama of Liberation: Part I. A Comparative Study of Aimé Césaire's Theater. Part II. A Translation of Césaire's* And the Dogs Were Silent. New York, NY: New York Univ; 1987. 213 pp. Notes. Biblio. [Ph.D. Dissertation, Univ. Microfilms Order No. AAC 8722756.] Lang.: Eng.

Martinique. 1946-1969. Critical studies. ▪Analysis of Césaire's first play *Et les Chiens se taisaient* and its affiliations with surrealism, the theories of Bertolt Brecht, and modern tragedy, and with respect to Césaire's dramatic vision as a whole with reference to his later works, *La Tragédie du roi Christophe*, *Une Saison au Congo*, and *Une Tempête.* Includes an original English translation of the play.

3270 Miller, Judith G. "Caribbean Women Playwrights: Madness, Memory, but Not Melancholia." *ThR.* 1998 Fall; 23(3): 225-232. Notes. Lang.: Eng.

Martinique. Guadeloupe. 1975-1998. Critical studies. ▪The interplay of physical bodies in the process of celebration in the plays of Simone Schwarz-Bart and Ina Césaire. Compares these works to those of Marguerite Duras.

3271 Upton, Carole-Anne. "The French-Speaking Caribbean: Journeying from the Native Land." 97-125 in Boon, Richard, ed.; Plastow, Jane, ed. *Theatre Matters: Performance and Culture on the World Stage.* Cambridge: Cambridge UP; 1998. 203 pp. (Cambridge Studies in Modern Theatre.) Notes. Index. Pref. Lang.: Eng.

Martinique. 1970-1995. Historical studies. ▪Political, ideological, and cultural identity in plays by Daniel Boukman.

3272 Arrizón, Alicia. "*Soldaderas* and the Staging of the Mexican Revolution." *TDR.* 1998 Spr; 42(1): 90-112. Notes. Biblio. Illus.: Photo. Pntg. Dwg. 5. Lang.: Eng.

Mexico. 1938. Critical studies. ▪Analysis of *Soldadera* by Josefina Niggli, with emphasis on its social and political ramifications, as well as audience reception in Mexico and the US.

3273 Bixler, Jacqueline E. "*Krísis*, Crisis, and the Politics of Representation." *Gestos.* 1998 Nov.; 13(26): 83-97. Notes. Biblio. Lang.: Eng.

Mexico. 1996. Critical studies. ▪The representation of current Mexican politics in Sabina Berman's *Krísis (Crisis).*

3274 Calderón, Luis Antonio. *El Miedo: Elemento de contacto existencialista en las obras dramáticas de Albert Camus y de Carlos Solórzano.* (Fear: Existentialist Point of Contact in the Dramatic Works of Albert Camus and Carlos Solórzano.) Athens, GA: Univ. of Georgia; 1988. 261 pp. Notes. Biblio. [Ph.D. Dissertation, Univ. Microfilms Order No. AAC 8823771.] Lang.: Spa.

Mexico. France. 1948-1955. Critical studies. ▪The conquering of fear as a key element in the postwar existentialist drama of Camus and Solórzano.

3275 Kelty, Mark James. *Jesusa Rodríguez: Mexico City's Postmodern/Permanent Revolutionary.* Columbia, MO: Univ. of Missouri; 1998. 256 pp. Notes. Biblio. [Ph.D. Dissertation, Univ. Microfilms Order No. AAC 9901247.] Lang.: Eng.

Mexico. 1970-1992. Critical studies. ▪Playwright/director/performer Jesusa Rodríguez's satirical treatment of Mexican society, politics, and government in her nativity pastoral, *La mano que mece el pesebre (The Hand that Rocks the Manger).*

3276 Moreno, Iani del Rosario. "La cultura 'Pulp' en dos obras: *Krísis* de Sabina Berman y *Pulp Fiction* de Quentin Tarantino." (The 'Pulp' Culture in Two Works: *Crisis* by Sabina Berman and *Pulp Fiction* by Quentin Tarantino.) *Gestos.* 1998 Nov.; 13(26): 67-82. Notes. Biblio. Lang.: Spa.

Mexico. USA. 1993-1996. Critical studies. ▪Comparison of Berman's play and Tarantino's film.

3277 Kirdjašov, V.F.; Merkuškina, L.G.; Poljakov, O.E. *Gorenie ščedroj duši: G.Ja. Merkuškin: Ličnost' i nasledie.* (Heart of a Generous Soul: G. Ja. Merkuškin: Identity and Inheritance.) Saransk: 1998. 264 pp. Lang.: Rus.

Mordovia. Histories-sources. ▪Materials on Mordovian playwright G. Ja. Merkuškin.

3278 Callens, Johan. *Acte(s) de présence: Teksten over Engelstalig in Vlaanderen en Nederland.* (Making an Apearance: Texts on Anglo-American Theatre in Flanders and the Netherlands.) Brussels: VUB Press; 1996. 199 pp. Lang.: Dut.

Netherlands. 1920-1998. Critical studies. ▪English-language plays on the Dutch and Flemish stage. Includes essays on O'Neill, Beckett, Pinter, Stein, Mamet, Shepard, Bond, Berkoff, and Jane Bowles.

3279 Rowell, Charles H. "An interview with Thea Doelwijt." *Callaloo.* 1998 Sum; 21(3): 611-613. Lang.: Eng.

Netherlands. Suriname. 1988. Histories-sources. ▪Interview with the Surinamese playwright regarding the differences between writing for a Dutch audience and for an audience in her native country.

3280 Simons, Johan. "Für ein Theater mitten in der Wirklichkeit." (For a Theatre in the Midst of Reality.) *dRAMATURg.* 1998; 1: 14-18. Illus.: Photo. B&W. 2. Lang.: Ger.

Netherlands: Amsterdam. 1985-1998. Histories-sources. ▪Director Simons, of Hollandia, an independent company, describes approaches to a theatre that reflects social and political debates. Describes the importance of choosing the right places and themes for a relevant theatre.

3281 Ranald, Margaret Loftus. "War, Male Contact Sports, and the Flight from Women." *ThR.* 1998 Spr; 23(1): 59-68. Notes. Lang.: Eng.

New Zealand. Europe. 1998. Critical studies. ▪The nature and role of women in the Shakespeare canon and in male contact sports, analyzed as a peacetime metaphor of war, where women are likewise excluded or circumscribed. Specifically considers playwright Greg McGee's play about rugby, *Foreskin's Lament.*

3282 Dunton, Chris. "*Sologa*, *Eneka*, and *The Supreme Commander*: The Theatre of Ken Saro-Wiwa." *RAL.* 1998 Spr; 29(1): 153-162. Notes. Pref. Biblio. Lang.: Eng.

Nigeria. 1971-1991. Critical studies. ▪Analysis of three unpublished plays of Saro-Wiwa: *The Supreme Commander*, *Eneka*, and *Dream of Sologa.*

DRAMA: —Plays/librettos/scripts

3283 Hogan, Patrick Colm. "Particular Myths, Universal Ethics: Wole Soyinka's *The Swamp Dwellers* in the New Nigeria." *MD.* 1998 Win; 41(4): 584-595. Notes. Lang.: Eng.
Nigeria. 1973. Critical studies. ■Soyinka's views on the cultural, ancestral, and sociological state of Nigeria as reflected in his play.

3284 Nwankwo, Nkeonye Caroline. *Drama as a Socio-Political Criticism in Nigeria: Wole Soyinka.* Los Angeles, CA: Univ. of California; 1987. 383 pp. Notes. Biblio. [Ph.D. Dissertation, Univ. Microfilms Order No. 8803653.] Lang.: Eng.
Nigeria. 1960-1979. Critical studies. ■Ideology, sociology and politics in the plays of Wole Soyinka, with attention to his use of satire as socio-political criticism. Works examined include *The Trials of Brother Jero, A Dance of the Forests, Kongi's Harvest, Madmen and Specialists, Jero's Metamorphosis* and *Opera Wonyosi.*

3285 Ogúndèjì, Philip Adédọ̀tun. "The Image of Ṣàngó in Duro Ladipọ's Plays." *RAL.* 1998 Sum; 29(2): 57-75. Notes. Pref. Biblio. Gloss. Lang.: Eng.
Nigeria. 1964-1970. Critical studies. ■Representation of the character of Ṣàngó in *Ọba Kó So (The King Did Not Hang), Ọ̀ṣun,* and *Ọbàtálá.*

3286 Osofisan, Femi. "'The Revolution as Muse': Drama as Surreptitious Insurrection in a Post-Colonial, Military State." 11-35 in Boon, Richard, ed.; Plastow, Jane, ed. *Theatre Matters: Performance and Culture on the World Stage.* Cambridge: Cambridge UP; 1998. 203 pp. (Cambridge Studies in Modern Theatre.) Notes. Index. Pref. Lang.: Eng.
Nigeria. 1978. Histories-sources. ■Propaganda tactics used by the author in his play *Once Upon Four Robbers,* among others, to influence and change cultural, social, and political perspectives of the ruling classes.

3287 Willingham, Camille Aljean. *The Tragedy of Uncertain Continuity: John Bekederemo and Wole Soyinka.* Providence, RI: Brown Univ; 1998. 163 pp. Notes. Biblio. [Ph.D. Dissertation, Univ. Microfilms Order No. AAC 9830562.] Lang.: Eng.
Nigeria. 1965-1998. Critical studies. ■The communal sense of ritual as a stylistic element in Bekederemo's *Song of a Goat* and *The Masquerade* and Soyinka's *The Strong Breed* and *Death and the King's Horseman.*

3288 Cirella, Anne Violette. *Avant-Gardism in Children's Theatre: The Use of Absurdist Techniques by Anglophone Children's Playwrights.* Austin, TX: Univ. of Texas; 1998. 245 pp. Biblio. Notes. [Ph.D. Dissertation, Univ. Microfilms Order No. AAC 9837931.] Lang.: Eng.
North America. Europe. 1896-1970. Critical studies. ■Compares the French theatre of the Absurd with the Anglophone Absurdist children's theatre of the 1960s. Considers the use of puppet theatre in Jarry's *Ubu Roi* and Aurand Harris's *Punch and Judy,* and the use of farce in Ionesco's *Les Chaises* and Mary Melwood's *The Tingalary Bird.*

3289 Edney, David. "Molière in North America: Problems of Translation and Adaptation." *MD.* 1998 Spr; 41(1): 60-76. Notes. Lang.: Eng.
North America. 1998. Critical studies. ■Argues that English-speaking translators of Molière in North America have led the audiences on that continent to view the playwright in a very different manner than their counterparts in France.

3290 Skloot, Robert. "'Where Does It Hurt?': Genocide, the Theatre and the Human Body." *ThR.* 1998 Spr; 23(1): 51-58. Notes. Lang.: Eng.
North America. UK-England. Argentina. 1998. Critical studies. ■The use of theatre to help create a world less violent and more protective of human life. Focuses on the concept of 'empathetic identification' and its use of pain as a frame for contemporary drama such as Griselda Gambaro's *El Campo (The Camp),* Arthur Kopit's *Indians,* and Peter Barnes's *Auschwitz.*

3291 Zlatescu, Andrei-Paul. *Prospero's Planet: Magic, Utopian and Allegorical Injunctions in the Rise of the Modern State.* London, ON: Univ. of Western Ontario; 1998. 125 pp. Biblio. Notes. [Ph.D. Dissertation, Univ. Microfilms Order No. AAC MQ30837.] Lang.: Eng.
North America. 1950-1995. Critical studies. ■Examines the statesman's role on the modern stage in terms of narrative strategies. Uses Shakespeare's *The Tempest* as a template to examine modern literary texts including plays.

3292 Baxter, Paul Sandvold. *Caesar Is my Captive: Hegel's Influence on Ibsen's Concept of Freedom.* Boston, MA: Boston Univ; 1998. 341 pp. Notes. Biblio. [Ph.D. Dissertation, Univ. Microfilms Order No. AAC 9811623.] Lang.: Eng.
Norway. Germany. 1870-1898. Critical studies. ■The influence of Hegelian philosophy on Ibsen's early epic play *Kejser og Galilaeer (The Emperor and the Galilean).*

3293 Elliott, Beverly Fritsch. *Ibsen's Women on Stage: Feminist and Anti-Feminist Reactions to Selected English Language Productions of* A Doll's House, Ghosts, *and* Hedda Gabler. Philadelphia, PA: Temple Univ; 1987. 326 pp. Biblio. Notes. [Ph.D. Dissertation, Univ. Microfilms Order No. 8711328.] Lang.: Eng.
Norway. 1879-1979. Critical studies. ■Argues that *A Doll's House (Et Dukkehjem), Ghosts (Gengangere),* and *Hedda Gabler* are feminist plays and have a bearing on the feminist movements in England and America. Focuses on English-language performances of Janet Achurch, Elizabeth Robins, Julia Cameron, Minnie Maddern Fiske, Alla Nazimova, Eva LeGallienne, Ruth Gordon, and others.

3294 Hawkins, Barrie. "*Hedda Gabler*: Eavesdropping on Real Events." *SATJ.* 1998 May/Sep.; 12(1/2): 109-136. Notes. Biblio. Lang.: Eng.
Norway. 1987. Critical studies. ■Analysis of Ibsen's play, with emphasis on his stage directions in the script.

3295 Leigh, James. "Ebb and Flow: Ibsen's *The Lady from the Sea* and the Possibility of Feminine Discourse." *MD.* 1998 Spr; 41(1): 119-133. Notes. Lang.: Eng.
Norway. 1888. Critical studies. ■The way in which the Norwegian language expresses male/female relationships in *Fruen fra havet,* with consideration of problems of translation into English.

3296 Markotic, Lorraine. "Epiphanic Transformations: Lou Andreas-Salomé's Reading of Nora, Rebecca and Ellida." *MD.* 1998 Fall; 41(3): 423-441. Notes. Lang.: Eng.
Norway. Germany. 1879-1906. Critical studies. ■Analysis of Andreas-Salomé's critical work *Henrik Ibsen's Frauen-Gestalten* (1906), focusing on his views on the central female characters in *A Doll's House (Et Dukkehjem), Rosmersholm,* and *The Lady from the Sea (Fruen fra havet).*

3297 Otten, Terry. "How Old Is Dr. Rank?" *MD.* 1998 Win; 41(4): 509-522. Notes. Lang.: Eng.
Norway. 1879. Critical studies. ■Analyzes the development of the character of Dr. Rank through Ibsen's revisions of *A Doll's House (Et Dukkehjem).*

3298 Stanton, Stephen S. "Trolls in Ibsen's Late Plays." *CompD.* 1998-99 Win; 32(4): 518-540. Notes. Lang.: Eng.
Norway. 1886-1894. Critical studies. ■Symbolic significance of trolls in Ibsen's *Little Eyolf (Lille Eyolf), Hedda Gabler, Rosmersholm, The Master Builder (Bygmester Solness),* and *The Lady from the Sea (Fruen fra havet).*

3299 Thresher, Tanya. *Seductive Strategies for Female Subjects: How Contemporary Scandinavian Women Dramatists Represent Woman on Stage.* Seattle, WA: Univ. of Washington; 1998. 204 pp. Biblio. Notes. [Ph.D. Dissertation, Univ. Microfilms Order No. AAC 9836264.] Lang.: Eng.
Norway. Sweden. Denmark. 1998. Critical studies. ■Seductive strategies that subvert hegemonic order in *Barock friise (Baroque Frieze)* by Cecilie Loveid, *Tant Blomma (Aunt Blomma)* by Kristina Lugn, and *Efter orgiet (After the Orgy)* by Suzanne Brogger.

3300 Timm, Mikael. "Är kulturen helt ofarlig?" (Is Culture Quite Harmless?)*Dramat.* 1998; 6(2): 20-21. Illus.: Photo. Color. Lang.: Swe.
Norway. 1882. ■A presentation of Henrik Ibsen as an author and as a man, with reference to his *En Folkefiende (An Enemy of the People)* and the critics of society.

3301 Chałupnik, Agata. "Sztandar ze spódnicy." (The Banner of the Skirt.) *DialogW.* 1998 Dec.; 12: 112-127. Illus.: Photo. Dwg. B&W. 8. Lang.: Pol.
Poland. 1885-1998. Critical studies. ■Feminist examination of the plays of Polish playwright Gabriela Zapolska, including *Moralność pani Duls-*

kiej (The Morality of Mrs. Dulska), Panna Maliczewska (Miss Maliczewska), Mężczyzna (The Man) and *Ich czworo (The Four of Them).*

3302 Ciechowicz, Jan. "Mickiewicz w badaniach teatrologicznych." (Mickiewicz in Theatre Research.) *DialogW.* 1998 May; 5: 117-130. Illus.: Photo. B&W. 4. Lang.: Pol.

Poland. 1843-1998. Critical studies. ■Examines current critical studies on playwright Adam Mickiewicz, especially on his most well-known work *Dziady (Forefathers' Eve).*

3303 Kuharski, Allen. "Performing History: A Translator's Introduction." *PerAJ.* 1998 Jan.; 20(58): 91-98. Notes. Illus.: Photo. B&W. 2. Lang.: Eng.

Poland. 1951-1998. Histories-sources. ■Translator relates the challenge of creating the English-language version of Witold Gombrowicz' unfinished play *History (Historia).* Includes background information on the play's own history.

3304 Masłowski, Michał. *Gest, symbol i rytuały polskiego teatru romantycznego.* (Gesture, Symbol and Rituals of the Polish Romantic Theatre.) Warsaw: Wydawnictwo Naukow PWN; 1998. 400 pp. Index. Pref. Biblio. Illus.: Photo. B&W. 15. Lang.: Pol.

Poland. 1832-1835. Critical studies. ■Anthropological analysis of the Polish national theatre style in Romantic dramas including *Dziady (Forefathers' Eve)* by Adam Mickiewicz, *Kordian (The Knot)* by Słowacki, and *Nie-boska komedia (The Un-Divine Comedy)* by Krasiński. Author specifically focuses on how this analysis can define and describe the Polish national theatre style.

3305 Pályi, András. *Suszterek és szalmabáb: Lengyel színházak, lengyel írók, lengyel sorsok.* (Shoemakers and a Man of Straw: Polish Theatres, Writers and Careers.) Pozsony: Kalligram; 1998. 638 pp. Index. Lang.: Hun.

Poland. 1960-1990. Critical studies. ■A volume of essays by the writer, translator, and critic the foremost expert of the Polish literature and theatre for three decades.

3306 Ratajczak, Dobrochna. "DOM emigracyjnego dramatu." (The Home of Drama in Exile.) 123-161 in Kalemba-Kasprzak, Elżbieta, ed.; Ratajczak, Dobrochna, ed. *Dramat i teatr emigracyjny po roku 1939.* Wroclaw: Wiedza o kulturze; 1998. 348 pp. Lang.: Pol.

Poland. UK-England. 1939-1984. Critical studies. ■The construction of home in Polish emigrant drama as a symbol of the lost country and the search for identity.

3307 Shmeruk, Chone. "Przegląd literatury dramatycznej w języku jidysz do I-ej wojny światowej." (Review of the Plays in Yiddish Up to World War I.) 31-51 in Kuligowska-Korzeniewska, Anna, ed.; Leyko, Małgorzata, ed. *Teatr żydowski w Polsce.* Lodz: Wydawnictwo Uniwersytetu Łódzkiego; 1998. 457 pp. Pref. Index. Illus.: Photo. B&W. 35. Lang.: Pol.

Poland. 1500-1914. Critical studies. ■Examines the influence of plays from the Enlightenment period on modern Jewish theatre in Yiddish, including the work of Abraham Goldfaden, Mendele Mojcher Sforim, Sholom Aleichem, and Icchok Lejbo Peretz.

3308 Sokół, Lech. "*Peer Gynt* jako wyzwanie." (*Peer Gynt* as a Challenge.) *DialogW.* 1998 Nov.; 11: 128-140. Illus.: Photo. B&W. 8. Lang.: Pol.

Poland. Norway. 1867-1967. Critical studies. ■The biographical background of Henrik Ibsen's *Peer Gynt*, said to be both a morality play and a realistic play, in light of the new Polish translation of the play by Zbigniew Krawczykowski, which presents Peer as a modern hero.

3309 Szpakowska, Małgorzata. "Starość? Nikt na to nie zasługuje." (Old Age? Nobody Deserves It.) *DialogW.* 1998 Apr.; 4: 145-158. Illus.: Photo. B&W. 6. Lang.: Pol.

Poland. 1945-1998. Critical studies. ■Examines the theme of old age in two plays by Tadeusz Różewicz: *Cmieszny staruszek (Funny Old Man)* and *Stara kobieta wysiaduje (Old Woman Breeds).*

3310 Wolitz, Seth. "Performing a Holocaust Play in Warsaw in 1963." 130-146 in Schumacher, Claude, ed. *Staging the Holocaust: The Shoah in Drama and Performance.* Cambridge: Cambridge UP; 1998. 355 pp. (Cambridge Studies in Modern Theatre.) Index. Notes. Biblio. Lang.: Eng.

Poland: Warsaw. 1963. Critical studies. ■The theme of political resistance in Mikhl Mirsky's *Der Kheshbn (The Final Reckoning)*, directed by Ida Kamińska at the Teatr Polski.

3311 Medina, Georgie. *La Mulatez en la Dramaturgía Puertorriqueña de Tapia y Rivera, Arrivi Alegría, y Rosario Quiles.* (The Mulatto in the Work of Puerto Rican Playwrights Alejandro Tapia y Rivera, Francisco Arrivi Alegría, and Rosario Quiles.) Lexington, KY: Univ. of Kentucky; 1998. 192 pp. Biblio. Notes. [Ph.D. Dissertation, Univ. Microfilms Order No. AAC 9907716.] Lang.: Spa.

Puerto Rico. 1850-1985. Critical studies. ■The theme of race-mixing and identity in Tapia y Rivera's *La cuarterona (The Quadroon)*, Francisco Arrivi Alegría's trilogy *Máscara puertorriqueña (Puerto Rican Mask)* and Rosario Quiles' *La movida de Victor Campolo (The Victor Campolo Scene)* and *Cimarron.*

3312 Roldan Rodriguez, Janet. *El Concepto Nación-Yo: Símbolo del Desencanto en la Dramaturgía de Roberto Ramos-Perea.* (The I-Nation Concept: Symbol of Disenchantment in the Drama of Roberto Ramos-Perea.) Mayaguez, PR: Univ. of Puerto Rico; 1998. 108 pp. Biblio. Notes. [M.A. Thesis, Univ. Microfilms Order No. AAC 1391412.] Lang.: Spa.

Puerto Rico. 1998. Critical studies. ■The 'nation-I' symbolism and the theme of disenchantment in the dramatic art of Roberto Ramos-Perea.

3313 Smith, Joseph Andrew. *The Translation of Tragedy into Imperial Rome: A Study of Seneca's* Hercules *and* Oedipus. Los Angeles, CA: Univ. of Southern California; 1998. 212 pp. Biblio. Notes. [Ph.D. Dissertation, Univ. Microfilms Order No. AAC 9902904.] Lang.: Eng.

Roman Empire. 4 B.C.-65 A.D. Critical studies. ■Study of two comparatively neglected tragedies of Seneca—*Hercules furens* and *Oedipus.* Explores how these plays reveal the culture of ancient Rome and examines the relationship between the literary traditions inherited by Seneca and the privileged audiences who came to the theatre to witness the Senecan transformation of these traditions.

3314 Tarján, Tamás. "Töprengésünk tüköre: Tanulmánykötet a drámaíró Tamásiról." (The Mirror of Meditation: A Volume of Essays on the Dramatist Áron Tamási.) *Sz.* 1998; 31(3): 45-46. Lang.: Hun.

Romania. 1907-1997. Critical studies. ■Review of a centennial collection of essays on the plays of Hungarian author Áron Tamási (1897-1966) who lived in Romania.

3315 Wutrich, Timothy Richard. *The Theater of Pain: Roman Tragic Theater from its Literary Origins to the Visual Spectacles of the Amphitheaters.* Medford, MA: Tufts Univ; 1988. 115 pp. Biblio. Notes. [Master's Thesis, Univ. Microfilms Order No. AAC 1332887.] Lang.: Eng.

Rome. 500 B.C.-476 A.D. Critical studies. ■Traces the development of Latin tragic theatre from its origins, through its literary period to its decline in the Roman arenas. Comparisons are made between illusionistic and actual representations of death in the theatre.

3316 "A.N. Ostrovskij." *Gubernskij dom.* 1998; 1-2: 1-96. Lang.: Rus.

Russia. Critical studies. ■Issue dedicated to playwright Aleksand'r Ostrovskij, on the occasion of his 175th birthday.

3317 An, Ben En. "Teatr A. Vampilova—nekotorye čerty dramaturgičeskoj poétiki." (The Theatre of A. Vampilov—Some Aspects of the Playwright's Art.) 140-150 in *Golosa molodych učenych.* Mosocw: 1998. Lang.: Rus.

Russia. 1998. Critical studies. ■Examines the work of playwright Aleksand'r Vampilov.

3318 Anašina, T. "Pejzaž v 'Drame na ochote' Čechova." (The Landscape in *Drama of the Hunting Trip* by Čechov.) 133-138 in *Molodye issledovateli Čechova.* Moscow: 1998. Lang.: Rus.

Russia. 1901. Critical studies. ■Analysis of the Čechov play.

3319 Boyle, Eloise M. *The Drama of Majakovskij: A Study of the Plays and Dramatic Elements in the Poetry of Vladimir Majakovskij.* Columbus, OH: Ohio State Univ; 1988. 201 pp.

Biblio. Notes. [Ph.D. Dissertation, Univ. Microfilms Order No. AAC 8812231.] Lang.: Eng.

Russia. 1910-1930. Critical studies. ■Focuses on Majakovskij's theatricalism and dramatic devices, verbal richness and complex structure.

3320 Čuvakov, V.N.,. *Leonid Nikolaevič Andreev: Bibliogr.* (Leonid Nikolajėvič Andrejėv: Bibliography.) Moscow: Nasledie; 1998. 608 pp. Lang.: Rus.

Russia. 1900-1919. Bibliographical studies. ■Bibliography of work by and about the playwright, including materials about productions of his plays in Russia.

3321 Desjatov, V.V. "Teatroterapija Gor'kogo: Simvoličeskaja psichodrama 'Voskresšij syn'." (Theatrical Therapy by Gorkij: Symbolic Psychodrama in *Reincarnated Son.*) 165-168 in *Gor'kovskie čtenija 1997 goda.* Nižni Novgorod: Izd-vo Nižegor. un-ta; 1998. Lang.: Rus.

Russia. 1930-1932. Critical studies. ■Analyzes Gorkij's theatricalization of life in his play.

3322 Gukovskij, G.A.; Zorin, A. *Russkaja literatura XVIII veka: Učebnik.* (Russian Literature of the 18th Century: Textbook.) Moscow: Aspekt Press; 1998. 453 pp. Lang.: Rus.

Russia. 1701-1800. Instructional materials. ■Overview of Russian literature of the eighteenth century, contains material regarding playwrights Denis Fonvizin and Vasilij Kapnist.

3323 Ivleva, T. "'Topor', srubivšij 'Višnevyj sad': (Kul'turno-ist. pročtenie p'esy A.P. Čechova)." (The Ax That Cut Down *The Cherry Orchard*: Cultural and Historical Reading of Čechov's Play.) 126-133 in *Molodye issledovateli Čechova.* Moscow: 1998. Lang.: Rus.

Russia. 1904. Critical studies. ■Analysis of *Višnëvyj sad (The Cherry Orchard)* by Anton Čechov.

3324 Kičin, V. "Ob jasnenie v ljubvi." (A Discussion About Love.) *MoskZ.* 1998; Sep-Oct: 34-37. Lang.: Rus.

Russia. 1940-1998. Biographical studies. ■Profile of playwright Emil Braginskij.

3325 Ključevskij, V.O. *O nravstvennosti i russkoj kul'ture.* (About Morals and Russian Culture.) Moscow: Izd-vo In-ta ros. istorii RAN; 1998. 348 pp. Lang.: Rus.

Russia. 1764-1869. Critical studies. ■Analysis of *Nedorosl (The Minor)* by Denis Fonvizin, *Voevoda* by Aleksand'r Ostrovskij, *Smert Ioanna Groznogo (The Death of Ivan the Terrible)* by Aleksej Tolstoj.

3326 Kočetkov, A.N. "Dramatičeskaja forma v perevode: 'Tri sestry' Čechova i 'Na dnė' Gor'kogo, perevod 'podteksta'." (Dramatical Form in Translation: Čechov's *Three Sisters* and Gorkij's *Lower Depths.*) 323-329 in *Gor'kovskie čtenija 1997 goda.* Nižn. Novgorod: Izd-vo Nižegor. un-ta; 1998. Lang.: Rus.

Russia. 1901-1902. Critical studies. ■Analysis of translations of the plays.

3327 Kononenko, Natalie O. "Clothes Unmake the Social Bandit: Sten'ka Razin and the Golyt'ba." 111-135 in Potter, Lois, ed. *Playing Robin Hood: The Legend as Performance in Five Centuries.* Newark, DE: Univ of Delaware P; 1998. 254 pp. Index. Notes. Biblio. Pref. Lang.: Eng.

Russia. 1620-1900. Critical studies. ■Analysis of the Russian legendary figure Stepan Razin, a real person who appears in Russian folktales, music, and plays, as a Robin Hood figure who robs from the rich and gives to the poor.

3328 Kulikova, E. "'Kuropatki' i 'solov'i': Dram. forma u Čechova i Meterlinka." ('Partridges' and 'Nightingales': Dramatic Forms Used by Čechov and Maeterlinck.) 253-260 in *Molodye issledovateli Čechova.* Moscow: 1998. Lang.: Rus.

Russia. Belgium. 1890-1949. Critical studies. ■Comparison of the dramatic styles of Maeterlinck and Čechov.

3329 Lenčevskij, Ju. "Patriarch otečestvennoj dramaturgii živet rjadom s nami: V.S. Rozovu ispolnilos' 85 let." (The Patriarch of Russian Playwriting Lives Nearby: On Viktor Rozov's 85th Birthday.) *Leningradskij prospekt.* 1998; 4: 42. Lang.: Rus.

Russia. 1913-1998. Biographical studies. ■Portrait of playwright Viktor Rozov.

3330 Moskwin, Andrej. "Recepcja dramatów Stanisława Przybyszewskiego w teatrze rosyjskim początku XX wieku." (The Reception of Stanisław Przybyszewski's Dramas in Russian Theatre at the Beginning of the Twentieth Century.) *PaT.* 1998; 47 (3-4): 410-450. Notes. Illus.: Sketches. Photo. Poster. B&W. 7. Lang.: Pol.

Russia: Moscow, St. Petersburg. 1901-1912. Historical studies. ■Examines the reception of the plays of Polish playwright Stanisław Przybyszewski in Russian theatre in the early twentieth century.

3331 Noriko, Agati. "Solenyj i drugie: (K vopr. o lit. citate v 'Trech sestrach')." (A Question about a Phrase in *Three Sisters*).) 177-182 in *Molodye issledovateli Čechova.* Moscow: 1998. Lang.: Rus.

Russia. 1901. Critical studies. ■Analysis of a phrase in Čechov's *Tri sestry (Three Sisters).*

3332 Pastušenko, L.M. *Iz istorii stanovlenija russkoj dramaturgii vtoroj poloviny XVIII veka: (M.M. Cheraskov).* (On the History of the Development of Russian Playwriting in the Second Half of the Eighteenth Century: M.M. Cheraskov.) Petropavlovsk-Kamčatskij: 1998. 120 pp. Lang.: Rus.

Russia. 1751-1799. Historical studies. ■Discusses the development of Russian playwriting from 1751-1799, with attention paid to Michajl Cheraskov.

3333 Podol'skaja, O. "Rečevoj portret Soni ('Djadja Vanja')." (Portrait of Sonya in *Uncle Vanya.*) 171-177 in *Molodye issledovateli Čechova.* Moscow: 1998. Lang.: Rus.

Russia. 1899. Critical studies. ■Analysis of the character Sonya in Čechov's play.

3334 Prokof'eva, N.N. "Otečestvennaja vojna 1812 goda i russkaja dramaturgija pervoj četverti XIX veka." (The Russian War of 1812 and Russian Playwriting in the First Quarter of the Nineteenth Century.) 195-218 in *Otečestvennaja vojna 1812 goda i russkaja literatura XIX veka.* Moscow: Nasledie; 1998. Lang.: Rus.

Russia. 1800-1825. Historical studies. ■Influence of the conflict on Russian playwrights in the early nineteenth century.

3335 Reid, John. "Matter and Spirit in *The Seagull.*" *MD.* 1998 Win; 41(4): 607-622. Notes. Lang.: Eng.

Russia. 1896. Critical studies. ■Analysis of Čechov's *Čajka*, with emphasis on his materialist views and the rejection of the ideological baggage of symbolism.

3336 Šejkina, M. "Vekovoj prototip: (Obraz Konstantina Trepleva v kul'ture rubeža vekov)." (Prototype of the Century: The Image of Konstantin Treplev in Turn-of-the-Century Culture.) 120-126 in *Molodye issledovateli Čechova.* Moscow: 1998. Lang.: Rus.

Russia. 1890-1910. Critical studies. ■Čechov's character Treplev in *Čajka (The Seagull)* as emblematic of Čechov's times.

3337 Seleznev, V. "'Vsjakoj drugoj ryby, krome krasnoj, on gnušaetsja...': (A. Potechin v sarat. gubernii)." (All Other Fish, Except Caviar, He Can't Stand...: A. Potechin in Saratov.) *Volga.* 1998; 11-12: 177-183. Lang.: Rus.

Russia: Saratov. 1850-1899. Biographical studies. ■Profile of playwright A. Potechin.

3338 Titkova, N. "Čechovskaja tradicija v poétike dramy M.A. Bulgakova." (The Čechovian Tradition in the Poetic Drama of M.A. Bulgakov.) 240-245 in *Molodye issledovateli Čechova.* Moscow: 1998. Lang.: Rus.

Russia. 1890-1936. Critical studies. ■Comparison of the work of Čechov and Bulgakov.

3339 Ušakov, S. "Bogatyr' russkoj sceny." (Hero of the Russian Stage.) *Nižnij Novgorod.* 1998; 9: 195-202. Lang.: Rus.

Russia. 1868-1945. Biographical studies. ■Profile of N.I. Sobol'ščikov-Samarin, actor and playwright.

3340 Zoščenko, V.V.; Filippov, G.V., ed. "Istorija odnoj p'esy: Iz vospominanij V.V. Zoščenko." (The History of a Play: From the Recollections of V.V. Zoščenko.) *R Lit.* 1998; 4: 185-195. Lang.: Rus.

Russia. 1998. Histories-sources. ■V.V. Zoščenko on his play, *Uvažaemyj tovarišč M.M. Zoščenko (The Respected M.M. Zoščenko).*

DRAMA: —Plays/librettos/scripts

3341 Žurčeva, O.V. "Dramaturgija M. Gor'kogo v kontekste 'Novoj dramy' rubeža XIX-XX vekov: (K post. probl.)." (The Playwriting of Maksim Gorkij in the Context of the New Drama in the Late Nineteenth and Early Twentieth Century.) 125-129 in *Gor'kovskie čtenija 1997 goda.* Nižni Novgorod: Izd-vo Nižegor. un-ta; 1998. Lang.: Rus.
Russia. 1890-1910. Critical studies. ■Finding Gorkij's place as playwright at the turn of the twentieth century.

3342 Plesch, Véronique. "Walls and Scaffolds: Pictorial and Dramatic Passion Cycles in the Duchy of Savoy." *CompD.* 1998 Sum; 32(2): 252-290. Notes. Illus.: Pntg. B&W. 4. Lang.: Eng.
Savoy. 1435-1505. Critical studies. ■Comparison of pictorial and staged versions, and their societal function, of the Passion in fifteenth- and early sixteenth-century Savoy.

3343 *Contemporary Slovenian Writers in Translation.* Ljubljana: Trubar Foundation; 1998. 63 pp. (Litterae Slovenicae. Special Edition.) Pref. Lang.: Eng.
Slovenia. 1960-1997. Bibliographical studies. ■A bibliography of the literary work of Slovenian writers, including playwrights, whose works have been translated and published abroad.

3344 Kermauner, Taras. *Duhovniki, meščani, delavci 2. Paternalizem in emancipacija.* (Priests, Citizens, Workers 2. Paternalism and Emancipation.) Ljubljana: SGFM; 1998. 233 pp. (Reconstruction and/or Reinterpretation of Slovene Drama.) Pref. Notes. Index. Tables. Gloss. Lang.: Slo.
Slovenia. 1897-1910. Critical studies. ■Analysis of social roles in Etbin Kristan's *Zvestoba (Fidelity)*, which presents examples of bourgeois capitalists, rebellious workers, and the clergy.

3345 Kermauner, Taras. *Svetost, čudež, žrtev. Knj. 1.* (Sanctity, Miracle, Victim. Book 1.) Ljubljana: SGFM; 1998. 272 pp. (Reconstruction and/or Reinterpretation of Slovene Drama.) Pref. Notes. Tables. Gloss. Lang.: Slo.
Slovenia. 1903-1994. Critical studies. ■Analyzes the theme of religion reflected in the presence of monasteries, the church, pilgrimage, and rites as the essential features of priesthood in selected Slovene plays.

3346 Kermauner, Taras. *Morala je amorala 1. Taščica ali noj?* (Morality Is Amorality 1. Robin or Ostrich?)Ljubljana: SGFM; 1998. 254 pp. (Reconstruction and/or Reinterpretation of Slovene Drama.) Notes. Tables. Gloss. Lang.: Slo.
Slovenia. 1946-1970. Critical studies. ■Analyzes the dramatic work of Igor Torkar. Using *Balada o taščici (Ballad of a Robin)*, author reveals the main structures of Torkar's work.

3347 Kermauner, Taras. *Dramatika narodno osvobodilnega boja 1. Naša sveta stvar (leva).* (The Drama of the Fight for National Liberation 1. The Sacred Cause of the Left.) Ljubljana: SGFM; 1998. 335 pp. (Reconstruction and/or Reinterpretation of Slovene Drama.) Notes. Tables. Gloss. Lang.: Slo.
Slovenia. 1943-1985. Critical studies. ■Examines the theme of an individual and his world as reflected in six Slovene plays written between 1943 and 1985. Plays discussed are *Večer pod Hmeljnikom (An Evening Under Hmeljnik)* by Edvard Kocbek, *Mati na pogorišču (Mother In a Gutted Ruin)* by Vasja Ocvirk, *Smrt dolgo po umiranju ali Marjetica (Death a Long Time After Dying, or Marjetica)* by Matjaž Kmecl, *Za koga naj še molim? (For Whom Shall I Still Pray?)* and *Justifikacija (The Execution)* by Tone Partljič, and *Žene na grobu (Women at the Grave)* by Božo Vodušek.

3348 Kermauner, Taras. *Blodnja. Knj. 3: Rabelj-žrtev.* (The Maze: Book 3: Hangman-Victim.) Ljubljana: SGFM; 1998. 261 pp. (Reconstruction and/or Reinterpretation of Slovene Drama.) Pref. Notes. Gloss. Lang.: Slo.
Slovenia. 1988. Critical studies. ■Analysis of Dane Zajc's play *Medeja (Medea).*

3349 Kermauner, Taras. *Trideseta leta. Leto 1940.* (The Thirties, Year 1940.) Ljubljana: SGFM; 1998. 248 pp. (Reconstruction and/or Reinterpretation of Slovene Drama.) Pref. Notes. Gloss. Lang.: Slo.
Slovenia. 1940. Critical studies. ■Analyzes the theme of peasantry in Slovene literature and particularly the idea of peasants in Slovene fascism, as reflected in *Zasad* by Stanko Kociper and *Stvar Jurija Trajbasa (The Case of Jurij Trabas)* by Vitomil Zupan, both pre-World War II plays.

3350 Kermauner, Taras. "Dramatika Primoža Kozaka." (The Dramatic Works of Primož Kozak.) *Sodobnost.* 1998; 904(6-7): 584-593. Lang.: Slo.
Slovenia. 1959-1969. Critical studies. ■The theme of political circumstances in Kozak's *Dialogi (Dialogues)*, *Afera (The Affair)*, *Kongres (The Congress)*, and *Legenda o svetem Che (The Legend of Saint Che).*

3351 Kermauner, Taras. *Duhovniki, plemiči, kmetje 1. Upornik človekoljub.* (Priests, Nobles, Peasants 1. Philanthropist Rebel.) Ljubljana: SGFM; 1998. 248 pp. (Reconstruction and/or Reinterpretation of Slovene Drama.) Index. Notes. Tables. Gloss. Lang.: Slo.
Slovenia. 1870. Critical studies. ■Detailed analysis of the unpublished anticlerical *Zoran ali Kmetska vojna na Slovenskem (Zoran or the Peasant War in Slovenia)* by Ivan Vrhovec.

3352 Kermauner, Taras. *Duhovniki, meščani, delavci 1. Klerikalizem in liberalizem.* (Priests, Citizens, Workers 1. Clericalism and Liberalism.) Ljubljana: Slovene Theatre and Film Museum; 1998. 283 pp. (Reconstruction and/or Reinterpretation of Slovene Drama.) Pref. Index. Notes. Tables. Gloss. Lang.: Slo.
Slovenia. 1897-1910. Critical studies. ■Analyzes social roles in *Grča (The Knot)* by Fran Govekar and *Sreče kolo (Wheel of Fortune)* by Anton Medved. Examines how the characters in these plays exist through the political and sociological ideologies of the time—liberalism and clericalism.

3353 Kermauner, Taras. *Duhovniki, meščani, delavci 3. Avtonomizem in kapitalizem.* (Priests, Citizens, Workers 3. Autonomism and Capitalism.) Ljubljana: SGFM; 1998. 278 pp. (Reconstruction and/or Reinterpretation of Slovene Drama.) Pref. Index. Notes. Tables. Gloss. Lang.: Slo.
Slovenia. 1897-1920. Critical studies. ■Analyzes social roles in *Kristalni Grad (The Crystal Castle)* by Anton Funtek, and *Pelinčkov gospod in njegova hiša (Master Pelinček and His House)* by Ivo Šorli.

3354 Kermauner, Taras. *Morala je amorala 2. Taščica — Noj.* (Morality Is Amorality 2: Robin — Ostrich.) Ljubljana: SGFM; 1998. 259 pp. (Reconstruction and/or Reinterpretation of Slovene Drama.) Pref. Notes. Tables. Gloss. Lang.: Slo.
Slovenia. 1946-1970. Critical studies. ■Further analysis of the work of playwright Igor Torkar. Author argues that the figures and names of the robin and the ostrich function as symbols in Torkar's *Balada o taščici (Ballad of a Robin)* and *Balada o črnem noju (Ballad of a Black Ostrich).*

3355 Maver, Aleš. "Med Jobom in Davidom." (Between Job and David.) *Dialogi.* 1998; 34(3-4): 32-46. Lang.: Slo.
Slovenia. 1925-1986. Biographical studies. ■Brief analysis of the life and work of Ivan Mrak, a prolific Slovene dramatist. He wrote thirty-seven dramas, mostly tragedies with religious contents.

3356 Maver, Aleš. "Čigav je meter našega sveta?" (Myth and Reality in Zajc's Drama *Grmače.*) *Dialogi.* 1998; 34(11-12): 39-53. Illus.: Photo. B&W. 2. Lang.: Slo.
Slovenia. 1991. Critical studies. ■Analysis of Dane Zajc's poetical drama, *Grmače*, a conflict between generations in a mythological context.

3357 Moder, Janko. "Namesto Župančiča." (Instead of Župančič.) *Sodobnost.* 1998; 1006(6-7): 527-534. Lang.: Slo.
Slovenia. 1900-1954. Critical studies. ■Examines the extensive translation work of playwright Oton Župančič.

3358 Poniž, Denis. "Oseba v dramah Ivana Mraka." (The Person in the Plays of Ivan Mrak.) 479-487 in Kovačič Peršin, Peter, ed. *Personalizem in odmevi na Slovenskem.* Ljubljana: Društvo 2000; 1998. 500 pp. (Literarni leksikon 44.) Lang.: Slo.
Slovenia. 1955. Critical studies. ■Examines the theme of religion in the theatre of Ivan Mrak, specifically the presence and the influence of Christ. Plays examined include the trilogy *Proces (The Trial)*, composed of the tragedies *Človek iz Kariota (Man from Kariot)*, *Veliki duhoven Kajfa (The High Priest Caiaphas)*, and *Prokurator Poncij Pilat (Procurator Pontius Pilate).*

DRAMA: —Plays/librettos/scripts

3359 Saksida, Igor. *Slovenska mladinska dramatika.* (Slovenian Youth Drama.) Maribor: Obzorja; 1998. 210 pp. Pref. Index. Biblio. Illus.: Dwg. B&W. 8. Lang.: Slo.
Slovenia. 1800-1997. Histories-specific. ■The first complete historical review and theoretical analysis of Slovene youth drama.

3360 Svetina, Ivo. "Veronika Deseniška ali vprašanje tragedije." (Veronica of Desenice or the Problem of Tragedy.) *Sodobnost.* 1998; 1006(6-7): 515-526. Lang.: Slo.
Slovenia. 1924. Critical studies. ■Analysis of the verse drama *Veronica of Desenice (Veronika Deseniška)* by Oton Župančič. Includes discussion of the play's reception upon publication.

3361 Colleran, Jeanne Marie. *The Dissenting Writer in South Africa: A Rhetorical Analysis of the Drama of Athol Fugard and the Short Fiction of Nadine Gordimer.* Columbus, OH: Ohio State Univ; 1988. 328 pp. Biblio. Notes. [Ph.D. Dissertation, Univ. Microfilms Order No. AAC 8824479.] Lang.: Eng.
South Africa, Republic of. 1958-1988. Critical studies. ■Focuses on how Fugard and Gordimer have overcome the strictures placed upon their art and created works that lodge an authentically felt and artfully constructed protest.

3362 Dickey, Jerry Richard. *The Artist as Rebel: The Development of Athol Fugard's Dramaturgy and the Influence of Albert Camus.* Bloomington, IN: Indiana Univ; 1987. 395 pp. Notes. Biblio. [Ph.D. Dissertation, Univ. Microfilms Order No. AAC 8717793.] Lang.: Eng.
South Africa, Republic of. 1960-1985. Critical studies. ■Analysis of *The Blood Knot, Hello and Goodbye, Boesman and Lena, Sizwe Bansi Is Dead, The Island, Dimetos, A Lesson from Aloes, Master Harold...and the boys* and *The Road to Mecca.*

3363 Gosher, Sydney Paul. *A Historical and Critical Survey of the South African One-Act Play Written in English.* Johannesburg: Univ. of South Africa; 1988. Biblio. Notes. [Ph.D. Dissertation.] Lang.: Eng.
South Africa, Republic of. 1950-1988. Histories-specific. ■The history of the South African one-act play in English. Includes discussion of the one-act's history in Western Europe and concludes with a discussion of its characteristics and criteria.

3364 Morgensen-Lindsay, Annissa Marie. *Post-Apartheid Fugard: Cross-Generation Attachment in Select Plays by Athol Fugard.* Bowling Green, OH: Bowling Green Univ; 1998. 291 pp. Notes. Biblio. [Ph.D. Dissertation, Univ. Microfilms Order No. AAC 9902347.] Lang.: Eng.
South Africa, Republic of. 1991-1998. Critical studies. ■A new post-apartheid examination of *Master Harold...and the boys, My Children! My Africa!, The Road to Mecca,* and *Valley Song.*

3365 Steadman, Ian. "Race Matters in South African Theatre." 55-75 in Boon, Richard, ed.; Plastow, Jane, ed. *Theatre Matters: Performance and Culture on the World Stage.* Cambridge: Cambridge UP; 1998. 203 pp. (Cambridge Studies in Modern Theatre.) Notes. Index. Pref. Lang.: Eng.
South Africa, Republic of. 1976-1996. Historical studies. ■The role of theatre in post-apartheid South Africa, with emphasis on *Shanti* by Mthuli ka Shezi, Matsemela Manaka's *Pula,* and others.

3366 Abraham, James Thorp. *'Los Españoles en Chile': A Distributed Multimedia Edition.* Tucson, AZ: Univ. of Arizona; 1998. 208 pp. Biblio. Notes. [Ph.D. Dissertation, Univ. Microfilms Order No. AAC 9829332.] Lang.: Eng.
Spain. 1665-1998. Critical studies. ■On the creation of a Web site of Francisco Ganzalez de Busto's *Los españoles en Chile,* which combines the 1665, the 1761, and the 1841 editions with digitized images from the earliest publication, a glossary, bibliography, and explanatory notes as well as representations of stage designs, costumes, blocking, machinery, historical materials, and related artistic works.

3367 Ames, Debra Collins. *The Function of Classical Allusions in the Theater of Lope de Vega.* Charlottesville, VA: Univ. of Virginia; 1987. 304 pp. Biblio. Notes. [Ph.D. Dissertation, Univ. Microfilms Order No. 8801123.] Lang.: Eng.
Spain. 1562-1635. Critical studies. ■Argues that classical allusions in Lope's theatre are used to characterize someone, add a humorous touch, or emphasize a theme, and to prefigure impending events.

3368 Bruls, Willem. "De martelaar van Granada. Op zoeu naar Federico García Lorca." (The Martyr of Granada: In Search of Federico García Lorca.) *Tmaker.* 1998; 2(5): 8-12. Illus.: Photo. B&W. 4. Lang.: Dut.
Spain. 1930-1998. Biographical studies. ■Critical biography of Lorca's life and works on the occasion of his 100th birthday (June 5, 1898).

3369 Burton, David G. "Juan de la Cueva." 87-95 in Parker, Mary, ed. *Spanish Dramatists of the Golden Age: A Bio-Bibliographical Sourcebook.* Westport, CT/London: Greenwood; 1998. 286 pp. Index. Notes. Biblio. Pref. Lang.: Eng.
Spain. 1543-1612. Critical studies. ■Life and career of poet and playwright Juan de la Cueva and his introduction of national themes into Spanish theatre. Major works analyzed include *Comedia de la muerte del rey don Sancho y reto de Zamora por don Diego Ordoñez (Comedy of the Death of King Sancho and the Challenge of Zamor by Don Diego Ordoñez).* Also includes critical response and select bibliography.

3370 Damiani, Bruno M. "Tirso de Molina (Gabriel Téllez)." 205-217 in Parker, Mary, ed. *Spanish Dramatists of the Golden Age: A Bio-Bibliographical Sourcebook.* Westport, CT/London: Greenwood; 1998. 286 pp. Index. Notes. Biblio. Pref. Lang.: Eng.
Spain. 1583-1648. Critical studies. ■Life and career of comic playwright Tirso de Molina. Covers major themes, his play *El burlador de Sevilla o El convidado de piedra (The Trickster of Seville or the Stone Guest),* among others. Also includes critical response and select bibliography.

3371 Delgado, Manuel. "Antonio Mira de Amescua." 107-123 in Parker, Mary, ed. *Spanish Dramatists of the Golden Age: A Bio-Bibliographical Sourcebook.* Westport, CT/London: Greenwood; 1998. 286 pp. Index. Notes. Biblio. Pref. Lang.: Eng.
Spain. 1574-1644. Critical studies. ■Playwright Antonio Mira de Amescua, his life as a priest, a lawyer, and a censor, and his close association with Lope de Vega. Major works examined include *La rueda de la fortuna.*

3372 Friedman, Edward H. "Miguel de Cervantes Saavedra." 63-74 in Parker, Mary, ed. *Spanish Dramatists of the Golden Age: A Bio-Bibliographical Sourcebook.* Westport, CT/London: Greenwood; 1998. 286 pp. Index. Notes. Biblio. Pref. Lang.: Eng.
Spain. 1547-1616. Critical studies. ■Life and career of Cervantes, analysis of the major themes in his dramatic work and in his novel *Don Quixote* and plays *El cerco de Numancia (The Siege of Numantia)* and *Los tratos de Argel (Commerce in Algiers).* Includes selected bibliography and critical response.

3373 Frye, Ellen Cressman. *The Development and Function of Dramatic Devices from Medieval to Golden Age Drama.* Philadelphia, PA: Univ. of Pennsylvania; 1998. 275 pp. Notes. Biblio. [Ph.D. Dissertation, Univ. Microfilms Order No. AAC 9829901.] Lang.: Eng.
Spain. 1550-1722. Critical studies. ■Examines the development, implementation and amplification of dramatic devices in Spanish medieval and Golden Age drama including soliloquies, monologues, asides, metatheatrical situations, prologues and epilogues. Argues that these devices foreground the interactive communicative nature of the actor-spectator relationship.

3374 García-Castañón, Santiago. "Francisco Antonio de Bances Candamo." 28-38 in Parker, Mary, ed. *Spanish Dramatists of the Golden Age: A Bio-Bibliographical Sourcebook.* Westport, CT/London: Greenwood; 1998. 286 pp. Index. Notes. Biblio. Pref. Lang.: Eng.
Spain. 1662-1704. Critical studies. ■Life and career of the poet and official court playwright. Examines major works and themes, critical response to his work, his own treatises as a dramatic critic, and a bibliography of plays and critical studies. Plays examined include *La piedra filosofal (The Philosopher's Stone).*

3375 Hernandez, Librada. *El teatro de José Echegaray: Un enigma crítico.* (The Theatre of José Echegaray: A Critical

DRAMA: —Plays/librettos/scripts

Enigma.) Los Angeles, CA: Univ. of California; 1987. 453 pp. Notes. Biblio. [Ph.D. Dissertation, Univ. Microfilms Order No. AAC 8719921.] Lang.: Eng.

Spain. 1874-1904. Critical studies. ■Critical re-examination of the theatre of José Echegaray. Argues that his work reveals an assimilation of many of the techniques being introduced into European theatre.

3376 Iglesias, Diane. "Luis Quiñones de Benavente." 140-144 in Parker, Mary, ed. *Spanish Dramatists of the Golden Age: A Bio-Bibliographical Sourcebook.* Westport, CT/London: Greenwood; 1998. 286 pp. Index. Notes. Biblio. Pref. Lang.: Eng.

Spain. 1600-1651. Critical studies. ■Life and career of priest Luis Quiñones de Benavente, author of short, dramatic sketches, or *entremeses.* Includes analysis of major themes in his work, critical response, and select bibliography.

3377 Ingber, Alix. "Lope Félix de Vega Carpio." 229-243 in Parker, Mary, ed. *Spanish Dramatists of the Golden Age: A Bio-Bibliographical Sourcebook.* Westport, CT/London: Greenwood; 1998. 286 pp. Index. Notes. Biblio. Pref. Lang.: Eng.

Spain. 1562-1635. Critical studies. ■Life and career of Lope de Vega, his prodigious output as a dramatist, and his major contributions to Spanish theatre (i.e., setting the three-act structure as its base structure). Analyzes themes in *El caballero de Olmedo (The Knight from Olmedo), Fuente ovejuna (The Sheep Well),* and others. Includes a select bibliography and criticism.

3378 Johnston, David. "Valle-Inclán: The Mirroring of the Esperpento." *MD.* 1998 Spr; 41(1): 30-48. Notes. Lang.: Eng.

Spain. 1936-1998. Critical studies. ■Difficulties of translating the plays of Valle-Inclán into English, and the playwright's relative obscurity in English-speaking countries.

3379 Kenworthy, Patricia. "Juan Pérez de Montalbán." 124-131 in Parker, Mary, ed. *Spanish Dramatists of the Golden Age: A Bio-Bibliographical Sourcebook.* Westport, CT/London: Greenwood; 1998. 286 pp. Index. Notes. Biblio. Pref. Lang.: Eng.

Spain. 1601-1638. Critical studies. ■Life and career of poet, priest, and playwright Juan Pérez de Montalbán, biographer of Lope de Vega. Includes analysis of *autos sacramentales,* critical response to his work, and a select bibliography.

3380 Kiosses, James T. *The Dynamics of the Imagery in the Theater of Federico García Lorca.* New York, NY: Columbia Univ; 1988. 397 pp. Biblio. Notes. [Ph.D. Dissertation, Univ. Microfilms Order No. AAC 8815676.] Lang.: Eng.

Spain. 1920-1936. Critical studies. ■Imagery, metaphorical language, and action in the plays of García Lorca.

3381 Klein, Richard Alan. *The Induction in Sixteenth-Century Spanish Drama: Problematizing the Boundaries of Illusion.* Princeton, NJ: Princeton Univ; 1998. 419 pp. Biblio. Notes. [Ph.D. Dissertation, Univ. Microfilms Order No. AAC 9901788.] Lang.: Eng.

Spain. 1500-1600. Critical studies. ■Argues that the induction, a type of dramatic prologue in Renaissance Spanish drama, dramatized, rather than expounded, some statement regarding the play it preceded and in many cases formed a symbolic equivalent to it.

3382 Leonard, Candyce. "Sex and Politics in the Theatre of Alfonso Armada." *WES.* 1998 Fall; 10(3): 101-106. Illus.: Photo. B&W. 5. Lang.: Eng.

Spain: Madrid. 1987-1998. Biographical studies. ■Profile of playwright/director Armada and his theatre company Koyaanisqatsi.

3383 Lihani, John. "Bartolomé de Torres Naharro." 218-228 in Parker, Mary, ed. *Spanish Dramatists of the Golden Age: A Bio-Bibliographical Sourcebook.* Westport, CT/London: Greenwood; 1998. 286 pp. Index. Notes. Biblio. Pref. Lang.: Eng.

Spain. 1480-1530. Critical studies. ■Playwright Bartolomé de Torres Naharro, also a priest, soldier, and court arranger for spectacles and entertainments. Analyzes major themes and works, including *Comedia Soldadesca (The Military Comedy), Comedia Jacinta (The Hyacinth Comedy)* and pastoral comedies, documentary, and fictional plays. Also includes a select bibliography and critical response to his work.

3384 Mujica, Barbara. "Guillén de Castro." 51-62 in Parker, Mary, ed. *Spanish Dramatists of the Golden Age: A Bio-Bibliographical Sourcebook.* Westport, CT/London: Greenwood; 1998. 286 pp. Index. Notes. Biblio. Pref. Lang.: Eng.

Spain. 1569-1631. Critical studies. ■Life and career of playwright Guillén de Castro, including analysis of major work and themes in *Las mocedades del Cid, I (The Youthful Deeds of El Cid, I).* Includes select bibliography and critical responses to his work.

3385 Mulroney, Diane Jean. *Re/presenting Gender: Four Women Dramatists of Seventeenth-Century Spain.* Madison, WI: Univ. of Wisconsin; 1998. 256 pp. Notes. Biblio. [Ph.D. Dissertation, Univ. Microfilms Order No. AAC 9826391.] Lang.: Eng.

Spain. 1605-1675. Critical studies. ■Feminist analysis of Leonor de la Cueva y Silva's *La firmeza en la ausencia (Constancy in Absence),* María de Zayas y Sotomayor's *Traición en la amistad (Treachery in Friendship),* Feliciana Enríquez de Guzmán's *Tragicomedia jardines y campos sabeos (Tragicomedy Gardens and Fields of Saba),* and Sor Marcela de San Félix's *Muerte del Apetito (Death of the Appetite).* Explores the cultural specifics of women's lives during the period and their confinement within home or convent, and argues that the plays provided women with a means by which they could express social criticism and challenge the status quo.

3386 Nordlund, David Earl. *Authority, Power, and Dramatic Genre in the Theatre of Federico García Lorca.* Los Angeles, CA: Univ. of California; 1998. 323 pp. Biblio. Notes. [Ph.D. Dissertation, Univ. Microfilms Order No. AAC 9818010.] Lang.: Eng.

Spain. 1920-1936. Critical studies. ■Different manifestations of authority and power in the theatre of García Lorca: familial, social/sexual, religious/spiritual, economic, and spatial.

3387 Parker, Mary. "Introduction: The Golden Age of Spanish Dramatists." 1-17 in Parker, Mary, ed. *Spanish Dramatists of the Golden Age: A Bio-Bibliographical Sourcebook.* Westport, CT/London: Greenwood; 1998. 286 pp. Index. Notes. Biblio. Pref. Lang.: Eng.

Spain. 1517-1681. Critical studies. ■Introductory article to collection of essays on Spanish Golden Age dramatists, providing historical and cultural context for the period.

3388 Parker, Mary. "Fernando de Rojas." 145-176 in Parker, Mary, ed. *Spanish Dramatists of the Golden Age: A Bio-Bibliographical Sourcebook.* Westport, CT/London: Greenwood; 1998. 286 pp. Index. Notes. Biblio. Pref. Lang.: Eng.

Spain. 1476-1541. Critical studies. ■Life and career of playwright and lawyer Fernando de Rojas. Includes discussion of major themes, his play *La Celestina,* critical response to his work, and a select bibliography.

3389 Parr, James A. "Juan Ruiz de Alarcón y Mendoza." 18-27 in Parker, Mary, ed. *Spanish Dramatists of the Golden Age: A Bio-Bibliographical Sourcebook.* Westport, CT/London: Greenwood; 1998. 286 pp. Index. Notes. Biblio. Pref. Lang.: Eng.

Spain. 1580-1639. Critical studies. ■Life and career of the playwright from his beginnings as a lawyer to his abandonment of theatre for a government position. Analyzes major works and themes and covers the critical response to his work.

3390 Peale, George. "Luis Vélez de Guevara." 244-256 in Parker, Mary, ed. *Spanish Dramatists of the Golden Age: A Bio-Bibliographical Sourcebook.* Westport, CT/London: Greenwood; 1998. 286 pp. Index. Notes. Biblio. Pref. Lang.: Eng.

Spain. 1578-1644. Critical studies. ■Life and career of playwright Luis Vélez de Guevara, themes in his plays and *autos sacramentales.* Includes critical response and select bibliography.

3391 Perez de Leon, Vicente. *Mood, Reform and Counter-Utopia in the* Entremeses *of Cervantes.* Bloomington, IN: Indiana Univ; 1998. 362 pp. Notes. Biblio. [Ph.D. Dissertation, Univ. Microfilms Order No. AAC 9834615.] Lang.: Spa.

Spain. 1600-1630. Critical studies. ■Argues that Cervantes' one-act plays, or interludes, were written as a reformist answer to the dramatic representations on the Spanish stage in the early seventeenth century and are marked by an interplay of historical, ideological, and artistic factors.

DRAMA: —Plays/librettos/scripts

3392 Perez-Rasilla Bayo, Eduardo. *El teatro policiaco de Jardiel Poncela y otros autores del teatro español de postguerra (1940-1969).* (Detective Theatre of Jardiel Poncela and Other Postwar Spanish Playwrights, 1940-1969.) Pamplona: Universidad de Navarra; 1988. 746 pp. Notes. Biblio. [Ph.D. Dissertation.] Lang.: Spa.

Spain. 1940-1969. Histories-specific. ■Focuses on the work of Jardiel Poncela and some of his influences including *An Inspector Calls* by Priestley.

3393 Rettig, Claes von. "Närvarande: Lorca." (Presenting: Lorca.) *Entré.* 1998; 25(3/4): 44-60. Illus.: Photo. Dwg. B&W. Lang.: Swe.

Spain. 1898-1936. Biographical studies. ■Federico García Lorca as playwright, poet, artist and actor.

3394 Satake, Kenichi. *Luz y oscuridad en el teatro de Calderón.* (Light and Darkness in the Theatre of Calderón.) Urbana-Champaign: Univ. of Illinois; 1988. 319 pp. Notes. Biblio. [Ph.D. Dissertation, Univ. Microfilms Order No. AAC 8908825.] Lang.: Spa.

Spain. 1600-1601. Critical studies. ■Different meanings and functions of light and dark imagery in Calderón's plays: the sowing of confusion in cloak-and-dagger comedies, egoism and altruism in tragedies of honor, paganism and Christianity in religious drama.

3395 Smith, Susan Manell. *The Colloquies of Sor Marcela de San Félix and the Tradition of Sacred Allegorical Drama.* Charlottesville, VA: Univ. of Virginia; 1998. 259 pp. Notes. Biblio. [Ph.D. Dissertation, Univ. Microfilms Order No. AAC 9840413.] Lang.: Eng.

Spain. 1595-1650. Critical studies. ■Explores the nature of faith in four sacred allegorical dramas by playwright/nun Sor Marcela de San Félix, daughter of Lope de Vega. Analyzes the Spanish sacred drama tradition and the works created by nuns and compares Marcela's plays with those of her father and her godfather, José de Valdivielso.

3396 Stoll, Anita K. "Francisco de Rojas Zorrilla." 177-187 in Parker, Mary, ed. *Spanish Dramatists of the Golden Age: A Bio-Bibliographical Sourcebook.* Westport, CT/London: Greenwood; 1998. 286 pp. Index. Notes. Biblio. Pref. Lang.: Eng.

Spain. 1607-1648. Critical studies. ■Life and career of playwright Francisco de Rojas Zorrilla including his collaboration with several dramatists, such as Luis Vélez de Guevara, his *autos sacramentales,* and his *Entre bobos anda el juego (A Fool's Game).* Includes critical response and select bibliography.

3397 Stroud, Matthew D. "Pedro Calderón de la Barca." 39-50 in Parker, Mary, ed. *Spanish Dramatists of the Golden Age: A Bio-Bibliographical Sourcebook.* Index. Notes. Biblio. Pref. Lang.: Eng.

Spain. 1600-1681. Critical studies. ■Examines the life and career of playwright Pedro Calderón de la Barca from his beginnings as a son of the nobility to his long involvement with the theatre, the church and court. Includes major works and themes, his *comedias* such as *El alcalde de Zalamea* and *La vida es sueño,* his *autos sacramentales,* and his mythological plays that were sung (similar to operas). Also includes critical responses to playwright as well as a selected bibliography.

3398 Sullivan, Michael R. *A Study of the Paired Sonnets in the Plays of Pedro Calderón de la Barca.* Columbia, MO: Univ. of Missouri; 1998. 253 pp. Notes. Biblio. [Ph.D. Dissertation, Univ. Microfilms Order No. AAC 9901291.] Lang.: Eng.

Spain. 1660-1722. Critical studies. ■Examines the paired sonnets embedded in playwright Calderón's dramatic texts.

3399 Throne, Stephanie Susanne. *Tainted Genders: Discourses of Power and Parenthood in Spanish Drama.* Ann Arbor, MI: Univ. of Michigan; 1998. 245 pp. Notes. Biblio. [Ph.D. Dissertation, Univ. Microfilms Order No. AAC 9825356.] Lang.: Eng.

Spain. 1908-1936. Critical studies. ■The image of woman on the Spanish stage in the works of Federico García Lorca, Jacinto Benavente y Martínez, Ramón María del Valle-Inclán, Halma Angélico (Margarita Francisca Clar Margarit), Concha Espina, Angélico del Diablo (Maria Palomeras Mallofre) and María Teresa Borragan.

3400 Trautmann, Gretchen. "Following the Lorquian Model: Parallels and Divergences between *La Casa de Bernarda Alba* and *António Marinheiro.*" *Gestos.* 1998 Nov.; 13(26): 57-65. Biblio. Lang.: Eng.

Spain. Portugal. 1919-1965. Critical studies. ■The influence of Lorca's *La Casa de Bernarda Alba (The House of Bernarda Alba)* on Bernardo Santareno's *António Marinheiro.*

3401 Velarde, Olga Angelica. *'La Vida es Sueño': Entre Calderón y Foucault.* London, ON: Univ. of Western Ontario; 1998. 122 pp. Biblio. Notes. [M.A. Thesis, Univ. Microfilms Order No. AAC MQ30831.] Lang.: Spa.

Spain. 1635. Critical studies. ■Analysis of characters and dramatic action in Calderon's *La vida es sueño (Life Is a Dream)* using Foucault's theory of power relations.

3402 Vicente, Arie I. *The Jewish Element in Spanish Contemporary Theatre: Myth, Demythologization and Integration.* University Park, PA: Pennsylvania State Univ; 1988. 318 pp. Notes. Biblio. [Ph.D. Dissertation, Univ. Microfilms Order No. AAC 8826834.] Lang.: Spa.

Spain. 1400-1950. Critical studies. ■Examines the implications of Jewish elements in Spanish theatre from the Middle Ages to the institution of democracy in post-Franquist Spain. Focuses on the myth of the Jewish character in the plays of Lope de Vega and the 'converso' character in theatre of Max Aub and Antonio Gala.

3403 Voros, Sharon D. "Lope de Rueda." 188-204 in Parker, Mary, ed. *Spanish Dramatists of the Golden Age: A Bio-Bibliographical Sourcebook.* Westport, CT/London: Greenwood; 1998. 286 pp. Index. Notes. Biblio. Pref. Lang.: Eng.

Spain. 1510-1565. Critical studies. ■Actor and playwright Lope de Rueda, creator of comic interludes, comedies, and colloquies. Also includes critical response and select bibliography.

3404 Weimer, Christopher B. "Andrés de Claramonte y Corroy." 75-86 in Parker, Mary, ed. *Spanish Dramatists of the Golden Age: A Bio-Bibliographical Sourcebook.* Westport, CT/London: Greenwood; 1998. 286 pp. Index. Notes. Biblio. Pref. Lang.: Eng.

Spain. 1580-1626. Critical studies. ■Life and career of playwright Andrés de Claramonte, including his beginnings as an actor and manager. Analyzes major themes in works such as *El secreto en la mujer* and *La infelice Dorotea,* as well as a select bibliography and critical response. Also argues that Claramonte may have written *La Estrella de Sevilla,* attributed to Tirso de Molina.

3405 Worley, Robert Donald, Jr. *Spain at the Confluence of Time and Eternity: National Mythopoeia in Three Autos by Calderón.* Waco, TX: Baylor Univ; 1998. 146 pp. Biblio. Notes. [M.A. Thesis, Univ. Microfilms Order No. AAC 1390601.] Lang.: Spa.

Spain. 1637-1671. Critical studies. ■Examines the role of Spanish Catholicism in three *autos sacramentales* by Calderón: *La Devoción de la misa (The Devotion of the Mass),* and *El santo rey don Fernando (The Holy King Don Fernando),* both first and second parts.

3406 Zimic, Stanislav. "Juan del Encina." 96-106 in Parker, Mary, ed. *Spanish Dramatists of the Golden Age: A Bio-Bibliographical Sourcebook.* Westport, CT/London: Greenwood; 1998. 286 pp. Index. Notes. Biblio. Pref. Lang.: Eng.

Spain. 1468-1529. Critical studies. ■Life and career of poet and court playwright Juan del Encina. Major works and themes are analyzed, as well as critical responses to his work and selected bibliography.

3407 Oller, Victor. "'Das Theater ist ein guter Ort für zweite Chancen'." ('Theatre Is a Good Place for Second Chances'.) *THeute.* 1998; 8/9: 62-64. Illus.: Photo. B&W. 2. Lang.: Ger.

Spain-Catalonia. 1963-1998. Histories-sources. ■Interview with playwright and director Sergi Belbel about his professional life, writing, his play *Morir (A Moment Before Dying)* and the current state of theatre in Spain.

3408 Amble, Lolo. "Dramatikern som skådespelare." (The Playwright As Actor.) *Dramat.* 1998; 6(3): 35-36. Illus.: Photo. B&W. Color. Lang.: Swe.

Sweden: Stockholm. 1990-1998. Histories-sources. ■Interview with the playwright, actor, and director Staffan Göthe about his activities and his

DRAMA: —Plays/librettos/scripts

new play *Ett Lysande elände (A Brilliant Misery)*, which he will direct as well as being one of the actors.

3409 Fransson, Emma. "Jag är ingen nöjd person." (I'm Not a Pleased Person.) *Tningen.* 1998; 21, is 4: 3-5. Illus.: Photo. Color. Lang.: Swe.

Sweden: Stockholm. Denmark: Copenhagen. 1995-1998. Histories-sources. ▪Interview with playwright Sofia Fredén about her background and her plays *Nya vänner och älskare (New Friends and Lovers)* staged by Katrine Wiederman at Dr Dante in Copenhagen, and *Diamanten (The Diamond).*

3410 Hagen, Eric. *The Concept of Time and Space in August Strindberg's 'A Dream Play'.* Ann Arbor, MI: Univ. of Michigan; 1988. 302 pp. Notes. Biblio. [Ph.D. Dissertation, Univ. Microfilms Order No. 8815280.] Lang.: Eng.

Sweden. 1901-1902. Critical studies. ▪Analysis of Strindberg's *Ett Drömspel* with emphasis on its dream-world structure and symbolism.

3411 Hallin, Ulrika. "Dramatikern och teatern." (The Playwright and the Theatre.) *Tningen.* 1998; 21(4): 12-14. Illus.: Photo. B&W. Lang.: Swe.

Sweden: Malmö, Gothenburg, Stockholm. 1994-1998. Critical studies. ▪Relations between the Swedish theatres and plays by the young Swedish generation, with references to Cristina Gottfridsson at Malmö Dramatiska Teater, Mattias Andersson at Backa Teater and Isa Shöier at Teaterkollektivet Rex.

3412 Larsson, Stellan. "Lycko-Per i villornas värld." (Lucky Per In the World of Illusions.) *Tningen.* 198; 21(1): 33-37. Illus.: Dwg. Photo. B&W. Lang.: Swe.

Sweden. 1912. Critical studies. ▪Folklore and occultism in August Strindberg's *Lycko-Pers resa (Lucky Per's Journey).*

3413 Sundberg, Björn. "I familjens rum." (In the Family's Circle.) *Tningen.* 1998; 21(5): 16-21. Illus.: Photo. B&W. Lang.: Swe.

Sweden. 1980-1998. Critical studies. ▪Comparison of Lars Norén's plays, especially *Och ge oss skuggorna (And Give Us the Shadows)* with O'Neill's *Long Day's Journey Into Night.*

3414 Tersman, Ninna. "Dramatik som slår omkring sig." (Plays That Lay About One.) *Tningen.* 1998; 21(2): 12-14. Illus.: Photo. B&W. Lang.: Swe.

Sweden: Stockholm. 1997-1998. Histories-sources. ▪Interview with playwright/director Kajsa Isakson about her plays *Box (Boxing), Rundgång, Undergång och Demedon (Vicious Circle, Extinction and Demedon)* and *För Vårt Högst Personliga Nöje (For Our Most Personal Pleasure)* which she directed for Teater Salieri.

3415 Wallström, Catharina. "Det som är värt att leva för är också värt att dö för." (That Which Is Worth Living For, Is Also Worth Dying For.) *Tningen.* 1998; 21(2): 7-11. Illus.: Photo. B&W. Color. Lang.: Swe.

Sweden: Gothenburg. 1980-1998. Histories-sources. ▪Interview with the playwright and director Petra Revenue about her life and career with reference to her plays *Älskad-Saknad (Loved-Regretted)* and the theatre group Teater Trixter.

3416 Walsh, Paul James. *August Strindberg and Dramatic Realism, 1872-1886.* Toronto, ON: Univ. of Toronto; 1988. n/a pp. Biblio. Notes. [Ph.D. Dissertation.] Lang.: Eng.

Sweden. 1872-1886. Critical studies. ▪Argues that Strindberg's realism differed markedly from that of his contemporaries by exploiting the tension between dramatic form and theatrical performance to disrupt audience expectations. Plays examined include *Mäster Olof (Master Olof)* and *Fadren (The Father).*

3417 Wille, Franz. "Der Berg bewegt sich." (The Mountain Is Moving.) *THeute.* 1998; 6: 49-51. Illus.: Photo. B&W. 3. Lang.: Ger.

Switzerland: Zurich. 1998. Critical studies. ▪Analyzes Thomas Hürlimann's *Das Lied der Heimat (The Song of the Homeland)* adapted from his short story *Dämmerschoppen* and its political background. Describes the performance directed by Werner Düggelin at Schauspielhaus Zurich.

3418 Said, Aleya A. "Wavering Identity: A Pirandellian Reading of Saadallah Wannus's *The King Is the King.*" *CompD.* 1998 Fall; 32(3): 347-361. Notes. Lang.: Eng.

Syria. 1977. Critical studies. ▪The mixture of Pirandellian thought, which stresses the slippery notion of reality, with a Brechtian perspective, which implies the possibility of understanding reality in *Al-Mawik Huwa Al-Mawik.*

3419 Gbanou, Sélom-Komlan. "Dramatic Esthetics in the Work of Sénouvo Agbota Zinsou." *RAL.* 1998 Fall; 29(3): 34-57. Notes. Pref. Biblio. Lang.: Eng.

Togo. 1984-1998. Critical studies. ▪Influences on, and artistic progress of, Togolese playwright Zinsou.

3420 "The Unbearable Lightness of Ayckbourn." *Econ.* 1998 Mar 7; 346(8058): 87-88. Illus.: Photo. B&W. 1. Lang.: Eng.

UK-England: London. 1998. Biographical studies. ▪Essay on the bittersweet comedies of the playwright Alan Ayckbourn, on the occasion of the opening of his latest *Things We Do for Love* at the Gielgud.

3421 "Travelling Through Life First Class." *Econ.* 1998 Apr 11; 347(8063): 67-68. Illus.: Photo. B&W. 1. Lang.: Eng.

UK-England. 1924-1998. Critical studies. ▪Discusses reasons for the recent return to fashionability of Noël Coward in the theatre.

3422 Baker-White, Robert. "Caryl Churchill's Natural Visions." 142-158 in Rabillard, Sheila, ed. *Essays on Caryl Churchill: Contemporary Representations.* Winnipeg, MB/Buffalo, NY: Blizzard; 1998. 224 pp. Biblio. Notes. Lang.: Eng.

UK-England. 1971-1989. Critical studies. ▪Playwright Caryl Churchill's exposure of 'imperialist landscapes' through the lens of ecological theory. Argues that Churchill uses the space of the stage to demonstrate the artificiality of oppositions between the 'human' and the 'natural' in *Cloud Nine, Icecream,* and *Not Not Not Not Not Enough Oxygen.*

3423 Baum, Rob K. "Travesty, Peterhood and the Flight of a Lost Girl." *NETJ.* 1998; 9: 71-97. Notes. Biblio. Lang.: Eng.

UK-England. 1908. Critical studies. ▪Colonialism and misogyny in J.M. Barrie's *Peter Pan.*

3424 Behrendt, Patricia Flanagan. *Brilliant Sins and Exquisite Amusements: Eros and Aesthetics in the Works of Oscar Wilde.* Lincoln, NB: Univ. of Nebraska; 1988. 268 pp. Notes. Biblio. [Ph.D. Dissertation, Univ. Microfilms Order No. 9022986.] Lang.: Eng.

UK-England. 1881-1898. Critical studies. ▪The relationship between Wilde's treatment of sexual subject matter and the development of his literary aesthetics from the early poetry through the social comedies which highlighted his career.

3425 Belford, Barbara. "On Becoming Oscar Wilde: Transformations Seen In a Biographer's Journal." *AImago.* 1997 Win; 54(4): 333-345. Biblio. Illus.: Photo. Diagram. B&W. 8. Lang.: Eng.

UK-England. USA. 1998. Histories-sources. ▪Biographer of Wilde relates her affinity with his negative attributes and addictive behaviors, and wonders whether or not this sympathy will color her approach to the writing of the biography.

3426 Bennett, Susan. "Growing Up on *Cloud Nine*: Gender, Sexuality, and Farce." 29-40 in Rabillard, Sheila, ed. *Essays on Caryl Churchill: Contemporary Representations.* Winnipeg, MB/Buffalo, NY: Blizzard; 1998. 224 pp. Biblio. Notes. Lang.: Eng.

UK-England. 1979. Critical studies. ▪How gender and sexuality operate in Caryl Churchill's *Cloud Nine* and how they affect audience reception of her work and the construction of canonicity.

3427 Berg, Fredric. "Structure and Philosophy in *Man and Superman* and *Major Barbara.*" 144-161 in Innes, Christopher, ed. *The Cambridge Companion to George Bernard Shaw.* Cambridge/New York: Cambridge UP; 1998. 343 pp. (Cambridge Companions to Literature.) Index. Biblio. Notes. Pref. Illus.: Photo. 3. Lang.: Eng.

UK-England. 1901-1905. Critical studies. ▪Dramatic structure and philosophical themes in George Bernard Shaw's *Man and Superman* and *Major Barbara.*

3428 Boon, Richard; Price, Amanda. "Maps of the World: 'Neo-Jacobeanism' and Contemporary British Theatre." *MD.* 1998 Win; 41 (4): 635-654. Notes. Lang.: Eng.

DRAMA: —Plays/librettos/scripts

UK-England. 1986-1998. Critical studies. ▪Influence of Jacobean theatre on contemporary British playwrights and directors, particularly Howard Brenton and Howard Barker.

3429 Bryden, Ronald. "The Roads to *Heartbreak House.*" 180-194 in Innes, Christopher, ed. *The Cambridge Companion to George Bernard Shaw.* Cambridge/New York: Cambridge UP; 1998. 343 pp. (Cambridge Companions to Literature.) Index. Biblio. Notes. Pref. Illus.: Photo. 1. Lang.: Eng.

UK-England. 1916-1919. Critical studies. ▪Examines the challenges experienced by George Bernard Shaw in writing *Heartbreak House*, as well as some of the influences on the play from his personal life.

3430 Burkman, Katherine H. "Harold Pinter's *Ashes to Ashes*: Rebecca and Devlin as Albert Speer." *PintR.* 1998: 86-96. Notes. Biblio. Lang.: Eng.

UK-England. 1996. Critical studies. ▪Analysis of the characters Rebecca and Devlin in Pinter's play as reflections of the personality of Hitler's Defense Minister.

3431 Callens, Johan. "Dansend in het zuur van zijn zonden: Steven Berkoff's *Decadence.*" (Dancing in the Heartburn of One's Sins: Steven Berkoff's *Decadence.*) *Documenta.* 1994; 12(2): 69-88. Lang.: Dut.

UK-England. 1981. Critical studies. ▪Analysis of Berkoff's play.

3432 Callens, Johan. "Van 'Angry Young Men' tot 'Angry Young Women': Brits theater en politiek engagement." (From 'Angry Young Men' to 'Angry Young Women': British Theatre and Political Commitment.) *Documenta.* 1997; 17(4): 221-240. Lang.: Dut.

UK-England. 1971-1997. Critical studies. ▪Political and social consciousness in the plays of Hare and Churchill.

3433 Callens, Johan. "Grens/Gevallen: Harold Pinter's *Moonlight.*" (Borderline Cases: Harold Pinter's *Moonlight.*) *Documenta.* 1994; 12(4): 215-248. Lang.: Dut.

UK-England. 1994. Critical studies. ▪Analysis of Pinter's play.

3434 Callens, Johan. "De zomer van Edward Bond." (Edward Bond's *Summer.*) *Etcetera.* 1984(6): 17-19. Lang.: Dut.

UK-England. 1982. Critical studies. ▪Analysis of Edward Bond's *Summer.*

3435 Chiba, Yoko. *W.B. Yeats and Noh: From* Japonisme *to Zen.* Toronto, ON: Univ. of Toronto; 1988. 437 pp. Notes. Biblio. [Ph.D. Dissertation, Univ. Microfilms Order No. AAC NN65838.] Lang.: Eng.

UK-England. 1853-1939. Critical studies. ▪Study of the influence of the *nō* theatre on playwright W.B. Yeats, in the context of *japonisme* and the aesthetic of Zen Buddhism.

3436 Cousin, Geraldine. "Owning the Disowned: *The Skriker* in the Context of Earlier Plays by Caryl Churchill." 189-205 in Rabillard, Sheila, ed. *Essays on Caryl Churchill: Contemporary Representations.* Winnipeg, MB/Buffalo, NY: Blizzard; 1998. 224 pp. Biblio. Notes. Lang.: Eng.

UK-England. 1994. Critical studies. ▪Compares Caryl Churchill's *The Skriker* to her earlier work and stresses inconsistencies of theme and technique.

3437 Crawford, Fred D., ed. *Shaw.* University Park, PA: Pennsylvania State UP; 1998. 247 pp. (Annual of Bernard Shaw Studies 18.) Illus.: Photo. Pntg. B&W. 8. Lang.: Eng.

UK-England. Ireland. 1886-1955. Critical studies. ▪Collection of essays discussing the life and work of George Bernard Shaw. Particulars examined are his family genealogy, his relationship with actress Sarah Bernhardt, his influence on Eugene O'Neill, his ideas on feminism, and background and analysis of his plays *You Never Can Tell, Man and Superman*, and *Pygmalion.*

3438 Davis, Tracy C. "Shaw's Interstices of Empire: Decolonizing at Home and Abroad." 218-239 in Innes, Christopher, ed. *The Cambridge Companion to George Bernard Shaw.* Cambridge/New York: Cambridge UP; 1998. 343 pp. (Cambridge Companions to Literature.) Index. Biblio. Notes. Pref. Illus.: Photo. 3. Lang.: Eng.

UK-England. 1895-1935. Critical studies. ▪The construction, use, and presence of colonialism in Shaw's plays, including *Caesar and Cleopatra, John Bull's Other Island, Saint Joan, Candida, Heartbreak House*, and *Too True to Be Good.*

3439 de Gay, Jane. "Playing (with) Shakespeare: Bryony Lavery's *Ophelia* and Jane Prendergast's *I, Hamlet.*" *NTQ.* 1998 May; 14(2): 125-138. Notes. Illus.: Photo. B&W. 4. [Issue 54.] Lang.: Eng.

UK-England. 1997. Critical studies. ▪Attitudes of contemporary feminist theatre artists towards Shakespeare as reflected in Lavery's and Prendergast's plays.

3440 Denison, Patricia Doreen. *Pinero in Perspective.* Charlottesville, VA: Univ. of Virginia; 1987. 338 pp. Notes. Biblio. [Ph.D. Dissertation, Univ. Microfilms Order No. AAC 8801129.] Lang.: Eng.

UK-England. 1890-1910. Critical studies. ▪Argues that playwright Arthur Wing Pinero was not a conventional conservative but an innovative playwright who manipulated 'comfortable conventions' of his day. Works examined include *The Profligate, The Second Mrs. Tanqueray, The Notorious Mrs. Ebbsmith, Trelawny of the 'Wells', The Gay Lord Quex*, and *His House in Order.*

3441 Downey, Katherine Brown. *Perverse Midrashim: Oscar Wilde's* Salomé, *André Gide's* Saül, *and Three Hundred Years' Censorship of Biblical Drama.* Dallas, TX: Univ. of Texas; 1998. 237 pp. Biblio. Notes. [Ph.D. Dissertation, Univ. Microfilms Order No. AAC 9901887.] Lang.: Eng.

UK-England. France. 1892-1898. Critical studies. ▪The theme of aberration in *Salomé* by Oscar Wilde and *Saül* by André Gide in the context of the history of the censorship of biblical drama.

3442 Dungate, Rod. "The Distorting Mirror." *PlPl.* Apr 1998; 521: 25-27. Illus.: Photo. B&W. 1. Lang.: Eng.

UK-England: Birmingham. 1998. Histories-sources. ▪Interview with playwright and teacher Rod Dungate on lack of arts funding for regional theatre playwrights.

3443 Esslin, Martin. "Mysterium Brecht." *DB.* 1998; 2: 31-33. Illus.: Photo. Graphs. B&W. 2. Lang.: Ger.

UK-England. North America. 1933-1998. Historical studies. ▪Perceptions of Bertolt Brecht's work in English-speaking countries for the last 65 years, the difficulties with translations, guest performances, influences on authors.

3444 Evans, T.F. "The Later Shaw." 240-260 in Innes, Christopher, ed. *The Cambridge Companion to George Bernard Shaw.* Cambridge/New York: Cambridge UP; 1998. 343 pp. (Cambridge Companions to Literature.) Index. Biblio. Notes. Pref. Illus.: Photo. 3. Lang.: Eng.

UK-England. 1923-1947. Critical studies. ▪Examines the later plays of George Bernard Shaw, including *Saint Joan, The Apple Cart, Too True to Be Good, On the Rocks, The Millionairess, 'In Good King Charles's Golden Days'* and *Buoyant Billions.*

3445 Everding, Robert G. "Shaw and the Popular Context." 309-333 in Innes, Christopher, ed. *The Cambridge Companion to George Bernard Shaw.* Cambridge/New York: Cambridge UP; 1998. 343 pp. (Cambridge Companions to Literature.) Index. Biblio. Notes. Pref. Illus.: Photo. 3. Lang.: Eng.

UK-England. 1890-1990. Critical studies. ▪The popularity of Shaw's plays on stage and on film. Considers musical adaptations such as *My Fair Lady*, by Alan Jay Lerner and Frederick Loewe, directed by George Cukor, based on Shaw's *Pygmalion*, as well as *Dear Liar* by Jerome Kilty, based on Shaw's correspondence with actress Mrs. Patrick Campbell.

3446 Freed, Donald. "An Interview with Michael Billington, Author of *The Life and Work of Harold Pinter.*" *PintR.* 1998: 123-136. Lang.: Eng.

UK-England. 1961-1997. Histories-sources. ▪Interview with the biographer of the playwright regarding Pinter's plays, politics, and future work.

3447 Gillen, Francis. "Pinter at Work: An Introduction to the First Draft of *The Homecoming* and Its Relationship to the Completed Drama." *PintR.* 1998: 31-47. Notes. Biblio. Lang.: Eng.

UK-England. 1964. Critical studies. ▪Comparative analysis of Harold Pinter's first draft of his play with the final version.

DRAMA: —Plays/librettos/scripts

3448 Girard, René; Luciani, Giovanni, transl. *Shakespeare. Il teatro dell'invidia.* (Shakespeare: The Theatre of Envy.) Milan: Adelphi; 1998. 578 pp. (Saggi, 28.) Index. Lang.: Ita.
UK-England. 1990. Critical studies. ■Italian translation of *Shakespeare. Les feux de l'envie* (Paris: Grasset, 1990).

3449 Golomb, Liorah Anne. "The Nesting Instinct: The Power of Family in Peter Barnes's *The Ruling Class* and *The Bewitched* (with additional dialogue by William Shakespeare)." *ET.* 1998; 17(1): 63-75. Notes. Biblio. Lang.: Eng.
UK-England. 1968-1974. Critical studies. ■Argues that Barnes's depiction of the struggle of the upper classes to maintain their position is similar to that depicted by Renaissance playwrights.

3450 Gordon, David J. "Shavian Comedy and the Shadow of Wilde." 124-143 in Innes, Christopher, ed. *The Cambridge Companion to George Bernard Shaw.* Cambridge/New York: Cambridge UP; 1998. 343 pp. (Cambridge Companions to Literature.) Index. Biblio. Notes. Pref. Illus.: Photo. 2. Lang.: Eng.
UK-England. 1885-1900. Critical studies. ■Comparative analysis of the comedy in the plays of George Bernard Shaw and Oscar Wilde.

3451 Gross, Robert. "Making Relations: *Icecream*'s Dramaturgy of Skepticism." 114-128 in Rabillard, Sheila, ed. *Essays on Caryl Churchill: Contemporary Representations.* Winnipeg, MB/Buffalo, NY: Blizzard; 1998. 224 pp. Biblio. Notes. Lang.: Eng.
UK-England. 1989. Critical studies. ■'Fragmentation' in Caryl Churchill's *Icecream* and its corresponding audience reception as a form of skepticism.

3452 Hall, Ann C. "Looking for Mr. Goldberg: Spectacle and Speculation in Harold Pinter's *The Birthday Party.*" *PintR.* 1998 : 48-56. Notes. Biblio. Lang.: Eng.
UK-England. 1958. Critical studies. ■Analysis of Pinter's play based on Jacques Lacan's theoretical distinction between 'look' and 'gaze'.

3453 Harless, Winston Neely. *Characterization in Selected One-Act Plays of George Bernard Shaw: A Display of Enthymematic Argument.* Columbus, OH: Ohio State Univ; 1988. 198 pp. Biblio. Notes. [Ph.D. Dissertation, Univ. Microfilms Order No. AAC 8824515.] Lang.: Eng.
UK-England. 1890-1945. Histories-specific. ■The nature of rhetorical arguments in *O'Flaherty, V.C., The Shewing-Up of Blanco Posnet, Augustus Does His Bit, The Six of Calais, The Man of Destiny,* and *Overruled.*

3454 Hauck, Christina. "'It Seems Queer': The Censorship of *Her Wedding Night.*" *MD.* 1998 Win; 41(4): 546-556. Notes. Lang.: Eng.
UK-England. 1917. Historical studies. ■Examines reasons for the censoring of an unpublished one-act play by Florence Bates, *Her Wedding Night.*

3455 Heine, Beate. "Die Realität in Splittern." (Reality in Splinters.) *DB.* 1998; 11: 20-22. Illus.: Photo. B&W. 4. Lang.: Ger.
UK-England. USA. 1998. Historical studies. ■Describes the current dramas and pieces from British and American theatre focusing on Marc Ravenhill's *Handbag*, Tim Luscombe's *The One You Love*, Patrick Marber's *Closer*, Sarah Kane's *Blasted*, Enda Walsh's *Disco Pigs.*

3456 Henderson, Heather. *'All Life Transfigured': Structural and Thematic Disillusionment in Shaw's 'Heartbreak House'.* New Haven, CT: Yale Univ; 1988. 273 pp. Notes. Biblio. [Ph.D. Dissertation, Univ. Microfilms Order No. AAC 8917185.] Lang.: Eng.
UK-England. 1920. Critical studies. ■Disillusionment in George Bernard Shaw's *Heartbreak House.*

3457 Innes, Christopher. "'Nothing but talk, talk, talk—Shaw talk': Discussion Plays and the Making of Modern Drama." 162-179 in Innes, Christopher, ed. *The Cambridge Companion to George Bernard Shaw.* Cambridge/New York: Cambridge UP; 1998. 343 pp. (Cambridge Companions to Literature.) Index. Biblio. Notes. Pref. Illus.: Photo. 2. Lang.: Eng.
UK-England. 1890-1910. Critical studies. ■Argues that the clash of opinion, reflected in the long discussions of the characters, replaces action in the plays of George Bernard Shaw, and that this technique influenced all of modern drama. Plays examined include *Getting Married* and *Misalliance.*

3458 Jenkins, Anthony. "Social Relations: An Overview." 14-28 in Rabillard, Sheila, ed. *Essays on Caryl Churchill: Contemporary Representations.* Winnipeg, MB/Buffalo, NY: Blizzard; 1998. 224 pp. Biblio. Notes. Lang.: Eng.
UK-England. 1975-1997. Critical studies. ■Examines the breadth of Caryl Churchill's work and suggests a new paradigm for analyzing the works, rather than Brechtian feminism. Argues that her work be thought of as cumulative and meditative, and suggests that this may lead to new emotional and psychological insights.

3459 Kaplan, Laurie. "*In the Native State/Indian Ink*: Footnoting the Footnotes on Empire." *MD.* 1998 Fall; 41(3): 337-346. Notes. Lang.: Eng.
UK-England. 1991-1995. Historical studies. ■Tom Stoppard's attitude toward misguided academics, and the difference between 'doers and thinkers,' as reflected in his radio play *In the Native State*, and the expansion of the idea in his stage version of the work as *Indian Ink.*

3460 Kelly, Katherine E. "Imprinting the Stage: Shaw and the Publishing Trade, 1883-1903." 25-54 in Innes, Christopher, ed. *The Cambridge Companion to George Bernard Shaw.* Cambridge/New York: Cambridge UP; 1998. 343 pp. (Cambridge Companions to Literature.) Index. Biblio. Notes. Pref. Illus.: Photo. Dwg. Sketches. 4. Lang.: Eng.
UK-England. 1883-1903. Critical studies. ■Shaw's advocacy for play publication as a way to establish both legal ownership and primary authorship. Argues that publication promoted the literary merits of drama and the author's right to it as property.

3461 Kern, Barbara Ellen Goldstein. *Transference in Selected Stage Plays of Harold Pinter.* Madison, NJ: Drew Univ; 1987. 224 pp. Notes. Biblio. [Ph.D. Dissertation, Univ. Microfilms Order No. AAC 8716914.] Lang.: Eng.
UK-England. 1960-1985. Critical studies. ■The presence of transference, the central concept in psychoanalysis, in Pinter's *The Room, A Slight Ache* and *Tea Party.*

3462 Knowles, Ronald. "From London: Harold Pinter 1996-97 and 1997-98." *PintR.* 1998: 165-185. Lang.: Eng.
UK-England: London. 1996-1998. Biographical studies. ■Review of Harold Pinter's activities and events related to his writings, primarily in London from 1996 through 1998. Includes his direction of Reginald Rose's *Twelve Angry Men* at the Comedy Theatre, and the premiere of his play *Ashes to Ashes* under his direction at the Lyttelton.

3463 Kritzer, Amelia Howe. "Systemic Poisons in Churchill's Recent Plays." 159-173 in Rabillard, Sheila, ed. *Essays on Caryl Churchill: Contemporary Representations.* Winnipeg, MB/Buffalo, NY: Blizzard; 1998. 224 pp. Biblio. Notes. Lang.: Eng.
UK-England. 1990-1997. Critical studies. ■Analyzes the politically, chemically, and emotionally 'poisoned' worlds in Caryl Churchill's most recent work, such as *Mad Forest, The Skriker* and *Lives of the Great Poisoners.* Argues that audiences become aware of their participation in the performance event and take responsibility for their roles in the theatrical and the wider environment.

3464 Kritzer, Amelia Howe. *Open Ended Inquiries: The Plays of Caryl Churchill.* Madison, WI: Univ. of Wisconsin; 1988. 556 pp. Biblio. Notes. [Ph.D. Dissertation, Univ. Microfilms Order No. AAC 8824097.] Lang.: Eng.
UK-England. 1959-1985. Critical studies. ■Survey and feminist analysis of the produced works of Caryl Churchill for radio, television, and the stage.

3465 Labre, Jean-François. "Le miroir assassin." (The Killing Mirror.) *ASO.* 1998 Sep/Oct.; 186: 106-113. Illus.: Photo. Dwg. B&W. 6. Lang.: Fre.
UK-England. France. 1854-1900. Biographical studies. ■The work of Oscar Wilde as playwright and author, with attention to his short story 'The Birthday of the Little Princess' which was adapted to operatic form in Zemlinsky's *Der Zwerg.*

3466 Lane, Harry. "Secrets as Strategies for Protection and Oppression in *Top Girls.*" 60-68 in Rabillard, Sheila, ed.

DRAMA: —Plays/librettos/scripts

Essays on Caryl Churchill: Contemporary Representations. Winnipeg, MB/Buffalo, NY: Blizzard; 1998. 224 pp. Biblio. Notes. Lang.: Eng.
UK-England. 1982. Critical studies. ■The function of secrets and information management in playwright Caryl Churchill's *Top Girls.* This analysis is said to disclose the political import of the play in light of its historical context.

3467 Lee, Josephine D. *Language and Action in the Plays of Wilde, Shaw and Stoppard.* Princeton, NJ: Princeton Univ; 1987. 212 pp. Notes. Biblio. [Ph.D. Dissertation, Univ. Microfilms Order No. AAC 8727368.] Lang.: Eng.
UK-England. 1890-1985. Critical studies. ■The relationship between linguistic style and action in Oscar Wilde's *The Importance of Being Earnest*, George Bernard Shaw's *Major Barbara, Man and Superman*, and *Heartbreak House*, and plays by Tom Stoppard.

3468 MacGregor, Catherine. "Undoing the Body Politic: Representing Rape in *Women Beware Women.*" *ThR.* 1998 Spr; 23(1): 14-23. Notes. Lang.: Eng.
UK-England. 1625-1986. Historical studies. ■Compares the original script of Thomas Middleton's *Women Beware Women* with its adaptation by Howard Barker. Uses a feminist perspective to analyze the two scripts, concentrating on the themes of lust and desire and the culmination of the plot in the rape of Bianca.

3469 Mackie, W. Craven. "Bunbury Pure and Simple." *MD.* 1998 Spr; 41(2): 327-330. Notes. Lang.: Eng.
UK-England: Worthing. 1894. Biographical studies. ■Focusing on Oscar Wilde's holiday in Worthing in 1894, where he was working on what would eventually be *The Importance of Being Earnest*, attempts to find the source of the name of the character of Bunbury.

3470 Marker, Frederick J. "Shaw's Early Plays." 103-123 in Innes, Christopher, ed. *The Cambridge Companion to George Bernard Shaw.* Cambridge/New York: Cambridge UP; 1998. 343 pp. (Cambridge Companions to Literature.) Index. Biblio. Notes. Pref. Illus.: Photo. 2. Lang.: Eng.
UK-England. 1892-1900. Critical studies. ■The influence of critic and friend William Archer on Shaw's *Widowers' Houses, The Philanderer*, and *Mrs. Warren's Profession.*

3471 McDonald, Jan. "Shaw and the Court Theatre." 261-282 in Innes, Christopher, ed. *The Cambridge Companion to George Bernard Shaw.* Cambridge/New York: Cambridge UP; 1998. 343 pp. (Cambridge Companions to Literature.) Index. Biblio. Notes. Pref. Illus.: Photo. 1. Lang.: Eng.
UK-England. 1904-1909. Critical studies. ■Examines George Bernard Shaw's association with the Court Theatre, its founders Harley Granville-Barker and J.E. Vedrenne, and its leading actress Lillah McCarthy. Also Shaw as director at the Court, and the influence of the Court 'experiment' on later British theatre.

3472 McGill, Rachael. "Coming Out." *PI.* 1998 Nov.; 14(2): 8-11, 29. Illus.: Photo. B&W. 4. Lang.: Eng.
UK-England. 1998. Histories-sources. ■Interview with playwright Jonathan Harvey regarding the transfer of his play *Guiding Star* from Liverpool's Everyman Theatre to a National Theatre production at the Cottesloe.

3473 McWilliam, G.H. "Pirandello in Inghilterra." (Pirandello in England.) *Ariel.* 1998; 13(1-2): 167-176. Notes. Lang.: Ita.
UK-England. 1924-1990. Historical studies. ■Argues that, in England, Pirandello's works are seldom performed and not always appreciated by the audience. Pirandello, however, is well known and studied by English scholars and university professors. This contradiction leads to an overly academic and intellectual approach to Pirandello's works.

3474 Melbourne, Lucy. "'Plotting the Apple of Knowledge': Tom Stoppard's *Arcadia* as Iterated Theatrical Algorithm." *MD.* 1998 Win; 41(4): 557-572. Notes. Lang.: Eng.
UK-England. 1993. Critical studies. ■Stoppard's theatrical use of mathematics in *Arcadia.*

3475 Merritt, Susan Hollis. "Harold Pinter Bibliography: 1994-1996." *PintR.* 1998: 186-218. Lang.: Eng.
UK-England. 1994-1996. Bibliographical studies. ■Bibliography of works by and about Harold Pinter published or performed 1994-96.

3476 Merschmeier, Michael. "Die Welt ist im Arsch." (The World Is Fucked Up.) *THeute.* 1998; 3: 50-54. Illus.: Photo. B&W. 3. Lang.: Ger.
UK-England. Germany. 1998. Critical studies. ■Analysis of Mark Ravenhill's *Shopping and Fucking*, a portrait of the playwright, and a critique of the production directed by Thomas Ostermeier at Deutsches Theater, Baracke.

3477 Morelli, Henriette Marguerite. *Somebody Sings: Brechtian Epic Devices in the Plays of Caryl Churchill.* Saskatoon, SK: Univ. of Saskatchewan; 1998. 261 pp. Notes. Biblio. [Ph.D. Dissertation, Univ. Microfilms Order No. AAC NQ27419.] Lang.: Eng.
UK-England. 1976-1986. Critical studies. ■Argues that as a socialist feminist, Churchill is attracted to epic theatre's counter-discursive, counter-hegemonic elements. Works analyzed include *Light Shining in Buckinghamshire, Vinegar Tom, Cloud Nine, Top Girls, Fen*, and *A Mouthful of Birds.*

3478 Murray, Thomas J. *J.M. Barrie and the Search for Self.* Cambridge, MA: Harvard Univ; 1988. 266 pp. Biblio. Notes. [Ph.D. Dissertation, Univ. Microfilms Order No. AAC 8908997.] Lang.: Eng.
UK-England. 1892-1937. Critical studies. ■Applies postmodern psychological theories of 'self-psychology' to plays and novels of J.M. Barrie.

3479 Oliva, Judy Lee. *Theatricalizing Politics: David Hare and a Tradition of British Political Drama.* Chicago, IL: Northwestern Univ; 1988. 386 pp. Biblio. Notes. [Ph.D. Dissertation, Univ. Microfilms Order No. AAC 8823016.] Lang.: Eng.
UK-England. 1969-1986. Critical studies. ■The theatricalization of social and political issues in the plays of David Hare.

3480 Parks, Barbara Louise. *George Bernard Shaw, Victorian, Modern, and Postmodern Prophet: A Rhetorical Analysis of Three Plays.* Los Angeles, CA: California State Univ; 1988. 115 pp. Notes. Biblio. [M.A. Thesis, Univ. Microfilms Order No. AAC 1338312.] Lang.: Eng.
UK-England. 1896-1908. Critical studies. ■The use of rhetoric in *Mrs. Warren's Profession, Candida*, and *Getting Married.* Argues that rhetorical examination of these plays reveals Shaw's perspectives on marriage, family life, religion, and the status of women.

3481 Peters, Sally. "Shaw's Life: A Feminist in Spite of Himself." 3-24 in Innes, Christopher, ed. *The Cambridge Companion to George Bernard Shaw.* Cambridge/New York: Cambridge UP; 1998. 343 pp. (Cambridge Companions to Literature.) Index. Biblio. Notes. Pref. Illus.: Photo. 2. Lang.: Eng.
UK-England. 1856-1950. Critical studies. ■Examines feminist presence in Shaw's dramatic criticism, plays, and novels and places his feminism in biographical and historical context.

3482 Ponnuswami, Meenakshi. "Celts and Celticists in Howard Brenton's *The Romans in Britain.*" *JDTC.* 1998 Spr; 12(2): 69-88 . Notes. Lang.: Eng.
UK-England. 1980-1981. Critical studies. ■Political and methodological implications of Brenton's reworking of the history of British colonialism in *The Romans in Britain.*

3483 Ponnuswami, Meenakshi. "Fanshen in the English Revolution: Caryl Churchill's *Light Shining in Buckinghamshire.*" 41-59 in Rabillard, Sheila, ed. *Essays on Caryl Churchill: Contemporary Representations.* Winnipeg, MB/Buffalo, NY: Blizzard; 1998. 224 pp. Biblio. Notes. Lang.: Eng.
UK-England. 1970-1976. Critical studies. ■Churchill's handling of source materials in *Light Shining in Buckinghamshire*, and how they operate in the 'countercultural' context in which the play was written.

3484 Poole, Gabrielle. *Byron's Heroes and the Byronic Hero.* Notre Dame, IN: Univ. of Notre Dame; 1998. 182 pp. Notes. Biblio. [Ph.D. Dissertation, Univ. Microfilms Order No. AAC 9835541.] Lang.: Eng.
UK-England. 1800-1824. Critical studies. ■Analysis of the relationship between the Byronic hero as Weberian ideal-type and the actual protagonists of Byron's works to reveal how Byron constructed the social, political, gender, and economic worlds of his texts.

DRAMA: —Plays/librettos/scripts

3485 Poole, Mary Margaret. *The Dynamic of Contradiction in Selected Plays of Edward Bond: A Study in Dramatic Technique.* Evanston, IL: Northwestern Univ; 1987. 268 pp. Biblio. Notes. [Ph.D. Dissertation, Univ. Microfilms Order No. AAC 8710374.] Lang.: Eng.

UK-England. 1962-1987. Critical studies. ■Examines the complex audience response effected through the technique of contradiction in the plays of Edward Bond. Argues that contradiction is essential to Bond's dramatic form.

3486 Powell, Kerry. "New Women, New Plays, and Shaw in the 1890s." 76-102 in Innes, Christopher, ed. *The Cambridge Companion to George Bernard Shaw.* Cambridge/New York: Cambridge UP; 1998. 343 pp. (Cambridge Companions to Literature.) Index. Biblio. Notes. Pref. Illus.: Photo. 2. Lang.: Eng.

UK-England. 1890-1900. Critical studies. ■The 'New Woman' in the English theatre in the 1890s, both as producers, actors, and directors and as characters in the 'new' theatre of Ibsen and Shaw, with emphasis on how Shaw used these new cultural roles for women in his plays and criticism. Plays examined include *Mrs. Warren's Profession, The Philanderer, Man and Superman, Heartbreak House,* and *You Never Can Tell.*

3487 Preusser, Gerhard. "Sex gestrichen—Sprache ist Macht." (Sex-Laden Language Is Power.) *THeute.* 1998; 6: 43-45. Illus.: Photo. B&W. 2. Lang.: Ger.

UK-England. Germany: Cologne, Bonn. 1998. Critical studies. ■Describes the perception of young British playwrights in Sarah Kane's *Phaedra's Love* directed by Ricarda Beilharz and John von Düffel at Schauspiel Bonn and David Harrower's *Knives in Hens* directed by Jacqueline Kornmüller at Schauspiel Köln.

3488 Raab, Michael. "Ein Königsdrama—very british." (A King's Drama—Very British.) *DB.* 1998; 11: 27-29. Illus.: Photo. B&W. 3. Lang.: Ger.

UK-England. 1994-1998. Critical studies. ■Portrait of English playwright Alan Bennett and his latest successful pieces *Writing Home, Talking Heads* and *The Madness of George III.*

3489 Rayner, Alice. "All Her Children: Caryl Churchill's Furious Ghosts." 206-224 in Rabillard, Sheila, ed. *Essays on Caryl Churchill: Contemporary Representations.* Winnipeg, MB/ Buffalo, NY: Blizzard; 1998. 224 pp. Biblio. Notes. Lang.: Eng.

UK-England. 1994. Critical studies. ■Argues that the language of 'encryption' in Caryl Churchill's *The Skriker,* instead of alienating audiences, allows access to the emotional 'loss' inherent in the play.

3490 Renton, Linda. "From Real to Real: Pinter and the Object of Desire in *Party Time* and *The Remains of the Day.*" *PintR.* 1998: 97-109. Notes. Biblio. Lang.: Eng.

UK-England. 1991-1996. Critical studies. ■Comparison of thematic content between Pinter's play *Party Time* and his screenplay for *The Remains of the Day.* Argues that his film scripts are extensions of his stage plays, exploring the relationship between internal desires and the external world.

3491 Runkel, Richard. *Theatre Workshop: Its Philosophy, Plays, Process and Productions.* Austin, TX: Univ. of Texas; 1987. 351 pp. Biblio. Notes. [Ph.D. Dissertation, Univ. Microfilms Order No. 8717524.] Lang.: Eng.

UK-England: London. 1945-1970. Critical studies. ■Analyzes the development of Theatre Workshop, founded by Ewan MacColl and Joan Littlewodd, emphasizing its theoretical bases as a means of understanding and evaluating the group's plays, its training and rehearsal methods, and its productions.

3492 Salamensky, Shelley Ilene. *The Wilde Word: Talk as Performance at the Fin de Siecle.* Cambridge, MA: Harvard Univ; 1998. 254 pp. Notes. Biblio. [Ph.D. Dissertation, Univ. Microfilms Order No. AAC 9838847.] Lang.: Eng.

UK-England. 1890-1900. Critical studies. ■'Talk' as structuring principle in the work and life of Oscar Wilde. Argues that discourse surrounding the word reflected anxiety about decadence, dissolution, sexuality, gender, law, transgression, and contagion in turn-of-the-century London.

3493 Selmon, Michael Layne. *Engendering Drama: Caryl Churchill and the Stages of Reform.* College Park, MD: Univ. of Maryland; 1988. 195 pp. Notes. Biblio. [Ph.D. Dissertation, Univ. Microfilms Order No. AAC 8827120.] Lang.: Eng.

UK-England. 1959-1987. Critical studies. ■Proposes a unifying context for Churchill's drama and analyzes her stage plays from *Having a Wonderful Time* to *Serious Money.*

3494 Sierz, Aleks. "Cool Britannia?: 'In-Yer-Face' Writing in the British Theatre Today." *NTQ.* 1998 Nov.; 14(4): 324-333. Notes. Biblio. Illus.: Photo. B&W. 4. [Issue 56.] Lang.: Eng.

UK-England. 1991-1998. Critical studies. ■Examines the rash of plays about sex, drugs, and violence—notably Irvine Welsh's *Trainspotting,* Jez Butterworth's *Mojo,* Mark Ravenhill's *Shopping and Fucking,* and Sarah Kane's *Blasted*—and asks whether they have anything in common beyond a flamboyant theatricality and a desperate need to shock.

3495 Sterner, Mark Hamilton. *Shaw's* Man and Superman *and the Theatre of Dialectics.* Austin, TX: Univ. of Texas; 1987. 304 pp. Biblio. Notes. [Ph.D. Dissertation, Univ. Microfilms Order No. 8717544.] Lang.: Eng.

UK-England. 1905. Critical studies. ■George Bernard Shaw's *Man and Superman* as a philosophical treatise in theatrical form.

3496 Tabert, Nils. "Moderne Märchen, die unsere ängste spiegeln." (Modern Fairytales That Reflect Our Fears.) *THeute.* 1998; Yb: 88-91. Illus.: Photo. B&W. 2. Lang.: Ger.

UK-England. 1998. Histories-sources. ■Interview with Mark Ravenhill who was chosen by critics of *Theater Heute* as playwright of the year about the reception of his play *Shopping and Fucking* by critics and audience in London.

3497 Thompson, Ann. "Teena Rochfort Smith, Frederick Furnivall, and the New Shakespeare Society's Four-Text Edition of *Hamlet.*" *SQ.* 1998 Sum; 49(2): 125-139. Notes. Illus.: Photo. B&W. 4. Lang.: Eng.

UK-England. 1882-1883. Historical studies. ■History of the New Shakespeare Society's unfinished four-text edition of *Hamlet,* the relationship between the Society's founder Furnivall and the text's young editor Smith who died before it could be completed.

3498 Waites, Aline. "John Hopkins—Playwright and Screenwriter: January 1931-23 July 1998." *PlPl.* 1998 Oct.; 527: 12. Lang.: Eng.

UK-England: London. USA: Hollywood, CA. 1931-1998. Biographical studies. ■Memories of career of stage and screen writer John Hopkins.

3499 Wang, H.C. *To Steal at Discretion: Stage Adaptations of Novels.* London: Unpublished PhD, Royal Holloway & Bedford New College, Univ. of London; 1996. Notes. Biblio. [Abstract in *Aslib Index to Theses* 47-5477.] Lang.: Eng.

UK-England. 1980-1995. Critical studies. ■Examines problems and strategies concerning the adaptation of novels for theatrical presentation and discusses in detail a variety of possible approaches.

3500 Weeks, Stephen Hyer. *Alternative Histories: British Historical Drama from the Left Since 1956.* Stanford, CA: Stanford Univ; 1988. 366 pp. Biblio. Notes. [Ph.D. Dissertation, Univ. Microfilms Order No. AAC 8826258.] Lang.: Eng.

UK-England. 1956-1988. Critical studies. ■How British historical drama has changed, with reference to John Arden, Margaretta D'Arcy, Peter Barnes, Edward Bond, Caryl Churchill, and Howard Barker.

3501 Weiss, Rudolf. "Harley Granville-Barker: The First English Chekhovian?" *NTQ.* 1998 Feb.; 14(1): 53-62. Notes. Biblio. [Issue 53.] Lang.: Eng.

UK-England, Russia. 1900-1946. Critical studies. ■The apparent lack of influence of Čechov on the plays of Granville-Barker.

3502 Weissengruber, Erik Paul. *Utopia and Politics in the Theatre of Howard Barker.* Minneapolis, MN: Univ. of Minnesota; 1998. 356 pp. Biblio. Notes. [Ph.D. Dissertation, Univ. Microfilms Order No. 9907526.] Lang.: Eng.

UK-England. 1960-1992. Critical studies. ■The evolution of political thought in Barker's *Crimes in Hot Countries, Victory: Choices in Reaction, Pity in History, The Castle,* and *Brutopia.*

3503 Wikander, Matthew H. "Reinventing the History Play: *Caesar and Cleopatra, Saint Joan,* and *'In Good King Charles's Golden Days'.*" 195-217 in Innes, Christopher, ed. *The Cambridge Companion to George Bernard Shaw.* Cambridge/ New York: Cambridge UP; 1998. 343 pp. (Cambridge Companions to Literature.) Index. Biblio. Notes. Pref. Illus.: Photo. 4. Lang.: Eng.

UK-England. 1899-1939. Critical studies. ■George Bernard Shaw's 're-invention' of the history play genre in the larger historical context of history plays in England since Shakespeare.

3504 Wilson, Ann. "Failure and the Limits of Representation in *The Skriker.*" 174-188 in Rabillard, Sheila, ed. *Essays on Caryl Churchill: Contemporary Representations.* Winnipeg, MB/Buffalo, NY: Blizzard; 1998. 224 pp. Biblio. Notes. Lang.: Eng.

UK-England. 1994. Critical studies. ■Argues that the 'failure' of Caryl Churchill's play with audiences and critics resulted from its dense nature, which tested the limits of representation and led to a lack of 'interpretive clarity.' Suggests new strategies for interpreting Churchill's work.

3505 Wing, Joylynn. "*Mad Forest* and the Interplay of Languages." 129-141 in Rabillard, Sheila, ed. *Essays on Caryl Churchill: Contemporary Representations.* Winnipeg, MB/ Buffalo, NY: Blizzard; 1998. 224 pp. Biblio. Notes. Lang.: Eng.

UK-England. 1990. Critical studies. ■Examines the performance of language in Caryl Churchill's *Mad Forest* and its effect on audiences. Argues that audiences have an equal responsibility to 'make meaning' out of the play.

3506 Wisenthal, J.L. "'Please remember, this is Italian opera': Shaw's Plays as Music-Drama." 283-308 in Innes, Christopher, ed. *The Cambridge Companion to George Bernard Shaw.* Cambridge/New York: Cambridge UP; 1998. 343 pp. (Cambridge Companions to Literature.) Index. Biblio. Notes. Pref. Illus.: Photo. 1. Lang.: Eng.

UK-England. 1888-1950. Critical studies. ■The presence of music in the plays of George Bernard Shaw, as well as his music criticism, and suggestions as to how orchestral music could be used in productions of Shaw's plays.

3507 Wixson, Christopher. "'Voiceless Presence': Desire, Deceit, and Harold Pinter's *The Collection.*" *PintR.* 1998: 57-73. Notes. Biblio. Lang.: Eng.

UK-England. 1975. Critical studies. ■Pinter's use of language to explore the nature of heterosexual and homosexual relations in his play.

3508 Wolf, Milton T., ed. *Shaw and Science Fiction.* University Park, PA: Pennsylvania State UP; 1997. 294 pp. (Annual of Bernard Shaw Studies 17.) Lang.: Eng.

UK-England. Ireland. 1887-1998. Critical studies. ■Collection of essays pertaining to George Bernard Shaw and his relationship to the literary genre of science fiction. Discusses its influence upon him, and his influence upon playwrights such as Čapek and Witkacy, and science fiction writers such as Ray Bradbury and Robert A. Heinlein. Examines Shaw's plays *Back to Methuselah, Don Juan in Hell, Saint Joan,* and *Man and Superman* for elements of the genre.

3509 Worth, Katharine. "Words for Music Perhaps." 9-20 in Bryden, Mary, ed. *Samuel Beckett and Music.* Oxford: Clarendon; 1998. 267 pp. Index. Notes. Biblio. Lang.: Eng.

UK-England. 1945-1995. Critical studies. ■The work of Humphrey Searle composing music for Samule Beckett's plays *Words and Music* and *Cascando.*

3510 Young, Stuart. "Fin-de-siècle Reflections and Revisions: Wertenbaker Challenges British Chekhov Tradition in *The Break of Day.*" *MD.* 1998 Fall; 41(3): 442-460. Notes. Lang.: Eng.

UK-England. Russia. 1901-1995. Critical studies. ■Examines the artistic license taken by Timberlake Wertenbaker in her adaptation of Čechov's *Three Sisters (Tri sestry), The Break of Day.*

3511 Doyle, Maria-Elena. *Challenging the Cathleen Paradigm: Rethinking Gender and Nationalism in Northern Irish Drama.* Los Angeles, CA: Univ. of California; 1998. 262 pp. Notes. Biblio. [Ph.D. Dissertation, Univ. Microfilms Order No. AAC 9906151.] Lang.: Eng.

UK-Ireland. 1902-1997. Critical studies. ■Examines the play *Cathleen ni Houlihan* by W.B. Yeats and Lady Gregory in light of its effect on dramatic production and gender in Northern Ireland, including plays by John Boyd, Anne Devlin, Terry Eagleton, Eva Gore-Booth, Seamus Heaney, Frank McGuinness, Bill Morrison, Stewart Parker, Tom Paulin, Christina Reid and David Rudkin.

3512 Hohenleitner, Kathleen. *'The Disquiet Between Two Aesthetics': Brian Friel's Plays and the Field Day Theatre Company.* Notre Dame, IN: Univ. of Notre Dame; 1998. 202 pp. Notes. Biblio. [Ph.D. Dissertation, Univ. Microfilms Order No. AAC 9823935.] Lang.: Eng.

UK-Ireland. 1980-1988. Critical studies. ■Examines the plays of Brian Friel from the foundation of the Field Day Theatre Company to his final Field Day play in 1988. Contrasts the cultural politics of Field Day's theatrical productions with the Field Day Anthology of Irish Writing.

3513 Findlay, Bill. "Silesian into Scots: Gerhart Hauptmann's *The Weavers.*" *MD.* 1998 Spr; 41(1): 90-104. Illus.: Photo. B&W. 3. Lang.: Eng.

UK-Scotland: Dundee, Glasgow. 1997. Histories-sources. ■Translator's account of difficulties faced translating Hauptmann's play into Scots dialect for the Dundee Repertory Theatre.

3514 McLaughlin, William J. *'Scotsmen in Hobnail Boots': An Analysis of the Original Works of Peter Barnes.* Pittsburgh, PA: Univ. of Pittsburgh; 1987. 281 pp. Biblio. Notes. [Ph.D. Dissertation, Univ. Microfilms Order No. AAC 8808337.] Lang.: Eng.

UK-Scotland. 1985. Critical studies. ■Analysis of three different versions of Barnes's *Red Noses.*

3515 "Robert Anderson." *DGQ.* 1998 Spr; 35(1): 4-15. Lang.: Eng.

USA. 1945-1998. Histories-sources. ■Interview with the playwright regarding his career in the theatre and his work as a screenwriter.

3516 "Douglas Carter Beane: From Boas to Bees." *DGQ.* 1998 Spr; 35(1): 28-34. Lang.: Eng.

USA. 1980-1998. Histories-sources. ■Interview with the playwright about his play *As Bees in Honey Drown,* screenplay *To Wong Foo, Thanks for Everything, Julie Newmar,* and his work as artistic director of the Drama Dept. theatre group.

3517 "Romulus Linney: 'A Few Things Are Not for Sale'." *SoTh.* 1998 Sum; 39(3): 20-23. Illus.: Photo. B&W. 1. Lang.: Eng.

USA: Birmingham, AL. 1998. Historical studies. ■The SETC All Convention address by playwright Romulus Linney.

3518 "The Word Made Flesh." *Econ.* 1998 Nov 7; 349(8093): 90. Illus.: Photo. B&W. 1. Lang.: Eng.

USA: New York, NY. UK-England: London. 1998. Critical studies. ■Discusses the nineties' vogue for stage adaptations of large novels, with emphasis on the London theatre company Shared Experience's adaptations of Tolstoy's *Anna Karenina* and George Eliot's *The Mill on the Floss* by Helen Edmundson and American artistic director Nancy Meckler and performed at BAM's Majestic Theatre.

3519 Anadolu-Okur, Nilgun. *Contemporary African-American Theatre: Afrocentricity in the Works of Larry Neal, Amiri Baraka, and Charles Fuller.* New York, NY/London: Garland; 1997. 199 pp. Notes. Biblio. Lang.: Eng.

USA. 1960-1998. Critical studies. ■African-American identity and the Afrocentric idea in the work of Neal, Baraka, and Fuller.

3520 Andreach, Robert J. "Ellen McLaughlin's *Iphigenia and Other Daughters*: A Classic Trilogy from a Contemporary Perspective." *CLS.* 1998; 35(4): 379-392. Notes. Lang.: Eng.

USA: New York, NY. 1995. Critical studies. ■Analysis of McLaughlin's adaptation and production of the *Oresteia,* using Euripedes' *Iphigenia in Aulis (Iphigéneia he en Aulíde)* and *Iphigenia in Tauris (Iphigéneia hé en Tauríde)* and Sophocles' *Elektra* staged at the Classic Stage Company.

3521 Applebaum, Susan Rae. *Mentor Mothers and Female Adolescent Protagonists: Rethinking Children's Theatre History Through Burnett's 'The Little Princess', Chorpenning's 'Cinderella', and Zeder's 'Mother Hicks'.* Evanston, IL: Northwestern Univ; 1998. 253 pp. Notes. Biblio. [Ph.D. Dissertation, Univ. Microfilms Order No. AAC 9832546.] Lang.: Eng.

USA. 1903-1983. Critical studies. ■Uses theories of feminist dramatic criticism, semiotics, and women's psychological development. Examines selected twentieth-century American women playwrights and their plays for young people, considering the intersection of children's theatre history and changing theorizations of the mother-daughter relationship at adolescence.

3522 Ardolino, Frank. "Irish Myth and Legends in *Long Day's Journey Into Night* and *A Moon for the Misbegotten.*" *EOR.* 1998 Spr/Fall; 22(1/2): 63-69. Biblio. Lang.: Eng.
USA. 1942-1956. Critical studies. ■Importance of O'Neill's Irish ancestry and use of Irish folklore in the two plays with emphasis on the conflicts between Shaughnessy and Harkel in *Long Day's Journey Into Night* and between Hogan and Harder in *A Moon for the Misbegotten.*

3523 Ards, Angela. "The Diaspora Comes to Dartmouth." *AmTh.* 1998 May/June; 15(5): 50-52. Illus.: Photo. B&W. 2. Lang.: Eng.
USA: Hanover, NH. 1998. Historical studies. ■Report on the National Black Theatre Summit held at Dartmouth College in March 1998. Includes comments from August Wilson and Ntozake Shange about the future of African-American theatre.

3524 Banks, Carol P. *Playwriting for Different Age Levels.* New York, NY: New York Univ; 1988. 279 pp. Notes. Biblio. [Ph.D. Dissertation, Univ. Microfilms Order No. 8825211.] Lang.: Eng.
USA. 1988. Empirical research. ■The theory and practice of writing plays for adults and for young audiences. Seeks to identify and overcome the limitations of young people's plays. Includes the author's experience of writing about two plays about Joan of Arc, one for adults and one for children.

3525 Barlow, Judith E. "O'Neill's Female Characters." 164-177 in Manheim, Michael, ed. *The Cambridge Companion to Eugene O'Neill.* Cambridge/New York, NY: Cambridge UP; 1998. 256 pp. (Cambridge Companions to Literature.) Index. Biblio. Notes. Lang.: Eng.
USA. 1920-1953. Critical studies. ■Feminist examination of the female characters in the plays of Eugene O'Neill, including *Bread and Butter, Before Breakfast, Beyond the Horizon, Strange Interlude, The Iceman Cometh, Mourning Becomes Electra, Desire Under the Elms*, and *Long Day's Journey Into Night.*

3526 Barto, Dan. *Owen Davis: From Melodrama to Realism.* New York, NY: New York Univ; 1987. 278 pp. Biblio. Notes. [Ph.D. Dissertation, Univ. Microfilms Order No. AAC 8803575.] Lang.: Eng.
USA. 1905-1923. Critical studies. ■Explores fifteen years in the career of American dramatist Owen Davis from the early melodramas based on spectacle to the realistic play *Icebound* (1923). Plays examined include *The Wishing Ring* (1910), *Driftwood* (1911), *Sinners* (1915), *Forever After* (1918), *No Place Like Home* (1920), and *The Detour* (1921).

3527 Berg, Allison; Taylor, Merideth. "Enacting Difference: Marita Bonner's *Purple Flower* and the Ambiguities of Race." *AfAmR.* 1998 Fall; 32(3): 469-480. Notes. Biblio. Lang.: Eng.
USA. 1927. Critical studies. ■Performance analysis of Bonner's play, with some historical background regarding the text.

3528 Berlin, Normand. "The Late Plays." 82-95 in Manheim, Michael, ed. *The Cambridge Companion to Eugene O'Neill.* Cambridge/New York, NY: Cambridge UP; 1998. 256 pp. (Cambridge Companions to Literature.) Index. Biblio. Notes. Lang.: Eng.
USA. 1939-1943. Critical studies. ■The late plays of Eugene O'Neill, including *The Iceman Cometh, Long Day's Journey Into Night, A Moon for the Misbegotten*, and *Hughie.* Analyzes O'Neill's elimination of complicated theatrical techniques, his new simplicity of story and characters, as well as his preoccupation with imagination and sound, silence, light and gesture.

3529 Bernstein, Samuel J. "*Hughie*: Inner Dynamics and Canonical Relevance." *EOR.* 1998 Spr/Fall; 22(1/2): 77-104. Biblio. Lang.: Eng.
USA. 1959. Critical studies. ■Analysis of O'Neill's one-act play and its place in his overall body of work.

3530 Berson, Misha. "The Demon in David Henry Hwang." *AmTh.* 1998 Apr.; 15(4): 14-18, 50-51. Illus.: Photo. B&W. 4. Lang.: Eng.
USA. 1980-1998. Histories-sources. ■Interview with playwright Hwang concerning the difference before and after one has one's first hit, and on his work in general.

3531 Berson, Misha. "Naomi Iizuka: Raising the Stakes." *AmTh.* 1998 Sep.; 15(7): 56-57. Illus.: Dwg. B&W. 2. Lang.: Eng.
USA. 1998. Biographical studies. ■Profile of playwright Naomi Iizuka.

3532 Bird, Robert R. *Remember Who Thou Art: Human Identity in Marlowe's* The Tragedy of Dido, Tamburlaine *I and II, and* Doctor Faustus*, and, Peer Evaluation in the Composition Classroom.* Pocatello, ID: Idaho State Univ; 1998. 60 pp. Notes. Biblio. [Ph.D. Dissertation, Univ. Microfilms Order No. AAC 9831979.] Lang.: Eng.
USA. 1997-1998. Critical studies. ■Examines themes of the constitution of 'self' and the implications of human identity in Christopher Marlowe's *The Tragedy of Dido, Tamburlaine* I and II, and *Doctor Faustus.* Positions argument within an empirical study of peer group evaluations in identifying primary traits in argumentative and explanatory writing and critical thinking skills.

3533 Black, Stephen A. "Episodes from a Life of O'Neill." *EOR.* 1998 Spr/Fall; 22(1/2): 6-22. Biblio. Lang.: Eng.
USA. 1911-1956. Biographical studies. ■Notes on the life and work of Eugene O'Neill focusing on his use of tragedy, his health condition, particularly the reason for his tremor, and the reasons for his discontinuing to write.

3534 Black, Stephen A. "'Celebrant of loss': Eugene O'Neill, 1888-1953." 4-17 in Manheim, Michael, ed. *The Cambridge Companion to Eugene O'Neill.* Cambridge/New York, NY: Cambridge UP; 1998. 256 pp. (Cambridge Companions to Literature.) Index. Biblio. Notes. Lang.: Eng.
USA. 1888-1953. Historical studies. ■Examines the early childhood home life of playwright Eugene O'Neill and its impact on his work.

3535 Bloch, Beverle Rochelle. *John Howard Lawson's* Processional*: Modernism in American Theatre in the Twenties.* Denver, CO: Univ. of Denver; 1988. 191 pp. Biblio. Notes. [Ph.D. Dissertation, Univ. Microfilms Order No. AAC 8827461.] Lang.: Eng.
USA. 1925. Critical studies. ■Examines Lawson's experimental play, first produced by the Theatre Guild, with respect to the use of unconventional forms, rejection of realism and expressionism, and stylized use of the presentational style of vaudeville, burlesque, and cabaret.

3536 Boan, Devon. "Call-and-Response: Parallel 'Slave Narrative' in August Wilson's *The Piano Lesson.*" *AfAmR.* 1998 Sum; 32 (2): 263-271. Notes. Biblio. Lang.: Eng.
USA. 1990. Critical studies. ■Communal and familial resonance of the African-American slave past in Wilson's play.

3537 Bruch, Debra Lynn. *A Method of Affective Analysis for the Drama.* Columbia, MO: Univ. of Missouri; 1987. 243 pp. Biblio. Notes. [Ph.D. Dissertation, Univ. Microfilms Order No. AAC 8728794.] Lang.: Eng.
USA. 1920-1975. Critical studies. ■Proposes a method of script analysis to isolate the dominant signals identifying a drama's organization of emotion. Applies technique to Peter Shaffer's *Equus*, Eugene O'Neill's *A Moon for the Misbegotten*, Edward Albee's *Who's Afraid of Virginia Woolf?*, and Samuel Beckett's *Waiting for Godot (En attendant Godot).*

3538 Byrd, Robert E., Jr. *Unseen Characters in Selected Plays of Eugene O'Neill, Tennessee Williams, and Edward Albee.* New York, NY: New York Univ; 1998. 549 pp. Notes. Biblio. [Ph.D. Dissertation, Univ. Microfilms Order No. AAC 9819852.] Lang.: Eng.
USA. 1915-1995. Critical studies. ■Argues that these playwrights used the traditional dramatic device of the unseen character in a new way, as a second order of reality that surrounds and touches the world of onstage action.

3539 Byun, Chang-Ku. *Impasse of the Romantic Imagination in the Plays of Tennessee Williams.* Tulsa, OK: Univ. of Tulsa; 1988. 228 pp. Biblio. Notes. [Ph.D. Dissertation, Univ. Microfilms Order No. AAC 8810990.] Lang.: Eng.

DRAMA: —Plays/librettos/scripts

USA. 1943-1970. Critical studies. ■Plays examined include *The Glass Menagerie*, *A Streetcar Named Desire*, *Suddenly Last Summer*, and *The Night of the Iguana*.

3540 Callens, Johan. "Sam Shepards verscheurde liefdes." (Sam Shepard's Split Loves.) *Etcetera*. 1986(13): 61-65. Lang.: Dut.

USA. 1979. Critical studies. ■Analysis of Sam Shepard's *Fool for Love*.

3541 Callens, Johan. *David Mamet*. Groningen: Samson Uitgeverij/Wolters-Noordhof; 1993. 26 pp. (Post-War Literatures in English: A Lexicon of Contemporary Authors.) Lang.: Eng.

USA. 1970-1993. Critical studies. ■Examines the work of David Mamet.

3542 Callens, Johan. "Watching the Myth Unfold: *The Prodigal*." 135-217 in Callens, Johan, ed. *Double Binds: Existentialist Inspiration and Generic Experimentation in the Early Work of Jack Richardson*. Amsterdam/Atlanta, GA: Editions Rodopi B.V.; 1993. 261 pp. Lang.: Eng.

USA. 1960. Critical studies. ■Analysis of Jack Richardson's *The Prodigal*, an adaptation of the *Oresteia* by Aeschylus.

3543 Callens, Johan. "Reciprocity and the Transformational Generation of Shepard and Chaikin's *Savage/Love*: A Text and Performance Analysis." 71-125 in Hellemans, Dina, ed.; Geerts, Ronald, ed. *Unwitting Influences in Theatre: Exchanges within Europe and Between Europe and the United States*. Brussels: VUB Press; 1996. 126 pp. (European Contributions to American Studies 38.) Lang.: Eng.

USA. 1991-1996. Critical studies. ■Analysis of the Chaikin/Shepard collaboration.

3544 Callens, Johan. "'Published and Unpublished Wars': Contextualizing Sam Shepard's *States of Shock*." 223-234 in Giorcelli, Christina, ed.; Kroes, Rob, ed.; Delaney, Kate, ed. *Living with America, 1946-1996*. Amsterdam: VU UP; 1997. 329 pp. (European Contributions to American Studies 38.) Lang.: Eng.

USA. 1965-1997. Critical studies. ■Examines the avant-garde and expressionistic elements in Shepard's play.

3545 Callens, Johan. "Sam Shepard's Inter/National Stage." 157-171 in Maufort, Marc, ed. *Staging Difference: Cultural Pluralism in American Theatre and Drama*. New York, NY: Peter Lang; 1995. (American University Studies 26: Theatre Arts 25.) Lang.: Eng.

USA. 1965-1995. Critical studies. ■Themes of national and international identity in the plays of Shepard, particularly *La Turista, Blue Bitch* and *Geography of a Horse Dreamer*.

3546 Callens, Johan. *Lanford Wilson*. Groningen: Martinus Nijhoff Uitgevers; 1995. 22 pp. (Post-War Literatures: A Lexicon of Contemporary Authors.) Lang.: Eng.

USA. 1960-1995. Critical studies. ■Examination of Wilson's plays.

3547 Callens, Johan. "'Lull us to sleep with tales of heroes ...': Mythologisering versus Ontmythologisering in Jack Richardson's *The Prodigal* (1960)." ('Lull us to sleep with tales of heroes ...': Mythification versus Demy(s)t(h)ification in Jack Richardson's *The Prodigal* (1960).) 93-104 in Vervliet, Raymond. *De mythe in de moderne literatuur*. Ghent: Flemish Association for General and Comparative Literary Theory; 1994. 139 pp. (Literary Theory 13.) Lang.: Dut.

USA. 1960. Critical studies. ■Richardson's use of mythology in his adaptation of the *Oresteia*.

3548 Callens, Johan. "Sam Shepard's *Operation Sidewinder*: The Needs and Risks of Revision(ism)." *American Studies/Amerikastudien*. 1993; 38(4): 549-565. Lang.: Eng.

USA. 1970. Critical studies. ■Analysis of Shepard's play.

3549 Callens, Johan. "'There Are Secret Signs We Know, We Two': Echoes from Homer in Jack Richardson's *The Prodigal*." *Neophilologus*. 1993; 77(3): 659-673. Lang.: Eng.

USA. 1960. Critical studies. ■Influence of Homer on Richardson's adaptation of the *Oresteia*.

3550 Callens, Johan. "Sam Shepard: portret van de kunstenaar als ontdekkingsreiziger." (Sam Shepard: Portrait of the Artist as an Explorer.) *De Vlaamse Gids*. 1992 May/June; 76(3): 23-32. Lang.: Dut.

USA. 1965-1992. Critical studies. ■Profile of the playwright and analysis of his work.

3551 Callens, Johan. "O'Neill: Het leven als tussenspel." (O'Neill: Life as an Interlude.) *Etcetera*. 1990; 30: 51-55. Lang.: Dut.

USA. 1926-1927. Critical studies. ■Analysis of Eugene O'Neill's *Strange Interlude*.

3552 Callens, Johan. "When the Center Cannot Hold, or the Problem of Mediation in Lanford Wilson's *The Mound Builders*." 201-226 in Debusscher, Gilbert; Schvey, Henry I.; Maufort, Marc. *New Essays on American Drama*. Amsterdam: Rodopi; 1989. 230 pp. (Costerus New Series Vol 76.) Lang.: Eng.

USA. 1976. Critical studies. ■Analysis of Wilson's play.

3553 Callens, Johan. *Sam Shepard*. Groningen: Samson Uitgeverij/Wolters-Noordhof; 1988. 13 pp. (Post-War Literatures in English: A Lexicon of Contemporary Authors.) Lang.: Eng.

USA. 1965-1988. Critical studies. ■Analysis of the plays of Sam Shepard.

3554 Callens, Johan. "'Allemaal mooie woorden: de eenden leggen de eieren' of David Mamets *Duck Variations*." (All the Smooth-Talking Drakes: The Ducks Lay the Eggs in David Mamet's *Duck Variations*.) *Documenta*. 1987; 5(4): 229-251. Lang.: Dut.

USA. 1976. Critical studies. ■Analysis of Mamet's play.

3555 Callens, Johan. "Macht en onmacht van de verbeelding: Globe speelt In het tuinhuis." (Power and Powerlessness of the Imagination: Globe Plays—*In the Summer House*.) 77-98 in van Berlaer-Hellemans, Dina; Van Kerkhoven, Marianne; Van den Dries, Luk. *Het teater zoekt ... zoek het teater. Aspekten van het eigentijdse teater in Vlaanderen 2*. Brussels: Vrije Universiteit of Brussels; 1986. 392 pp. (Studiereeks van de Vrije Universiteit 25.) Lang.: Dut.

USA. 1986. Critical studies. ■Analysis of Jane Bowles' play *In the Summer House*.

3556 Callens, Johan. "David Mamet: 'You've Gotta Be Where You Are'." *Etcetera*. 1985(11): 40-43. Lang.: Dut.

USA. 1983. Critical studies. ■Analysis of Mamet's *Glengarry Glen Ross*.

3557 Callens, Johan, ed. *Between the Margin and the Centre*. Reading: Harwood Academic; 1998. 98 pp. Lang.: Eng.

USA. 1965-1998. Critical studies. ■Collection of essays on the theatre of Sam Shepard.

3558 Cardullo, Bert. "The Blue Rose of St. Louis: Laura, Romanticism, and *The Glass Menagerie*." *JADT*. 1998 Spr; 10(2): 1-25. Notes. Lang.: Eng.

USA. 1944. Critical studies. ■Analysis of the character of Laura in Tennessee Williams' *The Glass Menagerie*. Focuses on Laura as a Romantic archetype of female fragility and draws parallels between Williams' work and other works of the Romantic genre.

3559 Carson, Rebecca. "The Transformation of History into Drama: The Women's History Play in America, 1900-1940." *TheatreS*. 1998; 43: 7-21. Notes. Illus.: Photo. B&W. 3. Lang.: Eng.

USA. 1900-1940. Critical studies. ■Analysis of three plays documenting events in the history of the women's movement: Josephine Preston Peabody's *Portrait of Mrs. W*, Maud Wood Park's *Lucy Stone: A Chronicle Play*, and Olivia Howard Dunbar's *Enter Women*.

3560 Cavander, Kenneth. "The Art & Craft of Jumping Fences." *AmTh*. 1998 Mar.; 15(3): 15-18, 52-54. Illus.: Photo. B&W. 8. Lang.: Eng.

USA. 1998. Critical studies. ■Discusses the pros and cons of writing for both the theatre and television.

3561 Chothia, Jean. "Trying to Write the Family Play: Autobiography and the Dramatic Imagination." 192-205 in Manheim, Michael, ed. *The Cambridge Companion to Eugene O'Neill*. Cambridge/New York, NY: Cambridge UP; 1998.

DRAMA: —Plays/librettos/scripts

256 pp. (Cambridge Companions to Literature.) Index. Biblio. Notes. Lang.: Eng.

USA. 1940-1995. Critical studies. ■How playwright Eugene O'Neill forged theatrical techniques suited to the writing of autobiographical drama throughout the latter part of the twentieth century, including its effects on the plays of Tennessee Williams, Arthur Miller, Edward Albee, and Sam Shepard.

3562 Codde, Philippe. "'Dat ole davil, sea': Cowardice and Redemption in Eugene O'Neill's *Anna Christie.*" *EOR.* 1998 Spr/Fall; 22(1/2): 23-32. Biblio. Lang.: Eng.

USA. 1921. Critical studies. ■Analysis of the play using Sartre's existentialist ideas of cowardice of identity, and the redemptive act of taking responsibility for one's actions.

3563 Cohn, Ruby. "Twice Translated Texts: Beckett into English and Chaikin into Theatre." *MD.* 1998 Spr; 41(1): 7-18. Notes. Lang.: Eng.

USA: New York, NY. 1995. Historical studies. ■Discusses Beckett's distaste for translating his texts. Includes information on Joseph Chaikin's adaptation of Beckett's *Texts for Nothing (Textes pour rien)*, in collaboration with Steve Kent, originally presented by the Public Theatre.

3564 Coleman, Stephen DuBois. "Joseph Edward Flies." *BlackM.* 1998 Jan/Feb.; 12(6): 6, 16. Lang.: Eng.

USA: New York, NY. 1997. Biographical studies. ■Profile of the playwright and actor whose play *Fly* is being presented by the American Place Theatre, directed by Wynn Handman.

3565 Collins, Marla del. *Communicating the Creative Process: A Non-Aristotelian Perspective on Eugene O'Neill and the Women in His Life.* New York, NY: New York Univ; 1998. 500 pp. Notes. Biblio. [Ph.D. Dissertation, Univ. Microfilms Order No. AAC 9832735.] Lang.: Eng.

USA. 1998. Histories-sources. ■The author's approach to creating the characters in her play *The Lovers and Others of Eugene O'Neill.*

3566 Connelly, Christopher Brian. *The Death of the American Dreamchild: The Parental Sacrifice of Sons and Daughters as a Subgenre of American Drama.* Athens, GA: Univ. of Georgia; 1998. 242 pp. Biblio. Notes. [Ph.D. Dissertation, Univ. Microfilms Order No. 9828374.] Lang.: Eng.

USA. 1910-1990. Critical studies. ■Argues that instead of an idealized parental self-sacrifice, American drama has a strong subgenre of plays that feature the symbolic and literal sacrifice of children.

3567 Corti, Lillian. "Countée Cullen's *Medea.*" *AfAmR.* 1998 Win; 32(4): 621-634. Biblio. Discography. Lang.: Eng.

USA. 1936. Critical studies. ■Analysis of Cullen's little-performed translation of Euripides' tragedy.

3568 Cote, John Louis. *Thirty-Two Qualities: The Principles of Artistry in Playwriting Stated or Implied in Fifteen Manuals.* Long Beach, CA: California State Univ; 1987. 152 pp. Notes. Biblio. [M.A. Thesis, Univ. Microfilms Order No. AAC 1330688.] Lang.: Eng.

USA. 1987. Critical studies. ■Analysis of playwriting principles found in manuals on the subject.

3569 Crawford, David Wright. *The Development of a Playwriting Philosophy as Demonstrated in the Writing of a Full-Length Script, 'Tangled Garden'.* Lubbock, TX: Texas Tech Univ; 1987. 195 pp. Biblio. Notes. [Ph.D. Dissertation, Univ. Microfilms Order No. 8713593.] Lang.: Eng.

USA. 1987. Histories-sources. ■The author's method of playwriting, followed by an original play.

3570 Crespy, David Allison. *Albarwild's Nexus of New Play Development: The Playwrights Unit, 1963 to 1971.* New York, NY: City Univ. of New York; 1998. 362 pp. Notes. Biblio. [Ph.D. Dissertation, Univ. Microfilms Order No. AAC 9908305.] Lang.: Eng.

USA. 1963-1971. Histories-specific. ■The founding of the Playwrights Unit, by playwrights Edward Albee, Richard Barr, and Clinton Wilder to nurture new play development through full production rather than staged readings and workshops. Playwrights whose work was produced include Louis Auchincloss, Mart Crowley, Gene Feist, John Guare, A.R. Gurney, LeRoi Jones (Amiri Baraka), Lee Kalcheim, Adrienne Kennedy, Terrence McNally, Leonard Melfi, Howard Moss, Sam Shepard, Megan Terry, Jean-Claude Van Itallie, Lanford Wilson, Doric Wilson, and Paul Zindel.

3571 Cummings, Scott T. "Psychic Space: The Interiors of Maria Irene Fornes." *JADT.* 1998 Spr; 10(2): 59-73. Notes. Lang.: Eng.

USA. 1977-1989. Critical studies. ■How playwright Fornes defines and uses theatrical space scenographically, dramatically, and thematically in her plays *Fefu and Her Friends, Mud, Abingdon Square, A Visit, Enter the Night, Sarita, The Conduct of Life*, and *And What of the Night?.*

3572 Davis, Tracy C. "A Feminist Boomerang: Eve Merriam's *The Club* (1976)." 146-165 in Colleran, Jeanne, ed.; Spencer, Jenny S., ed. *Staging Resistance: Essays on Political Theatre.* Ann Arbor, MI: Univ of Michigan P; 1998. 312 pp. (Theater: Theory/Text/Performance.) Notes. Index. Illus.: Dwg. 1. Lang.: Eng.

USA. 1976. Critical studies. ■Examines the gendered political critique in Eve Merriam's *The Club.*

3573 DeBaun, Linda Louise. *David Henry Hwang: The Fluid Mosaic of Identity.* Fullerton, CA: California State Univ; 1998. 47 pp. Notes. Biblio. [M.A. Thesis, Univ. Microfilms Order No. AAC 1390561.] Lang.: Eng.

USA. 1980-1998. Critical studies. ■Examines the work of playwright David Henry Hwang including his major themes, his identity as an Asian-American playwright, the influence of Sam Shepard on his work, and current directions of his playwriting career.

3574 DePaula, Paulo Spurgeon. *Theatre in Exile: The Cuban Theatre in Miami.* Kirksville, MO: Northeast Missouri State Univ; 1987. 123 pp. Biblio. Notes. [M.A. Thesis, Univ. Microfilms Order No. AAC 1330806.] Lang.: Eng.

USA: Miami, FL. 1985-1986. Critical studies. ■Analyzes the content of local Spanish-language plays, with reference to their social and political significance and how the plays assimilate into the American mainstream. Explores the work of local theatres as well as theatrical activities of the First Annual Hispanic Theatre Festival of Miami.

3575 Detsi, Zoe. "The Metaphors of Freedom: Republican Rhetoric and Gender Ideology in Mercy Otis Warren's Romantic Tragedies." *AmerD.* 1998 Fall; 8(1): 1-25. Notes. Biblio. Lang.: Eng.

USA. 1783-1785. Critical studies. ■How Warren used republican ideology to interweave political consciousness and women's social status in an attempt to reorient the ideas of freedom, democracy, and equality in post-revolutionary America in her tragedies *The Sack of Rome* and *The Ladies of Castile.*

3576 Dickey, Johanna Susan. *Strategies of Menace in the Plays of John Whiting, Harold Pinter and Sam Shepard.* Stanford, CA: Stanford Univ; 1988. 200 pp. Biblio. Notes. [Ph.D. Dissertation, Univ. Microfilms Order No. AAC 8906652.] Lang.: Eng.

USA. UK-England. 1960-1985. Critical studies. ■The nature and language of menace in these playwrights' works.

3577 Domina, Lynn. *Understanding* A Raisin in the Sun*: A Student Casebook to Issues, Sources, and Historical Documents.* Westport, CT/London: Greenwood; 1998. 158 pp. (Literature in Context.) Index. Biblio. Lang.: Eng.

USA. 1957-1997. Instructional materials. ■Collection of document excerpts to help students understand Lorraine Hansberry's *A Raisin in the Sun.* Includes a literary analysis of the play, documents on historical context of integration and segregation, Africa and African-Americans, the play and its relation to the Chicago literary tradition, gender in African-American relations, and contemporary race relations.

3578 Drukman, Steven. "Won't You Come Home, Edward Albee." *AmTh.* 1998 Dec.; 15(10): 16-20. Illus.: Photo. B&W. 5. Lang.: Eng.

USA: New York, NY, Hartford, CT. 1959-1998. Ctitical studies. ■Return to prominence of playwright Albee, with his new play *The Play About the Baby*, the Broadway revival of his *A Delicate Balance* directed by Gerald Gutierrez at Lincoln Center in 1996 and the Hartford Stage Company's staging of *Tiny Alice* in 1998 directed by Mark Lamos.

3579 Dugan, Olga. *Useful Drama: Variations on the Theme of Black Self-Determination in the Plays of Alice Childress,*

1949-1969. Rochester, NY: Univ. of Rochester; 1998. 281 pp. Notes. Biblio. [Ph.D. Dissertation, Univ. Microfilms Order No. AAC 9905371.] Lang.: Eng.

USA. 1949-1969. Critical studies. ▪Plays discussed include *Florence*, *Trouble in Mind*, *Wedding Band*, and *Wine in the Wilderness*.

3580 Duval, Elaine Isolyn. *Theatre and the Double: Revolutionary Consciousness in Baraka and Artaud.* Knoxville, TN: Univ. of Tennessee; 1988. 243 pp. Biblio. Notes. [Ph.D. Dissertation, Univ. Microfilms Order No. AAC 8904047.] Lang.: Eng.

USA. France. 1920-1970. Critical studies. ▪Revolutionary elements in the works of playwright/theorists Amiri Baraka and Antonin Artaud.

3581 Effiong, Philip Uko. "History, Myth, and Revolt in Lorraine Hansberry's *Les Blancs*." *AfAmR.* 1998 Sum; 32(2): 273-283. Notes. Biblio. Lang.: Eng.

USA. 1970. Critical studies. ▪Cultural analysis of Hansberry's play.

3582 Elam, Harry, Jr.; Rayner, Alice. "Body Parts: Between Story and Spectacle in *Venus* by Suzan-Lori Parks." 265-282 in Colleran, Jeanne, ed.; Spencer, Jenny S., ed. *Staging Resistance: Essays on Political Theatre.* Ann Arbor, MI: Univ of Michigan P; 1998. 312 pp. (Theater: Theory/Text/Performance.) Notes. Index. Illus.: Photo. 1. Lang.: Eng.

USA. 1996. Critical studies. ▪Race, gender, colonialism, and nationalism in Suzan-Lori Parks's *Venus*.

3583 Epperson, Jim. "Regional ACTF Features New Student Plays." *SoTh.* 1998 Sum; 39(3): 28-29. Illus.: Photo. B&W. 1. Lang.: Eng.

USA. 1998. Critical studies. ▪Reports on the Kennedy Center/American College Theatre Festival's showcase of new plays by students.

3584 Erickson, Jon. "The 'Mise en Scène' of the Non-Euclidean Character: Wellman, Jenkin and Strindberg." *MD.* 1998 Fall; 41(3): 355-370. Notes. Lang.: Eng.

USA. 1887-1998. Critical studies. ▪Influence of August Strindberg on characters in the plays of Len Jenkin and Mac Wellman.

3585 Evans, Don. "Langston Hughes: The Poet as Playwright: A Love-Hate Relationship." *AANYL.* 1995 July; 19(2): 7-16. Notes. Lang.: Eng.

USA: New York, NY. 1926-1967. Biographical studies. ▪Examines poet Hughes' unenthusiastic view of the theatre, even though he wrote several plays.

3586 Fenn, Jeffrey William. *Culture Under Stress: American Drama and the Vietnam War.* Vancouver, BC: Univ. of British Columbia; 1988. Notes. Biblio. [Ph.D. Dissertation.] Lang.: Eng.

USA. 1969-1987. Critical studies. ▪How the dramatic literature engendered by the Vietnam War in the 1960s and 1970s reflects the stresses and anxieties of contemporary American society. Investigates formative influences on the drama, the styles in which it emerged, and recurring themes and motifs.

3587 Fitzgerald, Brian. "Ghost, Writer." *EOR.* 1998 Spr/Fall; 22(1/2): 171-173. Lang.: Eng.

USA: Boston, MA. 1998. Historical studies. ▪Note on reports of Eugene O'Neill's ghost haunting Boston University's Shelton Hall.

3588 Fordyce, William. "Tennessee Williams's Tom Wingfield and Georg Kaiser's Cashier: A Contextual Comparison." *PLL.* 1998 Sum; 34(3): 250-272. Notes. Biblio. Lang.: Eng.

USA. Germany. 1912-1945. Critical studies. ▪Comparison of the lead characters from Williams' *The Glass Menagerie* and Kaiser's *Von Morgens bis Mitternacht (From Morn to Midnight)*, with an emphasis on their differences to clarify Williams's particular worldview.

3589 Fornes, Maria Irene; Parks, Suzan-Lori; Mann, Emily; MacLeod, Wendy; Yankowitz, Susan; Wasserstein, Wendy; Zimmerman, Mary. "Sources of Inspiration." *AmTh.* 1998 Sep.; 15(7): 32-33, 81-82. Illus.: Dwg. B&W. 1. Lang.: Eng.

USA. 1997. Histories-sources. ▪Female playwrights Wendy Wasserstein, Susan Yankowitz, Emily Mann, Suzan-Lori Parks, Maria Irene Fornes, Wendy MacLeod, and Mary Zimmerman share their backgrounds and influences writing for the theatre. Taken from their speeches at the Women's Project conference, New York, NY, November, 1997.

3590 Fox, Ann Margaret. *Open Houses: American Women Playwrights, Broadway Success, and Media Culture, 1906-1944.* Bloomington, IN: Indiana Univ; 1998. 212 pp. Biblio. Notes. [Ph.D. Dissertation, Univ. Microfilms Order No. 9907280.] Lang.: Eng.

USA. 1906-1944. Histories-specific. ▪Argues that the popular Broadway success of early American women playwrights, including Rachel Crothers, Sophie Treadwell, and Rose Franken, was dependent on the fact that female playwrights engaged a media culture traditionally opposed to women's emancipation.

3591 Frazier, Paul M. *Science Fiction Drama: The Present Seen Through the Future.* East Lansing, MI: Michigan State Univ; 1988. 93 pp. Notes. Biblio. [M.A. Thesis, Univ. Microfilms Order No. 1334441.] Lang.: Eng.

USA. 1945-1988. Histories-specific. ▪Focuses on literary merits as well as production possibilities of *Solitaire* by Robert Anderson, *A Bunch of the Gods Were Sitting Around One Day* by James Spencer, *To the Chicago Abyss* by Ray Bradbury, and *The Tin Can Riots* by Edward Bond.

3592 Frieze, James. "*Imperceptible Mutabilities in the Third Kingdom*: Suzan-Lori Parks and the Shared Struggle to Perceive." *MD.* 1998 Win; 41(4): 523-532. Notes. Lang.: Eng.

USA. 1995. Critical studies. ▪Analysis of time, perception, and identity in Parks' play.

3593 Gale, Steven H. "Introduction." *PintR.* 1998: xi-xiii. Lang.: Eng.

USA. 1997-1998. Critical studies. ▪Introductory overview to the subject of the volume, the life and work of Harold Pinter.

3594 Gallup, Donald. "'A Tale of Possessors Self-Dispossessed." 178-191 in Manheim, Michael, ed. *The Cambridge Companion to Eugene O'Neill.* Cambridge/New York, NY: Cambridge UP; 1998. 256 pp. (Cambridge Companions to Literature.) Index. Biblio. Notes. Lang.: Eng.

USA. 1945-1953. Critical studies. ▪Uses archival material from Eugene O'Neill's unfinished work diary to summarize unfinished 'cycle play' *A Tale of Possessors Self-Dispossessed.*

3595 Garrison, Gary Wayne. *Lanford Wilson's Use of Comedy and Humor.* Ann Arbor, MI: Univ. of Michigan; 1987. 210 pp. Biblio. Notes. [Ph.D. Dissertation, Univ. Microfilms Order No. AAC 8712119.] Lang.: Eng.

USA. 1961-1985. Critical studies. ▪Analysis of comedy and humor in the work of American playwright Lanford Wilson's *Ludlow Fair*, *The Hot l Baltimore*, *Fifth of July*, and *Talley's Folly*.

3596 Gelb, Arthur; Gelb, Barbara. "The Twisted Path to *More Stately Mansions*." *EOR.* 1998 Spr/Fall; 22(1/2): 105-109. Lang.: Eng.

USA. 1957-1964. Historical studies. ▪Account of the publication of the acting version of O'Neill's unfinished play, which was done against his dying wishes.

3597 Gelb, Barbara. "In Search of Memory." *EOR.* 1998 Spr/Fall; 22(1/2): 110-113. Lang.: Eng.

USA. 1954-1962. Histories-sources. ▪O'Neill biographer discusses the difficulty in tracking down people who knew his mother, Ella, to be interviewed for the biography.

3598 Gener, Randy. "Murphy Guyer: A Cleveland Romance." *AmTh.* 1998 Jan.; 15(1): 54-56. Illus.: Dwg. B&W. 2. Lang.: Eng.

USA: Cleveland, OH. 1998. Biographical studies. ▪Profile of playwright Murphy Guyer and his relationship with the Cleveland Playhouse.

3599 Gill, Glenda. "Love in Black and White: Miscegenation on the Stage." *JADT.* 1998 Fall; 10(3): 32-51. Notes. Illus.: Photo. 1. Lang.: Eng.

USA. 1909-1969. Critical studies. ▪Miscegenation in American drama, with attention to *The Nigger* by Edward Shelton, *All God's Chillun Got Wings* by Eugene O'Neill, *Wedding Band* by Alice Childress, and *The Great White Hope* by Howard Sackler.

3600 Goldfarb, Alvin. "Inadequate Memories: The Survivor in Plays by Mann, Kesselman, Lebow, and Baitz." 111-129 in Schumacher, Claude, ed. *Staging the Holocaust: The Shoah in Drama and Performance.* Cambridge: Cambridge UP;

DRAMA: —Plays/librettos/scripts

1998. 355 pp. (Cambridge Studies in Modern Theatre.) Index. Notes. Biblio. Lang.: Eng.

USA. 1970-1997. Critical studies. ■The survivor character in Emily Mann's *Annulla Allen: An Autobiography of a Survivor*, Wendy Kesselman's *I Love You, I Love You Not*, Barbara Lebow's *A Shayna Maidel*, and Jon Robin Baitz's *The Substance of Fire.*

3601 Goodfarb, Rowena Davis. *Heroic Gestures: Five Short Stories as Sources for the Plays of Tennessee Williams.* New York, NY: Fordham Univ; 1988. 257 pp. Biblio. Notes. [Ph.D. Dissertation, Univ. Microfilms Order No. AAC 8809471.] Lang.: Eng.

USA. 1943-1955. Critical studies. ■Examines five short stories of playwright Tennessee Williams for influences on his later plays.

3602 Gourdine, Angeletta KM. "The 'Drama' of Lynching in Two Black Women's Drama, or Relating Grimké's *Rachel* to Hansberry's *A Raisin in the Sun.*" *MD.* 1998 Win; 41(4): 533-545. Notes. Lang.: Eng.

USA. 1916-1958. Critical studies. ■The depiction of lynching as a dramatic strategy, with a comparison of its use by playwrights Angelina Weld Grimké and Lorraine Hansberry.

3603 Greeley, Lynne. *Spirals from the Matrix: The Feminist Plays of Martha Boesing, an Analysis.* College Park, MD: Univ. of Maryland; 1987. 340 pp. Notes. Biblio. [Ph.D. Dissertation, Univ. Microfilms Order No. AAC 8808555.] Lang.: Eng.

USA: Minneapolis, MN. 1974-1984. Historical studies. ■The plays of Martha Boesing and her association with the feminist theatre, At the Foot of the Mountain.

3604 Greene, Alexis. *Revolutions Off Off Broadway, 1959-1969: A Critical Study of Changes in Structure, Character, Language, and Theme in Experimental Drama in New York City.* New York, NY: City Univ. of New York; 1987. 224 pp. Notes. Biblio. [Ph.D. Dissertation, Univ. Microfilms Order No. AAC 8801716.] Lang.: Eng.

USA: New York, NY. 1959-1969. Historical studies. ■The 'revolutionary' nature of Off Broadway playwrights of the 1960s, including George Birimisa, Kenneth Bernard, Kenneth Brown, Rosalyn Drexler, Grant Duay, Tom Eyen, Maria Irene Fornes, Paul Foster, John Guare, A. R. Gurney, Jr., William M. Hoffman, Kenneth Koch, Charles Ludlam, Murray Mednick, Joel Oppenheimer, Rochelle Owens, Tom Sankey, Sam Shepard, David Starkweather, Ronald Tavel, Megan Terry, and Jean-Claude Van Itallie.

3605 Greenspan, Hank. "The Power and Limits of the Metaphor of Survivors' Testimony." 27-39 in Schumacher, Claude, ed. *Staging the Holocaust: The Shoah in Drama and Performance.* Cambridge: Cambridge UP; 1998. 355 pp. (Cambridge Studies in Modern Theatre.) Index. Notes. Biblio. Illus.: Photo. 1. Lang.: Eng.

USA. 1975-1995. Critical studies. ■Argues that survivors' testimony is used in Holocaust drama to force the spectator to ask 'how would I have behaved if ...'. Includes discussion of the author's own play *Remnants.*

3606 Haff, Stephen. "A Star Is Reborn." *AmTh.* 1998 Oct.; 15(8): 70-72. Illus.: Photo. B&W. 2. Lang.: Eng.

USA: New York, NY. 1940-1998. Historical studies. ■Analysis of production of *The Golden Door* by Sylvia Regan at the Tenement Museum under the direction of Jean Randich. The play is an abridged version of *Morning Star* which premiered on Broadway in 1940 and followed the fortunes of an immigrant family on New York's Lower East Side.

3607 Hall, Ann Christine. *'A Kind of Alaska': The Representation of Women in the Plays of Eugene O'Neill, Harold Pinter, and Sam Shepard.* Columbus, OH: Ohio State Univ; 1988. 237 pp. Notes. Biblio. [Ph.D. Dissertation, Univ. Microfilms Order No. AAC 8820302.] Lang.: Eng.

USA. UK-England. 1936-1985. Critical studies. ■Feminist Lacanian analysis of female presence/absence in Eugene O'Neill's *The Iceman Cometh*, *Long Day's Journey Into Night*, and *A Moon for the Misbegotten*, Pinter's *The Homecoming*, *No Man's Land*, and *A Kind of Alaska*, and Shepard's *Buried Child*, *True West*, and *A Lie of the Mind.*

3608 Hardin, Michael. "Fair Maiden and Dark Lady in *The Great God Brown*: Inverting the Standard Representations." *EOR.* 1998 Spr/Fall; 22(1/2): 41-47. Biblio. Lang.: Eng.

USA. 1926. Critical studies. ■O'Neill's gradual reversal of the roles of temptation and salvation traditionally played by the Black and white females in his play.

3609 Hays, Peter L. "Hemingway's 'A Clean, Well-Lighted Place' and O'Neill's *Iceman.*" *EOR.* 1998 Spr/Fall; 22(1/2): 70-76. Notes. Biblio. Lang.: Eng.

USA. 1939-1946. Critical studies. ■Comparison of Hemingway's short story with O'Neill's *The Iceman Cometh.*

3610 Heisserer, Gary Lawrence. *The Historical Drama of the Holocaust: Assessing the Transformation from Reality to Record.* Madison, WI: Univ. of Wisconsin; 1987. 494 pp. Notes. Biblio. [Ph.D. Dissertation, Univ. Microfilms Order No. AAC 8713157.] Lang.: Eng.

USA. Canada. Germany. 1950-1980. Critical studies. ■Analysis of Harold and Edith Lieberman's *Throne of Straw*, Gabriel Emanuel's *Children of Night*, Michael Brady's *Korczak's Children*, and Erwin Sylvanus' *Korczak und die Kinder (Korczak and the Children).*

3611 Herrington, Joan. "On August Wilson's *Jitney.*" *AmerD.* 1998 Fall; 8(1): 122-144. Notes. Biblio. Lang.: Eng.

USA. 1979. Critical studies. ■Analysis of Wilson's play.

3612 Herrington, Joan. "'Responsibility in Our Own Hands'." *JDTC.* 1998 Fall; 13(1): 87-99. Notes. Lang.: Eng.

USA. 1980-1997. Critical studies. ■Minority playwrights working in mainstream theatres: theoretical considerations. Uses the case of August Wilson as an example.

3613 Houppert, Karen. "Apologies to the Unborn." *AmTh.* 1998 Jan.; 15(1): 46-47. Illus.: Dwg. B&W. 2. Lang.: Eng.

USA. 1998. Critical studies. ■Analysis of Wendy MacLeod's play *The Water Children.*

3614 Howe, Tina. "Women's Work: White Gloves or Bare Hands?" *AmTh.* 1998 Sep.; 15(7): 27-29. Illus.: Photo. B&W. 1. Lang.: Eng.

USA: New York, NY. 1980-1997. Histories-sources. ■Excerpt from the playwright's keynote address to Women's Project conference on the difference between what is expected from men and women playwrights.

3615 Humphries, Eugenia. *Lorraine Hansberry: The Visionary American Playwright.* Stony Brook, NY: State Univ. of New York; 1988. 272 pp. Biblio. Notes. [Ph.D. Dissertation, Univ. Microfilms Order No. AAC 8915503.] Lang.: Eng.

USA. 1950-1965. Textual studies. ■Examination of the career of playwright Lorraine Hansberry.

3616 Hurt, James. "Arthur Kopit's *Wings* and the Languages of the Theatre." *AmerD.* 1998 Fall; 8(1): 75-94. Notes. Biblio. Lang.: Eng.

USA. 1978. Critical studies. ■Analysis of Kopit's play about a stroke victim, and the idiom Kopit chooses to present the inner life of the character theatrically.

3617 Huston-Findley, Shirley Annette. *Subverting the Dramatic Text: Folklore, Feminism, and the Images of Women in Three Canonical American Plays.* Columbia, MO: Univ. of Missouri; 1998. 211 pp. Biblio. Notes. [Ph.D. Dissertation, Univ. Microfilms Order No. 9901243.] Lang.: Eng.

USA. 1945-1965. Critical studies. ■Fairy-tale heroines in Alan Jay Lerner and Frederick Loewe's musical *My Fair Lady*, N. Richard Nash's *The Rainmaker*, and Tennessee Williams' *The Glass Menagerie.*

3618 Ivry, Benjamin. "Will the Real Anne Frank Please Stand Up." *AmTh.* 1998 Jan.; 15(1): 42-45. Illus.: Dwg. B&W. 2. Lang.: Eng.

USA: New York, NY. 1998. Critical studies. ■Report on the furor over the revised version of *The Diary of Anne Frank* by Frances Goodrich and Albert Hackett, adapted by Wendy Kesselman under the direction of James Lapine at the Music Box Theatre.

3619 Jackson, Shannon. "*White Noises*: On Performing White, On Writing Performance." *TDR.* 1998 Spr; 42(1): 49-55. Notes. Biblio. Illus.: Photo. B&W. 2. Lang.: Eng.

USA. 1998. Histories-sources. ■Introduction by the playwright to her solo piece, which she describes as a kind of response to Ntozake Shange's *spell #7.*

DRAMA: —Plays/librettos/scripts

3620 Jew, Kimberly May. *The Theatrical Experimentation of Elmer Rice.* New York, NY: New York Univ; 1998. 256 pp. Notes. Biblio. [Ph.D. Dissertation, Univ. Microfilms Order No. AAC 9832745.] Lang.: Eng.
USA. 1914-1963. Critical studies. ▪Examines the modernist formal and stylistic innovations in Rice's plays and delineates his contributions to an alternative American theatre.

3621 Jiggetts, Shelby. "Interview with Suzan-Lori Parks." *Callaloo.* 1996 Spr; 19(2): 309-317. Lang.: Eng.
USA. 1996. Histories-sources. ▪Interview with the playwright regarding on her influences and career.

3622 Johnson, Carla Jean. *A Tiger by the Tail: The Five Unfinished Versions of Tennessee Williams' Twenty-Seven Wagons Full of Cotton.* Notre Dame, IN: Univ. of Notre Dame; 1988. 245 pp. Biblio. Notes. [Ph.D. Dissertation, Univ. Microfilms Order No. AAC 8816740.] Lang.: Eng.
USA. 1936-1979. Textual studies. ▪Symbolic imagery in several versions of Williams's short story, the two one-act plays of the same name, the screenplay for *Baby Doll*, and the full-length play *Tiger Tail*, all based on the story.

3623 Johnson, Jeff. "Gendermandering: Stereotyping and Gender Role Reversal in the Major Plays of William Inge." *AmerD.* 1998 Spr; 7(2): 33-50. Biblio. Lang.: Eng.
USA. 1950-1958. Critical studies. ▪The subversion of sexual stereotypes in William Inge's *The Dark at the Top of the Stairs, Picnic, Bus Stop,* and *Come Back, Little Sheba.*

3624 Johnson, Jeff. "Sexual Symmetry and Moral Balance in William Inge's *Bus Stop.*" *JADT.* 1998 Fall; 10(3): 52-60. Notes. Lang.: Eng.
USA. 1955. Critical studies. ▪'Gender-bending' in the manipulation of sex and gender stereotypes in Inge's play.

3625 Johnson, Marcia V. "'The World in a Jug and the Stopper in (Her) Hand': *Their Eyes* as Blues Performance." *AfAmR.* 1998 Fall; 32(3): 401-414. Notes. Biblio. Discography. Lang.: Eng.
USA. 1920-1940. Critical studies. ▪Elements of blues music in the work of playwright Zora Neale Hurston, particularly her novel *Their Eyes Were Watching God.*

3626 Johnstone, Monica Carolyn. *Tennessee Williams and American Realism.* Berkeley, CA: Univ. of California; 1987. 217 pp. Notes. Biblio. [Ph.D. Dissertation, Univ. Microfilms Order No. 8813930.] Lang.: Eng.
USA. 1945-1986. Critical studies. ▪Realism and anti-realism in Tennessee Williams' *Battle of Angels, The Glass Menagerie, A Streetcar Named Desire, Cat on a Hot Tin Roof, Camino Real, The Night of the Iguana,* and others.

3627 Jones, Chris. "The Glory Years." *AmTh.* 1998 Nov.; 15(9): 20-22. Illus.: Photo. B&W. 2. Lang.: Eng.
USA. 1998. Critical studies. ▪Profile of Lanford Wilson and his new play *Book of Days.*

3628 Kaynar, Gad. "The Holocaust Experience through Theatrical Profanation." 53-69 in Schumacher, Claude, ed. *Staging the Holocaust: The Shoah in Drama and Performance.* Cambridge: Cambridge UP; 1998. 355 pp. (Cambridge Studies in Modern Theatre.) Index. Notes. Biblio. Illus.: Photo. 4. Lang.: Eng.
USA. 1980-1995. Critical studies. ▪Explores contemporary Holocaust drama through the lens of blasphemy and profanation, used in order to shock audiences.

3629 Kintz, Linda. "Chained to the Bed: Violence and Abortion in *Keely and Du.*" 186-212 in Colleran, Jeanne, ed.; Spencer, Jenny S., ed. *Staging Resistance: Essays on Political Theatre.* Ann Arbor, MI: Univ of Michigan P; 1998. 312 pp. (Theater: Theory/Text/Performance.) Notes. Index. Illus.: Photo. 1. Lang.: Eng.
USA. 1993. Critical studies. ▪Examines issues of gender and politics around the abortion debate in Jane Martin's *Keely and Du* with attention to both actual and symbolic violence in the play.

3630 Kohn, Rita. "The Business of Theatre for Young Audiences." *DGQ.* 1998 Spr; 35(1): 23-27. Lang.: Eng.
USA. 1998. Instructional materials. ▪Discussion on the best ways of approaching writing a play for companies geared to a youth audience.

3631 Konkle, Lincoln. "Puritan Paranoia: Tennessee Williams's *Suddenly Last Summer* as Calvinist Nightmare." *AmerD.* 1998 Spr; 7(2): 51-72. Notes. Biblio. Lang.: Eng.
USA. 1958. Critical studies. ▪Puritanism and predestination in Williams's play.

3632 Kovalenko, G.V. "Nekotorye aspekty nacional'nogo soznanija v zerkale teatra 1980-ch gg.: Deti Judžina O'Nila." (Some Aspects of National Understanding Seen Through the Mirror of Theatre in the 1980s: Children of Eugene O'Neill.) 205-230 in *Amerikanskij charakter.* Moscow: 1998. Lang.: Rus.
USA. 1980-1989. Critical studies. ▪Developments in drama and melodrama in the USA in the 1980s.

3633 Kraut, Anthea. "Reclaiming the Body: Representations of Black Dance in Three Plays by Zora Neale Hurston." *TheatreS.* 1998; 43: 23-36. Notes. Illus.: Pntg. B&W. 1. Lang.: Eng.
USA. 1925-1930. Critical studies. ▪Hurston's use of Black dance styles in her plays *Color Struck, The First One,* and *Mule Bone: A Comedy of Negro Life,* her unfinished theatrical collaboration with Langston Hughes.

3634 Kumar, Pranab. *Possessive Individualism and Self-Destruction: A Recurring Narrative in Selected Plays of Tennessee Williams.* East Lansing, MI: Michigan State Univ; 1998. 292 pp. Notes. Biblio. [Ph.D. Dissertation, Univ. Microfilms Order No. AAC 9839660.] Lang.: Eng.
USA. 1944-1980. Critical studies. ▪Possessive versus expressive individualism in the plays of Tennessee Williams.

3635 Lee, Josephine. "Pity and Terror as Public Acts: Reading Feminist Politics in the Plays of Maria Irene Fornes." 166-185 in Colleran, Jeanne, ed.; Spencer, Jenny S., ed. *Staging Resistance: Essays on Political Theatre.* Ann Arbor, MI: Univ of Michigan P; 1998. 312 pp. (Theater: Theory/Text/Performance.) Notes. Index. Lang.: Eng.
USA. 1975-1995. Critical studies. ▪The ways in which Fornes endows performative moments with immense political and feminist significance in her plays. Focuses on the use of empathy and emotional identification as a basis for politically effective theatre.

3636 Levine, Eric M. "Hidden Perspectivism: A Contemporary Approach to O'Neill's *Days Without End.*" *JADT.* 1998 Fall; 10(3) : 1-11. Notes. Lang.: Eng.
USA. 1934. Critical studies. ▪Nietzschean analysis of O'Neill's play as a metaphysical play requiring a non-realistic approach to production.

3637 Londré, Felicia Hardison. "Money Without Glory: Turn-of-the-Century America's Women Playwrights." 131-140 in Engle, Ron, ed.; Miller, Tice L., ed. *The American Stage: Social and Economic Issues from the Colonial Period to the Present.* Cambridge: Cambridge UP; 1993. 320 pp. Pref. Notes. Index. Lang.: Eng.
USA. 1890-1910. Historical studies. ▪The conservative social role of female playwrights even as they engaged in the supposedly masculine pursuit of earning large sums of money.

3638 Manheim, Michael. "Introduction." 1-3 in Manheim, Michael, ed. *The Cambridge Companion to Eugene O'Neill.* Cambridge/New York, NY: Cambridge UP; 1998. 256 pp. (Cambridge Companions to Literature.) Index. Biblio. Lang.: Eng.
USA. 1888-1953. Critical studies. ▪Introductory article to collection of essays on Eugene O'Neill, including historical and cultural context.

3639 Manheim, Michael. "The Stature of *Long Day's Journey Into Night.*" 206-216 in Manheim, Michael, ed. *The Cambridge Companion to Eugene O'Neill.* Cambridge/New York, NY: Cambridge UP; 1998. 256 pp. (Cambridge Companions to Literature.) Index. Biblio. Notes. Lang.: Eng.
USA. 1956. Critical studies. ▪Aspects of Eugene O'Neill's *Long Day's Journey Into Night* that constitute 'great' drama.

3640 Marre, Diana Katherine. *Traditions and Departures: Lorraine Hansberry and Black Americans in Theatre.* Berkeley,

DRAMA: —Plays/librettos/scripts

CA: Univ. of California; 1987. 451 pp. Notes. Biblio. [Ph.D. Dissertation, Univ. Microfilms Order No. 8726290.] Lang.: Eng.

USA. 1769-1986. Critical studies. ▪Political, historical and psychological influences on playwright Lorraine Hansberry, development of Black playwrights in American drama, and images of Black men and women by white playwrights.

3641 Maufort, Marc. "Exorcisms of the Past: Avatars of the O'Neillian Monologue in Modern American Drama." *EOR*. 1998 Spr/Fall; 22(1/2): 123-136. Notes. Lang.: Eng.

USA. 1911-1998. Critical studies. ▪The influence of Eugene O'Neill's novelistic style of monologue writing on later American playwrights, including Tennessee Williams, Edward Albee, and Sam Shepard.

3642 McConachie, Bruce A. "*The Dining Room*: A Tocquevillian Take on the Decline of WASP Culture." *JADT*. 1998 Win; 10(1): 39-50. Notes. Lang.: Eng.

USA. 1982-1984. Critical studies. ▪Examines the structuring of history and the roles played by gender and class in A.R. Gurney's *The Dining Room*.

3643 McFarland, Ron. "Dramatic Transformations of *Evangeline*." *AmerD*. 1998 Fall; 8(1): 26-49. Biblio. Lang.: Eng.

USA. Canada. 1860-1976. Historical studies. ▪History of dramatic adaptations of Henry Wadsworth Longfellow's poem *Evangeline*. Cited in article are various versions adapted by Mary O'Reilly, Olive M. Price, Thomas W. Broadhurst, John Goodwin and Edward Everett Rice, and Antonine Maillet's *Evangeline Deusse*.

3644 McNally, Terrence. "What I Know About Being a Playwright." *AmTh*. 1998 Nov.; 15(9): 25-26. Illus.: Dwg. B&W. 1. Lang.: Eng.

USA. 1998. Histories-sources. ▪Terrence McNally shares what he has learned in thirty-five years as a playwright.

3645 McNerney, Sheila. "Preston Jones and *A Texas Trilogy*: Regional Drama or the Drama of Regionalism?" *TheatreS*. 1998; 43 : 53-65. Notes. Illus.: Photo. B&W. 1. Lang.: Eng.

USA. 1977. Critical studies. ▪Analysis and defense of Jones' trilogy of plays about Texas, *Lu Ann Hampton Laverty Oberlander, The Last Meeting of the Knights of the White Magnolia*, and *The Oldest Living Graduate*.

3646 McNulty, Charles. "Lost and Found." *AmTh*. 1998 Nov.; 15(9): 16-17, 61. Illus.: Photo. B&W. 3. Lang.: Eng.

USA. 1998. Biographical studies. ▪Career of playwright W. David Hancock.

3647 Meserve, Walter J. "Social Awareness on Stage: Tensions Mounting, 1850-1859." 81-100 in Engle, Ron, ed.; Miller, Tice L., ed. *The American Stage: Social and Economic Issues from the Colonial Period to the Present*. Cambridge: Cambridge UP; 1993. 320 pp. Pref. Notes. Index. Lang.: Eng.

USA. 1850-1859. Historical studies. ▪The staging of social issues such as slavery, increased immigration, and crime.

3648 Midyett, Judith Ann. *The Comedy of Equitable Resolution: S.N. Behrman and Philip Barry*. Athens, GA: Univ. of Georgia; 1987. 190 pp. Notes. Biblio. [Ph.D. Dissertation, Univ. Microfilms Order No. AAC 8800285.] Lang.: Eng.

USA. 1920-1964. Critical studies. ▪The development of the comedies of manners of S. N. Behrman and Philip Barry: examines the political and socio-economic conditions at the time, the structural characteristics, the creation of special characters who push the action toward equitable resolution, and a particular use of location which aids the characters in accomplishing their goals.

3649 Miller, Arthur; Voznesenskij, A., transl. *Naplyvy vremeni: Istorija žizni.* (Tides of Time: The Story of Life.) Moscow: Progress; 1998. 592 pp. Lang.: Rus.

USA. 1915-1998. Biographical studies. ▪Translation of playwright Arthur Miller's autobiography *Timebends: A Life* (New York, NY: Grove, 1987).

3650 Milleret, Margo. "Girls Growing Up, Cultural Norms Breaking Down in Two Plays by Josefina López." *Gestos*. 1998 Nov. ; 13(26): 109-125. Biblio. Lang.: Eng.

USA. 1988-1989. Critical studies. ▪Analysis of *Simply Maria* and *Real Women Have Curves*.

3651 Molarsky, Mona. "A Feast of Lorca." *AmTh*. 1998 July/Aug.; 15(6): 52-53. Illus.: Photo. B&W. 2. Lang.: Eng.

USA: New York, NY. 1930-1998. Critical studies. ▪Background of Lorca's *The Public (El Público)* as the theatre company Repertorio Español prepares to give the play its New York premiere some seventy years after it was written, under the direction of René Buch.

3652 Montgomery, Benilde. "*Angels in America* as Medieval Mystery." *MD*. 1998 Win; 41(4): 596-606. Notes. Lang.: Eng.

USA. 1992-1994. Critical studies. ▪Influence of medieval mystery plays on Tony Kushner's *Angels in America*.

3653 Moore, Opal J. "Enter, the Tribe of Woman." *Callaloo*. 1996 Spr; 19(2): 340-347. Biblio. Lang.: Eng.

USA. 1996. Critical studies. ▪Analysis of *Diva Studies* by Elizabeth Alexander as an example of the role of female and Black writers in the new millennium.

3654 Murphy, Brenda. "O'Neill's America: The Strange Interlude Between the Wars." 135-147 in Manheim, Michael, ed. *The Cambridge Companion to Eugene O'Neill*. Cambridge/New York, NY: Cambridge UP; 1998. 256 pp. (Cambridge Companions to Literature.) Index. Biblio. Notes. Lang.: Eng.

USA. 1917-1940. Critical studies. ▪How the cultural mores of the period between the two World Wars worked to shape O'Neill's plays of that period, notably *Strange Interlude*.

3655 Murray, Frank J., Jr. *Speaking the Unspeakable: Theatrical Language in the Plays of Samuel Beckett and Sam Shepard*. Stanford, CA: Stanford Univ; 1988. 329 pp. Biblio. Notes. [Ph.D. Dissertation, Univ. Microfilms Order No. AAC 8826203.] Lang.: Eng.

USA. France. Ireland. 1950-1988. Critical studies. ▪The problematic relationship between words and other elements of expression in the plays of Samuel Beckett and Sam Shepard. Author uses theoretical insights drawn from semiology, phenomenology, hermeneutics, reader response theory, and performance theory.

3656 Nesmith, N. Graham. "John Henry Redwood: Firm Convictions." *AmTh*. 1998 Dec.; 15(10): 54-56. Illus.: Photo. B&W. 2. Lang.: Eng.

USA: Atlanta, GA. 1998. Biographical studies. ▪Profile of playwright Redwood and his play *The Old Settler*.

3657 Nickel, John. "Racial Degeneration and *The Hairy Ape*." *EOR*. 1998 Spr/Fall; 22(1/2): 33-40. Biblio. Notes. Lang.: Eng.

USA. 1922. Critical studies. ▪Argues that O'Neill's play is an attack on the then widely-held belief in the racial degeneration of the African-American race.

3658 Parker, Brian. "A Tentative Stemma for Drafts and Revisions of Tennessee Williams's *Suddenly Last Summer* (1958)." *MD*. 1998 Sum; 41(2): 303-326. Notes. Lang.: Eng.

USA. 1958. Textual studies. ▪Attempt to sequence Williams's drafts and revisions of his play. Includes a key to the archival material referred to in this stemma.

3659 Parker, Charles Leslie. *Men of Like Passions: Four Plays Based Upon Old Testament Accounts of the Hebrew Prophets*. Carbondale, IL: Southern Illinois Univ; 1987. 559 pp. Notes. Biblio. [Ph.D. Dissertation, Univ. Microfilms Order No. AAC 8728292.] Lang.: Eng.

USA. Europe. 1919-1970. Critical studies. ▪Analysis of Stefan Zweig's *Jeremias (Jeremiah)*, D. H. Lawrence's *David (for Samuel)*, Christopher Fry's *The Firstborn*, Martin Buber's *Elija*, Norman Nicholson's *The Old Man of the Mountains* and *Birth by Drowning*.

3660 Paulin, Diana R. "Performing Miscegenation: Rescuing *The White Slave* from the Threat of Interracial Desire." *JDTC*. 1998 Fall; 13(1): 71-86. Notes. Lang.: Eng.

USA. 1882. Critical studies. ▪Examines the way in which representation of Black/white unions in Bartley Campbell's play *The White Slave* invokes anxieties about the impact of interracial contact, while simultaneously rehearsing the multiple possibilities of these transgressive relationships.

3661 Pettinelli, Frances. *Tennessee Williams: A Study of the Dramaturgical Evolution of Three Later Plays, 1969-1978*. New York, NY: City Univ. of New York; 1988. 297 pp. Biblio.

Notes. [Ph.D. Dissertation, Univ. Microfilms Order No. AAC 8821111.] Lang.: Eng.

USA. 1969-1978. Critical studies. ■Examines the dramaturgical style of *The Two-Character Play*, *Small Craft Warnings*, and *Vieux Carre.* Argues that these later dramatic works illuminate Williams's earlier dramas.

3662 Phillip, Christine. "Interview with Elizabeth Alexander." *Callaloo.* 1996 Spr; 19(2): 493-507. Lang.: Eng.

USA. 1996. Histories-sources. ■Interview with the playwright concerning her work and philosophy, and her play *Diva Studies.*

3663 Poisson, Gary Arthur. *The Theme of Death, Symbolically and Motivationally, in the Plays of Eugene O'Neill.* Long Beach, CA: Univ. of California; 1987. 62 pp. Notes. Biblio. [M.A. Thesis, Univ. Microfilms Order No. 1330646.] Lang.: Eng.

USA. 1914-1950. Critical studies. ■Death in the plays of Eugene O'Neill with respect to symbolism and spirituality, and motivation and physicality.

3664 Preston, Deborah Elaine. *Epochs of Impossibility: A Marxian Theory of Dramatic Parody and Burlesque.* New Orleans, LA: Tulane Univ; 1998. 261 pp. Notes. Biblio. [Ph.D. Dissertation, Univ. Microfilms Order No. AAC 9906599.] Lang.: Eng.

USA. Europe. 1998. Critical studies. ■Marxist examination of dramatic parody and burlesque. Argues that history, politics, economics, class, and ideology all influence and shape the two genres.

3665 Prien, Helen Elizabeth. *The Enneagram and the Actor: Using a System of Personality Typology in Character Analysis.* Carbondale, IL: Southern Illinois Univ; 1998. 243 pp. Biblio. Notes. [Ph.D. Dissertation, Univ. Microfilms Order No. 9902736.] Lang.: Eng.

USA. 1998. Critical studies. ■Application of the enneagram system of personality typology to the character Martha in Edward Albee's *Who's Afraid of Virginia Woolf?.*

3666 Proehl, Geoffrey Scott. *Coming Home Again: American Family Drama and the Figure of the Prodigal.* Stanford, CA: Stanford Univ; 1988. 290 pp. Biblio. Notes. [Ph.D. Dissertation, Univ. Microfilms Order No. AAC 8826214.] Lang.: Eng.

USA. 1920-1985. Critical studies. ■The representation of the family in American drama, with reference to uses and conventions of the figure of the prodigal husband or son. Considers plays by Eugene O'Neill, Tennessee Williams, Arthur Miller, August Wilson, Sam Shepard, Christopher Durang and others.

3667 Ran, Faye. *The Tragicomic Vision—The Fool in Modern Drama, Film, and Literature.* New York, NY: Columbia Univ; 1988. 295 pp. Biblio. Notes. [Ph.D. Dissertation, Univ. Microfilms Order No. AAC 9102452.] Lang.: Eng.

USA. Germany. Italy. 1960-1968. Critical studies. ■The duality of the 'fool' character in contemporary theatre, film, and literature, with emphasis on Peter Handke's drama, *Kaspar*, Federico Fellini's film, *Juliet of the Spirits (Giuletta degli Spiriti)*, and Isaac Bashevis Singer's novel, *The Magician of Lublin.*

3668 Ranald, Margaret Loftus. "From Trial to Triumph: The Early Plays." 51-68 in Manheim, Michael, ed. *The Cambridge Companion to Eugene O'Neill.* Cambridge/New York, NY: Cambridge UP; 1998. 256 pp. (Cambridge Companions to Literature.) Index. Biblio. Notes. Illus.: Photo. 1. Lang.: Eng.

USA. 1915-1925. Critical studies. ■Themes in the early plays of Eugene O'Neill—the 'sea' plays, *The Emperor Jones*, *The Hairy Ape*, and *Desire Under the Elms.* Charts his continuing development as a playwright and themes of the supernatural, race relations, class divisions, and the dysfunctional family.

3669 Raymond, Gerard. "David Henry Hwang: Between East and West." *DGQ.* 1998 Spr; 35(1): 16-22. Lang.: Eng.

USA. 1980-1998. Histories-sources. ■Interview with the playwright regarding his career and artistic goals.

3670 Rees, Charles A. *Lady Bright and Her Children: Contemporary American Gay Drama.* Chattanooga, TN: Univ. of Tennessee; 1988. 180 pp. Biblio. Notes. [Ph.D. Dissertation, Univ. Microfilms Order No. AAC 8911754.] Lang.: Eng.

USA. 1960-1987. Critical studies. ■Examines American gay drama since 1960 and the impact of the AIDS crisis. Analyzes Lanford Wilson's *The Madness of Lady Bright* and *Fifth of July*, and Harvey Fierstein's *Safe Sex*, among others.

3671 Renner, Pamela. "The Mellowing of Miss Firecracker." *AmTh.* 1998 Nov.; 15(9): 18-19, 61. Illus.: Photo. B&W. 2. Lang.: Eng.

USA. 1998. Biographical studies. ■Profile of Beth Henley with emphasis on her evolution as a playwright.

3672 Richards, Jeffrey H. "How to Write an American Play: Murray's *Traveller Returned* and Its Source." *EAL.* 1998; 33(3): 277-290. Notes. Biblio. Lang.: Eng.

USA. 1771-1796. Critical studies. ■Argues that Judith Sargent Murray's play uses Richard Cumberland's comedy *The West Indian* as its source.

3673 Risdon, Michelle Elaine. *The Scene of the Crime: The True-Crime Docudrama in Contemporary Theatre.* Ann Arbor, MI: Univ. of Michigan; 1998. 341 pp. Biblio. Notes. [Ph.D. Dissertation, Univ. Microfilms Order No. 9840637.] Lang.: Eng.

USA. France. 1955-1996. Critical studies. ■Feminist analysis of true crimes and their transformations into a theatrical event. Plays discussed are Jean Genet's *Les Bonnes (The Maids)*, Wendy Kesselman's *My Sister in This House*, Sharon Pollock's *Blood Relations*, Marguerite Duras' *Les Viaducs de la Seine-et-Oise (The Viaducts of the Seine)*, and Rhodessa Jones' *Buried Fire.*

3674 Rizzo, Frank. "Raising Tennessee." *AmTh.* 1998 Oct.; 15(8): 20-25. Illus.: Photo. B&W. 5. Lang.: Eng.

USA. 1996-1998. Critical studies. ■Reasons for the recent renewal of interest in the work of Tennessee Williams.

3675 Robinson, James A. "The Middle Plays." 69-81 in Manheim, Michael, ed. *The Cambridge Companion to Eugene O'Neill.* Cambridge/New York, NY: Cambridge UP; 1998. 256 pp. (Cambridge Companions to Literature.) Index. Biblio. Notes. Lang.: Eng.

USA. 1925-1938. Critical studies. ■The middle period plays of Eugene O'Neill, including *The Great God Brown*, *Strange Interlude*, and *Mourning Becomes Electra*, and the historical and cultural contexts of O'Neill's solidified position as a major dramatist. Analyzes religious themes, new uses for masks and other theatrical techniques, and adaptations of European techniques.

3676 Rossini, John. "*Bandido!*: Melodrama, Stereotypes and the Construction of Ethnicity." *Gestos.* 1998 Apr.; 13(25): 127-141. Notes. Biblio. Illus.: Photo. B&W. 1. Lang.: Eng.

USA. 1986. Critical studies. ■Use of stereotypes and melodrama in constructing ethnic identity in Luis Valdez' play.

3677 Ryan, Steven Daniel. *David Mamet: Dramatic Craftsman.* New York, NY: Fordham Univ; 1988. 295 pp. Notes. Biblio. [Ph.D. Dissertation, Univ. Microfilms Order No. AAC 8818476.] Lang.: Eng.

USA. 1975-1987. Critical studies. ■Aphasic speech patterns in the plays of David Mamet. Argues that language is the defining element of Mamet's dramaturgy and serves as a poetic device through which the playwright portrays the world.

3678 Saddik, Annette J. "The (Un)Represented Fragmentation of the Body in Tennessee Williams's 'Desire and the Black Masseur' and *Suddenly Last Summer.*" *MD.* 1998 Fall; 41(3): 347-354. Notes. Lang.: Eng.

USA. 1946-1958. Critical studies. ■The fragmentation of social and psychological identity experienced through unrestricted, perverse desire in Williams' play and short story.

3679 Savran, David. "Driving Ms. Vogel." *AmTh.* 1998 Oct.; 15(8): 16-19, 96-106. Illus.: Photo. B&W. 5. Lang.: Eng.

USA: New York, NY. 1998. Histories-sources. ■Interview with playwright Paula Vogel about her writing and 1998's most produced play *How I Learned to Drive.*

3680 Schaeffer, Ira. *Rites of Passage in the Plays of David Mamet.* Providence, RI: Univ. of Rhode Island; 1998. 224 pp. Notes.

DRAMA: —Plays/librettos/scripts

Biblio. [Ph.D. Dissertation, Univ. Microfilms Order No. AAC 9902576.] Lang.: Eng.
USA. 1975-1995. Critical studies. ■The rite of passage as a means of transformation in *Lakeboat*, *American Buffalo*, *Disappearance of the Jews*, *Glengarry Glen Ross*, *Reunion*, *The Woods*, *Speed-the-Plow*, *The Shawl*, *Oleanna*, and *The Cryptogram*.

3681 Schempp, James I. "Getchell Winner: Criswell Moves from Backstage to Centerstage." *SoTh.* 1998 Fall; 39(4): 4-10. Illus.: Photo. B&W. 1. Lang.: Eng.
USA. 1998. Histories-sources. ■Interview with playwright Sheryle Criswell, winner of the 1998 Charles M. Getchell New Play Award for her play ... *Where Late the Sweet Birds Sang*.

3682 Schiavi, Michael R. *Staging Effeminacy in America*. New York, NY: New York Univ; 1998. 360 pp. Notes. Biblio. [Ph.D. Dissertation, Univ. Microfilms Order No. AAC 9831763.] Lang.: Eng.
USA. 1920-1998. Critcial studies. ■The representation of effeminacy in Eugene O'Neill's *Strange Interlude* and *Long Day's Journey Into Night*, Tennessee Williams' *The Glass Menagerie*, and *Kingdom of Earth*, Larry Kramer's *The Destiny of Me*, David Drake's *The Night Larry Kramer Kissed Me*, Split Britches and Bloolips' *Belle Reprieve*, Mart Crowley's *The Boys in the Band*, and Terrence McNally's *Love! Valour! Compassion!*.

3683 Schiffman, Jean. "Lillian Garrett-Groag: Playing with Fire." *AmTh.* 1998 Sep.; 15(7): 60-61. Illus.: Dwg. B&W. 1. Lang.: Eng.
USA: Los Angeles, CA. 1998. Biographical studies. ■Profile of Los Angeles-based playwright Garrett-Groag and her play *The Magic Fire*.

3684 Schneider, Robert. "Yasmina Reza in a Major Key." *AmTh.* 1998 Nov.; 15(9): 12-15. Illus.: Photo. B&W. 3. Lang.: Eng.
USA: New York, NY. France. 1998. Biographical studies. ■Profile of French playwright Yasmina Reza, with a focus on her play *'Art'*.

3685 Schulman, Sarah. "Tina Landau: The Rest Is Metaphor." *AmTh.* 1998 Sep.; 15(7): 68-69. Illus.: Photo. B&W. 1. Lang.: Eng.
USA. 1998. Histories-sources. ■Interview with director/playwright Landau on the respective strengths of working with words and working with images.

3686 Sharp, Allison Gappmayer. *Reflexive Drama, Coded Narrative, and Artistic Solipsism: Metadrama in Tennessee Williams' 'The Glass Menagerie', 'Suddenly Last Summer', and 'The Two-Character Play'*. College Park, MD: Univ. of Maryland; 1998. 262 pp. Notes. Biblio. [Ph.D. Dissertation, Univ. Microfilms Order No. AAC 9836480.] Lang.: Eng.
USA. 1944-1978. Histories-specific. ■Analyzes the metadramatic elements in three plays by Tennessee Williams.

3687 Shaughnessy, Edward L. "O'Neill's African and Irish-Americans: Stereotypes or 'Faithful Realism'." 148-163 in Manheim, Michael, ed. *The Cambridge Companion to Eugene O'Neill*. Cambridge/New York, NY: Cambridge UP; 1998. 256 pp. (Cambridge Companions to Literature.) Index. Biblio. Notes. Illus.: Photo. 1. Lang.: Eng.
USA. 1916-1953. Critical studies. ■Examines Eugene O'Neill's treatment of African-Americans and Irish-Americans, the two most frequently mentioned minority groups in his plays, especially *The Emperor Jones*, *All God's Chillun Got Wings*, *The Iceman Cometh*, *Long Day's Journey Into Night*, *The Hairy Ape*, *A Touch of the Poet*, and *A Moon for the Misbegotten*. Also discusses several original performers in these plays, including Charles Gilpin, Paul Robeson, Siobhan McKenna, Vincent Dowling and George M. Cohan.

3688 Sheehy, Henry. "Douglas Carter Beane." *AmTh.* 1998 May/June; 15(5): 48-49. Illus.: Photo. B&W. 1. Lang.: Eng.
USA. 1998. Biographical studies. ■Profile of playwright Beane, author of *As Bees in Honey Drown*.

3689 Siegal, Jessica. "Thulani Davis: Keeping It Real." *AmTh.* 1998 Sep.; 15(7): 57-58. Illus.: Dwg. B&W. 1. Lang.: Eng.
USA. 1998. Biographical studies. ■Profile of novelist and playwright Davis and her play about Zora Neale Hurston *Everybody's Ruby*.

3690 Silverstein, Marc. "'Any Baggage You Don't Claim, We Trash': Living With(in) History in *The Colored Museum*." *AmerD.* 1998 Fall; 8(1): 95-121. Notes. Biblio. Lang.: Eng.
USA. 1988. Critical studies. ■The contradictions of the African-American experience as reflected in George C. Wolfe's play.

3691 Singh, Yvonne Marie. *Stages in the Funnyhouse: The Dramaturgy of Adrienne Kennedy*. Ithaca, NY: Cornell Univ; 1998. 318 pp. Biblio. Notes. [Ph.D. Dissertation, Univ. Microfilms Order No. 9900031.] Lang.: Eng.
USA. 1964-1990. Critical studies. ■The dramaturgical evolution of Adrienne Kennedy, with reference to her plays *Funnyhouse of a Negro*, *A Movie Star Has to Star in Black and White*, and *The Ohio State Murders*.

3692 Splawn, P. Jane. "'Change the Joke(r) and Slip the Yoke': Boal's 'Joker' System in Ntozake Shange's *for colored girls . . . and spell #7*." *MD.* 1998 Fall; 41(3): 386-398. Notes. Lang.: Eng.
USA. 1977-1981. Critical studies. ■Examines the reinvention of Augusto Boal's 'Joker' system,' in which a central character acts as a master of ceremonies by inviting the audience to join in the action, in Shange's two plays.

3693 Sterling, Eric. "Protecting Home: Patriarchal Authority in August Wilson's *Fences*." *ET.* 1998; 17(1): 53-62. Notes. Biblio. Lang.: Eng.
USA. 1987. Critical studies. ■Examines social power and familial responsibility in August Wilson's *Fences*, especially through the use of baseball metaphors.

3694 Stucky, Nathan Paul. *Conversation Analysis and Performance: An Examination of Selected Plays by Sam Shepard*. Austin, TX: Univ. of Texas; 1988. 336 pp. Biblio. Notes. [Ph.D. Dissertation, Univ. Microfilms Order No. AAC 8816577.] Lang.: Eng.
USA. 1967-1985. Critical studies. ■The nature of language, in the plays of Sam Shepard, including *Curse of the Starving Class*, *Buried Child*, *True West*, and *A Lie of the Mind*.

3695 Tobin, Ronald W. *Tarte à la crème. Commedia e gastronomia nel teatro di Molière*. (Tarte à la Crème: Comedy and Gastronomy in Molière's Theatre.) Rome: Bulzoni; 1998. 237 pp. (Biblioteca Teatrale, 102.) Lang.: Ita.
USA. 1990-1998. Critical studies. ■Italian translation of *Tarte à la Crème* (Columbus: Ohio State UP, 1990).

3696 Tooks, Kim. "Kia Corthron: Staying On Track." *BlackM.* 1998 May/June; 13(1): 5-6, 15. Illus.: Photo. B&W. 1. Lang.: Eng.
USA. 1998. Historical studies. ■Interview with the playwright regarding her plays *Seeking the Genesis* and *Splash Hatch on the E Going Down*.

3697 Törnqvist, Egil. "O'Neill's Philosophical and Literary Paragons." 18-32 in Manheim, Michael, ed. *The Cambridge Companion to Eugene O'Neill*. Cambridge/New York, NY: Cambridge UP; 1998. 256 pp. (Cambridge Companions to Literature.) Index. Biblio. Lang.: Eng.
USA. 1888-1953. Critical studies. ■The European philosophers and playwrights—notably, Nietzsche, Ibsen, and Strindberg—who had the greatest influence on playwright Eugene O'Neill's intellectual and artistic development.

3698 Troiani, Elisa A. *The Players Come to the Americas: The Development of the Theatrical and Dramatic Traditions of the United States*. Toledo, OH: Univ. of Toledo; 1987. 444 pp. Biblio. Notes. [Ph.D. Dissertation, Univ. Microfilms Order No. 8722186.] Lang.: Eng.
USA. Argentina. 1600-1900. Historical studies. ■Compares and contrasts the dramatic traditions of Argentina and the United States, using a historical and literary approach. Traces the historical development of the two countries, and examines how the political, economic, and cultural characteristics of each country molded their theatre and drama.

3699 Tucker, Edward L. "Booth Tarkington, *The Country Cousin*, and Maud Howitt." *AmerD.* 1998 Fall; 8(1): 50-58. Notes. Biblio. Lang.: Eng.
USA. 1921. Historical studies. ■Describes the evolution of Tarkington's play, as well as his involvement in the casting of the show. Includes a let-

DRAMA: —Plays/librettos/scripts

ter from the playwright to actress Grace Elliston intended to persuade her to play the small but significant role of Maud Howitt.

3700 Turnbaugh, Douglas Blair. "James Purdy: Playwright." *PerAJ.* 1998 May; 20(2): 73-75. Illus.: Photo. B&W. 1. Lang.: Eng.

USA. 1957-1998. Critical studies. ■Touches on the theatrical output of the novelist, citing his plays *Souvenirs*, *Heatstroke*, and *Sun of the Sleepless.*

3701 Tyler, Kelsey Duane. *Shame and Tennessee Williams' 'A Streetcar Named Desire', 'Summer and Smoke', 'The Rose Tattoo', and 'The Night of the Iguana'.* East Lansing, MI: Michigan State Univ; 1998. 78 pp. Biblio. Notes. [M.A. Thesis, Univ. Microfilms Order No. 1390529.] Lang.: Eng.

USA. 1950-1970. Critical studies. ■Shame and the puritanical/sexual conflict in several works by Tennessee Williams.

3702 Ulrich, Judy A.P. *An Analysis of Selected Play Adaptations and the Original Version of 'The Adventures of Tom Sawyer'.* East Lansing, MI: Michigan State Univ; 1988. 306 pp. Notes. Biblio. [Ph.D. Dissertation, Univ. Microfilms Order No. 8912651.] Lang.: Eng.

USA. 1884-1983. Critical studies. ■Compares twenty-one adaptations of *The Adventures of Tom Sawyer* for young theatre audiences with respect to plot, character, and thematic and stylistic elements to their counterparts in the novel by Mark Twain.

3703 Voglino, Barbara. *The Evolution of Closure in the Plays of Eugene O'Neill.* New York, NY: Fordham Univ; 1998. 278 pp. Notes. Biblio. [Ph.D. Dissertation, Univ. Microfilms Order No. AAC 9816350.] Lang.: Eng.

USA. 1918-1950. Critical studies. ■Compares O'Neill's use of closure in three periods during his career. Plays examined include *Desire Under the Elms*, *The Iceman Cometh*, *Long Day's Journey Into Night*, and *A Moon for the Misbegotten.*

3704 Walker, Pierre A. "Zora Neale Hurston and the Post-Modern Self in *Dust Tracks on the Road.*" *AfAmR.* 1998 Fall; 32(3): 387-399. Notes. Biblio. Lang.: Eng.

USA. 1942. Critical studies. ■Analysis of Hurston's autobiography and its ambivalent reception by the critics of the day.

3705 Walton, Glenn. "Lill Women, Lill Men." *ArtsAtl.* 1998; 16(2): 41-43. Illus.: Photo. B&W. 2. Lang.: Eng.

USA: Halifax, NS. 1997-1998. Histories-sources. ■Interview with playwright/member of Parliament Wendy Lill, in which she discusses her recent play *Corker*, and her aspirations for a society built on a strong sense of community.

3706 Watermeier, Daniel J. "O'Neill and the Theatre of His Time." 33-50 in Manheim, Michael, ed. *The Cambridge Companion to Eugene O'Neill.* Cambridge/New York, NY: Cambridge UP; 1998. 256 pp. (Cambridge Companions to Literature.) Index. Biblio. Lang.: Eng.

USA. 1888-1953. Historical studies. ■The theatrical world in which playwright Eugene O'Neill grew up, including the work and career of his father, actor James O'Neill.

3707 Watson, John Clair. *The Ritual Plays of Peter Shaffer.* Eugene, OR: Univ. of Oregon; 1987. 235 pp. Biblio. Notes. [Ph.D. Dissertation, Univ. Microfilms Order No. AAC 8721260.] Lang.: Eng.

USA. 1975-1985. Critical studies. ■Modern theatrical ritual in the later plays of Peter Shaffer—*The Royal Hunt of the Sun*, *Equus*, and *Amadeus*—with emphasis on his unique structure, theme, character, and language.

3708 Wattenberg, Richard. "From 'Horse Opera' History to Hall of Mirrors: Luis Valdez's *Bandido!.*" *MD.* 1998 Fall; 41(3): 411-422. Notes. Lang.: Eng.

USA. 1982. Critical studies. ■Analysis of Valdez' play as a revision of the history of the 'Old West,' and as a challenge to Chicano stereotypes.

3709 Weaver, Michael S. "Genius and Alienation." *AANYL.* 1995 July; 19(2): 17-24. Biblio. Lang.: Eng.

USA. 1935. Critical studies. ■Analysis of Langston Hughes' play *Mulatto.*

3710 Wikander, Matthew H. "O'Neill and the Cult of Sincerity." 217-235 in Manheim, Michael, ed. *The Cambridge Companion to Eugene O'Neill.* Cambridge/New York, NY: Cambridge UP; 1998. 256 pp. (Cambridge Companions to Literature.) Index. Biblio. Notes. Lang.: Eng.

USA. 1997. Critical studies. ■Aspects of Eugene O'Neill's work that led to a repositioning of the playwright's place in the canon.

3711 Willingham, Ralph. *'Introduce Them to Harvey': Mary Chase and the Theatre.* Commerce, TX: East Texas State Univ; 1987. 198 pp. Biblio. Notes. [M.A. Thesis, Univ. Microfilms Order No. 1330331.] Lang.: Eng.

USA. 1944. Critical studies. ■Examines playwright Mary Chase and her theatrical career, and the impact of her most famous play *Harvey.*

3712 Wixson, Christopher. "Everyman and Superman: Assimilation, Ethnic Identity, and Elmer Rice's *Counsellor-at-Law.*" *AmerD.* 1998 Fall; 8(1): 59-74. Notes. Biblio. Lang.: Eng.

USA. 1931. Critical studies. ■Ideas of immigrant success, identity, and alienation in Rice's play.

3713 Wongchanta, Tipchan. *The Value of Open-Endedness and Undecidability of Meaning in the Plays of Sam Shepard.* Indiana, PA: Indiana Univ. of Pennsylvania; 1998. 267 pp. Notes. Biblio. [Ph.D. Dissertation, Univ. Microfilms Order No. AAC 9823514.] Lang.: Eng.

USA. 1966-1996. Critical studies. ■Themes and dramaturgical strategies in the plays of Sam Shepard.

3714 Wood, Jacqueline E. *Performance and African-American Women: Three Contemporary Dramatists.* Gainesville, FL: Univ. of Florida; 1998. 243 pp. Notes. Biblio. [Ph.D. Dissertation, Univ. Microfilms Order No. AAC 9906042.] Lang.: Eng.

USA. 1970-1998. Histories-specific. ■The development of theories of performance by playwrights Adrienne Kennedy, Ntozake Shange, and Suzan-Lori Parks.

3715 York, Julie. "Dueling with the Past." *AmTh.* 1998 July/Aug.; 15(6): 45-47. Illus.: Photo. B&W. 1. Lang.: Eng.

USA. 1998. Critical studies. ■Critique of Charles Smith's play *Les Trois Dumas.*

3716 Zesch, Lindy. "¡Viva Teatro!" *AmTh.* 1998 May/June; 15(5): 24-26. Illus.: Photo. B&W. 4. Lang.: Eng.

USA. 1998. Critical studies. ■Examines the availability of Latin theatre in world festivals, and the relative dearth of Hispanic representation in the arts in the USA.

3717 Zinman, Toby. "Amy Freed: On Desirability." *AmTh.* 1998 Sep.; 15(7): 66-67, 84-85. Illus.: Photo. B&W. 1. Lang.: Eng.

USA. 1998. Biographical studies. ■Career of playwright Freed, with comments on her most recent play *Freedomland.*

3718 Mulrine, Stephen. "*Moscow Stations*: From Novel to Play." *MD.* 1998 Spr; 41(1): 49-59. Notes. Lang.: Eng.

USSR. UK-England. 1973-1998. Histories-sources. ■Translator Mulrine gives an account of how he adapted Venedikt Erofeev's novel *Moskva-Petuškij* for the stage.

3719 Barnett, Dennis Carl. *The Worlds of Dušan Kovačevič: An Intersection of Dissident Texts.* Seattle, WA: Univ. of Washington; 1998. 424 pp. Notes. Biblio. [Ph.D. Dissertation, Univ. Microfilms Order No. AAC 9907877.] Lang.: Eng.

Yugoslavia. 1972-1997. Critical studies. ■How the formation and dissemination of Dušan Kovačevič's plays intersect with the prevalent political/cultural texts in Yugoslavia at the time. Also considers the resistance to Kovačevič's work in translation in the U.S. and England, and possible strategies for overcoming it.

3720 Gerold, László. *Drámakalauz.* (Drama Guide.) Újvidék: Fórum; 1998. 273 pp. Index. Notes. Lang.: Hun.

Yugoslavia: Subotica, Novi Sad. 1837-1998. Histories-specific. ■A collection of writings by the renowned theatre historian and critic on Hungarian dramatic art in Voivodship. Includes an outline of the history of drama in the region, essays on the post-war drama of Voivodship, and reviews of fifty stagings of forty dramas between 1967 and 1998.

3721 Jovičevič, Aleksandra; Martin, Christopher, transl. "Geschichten der Toten." (Stories of Dead Men.) *TZ.* 1998; 3 : 8-12. Illus.: Photo. B&W. 4. Lang.: Ger.

DRAMA: —Plays/librettos/scripts

Yugoslavia. 1991-1998. Historical studies. ■Analysis of the contemporary drama and the history of theatre in Yugoslavia in the political context. Reviews *Srpska drama (A Serbian Drama)* by Sinisa Kovačevič, *U potpalublju (In the Camp)* by Vladimir Arsenijevič, *Turneja (A Journey)* by Goran Markovič and others.

Reference materials

3722 Harner, James L., ed. "World Shakespeare Bibliography 1997." *SQ.* 1998; 49(5): 486-843. Index. Lang.: Eng.

1997. ■Bibliography of work pertaining to the study of William Shakespeare in 1997.

3723 Meserole, Harrison T., ed. "Shakespeare: Annotated World Bibliography for 1988." *SQ.* 1989 Win; 40(5): 522-962. Index. Lang.: Eng.

1988. ■1988 bibliography of materials pertaining to the study of Shakespeare.

3724 Meserole, Harrison T., ed. "Shakespeare: Annotated World Bibliography for 1987." *SQ.* 1988 Win; 39(5): 525-949. Lang.: Eng.

1987. ■1987 bibliography of materials pertaining to the study of Shakespeare.

3725 van Romondt, Alice C., ed. "Bibliography of Caribbean Literature in English from Suriname, the Netherlands Antilles, Aruba, and the Netherlands." *Callaloo.* 1998 Sum; 21(3): 703-713. Lang.: Eng.

Aruba. Suriname. Netherlands Antilles. Netherlands. 1998. ■Bibliography composed of Dutch-language drama, fiction, poetry, and critical studies written by, or pertaining to, Caribbean writers in former Dutch colonies in the western hemisphere.

3726 Castelli, Silvia. *Manoscritti teatrali della Biblioteca Riccardiana di Firenze.* (Theatrical Manuscripts of the Riccardi Library in Florence.) Florence: Edizioni Polistampa Firenze; 1998. 178 pp. Index. Illus.: Photo. Print. Color. 16. Lang.: Ita.

Italy: Florence. 1500-1700. ■Catalogue of the library's theatrical manuscripts.

3727 Gale, Shannon E. "*The Pinter Review*: Cumulative Author and Title Indices, 1992-1996." *PintR.* 1998: 219-223. Biblio. Index. Lang.: Eng.

UK-England. 1992-1996. ■Index to *The Pinter Review* (authors and titles) for the years 1992-1996.

Relation to other fields

3728 Fleissner, Robert F. "Shakespeare in the Land Down Under." *ShN.* 1998 Win; 48(4): 95, 106. Notes. Lang.: Eng.

Australia. 1998. Historical studies. ■State of Shakespeare studies and education in Australia.

3729 Detje, Robin. "Die Krankheit Kunst und das Spiel ohne Grenzen." (The Disease Art and the Play Without Borders.) *TZ.* 1998; 5: 7-9. Illus.: Photo. B&W. 3. Lang.: Ger.

Austria: Vienna. Germany. 1997-1998. Critical studies. ■The correlation between artist and reality, with respect to *Sportstück (Sport Play)* by Elfriede Jelinek and directed by Einar Schleef at Burgtheater (Vienna) and Christoph Schlingensief's action *Chance 2000* before the election in Germany.

3730 Weber, Manfred. "Morgen Sarajewo." (Morning Sarajevo.) *TZ.* 1998; 3: 20-21. Illus.: Photo. B&W. 2. Lang.: Ger.

Bosnia: Sarajevo. 1997-1998. Historical studies. ■Impressions from Sarajevo by Manfred Weber, theatre manager at Kleist Theater (Frankfurt/Oder). Describes his work on directing Georg Büchner's *Leonce und Lena* translated and adapted by Dĕvad Karahasan.

3731 Wuschek, Kay. "Der Rest ist Muskelkraft." (The Rest Is Muscle Power.) *TZ.* 1998; 5: 42-45. Illus.: Photo. B&W. 4. Lang.: Ger.

Bulgaria. 1997-1998. Historical studies. ■Impressions from Bulgaria: the economic and political-cultural conditions, and their effects on theatre and the efforts to reform theatre in 1997.

3732 Asselin, Olivier. "Le corps subtilisé: l'oeuvre d'art à l'ère de la photographie et du cinéma." (Spiriting Away the Body: Art in the Era of Photography and Cinema.) *JCT.* 1998; 88: 118-122. Notes. Illus.: Photo. B&W. 2. Lang.: Fre.

Canada. 1998. Critical studies. ■Impact of photography and cinema on theatre. Pertinence to theatre, with attention to the theories of Walter Benjamin.

3733 David, Gilbert. "L'offensive du théâtre théocentrique: Le messianisme des clercs entre la Crise et l'après-guerre." (The Theocentric Theatre Offensive: Messianism of Clerics Between the Crash and the Post-War Period.) *AnT.* Spr 1998; 23: 38-52. Notes. Biblio. Lang.: Fre.

Canada: Montreal, PQ. 1930-1950. Critical studies. ■Ideology in the discourse of Québécois priests producing amateur art theatre, particularly Émile Legault and Gustave Lamarche.

3734 Fouquet, Ludovic. "Clins d'oeil cinématographiques dans le théâtre de Robert Lepage." (Winks to Film in the Theatre of Robert Lepage.) *JCT.* 1998; 88: 131-139. Notes. Illus.: Photo. B&W. 6. Lang.: Fre.

Canada. 1990-1998. Critical studies. ■Uses of, and references to, cinema in theatrical productions of Robert Lepage.

3735 Guevara Salazar, Alberto José. *Playing in the Margins, an Ethnography in Two Acts: A 'Presentation' of a Performance of Social Action Theatre in Montreal.* North York, ON: York Univ; 1998. 156 pp. Notes. Biblio. [M.A. Thesis, Univ. Microfilms Order No. AAC MQ27396.] Lang.: Eng.

Canada: Montreal, PQ. 1995-1998. Critical studies. ■Analysis of the performative ethnography of play production by the social action theatre group Mise au Jeu Montréal to reveal cultural, social and political issues within the community.

3736 O'Farrell, Lawrence. "Theatre as Education: A Distinctively Canadian Approach to Secondary School Drama." *TRC.* 1998 Fall; 19(2): 116-124. Biblio. Lang.: Eng.

Canada. 1970-1998. Historical studies. ■Importance of process drama and collectively-created dramatic 'anthologies' in Canadian secondary school drama education.

3737 Vaïs, Michel. "Don Quichotte et l'invention artistique." (Don Quixote and Artistic Invention.) *JCT.* 1998; 89: 111-122. Notes. Illus.: Photo. Dwg. Pntg. B&W. 11. Lang.: Fre.

Canada. 1967-1998. Historical studies. ■Influence of Cervantes' *Don Quixote* on contemporary Québécois artists, with reference to Théâtre du Nouveau Monde's *Don Quichotte.*

3738 Vaïs, Michel. "Hommage à André Le Coz." (Homage to André Le Coz.) *JCT.* 1998; 86: 7-9. Illus.: Photo. B&W. 7. Lang.: Fre.

Canada: Montreal, PQ. 1952-1998. Biographical studies. ■Reviews career of Montreal-based photographer André Le Coz, whose lifework included some 150,000 photos of theatrical productions.

3739 Vaïs, Michel. "SOH CAH TOA ou Le théâtre au secours des maths." (SOH CAH TOA or Theatre to the Aid of Math.) *JCT.* 1998; 86: 158-161. Notes. Illus.: Photo. B&W. 3. Lang.: Fre.

Canada: Montreal, PQ. 1993-1998. Biographical studies. ■Performance skills used by actor/teacher Joe Cacchione in his primary school class.

3740 Berry, Edward. "Teaching Shakespeare in China." *SQ.* 1988 Sum; 39(2): 212-216. Notes. Lang.: Eng.

China, People's Republic of: Changsha. 1987. Histories-sources. ■Teacher relates his experiences teaching Shakespeare to two postgraduate classes at the Hunan Normal University in Changsha.

3741 Levith, Murray J. "The Paradox of Shakespeare in China." *ShN.* 1998 Sum; 48(2): 37-38, 42, 46, 48. Biblio. Lang.: Eng.

China, People's Republic of. 1990-1998. Critical studies. ■Examines the state of Shakespeare studies in China, and the Chinese love/hate relationship with this western cultural icon.

3742 Clark, Phyllis. "Sony Labou Tansi and Congolese Politics: An Interview with Jean Clotaire Hymboud." *RAL.* 1998 Sum; 29 (2): 183-192. Notes. Pref. Lang.: Eng.

Congo. 1996. Histories-sources. ■Interview with journalist Hymboud regarding playwright/novelist Tansi's role in the recent Congolese political developments.

3743 "Vaclav Havel, Westward Ho!" *Econ.* 1998 Apr 18; 347(8064): 49. Illus.: Sketches. B&W. 1. Lang.: Eng.

DRAMA: —Relation to other fields

Czech Republic. 1989-1998. Critical studies. ▪The influence of Havel, playwright and president of the Czech Republic, on the country's possible admission into the European Union.

3744 Mawdsley, Alice Lorraine Shoger. *Egypt's Eternal Drama: An Analysis of* The Triumph of Horus. Minneapolis, MN: Univ. of Minnesota; 1987. 270 pp. Biblio. Notes. [Ph.D. Dissertation, Univ. Microfilms Order No. AAC 8710306.] Lang.: Eng.
Egypt. 2500 B.C. Critical studies. ▪Analyzes the religious, political, and cultural institutions of the ancient Egyptian masterpiece *The Triumph of Horus.* Argues that the manuscript represents a dramatic synthesis of statement and expression for the ancient Egyptians.

3745 Barroll, Leeds. "A New History for Shakespeare and His Time." *SQ.* 1988 Win; 39(4): 441-464. Notes. Lang.: Eng.
England. 1580-1616. Critical studies. ▪New historicist's approach to interpret Shakespeare's relationship to his time.

3746 Buckridge, Patrick. "Christopher Hatton, Edward Dyer and the 'First Adonis'." *ERev.* 1998 Aut; 6(2): 15-30. Notes. Lang.: Eng.
England. 1590-1593. Historical studies. ▪Argues that Edward Dyer, not Shakespeare, is the author of the poem 'Venus and Adonis' and that the model for Adonis was Christopher Hatton, a favorite of the Queen. Hatton is also said to be the inspiration for Malvolio in Shakespeare's *Twelfth Night.*

3747 Fredricks, Daniel David. *Drama in the Life and Works of Thomas More.* Greensboro, NC: Univ. of North Carolina; 1988. 197 pp. Notes. Biblio. [Ph.D. Dissertation, Univ. Microfilms Order No. AAC 8822400.] Lang.: Eng.
England. 1550-1590. Critical studies. ▪Examines More's theatrical works as well as theatrical elements in his other writings, and argues that More's exposure to the theatre of his day influenced his philosophy and political life.

3748 Hope, Warren. "William Basse: Who Was He?" *ERev.* 1998 Aut; 6(2): 77-78. Notes. Append. Lang.: Eng.
England. 1602-1653. Biographical studies. ▪Background on the poet who wrote the poem in celebration of the playwright: 'Epitaph for Shakespeare'.

3749 Howard, Jean E. "Crossdressing, The Theatre, and Gender Struggle in Early Modern England." *SQ.* 1988 Win; 39(4): 418-440 . Notes. Lang.: Eng.
England. 1580-1620. Historical studies. ▪Argues that crossdressing threatened the normal social order based upon strict principles of hierarchy and subordination.

3750 King, Pamela M. "Corpus Christi Plays and the 'Bolton hours', 1: Tastes in Lay Piety and Patronage in Eighteenth-Century York." *MET.* 1996; 18: 46-62. Notes. Biblio. Lang.: Eng.
England: York. 1405-1500. Historical studies. ▪Examines the provenance of the *Bolton Book of Hours* (York Minister Library MS Additional 2) which contains full-page miniatures and historiated initials of many biblical scenes featured in the *York Cycle.* The former are essentially processional, while the function of the latter is narrative.

3751 Lester, Richard. "Why Was *Venus and Adonis* Published." *ERev.* 1998 Spr; 6(1): 67-72. Notes. Lang.: Eng.
England. 1589-1593. Historical studies. ▪Possible reasons for the poem's being published, if in fact it was actually the work of the Earl of Oxford.

3752 Sacks, David Harris. "Searching for 'Culture' in the English Renaissance." *SQ.* 1988 Win; 39(4): 465-488. Notes. Biblio. Lang.: Eng.
England. 1575-1630. Historical studies. ▪Attempts to identify what the populace of England considered to be 'culture', and their relationship to it.

3753 Schalkwyk, David. "What May Words Do? The Performative of Praise in Shakespeare's Sonnets." *SQ.* 1998 Fall; 49(3): 251-268. Notes. Lang.: Eng.
England. 1593-1599. Critical studies. ▪Performative analysis of Shakespeare's sonnets.

3754 Scofield, Martin. "Shakespeare and *Clarissa*: 'General Nature', Genre, and Sexuality." *ShS.* 1998; 51: 27-43. Notes. Lang.: Eng.
England. 1744-1747. Critical studies. ▪Comparison of Shakespeare with novelist Samuel Richardson, focusing on the mixture of comedy and tragedy in Richardson's novel.

3755 Tiffany, Grace. "Introduction." *CompD.* 1998 Spr; 32(1): v-ix. Lang.: Eng.
England. 1530-1607. Critical studies. ▪Introduction to the focus of *Comparative Drama* 32:1—drama and the English Reformation.

3756 Traub, Valerie. "Prince Hal's Falstaff: Positioning Psychoanalysis and the Female Reproductive Body." *SQ.* 1989 Win; 40 (4): 456-474. Notes. Biblio. Lang.: Eng.
England. 1589-1597. Critical studies. ▪Argues that Shakespearean drama, psychoanalysis, and early twentieth-century Vienna and Paris viewed the female reproductive body as 'grotesque'. Applies psychoanalytic theory to the characters of the *Henriad.*

3757 Welsh, Alexander. "History: or, The Difference Between Scott's Hamlet and Goethe's." *MLQ.* 1998 Sep.; 59(3): 313-343. Notes. Lang.: Eng.
England. Germany. 1776-1824. Critical studies. ▪Interpretations of the character from Shakespeare's play in two novels: Goethe's *Wilhelm Meisters Lehrjahre* and Walter Scott's *Redgauntlet.*

3758 Kaplan, Paul H.D. "The Earliest Images of Othello." *SQ.* 1988 Sum; 39(2): 171-186. Notes. Illus.: Dwg. B&W. 12. Lang.: Eng.
Europe. 1709-1804. Historical studies. ▪Depictions of the character Othello in the eighteenth and early nineteenth century in paintings and book illustrations.

3759 Burgoyne, Lynda. "Gertrude est morte cet après-midi et moi aussi." (Gertrude Died This Afternoon and So Did I.) *JCT.* 1998; 86: 165-168. Notes. Illus.: Photo. B&W. 2. Lang.: Fre.
France: Paris. 1874-1997. Biographical studies. ▪Remembrance of author Gertrude Stein, inspired by seeing Monique Lepeu's *Gertrude morte cet après midi (Gertrude Dead This Afternoon)* at the Détour Théâtre in Paris, 1997.

3760 Costaz, Gilles. "Die Wiederbelebung der Sozialmoral." (The Revival of Social Morality.) *TZ.* 1998; 5/Theater in Frankreich: 23-25. Lang.: Ger.
France. 1945-1998. Historical studies. ▪Describes the contemporary French theatre structures which were developed between state-subsidized theatre and private theatre by cultural policy.

3761 Kipling, Gordon. "Theatre as Subject and Object in Fouquet's *Martyrdom of St. Apollonia.*" *MET.* 1997; 19: 26-80. Notes. Illus.: Photo. B&W. 9. [Paper presented at the International Medieval Congress, Leeds, July 1997.] Lang.: Eng.
France. 1452-1577. Critical studies. ▪Argues against the traditional acceptance of Jean Fouquet's miniature as an accurate visual record of a play performance in the center of an open-air theatre in the round. Suggests that the theatre is Roman, that the narrative on which the illustration is based is a Roman tragedy, and that Fouquet's illustration is not a conventional devotional image, but an imaginary scene.

3762 Kipling, Gordon. "Fouquet, St. Apollonia, and the Motives of the Miniaturist's Art: A Reply to Graham Runnalls." *MET.* 1997; 19: 101-120. Notes. Lang.: Eng.
France: Tours. 1452-1577. Critical studies. ▪Response to Runnalls's article in the same issue of *MET* in which he argues that Jean Fouquet, painter of the miniature depicting the martyrdom of St. Apollonia, was an experienced man of the theatre and that a mystery play on this subject was performed in Tours.

3763 Runnalls, Graham. "Jean Fouquet's *Martyrdom of St. Apollonia* and the Medieval French Stage." *MET.* 1997; 19: 81-100. Notes. Lang.: Eng.
France. 1452-1577. Critical studies. ▪Argues that Jean Fouquet's miniature represents a fifteenth-century French mystery play in performance. Although not a realistic painting of a medieval theatre at work, it nevertheless gives a good indication of contemporary local practice.

3764 Dörr, Fritz. "'Da muss der Jude den Schaden bezahlen'." ('Then the Jew Must Pay the Damage'.) *THeute.* 1998; 12: 22-27. Illus.: Photo. B&W. 7. Lang.: Ger.

DRAMA: —Relation to other fields

Germany: Berlin. 1998. Histories-sources. ▪On the anniversary of the so-called 'Reichskristallnacht' on November 9, 1938, there was held a reading of the conversation among Nazi politicians in Göring's house, a document of German history, at Volksbühne Berlin.

3765 Greene, Shannon Keenan. *Dramatic Images: The Visual Performance of Gryphius' Tragedies.* Philadelphia, PA: Univ. of Pennsylvania; 1998. 221 pp. Notes. Biblio. [Ph.D. Dissertation, Univ. Microfilms Order No. AAC 9829906.] Lang.: Eng.

Germany. 1635-1664. Critical studies. ▪Examines the copper-plate engravings and etchings that illustrated the first editions of Andreas Gryphius' *Catharina von Georgien*, *Carolus Stuardus*, and *Papinianus*. Focuses on the performativity and theatricality of the artwork as extensions of Baroque tragedy.

3766 Herzinger, Richard. "Wem das Schicksal schlägt oder: Die Angst vor der Freiheit schafft Metaphysik." (For Whom Fate Comes: Or The Fear of Freedom Makes Metaphysics.) *THeute.* 1998; 1: 26-31. Illus.: Photo. B&W. 6. Lang.: Ger.

Germany: Berlin. 1989-1998. Critical studies. ▪Analyzes current public opinions about individualism and metaphysics in newspapers, theatres and politics. Relates changes in context of socialism since reunification to Einar Schleef's and Heiner Müller's work at Berliner Ensemble.

3767 Hesse, Ulrich. "'Wir müssen diese Ereignisse dem Zeitfluss entziehen und sie greifbar halten'." ('We Must Seize These Moments of Fleeting Time and Keep Them Concrete'.) *SuT.* 1998; 160: 13-19. Illus.: Photo. B&W. 4. Lang.: Ger.

Germany: Essen. 1985-1998. Histories-sources. ▪Interview with Frank Herdemerten, artistic director of the theatre company of Helmholtz-Gamnasium (Essen), on how to use play and acting in educating students about the Holocaust in Nazi Germany.

3768 Irmer, Thomas. "Lippenbekenntnisse." (Lip Service.) *TZ.* 1998; 4: 11-13. Illus.: Photo. B&W. 1. Lang.: Ger.

Germany: Berlin. 1998. Critical studies. ▪Describes *Die Berliner Ermittlung (The Berlin Investigation)*, a project by the conceptual artists Jochen Gerz and Esther Shalev-Gerz, co-produced by Hebbel-Theater, Berliner Ensemble and Volksbühne. Analyzes the interactive project of memorial and the reasons for going wrong.

3769 Pfister, Eva. "Von Sex zu Text—auf wessen Konto?" (From Sex to Text—In What Responsibility?)*DB.* 1998; 2: 46-47. Illus.: Photo. B&W. 2. Lang.: Ger.

Germany. 1926-1998. Biographical studies. ▪Bertolt Brecht's working methods between collectivity and exploitation as related in two books on the subject: John Fuegi's *Brecht & Co*, Hamburg 1997, and Sabine Kebir's *Ich fragte nicht nach meinem Anteil*, Berlin 1997.

3770 Radvan, Florian. "Überlegungen zur Wiederaufführung nationalsozialistischer Dramatik auf deutschen Bühnen: Hanns Johsts Schauspiel *Schlageter* (UA 1933) als Beispiel." (Reflections on a Revival of National Socialistic Drama on German Stages: Hanns Johst's *Schlageter*, First Performed 1933.) *FMT.* 1998; 13(2): 165-183. Lang.: Ger.

Germany: Uelzen, Wuppertal. 1977-1992. Critical studies. ▪Describes two adaptations of Hanns Johst's *Schlageter* performed by the theatre team of Lessing and Herzog Ernst Gymnasium (Uelzen) in 1977 and directed by Holk Freytag at Schauspiel Wuppertal in 1992. Discusses the need for a critical look at national socialist drama within the treatment of the historical national socialism.

3771 Wright, Stephen K. "Religious Drama, Civic Ritual, and the Police: The Semiotics of Public Safety in Late Medieval Germany." *TA.* 1998; 51: 1-14. Notes. Lang.: Eng.

Germany. 1234-1656. Historical studies. ▪Examines the relationship between ritual and power in late medieval Germany focusing on disruptive incidents during performances of religious drama—accidents, crime, fire—and the safety precautions taken by the plays' sponsors to prevent or control such occurrences.

3772 Luk, Yun Tong. "Post-Colonialism and Contemporary Hong Kong Theatre: Two Case Studies." *NTQ.* 1998 Nov.; 14(4): 366-372. Notes. Biblio. Illus.: Photo. B&W. 4. [Issue 56.] Lang.: Eng.

Hong Kong. 1984-1996. Historical studies. ▪Social and cultural significance of the productions *We're Hong Kong*, written and directed by Hardy Tsoi and staged in 1984 right after the Sino-British Joint Declaration, and *Tales of the Walled City* by Raymond To Kwak-wai, directed by Daniel S.P. Yang for Hong Kong Repertory, performed coincidentally with Hong Kong's reversion to Chinese rule.

3773 Nunns, Stephen. "Indonesian Playwright Faces Jail Term." *AmTh.* 1998 May/June; 15(5): 52. Illus.: Photo. B&W. 1. Lang.: Eng.

Indonesia: Jakarta. 1998. Historical studies. ▪Report on the arrest of playwright/activist Ratna Sarumpaet during a pro-democracy demonstration in Jakarta in March, now facing trial for holding a political meeting without a permit.

3774 Carlson, Marvin. "Italy's New Theatrical Legislation." *WES.* 1998 Win; 10(1): 59-60. Illus.: Photo. B&W. 2. Lang.: Eng.

Italy. 1998. Historical studies. ▪Presentation of acts of legislation pertaining to the place and role of the theatre in Italian society about to be enacted by the government.

3775 Feldman, Sharon. "National Theater/National Identity: Els Joglars and the Question of Cultural Politics in Catalonia." *Gestos.* 1998 Apr.; 13(25): 35-50. Notes. Biblio. Lang.: Eng.

Spain-Catalonia. 1962-1998. Critical studies. ▪The convergence of Catalan politics and culture, especially theatre, with emphasis on the work of the theatre company Els Joglars and its director Albert Boadella.

3776 Huss, Pia. "10 000 unga lär sig Shakespeare by heart." (Ten Thousand Youths Learn Shakespeare By Heart.) *Dramat.* 1998: vo 6(2): 44-46. Illus.: Photo. Color. Lang.: Swe.

Sweden. 1988-1998. Historical studies. ▪Presentation of a joint project by Kungliga Dramatiska Teatern in collaboration with schools and cultural organizations in which Donya Feuer and other actors read and act scenes by Shakespeare with undergraduates all over Sweden.

3777 Janzon, Mary Ulla-Britt. *Fjarde Klass pa teatern: tioåriga barns upplevelse av en teateruppsättning av Astrid Lindgren's Mio, Min Mio.* (The Fourth Form Goes to the Theatre: An Investigation of How Ten-Year-Old Children React to the Stage Version of Astrid Lindgren's *Mio, My Mio.*) Lund: Lunds Universitet; 1988. 192 pp. Biblio. Notes. [Ph.D. Dissertation.] Lang.: Swe.

Sweden. 1988. Empirical research. ▪The reactions of 614 randomly selected children to a stage production, with emphasis on how theatre affects the psychological developmental of children.

3778 Diamond, Catherine. "Darkening Clouds Over Istanbul: Turkish Theatre in a Changing Climate." *NTQ.* 1998 Nov.; 14(4): 334-350. Notes. Biblio. Illus.: Photo. B&W. 8. [Issue 56.] Lang.: Eng.

Turkey: Istanbul. 1994-1997. Historical studies. ▪Challenges facing Turkish theatre artists in a rapidly changing political scene, especially following the rise to power of the ruling Refah party, a pro-censorship military, and Muslim fundamentalists opposed to theatre in principle.

3779 Schwartz, Beth Carrol. *Virginia Woolf as a Reader of Shakespeare: The Drama Within the Fiction.* Ithaca, NY: Cornell Univ; 1987. 269 pp. Notes. Biblio. [Ph.D. Dissertation, Univ. Microfilms Order No. AAC 8708878.] Lang.: Eng.

UK-England. 1882-1941. Critical studies. ▪Shakespearean influence on four novels of Virginia Woolf: *Orlando*, *A Room of One's Own*, *The Waves*, and *Between the Acts.*

3780 Waites, Aline. "Here Comes Harry." *PlPl.* 1998/99 Dec/Jan.; 529: 27-28. Illus.: Photo. B&W. 1. Lang.: Eng.

UK-England: London. 1998. Histories-sources. ▪Actor-writer Steven Berkoff's ideas about theatre, and fictional actor 'Harry' in his recently-published short stories.

3781 Beer, Joseph Michael. *The Use of Religious Drama to Explore Faith and Morals.* Lancaster, PA: Lancaster Theological Seminary; 1998. 143 pp. Notes. Biblio. [Ph.D. Dissertation, Univ. Microfilms Order No. AAC 9829725.] Lang.: Eng.

USA. 1998. Histories-sources. ▪The creation and production of an original play by the author, *They Belong to God, Too!*, intended to help people with faith issues. Explores the impact of the play on an audience and reflects on the theological significance of such religious drama as well as its usefulness for ministry.

DRAMA: —Relation to other fields

3782 Bell, John. "Times Square: Public Space Disneyfied." *TDR.* 1998 Spr; 42(1): 24-33. Notes. Biblio. Illus.: Photo. B&W. 6. Lang.: Eng.
USA: New York, NY. 1997. Critical studies. ■The social significance of the Disney Corporation's current influence on Broadway theatre. Argues that theatre has become a theme park-style attraction rather than a place for artistic advancement.

3783 Benardo, Margot L. "The Political Geography of *Teatro Campesino* and the Construction of a Political Body." *Gestos.* 1998 Apr.; 13(25): 117-126. Notes. Biblio. Lang.: Eng.
USA. 1965-1970. Historical studies. ■Impact of Teatro Campesino's theatrical events, which were staged to raise the consciousness of Latino migrant workers, on the political landscape in the USA. Traces the transference from theatrical events to striker's actions and the news media between.

3784 Berson, Misha. "Witch Hunt in Washington State." *AmTh.* 1998 Feb.; 15(2): 52-57. Illus.: Photo. B&W. 1. Lang.: Eng.
USA: Seattle, WA. 1951. Historical studies. ■The blacklisting of Burton and Florence Bean James, the founders of the Seattle Repertory Playhouse, as a result of anti-Communist sentiment and action.

3785 Cherbo, Joni Maya. "Creative Synergy: Commercial and Not-for-Profit Live Theatre in America." *JAML.* 1998 Sum; 28(2): 129-142. Notes. Biblio. Tables. Lang.: Eng.
USA. 1998. Critical studies. ■Mutual influence of not-for-profit and commercial theatres and their role in American society.

3786 Cunningham, Karen. "Shakespeare, the Public, Public Education." *SQ.* 1998 Fall; 49(3): 293-298. Notes. Lang.: Eng.
USA. UK-England. 1998. Historical studies. ■Report on the state of Shakespearean studies in public education, and the public's perception of the changes being made in course curricula.

3787 Fuld, Catherine Elina. *Living in the Mists: Celtic and Pre-Celtic History as Healing Ritual-Theatre.* San Francisco, CA: California Institute of Integral Studies; 1998. 347 pp. Notes. Biblio. [M.A. Thesis, Univ. Microfilms Order No. AAC 1388765.] Lang.: Eng.
USA. 1997. Empirical research. ■Account of the creation and use of a full-length ritual-theatre piece, *Living in the Mists*, created by the author as an original drama therapy research project.

3788 Gable, Harvey L. "*Wieland, Othello, Genesis*, and the Floating City: The Sources of Charles Brockden Brown's *Wieland.*" *PLL.* 1998 Sum; 34(3): 301-318. Notes. Biblio. Lang.: Eng.
USA. England. 1604-1798. Critical studies. ■Argues that the early American novel *Wieland* is a conscious echo of Shakespeare's *Othello.*

3789 Harley, James. "The Art of Political Engagement: Governmental Response to *Paradise Now* in Europe and America." *TheatreS.* 1998; 43: 39-50. Notes. Illus.: Poster. B&W. 1. Lang.: Eng.
USA. Europe. 1968. Historical studies. ■Government efforts, both overt and covert, to suppress the highly politicized Living Theatre company's production of the collaboratively created *Paradise Now* while it toured in the United States and Europe.

3790 Henderson, Stephen. "Getting Them Hooked." *AmTh.* 1998 Dec.; 15(10): 60-63. Illus.: Photo. B&W. 3. Lang.: Eng.
USA. 1998. Critical studies. ■Arts education programs as a means to build audiences for the future, as well as present generations.

3791 Kaough, Judith Elaine Bishop. *Drama as Cross-Cultural Literature for Foreign Students in American Colleges: An Instructional Model.* Austin, TX: Univ. of Texas; 1987. 262 pp. Notes. Biblio. [Ph.D. Dissertation, Univ. Microfilms Order No. AAC 8728584.] Lang.: Eng.
USA. 1987. Empirical research. ■Proposes the inclusion of drama in the literature curriculum established for international students at the college level. Author conducted a research survey in educational methodology in a sophomore English class.

3792 McNulty, Charles. "The Last Temptation of MTC." *AmTh.* 1998 Dec.; 15(10): 64-67. Illus.: Photo. B&W. 1. Lang.: Eng.
USA: New York, NY. 1998. Historical studies. ■Report on the controversy surrounding the Manhattan Theatre Club's production of Terrence McNally's *Corpus Christi*, directed by Joe Mantello. The Catholic League objected to a gay Christ-like figure, leading to protests both pro and con on its opening night.

3793 Nunns, Stephen. "The NEA Four Go to Washington." *AmTh.* 1998 Jan.; 15(1): 70-71. Illus.: Dwg. B&W. 1. Lang.: Eng.
USA: Washington, DC. 1998. Historical studies. ■Report on the upcoming Supreme Court hearing as to whether the government can impose standards of 'decency' on artists who receive public money. The case is *The National Endowment for the Arts vs. Finley.*

Research/historiography

3794 Rozik, Eli. "Playscripts and Performance: The Same Side of Two Coins." *Gestos.* 1998 Nov.; 13(26): 11-24. Notes. Biblio. Lang.: Eng.
1998. Critical studies. ■Argues that play analysis and performance analysis are essentially the same, and the proper tasks of theatre research.

3795 Levin, Richard. "Another 'Source' for *The Alchemist* and Another Look at Source Studies." *ELR.* 1998 Spr; 28(2): 210-230. Notes. Pref. Illus.: Photo. B&W. 2. Lang.: Eng.
England. USA. 1610-1998. Critical studies. ■Suggests possible alternate or untried sources for Jonson's *The Alchemist*, and leads up to a critique of the academic discipline of source studies.

3796 Rodenhuis, Willem. "Spelen in Pompeius. Computersimulatie bij theateronderzoek." (Playing in Pompei: Computer Simulations and Theatre Research.) *Tmaker.* 1998; 2(2): 16-18. Illus.: Photo. B&W. 3. Lang.: Dut.
Europe. 1998. Histories-sources. ■Interview with Richard Beacham, a leader of the THEATRON project (Theatre history in Europe: Architectural and Textual Resources Online), which aims to use computer simulation and other technology for theatre research.

3797 "Marvin Carlson Donates Ibsen Collection to Ibsen Center." *INC.* 1998; 18: 3. Illus.: Photo. B&W. 1. Lang.: Eng.
Norway: Oslo. 1998. Historical studies. ■Report on Ibsen scholar Carlson's donation of his collection of memorabilia, letters, and programs from English-language productions of Ibsen's plays collected over forty years, to the Ibsen Center in Oslo.

3798 Callens, Johan. "Discovering Utopia: Drama on Drama in Contemporary British Theatre." 211-221 in Rothwell, Angela Downing, ed. *English Studies of the Complutense University.* Madrid: Complutense Univ; 1983. 260 pp. Lang.: Eng.
UK-England. Critical studies. ■Discusses the usefulness of the recently published tome *Drama on Drama: Theatricality on the Contemporary British Stage* (London: Macmillan, New York: St. Martin's Press, 1997), edited by Nicole Boireau.

3799 Cummings, Scott T. "Interactive Shakespeare." *TTop.* 1998 Mar.; 8(1): 93-112. Notes. Biblio. Append. Illus.: Photo. B&W. 4. Lang.: Eng.
USA: Cambridge, MA. 1991-1997. Histories-sources. ■Author's experience as consultant and contributor to the work of the computer-based Shakespeare Interactive Research Group at MIT. Focuses on theoretical and pedagogical issues raised by interactive technology that could revolutionize the teaching and study of Shakespeare.

Theory/criticism

3800 Dallet, Athenaide. "Invalid Representation and Despotism in the Theatre." *JDTC.* 1998 Fall; 13(1): 19-44. Notes. Lang.: Eng.
1998. Critical studies. ■Describes three kinds of representation in theatre—descriptive representation, symbolic representation and delegation, which theatre is said to share with government. Includes analysis of Weiss's *Marat/Sade*, Müller's *Der Auftrag*, and Massinger's *The Roman Actor.*

3801 Dawson, Anthony B. "*Measure for Measure*, New Historicism, and Theatrical Power." *SQ.* 1988 Fall; 39(3): 328-341. Notes. Lang.: Eng.
1988. Critical studies. ■Explores the new historicists' conception of power, its relation to the possibility of subversion or resistance, and its source in the present political and academic milieu. Focuses on Shakespeare's *Measure for Measure* to illustrate new historicism's validity as

a mode of interpretation and its antithetical relationship to traditional theatrical practice.

3802 Happé, Peter. "The English Cycle Plays: Contexts and Development." *EDAM.* 1998 Spr; 20(2): 71-87. Notes. Lang.: Eng.

1998. Critical studies. ■Critical evaluation of the scholarly work done with regards to English cycle plays.

3803 Kermode, Frank. "Explorations in Shakespeare's Language." *Raritan.* 1998 Sum; 18(1): 73-86. Notes. Lang.: Eng.

1998. Critical studies. ■Argues the need for accurate and imaginative critical readings of Shakespeare, fostered by William Empson's theory of ambiguity, to reinvigorate critical analysis of his work.

3804 Kralj, Lado. *Teorija drame.* (Theory of Drama.) Ljubljana: DZS; 1998. 196 pp. (Literarni leksikon, 44.) Index. Biblio. Lang.: Slo.

600 B.C.-1997 A.D. Critical studies. ■Examines the body of theoretical thinking from Aristotle to the present, specifically the methods, aims, functions, and characteristics of Western drama. The theoretical notions are discussed in relation to examples of dramatic literature from Sophocles to Ibsen, Mamet and Jovanovič, and especially, Shakespeare.

3805 Mercier, Martin. "Rhétorique et mise en scène théâtrale." (Rhetoric and Theatrical Staging.) *AnT.* Spr 1998; 24: 155-167. Notes. Biblio. Lang.: Fre.

1998. Critical studies. ■Proposes method of analyzing staging as rhetorical elocution of the director's interpretation.

3806 Parisious, Roger Nyle. "Occulist Influence on the Authorship Controversy." *ERev.* 1998 Spr; 6(1): 9-43. Notes. Lang.: Eng.

1591-1998. Historical studies. ■Examines the Tudor Rose, or royal birth, theory of the authorship of plays attributed to Shakespeare, an aspect of the Oxfordian hypothesis. Continued in 'Postscript to the Tudor Rose Theory' in *ERev* 6:2 (1998 Aut), 90-93.

3807 Tompkins, Joanne. "Inter-Referentiality: Interrogating Multicultural Australian Drama." 117-131 in Kelly, Veronica, ed. *Our Australian Theatre in the 1990s.* (Australian Playwrights 7.) Notes. Index. Biblio. Illus.: Photo. 1. Lang.: Eng.

Australia. 1990-1998. Critical studies. ■Critical examination of the rhetoric surrounding multiculturalism in Australian theatre.

3808 Bergeron, Serge. "Pour une méthode d'analyse de l'espace dans le texte dramatique." (For a Method of Analysis of Space in the Dramatic Text.) *AnT.* Spr 1998; 23: 133-145. Biblio. Lang.: Fre.

Canada. 1998. Critical studies. ■Proposes a comprehensive approach to analysing space through categorization of 'dramaturgical space' into physical space (location), dramatic space (characters) and textual space (discourse), with subdivisions in each category.

3809 Dufva, Annelie. "Jetlaggade kritiker." (Critics with Jet Lag.) *Tningen.* 1998; 21(4): 43-45. Illus.: Photo. B&W. Lang.: Swe.

Canada: Quebec, PQ. 1998. Historical studies. ■Report on a seminar, organized by International Association for Theatre Critics, for young critics: references several performances of the festival Carrefour and Robert Lepage.

3810 Steen, Shannon; Werry, Margaret. "Bodies, Technologies, and Subjectivities: The Production of Authority in Robert Lepage's *Elsinore.*" *ET.* 1998; 16(2): 139-151. Notes. Biblio. Lang.: Eng.

Canada. 1995-1996. Historical studies. ■The critical explosion that followed *Elsineur (Elsinore)*, Lepage's multimedia adaptation of *Hamlet.*

3811 Alexander, Catherine M.S. "Shakespeare and the Eighteenth Century: Criticism and Research." *ShS.* 1998; 51: 1-15. Notes. Illus.: Pntg. Dwg. B&W. 3. Lang.: Eng.

England. 1701-1800. Historical studies. ■Appraisal of eighteenth-century approaches to Shakespearean criticism and research.

3812 Dickson, Peter W. "Henry Peacham and the First Folio of 1623." *ERev.* 1998 Aut; 6(2): 55-76. Notes. Append. Lang.: Eng.

England. 1622-1623. Critical studies. ■Cites, as evidence in favor of the Oxfordian hypothesis of the authorship of Shakespearean plays, the compilation of great Elizabethan poets in Peachum's *Complete Gentlemen* (1623), in which Shakespeare's name is omitted while that of Edward de Devere, Earl of Oxford, is included.

3813 Kaplan, Philip Benjamin. *We All Expect a Gentle Answer:* The Merchant of Venice, *Anti-Semitism, and the Critics.* New Orleans, LA: Tulane Univ; 1998. 184 pp. Notes. Biblio. [Ph.D. Dissertation, Univ. Microfilms Order No. AAC 9906382.] Lang.: Eng.

England. 1596-1986. Critical studies. ■Examines the critical history of Shakespeare's *The Merchant of Venice* with respect to antisemitism.

3814 Finlayson, Rebecca Scott. *The Politics of Criticism: Poststructuralism and Early Modern Studies.* Atlanta, GA: Emory Univ.; 1998. 194 pp. Notes. Biblio. [Ph.D. Dissertation, Univ. Microfilms Order No. AAC 9830146.] Lang.: Eng.

Europe. North America. 1975-1997. Histories-specific. ■Survey of political criticism of early modern drama, particularly Shakespeare. Analyzes the ascension of political criticism by isolating exemplary, founding texts and chronicling the scholarship of the primary critics for each critical school within a larger discussion of its theoretical foundations.

3815 Kirkkopelto, Esa. "Teatterista taiteena." (Theatre as Art.) *Teat.* 1998; 53(5): 10-11. Illus.: Photo. B&W. 1. Lang.: Fin.

Finland. 1998. Histories-sources. ■Finnish director Kirkkopelto theorizes on the state of the theatre, and the difficulties in creating 'great' theatre that can be considered art.

3816 Serôdio, Maria Helena. "Theatre and Its Critics: A Positive Challenge." *NTQ.* 1998 Aug.; 14(3): 287-290. Notes. [Issue 55.] Lang.: Eng.

Finland: Helsinki. 1996. Historical studies. ■Report on the fourteenth Congress of the International Association of Theatre Critics, where the function and value of criticism in a time of media upheaval was debated.

3817 Banu, Georges. "Generationsschichten." (Layers of Generations.) *TZ.* 1998; 5/Theater in Frankreich: 4-7. Illus.: Photo. B&W. 6. Lang.: Ger.

France. 1960-1998. Historical studies. ■Describes the theatre in France from the point of view of the influences of theatre theorists from different generations that co-exist to this day.

3818 Finter, Helga. "Das Reale, der Körper und die soufflierten Stimmen: Artaud heute." (The Real, the Body and the Prompted Voices: Artaud Today.) *FMT.* 1998; 13(1): 3-17. Notes. Lang.: Ger.

France. 1945-1998. Critical studies. ■The meaning of Artaud's theatre of cruelty in the postwar era, with respect to the contemporary experimental theatre of Jan Fabre, Jan Lauwers and the Needcompany, and Robert Wilson.

3819 Laatto, Ritva. "Teema ja muunnelmia dramaatikon elämästä." (Theme and Variations on a Dramatist's Life.) *Teat.* 1998; 53(1): 33-35. Illus.: Photo. Color. B&W. 2. Lang.: Fin.

France. 1998. Critical studies. ■Analysis of plays by Eric-Emmanuel Schmitt, including *Variations énigmatiques (Enigma Variations), La Visiteuse (The Visitor),* and *La Nuit de Valognes (The Night of Valognes).*

3820 Rubidge, Bradley. "Catharsis through Admiration: Corneille, Le Moyne, and the Social Uses of Emotion." *MP.* 1998 Feb.; 95(3): 316-333. Notes. Lang.: Eng.

France. 1651-1653. Critical studies. ■Playwright Pierre Corneille's theory of catharsis, which he believed could be achieved through admiration of a character, rather than through compassion. Also discusses the Jesuit epic poet Pierre Le Moyne's views on reaching catharsis in reading epic poetry.

3821 "Unglücksfall? Kunsthuberndes Gewerbe? Schaubühnendämmerung? Grübers Iphigenie im Spiegel der Kritik." (Accident? Art and Craft? Twilight of Schaubühne? Grüber's Iphigenie as Seen by the Critics.) *THeute.* 1998; 4: 9-11. Illus.: Photo. B&W. 2. Lang.: Ger.

Germany. 1998. Critical studies. ■Compilation of current German critics (Peter Iden, Wolfgang Höbel, Roland Koberg, Petra Kohse, Sigrid Löffler, Gerhard Stadelmaier and C. Bernd Sucher) regarding Johann

DRAMA: —Theory/criticism

Wolfgang von Goethe's *Iphigenia auf Tauris* directed by Klaus Michael Grüber at Schaubühne.

3822 Rehm, Stefan Gerhard. *Emotion and Morality in the Tragic Theories of Lessing.* Kingston, ON: Queen's Univ; 1998. 263 pp. Notes. Biblio. [Ph.D. Dissertation, Univ. Microfilms Order No. AAC NQ27852.] Lang.: Eng.

Germany. 1760-1780. Critical studies. ▪Examines the relationship between emotion and morality in the tragic theory of Gotthold Ephraim Lessing. Argues that Lessing experimented with many different forms in order to prove the validity of the relationship and ultimately fails to link the two.

3823 Evola, Dario. "La scrittura scenica: uno sguardo critico nell'estetica delle mutazioni." (Scenic Writing: A Critical Look at the Aesthetics of Mutations.) *BiT.* 1998; 48: 33-54. Notes. Lang.: Ita.

Italy. 1965-1980. Critical studies. ▪Analysis of the work of critic Giuseppe Bartolucci, with respect to action in space, the presence of the body as perturbing factor, and the contamination of language.

3824 Pirandello, Luigi; Barbina, Alfred, ed. "Pirandello travestito da Rolando." (Pirandello Disguised as Roland.) *Ariel.* 1998; 13(1-2): 43-58. Notes. Lang.: Ita.

Italy. 1898. Critical studies. ▪Texts of two articles on French literature written for 'Rivista d'Italia' by Luigi Pirandello under the psuedonym Roland.

3825 Bobkova, Hana. "Nederlandse critici noemen geen uleuren toneelkritiek in de twintigste eeuw." (Dutch Critics Don't Mention Colors: Theatre Criticism in the 20th Century.) *Tmaker.* 1998; 2(4): 33-37. Illus.: Photo. B&W. 2. Lang.: Dut.

Netherlands. 1998. Critical studies. ▪Report on a symposium on theatre criticism held in March and an analysis of criticism in the Netherlands.

3826 Kalinowski, Daniel. *Koniec teatru alternatywnego?* (The End of Fringe Theatre?)Slupsk: Wydawnictwo Wyższej Szkoły Pedagogicznej w Słupsku; 1998. 129 pp. Notes. Pref. Append. Illus.: Graphs. B&W. 5. Lang.: Pol.

Poland. 1980-1995. Critical studies. ▪Collection of essays and critical sketches about the change in the political and social situation of Polish fringe theatre. Includes recollections of theatrical activity by directors and actors including Grotowski.

3827 Kozak, Krištof Jacek. *Estetski in idejni vplivi na predvojno dramsko in gledališko kritiko Josipa Vidmarja.* (The Artistic and Ideal Influences on the Pre-War Drama and Theatre Criticism of Josip Vidmar.) Ljubljana: Scientific Institute of the Faculty of Arts; 1998. 100 pp. (Razprave Filozofske fakultete.) Pref. Index. Biblio. Append. Lang.: Slo.

Slovenia. 1920-1941. Histories-specific. ▪Examines the critical writings of theatre practitioner Josip Vidmar, including influences on his aesthetic ideal for the theatre.

3828 Moravec, Dušan. "Župančičev gledališki esej." (Župančič and the Theatre Essay.) *Sodobnost.* 1998; 1006(6-7): 510-514. Lang.: Slo.

Slovenia. 1905-1949. Critical studies. ▪Examines the origin of the theatrical essay in Slovenia, emphasizing the importance of playwright Oton Župančič's early essays.

3829 Mrzel, Ludvik. *Gledališke kritike 1933-1939.* (Theatre Reviews 1933-1939.) Ljubljana: Slovenian Academy of Arts and Sciences; 1998. 173 pp. (Opera/Academia Scientiarum et Artium Slovenica. Classis II: Philologia et Litterae 46.) Pref. Index. Biblio. Lang.: Slo.

Slovenia: Ljubljana. 1933-1939. Critical studies. ▪Ludvik Mrzel's theatre reviews of Ljubljana National Theatre performances.

3830 Burningham, Bruce. "Barbarians at the Gates: The Invasive Discourse of Medieval Performance in Lope's *Arte nuevo.*" *TJ.* 1998 Oct.; 50(3): 289-302. Notes. Illus.: Photo. B&W. 2. Lang.: Eng.

Spain. 1600-1620. Critical studies. ▪Examines Lope de Vega's defense of the 'new art' of theatre against charges of barbarism and vulgarity, and association with itinerant fairground performers.

3831 García Santo-Tomás, Enrique. *Paradigmas de la recepción crítica: hacia una hermeneutica literaria del teatro de Lope de Vega (1609-1935).* (Paradigms of Critical Reception: Toward a Literary Hermeneutics of the Theatre of Lope de Vega, 1609-1935.) Providence, RI: Brown Univ; 1998. 273 pp. Biblio. Notes. [Ph.D. Dissertation, Univ. Microfilms Order No. AAC 9830439.] Lang.: Spa.

Spain. 1609-1935. Historical studies. ▪Examines the history of the critical reception of Lope de Vega's theatre masterworks in light of the aesthetics of reception and reader-response theory.

3832 Berst, Charles A. "New Theatres for Old." 55-75 in Innes, Christopher, ed. *The Cambridge Companion to George Bernard Shaw.* Cambridge/New York: Cambridge UP; 1998. 343 pp. (Cambridge Companions to Literature.) Index. Biblio. Notes. Pref. Illus.: Photo. 1. Lang.: Eng.

UK-England. 1891-1898. Critical studies. ▪George Bernard Shaw's *The Quintessence of Ibsen*, his defense not only of Ibsen, but of the 'new' theatre, and its impact on his *Plays Unpleasant*, published in 1898.

3833 Brook, Peter. *Lo spazio vuoto.* (The Empty Space.) Rome: Bulzoni; 1998. 148 pp. (Biblioteca Teatrale, 100.) Lang.: Ita.

UK-England. 1998. Critical studies. ▪Italian translation of the *The Empty Space* (London: Mc Gibbon & Kee, 1998).

3834 Gohar, Kourosh; Kim, Suzanne; Stuart, Ian. "A Discussion with Edward Bond." *JDTC.* 1998 Spr; 12(2): 57-68. Notes. Lang.: Eng.

UK-England. 1996-1998. Histories-sources. ▪Interview with playwright Edward Bond on the theoretical aspects of his career as well as the current state of theatre.

3835 Tanitch, Robert. "The School for Scandal." *PlPl.* 1998/99 Dec/Jan.; 529: 19. Lang.: Eng.

UK-England: Stratford. 1998. Reviews of performances. ▪Two contrasting reviews of RSC's production of Richard Sheridan's *The School for Scandal*, directed by Declan Donnellan, to illustrate subjectivity of criticism.

3836 Zarhy-Levo, Yael. "Theatrical Success: A Behind-the-Scenes Story." *THSt.* 1998; 53: 61-70. Notes. Lang.: Eng.

UK-England. 1950-1990. Historical studies. ▪Argues that critical acceptance of theatrical productions determines how theatrical history is constructed and reconstructed. Explores critical response to works of Tom Stoppard, Harold Pinter, Joe Orton, and Samuel Beckett.

3837 Ali, Mohamed El Shirbini Ahmed. *Eugene O'Neill and His Critics.* Albuquerque, NM: Univ. of New Mexico; 1998. 143 pp. Notes. Biblio. [Ph.D. Dissertation, Univ. Microfilms Order No. AAC 9839198.] Lang.: Eng.

USA. 1930-1997. Histories-specific. ▪Examines critical responses to playwright Eugene O'Neill's work. Focuses on early plays, Greek myth plays and language, development of women characters and naturalism, and late autobiographical plays.

3838 Bromels, John E. "Winning Review Examines *Carriage.*" *SoTh.* 1998 Sum; 39(3): 31. Lang.: Eng.

USA. 1998. Historical studies. ▪The author's winning critique of the 1998 Critics Institute competition, a review of Jerome Hairston's *Carriage.*

3839 Brooks, Robert E. *Creativity and the Cathartic Moment: Chaos Theory and the Art of Theatre.* Baton Rouge, LA: Louisiana State A&M; 1998. 222 pp. Biblio. Notes. [Ph.D. Dissertation, Univ. Microfilms Order No. 9902623.] Lang.: Eng.

USA. 1998. Histories-specific. ▪Argues that by illuminating the limitations of traditional Newtonian physics and Euclidean geometry, chaos theory conveys philosophical implications that transcend the scientific and provide suitable tools for describing cultural and artistic phenomena, including dramatic theory. Applies chaos theory to Aristotle's *Poetics*, Dryden's *An Essay of Dramatic Poesy*, Coleridge's *Biographia Literaria*, and Artaud's *Le Théâtre et son Double*, as well as the postmodern dramaturgy of Richard Foreman.

3840 Criswell, Sheryle. "The Dreaded 'C' Word: A Playwright Faces the Critics." *SoTh.* 1998 Fall; 39(4): 24-25. Illus.: Photo. B&W. 1. Lang.: Eng.

USA. 1998. Historical studies. ▪A new playwright faces the critics for the first time. Sheryle Criswell, author of ... *Where Late the Sweet Birds Sang*, discusses criticism of her play.

DRAMA: —Theory/criticism

3841 Diprima, Jay T. *Towards a Poetics of Monodrama in Performance: The History and Analysis of Critical Response to Monodramas on the Stages of New York City from 1952-1996.* New York, NY: New York Univ; 1998. 479 pp. Notes. Biblio. [Ph.D. Dissertation, Univ. Microfilms Order No. AAC 9832736.] Lang.: Eng.
USA: New York, NY. 1952-1996. Histories-specific. ■Analyzes the aesthetic criteria used by New York theatre critics in evaluating monodramas over the past forty-four years.

3842 Fishkin, Amy Lynne. *Michal: Voice of a Woman Towards a New Tradition of Reading and Writing the Self in the Hebrew Bible.* Atlanta, GA: Emory Univ; 1998. 129 pp. Notes. Biblio. [M.A. Thesis, Univ. Microfilms Order No. AAC 1389443.] Lang.: Eng.
USA. 1998. Histories- sources. ■The application of theatrical methodologies to character examination of biblical texts, specifically Michal in the Old Testament.

3843 Kolin, Philip C. "*Something Cloudy, Something Clear*: Tennessee Williams's Postmodern Memory Play." *JDTC.* 1998 Spr; 12 (2): 35-56. Notes. Illus.: Photo. B&W. 1. Lang.: Eng.
USA. 1980-1981. Critical studies. ■The postmodern as reflected in Tennessee Williams's play *Something Cloudy, Something Clear* and in its critical reception.

3844 London, Todd. "Shakespeare in a Strange Land." *AmTh.* 1998 July/Aug.; 15(6): 22-25, 63-66. Illus.: Photo. B&W. 4. Lang.: Eng.
USA. 1990-1998. Critical studies. ■American theatre's urge to make Shakespeare contemporary. Includes discussion of Al Pacino's film *Looking for Richard*, Ron Daniels' productions of *Richard II* and *Richard III*, George C. Wolfe's *Macbeth*, Joe Calarco's adaptation of *Romeo and Juliet* as *R and J*, and Baz Luhrmann's film version of *Romeo and Juliet.*

3845 Manheim, Michael. "O'Neill Criticism." 236-243 in Manheim, Michael, ed. *The Cambridge Companion to Eugene O'Neill.* Cambridge/New York, NY: Cambridge UP; 1998. 256 pp. (Cambridge Companions to Literature.) Index. Biblio. Lang.: Eng.
USA. 1997. Critical studies. ■Examines the body of O'Neill criticism and includes a select bibliography.

3846 Myung, Inn Seo. *The Dramatic and Theatrical Criticism of John Mason Brown.* Ann Arbor, MI: Univ. of Michigan; 1988. 253 pp. Notes. Biblio. [Ph.D. Dissertation, Univ. Microfilms Order No. 8812952.] Lang.: Eng.
USA. 1900-1969. Critical studies. ■Examines the theatrical aesthetics and criticism of John Mason Brown and evaluates Brown's position among other contemporary critics.

3847 O'Quinn, Jim. "Ross Wetzstoen: 1932-1998." *AmTh.* 1998 Apr.; 15(4): 41. Illus.: Photo. B&W. 1. Lang.: Eng.
USA. 1932-1998. Biographical studies. ■Obituary for Wetzstoen, theatre critic and inspiration for the creation of the Obie Awards.

3848 Walters, Scott Edward. *Completing the Circle: Lionel Trilling's Influence on the Criticism of Robert Brustein.* New York, NY: City Univ. of New York; 1998. 259 pp. Biblio. Notes. [Ph.D. Dissertation, Univ. Microfilms Order No. 9908377.] Lang.: Eng.
USA. 1960-1997. Historical studies. ■The influence of cultural and literary critic Lionel Trilling on director and theatre critic Robert Brustein in the context of middle-class American society, the effects of modernism on the aesthetic and moral sensibilities of American culture, the student revolts of the 1960s, and the rise of 'political correctness' in art and education.

3849 Worthen, W.B. "Deeper Meanings and Theatrical Technique: The Rhetoric of Performance Criticism." *SQ.* 1989 Win; 40(4): 441-455. Notes. Biblio. Lang.: Eng.
USA. 1989. Critical studies. ■Problems facing dramatic critics in relating the significance of the dramatic text to the practices of performance.

Training

3850 Ljadov, V.I.; Zinov'eva, A.G. *O M.O. Knebel'.* (On M.O. Knebel'.) Moscow: ; 1998. 206 pp. Lang.: Rus.
Russia. 1898-1989. Biographical studies. ■Profile of Marija Knebel', actress, director, and teacher.

3851 Kushner, Tony. "A Modest Proposal." *AmTh.* 1998 Jan.; 15(1): 20-22, 77-89. Illus.: Dwg. B&W. 1. Lang.: Eng.
USA. 1997. Histories-sources. ■Transcript of playwright Tony Kushner's keynote address before the annual conference of the Association of Theatre in Higher Education in August of 1997. Address focused on undergraduate theatre training, sex education, and cultural politics.

3852 Roach, Joseph. "The Future That Worked." *ThM.* 1998; 28(2): 19-26. Notes. Biblio. Illus.: Design. Dwg. B&W. 2. Lang.: Eng.
USSR. 1922-1929. Historical studies. ■Parallels between Leon Trotsky's ideas regarding the eventual synthesis of intellectual (including art) and physical work, and Mejerchol'd's theories of biomechanics in training actors.

MEDIA

General

Administation

3853 Feigenbaum, Harvey B. "Regulating the Media in the United States and France." *JAML.* 1998 Win; 28(4): 283-292. Notes. Tables. Lang.: Eng.
USA. France. 1912-1998. Historical studies. ■Comparison of the ways in which the United States and France intervene in their mass media industries.

Administration

3854 Robson, Christopher. "Fascinating Aida." *PlPl.* 1998 Sep.; 526: 14. Illus.: Photo. B&W. 1. Lang.: Eng.
UK-England. 1950-1998. Histories-sources. ■Film and television producer Aida Young on her career and future plans.

Design/technology

3855 Cashill, Robert. "In Memoriam: Scott Jason Jellen." *TCI.* 1998 Oct.; 32(9): 27-28. Lang.: Eng.
USA. 1973-1998. Biographical studies. ■Obituary for the film and television lighting technician, who was also owner and president of Liteworks Illumination and Power LLC.

Performance/production

3856 Laurendeau, Francine. "Ouvrir son corps: Entretien avec Jean-Louis Millette." (Opening One's Body: Interview with Jean-Louis Millette.) *JCT.* 1998; 88: 73-76. Illus.: Photo. B&W. 3. Lang.: Fre.
Canada: Montreal, PQ. 1965-1998. Histories-sources. ■Actor Jean-Louis Millette on acting for film and television.

3857 Laurendeau, Francine. "Un don et un abandon: Entretien avec Andrée Lachapelle." (A Gift and A Letting Go: Interview With Andrée Lachapelle.) *JCT.* 1998; 88: 68-72. Illus.: Photo. B&W. 2. Lang.: Fre.
Canada: Montreal, PQ. 1964-1998. Histories-sources. ■Actress Andrée Lachapelle on her work in film and for television.

3858 Troisi, Massimo. *Il mondo intero proprio.* (The Real Whole World.) Milan: Mondadori; 1998. 210 pp. (Biblioteca Umoristica Mondadori.) Biblio. Filmography. Lang.: Ita.
Italy. 1953-1994. Histories-sources. ■A collection of thoughts and witty remarks by the comic Neapolitan actor/director Massimo Troisi.

3859 Vasjuchin, V. "U neë liš' odin nedostatok: V ostal'nom ona bezuprečna." (She Only Has One Deficiency: Otherwise She Is Perfect.) *Ogonek.* 1998; 48: 32-39. Lang.: Rus.
Russia: Moscow. 1998. Biographical studies. ■Profile of stage and film actress Ljudmila Gurčenko.

3860 Boecking, Ulrike. "Die Kamera als Choreographin." (The Camera as Choreographer.) *Tanzd.* 1998; 41(2): 4-10. Illus.: Photo. B&W. 12. Lang.: Ger.
USA. Europe. 1920-1998. Historical studies. ■Relationship between film and dance from the American musical films with Gene Kelly and Fred

Astaire, the camera choreographies of Merce Cunningham, experimental work with film by European choreographers such as Maurice Béjart and Birgit Cullberg, and the current development of film and video dance.

Theory/criticism

3861 Militz, Klaus Ulrich. "Cause and Effect in Cross-Media Fertilization: The Impact of Historicity." *NTQ*. 1998 May; 14(2): 146-150. Notes. Biblio. [Issue 54.] Lang.: Eng.

Europe. 1963-1997. Critical studies. ■Modernist tradition of defining each art or medium in its own terms is criticized for an inherent essentialism. Proposes a less prescriptive approach concentrating on the interrelations between the audio-visual performance arts of film, television, and theatre.

Audio forms

Institutions

3862 Danielsen, Allan. "Bag højttaleren—Radioteatret i erne." (Behind the Loudspeaker—Radio Theatre in the Nineties.) *TE*. 1998 Feb.; 87: 31-33. Illus.: Photo. B&W. 3. Lang.: Dan.

Denmark. 1989-1998. Historical studies. ■Profile of Radioteatret, where a majority of the radio plays being produced are new Danish plays.

Performance/production

3863 Kostalanetz, Richard. "Audio Comedy in America: 1950 to the Present." *AmerD*. 1998 Spr; 7(2): 24-32. Lang.: Eng.

USA. 1950-1998. Historical studies. ■Analysis of the decline of radio comedy in the USA with the advent of television, with reference to the use of record albums by comedy performers Cheech & Chong and Firesign Theatre in the 1960s and 1970s.

3864 Miller, Edward D. *The Emergency Broadcast System: Panicked Bodies and Strange Voices in 30s America*. New York, NY: New York Univ; 1998. 335 pp. Notes. Biblio. [Ph.D. Dissertation, Univ. Microfilms Order No. AAC 9831741.] Lang.: Eng.

USA. 1929-1940. Histories-specific. ■The aesthetics of popular American radio in the 1930s. Analyzes President Roosevelt's 'Fireside Chats', news coverage of the explosion of the *Hindenburg*, and Mercury Theatre's *War of the Worlds* broadcast in the context of the growing importance of the disembodied voice and the impact of the medium of radio.

Plays/librettos/scripts

3865 Frost, Everett. "The Note Man on the Word Man: Morton Feldman on Composing the Music for Samuel Beckett: *Words and Music* in the Beckett Festival of Radio Plays." 47-55 in Bryden, Mary, ed. *Samuel Beckett and Music*. Oxford: Clarendon; 1998. 267 pp. Index. Notes. Biblio. Lang.: Eng.

Europe. 1987. Critical studies. ■Samuel Beckett's influence on composer Morton Feldman, with specific attention to Feldman's music for Beckett's play *Words and Music*.

3866 Nyytäjä, Outi. "Radioteatteri, vapauden viimeinen linnake." (Radio Theatre, Freedom's Last Bastion.) *Teat*. 1998 ; 53(1): 4-9. Illus.: Photo. Color. B&W. 3. Lang.: Fin.

Finland. 1998. Critical studies. ■Examines Finnish radio drama, arguing that the form is the last forum for Finnish playwrights to work on new and experimental texts.

3867 Bajama Griga, Stefano. "Beckett, *Tutti quelli che cadono* Esempio di struttura drammatica di ritorno all'origine." (Beckett, *All That Fall*: An Example of Dramatic Structure Returning to Its Origins.) *IlCast*. 1998; 11(31): 47-54. Biblio. Lang.: Ita.

Ireland. France. 1957. Critical studies. ■A brief analysis of Samuel Beckett's *All That Fall*.

3868 Bloom, J. *The Broken Yoke: A Dozen BBC Radio Plays About the Anglo-Irish Past and Present*. Exeter: Unpublished PhD, Univ. of Exeter; 1997. Notes. Biblio. [Absract in *Aslib Index to Theses*, 47-10562.] Lang.: Eng.

UK-England. Ireland. 1973-1986. Critical studies. ■Analysis of radio plays with Anglo-Irish themes with particular attention to Thomas Kilroy's *That Man Bracken*, David Rudkin's *Cries from Casement*, John Arden's *Pearl*, and Bill Morrison's *Maguire*.

Relation to other fields

3869 Greffard, Madeleine. "Le théâtre à la radio: un facteur de légitimation et de redéfinition." (Theatre on the Radio: A Legitimizing and Redefining Factor.) *AnT*. Spr 1998; 23: 53-73. Biblio. Notes. Lang.: Fre.

Canada. 1922-1952. Historical studies. ■Influence of radio drama production on professional theatre in Quebec from birth of commercial radio to advent of television.

Theory/criticism

3870 Meyer, Petra Maria. "'Encore—en corps—a corps': Antonin Artaud." *FMT*. 1998; 13(1): 18-41. Notes. Lang.: Ger.

France. 1920-1973. Critical studies. ■The use of voice in Artaud's radio project *Pour en finir avec le jugement de dieu (To Have Done with the Judgement of God)* and its influence on director Paul Pörtner's 'spontaneous theatre'.

Film

Administration

3871 Singer, Mark. "The Flick Factory." *NewY*. 1998 16 Mar.: 45-51. Illus.: Photo. B&W. 1. Lang.: Eng.

Israel. 1972-1998. Biographical studies. ■Profile of B-movie producer Avi Lerner.

3872 "Lord Grade." *Econ*. 1998 Dec 19; 349(8099): 122. Illus.: Photo. B&W. 1. Lang.: Eng.

UK-England. 1908-1998. Biographical studies. ■Obituary for the venerable producer and showman, Lew Grade.

3873 "America's Sorcerer." *Econ*. 1998 Jan 10; 346(8050): 71-73. Illus.: Photo. B&W. 1. Lang.: Eng.

USA. 1968-1998. Biographical studies. ■Influence, still being felt in the film industry, of Walt Disney, thirty years after his death. Contains sidebar regarding the California Institute of the Arts founded and endowed by Disney for potential animators.

3874 Regester, Charlene. "Headline to Headlights: Oscar Micheaux's Exploitation of the Rhinelander Case." *WJBS*. 1998 Fall; 22(3): 195-204. Notes. Biblio. Lang.: Eng.

USA. 1924. Historical studies. ■Account of how African-American filmmaker Micheaux exploited the publicity surrounding the Rhinelander-Jones interracial marriage court case, in which the couple's forced annulment was overturned and their union was legally validated, as a marketing tool to generate African-American audience interest.

3875 Stein, Jean. "West of Eden." *NewY*. 1998 23 Feb-2 Mar.: 150-170. Illus.: Photo. B&W. 6. Lang.: Eng.

USA: Hollywood, CA. 1918-1978. Histories-sources. ■Collection of interviews regarding the life of film producer Jack Warner of Warner Brothers.

Audience

3876 Giles, Jane. "Epilepsy: Performance, spectatorship & abjection." *PM*. 1988; 56/57: 26-27. Lang.: Eng.

1960-1988. Empirical research. ■Considers how the medium of film can prompt an epileptic seizure in a spectator, citing Flicker, by Tony Conrad, whose alternating transparent and opaque black frames caused one in fifteen thousand viewers to experience a seizure. Also refers to Paul Sharits' installation *Epileptic Seizure Comparison*.

3877 "Beloved It's Not." *Econ*. 1998 Nov 21; 349(8095): 86. Illus.: Photo. B&W. 1. Lang.: Eng.

USA. 1998. Critical studies. ■Discusses reasons for the failure of Jonathan Demme's *Beloved*, starring Oprah Winfrey, to achieve the expected audience appeal.

3878 Denby, David. "The Moviegoers." *NewY*. 1998 6 Apr.: 94-101. Illus.: Dwg. Color. 1. Lang.: Eng.

USA. 1998. Critical studies. ■The current state of film, film criticism, and the film audience, with emphasis on what the author calls the new corporate irony of contemporary commercial film and the generation gap between younger and older viewers.

Basic theatrical documents

3879 Beaufoy, Simon. "*The Full Monty*." *Scenario*. 1998 Spr; 4(1): 6-45. Illus.: Dwg. Color. 6. Lang.: Eng.

MEDIA: Film—Basic theatrical documents

UK-England. 1997. ■Text of the screenplay.

3880 Aronofsky, Darren. "*Pi.*" *Scenario.* 1998 Sum; 4(2): 62-90. Illus.: Pntg. Color. 4. Lang.: Eng.

USA. 1998. ■Text of screenplay.

3881 Bartel, Paul. "*The Secret Cinema.*" *Scenario.* 1998; 4(4): 166-174. Illus.: Pntg. Color. 1. Lang.: Eng.

USA. 1966. ■Screenplay for Bartel's thirty-minute film, which he remade in 1986 for Stephen Spielberg's television series *Amazing Stories.* Includes biographical information on Bartel's later career as a filmmaker.

3882 Condon, Bill. "*Gods and Monsters.*" *Scenario.* 1998; 4(4): 98-137. Illus.: Pntg. Color. 4. Lang.: Eng.

USA. 1998. ■Screenplay of the film, also directed by Condon, about the film director James Whale.

3883 Davidson, Adam. "*The Lunch Date.*" *Scenario.* 1998; 4(4): 162-165. Illus.: Pntg. Color. 1. Lang.: Eng.

USA. 1998. ■Screenplay of the Academy Award-winning twelve-minute film. Includes biographical information on Davidson.

3884 Frank, Scott. "*Out of Sight.*" *Scenario.* 1998 Sum; 4(2): 6-56. Illus.: Pntg. Color. 4. Lang.: Eng.

USA. 1998. ■Text of screenplay based on a novel by Elmore Leonard.

3885 Fuller, Sam. "*Pickup on South Street.*" *Scenario.* 1998; 4(3): 46-84. Illus.: Pntg. Color. 4. Lang.: Eng.

USA. 1953. ■Text of Fuller's 1953 Film.

3886 Fuller, Samuel. "*Shock Corridor.*" *Scenario.* 1998; 4(3): 100-140. Illus.: Pntg. Color. 4. Lang.: Eng.

USA. 1963. ■Text of Fuller's 1963 screenplay.

3887 Gorey, Edward. "*The Black Doll.*" *Scenario.* 1998 Spr; 4(1): 154-170. Lang.: Eng.

USA. 1973. ■Text of a first draft of Gorey's animated film, with numerous drawings by the author.

3888 Heil, Douglas. "*The First Wife*: A Screenplay." *JFV.* 1998 Fall; 50(3): 62-67. Lang.: Eng.

USA. 1998. ■Text of brief screenplay based on a short story by Colette. The play is complete but conceived as part of a larger project.

3889 Jones, William E. "*Finished.*" *PerAJ.* 1998 May; 20(2): 82-98. Illus.: Photo. B&W. 3. Lang.: Eng.

USA. 1997. ■Complete text of Jones's screenplay.

3890 LaGravenese, Richard. "*Living Out Loud.*" *Scenario.* 1998; 4(4): 12-52. Illus.: Pntg. Color. 4. Lang.: Eng.

USA. 1998. ■Text of the screenplay, which was also directed by the author.

3891 Lardner, Ring, Jr.; Trumbo, Dalton. "*The Fishermen of Beaudrais.*" *Scenario.* 1998 Sum; 4(2): 96-144. Illus.: Pntg. Sketches. B&W. Color. 8. Lang.: Eng.

USA. 1943-1998. ■Screenplay of the recently rereleased film.

3892 Lemmons, Kasi. "*Eve's Bayou.*" *Scenario.* 1998 Sum; 4(2): 152-191. Illus.: Pntg. Color. 4. Lang.: Eng.

USA. 1994-1998. ■Complete screenplay.

3893 Levin, Marc; Malone, Bonz; Sohn, Sonja; Stratton, Richard; Williams, Saul. "*Slam.*" *Scenario.* 1998; 4(3): 6-24. Illus.: Pntg. Color. 4. Lang.: Eng.

USA. 1998. ■Text of screenplay directed by Marc Levin.

3894 Lewin, Alex. "*Weeds.*" *Scenario.* 1998; 4(3): 142-180. Illus.: Pntg. Color. 4. Lang.: Eng.

USA. 1998. ■The winner of the *Scenario*/Writers Guild of America, East Foundation student screenplay competition.

3895 Lippy, Tod. "*Jim & Wanda.*" *Scenario.* 1998; 4(4): 175-182. Lang.: Eng.

USA. 1996. ■Screenplay for Lippy's short unproduced film.

3896 Mamet, David. "*The Spanish Prisoner.*" *Scenario.* 1998 Spr; 4(1): 102-149. Illus.: Photo. Color. 6. Lang.: Eng.

USA. 1998. ■Text of Mamet's screenplay.

3897 McMurtry, Larry; Bogdanovich, Peter. "*The Last Picture Show.*" *Scenario.* 1998; 4(4): 58-91. Illus.: Pntg. Color. 6. Lang.: Eng.

USA. 1971. ■Screenplay of the film, adapted and directed by Bogdanovich.

3898 Wilder, Gene; Brooks, Mel. "*Young Frankenstein.*" *Scenario.* 1998 Spr; 4(1): 50-94. Illus.: Pntg. Color. 4. Lang.: Eng.

USA. 1974. ■Complete screenplay.

Design/technology

3899 Calhoun, John. "Woop Woop De Doo." *TCI.* 1998 May; 32(5): 6-7. Illus.: Photo. Color. 1. Lang.: Eng.

Australia. 1998. Technical studies. ■Lizzy Gardiner's costumes for the movie *Welcome to Woop Woop* directed by Stephan Elliot.

3900 Calhoun, John. "A Study in Contrasts." *LDim.* 1998 Jan-Feb.; 22(1): 56-59, 94-96. Illus.: Photo. Color. 8. Lang.: Eng.

Australia. 1997. Critical studies. ■Examines the work of cinematographer Geoffrey Simpson on Gillian Armstrong's *Oscar and Lucinda* starring Ralph Fiennes and Cate Blanchett.

3901 Blake, Leslie (Hoban). "Faking It." *TCI.* 1998 Oct.; 32(9): 56-57. Illus.: Photo. Sketches. Color. 11. Lang.: Eng.

USA. 1998. Technical studies. ■Andrew Jackness' art deco influenced production design, and Juliet Polsca's costumes for the independent film *The Impostors,* directed by Stanley Tucci.

3902 Brody, Jeb. "Tony Walton, Production Designer." *Scenario.* 1998 Win; 4(4): 6-9. Illus.: Dwg. Photo. Pntg. Color. 16. Lang.: Eng.

USA. 1965-1998. Historical studies. ■Walton's work in the design of scenery and costumes for film productions.

3903 Calhoun, John. "Sight for Sore Eyes." *TCI.* 1998 Feb.; 32(2): 7-8. Illus.: Photo. Color. 1. Lang.: Eng.

USA: Hollywood, CA. 1998. Technical studies. ■Designer Tom Bronson's costumes for the Disney film *Mr. Magoo.*

3904 Calhoun, John. "Warning! Danger!" *TCI.* 1998 May; 32(5): 44-47. Illus.: Photo. Color. 12. Lang.: Eng.

USA: Hollywood, CA. 1998. Technical studies. ■Production designer Norman Garwood's concept for the film version of the 1960s television series *Lost in Space* directed by Stephen Hopkins.

3905 Calhoun, John. "Bette Noire." *TCI.* 1998 July; 32(7): 7-8. Illus.: Photo. Color. 1. Lang.: Eng.

USA: Hollywood, CA. 1998. Technical studies. ■First-time film director Des McAnuff's production design concept for the cinematic version of Honoré de Balzac's *Cousin Bette.*

3906 Calhoun, John. "Matthew Maraffi." *TCI.* 1998 Aug/Sep.; 32(8): 32-33. Illus.: Photo. B&W. 2. Lang.: Eng.

USA. 1998. Biographical studies. ■Profile of production designer for the black-and-white film *Pi* directed by Darren Aronofsky.

3907 Calhoun, John. "Forward Into the Past." *TCI.* 1998 Aug/Sep.; 32(8): 42-41. Illus.: Photo. Color. 7. Lang.: Eng.

USA: Hollywood, CA. 1998. Technical studies. ■Production designer Stuart Craig's visual concept for Jeremiah Chechik's film version of the 1960s British spy TV show *The Avengers.*

3908 Calhoun, John. "A Whale of a Tale." *TCI.* 1998 Nov.; 32(10): 7-9. Illus.: Photo. Color. 1. Lang.: Eng.

USA: Hollywood, CA. 1998. Technical studies. ■Richard Sherman's production design for Bill Condon's film *Gods and Monsters,* based on the life of director James Whale.

3909 Calhoun, John. "Black & White in Color." *TCI.* 1998 Nov.; 32(10): 48-51. Illus.: Photo. B&W. Color. 6. Lang.: Eng.

USA: Hollywood, CA. 1998. Technical studies. ■Design concept, emphasizing the look of 1950s television situation comedy, for the Gary Ross film *Pleasantville.* Discusses special effects, including techniques used by colorist Michael Southard, with costume design by Judianna Makovsky, and production design by Jeannine Oppewall.

3910 Calhoun, John. "Film: *Titanic.*" *TCI.* 1998 Jan.; 32(1): 24-29. Illus.: Photo. Color. 14. Lang.: Eng.

USA. 1997. Technical studies. ■Examines the technical designs of production designer Peter Lamont and visual historian Ken Marschall on the film *Titanic,* directed by James Cameron.

3911 Calhoun, John. "High Concept." *LDim.* 1998 June; 22(5): 51. Illus.: Photo. Color. 5. Lang.: Eng.

USA. 1998. Technical studies. ■Introductory article to an issue on film lighting.

MEDIA: Film—Design/technology

3912 Calhoun, John. "Volumes of Color." *LDim.* 1998 June; 22(5): 52-55, 84-87. Illus.: Photo. Color. 10. Lang.: Eng.
USA. 1998. Technical studies. ■Examines the lighting design of director of photography Elliot Davis for *Out of Sight*, directed by Steven Soderbergh and starring George Clooney and Jennifer Lopez.

3913 Calhoun, John. "A Bigger Flash." *LDim.* 1998 June; 22(5): 56-59, 91-93. Illus.: Photo. Lighting. Color. 5. Lang.: Eng.
USA. 1998. Technical studies. ■Examines the lighting design of Alexander Gruszynski on the film *54*, directed by Mark Christopher and starring Ryan Phillippe and Salma Hayek.

3914 Calhoun, John. "Military Maneuvers." *LDim.* 1998 July; 22(6): 68-77. Illus.: Photo. Color. 14. Lang.: Eng.
USA. 1998. Technical studies. ■Examines the lighting design of Jamie Anderson in the film *Small Soldiers*, directed by Joe Dante and featuring animatronic puppets and live actors.

3915 Calhoun, John. "Group Activities." *LDim.* 1998 Oct.; 22(9): 76-87. Illus.: Photo. B&W. 5. Lang.: Eng.
USA: Hollywood, CA. 1970-1998. Historical studies. ■Details the history of the Matthews Studio Group, a 'one-stop shop' for the lighting design industry. Founded in 1970, the company is experiencing steady growth.

3916 Cashill, Robert. "When Worlds Collide." *LDim.* 1998 July; 22(6): 44-47, 86-89. Illus.: Photo. Color. 6. Lang.: Eng.
USA. 1998. Technical studies. ■Examines the lighting design of John Schwartzman in the film *Armageddon*, directed by Michael Bays and starring Bruce Willis.

3917 Cashill, Robert. "Appetite for Destruction." *LDim.* 1998 June; 22(5): 60-65, 88-90. Illus.: Photo. Color. 8. Lang.: Eng.
USA. 1998. Technical studies. ■Examines the lighting design of Ueli Steiger on the film *Godzilla*, directed by Roland Emmerich and starring Matthew Broderick.

3918 Garrett, Michael. "Screen Gems." *LD&A.* 1998 Sep.; 28(9): 50-53. Illus.: Photo. Color. 6. Lang.: Eng.
USA. 1998. Technical studies. ■Examines the advances in motion picture lighting that have been achieved through techniques and processes that were pioneered for live performances.

3919 Johnson, David. "Life in a Fishbowl." *LDim.* 1998 June; 22(5): 70-73. Illus.: Photo. Color. 5. Lang.: Eng.
USA. 1998. Technical studies. ■Examines the lighting design of Peter Biziou on the film *The Truman Show*, directed by Peter Weir and starring Jim Carrey.

3920 Lavoie, Pierre. "Macbeth des ténèbres." (Shadowy Macbeth.) *JCT.* 1998; 88: 158. Illus.: Photo. B&W. 1. Lang.: Fre.
USA. 1948. Historical studies. ■Scenery as conveyor of spirit of play in Orson Welles' film adaptation of Shakespeare's *Macbeth.*

3921 Lazar, Wanda. "Sound for Film: Audio Education for Filmmakers." *JFV.* 1998 Fall; 50(3): 54-61. Notes. Lang.: Eng.
USA. 1998. Instructional materials. ■Model syllabus for a course or unit on sound in film.

3922 Slingerland, Amy L. "Top Secret." *LDim.* 1998 June; 22(5): 66-69, 94. Illus.: Photo. Color. 8. Lang.: Eng.
USA. 1998. Technical studies. ■Examines the lighting design of Ward Russell on the film *The X- Files*, directed by Rob Bowman and starring David Duchovny and Gillian Anderson.

Institutions

3923 Chin, Daryl; Qualls, Larry. "To Market, To Market." *PerAJ.* 1998 Jan.; 20(58): 38-43. Illus.: Photo. B&W. 2. Lang.: Eng.
Canada: Toronto, ON. 1997. Historical studies. ■Report on the 1997 Toronto Film Festival.

3924 Duckett, Josie W. "The Acapulco Black Film Festival." *PerAJ.* 1998 Jan.; 20(58): 44-47. Lang.: Eng.
Mexico: Acapulco. 1997. Historical studies. ■Report on the 1997 festival for Black filmmakers.

3925 Petrie, David Terry. *The Sundance Institute: The First Four Years.* Salt Lake City, UT: Brigham Young Univ; 1987. 293 pp. Notes. Biblio. [Ph.D. Dissertation, Univ. Microfilms Order No. 8710860.] Lang.: Eng.
USA: Sundance, CO. 1981-1984. Historical studies. ■History of the Sundance Institute for Film and Video, and its contributions to the production of independent American films.

Performance spaces

3926 Lampert-Gréaux, Ellen. "Orpheum Ascending." *TCI.* 1998 Oct.; 32(9): 54-55. Illus.: Photo. Color. 7. Lang.: Eng.
USA: Phoenix, AZ. 1929-1998. Critical studies. ■Appraisal of the architectural aspects of the recent restoration of the Orpheum Theatre movie palace, built in 1929.

Performance/production

3927 Hausmann, Vincent. "Cinematic Inscription of Otherness: Sounding a Critique of Subjectivity." *JFV.* 1998 Spr; 50(1): 20-41. Illus.: Photo. B&W. 4. Lang.: Eng.
1979-1998. Critical studies. ■Analysis of films by Bernardo Bertolucci: *La Luna, Stealing Beauty*, and *The Sheltering Sky.*

3928 Vaïs, Michel. "Robert Lepage: un homme de théâtre au cinéma." (Robert Lepage: A Man of the Theatre in Cinema.) *JCT.* 1998; 88: 123-130. Illus.: Photo. B&W. 8. Lang.: Fre.
Canada. 1995-1998. Historical studies. ■Theatre director Robert Lepage's work directing film: *Le Confessional (The Confessional*, 1995), *Le Polygraphe (The Polygraph*, 1996) and *Nō* (1998).

3929 Bren, Frank. "Connections and Crossovers: Cinema and Theatre in Hong Kong." *NTQ.* 1998 Feb.; 14(1): 63-74. Notes. Illus.: Photo. B&W. 9. [Issue 53.] Lang.: Eng.
China, People's Republic of: Hong Kong. 1941-1996. Historical studies. ■The history of the relationship between the theatre and film industries in Hong Kong.

3930 "Don't Say a Word." *Econ.* 1998 Jan 17; 346(3051): 77-78. Lang.: Eng.
Finland. 1988-1998. Biographical studies. ■Profile of minimalist film director Aki Kaurismaki, whose films contain almost no speech or sound.

3931 Bennett, Susan. "Godard and Lear: Trashing the Can(n)on." *ThS.* 1998 May; 39(1): 7-20. Notes. Lang.: Eng.
France. 1988. Critical studies. ■Jean-Luc Godard's modernist film *King Lear*, a film version of Shakespeare's play as essentially postmodern in its emphasis on commodity culture.

3932 Everett, Wendy. "Director as Composer: Marguerite Duras and the Musical Analogy." *LFQ.* 1998; 26(2): 124-129. Notes. Lang.: Eng.
France. 1974-1981. Critical studies. ■Function of music in films directed and scripted by Marguerite Duras, including *India Song* and *L'Homme atlantique.*

3933 Robson, Christopher. "Maurice Chevalier (1888-1972)—Everybody's Favourite Frenchman." *PlPl.* 1998 Nov.; 528: 21. Lang.: Eng.
France: Paris. USA. 1888-1972. Biographical studies. ■Life and film career of singer Maurice Chevalier.

3934 Perry, Maria. "Eva's Farewell." *PlPl.* 1998 Oct.; 527: 10. Lang.: Eng.
Hungary. UK-England: London. 1998. Historical studies. ■Circumstances surrounding the death of Hungarian film actress Eva Bartok, who starred in several cult fantasy movies.

3935 Lévesque, Solange. "'L'Étoile noire': Suzanne Cloutier chez Orson Welles." ('The Black Star': Suzanne Cloutier at the Hands of Orson Welles.) *JCT.* 1998; 88: 155-156. Illus.: Photo. B&W. 1. Lang.: Fre.
Italy. 1952. Historical studies. ■Surprising casting choice of Quebec-born francophone actress Suzanne Cloutier as Desdemona in Orson Welles' *Othello.*

3936 Mannelli, Valeria, ed. *Gian Maria Volonté. L'immagine e la memoria.* (Gian Maria Volonté: Image and Memory.) Ancona: Transeuropa; 1998. 126 pp. Biblio. Filmography. Illus.: Photo. B&W. 8. Lang.: Ita.
Italy. 1960-1994. Biographical studies. ■A collection of essays on the Italian cinema actor Gian Maria Volonté.

3937 "Akira Kurosawa." *Econ.* 1998 Sep 12; 348(8085): 100. Illus.: Photo. B&W. 1. Lang.: Eng.

MEDIA: Film—Performance/production

Japan. 1910-1998. Biographical studies. ■Obituary for the influential film director.

3938 Wynchank, Anny. "*Touki-Bouki*: The New Wave on the Cinematic Shores of Africa." *SATJ.* 1998 May/Sep.; 12(1/2): 53-72. Notes. Biblio. Lang.: Eng.

Senegal. 1973. Critical studies. ■Analysis of Djibril Diop Mambéty's film as a revolutionary landmark in West African cinema.

3939 Belzil, Patricia. "Brillants Bénédict et Béatrice." (Brilliant Benedict and Beatrice.) *JCT.* 1998; 88: 156-157. Illus.: Photo. B&W. 1. Lang.: Fre.

UK. 1993. Critical Studies. ■Casting and acting at heart of success of Kenneth Branagh's film adaptation of Shakespeare's *Much Ado About Nothing.*

3940 Hodgdon, Barbara. "Replicating Richard: Body Doubles, Body Politics." *TJ.* 1998 May; 50(2): 207-226. Notes. Illus.: Photo. B&W. 5. Lang.: Eng.

UK-England. USA. 1985-1998. Critical studies. ■Examines stage-to-film versions of *Richard III* to emphasize the effects of the body. Productions examined include Ian McKellen's, originally staged at the National Theatre, and Al Pacino's *Looking for Richard.*

3941 Robson, Christopher. "George Arliss (1868-1946)—The First Gentleman of the Screen." *PlPl.* Mar 1998; 520: 11. Illus.: Photo. B&W. 1. Lang.: Eng.

UK-England: London. 1868-1946. Biographical studies. ■Stage and screen career of actor George Arliss.

3942 "Sam Fuller in His Own Voice." *Scenario.* 1998; 4(3): 90-97. Illus.: Photo. B&W. Color. 9. Lang.: Eng.

USA. 1937-1994. Histories-sources. ■Excerpts from the film-maker's notes and diaries.

3943 "Samuel Fuller 1912-1997." *Scenario.* 1998; 4(3): 86-89. Illus.: Sketches. Photo. B&W. Color. 5. Lang.: Eng.

USA. 1912-1997. Biographical studies. ■Survey of Sam Fuller's career as a film maker.

3944 "Steven Soderbergh on *Out of Sight.*" *Scenario.* 1998 Sum; 4(2): 61, 202. Lang.: Eng.

USA. 1998. Histories-sources. ■Director's comments on the making of the film *Out of Sight*, based on the novel by Elmore Leonard and adapted by Scott Frank.

3945 "The White Dog Talks to Sam Fuller." *Scenario.* 1998; 4(3): 98-99. Illus.: Photo. B&W. 1. Lang.: Eng.

USA. 1982. Histories-sources. ■Film maker Sam Fuller 'interviews' a German shepherd that appeared in his film *White Dog* in order to express his own opinions about the film and racism.

3946 "Frank Sinatra." *Econ.* 1998 May 23; 347(8069): 82. Illus.: Photo. B&W. 1. Lang.: Eng.

USA. 1916-1998. Biographical studies. ■Obituary for the singer and film actor.

3947 "Maureen O'Sullivan." *Econ.* 1998 July 4; 348(8075): 87. Illus.: Photo. B&W. 1. Lang.: Eng.

USA. 1911-1998. Biographical studies. ■Obituary for the film actress, who was best known for playing Jane in *Tarzan.*

3948 "War Is Certainly Hell to Film." *Econ.* 1998 Aug 8; 348(8080): 69-70. Illus.: Photo. B&W. 2. Lang.: Eng.

USA: Hollywood, CA. 1998. Critical studies. ■Steven Spielberg's *Saving Private Ryan* and the recent unpopularity of war films. Includes sidebar review of the film.

3949 "Hate the Sin, Hate the Sinner." *Econ.* 1998 Oct 10; 349(8089): 92. Illus.: Photo. B&W. 1. Lang.: Eng.

USA. 1998. Critical studies. ■Analysis of Todd Solondz' film *Happiness*, in light of the United States' concern with curtailing the activities of pedophiles.

3950 Andersen, Kurt. "The Tom Hanks Phenomenon." *NewY.* 1998 7-14 Dec.: 104, 106, 115-128. Illus.: Photo. B&W. 2. Lang.: Eng.

USA. 1983-1998. Biographical studies. ■Profile of actor Tom Hanks.

3951 Hoberman, J. "Sam Fuller: Tabloid Artist." *Scenario.* 1998; 4(3): 4-5, 190-192. Illus.: Sketches. Photo. B&W. Color. 2. Lang.: Eng.

USA. 1937-1994. Biographical studies. ■The career of action film maker Sam Fuller.

3952 Kubek, Elizabeth. "'Spent for Us': Capra's Technologies of Mastery in *Lady for a Day.*" *JFV.* 1998 Sum; 50(2): 40-57. Notes. Lang.: Eng.

USA. 1933. Critical studies. ■Analysis of Frank Capra's film and its connection with maternal relationships in Capra's life.

3953 Lahr, John. "Personal History: The Lion and Me." *NewY.* 1998 Nov 16: 62-67. Illus.: Photo. B&W. 3. Lang.: Eng.

USA. 1895-1967. Histories-sources. ■The author's recollections of his father, actor Bert Lahr, with emphasis on the importance of Lahr's role as the Cowardly Lion in the 1939 film *The Wizard of Oz.*

3954 Nobile, Philip. "The Faking of Malcolm X." *Spy.* 1997 May/June; 11(2): 50-57. Illus.: Photo. B&W. 8. Lang.: Eng.

USA. 1992-1995. Historical studies. ■Report on director Spike Lee's numerous, and sometimes questionable, efforts to convince Muslim authorities to allow him to film scenes of *Malcolm X* in Mecca.

3955 Riva, M. *Moja mat' Marlen Ditrich.* (My Mother, Marlene Dietrich.) St. Petersburg: Mnibus Press; 1998. [2 vols.] Lang.: Rus.

USA. 1901-1992. Histories-sources. ■Biography of Marlene Dietrich, according to her daughter.

3956 Rosenbaum, Jonathan. "Mamet & Hitchcock: The Men Who Knew Too Much." *Scenario.* 1998 Spr; 4(1): 152-153, 179-180. Lang.: Eng.

USA. 1998. Critical studies. ■The influence of filmmaker Alfred Hitchcock on *The Spanish Prisoner*, written and directed by David Mamet.

3957 Ross, Alex. "The Nominees for the Music Oscar." *NewY.* 1998 9 Mar.: 82-86. Illus.: Dwg. Color. 1. Lang.: Eng.

USA. 1908-1998. Historical studies. ■Composers of Hollywood film scores.

3958 Rush, Michael. "The Enduring Avant-Garde: Jean-Luc Godard and William Kentridge." *PerAJ.* 1998 Sep.; 20(3): 48-52. Illus.: Photo. B&W. 2. Lang.: Eng.

USA: New York, NY. 1998. Historical studies. ■Report on separate retrospectives being held for the avant-garde filmmakers, Godard's at the Museum of Modern Art and Kentridge's at the Drawing Center.

3959 Slater, Thomas J. "June Mathis's *Classified*: One Woman's Response to Modernism." *JFV.* 1998 Sum; 50(2): 3-14. Notes. Illus.: Photo. B&W. 4. Lang.: Eng.

USA. 1916-1927. Historical studies. ■Feminist analysis of the work of Mathis, a highly influential screenwriter and producer, with emphasis on her 1925 film *Classified* and her later obscurity.

3960 Westerlund, Lennart. "De stora svarta talangerna i drömfabrikens skugga." (The Great Black Talent in the Shadow of the Dream Factory.) *Danst.* 1998; 8(1): 22-25. Illus.: Photo. B&W. Lang.: Swe.

USA. 1900-1957. Historical studies. ■The growing importance of Black artists in movie musicals during the first half of twentieth century, in spite of racial discrimination.

Plays/librettos/scripts

3961 Freund, Peter. "The Eye in the Object: Identification and Surveillance in Samuel Beckett's Screen Dramas." *JFV.* 1998 Spr; 50(1): 42-49. Illus.: Photo. B&W. 2. Lang.: Eng.

1966-1970. Critical studies. ■Analysis of Beckett's film scripts *Film* and *Eh Joe.*

3962 Schama, Simon. "Clio at the Multiplex." *NewY.* 1998 19 Jan.: 38-43. Illus.: Dwg. Color. 1. Lang.: Eng.

1963-1997. Critical studies. ■Critique of films on historical subjects, with particular attention to Stephen Spielberg's *Amistad.*

3963 Belzil, Patricia. "Contraintes et libertés de la scénarisation: Entretien avec Michel Marc Bouchard." (Constraints and Liberties of Scripting for Film: Interview with Michel Marc Bouchard.) *JCT.* 1998; 88: 46-67. Illus.: Photo. B&W. 17. Lang.: Fre.

Canada: Montreal, PQ. 1987-1998. Histories-sources. ■Playwright Michel Marc Bouchard on creating film adaptations of his plays *Les Feluettes (Lilies)* and *L'Histoire de l'oie (The Tale of Teeka).*

MEDIA: Film—Plays/librettos/scripts

3964 Lavoie, André. "Le cinéma québécois fait une scène." (Québécois Cinema Makes a Scene.) *JCT.* 1998; 88: 87-96. Notes. Illus.: Photo. B&W. 6. Lang.: Fre.
Canada. 1990-1998. Historical studies. ■Representations of theatre in Québécois films with special attention to Denis Arcand's *Jésus de Montréal (Jesus of Montreal).*

3965 Paventi, Eza. "Des histoires inventées: Rencontre avec André Forcier." (Made-Up Stories: Encounter with André Forcier.) *JCT.* 1998; 88: 97-101. Illus.: Photo. B&W. 3. Lang.: Fre.
Canada. 1998. Histories-sources. ■Québécois film-maker André Forcier on his employment of surrealism and metaphor in his films rather than insisting on realism.

3966 Raphael, Mitchel. "*Poor Super Man*: Brad Fraser's Leap from Playwright to Film Director." *PAC.* 1998; 31(3): 30-31. Illus.: Photo. B&W. 1. Lang.: Eng.
Canada. 1994-1998. Biographical studies. ■Brad Fraser directs a film adaptation of his stage play *Poor Superman.*

3967 Wickham, Philip. "De la scène à l'écran." (From Stage to Screen.) *JCT.* 1998; 88: 146-149. Notes. Illus.: Photo. Poster. B&W. 2. Lang.: Fre.
Canada. 1997. Critical studies. ■Transformation of *Cabaret neiges noires (Black Snow Cabaret),* co-written by Dominic Champagne, Jean-Frédéric Messier, Pascale Rafie and Jean-François Caron to make director Raymond Saint-Jean's film version.

3968 Ebrahim, Haseenah. "Afrocuban Religions in Sara Gómez's *One Way or Another* and Gloria Rolando's *Oggun.*" *WJBS.* 1998 Win; 22(4): 239-251. Notes. Biblio. Lang.: Eng.
Cuba. 1974-1991. Critical studies. ■The depiction of Afrocuban religions in Gómez's *De Cierta manera* and Rolando's *Oggun.*

3969 Morsberger, Katharine M.; Morsberger, Robert E. "Robin Hood on Film: Can We Ever Again 'Make Them Like They Used To'?" 205-231 in Potter, Lois, ed. *Playing Robin Hood: The Legend as Performance in Five Centuries.* Newark, DE: Univ of Delaware P; 1998. 254 pp. Index. Notes. Biblio. Pref. Illus.: Poster. 1. Lang.: Eng.
England. USA. 1920-1992. Critical studies. ■Comparison of major Robin Hood films with the plays of the 1590s in number and variety of interpretations. Films range from the Douglas Fairbanks 1922 epic to 1993's *Robin Hood: Men in Tights,* directed by Mel Brooks and featuring Roger Rees as the Sheriff.

3970 Jones, S.G. *Myth and tragedy: Representations of Joan of Arc in Film and Twentieth Century Theatre.* Bristol: Unpublished PhD, Univ. of Bristol; 1997. Notes. Biblio. [Absract in *Aslib Index to Theses,* 47-5469.] Lang.: Eng.
Europe. USA. 1900-1996. Critical studies. ■Considers the processes by which film and playtexts engage with the mythic figure of Joan of Arc, and among other things explores the semantic association between transgression and transcendence, and between the natural and unnatural.

3971 Lazaridès, Alexandre. "Théâtre et cinéma: l''irréductible différence'." (Theatre and Cinema: The 'Irreducible Difference'.) *JCT.* 1998; 88: 140-143. Notes. Illus.: Photo. B&W. 4. Lang.: Fre.
France. 1997. Critical studies. ■Analysis of two books about adapting theatre to film: *Le Film de Théâtre,* ed. Béatrice Picon-Vallin (Paris: CNRS, 1997) and *L'Adaptation. Du théâtre au cinéma* by André Helbo (Paris: Armand Colin, 1997).

3972 Micheli, Sergio. *Bertolt Brecht e il cinema di Weimar.* (Bertolt Brecht and Weimar's Cinema.) Florence: Manent; 1998. 174 pp. (Personaggi e interpreti, 3.) Pref. Index. Append. Illus.: Photo. Sketches. B&W. 10. Lang.: Ita.
Germany. 1919-1932. Critical studies. ■Examines the relationship between Bertolt Brecht and German cinema. Focuses on the scenario of the film *Kuhle Wampe, or To Whom Does the World Belong? (Kuhle Wampe oder Wem gehört die Welt)* written by Brecht with Ernst Ottwald.

3973 Kandé, Sylvie. "Look Homeward, Angel: Maroons and Mulattos in Haile Gerima's *Sankofa.*" *RAL.* 1998 Sum; 29(2): 128-146. Notes. Biblio. Pref. Lang.: Eng.
Ghana. 1993. Critical studies. ■Images of slavery and a new consciousness of African identity in Gerima's film.

3974 Piette, Alain. "The Face in the Mirror—Faust as Self-Deceived Actor." *LFQ.* 1998; 26(2): 136-141. Biblio. Illus.: Photo. B&W. 1. Lang.: Eng.
Hungary. 1981. Critical studies. ■Analysis of István Szabó's film *Mephisto,* a variation on the Faust myth.

3975 Špalikov, Gennadij. *Stichi. Pesni. Scenarii. Nabroski. Dnevniki. Pis'ma.* (Poems, Songs, Scenarios, Notes, Diaries, Letters.) Ekaterinburg: U-Faktorija; 1998. 656 pp. Lang.: Rus.
Russia. Histories-sources. ■Compiled writings, letters and diaries of of filmmaker Gennadij Špalikov.

3976 Špalikov, Gennadij; Fajt, Ju.A., ed. *Ja žil kak žil: Stichi. Proza. Dramaturgija. Dnevniki. Pis'ma.* (I Lived However I Lived: Poems, Drama, Diaries, Letters.) Moscow: Izdat. dom 'Podkova'; 1998. 526 pp. Lang.: Rus.
Russia. 1998. Histories-sources. ■Writings and reminiscences of actor/writer Gennadij Špalikov.

3977 Gugler, Josef; Diop, Oumar Cherif. "Ousmane Sembéne's *Xala*: The Novel, the Film, and Their Audiences." *RAL.* 1998 Sum; 29(2): 147-158. Notes. Pref. Biblio. Lang.: Eng.
Senegal. 1973-1974. Critical studies. ■Analyzes novelist and film director Sembéne's novel and movie discussing the differences between the two as well as the differences of the audiences of the two media.

3978 Willem, Linda M. "Almodóvar on the Verge of Cocteau's *La Voix humaine.*" *LFQ.* 1998; 26(2): 142-147. Notes. Biblio. Lang.: Eng.
Spain. France. 1981. Critical studies. ■Cocteau's one-act play as a source for Pedro Almodóvar in his film *Women on the Verge of a Nervous Breakdown (Mujeres al borde de un ataque de nervios).*

3979 "Writing *The Full Monty*: A Talk with Simon Beaufoy." *Scenario.* 1998 Spr; 4(1): 46-49, 180-184. Illus.: Dwg. B&W. 1. Lang.: Eng.
UK-England. 1997. Histories-sources. ■Interview with the author of *The Full Monty.*

3980 Abbotson, Susan C.W. "Stoppard's (Re)Vision of Rosencrantz and Guildenstern: A Lesson in Moral Responsibility." *EnSt.* 1998 Mar.; 79(2): 171-183. Notes. Lang.: Eng.
UK-England. 1967-1991. Critical studies. ■Analysis of Stoppard's film adaptation of his play *Rosencrantz and Guildenstern Are Dead.*

3981 Buchanan, J.R. *Visions of the Islands:* The Tempest *on film 1905-1991.* Oxford: Unpublished PhD, Univ. of Oxford; 1997. Notes. Biblio. [Abstract in *Aslib Index to Theses* 47-2825.] Lang.: Eng.
UK-England. USA. 1905-1991. Historcal studies. ■Chronologically organized critical production history of Shakespeare's play committed to film, examining especially the nature of the 'uninhabited island' as dramatic territory.

3982 Dodson, Mary Lynn. "*The French Lieutenant's Woman*: Pinter and Riesz's Adaptation of John Fowles' Adaptation." *LFQ.* 1998; 26(4): 296-303. Biblio. Illus.: Photo. B&W. 1. Lang.: Eng.
UK-England. USA. 1982. Critical studies. ■Analysis of Pinter's screenplay and Reisz's direction of the film version of Fowles' 1969 novel that emphasizes the book's sexual aspects.

3983 Evans, Nicola. "Games of Hide and Seek: Race, Gender and Drag in *The Crying Game* and *The Birdcage.*" *TextPQ.* 1998 July; 18(3): 199-216. Notes. Biblio. Lang.: Eng.
UK-England. USA. 1993-1996. Critical studies. ■Argues that contemporary film drag has become the vehicle for a new form of blackface for the nineties, disguised as 'subversive' performance. Cites examples in Neil Jordan's *The Crying Game* and Mike Nichol's *The Birdcage.*

3984 Gillen, Francis. "'My Dark Horse': Harold Pinter's Political Vision in His Screen Adaptation of Karen Blixen's *The Dreaming Child.*" *PintR.* 1998: 110-122. Notes. Biblio. Lang.: Eng.
UK-England. 1961-1997. Critical studies. ■Comparison of Isak Dinesen's short story and Pinter's screenplay adaptation to illustrate his belief that the playwright's imagination must be necessarily informed by a realistic political consciousness.

MEDIA: Film—Plays/librettos/scripts

3985 Hagen, W.S. "*Shadowlands* and the Redemption of Light." *LFQ.* 1998; 26(1): 10-15. Notes. Biblio. Illus.: Photo. B&W. 1. Lang.: Eng.

UK-England. 1993. Critical studies. ▪Analysis of Richard Attenborough's screen version of William Nicholson's adaptation of his own stage play.

3986 Martini, Emanuela. *Ombre che camminano: Shakespeare nel cinema.* (Walking Shadows: Shakespeare in the Cinema.) Torin: Lindau; 1998. 350 pp. Index. Biblio. Filmography. Lang.: Ita.

UK-England. 1900-1998. Critical studies. ▪Collection of essays on the cinematic adaptations of the theatre works of William Shakespeare.

3987 Murrell, Elizabeth. "History Revenged: Monty Python Translates Chrétien de Troyes's *Perceval, or the Story of the Grail* (Again)." *JFV.* 1998 Spr; 50(1): 50-62. Illus.: Photo. B&W. 1. Lang.: Eng.

UK-England. 1974. Critical studies. ▪Analysis of *Monty Python and the Holy Grail*, with attention to the way in which the film represents significant aspects of Chrétien's twelfth-century romance.

3988 Perlman, Doris. "50 Years After, *The Red Shoes* Dance On and On." *Dm.* 1998 Dec.; 72(12): 66-69. Illus.: Photo. Color. 4. Lang.: Eng.

UK-England. 1948. Critical studies. ▪Focuses on the continuing popularity of the Michael Powell-Emeric Pressburger film, often cited by dancers as the inspiration to make ballet a career.

3989 Sarris, Andrew. "An Archfiend Auteurist's Notes on Screenwriting." *Scenario.* 1998 Spr; 4(1): 4-5, 178. Illus.: Sketches. B&W. 1. Lang.: Eng.

UK-England. 1997. Critical studies. ▪Observations on screenwriting, with references to Simon Beaufoy's *The Full Monty.*

3990 Wickham, Philip. "L'homme dans l'oeuvre dans l'homme." (The Man in the Work in the Man.) *JCT.* 1998; 88: 151-153. Illus.: Photo. B&W. 1. Lang.: Fre.

UK-England. 1991. Historical studies. ▪Mixing of identities of Shakespeare and Prospero in Peter Greenaway's adaptation of Shakespeare's *The Tempest* as *Prospero's Books.*

3991 "Writing and Acting in *Young Frankenstein*: A Talk with Gene Wilder." *Scenario.* 1998 Spr; 4(1): 95-98, 184-188. Illus.: Dwg. B&W. 1. Lang.: Eng.

USA. 1998. Histories-sources. ▪Interview with actor and writer Gene Wilder about his work on *Young Frankenstein* and other collaborations with Mel Brooks.

3992 "Writing and Directing *Young Frankenstein*: A Talk with Mel Brooks." *Scenario.* 1998 Spr; 4(1): 99-101, 188-192. Illus.: Dwg. B&W. 1. Lang.: Eng.

USA. 1998. Histories-sources. ▪Interview with Brooks about his work on *Young Frankenstein.*

3993 "Writing and Directing *The Spanish Prisoner*: A Q&A with David Mamet." *Scenario.* 1998 Spr; 4(1): 150-152. Illus.: Dwg. B&W. 1. Lang.: Eng.

USA. 1998. Histories-sources. ▪Mamet's enigmatic answers to questions mailed to him about his work on *The Spanish Prisoner.*

3994 "Writing *The Black Doll*: A Talk with Edward Gorey." *Scenario.* 1998 Spr; 4(1): 171-177. Lang.: Eng.

USA. 1973-1997. Histories-sources. ▪Interview with Gorey about his animated film.

3995 "Adapting *Out of Sight*: A Talk with Scott Frank." *Scenario.* 1998 Sum; 4(2): 57-60, 199-202. Illus.: Sketches. B&W. 1. Lang.: Eng.

USA. 1998. Histories-sources. ▪Interview with the screenwriter about his film adaptation of a novel by Elmore Leonard.

3996 "Writing and Directing *Pi*: A Talk with Darren Aronofsky." *Scenario.* 1998 Sum; 4(2): 91-95, 202-204. Illus.: Sketches. B&W. 3. Lang.: Eng.

USA. 1998. Histories-sources. ▪Interview with the screenwriter and director.

3997 "Writing and Acting in *Slam*: A Talk with Sonja Sohn." *Scenario.* 1998; 4(3): 44-45, 189-190. Illus.: Sketches. B&W. 1. Lang.: Eng.

USA. 1998. Histories-sources. ▪Interview with Sohn on her role in creating the film *Slam.*

3998 "Writing *The Fishermen of Beaudrais*: A Talk with Ring Lardner Jr." *Scenario.* 1998 Sum; 4(2): 145-149, 205-206. Illus.: Sketches. Photo. B&W. 2. Lang.: Eng.

USA. 1943. Histories-sources. ▪Interview with the screenwriter about his collaboration with Dalton Trumbo on *The Fishermen of Beaudrais.*

3999 "Dalton Trumbo (1905-1976)." *Scenario.* 1998 Sum; 4(2): 150-151, 206-207. Lang.: Eng.

USA. 1905-1976. Biographical studies. ▪Profile of the screenwriter, with emphasis on his work on *The Fishermen of Beaudrais.* Includes excerpts from a 1969 interview with Gerald Pratley for *Cinema Canada.*

4000 "Writing and Directing *Eve's Bayou*: A Talk with Kasi Lemmons." *Scenario.* 1998 Sum; 4(2): 192-199. Illus.: Sketches. B&W. 1. Lang.: Eng.

USA. 1994-1998. Histories-sources. ▪Interview with screenwriter and director Kasi Lemmons.

4001 "Creating *Slam*: A Talk with Writer/Director Marc Levin, Writer/Producer Richard Stratton, Writer/Actor Bonz Malone." *Scenario.* 1998; 4(3): 35-41, 181-187. Illus.: Sketches. B&W. 3. Lang.: Eng.

USA. 1998. Histories-sources. ▪Interview with creators of the film *Slam.*

4002 "Writing and Acting in *Slam*: A Talk with Saul Williams." *Scenario.* 1998; 4(3): 42-43, 188-189. Illus.: Sketches. B&W. 1. Lang.: Eng.

USA. 1998. Histories-sources. ▪Interview with Williams on his role in creating the film *Slam.*

4003 "Is It Life or Is It Mamet?" *Econ.* 1998 Jan 31; 346(8053): 85-86. Illus.: Photo. B&W. 2. Lang.: Eng.

USA. 1998. Critical studies. ▪David Mamet's success as a screenwriter, with emphasis on his script for *Wag the Dog*, directed by Barry Levinson. Also notes his career as a film director.

4004 "It's Stupidity, Stupid." *Econ.* 1998 Sep 5; 348(8084): 79-80. Illus.: Photo. B&W. 1. Lang.: Eng.

USA. 1998. Critical studies. ▪Reasons for the popularity of crude comedy in recent American cinema, exemplified by the Farrelly Brothers' *There's Something About Mary.*

4005 Beard, John. "Science Fiction Films of the Eighties: 'Fin de Siècle' Before Its Time." *JPC.* 1998 Sum; 32(1): 1-13. Biblio. Lang.: Eng.

USA. 1981-1990. Critical studies. ▪Examines the predominance of the apocalyptic view of the future in science-fiction films during the 1980s.

4006 Begley, Varun. "On Adaptation: David Mamet and Hollywood." *ET.* 1998; 16(2): 165-176. Notes. Biblio. Lang.: Eng.

USA: Los Angeles, CA. 1980-1998. Critical studies. ▪Examines the creative expression in the commercial films of playwright David Mamet, including *Speed-the-Plow, About Last Night*, and *Sexual Perversity in Chicago.*

4007 Callens, Johan. "An American Abroad or Sam Shepard's Bodyguard." 183-202 in Versluys, Kristiaan, ed. *The Insular Dream: Obsession and Resistance.* Amsterdam: Free UP; 1995. 384 pp. (European Contributions to American Studies 35.) Lang.: Eng.

USA. 1970-1995. Critical studies. ▪Shepard's take on English and American national characteristics in *The Bodyguard*, his screen adaptation of Middleton and Rowley's *The Changeling.*

4008 Callens, Johan. "Through the Windows of Perception: Shepard's *Fool for Love* on the Screen." 83-112 in Callens, Johan. *American Literature and the Arts.* Brussels: VUB Press; 1991. 127 pp. Lang.: Eng.

USA. 1979. Critical studies. ▪Analysis of the screen version of *Fool for Love.*

4009 Carpenter, Mark Peter. *'Uneasy Lies the Head that Wears the Crown': The Gangster Genre, Shakespearean Tragedy, and the* Godfather *Trilogy.* North York, ON: York Univ; 1998. 201 pp. Notes. Biblio. [M.F.A. Thesis, Univ. Microfilms Order No. AAC MQ27330.] Lang.: Eng.

USA. 1971-1991. Critical studies. ▪Applies Robert Warshow's theoretical analysis to Francis Ford Coppola's *Godfather* trilogy and examines

MEDIA: Film—Plays/librettos/scripts

its links to tragedy and Shakespeare's *Henry IV, Parts 1 and 2* and *King Lear.*

4010 Gilmour, Heather. "Different, Except in a Different Way: Marriage, Divorce, and Gender in the Hollywood Comedy of Remarriage." *JFV.* 1998 Sum; 50(2): 26-39. Notes. Illus.: Photo. B&W. 2. Lang.: Eng.
USA. 1935-1942. Critical studies. ▪Includes brief discussion of several films, with more extensive analysis of *Bringing Up Baby* (1938) and *Love Crazy* (1941).

4011 Godin, Diane. "Le cinéma et son double." (Cinema and its Double.) *JCT.* 1998; 88: 102-107. Notes. Illus.: Photo. B&W. 4. Lang.: Fre.
USA. 1978. Critical studies. ▪Theatre and theatricality in director John Cassavetes' film *Opening Night.*

4012 Godin, Diane. "Richard III devant la caméra." (Richard III in Front of the Camera.) *JCT.* 1998; 88: 153-155. Illus.: Photo. B&W. 2. Lang.: Fre.
USA. UK-England. 1995-1996. Critical studies. ▪Similarities in two film adaptations of Shakespeare's *Richard III*: director Richard Loncraine's version and actor Al Pacino's *Looking for Richard.*

4013 Kaufman, Millard. "Recollection Without Tranquility." *Scenario.* 1998; 4(4): 10. Illus.: Dwg. B&W. 1. Lang.: Eng.
USA. 1917-1998. Histories-sources. ▪Kaufman's screenwriting experiences with emphasis on the 1950s.

4014 Lavoie, Pierre. "'Mort, où est ta victoire?'." ('Death, Where Is Thy Victory?'.) *JCT.* 1998; 88: 159. Illus.: Photo. B&W. 1. Lang.: Fre.
USA. 1971. Historical studies. ▪Theme of murder in Roman Polanski's adaptation of Shakespeare's *Macbeth.*

4015 Leight, Warren. "Movie Prison." *Scenario.* 1998; 4(4): 11, 192. Illus.: Sketches. B&W. 1. Lang.: Eng.
USA. 1998. Histories-sources. ▪Humorous account of the author's experiences writing for film, with reference to denial, anger, bargaining, and acceptance.

4016 Lesage, Marie-Christine. "Roméo selon Baz Luhrmann." (Romeo According to Baz Luhrmann.) *JCT.* 1998; 88: 150-151. Illus.: Photo. B&W. 1. Lang.: Fre.
USA. 1996. Critical studies. ▪Modernization and derision mix with tragedy in director Baz Luhrmann's adaptation of Shakespeare's *Romeo and Juliet.*

4017 McKelly, James C. "The Double Truth, Ruth: *Do the Right Thing* and the Culture of Ambiguity." *AfAmR.* 1998 Sum; 32(2): 215-227. Biblio. Lang.: Eng.
USA. 1989. Critical studies. ▪Ethical paradoxes facing African-Americans as reflected in Spike Lee's film.

4018 McMurtry, Larry. "Larry McMurtry on The Last Picture Show." *Scenario.* 1998; 4(4): 97. Lang.: Eng.
USA. 1971. Histories-sources. ▪Excerpts dealing with *The Last Picture Show* by McMurtry and Peter Bogdanovich from McMurtry's *Flim-Flam: Essays on Hollywood.*

4019 Nocenti, Annie. "Writing and Directing *Living Out Loud*: A Talk with Richard LaGravenese." *Scenario.* 1998; 4(4): 53-57, 183-186. Lang.: Eng.
USA. 1998. Histories-sources. ▪Interview with LaGravenese about the film, based on two short stories by Čechov, that he wrote and directed.

4020 Nocenti, Annie. "Adapting and Directing *The Last Picture Show*: A Talk with Peter Bogdanovich." *Scenario.* 1998; 4(4): 92-96, 186-190. Lang.: Eng.
USA. 1971-1998. Histories-sources. ▪Interview with Bogdanovich about his film adaptation of *The Last Picture Show* by Larry McMurtry.

4021 Nocenti, Annie. "Writing and Directing *Gods and Monsters*: A Talk with Bill Condon." *Scenario.* 1998; 4(4): 138-143, 190-191. Illus.: Sketches. B&W. 1. Lang.: Eng.
USA. 1998. Histories-sources. ▪Interview with Condon regarding his film about director James Whale.

4022 Prats, Armando José. "The Image of the Other and the Other *Dances With Wolves*: The Refigured Indian and the Textual Supplement." *JFV.* 1998 Spr; 50(1): 3-19. Illus.: Photo. B&W. 3. Lang.: Eng.
USA. 1990-1993. Critical studies. ▪Comparison of Kevin Costner's film *Dances With Wolves* and the five-hour ABC mini-series version aired in 1993.

4023 Roulston, Helen H. "Opera in Gangster Movies: From Capone to Coppola." *JPC.* 1998 Sum; 32(1): 99-111. Notes. Biblio. Lang.: Eng.
USA. 1932-1990. Critical studies. ▪Significance of opera in American gangster films, including Howard Hawks's *Scarface*, Brian DePalma's *The Untouchables*, Francis Ford Coppola's *Godfather III*, Richard Wilson's *Al Capone*, and Billy Wilder's *Some Like It Hot.*

4024 Rutter, Carol Chillington. "Snatched Bodies: Ophelia in the Grave." *SQ.* 1998 Fall; 49(3): 299-319. Notes. Lang.: Eng.
USA. UK-England. USSR. 1947-1990. Critical studies. ▪Interpretation of Ophelia in film versions of Shakespeare's *Hamlet* by Laurence Olivier, Grigorij Kozincev, and Franco Zeffirelli.

4025 Server, Lee. "Comrades in Arms." *Scenario.* 1998 Sum; 4(2): 4-5, 207-208. Illus.: Sketches. B&W. 1. Lang.: Eng.
USA. 1943-1998. Critical studies. ▪Introduction and background on the screenplay of *The Fishermen of Beaudrais* by Ring Lardner, Jr., and Dalton Trumbo, to be rereleased.

4026 Server, Lee. "Big Talk: Screenwriting in Pre-Code Hollywood, 1927-1934." *Scenario.* 1998; 4(4): 144-160. Lang.: Eng.
USA. 1927-1934. Historical studies. ▪The subjects of films before the introduction of the severely limiting Motion Picture Production Code, which included social and economic realities such as the condition of immigrants, drug use, rape, adultery, unwed pregnancy, and homosexuality.

4027 Stenberg, Douglas G. "Who Shot the Seagull? Anton Chekhov's Influence on Woody Allen's *Bullets Over Broadway.*" *LFQ.* 1998; 26(3): 204-213. Notes. Biblio. Illus.: Photo. B&W. 1. Lang.: Eng.
USA. 1994. Critical studies. ▪Comparison of Allen's film with Čechov's *Čajka (The Seagull).*

4028 Templeton, Alice. "The Confessing Animal in *sex, lies, and videotape.*" *JFV.* 1998 Sum; 50(2): 15-25. Notes. Illus.: Photo. B&W. 1. Lang.: Eng.
USA. 1989. Critical studies. ▪Analysis of Steven Soderbergh's film with emphasis on Foucault's notion of man as a confessing animal.

4029 Thaggert, Miriam. "Divided Images: Black Female Spectatorship and John Stahl's *Imitation of Life.*" *AfAmR.* 1998 Fall; 32(3): 481-491. Notes. Biblio. Lang.: Eng.
USA: Hollywood, CA. 1934. Critical studies. ▪Feminist analysis of John Stahl's cinematic adaptation of the Fannie Hurst novel, with an eye toward Black female viewer response.

4030 Tolchinsky, David E. "*The First Wife*: An Adaptation of Colette's *The Other Wife.*" *JFV.* 1998 Fall; 50(3): 68-71. Notes. Lang.: Eng.
USA. 1998. Critical studies. ▪Analysis of Douglas Heil's screenplay *The First Wife.*

4031 Vigeant, Louise. "Scènes de la vie de ville." (Scenes from City Life.) *JCT.* 1998; 88: 108-110. Notes. Illus.: Photo. B&W. 3. Lang.: Fre.
USA. 1994. Critical studies. ▪Blurring of fiction and reality in Louis Malle's 1994 film *Vanya on 42nd Street*, presenting a rehearsal of Čechov's *Uncle Vanya.*

4032 Winkler, Martin M. "The Roman Empire in American Cinema After 1945." *ClassJ.* 1998 Dec/Jan.; 93(2): 167-196. Notes. Biblio. Filmography. Lang.: Eng.
USA. 1945-1998. Critical studies. ▪Divergent views of the Roman Empire in post-World War II American movies.

Reference materials

4033 Razzakov, F. *Dos'e na zvezd (teatra i kino).* (The Story of the Stars of Stage and Cinema.) Moscow: ÉKSMO-Press; 1998. 752 pp. Lang.: Rus.
Russia. 1998. Biographical studies. ▪Profiles of stage and film actors.

MEDIA: Film

Relation to other fields

4034 Eyoh, Dickson. "Social Realist Cinema and Representations of Power in African Nationalist Discourse." *RAL.* 1998 Sum; 29 (2): 112-127. Notes. Biblio. Lang.: Eng.
Africa. 1990-1998. Critical studies. ■Development of political power and nationalist identity reflected in African film since the beginning of the 1990s.

4035 Frost, Derek Trowbridge. "Parallel Worlds, Convergent Aesthetics: Cabrera Infante's *Tres tristes tigres* and Fellini's *La dolce vita.*" *RomN.* 1997 Fall; 38(1): 3-14. Biblio. Lang.: Eng.
Spain. Italy. 1960-1967. Critical studies. ■Influence of Fellini's film on film critic Cabrera Infante's novel *Three Sad Tigers (Tres triste tigres).*

4036 "Mr. Bond." *Econ.* 1998 Feb 28; 346(8057): 61. Illus.: Photo. B&W. 1. Lang.: Eng.
UK. 1998. Historical studies. ■Reasons for refusing a knighthood to film star Sean Connery, including politicians' fear of enhancing Connery's political stand supporting Scottish nationalism.

4037 Beene, Geoffrey; Kalin, Tom; Mirabella, Grace; Yokobosky, Matthew. "Fashion and Film: A Symposium." *PerAJ.* 1998 Sep.; 20(3): 12-21. Illus.: Photo. B&W. 3. Lang.: Eng.
USA: New York, NY. 1997. Histories-sources. ■Transcript of a symposium held at the Whitney Museum of American Art regarding the mutual influence of fashion and film. The participants are actor/director Kalins, magazine editor Mirabella, fashion designer Beene, and curator of the museum's film and video collection Yokobosky.

4038 Springhall, John. "Censoring Hollywood: Youth, Moral Panic, and Crime/Gangster Movies of the 1930s." *JPC.* 1998 Win; 32 (3): 135-154. Notes. Biblio. Lang.: Eng.
USA. 1931-1940. Historical studies. ■Examines the public concern over the moral corruption of the country's youth because of gangster/crime films, leading to the toning down of the genre.

4039 Kenez, Peter. "Jewish Themes in Stalinist Films." *JPC.* 1998 Spr; 31(4): 159-169. Notes. Biblio. Lang.: Eng.
USSR. 1924-1953. Historical studies. ■Changing treatment of Jews in Soviet cinema during the reign of Stalin.

Theory/criticism

4040 Popovich, George Lee. *Structural Analyses of Selected Modern Science Fiction Films.* Columbus, OH: Ohio State Univ; 1987. 450 pp. Biblio. Notes. [Ph.D. Dissertation, Univ. Microfilms Order No. AAC 8717704.] Lang.: Eng.
USA. 1960-1981. Critical studies. ■Analysis of critical approaches to science-fiction films. Posits twelve categories of science-fiction films and reviews the critical methodologies applied to specific films.

Training

4041 Rustan, John. "Media Acting: An Affordable Reality with Portable Equipment." *TTop.* 1998 Sep.; 8(2): 205-218. Notes. Biblio. Append. Lang.: Eng.
USA. 1994-1998. Instructional materials. ■Provides a step-by-step approach and class outline for theatre departments contemplating the addition of media acting to their current curricula.

Mixed media

Performance/production

4042 Morgan, Robert C. "The Story of the Other." *PerAJ.* 1998 Jan.; 20(58): 55-60. Illus.: Photo. B&W. 3. Lang.: Eng.
France: Lyon. 1997. Historical studies. ■Report on the mixed media art biennial in Lyon.

4043 Sapienza, Annamaria. "The Theatrical Company of Giorgio Barberio Corsetti." *WES.* 1998 Win; 10(1): 67-72. Illus.: Photo. B&W. 3. Lang.: Eng.
Italy: Rome, Milan. 1985-1998. Historical studies. ■Profile of Corsetti, director of his own theatre company, with emphasis on his use of multimedia, including a collaboration with audio-visual installation company Studio Azzuro.

4044 O'Pray, Michael. "Tina Keane." *PM.* 1988; 53: 10-13. Illus.: Photo. B&W. 6. Lang.: Eng.
UK-England. 1970-1988. Biographical studies. ■Influences on the work of mixed media artist Keane, whose combined use of film, objects, and performance has been highly influential in the women's art movement.

4045 Dalton, Jennifer. "Ebon Fisher's AlulA Dimension." *PerAJ.* 1998 Jan.; 20(58): 62-70. Notes. Illus.: Photo. B&W. 8. Lang.: Eng.
USA. 1998. Critical studies. ■Defines the work of mixed media artist Fisher who uses a conglomerate of media (film, video, computers) to create what he calls 'media organisms'.

4046 Hood, Woodrow. "'The Reason I've Been Talking About All of These Dead People': Cultural Resistance in Laurie Anderson's *Nerve Bible.*" *JDTC.* 1998 Fall; 13(1): 161-175. Notes. Lang.: Eng.
USA. 1995. Critical studies. ■Examines the theoretical implications of Laurie Anderson's use of media technology to maintain audience attention while she uses content to engage audiences critically.

Plays/librettos/scripts

4047 Paventi, Eva. "Le langage pour le dire: Carole Nadeau." (The Language to Tell It With: Carole Nadeau.) *JCT.* 1998; 86: 17-22. Notes. Illus.: Photo. B&W. 3. Lang.: Fre.
Canada: Quebec, PQ, Montreal, PQ. 1998. Biographical studies. ■Integration of media arts in director/playwright Carole Nadeau's creations: *Chaos K.O. Chaos, Contes pour l'oeil avide (Stories For the Avid Eye), Rouge (Red)* and *La Peau des Yeux (The Skin of the Eyes).*

Theory/criticism

4048 Hussey, Michael J.; Staub, August W. "Saints and Cyborgs: Mystical Performance Spaces (Re)visioned." *JDTC.* 1998 Fall; 13(1): 177-182. Notes. Lang.: Eng.
North America. 1998. Critical studies. ■Examines the use of cyberspace as a site for performance. Contrasts the limited space of medieval theatre with unlimited video space.

Video forms

Design/technology

4049 Boepple, Leanne. "In Memoriam: William Greenfield." *TCI.* 1998 May; 32(5): 16. Lang.: Eng.
USA. 1930-1998. Biographical studies. ■Obituary for the veteran television lighting designer.

4050 Calhoun, John. "Burmans Take On ..." *TCI.* 1998 Mar.; 32(3): 32-33. Illus.: Photo. B&W. Color. 12. Lang.: Eng.
USA: Hollywood, CA. 1998. Technical studies. ■Profile of married make-up artists Tom Burman and Bari Dreiband-Burman, who develop special make-up effects for television and film.

4051 Calhoun, John. "World Gone CAD!" *TCI.* 1998 Mar.; 32(3): 38-41. Illus.: Photo. Design. Dwg. Photo. B&W. Color. 22. Lang.: Eng.
USA: Hollywood, CA. 1998. Technical studies. ■Increasing use of computer-aided design tools in the area of television production design.

4052 Calhoun, John. "Merlin Mesmerizes Emmy." *TCI.* 1998 Nov.; 32(10): 19. Lang.: Eng.
USA: Pasadena, CA. 1998. Technical studies. ■Report on the technical achievement and production design awards garnered by the television mini-series *Merlin,* with a quick rundown of other technical awards handed out at the Primetime Creative Emmy Awards.

4053 Calhoun, John. "An Otherworldly World." *TCI.* 1998 Dec.; 32(11): 5-8. Illus.: Photo. Color. 4. Lang.: Eng.
USA. 1998. Technical studies. ■Shawn Dudley's costumes for a masquerade ball scene in the soap opera *Another World.*

4054 Calhoun, John. "Order in the Court." *LDim.* 1998 Oct.; 22(9): 62-65. Illus.: Photo. Lighting. B&W. 9. Lang.: Eng.
USA. 1998. Historical studies. ■Reports on director of photography Billy Dickson's new lighting design for television's *Ally MacBeal,* created by David E. Kelley.

4055 Cashill, Robert. "Purchasing Power." *LDim.* 1998 Apr.; 22(3): 40-43, 87, 89. Notes. Illus.: Photo. Lighting. 4. Lang.: Eng.
USA: West Chester, PA. 1998. Technical studies. ■Examines the lighting design by Chuck Lester for QVC Studio Park, the cable television home

MEDIA: Video forms—Design/technology

shopping network, with emphasis on the unique requirements of lighting a 24-hour television event.

4056 McHugh, Catherine. "Rich Claffey and Marty Fuller." *TCI*. 1998 May; 32(5): 24-25. Illus.: Photo. Color. 1. Lang.: Eng.
USA: New York, NY. 1998. Biographical studies. ■Profile of head electrician Claffey and head carpenter Fuller for 1998 Grammy Awards telecast held at Radio City Music Hall.

Performance/production

4057 Ovčinnikova, S. "Stradanija teatra na TV." (The Suffering of Theatre on TV.) *TeatZ*. 1998; 4: 28-30. Lang.: Rus.
1998. Critical studies. ■Examines the lack of emotional impact of theatrical productions broadcast on television.

4058 Lévesque, Solange. "Fassbinder: du théâtre à un cinéma théâtral." (Fassbinder: From Theatre to Theatrical Cinema.) *JCT*. 1998; 88: 111-113. Illus.: Photo. B&W. 5. Lang.: Fre.
East Germany: Berlin. 1969-1982. Biographical studies. ■Theatrical influences on work of director Rainer Werner Fassbinder, with special attention to his televised mini-series *Berlin Alexanderplatz*.

4059 Rosiny, Claudia. "Bewegungszeit und Zeit in Bewegung." (Time of Movement and Time in Movement.) *Tanzd*. 1998; 41(2): 10-13. Notes. Illus.: Photo. B&W. 3. Lang.: Ger.
Europe. 1970-1998. Critical studies. ■Analyzes specific time aspects used in video dance. Describes the typical characteristics of slow-motion, time-lapse and other effects that enhance video dance.

4060 "One German at Least Is Retiring." *Econ*. 1998 Jan 3; 346(8049): 48. Illus.: Sketches. B&W. 1. Lang.: Eng.
Germany. 1998. Historical studies. ■Acknowledgement of the final episode for Germany's most popular TV show, *Derrick*, signing off after twenty-three years on the air.

4061 Schmoll, Linda Brigitte. *Goethe on Film: Television Adaptations of 'Goetz von Berlichingen', 'Egmont', and 'Stella'*. Waterloo, ON: Univ. of Waterloo; 1998. 212 pp. Notes. Biblio. [Ph.D. Dissertation, Univ. Microfilms Order No. AAC NQ30642.] Lang.: Eng.
Germany. 1965-1997. Historical studies. ■Analysis of six film adaptations of works by Goethe, considered as important works in Goethe reception studies: Gert Westphal's and Wolfgang Liebeneiner's versions of *Götz von Berlichingen*, Helmut Schiemann's and Franz Peter Wirth's films of *Egmont* and Franz Joseph Wild's and Thomas Langhoff's productions of *Stella*.

4062 Marzullo, Gigi. *Stelle di notte. Ventidue donne di raccontano. Sottovoce.* (Night Stars: Twenty-two Women Tell About Themselves, In a Low Voice.) Venice and Rome: Marsilio, RAI-ERI; 1998. 190 pp. (Gli specchi della memoria.) Pref. Lang.: Ita.
Italy. 1998. Histories-sources. ■Twenty-two television interviews of Italian actresses and famous women.

4063 Menduni, Enrico. *La televisione.* (Television.) Bologna: Il Mulino; 1998. 127 pp. (Farsi un'idea 17.) Lang.: Ita.
Italy. 1940-1998. Historical studies. ■A brief history of television in Europe and in the world. Its strong impact on culture and social behavior.

4064 Cook, Hardy Merrill, III. *Reading Shakespeare on Television.* College Park, MD: Univ. of Maryland; 1988. 330 pp. Biblio. Notes. [Ph.D. Dissertation, Univ. Microfilms Order No. AAC 8827056.] Lang.: Eng.
UK-England. 1982-1983. Critical studies. ■Explores the elements unique to two recent productions of Shakespeare's *King Lear* conceived for television: Jonathan Miller's for the BBC series and Michael Elliott's for Granada Television.

4065 de Gay, Jane. "Colour Me Beautiful? Clothes Consciousness in the Open University/BBC Video Production of *Top Girls*." 102-113 in Rabillard, Sheila, ed. *Essays on Caryl Churchill: Contemporary Representations.* Winnipeg, MB/ Buffalo, NY: Blizzard; 1998. 224 pp. Biblio. Notes. Illus.: Photo. 6. Lang.: Eng.
UK-England. 1982-1991. Critical studies. ■Analyzes the language of costume in the video production of Caryl Churchill's *Top Girls* as an articulation of specific fashion 'dialects.' Video produced by BBC/Open University, directed by Max Stafford-Clark, and featuring Fiona Shaw.

4066 Tanitch, Robert. "Sir Simon Canterville." *PlPl*. Mar 1998; 520: 9. Illus.: Photo. B&W. 1. Lang.: Eng.
UK-England. USA. 1943-1998. Historical studies. ■Four actors' interpretations of title character of Oscar Wilde's *The Canterville Ghost*: Charles Laughton in Jules Dassin's film version, Sir John Gielgud in Paul Bogart's television version, Patrick Stewart in Syd Macartney's television version and Ian Richardson in Crispin Reece's television version.

4067 "'Buffalo Bob' Smith." *PuJ*. 1998 Fall; 50(1): 34. Lang.: Eng.
USA. 1918-1998. Biographical studies. ■Obituary for Smith who was host of *The Howdy Doody Show*.

4068 Brook, Vincent. "Checks and Imbalances: Political Economy and the Rise and Fall of *East Side/West Side*." *JFV*. 1998 Fall; 50(3): 24-39. Notes. Illus.: Photo. B&W. 4. Lang.: Eng.
USA. 1963-1964. Historical studies. ■Social commentary on the short-lived television series *East Side/West Side*, including background information on network policies.

4069 Fink, Edward J. "Television Music: Automaticity and the Case of Mike Post." *JFV*. 1998 Fall; 50(3): 40-53. Notes. Tables. Append. Illus.: Photo. B&W. 1. Lang.: Eng.
USA. 1998. Historical studies. ■The theory and practice of scoring a television production, with specific reference to the work of composer Mike Post.

4070 Halley, Richard. "Television: Wayne Martin and the 'Lil' Iguana'." *PuJ*. 1998 Fall; 50(1): 31. Illus.: Photo. B&W. 1. Lang.: Eng.
USA: Boston, MA. 1998. Biographical studies. ■Profile of puppeteer Martin, who has been chosen to voice and manipulate a Boston television children's character, Lil' Iguana.

4071 Kieth, Chris. "Image After Image: The Video Art of Bill Viola." *PerAJ*. 1998 May; 20(2): 1-16. Notes. Illus.: Photo. B&W. 8. Lang.: Eng.
USA: New York, NY. 1976-1998. Critical studies. ■Analysis of video artist Bill Viola's work on the occasion of a retrospective at the Whitney Museum of American Art.

4072 Messmore, Francis B. *An Exploratory Investigation of Below-the-Line Cost Components for Soap Opera Production in New York City.* New York, NY: Pace Univ; 1988. 218 pp. Biblio. Notes. [Ph.D. Dissertation, Univ. Microfilms Order No. AAC 8914658.] Lang.: Eng.
USA: New York, NY. 1950-1988. Histories-specific. ■Managerial analysis of the New York daytime serial industry. Suggests production costs could be better controlled by centralizing production facilities.

Plays/librettos/scripts

4073 Dmitriev, L.A. *Zakony dramaturgii: Teorija i metod tvorčestva.* (The Rules of Playwriting: Theory and Method of the Art.) Moscow: Dialog-MGU; 1998. 124 pp. Lang.: Rus.
1998. Instructional materials. ■Beginner's guide to the art of television playwriting and journalism.

4074 Lévesque, Solange. "L'autonomie d'une oeuvre." (Autonomy of a Work of Art.) *JCT*. 1998; 88: 144-145. Illus.: Photo. B&W. 2. Lang.: Fre.
Canada. 1998. Critical studies. ■Director Francis Leclerc's successes and failures creating a 62-minute video condensation of Robert Lepage's epic *Les Sept Branches de la rivière Ota (The Seven Streams of the River Ota)*.

4075 Murphy, Sarah. "Drama as Docufiction." *CTR*. 1998 Spr; 94: 36-41. Illus.: Photo. B&W. 2. Lang.: Eng.
Canada. 1989-1995. Histories-sources. ■Writer/director Leila Sujir on treatment of issues such as racism and immigration in her video *The Dreams of the Night Cleaners*, along with excerpts from the script.

4076 Herren, Graley V. "Unfamiliar Chambers: Power and Pattern in Samuel Beckett's *Ghost Trio*." *JBeckS*. 1998 Sum; 8(1): 72-100. Notes. Lang.: Eng.
France. Ireland. 1976. Critical studies. ■Power and status in Beckett's teleplay.

MEDIA: Video forms—Plays/librettos/scripts

4077 Herren, Graley V. *The Ghost in the Machine: A Study of Samuel Beckett's Teleplays.* Gainesville, FL: Florida State Univ; 1998. 229 pp. Notes. Biblio. [Ph.D. Dissertation, Univ. Microfilms Order No. AAC 9903597.] Lang.: Eng.
France. 1965-1989. Critical studies. ▪Examines the teleplays of Samuel Beckett: *Eh Joe, Ghost Trio, ... but the clouds ..., Quad,* and *Nacht und Träume.* Focuses on how the playwright adapted his work for the limits and potentials of television.

4078 Eisen, Kurt. "O'Neill on Screen." 116-134 in Manheim, Michael, ed. *The Cambridge Companion to Eugene O'Neill.* Cambridge/New York, NY: Cambridge UP; 1998. 256 pp. (Cambridge Companions to Literature.) Index. Biblio. Notes. Illus.: Photo. 2. Lang.: Eng.
USA. 1935-1988. Critical studies. ▪The expanding production history of the plays of Eugene O'Neill in film and television.

4079 Schely-Newman, Esther. "Performing Access: Tim Miller, Larry Sanders, and Jay Leno." *TextPQ.* 1998 Apr.; 18(2): 137-146. Biblio. Lang.: Eng.
USA. 1995. Critical studies. ▪Analysis of the script for the 'Performance Artist' episode of *The Larry Sanders Show.* Gay performer Tim Miller contributed to the script, and on the show is seen performing his *My Queer Body* on Jay Leno's *Tonight Show.* Discusses the political and cultural implications of the episode in light of Miller losing his NEA grants because of Congressional pressure.

4080 Worland, Rick. "The Other Living-Room War: Prime Time Combat Series, 1962-1975." *JFV.* 1998 Fall; 50(3): 3-23. Notes. Illus.: Photo. B&W. 2. Lang.: Eng.
USA. 1962-1975. Critical studies. ▪History of television series dealing with World War II and the Korean war.

Relation to other fields

4081 Haynes, Jonathan; Onookome, Okome. "Evolving Popular Media: Nigerian Video Films." *RAL.* 1998 Fall; 29(3): 106-128. Notes. Biblio. Lang.: Eng.
Nigeria. 1992-1998. Historical studies. ▪Discusses the collapse of the Nigerian film industry and the boom in production of movies with video recorders.

4082 "'Seinfield,' LA's Trojan Horse." *Econ.* 1998 Apr 11; 347(8063): 24. Illus.: Sketches. B&W. 1. Lang.: Eng.
USA. 1998. Critical studies. ▪Light comparison of the socioeconomic differences between New York and Los Angeles, using the TV sitcom *Seinfeld.*

4083 Nadel, Alan. "The New Frontier, the Old West, and the Free World: The Cultural Politics of 'Adult Western' TV Dramas." *AmerD.* 1998 Spr; 7(2): 1-23. Notes. Biblio. Lang.: Eng.
USA. 1957-1960. Historical studies. ▪The changing sociopolitical landscape of the United States as reflected in television westerns of the late 1950s.

4084 Watson, Ian. "News, Television, and Performance: The Case of the Los Angeles Riots." *NTQ.* 1998 Aug.; 14(3): 210-219. Biblio. [Issue 55.] Lang.: Eng.
USA: Los Angeles, CA. 1992. Critical studies. ▪Considers to what extent a news event is shaped by the medium of television, using as an example the six days of riots in Los Angeles after the acquittal of police officers charged in the beating of Rodney King.

MIME

General

Performance/production

4085 Bannerman, Eugen; Pecknold, Adrian. "The Canadian Mime Theatre: A Thirty-Year Retrospective." *CTR.* Fall 1998; 96: 83-86 . Illus.: Photo. B&W. 1. Lang.: Eng.
Canada: Niagara-on-the-Lake, ON. 1940-1978. Histories-sources. ▪Adrian Pecknold's background as a *commedia dell'arte* performer and mime, and his work with the Canadian Mime Theatre (Niagara-on-the-Lake, ON, 1969-78).

4086 Král, Karel. "Ctibor Turba and the Alfreds/Ctibor Turba et ses Alfred." *CzechT.* 1998 June; 14: 39-44. Illus.: Photo. B&W. 5. Lang.: Eng, Fre.
Czech Republic. 1966-1998. Historical studies. ▪Portrait of mime, director, educationalist and playwright Ctibor Turba and mime theatre Alfred ve dvoře.

4087 Åkesson, Birgit. "Jean-Gaspard Deburau, den franska mimen och pantomimen." (Jean-Gaspard Deburau, the French Mime and Pantomime.) *Danst.* 1998; 8(4): 9-11. Illus.: Dwg. B&W. Lang.: Swe.
France. 1700-1998. Critical studies. ▪Regards the merits of mime versus pantomime, with reference to Jean-Gaspard Deburau.

4088 Marc, Yves; Leabhart, Sally, transl. "Disciples and Traitors: Such a Shame, Too Bad, So Much the Better..." *MimeJ.* 1998 ; 19: 68-75. Illus.: Photo. B&W. 2. Lang.: Eng.
France: Paris. 1998. Histories-sources. ▪The author, one of the artistic directors of Théâtre du Movement, on the influence of Etienne Decroux.

4089 Mingalon, Jean-Louis; Leabhart, Sally, transl. "An Interview with Marie-Hélène Dasté." *MimeJ.* 1998; 19: 10-27. Illus.: Photo. B&W. 7. Lang.: Eng.
France: Paris. 1913-1992. Histories-sources. ▪Interview in which Dasté speaks about her father Jacques Copeau, his Vieux Colombier school, which she attended, and the school's mission.

4090 Soum, Corinne; Leabhart, Sally, transl.; Leabhart, Thomas, transl. "A Little History of a Great Transmission or Simplon's Tunnel." *MimeJ.* 1998; 19: 52-67. Notes. Biblio. Illus.: Photo. B&W. 3. Lang.: Eng.
France: Paris. UK-England: London. 1968-1998. Histories-sources. ▪Etienne Decroux's longtime assistant, now director of Théâtre de l'Ange Fou in London, relates her experiences with the master and his influence upon her artistic mission.

4091 Leabhart, Thomas. "Does Etienne Decroux's 'Great Project' Exist?" *MimeJ.* 1998; 19: 110-133. Illus.: Photo. B&W. 7. Lang.: Eng.
USA. France. 1920-1998. Critical studies. ▪Meditation on Decroux's concept of the actor being central to the dramatic form as opposed to playwright and text. Corollaries are also drawn between his work and that of Jerzy Grotowski.

4092 Sims, Caitlin; Caravaglia, Tom, photo. "A Meeting of Like Mimes." *Dm.* 1998 Mar.; 72(3): 76-78. Illus.: Photo. Color. 2. Lang.: Eng.
USA: New York, NY. 1998. Historical studies. ▪Report on a photo session involving Marcel Marceau and Bill Irwin, with attention to the similarities and differences between the two.

English pantomime

Performance/production

4093 O'Brien, John. "Harlequin Britain: Eighteenth-Century Pantomime and the Cultural Location of Entertainment(s)." *TJ.* 1998 Dec.; 50(4): 489-510. Notes. Illus.: Dwg. B&W. 1. Lang.: Eng.
England. 1700-1800. Critical studies. ▪Focuses on scenery, stage effects and the performers' bodies to analyze cultural anxieties about the materiality of the stage and what these elements reveal about the genre's relation to imperialism. Takes David Garrick's Christmas pantomime, *Harlequin's Invasion,* as a paradigm for the study.

Pantomime

Performance/production

4094 Perroux, Alain. "'L'Anniversaire de l'infante' de Franz Schreker." (Franz Schreker's *Birthday of the Princess.*) *ASO.* 1998 Sep/Oct.; 186: 91. Illus.: Photo. B&W. 1. Lang.: Fre.
Germany. 1908-1923. Historical studies. ▪Brief description of Schreker's pantomime, based on Oscar Wilde's short story *The Birthday of the Little Princess,* with reference to the operatic adaptation *Der Zwerg* by Alexander Zemlinsky, libretto by Georg C. Klaren, based on the same source. Reference to Schreker's later suite for orchestra derived from the pantomime.

MIXED ENTERTAINMENT

General

Design/technology

4095 McHugh, Catherine. "Presenting the Piano Men: Steve Cohen Grandly Produces Billy Joel's and Elton John's Solo Tours, Then Sets Them Up *Face to Face*." *LDim.* 1998 July; 22(6): 48-53, 97-102. Illus.: Photo. Lighting. Color. 9. Lang.: Eng.

Australia. 1998. Technical studies. ■Examines the lighting design of Steve Cohen for the *Face to Face* Australian tour of pop performers Billy Joel and Elton John.

4096 Moles, Steve. "Genesis Begins Again." *TCI.* 1998 May; 32(5): 9-11. Illus.: Photo. Color. 1. Lang.: Eng.

Europe. 1998. Technical studies. ■Stripped-back production design for the European tour of the rock group Genesis.

4097 McHugh, Catherine. "It's a Spiceworld After All." *TCI.* 1998 Dec.; 32(11): 4-5. Illus.: Photo. Color. 2. Lang.: Eng.

UK-England. 1998. Technical studies. ■Mike Dolling's sound design and Pete Barnes' lighting concept for the 1998 tour of the teeny-bopper vocal group The Spice Girls.

4098 French, Liz. "In Memoriam: Frederic Paddock Hope." *TCI.* 1998 Apr.; 32(4): 12-13. Lang.: Eng.

USA. 1930-1998. Biographical studies. ■Obituary for one of the original master planners for Walt Disney World.

4099 McHugh, Catherine. "Double Header: How Two Lighting Designers Used One Lighting System to Create Two Distinct Shows for the B-52s/Pretenders Tour." *LDim.* 1998 Nov.; 22(10): 80-85, 174-175. Illus.: Photo. Lighting. B&W. 5. Lang.: Eng.

USA. 1998. Historical studies. ■Lighting designers Norman Schwab and Alan Parker's views on the challenges inherent in designing lighting for the concert.

4100 McHugh, Catherine. "Tom Strahan/Scale Design." *TCI.* 1998 Nov.; 32(10): 34-39. Illus.: Photo. Color. B&W. 5. Lang.: Eng.

USA: San Francisco, CA. 1976-1998. Technical studies. ■Profile of scenic designer for rock concerts and corporate events, Strahan, and his company Scale Design.

4101 McHugh, Catherine. "Power and Beauty." *LDim.* 1998 Jan-Feb.; 22(1): 50-55, 87-92. Illus.: Photo. Lighting. Color. 15. Lang.: Eng.

USA. 1997-1998. Critical studies. ■Examines the lighting design work of Graeme Nicol on two touring productions organized by pop singer Sarah McLachlan: her *Surfacing* tour and the all-women's *Lilith Fair* festival.

4102 McHugh, Catherine. "Dance Partners." *LDim.* 1998 Jan-Feb.; 22(1): 60-67. Illus.: Photo. Lighting. Color. 7. Lang.: Eng.

USA. 1997. Critical studies. ■Examines the work of lighting designers Steve Cohen and Curry Grant on pop music group Fleetwood Mac's reunion tour.

4103 McHugh, Catherine. "Bridges to Babylon." *LDim.* 1998 Mar.; 22(2): 54-59, 86-94. Illus.: Photo. Sketches. 13. Lang.: Eng.

USA. 1997-1998. Critical studies. ■Examines the work of lighting designer Patrick Woodroffe and set architect Mark Fisher on the Rolling Stones' *Bridges to Babylon* tour.

4104 McHugh, Catherine. "The Cats Came Back." *LDim.* 1998 Apr.; 22(3): 44-49, 77-80. Notes. Illus.: Photo. Lighting. 10. Lang.: Eng.

USA. 1998. Technical studies. ■Examines the lighting design and requirements by Jim Chapman for the rock group Aerosmith's *Nine Lives* tour.

4105 McHugh, Catherine. "Tailor Made: LD Howard Ungerleider Gives Van Halen's Current Tour a Custom Fit." *LDim.* 1998 July; 22(6): 66-69, 102-104. Illus.: Photo. Lighting. Color. 5. Lang.: Eng.

USA. 1998. Technical studies. ■Examines the lighting design by Howard Ungerleider for the Van Halen pop music tour.

4106 McHugh, Catherine. "Power Pop that Rocks: Lighting Designer Stan Crocker Applies Some Hard Edges to Hanson's *Albertane* Tour." *LDim.* 1998 Oct.; 22(9): 66-69. Illus.: Photo. Lighting. B&W. 7. Lang.: Eng.

USA. 1998. Historical studies. ■Lighting designer Stan Crocker on his design for pop rock group Hanson's *Albertane* tour.

4107 McHugh, Catherine. "Second Coming: Building on Last Summer's Success, the Lilith Fair Continues to Celebrate." *LDim.* 1998 Nov.; 22(10): 102-106. Illus.: Photo. Lighting. B&W. 7. Lang.: Eng.

USA. 1998. Historical studies. ■Recounts lighting designer Graeme B. Nicol's experiences lighting the second Lilith Fair tour.

4108 Moen, Debi. "Rimes and Reason." *LD&A.* 1998 Sep.; 28(9): 46-49. Illus.: Photo. Color. 6. Lang.: Eng.

USA. 1998. Technical studies. ■Peter Morse's lighting for country singers LeAnn Rimes and Bryan White's 1998 concert tour.

4109 Mumm, Robert C. "Disney's Light Magic." *TD&T.* 1998 Win; 34(1): 18-26. Illus.: Photo. Diagram. Lighting. Color. 9. Lang.: Eng.

USA: Anaheim, CA. 1998. Technical studies. ■Show control, light plot, sound equipment, and floats for the 'Light Magic' show presented at Disneyland.

4110 Rubin, Judith. "Landmark Entertainment Group." *TCI.* 1998 Nov.; 32(10): 40-43. Illus.: Photo. Color. 7. Lang.: Eng.

USA: Hollywood, CA. 1970-1998. Historical studies. ■Profile of the company specializing in theme-park attractions.

Institutions

4111 Behrendt, Eva. "'Stoppt den Castorf'." ('Stop Castorf'.) *TZ.* 1998; 6: 34-37. Illus.: Photo. B&W. 4. Lang.: Ger.

Germany: Giessen. 1982-1998. Historical studies. ■Describes the institute 'Angewandte Theaterwissenschaft' and its yearly festival 'diskurs' where directors and groups from so-called Giessener School present their performances between culture industry and free scene.

4112 McConachie, Bruce A. "Museum Theatre and the Problem of Respectability for Mid-Century Urban Americans." 65-80 in Engle, Ron, ed.; Miller, Tice L., ed. *The American Stage: Social and Economic Issues from the Colonial Period to the Present.* Cambridge: Cambridge UP; 1993. 320 pp. Pref. Notes. Index. Lang.: Eng.

USA: New York, NY. 1840-1880. Historical studies. ■Examines how the theatre responded to social tensions and issues such as the rise of respectability, through the prism of P.T. Barnum's American Museum and the construction of respectable modes of entertainment.

4113 Von Geldern, James R. *Festivals of the Revolution, 1917-1920: Art and Theater in the Formation of Soviet Culture.* Providence, RI: Brown Univ; 1987. 171 pp. Notes. Biblio. [Ph.D. Dissertation, Univ. Microfilms Order No. AAC 8715579.] Lang.: Eng.

USSR. 1917-1920. Historical studies. ■The political intent and creative cultural environments of the mass festivals of the newly formed Soviet Union.

Performance spaces

4114 Nobling, Torsten. "Nalen: Där allting händer och mycket fötter." (Nalen: Where Everything Happens and Many Feet.) *ProScen.* 1998; 22(4): 14-17. Illus.: Photo. Plan. B&W. Color. Lang.: Swe.

Sweden: Stockholm. 1889-1998. Historical studies. ■Presentation of the old dance palace, with reference to its history as a temple of jazz, and now the restoration to former beauty under the name Nationalpalatset.

4115 French, Liz. "Merv Is So Money." *TCI.* 1998 Nov.; 32(10): 14-19. Illus.: Photo. Color. 1. Lang.: Eng.

USA: Los Angeles, CA. 1998. Critical studies. ■Report on Merv Griffin's new supper and swing music venue, the Coconut Club, with an appraisal of its sound, stage, lighting aspects.

MIXED ENTERTAINMENT: General

Performance/production

4116 Seitinger, Astrid. "Strassentheater–Schmelztiegel der Formen." (Street Theatre–a Melting Pot of Forms.) *MuK.* 1998; 40 (2-4): 67-75. Notes. Lang.: Ger.
Austria. 1953-1998. Critical studies. ■Defines street theatre as outdoor theatre using different forms to attract the audience. Describes the performer Alain Stan and the street theatre 'vis plastica'.

4117 Cashman, Cheryl. "Clown Noir." *CTR.* 1998 Sum; 95: 70-78. Illus.: Photo. B&W. 9. Lang.: Eng.
Canada. 1980-1998. Historical studies. ■Canada's dark clowns and buffoons in the traditions of clown teacher Richard Pochinko and buffoon teacher Philippe Gaulier.

4118 Wickham, Philip. "Huy-Phong Doàn: Poursuivre une tradition antique dans la modernité." (Huy-Phong Doàn: Pursuing an Ancient Tradition in Modernity.) *JCT.* 1998; 87: 175-180. Illus.: Photo. B&W. 4. Lang.: Fre.
Canada: Montreal, PQ. 1992-1998. Biographical studies. ■Huy-Phong Doàn's background in martial arts and stage combat, culminating in directing *La Légende du manuel sacré (The Legend of the Sacred Handbook)*, produced by Voies Obscures, an adaptation of Jin Yong's *The Joke of Life.*

4119 Rohlehr, Gordon. "'We Getting the Kaiso We Deserve': Calypso and the World Music Market." *TDR.* 1998 Fall; 42(3): 82-95. Notes. Illus.: Photo. B&W. 4. Lang.: Eng.
Caribbean. 1933-1998. Historical studies. ■Discusses the history of calypso music and its present place in the world market. Includes the lyrics to three songs of different periods: 'Graf Zeppelin' (1933), 'The Yankee Gone' (1956), and 'Calypso Music' (1987).

4120 Johansson, Kerstin. "Amaryllis på Tropicana." (Amaryllis at the Tropicana.) *Danst.* 1998; 8(6): 44-45. Illus.: Photo. Color. Lang.: Swe.
Cuba: Havana. 1939. Historical studies. ■Report on the Tropicana show, with an interview with one of the dancers, Amaryllis Pons.

4121 Baldwin, Elizabeth. "John Seckerston: The Earl of Derby's Bearward." *MET.* 1998; 20: 95-103. Notes. Lang.: Eng.
England. 1517-1616. Historical studies. ■Assesses records relating to John Seckerston (aka Sakarston, Sackerson, or Secaston) to determine whether the man described as 'the Earl of Derby's bearward' was also the wealthy innkeeper of the Bear Inn at Nantwich.

4122 Butterworth, Philip. "Royal Firework Theatre: The Fort Holding, Part III." *RORD.* 1998; 37: 99-112. Notes. Biblio. Illus.: Dwg. B&W. 2. Lang.: Eng.
England. 1501-1600. Historical studies. ■Development of the sixteenth-century pyrotechnical form of entertainment known as 'fort holding'.

4123 Goslar, Lotte. "From Dresden to Hollywood." *Dm.* 1998 Feb.; 72(2): 78-81. Illus.: Photo. B&W. 6. Lang.: Eng.
Germany: Dresden. USA: Los Angeles, CA. 1907-1997. Histories-sources. ■Excerpts from the autobiography of the comic dance performer, *What's So Funny?* (Amsterdam: Harwood Academic, 1998). Focuses on her L.A.-based troupe the Pantomime Circus.

4124 Koegler, Horst. "Lotte Goslar." *Dm.* 1998 Jan.; 72(1): 122-123. Illus.: Photo. B&W. 1. Lang.: Eng.
Germany. USA. 1907-1997. Biographical studies. ■Obituary for Goslar, a comic dance performer who was born in Germany and fled the Nazis in World War II. Her act included elements of cabaret, mime, and dance.

4125 Croce, Marcella. *Manifestations of the Chivalric Tradition in Sicily.* Madison, WI: Univ. of Wisconsin; 1988. 359 pp. Notes. Biblio. [Ph.D. Dissertation, Univ. Microfilms Order No. AAC 8820040.] Lang.: Ita.
Italy. 1500-1985. Histories-specific. ■The development and diffusion of the chivalric tradition in Sicily over the centuries, with detailed analyses of its manifestations in storytelling, folk poetry, puppet shows, folk festivals and art.

4126 Viazzi, Cesare. *Le maschere genovesi. Dal Signor Regina al Gabibbo.* (Genovese Masks: From Mister Regina to Gabibbo.) Genoa: De Ferrari; 1998. 71 pp. Pref. Illus.: Photo. Sketches. Print. B&W. 4. Lang.: Ita.
Italy: Genoa. 1700-1998. Histories-reconstruction. ■A brief reconstruction of the characters and masks belonging to the Genoese theatre tradition.

4127 Lahr, John. "The Izzard King." *NewY.* 1998 6 Apr.: 80-85. Illus.: Photo. Color. 1. Lang.: Eng.
North America. UK-England. 1998. Historical studies. ■The North American tour of English comedian Eddie Izzard.

4128 Harley, James. "The Aesthetics of Death: The Theatrical Elaboration of Ancient Roman Blood Spectacles." *THSt.* 1998; 53: 89-98. Notes. Lang.: Eng.
Roman Empire. Historical studies. ■Examines the dramatic and performative aspects of 'blood spectacles' in the Roman era, and attempts to elucidate an aesthetic for this form, in relation to other popular Roman theatrical entertainments.

4129 Gaganova, A. "Star'e berem!: Žiteli Jaroslavlja pomogajut fokusniku Dž. Mostoslavskomu sozdat' vtoroj častnyj muzej." (We Are Taking the Old Stuff! The Viewers from Yaroslav Are Helping the Magician Dž. Mostoslavskij To Create the Second Private Museum.) *Lica.* 1998; Sent.: 66-71. Lang.: Rus.
Russia: Yaroslav. 1998. Biographical studies. ■Illusionist Dž. Mostoslavskij.

4130 Zubanova, L. "Valerij Meladze: 'Ja nikogda ne umel otkazyvat' ljudjam'." (Valerij Meladze: 'I Never Could Say No to People'.) *Avtograf.* 1998; 3: 64-65. Lang.: Rus.
Russia. 1998. Biographical studies. ■Profile of singer Valerij Meladze.

4131 Zubcova, Ja. "Valera, Ira, ogon', voda i mednye truby." (Valera, Ira, Fire, Water, and Copper Pipes.) *Domovoj.* 1998; 7: 20-27. Lang.: Rus.
Russia. 1998. Histories-sources. ■Singer Valerij Meladze about himself and his work.

4132 Crocker, Nicole Amanda. *From the Provinces: The Representation of Regional Identity in the British Music Hall, 1880-1914.* Kingston, ON: Queen's Univ. at Kingston; 1998. 192 pp. Notes. Biblio. [M.A. Thesis, Univ. Microfilms Order No. AAC MQ31193.] Lang.: Eng.
UK-England. 1880-1914. Histories-specific. ■Analyzes the portrayal of Irish, Scottish, English, and Welsh character identities in music hall song, costume and performance.

4133 Spier, Steven. "*Tight Roaring Circle*: Organizing the Organization of Bodies in Space." *NTQ.* 1998 Aug.; 14(3): 202-209 . Notes. Biblio. Illus.: Photo. B&W. 5. [Issue 55.] Lang.: Eng.
UK-England: London. 1993-1997. Critical studies. ■Analysis of the collaborative art installation *Tight Roaring Circle* by Joel Ryan, Dana Casperson, and William Forsythe which included elements of choreography, music, and input from the audience and curators at The Round House, where it was shown.

4134 Bowman, Ruth Laurion. "Performing Social Rubbish: Humbug and Romance in the American Market Place." 121-141 in Pollock, Della, ed. *Exceptional Spaces: Essays in Performance and History.* Chapel Hill, NC/London: Univ of North Carolina P; 1998. 394 pp. Index. Notes. Lang.: Eng.
USA. 1850-1890. Critical studies. ■Examines the American marketplace of the nineteenth century as a broadscale market economy structured by performance for pleasure and profit, with reference to P.T. Barnum's American Museum, and as reflected in Hawthorne's novel *The House of the Seven Gables.*

4135 Canning, Charlotte. "The Platform vs. the Stage: The Circuit Chautauqua's Antitheatrical Theatre." *TJ.* 1998 Oct.; 50(3) : 303-318. Notes. Illus.: Photo. B&W. 2. Lang.: Eng.
USA. 1913-1930. Critical studies. ■Examines the antitheatrical nature of the Circuit Chautauqua located in its demonization of 'common' and female performance.

4136 Davis, C.B. "Reading the Ventriloquist's Lips: The Performance Genre Behind the Metaphor." *TDR.* 1998 Win; 42(4): 133-156. Notes. Biblio. Illus.: Photo. B&W. 6. Lang.: Eng.
USA. 1998. Critical studies. ■Semiotic study of ventriloquism as a link between voice and identity and its use as a metaphor of representation.

MIXED ENTERTAINMENT: General—Performance/production

4137 Harrison-Pepper, Sally. *Drawing a Circle in the Square: Street Performing in New York City's Washington Square Park, 1980-1984.* New York, NY: New York Univ; 1987. 303 pp. Biblio. Notes. [Ph.D. Dissertation, Univ. Microfilms Order No. AAC 8712749.] Lang.: Eng.

USA: New York, NY. 1980-1984. Empirical research. ▪Complex study of the street performers of Washington Square Park. Through a combination of fieldwork and text-based research, author describes the expressions of street performance in a specific outdoor environment, and the relationships between outdoor performance and urban culture.

4138 Heaton, Daniel W. "Twenty Fragments: The 'Other', Gazing Back or Touring Juanita." *TextPQ.* 1998 July; 18(3): 248-261. Notes. Biblio. Illus.: Photo. B&W. 1. Lang.: Eng.

USA: New Orleans, LA. 1995. Histories-sources. ▪First-person account of a 'critical ethnographer's' experience living as the opposite sex, infiltrating New Orleans' French Quarter in female drag as a hairdresser.

4139 Jaeger, Ernest. *The Performer at Society's Footsteps: Conversations with Contemporary Street Performers.* New Brunswick, NJ: Rutgers Univ; 1988. 338 pp. Biblio. Notes. [Ph.D. Dissertation, Univ. Microfilms Order No. AAC 8911235.] Lang.: Eng.

USA. 1980-1987. Empirical research. ▪Qualitative and quantitative analysis of personality traits, background characteristics and attitudes toward performance shared among street performers.

4140 Lesser, Joseph Leroy. *Top Banana Joey Faye: The Evolution of a Burlesque Comedian.* New York, NY: New York Univ; 1987. 393 pp. Biblio. Notes. [Ph.D. Dissertation, Univ. Microfilms Order No. AAC 8720128.] Lang.: Eng.

USA. 1925-1960. Historical studies. ▪Describes and analyzes the personal, socio-economic, and theatrical elements that shaped Joey Faye into a Depression 'Runyonesque' character-type in the American burlesque theatre.

4141 Levine, Mark. "The Juggler." *NewY.* 1998 7-14 Dec.: 72-80. Illus.: Photo. B&W. 1. Lang.: Eng.

USA. 1955-1998. Biographical studies. ▪Profile of juggler Michael Moschen, a MacArthur fellow and former partner of Penn Jillette of Penn & Teller.

4142 McConachie, Brian. "Slavery and Authenticity: Performing a Slave Auction at Colonial Williamsburg." *TA.* 1998; 51: 71-81 . Notes. Lang.: Eng.

USA: Williamsburg, VA. 1994. Critical studies. ▪Verisimilitude of a mock estate auction involving the sale of four slaves at the reconstructed colonial American town.

4143 McGee, Randall. "Building Bridges." *PuJ.* 1998 Win; 50(2): 16-17. Illus.: Dwg. B&W. 8. Lang.: Eng.

USA: Las Vegas, NV. 1998. Historical studies. ▪Report on the Second Annual Vegas Ventriloquist Convention.

4144 McNamara, Brooks. "'For Laughing Purposes Only': The Literature of American Popular Entertainment." 141-158 in Engle, Ron, ed.; Miller, Tice L., ed. *The American Stage: Social and Economic Issues from the Colonial Period to the Present.* Cambridge: Cambridge UP; 1993. 320 pp. Pref. Notes. Index. Illus.: Photo. 2. Lang.: Eng.

USA. 1870-1910. Historical studies. ▪The publication of minstrel guides, gag books, joke books, sketches, and short plays as a reflection of social concerns.

4145 Morrow, Lee Alan. *Elsie Janis: A Compensatory Biography.* Chicago, IL: Northwestern Univ; 1988. 360 pp. Biblio. Notes. [Ph.D. Dissertation, Univ. Microfilms Order No. AAC 8823011.] Lang.: Eng.

USA. 1896-1941. Biographical studies. ▪The many forms of popular entertainment performed by vaudeville stage and screen performer Elsie Janis, from musical theatre to vaudeville, early film, radio, and wartime entertainment.

4146 Singer, Stanford Paul. *Vaudeville West: To Los Angeles and the Final Stages of Vaudeville.* Los Angeles, CA: Univ. of California; 1987. 248 pp. Notes. Biblio. [Ph.D. Dissertation, Univ. Microfilms Order No. 8802501.] Lang.: Eng.

USA: Los Angeles, CA. 1850-1934. Historical studies. ▪The history and significance of the West Coast vaudeville centers from 1850 to 1934, with particular focus on Los Angeles and its vaudeville theatres.

4147 Snow, Stephen Eddy. *Theatre of the Pilgrims: Documentation and Analysis of a 'Living History' Performance in Plymouth, Massachusetts.* New York, NY: New York Univ; 1987. 434 pp. Biblio. Notes. [Ph.D. Dissertation, Univ. Microfilms Order No. AAC 8801571.] Lang.: Eng.

USA: Plymouth, MA. 1950-1987. Historical studies. ▪First-person role-playing at Plimoth Plantation as a form of environmental theatre.

4148 Stockman, Todd. "Stanley Burns." *PuJ.* 1998 Win; 50(2): 34. Illus.: Photo. B&W. 1. Lang.: Eng.

USA: New York, NY. 1919-1998. Biographical studies. ▪Obituary for the long-time ventriloquist.

4149 Stockman, Todd. "Bob McAllister." *PuJ.* 1998 Win; 50(2): 36. Lang.: Eng.

USA. 1935-1998. Biographical studies. ▪Obituary for the ventriloquist/magician. He was also host of the children's television show *Wonderama.*

Relation to other fields

4150 Oberander, Thomas; Janzon, Leif, transl. "Bäst före 2000—allt nytt: konst, generation, århundrade." (Best Before 2000—All New: Art, Generation, Century.) *Entré.* 1998; 25(1): 30-35. Illus.: Photo. B&W. Lang.: Swe.

Europe. 1995-1998. Critical studies. ▪Investigation of the new cultural trends of the new generation, with references to Karel du Bar's open living room and the British group Forced Entertainment's performances with ever-changing costumes and attitudes.

Theory/criticism

4151 Concannon, Kevin Christopher. *Yoko Ono's* Cut Piece*: A Reconsideration.* Richmond, VA: Virginia Commonwealth Univ; 1998. 106 pp. Notes. Biblio. [M.A. Thesis, Univ. Microfilms Order No. AAC 1390581.] Lang.: Eng.

USA. 1964-1998. Histories-specific. ▪Examines reasons for the recent critical framing of Yoko Ono's 1964 performance work, *Cut Piece,* within the terms of feminist and reception discourse.

Cabaret

Basic theatrical documents

4152 Potak, Philip D. *The Production of a Cabaret Revue: 'Carnival Knowledge, or What Did You Do with the Money?'.* Garden City, NY: Adelphi Univ; 1988. 97 pp. Biblio. Notes. [Master's Thesis, Univ. Microfilms Order No. AAC 1332257.] Lang.: Eng.

USA. 1988. ▪Text of an original cabaret revue.

Performance/production

4153 Kift, Roy. "Reality and Illusion in the Theresienstadt Cabaret." 147-168 in Schumacher, Claude, ed. *Staging the Holocaust: The Shoah in Drama and Performance.* Cambridge: Cambridge UP; 1998. 355 pp. (Cambridge Studies in Modern Theatre.) Index. Notes. Biblio. Illus.: Photo. 4. Lang.: Eng.

Czechoslovakia: Terezin. 1944. Historical studies. ▪Examines the varied cabaret performances staged by and for the inmates of the Theresienstadt concentration camp.

4154 Kiec, Izolda. "Kabaret Serio. O scenkach, teatrzykach I rewiach emigracji polskiej po 1939." (The Serious Cabaret: On Small Theatres and Varieties of the Polish Emigration after 1939.) 161-191 in Kalemba-Kasprzak, Elżbieta, ed.; Ratajczak, Dobrochna, ed. *Dramat i teatr emigracyjny po roku 1939.* Wroclaw: Wiedza o kulturze; 1998. 348 pp. (Dramat w teatrze. Teatr w dramacie 15.) Lang.: Pol.

Europe. 1939-1998. Historical studies. ▪Theatre groups and their satirical performances accompanied Polish soldiers at different fronts of World War II. This article describes their activity as well as the productions of the Polish cabarets in London after the war.

MIXED ENTERTAINMENT: Cabaret—Performance/production

4155 Zaich, Katja B. "Operette am Rande des Grabes." (Operetta on the Edge of the Grave.) *THeute.* 1998; 8/9: 38-43. Illus.: Photo. B&W. 9. Lang.: Ger.
Netherlands. 1940-1944. Historical studies. ▪Describes the engagement of emigrants from Nazi Germany who played cabaret and revue in Netherlands under German occupation.

4156 Chojka, Joanna. "Wąchanie czasu. STS kontra BIM-BOM." (Smelling the Time: STS Versus BIM-BOM.) *DialogW.* 1998 Apr.; 4: 98-109. Illus.: Photo. Sketches. Poster. B&W. 7. Lang.: Pol.
Poland: Warsaw, Gdańsk. 1954-1959. Historical studies. ▪Examines two student theatre groups producing cabaret performances: the STS in Warsaw and BIM-BOM in Gdańsk.

4157 Kuligowska-Korzeniewska, Anna. "Kabaret za murem." (Cabaret Behind the Wall.) *DialogW.* 1998 Jan.; 1: 105-115. Illus.: Photo. B&W. 3. Lang.: Pol.
Poland: Warsaw. 1939-1988. Historical studies. ▪Kabaret za murem and its Jewish artists, who performed in the Warsaw ghetto during World War II, and its use as a historical subject in plays such as Jacek Buras' *Gwiazda za murem (The Star Behind the Wall)* and Henryk Grynberg's *Kabaret po tamtej stronie (Cabaret on the Other side).*

4158 Norris, James. "Knocking On Doors." *PlPl.* 1998 Aug.; 525: 26-27. Illus.: Photo. B&W. 1. Lang.: Eng.
USA. 1998. Histories-sources. ▪Singer Lorna Luft on her career, her view of fellow singers and the music industry.

Carnival

Design/technology

4159 Scarsella, Alessandro. *Le maschere veneziane. Le fantastiche e tradizionali figure del Carnevale più antico del mondo.* (Venetian Masks: The Traditional and Fantastical Figures of the Oldest Carnival in the World.) Rome: Newton & Compton; 1998. 65 pp. (Italia Tascabile 31.) Biblio. Append. Illus.: Dwg. Lang.: Ita.
Italy: Venice. 1500-1650. Histories-specific. ▪The use of the masks in Venice and the characters belonging to the tradition of the *commedia dell'arte.*

4160 Riggio, Milla C.; Cupid, John, intro. "Geraldo Andrew Vieira: Making *Mas.*" *TDR.* 1998 Fall; 42(3): 194-202. Illus.: Photo. B&W. 8. Lang.: Eng.
Trinidad and Tobago. 1952-1996. Histories-sources. ▪Interview with leading designer of carnival costumes and scenery regarding his work in the *mas* genre.

Institutions

4161 Bénard, Johanne. "Un public amusé?: À propos du 10e festival des arts de la rue de Kingston (the 10th Annual Kingston Buskers Rendez-vous)." (An Amused Public?: About the 10th Annual Kingston Buskers Rendez-vous.) *JCT.* 1998; 89: 124-127. Notes. Illus.: Photo. Poster. B&W. 9. Lang.: Fre.
Canada: Kingston, ON. 1998. Critical studies. ▪10th Annual Kingston Buskers Rendez-vous examined through the optic of Mikhaïl Bakhtin's idea of carnival.

Performance/production

4162 Giurgea, Adrian. *Theatre of the Flesh: The Carnival of Venice and the Theatre of the World.* Los Angeles, CA: Univ. of California; 1987. 754 pp. Notes. Biblio. [Ph.D. Dissertation, Univ. Microfilms Order No. 8721030.] Lang.: Eng.
Italy: Venice. 1600-1985. Critical studies. ▪Describes the Carnival of Venice and presents a historical overview of Venice's 'theatrical constitution'. Provides commentary and interpretation.

4163 Tereščenko, V. "Forma skuki." (The Form of Boredom.) *Ogonek.* 1998; 9: 52-53. Lang.: Rus.
Italy: Venice. Historical studies. ▪History of Venetian carnival.

4164 Bellour, Helene; Kinser, Samuel. "Amerindian Masking in Trinidad's Carnival: The House of Black Elk in San Fernando." *TDR.* 1998 Fall; 42(3): 147-169. Notes. Illus.: Photo. Dwg. B&W. 16. Lang.: Eng.
Trinidad and Tobago: San Fernando. 1700-1950. Historical studies. ▪History of the influence of Amerindians on the Trinidad Carnival, with emphasis on the masks used in the parades. Uses the parades during Carnival 1996 in San Fernando.

4165 Delano, Pablo. "Images of Trinidad: Carnival 1997." *TDR.* 1998 Fall; 42(3): 74-81. Notes. Illus.: Photo. B&W. 12. Lang.: Eng.
Trinidad and Tobago. 1997. Historical studies. ▪Collection of photographs taken throughout Trinidad and Tobago during carnival.

4166 Elder, J.D.; Hall, Tony. "Cannes Brûlées." *TDR.* 1998 Fall; 42(3): 38-43. Illus.: Photo. Diagram. B&W. 2. Lang.: Eng.
Trinidad and Tobago. 1998. Critical studies. ▪The role of women in the *Canboulay* (cannes brûlées) ceremony as a Black artistic institution in Trinidad and Tobago, defined as a multimedia symbolic ceremony combining elements of music, poetics, dance, theatre, and acrobatics. Contains sidebar interview with *Canboulay* musician Lennox Pierre on the role of women in the performance.

4167 Hall, Tony. "'They Want to See George Band': Tobago *Mas* According to George Leacock." *TDR.* 1998 Fall; 42(3): 44-53. Notes. Lang.: Eng.
Trinidad and Tobago. 1923-1998. Histories-sources. ▪Interview with carnival *mas* music performer George Leacock regarding his experiences playing at carnival and his reasons for becoming a *mas* performer.

4168 Honoré, Brian. "The Midnight Robber: Master of Metaphor, Baron of Bombast." *TDR.* 1998 Fall; 42(3): 124-131. Notes. Illus.: Photo. B&W. 4. Lang.: Eng.
Trinidad and Tobago. 1900-1998. Historical studies. ▪Rise, decline and eventual reemergence of the popular Trinidad carnival character of the Midnight Robber. During Carnival many dress as this character and perform in duels of words, often set to music.

4169 Johnson, Kim; Gay, Derek; Smith, Armin. "Notes on Pans." *TDR.* 1998 Fall; 42(3): 61-73. Illus.: Photo. B&W. 6. Lang.: Eng.
Trinidad and Tobago: Port of Spain. 1777-1998. Historical studies. ▪History of the steeldrum (pan): contains two sidebars, one with a chronology of instrumental development in Trinidad and Tobago with diagrams, and the other focused on the annual steelband festival, championed by musician Armin Smith.

4170 Stegassy, Ruth. "John Cupid: We Have Been Called." *TDR.* 1998 Fall; 42(3): 96-107. Notes. Illus.: Photo. B&W. 6. Lang.: Eng.
Trinidad and Tobago. 1998. Histories-sources. ▪Interview with Cupid of the National Carnival Commission about the important place of carnival in the social fabric of Trinidad and Tobago as the one thing that unites all its varied religions and cultures.

4171 Walsh, Martin W. "Jouvay Mornin' with the Merry Darevils: A Small Neighborhood Band on Carnival Monday." *TDR.* 1998 Fall ; 42(3): 132-146. Notes. Illus.: Photo. B&W. 7. Lang.: Eng.
Trinidad and Tobago: Port of Spain. 1996. Historical studies. ▪Follows the routine of a band of *jouvay* musicians as they prepare for, and then perform, on Carnival Monday.

Plays/librettos/scripts

4172 Schechner, Richard; Riggio, Milla C. "Peter Minshall: A Voice to Add to the Song of the Universe." *TDR.* 1998 Fall; 42 (3): 170-193. Illus.: Photo. Dwg. Sketches. B&W. 17. Lang.: Eng.
Trinidad and Tobago: Port of Spain. 1974-1997. Histories-sources. ▪Interview with the prolific creator/director of carnival *mas* and theatrical pieces, as well as being a set and costume designer, regarding his love affair with the genre *mas.* Contains a chronology of all his work in both carnival and theatre and a synopsis of his two-act *mas, River.*

Reference materials

4173 Martin, Carol. "Trinidad Carnival Glossary." *TDR.* 1998 Fall; 42(3): 220-235. Illus.: Photo. B&W. 23. Lang.: Eng.
Trinidad and Tobago. 1998. ▪Glossary of terms and phrases specific to carnival in Trinidad.

MIXED ENTERTAINMENT: Carnival

Relation to other fields

4174 Chang, Carlisle. "Chinese in Trinidad Carnival." *TDR.* 1998 Fall; 42(3): 213-219. Illus.: Photo. B&W. 7. Lang.: Eng.
Trinidad and Tobago. China. 1808-1998. Historical studies. ■Chinese cultural influence upon Trinidad Carnival.

4175 Liverpool, Hollis Urban. "Origins of Ritual and Customs in the Trinidad Carnival: African or European." *TDR.* 1998 Fall; 42(3): 24-37. Notes. Illus.: Photo. Sketches. B&W. 3. Lang.: Eng.
Trinidad and Tobago. 1501-1998. Historical studies. ■Examines the customs and rituals of Trinidadian Carnival in order to ascertain whether its roots are to be found in the Europeans who settled there or the Africans who arrived as slaves.

4176 Lovelace, Earl. "The Emancipation-Jouvay Tradition and the Almost Loss of Pain." *TDR.* 1998 Fall; 42(3): 54-60. Illus.: Photo. B&W. 3. Lang.: Eng.
Trinidad and Tobago: Port of Spain. 1838-1998. Historical studies. ■Roots of the *jouvay* ceremony on Carnival Sunday in Trinidad and Tobago as a celebration of emancipation. Discusses reasons for its near disappearance in the 1950s and 60s, and its revitalization today.

4177 Riggio, Milla C. "Resistance and Integrity: Carnival in Trinidad and Tobago." *TDR.* 1998 Fall; 42(3): 7-23. Notes. Illus.: Photo. B&W. 8. Lang.: Eng.
Trinidad and Tobago. 1889-1998. Critical studies. ■Importance of carnival to the identity of the people of these two southernmost islands of the Caribbean. Emphasizes the multicultural populace and how carnival facilitates assimilation. Also serves as an introduction to the theme of *TDR* 42:3, Carnival.

4178 Sankeralli, Burton. "Indian Presence in Carnival." *TDR.* 1998 Fall; 42(3): 203-212. Notes. Illus.: Photo. B&W. 7. Lang.: Eng.
Trinidad and Tobago. India. 1845-1998. Historical studies. ■Influence of the Indian community on Trinidad Carnival since their first arrival as indentured immigrants in 1845.

Circus

Performance/production

4179 Gesmer, Daniel; Seib, Al, photo. "Ringmistress of Cirque du Soleil." *Dm.* 1998 July; 72(7): 50-54. Illus.: Photo. Color. B&W. 5. Lang.: Eng.
Canada: Montreal, PQ. 1987-1998. Biographical studies. ■Profile of choreographer Debra Brown and her work with the circus troupe.

4180 Little, William Kenneth. *Inventing Circus Clowns: The Irony of Parody and Pastiche in the Modern European Circus.* Charlottesville, VA: Univ. of Virginia; 1988. 565 pp. Biblio. Notes. [Ph.D. Dissertation, Univ. Microfilms Order No. AAC 8909574.] Lang.: Eng.
Europe. 1950-1987. Historical studies. ■The use of spectacle in the modern world and the nature of clown performance in the creation of the modern variety circus.

4181 Vuori, Suna. "Sirkus tunkee salonkiin." (Circus Is Pushing Itself Into the Salon.) *Teat.* 1998; 53(2): 4-6. Illus.: Photo. Color. 1. Lang.: Fin.
Finland. 1980-1998. Historical studies. ■Focuses on the changing definition of circus performance as it becomes less reliant on traditional animal-based acts and veers toward a more sophisticated spectacle.

4182 Sörenson, Margareta. "Något har hänt i manegen." (Something Has Occurred In the Ring.) *Danst.* 1998; 8(5): 19-20. Illus.: Photo. B&W. Lang.: Swe.
France. Sweden. 1990-1998. ■Survey of the 'new circus' with references to Cirque Invisible, Cirkus Cirkör, Zingaro and Cirque Plume.

4183 Gneušev, V. "Ljudjam nužno semejnoe šou." (People Need a Family Show.) *MoskZ.* 1998; Oct-Nov: 82-85. Lang.: Rus.
Russia: Moscow. 1998. ■The art of the circus according to V. Gneušev, producer of the Circus at Cvetnoj Boulevard.

4184 Nikulin, Ju. V. *Počti ser'ezno...* (Almost Seriously...)Moscow: Vagrius; 1998. 574 pp. (Moj dvadcatyj vek.) Lang.: Rus.
Russia: Moscow. 1998. Histories-sources. ■Recollections of Jurij Nikulin, film actor and clown, and director of the Nikulina na Cvetnom bul'vare Circus.

4185 Myrvold, Paul. *High Wire: Risk and the Art of Tightrope Walking.* San Jose, CA: San Jose State Univ; 1998. 166 pp. Notes. Biblio. [M.A. Thesis, Univ. Microfilms Order No. AAC 1389667.] Lang.: Eng.
USA. 1985-1997. Histories-specific. ■Physical risk as an aesthetic element in performances of Philippe Petit, Jay Cochrane, the Flying Wallendas, and the author.

Commedia dell'arte

Performance/production

4186 Holm, Bent. "Harlequin, Holberg and the (In)visible Masks: *Commedia dell'arte* in Eighteenth-Century Denmark." *ThR.* 1998 Sum; 23(2): 159-166. Notes. Lang.: Eng.
Denmark: Copenhagen. 1700-1750. Historical studies. ■The influence of *commedia* masks on the first Scandinavian theatre company, founded by French actor René Magnon de Montaigu and Danish playwright Ludvig Holberg at the Lille Grønnegade Teater.

4187 Anderson, Michael. "The Idea of *Commedia* in the Twentieth Century." *ThR.* 1998 Sum; 23(2): 167-173. Notes. Lang.: Eng.
Europe. 1860-1950. Historical studies. ■The symbiotic relationship between scholarly research and practical experiment in modern revivals of *commedia.* Considers the role of Edward Gordon Craig and Constant Mic, their influence on directors V.E. Mejerchol'd and Jacques Copeau, and the spread of the revival to England through Copeau's student Michel Saint-Denis.

4188 Katritzky, M.A. "The *Commedia dell'arte*: An Introduction." *ThR.* 1998 Sum; 23(2): 99-103. Notes. Lang.: Eng.
Europe. North America. 1550-1950. Historical studies. ■Introductory essay to an issue devoted to *commedia dell'arte,* including a short history of the form and its major players.

4189 Marks, Jonathan. "The Charlatans of the Pont-Neuf." *ThR.* 1998 Sum; 23(2): 133-141. Notes. Lang.: Eng.
France. Italy. 1600-1700. Historical studies. ■Argues that the entertainments offered on the outdoor stages of the French and Italian charlatans are an integral part of the *commedia,* and that an understanding of these street performers is essential to an understanding of the development of French comedy.

4190 Aliverti, Maria Ines. "An Unknown Portrait of Tiberio Fiorilli." *ThR.* 1998 Sum; 23(2): 127-132. Notes. Illus.: Photo. Dwg. Color. B&W. 10. Lang.: Eng.
Italy. 1625-1700. Historical studies. ■Examines a painting, recently discovered and thought to be that of *commedia* performer Tiberio Fiorilli, with attention to the significance of his stage costumes, his skill in portraying the passions, and wider cultural issues.

4191 Katritzky, M.A. "Was *Commedia dell'arte* Performed by Mountebanks? *Album amicorum* Illustrations and Thomas Platter's Description of 1598." *ThR.* 1998 Sum; 23(2): 104-126. Notes. Append. Illus.: Pntg. Dwg. 6. Lang.: Eng.
Italy. France: Avignon. 1550-1620. Historical studies. ■Examines aspects of early modern mountebank activity for evidence of *commedia* performances. Specifically focuses on writer Thomas Platter's lengthy account of an Italian mountebank troupe performing in Avignon, as well as pictures of mountebanks in *alba amicorum.*

4192 Molinari, Cesare. "Actor-authors of the *Commedia dell'arte*: The Dramatic Writings of Flaminio Scala and Giambattista Andreini." *ThR.* 1998 Sum; 23(2): 142-151. Notes. Lang.: Eng.
Italy. 1600-1700. Historical studies. ■Examines the literary output such as treatises, *zibaldone,* poems, and orations, as well as scenarios, of the early *comici dell'arte,* including the work of Flaminio Scala and Giambattista Andreini. Argues that the best of these writings transcend their stereotyped characterization.

4193 Beale, Geoff; Gayton, Howard. "The Drive to Communicate—The Use of Language in *Commedia* *dell'arte.*" *ThR.* 1998 Sum; 23 (2): 1740-178. Notes. Illus.: Photo. B&W. 2. Lang.: Eng.

UK-England: London. 1991-1998. Histories-sources. ■The authors, co-artistic directors and founders of Ophaboom Theatre, discuss insights gained from their use of language in performing to both English-speaking and non-English-speaking audiences and the implications for the development and impact of effective forms of communication in *commedia* and its revival.

Court entertainment

Audience

4194 Carpenter, Sarah. "The Sixteenth-Century Court Audience: Performers and Spectators." *MET.* 1997; 19: 3-14. Notes. [Paper presented at SITM Triennial Colloquium, University of Odense, August 1997.] Lang.: Eng.

England: Greenwich. 1527. Historical studies. ■The complex role of the audience in the festivities mounted by Henry VIII, for ambassadors from the king of France. Argues that the political and personal relationships among the members of the carefully chosen audience are what constitute and give meaning to the entertainment.

4195 Somerset, Alan. "'Beginning in the Middle ...': Warwickshire Locations and Families, as Audiences from Early Modern Music and Drama." *MET.* 1998; 20: 77-94. Notes. [Paper presented at SITM Triennial Colloquium, University of Odense, August 1997.] Lang.: Eng.

England. 1431-1635. Historical studies. ■Differences between influential families in their employment of entertainers: for the great and titled, life consisted of public performance and ceremony, while for the rich and powerful gentry, entertainments provided occasions for display and opportunities to strengthen bonds of patronage and power.

Performance/production

4196 Hammer, Paul E.J. "Upstaging the Queen: the Earl of Essex, Francis Bacon and the Accession Day Celebrations of 1595." 41-66 in Bevington, David, ed.; Holbrook, Peter, ed. *The Politics of the Stuart Court Masque.* Cambridge/New York, NY: Cambridge UP; 1998. 335 pp. Index. Notes. Lang.: Eng.

England. 1595. Critical studies. ■Argues that the masques used in Accession Day celebrations reveal political tensions between Elizabeth I and the Earl of Essex, who was attempting to 'upstage' the queen through a campaign of 'self-promotion' (assisted by Francis Bacon).

4197 Lindley, David. "The Politics of Music in the Masque." 273-295 in Bevington, David, ed.; Holbrook, Peter, ed. *The Politics of the Stuart Court Masque.* Cambridge/New York, NY: Cambridge UP; 1998. 335 pp. Index. Notes. Lang.: Eng.

England. 1620-1634. Critical studies. ■Argues that music, as a marker of sophistication, could be manipulated and used for political leverage.

4198 Ravelhofer, Barbara. "'Virgin Wax' and 'Hairy Men-Monsters': Unstable Movement Codes in the Stuart Masque." 244-272 in Bevington, David, ed.; Holbrook, Peter, ed. *The Politics of the Stuart Court Masque.* Cambridge/New York, NY: Cambridge UP; 1998. 335 pp. Index. Notes. Illus.: Photo. 3. Lang.: Eng.

England. 1610-1642. Critical studies. ■How spectacle and dance movement in masques related to the complex negotiation of political and social dialogue. Suggests that 'movement codes' were highly unstable and could be easily manipulated for political effect.

4199 Leslie, Michael. "'Something Nasty in the Wilderness': Entertaining Queen Elizabeth on Her Progress." *MRDE.* 1998; 10: 47-72. Notes. Lang.: Eng.

UK-England: Sheffield. 1954. Historical studies. ■Critical account of Sir William Empson's controversial presentation of his *The Masque of Steel* for Queen Elizabeth II's visit to Sheffield not long after her coronation.

Plays/librettos/scripts

4200 Barroll, Leeds. "Inventing the Stuart Masque." 121-143 in Bevington, David, ed.; Holbrook, Peter, ed. *The Politics of the Stuart Court Masque.* Cambridge/New York, NY: Cambridge UP; 1998. 335 pp. Index. Notes. Lang.: Eng.

England. 1604-1605. Critical studies. ■Gender and politics in Samuel Daniel's *Vision of the Twelve Goddesses*, commissioned by Queen Anne, and in *The Masque of Blackness* by Ben Jonson, with their many female roles that are central both spatially and thematically.

4201 Bevington, David; Holbrook, Peter. "Introduction." 6-17 in Bevington, David, ed.; Holbrook, Peter, ed. *The Politics of the Stuart Court Masque.* Cambridge/New York, NY: Cambridge UP; 1998. 335 pp. Index. Notes. Lang.: Eng.

England. 1610-1642. Critical studies. ■Introductory essay on the interdisciplinary study of the historical and critical aspects of politics in Stuart Court masques. Essays focus on literary aspects more than on performance.

4202 Bevington, David. "*The Tempest* and the Jacobean Court Masque." 218-243 in Bevington, David, ed.; Holbrook, Peter, ed. *The Politics of the Stuart Court Masque.* Cambridge/New York, NY: Cambridge UP; 1998. 335 pp. Index. Notes. Lang.: Eng.

England. 1613. Critical studies. ■Compares the masque written into Shakespeare's *The Tempest* with Thomas Campion's *The Lord's Masque*, both written specifically for the marriage of James's daughter Elizabeth. Suggests that Shakespeare wanted to show a masque to the popular paying audience, and thus, knew its political potential, while Campion celebrates the absolutism of the monarchy.

4203 Bishop, Tom. "The Gingerbread Host: Tradition and Novelty in the Jacobean Masque." 88-120 in Bevington, David, ed.; Holbrook, Peter, ed. *The Politics of the Stuart Court Masque.* Cambridge/New York, NY: Cambridge UP; 1998. 335 pp. Index. Notes. Lang.: Eng.

England. 1611. Critical studies. ■Political tension between King James I and his heir apparent Prince Henry reflected in Ben Jonson's masque *Oberon.*

4204 Butler, Martin. "Courtly Negotiations." 20-40 in Bevington, David, ed.; Holbrook, Peter, ed. *The Politics of the Stuart Court Masque.* Cambridge/New York, NY: Cambridge UP; 1998. 335 pp. Index. Notes. Lang.: Eng.

England. 1611. Critical studies. ■Examines the masque as an instrument of royal policy, yet also addresses its subversive potential. Concentrates on Ben Jonson's masque, *Oberon.*

4205 Craig, Hugh. "Jonson, the Antimasque and the 'Rules of Flattery'." 176-196 in Bevington, David, ed.; Holbrook, Peter, ed. *The Politics of the Stuart Court Masque.* Cambridge/New York, NY: Cambridge UP; 1998. 335 pp. Index. Notes. Lang.: Eng.

England. 1612-1632. Critical studies. ■Examines the antimasques of Ben Jonson, especially *Time Vindicated*, as sites of contestation and potential political subversion, where 'holiday misrule' was the norm.

4206 Holbrook, Peter. "Jacobean Masques and the Jacobean Peace." 67-87 in Bevington, David, ed.; Holbrook, Peter, ed. *The Politics of the Stuart Court Masque.* Cambridge, NY/New York: Cambridge UP; 1998. 335 pp. Index. Notes. Lang.: Eng.

England. 1604-1609. Critical studies. ■Examines the political and ideological struggle between Queen Anne and King James I as reflected in Samuel Daniel's masque *Vision of the Twelve Goddesses* and Ben Jonson's *The Masque of Queens.*

4207 Lewalski, Barbara K. "Milton's *Comus* and the Politics of Masquing." 296-320 in Bevington, David, ed.; Holbrook, Peter, ed. *The Politics of the Stuart Court Masque.* Cambridge/New York, NY: Cambridge UP; 1998. 335 pp. Index. Notes. Lang.: Eng.

England. 1634-1635. Critical studies. ■Examines Milton's masque *Comus* in the context of the tensions of the new Stuart court of Charles I and the resulting political and social unrest and upheaval. Argues that *Comus* is a 'reformed' masque that reflects Puritan religious and political sensibilities.

4208 Orgel, Stephen. "Marginal Jonson." 144-175 in Bevington, David, ed.; Holbrook, Peter, ed. *The Politics of the Stuart Court Masque.* Cambridge/New York, NY: Cambridge UP; 1998. 335 pp. Index. Notes. Illus.: Sketches. Dwg. 17. Lang.: Eng.

MIXED ENTERTAINMENT: Court entertainment—Plays/librettos/scripts

England. 1605-1611. Critical studies. ▪Political power, gender, and race in Ben Jonson's *The Masque of Blackness*, among others, said to be testaments to Queen Anne's power and her transgression of normal gender roles. Also examines costuming.

4209 Raylor, Timothy. "The Design and Authorship of *The Essex House Masque*." *MRDE*. 1998; 10: 218-237. Notes. Lang.: Eng.

England. 1621. Textual studies. ▪Attempts to ascertain authorship of the recently discovered libretto for the the masque, and to identify the designer of the entertainment, which was presented for the visiting French ambassador at Essex House.

Relation to other fields

4210 Bauer, Gerald M. "Theatrale Repräsentation am Leopoldinischen Kaiserhof." (Theatrical Representation at 'Leopoldinischen Kaiserhof'.) *MuK*. 1998; 40(2-4): 157-168. Notes. Lang.: Ger.

Austria: Vienna. 1650-1699. Historical studies. ▪Analyzes the the role of theatre and art in the age of court and how forms of expression reflected the everyday life of the Austrian court.

4211 Lucas, Scott. "Conspiracy and Court Revels: Were the 1551-52 Christmas Revels a Plot Against Protector Somerset." *MRDE*. 1998; 10: 19-46. Notes. Lang.: Eng.

England. 1551-1552. Historical studies. ▪Argues that the Christmas revels, organized and presented by poet George Ferrers, purposely created an atmosphere of distraction for King Edward IV, while the enemies of his uncle, the Duke of Somerset, hurried along the execution of the former Lord Protector.

Theory/criticism

4212 Marcus, Leah S. "Valediction." 321-326 in Bevington, David, ed.; Holbrook, Peter, ed. *The Politics of the Stuart Court Masque*. Cambridge/New York, NY: Cambridge UP; 1998. 335 pp. Index. Notes. Lang.: Eng.

UK-England. 1970-1995. Critical studies. ▪Historical and theoretical essay on why the Stuart masque has been of interest to contemporary scholars. Examines scholarship of the 1970s to the 90s to answer questions of popularity.

Pageants/parades

Performance/production

4213 Kaplan, Joel. "Staging the *York*: *Creation* and *Hortulanus*, Toronto 1997." *MET*. 1997; 19: 129-143. Notes. Illus.: Photo. Dwg. B&W. 6. Lang.: Eng.

Canada: Toronto, ON. 1998. Histories-sources. ▪The director of two of the *York Cycle* plays presented in Toronto, discusses his approach and technical solutions.

4214 Potter, Bob. "The *York* Plays, University of Toronto, 20 June 1997." *MET*. 1997; 19: 121-128. Lang.: Eng.

Canada: Toronto, ON. 1998. Historical studies. ▪Examines the complete, single-day processional staging of the *York Cycle* plays, the first to be staged since the Middle Ages. The entire forty-seven plays were presented in separate productions in Canada, the USA, and the United Kingdom on wagons moving between four performance spaces. Casting was multicultural and many female actors took over men's roles. The diversity of the casts was mirrored in the composition of the audience.

4215 Wright, Nancy E. "'Rival Traditions': Civic and Courtly Ceremonies in Jacobean London." 197-217 in Bevington, David, ed.; Holbrook, Peter, ed. *The Politics of the Stuart Court Masque*. Cambridge/New York, NY: Cambridge UP; 1998. 335 pp. Index. Notes. Lang.: Eng.

England. 1605-1610. Critical studies. ▪Argues that public ceremonial traditions, like the Lord Mayor's Show, reveal negotiations of differences and conflicts in a changing social and political order and that court presence at the symbolic civic spectacles was crucial.

4216 Mellen, Peter J. *The Third Reich Examined as the Dramatic Illusion of Ritual Performance*. Bowling Green, OH: Bowling Green State Univ; 1988. 353 pp. Notes. Biblio. [Ph.D. Dissertation, Univ. Microfilms Order No. AAC 8914717.] Lang.: Eng.

Germany. 1938-1945. Histories-specific. ▪Examines the role played by ritual myth in the formation and maintenance of Germany's Third Reich. Compares the form and function of classic models of ritual myth, with the Nazi world view as it was articulated and disseminated in selected public performances, such as the Nuremburg Party Rallies.

4217 Cremona, Vicki Ann. "Re-enacting the Passion during the Holy Week Rituals in Malta." *TA*. 1998; 51: 32-53. Notes. Illus.: Photo. B&W. 6. Lang.: Eng.

Malta. 1998. Historical studies. ▪Description of the rituals of Holy Week, including the re-enactment of the Passion of Christ.

4218 Harris, Max. "Fireworks, Turks, and Long-Necked Mules: Pyrotechnic Theater in Germany and Catalonia." *CompD*. 1998 Fall; 32(3): 362-388. Notes. Illus.: Photo. Dwg. B&W. 7. Lang.: Eng.

Spain-Catalonia: Berga. Germany: Trent. 1549-1996. Historical studies. ▪Similarities between the present-day *Corpus Christi* festival held in Berga, called the *Patum*, and a description of a similar entertainment held in Trent in the sixteenth century, including the pyrotechnical aspects, the mock battles, fireworks displays, and monsters and dragons.

4219 Harris, Max. "The Impotence of Dragons." *TDR*. 1998 Fall; 42(3): 108-123. Notes. Illus.: Photo. B&W. 9. Lang.: Eng.

Trinidad and Tobago: Paramin. 1997. Historical studies. ▪Description of the parade of devils, imps, and beasts held on Carnival Monday on Paramin Mountain near the village of the same name.

4220 Citron, Atay. "Ben Hecht's Pageant-Drama: *A Flag Is Born*." 70-93 in Schumacher, Claude, ed. *Staging the Holocaust: The Shoah in Drama and Performance*. Cambridge: Cambridge UP; 1998. 355 pp. (Cambridge Studies in Modern Theatre.) Index. Notes. Biblio. Illus.: Photo. 4. Lang.: Eng.

USA: New York, NY. 1946. Historical studies. ▪Investigates events surrounding the staging and performance of a propaganda pageant, *A Flag Is Born* by Ben Hecht, which galvanized American Jews to actively support displaced persons and campaign for a Jewish homeland.

4221 Ferre, Craig. *A History of the Polynesian Cultural Center's 'Night Show': 1963-1983*. Laie, HI: Brigham Young Univ; 1988. 363 pp. Notes. Biblio. [Ph.D. Dissertation, Univ. Microfilms Order No. AAC 8821897.] Lang.: Eng.

USA: Laie, HI. 1963-1983. Histories-specific. ▪The history of the feature dramatic presentation of the Polynesian Cultural Center, the Night Show, and its purposes—to display and preserve authentic Polynesian culture and to provide work for the students of neighboring BYU-Hawaii.

4222 Jones, Jennifer. "The Beauty Queen as Deified Sacrificial Victim." *THSt*. 1998; 53: 99-106. Notes. Lang.: Eng.

USA. 1920-1968. Historical studies. ▪How beauty pageants objectify young women and require them to participate in a competitive rather than cooperative relationship. Also considers the connection between the rise of women's social and political power and the emergence of a national beauty ritual.

4223 Stephenson, Tracy. "My Silence Speaks Volumes: Mickey Mouse and the Ideology of an Icon." *TA*. 1998; 51: 54-70. Notes. Lang.: Eng.

USA: Orlando, FL. 1998. Histories-sources. ▪First-hand account of the experience of portraying Mickey Mouse at Walt Disney World.

Plays/librettos/scripts

4224 Knight, Alan E. "The Roman *Saint's Plays* of Lille." *MET*. 1997; 19: 15-25. Notes. [Paper presented at SITM Triennial Colloquium, University of Odense, August 1997.] Lang.: Eng.

Belgium: Lille. 1450-1499. Historical studies. ▪Analogies to saint's plays in four plays based on Roman history that were presented at the annual procession in honor of the Virgin Mary and intended to provide spectators with examples of virtuous or vicious behavior.

4225 Bergeron, David M. "Stuart Civic Pageants and Textual Performance." *RenQ*. 1998 Spr; 51(1): 162-183. Notes. Biblio. Lang.: Eng.

England. 1604-1637. Critical studies. ▪Analysis of extant printed texts of Jacobean and Carolinean 'Lord Mayor's Shows'.

MIXED ENTERTAINMENT: Pageants/parades

Relation to other fields

4226 Mills, David. "Who Are Our Customers?: The Audience for Chester's Plays." *MET.* 1998; 20: 104-117. Notes. [Paper presented at SITM Triennial Colloquium, University of Odense, August 1997.] Lang.: Eng.

England: Chester. 1521-1678. Historical studies. ■Considers the commercial aspect of Chester's Whitsun plays and concludes that despite claims made for religious edification and social cohesion, the main justification for their performance was economic self-interest. Ultimately, the production costs proved to be too high and the Whitsun cycle was replaced by the Midsummer show, which provided a more cost-effective alternative.

4227 Pasero, Nicolò, ed.; Tinterri, Alessandro, ed. *La piazza del popolo.* (The People's Square.) Rome: Meltemi; 1998. 163 pp. Lang.: Ita.

Italy. 1933-1975. Critical studies. ■The importance of the square in open-air entertainments and political and religious processions. The relationship between masses and public representations.

4228 Hall, Ardencie. *New Orleans Jazz Funerals: Transition to the Ancestors.* New York, NY: New York Univ; 1998. 298 pp. Notes. Biblio. [Ph.D. Dissertation, Univ. Microfilms Order No. AAC 9831721.] Lang.: Eng.

USA: New Orleans, LA. 1900-1990. Histories-specific. ■Examines jazz funerals as an African retention and as a sign of resistance against the dominant structure, while providing a model for how the event might be adapted for the theatre in the future.

Performance art

Administration

4229 Rogers, Steve. "From Rag-Bag to Riches." *PM.* 1988; 53: 7-8. Illus.: Photo. B&W. 3. Lang.: Eng.

UK-England: Brighton. 1967-1988. Histories-sources. ■History of the Brighton Festival, and a discussion about its programming with the festival's director Gavin Henderson.

Audience

4230 Watson, Gray. "A Matter of Content." *PM.* 1988; 55: 22-25. Notes. [Cover title: *Edge 88.*] Lang.: Eng.

Europe. 1960-1988. Critical studies. ■Examines why performance art prompts negative reactions, citing its content and manner of presentation as the main reasons, and argues that artists must overcome this phenomenon to increase the relevance of the art form.

4231 Gaskell, Ivan. "Free State." *PM.* 1990; 60: 31-35. Illus.: Photo. B&W. 2. Lang.: Eng.

Netherlands: Arnhem. 1989. Histories-sources. ■Conversation with performer Tim Brennan regarding audience reaction to his piece during the International Audio Visual Experimental Festival, in which he occupied a low, barrel-vaulted brick cellar for several hours at a time over a three day period. Refers to discussions Brennan had during the piece with video artist Susan Brind and sculptor Simon Penny about the circumstances of the work that became part of the piece itself.

Institutions

4232 Borello, Christine. "Un théâtre de recherche sur la perception: Portrait d'Arbo Cyber, théâtre (?)." (An Experimental Theatre of Perception: Portrait of Arbo Cyber, théâtre (?).) *JCT.* 1998; 86: 101-105. Notes. Illus.: Photo. B&W. 3. Lang.: Fre.

Canada: Quebec, PQ. 1985-1998. Historical studies. ■Arbo Cyber, théâtre (?) subverts theatre through use of recorded media and unusual forms of presentation.

4233 Landry, Pascale; Morin, Émile. "Méthode d'assemblage: Productions Recto-Verso." (Method of Assembly: Productions Recto-Verso.) *JCT.* 1998; 86: 99-100. Illus.: Photo. B&W. 1. Lang.: Fre.

Canada: Quebec, PQ. 1996. Histories-sources. ■Scenographer Émile Morin and performance artist/actress Pascale Landry outline principles guiding creations of their production company, Productions Recto-Verso and their latest show, *Un paysage/Eine Landschaft/A Landscape.*

4234 Tiedemann, Kathrin. "Die Beweglichkeit der Sinne." (The Flexibility of Senses.) *dRAMATURg.* 1998; 2: 23-29. Illus.: Photo. B&W. 1. Lang.: Ger.

Germany: Franfurt. 1993-1998. Critical studies. ■Describes border crossings between arts and media according to independent director Helena Waldmann and her company, Showcase Beat le Mot. Discusses the changing perception of audience.

4235 Barker, Peter. "Edge 88." *PM.* 1988(56/57): 34-35. Illus.: Photo. B&W. 21. Lang.: Eng.

UK-England: London. 1988. Historical studies. ■Illustrated record of Britain's first biennial experimental festival, Edge 88.

4236 Kershaw, Baz. "Between Wordsworth and Windscale." *PM.* 1988; 54: 7-12. Notes. Illus.: Photo. B&W. 7. Lang.: Eng.

UK-England: Ulverston. 1968-1988. Histories-sources. ■Interview with John Fox, founder of Welfare State International, one of the oldest performance art companies in Britain, regarding the company's mission.

4237 Hughes, David. "Locating Goat Island: Conversations with Matthew Goulish and Lin Hixson." *PM.* 1990(61): 11-17. Illus.: Photo. B&W. 4. Lang.: Eng.

USA: Chicago, IL. 1990. Histories-sources. ■Interview with Goulish and Hixson, the performer/directors of the Goat Island performance company about their mission and political and theoretical postions.

Performance/production

4238 Allthorpe-Guyton, Marjorie. "Artist's notes." *PM.* 1988; 55: 26-69. Biblio. Illus.: Photo. B&W. 23. [Cover title: *Edge 88.*] Lang.: Eng.

1963-1988. Biographical studies. ■Short biographies of twenty-six performance artists throughout the world, with a chronology and a list of the distinguishing features of their work. Helen Chadwick, Ian Breakwell, Rose Gerard, Stuart Brisley, Vera Frenkel are a few of the artists covered.

4239 Kaye, Nick. "Breaking Up the Frame." *PM.* 1988; 56/57: 23-25. Biblio. Illus.: Sketches. B&W. 1. Lang.: Eng.

Austria: Vienna. Italy. 1960-1977. Critical Studies. ■Challenges to conventional aesthetic values and definitions in the work of performers Vito Acconci and Hermann Nitsch. Discusses their violation of social and moral taboos in which the performance of personally painful or bloody acts are transformed into public ritual.

4240 Iles, Charles. "Taking a Line for a Walk." *PM.* 1988; 53: 14-19. Illus.: Photo. B&W. 5. Lang.: Eng.

Europe. China, People's Republic of. 1970-1988. Historical studies. ■Analyzes the work of performance artists Marina Abramovič and Ulay and their latest collaboration which involves a walk from either end of the Great Wall of China.

4241 Caton, Shaun. "A Profile of Egon Schrick." *PM.* 1989/90; 59: 24-29. Illus.: Photo. B&W. 5. Lang.: Eng.

Germany. 1976-1987. Biographical studies. ■Profile of performance artist Schrick, trained as an artist and and architect, who turned to performance art in the piece *Aktionismus.*

4242 Shimizu, Tetsuo. "The Impossibility of Art." *PerAJ.* 1998 May; 20(2): 54-56. Illus.: Photo. B&W. 1. Lang.: Eng.

Japan. 1996-1998. Critical studies. ■Visual artist Rei Naito's use of her body and movement in her latest exhibition to address issues of anonymity and the artist.

4243 Blumberg, Marcia. "Domestic Place as Contestatory Space: The Kitchen as Catalyst and Crucible." *NTQ.* 1998 Aug.; 14(3): 195-201. Notes. Biblio. [Issue 55.] Lang.: Eng.

UK-England. South Africa, Republic of. 1990-1992. Historical studies. ■The subversion of kitchen-related gender roles in *Kitchen Show* and *Cook Dems* by Bobby Baker and *Kitchen Blues* by Jeanne Goosen.

4244 Campbell, Patrick; Spackman, Helen. "Surviving the Performance: Interview with Franko B." *TDR.* 1998 Win; 42(4): 67-74. Illus.: Photo. B&W. 4. Lang.: Eng.

UK-England. 1998. Histories-sources. ■Interview with the performance artist on the difficulty of his demanding physical performance style.

4245 Hill, Leslie. "'Push the Boat Out': Site-Specific and Cyberspatial." *NTQ.* 1998 Feb.; 14(1): 43-52. Notes. Illus.: Photo. B&W. 2. [Issue 53.] Lang.: Eng.

MIXED ENTERTAINMENT: Performance art—Performance/production

UK-England: London. USA. 1995-1997. Histories-sources. ▪Performance artist Leslie Hill's site-specific piece *Push the Boat Out* at the Institute of Contemporary Arts and the potential of new technologies in the creation and documentation of live art.

4246 Rogers, Steve. "Showing the Wires." *PM.* 1988(56/57): 9-14. Illus.: Photo. B&W. 9. Lang.: Eng.

UK-England: London. 1980-1988. Histories-sources. ▪Julian Maynard Smith discusses his performance group, Station House Opera, his performance pieces *Cuckoo* and *Split Second Paradise*, and his attempts to extend the boundaries of theatre by subverting formal structure.

4247 Rogers, Steve. "Life After Living." *PM.* 1988; 52: 10-11. Illus.: Photo. Dwg. B&W. 4. Lang.: Eng.

UK-England. USA. 1987-1988. Biographical studies. ▪The 'living paintings' of performer Steven Taylor Woodrow, and the resentment of some artists and dealers as a result of his success.

4248 Dickson, Malcolm. "All the Rage." *PM.* 1988; 54: 24-27. Notes. Illus.: Photo. B&W. 6. Lang.: Eng.

UK-Scotland. 1960-1988. Historical studies. ▪Examination of the Scottish performance art scene: its history and the problems surrounding it.

4249 Carter, Cassie Elaine. *'Woman, Red in Tooth and Claw': Angry Essentialism, Abjection, and Visionary Liberation in Women's Performances.* Bowling Green, OH: Bowling Green Univ; 1998. 234 pp. Notes. Biblio. [Ph.D. Dissertation, Univ. Microfilms Order No. AAC 9902335.] Lang.: Eng.

USA. 1981-1998. Critical studies. ▪Angry Essentialism, a feminist performance trend that emerged during the 1980s, as a problematic intersection of a variety of feminist and avant-garde ideals. Focuses on performance artists Karen Finley and Holly Hughes and the criticism of their work.

4250 Chin, Daryl. "Models of Fashion." *PerAJ.* 1998 Sep.; 20(3): 22-25. Lang.: Eng.

USA. 1996-1998. Critical studies. ▪Argues that the current young generation of performance artists is unaware of its antecedents in the avant-garde of the 1960s and 1970s, with reference to *Beige* and *Show* by Vanessa Beecroft.

4251 Durland, Steven. "Three Points in a Circle: Three Decades of Experiment in the US and Canada." *PM.* 1988; 55: 17-21. Notes. [Cover title: *Edge 88.*] Lang.: Eng.

USA. Canada. 1960-1988. Historical studies. ▪Survey of the work of performance artists: Carolee Schneemann, Paul Wong, and Mark Pauline and Matt Heckert.

4252 Frieze, James. "Making Space/Losing Face: Mimi Goese and the Penultimate Dis-." *PerAJ.* 1998 Sep.; 20(3): 1-9. Notes. Illus.: Photo. B&W. 2. Lang.: Eng.

USA. 1982-1998. Critical studies. ▪Examines the work of performance artist Goese, said to join the incompatible, leading to chaos.

4253 Goldberg, RoseLee. "The Provocateurs." *AmTh.* 1998 Dec.; 15(10): 22-24. Illus.: Photo. B&W. 6. Lang.: Eng.

USA. 1960-1998. Historical studies. ▪Excerts from RoseLee Goldberg's book *Performance: Live Art Since 1960*, a pictorial history with text of performance art, focusing on the highlights of the genre.

4254 Kaye, Nick. "Ritualism and Renewal: Reconsidering the Image of the Shaman." *PM.* 1989/90; 59: 30-45. Notes. Illus.: Photo. B&W. 8. Lang.: Eng.

USA. Germany. Netherlands. 1964-1985. Critical studies. ▪Re-examines the important performance pieces of Joseph Beuys, Marina Abramovič, and Ulay.

4255 Kirshenblatt-Gimblett, Barbara. "The Ethnographic Burlesque." *TDR.* 1998 Sum; 42(2): 175-180. Notes. Biblio. Lang.: Eng.

USA. 1995. Critical studies. ▪Analysis of Guillermo Gómez-Peña and Coco Fusco's performance piece *The Couple in the Cage.*

4256 Matthews, Lydia. "Camp Out: DIWA Arts and the Bayanihan Spirit." *TDR.* 1998 Win; 42(4): 115-132. Notes. Biblio. Illus.: Photo. B&W. 9. Lang.: Eng.

USA: San Francisco, CA. 1994-1996. Historical studies. ▪Report on a series of performance installations conceived by DIWA Arts entitled *Santa Cruzan/Flores de Mayo* that focused on the Filipino immigrant experience in the San Francisco Bay Area.

4257 Peterson, Willam. "Of Cats, Dreams and Interior Knowledge: An Interview with Carolee Schneemann." *PM.* 1989/90; 59: 10-23. Illus.: Photo. B&W. 7. Lang.: Eng.

USA. 1964-1989. Histories-sources. ▪Interview with performance artist Schneemann about the inspiration she derives from dreams, Egyptian and Tantric mythology in creating an erotic, ecstatic art, and her works *Cat Scan* and *Fresh Blood—A Dream Morphology.*

4258 Quasha, George; Stein, Charles. "Liminal Performance: Gary Hill." *PerAJ.* 1998 Jan.; 20(58): 1-25. Biblio. Illus.: Photo. B&W. 4. Lang.: Eng.

USA. 1969-1998. Histories-sources. ▪Interview with video and installation artist Hill regarding his artistic goals, his work, his influences, and his openness to collaboration with artists from other disciplines.

4259 Taylor, Diana. "A Savage Performance: Guillermo Gómez-Peña and Coco Fusco's 'Couple in a Cage'." *TDR.* 1998 Sum; 42(2): 160-175. Notes. Biblio. Illus.: Poster. B&W. 1. Lang.: Eng.

USA. 1992-1995. Critical studies. ▪Background of the two performance artists' piece, *The Couple in the Cage*, in which they toured together locked in a cage.

4260 Thorne, Simon; Mackenzie, Phillip. "Playing with Richard Schechner." *PM.* 1988; 56/57: 20-22. Lang.: Eng.

USA. 1987. Histories-sources. ▪Excerpts from conversations with director Schechner taped over five days as he prepares to present a performance of *Man Act.*

Plays/librettos/scripts

4261 Campbell, Patrick; Spackman, Helen. "With/out Anaesthetic: Terrible Beauty of Franko B." *TDR.* 1998 Win; 42(4): 56-67. Notes. Biblio. Illus.: Photo. B&W. 6. Lang.: Eng.

UK-England. 1996-1998. Critical studies. ▪Analysis of the work of performance artist Franko B., with emphasis on how the AIDS pandemic informs his oeuvre, particularly *Mama I Can't Sing* and *I'm Not Your Baby.*

4262 Cheng, Meiling. "Les Demoiselles d/L.A.: Sacred Nature Girls' *Untitled Flesh.*" *TDR.* 1998 Sum; 42(2): 70-97. Notes. Biblio. Illus.: Photo. Pntg. B&W. 8. Lang.: Eng.

USA: Los Angeles, CA. 1994-1997. Critical studies. ▪History of the Sacred Naked Nature Girls all-female performance group and their all-nude work *Untitled Flesh.*

4263 Dickinson, Joan; Mallozzi, Dawn; Moore, Iris. "*Hunter's Moon* and *Flower*: Two Performances by Joan Dickinson." *TDR.* 1998 Win; 42(4): 14-36. Illus.: Photo. Dwg. B&W. 18. Lang.: Eng.

USA. 1997-1998. Histories-sources. ▪Developed from a series of conversations between the writer Dickinson and the performers Mallozzi and Moore over the course of several months as they put together the two video performance pieces. Includes synopses of both works and the lyrics to Dickinson's verse 'Ode to a Feisty Bearded Clam'.

Relation to other fields

4264 Allthorpe-Guyton, Marjorie. "The Big Dipper: The Legacy of Arte Povera." *PM.* 1989; 58: 22-29. Notes. Illus.: Photo. B&W. 4. Lang.: Eng.

Italy. 1967-1985. Historical studies. ▪Analyzes the growth of the Arte Povera movement, named by the critic Germano Celant, with special reference to director/artist Michelangelo Pistoletti's collaboration with actors and playwrights.

4265 Anderson, Simon. "Flux-Hunting: The Uncertain in Pursuit of the Incomprehensible." *PM.* 1989; 58: 11-22. Illus.: Photo. B&W. 7. Lang.: Eng.

USA. Europe. 1961-1979. Historical studies. ▪Recounts the spread of the philosophy Fluxus, a way of thinking about art's relationship to society, which was devised by George Maciunas, and other artists in different fields.

4266 Stuckert, Heike. "Dieses Gefühl von Demut." (That Humble Feeling.) 34-49 in Pochhammer, Sabine, ed. *Utopie: Spiritualität? Spiritualité: une utopie?/Utopia: Spirituality? Spirituality: A Utopia?.* Berlin: Theaterschrift c/o Künstlerhaus

Bethanien; 1998. 173 pp. (Theaterschrift 13.) Illus.: Photo. B&W. 2. Lang.: Ger, Fre, Dut, Eng.
USA. Germany. 1997-1998. Histories-sources. ■An interview with the performance artist Shelley Hirsch about her piece *For Jerry—Part I*, an homage to performer Jerry Hunt. Describes the links between spirituality and modern technology and the use of magical and ritualistic qualities of electronics based on her own work and that of Jerry Hunt.

Research/historiography

4267 Kaye, Nick. "Documenting Performance Art." *PM.* 1988; 53: 30-31. Illus.: Photo. B&W. 2. Lang.: Eng.
1950-1988. Historical studies. ■Consideration of how performance art can best be documented when traditional means of verbal descriptions and filmed records fail to convey the special use of place, space, and time, or the tensions between performers, audience, and objects.

Theory/criticism

4268 Gaynor, Mark. "A Question of Difference." *PM.* 1988; 56/57: 31-32. Illus.: Photo. B&W. 2. Lang.: Eng.
UK-England. 1988. Critical studies. ■Report on the Eighth National Review of Live Art.

4269 Herbert, Simon. "Somebody Should Tell the Emperor." *PM.* 1988; 54: 19-21. Illus.: Photo. B&W. 4. Lang.: Eng.
UK-England. 1960-1988. Critical studies. ■Argues that modern performance art has lost its true experimental character, and is likely to come packaged with program notes for its audience. Asserts that performance art's audience is far too lenient in its critical appraisal.

4270 Hughes, David. "Window on Performance: The Poetics of Space." *PM.* 1989/90; 59: 46-57. Notes. Illus.: Photo. B&W. 5. Lang.: Eng.
USA. Poland. 1952-1984. Critical studies. ■Discusses the 'poetics of space' (an impulse to move from the logic of the line, or of the flat plane into space) from its definition by Charles Olson, and its emergence in the work of John Cage and Tadeusz Kantor, to its theoretical dimension in some post-structuralist writings.

Variety acts

Administration

4271 Hanna, Judith Lynne. "Undressing the First Amendment and Corsetting the Striptease Dancer." *TDR.* 1998 Sum; 42(2): 38-69 . Notes. Biblio. Tables. Illus.: Photo. B&W. 14. Lang.: Eng.
USA. 1998. Critical studies. ■Political and legal aspects of exotic dance clubs with emphasis on the first amendment rights of the dancers and clubs and negative community reaction.

Institutions

4272 Dženikaeva, L. "Nartam žit'!" (Long Live Narty!)*Dar'jal.* 1998; 5: 290-299. Lang.: Rus.
Russia: Vladikavkaz. 1998. Historical studies. ■History of A. Dživaev's theatre of horses, 'Narty'.

Performance spaces

4273 Sommaiolo, Paolo. *Il Café-Chantant. Artisti e ribalte nella Napoli Belle Epoque.* (The Café-Chantant. Artists and Stages During the Belle Epoque in Naples.) Napoli: Tempolungo; 1998. 286 pp. Lang.: Ita.
Italy: Naples. 1880-1915. Historical studies. ■The artistic history of the *café chantant* in Naples.

Performance/production

4274 Svečnikov, V. *Teorija i praktika sceničeskoj magii.* (Theory and Practice of Stage Magic.) Saratov: 1998. 200 pp. Lang.: Rus.
1998. Critical studies. ■Analysis of illusion, using examples from the works of David Copperfield and Lance Barton.

4275 Fano, Nicola. *De Rege varietà. Biografia probabile di un duo comico.* (De Rege Variety Theatre. A Probable Biography of Two Comic Actors.) Milan: Baldini & Castoldi; 1998. 184 pp. (Storia della storia d'Italia, 45.) Illus.: Photo. B&W. 8. Lang.: Ita.
Italy. 1891-1948. Biographical studies. ■Biography of comic actors Guido and Giorgio De Rege, who were very popular in the variety theatre of the 1930s.

4276 "Ne choču videt' svoj pamjatnik." (I Do Not Want To See My Monument.) *MoskZ.* 1998; Apr: 73-75. Lang.: Rus.
Russia. 1998. Histories-sources. ■Interview with actor R. Karcev.

4277 Chazanov, G. "'Čelovečeskomu organizmu vovse ne objazatel'no nosit' galstuk ot Versače'." (A Person's Body Doesn't Need to Wear a Tie Made by Versace.) *Ogonek.* 1998; 47: 50-52. Lang.: Rus.
Russia: Moscow. Histories-sources. ■Director of Moscow's Theatre of Stage Performance (Teat'r Estrady) talks about theatre and stage genres.

4278 Hughes, Howard; Benn, Danielle. "Holiday Entertainment in a British Seaside Resort Town." *JAML.* 1998 Win; 28(4): 295-306. Notes. Biblio. Lang.: Eng.
UK-England. 1950-1998. Historical studies. ■Reasons for the decline of live entertainment in seaside resort towns in Great Britain.

4279 Robson, Christopher. "Will Rogers (1879-1935) Unique American Folk Hero." *PlPl.* May 1998; 522: 15. Illus.: Photo. B&W. 1. Lang.: Eng.
UK-England: London. 1879-1935. Biographical studies. ■Career and private life of entertainer Will Rogers.

4280 Robson, Christopher. "Al Jolson (1886-1990)—The World's Greatest Entertainer." *PlPl.* Feb 1998; 519: 28. Lang.: Eng.
USA. 1886-1950. Biographical studies. ■Life of Al Jolson and his career on stage, screen and radio.

4281 Rodger, Gillian Margaret. *Male Impersonation on the North American Variety and Vaudeville Stage, 1868-1930.* Pittsburgh, PA: Univ. of Pittsburgh; 1998. 428 pp. Notes. Biblio. [Ph.D. Dissertation, Univ. Microfilms Order No. AAC 9906325.] Lang.: Eng.
USA. 1868-1930. Histories-specific. ■Concentrates on the most successful male impersonators active in variety and vaudeville and describes their performance style, including vocal range, repertoire and conventions of performance.

4282 Solomon, Alisa. "Five Lesbian Brothers: No Whining!" *AmTh.* 1998 Sep.; 15(7): 61-62. Illus.: Dwg. B&W. 1. Lang.: Eng.
USA: New York, NY. 1989-1998. Historical studies. ■Brief history of the satiric comedy troupe and their roots at the WOW Café.

Relation to other fields

4283 Horrall, A.J. *Music-hall, Transportation and Sport: Up-to-Dateness in London Popular Culture c. 1890-1914.* Cambridge: Unpublished PhD, Univ. of Cambridge; 1998. Notes. Biblio. [Abstract in *Aslib Index to Theses* 47-5468.] Lang.: Eng.
UK-England: London. 1890-1914. Historical studies. ■How 'up-to-dateness' required artists to continually adjust their acts to reflect the latest popular crazes, which allowed performers not related to the stage, such as cyclists, motorists, pilots, diabolists, and athletes to pursue careers in the music halls in both sketches and solo pieces.

4284 Waites, Aline. "The Tavern Music Hall." *PlPl.* Mar 1998; 520: 7. Lang.: Eng.
UK-England: London. 1843-1998. Historical studies. ■Historical origins of London's music halls and segregation of variety acts from legitimate theatre.

4285 Liepe-Levinson, Katherine. "Striptease: Desire, Mimetic Jeopardy, and Performing Spectators." *TDR.* 1998 Sum; 42(2): 9-37. Notes. Biblio. Illus.: Photo. Poster. B&W. 14. Lang.: Eng.
USA. 1992-1998. Critical studies. ■Field study of white, middle-class, male/female heterosexual striptease events focusing on the strip show's concurrent upholding and breaking of conventional sex roles in terms of the participation of the spectator.

MUSIC-DRAMA

General

Administration

4286 Blankemeyer, Silke. "So gehört's." (So It Goes.) *DB.* 1998; 6: 40-41. Illus.: Photo. B&W. 3. Lang.: Ger.

Germany: Essen. 1997-1998. Historical studies. ▪Portrait of Stefan Soltesz, theatre-manager and music director at Aalto-Musiktheater and his first season at the house.

Basic theatrical documents

4287 Demarcy, Richard. "*Ubu déchaîné.*" (Ubu Unchained.) *AST.* 1998 1 Apr.; 1027: 2-37. Illus.: Photo. B&W. 14. Lang.: Fre.

Benin. France. 1998. ▪Text of Demarcy's play, inspired by Alfred Jarry, as produced by Sanza Théâtre of Benin, directed and choreographed by Demarcy and Vincent Mambachaka. Includes profiles of the author and Sanza Théâtre and an essay on the play.

4288 Brenk, Tomaž; Kasjak, Mojca. *Emanacije. (Emanations.)* Maribor: Mladinski kulturni center; 1998. 8 pp. Lang.: Eng, Slo.

Slovenia. 1997. ▪Text of the musical play *Emanations (Emanacije)*, by Tomaž Brenk, including choreography by Mojca Kasjak.

Design/technology

4289 Wolf, Matt. "Shearing *Samson.*" *OpN.* 1998 Feb 28; 62(12): 24-27. Illus.: Design. Photo. Color. 5. Lang.: Eng.

UK-England. USA. 1954-1998. Biographical studies. ▪The scenic design history of Richard Hudson, which includes *The Lion King* on Broadway as well as the new Metropolitan Opera production of *Samson et Dalila* by Camille Saint-Saëns.

4290 Lampert-Gréaux, Ellen. "Spanish Steps." *TCI.* 1998 May; 32(5): 7-8. Illus.: Photo. Color. 1. Lang.: Eng.

USA: Washington, DC. 1998. Technical studies. ▪Joan Sullivan's lighting for the Washington Opera's production of *Doña Francisquita*, the Amadeo Vives *zarzuela.*

Institutions

4291 Brandenburg, Detlef. "Aufbruch zur 'Zweiten Moderne'." (The Emergence Towards the 'Second Modern Age'.) *DB.* 1998; 3: 30-33. Illus.: Photo. B&W. 4. Lang.: Ger.

Germany: Munich. 1998. Histories-sources. ▪Interview with Peter Ruzicka, responsible for the festival of the 6th Münchener Biennale, about program, concepts and advertising.

4292 Davidson, Clifford; Davidson, Audrey Ekdahl. *Performing Medieval Music Drama.* Kalamazoo, MI: Medieval Institute Publications; 1998. 50 pp. Notes. Illus.: Photo. B&W. 4. Lang.: Eng.

USA: Kalamazoo, MI. 1968-1991. Historical studies. ▪History of the Society for Old Music, dedicated to the performance of medieval religious drama.

Performance/production

4293 Brandenburg, Detlef. "Streifzüge unter dem Wind." (Expeditions Under Wind.) *DB.* 1998; 11: 42-47. Illus.: Photo. B&W. 6. Lang.: Ger.

Germany: Lübeck, Hamburg, Bremen, Kiel. 1998. Reviews of performances. ▪Impressions from current theatre situation in North Germany: Robert Wilson's *The Black Rider* directed by Christian von Götz at Theater Lübeck, Giuseppe Verdi's *Otello* directed by Andrej Woron at Bremer Theater, Gian Francesco Malipiero's *I Capricci di Callot* directed by Katja Czellnik at Bühnen der Landeshauptstadt Kiel and Alban Berg's *Wozzeck* directed by Peter Konwitschny at Staatsoper Hamburg.

4294 Davidson, Audrey Ekdahl. "Sequentia's New *Ordo Virtutum.*" *EDAM.* 1998 Fall; 21(1): 28-30. Lang.: Eng.

Germany. 1997. Critical studies. ▪Virtues of the early music ensemble Sequentia's re-recording of Hildegard of Bingen's *Ordo Virtutum.*

4295 Hammarlund, Jan. "Om Brecht och sångstämman: Den oväntade ömsintheten." (About Brecht and the Vocal Part: The Unexpected Tenderness of Heart.) *MuD.* 1998; 20(4): 14-17. Illus.: Photo. B&W. Lang.: Swe.

Germany. 1920-1998. Critical studies. ▪The singing praxis of the songs of Brecht's plays, with references to Lotte Lenya, Kurt Weill, Hanns Eisler and Paul Dessau.

4296 Mazanec, Brigitta. "Ein Magier des Klanges und der Farben." (A Magician of Sound and Colors.) *DB.* 1998; 6: 42-44. Illus.: Photo. B&W. 4. Lang.: Ger.

Germany: Kassel. 1997-1998. Historical studies. ▪Portrait of Roberto Paternostro and his start as music director at Staatstheater Kassel in context of financial crisis und increasing budget cuts.

4297 Reininghaus, Frieder. "'Glotzt nicht so romantisch'." ('Don't Stare So Romantically'.) *DB.* 1998; 2: 44-45. Illus.: Photo. B&W. 2. Lang.: Ger.

Germany. 1928-1998. Historical studies. ▪Describes the relationship between composers and Bertolt Brecht's work from Kurt Weill and Hanns Eisler to Heiner Goebbels.

4298 Eősze, László; Mezey, Béla, photo. "Felújítás az Operaházban: *Székely fonó.*" (Revival at the Opera House: Zoltán Kodály: *The Székler Spinnery.*) *ZZT.* 1998; 5(2): 4-5. Illus.: Photo. B&W. 1. Lang.: Hun.

Hungary: Budapest. 1998. Reviews of performances. ▪Imre Kerényi's revival of Kodály's musical play at the Hungarian State Opera House.

4299 Szomory, György. "Dalok az összetartozásról s a közösség összetartó erejéről: Beszélgetés Kerényi Imrével, a *Székely fonó* rendezőjével." (Songs about Unity, the Power of the Community: A Conversation with Imre Kerényi, Stage Director of *The Székler Spinnery.*) *OperaL.* 1998; 7(2): 2-12. Illus.: Photo. B&W. 1. Lang.: Hun.

Hungary: Budapest. 1997. Histories-sources. ▪Interview with the director of Zoltán Kodály's only work for the stage at the Budapest Opera House. Describes the work, a presentation of the folk songs and ballads of the Hungarians of Eastern Transylvania in an orchestral setting.

4300 Guccini, Gerardo, ed. *Le opere senza canto di Giovanni Tamborrino. Drammaturgie e ricerche alla confluenza dei teatri.* (The Operas without Song of Giovanni Tamborrino: Dramaturgies and Research at the Confluence of Theatres.) Bologna: CLUEB; 1998. 158 pp. (Alma Materiali.) Pref. Notes. Illus.: Photo. Print. B&W. Lang.: Ita.

Italy. Critical studies. ▪Essays on the dramaturgy of composer Giovanni Tamborrino, in collaboration with some actors, creating a theatre for music.

4301 Žučkov, V. "Nezabyvaemye mgnovenija." (Unforgettable Moments.) *Nižnij Novgorod.* 1998; 9: 208-212. Lang.: Rus.

Russia: Nizhni Novgorod. 1998. Biographical studies. ▪Profile of singer I.S. Kozlovskij in a touring production.

4302 Zykina, L.G. *Tečet moja Volga...* (My River, Volga, Flows...) Moscow: Novosti; 1998. 416 pp. Lang.: Rus.

Russia. Histories-sources. ▪Singer Ljudmila Zykina on her career and her art.

4303 Midgette, Anne. "Voice Talk: Choosing a voice teacher is the most important decision a young singer has to make..." *OpN.* 1998 Sep.; 63(3): 20-22. Illus.: Photo. B&W. 4. Lang.: Eng.

USA. 1998. Critical studies. ▪Anne Midgette discusses with voice teacher William Schuman of the Academy of Vocal Arts the technical differences between singing opera and Broadway.

4304 Morris, Mark; Brazil, Tom, photo. "*Platée.*" *BR.* 1998 Sum; 26(2): 43-58. Illus.: Photo. B&W. 39. Lang.: Eng.

USA: Berkeley, CA. 1998. Historical studies. ▪Photographic essay of a performance of director/choreographer Mark Morris' production of *Platée*, a lyric comedy with music by Jean-Philippe Rameau and libretto by Adrien-Joseph Le Valois d'Orville. Morris supplies synopses for each act.

Plays/librettos/scripts

4305 Barlow, Clarence. "Songs Within Words: The Programme *TXMS* and the Performance of *Ping* on the Piano." 233-240 in Bryden, Mary, ed. *Samuel Beckett and Music.* Oxford: Clarendon; 1998. 267 pp. Index. Notes. Biblio. Illus.: Dwg. 2. Lang.: Eng.

MUSIC-DRAMA: General—Plays/librettos/scripts

1971-1972. Histories-sources. ■The author's development of a computer program to create 'abstract' music to which a prose text from Samuel Beckett's *Ping* was set.

4306 Kim, Earl. "A Note: *Dead Calm*." 257-258 in Bryden, Mary, ed. *Samuel Beckett and Music*. Oxford: Clarendon; 1998. 267 pp. Index. Notes. Biblio. Illus.: Diagram. 1. Lang.: Eng.

1945-1995. Histories-sources. ■Composer Earl Kim provides a musical example from his piece *Dead Calm*, inspired by playwright Samuel Beckett's novel, *Watt*.

4307 Frenquellucci, Chiara. *A Passion to Amuse: Girolamo Gigli's Theatre and Prose*. Cambridge, MA: Harvard Univ; 1998. 234 pp. Notes. Biblio. [Ph.D. Dissertation, Univ. Microfilms Order No. AAC 9832367.] Lang.: Eng.

Italy. 1660-1722. Critical studies. ■Reassessment of writer Girolamo Gigli's original contributions to the theatre and to narrative prose. Author focuses on his musical dramas examining his use of parody, mythology, and *commedia* in *La Dirindina* and *La sorellina di Don Pilone (Don Pilone's Little Sister)*.

4308 Bosseur, Jean-Yves; Bryden, Mary, transl. "Between Word and Silence: *Bing*." 241-248 in Bryden, Mary, ed. *Samuel Beckett and Music*. Oxford: Clarendon; 1998. 267 pp. Index. Notes. Biblio. Illus.: Sketches. 1. Lang.: Eng.

USA. 1986. Histories-sources. ■The author's French adaptation, *Bing*, of Roger Reynold's *Ping*, itself a musical adaptation of a prose work by Samuel Beckett.

4309 Reynolds, Roger. "The Indifference of the Broiler to the Broiled." 195-212 in Bryden, Mary, ed. *Samuel Beckett and Music*. Oxford: Clarendon; 1998. 267 pp. Index. Notes. Biblio. Illus.: Photo. Diagram. 6. Lang.: Eng.

USA. 1968-1976. Histories-sources. ■The author's use of texts by Samuel Beckett in his musical works *Ping*, based on a short prose text by Beckett, and *A Merciful Coincidence*, based on text from a Beckett novel, *Watt*.

Theory/criticism

4310 Hiss, Guido. "Theater im Fin de Siècle." (Theatre in the Fin de Siècle.) *dRAMATURg*. 1998; 2: 11-22. Illus.: Photo. B&W. 1. Lang.: Ger.

Germany: Berlin. 1993-1998. Critical studies. ■Analyzes the music concept of Christoph Marthaler beyond classic opera and beyond spoken theatre. Describes *Murx den Europäer! Murx ihn! Murx ihn! Murx ihn ab! (Kill the European! Kill Him! Kill Him! Kill Him Off!)* in the tradition of dadaism and symbolism and summarizes the specific aesthetics and problems of his performances.

Chinese opera

Performance/production

4311 Vinogradova, T.I. "Dinastija Čžou v interpretacii pekinskoj muzykal'noj dramy i teatral'noj kartiny." (The Chou Dynasty, as Interpreted in Peking Musical Drama and in Theatrical Paintings.) 403-409 in *Dvadcat' vos'maja naučnaja konferencija 'Obščestvo i gosudarstvo v Kitae'*. Moscow: 1998. Lang.: Rus.

China. 1027-771 B.C. Historical studies. ■Representation of the Chou dynasty in its operas and pictorial arts.

4312 Wang, Hsiao-Mei. *The Characterization of* Sheng *and* Dan *Roles in Chinese Opera*. Denton, TX: Univ. of North Texas; 1987. 347 pp. Biblio. Notes. [M.A. Thesis, Univ. Microfilms Order No. 1331314.] Lang.: Eng.

China. 1500-1980. Historical studies. ■Examines principles of characterization governing the *sheng* (male) and the *dan* (female) roles in Chinese opera.

4313 Chan, Sau Y. "Exploding the Belly: Improvisation in Cantonese Opera." 199-218 in Nettl, Bruno, ed.; Russell, Melinda, ed. *In the Course of Performance: Studies in the World of Musical Improvisation*. (Chicago Studies in Ethnomusicology.) Notes. Index. Biblio. Tables. Lang.: Eng.

China, People's Republic of. 1920-1997. Historical studies. ■Examines the ways in which the concept of improvisation can be used to shed light on the structure of an entire musical genre, such as Chinese opera.

4314 Ram, Jane. "Some Enchanted Evenings." *OpN*. 1998 June; 62(17): 22-24. Illus.: Photo. Design. 3. Lang.: Eng.

China, People's Republic of. 1998. Critical studies. ■Preview of guest performance of *The Peony Pavilion (Mudan ting)*, a Ming Dynasty Kungju opera composed by Tang Xianzu (1550-1617). Includes introduction to plot and style, including cross-gender casting.

Plays/librettos/scripts

4315 Lu, Tina. *Persons, Personae, Personages: Identity in* Mudan Ting *and* Taohua Shan. Cambridge, MA: Harvard Univ; 1998. 485 pp. Biblio. Notes. [Ph.D. Dissertation, Univ. Microfilms Order No. AAC 9832434.] Lang.: Eng.

China. 1575-1675. Critical studies. ■Examines personal identity in two Chinese plays: *Mudan ting (The Peony Pavilion)* by Tang Xianzu and *Taohua shan (The Peach Blossom Fan)* by Kong Shangren.

Musical theatre

Administration

4316 Stähr, Susanne. "Monokultur für Säulenheilige." (Monoculture for Repentant.) *DB*. 1998; 5: 21-24. Illus.: Photo. Graphs. B&W. 5. Lang.: Ger.

Germany. 1986-1998. Critical studies. ■Compares different conditions facing musical companies and municipal and state theatres concerning producing, pricing, marketing, and communications.

4317 "Disney's High Kicks on Broadway." *Econ*. 1998 May 23; 347(8069): 77-78. Lang.: Eng.

USA: New York, NY. 1996-1998. Critical studies. ■Influence of the Disney Corporation on Broadway musicals in light of the successes of *The Lion King*, directed by Julie Taymor at the New Amsterdam Theatre, and *Beauty and the Beast*, directed by Robert Jess Roth at the Palace Theatre.

4318 Eisenberg, Alan. "Executive Director Goes on the Road with *Cats*." *EN*. 1998 June; 83(5): 4-6. Illus.: Photo. Dwg. 6. Lang.: Eng.

USA: New York, NY. 1998. Historical studies. ■Alan Eisenberg, executive director of Actors' Equity, recounts his experience with bus-and-truck touring company of *Cats*.

4319 Moore, Dick. "Minimums Up in RMTA." *EN*. 1998 Jan/Feb.; 83(1): 5. Lang.: Eng.

USA. 1998. Historical studies. ■Reports on the new three-year Resident Musical Theatre Association contract which features improved salaries and payments.

4320 Moore, Dick. "Meet Rebecca Spencer: First time on Broadway, First Time as a Deputy." *EN*. 1998 May; 83(4): 2. Illus.: Photo. 1. Lang.: Eng.

USA: New York, NY. 1998. Historical studies. ■Chorus member Rebecca Spencer relates her experience as a first-time Equity Deputy in a Broadway musical, *Jekyll & Hyde* by Frank Wildhorn.

4321 Nunns, Stephen. "Another *Rent* Strike." *AmTh*. 1998 July/Aug.; 15(6): 55. Lang.: Eng.

USA: New York, NY. 1998. Historical studies. ■Note on the legal battle over the ownership of the rights to *Rent* between the estate of playwright Jonathan Larson and dramaturg Lynn Thomson.

4322 Nunns, Stephen. "Rent Control." *AmTh*. 1998 Nov.; 15(9): 60. Lang.: Eng.

USA: New York, NY. 1998. Critical studies. ■Report on the settlement between dramaturg Lynn Thomson and the estate of playwright Jonathan Larson regarding ownership to the rights of Larson's musical *Rent*. Thomson claimed 16 percent ownership.

Basic theatrical documents

4323 Tarleton, Angela Brannon. *Raven's Song: An Original Musical*. Denton, TX: Univ. of North Texas; 1988. 135 pp. Biblio. Notes. [M.A. Thesis, Univ. Microfilms Order No. AAC 1333569.] Lang.: Eng.

USA. 1988. ■Text of original play.

Design/technology

4324 Gornall, Nick. "Joe Control." *TCI*. 1998 May; 32(5): 50. Illus.: Photo. Diagram. Color. 2. Lang.: Eng.

MUSIC-DRAMA: Musical theatre—Design/technology

Netherlands: Amsterdam. 1998. Technical studies. ■Report on the system, called Avenger's Conductor, designed by Sierk Janszen to operate the complex technical elements of light, sound, and special effects involved in the production of *Joe—The Musical* by Ad and Koen van Dijk, directed by Pieter van de Waterbeemd at the Koninklijk Theater Carré.

4325 Johnson, David; Lampert-Gréaux, Ellen. "You've Never Seen Anything Like It." *TCI.* 1998 Nov.; 32(10): 56-67. Illus.: Photo. Design. Dwg. Sketches. B&W. Color. 19. Lang.: Eng.

UK-England: London. 1998. Technical studies. ■Paul Arditti and Richard Ryan's sound design, Hugh Vanstone's lighting, Mark Thompson's sets, and the nearly one-hundred animals provided by the Jim Henson Creature Shop for Steven Pimlott's production of Leslie Bricusse's *Doctor Doolittle* at the Apollo Hammersmith. Includes a list of the crews and equipment employed for the show.

4326 Moles, Steven. "London Razzle Dazzle." *TCI.* 1998 Mar.; 32(3): 9-10. Illus.: Photo. Color. 1. Lang.: Eng.

UK-England: London. 1998. Technical studies. ■Rick Clark's sound design for the London production of Kander and Ebb's *Chicago* at the Adelphi directed by Walter Bobbie.

4327 Moles, Steven. "No Kidding Around." *TCI.* 1998 Apr.; 32(4): 10-11. Illus.: Photo. Photo. B&W. 1. Lang.: Eng.

UK-England: London. 1997. Technical studies. ■Thomas Ashbee's sound design for *Bugsy Malone* by Paul Williams and Alan Parker, directed by Russell Labey and Jeremy James Taylor at the Queen's Theatre.

4328 Barbour, David. "The Rythym of Light." *TCI.* 1998 Apr.; 32(4): 44. Illus.: Photo. Color. 1. Lang.: Eng.

USA: New York, NY. 1998. Technical studies. ■Jules Fisher and Peggy Eisenhauer's lighting design for *Ragtime* at the Ford Center for the Performing Arts, with a sidebar concerning the projections for the musical designed by Wendall K. Harrington.

4329 Barbour, David. "Side by Side." *TCI.* 1998 Feb.; 32(2): 6-7. Illus.: Photo. Color. 1. Lang.: Eng.

USA: New York, NY. 1998. Technical studies. ■Tom Clark's sound design for Henry Krieger and Bill Russell's musical *Side Show* directed by Robert Longbottom at the Richard Rodgers Theatre.

4330 Barbour, David. "Boy's Life." *TCI.* 1998 Mar.; 32(3): 7-9. Illus.: Dwg. Color. 1. Lang.: Eng.

USA: Minneapolis, MN. 1998. Technical studies. ■Campbell Baird's costume design for a new version of *Peter Pan* (book and lyrics by Timothy Mason, music by Hiram Titus) premiere performances by the Children's Theatre Company of Minneapolis directed by Wendy Lehr.

4331 Barbour, David. "Scarlet Fever." *TCI.* 1998 Mar.; 32(3): 34-37. Illus.: Photo. Design. Dwg. Color. 12. Lang.: Eng.

USA: New York, NY. 1998. Technical studies. ■Andrew Jackness' sets and Jane Greenwood's costumes for *The Scarlet Pimpernel*, music by Frank Wildhorn, book and lyrics by Nan Knighton, directed by Robert Longbottom at the Minskoff Theatre.

4332 Barbour, David. "There Is Nothing Like a Dame." *TCI.* 1998 Aug/Sep.; 32(8): 9-10. Illus.: Dwg. Color. 1. Lang.: Eng.

USA: San Francisco, CA. 1998. Technical studies. ■Costume designs for *Dames at Sea*, by George Haimsohn and Robin Miller, music by Jim Wise, by Michael Bottari and Donald Case. The show was performed at the Marine Memorial Theatre under the direction of Scott Thompson.

4333 Barbour, David. "Accessorize for Success." *TCI.* 1998 Aug/Sep.; 32(8): 12-13. Illus.: Sketches. B&W. 1. Lang.: Eng.

USA: New York, NY. 1998. Technical studies. ■Jonathan Bixby and George A. Gale's costumes for the revival of the Moss Hart-Irving Berlin revue *As Thousands Cheer*, directed by Christopher Ashley for the Drama Dept. at Greenwich House Theatre.

4334 Barbour, David. "High-Wire Walking." *TCI.* 1998 Oct.; 32(9): 21-23. Illus.: Photo. Color. 1. Lang.: Eng.

USA: East Haddam, CT. 1998. Technical studies. ■Neil Patel's circus-themed scenic design for the musical *Mirette*, book by Elizabeth Diggs, music by Harvey Schmidt, lyrics by Tom Jones, and directed by Andre Ernotte at the Goodspeed Opera House.

4335 Barbour, David. "Beautiful Girls." *LDim.* 1998 July; 22(6): 54-57, 90-91. Illus.: Photo. Lighting. Color. 5. Lang.: Eng.

USA: Millburn, NJ. 1998. Technical studies. ■Examines the lighting design by Mark Stanley for the musical *Follies*, by Stephen Sondheim and James Goldman, directed by Robert Johanson at the Paper Mill Playhouse and starring Kaye Ballard.

4336 Boepple, Leanne. "Rite of Passage." *LDim.* 1998 Mar.; 22(2): 48-52, 83-86. Illus.: Photo. Lighting. Color. 12. Lang.: Eng.

USA: New York, NY. 1997-1998. Critical studies. ■Examines the lighting design of Donald Holder in Julie Taymor's Broadway production of *The Lion King*, at the New Amsterdam Theatre, based on the Disney animated movie of the same name, with music and lyrics by Elton John.

4337 Essig, Linda. "*A Chorus Line* Revisited." *TD&T.* 1998 Win; 34(1): 12-16. Notes. Illus.: Photo. Color. 1. Lang.: Eng.

USA: New York, NY. 1974-1975. Technical studies. ■Lighting design and preset control board design, by Tharon Musser and Jane Reisman respectively, for the groundbreaking musical, which inaugurated the era of digital lighting control.

4338 Johnson, David. "The People Call It Ragtime." *TCI.* 1998 Apr.; 32(4): 40-43, 59-60. Illus.: Photo. Design. Dwg. Color. 8. Lang.: Eng.

USA: New York, NY. 1998. Technical studies. ■Eugene Lee's scenic design and Santo Loquasto's costumes for the Broadway premiere of the musical *Ragtime* based on E.L. Doctorow's novel with book by Terrence McNally, music and lyrics by Stephen Flaherty and Lynn Ahrens, and directed by Frank Galati at the Ford Center for the Performing Arts.

4339 Johnson, David. "Tale of the Cape." *TCI.* 1998 May; 32(5): 42-43. Illus.: Photo. Color. 4. Lang.: Eng.

USA: New York, NY. 1998. Technical studies. ■Peter J. Fitzgerald's sound design for the Paul Simon/Derek Walcott musical *The Capeman*, directed and choreograghed by Mark Morris at the Marquis Theatre. Includes partial list of sound equipment used.

4340 Lahr, John. "Skeleton of the New." *NewY.* 1998 5 Jan.: 56-61. Illus.: Pntg. Photo. Sketches. Color. 5. Lang.: Eng.

USA. 1997-1998. Historical studies. ■Analysis of Eugene Lee's set design for the musical *Ragtime*, directed by Frank Galati at the Ford Center in New York.

4341 Lampert-Gréaux, Ellen. "Syncopated Rythyms." *TCI.* 1998 Apr.; 32(4): 45, 59. Illus.: Photo. B&W. Color. 2. Lang.: Eng.

USA: New York, NY. 1998. Technical studies. ■Jonathan Deans' sound design for the Broadway premiere of the musical *Ragtime* at the Ford Center for the Performing Arts.

4342 Lampert-Gréaux, Ellen; Johnson, David; Boepple, Leanne. "It's Good to Be King." *TCI.* 1998 Mar.; 32(3): 42-48. Illus.: Photo. Design. Dwg. Photo. B&W. Color. 23. Lang.: Eng.

USA: New York, NY. 1998. Technical studies. ■Julie Taymor's masks and costumes for the Broadway musical version of the Disney film *The Lion King*, music by Elton John, lyrics by Tim Rice, directed by Taymor at the New Amsterdam Theatre. Includes two sidebars concerning Don Holder's light design and Tony Meola's sound design, and a list of production houses and equipment employed in the fabrication of sets, costumes, lights and sound.

4343 Lampert-Gréaux, Ellen. "Period Light, Something Old, Something New, Real Sound." *TCI.* 1998 July; 32(7): 40-41. Illus.: Photo. Color. 7. Lang.: Eng.

USA: New York, NY. 1998. Technical studies. ■Peggy Eisenhauer's lights, William Ivey Long's costumes, and Brian Ronana's sound design for Sam Mendes' production of *Cabaret* at the Kit Kat Klub, formerly the Henry Miller Theatre.

4344 Lampert-Gréaux, Ellen. "Life As a Cabaret." *LDim.* 1998 July; 22(6): 58-63, 102. Illus.: Photo. Lighting. Color. 8. Lang.: Eng.

USA: New York, NY. 1998. Technical studies. ■Examines the lighting design of Peggy Eisenhauer and Mike Baldassari for John Kander and Fred Ebb's *Cabaret*, directed by Sam Mendes at the Roundabout Theatre and starring Natasha Richardson and Alan Cummings.

4345 Newman, Mark A. "Dynamic Duo." *LD&A.* 1998 Sep.; 28(9): 42-45. Illus.: Photo. Color. 7. Lang.: Eng.

MUSIC-DRAMA: Musical theatre—Design/technology

USA: New York, NY. 1998. Technical studies. ■Beverly Emmons' light design for *Jekyll & Hyde* by Frank Wildhorn and Leslie Bricusse and directed by Robin Phillips at the Plymouth Theatre.

Institutions

4346 Lane, Harry; Hopkinson, Claire; Strongman, Wayne. "Life Beyond the Premiere: Process and Purpose at Tapestry Music Theatre." *CTR*. Fall 1998; 96: 50-55. Illus.: Photo. B&W. 6. Lang.: Eng.

Canada: Toronto, ON. 1985-1998. Histories-sources. ■Artistic director Wayne Strongman and general manager/producer Claire Hopkinson explain Tapestry Music Theatre's mandate and method of producing and sustaining new Canadian music theatre.

4347 Brandenburg, Detlef. "'Schöne Neue Musik!'." ('Fine New Music!'.) *DB*. 1998; 8: 48-50. Illus.: Photo. B&W. 2. Lang.: Ger.

Germany: Wiesbaden. 1986-1998. Histories-sources. ■Interview with singer Carla Henius about new music and the musik-theater-werkstatt festival which she has managed since 1986 at Hessisches Staatstheater Wiesbaden.

4348 Mazanec, Brigitta. "In der Tradition die Utopie finden." (To Find an Utopia in Tradition.) *DB*. 1998; 8: 51-53. Illus.: Photo. B&W. 3. Lang.: Ger.

Germany: Wiesbaden. 1998. Historical studies. ■Portrait of Ernst August Klötzke and his future plans as manager of musik-theater-werkstatt festival at Hessisches Staatstheater Wiesbaden.

4349 Ångström, Anna. "De får jobb innan skolan är slut." (They Got a Job Before School Was Out.) *Danst*. 1998 ; 8(2): 8-9. Illus.: Photo. Color. Lang.: Swe.

Sweden: Gothenburg. 1984-1998. Histories-sources. ■Description of the musical theatre course at Balettakademien, with an interview with the director Lars Anderstam.

Performance spaces

4350 Barbour, David. "The Kit Kat Klub Revisited." *TCI*. 1998 July; 32(7): 38-39. Illus.: Photo. Color. 2. Lang.: Eng.

USA: New York, NY. 1998. Technical studies. ■Transformation of the old Henry Miller Theatre, by set designer Robert Brill, into the site-specific space for Sam Mendes' production of Kander and Ebb's *Cabaret*. The old theatre has been renamed the Kit Kat Klub.

Performance/production

4351 Chlebnikova, M. "Nam vse daetsja svyše." (Our Fate Comes from God.) *Smena*. 1998; 3: 116-119. Lang.: Rus.

1998. Histories-sources. ■Singer M. Chlebnikova on her career.

4352 Mercado, Mario R. "A Voice Apart." *OpN*. 1998 Nov.; 63(5): 38-45, 83. Illus.: Photo. B&W. Color. 12. Lang.: Eng.

Austria: Vienna. 1898-1981. Biographical studies. ■The career of Viennese soprano Lotte Lenya, wife of the composer Kurt Weill, whose work she introduced and immortalized in performance.

4353 Vasil'ev, A. "Slovo na pačke." (A Word in a Box.) *Persona*. 1998; 4: 51-53. Lang.: Rus.

Bulgaria. 1998. Histories-sources. ■Musical theatre performer, L. Ivanova, on contemporary theatre in Bulgaria.

4354 "Lenya: In Praise of a Career." *KWN*. 1998 Fall; 16(2): 3. Illus.: Photo. B&W. 5. Lang.: Eng.

Germany. 1928-1966. Histories-sources. ■Quotes from theatre critics in praise of the performance style of singer/actress Lotte Lenya.

4355 "I Remember Lenya ..." *KWN*. 1998 Fall; 16(2): 4-7. Illus.: Photo. B&W. 6. Lang.: Eng.

Germany. 1928-1981. Histories-sources. ■Reminiscences of friends, neighbors, and colleagues of singer/actress Lotte Lenya, including actors Scott Merrill, Dolores Sutton, and Michael Wager, composers John Kander and John Cacavas, producers Hank Kaufman and Stanley Chase, director Carmen Capalbo, lyricist Fred Ebb, and *Cabaret* book writer Joe Masteroff.

4356 Burckhardt, Barbara. "Das Theater der Klone." (Theatre of Clones.) *THeute*. 1998; 3: 17-19. Illus.: Photo. B&W. 2. Lang.: Ger.

Germany: Berlin. 1998. Critical studies. ■Analyzes *Der Ozeanflug* directed by Robert Wilson using Bertolt Brecht's play, with music by Kurt Weill, and compiling it with texts by Heiner Müller and Dostojėvskij.

4357 Hamilton, David. "Listening to Lenya." *KWN*. 1998 Fall; 16(2): 8-12. Illus.: Photo. B&W. 6. Lang.: Eng.

Germany. 1929-1965. Critical studies. ■Analysis of Lotte Lenya's singing style on the release of a centenary package of her recordings.

4358 Csáki, Judit; Ilovszky, Béla, photo. "Big Mac: Brecht-Weill: *Koldusopera*." (Big Mac: Bertolt Brecht-Kurt Weill: *The Three Penny Opera*.) *Sz*. 1998; 31(12): 19-21. Illus.: Photo. B&W. 1. Lang.: Hun.

Hungary: Veszprém. 1998. Reviews of performances. ■*Die Dreigroschenoper* at the Petőfi Theatre, Veszprém, directed by László Vándorfi.

4359 Hollósi, Zsolt; Veréb, Simon, photo. "Szegedi Szabadtéri Játékok: *Háry János*." (Szeged Open-Air Festival: *Háry János*.) *OperaL*. 1998; 7(4): 20-21. Illus.: Photo. Color. 6. Lang.: Hun.

Hungary: Szeged. 1998. Reviews of performances. ■A pictorial account of one of the summer productions at this year's Szeged Open-Air Festival, the premiere of Zoltán Kodály's musical play.

4360 Karsai, György; Fábián, József, photo.; Ilovszky, Béla, photo. "Két musical-bemutató." (Two Musical Premieres.) *Sz*. 1998; 31(2): 41-45. Illus.: Photo. B&W. 3. Lang.: Hun.

Hungary: Budapest. 1997. Reviews of performances. ■Two new Hungarian musical plays: *A kiátkozott (The Outcast)* by Levente Szörényi and János Bródy directed by István Iglódi at the National Theatre and *Will Shakespeare avagy akit akartok (Will Shakespeare: or, Whom You Will)* by Mátyás Várkonyi and János Bródy directed by Viktor Nagy at the Madách Theatre.

4361 Mátai, Györgyi. "*West Side Story* Veszprémből." (*West Side Story* from Veszprém.) *Tanc*. 1998; 29 (4): 20. Illus.: Photo. B&W. 1. Lang.: Hun.

Hungary: Veszprém. 1998. Reviews of performances. ■Bernstein's musical at an open-air stage, Budai Parkszínpad presented by the Petőfi Theatre of Veszprém as a guest performance directed by László Vándorfi.

4362 Sándor, L. István; Koncz, Zsuzsa, photo.; Veréb, Simon, photo. "Brecht itt, Weill ott: Két *Koldusopera*-előadás." (Brecht Here, Weill There: Two Productions of *The Three Penny Opera*.) *Sz*. 1998; 31(5): 30-35. Illus.: Photo. B&W. 5. Lang.: Hun.

Hungary: Budapest, Szeged. 1998. Reviews of performances. ■A comparative analysis of two productions of *Die Dreigroschenoper* by Brecht-Weill: at the New Theatre directed by Eszter Novák and at the Szeged National Theatre directed by János Szikora.

4363 Henderson, Stephen. "Annie Get Your Shogun." *AmTh*. 1998 Feb.; 15(2): 58-64. Illus.: Photo. B&W. 4. Lang.: Eng.

Japan: Tokyo. 1963-1998. Historical studies. ■History of the popularity of the American musical on the Japanese stage.

4364 Killick, Andrew Peter. *The Invention of Traditional Korean Opera and the Problem of the Traditionesque:* Ch'angguk *and Its Relation to* P'ansori *Narratives*. Seattle, WA: Univ. of Washington; 1998. 560 pp. Notes. Biblio. [Ph.D. Dissertation, Univ. Microfilms Order No. AAC 9826339.] Lang.: Eng.

Korea. 1900-1998. Histories-specific. ■The evolution of the Korean musical story-telling form *p'ansori*, prized as 'traditional art,' into a uniquely Korean form of modern opera, known as *ch'angguk*. Author examines the cultural struggle over this evolution as well as the musical evolution itself.

4365 Žigarev, A. *Anna German*. Smolensk: Rusič; 1998. 430 pp. (Ženščina-mif.) Lang.: Rus.

Poland. 1998. Biographical studies. ■Biography of Polish musical theatre performer Anna German.

4366 Dolina, Larisa. "Volšebnyj zont." (The Magical Umbrella.) *Smena*. 1998; 1: 268-272. Lang.: Rus.

Russia: Moscow. Histories-sources. ■Singer Larisa Dolina on her life and career.

MUSIC-DRAMA: Musical theatre—Performance/production

4367 Orbakajte, Kristina. "Tak že, kak vse, kak vse, kak vse." (Just Like Everyone Else.) *Domovoj.* 1998; 8-9: 78-83. Lang.: Rus.

Russia: Moscow. 1998. Histories-sources. ▪Musical performer Kristina Orbakajte, about herself, her tastes, her life style.

4368 Tal'kova, O. Ju. *Ja voskresnu i spoju...: Iz vospominanij mamy I. Tal'kova.* (I Will Come Back to Life and Sing...: From a Recollection of the Mother of Tal'kov.) Moscow: Firma 'Alesja'; 1998. 208 pp. Lang.: Rus.

Russia. 1998. Histories-sources. ▪Profile of singer I. Tal'kov by his mother.

4369 Bevan, Anthony. "What a Trooper." *PlPl.* Aug 1998; 525: 32. Lang.: Eng.

UK-England: Basingstoke. 1998. Histories-sources. ▪Applauds actors' handling of a mishap during a production of *Phantom of the Opera.*

4370 Eccles, Christine. "Back to the 1970s." *PI.* 1998 Oct.; 14(1): 10-11. Illus.: Photo. B&W. 1. Lang.: Eng.

UK-England. 1998. Histories-sources. ▪Interview with Shane Ritchie, actor, and Jon Conway, coauthor and director of the musical *Boogie Nights.*

4371 Olenin, A. "Zastenčivyj d'javol Élton Džon." (Elton John Is a Shy Devil.) *MoskZ.* 1998; Oct-Nov: 71-73. Lang.: Rus.

UK-England. 1998. Biographical studies. ▪Profile of British rock star turned musical theatre composer Elton John.

4372 Taylor, John Russel. "Gillian Lynne." *PlPl.* Feb 1998; 519: 15. Lang.: Eng.

UK-England: London. USA: New York, NY. 1951-1998. Histories-sources. ▪Gillian Lynne's transition from performance to directing and choreographing in London and on Broadway, based on information given in an interview.

4373 Wolf, Matt. "West End Cowboys." *AmTh.* 1998 Nov.; 15(9): 50-53. Illus.: Photo. B&W. 2. Lang.: Eng.

UK-England: London. 1998. Critical studies. ▪The popular and critical success of the revival of the American musical *Oklahoma!* on the London stage, directed by Trevor Nunn at the new Olivier Theatre, at the expense of homegrown musicals.

4374 Anthony, Eugene. "Choreography: You Can Present a 'Perfect' Broadway Musical Using Actors Who Move Well." *SoTh.* 1998 Spr; 39(2): 4-8. Illus.: Photo. 2. Lang.: Eng.

USA. 1998. Instructional materials. ▪Provides tips and advice on how to stage a musical theatre production successfully when few, if any, trained dancers are available.

4375 Békés, Pál. "Más kor, más kór: Jonathan Larson: *Rent.*" (Another Age, Another Disease: Jonathan Larson: *Rent.*) *Sz.* 1998; 31(4): 43-44. Illus.: Photo. B&W. 1. Lang.: Hun.

USA: New York, NY. 1990. Reviews of performances. ▪While appreciating the play by composer-librettist Jonathan Larson and its production the Hungarian playwright also sketches its socio-cultural background.

4376 Blier, Steven; Diggans, Elizabeth, illus. "'You Say Ee-ther...'." *OpN.* 1998 Aug.; 63(2): 16-17. Illus.: Dwg. Pntg. 1. Lang.: Eng.

USA. 1896-1998. Critical studies. ▪Comments on the work of the two Gershwin brothers arising from a visit to the exhibition of Gershwin memorabilia at the Rose Museum, Carnegie Hall.

4377 Bramley, Ian. "It's Showtime, Folks!" *DTJ.* 1998; 14(2): 22-25. Notes. Illus.: Photo. B&W. 1. Lang.: Eng.

USA. 1953-1987. Critical studies. ▪Bob Fosse's choreographic style and its development.

4378 Carter, Marva Griffin. *The Life and Music of Will Marion Cook.* Urbana-Champaign, IL: Univ. of Illinois; 1988. 651 pp. Notes. Biblio. [Ph.D. Dissertation, Univ. Microfilms Order No. AAC 8908642.] Lang.: Eng.

USA. 1898-1950. Biographical studies. ▪Focuses on Cook's creative output as a musical theatre composer including his work with Bert Williams and George F. Walker on *In Dahomey.*

4379 Copeland, Philip Larue. *The Role of Drama and Spirituality in the Music of Leonard Bernstein.* Louisville, KY: Southern Baptist Theological Seminary; 1998. 221 pp. Notes. Biblio. [D.M.A. Dissertation, Univ. Microfilms Order No. AAC 9903146.] Lang.: Eng.

USA. 1965-1990. Historical studies. ▪Explores the previously overlooked role of drama and spirituality in the dramatic music of Leonard Bernstein with special focus on his symphonies and the theatrical techniques employed in his music.

4380 de Lappe, Gemze. "A Half Century with Agnes." *Dm.* 1998 Jan.; 72(1): 66-69. Illus.: Photo. B&W. 4. Lang.: Eng.

USA: New York, NY. 1943-1998. Histories-sources. ▪Dancer de Lappe relates her experience dancing in musicals for choreographer Agnes De Mille.

4381 Elwell, Jeffery Scott. "Secondary: Hattiesburg High Students Share the Magic of Oz on a Mystical Journey to the Fringe." *SoTh.* 1998 Win; 39(1): 22-28. Illus.: Photo. 6. Lang.: Eng.

USA: Hattiesburg, MS. UK-Scotland: Edinburgh. 1996. Historical studies. ▪Students from a Mississippi high school take their production of *The Wiz,* book by William Brown, music by Charlie Smalls, to the Edinburgh Festival to participate in the American high school portion of the Fringe Festival.

4382 Flatow, Sheryl. "Who Could Ask for Anything More: A Selective Guide to Gershwin Recordings." *OpN.* 1998 Aug.; 63(2): 24-27, 52. Illus.: Photo. B&W. 9. Lang.: Eng.

USA. 1998. Critical studies. ▪Critical comments on the many recordings of George Gershwin's non-concert music available on compact disc.

4383 Frielinghaus, Helmut. "Bitte recht freundlich!" (Smile Please.) *THeute.* 1998; 10: 38-41. Illus.: Photo. B&W. 3. Lang.: Ger.

USA: New York. 1998. Critical studies. ▪Describes the current musical performances on-and-off-Broadway: *Cabaret* after Christopher Isherwood directed by Rob Marshall and Sam Mendes, John Cameron Mitchell's and Stephen Trask's *Hedwig and the Angry Inch,* William Shakespeare's *Cymbeline* directed by Andrei Serban.

4384 Hill, Errol. "The Hyers Sisters: Pioneers in Black Musical Comedy." 115-130 in Engle, Ron, ed.; Miller, Tice L., ed. *The American Stage: Social and Economic Issues from the Colonial Period to the Present.* Cambridge: Cambridge UP; 1993. 320 pp. Pref. Notes. Index. Lang.: Eng.

USA. 1870-1902. Historical studies. ▪The contribution of African-American sister performers Emma Louise and Anna Madah Hyers to American musical comedy.

4385 Hulbert, Dan. "Safety First." *AmTh.* 1998 Dec.; 15(10): 52-53. Illus.: Photo. B&W. 1. Lang.: Eng.

USA: Atlanta, GA. 1998. Reviews of performances. ▪The premiere of *Elaborate Lives: The Legend of Aida,* music by Elton John, lyrics by Tim Rice, book by Linda Woolverton, at the Alliance Theatre under the direction of Robert Jess Roth and produced by the Disney Company.

4386 Moore, Dick. "BC/EFA, AmFAR Present All-Star Charity." *EN.* 1998 Sep.; 83(7): 2. Illus.: Photo. 1. Lang.: Eng.

USA: New York, NY. 1998. Historical studies. ▪Reports on a Broadway Cares/Equity Fights AIDS benefit performance of Cy Coleman's *Sweet Charity,* presented in conjunction with the American Foundation for AIDS Research. Coleman and performer Gwen Verdon, star of the original 1966 production, led a staged, concert version of the piece.

4387 Oseland, James. "Defending *The Capeman.*" *AmTh.* 1998 Apr.; 15(4): 31. Illus.: Photo. B&W. 1. Lang.: Eng.

USA: New York, NY. 1998. Critical studies. ▪One critic's rebuttal to the negative reviews given to the Paul Simon-Derek Walcott musical directed by Jerry Zaks at the Marquis.

4388 Payne-Carter, David. *Gower Champion and the American Musical Theatre.* New York, NY: New York Univ; 1987. 542 pp. Biblio. Notes. [Ph.D. Dissertation, Univ. Microfilms Order No. AAC 8801561.] Lang.: Eng.

USA: New York, NY. 1936-1980. Historical studies. ▪Examines the career of dancer/choreographer/director Gower Champion. Focuses on his training and his work on Broadway.

Plays/librettos/scripts

4389 Bell, Karen. "Leslie Arden." *PAC.* 1998; 31(3): 14-16. Illus.: Photo. B&W. 2. Lang.: Eng.

MUSIC-DRAMA: Musical theatre—Plays/librettos/scripts

Canada. 1993-1998. Biographical studies. ▪Recounts the career of performer/director/writer Leslie Arden, especially her current work writing the music, lyrics, and story for *The House of Martin Guerre*, which won the Dora award for best new musical and was directed by Anna Teresa Cascio.

4390 Atkins, Madeline Smith. *The Importance of Music in London's Eighteenth Century Popular Theatre.* New York, NY: St. John's Univ; 1998. 196 pp. Notes. Biblio. [Ph.D. Dissertation, Univ. Microfilms Order No. AAC 9821681.] Lang.: Eng.

England. 1728-1780. Critical studies. ▪Analyzes the evolution of music, especially the ballad opera genre, in English popular theatre. Examines John Gay's *The Beggar's Opera*, Charles Coffey's *The Beggar's Wedding* and *The Devil to Pay*, Thomas Arne's *Thomas and Sally* and *Love in a Village*, Samuel Arnold's *The Maid of the Mill*, the Linleys' *The Duenna*, Kane O'Hara's burlettas *Midas* and *The Golden Pippin*, and George Colman's *The Portrait.*

4391 Fischer, Gerhard. "'Karnevalistisches Weltempfinden' und Dramaturgie der sozialen Integration: Die Komödienästhetik Volker Ludwigs." ('Carnivalesque World Feeling' and Dramaturgy of Social Integration: Volker Ludwig's Comic Aesthetics.) *FMT.* 1998; 13(2): 184-194. Lang.: Ger.

Germany: Berlin. 1968-1998. Historical studies. ▪Analysis of the plays of Volker Ludwig through the lens of the theories of Mikhail Bakhtin, particularly his view of the nature of laughter. Also looks at his new musical *Line1.*

4392 Pollock, Adam. "A Question of Baloney: The Search for a Lost Translation of *The Seven Deadly Sins.*" *KWN.* 1998 Spr; 16 (1): 12-13. Illus.: Photo. B&W. 1. Lang.: Eng.

Germany. UK-England. 1933-1998. Histories-sources. ▪Author's experience tracking down impresario Edward James' translation of Brecht and Weill's play.

4393 Wille, Frank. "Lerne hoffen ohne zu lügen." (Learn to Hope Without Lying.) *THeute.* 1998; 1: 43-45. Illus.: Photo. B&W. 3. Lang.: Ger.

Germany: Berlin. 1997-1998. Critical studies. ▪Analysis of playwright/theatre-manager Volker Ludwig's children's piece with music *Café Mitte (Café Center)* performed at GRIPS and directed by Rüdiger Wandel.

4394 Jaffer, Kay. "Notions of Coloured Identities in Cape Flats Theatre: A Look at Taliep Petersen's *District Six—The Musical.*" *SATJ.* 1998 May/Sep.; 12(1/2): 91-107. Notes. Biblio. Lang.: Eng.

South Africa, Republic of. 1987. Critical studies. ▪Impact of Petersen's musical on contemporary South African theatre.

4395 Farrelly, Mark. "Rising from the Ashes of the Blacklist: Earl Robinson and Waldo Salt's *Sandhog*, A Worker's Musical." *AmerD.* 1998 Spr; 7(2): 73-91. Notes. Biblio. Lang.: Eng.

USA. 1954. Historical studies. ▪Story behind blacklisted writers Earl Robinson and Waldo Salt's worker's musical *Sandhog.*

4396 Julian, Patrick. "Let the Orchestra Go, but Carry the Gallery: The Mythic Portrayal of FDR in *I'd Rather Be Right.*" *NETJ.* 1998; 9: 49-69. Biblio. Lang.: Eng.

USA. 1937. Critical studies. ▪Investigates the portrayal of President Franklin D. Roosevelt in Kaufman and Hart's musical.

4397 Orchard, Lee Frederick. *Stephen Sondheim and the Disintegration of the American Dream: A Study of the Work of Stephen Sondheim from 'Company' to 'Sunday in the Park with George'.* Salem, OR: Univ. of Oregon; 1988. 695 pp. Biblio. Notes. [Ph.D. Dissertation, Univ. Microfilms Order No. AAC 8814194.] Lang.: Eng.

USA. 1970-1984. Historical studies. ▪The theme of the disintegration of the American dream in Stephen Sondheim's *Company, Follies, A Little Night Music, Pacific Overtures, Sweeney Todd, Merrily We Roll Along,* and *Sunday in the Park with George.*

4398 Pen, Polly, ed. "New Voices in Musical Theatre." *DGQ.* 1998 Spr; 35(1): 35-47. Lang.: Eng.

USA: New York, NY. 1998. Histories-sources. ▪Edited transcript of a panel discussion on musical theatre held in New York. Panelists include librettist-lyricists Brian Crawley, Cornelius Eady, and Sarah Schlesinger, and composers Michael John LaChiusa, Jeanine Tesori, and Diedre Murray.

4399 Secrest, Meryle. "How Rose Got Her Turn." *AmTh.* 1998 May/June; 15(5): 18-21. Illus.: Photo. B&W. 2. Lang.: Eng.

USA: New York, NY. 1956-1959. Biographical studies. ▪Excerpt from *Stephen Sondheim*, Secrest's biography of the composer/lyricist, focusing on the creation of the musical *Gypsy.*

4400 Shteir, Rachel. "Betty Comden: That Ol' Zappo Punch." *AmTh.* 1998 Sep.; 15(7): 76-77. Illus.: Photo. B&W. 1. Lang.: Eng.

USA. 1938-1998. Biographical studies. ▪Profile of Broadway musical and film lyricist and librettist Betty Comden.

4401 Zinman, Toby. "Sometimes More Is Less: Fellini's *Otto e mezzo* to Kopit's *Nine.*" *MD.* 1998 Spr; 41(1): 146-156. Notes. Lang.: Eng.

USA. 1963-1982. Critical studies. ▪Comparison of Arthur Kopit's book for *Nine*, music and lyrics by Maury Yeston, with its source, Federico Fellini's *8 1/2.*

Relation to other fields

4402 Humfeld, Nancy Jo. *Music Theatre: A Synthesized Program.* Carbondale, IL: Southern Illinois Univ; 1987. 348 pp. Notes. Biblio. [Ph.D. Dissertation, Univ. Microfilms Order No. AAC 8805838.] Lang.: Eng.

USA. 1987. Empirical research. ▪Study of interdisciplinary approaches to teaching music theatre. Author conducted a survey of fourteen universities to examine two specialized courses created for use in a musical theatre degree—music theatre history and music theatre literature.

Theory/criticism

4403 Kennedy, William Bruce. *Rhyme and Reason: An Evaluation of Lehman Engel's Contribution to the Criticism of Music Theatre.* Kent, OH: Kent State Univ; 1987. 321 pp. Notes. Biblio. [Ph.D. Dissertation, Univ. Microfilms Order No. AAC 8806530.] Lang.: Eng.

USA. 1940-1982. Critical studies. ▪Explores the career of musical director/conductor Aaron Lehman Engel. Focuses on Engel's theoretical writings and their contribution to the genre of musical theatre.

Opera

Administration

4404 Baisch, Axel. "Hohe Ziele, harte Zahlen." (High Aims, Hard Numbers.) *DB.* 1998; 5: 43-45. Illus.: Photo. B&W. 4. Lang.: Ger.

Germany: Duisburg. 1996-1998. Histories-sources. ▪How Deutsche Oper am Rhein has converted its marketing concepts into practice.

4405 Hessler, Ulrike. "Markenzeichen: Abenteuerlust." (Corporate Identity: Thirst for Adventure.) *DB.* 1998; 5: 30-33. Illus.: Photo. B&W. 6. Lang.: Ger.

Germany: Munich. 1993-1998. Histories-sources. ▪Hessler, the manager of the public relations department, describes the plans to create a new image of Bayerische Staatsoper.

4406 Buchau, Stephanie von. "Coda: Pitch Problems." *OpN.* 1998 Mar 28; 62(14): 54. Illus.: Photo. B&W. Color. 2. Lang.: Eng.

USA. 1998. Critical studies. ▪Speculations on the future marketing of opera, noting that younger audiences may be attracted by opera's sexuality and an irreverent treatment of tradition.

4407 Mitchell, Emily; Bergman, Beth, photo.; Needham, Mark, photo. "Standing Room Only." *OpN.* 1998 Dec.; 63(6): 28-31. Illus.: Photo. Color. 12. Lang.: Eng.

USA: New York, NY. 1998. Historical studies. ▪The effect of standing-room-only practices at the Metropolitan Opera.

4408 Moore, Dick. "Rosetta LeNoire Award Presented at Western Meeting." *EN.* 1998 May; 83(4): 1. Lang.: Eng.

USA: Sacramento, CA. 1998. Historical studies. ▪Reports on the presentation of the annual Rosetta LeNoire Award to Leland Ball and the Sacramento Light Opera Association.

MUSIC-DRAMA: Opera

Audience

4409 Campos, Rémy. "Delibes, entre passé et avenir." (Delibes Between Past and Future.) *ASO.* 1998 Mar/Apr.; 183: 60-61. Notes. Lang.: Fre.

1900-1996. Historical studies. ▪The negative influence of Wagnerianism on the reception of Delibes' opera *Lakmé.*

4410 Krämer, Timm. "Ist der *Parsifal* zu lang?" (Is *Parsifal* Too Long?)*DB.* 1998; 9: 24-27. Illus.: Photo. B&W. 4. Lang.: Ger.

Germany. 1998. Critical studies. ▪Describes the current relationship between opera performances and young audiences. Suggests presentations that are better oriented to young people's needs.

4411 Solie, Ruth A. "Fictions of the Opera Box." 185-208 in Dellamora, Richard, ed.; Fischlin, Daniel, ed. *The Work of Opera: Genre, Nationhood, and Sexual Difference.* New York, NY: Columbia UP; 1997. 350 pp. Notes. Index. Biblio. Lang.: Eng.

USA. 1890-1910. Historical studies. ▪The Metropolitan Opera's famous 'golden horseshoe' as a site where social warfare was waged through the prism of gender between the patricians and the *nouveaux riches* of New York society. Argues that women were the bearers of high culture.

Basic theatrical documents

4412 Berg, Alban; Banoun, Bernard, transl.; Condé, Gérard, ed. "*Lulu.*" *ASO.* 1998 Jan/Feb.; 181/182: 7-152. Notes. Lang.: Fre, Ger.

Austria. 1935. ▪Complete text, in the original German and in French translation, of the libretto of Berg's opera, based on two plays by Frank Wedekind. Includes a summary of the plot, detailed musical analysis of numerous passages, commentary on the work, and many photos from various productions.

4413 Clarke, George Elliot. "Beatrice Chancy: A Libretto in Four Acts." *CTR.* Fall 1998; 96: 62-77. LI. Illus.: Photo. B&W. 7. Lang.: Eng.

Canada: Toronto, ON. 1998. ▪Complete libretto by George Elliot Clarke of opera *Beatrice Chancy* (music by James Rolfe), which premiered at Music Gallery, Toronto ON (Queen of Puddings Music Theatre Company, directed by Michael Cavanagh, 1998). Includes introduction and lists of historical and artistic sources of inspiration.

4414 Rolfe, James. "Some thoughts on the opera *Beatrice Chancy* (with excerpts from the score)." *CTR.* Fall 1998; 96: 78-82. Illus.: Photo. B&W. 1. Lang.: Eng.

Canada: Toronto, ON. 1998. ▪Excerpts from the opera *Beatrice Chancy,* libretto by George Elliot Clarke and music by Rolfe, with additional text on composers' challenges and techniques of writing music.

4415 Delibes, Léo; Gondinet, Edmond; Gille, Philippe; Campos, Rémy, ed. "*Lakmé.*" *ASO.* 1998 Mar/Apr.; 183: 3-54 . Notes. Illus.: Photo. B&W. Lang.: Fre.

France. 1883. ▪Complete libretto with a plot summary, extensive commentary on the music and plot, numerous illustrations.

4416 Massenet, Jules; Milliet, Paul; Grémont, Henri; Zanardini, Angelo; Condé, Gérard, ed. "*Hérodiade.*" *ASO.* 1998 Nov/Dec.; 187: 68-115. Notes. Illus.: Photo. Dwg. B&W. 21. Lang.: Fre.

France. 1881. ▪Libretto for Massenet's opera with extensive musicological and textual commentary by the editor.

4417 Massenet, Jules; Gallet, Louis; Condé, Gérard, ed. "*Le Roi de Lahore.*" (The King of Lahore.) *ASO.* 1998 Nov/Dec.; 187: 3-45. Illus.: Photo. Dwg. B&W. 11. Lang.: Fre.

France. 1877. ▪Gallet's libretto for the opera by Massenet. Includes detailed musicological and textual analysis by the editor.

4418 Offenbach, Jacques; Crémieux, Hector; Halévy, Ludovic; Campos, Rémy, ed. "*Orphée aux Enfers.*" (Orpheus in the Underworld.) *ASO.* 1998 July/Aug.; 185: 3-67. Notes. Illus.: Photo. B&W. Lang.: Fre.

France. 1874. ▪Full text of the libretto with numerous illustrations and extensive commentary.

4419 Zemlinsky, Alexander; Meyerfeld, Max; Perroux, Alain, ed.; Banoun, Bernard, transl. "*Une Tragédie Florentine.*" (A Florentine Tragedy.) *ASO.* 1998 Sep/Oct.; 186: 3-35. Notes. Illus.: Photo. Dwg. B&W. Lang.: Ger, Fre.

Germany. 1917. ▪Text of Meyerfeld's libretto for Zemlinsky's opera *Eine florentinische Tragödie,* based on his translation of Oscar Wilde's play *A Florentine Tragedy.* Includes French translation, many illustrations and detailed commentary on the plot and music.

4420 Zemlinsky, Alexander; Klaren, Georg C.; Perroux, Alain, ed. "*Le Nain.*" (The Dwarf.) *ASO.* 1998 Sep/Oct.; 186: 46-86. Notes. Illus.: Photo. Dwg. B&W. Lang.: Fre, Ger.

Germany. 1922. ▪Klaren's libretto for Zemlinsky's opera *Der Zwerg,* based on a short story by Oscar Wilde (*The Birthday of the Little Princess,* 1889). Includes detailed commentary on the music and the plot, numerous illustrations, and French translation of the libretto.

4421 Rossini, Gioacchino; Rossini, Gaetano; Colas, Damien, ed. "*Sémiramis.*" *ASO.* 1998 May/June; 184: 2-71. Notes. Illus.: Photo. Dwg. B&W. Lang.: Fre, Ita.

Italy. 1823. ▪Complete text of the libretto by Gaetano Rossini to Gioacchino Rossini's opera *Semiramide,* based on *Sémiramis* by Voltaire, in Italian with a facing French translation, and including numerous illustrations as well as extensive commentary.

4422 Golove, Jonathan. *Red Harvest: An Opera with Libretto Adapted from the Novel by Dashiell Hammett.* Buffalo, NY: State Univ. of New York; 1998. 86 pp. Notes. Biblio. [Ph.D. Dissertation, Univ. Microfilms Order No. AAC 9905262.] Lang.: Eng.

USA. 1940-1950. ▪Text and libretto of *Red Harvest,* commissioned by the Académie Européene de Musique, which gave the work its premiere at the 1998 Festival International d'Art Lyrique d'Aix-en-Provence.

4423 Warfield, Jean Mae. *Christina's Opera: A Full Length Ballad Opera About Christina, Queen of Sweden.* New York, NY: New York Univ; 1988. 324 pp. Biblio. Notes. [Ph.D. Dissertation, Univ. Microfilms Order No. AAC 8910648.] Lang.: Eng.

USA. 1988. ▪Libretto for *Christina, Queen of Sweden* by Jean Mae Warfield.

Design/technology

4424 Adams, Stephen. "An Audience of Trees: R. Murray Schaffer's *The Princess of the Stars.*" *CTR.* Fall 1998; 96: 44-49. Notes. Biblio. Illus.: Dwg. Photo. B&W. 7. Lang.: Eng.

Canada. 1981-1997. Critical studies. ▪Ideological, aesthetic and technological challenges of R. Murray Schaffer's environmental opera *The Princess of the Starts,* designed to be performed on a lake in the woods.

4425 Rewa, Natalie. "Scenographic Stories: Design in Contemporary Opera Performance." *CTR.* 1998 Fall; 96: 9-17. Notes. Illus.: Photo. B&W. 19. Lang.: Eng.

Canada: Toronto, ON. 1983-1998. Historical studies. ▪Innovative use of visual symbols in the scenography of various experimental opera companies in Canada, particularly on the Toronto stage.

4426 Rewa, Natalie. "Michael Levine: The Process to See." *CTR.* Win 1998; 97: 41-47. Illus.: Photo. B&W. 10. Lang.: Eng.

Canada: Toronto, ON. 1988-1998. Biographical studies. ▪Design process and innovative visuals of opera scenographer Michael Levine, both in Canada for the Canadian Opera Company and abroad, often in collaboration with director Robert Carson.

4427 Rickerd, Julie Rekai. "Gretel Expectations." *TCI.* 1998 Apr.; 32(4): 24-26. Illus.: Photo. B&W. Color. 6. Lang.: Eng.

Canada: Toronto, ON. 1998. Technical studies. ▪Maurice Sendak's set design for the Canadian Opera Company's production of Humperdinck's opera *Hänsel und Gretel* directed by Frank Corsaro.

4428 Abel, Iris. "Oper in der Manege." (Opera in a Circus Ring.) *BtR.* 1998; 5: 24-25. Illus.: Photo. Color. 5. Lang.: Ger.

Germany: Berlin. 1998. Technical studies. ▪Technical aspects of *Die Zauberflöte* by Mozart, directed by George Tabori in a circus ring.

4429 Loney, Glenn. "The Way We Wernicke." *TCI.* 1998 Nov.; 32(10): 12-14. Illus.: Photo. Color. 1. Lang.: Eng.

Germany: Munich. 1998. Technical studies. ▪Herbert Wernicke's set and costume designs for Richard Strauss's *Elektra* at the Staatsoper in Munich directed by Wernicke.

4430 Rickerd, Julie Rekai. "Birds of a Feather." *TCI.* 1998 Aug/Sep.; 32(8): 13-14. Illus.: Photo. Color. 1. Lang.: Eng.

MUSIC-DRAMA: Opera—Design/technology

Germany: Berlin. 1998. Technical studies. ■Director/designer Robert Wilson's set design, in collaboration with Vera Dobroschke, for his production of Brecht's *Der Ozeanflug* at Berliner Ensemble.

4431 Winkelsesser, Karin. "Ein Traum–was sonst?" (A Dream–What Else?)*BtR.* 1998; 1: 18-21. Illus.: Design. Photo. Color. 4. Lang.: Ger.

Germany: Berlin. 1997. Technical studies. ■Describes Hans Werner Henze's *Der Prinz von Homburg* after Heinrich von Kleist directed by Götz Friedrich at Deutsche Oper Berlin from the point of view of the lighting concept and its integration into the fabric of the production. Includes an interview with the lighting worker Ulrich Niepel.

4432 Cenner, Mihály. "'A jelmez a szereplő lelki ruhája': Márk Tivadar köszöntése." ('Costumes are the Mental Clothes of the Performers': Saluting Tivadar Márk.) *OperaL.* 1998; 7(3): 2-3. Illus.: Photo. B&W. 1. Lang.: Hun.

Hungary. 1908-1998. Biographical studies. ■Profile of the costume designer on the occasion of his ninetieth birthday and the sixtieth anniversary of his appointment as life member of the Hungarian State Opera House.

4433 Baker, Evan. "Verdi's Operas and Giuseppe Bertoja's Designs at the Gran Teatro La Fenice, Venice." 209-240 in Radice, Mark A., ed. *Opera in Context: Essays on Historical Staging from the Late Renaissance to the Time of Puccini.* Portland, OR: Amadeus P; 1998. 410 pp. Notes. Index. Tables. Biblio. Illus.: Plan. Dwg. Sketches. Design. 14. Lang.: Eng.

Italy: Venice. 1840-1870. Historical studies. ■The professional relationship between opera composer Giuseppe Verdi and scenic/theatre designer Giuseppe Bertoja at La Fenice. Argues that Bertoja and his designs may have influenced Verdi's development of his operas.

4434 Clark, Mike. "Turandot Turnaround." *TCI.* 1998 Feb.; 32(2): 16-17. Illus.: Photo. Color. 1. Lang.: Eng.

Italy: Rome. 1998. Technical studies. ■Description of sound system, designed by Daniele Tramontani, used for the Rome Opera production of Puccini's *Turandot* staged at the Olympic soccer stadium. Briefly notes lighting design by Giorgio Nisi.

4435 Clark, Mike. "Milanese Macbeth." *TCI.* 1998 July; 32(7): 10-11. Illus.: Dwg. Color. 2. Lang.: Eng.

Italy: Milan. 1998. Technical studies. ■Lighting design of Thomas Webster for Teatro alla Scala's mounting of Verdi's *Macbeth* directed by Graham Vick.

4436 Ossi, Massimo. "*Dalle macchine...la maraviglia*: Bernardo Buontalenti's *Il rapimento di Cefalo* at the Medici Theater in 1600." 15-36 in Radice, Mark A., ed. *Opera in Context: Essays on Historical Staging from the Late Renaissance to the Time of Puccini.* Portland, OR: Amadeus P; 1998. 410 pp. Notes. Index. Tables. Biblio. Illus.: Plan. Dwg. 3. Lang.: Eng.

Italy: Florence. 1600. Historical studies. ■The use of theatrical machines, or *maraviglia*, in Italian Renaissance theatre, with emphasis on Buontalenti's production of *Il Rapimento di Cefalo* by Gabriello Chiabrera (libretto) and Guilio Caccini (music), with additional music by Ottavio Rinuccini.

4437 Chmeleva, N. "Chudožniki Mamontovskoj opery." (The Artists of Mamontovskaja Opera.) *Naše nasledie.* 1998; 46: 128-136. Lang.: Rus.

Russia: Moscow. 1875-1925. Biographical studies. ■Profiles of designers of the opera house.

4438 Mut'ja, N.N. "Éskizy V. Gartmana k opere M.I. Glinki 'Ruslan i Ljudmila'." (V. Gartman's Sketches for M.I. Glinka's Opera *Ruslan and Ljudmila.*) 30-38 in *K issledovaniju russkogo izobrazitel'nogo iskusstva.* St. Petersburg: 1998. Lang.: Rus.

Russia: St. Petersburg. 1876. Technical studies. ■The architect's sketches for the production at the Mariinskij Theatre.

4439 Tranberg, Sören; Nygren, Per. "Kaos är granne med Mörk." (Chaos Is Neighbour To Mörk.) *MuD.* 1998; 20(2) : 16-17. Illus.: Photo. B&W. Lang.: Swe.

Sweden: Stockholm. France: Paris. 1957-1998. Biographical studies. ■Profile of scenographer Lennart Mörk, with reference to his design to Stein Winge's production of Wagner's *Tristan und Isolde* at l'Opéra-Bastille.

4440 Barbour, David. "Pioneer Women." *TCI.* 1998 July; 32(7): 9-10. Illus.: Dwg. Color. 2. Lang.: Eng.

USA: New York, NY. 1998. Technical studies. ■Marie Anne Chiment's costumes and set design for Paula M. Kimper's opera *Patience and Sarah* directed by Douglas Moser at the Lincoln Center Festival.

4441 Dunham, Richard E. "Jennifer Tipton: Lighting Designer." *TD&T.* 1998 Sum; 34(3): 19-31. Illus.: Photo. Lighting. Color. B&W. 8. Lang.: Eng.

USA: New York, NY. 1998. Biographical studies. ■Profile of designer Tipton with focus on her light design for the Metropolitan Opera's *The Rake's Progress* by Igor Stravinskij, directed by James Levine.

4442 Knox, Robert Erskine, Jr. *Aeolus Appeased: A Modern Scenographic Concept.* Carbondale, IL: Southern Illinois Univ; 1988. 224 pp. Biblio. Notes. [Ph.D. Dissertation, Univ. Microfilms Order No. AAC 9117449.] Lang.: Eng.

USA. 1988. Histories-specific. ■Documents a scenographer's approach to creating a viable production concept for an earlier period musical-theatrical work that will ultimately engage and edify a modern American audience, using the *dramma per musica*, *Aeolus Appeased*, by J. S. Bach and C. F. Henrici as an example.

4443 Loney, Glenn. "Dangerous Women." *TCI.* 1998 Oct.; 32(9): 10-12. Illus.: Photo. Dwg. Color. 2. Lang.: Eng.

USA: San Francisco, CA. 1998. Technical studies. ■Robert Perdziola's sets for the production of Monteverdi's *L'Incoronazione di Poppea*, Bob Mackie's costumes for Alban Berg's *Lulu*, and Michael Yeargen's sets for Bizet's *Carmen*, all staged by Christopher Alden at the San Francisco Opera.

4444 Smith, Cary. "Onward Tristan Soldiers." *TCI.* 1998 Nov.; 32(10): 6-7. Illus.: Photo. Color. 2. Lang.: Eng.

USA: Seattle, WA. 1998. Technical studies. ■Alison Chitty's sets and Mimi Jordan Sherin's lights for the Seattle Opera's production of Wagner's *Tristan und Isolde*, directed by Francesca Zambello.

Institutions

4445 Sevilla-Gonzaga, Marylis, comp. "Voices of Summer." *OpN.* 1998 May; 62(16): 32-34, 36-39, 41-46. Illus.: Photo. B&W. Color. 10. Lang.: Eng.

1998. Histories-sources. ■List of summer 1998 opera festivals in Europe, Scandinavia, Russia, Turkey.

4446 Clark, Caryl. "The Heroic Success of Opera Atelier." *CTR.* Fall 1998; 96: 56-61. Illus.: Dwg. Photo. B&W. 9. Lang.: Eng.

Canada: Toronto, ON. 1985-1998. Historical studies. ■Efforts of Opera Atelier at bringing Baroque opera to a contemporary audience, from school children to general audiences, with appendix listing Opera Atelier's productions to date.

4447 Knowles, Richard Paul. "Marketing and Meaning at the COC." *CTR.* Fall 1998; 96: 23-33. Notes. Biblio. Illus.: Photo. B&W. 22. Lang.: Eng.

Canada: Toronto, ON. 1996-1998. Critical studies. ■Materialist analysis of marketing techniques used by Toronto's Canadian Opera Company.

4448 Ram, Jane. "Letter from Shanghai." *OpN.* 1998 Sep.; 63(3): 114-116. Illus.: Photo. Color. 1. Lang.: Eng.

China, People's Republic of: Shanghai. 1998. Historial studies. ■The opening of the Grand Theatre in Shanghai with *Aida* and *Faust* produced by European companies.

4449 Sørensen, Lilo. "Fra rugekasse til spotlys." (From the Breeding Ground to the Spotlight.) *TE.* 1998 Apr.; 88: 32-34. Illus.: Photo. B&W. 2. Lang.: Dan.

Denmark. 1956-1998. Historical studies. ■A history of opera education in Denmark, focusing on Det Kongelige Teater's Opera Akademiet.

4450 Heed, Sven Åke. "Nytändning i Aix." (New Life For Aix.) *MuD.* 1998; 20(4): 22-25. Illus.: Photo. B&W. Color. Lang.: Swe.

France: Aix-en-Provence. 1998. Historical studies. ■Report from the Festival d'Aix-en-Provence, with reference to Peter Brook's staging of Mozart's *Don Giovanni.*

MUSIC-DRAMA: Opera—Institutions

4451 "Dallas am Main." *Econ.* 1998 May 9; 347(8067): 84. Illus.: Dwg. B&W. 1. Lang.: Eng.
Germany: Bayreuth. 1998. Critical studies. ■Report on the troubles faced by artistic director/administrator of the Bayreuth Festival, Wolfgang Wagner, due to two new books by Wagner family members.

4452 "Athens Beats Sparta By an Ear." *Econ.* 1998 Aug 15; 348(8081): 69-70. Illus.: Photo. B&W. 2. Lang.: Eng.
Germany: Bayreuth. Austria: Salzburg. 1998. Critical studies. ■Comparison of the 1998 seasons at the Salzburg and Bayreuth opera festivals.

4453 Baker, Evan. "The Dresden International Music Festival." *WES.* 1998 Fall; 10(3): 71-76. Illus.: Photo. B&W. 4. Lang.: Eng.
Germany: Dresden. 1998. Historical studies. ■Report on the 1998 festival of opera in Dresden.

4454 Balogh, Anikó. "Mesék a Zöld dombról: Wagner *Ring* je Bayreuthban." (Tales of the Green Hill: Wagner's *Ring* in Bayreuth.) *OperaL.* 1998; 7(1): 31-33. Lang.: Hun.
Germany: Bayreuth. 1997-1998. Reviews of performances. ■Detailed description of experiences gained at four evenings of the *Ring* production, staged by Alfred Kirchner at the Bayreuth Festival.

4455 Blankemeyer, Silke. "Nachtigall gwinnt junges Publikum für die Oper." (Nightingale Wins Young Audience Over to Opera.) *DB.* 1998; 9: 20-21. Illus.: Photo. B&W. 2. Lang.: Ger.
Germany: Cologne. 1996-1998. Historical studies. ■Portrait of the children's opera Yakult Halle, a department of Bühnen der Stadt Köln.

4456 Brandenburg, Detlef. "In der Ferne die Moderne." (In the Distance the Modern Age.) *DB.* 1998; 6: 16-19. Illus.: Photo. B&W. 6. Lang.: Ger.
Germany: Munich. 1998. Historical studies. ■Impressions from the 6th Münchener Biennale festival.

4457 Loney, Glenn. "Festival Season in Munich." *WES.* 1998 Spr; 10(2): 25-40. Illus.: Photo. B&W. 8. Lang.: Eng.
Germany: Munich. 1998. Historical studies. ■Survey of the opera festival season in Munich.

4458 Rohde, Frank. "Kinder lieben Oper." (Children Love Opera.) *SuT.* 1998; 160: 6-7. Illus.: Photo. B&W. 1. Lang.: Ger.
Germany: Cologne. 1996-1998. Historical studies. ■Profile of Günter Krämer, general manager of Bühnen der Stadt Köln, and the children's opera he introduced to the institution in 1996.

4459 Thöming, Anja-Rose. "Ist Regie lehrbar?" (Is Direction Teachable?)*DB.* 1998; 1: 22-26. Illus.: Photo. B&W. 6. Lang.: Ger.
Germany: Hamburg. 1988-1998. Historical studies. ■Reflects with three colleagues about the sense of the training at the course in music theatre studies at Hochschule für Musik und Theater, including short portraits of the directors Barbara Giese, Kay Kuntze and Holger Müller-Brandes.

4460 Réfi, Zszuzsanna. "Új operatagozattal bővül a magyar dalszínházak sora." (New Opera Ensemble Among Hungarian Musical Theatres.) *ZZT.* 1998; 5(4): 26-27. Illus.: Photo. B&W. 2. Lang.: Hun.
Hungary: Miskolc. 1998. Critical studies. ■Creation of an opera company at the Miskolc National Theatre for producing more musical performances.

4461 Rigó, Béla. "Világsztárok kerestetnek: énekverseny Budapesten." (Looking for Wolrd Stars: The Budapest Singing Contest.) *OperaL.* 1998; 7(5): 25-29. Illus.: Photo. B&W. 5. Lang.: Hun.
Hungary: Budapest. 1998. Historical studies. ■Account of the 4th International Singing Contest in which the two ensembles formed from the winners and the runners-up appeared in four full performances before audiences of Puccini's *La Bohème.* Notes the large number of contestants and winners from Asia.

4462 Hastings, Stephen. "Letter from Pesaro." *OpN.* 1998 Dec.; 63(6): 52-53. Illus.: Photo. B&W. Color. 2. Lang.: Eng.
Italy: Pesaro. 1792-1998. Historical studies. ■The opera festival held since 1992 in Pesaro, the birthplace of Gioacchino Rossini.

4463 Sorokina, I.; Sedov, Ja. "Akademija ital'janskoj opery: V 20 v. La Skala—i sovrem. teatr, i muzej muzyki." (The Academy of the Italian Opera: Twentieth Century. La Scala: Modern Theatre, and the Museum of Music.) *Itogi.* 1998; 5: 73-76. Lang.: Rus.
Italy: Milan. Historical studies. ■Contemporary theatre and opera at Teatro alla Scala.

4464 Kitagava, T. "Svoj dom est' teper' i u japonskoj opery." (The Japanese Opera Now Has Its Own Opera House.) *Znakom'tes' Japonija.* 1998; 4: 30-31. Lang.: Rus.
Japan: Tokyo. 1998. Historical studies. ■Profile of the new national theatre, Shinkokuritsu Gekyo, which now includes an opera house.

4465 Tranberg, Sören. "Johohoe! Vi skall visst ha ett operahus..." (We Shall Certainly Get an Operahouse.) *MuD.* 1998; 20 (3): 7. Illus.: Photo. Color. Lang.: Swe.
Norway: Oslo. 1998. Histories-sources. ■Interview with the director of Den Norske Opera, Bjørn Simensen about the postponed building of a new operahouse, the future plans and the urge for a realistic funding.

4466 *Bol'šoj teat'r. Sezon 222, 1997-1998.* (Bolšoj Theatre: 222nd Season, 1997-1998.) Moscow: 1998. 24 pp. Lang.: Rus.
Russia: Moscow. 1997-1998. Historical studies. ■Overview of the 1997-98 production season.

4467 Aronsson, Katarina. "Champagne, choklad och Coca-Cola." (Champagne, Chocolate And Coca-Cola.) *MuD.* 1998; 20(1): 30-31. Illus.: Photo. B&W. Lang.: Swe.
Russia: Moscow. 1997. Historical studies. ■Presentation of the Bolšoj of today and the new, more experimental, opera company Moskovskij Muzykal'nyj Teat'r Gelikon, with references to Aleksand'r Lazarjév's production of *Kniaz Igor (Prince Igor)* and Dmitrij Bertman's production of Čajkovskij's *Eugene Onegin.*

4468 Bertman, D. "Opera—bessmertna. Kak Kaščej!" (Opera Lives Forever. Like Kaščej!)*NV.* 1998; 38: 37-39. Lang.: Rus.
Russia: Moscow. 1998. Historical studies. ■Profile of Moskovskij Muzykal'nyj Teat'r Gelikon and Dmitrij Bertman, artistic director.

4469 Larina, S. "Naš Puškin." (Our Puškin.) *Nižnij Novgorod.* 1998; 9: 214-219. Lang.: Rus.
Russia: Nizhni Novgorod. 1998. Historical studies. ■Account of the Boldinia Opera and Ballet Festival honoring the memory of Aleksand'r Puškin.

4470 Loomis, George W. "Banda Slavonia: The Kirov Comes to the Met." *OpN.* 1998 Apr 11; 62(15): 26-27, 61. Illus.: Photo. B&W. Color. 6. Lang.: Eng.
Russia: St. Petersburg. 1997. Historical studies. ■Evaluation of the Kirov Opera before it visits the Metropolitan Opera in the summer of 1998.

4471 Ross, Alex. "Valery Gergiev in New York." *NewY.* 1998 20 Apr.: 86-93. Illus.: Photo. B&W. 1. Lang.: Eng.
Russia: St. Petersburg. 1998. Historical studies. ■The world tour of the Kirov Opera, headed by Valerij Gergiev.

4472 Eriksson, Torbjörn. "Stockholms Operamathus." (The Opera and Food-House of Stockholm.) *MuD.* 1998; 20(1): 11. Illus.: Photo. B&W. Lang.: Swe.
Sweden: Stockholm. 1997. Historical studies. ■Profile of Regina, Stockholms Operamathus, where opera and food are served under the guidance of Hans Ramberg and his wife, the soprano Charlotta Huldt-Ramberg.

4473 Lindblad, Katarina. "Om droppen som fick bägaren att rinna över." (About the Last Straw.) *MuD.* 1998; 20(5): 8-10. Illus.: Photo. B&W. Lang.: Swe.
Sweden: Umeå. 1998. Historical studies. ■Report about the problems of the administration of Norrlandsoperan, with references to the former managing director Ingemar Sjölander and the artistic director Jonas Forssell.

4474 "Only Fools and Horses." *Econ.* 1998 July 4; 348(8075): 84. Illus.: Photo. B&W. 1. Lang.: Eng.
UK-England: London. 1993-1998. Historical studies. ■The effects of the six-part television documentary *The House* on the Royal Opera House, including staff changes and resistance to filming a seventh part.

MUSIC-DRAMA: Opera—Institutions

4475 Allison, John. "London Guardian." *OpN.* 1998 May; 62(16): 20-21. Illus.: Photo. Color. 3. Lang.: Eng.
UK-England: London. 1997-1998. Biographical studies. ▪Paul Daniel, appointed 1997 as music director of the English National Opera, and his achievements.

4476 Guinther, Louise T. "'This Earth, This Realm, This England'." *OpN.* 1998 May; 62(16): 22-24, 26, 28. Illus.: Photo. Color. 4. Lang.: Eng.
UK-England. 1998. Historical studies. ▪English summer opera festivals: the Aldeburgh Festival, Glyndebourne Opera, and Garsington Festival.

4477 Hall, George. "This Old House." *OpN.* 1998 May; 62(16): 14. Illus.: Photo. B&W. Color. 2. Lang.: Eng.
UK-England: London. 1732-1998. Historical studies. ▪Brief history of the Royal Opera House, Covent Garden.

4478 Hall, George. "Opera Watch: Nightmare on Floral Street." *OpN.* 1998 Nov.; 63(5): 10. Illus.: Photo. Color. 3. Lang.: Eng.
UK-England: London. 1998. Historical studies. ▪Royal Opera House, Covent Garden's cancellation of its April-July 1999 performances, originally scheduled for the newly rebuilt Sadler's Wells Theatre, for financial reasons.

4479 Sutcliffe, Tom. "London Under Siege." *OpN.* 1998 May; 62(16): 10-12, 14, 16-17. Illus.: Photo. Color. B&W. 12. Lang.: Eng.
UK-England: London. 1988-1998. Historical studies. ▪The historical, political, architectural and economic situation of the Royal Opera House, Covent Garden (built 1857), currently under reconstruction, and the English National Opera at the London Coliseum (built 1904). It has been suggested that the National Opera share the use of the Royal Opera House.

4480 "Meanwhile, Up North." *OpN.* 1998 May; 62(16): 16. Illus.: Photo. Color. 1. Lang.: Eng.
UK-Scotland: Edinburgh. 1963-1998. Historical studies. ▪Brief history of the Scottish Opera.

4481 Alipio, Amy. "Patti's Palace." *OpN.* 1998 May; 62(16): 40. Illus.: Photo. B&W. 2. Lang.: Eng.
UK-Wales: Brecon. 1843-1919. Historical studies. ▪The Neath Opera Group's annual two-week festival in a small theatre in the castle Craig-y-Nos, which was owned by soprano Adelina Patti. Plans are under way to establish a full time music center there.

4482 "SummerMusic: Warm-Weather Opera Festivals Around North America." *OpN.* 1998 May; 62(16): 36-45. Illus.: Photo. Color. 10. Lang.: Eng.
USA. 5/1998-9/1998. Histories-sources. ▪Alphabetical listing of opera festival performance timetables throughout the United States in summer 1998.

4483 Baker, David J. "A Singer's Diary: Back to School." *OpN.* 1998 Sep.; 63(3): 14, 16-17. Illus.: Photo. Color. 2. Lang.: Eng.
USA: New Haven, CT. 1998. Histories-sources. ▪Students Maksim Zhdanovskhikh (Russian baritone age 28) and Mary Petro (American soprano age 26) discuss their expenses and training experience as graduate students at the Yale University School of Music.

4484 DeCarlo, Tessa. "In a Week, Maybe Two, They'll Make You a Star." *OpN.* 1998 Mar 28; 62(14): 30-31, 53. Lang.: Eng.
USA: San José, CA. 1980-1998. Historical studies. ▪American mezzo-soprano, Irene Dalis, now in retirement from the Metropolitan Opera House, is in charge of Opera San Jose. She is on the faculty of San Jose State University, her alma mater.

4485 Grant, James. "Twilight Times." *OpN.* 1998 June; 62(17): 28-30. Illus.: Photo. B&W. Color. 7. Lang.: Eng.
USA. 1960-1998. Historical studies. ▪Profiles of the retiring artistic directors of Lyric Opera of Kansas City (Russell Patterson) and Arizona Opera (Glyn Ross).

4486 Harris, Charlotte Daniels. *A History of the Metropolitan Opera Guild and Its Educational Program, 1935-1936 through 1974-1975.* New York, NY: Columbia Univ. Teachers College; 1988. 570 pp. Biblio. Notes. [Ph.D. Dissertation, Univ. Microfilms Order No. AAC 8906459.] Lang.: Eng.
USA. 1935-1975. Histories-specific. ▪Includes information concerning the development of the organization, performances, meetings, rehearsals, lectures, education courses, and radio broadcasts.

4487 Paller, Rebecca. "A Singer's Diary: Shoestring Opera." *OpN.* 1998 Nov.; 63(5): 16-17. Illus.: Photo. Color. 1. Lang.: Eng.
USA: New York, NY. 1995-1998. Historical studies. ▪The origin of the coOPERAtive opera of New York, founded by Sarah Jamison, which numbers thirty singers. Lists some of the personnel and performances.

4488 Peters, Alton E. "Metropolitan Opera Guild Annual Report." *OpN.* 1998 Nov.; 63(5): 60, 82. Lang.: Eng.
USA: New York, NY. 1997-1998. Histories-sources. ▪Annual report by the president of the Metropolitan Opera Guild.

4489 Story, Rosalyn M. "Up from Houston." *OpN.* 1998 Jan 3; 62(8): 24-25, 52. Illus.: Photo. Color. 2. Lang.: Eng.
USA: Houston, TX. 1977-1998. Historical studies. ▪The training practices of the Houston Opera Studio, David Gockley, co-founder, for people of varied voices, many of whom become opera stars.

4490 West, William D. "A Tale of Three Cities." *OpN.* 1998 Aug.; 63(2): 32-33. Illus.: Photo. B&W. 4. Lang.: Eng.
USA: Binghamton, NY. 1949-1998. Historical studies. ▪The history of the Tri-Cities Opera, founded by Peyton Hibbitt and Carmen Savoca. The artistic director elect is Duane Skrabalak.

Performance spaces

4491 Nielsen, Ulf. "Magnifik Lucia intog danskt dagbrott." (A Magnificent Lucia Held in a Danish Open-Cast Mine.) *ProScen.* 1998; 22(4): 24-28. Illus.: Photo. Lighting. B&W. Color. Lang.: Swe.
Denmark: Hedeland. 1997. Technical studies. ▪Report about the technical side of Malmö Musikteater's production of Donizetti's *Lucia di Lammermoor* at Hedeland amfiteater.

4492 Baker, Evan. "Richard Wagner and His Search for the Ideal Theatrical Space." 241-278 in Radice, Mark A., ed. *Opera in Context: Essays on Historical Staging from the Late Renaissance to the Time of Puccini.* Portland, OR: Amadeus P; 1998. 410 pp. Notes. Index. Tables. Biblio. Illus.: Plan. Dwg. Photo. Design. 14. Lang.: Eng.
Europe. 1835-1885. Historical studies. ▪Wagner's quest for the 'perfect' theatrical space in which to stage his operas, culminating in his personally designed Bayreuther Festspielhaus. Charts his experiences at different theatres in Germany, France, and Italy, and applies his analysis to the premiere performance of *Parsifal*, written expressly for Bayreuth.

4493 Coeyman, Barbara. "Opera and Ballet in Seventeenth-Century French Theaters: Case Studies of the Salle des Machines and the Palais Royal Theater." 37-72 in Radice, Mark A., ed. *Opera in Context: Essays on Historical Staging from the Late Renaissance to the Time of Puccini.* Portland, OR: Amadeus P; 1998. 410 pp. Notes. Index. Tables. Biblio. Illus.: Plan. Dwg. Sketches. Diagram. 5. Lang.: Eng.
France: Paris. 1640-1690. Historical studies. ▪Examines French Baroque opera through its two primary theatrical spaces, the Salle des Machines and the Palais Royal. Investigates how the spaces influenced the style of the operas performed there.

4494 Wilkins, Stephen. "Paradise Found: The Salle le Peletier and French Grand Opera." 171-208 in Radice, Mark A., ed. *Opera in Context: Essays on Historical Staging from the Late Renaissance to the Time of Puccini.* Portland, OR: Amadeus P; 1998. 410 pp. Notes. Index. Tables. Biblio. Illus.: Plan. Dwg. Sketches. Design. Diagram. 11. Lang.: Eng.
France: Paris. 1823-1873. Historical studies. ▪The impact of the newly renovated Salle le Peletier (also known as the Opéra de Paris) on the development of French grand opera. Considers the new scenery designs and structure of the house, as well as the stage machinery.

4495 Kandell, Jonathan; Jamieson, Nigel. "Raising the Roof: Barcelona and Venice Rebuild Their Fabled Opera Houses." *OpN.* 1998 Nov.; 63(5): 32-36. Illus.: Photo. Color. 6. Lang.: Eng.

MUSIC-DRAMA: Opera—Performance spaces

Spain: Barcelona. Italy: Venice. 1994-1998. Historical studies. ▪The restoration of the Gran Teatro del Liceu of Barcelona and Teatro La Fenice in Venice.

4496 Rubio, José Luis. "¡Viva! Teatro Real." *OpN.* 1998 Jan 17; 62(9): 40-41. Illus.: Photo. Color. 4. Lang.: Eng.

Spain: Madrid. 1988-1997. Historical studies. ▪Photographs of the interior and exterior of the newly remodeled Teatro Real, in Madrid.

4497 Edström, Per Simon. "Dalhallas naturakustik eller hur en idé växte fram och sedan förvanskades." (The Natural Acoustic of Dalhalla, or How an Idea Develops and Then Distorts.) *ProScen.* 1998; 22(5): 26-30: ia. Illus.: Dwg. Photo. B&W. Color. Lang.: Swe.

Sweden: Rättvik. 1997. Technical studies. ▪Presentation of how to build an ideal acoustic stage for opera in the lime-stone quarry at Dalhalla, with reference to Vitruvius' tract *De architectura.*

4498 Gademan, Göran. "Dionysos i frack." (Dionysus in Tails.) *MuD.* 1998; 20(4): 12-13, 41. Illus.: Photo. B&W. Lang.: Swe.

Sweden: Stockholm. 1898. Historical studies. ▪The inauguration of the house of Kungliga Operan a hundred years ago, with reference to the reviews.

4499 Lampert-Gréaux, Ellen. "Raising the Roof." *TCI.* 1998 Aug/Sep.; 32(8): 34-36. Illus.: Photo. Plan. Color. 6. Lang.: Eng.

USA: Santa Fe, NM. 1991-1998. Critical studies. ▪Report on the newly-renovated open-air theatre for the Santa Fe Opera.

4500 Maiman, William L. "A Touring Stage for Houston Grand Opera." *TCI.* 1998 Nov.; 32(10): 31-33. Illus.: Photo. Color. 3. Lang.: Eng.

USA: Houston, TX. 1998. Technical studies. ▪Description of the Multimedia Modular Stage, designed by Ken Foy, for the touring requirements of the Houston Grand Opera.

4501 Wengrow, Arnold. "Small Town Venue Gets a Big City Shine." *TCI.* 1998 Oct.; 32(9): 19-21. Illus.: Photo. Color. 1. Lang.: Eng.

USA: Newberry, SC. 1998. Critical studies. ▪Appraisal of the newly-renovated Newberry Opera House.

Performance/production

4502 Blair, Steven. "The Carmen Challenge." *OpN.* 1998 Dec.; 63(6): 22-26. Illus.: Photo. B&W. Color. 8. Lang.: Eng.

1875-1998. Historical studies. ▪An account of performers' approaches to the role of Carmen, in the opera of that name by Georges Bizet. Illustrations demonstrate the work of Risë Stevens, Fiorenza Cossotto, Régine Crespin, Grace Bumbry, Marilyn Monroe, Agnes Baltsa, Denyce Graves, Lorraine Hunt, Emily Golden.

4503 Cometta, Sandro; Soldini, Elisabetta. "Videographie." (Videography.) *ASO.* 1998 May/June; 184: 96-99. Illus.: Photo. B&W. 5. Lang.: Fre.

1980-1991. Historical studies. ▪Description of three videotaped performances of Rossini's *Semiramide.*

4504 Cometta, Sandro; Soldini, Elisabetta. "Discographie." (Discography.) *ASO.* 1998 May/June; 184: 88-94. Illus.: Photo. B&W. 3. Lang.: Fre.

1962-1992. Historical studies. ▪Table of recorded performances of Rossini's *Semiramide* with discussion of each recording.

4505 Dutronc, Jean-Louis. "Mémoire de Lakmé." (Memory of Lakmé.) *ASO.* 1998 Mar/Apr.; 183: 74-77. Illus.: Photo. B&W. 4. Lang.: Fre.

1932-1995. Histories-sources. ▪The author's personal appreciation of seven interpreters of the title role in Delibes' *Lakmé*: Lily Pons, Mado Robin, Joan Sutherland, Mady Mesplé, Christiane Eda-Pierre, Mariella Devia, and Natalie Dessay.

4506 Flinois, Pierre. "Discographie." (Discography.) *ASO.* 1998 Sep/Oct.; 186: 42-43. Lang.: Fre.

1980-1997. Historical studies. ▪Listing and discussion of four recordings of Zemlinsky's *Eine florentinische Tragödie.*

4507 Flinois, Pierre. "Discographie." (Discography.) *ASO.* 1998 Sep/Oct.; 186: 92-93. Lang.: Fre.

1983-1996. Historical studies. ▪Listing and discussion of recordings of Zemlinsky's *Der Zwerg.*

4508 Flinois, Pierre. "Discographie." (Discography.) *ASO.* 1998 Jan/Feb.; 181/182: 198-205. Lang.: Fre.

1935-1998. Historical studies. ▪Discography of productions of Alban Berg's *Lulu.*

4509 Flinois, Pierre. "Visages de Lulu." (Faces of Lulu.) *ASO.* 1998 Jan/Feb.; 181/182: 184-193. Illus.: Photo. B&W. 9. Lang.: Fre.

1937-1996. Historical studies. ▪Significant interpreters of the title role of Alban Berg's *Lulu.*

4510 Hastings, Stephen. "That's Italian?...What's Left of Classic Singing Traditions of Italy." *OpN.* 1998 Mar 28; 62(14): 16-19, 20-21. Illus.: Photo. B&W. Color. 8. Lang.: Eng.

1998. Critical studies. ▪Comparison of present-day opera singers with the great names of the past.

4511 Perroux, Alain. "Discographie." (Discography.) *ASO.* 1998 July/Aug.; 185: 92-96. Illus.: Dwg. B&W. 1. Lang.: Fre.

1953-1997. Historical studies. ▪Listing and discussion of recorded performances of Offenbach's *Orphée aux Enfers.*

4512 Rauch, Rudolph S. "'Three-Cornered Hat'." *OpN.* 1998 Sep.; 63(3): 24-32. Illus.: Photo. B&W. Color. 7. Lang.: Eng.

1941-1998. Biographical studies. ▪In celebration of the thirtieth anniversary of his debut at the Metropolitan Opera, tenor Plácido Domingo discusses opera as an art form, his many roles, his work as a conductor and opera administrator, and his opera scholarship.

4513 Rosenfeld, Lorraine. "The 1988-99 *Opera News* International Forecast." *OpN.* 1998 Sep.; 63(3): 57-62, 64-81. Lang.: Eng.

1998. Histories-sources. ▪List of 1998-99 opera productions planned throughout the world.

4514 Soldini, Elisabetta. "L'oeuvre à l'affiche." (The Work on Stage.) *ASO.* 1998 Sep/Oct.; 186: 94-95. Illus.: Photo. Dwg. B&W. 2. Lang.: Fre.

1922-1998. Historical studies. ▪Performances worldwide of Zemlinsky's *Der Zwerg.*

4515 Soldini, Elisabetta. "L'oeuvre à l'affiche." (The Work on Stage.) *ASO.* 1998 Sep/Oct.; 186: 44-45. Illus.: Photo. B&W. 2. Lang.: Fre.

1917-1996. Historical studies. ▪Details of productions worldwide of Zemlinsky's *Eine florentinische Tragödie.*

4516 Soldini, Elisabetta. "L'oeuvre à l'affiche." (The Work on Stage.) *ASO.* 1998 July/Aug.; 185: 104-109. Illus.: Dwg. Photo. B&W. 10. Lang.: Fre.

1858-1997. Historical studies. ▪Productions of Offenbach's *Orphée aux Enfers* worldwide.

4517 Soldini, Elisabetta. "L'oeuvre à l'affiche." (The Work on Stage.) *ASO.* 1998 May/June; 184: 100-107. Illus.: Dwg. Photo. B&W. 15. Lang.: Fre.

1823-1998. Historical studies. ▪Details of performances worldwide of Rossini's *Semiramide.*

4518 Soldini, Elisabetta. "L'oeuvre à l'affiche." (The Work on Stage.) *ASO.* 1998 Jan/Feb.; 181/182: 206-213. Illus.: Photo. B&W. 12. Lang.: Fre.

1935-1998. Historical studies. ▪Table of productions of Berg's *Lulu* including date, place, cast, conductor, director, etc.

4519 Soldini, Elisabetta. "L'oeuvre à l'affiche." (The Work on Stage.) *ASO.* 1998 Mar/Apr.; 183: 88-95. Illus.: Photo. Dwg. B&W. 16. Lang.: Fre.

1883-1997. Historical studies. ▪Details on performances of Delibes' opera *Lakmé* worldwide.

4520 Soldini, Elisabetta, comp. "L'oeuvre à l'affiche." (The Work on Stage.) *ASO.* 1998 Nov/Dec.; 187: 128-133. Illus.: Photo. B&W. 11. Lang.: Fre.

1881-1995. Historical studies. ▪Productions of Massenet's *Hérodiade* in French and Italian.

4521 Soldini, Elisabetta, comp. "L'oeuvre à l'affiche." (The Work on Stage.) *ASO.* 1998 Nov/Dec.; 187: 64-67. Illus.: Photo. Dwg. B&W. 13. Lang.: Fre.

MUSIC-DRAMA: Opera—Performance/production

1877-1923. Historical studies. ■Calendar of premieres of Massenet's *Le Roi de Lahore* in both French and Italian.

4522 Stearns, David Patrick. "And Then There Were None?" *OpN.* 1998 Oct.; 63(4): 36, 38-41. Illus.: Photo. Color. 13. Lang.: Eng.

1988-1998. Historical studies. ■Discussion and evaluation of recordings by star singers and video records of complete operas.

4523 van Moere, Didier. "Discographie." (Discography.) *ASO.* 1998 Nov/Dec.; 187: 122-127. Illus.: Poster. B&W. 1. Lang.: Fre.

1974-1994. Historical studies. ■Details on complete recordings of Massenet's opera *Hérodiade.*

4524 van Moere, Didier. "Discographie." (Discography.) *ASO.* 1998 Mar/Apr.; 183: 82-87. Illus.: Photo. B&W. 3. Lang.: Fre.

1941-1998. Critical studies. ■Listing of integral recordings of Delibes' *Lakmé* with discussion of each recording.

4525 van Moere, Didier. "Discographie." (Discography.) *ASO.* 1998 Nov/Dec.; 187: 60-62. Notes. Illus.: Photo. B&W. 1. Lang.: Fre.

1979. Historical studies. ■Describes the single complete recording of Massenet's *Le Roi de Lahore*, as well as the vocal requirements of the major roles.

4526 Kellow, Brian. "Return Engagement." *OpN.* 1998 Mar 28; 62(14): 8-10. Illus.: Photo. B&W. Color. 3. Lang.: Eng.

Australia. 1998. Histories-sources. ■Profile, interview with Australian soprano Joan Sutherland.

4527 Brandenburg, Detlef. "Salzburg oblige." (Salzburg Obliges.) *DB.* 1998; 9: 10-14. Illus.: Photo. B&W. 4. Lang.: Ger.

Austria: Salzburg. 1998. Reviews of performances. ■Impressions from the music program of Salzburger Festspiele. Reviews Kurt Weill's and Bertolt Brechts's *Aufstieg und Fall der Stadt Mahagonny* directed by Peter Zadek, Leoš Janáček's *Kát'a Kabanová* directed by Christoph Marthaler, and Giuseppe Verdi's *Don Carlo* directed by Herbert Wernicke.

4528 Cole, Malcolm S. "Mozart and Two Theaters in Josephinian Vienna." 111-146 in Radice, Mark A., ed. *Opera in Context: Essays on Historical Staging from the Late Renaissance to the Time of Puccini.* Portland, OR: Amadeus P; 1998. 410 pp. Notes. Index. Tables. Biblio. Illus.: Plan. Dwg. Sketches. Diagram. 8. Lang.: Eng.

Austria: Vienna. 1782-1791. Historical studies. ■Examines three different productions of Mozart's operas during his lifetime in two different Viennese theatres to reveal information on operatic conditions and traditions. The productions are: *Die Entführung aus dem Serail* at the Burgtheater, *Le nozze di Figaro*, also at the Burgtheater, and *Die Zauberflöte* at the Freihaus Theater.

4529 Hamilton, David. "Wiener Blut." *OpN.* 1998 Dec.; 63(6): 42-47. Illus.: Photo. B&W. 10. Lang.: Eng.

Austria: Vienna. 1945-1955. Critical studies. ■Analysis of the postwar Viennese style of performing Mozart's operas, questioning whether that style was really a new departure. Includes discussion of the political significance of performances of Mozart and Beethoven in postwar Vienna.

4530 Jürgensen, Knud Arne. "Profeten i Wien—upptakt till en Meyerbeer-renässans." (The Prophet in Vienna—Prelude To a Renaissance For Meyerbeer.) *MuD.* 1998; 20(4): 26-28. Illus.: Dwg. Photo. B&W. Color. Lang.: Swe.

Austria: Vienna. 1998. Historical studies. ■Report from a symposium about Meyerbeer, organised by Theatermuseum in Vienna, with reference to Hans Neuenfels' staging of *Le Prophète* at Staatsoper.

4531 Koltai, Tamás. "A színész énekel: Opera-előadások Salzburgban." (The Actor Is Singing: Opera Performances in Salzburg.) *Sz.* 1998; 31(12): 42-44. Illus.: Photo. B&W. 2. Lang.: Hun.

Austria: Salzburg. 1998. Reviews of performances. ■Mozart's *Le Nozze di Figaro* directed by Luc Bondy, Verdi's *Don Carlos* directed by Herbert Wernicke, Messiaen's *Saint-François d'Assise* directed by Peter Sellars, and Brecht and Weill's *Aufsteig und Fall der Stadt Mahagonny* directed by Peter Zadek.

4532 Loney, Glenn. "Montemezzi's *Love of Three Kings* at the 1998 Bregenz Festival." *WES.* 1998 Fall; 10(3): 67-70. Illus.: Photo. B&W. 1. Lang.: Eng.

Austria: Bregenz. 1998. Critical studies. ■Analysis of designer/director Philippe Arlaud's production of Montemezzi's opera *L'amore dei tre re* at the 1998 Bregenz Festival.

4533 Schoenberg, Arnold. "Lettre de refus." (Letter of Refusal.) *ASO.* 1998 Jan/Feb.; 181/182: 168-169. Illus.: Photo. B&W. 1. Lang.: Fre.

Austria. 1935. Histories-sources. ■Schoenberg's explanation of his refusal to complete Alban Berg's unfinished opera *Lulu* at the request of Berg's widow, because of anti-Semitic language in the libretto.

4534 Dokučaeva, A. "Opery i dramy čety Abdrazakovych." (Abdrazakov's Opera and Drama.) *Bel'skie prostory.* 1998; 12: 184-190. Lang.: Rus.

Bashkir. 1998. Biographical studies. ■Profile of opera singers, E. Kočetova and A. Abdrazakov.

4535 "Orphée vu par la presse." (Orpheus Seen by the Press.) *ASO.* 1998 July/Aug.; 185: 98-103. Illus.: Photo. B&W. 9. Lang.: Fre.

Belgium. Switzerland. France. 1997. Critical studies. ■Press reactions to three productions of Offenbach's *Orphée aux Enfers*: directed by Herbert Wernicke at Théâtre de la Monnaie (Brussels), and by Laurent Pelly both at the Grand Théâtre of Geneva and the Opéra de Lyon.

4536 Scott, Michael. "Miss Gorr to You: ... the Career of the Incomparable Rita Gorr." *OpN.* 1998 Feb 28; 62(12): 14-17. Illus.: Photo. B&W. 7. Lang.: Eng.

Belgium. 1998. Histories-sources. ■Profile, interview with Belgian mezzo soprano Rita Gorr.

4537 George, David S. "*Mattogrosso*: The Postmodernist Stage in Brazil." *MD.* 1998 Fall; 41(3): 474-482. Notes. Lang.: Eng.

Brazil: Rio de Janeiro. 1989. Critical studies. ■Analysis of Ópera Seca's production *Mattogrosso* created by its artistic director, Gerald Thomas, in collaboration with composer Philip Glass and designer Daniela Thomas.

4538 Buchau, Stephanie von. "Canadian Troubadour: Tenor Richard Margison Takes on *Il Trovatore* at the Met." *OpN.* 1998 Feb 14; 62(11): 26-27. Illus.: Photo. Color. 2. Lang.: Eng.

Canada. 1998. Histories-sources. ■Interview with Canadian tenor Richard Margison.

4539 Gurewitsch, Matthew. "Ben Heppner Towers Over the Rest of Today's Young Heldentenors." *OpN.* 1998 Apr 11; 62(15): 8-10, 12. Illus.: Photo. Color. 5. Lang.: Eng.

Canada. 1998. Biographical studies. ■Profile, interview with Canadian *Heldentenor* Ben Heppner.

4540 Hamilton, Stuart; Kehler, Grace. "Canadian Operatic Voices." *CTR.* 1998 Fall; 96: 18-22. Illus.: Photo. B&W. 3. Lang.: Eng.

Canada. 1998. Histories-sources. ■Interview with vocal coach Stuart Hamilton on Canada's operatic scene and opportunities for new and established Canadian opera singers.

4541 "One Country, Two Turandots." *Econ.* 1998 Sep 19; 348(8086): 101-102. Illus.: Photo. B&W. 2. Lang.: Eng.

China, People's Republic of: Beijing. 1998. Critical studies. ■Cultural politics surrounding two rival productions of Puccini's *Turandot*, Zhang Yimou's within the walls of the Forbidden City and Zigong Sichuan Opera Company's directed by Wei Mingren.

4542 Grant, James. "Bringing *Turandot* Home." *OpN.* 1998 Aug.; 63(2): 28-29. Illus.: Photo. Color. 4. Lang.: Eng.

China, People's Republic of: Beijing. 1998. Historical studies. ■The planned production of Puccini's *Turandot* at the People's Cultural Palace in Beijing by the Maggio Musicale Fiorentino orchestra and chorus, directed by Zubin Mehta.

4543 Herman, Josef. "Repertoire Innovations in Czech Opera/Du nouveau à l'Opéra." *CzechT.* 1998 June; 14: 56-60. Illus.: Photo. B&W. 4. Lang.: Eng, Fre.

Czech Republic. 1997. Historical studies. ■Review of the 1997 Czech opera season.

MUSIC-DRAMA: Opera—Performance/production

4544 Sevilla-Gonzaga, Marylis. "Sound Bites: Gert Henning-Jensen." *OpN.* 1998 Apr 11; 62(15): 34-35. Illus.: Photo. Color. 1. Lang.: Eng.

Denmark. 1992-1998. Biographical studies. ■Brief account of the career of Danish tenor Gert Henning-Jensen.

4545 Cervantes, Xavier. "'Tuneful Monsters': The Castrati and the London Operatic Public 1667-1737." *Restor.* 1998 Sum; 13(1) : 1-24. Notes. Lang.: Eng.

England: London. 1667-1737. Historical studies. ■Public response to *castrati* performance in operas performed in Restoration London.

4546 Cowgill, Rachel. "Regendering the Libertine, or, the Taming of the Rake: Lucy Vestris as Don Giovanni on the Early Nineteenth-Century London Stage." *COJ.* 1998; 10(1): 45-66. Notes. Illus.: Handbill. Dwg. Print. B&W. 6. Lang.: Eng.

England: London. 1842. Historical studies. ■The impact of Lucy Vestris in the travesty role of Don Giovanni in a comic sequel to Mozart andDda Ponte's opera, William Thomas Moncrieff's *Giovanni in London, or The Libertine Reclaimed.* The article raises issues of lesbianism, transvestism, and female challenges to male dominance.

4547 Girdham, Jane Catherine. *Stephen Storace and the English Opera Tradition of the Late Eighteenth Century.* Philadelphia, PA: Univ. of Pennsylvania; 1988. 695 pp. Notes. Biblio. [Ph.D. Dissertation, Univ. Microfilms Order No. AAC 8824742.] Lang.: Eng.

England: London. 1762-1796. Histories-specific. ■Examines the operas of Stephen Storace, house composer at Drury Lane, and analyzes their close relationship to continental genres, as well as their representative status in the London theatrical repertoire.

4548 Radice, Mark A. "Theater Architecture at the Time of Henry Purcell and Its Influence on His 'Dramatick Operas'." 73-94 in Radice, Mark A., ed. *Opera in Context: Essays on Historical Staging from the Late Renaissance to the Time of Puccini.* Portland, OR: Amadeus P; 1998. 410 pp. Notes. Index. Tables. Biblio. Illus.: Plan. Dwg. Sketches. Diagram. 7. Lang.: Eng.

England: London. 1659-1695. Historical studies. ■The influence of English theatre architecture on the staging and the content of Purcell's operas.

4549 Stahura, Mark. "Handel's Haymarket Theatre." 95-110 in Radice, Mark A., ed. *Opera in Context: Essays on Historical Staging from the Late Renaissance to the Time of Puccini.* Portland, OR: Amadeus P; 1998. 410 pp. Notes. Index. Tables. Biblio. Illus.: Plan. 1. Lang.: Eng.

England: London. 1710-1739. Historical studies. ■How the theatrical space of the Haymarket Theatre, home of composer George Frideric Handel, influenced Handel's opera. Uses Handel's *Rinaldo* (Giacomo Rossi, librettist) as a case study.

4550 Appia, Adolphe; Koncut, Suzana, transl. *Glasba, igralec, prostor.* (The Music, the Actor, the Space.) Ljubljana: Mestno gledališče ljubljansko; 1998. 356 pp. (Knjižnica Mestnega gledališča ljubljanskega 126.) Pref. Illus.: Photo. B&W. 2. Lang.: Slo.

Europe. 1892. Histories-specific. ■Translation of *La mise en scène du drame Wagnérian.*

4551 Chailly, Riccardo. "Riccardo Chailly: 'Il est proche de ma sensibilité'." (Riccardo Chailly: He Is Close to My Own Sensibility.) *ASO.* 1998 Sep/Oct.; 186: 114-115. Illus.: Photo. B&W. 1. Lang.: Fre.

Europe. 1998. Histories-sources. ■The conductor's reaction to the work of Alexander Zemlinsky.

4552 Dellamora, Richard; Fischlin, Daniel. "Introduction." 1-26 in Dellamora, Richard, ed.; Fischlin, Daniel, ed. *The Work of Opera: Genre, Nationhood, and Sexual Difference.* New York, NY: Columbia UP; 1997. 350 pp. Index. Lang.: Eng.

Europe. North America. 1998. Historical studies. ■Introductory essay for a book on opera, national ideologies, and sexualities.

4553 Green, London. "Callas and *Lucia.*" *OQ.* 1998 Spr; 14(3): 65-71. Notes. Illus.: Photo. B&W. 2. Lang.: Eng.

Europe. 1953-1959. Critical studies. ■Maria Callas' performances singing Donizetti's *Lucia di Lammermoor.* Credits her with establishing the opera's importance in the latter half of the twentieth-century.

4554 Hermansson, Jan. "Frun fortsätter." (The Woman Goes On.) *MuD.* 1998; 20(2): 20-21. Illus.: Photo. B&W. Lang.: Swe.

Europe. 1954. Critical studies. ■Critique of seven recordings of Richard Strauss' *Die Frau ohne Schatten.*

4555 Honolka, K. *Velikie primadonny.* (The Great Soloists.) Moscow: Agraf; 1998. 320 pp. (Volšebnaja flejta.) Lang.: Rus.

Europe. North America. 1650-1950. Historical studies. ■Great female opera singers. Translation of *Die grossen Primadonnen* (Stuttgart: Cotta, 1960).

4556 Koek, Ariane. "Harpo's Challenge: Performance Art & the Reinvigoration of Opera." *PM.* 1989/90(59): 60-65. Notes. Illus.: Photo. B&W. 6. Lang.: Eng.

Europe. 1964-1989. Critical studies. ■The use of performance art to rejuvenate opera and make it a more pluralistic art form.

4557 McKee, David; Rishoi, Niel; Green, London; Glasow, E. Thomas. "Videos." *OQ.* 1998 Spr; 14(3): 86-101. Notes. Lang.: Eng.

Europe. USA. 1980-1998. Critical studies. ■A rating of six Donizetti opera videos: *Lucia di Lammermoor* directed by Frank Dunlop, *Lucrezia Borgia* and *Mary Stuart* both directed by John Copley, *Roberto Devereux* directed by Tito Capobianco, *Linda di Chamounix* directed by Daniel Schmid, and *La Favorite* with no director credited.

4558 Reininghaus, Frieder. "Verstand. Anmut. Würde..." (Reason. Grace. Dignity...)*DB.* 1998; 6: 20-23. Illus.: Photo. B&W. 3. Lang.: Ger.

Europe. 1989-1998. Historical studies. ■Portrait of opera director Robert Carson, his working methods and close cooperation with set designers for performances in opera houses in Europe.

4559 Smith, Patrick J. "Midnight Chill." *OpN.* 1998 Jan 17; 62(9): 20-21. Illus.: Photo. Color. 1. Lang.: Eng.

Europe. 1951. Critical studies. ■The atmospheric use of the harpsichord in the graveyard scene of *The Rake's Progress* by Igor F. Stravinskij.

4560 Stearns, David Patrick. "20/20 Revision." *OpN.* 1998 Dec.; 63(6): 38-41. Illus.: Photo. Color. 2. Lang.: Eng.

Finland. 1998. Histories-sources. ■Interview with conductor Esa-Pekka Salonen.

4561 "Jacques Offenbach: Repères chronologiques." *ASO.* 1998 July/Aug.; 185: 78-79. Lang.: Fre.

France. 1819-1880. Biographical studies. ■Brief chronology of the life of the composer.

4562 "James Conlon: '...j'aime cette musique!'." (James Conlon: I Love This Music.) *ASO.* 1998 Sep/Oct.; 186: 116-117. Illus.: Photo. B&W. 1. Lang.: Fre.

France: Paris. 1998. Histories-sources. ■The conductor on his 1998 production of Alexander Zemlinsky's opera *Der Zwerg* at the Palais Garnier.

4563 "Sunny Singing." *Econ.* 1998 Aug 1; 348(8079): 72-73. Lang.: Eng.

France: Aix-en-Provence. 1998. Historical studies. ■Report on the 1998 opera festival in Aix-en-Provence.

4564 Bergström, Gunnel. "Peter Mattei om Don Giovanni." (Peter Mattei on Don Giovanni.) *MuD.* 1998; 20(3): 24-25. Illus.: Photo. B&W. Lang.: Swe.

France: Aix-en-Provence. 1985-1998. Histories-sources. ■Interview with the singer Peter Mattei about his background, with reference to Mozart's *Don Giovanni* in the production of Peter Brook.

4565 Berlioz, Hector; Glasow, E. Thomas, transl. "Berlioz on the Premiere of *La Favorite.*" *OQ.* 1998 Spr; 14(3): 33-43. Notes. Illus.: Sketches. B&W. 4. Lang.: Eng.

France: Paris. 1840. Critical studies. ■New translation of Berlioz' review of the premiere of Donizetti's opera at the Paris Opéra. Includes brief background introduction by the translator.

4566 Blier, Steven. "The Secret of Samson's Strength." *OpN.* 1998 Feb 28; 62(12): 8-10,12. Illus.: Photo. B&W. Color. 7. Lang.: Eng.

MUSIC-DRAMA: Opera—Performance/production

France. Germany. USA. 1877-1998. Historical studies. ▪The performance history of *Samson et Dalila* by Camille Saint-Saëns, said to have continued success despite being unstageable.

4567 Boulez, Pierre. "Court post-scriptum sur la fidelité." (Short Post-Script on Fidelity.) *ASO*. 1998 Jan/Feb.; 181/182 : 194-197. Lang.: Fre.
France: Paris. 1979. Critical studies. ▪Conductor's response to criticism of a production of Alban Berg's *Lulu* directed by Patrice Chéreau.

4568 Condé, Gérard. "Les Aventures du Roi de Lahore." (The Adventures of the King of Lahore.) *ASO*. 1998 Nov/Dec.; 187: 46-53. Notes. Illus.: Dwg. B&W. 4. Lang.: Fre.
France. 1877. Historical studies. ▪On the creation of Massenet's opera *Le Roi de Lahore*.

4569 Croydon, Margaret. "Peter Brook's Return to Opera. Mozart's *Don Giovanni* at Aix-en-Provence." *WES*. 1998 Fall; 10(3): 63-66. Illus.: Photo. B&W. 1. Lang.: Eng.
France: Aix-en-Provence. 1998. Critical studies. ▪Analysis of Brook's production of Mozart's opera at the Aix-en- Provence Music Festival.

4570 Dessay, Natalie. "Rencontre avec Natalie Dessay: Y-a-t-il une vie après l'air des clochettes?" (Meeting with Natalie Dessay: Is There Life After the Bell Song?)*ASO*. 1998 Mar/Apr.; 183: 80-81. Lang.: Fre.
France: Paris. 1995. Histories-sources. ▪Dessay's thoughts on Delibes' opera *Lakmé*, with reference to her role in the 1995 Opéra-Comique production directed by Gilbert Blin.

4571 Fraison, Laurent. "Deux genèses pour un double chef-d'oeuvre." (Two Beginnings for a Double Masterpiece.) *ASO*. 1998 July/Aug.; 185: 68-77. Notes. Illus.: Photo. Dwg. B&W. 9. Lang.: Fre.
France. 1858-1874. Historical studies. ▪Offenbach's recasting of his two-act opera into the four-act *Orphée aux Enfers*.

4572 Hansen, Jack Winsor. "Sibyl Sanderson's Influence on *Manon*." *OQ*. 1998-1999 Win; 15(1): 38-48. Notes. Illus.: Photo. B&W. 3. Lang.: Eng.
France. 1885-1903. Historical studies. ▪Modifications made by Jules Massenet to his opera to accommodate Sanderson, the first singer he met capable of performing the lead, allowing for the first revivals of the opera since the death of singer Marie Heilbronn.

4573 Mesplé, Mady. "Rencontre avec Mady Mesplé: 'Lakmé a accompagné ma vie'." (Meeting with Mady Mesplé: Lakmé Has Accompanied My Life.) *ASO*. 1998 Mar/Apr.; 183: 78-79. Lang.: Fre.
France. 1961-1997. Histories-sources. ▪Opera singer recalls singing the title role in Delibes' *Lakmé* throughout her career.

4574 Morgan, Kenneth. "Georges Thill." *OQ*. 1998-1999 Win; 15(1): 72-86. Notes. Illus.: Photo. B&W. 1. Lang.: Eng.
France. 1897-1984. Biographical studies. ▪Life and career of French tenor Thill.

4575 Myers, Eric. "Sound Bites: Natalie Dessay." *OpN*. 1998 Jan 31; 62(10): 38-39. Illus.: Photo. Color. 1. Lang.: Eng.
France. 1998. Histories-sources. ▪Brief profile, interview with French soprano Natalie Dessay.

4576 Scherer, Barrymore Laurence. "Song of the Orient." *OpN*. 1998 Feb 28; 62(12): 18-20,22-23. Illus.: Pntg. Color. 5. Lang.: Eng.
France. 1872-1911. Historical studies. ▪The use of oriental themes by Camille Saint-Saëns in his instrumental works and operas, including *Samson et Dalila*.

4577 Steiner, George. "Letter from Lyons." *OpN*. 1998 Feb 14; 62(11): 49-50. Illus.: Photo. Color. 1. Lang.: Eng.
France: Lyons. 1997. Critical studies. ▪A review of the Opéra de Lyon production of *Doktor Faust* by Ferruccio Busoni staged by Pierre Strosser.

4578 Baker, David J. "At Odds: *Capriccio*'s Music Frequently Contradicts Its Text." *OpN*. 1998 Jan 31; 62(10): 16-19, 55. Illus.: Photo. B&W. Color. 5. Lang.: Eng.
Germany. 1942-1998. Critical studies. ▪Argues that Richard Strauss deliberately creates a discrepancy between words and music in *Capriccio*, described as an 'opera about opera'.

4579 Blankemeyer, Silke. "Neue Wege im Musiktheater." (New Ways in Music Theatre.) *DB*. 1998; 3: 42-44. Illus.: Dwg. Photo. B&W. 5. Lang.: Ger.
Germany. 1998. Historical studies. ▪Impressions from Sechs-Tage-Oper (Six Days of Opera), the first international festival of the independent music theatre scene in Rhineland.

4580 Blankemeyer, Silke. "Vom Traumschiff zum Panzerkreuzer." (From Dream Ship to Battleship.) *DB*. 1998; 8: 23-25. Illus.: Photo. B&W. 4. Lang.: Ger.
Germany: Munich, Duisberg. 1998. Critical studies. ▪Compares the political dimensions of Richard Wagner's *Tristan und Isolde* directed by Peter Konwitschny at Bayerische Staatsoper and directed by Werner Schroeter at Deutsche Oper am Rhein.

4581 Bomberger, E. Douglas. "The Neues Schauspielhaus in Berlin and the Premiere of Carl Maria von Weber's *Der Freischütz*." 147-170 in Radice, Mark A., ed. *Opera in Context: Essays on Historical Staging from the Late Renaissance to the Time of Puccini*. Portland, OR: Amadeus P; 1998. 410 pp. Notes. Index. Tables. Biblio. Illus.: Plan. Dwg. Sketches. Diagram. 10. Lang.: Eng.
Germany: Berlin. 1821. Historical studies. ▪The premiere of Carl Maria von Weber's *Der Freischütz* (librettist, Johann Friedrich Kind), the first opera produced in Berlin's Neues Schauspielhaus. Argues that the new theatre's innovations in theatrical construction contributed to the opera's success.

4582 Brandenburg, Detlef. "Auf der Suche nach dem Code." (Looking For the Code.) *DB*. 1998; 3: 22-26. Illus.: Photo. B&W. 5. Lang.: Ger.
Germany: Munich. 1998. Histories-sources. ▪Interview with composer Manfred Trojahn on occasion of the first performance of his opera *Was ihr wollt*, based on Shakespeare's *Twelfth Night*, directed by Peter Mussbach at Bayerische Staatsoper.

4583 Brandenburg, Detlef. "Durch Räume gehen." (Going Through Rooms.) *DB*. 1998; 10: 10-14. Illus.: Photo. B&W. 6. Lang.: Ger.
Germany: Oldenburg, Kiel. 1996-1998. Historical studies. ▪Portrait of the opera director Katja Czellnik and her working methods concerning directions of Claude Debussy's *Pelléas et Mélisande* at Oldenburgisches Staatstheater, Wilfried Hiller's *Der Rattenfänger* and Ruggiero Leoncavallo's *Edipo Re* and *Pagliacci* at Bühnen der Landeshauptstadt Kiel.

4584 Brandenburg, Detlef. "Brüder, zur Sonne–zu Gott?" (Brother, to the Sun–to God?)*DB*. 1998; 12: 10-13. Illus.: Photo. B&W. 3. Lang.: Ger.
Germany: Stuttgart, Leipzig. 1998. Reviews of performances. ▪Reviews Luigi Nono's *Al gran sole carico d'amore* directed by Martin Kušej at Staatstheater Stuttgart and Olivier Messiaen's *Saint-François d'Assise* directed by Gottfried Pilz at Oper Leipzig. Analyzes the concepts in context of increasing budget cuts.

4585 Buller, Jeffrey L. "Spectacle in the *Ring*." *OQ*. 1998 Sum; 14(4): 41-57. Lang.: Eng.
Germany. 1869-1876. Critical studies. ▪Importance of visual spectacle to performance of Wagner's *Der Ring des Nibelungen*.

4586 Carlson, Marvin. "Aleatory Art and the Frankfurt Police." *TA*. 1998; 51: 27-31. Notes. Lang.: Eng.
Germany: Frankfurt. 1987. Historical studies. ▪Police involvement in a performance of John Cage's *Europeras 1 and 2* at the Frankfurter Theater.

4587 Crutchfield, Will. "Her Way." *OpN*. 1998 Nov.; 63(5): 54-59. Illus.: Photo. B&W. 5. Lang.: Eng.
Germany. 1848-1929. Biographical studies. ▪Evaluation of the strengths and weaknesses of soprano Lilli Lehmann, the pioneering singer of operatic roles written by Richard Wagner.

4588 Eaton, Jonathan. "*Die Bürgschaft* Then and Now." *KWN*. 1998 Spr; 16(1): 4-11. Illus.: Photo. Sketches. B&W. 8. Lang.: Eng.
Germany: Berlin, Bielefeld. 1931-1998. Historical studies. ▪Overview of the performance history of the Kurt Weill-Caspar Neher opera: its premiere at the Berlin Opera House in 1932, directed by Carl Ebert, Ebert's revival in 1957 at the Städtische Oper in Berlin, Jonathon Eaton's present

MUSIC-DRAMA: Opera—Performance/production

day production at Bühne der Stadt, Bielefeld. Includes review of the Bielefeld production, and a letter by Weill regarding his opera.

4589 Eckert, Nora. "Oper als Sehnsucht nach dem Eigenen." (Opera as Longing for One's Own.) *TZ*. 1998; 4: 46-48. Illus.: Photo. B&W. 4. Lang.: Ger.
Germany: Nuremberg. 1996-1998. Biographical studies. ■Barbara Beyer's directing approach to operas with respect to Mozart's *Die Entführung aus dem Serail (The Abduction from the Seraglio)* in 1996 and Beethoven's *Fidelio* in 1997 at Städtische Bühnen (Nuremberg).

4590 Eriksson, Torbjörn. "'Jag gillar roller med utanförskap'." (I Like the Role of the Outsider.) *MuD*. 1998; 20(1): 8-9. Illus.: Photo. B&W. Lang.: Swe.
Germany. Sweden. 1988-1998. Histories-sources. ■Interview with the singer Krister St. Hill about his career from musical artist to opera singer, with reference to his part in Michael Tippett's *New Year*.

4591 Eriksson, Torbjörn. "Den nye Lander." (The New Lander.) *MuD*. 1998; 20(1): 10. Illus.: Photo. B&W. Lang.: Swe.
Germany. Austria. Sweden. 1981-1998. Biographical studies. ■Profile of the singer Thomas Lander, with reference to his career in Germany and Austria, and his return to Sweden.

4592 Feller, Elisabeth. "Der Klang eines Stückes." (The Sound of a Play.) *DB*. 1998; 5: 10-13. Illus.: Photo. B&W. 4. Lang.: Ger.
Germany: Stuttgart. Switzerland: Basel. 1998. Histories-sources. ■Interview with director Jossi Wieler on his production of Handel's *Alcina* at Staatstheater Stuttgart and the differences between directing drama or opera. Includes a critique of his production of Mozart's *Die Entführung aus dem Serail* at Theater Basel.

4593 Guinther, Louise T. "Head, Body and Heart." *OpN*. 1998 Jan 31; 62(10): 24-28. Illus.: Photo. B&W. Color. 6. Lang.: Eng.
Germany. 1998. Histories-sources. ■Profile, interview with German baritone Wolfgang Brendel.

4594 Halbreich, Harry. "Zemlinsky, le crépusculaire." (Zemlinsky the Shadowy.) *ASO*. 1998 Sep/Oct.; 186: 98-103. Illus.: Dwg. Photo. B&W. 4. Lang.: Fre.
Germany. 1871-1942. Biographical studies. ■Life of composer and conductor Alexander Zemlinsky.

4595 Hatch, Christopher. "The Wondrous Trumpet Call in Beethoven's *Fidelio*." *OQ*. 1998-1999 Win; 15(1): 5-17. Notes. Lang.: Eng.
Germany. 1814. Critical studies. ■Analysis of Beethoven's opera, particularly the trumpet call in Act 2, Scene 1.

4596 Kranz, Dieter. "Der absolute Blick." (The Absolute Look.) *DB*. 1998; 8: 26-30. Illus.: Photo. B&W. 7. Lang.: Ger.
Germany. 1970-1996. Biographical studies. ■Retrospective of the director Ruth Berghaus, her working methods and aesthetics including statements by conductor Michael Gielen, singer Anja Silja and festival-manager Gérard Mortier.

4597 Kranz, Dieter. "Die Lust zur Verantwortung." (Fancying Responsibility.) *DB*. 1998; 8: 36-37. Illus.: Photo. B&W. 2. Lang.: Ger.
Germany: Meiningen. 1991-1998. Biographical studies. ■Portrait of director Christine Mielitz, her works at Komische Oper Berlin, international directions and new plans as theatre-manager in Meiningen.

4598 Lennartz, Knut. "Jahre in Bielefeld." (Years in Bielefeld.) *DB*. 1998; 6: 10-15. Illus.: Photo. B&W. 1. Lang.: Ger.
Germany: Bielefeld. 1975-1998. Histories-sources. ■Interview with the director and theatre-manager Heiner Bruns who managed Städtische Bühnen Bielefeld for twenty-three years about concepts and successes with music theatre.

4599 Machrova, É.V.; Mosolova, L.M., ed. *Opernyj teat'r v kul'ture Germanii vtoroj poloviny XX veka*. (The Theatre of Opera in the Culture of Germany during the Second Half of the Twentieth Century.) St.Petersburg: RGPU; 1998. 264 pp. Lang.: Rus.
Germany. 1950-1998. Historical studies. ■History of opera in late twentieth-century Germany.

4600 Mazanec, Brigitta. "Der Reiz der anderen Form." (The Attraction of a Different Form.) *DB*. 1998; 8: 20-22. Illus.: Photo. B&W. 3. Lang.: Ger.
Germany. 1986-1998. Historical studies. ■Portrait of director Herbert Wernicke, his working methods and concepts of opera.

4601 O'Connor, Patrick. "The Lieder Zone." *OpN*. 1998 Oct.; 63(4): 18-20, 22. Illus.: Photo. B&W. Color. 8. Lang.: Eng.
Germany. UK-England. 1998. Critical studies. ■Lieder recordings of Robert Schumann's *Dichterliebe* and *Liederkreis* by English tenor Ian Bostridge, accompanied by Julius Drake, and German baritone Matthias Goerne, accompanied by Vladimir Ashkenazy.

4602 Peter, Wolf-Dieter. "Anderer Wagner, anderes Bayreuth...?" (A Different Wagner, a Different Bayreuth...?)*DB*. 1998; 8: 31-33. Illus.: Photo. B&W. 1. Lang.: Ger.
Germany: Bayreuth. 1901-1981. Critical studies. ■Portrait of Franz Wilhelm Beidler, a grandchild of Richard Wagner, and his concepts of a different Bayreuther Festspiele, with respect to new publications of Franz Wilhelm Beidler's works edited by Dieter Borchmeyer.

4603 Sandgren, Maria. "Podiumangst i Berlin." (Stage Fright in Berlin.) *MuD*. 1998; 20(5): 16-17. Illus.: Photo. B&W. Lang.: Swe.
Germany: Berlin. 1998. Historical studies. ■Report from a seminar on stage fright or psychological problems of musicians and singers.

4604 Schoenberg, Arnold. "'Zemlinsky peut attendre' (1921)." (Zemlinsky Can Wait, 1921.) *ASO*. 1998 Sep/Oct.; 186: 104-105. Illus.: Photo. B&W. 1. Lang.: Fre.
Germany. 1921. Histories-sources. ■Schoenberg's opinion of Alexander Zemlinsky, who was his teacher, friend, and later brother-in-law.

4605 Shafer, Yvonne. "Interview with Christine Mielitz." *WES*. 1998 Spr; 10(2): 59-64. Illus.: Photo. B&W. 4. Lang.: Eng.
Germany: Berlin. 1979-1997. Histories-sources. ■Interview with Mielitz regarding her career as an opera director, and her work as an assistant to director Harry Kupfer.

4606 Simon, John. "Testament: ... *Capriccio*, Strauss' 'Last Word on Opera'." *OpN*. 1998 Jan 31; 62(10): 8-10, 54. Illus.: Photo. B&W. 6. Lang.: Eng.
Germany. 1942. Critical studies. ■Examination and criticism of the fifteenth and last opera by Richard Strauss, with libretto by Clemens Krauss, who also conducted the premiere. Stefan Zweig (the usual Strauss librettist) discovered the idea, but as a proscribed Jew could not write it.

4607 Stähr, Susanne. "Die Dinge in ihrer Rohform." (The Things in Their Rough Form.) *DB*. 1998; 3: 27-29. Illus.: Photo. B&W. 2. Lang.: Ger.
Germany. 1990-2001. Historical studies. ■Portrait of young composer Matthias Pintscher and his new opera *Thomas Chatterton* after Hans Henny Jahnn's drama.

4608 Sündermann, Anja. "Theater ist kein Spass." (Theatre Is No Fun.) *DB*. 1998; 1: 35-36. Illus.: Photo. B&W. 1. Lang.: Ger.
Germany: Hamburg. 1991-1998. Histories-sources. ■Director Sündermann her experiences directing her first project after ending her studies, Giuseppe Verdi's *Rigoletto* at Volkstheater Rostock, and describes her process.

4609 Teschke, Holger; Lindman, Magnus, transl. "Lyssna med kroppen, tala med kroppen." (Listen with the Body, Speak with the Body.) *Tningen*. 1998; 21(3): 5-7. Illus.: Photo. Color. Lang.: Swe.
Germany: Berlin. 1970-1998. Histories-sources. ■Interview with Robert Wilson about his method of producing theatre with references to Bertolt Brecht and *Der Ozeanflug*.

4610 Thomason, Paul. "*Lohengrin*'s Line." *OpN*. 1998 Mar 14; 62(13): 14, 16, 18-19. Illus.: Photo. B&W. Color. 8. Lang.: Eng.
Germany: Bayreuth. 1850-1998. Historical studies. ■Historical account of Wagnerian singers, with special attention to the romantic performance of *Lohengrin* at the Bayreuther Festspiele, 1936.

4611 Ueding, Cornelie. "'No Homeland in the World'." *DB*. 1998; 1: 38-39. Illus.: Photo. B&W. 3. Lang.: Ger.

MUSIC-DRAMA: Opera—Performance/production

Germany: Stuttgart. 1959-1998. Biographical studies. ▪Portrait of the opera director Inge Levant and her working method, with respect to her productions of Strauss's *Salome* and Mussorgskij's *Boris Godunov* at Staatstheater Stuttgart.

4612 Wille, Franz. "Klänge der Heimat." (Sounds of Home.) *THeute.* 1998; 1: 18-20. Illus.: Photo. B&W. 3. Lang.: Ger.

Germany: Hamburg. 1997-1998. Critical studies. ▪Analyzes Frank Castorf's view on Johann Strauss' *Die Fledermaus* performed at Schauspielhaus Hamburg.

4613 Zemlinsky, Alexander. "Lettre à Alma Mahler (mai 1917)." (Letter to Alma Mahler, May 1917.) *ASO.* 1998 Sep/Oct.; 186 : 40-41. Illus.: Photo. B&W. 2. Lang.: Fre.

Germany. 1917. Histories-sources. ▪French translation of the composer's letter to Alma Mahler regarding his opera *Eine florentinische Tragödie.*

4614 McKee, David. "Wieland's Way." *OpN.* 1998 Mar 14; 62(13): 26-27. Illus.: Photo. B&W. 3. Lang.: Eng.

Germany, West: Bayreuth. 1966. Historical studies. ▪Wieland Wagner's production of *Lohengrin* by Richard Wagner at the Bayreuther Festspiele.

4615 Albert, István. "Operaprimadonna–a két háború között: Németh Mária." (An Opera Primadonna Between the Two World Wars: Mária Németh.) *OperaL.* 1998; 7(3): 23-24. Illus.: Photo. B&W. 1. Lang.: Hun.

Hungary. Austria: Vienna. 1898-1967. Biographical studies. ▪Profile of the famous soprano.

4616 Albert, István. "Karkötelezett segédszínészből tenorsztár: Kortársai Környey Béláról." (Star Tenor from the Chorus: Contemporaries Remember Béla Környey.) *OperaL.* 1998; 7(5): 7-9. Illus.: Photo. B&W. 4. Lang.: Hun.

Hungary. 1875-1925. Biographical studies. ▪Life and career of the famous Bohemian-born tenor of the Opera House. Originally a baritone, he became a tenor.

4617 Bónis, Ferenc. "Találkozások Ránki Györggyel: A zeneszerző születésének évfordulójára." (My Meetings with György Ránki: On the Anniversary of the Composer's Birth.) *OperaL.* 1998; 7 (1): 18-20. Illus.: Photo. B&W. 2. Lang.: Hun.

Hungary. 1907-1992. Biographical studies. ▪Memory of the composer on the occasion of the 90th anniversary of his birth. Besides piano pieces, cantatas, music for films and radio plays he composed parodies and even operas.

4618 Boros, Attila. "Huszonöt éve a pályán: Gáti István." (István Gáti: Twenty-Five Years on the Stage.) *OperaL.* 1998; 7(3): 16-20. Illus.: Photo. B&W. 3. Lang.: Hun.

Hungary. 1971-1998. Histories-sources. ▪Interview with István Gáti, an outstanding baritone of the Hungarian Opera House, about his preference for Mozart roles and his performances all over the world.

4619 Csák, P. Judit. "Beszélgetés Kerényi Miklós Gáborral: Az Álarcosbálról, a megrendezett nyitányról, az operáról a videoklip korában." (An Interview with the director of Verdi's *The Masked Ball* about the staged overture and opera in the age of the video clip.) *OperaL.* 1998; 7(4): 4-8. Lang.: Hun.

Hungary: Budapest. 1998. Histories-sources. ▪Interview with Miklós Gábor Kerényi, director of *Un Ballo in Maschera* at the Szeged Open-Air Festival and the Budapest Opera House.

4620 Dalos, László. "A karakter-tenor: Múltidézés Palcsó Sándorral." (The Character-Tenor: Waking Memories of the Past with Sándor Palcsó.) *OperaL.* 1998; 7(4): 8-13. Illus.: Photo. B&W. 6. Lang.: Hun.

Hungary. 1929-1998. Histories-sources. ▪Interview with the retired tenor who specialized in comprimario roles.

4621 Hollósi, Zsolt. "Az elfeledett *Stiffelio*: Verdi - opera magyarországi bemutatója." (The Forgotten *Stiffelio*: The Hungarian Premiere of Verdi's Opera.) *OperaL.* 1998; 7(4): 34. Illus.: Photo. Color. 1. Lang.: Hun.

Hungary: Szeged. 1998. Reviews of performances. ▪The Hungarian premiere of Verdi's *Stiffelio* in a concert performance by the opera ensemble of the Szeged National Theatre.

4622 Hollósi, Zsolt; Veréb, Simon, photo. "*Don Giovanni.*" *OperaL.* 1998; 31(7): 11-13. Illus.: Photo. Color. 6. Lang.: Hun.

Hungary: Szeged. 1998. Histories-sources. ▪Interview with the conductor and musical director of Szeged National Theatre, Tamás Pál, on the occasion of the first night of Mozart's masterpiece. Director János Szikora staged the original version as premiered in Prague, October 29, 1787.

4623 Huszár, Klára. "Búcsú Orosz Júliától." (Farewell to Júlia Orosz.) *OperaL.* 1998; 7(1): 2-3. Illus.: Photo. B&W. 1. Lang.: Hun.

Hungary. 1908-1997. Biographical studies. ▪The death at the age of 90 of soprano Júlia Orosz.

4624 Huszár, Klára. "Emlékezés Radnai Györgyre." (György Radnai–Commemoration.) *OperaL.* 1998; 7(2): 22-25. Illus.: Photo. B&W. 3. Lang.: Hun.

Hungary. 1920-1977. Biographical studies. ▪Profile of the Budapest Opera baritone who participated in the 'Opera on Rails' touring performances in the Hungarian provinces during the 1950s.

4625 Kertész, Iván; Vajda, M. Pál, photo. "Laczó István emlékezete." (Commemorating István Laczó.) *OperaL.* 1998; 7(1): 28-30. Illus.: Photo. B&W. 1. Lang.: Hun.

Hungary. 1904-1965. Biographical studies. ▪Memory of the well-known tenor, who was 'discovered' by Pietro Mascagni while working as an architect.

4626 Kertész, Iván. "Az Operaház örökös tagjai: Haselbeck Olga." (Life Members of the Opera House: Olga Haselbeck.) *OperaL.* 1998; 7(1): 21-22. Illus.: Photo. B&W. 3. Lang.: Hun.

Hungary. 1884-1961. Biographical studies. ▪Profile of the soprano who sang the role of Judet in the premiere of Bartók's *A kékszakállú herceg vára (Bluebeard's Castle)* in 1918.

4627 Kertész, Iván. "Anday Piroska emlékezet." (Remembering Piroska Anday.) *OperaL.* 1998; 7(2): 30-31. Illus.: Photo. B&W. 1. Lang.: Hun.

Hungary: Budapest. Austria: Vienna. 1903-1977. Biographical studies. ▪Profile of the world-famous Hungarian soprano most of whose career took place at the Vienna Staatsoper.

4628 Kertész, Iván. "Bende Zsolt." (Zsolt Bende.) *OperaL.* 1998; 7(4): 2-3. Illus.: Photo. B&W. 1. Lang.: Hun.

Hungary. 1926-1998. Biographical studies. ▪Obituary for the baritone, a thirty-year member of the Hungarian State Opera House.

4629 Koltai, Tamás; Kallus, György, photo. "A színészkirály: Verdi: *Az álarcosbál.*" (The Actor King: Giuseppe Verdi: *Un Ballo in Maschera.*) *Sz.* 1998; 31(12): 32-34. Illus.: Photo. B&W. 1. Lang.: Hun.

Hungary: Budapest. 1998. Reviews of performances. ▪Verdi's opera at the Hungarian State Opera House (as replaced in its original Swedish setting) directed by Miklós Gábor Kerényi.

4630 Koltai, Tamás; Koncz, Zsuzsa, photo. "Életminőségek szembesítése: Szikora János *A varázsfuvolá*ról." (Confronting Qualities of Life: János Szikora on Mozart's *The Magic Flute.*) *OperaL.* 1998; 7 (3): 4-7. Illus.: Photo. B&W. 1. Lang.: Hun.

Hungary: Budapest. 1998. Histories-sources. ▪Interview with stage director János Szikora on his production of *Die Zauberflöte* at the Budapest Opera House at the Thália Theatre. Szikora has also written a play on the subject.

4631 Márok, Tamás; Kallus, György, photo.; Veréb, Simon, photo. "A tiszta eszme unalma: Két Mozart Szikorától." (The Boredom of the Clear Mind: Two Mozart Productions Directed by János Szikora.) *Sz.* 1998; 31(12): 34-36. Illus.: Photo. B&W. 2. Lang.: Hun.

Hungary: Budapest. Hungary: Szeged. 1998. Reviews of performances. ▪Two revivals of *Die Zauberflöte*: the guest production of the Opera House at the Thália Theatre, Budapest and at the Szeged National Theatre, both directed by János Szikora.

4632 Mátai, Györgyi. "Bemutatjuk Fekete Veronikát." (Introducing Veronika Fekete.) *OperaL.* 1998; 7(2): 26-29. Illus.: Photo. B&W. 5. Lang.: Hun.

MUSIC-DRAMA: Opera—Performance/production

Hungary. 1958-1998. Histories-sources. ■Profile of Budapest Opera soprano best known for her performance as the Queen of Night in Mozart's *Die Zauberflöte.*

4633 Mátai, Györgyi. "Melis György 75. születésnapjára." (75th Birthday of György Melis.) *OperaL.* 1998; 7(5): 5-7. Illus.: Photo. B&W. 1. Lang.: Hun.

Hungary. 1923-1998. Historical studies. ■The celebration of the 75th birthday baritone György Melis by the ensemble of the Budapest Opera House with a gala performance of *Così fan tutte* in which Melis sang the part of Don Alfonso.

4634 Ménes, Aranka. "Látogatóban Antalffy Albertnél." (Paying a Visit to Albert Antalffy.) *OperaL.* 1998; 7 (3): 25-28. Illus.: Photo. B&W. 4. Lang.: Hun.

Hungary. Austria: Mödling. 1924-1998. Histories-sources. ■Interview with the retired bass of the Budapest Opera House, who has been teaching at the Beethoven Musikhochschule for almost twenty years.

4635 Réfi, Zsuzsanna. "'Kövessük Wagner gondolatait és ne tévedjünk el'." ('Follow Wagner's Thoughts and Do Not Miss the Way'.) *ZZT.* 1998; 5(3): . Illus.: Photo. B&W. 1. Lang.: Hun.

Hungary: Budapest. 1998. Histories-sources. ■Director Viktor Nagy introduces the *Ring* cycle after the premiere of the final part of Wagner's tetralogy at the Budapest Opera House.

4636 Réfi, Zsuzsanna. "A svéd *Álarcosbál* az Operaházban: Kerényi Miklós Gábor kedvenc darabja." (The Swedish Version of Verdi's *The Masked Ball* at the Opera House: Miklós Gábor Kerényi's Favorite Opera.) *ZZT.* 1998; 5(4): 6-7. Illus.: Photo. B&W. 1. Lang.: Hun.

Hungary: Budapest, Szeged. 1998. Histories-sources. ■The director of Verdi's *Un Ballo in maschera* discusses the different stagings used at the opera's production at the Szeged Open-Air Festival in July and at the Budapest Opera House in September.

4637 Sándor, Judit. "A nadrágszerepekről." (On Male Roles.) *ZZT.* 1998; 5(1): 32-34. Illus.: Photo. B&W. 2. Lang.: Hun.

Hungary. 1948-1998. Histories-sources. ■Recollection of opera singer Judit Sándor on her male roles.

4638 Sediánszky, Nóra; Földi, Imre, photo. "Figaro itt, Figaro ott: Mozart operája." (Figaro Here, Figaro There: Mozart's Opera.) *Sz.* 1998; 31(12): 37-38. Illus.: Photo. B&W. 1. Lang.: Hun.

Hungary: Budapest. 1998. Reviews of performances. ■Mozart's *Le Nozze di Figaro* at the Hungarian State Opera House directed by Judit Galgóczy.

4639 Szegvári, Katalin. *Melis György.* (György Melis.) Budapest: Pallas Stúdió; 1998. 48 pp. (örökös tagság.) Append. Illus.: Photo. B&W. 60. Lang.: Hun, Eng.

Hungary. 1923-1998. Histories-sources. ■An album on the life and career of the baritone of the Hungarian State Opera House, recently awarded the honor of 'life-membership'.

4640 Szomory, György. "'Hiszek a művészet felemelő erejében': Találkozás Polgár Lászlóval." ('I Believe in the Elevating Power of Art': Meeting László Polgár.) *OperaL.* 1998; 7(2): 13-19. Illus.: Photo. B&W. 8. Lang.: Hun.

Hungary. Switzerland: Zurich. 1947-1998. Histoires- sources. ■Interview with the popular Hungarian bass, a mamber of both the Hungarian State opera House and the Zurich Opera House.

4641 Szomory, György. "Ismerni a figura lelki mozgatóit: Beszélgetés Tréfás Györggyel." (You Have to Know the Spiritual and Mental Motivation of a Character: A Conversation with György Tréfás.) *OperaL.* 1998; 7(5): 10-18. Illus.: Photo. B&W. 4. Lang.: Hun.

Hungary: Debrecen. 1931-1998. Histories-sources. ■Inteview with the bass György Tréfás, who has been a member of the opera ensemble of the Debrecen Csokonai Theatre for more than four and a half decades.

4642 Wilheim, András; Kallus, György, photo. "Műfajtörténeti panoptikum: Ligeti györgy: *Le Grand Macabre.*" (Historical Waxwork of a Genre: György Ligeti: *Le Grand Macabre.*) *Sz.* 1998; 31(12): 31-32. Illus.: Photo. B&W. 1. Lang.: Hun.

Hungary: Budapest. 1998. Reviews of performances. ■György Ligeti's opera at the Thália Theatre directed by Balázs Kovalik.

4643 Wirthmann, Julianna. "'Megtaláltam az utamat': Beszélgetés Temesi Máriával." ('I Have Found My Way': Interview with Mária Temesi.) *OperaL.* 1998; 7(1): 23-27. Illus.: Photo. B&W. 5. Lang.: Hun.

Hungary. 1977-1998. Histories-sources. ■The leading mezzo-soprano of the Budapest Opera who performs Italian and German dramatic soprano parts and also in oratorios.

4644 Zala, Szilárd Zoltán; Szoboszlai, Gábor, photo.; Korniss, Péter, photo. "Cselédlépcső a Walhallába: Wagner: *Ring* tetralógia." (Backstairs at Valhalla: Richard Wagner: *Ring* tetralogy.) *Sz.* 1998; 31(12): 38-41. Illus.: Photo. B&W. 3. Lang.: Hun.

Hungary: Budapest. 1998. Reviews of performances. ■Wagner's *Ring des Nibelungen* at the Hungarian State Opera House.

4645 Walsh, Basil F. "Catherine Hayes: An Early Donizetti Prima Donna." *OQ.* 1998 Spr; 14(3): 44-54. Notes. Tables. Illus.: Pntg. B&W. 1. Lang.: Eng.

Ireland. Italy. 1839-1861. Biographical studies. ■Career of singer Hayes, particularly singing the female leads in such Donizetti operas as *Maria di Rohan, Linda di Chamounix, Lucia di Lammermoor*, and *Olivo e Pasquale.*

4646 "'Mat' durakov vsegda beremenna'." (The Mother of Stupid People Is Always Pregnant.) *NV.* 1998; 40: 40-42. Lang.: Rus.

Italy. 1998. Histories-sources. ■Interview with Italian opera singer Luigi Cucci on his art.

4647 Ashbrook, William; Guccini, Gerardo. *Mefistofele di Arrigo Boito.* (*Mephistopheles* by Arrigo Boito.) Milan: Ricordi; 1998. 318 pp. (Musica e Spettacolo.) Biblio. Notes. Illus.: Sketches. Photo. Dwg. Plan. 71. Lang.: Ita.

Italy. 1871-1881. Histories-reconstruction. ■Reconstruction of the final version of Boito's *Mefistofele* at the Teatro alla Scala in Milan on 25 May 1881. Includes the scenic disposition by Boito himself.

4648 Castiglioni, Elisabetta. "Luca Ronconi e la regia lirica." (Luca Ronconi and Lyric Direction.) *BiT.* 1998; 45/47: 35-81. Notes. Illus.: Sketches. 3. Lang.: Ita.

Italy. 1974-1992. Critical studies. ■Analysis of the works of the Italian theatre director Luca Ronconi as director of opera. This essay underlines the working methods used by one of the most original directors of the European theatre.

4649 Crutchfield, Will. "Dark Shadows." *OpN.* 1998 July; 63(1): 32-35. Illus.: Pntg. Color. B&W. 3. Lang.: Eng.

Italy. UK-England. 1797-1998. Critical studies. ■A critical/historical interpretation of Donizetti's *Lucrezia Borgia*, which is to be conducted by the author at the 1998 Caramoor International Musical Festival. Includes a painting by Frank Cadogan Cowper of the historical Lucrezia Borgia.

4650 Dennis, Robert J. "Setting the Record(s) Straight: *Don Carlos* and Textual Harassment." *OQ.* 1998 Sum; 14(4): 71-81. Discography. Lang.: Eng.

Italy. Europe. 1866-1998. Critical studies. ■Categorizes recordings of Verdi's opera according to three versions created by the composer.

4651 Eősze, László. "Négyszáz éves az opera." (The 400th Anniversary of Opera Art.) *OperaL.* 1998; 7 (1): 16-17. Lang.: Hun.

Italy: Florence. 1598. Historical studies. ■Commemorates what is considered by musicologists to be the first opera: *Daphne*, by Jacopo Peri and Ottavio Rinuccini, which probably premiered in Florence in February 1598. Only a few fragments of the composition survived.

4652 Eősze, László. "Operaritkaság: *Stiffelio*: Egy bukott Verdi-opera?" (An Opera Rarity: *Stiffelio*: A Verdi Opera Flop?) *OperaL.* 1998; 7(3): 20-22. Lang.: Hun.

Italy. 1850-1998. Historical studies. ■Overview of the production history of Verdi's rarely performed *Stiffelio* (libretto by Piave) on the occasion of its live broadcast in Hungary from the Metropolitan Opera in New York.

4653 Eriksson, Torbjörn. "Tenor med opera som schlager." (A Tenor With Opera As a Popular Song.) *MuD.* 1998; 20(2): 31. Illus.: Photo. B&W. Lang.: Swe.

Italy. 1985-1998. Biographical studies. ■Profile of tenor Andrea Bocelli.

MUSIC-DRAMA: Opera—Performance/production

4654 Freeman, John W. "The Real Salieri." *OpN.* 1998 Mar 28; 62(14): 26-28. Illus.: Photo. B&W. Color. 6. Lang.: Eng.

Italy: Milan. 1799-1998. Biographical studies. ■The work of composer Antonio Salieri, whose *Falstaff* has been revived by La Società dell'Opera Buffa, directed by Beni Montresor.

4655 Garlato, Rita. *Repertorio metrico verdiano.* (Metric Repertory of Giuseppe Verdi.) Venice: Marsilio; 1998. 316 pp. (Saggi Marsilio.) Pref. Biblio. Lang.: Ita.

Italy. 1813-1901. Critical studies. ■Examines the metrics applied by musician Giuseppe Verdi in his musical dramaturgy.

4656 Glasow, E. Thomas. "Quarter Notes." *OQ.* 1998 Spr; 14(3): 1-10. Notes. Illus.: Photo. Pntg. Dwg. B&W. 3. Lang.: Eng.

Italy. 1797-1848. Biographical studies. ■Introduction to the focus of *OQ* 14:3, the life and work of composer Gaetano Donizetti.

4657 Graune, Erik. "Gud är Puccini och Muti är hans profet." (God Is Puccini and Muti His Prophet.) *MuD.* 1998; 20(5) : 20-21. Illus.: Photo. B&W. Lang.: Swe.

Italy: Milan. 1980-1998. Historical studies. ■Report from La Scala and the work of Riccardo Muti, with reference to Puccini's *Manon Lescaut* staged by Liliana Cavani.

4658 Hoelterhoff, Manuela. "Chasing the Anti-Diva." *NewY.* 1998 24-31 Aug.: 89-95. Illus.: Pntg. Color. 1. Lang.: Eng.

Italy. 1995-1998. Biographical studies. ■Profile of opera star Cecilia Bartoli, based on several meetings with the author.

4659 Kaufman, Tom. "A Performance History of *Aureliano in Palmira.*" *OQ.* 1998-1999 Win; 15(1): 33-37. Tables. Lang.: Eng.

Italy. Europe. 1813-1996. Historical studies. ■Chronology of all performances of Rossini's *opera seria* throughout Europe and Italy since its premiere in 1813.

4660 Leve, James Samuel. *Humor and Intrigue: A Comparative Study of Comic Opera in Florence and Rome During the Late Seventeenth Century.* New Haven, CT: Yale Univ; 1998. 721 pp. Notes. Biblio. [Ph.D. Dissertation, Univ. Microfilms Order No. AAC 9835278.] Lang.: Eng.

Italy: Florence, Rome. 1665-1700. Histories-specific. ■The different evolution and eventual convergence of comic opera in Florence and Rome in the work of composers Giovanni Andrea Moniglia, Jacopo Melani, Pietro Susini, Giovanni Cosimo Villifranchi, and Filippo Acciaiuoli.

4661 Midgette, Anne. "Bloodline: How Azucena Gave Birth to the 'Verdi Mezzo'." *OpN.* 1998 Feb 14; 62(11): 28-31. Illus.: Photo. B&W. Color. 3. Lang.: Eng.

Italy. 1853. Critical studies. ■The role of Azucena in *Il Trovatore* as an example of the important mezzo soprano roles created by Giuseppe Verdi in collaboration with his librettist Salvatore Cammarano.

4662 Midgette, Anne. "In Search of Pavarotti." *OpN.* 1998 Nov.; 63(5): 22-30. Illus.: Photo. B&W. Color. 18. Lang.: Eng.

Italy. 1935-1998. Histories-sources. ■Interview with tenor Luciano Pavarotti with notes on his learning process. Personal details as well as his training are included, along with difficulties in achieving a meeting.

4663 Tranberg, Sören. "Musa i magiskt gränsland." (A Muse in a Magical Borderland.) *MuD.* 1998; 20(4): 10-11. Illus.: Photo. B&W. Color. Lang.: Swe.

Italy. 1997. Histories-sources. ■Interview with Cecilia Bartoli about her career, with reference to her change of repertory to more soprano parts.

4664 Kong, Eunah. *Music at the Interface of Cultural Identity: Opera of Korea, 1948 to Present.* Los Angeles, CA: Univ. of California; 1998. 311 pp. Notes. Biblio. [Ph.D. Dissertation, Univ. Microfilms Order No. AAC 9906058.] Lang.: Eng.

Korea. 1948-1998. Critical studies. ■Explores the history of Western opera in Korea and the creation of a contemporary Korean opera that combines traditional and Western elements. Focuses on *ch'angjak* operas, works by Korean composers which include elements of Korea's national identity incorporated into a primarily Western musical framework.

4665 Tranberg, Sören. "Favoritroll—alltid den för tillfället aktuella." (Favorite Part—Always the One That Is Current for the Moment.) *MuD.* 1998; 20(4): 18-20. Illus.: Photo. B&W. Lang.: Swe.

Norway. Sweden. 1980-1998. Histories-sources. ■Interview with the opera singer Anne Bolstad about her background and career, with reference to Musikteatern i Värmland and her parts in *Peter Grimes* and *Salome* at GöteborgsOperan.

4666 Csák, P. Judit. "Operabemutató Kolozsvárott: Lajtha László: *A kék kalap.*" (Opera Premiere at Cluj/Kolozsvár: László Lajtha: *The Blue Hat.*) *ZZT.* 1998; 5(2): 14-15. Illus.: Photo. B&W. 1. Lang.: Hun.

Romania: Cluj-Napoca. Hungary. 1998. Reviews of performances. ■The opening of Lajtha's comic opera *Le chapeau bleu* at the Hungarian State Opera of Kolozsvár/Cluj-Napoca, performed in Hungarian. Includes the history of the composition.

4667 Jánosi, Ildikó; Strassburger, Alexandra, photo. "Bemutatjuk: Lory Andreát." (Introducing Andrea Lory.) *OperaL.* 1998; 7(4): 36-37. Illus.: Photo. B&W. 1. Lang.: Hun.

Romania: Iasi. Hungary. 1998. 19-1998. Histories-sources. ■Interview with the young Budapest Opera House soprano who studied and made her début in Romania.

4668 Solymosi Tari, Emőke. "*A kék kalap*: Lajtha László vígoperájának színpadi világpremierje Kolozsvárott." (*The Blue Hat*: World Premiere of the Comic Opera by László Lajtha at Kolozsvár/Cluj.) *OperaL.* 1998; 7(3): 7-16. Illus.: Photo. B&W. 2. Lang.: Hun.

Romania: Cluj-Napoca. Hungary. 1948-1998. Reviews of performances. ■*Le chapeau bleu*, a comic opera by Lajtha, a contemporary of Bartók and Kodály, staged in Hungarian (as *A kék Kalap*) by Zs. József Katona for the Kolszsvár Hungarian Opera ensemble. Libretto by Salvador de Madriaga, translation into Hungarian by Frigyes Rona and László Dalos. The work is said to evoke the seventeenth century and the *commedia dell'arte.*

4669 "Fedor Ivanovič Šaljapin, 1873-1938." *Vjatka.* 1998; 1: 4-48. Lang.: Rus.

Russia. 1873-1938. Biographical studies. ■Issue devoted to the opera singer.

4670 "Perepiska N.A. Rimskogo-Korsakova s N.I. Zabeloj-Vrubel'." (The Correspondence Between N.A. Rimskij-Korsakov and N.I. Zabela-Vrubel'.) *Novyj žurnal.* 1998; 2: 96-111. Lang.: Rus.

Russia. 1868-1913. Histories-sources. ■Correspondence between the composer and opera singer Nadežda Zabela-Vrubel'.

4671 "Samyj neobchodimyj spektakl'." (The Necessary Play.) *Žurnal ljubitelej iskusstv.* 1998; 1: 18-19. Lang.: Rus.

Russia: St. Petersburg. 1998. Critical studies. ■A new presentation of Čajkovskij's opera, *Eugene Onegin*, directed by A. Stepanov at the Rimskij-Korsakov Theatre.

4672 "Fëdor Šaljapin." *Kazan'.* 1998; 4: 70-105. Lang.: Rus.

Russia. 1873-1938. Biographical studies. ■Life and work of singer Fëdor Šaljapin.

4673 Abramovskij, G. *Opernoe tvorčestvo A.N. Serova.* (The Operatic Art of A.N. Serov.) St. Petersburg: Kanon; 1998. 180 pp. Lang.: Rus.

Russia. 1820-1871. Biographical studies. ■Profile of singer Aleksand'r Serov.

4674 Allison, John. "Russian Evolution." *OpN.* 1998 Jan 3; 62(8): 22. Illus.: Photo. Color. 1. Lang.: Eng.

Russia. 1959-1998. Biographical studies. ■A brief discussion of the career of Russian tenor Sergej Larin who was trained in Latvia.

4675 Arifdžanov, R. "Skripka, i nemnožko grustno." (A Violin, and a Little Bit of Sadness.) *Persona.* 1998; 4: 30-33. Lang.: Rus.

Russia. 1998. Biographical studies. ■Profile of opera singers Tamara Sinjavskaja and Muslim Magomaev.

4676 Bachrevskij, V. "Sotvorenie Šaljapina." (The Creation of Šaljapin.) *Nižnij Novgorod.* 1998; 9: 202-208. Lang.: Rus.

Russia: Nizhni Novgorod. 1890-1899. Biographical studies. ■Profile of Fëdor Šaljapin at the beginning of his career.

4677 Calobanova, V. "Duša prosila muzyki." (The Soul Was Asking for Music.) *Neva.* 1998; 6: 209-214. Lang.: Rus.

MUSIC-DRAMA: Opera—Performance/production

Russia: Leningrad. 1998. Biographical studies. ■Profile of opera singer N.K. Pečkovskij.

4678 Garanina, S. "Poslednij tragik: (Istorija perv. monogr. o F.I. Šaljapine)." (The Last Tragic Hero: History of the First Monograph about Šaljapin.) 77-84 in *Knigočej.* Moscow: Libereja-Bibinform; 1998. Lang.: Rus.

Russia. 1916. Critical studies. ■Critical appraisal of the first book on the singer: *F.I. Šaljapin* by E. Stark (Petrograd, 1916).

4679 Goder, D. "Ten' opery: Mosk. teatr Ten' dokazyvaet, čto do togo kak tancevat' 'Lebedinoe ozero' P. Čajkovskogo ego peli." (*The Shadow of the Opera*: Moscow's Theatre Ten' Proves That Čajkovskij's *Swan Lake* Was Sung Before It Was Danced.) *Itogi.* 1998; 40: 61-62. Lang.: Rus.

Russia: Moscow. 1998. Historical studies. ■Performance of *Ten' opery (The Shadow of the Opera)* by the puppet theatre Teat'r Ten', directed by Maja Krasnopol'skaya and Ilja Épel'baum.

4680 Goder, D. "Kto možet sravnit'sja...: I. Épel'baum i M. Krasnopol'skaja v svoem semejnom kukol'nom teatre Ten' predstavili 'Iolantu' Čajkovskogo." (Who Can Compare...: I. Épel'baum and M. Krasnopol'skaja in Their Family Puppet Theater, Ten, Present *Iolanta* by Čajkovskij.) *Itogi.* 1998; 46: 73-74. Lang.: Rus.

Russia: Moscow. Critical studies. ■Ten' Puppet Theatre's production of Čajkovskij's opera *Iolanta.*

4681 Il'in, I.A. "Chudožestvennoe prizvanie Šaljapina." (The Artistic Vocation of Šaljapin.) 415-450 in *Sobranie sočinenij.* Moscow: Rus. kniga; 1998. [Vol. 7.] Lang.: Rus.

Russia. 1873-1938. Biographical studies. ■The life of the opera singer Fëdor Šaljapin.

4682 Katz, Robert Scott. *'Persephone' and Mythic Elements in Stravinsky's Theatre Works.* Austin, TX: Univ. of Texas at Austin; 1998. 207 pp. Notes. Biblio. [Ph.D. Dissertation, Univ. Microfilms Order No. AAC 9905767.] Lang.: Eng.

Russia. 1934. Historical studies. ■The importance of myth and folklore as a subject for many of Stravinskij's works for the stage, and his style of theatrical production, with emphasis on the melodramatic *Perséphone,* libretto by André Gide.

4683 Markina, I. "Novaja zvezda russkoj opery." (The New Star of Russian Opera.) *Vstreča.* 1998; 5: 16-17. Lang.: Rus.

Russia: Moscow. Biographical studies. ■Profile of V. Bukin, singer and soloist of the Bolšoj Theatre.

4684 Mincaev, M. "Bol'šoj teatr—delo moej žizni." (Bolšoj Theatre—My Whole Life.) *Vajnach segodnja.* 1998; 1-3: 65-70. Lang.: Rus.

Russia: Moscow. 1998. Histories-sources. ■Bolšoj Opera singer M. Mincaev on his career.

4685 Peters, Margot. "The Voice of the Father: My Father Boris Godunov." *OpN.* 1998 Jan 3; 62(8): 8-10. Illus.: Photo. B&W. 4. Lang.: Eng.

Russia. 1873-1938. Histories-sources. ■The author's reminiscences of fatherless childhood playing old records of *Boris Godunov* featuring Russian basso Fëdor Šaljapin.

4686 Petrovskaja, I.F. "K istorii opernogo teatra v Peterburge v 1801-1840 gg." (Dedicated to the History of Opera in Petersburg, 1801-1840.) 191-206 in *Pamjatniki kul'tury.* Moscow: Nauka; 1998. Lang.: Rus.

Russia: St. Petersburg. 1801-1840. Historical studies. ■Examines the early nineteenth-century opera of St. Petersburg.

4687 Sadyrin, B.V. *Vjatskij Šaljapin.* (Vjatka's Šaljapin.) Kirov: 1998. 256 pp. Lang.: Rus.

Russia: Vjatka. 1873-1938. Biographical studies. ■Roots of Fëdor Šaljapin, his relatives and close friends in Vjatka.

4688 Sedov, A. "Pravoslavnyj pevec." (Slav Singer.) *Vstreča.* 1998; 6: 29-33. Lang.: Rus.

Russia. 1873-1938. Biographical studies. ■Career of Fëdor Šaljapin.

4689 Sedov, A. "Genij, zabytyj rodinoj." (Genius, Forgotten by His Home Town.) *Vstreča.* 1998; 10-11: 41-44. Lang.: Rus.

Russia. 1998. Biographical studies. ■Profile of D.A. Smirnov, Russian opera singer.

4690 Sedov, Ja. "Svet i teni 'Chrustal'nogo dvorca'." (Light and Shadows of the Crystal Palace.) *Itogi.* 1998; 6: 70-72. Lang.: Rus.

Russia: Moscow. 1997. Historical studies. ■Overview of the Mariinskij theatre tour.

4691 Silant'eva, I.I. "Knigi v žizni velikogo artista." (Books in the Life of the Great Artist.) *Mir bibliografii.* 1998; 1: 36-37. Lang.: Rus.

Russia. 1873-1938. Biographical studies. ■The role of books in the life and career of singer Fëdor Šaljapin.

4692 Syčeva, L. "Bol'šoj bas Bol'šogo..." (The Big Bass Voice of a Big Man...)*Slovo.* 1998; 5: 20-22. Lang.: Rus.

Russia: Moscow. 1998. Biographical studies. ■Profile of Bolšoj Opera singer, V. Matorin.

4693 Zarubin, V.I. *Bol'šoj teat'r: Perv. postanovki na rus. scene, 1825-1997.* (Bolšoj Theatre: Premieres on the Russian Stage, 1825-1997.) Moscow: Éllis Lak; 1998. 432 pp. Lang.: Rus.

Russia: Moscow. 1825-1997. Historical studies. ■Account of premieres of ballet and opera on the Bolšoj stage.

4694 Lee, Tong Soon. *Performing Chinese Street Opera and Constructing National Culture in Singapore.* Pittsburgh, PA: Univ. of Pittsburgh; 1998. 299 pp. Notes. Biblio. [Ph.D. Dissertation, Univ. Microfilms Order No. AAC 9906315.] Lang.: Eng.

Singapore. 1965-1998. Historical studies. ■Explores the varied meanings of Chinese street opera, produced and defined through interactions between traditions of professional and amateur operatic practices, and the official cultural mechanisms that regulate it.

4695 Rishoi, Niel. "Donizetti *Kammersängerin*: An Interview with Edita Gruberova." *OQ.* 1998 Spr; 14(3): 72-81. Illus.: Photo. B&W. 6. Lang.: Eng.

Slovakia. 1975-1998. Histories-sources. ■Interview with the Slovakian soprano, one of the foremost interpreters of the work of Donizetti, regarding her career and the composer.

4696 Klančnik Kocutar, Katarina. "Ondina Otta Klasine." *Dialogi.* 1998; 34(1-2): 3-10. Illus.: Photo. B&W. 3. Lang.: Slo.

Slovenia. 1946-1998. Histories-sources. ■Interview with Slovene soprano Ondina Otta Klasine about her life and career.

4697 Bergström, Gunnel. "'Bel canto bör inte alltid vara bello'." (Bel Canto Mustn't Always Be Bel.) *MuD.* 1998; 20 (1): 12-14. Illus.: Photo. B&W. Color. Lang.: Swe.

Sweden: Stockholm. 1982-1998. Histories-sources. ■Interview with the soprano Lena Nordin about bel canto and her studying of Norma for Ann-Margret Pettersson's production of *Norma* at Kungliga Operan.

4698 Bergström, Gunnel. "Jag—en gnolare." (I'm a Hummer.) *MuD.* 1998; 20(2): 12-15. Illus.: Photo. Color. Lang.: Swe.

Sweden. 1960-1998. Histories-sources. ■Interview with the singer Mikael Samuelsson about his background and attitude to the text versus singing, with reference to his interpretation of Schubert's *Die Winterreise.*

4699 Eriksson, Torbjörn; Stensson, Ola. "Två röster om *Staden.*" (Two Views on *Staden.*) *MuD.* 1998; 20(5: pp 18). Illus.: Photo. Color. Lang.: Swe.

Sweden: Stockholm. 1998. Critical studies. ■Two views on Sven-David Sandström's and Katarina Frostensson's *Staden* at Kungliga Operan, staged by Lars Rudolfsson.

4700 Sandgren, Maria. "Skratta Pajazzo!" (Laugh Pagliacci!) *MuD.* 1998; 20(1): 20-22. Illus.: Dwg. B&W. Lang.: Swe.

Sweden. 1997. Critical studies. ■The singer's relation to the voice and body, with reference to a thesis in progress within the project 'Expressive creation in music, dance, speech and body language'.

4701 Sjöberg, Lars. "Att blunda för trams." (To Wink at Rubbish.) *MuD.* 1998; 20(4): 21. Illus.: Photo. B&W. Lang.: Swe.

Sweden: Stockholm. 1998. Critical studies. ■A critical opinion about Johannes Schaaf's production of Verdi's *Otello* at Kungliga Operan.

4702 Schreiber, Ulrich. "Sinn-Spiele mit Einsatz." (Sense-Games with Stakes.) *THeute.* 1998; Yb: 108-123. Illus.: Photo. B&W. 8. Lang.: Ger.

MUSIC-DRAMA: Opera—Performance/production

Switzerland: Basel. Germany: Stuttgart, Berlin, Hamburg. France: Strasbourg. 1997-1998. Reviews of performances. ■Reviews Johann Strauss' *Die Fledermaus* directed by Frank Castorf at Deutsches Schauspielhaus Hamburg, Mozart's *Die Entführung aus dem Serail* directed by Hans Neuenfels at Staatsoper Stuttgart, Mozart's *Don Giovanni* directed by Achim Freyer at Opéra National du Rhin Strasbourg, Christoph Marthaler's *The Unanswered Question* at Theater Basel, Beethoven's *Fidelio* directed by Martin Kušej at Württembergische Staatsoper Stuttgart and Offenbach's *La vie parisienne* directed by Christoph Marthaler at Volksbühne.

4703 "George Lloyd." *Econ.* 1998 July 18; 348(8077): 77. Illus.: Photo. B&W. 1. Lang.: Eng.

UK-England. 1913-1998. Biographical studies. ■Obituary for the conductor/composer.

4704 Driscoll, F. Paul. "The English Beat." *OpN.* 1998 Jan 31; 62(10): 12-15. Illus.: Photo. Color. 3. Lang.: Eng.

UK-England. USA. 1998. Biographical studies. ■Profile, interview and analysis of the work of English conductor Andrew Davis, about to conduct *Capriccio* by Richard Strauss at the Metropolitan Opera and to become music director and principal conductor at the Lyric Opera of Chicago.

4705 Sutcliffe, Tom. "British Journal." *OpN.* 1998 Jan 31; 62(10): 56-57. Illus.: Photo. Color. 2. Lang.: Eng.

UK-England. 1997. Critical studies. ■Critical comments on the state of opera in England, including the government suggestion that the English National Opera cohabit with the Royal Opera and Ballet at the newly refurbished Covent Garden Opera House to reopen in 1999. Particular note is taken of the *Falstaff*, production borrowed from Opera North, and *The Turn of the Screw* staged by Deborah Warner.

4706 Canning, Hugh. "Competing in Cardiff." *OpN.* 1998 May; 62(16): 30-31. Illus.: Photo. Color. 3. Lang.: Eng.

UK-Wales: Cardiff. 1997. Historical studies. ■An account of the 1997 singing competition and its winners.

4707 Kellow, Brian. "Prince of Wales." *OpN.* 1998 Dec.; 63(6): 16-21, 111, 116. Illus.: Photo. B&W. Color. 8. Lang.: Eng.

UK-Wales. 1965-1998. Biographical studies. ■The life, training, and career of tenor Bryn Terfel.

4708 "In Memoriam: Randolph Symonette, 1910-98. Todd Duncan, 1903-1998." *KWN.* 1998 Spr; 16(1): 3. Illus.: Photo. B&W. 2. Lang.: Eng.

USA. 1998. Biographical studies. ■Obituaries for the two opera baritones who also performed in many Broadway musicals.

4709 "Radio Broadcast Performances." *OpN.* 1998; 62. Illus.: Design. Diagram. Dwg. Photo. Color. B&W. [*Le Nozze di Figaro* (May): 49, *Nabucco* (May): 50, *Amistad* (May): 50, *La Bohème* (May): 51, *Idomeneo* (May):51, *Les Pêcheurs de Perles* (June): 47, *Peter Grimes* (June): 48, *Madama Butterfly* (June): 48.] Lang.: Eng.

USA: Chicago, IL. 1998. Histories-sources. ■Photographs, lists of principals, conductors, production staff, Lyric Opera of Chicago radio broadcast performances.

4710 "Telecast Performance." *OpN.* 1998; 61. Illus.: Design. Diagram. Dwg. Photo. Color. B&W. [*Paul Bunyan* (Apr 11): 61.] Lang.: Eng.

USA: New York, NY. 1998. Histories-sources. ■Photograph, list of principals, conductor, production staff, Metropolitan Opera telecast performance.

4711 "Elliott Carter: No Time for Nostalgia." *Econ.* 1998 June 27; 347(8074): 89. Illus.: Photo. B&W. 1. Lang.: Eng.

USA. 1908-1998. Biographical studies. ■Tribute to composer Carter as he approaches his ninetieth birthday and embarks on writing his first (as yet unnamed) opera.

4712 Baker, David J. "Night and Day." *OpN.* 1998 Feb 14; 62(11): 20-25,48. Illus.: Photo. Color. 6. Lang.: Eng.

USA. 1998. Biographical studies. ■Profile and interview with American coloratura soprano June Anderson.

4713 Barda, Clive; Bergmann, Beth; Johnson, Rolfe; Davidson, Erika; Elbers, Johan; Schiller, Beatriz; Reilly, John. "Radio Broadcast Performances." *OpN.* 1998; 62. Illus.: Design. Diagram. Dwg. Photo. Color. B&W. [*Boris Godunov* (Jan 3): 30-33, *Peter Grimes* (Jan 3): 34-37, *The Rake's Progress* (Jan 17): 28-31, *La Cenerentola* (Jan 17): 32-35, *Capriccio* (Jan 31): 40-43, *Les Contes d'Hoffman* (Jan 31): 44-47, *Il Trovatore* (Feb 14): 32-35, *Die Zauberflöte* (Feb 14): 36-39, *Samson et Dalila* (Feb 28): 28-33, *Madama Butterfly* (Feb 28): 34-37, *L'Elisir d'Amore* (Mar 14): 32-35, *Lohengrin* (Mar 14): 36-39, *Roméo et Juliette* (Mar 28): 34-37, *Stiffelio* (Mar 28): 38-41, *Die Meistersinger von Nürnberg* (Apr 11): 36- 39, *Věc Makropulos* (Apr 11): 40-43.] Lang.: Eng.

USA: New York, NY. 1998. Histories-sources. ■Photographs, lists of principals, conductors, production staff, biographies, synopses, discographies for Metropolitan Opera radio broadcast performances.

4714 Bergman, Beth. "Telecast Performance." *OpN.* 1998; 63. Illus.: Design. Diagram. Dwg. Photo. Color. B&W. [*Samson et Dalila* (Sep): 113.] Lang.: Eng.

USA: New York, NY. 1998. Histories-sources. ■Photograph, list of principals, conductor, production staff, Metropolitan Opera telecast performance.

4715 Coleman, Emily. "Grace Moore." *OpN.* 1998 Sep.; 63(3): 88-93, 118. . Illus.: Photo. B&W. 11. Lang.: Eng.

USA. 1901-1947. Biographical studies. ■The career of American soprano Grace Moore.

4716 Davison, Peter; Acheson, James; Hamilton, David; Guinther, Louise. "Radio Broadcast Performances." *OpN.* 1998; 63. Illus.: Design. Diagram. Dwg. Photo. Color. B&W. [*Le Nozze di Figaro* (Dec): 58-61, *Carmen* (Dec): 62-67, *La Traviata (Dec): 68-71, Die Zauberflöte* (Dec): 72-78.] Lang.: Eng.

USA: New York, NY. 1998. Histories-sources. ■Photographs, lists of principals, conductors, production staff, biographies, synopses, discographies, Metropolitan Opera radio broadcast performances.

4717 Driscoll, F. Paul. "Burning Bright." *OpN.* 1998 Mar 14; 62(13): 8-13. Illus.: Photo. Color. 8. Lang.: Eng.

USA. 1998. Biographical studies. ■Profile, interview with American dramatic soprano Deborah Voigt.

4718 Driscoll, F. Paul. "Going to the Opera ... with Joyce Carol Oates." *OpN.* 1998 Jan 3; 62(8): 26-29. Illus.: Photo. B&W. Color. 2. Lang.: Eng.

USA: New York, NY. 1997. Histories-sources. ■Novelist Joyce Carol Oates on her opera knowledge and her reaction to the Metropolitan Opera's new production of *Wozzeck* by Alban Berg.

4719 Driscoll, F. Paul. "Going to the Opera...with Ira Siff." *OpN.* 1998 June; 62(17): 32-35. Illus.: Photo. B&W. Color. 3. Lang.: Eng.

USA: New York, NY. 1998. Histories-sources. ■Ira Siff is the alter ego of Mme Vera Galupe-Borszkh, the founder and artistic director of La Gran Scena operatic company. He analyzes the career of his company and discusses important performers at the Metropolitan Opera. He also discusses the current performance of *Don Carlo* by Giuseppe Verdi.

4720 Driscoll, F. Paul; Zuba, Manya; Midgette, Anne. "*Liederabend*: A Look at the Best of the Current Crop of Lieder Artists." *OpN.* 1998 Oct.; 63(4): 24-26. Illus.: Photo. Color. 4. Lang.: Eng.

USA. Slovenia. Austria. 1998. Critical studies. ■Reviews of *Lieder* recordings by Wolfgang Holzmair, Marjana Lipovšek, and Christoph Prégardien.

4721 Giles, Patrick. "Magnificent Obsession." *OpN.* 1998 Oct.; 63(4): 28-30, 32-35. Illus.: Photo. Color. 8. Lang.: Eng.

USA. UK-England. 1900-1998. Historical studies. ■Discussion of the recorded operatic holdings of American and British collectors.

4722 Guinther, Louise T. "Reprise: James Johnson Returns to the Role of Hans Sachs for the First Time in Nineteen Years." *OpN.* 1998 Apr 11; 62(15): 32. Illus.: Photo. Color. 1. Lang.: Eng.

USA. 1998. Biographical studies. ■Brief account of the career of New Orleans bass James Johnson prior to his Metropolitan Opera Performance as Hans Sachs in *Die Meistersinger von Nürnberg.*

4723 Guinther, Louise T. "Golden Boy." *OpN.* 1998 Nov.; 63(5): 50-53. Illus.: Photo. Color. 3. Lang.: Eng.

MUSIC-DRAMA: Opera—Performance/production

USA. 1971-1998. Biographical studies. ■Baritone Nathan Gunn, who won the Metropolitan Opera National Council Auditions (1994), has sung frequently at Glimmerglass Opera and now moves to the Metropolitan Opera.

4724 Herx, Stephen. "Marcella Sembrich and Three Great Events at the Metropolitan." *OQ.* 1998-1999 Win; 15(1): 49-71. Notes. Tables. Illus.: Photo. Poster. Sketches. B&W. 5. Lang.: Eng.

USA: New York, NY. 1883-1909. Biographical studies. ■Soprano Sembrich's debut at the Metropolitan Opera House, her performance at the Henry Abbey (director of the Met) benefit at the close of the 1883-84 season, and her farewell gala in 1909.

4725 Hilferty, Robert. "Women in Love." *OpN.* 1998 June; 62(17): 26. Illus.: Photo. B&W. 2. Lang.: Eng.

USA. 1969-1998. Historical studies. ■The history of the opera *Patience and Sarah*, written by Paula Kimper and Wende Persons, based on the 1969 novel by Isabel Miller on romantic love between two women. To be presented by the Lincoln Center Festival in July 1998.

4726 Honig, Joel. "Whatever Happened to *Capriccio*'s Unanswered Question?" *OpN.* 1998 Jan 31; 62(10): 20-22. Illus.: Dwg. 1. Lang.: Eng.

USA. 1942-1998. Critical studies. ■Critique of current trends in opera production, including an emphasis on 'directorial concepts and conceits' and projected titles in opera houses. Refers to *Capriccio* by Richard Strauss, and numerous other operas, past and present.

4727 Kaup-Hasler, Veronica; Klingan, Katrin. "Das Recht zu hoffen." (The Right to Hope.) 78-97 in Pochhammer, Sabine, ed. *Utopie: Spiritualität? Spiritualité: une utopie?/Utopia: Spirituality? Spirituality: A Utopia?.* Berlin: Theaterschrift c/o Künstlerhaus Bethanien; 1998. 173 pp. (Theaterschrift 13.) Illus.: Photo. B&W. 5. Lang.: Ger, Fre, Dut, Eng.

USA. 1990-1998. Histories-sources. ■An interview with director Peter Sellars about spirituality on stage and his upcoming projects.

4728 Keller, James M. "Voice Talk: Breathing Lessons." *OpN.* 1998 Nov.; 63(5): 18-21. Illus.: Photo. Color. 3. Lang.: Eng.

USA: New York, NY. 1998. Histories-sources. ■Interview with soprano Joan Sutherland, giving a master class in New York, about breathing and breath support.

4729 Kellow, Brian. "The Defiant One." *OpN.* 1998 Aug.; 63(2): 10-12, 14-15. Illus.: Photo. Color. 7. Lang.: Eng.

USA. 1998. Biographical studies. ■Profile, interview, biography of dramatic soprano Alessandra Marc (born Judith Borden).

4730 Kerner, Leighton. "Wheel of Fortune." *OpN.* 1998 Mar 28; 62(14): 12-14, 50. Illus.: Photo. B&W. Color. 7. Lang.: Eng.

USA: New York, NY. 1850-1998. Historical studies. ■New York productions of the operas *Stiffelio* by Giuseppe Verdi (1850) and *Roméo et Juliette* by Charles Gounod (1867). Until the current season, *Stiffelio* was totally forgotten, and *Roméo et Juliette* had long been absent from the Metropolitan Opera House and New York City Opera.

4731 Loomis, George W. "Shadow and Light." *OpN.* 1998 Apr 11; 62(15): 28-31. Illus.: Photo. Design. 4. Lang.: Eng.

USA: New York, NY. 1998. Critical studies. ■Introduction to the Kirov Opera's guest performances at the Metropolitan Opera: Čajkovskij's *Mazeppa* (libretto based on Puškin's *Poltava*) and Prokofjėv's *Betrothal in a Monastery (Obručinnie v monastïre)*, based on Sheridan's *The Duenna*.

4732 Marx, Robert. "Wilson, Wagner, and the Met." *PerAJ.* 1998 Sep.; 20(3): 40-47. Illus.: Photo. B&W. 3. Lang.: Eng.

USA: New York, NY. 1998. Critical studies. ■Analysis of Robert Wilson's production of Wagner's *Lohengrin* at the Metropolitan Opera.

4733 Matt, Wolff. "Transplant Specialist." *OpN.* 1998 Jan 17; 62(9): 16-19. Illus.: Photo. Color. 6. Lang.: Eng.

USA: New York, NY. 1998. Critical studies. ■An account of Jonathan Miller's work on the Metropolitan Opera production of *The Rake's Progress* by Stravinskij.

4734 May, Thomas. "Meister Builder." *OpN.* 1998 Mar 14; 62(13): 28, 30. Illus.: Photo. B&W. Color. 3. Lang.: Eng.

USA: Washington, DC. 1993-1998. Biographical studies. ■Profile of Heinz Fricke, music director of the Washington Opera, of which Plácido Domingo is now artistic director.

4735 McKee, David. "Sound Bites: Mary Mills." *OpN.* 1998 Jan.; 62(8): 38-39. Illus.: Photo. Color. 2. Lang.: Eng.

USA. 1998. Historical studies. ■Comments on the amusing mishaps experienced by American soprano Mary Mills.

4736 Melick, Jennifer. "Sound Bites: Rodney Gilfry." *OpN.* 1998 Sep.; 63(3): 18-19. Illus.: Photo. Color. 2. Lang.: Eng.

USA. 1998. Biographical studies. ■American baritone Rodney Gilfry speaks of his work at the San Francisco Opera and elsewhere, with emphasis on his role as Stanley Kowalski in the forthcoming world premiere in the opera adaptation by André Previn of the play *A Streetcar Named Desire by Tennessee Williams.*

4737 Mermelstein, David. "Getting Rossini Right." *OpN.* 1998 Jan 17; 62(9): 26-27. Illus.: Photo. B&W. 1. Lang.: Eng.

USA: Chicago, IL. 1998. Critical studies. ■The work of musicologist Philip Gossett of the University of Chicago on the current Metropolitan Opera production of *La Cenerentola* by Gioacchino Rossini in collaboration with conductor Alberto Zedda.

4738 Mermelstein, David; Heliotis, Harry, photo. "Sound Bites: Tracey Welborn." *OpN.* 1998 Feb 28; 62(12): 28-29. Illus.: Photo. Color. 2. Lang.: Eng.

USA. 1962-1998. Biographical studies. ■Brief biography of American tenor Tracey Welborn.

4739 Midgette, Anne. "A Natural Artifice." *OpN.* 1998 Mar 14; 62(13): 20-22. Illus.: Photo. Color. 6. Lang.: Eng.

USA: New York, NY. 1976-1998. Historical studies. ■The production style of director Robert Wilson, with emphasis on his production of Wagner's *Lohengrin* at the Metropolitan Opera.

4740 Minter, Drew. "Baroque Dialogue." *OpN.* 1998 Oct.; 63(4): 54-59. Illus.: Photo. Color. 2. Lang.: Eng.

USA. UK-England. 1998. Histories-sources. ■American countertenor Drew Minter interviews conductor Nicholas McGegan.

4741 Mitchell, Emily; Bergman, Beth. "The Longest Day." *OpN.* 1998 Sep.; 63(3): 82-84, 86-87. Illus.: Photo. Color. 13. Lang.: Eng.

USA: New York, NY. 1997-1998. Historical studies. ■A detailed account of organizing two performances at the Metropolitan Opera, with *Die Meistersinger* at noon and *The Makropulos Case* at 8:30.

4742 Myers, Eric. "Making *Streetcar* Sing." *OpN.* 1998 Sep.; 63(3): 34-40. Illus.: Photo. B&W. Color. 10. Lang.: Eng.

USA: San Francisco. 1998. Historical studies. ■André Previn's opera *A Streetcar Named Desire*, based on the play by Tennessee Williams, with libretto by Philip Littell.

4743 Paller, Rebecca. "Hot Tickets!...American Opera Companies Are Treating the Century to a Spectacular Sendoff." *OpN.* 1998 Sep.; 63(3): 43-55. Illus.: Photo. B&W. Color. 17. Lang.: Eng.

USA. Canada. 1998. Historical studies. ■Proposals for productions at major opera houses in the U.S. and Canada until the end of the century.

4744 Paris, Barry. "First Bass." *OpN.* 1998 Jan 3; 62(8): 12-17. Illus.: Photo. Color. B&W. 8. Lang.: Eng.

USA. 1940-1998. Biographical studies. ■A critical and biographical account of the career of American bass Samuel Ramey, singing *Boris Godunov, Il Barbiere di Siviglia* and *The Rake's Progress* at the Metropolitan Opera.

4745 Roach, Joseph. "Barnumizing Diaspora: The 'Irish Skylark' Does New Orleans." *TJ.* 1998 Mar.; 50(1): 39-52. Notes. Lang.: Eng.

USA: New Orleans, LA. 1852. Critical studies. ■The marketing of Irish opera singer Catherine Hayes's performances in New Orleans, which played on Irish suffering during the Potato Famine. Contrasts the empathetic reaction of audiences to the performances with the reaction to actual Irish immigrants.

4746 Sabrey-Saperstein, Sheila. *Opera-in-English: The Popularization of Foreign Opera in America.* Evanston, IL: Northwestern Univ; 1988. 194 pp. Biblio. Notes. [Ph.D.

MUSIC-DRAMA: Opera—Performance/production

Dissertation, Univ. Microfilms Order No. AAC 8811506.] Lang.: Eng.
USA. 1850-1985. Historical studies. ■The efforts of the Opera-in-English movement, with consideration of the history of opera in the US, the televised opera, and the use of superimposed 'titles' in the opera house, and the work of regional companies who perform operas in English.

4747 Sandla, Robert. "Lady of the Lamps." *OpN.* 1998 Jan 17; 62(9): 18. Illus.: Photo. Color. 1. Lang.: Eng.
USA. 1937-1998. Biographical studies. ■Brief account of the career of American lighting expert Jennifer Tipton, and her current work at the Metropolitan Opera on *The Rake's Progress* by Igor Stravinskij, directed by Jonathan Miller.

4748 Scarnati, Blase Samuel, Jr. *Bellini's* La Sonnambula *in America and the Gendered Gaze.* Pittsburgh, PA: Univ. of Pittsburgh; 1998. 250 pp. Notes. Biblio. [Ph.D. Dissertation, Univ. Microfilms Order No. AAC 9837599.] Lang.: Eng.
USA. 1835-1860. Historical studies. ■Feminist study of performances of Vincenzo Bellini's *La Sonnambula.* Uses feminist film theory to articulate a model of the gendered gaze and focuses on Bellini's use of the verbal double entendre, sexual colloquialisms, male sexual codes, and visual cues tailored for men, and the differing reception by male and female audiences.

4749 Schiff, David. "Learning from Britten." *OpN.* 1998 Jan 3; 62(8): 18-21. Illus.: Photo. B&W. Color. 7. Lang.: Eng.
USA: New York, NY. 1945-1998. Historical studies. ■Operas by Benjamin Britten which have entered the repertory of the Metropolitan Opera include *Peter Grimes, Billy Budd, A Midsummer Night's Dream* and *Death in Venice.* The New York City Opera also include *Paul Bunyan* and *The Turn of the Screw.*

4750 Schwarz, J. Robert. "Bad Boy Makes Good." *OpN.* 1998 Mar 28; 62(14): 22-25. Illus.: Dwg. Poster. Photo. BE. 5. Lang.: Eng.
USA. 1900-1959. Historical studies. ■The career of American composer George Antheil, with emphasis on his political opera *Transatlantic* (1930).

4751 Sevilla-Gonzaga, Marylis. "Take-off." *OpN.* 1998 June; 62(17): 8-11. Illus.: Photo. B&W. 5. Lang.: Eng.
USA: New York, NY. 1998. Biographical studies. ■The development of American baritone Dwayne Croft, Metropolitan Opera.

4752 Smith, Patrick J. "A Night to Remember." *OpN.* 1998 Mar 14; 62(13): 4. Lang.: Eng.
USA: New York, NY. 1998. Biographical studies. ■Very brief account of the career and debut of American tenor Anthony Dean Griffey at the Metropolitan Opera.

4753 Thomason, Paul. "The Problem with *Porgy and Bess.*" *OpN.* 1998 Aug.; 63(2): 18-22. Illus.: Photo. Color. 8. Lang.: Eng.
USA. 1937. Critical studies. ■Analysis of the musical qualities of *Porgy and Bess* composed by George Gershwin, with lyrics by his brother Ira Gershwin.

4754 Thomason, Paul. "*La* Div-*ina*: Barbara Bonney, the Thinking Man's Ingenue." *OpN.* 1998 Feb 14; 62(11): 8-10, 12-13. Illus.: Photo. Color. 5. Lang.: Eng.
USA. 1998. Biographical studies. ■Profile, interview with American soprano Barbara Bonney specializing in ingenue roles.

4755 Thomason, Paul. "Summers Time." *OpN.* 1998 Nov.; 63(5): 46-49. Illus.: Photo. Color. B&W. 2. Lang.: Eng.
USA. 1990-1998. Biographical studies. ■Patrick Summers, still in his early thirties, has been a conductor at San Francisco Opera since 1990, and now moves to Houston Grand Opera as music director. He also conducts *Die Fledermaus* at the Metropolitan Opera of New York this Christmas.

4756 Wynne, Peter. "Video Days: A Historical Survey of Opera on Television." *OpN.* 1998 June; 62(17): 2-14, 16, 18, 20. Illus.: Photo. B&W. 8. Lang.: Eng.
USA: New York, NY. 1939-1980. Historical studies. ■Commercial TV opera broadcasts in the New York area.

Plays/librettos/scripts

4757 Scherer, Barrymore Laurence. "Rags to Riches." *OpN.* 1998 Jan 17; 62(9): 22-25. Illus.: Photo. B&W. Color. 8. Lang.: Eng.
1817-1998. Critical studies. ■Treatments of the Cinderella story, with emphasis on Rossini's *Cenerentola.* Argues that Rossini's treatment is more successful than those by Walt Disney, Rodgers and Hammerstein, and Massenet (*Cendrillon*).

4758 Yon, Jean-Claude. "Les métamorphoses d'Orphée." (The Metamorphoses of Orpheus.) *ASO.* 1998 July/Aug.; 185: 80-87 . Notes. Illus.: Photo. Dwg. Poster. B&W. 8. Lang.: Fre.
1600-1986. Historical studies. ■Various operatic treatments of the myth of Orpheus, both in librettos and in stagings, with attention to Offenbach's *Orphée aux Enfers.*

4759 Black, Leo. "Schubert and *Fierrabras*: A Mind in Ferment." *OQ.* 1998 Sum; 14(4): 17-39. Notes. Lang.: Eng.
Austria. 1823. Critical studies. ■In-depth analysis of Schubert's never performed opera.

4760 Jameux, Dominique. "Abécédaire Lulu." (The Lulu Alphabet.) *ASO.* 1998 Jan/Feb.; 181/182: 154-166. Lang.: Fre.
Austria. 1935. Instructional materials. ■Dictionary of characters, musical themes, treatments, productions, etc., of Alban Berg's *Lulu.*

4761 Bennett, Susan. "'Don't Look Back': *Jackie O* in Banff." *CTR.* Fall 1998; 96: 39-43. Notes. Biblio. Illus.: Photo. B&W. 4. Lang.: Eng.
Canada: Banff, AB. USA: Houston, TX. 1997. Critical studies. ■Popular culture and celebrity in Wayne Koestenbaum and Michael Daugherty's *Jackie O,* and impact of production contexts of Houston Grand Opera world premiere and Banff Centre for the Arts Canadian premiere (both directed by Nicholas Muni, 1997).

4762 Hepburn, Allan. "Perfectly Normal: Queer Opera in Canada." *CTR.* Fall 1998; 96: 34-38. Notes. Biblio. Illus.: Photo. B&W. 2. Lang.: Eng.
Canada. 1970-1998. Critical studies. ■Homosexuality in Canadian operas such as Harry Somers and Rod Anderson's *Mario and the Magician,* Atom Egoyan and Rodney Sharman's *Elsewhereness* and Brad Walton's *The Loves of Wayne Gretzky.*

4763 Hutcheon, Linda; Hutcheon, Michael. "Imagined Communities: Postnational Canadian Opera." 235-252 in Dellamora, Richard, ed.; Fischlin, Daniel, ed. *The Work of Opera: Genre, Nationhood, and Sexual Difference.* New York, NY: Columbia UP; 1997. 350 pp. Notes. Index. Lang.: Eng.
Canada. 1965-1992. Historical studies. ■State patronage and ethnic and linguistic chauvinism and xenophobia in Canadian opera, with emphasis on *Mario the Magician* by Harry Somers and Rod Anderson.

4764 Hutcheon, Linda; Hutcheon, Michael. "Opera and National Identity: New Canadian Opera." *CTR.* 1998 Fall; 96: 5-8. Notes. Biblio. Illus.: Photo. B&W. 3. Lang.: Eng.
Canada. 1967-1998. Critical studies. ■Nationalism and treatment of national concerns in Canadian operas since 1967.

4765 Thomason, Paul; Hilferty, Robert. "*Makropulos*: The Case for—and Against." *OpN.* 1998 Apr 11; 62(15): 20-22, 24. Illus.: Photo. B&W. Color. 4. Lang.: Eng.
Czechoslovakia. 1922-1998. Critical studies. ■A debate between two critics concerning the nature of the opera *Věc Makropulos* by Leoś Janáček, libretto by Karel Čapek.

4766 Gilman, Todd S. "The Italian (Castrato) in London." 49-70 in Dellamora, Richard, ed.; Fischlin, Daniel, ed. *The Work of Opera: Genre, Nationhood, and Sexual Difference.* New York, NY: Columbia UP; 1997. 350 pp. Notes. Index. Lang.: Eng.
England: London. 1710-1740. Historical studies. ■Argues that the attacks on Italian *castrati* singers in English pamphlet literature are explained by anxiety and fear over the *castrato*'s transgression of conventional sexual norms that defined English citizenship.

4767 Hume, Robert D. "The Politics of Opera in Late Seventeenth-Century London." *COJ.* 1998; 10(1): 15-43. Notes. Tables. Lang.: Eng.

MUSIC-DRAMA: Opera—Plays/librettos/scripts

England: London. 1620-1711. Critical studies. ▪The relative absence of political allegory in English opera compared with previous and contemporary plays, masques, and European operas. Dryden and Purcell's *King Arthur* is cited as an example of the closest proven instance of intentional use of allegory.

4768 Albèra, Philippe; Bryden, Mary, transl. "Beckett and Holliger." 87-97 in Bryden, Mary, ed. *Samuel Beckett and Music.* Oxford: Clarendon; 1998. 267 pp. Index. Notes. Biblio. Lang.: Eng.

Europe. 1992. Histories-sources. ▪Includes an interview with composer Heinz Holliger on his operatic adaptation of Beckett's *What Where.*

4769 Fournier, Edith; Bryden, Mary, transl. "Marcel Mihalovici and Samuel Beckett: Musicians of Return." 131-139 in Bryden, Mary, ed. *Samuel Beckett and Music.* Oxford: Clarendon; 1998. 267 pp. Index. Notes. Biblio. Lang.: Eng.

Europe. 1965. Critical studies. ▪Mihalovici's operatic adaptation of Beckett's *Krapp's Last Tape* into the musical piece, *Krapp.*

4770 Joe, Jeongwon. *Opera on Film, Film in Opera: Postmodern Implications of the Cinematic Influence on Opera.* Evanston, IL: Northwestern Univ; 1998. 324 pp. Notes. Biblio. [Ph.D. Dissertation, Univ. Microfilms Order No. AAC 9832617.] Lang.: Eng.

Europe. North America. 1904-1994. Histories-specific. ▪The reciprocal influence of opera and film, including Georges Méliès's *La Damnation du Docteur Faust*, a thirteen-minute silent film based on Gounod's opera *Faust*, Ingmar Bergman's *Trollflöjten (The Magic Flute)*, Hans-Jurgen Syberberg's *Parsifal*, Don Boyd's *Aria*, and Philip Glass's *La Belle et la Bête.*

4771 Kopelson, Kevin. "Metropolitan Opera/Suburban Identity." 297-313 in Dellamora, Richard, ed.; Fischlin, Daniel, ed. *The Work of Opera: Genre, Nationhood, and Sexual Difference.* New York, NY: Columbia UP; 1997. 350 pp. Notes. Index. Lang.: Eng.

Europe. North America. 1985-1995. Historical studies. ▪The AIDS epidemic as seen in contemporary operas that are openly gay. Argues that opera signals the gap between homosexual fantasies of escape from the American hinterlands and the dream of 'genuine' citizenship in a metropolitan culture.

4772 Laws, Catherine. "Morton Feldman's *Neither*: A Musical Translation of Beckett's Text." 57-85 in Bryden, Mary, ed. *Samuel Beckett and Music.* Oxford: Clarendon; 1998. 267 pp. Index. Notes. Biblio. Illus.: Sketches. 4. Lang.: Eng.

Europe. 1976-1977. Critical studies. ▪Analysis of Feldman's one-act opera *Neither*, based on a text specifically requested for that purpose and supplied by Beckett.

4773 Lister, Linda Joanne. *Realizing Rosina: Operatic Characterizations of Beaumarchais's Heroine.* Greensboro, NC: Univ. of North Carolina; 1998. 141 pp. Notes. Biblio. [D.M.A. Thesis, Univ. Microfilms Order No. AAC 9833411.] Lang.: Eng.

Europe. North America. 1784-1991. Histories-specific. ▪Operatic realizations of the character of Rosina from the trilogy of plays (*Le Barbier de Séville, Le Mariage de Figaro*, and *La Mère Coupable*) by Beaumarchais. Focuses on the following operas: Paisiello's *Il barbiere di Siviglia*, Mozart's *Le Nozze di Figaro*, Rossini's *Il barbiere di Siviglia*, Milhaud's *La Mère Coupable*, Hiram Titus's *Rosina*, and John Corigliano's *The Ghosts of Versailles.*

4774 Malm, Anna Stina. "Modern opera: Från non sens till sens." (Modern Opera: From Nonsense To Sense.) *MuD.* 1998; 20(4) : 36-37, 40. Illus.: Photo. B&W. Lang.: Swe.

Europe. 1912-1998. Historical studies. ▪Twentieth-century opera and the attitude toward text and conventional story-line.

4775 Schmitz-Gielsdorf, Uwe. "Der Text als Suppenwürfel." (The Text as Bouillon Cube.) *DB.* 1998; 3: 45-47. Illus.: Dwg. Photo. B&W. 3. Lang.: Ger.

Europe. 1800-1998. Historical studies. ▪Notes on the question of how to write a libretto, with reference to the recently published book *Das Libretto—Theorie und Geschichte einer musikoliterarischen Gattung (The Libretto—Theory and History of a Musical-Literary Genre)* by Albert Gier.

4776 Szendy, Peter; Heath, Veronica, transl. "End Games." 99-129 in Bryden, Mary, ed. *Samuel Beckett and Music.* Oxford: Clarendon; 1998. 267 pp. Index. Notes. Biblio. Illus.: Sketches. 20. Lang.: Eng.

Europe. 1976-1988. Critical studies. ▪Composer Heinz Holliger's operatic adaptations of Samuel Beckett's *What Where* and *Va-et-vient (Come and Go).*

4777 Weber, Brigitta; Garforth, Julian, transl. "*That Time*: Samuel Beckett and Wolfgang Fortner." 141-158 in Bryden, Mary, ed. *Samuel Beckett and Music.* Oxford: Clarendon; 1998. 267 pp. Index. Notes. Biblio. Illus.: Sketches. 7. Lang.: Eng.

Europe. 1974-1977. Critical studies. ▪Wolfgang Fortner's operatic adaptation of Beckett's *That Time.*

4778 Branger, Jean-Christophe. "Histoire d'une collaboration artistique: Louis Gallet et Jules Massenet." (History of an Artistic Collaboration: Louis Gallet and Jules Massenet.) *ASO.* 1998 Nov/Dec.; 187: 54-59. Notes. Illus.: Photo. Dwg. B&W. 2. Lang.: Fre.

France. 1877-1894. Historical studies. ▪The collaboration of composer Jules Massenet and librettist Louis Gallet on the operas *Le Roi de Lahore* and *Thaïs.*

4779 Brèque, Jean-Michel. "Loin de Flaubert, très loin des Évangiles." (Far from Flaubert, Very Far from the Bible.) *ASO.* 1998 Nov/Dec.; 187: 116-121. Notes. Illus.: Dwg. B&W. 4. Lang.: Fre.

France. 1881. Critical studies. ▪Compares the libretto for Massenet's opera *Hérodiade* to its literary sources, including the short story *Hérodias* by Flaubert, and finds the music superior to the book.

4780 Burgess, Geoffrey. "'Le théâtre ne change qu'à la troisième scène': The Hand of the author and Unity of Place in Act V of *Hippolyte et Aricie.*" *COJ.* 1998; 10(3): 275-287. Notes. [Paper from symposium on Pelligrin and Rameau's *Hippolyte et Aricie.*] Lang.: Eng.

France. 1733. Critical studies. ▪The unity of place and political self-censorship in the libretto by Simon-Joseph Pelligrin for *Hippolyte et Aricie* by Rameau.

4781 Clay, Simone Monnier. *Henri Meilhac—Ludovic Halévy: Des Bouffes-Parisiens à L'Opéra-Comique.* (Henri Meilhac and Ludovic Halévy: From the Bouffes-Parisiens to the Opéra-Comique.) Davis, CA: Univ. of California; 1987. 279 pp. Notes. Biblio. [Ph.D. Dissertation, Univ. Microfilms Order No. AAC 8809743.] Lang.: Fre.

France. 1800-1900. Critical studies. ▪Examines the contributions of Henri Meilhac and Ludovic Halévy to the formation of the French libretto.

4782 Condé, Gérard. "Comme dans un rêve." (As in a Dream.) *ASO.* 1998 Mar/Apr.; 183: 56-59. Illus.: Photo. B&W. 2. Lang.: Fre.

France. 1883. Critical studies. ▪Analysis of Delibes' opera *Lakmé*, libretto by Edmond Gondinet and Philippe Gille.

4783 Dill, Charles. "Pelligrin, Opera, and Tragedy." *COJ.* 1998; 10(3): 247-257. Notes. [Paper from symposium on Pelligrin and Rameau's *Hippolyte et Aricie.*] Lang.: Eng.

France. 1635-1774. Critical studies. ▪Compares Pelligrin's and Voltaire's ideas for the reform of opera libretti through the use of themes from Greek tragedy to endow opera with a didactic function. Examines excerpts from the libretti of several operas with particular attention to Pelligrin and Rameau's *Hippolyte et Aricie.*

4784 Lacombe, Hervé. "Lakmé ou la fabrique de l'exotisme." (Lakmé or the Manufacture of Exoticism.) *ASO.* 1998 Mar/Apr.; 183: 68-73. Notes. Illus.: Dwg. B&W. 3. Lang.: Fre.

France. 1853-1883. Historical studies. ▪Proposes, as a source for the libretto by Edmond Gondinet and Philippe Gille to Delibes' opera *Lakmé*, the writings of Théodore Pavie, a translator of orientalia, including stories from India.

4785 Martinoty, Jean-Louis. "Offenbach ou la provocation pour rire." (Offenbach and Provocation for the Fun of It.) *ASO.* 1998 July/Aug.; 185: 88-91. Notes. Illus.: Dwg. Poster. B&W. 2. Lang.: Fre.

MUSIC-DRAMA: Opera—Plays/librettos/scripts

France. 1874. Critical studies. ▪Humor and parody in Offenbach's opera *Orphée aux Enfers.*

4786 McClary, Susan. "Structures of Identity and Difference in Bizet's *Carmen.*" 115-129 in Dellamora, Richard, ed.; Fischlin, Daniel, ed. *The Work of Opera: Genre, Nationhood, and Sexual Difference.* New York, NY: Columbia UP; 1997. 350 pp. Notes. Index. Biblio. Lang.: Eng.

France. 1870-1879. Critical studies. ▪The theme of imperial ambition and gender roles in Bizet's *Carmen.*

4787 Miller, Felicia. "*Farinelli*'s Electronic Hermaphrodite and the Contralto Tradition." 73-92 in Dellamora, Richard, ed.; Fischlin, Daniel, ed. *The Work of Opera: Genre, Nationhood, and Sexual Difference.* New York, NY: Columbia UP; 1997. 350 pp. Notes. Index. Lang.: Eng.

France. Italy. 1994. Critical studies. ▪Gender and the creation of national identity in opera, with respect to Gérard Corbiau's film *Farinelli, Il Castrato.* Compares the celebrity of eighteenth-century *castrato* Farinelli with the cross-dressed singing of nineteenth-century contralto Pauline Viardot and the technological 'morphing' of a coloratura soprano and a countertenor to simulate the effect of *castrato* vocalization in the film.

4788 Norman, Buford. "Remaking a Cultural Icon: *Phèdre* and the Operatic Stage." *COJ.* 1998; 10(3): 225-245. Notes. Append. [Paper from symposium on Pelligrin and Rameau's *Hippolyte et Aricie.*] Lang.: Eng.

France. 1660-1733. Critical studies. ▪Analysis of Simon-Joseph Pelligrin's libretto for Rameau's *Hippolyte et Aricie* with respect to borrowings from Racine's *Phèdre.*

4789 Phillips-Matz, Mary Jane. "Artist's Model." *OpN.* 1998 Dec.; 63(6): 34-36. Illus.: Photo. B&W. 2. Lang.: Eng.

France. Italy. 1848-1853. Biographical studies. ▪Profile of Alphonsine Duplessis, the mistress of Dumas *fils*, who was the model for the character Marguerite Gautier in his novel and stage play *La Dame aux Caméllias (Camille)*, which in turn inspired the libretto for Verdi's *La Traviata.*

4790 Rosow, Lois. "Structure and Expression in the Scenes of Rameau's *Hippolyte et Aricie.*" *COJ.* 1998; 10(3): 259-273. Notes. Append. [Paper from symposium on Pelligrin and Rameau's *Hippolyte et Aricie.*] Lang.: Eng.

France. 1733. Critical studies. ▪Examination of how Pelligrin's libretto may have shaped Rameau's music in *Hippolyte et Aricie.*

4791 Amzoll, Stefan. "Heldendämmerung." (Twilight of the Heroes.) *TZ.* 1998; 2: 56-59. Lang.: Ger.

Germany. 1998. Critical studies. ▪Function of the hero in contemporary opera in a political context with regards to Robert Wilson's production of *Saints and Singing* by Gertrude Stein and Hans Peter Kuhn at Hebbel-Theater and *Der Ozeanflug* by Bertolt Brecht, Paul Hindemith, Kurt Weill, and Paul Dessau at Berliner Ensemble, and John Dew's production of *Kniefall in Warschau* by Gerhard Rosenfeld at Städtische Bühnen Dortmund. Continued in *TZ* (1998) 3, 58-60, with discussion of the anti-hero in Harry Kupfer's production of Beethoven's *Fidelio* at Komische Oper Berlin and Marcus Lobbes' production of *Hyperion* by Bruno Maderna at Hamburgische Staatsoper.

4792 Baker, David J. "No Laughing Matter: Where Is the Comedy in *Die Meistersinger*?" *OpN.* 1998 Apr 11; 62(15): 14-16, 18. Illus.: Photo. B&W. 6. Lang.: Eng.

Germany. 1868-1998. Critical studies. ▪Comic and tragic elements in the opera *Die Meistersinger von Nürnberg* by Richard Wagner.

4793 Barilier, Etienne. "La quatrième étape: Sur la 'perversité de l'Infante'." (The Fourth Stage: On the 'Perversity' of the Princess.) *ASO.* 1998 Sep/Oct.; 186: 88-90. Illus.: Dwg. B&W. 1. Lang.: Fre.

Germany. 1922. Critical studies. ▪Analysis of Alexander Zemlinsky's *Der Zwerg*, libretto by Georg C. Klaren, based on a short story by Oscar Wilde.

4794 Gurewitsch, Matthew. "Her Brother's Keeper." *OpN.* 1998 Mar 14; 62(13): 24-25, 57. Illus.: Photo. B&W. 2. Lang.: Eng.

Germany. 1850-1998. Critical studies. ▪The brother-sister bond of Gottfried and Elsa in *Lohengrin* by Richard Wagner.

4795 Hermansson, Jan. "Kvinnan utan skugga." (The Woman Without a Shadow.) *MuD.* 1998; 20: is 1: 15-19. Illus.: Photo. B&W. Color. Lang.: Swe.

Germany. 1917-1998. Critical studies. ▪Analysis of Richard Strauss' and Hugo von Hofmannsthal's *Die Frau ohne Schatten*, with reference to the part of the Nurse and Giuseppe Sinopoli's production at Sächsische Staatsoper.

4796 Kramer, Lawrence. "The Waters of Prometheus: Nationalism and Sexuality in Wagner's *Ring.*" 131-160 in Dellamora, Richard, ed.; Fischlin, Daniel, ed. *The Work of Opera: Genre, Nationhood, and Sexual Difference.* New York, NY: Columbia UP; 1997. 350 pp. Notes. Index. Lang.: Eng.

Germany. 1870-1880. Critical studies. ▪The dialectic between nationalism and eroticism in Wagner's *Ring* cycle.

4797 Locke, Ralph P. "Constructing the Oriental 'Other': Saint-Saëns's *Samson et Dalila.*" 161-184 in Dellamora, Richard, ed.; Fischlin, Daniel, ed. *The Work of Opera: Genre, Nationhood, and Sexual Difference.* New York, NY: Columbia UP; 1997. 350 pp. Notes. Index. Illus.: Photo. 2. Lang.: Eng.

Germany. 1868-1877. Critical studies. ▪Examines Orientalism and the 'other' in the gendered construction of nationalism in Camille Saint-Saëns's *Samson et Dalila.*

4798 Merlin, Christian. "Frank Wedekind à l'opéra de 'La Boîte de Pandore' à 'Lulu.'" (Frank Wedekind at the Opera: From *Pandora's Box* to *Lulu.*) *ASO.* 1998 Jan/Feb.; 181/182: 172-180. Illus.: Dwg. Photo. Poster. Plan. B&W. 4. Lang.: Fre.

Germany. Austria. 1895-1935. Historical studies. ▪Wedekind's two Lulu plays *Erdgeist (Earth Spirit)* and *Die Büchse der Pandora (Pandora's Box)* and their adaptation by Alban Berg in his opera *Lulu.*

4799 Wagner, Gottfried; Rosetti Wagner, Teresina, transl. *Il crepuscolo dei Wagner.* (Twilight of the Wagners.) Milan: Il Saggiatore; 1998. 347 pp. Pref. Index. Illus.: Photo. B&W. 4. Lang.: Ita.

Germany. 1923-1995. Biographical studies. ▪Italian translation of *Wer nicht mit dem Wolf heult*, on the life of composer Richard Wagner (Cologne: Verlag Kiepenheuer & Witsch, 1997).

4800 Sólyom, György. "Mítosz—zenedráma—lágdráma: *A Nibelung gyűrűje* felújítása elé, 5.—Harmadik nap: *Az istenek alkonya.*" (Myth, Musical Drama, World Drama: The Revival of *The Ring of the Nibelungen*, 5. Third Day: *The Twilight of the Gods.*) *OperaL.* 1998; 7(2): 20-22. Lang.: Hun.

Hungary: Budapest. 1998. Critical studies. ▪An outline of the opera by musicologist on the occasion of the revival of the fourth piece of Wagner's *Ring* cycle *Götterdämmerung* directed by Viktor Nagy with a double cast at the Budapest Opera House in May.

4801 Szokolay, Sándor. "A *Szávitri* világa." (The World of *Szávitri.*) *ZZT.* 1998; 5(3): 9-10. Illus.: Photo. B&W. 1. Lang.: Hun.

Hungary: Budapest. 1998. Histories-sources. ▪The composer talks about the libretto of his new opera.

4802 Ashbrook, William. "The Evolution of the Donizettian Tenor-Persona." *OQ.* 1998 Spr; 14(3): 24-32. Notes. Illus.: Pntg. Dwg. B&W. 4. Lang.: Eng.

Italy. 1816-1845. Critical studies. ▪Analysis of how Donizetti's use of the tenor developed throughout his career. Cites examples from *Dom Sébastien, roi de Portugal, Lucia di Lammermoor*, and *Il furioso all'isola di San Domingo* among others.

4803 Coelho, Victor Anand. "Kapsberger's *Apotheosis ... of Francis Xavier* (1622) and the Conquering of India." 27-47 in Dellamora, Richard, ed.; Fischlin, Daniel, ed. *The Work of Opera: Genre, Nationhood, and Sexual Difference.* New York, NY: Columbia UP; 1997. 350 pp. Notes. Index. Lang.: Eng.

Italy: Rome. 1622. Historical studies. ▪Examines a long-forgotten Jesuit musical piece *The Apotheosis or Consecration of Saints Ignatius Loyola and Francis Xavier* (composer, Giovanni Girolamo Kapsberger, librettist Orazio Grassi), for the relation of empire to colony in the gendered relationship of Portugal to India.

MUSIC-DRAMA: Opera—Plays/librettos/scripts

4804 Gentry, Theodore L. "Musical Symbols of Death in *Tosca.*" *OQ.* 1998 Sum; 14(4): 59-69. Notes. Lang.: Eng.
Italy. 1900. Critical studies. ■Puccini's use of drum rolls and whole-tone scales to symbolize death and doom in his dark opera.

4805 Gosset, Philip; Glasow, E. Thomas, transl. "Donizetti: European Composer." *OQ.* 1998 Spr; 14(3): 11-16. Notes. Illus.: Pntg. B&W. 1. Lang.: Eng.
Italy. Europe. 1835-1848. Biographical studies. ■Examines the composer's work outside of his native Italy, and the influence of French, German, and English literature on his work.

4806 Lindner, Thomas. "Rossini's *Aureliano in Palmira*: A Descriptive Analysis." *OQ.* 1998-1999 Win; 15(1): 18-32. Notes. Tables. Illus.: Pntg. B&W. 1. Lang.: Eng.
Italy. 1813. Textual studies. ■Step-by-step analysis of Rossini's two-act *opera seria.* Breaks down the libretto (by Felice Romani), music, and background of the piece.

4807 Marinelli, David Newton. *Carlo Goldoni as Experimental Librettist: The 'Drammi giocosi' of 1750.* New Brunswick, NJ: Rutgers Univ; 1988. 214 pp. Notes. Biblio. [Ph.D. Dissertation, Univ. Microfilms Order No. AAC 8914259.] Lang.: Eng.
Italy. 1748-1762. Critical studies. ■Goldoni's creation of the full-length comic opera libretto, the 'dramma giocoso.' Compares the formal parameters of the form with a group of early, transitional libretti.

4808 Phillips-Matz, Mary Jane. "Wild Thing." *OpN.* 1998 Feb 14; 62(11): 14-16,18-19. Illus.: Dwg. B&W. 3. Lang.: Eng.
Italy. 1853-1998. Critical studies. ■The importance of the mezzo soprano character Azucena in *Il Trovatore* by Giuseppe Verdi.

4809 Rosenberg, Charles George; Illo, John, ed. "Donizetti in Decline: Another Memoir." *OQ.* 1998 Spr; 14(3): 55-64. Notes. Lang.: Eng.
Italy. 1845-1848. Histories-sources. ■Account from journalist and music critic Rosenberg's memoir pertaining to his dealings with Donizetti while Donizetti was suffering from the latter stages of syphillis. Includes background introduction by the editor.

4810 Roux, Georges. "Légende d'une reine d'Orient." (Legend of a Queen of the Orient.) *ASO.* 1998 May/June; 184: 84-87. Illus.: Dwg. B&W. 3. Lang.: Fre.
Italy. 1823. Historical studies. ■Background information on the title character of Rossini's opera *Semiramide.*

4811 Sapienza, Annamaria. "La parodia dell'opera lirica nell'ottocento napoletano. Nove libretti del Conservatorio di San Pietro a Majella." (The Opera Parody in Naples in the Nineteenth Century: Nine Librettos Belonging to the Conservatory of San Pietro a Maiella.) *IlCast.* 1998; 11(31): 89-123. Notes. Lang.: Ita.
Italy: Naples. 1813-1875. Critical studies. ■Analysis of the librettos of the parodies of the most celebrated Italian operas then being performed in the royal theatres of San Carlo and Fondo in Naples.

4812 Senici, Emanuele Giuseppe. *Virgins of the Rocks: Alpine Landscape and Female Purity in Early Nineteenth-Century Italian Opera.* Ithaca, NY: Cornell Univ; 1998. 306 pp. Notes. Biblio. [Ph.D. Dissertation, Univ. Microfilms Order No. AAC 9839912.] Lang.: Eng.
Italy. 1800-1850. Critical studies. ■The virginal heroine in Alpine settings in operas of Vincenzo Bellini (*La Sonnambula*), Gaetano Donizetti (*Linda di Chamounix*) and Giuseppe Verdi (*Luisa Miller*). Focuses on questions of class, politics, and gender.

4813 Smith, Patricia Juliana. "'O Patria Mia': Female Homosociality and the Gendered Nation in Bellini's *Norma* and Verdi's *Aida.*" 93-114 in Dellamora, Richard, ed.; Fischlin, Daniel, ed. *The Work of Opera: Genre, Nationhood, and Sexual Difference.* New York, NY: Columbia UP; 1997. 350 pp. Notes. Index. Lang.: Eng.
Italy. 1831-1871. Critical studies. ■Argues that both operas turn on the desire between women, mediated by a man, and present a form of national identity often at odds with the politics of empire and the modern nation-state.

4814 Treadwell, Nina. "Female Operatic Cross-Dressing: Bernardo Saddumene's Libretto for Leonardo Vinci's *Li Zite 'n Galera.*" *COJ.* 1998; 10(2): 131-156. Notes. Illus.: Diagram. B&W. 1. Lang.: Eng.
Italy: Naples, Venice. 1601-1800. Critical studies. ■Searches for instances of cross-dressing in the opera genres *commedia per musica* and Venetian *opera seria,* using Saddumene's libretto to cite examples of the phenomenon.

4815 Kuz'mina, N.I.,. *Puškin v russkoj opere: 'Kamennyj gost' Dargomyžskogo, 'Zolotoj petušok' Rimskogo-Korsakova.* (Puškin in Russian Opera: *Kamennyj gost* by Dargomyžskij, *Le Coq d'Or* by Rimskij-Korsakov.) St. Petersburg: 1998. 400 pp. Lang.: Rus.
Russia. 1799-1869. Critical studies. ■Comparative analysis of the problems presented to composers setting text for operas.

4816 O'Malley, Lurana Donnels. "Catherine the Great's Operatic Splendour at Court: *The Beginning of Oleg's Reign.*" *ET.* 1998; 17(1): 33-51. Notes. Biblio. Illus.: Photo. B&W. 1. Lang.: Eng.
Russia. 1768-1794. Critical studies. ■Loosely inspired by Shakespeare, Catherine wrote *Oleg* to support her political ambitions for Constantinople and to encourage a cultural connection with Greece.

4817 Šafer, N. "Bulgakov—Librettist." 3-22 in *Opernye libretto.* Pavlodar: 1998. Lang.: Rus.
Russia. Critical studies. ■Analysis of playwright Michajl Bulgakov as a librettist.

4818 Sajmon, G.U. *Sto velikich oper i ich sjužety. Majkapar A. Šedevry russkoj opery.* (One Hundred Great Operas and Their Plots: The Best of Russian Operas.) Moscow: Kron-press; 1998. 864 pp. (Akademija.) Lang.: Rus.
Russia. 1998. Critical studies. ■Scenarios of one hundred operas: includes a history of the genre.

4819 Johnson, Warren. "Carmen and Exotic Nationalism: España à la Française." *RomN.* 1997 Fall; 38(1): 45-60. Notes. Biblio. Lang.: Eng.
Spain. France. 1845. Critical studies. ■Representations of Spain as exotic locale and its significance in Bizet's opera *Carmen* and its source, Prosper Mérimée's short story.

4820 Macedo, Catherine. "Between Opera and Reality: The Barcelona Parsifal." *COJ.* 1998; 10(1): 97-109. Notes. Lang.: Eng.
Spain-Catalonia: Barcelona. 1841-1914. Historical studies. ■Political resonance of the works of Wagner on the imagination of Catalonians, who viewed *Parsifal,* in particular, as symbolic of their desire for political autonomy. Includes a review of Miquel Domènech's book on the first performance of *Parsifal* in the region, *L'Apothose musique de la religion Catholique: Parsifal de Wagner.*

4821 Eriksson, Torbjörn. "Snart stundar *Staden.*" (Soon Will *Staden* Be at Hand.) *MuD.* 1998; 20(3): 8-9, 50. Illus.: Photo. B&W. Color. Lang.: Swe.
Sweden: Stockholm. 1998. Histories-sources. ■Interview with the composer Sven-David Sandström about his new opera *Staden* and co-operation with the poet Katarina Frostensson.

4822 Ellis, Jim. "Strange Meeting: Wilfred Owen, Benjamin Britten, Derek Jarman, and the *War Requiem.*" 277-296 in Dellamora, Richard, ed.; Fischlin, Daniel, ed. *The Work of Opera: Genre, Nationhood, and Sexual Difference.* New York, NY: Columbia UP; 1997. 350 pp. Notes. Index. Lang.: Eng.
UK-England. 1968-1988. Historical studies. ■Derek Jarman's film adaptation of *War Requiem* and the opera *Owen Wingrave,* both by Benjamin Britten, and the anti-war poetry of Wilfred Owen, with attention to same-sex gender ideology in the hostile environment of 1980s England.

4823 Fischlin, Daniel. "'Eros Is in the Word': Music, Homoerotic Desire, and the Psychopathologies of Fascism, or The 'Strangely Fruitful Intercourse' of Thomas Mann and Benjamin Britten." 209-233 in Dellamora, Richard, ed.; Fischlin, Daniel, ed. *The Work of Opera: Genre, Nationhood, and Sexual Difference.* New York, NY: Columbia UP; 1997. 350 pp. Notes. Index. Lang.: Eng.

MUSIC-DRAMA: Opera—Plays/librettos/scripts

UK-England. 1912-1992. Historical studies. ■Issues of gender, sexuality, and national identity in Benjamin Britten's last opera *Death in Venice*, adapted from Thomas Mann's short novel.

4824 Hamilton, David. "The *Rake* Decoded." *OpN.* 1998 Jan 17; 62(9): 12-15. Illus.: Photo. Dwg. B&W. Color. 6. Lang.: Eng.

UK-England. 1971. Historical studies. ■The libretto by W.H. Auden and Chester Kallman for *The Rake's Progress* by Stravinskij.

4825 Marx, Robert. "Auden in Opera: The Libretto as Poetic Style." *OpN.* 1998 Jan 17; 62(9): 8-11. Illus.: Photo. B&W. 4. Lang.: Eng.

UK-England. 1907-1973. Biographical studies. ■Poet W.H. Auden's work on opera librettos in collaboration with Chester Kallman from the late 1940s until his death in 1973, including works by Stravinskij, Henze, Brecht, and Britten, as well as opera translations for television and stage performances of operas by Mozart and Kurt Weill and some unused lyrics for Broadway's *Man of La Mancha.*

4826 "Daniel Barenboim and Edward Said: A Conversation." *Raritan.* 1998 Sum; 18(1): 1-31. Lang.: Eng.

USA: New York, NY. Germany. 1995. Histories-sources. ■Transcript of a discussion between pianist and conductor Barenboim and Professor Said before an audience at Columbia University regarding the life and work of composer Richard Wagner.

4827 Honig, Joel. "Once Is Not Enough." *OpN.* 1998 Oct.; 63(4): 48-53. Illus.: Photo. B&W. 4. Lang.: Eng.

USA. 1931-1998. Historical studies. ■Eugene O'Neill's 1931 drama *Mourning Becomes Electra*, and its operatic adaptation by Marvin David Levy, performed at the Metropolitan Opera (1967). It very had few revivals but was reedited by the composer for performance by the Lyric Opera of Chicago in 1998.

4828 Leonardi, Susan J.; Pope, Rebecca A. "Divas and Disease, Mourning and Militancy: Diamanda Galas' Operatic *Plague Mass.*" 315-333 in Dellamora, Richard, ed.; Fischlin, Daniel, ed. *The Work of Opera: Genre, Nationhood, and Sexual Difference.* New York, NY: Columbia UP; 1997. 350 pp. Notes. Index. Lang.: Eng.

USA. 1991. Historical studies. ■The militant response to the AIDS epidemic in Galas' operatic piece.

4829 Edwards, Paul. "'Lost Children': Shostakovich and *Lady Macbeth.*" *TextPQ.* 1998 July; 18(3): 157-198. Notes. Biblio. Lang.: Eng.

USSR. 1930-1932. Critical studies. ■Analysis of Šostakovič's opera *Ledi Makbet Mtsenskogo Uezda* combining the interpretive approaches of the biographical, intertextual, formal and Bakhtinian dialogics to suggest new answers to old questions regarding the work.

Reference materials

4830 Druskin, M., ed. *111 oper: Sprav.-putevoditel'.* (300 Operas: Directory—Guide.) St. Petersburg: Kul'tInformPress; 1998. 688 pp. Lang.: Rus.

1998. ■Guide to opera: includes notes on the music and librettos, in addition to the plot descriptions.

4831 Glasow, E. Thomas, ed. "Recordings." *OQ.* 1998 Spr; 14(3): 103-208. Notes. Illus.: Photo. Pntg. B&W. 4. Lang.: Eng.

Europe. North America. 1998. ■Discography of Donizetti operatic recordings currently in print, or out-of-print recordings about to be reissued. Some items in the discography contain brief reviews.

4832 Mátyus, Zsuzsa, comp., ed.; Mezey, Béla, photo. *Magyar Állami Operaház 113. évad, 1996-1997.* (Hungarian State Opera House 113th Season, 1996-1997.) Budapest: Magyar Állami Operaház; 1997. 148 pp. Illus.: Photo. Poster. B&W. Color. 135. Lang.: Hun.

Hungary: Budapest. 1996-1997. ■A richly illustrated annual of the activity of Budapest's Opera House summing up the premieres, revivals, guest performances, competitions and other events with collection of data on the company.

4833 Lindner, Thomas. "An Integral Catalog of Donizetti's Operatic Works." *OQ.* 1998 Spr; 14(3): 17-23. Notes. Illus.: Photo. B&W. 1. Lang.: Eng.

Italy. Europe. 1816-1845. Historical studies. ■Comprehensive catalogue of the composer's completed and performed operas, unfinished operas, fragments, dubia, scene liriche, and cantatas.

4834 Milnes, Rodney, ed. *Opera Index 1998.* London: Opera; 1998. 93 pp. Lang.: Eng.

UK-England. Europe. USA. 1998. ■General subject index to volume 49 of *Opera*, with additional separate indices to operas, artists, and contributors.

Research/historiography

4835 Della Seta, Fabrizio. "Some Difficulties in the Historiography of Italian Opera." *COJ.* 1998; 10(1): 3-13. Notes. Lang.: Eng.

Italy. 1601-1998. Critical studies. ■Argues that recent analytical methods are more appropriate to the historiography of seventeenth-century Italian opera than the application of Wagnerian principles. Refers to the work of Carl Dahlhaus, Harold Powers, and Lorenzo Bianconi.

Theory/criticism

4836 Levin, David J. "Response to James Treadwell." *COJ.* 1998; 10(3): 307-311. Notes. Lang.: Eng.

Europe. 1987-1998. Critical studies. ■Defends and amends theories expressed in his 'Reading a Staging/Staging a Reading' (*COJ*, 9:1) with regard to the need for a critical vocabulary with which to read operatic productions in reaction to James Treadwell's criticism in 'Restaging a Reading' (*COJ*, 10:2).

4837 Treadwell, James. "Reading and Staging Again." *COJ.* 1998; 10(2): 205-220. Notes. Lang.: Eng.

Europe. 1965-1998. Critical studies. ■Criticizes David J. Levin's article 'Reading a Staging/Staging a Reading' (*COJ*, 9:1), which proposes an approach to evaluating the work of opera directors, with particular attention to traditional versus radical versions of Wagner's operas. Argues that Levin's methods and results and do not take into account audience attitudes, interpretation, and prior experience, and that the study of staging is ultimately an exploration of the continuing history of interpretation itself.

4838 Schmidgall, Gary. "Arcibravo, GBS!" *OQ.* 1998 Sum; 14(4): 5-15. Notes. Lang.: Eng.

UK-England: London. 1887-1894. Critical studies. ■Honorific for the seven years playwright George Bernard Shaw spent writing music criticism for several London magazines.

4839 Sutcliffe, Tom. "The Cooling of Britannia." *OpN.* 1998 July; 63(1): 30-31. Illus.: Photo. Color. 1. Lang.: Eng.

UK-England. 1985-1999. Historical studies. ■Changes in selectivity in review policies of operas and orchestras in *The Times*, *The Daily Telegraph, The Manchester Times, The Financial Times.*

4840 Bernheimer, Martin. "Tough Guy." *OpN.* 1998 July; 63(1): 22-23. Lang.: Eng.

USA. 1965-1996. Histories-sources. ■Pulitzer Prize-winning music critic for *The Saturday Review* and *Los Angeles Times* on his career.

4841 Buchau, Stephanie von. "Nothing Afloat—Barely." *OpN.* 1998 July; 63(1): 24-25. Illus.: Dwg. Color. 1. Lang.: Eng.

USA. 1998. Histories-sources. ■The author's work as a music critic.

4842 Coleman, Emily. "Glory Days." *OpN.* 1998 July; 63(1): 16-19, 52. Illus.: Photo. B&W. Color. 9. Lang.: Eng.

USA. 1942-1964. Histories-sources. ■The author recalls the wide-ranging arts coverage of *Newsweek* during her editorial tenure there and the large number of composers, singers, dancers and theatrical figures she met.

4843 Gross, Robert. "*Iphigénie en Tauride.* By Christoph Willibald Gluck. Glimmerglass Opera, Cooperstown, New York. 19 August 1997." *JDTC.* 1998 Fall; 13(1): 183-186. Notes. Illus.: Photo. B&W. 1. Lang.: Eng.

USA: Cooperstown, NY. 1997. Critical studies. ■The role of gender in *Iphigénie en Tauride*, directed at Glimmerglass Opera by Francesca Zambello.

4844 Johnson, Chelsey. "Backtalk." *OpN.* 1998 July; 63(1): 26-29. Illus.: Photo. B&W. 12. Lang.: Eng.

USA. 1998. Histories-sources. ■The damaging effect of unfair reviews on performers and conductors, as described by conductors/music directors

MUSIC-DRAMA: Opera—Theory/criticism

John Nelson (Ensemble Orchestral de Paris), Yves Abel (L'Opéra Français de New York), Patrick Summers (Houston Grand Opera), Martina Arroyo (Indiana University School of Music), and singers Sharon Sweet, Jerry Hadley, Alessandra Marc, Chris Merritt, Richard Leech, Paul Plishka, Dolora Zajick, and Jennifer Larmore.

4845 Keller, James M.; Kapusta, Janusz, illus. "Endangered Species: Are Informed Music Critics a Dying Breed?" *OpN.* 1998 July; 63(1): 8-10. Illus.: Pntg. 3. Lang.: Eng.

USA. Canada. 1998. Critical studies. ■Comments on the current state of music criticism, suggesting that it should be more than merely descriptions of scenery.

4846 Page, Tim. "Critical List." *OpN.* 1998 July; 63(1): 20. Lang.: Eng.

USA. 1940-1998. Critical studies. ■Pulitzer Prize-winning classical music critic for the *Washington Post* offers advice to writers: get the facts, cover the news, keep a good critical position, be honest in opinion, and be courteous.

4847 Rockwell, John. "The Vanishing Arts." *OpN.* 1998 July; 63(1): 12-15. Illus.: Dwg. 2. Lang.: Eng.

USA. 1988-1999. Critical studies. ■Critic's personal evaluation of newspaper criticism of classical music appearing in *The Oakland Tribune*, *The Los Angeles Times*, and *The New York Times*. Suggestions for improvement.

Training

4848 Tranberg, Sören. "Skola med Falstaff i fokus." (A School With Falstaff at the Center.) *MuD.* 1998; 20(2): 7-11. Illus.: Photo. B&W. Lang.: Swe.

Sweden: Gothenburg. 1960-1998. Histories-sources. ■Interview with Harald Ek, the director of the Teater- & Operahögskolan, about the training of the young singers today compared with the sixties, with references to Walter Felsenstein, the student production by Vernon Mound of Verdi's *Falstaff*, and interviews with the singers Karin Blomgren, Mattias Danielsson, Victoria Granlund and Håkan Starkenberg and the designer Janna Holmstedt.

4849 Adams, William Jenkins. *An Introduction to Acting Training for the Developing Character Tenor.* Coral Gables, FL: Univ. of Miami; 1998. 113 pp. Notes. Biblio. [D.M.A. Thesis, Univ. Microfilms Order No. AAC 9904644.] Lang.: Eng.

USA. 1998. Instructional materials. ■Uses the role of King Kaspar from Gian Carlo Menotti's *Amahl and the Night Visitors* to demonstrate a method of actor training for the opera singer.

Operetta

Audience

4850 "Weeping Fans." *Econ.* 1998 Oct 31; 349(8092): 92. Lang.: Eng.

Austria: Vienna. 1898-1998. Historical studies. ■The decline in popularity of operetta on the Viennese stage and the need to attract a new audience.

4851 Clason, Mathias. "Den Erotiska Rytmen—operettens hemliga vapen?" (The Erotic Rhythm—the Secret Weapon of Operetta?)*MuD.* 1998; 20(3): 16-17. Illus.: Dwg. Photo. B&W. Lang.: Swe.

France. Germany. USA. 1860-1998. Critical studies. ■Discusses the dim view of operetta by contemporary audiences.

Performance/production

4852 Hagman, Bertil. "'Jag mötte Lehár'." (I Met Lehár.) *MuD.* 1998; 20(3): 20-21. Illus.: Dwg. B&W. Lang.: Swe.

Austria: Vienna. 1936. Histories-sources. ■Some personal memories of Franz Lehár, with reference to his palace in Vienna.

4853 Clason, Mathias. "Oh! Offenbach." *MuD.* 1998; 20(5): 12-13. Illus.: Photo. B&W. Lang.: Swe.

France. UK-England. 1950. Critical studies. ■Survey of recordings of the operettas by Offenbach.

4854 Gademan, Göran. "Operett som i Offenbach." (Operetta à la Offenbach.) *MuD.* 1998; 20(3): 18-19. Illus.: Dwg. Photo. B&W. Color. Lang.: Swe.

France. 1819-1880. Biographical studies. ■Profile of composer Jacques Offenbach.

4855 Yon, Jean-Claude. "Delibes avant *Lakmé*." (Delibes Before *Lakmé*.) *ASO.* 1998 Mar/Apr.; 183: 62-67. Notes. Illus.: Photo. Dwg. B&W. 2. Lang.: Fre.

France. 1856-1883. Historical studies. ■Léo Delibes as a composer of operetta.

4856 Streisand, Marianne. "Bitterfeld 3." *TZ.* 1998; 6: 47-49. Illus.: Photo. B&W. 2. Lang.: Ger.

Germany: Bitterfeld. 1998. Critical studies. ■Peter Hacks's adaptation of *Orphée aux Enfers (Orpheus in the Underworld)* after Calzabigi, Crémieux, and Halévy, composed by Jacques Offenbach, performed in Bitterfeld, directed by Jens Mehrle and Stefan Nolte, with professional and amateur performers, in the context of its production at Kulturpalast at the conferences of 'Bitterfelder Weg'.

4857 Abenius, Folke. "'Kanske var det skrattet'." (Maybe It Was the Laugh.) *MuD.* 1998; 20(3): 22-23, 38. Illus.: Dwg. Photo. B&W. Color. Lang.: Swe.

Sweden. Germany. Austria. 1960-1998. Critical studies. ■The problem of staging operettas on the contemporary stage.

4858 Gademan, Göran. "Så blev narren rumsren." (Thus Was the Fool On the Level.) *MuD.* 1998; 20(4): 60-61. Illus.: Dwg. Photo. B&W. Lang.: Swe.

Sweden: Stockholm. 1860-1928. Critical studies. ■The operettas of Offenbach at Kungliga Operan, and the critical reactions from the audience.

4859 Tranberg, Sören. "Nicolai Gedda: Operett som bel canto." (Nicolai Gedda: The Operetta As Bel Canto.) *MuD.* 1998; 20 (3): 10-14. Illus.: Photo. B&W. Color. Lang.: Swe.

UK-England: London. Germany, West: Munich. 1952-1984. Histories-sources. ■Interview with Nicolai Gedda about the art of singing operetta, with references to his recordings and Walter Legge.

4860 Voigt, Thomas. "Elisabeth Schwarzkopf: Hela skillnaden ligger i hur." (Elisabeth Schwarzkopf: The Whole Difference Is How.) *MuD.* 1998; 20(3): 15. Illus.: Photo. B&W. Lang.: Swe.

UK-England. Austria. 1950-1998. Histories-sources. ■Interview with Elisabeth Schwarzkopf about the art of singing operetta.

Plays/librettos/scripts

4861 Hoffman, Cheryl Conover. *A Study of the Women in W.S. Gilbert's* Patience, Iolanthe, *and* Princess Ida*: Or, the Folly of Being Feminist.* Morgantown, WV: West Virginia Univ; 1988. 215 pp. Notes. Biblio. [Ph.D. Dissertation, Univ. Microfilms Order No. AAC 8905150.] Lang.: Eng.

UK-England. 1880-1890. Critical studies. ■The construction of the conflict between men and women in the librettos of W.S. Gilbert and his trivialization of feminism.

4862 Sweeney, Megan. "Two Unpublished Letters from Lady Morgan to Richard Jones." *ELN.* 1998 Mar.; 35(3): 40-52. Notes. Pref. Lang.: Eng.

UK-Ireland. 1807. Biographical studies. ■Analysis of the correspondence between Lady Morgan and actor Richard Jones regarding her comic operetta *The First Attempt.*

PUPPETRY

General

Administration

4863 Arciero, Pam. "Help! I Have a Contract, Now What? Or Eek! I Have No Work, Will an Agent Help?" *PuJ.* 1998 Win; 50(2): 12 . Illus.: Photo. B&W. 1. Lang.: Eng.

USA. 1998. Instructional materials. ■Tips on marketing strategies for the puppeteer looking to work in film and television.

4864 Dannenhauer, Mark. "The Pricing of Puppetry." *PuJ.* 1998 Fall; 50(1): 13. Illus.: Dwg. B&W. 1. Lang.: Eng.

USA. 1998. Instructional materials. ■Puppeteer's advice on how much to charge for services.

PUPPETRY: General

Basic theatrical documents

4865 Androjna, Irena. "*Pospravljica.*" (Tidying Up.) *Lutka.* 1998; 54: 29-50. Lang.: Slo.
Slovenia. 1997. ■Text of a puppet play for children.

4866 Combač, Borut. "*Kdo je navil rumeno budilko?.*" (Who Set the Yellow Alarm Clock?)*Lutka.* 1998; 54: 53-63. Illus.: Photo. B&W. 3. Lang.: Slo.
Slovenia. 1997. ■Playtext of *Kdo je navil rumeno budilko? (Who Set the Yellow Alarm Clock?)* by Borut Combač.

Design/technology

4867 Hogan, Jane. "Twist & Shout." *TCI.* 1998 Aug/Sep.; 32(8): 19-21. Illus.: Photo. Color. 1. Lang.: Eng.
USA: New York, NY. 1998. Technical studies. ■Collaboration of puppteer Basil Twist with lighting designer Andrew Hill on Twist's creation *Symphonie Fantastique*, set to music of Berlioz, which is set in a five-hundred-gallon aquarium at the new Dorothy B. Williams Theatre.

4868 Latshaw, George. "The Handle Bag Puppet." *PuJ.* 1998 Fall; 50(1): 18-20. Illus.: Photo. Diagram. 2. Lang.: Eng.
USA. 1998. Instructional materials. ■Instructions on how to make a puppet out of an ordinary bag with a handle.

4869 Patton, Roy; Patton, Harry J., photo. "Pattons on Parade." *PuJ.* 1998 Fall; 50(1): 6-7. Illus.: Photo. B&W. 8. Lang.: Eng.
USA. 1998. Instructional materials. ■Illustrated guide to constructing miniature figures out of pipe cleaners and balsa wood, and costume them with yarn, paper clips, ribbon, etc.

Institutions

4870 Morrow, Jim. "Mermaid Theatre and its Place in Canadian Puppetry." *CTR.* 1998 Sum; 94: 13-16. Illus.: Photo. B&W. 2. Lang.: Eng.
Canada: Wolfville, NS. 1972-1998. Histories-sources. ■Evolution of Mermaid Theatre and its techniques of puppetry, according to associate director and designer, Jim Morrow.

4871 *Teatr kukol 'Ognivo'. (g. Mytišči - Moskva): Teatr. stranicy.* (The 'Ognivo' Puppet Theatre (Mytišči-Moscow): Theatrical Pages.) Rjazan': Uzoroč'e; 1998. 16 pp. Lang.: Rus.
Russia: Mytišchi. 1998. Historical studies. ■Profile of 'Ognivo' puppet theatre.

4872 Poljakova, O.; Fajnštejn, F. *Rešenija sceničeskogo prostranstva: Spektakli gos. akademičeskogo central'nogo teatra kukol.* (Decisions on How To Set Up the Stage: Plays of the National Academic Central Puppet Theatre.) Moscow: STD RSFSR; 1998. 115 pp. Lang.: Rus.
Russia: Moscow. 1998. Historical studies. ■Profile of the National Puppet Theatre.

4873 Kosi, Tina; Vevar, Rok. "Ob 50. Obletnici LGL." (On the 50th Anniversary of LGL.) *Lutka.* 1998; 54: 4-20. Illus.: Photo. B&W. 4. Lang.: Slo.
Slovenia: Ljubljana. 1968-1997. Historical studies. ■Reports on the fiftieth anniversary of the founding of the Lutkovno Gledališče Ljubljana (The Puppet Theatre of Ljubljana). The authors, artistic directors of LGL, discuss their working concepts, the different problems with texts and their opinions on the puppet theatre today.

4874 Loboda, Matjaž. *Petdeset let Lutkovnega gledališča Ljubljana.* (Fifty Years of Ljubljana Puppet Theatre.) Ljubljana: LGL; 1998. 28 pp. Illus.: Photo. Color. B&W. 8. Lang.: Slo.
Slovenia: Ljubljana. 1948-1998. Histories-specific. ■A historical presentation of the professional development of the Lutkovno Gledališče Ljubljana (Ljubljana Puppet Theatre).

4875 Sever, Boštjan, ed. *KiselFestival '98.* Kranj: Puppet Theatre; 1998. 27 pp. Illus.: Photo. Dwg. B&W. 7. [Festival of Living Culture.] Lang.: Slo.
Slovenia: Kranj. 1998. Histories-sources. ■The program of the Kisel Festival '98, a festival of living culture which presented twenty-four theatrical pieces for children and adults, of which twelve were puppet shows.

4876 "Print." *PuJ.* 1998 Fall; 50(1): 24-28. Illus.: Photo. B&W. 2. Lang.: Eng.
USA. 1948-1998. Historical studies. ■*Puppetry Journal* celebrates its fiftieth anniversary. Continued in *PuJ* 50:2 (1998 Win) pp. 25-31.

4877 Bartha, Anikó. "Bread and Puppet." *Vilag.* 1998 Win; 12: 159-160. Lang.: Hun.
USA: Plainfield, VT. 1963-1998. Historical studies. ■Report on the activity of the puppet ensemble. The most important event in the life of the theatre is the annual two-day festival entitled 'Our Domestic Resurrection' focusing on a theme. This year's topic related to the anniversary of Bertolt Brecht's birth.

4878 Bell, John. "Beyond the Cold War: Bread and Puppet Theatre and the New World Order." 31-53 in Colleran, Jeanne, ed.; Spencer, Jenny S., ed. *Staging Resistance: Essays on Political Theatre.* Ann Arbor, MI: Univ of Michigan P; 1998. 312 pp. (Theater: Theory/Text/Performance.) Notes. Index. Illus.: Photo. 3. Lang.: Eng.
USA: Plainfield, VT. 1990-1997. Historical studies. ■Argues that the traditionally low status of puppetry, and the use of imagery and spectacle has allowed Bread and Puppet Theatre to accommodate a postmodernist theatre practice that resists closure and articulates a clear political position.

4879 Cleary, Beth. "Negation Strategies: The Bread and Puppet Theatre and Performance Practice." *NETJ.* 1998; 9: 23-48. Notes. Biblio. Illus.: Photo. B&W. 5. Lang.: Eng.
USA: Plainfield, VT. 1991. Critical studies. ■Using the Bread and Puppet Theatre's 1991 pageant *The Triumph of Capitalism*, illustrates the group's political performance aesthetic.

4880 Henk, Nancy B. "The Detroit Institute of Arts: A Renaissance of Puppet Activity." *PuJ.* 1998 Win; 50(2): 10-12. Illus.: Photo. B&W. 4. Lang.: Eng.
USA: Detroit, MI. 1998. Historical studies. ■Report on the state of the collection of puppets held by the Detroit museum.

4881 Lach, Elizabeth. "Puppets: A Handful of Magic." *PuJ.* 1998 Fall; 50(1): 8-10. Illus.: Photo. B&W. 4. Lang.: Eng.
USA: Chicago, IL. Mexico: Mexico City. 1998. Historical studies. ■Inventory of puppetry exhibits on view at the Chicago Children's Museum's 'Puppets: A Handful of Magic' on loan courtesy of Mexico City's Papalote Museo del Niño.

4882 Molarsky, Mona. "Attack of the Killer Puppets." *AmTh.* 1998 Dec.; 15(10): 48-51. Illus.: Photo. B&W. 2. Lang.: Eng.
USA: New York, NY. 1998. Historical studies. ■Report on the fourth International Festival of Puppet Theatre held in New York City in September of 1998.

4883 Thompson, Fred; Hunter, Kurt, photo. "Don't Try to Force the Frog! Or, Zen and the Art of Puppetry." *PuJ.* 1998 Win; 50 (2): 13-15. Illus.: Photo. B&W. 4. Lang.: Eng.
USA: Storrs, CT. 1998. Historical studies. ■Report on the Third International Academy of String Puppetry held at the University of Connecticut.

Performance/production

4884 Raugul, E.; Kozyreva, M. *Teatr v čemodane.* (Theatre in a Suitcase.) St. Petersburg: Litera; 1998. 178 pp. (Akademija uvlečenij.) Lang.: Rus.
1998. Instructional materials. ■Self-help guide for creating home theatre: fabrication and movement of puppets, costume design, and storywriting.

4885 Varl, Breda. *Igrajmo se z lutkami.* (Let's Play with Puppets.) Celovec, Dunaj and Ljubljana: Mohorjeva družba; 1998. 123 pp. Illus.: Dwg. Photo. Color. B&W. 35. Lang.: Slo.
Austria. Slovenia. 1993-1997. Instructional materials. ■The puppet work of Slovene children in an Austrian summer arts and handicrafts camp. The book is a compendium of puppetry made by the children, with drawings, photos, and working instructions.

4886 Duchscherer, Brian. "Playing With Dolls: A Personal Reflection on a Career." *CTR.* 1998 Sum; 95: 21-23. Illus.: Photo. B&W. 3. Lang.: Eng.
Canada. 1980-1998. Histories-sources. ■Interview with puppet animator Brian Duchscherer on his fascination with animated puppets, and puppet animation in Canadian film.

4887 Mirbt, Felix. "My Story." *CTR.* 1998 Sum; 95: 4-9. Illus.: Photo. B&W. 7. Lang.: Eng.

PUPPETRY: General—Performance/production

Canada. Germany: Berlin. 1945-1998. Histories-sources. ▪Two intermingled texts: puppeteer Felix Mirbt's techniques including his use of visible actors as puppet manipulators, and Mirbt's childhood memories of WWII Germany which he intends to mix with his work.

4888 Scott, Shelley. "A Family of Puppeteers: An Interview with Nina Keogh about Puppets on Television." *CTR.* 1998 Sum; 95: 24-30. Illus.: Photo. B&W. 2. Lang.: Eng.

Canada: Toronto, ON. 1953-1998. Histories-sources. ▪Nina Keogh on her experience as a third-generation puppeteer and puppet maker working almost exclusively in television.

4889 Motýlová, Hermína. "Čtyřicetpět let ostravského Divadlo loutek." (Forty-Five Years of the Ostrava Puppet Theatre.) *Loutkář.* 1998; 11-12: 272-278. Biblio. Illus.: Photo. B&W. 15. Lang.: Cze.

Czech Republic: Ostrava. 1953-1998. Historical studies. ▪Portrait of the Ostrava Puppet Theatre, with a picture gallery.

4890 Rogerson, Margaret. "English Puppets and the Survival of Religious Theatre." *TN.* 1998; 52(2): 91-111. Notes. Lang.: Eng.

England: London. 1500-1780. Historical studies. ▪How London's puppet theatres and travelling puppeteers kept medieval English religious theatre alive.

4891 Obernauer, Gréta. "Bábtáncoltató betlehemezés Közép-Kelet- Európában." (The 'Bethlehem-play' Tradition with Dancing Puppets in Central and Eastern Europe.) *Vilag.* 1998 Win; 12: 110-117. Biblio. Notes. Lang.: Hun.

Europe. 1700-1990. Historical studies. ▪Survey of a special branch of puppetry based on the folklore of the Christmas season including German, Czech, Slovak, Polish, Ukrainian and Romanian traditions.

4892 Engel, Gert. "'Mit den Dingen spielen, bis ein Kunstwerk daraus wird'." ('To Play with Something Until It Becomes a Work of Art'.) *TZ.* 1998; 5/Theater in Frankreich: 44-46. Illus.: Dwg. Photo. B&W. 7. Lang.: Ger.

France. 1970-1998. Historical studies. ▪The variety of puppetry in France and the artistic influence of puppeteers Jean-Pierre Larroche, Philippe Genty, Jean-Paul Céalis.

4893 Lakos, Anna, comp. "Madách Imre: *Az ember tragédiájá*-nak bábelőadása Colmarban." (Imre Madách: *The Tragedy of Man* in a Puppet Theatre in Colmar.) *Vilag.* 1998 Win; 12: 142-143. Lang.: Hun.

France: Colmar. 1998. Reviews of performances. ▪One of the classic Hungarian dramas on puppet stage directed by Grégoire Callies, director of TJP Strasbourg, Centre dramatique National d'Alsace.

4894 Aguigah, René. "Zeit-Suche-Geschichte(n)." (Time-Search-Stories (History).) *TZ.* 1998; 4: 64-66. Illus.: Photo. B&W. 5. Lang.: Ger.

Germany: Bochum. 1998. Historical studies. ▪Profile of the Fidena (Figurentheater der Nationen), a puppet festival managed by Silvia Brendenal. Includes reviews of several productions.

4895 Kozień, Lucyna, ed.; Waszkiel, Marek, ed. *100 przedstawień teatru lalek. Antologia recenzji, 1945-1996.* (100 Puppet Theatre Performances: Anthology of Reviews, 1945-1996.) Lodz: Pracownia Documentacji Teatru Lalek przy Teatrze Lalek 'Arlekin' w Łodzi; 1998. 320 pp. (O teatrze lalek.) Notes. Pref. Index. Illus.: Photo. B&W. 1. Lang.: Pol.

Poland. 1945-1996. Reviews of performances. ▪Anthology of reviews of best Polish puppet theatre performances produced by professional theatres both for children and for adults.

4896 Olesiewicz, Marek. "Wileńskie Szopki Akademickie 1921-1933. Jako świadectwo zbiorowego życia." (Academic Nativity Performances in Vilna, 1921-1933: As a Testimony of a Community's Life.) 47-54 in Kozłowska, Mirosława, ed. *Wilno teatralne.* Warsaw: Ogólnopolski Klub Miłośników Litwy; 1998. 478 pp. Lang.: Pol.

Poland: Vilna. 1921-1933. Historical studies. ▪Argues that Nativity puppet theatre performances in the Vilna academic community were a form of cabaret because puppets representing contemporary local personages appeared along with the traditional figures in the Nativity crèche.

4897 Andreeva, T.P. "Net 'Gullivera'? Est' 'Gulliver'!: K 50-letiju so dnja obrazovanija Kurgan. teatra kukol." (No Gulliver? Gulliver Is Here!: 50th Anniversary of Kurgan's Puppet Theatre.) *Nauka i obrazovanie Zaural'ja.* 1998; 2(3): 181-189. Lang.: Rus.

Russia: Kurgan. 1948-1998. ▪Description of 50th anniversary celebration of Kurgan's Puppet Theatre.

4898 Francis, Penny; Jurkowski, Henryk; Klep, Mihael, transl. *Zgodovina evropskega lutkarstva. Knj. 1: Od svojih začetkov do konca devetnajstega stoletja.* (History of European Puppetry. Book 1: From the Origins to the End of the Nineteenth Century.) Novo mesto: Kulturno umetniško društvo Klemenčičevi dnevi; 1998. 429 pp. Index. Biblio. Lang.: Slo.

Slovenia. 600 B.C.-1890 A.D. Histories-general. ▪A world history of puppet theatre translated into Slovene.

4899 Radeščsek, Borko. "Ponovno po triindvajsetih letih ali prispevek k zgodovini slovenskega lutkovnega filma." (Twenty-Three Years or A Contribution to the History of Slovene Puppet Film.) *Lutka.* 1998; 54: 65-66. Lang.: Slo.

Slovenia. 1947-1997. Historical studies. ▪On the history of Slovene puppet film, culminating in the latest by Eka Vogelnik, *One Tolar Saved Today (En prišparan tolar danes).*

4900 "Opera for a Kids Division—It's OK." *PuJ.* 1998 Fall; 50(1): 15-16. Illus.: Photo. B&W. 2. Lang.: Eng.

USA: Boston, MA. 1998. Historical studies. ▪Preview of the New England Marionettes' Opera for Kids Division's adaptation of Mozart's *The Magic Flute (Die Zauberflöte)* by Susan Hammond at the Emerson Majestic Theatre.

4901 "Mary Churchill." *PuJ.* 1998 Fall; 50(1): 33-34. Illus.: Photo. B&W. 2. Lang.: Eng.

USA. 1930-1997. Biographical studies. ▪Obituary for puppeteer Churchill.

4902 Abrams, Steve. "Duke Kraus." *PuJ.* 1998 Win; 50(2): 36. Lang.: Eng.

USA. 1937-1998. Biographical studies. ▪Obituary for the comedic puppeteer.

4903 Abrams, Steve; Jones, Kenneth Lee; Kurten, Allelu. "All Around the Town." *PuJ.* 1998 Win; 50(2): 2-8. Illus.: Photo. Maps. B&W. 8. Lang.: Eng.

USA: New York, NY. 1998. Historical studies. ▪Report on the Fourth Annual Jim Henson Festival.

4904 Kurten, Allelu. "Basil Twist's *Symphonie Fantastique.*" *PuJ.* 1998 Fall; 50(1): 12. Illus.: Photo. B&W. 1. Lang.: Eng.

USA: New York, NY. 1998. Reviews of performances. ▪Twist's interpretation of the Berlioz symphony, manipulating mylar strips, cloth, and feathers to the music.

4905 Mallard, Sidney. "Preview: Festival of the Millenium." *PuJ.* 1998 Fall; 50(1): 3-5. Illus.: Photo. B&W. 3. Lang.: Eng.

USA: Seattle, WA. 1999. Historical studies. ▪Preview of what is to be offered at the 1999 Puppeteers of America Festival to be held in Seattle, WA.

4906 Molarsky, Mona. "Ralph Lee." *AmTh.* 1998 Apr.; 15(4): 32-34. Illus.: Photo. B&W. 4. Lang.: Eng.

USA. 1974-1998. Biographical studies. ▪Profile of master puppeteer Ralph Lee.

4907 Stockman, Todd. "Cal Schumann." *PuJ.* 1998 Win; 50(2): 36. Lang.: Eng.

USA. 1930-1998. Biographical studies. ▪Obituary for the television puppeteer.

4908 Stockman, Todd. "Bob Mason." *PuJ.* 1998 Win; 50(2): 35. Lang.: Eng.

USA. 1924-1998. Biographical studies. ▪Obituary for the veteran puppeteer.

4909 Stockman, Todd. "Shari Lewis." *PuJ.* 1998 Win; 50(2): 34-35. Illus.: Photo. B&W. 1. Lang.: Eng.

USA. 1933-1998. Biographical studies. ▪Obituary for the beloved television puppeteer.

4910 Wallace, Lea. "Gia Wallace Brown." *PuJ.* 1998 Win; 50(2): 36. Illus.: Photo. B&W. 1. Lang.: Eng.

USA. 1929-1998. Biographical studies. ▪Obituary for puppeteer and one of the founding members of the Puppetry Guild of Greater New York.

PUPPETRY: General

Plays/librettos/scripts

4911 Székely, György. "Doktor Faustus és Kasperl." (Doctor Faustus and Kasperl.) *Vilag.* 1998 Win; 12: 76-92. Notes. Lang.: Hun.

1578-1945. Historical studies. ■Survey of various adaptations of the Faustus theme including the versions on puppet stage.

4912 Bleu, Loup. "Lettre du Loup Bleu à Maître Melançon." (Lettre from Loup Bleu to Master Melançon.) *JCT.* 1998; 86: 139-141. Illus.: Photo. B&W. 3. Lang.: Fre.

Canada: Quebec, PQ. 1997. Histories-sources. ■Response to 'Moderniser les Lumières?', article in *Jeu* no. 83 by Benoît Melançon, which had criticized Sous-Marin Jaune's loose, puppet-show adaptation of Voltaire's *Candide.*

4913 Coetzee, Yvette. "Visibly Invisible." *SATJ.* 1998 May/Sep.; 12(1/2): 35-51. Notes. Biblio. Lang.: Eng.

South Africa, Republic of. 1997. Critical studies. ■How shifting the conventions of the traditionally invisible puppeteer allows for more dimension in both the puppeteer-puppet relationship and the creation of theatrical meaning in *Ubu & the Truth Commission* by William Kentridge.

Reference materials

4914 Vranc, Danilo. *Repertoarni kažipot za lutkarje, lutkovne skupine ali lutkovna gledališča.* (Repertory Directory for Puppeteers, Puppetry Groups and Puppetry Theatres.) Maribor: Zveza kulturnih društev; 1998. 49 pp. Index. Lang.: Slo.

Slovenia. 1942-1997. Bibliographical studies. ■A new, revised, and enlarged edition of a basic bibliography of scripts for puppet theatre in Slovenia.

Relation to other fields

4915 "Puppetry in Education." *CTR.* 1998 Sum; 95: 10-12. Illus.: Photo. B&W. 2. Lang.: Eng.

Canada. 1994-1998. Histories-sources. ■Interview with puppeteer Ken McKay on his experiences leading puppet-making and puppeteering workshops in schools.

Marionettes

Administration

4916 Mavrinskaja, L. "Natjanutye struny duši." (The Taut Strings of the Soul.) *Avtograf.* 1998; 3: 49-52. Lang.: Rus.

Russia. 1998. Biographical studies. ■Profile of V. Vol'chovskij, puppet theatre producer.

Basic theatrical documents

4917 Burkett, Ronnie. "*Tinka's New Dress.*" *CTR.* 1998 Sum; 95: 38-69. Illus.: Photo. B&W. 6. Lang.: Eng.

Canada: Winnipeg, MB. 1994. ■Playtext of puppeteer Ronnie Burkett's touring show, premiered at Manitoba Theatre Centre (Winnipeg, MB, 1994).

Design/technology

4918 Cheatle, Esther. "The Balance Line: Use It for Good Marionette Posture." *PuJ.* 1998 Win; 50(2): 32. Biblio. Illus.: Diagram. B&W. 1. Lang.: Eng.

USA. 1998. Technical studies. ■Stresses importance of a balance line to enhance a marionette's manipulative performance.

Institutions

4919 Coad, Luman. "Movement—Puppet Sized." *CTR.* 1998 Sum; 94: 17-20. Biblio. Illus.: Dwg. Photo. B&W. 5. Lang.: Eng.

Canada: Vancouver, BC. 1966-1998. Histories-sources. ■Limitations and possibilities of hand puppets, rod puppets and marionettes, and history of Coad Canada Puppets, Vancouver-based touring puppet theatre company comprising puppeteers Luman and Arlyn Coad.

Performance/production

4920 Nicholls, Liz. "World on a String." *CTR.* 1998 Sum; 95: 31-37. Illus.: Photo. B&W. 4. Lang.: Eng.

Canada: Calgary, AB, Winnipeg, MB. 1970-1998. Biographical studies. ■Career of puppeteer/playwright Ronnie Burkett.

4921 Tóth, Hajnalka. "A teatro dei pupi hagyománya Szicíliában." (The Tradition of the 'teatro dei pupi' in Sicily.) *Vilag.* 1998 Win; 12: 93-109. Notes. Lang.: Hun.

Sicily. 1646-1996. Historical studies. ■The history of this branch of puppetry, significant form in South Italy from its ancient tradition to the present.

Plays/librettos/scripts

4922 McCarthy, James. "Militant Marionettes: Two Lost Puppet Plays of the Spanish Civil War, 1936-39." *ThR.* 1998 Spr; 23(1): 44-50. Notes. Lang.: Eng.

Spain. 1936-1939. Critical studies. ■The use of puppet theatre as antifascist propaganda in the Spanish Civil War. Focuses on two such plays, *Radio Sevilla (Radio Seville)* and *Los salvadores de España (The Saviors of Spain)*, both by Rafael Alberti.

Muppets

Performance/production

4923 Kearns, Gail. "*Sesame Street* Comes Home!" *PuJ.* 1998 Win; 50(2): 18-19. Illus.: Photo. B&W. 1. Lang.: Eng.

USA. 1968-1998. Historical studies. ■Report on a conference panel discussion on the impact of *Sesame Street* held at Harvard University.

Shadow puppets

Performance/production

4924 Mrazek, Jan. *Phenomenology of a Puppet Theatre: Contemplations on the Performance Technique of Contemporary Javanese Wayang Kulit.* Ithaca, NY: Cornell Univ; 1998. 973 pp. Notes. Biblio. [Ph.D. Dissertation, Univ. Microfilms Order No. AAC 9818296.] Lang.: Eng.

Indonesia. 1700-1998. Critical studies. ■The complex interaction of performative elements in *wayang kulit* shadow puppet theatre including puppets, puppeteers, dance-like movement, complex orchestral music, and theatrical language.

4925 Weiss, Sarah. *Paradigms and Anomalies: Female-Style Genderan and the Aesthetics of Central Javanese Wayang.* New York, NY: New York Univ; 1998. 529 pp. Notes. Biblio. [Ph.D. Dissertation, Univ. Microfilms Order No. AAC 9819809.] Lang.: Eng.

Indonesia. 1650-1998. Histories-specific. ■A study of the gender-construction and aesthetics of the so-called female style of gender playing, *genderan*, during the all-night performance of shadow-puppet theatre.

4926 Sitar, Jelena. "Kaj je važno na potovanju?" (What Is Important When You Travel?)*Lutka.* 1998; 54: 68-70. Illus.: Photo. B&W. 3. Lang.: Slo.

Slovenia: Ribnica. 1997. Histories-sources. ■Reports on a puppet workshop for refugee children from Bosnia, held in Ribnica, and led by the author and Igor Cvetko. The result of the workshop was a performance with shadow puppets.

SUBJECT INDEX

A Flor da pele (Skin Deep)
Plays/librettos/scripts
Cruelty and the absurd in theatre of Latin American playwrights. Latin America. 1960-1980. Lang.: Eng. 3267
A.Artist.Associati (Rome)
Performance/production
Productions by Toni Bertorelli and Alfiero Alfieri. Italy: Rome. 1997. Lang.: Eng. 2175
A.D. Players (Houston, TX)
Institutions
Jeannette Clift George and the A.D. Players. USA: Houston, TX. 1967-1997. Lang.: Eng. 1785
Aalborg Teater
Administration
Interview with Malene Schwartz, manager of Aalborg Teater. Denmark: Aalborg. 1993-1998. Lang.: Dan. 5
Aalto-Musiktheater (Essen)
Administration
Stefan Soltesz's administration at Aalto-Musiktheater. Germany: Essen. 1997-1998. Lang.: Ger. 4286
Abba, Marta
Plays/librettos/scripts
Analysis of correspondence between Pirandello and Marta Abba. Italy. 1925-1936. Lang.: Ita. 3222
Pirandello's fictional characters and his relationship with actress Marta Abba. Italy. 1925-1936. Lang.: Ita. 3229
Luigi Pirandello's letters to Marta Abba. Italy. 1925-1936. Lang.: Ita. 3230
Marta Abba and Pirandellian dramaturgy. Italy. Lang.: Ita. 3232
An anecdote of Silvio D'Amico regarding Pirandello and Abba. Italy: Rome. 1933. Lang.: Ita. 3233
Marta Abba and the characters of Pirandello's plays. Italy. 1925-1936. Lang.: Ita. 3245
Pirandello, Abba, and the Teatro d'Arte. Italy: Rome. 1925-1927. Lang.: Ita. 3248
Correspondence of playwright Luigi Pirandello and actress Marta Abba. Italy. 1925-1936. Lang.: Ita. 3255
Abbey Theatre (Dublin)
Audience
Nationalist response to the premiere of Synge's *Playboy of the Western World.* Ireland: Dublin. 1907. Lang.: Eng. 1404
Performance/production
Recent productions in Ireland of plays by Eugene O'Neill. Ireland: Dublin. UK-Ireland: Belfast. 1989-1998. Lang.: Eng. 2154
Collection of newspaper reviews by London theatre critics. UK-England. 1998. Lang.: Eng. 2489
Plays/librettos/scripts
Recent history in Irish theatre and drama. Ireland: Dublin. UK-Ireland: Belfast. 1993-1996. Lang.: Eng. 3212
Theory/criticism
Political interpretations of Irish literary theatre. Ireland. 1897-1996. Lang.: Eng. 846
Abbey, Henry
Performance/production
Soprano Marcella Sembrich's performances at the Metropolitan Opera. USA: New York, NY. 1883-1909. Lang.: Eng. 4724
Abbott, June
Performance/production
Collection of newspaper reviews by London theatre critics. UK-England: London. 1998. Lang.: Eng. 2441
Abdrazakov, A.
Performance/production
Opera singers E. Kočetova and A. Abdrazakov. Bashkir. 1998. Lang.: Rus. 4534
Abduction from the Seraglio, The
SEE
Entführung aus dem Serail, Die.
Abel, Yves
Theory/criticism
Performers and conductors complain about unfair reviews. USA. 1998. Lang.: Eng. 4844
Abingdon Square
Plays/librettos/scripts
Theatrical space in plays of Maria Irene Fornes. USA. 1977-1989. Lang.: Eng. 3571
Åbo Svenska Teater (Turku)
Performance/production
Swedish and bilingual Finnish-Swedish theatre. Finland: Turku, Vaasa. 1998. Lang.: Eng, Fre. 1913
About Last Night
Plays/librettos/scripts
Analysis of films of David Mamet. USA: Los Angeles, CA. 1980-1998. Lang.: Eng. 4006
About the Boy
Performance/production
Collection of newspaper reviews by London theatre critics. UK-England: London. 1998. Lang.: Eng. 2549
Abraha, Afewerki
Plays/librettos/scripts
Theatre as cultural weapon and military education in the Eritrean war. Eritrea. 1980-1984. Lang.: Eng. 3048
Abramovič, Marina
Performance/production
The performance of sacrifice on stage. France. Germany. 1900-1998. Lang.: Ger. 530
Recent collaboration of performance artists Marina Abramowič and Ulay. Europe. China, People's Republic of. 1970-1988. Lang.:Eng. 4240
Reexamination of the performance art of Beuys, Abramovič, and Ulay. USA. Germany. Netherlands. 1964-1985. Lang.: Eng. 4254
Abramowitsch-Sorel, Ruth
Performance/production
Dancer, choreographer, and teacher Ruth Abramowitsch-Sorel. Poland. 1907-1974. Lang.: Ger. 1296
AbsoluTheatre (Montreal, PQ)
Plays/librettos/scripts
The use of collage in contemporary productions involving Greek myths. Canada: Montreal, PQ. 1998. Lang.: Fre. 2814
Absurdist theatre
Plays/librettos/scripts
Beckett's influence on *Che zhan (The Bus Stop)* by Gao Xingjian. China, People's Republic of. 1983. Lang.: Eng. 2844
The theatre of Eugène Ionesco. France. 1912-1994. Lang.: Ita. 3079

Absurdist theatre — cont'd

Analysis of *Le Roi se meurt (Exit the King)* by Eugène Ionesco. France. 1962. Lang.: Eng. 3080
The speaking subject in plays of Beckett and Stoppard. France. Ireland. UK-England. 1945-1998. Lang.: Ger. 3098
Obituary for playwright Samuel Beckett. Ireland. France. 1906-1989. Lang.: Dut. 3199
Conversations with playwright Samuel Beckett. Ireland. France. 1998. Lang.: Ita. 3205
Absurdism in children's theatre. North America. Europe. 1896-1970. Lang.: Eng. 3288

Abundance
Performance/production
The collaborative process at Catalyst Theatre. Canada: Edmonton, AB. 1986-1998. Lang.: Eng. 504

Academy of Vocal Arts (Philadelphia, PA)
Performance/production
William Schuman on the differences between operatic and Broadway theatre singing. USA. 1998. Lang.: Eng. 4303

Acciaiuoli, Filippo
Performance/production
The evolution of comic opera. Italy: Florence, Rome. 1665-1700. Lang.: Eng. 4660

Accidental Death of an Anarchist
SEE
Morte accidentale di un anarchico.

Acconci, Vito
Performance/production
Performance artists Vito Acconci and Hermann Nitsch. Austria: Vienna. Italy. 1960-1977. Lang.: Eng. 4239

According to Mark
Performance/production
Collection of newspaper reviews by London theatre critics. UK-England: London. 1998. Lang.: Eng. 2517

Achurch, Janet
Plays/librettos/scripts
Feminism and plays of Henrik Ibsen. Norway. 1879-1979. Lang.: Eng. 3293

Ackland, Rodney
Performance/production
Collection of newspaper reviews by London theatre critics. UK-England: London. 1998. Lang.: Eng. 2493

Acosta, Carlos
Performance/production
Dancer Carlos Acosta of Royal Ballet and Houston Ballet. USA: Houston, TX. UK-England: London. 1993-1998. Lang.: Eng. 1190

Across the Bridge
Performance/production
Collection of newspaper reviews by London theatre critics. UK-England: London. 1998. Lang.: Eng. 2467

Ács, János
Performance/production
János Acs' *A mennyei híd (The Heavenly Bridge)* directed by Gábor Cziezel. Hungary: Debrecen. 1998. Lang.: Hun. 2069
Review of Molnár's *Az üvegcipő (The Glass Slipper)*, Új Színház. Hungary: Budapest. 1997. Lang.: Hun. 2094
Plays/librettos/scripts
New Hungarian translations of Shakespeare. Hungary. 1990-1998. Lang.: Hun. 3187

Acting
SEE ALSO
Training, actor.
Behavior/psychology, actor.
Administration
Performance in fundraising. USA: New York, NY. 1998. Lang.: Eng. 34
Preparations for the centennial of actor and singer Paul Robeson. USA. 1898-1998. Lang.: Eng. 61
Interview with actors on Equity. USA: New York, NY. 1998. Lang.: Eng. 75
The debate on organizing non-union tours of theatrical production. USA: New York, NY. 1998. Lang.: Eng. 88
Equity seminar for young performers and their families. USA: New York, NY. 1998. Lang.: Eng. 114
The creation of Actors' Equity in response to abusive working conditions. USA: New York, NY. 1913. Lang.: Eng. 127
The campaign to ban child performers in New York City. USA: New York, NY. 1874-1919. Lang.: Eng. 139
Equity Executive Director Alan Eisenberg's experience with a touring production of *Cats*. USA: New York, NY. 1998. Lang.: Eng. 4318
Basic theatrical documents
Theatrical and other writings of actor Leonid Filatov. Russia: Moscow. 1998. Lang.: Rus. 163
English translation of *Takatoki* by Mokuami Kawatake. Japan. 1884-1998. Lang.: Eng. 1361
Dutch translations of women's monologues by Dario Fo. Italy. 1998. Lang.: Dut. 1440
Songs and poems of Vladimir Vysockij. Russia: Moscow. 1938-1980. Lang.: Rus. 1453
Design/technology
The influence of Dalcroze's eurhythmics on designer Adolphe Appia. Switzerland. 1906-1915. Lang.: Eng. 228
Job-hunting advice for costumers and theatrical professionals. USA. 1998. Lang.: Eng. 259
Geraldo Andrew Vieira, carnival costumer and performer. Trinidad and Tobago. 1952-1996. Lang.: Eng. 4160
Institutions
History of the Ligue Nationale de l'Improvisation. Canada: Montreal, PQ. 1979-1997. Lang.: Fre. 339
Profile of Acteurs Associés, an alternative to agencies. Canada. 1995-1998. Lang.: Fre. 343
The all-female Takarazuka Revue Company. Japan. 1914-1988. Lang.: Eng. 368
The work of performance troupe Goat Island. USA: Chicago, IL. 1987-1998. Lang.: Eng. 395
Preview of SETC convention. USA: Birmingham, AL. 1998. Lang.: Eng. 405
The relationship between theatrical artists and theatrical institutions. USA: Tarrytown, NY. 1998. Lang.: Eng. 421
Estonian theatre and actors before and after the end of Soviet rule. Estonia. 1985-1998. Lang.: Swe, Eng, Ger. 1600
Profile of the Swedish Institute of Acting at the Finnish Theatre Academy. Finland: Helsinki. 1908-1998. Lang.: Eng, Fre. 1603
Experiential memory work and acting at Theater Jugend Club. Germany: Nordhausen. 1995-1998. Lang.: Ger. 1629
Carlo Quartucci's acting workshop on Shakespeare's *Macbeth*. Italy: Rome. 1991-1992. Lang.: Ita. 1674
Theatre schools: production of showcases for graduating students. UK-England: London. 1998. Lang.: Eng. 1746
Interview with Robert Lewis on the founding of Actors Studio. USA: New York, NY. 1997. Lang.: Eng. 1766
Arthur Penn and Actors Studio. USA: New York, NY. 1997. Lang.: Eng. 1767
Interview with Matthew Goulish and Lin Hixson of Goat Island. USA: Chicago, IL. 1990. Lang.: Eng. 4237
Performance spaces
History and nature of German open-air theatre. Germany. 1700-1994. Lang.: Eng. 442
Performance/production
Speech-act theory and the actor. 1998. Lang.: Eng. 481
Differences between nudity onstage and on screen. Canada: Montreal, PQ. 1995-1997. Lang.: Fre. 499
Social criticism and alternative theatre in Quebec and Newfoundland. Canada. 1970-1985. Lang.: Eng. 500
Interview with actress Andrée Lachapelle. Canada: Montreal, PQ. 1950-1998. Lang.: Fre. 502
Opportunities for South Asian actors. Canada: Toronto, ON. 1997. Lang.: Eng. 508
Interview with actress Tammi Øst. Denmark. 1982-1998. Lang.: Dan. 514
The Cibber family: private life as public spectacle. England. 1713-1760. Lang.: Eng. 517
Estonian artists as war refugees in Sweden. Estonia. Sweden. 1939-1945. Lang.: Swe, Eng, Ger. 519
Handbook and training exercises for actors. Europe. 1998. Lang.: Ita. 520
Empathy and distancing in theatre education. Europe. 1998. Lang.: Fin. 523
Directing and intercultural theatre. Europe. 1930-1998. Lang.: Ger. 524
The disappearance of the diva in the modern world. Europe. USA. 1890-1998. Lang.: Swe. 525

Acting — cont'd

The 'grande coquette' on the Parisian stage. France: Paris. 1885-1925. Lang.: Eng. 531

Working-class theatre and censorship. France: Paris. 1800-1862. Lang.: Eng. 533

The nature of acting in German Expressionist production. Germany. 1916-1921. Lang.: Eng. 536

Catalogue of an exhibition on actor Totò. Italy: Naples. 1898-1998. Lang.: Ita. 542

Sketches and caricatures of dialect actor Gilberto Govi. Italy: Genoa. 1885-1966. Lang.: Ita. 543

A conversation with actor and director Carmelo Bene. Italy. 1998. Lang.: Ita. 544

Actor Angelo Musco. Italy. 1872-1937. Lang.: Ita. 549

Catalogue of an exhibition devoted to actress Anna Proclemer. Italy. 1923-1998. Lang.: Ita. 552

Early modern French and Italian actresses. Italy. France. 1550-1750. Lang.: Eng. 553

Lithuanian theatre education and the visit of Tadashi Suzuki. Lithuania. 1998. Lang.: Fin. 559

The symposium on acting at Theaterfestival. Netherlands: Amsterdam. 1998. Lang.: Dut. 562

Coping with stage fright. Netherlands. 1998. Lang.: Dut. 566

Actor Arkadij Rajkin. Russia. 1998. Lang.: Rus. 579

Memoirs of actress Tatjana Okunevskaja. Russia. 1998. Lang.: Rus. 582

Memoirs of actor Arkadij Rajkin. Russia. 1998. Lang.: Rus. 583

Anecdotes by and about actress Faina Ranevskaja. Russia. 1896-1984. Lang.: Rus. 584

Actress/director Alla Nazimova. Russia. USA. 1878-1945. Lang.: Eng. 585

Interview with actor Jėvgenij Vesnik. Russia: Moscow. 1998. Lang.: Rus. 586

Notes and essays on dancers and actors of the nineties. Russia. 1995-1999. Lang.: Rus. 587

Polde Bibič on other Slovene actors. Slovenia. 1945-1997. Lang.: Slo. 591

European influences on Slovene performance. Slovenia. 1994-1997. Lang.: Slo. 594

Interview with actress Milena Zupančič. Slovenia. 1960-1997. Lang.: Slo. 596

Performer, writer, director Elsie Janis and the 'gay sensibility'. UK-England. 1889-1956. Lang.: Eng. 612

Audience reaction to actress Adah Isaacs Menken. USA. 1835-1869. Lang.: Eng. 619

Psychoanalytic study of the actor. USA. 1988. Lang.: Eng. 621

Postmodern acting theory. USA. 1988. Lang.: Eng. 622

Directing and design to accommodate the disabled in performance. USA. 1988. Lang.: Eng. 623

Actor-training project involving character development in drama and musical theatre. USA. 1987. Lang.: Eng. 625

Character development in drama and musical theatre: actor-training project. USA. 1987. Lang.: Eng. 626

The application of Laban Movement Studies to actor training. USA. 1997-1998. Lang.: Eng. 628

The effect of a heterogeneous audience on performance anxiety. USA. 1987. Lang.: Eng. 630

The life and career of singer Paul Robeson. USA. 1998. Lang.: Eng. 631

A model for systematic analysis of vocal performance. USA. 1988-1997. Lang.: Eng. 636

Analysis of character development for acting degree. USA: Long Beach, CA. 1988. Lang.: Eng. 637

Actor training and psychotherapy-derived techniques. USA. 1988. Lang.: Eng. 639

The Field frontier acting family. USA. 1830-1860. Lang.: Eng. 641

Sociolinguistics, gender, and the actor. USA. 1997-1998. Lang.: Eng. 642

Current news about the theatre and its people. USA: New York, NY. 1998. Lang.: Eng. 658

Photo essay on celebration of Paul Robeson. USA: New York, NY. 1998. Lang.: Eng. 660

Short news takes on current theatre events. USA: New York, NY. 1998. Lang.: Eng. 661

The Alba Emoting system of actor training. USA. 1995-1998. Lang.: Eng. 668

Character development in dramas and musicals. USA. 1987. Lang.: Eng. 670

Actor-training project in character development. USA. 1987. Lang.: Eng. 671

Actor Edwin Forrest and the construction of masculinity. USA. 1806-1872. Lang.: Eng. 674

History of movement training for the actor. USA. 1910-1985. Lang.: Eng. 675

Creativity and ego identity in actors. USA. 1984-1987. Lang.: Eng. 678

The role of acting in preparing a homily. USA. 1997. Lang.: Eng. 679

Gender and the career of actress Charlotte Cushman. USA. 1816-1876. Lang.: Eng. 680

San Francisco's professional theatre. USA: San Francisco, CA. 1850-1860. Lang.: Eng. 682

Character development from the actor's point of view. USA. 1987. Lang.: Eng. 686

Performer, director, and artist Wolfgang Martin Schede. Germany. 1898-1975. Lang.: Ger. 929

Analysis of *kyōgen* performance. Japan. 1400-1700. Lang.: Eng. 1351

Female performers of the formerly all-male genre *randai*. Sumatra. 1980-1998. Lang.: Eng. 1354

The performance of *onnagata* Tamasaburō in *Elizabeth* by Francisco Ors. Japan: Tokyo. 1993-1995. Lang.: Eng. 1362

Feminist analysis of female roles in *kabuki*. Japan. 1600-1900. Lang.: Eng. 1363

The role of the *onnagata* heroine in late eighteenth-century *kabuki*. Japan. 1770-1800. Lang.: Eng. 1364

Psychotherapy and the actor. 1998. Lang.: Rus. 1812

Women's roles in Shakespeare. 1600-1998. Lang.: Ger. 1813

The training of actors in Asian performance styles. Australia: Brisbane. 1992-1998. Lang.: Eng. 1817

Actor Helmuth Lohner's stint as administrative director of Theater in der Josefstadt. Austria: Vienna. 1960-1998. Lang.: Ger. 1819

Actors Gert Voss and Ignaz Kirchner on George Tabori's production of *Fin de partie (Endgame)*. Austria: Vienna. 1998. Lang.: Ger. 1821

Gert Voss and Ignaz Kirchner, *Theater Heute*'s actors of the year. Austria: Vienna. 1988-1998. Lang.: Ger. 1823

César Brie and *La pista del cabeceo (The Land of Nod)*. Bolivia. 1970-1985. Lang.: Ita. 1829

Interview with actor Gérard Poirier. Canada: Montreal, PQ. 1942-1998. Lang.: Fre. 1834

Actor Jack Robitaille. Canada: Quebec, PQ. 1998. Lang.: Fre. 1835

Voice teachers Alex Bulmer and Kate Lynch. Canada: Toronto, ON. UK-England: London. 1986-1998. Lang.: Eng. 1837

Actress Anne-Marie Cadieux on working in theatre and in film. Canada: Montreal, PQ. 1998. Lang.: Fre. 1838

Analysis of a student production of Caryl Churchill's *Cloud Nine*. Canada. 1997. Lang.: Eng. 1840

Interview with actor William Hutt. Canada: Stratford, ON. 1962-1996. Lang.: Eng. 1844

Marie-Ginette Guay's wordless performance in Franz Xaver Kroetz's *Wunschkonzert (Request Concert)*. Canada: Quebec, PQ. 1995-1997. Lang.: Fre. 1847

Problems of post-secondary theatre training. Canada: Edmonton, AB. 1919-1998. Lang.: Eng. 1848

Actor Mervyn Blake. Canada: Stratford, ON. 1933-1998. Lang.: Eng. 1851

Interview with actor Jacques Leblanc. Canada: Quebec, PQ. 1980-1998. Lang.: Fre. 1853

Interview with actor/director Paul Hébert. Canada: Quebec, PQ. 1952-1998. Lang.: Fre. 1854

Actor William Hutt. Canada: Stratford, ON. USA. 1953-1998. Lang.: Eng. 1858

Interview with actress Denise Gagnon. Canada: Quebec, PQ. 1958-1998. Lang.: Fre. 1864

The performances of Frances Hyland, Kate Reid, and Martha Henry in *The Cherry Orchard*. Canada: Stratford, ON. 1965. Lang.: Eng. 1865

Acting in the private theatre of the Ming Dynasty. China. 1368-1644. Lang.: Eng. 1872

Acting — cont'd

Interview with actor Jiří Pecha. Czech Republic. 1967-1998. Lang.: Cze. 1882

Actor Jan Nebeský. Czech Republic. 1982-1997. Lang.: Eng, Fre. 1883

Actor/director Jaroslav Dušek of Divadlo Vizita. Czech Republic: Prague. 1987-1998. Lang.: Cze. 1884

The director's role in the development of good acting. Denmark. 1998. Lang.: Dan. 1887

Director Jonathan Paul Cook on developing talent in an ensemble. Denmark. 1997-1998. Lang.: Dan. 1888

Actress Ghita Nørby on adapting to various performance spaces. Denmark. 1970-1998. Lang.: Dan. 1889

Actress/writer Charlotte Cibber Charke. England. 1713-1760. Lang.: Eng. 1891

The activities of actor Edward Alleyn in retirement. England: London. 1597-1600. Lang.: Eng. 1894

Images associated with actress Charlotte Cibber Charke. England. 1713-1760. Lang.: Eng. 1896

The feud between David Garrick and Charles Macklin. England: London. 1743-1777. Lang.: Eng. 1897

Contemporary remarks on the styles and manners of actors. England: London. 1740-1779. Lang.: Eng. 1898

Rowe's Jane Shore as a major role for actresses. England. 1714. Lang.: Eng. 1899

The resurgence of interest in actress Charlotte Cibber Charke. England. 1713-1760. Lang.: Eng. 1901

Shakespearean production and the theatrical portrait collection of the Garrick Club. England: London. 1702-1814. Lang.: Eng. 1903

Feminist analysis of the life of actress Charlotte Cibber Charke. England. 1713-1760. Lang.: Eng. 1904

Rehearsal practices in British professional theatre. England. 1500-1700. Lang.: Eng. 1905

Actress Charlotte Cibber Charke and cross-dressing. England. 1713-1760. Lang.: Eng. 1906

Press responses to the autobiography of actress Charlotte Cibber Charke. England. 1713-1760. Lang.: Eng. 1908

Casting and performance in eighteenth-century productions of *Othello*. England. 1777-1800. Lang.: Eng. 1909

Actor Lasse Pöysti. Finland. 1944-1998. Lang.: Eng, Fre. 1917

Interview with acting teacher Kari Väänänen. Finland. 1998. Lang.: Fin. 1918

The classic French tradition of declaiming text. France. 1657-1749. Lang.: Fre. 1923

Movement training for actors in plays of Molière. France. 1622-1673. Lang.: Eng. 1938

Letters of actress Adrienne Lecouvreur. France. 1720-1730. Lang.: Ita. 1940

The performances of Lucinda Childs and Michel Piccoli in *La Maladie de la Mort (The Sickness of Death)*, directed by Robert Wilson. France: Paris. 1997. Lang.: Eng. 1942

Interview with actress Lucinda Childs. France: Paris. 1976-1997. Lang.: Eng. 1943

Interview with actress Fanny Ardant. France: Paris. 1990-1998. Lang.: Swe. 1944

Interview with actor Vachtang Kikabidze. Georgia. 1998. Lang.: Rus. 1947

The career of actor Bernhard Minetti. Germany. 1905-1998. Lang.: Ger. 1949

Mei Lanfang's influence on Bertolt Brecht. Germany. China. 1935. Lang.: Eng. 1951

Christoph Schlingensief's project with the homeless at Deutsches Schauspielhaus. Germany: Hamburg. 1998. Lang.: Ger. 1961

Matthias Matschke, *Theater Heute*'s young actor of the year. Germany: Berlin. 1985-1997. Lang.: Ger. 1963

Thomas Langhoff's production of Brecht's *Der Kaukasische Kreidekreis (The Caucasian Chalk Circle)* at Deutsches Theater. Germany: Berlin. 1998. Lang.: Ger. 1965

Natali Seelig, *Theater Heute*'s actress of the year. Germany: Munich. 1991-1998. Lang.: Ger. 1966

Actress Christine Hoppe. Germany: Dresden. 1993-1998. Lang.: Ger. 1973

Comparison of two productions of Shakespeare's *Richard III*. Germany: Munich. 1996-1997. Lang.: Ger. 1976

Actress Ilse Ritter. Germany. 1944-1998. Lang.: Ger. 1980

Actress Stephanie Eidt. Germany. 1990-1998. Lang.: Ger. 1982

Actor Herbert Fritsch. Germany. 1992-1998. Lang.: Ger. 1985

Director and actor Christoph Schlingensief. Germany. 1993-1998. Lang.: Ger. 1988

Interview with actor Ekkehard Schall. Germany: Berlin. 1959-1998. Lang.: Ger. 1990

Tribute to the late actor Bernhard Minetti. Germany. 1905-1998. Lang.: Ger. 1992

Actor Oliver Bässler. Germany: Cottbus. 1985-1998. Lang.: Ger. 1995

Actress Maike Bollow. Germany: Hannover. 1991-1998. Lang.: Ger. 2006

Deconstructionist analysis of acting in the theatre of Bertolt Brecht. Germany. 1922-1956. Lang.: Eng. 2007

Interview with actor Klaus Piontek. Germany: Berlin. 1962-1998. Lang.: Ger. 2008

Actor Bernhard Minetti. Germany. 1905-1998. Lang.: Ger. 2015

English actors in Kassel. Germany: Kassel. 1592-1620. Lang.: Eng. 2016

The collaboration of choreographer Lucinda Childs and director Robert Wilson on *La Maladie de la Mort*. Germany. 1992-1997. Lang.: Eng. 2019

Realism in acting death scenes. Germany. 1727-1767. Lang.: Ger. 2023

Interview with actor/director Johanna Schall. Germany, East. 1980-1995. Lang.: Eng. 2045

Actor/director Katja Paryla. Germany, East. 1975-1995. Lang.: Eng. 2046

Actor/director Ursula Karusseit. Germany, East. 1977-1995. Lang.: Eng. 2047

Shakespearean production and the GDR's 'existential crisis'. Germany, East. 1976-1980. Lang.: Eng. 2051

Reviews and photos from the career of the late actor Miklós Gábor. Hungary. 1948-1998. Lang.: Hun. 2055

Interview with actor István Holl. Hungary. 1960-1998. Lang.: Hun. 2059

Interview with actress Kati Lázár. Hungary. 1998. Lang.: Hun. 2062

Excerpts from the diary of singer and actress Ilka Markovits. Hungary. 1839-1915. Lang.: Hun. 2064

Interview with actor Tibor Szervét. Hungary. 1988-1998. Lang.: Hun. 2071

Interview with actor György Gazsó. Hungary. 1980-1998. Lang.: Hun. 2072

Excerpt from an illustrated novel by actor Miklós Gábor. Hungary. 1971. Lang.: Hun. 2076

Review of biographies of actors Ádám Szirtes and Éva Ruttkai. Hungary. 1998. Lang.: Hun. 2077

Obituary for actor Miklós Gábor. Hungary. 1919-1998. Lang.: Hun. 2093

Interview with Péter Blaskó. Hungary. 1970-1998. Lang.: Hun. 2119

Director József Ruszt recalls actor Miklós Gábor. Hungary. 1919-1998. Lang.: Hun. 2120

Mari Törőcsik's performance in Ostrovskij's *Guilty Though Innocent* directed by Vasiljév. Hungary: Szolnok. 1997. Lang.: Hun. 2125

Actress Mária Mezei. Hungary. 1945-1983. Lang.: Hun. 2140

Tribute to the late actress and director Erzsébet Gaál. Hungary. 1951-1998. Lang.: Hun. 2141

Profile of actor-director Erzsébet Gaál. Hungary. 1951-1998. Lang.: Hun. 2147

Obituary for actor and director Śombhu Mitra. India. 1914-1997. Lang.: Eng. 2151

Laura Curano's solo piece *Olivetti*. Italy: Calabria. 1998. Lang.: Eng. 2156

The cult of actor Totò after his death. Italy: Naples. 1967-1997. Lang.: Ita. 2164

The actor/clown team of Claudio Remondi and Riccardo Caporossi. Italy. 1971-1998. Lang.: Eng. 2176

Actress Giacinta Pezzana. Italy. 1841-1919. Lang.: Ita. 2177

Giorgio Strehler of Piccolo Teatro. Italy: Milan. 1921-1997. Lang.: Ger. 2181

Acting — cont'd

Tadashi Suzuki's method of actor training. Japan. 1998. Lang.: Eng. 2191

Articles on stage and film actors and other celebrities. Latvia. 1998. Lang.: Rus. 2197

Memoirs of actor and director Egbert van Paridon. Netherlands. 1920-1990. Lang.: Dut. 2204

Speaking styles of selected actors reading Shakespeare's *Henry V*. North America. UK-England. 1998. Lang.: Eng. 2208

Actor Jan Kreczmar. Poland: Warsaw, Lvov. 1939-1945. Lang.: Pol. 2216

Tadeusz Kantor's directorial process. Poland: Cracow. 1987. Lang.: Eng. 2217

Analysis of productions of *Dziady (Forefather's Eve)* by Adam Mickiewicz. Poland. 1901-1995. Lang.: Pol. 2220

Actor/director Aleksander Zelwerowicz. Poland: Vilna. 1929-1931. Lang.: Pol. 2223

Interview with director Andrzej Wajda. Poland. 1960-1998. Lang.: Fin. 2224

Account of an exhibition devoted to Russian actors. Russia: St. Petersburg. 1785-1917. Lang.: Rus. 2231

Interview with actor Armen Džigarchanjan. Russia: Moscow. 1998. Lang.: Rus. 2232

Memoirs of actresses Olga Aroseva and V.A. Maksimova. Russia: Moscow. 1998. Lang.: Rus. 2234

Actor Vladislav Stržel'čik. Russia: St. Petersburg. 1998. Lang.: Rus. 2235

Interview with Moscow Art Theatre actress G. Kalinovskaja. Russia: Moscow. 1998. Lang.: Rus. 2238

Actors of the Adygeian Drama Theatre. Russia: Majkop. 1998. Lang.: Rus. 2239

Major Russian actresses and ballerinas of the nineteenth and twentieth centuries. Russia. 1800-1998. Lang.: Rus. 2240

Memoirs of actor Georgij Burkov. Russia. 1933-1990. Lang.: Rus. 2241

Actress Elina Bystrickaja. Russia: Moscow. 1998. Lang.: Rus. 2242

Memoirs of actress Ol'ga Čechova. Russia. 1917-1980. Lang.: Rus. 2243

Serf actors from Saratov in the theatre of Czar Alexander I. Russia: St. Petersburg. 1805. Lang.: Rus. 2246

Memoirs of actor Oleg Dal'. Russia: Moscow. 1998. Lang.: Rus. 2247

Actor Nikolaj K. Simonov. Russia: St. Petersburg. 1998. Lang.: Rus. 2248

Actress Alla S. Demidova. Russia. 1998. Lang.: Rus. 2249

Journal of actress Tatjana Doronina. Russia: Moscow. 1998. Lang.: Rus. 2252

Actress and director Tatjana Doronina of Moscow Art Theatre. Russia: Moscow. Lang.: Rus. 2253

Actress Tatjana Doronina. Russia. 1998. Lang.: Rus. 2254

Memoirs of Moscow Art Theatre actress Tatjana Doronina. Russia: Moscow. 1998. Lang.: Rus. 2255

Mother and daughter actresses Nina and E. Dobyševa. Russia: Moscow. 1998. Lang.: Rus. 2256

Memoirs of actor Lev Durov. Russia: Moscow. 1998. Lang.: Rus. 2257

Moscow Art Theatre actor Viktor Gvozdickij. Russia: Moscow. 1998. Lang.: Rus. 2259

Interview with director Lev Dodin. Russia. 1997. Lang.: Fre. 2260

Actress Margarita Terechova. Russia. Spain. 1998. Lang.: Rus. 2261

Profiles of major theatrical figures. Russia. 1950-1998. Lang.: Rus. 2263

Solomon Michoëls of Moscow's Jewish Theatre. Russia: Moscow. 1998. Lang.: Rus. 2264

Actor Juri Nazarov. Russia. 1998. Lang.: Rus. 2275

Actor E. Mjazinoj. Russia. 1998. Lang.: Rus. 2277

Sergej Bezrukov's creation of the character of poet Sergej Esenin. Russia: Moscow. 1998. Lang.: Rus. 2278

Moscow Art Theatre actress G. Kalinovskaja. Russia: Moscow. 1998. Lang.: Rus. 2280

Actress E. Majorova and her husband, scenographer S. Šerstjuk. Russia: Moscow. 1998. Lang.: Rus. 2283

Student performances in the State University's theatre. Russia: Moscow. 1998. Lang.: Rus. 2284

Actor Anatolij Ktorov. Russia: Moscow. 1998. Lang.: Rus. 2286

Religion and actor Oleg Borisov. Russia: St. Petersburg. 1998. Lang.: Rus. 2287

Actor Nikolaj Simonov. Russia: St. Petersburg. 1998. Lang.: Rus. 2289

Profile of stage and film actor Armen B. Džigarchanjan. Russia: Moscow. 1998. Lang.: Rus. 2290

Biographical information on actor Vladimir Vysockij. Russia: Moscow. 1938-1980. Lang.: Rus. 2291

Memoirs of actor A.P. Ktorov. Russia: Moscow. 1998. Lang.: Rus. 2292

The murder of actor and director Solomon Michoëls. Russia: Moscow. 1948. Lang.: Rus. 2293

Memoirs of actress I.V. Makarova. Russia: Moscow. 1998. Lang.: Rus. 2294

Actor Sergej Makoveckij. Russia: Moscow. 1998. Lang.: Rus. 2295

Analysis of Čechov's *Platonov* and *Lešji (The Wood Demon)*. Russia. 1878-1889. Lang.: Eng. 2297

Actress Pavlina Konopčuk. Russia. 1998. Lang.: Rus. 2298

Actress Farida Muminova. Russia: Magnitogorsk. 1998. Lang.: Rus. 2299

Serf actor Michajl Ščepkin. Russia: Samara. 1788-1863. Lang.: Rus. 2300

Actress Inna Čurikova. Russia: Moscow. 1998. Lang.: Rus. 2301

Actress Tatjana Doronina. Russia: Moscow. 1998. Lang.: Rus. 2302

Actor Oleg Menšikov. Russia: Moscow. Russia. 1998. Lang.: Rus. 2304

The final months of actor Vladimir Vysockij. Russia: Moscow. 1980. Lang.: Rus. 2307

Actor Andrej Mironov. Russia: Moscow. 1998. Lang.: Rus. 2308

Children's theatre actor Gennadij Pečnikov. Russia: Moscow. 1998. Lang.: Rus. 2310

Actor Lenid Leonidov. Russia: Moscow. 1873-1941. Lang.: Rus. 2312

Actor G.I Sal'nikov. Russia: Saratov. 1998. Lang.: Rus. 2315

Dictionary of Russian stage actors. Russia. 1998. Lang.: Rus. 2317

Actress I.S. Savvina. Russia: Moscow. 1998. Lang.: Rus. 2318

Singer and actress Faina Ranevskaja. Russia. 1896-1984. Lang.: Rus. 2319

Biography of actress Faina Ranevskaja. Russia. 1896-1984. Lang.: Rus. 2320

Memoirs of actor Innokentij Smoktunovskij. Russia: Moscow. 1998. Lang.: Rus. 2323

Letters of K.S. Stanislavskij. Russia. 1906-1917. Lang.: Rus. 2327

Italian translation of letters written by K.S. Stanislavskij. Russia. 1919-1938. Lang.: Ita. 2328

Actor/director Pavel Medvedev. Russia. 1851-1899. Lang.: Rus. 2330

The funeral of actor and playwright Vladimir Vysockij. Russia: Moscow. 1980. Lang.: Rus. 2333

Actress M. Vertinskaja on her father, singer Aleksand'r Vertinskij. Russia: Moscow. 1998. Lang.: Rus. 2334

Memoirs of Malyj Theatre actor E. Ja. Vesnik. Russia: Moscow. 1998. Lang.: Rus. 2336

Actor Vladimir Vinokur. Russia. 1998. Lang.: Rus. 2337

Vagant, a journal dedicated to the work of actor Vladimir Vysockij. Russia: Moscow. 1998. Lang.: Rus. 2339

Actor Sergej Bezrukov. Russia: Moscow. Lang.: Rus. 2341

Slovene translation of Cicely Berry's work on vocal training for the actor. Slovenia. UK-England. 1973-1993. Lang.: Slo. 2344

Actresses and female managers in Spanish theatre. Spain. 1600-1700. Lang.: Eng. 2357

Swedish actors who have won the O'Neill Prize. Sweden: Stockholm. 1956-1998. Lang.: Swe. 2365

Photographs of Dramaten actors. Sweden: Stockholm. 1998. Lang.: Swe. 2366

Interview with actor Dan Ekborg. Sweden: Stockholm. 1998. Lang.: Swe. 2367

Seven critics on their favorite character or portrayal. Sweden. 1950. Lang.: Swe. 2369

Interview with actress Anna Pettersson. Sweden: Stockholm. 1988-1998. Lang.: Swe. 2371

Interview with actress and director Anna Takanen. Sweden: Stockholm. 1994-1998. Lang.: Swe. 2372

Acting — cont'd

Actor Erland Josephson on his profession. Sweden. 1945-1998. Lang.: Swe. 2379

Interviews with actresses of three generations on female roles. Sweden: Stockholm. 1945-1998. Lang.: Swe. 2380

Interviews with actors Lil Terselius and Björn Granath. Sweden: Stockholm. 1998. Lang.: Swe. 2381

Interview with actor/director Stefan Larsson. Sweden: Stockholm. 1984-1998. Lang.: Swe. 2382

Interviews with actors Börje Ahlstedt and Krister Henriksson. Sweden: Stockholm. 1962-1998. Lang.: Swe. 2383

Gerthi Kulle's role in Brecht's *Der Gute Mensch von Sezuan (The Good Person of Szechwan)* at Dramaten. Sweden: Stockholm. 1998. Lang.: Swe. 2384

Changing attitudes toward the acting profession. Sweden. 1800-1998. Lang.: Swe. 2387

Interview with actor Jan-Olof Strandberg. Sweden: Stockholm, Gothenburg, Uppsala. 1948-1998. Lang.: Swe. 2390

Interview with actors in Feydeau's *La Puce à l'Oreille (A Flea in Her Ear)* at Dramaten. Sweden: Stockholm. 1998. Lang.: Swe. 2396

Katharina Thalbach in Brecht's *Die heilige Johanna der Schlachthöfe (Saint Joan of the Stockyards)* directed by Benno Besson. Switzerland: Zurich. 1998. Lang.: Ger. 2400

Actress G. Isangulova. Tatarstan: Kazan. 1998. Lang.: Rus. 2404

Profile of actress S. Gizzatulina-Volžskaja. Tatarstan. 1998. Lang.: Rus. 2405

The future of English repertory companies. UK-England: London. 1998. Lang.: Eng. 2563

Interview with actor Saeed Jaffrey. UK-England. USA. India. 1950-1998. Lang.: Eng. 2589

Actor and playwright George Dibdin Pitt. UK-England: London. 1806-1808. Lang.: Eng. 2592

Susan Brown on her role in *Richard III* at RSC. UK-England: London, Stratford. 1995-1996. Lang.: Eng. 2593

Interview with Katie Mitchell on directing plays of Beckett. UK-England. 1998. Lang.: Eng. 2594

Actor Daniel Massey. UK-England: London. 1968-1998. Lang.: Eng. 2595

Actress Betty Marsden. UK-England: London. 1930-1998. Lang.: Eng. 2596

Career of actress Joan Hickson. UK-England: London. 1927-1998. Lang.: Eng. 2597

Career of actor Marius Goring. UK-England: London. 1930-1998. Lang.: Eng. 2598

Acting career of Michael Denison. UK-England: London. 1936-1998. Lang.: Eng. 2599

Julian Glover on his performance in *Romeo and Juliet* for RSC. UK-England: London, Stratford. 1995-1996. Lang.: Eng. 2606

Actor and director Harold French. UK-England: London. 1900-1998. Lang.: Eng. 2614

Excerpts from Johanna Schopenhauer's journal relating to London theatre. UK-England: London. Germany. 1803-1805. Lang.: Eng. 2615

Derek Jacobi on playing Macbeth for the RSC. UK-England: London, Stratford. 1993-1994. Lang.: Eng. 2616

Paul Jesson's role in *Henry VIII* at RSC. UK-England: London, Stratford. 1996-1997. Lang.: Eng. 2617

Jane Lapotaire on her performance in *Henry VIII* at RSC. UK-England: London, Stratford. 1996-1997. Lang.: Eng. 2619

Christopher Luscombe on acting in RSC productions. UK-England: London, Stratford. 1993-1994. Lang.: Eng. 2620

Interview with actor Eddie Marsan. UK-England: London. 1990-1998. Lang.: Eng. 2622

Richard McCabe on his role in *The Winter's Tale* at RSC. UK-England: London, Stratford. 1992-1993. Lang.: Eng. 2623

John Nettles on his role in an RSC production of *Julius Caesar*. UK-England: London, Stratford. 1995. Lang.: Eng. 2625

Profile of actor Tom Conti. UK-England. 1998. Lang.: Eng. 2629

Actor Leslie Howard. UK-England: London. USA: New York, NY. 1893-1943. Lang.: Eng. 2631

Actor Charles Laughton. UK-England: London. USA: Hollywood, CA. 1899-1962. Lang.: Eng. 2632

Actor Robert Donat. UK-England: London. 1905-1958. Lang.: Eng. 2633

Michael Siberry on performing in an RSC production of *The Taming of the Shrew*. UK-England: London, Stratford. 1995-1996. Lang.:Eng. 2637

Royal Shakespeare Company actors on their performances as Shakespearean characters. UK-England: London, Stratford. 1992-1997. Lang.: Eng. 2638

David Tennant on his performance in *As You Like It* at RSC. UK-England: London, Stratford. 1996-1997. Lang.: Eng. 2640

David Troughton on playing Shakespeare's *Richard III*. UK-England: London, Stratford. 1995-1996. Lang.: Eng. 2642

Philip Voss on his role in *Coriolanus* at RSC. UK-England: London, Stratford. 1994. Lang.: Eng. 2643

Actor Michael Williams. UK-England: London. 1950-1998. Lang.: Eng. 2644

Possible castings for Beckett's *En attendant Godot (Waiting for Godot)*. UK-England. 1998. Lang.: Eng. 2645

Actor George Grizzard. UK-England: London. USA: New York, NY. 1954-1998. Lang.: Eng. 2646

Types of actors and their relationship with directors. UK-England. Sweden. 1950-1998. Lang.: Swe. 2648

Actor Ian Richardson. UK-Scotland: Edinburgh. UK-England: London. 1945-1998. Lang.: Eng. 2652

Obituaries for Joseph Maher, Warren Kliewer, and E.G. Marshall. USA. 1912-1998. Lang.: Eng. 2655

Acting couple Alfred Lunt and Lynn Fontanne: 'idealized heterosexuality'. USA. 1887-1983. Lang.: Eng. 2656

Research on the importance of vocal training for the actor. USA. 1986-1987. Lang.: Eng. 2657

An approach to playing Malvolio in Shakespeare's *Twelfth Night*. USA. 1987. Lang.: Eng. 2659

Acting analysis of character development. USA: Long Beach, CA. 1988. Lang.: Eng. 2662

Account of an actor-training project focused on character development. USA. 1987. Lang.: Eng. 2664

Creating the character Alma in Tennessee Williams' *Summer and Smoke*. USA. 1997. Lang.: Eng. 2665

Actress Audra McDonald. USA. 1993-1998. Lang.: Eng. 2669

Actor Arthur French. USA: New York, NY. 1962-1998. Lang.: Eng. 2671

Actors and directors on the late plays of Tennessee Williams. USA. 1966-1981. Lang.: Eng. 2675

Interview with actor Peter Riegert. USA: New York, NY. 1998. Lang.: Eng. 2676

The 'viewpoint theory' of actor training. USA. 1998. Lang.: Eng. 2677

Actor-training and character development. USA. 1987. Lang.: Eng. 2679

Creating the role of Biagio Buonaccorsi in Robert Cohen's *The Prince*. USA. 1997. Lang.: Eng. 2686

Actress Frances Sternhagen. USA. 1998. Lang.: Eng. 2687

Robert Wilson's work with actors on a production of *Danton's Death (Dantons Tod)*. USA: Houston, TX. 1997. Lang.: Eng. 2688

Actress Ruby Dee. USA. 1998. Lang.: Eng. 2689

An approach to playing Babe Botrelle in Beth Henley's *Crimes of the Heart*. USA. 1987. Lang.: Eng. 2690

The career of gay actor Monty Woolley. USA. 1888-1963. Lang.: Eng. 2691

Ruth Maleczech of Mabou Mines. USA: New York, NY. 1970-1998. Lang.: Eng. 2694

Interview with actress Phylicia Rashad. USA: Atlanta, GA. 1998. Lang.: Eng. 2695

Irish and Irish-American characters on the stages of the Midwest. USA. 1875-1915. Lang.: Eng. 2696

An approach to playing Jamie in O'Neill's *Long Day's Journey Into Night*. USA. 1987. Lang.: Eng. 2697

George Crichton Miln's touring Shakespearean company in Japan. USA: Chicago, IL. Japan: Yokohama. 1882. Lang.: Eng. 2702

John Barton's workshop on Shakespearean performance. USA: New York, NY. 1998. Lang.: Eng. 2704

Director Charles Marowitz on the actor's calling. USA. UK-England. 1958-1998. Lang.: Eng. 2706

Acting — cont'd

Creating the role of Julien Davis Cornell in *The Trial of Ezra Pound.* USA: Long Beach, CA. 1997. Lang.: Eng. 2712

Culture Clash and their production of Aristophanes' *Birds.* USA: Berkeley, CA. 1984-1998. Lang.: Eng. 2713

Actors Helen Carey and Max Wright, winners of Joe A. Callaway Award. USA. 1998. Lang.: Eng. 2716

Report on speech by actor Eli Wallach to Actors' Equity meeting. USA. 1998. Lang.: Eng. 2717

Elizabeth Perry's one-woman show *Sun Flower* about Elizabeth Cady Stanton. USA: New York, NY. 1998. Lang.: Eng. 2718

Julyana Soelistyo and Sam Trammel, winners of the Derwent Award. USA: New York, NY. 1998. Lang.: Eng. 2719

Excerpt from a speech by actor Robert Prosky. USA: Washington, DC. 1998. Lang.: Eng. 2720

Actress Caroline Nesbitt on giving up her theatrical career. USA: New York, NY. 1998. Lang.: Eng. 2723

Actors and the psychology of identity. USA. 1959-1998. Lang.: Eng. 2724

Obituaries for Ellis Rabb, Giorgio Strehler, and David Mark Cohen. USA. 1930-1997. Lang.: Eng. 2725

Creating the character Marlene in Caryl Churchill's *Top Girls.* USA. 1997. Lang.: Eng. 2730

Actor Tomasso Salvini. USA. Italy. 1856-1915. Lang.: Eng. 2731

Actor John Barrymore. USA: New York, NY. 1882-1942. Lang.: Eng. 2732

Actor Paul Muni. USA: New York, NY. 1895-1998. Lang.: Eng. 2733

Actress Marie Dressler. USA: New York, NY. 1869-1934. Lang.: Eng. 2734

Interview with actress Kate Valk. USA: New York, NY. 1979-1998. Lang.: Eng. 2736

Directorial style of JoAnne Akalaitis. USA. 1982-1998. Lang.: Eng. 2737

Actress Lori Holt. USA: San Francisco, CA. 1978-1998. Lang.: Eng. 2740

The 'scientific perspective' of director David Belasco. USA. 1882-1931. Lang.: Eng. 2741

Character development in drama. USA. 1987. Lang.: Eng. 2743

Jane Alexander's return to acting after chairing the NEA. USA. 1998. Lang.: Eng. 2744

Actress and teacher Uta Hagen. USA. 1998. Lang.: Eng. 2745

Actor's analysis of character development. USA. 1987. Lang.: Eng. 2746

Obituary for actor Leverne Summers. USA: New York, NY. 1998. Lang.: Eng. 2748

Obituary for actress Theresa Merritt. USA: New York, NY. 1998. Lang.: Eng. 2749

Profile of performer and activist Paul Robeson. USA. 1898-1959. Lang.: Eng. 2750

Creating the role of Mrs. Scully in Shirley Gee's *Warrior.* USA: Long Beach, CA. 1997. Lang.: Eng. 2753

Careeer of actress Tsai Chin. USA. 1959-1998. Lang.: Eng. 2754

Creating the role of Billy Cuttle in Shirley Gee's *Warrior.* USA: Long Beach, CA. 1997. Lang.: Eng. 2758

Interview with actor Patrick Stewart. USA: Washington, DC. 1998. Lang.: Eng. 2760

The development of character in an actor training project. USA. 1987. Lang.: Eng. 2761

Director Mel Gordon on Mejerchol'd's influence. USSR. 1920-1931. Lang.: Eng. 2765

Interview with film and television actor Jean-Louis Millette. Canada: Montreal, PQ. 1965-1998. Lang.: Fre. 3856

Interview with film and television actress Andrée Lachapelle. Canada: Montreal, PQ. 1964-1998. Lang.: Fre. 3857

Humorous anecdotes by actor/director Massimo Troisi. Italy. 1953-1994. Lang.: Ita. 3858

Actress Ljudmila Gurčenko. Russia: Moscow. 1998. Lang.: Rus. 3859

The death of actress Eva Bartok. Hungary. UK-England: London. 1998. Lang.: Eng. 3934

Suzanne Cloutier's role in Shakespeare's *Othello,* directed by Orson Welles. Italy. 1952. Lang.: Fre. 3935

Essays on actor Gian Maria Volonté. Italy. 1960-1994. Lang.: Ita. 3936

Analysis of casting and acting in Kenneth Branagh's film adaptation of *Much Ado About Nothing.* UK. 1993. Lang.: Fre. 3939

Actor George Arliss. UK-England: London. 1868-1946. Lang.: Eng. 3941

Obituary for singer and actor Frank Sinatra. USA. 1916-1998. Lang.: Eng. 3946

Obituary for actress Maureen O'Sullivan. USA. 1911-1998. Lang.: Eng. 3947

Profile of actor Tom Hanks. USA. 1983-1998. Lang.: Eng. 3950

Actor Bert Lahr. USA. 1895-1967. Lang.: Eng. 3953

Biography of film star Marlene Dietrich by her daughter. USA. 1901-1992. Lang.: Rus. 3955

The importance of Black performers in American musical films. USA. 1900-1957. Lang.: Swe. 3960

Interviews with Italian actresses. Italy. 1998. Lang.: Ita. 4062

Actors' interpretations of the title role in Oscar Wilde's *The Canterville Ghost.* UK-England. USA. 1943-1998. Lang.: Eng. 4066

Obituary for 'Buffalo Bob' Smith, former host of *The Howdy Doody Show.* USA. 1918-1998. Lang.: Eng. 4067

Adrian Pecknold and the Canadian Mime Theatre. Canada: Niagara-on-the-Lake, ON. 1940-1978. Lang.: Eng. 4085

Interview with Marie-Hélène Dasté, daughter of Jacques Copeau. France: Paris. 1913-1992. Lang.: Eng. 4089

Etienne Decroux's concept of actor-centered theatre. USA. France. 1920-1998. Lang.: Eng. 4091

A photo session involving mimes Marcel Marceau and Bill Irwin. USA: New York, NY. 1998. Lang.: Eng. 4092

The cultural background of eighteenth-century British pantomime. England. 1700-1800. Lang.: Eng. 4093

Austrian street theatre. Austria. 1953-1998. Lang.: Ger. 4116

The figure of the Midnight Robber in Trinidadian carnival. Trinidad and Tobago. 1900-1998. Lang.: Eng. 4168

Memoirs of film actor and clown Jurij Nikulin. Russia: Moscow. 1998. Lang.: Rus. 4184

A painting of *commedia dell'arte* performer Tiberio Fiorilli. Italy. 1625-1700. Lang.: Eng. 4190

Mountebanks and the performance of *commedia dell'arte.* Italy. France: Avignon. 1550-1620. Lang.: Eng. 4191

Portraying Mickey Mouse at Walt Disney World. USA: Orlando, FL. 1998. Lang.: Eng. 4223

Performance artists Vito Acconci and Hermann Nitsch. Austria: Vienna. Italy. 1960-1977. Lang.: Eng. 4239

Interview with performance artist Franko B. UK-England. 1998. Lang.: Eng. 4244

Performance artist Mimi Goese. USA. 1982-1998. Lang.: Eng. 4252

Excerpts from a pictorial history of performance art. USA. 1960-1998. Lang.: Eng. 4253

Variety actors Guido and Giorgio De Rege. Italy. 1891-1948. Lang.: Ita. 4275

Interview with actor R. Karcev. Russia. 1998. Lang.: Rus. 4276

G. Chazanov of Teat'r Estrady. Russia: Moscow. Lang.: Rus. 4277

Career of entertainer Al Jolson. USA. 1886-1950. Lang.: Eng. 4280

Excerpts from critical reviews of singer and actress Lotte Lenya. Germany. 1928-1966. Lang.: Eng. 4354

Friends and colleagues recall singer Lotte Lenya. Germany. 1928-1981. Lang.: Eng. 4355

Actors' handling of a mishap on stage during a production of *The Phantom of the Opera.* UK-England: Basingstoke. 1998. Lang.: Eng. 4369

Interview with Shane Ritchie and Jon Conway about the musical *Boogie Nights.* UK-England. 1998. Lang.: Eng. 4370

Staging a musical without professional dancers. USA. 1998. Lang.: Eng. 4374

The Hyers sisters and Black musical comedy. USA. 1870-1902. Lang.: Eng. 4384

Lucy Vestris in *Giovanni in London.* England: London. 1842. Lang.: Eng. 4546

Puppeteer Felix Mirbt. Canada. Germany: Berlin. 1945-1998. Lang.: Eng. 4887

Acting — cont'd

Plays/librettos/scripts
Theatre artist Elizabeth Sterling Haynes and Alberta theatre. Canada. 1916-1957. Lang.: Eng. 2799
Playwright, actor, and director Charles Follini. Canada. 1972-1998. Lang.: Eng. 2818
Director Djanet Sears and actor Alison Sealy Smith on all-Black theatre. Canada: Toronto, ON. 1998. Lang.: Eng. 2826
The character Honeywood in Goldsmith's *The Good Natur'd Man*. England. 1767-1768. Lang.: Eng. 3045
The women in Shakespeare's *Hamlet*. England. 1600-1601. Lang.: Eng. 3046
Insanity in nineteenth- and twentieth-century theatre. Europe. 1880-1970. Lang.: Eng. 3050
Actor and playwright Curt Goetz and Nazi attitudes toward theatre. Germany. 1933-1944. Lang.: Eng. 3139
Analysis of scripts by Eleanora Duse. Italy. 1858-1924. Lang.: Ita. 3228
Reactions to the awarding of the Nobel Prize to satirical playwright Dario Fo. Italy. 1998. Lang.: Eng. 3242
Marta Abba and the characters of Pirandello's plays. Italy. 1925-1936. Lang.: Ita. 3245
Pirandello, Abba, and the Teatro d'Arte. Italy: Rome. 1925-1927. Lang.: Ita. 3248
Essays on actor, director, and playwright Eduardo De Filippo. Italy. 1900-1984. Lang.: Ita. 3254
Actor and playwright N.I. Sobol'ščikov-Samarin. Russia. 1868-1945. Lang.: Rus. 3339
Interview with Staffan Göthe, author, director, and one of the actors of *Ett Lysand elände (A Brilliant Misery)*. Sweden: Stockholm. 1990-1998. Lang.: Swe. 3408
Playwright and actor Joseph Edward. USA: New York, NY. 1997. Lang.: Eng. 3564
The enneagram system applied to Albee's *Who's Afraid of Virginia Woolf?*. USA. 1998. Lang.: Eng. 3665
African- and Irish-Americans in the plays of Eugene O'Neill. USA. 1916-1953. Lang.: Eng. 3687
Playwright Eugene O'Neill's theatrical milieu. USA. 1888-1953. Lang.: Eng. 3706
Interview with actor and screenwriter Gene Wilder. USA. 1998. Lang.: Eng. 3991
Interview with creators of the film *Slam*. USA. 1998. Lang.: Eng. 4001

Reference materials
Yearbook of Slovene theatre. Slovenia. 1996-1997. Lang.: Slo. 708
Russian actors and film stars. Russia. 1998. Lang.: Rus. 4033

Relation to other fields
Plastic-cognitive therapy and the actor. 1998. Lang.: Rus. 713
Humanist ideology and the imaginary stage. Europe. 1549-1629. Lang.: Eng. 731
Developmental differences in adolescents' ability to enact character. USA. 1988. Lang.: Eng. 782
Factors influencing actors' ability to exit a role. USA. 1998. Lang.: Eng. 784
The University of Louisville's African-American Theatre Program. USA: Louisville, KY. 1998. Lang.: Eng. 790
Student responses to the autobiography of actress Charlotte Cibber Charke. USA. 1998. Lang.: Eng. 800
The use of performance skills in the primary school classroom. Canada: Montreal, PQ. 1993-1998. Lang.: Fre. 3739

Research/historiography
Critique of the biases of theatre history toward the exceptional. Poland. 1865-1998. Lang.: Pol. 822

Theory/criticism
Excerpts from diary of theatre critic Andrej Inkret. Slovenia. 1992-1995. Lang.: Slo. 857
American acting theory. USA. 1923-1973. Lang.: Eng. 866
Theatrical dancing and the performance aesthetics of Wilde, Yeats, and Shaw. UK-England. Ireland. 1890-1950. Lang.: Eng. 1012
Representation and delegation in theatre. 1998. Lang.: Eng. 3800
Italian translation of *The Empty Space* by Peter Brook. UK-England. 1998. Lang.: Ita. 3833
Text and performance in drama criticism. USA. 1989. Lang.: Eng. 3849

Training
Director Walter Pfaff on the influence of Jerzy Grotowski. Poland. Germany. 1998. Lang.: Eng. 876
Details of a media acting curriculum. USA. 1994-1998. Lang.: Eng. 4041
Actor training for the character tenor. USA. 1998. Lang.: Eng. 4849

Action

Performance/production
De Zaak's production of *Action* by Sam Shepard. Netherlands: Rotterdam. 1988. Lang.: Dut. 2201

Action-Theater (Munich)

Institutions
Gunnar Martin Aronsson of TeaterX2 recalls Action-Theater. Sweden: Stockholm. Germany: Munich. 1968-1998. Lang.: Swe. 1722

Actor-managers

Performance/production
Rehearsal practices in British professional theatre. England. 1500-1700. Lang.: Eng. 1905

Actor's Company (London)

Performance/production
Correspondence of George Devine and Michel Saint-Denis. UK-England: London. 1939-1945. Lang.: Eng. 2630

Actors Studio (New York, NY)

Institutions
Interview with Robert Lewis on the founding of Actors Studio. USA: New York, NY. 1997. Lang.: Eng. 1766
Arthur Penn and Actors Studio. USA: New York, NY. 1997. Lang.: Eng. 1767

Actors' Equity Association (Canada)

Administration
Negotiations between US and Canadian Equity. USA. Canada. 1998. Lang.: Eng. 54

Actors' Equity Association (USA)

Administration
Changes in income tax regulations and effect on theatre workers. USA. 1998. Lang.: Eng. 40
Carol Waaser, Eastern Region Equity Director. USA: New York, NY. 1998. Lang.: Eng. 47
Equity Council member Tom Joyce. USA: Chicago, IL. 1998. Lang.: Eng. 48
Theatre and Equity business in the Atlanta area. USA: Atlanta, GA. 1998. Lang.: Eng. 49
Equity activity in central Texas. USA: Austin, TX, San Antonio, TX. 1998. Lang.: Eng. 50
Report of Equity Executive Director on finance and organization. USA. 1998. Lang.: Eng. 51
Reports on the 10th Anniversary of Broadway Cares/Equity Fights AIDS. USA: New York, NY. 1998. Lang.: Eng. 52
Equity's support of air-rights proposal of Broadway Initiative. USA. 1998. Lang.: Eng. 53
Negotiations between US and Canadian Equity. USA. Canada. 1998. Lang.: Eng. 54
Equity Executive Director's investigation into union issues. USA. 1998. Lang.: Eng. 55
Jack Goldstein's departure from Equity to head Theatre Development Fund. USA: New York, NY. 1998. Lang.: Eng. 56
Changes to Equity's theatre bonding policy. USA. 1998. Lang.: Eng. 57
Benefits to performers of Taxpayer Relief Act. USA. 1998. Lang.: Eng. 58
Report on Equity's Off-Broadway contract agreement. USA. 1998. Lang.: Eng. 60
Equity's new contract with East West Players. USA: Los Angeles, CA. 1998. Lang.: Eng. 62
Equity agreement on New Orleans working conditions. USA: New Orleans, LA. 1998. Lang.: Eng. 63
Equity's business theatre contract. USA: New York, NY. 1998. Lang.: Eng. 64
Changes in Equity's health insurance coverage. USA: New York, NY. 1998. Lang.: Eng. 65
Equity agreement with Second City. USA: Chicago, IL, Detroit, MI. 1998. Lang.: Eng. 66
Effect on Actors Federal Credit Unions of a recent Supreme Court ruling. USA: New York, NY. 1998. Lang.: Eng. 67
Actors' Fund annual benefit for women's health. USA: New York, NY. 1998. Lang.: Eng. 68
Jekyll and Hyde restaurants sign Equity contract. USA: New York, NY. 1998. Lang.: Eng. 69

Actors' Equity Association (USA) — cont'd

Report on credit union legislation. USA: New York, NY. 1998. Lang.: Eng. 70
Record of Equity Council vote. USA: New York, NY. 1998. Lang.: Eng. 71
Report on Easter Bonnet fundraiser for AIDS. USA: New York, NY. 1998. Lang.: Eng. 72
Interview with actors on Equity. USA: New York, NY. 1998. Lang.: Eng. 75
Report on 'Broadway Bares' benefit for AIDS. USA: New York, NY. 1998. Lang.: Eng. 76
Issues of concern to Equity members in current Broadway shows. USA: New York, NY. 1998. Lang.: Eng. 77
The launch of the Equity website. USA: New York, NY. 1998. Lang.: Eng. 78
Negotiations with Equity dinner theatres. USA: New York, NY. 1998. Lang.: Eng. 79
John Holly, Western Regional Director of Equity. USA: New York, NY. 1998. Lang.: Eng. 80
Annual report of the Equity pension fund. USA: New York, NY. 1998. Lang.: Eng. 81
Profiles of Equity council members. USA: New York, NY. 1998. Lang.: Eng. 82
Effect of recent legislation on the Actors Federal Credit Union. USA: New York, NY. 1998. Lang.: Eng. 83
The work of an Equity Stage Manager. USA: New York, NY. 1998. Lang.: Eng. 84
Equity's Stage Reading Guidelines. USA: New York, NY. 1998. Lang.: Eng. 85
Changes in Equity's bonding policy for regional theatres. USA: New York, NY. 1998. Lang.: Eng. 86
Complaints against an Equity Councillor and the 1998 Council election. USA: New York, NY. 1998. Lang.: Eng. 87
The debate on organizing non-union tours of theatrical production. USA: New York, NY. 1998. Lang.: Eng. 88
City Council's approval of a plan to sell theatres' air rights to developers. USA: New York, NY. 1998. Lang.: Eng. 89
Current news on the theatre and Equity business. USA: New York, NY. 1998. Lang.: Eng. 90
The waiting period before Equity health benefits take effect. USA: New York, NY. 1998. Lang.: Eng. 91
Kathryn Lamkey, Director of Equity's Central Regional Office. USA: Chicago, IL. 1998. Lang.: Eng. 92
Securing sick pay and worker's compensation for an on-the-job injury. USA: New York, NY. 1998. Lang.: Eng. 93
Equity's National Council elections. USA: New York, NY. 1998. Lang.: Eng. 94
The Palm View residence for people with AIDS. USA: Hollywood, CA. 1998. Lang.: Eng. 95
Working conditions and requirements of stage managers. USA: New York, NY. 1998. Lang.: Eng. 96
Summary of Equity's accomplishments in 1998. USA: New York, NY. 1998. Lang.: Eng. 97
Equity's approval of a contract for the Chicago area. USA: Chicago, IL. 1998. Lang.: Eng. 98
Profile of Equity administrator Guy Pace. USA: New York, NY. 1998. Lang.: Eng. 99
Equity's First Vice-President Patrick Quinn. USA: New York, NY. 1998. Lang.: Eng. 100
Shubert Alley's breast cancer screening program. USA: New York, NY. 1998. Lang.: Eng. 101
The merger plan of the Screen Actors Guild and the American Federation of Television and Radio Artists. USA: New York, NY. 1998. Lang.: Eng. 102
Equity's casting website. USA: New York, NY. 1998. Lang.: Eng. 103
Conductor Leonard dePaur, winner of the Paul Robeson Award. USA: New York, NY. 1910-1998. Lang.: Eng. 104
The loss of medical coverage for Equity dependents over nineteen years of age. USA: New York, NY. 1998. Lang.: Eng. 105
Equity debate on member behavior when not under Equity contract. USA: New York, NY. 1998. Lang.: Eng. 106
Actress Helen Hunt's support of Equity's holiday basket program for people with AIDS. USA: New York, NY. 1986-1998. Lang.: Eng. 107
Equity's approval of Cabaret and Small Professional Theatre contracts. USA: New York, NY. 1998. Lang.: Eng. 108
Flea Market fundraiser for AIDS. USA: New York, NY. 1998. Lang.: Eng. 109
Record-breaking Equity membership in LA area. USA: Los Angeles, CA. 1998. Lang.: Eng. 110
Equity seminar on finding an agent. USA: New York, NY. 1998. Lang.: Eng. 111
Report on Equity deputy meetings. USA. 1998. Lang.: Eng. 112
Interview with father and daughter serving on Equity council. USA: New York, NY. 1998. Lang.: Eng. 113
Equity seminar for young performers and their families. USA: New York, NY. 1998. Lang.: Eng. 114
Survey of Equity membership and employment data. USA: New York, NY. 1998. Lang.: Eng. 115
The creation of Actors' Equity in response to abusive working conditions. USA: New York, NY. 1913. Lang.: Eng. 127
The campaign to ban child performers in New York City. USA: New York, NY. 1874-1919. Lang.: Eng. 139
Equity Executive Director Alan Eisenberg's experience with a touring production of *Cats*. USA: New York, NY. 1998. Lang.: Eng. 4318
Performer Rebecca Spencer's experience as an Equity Deputy. USA: New York, NY. 1998. Lang.: Eng. 4320

Institutions
Theatrical activity in Cleveland's Playhouse Square. USA: Cleveland, OH. 1998. Lang.: Eng. 416
The new home of Chicago Shakespeare Theatre, formerly Shakespeare Repertory Theatre. USA: Chicago, IL. 1998. Lang.: Eng. 1775

Performance/production
Recent news on the international theatre scene. 1998. Lang.: Eng. 482
Actress Betty Buckley's performance in AIDS fundraiser. Switzerland: Geneva. 1998. Lang.: Eng. 603
Announcement of Equity's young performers seminar series. USA: New York, NY. 1998. Lang.: Eng. 656
Equity's free seminar series for young performers and their families. USA: New York, NY. 1998. Lang.: Eng. 657
Current news about the theatre and its people. USA: New York, NY. 1998. Lang.: Eng. 658
Short news takes on current theatre events. USA: New York, NY. 1998. Lang.: Eng. 661
Report on speech by actor Eli Wallach to Actors' Equity meeting. USA. 1998. Lang.: Eng. 2717
AIDS-benefit performance of the musical *Sweet Charity*. USA: New York, NY. 1998. Lang.: Eng. 4386

Actors' Fund of America (New York, NY)

Administration
Actors' Fund annual benefit for women's health. USA: New York, NY. 1998. Lang.: Eng. 68
The Palm View residence for people with AIDS. USA: Hollywood, CA. 1998. Lang.: Eng. 95

Actors' Theatre of Louisville (Louisville, KY)

Institutions
Productions of Actors' Theatre Humana Festival. USA: Louisville, KY. 1998. Lang.: Eng. 1779

Performance/production
Reviews of Actors' Theatre productions. USA: Louisville, KY. 1998. Lang.: Eng. 2727

Actors' Workshop (San Francisco, CA)

Performance/production
The multifaceted nature of early nonprofit regional theatre. USA. 1940-1960. Lang.: Eng. 2705

Adagio Hammerklavier

Performance/production
Ballets of Hans van Manen. Netherlands. 1951-1998. Lang.: Eng. 1120

Adam Geist

Institutions
New plays by Dea Loher at Staatsschauspiel Hannover. Germany: Hannover. 1992-1998. Lang.: Ger. 1643

Plays/librettos/scripts
Analysis of plays by Dea Loher, directed by Andreas Kriegenburg. Germany: Hannover. 1998. Lang.: Ger. 3130
The collaboration of playwright Dea Loher and director Andreas Kriegenburg. Germany: Hannover, Munich. 1990-1998. Lang.: Ger. 3151

***Adam Geist* — cont'd**

Marginal notes by Dea Loher on her plays. Germany. 1991-1998. Lang.: Ger. 3162

Interview with playwright Dea Loher. Germany. 1964-1998. Lang.: Ger. 3173

Adam le Bossu

SEE

Adam de la Halle.

Adam quoiś

Plays/librettos/scripts

The Holocaust in environmental theatre of Armand Gatti. France. 1989-1993. Lang.: Eng. 3097

Adam, Adolphe

Performance/production

Premiere of Sylvie Guillem's new choreography for Adolphe Adam's *Giselle.* Finland: Helsinki. 1998. Lang.: Hun. 1068

The Budapest Opera House's new production of *Giselle.* Hungary: Budapest. 1998. Lang.: Hun. 1094

Adame Miroir

Plays/librettos/scripts

Analysis of Jean Genet's dance work *Adame Miroir.* France. 1949. Lang.: Ita. 993

Adamo (Adam)

Performance/production

Analysis of religious theatre of Giambattista Andreini. Italy. 1576-1654. Lang.: Eng. 2190

Adams, John

Performance/production

Collection of newspaper reviews by London theatre critics. UK-England: London. 1998. Lang.: Eng. 2568

Adams, Judith

Performance/production

Collection of newspaper reviews by London theatre critics. UK-England: London. 1998. Lang.: Eng. 2420

Adams, Kevin

Design/technology

Lighting designer Kevin Adams. USA. 1979-1998. Lang.: Eng. 258

Adamson, Eve

Performance/production

Actors and directors on the late plays of Tennessee Williams. USA. 1966-1981. Lang.: Eng. 2675

Reviews of productions of plays by Ibsen. USA: New York, NY. Norway: Oslo. 1998. Lang.: Eng. 2747

Adaptations

Basic theatrical documents

English translation of *Kanadehon Hamlet* by Harue Tsutsumi. Japan. 1997. Lang.: Eng. 1360

English translation of Mejerchol'd's adaptation of *Revizor (The Inspector General)* by Gogol. Russia. USSR. 1838-1926. Lang.: Eng. 1450

Design/technology

Scenery in Orson Welles' film adaptation of Shakespeare's *Macbeth.* USA. 1948. Lang.: Fre. 3920

Performance/production

Dance adaptations of Shakespeare's *Hamlet.* Germany: Bremen, Weimar. 1996-1997. Lang.: Ger. 930

Interview with ballerina Katalin Hágai. Hungary. 1961-1998. Lang.: Hun. 1096

Analysis of the ballet *Berthalda en Hildebrand (Berthalda and Hildebrand).* Netherlands: Amsterdam. 1849. Lang.: Ger. 1122

Stage adaptations of literary classics and the effect on audiences. 1998. Lang.: Rus. 1811

List of French-language productions of Shakespeare. Canada: Montreal, PQ, Quebec, PQ. 1945-1998. Lang.: Fre. 1841

French Canadian translations/adaptations of Shakespeare. Canada: Montreal, PQ. 1988. Lang.: Fre. 1855

Interview with director Dominic Champagne. Canada: Montreal, PQ. 1998. Lang.: Fre. 1860

Robert Gurik's adaptation of Shakespeare's *Hamlet.* Canada: Montreal, PQ, London, ON. 1968. Lang.: Fre. 1866

Irondale Ensemble's production of *Leben des Galilei (The Life of Galileo)* by Bertolt Brecht. Canada: Halifax, NS. 1998. Lang.: Eng. 1869

Pierre Benoît's music for *Don Quichotte* at Théâtre du Nouveau Monde. Canada: Montreal, PQ. 1995-1998. Lang.: Fre. 1870

The adaptation of classic Czech works to the stage. Czech Republic: Prague, Brno. 1990-1998. Lang.: Cze. 1877

Music for London Shakespearean productions. England: London. 1660-1830. Lang.: Eng. 1900

The performances of Lucinda Childs and Michel Piccoli in *La Maladie de la Mort (The Sickness of Death),* directed by Robert Wilson. France: Paris. 1997. Lang.: Eng. 1942

Interview with actress Lucinda Childs. France: Paris. 1976-1997. Lang.: Eng. 1943

German productions of adaptations of *A Clockwork Orange* by Anthony Burgess. Germany: Dresden, Hamburg, Stendal. 1998. Lang.: Ger. 1972

The collaboration of choreographer Lucinda Childs and director Robert Wilson on *La Maladie de la Mort.* Germany. 1992-1997. Lang.: Eng. 2019

Interview with playwright Heiner Müller about his adaptations of Shakespeare. Germany, East. 1965-1990. Lang.: Eng. 2039

Adaptations of Shakespeare in productions of Bertolt Brecht and Heiner Müller. Germany, East. 1945-1990. Lang.: Eng. 2049

Brecht's *Der Kaukasische Kreidkreis (The Caucasian Chalk Circle)* adapted and directed by János Mohácsi. Hungary: Nyíregyháza. 1998. Lang.: Hun. 2127

Iraqi productions of Shakespeare. Iraq. 1880-1988. Lang.: Eng. 2152

Luca Ronconi's stage adaptation of *The Brothers Karamazov.* Italy: Rome. 1997. Lang.: Eng. 2188

Romeo Castellucci's adaptation of the *Oresteia* by Aeschylus. Italy: Cesena. 1997. Lang.: Eng. 2189

Andrej Žitinkin directs *Confessions of Felix Krull, Confidence Man,* adapted from Thomas Mann. Russia: Moscow. 1998. Lang.: Rus. 2335

Athol Fugard and the *Oresteia* of Aeschylus. South Africa, Republic of: Cape Town. 1978. Lang.: Eng. 2354

Theatrical adaptations of children's stories by Astrid Lindgren. Sweden: Stockholm. 1998. Lang.: Eng. 2374

Teater UNO's stage adaptation of *L'Étranger (The Stranger)* by Albert Camus. Sweden: Gothenburg. 1998. Lang.: Swe. 2395

Volker Hesse's production of *Die schwarze Spinne (The Black Spider)* by Urs Widmer. Switzerland: Zurich. 1998. Lang.: Ger. 2402

The influence of collage on director Charles Marowitz. UK-England. USA. 1962-1979. Lang.: Eng. 2624

Twentieth-century productions of Euripidean tragedy. USA. 1915-1969. Lang.: Eng. 2678

Brief productions of Shakespeare, Shaw, and Marlowe at the World's Fair. USA: Chicago, IL. 1934. Lang.: Eng. 2701

Comparison of productions of Ibsen's *Peer Gynt.* USA: Providence, RI, New York, NY, Washington, DC, Nacogdoches, TX. 1998. Lang.: Eng. 2711

Culture Clash and their production of Aristophanes' *Birds.* USA: Berkeley, CA. 1984-1998. Lang.: Eng. 2713

Postmodernism in Jean-Luc Godard's film adaptation of Shakespeare's *King Lear.* France. 1988. Lang.: Eng. 3931

Suzanne Cloutier's role in Shakespeare's *Othello,* directed by Orson Welles. Italy. 1952. Lang.: Fre. 3935

Analysis of casting and acting in Kenneth Branagh's film adaptation of *Much Ado About Nothing.* UK. 1993. Lang.: Fre. 3939

Television adaptations of works by Goethe. Germany. 1965-1997. Lang.: Eng. 4061

Director and martial artist Huy-Phong Doàn's *La Légende du manuel sacré (The Legend of the Sacred Handbook).* Canada: Montreal, PQ. 1992-1998. Lang.: Fre. 4118

A puppet production of Madách's *Az ember tragédiája (The Tragedy of Man).* France: Colmar. 1998. Lang.: Hun. 4893

New England Marionettes' production of Mozart's *Die Zauberflöte.* USA: Boston, MA. 1998. Lang.: Eng. 4900

Plays/librettos/scripts

Analysis of Elfriede Jelinek's adaptation of *Et Dukkehjem (A Doll's House)* by Ibsen. Austria. 1979. Lang.: Eng. 2782

Recent productions directed by Frank Castorf. Austria: Vienna. 1998. Lang.: Ger. 2788

French translations of Shakespeare by Antonine Maillet and Jean-Louis Roux. Canada: Montreal, PQ. 1988-1993. Lang.: Fre. 2793

Michel Tremblay's adaptation of *Mistero Buffo* by Dario Fo. Canada: Montreal, PQ. 1969-1973. Lang.: Fre. 2795

Analysis of *Queen Lear* by Beau Coleman. Canada: Edmonton, AB. 1995-1997. Lang.: Eng. 2800

Adaptations — cont'd

Cervantes' *Don Quixote* and Wadji Mouawad's adaptation, *Don Quichotte.* Canada: Montreal, PQ. 1998. Lang.: Fre. 2803

The character Sancho in Wadji Mouawad's *Don Quichotte (Don Quixote).* Canada: Montreal, PQ. 1998. Lang.: Fre. 2807

Vie et mort du Roi Boiteux (Life and Death of the Lame King), Jean-Pierre Ronfard's adaptation of *Richard III.* Canada. 1981. Lang.: Fre. 2813

The contrast of form and content in Théâtre du Nouveau Monde's *Don Quichotte.* Canada: Montreal, PQ. 1998. Lang.: Fre. 2815

Normand Chaurette's translations of *As You Like It* by Shakespeare. Canada: Montreal, PQ. 1989-1994. Lang.: Fre. 2824

Wonderbolt Circus's *Maid of Avalon*, a loose adaptation of *Der Gute Mensch von Sezuan (The Good Person of Szechwan)* by Brecht.Canada: St. John's, NF. 1950-1998. Lang.: Eng. 2825

Don Quichotte, an adaptation of Cervantes' *Don Quixote* by Wadji Mouawad. Canada: Montreal, PQ. 1998. Lang.: Fre. 2830

Young People's Theatre's adaptation of *Anne of Green Gables.* Canada: Toronto, ON. 1911-1998. Lang.: Eng. 2832

Horace Walpole's *The Dear Witches* and Shakespeare's *Macbeth.* England. 1743. Lang.: Eng. 2857

Analysis of Dryden and Davenant's *Enchanted Island.* England. 1674. Lang.: Eng. 2873

The defense of prostitution in Lillo's *Marina.* England. 1738. Lang.: Eng. 2887

Shakespeare, Branagh, and the concept of the author. England. 1590-1998. Lang.: Eng. 2958

The obedient daughter in adaptations of Shakespeare's plays. England. 1701-1800. Lang.: Eng. 2969

Analysis of *Marina*, George Lillo's adaptation of Shakespeare's *Pericles.* England. 1738. Lang.: Eng. 2971

Don Quixote, Lewis Theobald's *The Double Falsehood* and the lost *Cardenio* of Shakespeare and Fletcher. England. Spain. 1610-1727. Lang.: Eng. 3001

Political context of Charles Johnson's *Love in a Forest*, an adaptation of *As You Like It.* England. 1723. Lang.: Eng. 3013

The character Medea in European drama. Europe. 450 B.C.-1998 A.D. Lang.: Ger. 3063

Brecht's *Leben des Galilei (The Life of Galileo)* as an adaptation of Shakespeare's *Hamlet.* Germany. 1600-1932. Lang.: Eng. 3160

Adaptations of Greek tragedy by contemporary Irish writers. Ireland. UK-Ireland. 1984-1998. Lang.: Eng. 3214

Shakespeare and the feminist theatre of Bryony Lavery and Jane Prendergast. UK-England. 1997. Lang.: Eng. 3439

Popular adaptations of the works of George Bernard Shaw. UK-England. 1890-1990. Lang.: Eng. 3445

Analysis of *In the Native State* and *Indian Ink* by Tom Stoppard. UK-England. 1991-1995. Lang.: Eng. 3459

Rape in Middleton's *Women Beware Women* and its adaptation by Howard Barker. UK-England. 1625-1986. Lang.: Eng. 3468

The adaptation of novels for the stage. UK-England. 1980-1995. Lang.: Eng. 3499

The Break of Day, Timberlake Wertenbaker's adaptation of Čechov's *Three Sisters.* UK-England. Russia. 1901-1995. Lang.: Eng. 3510

Shared Experience's stage adaptations of nineteenth-century novels. USA: New York, NY. UK-England: London. 1998. Lang.: Eng. 3518

Ellen McLaughlin's *Iphigenia and Other Daughters* at CSC Repertory. USA: New York, NY. 1995. Lang.: Eng. 3520

Analysis of the plays of David Mamet. USA. 1970-1993. Lang.: Eng. 3541

Analysis of *The Prodigal* by Jack Richardson. USA. 1960. Lang.: Eng. 3542

The Prodigal, Jack Richardson's adaptation of *The Oresteia.* USA. 1960. Lang.: Dut. 3547

Homeric influences on *The Prodigal* by Jack Richardson. USA. 1960. Lang.: Eng. 3549

Joseph Chaikin's adaptation of *Textes pour rien (Texts for Nothing)* by Samuel Beckett. USA: New York, NY. 1995. Lang.: Eng. 3563

Jean Randich's production of *The Golden Door* by Sylvia Regan, Tenement Museum. USA: New York, NY. 1940-1998. Lang.: Eng. 3606

Reactions to the revised version of *The Diary of Anne Frank.* USA: New York, NY. 1998. Lang.: Eng. 3618

Dramatic adaptations of Henry Wadsworth Longfellow's poem *Evangeline.* USA. Canada. 1860-1976. Lang.: Eng. 3643

Stage adaptations of Mark Twain's *Adventures of Tom Sawyer.* USA. 1884-1983. Lang.: Eng. 3702

Stephen Mulrine's translation and stage adaptation of *Moscow Stations* by Venedikt Erofeev. USSR. UK-England. 1973-1998. Lang.: Eng. 3718

Interview with playwright and scriptwriter Michel Marc Bouchard. Canada: Montreal, PQ. 1987-1998. Lang.: Fre. 3963

Raymond Saint-Jean's film adaptation of *Cabaret neiges noires (Black Snow Cabaret).* Canada. 1997. Lang.: Fre. 3967

Representations of Joan of Arc in film and theatre. Europe. USA. 1900-1996. Lang.: Eng. 3970

Problems of adapting theatre to film. France. 1997. Lang.: Fre. 3971

Ousmane Sembéne's film adaptation of his own novel *Xala.* Senegal. 1973-1974. Lang.: Eng. 3977

Tom Stoppard's film adaptation of his own *Rosencrantz and Guildenstern Are Dead.* UK-England. 1967-1991. Lang.: Eng. 3980

Shakespeare's *The Tempest* on film. UK-England. USA. 1905-1991. Lang.: Eng. 3981

The film adaptation by Harold Pinter and Karel Reisz of *The French Lieutenant's Woman* by John Fowles. UK-England. USA. 1982. Lang.: Eng. 3982

Harold Pinter's screenplay adaptation of *The Dreaming Child* by Isak Dinesen. UK-England. 1961-1997. Lang.: Eng. 3984

Richard Attenborough's film adaptation of *Shadowlands* by William Nicholson. UK-England. 1993. Lang.: Eng. 3985

Film adaptations of Shakespeare's plays. UK-England. 1900-1998. Lang.: Ita. 3986

Analysis of Peter Greenaway's film *Prospero's Books.* UK-England. 1991. Lang.: Fre. 3990

Interview with screenwriter Scott Frank. USA. 1998. Lang.: Eng. 3995

The Bodyguard, Sam Shepard's screen adaptation of *The Changeling* by Middleton and Rowley. USA. 1970-1995. Lang.: Eng. 4007

Film adaptations of Shakespeare's *Richard III* by Richard Loncraine and Al Pacino. USA. UK-England. 1995-1996. Lang.: Fre. 4012

Roman Polanski's film adaptation of Shakespeare's *Macbeth.* USA. 1971. Lang.: Fre. 4014

Baz Luhrmann's film adaptation of Shakespeare's *Romeo and Juliet.* USA. 1996. Lang.: Fre. 4016

Film interpretations of Ophelia in Shakespeare's *Hamlet.* USA. UK-England. USSR. 1947-1990. Lang.: Eng. 4024

John Stahl's film adaptation of *Imitation of Life* by Fannie Hurst. USA: Hollywood, CA. 1934. Lang.: Eng. 4029

Analysis of Douglas Heil's screenplay *The First Wife.* USA. 1998. Lang.: Eng. 4030

Analysis of Louis Malle's film *Vanya on 42nd Street.* USA. 1994. Lang.: Fre. 4031

Francis Leclerc's video adaptation of *Les Sept Branches de la Rivière Ota (The Seven Streams of the River Ota)* by Robert Lepage. Canada. 1998. Lang.: Fre. 4074

Samuel Beckett's short story *Bing* as adapted by Roger Reynolds and Jean-Yves Bosseur. USA. 1986. Lang.: Eng. 4308

Arthur Kopit's *Nine*, a musical adaptation of Fellini's *8 1/2.* USA. 1963-1982. Lang.: Eng. 4401

Heinz Holliger's operatic adaptation of Samuel Beckett's *What Where.* Europe. 1992. Lang.: Eng. 4768

Marcel Mihalovici's operatic adaptation of *Krapp's Last Tape* by Samuel Beckett. Europe. 1965. Lang.: Eng. 4769

Operatic adaptations of Beckett's plays by Heinz Holliger. Europe. 1976-1988. Lang.: Eng. 4776

Composer Wolfgang Fortner's adaptation of *That Time* by Samuel Beckett. Europe. 1974-1977. Lang.: Eng. 4777

Racine's *Phèdre* as a source for *Hippolyte et Aricie* by Rameau and Pelligrin. France. 1660-1733. Lang.: Eng. 4788

Wedekind's Lulu plays and their adaptation by Berg. Germany. Austria. 1895-1935. Lang.: Fre. 4798

Operas of Dargomyžskij and Rimskij-Korsakov on texts of Puškin. Russia. 1799-1869. Lang.: Rus. 4815

Derek Jarman's adaptation of works by Benjamin Britten and Wilfred Owen. UK-England. 1968-1988. Lang.: Eng. 4822

Adaptations — cont'd

Analysis of Benjamin Britten's opera *Death in Venice*. UK-England. 1912-1992. Lang.: Eng. 4823
Marvin David Levy's operatic adaptation of *Mourning Becomes Electra* by Eugene O'Neill. USA. 1931-1998. Lang.: Eng. 4827
Puppet adaptations of the story of Faust. 1578-1945. Lang.: Hun. 4911
Response to criticism of Théâtre du Sous-Marin Jaune's adaptation of Voltaire's *Candide*. Canada: Quebec, PQ. 1997. Lang.: Fre. 4912
Relation to other fields
The influence of Cervantes' *Don Quixote* on contemporary Quebec artists. Canada. 1967-1998. Lang.: Fre. 3737
Theory/criticism
The urge to make Shakespeare contemporary. USA. 1990-1998. Lang.: Eng. 3844

Adelphi Theatre (London)
Design/technology
Sound design for the London production of *Chicago*. UK-England: London. 1998. Lang.: Eng. 4326

Administration
SEE ALSO
Classed Entries.
Institutions
The directorship of Ferdinand Rieser at Zürcher Schauspielhaus. Switzerland: Zurich. 1926-1938. Lang.: Ger. 387
Profile of TAXI Children's Theatre. USA: Louisville, KY. 1992-1998. Lang.: Eng. 390
Graphic design and the theatrical evolution of Arena Stage. USA: Washington, DC. 1950-1987. Lang.: Eng. 414
Systems analysis of the Southwest Theatre Association. USA. 1988. Lang.: Eng. 418
The relationship between theatrical artists and theatrical institutions. USA: Tarrytown, NY. 1998. Lang.: Eng. 421
The Shuberts vs. the Syndicate. USA: New York, NY. 1976-1998. Lang.: Eng. 427
The present state of the Royal Ballet under Michael Kaiser. UK-England: London. 1998. Lang.: Hun. 1054
The Mummers' Troupe and the Canada Council. Canada: St. John's, NF. 1972-1982. Lang.: Eng. 1581
The fate of the Berliner Ensemble after the resignation of artistic director Manfred Wekwerth. Germany: Berlin. 1991-1998. Lang.:Ger. 1625
The future of Schaubühne after the resignation of artistic director Andrea Breth. Germany: Berlin. 1997. Lang.: Ger. 1633
Profile of Theater in der Fabrik. Germany: Dresden. 1993-1998. Lang.: Ger. 1644
Problems of management and repertory at Berliner Ensemble. Germany: Berlin. 1992-1998. Lang.: Ger. 1656
Profile of Watermill Theatre. UK-England: Newbury. 1998. Lang.: Eng. 1744
Interview with singer Carla Henius, manager of musik-theater-werkstatt festival. Germany: Wiesbaden. 1986-1998. Lang.: Ger. 4347
Problems of administration at Norrlandsoperan. Sweden: Umeå. 1998. Lang.: Swe. 4473
Effects of a TV documentary on the Royal Opera House. UK-England: London. 1993-1998. Lang.: Eng. 4474
Performance spaces
The architectural and administrative history of Redoutentheater. Austria: Vienna. 1918-1992. Lang.: Ger. 433
Performance/production
Actor Helmuth Lohner's stint as administrative director of Theater in der Josefstadt. Austria: Vienna. 1960-1998. Lang.: Ger. 1819
The career of director Claus Peymann. Germany. 1960-1984. Lang.: Eng. 2014
Relation to other fields
The movement of performing artists between economic sectors. USA. 1998. Lang.: Eng. 793

Adshead, Kay
Performance/production
Collection of newspaper reviews by London theatre critics. UK-England: London. 1998. Lang.: Eng. 2427
Collection of newspaper reviews by London theatre critics. UK-England: London. 1998. Lang.: Eng. 2483

Adventures in a Yorkshire Landscape
Performance/production
Collection of newspaper reviews by London theatre critics. UK-England: London. 1998. Lang.: Eng. 2585

Adventures of Robyn Hood, The
Performance/production
Collection of newspaper reviews by London theatre critics. UK-England: London. 1998. Lang.: Eng. 2555

Adventures of Tom Sawyer, The
Plays/librettos/scripts
Stage adaptations of Mark Twain's *Adventures of Tom Sawyer*. USA. 1884-1983. Lang.: Eng. 3702

Advertising
Administration
The role of government in audience and marketing development for arts organizations. 1996. Lang.: Eng. 1
Marketing, advertising, and sponsorship of German theatre. Germany. 1998. Lang.: Ger. 7
Cooperation of theatres and tourist organizations. Germany. 1993-1998. Lang.: Ger. 10
Changes in arts marketing strategies. USA. 1977-1997. Lang.: Eng. 126
Oscar Micheaux's use of an interracial marriage case as a publicity tool for his films. USA. 1924. Lang.: Eng. 3874
Various conditions affecting production, pricing, marketing and communication in German theatre. Germany. 1986-1998. Lang.: Ger. 4316
Institutions
Marketing techniques of Canadian Opera Company. Canada: Toronto, ON. 1996-1998. Lang.: Eng. 4447

Adygejskij Gosudarstvénnyj Dramatičeskij Teat'r (Majkop)
Performance/production
Actors of the Adygeian Drama Theatre. Russia: Majkop. 1998. Lang.: Rus. 2239

Aeolus Appeased
Design/technology
Scenographic concept for the *dramma per musica*, *Aeolus Appeased*. USA. 1988. Lang.: Eng. 4442

Aerialists
Institutions
Report on festival of physical theatre. Germany: Munich. 1997. Lang.: Eng. 1664
Performance/production
Changes in the nature of circus performance. Finland. 1980-1998. Lang.: Fin. 4181
Physical risk and its aesthetics in aerialist performance. USA. 1985-1997. Lang.: Eng. 4185

Aerowaves (London)
Performance/production
Seminar on auditions for choreographers for Resolution dance festival. UK-England: London. Belgium: Brussels. 1998. Lang.: Swe. 1314

Aeschylus
Performance/production
Romeo Castellucci's adaptation of the *Oresteia* by Aeschylus. Italy: Cesena. 1997. Lang.: Eng. 2189
Athol Fugard and the *Oresteia* of Aeschylus. South Africa, Republic of: Cape Town. 1978. Lang.: Eng. 2354
Collection of newspaper reviews by London theatre critics. UK-England: London. 1998. Lang.: Eng. 2520
Collection of newspaper reviews by London theatre critics. UK-England: London. 1998. Lang.: Eng. 2545
Plays/librettos/scripts
The use of collage in contemporary productions involving Greek myths. Canada: Montreal, PQ. 1998. Lang.: Fre. 2814
Electra and Orestes in plays of Aeschylus, Euripides, and Sophocles. Greece. 438-411 B.C. Lang.: Eng. 3184
Civic discourse and civil discord in Greek tragedy. Greece. 475-400 B.C. Lang.: Eng. 3185
Adaptations of Greek tragedy by contemporary Irish writers. Ireland. UK-Ireland. 1984-1998. Lang.: Eng. 3214
Ellen McLaughlin's *Iphigenia and Other Daughters* at CSC Repertory. USA: New York, NY. 1995. Lang.: Eng. 3520
Analysis of *The Prodigal* by Jack Richardson. USA. 1960. Lang.: Eng. 3542
The Prodigal, Jack Richardson's adaptation of *The Oresteia*. USA. 1960. Lang.: Dut. 3547
Homeric influences on *The Prodigal* by Jack Richardson. USA. 1960. Lang.: Eng. 3549

Aesthetics
Audience
The aesthetics of audience-performer interaction in the theatrical event. USA. 1970-1981. Lang.: Eng. 160

Aesthetics — cont'd

Design/technology
An ontological approach to the aesthetics of scenography. USA. 1987. Lang.: Eng. 298
Performance/production
Characteristics and development of ritual theatre. Slovenia. 1960-1998. Lang.: Slo. 592
Director Jacques Copeau and his theatrical aesthetic. France. 1913-1920. Lang.: Eng. 1941
Interview with director Stefan Pucher. Germany. 1998. Lang.: Ger. 1999
Mejerchol'd's relationship with Lunačarskij. USSR. 1890-1931. Lang.: Eng. 2768
Plays/librettos/scripts
Aesthetic peculiarities of *Baal* by Bertolt Brecht. Germany. 1918-1922. Lang.: Hun. 3146
Relation to other fields
Symposium on fashion and film. USA: New York, NY. 1997. Lang.: Eng. 4037
Theory/criticism
Children's theatre and contemporary aesthetics. Canada: Montreal, PQ. 1998. Lang.: Fre. 833
Round-table discussion on theatre and impurity. Canada: Quebec, PQ. 1998. Lang.: Fre. 835
Society's fundamental need for theatre. Finland. 1998. Lang.: Fin. 840
Hungarian translation of Volker Klotz on theatre aesthetics. Germany. 1995. Lang.: Hun. 842
Theatre and 'a theory of looking'. North America. 1998. Lang.: Eng. 851
Roman Ingarden, phenomenology, and theatre. Poland. 1998. Lang.: Pol. 855
Essay on theatre and reception theory. Poland. 1998. Lang.: Pol. 856
Essay on dance as an art form. 1997. Lang.: Eng. 1005
The influence of Symbolism on European dance. Europe. 1895-1939. Lang.: Eng. 1007
Analysis of choreography by Merce Cunningham. USA. 1998. Lang.: Eng. 1340
Director Esa Kirkkopelto on theatre as great art. Finland. 1998. Lang.: Fin. 3815
The persistent influence of generations of theory on French theatre. France. 1960-1998. Lang.: Ger. 3817
Artaud's theatre of cruelty and contemporary experimental theatre. France. 1945-1998. Lang.: Ger. 3818
The work of theatre critic Giuseppe Bartolucci. Italy. 1965-1980. Lang.: Ita. 3823
Critique of the modernist tradition of defining each medium in its own terms. Europe. 1963-1997. Lang.: Eng. 3861
The influence of Antonin Artaud on director Paul Pörtner. France. 1920-1973. Lang.: Ger. 3870
Performance art and the 'poetics of space'. USA. Poland. 1952-1984. Lang.: Eng. 4270
The music-theatre concept of Christoph Marthaler. Germany: Berlin. 1993-1998. Lang.: Ger. 4310
Training
Mejerchol'd, actor training, and Trotsky. USSR. 1922-1929. Lang.: Eng. 3852

Afera (Affair, The)
Plays/librettos/scripts
Analysis of plays by Primož Kozak. Slovenia. 1959-1969. Lang.: Slo. 3350

Affabulazione (Fables)
Plays/librettos/scripts
Theory and practice in the work of director Pier Paolo Pasolini. Italy. 1960-1970. Lang.: Eng. 3264

Affaire de la rue de Lourcine, L' (Rue de Lourcine Affair, The)
Institutions
Productions of Bochumer Schauspielhaus. Germany: Bochum. 1998. Lang.: Ger. 1655

Àfrica 30
Basic theatrical documents
Text of *Àfrica 30* by Mercè Sarrias Fornés. Spain-Catalonia. 1997. Lang.: Cat. 1467

African Company Presents Richard III, The
Performance/production
Collection of newspaper reviews by London theatre critics. UK-England: London. 1998. Lang.: Eng. 2487

African-American theatre
SEE ALSO
Black theatre.
Administration
Preparations for the centennial of actor and singer Paul Robeson. USA. 1898-1998. Lang.: Eng. 61
Christine Melton on the production of her play *Still Life Goes On*. USA: New York, NY. 1997. Lang.: Eng. 1398
Interview with Carrie Jackson, executive director of AUDELCO. USA: New York, NY. 1998. Lang.: Eng. 1399
Basic theatrical documents
Texts of plays by Eddie Paul Bradley, Jr. USA. 1998. Lang.: Eng. 1482
Text of *Insurrection: Holding History* by Robert O'Hara. USA. 1998. Lang.: Eng. 1500
Institutions
Report on the National Black Theatre Festival. USA: Winston-Salem, NC. 1997. Lang.: Eng. 1763
Report on the second National Black Theatre Summit. USA: Atlanta, GA. 1998. Lang.: Eng. 1773
Report on National Black Theatre Summit. USA: Dartmouth, NH. 1998. Lang.: Eng. 1782
Playwright Garland Lee on the National Black Theatre Summit. USA: Dartmouth, NH. 1998. Lang.: Eng. 1786
Report on the National Black Theatre Festival. USA: Winston-Salem, NC. 1997. Lang.: Eng. 1787
Performance/production
The life and career of singer Paul Robeson. USA. 1998. Lang.: Eng. 631
Conference on African-American theatre convened by playwright August Wilson. USA: Hanover, NH. 1998. Lang.: Eng. 659
Photo essay on celebration of Paul Robeson. USA: New York, NY. 1998. Lang.: Eng. 660
African-American dance. USA. 1960-1997. Lang.: Eng. 986
Dancer Albert Evans of New York City Ballet. USA: New York, NY. 1987-1998. Lang.: Eng. 1181
Actor Arthur French. USA: New York, NY. 1962-1998. Lang.: Eng. 2671
Alternative theatre and the Black audience. USA. 1998. Lang.: Eng. 2682
Obituary for actor Leverne Summers. USA: New York, NY. 1998. Lang.: Eng. 2748
Obituary for actress Theresa Merritt. USA: New York, NY. 1998. Lang.: Eng. 2749
Profile of performer and activist Paul Robeson. USA. 1898-1959. Lang.: Eng. 2750
The importance of Black performers in American musical films. USA. 1900-1957. Lang.: Swe. 3960
The Hyers sisters and Black musical comedy. USA. 1870-1902. Lang.: Eng. 4384
Plays/librettos/scripts
Afrocentricity in plays of Charles Fuller, Amiri Baraka, and Larry Neal. USA. 1960-1998. Lang.: Eng. 3519
Account of National Black Theatre Summit. USA: Hanover, NH. 1998. Lang.: Eng. 3523
Analysis of *The Purple Flower* by Marita Bonner. USA. 1927. Lang.: Eng. 3527
Analysis of *The Piano Lesson* by August Wilson. USA. 1990. Lang.: Eng. 3536
Playwright and actor Joseph Edward. USA: New York, NY. 1997. Lang.: Eng. 3564
Analysis of Countée Cullen's translation of Euripides' *Medea*. USA. 1936. Lang.: Eng. 3567
Student casebook on *A Raisin in the Sun* by Lorraine Hansberry. USA. 1957-1997. Lang.: Eng. 3577
Black self-determination in the plays of Alice Childress. USA. 1949-1969. Lang.: Eng. 3579
Analysis of *Les Blancs* by Lorraine Hansberry. USA. 1970. Lang.: Eng. 3581
Poet Langston Hughes and the theatre. USA: New York, NY. 1926-1967. Lang.: Eng. 3585
Analysis of *Imperceptible Mutabilities in the Third Kingdom* by Suzan-Lori Parks. USA. 1995. Lang.: Eng. 3592
Lynching in plays of Angelina Weld Grimké and Lorraine Hansberry. USA. 1916-1958. Lang.: Eng. 3602

African-American theatre — cont'd

Analysis of *Jitney* by August Wilson. USA. 1979. Lang.: Eng. 3611
Playwright Lorraine Hansberry. USA. 1950-1965. Lang.: Eng. 3615
Interview with playwright Suzan-Lori Parks. USA. 1996. Lang.: Eng. 3621
Blues music in the writings of Zora Neale Hurston. USA. 1920-1940. Lang.: Eng. 3625
Black dance in plays of Zora Neale Hurston. USA. 1925-1930. Lang.: Eng. 3633
Lorraine Hansberry and Black Americans in theatre. USA. 1769-1986. Lang.: Eng. 3640
Analysis of *Diva Studies* by Elizabeth Alexander. USA. 1996. Lang.: Eng. 3653
Interview with playwright Elizabeth Alexander. USA. 1996. Lang.: Eng. 3662
Novelist and playwright Thulani Davis. USA. 1998. Lang.: Eng. 3689
Analysis of *The Colored Museum* by George C. Wolfe. USA. 1988. Lang.: Eng. 3690
The dramaturgical evolution of playwright Adrienne Kennedy. USA. 1964-1990. Lang.: Eng. 3691
Analysis of *Fences* by August Wilson. USA. 1987. Lang.: Eng. 3693
Interview with playwright Kia Corthon. USA. 1998. Lang.: Eng. 3696
The critical reception of Zora Neale Hurston's autobiography. USA. 1942. Lang.: Eng. 3704
Analysis of *Mulatto* by Langston Hughes. USA. 1935. Lang.: Eng. 3709
Playwrights Adrienne Kennedy, Ntozake Shange, and Suzan-Lori Parks. USA. 1970-1998. Lang.: Eng. 3714

Relation to other fields
Teaching African-American performance and the meaning of race. USA. 1996-1997. Lang.: Eng. 783
The University of Louisville's African-American Theatre Program. USA: Louisville, KY. 1998. Lang.: Eng. 790
Detroit's Black theatres and training opportunities for high school students. USA: Detroit, MI. 1984-1987. Lang.: Eng. 813
Analysis of the jazz funeral. USA: New Orleans, LA. 1900-1990. Lang.: Eng. 4228

After Darwin
Performance/production
Collection of newspaper reviews by London theatre critics. UK-England: London. 1998. Lang.: Eng. 2470

After the Orgy
Performance/production
Collection of newspaper reviews by London theatre critics. UK-England: London. 1998. Lang.: Eng. 2448

Aftershocks
Plays/librettos/scripts
The community play *Aftershocks.* Australia: Newcastle, NSW. 1990-1998. Lang.: Eng. 2774

Agatha
Plays/librettos/scripts
Space and pre-verbal memory in later works of Marguerite Duras. France. 1970-1982. Lang.: Eng. 3106

Âge d'or, L' (Golden Age, The)
Institutions
Theatrical space in productions of Ariane Mnouchkine. France: Paris. 1970-1995. Lang.: Eng. 1607

Age of Anxiety, The
Performance/production
Synopses of lost choreographies by Jerome Robbins. USA: New York, NY. 1949-1952. Lang.: Eng. 1166

Agents
Administration
The lesbian relationship of agent Elisabeth Marbury and designer Elsie de Wolfe. USA. 1886-1933. Lang.: Eng. 44
Equity seminar on finding an agent. USA: New York, NY. 1998. Lang.: Eng. 111
Theatrical agent Margaret Ramsey. UK-England: London. 1908-1991. Lang.: Ger. 1394

Institutions
The Shuberts vs. the Syndicate. USA: New York, NY. 1976-1998. Lang.: Eng. 427
Theatre schools: production of showcases for graduating students. UK-England: London. 1998. Lang.: Eng. 1746

Ágh, Márton
Design/technology
Survey of an exhibition of Hungarian scene design. Hungary: Budapest. 1998. Lang.: Hun. 195
Catalogue of an exhibition devoted to Hungarian theatre and film. Hungary: Budapest. 1998. Lang.: Hun. 197

Agon
Performance/production
New York performances of the San Francisco Ballet. USA: New York, NY. 1998. Lang.: Eng. 1170

Agrippina
Plays/librettos/scripts
Representation of the virginal body on the German stage. Germany. 1600-1800. Lang.: Ger. 3171

Ah, Wilderness!
Performance/production
Julyana Soelistyo and Sam Trammel, winners of the Derwent Award. USA: New York, NY. 1998. Lang.: Eng. 2719

Ahačič, Draga
Performance/production
Theatre as a phenomenon of language. Slovenia. 1997. Lang.: Slo. 590

Ahl Al-kahf (People of the Cave, The)
Basic theatrical documents
English translations of plays by Tawfiq Al-Hakim. Egypt. 1930-1945. Lang.: Eng. 1416

Ahlfors, Bengt
Performance/production
Swedish and bilingual Finnish-Swedish theatre. Finland: Turku, Vaasa. 1998. Lang.: Eng, Fre. 1913

Plays/librettos/scripts
Recent drama and revue in Swedish. Finland. 1998. Lang.: Eng, Fre. 3069

Ahlstedt, Börje
Performance/production
Interviews with actors Börje Ahlstedt and Krister Henriksson. Sweden: Stockholm. 1962-1998. Lang.: Swe. 2383

Ähnlichen, Die (Lookalikes)
Plays/librettos/scripts
New directions in the plays of Botho Strauss. Europe. 1971-1998. Lang.: Ger. 3067

Ahrens, Lynn
Design/technology
Lighting and projections for the musical *Ragtime.* USA: New York, NY. 1998. Lang.: Eng. 4328
Technical designs for *Ragtime* at the Ford Center. USA: New York, NY. 1998. Lang.: Eng. 4338
Sound design for the Broadway premiere of the musical *Ragtime.* USA: New York, NY. 1998. Lang.: Eng. 4341

Aichinger, Ilsa
Performance/production
Collection of newspaper reviews by London theatre critics. UK-England: London. 1998. Lang.: Eng. 2564

Aida
SEE ALSO
Elaborate Lives: The Legend of Aida.

Performance/production
The premiere of the musical *Elaborate Lives: The Legend of Aida.* USA: Atlanta, GA. 1998. Lang.: Eng. 4385

Plays/librettos/scripts
Gender in Bellini's *Norma* and Verdi's *Aida.* Italy. 1831-1871. Lang.: Eng. 4813

AIDS
Administration
Reports on the 10th Anniversary of Broadway Cares/Equity Fights AIDS. USA: New York, NY. 1998. Lang.: Eng. 52
Report on Easter Bonnet fundraiser for AIDS. USA: New York, NY. 1998. Lang.: Eng. 72
Report on 'Broadway Bares' benefit for AIDS. USA: New York, NY. 1998. Lang.: Eng. 76
The Palm View residence for people with AIDS. USA: Hollywood, CA. 1998. Lang.: Eng. 95
Actress Helen Hunt's support of Equity's holiday basket program for people with AIDS. USA: New York, NY. 1986-1998. Lang.: Eng. 107
Flea Market fundraiser for AIDS. USA: New York, NY. 1998. Lang.: Eng. 109

Performance/production
Actress Betty Buckley's performance in AIDS fundraiser. Switzerland: Geneva. 1998. Lang.: Eng. 603
Interview with choreographer Bill T. Jones. USA. 1990-1998. Lang.: Eng. 1316
Defense of Bill T. Jones' dance piece *Still/Here.* USA. 1994. Lang.: Eng. 1318

AIDS — cont'd

AIDS-benefit performance of the musical *Sweet Charity*. USA: New York, NY. 1998. Lang.: Eng. 4386
Plays/librettos/scripts
American gay drama and the impact of AIDS. USA. 1960-1987. Lang.: Eng. 3670
AIDS and the work of performance artist Franko B. UK-England. 1996-1998. Lang.: Eng. 4261
The AIDS epidemic in contemporary opera. Europe. North America. 1985-1995. Lang.: Eng. 4771
Analysis of *Plague Mass* by Diamanda Galas. USA. 1991. Lang.: Eng. 4828

Ailey, Alvin
Institutions
The fortieth anniversary of Alvin Ailey American Dance Company. USA: New York, NY. 1958-1998. Lang.: Eng. 1255
Relation to other fields
American modern dance and gay culture. USA. 1933-1998. Lang.: Eng. 1337

Ajtekova, M.
Performance/production
Actors of the Adygeian Drama Theatre. Russia: Majkop. 1998. Lang.: Rus. 2239

Akademia Ruchu (Warsaw)
Performance/production
Productions of the festival of experimental theatre. Poland: Cracow. 1998. Lang.: Ger. 2225

Akademičeskij Dramatičeskij Teat'r im. N.G. Černyševskogo (Saratov)
Performance/production
Actor G.I Sal'nikov. Russia: Saratov. 1998. Lang.: Rus. 2315

Akademičeskij Teat'r Dramy im. A.S. Puškina (St. Petersburg)
Performance/production
Actor Nikolaj Simonov. Russia: St. Petersburg. 1998. Lang.: Rus. 2289

Akademičeskij Teat'r Junogo Zritelja im. Ju. P. Kiseleva (Saratov)
Institutions
Profile of the Kiselev Youth Theatre. Russia: Saratov. 1998. Lang.: Rus. 1711

Akademičeskij Teat'r Opery i Baleta im. S.M. Kirova (St. Petersburg)
Design/technology
Scene designs for *Ruslan i Ljudmila* by V. Gartman. Russia: St. Petersburg. 1876. Lang.: Rus. 4438
Institutions
Preview of the Kirov Opera's visit to the Metropolitan Opera. Russia: St. Petersburg. 1997. Lang.: Eng. 4470
The world tour of the Kirov Opera, headed by Valerij Gergiev. Russia: St. Petersburg. 1998. Lang.: Eng. 4471
Performance/production
Guest performances of dancers and ballet masters of the Kirov and Bolšoj ballets. Hungary. 1975-1978. Lang.: Hun. 1086
Choreographer Boris Ejfman. Russia: St. Petersburg. 1972-1998. Lang.: Eng. 1126
Boris Asafjev's ballet *Bachčisarajskij fontan* directed by R. Zacharov at the Mariinskij. Russia: St. Petersburg. 1934. Lang.: Rus. 1134
I. Igin's *Czars*, a biography of dancers Konstantin Sergejév and Natalija Dudinskaja. Russia: Leningrad. 1940. Lang.: Rus. 1138
Ballerina Alla Osipenko. Russia. 1932-1998. Lang.: Eng. 1139
Ballerina Uljana Lopatkina. Russia: St. Petersburg. 1998. Lang.: Rus. 1140
Ballet dancer Uljana Lopatkina. Russia: St. Petersburg. Lang.: Rus. 1146
Interview with composer Paul Schmidt. USA: New Haven, CT. 1998. Lang.: Eng. 2660
Yale Drama Department's reconstruction of Gogol's *Revizor (The Inspector General)* as staged by Mejerchol'd. USA: New Haven, CT. 1997. Lang.: Eng. 2668
The tour of the Mariinskij Theatre. Russia: Moscow. 1997. Lang.: Rus. 4690
Guest performances of the Kirov Opera at the Metropolitan.. USA: New York, NY. 1998. Lang.: Eng. 4731

Akademietheater (Vienna)
Performance/production
Premieres of new plays. Austria: Vienna. 1998. Lang.: Ger. 1820
Actors Gert Voss and Ignaz Kirchner on George Tabori's production of *Fin de partie (Endgame)*. Austria: Vienna. 1998. Lang.: Ger. 1821
Gert Voss and Ignaz Kirchner, *Theater Heute*'s actors of the year. Austria: Vienna. 1988-1998. Lang.: Ger. 1823

Akalaitis, JoAnne
Performance/production
Statements of women directors on their work. USA. 1996. Lang.: Eng. 2674
Directorial style of JoAnne Akalaitis. USA. 1982-1998. Lang.: Eng. 2737

Akarova (Acarin, Marguerite)
Performance spaces
Dancers and performance space. Europe. 1895-1937. Lang.: Ger. 909

Åkerlund, Susanna
Performance/production
Interview with *butō* dancer Susanna Åkerlund. Sweden. Japan. 1990-1998. Lang.: Swe. 1300

Åkesson, Birgit
Performance/production
Interview with choreographer Birgit Åkesson. Sweden. Africa. Asia. 1908. Lang.: Swe. 963
Dancer Birgit Åkesson. Sweden: Stockholm. 1908-1998. Lang.: Ger. 1303

Aktionismus (Actionism)
Performance/production
Performance artist Egon Schrick. Germany. 1976-1987. Lang.: Eng. 4241

Al Capone
Plays/librettos/scripts
Opera in American gangster films. USA. 1932-1990. Lang.: Eng. 4023

Al gran sole carico d'amore
Performance/production
Review of opera productions. Germany: Stuttgart, Leipzig. 1998. Lang.: Ger. 4584

Al-Bayaty, Farah
Performance/production
Interview with dancer Farah Al-Bayaty. Sweden: Gothenburg. Iraq. 1983-1998. Lang.: Swe. 967

Al-Hakim, Tawfiq
Basic theatrical documents
English translations of plays by Tawfiq Al-Hakim. Egypt. 1930-1945. Lang.: Eng. 1416

Al-Mawik Huwa Al-Mawik (King Is the King, The)
Plays/librettos/scripts
Analysis of *Al-Mawik Huwa Al-Mawik (The King Is the King)* by Saadallah Wannus. Syria. 1977. Lang.: Eng. 3418

Alabama Shakespeare Festival (Montgomery, AL)
Institutions
Profile of Alabama Shakespeare Festival. USA: Montgomery, AL. 1972-1998. Lang.: Eng. 1784

Alain und Elise
Plays/librettos/scripts
Mythological figures in late plays of Georg Kaiser. Germany. 1914-1940. Lang.: Ger. 3143

Alarms and Excursions
Performance/production
Collection of newspaper reviews by London theatre critics. UK-England: London. 1998. Lang.: Eng. 2505

Albany Theatre (London)
Performance/production
Collection of newspaper reviews by London theatre critics. UK-England: London. 1998. Lang.: Eng. 2528
Collection of newspaper reviews by London theatre critics. UK-England: London. 1998. Lang.: Eng. 2557
Collection of newspaper reviews by London theatre critics. UK-England: London. 1998. Lang.: Eng. 2580

Albee, Edward
Institutions
Profile of Württembergische Landesbühne. Germany: Esslingen. 1996-1997. Lang.: Ger. 1639
Performance/production
Collection of newspaper reviews by London theatre critics. UK-England: London. 1998. Lang.: Eng. 2491
Plays/librettos/scripts
Adoption narratives in novels, plays, and films. USA. 1960-1997. Lang.: Eng. 691
Aggressive language in modern drama. Europe. USA. 1960-1985. Lang.: Eng. 3055
A method of analysis for the drama. USA. 1920-1975. Lang.: Eng. 3537
The unseen character in plays of O'Neill, Albee, and Tennessee Williams. USA. 1915-1995. Lang.: Eng. 3538

Albee, Edward — cont'd
Eugene O'Neill and the creation of autobiographical drama. USA. 1940-1995. Lang.: Eng. 3561
History of the Playwrights Unit. USA. 1963-1971. Lang.: Eng. 3570
Recent productions of plays by Edward Albee. USA: New York, NY, Hartford, CT. 1959-1998. Lang.: Eng. 3578
Influence of the novelistic monologues of Eugene O'Neill. USA. 1911-1998. Lang.: Eng. 3641
The enneagram system applied to Albee's *Who's Afraid of Virginia Woolf?*. USA. 1998. Lang.: Eng. 3665

Alberola, Carles
Basic theatrical documents
Text of *Mandíbula afilada (Sharp Chin)* by Carles Alberola. Spain. 1997. Lang.: Eng. 1463

Albers, Kenneth
Design/technology
Costume designs for Oregon Shakespeare Festival productions. USA: Ashland, OR. 1998. Lang.: Eng. 1543

Albert, Lyle Victor
Performance/production
Productions of children's theatre festival. Canada: Montreal, PQ. 1998. Lang.: Fre. 503

Alberti, Leone Battista
Relation to other fields
Renaissance architect Leone Battista Alberti and theatre design. Italy. 1440-1470. Lang.: Eng. 751

Alberti, Rafael
Plays/librettos/scripts
Antifascist puppet plays by Rafael Alberti. Spain. 1936-1939. Lang.: Eng. 4922

Albery Theatre (London)
Performance/production
Collection of newspaper reviews by London theatre critics. UK-England: London. 1998. Lang.: Eng. 2494
Collection of newspaper reviews by London theatre critics. UK-England: London. 1998. Lang.: Eng. 2534
Interview with actress Fiona Shaw. UK-England. 1995-1997. Lang.: Eng. 2607

Alcalde de Zalamea, El (Mayor of Zalamea, The)
Plays/librettos/scripts
Life and career of playwright Pedro Calderón de la Barca. Spain. 1600-1681. Lang.: Eng. 3397

Alchemist, The
Plays/librettos/scripts
The control of time in Renaissance English drama. England. 1590-1620. Lang.: Eng. 2883
Women's use of wit in response to men in English popular culture. England. 1590-1630. Lang.: Eng. 2884
Research/historiography
Jonson's *The Alchemist* and source studies. England. USA. 1610-1998. Lang.: Eng. 3795

Alcina
Performance/production
Interview with opera director Jossi Wieler. Germany: Stuttgart. Switzerland: Basel. 1998. Lang.: Ger. 4592

Aldwych Theatre (London)
Performance/production
Collection of newspaper reviews by London theatre critics. UK-England: London. 1998. Lang.: Eng. 2425
Collection of newspaper reviews by London theatre critics. UK-England: London. 1998. Lang.: Eng. 2569

Alegria
Performance/production
Collection of newspaper reviews by London theatre critics. UK-England: London. 1998. Lang.: Eng. 2564

Aleichem, Sholom
Plays/librettos/scripts
Enlightenment influences on modern Jewish theatre. Poland. 1500-1914. Lang.: Pol. 3307

Alenikoff, Frances
Performance/production
Dancer Frances Alenikoff. USA: New York, NY. 1960-1998. Lang.: Eng. 1324

Alessandro
Plays/librettos/scripts
Analysis of plays by Alessandro Piccolomini. Italy. 1508-1578. Lang.: Eng. 3244

Alex Theatre (Los Angeles, CA)
Performance spaces
Profiles of Southern California theatres. USA. 1998. Lang.: Eng. 473

Alexander, Bill
Institutions
Interview with Bill Alexander, artistic director of Birmingham Repertory Theatre. UK-England: Birmingham. 1998. Lang.: Eng. 1740
Performance/production
Collection of newspaper reviews by London theatre critics. UK-England: London. 1998. Lang.: Eng. 2557

Alexander, Elizabeth
Basic theatrical documents
Excerpt from *Diva Studies* by Elizabeth Alexander. USA. 1996. Lang.: Eng. 1480
Plays/librettos/scripts
Analysis of *Diva Studies* by Elizabeth Alexander. USA. 1996. Lang.: Eng. 3653
Interview with playwright Elizabeth Alexander. USA. 1996. Lang.: Eng. 3662

Alexander, F.M.
Performance/production
History of movement training for the actor. USA. 1910-1985. Lang.: Eng. 675

Alexander, Jane
Performance/production
Jane Alexander's return to acting after chairing the NEA. USA. 1998. Lang.: Eng. 2744

Alexandrowicz, Conrad
Basic theatrical documents
Text of *The Wines of Tuscany* by Conrad Alexandrowicz. Canada: Vancouver, BC. 1996. Lang.: Eng. 1344
Plays/librettos/scripts
Conrad Alexandrowicz on his dance-theatre piece *The Wines of Tuscany*. Canada: Vancouver, BC. 1992-1996. Lang.: Eng. 1356

Alfieri, Alfiero
Performance/production
Productions by Toni Bertorelli and Alfiero Alfieri. Italy: Rome. 1997. Lang.: Eng. 2175

Alfieri, Vittorio
Performance/production
Collection of newspaper reviews by London theatre critics. UK-England. 1998. Lang.: Eng. 2497

Alföldi, Róbert
Institutions
Theatre critics' awards 97-98. Hungary. 1997-1998. Lang.: Hun. 355
Performance/production
Interview with actor and director Róbert Alföldi. Hungary: Budapest. 1998. Lang.: Hun. 2056
Review of Róbert Alföldi's *Phaedra-story*. Hungary: Budapest. 1997. Lang.: Hun. 2102
Round-table discussion on Tivoli Theatre's production of *The Merchant of Venice*. Hungary. 1986-1997. Lang.: Hun. 2109
Shakespeare's *The Merchant of Venice* directed by Róbert Alföldi. Hungary: Budapest. 1998. Lang.: Hun. 2111
Plays/librettos/scripts
New Hungarian translations of Shakespeare. Hungary. 1990-1998. Lang.: Hun. 3187
Analysis of Imre Szabó Stein's new translation of Shakespeare's *The Merchant of Venice*. Hungary: Budapest. 1998. Lang.: Hun. 3188

Alfonso, Santiago
Performance/production
Collection of newspaper reviews by London theatre critics. UK-England: London. 1998. Lang.: Eng. 2429

Alfred Stieglitz Loves O'Keeffe
Basic theatrical documents
French translation of *Alfred Stieglitz Loves O'Keeffe* by Lanie Robertson. USA. France. 1987-1997. Lang.: Fre. 1505

Alfred ve dvoře (Prague)
Performance/production
Ctibor Turba and his mime theatre Alfred ve dvoře. Czech Republic. 1966-1998. Lang.: Eng, Fre. 4086

Alfreds, Mike
Performance/production
Collection of newspaper reviews by London theatre critics. UK-England: London. 1998. Lang.: Eng. 2423

Alhanko, Anneli
Performance/production
Interview with ballerina Anneli Alhanko. Sweden: Stockholm. 1963. Lang.: Swe. 1151

Ali, Lugman
Performance/production
Collection of newspaper reviews by London theatre critics. UK-England: London. 1998. Lang.: Eng. 2501

Ali, Tariq
Performance/production
Collection of newspaper reviews by London theatre critics. UK-England: London. 1998. Lang.: Eng. 2532

Alice
Performance/production
Collection of newspaper reviews by London theatre critics. UK-England: London. 1998. Lang.: Eng. 2477

Alice in Bed
Performance/production
Documentary theatre and the politics of representation. USA. 1966-1993. Lang.: Eng. 2728

Alien Boy
Basic theatrical documents
Text of three monologues by Will Scheffer. USA. 1997. Lang.: Eng. 1509

Alien/A(c)tion
Performance/production
The choreography of William Forsythe and the painting of Marcel Duchamp. Germany. France. 1915-1998. Lang.: Eng. 1280

All God's Chillun Got Wings
Performance/production
Aleksand'r Tairov's productions of plays by Eugene O'Neill. USSR. 1926-1929. Lang.: Eng. 2769
Plays/librettos/scripts
Miscegenation in American drama. USA. 1909-1969. Lang.: Eng. 3599
African- and Irish-Americans in the plays of Eugene O'Neill. USA. 1916-1953. Lang.: Eng. 3687

All Over Lovely
Performance/production
Collection of newspaper reviews by London theatre critics. UK-England: London. 1998. Lang.: Eng. 2546

All Talk
Performance/production
Collection of newspaper reviews by London theatre critics. UK-England: London. 1998. Lang.: Eng. 2475

All That Fall
Plays/librettos/scripts
Analysis of Samuel Beckett's radio play *All That Fall*. Ireland. France. 1957. Lang.: Ita. 3867

All Whispers/No Words
Plays/librettos/scripts
Interview with playwright/director Sheila James. Canada: Toronto, ON. 1990-1998. Lang.: Eng. 2809

All's Well That Ends Well
Performance/production
Brief productions of Shakespeare, Shaw, and Marlowe at the World's Fair. USA: Chicago, IL. 1934. Lang.: Eng. 2701
Plays/librettos/scripts
A possible source for the character Young Bertram in Shakespeare's *All's Well That Ends Well*. England. 1602-1603. Lang.: Eng. 2901
Closure and the happy ending in Shakespeare's *All's Well That Ends Well*. England. 1602-1603. Lang.: Eng. 3030

Állami Magyar Opera (Cluj-Napoca)
Performance/production
A production of László Lajtha's comic opera *Le chapeau bleu*. Romania: Cluj-Napoca. Hungary. 1998. Lang.: Hun. 4666
Production of László Lajtha's comic opera *Le chapeau bleu*. Romania: Cluj-Napoca. Hungary. 1948-1998. Lang.: Hun. 4668

Állami Magyar Színház (Cluj-Napoca)
Institutions
Hungarian dramatic art in Transylvania. Romania: Cluj-Napoca, Satu Mare. Hungary. 1965-1989. Lang.: Hun. 378
History of annual festival of Hungarian-language theatre. Hungary: Kisvárda. 1989-1998. Lang.: Hun. 1669
History of Hungarian-language theatre in Transylvania. Romania. Hungary. 1919-1992. Lang.: Hun, Rom. 1693
Performance/production
Review of Madách's *Tragedy of Man* at the Hungarian Theatre of Kolozsvár. Hungary. Romania: Cluj-Napoca. 1997. Lang.: Hun. 2065

Allcott, A.M.
Performance/production
Performativity in postmodern 'queer' works. USA. 1985-1995. Lang.: Eng. 616

Allen Theatre (Cleveland, OH)
Institutions
Theatrical activity in Cleveland's Playhouse Square. USA: Cleveland, OH. 1998. Lang.: Eng. 416

Allen, Greg
Performance/production
Performativity in postmodern 'queer' works. USA. 1985-1995. Lang.: Eng. 616

Allen, Jay Presson
Performance/production
Collection of newspaper reviews by London theatre critics. UK-England: London. 1998. Lang.: Eng. 2423

Allen, Maud
Performance/production
Modern dance and the female body. USA. Europe. 1900-1930. Lang.: Eng. 1321

Allen, Michèle
Performance/production
French Canadian translations/adaptations of Shakespeare. Canada: Montreal, PQ. 1988. Lang.: Fre. 1855

Allen, Paul
Performance/production
Collection of newspaper reviews by London theatre critics. UK-England: London. 1998. Lang.: Eng. 2414

Allen, Woody
Plays/librettos/scripts
Čechov's influence on Woody Allen's film *Bullets Over Broadway*. USA. 1994. Lang.: Eng. 4027

Alley Theatre (Houston, TX)
Design/technology
Set design for Tennessee Williams' *Not About Nightingales* at the National. UK-England: London. 1998. Lang.: Eng. 1526
Performance/production
Robert Wilson's work with actors on a production of *Danton's Death (Dantons Tod)*. USA: Houston, TX. 1997. Lang.: Eng. 2688
The multifaceted nature of early nonprofit regional theatre. USA. 1940-1960. Lang.: Eng. 2705
Trevor Nunn's production of *Not About Nightingales* by Tennessee Williams, Alley Theatre. USA: Houston, TX. 1998. Lang.: Eng. 2729

Alleyn, Edward
Performance/production
The activities of actor Edward Alleyn in retirement. England: London. 1597-1600. Lang.: Eng. 1894

Alliance Theatre (Atlanta, GA)
Performance/production
Interview with actress Phylicia Rashad. USA: Atlanta, GA. 1998. Lang.: Eng. 2695
The premiere of the musical *Elaborate Lives: The Legend of Aida*. USA: Atlanta, GA. 1998. Lang.: Eng. 4385

Alliger, Jeremy
Performance/production
Collection of newspaper reviews by London theatre critics. UK-England. 1998. Lang.: Eng. 2497

Alloula, Abdekader
Performance/production
Survey of contemporary Algerian theatre. Algeria. 1962-1998. Lang.: Swe. 1814

Allrakärasta syster (My Dearest Sister)
Performance/production
Theatrical adaptations of children's stories by Astrid Lindgren. Sweden: Stockholm. 1998. Lang.: Eng. 2374

Allrakäraste syster (My Dearest Sister)
Performance/production
Interview with children's theatre director Marie Feldtmann. Sweden: Stockholm. 1996-1998. Lang.: Swe. 2388

Alltagsgeschichten (Daily Stories)
Plays/librettos/scripts
Recent productions directed by Frank Castorf. Austria: Vienna. 1998. Lang.: Ger. 2788

Ally MacBeal
Design/technology
Lighting design for TV series *Ally MacBeal*. USA. 1998. Lang.: Eng. 4054

Almeida Theatre (London)
Performance/production
Collection of newspaper reviews by London theatre critics. UK-England: London. 1998. Lang.: Eng. 2459
Collection of newspaper reviews by London theatre critics. UK-England: London. 1998. Lang.: Eng. 2491
Collection of newspaper reviews by London theatre critics. UK-England. 1998. Lang.: Eng. 2504
Collection of newspaper reviews by London theatre critics. UK-England: London. 1998. Lang.: Eng. 2522

Almeida Theatre (London) — cont'd

Collection of newspaper reviews by London theatre critics. UK-England: London. 1998. Lang.: Eng. 2543

Collection of newspaper reviews by London theatre critics. UK-England: London. 1998. Lang.: Eng. 2588

Almodóvar, Pedro

Plays/librettos/scripts

The influence of Jean Cocteau on filmmaker Pedro Almodóvar. Spain. France. 1981. Lang.: Eng. 3978

Alonso, Alicia

Institutions

Interview with Alicia Alonso of Ballet Nacional de Cuba. Cuba: Havana. 1948-1998. Lang.: Swe. 1036

Performance/production

Interviews with dancers about performance. UK-England. USA. Cuba. 1942-1989. Lang.: Eng. 1162

Alpenkönig und Der Menschenfiend, Der (King of the Alps and the Misanthrope, The)

Institutions

Peter Stein's last season as director at the Salzburg Festival. Austria: Salzburg. 1997. Lang.: Eng. 336

Älskad-Saknad (Loved-Regretted)

Plays/librettos/scripts

Interview with playwright-director Petra Revenue. Sweden: Gothenburg. 1980-1998. Lang.: Swe. 3415

Alte Meister (Old Masters)

Performance/production

Adaptations and performances of *Alte Meister (Old Masters)* by Thomas Bernhard. Germany. 1997-1998. Lang.: Ger. 1996

Alternative theatre

SEE ALSO

Experimental theatre.

Avant-garde theatre.

Institutions

István Paál's Egyetemi Színpad. Hungary: Szeged. 1960-1998. Lang.: Hun. 361

Interview with director János Regős of Szkéné Színház. Hungary: Budapest. 1979-1998. Lang.: Hun. 362

History of Szkéné Színház. Hungary: Budapest. 1963-1995. Lang.: Hun. 1668

History of Squat Theatre. Hungary. USA: New York, NY. 1969-1981. Lang.: Ita. 1670

Tamás Fodor's Stúdió K. Hungary: Budapest. 1971-1997. 1971-1997. Lang.: Hun. 1671

Theatre selections at the 1998 Edinburgh Festival and Edinburgh Fringe Festival. UK-England: London. 1998. Lang.: Eng. 1743

Funding status of London's fringe theatres. UK-England: London. 1998. Lang.: Eng. 1748

Performance/production

Truth and authenticity in *M.T.M.* by La Fura dels Baus. Spain: Barcelona. 1983-1998. Lang.: Eng. 598

Sándor Lajos' *Szűrővizsgálat (Screen Test)* directed by Tamás Fodor. Hungary: Budapest. 1998. Lang.: Hun. 2103

Profile of actor-director Erzsébet Gaál. Hungary. 1951-1998. Lang.: Hun. 2147

Alternative theatre and the Black audience. USA. 1998. Lang.: Eng. 2682

Relation to other fields

The quality of Berlin's independent theatres. Germany: Berlin. 1998. Lang.: Ger. 748

Alvin Ailey American Dance Theatre (New York, NY)

Institutions

The fortieth anniversary of Alvin Ailey American Dance Company. USA: New York, NY. 1958-1998. Lang.: Eng. 1255

Älvsborgsteatern (Borås)

Institutions

Interview with Ronnie Hallgren of Älvsborgsteatern about theatre for youth. Sweden: Borås. 1994-1998. Lang.: Swe. 1726

Profile of children's and youth theatre Älvsborgsteatern. Sweden: Borås. 1995-1998. Lang.: Swe. 1731

Am Ziel (To the Goal)

Basic theatrical documents

Catalan translation of *Am Ziel (To the Goal)* by Thomas Bernhard. Austria. 1981. Lang.: Cat. 1407

Amacher, Maryanne

Performance/production

Interview with dancer/choreographer Merce Cunningham. USA. 1960-1998. Lang.: Eng. 1186

Amadeus

Performance/production

Collection of newspaper reviews by London theatre critics. UK-England: London. 1998. Lang.: Eng. 2528

Plays/librettos/scripts

Theatrical ritual in plays of Peter Shaffer. USA. 1975-1985. Lang.: Eng. 3707

Amagacu, Usio

Performance/production

Guest performance of Sankai Juku *butō* company. Hungary: Budapest. 1998. Lang.: Hun. 941

Amahl and the Night Visitors

Training

Actor training for the character tenor. USA. 1998. Lang.: Eng. 4849

Amateur theatre

Institutions

L.L. Vasil'čikova's amateur theatre group. France: Paris. 1930-1939. Lang.: Rus. 1616

Experiential memory work and acting at Theater Jugend Club. Germany: Nordhausen. 1995-1998. Lang.: Ger. 1629

Holocaust education and Thalia Treffpunkt. Germany: Hamburg. 1988-1998. Lang.: Ger. 1630

History of Szkéné Színház. Hungary: Budapest. 1963-1995. Lang.: Hun. 1668

Eighteenth-century amateur theatre in Vilna. Poland: Vilna. 1732-1798. Lang.: Pol. 1691

Swiss theatre clubs for children and youth. Switzerland. 1998. Lang.: Ger, Fre. 1735

Children's theatre festival Spilplätz. Switzerland: Basel. 1998. Lang.: Ger. 1736

Performance/production

Garrison and amateur theatricals during the British regime. Canada: Quebec, PQ, Kingston, ON. 1763-1867. Lang.: Eng. 505

Norwich's unregulated entertainers. England: Norwich. 1530-1624. Lang.: Eng. 1907

South African amateur theatre. South Africa, Republic of. 1861-1982. Lang.: Afr. 2352

A rare production of Eugene O'Neill's *Lazarus Laughed*. USA: Detroit, MI. 1963. Lang.: Eng. 2673

Irish and Irish-American characters on the stages of the Midwest. USA. 1875-1915. Lang.: Eng. 2696

Chinese street opera and nation-building. Singapore. 1965-1998. Lang.: Eng. 4694

A production of Offenbach's *Orphée aux Enfers* directed by Jens Mehrle and Stefan Nolte. Germany: Bitterfeld. 1998. Lang.: Ger. 4856

Reference materials

Yearbook of Slovene theatre. Slovenia. 1996-1997. Lang.: Slo. 708

Relation to other fields

Locating and defining the 'unincorporated' arts. USA. 1998. Lang.: Eng. 806

Amateur art theatre produced by Quebec priests. Canada: Montreal, PQ. 1930-1950. Lang.: Fre. 3733

Use of theatre in Holocaust education. Germany: Essen. 1985-1998. Lang.: Ger. 3767

Interactions between commercial and not-for-profit theatre. USA. 1998. Lang.: Eng. 3785

Amber Room, The

Performance/production

Collection of newspaper reviews by London theatre critics. UK-England: London. 1998. Lang.: Eng. 2439

Ambrosone, John

Design/technology

Lighting design for Mamet's *The Old Neighborhood* directed by Scott Zigler. USA: New York, NY. 1998. Lang.: Eng. 1547

Ambrus, Mária

Design/technology

Survey of an exhibition of Hungarian scene design. Hungary: Budapest. 1998. Lang.: Hun. 195

An exhibition of sets and environments by Hungarian designers. Hungary: Budapest. 1998. Lang.: Hun. 196

Catalogue of an exhibition devoted to Hungarian theatre and film. Hungary: Budapest. 1998. Lang.: Hun. 197

Amends for Ladies

Plays/librettos/scripts

The treatment of single women in early Stuart drama. England. 1604-1608. Lang.: Eng. 2979

American Ballet Theatre (New York, NY)
Institutions
American Ballet Theatre and diminishing government support. USA: New York, NY. 1998. Lang.: Eng. 1059
Profile of the American Ballet Theatre. USA: New York, NY. 1998. Lang.: Hun. 1061
Performance/production
Dancer Yan Chen of American Ballet Theatre. USA: New York, NY. 1981-1998. Lang.: Eng. 1176
Theory/criticism
Comparison of critical reviews of dance performances. USA: New York, NY. 1992. Lang.: Eng. 1201
American Buffalo
Plays/librettos/scripts
Rites of passage in the plays of David Mamet. USA. 1975-1995. Lang.: Eng. 3680
American Conservatory Theatre (San Francisco, CA)
Institutions
Women in top management of American Conservatory Theatre. USA: San Francisco, CA. 1992-1998. Lang.: Eng. 1781
Performance/production
Careeer of actress Tsai Chin. USA. 1959-1998. Lang.: Eng. 2754
American Federation of Television and Radio Artists (USA)
Administration
The merger plan of the Screen Actors Guild and the American Federation of Television and Radio Artists. USA: New York, NY. 1998. Lang.: Eng. 102
American Hero Entertains, An
Performance/production
Collection of newspaper reviews by London theatre critics. UK-England: London. 1998. Lang.: Eng. 2463
American Museum (New York, NY)
Institutions
Respectability and museum theatre. USA: New York, NY. 1840-1880. Lang.: Eng. 4112
Performance/production
Performance and the nineteenth-century economy. USA. 1850-1890. Lang.: Eng. 4134
American Place Theatre (New York, NY)
Institutions
History of the Women's Project of the American Place Theatre. USA: New York, NY. 1978-1979. Lang.: Eng. 1791
Plays/librettos/scripts
Playwright and actor Joseph Edward. USA: New York, NY. 1997. Lang.: Eng. 3564
American Repertory Dance Company (Los Angeles, CA)
Institutions
Profile of American Repertory Dance Company. USA: Los Angeles, CA. 1994-1998. Lang.: Eng. 1256
American Repertory Theatre (Cambridge, MA)
Design/technology
Set and lighting designs for *The Taming of the Shrew*, American Repertory Theatre. USA: Cambridge, MA. 1998. Lang.: Eng. 1559
Performance/production
Interview with director Peter Sellars. USA: Cambridge, MA. 1980-1981. Lang.: Eng. 2661
American Repertory Theatre (New York, NY)
Administration
Producer Cheryl Crawford and her contributions to the American stage. USA. 1930-1965. Lang.: Eng. 1396
Institutions
The economic failure of the American Repertory Theatre. USA: New York, NY. 1946-1947. Lang.: Eng. 1790
Âmes mortes, Les (Dead Souls, The)
Plays/librettos/scripts
Analysis of plays by Gilles Maheu. Canada: Montreal, PQ. 1994-1998. Lang.: Fre. 1357
Amistad
Performance/production
Background material on Lyric Opera of Chicago radio broadcast performances. USA: Chicago, IL. 1998. Lang.: Eng. 4709
Plays/librettos/scripts
Spielberg's *Amistad* and historical films. 1963-1997. Lang.: Eng. 3962
Amodio, Amedeo
Performance/production
Amedeo Amodio's new choreography for Čajkovskij's *The Nutcracker*. Italy: Rome. 1998. Lang.: Hun. 1118
Amor Costante (Faithful Love)
Plays/librettos/scripts
Analysis of plays by Alessandro Piccolomini. Italy. 1508-1578. Lang.: Eng. 3244
Amor de don Perlimplín con Belisa en su jardín (Don Perlimplin's Love with Belisa in Her Garden)
Performance/production
Collection of newspaper reviews by London theatre critics. UK-England: London. 1998. Lang.: Eng. 2499
Amor und Psyche (Cupid and Psyche)
Performance/production
Collaborative Symbolist dance/theatre projects. Europe. USA. 1916-1934. Lang.: Eng. 1268
Amore dei tre re, L'
Performance/production
Montemezzi's *L'amore dei tre re*, directed and designed by Philippe Arlaud. Austria: Bregenz. 1998. Lang.: Eng. 4532
Amour médecin, L' (Doctor Love)
Plays/librettos/scripts
Analysis of medical plays by Molière. France. 1660-1722. Lang.: Eng. 3078
Amphitheatres/arenas
Performance spaces
The feasibility of a floating open-air theatre. Europe. 1998. Lang.: Swe. 436
Städtische Bühnen's alternative venue, a velodrome. Germany: Regensburg. 1898-1998. Lang.: Ger. 439
Michael Marmarinos' production of Sophocles' *Electra* at the Epidauros amphitheatre. Greece: Epidauros. 1938-1998. Lang.: Ger. 445
Malmö Musikteater's production of *Lucia di Lammermoor* at Hedeland Amfiteater. Denmark: Hedeland. 1997. Lang.: Swe. 4491
The building of an ideal operatic stage in a disused limestone quarry. Sweden: Rättvik. 1997. Lang.: Swe. 4497
Amusement parks
Design/technology
Lighting design and equipment in various Las Vegas spaces. USA: Las Vegas, NV. 1998. Lang.: Eng. 276
Sound, lighting, and scenic elements of *Star Trek: The Next Generation* at the Las Vegas Hilton. USA: Las Vegas, NV. 1998. Lang.: Eng. 320
Frederic Paddock Hope, planner of Walt Disney World. USA. 1930-1998. Lang.: Eng. 4098
Lighting and sound control for the Disneyland 'Light Magic' show. USA: Anaheim, CA. 1998. Lang.: Eng. 4109
Landmark Entertainment Group, specializing in theme-park design. USA: Hollywood, CA. 1970-1998. Lang.: Eng. 4110
Performance/production
Portraying Mickey Mouse at Walt Disney World. USA: Orlando, FL. 1998. Lang.: Eng. 4223
Amy's View
Performance/production
Collection of newspaper reviews by London theatre critics. UK-England: London. 1998. Lang.: Eng. 2569
Anahory, Oro
Plays/librettos/scripts
Round-table discussion on story-telling and theatre. Canada: Montreal, PQ. 1998. Lang.: Fre. 688
Ananiašvili, Nina
Performance/production
Ballerina Nina Ananiašvili. Russia. 1998. Lang.: Rus. 1142
Dancer Nina Ananiašvili. USA: Houston, TX. 1986-1998. Lang.: Eng. 1193
Anatol
Basic theatrical documents
Catalan translation of *Anatol* and *Anatols Grössenwahn (The Megalomania of Anatol)* by Arthur Schnitzler. Austria. 1889. Lang.: Cat. 1408
Anatols Grössenwahn (Megalomania of Anatol, The)
Basic theatrical documents
Catalan translation of *Anatol* and *Anatols Grössenwahn (The Megalomania of Anatol)* by Arthur Schnitzler. Austria. 1889. Lang.: Cat. 1408
Ancient Greek theatre
SEE ALSO
Geographical-Chronological Index under Greece 600 BC-100 AD.
Performance/production
Early theatre. Ancient Greece. Roman Empire. India. Egypt. Lang.: Rus. 484
Renaissance ideas about classical Greek staging. Europe. 1400-1600. Lang.: Slo. 521
A dancer's experience of and investigations into ecstasy. USA. Germany. 1969-1990. Lang.: Eng. 673

Ancient Greek theatre — cont'd

Massimo Castri's production of Euripides' *Electra.* Italy: Spoleto. 1993. Lang.: Ita. 2179

Twentieth-century productions of Euripidean tragedy. USA. 1915-1969. Lang.: Eng. 2678

Plays/librettos/scripts

The use of collage in contemporary productions involving Greek myths. Canada: Montreal, PQ. 1998. Lang.: Fre. 2814

Hermes in the Greek theatre devoted to Dionysus. Greece. 600-411 B.C. Lang.: Eng. 3179

The playwright Euripides as a character in *Thesmophoriazusae* of Aristophanes. Greece. 438-411 B.C. Lang.: Eng. 3181

Myth and technique in Greek tragedy. Greece. 490-406 B.C. Lang.: Ita. 3182

The subversion of tragic forms in comic plays of Menander. Greece. 342-291 B.C. Lang.: Eng. 3183

Electra and Orestes in plays of Aeschylus, Euripides, and Sophocles. Greece. 438-411 B.C. Lang.: Eng. 3184

Civic discourse and civil discord in Greek tragedy. Greece. 475-400 B.C. Lang.: Eng. 3185

Ancient Roman theatre

Performance/production

Early theatre. Ancient Greece. Roman Empire. India. Egypt. Lang.: Rus. 484

Aesthetic analysis of ancient Roman 'blood spectacles'. Roman Empire. Lang.: Eng. 4128

Plays/librettos/scripts

Analysis of Seneca's *Oedipus* and *Hercules furens.* Roman Empire. 4 B. C.-65 A.D. Lang.: Eng. 3313

Roman tragic theatre from literary origins to the Roman arena. Rome. 500 B.C.-476 A.D. Lang.: Eng. 3315

And the Snake Sheds Its Skin

Performance/production

Collection of newspaper reviews by London theatre critics. UK-England: London. 1998. Lang.: Eng. 2457

And What of the Night?

Plays/librettos/scripts

Theatrical space in plays of Maria Irene Fornes. USA. 1977-1989. Lang.: Eng. 3571

Andarse por las ramas (Beating Around the Bush)

Plays/librettos/scripts

Cruelty and the absurd in theatre of Latin American playwrights. Latin America. 1960-1980. Lang.: Eng. 3267

Anday, Piroska

Performance/production

Profile of soprano Piroska Anday. Hungary: Budapest. Austria: Vienna. 1903-1977. Lang.: Hun. 4627

Andersen, Hans Christian

Performance/production

Collection of newspaper reviews by London theatre critics. UK-England: London. 1998. Lang.: Eng. 2556

Collection of newspaper reviews by London theatre critics. UK-England: London. 1998. Lang.: Eng. 2567

Anderson, Abigail

Performance/production

Collection of newspaper reviews by London theatre critics. UK-England: London. 1998. Lang.: Eng. 2541

Anderson, Adele

Performance/production

Collection of newspaper reviews by London theatre critics. UK-England: London. 1998. Lang.: Eng. 2568

Anderson, Gordon

Performance/production

Collection of newspaper reviews by London theatre critics. UK-England: London. 1998. Lang.: Eng. 2418

Collection of newspaper reviews by London theatre critics. UK-England: London. 1998. Lang.: Eng. 2517

Anderson, Jamie

Design/technology

Lighting design for Joe Dante's film *Small Soldiers.* USA. 1998. Lang.: Eng. 3914

Anderson, June

Performance/production

Coloratura soprano June Anderson. USA. 1998. Lang.: Eng. 4712

Anderson, Laurie

Performance/production

Theoretical implications of Laurie Anderson's use of media technology. USA. 1995. Lang.: Eng. 4046

Anderson, Lea

Performance/production

The body and personality of the dancer as the source of the physical vocabulary of dance. Europe. 1989. Lang.: Eng. 1269

Analysis of *The Featherstonehaughs Draw on the Sketchbooks of Egon Schiele* by choreographer Lea Anderson. UK-England: London. 1998. Lang.: Eng. 1315

Anderson, Paul

Design/technology

Technical designs for *The Chairs (Les Chaises),* Théâtre de Complicité. UK-England: London. 1998. Lang.: Eng. 1524

Anderson, Robert

Plays/librettos/scripts

Interview with playwright and screenwriter Robert Anderson. USA. 1945-1998. Lang.: Eng. 3515

Science fiction drama since World War II. USA. 1945-1988. Lang.: Eng. 3591

Anderson, Rod

Plays/librettos/scripts

Homosexuality in Canadian opera. Canada. 1970-1998. Lang.: Eng. 4762

Analysis of the opera *Mario the Magician* by Harry Somers and Rod Anderson. Canada. 1965-1992. Lang.: Eng. 4763

Andersson, Bengt

Performance/production

Interview with Bengt Andersson, artistic director of Teater Tre. Sweden. 1983-1998. Lang.: Swe. 601

Andersson, Benny

Performance spaces

The rebuilding of the stage at Cirkus to accommodate a production of *Kristina från Duvemåla (Kristina of Duvemåla).*Sweden: Stockholm. 1995. Lang.: Swe. 1804

Andersson, Mattias

Plays/librettos/scripts

Swedish theatres and young Swedish playwrights. Sweden: Malmö, Gothenburg, Stockholm. 1994-1998. Lang.: Swe. 3411

Anderstam, Lars

Institutions

The musical theatre program at Balettakademien. Sweden: Gothenburg. 1984-1998. Lang.: Swe. 4349

Andonyadis, Nephelie

Design/technology

Set design for a University of Michigan production of *Henry V.* USA: Ann Arbor, MI. 1998. Lang.: Eng. 1557

Andrea, Tony

Design/technology

The 1998 USITT expo. USA: Long Beach, CA. 1998. Lang.: Eng. 251

Andreeva, M.F.

Performance/production

Major Russian actresses and ballerinas of the nineteenth and twentieth centuries. Russia. 1800-1998. Lang.: Rus. 2240

Andreini, Giambattista

Performance/production

Analysis of religious theatre of Giambattista Andreini. Italy. 1576-1654. Lang.: Eng. 2190

Dramatic writings of Flaminio Scala and Giambattista Andreini. Italy. 1600-1700. Lang.: Eng. 4192

Andreini, Isabella

Performance/production

Early modern French and Italian actresses. Italy. France. 1550-1750. Lang.: Eng. 553

Andrejév, Leonid Nikolajévič

Plays/librettos/scripts

Bibliography relating to plays of Andrejév and their productions. Russia. 1900-1919. Lang.: Rus. 3320

Androjna, Irena

Basic theatrical documents

Text of puppet play for children, *Pospravljica (Tidying Up)* by Irena Androjna. Slovenia. 1997. Lang.: Slo. 4865

Aneks (Annex)

Basic theatrical documents

Plays and screenplays by Vili Ravnjak. Slovenia. 1991-1997. Lang.: Slo. 1460

Ängel och den blå hästen (Angel and the Blue Horse)

Performance/production

Interview with children's theatre director Marie Feldtmann. Sweden: Stockholm. 1996-1998. Lang.: Swe. 2388

Angélico, Halma (Margarit, Margarita Francisca Clar)

Plays/librettos/scripts

The image of women on the Spanish stage. Spain. 1908-1936. Lang.: Eng. 3399

Angels and Saints
Performance/production
Collection of newspaper reviews by London theatre critics. UK-England: London. 1998. Lang.: Eng. 2550
Angels in America
Performance/production
Contemporary queer politics and the production of gay and lesbian theatre. USA. 1970-1997. Lang.: Eng. 2710
Plays/librettos/scripts
The medieval mystery play and Tony Kushner's *Angels in America*. USA. 1992-1994. Lang.: Eng. 3652
Angiolini, Gasparo
Theory/criticism
Gasparo Angiolini and eighteenth-century dance. Italy. 1761-1765. Lang.: Eng. 1199
Angus, Eric
Performance/production
Collection of newspaper reviews by London theatre critics. UK-England: London. 1998. Lang.: Eng. 2553
Anhaltinisches Theater (Dessau)
Performance/production
The performance of Shakespeare in the former East Germany. Germany: Rostock, Leipzig, Berlin, Dessau. 1996-1997. Lang.: Ger. 1974
Animal acts
Institutions
Popular entertainment at the New Haven Assembly Hall and Columbian Museum and Gardens. USA: New Haven, CT. 1796-1820. Lang.: Eng. 394
A. Dživaev's equestrian theatre Konnyj Teat'r 'Narty'. Russia: Vladikavkaz. 1998. Lang.: Rus. 4272
Performance spaces
Evidence that Davies' bear-baiting ring may have been a restoration of the Hope Theatre. England: London. 1647-1682. Lang.: Eng. 435
Performance/production
Analysis of records relating to the Earl of Derby's 'bearward'. England. 1517-1616. Lang.: Eng. 4121
Changes in the nature of circus performance. Finland. 1980-1998. Lang.: Fin. 4181
Animal Crackers
Performance/production
Collection of newspaper reviews by London theatre critics. UK-England: London. 1998. Lang.: Eng. 2420
Animal Instincts: Tales of Flesh and Tales of Blood
Performance/production
Analysis of Rae C. Wright's solo performance piece *Animal Instincts*. USA: New York, NY. 1997. Lang.: Eng. 2684
Animals of Farthing Wood, The
Performance/production
Collection of newspaper reviews by London theatre critics. UK-England: London. 1998. Lang.: Eng. 2556
Animation
Administration
The influence of Walt Disney on the film industry. USA. 1968-1998. Lang.: Eng. 3873
Performance/production
Interview with puppet animator Brian Duchscherer. Canada. 1980-1998. Lang.: Eng. 4886
Änlichen, Die (Lookalikes)
Performance/production
Collection of newspaper reviews by London theatre critics. UK-England: London. 1998. Lang.: Eng. 2488
Anna Christie
Performance/production
Recent productions in Ireland of plays by Eugene O'Neill. Ireland: Dublin. UK-Ireland: Belfast. 1989-1998. Lang.: Eng. 2154
Notable productions of plays by Eugene O'Neill. USA. 1916-1996. Lang.: Eng. 2752
Plays/librettos/scripts
Existential analysis of Eugene O'Neill's *Anna Christie*. USA. 1921. Lang.: Eng. 3562
Anna Karenina
Performance/production
Lilla Pártay's ballet adaptation of *Anna Karenina*. Hungary. 1991-1998. Lang.: Hun. 1090
Collection of newspaper reviews by London theatre critics. UK-England: London. 1998. Lang.: Eng. 2506
Plays/librettos/scripts
Shared Experience's stage adaptations of nineteenth-century novels. USA: New York, NY. UK-England: London. 1998. Lang.: Eng. 3518
Anna Utcai Nyári Játékok (Pécs)
Performance/production
Open-air dance performances. Hungary: Pécs. 1998. Lang.: Hun. 1292
Annan Teater, En (Gothenburg)
Institutions
Interview with Rolf Sossna of En Annan Teater. Sweden: Gothenburg. 1992-1998. Lang.: Swe. 1734
Anne
Plays/librettos/scripts
Young People's Theatre's adaptation of *Anne of Green Gables*. Canada: Toronto, ON. 1911-1998. Lang.: Eng. 2832
Annie
Performance/production
Collection of newspaper reviews by London theatre critics. UK-England: London. 1998. Lang.: Eng. 2514
Annie Mae's Movement
Plays/librettos/scripts
Dramaturg's experience working on a play by Yvette Nolan. Canada. 1997-1998. Lang.: Eng. 2827
Annulla Allen: An Autobiography
Plays/librettos/scripts
The survivor character in contemporary American drama. USA. 1970-1997. Lang.: Eng. 3600
Anomalie-Cirque Compagnie (Paris)
Performance/production
Comparison of text-based and visual productions. France. 1998. Lang.: Fre. 1939
Another World
Design/technology
Costumes for a masked ball scene in the TV series *Another World*. USA. 1998. Lang.: Eng. 4053
Anouilh, Jean
Performance/production
Collection of newspaper reviews by London theatre critics. UK-England: London. 1998. Lang.: Eng. 2413
Collection of newspaper reviews by London theatre critics. UK-England: London. 1998. Lang.: Eng. 2548
Plays/librettos/scripts
The rebel in modern drama. Europe. 1950-1988. Lang.: Eng. 3053
ANTA
SEE
American National Theatre and Academy.
Antal, Csaba
Design/technology
Survey of an exhibition of Hungarian scene design. Hungary: Budapest. 1998. Lang.: Hun. 195
An exhibition of sets and environments by Hungarian designers. Hungary: Budapest. 1998. Lang.: Hun. 196
Catalogue of an exhibition devoted to Hungarian theatre and film. Hungary: Budapest. 1998. Lang.: Hun. 197
Antalffy, Albert
Performance/production
Interview with bass Albert Antalffy. Hungary. Austria: Mödling. 1924-1998. Lang.: Hun. 4634
Antheil, George
Performance/production
Opera composer George Antheil. USA. 1900-1959. Lang.: Eng. 4750
Anthropology
Performance/production
Account of the theatre anthropology workshop. Austria: Vienna. 1989-1998. Lang.: Hun. 494
Ritual in the theatre of Jerzy Grotowski. Poland. 1960-1975. Lang.: Pol. 2221
African ritual in the work of director and playwright Brett Bailey. South Africa, Republic of. 1997-1998. Lang.: Eng. 2349
Amerindian influence on Trinidadian carnival. Trinidad and Tobago: San Fernando. 1700-1950. Lang.: Eng. 4164
Plays/librettos/scripts
The Polish national style in Romantic dramas. Poland. 1832-1835. Lang.: Pol. 3304
Relation to other fields
The differences between theatre and ritual. 1998. Lang.: Ger. 711
Analysis of anti-theatricalism. England. 1579-1642. 726
Humanist ideology and the imaginary stage. Europe. 1549-1629. Lang.: Eng. 731
Performance ethnography of social action theatre Mise au Jeu Montréal. Canada: Montreal, PQ. 1995-1998. Lang.: Eng. 3735

Anthropology — cont'd

Chinese influence on Trinidadian carnival. Trinidad and Tobago. China. 1808-1998. Lang.: Eng. 4174

African and European influences on Trinidadian carnival. Trinidad and Tobago. 1501-1998. Lang.: Eng. 4175

The *jouvay* ceremony of Trinidadian carnival. Trinidad and Tobago: Port of Spain. 1838-1998. Lang.: Eng. 4176

Carnival, cultural identity, and assimilation. Trinidad and Tobago. 1889-1998. Lang.: Eng. 4177

Indian influence on Trinidadian carnival. Trinidad and Tobago. India. 1845-1998. Lang.: Eng. 4178

Theory/criticism

Survey of theatre studies as cultural studies. USA. UK-England. France. 1957-1998. Lang.: Ger. 865

Antigone

Performance/production

Collection of newspaper reviews by London theatre critics. UK-England: London. 1998. Lang.: Eng. 2441

Plays/librettos/scripts

The rebel in modern drama. Europe. 1950-1988. Lang.: Eng. 3053

Adaptations of Greek tragedy by contemporary Irish writers. Ireland. UK-Ireland. 1984-1998. Lang.: Eng. 3214

Antimasque

Plays/librettos/scripts

Ben Jonson's antimasques. England. 1612-1632. Lang.: Eng. 4205

Antonio and Mellida

Plays/librettos/scripts

The politics of gender in the plays of John Marston. England. 1599-1634. Lang.: Eng. 3009

António Marinheiro

Plays/librettos/scripts

The influence of Federico García Lorca on playwright Bernardo Santareno. Spain. Portugal. 1919-1965. Lang.: Eng. 3400

Antonio, Maria Oliver

Performance/production

The body and personality of the dancer as the source of the physical vocabulary of dance. Europe. 1989. Lang.: Eng. 1269

Antonio's Revenge

Plays/librettos/scripts

The politics of gender in the plays of John Marston. England. 1599-1634. Lang.: Eng. 3009

Antony and Cleopatra

Performance/production

The performance of Shakespeare in the former East Germany. Germany: Rostock, Leipzig, Berlin, Dessau. 1996-1997. Lang.: Ger. 1974

Collection of newspaper reviews by London theatre critics. UK-England: London. 1998. Lang.: Eng. 2523

Plays/librettos/scripts

Game theory analysis of Shakespeare's *Antony and Cleopatra*. England. 1607. Lang.: Eng. 2879

'Demonic' women in Shakespeare's tragedies. England. 1590-1613. Lang.: Eng. 2999

Apocalyptica

Performance/production

Collection of newspaper reviews by London theatre critics. UK-England: London. 1998. Lang.: Eng. 2434

Apollo

Performance/production

Interviews with dancers about performance. UK-England. USA. Cuba. 1942-1989. Lang.: Eng. 1162

Apollo Theatre (London)

Design/technology

Technical designs for the musical *Doctor Doolittle* directed by Steven Pimlott. UK-England: London. 1998. Lang.: Eng. 4325

Performance/production

Collection of newspaper reviews by London theatre critics. UK-England: London. 1998. Lang.: Eng. 2508

Collection of newspaper reviews by London theatre critics. UK-England: London. 1998. Lang.: Eng. 2546

Collection of newspaper reviews by London theatre critics. UK-England: London. 1998. Lang.: Eng. 2552

Profile of actor Tom Conti. UK-England. 1998. Lang.: Eng. 2629

Apollók és Vénuszok (Apollos and Venuses)

Performance/production

New work of Budapest Táncszínház. Hungary: Budapest. 1998. Lang.: Hun. 1294

Appen, Karl

Performance/production

Thomas Langhoff's production of Brecht's *Der Kaukasische Kreidekreis (The Caucasian Chalk Circle)* at Deutsches Theater. Germany: Berlin. 1998. Lang.: Ger. 1965

Appia, Adolphe

Design/technology

The influence of Dalcroze's eurhythmics on designer Adolphe Appia. Switzerland. 1906-1915. Lang.: Eng. 228

Performance/production

Slovene translation of Adolphe Appia on staging Wagner. Europe. 1892. Lang.: Slo. 4550

Apple Cart, The

Plays/librettos/scripts

Analysis of the later plays of George Bernard Shaw. UK-England. 1923-1947. Lang.: Eng. 3444

Apprenticeship

Design/technology

The experience of a costumer from Suomen Kansallisteatteri at Stockholms Stadsteatern. Finland: Helsinki. Sweden: Stockholm. 1996-1998. Lang.: Swe. 1519

Après moi

Performance/production

Productions of Szegedi Kortárs Balett. Hungary: Szeged. 1998. Lang.: Hun. 1102

Après-midi d'un faune, L'

Performance/production

Yvette Bozsik's new choreography for Debussy's *L'après-midi d'un faune*. Hungary: Budapest. 1997. Lang.: Hun. 940

Arabian Nights

Performance/production

Collection of newspaper reviews by London theatre critics. UK-England: London. 1998. Lang.: Eng. 2555

Arbo Cyber, théâtre (?) (Quebec, PQ)

Institutions

Profile of Arbo Cyber, théâtre (?). Canada: Quebec, PQ. 1985-1998. Lang.: Fre. 4232

Árbol, El (Tree, The)

Plays/librettos/scripts

Cruelty and the absurd in theatre of Latin American playwrights. Latin America. 1960-1980. Lang.: Eng. 3267

Arcadia

Performance/production

Tom Stoppard's *Arcadia* as directed by Tamás Ascher. Hungary: Budapest. 1998. Lang.: Hun. 2058

Review of Tom Stoppard's *Arcadia* directed by Tamás Ascher. Hungary: Budapest. 1998. Lang.: Hun. 2133

Plays/librettos/scripts

Analysis of Tom Stoppard's *Arcadia*. UK-England. 1993. Lang.: Eng. 3474

Arcand, Denis

Plays/librettos/scripts

Representations of theatre in the film *Jésus de Montréal*. Canada. 1990-1998. Lang.: Fre. 3964

Archer, Kenneth

Performance/production

The reconstruction of Jean Börlin's ballet *Dervisher*. Sweden: Stockholm. 1997. Lang.: Eng. 1150

Arches Theatre (Glasgow)

Performance/production

Collection of newspaper reviews by London theatre critics. UK. 1998. Lang.: Eng. 2407

Architecture

Design/technology

Survey of lighting equipment, design, and information. North America. 1998. Lang.: Eng. 209

The 1998 TCI awards. USA. 1998. Lang.: Eng. 243

Lighting design and equipment in various Las Vegas spaces. USA: Las Vegas, NV. 1998. Lang.: Eng. 276

Design for houses of worship, including their adaptation for performance and exhibitions. USA: Long Beach, CA. 1998. Lang.: Eng. 290

Lighting design for Mohegan Sun Casino. USA: Uncasville, CT. 1998. Lang.: Eng. 307

Sound, lighting, and scenic elements of *Star Trek: The Next Generation* at the Las Vegas Hilton. USA: Las Vegas, NV. 1998. Lang.: Eng. 320

Institutions

The new home of Chicago Shakespeare Theatre, formerly Shakespeare Repertory Theatre. USA: Chicago, IL. 1998. Lang.: Eng. 1775

Architecture — cont'd

Performance spaces
The architectural and administrative history of Redoutentheater. Austria: Vienna. 1918-1992. Lang.: Ger. 433
The feasibility of a floating open-air theatre. Europe. 1998. Lang.: Swe. 436
Brief history of theatre architecture. Europe. 340 B.C.-1998 A.D. Lang.: Dan. 437
The construction of a theatre for *Beauty and the Beast.* Germany: Stuttgart. 1997. Lang.: Ger. 444
Ferenc Bán's architectural design for Hungary's new National Theatre. Hungary: Budapest. 1998. Lang.: Hun. 446
Account of the competition for the design of the new National Theatre. Hungary: Budapest. 1996-1997. Lang.: Hun. 448
Interview with architect Miklós Ölveczky about Hungary's new National Theatre. Hungary. Norway. 1998. Lang.: Hun. 449
Architectural critique of the new Ford Center. USA: New York, NY. 1998. Lang.: Eng. 468
Seattle's new and renovated theatres. USA: Seattle, WA. 1998. Lang.: Eng. 475
Architectural critique of the restored New Amsterdam Theatre. USA: New York, NY. 1998. Lang.: Eng. 476
The architecture of the Bass Performance Hall. USA: Ft. Worth, TX. 1998. Lang.: Eng. 477
The renovation of Times Square. USA: New York, NY. 1998. Lang.: Eng. 479
Analysis of a sketch of the Swan Theatre. England: London. 1596. Lang.: Eng. 1801
The restoration of the Orpheum Theatre. USA: Phoenix, AZ. 1929-1998. Lang.: Eng. 3926
The influence of the Salle le Peletier on French grand opera. France: Paris. 1823-1873. Lang.: Eng. 4494
The building of an ideal operatic stage in a disused limestone quarry. Sweden: Rättvik. 1997. Lang.: Swe. 4497
Sante Fe Opera's newly renovated open-air theatre. USA: Santa Fe, NM. 1991-1998. Lang.: Eng. 4499
The newly renovated Newberry Opera House. USA: Newberry, SC. 1998. Lang.: Eng. 4501

Performance/production
English theatre architecture and the operas of Henry Purcell. England: London. 1659-1695. Lang.: Eng. 4548
Weber's *Der Freischütz* and the Neues Schauspielhaus. Germany: Berlin. 1821. Lang.: Eng. 4581

Relation to other fields
The design firm Yabu Pushelberg. Canada: Toronto, ON. 1998. Lang.: Eng. 718
Renaissance architect Leone Battista Alberti and theatre design. Italy. 1440-1470. Lang.: Eng. 751
Tourism and the development of theatre districts. USA: New York, NY. Germany: Berlin. 1998. Lang.: Eng. 807
The changing face of Times Square and its effect on the local community. USA: New York, NY. 1998. Lang.: Eng. 812

Archives/libraries

Design/technology
Catalog of the Tobin scenography collection. USA. Europe. 1500-1900. Lang.: Eng. 272

Institutions
Restoration of the Burcardo Palace, which includes a theatrical museum. Italy: Rome. 1998. Lang.: Ita. 366
Shubert archivist on her work. USA: New York, NY. 1987-1998. Lang.: Eng. 398
Assistant archivist on the Shubert archive. USA: New York, NY. 1984-1998. Lang.: Eng. 401
The early years of the Shubert archive. USA: New York, NY. 1976-1987. Lang.: Eng. 409
Brooks McNamara, founder and director of the Shubert archive. USA: New York, NY. 1976-1998. Lang.: Eng. 413
Brooks McNamara on the Shubert archive of which he is director. USA: New York, NY. 1976-1998. Lang.: Eng. 415
The temporary relocation of the New York Public Library for the Performing Arts. USA: New York, NY. 1998. Lang.: Eng. 419
The twentieth anniversary of the Shubert archive newsletter *The Passing Show.* USA: New York, NY. 1949-1998. Lang.: Eng. 425
Working at the Shubert archive. USA: New York, NY. 1988-1998. Lang.: Eng. 426

Performance/production
The Murray Louis/Alwin Nikolais dance archive. USA: Athens, OH. 1950-1998. Lang.: Eng. 1331

Plays/librettos/scripts
Eugene O'Neill's unfinished *A Tale of Possessors Self-Dispossessed.* USA. 1945-1953. Lang.: Eng. 3594

Reference materials
Catalogue of a Riccardi Library exhibition of theatrical manuscripts. Italy. 1998-1999. Lang.: Ita. 703
Index of the first twenty volumes of *The Passing Show.* USA: New York, NY. 1976-1998. Lang.: Eng. 709
Catalogue of early theatre manuscripts of the Riccardi Library. Italy: Florence. 1500-1700. Lang.: Ita. 3726

Research/historiography
German holdings of St. Petersburg's National Theatre Library. Russia: St. Petersburg. 1998. Lang.: Rus. 823
The current state of research on Polish theatre in exile. UK-England: London. 1939-1998. Lang.: Pol. 824
The Marvin Carlson collection of materials at the Ibsen Center. Norway: Oslo. 1998. Lang.: Eng. 3797

Ardant, Fanny

Performance/production
Interview with actress Fanny Ardant. France: Paris. 1990-1998. Lang.: Swe. 1944

Arden of Faversham

Plays/librettos/scripts
Language, rank, and sexuality in the anonymous *Arden of Faversham.* England. 1592. Lang.: Eng. 2986

Arden Theatre Company (Philadelphia, PA)

Performance spaces
The renovation of Arden Theatre Company's F. Otto Haas Theatre. USA: Philadelphia, PA. 1998. Lang.: Eng. 469

Arden, Anabel

Performance/production
The function of sound in productions of *India Song* by Marguerite Duras. France. UK-Wales: Mold. 1973-1993. Lang.: Eng. 1945

Arden, John

Plays/librettos/scripts
British historical drama. UK-England. 1956-1988. Lang.: Eng. 3500
BBC radio plays with Anglo-Irish themes. UK-England. Ireland. 1973-1986. Lang.: Eng. 3868

Arden, Leslie

Plays/librettos/scripts
Leslie Arden's career in musical theatre. Canada. 1993-1998. Lang.: Eng. 4389

Arditti, Paul

Design/technology
Technical designs for *The Chairs (Les Chaises)*, Théâtre de Complicité. UK-England: London. 1998. Lang.: Eng. 1524
Technical designs for the musical *Doctor Doolittle* directed by Steven Pimlott. UK-England: London. 1998. Lang.: Eng. 4325

Are You Now or Have You Ever Been

Performance/production
Documentary theatre and the politics of representation. USA. 1966-1993. Lang.: Eng. 2728

Arena Stage (Washington, DC)

Institutions
Graphic design and the theatrical evolution of Arena Stage. USA: Washington, DC. 1950-1987. Lang.: Eng. 414
Director Molly Smith, new artistic director of Arena Stage. USA: Washington, DC. 1998. Lang.: Eng. 1789

Performance/production
The multifaceted nature of early nonprofit regional theatre. USA. 1940-1960. Lang.: Eng. 2705

Arenas

Design/technology
Lighting design for musical performance and sports at the Nashville arena. USA: Nashville, TN. 1998. Lang.: Eng. 317

Arendt, Paul

Performance/production
Collection of newspaper reviews by London theatre critics. UK-England: London. 1998. Lang.: Eng. 2430

Aretino, Pietro

Plays/librettos/scripts
The comedies of Pietro Aretino. Italy. 1534-1556. Lang.: Eng. 3251

Argentina, La (Merce, Antonia)
Performance/production
Dancer Antonia Merce, La Argentina. France. Spain. 1888-1936. Lang.: Eng. 922
Aria
Plays/librettos/scripts
The reciprocal influence of opera and film. Europe. North America. 1904-1994. Lang.: Eng. 4770
Ariosto, Ludovico
Plays/librettos/scripts
Ludic aspects of Italian Renaissance theatre. Italy. 1500-1700. Lang.: Ita. 3240
Aristophanes
Basic theatrical documents
Catalan translation of Aristophanes' *Lysistrata*. Greece. 435 B.C. Lang.: Cat. 1438
Performance/production
Collection of newspaper reviews by London theatre critics. UK-England: London. 1998. Lang.: Eng. 2441
Culture Clash and their production of Aristophanes' *Birds*. USA: Berkeley, CA. 1984-1998. Lang.: Eng. 2713
Plays/librettos/scripts
The playwright Euripides as a character in *Thesmophoriazusae* of Aristophanes. Greece. 438-411 B.C. Lang.: Eng. 3181
Aristoteles
Theory/criticism
Aristotelian approach to Deaf performance. USA. 1988. Lang.: Eng. 861
Theatrical theory and practice. 600 B.C.-1997 A.D. Lang.: Slo. 3804
Chaos theory and its application to theatre and drama theory. USA. 1998. Lang.: Eng. 3839
Aristotle
SEE
Aristoteles.
Arizona Opera (Phoenix, AZ)
Institutions
Retiring artistic directors of regional opera companies, Russell Patterson and Glyn Ross. USA. 1960-1998. Lang.: Eng. 4485
Arizona Theatre Company (Phoenix & Tuscon, AZ)
Institutions
Cooperation between Childsplay and the Arizona Theatre Company. USA: Tempe, AZ, Tucson, AZ, Phoenix, AZ. 1995-1998. Lang.: Eng. 1756
Arkin, Alan
Design/technology
Michael McGarty's set design for Elaine May and Alan Arkin's *Power Plays*. USA: New York, NY. 1998. Lang.: Eng. 1542
Árkosi, Árpád
Performance/production
Two Hungarian productions of Čechov's *Tri sestry (Three Sisters)*. Hungary: Veszprém, Szeged. 1998. Lang.: Hun. 2135
Arlaud, Philippe
Performance/production
Montemezzi's *L'amore dei tre re*, directed and designed by Philippe Arlaud. Austria: Bregenz. 1998. Lang.: Eng. 4532
Arliss, George
Performance/production
Actor George Arliss. UK-England: London. 1868-1946. Lang.: Eng. 3941
Armada, Alfonso
Plays/librettos/scripts
Playwright/director Alfonso Armada. Spain: Madrid. 1987-1998. Lang.: Eng. 3382
Armageddon
Design/technology
Lighting design for Michael Bays' film *Armageddon*. USA. 1998. Lang.: Eng. 3916
Armfield, Neil
Design/technology
Lighting designer Mark Howett's work for Black Swan Theatre Company. Australia: Fremantle. 1998. Lang.: Eng. 1513
Arms and the Man
Basic theatrical documents
Catalan translation of *Arms and the Man* by George Bernard Shaw. UK-England. 1894. Lang.: Cat. 1478
Armstrong, Gillian
Design/technology
Geoffrey Simpson's cinematography for Gillian Armstrong's *Oscar and Lucinda*. Australia. 1997. Lang.: Eng. 3900
Armstrong, Gordon
Plays/librettos/scripts
Review of collections of plays with gay themes. Canada. 1996. Lang.: Eng. 2802
Armstrong, Michael
Performance/production
Collection of newspaper reviews by London theatre critics. UK-England: London. 1998. Lang.: Eng. 2470
Arne, Thomas
Plays/librettos/scripts
Music and the ballad opera in English popular theatre. England. 1728-1780. Lang.: Eng. 4390
Arnold, Samuel
Plays/librettos/scripts
Music and the ballad opera in English popular theatre. England. 1728-1780. Lang.: Eng. 4390
Aronin, Marc J.
Basic theatrical documents
Text of *Like Father, Like Son* by Marc J. Aronin. USA. 1987. Lang.: Eng. 1481
Aronofsky, Darren
Basic theatrical documents
Screenplay of *Pi* by Darren Aronofsky. USA. 1998. Lang.: Eng. 3880
Design/technology
Matthew Maraffi, production for the film *Pi*. USA. 1998. Lang.: Eng. 3906
Plays/librettos/scripts
Interview with Darren Aronofsky, writer and director of the film *Pi*. USA. 1998. Lang.: Eng. 3996
Aronsson, Gunnar Martin
Institutions
Gunnar Martin Aronsson of TeaterX2 recalls Action-Theater. Sweden: Stockholm. Germany: Munich. 1968-1998. Lang.: Swe. 1722
Aroseva, Olga
Performance/production
Memoirs of actresses Olga Aroseva and V.A. Maksimova. Russia: Moscow. 1998. Lang.: Rus. 2234
Arrabal, Fernando
Performance/production
Collection of newspaper reviews by London theatre critics. UK-England. 1998. Lang.: Eng. 2485
Arrête de rêver, l'Étrangère (Stop Dreaming, Stranger)
Basic theatrical documents
Text of *Arrête de rêver, l'Étrangère (Stop Dreaming, Stranger)*. Switzerland. 1998. Lang.: Fre. 1469
Arrighi, Cletto
Plays/librettos/scripts
Playwright Cletto Arrighi and Milanese theatrical life. Italy: Milan. 1869-1876. Lang.: Ita. 3220
Arrivederci Barnsley
Performance/production
Collection of newspaper reviews by London theatre critics. UK-England: London. 1998. Lang.: Eng. 2475
Arrivi Alegría, Francisco
Plays/librettos/scripts
The mulatto in Puerto Rican drama. Puerto Rico. 1850-1985. Lang.: Spa. 3311
Arroyo, Martina
Theory/criticism
Performers and conductors complain about unfair reviews. USA. 1998. Lang.: Eng. 4844
Arsand, Uwe
Design/technology
Lighting in contemporary theatre. Germany. 1998. Lang.: Ger. 192
Arsenic and Old Lace
Performance/production
Rehearsals of Christoph Marthaler's production of *Arsenic and Old Lace* by Joseph Kesselring. Germany: Hamburg. 1998. Lang.: Ger. 1953
Christoph Marthaler's approach to directing Joseph Kesselring's *Arsenic and Old Lace*. Germany: Hamburg. 1998. Lang.: Ger. 1956
Arsenijevič, Vladimir
Plays/librettos/scripts
Contemporary drama of the former Yugoslavia in its political context. Yugoslavia. 1991-1998. Lang.: Ger. 3721
Årsta Teater (Stockholm)
Performance/production
Interview with community theatre director Kent Ekberg. Sweden: Stockholm. 1973-1998. Lang.: Swe. 2385
'Art'
Design/technology
Lighting designer Hugh Vanstone. USA: New York, NY. 1998. Lang.: Eng. 1554

'Art' — cont'd

Plays/librettos/scripts
Playwright Yasmina Reza. USA: New York, NY. France. 1998. Lang.: Eng. 3684

Art's Bridge (Chicago, IL)
Administration
'Arts incubator' organization Art's Bridge. USA: Chicago, IL. 1986-1998. Lang.: Eng. 120

Artaud, Antonin
Institutions
Polish experimental theatre training. Poland: Cracow, Wrocław, Warsaw. 1930-1998. Lang.: Pol. 1685
Performance/production
Directing and intercultural theatre. Europe. 1930-1998. Lang.: Ger. 524
Antonin Artaud's journey to Mexico. France. Mexico. 1936-1937. Lang.: Eng. 1922
Plays/librettos/scripts
Insanity in nineteenth- and twentieth-century theatre. Europe. 1880-1970. Lang.: Eng. 3050
Antonin Artaud's years in a mental hospital. France. 1896-1948. Lang.: Ita. 3113
Revolutionary elements in plays and theory of Baraka and Artaud. USA. France. 1920-1970. Lang.: Eng. 3580
Theory/criticism
Artaud's theatre of cruelty and contemporary experimental theatre. France. 1945-1998. Lang.: Ger. 3818
Chaos theory and its application to theatre and drama theory. USA. 1998. Lang.: Eng. 3839
The influence of Antonin Artaud on director Paul Pörtner. France. 1920-1973. Lang.: Ger. 3870

Arte Povera
Relation to other fields
The Arte Povera movement. Italy. 1967-1985. Lang.: Eng. 4264

Article XXIV
Performance/production
Producing Howard Burman's *Article XXIV* at the Shanghai Theatre Academy. China, People's Republic of: Shanghai. 1995. Lang.: Eng. 511

Artisjus (Budapest)
Administration
Round-table on author's rights. Hungary. 1990-1998. Lang.: Hun. 16

Arts Council of Canada (Canada)
SEE
Canada Council.

Arts Theatre (London)
Performance/production
Collection of newspaper reviews by London theatre critics. UK-England: London. 1998. Lang.: Eng. 2416
Collection of newspaper reviews by London theatre critics. UK-England: London. 1998. Lang.: Eng. 2428
Collection of newspaper reviews by London theatre critics. UK-England: London. 1998. Lang.: Eng. 2479
Collection of newspaper reviews by London theatre critics. UK-England: London. 1998. Lang.: Eng. 2484
Collection of newspaper reviews by London theatre critics. UK-England: London. 1998. Lang.: Eng. 2512
Collection of newspaper reviews by London theatre critics. UK-England: London. 1998. Lang.: Eng. 2537

Artus Táncegyüttes (Budapest)
Performance/production
Artus Táncegyüttes' new production *Csillagőrlő (Starmill)*. Hungary: Budapest. 1998. Lang.: Hun. 948

Árvai, György
Design/technology
An exhibition of sets and environments by Hungarian designers. Hungary: Budapest. 1998. Lang.: Hun. 196
Catalogue of an exhibition devoted to Hungarian theatre and film. Hungary: Budapest. 1998. Lang.: Hun. 197
Performance/production
Visual dance productions by Cie, 2 in 1. Hungary: Budapest. 1998. Lang.: Hun. 942

Arvisura Színházi Társaság (Budapest)
Performance/production
István Somogyi's productions of *Magyar Elektra* by Péter Bornemisza. Hungary: Budapest. 1988-1998. Lang.: Hun. 2114
Two productions by István Somogyi of Bornemisza's *Magyar Elektra*. Hungary: Budapest. 1988-1998. Lang.: Hun. 2148

As Bees in Honey Drown
Plays/librettos/scripts
Interview with playwright Douglas Carter Beane. USA. 1980-1998. Lang.: Eng. 3516
Playwright Douglas Carter Beane. USA. 1998. Lang.: Eng. 3688

As I Lay Dying
Performance/production
Collection of newspaper reviews by London theatre critics. UK-England: London. 1998. Lang.: Eng. 2413

As Thousands Cheer
Design/technology
Costume design for revival of *As Thousands Cheer* by Drama Dept. USA: New York, NY. 1998. Lang.: Eng. 4333

As You Like It
Performance/production
Shakespeare performance on the Rhine and the Ruhr. Germany: Cologne, Bochum, Düsseldorf. 1996-1997. Lang.: Ger. 1962
Contemporary Polish productions of Shakespeare. Poland. 1990-1998. Lang.: Pol. 2213
Collection of newspaper reviews by London theatre critics. UK-England: London. 1998. Lang.: Eng. 2496
Collection of newspaper reviews by London theatre critics. UK-England: London. 1998. Lang.: Eng. 2523
Interview with actress Fiona Shaw. UK-England. 1995-1997. Lang.: Eng. 2607
David Tennant on his performance in *As You Like It* at RSC. UK-England: London, Stratford. 1996-1997. Lang.: Eng. 2640
Brief productions of Shakespeare, Shaw, and Marlowe at the World's Fair. USA: Chicago, IL. 1934. Lang.: Eng. 2701
Plays/librettos/scripts
Normand Chaurette's translations of *As You Like It* by Shakespeare. Canada: Montreal, PQ. 1989-1994. Lang.: Fre. 2824
Characters named Rosalind in Shakespeare's *As You Like It* and elsewhere. England. 1579-1600. Lang.: Eng. 2951
The two Jaques in Shakespeare's *As You Like It*. England. 1599-1600. Lang.: Eng. 2970
Political context of Charles Johnson's *Love in a Forest*, an adaptation of *As You Like It*. England. 1723. Lang.: Eng. 3013

Asafjev, Boris Vladimirovič
Performance/production
Boris Asafjev's ballet *Bachčisarajskij fontan* directed by R. Zacharov at the Mariinskij. Russia: St. Petersburg. 1934. Lang.: Rus. 1134

Åsberg, Margaretha
Performance/production
Dancer Anja Birnbaum. Sweden: Stockholm. 1984-1998. Lang.: Swe. 1299

Ascenseur, L' (Elevator, The)
Basic theatrical documents
Text of *L'Ascenseur (The Elevator)* by Gérard Levoyer. France. 1984-1987. Lang.: Fre. 1431

Ascher, Tamás
Performance/production
Tom Stoppard's *Arcadia* as directed by Tamás Ascher. Hungary: Budapest. 1998. Lang.: Hun. 2058
Review of Tom Stoppard's *Arcadia* directed by Tamás Ascher. Hungary: Budapest. 1998. Lang.: Hun. 2133
Interview with director Tamás Ascher on director training. Hungary. 1960-1990. Lang.: Hun. 2146

Ashbee, Thomas
Design/technology
Sound design for the musical *Bugsy Malone*. UK-England: London. 1997. Lang.: Eng. 4327

Ashe, Rosemary
Performance/production
Collection of newspaper reviews by London theatre critics. UK-England: London. 1998. Lang.: Eng. 2517

Ashes
Performance/production
Career of director Lynne Meadow. USA: New York, NY. 1972-1985. Lang.: Eng. 2708

Ashes to Ashes
Institutions
Productions of Bochumer Schauspielhaus. Germany: Bochum. 1998. Lang.: Ger. 1655
Performance/production
Harold Pinter's production of his play *Ashes to Ashes* at the Pinter festival. Spain-Catalonia: Barcelona. 1996. Lang.: Eng. 2364
Collection of newspaper reviews by London theatre critics. UK-England: London. 1998. Lang.: Eng. 2422
Plays/librettos/scripts
Analysis of *Ashes to Ashes* by Harold Pinter. UK-England. 1996. Lang.: Eng. 3430

***Ashes to Ashes* — cont'd**

Theatrical activities of Harold Pinter. UK-England: London. 1996-1998. Lang.: Eng. 3462

Ashkenazy, Vladimir
Performance/production
Recordings of *Lieder* by Schumann. Germany. UK-England. 1998. Lang.: Eng. 4601

Ashley, Christopher
Design/technology
Costume design for revival of *As Thousands Cheer* by Drama Dept. USA: New York, NY. 1998. Lang.: Eng. 4333

Ashley, Elizabeth
Performance/production
Actors and directors on the late plays of Tennessee Williams. USA. 1966-1981. Lang.: Eng. 2675

Ashley, Jonathan
Performance/production
Collection of newspaper reviews by London theatre critics. UK-England: London. 1998. Lang.: Eng. 2451

Ashley, Merrill
Performance/production
Panel discussion on Balanchine's *Jewels*. USA: New York, NY. 1967. Lang.: Eng. 1188

Ashman, Howard
Administration
The Disney Corporation's Broadway musicals. USA: New York, NY. 1996-1998. Lang.: Eng. 4317
Performance spaces
The construction of a theatre for *Beauty and the Beast*. Germany: Stuttgart. 1997. Lang.: Ger. 444

Ashton, Frederick
Performance/production
La Fille mal Gardée at Erkel Színház. Hungary: Budapest. 1997. Lang.: Hun. 1087

Annabel Farjeon on dancing for Ninette de Valois and Frederick Ashton. UK-England: London. 1930-1940. Lang.: Eng. 1158
Theory/criticism
Comparison of critical reviews of dance performances. USA: New York, NY. 1992. Lang.: Eng. 1201

Así que Pasen Cinco Años: Leyenda del Tiempo (Once Five Years Pass: Legend of Time)
Performance/production
Collection of newspaper reviews by London theatre critics. UK-England: London. 1998. Lang.: Eng. 2586

Asian-American theatre
Theory/criticism
Theory and Asian-American theatre. USA: Minneapolis, MN. 1994-1995. Lang.: Eng. 869

Asmussen, Peter
Plays/librettos/scripts
Interview with playwright Peter Asmussen. Denmark: Copenhagen. 1989-1998. Lang.: Swe. 2853

Asociación Cubana de Ingenieros y Técnicos de los Artes Escénicas (ACITAE)
Design/technology
Report from the meeting of Asociación Cubana de Ingenieros y Técnicos de los Artes Escénicas (ACITAE). Cuba: Havana. 1998. Lang.: Swe. 171

Aspern Papers, The
Performance/production
Collection of newspaper reviews by London theatre critics. UK-England: London. 1998. Lang.: Eng. 2409

Asselin, Jean
Performance/production
French Canadian translations/adaptations of Shakespeare. Canada: Montreal, PQ. 1988. Lang.: Fre. 1855

Assunção, Leilah
Plays/librettos/scripts
Cruelty and the absurd in theatre of Latin American playwrights. Latin America. 1960-1980. Lang.: Eng. 3267

Astaire, Fred
Performance/production
Analysis of the *Night and Day* dance sequence of *The Gay Divorcee*. USA: Hollywood, CA. 1934. Lang.: Eng. 977

Choreography in the musical film *The Bandwagon*. USA. 1953. Lang.: Eng. 982

Dance on screen. USA. Europe. 1920-1998. Lang.: Ger. 3860

Astor Place Theatre (New York, NY)
Design/technology
Sound design for Blue Man Group's Chicago production of *Tubes*. USA: Chicago, IL. 1996-1997. Lang.: Eng. 261

At the Foot of the Mountain (Minneapolis, MN)
Plays/librettos/scripts
Feminist theatre of Martha Boesing. USA: Minneapolis, MN. 1974-1984. Lang.: Eng. 3603

At the Hawk's Well
Performance/production
Collaborative Symbolist dance/theatre projects. Europe. USA. 1916-1934. Lang.: Eng. 1268

Collection of newspaper reviews by London theatre critics. UK-England: London. 1998. Lang.: Eng. 2458
Relation to other fields
The 'bird-woman' folktale in Southeast Asian shamanic healing rituals. Ireland. Thailand. Malaysia. Lang.: Eng. 1358

Atelier de recherche théâtrale l'Eskabel (Montreal, PQ)
Institutions
Jacques Crête and Atelier de recherche théâtrale l'Eskabel. Canada: Montreal, PQ. 1971-1989. Lang.: Eng. 1590

Atelier Théâtre des Compagnons (Paris)
Basic theatrical documents
French translation of *Tres diamantes y una mujer (Three Diamonds and One Woman)* by Alejandro Casona. Spain. France. 1959-1998. Lang.: Fre. 1464

Atelier, L' (Workshop, The)
Plays/librettos/scripts
Analysis of Holocaust plays by Jean-Claude Grumberg. France. 1974-1991. Lang.: Eng. 3108

Atelier, Théâtre de l' (Paris)
SEE
Théâtre de l'Atelier.

Athalie
Plays/librettos/scripts
The ritual structure of Racine's *Athalie*. France. 1691. Lang.: Eng. 3099

Atlan, Liliane
Plays/librettos/scripts
Analysis of *Un opéra pour Terezin (An Opera for Terezin)* by Liliane Atlan. France. 1986. Lang.: Eng. 3105

Attar, Faridu'd-Din
Performance/production
Collection of newspaper reviews by London theatre critics. UK-England: London. 1998. Lang.: Eng. 2501

Attar's Conference of the Birds
Performance/production
Collection of newspaper reviews by London theatre critics. UK-England: London. 1998. Lang.: Eng. 2501

Attempts on Her Life
Institutions
Profile of new venue, Bayerisches Staatsschauspiel, Marstall. Germany: Munich. 1993-1998. Lang.: Ger. 1660
Performance/production
Recent productions of Schauspiel Leipzig. Germany: Leipzig. 1997-1998. Lang.: Ger. 2011

Attenborough, Richard
Plays/librettos/scripts
Richard Attenborough's film adaptation of *Shadowlands* by William Nicholson. UK-England. 1993. Lang.: Eng. 3985

Attila József Theatre
SEE
József Attila Színház.

Aub, Max
Performance/production
Juan Carlos Pérez de la Fuente's production of *San Juan* by Max Aub. Spain: Madrid. 1998. Lang.: Eng. 2363
Plays/librettos/scripts
Jewish characters in Spanish drama. Spain. 1400-1950. Lang.: Spa. 3402

Auchincloss, Louis
Plays/librettos/scripts
History of the Playwrights Unit. USA. 1963-1971. Lang.: Eng. 3570

Auden, Wystan Hugh
Plays/librettos/scripts
The libretto of *The Rake's Progress* by W.H. Auden and Chester Kallman. UK-England. 1971. Lang.: Eng. 4824

W.H. Auden as an opera librettist and translator. UK-England. 1907-1973. Lang.: Eng. 4825

Audergon, Arlene
Performance/production
The Creative Surges actor-training seminar. UK-England: Ipswich. 1998. Lang.: Eng. 606

Audergon, Jean-Claude
Performance/production
The Creative Surges actor-training seminar. UK-England: Ipswich. 1998. Lang.: Eng. 606

Audience
SEE ALSO
Behavior/psychology, audience.
Classed Entries.
Administration
Marketing, advertising, and sponsorship of German theatre. Germany. 1998. Lang.: Ger. 7
Wolfgang Gropper, director of Staatstheater Braunschweig. Germany: Braunschweig. 1997-1998. Lang.: Ger. 8
Speculation on the future effects of technology and ethnic diversity on theatre. USA. 1990-1993. Lang.: Eng. 42
Ernö Weil, manager of Theater Pforzheim. Germany: Pforzheim. 1997-1998. Lang.: Ger. 1380
Interview with Carrie Jackson, executive director of AUDELCO. USA: New York, NY. 1998. Lang.: Eng. 1399
Oscar Micheaux's use of an interracial marriage case as a publicity tool for his films. USA. 1924. Lang.: Eng. 3874
Audience
Operetta and the contemporary audience. France. Germany. USA. 1860-1998. Lang.: Swe. 4851
Design/technology
Set designer Jean-Guy Lecat and his work with Peter Brook. France. Denmark. 1975-1998. Lang.: Dan. 182
Institutions
Festivals of theatre by and for youth. Germany: Dresden, Stuttgart. 1998. Lang.: Ger. 349
The relationship between theatrical artists and theatrical institutions. USA: Tarrytown, NY. 1998. Lang.: Eng. 421
Appealing to the youth audience at Theater Dresden. Germany: Dresden. 1997-1998. Lang.: Ger. 1631
Profile of Nordhessisches Landestheater Marburg. Germany: Marburg. 1997-1998. Lang.: Ger. 1653
Badische Landesbühne and the problem of declining audiences. Germany: Bruchsal. 1993-1998. Lang.: Ger. 1662
History of the Scottish National Players. UK-Scotland. 1913-1934. Lang.: Eng. 1752
Cooperation between Childsplay and the Arizona Theatre Company. USA: Tempe, AZ, Tucson, AZ, Phoenix, AZ. 1995-1998. Lang.: Eng. 1756
Profile of Manbites Dog and its topical and controversial productions. USA: Durham, NC. 1989-1998. Lang.: Eng. 1758
Performance spaces
History and nature of German open-air theatre. Germany. 1700-1994. Lang.: Eng. 442
Speculations on the theatre of John Rastell. England: London. 1524-1530. Lang.: Eng. 1799
Performance/production
Multiculturalism and the site-specificity of theatre. Asia. North America. Europe. 1976-1997. Lang.: Eng. 485
The performance of sacrifice on stage. France. Germany. 1900-1998. Lang.: Ger. 530
History of Arabic theatre. Middle East. 225-1995. Lang.: Eng. 561
Survey of London and Paris productions. UK-England: London. France: Paris. 1998. Lang.: Eng. 607
The success of dance extravaganzas and solo performance at the expense of traditional shows. USA: New York, NY. 1994-1998. Lang. :Eng. 645
San Francisco's professional theatre. USA: San Francisco, CA. 1850-1860. Lang.: Eng. 682
Baroque ballet at the Jesuit College of Clermont/Louis le Grand. France: Paris. 1660-1761. Lang.: Eng. 1076
The Nutcracker at the Budapest Opera House. Hungary: Budapest. 1998. Lang.: Hun. 1115
Stage adaptations of literary classics and the effect on audiences. 1998. Lang.: Rus. 1811
Shaw's *Major Barbara* at the People's Arts Theatre. China, People's Republic of: Beijing. 1991. Lang.: Eng. 1874
Contemporary Dutch theatre. Netherlands. 1990-1998. Lang.: Dut. 2205
Excerpts from Johanna Schopenhauer's journal relating to London theatre. UK-England: London. Germany. 1803-1805. Lang.: Eng. 2615
Semiotic analysis of Peter Hall's National Theatre production of Shakespeare's *Coriolanus*. UK-England. 1985. Lang.: Eng. 2647
Alternative theatre and the Black audience. USA. 1998. Lang.: Eng. 2682
Interview with director Richard Foreman. USA: New York, NY. 1975-1990. Lang.: Eng. 2700
The success of a revival of *Oklahoma!* at the Olivier. UK-England: London. 1998. Lang.: Eng. 4373
Opera in German culture. Germany. 1950-1998. Lang.: Rus. 4599
Plays/librettos/scripts
Analysis of scenic transitions in the plays of Shakespeare. England. 1590-1613. Lang.: Eng. 2875
Game theory analysis of Shakespeare's *Antony and Cleopatra*. England. 1607. Lang.: Eng. 2879
Shakespeare and the creation of a theatre audience. England. 1600-1616. Lang.: Eng. 3017
Interview with playwright Thea Doelwijt. Netherlands. Suriname. 1988. Lang.: Eng. 3279
Analysis of Seneca's *Oedipus* and *Hercules furens*. Roman Empire. 4 B.C.-65 A.D. Lang.: Eng. 3313
Boal's 'joker system' in plays of Ntozake Shange. USA. 1977-1981. Lang.: Eng. 3692
Theatricality and the printed texts of civic pageants. England. 1604-1637. Lang.: Eng. 4225
Relation to other fields
'Up-to-dateness' on the music hall stage. UK-England: London. 1890-1914. Lang.: Eng. 4283
Analysis of striptease events. USA. 1992-1998. Lang.: Eng. 4285
Theory/criticism
Evaluating the work of opera directors. Europe. 1965-1998. Lang.: Eng. 4837

Audience composition
Administration
Marketing analysis and plan for Texas Tech University Theatre's subscription campaign. USA: Lubbock, TX. 1997-1998. Lang.: Eng. 46
Audience
Analysis of audience composition at London theatres. England: London. 1835-1861. Lang.: Eng. 147
Gender-related social issues, theatre, and historiography. USA. 1830-1860. Lang.: Eng. 157
George Pierce Baker's 47 Workshop and the construction of the audience. USA: Cambridge, MA. 1918-1924. Lang.: Eng. 159
The popularity of *nō* among all the classes during the Edo period. Japan. 1603-1868. Lang.: Eng. 1371
Popularity of *nō* plays among common audiences. Japan: Edo. 1603-1868. Lang.: Eng. 1372
Performance/production
The staging of the complete *York Cycle* by the University of Toronto. Canada: Toronto, ON. 1998. Lang.: Eng. 4214

Audience development
Administration
The role of government in audience and marketing development for arts organizations. 1996. Lang.: Eng. 1
Ways to attract new young audiences to theatre. Sweden: Stockholm. 1995-1998. Lang.: Swe. 21
Finding a reliable sample frame for potential audience data collection. USA. 1997. Lang.: Eng. 39
Audience
The role of *Theatre Arts Monthly* in the development of the American audience. USA. 1916-1940. Lang.: Eng. 158
Diaghilev's strategies of audience development. France: Paris. 1906-1914. Lang.: Eng. 1028
The decline in popularity of operetta. Austria: Vienna. 1898-1998. Lang.: Eng. 4850
Relation to other fields
Arts education as audience-building. USA. 1998. Lang.: Eng. 3790

Audience Development, Inc. (AUDELCO, New York, NY)
Administration
Interview with Carrie Jackson, executive director of AUDELCO. USA: New York, NY. 1998. Lang.: Eng. 1399

Audience participation
Performance/production
Preparing a production of Brian Way's participatory *The Mirrorman*. USA. 1987. Lang.: Eng. 633

Audience reactions/comments
Administration
Audience questionnaire for use in theatrical marketing. Germany. 1998. Lang.: Ger. 12
Audience
Theatrical production and reception. Canada. 1988. Lang.: Eng. 146

Audience reactions/comments — cont'd

The fickleness of theatrical audiences. Finland. 1998. Lang.: Fin. 148
Seven theatre-goers on their reasons for attending a performance. Finland. 1998. Lang.: Fin. 149
The relationship between theatres and the youth audience. Germany. 1998. Lang.: Ger. 152
The interpretation of audience research data to yield marketing strategies. Germany: Berlin. 1993-1998. Lang.: Ger. 153
Ten-year study of audience response to Dutch theatre festivals. Netherlands. 1987-1996. Lang.: Dut. 155
Gender-related social issues, theatre, and historiography. USA. 1830-1860. Lang.: Eng. 157
Analysis of the teenage-girl audience. USA. UK-England. 1950-1970. Lang.: Ger. 161
Audience response to the structuring of its expectations. USA: Madison, WI. 1993-1997. Lang.: Eng. 162
New York reaction to visiting British dance companies. USA: New York, NY. 1997-1998. Lang.: Eng. 1246
Audience assumptions about the York *Resurrection.* England: York. 1275-1541. Lang.: Eng. 1400
Audience response to *Vor Sonnenaufgang (Before Sunrise)* by Gerhart Hauptmann. Germany: Berlin. 1889-1890. Lang.: Eng. 1402
Audience response to Bronnen's *Der Vatermord (Parricide)* and German culture. Germany: Frankfurt. 1922. Lang.: Eng. 1403
Nationalist response to the premiere of Synge's *Playboy of the Western World.* Ireland: Dublin. 1907. Lang.: Eng. 1404
Reactions to Norén's *Personkrets 3:1 (Circle 3:1)* at Dramaten. Sweden: Stockholm. 1998. Lang.: Swe. 1405
Jonathan Demme's film adaptation of *Beloved* by Toni Morrison. USA. 1998. Lang.: Eng. 3877
The current state of film, film criticism, and the audience. USA. 1998. Lang.: Eng. 3878
The negative reaction to performance art. Europe. 1960-1988. Lang.: Eng. 4230
Interview with performance artist Tim Brennan. Netherlands: Arnhem. 1989. Lang.: Eng. 4231
The negative influence of Wagnerianism on the reception of Delibes' opera *Lakmé.* 1900-1996. Lang.: Fre. 4409
Operetta and the contemporary audience. France. Germany. USA. 1860-1998. Lang.: Swe. 4851

Design/technology
The effect of lighting on the relationship between stage and audience. UK-England. 1820-1906. Lang.: Eng. 231
Panel discussion of sound designers. USA. 1998. Lang.: Eng. 287

Institutions
The work of performance troupe Goat Island. USA: Chicago, IL. 1987-1998. Lang.: Eng. 395
Polish guest performances of HaBimah. Poland. 1926-1938. Lang.: Pol. 1689
Experimental performances of Helena Waldmann and Showcase Beat le Mot. Germany: Franfurt. 1993-1998. Lang.: Ger. 4234

Performance/production
Playwright Rana Bose on memorable performances. Canada: Montreal, PQ. 1959-1998. Lang.: Eng. 498
Practical issues of cultural exchange: the Cry of Asia! tour. France. Philippines. 1988-1990. Lang.: Eng. 535
Dutch reception of the work of Bertolt Brecht. Netherlands. 1940-1998. Lang.: Dut. 564
Audience reaction to actress Adah Isaacs Menken. USA. 1835-1869. Lang.: Eng. 619
A personal response to Pina Bausch's dance theatre. Germany: Wuppertal. 1982-1998. Lang.: Eng. 1277
Michel Laprise's *Masculin/Féminin (Male/Female),* presented to audiences segregated by sex. Canada: Montreal, PQ. 1998. Lang.: Fre. 1867
Peter Zadek's production of Čechov's *Višnëvyj sad (The Cherry Orchard).* Germany. Netherlands. 1998. Lang.: Dut. 1954
Alexander Stillmark's production of *Bruder Eichmann (Brother Eichmann)* by Heinar Kipphardt. Germany: Berlin. 1984-1992. Lang.: Eng. 2022
Playwright Theresia Walser on children's reactions to Christmas plays. Germany. Switzerland. 1997. Lang.: Ger. 2027
Interview with playwright Heiner Müller about his adaptations of Shakespeare. Germany, East. 1965-1990. Lang.: Eng. 2039
Shakespeare in the GDR: producer and critic B.K. Tragelehn. Germany, East. 1950-1990. Lang.: Eng. 2040
Interview with actor/director Johanna Schall. Germany, East. 1980-1995. Lang.: Eng. 2045
Pirandello on the Greek stage. Greece. 1914-1995. Lang.: Ita. 2054
Massimo Castri's production of Euripides' *Electra.* Italy: Spoleto. 1993. Lang.: Ita. 2179
Slovenian reception of Austrian drama. Slovenia. Austria. 1867-1997. Lang.: Ger. 2347
The collaborative art installation *Tight Roaring Circle.* UK-England: London. 1993-1997. Lang.: Eng. 4133
Response to *castrato* performances. England: London. 1667-1737. Lang.: Eng. 4545
Audience reaction to Irish opera singer Catherine Hayes. USA: New Orleans, LA. 1852. Lang.: Eng. 4745
Reactions to Offenbach operettas at Kungliga Operan. Sweden: Stockholm. 1860-1928. Lang.: Swe. 4858

Plays/librettos/scripts
The community play *Aftershocks.* Australia: Newcastle, NSW. 1990-1998. Lang.: Eng. 2774
Recognition, repression, and ideology in Restoration drama. England: London. 1660-1680. Lang.: Eng. 2918
Analysis of Shakespeare's *Julius Caesar.* England. 1599. Lang.: Eng. 2948
Analysis of *Soldadera* by Josefina Niggli. Mexico. 1938. Lang.: Eng. 3272
North American translations and adaptations of Molière. North America. 1998. Lang.: Eng. 3289
Dramatic devices in early Spanish drama. Spain. 1550-1722. Lang.: Eng. 3373
Gender and sexuality in Caryl Churchill's *Cloud Nine.* UK-England. 1979. Lang.: Eng. 3426
Fragmentation and skepticism in Caryl Churchill's *Icecream.* UK-England. 1989. Lang.: Eng. 3451
Systemic poisons in plays of Caryl Churchill. UK-England. 1990-1997. Lang.: Eng. 3463
Pirandello, English theatre, and English scholarship. UK-England. 1924-1990. Lang.: Ita. 3473
Contradiction in the plays of Edward Bond. UK-England. 1962-1987. Lang.: Eng. 3485
Analysis of *The Skriker* by Caryl Churchill. UK-England. 1994. Lang.: Eng. 3489
The critical and popular failure of *The Skriker* by Caryl Churchill. UK-England. 1994. Lang.: Eng. 3504
Shocking the audience in Holocaust theatre. USA. 1980-1995. Lang.: Eng. 3628
The recent renewal of interest in the plays of Tennessee Williams. USA. 1996-1998. Lang.: Eng. 3674
Ousmane Sembéne's film adaptation of his own novel *Xala.* Senegal. 1973-1974. Lang.: Eng. 3977
John Stahl's film adaptation of *Imitation of Life* by Fannie Hurst. USA: Hollywood, CA. 1934. Lang.: Eng. 4029
The relative absence of political allegory in English opera. England: London. 1620-1711. Lang.: Eng. 4767

Relation to other fields
Catharsis and contemporary theatre. USA. 1998. Lang.: Eng. 795
Drama therapy and forgiveness. USA. 1998. Lang.: Eng. 804
The use of original theatrical productions in the ministry. USA. 1998. Lang.: Eng. 3781
The gangster film and public concern about moral corruption. USA. 1931-1940. Lang.: Eng. 4038

Theory/criticism
Theatre reviewers and popular entertainment. USA. 1975-1997. Lang.: Eng. 868
Activist political theatre and Western democracy. USA. 1985-1997. Lang.: Eng. 870
Critical response to *Elsineur (Elsinore),* Robert Lepage's multimedia adaptation of *Hamlet.* Canada. 1995-1996. Lang.: Eng. 3810

Audience-performer relationship

Administration
The star system and Danish theatre. Denmark. 1930-1997. Lang.: Dan. 1377

Audience-performer relationship — cont'd

Audience
The role of the audience in performance. Finland. 1998. Lang.: Fin. 150
The importance of independent theatre for children. Germany: Hannover. 1998. Lang.: Ger. 151
The aesthetics of audience-performer interaction in the theatrical event. USA. 1970-1981. Lang.: Eng. 160
Analysis of the teenage-girl audience. USA. UK-England. 1950-1970. Lang.: Ger. 161
Children's theatre and cultural exchange. Germany: Flensburg. 1998. Lang.: Ger. 1401
The prompting of epileptic seizures by film. 1960-1988. Lang.: Eng. 3876
The complex role of the audience in court entertainment. England: Greenwich. 1527. Lang.: Eng. 4194
Social uses of entertainment in Warwickshire. England. 1431-1635. Lang.: Eng. 4195
Opera and the young audience. Germany. 1998. Lang.: Ger. 4410
Institutions
Anna Deavere Smith on the Institute on the Arts and Civic Dialogue. USA: Cambridge, MA. 1998. Lang.: Eng. 399
The new children's theatre at Schauburg. Germany: Munich. 1998. Lang.: Ger. 1657
Performance spaces
Theatre SKAM's production of *Louis and Dave* in a Plymouth Volaré. Canada: Victoria, BC. 1996. Lang.: Eng. 1797
Performance/production
Differences between nudity onstage and on screen. Canada: Montreal, PQ. 1995-1997. Lang.: Fre. 499
The effect of a heterogeneous audience on performance anxiety. USA. 1987. Lang.: Eng. 630
Analysis of *kyōgen* performance. Japan. 1400-1700. Lang.: Eng. 1351
Interview with actor/director Johanna Schall. Germany, East. 1980-1995. Lang.: Eng. 2045
Analysis of Rae C. Wright's solo performance piece *Animal Instincts*. USA: New York, NY. 1997. Lang.: Eng. 2684
Interview with actor Patrick Stewart. USA: Washington, DC. 1998. Lang.: Eng. 2760
Performance artists Vito Acconci and Hermann Nitsch. Austria: Vienna. Italy. 1960-1977. Lang.: Eng. 4239
Performance artist Egon Schrick. Germany. 1976-1987. Lang.: Eng. 4241
Plays/librettos/scripts
Dramatic devices in early Spanish drama. Spain. 1550-1722. Lang.: Eng. 3373
Analysis of *Mad Forest* by Caryl Churchill. UK-England. 1990. Lang.: Eng. 3505
Research/historiography
Problem of documentary performance art. 1950-1988. Lang.: Eng. 4267
Theory/criticism
Criticism of performance art as no longer truly experimental. UK-England. 1960-1988. Lang.: Eng. 4269

Audini, Lawrence
Performance/production
Collection of newspaper reviews by London theatre critics. UK-England: London. 1998. Lang.: Eng. 2577

Audio forms
SEE ALSO
Classed Entries under MEDIA—Audio forms.
Institutions
Theatre and land use in midtown Manhattan. USA: New York, NY. 1925-1928. Lang.: Eng. 430
History of Mercury Theatre. USA: New York, NY. 1937-1942. Lang.: Eng. 1776
Performance/production
Multimedia and the productions of Giorgio Barberio Corsetti. Italy: Rome, Milan. 1985-1998. Lang.: Eng. 4043
Popular entertainer Elsie Janis. USA. 1896-1941. Lang.: Eng. 4145
Career of entertainer Al Jolson. USA. 1886-1950. Lang.: Eng. 4280
The music of George Gershwin available on compact disc. USA. 1998. Lang.: Eng. 4382
Audio and video recordings of opera stars and complete operas. 1988-1998. Lang.: Eng. 4522
Background material on Lyric Opera of Chicago radio broadcast performances. USA: Chicago, IL. 1998. Lang.: Eng. 4709
Background material on Metropolitan Opera radio broadcast performances. USA: New York, NY. 1998. Lang.: Eng. 4713
Background material on Metropolitan Opera radio broadcast performances. USA: New York, NY. 1998. Lang.: Eng. 4716
Operatic holdings of American and British record collectors. USA. UK-England. 1900-1998. Lang.: Eng. 4721
Plays/librettos/scripts
Radio, television, and stage plays of Caryl Churchill. UK-England. 1959-1985. Lang.: Eng. 3464
Reference materials
Discography of operas by Donizetti. Europe. North America. 1998. Lang.: Eng. 4831
Theory/criticism
Critique of dance criticism. UK-England: London. 1989. Lang.: Eng. 1339

Auditions
Administration
Survey of dance audition practices in Swedish schools and theatres. Sweden. 1990-1998. Lang.: Swe. 882
Performance/production
Auditioning for an Irene Ryan Scholarship. USA. 1998. Lang.: Eng. 635
Seminar on auditions for choreographers for Resolution dance festival. UK-England: London. Belgium: Brussels. 1998. Lang.: Swe. 1314

Auditorium
Design/technology
The effect of lighting on the relationship between stage and audience. UK-England. 1820-1906. Lang.: Eng. 231
Performance spaces
Brief history of theatre architecture. Europe. 340 B.C.-1998 A.D. Lang.: Dan. 437
The architecture of the Bass Performance Hall. USA: Ft. Worth, TX. 1998. Lang.: Eng. 477
Quebec's performance spaces. Canada: Quebec, PQ. 1992-1998. Lang.: Fre. 1795
The newly renovated Newberry Opera House. USA: Newberry, SC. 1998. Lang.: Eng. 4501

Aufstieg und Fall der Stadt Mahagonny (Rise and Fall of the City of Mahagonny)
Basic theatrical documents
Catalan translations of plays by Bertolt Brecht (volume 1). Germany. 1919-1954. Lang.: Cat. 1437
Performance/production
Review of Salzburger Festspiele performances. Austria: Salzburg. 1998. Lang.: Ger. 4527
Opera productions of the Salzburg Festival. Austria: Salzburg. 1998. Lang.: Hun. 4531

Auftrag, Der (Mission, The)
Theory/criticism
Representation and delegation in theatre. 1998. Lang.: Eng. 3800

Augustus Does His Bit
Plays/librettos/scripts
Rhetorical arguments in one-act plays of Shaw. UK-England. 1890-1945. Lang.: Eng. 3453

Augustynowicz, Anna
Performance/production
Director Anna Augustynowicz. Poland: Szczecin. 1989-1998. Lang.: Pol. 2214
The new generation of Polish directors. Poland. 1989-1998. Lang.: Pol. 2219

Auletta, Robert
Performance/production
Theatre Magazine's anniversary issue. USA. 1968-1998. Lang.: Eng. 617

Aureliano in Palmira
Performance/production
Performance history of Rossini's *Aureliano in Palmira*. Italy. Europe. 1813-1996. Lang.: Eng. 4659
Plays/librettos/scripts
Analysis of the opera *Aureliano in Palmira* by Rossini and Romani. Italy. 1813. Lang.: Eng. 4806

Auschwitz
Plays/librettos/scripts
Genocide, theatre, and the human body. North America. UK-England. Argentina. 1998. Lang.: Eng. 3290

Ausnahme und die Regel, Die (Exception and the Rule, The)
Performance/production
One-act plays by Brecht directed by József Jámbor. Hungary: Debrecen. 1998. Lang.: Hun. 2131
Plays/librettos/scripts
Analysis of *Die Ausnahme und die Regel (The Exception and the Rule)* by Bertolt Brecht. Germany. 1938. Lang.: Swe. 3133

Austrian Federal Theatres
SEE
Österreichische Bundestheater.
Autos sacramentales
Plays/librettos/scripts
Playwright Juan Pérez de Montalbán. Spain. 1601-1638. Lang.: Eng. 3379
Playwright Luis Vélez de Guevara. Spain. 1578-1644. Lang.: Eng. 3390
Autumn's Song
Basic theatrical documents
Texts of plays by Eddie Paul Bradley, Jr. USA. 1998. Lang.: Eng. 1482
Avant-garde theatre
SEE ALSO
Experimental theatre.
Alternative theatre.
Shōgekijō undō.
Design/technology
Avant-garde Russian women artist/designers. Russia. USSR. 1880-1949. Lang.: Eng. 214
Institutions
The avant-garde theatre festival Theaterformen. Germany: Braunschweig, Hannover. 1998. Lang.: Ger. 351
Jacques Crête and Atelier de recherche théâtrale l'Eskabel. Canada: Montreal, PQ. 1971-1989. Lang.: Eng. 1590
History of Squat Theatre. Hungary. USA: New York, NY. 1969-1981. Lang.: Ita. 1670
Performance/production
Social criticism and alternative theatre in Quebec and Newfoundland. Canada. 1970-1985. Lang.: Eng. 500
The influence of experimental performance on contemporary drama. Europe. USA. 1960-1987. Lang.: Eng. 526
The dynamics and contradictions of avant-garde theatre. Italy. 1960-1985. Lang.: Ita. 554
The use of closed circuit television in avant-garde theatre performance. USA: New York, NY. 1978-1986. Lang.: Eng. 662
The Living Theatre's *Paradise Now*—creation and production. USA. 1951-1968. Lang.: Eng. 667
Avant-garde dancer Anna Huber. Germany: Berlin. 1994-1998. Lang.: Ger. 1286
Dancer Frances Alenikoff. USA: New York, NY. 1960-1998. Lang.: Eng. 1324
The development of Toronto's alternative theatres. Canada: Toronto, ON. 1968-1975. Lang.: Eng. 1850
Hauptmann's *Fuhrmann Henschel (Drayman Henschel)* and realism. Germany. 1899-1933. Lang.: Eng. 1970
Spirituality and the theatre of Jerzy Grotowski. Poland. 1958-1998. Lang.: Ger, Fre, Dut, Eng. 2226
Avant-garde American women directors' productions of *Doctor Faustus Lights the Lights* by Gertrude Stein. USA. 1940-1995. Lang.:Eng. 2735
Mejerchol'd's relationship with Lunačarskij. USSR. 1890-1931. Lang.: Eng. 2768
Retrospectives of filmmakers Jean-Luc Godard and William Kentridge. USA: New York, NY. 1998. Lang.: Eng. 3958
The feminist performance trend Angry Essentialism. USA. 1981-1998. Lang.: Eng. 4249
Contemporary performance art's ignorance of its avant-garde antecedents. USA. 1996-1998. Lang.: Eng. 4250
Plays/librettos/scripts
Insanity in nineteenth- and twentieth-century theatre. Europe. 1880-1970. Lang.: Eng. 3050
Playwrights Annibale Ruccello, Enzo Moscato, and Manlio Santanelli. Italy: Naples. 1980-1989. Lang.: Eng. 3261
Analysis of *States of Shock* by Sam Shepard. USA. 1965-1997. Lang.: Eng. 3544
Experimental theatre of Elmer Rice. USA. 1914-1963. Lang.: Eng. 3620
Relation to other fields
Survey of Czech avant-garde theatre and socialist realism. Czech Republic. 1925-1950. Lang.: Cze. 721
Theory/criticism
Politics, tradition, and avant-garde theatre. Italy. 1985. Lang.: Ita. 847
Avant-garde theatre and technology. Italy. 1998. Lang.: Ita. 848
Changes in the social and political situation of Polish fringe theatre. Poland. 1980-1995. Lang.: Pol. 3826
The influence of Antonin Artaud on director Paul Pörtner. France. 1920-1973. Lang.: Ger. 3870
Avengers, The
Design/technology
Production design for the film *The Avengers.* USA: Hollywood, CA. 1998. Lang.: Eng. 3907
Avian, Bob
Performance/production
Collection of newspaper reviews by London theatre critics. UK-England: London, Scarborough. 1998. Lang.: Eng. 2426
Avni, Ran
Institutions
History of the Jewish Repertory Theatre. USA: New York, NY. 1974-1984. Lang.: Eng. 1757
Awards
Administration
Conductor Leonard dePaur, winner of the Paul Robeson Award. USA: New York, NY. 1910-1998. Lang.: Eng. 104
Leland Ball of Sacramento Light Opera Association, winner of Rosetta LeNoire Award. USA: Sacramento, CA. 1998. Lang.: Eng. 4408
Basic theatrical documents
Russian translations of plays by Nobel Prize winners. Italy. 1848-1998. Lang.: Rus. 1446
Design/technology
The 1998 TCI awards. USA. 1998. Lang.: Eng. 243
Imero Fiorentino, USITT's most distinguished lighting designer of 1997. USA. 1998. Lang.: Eng. 291
Design awards for the TV mini-series *Merlin.* USA: Pasadena, CA. 1998. Lang.: Eng. 4052
Profile of technicians for Grammy Awards television broadcast. USA: New York, NY. 1998. Lang.: Eng. 4056
Institutions
Theatre critics' awards 97-98. Hungary. 1997-1998. Lang.: Hun. 355
History of annual festival of Hungarian-language theatre. Hungary: Kisvárda. 1989-1998. Lang.: Hun. 1669
Impressions from the 'Golden Mask' festival. Russia: Minusinsk. 1998. Lang.: Ger. 1701
Performance/production
Gert Voss and Ignaz Kirchner, *Theater Heute*'s actors of the year. Austria: Vienna. 1988-1998. Lang.: Ger. 1823
Profile of Thomas Ostermeier, *Theater Heute*'s young director of the year. Germany: Berlin. 1997-1998. Lang.: Ger. 1959
Matthias Matschke, *Theater Heute*'s young actor of the year. Germany: Berlin. 1985-1997. Lang.: Ger. 1963
Natali Seelig, *Theater Heute*'s actress of the year. Germany: Munich. 1991-1998. Lang.: Ger. 1966
Kortner-award winners Anna Viebrock and Christoph Marthaler. Germany: Berlin. 1997. Lang.: Ger. 1968
Swedish actors who have won the O'Neill Prize. Sweden: Stockholm. 1956-1998. Lang.: Swe. 2365
Actors Helen Carey and Max Wright, winners of Joe A. Callaway Award. USA. 1998. Lang.: Eng. 2716
Julyana Soelistyo and Sam Trammel, winners of the Derwent Award. USA: New York, NY. 1998. Lang.: Eng. 2719
Excerpt from a speech by actor Robert Prosky. USA: Washington, DC. 1998. Lang.: Eng. 2720
Plays/librettos/scripts
Playwright Volker Lüdecke. Germany: Kaiserslautern. 1992-1998. Lang.: Ger. 3141
Ivan Nagel's speech on awarding the Büchner Prize to playwright Elfriede Jelinek. Germany. 1998. Lang.: Ger. 3154
Reactions to the awarding of the Nobel Prize to satirical playwright Dario Fo. Italy. 1998. Lang.: Eng. 3242
Playwright Dario Fo. Italy. 1998. Lang.: Eng. 3243
Interview with playwright Mark Ravenhill. UK-England. 1998. Lang.: Ger. 3496
Interview with playwright Sheryle Criswell. USA. 1998. Lang.: Eng. 3681
Theory/criticism
Obituary for critic Ross Wetzstoen, who inspired the Obie Awards. USA. 1932-1998. Lang.: Eng. 3847
Awards, Antoinette Perry
Administration
History of the Tony Awards. USA: New York, NY. 1950-1998. Lang.: Eng. 74

Ayckbourn, Alan
Administration
Theatrical agent Margaret Ramsey. UK-England: London. 1908-1991. Lang.: Ger. 1394
Basic theatrical documents
French translation of *Time of My Life* by Alan Ayckbourn. UK-England. France. 1993-1998. Lang.: Fre. 1471
Performance/production
Collection of newspaper reviews by London theatre critics. UK-England: London, Scarborough. 1998. Lang.: Eng. 2426
Collection of newspaper reviews by London theatre critics. UK-England: London. 1998. Lang.: Eng. 2438
Plays/librettos/scripts
The comedies of Alan Ayckbourn. UK-England: London. 1998. Lang.: Eng. 3420

B., Franko
Performance/production
Interview with performance artist Franko B. UK-England. 1998. Lang.: Eng. 4244
Plays/librettos/scripts
AIDS and the work of performance artist Franko B. UK-England. 1996-1998. Lang.: Eng. 4261

Baal
Basic theatrical documents
Catalan translations of plays by Bertolt Brecht (volume 1). Germany. 1919-1954. Lang.: Cat. 1437
Performance/production
Interview with directors János Szász and Árpád Schilling. Hungary. 1998. Lang.: Hun. 2129
Chris Vorster's production of *Baal* by Bertolt Brecht. South Africa, Republic of: Capetown. 1998. Lang.: Eng. 2350
Plays/librettos/scripts
Aesthetic peculiarities of *Baal* by Bertolt Brecht. Germany. 1918-1922. Lang.: Hun. 3146

Babarczy, László
Performance/production
Ferenc Deák's *Fojtás (Tamping)* directed by László Babarczy. Hungary: Kaposvár. 1998. Lang.: Hun. 2117
László Babarczy's production of *Pepe* by Andor Szilágy. Serbia: Novi Sad. 1998. Lang.: Hun. 2342

Babe XXX
Performance/production
Collection of newspaper reviews by London theatre critics. UK-England: London. 1998. Lang.: Eng. 2530

Babička (Grandmother)
Performance/production
The adaptation of classic Czech works to the stage. Czech Republic: Prague, Brno. 1990-1998. Lang.: Cze. 1877

Baby Doll
Plays/librettos/scripts
Tennessee Williams's short story *Twenty-Seven Wagons Full of Cotton* and the plays based on it. USA. 1936-1979. Lang.: Eng. 3622

Babysitters
Performance/production
Collection of newspaper reviews by London theatre critics. UK-England: London. 1998. Lang.: Eng. 2506

Bacchae, The
SEE
Bákchai.

Bach, Johann Sebastian
Design/technology
Scenographic concept for the *dramma per musica*, *Aeolus Appeased.* USA. 1988. Lang.: Eng. 4442
Performance/production
Premieres of choreographies by Danny Rosseel. Belgium: Antwerp. Netherlands: Amsterdam. 1998. Lang.: Hun. 1065
Antal Fodor's ballet *A Próba (The Rehearsal).* Hungary: Budapest. 1998. Lang.: Hun. 1111
Collection of newspaper reviews by London theatre critics. UK-Scotland: Edinburgh. 1998. Lang.: Eng. 2650

Bachmann, Stefan
Administration
Theater Basel under the direction of Stefan Bachmann. Switzerland: Basel. 1996-1998. Lang.: Ger. 1391
Institutions
Productions of Salzburger Festspiele. Austria: Salzburg. 1998. Lang.: Ger. 1571
Stefan Bachmann of Basler Theater. Switzerland: Basel. 1998. Lang.: Ger. 1737
Performance/production
Two productions of Brecht's *Der Kaukasische Kreidekreis (The Caucasian Chalk Circle).* Germany: Berlin, Hamburg. 1998. Lang.: Ger. 1957
Recent German productions of plays by Bertolt Brecht. Germany: Hamburg, Berlin. 1997. Lang.: Swe. 1977
Stefan Bachmann's production of Shakespeare's *Troilus and Cressida.* Switzerland: Basle. 1998. Lang.: Ger. 2399
Reviews of plays by Wolfgang Bauer and Thomas Bernhard. Switzerland: Basel. Austria: Vienna. 1998. Lang.: Ger. 2403

Back to Methuselah
Performance/production
Collection of newspaper reviews by London theatre critics. UK-England: London. 1998. Lang.: Eng. 2524
Plays/librettos/scripts
George Bernard Shaw and science fiction. UK-England. Ireland. 1887-1998. Lang.: Eng. 3508

Backa Teater (Gothenburg)
Plays/librettos/scripts
Swedish theatres and young Swedish playwrights. Sweden: Malmö, Gothenburg, Stockholm. 1994-1998. Lang.: Swe. 3411

Backlund, Thomas
Performance/production
Swedish and bilingual Finnish-Swedish theatre. Finland: Turku, Vaasa. 1998. Lang.: Eng, Fre. 1913

Backroom, The
Performance/production
Collection of newspaper reviews by London theatre critics. UK-England: London. 1998. Lang.: Eng. 2550

Backstage
SEE
Support areas.

Backstage, Stadsteater (Stockholm)
Performance/production
Dr. Kokos Kärlekslaboratorium (Dr. Koko's Laboratory of Love) at Backstage, Stockholms Stadsteater. Sweden: Stockholm. 1998. Lang.: Swe. 2378

Bacon, Gloria
Performance/production
Interview with dancer and choreographer Gloria Bacon. Nicaragua. 1979-1998. Lang.: Swe. 958

Bad Faith
Performance/production
Collection of newspaper reviews by London theatre critics. UK-England: London. 1998. Lang.: Eng. 2569

Bad Weather
Performance/production
Collection of newspaper reviews by London theatre critics. UK-England: London, Stratford, Derby. 1998. Lang.: Eng. 2417

Badische Landesbühne (Bruchsal)
Administration
Interviews with theatre managers regarding the changing cultural landscape. Germany: Bruchsal, Esslingen, Tübingen. 1998. Lang.: Ger. 1381
Institutions
Badische Landesbühne and the problem of declining audiences. Germany: Bruchsal. 1993-1998. Lang.: Ger. 1662

Badisches Staatstheater (Karlsruhe)
Institutions
Interview with Pavel Fieber, manager of Badisches Staatstheater Karlsruhe. Germany: Karlsruhe. 1997-1998. Lang.: Ger. 1649
Plays/librettos/scripts
Recent German productions of Brecht's plays. Germany. 1998. Lang.: Ger. 3150

Bagó, Bertalan
Performance/production
Three Hungarian productions of Shakespeare's *Richard III.* Hungary: Budapest, Zsámbék, Szeged. 1997. Lang.: Hun. 2121

Bagossy, László
Performance/production
Thomas Bernhard's *Ritter, Dene, Voss* at Bárka Színház. Hungary: Budapest. 1997. Lang.: Hun. 2087
Performances at the new Bárka Színház. Hungary: Budapest. 1997. Lang.: Hun. 2097
Lajos Parti Nagy's *Ibusár* directed by János Mikuli. Hungary: Kecskemét, Pécs. 1998. Lang.: Hun. 2110

Bailey Chubb, Katherine
Performance/production
Collection of newspaper reviews by London theatre critics. UK-England: London. 1998. Lang.: Eng. 2432

Bailey, Adrian
Performance/production
Collection of newspaper reviews by London theatre critics. UK-England: London. 1998. Lang.: Eng. 2475
Bailey, Brett
Performance/production
African ritual in the work of director and playwright Brett Bailey. South Africa, Republic of. 1997-1998. Lang.: Eng. 2349
Bailey, Ian
Performance/production
Collection of newspaper reviews by London theatre critics. UK-England: London. 1998. Lang.: Eng. 2463
Bailey, Kim
Performance/production
Collection of newspaper reviews by London theatre critics. UK-England: London. 1998. Lang.: Eng. 2477
Bailey, Lucy
Institutions
The inaugural season of Shakespeare's Globe Theatre. UK-England: London. 1997-1998. Lang.: Eng. 1741
Performance/production
Collection of newspaper reviews by London theatre critics. UK-England: London. 1998. Lang.: Eng. 2496
The inaugural season of Shakespeare's Globe Theatre. UK-England: London. 1997. Lang.: Eng. 2601
Baird, Campbell
Design/technology
Professional theatrical designers on design training. USA. 1998. Lang.: Eng. 252
Costume design for a new version of *Peter Pan* at Children's Theatre Company. USA: Minneapolis, MN. 1998. Lang.: Eng. 4330
Baitz, Jon Robin
Design/technology
Set designs by Santo Loquasto at Manhattan Theatre Club. USA: New York, NY. 1998. Lang.: Eng. 1536
Plays/librettos/scripts
The survivor character in contemporary American drama. USA. 1970-1997. Lang.: Eng. 3600
Bakathir, Ali Ahmad
Basic theatrical documents
English translation and analysis of two plays by Ali Ahmad Bakathir. Egypt. 1908-1969. Lang.: Eng. 1417
Bákchai (Bacchae, The)
Performance/production
Twentieth-century productions of Euripidean tragedy. USA. 1915-1969. Lang.: Eng. 2678
Training
Anne-Lise Gabold's use of the methods of Tadashi Suzuki in her production of Euripides' *Bákchai (The Bacchae)*. Japan. Denmark: Copenhagen. 1960-1998. Lang.: Dan. 1359
Baker, Bobby
Performance/production
The kitchen in performance art of Bobby Baker and Jeanne Goosen. UK-England. South Africa, Republic of. 1990-1992. Lang.: Eng. 4243
Baker, George Pierce
Audience
George Pierce Baker's 47 Workshop and the construction of the audience. USA: Cambridge, MA. 1918-1924. Lang.: Eng. 159
Baker, James A.
Performance/production
Collection of newspaper reviews by London theatre critics. UK-England: London. 1998. Lang.: Eng. 2422
Baker, Shelley
Institutions
Interview with members of dance group Creative Independent Artists. UK-Scotland: Glasgow. 1996-1998. Lang.: Eng. 904
Baker, Thomas
Performance/production
Collection of newspaper reviews by London theatre critics. UK-England. 1998. Lang.: Eng. 2485
Bakkum, Tryntsje
Design/technology
Profiles of young theatrical designers. Netherlands. 1990-1998. Lang.: Dut. 207
Balada o črnem noju (Ballad of a Black Ostrich)
Plays/librettos/scripts
Analysis of plays by Igor Torkar. Slovenia. 1946-1970. Lang.: Slo. 3354
Balada o taščici (Ballad of a Robin)
Plays/librettos/scripts
Analysis of *Balada o taščici (Ballad of a Robin)* by Igor Torkar. Slovenia. 1946-1970. Lang.: Slo. 3346
Analysis of plays by Igor Torkar. Slovenia. 1946-1970. Lang.: Slo. 3354
Balagna, Olivier
Institutions
New plays by Dea Loher at Staatsschauspiel Hannover. Germany: Hannover. 1992-1998. Lang.: Ger. 1643
Plays/librettos/scripts
The language of Dea Loher's *Tätowierung (Tattoo)*. Germany. 1995-1998. Lang.: Ger. 3126
Balanchine, George
Performance/production
Balanchine's choreography for Bizet's *Symphony in C*. France: Paris. 1947-1948. Lang.: Eng. 1079
Review of one-act ballets by Balanchine. Hungary: Budapest. 1997. Lang.: Hun. 1105
Interviews with dancers about performance. UK-England. USA. Cuba. 1942-1989. Lang.: Eng. 1162
Synopses of lost choreographies by Jerome Robbins. USA: New York, NY. 1949-1952. Lang.: Eng. 1166
New York performances of the San Francisco Ballet. USA: New York, NY. 1998. Lang.: Eng. 1170
Ballerina Alexandra Danilova on Balanchine's *Raymonda*. USA: New York, NY. 1946. Lang.: Eng. 1172
Balanchine's choreography to Čajkovskij's *Themes and Variations*. USA. 1960-1998. Lang.: Eng. 1179
Interview with choreographer John Taras. USA: New York, NY. 1919-1998. Lang.: Hun. 1187
Panel discussion on Balanchine's *Jewels*. USA: New York, NY. 1967. Lang.: Eng. 1188
Theory/criticism
The use of different analytical strategies to obtain multiple readings of dance performance. USA. Europe. 1946-1982. Lang.: Eng. 1200
Comparison of critical reviews of dance performances. USA: New York, NY. 1992. Lang.: Eng. 1201
Training
Balanchine's ballet mistress on his training methods. USA. 1947-1998. Lang.: Eng. 1214
Balázsovits, Lajos
Institutions
Interviews with the jury who selected the National Theatre Festival presentations. Hungary. 1996-1997. Lang.: Hun. 363
Bald Soprano, The
SEE
Cantatrice chauve, La.
Baldassari, Mike
Design/technology
Lighting design for Sam Mendes' production of *Cabaret*. USA: New York, NY. 1998. Lang.: Eng. 4344
Balderston, John L.
Design/technology
Magical stage effects in 'vampire' plays. USA. 1820-1977. Lang.: Eng. 1548
Baldinu, Pichon
Institutions
Report on festival of physical theatre. Germany: Munich. 1997. Lang.: Eng. 1664
Bale, John
Performance/production
Music in Tudor drama. England. 1497-1569. Lang.: Eng. 1902
Plays/librettos/scripts
John Bale's characters Sodomy and Idolatry. England. 1536-1546. Lang.: Eng. 2914
Balettakademien (Gothenburg)
Institutions
Interview with dance teacher Lia Schubert. Sweden: Stockholm, Gothenburg. 1935-1998. Lang.: Swe. 900
The musical theatre program at Balettakademien. Sweden: Gothenburg. 1984-1998. Lang.: Swe. 4349
Training
Memoirs of dance teacher Lia Schubert. Sweden: Malmö, Stockholm, Gothenburg. 1950-1998. Lang.: Swe. 1021
Balettakademien (Stockholm)
Institutions
Interview with dance teacher Lia Schubert. Sweden: Stockholm, Gothenburg. 1935-1998. Lang.: Swe. 900
History of Ballettakademian, Lillemor Lundberg, artistic director. Sweden: Stockholm. 1957-1998. Lang.: Swe. 901

Balettakademien (Stockholm) — cont'd

Training
Memoirs of dance teacher Lia Schubert. Sweden: Malmö, Stockholm, Gothenburg. 1950-1998. Lang.: Swe. 1021

Balikó, Tamás
Performance/production
Two Hungarian productions of Arthur Miller's *Death of a Salesman.* Hungary: Pécs, Szeged. 1998. Lang.: Hun. 2123

Bálint, András
Performance/production
Review of András Bálint's one-man show *INRI.* Hungary: Budapest. 1997. Lang.: Hun. 2073

Ball, Leland
Administration
Leland Ball of Sacramento Light Opera Association, winner of Rosetta LeNoire Award. USA: Sacramento, CA. 1998. Lang.: Eng. 4408

Ballad of Bony Lairt, The
Performance/production
Collection of newspaper reviews by London theatre critics. UK-England: London. 1998. Lang.: Eng. 2427

Ballad of Sam Bass, The
Basic theatrical documents
Text of *The Ballad of Sam Bass* by William Johnson Evarts. USA. 1988. Lang.: Eng. 1484

Ballad opera
Plays/librettos/scripts
Music and the ballad opera in English popular theatre. England. 1728-1780. Lang.: Eng. 4390

Ballade
Performance/production
Synopses of lost choreographies by Jerome Robbins. USA: New York, NY. 1949-1952. Lang.: Eng. 1166

Ballade von der Stadt, Die (Ballad of the City, The)
Plays/librettos/scripts
Social criticism in Viennese Expressionist drama. Austria: Vienna. 1907-1922. Lang.: Ger. 2779

Ballet
SEE ALSO
Classed Entries under DANCE—Ballet.

Training, ballet.

Design/technology
New lighting equipment of Lithuanian Opera and Ballet Theatre. Lithuania: Vilnius. 1974-1998. Lang.: Swe, Eng, Ger. 205

Institutions
The Bolšoj Theatre's 222nd season. Russia: Moscow. 1997-1998. Lang.: Rus. 4466

The Boldina Opera and Ballet festival honoring Puškin. Russia: Nizhni Novgorod. 1998. Lang.: Rus. 4469

Performance/production
The performance of sacrifice on stage. France. Germany. 1900-1998. Lang.: Ger. 530

Survey of Berlin productions in the holiday season. Germany: Berlin. 1997-1998. Lang.: Eng. 538

Onstage costume changes. Japan. Russia. Denmark. 1752-1998. Lang.: Swe. 556

Notes and essays on dancers and actors of the nineties. Russia. 1995-1999. Lang.: Rus. 587

Brief history of Slovene theatre. Slovenia. 1867-1997. Lang.: Slo. 595

Interview with Bengt Andersson, artistic director of Teater Tre. Sweden. 1983-1998. Lang.: Swe. 601

Director and choreographer Jerome Robbins. USA. 1919-1998. Lang.: Eng. 975

The possibilities for creativity in the reconstruction of dance choreographies. 1998. Lang.: Eng. 1258

The importance of reconstructing and preserving choreographies. 1998. Lang.: Eng. 1259

The body and personality of the dancer as the source of the physical vocabulary of dance. Europe. 1989. Lang.: Eng. 1269

Premieres of the Bolšoj Theatre. Russia: Moscow. 1825-1997. Lang.: Rus. 4693

Plays/librettos/scripts
The character of Ivan the Terrible. USSR. 1800-1965. Lang.: Eng. 692

The popularity and influence of the ballet film *The Red Shoes.* UK-England. 1948. Lang.: Eng. 3988

Reference materials
Yearbook of Slovene theatre. Slovenia. 1996-1997. Lang.: Slo. 708

Popular history of world dance. 2000 B.C.-1990 A.D. Lang.: Slo. 994

History of dance and ballet. 2000 B.C.-1990 A.D. Lang.: Slo. 995

Yearbook of the Hungarian State Opera House. Hungary: Budapest. 1996-1997. Lang.: Hun. 4832

Ballet Folklórico de México (Mexico City)
Performance/production
Performances of the Ballet Folklórico de México and the Guangdong Dance Company. USA: Washington, DC. 1997. Lang.: Hun. 1241

Ballet Gulbenkian (Lisbon)
Performance/production
Comparison of performances by Rosas and Ballet Gulbenkian. Hungary: Budapest. 1992-1994. Lang.: Hun. 939

Ballet Nacional de Cuba (Havana)
Institutions
Interview with Alicia Alonso of Ballet Nacional de Cuba. Cuba: Havana. 1948-1998. Lang.: Swe. 1036

Performance/production
Interviews with dancers about performance. UK-England. USA. Cuba. 1942-1989. Lang.: Eng. 1162

BalletMet (Columbus, OH)
Institutions
Profile of BalletMet. USA: Columbus, OH. 1978-1998. Lang.: Eng. 1062

Ballets Africains, Les (Guinea)
Performance/production
Performances of Joaquím Cortez's flamenco troupe and the Ballets Africains of Guinea. UK-England: London. 1997. Lang.: Hun. 1238

Ballets Contemporains de la Belgique (Ghent)
Performance/production
Interview with choreographer Alain Platel. Belgium: Ghent. 1984-1998. Lang.: Eng. 1261

Ballets Russes (Paris)
Audience
Diaghilev's strategies of audience development. France: Paris. 1906-1914. Lang.: Eng. 1028

Institutions
Display of objects related to guest performances of the Ballets Russes. Germany: Berlin. 1910-1914. Lang.: Hun. 1040

Performance/production
Masculinity in ballet. France: Paris. 1908-1915. Lang.: Eng. 1070

Ballets Suédois (Paris)
Performance/production
Collaborative Symbolist dance/theatre projects. Europe. USA. 1916-1934. Lang.: Eng. 1268

Ballets Trockadero de Monte Carlo, Les (New York, NY)
Performance/production
Interview with dancer/choreographer Elena Kunikova on her work with Les Ballets Trockadero. USA: New York, NY. 1997. Lang.: Eng. 1180

Ballett Frankfurt
Performance/production
Choreographer William Forsythe. Germany: Frankfurt. 1973-1998. Lang.: Eng. 1081

Choreographer William Forsythe, director of Ballett Frankfurt. Germany: Frankfurt. 1949-1998. Lang.: Eng. 1084

The choreography of William Forsythe and the painting of Marcel Duchamp. Germany. France. 1915-1998. Lang.: Eng. 1280

William Forsythe of Ballett Frankfurt. Germany: Frankfurt. 1984-1998. Lang.: Ger. 1284

Ballo in Maschera, Un
Performance/production
Interview with Miklós Gábor Kerényi on directing Verdi's *Un Ballo in Maschera.* Hungary: Budapest. 1998. Lang.: Hun. 4619

Verdi's *Un Ballo in Maschera* at the Hungarian State Opera House. Hungary: Budapest. 1998. Lang.: Hun. 4629

Interview with Miklós Gábor Kerényi on his production of *Un Ballo in maschera.* Hungary: Budapest, Szeged. 1998. Lang.: Hun. 4636

Ballroom dancing
Performance spaces
The former dance palace Nalen, now restored as Nationalpalatset. Sweden: Stockholm. 1889-1998. Lang.: Swe. 4114

Performance/production
The influence of tango on world dance. Argentina. Lang.: Rus. 1223

Balls
Performance/production
Collection of newspaper reviews by London theatre critics. UK-England: London. 1998. Lang.: Eng. 2449

Baltsa, Agnes
Performance/production
Singers' approaches to the title role in Bizet's *Carmen.* 1875-1998. Lang.: Eng. 4502

Balzac, Honoré de
Design/technology
Des McAnuff's design concept for his film *Cousin Bette*. USA: Hollywood, CA. 1998. Lang.: Eng. 3905
Plays/librettos/scripts
Criticism of the creation of literary 'genealogies' for dramatic characters. Ireland. France. 1953-1998. Lang.: Swe. 3211
BAM
SEE
Brooklyn Academy of Music.
Bán, Ferenc
Performance spaces
Ferenc Bán's architectural design for Hungary's new National Theatre. Hungary: Budapest. 1998. Lang.: Hun. 446
Account of the competition for the design of the new National Theatre. Hungary: Budapest. 1996-1997. Lang.: Hun. 448
Bance, Georgia
Performance/production
Collection of newspaper reviews by London theatre critics. UK-England: London. 1998. Lang.: Eng. 2458
Bances Candamo, Francisco Antonio de
Plays/librettos/scripts
Life and career of playwright Francisco Antonio de Bances Candamo. Spain. 1662-1704. Lang.: Eng. 3374
Bancil, Parv
Performance/production
Collection of newspaper reviews by London theatre critics. UK-England: London. 1998. Lang.: Eng. 2427
Collection of newspaper reviews by London theatre critics. UK-England: London. 1998. Lang.: Eng. 2532
Band Wagon, The
Performance/production
Choreography in the musical film *The Bandwagon*. USA. 1953. Lang.: Eng. 982
Band, The
Institutions
Profile of Nordhessisches Landestheater Marburg. Germany: Marburg. 1997-1998. Lang.: Ger. 1653
Bandele, Biyi
Performance/production
Collection of newspaper reviews by London theatre critics. UK-England: London. 1998. Lang.: Eng. 2515
Bandido!
Plays/librettos/scripts
Analysis of *Bandido!* by Luis Valdez. USA. 1986. Lang.: Eng. 3676
Analysis of *Bandido!* by Luis Valdez. USA. 1982. Lang.: Eng. 3708
Banks, Carol P.
Plays/librettos/scripts
The theory and practice of playwriting for different age groups. USA. 1988. Lang.: Eng. 3524
Banks, Greg
Performance/production
Collection of newspaper reviews by London theatre critics. UK-England: London. 1998. Lang.: Eng. 2410
Bannerman, Celia
Performance/production
Collection of newspaper reviews by London theatre critics. UK-England: London. 1998. Lang.: Eng. 2421
Bannister, Kate
Performance/production
Collection of newspaper reviews by London theatre critics. UK-England: London. 1998. Lang.: Eng. 2490
Bara, Charlotte
Performance spaces
Dancers and performance space. Europe. 1895-1937. Lang.: Ger. 909
Barabás, Olga
Performance/production
Molière's *Dom Juan* directed by Olga Barabás. Hungary. Romania: Sfântu-Gheorghe. 1998. Lang.: Hun. 2063
Barabbas
Performance/production
Collection of newspaper reviews by London theatre critics. UK-England: London. 1998. Lang.: Eng. 2581
Baraka, Imamu Amiri (Jones, LeRoi)
Plays/librettos/scripts
Afrocentricity in plays of Charles Fuller, Amiri Baraka, and Larry Neal. USA. 1960-1998. Lang.: Eng. 3519
History of the Playwrights Unit. USA. 1963-1971. Lang.: Eng. 3570
Revolutionary elements in plays and theory of Baraka and Artaud. USA. France. 1920-1970. Lang.: Eng. 3580
Baranova, Irina
Performance/production
Tributes to ballerina Alexandra Danilova. USA: New York, NY. 1997. Lang.: Eng. 1165
Barba, Eugenio
Institutions
The eleventh session of the International School of Theatre Anthropology. Portugal: Lisbon. Denmark: Holstebro. 1998. Lang.: Eng. 376
Performance/production
Directing and intercultural theatre. Europe. 1930-1998. Lang.: Ger. 524
Eugenio Barba's *Oxyrhyncus Evangeliet*, Odin Teatret. USA. 1988. Lang.: Eng. 646
Acting and directing influences on Eugenio Barba. Denmark: Holstebro. 1997. Lang.: Eng. 1886
Barber of Seville, The (opera)
SEE
Barbiere di Siviglia, Il.
Barber, Emily
Performance/production
Collection of newspaper reviews by London theatre critics. UK-England: London. 1998. Lang.: Eng. 2522
Barber, Samuel
Performance/production
A performance by Mikhail Baryshnikov and the White Oak Dance Project. USA: Washington, DC. 1990-1998. Lang.: Hun. 1194
Barbers of Surreal, The
Performance/production
Collection of newspaper reviews by London theatre critics. UK-England: London. 1998. Lang.: Eng. 2436
Barbican Centre (London)
Administration
Interview with John Tusa, managing director of the Barbican Centre. UK-England: London. 1996-1998. Lang.: Eng. 24
Attempts to diversify offerings of the Barbican Centre. UK-England: London. 1998. Lang.: Eng. 25
Barbican Theatre (London)
SEE ALSO
Royal Shakespeare Company.
Performance/production
Collection of newspaper reviews by London theatre critics. UK-England: London. 1998. Lang.: Eng. 2409
Collection of newspaper reviews by London theatre critics. UK-England: London. 1998. Lang.: Eng. 2420
Collection of newspaper reviews by London theatre critics. UK-England: London. 1998. Lang.: Eng. 2424
Collection of newspaper reviews by London theatre critics. UK-England: London. 1998. Lang.: Eng. 2476
Collection of newspaper reviews by London theatre critics. UK-England: London. 1998. Lang.: Eng. 2484
Collection of newspaper reviews by London theatre critics. UK-England: London. 1998. Lang.: Eng. 2496
Collection of newspaper reviews by London theatre critics. UK-England: London. 1998. Lang.: Eng. 2503
Collection of newspaper reviews by London theatre critics. UK-England: London. 1998. Lang.: Eng. 2512
Collection of newspaper reviews by London theatre critics. UK-England: London. 1998. Lang.: Eng. 2520
Collection of newspaper reviews by London theatre critics. UK-England: London. 1998. Lang.: Eng. 2531
Collection of newspaper reviews by London theatre critics. UK-England: London. 1998. Lang.: Eng. 2551
Collection of newspaper reviews by London theatre critics. UK-England: London. 1998. Lang.: Eng. 2571
Collection of newspaper reviews by London theatre critics. UK-England: London. 1998. Lang.: Eng. 2588
Reviews of recent London performances. UK-England: London. 1998. Lang.: Ger. 2591
Barbier de Séville, Le (Barber of Seville, The)
Plays/librettos/scripts
Operatic realizations of Beaumarchais' character Rosina. Europe. North America. 1784-1991. Lang.: Eng. 4773
Barbiere di Siviglia, Il
Performance/production
Bass Samuel Ramey. USA. 1940-1998. Lang.: Eng. 4744

***Barbiere di Siviglia, Il* — cont'd**

Plays/librettos/scripts
Operatic realizations of Beaumarchais' character Rosina. Europe. North America. 1784-1991. Lang.: Eng. 4773

Barbiere di Siviglia, Il (by Paisiello)
Plays/librettos/scripts
Operatic realizations of Beaumarchais' character Rosina. Europe. North America. 1784-1991. Lang.: Eng. 4773

Bárdy, Margit
Design/technology
Costume designer Margit Bárdy. Hungary. Germany: Munich. 1929-1997. Lang.: Hun. 193

Barenboim, Daniel
Plays/librettos/scripts
Daniel Barenboim and Edward Said on composer Richard Wagner. USA: New York, NY. Germany. 1995. Lang.: Eng. 4826

Bargagli, Girolamo
Plays/librettos/scripts
Ludic aspects of Italian Renaissance theatre. Italy. 1500-1700. Lang.: Ita. 3240

Bargum, Johan
Plays/librettos/scripts
Recent drama and revue in Swedish. Finland. 1998. Lang.: Eng, Fre. 3069

Bariona
Plays/librettos/scripts
Analysis of *Bariona* by Jean-Paul Sartre. France. 1940-1945. Lang.: Eng. 3093

Bárka Színház (Budapest)
Performance/production
Péter Kárpáti's *Díszelőadás (Gala Performance)* directed by Balázs Simon. Hungary: Budapest. 1998. Lang.: Hun. 2057

Thomas Bernhard's *Ritter, Dene, Voss* at Bárka Színház. Hungary: Budapest. 1997. Lang.: Hun. 2087

Performances at the new Bárka Színház. Hungary: Budapest. 1997. Lang.: Hun. 2097

Lorca's *Doña Rosita* directed by Gergő Kaszás. Hungary: Budapest. 1998. Lang.: Hun. 2099

Csaba Kiss's adaptation of Shakespeare's chronicle plays at Bárka Színház. Hungary: Győr. 1997. Lang.: Hun. 2101

István Tasnádi's *Titanic vízirevü (Titanic Water Show)* at Bárka Színház. Hungary: Budapest. 1998. Lang.: Hun. 2144

Barker, Cary
Administration
Interview with actors on Equity. USA: New York, NY. 1998. Lang.: Eng. 75

Barker, Howard
Performance/production
Collection of newspaper reviews by London theatre critics. UK-England. 1998. Lang.: Eng. 2504

Collection of newspaper reviews by London theatre critics. UK-England: London. 1998. Lang.: Eng. 2505

Plays/librettos/scripts
The influence of Jacobean theatre on contemporary plays and productions. UK-England. 1986-1998. Lang.: Eng. 3428

Rape in Middleton's *Women Beware Women* and its adaptation by Howard Barker. UK-England. 1625-1986. Lang.: Eng. 3468

British historical drama. UK-England. 1956-1988. Lang.: Eng. 3500

Political thought in plays of Howard Barker. UK-England. 1960-1992. Lang.: Eng. 3502

Barker, Ronnie
Performance/production
Collection of newspaper reviews by London theatre critics. UK-England: London. 1998. Lang.: Eng. 2513

Barlow, Clarence
Plays/librettos/scripts
Clarence Barlow's abstract musical setting of a prose text by Samuel Beckett. 1971-1972. Lang.: Eng. 4305

Barlow, Patrick
Performance/production
Collection of newspaper reviews by London theatre critics. UK-England: London. 1998. Lang.: Eng. 2495

Collection of newspaper reviews by London theatre critics. UK-England: London. 1998. Lang.: Eng. 2540

Barnes, Djuna
Performance/production
The first wave of American feminist theatre. USA. 1890-1930. Lang.: Eng. 648

Barnes, Jason
Design/technology
Jason Barnes, production manager of the Royal National Theatre. UK-England: London. 1973-1998. Lang.: Eng. 1527

Barnes, Pete
Design/technology
Sound design for The Spice Girls tour. UK-England. 1998. Lang.: Eng. 4097

Barnes, Peter
Performance/production
Collection of newspaper reviews by London theatre critics. UK-England: London. 1998. Lang.: Eng. 2427

Plays/librettos/scripts
Gender and madness in modern drama. Europe. 1880-1969. Lang.: Eng. 3061

Genocide, theatre, and the human body. North America. UK-England. Argentina. 1998. Lang.: Eng. 3290

Plays of Peter Barnes compared to those of Renaissance dramatists. UK-England. 1968-1974. Lang.: Eng. 3449

British historical drama. UK-England. 1956-1988. Lang.: Eng. 3500

Analysis of *Red Noses* by Peter Barnes. UK-Scotland. 1985. Lang.: Eng. 3514

Barnet (Child, The)
Performance/production
Collection of newspaper reviews by London theatre critics. UK-England: London. 1998. Lang.: Eng. 2582

Barnett, Robby
Performance/production
Comparison of productions of Ibsen's *Peer Gynt*. USA: Providence, RI, New York, NY, Washington, DC, Nacogdoches, TX. 1998. Lang.: Eng. 2711

Barnum, Phineas T.
Institutions
Respectability and museum theatre. USA: New York, NY. 1840-1880. Lang.: Eng. 4112

Performance/production
Performance and the nineteenth-century economy. USA. 1850-1890. Lang.: Eng. 4134

Barock friise (Baroque Frieze)
Plays/librettos/scripts
Female characters in plays by Scandinavian women. Norway. Sweden. Denmark. 1998. Lang.: Eng. 3299

Baron's Court Theatre (London)
Performance/production
Collection of newspaper reviews by London theatre critics. UK-England: London. 1998. Lang.: Eng. 2457

Collection of newspaper reviews by London theatre critics. UK-England: London. 1998. Lang.: Eng. 2517

Baroni, Guido
Design/technology
Theatrical lighting design of Guido and Lucilla Baroni. Italy. 1946-1998. Lang.: Eng. 201

Baroni, Lucilla
Design/technology
Theatrical lighting design of Guido and Lucilla Baroni. Italy. 1946-1998. Lang.: Eng. 201

Baroque opera
Institutions
Profile of Opera Atelier. Canada: Toronto, ON. 1985-1998. Lang.: Eng. 4446

Performance spaces
Baroque opera and ballet at the Salle des Machines and the Palais Royal. France: Paris. 1640-1690. Lang.: Eng. 4493

Performance/production
The influence of the Haymarket Theatre on Handelian opera. England: London. 1710-1739. Lang.: Eng. 4549

Baroque theatre
SEE ALSO
Geographical-Chronological Index under Europe, and other European countries, 1594-1702.

Barr, Richard
Plays/librettos/scripts
History of the Playwrights Unit. USA. 1963-1971. Lang.: Eng. 3570

Barr, Sara
Performance/production
Collection of newspaper reviews by London theatre critics. UK-England: London. 1998. Lang.: Eng. 2549

Barraca, La (Bologna)
Institutions
The quality of theatre for children and youth. Italy: Bologna. Sweden: Stockholm. Germany. 1998. Lang.: Ger. 367

Barrie, James M.
Performance/production
Collection of newspaper reviews by London theatre critics. UK-England: London. 1998. Lang.: Eng. 2555
Plays/librettos/scripts
Colonialism and misogyny in J.M. Barrie's *Peter Pan.* UK-England. 1908. Lang.: Eng. 3423
Psychology and the self in works of J.M. Barrie. UK-England. 1892-1937. Lang.: Eng. 3478
Barrie, Tom
Basic theatrical documents
Text of *Example: The Case of Craig and Bentley* adapted by Tom Barrie. UK-England. 1998. Lang.: Eng. 1472
Performance/production
Collection of newspaper reviews by London theatre critics. UK-England: London. 1998. Lang.: Eng. 2528
Collection of newspaper reviews by London theatre critics. UK-England: London. 1998. Lang.: Eng. 2554
Barry, Kieron
Performance/production
Collection of newspaper reviews by London theatre critics. UK-England: London. 1998. Lang.: Eng. 2521
Barry, Philip
Plays/librettos/scripts
The comedies of manners of S.N. Behrman and Philip Barry. USA. 1920-1964. Lang.: Eng. 3648
Barry, Sebastian
Performance/production
Collection of newspaper reviews by London theatre critics. UK-England: London. 1998. Lang.: Eng. 2461
Plays/librettos/scripts
Contemporary Irish playwrights. Ireland. 1998. Lang.: Eng. 3207
Barrymore, John
Performance/production
Actor John Barrymore. USA: New York, NY. 1882-1942. Lang.: Eng. 2732
Bartel, Paul
Basic theatrical documents
Screenplay for *The Secret Cinema* by Paul Bartel. USA. 1966. Lang.: Eng. 3881
Bartenieff, Irmgard
Training
The development of Irmgard Bartenieff's corrective physical training methods. USA. 1925-1981. Lang.: Ger. 1024
Bartered Bride, The
SEE
Prodana Nevěsta.
Bartlett, Neil
Performance/production
Collection of newspaper reviews by London theatre critics. UK-England: London. 1998. Lang.: Eng. 2500
Collection of newspaper reviews by London theatre critics. UK-England: London. 1998. Lang.: Eng. 2556
Collection of newspaper reviews by London theatre critics. UK-England: London. 1998. Lang.: Eng. 2584
Bartók Kamaraszínház (Dunaújváros)
Performance/production
One-act comedies by Čechov directed by Péter Valló. Hungary: Dunaújváros. 1998. Lang.: Hun. 2080
Bartók, Béla
Performance/production
Bartók's *A csodálatos mandarin (The Miraculous Mandarin)* choreographed by Gyula Harangozó. Hungary: Budapest. 1998.Lang.: Hun. 1088
Productions of the Magyar Fesztival Balett choreographed by Iván Markó. Hungary: Budapest. 1998. Lang.: Hun. 1097
Bartók's *A fából faragott királyfi (The Wooden Prince)* choreographed by László Seregi. Hungary: Budapest. 1998. Lang.: Hun. 1103
Soprano Olga Haselbeck. Hungary. 1884-1961. Lang.: Hun. 4626
Bartok, Eva
Performance/production
The death of actress Eva Bartok. Hungary. UK-England: London. 1998. Lang.: Eng. 3934
Bartoli, Cecilia
Performance/production
Profile of opera star Cecilia Bartoli. Italy. 1995-1998. Lang.: Eng. 4658
Interview with singer Cecilia Bartoli. Italy. 1997. Lang.: Swe. 4663
Barton, Bruce
Performance/production
Analysis of *1837: The Farmer's Revolt* directed by Bruce Barton of Carrefour Theatre. Canada: Charlottetown, PE. 1998. Lang.: Eng. 1856
Barton, John
Performance/production
Three productions of Shakespeare's *Richard III.* UK-England. 1973-1984. Lang.: Eng. 2612
John Barton's workshop on Shakespearean performance. USA: New York, NY. 1998. Lang.: Eng. 2704
Barton, Lance
Performance/production
The theory and practice of stage magic. 1998. Lang.: Rus. 4274
Baryshnikov, Mikhail
Institutions
Profile of the American Ballet Theatre. USA: New York, NY. 1998. Lang.: Hun. 1061
Performance/production
Ballet soloist Mikhail Baryshnikov. Latvia. USA. 1948-1997. Lang.: Eng. 1119
Russian émigré ballet dancers. Russia: St. Petersburg. Lang.: Rus. 1129
Collaboration of the Bolšoj and Mariinskij ballet troupes. Russia: Moscow, St. Petersburg. 1998. Lang.: Rus. 1135
Russsian-born dancer Mikhail Baryshnikov. USA. 1998. Lang.: Rus. 1169
Dancer/choreographer Mikhail Baryshnikov. USA. USSR. 1966-1998. Lang.: Eng. 1189
A performance by Mikhail Baryshnikov and the White Oak Dance Project. USA: Washington, DC. 1990-1998. Lang.: Hun. 1194
Dancer/choreographer Mikhail Baryshnikov. USSR. USA. 1969-1998. Lang.: Eng. 1196
Baškirskij Akademičeskij Teat'r Dramy (Ufa)
Performance/production
Rijfkat Israfilov's production of *Bibinur, ah, Bibinur!*. Bashkir: Ufa. 1998. Lang.: Rus. 1827
Basler Theater (Basel)
Administration
Theater Basel under the direction of Stefan Bachmann. Switzerland: Basel. 1996-1998. Lang.: Ger. 1391
Institutions
Stefan Bachmann of Basler Theater. Switzerland: Basel. 1998. Lang.: Ger. 1737
Performance/production
Stefan Bachmann's production of Shakespeare's *Troilus and Cressida.* Switzerland: Basle. 1998. Lang.: Ger. 2399
Reviews of plays by Wolfgang Bauer and Thomas Bernhard. Switzerland: Basel. Austria: Vienna. 1998. Lang.: Ger. 2403
Interview with opera director Jossi Wieler. Germany: Stuttgart. Switzerland: Basel. 1998. Lang.: Ger. 4592
Reviews of recent opera productions. Switzerland: Basel. Germany: Stuttgart, Berlin, Hamburg. France: Strasbourg. 1997-1998. Lang.: Ger. 4702
Bass Performance Hall (Ft. Worth, TX)
Performance spaces
The architecture of the Bass Performance Hall. USA: Ft. Worth, TX. 1998. Lang.: Eng. 477
Bassano, Enrico
Plays/librettos/scripts
Analysis of plays of Enrico Bassano. Italy. 1899-1979. Lang.: Ita. 3226
Basset Table, The
Performance/production
Collection of newspaper reviews by London theatre critics. UK-England: London. 1998. Lang.: Eng. 2419
Basshe, Em Jo
Institutions
The New Playwrights Theatre Company. USA: New York, NY. 1927-1929. Lang.: Eng. 410
Bässler, Oliver
Performance/production
Actor Oliver Bässler. Germany: Cottbus. 1985-1998. Lang.: Ger. 1995
Bat (Berlin)
Institutions
Director training at Ernst-Busch-Schule and some of its graduates. Germany: Berlin. 1972-1998. Lang.: Ger. 1648
Performance/production
Comparison of productions of Brecht's *Die Massnahme (The Measures Taken).* Germany: Berlin, Wuppertal. 1995-1998. Lang.: Ger. 1950

Bates, Florence
Plays/librettos/scripts
The censorship of the unpublished *Her Wedding Night* by Florence Bates. UK-England. 1917. Lang.: Eng. 3454
Bates, Terry John
Performance/production
Collection of newspaper reviews by London theatre critics. UK-England: London. 1998. Lang.: Eng. 2480
Batsheva Dance Company
Institutions
Productions of Gothenburg's Dance and Theatre Festival. Sweden: Gothenburg. 1998. Lang.: Swe. 1253
Battersea Arts Centre (London)
Performance/production
Collection of newspaper reviews by London theatre critics. UK-England: London. 1998. Lang.: Eng. 2424
Collection of newspaper reviews by London theatre critics. UK-England: London, Scarborough. 1998. Lang.: Eng. 2426
Collection of newspaper reviews by London theatre critics. UK-England: London. 1998. Lang.: Eng. 2427
Collection of newspaper reviews by London theatre critics. UK-England: London. 1998. Lang.: Eng. 2430
Collection of newspaper reviews by London theatre critics. UK-England: London. 1998. Lang.: Eng. 2440
Collection of newspaper reviews by London theatre critics. UK-England: London. 1998. Lang.: Eng. 2446
Collection of newspaper reviews by London theatre critics. UK-England: London. 1998. Lang.: Eng. 2448
Collection of newspaper reviews by London theatre critics. UK-England: London. 1998. Lang.: Eng. 2499
Collection of newspaper reviews by London theatre critics. UK-England: London. 1998. Lang.: Eng. 2525
Collection of newspaper reviews by London theatre critics. UK-England: London. 1998. Lang.: Eng. 2532
Collection of newspaper reviews by London theatre critics. UK-England: London. 1998. Lang.: Eng. 2535
Collection of newspaper reviews by London theatre critics. UK-England: London. 1998. Lang.: Eng. 2542
Collection of newspaper reviews by London theatre critics. UK-England: London. 1998. Lang.: Eng. 2548
Collection of newspaper reviews by London theatre critics. UK-England: London. 1998. Lang.: Eng. 2554
Collection of newspaper reviews by London theatre critics. UK-England: London. 1998. Lang.: Eng. 2564
Collection of newspaper reviews by London theatre critics. UK-England: London. 1998. Lang.: Eng. 2568
Collection of newspaper reviews by London theatre critics. UK-England: London. 1998. Lang.: Eng. 2572
Collection of newspaper reviews by London theatre critics. UK-England: London. 1998. Lang.: Eng. 2574
Collection of newspaper reviews by London theatre critics. UK-England: London. 1998. Lang.: Eng. 2576
Collection of newspaper reviews by London theatre critics. UK-England: London. 1998. Lang.: Eng. 2578
Collection of newspaper reviews by London theatre critics. UK-England: London. 1998. Lang.: Eng. 2580
Collection of newspaper reviews by London theatre critics. UK-England: London. 1998. Lang.: Eng. 2583
Battersea Latchmere Theatre (London)
SEE
Latchmere Theatre (London).
Battistoni, Carlo
Performance/production
Piccolo Teatro after the death of director Giorgio Strehler. Italy: Milan. 1947-1998. Lang.: Hun. 2186
Battle of Angels
Plays/librettos/scripts
Realism and anti-realism in plays of Tennessee Williams. USA. 1945-1986. Lang.: Eng. 3626
Bauer, Sabine
Performance/production
Collection of newspaper reviews by London theatre critics. UK-England: London. 1998. Lang.: Eng. 2481
Bauer, Wolfgang
Performance/production
Reviews of plays by Wolfgang Bauer and Thomas Bernhard. Switzerland: Basel. Austria: Vienna. 1998. Lang.: Ger. 2403
Baumbauer, Frank
Administration
Interview with Frank Baumbauer of Deutsches Schauspielhaus Hamburg. Germany: Hamburg. 1993-2000. Lang.: Ger. 11
Bausch, Pina
Design/technology
Set and costume designer Frank Leimbach and his work with choreographers. Germany. 1991-1998. Lang.: Ger. 1247
Institutions
Profile of Pina Bausch and her Tanztheater. Germany: Wuppertal. 1977-1998. Lang.: Eng. 893
Performance/production
Dancer/choreographer Pina Bausch. Germany: Wuppertal. 1973-1997. Lang.: Eng. 932
Nudity in dance theatre. Europe. 1970-1998. Lang.: Ger. 1270
A personal response to Pina Bausch's dance theatre. Germany: Wuppertal. 1982-1998. Lang.: Eng. 1277
Analysis of *Nur du (Only You)* by choreographer Pina Bausch. Germany: Wuppertal. 1997. Lang.: Eng. 1278
Interview with dancer and choreographer Pina Bausch. Germany: Wuppertal. 1973-1998. Lang.: Ger. 1279
Portrait of choreographer/director Pina Bausch. Germany: Wuppertal. 1973-1998. Lang.: Ger. 1281
Analysis of Pina Bausch's dance work *Masuca Fogo*. Germany: Wuppertal. 1998. Lang.: Ger. 1282
Reactions to guest performances of dancer/choreographer Pina Bausch. Sweden: Stockholm. 1998. Lang.: Swe. 1301
Stockholm's year as Cultural Capital of Europe. Sweden: Stockholm. 1766-1998. Lang.: Eng. 2394
Training
Dance training at Folkwang Hochschule. Germany: Essen. 1996-1998. Lang.: Hun. 1341
Bavarian State Opera
SEE
Bayerische Staatsoper.
Bayerische Staatsballett (München)
Performance/production
Bayerische Staatsballett's guest performances at Budapest Opera House. Hungary: Budapest. 1998. Lang.: Hun. 1092
Bayerische Staatsballett (Munich)
Administration
Interview with Ivan Liška, new director of Bayerische Staatsballett. Germany: Munich. 1998. Lang.: Hun. 1026
Bayerische Staatsoper (Munich)
Administration
Bayerische Staatsoper's new marketing concept. Germany: Munich. 1993-1998. Lang.: Ger. 4405
Performance/production
Productions of Wagner's *Tristan und Isolde* by Peter Konwitschny and Werner Schroeter. Germany: Munich, Duisberg. 1998. Lang.: Ger. 4580
Interview with opera composer Manfred Trojahn. Germany: Munich. 1998. Lang.: Ger. 4582
Bayerische Theaterakademie/Hochschule für Musik (Munich)
Institutions
Profile of Munich's theatre training institutions. Germany: Munich. 1998. Lang.: Ger. 348
The curriculum at Bayerische Theaterakademie. Germany: Munich. 1985-1998. Lang.: Ger. 1659
Bayerisches Staatsschauspiel (Munich)
Plays/librettos/scripts
The collaboration of playwright Dea Loher and director Andreas Kriegenburg. Germany: Hannover, Munich. 1990-1998. Lang.: Ger. 3151
The development of *Blaubart—Hoffnung der Frauen (Bluebeard—Hope of Women)* by Dea Loher. Germany: Munich. 1998. Lang.: Ger. 3164
Bayerisches Staatsschauspiel, Marstall (Munich)
Institutions
Survey of Munich's theatre scene. Germany: Munich. 1997. Lang.: Ger. 1626
Profile of new venue, Bayerisches Staatsschauspiel, Marstall. Germany: Munich. 1993-1998. Lang.: Ger. 1660
Bayerisches Staatsschauspiel, Residenztheater (Munich)
Performance/production
Natali Seelig, *Theater Heute*'s actress of the year. Germany: Munich. 1991-1998. Lang.: Ger. 1966
Comparison of two productions of Shakespeare's *Richard III*. Germany: Munich. 1996-1997. Lang.: Ger. 1976

Bayerisches Staatsschauspiel, Residenztheater (Munich) — cont'd

Andreas Kriegenburg's production of Büchner's *Leonce und Lena*. Germany: Munich. 1998. Lang.: Ger. 2020

Roberto Ciulli's production of *Doña Rosita la Soltera (Doña Rosita the Spinster)* by Federico García Lorca. Germany: Munich. 1998. Lang.: Ger. 2021

Baynham, Peter

Performance/production

Collection of newspaper reviews by London theatre critics. UK-England: London. 1998. Lang.: Eng. 2513

Bayreuther Festspiele (Bayreuth)

Institutions

Effect of Wagner family memoirs on the Bayreuth Festival. Germany: Bayreuth. 1998. Lang.: Eng. 4451

Comparison of Salzburg and Bayreuth festival seasons. Germany: Bayreuth. Austria: Salzburg. 1998. Lang.: Eng. 4452

Review of Wagner's *Ring* cycle at the Bayreuth Festival. Germany: Bayreuth. 1997-1998. Lang.: Hun. 4454

Performance spaces

Opera composer Richard Wagner and performance space. Europe. 1835-1885. Lang.: Eng. 4492

Performance/production

Iván Markó's choreography for Bayreuth Festival productions. Germany: Bayreuth. Hungary. 1998. Lang.: Hun. 1083

F.W. Beidler's ideas for a different Bayreuth Festival. Germany: Bayreuth. 1901-1981. Lang.: Ger. 4602

Historical overview of Wagnerian singing. Germany: Bayreuth. 1850-1998. Lang.: Eng. 4610

The influence of Wieland Wagner's production of *Lohengrin*. Germany, West: Bayreuth. 1966. Lang.: Eng. 4614

Bays, Michael

Design/technology

Lighting design for Michael Bays' film *Armageddon*. USA. 1998. Lang.: Eng. 3916

BDT

SEE

Bolšoj Dramatičeskij Teat'r.

Be My Baby

Performance/production

Collection of newspaper reviews by London theatre critics. UK-England: London. 1998. Lang.: Eng. 2550

Beacham, Richard

Research/historiography

The THEATRON theatre history project. Europe. 1998. Lang.: Dut. 3796

Beachum, Richard

Performance/production

Theatre Magazine's anniversary issue. USA. 1968-1998. Lang.: Eng. 617

Beale, Geoff

Performance/production

Ophaboom Theatre's experience in recreating *commedia dell'arte*. UK-England: London. 1991-1998. Lang.: Eng. 4193

Beane, Douglas Carter

Plays/librettos/scripts

Interview with playwright Douglas Carter Beane. USA. 1980-1998. Lang.: Eng. 3516

Playwright Douglas Carter Beane. USA. 1998. Lang.: Eng. 3688

Beardsmore-Billings, Hugh

Performance/production

Collection of newspaper reviews by London theatre critics. UK-England: London. 1998. Lang.: Eng. 2479

Beast on the Moon

Basic theatrical documents

French translation of *Beast on the Moon* by Richard Kalinoski. USA. France. 1995-1997. Lang.: Fre. 1491

Beatrice Chancy

Basic theatrical documents

Text of libretto for *Beatrice Chancy*. Canada: Toronto, ON. 1998. Lang.: Eng. 4413

James Rolfe on his opera *Beatrice Chancy*. Canada: Toronto, ON. 1998. Lang.: Eng. 4414

Beaufoy, Simon

Basic theatrical documents

Text of Simon Beaufoy's screenplay *The Full Monty*. UK-England. 1997. Lang.: Eng. 3879

Plays/librettos/scripts

Interview with Simon Beaufoy, author of *The Full Monty*. UK-England. 1997. Lang.: Eng. 3979

Observations on screenwriting and Beaufoy's *The Full Monty*. UK-England. 1997. Lang.: Eng. 3989

Beaumarchais, Pierre-Augustin Caron de

Plays/librettos/scripts

Desire in *Le Mariage de Figaro (The Marriage of Figaro)* by Beaumarchais. France. 1784. Lang.: Eng. 3095

Operatic realizations of Beaumarchais' character Rosina. Europe. North America. 1784-1991. Lang.: Eng. 4773

Beaumont, Francis

Performance/production

Review of the opening season of Shakespeare's Globe Theatre. UK-England: London. 1997. Lang.: Eng. 2602

Plays/librettos/scripts

Playwriting and publishing for the London stage. England. 1590-1650. Lang.: Eng. 2881

Plague imagery in Jacobean tragedy. England. 1618-1642. Lang.: Eng. 2889

The murders of royal women in plays of Shakespeare and Beaumont and Fletcher. England. 1609-1610. Lang.: Eng. 2894

Casuistry and early modern English tragedy. England. 1600-1671. Lang.: Eng. 2980

Beaumont, Hugh Morgan Griffiths

Administration

The 'Group of Four' at the Lyric Hammersmith and the concept of a national theatre. UK-England: London. 1945-1956. Lang.: Eng. 1392

Beaumont, William

Institutions

The inaugural season of Shakespeare's Globe Theatre. UK-England: London. 1997-1998. Lang.: Eng. 1741

Performance/production

The inaugural season of Shakespeare's Globe Theatre. UK-England: London. 1997. Lang.: Eng. 2601

Beauty and the Beast

Administration

The Disney Corporation's Broadway musicals. USA: New York, NY. 1996-1998. Lang.: Eng. 4317

Performance spaces

The construction of a theatre for *Beauty and the Beast*. Germany: Stuttgart. 1997. Lang.: Ger. 444

Beauty Queen of Leenane, The

Design/technology

Set designs of Francis O'Connor. USA: New York, NY. 1998. Lang.: Eng. 1541

Performance/production

Productions of director Peter Wittenberg. Germany: Munich, Bonn. 1998. Lang.: Ger. 2013

Plays/librettos/scripts

Playwright Martin McDonagh. Ireland. 1998. Lang.: Eng. 3216

Bechtolf, Sven-Eric

Performance/production

German directors about the meaning of Brecht today. Germany. 1998. Lang.: Ger. 1948

Shakespearean productions in northern Germany. Germany: Hamburg. 1996-1997. Lang.: Ger. 1978

Beck-Friis, Regina

Performance/production

Stockholm's year as Cultural Capital of Europe. Sweden: Stockholm. 1766-1998. Lang.: Eng. 2394

Beck, Julian

Institutions

European activities of the Living Theatre. Europe. USA. 1964-1983. Lang.: Ita. 1602

Performance/production

Theatre Magazine's anniversary issue. USA. 1968-1998. Lang.: Eng. 617

The Living Theatre's *Paradise Now*—creation and production. USA. 1951-1968. Lang.: Eng. 667

Relation to other fields

Government response to Living Theatre's *Paradise Now*. USA. Europe. 1968. Lang.: Eng. 3789

Becker, Danny

Performance/production

Collection of newspaper reviews by London theatre critics. UK-England: London. 1998. Lang.: Eng. 2470

Becker, Rob

Performance/production

The success of dance extravaganzas and solo performance at the expense of traditional shows. USA: New York, NY. 1994-1998. Lang. :Eng. 645

Beckett, Samuel
Basic theatrical documents
Russian translations of plays by Nobel Prize winners. Italy. 1848-1998. Lang.: Rus. 1446
Performance/production
The influence of experimental performance on contemporary drama. Europe. USA. 1960-1987. Lang.: Eng. 526
Actors Gert Voss and Ignaz Kirchner on George Tabori's production of *Fin de partie (Endgame)*. Austria: Vienna. 1998. Lang.: Ger. 1821
Gert Voss and Ignaz Kirchner, *Theater Heute*'s actors of the year. Austria: Vienna. 1988-1998. Lang.: Ger. 1823
Samuel Beckett's plays in production. France. 1950-1980. Lang.: Eng. 1936
Seven critics on their favorite character or portrayal. Sweden. 1950. Lang.: Swe. 2369
Collection of newspaper reviews by London theatre critics. UK-England: London. 1998. Lang.: Eng. 2442
Collection of newspaper reviews by London theatre critics. UK-England: London. 1998. Lang.: Eng. 2511
Collection of newspaper reviews by London theatre critics. UK-England: London. 1998. Lang.: Eng. 2547
Collection of newspaper reviews by London theatre critics. UK-England: London. 1998. Lang.: Eng. 2578
Interview with Katie Mitchell on directing plays of Beckett. UK-England. 1998. Lang.: Eng. 2594
The change in Shakespearean production. UK-England. 1960-1980. Lang.: Eng. 2628
Possible castings for Beckett's *En attendant Godot (Waiting for Godot)*. UK-England. 1998. Lang.: Eng. 2645
Plays/librettos/scripts
Beckett's influence on *Che zhan (The Bus Stop)* by Gao Xingjian. China, People's Republic of. 1983. Lang.: Eng. 2844
Recognition in plays of Čechov, Shakespeare, and Beckett. England. France. Russia. 1596-1980. Lang.: Eng. 2949
Insanity in nineteenth- and twentieth-century theatre. Europe. 1880-1970. Lang.: Eng. 3050
The clown as a character in modern drama. Europe. 1915-1995. Lang.: Eng. 3056
The devouring woman in plays of Racine, Kleist, Ibsen, and Beckett. Europe. 1760-1992. Lang.: Eng. 3058
The influence Dryden and Johnson's theories on self-translated works of Samuel Beckett. France. Ireland. 1957-1976. Lang.: Eng. 3077
The influence of eighteenth-century philosophy on the work of Samuel Beckett. France. Ireland. 1935-1993. Lang.: Eng. 3084
Authority, truth, and the allegory of the cave in works of Samuel Beckett. France. Ireland. 1953-1986. Lang.: Eng. 3085
Analysis of *En attendant Godot (Waiting for Godot)* and *Rockaby* by Samuel Beckett. France. Ireland. 1953-1981. Lang.: Eng. 3087
The speaking subject in plays of Beckett and Stoppard. France. Ireland. UK-England. 1945-1998. Lang.: Ger. 3098
Humor in the works of Samuel Beckett. France. Ireland. 1953-1986. Lang.: Eng. 3110
Beckett's *Happy Days* as a rewriting of *Lady Chatterley's Lover*. France. Ireland. UK-England. 1961. Lang.: Eng. 3120
Composer Philip Glass on Beckett's influence on his work. Ireland. France. USA. 1965-1995. Lang.: Eng. 3194
Composer Luciano Berio on Beckett's influence on his work. Ireland. France. Italy. 1965-1985. Lang.: Eng. 3195
Music in the early life of Samuel Beckett. Ireland. 1912-1945. Lang.: Eng. 3196
Music and Samuel Beckett. Ireland. France. 1945-1990. Lang.: Eng. 3198
Obituary for playwright Samuel Beckett. Ireland. France. 1906-1989. Lang.: Dut. 3199
Beckett's character Winnie in *Happy Days*. Ireland. France. 1960-1963. Lang.: Ita. 3200
Melanie Daiken's musical settings of texts by Samuel Beckett. Ireland. France. 1945-1995. Lang.: Eng. 3201
Playwright Samuel Beckett's love of music. Ireland. France. 1955-1995. Lang.: Eng. 3204
Conversations with playwright Samuel Beckett. Ireland. France. 1998. Lang.: Ita. 3205
Music in Samuel Beckett's novel *Proust*. Ireland. France. 1931. Lang.: Eng. 3208
Analysis of Samuel Beckett's later plays. Ireland. France. 1950-1989. Lang.: Eng. 3210
Criticism of the creation of literary 'genealogies' for dramatic characters. Ireland. France. 1953-1998. Lang.: Swe. 3211
Beckett's work analyzed in terms of musical serialism. Ireland. France. 1945-1995. Lang.: Eng. 3215
Composer Giacomo Manzoni and his work *Words by Beckett (Parole da Beckett)*. Italy. 1970-1971. Lang.: Eng. 3250
English-language plays on the Dutch and Flemish stage. Netherlands. 1920-1998. Lang.: Dut. 3278
Samuel Beckett's influence on composer Humphrey Searle. UK-England. 1945-1995. Lang.: Eng. 3509
A method of analysis for the drama. USA. 1920-1975. Lang.: Eng. 3537
Joseph Chaikin's adaptation of *Textes pour rien (Texts for Nothing)* by Samuel Beckett. USA: New York, NY. 1995. Lang.: Eng. 3563
Language and other elements of expression in plays of Beckett and Shepard. USA. France. Ireland. 1950-1988. Lang.: Eng. 3655
Morton Feldman's musical setting for Samuel Beckett's radio play *Words and Music*. Europe. 1987. Lang.: Eng. 3865
Analysis of Samuel Beckett's radio play *All That Fall*. Ireland. France. 1957. Lang.: Ita. 3867
Analysis of filmscripts by Samuel Beckett. 1966-1970. Lang.: Eng. 3961
Analysis of *Ghost Trio* by Samuel Beckett. France. Ireland. 1976. Lang.: Eng. 4076
Analysis of television plays by Samuel Beckett. France. 1965-1989. Lang.: Eng. 4077
Clarence Barlow's abstract musical setting of a prose text by Samuel Beckett. 1971-1972. Lang.: Eng. 4305
Earl Kim's musical piece *Dead Calm*, based on a text by Samuel Beckett. 1945-1995. Lang.: Eng. 4306
Samuel Beckett's short story *Bing* as adapted by Roger Reynolds and Jean-Yves Bosseur. USA. 1986. Lang.: Eng. 4308
Roger Reynolds' musical settings of texts by Samuel Beckett. USA. 1968-1976. Lang.: Eng. 4309
Heinz Holliger's operatic adaptation of Samuel Beckett's *What Where*. Europe. 1992. Lang.: Eng. 4768
Marcel Mihalovici's operatic adaptation of *Krapp's Last Tape* by Samuel Beckett. Europe. 1965. Lang.: Eng. 4769
The opera *Neither* by Morton Feldman and Samuel Beckett. Europe. 1976-1977. Lang.: Eng. 4772
Operatic adaptations of Beckett's plays by Heinz Holliger. Europe. 1976-1988. Lang.: Eng. 4776
Composer Wolfgang Fortner's adaptation of *That Time* by Samuel Beckett. Europe. 1974-1977. Lang.: Eng. 4777
Relation to other fields
Analysis of Samuel Beckett's novel *Murphy*. France. Ireland. 1935. Lang.: Eng. 733
Theory/criticism
Theatrical reviews and the nature of theatrical success. UK-England. 1950-1990. Lang.: Eng. 3836

Beecroft, Vanessa
Performance/production
Contemporary performance art's ignorance of its avant-garde antecedents. USA. 1996-1998. Lang.: Eng. 4250

Been So Long
Performance/production
Collection of newspaper reviews by London theatre critics. UK-England: London. 1998. Lang.: Eng. 2458

Beer, Joseph Michael
Relation to other fields
The use of original theatrical productions in the ministry. USA. 1998. Lang.: Eng. 3781

Beethoven, Ludwig van
Performance/production
The work of opera director Barbara Beyer. Germany: Nuremberg. 1996-1998. Lang.: Ger. 4589
Analysis of a scene from Beethoven's *Fidelio*. Germany. 1814. Lang.: Eng. 4595
Reviews of recent opera productions. Switzerland: Basel. Germany: Stuttgart, Berlin, Hamburg. France: Strasbourg. 1997-1998. Lang.: Ger. 4702

Beethoven, Ludwig van — cont'd

Plays/librettos/scripts
Hero and anti-hero in contemporary opera production. Germany. 1998. Lang.: Ger. 4791

Beevers, Geoffrey
Performance/production
Collection of newspaper reviews by London theatre critics. UK-England: London. 1998. Lang.: Eng. 2459

Before Breakfast
Plays/librettos/scripts
Female characters in Eugene O'Neill's plays. USA. 1920-1953. Lang.: Eng. 3525

Bėg (Flight)
Performance/production
Collection of newspaper reviews by London theatre critics. UK-England: London. 1998. Lang.: Eng. 2586

Beggar's Opera, The
Plays/librettos/scripts
Music and the ballad opera in English popular theatre. England. 1728-1780. Lang.: Eng. 4390

Beggar's Wedding, The
Plays/librettos/scripts
Music and the ballad opera in English popular theatre. England. 1728-1780. Lang.: Eng. 4390

Beginning of Oleg's Reign, The
Plays/librettos/scripts
Analysis of Catherine the Great's opera *The Beginning of Oleg's Reign.* Russia. 1768-1794. Lang.: Eng. 4816

Behan, Brendan
Plays/librettos/scripts
Music and song in plays of Brendan Behan. Ireland. 1954-1958. Lang.: Eng. 3206

Behavior/psychology, actor
Audience
The aesthetics of audience-performer interaction in the theatrical event. USA. 1970-1981. Lang.: Eng. 160
Performance/production
Coping with stage fright. Netherlands. 1998. Lang.: Dut. 566
Psychoanalytic study of the actor. USA. 1988. Lang.: Eng. 621
The effect of a heterogeneous audience on performance anxiety. USA. 1987. Lang.: Eng. 630
Actors and the psychology of identity. USA. 1959-1998. Lang.: Eng. 2724

Behavior/psychology, dancer
Relation to other fields
A warning to dancers not to become malnourished. Sweden. 1998. Lang.: Swe. 998

Behavior/psychology, singer
Performance/production
Stage fright and other psychological problems of singers and musicians. Germany: Berlin. 1998. Lang.: Swe. 4603

Behn, Aphra
Plays/librettos/scripts
Feminism and seventeenth-century city comedy. England. 1600-1700. Lang.: Eng. 3000
Sexual politics in *The Rover* by Aphra Behn. England. 1677. Lang.: Eng. 3031

Behrman, S.N.
Plays/librettos/scripts
The comedies of manners of S.N. Behrman and Philip Barry. USA. 1920-1964. Lang.: Eng. 3648

Beidler, Franz Wilhelm
Performance/production
F.W. Beidler's ideas for a different Bayreuth Festival. Germany: Bayreuth. 1901-1981. Lang.: Ger. 4602

Beier, Karin
Performance/production
German productions of adaptations of *A Clockwork Orange* by Anthony Burgess. Germany: Dresden, Hamburg, Stendal. 1998. Lang.: Ger. 1972
Shakespearean productions in northern Germany. Germany: Hamburg. 1996-1997. Lang.: Ger. 1978
German productions of Shakespeare. Germany: Leipzig, Hamburg, Berlin. 1998. Lang.: Ger. 2033

Beige
Performance/production
Contemporary performance art's ignorance of its avant-garde antecedents. USA. 1996-1998. Lang.: Eng. 4250

Beijing opera
SEE ALSO
Chinese opera.

Beilharz, Ricarda
Plays/librettos/scripts
Analysis of plays by Sarah Kane and David Harrower, recently produced in Germany. UK-England. Germany: Cologne, Bonn. 1998. Lang.: Ger. 3487

Being Sellars
Performance/production
Collection of newspaper reviews by London theatre critics. UK-England: London. 1998. Lang.: Eng. 2545

Béjart, Armande
Performance/production
Early modern French and Italian actresses. Italy. France. 1550-1750. Lang.: Eng. 553

Béjart, Maurice
Performance/production
Choreographer Maurice Béjart. France. 1927-1998. Lang.: Rus. 1077
Hungarian guest performances of world ballet stars. Hungary: Budapest. 1975-1978. Lang.: Hun. 1085
Dance on screen. USA. Europe. 1920-1998. Lang.: Ger. 3860

Beke, Sándor
Performance/production
Madách's *Tragedy of Man* directed by Sándor Beke. Hungary: Eger. 1998. Lang.: Hun. 2090

Bekederemo, John
Plays/librettos/scripts
Ritual in plays of John Bekederemo and Wole Soyinka. Nigeria. 1965-1998. Lang.: Eng. 3287

Békés, Pál
Performance/production
Pál Békés' *Pincejáték (Cellar Play)* directed by Zoltán Ternyák. Hungary: Budapest. 1997. Lang.: Hun. 2078

Belasco, David
Design/technology
Lighting and realism in opera and theatre: Belasco and Puccini. Italy. USA. 1890-1910. Lang.: Eng. 203
Performance/production
The 'scientific perspective' of director David Belasco. USA. 1882-1931. Lang.: Eng. 2741

Belbel, Sergi
Plays/librettos/scripts
Hasko Weber's production of *Morir (A Moment Before Dying)* by Sergi Belbel. Germany: Dresden. 1998. Lang.: Ger. 3132
Interview with playwright Sergi Belbel. Spain-Catalonia. 1963-1998. Lang.: Ger. 3407

Belfry Theatre Company (Victoria, BC)
Institutions
Profile of Belfry Theatre Company. Canada: Victoria, BC. 1974-1998. Lang.: Eng. 1583

Belgrade Theatre (London)
Basic theatrical documents
Text of *Example: The Case of Craig and Bentley* adapted by Tom Barrie. UK-England. 1998. Lang.: Eng. 1472

Bell, Christopher
Performance/production
Multiculturalism and Italo-Australian theatre. Australia. 1990-1998. Lang.: Eng. 490

Bell, David
Design/technology
Dex Edwards' set design for *The Comedy of Errors*, Shakespeare Repertory Company. USA: Chicago, IL. 1998. Lang.: Eng. 1560

Bell, Mary Hayley
Performance/production
Collection of newspaper reviews by London theatre critics. UK-England: London. 1998. Lang.: Eng. 2425

Bell, Suzanne
Performance/production
Collection of newspaper reviews by London theatre critics. UK-England: London. 1998. Lang.: Eng. 2411
Collection of newspaper reviews by London theatre critics. UK-England: London. 1998. Lang.: Eng. 2478

Belle et la Bête, La (Beauty and the Beast)
Plays/librettos/scripts
The reciprocal influence of opera and film. Europe. North America. 1904-1994. Lang.: Eng. 4770

Belle Fontaine
Performance/production
Collection of newspaper reviews by London theatre critics. UK-England: London. 1998. Lang.: Eng. 2550

Belle of Belfast City, The
Plays/librettos/scripts
Recent history in Irish theatre and drama. Ireland: Dublin. UK-Ireland: Belfast. 1993-1996. Lang.: Eng. 3212
Belle Reprieve
Plays/librettos/scripts
Effeminacy on the American stage. USA. 1920-1998. Lang.: Eng. 3682
Bellini, Vincenzo
Performance/production
Review of one-act ballets by Balanchine. Hungary: Budapest. 1997. Lang.: Hun. 1105
Interview with soprano Lena Nordin. Sweden: Stockholm. 1982-1998. Lang.: Swe. 4697
Gendered readings of Bellini's *La Sonnambula* in performance. USA. 1835-1860. Lang.: Eng. 4748
Plays/librettos/scripts
Virginal heroines in Alpine settings in operas of Bellini, Donizetti, and Verdi. Italy. 1800-1850. Lang.: Eng. 4812
Gender in Bellini's *Norma* and Verdi's *Aida*. Italy. 1831-1871. Lang.: Eng. 4813
Beloved
Audience
Jonathan Demme's film adaptation of *Beloved* by Toni Morrison. USA. 1998. Lang.: Eng. 3877
Below the Belt
Institutions
English-language plays at Berlin Festwochen. Germany: Berlin. 1998. Lang.: Ger. 1623
Belvoir Street Theatre (Sidney)
Performance/production
Contemporary Asian-Australian theatre. Australia. 1990-1998. Lang.: Eng. 488
Ben-Tovim, Ruth
Performance/production
Collection of newspaper reviews by London theatre critics. UK-England: London. 1998. Lang.: Eng. 2548
Benaïssa, Slimane
Performance/production
Survey of contemporary Algerian theatre. Algeria. 1962-1998. Lang.: Swe. 1814
Benavente, Jacinto
Basic theatrical documents
Russian translations of plays by Nobel Prize winners. Italy. 1848-1998. Lang.: Rus. 1446
Plays/librettos/scripts
The image of women on the Spanish stage. Spain. 1908-1936. Lang.: Eng. 3399
Bende, Zsolt
Performance/production
Obituary for baritone Zsolt Bende. Hungary. 1926-1998. Lang.: Hun. 4628
Bene, Carmelo
Performance/production
A conversation with actor and director Carmelo Bene. Italy. 1998. Lang.: Ita. 544
Book-length interview with director Carmelo Bene. Italy. 1937-1998. Lang.: Ita. 2167
Benecke, Patricia
Performance/production
Collection of newspaper reviews by London theatre critics. UK-England: London. 1998. Lang.: Eng. 2493
Benedict, Peter
Performance/production
Collection of newspaper reviews by London theatre critics. UK-England: London. 1998. Lang.: Eng. 2446
Benefits
Administration
Actors' Fund annual benefit for women's health. USA: New York, NY. 1998. Lang.: Eng. 68
Report on 'Broadway Bares' benefit for AIDS. USA: New York, NY. 1998. Lang.: Eng. 76
Performance/production
AIDS-benefit performance of the musical *Sweet Charity*. USA: New York, NY. 1998. Lang.: Eng. 4386
Bennet, Michael
Design/technology
Digital lighting control for *A Chorus Line*. USA: New York, NY. 1974-1975. Lang.: Eng. 4337
Bennett, Alan
Performance/production
Collection of newspaper reviews by London theatre critics. UK-England: London. 1998. Lang.: Eng. 2545
Plays/librettos/scripts
Playwright Alan Bennett. UK-England. 1994-1998. Lang.: Ger. 3488
Benoit, Jean-Louis
Performance/production
Social context of French and Canadian productions of *Les Fourberies de Scapin* by Molière. Canada: Montreal, PQ. France: Paris. 1998. Lang.: Fre. 1842
Benoît, Pierre
Performance/production
Pierre Benoît's music for *Don Quichotte* at Théâtre du Nouveau Monde. Canada: Montreal, PQ. 1995-1998. Lang.: Fre. 1870
Benson, David
Performance/production
Collection of newspaper reviews by London theatre critics. UK-England: London. 1998. Lang.: Eng. 2428
Benson, Susan
Design/technology
Professional theatrical designers on design training. USA. 1998. Lang.: Eng. 252
Bent, Simon
Performance/production
Collection of newspaper reviews by London theatre critics. UK-England: London. 1998. Lang.: Eng. 2468
Bentley, Eric
Performance/production
Documentary theatre and the politics of representation. USA. 1966-1993. Lang.: Eng. 2728
Benua, Aleksand'r Nikolajėvič
SEE
Benois, Alexandre.
Beothuk Street Players (St. John's, NF)
Performance/production
Beothuk Street Players' production of *Faces in the Rock* by Fred Hawksley. Canada: St. John's, NF. 1998. Lang.: Eng. 1863
Beran, Josef
Plays/librettos/scripts
New direction in Czech playwriting. Czech Republic. 1990-1997. Lang.: Cze. 2850
Beregszászi Illyés Gyula Magyar Nemzeti Színház
SEE
Illyés Gyula Magyar Nemzeti Színház (Beregovo).
Berg, Alban
Basic theatrical documents
Complete libretto of Alban Berg's *Lulu*. Austria. 1935. Lang.: Fre, Ger. 4412
Design/technology
Set and costume design for San Francisco Opera productions. USA: San Francisco, CA. 1998. Lang.: Eng. 4443
Institutions
Peter Stein's last season as director at the Salzburg Festival. Austria: Salzburg. 1997. Lang.: Eng. 336
Performance/production
Music theatre production in northern Germany. Germany: Lübeck, Hamburg, Bremen, Kiel. 1998. Lang.: Ger. 4293
Discography of productions of Alban Berg's *Lulu*. 1935-1998. Lang.: Fre. 4508
Significant interpreters of the title role of Alban Berg's *Lulu*. 1937-1996. Lang.: Fre. 4509
Productions of Berg's *Lulu*. 1935-1998. Lang.: Fre. 4518
Arnold Schoenberg's refusal to complete Alban Berg's unfinished opera *Lulu*. Austria. 1935. Lang.: Fre. 4533
Conductor Pierre Boulez on Patrice Chéreau's production of *Lulu* by Alban Berg. France: Paris. 1979. Lang.: Fre. 4567
Novelist Joyce Carol Oates' reaction to Berg's *Wozzeck* at the Metropolitan Opera. USA: New York, NY. 1997. Lang.: Eng. 4718
Plays/librettos/scripts
Dictionary of Alban Berg's *Lulu*. Austria. 1935. Lang.: Fre. 4760
Wedekind's Lulu plays and their adaptation by Berg. Germany. Austria. 1895-1935. Lang.: Fre. 4798
Berg, Gunilla
Performance/production
Seven critics on their favorite character or portrayal. Sweden. 1950. Lang.: Swe. 2369

Bergen, Jim van
Design/technology
Sound design for Blue Man Group's Chicago production of *Tubes*. USA: Chicago, IL. 1996-1997. Lang.: Eng. 261
Panel discussion of sound designers. USA. 1998. Lang.: Eng. 287

Berger, Fabienne
Performance/production
Yvette Bozsik's *Nevess remegve (Emlék) (Laugh Tremble–Memory)* at Trafó. Hungary: Budapest. 1998. Lang.: Hun. 1293

Berggren, Britt-Marie
Training
Britt-Marie Berggren's dancing school for children. Sweden: Stockholm. 1946. Lang.: Swe. 1020

Berggren, Janni
Performance/production
Interview with Flamenco dancer Janni Berggren. Sweden. Spain. 1970. Lang.: Swe. 1237

Berghaus, Ruth
Performance/production
Director Ruth Berghaus. Germany. 1970-1996. Lang.: Ger. 4596

Bergman, Ingmar
Design/technology
Interview with set designer Lennart Mörk. Sweden: Stockholm. France: Paris. 1958-1998. Lang.: Swe. 222
Plays/librettos/scripts
The reciprocal influence of opera and film. Europe. North America. 1904-1994. Lang.: Eng. 4770
Theory/criticism
Essay on the nature of talent. Denmark. Sweden. UK-England. 1847-1987. Lang.: Dan. 838

Bergwerk, Das (Mine, The)
Plays/librettos/scripts
Social criticism in Viennese Expressionist drama. Austria: Vienna. 1907-1922. Lang.: Ger. 2779

Berio, Luciano
Plays/librettos/scripts
Composer Luciano Berio on Beckett's influence on his work. Ireland. France. Italy. 1965-1985. Lang.: Eng. 3195

Berkoff, Steven
Performance/production
Collection of newspaper reviews by London theatre critics. UK-England: London. 1998. Lang.: Eng. 2524
Collection of newspaper reviews by London theatre critics. UK-England: London. 1998. Lang.: Eng. 2550
Plays/librettos/scripts
English-language plays on the Dutch and Flemish stage. Netherlands. 1920-1998. Lang.: Dut. 3278
Analysis of *Decadence* by Steven Berkoff. UK-England. 1981. Lang.: Dut. 3431
Relation to other fields
Interview with actor/writer Steven Berkoff, creator of actor character 'Harry'. UK-England: London. 1998. Lang.: Eng. 3780

Berlin Alexanderplatz
Performance/production
Theatrical influences on director Rainer Werner Fassbinder. East Germany: Berlin. 1969-1982. Lang.: Fre. 4058

Berlin, Irving
Design/technology
Costume design for revival of *As Thousands Cheer* by Drama Dept. USA: New York, NY. 1998. Lang.: Eng. 4333

Berliner Ensemble (Berlin)
Design/technology
Scenographer and now director Klaus Noack. Germany. 1953. Lang.: Ger. 190
Lighting in contemporary theatre. Germany. 1998. Lang.: Ger. 192
Robert Wilson and Vera Dobroschke's design for Brecht's *Ozeanflug*. Germany: Berlin. 1998. Lang.: Eng. 4430
Institutions
The fate of the Berliner Ensemble after the resignation of artistic director Manfred Wekwerth. Germany: Berlin. 1991-1998. Lang.:Ger. 1625
Problems of management and repertory at Berliner Ensemble. Germany: Berlin. 1992-1998. Lang.: Ger. 1656
Performance/production
Comparison of productions of Brecht's *Die Massnahme (The Measures Taken)*. Germany: Berlin, Wuppertal. 1995-1998. Lang.: Ger. 1950
Interview with director Jochen Gerz. Germany: Berlin. 1998. Lang.: Ger, Fre, Dut, Eng. 1967
Bertolt Brecht's production of his *Mutter Courage (Mother Courage)*. Germany: Berlin. 1947-1956. Lang.: Ger. 1975
Interview with director Benno Besson. Germany: Berlin. 1947-1998. Lang.: Ger. 1981
Reviews of productions of plays by Brecht. Germany. 1998. Lang.: Ger. 1986
Interview with director Matthias Langhoff. Germany: Berlin. 1945-1998. Lang.: Ger. 1987
Interview with actor Ekkehard Schall. Germany: Berlin. 1959-1998. Lang.: Ger. 1990
Swedish directors on recent Berlin productions. Germany: Berlin. 1998. Lang.: Swe. 2012
Plays/librettos/scripts
Recent German productions of Brecht's plays. Germany. 1998. Lang.: Ger. 3150
Brecht, copyright, and contemporary perceptions. Germany: Berlin. 1898-1998. Lang.: Ger. 3153
Hero and anti-hero in contemporary opera production. Germany. 1998. Lang.: Ger. 4791
Relation to other fields
Current attitudes toward socialism, individualism, and metaphysics in German culture, including theatre. Germany: Berlin. 1989-1998. Lang.: Ger. 3766
Die Berliner Ermittlung (The Berlin Investigation), an interactive theatre project by Jochen Gerz and Esther Shalev-Gerz. Germany: Berlin. 1998. Lang.: Ger. 3768

Berliner Ermittlung, Die (Berlin Investigation, The)
Performance/production
Interview with director Jochen Gerz. Germany: Berlin. 1998. Lang.: Ger, Fre, Dut, Eng. 1967
Relation to other fields
Die Berliner Ermittlung (The Berlin Investigation), an interactive theatre project by Jochen Gerz and Esther Shalev-Gerz. Germany: Berlin. 1998. Lang.: Ger. 3768

Berliner, Charles
Design/technology
Costume designs for Oregon Shakespeare Festival productions. USA: Ashland, OR. 1998. Lang.: Eng. 1543

Berlioz, Hector
Design/technology
Lighting design for Basil Twist's puppet production *Symphonie Fantastique*. USA: New York, NY. 1998. Lang.: Eng. 4867
Performance/production
Hector Berlioz's review of Donizetti's *La Favorite*. France: Paris. 1840. Lang.: Eng. 4565
Basil Twist's puppetry interpretation of Berlioz's *Symphonie Fantastique*. USA: New York, NY. 1998. Lang.: Eng. 4904

Berman, Sabina
Basic theatrical documents
English translation of *The Mustache* by Sabine Berman. Mexico. 1992. Lang.: Eng. 1447
Plays/librettos/scripts
Analysis of *Krísis (Crisis)* by Sabina Berman. Mexico. 1996. Lang.: Eng. 3273
Comparison between *Krísis (Crisis)* by Sabina Berman and Quentin Tarantino's film *Pulp Fiction*. Mexico. USA. 1993-1996. Lang.: Spa. 3276

Bernard, Emma
Performance/production
Collection of newspaper reviews by London theatre critics. UK-England: London, Scarborough. 1998. Lang.: Eng. 2426

Bernard, Kenneth
Plays/librettos/scripts
Revolutionary Off Broadway playwriting. USA: New York, NY. 1959-1969. Lang.: Eng. 3604

Bernard, Penny
Performance/production
Collection of newspaper reviews by London theatre critics. UK-England: London, Stratford, Derby. 1998. Lang.: Eng. 2417

Berndt, Fred
Performance/production
Comparison of productions of *The Lisbon Traviata* by Terrence McNally. Germany: Berlin, Essen. 1998. Lang.: Ger. 2005

Bernhard-Dramolette (Bernhard's Small Dramas)
Performance/production
Reviews of plays by Wolfgang Bauer and Thomas Bernhard. Switzerland: Basel. Austria: Vienna. 1998. Lang.: Ger. 2403

Bernhard, Thomas
Basic theatrical documents
Catalan translation of *Am Ziel (To the Goal)* by Thomas Bernhard. Austria. 1981. Lang.: Cat. 1407
Institutions
The current state of Theater Bielefeld. Germany: Bielefeld. 1998. Lang.: Ger. 1621
The aesthetic perspectives of the ensemble at Münchner Kammerspiele. Germany: Munich. 1997-1998. Lang.: Ger. 1666
Performance/production
Adaptations and performances of *Alte Meister (Old Masters)* by Thomas Bernhard. Germany. 1997-1998. Lang.: Ger. 1996
Thomas Bernhard's *Ritter, Dene, Voss* at Bárka Színház. Hungary: Budapest. 1997. Lang.: Hun. 2087
Performances at the new Bárka Színház. Hungary: Budapest. 1997. Lang.: Hun. 2097
Reviews of plays by Wolfgang Bauer and Thomas Bernhard. Switzerland: Basel. Austria: Vienna. 1998. Lang.: Ger. 2403
Plays/librettos/scripts
Thomas Bernhard's Holocaust play, *Heldenplatz (Heroes' Square)*. Austria. 1988. Lang.: Eng. 2784

Bernhardt, Sarah
Administration
Sarah Bernhardt's farewell tour and its revenues. USA. 1905-1906. Lang.: Eng. 28
Performance/production
The disappearance of the diva in the modern world. Europe. USA. 1890-1998. Lang.: Swe. 525
Plays/librettos/scripts
George Bernard Shaw: life, work, influences. UK-England. Ireland. 1886-1955. Lang.: Eng. 3437

Bernie Spain Gardens (London)
Performance/production
Collection of newspaper reviews by London theatre critics. UK-England: London. 1998. Lang.: Eng. 2461

Bernstein, Elsa
Plays/librettos/scripts
Power, gender relations, and communication in German drama. Germany. 1776-1989. Lang.: Ger. 3138
Women in German turn-of-the-century drama. Germany. 1890-1910. Lang.: Eng. 3158

Bernstein, Leonard
Design/technology
Costume designs by Irene Sharaff. USA. 1933-1976. Lang.: Eng. 277
Performance/production
Choreographer John Neumeier. Germany: Hamburg. USA: New York, NY. 1998. Lang.: Eng. 1082
Collection of newspaper reviews by London theatre critics. UK-England: London. 1998. Lang.: Eng. 2516
An open-air production of *West Side Story* directed by László Vándorfi. Hungary: Veszprém. 1998. Lang.: Hun. 4361
Drama and spirituality in the music of Leonard Bernstein. USA. 1965-1990. Lang.: Eng. 4379

Berry, Cicely
Performance/production
Slovene translation of Cicely Berry's work on vocal training for the actor. Slovenia. UK-England. 1973-1993. Lang.: Slo. 2344

Berry, Gabriel
Design/technology
Professional theatrical designers on design training. USA. 1998. Lang.: Eng. 252

Berthalda en Hildebrand of de Waternimf (Berthalda and Hildebrand, or the Water Nymph)
Performance/production
Analysis of the ballet *Berthalda en Hildebrand (Berthalda and Hildebrand)*. Netherlands: Amsterdam. 1849. Lang.: Ger. 1122

Berthier, Robert
Performance/production
Hungarian student's training at Jeune Ballet de France. France: Paris. 1996-1998. Lang.: Hun. 1075

Bertman, Dmitrij
Institutions
The Bolšoj Ballet and the experimental company Gelikon. Russia: Moscow. 1997. Lang.: Swe. 4467
Portrait of Dmitrij Bertman, artistic director of Moskovskij Muzykal'nyj Teat'r Gelikon. Russia: Moscow. 1998. Lang.: Rus. 4468

Bertoja, Giuseppe
Design/technology
Verdi's operas and the influence of La Fenice scene designer Giuseppe Bertoja. Italy: Venice. 1840-1870. Lang.: Eng. 4433

Bertolucci, Bernardo
Performance/production
Analysis of films by Bernardo Bertolucci. 1979-1998. Lang.: Eng. 3927

Bertorelli, Toni
Performance/production
Productions by Toni Bertorelli and Alfiero Alfieri. Italy: Rome. 1997. Lang.: Eng. 2175

Besset, Jean-Marie
Performance/production
Collection of newspaper reviews by London theatre critics. UK-England: London. 1998. Lang.: Eng. 2469

Besson, Benno
Performance/production
Interview with director Benno Besson. Germany: Berlin. 1947-1998. Lang.: Ger. 1981
Interview with director Alexander Lang. Germany, East. 1970-1990. Lang.: Eng. 2037
Shakespearean production and the GDR's 'existential crisis'. Germany, East. 1976-1980. Lang.: Eng. 2051
Katharina Thalbach in Brecht's *Die heilige Johanna der Schlachthöfe (Saint Joan of the Stockyards)* directed by Benno Besson. Switzerland: Zurich. 1998. Lang.: Ger. 2400

Bessy, Claude
Training
Gala concert of the Paris Opera ballet school. France: Paris. 1998. Lang.: Hun. 1205

Best of Times: The Showtunes of Jerry Herman, The
Performance/production
Collection of newspaper reviews by London theatre critics. UK-England: London. 1998. Lang.: Eng. 2483
Collection of newspaper reviews by London theatre critics. UK-England: London. 1998. Lang.: Eng. 2544

Besy (Possessed, The)
Performance/production
Collection of newspaper reviews by London theatre critics. UK-England: London. 1998. Lang.: Eng. 2424

Betrayal
Performance/production
Collection of newspaper reviews by London theatre critics. UK-England: London. 1998. Lang.: Eng. 2546

Betrayal of Nora Blake, The
Performance/production
Collection of newspaper reviews by London theatre critics. UK-England: London. 1998. Lang.: Eng. 2499

Betrothal in a Monastery
SEE
Obručinie v monastïre.

Betti, Ugo
Performance/production
Collection of newspaper reviews by London theatre critics. UK-England: London. 1998. Lang.: Eng. 2534

Bettler, oder Der tote Hund, Der (Beggar or the Dead Dog, The)
Performance/production
One-act plays by Brecht directed by József Jámbor. Hungary: Debrecen. 1998. Lang.: Hun. 2131

Bettler, oder Der tote Hund, Der (The Beggar, or the Dead Dog, The)
Basic theatrical documents
Catalan translations of plays by Bertolt Brecht (volume 1). Germany. 1919-1954. Lang.: Cat. 1437

Between Two Women
SEE
Fausse suivante, La.

Beuys, Joseph
Performance/production
Reexamination of the performance art of Beuys, Abramovič, and Ulay. USA. Germany. Netherlands. 1964-1985. Lang.: Eng. 4254

Bewitched, The
Plays/librettos/scripts
Plays of Peter Barnes compared to those of Renaissance dramatists. UK-England. 1968-1974. Lang.: Eng. 3449

Beyer, Barbara
Performance/production
The work of opera director Barbara Beyer. Germany: Nuremberg. 1996-1998. Lang.: Ger. 4589

Beyond Ecstasy
Performance/production
Collection of newspaper reviews by London theatre critics. UK-England: London. 1998. Lang.: Eng. 2447

Beyond the Horizon
Design/technology
Set design for Chain Lightning Theatre's production of *Beyond the Horizon* by Eugene O'Neill. USA: New York, NY. 1998. Lang.: Eng. 1551
Plays/librettos/scripts
Female characters in Eugene O'Neill's plays. USA. 1920-1953. Lang.: Eng. 3525

Bez viny vinovatjė (Guilty Though Innocent)
Performance/production
Interviews with actors on Anatolij Vasiljėv's guest direction at Szigligeti Theatre. Hungary: Szolnok. 1998. Lang.: Hun. 2061
A.A. Vasiljėv's production of *Bez viny vinovatjė (Guilty Though Innocent)* by Ostrovskij. Hungary: Szolnok. 1998. Lang.:Hun. 2096
Symbolism in Anatolij Vasiljėv's production of *Guilty Though Innocent* by Ostrovskij. Hungary: Szolnok. 1998. Lang.: Hun. 2098
Mari Törőcsik's performance in Ostrovskij's *Guilty Though Innocent* directed by Vasiljėv. Hungary: Szolnok. 1997. Lang.: Hun. 2125

Bezace, Didier
Performance/production
Comparison of text-based and visual productions. France. 1998. Lang.: Fre. 1939

Bezencon, Hélène
Basic theatrical documents
Text of *Arrête de rêver, l'Étrangère (Stop Dreaming, Stranger)*. Switzerland. 1998. Lang.: Fre. 1469

Bezerédi, Zoltán
Institutions
Theatre critics' awards 97-98. Hungary. 1997-1998. Lang.: Hun. 355

Bezrukov, Sergej
Performance/production
Sergej Bezrukov's creation of the character of poet Sergej Esenin. Russia: Moscow. 1998. Lang.: Rus. 2278
Actor Sergej Bezrukov. Russia: Moscow. Lang.: Rus. 2341

Bhaggiyadatta, Krisanthra Sri
Plays/librettos/scripts
Political community theatre by South Indian emigrants. Canada: Toronto, ON, Montreal, PQ. India. 1984-1998. Lang.: Eng. 2821

Bharadwaj, Radha
Performance/production
Collection of newspaper reviews by London theatre critics. UK-England: London. 1998. Lang.: Eng. 2480

Bharata natyam
Performance/production
Obituary for dancer Sanjukta Panigrahi. India. 1944-1997. Lang.: Eng. 1230
Rival styles in *bharata natyam* performance. India. 1930-1990. Lang.: Eng. 1348
Classical Indian dance performer Malavika Sarukkai. India. 1998. Lang.: Rus. 1349

Bhuchara, Sudha
Performance/production
Collection of newspaper reviews by London theatre critics. UK-England: London. 1998. Lang.: Eng. 2541

Bianchi, Rosemary
Performance/production
Collection of newspaper reviews by London theatre critics. UK-England: London. 1998. Lang.: Eng. 2418

Bibapoh
Performance/production
Premieres of new plays. Austria: Vienna. 1998. Lang.: Ger. 1820

Bibbiena, Bernardo Dovizi da
Plays/librettos/scripts
Ludic aspects of Italian Renaissance theatre. Italy. 1500-1700. Lang.: Ita. 3240

Bibel, Die (Bible, The)
Basic theatrical documents
Catalan translations of plays by Bertolt Brecht (volume 1). Germany. 1919-1954. Lang.: Cat. 1437

Bibič, Polde
Performance/production
Polde Bibič on other Slovene actors. Slovenia. 1945-1997. Lang.: Slo. 591

Bibinur, ah, Bibinur!
Performance/production
Rijfkat Israfilov's production of *Bibinur, ah, Bibinur!*. Bashkir: Ufa. 1998. Lang.: Rus. 1827

Bibliographies
Performance/production
Pirandello on the Russian stage. Russia. 1905-1989. Lang.: Ita. 2250
The popular theatre genre *teatro por horas*. Spain. 1867-1922. Lang.: Eng. 2361
Plays/librettos/scripts
Bibliography of Holocaust drama. Europe. North America. 1933-1997. Lang.: Eng. 3054
Annual bibliography of modern drama studies. Europe. North America. 1899-1998. Lang.: Eng. 3060
Bibliography of Slovene writers and playwrights in translation. Slovenia. 1960-1997. Lang.: Eng. 3343
Bibliography of works by or about Harold Pinter. UK-England. 1994-1996. Lang.: Eng. 3475
Reference materials
Yearbook of Slovene theatre. Slovenia. 1996-1997. Lang.: Slo. 708
Bibliography of books on popular entertainment. USA. 1990-1997. Lang.: Eng. 710
Annual bibliography of Shakespeare studies. 1997. Lang.: Eng. 3722
Annual Shakespeare bibliography. 1988. Lang.: Eng. 3723
Annual Shakespeare studies bibliography. 1987. Lang.: Eng. 3724
Bibliography of Dutch-language Caribbean literature. Aruba. Suriname. Netherlands Antilles. Netherlands. 1998. Lang.: Eng. 3725
Bibliography of scripts for Slovene puppet theatre. Slovenia. 1942-1997. Lang.: Slo. 4914
Research/historiography
List of current doctoral dissertations in progress. USA. 1998. Lang.: Eng. 828
Bibliography of important works on American theatre. USA. 1960-1990. Lang.: Eng. 829
Theory/criticism
Summary of Eugene O'Neill criticism. USA. 1997. Lang.: Eng. 3845

Biedermann und die Brandstifter (Firebugs, The)
Performance/production
Collection of newspaper reviews by London theatre critics. UK-England: London. 1998. Lang.: Eng. 2442

Bieito, Calixto
Performance/production
Collection of newspaper reviews by London theatre critics. UK-England: London. 1998. Lang.: Eng. 2488

Bielemeier, Gregg
Performance/production
Mary Oslund and Gregg Bielemeier of Conduit. USA: Portland, OR. 1995-1998. Lang.: Eng. 1333

Biene, Die (Bee, The)
Performance/production
Collaborative Symbolist dance/theatre projects. Europe. USA. 1916-1934. Lang.: Eng. 1268

Bienvenue, Yvan
Plays/librettos/scripts
Round-table discussion on story-telling and theatre. Canada: Montreal, PQ. 1998. Lang.: Fre. 688

Biereye, Margarethe
Institutions
Margarethe Biereye and David Johnston of the touring company Ton und Kirschen. Germany: Glindow. 1992-1997. Lang.: Eng. 1624

Big Idea, The
Performance/production
Collection of newspaper reviews by London theatre critics. UK-England: London. 1998. Lang.: Eng. 2427

Biggins, Jonathan
Performance/production
Collection of newspaper reviews by London theatre critics. UK-England: London. 1998. Lang.: Eng. 2545

Bildmakarna (Image Makers, The)
Performance/production
Reviews of two plays by Per Olov Enquist. Hungary: Budapest. 1998. Lang.: Hun. 2089

Bill T. Jones/Arnie Zane Dance Company (New York, NY)
Performance/production
Interview with choreographer Bill T. Jones. USA. 1990-1998. Lang.: Eng. 1316

Billy Budd
Performance/production
Operas by Benjamin Britten in the repertory of the Metropolitan and the New York City Opera. USA: New York, NY. 1945-1998. Lang.:Eng. 4749

Billy Liar
Performance/production
Collection of newspaper reviews by London theatre critics. UK-England: London. 1998. Lang.: Eng. 2502
Biloxi Blues
Performance/production
Collection of newspaper reviews by London theatre critics. UK-England: London. 1998. Lang.: Eng. 2484
BIM-BOM (Gdańsk)
Performance/production
Profiles of student cabaret groups. Poland: Warsaw, Gdańsk. 1954-1959. Lang.: Pol. 4156
Bing
Plays/librettos/scripts
Samuel Beckett's short story *Bing* as adapted by Roger Reynolds and Jean-Yves Bosseur. USA. 1986. Lang.: Eng. 4308
Bing, Rudolf
Administration
The 'Group of Four' at the Lyric Hammersmith and the concept of a national theatre. UK-England: London. 1945-1956. Lang.: Eng. 1392
Binkley, Howell
Design/technology
Lighting design for *Never the Sinner* by John Logan, directed by Ethan McSweeney. USA: New York, NY. 1998. Lang.: Eng. 1534
Binning, Sadhu
Institutions
Sadhu Binning on his politically-oriented theatre group Vancouver Sath. Canada: Vancouver, BC. 1972-1989. Lang.: Eng. 1577
Birch, Michael
Performance/production
Michael Birch's production of *Vanity Fair*. UK-England: Leeds. 1997. Lang.: Eng. 2600
Birch, Patricia
Performance/production
Collection of newspaper reviews by London theatre critics. UK-England: London. 1998. Lang.: Eng. 2567
Bird's Nest Theatre (London)
Performance/production
Collection of newspaper reviews by London theatre critics. UK-England: London. 1998. Lang.: Eng. 2421
Collection of newspaper reviews by London theatre critics. UK-England: London. 1998. Lang.: Eng. 2502
Birdcage, The
Plays/librettos/scripts
Transvestism in contemporary film as the 'blackface' of the nineties. UK-England. USA. 1993-1996. Lang.: Eng. 3983
Birds
SEE
Ornithes.
SEE ALSO
Aves.
Birimisa, George
Plays/librettos/scripts
Revolutionary Off Broadway playwriting. USA: New York, NY. 1959-1969. Lang.: Eng. 3604
Birmingham Children's Theatre (Birmingham, AL)
Institutions
Profile of Birmingham Children's Theatre. USA: Birmingham, AL. 1947-1998. Lang.: Eng. 412
Birmingham Repertory Theatre
Institutions
Interview with Bill Alexander, artistic director of Birmingham Repertory Theatre. UK-England: Birmingham. 1998. Lang.: Eng. 1740
Performance/production
Collection of newspaper reviews by London theatre critics. UK-England: Leeds, Manchester. 1998. Lang.: Eng. 2433
Collection of newspaper reviews by London theatre critics. UK-England: Stratford, Birmingham. 1998. Lang.: Eng. 2536
Birnbaum, Anja
Performance/production
Dancer Anja Birnbaum. Sweden: Stockholm. 1984-1998. Lang.: Swe. 1299
Birth by Drowning
Plays/librettos/scripts
Analysis of plays based on the Hebrew prophets. USA. Europe. 1919-1970. Lang.: Eng. 3659
Birthday Party, The
Plays/librettos/scripts
Lacanian analysis of *The Birthday Party* by Harold Pinter. UK-England. 1958. Lang.: Eng. 3452
Bischoff, Thomas
Performance/production
Recent productions of Schauspiel Leipzig. Germany: Leipzig. 1997-1998. Lang.: Ger. 2011
Biswas, Neil
Performance/production
Collection of newspaper reviews by London theatre critics. UK-England: London. 1998. Lang.: Eng. 2525
Bit of Rough, A
Performance/production
Collection of newspaper reviews by London theatre critics. UK-England: London. 1998. Lang.: Eng. 2581
Bitter Sauce
Performance/production
Collection of newspaper reviews by London theatre critics. UK-England: London. 1998. Lang.: Eng. 2498
Bitteren Tränen der Petra von Kant, Die (Bitter Tears of Petra von Kant, The)
Plays/librettos/scripts
Homosexuality on the German stage. Germany. 1920-1980. Lang.: Eng. 3147
Bixby, Jonathan
Design/technology
Costume design for revival of *As Thousands Cheer* by Drama Dept. USA: New York, NY. 1998. Lang.: Eng. 4333
Bizet, Georges
Design/technology
Set and costume design for San Francisco Opera productions. USA: San Francisco, CA. 1998. Lang.: Eng. 4443
Performance/production
Balanchine's choreography for Bizet's *Symphony in C*. France: Paris. 1947-1948. Lang.: Eng. 1079
Review of one-act ballets by Balanchine. Hungary: Budapest. 1997. Lang.: Hun. 1105
Singers' approaches to the title role in Bizet's *Carmen*. 1875-1998. Lang.: Eng. 4502
Background material on Lyric Opera of Chicago radio broadcast performances. USA: Chicago, IL. 1998. Lang.: Eng. 4709
Background material on Metropolitan Opera radio broadcast performances. USA: New York, NY. 1998. Lang.: Eng. 4716
Plays/librettos/scripts
Ambition and gender in Bizet's *Carmen*. France. 1870-1879. Lang.: Eng. 4786
Spain as an exotic locale in Bizet's *Carmen* and its source. Spain. France. 1845. Lang.: Eng. 4819
Biziou, Peter
Design/technology
Lighting design for Peter Weir's film *The Truman Show*. USA. 1998. Lang.: Eng. 3919
Bjarke, Kim
Performance/production
The director's role in the development of good acting. Denmark. 1998. Lang.: Dan. 1887
Björk, Anita
Performance/production
Interviews with actresses of three generations on female roles. Sweden: Stockholm. 1945-1998. Lang.: Swe. 2380
Björklund Dahlgren, Cecilia
Institutions
Joint project to promote dance throughout Sweden. Sweden. 1974-1998. Lang.: Swe. 899
Black Books
Performance/production
Collection of newspaper reviews by London theatre critics. UK-England: London. 1998. Lang.: Eng. 2475
Black Comedy
Performance/production
Collection of newspaper reviews by London theatre critics. UK-England: London. 1998. Lang.: Eng. 2463
Black Doll, The
Basic theatrical documents
Text of *The Black Doll* by Edward Gorey. USA. 1973. Lang.: Eng. 3887
Plays/librettos/scripts
Interview with Edward Gorey about his animated film *The Black Doll*. USA. 1973-1997. Lang.: Eng. 3994
Black Rider, The
Performance/production
Music theatre production in northern Germany. Germany: Lübeck, Hamburg, Bremen, Kiel. 1998. Lang.: Ger. 4293

Black Swan Theatre Company (Freemantle)
Design/technology
Lighting designer Mark Howett's work for Black Swan Theatre Company. Australia: Fremantle. 1998. Lang.: Eng. 1513
Black theatre
SEE ALSO
African-American theatre.
Institutions
Report on Black film festival. Mexico: Acapulco. 1997. Lang.: Eng. 3924
Performance/production
Afro-Cuban identity in Cuban theatre and popular arts. Cuba. 1959-1996. Lang.: Spa. 513
Collection of newspaper reviews by London theatre critics. UK-England. 1998. Lang.: Eng. 2527
Plays/librettos/scripts
Director Djanet Sears and actor Alison Sealy Smith on all-Black theatre. Canada: Toronto, ON. 1998. Lang.: Eng. 2826
Black, Michael
Performance/production
Collection of newspaper reviews by London theatre critics. UK-England: London. 1998. Lang.: Eng. 2439
Blackfriars Theatre (London)
Performance spaces
Evidence of theatre closings in a Folger Library manuscript. England: London. 1650. Lang.: Eng. 1798
Blackley, Stuart
Plays/librettos/scripts
Review of collections of plays with gay themes. Canada. 1996. Lang.: Eng. 2802
Blacks, The
SEE
Nègres, Les.
Blair, D. Bartlett
Design/technology
The 1998 USITT expo. USA: Long Beach, CA. 1998. Lang.: Eng. 251
Blake, Howard
Performance/production
Collection of newspaper reviews by London theatre critics. UK-England: London. 1998. Lang.: Eng. 2557
Blake, Mervyn
Performance/production
Actor Mervyn Blake. Canada: Stratford, ON. 1933-1998. Lang.: Eng. 1851
Blakemore, Michael
Performance/production
Collection of newspaper reviews by London theatre critics. UK-England: London. 1998. Lang.: Eng. 2501
Collection of newspaper reviews by London theatre critics. UK-England: London. 1998. Lang.: Eng. 2505
Blancs, Les
Plays/librettos/scripts
Analysis of *Les Blancs* by Lorraine Hansberry. USA. 1970. Lang.: Eng. 3581
Blaskó, Borbála
Training
Dance training at Folkwang Hochschule. Germany: Essen. 1996-1998. Lang.: Hun. 1341
Blaskó, Péter
Performance/production
Interview with Péter Blaskó. Hungary. 1970-1998. Lang.: Hun. 2119
Blast from the Past
Performance/production
Collection of newspaper reviews by London theatre critics. UK-England. 1998. Lang.: Eng. 2456
Blasted
Plays/librettos/scripts
German view of English and American drama. UK-England. USA. 1998. Lang.: Ger. 3455
Sex, drugs, and violence in contemporary British drama. UK-England. 1991-1998. Lang.: Eng. 3494
Blau, Herbert
Performance/production
The multifaceted nature of early nonprofit regional theatre. USA. 1940-1960. Lang.: Eng. 2705
Blaubart—Hoffnung der Frauen (Bluebeard—Hope of Women)
Plays/librettos/scripts
The development of *Blaubart—Hoffnung der Frauen (Bluebeard—Hope of Women)* by Dea Loher. Germany: Munich. 1998. Lang.: Ger. 3164
Blaubart—Hoffnung der Frauen (Bluebeard—Hope Of Women)
Plays/librettos/scripts
The collaboration of playwright Dea Loher and director Andreas Kriegenburg. Germany: Hannover, Munich. 1990-1998. Lang.: Ger. 3151
Blavatsky's Tower
Performance/production
Collection of newspaper reviews by London theatre critics. UK-England: London. 1998. Lang.: Eng. 2449
Blench, Julian
Performance/production
Collection of newspaper reviews by London theatre critics. UK-England: London. 1998. Lang.: Eng. 2465
Bleont, Beatrice
Performance/production
Events of the Zsámbék theatre festival. Hungary: Zsámbék. 1998. Lang.: Hun. 2126
Blessed, Brian
Performance/production
Collection of newspaper reviews by London theatre critics. UK-England: London. 1998. Lang.: Eng. 2424
Blinde Göttin, Die (Blind Goddess, The)
Plays/librettos/scripts
Analysis of revisions of plays by Ernst Toller. Germany. 1920-1939. Lang.: Eng. 3172
Blinden von Kilcrobally, Die (Blind Men of Kilcrobally, The)
Performance/production
Premieres of new plays. Austria: Vienna. 1998. Lang.: Ger. 1820
Bloch, Rüdiger
Administration
Rüdiger Bloch, manager of West Pomeranian theatres. Germany: Greifswald, Straslund. 1997-1998. Lang.: Ger. 1384
Blok, Aleksand'r Aleksandrovič
Performance/production
Mikle Mizjukov's production of *Pesn' sud'by (The Song of Fate)* by Blok. Russia: Moscow. 1998. Lang.: Rus. 2276
Blom, Maria
Performance/production
Dr. Kokos Kärlekslaboratorium (Dr. Koko's Laboratory of Love) at Backstage, Stockholms Stadsteater. Sweden: Stockholm. 1998. Lang.: Swe. 2378
Blomgren, Karin
Training
Singer training at Teater- & Operahögskolan. Sweden: Gothenburg. 1960-1998. Lang.: Swe. 4848
Blomqvist, Arn-Henrik
Performance/production
Swedish and bilingual Finnish-Swedish theatre. Finland: Turku, Vaasa. 1998. Lang.: Eng, Fre. 1913
Blood and Iron
Performance/production
Collection of newspaper reviews by London theatre critics. UK-England: London. 1998. Lang.: Eng. 2491
Blood Brothers
Performance/production
Collection of newspaper reviews by London theatre critics. UK-England: London. 1998. Lang.: Eng. 2480
Blood Knot, The
Plays/librettos/scripts
The influence of Albert Camus on playwright Athol Fugard. South Africa, Republic of. 1960-1985. Lang.: Eng. 3362
Blood Relations
Plays/librettos/scripts
The representation of true crime in modern drama. USA. France. 1955-1996. Lang.: Eng. 3673
Blood Ugly
Performance/production
Collection of newspaper reviews by London theatre critics. UK-England: London. 1998. Lang.: Eng. 2550
Bloody Chamber, The
Performance/production
Collection of newspaper reviews by London theatre critics. UK-England: London. 1998. Lang.: Eng. 2437
Bloolips (London)
Plays/librettos/scripts
Effeminacy on the American stage. USA. 1920-1998. Lang.: Eng. 3682
Bloomfield, Nicholas
Performance/production
Collection of newspaper reviews by London theatre critics. UK-England: London. 1998. Lang.: Eng. 2500

Bloomsbury Theatre (London)
Performance/production
Collection of newspaper reviews by London theatre critics. UK-England: London. 1998. Lang.: Eng. 2490
Bloudění (Wandering)
Performance/production
The adaptation of classic Czech works to the stage. Czech Republic: Prague, Brno. 1990-1998. Lang.: Cze. 1877
Blue Bitch
Plays/librettos/scripts
National identity in plays of Sam Shepard. USA. 1965-1995. Lang.: Eng. 3545
Blue Jam
Performance/production
Collection of newspaper reviews by London theatre critics. UK-England: London, Scarborough. 1998. Lang.: Eng. 2426
Blue Man Group (New York, NY)
Design/technology
Sound design for Blue Man Group's Chicago production of *Tubes*. USA: Chicago, IL. 1996-1997. Lang.: Eng. 261
Blue Room, The
Performance/production
Collection of newspaper reviews by London theatre critics. UK-England: London. 1998. Lang.: Eng. 2509
Blue Window
Performance/production
Collection of newspaper reviews by London theatre critics. UK-England: London. 1998. Lang.: Eng. 2581
Bluebeard's Castle
SEE
Kékszakállú herceg vára, A.
Bluebird
Performance/production
Collection of newspaper reviews by London theatre critics. UK-England: London. 1998. Lang.: Eng. 2549
Blumenthal, Mara
Design/technology
Costume designer Mara Blumenthal. Canada. 1992-1998. Lang.: Eng. 170
Bluthal, Lisa
Performance/production
Collection of newspaper reviews by London theatre critics. UK-England: London. 1998. Lang.: Eng. 2539
Boadella, Albert
Relation to other fields
Catalonian cultural politics and Els Joglars. Spain-Catalonia. 1962-1998. Lang.: Eng. 3775
Boal, Augusto
Performance/production
Cultural identity and Brazilian theatre. Brazil. 1980-1995. Lang.: Eng. 496
French political theatre: Boal and Mnouchkine. France. 1990-1996. Lang.: Eng. 529
Interview with director Augusto Boal. Brazil: Rio de Janeiro. 1992-1996. Lang.: Eng. 1833
Plays/librettos/scripts
Boal's 'joker system' in plays of Ntozake Shange. USA. 1977-1981. Lang.: Eng. 3692
Relation to other fields
Theatre of the Oppressed and racism in high schools. Canada. 1991-1998. Lang.: Eng. 717
Boards of directors
Administration
Obituary for Tom Dent, former chairman of the Free Southern Theatre board. USA: New Orleans, LA. 1998. Lang.: Eng. 1395
Bobbie, Walter
Design/technology
Sound design for the London production of *Chicago*. UK-England: London. 1998. Lang.: Eng. 4326
Boccaccio, Giovanni
Performance/production
The ballet adaptation of the *Decameron* performed by Veszprém Dance Workshop. Hungary: Veszprém. 1998. Lang.: Hun. 1108
Bocelli, Andrea
Performance/production
Profile of tenor Andrea Bocelli. Italy. 1985-1998. Lang.: Swe. 4653
Bochumer Schauspielhaus (Bochum)
Institutions
Productions of Bochumer Schauspielhaus. Germany: Bochum. 1998. Lang.: Ger. 1655
Performance/production
Shakespeare performance on the Rhine and the Ruhr. Germany: Cologne, Bochum, Düsseldorf. 1996-1997. Lang.: Ger. 1962
Recent productions of Bochumer Schauspielhaus. Germany: Bochum. 1998. Lang.: Ger. 2009
Bodas de sangre (Blood Wedding)
Performance/production
Hanne Tierney's adaptation of *Bodas de sangre (Blood Wedding)* by García Lorca. USA. 1997. Lang.: Eng. 647
Bodinetz, Gemma
Performance/production
Collection of newspaper reviews by London theatre critics. UK-England: London. 1998. Lang.: Eng. 2440
Collection of newspaper reviews by London theatre critics. UK-England: London. 1998. Lang.: Eng. 2475
Collection of newspaper reviews by London theatre critics. UK-England: London. 1998. Lang.: Eng. 2540
Collection of newspaper reviews by London theatre critics. UK-England: London. 1998. Lang.: Eng. 2560
Analysis of recent New York productions. USA: New York, NY. 1997-1998. Lang.: Eng. 2759
Bodor, Johanna
Performance/production
Interview with ballet dancer Johanna Bodor. Hungary. 1984-1998. Lang.: Hun. 1098
Bodow, Steve
Performance/production
Analysis of recent New York productions. USA: New York, NY. 1997-1998. Lang.: Eng. 2759
Body
Performance/production
Guest performance of Théâtre du Plantin, a company for developmentally disabled actors. Hungary: Budapest. 1983-1998. Lang.: Hun. 2081
Bodyguard, The
Plays/librettos/scripts
The Bodyguard, Sam Shepard's screen adaptation of *The Changeling* by Middleton and Rowley. USA. 1970-1995. Lang.: Eng. 4007
Boesing, Martha
Plays/librettos/scripts
Feminist theatre of Martha Boesing. USA: Minneapolis, MN. 1974-1984. Lang.: Eng. 3603
Boesman and Lena
Performance/production
Market Theatre productions of plays by Athol Fugard. South Africa, Republic of. 1993-1994. Lang.: Eng. 2351
Plays/librettos/scripts
The influence of Albert Camus on playwright Athol Fugard. South Africa, Republic of. 1960-1985. Lang.: Eng. 3362
Bogart, Anne
Performance/production
The 'viewpoint theory' of actor training. USA. 1998. Lang.: Eng. 2677
Bogart, Paul
Performance/production
Actors' interpretations of the title role in Oscar Wilde's *The Canterville Ghost*. UK-England. USA. 1943-1998. Lang.: Eng. 4066
Bogatyrëv, Pëtr Grigorevič
Theory/criticism
Hungarian translation of Pëtr Bogatyrëv's essay on the costume as sign. USSR. 1893-1971. Lang.: Hun. 871
Bogdanov, Michael
Performance/production
Collection of newspaper reviews by London theatre critics. UK-England: London. 1998. Lang.: Eng. 2523
Bogdanovich, Peter
Basic theatrical documents
Screenplay of *The Last Picture Show* by Larry McMurtry and Peter Bogdanovich. USA. 1971. Lang.: Eng. 3897
Plays/librettos/scripts
Larry McMurtry on *The Last Picture Show*. USA. 1971. Lang.: Eng. 4018
Interview with director Peter Bogdanovich. USA. 1971-1998. Lang.: Eng. 4020
Böge, Harriet Maria
Performance/production
Impressions from Podewil theatre workshop. Germany: Berlin. 1998. Lang.: Ger. 2024
Bogosian, Eric
Design/technology
Technical designs for *Griller* by Eric Bogosian. USA: Chicago, IL. 1998. Lang.: Eng. 1558

Bogosian, Eric — cont'd

Performance/production
Collection of newspaper reviews by London theatre critics. UK-England: London. 1998. Lang.: Eng. 2498

(Bogus) People's Poem, The
Performance/production
Collection of newspaper reviews by London theatre critics. UK-England: London. 1998. Lang.: Eng. 2427

Bohème, La
Institutions
The fourth international singing contest. Hungary: Budapest. 1998. Lang.: Hun. 4461
Performance/production
Background material on Lyric Opera of Chicago radio broadcast performances. USA: Chicago, IL. 1998. Lang.: Eng. 4709

Böhnisch, Siemke
Theory/criticism
A theory of authenticity in the theatre. Germany. 1992. Lang.: Hun. 841

Boi imeli mestnoe zančenie (Battles Had Localized, The)
Performance/production
K. Dubinin's production of *Boi imeli mestnoe zančenie (The Battles Had Localized)* based on work of Viačeslav Kondratjėv. Russia: Volgograd. Lang.: Rus. 2331

Boito, Arrigo
Performance/production
Reconstruction of the premiere of Boito's *Mefistofele.* Italy. 1871-1881. Lang.: Ita. 4647

Bollow, Maike
Performance/production
Actress Maike Bollow. Germany: Hannover. 1991-1998. Lang.: Ger. 2006

Bolme, Tomas
Administration
Interview with Tomas Bolme, director of the Swedish actors' union. Sweden: Stockholm. 1970-1998. Lang.: Swe. 1388

Bolond Helga (Foolish Helga)
Performance/production
Review of Darvasi's *Bolond Helga (Foolish Helga)*, Csokonai Theatre. Hungary: Debrecen. 1997. Lang.: Hun. 2122

Bolshoi Theatre (Leningrad/St. Petersburg)
SEE
Bolšoj Dramatičėskij Teat'r.

Bolshoi Theatre (Moscow)
SEE
Gosudarstvėnnyj Akademičėskij Bolšoj Teat'r.

Bolstad, Anne
Performance/production
Interview with opera singer Anne Bolstad. Norway. Sweden. 1980-1998. Lang.: Swe. 4665

Bolt, Robert
Administration
Theatrical agent Margaret Ramsey. UK-England: London. 1908-1991. Lang.: Ger. 1394

Bolzer, Bernard
Basic theatrical documents
Text of *Mendiants d'amour (Beggars of Love)* by Gérard Levoyer. France. 1998. Lang.: Fre. 1430

Bond, Edward
Administration
Theatrical agent Margaret Ramsey. UK-England: London. 1908-1991. Lang.: Ger. 1394
Performance/production
Survey of Parisian productions. France: Paris. 1997-1998. Lang.: Eng. 1937
Plays/librettos/scripts
Aggressive language in modern drama. Europe. USA. 1960-1985. Lang.: Eng. 3055

English-language plays on the Dutch and Flemish stage. Netherlands. 1920-1998. Lang.: Dut. 3278

Analysis of Edward Bond's *Summer.* UK-England. 1982. Lang.: Dut. 3434

Contradiction in the plays of Edward Bond. UK-England. 1962-1987. Lang.: Eng. 3485

British historical drama. UK-England. 1956-1988. Lang.: Eng. 3500

Science fiction drama since World War II. USA. 1945-1988. Lang.: Eng. 3591
Theory/criticism
Interview with playwright Edward Bond. UK-England. 1996-1998. Lang.: Eng. 3834

Bonds, Alexandra
Design/technology
The 1998 USITT expo. USA: Long Beach, CA. 1998. Lang.: Eng. 251

Bondy, Luc
Performance/production
Luc Bondy's production of Horváth's *Figaro lässt sich scheiden (Figaro Gets Divorced).* Austria: Vienna. 1998. Lang.: Ger. 1822

Collection of newspaper reviews by London theatre critics. UK-Scotland: Edinburgh. 1998. Lang.: Eng. 2650

Opera productions of the Salzburg Festival. Austria: Salzburg. 1998. Lang.: Hun. 4531

Bone Room, The
Performance/production
Collection of newspaper reviews by London theatre critics. UK-England: London. 1998. Lang.: Eng. 2420

Bonin, Laure
Basic theatrical documents
Text of *Pour la galerie (For the Gallery)* by Claude d'Anna and Laure Bonin. France. 1998. Lang.: Fre. 1424

Bonner, Marita
Performance/production
The first wave of American feminist theatre. USA. 1890-1930. Lang.: Eng. 648
Plays/librettos/scripts
Analysis of *The Purple Flower* by Marita Bonner. USA. 1927. Lang.: Eng. 3527

Bonnes, Les (Maids, The)
Plays/librettos/scripts
The representation of true crime in modern drama. USA. France. 1955-1996. Lang.: Eng. 3673

Bonney, Barbara
Performance/production
Soprano Barbara Bonney. USA. 1998. Lang.: Eng. 4754

Boogie Nights
Performance/production
Collection of newspaper reviews by London theatre critics. UK-England: London. 1998. Lang.: Eng. 2526

Interview with Shane Ritchie and Jon Conway about the musical *Boogie Nights.* UK-England. 1998. Lang.: Eng. 4370

Book of Days
Plays/librettos/scripts
Lanford Wilson's *Book of Days.* USA. 1998. Lang.: Eng. 3627

Boone, Vicky
Institutions
Vicky Boone, artistic director of Frontera Theatre. USA: Austin, TX. 1998. Lang.: Eng. 1759

Booth Theatre (New York, NY)
Design/technology
Lighting design for Mamet's *The Old Neighborhood* directed by Scott Zigler. USA: New York, NY. 1998. Lang.: Eng. 1547

Booth, Anthony
Performance/production
Collection of newspaper reviews by London theatre critics. UK-England: London. 1998. Lang.: Eng. 2487

Boothe, Clare
SEE
Luce, Clare Boothe.

Borchert, Wolfgang
Performance/production
Collection of newspaper reviews by London theatre critics. UK-England: London. 1998. Lang.: Eng. 2418

Borden, Lizzie
Relation to other fields
Actress Nance O'Neil and her friendship with Lizzie Borden. USA. 1874-1965. Lang.: Eng. 799

Borderers, The
Plays/librettos/scripts
The feminine ideal in the drama of English Romantic poets. England. 1794-1840. Lang.: Eng. 2886

Borge, Runar
Performance/production
Collection of newspaper reviews by London theatre critics. UK-England: London. 1998. Lang.: Eng. 2525

Boris Godunov
Performance/production
Opera director Inge Levant. Germany: Stuttgart. 1959-1998. Lang.: Ger. 4611

Personal recollections of Šaljapin singing on recordings of *Boris Godunov.* Russia. 1873-1938. Lang.: Eng. 4685

***Boris Godunov* — cont'd**

Background material on Metropolitan Opera radio broadcast performances. USA: New York, NY. 1998. Lang.: Eng. 4713

Bass Samuel Ramey. USA. 1940-1998. Lang.: Eng. 4744

Borisov, Oleg

Performance/production

Religion and actor Oleg Borisov. Russia: St. Petersburg. 1998. Lang.: Rus. 2287

Borissova, Galina

Performance/production

Profile of choreographer Galina Borissova. Bulgaria. 1998. Lang.: Dut. 1262

Börlin, Jean

Performance/production

The reconstruction of Jean Börlin's ballet *Dervisher*. Sweden: Stockholm. 1997. Lang.: Eng. 1150

Collaborative Symbolist dance/theatre projects. Europe. USA. 1916-1934. Lang.: Eng. 1268

Millicent Hodson and Kenneth Archer's revival of Jean Börlin's ballet *Dervisher*. UK-England: London. Sweden: Stockholm. 1920-1998. Lang.: Swe. 1311

Bornemisza, Péter

Performance/production

István Somogyi's productions of *Magyar Elektra* by Péter Bornemisza. Hungary: Budapest. 1988-1998. Lang.: Hun. 2114

Two productions by István Somogyi of Bornemisza's *Magyar Elektra*. Hungary: Budapest. 1988-1998. Lang.: Hun. 2148

Borodin, Aleksand'r Porfirjévič

Institutions

The Bolšoj Ballet and the experimental company Gelikon. Russia: Moscow. 1997. Lang.: Swe. 4467

Borovskij, David

Design/technology

Scene design and the plays of Ostrovskij. Russia. 1998. Lang.: Rus. 1523

Borragan, Maria Teresa

Plays/librettos/scripts

The image of women on the Spanish stage. Spain. 1908-1936. Lang.: Eng. 3399

Bose, Rana

Basic theatrical documents

Text of *Five or Six Characters in Search of Toronto* by Rana Bose. Canada: Toronto, ON. 1993. Lang.: Eng. 1409

Performance/production

Playwright Rana Bose on memorable performances. Canada: Montreal, PQ. 1959-1998. Lang.: Eng. 498

Plays/librettos/scripts

Interview with playwright Rana Bose. Canada: Montreal, PQ. India: Calcutta. 1950-1998. Lang.: Eng. 2820

Bosse, Jürgen

Performance/production

Comparison of productions of *The Lisbon Traviata* by Terrence McNally. Germany: Berlin, Essen. 1998. Lang.: Ger. 2005

Bosseur, Jean-Yves

Plays/librettos/scripts

Samuel Beckett's short story *Bing* as adapted by Roger Reynolds and Jean-Yves Bosseur. USA. 1986. Lang.: Eng. 4308

Boston Lyric Opera (Boston, MA)

Performance/production

Major opera houses' proposals for productions to the end of the century. USA. Canada. 1998. Lang.: Eng. 4743

Bostridge, Ian

Performance/production

Recordings of *Lieder* by Schumann. Germany. UK-England. 1998. Lang.: Eng. 4601

Bottari, Michael

Design/technology

Costume design for *Dames at Sea*, Marine Memorial Theatre. USA: San Francisco, CA. 1998. Lang.: Eng. 4332

Bottega del caffè, La (Coffee Shop, The)

Basic theatrical documents

Catalan translation of *La Bottega del caffè (The Coffee Shop)* by Carlo Goldoni. Italy. 1750. Lang.: Cat. 1444

Bottoms, Stephen J.

Performance/production

A production of Susan Glaspell's experimental play *The Verge*. UK-Scotland: Glasgow. 1996. Lang.: Eng. 2651

Boublil, Alain

Performance/production

Collection of newspaper reviews by London theatre critics. UK-England: Leeds, Manchester. 1998. Lang.: Eng. 2559

Bouchard, Michel Marc

Plays/librettos/scripts

Interview with playwright and scriptwriter Michel Marc Bouchard. Canada: Montreal, PQ. 1987-1998. Lang.: Fre. 3963

Boucicault, Dion

Performance/production

Boucicault's *The Octoroon* and the performance of race, gender, and power. USA. 1800-1860. Lang.: Eng. 669

Irish and Irish-American characters on the stages of the Midwest. USA. 1875-1915. Lang.: Eng. 2696

Actors Helen Carey and Max Wright, winners of Joe A. Callaway Award. USA. 1998. Lang.: Eng. 2716

Joe Dowling's production of *London Assurance* by Dion Boucicault. USA. 1997. Lang.: Eng. 2755

Bouffes du Nord (Paris)

SEE

Théâtre aux Bouffes du Nord.

Boukman, Daniel

Plays/librettos/scripts

Caribbean identity in plays of Daniel Boukman. Martinique. 1970-1995. Lang.: Eng. 3271

Boulez, Pierre

Performance/production

Conductor Pierre Boulez on Patrice Chéreau's production of *Lulu* by Alban Berg. France: Paris. 1979. Lang.: Fre. 4567

Bounce (Stockholm)

Performance/production

Interview with dancer Jennie Widegren. Sweden: Stockholm. 1995-1998. Lang.: Swe. 1306

Bound Man, The

Performance/production

Collection of newspaper reviews by London theatre critics. UK-England: London. 1998. Lang.: Eng. 2564

Bourne, Matthew

Design/technology

Interview with lighting designer Rick Fisher. UK-England. 1998. Lang.: Eng. 1030

Technical designs for Matthew Bourne's productions of ballets by Čajkovskij and Prokofjev. UK-England: London. 1998. Lang.: Eng. 1031

Performance/production

Narrative in choreographies of Matthew Bourne and Mark Murphy. UK-England. 1998. Lang.: Eng. 1156

Analysis of choreographies of Matthew Bourne. UK-England: London. 1996-1997. Lang.: Eng. 1157

Matthew Bourne's choreography for *Swan Lake*. UK-England. 1998. Lang.: Eng. 1159

Interview with choreographer Matthew Bourne. UK-England. 1998. Lang.: Eng. 1160

Matthew Bourne's dance piece *Cinderella* to music of Prokofjév. UK-England: London. 1998. Lang.: Eng. 1161

Bournonville, August

Performance/production

Onstage costume changes. Japan. Russia. Denmark. 1752-1998. Lang.: Swe. 556

Bowler Hat, The

Performance/production

Collection of newspaper reviews by London theatre critics. UK-England: London. Lang.: Eng. 2408

Bowles, Jane

Plays/librettos/scripts

English-language plays on the Dutch and Flemish stage. Netherlands. 1920-1998. Lang.: Dut. 3278

Analysis of Jane Bowles' play *In the Summer House*. USA. 1986. Lang.: Dut. 3555

Bowman, Rob

Design/technology

Lighting design for Rob Bowman's film *The X-Files*. USA. 1998. Lang.: Eng. 3922

Box (Boxing)

Plays/librettos/scripts

Interview with playwright-director Kajsa Isakson. Sweden: Stockholm. 1997-1998. Lang.: Swe. 3414

Boyd, Don

Plays/librettos/scripts

The reciprocal influence of opera and film. Europe. North America. 1904-1994. Lang.: Eng. 4770

Boyd, John
Plays/librettos/scripts
Gender and nationalism in Northern Irish drama. UK-Ireland. 1902-1997. Lang.: Eng. 3511
Boyd, Michael
Design/technology
Set and costume design for *The Spanish Tragedy* at RSC. UK-England: London. 1998. Lang.: Eng. 1525
Performance/production
Collection of newspaper reviews by London theatre critics. UK. 1998. Lang.: Eng. 2407
Collection of newspaper reviews by London theatre critics. UK-England: London. 1998. Lang.: Eng. 2538
Collection of newspaper reviews by London theatre critics. UK-England. 1998. Lang.: Eng. 2558
Collection of newspaper reviews by London theatre critics. UK-England: London. 1998. Lang.: Eng. 2588
Report on several English performances. UK-England: London, Stratford. 1998. Lang.: Swe. 2634
Boys in the Band, The
Plays/librettos/scripts
Effeminacy on the American stage. USA. 1920-1998. Lang.: Eng. 3682
Bozsik Yvette Társulat (Budapest)
Performance/production
The premiere of *Kabaré (Cabaret)* choreographed by Yvette Bozsik. Hungary: Budapest. 1998. Lang.: Hun. 945
Yvette Bozsik's *Nevess remegve (Emlék) (Laugh Tremble—Memory)* at Trafó. Hungary: Budapest. 1998. Lang.: Hun. 1293
Bozsik, Yvette
Performance/production
Round-table discussion on dance and movement. Hungary. 1998. Lang.: Hun. 938
Yvette Bozsik's new choreography for Debussy's *L'après-midi d'un faune*. Hungary: Budapest. 1997. Lang.: Hun. 940
The premiere of *Kabaré (Cabaret)* choreographed by Yvette Bozsik. Hungary: Budapest. 1998. Lang.: Hun. 945
Yvette Bozsik's *Nevess remegve (Emlék) (Laugh Tremble—Memory)* at Trafó. Hungary: Budapest. 1998. Lang.: Hun. 1293
Training
Dance training at Folkwang Hochschule. Germany: Essen. 1996-1998. Lang.: Hun. 1341
Bozzone, Bill
Performance/production
Collection of newspaper reviews by London theatre critics. UK-England: London. 1998. Lang.: Eng. 2543
Bracco, Roberto
Plays/librettos/scripts
Italian realist drama. Italy. 1860-1918. Lang.: Eng. 3260
Brad, Walton
Plays/librettos/scripts
Homosexuality in Canadian opera. Canada. 1970-1998. Lang.: Eng. 4762
Bradbury, Ray
Plays/librettos/scripts
Science fiction drama since World War II. USA. 1945-1988. Lang.: Eng. 3591
Bradley, Eddie Paul, Jr.
Basic theatrical documents
Texts of plays by Eddie Paul Bradley, Jr. USA. 1998. Lang.: Eng. 1482
Bradley, Jyll
Performance/production
Collection of newspaper reviews by London theatre critics. UK-England: London, Scarborough. 1998. Lang.: Eng. 2426
Bradwell, Mike
Performance/production
Collection of newspaper reviews by London theatre critics. UK-England: London. 1998. Lang.: Eng. 2502
Collection of newspaper reviews by London theatre critics. UK-England: London. 1998. Lang.: Eng. 2537
Brady, Michael
Plays/librettos/scripts
Analysis of historical drama of the holocaust. USA. Canada. Germany. 1950-1980. Lang.: Eng. 3610
Bragaglia, Anton Giulio
Reference materials
Index to performing arts articles in Bragaglia's *Chronache d'attualità*. Italy: Rome. 1916-1922. Lang.: Ita. 704
Braginskij, Emil
Plays/librettos/scripts
Playwright Emil Braginskij. Russia. 1940-1998. Lang.: Rus. 3324
Braine, John
Performance/production
Collection of newspaper reviews by London theatre critics. UK-England: London. 1998. Lang.: Eng. 2477
Branagh, Kenneth
Performance/production
Analysis of casting and acting in Kenneth Branagh's film adaptation of *Much Ado About Nothing*. UK. 1993. Lang.: Fre. 3939
Plays/librettos/scripts
Shakespeare, Branagh, and the concept of the author. England. 1590-1998. Lang.: Eng. 2958
Brand
Institutions
Survey of annual Ibsen festival. Norway: Oslo. 1998. Lang.: Eng. 1683
Performance/production
Report from Ibsen festival. Norway: Oslo. 1998. Lang.: Swe. 2211
Branth, Janicke
Plays/librettos/scripts
Dramaturgs on recognizing talented new playwrights. Denmark. 1998. Lang.: Dan. 2854
Brassed Off
Performance/production
Collection of newspaper reviews by London theatre critics. UK-England: London. 1998. Lang.: Eng. 2414
Bratja Karamazov (Brothers Karamazov, The)
Performance/production
Luca Ronconi's stage adaptation of *The Brothers Karamazov*. Italy: Rome. 1997. Lang.: Eng. 2188
Braun, Matthias
Plays/librettos/scripts
The character Medea in European drama. Europe. 450 B.C.-1998 A.D. Lang.: Ger. 3063
Braunek, Manfred
Institutions
Director training at Universität und Musikhochschule. Germany: Hamburg. 1988-1998. Lang.: Ger. 1658
Braunschweig, Stéphane
Performance/production
Recent Paris productions. France: Paris. 1997-1998. Lang.: Ger. 1933
French production of *Im Dickicht der Städte (In the Jungle of Cities)* by Bertolt Brecht. France. 1997-1998. Lang.: Ger. 1946
Collection of newspaper reviews by London theatre critics. UK-England: London. 1998. Lang.: Eng. 2496
Brawn, Geoffrey
Performance/production
Collection of newspaper reviews by London theatre critics. UK-England: London. 1998. Lang.: Eng. 2557
Bread and Butter
Plays/librettos/scripts
Female characters in Eugene O'Neill's plays. USA. 1920-1953. Lang.: Eng. 3525
Bread and Puppet Theatre (Plainfield, VT)
Institutions
Profile of the Bread and Puppet Theatre. USA: Plainfield, VT. 1963-1998. Lang.: Hun. 4877
Bread and Puppet Theatre's postmodern puppetry. USA: Plainfield, VT. 1990-1997. Lang.: Eng. 4878
The political performance aesthetic of Bread and Puppet Theatre. USA: Plainfield, VT. 1991. Lang.: Eng. 4879
Break of Day, The
Plays/librettos/scripts
The Break of Day, Timberlake Wertenbaker's adaptation of Čechov's *Three Sisters*. UK-England. Russia. 1901-1995. Lang.: Eng. 3510
Breakfast Soldiers, The
Performance/production
Collection of newspaper reviews by London theatre critics. UK-England: London. 1998. Lang.: Eng. 2411
Breakwell, Ian
Performance/production
Brief biographies of performance artists. 1963-1988. Lang.: Eng. 4238
Brecht on Brecht
Performance/production
Semiotic analysis of the nature of theatrical directing. USA. 1988. Lang.: Eng. 650
Brecht, Bertolt
Audience
Theatrical production and reception. Canada. 1988. Lang.: Eng. 146

Brecht, Bertolt — cont'd

Basic theatrical documents
Catalan translations of plays by Bertolt Brecht (volume 1). Germany. 1919-1954. Lang.: Cat. 1437

Design/technology
Costume designer Isabelle Larivière. Canada: Quebec, PQ. 1994-1995. Lang.: Fre. 1514

An exhibition of sets by Caspar Neher for the plays of Bertolt Brecht. Germany: Berlin. 1998. Lang.: Eng. 1522

Robert Wilson and Vera Dobroschke's design for Brecht's *Ozeanflug*. Germany: Berlin. 1998. Lang.: Eng. 4430

Performance/production
Dutch reception of the work of Bertolt Brecht. Netherlands. 1940-1998. Lang.: Dut. 564

Review of Brazilian performances of plays by Brecht. Brazil: São Paulo. 1998. Lang.: Ger. 1832

Irondale Ensemble's production of *Leben des Galilei (The Life of Galileo)* by Bertolt Brecht. Canada: Halifax, NS. 1998. Lang.: Eng. 1869

Approaches to staging Brecht's plays, based on compiled reviews. Europe. 1961-1997. Lang.: Ger. 1910

The rise of the modern Shakespearean director. Europe. 1878-1995. Lang.: Eng. 1911

Recent Paris productions. France: Paris. 1997-1998. Lang.: Ger. 1933

French productions of German plays. France. 1998. Lang.: Ger. 1935

French production of *Im Dickicht der Städte (In the Jungle of Cities)* by Bertolt Brecht. France. 1997-1998. Lang.: Ger. 1946

German directors about the meaning of Brecht today. Germany. 1998. Lang.: Ger. 1948

Comparison of productions of Brecht's *Die Massnahme (The Measures Taken)*. Germany: Berlin, Wuppertal. 1995-1998. Lang.: Ger. 1950

Mei Lanfang's influence on Bertolt Brecht. Germany. China. 1935. Lang.: Eng. 1951

Erwin Piscator and Brecht's *Schwejk im zweiten Weltkrieg (Schweik in the Second World War)*. Germany: Berlin. 1928. Lang.: Ger. 1952

Two productions of Brecht's *Der Kaukasische Kreidekreis (The Caucasian Chalk Circle)*. Germany: Berlin, Hamburg. 1998. Lang.: Ger. 1957

Thomas Langhoff's production of Brecht's *Der Kaukasische Kreidekreis (The Caucasian Chalk Circle)* at Deutsches Theater. Germany: Berlin. 1998. Lang.: Ger. 1965

Bertolt Brecht's production of his *Mutter Courage (Mother Courage)*. Germany: Berlin. 1947-1956. Lang.: Ger. 1975

Recent German productions of plays by Bertolt Brecht. Germany: Hamburg, Berlin. 1997. Lang.: Swe. 1977

Interview with director Benno Besson. Germany: Berlin. 1947-1998. Lang.: Ger. 1981

Reviews of productions of plays by Brecht. Germany. 1998. Lang.: Ger. 1986

Interview with director Matthias Langhoff. Germany: Berlin. 1945-1998. Lang.: Ger. 1987

Interview with actor Ekkehard Schall. Germany: Berlin. 1959-1998. Lang.: Ger. 1990

Deconstructionist analysis of acting in the theatre of Bertolt Brecht. Germany. 1922-1956. Lang.: Eng. 2007

Recent productions of Bochumer Schauspielhaus. Germany: Bochum. 1998. Lang.: Ger. 2009

Recent productions of plays by Bertolt Brecht. Germany. 1997-1998. Lang.: Ger. 2028

Productions of plays by Shakespeare, Brecht, and Camus. Germany. 1998. Lang.: Ger. 2032

Gender and Shakespearean production in the GDR. Germany, East. 1982-1990. Lang.: Eng. 2044

Adaptations of Shakespeare in productions of Bertolt Brecht and Heiner Müller. Germany, East. 1945-1990. Lang.: Eng. 2049

Brecht's *Die Heilige Johanna der Schlachthöfe (Saint Joan of the Stockyards)* directed by Sándor Zsóter. Hungary: Miskolc. 1998. Lang.: Hun. 2084

Brecht's *Der Kaukasische Kreidkreis (The Caucasian Chalk Circle)* adapted and directed by János Mohácsi. Hungary: Nyíregyháza. 1998. Lang.: Hun. 2127

Interview with directors János Szász and Árpád Schilling. Hungary. 1998. Lang.: Hun. 2129

One-act plays by Brecht directed by József Jámbor. Hungary: Debrecen. 1998. Lang.: Hun. 2131

Giorgio Strehler's productions of plays by Bertolt Brecht. Italy: Milan. 1956-1998. Lang.: Swe. 2171

Productions of plays by Brecht and Shakespeare at the Hungarian theatre of Satu Mare. Romania: Satu Mare. 1998. Lang.: Hun. 2228

The Russian-German theatrical relationship. Russia. Germany. 1920-1949. Lang.: Rus. 2285

Chris Vorster's production of *Baal* by Bertolt Brecht. South Africa, Republic of: Capetown. 1998. Lang.: Eng. 2350

Gerthi Kulle's role in Brecht's *Der Gute Mensch von Sezuan (The Good Person of Szechwan)* at Dramaten. Sweden: Stockholm. 1998. Lang.: Swe. 2384

Interview with community theatre director Kent Ekberg. Sweden: Stockholm. 1973-1998. Lang.: Swe. 2385

Katharina Thalbach in Brecht's *Die heilige Johanna der Schlachthöfe (Saint Joan of the Stockyards)* directed by Benno Besson. Switzerland: Zurich. 1998. Lang.: Ger. 2400

Collection of newspaper reviews by London theatre critics. UK-England: London. 1998. Lang.: Eng. 2522

The change in Shakespearean production. UK-England. 1960-1980. Lang.: Eng. 2628

Interview with director Simon McBurney. UK-England: London. 1997. Lang.: Swe. 2641

Brecht and the vocal role. Germany. 1920-1998. Lang.: Swe. 4295

Composers and the work of Bertolt Brecht. Germany. 1928-1998. Lang.: Ger. 4297

Robert Wilson's production of Brecht's *Der Ozeanflug*. Germany: Berlin. 1998. Lang.: Ger. 4356

Brecht and Weill's *Die Dreigroschenoper (The Three Penny Opera)* directed by László Vándorfi. Hungary: Veszprém.1998. Lang.: Hun. 4358

Two Hungarian productions of *Die Dreigroschenoper (The Three Penny Opera)*. Hungary: Budapest, Szeged. 1998. Lang.: Hun. 4362

Review of Salzburger Festspiele performances. Austria: Salzburg. 1998. Lang.: Ger. 4527

Opera productions of the Salzburg Festival. Austria: Salzburg. 1998. Lang.: Hun. 4531

Interview with director Robert Wilson. Germany: Berlin. 1970-1998. Lang.: Swe. 4609

Plays/librettos/scripts
Wonderbolt Circus's *Maid of Avalon*, a loose adaptation of *Der Gute Mensch von Sezuan (The Good Person of Szechwan)* by Brecht.Canada: St. John's, NF. 1950-1998. Lang.: Eng. 2825

The recent revival of interest in works of Bertolt Brecht. Europe. 1998. Lang.: Eng. 3049

The rebel in modern drama. Europe. 1950-1988. Lang.: Eng. 3053

The clown as a character in modern drama. Europe. 1915-1995. Lang.: Eng. 3056

Gender and madness in modern drama. Europe. 1880-1969. Lang.: Eng. 3061

The influence of Bertolt's Brecht. Europe. 1898-1998. Lang.: Swe. 3068

German playwrights on the meaning of Brecht today. Germany. 1998. Lang.: Ger. 3123

Musicological perspective on *Die Massnahme (The Measures Taken)* by Brecht and Eisler. Germany: Berlin. 1929-1998. Lang.: Ger. 3125

The relevance of Bertolt Brecht in his centennial year. Germany. 1998. Lang.: Eng. 3128

Analysis of *Die Ausnahme und die Regel (The Exception and the Rule)* by Bertolt Brecht. Germany. 1938. Lang.: Swe. 3133

The meanings of the cigar in the appearance and works of Heiner Müller and Bertolt Brecht. Germany. 1930-1997. Lang.: Swe. 3134

The relevance of Bertolt Brecht in reunified Germany. Germany. 1934-1998. Lang.: Ger. 3135

Playwright Bertolt Brecht. Germany. 1898-1956. Lang.: Rus. 3140

The significance of Bertolt Brecht to theatre in the late twentieth century. Germany. USA. 1898-1998. Lang.: Eng. 3142

Brecht's working methods as a playwright as documented in annotated editions of his plays. Germany. 1998. Lang.: Ger. 3144

Aesthetic peculiarities of *Baal* by Bertolt Brecht. Germany. 1918-1922. Lang.: Hun. 3146

Reevaluation of the legacy of Bertolt Brecht. Germany. 1898-1998. Lang.: Swe. 3149

Brecht, Bertolt — cont'd

Recent German productions of Brecht's plays. Germany. 1998. Lang.: Ger. 3150
Brecht, copyright, and contemporary perceptions. Germany: Berlin. 1898-1998. Lang.: Ger. 3153
Late twentieth-century view of playwright Bertolt Brecht. Germany. 1898-1956. Lang.: Fin. 3155
Brecht's *Leben des Galilei (The Life of Galileo)* as an adaptation of Shakespeare's *Hamlet.* Germany. 1600-1932. Lang.: Eng. 3160
Analysis of *Mann ist Mann (A Man's a Man)* by Bertolt Brecht. Germany. 1926. Lang.: Swe. 3165
Brecht and the city as an expressionistic setting. Germany. USA. 1923-1926. Lang.: Eng. 3168
The diminishing importance of Bertolt Brecht in reunified Germany. Germany. 1989-1998. Lang.: Ger. 3170
Brecht and the translation of Shakespeare into German. Germany, East. 1945-1990. Lang.: Eng. 3177
Analysis and translation of *Et les Chiens se taisaient (And the Dogs Were Silent)* by Aimé Césaire. Martinique. 1946-1969. Lang.: Eng. 3269
Analysis of *Al-Mawik Huwa Al-Mawik (The King Is the King)* by Saadallah Wannus. Syria. 1977. Lang.: Eng. 3418
Perceptions of Bertolt Brecht in the English-speaking world. UK-England. North America. 1933-1998. Lang.: Ger. 3443
Bertolt Brecht and German cinema. Germany. 1919-1932. Lang.: Ita. 3972
The search for a lost translation of *The Seven Deadly Sins* by Brecht and Weill. Germany. UK-England. 1933-1998. Lang.: Eng. 4392
Hero and anti-hero in contemporary opera production. Germany. 1998. Lang.: Ger. 4791
W.H. Auden as an opera librettist and translator. UK-England. 1907-1973. Lang.: Eng. 4825

Relation to other fields
The rise and fall of German political theatre. Germany. 1928-1998. Lang.: Ger. 745
Bertolt Brecht's working methods as described in recent books. Germany. 1926-1998. Lang.: Ger. 3769

Theory/criticism
Hungarian translation of Brecht's article on the alienation effect in Chinese theatre. China. 1910-1950. Lang.: Hun. 836

Bremer Theater (Bremen)
Performance/production
Dance adaptations of Shakespeare's *Hamlet.* Germany: Bremen, Weimar. 1996-1997. Lang.: Ger. 930
Music theatre production in northern Germany. Germany: Lübeck, Hamburg, Bremen, Kiel. 1998. Lang.: Ger. 4293

Brendan's Visit
Performance/production
Collection of newspaper reviews by London theatre critics. UK-England: London. 1998. Lang.: Eng. 2570

Brendel, Wolfgang
Performance/production
Baritone Wolfgang Brendel. Germany. 1998. Lang.: Eng. 4593

Brendenal, Silvia
Performance/production
Profile of the Fidena puppet festival. Germany: Bochum. 1998. Lang.: Ger. 4894

Brenk, Tomaž
Basic theatrical documents
Text of the musical play *Emanacije (Emanations)* by Tomaž Brenk and Mojca Kasjak. Slovenia. 1997. Lang.: Eng, Slo. 4288

Brennan, Tim
Audience
Interview with performance artist Tim Brennan. Netherlands: Arnhem. 1989. Lang.: Eng. 4231

Brenner, John
Performance/production
Collection of newspaper reviews by London theatre critics. UK-England: London. 1998. Lang.: Eng. 2415

Brenner, Matthias
Institutions
Contemporary drama at Schauspiel Leipzig. Germany: Leipzig. 1998. Lang.: Ger. 1661

Brenton, Howard
Performance/production
Collection of newspaper reviews by London theatre critics. UK. 1998. Lang.: Eng. 2407
Collection of newspaper reviews by London theatre critics. UK-England: London. 1998. Lang.: Eng. 2532

Plays/librettos/scripts
The influence of Jacobean theatre on contemporary plays and productions. UK-England. 1986-1998. Lang.: Eng. 3428
Analysis of *The Romans in Britain* by Howard Brenton. UK-England. 1980-1981. Lang.: Eng. 3482

Breth, Andrea
Institutions
The future of Schaubühne after the resignation of artistic director Andrea Breth. Germany: Berlin. 1997. Lang.: Ger. 1633
Performance/production
Political changes reflected in Berlin theatre productions. Germany: Berlin. 1998. Lang.: Ger. 1958

Briar Street Theatre (Chicago, IL)
Design/technology
Sound design for Blue Man Group's Chicago production of *Tubes.* USA: Chicago, IL. 1996-1997. Lang.: Eng. 261

Bricusse, Leslie
Design/technology
Technical designs for the musical *Doctor Doolittle* directed by Steven Pimlott. UK-England: London. 1998. Lang.: Eng. 4325
Lighting design for *Jekyll & Hyde* directed by Robin Phillips. USA: New York, NY. 1998. Lang.: Eng. 4345
Performance/production
Collection of newspaper reviews by London theatre critics. UK-England: London. 1998. Lang.: Eng. 2472

Bride, Greg
Institutions
Street theatre company Scaffold Theatre Project. Canada: Hamilton, ON. 1995-1998. Lang.: Eng. 1593

Bridewell Theatre (London)
Performance/production
Collection of newspaper reviews by London theatre critics. UK-England: London. 1998. Lang.: Eng. 2442
Collection of newspaper reviews by London theatre critics. UK-England: London. 1998. Lang.: Eng. 2470
Collection of newspaper reviews by London theatre critics. UK-England: London. 1998. Lang.: Eng. 2483
Collection of newspaper reviews by London theatre critics. UK-England: London. 1998. Lang.: Eng. 2501
Collection of newspaper reviews by London theatre critics. UK-England: London. 1998. Lang.: Eng. 2512
Collection of newspaper reviews by London theatre critics. UK-England: London. 1998. Lang.: Eng. 2521
Collection of newspaper reviews by London theatre critics. UK-England: London. 1998. Lang.: Eng. 2549
Collection of newspaper reviews by London theatre critics. UK-England: London. 1998. Lang.: Eng. 2562
Collection of newspaper reviews by London theatre critics. UK-England: London. 1998. Lang.: Eng. 2584

Bridge, Richard
Performance/production
Collection of newspaper reviews by London theatre critics. UK-England: London. 1998. Lang.: Eng. 2437

Brie, César
Performance/production
César Brie and *La pista del cabeceo (The Land of Nod).* Bolivia. 1970-1985. Lang.: Ita. 1829

Brief Lives
Performance/production
Collection of newspaper reviews by London theatre critics. UK-England: London. 1998. Lang.: Eng. 2445
Actor Michael Williams. UK-England: London. 1950-1998. Lang.: Eng. 2644

Briggs, Raymond
Performance/production
Collection of newspaper reviews by London theatre critics. UK-England: London. 1998. Lang.: Eng. 2557

Brill, Robert
Performance spaces
The creation of a site-specific performance space for Sam Mendes' production of *Cabaret.* USA: New York, NY. 1998. Lang.: Eng. 4350

Brinberg, Steven
Performance/production
Collection of newspaper reviews by London theatre critics. UK-England: London. 1998. Lang.: Eng. 2531

Brind, Susan
Audience
Interview with performance artist Tim Brennan. Netherlands: Arnhem. 1989. Lang.: Eng. 4231
Bringing Up Baby
Plays/librettos/scripts
Marriage, divorce, and gender in the Hollywood comedy of remarriage. USA. 1935-1942. Lang.: Eng. 4010
Brisley, Stuart
Performance/production
Brief biographies of performance artists. 1963-1988. Lang.: Eng. 4238
Britannicus
Performance/production
Collection of newspaper reviews by London theatre critics. UK-England: London. 1998. Lang.: Eng. 2534
British Broadcasting Corporation (BBC, London)
Plays/librettos/scripts
BBC radio plays with Anglo-Irish themes. UK-England. Ireland. 1973-1986. Lang.: Eng. 3868
Britten, Benjamin
Performance/production
Interview with opera singer Anne Bolstad. Norway. Sweden. 1980-1998. Lang.: Swe. 4665
The current state of opera in England. UK-England. 1997. Lang.: Eng. 4705
Background material on Lyric Opera of Chicago radio broadcast performances. USA: Chicago, IL. 1998. Lang.: Eng. 4709
Background material on telecast performance of Britten's *Paul Bunyan* at New York City Opera. USA: New York, NY. 1998. Lang.: Eng. 4710
Background material on Metropolitan Opera radio broadcast performances. USA: New York, NY. 1998. Lang.: Eng. 4713
Operas by Benjamin Britten in the repertory of the Metropolitan and the New York City Opera. USA: New York, NY. 1945-1998. Lang.:Eng. 4749
Plays/librettos/scripts
Derek Jarman's adaptation of works by Benjamin Britten and Wilfred Owen. UK-England. 1968-1988. Lang.: Eng. 4822
Analysis of Benjamin Britten's opera *Death in Venice*. UK-England. 1912-1992. Lang.: Eng. 4823
W.H. Auden as an opera librettist and translator. UK-England. 1907-1973. Lang.: Eng. 4825
Britten, Tony
Performance/production
Collection of newspaper reviews by London theatre critics. UK-England: London. 1998. Lang.: Eng. 2420
Britton, Tim
Performance/production
Collection of newspaper reviews by London theatre critics. UK-England: London. 1998. Lang.: Eng. 2436
Brixton Shaw Theatre (London)
Performance/production
Collection of newspaper reviews by London theatre critics. UK-England: London. 1998. Lang.: Eng. 2447
Brizell, Cindy
Performance/production
Theatre Magazine's anniversary issue. USA. 1968-1998. Lang.: Eng. 617
Broadhurst Theatre (New York, NY)
Design/technology
Recent work of lighting designer Brian MacDevitt. USA: New York, NY. 1997. Lang.: Eng. 1530
Broadhurst, Thomas
Plays/librettos/scripts
Dramatic adaptations of Henry Wadsworth Longfellow's poem *Evangeline*. USA. Canada. 1860-1976. Lang.: Eng. 3643
Broadway Cares/Equity Fights AIDS (New York, NY)
Administration
Reports on the 10th Anniversary of Broadway Cares/Equity Fights AIDS. USA: New York, NY. 1998. Lang.: Eng. 52
Report on Easter Bonnet fundraiser for AIDS. USA: New York, NY. 1998. Lang.: Eng. 72
Report on 'Broadway Bares' benefit for AIDS. USA: New York, NY. 1998. Lang.: Eng. 76
The Palm View residence for people with AIDS. USA: Hollywood, CA. 1998. Lang.: Eng. 95
Flea Market fundraiser for AIDS. USA: New York, NY. 1998. Lang.: Eng. 109
Performance/production
Actress Betty Buckley's performance in AIDS fundraiser. Switzerland: Geneva. 1998. Lang.: Eng. 603
AIDS-benefit performance of the musical *Sweet Charity*. USA: New York, NY. 1998. Lang.: Eng. 4386
Broadway theatre
Administration
Actors' Fund annual benefit for women's health. USA: New York, NY. 1998. Lang.: Eng. 68
Report on Easter Bonnet fundraiser for AIDS. USA: New York, NY. 1998. Lang.: Eng. 72
The debate on the rezoning of the New York theatre district. USA: New York, NY. 1998. Lang.: Eng. 73
History of the Tony Awards. USA: New York, NY. 1950-1998. Lang.: Eng. 74
Report on 'Broadway Bares' benefit for AIDS. USA: New York, NY. 1998. Lang.: Eng. 76
Issues of concern to Equity members in current Broadway shows. USA: New York, NY. 1998. Lang.: Eng. 77
City Council's approval of a plan to sell theatres' air rights to developers. USA: New York, NY. 1998. Lang.: Eng. 89
The Disney Corporation's Broadway musicals. USA: New York, NY. 1996-1998. Lang.: Eng. 4317
Performer Rebecca Spencer's experience as an Equity Deputy. USA: New York, NY. 1998. Lang.: Eng. 4320
Design/technology
Lighting designer Kevin Adams. USA. 1979-1998. Lang.: Eng. 258
Costume designer Jeanne Button. USA. 1965-1998. Lang.: Eng. 260
Lighting designer Kenneth Posner. USA. 1998. Lang.: Eng. 1545
Lighting designer Hugh Vanstone. USA: New York, NY. 1998. Lang.: Eng. 1554
Sound design for the London production of *Chicago*. UK-England: London. 1998. Lang.: Eng. 4326
Donald Holder's lighting design for *The Lion King*. USA: New York, NY. 1997-1998. Lang.: Eng. 4336
Lighting design for *Jekyll & Hyde* directed by Robin Phillips. USA: New York, NY. 1998. Lang.: Eng. 4345
Performance spaces
Theatre space and performance. USA: New York, NY. 1925-1985. Lang.: Eng. 464
The renovation of Times Square. USA: New York, NY. 1998. Lang.: Eng. 479
Performance/production
The success of dance extravaganzas and solo performance at the expense of traditional shows. USA: New York, NY. 1994-1998. Lang. :Eng. 645
German impressions of recent New York theatre. USA: New York, NY. 1998. Lang.: Ger. 655
Dance director Seymour Felix. USA. 1918-1953. Lang.: Eng. 976
The influence of *The Little Princess* on popular theatre and culture. USA. 1903. Lang.: Eng. 2658
Attempted censorship of productions. USA. 1900-1905. Lang.: Eng. 2698
Julyana Soelistyo and Sam Trammel, winners of the Derwent Award. USA: New York, NY. 1998. Lang.: Eng. 2719
The 'scientific perspective' of director David Belasco. USA. 1882-1931. Lang.: Eng. 2741
The Broadway directing career of George M. Cohan. USA. 1900-1950. Lang.: Eng. 2751
William Schuman on the differences between operatic and Broadway theatre singing. USA. 1998. Lang.: Eng. 4303
Musical performances on and off Broadway. USA: New York. 1998. Lang.: Ger. 4383
AIDS-benefit performance of the musical *Sweet Charity*. USA: New York, NY. 1998. Lang.: Eng. 4386
Gower Champion's work in musical theatre. USA: New York, NY. 1936-1980. Lang.: Eng. 4388
Obituaries of singers Randolph Symonette and Todd Duncan. USA. 1998. Lang.: Eng. 4708
Plays/librettos/scripts
Playwright Martin McDonagh. Ireland. 1998. Lang.: Eng. 3216
The Broadway success of women playwrights. USA. 1906-1944. Lang.: Eng. 3590

Broadway theatre — cont'd

Jean Randich's production of *The Golden Door* by Sylvia Regan, Tenement Museum. USA: New York, NY. 1940-1998. Lang.: Eng. 3606

Lyricist and librettist Betty Comden. USA. 1938-1998. Lang.: Eng. 4400

Relation to other fields

Tourism and the development of theatre districts. USA: New York, NY. Germany: Berlin. 1998. Lang.: Eng. 807

The changing face of Times Square and its effect on the local community. USA: New York, NY. 1998. Lang.: Eng. 812

The social significance of the Disney Corporation's influence on Broadway theatre. USA: New York, NY. 1997. Lang.: Eng. 3782

Interactions between commercial and not-for-profit theatre. USA. 1998. Lang.: Eng. 3785

Brochen, Julie

Performance/production

Recent Paris productions. France: Paris. 1997-1998. Lang.: Ger. 1933

Brodauf, Angela

Performance/production

Director Angela Brodauf. Germany: Dortmund. 1984-1998. Lang.: Ger. 1989

Bródy, János

Performance/production

Reviews of new Hungarian musicals. Hungary: Budapest. 1997. Lang.: Hun. 4360

Brogger, Suzanne

Plays/librettos/scripts

Female characters in plays by Scandinavian women. Norway. Sweden. Denmark. 1998. Lang.: Eng. 3299

Bronnen, Arnolt

Audience

Audience response to Bronnen's *Der Vatermord (Parricide)* and German culture. Germany: Frankfurt. 1922. Lang.: Eng. 1403

Plays/librettos/scripts

Social criticism in Viennese Expressionist drama. Austria: Vienna. 1907-1922. Lang.: Ger. 2779

Bronson, Tom

Design/technology

Costuming for the film *Mr. Magoo*. USA: Hollywood, CA. 1998. Lang.: Eng. 3903

Brook, Irina

Basic theatrical documents

French translation of *Beast on the Moon* by Richard Kalinoski. USA. France. 1995-1997. Lang.: Fre. 1491

Brook, Peter

Design/technology

Set designer Jean-Guy Lecat and his work with Peter Brook. France. Denmark. 1975-1998. Lang.: Dan. 182

Institutions

Peter Brook's production of Mozart's *Don Giovanni* at the Aix festival. France: Aix-en-Provence. 1998. Lang.: Swe. 4450

Performance/production

Directing and intercultural theatre. Europe. 1930-1998. Lang.: Ger. 524

Peter Brook's *The Mahabharata*, and problems of intercultural performance. France. 1988-1992. Lang.: Eng. 1925

Peter Brook's *Je suis un phénomène (I Am a Phenomenon)* at Bouffes du Nord. France: Paris. 1998. Lang.: Hun. 1930

Peter Brook's *Je suis un phénomène (I Am a Phenomenon)*. France: Paris. 1998. Lang.: Ger. 1934

The evolution of the contemporary Shakespearean director. North America. Europe. 1967-1998. Lang.: Eng. 2207

Modernist and postmodernist Shakespearean production. UK-England. Canada. 1966-1996. Lang.: Eng. 2618

Interview with singer Peter Mattei. France: Aix-en-Provence. 1985-1998. Lang.: Swe. 4564

Peter Brook's *Don Giovanni* at the Aix Festival. France: Aix-en-Provence. 1998. Lang.: Eng. 4569

Theory/criticism

Essay on the nature of talent. Denmark. Sweden. UK-England. 1847-1987. Lang.: Dan. 838

Italian translation of *The Empty Space* by Peter Brook. UK-England. 1998. Lang.: Ita. 3833

Training

Actor/director Jean-Paul Denizon and his workshops on Peter Brook's approach to theatre. France. 1980-1998. Lang.: Ita. 873

Brooklyn Academy of Music (BAM, New York, NY)

Design/technology

Design concept for Ralph Lemon's dance piece *Geography* at BAM. USA: New York, NY. 1998. Lang.: Eng. 1248

Lighting designer Hugh Vanstone. USA: New York, NY. 1998. Lang.: Eng. 1554

Plays/librettos/scripts

Shared Experience's stage adaptations of nineteenth-century novels. USA: New York, NY. UK-England: London. 1998. Lang.: Eng. 3518

Brooks, Andrea

Performance/production

Collection of newspaper reviews by London theatre critics. UK-England: London, Scarborough. 1998. Lang.: Eng. 2426

Collection of newspaper reviews by London theatre critics. UK-England: London. 1998. Lang.: Eng. 2572

Brooks, Daniel

Plays/librettos/scripts

Analysis of *The Noam Chomsky Lectures* by Daniel Brooks and Guillermo Verdecchio. Canada: Toronto, ON. 1990-1991. Lang.: Eng. 2797

Analysis of Daniel MacIvor's *Monster* as directed by Daniel Brooks. Canada: Toronto, ON. 1998. Lang.: Eng. 2834

Brooks, Mel

Basic theatrical documents

Text of *Young Frankenstein* by Gene Wilder and Mel Brooks. USA. 1974. Lang.: Eng. 3898

Plays/librettos/scripts

Robin Hood on film. England. USA. 1920-1992. Lang.: Eng. 3969

Interview with actor and screenwriter Gene Wilder. USA. 1998. Lang.: Eng. 3991

Interview with director and screenwriter Mel Brooks. USA. 1998. Lang.: Eng. 3992

Brossner, Lars-Erik

Performance/production

Conference on theatre for children ages 2-4. Sweden: Stockholm. 1998. Lang.: Swe. 2368

Brothers Karamazov, The

SEE

Bratja Karamazov.

Brotherston, Lez

Design/technology

Technical designs for Matthew Bourne's productions of ballets by Čajkovskij and Prokofjév. UK-England: London. 1998. Lang.: Eng. 1031

Brown, Carlyle

Performance/production

Collection of newspaper reviews by London theatre critics. UK-England: London. 1998. Lang.: Eng. 2487

Brown, Debra

Performance/production

Choreographer Debra Brown of Cirque du Soleil. Canada: Montreal, PQ. 1987-1998. Lang.: Eng. 4179

Brown, Eleanor

Performance/production

Collection of newspaper reviews by London theatre critics. UK-England: London. Lang.: Eng. 2408

Brown, Ian

Performance/production

Collection of newspaper reviews by London theatre critics. UK-England: London. 1998. Lang.: Eng. 2410

Collection of newspaper reviews by London theatre critics. UK-England: Leeds, Manchester. 1998. Lang.: Eng. 2433

Collection of newspaper reviews by London theatre critics. UK-England: London. 1998. Lang.: Eng. 2450

Collection of newspaper reviews by London theatre critics. UK-England: London. 1998. Lang.: Eng. 2549

Collection of newspaper reviews by London theatre critics. UK-England: London. 1998. Lang.: Eng. 2568

Brown, John Mason

Theory/criticism

Theatre critic John Mason Brown. USA. 1900-1969. Lang.: Eng. 3846

Brown, Kenneth

Performance/production

Theatre Magazine's anniversary issue. USA. 1968-1998. Lang.: Eng. 617

Plays/librettos/scripts

Revolutionary Off Broadway playwriting. USA: New York, NY. 1959-1969. Lang.: Eng. 3604

Brown, Michael

Design/technology

Lighting designer Michael Brown. USA. 1998. Lang.: Eng. 282

Brown, Susan

Performance/production

Susan Brown on her role in *Richard III* at RSC. UK-England: London, Stratford. 1995-1996. Lang.: Eng. 2593

Brown, William
Performance/production
High-school students' production of *The Wiz* at the Edinburgh Fringe Festival. USA: Hattiesburg, MS. UK-Scotland: Edinburgh. 1996. Lang.: Eng. 4381

Browne, Robert
Performance/production
English actors in Kassel. Germany: Kassel. 1592-1620. Lang.: Eng. 2016

Browning, Maurice
Performance/production
Collection of newspaper reviews by London theatre critics. UK-England: London. 1998. Lang.: Eng. 2557

Browning, Robert
Plays/librettos/scripts
The influence of Webster, Middleton, and Shakespeare on the poetry of Robert Browning. England. 1590-1889. Lang.: Eng. 2906

Bruce, Christopher
Performance/production
Interview with choreographer Christopher Bruce of the Rambert Dance Company. UK-England: London. 1998. Lang.: Hun. 1163

Bruce, Deborah
Performance/production
Collection of newspaper reviews by London theatre critics. UK-England: London. 1998. Lang.: Eng. 2427

Bruckner, Ferdinand
Plays/librettos/scripts
Homosexuality on the German stage. Germany. 1920-1980. Lang.: Eng. 3147

Bruder Eichmann (Brother Eichmann)
Performance/production
Alexander Stillmark's production of *Bruder Eichmann (Brother Eichmann)* by Heinar Kipphardt. Germany: Berlin. 1984-1992. Lang.: Eng. 2022

Bruncken, Thirza
Institutions
New productions of Düsseldorfer Schauspielhaus. Germany: Dusseldorf. 1998. Lang.: Ger. 1654

Brunel, Johnny
Performance/production
Collection of newspaper reviews by London theatre critics. UK-England: London. 1998. Lang.: Eng. 2532

Bruns, Heiner
Performance/production
Interview with director Heiner Bruns of Städtische Bühnen Bielefeld. Germany: Bielefeld. 1975-1998. Lang.: Ger. 4598

Brus, Roland
Performance/production
A production of Schiller's *Die Räuber (The Robbers)* performed by prisoners. Germany: Berlin. 1997. Lang.: Ger. 2025

Bruscambille
SEE
Gracieux, Jean.

Brustein, Robert
Theory/criticism
The influence of Lionel Trilling on criticism of Robert Brustein. USA. 1960-1997. Lang.: Eng. 3848

Brutahlia Teatret (Copenhagen)
Performance/production
Director Jonathan Paul Cook on developing talent in an ensemble. Denmark. 1997-1998. Lang.: Dan. 1888

Brutopia
Plays/librettos/scripts
Political thought in plays of Howard Barker. UK-England. 1960-1992. Lang.: Eng. 3502

Bryden, Bill
Performance/production
Collection of newspaper reviews by London theatre critics. UK-England: Stratford, Birmingham. 1998. Lang.: Eng. 2536

Brytpunkt (Sweden)
Administration
Ways to attract new young audiences to theatre. Sweden: Stockholm. 1995-1998. Lang.: Swe. 21

Brzoza, Zbigniew
Performance/production
The new generation of Polish directors. Poland. 1989-1998. Lang.: Pol. 2219

Buber, Martin
Plays/librettos/scripts
Analysis of plays based on the Hebrew prophets. USA. Europe. 1919-1970. Lang.: Eng. 3659

Buc, George
Plays/librettos/scripts
The authorship of *George a Greene*. England. 1593-1599. Lang.: Eng. 2989

Buch, René
Plays/librettos/scripts
Background on Lorca's *El Público (The Public)*, about to have its New York premiere. USA: New York, NY. 1930-1998. Lang.: Eng. 3651

Büchner, Georg
Institutions
Productions by Stefan Bachmann and Robert Wilson at the Salzburg Festival. Austria: Salzburg. 1998. Lang.: Hun. 1570

Productions of Salzburger Festspiele. Austria: Salzburg. 1998. Lang.: Ger. 1571

Productions of the Salzburg Festival. Austria: Salzburg. 1998. Lang.: Ger. 1573

Performance/production
Director Armin Petras. Germany: Nordhausen. 1970-1998. Lang.: Ger. 2001

Andreas Kriegenburg's production of Büchner's *Leonce und Lena*. Germany: Munich. 1998. Lang.: Ger. 2020

Robert Wilson's work with actors on a production of *Danton's Death (Dantons Tod)*. USA: Houston, TX. 1997. Lang.: Eng. 2688

Plays/librettos/scripts
Gender and madness in modern drama. Europe. 1880-1969. Lang.: Eng. 3061

Relation to other fields
Manfred Weber on directing Děvad Karahasan's translation of *Leonce und Lena* by Büchner. Bosnia: Sarajevo. 1997-1998. Lang.: Ger. 3730

Büchse der Pandora, Die (Pandora's Box)
Plays/librettos/scripts
A private performance of *Die Büchse der Pandora (Pandora's Box)* by Frank Wedekind. Austria: Vienna. 1905. Lang.: Fre. 2783

Excerpt of Frank Wedekind's preface to *Die Büchse der Pandora (Pandora's Box)*. Germany. 1906. Lang.: Fre. 3169

Buckley, Betty
Performance/production
Actress Betty Buckley's performance in AIDS fundraiser. Switzerland: Geneva. 1998. Lang.: Eng. 603

Bucz, Hunor
Performance/production
Two productions of Csokonai Vitéz's *Karnyóné és a két szeleburdiak (Mrs. Karnyó and the Two Feather-Brains)*. Hungary: Budapest. 1998. Lang.: Hun. 2113

Budapest Opera
SEE
Magyar Állami Operaház.

Budapest Táncszínház (Budapest)
Performance/production
New work of Budapest Táncszínház. Hungary: Budapest. 1998. Lang.: Hun. 1294

Budapesti Kamaraszínház (Budapest)
Performance/production
Two productions of Shakespeare's *Richard III* by József Ruszt. Hungary: Budapest. Hungary: Kecskemét. 1973-1997. Lang.: Hun. 2070

Interview with director József Ruszt. Hungary. 1963-1997. Lang.: Hun. 2115

Three Hungarian productions of Shakespeare's *Richard III*. Hungary: Budapest, Zsámbék, Szeged. 1997. Lang.: Hun. 2121

Buddies in Bad Times Theatre (Toronto, ON)
Plays/librettos/scripts
R.M. Vaughan's *Camera, Woman* at Buddies in Bad Times. Canada: Toronto, ON. 1998. Lang.: Eng. 2835

Buenaventura, Enrique
Plays/librettos/scripts
New Theatre of Buenaventura, Reyes, and Niño. Colombia. 1950-1985. Lang.: Spa. 2846

Politics and violence in *Los papeles del infierno (Leaflets from Hell)* by Enrique Buenaventura. Colombia. 1970-1985. Lang.: Spa. 2847

Buff
Performance/production
Collection of newspaper reviews by London theatre critics. UK-England: London. 1998. Lang.: Eng. 2422

Buffini, Moira
Performance/production
Collection of newspaper reviews by London theatre critics. UK-England: London. 1998. Lang.: Eng. 2449

Bugeau, Christian
Basic theatrical documents
Text of *Soleil pour deux (Sun for Two)* by Pierre Sauvil. France. 1998. Lang.: Fre. 1434
Bugsy Malone
Design/technology
Sound design for the musical *Bugsy Malone*. UK-England: London. 1997. Lang.: Eng. 4327
Bühne der Stadt (Bielefeld)
Performance/production
Production history of *Die Bürgschaft* by Kurt Weill and Casper Neher. Germany: Berlin, Bielefeld. 1931-1998. Lang.: Eng. 4588
Bühnen der Landeshauptstadt (Kiel)
Performance/production
Music theatre production in northern Germany. Germany: Lübeck, Hamburg, Bremen, Kiel. 1998. Lang.: Ger. 4293
Opera director Katja Czellnik. Germany: Oldenburg, Kiel. 1996-1998. Lang.: Ger. 4583
Bühnen der Stadt Köln (Cologne)
Institutions
Children's opera company Yakult Halle. Germany: Cologne. 1996-1998. Lang.: Ger. 4455
Günter Krämer and children's opera. Germany: Cologne. 1996-1998. Lang.: Ger. 4458
Bukin, V.
Performance/production
Bolšoj Opera star V. Bukin. Russia: Moscow. Lang.: Rus. 4683
Bulgakov, Michajl Afanasjévič
Performance/production
Review of Bulgakov's *Ivan Vasiljévič* directed by János Mohácsi. Hungary: Kaposvár. 1998. Lang.: Hun. 2095
Collection of newspaper reviews by London theatre critics. UK-England: London. 1998. Lang.: Eng. 2507
Collection of newspaper reviews by London theatre critics. UK-England: London. 1998. Lang.: Eng. 2586
Plays/librettos/scripts
Comparison of the plays of Čechov and Bulgakov. Russia. 1890-1936. Lang.: Rus. 3338
Opera librettos of playwright Michajl Bulgakov. Russia. Lang.: Rus. 4817
Bulldog Theatre Company (New York, NY)
Performance/production
Reviews of productions of plays by Ibsen. USA: New York, NY. Norway: Oslo. 1998. Lang.: Eng. 2747
Bullen, Geoff
Performance/production
Collection of newspaper reviews by London theatre critics. UK-England: London. 1998. Lang.: Eng. 2477
Bullet, The
Performance/production
Collection of newspaper reviews by London theatre critics. UK-England: London. 1998. Lang.: Eng. 2454
Bullets Over Broadway
Plays/librettos/scripts
Čechov's influence on Woody Allen's film *Bullets Over Broadway*. USA. 1994. Lang.: Eng. 4027
Bulmer, Alex
Performance/production
Voice teachers Alex Bulmer and Kate Lynch. Canada: Toronto, ON. UK-England: London. 1986-1998. Lang.: Eng. 1837
Bumba-meu-boi
Performance/production
Northern Brazilian folk theatre forms. Brazil. 1972-1997. Lang.: Eng. 497
Bumbry, Grace
Performance/production
Singers' approaches to the title role in Bizet's *Carmen*. 1875-1998. Lang.: Eng. 4502
Bunch of the Gods Were Sitting Around One Day, A
Plays/librettos/scripts
Science fiction drama since World War II. USA. 1945-1988. Lang.: Eng. 3591
Buontalenti, Bernardo
Design/technology
Stage machinery in *Il Rapimento di Cefalo* staged by Bernardo Buontalenti. Italy: Florence. 1600. Lang.: Eng. 4436
Buoyant Billions
Plays/librettos/scripts
Analysis of the later plays of George Bernard Shaw. UK-England. 1923-1947. Lang.: Eng. 3444
Buras, Jacek
Performance/production
The Jewish Kabaret za murem and its treatment in Polish theatre. Poland: Warsaw. 1939-1988. Lang.: Pol. 4157
Burbridge, Paul
Performance/production
Collection of newspaper reviews by London theatre critics. UK-England: London. 1998. Lang.: Eng. 2442
Burgers, Marianne
Design/technology
Profiles of young theatrical designers. Netherlands. 1990-1998. Lang.: Dut. 207
Burgess, Anthony
Performance/production
German productions of adaptations of *A Clockwork Orange* by Anthony Burgess. Germany: Dresden, Hamburg, Stendal. 1998. Lang.: Ger. 1972
Burgess, Melvin
Performance/production
Collection of newspaper reviews by London theatre critics. UK-England: London. 1998. Lang.: Eng. 2580
Burghofbühne (Wesel)
Administration
Theatrical marketing in North Rhine-Westphalia. Germany. 1994-1998. Lang.: Ger. 6
Bürgschaft, Die
Performance/production
Production history of *Die Bürgschaft* by Kurt Weill and Casper Neher. Germany: Berlin, Bielefeld. 1931-1998. Lang.: Eng. 4588
Burgtheater (Vienna)
Performance/production
Analysis of *Sportstück (Sport Play)* by Elfriede Jelinek. Austria: Vienna. 1998. Lang.: Ger. 1818
Premieres of new plays. Austria: Vienna. 1998. Lang.: Ger. 1820
Premieres of plays on the Nazi theme. Germany: Darmstadt. Austria: Vienna. 1998. Lang.: Ger. 2030
Reviews of plays by Wolfgang Bauer and Thomas Bernhard. Switzerland: Basel. Austria: Vienna. 1998. Lang.: Ger. 2403
Mozart's operas and contemporary Viennese performance spaces. Austria: Vienna. 1782-1791. Lang.: Eng. 4528
Plays/librettos/scripts
Thomas Bernhard's Holocaust play, *Heldenplatz (Heroes' Square)*. Austria. 1988. Lang.: Eng. 2784
Analysis of plays by Carl Zuckmayer. Austria: Vienna. 1925-1938. Lang.: Ger. 2785
Recent productions directed by Frank Castorf. Austria: Vienna. 1998. Lang.: Ger. 2788
Relation to other fields
The artist and the world in recent productions. Austria: Vienna. Germany. 1997-1998. Lang.: Ger. 3729
Buried Child
Plays/librettos/scripts
Female presence/absence in plays of O'Neill, Pinter, and Shepard. USA. UK-England. 1936-1985. Lang.: Eng. 3607
Language in the plays of Sam Shepard. USA. 1967-1985. Lang.: Eng. 3694
Buried Fire
Plays/librettos/scripts
The representation of true crime in modern drama. USA. France. 1955-1996. Lang.: Eng. 3673
Burkett, Ronnie
Basic theatrical documents
Text of *Tinka's New Dress* by puppeteer Ronnie Burkett. Canada: Winnipeg, MB. 1994. Lang.: Eng. 4917
Performance/production
Productions of children's theatre festival. Canada: Montreal, PQ. 1998. Lang.: Fre. 503
Puppeteer Ronnie Burkett. Canada: Calgary, AB, Winnipeg, MB. 1970-1998. Lang.: Eng. 4920
Burkov, Georgij Ivanovič
Performance/production
Memoirs of actor Georgij Burkov. Russia. 1933-1990. Lang.: Rus. 2241
Burlador de Sevilla y convidado de piedra, El (Trickster of Seville and the Stone Guest, The)
Plays/librettos/scripts
Playwright Tirso de Molina. Spain. 1583-1648. Lang.: Eng. 3370
Burlesque
SEE ALSO
Classed Entries under MIXED ENTERTAINMENT—Variety acts.

Burlesque — cont'd

Performance/production
Burlesque comedian Joey Faye. USA. 1925-1960. Lang.: Eng. 4140
Plays/librettos/scripts
Analysis of *Processional* by John Howard Lawson. USA. 1925. Lang.: Eng. 3535
Marxian analysis of dramatic parody and burlesque. USA. Europe. 1998. Lang.: Eng. 3664

Burman, Tom
Design/technology
TV and film make-up artists Tom Burman and Bari Dreiband-Burman. USA: Hollywood, CA. 1998. Lang.: Eng. 4050

Burnett, Frances Hodgson
Performance/production
The influence of *The Little Princess* on popular theatre and culture. USA. 1903. Lang.: Eng. 2658
Plays/librettos/scripts
Feminist analysis of plays for young people by women playwrights. USA. 1903-1983. Lang.: Eng. 3521

Burns, Nina
Performance/production
Collection of newspaper reviews by London theatre critics. UK-England: London. 1998. Lang.: Eng. 2568

Burns, Stanley
Performance/production
Obituary for ventriloquist Stanley Burns. USA: New York, NY. 1919-1998. Lang.: Eng. 4148

Buroch, Dieter
Performance spaces
Profile of the theatrical venue Mousonturm. Germany: Franfurt. 1978-1998. Lang.: Ger. 441

Burroughs, William S.
Performance/production
Music theatre production in northern Germany. Germany: Lübeck, Hamburg, Bremen, Kiel. 1998. Lang.: Ger. 4293

Burrows, James
Performance/production
Collection of newspaper reviews by London theatre critics. UK-England: London. 1998. Lang.: Eng. 2476

Burstin, Michel
Basic theatrical documents
French translation of *The Primary English Class* by Israel Horovitz. USA. France. 1996. Lang.: Fre. 1489

Burton, Gail
Performance/production
Contemporary queer politics and the production of gay and lesbian theatre. USA. 1970-1997. Lang.: Eng. 2710

Burton, Richard
Performance/production
Speaking styles of selected actors reading Shakespeare's *Henry V*. North America. UK-England. 1998. Lang.: Eng. 2208

Burton, Robert
Basic theatrical documents
Critical edition and English translation of Robert Burton's *Philosophaster*. England. 1606-1618. Lang.: Eng. 1418

Bus Stop
Plays/librettos/scripts
Gender-role reversal in plays of William Inge. USA. 1950-1958. Lang.: Eng. 3623
Analysis of *Bus Stop* by William Inge. USA. 1955. Lang.: Eng. 3624

Bush Theatre (London)
Performance/production
Collection of newspaper reviews by London theatre critics. UK-England: London. 1998. Lang.: Eng. 2445
Collection of newspaper reviews by London theatre critics. UK-England: London. 1998. Lang.: Eng. 2465
Collection of newspaper reviews by London theatre critics. UK-England: London. 1998. Lang.: Eng. 2468
Collection of newspaper reviews by London theatre critics. UK-England: London. 1998. Lang.: Eng. 2495
Collection of newspaper reviews by London theatre critics. UK-England: London. 1998. Lang.: Eng. 2502
Collection of newspaper reviews by London theatre critics. UK-England: London. 1998. Lang.: Eng. 2515
Collection of newspaper reviews by London theatre critics. UK-England: London. 1998. Lang.: Eng. 2537
Collection of newspaper reviews by London theatre critics. UK-England: London. 1998. Lang.: Eng. 2566
Collection of newspaper reviews by London theatre critics. UK-England: London. 1998. Lang.: Eng. 2583

Bushell-Mingo, Josette
Performance/production
Collection of newspaper reviews by London theatre critics. UK-England: London. 1998. Lang.: Eng. 2453
Collection of newspaper reviews by London theatre critics. UK-England: London. 1998. Lang.: Eng. 2515

Busoni, Ferruccio
Performance/production
Review of Pierre Strosser's staging of Busoni's *Doktor Faust*. France: Lyons. 1997. Lang.: Eng. 4577

Bussy D'Ambois
Plays/librettos/scripts
Historical allusion in Chapman's *Bussy d'Ambois*. England. 1604. Lang.: Eng. 2867

... but the clouds ...
Plays/librettos/scripts
Analysis of television plays by Samuel Beckett. France. 1965-1989. Lang.: Eng. 4077

Butcher, Rosemary
Performance/production
Choreographer Rosemary Butcher on her return to New York. USA: New York, NY. 1969-1998. Lang.: Eng. 979

Butō
Performance/production
Guest performance of Sankai Juku *butō* company. Hungary: Budapest. 1998. Lang.: Hun. 941
Program of *butō* festival, Szkéné Theatre. Hungary: Budapest. 1997. Lang.: Hun. 950
Interview with *butō* dancer Susanna Åkerlund. Sweden. Japan. 1990-1998. Lang.: Swe. 1300
The training of actors in Asian performance styles. Australia: Brisbane. 1992-1998. Lang.: Eng. 1817

Butterworth, Jez
Plays/librettos/scripts
Sex, drugs, and violence in contemporary British drama. UK-England. 1991-1998. Lang.: Eng. 3494

Butti, E.A.
Plays/librettos/scripts
Italian realist drama. Italy. 1860-1918. Lang.: Eng. 3260

Button, Jeanne
Design/technology
Costume designer Jeanne Button. USA. 1965-1998. Lang.: Eng. 260

Bye Bye Blackbird
Performance/production
Collection of newspaper reviews by London theatre critics. UK-England: London. 1998. Lang.: Eng. 2522

Bygmester Solness (Master Builder, The)
Plays/librettos/scripts
Trolls in the late plays of Ibsen. Norway. 1886-1894. Lang.: Eng. 3298

Byrd, Betty
Performance/production
Tap dance team of Betty Byrd and Danny Hoctor. USA. 1959-1998. Lang.: Eng. 983

Byrne, David
Performance/production
Critique of Twyla Tharp's *The Catherine Wheel*. USA: New York, NY. 1981. Lang.: Eng. 980

Byrne, Grainne
Performance/production
Collection of newspaper reviews by London theatre critics. UK-England: London. 1998. Lang.: Eng. 2534

Byron, George Gordon, Lord
Plays/librettos/scripts
Byron's heroes and the Byronic hero. UK-England. 1800-1824. Lang.: Eng. 3484

Bystrickaja, Elina A.
Performance/production
Actress Elina Bystrickaja. Russia: Moscow. 1998. Lang.: Rus. 2242

B22
Performance/production
Collection of newspaper reviews by London theatre critics. UK-England: London. 1998. Lang.: Eng. 2549

B3 Team, The
Performance/production
Collection of newspaper reviews by London theatre critics. UK-England: London. 1998. Lang.: Eng. 2463

c.t. 201 (Cologne)
Performance/production
The Cologne theatre scene. Germany: Cologne. 1985-1997. Lang.: Ger. 1964

Caballero de Olmedo, El (Knight from Olmedo, The)
Plays/librettos/scripts
Playwright Lope de Vega. Spain. 1562-1635. Lang.: Eng. 3377

Cabaret
Design/technology
Technical designs for Sam Mendes' production of *Cabaret*. USA: New York, NY. 1998. Lang.: Eng. 4343
Lighting design for Sam Mendes' production of *Cabaret*. USA: New York, NY. 1998. Lang.: Eng. 4344
Institutions
Profile of Watermill Theatre. UK-England: Newbury. 1998. Lang.: Eng. 1744
Performance spaces
The creation of a site-specific performance space for Sam Mendes' production of *Cabaret*. USA: New York, NY. 1998. Lang.: Eng. 4350
Performance/production
Friends and colleagues recall singer Lotte Lenya. Germany. 1928-1981. Lang.: Eng. 4355
Musical performances on and off Broadway. USA: New York. 1998. Lang.: Ger. 4383

Cabaret
SEE ALSO
Classed Entries under MIXED ENTERTAINMENT—Cabaret.
Performance/production
Performance culture in prerevolutionary Russia. Russia. 1910-1915. Lang.: Eng. 580
The influence of exhibition ballroom dance on theatrical entertainments. USA. 1910-1925. Lang.: Eng. 985
Comic dance performer Lotte Goslar. Germany. USA. 1907-1997. Lang.: Eng. 4124
Nativity puppet plays as a form of cabaret. Poland: Vilna. 1921-1933. Lang.: Pol. 4896
Plays/librettos/scripts
Analysis of *Processional* by John Howard Lawson. USA. 1925. Lang.: Eng. 3535

Cabaret neiges noires (Black Snow Cabaret)
Plays/librettos/scripts
Raymond Saint-Jean's film adaptation of *Cabaret neiges noires (Black Snow Cabaret)*. Canada. 1997. Lang.: Fre. 3967

Cablegs
Performance/production
Analysis of recent New York productions. USA: New York, NY. 1997-1998. Lang.: Eng. 2759

Cabot, Michael
Performance/production
Collection of newspaper reviews by London theatre critics. UK-England: London. 1998. Lang.: Eng. 2481
Collection of newspaper reviews by London theatre critics. UK-England: London. 1998. Lang.: Eng. 2486

Cabrera Infante, Guillermo
Relation to other fields
The influence of Fellini's *La Dolce Vita* on a novel of film critic Guillermo Cabrera Infante. Spain. Italy. 1960-1967. Lang.: Eng. 4035

Caccini, Giulio
Design/technology
Stage machinery in *Il Rapimento di Cefalo* staged by Bernardo Buontalenti. Italy: Florence. 1600. Lang.: Eng. 4436

Cacvas, John
Performance/production
Friends and colleagues recall singer Lotte Lenya. Germany. 1928-1981. Lang.: Eng. 4355

Cadieux, Anne-Marie
Performance/production
Actress Anne-Marie Cadieux on working in theatre and in film. Canada: Montreal, PQ. 1998. Lang.: Fre. 1838

Caesar and Cleopatra
Performance/production
The performance of Shakespeare in the former East Germany. Germany: Rostock, Leipzig, Berlin, Dessau. 1996-1997. Lang.: Ger. 1974
Plays/librettos/scripts
Colonialism in the plays of George Bernard Shaw. UK-England. 1895-1935. Lang.: Eng. 3438
George Bernard Shaw and the history-play tradition. UK-England. 1899-1939. Lang.: Eng. 3503

Café Mitte (Café Center)
Plays/librettos/scripts
Analysis of *Café Mitte (Café Center)* by Volker Ludwig. Germany: Berlin. 1997-1998. Lang.: Ger. 4393

Café Müller
Performance/production
Reactions to guest performances of dancer/choreographer Pina Bausch. Sweden: Stockholm. 1998. Lang.: Swe. 1301
Stockholm's year as Cultural Capital of Europe. Sweden: Stockholm. 1766-1998. Lang.: Eng. 2394

Caffe Cino (New York, NY)
Institutions
Producer Joseph Cino and Off-off Broadway theatre. USA: New York, NY. 1931-1967. Lang.: Eng. 404

Cage Without Bars, A
Performance/production
Collection of newspaper reviews by London theatre critics. UK-England: London. 1998. Lang.: Eng. 2444

Cage, John
Performance/production
Interview with choreographer Merce Cunningham. USA. 1944-1998. Lang.: Eng. 1326
The police and John Cage's *Europeras 1 and 2* at Frankfurter Theater. Germany: Frankfurt. 1987. Lang.: Eng. 4586
Theory/criticism
Performance art and the 'poetics of space'. USA. Poland. 1952-1984. Lang.: Eng. 4270

Cage, The
Performance/production
New York performances of the San Francisco Ballet. USA: New York, NY. 1998. Lang.: Eng. 1170

Cagnotte, La (Pots of Money)
Performance/production
Seven critics on their favorite character or portrayal. Sweden. 1950. Lang.: Swe. 2369

Caird, John
Performance/production
Collection of newspaper reviews by London theatre critics. UK-England: London. 1998. Lang.: Eng. 2555

Cairns, Anthony
Performance/production
Collection of newspaper reviews by London theatre critics. UK-England: London. 1998. Lang.: Eng. 2465

Čajka (Seagull, The)
Basic theatrical documents
Catalan translations of the complete plays of Anton Čechov. Russia. 1884-1904. Lang.: Cat. 1449
Institutions
The aesthetic perspectives of the ensemble at Münchner Kammerspiele. Germany: Munich. 1997-1998. Lang.: Ger. 1666
Performance/production
Collection of newspaper reviews by London theatre critics. UK-England: London. 1998. Lang.: Eng. 2542
Plays/librettos/scripts
Analysis of *Čajka (The Seagull)* by Anton Čechov. Russia. 1896. Lang.: Eng. 3335
Čechov's character Treplev. Russia. 1890-1910. Lang.: Rus. 3336
Čechov's influence on Woody Allen's film *Bullets Over Broadway*. USA. 1994. Lang.: Eng. 4027

Čajkovskij, Pëtr Iljič
Design/technology
Rapid on-stage costume changes in dance. Russia. Sweden. Japan. 1840-1998. Lang.: Swe. 889
Interview with lighting designer Rick Fisher. UK-England. 1998. Lang.: Eng. 1030
Technical designs for Matthew Bourne's productions of ballets by Čajkovskij and Prokofjev. UK-England: London. 1998. Lang.: Eng. 1031
Technical designs for Čajovskij's *Sneguročka*, Houston Ballet. USA: Houston, TX. 1998. Lang.: Eng. 1033
Lighting design for Čajkovskij's *Sneguročka (The Snow Maiden)* at Houston Ballet. USA: Houston, TX. 1998. Lang.: Eng. 1035
Institutions
The current state of Theater Bielefeld. Germany: Bielefeld. 1998. Lang.: Ger. 1621
The Bolšoj Ballet and the experimental company Gelikon. Russia: Moscow. 1997. Lang.: Swe. 4467

Čajkovskij, Pëtr Iljič — cont'd

Performance/production
Nureyev's *Swan Lake* at Staatsoper. Austria: Vienna. 1998. Lang.: Hun. 1064
Review of one-act ballets by Balanchine. Hungary: Budapest. 1997. Lang.: Hun. 1105
The Nutcracker at the Budapest Opera House. Hungary: Budapest. 1998. Lang.: Hun. 1115
Amedeo Amodio's new choreography for Čajkovskij's *The Nutcracker.* Italy: Rome. 1998. Lang.: Hun. 1118
Analysis of choreographies of Matthew Bourne. UK-England: London. 1996-1997. Lang.: Eng. 1157
Matthew Bourne's choreography for *Swan Lake.* UK-England. 1998. Lang.: Eng. 1159
Balanchine's choreography to Čajkovskij's *Themes and Variations.* USA. 1960-1998. Lang.: Eng. 1179
Dancer Nina Ananiašvili. USA: Houston, TX. 1986-1998. Lang.: Eng. 1193
Čajkovskij's *Eugene Onegin* directed by A. Stepanov. Russia: St. Petersburg. 1998. Lang.: Rus. 4671
Ten' Puppet Theatre's production of Čajkovskij's opera *Iolanta.* Russia: Moscow. Lang.: Rus. 4680
Guest performances of the Kirov Opera at the Metropolitan.. USA: New York, NY. 1998. Lang.: Eng. 4731

Calandria, La
Plays/librettos/scripts
Ludic aspects of Italian Renaissance theatre. Italy. 1500-1700. Lang.: Ita. 3240

Calarco, Joe
Theory/criticism
The urge to make Shakespeare contemporary. USA. 1990-1998. Lang.: Eng. 3844

Calderon
Plays/librettos/scripts
Theory and practice in the work of director Pier Paolo Pasolini. Italy. 1960-1970. Lang.: Eng. 3264

Calderón de la Barca, Pedro
Performance/production
Calderón's *La cisma de Inglaterra (The Schism of England)* directed by Péter Telihay. Hungary: Budapest. 1997. Lang.: Hun. 2137
Collection of newspaper reviews by London theatre critics. UK-England: London. 1998. Lang.: Eng. 2441
Collection of newspaper reviews by London theatre critics. UK-England: London. 1998. Lang.: Eng. 2488
José Rivera's production of *La Vida es sueño (Life Is a Dream),* Hartford Stage. USA: Hartford, CT. 1998. Lang.: Eng. 2722
Plays/librettos/scripts
Light/dark imagery in Calderón's plays. Spain. 1600-1601. Lang.: Spa. 3394
Life and career of playwright Pedro Calderón de la Barca. Spain. 1600-1681. Lang.: Eng. 3397
Analysis of sonnets in the plays of Calderón. Spain. 1660-1722. Lang.: Eng. 3398
Power relations in Calderón's *La Vida es Sueño (Life Is a Dream).* Spain. 1635. Lang.: Spa. 3401
Spanish Catholicism and the *autos sacramentales* of Calderón. Spain. 1637-1671. Lang.: Spa. 3405

Caldwell, Zoe
Performance/production
Actors and directors on the late plays of Tennessee Williams. USA. 1966-1981. Lang.: Eng. 2675

California Repertory Company (Long Beach, CA)
Performance/production
Creating the role of Biagio Buonaccorsi in Robert Cohen's *The Prince.* USA. 1997. Lang.: Eng. 2686

Caligula
Performance/production
Productions of plays by Shakespeare, Brecht, and Camus. Germany. 1998. Lang.: Ger. 2032
Collection of newspaper reviews by London theatre critics. UK-Scotland: Edinburgh. 1998. Lang.: Eng. 2650
Plays/librettos/scripts
The sources of Camus's *Caligula.* France. 1937-1958. Lang.: Ita. 3116

Call, Daniel
Performance/production
Director Angela Brodauf. Germany: Dortmund. 1984-1998. Lang.: Ger. 1989
Recent productions of Schauspiel Leipzig. Germany: Leipzig. 1997-1998. Lang.: Ger. 2011
Plays/librettos/scripts
German playwrights on the meaning of Brecht today. Germany. 1998. Lang.: Ger. 3123

Callas, Maria
Performance/production
The disappearance of the diva in the modern world. Europe. USA. 1890-1998. Lang.: Swe. 525
Maria Callas and Donizetti's *Lucia di Lammermoor.* Europe. 1953-1959. Lang.: Eng. 4553

Callies, Grégoire
Performance/production
A puppet production of Madách's *Az ember tragédiája (The Tragedy of Man).* France: Colmar. 1998. Lang.: Hun. 4893

Camacho, Francisco
Performance/production
Politics, culture, and Portuguese dance and choreography. Portugal. 1998. Lang.: Eng. 959

Cambell, Ken
Performance/production
Collection of newspaper reviews by London theatre critics. UK-England: London. 1998. Lang.: Eng. 2518

Cambyses, King of Persia
Performance/production
Music in Tudor drama. England. 1497-1569. Lang.: Eng. 1902

Camera, Woman
Plays/librettos/scripts
R.M. Vaughan's *Camera, Woman* at Buddies in Bad Times. Canada: Toronto, ON. 1998. Lang.: Eng. 2835

Cameron, James
Design/technology
Technical designs for the film *Titanic.* USA. 1997. Lang.: Eng. 3910

Cameron, Julia
Plays/librettos/scripts
Feminism and plays of Henrik Ibsen. Norway. 1879-1979. Lang.: Eng. 3293

Cameron, Linda
Administration
Profiles of Equity council members. USA: New York, NY. 1998. Lang.: Eng. 82

Caminho de volta (Return Trip)
Plays/librettos/scripts
Cruelty and the absurd in theatre of Latin American playwrights. Latin America. 1960-1980. Lang.: Eng. 3267

Camino Real
Performance/production
Collection of newspaper reviews by London theatre critics. UK-England: London. 1998. Lang.: Eng. 2435
Plays/librettos/scripts
Realism and anti-realism in plays of Tennessee Williams. USA. 1945-1986. Lang.: Eng. 3626

Cammarano, Salvatore
Performance/production
Verdi's important mezzo soprano roles, including Azucena in *Il Trovatore.* Italy. 1853. Lang.: Eng. 4661

Campbell Park Theatre (Milton Keynes)
Performance/production
Collection of newspaper reviews by London theatre critics. UK-England. 1998. Lang.: Eng. 2456

Campbell, Bartley
Plays/librettos/scripts
Analysis of *The White Slave* by Bartley Campbell. USA. 1882. Lang.: Eng. 3660

Campbell, Daisy
Performance/production
Collection of newspaper reviews by London theatre critics. UK-England: London. 1998. Lang.: Eng. 2518

Campbell, Ken
Institutions
Profile of Nordhessisches Landestheater Marburg. Germany: Marburg. 1997-1998. Lang.: Ger. 1653
Performance/production
Collection of newspaper reviews by London theatre critics. UK-England: London. 1998. Lang.: Eng. 2471

Campbell, Mrs. Patrick (Tanner, Beatrice Stella)
Plays/librettos/scripts
Popular adaptations of the works of George Bernard Shaw. UK-England. 1890-1990. Lang.: Eng. 3445

Campion, Thomas
Plays/librettos/scripts
Shakespeare's *The Tempest* and Thomas Campion's *The Lord's Masque*. England. 1613. Lang.: Eng. 4202
Campo, El (Camp, The)
Plays/librettos/scripts
Cruelty and the absurd in theatre of Latin American playwrights. Latin America. 1960-1980. Lang.: Eng. 3267
Genocide, theatre, and the human body. North America. UK-England. Argentina. 1998. Lang.: Eng. 3290
Camus, Albert
Performance/production
Productions of plays by Shakespeare, Brecht, and Camus. Germany. 1998. Lang.: Ger. 2032
Teater UNO's stage adaptation of *L'Étranger (The Stranger)* by Albert Camus. Sweden: Gothenburg. 1998. Lang.: Swe. 2395
Collection of newspaper reviews by London theatre critics. UK-Scotland: Edinburgh. 1998. Lang.: Eng. 2650
Plays/librettos/scripts
The sources of Camus's *Caligula*. France. 1937-1958. Lang.: Ita. 3116
The postwar existentialist drama of Albert Camus and Carlos Solórzano. Mexico. France. 1948-1955. Lang.: Spa. 3274
The influence of Albert Camus on playwright Athol Fugard. South Africa, Republic of. 1960-1985. Lang.: Eng. 3362
Canac-Marquis, Normand
Plays/librettos/scripts
Quebecois drama and the influence of visual arts. Canada. 1980-1990. Lang.: Fre. 2816
Canadian Mime Theatre (Niagara-on-the-Lake, ON)
Performance/production
Adrian Pecknold and the Canadian Mime Theatre. Canada: Niagara-on-the-Lake, ON. 1940-1978. Lang.: Eng. 4085
canadian monsoon, a
Basic theatrical documents
Excerpt from *a canadian monsoon* by Sheila James. Canada: Toronto, ON. 1993-1996. Lang.: Eng. 1411
Plays/librettos/scripts
Interview with playwright/director Sheila James. Canada: Toronto, ON. 1990-1998. Lang.: Eng. 2809
Canadian Opera Company (Toronto, ON)
Design/technology
Opera scenographer Michael Levine. Canada: Toronto, ON. 1988-1998. Lang.: Eng. 4426
Maurice Sendak's set design for *Hänsel und Gretel*, Canadian Opera Company. Canada: Toronto, ON. 1998. Lang.: Eng. 4427
Institutions
Marketing techniques of Canadian Opera Company. Canada: Toronto, ON. 1996-1998. Lang.: Eng. 4447
Canadian Theatre of the Deaf (Canada)
Performance/production
The failure of the Canadian Theatre of the Deaf. Canada. 1965-1998. Lang.: Eng. 507
Canal Cafe (London)
Performance/production
Collection of newspaper reviews by London theatre critics. UK-England: London. 1998. Lang.: Eng. 2411
Collection of newspaper reviews by London theatre critics. UK-England: London. 1998. Lang.: Eng. 2416
Collection of newspaper reviews by London theatre critics. UK-England: London. 1998. Lang.: Eng. 2430
Collection of newspaper reviews by London theatre critics. UK-England: London. 1998. Lang.: Eng. 2483
Collection of newspaper reviews by London theatre critics. UK-England: London. 1998. Lang.: Eng. 2514
Collection of newspaper reviews by London theatre critics. UK-England: London. 1998. Lang.: Eng. 2539
Collection of newspaper reviews by London theatre critics. UK-England: London. 1998. Lang.: Eng. 2550
Collection of newspaper reviews by London theatre critics. UK-England: London. 1998. Lang.: Eng. 2570
Canboulay
Performance/production
Women in the *canboulay* ceremony. Trinidad and Tobago. 1998. Lang.: Eng. 4166
Candelaria, La (Bogotá)
SEE
Teatro La Candelaria.
Candida
Performance/production
Collection of newspaper reviews by London theatre critics. UK-England: London. 1998. Lang.: Eng. 2449
Plays/librettos/scripts
Colonialism in the plays of George Bernard Shaw. UK-England. 1895-1935. Lang.: Eng. 3438
Rhetorical analysis of plays by George Bernard Shaw. UK-England. 1896-1908. Lang.: Eng. 3480
Candide
Plays/librettos/scripts
Response to criticism of Théâtre du Sous-Marin Jaune's adaptation of Voltaire's *Candide*. Canada: Quebec, PQ. 1997. Lang.: Fre. 4912
Canterbury Tales
Performance/production
Collection of newspaper reviews by London theatre critics. UK-England: London. 1998. Lang.: Eng. 2577
Canterville Ghost, The
Performance/production
Actors' interpretations of the title role in Oscar Wilde's *The Canterville Ghost*. UK-England. USA. 1943-1998. Lang.: Eng. 4066
Cantin, Ado
Design/technology
Set designer and builder Ado Cantin. Italy: Verona. 1967-1998. Lang.: Eng. 200
Cap with Bells, The
SEE
Berretto a sonagli, Il.
Capalbo, Carmen
Performance/production
Friends and colleagues recall singer Lotte Lenya. Germany. 1928-1981. Lang.: Eng. 4355
Čapek, Karel
Plays/librettos/scripts
George Bernard Shaw and science fiction. UK-England. Ireland. 1887-1998. Lang.: Eng. 3508
Analysis of Janáček's *Věc Makropulos*. Czechoslovakia. 1922-1998. Lang.: Eng. 4765
Capeman, The
Design/technology
Sound design for the musical *The Capeman*. USA: New York, NY. 1998. Lang.: Eng. 4339
Performance/production
Response to negative criticism of *The Capeman*. USA: New York, NY. 1998. Lang.: Eng. 4387
Capitaine Bringuier
Basic theatrical documents
Text of *Capitaine Bringuier* by Pascal Lainé. France. 1998. Lang.: Fre. 1429
Capobianco, Tito
Performance/production
Evaluation of video performances of Donizetti's operas. Europe. USA. 1980-1998. Lang.: Eng. 4557
Caporossi, Riccardo
Performance/production
The theatre of Claudio Remondi and Riccardo Caporossi. Italy. 1970-1995. Lang.: Ita. 2169
The actor/clown team of Claudio Remondi and Riccardo Caporossi. Italy. 1971-1998. Lang.: Eng. 2176
Capra, Frank
Performance/production
Analysis of Frank Capra's film *Lady for a Day*. USA. 1933. Lang.: Eng. 3952
Capricci di Callot, I
Performance/production
Music theatre production in northern Germany. Germany: Lübeck, Hamburg, Bremen, Kiel. 1998. Lang.: Ger. 4293
Capriccio
Performance/production
Analysis of Richard Strauss's opera *Capriccio*. Germany. 1942-1998. Lang.: Eng. 4578
Analysis of Richard Strauss's *Capriccio*. Germany. 1942. Lang.: Eng. 4606
Conductor Andrew Davis. UK-England. USA. 1998. Lang.: Eng. 4704
Background material on Metropolitan Opera radio broadcast performances. USA: New York, NY. 1998. Lang.: Eng. 4713
Critique of current trends in opera production. USA. 1942-1998. Lang.: Eng. 4726

Caprice, Un (Caprice, A)
Plays/librettos/scripts
Fidelity in two plays of Musset. France. 1835-1837. Lang.: Eng. 3102
Captives of the Faceless Drummer
Plays/librettos/scripts
Language and rhetoric in plays of George Ryga. Canada. 1967-1985. Lang.: Eng. 2792
Car, Evgen
Basic theatrical documents
Text of Evgen Car's monologue *Poredušov Janoš.* Slovenia. 1968-1998. Lang.: Slo. 1454
Caracal, De (Caracal, The)
Performance/production
Collection of newspaper reviews by London theatre critics. UK-England: London. 1998. Lang.: Eng. 2462
Carbone 14 (Montreal, PQ)
Plays/librettos/scripts
Analysis of plays by Gilles Maheu. Canada: Montreal, PQ. 1994-1998. Lang.: Fre. 1357
Card Index
SEE
Kartoteka.
Carden, William
Design/technology
Lighting design for Donald Margulies' *Collected Stories*, directed by William Carden. USA: New York, NY. 1998. Lang.: Eng. 1544
Cardenio
Plays/librettos/scripts
Don Quixote, Lewis Theobald's *The Double Falsehood* and the lost *Cardenio* of Shakespeare and Fletcher. England. Spain. 1610-1727. Lang.: Eng. 3001
Cardy, Geraint
Performance/production
Collection of newspaper reviews by London theatre critics. UK-England: London. 1998. Lang.: Eng. 2494
Carey, Helen
Performance/production
Actors Helen Carey and Max Wright, winners of Joe A. Callaway Award. USA. 1998. Lang.: Eng. 2716
Carmen
Design/technology
Set and costume design for San Francisco Opera productions. USA: San Francisco, CA. 1998. Lang.: Eng. 4443
Performance/production
Singers' approaches to the title role in Bizet's *Carmen.* 1875-1998. Lang.: Eng. 4502
Background material on Metropolitan Opera radio broadcast performances. USA: New York, NY. 1998. Lang.: Eng. 4716
Plays/librettos/scripts
Ambition and gender in Bizet's *Carmen.* France. 1870-1879. Lang.: Eng. 4786
Spain as an exotic locale in Bizet's *Carmen* and its source. Spain. France. 1845. Lang.: Eng. 4819
Carmina Burana
Administration
Stockholm's debut as cultural capital of Europe. Sweden: Stockholm. 1998. Lang.: Dan. 22
Performance/production
Premieres of choreographies by Danny Rosseel. Belgium: Antwerp. Netherlands: Amsterdam. 1998. Lang.: Hun. 1065
Carnival
SEE ALSO
Classed Entries under MIXED ENTERTAINMENT—Carnival.
Performance/production
Afro-Cuban identity in Cuban theatre and popular arts. Cuba. 1959-1996. Lang.: Spa. 513
The carnival parade of devils and imps. Trinidad and Tobago: Paramin. 1997. Lang.: Eng. 4219
Carnival Knowledge, or What Did You Do with the Money?
Basic theatrical documents
Text of cabaret revue *Carnival Knowledge* by Philip D. Potak. USA. 1988. Lang.: Eng. 4152
Carolus Stuardus
Relation to other fields
Analysis of illustrations of first editions of tragedies by Gryphius. Germany. 1635-1664. Lang.: Eng. 3765
Caron, Jean-François
Plays/librettos/scripts
Raymond Saint-Jean's film adaptation of *Cabaret neiges noires (Black Snow Cabaret).* Canada. 1997. Lang.: Fre. 3967
Carosello Napoletano (Neapolitan Carousel)
Performance/production
Ettore Giannini's film and stage work *Carosello Napoletano (Neapolitan Carousel).* Italy. 1950. Lang.: Ita. 546
Carp, Stefanie
Performance/production
Christoph Schlingensief's project with the homeless at Deutsches Schauspielhaus. Germany: Hamburg. 1998. Lang.: Ger. 1961
Adaptations and performances of *Alte Meister (Old Masters)* by Thomas Bernhard. Germany. 1997-1998. Lang.: Ger. 1996
Carpenter Performing Arts Center (Long Beach, CA)
Administration
Target marketing and successful ticket sales. USA: Long Beach, CA. 1996-1998. Lang.: Eng. 37
Carr, Ashley
Performance/production
Creating the role of Biagio Buonaccorsi in Robert Cohen's *The Prince.* USA. 1997. Lang.: Eng. 2686
Carr, Marina
Plays/librettos/scripts
Contemporary Irish playwrights. Ireland. 1998. Lang.: Eng. 3207
Carrefour Theatre (Charlottetown, PE)
Performance/production
Analysis of *1837: The Farmer's Revolt* directed by Bruce Barton of Carrefour Theatre. Canada: Charlottetown, PE. 1998. Lang.: Eng. 1856
Carriage
Theory/criticism
Winning essay of Critics Institute Competition on *Carriage* by Jerome Hairston. USA. 1998. Lang.: Eng. 3838
Carrió, Racquel
Performance/production
Collection of newspaper reviews by London theatre critics. UK-England: London. 1998. Lang.: Eng. 2477
Carroll, Jacqui
Performance/production
The training of actors in Asian performance styles. Australia: Brisbane. 1992-1998. Lang.: Eng. 1817
Carroll, Lewis (Dodgson, Charles Lutwidge)
Performance/production
Collection of newspaper reviews by London theatre critics. UK-England: London. 1998. Lang.: Eng. 2477
Carroll, Tim
Performance/production
Collection of newspaper reviews by London theatre critics. UK-England: London. 1998. Lang.: Eng. 2583
Carrott, Jasper
Performance/production
Collection of newspaper reviews by London theatre critics. UK-England: London. 1998. Lang.: Eng. 2518
Carrousel Theater (Berlin)
Institutions
Children's theatres GRIPS and Carrousel. Germany: Berlin. 1998. Lang.: Ger. 347
History of Carrousel Theater, formerly Theater der Freundschaft. Germany: Berlin. 1950-1998. Lang.: Ger. 1628
Carson, Robert
Design/technology
Opera scenographer Michael Levine. Canada: Toronto, ON. 1988-1998. Lang.: Eng. 4426
Performance/production
Opera director Robert Carson. Europe. 1989-1998. Lang.: Ger. 4558
Carter, Angela
Performance/production
Collection of newspaper reviews by London theatre critics. UK-England: London. 1998. Lang.: Eng. 2437
Collection of newspaper reviews by London theatre critics. UK-England: London. 1998. Lang.: Eng. 2556
Carter, Elliott
Performance/production
Profile of composer Elliott Carter. USA. 1908-1998. Lang.: Eng. 4711
Carter, Richard
Performance/production
Collection of newspaper reviews by London theatre critics. UK-England: London. 1998. Lang.: Eng. 2491
Cartwright, Jim
Performance/production
Collection of newspaper reviews by London theatre critics. UK-England: London. 1998. Lang.: Eng. 2450

Carvalho, Sergio
Performance/production
Review of Brazilian performances of plays by Brecht. Brazil: São Paulo. 1998. Lang.: Ger. 1832
Cary, Elizabeth
Plays/librettos/scripts
Women's use of wit in response to men in English popular culture. England. 1590-1630. Lang.: Eng. 2884
Marriage and patriarchy in *The Tragedy of Mariam* by Elizabeth Cary. England. 1613. Lang.: Eng. 2893
Feminist analysis of *The Tragedy of Mariam* by Elizabeth Cary. England. 1602-1612. Lang.: Eng. 3019
Casa de Bernarda Alba, La (House of Bernarda Alba, The)
Plays/librettos/scripts
The influence of Federico García Lorca on playwright Bernardo Santareno. Spain. Portugal. 1919-1965. Lang.: Eng. 3400
Casanova, Giacomo
Reference materials
Catalog of an exhibition devoted to dramatist Giacomo Casanova. Italy: Venice. 1725-1798. Lang.: Ita. 701
Cascando
Plays/librettos/scripts
Samuel Beckett's influence on composer Humphrey Searle. UK-England. 1945-1995. Lang.: Eng. 3509
Cascio, Anna Teresa
Plays/librettos/scripts
Leslie Arden's career in musical theatre. Canada. 1993-1998. Lang.: Eng. 4389
Case, Donald
Design/technology
Costume design for *Dames at Sea*, Marine Memorial Theatre. USA: San Francisco, CA. 1998. Lang.: Eng. 4332
Caserne, La (Quebec, PQ)
Design/technology
Set design for Robert Lepage's *Geometry of Miracles*. Canada: Quebec, PQ. 1998. Lang.: Eng. 1516
Casona, Alejandro
Basic theatrical documents
French translation of *Tres diamantes y una mujer (Three Diamonds and One Woman)* by Alejandro Casona. Spain. France. 1959-1998. Lang.: Fre. 1464
Casperson, Dana
Performance/production
The collaborative art installation *Tight Roaring Circle*. UK-England: London. 1993-1997. Lang.: Eng. 4133
Cassaria
Plays/librettos/scripts
Ludic aspects of Italian Renaissance theatre. Italy. 1500-1700. Lang.: Ita. 3240
Cassavetes, John
Plays/librettos/scripts
Theatricality in John Cassavetes' film *Opening Night*. USA. 1978. Lang.: Fre. 4011
Cassiers, Guy
Performance/production
The use of television in theatrical space. Netherlands. USA. 1970-1998. Lang.: Dut. 2206
Casson, Lewis
Performance/production
Experimental Shakespeare production at the Gaiety Theatre. UK-England: Manchester. 1908-1915. Lang.: Eng. 2605
Castellucci, Romeo
Institutions
Italian experimental theatre at Spielart '97. Germany: Munich. Italy. 1997. Lang.: Eng. 1619
Performance/production
Romeo Castellucci's adaptation of the *Oresteia* by Aeschylus. Italy: Cesena. 1997. Lang.: Eng. 2189
Casting
Administration
Equity's casting website. USA: New York, NY. 1998. Lang.: Eng. 103
Equity seminar on finding an agent. USA: New York, NY. 1998. Lang.: Eng. 111
Survey of dance audition practices in Swedish schools and theatres. Sweden. 1990-1998. Lang.: Swe. 882
Institutions
Profile of Acteurs Associés, an alternative to agencies. Canada. 1995-1998. Lang.: Fre. 343
Performance/production
Analysis of a student production of Caryl Churchill's *Cloud Nine*. Canada. 1997. Lang.: Eng. 1840
Casting and performance in eighteenth-century productions of *Othello*. England. 1777-1800. Lang.: Eng. 1909
Possible castings for Beckett's *En attendant Godot (Waiting for Godot)*. UK-England. 1998. Lang.: Eng. 2645
Suzanne Cloutier's role in Shakespeare's *Othello*, directed by Orson Welles. Italy. 1952. Lang.: Fre. 3935
Analysis of casting and acting in Kenneth Branagh's film adaptation of *Much Ado About Nothing*. UK. 1993. Lang.: Fre. 3939
The staging of the complete *York Cycle* by the University of Toronto. Canada: Toronto, ON. 1998. Lang.: Eng. 4214
Plays/librettos/scripts
The development and casting of Booth Tarkington's *The Country Cousin*. USA. 1921. Lang.: Eng. 3699
Castle Theatre (Budapest)
SEE
Várszinház.
Castle Theatre (Gyula)
SEE
Gyulai Várszinház.
Castle Theatre (Kisvárda)
SEE
Kisvárdai Várszinház.
Castle Theatre (Kőszeg)
SEE
Kőszegi Várszinház.
Castle, The
Plays/librettos/scripts
Political thought in plays of Howard Barker. UK-England. 1960-1992. Lang.: Eng. 3502
Castledine, Annie
Performance/production
The function of sound in productions of *India Song* by Marguerite Duras. France. UK-Wales: Mold. 1973-1993. Lang.: Eng. 1945
Collection of newspaper reviews by London theatre critics. UK-England: London. 1998. Lang.: Eng. 2511
Collection of newspaper reviews by London theatre critics. UK-England: London. 1998. Lang.: Eng. 2560
Castorf, Frank
Administration
Theatre directors on the future of subsidized theatre. Switzerland: Zurich. Germany: Hannover, Berlin. 1998. Lang.: Ger. 1390
Theater Basel under the direction of Stefan Bachmann. Switzerland: Basel. 1996-1998. Lang.: Ger. 1391
Performance/production
Recent German productions of plays by Bertolt Brecht. Germany: Hamburg, Berlin. 1997. Lang.: Swe. 1977
Political context of Frank Castorf's production of *Les Mains Sales (Dirty Hands)* by Sartre. Germany: Berlin. 1998. Lang.: Ger. 2002
Theatre, society, and directors Frank Castorf, Peter Stein, and Einar Schleef. Germany. 1998. Lang.: Ger. 2029
Interview with director Frank Castorf. Germany, East. 1980-1990. Lang.: Eng. 2041
Frank Castorf's production of Strauss's *Die Fledermaus*. Germany: Hamburg. 1997-1998. Lang.: Ger. 4612
Reviews of recent opera productions. Switzerland: Basel. Germany: Stuttgart, Berlin, Hamburg. France: Strasbourg. 1997-1998. Lang.: Ger. 4702
Plays/librettos/scripts
Recent productions directed by Frank Castorf. Austria: Vienna. 1998. Lang.: Ger. 2788
Frank Castorf's production of Sartre's *Les Mains Sales (Dirty Hands)* and the civil war in Yugoslavia. Germany: Berlin. 1998. Lang.: Ger. 3129
Relation to other fields
Frank Castorf of Volksbühne and the object and possibilities of contemporary theatre. Germany: Berlin. 1998. Lang.: Ger. 747
Castrati
Performance/production
Response to *castrato* performances. England: London. 1667-1737. Lang.: Eng. 4545
Plays/librettos/scripts
Attacks on *castrati* in English pamphlets. England: London. 1710-1740. Lang.: Eng. 4766

***Castrati* — cont'd**

The *castrato*, the contralto, and the film *Farinelli*. France. Italy. 1994. Lang.: Eng. 4787

Castri, Massimo
Performance/production
Excerpts from the notebooks of director Massimo Castri. Italy: Prato. 1996. Lang.: Ita. 2162
Massimo Castri's production of Euripides' *Electra*. Italy: Spoleto. 1993. Lang.: Ita. 2179

Castro, Consuelo de
Plays/librettos/scripts
Cruelty and the absurd in theatre of Latin American playwrights. Latin America. 1960-1980. Lang.: Eng. 3267

Castro, Guillén de
Plays/librettos/scripts
Life and career of playwright Guillén de Castro. Spain. 1569-1631. Lang.: Eng. 3384

Cat on a Hot Tin Roof
Plays/librettos/scripts
Realism and anti-realism in plays of Tennessee Williams. USA. 1945-1986. Lang.: Eng. 3626

Cat Scan
Performance/production
Interview with performance artist Carolee Schneemann. USA. 1964-1989. Lang.: Eng. 4257

Català, Víctor
SEE
Albert, Caterina.

Catalogues
Design/technology
Catalogue of an exhibition on scenography of Galileo Chini. Italy. 1908-1956. Lang.: Ita. 199
Catalogue of an exhibition devoted to choreography of Diaghilev. Russia: St. Petersburg. 1998. Lang.: Rus. 1029
Performance/production
Catalogue of an exhibition devoted to actress Anna Proclemer. Italy. 1923-1998. Lang.: Ita. 552
Reference materials
Catalog of an exhibition devoted to dramatist Giacomo Casanova. Italy: Venice. 1725-1798. Lang.: Ita. 701
Catalogue of a Riccardi Library exhibition of theatrical manuscripts. Italy. 1998-1999. Lang.: Ita. 703
Catalogue of early theatre manuscripts of the Riccardi Library. Italy: Florence. 1500-1700. Lang.: Ita. 3726
Catalogue of the work of Donizetti. Italy. Europe. 1816-1845. Lang.: Eng. 4833

Catalyst Theatre (Edmonton, AB)
Performance/production
The collaborative process at Catalyst Theatre. Canada: Edmonton, AB. 1986-1998. Lang.: Eng. 504

Catesby, Deborah
Performance/production
Collection of newspaper reviews by London theatre critics. UK-England: London. 1998. Lang.: Eng. 2419

Catharina von Georgien
Plays/librettos/scripts
Representation of the virginal body on the German stage. Germany. 1600-1800. Lang.: Ger. 3171
Relation to other fields
Analysis of illustrations of first editions of tragedies by Gryphius. Germany. 1635-1664. Lang.: Eng. 3765

Cathédrale..., La (Cathedral..., The)
Plays/librettos/scripts
On the text and staging of *La Cathédrale...* by Jean Depréz (Laurette Laroque). Canada: Montreal, PQ. 1949. Lang.: Fre. 2823

Catherine Wheel, The
Performance/production
Critique of Twyla Tharp's *The Catherine Wheel*. USA: New York, NY. 1981. Lang.: Eng. 980

Catherine, Empress of Russia
Plays/librettos/scripts
Analysis of Catherine the Great's opera *The Beginning of Oleg's Reign*. Russia. 1768-1794. Lang.: Eng. 4816

Catherine, Lucy
Performance/production
Collection of newspaper reviews by London theatre critics. UK-England: London. 1998. Lang.: Eng. 2465

Cathleen ni Houlihan
Plays/librettos/scripts
Gender and nationalism in Northern Irish drama. UK-Ireland. 1902-1997. Lang.: Eng. 3511

Cats
Administration
Equity Executive Director Alan Eisenberg's experience with a touring production of *Cats*. USA: New York, NY. 1998. Lang.: Eng. 4318

Caucasian Chalk Circle, The
SEE
Kaukasische Kreidekreis, Der.

Caufield, Carl
Performance/production
Collection of newspaper reviews by London theatre critics. UK-England: London. 1998. Lang.: Eng. 2545

Cause Célèbre
Performance/production
Collection of newspaper reviews by London theatre critics. UK-England: London. 1998. Lang.: Eng. 2584

Cavanagh, Michael
Basic theatrical documents
Text of libretto for *Beatrice Chancy*. Canada: Toronto, ON. 1998. Lang.: Eng. 4413

Cavani, Liliana
Performance/production
Productions of Puccini operas at La Scala. Italy: Milan. 1980-1998. Lang.: Swe. 4657

Cavendish, Margaret
Plays/librettos/scripts
Restoration playwright Margaret Cavendish. England. 1645-1662. Lang.: Eng. 3002

Cawdron, Nick
Performance/production
Collection of newspaper reviews by London theatre critics. UK-England: London. 1998. Lang.: Eng. 2476

Ce qui arrive et ce qu'on attend (What You Get and What You Expect)
Performance/production
Collection of newspaper reviews by London theatre critics. UK-England: London. 1998. Lang.: Eng. 2469

Céalis, Jean-Paul
Performance/production
The present state of French puppetry. France. 1970-1998. Lang.: Ger. 4892

Cecchi, Carlo
Performance/production
Italian productions of plays by Harold Pinter. Italy. 1997. Lang.: Eng. 2165

Čechov, Anton Pavlovič
Basic theatrical documents
Catalan translations of the complete plays of Anton Čechov. Russia. 1884-1904. Lang.: Cat. 1449
Design/technology
The work of scene designer Libor Fára. Czech Republic: Prague. 1950-1981. Lang.: Cze. 1518
Institutions
The aesthetic perspectives of the ensemble at Münchner Kammerspiele. Germany: Munich. 1997-1998. Lang.: Ger. 1666
Moscow Art Theatre's production of Čechov's *Tri sestry (Three Sisters)*. Russia: Moscow. 1901-1998. Lang.: Eng. 1713
Performance/production
The performances of Frances Hyland, Kate Reid, and Martha Henry in *The Cherry Orchard*. Canada: Stratford, ON. 1965. Lang.: Eng. 1865
Peter Zadek's production of Čechov's *Višnëvyj sad (The Cherry Orchard)*. Germany. Netherlands. 1998. Lang.: Dut. 1954
Political changes reflected in Berlin theatre productions. Germany: Berlin. 1998. Lang.: Ger. 1958
Čechov's one-act plays at Thália Színház. Hungary. Slovakia: Košice. 1998. Lang.: Hun. 2075
One-act comedies by Čechov directed by Péter Valló. Hungary: Dunaújváros. 1998. Lang.: Hun. 2080
Čechov's *Platonov* as adapted and directed by Erzsébet Gaál. Hungary: Budapest. 1997. Lang.: Hun. 2082
One-act plays of Čechov by the Illyés Gyula National Theatre. Hungary. Ukraine: Beregovo. 1997. Lang.: Hun. 2104
Čechov's *Diadia Vania (Uncle Vanya)* directed by János Szász. Hungary: Nyíregyháza. 1998. Lang.: Hun. 2124
Two Hungarian productions of Čechov's *Tri sestry (Three Sisters)*. Hungary: Veszprém, Szeged. 1998. Lang.: Hun. 2135
A century of Čechov productions by the Moscow Art Theatre. Russia: Moscow. 1898-1998. Lang.: Rus. 2288

Čechov, Anton Pavlovič — cont'd

Analysis of Čechov's *Platonov* and *Lešji (The Wood Demon)*. Russia. 1878-1889. Lang.: Eng. 2297
Productions of international Čechov festival. Russia: Moscow. 1998. Lang.: Swe. 2306
Collection of newspaper reviews by London theatre critics. UK-England: London, Stratford, Derby. 1998. Lang.: Eng. 2417
Collection of newspaper reviews by London theatre critics. UK-England: London. 1998. Lang.: Eng. 2453
Collection of newspaper reviews by London theatre critics. UK-England: Stratford, Birmingham. 1998. Lang.: Eng. 2536
Collection of newspaper reviews by London theatre critics. UK-England: London. 1998. Lang.: Eng. 2542
Career of director Lynne Meadow. USA: New York, NY. 1972-1985. Lang.: Eng. 2708
Actors Helen Carey and Max Wright, winners of Joe A. Callaway Award. USA. 1998. Lang.: Eng. 2716

Plays/librettos/scripts
Recognition in plays of Čechov, Shakespeare, and Beckett. England. France. Russia. 1596-1980. Lang.: Eng. 2949
Robert Musil and the 'crisis of modern drama'. Europe. 1880-1930. Lang.: Eng. 3062
Analysis of Čechov's *Drame na ochote (Drama of the Hunting Trip)*. Russia. 1901. Lang.: Rus. 3318
Analysis of Čechov's *Višnëvyj sad (The Cherry Orchard)*. Russia. 1904. Lang.: Rus. 3323
Translations of Čechov's *Three Sisters* and Gorkij's *The Lower Depths*. Russia. 1901-1902. Lang.: Rus. 3326
The dramatic styles of Maurice Maeterlinck and Anton Čechov. Russia. Belgium. 1890-1949. Lang.: Rus. 3328
Linguistic questions in Čechov's *Tri sestry (Three Sisters)*. Russia. 1901. Lang.: Rus. 3331
The character Sonya in Čechov's *Diadia Vania (Uncle Vanya)*. Russia. 1899. Lang.: Rus. 3333
Analysis of *Čajka (The Seagull)* by Anton Čechov. Russia. 1896. Lang.: Eng. 3335
Čechov's character Treplev. Russia. 1890-1910. Lang.: Rus. 3336
Comparison of the plays of Čechov and Bulgakov. Russia. 1890-1936. Lang.: Rus. 3338
Comparison of plays by Harley Granville-Barker and Anton Čechov. UK-England. Russia. 1900-1946. Lang.: Eng. 3501
The Break of Day, Timberlake Wertenbaker's adaptation of Čechov's *Three Sisters*. UK-England. Russia. 1901-1995. Lang.: Eng. 3510
Interview with screenwriter and director Richard LaGravenese. USA. 1998. Lang.: Eng. 4019
Čechov's influence on Woody Allen's film *Bullets Over Broadway*. USA. 1994. Lang.: Eng. 4027
Analysis of Louis Malle's film *Vanya on 42nd Street*. USA. 1994. Lang.: Fre. 4031

Čechova, Ol'ga Konstantinovna
Performance/production
Memoirs of actress Ol'ga Čechova. Russia. 1917-1980. Lang.: Rus. 2243

Celestina, La
Performance/production
Interviews with actors Lil Terselius and Björn Granath. Sweden: Stockholm. 1998. Lang.: Swe. 2381
Interview with director Robert Lepage. Sweden: Stockholm. Canada: Montreal, PQ. 1997. Lang.: Swe. 2397
Plays/librettos/scripts
Playwright Fernando de Rojas. Spain. 1476-1541. Lang.: Eng. 3388

Celle-là (That One)
Plays/librettos/scripts
Quebecois drama and the influence of visual arts. Canada. 1980-1990. Lang.: Fre. 2816

Cemetery Club, The
Performance/production
Collection of newspaper reviews by London theatre critics. UK-England: London. 1998. Lang.: Eng. 2491

Cenci, The
Plays/librettos/scripts
The feminine ideal in the drama of English Romantic poets. England. 1794-1840. Lang.: Eng. 2886

Cendres de cailloux (Ashes and Stone)
Performance/production
Collection of newspaper reviews by London theatre critics. UK-England: London. 1998. Lang.: Eng. 2416

Cendrillon
Plays/librettos/scripts
Treatments of the Cinderella theme, with emphasis on *La Cenerentola* by Rossini. 1817-1998. Lang.: Eng. 4757

Cenerentola, La
Performance/production
Background material on Metropolitan Opera radio broadcast performances. USA: New York, NY. 1998. Lang.: Eng. 4713
Musicological preparation for the Metropolitan Opera production of Rossini's *La Cenerentola*. USA: Chicago, IL. 1998. Lang.: Eng. 4737
Plays/librettos/scripts
Treatments of the Cinderella theme, with emphasis on *La Cenerentola* by Rossini. 1817-1998. Lang.: Eng. 4757

Censorship
Administation
American and French regulation of mass media. USA. France. 1912-1998. Lang.: Eng. 3853
Administration
The cancellation of Kansas University's cultural exchange program with Eastern Europe. USA: Lawrence, KS. Europe. 1964-1969. Lang.: Eng. 131
Censorship and Russian and East European theatre and film. USSR. Europe. 1963-1980. Lang.: Eng. 145
The First Amendment and the striptease dancer. USA. 1998. Lang.: Eng. 4271
Institutions
The first decade of Ljubljana's municipal theatre, Mestno gledališče ljubljansko. Slovenia: Ljubljana. 1951-1961. Lang.: Slo. 1718
Performance/production
Working-class theatre and censorship. France: Paris. 1800-1862. Lang.: Eng. 533
Theatre Magazine's anniversary issue. USA. 1968-1998. Lang.: Eng. 617
Interview with director Alexander Weigel. Germany, East. 1970-1990. Lang.: Eng. 2042
Gender and Shakespearean production in the GDR. Germany, East. 1982-1990. Lang.: Eng. 2044
Resistance to a Boston production of Eugene O'Neill's *Strange Interlude*. USA: Boston, MA. 1929. Lang.: Eng. 2693
Attempted censorship of productions. USA. 1900-1905. Lang.: Eng. 2698
New York City's attempt to impose censorship on theatre productions. USA: New York, NY. 1900-1927. Lang.: Eng. 2699
Plays/librettos/scripts
'Underground realism' in contemporary Chinese drama. China, People's Republic of: Shanghai. 1993-1996. Lang.: Eng. 2845
Politics, censorship, and the 'authorial' studio theatre. Czechoslovakia. 1968-1989. Lang.: Eng. 2852
Flemish immigrants in English Renaissance drama. England. 1515-1635. Lang.: Eng. 2976
Possible censorship of *The Tragedy of Philotas* by Samuel Daniel. England. 1605. Lang.: Eng. 2996
Actor and playwright Curt Goetz and Nazi attitudes toward theatre. Germany. 1933-1944. Lang.: Eng. 3139
Wilde, Gide, and the censorship of Biblical drama. UK-England. France. 1892-1898. Lang.: Eng. 3441
The censorship of the unpublished *Her Wedding Night* by Florence Bates. UK-England. 1917. Lang.: Eng. 3454
Screenwriting before the Motion Picture Production Code. USA. 1927-1934. Lang.: Eng. 4026
Analysis of performance art on *The Larry Sanders Show*. USA. 1995. Lang.: Eng. 4079
Relation to other fields
Contestatory playwriting under dictatorship. South Africa, Republic of. Spain. Chile. 1939-1994. Lang.: Eng. 765
The arrest of playwright and activist Ratna Sarumpaet. Indonesia: Jakarta. 1998. Lang.: Eng. 3773
Challenges facing Turkish theatre artists. Turkey: Istanbul. 1994-1997. Lang.: Eng. 3778
Government response to Living Theatre's *Paradise Now*. USA. Europe. 1968. Lang.: Eng. 3789
Controversy over Terrence McNally's *Corpus Christi*, Manhattan Theatre Club. USA: New York, NY. 1998. Lang.: Eng. 3792
The upcoming Supreme Court hearing on the government's right to impose decency standards on arts grants. USA: Washington, DC. 1998. Lang.: Eng. 3793

Censorship — cont'd

The gangster film and public concern about moral corruption. USA. 1931-1940. Lang.: Eng. 4038

Centaur Theatre (Montreal, PQ)
Performance/production
English and French-language productions of *Picasso at the Lapin Agile* by Steve Martin. Canada: Montreal, PQ. 1997. Lang.: Fre. 1836

Center for Theatrical Practice (Gardzienice)
SEE
Ośrodek Praktyk Teatralnych.

Centlivre, Susannah
Performance/production
Collection of newspaper reviews by London theatre critics. UK-England: London. 1998. Lang.: Eng. 2419

Central Puppet Theatre (Moscow)
SEE
Gosudarstvénnyj Centralnyj Teat'r Kukol.

Central'nyj Detskij Teat'r (Moscow)
Performance/production
Children's theatre actor Gennadij Pečnikov. Russia: Moscow. 1998. Lang.: Rus. 2310

Central'nyj Teat'r Rossijskoj Armii (Moscow)
Performance/production
Recent Russian productions of Shakespeare's *Hamlet.* Russia: Moscow. 1998. Lang.: Rus. 2268

Centre Chorégraphique National d'Orléans
Institutions
Interview with Josef Nadj, choreographer. France. 1990-1998. Lang.: Hun. 892

Centre d'Information Professionnelle aux Techniques du Spectacle (Paris)
Design/technology
Account of ACTSAFE conference on theatre safety. France: Paris. 1998. Lang.: Swe. 181

Centre Dramatique d'Orléans
Plays/librettos/scripts
Olivier Py, actor, playwright, director, and head of the Centre Dramatique d'Orléans. France: Orléans. 1966-1998. Lang.: Ger. 3073

Centre dramatique National d'Alsace (Strasbourg)
Performance/production
A puppet production of Madách's *Az ember tragédiája (The Tragedy of Man).* France: Colmar. 1998. Lang.: Hun. 4893

Centro Teatro Ateneo (Rome)
Performance/production
Roman theatre, traditional and experimental. Italy: Rome. 1994-1998. Lang.: Eng. 2187

Century Center for the Performing Arts (New York, NY)
Performance/production
Reviews of productions of plays by Ibsen. USA: New York, NY. Norway: Oslo. 1998. Lang.: Eng. 2747

Cerco de Numancia, El (Siege of Numantia, The)
Plays/librettos/scripts
Life and career of dramatist Miguel de Cervantes. Spain. 1547-1616. Lang.: Eng. 3372

Černikov, O.
Institutions
The Vienna-based foundation for the development of Moscow's Bolšoj Theatre. Austria: Vienna. 1998. Lang.: Rus. 335

Černobrivkina, T.
Performance/production
Ballet soloist T. Černobrivkina. Russia: Moscow. 1998. Lang.: Rus. 1130

Černyševskij Opera Theatre
SEE
Teat'r Opery i Baleta im. N. Černyševskogo.

Cervantes Saavedra, Miguel de
Performance/production
Interview with director Dominic Champagne. Canada: Montreal, PQ. 1998. Lang.: Fre. 1860

Pierre Benoît's music for *Don Quichotte* at Théâtre du Nouveau Monde. Canada: Montreal, PQ. 1995-1998. Lang.: Fre. 1870

Plays/librettos/scripts
Cervantes' *Don Quixote* and Wadji Mouawad's adaptation, *Don Quichotte.* Canada: Montreal, PQ. 1998. Lang.: Fre. 2803

The character Sancho in Wadji Mouawad's *Don Quichotte (Don Quixote).* Canada: Montreal, PQ. 1998. Lang.: Fre. 2807

The contrast of form and content in Théâtre du Nouveau Monde's *Don Quichotte.* Canada: Montreal, PQ. 1998. Lang.: Fre. 2815

Don Quichotte, an adaptation of Cervantes' *Don Quixote* by Wadji Mouawad. Canada: Montreal, PQ. 1998. Lang.: Fre. 2830

Don Quixote, Lewis Theobald's *The Double Falsehood* and the lost *Cardenio* of Shakespeare and Fletcher. England. Spain. 1610-1727. Lang.: Eng. 3001

Martial law and Renaissance drama and fiction. Europe. 1563-1753. Lang.: Eng. 3059

Life and career of dramatist Miguel de Cervantes. Spain. 1547-1616. Lang.: Eng. 3372

Analysis of the interludes of Cervantes. Spain. 1600-1630. Lang.: Spa. 3391

Relation to other fields
The influence of Cervantes' *Don Quixote* on contemporary Quebec artists. Canada. 1967-1998. Lang.: Fre. 3737

Césaire, Aimé
Performance/production
Collection of newspaper reviews by London theatre critics. UK-England: London. 1998. Lang.: Eng. 2509

Plays/librettos/scripts
Analysis and translation of *Et les Chiens se taisaient (And the Dogs Were Silent)* by Aimé Césaire. Martinique. 1946-1969. Lang.: Eng. 3269

Césaire, Ina
Plays/librettos/scripts
Postcolonialism, ethnicity, and feminism in French and Caribbean plays. France. Martinique. Guadeloupe. 1960-1990. Lang.: Eng. 3104

Celebration and the body in plays of Ina Césaire and Simone Schwarz-Bart. Martinique. Guadeloupe. 1975-1998. Lang.: Eng. 3270

Ch'angguk
Performance/production
The evolution of Korean *p'ansori* as modern Korean opera, *ch'angguk.* Korea. 1900-1998. Lang.: Eng. 4364

Ch'angjak
Performance/production
Traditional and Western elements in Korean opera. Korea. 1948-1998. Lang.: Eng. 4664

Chabrol, Claude
Performance/production
Dancer and choreographer Brygida Ochaim. Germany. France. 1970-1998. Lang.: Ger. 1283

Chadwick, Helen
Performance/production
Brief biographies of performance artists. 1963-1988. Lang.: Eng. 4238

Chadwick, Maureen
Performance/production
Collection of newspaper reviews by London theatre critics. UK-England: London. 1998. Lang.: Eng. 2440

Chaikin, Joseph
Design/technology
Set design for Joseph Chaikin's production of two one-acts by Arthur Miller. USA: New york, NY. 1998. Lang.: Eng. 1532

Performance/production
Theatre Magazine's anniversary issue. USA. 1968-1998. Lang.: Eng. 617

Plays/librettos/scripts
Analysis of *Savage/Love* by Joseph Chaikin and Sam Shepard. USA. 1991-1996. Lang.: Eng. 3543

Joseph Chaikin's adaptation of *Textes pour rien (Texts for Nothing)* by Samuel Beckett. USA: New York, NY. 1995. Lang.: Eng. 3563

Chailly, Riccardo
Performance/production
Conductor Riccardo Chailly on composer Alexander Zemlinsky. Europe. 1998. Lang.: Fre. 4551

Chain Lightning Theatre (New York, NY)
Design/technology
Set design for Chain Lightning Theatre's production of *Beyond the Horizon* by Eugene O'Neill. USA: New York, NY. 1998. Lang.: Eng. 1551

Institutions
Interview with Kricker James and Claire Higgins of Chain Lightning Theatre. USA: New York, NY. 1991-1998. Lang.: Eng. 1780

Chairs for Jacob
Performance/production
Performativity in postmodern 'queer' works. USA. 1985-1995. Lang.: Eng. 616

Chaises, Les (Chairs, The)
Design/technology
Technical designs for *The Chairs (Les Chaises)*, Théâtre de Complicité. UK-England: London. 1998. Lang.: Eng. 1524

Plays/librettos/scripts
Absurdism in children's theatre. North America. Europe. 1896-1970. Lang.: Eng. 3288

Chalem, Denise
Plays/librettos/scripts
Food and alienation in plays of Chantal Chawaf and Denise Chalem. France. 1970-1989. Lang.: Eng. 3072
Chalmers, Robin
Performance/production
Collection of newspaper reviews by London theatre critics. UK-England: London. 1998. Lang.: Eng. 2570
Chamber Theatre (Moscow)
SEE
Kamernyj Teat'r.
Chamber Theatre (Munich)
SEE
Münchner Kammerspiele.
Chamber Theatre (Pest)
SEE
Kamaraszinház.
Chamber Theatre (Sopot)
SEE
Teatr Wybrzeżne.
Chamber Theatre (Tel Aviv)
SEE
Kameri.
Chambers, David
Performance/production
Interview with composer Paul Schmidt. USA: New Haven, CT. 1998. Lang.: Eng. 2660
Yale Drama Department's reconstruction of Gogol's *Revizor (The Inspector General)* as staged by Mejerchol'd. USA: New Haven, CT. 1997. Lang.: Eng. 2668
Champa, Russell H.
Design/technology
Design concept for Amy Freed's *The Psychic Life of Savages*, Wilma Theatre. USA: Philadelphia, PA. 1998. Lang.: Eng. 1555
Champagne, Dominic
Performance/production
Interview with director Dominic Champagne. Canada: Montreal, PQ. 1998. Lang.: Fre. 1860
Pierre Benoît's music for *Don Quichotte* at Théâtre du Nouveau Monde. Canada: Montreal, PQ. 1995-1998. Lang.: Fre. 1870
Plays/librettos/scripts
Cervantes' *Don Quixote* and Wadji Mouawad's adaptation, *Don Quichotte*. Canada: Montreal, PQ. 1998. Lang.: Fre. 2803
The character Sancho in Wadji Mouawad's *Don Quichotte (Don Quixote)*. Canada: Montreal, PQ. 1998. Lang.: Fre. 2807
The contrast of form and content in Théâtre du Nouveau Monde's *Don Quichotte*. Canada: Montreal, PQ. 1998. Lang.: Fre. 2815
Don Quichotte, an adaptation of Cervantes' *Don Quixote* by Wadji Mouawad. Canada: Montreal, PQ. 1998. Lang.: Fre. 2830
Raymond Saint-Jean's film adaptation of *Cabaret neiges noires (Black Snow Cabaret)*. Canada. 1997. Lang.: Fre. 3967
Champagne, Gilles
Design/technology
Set designer Jean Hazel. Canada: Quebec, PQ. 1985-1998. Lang.: Fre. 1515
Performance/production
Marie-Ginette Guay's wordless performance in Franz Xaver Kroetz's *Wunschkonzert (Request Concert)*. Canada: Quebec, PQ. 1995-1997. Lang.: Fre. 1847
Champion, Gower
Performance/production
Gower Champion's work in musical theatre. USA: New York, NY. 1936-1980. Lang.: Eng. 4388
Champion, Kate
Performance/production
Collection of newspaper reviews by London theatre critics. UK-England. 1998. Lang.: Eng. 2510
Champmeslé, Marie
Performance/production
Early modern French and Italian actresses. Italy. France. 1550-1750. Lang.: Eng. 553
Chance 2000
Relation to other fields
The artist and the world in recent productions. Austria: Vienna. Germany. 1997-1998. Lang.: Ger. 3729
Chang, Tisa
Performance/production
Statements of women directors on their work. USA. 1996. Lang.: Eng. 2674
Changeling, The
Performance/production
Collection of newspaper reviews by London theatre critics. UK-England: London. 1998. Lang.: Eng. 2424
Plays/librettos/scripts
The Bodyguard, Sam Shepard's screen adaptation of *The Changeling* by Middleton and Rowley. USA. 1970-1995. Lang.: Eng. 4007
Changing of the Guard, The
Performance/production
Collection of newspaper reviews by London theatre critics. UK-England: London. 1998. Lang.: Eng. 2506
Channer, Lisa
Performance/production
Theatre Magazine's anniversary issue. USA. 1968-1998. Lang.: Eng. 617
Chant, Le (Chant, The)
Plays/librettos/scripts
The Holocaust in environmental theatre of Armand Gatti. France. 1989-1993. Lang.: Eng. 3097
Chaos debout
Institutions
Impressions from the Avignon theatre festival. France: Avignon. 1998. Lang.: Ger. 1612
Chaos K.O. Chaos
Plays/librettos/scripts
Mixed media in theatre productions of Carole Nadeau. Canada: Quebec, PQ, Montreal, PQ. 1998. Lang.: Fre. 4047
Chapeau bleu, Le
Performance/production
A production of László Lajtha's comic opera *Le chapeau bleu*. Romania: Cluj-Napoca. Hungary. 1998. Lang.: Hun. 4666
Production of László Lajtha's comic opera *Le chapeau bleu*. Romania: Cluj-Napoca. Hungary. 1948-1998. Lang.: Hun. 4668
Chapman, George
Plays/librettos/scripts
Historical allusion in Chapman's *Bussy d'Ambois*. England. 1604. Lang.: Eng. 2867
Plague imagery in Jacobean tragedy. England. 1618-1642. Lang.: Eng. 2889
Influences on *'Tis Pity She's a Whore* by John Ford. England. 1587-1631. Lang.: Eng. 2937
The malcontent scholar in Elizabethan and Jacobean theatre. England. 1590-1642. Lang.: Eng. 3003
Chapman, Harry
Performance/production
Collection of newspaper reviews by London theatre critics. UK-England: London. 1998. Lang.: Eng. 2586
Chapman, Jim
Design/technology
Jim Chapman's lighting design for rock music tour. USA. 1998. Lang.: Eng. 4104
Chapman, Ribas
Performance/production
Collection of newspaper reviews by London theatre critics. UK-England: London. 1998. Lang.: Eng. 2586
Charabanc Theatre Company (Belfast)
Plays/librettos/scripts
Recent history in Irish theatre and drama. Ireland: Dublin. UK-Ireland: Belfast. 1993-1996. Lang.: Eng. 3212
Characters/roles
Performance/production
The 'grande coquette' on the Parisian stage. France: Paris. 1885-1925. Lang.: Eng. 531
Harlequin as a character in ballet. France. 1550-1965. Lang.: Eng. 1069
Women's roles in Shakespeare. 1600-1998. Lang.: Ger. 1813
Casting and performance in eighteenth-century productions of *Othello*. England. 1777-1800. Lang.: Eng. 1909
The evolution of the character Feste in productions of Shakespeare's *Twelfth Night*. UK-England. 1773-1988. Lang.: Eng. 2611
Irish and Irish-American characters on the stages of the Midwest. USA. 1875-1915. Lang.: Eng. 2696
Characters and masks of the Genoese theatre tradition. Italy: Genoa. 1700-1998. Lang.: Ita. 4126
The figure of the Midnight Robber in Trinidadian carnival. Trinidad and Tobago. 1900-1998. Lang.: Eng. 4168
Characterization of male and female roles in Chinese opera. China. 1500-1980. Lang.: Eng. 4312

Characters/roles — cont'd

Interview with opera singer Judit Sándor on her male roles. Hungary. 1948-1998. Lang.: Hun. 4637

Plays/librettos/scripts

Stage devils in English Reformation plays. England. 1530-1583. Lang.: Eng. 2899

Characters named Rosalind in Shakespeare's *As You Like It* and elsewhere. England. 1579-1600. Lang.: Eng. 2951

'Demonic' women in Shakespeare's tragedies. England. 1590-1613. Lang.: Eng. 2999

The malcontent scholar in Elizabethan and Jacobean theatre. England. 1590-1642. Lang.: Eng. 3003

The 'troubler' personality in Shakespeare's *Henry IV, Part One*. England. 1596-1597. Lang.: Eng. 3032

The interaction of other characters with Shakespeare's tragic heroes. England. 1590-1613. Lang.: Eng. 3037

The rebel in modern drama. Europe. 1950-1988. Lang.: Eng. 3053

The clown as a character in modern drama. Europe. 1915-1995. Lang.: Eng. 3056

The character Medea in European drama. Europe. 450 B.C.-1998 A.D. Lang.: Ger. 3063

Analysis of the 'Russian Robin Hood' Stepan Razin. Russia. 1620-1900. Lang.: Eng. 3327

Jewish characters in Spanish drama. Spain. 1400-1950. Lang.: Spa. 3402

The unseen character in plays of O'Neill, Albee, and Tennessee Williams. USA. 1915-1995. Lang.: Eng. 3538

The return of the prodigal in American drama. USA. 1920-1985. Lang.: Eng. 3666

The fool character in works of Handke, Fellini, and Singer. USA. Germany. Italy. 1960-1968. Lang.: Eng. 3667

Representations of Joan of Arc in film and theatre. Europe. USA. 1900-1996. Lang.: Eng. 3970

Operatic realizations of Beaumarchais' character Rosina. Europe. North America. 1784-1991. Lang.: Eng. 4773

The use of the tenor in operas of Donizetti. Italy. 1816-1845. Lang.: Eng. 4802

Relation to other fields

Literary influences of the characters Faust, Don Juan, Don Quixote, and Robinson Crusoe. Europe. 1587-1998. Lang.: Ita. 730

Factors influencing actors' ability to exit a role. USA. 1998. Lang.: Eng. 784

Shakespeare's Hamlet in novels of Goethe and Scott. England. Germany. 1776-1824. Lang.: Eng. 3757

Depictions of Shakespeare's Othello. Europe. 1709-1804. Lang.: Eng. 3758

Charisse, Cyd

Performance/production

Choreography in the musical film *The Bandwagon*. USA. 1953. Lang.: Eng. 982

Charke, Charlotte Cibber

Performance/production

The Cibber family: private life as public spectacle. England. 1713-1760. Lang.: Eng. 517

Actress/writer Charlotte Cibber Charke. England. 1713-1760. Lang.: Eng. 1891

Images associated with actress Charlotte Cibber Charke. England. 1713-1760. Lang.: Eng. 1896

The resurgence of interest in actress Charlotte Cibber Charke. England. 1713-1760. Lang.: Eng. 1901

Feminist analysis of the life of actress Charlotte Cibber Charke. England. 1713-1760. Lang.: Eng. 1904

Actress Charlotte Cibber Charke and cross-dressing. England. 1713-1760. Lang.: Eng. 1906

Press responses to the autobiography of actress Charlotte Cibber Charke. England. 1713-1760. Lang.: Eng. 1908

Plays/librettos/scripts

Cross-dressing in Shakespeare's *The Merchant of Venice* and in the autobiography of actress Charlotte Cibber Charke. England. 1713-1760. Lang.: Eng. 2891

Relation to other fields

Student responses to the autobiography of actress Charlotte Cibber Charke. USA. 1998. Lang.: Eng. 800

Charleston Theatre (Charleston, SC)

Administration

Theatre manager Charles H. Gilfert. USA: Charleston, SC. 1817-1822. Lang.: Eng. 135

Charlotte's Web

Performance/production

Collection of newspaper reviews by London theatre critics. UK-England: London. 1998. Lang.: Eng. 2550

Charlton, James Martin

Performance/production

Collection of newspaper reviews by London theatre critics. UK-England: London. 1998. Lang.: Eng. 2421

Collection of newspaper reviews by London theatre critics. UK-England: London. 1998. Lang.: Eng. 2517

Charnin, Martin

Performance/production

Collection of newspaper reviews by London theatre critics. UK-England: London. 1998. Lang.: Eng. 2514

Charnock, Nigel

Performance/production

Collection of newspaper reviews by London theatre critics. UK-England: London. 1998. Lang.: Eng. 2428

Chartrand, Simone

Plays/librettos/scripts

Philippe Soldevila on his *Le miel est plus doux que sang (Honey Is Milder than Blood)*. Canada: Quebec, PQ. 1995. Lang.: Fre. 2796

Chase, Lucia

Institutions

Profile of the American Ballet Theatre. USA: New York, NY. 1998. Lang.: Hun. 1061

Chase, Mary

Plays/librettos/scripts

Playwright Mary Chase, author of *Harvey*. USA. 1944. Lang.: Eng. 3711

Chase, Stanley

Performance/production

Friends and colleagues recall singer Lotte Lenya. Germany. 1928-1981. Lang.: Eng. 4355

Chaste Maid in Cheapside, A

Performance/production

The inaugural season of Shakespeare's Globe Theatre. UK-England: London. 1997. Lang.: Eng. 2601

Review of the opening season of Shakespeare's Globe Theatre. UK-England: London. 1997. Lang.: Eng. 2602

Chastity Belts

Plays/librettos/scripts

Mennonite drama of Veralyn Warkentin and Vern Thiessen. Canada. 1890-1997. Lang.: Eng. 2829

Chasza family

Performance/production

Vilna's Yiddish theatre companies. Poland: Vilna, Cracow. 1918-1939. Lang.: Pol. 2212

Chaucer in the Sky with Diamonds

Performance/production

Collection of newspaper reviews by London theatre critics. UK-England: London. 1998. Lang.: Eng. 2577

Chaucer, Geoffrey

Performance/production

Collection of newspaper reviews by London theatre critics. UK-England: London. 1998. Lang.: Eng. 2577

Chaurette, Normand

Plays/librettos/scripts

Normand Chaurette's translations of *As You Like It* by Shakespeare. Canada: Montreal, PQ. 1989-1994. Lang.: Fre. 2824

Chawaf, Chantal

Plays/librettos/scripts

Food and alienation in plays of Chantal Chawaf and Denise Chalem. France. 1970-1989. Lang.: Eng. 3072

Chazanov, G.

Performance/production

G. Chazanov of Teat'r Estrady. Russia: Moscow. Lang.: Rus. 4277

Che zhan (Bus Stop, The)

Basic theatrical documents

Anthology of contemporary Chinese drama. China, People's Republic of. 1979-1986. Lang.: Eng. 1414

Plays/librettos/scripts

Beckett's influence on *Che zhan (The Bus Stop)* by Gao Xingjian. China, People's Republic of. 1983. Lang.: Eng. 2844

Cheats, The

Plays/librettos/scripts

Analysis of Restoration anti-Puritan comedies. England. 1661-1663. Lang.: Eng. 2907

Chechik, Jeremiah

Design/technology

Production design for the film *The Avengers*. USA: Hollywood, CA. 1998. Lang.: Eng. 3907

Check-up
Performance/production
Survey of Parisian productions. France: Paris. 1997-1998. Lang.: Eng. 1937

Chedid, Andrée
Plays/librettos/scripts
Analysis of *Les Nombres (The Numbers)* by Andrée Chedid. France. 1965. Lang.: Eng. 3090

Cheek by Jowl (London)
Performance/production
Interview with actress Fiona Shaw. UK-England. 1995-1997. Lang.: Eng. 2607

Chegança
Performance/production
Northern Brazilian folk theatre forms. Brazil. 1972-1997. Lang.: Eng. 497

Chekhov, Anton
SEE
Čechov, Anton Pavlovič.

Chekhov, Michael
SEE
Čechov, Michajl A.

Chelsea Theatre Center (New York, NY)
Institutions
History of the Chelsea Theatre Center. USA: New York, NY. 1965-1988. Lang.: Eng. 417

Chelsea Theatre Centre (London)
Performance/production
Collection of newspaper reviews by London theatre critics. UK-England: London. 1998. Lang.: Eng. 2581

Chemistry of Change, The
Basic theatrical documents
Text of *The Chemistry of Change* by Marlane Meyer. USA. 1998. Lang.: Eng. 1497

Chen, Yan
Performance/production
Dancer Yan Chen of American Ballet Theatre. USA: New York, NY. 1981-1998. Lang.: Eng. 1176

Chen, Zidu
Basic theatrical documents
Anthology of contemporary Chinese drama. China, People's Republic of. 1979-1986. Lang.: Eng. 1414

Cheraskov, Michajl Matvejevič
Plays/librettos/scripts
Playwright Michajl Cheraskov and late eighteenth-century drama. Russia. 1751-1799. Lang.: Rus. 3332

Cherbonnier, Philippe
Performance/production
Collection of newspaper reviews by London theatre critics. UK-England: London. 1998. Lang.: Eng. 2538

Chéreau, Patrice
Performance/production
Conductor Pierre Boulez on Patrice Chéreau's production of *Lulu* by Alban Berg. France: Paris. 1979. Lang.: Fre. 4567

Chérif, Ziani
Performance/production
Survey of contemporary Algerian theatre. Algeria. 1962-1998. Lang.: Swe. 1814

Cherns, Penny
Performance/production
Collection of newspaper reviews by London theatre critics. UK-England: London. Lang.: Eng. 2408

Collection of newspaper reviews by London theatre critics. UK-England: London. 1998. Lang.: Eng. 2553

Cherry Orchard, The
SEE
Višnëvyj sad.

Chester Cycle
Plays/librettos/scripts
The Easter play tradition. England. 1180-1557. Lang.: Eng. 2942

The Expositor character of the Chester Cycle. England. 1400-1500. Lang.: Eng. 3033

Relation to other fields
Economic forces and the Chester Whitsun plays. England: Chester. 1521-1678. Lang.: Eng. 4226

Chettle, Henry
Plays/librettos/scripts
Women's use of wit in response to men in English popular culture. England. 1590-1630. Lang.: Eng. 2884

Henry Chettle's supposed apology to Shakespeare. England: London. 1592-1607. Lang.: Eng. 2915

Chevalier, Maurice
Performance/production
Life and film career of singer Maurice Chevalier. France: Paris. USA. 1888-1972. Lang.: Eng. 3933

Chiabrera, Gabriello
Design/technology
Stage machinery in *Il Rapimento di Cefalo* staged by Bernardo Buontalenti. Italy: Florence. 1600. Lang.: Eng. 4436

Chicago
Design/technology
Sound design for the London production of *Chicago*. UK-England: London. 1998. Lang.: Eng. 4326

Chicago Shakespeare Theatre
SEE ALSO
Shakespeare Repertory Theatre.

Chicago Shakespeare Theatre (Chicago, IL)
Institutions
The new home of Chicago Shakespeare Theatre, formerly Shakespeare Repertory Theatre. USA: Chicago, IL. 1998. Lang.: Eng. 1775

Chicano theatre
SEE ALSO
Hispanic theatre.

Ethnic theatre.

Plays/librettos/scripts
Analysis of *Bandido!* by Luis Valdez. USA. 1982. Lang.: Eng. 3708

Chichester Festival Theatre
Institutions
Interview with Andrew Welch, new director of Chichester Festival. UK-England: Chichester. 1998. Lang.: Eng. 1745

Performance/production
Collection of newspaper reviews by London theatre critics. UK-England. 1998. Lang.: Eng. 2485

Collection of newspaper reviews by London theatre critics. UK-England. 1998. Lang.: Eng. 2504

Collection of newspaper reviews by London theatre critics. UK-England. 1998. Lang.: Eng. 2510

Chikamatsu, Monzaemon
Performance/production
The role of the *onnagata* heroine in late eighteenth-century *kabuki*. Japan. 1770-1800. Lang.: Eng. 1364

Chikera, Ruwanthie de
Performance/production
Collection of newspaper reviews by London theatre critics. UK-England: London. 1998. Lang.: Eng. 2549

Children of Night
Plays/librettos/scripts
Analysis of historical drama of the holocaust. USA. Canada. Germany. 1950-1980. Lang.: Eng. 3610

Children's dance
Performance/production
Report on children's dance festival. Sweden: Malmö. Denmark: Copenhagen. 1997. Lang.: Swe. 966

Training
Interview with dance teacher Maria Llerena. Sweden: Stockholm. 1966-1998. Lang.: Swe. 1018

Interview with children's dance teacher Yvonne Jahn-Olsson. Sweden: Stockholm. 1945-1998. Lang.: Swe. 1019

Britt-Marie Berggren's dancing school for children. Sweden: Stockholm. 1946. Lang.: Swe. 1020

Children's theatre
Administration
Ways to attract new young audiences to theatre. Sweden: Stockholm. 1995-1998. Lang.: Swe. 21

Equity seminar for young performers and their families. USA: New York, NY. 1998. Lang.: Eng. 114

Audience
The importance of independent theatre for children. Germany: Hannover. 1998. Lang.: Ger. 151

The relationship between theatres and the youth audience. Germany. 1998. Lang.: Ger. 152

Children's theatre and cultural exchange. Germany: Flensburg. 1998. Lang.: Ger. 1401

Opera and the young audience. Germany. 1998. Lang.: Ger. 4410

Basic theatrical documents
Text of *Le Roi Hâtif (King Hasty)* by Françoise Gerbaulet. France. 1993-1998. Lang.: Fre. 1425

Children's theatre — cont'd

Texts of Slovene youth theatre plays. Slovenia. 1800-1988. Lang.: Slo. 1462

Text of puppet play for children, *Pospravljica (Tidying Up)* by Irena Androjna. Slovenia. 1997. Lang.: Slo. 4865

Design/technology

Costume design for a new version of *Peter Pan* at Children's Theatre Company. USA: Minneapolis, MN. 1998. Lang.: Eng. 4330

Institutions

Account of children's theatre festival. Canada: Montreal, PQ. 1998. Lang.: Fre. 337

Children's theatres GRIPS and Carrousel. Germany: Berlin. 1998. Lang.: Ger. 347

Festivals of theatre by and for youth. Germany: Dresden, Stuttgart. 1998. Lang.: Ger. 349

Independent children's theatre workshop. Germany: Hannover. 1998. Lang.: Ger. 352

The quality of theatre for children and youth. Italy: Bologna. Sweden: Stockholm. Germany. 1998. Lang.: Ger. 367

Annual festival of theatre performed by children. Russia: Kaluga. 1998. Lang.: Rus. 382

Profile of TAXI Children's Theatre. USA: Louisville, KY. 1992-1998. Lang.: Eng. 390

Profile of Birmingham Children's Theatre. USA: Birmingham, AL. 1947-1998. Lang.: Eng. 412

History of Carrousel Theater, formerly Theater der Freundschaft. Germany: Berlin. 1950-1998. Lang.: Ger. 1628

Appealing to the youth audience at Theater Dresden. Germany: Dresden. 1997-1998. Lang.: Ger. 1631

Profile of Junges Theater. Germany: Göttingen. 1996-1998. Lang.: Ger. 1636

Profile of the children's theatre Schauburg, George Podt, artistic director. Germany: Munich. 1993-1998. Lang.: Ger. 1640

Children's theatre festivals in Baden-Württemberg. Germany: Stuttgart. 1998. Lang.: Ger. 1641

German-Danish children's theatre festival. Germany. Denmark. 1998. Lang.: Ger. 1642

The new children's theatre at Schauburg. Germany: Munich. 1998. Lang.: Ger. 1657

Profile of the Kiselev Youth Theatre. Russia: Saratov. 1998. Lang.: Rus. 1711

Interview with Ronnie Hallgren of Älvsborgsteatern about theatre for youth. Sweden: Borås. 1994-1998. Lang.: Swe. 1726

Profile of Teater 23. Sweden: Malmö. 1959-1998. Lang.: Swe. 1727

Profile of children's and youth theatre Älvsborgsteatern. Sweden: Borås. 1995-1998. Lang.: Swe. 1731

Elsa Olenius and Vår Teater. Sweden: Stockholm. 1942-1980. Lang.: Swe. 1732

Swiss theatre clubs for children and youth. Switzerland. 1998. Lang.: Ger, Fre. 1735

Children's theatre festival Spilplätz. Switzerland: Basel. 1998. Lang.: Ger. 1736

Cooperation between Childsplay and the Arizona Theatre Company. USA: Tempe, AZ, Tucson, AZ, Phoenix, AZ. 1995-1998. Lang.: Eng. 1756

History of Palo Alto Children's Theatre. USA: Palo Alto, CA. 1932-1997. Lang.: Eng. 1778

Children's opera company Yakult Halle. Germany: Cologne. 1996-1998. Lang.: Ger. 4455

Günter Krämer and children's opera. Germany: Cologne. 1996-1998. Lang.: Ger. 4458

Program of the Kisel Festival, including theatrical and puppet productions. Slovenia: Kranj. 1998. Lang.: Slo. 4875

Performance/production

The current state of Australian theatre for youth. Australia. 1990-1998. Lang.: Eng. 489

Ethnicity, community youth theatre, and the dramaturg. Bosnia. 1996-1998. Lang.: Eng. 495

Productions of children's theatre festival. Canada: Montreal, PQ. 1998. Lang.: Fre. 503

Review of recent works on children's and youth theatre. Germany. 1579-1998. Lang.: Ger. 537

Interview with Bengt Andersson, artistic director of Teater Tre. Sweden. 1983-1998. Lang.: Swe. 601

Preparing a production of Brian Way's participatory *The Mirrorman.* USA. 1987. Lang.: Eng. 633

Announcement of Equity's young performers seminar series. USA: New York, NY. 1998. Lang.: Eng. 656

Dance improvisation with children. France. 1998. Lang.: Fre. 1275

Playwright Theresia Walser on children's reactions to Christmas plays. Germany. Switzerland. 1997. Lang.: Ger. 2027

Israeli children's theatre. Israel. 1993-1998. Lang.: Ger. 2155

The development of Dutch theatre for children. Netherlands. 1800-1995. Lang.: Dut. 2203

Children's theatre director E. Padve. Russia: St. Petersburg. 1998. Lang.: Rus. 2262

Director Kama Ginkas of Teat'r Junogo Zritelja. Russia. 1998. Lang.: Rus. 2265

Children's theatre actor Gennadij Pečnikov. Russia: Moscow. 1998. Lang.: Rus. 2310

Conference on theatre for children ages 2-4. Sweden: Stockholm. 1998. Lang.: Swe. 2368

Theatrical adaptations of children's stories by Astrid Lindgren. Sweden: Stockholm. 1998. Lang.: Eng. 2374

Overview of children's theatre performances. Sweden. 1998. Lang.: Swe. 2376

Interview with children's theatre director Marie Feldtmann. Sweden: Stockholm. 1996-1998. Lang.: Swe. 2388

Stockholm's children's theatre scene. Sweden: Stockholm. 1998. Lang.: Ger. 2389

Puppeteer Wayne Martin. USA: Boston, MA. 1998. Lang.: Eng. 4070

Children's puppet work. Austria. Slovenia. 1993-1997. Lang.: Slo. 4885

Collection of reviews of puppet performances. Poland. 1945-1996. Lang.: Pol. 4895

Plays/librettos/scripts

Young People's Theatre's adaptation of *Anne of Green Gables.* Canada: Toronto, ON. 1911-1998. Lang.: Eng. 2832

Playwright Hans Zimmer. Germany: Hannover. 1993-1998. Lang.: Ger. 3136

Children's theatre at GRIPS. Germany: Berlin. 1966-1998. Lang.: Ger. 3152

Absurdism in children's theatre. North America. Europe. 1896-1970. Lang.: Eng. 3288

History and analysis of Slovene youth drama. Slovenia. 1800-1997. Lang.: Slo. 3359

The theory and practice of playwriting for different age groups. USA. 1988. Lang.: Eng. 3524

Writing for the youth audience. USA. 1998. Lang.: Eng. 3630

Stage adaptations of Mark Twain's *Adventures of Tom Sawyer.* USA. 1884-1983. Lang.: Eng. 3702

Analysis of *Café Mitte (Café Center)* by Volker Ludwig. Germany: Berlin. 1997-1998. Lang.: Ger. 4393

Reference materials

Yearbook of Italian children's theatre. Italy. 1998-1999. Lang.: Ita. 700

Relation to other fields

Developmental differences in adolescents' ability to enact character. USA. 1988. Lang.: Eng. 782

Theatre and the psychological development of children. Sweden. 1988. Lang.: Swe. 3777

Theory/criticism

Children's theatre and contemporary aesthetics. Canada: Montreal, PQ. 1998. Lang.: Fre. 833

Feminism and children's theatre. North America. 1997-1998. Lang.: Eng. 852

JDTC's ongoing discussion of feminism and children's theatre. North America. 1997-1998. Lang.: Eng. 853

Children's Theatre Company (Minneapolis, MN)

Design/technology

Costume design for a new version of *Peter Pan* at Children's Theatre Company. USA: Minneapolis, MN. 1998. Lang.: Eng. 4330

Childress, Alice

Plays/librettos/scripts

Black self-determination in the plays of Alice Childress. USA. 1949-1969. Lang.: Eng. 3579

Miscegenation in American drama. USA. 1909-1969. Lang.: Eng. 3599

Childs, Lucinda

Performance/production

The performances of Lucinda Childs and Michel Piccoli in *La Maladie de la Mort (The Sickness of Death),* directed by Robert Wilson. France: Paris. 1997. Lang.: Eng. 1942

Childs, Lucinda — cont'd

Interview with actress Lucinda Childs. France: Paris. 1976-1997. Lang.: Eng. 1943

The collaboration of choreographer Lucinda Childs and director Robert Wilson on *La Maladie de la Mort*. Germany. 1992-1997. Lang.: Eng. 2019

Childsplay (Tempe, AZ)

Institutions

Cooperation between Childsplay and the Arizona Theatre Company. USA: Tempe, AZ, Tucson, AZ, Phoenix, AZ. 1995-1998. Lang.: Eng. 1756

Chilton, Charles

Performance/production

Collection of newspaper reviews by London theatre critics. UK-England. 1998. Lang.: Eng. 2456

Collection of newspaper reviews by London theatre critics. UK-England: London. 1998. Lang.: Eng. 2461

Collection of newspaper reviews by London theatre critics. UK-England: London. 1998. Lang.: Eng. 2482

Chiment, Marie Anne

Design/technology

Professional theatrical designers on design training. USA. 1998. Lang.: Eng. 252

Set and costume design for *Patience and Sarah* at Lincoln Center. USA: New York, NY. 1998. Lang.: Eng. 4440

Chimes at Midnight

Performance/production

Collection of newspaper reviews by London theatre critics. UK-England. 1998. Lang.: Eng. 2485

Chin, Tsai

Performance/production

Careeer of actress Tsai Chin. USA. 1959-1998. Lang.: Eng. 2754

Chinese opera

SEE ALSO

Classed Entries under MUSIC-DRAMA—Chinese opera.

Chini, Galileo

Design/technology

Catalogue of an exhibition on scenography of Galileo Chini. Italy. 1908-1956. Lang.: Ita. 199

Chisenhale Dance Space (London)

Administration

How Chisenhale Dance Space coped with loss of funding. UK-England: London. 1998. Lang.: Eng. 885

Chitty, Alison

Design/technology

Technical designs for *Tristan und Isolde* at Seattle Opera. USA: Seattle, WA. 1998. Lang.: Eng. 4444

Chlebnikova, M.

Performance/production

Musical theatre actress M. Chlebnikova. 1998. Lang.: Rus. 4351

Choephoroi (Libation Bearers, The)

Plays/librettos/scripts

Electra and Orestes in plays of Aeschylus, Euripides, and Sophocles. Greece. 438-411 B.C. Lang.: Eng. 3184

Choirboys

Performance/production

Collection of newspaper reviews by London theatre critics. UK-England: London. 1998. Lang.: Eng. 2457

Collection of newspaper reviews by London theatre critics. UK-England: London. 1998. Lang.: Eng. 2492

Chong, Ping

Theory/criticism

Theory and Asian-American theatre. USA: Minneapolis, MN. 1994-1995. Lang.: Eng. 869

Chong, Thomas

Performance/production

The decline of radio comedy and the use of record albums by some comedians. USA. 1950-1998. Lang.: Eng. 3863

Choreography

Basic theatrical documents

Score of Yu-Chun Kuo's concerto for dance and music, *Ring*. USA. 1988. Lang.: Eng. 887

Text of the musical play *Emanacije (Emanations)* by Tomaž Brenk and Mojca Kasjak. Slovenia. 1997. Lang.: Eng, Slo. 4288

Design/technology

New stage technology and the dance performance. 1998. Lang.: Eng. 888

Catalogue of an exhibition devoted to choreography of Diaghilev. Russia: St. Petersburg. 1998. Lang.: Rus. 1029

Technical designs for Matthew Bourne's productions of ballets by Čajkovskij and Prokofjėv. UK-England: London. 1998. Lang.: Eng. 1031

Set and costume designer Frank Leimbach and his work with choreographers. Germany. 1991-1998. Lang.: Ger. 1247

Institutions

The work of young choreographers at the Councours de Bagnolet. France: Bagnolet. 1998. Lang.: Swe. 891

Profile of Pina Bausch and her Tanztheater. Germany: Wuppertal. 1977-1998. Lang.: Eng. 893

Interview with members of dance group Creative Independent Artists. UK-Scotland: Glasgow. 1996-1998. Lang.: Eng. 904

The Walker Arts Center's exhibition on dance. USA: Minneapolis, MN. 1998. Lang.: Eng. 905

Amanda Miller and her ballet company Pretty Ugly. Germany: Freiburg. 1984-1998. Lang.: Ger. 1039

Peter Martins, artistic director of New York City Ballet. USA: New York, NY. 1983-1998. Lang.: Eng. 1057

Profile of dance company Nye Carte Blanche. Norway: Bergen. 1990-1998. Lang.: Swe. 1251

Profile of American Repertory Dance Company. USA: Los Angeles, CA. 1994-1998. Lang.: Eng. 1256

Performance/production

Hanne Tierney's adaptation of *Bodas de sangre (Blood Wedding)* by García Lorca. USA. 1997. Lang.: Eng. 647

The dancer-choreographer relationship. Finland. 1998. Lang.: Fin. 916

The contribution of unaffiliated dancers and choreographers. Finland. 1998. Lang.: Fin. 917

Interview with dance notator Päivi Eskelinen. Finland. 1998. Lang.: Fin. 920

Dance on Finnish television. Finland. 1998. Lang.: Fin. 921

Choreographer Koffi Koko. France: Paris. Benin. 1990-1998. Lang.: Eng. 923

Choreographer Josef Nadj and his company Théâtre du Signe. France. 1987-1998. Lang.: Hun. 924

The publication of a work by eighteenth-century dancing master C.J. von Feldtenstein. Germany: Braunschweig. 1767-1775. Lang.: Hun. 927

Performer, director, and artist Wolfgang Martin Schede. Germany. 1898-1975. Lang.: Ger. 929

Dance adaptations of Shakespeare's *Hamlet*. Germany: Bremen, Weimar. 1996-1997. Lang.: Ger. 930

The wide diversity of Jewish choreographers. Germany: Munich. 1998. Lang.: Ger. 931

Dancer/choreographer Pina Bausch. Germany: Wuppertal. 1973-1997. Lang.: Eng. 932

Recent dance performances in Berlin. Germany: Berlin. 1998. Lang.: Ger. 933

Interview with choreographer Renate Schottelius. Germany. 1936-1998. Lang.: Ger. 934

Yvette Bozsik's new choreography for Debussy's *L'après-midi d'un faune*. Hungary: Budapest. 1997. Lang.: Hun. 940

Guest performance of Sankai Juku *butō* company. Hungary: Budapest. 1998. Lang.: Hun. 941

Visual dance productions by Cie, 2 in 1. Hungary: Budapest. 1998. Lang.: Hun. 942

The premiere of *Kabaré (Cabaret)* choreographed by Yvette Bozsik. Hungary: Budapest. 1998. Lang.: Hun. 945

Ildikó Mándy's *X.Y.Z.*, a film-dance theatre piece. Hungary: Budapest. 1998. Lang.: Hun. 947

Sanjukta Panigrahi, dancer, choreographer, and co-founder of ISTA. India. 1944-1997. Lang.: Eng. 952

Dancer, choreographer, and teacher Amos Hetz. Israel: Jerusalem. 1978-1998. Lang.: Ger. 953

Interview with dancer and choreographer Gloria Bacon. Nicaragua. 1979-1998. Lang.: Swe. 958

Politics, culture, and Portuguese dance and choreography. Portugal. 1998. Lang.: Eng. 959

Interview with choreographer Kasjan Golejzovskij. Russia. 1892-1970. Lang.: Rus. 960

Choreographers and theorists E.V. Javorskij and N.S. Poznjakov. Russia: Moscow. 1920-1939. Lang.: Rus. 961

Choreography — cont'd

Interview with choreographer Birgit Åkesson. Sweden. Africa. Asia. 1908. Lang.: Swe. 963

Lois Weaver's *Faith and Dancing* and the CD-ROM in interactive performance. UK-England. USA. 1996. Lang.: Eng. 971

National identity and the choreography of Shobana Jeyasingh. UK-England. 1991-1994. Lang.: Eng. 972

Hip-hop choreographer Jonzi D. UK-England: London. 1998. Lang.: Eng. 973

Digital dance. UK-England. 1998. Lang.: Eng. 974

Director and choreographer Jerome Robbins. USA. 1919-1998. Lang.: Eng. 975

Analysis of the *Night and Day* dance sequence of *The Gay Divorcee.* USA: Hollywood, CA. 1934. Lang.: Eng. 977

Choreographer Rosemary Butcher on her return to New York. USA: New York, NY. 1969-1998. Lang.: Eng. 979

The receding place of dance in American culture. USA: New York, NY. 1996-1997. Lang.: Eng. 981

Choreography in the musical film *The Bandwagon.* USA. 1953. Lang.: Eng. 982

Software for choreography. USA. 1998. Lang.: Eng. 984

Jazz dancer and choreographer Mia Michaels. USA. 1998. Lang.: Eng. 987

Jazz dancer and choreographer Gus Giordano. USA: Chicago, IL. 1962-1998. Lang.: Eng. 988

Prokofjév's *Romeo and Juliet*, choreographed by Cranko, Wiener Staatsoper. Austria: Vienna. 1998. Lang.: Hun. 1063

Premieres of choreographies by Danny Rosseel. Belgium: Antwerp. Netherlands: Amsterdam. 1998. Lang.: Hun. 1065

Premiere of Sylvie Guillem's new choreography for Adolphe Adam's *Giselle.* Finland: Helsinki. 1998. Lang.: Hun. 1068

Choreographer Maurice Béjart. France. 1927-1998. Lang.: Rus. 1077

Balanchine's choreography for Bizet's *Symphony in C.* France: Paris. 1947-1948. Lang.: Eng. 1079

Choreographer William Forsythe. Germany: Frankfurt. 1973-1998. Lang.: Eng. 1081

Choreographer John Neumeier. Germany: Hamburg. USA: New York, NY. 1998. Lang.: Eng. 1082

Choreographer William Forsythe, director of Ballett Frankfurt. Germany: Frankfurt. 1949-1998. Lang.: Eng. 1084

Lilla Pártay's ballet adaptation of *Anna Karenina.* Hungary. 1991-1998. Lang.: Hun. 1090

Choreographer László Seregi. Hungary: Budapest. 1949-1998. Lang.: Hun. 1100

Interview with choreographer Iván Markó. Hungary: Budapest. 1998. Lang.: Hun. 1101

Productions of Szegedi Kortárs Balett. Hungary: Szeged. 1998. Lang.: Hun. 1102

Choreographer Gyula Harangozó and the Hungarian National Ballet. Hungary. 1908-1998. Lang.: Hun. 1104

Review of one-act ballets by Balanchine. Hungary: Budapest. 1997. Lang.: Hun. 1105

The ballet adaptation of the *Decameron* performed by Veszprém Dance Workshop. Hungary: Veszprém. 1998. Lang.: Hun. 1108

Ballets of Hans van Manen. Netherlands. 1951-1998. Lang.: Eng. 1120

Analysis of the ballet *Berthalda en Hildebrand (Berthalda and Hildebrand).* Netherlands: Amsterdam. 1849. Lang.: Ger. 1122

The artistic life of dancer Vaclav Nižinskij. Poland. Russia. France. 1881-1953. Lang.: Pol. 1123

Choreographer Boris Ejfman. Russia: St. Petersburg. 1972-1998. Lang.: Eng. 1126

Diaghilev recalled by his stepmother. Russia. 1872-1929. Lang.: Rus. 1132

Boris Asafjev's ballet *Bachčisarajskij fontan* directed by R. Zacharov at the Mariinskij. Russia: St. Petersburg. 1934. Lang.: Rus. 1134

Bolšoj Ballet director Jurij Grigorovič. Russia: Moscow. 1998. Lang.: Rus. 1141

Bolšoj ballet master and choreographer Vladimir Vasiljév. Russia: Moscow. 1998. Lang.: Rus. 1147

The influence of Russian dancers and choreographers on world ballet. Russia. 1901-1998. Lang.: Eng. 1149

The reconstruction of Jean Börlin's ballet *Dervisher.* Sweden: Stockholm. 1997. Lang.: Eng. 1150

The lack of new ballets. UK-England. 1998. Lang.: Eng. 1155

Narrative in choreographies of Matthew Bourne and Mark Murphy. UK-England. 1998. Lang.: Eng. 1156

Analysis of choreographies of Matthew Bourne. UK-England: London. 1996-1997. Lang.: Eng. 1157

Annabel Farjeon on dancing for Ninette de Valois and Frederick Ashton. UK-England: London. 1930-1940. Lang.: Eng. 1158

Matthew Bourne's choreography for *Swan Lake.* UK-England. 1998. Lang.: Eng. 1159

Interview with choreographer Matthew Bourne. UK-England. 1998. Lang.: Eng. 1160

Matthew Bourne's dance piece *Cinderella* to music of Prokofjév. UK-England: London. 1998. Lang.: Eng. 1161

Interview with choreographer Christopher Bruce of the Rambert Dance Company. UK-England: London. 1998. Lang.: Hun. 1163

Synopses of lost choreographies by Jerome Robbins. USA: New York, NY. 1949-1952. Lang.: Eng. 1166

Choreographer Jerome Robbins. USA. 1918-1998. Lang.: Eng. 1167

Russsian-born dancer Mikhail Baryshnikov. USA. 1998. Lang.: Rus. 1169

New York performances of the San Francisco Ballet. USA: New York, NY. 1998. Lang.: Eng. 1170

Ballerina Kristina Fernandez on working with choreographer Jerome Robbins. USA. 1998. Lang.: Eng. 1171

Ballerina Alexandra Danilova on Balanchine's *Raymonda.* USA: New York, NY. 1946. Lang.: Eng. 1172

Playwright Jess Gregg's relationship with choreographer Agnes De Mille. USA: New York, NY. 1961-1998. Lang.: Eng. 1178

Balanchine's choreography to Čajkovskij's *Themes and Variations.* USA. 1960-1998. Lang.: Eng. 1179

Interview with dancer/choreographer Elena Kunikova on her work with Les Ballets Trockadero. USA: New York, NY. 1997. Lang.: Eng. 1180

Recollections of ballerina Margot Fonteyn. USA. Panama. 1946-1998. Lang.: Eng. 1182

Ballerina Tanaquil LeClerq on working with choreographer Jerome Robbins. USA. 1940-1998. Lang.: Eng. 1185

Interview with dancer/choreographer Merce Cunningham. USA. 1960-1998. Lang.: Eng. 1186

Interview with choreographer John Taras. USA: New York, NY. 1919-1998. Lang.: Hun. 1187

Panel discussion on Balanchine's *Jewels.* USA: New York, NY. 1967. Lang.: Eng. 1188

Dancer/choreographer Mikhail Baryshnikov. USA. USSR. 1966-1998. Lang.: Eng. 1189

The creation of the religious ballet *A Dancer's Christmas.* USA: Boston, MA. 1980-1998. Lang.: Eng. 1192

Dancer Nina Ananiašvili. USA: Houston, TX. 1986-1998. Lang.: Eng. 1193

Dancer/choreographer Mikhail Baryshnikov. USSR. USA. 1969-1998. Lang.: Eng. 1196

Fáklya Horvát Táncegyüttes' folk dance production *Napmadarak (Sunbirds).* Hungary. 1998. Lang.: Hun. 1227

Folk dance program in honor of choreographer István Molnár. Hungary: Budapest. 1930-1998. Lang.: Hun. 1229

Choreographer Igor Moisejév. Russia: Moscow. 1998. Lang.: Rus. 1231

Tatar folk dance in Siberia. Russia. 1998. Lang.: Rus. 1232

Memoirs of choreographer Igor Moisejév. Russia: Moscow. 1926-1998. 1920-1940. Lang.: Rus. 1233

Flamenco dancer and choreographer Carlota Santana. USA: New York, NY. 1998. Lang.: Eng. 1239

Rosalie Jones of Native American dance company Daystar. USA: Santa Fe, NM. 1966-1998. Lang.: Eng. 1240

The possibilities for creativity in the reconstruction of dance choreographies. 1998. Lang.: Eng. 1258

The importance of reconstructing and preserving choreographies. 1998. Lang.: Eng. 1259

Dancer/choreographer Anne Teresa De Keersmaeker. Belgium: Brussels. 1981-1998. Lang.: Eng. 1260

Choreography — cont'd

Interview with choreographer Alain Platel. Belgium: Ghent. 1984-1998. Lang.: Eng. 1261
Survey of women's dance and choreography of the season. Canada: Montreal, PQ. 1998. Lang.: Fre. 1263
The current status of Czech dance and choreography. Czech Republic. 1998. Lang.: Cze. 1265
Choreographers Monika Rebcová, Petr Tyc, and Petr Zuska. Czech Republic: Prague. 1997. Lang.: Eng, Fre. 1266
The body and personality of the dancer as the source of the physical vocabulary of dance. Europe. 1989. Lang.: Eng. 1269
Nudity in dance theatre. Europe. 1970-1998. Lang.: Ger. 1270
Director and choreographer Nada Kokotovic. Europe. 1978-1998. Lang.: Ger. 1272
Dance improvisation with children. France. 1998. Lang.: Fre. 1275
The collaboration of choreographers Claire Russ and Anne-Marie Pascoli. France. UK-England. 1994-1998. Lang.: Eng. 1276
A personal response to Pina Bausch's dance theatre. Germany: Wuppertal. 1982-1998. Lang.: Eng. 1277
Analysis of *Nur du (Only You)* by choreographer Pina Bausch. Germany: Wuppertal. 1997. Lang.: Eng. 1278
Interview with dancer and choreographer Pina Bausch. Germany: Wuppertal. 1973-1998. Lang.: Ger. 1279
The choreography of William Forsythe and the painting of Marcel Duchamp. Germany. France. 1915-1998. Lang.: Eng. 1280
Portrait of choreographer/director Pina Bausch. Germany: Wuppertal. 1973-1998. Lang.: Ger. 1281
Analysis of Pina Bausch's dance work *Masuca Fogo*. Germany: Wuppertal. 1998. Lang.: Ger. 1282
Dancer and choreographer Brygida Ochaim. Germany. France. 1970-1998. Lang.: Ger. 1283
William Forsythe of Ballett Frankfurt. Germany: Frankfurt. 1984-1998. Lang.: Ger. 1284
Interview with choreographer Sasha Waltz. Germany: Berlin. 1998. Lang.: Ger. 1285
Dancer, choreographer, and teacher Hellmut Gottschild. Germany. USA. 1936-1998. Lang.: Ger. 1287
Dancer/choreographer Ralf Jaroschinski. Germany: Hannover. 1966-1998. Lang.: Ger. 1288
Interview with dancer, choreographer, and teacher Lilian Karina. Germany. 1911-1998. Lang.: Ger. 1289
Mary Wigman's summary of her work in choreography and dance training. Germany: Dresden. 1925. Lang.: Ger. 1290
Interview with dancer and choreographer Hedvig Fekete. Hungary: Budapest. 1998. Lang.: Hun. 1291
Utolsó kontrasztok (Last Contrasts) choreographed by István Orsovszky. Hungary: Zalaegerszeg. 1998. Lang.: Hun. 1295
Dancer, choreographer, and teacher Ruth Abramowitsch-Sorel. Poland. 1907-1974. Lang.: Ger. 1296
Boris Ejfman's Teat'r Sovremennogo Baleta. Russia: St. Petersburg. 1998. Lang.: Rus. 1298
Reactions to guest performances of dancer/choreographer Pina Bausch. Sweden: Stockholm. 1998. Lang.: Swe. 1301
Dancer/choreographer Birgit Cullberg. Sweden: Stockholm. 1908-1998. Lang.: Ger. 1302
Choreographer Wayne McGregor and his work with Swedish students. Sweden: Husby. 1998. Lang.: Swe. 1304
Dancer/choreographer Rosemary Lee. UK-England: London. 1989-1998. Lang.: Eng. 1307
Interview with choreographer Keely Garfield. UK-England. 1998. Lang.: Eng. 1308
Performer/choreographer Wendy Houstoun. UK-England. 1989-1998. Lang.: Eng. 1309
Interview with dancer and choreographer Michael Clark. UK-England. 1995-1998. Lang.: Eng. 1312
Interview with Lloyd Newson of DV8 Physical Theatre. UK-England: London. 1995-1998. Lang.: Swe. 1313
Seminar on auditions for choreographers for Resolution dance festival. UK-England: London. Belgium: Brussels. 1998. Lang.: Swe. 1314
Analysis of *The Featherstonehaughs Draw on the Sketchbooks of Egon Schiele* by choreographer Lea Anderson. UK-England: London. 1998. Lang.: Eng. 1315
Interview with choreographer Bill T. Jones. USA. 1990-1998. Lang.: Eng. 1316
Analysis of the choreography of Mark Morris. USA. 1980-1997. Lang.: Eng. 1317
Defense of Bill T. Jones' dance piece *Still/Here*. USA. 1994. Lang.: Eng. 1318
Choreographer Bill Cratty. USA. 1974-1998. Lang.: Eng. 1320
The influence of Merce Cunningham on choreographer Emma Diamond. USA. 1988-1998. Lang.: Eng. 1322
Choreographer Meredith Monk. USA: New York, NY. 1964-1998. Lang.: Eng. 1325
Interview with choreographer Merce Cunningham. USA. 1944-1998. Lang.: Eng. 1326
Recent work of choreographer Twyla Tharp. USA: New York, NY. 1988-1998. Lang.: Eng. 1328
Dancer/choreographer David Parsons. USA: New York, NY. 1998. Lang.: Eng. 1329
Choreographer Mark Dendy. USA: New York, NY. 1980-1998. Lang.: Eng. 1330
The Murray Louis/Alwin Nikolais dance archive. USA: Athens, OH. 1950-1998. Lang.: Eng. 1331
Interview with choreographer Javier De Frutos. USA. 1990-1998. Lang.: Eng. 1332
Mary Oslund and Gregg Bielemeier of Conduit. USA: Portland, OR. 1995-1998. Lang.: Eng. 1333
Analysis of dance trilogy by choreographer Neil Greenberg. USA. 1994-1998. Lang.: Eng. 1334
Choreographer Paul Taylor. USA. 1977-1998. Lang.: Eng. 1335
The theory of movement in *Les Enfants Terribles*, adapted to dance-opera by Philip Glass and Susan Marshall. North America. 1997. Lang.: Eng. 1353
Interview with choreographer Runa Singha. Canada: Toronto, ON. 1970-1998. Lang.: Eng. 1368
Dance on screen. USA. Europe. 1920-1998. Lang.: Ger. 3860
Time aspects of video dance. Europe. 1970-1998. Lang.: Ger. 4059
Choreographer Debra Brown of Cirque du Soleil. Canada: Montreal, PQ. 1987-1998. Lang.: Eng. 4179
Gillian Lynne, director and choreographer. UK-England: London. USA: New York, NY. 1951-1998. Lang.: Eng. 4372
Staging a musical without professional dancers. USA. 1998. Lang.: Eng. 4374
The development of Bob Fosse's choreographic style. USA. 1953-1987. Lang.: Eng. 4377
Dancer Gemze de Lappe's work with choreographer Agnes De Mille. USA: New York, NY. 1943-1998. Lang.: Eng. 4380
Gower Champion's work in musical theatre. USA: New York, NY. 1936-1980. Lang.: Eng. 4388
Premieres of the Bolšoj Theatre. Russia: Moscow. 1825-1997. Lang.: Rus. 4693

Plays/librettos/scripts
Conrad Alexandrowicz on his dance-theatre piece *The Wines of Tuscany*. Canada: Vancouver, BC. 1992-1996. Lang.: Eng. 1356

Reference materials
Encyclopedia of Slovene folk dance. Slovenia. 1997. Lang.: Slo. 1243

Research/historiography
Interview with dance historian Ann Hutchinson Guest on dance notation. USA. 1998. Lang.: Eng. 1004

Theory/criticism
The influence of Symbolism on European dance. Europe. 1895-1939. Lang.: Eng. 1007
The nature of the body in dance. North America. Europe. 1998. Lang.: Eng. 1010
Critique of dance criticism. UK-England: London. 1989. Lang.: Eng. 1339

Chorpenning, Charlotte

Plays/librettos/scripts
Feminist analysis of plays for young people by women playwrights. USA. 1903-1983. Lang.: Eng. 3521

Chorus Line, A

Design/technology
Digital lighting control for *A Chorus Line*. USA: New York, NY. 1974-1975. Lang.: Eng. 4337

Chrimekundan
Basic theatrical documents
Slovene translations of Tibetan plays. Tibet. 1400-1990. Lang.: Slo. 1470
Christiani Wallace Brothers Combined
SEE
Wallace Brothers Circus.
Christina, Queen of Sweden
Basic theatrical documents
Libretto for *Christina, Queen of Sweden.* USA. 1988. Lang.: Eng. 4423
Christliche Ritter, Der (Christian Knights, The)
Plays/librettos/scripts
Morality plays of the Reformation. Germany. 1550-1584. Lang.: Eng. 3163
Christopher, Mark
Design/technology
Lighting design for Mark Christopher's film *54.* USA. 1998. Lang.: Eng. 3913
Christopher, Stephen
Performance/production
Collection of newspaper reviews by London theatre critics. UK-England: London. 1998. Lang.: Eng. 2437
Chroniques des jours entiers, des nuits entières (Whole Days, Whole Nights)
Institutions
Interview with playwright, director, and film-maker Xavier Durringer. France: Paris. 1988-1998. Lang.: Ger. 1609
Chrysanthemum and the Rose, The
Performance/production
Theatrical component of Japan's UK98 Festival. Japan: Tokyo. 1994-1998. Lang.: Eng. 2192
Chubb, Justin
Performance/production
Collection of newspaper reviews by London theatre critics. UK-England: London. 1998. Lang.: Eng. 2476
Churchill, Caryl
Performance/production
Analysis of a student production of Caryl Churchill's *Cloud Nine.* Canada. 1997. Lang.: Eng. 1840
Collection of newspaper reviews by London theatre critics. UK-England: London. 1998. Lang.: Eng. 2452
Collection of newspaper reviews by London theatre critics. UK-England: London. 1998. Lang.: Eng. 2462
Collection of newspaper reviews by London theatre critics. UK-England: London. 1998. Lang.: Eng. 2537
Analysis of two productions of Caryl Churchill's *Top Girls.* UK-England. 1982-1991. Lang.: Eng. 2608
Creating the character Marlene in Caryl Churchill's *Top Girls.* USA. 1997. Lang.: Eng. 2730
The language of costume in a video production of Caryl Churchill's *Top Girls.* UK-England. 1982-1991. Lang.: Eng. 4065
Plays/librettos/scripts
Ecology and the plays of Caryl Churchill. UK-England. 1971-1989. Lang.: Eng. 3422
Gender and sexuality in Caryl Churchill's *Cloud Nine.* UK-England. 1979. Lang.: Eng. 3426
Analysis of plays by David Hare and Caryl Churchill. UK-England. 1971-1997. Lang.: Dut. 3432
Caryl Churchill's *The Skriker* compared to her earlier plays. UK-England. 1994. Lang.: Eng. 3436
Fragmentation and skepticism in Caryl Churchill's *Icecream.* UK-England. 1989. Lang.: Eng. 3451
A paradigm for analysis of works by Caryl Churchill. UK-England. 1975-1997. Lang.: Eng. 3458
Systemic poisons in plays of Caryl Churchill. UK-England. 1990-1997. Lang.: Eng. 3463
Radio, television, and stage plays of Caryl Churchill. UK-England. 1959-1985. Lang.: Eng. 3464
Secrets in Caryl Churchill's *Top Girls.* UK-England. 1982. Lang.: Eng. 3466
Brechtian epic devices in the theatre of Caryl Churchill. UK-England. 1976-1986. Lang.: Eng. 3477
Analysis of *Light Shining in Buckinghamshire* by Caryl Churchill. UK-England. 1970-1976. Lang.: Eng. 3483
Analysis of *The Skriker* by Caryl Churchill. UK-England. 1994. Lang.: Eng. 3489
The plays of Caryl Churchill. UK-England. 1959-1987. Lang.: Eng. 3493
British historical drama. UK-England. 1956-1988. Lang.: Eng. 3500
The critical and popular failure of *The Skriker* by Caryl Churchill. UK-England. 1994. Lang.: Eng. 3504
Analysis of *Mad Forest* by Caryl Churchill. UK-England. 1990. Lang.: Eng. 3505
Churchill, Mary
Performance/production
Obituary for puppeteer Mary Churchill. USA. 1930-1997. Lang.: Eng. 4901
Churney, Russell
Performance/production
Collection of newspaper reviews by London theatre critics. UK-England: London. 1998. Lang.: Eng. 2556
Chybowski, Michael
Design/technology
Set and lighting designs for *The Taming of the Shrew,* American Repertory Theatre. USA: Cambridge, MA. 1998. Lang.: Eng. 1559
Cibber, Colley
Performance/production
The Cibber family: private life as public spectacle. England. 1713-1760. Lang.: Eng. 517
Cibber, Theophilus
Performance/production
The Cibber family: private life as public spectacle. England. 1713-1760. Lang.: Eng. 517
Ciconi, Teobaldo
Plays/librettos/scripts
Italian realist drama. Italy. 1860-1918. Lang.: Eng. 3260
Cid, Le (Cid, The)
Institutions
Impressions from the Avignon theatre festival. France: Avignon. 1998. Lang.: Ger. 1612
Cie, 2 in 1 (Budapest)
Performance/production
Visual dance productions by Cie, 2 in 1. Hungary: Budapest. 1998. Lang.: Hun. 942
Cieplak, Piotr
Performance/production
The new generation of Polish directors. Poland. 1989-1998. Lang.: Pol. 2219
Cierta manera, De (One Way or Another)
Plays/librettos/scripts
Afrocuban religion in Cuban films. Cuba. 1974-1991. Lang.: Eng. 3968
Cieślak, Piotr
Performance/production
Contemporary Polish productions of Shakespeare. Poland. 1990-1998. Lang.: Pol. 2213
Cimarron
Plays/librettos/scripts
The mulatto in Puerto Rican drama. Puerto Rico. 1850-1985. Lang.: Spa. 3311
Cinderella
Performance/production
Matthew Bourne's dance piece *Cinderella* to music of Prokofjév. UK-England: London. 1998. Lang.: Eng. 1161
Collection of newspaper reviews by London theatre critics. UK-England: London. 1998. Lang.: Eng. 2556
Collection of newspaper reviews by London theatre critics. UK-England: London. 1998. Lang.: Eng. 2557
Plays/librettos/scripts
Feminist analysis of plays for young people by women playwrights. USA. 1903-1983. Lang.: Eng. 3521
Treatments of the Cinderella theme, with emphasis on *La Cenerentola* by Rossini. 1817-1998. Lang.: Eng. 4757
***Cinderella* by Kalmár**
SEE
Hamupipőke.
Cine Mexico (Chicago, IL)
SEE
Congress Theatre.
Cinematography
Design/technology
Geoffrey Simpson's cinematography for Gillian Armstrong's *Oscar and Lucinda.* Australia. 1997. Lang.: Eng. 3900
Cino, Joseph
Institutions
Producer Joseph Cino and Off-off Broadway theatre. USA: New York, NY. 1931-1967. Lang.: Eng. 404

Činoherní klub (Prague)
Design/technology
The work of scene designer Libor Fára. Czech Republic: Prague. 1950-1981. Lang.: Cze. 1518
Cinzio
SEE
Giraldi Cinthio, Giovanni Battista.
Circle in the Square (New York, NY)
Performance spaces
Theatre space and performance. USA: New York, NY. 1925-1985. Lang.: Eng. 464
Performance/production
Notable productions of plays by Eugene O'Neill. USA. 1916-1996. Lang.: Eng. 2752
Circle Repertory (New York, NY)
Performance spaces
Theatre space and performance. USA: New York, NY. 1925-1985. Lang.: Eng. 464
Performance/production
The collaboration of playwright Lanford Wilson and director Marshall W. Mason. USA: New York, NY. 1978-1986. Lang.: Eng. 2756
Circle Theatre (Budapest)
SEE
Körszinház.
Circuit Chautauqua (USA)
Performance/production
Antitheatricalism in the Circuit Chautauqua. USA. 1913-1930. Lang.: Eng. 4135
Circus
SEE ALSO
Classed Entries under MIXED ENTERTAINMENT—Circus.
Performance/production
Recent developments in Australian 'physical theatre'. Australia. 1990-1998. Lang.: Eng. 492
Onstage costume changes. Japan. Russia. Denmark. 1752-1998. Lang.: Swe. 556
Circus Space (London)
Performance/production
Collection of newspaper reviews by London theatre critics. UK-England: London. 1998. Lang.: Eng. 2580
Cirkus (Stockholm)
Performance spaces
The rebuilding of the stage at Cirkus to accommodate a production of *Kristina från Duvemåla (Kristina of Duvemåla)*.Sweden: Stockholm. 1995. Lang.: Swe. 1804
Cirkus Cirkör (Stockholm)
Performance/production
Analysis of the 'new circus'. France. Sweden. 1990-1998. Lang.: Swe. 4182
Cirkus Schumann (Berlin)
Performance spaces
Non-traditional theatrical space. Germany. France. UK-England. 1898-1998. Lang.: Dan. 443
Cirque du Soleil (Montreal, PQ)
Performance/production
Collection of newspaper reviews by London theatre critics. UK-England: London. 1998. Lang.: Eng. 2564
Choreographer Debra Brown of Cirque du Soleil. Canada: Montreal, PQ. 1987-1998. Lang.: Eng. 4179
Cirque Invisible (Paris)
Performance/production
Analysis of the 'new circus'. France. Sweden. 1990-1998. Lang.: Swe. 4182
Cirque Plume (Paris)
Performance/production
Analysis of the 'new circus'. France. Sweden. 1990-1998. Lang.: Swe. 4182
Cisma de Inglaterra, La (Schism of England, The)
Performance/production
Calderón's *La cisma de Inglaterra (The Schism of England)* directed by Péter Telihay. Hungary: Budapest. 1997. Lang.: Hun. 2137
City Center (New York, NY)
Performance/production
New York performances of the San Francisco Ballet. USA: New York, NY. 1998. Lang.: Eng. 1170
Ballerina Alexandra Danilova on Balanchine's *Raymonda*. USA: New York, NY. 1946. Lang.: Eng. 1172
Dancer/choreographer David Parsons. USA: New York, NY. 1998. Lang.: Eng. 1329
City Center Theatre (New York, NY)
SEE ALSO
Manhattan Theatre Club.
City of Angels
Performance/production
Collection of newspaper reviews by London theatre critics. UK-England: London. 1998. Lang.: Eng. 2516
City Theatre (Helsinki)
SEE
Helsingin Kaupunginteatteri.
Ciulli, Roberto
Performance/production
Roberto Ciulli's production of *Doña Rosita la Soltera (Doña Rosita the Spinster)* by Federico García Lorca. Germany: Munich. 1998. Lang.: Ger. 2021
Civanyan, Eric
Basic theatrical documents
French translation of *Funny Money* by Ray Cooney. UK-England. France. 1995-1997. Lang.: Fre. 1473
Cixous, Hélène
Performance/production
Reviews of productions by Wilson, Greenaway, and Mnouchkine. France: Paris. 1997-1998. Lang.: Eng. 1926
Survey of Parisian productions. France: Paris. 1997-1998. Lang.: Eng. 1937
Plays/librettos/scripts
Poetic identity in plays of Hélène Cixous. France. 1988-1994. Lang.: Eng. 3083
Bisexuality in *Le Nom d'Oedipe (The Name of Oedipus)* by Hélène Cixous. France. 1978. Lang.: Eng. 3089
Postcolonialism, ethnicity, and feminism in French and Caribbean plays. France. Martinique. Guadeloupe. 1960-1990. Lang.: Eng. 3104
Clack, Les
Performance/production
Survey of Parisian productions. France: Paris. 1997-1998. Lang.: Eng. 1937
Clacson, trombette e pernacchi (Klaxons, Trumpets and Raspberries)
Performance/production
Collection of newspaper reviews by London theatre critics. UK-England: London. 1998. Lang.: Eng. 2565
Claffey, Rich
Design/technology
Profile of technicians for Grammy Awards television broadcast. USA: New York, NY. 1998. Lang.: Eng. 4056
Clandestine Marriage, The
Plays/librettos/scripts
Analysis of *The Clandestine Marriage* by David Garrick. England. 1766. Lang.: Eng. 2926
Claramonte y Corroy, Andrés de
Plays/librettos/scripts
Playwright Andrés de Claramonte. Spain. 1580-1626. Lang.: Eng. 3404
Clarence B. Hilberry Repertory Theatre (Detroit, MI)
Institutions
The training program of the Clarence B. Hilberry Repertory Theatre. USA: Detroit, MI. 1963-1973. Lang.: Eng. 408
Clark, Anthony
Performance/production
Collection of newspaper reviews by London theatre critics. UK-England: Leeds, Manchester. 1998. Lang.: Eng. 2433
Clark, Boyd
Performance/production
Collection of newspaper reviews by London theatre critics. UK-England: London. 1998. Lang.: Eng. 2576
Clark, Michael
Performance/production
Interview with dancer and choreographer Michael Clark. UK-England. 1995-1998. Lang.: Eng. 1312
Clark, Rick
Design/technology
Sound design for the London production of *Chicago*. UK-England: London. 1998. Lang.: Eng. 4326
Clark, Stephen
Performance/production
Collection of newspaper reviews by London theatre critics. UK-England: London. 1998. Lang.: Eng. 2470
Collection of newspaper reviews by London theatre critics. UK-England: London. 1998. Lang.: Eng. 2500
Collection of newspaper reviews by London theatre critics. UK-England: London. 1998. Lang.: Eng. 2549

Clark, Stephen — cont'd

Collection of newspaper reviews by London theatre critics. UK-England: Leeds, Manchester. 1998. Lang.: Eng. 2559

Clark, Tom
Design/technology
Sound design for *Side Show* at Richard Rodgers Theatre. USA: New York, NY. 1998. Lang.: Eng. 4329

Clarke, George Elliot
Basic theatrical documents
Text of libretto for *Beatrice Chancy*. Canada: Toronto, ON. 1998. Lang.: Eng. 4413
James Rolfe on his opera *Beatrice Chancy*. Canada: Toronto, ON. 1998. Lang.: Eng. 4414

Classic Stage Company
SEE
CSC Repertory.

Classified
Performance/production
Screenwriter and producer June Mathis. USA. 1916-1927. Lang.: Eng. 3959

Claudel, Paul
Performance/production
Collaborative Symbolist dance/theatre projects. Europe. USA. 1916-1934. Lang.: Eng. 1268

Claus, Hugo
Plays/librettos/scripts
The nature of conflict in the plays of Hugo Claus. France. 1950-1988. Lang.: Eng. 3121

Cleansed
Performance/production
Collection of newspaper reviews by London theatre critics. UK-England: London. 1998. Lang.: Eng. 2467
Reviews of recent London performances. UK-England: London. 1998. Lang.: Ger. 2591

Cleary, Ann
Performance/production
Collection of newspaper reviews by London theatre critics. UK-England: London. 1998. Lang.: Eng. 2554

Cleo, Camping, Emmanuelle and Dick
Performance/production
Collection of newspaper reviews by London theatre critics. UK-England: London. 1998. Lang.: Eng. 2508

Cleopatra. Ein Spiel zwischen Liebe und Macht (Cleopatra: A Play Between Love and Power)
Performance/production
The performance of Shakespeare in the former East Germany. Germany: Rostock, Leipzig, Berlin, Dessau. 1996-1997. Lang.: Ger. 1974

Cleveland Playhouse (Cleveland, OH)
Plays/librettos/scripts
Playwright Murphy Guyer and the Cleveland Playhouse. USA: Cleveland, OH. 1998. Lang.: Eng. 3598

Cleveland San Jose Ballet (Cleveland, OH)
Administration
Financially troubled Ohio ballet companies. USA: Cleveland, OH, Akron, OH. 1998. Lang.: Eng. 1027
Design/technology
Marilyn Lowey's lighting design for Cleveland San Jose Ballet. USA: Cleveland, OH. 1997. Lang.: Eng. 1034

Clever, Edith
Plays/librettos/scripts
New directions in the plays of Botho Strauss. Europe. 1971-1998. Lang.: Ger. 3067

Clifford, Sara
Performance/production
Collection of newspaper reviews by London theatre critics. UK-England: London. 1998. Lang.: Eng. 2511

Clifton, Piers
Performance/production
Collection of newspaper reviews by London theatre critics. UK-England: London. 1998. Lang.: Eng. 2503

Clink Theatre (London)
Performance/production
Collection of newspaper reviews by London theatre critics. UK-England: London. 1998. Lang.: Eng. 2571

Clizia
Plays/librettos/scripts
Analysis of Machiavelli's *Clizia*. Italy. 1525. Lang.: Eng. 3257

Clockwork Orange 2004, A
Performance/production
German productions of adaptations of *A Clockwork Orange* by Anthony Burgess. Germany: Dresden, Hamburg, Stendal. 1998. Lang.: Ger. 1972

Clockwork Orange, A
Performance/production
German productions of adaptations of *A Clockwork Orange* by Anthony Burgess. Germany: Dresden, Hamburg, Stendal. 1998. Lang.: Ger. 1972

Closer
Performance/production
Political changes reflected in Berlin theatre productions. Germany: Berlin. 1998. Lang.: Ger. 1958
Interview with actor/director Stefan Larsson. Sweden: Stockholm. 1984-1998. Lang.: Swe. 2382
Collection of newspaper reviews by London theatre critics. UK-England: London. 1998. Lang.: Eng. 2452
Report on several English performances. UK-England: London, Stratford. 1998. Lang.: Swe. 2634
Plays/librettos/scripts
German view of English and American drama. UK-England. USA. 1998. Lang.: Ger. 3455

Closer Than Ever
Performance/production
Collection of newspaper reviews by London theatre critics. UK-England: London. 1998. Lang.: Eng. 2476

Closet drama
Plays/librettos/scripts
Survey of recent studies on closet drama. Europe. North America. 1998. Lang.: Eng. 3065

Closet Land
Performance/production
Collection of newspaper reviews by London theatre critics. UK-England: London. 1998. Lang.: Eng. 2480

Cloud Nine
Performance/production
Analysis of a student production of Caryl Churchill's *Cloud Nine*. Canada. 1997. Lang.: Eng. 1840
Collection of newspaper reviews by London theatre critics. UK-England: London. 1998. Lang.: Eng. 2452
Plays/librettos/scripts
Ecology and the plays of Caryl Churchill. UK-England. 1971-1989. Lang.: Eng. 3422
Gender and sexuality in Caryl Churchill's *Cloud Nine*. UK-England. 1979. Lang.: Eng. 3426
Brechtian epic devices in the theatre of Caryl Churchill. UK-England. 1976-1986. Lang.: Eng. 3477

Cloudstreet
Design/technology
Lighting designer Mark Howett's work for Black Swan Theatre Company. Australia: Fremantle. 1998. Lang.: Eng. 1513

Cloutier, Suzanne
Performance/production
Suzanne Cloutier's role in Shakespeare's *Othello*, directed by Orson Welles. Italy. 1952. Lang.: Fre. 3935

Človek iz Kariota (Man from Kariot)
Plays/librettos/scripts
Religion and the individual in plays of Ivan Mrak. Slovenia. 1955. Lang.: Slo. 3358

Človek, ki je umoril Boga (Man Who Killed God, The)
Basic theatrical documents
Text of plays by Branko Rozman. Slovenia. 1990-1997. Lang.: Slo. 1461

Clownin, Die (Clowness, The)
Performance/production
Collection of newspaper reviews by London theatre critics. UK-England: London. 1998. Lang.: Eng. 2481

Clowning
Institutions
Report on a seminar on mime, illusionism, *commedia* and clowning in dance. Sweden: Stockholm. 1998. Lang.: Swe. 386
Performance/production
The actor/clown team of Claudio Remondi and Riccardo Caporossi. Italy. 1971-1998. Lang.: Eng. 2176
Clown teachers Richard Pochinko and Philippe Gaulier. Canada. 1980-1998. Lang.: Eng. 4117
The clown and the modern variety circus. Europe. 1950-1987. Lang.: Eng. 4180
Memoirs of film actor and clown Jurij Nikulin. Russia: Moscow. 1998. Lang.: Rus. 4184

Club Tropicana
Performance/production
Collection of newspaper reviews by London theatre critics. UK-England: London. 1998. Lang.: Eng. 2429

Club, The
Plays/librettos/scripts
Gendered political critique in *The Club* by Eve Merriam. USA. 1976. Lang.: Eng. 3572
Clue in the Old Birdbath
Performance/production
Contemporary queer politics and the production of gay and lesbian theatre. USA. 1970-1997. Lang.: Eng. 2710
Clune, Jackie
Performance/production
Collection of newspaper reviews by London theatre critics. UK-England: London. 1998. Lang.: Eng. 2508
Clurman, Harold
Performance/production
The idea of Hollywood in theatre autobiographies. USA. 1950-1990. Lang.: Eng. 665
Director Harold Clurman's reaction to Mejerchol'd's *Revizor (The Inspector General)*. USSR: Moscow. 1935. Lang.: Eng. 2764
Cmieszny staruszek (Funny Old Man)
Plays/librettos/scripts
Old age in plays of Różewicz. Poland. 1945-1998. Lang.: Pol. 3309
Coad Canada Puppets (Vancouver, BC)
Institutions
Luman Coad on the work of Coad Canada Puppets. Canada: Vancouver, BC. 1966-1998. Lang.: Eng. 4919
Coad, Arlyn
Institutions
Luman Coad on the work of Coad Canada Puppets. Canada: Vancouver, BC. 1966-1998. Lang.: Eng. 4919
Coad, Luman
Institutions
Luman Coad on the work of Coad Canada Puppets. Canada: Vancouver, BC. 1966-1998. Lang.: Eng. 4919
Cochrane Theatre (London)
Performance/production
Collection of newspaper reviews by London theatre critics. UK-England: London. 1998. Lang.: Eng. 2507
Cochrane, Jay
Performance/production
Physical risk and its aesthetics in aerialist performance. USA. 1985-1997. Lang.: Eng. 4185
Cockpit Theatre (London)
Performance/production
Collection of newspaper reviews by London theatre critics. UK-England: London. 1998. Lang.: Eng. 2480
Collection of newspaper reviews by London theatre critics. UK-England: London. 1998. Lang.: Eng. 2570
Coconut Club (Los Angeles, CA)
Performance spaces
The supper and swing-music venue the Coconut Club. USA: Los Angeles, CA. 1998. Lang.: Eng. 4115
Cocteau, Jean
Performance/production
The theory of movement in *Les Enfants Terribles*, adapted to dance-opera by Philip Glass and Susan Marshall. North America. 1997. Lang.: Eng. 1353
Plays/librettos/scripts
The influence of Jean Cocteau on filmmaker Pedro Almodóvar. Spain. France. 1981. Lang.: Eng. 3978
Cocu imaginaire, Le
SEE ALSO
Sganarelle.
Codco (St. John's, NF)
Performance/production
Social criticism and alternative theatre in Quebec and Newfoundland. Canada. 1970-1985. Lang.: Eng. 500
Coffey, Charles
Plays/librettos/scripts
Music and the ballad opera in English popular theatre. England. 1728-1780. Lang.: Eng. 4390
Cogdale, Barcy
Performance/production
Collection of newspaper reviews by London theatre critics. UK-England: London. 1998. Lang.: Eng. 2425
Cohan, George M.
Performance/production
The Broadway directing career of George M. Cohan. USA. 1900-1950. Lang.: Eng. 2751
Plays/librettos/scripts
African- and Irish-Americans in the plays of Eugene O'Neill. USA. 1916-1953. Lang.: Eng. 3687
Cohen, David Mark
Performance/production
Obituaries for Ellis Rabb, Giorgio Strehler, and David Mark Cohen. USA. 1930-1997. Lang.: Eng. 2725
Cohen, Douglas J.
Performance/production
Collection of newspaper reviews by London theatre critics. UK-England: London. 1998. Lang.: Eng. 2479
Cohen, Robert
Design/technology
Scenery by Yevgenia Nayberg for Robert Cohen's *The Prince*. USA: Long Beach, CA. 1997. Lang.: Eng. 1561
Performance/production
New productions of Győri Balett. Hungary: Budapest. 1998. Lang.: Hun. 1095
Collection of newspaper reviews by London theatre critics. UK-England: London. 1998. Lang.: Eng. 2463
Creating the role of Biagio Buonaccorsi in Robert Cohen's *The Prince*. USA. 1997. Lang.: Eng. 2686
Cohen, Steve
Design/technology
Steve Cohen's lighting design for pop music tour. Australia. 1998. Lang.: Eng. 4095
Pop music lighting design of Steve Cohen and Curry Grant. USA. 1997. Lang.: Eng. 4102
Colas, Hubert
Performance/production
French production of *Im Dickicht der Städte (In the Jungle of Cities)* by Bertolt Brecht. France. 1997-1998. Lang.: Ger. 1946
Cold Draft on Tap
Performance/production
Collection of newspaper reviews by London theatre critics. UK-England: London. 1998. Lang.: Eng. 2460
Coleman, Beau
Plays/librettos/scripts
Analysis of *Queen Lear* by Beau Coleman. Canada: Edmonton, AB. 1995-1997. Lang.: Eng. 2800
Coleman, Cy
Performance/production
Collection of newspaper reviews by London theatre critics. UK-England: London. 1998. Lang.: Eng. 2410
Collection of newspaper reviews by London theatre critics. UK-England: London. 1998. Lang.: Eng. 2516
AIDS-benefit performance of the musical *Sweet Charity*. USA: New York, NY. 1998. Lang.: Eng. 4386
Coleman, Emily
Performance/production
Tributes to ballerina Alexandra Danilova. USA: New York, NY. 1997. Lang.: Eng. 1165
Coleridge, Samuel Taylor
Plays/librettos/scripts
The feminine ideal in the drama of English Romantic poets. England. 1794-1840. Lang.: Eng. 2886
Theory/criticism
Chaos theory and its application to theatre and drama theory. USA. 1998. Lang.: Eng. 3839
Colicos, John
Performance/production
The Stratford Festival production of Shakespeare's *King Lear*. Canada: Stratford, ON. 1964. Lang.: Eng. 506
Coliseo de la Cruz (Madrid)
Performance spaces
History of the Coliseo de la Cruz. Spain: Madrid. 1737-1859. Lang.: Eng. 457
Collected Stories
Design/technology
Lighting design for Donald Margulies' *Collected Stories*, directed by William Carden. USA: New York, NY. 1998. Lang.: Eng. 1544
Collection, The
Performance/production
Collection of newspaper reviews by London theatre critics. UK-England: London. 1998. Lang.: Eng. 2561
Recent productions of plays by Harold Pinter at Donmar Warehouse. UK-England: London. 1998. Lang.: Eng. 2609
Plays/librettos/scripts
Analysis of *The Collection* by Harold Pinter. UK-England. 1975. Lang.: Eng. 3507

College of Theatre Arts (Warsaw)
SEE
Panstova Akademia Sztuk Teatralnych.
Collins, Brendan
Institutions
The 225th anniversary of the Royal Swedish Ballet. Sweden: Stockholm. 1773-1998. Lang.: Eng. 1048
Collins, John
Performance/production
Analysis of recent New York productions. USA: New York, NY. 1997-1998. Lang.: Eng. 2759
Collins, Marla del
Plays/librettos/scripts
Marla del Collins on her play *The Lovers and Others of Eugene O'Neill*. USA. 1998. Lang.: Eng. 3565
Colman, George
Plays/librettos/scripts
Music and the ballad opera in English popular theatre. England. 1728-1780. Lang.: Eng. 4390
Color Struck
Plays/librettos/scripts
Black dance in plays of Zora Neale Hurston. USA. 1925-1930. Lang.: Eng. 3633
Color Struck and Weary Blues
Basic theatrical documents
Texts of plays about Zora Neale Hurston by Barbara Waddell Speisman. USA. 1988. Lang.: Eng. 1510
Colorado Ballet (Denver, CO)
Performance/production
Dancer Koichi Kubo of Colorado Ballet. USA: Denver, CO. 1991-1998. Lang.: Eng. 1174
Colored Museum, The
Plays/librettos/scripts
Analysis of *The Colored Museum* by George C. Wolfe. USA. 1988. Lang.: Eng. 3690
Colosseo (Rome)
Performance/production
Roman theatre, traditional and experimental. Italy: Rome. 1994-1998. Lang.: Eng. 2187
Combač, Borut
Basic theatrical documents
Text of Borut Combač's puppet play *Kdo je navil rumeno budilko? (Who Set the Yellow Alarm Clock)?*. Slovenia. 1997. Lang.: Slo. 4866
Combat de nègre et de chiens (Struggle of the Dogs and the Black)
Performance/production
Productions of plays by Bernard-Marie Koltès. Canada: Montreal, PQ. 1991-1997. Lang.: Fre. 1862
Combe, Debbie
Performance/production
Collection of newspaper reviews by London theatre critics. UK-England: London. 1998. Lang.: Eng. 2469
Comden, Betty
Plays/librettos/scripts
Lyricist and librettist Betty Comden. USA. 1938-1998. Lang.: Eng. 4400
Come Back, Little Sheba
Plays/librettos/scripts
Gender-role reversal in plays of William Inge. USA. 1950-1958. Lang.: Eng. 3623
Comedia de la muerte del rey don Sancho (Comedy of the Death of King Sancho, The)
Plays/librettos/scripts
Playwright Juan de la Cueva. Spain. 1543-1612. Lang.: Eng. 3369
Comedia Jacinta (Hyacinth Comedy, The)
Plays/librettos/scripts
Playwright Bartolomé de Torres Naharro. Spain. 1480-1530. Lang.: Eng. 3383
Comedia Soldadesca (Military Comedy, The)
Plays/librettos/scripts
Playwright Bartolomé de Torres Naharro. Spain. 1480-1530. Lang.: Eng. 3383
Comédie de Saint-Étienne
Basic theatrical documents
Text of *La Médée de Saint-Médard (The Medea of Saint-Medard)* by Anca Visdei. France. 1998. Lang.: Fre. 1436
Comédie-Française (Paris)
Administration
Interview with Jean-Pierre Miquel, managing director of the Comédie-Française. France. 1998. Lang.: Hun. 1378
Design/technology
The representation of history through costume in productions of the Comédie-Française. France: Paris. 1815-1830. Lang.: Eng. 1520
Institutions
Interview with Jean-Pierre Miquel, director of the Comédie-Française. France: Paris. 1993-1998. Lang.: Eng. 1613
Performance/production
Social context of French and Canadian productions of *Les Fourberies de Scapin* by Molière. Canada: Montreal, PQ. France: Paris. 1998. Lang.: Fre. 1842
Comedy
Basic theatrical documents
Catalan translation of *Les Femmes savantes (The Learned Ladies)* by Molière. France. 1672. Lang.: Cat. 1433
Text of *Mandibula afilada (Sharp Chin)* by Carles Alberola. Spain. 1997. Lang.: Eng. 1463
Performance/production
Analysis of transformative comedy. USA. 1975-1988. Lang.: Eng. 666
The popular comic art-form *rakugo*. Japan. 1600-1980. Lang.: Eng. 2195
Actor/director Aleksander Zelwerowicz. Poland: Vilna. 1929-1931. Lang.: Pol. 2223
Humorous anecdotes by actor/director Massimo Troisi. Italy. 1953-1994. Lang.: Ita. 3858
The decline of radio comedy and the use of record albums by some comedians. USA. 1950-1998. Lang.: Eng. 3863
Lotte Goslar's Pantomime Circus. Germany: Dresden. USA: Los Angeles, CA. 1907-1997. Lang.: Eng. 4123
Comic dance performer Lotte Goslar. Germany. USA. 1907-1997. Lang.: Eng. 4124
The North American tour of English comedian Eddie Izzard. North America. UK-England. 1998. Lang.: Eng. 4127
Commedia dell'arte and the street performances of charlatans. France. Italy. 1600-1700. Lang.: Eng. 4189
Variety actors Guido and Giorgio De Rege. Italy. 1891-1948. Lang.: Ita. 4275
Profile of the satiric comedy troupe Five Lesbian Brothers. USA: New York, NY. 1989-1998. Lang.: Eng. 4282
Plays/librettos/scripts
Comic roles in the early Song play *Zhang Xie Zhuangyuan (Top Graduate Zhang Xie)*. China. 960-1127. Lang.: Eng. 2840
Analysis of Restoration anti-Puritan comedies. England. 1661-1663. Lang.: Eng. 2907
Comedy and farce in Finnish theatre and film. Finland. 1950-1998. Lang.: Fin. 3070
Humor in the works of Samuel Beckett. France. Ireland. 1953-1986. Lang.: Eng. 3110
The subversion of tragic forms in comic plays of Menander. Greece. 342-291 B.C. Lang.: Eng. 3183
Playwright Dario Fo. Italy. 1998. Lang.: Eng. 3243
Analysis of plays by Alessandro Piccolomini. Italy. 1508-1578. Lang.: Eng. 3244
The comedy of George Bernard Shaw and Oscar Wilde. UK-England. 1885-1900. Lang.: Eng. 3450
Comedy and humor in plays of Lanford Wilson. USA. 1961-1985. Lang.: Eng. 3595
The popularity of crude comedy in recent American films. USA. 1998. Lang.: Eng. 4004
Marriage, divorce, and gender in the Hollywood comedy of remarriage. USA. 1935-1942. Lang.: Eng. 4010
Comedy in the plays and musicals of Volker Ludwig. Germany: Berlin. 1968-1998. Lang.: Ger. 4391
Relation to other fields
Novelist Samuel Richardson compared to Shakespeare. England. 1744-1747. Lang.: Eng. 3754
Comedy Concernynge Thre Lawes, of Nature, Moses, and Christ, A
Plays/librettos/scripts
John Bale's characters Sodomy and Idolatry. England. 1536-1546. Lang.: Eng. 2914
Comedy of Errors, The
Design/technology
Costume designs for Oregon Shakespeare Festival productions. USA: Ashland, OR. 1998. Lang.: Eng. 1543
Dex Edwards' set design for *The Comedy of Errors*, Shakespeare Repertory Company. USA: Chicago, IL. 1998. Lang.: Eng. 1560
Performance/production
Collection of newspaper reviews by London theatre critics. UK-England: London. 1998. Lang.: Eng. 2415

***Comedy of Errors, The* — cont'd**

Brief productions of Shakespeare, Shaw, and Marlowe at the World's Fair. USA: Chicago, IL. 1934. Lang.: Eng. 2701

Plays/librettos/scripts

The 'unruly' speech of Ariana in Shakespeare's *Comedy of Errors*. England. 1590-1593. Lang.: Eng. 2924

Comedy Theatre (Budapest)

SEE

Vigszinház.

Comedy Theatre (London)

Performance/production

Collection of newspaper reviews by London theatre critics. UK-England: London. 1998. Lang.: Eng. 2463

Collection of newspaper reviews by London theatre critics. UK-England: London. 1998. Lang.: Eng. 2540

Plays/librettos/scripts

Theatrical activities of Harold Pinter. UK-England: London. 1996-1998. Lang.: Eng. 3462

Comic opera

Performance/production

The evolution of comic opera. Italy: Florence, Rome. 1665-1700. Lang.: Eng. 4660

Comic Potential

Performance/production

Collection of newspaper reviews by London theatre critics. UK-England: London, Scarborough. 1998. Lang.: Eng. 2426

Commedia dell'arte

SEE ALSO

Classed Entries under MIXED ENTERTAINMENT—*Commedia dell'arte*.

Design/technology

Masks in Venetian carnival. Italy: Venice. 1500-1650. Lang.: Ita. 4159

Institutions

Report on a seminar on mime, illusionism, *commedia* and clowning in dance. Sweden: Stockholm. 1998. Lang.: Swe. 386

Performance/production

Early modern French and Italian actresses. Italy. France. 1550-1750. Lang.: Eng. 553

Harlequin as a character in ballet. France. 1550-1965. Lang.: Eng. 1069

Amedeo Amodio's new choreography for Čajkovskij's *The Nutcracker*. Italy: Rome. 1998. Lang.: Hun. 1118

Adrian Pecknold and the Canadian Mime Theatre. Canada: Niagara-on-the-Lake, ON. 1940-1978. Lang.: Eng. 4085

Production of László Lajtha's comic opera *Le chapeau bleu*. Romania: Cluj-Napoca. Hungary. 1948-1998. Lang.: Hun. 4668

Plays/librettos/scripts

Yearbook of Pirandello studies. Italy. 1589-1926. Lang.: Eng. 3247

The theatre of Girolamo Gigli. Italy. 1660-1722. Lang.: Eng. 4307

Commedia per musica

Plays/librettos/scripts

Female operatic cross-dressing. Italy: Naples, Venice. 1601-1800. Lang.: Eng. 4814

Committee, The

Plays/librettos/scripts

Analysis of Restoration anti-Puritan comedies. England. 1661-1663. Lang.: Eng. 2907

Community relations

Administration

Performance in fundraising. USA: New York, NY. 1998. Lang.: Eng. 34

Arts and culture indicators in community building. USA. 1996-1998. Lang.: Eng. 38

The use of impact analysis in the arts. USA. 1998. Lang.: Eng. 138

The campaign to ban child performers in New York City. USA: New York, NY. 1874-1919. Lang.: Eng. 139

How Chisenhale Dance Space coped with loss of funding. UK-England: London. 1998. Lang.: Eng. 885

Interview with Carrie Jackson, executive director of AUDELCO. USA: New York, NY. 1998. Lang.: Eng. 1399

The First Amendment and the striptease dancer. USA. 1998. Lang.: Eng. 4271

Institutions

Anna Deavere Smith on the Institute on the Arts and Civic Dialogue. USA: Cambridge, MA. 1998. Lang.: Eng. 399

Profile of Belfry Theatre Company. Canada: Victoria, BC. 1974-1998. Lang.: Eng. 1583

Teater NOR and its relationship with the community. Norway: Stamsund. 1998. Lang.: Eng. 1680

East Bay Center for the Performing Arts and the revival of a community. USA: Richmond, CA. 1958-1998. Lang.: Eng. 1764

Performance spaces

Community efforts to save the Emerson Majestic and Rialto theatres. USA: Boston, MA, Chicago, IL. 1988-1998. Lang.: Eng. 474

Relation to other fields

The arts as a sector in American life. USA. 1997-1998. Lang.: Eng. 775

Community theatre

Administration

Participants in rural community theatre. USA. 1986. Lang.: Eng. 30

Institutions

History of Virginia Museum Theatre. USA: Richmond, VA. 1955-1987. Lang.: Eng. 406

Profile of Women's Circus. Australia: Melbourne. 1990-1998. Lang.: Eng. 1568

Performance/production

Ethnicity, community youth theatre, and the dramaturg. Bosnia. 1996-1998. Lang.: Eng. 495

The dramaturg in the community theatre. North America. Asia. South America. 1990-1998. Lang.: Eng. 570

Culture and the opera house in Appalachia. USA. 1875-1925. Lang.: Eng. 629

The student-created community theatre piece *Walk Together Children*. USA. 1996-1997. Lang.: Eng. 652

Maryat Lee and the creation of the street theatre piece *Dope!*. USA: New York, NY. 1949-1951. Lang.: Eng. 663

Analysis of *1837: The Farmer's Revolt* directed by Bruce Barton of Carrefour Theatre. Canada: Charlottetown, PE. 1998. Lang.: Eng. 1856

Interview with community theatre director Kent Ekberg. Sweden: Stockholm. 1973-1998. Lang.: Swe. 2385

Contemporary queer politics and the production of gay and lesbian theatre. USA. 1970-1997. Lang.: Eng. 2710

Plays/librettos/scripts

The community play *Aftershocks*. Australia: Newcastle, NSW. 1990-1998. Lang.: Eng. 2774

Political community theatre by South Indian emigrants. Canada: Toronto, ON, Montreal, PQ. India. 1984-1998. Lang.: Eng. 2821

Analysis of Daniel MacIvor's *Monster* as directed by Daniel Brooks. Canada: Toronto, ON. 1998. Lang.: Eng. 2834

Robin Hood and Elizabethan theatre. England. 1588-1601. Lang.: Eng. 2902

Analysis of *Downfall of Robert Earl of Huntingdon* by Anthony Munday. England. 1598-1599. Lang.: Eng. 3018

Reference materials

Yearbook of Slovene theatre. Slovenia. 1996-1997. Lang.: Slo. 708

Relation to other fields

Locating and defining the 'unincorporated' arts. USA. 1998. Lang.: Eng. 806

Theory/criticism

Theory and Asian-American theatre. USA: Minneapolis, MN. 1994-1995. Lang.: Eng. 869

Compagnie Hercub' (Paris)

Basic theatrical documents

French translation of *Lebensraum* by Israel Horovitz. USA. France. 1996-1997. Lang.: Fre. 1488

French translation of *The Primary English Class* by Israel Horovitz. USA. France. 1996. Lang.: Fre. 1489

Compagnie l'Envers du Décor (Paris)

Performance/production

Comparison of text-based and visual productions. France. 1998. Lang.: Fre. 1939

Compagnons du Saint-Laurent (Montreal, PQ)

Institutions

Analysis of the bulletin of theatre company Les Compagnons du Saint-Laurent. Canada: Montreal, PQ. 1944-1947. Lang.: Fre. 1585

Companhia do Latão (São Paolo)

Performance/production

Review of Brazilian performances of plays by Brecht. Brazil: São Paulo. 1998. Lang.: Ger. 1832

Company

Plays/librettos/scripts

The disintegration of the American dream in works of Stephen Sondheim. USA. 1970-1984. Lang.: Eng. 4397

Competitions

Design/technology

Winners of American College Theatre Festival design competitions. USA. 1998. Lang.: Eng. 279

Competitions — cont'd

Set and costume designer Eduardo Sicangco, judge of SETC design competition. USA: Birmingham, AL. 1998. Lang.: Eng. 292

Institutions

The work of young choreographers at the Councours de Bagnolet. France: Bagnolet. 1998. Lang.: Swe. 891

Account of the eighth international ballet competition. France: Paris. 1998. Lang.: Hun. 1038

The third international Nureyev ballet competition. Hungary: Budapest. 1998. Lang.: Hun. 1044

Report on folk dance festival and competition. Russia: Voskresensk. 1998. Lang.: Rus. 1222

The fourth international singing contest. Hungary: Budapest. 1998. Lang.: Hun. 4461

Performance/production

The biennial Singer of the World contest. UK-Wales: Cardiff. 1997. Lang.: Eng. 4706

Theory/criticism

Winning essay of Critics Institute Competition on *Carriage* by Jerome Hairston. USA. 1998. Lang.: Eng. 3838

Compleat Works of Wllm Shkspr, Abridged, The

SEE ALSO

Complete Works of William Shakespeare (Abridged), The.

Composing

Design/technology

The 1998 TCI awards. USA. 1998. Lang.: Eng. 243

Performance/production

Interview with composer Paul Schmidt. USA: New Haven, CT. 1998. Lang.: Eng. 2660

Composers of Hollywood film scores. USA. 1908-1998. Lang.: Eng. 3957

The theory and practice of scoring a television production. USA. 1998. Lang.: Eng. 4069

Composers and the work of Bertolt Brecht. Germany. 1928-1998. Lang.: Ger. 4297

Giovanni Tamborrino's opera without song. Italy. Lang.: Ita. 4300

Elton John as musical theatre composer. UK-England. 1998. Lang.: Rus. 4371

The songs of George and Ira Gershwin. USA. 1896-1998. Lang.: Eng. 4376

Musical theatre composer Will Marion Cook. USA. 1898-1950. Lang.: Eng. 4378

Arnold Schoenberg's refusal to complete Alban Berg's unfinished opera *Lulu.* Austria. 1935. Lang.: Fre. 4533

The English operas of Stephen Storace. England: London. 1762-1796. Lang.: Eng. 4547

The use of the harpsichord in Stravinskij's opera *The Rake's Progress.* Europe. 1951. Lang.: Eng. 4559

Chronology of the life of composer Jacques Offenbach. France. 1819-1880. Lang.: Fre. 4561

The creation of Massenet's opera *Le Roi de Lahore.* France. 1877. Lang.: Fre. 4568

Offenbach's *Orphée aux Enfers* from two acts to four. France. 1858-1874. Lang.: Fre. 4571

Massenet's revisions to *Manon* for performance by Sybil Sanderson. France. 1885-1903. Lang.: Eng. 4572

Oriental themes in operas and instrumental works of Saint-Saëns. France. 1872-1911. Lang.: Eng. 4576

Analysis of Richard Strauss's opera *Capriccio.* Germany. 1942-1998. Lang.: Eng. 4578

Interview with opera composer Manfred Trojahn. Germany: Munich. 1998. Lang.: Ger. 4582

Life of composer and conductor Alexander Zemlinsky. Germany. 1871-1942. Lang.: Fre. 4594

Analysis of a scene from Beethoven's *Fidelio.* Germany. 1814. Lang.: Eng. 4595

Arnold Schoenberg on composer Alexander Zemlinsky. Germany. 1921. Lang.: Fre. 4604

Analysis of Richard Strauss's *Capriccio.* Germany. 1942. Lang.: Eng. 4606

Composer Matthias Pintscher and his opera *Thomas Chatterton.* Germany. 1990-2001. Lang.: Ger. 4607

A letter from composer Alexander Zemlinsky to Alma Mahler. Germany. 1917. Lang.: Fre. 4613

Analysis of Donizetti's opera *Lucrezia Borgia.* Italy. UK-England. 1797-1998. Lang.: Eng. 4649

Recordings of the different versions of Verdi's *Don Carlos.* Italy. Europe. 1866-1998. Lang.: Eng. 4650

Antonio Salieri and his opera *Falstaff,* recently revived. Italy: Milan. 1799-1998. Lang.: Eng. 4654

Verdi's metrics. Italy. 1813-1901. Lang.: Ita. 4655

The life and work of composer Gaetano Donizetti. Italy. 1797-1848. Lang.: Eng. 4656

Verdi's important mezzo soprano roles, including Azucena in *Il Trovatore.* Italy. 1853. Lang.: Eng. 4661

Obituary for conductor/composer George Lloyd. UK-England. 1913-1998. Lang.: Eng. 4703

Profile of composer Elliott Carter. USA. 1908-1998. Lang.: Eng. 4711

André Previn's opera *A Streetcar Named Desire.* USA: San Francisco. 1998. Lang.: Eng. 4742

Opera composer George Antheil. USA. 1900-1959. Lang.: Eng. 4750

Musical analysis of Gershwin's *Porgy and Bess.* USA. 1937. Lang.: Eng. 4753

Personal recollection of composer Franz Lehár. Austria: Vienna. 1936. Lang.: Swe. 4852

Opera composer Jacques Offenbach. France. 1819-1880. Lang.: Swe. 4854

Léo Delibes as a composer of operetta. France. 1856-1883. Lang.: Fre. 4855

Plays/librettos/scripts

Composer Philip Glass on Beckett's influence on his work. Ireland. France. USA. 1965-1995. Lang.: Eng. 3194

Composer Luciano Berio on Beckett's influence on his work. Ireland. France. Italy. 1965-1985. Lang.: Eng. 3195

Melanie Daiken's musical settings of texts by Samuel Beckett. Ireland. France. 1945-1995. Lang.: Eng. 3201

Composer Giacomo Manzoni and his work *Words by Beckett (Parole da Beckett).* Italy. 1970-1971. Lang.: Eng. 3250

Morton Feldman's musical setting for Samuel Beckett's radio play *Words and Music.* Europe. 1987. Lang.: Eng. 3865

Clarence Barlow's abstract musical setting of a prose text by Samuel Beckett. 1971-1972. Lang.: Eng. 4305

Earl Kim's musical piece *Dead Calm,* based on a text by Samuel Beckett. 1945-1995. Lang.: Eng. 4306

Samuel Beckett's short story *Bing* as adapted by Roger Reynolds and Jean-Yves Bosseur. USA. 1986. Lang.: Eng. 4308

Roger Reynolds' musical settings of texts by Samuel Beckett. USA. 1968-1976. Lang.: Eng. 4309

Panel discussion on contemporary musical theatre. USA: New York, NY. 1998. Lang.: Eng. 4398

Heinz Holliger's operatic adaptation of Samuel Beckett's *What Where.* Europe. 1992. Lang.: Eng. 4768

Marcel Mihalovici's operatic adaptation of *Krapp's Last Tape* by Samuel Beckett. Europe. 1965. Lang.: Eng. 4769

The opera *Neither* by Morton Feldman and Samuel Beckett. Europe. 1976-1977. Lang.: Eng. 4772

Operatic adaptations of Beckett's plays by Heinz Holliger. Europe. 1976-1988. Lang.: Eng. 4776

Composer Wolfgang Fortner's adaptation of *That Time* by Samuel Beckett. Europe. 1974-1977. Lang.: Eng. 4777

Collaboration of composer Jules Massenet and librettist Louis Gallet. France. 1877-1894. Lang.: Fre. 4778

Musical representation of death in Puccini's *Tosca.* Italy. 1900. Lang.: Eng. 4804

Composer Gaetano Donizetti. Italy. Europe. 1835-1848. Lang.: Eng. 4805

Analysis of the opera *Aureliano in Palmira* by Rossini and Romani. Italy. 1813. Lang.: Eng. 4806

Daniel Barenboim and Edward Said on composer Richard Wagner. USA: New York, NY. Germany. 1995. Lang.: Eng. 4826

Computers—administration

Administration

Adelaide Festival Centre Trust's database for tracking economics and cultural impact of events. Australia: Adelaide. 1991-1998. Lang.: Eng. 3

Fundraising on the World Wide Web. USA. 1998. Lang.: Eng. 41

Computers—administration — cont'd

Equity's casting website. USA: New York, NY. 1998. Lang.: Eng. 103
Guide to software for nonprofits. USA. 1998. Lang.: Eng. 118
The importance of maintaining an up-to-date fundraising data base. USA. 1998. Lang.: Eng. 130

Computers—choreography
Performance/production
Software for choreography. USA. 1998. Lang.: Eng. 984

Computers—design/technology
Design/technology
Essay on lighting technology and the computer. Sweden. USA. 1992-1997. Lang.: Swe. 224
Survey of lighting-design software manufacturers. USA. 1998. Lang.: Eng. 245
Review of new lighting software. USA. 1998. Lang.: Eng. 273
The Datatron control system for visual projections. USA. 1998. Lang.: Eng. 304
Computer graphics as a lighting design tool. USA: Lawrence, KS. 1998. Lang.: Eng. 311
Recommendation for inexpensive digital noise-reduction software. USA. 1998. Lang.: Eng. 319
Comparison of computer-assisted and traditional scenery and lighting design. USA. 1980-1987. Lang.: Eng. 324
Virtual reality technology for set design. USA: Lawrence, KS. 1997. Lang.: Eng. 1562
Lighting design for Joe Dante's film *Small Soldiers*. USA. 1998. Lang.: Eng. 3914
Computer-aided design in TV production. USA: Hollywood, CA. 1998. Lang.: Eng. 4051
Training
The use of computer animation techniques in design training. USA: Athens, GA. 1988-1998. Lang.: Eng. 878

Computers—ethernet
Design/technology
Ethernet computer connections between lighting systems of two theatres at Herberger Theatre Center. USA: Phoenix, AZ. 1998. Lang.: Eng. 294

Computers—internet
Administration
Fundraising on the World Wide Web. USA. 1998. Lang.: Eng. 41
The launch of the Equity website. USA: New York, NY. 1998. Lang.: Eng. 78
The publicizing of financial information about nonprofit arts organizations. USA. 1998. Lang.: Eng. 137
Design/technology
The application of new media for theatrical use. Europe. 1998. Lang.: Ger. 176
Recommendation for inexpensive digital noise-reduction software. USA. 1998. Lang.: Eng. 319
Institutions
Directory of Italian theatre websites. Italy. 1998. Lang.: Eng. 1675
Performance/production
Performance artist Leslie Hill's *Push the Boat Out*. UK-England: London. USA. 1995-1997. Lang.: Eng. 4245

Computers—performance/production
Performance/production
Barry Edwards on his theatrical movement work with OPTIK. UK-England: London. 1997-1998. Lang.: Eng. 609
Dancer Susan Kozel on performing in Paul Sermon's *Telematic Dreaming*. Netherlands: Amsterdam. 1997. Lang.: Eng. 956
Lois Weaver's *Faith and Dancing* and the CD-ROM in interactive performance. UK-England. USA. 1996. Lang.: Eng. 971
Mixed media artist Ebon Fisher. USA. 1998. Lang.: Eng. 4045
Plays/librettos/scripts
Clarence Barlow's abstract musical setting of a prose text by Samuel Beckett. 1971-1972. Lang.: Eng. 4305
The *castrato*, the contralto, and the film *Farinelli*. France. Italy. 1994. Lang.: Eng. 4787
Theory/criticism
Cyberspace as performance site. North America. 1998. Lang.: Eng. 4048

Computers—research/historiography
Plays/librettos/scripts
Description of a Web site devoted to *Los españoles en Chile* by Francisco Ganzalez de Busto. Spain. 1665-1998. Lang.: Eng. 3366
Research/historiography
The use of 'Literature Online' for editing and attribution studies. UK-England. 1998. Lang.: Eng. 825
The THEATRON theatre history project. Europe. 1998. Lang.: Dut. 3796
The Shakespeare Interactive Research Group. USA: Cambridge, MA. 1991-1997. Lang.: Eng. 3799

Comsomol Theatre
SEE
Teat'r im. Leninskogo Komsomola.

Comus
Plays/librettos/scripts
Puritanism and Milton's *Comus*. England. 1634-1635. Lang.: Eng. 4207

Comyn, Annabelle
Performance/production
Collection of newspaper reviews by London theatre critics. UK-England: London. 1998. Lang.: Eng. 2549

Condé, Maryse
Plays/librettos/scripts
Analysis of plays by Maryse Condé. Guadeloupe. 1965-1996. Lang.: Eng. 3186

Condon, Bill
Basic theatrical documents
Screenplay of *Gods and Monsters* by Bill Condon. USA. 1998. Lang.: Eng. 3882
Design/technology
Production design for Bill Condon's film *Gods and Monsters*. USA: Hollywood, CA. 1998. Lang.: Eng. 3908
Plays/librettos/scripts
Interview with film-maker Bill Condon. USA. 1998. Lang.: Eng. 4021

Conduct of Life, The
Plays/librettos/scripts
Theatrical space in plays of Maria Irene Fornes. USA. 1977-1989. Lang.: Eng. 3571

Conducting
Administration
Conductor Leonard dePaur, winner of the Paul Robeson Award. USA: New York, NY. 1910-1998. Lang.: Eng. 104
Performance/production
Tenor and artistic director of Washington Opera Plácido Domingo. 1941-1998. Lang.: Eng. 4512
Conductor Riccardo Chailly on composer Alexander Zemlinsky. Europe. 1998. Lang.: Fre. 4551
Interview with conductor Esa-Pekka Salonen. Finland. 1998. Lang.: Eng. 4560
Interview with Tamás Pál, conductor and musical director of Szeged National Theatre. Hungary: Szeged. 1998. Lang.: Hun. 4622
Conductor Andrew Davis. UK-England. USA. 1998. Lang.: Eng. 4704
Heinz Fricke, music director of Washington Opera. USA: Washington, DC. 1993-1998. Lang.: Eng. 4734
Interview with conductor Nicholas McGegan. USA. UK-England. 1998. Lang.: Eng. 4740
Opera conductor Patrick Summers. USA. 1990-1998. Lang.: Eng. 4755

Conduit (Portland, OR)
Performance/production
Mary Oslund and Gregg Bielemeier of Conduit. USA: Portland, OR. 1995-1998. Lang.: Eng. 1333

Conference of the Birds, The
SEE
Aves.

Conferences
Administration
Symposium on the position of young theatre professionals. Netherlands. 1998. Lang.: Dut. 1387
Design/technology
Report from the meeting of Asociación Cubana de Ingenieros y Técnicos de los Artes Escénicas (ACITAE). Cuba: Havana. 1998. Lang.: Swe. 171
Account of ACTSAFE conference on theatre safety. France: Paris. 1998. Lang.: Swe. 181
Impressions from the Salon de Théâtre. France: Paris. 1998. Lang.: Ger. 183
Survey of Light Fair. Germany: Hannover. 1998. Lang.: Eng. 186
OISTAT meeting on technician training. Netherlands: Amsterdam. 1998. Lang.: Swe. 206
Survey of NoTT98 at Oslo. Norway: Oslo. 1998. Lang.: Nor. 210
Lighting operators' conference regarding controls at Dansens Hus. Sweden: Stockholm. 1998. Lang.: Swe. 223
The combined conference and fair, Nordisk TeaterTeknik (NoTT). Sweden: Stockholm, Gothenburg. 1983-1998. Lang.: Swe. 227

Conferences — cont'd

Exhibits at PLASA show. UK-England: London. 1998. Lang.: Eng. 229
Report on PLASA trade show. UK-England: London. 1998. Lang.: Eng. 230
Report on PLASA light and sound equipment trade show. UK-England: London. 1998. Lang.: Swe. 236
Calendar of events at LDI98 trade show. USA: Las Vegas, NV. 1998. Lang.: Eng. 240
List of exhibitors at LDI convention. USA: Phoenix, AZ. 1998. Lang.: Eng. 244
Workshops of LDI expo. USA: Phoenix, AZ. 1998. Lang.: Eng. 248
The 1998 USITT expo. USA: Long Beach, CA. 1998. Lang.: Eng. 251
Report on lighting designers' conference. USA: New York, NY. 1997. Lang.: Eng. 254
Job-hunting advice for costumers and theatrical professionals. USA. 1998. Lang.: Eng. 259
Preview of Lightfair seminar. USA: Las Vegas, NV. 1998. Lang.: Eng. 278
Winners of American College Theatre Festival design competitions. USA. 1998. Lang.: Eng. 279
NSCA sound products and technology trade show. USA: Las Vegas, NV. 1998. Lang.: Eng. 288
Report on AES trade show. USA: San Francisco, CA. 1998. Lang.: Eng. 289
Set and costume designer Eduardo Sicangco, judge of SETC design competition. USA: Birmingham, AL. 1998. Lang.: Eng. 292
Report on annual USITT conference. USA: Long Beach, CA. 1998. Lang.: Eng. 302
Preview of LDI convention. USA: Phoenix, AZ. 1998. Lang.: Eng. 305
Lighting designer John Osborne. USA. 1998. Lang.: Eng. 310
Former student on learning lighting design. USA: Las Vegas, NV. 1997. Lang.: Eng. 316
Lighting designer Tharon Musser. USA. 1965-1998. Lang.: Eng. 326

Institutions
Festivals of theatre by and for youth. Germany: Dresden, Stuttgart. 1998. Lang.: Ger. 349
Festival of Hungarian-language theatres abroad. Hungary: Kisvárda. 1998. Lang.: Hun. 357
Report on Vachtangov School conference. Russia: Moscow. 1990-1998. Lang.: Rus. 380
Report on a seminar on mime, illusionism, *commedia* and clowning in dance. Sweden: Stockholm. 1998. Lang.: Swe. 386
Photographic essay on SETC convention. USA: Birmingham, AL. 1998. Lang.: Eng. 389
Program of the Hungarian Centre of OISTAT's conference. USA: Pittsburgh, PA. 1997. Lang.: Hun. 392
Convention of the Southeastern Theatre Conference. USA: Birmingham, AL. 1998. Lang.: Eng. 402
Preview of SETC convention. USA: Birmingham, AL. 1998. Lang.: Eng. 405
Report on biennial dance conference. Sweden: Stockholm. 1998. Lang.: Swe. 902
Report on the Cairo festival and symposia on women's theatre. Egypt: Cairo. 1997. Lang.: Eng. 1597
Ibsen Society of America's celebration of the centennial of *Når vi døde vågner (When We Dead Awaken)*. USA: New York, NY. 1998. Lang.: Eng. 1755
Report on the second National Black Theatre Summit. USA: Atlanta, GA. 1998. Lang.: Eng. 1773
Report on National Black Theatre Summit. USA: Dartmouth, NH. 1998. Lang.: Eng. 1782
Playwright Garland Lee on the National Black Theatre Summit. USA: Dartmouth, NH. 1998. Lang.: Eng. 1786
Report on Academy of String Puppetry Conference. USA: Storrs, CT. 1998. Lang.: Eng. 4883

Performance spaces
Conference on the need for new dance performance space. UK-Scotland: Glasgow. 1998. Lang.: Eng. 910

Performance/production
'The Speaking Body' museum installation, site of theatre anthropology seminars. Austria: Vienna. Switzerland: Zurich. 1996-1998. Lang.: Eng. 493
Account of the 1998 International European Theatre Meeting. Europe. 1990-1998. Lang.: Eng. 522
The symposium on acting at Theaterfestival. Netherlands: Amsterdam. 1998. Lang.: Dut. 562
Conference on African-American theatre convened by playwright August Wilson. USA: Hanover, NH. 1998. Lang.: Eng. 659
Director Gerald Freedman on 'real' theatre. USA: Birmingham, AL. 1998. Lang.: Eng. 684
Seminar on auditions for choreographers for Resolution dance festival. UK-England: London. Belgium: Brussels. 1998. Lang.: Swe. 1314
Report on international conference devoted to the work of Vladimir Vysockij. Russia: Moscow. 1998. Lang.: Rus. 2313
Indian theatre in South Africa. South Africa, Republic of. 1900-1998. Lang.: Eng. 2356
Conference on theatre for children ages 2-4. Sweden: Stockholm. 1998. Lang.: Swe. 2368
Report on ventriloquist's convention. USA: Las Vegas, NV. 1998. Lang.: Eng. 4143
Hans Neuenfels's production of Meyerbeer's *Le Prophète*. Austria: Vienna. 1998. Lang.: Swe. 4530
Stage fright and other psychological problems of singers and musicians. Germany: Berlin. 1998. Lang.: Swe. 4603
The influence of *Sesame Street*. USA. 1968-1998. Lang.: Eng. 4923

Plays/librettos/scripts
Playwright Romulus Linney's address to SETC convention. USA: Birmingham, AL. 1998. Lang.: Eng. 3517
Account of National Black Theatre Summit. USA: Hanover, NH. 1998. Lang.: Eng. 3523
Women playwrights' addresses to the Women's Project conference. USA. 1997. Lang.: Eng. 3589
Playwright Tina Howe on gender expectations on playwrights. USA: New York, NY. 1980-1997. Lang.: Eng. 3614

Research/historiography
New approaches to theatre studies and performance analysis. UK-England: Bristol. 1998. Lang.: Eng. 826
Symposium on Dutch dance history and historiography. Netherlands. 1990-1998. Lang.: Dut. 1002

Theory/criticism
Theatre criticism as it is taught to students. USA: Birmingham, AL. 1998. Lang.: Eng. 864
Report on *kabuki* conference. Japan: Tokyo. 1996. Lang.: Eng. 1367
Report on a seminar for young theatre critics. Canada: Quebec, PQ. 1998. Lang.: Swe. 3809
Report on congress of International Association of Theatre Critics. Finland: Helsinki. 1996. Lang.: Eng. 3816
Dutch theatre criticism. Netherlands. 1998. Lang.: Dut. 3825
Report on the Eighth National Review of Live Art. UK-England. 1988. Lang.: Eng. 4268

Confessional, Le (Confessional, The)
Performance/production
Cinematic work of director Robert Lepage. Canada. 1995-1998. Lang.: Fre. 3928

Confidential Clerk, The
Performance/production
Collection of newspaper reviews by London theatre critics. UK-England: London. 1998. Lang.: Eng. 2474

Congdon, Constance
Performance/production
Collection of newspaper reviews by London theatre critics. UK-England: London. 1998. Lang.: Eng. 2566

Congreve, William
Plays/librettos/scripts
Motherhood in Restoration comedy. England. 1642-1729. Lang.: Eng. 2864
Confessional theatre in the Restoration period. England. 1690-1700. Lang.: Eng. 2991

Conlon, James
Performance/production
Conductor James Conlon on his production of Zemlinsky's *Der Zwerg*. France: Paris. 1998. Lang.: Fre. 4562

Connelly Theatre (New York, NY)
Design/technology
Set design for Chain Lightning Theatre's production of *Beyond the Horizon* by Eugene O'Neill. USA: New York, NY. 1998. Lang.: Eng. 1551

Connery, Sean
Relation to other fields
Politics, knighthood, and actor Sean Connery. UK. 1998. Lang.: Eng. 4036
Conrad, Tony
Audience
The prompting of epileptic seizures by film. 1960-1988. Lang.: Eng. 3876
Conservatoire d'art dramatique de Québec
Institutions
Training methods of the Conservatoire d'art dramatique de Québec. Canada: Quebec, PQ. 1998. Lang.: Fre. 1578
Construction, puppet
Design/technology
Use of a balance line in marionette construction. USA. 1998. Lang.: Eng. 4918
Construction, theatre
Performance spaces
The construction of a theatre for *Beauty and the Beast*. Germany: Stuttgart. 1997. Lang.: Ger. 444
The construction of the Grand Théâtre de Genève. Switzerland: Geneva. 1984-1998. Lang.: Ger. 459
Contemporary Theatre, A (Seattle, WA)
Performance spaces
Seattle's new and renovated theatres. USA: Seattle, WA. 1998. Lang.: Eng. 475
Contes d'Hoffmann, Les
Performance/production
Background material on Metropolitan Opera radio broadcast performances. USA: New York, NY. 1998. Lang.: Eng. 4713
Contes pour l'oeil avide (Stories for the Avid Eye)
Plays/librettos/scripts
Mixed media in theatre productions of Carole Nadeau. Canada: Quebec, PQ, Montreal, PQ. 1998. Lang.: Fre. 4047
Conti, Tom
Basic theatrical documents
Text of *Jesus, My Boy* by John Dowie. UK-England. 1998. Lang.: Eng. 1474
Performance/production
Profile of actor Tom Conti. UK-England. 1998. Lang.: Eng. 2629
Contracts
Administration
Negotiations between US and Canadian Equity. USA. Canada. 1998. Lang.: Eng. 54
Report on Equity's Off-Broadway contract agreement. USA. 1998. Lang.: Eng. 60
Equity's new contract with East West Players. USA: Los Angeles, CA. 1998. Lang.: Eng. 62
Equity's business theatre contract. USA: New York, NY. 1998. Lang.: Eng. 64
Equity agreement with Second City. USA: Chicago, IL, Detroit, MI. 1998. Lang.: Eng. 66
Jekyll and Hyde restaurants sign Equity contract. USA: New York, NY. 1998. Lang.: Eng. 69
Issues of concern to Equity members in current Broadway shows. USA: New York, NY. 1998. Lang.: Eng. 77
Negotiations with Equity dinner theatres. USA: New York, NY. 1998. Lang.: Eng. 79
John Holly, Western Regional Director of Equity. USA: New York, NY. 1998. Lang.: Eng. 80
Complaints against an Equity Councillor and the 1998 Council election. USA: New York, NY. 1998. Lang.: Eng. 87
Equity's approval of a contract for the Chicago area. USA: Chicago, IL. 1998. Lang.: Eng. 98
Equity's approval of Cabaret and Small Professional Theatre contracts. USA: New York, NY. 1998. Lang.: Eng. 108
Equity's contract with Resident Musical Theatre Association. USA. 1998. Lang.: Eng. 4319
Marketing strategies for puppetry in film and TV. USA. 1998. Lang.: Eng. 4863
Contrast, The
Performance/production
Collection of newspaper reviews by London theatre critics. UK-England: London. 1998. Lang.: Eng. 2507
Conversations with My Agent
Performance/production
Collection of newspaper reviews by London theatre critics. UK-England: London. 1998. Lang.: Eng. 2517
Conway, Jon
Performance/production
Collection of newspaper reviews by London theatre critics. UK-England: London. 1998. Lang.: Eng. 2526
Interview with Shane Ritchie and Jon Conway about the musical *Boogie Nights*. UK-England. 1998. Lang.: Eng. 4370
Cooder, Ry
Performance/production
Productions of Szegedi Kortárs Balett. Hungary: Szeged. 1998. Lang.: Hun. 1102
Coogan, Steve
Performance/production
Collection of newspaper reviews by London theatre critics. UK-England: London. 1998. Lang.: Eng. 2513
Cook Dems
Performance/production
The kitchen in performance art of Bobby Baker and Jeanne Goosen. UK-England. South Africa, Republic of. 1990-1992. Lang.: Eng. 4243
Cook, Caroline Burns
Performance/production
Collection of newspaper reviews by London theatre critics. UK-England: London. 1998. Lang.: Eng. 2517
Cook, Jonathan Paul
Performance/production
Director Jonathan Paul Cook on developing talent in an ensemble. Denmark. 1997-1998. Lang.: Dan. 1888
Cook, Will Marion
Performance/production
Musical theatre composer Will Marion Cook. USA. 1898-1950. Lang.: Eng. 4378
Cooke, Dominic
Performance/production
Collection of newspaper reviews by London theatre critics. UK-England: London. 1998. Lang.: Eng. 2454
Collection of newspaper reviews by London theatre critics. UK-England: London. 1998. Lang.: Eng. 2555
Cool Heat Urban Beat
Performance/production
Collection of newspaper reviews by London theatre critics. UK-England. 1998. Lang.: Eng. 2497
Cooney, Ray
Basic theatrical documents
French translation of *Funny Money* by Ray Cooney. UK-England. France. 1995-1997. Lang.: Fre. 1473
Coonrod, Karin
Design/technology
Costume design for *Christmas with the Ivanovs*, CSC Repertory. USA: New York, NY. 1998. Lang.: Eng. 1533
CoOPERAtive Opera Company of New York (New York, NY)
Institutions
Profile of CoOPERAtive Opera Company of New York. USA: New York, NY. 1995-1998. Lang.: Eng. 4487
Cope, Louise
Performance/production
Collection of newspaper reviews by London theatre critics. UK-England: London. 1998. Lang.: Eng. 2454
Copeau, Jacques
Performance/production
The rise of the modern Shakespearean director. Europe. 1878-1995. Lang.: Eng. 1911
Director Jacques Copeau and his theatrical aesthetic. France. 1913-1920. Lang.: Eng. 1941
Interview with Marie-Hélène Dasté, daughter of Jacques Copeau. France: Paris. 1913-1992. Lang.: Eng. 4089
Commedia dell'arte and twentieth-century theatre. Europe. 1860-1950. Lang.: Eng. 4187
Copelin, David
Performance/production
Theatre Magazine's anniversary issue. USA. 1968-1998. Lang.: Eng. 617
Copeman, Peter
Performance/production
Contemporary Asian-Australian theatre. Australia. 1990-1998. Lang.: Eng. 488
Copenhagen
Performance/production
Collection of newspaper reviews by London theatre critics. UK-England: London. 1998. Lang.: Eng. 2501
Copley, John
Performance/production
Evaluation of video performances of Donizetti's operas. Europe. USA. 1980-1998. Lang.: Eng. 4557

Copperfield, David
Performance/production
The theory and practice of stage magic. 1998. Lang.: Rus. 4274
Coppola, Francis Ford
Plays/librettos/scripts
Gangster film and Shakespearean tragedy. USA. 1971-1991. Lang.: Eng. 4009
Opera in American gangster films. USA. 1932-1990. Lang.: Eng. 4023
Copyright
Administration
Round-table on author's rights. Hungary. 1990-1998. Lang.: Hun. 16
The legal battle over copyright of the musical *Rent*. USA: New York, NY. 1998. Lang.: Eng. 4321
The settlement of a copyright case regarding the musical *Rent*. USA: New York, NY. 1998. Lang.: Eng. 4322
Plays/librettos/scripts
The playwright and the play development process. Canada. 1998. Lang.: Eng. 2811
Brecht, copyright, and contemporary perceptions. Germany: Berlin. 1898-1998. Lang.: Ger. 3153
Coq d'Or, Le
Plays/librettos/scripts
Operas of Dargomyžskij and Rimskij-Korsakov on texts of Puškin. Russia. 1799-1869. Lang.: Rus. 4815
Corbiau, Gérard
Plays/librettos/scripts
The *castrato*, the contralto, and the film *Farinelli*. France. Italy. 1994. Lang.: Eng. 4787
Cording, John
Performance/production
Collection of newspaper reviews by London theatre critics. UK-England: London. 1998. Lang.: Eng. 2457
Corigliano, John
Plays/librettos/scripts
Operatic realizations of Beaumarchais' character Rosina. Europe. North America. 1784-1991. Lang.: Eng. 4773
Coriolanus
Performance/production
Philip Voss on his role in *Coriolanus* at RSC. UK-England: London, Stratford. 1994. Lang.: Eng. 2643
Semiotic analysis of Peter Hall's National Theatre production of Shakespeare's *Coriolanus*. UK-England. 1985. Lang.: Eng. 2647
Plays/librettos/scripts
The interaction of other characters with Shakespeare's tragic heroes. England. 1590-1613. Lang.: Eng. 3037
Corke, Gareth
Performance/production
Collection of newspaper reviews by London theatre critics. UK-England: London. 1998. Lang.: Eng. 2512
Corker
Plays/librettos/scripts
Analysis of *Corker* by Wendy Lill. Canada: Halifax, NS. 1994-1998. Lang.: Eng. 2836
Interview with playwright/MP Wendy Lill. USA: Halifax, NS. 1997-1998. Lang.: Eng. 3705
Corneille, Pierre
Institutions
Impressions from the Avignon theatre festival. France: Avignon. 1998. Lang.: Ger. 1612
Plays/librettos/scripts
The character Medea in European drama. Europe. 450 B.C.-1998 A.D. Lang.: Ger. 3063
Analysis of plays by Pierre Corneille. France. 1643-1652. Lang.: Eng. 3112
Theory/criticism
The plays of Corneille and catharsis through admiration. France. 1651-1653. Lang.: Eng. 3820
Cornell, Katharine
Performance/production
The marriage of theatre artists Katharine Cornell and Guthrie McClintic. USA. 1893-1974. Lang.: Eng. 634
Relation to other fields
Fitzroy Davis's theatre novel *Quicksilver*. USA. 1930-1940. Lang.: Eng. 810
Coronation of Poppea, The
SEE
Incoronazione di Poppea, L'.
Corroboree
Performance/production
Performance space in Aboriginal *corroboree*. Australia. 800 B.C.-1988 A.D. Lang.: Eng. 487
Corsaro, Frank
Design/technology
Maurice Sendak's set design for *Hänsel und Gretel*, Canadian Opera Company. Canada: Toronto, ON. 1998. Lang.: Eng. 4427
Corsetti, Giorgio Barberio
Performance/production
Multimedia and the productions of Giorgio Barberio Corsetti. Italy: Rome, Milan. 1985-1998. Lang.: Eng. 4043
Cortez, Joaquím
Performance/production
Performances of Joaquím Cortez's flamenco troupe and the Ballets Africains of Guinea. UK-England: London. 1997. Lang.: Hun. 1238
Corthron, Kia
Plays/librettos/scripts
Interview with playwright Kia Corthon. USA. 1998. Lang.: Eng. 3696
Cortigiana, La (Courtesan, The)
Plays/librettos/scripts
The comedies of Pietro Aretino. Italy. 1534-1556. Lang.: Eng. 3251
Così
Plays/librettos/scripts
Australian plays about the war in Vietnam. Australia. 1990-1998. Lang.: Eng. 2776
Cosí è (se vi pare) (Right You Are, If You Think You Are)
Plays/librettos/scripts
Yearbook of Pirandello studies. Italy. 1589-1926. Lang.: Eng. 3247
Così fan tutte
Performance/production
Baritone György Melis and the performance in celebration of his 75th birthday. Hungary. 1923-1998. Lang.: Hun. 4633
Cosier, E. David
Design/technology
Set design for Joseph Chaikin's production of two one-acts by Arthur Miller. USA: New york, NY. 1998. Lang.: Eng. 1532
Cosmic Illusions (Amsterdam)
Institutions
Interview with founders of Dutch multicultural group Cosmic Illusions. Netherlands: Amsterdam. Netherlands Antilles. 1988. Lang.:Eng. 1679
Cossotto, Fiorenza
Performance/production
Singers' approaches to the title role in Bizet's *Carmen*. 1875-1998. Lang.: Eng. 4502
Costi, Angela
Basic theatrical documents
Text of *Panayiotis* by Angela Costi. Australia. 1997. Lang.: Eng. 1406
Costner, Kevin
Plays/librettos/scripts
Comparison of film and television versions of *Dances With Wolves*. USA. 1990-1993. Lang.: Eng. 4022
Costuming
Design/technology
A staged costume exhibition. 1998. Lang.: Swe. 167
Costume designer Mara Blumenthal. Canada. 1992-1998. Lang.: Eng. 170
Costume designs of Kateřina Štefková and Zuzana Štefunková. Czech Republic. 1990-1998. Lang.: Eng, Fre. 172
Costume practice and training in the U.S. and eastern Europe. Europe. USA. 1945-1998. Lang.: Ger. 177
Interview with costume designer Maija Pekkanen. Finland. 1998. Lang.: Fin. 179
Impressions from the Salon de Théâtre. France: Paris. 1998. Lang.: Ger. 183
The work of costume designer Robert Ebeling. Germany. 1995-1998. Lang.: Ger. 185
Careers in technical theatre. Germany. Austria. 1998. Lang.: Ger. 189
Scenographer and now director Klaus Noack. Germany. 1953. Lang.: Ger. 190
Costume designer Margit Bárdy. Hungary. Germany: Munich. 1929-1997. Lang.: Hun. 193
Set and costume designs of Péter Makai. Hungary. 1957-1991. Lang.: Hun. 194
Profiles of young theatrical designers. Netherlands. 1990-1998. Lang.: Dut. 207

Costuming — cont'd

Avant-garde Russian women artist/designers. Russia. USSR. 1880-1949. Lang.: Eng. 214
Dancer Isadora Duncan's influence on the designs of Edward Gordon Craig. UK-England. 1904-1905. Lang.: Eng. 237
Guide to theatrical design manufacturers and equipment. USA. 1998. Lang.: Eng. 241
The 1998 USITT expo. USA: Long Beach, CA. 1998. Lang.: Eng. 251
Professional theatrical designers on design training. USA. 1998. Lang.: Eng. 252
Costumer Paul Reinhardt. USA. 1998. Lang.: Eng. 253
Job-hunting advice for costumers and theatrical professionals. USA. 1998. Lang.: Eng. 259
Costume designer Jeanne Button. USA. 1965-1998. Lang.: Eng. 260
Costumer Kermit Love. USA. 1935-1998. Lang.: Eng. 271
Costume designs by Irene Sharaff. USA. 1933-1976. Lang.: Eng. 277
Costume designer Robert Mackintosh. USA. 1926-1998. Lang.: Eng. 284
Constructing collapsible changing booths for actors. USA. 1998. Lang.: Eng. 295
Creating stage jewelry from polymer clays. USA. 1998. Lang.: Eng. 306
Students' recreation of paintings on stage. USA: Huntington, WV. 1996-1997. Lang.: Eng. 313
Costume designer Catherine Zuber. USA. 1998. Lang.: Eng. 315
Creativity and beauty in theatrical design. USA. 1998. Lang.: Eng. 322
Index to *Technical Brief* volumes 11-17. USA. 1998. Lang.: Eng. 323
Rapid on-stage costume changes in dance. Russia. Sweden. Japan. 1840-1998. Lang.: Swe. 889
Catalogue of an exhibition devoted to choreography of Diaghilev. Russia: St. Petersburg. 1998. Lang.: Rus. 1029
Technical designs for Matthew Bourne's productions of ballets by Čajkovskij and Prokofjév. UK-England: London. 1998. Lang.: Eng. 1031
Costume design for the ballet *Cyrano de Bergerac*. USA: San Francisco, CA. 1998. Lang.: Eng. 1032
Set and costume designer Frank Leimbach and his work with choreographers. Germany. 1991-1998. Lang.: Ger. 1247
Design concept for Ralph Lemon's dance piece *Geography* at BAM. USA: New York, NY. 1998. Lang.: Eng. 1248
Costume designer Isabelle Larivière. Canada: Quebec, PQ. 1994-1995. Lang.: Fre. 1514
The experience of a costumer from Suomen Kansallisteatteri at Stockholms Stadsteatern. Finland: Helsinki. Sweden: Stockholm. 1996-1998. Lang.: Swe. 1519
The representation of history through costume in productions of the Comédie-Française. France: Paris. 1815-1830. Lang.: Eng. 1520
Set and costume design for *The Spanish Tragedy* at RSC. UK-England: London. 1998. Lang.: Eng. 1525
Costume design for *Christmas with the Ivanovs*, CSC Repertory. USA: New York, NY. 1998. Lang.: Eng. 1533
Costume design for Feydeau's *A Flea in Her Ear (La Puce à l'Oreille)*, Roundabout Theatre Company. USA: New York, NY. 1998. Lang.: Eng. 1537
Costume designs for Oregon Shakespeare Festival productions. USA: Ashland, OR. 1998. Lang.: Eng. 1543
Costume designer Catherine Zuber. USA. 1998. Lang.: Eng. 1549
Design concept for Amy Freed's *The Psychic Life of Savages*, Wilma Theatre. USA: Philadelphia, PA. 1998. Lang.: Eng. 1555
The design concept for Nicholas Hytner's production of Shakespeare's *Twelfth Night*. USA: New York, NY. 1998. Lang.: Eng. 1556
Costumes for the film *Welcome to Woop Woop*. Australia. 1998. Lang.: Eng. 3899
Technical designs for Stanley Tucci's film *The Impostors*. USA. 1998. Lang.: Eng. 3901
Film design work of Tony Walton. USA. 1965-1998. Lang.: Eng. 3902
Costuming for the film *Mr. Magoo*. USA: Hollywood, CA. 1998. Lang.: Eng. 3903
Production design for Gary Ross's film *Pleasantville*. USA: Hollywood, CA. 1998. Lang.: Eng. 3909
Design awards for the TV mini-series *Merlin*. USA: Pasadena, CA. 1998. Lang.: Eng. 4052
Costumes for a masked ball scene in the TV series *Another World*. USA. 1998. Lang.: Eng. 4053
Geraldo Andrew Vieira, carnival costumer and performer. Trinidad and Tobago. 1952-1996. Lang.: Eng. 4160
Costume design for a new version of *Peter Pan* at Children's Theatre Company. USA: Minneapolis, MN. 1998. Lang.: Eng. 4330
Technical designs for *The Scarlet Pimpernel* directed by Robert Longbottom. USA: New York, NY. 1998. Lang.: Eng. 4331
Costume design for *Dames at Sea*, Marine Memorial Theatre. USA: San Francisco, CA. 1998. Lang.: Eng. 4332
Costume design for revival of *As Thousands Cheer* by Drama Dept. USA: New York, NY. 1998. Lang.: Eng. 4333
Technical designs for *Ragtime* at the Ford Center. USA: New York, NY. 1998. Lang.: Eng. 4338
Technical designs for the Broadway production of *The Lion King*. USA: New York, NY. 1998. Lang.: Eng. 4342
Technical designs for Sam Mendes' production of *Cabaret*. USA: New York, NY. 1998. Lang.: Eng. 4343
Geogre Tabori's production of Mozart's *Die Zauberflöte* in a circus ring. Germany: Berlin. 1998. Lang.: Ger. 4428
Herbert Wernicke's set and costume designs for his own production of Strauss's *Elektra*. Germany: Munich. 1998. Lang.: Eng. 4429
Profile of costume designer Tivadar Márk. Hungary. 1908-1998. Lang.: Hun. 4432
Set and costume design for *Patience and Sarah* at Lincoln Center. USA: New York, NY. 1998. Lang.: Eng. 4440
Set and costume design for San Francisco Opera productions. USA: San Francisco, CA. 1998. Lang.: Eng. 4443

Performance spaces
The construction of a theatre for *Beauty and the Beast*. Germany: Stuttgart. 1997. Lang.: Ger. 444

Performance/production
Representation of the historical past on the French stage. France. 1810-1820. Lang.: Eng. 527
History of Korean dance. Korea. 1600-1985. Lang.: Eng. 954
Director, costumer, and mask-maker Julie Taymor. USA. 1980-1998. Lang.: Eng. 2685
The language of costume in a video production of Caryl Churchill's *Top Girls*. UK-England. 1982-1991. Lang.: Eng. 4065
Representations of regional identity in music hall. UK-England. 1880-1914. Lang.: Eng. 4132
A painting of *commedia dell'arte* performer Tiberio Fiorilli. Italy. 1625-1700. Lang.: Eng. 4190
Guide to home puppet theatre. 1998. Lang.: Rus. 4884

Plays/librettos/scripts
Description of a Web site devoted to *Los españoles en Chile* by Francisco Ganzalez de Busto. Spain. 1665-1998. Lang.: Eng. 3366
Interview with Peter Minshall, creator of theatre pieces and carnival performances. Trinidad and Tobago: Port of Spain. 1974-1997. Lang.: Eng. 4172
Power, gender, and race in *The Masque of Blackness* by Ben Jonson. England. 1605-1611. Lang.: Eng. 4208
The design and authorship of *The Essex House Masque*. England. 1621. Lang.: Eng. 4209

Relation to other fields
Analysis of anti-theatricalism. England. 1579-1642. 726

Theory/criticism
Hungarian translation of Pëtr Bogatyrëv's essay on the costume as sign. USSR. 1893-1971. Lang.: Hun. 871

Côté, Lorraine

Plays/librettos/scripts
Interview with playwright Michel Vinaver. Canada: Quebec, PQ. 1969-1998. Lang.: Fre. 2831

Cottesloe Theatre (London)

Design/technology
Set design for Tennessee Williams' *Not About Nightingales* at the National. UK-England: London. 1998. Lang.: Eng. 1526

Performance/production
Collection of newspaper reviews by London theatre critics. UK-England: London. 1998. Lang.: Eng. 2435
Collection of newspaper reviews by London theatre critics. UK-England: London. 1998. Lang.: Eng. 2461
Collection of newspaper reviews by London theatre critics. UK-England: London. 1998. Lang.: Eng. 2471

Cottesloe Theatre (London) — cont'd

Collection of newspaper reviews by London theatre critics. UK-England: London. 1998. Lang.: Eng. 2501
Collection of newspaper reviews by London theatre critics. UK-England: London. 1998. Lang.: Eng. 2514
Collection of newspaper reviews by London theatre critics. UK-England: London. 1998. Lang.: Eng. 2540
Collection of newspaper reviews by London theatre critics. UK-England: London. 1998. Lang.: Eng. 2567
Plays/librettos/scripts
Interview with playwright Jonathan Harvey. UK-England. 1998. Lang.: Eng. 3472

Cottis, David
Performance/production
Collection of newspaper reviews by London theatre critics. UK-England: London. 1998. Lang.: Eng. 2576

Coulbois, Jean-Claude
Performance/production
Jean-Claude Coulbois on filming theatrical productions. Canada: Montreal, PQ. 1996-1998. Lang.: Fre. 1839

Counsellor-at-Law
Plays/librettos/scripts
Analysis of *Counsellor-at-Law* by Elmer Rice. USA. 1931. Lang.: Eng. 3712

Count Dracula
Design/technology
Magical stage effects in 'vampire' plays. USA. 1820-1977. Lang.: Eng. 1548

Counter Offence
Plays/librettos/scripts
Political community theatre by South Indian emigrants. Canada: Toronto, ON, Montreal, PQ. India. 1984-1998. Lang.: Eng. 2821

Country Cousin, The
Plays/librettos/scripts
The development and casting of Booth Tarkington's *The Country Cousin*. USA. 1921. Lang.: Eng. 3699

Country Mouse and the City Mouse, The
Basic theatrical documents
Text of *The Country Mouse and the City Mouse* by Robert Charles Lunde. USA. 1986. Lang.: Eng. 1495

Country Wife, The
Performance/production
Collection of newspaper reviews by London theatre critics. UK-England: London. 1998. Lang.: Eng. 2481

Couple in the Cage, The
Performance/production
Analysis of Guillermo Gómez-Peña and Coco Fusco's performance piece *The Couple in the Cage*. USA. 1995. Lang.: Eng. 4255
Background on *The Couple in the Cage* by Guillermo Gómez-Peña and Coco Fusco. USA. 1992-1995. Lang.: Eng. 4259

Courier, The
Plays/librettos/scripts
Mennonite drama of Veralyn Warkentin and Vern Thiessen. Canada. 1890-1997. Lang.: Eng. 2829

Court entertainment
SEE ALSO
Classed Entries under MIXED ENTERTAINMENT—Court entertainment.
Performance/production
Dance culture and the court of King Mátyás. Hungary. 1413-1485. Lang.: Hun. 943
Plays/librettos/scripts
Playwright Bartolomé de Torres Naharro. Spain. 1480-1530. Lang.: Eng. 3383

Court Theatre (Chicago, IL)
Institutions
Charles Newell, artistic director of the Court Theatre. USA: Chicago, IL. 1998. Lang.: Eng. 1792

Court Theatre (London)
SEE ALSO
Royal Court Theatre.
Plays/librettos/scripts
George Bernard Shaw's involvement with the Court Theatre. UK-England. 1904-1909. Lang.: Eng. 3471

Courtyard Theatre (Leeds)
Performance/production
Collection of newspaper reviews by London theatre critics. UK-England: Leeds, Manchester. 1998. Lang.: Eng. 2433
Collection of newspaper reviews by London theatre critics. UK-England: London. 1998. Lang.: Eng. 2441
Collection of newspaper reviews by London theatre critics. UK-England. 1998. Lang.: Eng. 2485
Collection of newspaper reviews by London theatre critics. UK-England: London. 1998. Lang.: Eng. 2542
Collection of newspaper reviews by London theatre critics. UK-England: Leeds, Manchester. 1998. Lang.: Eng. 2559

Cousin Bette
Design/technology
Des McAnuff's design concept for his film *Cousin Bette*. USA: Hollywood, CA. 1998. Lang.: Eng. 3905

Covenant Players (Camarillo, CA)
Institutions
History of Christian theatre company, the Covenant Players. USA: Camarillo, CA. 1988. Lang.: Eng. 429

Covent Garden Theatre (London)
Performance/production
Excerpts from Johanna Schopenhauer's journal relating to London theatre. UK-England: London. Germany. 1803-1805. Lang.: Eng. 2615
Possible illustrations of Dibdin's *Harlequin and Mother Goose* at Covent Garden. UK-England: London. 1806-1808. Lang.: Eng. 2639

Covent Garden, Theatre Royal (London)
SEE ALSO
Royal Opera House, Covent Garden.

Coward, Noël
Performance/production
Collection of newspaper reviews by London theatre critics. UK-England: Leeds, Manchester. 1998. Lang.: Eng. 2559
Plays/librettos/scripts
The renewed popularity of works by Noël Coward. UK-England. 1924-1998. Lang.: Eng. 3421

Cowie, Andrew
Performance/production
Collection of newspaper reviews by London theatre critics. UK-England: London. 1998. Lang.: Eng. 2534

Cowie, Michael
Performance/production
Collection of newspaper reviews by London theatre critics. UK-England: London. 1998. Lang.: Eng. 2562

Cowley, Abraham
Plays/librettos/scripts
Analysis of Restoration anti-Puritan comedies. England. 1661-1663. Lang.: Eng. 2907

Cowley, Michael
Performance/production
Collection of newspaper reviews by London theatre critics. UK-England: London. 1998. Lang.: Eng. 2480

Cows Are Mad, The
Performance/production
Collection of newspaper reviews by London theatre critics. UK-England: London. 1998. Lang.: Eng. 2427

Craig, Catriona
Performance/production
Collection of newspaper reviews by London theatre critics. UK-England: London. 1998. Lang.: Eng. 2537

Craig, Edward Gordon
Design/technology
Dancer Isadora Duncan's influence on the designs of Edward Gordon Craig. UK-England. 1904-1905. Lang.: Eng. 237
Performance spaces
Non-traditional theatrical space. Germany. France. UK-England. 1898-1998. Lang.: Dan. 443
Performance/production
The rise of the modern Shakespearean director. Europe. 1878-1995. Lang.: Eng. 1911
Commedia dell'arte and twentieth-century theatre. Europe. 1860-1950. Lang.: Eng. 4187

Craig, Ryan
Performance/production
Collection of newspaper reviews by London theatre critics. UK-England: London. 1998. Lang.: Eng. 2482

Craig, Stuart
Design/technology
Production design for the film *The Avengers*. USA: Hollywood, CA. 1998. Lang.: Eng. 3907

Craig, Ted
Performance/production
Collection of newspaper reviews by London theatre critics. UK-England: London. 1998. Lang.: Eng. 2554

Crane Made Theater (Mostar)
Performance/production
The development of *Letters, or Where Does the Postman Go When All the Street Names Are Changed*, based on experiences of residents of Mostar. Bosnia-Herzegovina: Mostar. 1997. Lang.: Eng. 1831
Crane, David
Performance/production
Collection of newspaper reviews by London theatre critics. UK-England: London. 1998. Lang.: Eng. 2492
Cranko, John
Performance/production
Prokofjév's *Romeo and Juliet*, choreographed by Cranko, Wiener Staatsoper. Austria: Vienna. 1998. Lang.: Hun. 1063
Bayerische Staatsballett's guest performances at Budapest Opera House. Hungary: Budapest. 1998. Lang.: Hun. 1092
Cratty, Bill
Performance/production
Choreographer Bill Cratty. USA. 1974-1998. Lang.: Eng. 1320
Crave
Performance/production
Collection of newspaper reviews by London theatre critics. UK-England: London. 1998. Lang.: Eng. 2493
Craven, Mark
Performance/production
Collection of newspaper reviews by London theatre critics. UK-England: London. 1998. Lang.: Eng. 2507
Craven, Tony
Performance/production
Collection of newspaper reviews by London theatre critics. UK-England: London. 1998. Lang.: Eng. 2520
Crawford, Cheryl
Administration
Producer Cheryl Crawford, gender and sexuality. USA. 1902-1986. Lang.: Eng. 116
Producer Cheryl Crawford and her contributions to the American stage. USA. 1930-1965. Lang.: Eng. 1396
Performance/production
The idea of Hollywood in theatre autobiographies. USA. 1950-1990. Lang.: Eng. 665
Crawford, Dan
Institutions
History of the King's Head Theatre and pub. UK-England: London. 1970-1998. Lang.: Eng. 1747
Performance/production
Collection of newspaper reviews by London theatre critics. UK-England: London. 1998. Lang.: Eng. 2513
Crawford, David Wright
Plays/librettos/scripts
Text of *Tangled Garden* by David Wright Crawford with documentation of the author's method. USA. 1987. Lang.: Eng. 3569
Crawley, Brian
Plays/librettos/scripts
Panel discussion on contemporary musical theatre. USA: New York, NY. 1998. Lang.: Eng. 4398
Craze, Tony
Performance/production
Collection of newspaper reviews by London theatre critics. UK-England: London. 1998. Lang.: Eng. 2427
Crea, Teresa
Performance/production
Multiculturalism and Italo-Australian theatre. Australia. 1990-1998. Lang.: Eng. 490
Creative drama
SEE ALSO
Children's theatre.
Creative Independent Artists (Glasgow)
Institutions
Interview with members of dance group Creative Independent Artists. UK-Scotland: Glasgow. 1996-1998. Lang.: Eng. 904
Cregan, David
Performance/production
Collection of newspaper reviews by London theatre critics. UK-England: London. 1998. Lang.: Eng. 2557
Crémieux, Hector
Basic theatrical documents
Text of Offenbach's *Orphée aux Enfers*. France. 1874. Lang.: Fre. 4418
Crespin, Régine
Performance/production
Singers' approaches to the title role in Bizet's *Carmen*. 1875-1998. Lang.: Eng. 4502
Cresswell, Luke
Performance/production
Collection of newspaper reviews by London theatre critics. UK-England: London. 1998. Lang.: Eng. 2544
Crête, Jacques
Institutions
Jacques Crête and Atelier de recherche théâtrale l'Eskabel. Canada: Montreal, PQ. 1971-1989. Lang.: Eng. 1590
Cri du caméléon, Le (Call of the Chameleon, The)
Performance/production
Comparison of text-based and visual productions. France. 1998. Lang.: Fre. 1939
Cries from Casement
Plays/librettos/scripts
BBC radio plays with Anglo-Irish themes. UK-England. Ireland. 1973-1986. Lang.: Eng. 3868
Crime and Punishment
SEE ALSO
Prestuplenijè i nakazanijè.
Performance/production
Collection of newspaper reviews by London theatre critics. UK-England: London. 1998. Lang.: Eng. 2493
Crimes in Hot Countries
Plays/librettos/scripts
Political thought in plays of Howard Barker. UK-England. 1960-1992. Lang.: Eng. 3502
Crimes of the Heart
Performance/production
Collection of newspaper reviews by London theatre critics. UK-England: London. 1998. Lang.: Eng. 2539
An approach to playing Babe Botrelle in Beth Henley's *Crimes of the Heart*. USA. 1987. Lang.: Eng. 2690
Crimp, Martin
Institutions
Profile of new venue, Bayerisches Staatsschauspiel, Marstall. Germany: Munich. 1993-1998. Lang.: Ger. 1660
Performance/production
Recent productions of Schauspiel Leipzig. Germany: Leipzig. 1997-1998. Lang.: Ger. 2011
Cripple of Inishmaan, The
Plays/librettos/scripts
Playwright Martin McDonagh. Ireland. 1998. Lang.: Eng. 3216
Crisp, Sharon
Performance/production
Collection of newspaper reviews by London theatre critics. UK-England: London. 1998. Lang.: Eng. 2471
Criswell, Sheryle
Basic theatrical documents
Text of ... *Where Late the Sweet Birds Sang* by Sheryle Criswell. USA. 1998. Lang.: Eng. 1483
Plays/librettos/scripts
Interview with playwright Sheryle Criswell. USA. 1998. Lang.: Eng. 3681
Theory/criticism
Playwright Sheryle Criswell on criticism of her work. USA. 1998. Lang.: Eng. 3840
Criterion Center (New York, NY)
SEE ALSO
Roundabout Theatre Company.
Criticism
SEE
Theory/criticism.
Croatian National Theatre (Drama and Opera)
SEE
Hravatsko Narodno Kazalište.
Crocker, Stan
Design/technology
Stan Crocker's lighting design for pop rock group tour. USA. 1998. Lang.: Eng. 4106
Croft, Dwayne
Performance/production
Baritone Dwayne Croft. USA: New York, NY. 1998. Lang.: Eng. 4751
Croghan, Declan
Performance/production
Collection of newspaper reviews by London theatre critics. UK-England: London. 1998. Lang.: Eng. 2457
Collection of newspaper reviews by London theatre critics. UK-England: London. 1998. Lang.: Eng. 2492

Croghan, Declan — cont'd

Collection of newspaper reviews by London theatre critics. UK-England: London. 1998. Lang.: Eng. 2506

Croiter, Jeff
Design/technology
Professional theatrical designers on design training. USA. 1998. Lang.: Eng. 252

Croose, Jonathan
Performance/production
Collection of newspaper reviews by London theatre critics. UK-England: London. 1998. Lang.: Eng. 2447

Cropper, Anna
Performance/production
Collection of newspaper reviews by London theatre critics. UK-England: London. 1998. Lang.: Eng. 2467

Cross, Felix
Performance/production
Collection of newspaper reviews by London theatre critics. UK-England: London. 1998. Lang.: Eng. 2515
Collection of newspaper reviews by London theatre critics. UK-England: London. 1998. Lang.: Eng. 2572

Crothers, Rachel
Plays/librettos/scripts
The Broadway success of women playwrights. USA. 1906-1944. Lang.: Eng. 3590

Crouch, Julian
Performance/production
Collection of newspaper reviews by London theatre critics. UK-England: London. 1998. Lang.: Eng. 2465
Collection of newspaper reviews by London theatre critics. UK-England: London. 1998. Lang.: Eng. 2556

Croucher, Brian
Performance/production
Collection of newspaper reviews by London theatre critics. UK-England: London. 1998. Lang.: Eng. 2464

Crow, Laura
Design/technology
The 1998 USITT expo. USA: Long Beach, CA. 1998. Lang.: Eng. 251

Crowley, Bob
Design/technology
The design concept for Nicholas Hytner's production of Shakespeare's *Twelfth Night*. USA: New York, NY. 1998. Lang.: Eng. 1556

Crowley, John
Performance/production
Collection of newspaper reviews by London theatre critics. UK-England: London. 1998. Lang.: Eng. 2423
Collection of newspaper reviews by London theatre critics. UK-England: London. 1998. Lang.: Eng. 2543
Collection of newspaper reviews by London theatre critics. UK-England: London. 1998. Lang.: Eng. 2551

Crowley, Mart
Plays/librettos/scripts
History of the Playwrights Unit. USA. 1963-1971. Lang.: Eng. 3570
Effeminacy on the American stage. USA. 1920-1998. Lang.: Eng. 3682

Crowns and Anchors
Plays/librettos/scripts
Review of collections of plays with gay themes. Canada. 1996. Lang.: Eng. 2802

Croydon Warehouse (London)
Performance/production
Collection of newspaper reviews by London theatre critics. UK-England: London. 1998. Lang.: Eng. 2421
Collection of newspaper reviews by London theatre critics. UK-England: London. 1998. Lang.: Eng. 2438
Collection of newspaper reviews by London theatre critics. UK-England: London. 1998. Lang.: Eng. 2465
Collection of newspaper reviews by London theatre critics. UK-England: London. 1998. Lang.: Eng. 2499
Collection of newspaper reviews by London theatre critics. UK-England: London. 1998. Lang.: Eng. 2507
Collection of newspaper reviews by London theatre critics. UK-England: London. 1998. Lang.: Eng. 2515
Collection of newspaper reviews by London theatre critics. UK-England: London. 1998. Lang.: Eng. 2521
Collection of newspaper reviews by London theatre critics. UK-England: London. 1998. Lang.: Eng. 2554
Collection of newspaper reviews by London theatre critics. UK-England: London. 1998. Lang.: Eng. 2577

Crucible, The
Performance/production
Review of Arthur Miller's *The Crucible* directed by Péter Rudolf. Hungary: Budapest. 1998. Lang.: Hun. 2068

Crutch, The
Performance/production
Collection of newspaper reviews by London theatre critics. UK-England: London. 1998. Lang.: Eng. 2549

Cry If I Want To
Performance/production
Collection of newspaper reviews by London theatre critics. UK-England: London. 1998. Lang.: Eng. 2427

Crying Game, The
Plays/librettos/scripts
Transvestism in contemporary film as the 'blackface' of the nineties. UK-England. USA. 1993-1996. Lang.: Eng. 3983

Cryptogram, The
Plays/librettos/scripts
Rites of passage in the plays of David Mamet. USA. 1975-1995. Lang.: Eng. 3680

Crystal Clear
Performance/production
Collection of newspaper reviews by London theatre critics. UK-England: London. 1998. Lang.: Eng. 2464

Csanádi, Judit
Design/technology
Survey of an exhibition of Hungarian scene design. Hungary: Budapest. 1998. Lang.: Hun. 195
An exhibition of sets and environments by Hungarian designers. Hungary: Budapest. 1998. Lang.: Hun. 196
Catalogue of an exhibition devoted to Hungarian theatre and film. Hungary: Budapest. 1998. Lang.: Hun. 197

CSC Repertory (New York, NY)
Design/technology
Costume design for *Christmas with the Ivanovs*, CSC Repertory. USA: New York, NY. 1998. Lang.: Eng. 1533
Performance spaces
Theatre space and performance. USA: New York, NY. 1925-1985. Lang.: Eng. 464
Plays/librettos/scripts
Ellen McLaughlin's *Iphigenia and Other Daughters* at CSC Repertory. USA: New York, NY. 1995. Lang.: Eng. 3520

Cseke, Péter
Performance/production
Two productions of Ernő Szép's *Vőlegény (The Fiancé)*. Hungary: Nyíregyháza. Hungary: Győr. 1998.Lang.: Hun. 2118

Csiky Gergely Színház (Kaposvár)
Institutions
Theatre critics' awards 97-98. Hungary. 1997-1998. Lang.: Hun. 355
Performance/production
Interview with director János Mohácsi. Hungary. 1998. Lang.: Hun. 2060
Interview with actress Kati Lázár. Hungary. 1998. Lang.: Hun. 2062
Goldoni's *La Locandiera* directed by Lászlo Keszég. Hungary: Kaposvár. 1998. Lang.: Hun. 2092
Review of Bulgakov's *Ivan Vasiljèvič* directed by János Mohácsi. Hungary: Kaposvár. 1998. Lang.: Hun. 2095
Ferenc Deák's *Fojtás (Tamping)* directed by László Babarczy. Hungary: Kaposvár. 1998. Lang.: Hun. 2117
Productions of plays by Koljada and Jerofejèv at Csiky Gergely Theatre. Hungary: Kaposvár. 1998. Lang.: Hun. 2149

Csiky Gergely Színház (Timişoara)
Institutions
History of annual festival of Hungarian-language theatre. Hungary: Kisvárda. 1989-1998. Lang.: Hun. 1669
History of Hungarian-language theatre in Transylvania. Romania. Hungary. 1919-1992. Lang.: Hun, Rom. 1693

Csillagőrlő (Starmill)
Performance/production
Artus Táncegyüttes' new production *Csillagőrlő (Starmill)*. Hungary: Budapest. 1998. Lang.: Hun. 948

Csiszár, Imre
Performance/production
Review of Madách's *Tragedy of Man* at the Hungarian Theatre of Kolozsvár. Hungary. Romania: Cluj-Napoca. 1997. Lang.: Hun. 2065
Reviews of two plays by Per Olov Enquist. Hungary: Budapest. 1998. Lang.: Hun. 2089
Three Hungarian productions of plays by Molière. Hungary: Szentendre, Kapolcs, Kőszeg. 1998. Lang.: Hun. 2142

Csizmadia, Tibor
Plays/librettos/scripts
New Hungarian translations of Shakespeare. Hungary. 1990-1998. Lang.: Hun. 3187
Csodálatos mandarin, A (Miraculous Mandarin, The)
Performance/production
Bartók's *A csodálatos mandarin (The Miraculous Mandarin)* choreographed by Gyula Harangozó. Hungary: Budapest. 1998.Lang.: Hun. 1088
Csokonai Színház (Debrecen)
Performance/production
János Acs' *A mennyei hid (The Heavenly Bridge)* directed by Gábor Cziezel. Hungary: Debrecen. 1998. Lang.: Hun. 2069
Interview with bass György Tréfás. Hungary: Debrecen. 1931-1998. Lang.: Hun. 4641
Csokonai Színház, Horváth Árpád Stúdiószínház (Debrecen)
Performance/production
Review of Darvasi's *Bolond Helga (Foolish Helga)*, Csokonai Theatre. Hungary: Debrecen. 1997. Lang.: Hun. 2122
One-act plays by Brecht directed by József Jámbor. Hungary: Debrecen. 1998. Lang.: Hun. 2131
Csokonai Vitéz, Mihály
Performance/production
Two productions of Csokonai Vitéz's *Karnyóné és a két szeleburdiak (Mrs. Karnyó and the Two Feather-Brains)*. Hungary: Budapest. 1998. Lang.: Hun. 2113
Csokor, Franz
Plays/librettos/scripts
Social criticism in Viennese Expressionist drama. Austria: Vienna. 1907-1922. Lang.: Ger. 2779
Cuarterona, La (Quatroon, The)
Plays/librettos/scripts
The mulatto in Puerto Rican drama. Puerto Rico. 1850-1985. Lang.: Spa. 3311
Cucci, Luigi
Performance/production
Opera singer Luigi Cucci. Italy. 1998. Lang.: Rus. 4646
Cuckoo
Performance/production
Interview with performance artist Julian Maynard Smith. UK-England: London. 1980-1988. Lang.: Eng. 4246
Cueva y Silva, Leonor de la
Plays/librettos/scripts
Feminist analysis of seventeenth-century plays by women. Spain. 1605-1675. Lang.: Eng. 3385
Cueva, Juan de la
Plays/librettos/scripts
Playwright Juan de la Cueva. Spain. 1543-1612. Lang.: Eng. 3369
Cukor, George
Plays/librettos/scripts
Popular adaptations of the works of George Bernard Shaw. UK-England. 1890-1990. Lang.: Eng. 3445
Cullberg, Birgit
Design/technology
Rapid on-stage costume changes in dance. Russia. Sweden. Japan. 1840-1998. Lang.: Swe. 889
Performance/production
Dancer/choreographer Birgit Cullberg. Sweden: Stockholm. 1908-1998. Lang.: Ger. 1302
Dancer Ana Laguna of Cullbergbaletten. Sweden: Stockholm. 1974-1998. Lang.: Swe. 1305
Dance on screen. USA. Europe. 1920-1998. Lang.: Ger. 3860
Cullbergbaletten (Stockholm)
Performance/production
Dancer Ana Laguna of Cullbergbaletten. Sweden: Stockholm. 1974-1998. Lang.: Swe. 1305
Training
Memoirs of dance teacher Lia Schubert. Sweden: Malmö, Stockholm, Gothenburg. 1950-1998. Lang.: Swe. 1021
Cullen, Countée
Plays/librettos/scripts
Analysis of Countée Cullen's translation of Euripides' *Medea*. USA. 1936. Lang.: Eng. 3567
Culling, David
Performance/production
Collection of newspaper reviews by London theatre critics. UK-England: London. 1998. Lang.: Eng. 2421
Cultural policy
Administration
Comparative analysis of national cultural policies. Canada. France. Germany. Norway. 1905-1998. Lang.: Eng. 4
Interview with Frank Baumbauer of Deutsches Schauspielhaus Hamburg. Germany: Hamburg. 1993-2000. Lang.: Ger. 11
The system of subsidized theatre in Germany, and suggestions for changing it. Germany. 1989-1998. Lang.: Ger. 13
New funding options for Romanian arts groups. Romania. 1989-1998. Lang.: Eng. 20
Alternative methods of measuring the success and failure of cultural institutions. USA. 1998. Lang.: Eng. 36
The nomination of William J. Ivey as head of NEA. USA. 1998. Lang.: Eng. 59
The commitment to arts funding by cities that sponsor major league sports. USA. 1989-1998. Lang.: Eng. 125
The effect of outcome analysis and impact studies on cultural policy. USA. 1998. Lang.: Eng. 136
American and Japanese cultural policy. USA. Japan. 1949-1998. Lang.: Eng. 141
Current thinking on the impact of the arts. USA. 1998. Lang.: Eng. 142
Riksteatern and Dansens Hus' Dansbiennal 98 meeting with government officials. Sweden. 1998. Lang.: Swe. 881
Sweden's new dance funding program. Sweden. 1998. Lang.: Swe. 883
Arts Minister on the current state of dance, training, and funding. UK-England. 1998. Lang.: Eng. 884
Interviews with theatre managers regarding the changing cultural landscape. Germany: Bruchsal, Esslingen, Tübingen. 1998. Lang.: Ger. 1381
The closing of Göteborgs Stadsteatern. Sweden. 1974-1997. Lang.: Dan. 1389
Institutions
Proposal for changes in the mission of the National Endowment for the Arts. USA. 1998. Lang.: Eng. 397
The Mummers' Troupe and the Canada Council. Canada: St. John's, NF. 1972-1982. Lang.: Eng. 1581
Interview with director and dramaturg of Staatstheater Stuttgart. Germany: Stuttgart. 1993-1998. Lang.: Ger. 1632
The National Theatre's experiment in artistic renewal. Hungary: Budapest. 1979-1982. Lang.: Hun. 1672
Performance/production
Czech theatre after the end of Communist rule. Czech Republic. 1989-1998. Lang.: Eng, Fre. 1876
Roman theatre, traditional and experimental. Italy: Rome. 1994-1998. Lang.: Eng. 2187
Mejerchol'd's production of Gogol's *Revizor (The Inspector General)*. USSR: Moscow. 1926. Lang.: Eng. 2763
Mejerchol'd's relationship with Lunačarskij. USSR. 1890-1931. Lang.: Eng. 2768
Plays/librettos/scripts
Actor and playwright Curt Goetz and Nazi attitudes toward theatre. Germany. 1933-1944. Lang.: Eng. 3139
Relation to other fields
Postwar Austrian cultural and theatrical identity. Austria. 1945-1998. Lang.: Ger. 715
Theatre in Danish cultural policy. Denmark. 1990-1998. Lang.: Dan. 724
The evaluation of theatrical quality in the Århus area. Denmark: Århus. 1993-1998. Lang.: Dan. 725
French theatre and the influence of the right wing. France. 1995-1998. Lang.: Ger. 734
Government and budget cuts in German theatres. Germany: Bochum, Cologne. 1991-1998. Lang.: Ger. 738
The national movement, cultural policy, and German regional theatre. Germany: Eisleben. 1998. Lang.: Ger. 740
Political and cultural situation of Frankfurt theatres. Germany: Frankfurt. 1997-1999. Lang.: Ger. 744
The debate over whether Germany needs a national cultural minister. Germany. 1998. Lang.: Ger. 746
German politicians interviewed on cultural policy. Germany. 1998. Lang.: Ger. 749
The effect of social and political change on Slovakian theatre. Slovakia. 1989-1998. Lang.: Ger. 763
Stockholm's cultural facilities. Sweden: Stockholm. 1998. Lang.: Eng. 766
The current status of English cultural policy. UK-England. 1997-1998. Lang.: Ger. 769

Cultural policy — cont'd

European fears of American cultural hegemony. USA. Europe. 1998. Lang.: Eng. 773
Conditions of Bulgarian theatre and reform efforts. Bulgaria. 1997-1998. Lang.: Ger. 3731
Cultural policy and French theatre structures. France. 1945-1998. Lang.: Ger. 3760
New Italian theatrical legislation. Italy. 1998. Lang.: Eng. 3774
Catalonian cultural politics and Els Joglars. Spain-Catalonia. 1962-1998. Lang.: Eng. 3775
Training
Playwright Tony Kushner's address to the Association of Theatre in Higher Education. USA. 1997. Lang.: Eng. 3851

Culture Clash (San Francisco, CA)
Performance/production
Culture Clash and their production of Aristophanes' *Birds*. USA: Berkeley, CA. 1984-1998. Lang.: Eng. 2713

Cumberland, Richard
Plays/librettos/scripts
The obedient daughter in adaptations of Shakespeare's plays. England. 1701-1800. Lang.: Eng. 2969
Judith Sargent Murray's *Traveller Returned* and its source. USA. 1771-1796. Lang.: Eng. 3672

Cunning Little Vixen, The
SEE
Příhody lišky bystroušky.

Cunningham, Glen
Design/technology
Lighting designer Glen Cunningham. USA. 1956-1998. Lang.: Eng. 301

Cunningham, Merce
Performance/production
Interview with dancer/choreographer Merce Cunningham. USA. 1960-1998. Lang.: Eng. 1186
Interview with choreographer Keely Garfield. UK-England. 1998. Lang.: Eng. 1308
The influence of Merce Cunningham on choreographer Emma Diamond. USA. 1988-1998. Lang.: Eng. 1322
Interview with choreographer Merce Cunningham. USA. 1944-1998. Lang.: Eng. 1326
Dance on screen. USA. Europe. 1920-1998. Lang.: Ger. 3860
Relation to other fields
American modern dance and gay culture. USA. 1933-1998. Lang.: Eng. 1337
Theory/criticism
Critique of dance criticism. UK-England: London. 1989. Lang.: Eng. 1339
Analysis of choreography by Merce Cunningham. USA. 1998. Lang.: Eng. 1340

Cupid, John
Performance/production
Carnival as a unifying force. Trinidad and Tobago. 1998. Lang.: Eng. 4170

Curano, Laura
Performance/production
Laura Curano's solo piece *Olivetti*. Italy: Calabria. 1998. Lang.: Eng. 2156

Cure at Troy, The
Plays/librettos/scripts
Adaptations of Greek tragedy by contemporary Irish writers. Ireland. UK-Ireland. 1984-1998. Lang.: Eng. 3214

Čurikova, Inna
Performance/production
Actress Inna Čurikova. Russia: Moscow. 1998. Lang.: Rus. 2301

Curran, Lee
Institutions
Interview with members of dance group Creative Independent Artists. UK-Scotland: Glasgow. 1996-1998. Lang.: Eng. 904

Currie, Mark Stuart
Performance/production
Collection of newspaper reviews by London theatre critics. UK-England: London. 1998. Lang.: Eng. 2420

Curry, Rob
Performance/production
Collection of newspaper reviews by London theatre critics. UK-England: London. 1998. Lang.: Eng. 2577

Curse of the Starving Class
Plays/librettos/scripts
Language in the plays of Sam Shepard. USA. 1967-1985. Lang.: Eng. 3694

Curse of Tittikhamon, The
Performance/production
Collection of newspaper reviews by London theatre critics. UK-England: London. 1998. Lang.: Eng. 2470

Curtis, Adam
Performance/production
Collection of newspaper reviews by London theatre critics. UK-England: London. 1998. Lang.: Eng. 2571

Cusack, Dymphna
Plays/librettos/scripts
Analysis of plays by Dymphna Cusack. Australia. 1927-1959. Lang.: Eng. 2777

Cush, Geoffrey
Performance/production
Collection of newspaper reviews by London theatre critics. UK-England: London. 1998. Lang.: Eng. 2446

Cushman, Charlotte
Performance/production
Gender and the career of actress Charlotte Cushman. USA. 1816-1876. Lang.: Eng. 680

Cusick, Michael
Design/technology
New sound and video system in the performance space of Luxor Hotel and Casino. USA: Las Vegas, NV. 1998. Lang.: Eng. 285

Cut Piece
Theory/criticism
Analysis of Yoko Ono's performance work *Cut Piece*. USA. 1964-1998. Lang.: Eng. 4151

Cutter of Coleman Street
Plays/librettos/scripts
Analysis of Restoration anti-Puritan comedies. England. 1661-1663. Lang.: Eng. 2907

Cvetko, Igor
Performance/production
Account of shadow-puppet workshop for Bosnian refugee children. Slovenia: Ribnica. 1997. Lang.: Slo. 4926

Cycle des rois, Le (Kings Cycle, The)
Performance/production
French Canadian translations/adaptations of Shakespeare. Canada: Montreal, PQ. 1988. Lang.: Fre. 1855

Cycle plays
Plays/librettos/scripts
Wonder and recognition in medieval and Renaissance drama. England. 1400-1612. Lang.: Eng. 2874
The Easter play tradition. England. 1180-1557. Lang.: Eng. 2942
Eugene O'Neill's unfinished *A Tale of Possessors Self-Dispossessed*. USA. 1945-1953. Lang.: Eng. 3594
Theory/criticism
Evaluation of scholarship on English cycle plays. 1998. Lang.: Eng. 3802

Cymbeline
Design/technology
Costume designs for Oregon Shakespeare Festival productions. USA: Ashland, OR. 1998. Lang.: Eng. 1543
Lighting designer Hugh Vanstone. USA: New York, NY. 1998. Lang.: Eng. 1554
Performance/production
Collection of newspaper reviews by London theatre critics. UK-England: London. 1998. Lang.: Eng. 2571
Musical performances on and off Broadway. USA: New York. 1998. Lang.: Ger. 4383
Plays/librettos/scripts
The murders of royal women in plays of Shakespeare and Beaumont and Fletcher. England. 1609-1610. Lang.: Eng. 2894
Sources of the wager scene in Shakespeare's *Cymbeline*. England. 1609-1610. Lang.: Eng. 2910

Cyrano
Performance/production
Interview with director Anders Paulin. Sweden: Malmö. 1997-1998. Lang.: Swe. 2377

Cyrano de Bergerac
Design/technology
Costume design for the ballet *Cyrano de Bergerac*. USA: San Francisco, CA. 1998. Lang.: Eng. 1032

Czeizel, Gábor
Performance/production
János Acs' *A mennyei híd (The Heavenly Bridge)* directed by Gábor Cziezel. Hungary: Debrecen. 1998. Lang.: Hun. 2069
Review of Darvasi's *Bolond Helga (Foolish Helga)*, Csokonai Theatre. Hungary: Debrecen. 1997. Lang.: Hun. 2122

Czellnik, Katja
Performance/production
Music theatre production in northern Germany. Germany: Lübeck, Hamburg, Bremen, Kiel. 1998. Lang.: Ger. 4293
Opera director Katja Czellnik. Germany: Oldenburg, Kiel. 1996-1998. Lang.: Ger. 4583
D, Jonzi
Performance/production
Hip-hop choreographer Jonzi D. UK-England: London. 1998. Lang.: Eng. 973
d'Anna, Claude
Basic theatrical documents
Text of *Pour la galerie (For the Gallery)* by Claude d'Anna and Laure Bonin. France. 1998. Lang.: Fre. 1424
D'Annunzio, Gabriele
Performance/production
Robert Wilson's dance adaptation of *Le Martyre de Saint Sébastien* by D'Annunzio. France: Paris. 1988. Lang.: Ita. 1074
Collaborative Symbolist dance/theatre projects. Europe. USA. 1916-1934. Lang.: Eng. 1268
Collection of newspaper reviews by London theatre critics. UK-England: London. 1998. Lang.: Eng. 2517
Plays/librettos/scripts
Sketches and drafts of works by Gabriele D'Annunzio. Italy. 1888-1892. Lang.: Ita. 3234
Analysis of plays by Gabriele D'Annunzio. Italy. 1863-1938. Lang.: Ita. 3263
D'Arcier, Bernard Faivre
Performance/production
The Avignon Festival under the direction of Bernard Faivre D'Arcier. France: Avignon. 1998. Lang.: Ger. 1927
D'Arcy, Margaretta
Plays/librettos/scripts
British historical drama. UK-England. 1956-1988. Lang.: Eng. 3500
Da Da Kamera Canadian Stage Theatre (Toronto, ON)
Plays/librettos/scripts
Analysis of Daniel MacIvor's *Monster* as directed by Daniel Brooks. Canada: Toronto, ON. 1998. Lang.: Eng. 2834
Da Ponte, Lorenzo
Performance/production
Lucy Vestris in *Giovanni in London.* England: London. 1842. Lang.: Eng. 4546
da Silva, Joël
Plays/librettos/scripts
Round-table discussion on story-telling and theatre. Canada: Montreal, PQ. 1998. Lang.: Fre. 688
Dagenais, Pierre
Performance/production
Pierre Dagenais and his company L'Équipe. Canada: Montreal, PQ. 1933-1990. Lang.: Fre. 1846
Dahlberg, Ingrid
Institutions
Interview with Ingrid Dahlberg, manager of Dramaten. Sweden: Stockholm. 1996-1998. Lang.: Swe. 1730
Daiken, Melanie
Plays/librettos/scripts
Melanie Daiken's musical settings of texts by Samuel Beckett. Ireland. France. 1945-1995. Lang.: Eng. 3201
Dal', Oleg
Performance/production
Memoirs of actor Oleg Dal'. Russia: Moscow. 1998. Lang.: Rus. 2247
Dalateatern (Falun)
Institutions
Swedish-Lithuanian theatrical exchange. Lithuania: Valmeira. Sweden: Falun. 1996. Lang.: Swe, Eng, Ger. 1677
Daldry, Stephen
Performance/production
Collection of newspaper reviews by London theatre critics. UK-England: London. 1998. Lang.: Eng. 2495
Dale-Jones, Shôn
Performance/production
Collection of newspaper reviews by London theatre critics. UK-England: London. 1998. Lang.: Eng. 2445
Daley, Dona
Performance/production
Collection of newspaper reviews by London theatre critics. UK-England: London. 1998. Lang.: Eng. 2427
Dalis, Irene
Institutions
Mezzo soprano Irene Dalis, now in charge of Opera San Jose. USA: San José, CA. 1980-1998. Lang.: Eng. 4484
Dallas Opera (Dallas TX)
Performance/production
Major opera houses' proposals for productions to the end of the century. USA. Canada. 1998. Lang.: Eng. 4743
Dallos, Chris
Design/technology
Lighting design for Donald Margulies' *Collected Stories*, directed by William Carden. USA: New York, NY. 1998. Lang.: Eng. 1544
Dalos, László
Performance/production
Production of László Lajtha's comic opera *Le chapeau bleu.* Romania: Cluj-Napoca. Hungary. 1948-1998. Lang.: Hun. 4668
Daly, Arnold
Performance/production
Attempted censorship of productions. USA. 1900-1905. Lang.: Eng. 2698
New York City's attempt to impose censorship on theatre productions. USA: New York, NY. 1900-1927. Lang.: Eng. 2699
Daly, Augustin
Plays/librettos/scripts
Analysis of *The Foresters* by Alfred, Lord Tennyson. England. USA. 1700-1910. Lang.: Eng. 2998
Dame aux Camélias, La (Camille)
Plays/librettos/scripts
The inspiration for Dumas *fils*' Marguerite Gautier and Verdi's Violetta. France. Italy. 1848-1853. Lang.: Eng. 4789
Dame Blanche (Montmorency, PQ)
Performance spaces
The Dame Blanche theatre. Canada: Quebec, PQ. 1982-1998. Lang.: Fre. 1796
Damerius, Frank
Institutions
Profile of Nordhessisches Landestheater Marburg. Germany: Marburg. 1997-1998. Lang.: Ger. 1653
Dames at Sea
Design/technology
Costume design for *Dames at Sea*, Marine Memorial Theatre. USA: San Francisco, CA. 1998. Lang.: Eng. 4332
Damnation du Docteur Faust, La (Damnation of Dr. Faust, The)
Plays/librettos/scripts
The reciprocal influence of opera and film. Europe. North America. 1904-1994. Lang.: Eng. 4770
Damon and Pythias
Performance/production
Gaynor Macfarlane's production of Edwards' *Damon and Pythias* at Shakespeare's Globe. UK-England: London. 1996. Lang.: Eng. 2613
Dance
SEE
Dancing.
Dance of Death, The
SEE
Dödsdansen.
Dance of the Forest, A
Plays/librettos/scripts
Political satire in the plays of Wole Soyinka. Nigeria. 1960-1979. Lang.: Eng. 3284
Dance therapy
Relation to other fields
Dancer, teacher, and healing facilitator Anna Halprin of Tamalpa Institute. USA: Kentfield, CA. 1978-1998. Lang.: Ger. 1338
Training
The development of Irmgard Bartenieff's corrective physical training methods. USA. 1925-1981. Lang.: Ger. 1024
Dance-Drama
SEE ALSO
Classed Entries under DANCE-DRAMA.
Dancer's Christmas, A
Performance/production
The creation of the religious ballet *A Dancer's Christmas.* USA: Boston, MA. 1980-1998. Lang.: Eng. 1192
Dancing
SEE ALSO
Training, dance.
Choreography.
Classed Entries under DANCE.
Administration
Interviews with German theatre and film directors. Germany. 1998. Lang.: Ger. 1385
Design/technology
Dancer Isadora Duncan's influence on the designs of Edward Gordon Craig. UK-England. 1904-1905. Lang.: Eng. 237

Dancing — cont'd

Performance/production
Report on festival of performing and visual arts. France: Paris. 1997. Lang.: Eng. 532
Interview with Bengt Andersson, artistic director of Teater Tre. Sweden. 1983-1998. Lang.: Swe. 601
The success of dance extravaganzas and solo performance at the expense of traditional shows. USA: New York, NY. 1994-1998. Lang. :Eng. 645
A dancer's experience of and investigations into ecstasy. USA. Germany. 1969-1990. Lang.: Eng. 673
Dance and improvisation. Lang.: Rus. 911
Western ballet's influence on Indian classical dancer Ram Gopal. Europe. India. 1930-1960. Lang.: Ita. 915
Interview with dancer Mária Tatai. Hungary. 1981-1998. Lang.: Hun. 935
Dance director Seymour Felix. USA. 1918-1953. Lang.: Eng. 976
Interview with dancer and ballet mistress Márta Metzger. Budapest. 1968-1998. Lang.: Hun. 1066
Ballerina Marie Taglioni. France. 1804-1836. Lang.: Hun. 1071
Ballet dancer K. Kastal'skaja. France: Lyon. 1998. Lang.: Rus. 1073
Iván Markó's choreography for Bayreuth Festival productions. Germany: Bayreuth. Hungary. 1998. Lang.: Hun. 1083
Bayerische Staatsballett's guest performances at Budapest Opera House. Hungary: Budapest. 1998. Lang.: Hun. 1092
Interview with ballerina Katalin Hágai. Hungary. 1961-1998. Lang.: Hun. 1096
A gala performance at the Magyar Állami Operaház. Hungary: Budapest. 1998. Lang.: Hun. 1099
Interview with dancer Katalin Hágai. Hungary. 1998. Lang.: Hun. 1107
Interview with ballerina Adél Orosz. Hungary. 1954-1998. Lang.: Hun. 1112
Obituary for ballerina Galina Ulanova. Russia. 1910-1998. Lang.: Eng. 1125
Obituary for ballerina Galina Ulanova. Russia. 1910-1998. Lang.: Eng. 1127
Choreographer Marius Petipa and his wife, ballerina Marie Surovščikova. Russia. Lang.: Rus. 1128
Russian émigré ballet dancers. Russia: St. Petersburg. Lang.: Rus. 1129
Biography of ballerina Maja Pliseckaja. Russia. 1925-1994. Lang.: Rus. 1131
Collaboration of the Bolšoj and Mariinskij ballet troupes. Russia: Moscow, St. Petersburg. 1998. Lang.: Rus. 1135
Ballerina Natalija Ledovskaja. Russia: Moscow. 1998. Lang.: Rus. 1136
Ballerina Alla Osipenko. Russia. 1932-1998. Lang.: Eng. 1139
Ballerina Uljana Lopatkina. Russia: St. Petersburg. 1998. Lang.: Rus. 1140
Ballerina Maja Pliseckaja and her husband, composer Rodion Ščedrin. Russia: Moscow. 1998. Lang.: Rus. 1143
Memoirs of ballerina Maja Pliseckaja. Russia. 1998. Lang.: Rus. 1145
Ballet dancer Uljana Lopatkina. Russia: St. Petersburg. Lang.: Rus. 1146
Profile of ballerinas Uljana Lopatkina and Diana Višneva. Russia: St. Petersburg. 1998. Lang.: Rus. 1148
Tributes to ballerina Alexandra Danilova. USA: New York, NY. 1997. Lang.: Eng. 1165
Recollections of ballerina Margot Fonteyn. USA. Panama. 1946-1998. Lang.: Eng. 1182
Interview with dancer Julie Kent. USA. 1998. Lang.: Eng. 1184
David Parsons Dance Company's *Fill the Woods with Light*. USA: Washington, DC. 1998. Lang.: Hun. 1195
Dancer/choreographer Mikhail Baryshnikov. USSR. USA. 1969-1998. Lang.: Eng. 1196
The influence of tango on world dance. Argentina. Lang.: Rus. 1223
Obituary for dancer Sanjukta Panigrahi. India. 1944-1997. Lang.: Eng. 1230
Survey of women's dance and choreography of the season. Canada: Montreal, PQ. 1998. Lang.: Fre. 1263
Profile of the Festival international de nouvelle danse. Canada: Montreal, PQ. 1997. Lang.: Fre. 1264
Dancer Isadora Duncan's relationship with poet Sergej Esenin. Russia. 1919-1925. Lang.: Rus. 1297
Interview with choreographer Keely Garfield. UK-England. 1998. Lang.: Eng. 1308
Dancer Frances Alenikoff. USA: New York, NY. 1960-1998. Lang.: Eng. 1324
Shakespeare and traditional Asian theatrical forms. China, People's Republic of. India. Japan. 1981-1997. Lang.: Eng. 1346
Rival styles in *bharata natyam* performance. India. 1930-1990. Lang.: Eng. 1348
Classical Indian dance performer Malavika Sarukkai. India. 1998. Lang.: Rus. 1349
Analysis of Korean mask-dance theatre form *hahoe pyolsin-kut*. Korea. 1150-1928. Lang.: Eng. 1352
Kathak dancer Lakhiya Kumudini. India. 1998. Lang.: Rus. 1369
Acting in the private theatre of the Ming Dynasty. China. 1368-1644. Lang.: Eng. 1872
Interview with actress Lucinda Childs. France: Paris. 1976-1997. Lang.: Eng. 1943
Report from a symposium on traditional Korean theatre. Korea. Germany: Berlin. 1980-1998. Lang.: Ger, Fre, Dut, Eng. 2196
Using Renaissance dance in Shakespearean productions. USA. 1998. Lang.: Eng. 2692
Dance on screen. USA. Europe. 1920-1998. Lang.: Ger. 3860
The importance of Black performers in American musical films. USA. 1900-1957. Lang.: Swe. 3960
Time aspects of video dance. Europe. 1970-1998. Lang.: Ger. 4059
The Tropicana night club show. Cuba: Havana. 1939. Lang.: Swe. 4120
The collaborative art installation *Tight Roaring Circle*. UK-England: London. 1993-1997. Lang.: Eng. 4133
Carnival as a unifying force. Trinidad and Tobago. 1998. Lang.: Eng. 4170
Masque, movement, and social and political negotiations. England. 1610-1642. Lang.: Eng. 4198
Performance artist Mimi Goese. USA. 1982-1998. Lang.: Eng. 4252
Gower Champion's work in musical theatre. USA: New York, NY. 1936-1980. Lang.: Eng. 4388

Reference materials
Index to performing arts articles in Bragaglia's *Chronache d'attualità*. Italy: Rome. 1916-1922. Lang.: Ita. 704

Relation to other fields
The theatrical nature of Salvation Army activities. USA. 1865-1950. Lang.: Eng. 796
Drama therapy, personal narrative, and performance. USA. 1998. Lang.: Eng. 797
Non-Western dance forms in the teaching of theatre arts. USA: Davis, CA. 1990-1997. Lang.: Eng. 809
Theatrical activities of the Mormon Church. USA. 1977-1986. Lang.: Eng. 811
The effect of emigration on Russian dance. Russia. Lang.: Rus. 1197

Theory/criticism
Theatrical dancing and the performance aesthetics of Wilde, Yeats, and Shaw. UK-England. Ireland. 1890-1950. Lang.: Eng. 1012

Dancing at Lughnasa

Performance/production
Collection of newspaper reviews by London theatre critics. UK-England: London. 1998. Lang.: Eng. 2484

Daneau, Normand

Theory/criticism
Round-table discussion on theatre and impurity. Canada: Quebec, PQ. 1998. Lang.: Fre. 835

Dangerous Woman, A

Performance/production
Collection of newspaper reviews by London theatre critics. UK-England: London. 1998. Lang.: Eng. 2415

Daniel, Paul

Institutions
Paul Daniel, music director of the English National Opera. UK-England: London. 1997-1998. Lang.: Eng. 4475

Daniel, Samuel

Plays/librettos/scripts
Possible censorship of *The Tragedy of Philotas* by Samuel Daniel. England. 1605. Lang.: Eng. 2996

Daniel, Samuel — cont'd
Gender and politics in masques of Ben Jonson and Samuel Daniel. England. 1604-1605. Lang.: Eng. 4200
Political and ideological struggles in Jacobean masques. England. 1604-1609. Lang.: Eng. 4206
Daniels, Ron
Design/technology
Technical designs for Off Broadway Shakespearean productions. USA: New York, NY. 1998. Lang.: Eng. 1539
Theory/criticism
The urge to make Shakespeare contemporary. USA. 1990-1998. Lang.: Eng. 3844
Danielsson, Bente
Institutions
Profile of independent feminist theatre Kvinnliga Dramatiska Teatern. Sweden: Stockholm. 1997-1998. Lang.: Swe. 1725
Danielsson, Mattias
Training
Singer training at Teater- & Operahögskolan. Sweden: Gothenburg. 1960-1998. Lang.: Swe. 4848
Danilova, Alexandra
Performance/production
Tributes to ballerina Alexandra Danilova. USA: New York, NY. 1997. Lang.: Eng. 1165
Ballerina Alexandra Danilova on Balanchine's *Raymonda*. USA: New York, NY. 1946. Lang.: Eng. 1172
Danis, Daniel
Performance/production
Collection of newspaper reviews by London theatre critics. UK-England: London. 1998. Lang.: Eng. 2416
Plays/librettos/scripts
Quebecois drama and the influence of visual arts. Canada. 1980-1990. Lang.: Fre. 2816
Danovski, Ana Gabriela
Performance/production
Guest performance of Oleg Danovski Dance Theatre. Hungary: Budapest. 1998. Lang.: Hun. 1109
Danovski, Oleg
Performance/production
Guest performance of Oleg Danovski Dance Theatre. Hungary: Budapest. 1998. Lang.: Hun. 1109
Dans la solitude des champs de coton (In the Solitude of the Cotton Fields)
Performance/production
Productions of plays by Bernard-Marie Koltès. Canada: Montreal, PQ. 1991-1997. Lang.: Fre. 1862
Dansens Hus (Stockholm)
Administration
Riksteatern and Dansens Hus' Dansbiennal 98 meeting with government officials. Sweden. 1998. Lang.: Swe. 881
Design/technology
Lighting operators' conference regarding controls at Dansens Hus. Sweden: Stockholm. 1998. Lang.: Swe. 223
Institutions
Joint project to promote dance throughout Sweden. Sweden. 1974-1998. Lang.: Swe. 899
Danshögskolan (Stockholm)
Institutions
Appeal for more varied dance training. Sweden. 1998. Lang.: Swe. 903
Dante, Joe
Design/technology
Lighting design for Joe Dante's film *Small Soldiers*. USA. 1998. Lang.: Eng. 3914
Dantons Tod (Danton's Death)
Institutions
Productions by Stefan Bachmann and Robert Wilson at the Salzburg Festival. Austria: Salzburg. 1998. Lang.: Hun. 1570
Productions of Salzburger Festspiele. Austria: Salzburg. 1998. Lang.: Ger. 1571
Productions of the Salzburg Festival. Austria: Salzburg. 1998. Lang.: Ger. 1573
Performance/production
Director Armin Petras. Germany: Nordhausen. 1970-1998. Lang.: Ger. 2001
Robert Wilson's work with actors on a production of *Danton's Death (Dantons Tod)*. USA: Houston, TX. 1997. Lang.: Eng. 2688
Danz, Sanne
Design/technology
Profiles of young theatrical designers. Netherlands. 1990-1998. Lang.: Dut. 207
Danza Contemporánea de Cuba (Havana)
Institutions
Contemporary Cuban dance. Cuba: Havana. 1959-1998. Lang.: Swe. 1250
Danza Nacional (Havana)
Institutions
Contemporary Cuban dance. Cuba: Havana. 1959-1998. Lang.: Swe. 1250
Daphne
Performance/production
Peri and Rinuccini's *Daphne*, the first opera. Italy: Florence. 1598. Lang.: Hun. 4651
Dargomyžskij, Aleksand'r Sergejėvič
Plays/librettos/scripts
Operas of Dargomyžskij and Rimskij-Korsakov on texts of Puškin. Russia. 1799-1869. Lang.: Rus. 4815
Darja
Plays/librettos/scripts
Playwright Volker Lüdecke. Germany: Kaiserslautern. 1992-1998. Lang.: Ger. 3141
Dark at the Top of the Stairs, The
Plays/librettos/scripts
Gender-role reversal in plays of William Inge. USA. 1950-1958. Lang.: Eng. 3623
Dark House, The
Performance/production
Collection of newspaper reviews by London theatre critics. UK-England: London. 1998. Lang.: Eng. 2411
Dark Lady, The
Performance/production
Brief productions of Shakespeare, Shaw, and Marlowe at the World's Fair. USA: Chicago, IL. 1934. Lang.: Eng. 2701
Darke, Nick
Performance/production
Collection of newspaper reviews by London theatre critics. UK-England: London. 1998. Lang.: Eng. 2440
Collection of newspaper reviews by London theatre critics. UK-England: London. 1998. Lang.: Eng. 2513
Darkness Visible
Performance/production
Collection of newspaper reviews by London theatre critics. UK-England: London. 1998. Lang.: Eng. 2575
Darvasi, László
Performance/production
Review of Darvasi's *Bolond Helga (Foolish Helga)*, Csokonai Theatre. Hungary: Debrecen. 1997. Lang.: Hun. 2122
Darwall-Smith, Emma
Performance/production
Collection of newspaper reviews by London theatre critics. UK-England: London. 1998. Lang.: Eng. 2524
Darwin Theatre Group
Performance/production
Analysis of performance pieces reacting to the Australian bicentenary. Australia: Darwin, Sydney. 1988. Lang.: Eng. 1815
Plays/librettos/scripts
Australian plays about the war in Vietnam. Australia. 1990-1998. Lang.: Eng. 2776
Dashwood, Robin
Performance/production
Collection of newspaper reviews by London theatre critics. UK-England: London. 1998. Lang.: Eng. 2465
Dassin, Jules
Performance/production
Actors' interpretations of the title role in Oscar Wilde's *The Canterville Ghost*. UK-England. USA. 1943-1998. Lang.: Eng. 4066
Dasté, Marie-Hélène
Performance/production
Interview with Marie-Hélène Dasté, daughter of Jacques Copeau. France: Paris. 1913-1992. Lang.: Eng. 4089
Databases
Research/historiography
The use of 'Literature Online' for editing and attribution studies. UK-England. 1998. Lang.: Eng. 825
Daugherty, Michael
Plays/librettos/scripts
The American and Canadian premieres of *Jackie O*. Canada: Banff, AB. USA: Houston, TX. 1997. Lang.: Eng. 4761
Daughter of the Poet, The
Performance/production
Collection of newspaper reviews by London theatre critics. UK-England: London. 1998. Lang.: Eng. 2464

Daughters
Performance/production
Collection of newspaper reviews by London theatre critics. UK-England: London. 1998. Lang.: Eng. 2549

Daumas, Adrían
Performance/production
Productions of Shakespeare's *Twelfth Night* at the Madrid Theatre Festival. Spain: Madrid. 1996-1997. Lang.: Eng. 2359

Davant l'Empire (Inside the Empire)
Basic theatrical documents
Text of *Davant l'Empire (Inside the Empire)* by Octavi Egea. Spain-Catalonia. 1999. Lang.: Cat. 1465

Davenant, William
Plays/librettos/scripts
Analysis of Dryden and Davenant's *Enchanted Island.* England. 1674. Lang.: Eng. 2873

Davey, Patrick
Performance/production
Collection of newspaper reviews by London theatre critics. UK-England: London. 1998. Lang.: Eng. 2537

Davey, Sarah
Performance/production
Collection of newspaper reviews by London theatre critics. UK-England: London. 1998. Lang.: Eng. 2483

David (for Samuel)
Plays/librettos/scripts
Analysis of plays based on the Hebrew prophets. USA. Europe. 1919-1970. Lang.: Eng. 3659

David Copperfield
Performance/production
Collection of newspaper reviews by London theatre critics. UK-England: London. 1998. Lang.: Eng. 2531

David Parsons Dance Company (New York, NY)
Performance/production
David Parsons Dance Company's *Fill the Woods with Light.* USA: Washington, DC. 1998. Lang.: Hun. 1195

Davidson, Adam
Basic theatrical documents
Screenplay of *The Lunch Date* by Adam Davidson. USA. 1998. Lang.: Eng. 3883

Davidson, Ruth
Performance/production
Dancers Tina Fehlandt and Ruth Davidson of Mark Morris Dance Group. USA: New York, NY. 1980-1998. Lang.: Eng. 1327

Davies, Alan
Performance/production
Collection of newspaper reviews by London theatre critics. UK-England: London. 1998. Lang.: Eng. 2429

Davies, Howard
Performance/production
Collection of newspaper reviews by London theatre critics. UK-England: London. 1998. Lang.: Eng. 2459
Collection of newspaper reviews by London theatre critics. UK-England: London. 1998. Lang.: Eng. 2491
Collection of newspaper reviews by London theatre critics. UK-England: London. 1998. Lang.: Eng. 2586

Davies, Paul
Performance/production
Collection of newspaper reviews by London theatre critics. UK-England: London. 1998. Lang.: Eng. 2448

Davies, Siobhan
Theory/criticism
The use of different analytical strategies to obtain multiple readings of dance performance. USA. Europe. 1946-1982. Lang.: Eng. 1200

Davies, Thomas
Performance spaces
Evidence that Davies' bear-baiting ring may have been a restoration of the Hope Theatre. England: London. 1647-1682. Lang.: Eng. 435

Davis, Andrew
Performance/production
Conductor Andrew Davis. UK-England. USA. 1998. Lang.: Eng. 4704

Davis, Anthony
Performance/production
Background material on Lyric Opera of Chicago radio broadcast performances. USA: Chicago, IL. 1998. Lang.: Eng. 4709

Davis, Donald
Performance/production
Obituaries for Roger L. Stevens, Kenneth Frankel, Donald Davis, and Edith Oliver. USA. Canada. 1910-1998. Lang.: Eng. 2742

Davis, Elliot
Design/technology
Lighting design for Steven Soderbergh's film *Out of Sight.* USA. 1998. Lang.: Eng. 3912

Davis, Harry
Administration
Theatre manager and entrepreneur Harry Davis. USA: Pittsburgh, PA. 1893-1927. Lang.: Eng. 134

Davis, Julia
Performance/production
Collection of newspaper reviews by London theatre critics. UK-England: London. 1998. Lang.: Eng. 2513

Davis, Owen
Plays/librettos/scripts
The development of playwright Owen Davis. USA. 1905-1923. Lang.: Eng. 3526

Davis, Thulani
Plays/librettos/scripts
Novelist and playwright Thulani Davis. USA. 1998. Lang.: Eng. 3689

Dawson, Andrew
Performance/production
Collection of newspaper reviews by London theatre critics. UK-England: London. 1998. Lang.: Eng. 2556

Dawson, Peter
Performance/production
Collection of newspaper reviews by London theatre critics. UK-England: London. 1998. Lang.: Eng. 2449

Day at Musemeci's, A
Basic theatrical documents
Text of *A Day at Musemeci's* by Scott R. Ritter. USA. 1987. Lang.: Eng. 1503

Day I Stood Still, The
Performance/production
Collection of newspaper reviews by London theatre critics. UK-England: London. 1998. Lang.: Eng. 2567

Day, Greg
Performance/production
Collection of newspaper reviews by London theatre critics. UK-England: London. 1998. Lang.: Eng. 2520

Days Without End
Plays/librettos/scripts
Analysis of *Days Without End* by Eugene O'Neill. USA. 1934. Lang.: Eng. 3636

Daystar (Santa Fe, NM)
Performance/production
Rosalie Jones of Native American dance company Daystar. USA: Santa Fe, NM. 1966-1998. Lang.: Eng. 1240

De Antonis, Pasquale
Relation to other fields
Catalogue of an exhibition of theatre photography by Pasquale De Antonis. Italy. 1908-1998. Lang.: Ita. 752

de Baan, Peter
Performance/production
De Zaak's production of *Action* by Sam Shepard. Netherlands: Rotterdam. 1988. Lang.: Dut. 2201

De Beauvoir, Simone
SEE
Beauvoir, Simone de.

De Bosio, Gianfranco
Performance/production
Gianfranco De Bosio's production of *Se questo è un uomo (If This Is a Man)* by Primo Levi. Italy: Turin. 1963-1966. Lang.: Eng. 2168

de Castro, Angela
Performance/production
Collection of newspaper reviews by London theatre critics. UK-England: London. 1998. Lang.: Eng. 2421

De Chirico, Giorgio
Design/technology
New edition of the autobiography of painter and scenographer Giorgio De Chirico. Italy. 1888-1978. Lang.: Ita. 202

De Filippo, Eduardo
Performance/production
Collection of newspaper reviews by London theatre critics. UK-England. 1998. Lang.: Eng. 2504
Collection of newspaper reviews by London theatre critics. UK-England: London. 1998. Lang.: Eng. 2518
Plays/librettos/scripts
Essays on actor, director, and playwright Eduardo De Filippo. Italy. 1900-1984. Lang.: Ita. 3254

De Frutos, Javier
Performance/production
Choreography of Javier De Frutos at the Dance Umbrella Festival. UK-England: London. 1998. Lang.: Hun. 970
Interview with choreographer Javier De Frutos. USA. 1990-1998. Lang.: Eng. 1332
de Gouges, Olympe
Plays/librettos/scripts
Olympe de Gouges and the theatre of the French Revolution. France. 1789-1795. Lang.: Fre. 3109
de Haan, Christopher
Performance/production
Theatre Magazine's anniversary issue. USA. 1968-1998. Lang.: Eng. 617
de Helen, Sandra
Performance/production
Contemporary queer politics and the production of gay and lesbian theatre. USA. 1970-1997. Lang.: Eng. 2710
de Jong, Anis
Performance/production
The work of Theatergroep Delta. Netherlands: Amsterdam. 1983-1998. Lang.: Dut. 2200
de Jonge, Dorien
Design/technology
Profiles of young theatrical designers. Netherlands. 1990-1998. Lang.: Dut. 207
de Josselin De Jong, Laura
Design/technology
Profiles of young theatrical designers. Netherlands. 1990-1998. Lang.: Dut. 207
De Keersmaeker, Anne Teresa
Performance/production
Dancer/choreographer Anne Teresa De Keersmaeker. Belgium: Brussels. 1981-1998. Lang.: Eng. 1260
De La Guarda (Buenos Aires)
Institutions
Report on festival of physical theatre. Germany: Munich. 1997. Lang.: Eng. 1664
de la Motte Fouqué, Friedrich
Performance/production
Analysis of the ballet *Berthalda en Hildebrand (Berthalda and Hildebrand).* Netherlands: Amsterdam. 1849. Lang.: Ger. 1122
de la Parra, Marco Antonio
Plays/librettos/scripts
Visual imagery in *El padre muerto (The Dead Father)* by Marco Antonio de la Parra. Chile. 1993. Lang.: Eng. 2839
de Lappe, Gemze
Performance/production
Dancer Gemze de Lappe's work with choreographer Agnes De Mille. USA: New York, NY. 1943-1998. Lang.: Eng. 4380
De Mille, Agnes
Performance/production
Playwright Jess Gregg's relationship with choreographer Agnes De Mille. USA: New York, NY. 1961-1998. Lang.: Eng. 1178
Dancer Gemze de Lappe's work with choreographer Agnes De Mille. USA: New York, NY. 1943-1998. Lang.: Eng. 4380
De Molina, Tirso
SEE
Molina, Tirso de.
de Palm, Norman
Institutions
Interview with founders of Dutch multicultural group Cosmic Illusions. Netherlands: Amsterdam. Netherlands Antilles. 1988. Lang.:Eng. 1679
De Rege, Giorgio
Performance/production
Variety actors Guido and Giorgio De Rege. Italy. 1891-1948. Lang.: Ita. 4275
De Rege, Guido
Performance/production
Variety actors Guido and Giorgio De Rege. Italy. 1891-1948. Lang.: Ita. 4275
de Ridder, Annelies
Design/technology
Profiles of young theatrical designers. Netherlands. 1990-1998. Lang.: Dut. 207
de Rooy, Felix
Institutions
Interview with founders of Dutch multicultural group Cosmic Illusions. Netherlands: Amsterdam. Netherlands Antilles. 1988. Lang.:Eng. 1679
de Silva, David
Performance/production
Collection of newspaper reviews by London theatre critics. UK-England: London. 1998. Lang.: Eng. 2525
de Valois, Ninette
Performance/production
Annabel Farjeon on dancing for Ninette de Valois and Frederick Ashton. UK-England: London. 1930-1940. Lang.: Eng. 1158
Collaborative Symbolist dance/theatre projects. Europe. USA. 1916-1934. Lang.: Eng. 1268
De Verna, Francis P.
Design/technology
Lighting expert Francis P. De Verna. USA. 1928-1998. Lang.: Eng. 257
de Wolfe, Elsie
Administration
The lesbian relationship of agent Elisabeth Marbury and designer Elsie de Wolfe. USA. 1886-1933. Lang.: Eng. 44
Dead Calm
Plays/librettos/scripts
Earl Kim's musical piece *Dead Calm,* based on a text by Samuel Beckett. 1945-1995. Lang.: Eng. 4306
Dead Class, The
SEE
Umerla Klasa.
Dead End Kids
Performance/production
Documentary theatre and the politics of representation. USA. 1966-1993. Lang.: Eng. 2728
Dead Funny
Performance/production
Collection of newspaper reviews by London theatre critics. UK-England. 1998. Lang.: Eng. 2497
Dead Indians
Plays/librettos/scripts
Review of collections of plays with gay themes. Canada. 1996. Lang.: Eng. 2802
Dead Man Walking
Institutions
The partnership between San Francisco Opera and Chase Manhattan Bank. USA: San Francisco, CA, New York, NY. 1998. Lang.: Eng. 423
Dead Meat
Performance/production
Collection of newspaper reviews by London theatre critics. UK-England: London. 1998. Lang.: Eng. 2471
Dead Monkey, The
Performance/production
Collection of newspaper reviews by London theatre critics. UK-England: London. 1998. Lang.: Eng. 2440
Collection of newspaper reviews by London theatre critics. UK-England: London. 1998. Lang.: Eng. 2513
Dead on the Ground
Performance/production
Collection of newspaper reviews by London theatre critics. UK-England: London. 1998. Lang.: Eng. 2445
Dead White Males
Plays/librettos/scripts
Analysis of *Dead White Males* by David Williamson. Australia. 1995. Lang.: Eng. 2773
Deaf theatre
Performance/production
The failure of the Canadian Theatre of the Deaf. Canada. 1965-1998. Lang.: Eng. 507
Interview with Deaf dancer Juho Saarinen. Finland. 1998. Lang.: Fin. 1273
Theory/criticism
Aristotelian approach to Deaf performance. USA. 1988. Lang.: Eng. 861
Deák, Ferenc
Performance/production
Ferenc Deák's *Fojtás (Tamping)* directed by László Babarczy. Hungary: Kaposvár. 1998. Lang.: Hun. 2117
Deane, Hamilton
Design/technology
Magical stage effects in 'vampire' plays. USA. 1820-1977. Lang.: Eng. 1548
Deans, Jonathan
Design/technology
Sound design for the Broadway premiere of the musical *Ragtime.* USA: New York, NY. 1998. Lang.: Eng. 4341

Dear Conjunction Theatre (Paris)
Performance/production
Survey of Parisian productions. France: Paris. 1997-1998. Lang.: Eng. 1937
Dear Liar
Plays/librettos/scripts
Popular adaptations of the works of George Bernard Shaw. UK-England. 1890-1990. Lang.: Eng. 3445
Dear Witches, The
Plays/librettos/scripts
Horace Walpole's *The Dear Witches* and Shakespeare's *Macbeth*. England. 1743. Lang.: Eng. 2857
Death and the King's Horseman
Plays/librettos/scripts
Ritual in plays of John Bekederemo and Wole Soyinka. Nigeria. 1965-1998. Lang.: Eng. 3287
Death and the Maiden
SEE ALSO
Muerte y la doncella, La.
Death at Balibo
Performance/production
Analysis of performance pieces reacting to the Australian bicentenary. Australia: Darwin, Sydney. 1988. Lang.: Eng. 1815
Death by Heroine
Performance/production
Collection of newspaper reviews by London theatre critics. UK-England: London. 1998. Lang.: Eng. 2582
Death in Venice
Performance/production
Operas by Benjamin Britten in the repertory of the Metropolitan and the New York City Opera. USA: New York, NY. 1945-1998. Lang.:Eng. 4749
Plays/librettos/scripts
Analysis of Benjamin Britten's opera *Death in Venice*. UK-England. 1912-1992. Lang.: Eng. 4823
Death of a Salesman
Performance/production
Two Hungarian productions of Arthur Miller's *Death of a Salesman*. Hungary: Pécs, Szeged. 1998. Lang.: Hun. 2123
Seven critics on their favorite character or portrayal. Sweden. 1950. Lang.: Swe. 2369
Death of Cúchulain, The
Performance/production
Collection of newspaper reviews by London theatre critics. UK-England: London. 1998. Lang.: Eng. 2458
Deburau, Jean-Gaspard
Performance/production
Mime, pantomime, and the work of Jean-Gaspard Deburau. France. 1700-1998. Lang.: Swe. 4087
Debussy, Claude
Performance/production
Yvette Bozsik's new choreography for Debussy's *L'après-midi d'un faune*. Hungary: Budapest. 1997. Lang.: Hun. 940
Robert Wilson's dance adaptation of *Le Martyre de Saint Sébastien* by D'Annunzio. France: Paris. 1988. Lang.: Ita. 1074
Collaborative Symbolist dance/theatre projects. Europe. USA. 1916-1934. Lang.: Eng. 1268
Opera director Katja Czellnik. Germany: Oldenburg, Kiel. 1996-1998. Lang.: Ger. 4583
Decadence
Plays/librettos/scripts
Analysis of *Decadence* by Steven Berkoff. UK-England. 1981. Lang.: Dut. 3431
Decir sí (To Say Yes)
Plays/librettos/scripts
Cruelty and the absurd in theatre of Latin American playwrights. Latin America. 1960-1980. Lang.: Eng. 3267
Deconstruction
Performance/production
Deconstructionist analysis of acting in the theatre of Bertolt Brecht. Germany. 1922-1956. Lang.: Eng. 2007
Decroux, Etienne
Performance/production
Yves Marc on Etienne Decroux. France: Paris. 1998. Lang.: Eng. 4088
Corinne Soum, former assistant to Etienne Decroux. France: Paris. UK-England: London. 1968-1998. Lang.: Eng. 4090
Etienne Decroux's concept of actor-centered theatre. USA. France. 1920-1998. Lang.: Eng. 4091
Dedekind, Friedrich
Plays/librettos/scripts
Morality plays of the Reformation. Germany. 1550-1584. Lang.: Eng. 3163
Dee, Ruby
Performance/production
Actress Ruby Dee. USA. 1998. Lang.: Eng. 2689
Deep Space
Performance/production
Collection of newspaper reviews by London theatre critics. UK-England: London. 1998. Lang.: Eng. 2445
Definitions of Intimacy
Performance/production
Collection of newspaper reviews by London theatre critics. UK-England: London. 1998. Lang.: Eng. 2455
Dehler, Peter
Institutions
Profile of Nordhessisches Landestheater Marburg. Germany: Marburg. 1997-1998. Lang.: Ger. 1653
Deirdre
Performance/production
Directing a student production of Yeats's *Deirdre*. USA: Louisville, KY. 1988. Lang.: Eng. 2738
Dekameron (Decameron)
Performance/production
The ballet adaptation of the *Decameron* performed by Veszprém Dance Workshop. Hungary: Veszprém. 1998. Lang.: Hun. 1108
Dekker, John
Plays/librettos/scripts
Comic scenes and characters in the Elizabethan history play. England. 1590-1618. Lang.: Eng. 2955
Dekker, Thomas
Performance/production
Collection of newspaper reviews by London theatre critics. UK-England: London. 1998. Lang.: Eng. 2486
Plays/librettos/scripts
Women's use of wit in response to men in English popular culture. England. 1590-1630. Lang.: Eng. 2884
The representation of historical female characters on the Renaissance stage. England. 1580-1615. Lang.: Eng. 2922
Analysis of *The Witch of Edmonton* by Ford, Dekker, and Rowley. England. 1621. Lang.: Eng. 2928
Protestant belief and English Reformation drama. England. 1535-1607. Lang.: Eng. 2972
Sociological analysis of *The Shoemaker's Holiday* by Thomas Dekker. England. 1600. Lang.: Eng. 2973
Flemish immigrants in English Renaissance drama. England. 1515-1635. Lang.: Eng. 2976
The treatment of single women in early Stuart drama. England. 1604-1608. Lang.: Eng. 2979
The skull in plays of Shakespeare, Dekker, and Tourneur. England. 1606. Lang.: Eng. 3026
Del Valle-Inclán, Ramón
SEE
Valle-Inclán, Ramón María del.
Delamere, Robert
Performance/production
Collection of newspaper reviews by London theatre critics. UK-England: London. 1998. Lang.: Eng. 2443
Delaney
Performance/production
Collection of newspaper reviews by London theatre critics. UK-England: London. Lang.: Eng. 2408
Delaunay, Sonia
Design/technology
Avant-garde Russian women artist/designers. Russia. USSR. 1880-1949. Lang.: Eng. 214
Delbo, Charlotte
Plays/librettos/scripts
The Holocaust in plays of Charlotte Delbo. France. 1913-1985. Lang.: Eng. 3115
Delibes, Léo
Audience
The negative influence of Wagnerianism on the reception of Delibes' opera *Lakmé*. 1900-1996. Lang.: Fre. 4409
Basic theatrical documents
Libretto of *Lakmé* by Léo Delibes, Edmond Gondinet, and Philippe Gille. France. 1883. Lang.: Fre. 4415

Delibes, Léo — cont'd

Performance/production
Interpreters of the title role in Delibes' opera *Lakmé*. 1932-1995. Lang.: Fre. 4505
Performances of Delibes' *Lakmé*. 1883-1997. Lang.: Fre. 4519
Recordings of Delibes' *Lakmé*. 1941-1998. Lang.: Fre. 4524
Natalie Dessay's role in Gilbert Blin's production of *Lakmé*. France: Paris. 1995. Lang.: Fre. 4570
Soprano Mady Mesplé on Delibes' *Lakmé*. France. 1961-1997. Lang.: Fre. 4573
Léo Delibes as a composer of operetta. France. 1856-1883. Lang.: Fre. 4855
Plays/librettos/scripts
Analysis of Delibes' opera *Lakmé*. France. 1883. Lang.: Fre. 4782
The source of the libretto for Delibes' *Lakmé*. France. 1853-1883. Lang.: Fre. 4784

Delicate Balance, A
Plays/librettos/scripts
Recent productions of plays by Edward Albee. USA: New York, NY, Hartford, CT. 1959-1998. Lang.: Eng. 3578

Delincuentes, Los (Criminals, The)
Performance/production
Collection of newspaper reviews by London theatre critics. UK-England: London. 1998. Lang.: Eng. 2450

Delitto all'Isola delle Capre (Crime on Goat Island)
Performance/production
Collection of newspaper reviews by London theatre critics. UK-England: London. 1998. Lang.: Eng. 2534

Dell, Patricia
Administration
Interview with actors on Equity. USA: New York, NY. 1998. Lang.: Eng. 75

Delsarte, François
Performance/production
History of movement training for the actor. USA. 1910-1985. Lang.: Eng. 675

Demande d'emploi, La (Interview, The)
Plays/librettos/scripts
Interview with playwright Michel Vinaver. Canada: Quebec, PQ. 1969-1998. Lang.: Fre. 2831

Demarcy-Mota, François
Basic theatrical documents
French translation of Shakespeare's *Love's Labour's Lost*. England. France. 1594-1998. Lang.: Fre. 1419

Demarcy, Richard
Basic theatrical documents
Text of *Ubu déchaîné (Ubu Unchained)* by Richard Demarcy. Benin. France. 1998. Lang.: Fre. 4287

Demidova, Alla S.
Performance/production
Actress Alla S. Demidova. Russia. 1998. Lang.: Rus. 2249

Demme, Jonathan
Audience
Jonathan Demme's film adaptation of *Beloved* by Toni Morrison. USA. 1998. Lang.: Eng. 3877

Demon Headmaster, The
Performance/production
Collection of newspaper reviews by London theatre critics. UK-England: London. 1998. Lang.: Eng. 2553

Demons and Dybbuks
Performance/production
Collection of newspaper reviews by London theatre critics. UK-England: London. 1998. Lang.: Eng. 2423

Denard, Michael
Performance/production
Hungarian guest performances of world ballet stars. Hungary: Budapest. 1975-1978. Lang.: Hun. 1085

Dendy, Mark
Performance/production
Choreographer Mark Dendy. USA: New York, NY. 1980-1998. Lang.: Eng. 1330

Denison, Michael
Performance/production
Acting career of Michael Denison. UK-England: London. 1936-1998. Lang.: Eng. 2599

Denizon, Jean-Paul
Training
Actor/director Jean-Paul Denizon and his workshops on Peter Brook's approach to theatre. France. 1980-1998. Lang.: Ita. 873

Dennewitz, Ekkehard
Institutions
Profile of Nordhessisches Landestheater Marburg. Germany: Marburg. 1997-1998. Lang.: Ger. 1653

Denoncourt, Serge
Design/technology
Costume designer Isabelle Larivière. Canada: Quebec, PQ. 1994-1995. Lang.: Fre. 1514

Dent, Tom
Administration
Obituary for Tom Dent, former chairman of the Free Southern Theatre board. USA: New Orleans, LA. 1998. Lang.: Eng. 1395

Depardon, Raymond
Performance/production
Productions of the Paris Festival d'Automne. France: Paris. 1998. Lang.: Fre. 1931

dePaur, Leonard
Administration
Conductor Leonard dePaur, winner of the Paul Robeson Award. USA: New York, NY. 1910-1998. Lang.: Eng. 104

Derby Day
Performance/production
Collection of newspaper reviews by London theatre critics. UK-England: London. 1998. Lang.: Eng. 2422

Derby Playhouse
Performance/production
Collection of newspaper reviews by London theatre critics. UK-England: London, Stratford, Derby. 1998. Lang.: Eng. 2417

Dernière bande, La
SEE
Krapp's Last Tape.

Derrick
Performance/production
The popular German TV show *Derrick*. Germany. 1998. Lang.: Eng. 4060

Dervisher
Performance/production
The reconstruction of Jean Börlin's ballet *Dervisher*. Sweden: Stockholm. 1997. Lang.: Eng. 1150
Millicent Hodson and Kenneth Archer's revival of Jean Börlin's ballet *Dervisher*. UK-England: London. Sweden: Stockholm. 1920-1998. Lang.: Swe. 1311

Des Lauriers
SEE
Gracieux, Jean.

Design/technology
SEE ALSO
Classed Entries.
Performance/production
László Márkus, one-time director of the Budapest Opera House. Hungary. 1881-1948. Lang.: Hun. 540
Directing and design to accommodate the disabled in performance. USA. 1988. Lang.: Eng. 623
The methodology of director Robert Lepage. Canada: Toronto, ON. 1992. Lang.: Eng. 1845
Profiles of major theatrical figures. Russia. 1950-1998. Lang.: Rus. 2263
Directorial style of JoAnne Akalaitis. USA. 1982-1998. Lang.: Eng. 2737
Director Joel Kaplan on his production of the *York Cycle*. Canada: Toronto, ON. 1998. Lang.: Eng. 4213

deSingel (Antwerp)
Performance/production
Robert Wilson's production of *Doctor Faustus Lights the Lights* by Gertrude Stein. Belgium: Antwerp. 1992. Lang.: Fle. 1828

Desire Under the Elms
Performance/production
Aleksand'r Tairov's productions of plays by Eugene O'Neill. USSR. 1926-1929. Lang.: Eng. 2769
Plays/librettos/scripts
Female characters in Eugene O'Neill's plays. USA. 1920-1953. Lang.: Eng. 3525
Themes of Eugene O'Neill's early plays. USA. 1915-1925. Lang.: Eng. 3668
Closure in plays of Eugene O'Neill. USA. 1918-1950. Lang.: Eng. 3703

Desperate Optimists (London)
Performance/production
Collection of newspaper reviews by London theatre critics. UK-England: London. 1998. Lang.: Eng. 2565

Despres, Suzanne
Performance/production
The 'grande coquette' on the Parisian stage. France: Paris. 1885-1925. Lang.: Eng. 531
Despréz, Jean (Laroque, Laurette)
Plays/librettos/scripts
On the text and staging of *La Cathédrale...* by Jean Depréz (Laurette Laroque). Canada: Montreal, PQ. 1949. Lang.: Fre. 2823
Desquite, El (Getting Even)
Performance/production
Theatrical construction of Chilean national identity and history. Chile. 1990-1998. Lang.: Spa. 510
Dessau, Paul
Performance/production
Thomas Langhoff's production of Brecht's *Der Kaukasische Kreidekreis (The Caucasian Chalk Circle)* at Deutsches Theater. Germany: Berlin. 1998. Lang.: Ger. 1965
Productions of plays by Brecht and Shakespeare at the Hungarian theatre of Satu Mare. Romania: Satu Mare. 1998. Lang.: Hun. 2228
Brecht and the vocal role. Germany. 1920-1998. Lang.: Swe. 4295
Plays/librettos/scripts
Hero and anti-hero in contemporary opera production. Germany. 1998. Lang.: Ger. 4791
Dessay, Natalie
Performance/production
Interpreters of the title role in Delibes' opera *Lakmé*. 1932-1995. Lang.: Fre. 4505
Natalie Dessay's role in Gilbert Blin's production of *Lakmé*. France: Paris. 1995. Lang.: Fre. 4570
Soprano Natalie Dessay. France. 1998. Lang.: Eng. 4575
Destiny of Me, The
Plays/librettos/scripts
Effeminacy on the American stage. USA. 1920-1998. Lang.: Eng. 3682
Deszcz, Katarzyna
Performance/production
Collection of newspaper reviews by London theatre critics. UK-England: London. 1998. Lang.: Eng. 2534
Détour Théâtre (Paris)
Relation to other fields
Author Gertrude Stein, subject of *Gertrude morte cet après-midi (Gertrude Dead This Afternoon)* by Monique Lepeu. France: Paris. 1874-1997. Lang.: Fre. 3759
Detour, The
Plays/librettos/scripts
The development of playwright Owen Davis. USA. 1905-1923. Lang.: Eng. 3526
Deutsch Sorbisches Volkstheater (Bautzen)
Institutions
Profiles of theatres in Saxony. Germany: Zittau, Bautzen, Görlitz. 1997-1998. Lang.: Ger. 1650
Deutsche Oper (Berlin)
Design/technology
Lighting for Henze's opera *Der Prinz von Homburg* at Deutsche Oper Berlin. Germany: Berlin. 1997. Lang.: Ger. 4431
Deutsche Oper am Rhein (Duisburg)
Administration
Marketing practices of Deutsche Oper am Rhein. Germany: Duisburg. 1996-1998. Lang.: Ger. 4404
Performance/production
Productions of Wagner's *Tristan und Isolde* by Peter Konwitschny and Werner Schroeter. Germany: Munich, Duisberg. 1998. Lang.: Ger. 4580
Deutsche Theatertechnische Gesellschaft (Munich)
Design/technology
Account of ACTSAFE conference on theatre safety. France: Paris. 1998. Lang.: Swe. 181
Deutsches Nationaltheater (Weimar)
Institutions
The proposed merger of Deutsches Nationaltheater Weimar and Theater Erfurt. Germany: Weimar, Erfurt. 1998. Lang.: Ger. 354
Performance/production
Dance adaptations of Shakespeare's *Hamlet*. Germany: Bremen, Weimar. 1996-1997. Lang.: Ger. 930
Deutsches Schauspielhaus (Hamburg)
Administration
Interview with Frank Baumbauer of Deutsches Schauspielhaus Hamburg. Germany: Hamburg. 1993-2000. Lang.: Ger. 11
Performance/production
Rehearsals of Christoph Marthaler's production of *Arsenic and Old Lace* by Joseph Kesselring. Germany: Hamburg. 1998. Lang.: Ger. 1953
Christoph Marthaler's approach to directing Joseph Kesselring's *Arsenic and Old Lace*. Germany: Hamburg. 1998. Lang.: Ger. 1956
Two productions of Brecht's *Der Kaukasische Kreidekreis (The Caucasian Chalk Circle)*. Germany: Berlin, Hamburg. 1998. Lang.: Ger. 1957
Christoph Schlingensief's project with the homeless at Deutsches Schauspielhaus. Germany: Hamburg. 1998. Lang.: Ger. 1961
German productions of adaptations of *A Clockwork Orange* by Anthony Burgess. Germany: Dresden, Hamburg, Stendal. 1998. Lang.: Ger. 1972
Shakespearean productions in northern Germany. Germany: Hamburg. 1996-1997. Lang.: Ger. 1978
Actor Herbert Fritsch. Germany. 1992-1998. Lang.: Ger. 1985
Adaptations and performances of *Alte Meister (Old Masters)* by Thomas Bernhard. Germany. 1997-1998. Lang.: Ger. 1996
German productions of Shakespeare. Germany: Leipzig, Hamburg, Berlin. 1998. Lang.: Ger. 2033
Recent productions of Deutsches Schauspielhaus. Germany: Hamburg. 1998. Lang.: Ger. 2034
Frank Castorf's production of Strauss's *Die Fledermaus*. Germany: Hamburg. 1997-1998. Lang.: Ger. 4612
Reviews of recent opera productions. Switzerland: Basel. Germany: Stuttgart, Berlin, Hamburg. France: Strasbourg. 1997-1998. Lang.: Ger. 4702
Deutsches Theater (Berlin)
Audience
The relationship between theatres and the youth audience. Germany. 1998. Lang.: Ger. 152
Performance/production
Two productions of Brecht's *Der Kaukasische Kreidekreis (The Caucasian Chalk Circle)*. Germany: Berlin, Hamburg. 1998. Lang.: Ger. 1957
Thomas Langhoff's production of Brecht's *Der Kaukasische Kreidekreis (The Caucasian Chalk Circle)* at Deutsches Theater. Germany: Berlin. 1998. Lang.: Ger. 1965
Reviews of productions of plays by Brecht. Germany. 1998. Lang.: Ger. 1986
Interview with actor Klaus Piontek. Germany: Berlin. 1962-1998. Lang.: Ger. 2008
German productions of Shakespeare. Germany: Leipzig, Hamburg, Berlin. 1998. Lang.: Ger. 2033
Shakespearean production and the GDR's 'existential crisis'. Germany, East. 1976-1980. Lang.: Eng. 2051
Deutsches Theater, Baracke (Berlin)
Administration
Interview with Thomas Ostermeier, artistic director of Schaubühne. Germany: Berlin. 1996-1998. Lang.: Ger. 1386
Theatre directors on the future of subsidized theatre. Switzerland: Zurich. Germany: Hannover, Berlin. 1998. Lang.: Ger. 1390
Institutions
Profile of Deutsches Theater, Baracke. Germany: Berlin. 1996-1998. Lang.: Ger. 1637
Performance/production
Political changes reflected in Berlin theatre productions. Germany: Berlin. 1998. Lang.: Ger. 1958
Profile of Thomas Ostermeier, *Theater Heute*'s young director of the year. Germany: Berlin. 1997-1998. Lang.: Ger. 1959
Recent German productions of plays by Bertolt Brecht. Germany: Hamburg, Berlin. 1997. Lang.: Swe. 1977
Director Thomas Ostermeier. Germany: Berlin. 1996-1998. Lang.: Swe. 1998
Plays/librettos/scripts
Interview with director Thomas Ostermeier. Germany: Berlin. 1996-1998. Lang.: Ger. 3124
Mark Ravenhill's *Shopping and Fucking* and its production by Thomas Ostermeier. UK-England. Germany. 1998. Lang.: Ger. 3476
Deutsches Theater, Kammerspiele (Berlin)
Performance/production
Adaptations and performances of *Alte Meister (Old Masters)* by Thomas Bernhard. Germany. 1997-1998. Lang.: Ger. 1996
Devia, Mariella
Performance/production
Interpreters of the title role in Delibes' opera *Lakmé*. 1932-1995. Lang.: Fre. 4505
Devil to Pay, The
Plays/librettos/scripts
Music and the ballad opera in English popular theatre. England. 1728-1780. Lang.: Eng. 4390

Devils, The
SEE ALSO
Besy.

Devine, Robert
Performance/production
Correspondence of George Devine and Michel Saint-Denis. UK-England: London. 1939-1945. Lang.: Eng. 2630

Devlin, Anne
Plays/librettos/scripts
Gender and nationalism in Northern Irish drama. UK-Ireland. 1902-1997. Lang.: Eng. 3511

Devoción de la misa, La (Devotion of the Mass, The)
Plays/librettos/scripts
Spanish Catholicism and the *autos sacramentales* of Calderón. Spain. 1637-1671. Lang.: Spa. 3405

Dew, John
Plays/librettos/scripts
Hero and anti-hero in contemporary opera production. Germany. 1998. Lang.: Ger. 4791

Dewhurst, Keith
Performance/production
Collection of newspaper reviews by London theatre critics. UK-England: London. 1998. Lang.: Eng. 2556

Di Cori, Ferruccio
Training
Ferruccio Di Cori's improvisational workshops for actors and directors. Italy: Rome. 1994-1996. Lang.: Ita. 874

Diablo, Angélico del (Palomeras Mallofre, María)
Plays/librettos/scripts
The image of women on the Spanish stage. Spain. 1908-1936. Lang.: Eng. 3399

Diadia Vania (Uncle Vanya)
Basic theatrical documents
Catalan translations of the complete plays of Anton Čechov. Russia. 1884-1904. Lang.: Cat. 1449
Institutions
Theatre critics' awards 97-98. Hungary. 1997-1998. Lang.: Hun. 355
Performance/production
Political changes reflected in Berlin theatre productions. Germany: Berlin. 1998. Lang.: Ger. 1958
Interview with actor Tibor Szervét. Hungary. 1988-1998. Lang.: Hun. 2071
Čechov's *Diadia Vania (Uncle Vanya)* directed by János Szász. Hungary: Nyíregyháza. 1998. Lang.: Hun. 2124
Collection of newspaper reviews by London theatre critics. UK-England: London. 1998. Lang.: Eng. 2453
Plays/librettos/scripts
The character Sonya in Čechov's *Diadia Vania (Uncle Vanya).* Russia. 1899. Lang.: Rus. 3333
Analysis of Louis Malle's film *Vanya on 42nd Street.* USA. 1994. Lang.: Fre. 4031

Diaghilev, Sergei Pavlovič
Audience
Diaghilev's strategies of audience development. France: Paris. 1906-1914. Lang.: Eng. 1028
Design/technology
Catalogue of an exhibition devoted to choreography of Diaghilev. Russia: St. Petersburg. 1998. Lang.: Rus. 1029
Institutions
Display of objects related to guest performances of the Ballets Russes. Germany: Berlin. 1910-1914. Lang.: Hun. 1040
Performance/production
Diaghilev recalled by his stepmother. Russia. 1872-1929. Lang.: Rus. 1132

Dialogi (Dialogues)
Plays/librettos/scripts
Analysis of plays by Primož Kozak. Slovenia. 1959-1969. Lang.: Slo. 3350

Dialogo de la Bella Creanza de le Donne, o Raffaella (Dialogue on the Fine Manners of Women, or Raffaella)
Plays/librettos/scripts
Analysis of plays by Alessandro Piccolomini. Italy. 1508-1578. Lang.: Eng. 3244

Diamanten (Diamond, The)
Plays/librettos/scripts
Interview with playwright Sofia Fredén. Sweden: Stockholm. Denmark: Copenhagen. 1995-1998. Lang.: Swe. 3409

Diamond, Emma
Performance/production
The influence of Merce Cunningham on choreographer Emma Diamond. USA. 1988-1998. Lang.: Eng. 1322

Diamond, Liz
Performance/production
Statements of women directors on their work. USA. 1996. Lang.: Eng. 2674

Diary of a Scoundrel
SEE
Na vsiakogo mudreca dovolno prostoty.

Diary of Anne Frank, The
Design/technology
Recent work of lighting designer Brian MacDevitt. USA: New York, NY. 1997. Lang.: Eng. 1530
Sound design for *The Diary of Anne Frank* directed by James Lapine. USA: New York, NY. 1998. Lang.: Eng. 1553
Performance/production
Student production of *The Diary of Anne Frank.* USA. 1955. Lang.: Eng. 2703
Plays/librettos/scripts
Reactions to the revised version of *The Diary of Anne Frank.* USA: New York, NY. 1998. Lang.: Eng. 3618

Diavolo con le zinne, Il (Devil with Breasts, The)
Plays/librettos/scripts
Profile of playwright, director, and actor Dario Fo. Italy. 1997-1998. Lang.: Ger. 3231

Dibdin, Thomas
Performance/production
Possible illustrations of Dibdin's *Harlequin and Mother Goose* at Covent Garden. UK-England: London. 1806-1808. Lang.: Eng. 2639

Dick Whittington
Performance/production
Collection of newspaper reviews by London theatre critics. UK-England. 1998. Lang.: Eng. 2558

Dick, Fergus
Performance/production
New London venues and productions. UK-England: London. 1994-1998. Lang.: Eng. 605

Dickens, Charles
Performance/production
Collection of newspaper reviews by London theatre critics. UK-England: London. 1998. Lang.: Eng. 2531

Dickinson, Joan
Plays/librettos/scripts
Account of performances by Joan Dickinson. USA. 1997-1998. Lang.: Eng. 4263

Dickson, Billy
Design/technology
Lighting design for TV series *Ally MacBeal.* USA. 1998. Lang.: Eng. 4054

Dictionaries
Reference materials
Italian translation of Patrice Pavis' *Dictionnaire du théâtre.* Lang.: Ita. 694
Dictionary of history and the arts. Lang.: Ita. 695
Performing arts dictionary. Italy. 1900-1998. Lang.: Ita. 702

Did You Hear the One about the Irishman
Plays/librettos/scripts
Recent history in Irish theatre and drama. Ireland: Dublin. UK-Ireland: Belfast. 1993-1996. Lang.: Eng. 3212

Dietrich, Marlene
Performance/production
The disappearance of the diva in the modern world. Europe. USA. 1890-1998. Lang.: Swe. 525
Biography of film star Marlene Dietrich by her daughter. USA. 1901-1992. Lang.: Rus. 3955

Dietz, Howard
Performance/production
Choreography in the musical film *The Bandwagon.* USA. 1953. Lang.: Eng. 982

Dificultat pel domini de la casa (Difficulties of Running the House)
Basic theatrical documents
Text of plays by Josep M. Muñoz Pujol. Spain-Catalonia. 1995. Lang.: Cat. 1466

Digging for Ladies
Performance/production
Collection of newspaper reviews by London theatre critics. UK-England: London, Scarborough. 1998. Lang.: Eng. 2426

Diggs, Elizabeth
Design/technology
Neil Patel's scene design for *Mirette,* Goodspeed Opera House. USA: East Haddam, CT. 1998. Lang.: Eng. 4334

Dillon, David
Performance/production
Collection of newspaper reviews by London theatre critics. UK-England: London. 1998. Lang.: Eng. 2512
Dimetos
Plays/librettos/scripts
The influence of Albert Camus on playwright Athol Fugard. South Africa, Republic of. 1960-1985. Lang.: Eng. 3362
Dinesen, Isak (Blixen, Karen)
Plays/librettos/scripts
Harold Pinter's screenplay adaptation of *The Dreaming Child* by Isak Dinesen. UK-England. 1961-1997. Lang.: Eng. 3984
Dining Room, The
Plays/librettos/scripts
Analysis of *The Dining Room* by A.R. Gurney. USA. 1982-1984. Lang.: Eng. 3642
Dinner theatre
Administration
Negotiations with Equity dinner theatres. USA: New York, NY. 1998. Lang.: Eng. 79
Performance spaces
The present status of dinner theatre. USA. 1998. Lang.: Eng. 471
Dinner with Friends
Performance/production
Reviews of Actors' Theatre productions. USA: Louisville, KY. 1998. Lang.: Eng. 2727
Dionysus in 69
Performance/production
Twentieth-century productions of Euripidean tragedy. USA. 1915-1969. Lang.: Eng. 2678
DiPalma, Brian
Plays/librettos/scripts
Opera in American gangster films. USA. 1932-1990. Lang.: Eng. 4023
Diplomatist's Wife in Japan, A
Performance/production
Theatrical component of Japan's UK98 Festival. Japan: Tokyo. 1994-1998. Lang.: Eng. 2192
Directing
Audience
Jonathan Demme's film adaptation of *Beloved* by Toni Morrison. USA. 1998. Lang.: Eng. 3877
Design/technology
Scenographer and now director Klaus Noack. Germany. 1953. Lang.: Ger. 190
Lighting in contemporary theatre. Germany. 1998. Lang.: Ger. 192
Handbook on stage spaces and physical elements. Slovenia. 1997. Lang.: Slo. 219
The 1998 TCI awards. USA. 1998. Lang.: Eng. 243
Set design for Joseph Chaikin's production of two one-acts by Arthur Miller. USA: New york, NY. 1998. Lang.: Eng. 1532
Des McAnuff's design concept for his film *Cousin Bette.* USA: Hollywood, CA. 1998. Lang.: Eng. 3905
Opera scenographer Michael Levine. Canada: Toronto, ON. 1988-1998. Lang.: Eng. 4426
Robert Wilson and Vera Dobroschke's design for Brecht's *Ozeanflug.* Germany: Berlin. 1998. Lang.: Eng. 4430
Institutions
Peter Stein's last season as director at the Salzburg Festival. Austria: Salzburg. 1997. Lang.: Eng. 336
The relationship between theatrical artists and theatrical institutions. USA: Tarrytown, NY. 1998. Lang.: Eng. 421
Gunnar Martin Aronsson of TeaterX2 recalls Action-Theater. Sweden: Stockholm. Germany: Munich. 1968-1998. Lang.: Swe. 1722
Interview with Matthew Goulish and Lin Hixson of Goat Island. USA: Chicago, IL. 1990. Lang.: Eng. 4237
Performance spaces
The creation of a site-specific performance space for Sam Mendes' production of *Cabaret.* USA: New York, NY. 1998. Lang.: Eng. 4350
Performance/production
Guide to directing sports shows and other entertainments. Lang.: Rus. 480
Directing and intercultural theatre. Europe. 1930-1998. Lang.: Ger. 524
László Márkus, one-time director of the Budapest Opera House. Hungary. 1881-1948. Lang.: Hun. 540
A conversation with actor and director Carmelo Bene. Italy. 1998. Lang.: Ita. 544
Ettore Giannini's film and stage work *Carosello Napoletano (Neapolitan Carousel).* Italy. 1950. Lang.: Ita. 546
Tadashi Suzuki and Suzuki Company of Toga. Japan. 1939-1984. Lang.: Eng. 555
Collaboration of Jewish and Polish theatres in the interwar period. Poland: Warsaw. 1923-1937. Lang.: Pol. 574
Early work of Jerzy Grotowski. Poland: Cracow. 1951-1959. Lang.: Pol. 575
Actress/director Alla Nazimova. Russia. USA. 1878-1945. Lang.: Eng. 585
Interview with Bengt Andersson, artistic director of Teater Tre. Sweden. 1983-1998. Lang.: Swe. 601
Barry Edwards on his theatrical movement work with OPTIK. UK-England: London. 1997-1998. Lang.: Eng. 609
Performer, writer, director Elsie Janis and the 'gay sensibility'. UK-England. 1889-1956. Lang.: Eng. 612
Directing and design to accommodate the disabled in performance. USA. 1988. Lang.: Eng. 623
Preparing a production of Brian Way's participatory *The Mirrorman.* USA. 1987. Lang.: Eng. 633
Semiotic analysis of the nature of theatrical directing. USA. 1988. Lang.: Eng. 650
Proposal for a college course in directing. USA: Brevard, NC. 1997-1998. Lang.: Eng. 683
Director Gerald Freedman on 'real' theatre. USA: Birmingham, AL. 1998. Lang.: Eng. 684
Performer, director, and artist Wolfgang Martin Schede. Germany. 1898-1975. Lang.: Ger. 929
Dance director Seymour Felix. USA. 1918-1953. Lang.: Eng. 976
Directing the documentary-based performance project *The Worst Woman in the World.* Australia. 1994. Lang.: Eng. 1816
Pirandello's theatre on the Austrian stage. Austria. 1924-1989. Lang.: Ita. 1825
Robert Wilson's production of *Doctor Faustus Lights the Lights* by Gertrude Stein. Belgium: Antwerp. 1992. Lang.: Fle. 1828
Interview with director Aleš Kurt. Bosnia: Sarajevo. 1998. Lang.: Hun. 1830
Interview with director Augusto Boal. Brazil: Rio de Janeiro. 1992-1996. Lang.: Eng. 1833
Pierre Dagenais and his company L'Équipe. Canada: Montreal, PQ. 1933-1990. Lang.: Fre. 1846
Student production of Ford's *'Tis Pity She's a Whore.* Canada. 1997. Lang.: Eng. 1849
Interview with actor/director Paul Hébert. Canada: Quebec, PQ. 1952-1998. Lang.: Fre. 1854
Student production of *Les Femmes savantes (The Learned Ladies)* by Molière. Canada: Calgary, AB. 1997. Lang.: Eng. 1859
Directing shows with three-week rehearsal time at Eastern Front Theatre. Canada: Dartmouth, NS. 1980-1998. Lang.: Eng. 1868
Director Serge Ouaknine and his use of visual aids. Canada: Montreal, PQ. 1968-1998. Lang.: Fre. 1871
The director in Slovene and Croatian theatre. Croatia. Slovenia. 1800-1998. Lang.: Rus. 1875
Interview with director Jakub Krofta. Czech Republic. 1973-1998. Lang.: Cze. 1878
Interview with director Josef Krofta of Divadlo Drak. Czech Republic: Hradec. 1990-1998. Lang.: Cze. 1879
Interview with director Vladimír Morávek. Czech Republic: Hradec. 1985-1998. Lang.: Cze. 1880
Actor/director Jaroslav Dušek of Divadlo Vizita. Czech Republic: Prague. 1987-1998. Lang.: Cze. 1884
Acting and directing influences on Eugenio Barba. Denmark: Holstebro. 1997. Lang.: Eng. 1886
The director's role in the development of good acting. Denmark. 1998. Lang.: Dan. 1887
Director Jonathan Paul Cook on developing talent in an ensemble. Denmark. 1997-1998. Lang.: Dan. 1888
The rise of the modern Shakespearean director. Europe. 1878-1995. Lang.: Eng. 1911
Interview with director Esa Leskinen. Finland. 1998. Lang.: Fin. 1916

Directing — cont'd

Interview with director Kristian Smeds. Finland. 1998. Lang.: Eng. 1919

Antonin Artaud's journey to Mexico. France. Mexico. 1936-1937. Lang.: Eng. 1922

Reviews of productions by Wilson, Greenaway, and Mnouchkine. France: Paris. 1997-1998. Lang.: Eng. 1926

Director Jacques Copeau and his theatrical aesthetic. France. 1913-1920. Lang.: Eng. 1941

German directors about the meaning of Brecht today. Germany. 1998. Lang.: Ger. 1948

Daniel Karasek, drama director at Hessisches Staatstheater. Germany: Wiesbaden. 1997-1998. Lang.: Ger. 1955

Christoph Marthaler's approach to directing Joseph Kesselring's *Arsenic and Old Lace*. Germany: Hamburg. 1998. Lang.: Ger. 1956

Profile of Thomas Ostermeier, *Theater Heute*'s young director of the year. Germany: Berlin. 1997-1998. Lang.: Ger. 1959

Kortner-award winners Anna Viebrock and Christoph Marthaler. Germany: Berlin. 1997. Lang.: Ger. 1968

Bertolt Brecht's production of his *Mutter Courage (Mother Courage)*. Germany: Berlin. 1947-1956. Lang.: Ger. 1975

Comparison of two productions of Shakespeare's *Richard III*. Germany: Munich. 1996-1997. Lang.: Ger. 1976

Director Thomas Ostermeier. Germany. 1997-1998. Lang.: Dan. 1979

Actress Ilse Ritter. Germany. 1944-1998. Lang.: Ger. 1980

Interview with director Matthias Langhoff. Germany: Berlin. 1945-1998. Lang.: Ger. 1987

Director and actor Christoph Schlingensief. Germany. 1993-1998. Lang.: Ger. 1988

Director Thomas Ostermeier. Germany: Berlin. 1996-1998. Lang.: Swe. 1998

Interview with director Stefan Pucher. Germany. 1998. Lang.: Ger. 1999

Director Christina Emig-Könning. Germany: Rostock. 1995-1997. Lang.: Ger. 2000

Productions of Horváth's *Geschichten aus dem Wienerwald (Tales from the Vienna Woods)*. Germany: Hamburg, Hannover. Austria: Vienna. 1998. Lang.: Ger. 2003

Recent productions of Bochumer Schauspielhaus. Germany: Bochum. 1998. Lang.: Ger. 2009

Interview with director Andreas Kriegenburg. Germany. 1992-1998. Lang.: Ger. 2010

Swedish directors on recent Berlin productions. Germany: Berlin. 1998. Lang.: Swe. 2012

Productions of director Peter Wittenberg. Germany: Munich, Bonn. 1998. Lang.: Ger. 2013

The career of director Claus Peymann. Germany. 1960-1984. Lang.: Eng. 2014

Interview with director Bernd Wilms. Germany: Berlin. 1998. Lang.: Swe. 2018

The collaboration of choreographer Lucinda Childs and director Robert Wilson on *La Maladie de la Mort*. Germany. 1992-1997. Lang.: Eng. 2019

The work of director Einar Schleef. Germany: Düsseldorf. 1998. Lang.: Ger. 2026

Theatre, society, and directors Frank Castorf, Peter Stein, and Einar Schleef. Germany. 1998. Lang.: Ger. 2029

Interview with director Christoph Schroth. Germany, East. 1970-1990. Lang.: Eng. 2035

Interview with director Adolf Dresen. Germany, East. 1965-1985. Lang.: Eng. 2036

Interview with director Alexander Lang. Germany, East. 1970-1990. Lang.: Eng. 2037

Interview with director Thomas Langhoff. Germany, East. 1970-1990. Lang.: Eng. 2038

Interview with director Frank Castorf. Germany, East. 1980-1990. Lang.: Eng. 2041

Interview with director Alexander Weigel. Germany, East. 1970-1990. Lang.: Eng. 2042

Directors Manfred Wekwerth and Robert Weimann on Brecht and Shakespeare. Germany, East. 1945-1990. Lang.: Eng. 2043

Interview with actor/director Johanna Schall. Germany, East. 1980-1995. Lang.: Eng. 2045

Actor/director Katja Paryla. Germany, East. 1975-1995. Lang.: Eng. 2046

Actor/director Ursula Karusseit. Germany, East. 1977-1995. Lang.: Eng. 2047

Director Robert Weimann on East German Shakespeare production. Germany, East. 1945-1995. Lang.: Eng. 2053

Interview with actor and director Róbert Alföldi. Hungary: Budapest. 1998. Lang.: Hun. 2056

Interview with director János Mohácsi. Hungary. 1998. Lang.: Hun. 2060

Two productions of Shakespeare's *Richard III* by József Ruszt. Hungary: Budapest. Hungary: Kecskemét. 1973-1997. Lang.: Hun. 2070

Interview with director Csaba Kiss. Hungary. 1990-1998. Lang.: Hun. 2112

Interview with director József Ruszt. Hungary. 1963-1997. Lang.: Hun. 2115

Interview with directors Gábor Székely and Eszter Novák. Hungary: Budapest. 1998. Lang.: Hun. 2128

Interview with directors János Szász and Árpád Schilling. Hungary. 1998. Lang.: Hun. 2129

Interview with director Péter Telihay. Hungary. 1993-1998. Lang.: Hun. 2130

Tribute to the late actress and director Erzsébet Gaál. Hungary. 1951-1998. Lang.: Hun. 2141

Obituary for director István Paál. Hungary: Szolnok. 1942-1998. Lang.: Hun. 2143

Interview with director Tamás Ascher on director training. Hungary. 1960-1990. Lang.: Hun. 2146

Profile of actor-director Erzsébet Gaál. Hungary. 1951-1998. Lang.: Hun. 2147

Obituary for actor and director Śombhu Mitra. India. 1914-1997. Lang.: Eng. 2151

Dario Fo and Giorgio Strehler honored at Venice Biennale. Italy: Venice. 1947-1998. Lang.: Eng. 2163

Interview with director Mario Martone. Italy: Naples. 1977-1997. Lang.: Eng. 2166

Book-length interview with director Carmelo Bene. Italy. 1937-1998. Lang.: Ita. 2167

Essays on director Giorgio Strehler. Italy. 1936-1996. Lang.: Ita. 2173

The ideas and productions of director Giorgio Strehler. Italy. 1940-1998. Lang.: Swe. 2180

Giorgio Strehler of Piccolo Teatro. Italy: Milan. 1921-1997. Lang.: Ger. 2181

Luca Ronconi's production of *Mourning Becomes Electra* by Eugene O'Neill. Italy: Rome. 1996-1997. Lang.: Eng. 2183

Interview with director Giorgio Strehler. Italy: Milan. 1993. Lang.: Hun. 2185

Piccolo Teatro after the death of director Giorgio Strehler. Italy: Milan. 1947-1998. Lang.: Hun. 2186

Luca Ronconi's stage adaptation of *The Brothers Karamazov*. Italy: Rome. 1997. Lang.: Eng. 2188

Report from a symposium on traditional Korean theatre. Korea. Germany: Berlin. 1980-1998. Lang.: Ger, Fre, Dut, Eng. 2196

Director Eimuntus Nekrošius. Lithuania. 1952-1998. Lang.: Pol. 2198

Memoirs of actor and director Egbert van Paridon. Netherlands. 1920-1990. Lang.: Dut. 2204

The evolution of the contemporary Shakespearean director. North America. Europe. 1967-1998. Lang.: Eng. 2207

Interview with director Stein Winge. Norway: Oslo. 1988-1998. Lang.: Eng. 2210

Contemporary Polish productions of Shakespeare. Poland. 1990-1998. Lang.: Pol. 2213

Director Anna Augustynowicz. Poland: Szczecin. 1989-1998. Lang.: Pol. 2214

Tadeusz Kantor's directorial process. Poland: Cracow. 1987. Lang.: Eng. 2217

The new generation of Polish directors. Poland. 1989-1998. Lang.: Pol. 2219

Ritual in the theatre of Jerzy Grotowski. Poland. 1960-1975. Lang.: Pol. 2221

Actor/director Aleksander Zelwerowicz. Poland: Vilna. 1929-1931. Lang.: Pol. 2223

Directing — cont'd

Interview with director Andrzej Wajda. Poland. 1960-1998. Lang.: Fin. 2224

Spirituality and the theatre of Jerzy Grotowski. Poland. 1958-1998. Lang.: Ger, Fre, Dut, Eng. 2226

Director György Harag. Romania. Hungary. 1925-1985. Lang.: Hun. 2229

Director V.E. Mejerchol'd. Russia. 1900-1940. Lang.: Rus. 2230

Russian reception and interpretation of the work of Jerzy Grotowski. Russia. 1913-1998. Lang.: Pol. 2236

Interview with director Roman Viktjuk. Russia: Moscow. 1998. Lang.: Rus. 2244

Director Anatolij Efros. Russia: Moscow. 1998. Lang.: Rus. 2251

Biography of director V.E. Mejerchol'd. Russia. 1874-1940. Lang.: Rus. 2258

Interview with director Lev Dodin. Russia. 1997. Lang.: Fre. 2260

Children's theatre director E. Padve. Russia: St. Petersburg. 1998. Lang.: Rus. 2262

Profiles of major theatrical figures. Russia. 1950-1998. Lang.: Rus. 2263

Solomon Michoėls of Moscow's Jewish Theatre. Russia: Moscow. 1998. Lang.: Rus. 2264

Director Kama Ginkas of Teat'r Junogo Zritelja. Russia. 1998. Lang.: Rus. 2265

Roman Viktjuk's production of *Salomé* by Oscar Wilde. Russia: Moscow. 1998. Lang.: Rus. 2266

Oleg Menšikov's production of *Gore ot uma (Wit Works Woe)* by Gribojėdov. Russia: Moscow. 1998. Lang.: Rus. 2267

Producer and director Boris Golubovskij. Russia. 1998. Lang.: Rus. 2271

Interview with director Andrej Gončarov. Russia: Moscow. 1998. Lang.: Rus. 2272

Director Anatolij Efros. Russia: Moscow. 1998. Lang.: Rus. 2273

Michajl Mokejėv's production of Shakespeare's *Romeo and Juliet.* Russia: Belgorod. 1998. Lang.: Rus. 2274

Memoirs of director and playwright Nikolaj Jėvrejnov. Russia. 1879-1953. Lang.: Rus. 2279

A friend's view of director Pëtr Fomenko. Russia: Moscow. 1998. Lang.: Rus. 2281

Director Anatolij Vasiljėv. Russia. 1942-1998. Lang.: Hun. 2282

The Russian-German theatrical relationship. Russia. Germany. 1920-1949. Lang.: Rus. 2285

Autobiographical writings by director V.E. Mejerchol'd. Russia. 1891-1903. Lang.: Rus. 2296

Review of a Hungarian edition of writings by director A.A. Vasiljėv. Russia: Moscow. 1998. Lang.: Hun. 2321

Director Sergej Rudzinskij. Russia: Omsk. 1998. Lang.: Rus. 2325

Director Jurij Solomin of Malyj Teat'r. Russia: Moscow. 1998. Lang.: Rus. 2326

Actor/director Pavel Medvedev. Russia. 1851-1899. Lang.: Rus. 2330

Director Andrej Žitinkin. Russia: Moscow. 1998. Lang.: Rus. 2338

African ritual in the work of director and playwright Brett Bailey. South Africa, Republic of. 1997-1998. Lang.: Eng. 2349

The absence of research on South African directing. South Africa, Republic of. 1998. Lang.: Eng. 2355

Harold Pinter's production of his play *Ashes to Ashes* at the Pinter festival. Spain-Catalonia: Barcelona. 1996. Lang.: Eng. 2364

Interview with actress and director Anna Takanen. Sweden: Stockholm. 1994-1998. Lang.: Swe. 2372

Interview with director Anders Paulin. Sweden: Malmö. 1997-1998. Lang.: Swe. 2377

Interviews with actors Lil Terselius and Björn Granath. Sweden: Stockholm. 1998. Lang.: Swe. 2381

Interview with actor/director Stefan Larsson. Sweden: Stockholm. 1984-1998. Lang.: Swe. 2382

Interview with community theatre director Kent Ekberg. Sweden: Stockholm. 1973-1998. Lang.: Swe. 2385

Interview with children's theatre director Marie Feldtmann. Sweden: Stockholm. 1996-1998. Lang.: Swe. 2388

Interview with director Robert Lepage. Sweden: Stockholm. Canada: Montreal, PQ. 1997. Lang.: Swe. 2397

Actor/director Margaret Webster, gender and sexuality. UK-England. USA. 1905-1972. Lang.: Eng. 2590

Interview with Katie Mitchell on directing plays of Beckett. UK-England. 1998. Lang.: Eng. 2594

Michael Birch's production of *Vanity Fair.* UK-England: Leeds. 1997. Lang.: Eng. 2600

Experimental Shakespeare production at the Gaiety Theatre. UK-England: Manchester. 1908-1915. Lang.: Eng. 2605

Three productions of Shakespeare's *Richard III.* UK-England. 1973-1984. Lang.: Eng. 2612

Actor and director Harold French. UK-England: London. 1900-1998. Lang.: Eng. 2614

Modernist and postmodernist Shakespearean production. UK-England. Canada. 1966-1996. Lang.: Eng. 2618

Richard Olivier's production of Shakespeare's *The Merchant of Venice.* UK-England: London. 1998. Lang.: Eng. 2621

The influence of collage on director Charles Marowitz. UK-England. USA. 1962-1979. Lang.: Eng. 2624

Trevor Nunn's production of *An Enemy of the People* by Ibsen. UK-England: London. 1998. Lang.: Eng. 2627

Correspondence of George Devine and Michel Saint-Denis. UK-England: London. 1939-1945. Lang.: Eng. 2630

Interview with director Simon McBurney. UK-England: London. 1997. Lang.: Swe. 2641

Types of actors and their relationship with directors. UK-England. Sweden. 1950-1998. Lang.: Swe. 2648

A production of Susan Glaspell's experimental play *The Verge.* UK-Scotland: Glasgow. 1996. Lang.: Eng. 2651

Obituaries for Joseph Maher, Warren Kliewer, and E.G. Marshall. USA. 1912-1998. Lang.: Eng. 2655

Interview with composer Paul Schmidt. USA: New Haven, CT. 1998. Lang.: Eng. 2660

Interview with director Peter Sellars. USA: Cambridge, MA. 1980-1981. Lang.: Eng. 2661

Analysis of the Wooster Group's *Fish Story* directed by Elizabeth LeCompte. USA: New York, NY. 1990-1996. Lang.: Eng. 2667

Director Michael Mayer. USA. 1998. Lang.: Eng. 2670

Statements of women directors on their work. USA. 1996. Lang.: Eng. 2674

Actors and directors on the late plays of Tennessee Williams. USA. 1966-1981. Lang.: Eng. 2675

Directors' nonverbal behavior in rehearsal. USA. 1987. Lang.: Eng. 2680

Richard Foreman's notes for a production of his *Pearls for Pigs.* USA: Hartford, CT. 1997. Lang.: Eng. 2681

Tribute to late director José Quintero. USA. 1924-1998. Lang.: Eng. 2683

Director, costumer, and mask-maker Julie Taymor. USA. 1980-1998. Lang.: Eng. 2685

Robert Wilson's work with actors on a production of *Danton's Death (Dantons Tod).* USA: Houston, TX. 1997. Lang.: Eng. 2688

The career of gay actor Monty Woolley. USA. 1888-1963. Lang.: Eng. 2691

Using Renaissance dance in Shakespearean productions. USA. 1998. Lang.: Eng. 2692

Interview with director Richard Foreman. USA: New York, NY. 1975-1990. Lang.: Eng. 2700

Student production of *The Diary of Anne Frank.* USA. 1955. Lang.: Eng. 2703

Director Charles Marowitz on the actor's calling. USA. UK-England. 1958-1998. Lang.: Eng. 2706

Director Garland Wright. USA. 1946-1998. Lang.: Eng. 2707

Career of director Lynne Meadow. USA: New York, NY. 1972-1985. Lang.: Eng. 2708

Director Mary Hausch of Hippodrome State Theatre. USA: Gainesville, FL. 1973-1998. Lang.: Eng. 2709

Obituaries for Ellis Rabb, Giorgio Strehler, and David Mark Cohen. USA. 1930-1997. Lang.: Eng. 2725

Avant-garde American women directors' productions of *Doctor Faustus Lights the Lights* by Gertrude Stein. USA. 1940-1995. Lang.:Eng. 2735

Directorial style of JoAnne Akalaitis. USA. 1982-1998. Lang.: Eng. 2737

Directing a student production of Yeats's *Deirdre.* USA: Louisville, KY. 1988. Lang.: Eng. 2738

Directing — cont'd

The 'scientific perspective' of director David Belasco. USA. 1882-1931. Lang.: Eng. 2741

The Broadway directing career of George M. Cohan. USA. 1900-1950. Lang.: Eng. 2751

The collaboration of playwright Lanford Wilson and director Marshall W. Mason. USA: New York, NY. 1978-1986. Lang.: Eng. 2756

The development of the character Khlezstakov in Gogol's *Revizor (The Inspector General)* in productions by Mejerchol'd. USSR. 1926-1939. Lang.: Eng. 2762

Mejerchol'd's production of Gogol's *Revizor (The Inspector General)*. USSR: Moscow. 1926. Lang.: Eng. 2763

Director Harold Clurman's reaction to Mejerchol'd's *Revizor (The Inspector General)*. USSR: Moscow. 1935. Lang.: Eng. 2764

Director Mel Gordon on Mejerchol'd's influence. USSR. 1920-1931. Lang.: Eng. 2765

Mejerchol'd's denial of charges that he was a counter-revolutionary. USSR: Moscow. 1940. Lang.: Eng. 2767

Mejerchol'd's relationship with Lunačarskij. USSR. 1890-1931. Lang.: Eng. 2768

Aleksand'r Tairov's productions of plays by Eugene O'Neill. USSR. 1926-1929. Lang.: Eng. 2769

Humorous anecdotes by actor/director Massimo Troisi. Italy. 1953-1994. Lang.: Ita. 3858

Cinematic work of director Robert Lepage. Canada. 1995-1998. Lang.: Fre. 3928

Minimalist film director Aki Kaurismaki. Finland. 1988-1998. Lang.: Eng. 3930

Music in films of Marguerite Duras. France. 1974-1981. Lang.: Eng. 3932

Obituary for film director Akira Kurosawa. Japan. 1910-1998. Lang.: Eng. 3937

Analysis of *Touki-Bouki (The Hyena's Travels)* by Djibril Diop Mambéty. Senegal. 1973. Lang.: Eng. 3938

Steven Soderbergh on directing *Out of Sight*. USA. 1998. Lang.: Eng. 3944

Spielberg's *Saving Private Ryan* and the war film. USA: Hollywood, CA. 1998. Lang.: Eng. 3948

Analysis of Todd Solondz' film *Happiness*. USA. 1998. Lang.: Eng. 3949

Spike Lee's unsuccessful efforts to film parts of *Malcolm X* in Mecca. USA. 1992-1995. Lang.: Eng. 3954

Hitchcock's influence on *The Spanish Prisoner* by David Mamet. USA. 1998. Lang.: Eng. 3956

Retrospectives of filmmakers Jean-Luc Godard and William Kentridge. USA: New York, NY. 1998. Lang.: Eng. 3958

Multimedia and the productions of Giorgio Barberio Corsetti. Italy: Rome, Milan. 1985-1998. Lang.: Eng. 4043

Theatrical influences on director Rainer Werner Fassbinder. East Germany: Berlin. 1969-1982. Lang.: Fre. 4058

Yves Marc on Etienne Decroux. France: Paris. 1998. Lang.: Eng. 4088

Corinne Soum, former assistant to Etienne Decroux. France: Paris. UK-England: London. 1968-1998. Lang.: Eng. 4090

Director and martial artist Huy-Phong Doàn's *La Légende du manuel sacré (The Legend of the Sacred Handbook)*. Canada: Montreal, PQ. 1992-1998. Lang.: Fre. 4118

Commedia dell'arte and twentieth-century theatre. Europe. 1860-1950. Lang.: Eng. 4187

Director Joel Kaplan on his production of the *York Cycle*. Canada: Toronto, ON. 1998. Lang.: Eng. 4213

Interview with performance artist Julian Maynard Smith. UK-England: London. 1980-1988. Lang.: Eng. 4246

Interview with director Richard Schechner. USA. 1987. Lang.: Eng. 4260

G. Chazanov of Teat'r Estrady. Russia: Moscow. Lang.: Rus. 4277

Robert Wilson's production of Brecht's *Der Ozeanflug*. Germany: Berlin. 1998. Lang.: Ger. 4356

Interview with Shane Ritchie and Jon Conway about the musical *Boogie Nights*. UK-England. 1998. Lang.: Eng. 4370

Gillian Lynne, director and choreographer. UK-England: London. USA: New York, NY. 1951-1998. Lang.: Eng. 4372

Gower Champion's work in musical theatre. USA: New York, NY. 1936-1980. Lang.: Eng. 4388

Montemezzi's *L'amore dei tre re*, directed and designed by Philippe Arlaud. Austria: Bregenz. 1998. Lang.: Eng. 4532

Ópera Seca's *Mattogrosso*. Brazil: Rio de Janeiro. 1989. Lang.: Eng. 4537

Slovene translation of Adolphe Appia on staging Wagner. Europe. 1892. Lang.: Slo. 4550

Opera director Robert Carson. Europe. 1989-1998. Lang.: Ger. 4558

Peter Brook's *Don Giovanni* at the Aix Festival. France: Aix-en-Provence. 1998. Lang.: Eng. 4569

Opera director Katja Czellnik. Germany: Oldenburg, Kiel. 1996-1998. Lang.: Ger. 4583

Production history of *Die Bürgschaft* by Kurt Weill and Casper Neher. Germany: Berlin, Bielefeld. 1931-1998. Lang.: Eng. 4588

The work of opera director Barbara Beyer. Germany: Nuremberg. 1996-1998. Lang.: Ger. 4589

Interview with opera director Jossi Wieler. Germany: Stuttgart. Switzerland: Basel. 1998. Lang.: Ger. 4592

Director Ruth Berghaus. Germany. 1970-1996. Lang.: Ger. 4596

Opera director Christine Mielitz. Germany: Meiningen. 1991-1998. Lang.: Ger. 4597

Interview with director Heiner Bruns of Städtische Bühnen Bielefeld. Germany: Bielefeld. 1975-1998. Lang.: Ger. 4598

Opera director Herbert Wernicke. Germany. 1986-1998. Lang.: Ger. 4600

Interview with opera director Christine Mielitz. Germany: Berlin. 1979-1997. Lang.: Eng. 4605

Interview with director Robert Wilson. Germany: Berlin. 1970-1998. Lang.: Swe. 4609

Interview with Miklós Gábor Kerényi on directing Verdi's *Un Ballo in Maschera*. Hungary: Budapest. 1998. Lang.: Hun. 4619

Robert Wilson's production of Wagner's *Lohengrin*. USA: New York, NY. 1998. Lang.: Eng. 4732

Plays/librettos/scripts

Playwright, dramaturg, and director Thomas Jonigk on contemporary theatre. Austria: Vienna. 1998. Lang.: Ger. 2781

Theatre artist Elizabeth Sterling Haynes and Alberta theatre. Canada. 1916-1957. Lang.: Eng. 2799

Playwright, actor, and director Charles Follini. Canada. 1972-1998. Lang.: Eng. 2818

Director Djanet Sears and actor Alison Sealy Smith on all-Black theatre. Canada: Toronto, ON. 1998. Lang.: Eng. 2826

Playwright/director J.A. Pitínský (Zdeněk Petrželka). Czech Republic. 1995-1997. Lang.: Eng, Fre. 2851

Antonin Artaud's years in a mental hospital. France. 1896-1948. Lang.: Ita. 3113

Plays and performance, playwrights and directors. Germany: Hannover. 1998. Lang.: Ger. 3145

The collaboration of playwright Dea Loher and director Andreas Kriegenburg. Germany: Hannover, Munich. 1990-1998. Lang.: Ger. 3151

Director and playwright Pier Paolo Pasolini. Italy. 1922-1975. Lang.: Ita. 3227

The collaboration of playwright Curzio Malaparte and director Guido Salvini. Italy. 1905-1956. Lang.: Ita. 3239

Essays on actor, director, and playwright Eduardo De Filippo. Italy. 1900-1984. Lang.: Ita. 3254

Playwright/director Alfonso Armada. Spain: Madrid. 1987-1998. Lang.: Eng. 3382

Interview with Staffan Göthe, author, director, and one of the actors of *Ett Lysand elände (A Brilliant Misery)*. Sweden: Stockholm. 1990-1998. Lang.: Swe. 3408

Interview with playwright-director Kajsa Isakson. Sweden: Stockholm. 1997-1998. Lang.: Swe. 3414

Interview with playwright-director Petra Revenue. Sweden: Gothenburg. 1980-1998. Lang.: Swe. 3415

The influence of Jacobean theatre on contemporary plays and productions. UK-England. 1986-1998. Lang.: Eng. 3428

Theatrical activities of Harold Pinter. UK-England: London. 1996-1998. Lang.: Eng. 3462

George Bernard Shaw's involvement with the Court Theatre. UK-England. 1904-1909. Lang.: Eng. 3471

Directing — cont'd

Ellen McLaughlin's *Iphigenia and Other Daughters* at CSC Repertory. USA: New York, NY. 1995. Lang.: Eng. 3520
Interview with playwright and director Tina Landau. USA. 1998. Lang.: Eng. 3685
Brad Fraser's direction of a film version of his *Poor Superman*. Canada. 1994-1998. Lang.: Eng. 3966
Interview with director and screenwriter Mel Brooks. USA. 1998. Lang.: Eng. 3992
Mail interview with David Mamet about *The Spanish Prisoner*. USA. 1998. Lang.: Eng. 3993
Interview with Darren Aronofsky, writer and director of the film *Pi*. USA. 1998. Lang.: Eng. 3996
Interview with creators of the film *Slam*. USA. 1998. Lang.: Eng. 4001
David Mamet's success as a screenwriter and film director. USA. 1998. Lang.: Eng. 4003
Interview with screenwriter and director Richard LaGravenese. USA. 1998. Lang.: Eng. 4019
Interview with director Peter Bogdanovich. USA. 1971-1998. Lang.: Eng. 4020
Interview with film-maker Bill Condon. USA. 1998. Lang.: Eng. 4021
John Stahl's film adaptation of *Imitation of Life* by Fannie Hurst. USA: Hollywood, CA. 1934. Lang.: Eng. 4029
Interview with Peter Minshall, creator of theatre pieces and carnival performances. Trinidad and Tobago: Port of Spain. 1974-1997. Lang.: Eng. 4172

Reference materials
Yearbook of Slovene theatre. Slovenia. 1996-1997. Lang.: Slo. 708

Relation to other fields
References to film in theatre of Robert Lepage. Canada. 1990-1998. Lang.: Fre. 3734
The Arte Povera movement. Italy. 1967-1985. Lang.: Eng. 4264

Theory/criticism
Excerpts from diary of theatre critic Andrej Inkret. Slovenia. 1992-1995. Lang.: Slo. 857
Analysis of staging as the rhetorical elocution of directorial interpretation. 1998. Lang.: Fre. 3805
Director Esa Kirkkopelto on theatre as great art. Finland. 1998. Lang.: Fin. 3815
Italian translation of *The Empty Space* by Peter Brook. UK-England. 1998. Lang.: Ita. 3833
Text and performance in drama criticism. USA. 1989. Lang.: Eng. 3849
The need for a critical vocabulary to evaluate operatic productions. Europe. 1987-1998. Lang.: Eng. 4836
Evaluating the work of opera directors. Europe. 1965-1998. Lang.: Eng. 4837

Training
Director Walter Pfaff on the influence of Jerzy Grotowski. Poland. Germany. 1998. Lang.: Eng. 876
Standards for future directors and teachers of directing. Russia. 1998. Lang.: Rus. 877

Directories

Design/technology
Guide to theatrical design manufacturers and equipment. USA. 1998. Lang.: Eng. 241
USITT membership directory. USA. 1998-1999. Lang.: Eng. 250

Institutions
Directory of theatre festivals. 1998. Lang.: Eng. 1566
Directory of Italian theatre websites. Italy. 1998. Lang.: Eng. 1675

Dirindina, La

Plays/librettos/scripts
The theatre of Girolamo Gigli. Italy. 1660-1722. Lang.: Eng. 4307

Disappearance of the Jews

Plays/librettos/scripts
Rites of passage in the plays of David Mamet. USA. 1975-1995. Lang.: Eng. 3680

Disch, Matthias

Institutions
Experiential memory work and acting at Theater Jugend Club. Germany: Nordhausen. 1995-1998. Lang.: Ger. 1629

Disco Pigs

Institutions
English-language plays at Berlin Festwochen. Germany: Berlin. 1998. Lang.: Ger. 1623

Performance/production
Political changes reflected in Berlin theatre productions. Germany: Berlin. 1998. Lang.: Ger. 1958
Collection of newspaper reviews by London theatre critics. UK-England: London. 1998. Lang.: Eng. 2416

Plays/librettos/scripts
German view of English and American drama. UK-England. USA. 1998. Lang.: Ger. 3455

Disco Project, The

Performance/production
Analysis of dance trilogy by choreographer Neil Greenberg. USA. 1994-1998. Lang.: Eng. 1334

Discographies

Performance/production
Recordings of Rossini's *Semiramide*. 1962-1992. Lang.: Fre. 4504
Recordings of Zemlinsky's *Eine florentinische Tragödie*. 1980-1997. Lang.: Fre. 4506
Discography of productions of Alban Berg's *Lulu*. 1935-1998. Lang.: Fre. 4508
Discography of Offenbach's *Orphée aux Enfers*. 1953-1997. Lang.: Fre. 4511
Recordings of Delibes' *Lakmé*. 1941-1998. Lang.: Fre. 4524

Reference materials
Discography of operas by Donizetti. Europe. North America. 1998. Lang.: Eng. 4831

Disney Corporation (Hollywood, CA)

Administration
The influence of Walt Disney on the film industry. USA. 1968-1998. Lang.: Eng. 3873
The Disney Corporation's Broadway musicals. USA: New York, NY. 1996-1998. Lang.: Eng. 4317

Design/technology
Costuming for the film *Mr. Magoo*. USA: Hollywood, CA. 1998. Lang.: Eng. 3903
Lighting and sound control for the Disneyland 'Light Magic' show. USA: Anaheim, CA. 1998. Lang.: Eng. 4109
Donald Holder's lighting design for *The Lion King*. USA: New York, NY. 1997-1998. Lang.: Eng. 4336
Technical designs for the Broadway production of *The Lion King*. USA: New York, NY. 1998. Lang.: Eng. 4342

Performance spaces
The construction of a theatre for *Beauty and the Beast*. Germany: Stuttgart. 1997. Lang.: Ger. 444

Performance/production
Portraying Mickey Mouse at Walt Disney World. USA: Orlando, FL. 1998. Lang.: Eng. 4223
The premiere of the musical *Elaborate Lives: The Legend of Aida*. USA: Atlanta, GA. 1998. Lang.: Eng. 4385

Relation to other fields
The social significance of the Disney Corporation's influence on Broadway theatre. USA: New York, NY. 1997. Lang.: Eng. 3782

Disney, Walt

Administration
The influence of Walt Disney on the film industry. USA. 1968-1998. Lang.: Eng. 3873

Distel, Die (Berlin)

Performance/production
Swedish directors on recent Berlin productions. Germany: Berlin. 1998. Lang.: Swe. 2012

District Six—The Musical

Plays/librettos/scripts
The influence of Taliep Petersen's musical *District Six*. South Africa, Republic of. 1987. Lang.: Eng. 4394

Díszelőadás (Gala Performance)

Performance/production
Péter Kárpáti's *Díszelőadás (Gala Performance)* directed by Balázs Simon. Hungary: Budapest. 1998. Lang.: Hun. 2057
Performances at the new Bárka Színház. Hungary: Budapest. 1997. Lang.: Hun. 2097

Diva Studies

Basic theatrical documents
Excerpt from *Diva Studies* by Elizabeth Alexander. USA. 1996. Lang.: Eng. 1480

Plays/librettos/scripts
Analysis of *Diva Studies* by Elizabeth Alexander. USA. 1996. Lang.: Eng. 3653
Interview with playwright Elizabeth Alexander. USA. 1996. Lang.: Eng. 3662

Divadlo Drak (Hradec)
Performance/production
Interview with director Josef Krofta of Divadlo Drak. Czech Republic: Hradec. 1990-1998. Lang.: Cze. 1879
Divadlo Husa na Provázku (Brno)
Performance/production
The adaptation of classic Czech works to the stage. Czech Republic: Prague, Brno. 1990-1998. Lang.: Cze. 1877
Divadlo Jokai (Komarno)
SEE
Jókai Színház.
Divadlo loutek (Ostrava)
Performance/production
Profile of puppet theatre Divadlo loutek Ostrava. Czech Republic: Ostrava. 1953-1998. Lang.: Cze. 4889
Divadlo Na zábradlí (Prague)
Design/technology
The work of scene designer Libor Fára. Czech Republic: Prague. 1950-1981. Lang.: Cze. 1518
Divadlo Vizita (Prague)
Performance/production
Actor/director Jaroslav Dušek of Divadlo Vizita. Czech Republic: Prague. 1987-1998. Lang.: Cze. 1884
DIWA Arts (San Francisco, CA)
Performance/production
The performance installations *Santa Cruzan/Flores de Mayo* by DIWA Arts. USA: San Francisco, CA. 1994-1996. Lang.: Eng. 4256
Dixon's Place (New York, NY)
Performance/production
Analysis of Rae C. Wright's solo performance piece *Animal Instincts*. USA: New York, NY. 1997. Lang.: Eng. 2684
Dmitriev, Vladimir
Design/technology
Scene design and the plays of Ostrovskij. Russia. 1998. Lang.: Rus. 1523
DMO, The
Plays/librettos/scripts
Political community theatre by South Indian emigrants. Canada: Toronto, ON, Montreal, PQ. India. 1984-1998. Lang.: Eng. 2821
Do the Right Thing
Plays/librettos/scripts
Analysis of Spike Lee's film *Do the Right Thing*. USA. 1989. Lang.: Eng. 4017
Do You Come Here Often?
Performance/production
Collection of newspaper reviews by London theatre critics. UK-England: London. 1998. Lang.: Eng. 2564
Doàn, Huy-Phong
Performance/production
Director and martial artist Huy-Phong Doàn's *La Légende du manuel sacré (The Legend of the Sacred Handbook)*. Canada: Montreal, PQ. 1992-1998. Lang.: Fre. 4118
Dobbins, Ray
Performance/production
Collection of newspaper reviews by London theatre critics. UK-England: London. 1998. Lang.: Eng. 2579
Dobell, Linda
Performance/production
Collection of newspaper reviews by London theatre critics. UK-England: London. 1998. Lang.: Eng. 2581
Dobroschke, Vera
Design/technology
Robert Wilson and Vera Dobroschke's design for Brecht's *Ozeanflug*. Germany: Berlin. 1998. Lang.: Eng. 4430
Doctor Doolittle
Design/technology
Technical designs for the musical *Doctor Doolittle* directed by Steven Pimlott. UK-England: London. 1998. Lang.: Eng. 4325
Performance/production
Collection of newspaper reviews by London theatre critics. UK-England: London. 1998. Lang.: Eng. 2472
Doctor Faustus
Institutions
Profile of theatre company Teatr St I Witkiewicza. Poland: Zakopane. 1989. Lang.: Eng. 1684
Performance/production
Brief productions of Shakespeare, Shaw, and Marlowe at the World's Fair. USA: Chicago, IL. 1934. Lang.: Eng. 2701
Plays/librettos/scripts
Marlowe's tragedies and peer evaluation in the composition classroom. USA. 1997-1998. Lang.: Eng. 3532
Doctor Faustus Lights the Lights
Performance/production
Robert Wilson's production of *Doctor Faustus Lights the Lights* by Gertrude Stein. Belgium: Antwerp. 1992. Lang.: Fle. 1828
Avant-garde American women directors' productions of *Doctor Faustus Lights the Lights* by Gertrude Stein. USA. 1940-1995. Lang.:Eng. 2735
Interview with actress Kate Valk. USA: New York, NY. 1979-1998. Lang.: Eng. 2736
Analysis of recent New York productions. USA: New York, NY. 1997-1998. Lang.: Eng. 2759
Doctor's Dilemma, The
Performance/production
Collection of newspaper reviews by London theatre critics. UK-England. 1998. Lang.: Eng. 2504
Doctorow, E.L.
Design/technology
Lighting and projections for the musical *Ragtime*. USA: New York, NY. 1998. Lang.: Eng. 4328
Technical designs for *Ragtime* at the Ford Center. USA: New York, NY. 1998. Lang.: Eng. 4338
Sound design for the Broadway premiere of the musical *Ragtime*. USA: New York, NY. 1998. Lang.: Eng. 4341
Documentary theatre
Performance/production
Productions of the Federal Theatre Project's Living Newspapers. USA: New York, NY. 1935-1939. Lang.: Eng. 643
Documentary theatre and the politics of representation. USA. 1966-1993. Lang.: Eng. 2728
Dodin, Lev Abramovič
Performance/production
Interview with director Lev Dodin. Russia. 1997. Lang.: Fre. 2260
Productions of international Čechov festival. Russia: Moscow. 1998. Lang.: Swe. 2306
Collection of newspaper reviews by London theatre critics. UK-England: London. 1998. Lang.: Eng. 2424
Dödsdansen (Dance of Death, The)
Performance/production
Collection of newspaper reviews by London theatre critics. UK-England: London. 1998. Lang.: Eng. 2453
Doelwijt, Thea
Plays/librettos/scripts
Interview with playwright Thea Doelwijt. Netherlands. Suriname. 1988. Lang.: Eng. 3279
Doesipuri
Performance/production
Historical, political, and aesthetic context of *madang* theatre. Korea. 1976-1998. Lang.: Ger. 557
Dog in the Manger, The
SEE
Perro del hortelano, El.
Dojoji
Performance/production
Onstage costume changes. Japan. Russia. Denmark. 1752-1998. Lang.: Swe. 556
Doktor Faust
Performance/production
Review of Pierre Strosser's staging of Busoni's *Doktor Faust*. France: Lyons. 1997. Lang.: Eng. 4577
Dolan, Chris
Performance/production
Collection of newspaper reviews by London theatre critics. UK-England: London. 1998. Lang.: Eng. 2439
Dolce vita, La
Relation to other fields
The influence of Fellini's *La Dolce Vita* on a novel of film critic Guillermo Cabrera Infante. Spain. Italy. 1960-1967. Lang.: Eng. 4035
Dolder, Peter
Administration
Interviews with theatre managers regarding the changing cultural landscape. Germany: Bruchsal, Esslingen, Tübingen. 1998. Lang.: Ger. 1381
Institutions
German theatres' responses to threatened closings and mergers. Germany: Esslingen, Tübingen. 1998. Lang.: Ger. 1665
Dolina, Larisa
Performance/production
Singer Larisa Dolina. Russia: Moscow. Lang.: Rus. 4366

Doll's House, A
SEE
Dukkehjem, Et.
Dolling, Mike
Design/technology
Sound design for The Spice Girls tour. UK-England. 1998. Lang.: Eng. 4097
Dom Juan (Don Juan)
Performance/production
Molière's *Dom Juan* directed by Olga Barabás. Hungary. Romania: Sfântu-Gheorghe. 1998. Lang.: Hun. 2063
Events of the Zsámbék theatre festival. Hungary: Zsámbék. 1998. Lang.: Hun. 2126
Dom Sébastien, roi de Portugal
Plays/librettos/scripts
The use of the tenor in operas of Donizetti. Italy. 1816-1845. Lang.: Eng. 4802
Domingo, Plácido
Performance/production
Tenor and artistic director of Washington Opera Plácido Domingo. 1941-1998. Lang.: Eng. 4512
Heinz Fricke, music director of Washington Opera. USA: Washington, DC. 1993-1998. Lang.: Eng. 4734
Don Carlo
Performance/production
Review of Salzburger Festspiele performances. Austria: Salzburg. 1998. Lang.: Ger. 4527
Interview with Ira Siff of La Gran Scena. USA: New York, NY. 1998. Lang.: Eng. 4719
Don Carlos
Performance/production
Opera productions of the Salzburg Festival. Austria: Salzburg. 1998. Lang.: Hun. 4531
Recordings of the different versions of Verdi's *Don Carlos*. Italy. Europe. 1866-1998. Lang.: Eng. 4650
Don Giovanni
Institutions
Peter Brook's production of Mozart's *Don Giovanni* at the Aix festival. France: Aix-en-Provence. 1998. Lang.: Swe. 4450
Performance/production
Lucy Vestris in *Giovanni in London*. England: London. 1842. Lang.: Eng. 4546
Interview with singer Peter Mattei. France: Aix-en-Provence. 1985-1998. Lang.: Swe. 4564
Peter Brook's *Don Giovanni* at the Aix Festival. France: Aix-en-Provence. 1998. Lang.: Eng. 4569
Reviews of recent opera productions. Switzerland: Basel. Germany: Stuttgart, Berlin, Hamburg. France: Strasbourg. 1997-1998. Lang.: Ger. 4702
Don Juan
Performance/production
Stockholm's year as Cultural Capital of Europe. Sweden: Stockholm. 1766-1998. Lang.: Eng. 2394
Don Juan by Molière
SEE
Dom Juan.
Don Juan by Tirso de Molina
SEE
Burlador de Sevilla, El.
Don Juan in Hell
Plays/librettos/scripts
George Bernard Shaw and science fiction. UK-England. Ireland. 1887-1998. Lang.: Eng. 3508
Don Quichotte (Don Quixote)
Performance/production
Interview with director Dominic Champagne. Canada: Montreal, PQ. 1998. Lang.: Fre. 1860
Pierre Benoît's music for *Don Quichotte* at Théâtre du Nouveau Monde. Canada: Montreal, PQ. 1995-1998. Lang.: Fre. 1870
Plays/librettos/scripts
Cervantes' *Don Quixote* and Wadji Mouawad's adaptation, *Don Quichotte*. Canada: Montreal, PQ. 1998. Lang.: Fre. 2803
The character Sancho in Wadji Mouawad's *Don Quichotte (Don Quixote)*. Canada: Montreal, PQ. 1998. Lang.: Fre. 2807
The contrast of form and content in Théâtre du Nouveau Monde's *Don Quichotte*. Canada: Montreal, PQ. 1998. Lang.: Fre. 2815
Don Quichotte, an adaptation of Cervantes' *Don Quixote* by Wadji Mouawad. Canada: Montreal, PQ. 1998. Lang.: Fre. 2830
Don Quixote
Performance/production
Irma Nioradze in a performance of *Don Quixote* choreographed by Marius Petipa. Hungary: Budapest. 1998. Lang.: Hun. 1093
Relation to other fields
The influence of Cervantes' *Don Quixote* on contemporary Quebec artists. Canada. 1967-1998. Lang.: Fre. 3737
Don Sanche
Plays/librettos/scripts
Analysis of plays by Pierre Corneille. France. 1643-1652. Lang.: Eng. 3112
Don the Burp
Performance/production
Collection of newspaper reviews by London theatre critics. UK-England: London. 1998. Lang.: Eng. 2579
Don't Laugh It's My Life
Performance/production
Collection of newspaper reviews by London theatre critics. UK-England: London. 1998. Lang.: Eng. 2576
Doña Francisquita
Design/technology
Lighting for Washington Opera's production of *Doña Francisquita*. USA: Washington, DC. 1998. Lang.: Eng. 4290
Doña Rosita la Soltera (Doña Rosita the Spinster)
Performance/production
Roberto Ciulli's production of *Doña Rosita la Soltera (Doña Rosita the Spinster)* by Federico García Lorca. Germany: Munich. 1998. Lang.: Ger. 2021
Lorca's *Doña Rosita* directed by Gergő Kaszás. Hungary: Budapest. 1998. Lang.: Hun. 2099
Donat, Robert
Performance/production
Actor Robert Donat. UK-England: London. 1905-1958. Lang.: Eng. 2633
Donavan, Maripat
Performance/production
Collection of newspaper reviews by London theatre critics. UK-England: London. 1998. Lang.: Eng. 2553
Donizetti, Gaetano
Performance spaces
Malmö Musikteater's production of *Lucia di Lammermoor* at Hedeland Amfiteater. Denmark: Hedeland. 1997. Lang.: Swe. 4491
Performance/production
Maria Callas and Donizetti's *Lucia di Lammermoor*. Europe. 1953-1959. Lang.: Eng. 4553
Evaluation of video performances of Donizetti's operas. Europe. USA. 1980-1998. Lang.: Eng. 4557
Hector Berlioz's review of Donizetti's *La Favorite*. France: Paris. 1840. Lang.: Eng. 4565
Soprano Catherine Hayes. Ireland. Italy. 1839-1861. Lang.: Eng. 4645
Analysis of Donizetti's opera *Lucrezia Borgia*. Italy. UK-England. 1797-1998. Lang.: Eng. 4649
The life and work of composer Gaetano Donizetti. Italy. 1797-1848. Lang.: Eng. 4656
Interview with soprano Edita Gruberova. Slovakia. 1975-1998. Lang.: Eng. 4695
Background material on Metropolitan Opera radio broadcast performances. USA: New York, NY. 1998. Lang.: Eng. 4713
Plays/librettos/scripts
The use of the tenor in operas of Donizetti. Italy. 1816-1845. Lang.: Eng. 4802
Composer Gaetano Donizetti. Italy. Europe. 1835-1848. Lang.: Eng. 4805
Contemporary account of the last years of composer Gaetano Donizetti. Italy. 1845-1848. Lang.: Eng. 4809
Virginal heroines in Alpine settings in operas of Bellini, Donizetti, and Verdi. Italy. 1800-1850. Lang.: Eng. 4812
Reference materials
Discography of operas by Donizetti. Europe. North America. 1998. Lang.: Eng. 4831
Catalogue of the work of Donizetti. Italy. Europe. 1816-1845. Lang.: Eng. 4833
Donmar Warehouse (London)
Institutions
Caro Newling, executive producer of Donmar Warehouse. UK-England: London. 1998. Lang.: Eng. 1742

Donmar Warehouse (London) — cont'd

Performance/production
Collection of newspaper reviews by London theatre critics. UK-England: London. 1998. Lang.: Eng. 2423
Collection of newspaper reviews by London theatre critics. UK-England: London. 1998. Lang.: Eng. 2434
Collection of newspaper reviews by London theatre critics. UK-England: London. 1998. Lang.: Eng. 2443
Collection of newspaper reviews by London theatre critics. UK-England: London. 1998. Lang.: Eng. 2454
Collection of newspaper reviews by London theatre critics. UK-England: London. 1998. Lang.: Eng. 2509
Collection of newspaper reviews by London theatre critics. UK-England: London. 1998. Lang.: Eng. 2543
Collection of newspaper reviews by London theatre critics. UK-England: London. 1998. Lang.: Eng. 2561
Recent productions of plays by Harold Pinter at Donmar Warehouse. UK-England: London. 1998. Lang.: Eng. 2609

Donnellan, Declan
Institutions
Impressions from the Avignon theatre festival. France: Avignon. 1998. Lang.: Ger. 1612
Performance/production
Guest performances in Moscow. Russia: Moscow. 1998. Lang.: Rus. 2269
Collection of newspaper reviews by London theatre critics. UK-England: London. 1998. Lang.: Eng. 2413
Collection of newspaper reviews by London theatre critics. UK-England: Stratford. 1998. Lang.: Eng. 2529
Collection of newspaper reviews by London theatre critics. UK-England: London. 1998. Lang.: Eng. 2531
Interview with actress Fiona Shaw. UK-England. 1995-1997. Lang.: Eng. 2607
Theory/criticism
Contrasting reviews of Declan Donnellan's RSC production of *The School for Scandal*. UK-England: Stratford. 1998. Lang.: Eng. 3835

Donnelly, John
Performance/production
Collection of newspaper reviews by London theatre critics. UK-England: London. 1998. Lang.: Eng. 2578

Doongaji House
Plays/librettos/scripts
Diaspora and home in postcolonial Indian drama. India. 1978-1985. Lang.: Eng. 3193

Dope!
Performance/production
Maryat Lee and the creation of the street theatre piece *Dope!*. USA: New York, NY. 1949-1951. Lang.: Eng. 663

Doppio Teatro (Melbourne)
Performance/production
Multiculturalism and Italo-Australian theatre. Australia. 1990-1998. Lang.: Eng. 490

Doran, Gregory
Performance/production
Collection of newspaper reviews by London theatre critics. UK-England: London. 1998. Lang.: Eng. 2463
Collection of newspaper reviews by London theatre critics. UK-England: London. 1998. Lang.: Eng. 2551
Collection of newspaper reviews by London theatre critics. UK-England: London. 1998. Lang.: Eng. 2587
Paul Jesson's role in *Henry VIII* at RSC. UK-England: London, Stratford. 1996-1997. Lang.: Eng. 2617
Jane Lapotaire on her performance in *Henry VIII* at RSC. UK-England: London, Stratford. 1996-1997. Lang.: Eng. 2619

Dorfman, Ariel
Performance/production
Collection of newspaper reviews by London theatre critics. UK-England: London. 1998. Lang.: Eng. 2577

Dorn, Dieter
Institutions
The aesthetic perspectives of the ensemble at Münchner Kammerspiele. Germany: Munich. 1997-1998. Lang.: Ger. 1666

Doronina, Tatjana
Institutions
Moscow Art Theatre's two theatres and their artistic directors. Russia: Moscow. 1998. Lang.: Rus. 1698
Performance/production
Journal of actress Tatjana Doronina. Russia: Moscow. 1998. Lang.: Rus. 2252
Actress and director Tatjana Doronina of Moscow Art Theatre. Russia: Moscow. Lang.: Rus. 2253
Actress Tatjana Doronina. Russia. 1998. Lang.: Rus. 2254
Memoirs of Moscow Art Theatre actress Tatjana Doronina. Russia: Moscow. 1998. Lang.: Rus. 2255
Actress Tatjana Doronina. Russia: Moscow. 1998. Lang.: Rus. 2302

Dorothy B. Williams Theatre (New York, NY)
Design/technology
Lighting design for Basil Twist's puppet production *Symphonie Fantastique*. USA: New York, NY. 1998. Lang.: Eng. 4867

Dorst, Tankred
Administration
Interview with Tankred Dorst and Hannah Hurtzig of the Bonner Biennale festival. Germany: Bonn. 1998. Lang.: Ger. 1379
Performance/production
Productions of Tankred Dorst's *Was sollen wir tun (What Shall We Do)*. Germany: Dresden, Bonn. 1997-1998. Lang.: Ger. 1971
Plays/librettos/scripts
Family conflict in *Was sollen wir tun (What Shall We Do)* by Tankred Dorst and *Die Hamletmaschine (Hamletmachine)* by Heiner Müller. Germany. 1997-1998. Lang.: Ger. 3148

Dőry, Virág
Institutions
Theatre critics' awards 97-98. Hungary. 1997-1998. Lang.: Hun. 355

Dos Passos, John
Institutions
The New Playwrights Theatre Company. USA: New York, NY. 1927-1929. Lang.: Eng. 410
Performance/production
Aleksand'r Tairov's production of *Fortune Heights* by John Dos Passos. USA. 1930-1935. Lang.: Rus. 2739

Dossier: Ronald Akkerman
Performance/production
Collection of newspaper reviews by London theatre critics. UK-England: London. 1998. Lang.: Eng. 2462

Dostojėvskij, Fëdor Michajlovič
Performance/production
Dostojėvskij's *Crime and Punishment* directed by Géza Tordy. Hungary: Győr. 1998. Lang.: Hun. 2100
Luca Ronconi's stage adaptation of *The Brothers Karamazov*. Italy: Rome. 1997. Lang.: Eng. 2188
Collection of newspaper reviews by London theatre critics. UK-England: London. 1998. Lang.: Eng. 2424
Collection of newspaper reviews by London theatre critics. UK-England: London. 1998. Lang.: Eng. 2493
Robert Wilson's production of Brecht's *Der Ozeanflug*. Germany: Berlin. 1998. Lang.: Ger. 4356

Dostoyevsky, Fyodor
SEE
Dostojėvskij, Fëdor Michajlovič.

Doty, Johnna
Design/technology
Panel discussion of sound designers. USA. 1998. Lang.: Eng. 287

Double Falsehood, The
Plays/librettos/scripts
Don Quixote, Lewis Theobald's *The Double Falsehood* and the lost *Cardenio* of Shakespeare and Fletcher. England. Spain. 1610-1727. Lang.: Eng. 3001

Douglas, Paul
Training
The use of martial arts in dance training. UK-England. 1998. Lang.: Eng. 1022

Dowie, Claire
Performance/production
Collection of newspaper reviews by London theatre critics. UK-England: London. 1998. Lang.: Eng. 2546
Collection of newspaper reviews by London theatre critics. UK-England: London. 1998. Lang.: Eng. 2581

Dowie, John
Basic theatrical documents
Text of *Jesus, My Boy* by John Dowie. UK-England. 1998. Lang.: Eng. 1474
Performance/production
Collection of newspaper reviews by London theatre critics. UK-England: London. 1998. Lang.: Eng. 2552

Dowie, John — cont'd

Profile of actor Tom Conti. UK-England. 1998. Lang.: Eng. 2629

Dowling, Joe
Performance/production
Joe Dowling's production of *London Assurance* by Dion Boucicault. USA. 1997. Lang.: Eng. 2755

Dowling, Vincent
Plays/librettos/scripts
African- and Irish-Americans in the plays of Eugene O'Neill. USA. 1916-1953. Lang.: Eng. 3687

Downes, Cathy
Performance/production
Collection of newspaper reviews by London theatre critics. UK-England: London. 1998. Lang.: Eng. 2503

Downfall of Robert Earl of Huntingdon
Plays/librettos/scripts
Analysis of *Downfall of Robert Earl of Huntingdon* by Anthony Munday. England. 1598-1599. Lang.: Eng. 3018

Dowse, Pippa
Performance/production
Collection of newspaper reviews by London theatre critics. UK-England: London. 1998. Lang.: Eng. 2502

Doyle, John
Institutions
Profile of Watermill Theatre. UK-England: Newbury. 1998. Lang.: Eng. 1744

Doyle, Patricia
Performance/production
Collection of newspaper reviews by London theatre critics. UK-England: London. 1998. Lang.: Eng. 2462

Doyle, Richard
Performance/production
Collection of newspaper reviews by London theatre critics. UK-England: London. 1998. Lang.: Eng. 2526

Dózsa, Imre
Institutions
Interview with Imre Dózsa, general director of Magyar Táncművészeti Főiskola. Hungary. 1998. Lang.: Hun. 894

Interview with Imre Dózsa, managing director of Táncművészeti Főiskola. Hungary: Budapest. 1998. Lang.: Hun. 897

Dr Dante (Copenhagen)
Plays/librettos/scripts
Interview with playwright Sofia Fredén. Sweden: Stockholm. Denmark: Copenhagen. 1995-1998. Lang.: Swe. 3409

Dr. Kokos Kärlekslaboratorium (Dr. Koko's Laboratory of Love)
Performance/production
Dr. Kokos Kärlekslaboratorium (Dr. Koko's Laboratory of Love) at Backstage, Stockholms Stadsteater. Sweden: Stockholm. 1998. Lang.: Swe. 2378

Dracula
Design/technology
Magical stage effects in 'vampire' plays. USA. 1820-1977. Lang.: Eng. 1548

Performance/production
Collection of newspaper reviews by London theatre critics. UK-England: London. 1998. Lang.: Eng. 2579

Drag King
Performance/production
Collection of newspaper reviews by London theatre critics. UK-England: London. 1998. Lang.: Eng. 2550

Dragone, Franco
Performance/production
Collection of newspaper reviews by London theatre critics. UK-England: London. 1998. Lang.: Eng. 2564

Dragonfly of Chicoutimi, The
Plays/librettos/scripts
Analysis of works by Larry Tremblay. Canada: Montreal, PQ. 1995-1998. Lang.: Fre. 2804

Drake, David
Plays/librettos/scripts
Effeminacy on the American stage. USA. 1920-1998. Lang.: Eng. 3682

Drake, Julius
Performance/production
Recordings of *Lieder* by Schumann. Germany. UK-England. 1998. Lang.: Eng. 4601

Drama Dept. (New York, NY)
Design/technology
Costume design for revival of *As Thousands Cheer* by Drama Dept. USA: New York, NY. 1998. Lang.: Eng. 4333

Plays/librettos/scripts
Interview with playwright Douglas Carter Beane. USA. 1980-1998. Lang.: Eng. 3516

Drama therapy
Relation to other fields
Drama therapy as a tool in the treatment of psychosis. USA. 1998. Lang.: Eng. 778

Spiritual practice and drama therapy. USA. 1998. Lang.: Eng. 786

Drama therapy, personal narrative, and performance. USA. 1998. Lang.: Eng. 797

Therapeutic *nō* theatre for the mentally retarded. USA. 1998. Lang.: Eng. 798

Drama therapy and forgiveness. USA. 1998. Lang.: Eng. 804

The integration of Buddhism in drama therapy. USA. 1998. Lang.: Eng. 808

The creation and use of ritual theatre for drama therapy. USA. 1997. Lang.: Eng. 3787

Dramaten (Royal Dramatic Theatre of Stockholm)
SEE
Kungliga Dramatiska Teatern.

Dramatiska Teater (Malmö)
Institutions
Investing in culture in Malmö, formerly an industrial city. Sweden: Malmö. 1995-1998. Lang.: Swe. 1723

Performance/production
Keve Hjelm's production of *Ett Drömspel (A Dream Play)* by Strindberg. Sweden: Malmö. 1998. Lang.: Eng. 2373

Interview with director Anders Paulin. Sweden: Malmö. 1997-1998. Lang.: Swe. 2377

Plays/librettos/scripts
Swedish theatres and young Swedish playwrights. Sweden: Malmö, Gothenburg, Stockholm. 1994-1998. Lang.: Swe. 3411

Dramaturgs
Administration
Dramaturg Hans-Peter Frings on his role in the theatre. Germany: Magdeburg. 1990-1998. Lang.: Ger. 1382

Dramaturg Dirk Olaf Hanke on the dramaturg's complex role. Germany: Konstanz. 1998. Lang.: Ger. 1383

The settlement of a copyright case regarding the musical *Rent*. USA: New York, NY. 1998. Lang.: Eng. 4322

Institutions
Interview with director and dramaturg of Staatstheater Stuttgart. Germany: Stuttgart. 1993-1998. Lang.: Ger. 1632

Profile of Deutsches Theater, Baracke. Germany: Berlin. 1996-1998. Lang.: Ger. 1637

Performance/production
Ethnicity, community youth theatre, and the dramaturg. Bosnia. 1996-1998. Lang.: Eng. 495

The dramaturg and feminist theory and practice. North America. 1998. Lang.: Eng. 568

The dramaturg in the community theatre. North America. Asia. South America. 1990-1998. Lang.: Eng. 570

Theory and the role of the dramaturg. North America. 1998. Lang.: Eng. 572

The development of *Letters, or Where Does the Postman Go When All the Street Names Are Changed*, based on experiences of residents of Mostar. Bosnia-Herzegovina: Mostar. 1997. Lang.: Eng. 1831

The role of the dramaturg in script development and production. Finland. 1998. Lang.: Fin. 1914

Christoph Schlingensief's project with the homeless at Deutsches Schauspielhaus. Germany: Hamburg. 1998. Lang.: Ger. 1961

Gender and Shakespearean production in the GDR. Germany, East. 1982-1990. Lang.: Eng. 2044

Oton Župančič and the Slovene stage language consultant. Slovenia. 1912-1927. Lang.: Slo. 2345

The Slovene language consultant (*lektor*). Slovenia. 1995-1997. Lang.: Slo. 2348

Plays/librettos/scripts
Playwright, dramaturg, and director Thomas Jonigk on contemporary theatre. Austria: Vienna. 1998. Lang.: Ger. 2781

Dramaturg's experience working on a play by Yvette Nolan. Canada. 1997-1998. Lang.: Eng. 2827

Dramaturgs on recognizing talented new playwrights. Denmark. 1998. Lang.: Dan. 2854

Dramaturgs — cont'd

Relation to other fields
Politics and the dramaturg. North America. 1990-1998. Lang.: Eng. 754
Drame na ochote (Drama of the Hunting Trip)
Plays/librettos/scripts
Analysis of Čechov's *Drame na ochote (Drama of the Hunting Trip)*. Russia. 1901. Lang.: Rus. 3318
Drammens Teater (Drammen)
Performance spaces
The reconstruction of Drammens Teater after a fire. Norway: Drammen. 1993-1998. Lang.: Swe. 1803
Drang, Der (Crowd, The)
Performance/production
Interview with director Anders Paulin. Sweden: Malmö. 1997-1998. Lang.: Swe. 2377
Draussen vor der Tur (Man Outside, The)
Performance/production
Collection of newspaper reviews by London theatre critics. UK-England: London. 1998. Lang.: Eng. 2418
Dream Catching
Performance/production
New London venues and productions. UK-England: London. 1994-1998. Lang.: Eng. 605
Dream of Sologa
Plays/librettos/scripts
Analysis of unpublished plays by Ken Saro-Wiwa. Nigeria. 1971-1991. Lang.: Eng. 3282
Dream on Monkey Mountain
Plays/librettos/scripts
Theatre and the creation of a new nationalism. Canada. Saint Lucia. 1980-1995. Lang.: Eng. 2808
Dreaming Child, The
Plays/librettos/scripts
Harold Pinter's screenplay adaptation of *The Dreaming Child* by Isak Dinesen. UK-England. 1961-1997. Lang.: Eng. 3984
Dreaming of the Bones, The
Performance/production
Collection of newspaper reviews by London theatre critics. UK-England: London. 1998. Lang.: Eng. 2420
Dreams
Basic theatrical documents
Text of *Dreams* by Kathleen Kristy-Brooks. USA. 1988. Lang.: Eng. 1493
Dreams of the Night Cleaners, The
Plays/librettos/scripts
Leila Sujir's video *The Dreams of the Night Cleaners*. Canada. 1989-1995. Lang.: Eng. 4075
Dreiband-Burman, Bari
Design/technology
TV and film make-up artists Tom Burman and Bari Dreiband-Burman. USA: Hollywood, CA. 1998. Lang.: Eng. 4050
Dreigroschenoper, Die (Three Penny Opera, The)
Basic theatrical documents
Catalan translations of plays by Bertolt Brecht (volume 1). Germany. 1919-1954. Lang.: Cat. 1437
Performance/production
Recent productions of Bochumer Schauspielhaus. Germany: Bochum. 1998. Lang.: Ger. 2009
Giorgio Strehler's productions of plays by Bertolt Brecht. Italy: Milan. 1956-1998. Lang.: Swe. 2171
Interview with community theatre director Kent Ekberg. Sweden: Stockholm. 1973-1998. Lang.: Swe. 2385
Brecht and Weill's *Die Dreigroschenoper (The Three Penny Opera)* directed by László Vándorfi. Hungary: Veszprém.1998. Lang.: Hun. 4358
Two Hungarian productions of *Die Dreigroschenoper (The Three Penny Opera)*. Hungary: Budapest, Szeged. 1998. Lang.: Hun. 4362
Dresen, Adolf
Performance/production
Interview with director Adolf Dresen. Germany, East. 1965-1985. Lang.: Eng. 2036
The political and social climate of East German theatre in the sixties. Germany, East. 1960-1970. Lang.: Eng. 2052
Dresken, William K.
Performance/production
Collection of newspaper reviews by London theatre critics. UK-England: London. 1998. Lang.: Eng. 2492
Dresser, Richard
Design/technology
Set design for *Gun Shy* by Richard Dresser at Playwrights Horizons. USA: New York, NY. 1998. Lang.: Eng. 1535
Institutions
English-language plays at Berlin Festwochen. Germany: Berlin. 1998. Lang.: Ger. 1623
Dressler, Marie
Performance/production
Actress Marie Dressler. USA: New York, NY. 1869-1934. Lang.: Eng. 2734
Drexler, Rosalyn
Plays/librettos/scripts
Revolutionary Off Broadway playwriting. USA: New York, NY. 1959-1969. Lang.: Eng. 3604
Dreyfus
Plays/librettos/scripts
Analysis of Holocaust plays by Jean-Claude Grumberg. France. 1974-1991. Lang.: Eng. 3108
Driftwood
Plays/librettos/scripts
The development of playwright Owen Davis. USA. 1905-1923. Lang.: Eng. 3526
Drill Hall Theatre (London)
Performance/production
Collection of newspaper reviews by London theatre critics. UK-England: London. 1998. Lang.: Eng. 2420
Collection of newspaper reviews by London theatre critics. UK-England: London. 1998. Lang.: Eng. 2425
Collection of newspaper reviews by London theatre critics. UK-England: London. 1998. Lang.: Eng. 2457
Collection of newspaper reviews by London theatre critics. UK-England: London. 1998. Lang.: Eng. 2477
Collection of newspaper reviews by London theatre critics. UK-England: London. 1998. Lang.: Eng. 2508
Collection of newspaper reviews by London theatre critics. UK-England: London. 1998. Lang.: Eng. 2511
Collection of newspaper reviews by London theatre critics. UK-England: London. 1998. Lang.: Eng. 2531
Collection of newspaper reviews by London theatre critics. UK-England: London. 1998. Lang.: Eng. 2546
Collection of newspaper reviews by London theatre critics. UK-England: London. 1998. Lang.: Eng. 2555
Collection of newspaper reviews by London theatre critics. UK-England: London. 1998. Lang.: Eng. 2560
Collection of newspaper reviews by London theatre critics. UK-England: London. 1998. Lang.: Eng. 2581
Drimeh Kundan
Performance/production
Analysis of Tibetan Buddhist drama. Tibet. 1500-1984. Lang.: Eng. 1355
Drobner, Boleslaw
Performance/production
Postwar Polish theatre, culture, and politics. Poland. 1945-1950. Lang.: Eng. 573
Drobyševa, E.
Performance/production
Mother and daughter actresses Nina and E. Dobyševa. Russia: Moscow. 1998. Lang.: Rus. 2256
Drobyševa, Nina
Performance/production
Mother and daughter actresses Nina and E. Dobyševa. Russia: Moscow. 1998. Lang.: Rus. 2256
Drömspel, Ett (Dream Play, A)
Institutions
Interview with Rolf Sossna of En Annan Teater. Sweden: Gothenburg. 1992-1998. Lang.: Swe. 1734
Performance/production
Keve Hjelm's production of *Ett Drömspel (A Dream Play)* by Strindberg. Sweden: Malmö. 1998. Lang.: Eng. 2373
Plays/librettos/scripts
Time and space in *Ett Drömspel (A Dream Play)* by August Strindberg. Sweden. 1901-1902. Lang.: Eng. 3410
Drottningholms Slottsteater (Stockholm)
Performance spaces
Excerpts from the diary of the builder of Drottningholms Slottsteater. Sweden: Stockholm. 1755-1766. Lang.: Swe. 458
Performance/production
Stockholm's year as Cultural Capital of Europe. Sweden: Stockholm. 1766-1998. Lang.: Eng. 2394
Druce, Dominic
Performance/production
Collection of newspaper reviews by London theatre critics. UK-England: London. 1998. Lang.: Eng. 2516

Drury Lane Theatre (London)
Performance/production
Excerpts from Johanna Schopenhauer's journal relating to London theatre. UK-England: London. Germany. 1803-1805. Lang.: Eng. 2615
The English operas of Stephen Storace. England: London. 1762-1796. Lang.: Eng. 4547
Dry Lips Oughta Move to Kapuskasing
Plays/librettos/scripts
Theatre and the creation of a new nationalism. Canada. Saint Lucia. 1980-1995. Lang.: Eng. 2808
Dryden, Deborah M.
Design/technology
Costume designs for Oregon Shakespeare Festival productions. USA: Ashland, OR. 1998. Lang.: Eng. 1543
Dryden, John
Basic theatrical documents
Analysis of Smock Alley promptbook for Dryden's *Tyrannick Love*. Ireland: Dublin. 1669-1684. Lang.: Eng. 1439
Plays/librettos/scripts
Analysis of Dryden and Davenant's *Enchanted Island*. England. 1674. Lang.: Eng. 2873
Recognition, repression, and ideology in Restoration drama. England: London. 1660-1680. Lang.: Eng. 2918
The influence Dryden and Johnson's theories on self-translated works of Samuel Beckett. France. Ireland. 1957-1976. Lang.: Eng. 3077
The relative absence of political allegory in English opera. England: London. 1620-1711. Lang.: Eng. 4767
Theory/criticism
Chaos theory and its application to theatre and drama theory. USA. 1998. Lang.: Eng. 3839
Du Bar, Karel
Relation to other fields
Cultural trends of the younger generation. Europe. 1995-1998. Lang.: Swe. 4150
Duay, Grant
Plays/librettos/scripts
Revolutionary Off Broadway playwriting. USA: New York, NY. 1959-1969. Lang.: Eng. 3604
DubbelJoint Productions (Dublin)
Performance/production
Recent productions in Ireland of plays by Eugene O'Neill. Ireland: Dublin. UK-Ireland: Belfast. 1989-1998. Lang.: Eng. 2154
Duberman, Martin
Performance/production
Documentary theatre and the politics of representation. USA. 1966-1993. Lang.: Eng. 2728
Dubinin, K.
Performance/production
K. Dubinin's production of *Boi imeli mestnoe zančenie (The Battles Had Localized)* based on work of Viačeslav Kondratjėv. Russia: Volgograd. Lang.: Rus. 2331
Dubois, René-Daniel
Plays/librettos/scripts
Quebecois plays about the crisis of October 1970. Canada. 1970-1990. Lang.: Fre, Eng. 2812
Duchess of Malfi, The
Performance/production
Collection of newspaper reviews by London theatre critics. UK-England: London. 1998. Lang.: Eng. 2432
Denise Gillman's production of Webster's *The Duchess of Malfi*, Theatre of NOTE. USA: Los Angeles, CA. 1998. Lang.: Eng. 2714
Plays/librettos/scripts
Feminist analysis of Webster's *The Duchess of Malfi*. England. 1613. Lang.: Eng. 2931
Authority and medicine in Webster's *The Duchess of Malfi*. England. 1613. Lang.: Eng. 2947
Duchess Theatre (London)
Performance/production
Collection of newspaper reviews by London theatre critics. UK-England: London. 1998. Lang.: Eng. 2419
Collection of newspaper reviews by London theatre critics. UK-England: London. 1998. Lang.: Eng. 2429
Collection of newspaper reviews by London theatre critics. UK-England: London. 1998. Lang.: Eng. 2445
Duchscherer, Brian
Performance/production
Interview with puppet animator Brian Duchscherer. Canada. 1980-1998. Lang.: Eng. 4886
Duck Barton—Special Agent
Performance/production
Collection of newspaper reviews by London theatre critics. UK-England: London. 1998. Lang.: Eng. 2554
Duck Variations
Plays/librettos/scripts
Analysis of *Duck Variations* by David Mamet. USA. 1976. Lang.: Dut. 3554
Duclos, Philippe
Performance/production
French production of *Im Dickicht der Städte (In the Jungle of Cities)* by Bertolt Brecht. France. 1997-1998. Lang.: Ger. 1946
Dudesche Schlomer, De
Plays/librettos/scripts
Morality plays of the Reformation. Germany. 1550-1584. Lang.: Eng. 3163
Dudinskaja, Natalija Michajlovna
Performance/production
I. Igin's *Czars*, a biography of dancers Konstantin Sergejėv and Natalija Dudinskaja. Russia: Leningrad. 1940. Lang.: Rus. 1138
Dudley, Shawn
Design/technology
Costumes for a masked ball scene in the TV series *Another World*. USA. 1998. Lang.: Eng. 4053
Due gemelli Veneziani, I (Venetian Twins, The)
Performance/production
Collection of newspaper reviews by London theatre critics. UK-England: London. 1998. Lang.: Eng. 2474
Duenna, The
Performance/production
Guest performances of the Kirov Opera at the Metropolitan.. USA: New York, NY. 1998. Lang.: Eng. 4731
Plays/librettos/scripts
Music and the ballad opera in English popular theatre. England. 1728-1780. Lang.: Eng. 4390
Duets
Theory/criticism
The use of different analytical strategies to obtain multiple readings of dance performance. USA. Europe. 1946-1982. Lang.: Eng. 1200
Düffel, John von
Plays/librettos/scripts
Analysis of plays by Sarah Kane and David Harrower, recently produced in Germany. UK-England. Germany: Cologne, Bonn. 1998. Lang.: Ger. 3487
Duffield, Christine P.
Design/technology
The 1998 USITT expo. USA: Long Beach, CA. 1998. Lang.: Eng. 251
Duffield, Neil
Performance/production
Collection of newspaper reviews by London theatre critics. UK-England: London. 1998. Lang.: Eng. 2556
Düggelin, Werner
Plays/librettos/scripts
Thomas Hürlimann's *Das Lied der Heimat (The Song of the Homeland)* and its production by Werner Düggelin. Switzerland: Zurich. 1998. Lang.: Ger. 3417
Duke of York's Theatre (London)
Performance/production
Collection of newspaper reviews by London theatre critics. UK-England: London. 1998. Lang.: Eng. 2495
Dukkehjem, Et (Doll's House, A)
Performance/production
Reviews of productions of plays by Ibsen. USA: New York, NY. Norway: Oslo. 1998. Lang.: Eng. 2747
Plays/librettos/scripts
Analysis of Elfriede Jelinek's adaptation of *Et Dukkehjem (A Doll's House)* by Ibsen. Austria. 1979. Lang.: Eng. 2782
Feminism and plays of Henrik Ibsen. Norway. 1879-1979. Lang.: Eng. 3293
Andreas-Salomé's view of Ibsen's female characters. Norway. Germany. 1879-1906. Lang.: Eng. 3296
The development of the character Dr. Rank in Ibsen's *Et Dukkehjem (A Doll's House)*. Norway. 1879. Lang.: Eng. 3297
Dumas, Alexandre *(fils)*
Performance/production
The 'grande coquette' on the Parisian stage. France: Paris. 1885-1925. Lang.: Eng. 531
Plays/librettos/scripts
The inspiration for Dumas *fils*' Marguerite Gautier and Verdi's Violetta. France. Italy. 1848-1853. Lang.: Eng. 4789

Dumas, Alexandre *(père)*
Design/technology
Magical stage effects in 'vampire' plays. USA. 1820-1977. Lang.: Eng. 1548
Dumb Type Theatre (London)
Performance/production
Collection of newspaper reviews by London theatre critics. UK-England: London. 1998. Lang.: Eng. 2512
Dun, Tan
Performance/production
Collection of newspaper reviews by London theatre critics. UK-England: London. 1998. Lang.: Eng. 2503
Dunbar, Olivia Howard
Plays/librettos/scripts
Analysis of plays about the women's movement. USA. 1900-1940. Lang.: Eng. 3559
Duncan, Isadora
Design/technology
Dancer Isadora Duncan's influence on the designs of Edward Gordon Craig. UK-England. 1904-1905. Lang.: Eng. 237
Performance/production
Dancer Isadora Duncan's relationship with poet Sergej Esenin. Russia. 1919-1925. Lang.: Rus. 1297
Modern dance and the female body. USA. Europe. 1900-1930. Lang.: Eng. 1321
Duncan, Martin
Performance/production
Collection of newspaper reviews by London theatre critics. UK-England: London. 1998. Lang.: Eng. 2495
Collection of newspaper reviews by London theatre critics. UK-England: London. 1998. Lang.: Eng. 2540
Duncan, Todd
Performance/production
Obituaries of singers Randolph Symonette and Todd Duncan. USA. 1998. Lang.: Eng. 4708
Dundee Repertory Theatre (Dundee & Glasgow)
Plays/librettos/scripts
Translating Hauptmann's *Die Weber (The Weavers)* into Scots dialect. UK-Scotland: Dundee, Glasgow. 1997. Lang.: Eng. 3513
Dungate, Rod
Plays/librettos/scripts
Interview with playwright Rod Dungate. UK-England: Birmingham. 1998. Lang.: Eng. 3442
Theory/criticism
Contrasting reviews of Declan Donnellan's RSC production of *The School for Scandal.* UK-England: Stratford. 1998. Lang.: Eng. 3835
Dunlop, Frank
Performance/production
Evaluation of video performances of Donizetti's operas. Europe. USA. 1980-1998. Lang.: Eng. 4557
Dunmore, Simon
Performance/production
Collection of newspaper reviews by London theatre critics. UK-England: London. 1998. Lang.: Eng. 2412
Collection of newspaper reviews by London theatre critics. UK-England: London. 1998. Lang.: Eng. 2491
Dunn, Nell
Performance/production
Collection of newspaper reviews by London theatre critics. UK-England: London. 1998. Lang.: Eng. 2530
Dünsser, Crescentia
Administration
Interviews with German theatre and film directors. Germany. 1998. Lang.: Ger. 1385
Dunster, Mathew
Performance/production
Collection of newspaper reviews by London theatre critics. UK-England: London. 1998. Lang.: Eng. 2443
Durang, Christopher
Plays/librettos/scripts
The return of the prodigal in American drama. USA. 1920-1985. Lang.: Eng. 3666
Duras, Marguerite
Performance/production
Reviews of productions by Wilson, Greenaway, and Mnouchkine. France: Paris. 1997-1998. Lang.: Eng. 1926
The performances of Lucinda Childs and Michel Piccoli in *La Maladie de la Mort (The Sickness of Death)*, directed by Robert Wilson. France: Paris. 1997. Lang.: Eng. 1942
Interview with actress Lucinda Childs. France: Paris. 1976-1997. Lang.: Eng. 1943
The function of sound in productions of *India Song* by Marguerite Duras. France. UK-Wales: Mold. 1973-1993. Lang.: Eng. 1945
The collaboration of choreographer Lucinda Childs and director Robert Wilson on *La Maladie de la Mort.* Germany. 1992-1997. Lang.: Eng. 2019
Music in films of Marguerite Duras. France. 1974-1981. Lang.: Eng. 3932
Plays/librettos/scripts
Insanity in nineteenth- and twentieth-century theatre. Europe. 1880-1970. Lang.: Eng. 3050
Analysis of plays by Marguerite Duras and Marie Redonnet. France. 1977-1992. Lang.: Eng. 3071
Verbal and non-verbal communication in the theatre of Marguerite Duras. France. 1914-1985. Lang.: Eng. 3094
Narrative and form as theatrical media in the plays of Marguerite Duras. France. 1914-1986. Lang.: Eng. 3101
Space and pre-verbal memory in later works of Marguerite Duras. France. 1970-1982. Lang.: Eng. 3106
Response to the structures of male oppression in plays of Yourcenar, Sarraute, and Duras. France. 1975-1995. Lang.: Fre. 3119
Celebration and the body in plays of Ina Césaire and Simone Schwarz-Bart. Martinique. Guadeloupe. 1975-1998. Lang.: Eng. 3270
The representation of true crime in modern drama. USA. France. 1955-1996. Lang.: Eng. 3673
Durif, Eugène
Performance/production
Comparison of text-based and visual productions. France. 1998. Lang.: Fre. 1939
Theory/criticism
Round-table discussion on theatre and impurity. Canada: Quebec, PQ. 1998. Lang.: Fre. 835
Dúró, Győző
Performance/production
The ballet adaptation of the *Decameron* performed by Veszprém Dance Workshop. Hungary: Veszprém. 1998. Lang.: Hun. 1108
Durov, Lev
Performance/production
Memoirs of actor Lev Durov. Russia: Moscow. 1998. Lang.: Rus. 2257
Durringer, Xavier
Institutions
Interview with playwright, director, and film-maker Xavier Durringer. France: Paris. 1988-1998. Lang.: Ger. 1609
Impressions from the Avignon theatre festival. France: Avignon. 1998. Lang.: Ger. 1612
Durych, Jaroslav
Performance/production
The adaptation of classic Czech works to the stage. Czech Republic: Prague, Brno. 1990-1998. Lang.: Cze. 1877
Duse, Eleonora
Plays/librettos/scripts
Analysis of scripts by Eleanora Duse. Italy. 1858-1924. Lang.: Ita. 3228
Dušek, Jan
Design/technology
Action design scenographer Jan Dušek. Czech Republic: Prague. 1970-1998. Lang.: Eng. 173
Dušek, Jaroslav
Performance/production
Actor/director Jaroslav Dušek of Divadlo Vizita. Czech Republic: Prague. 1987-1998. Lang.: Cze. 1884
Düsseldorfer Schauspielhaus (Dusseldorf)
Institutions
New productions of Düsseldorfer Schauspielhaus. Germany: Dusseldorf. 1998. Lang.: Ger. 1654
Performance/production
Shakespeare performance on the Rhine and the Ruhr. Germany: Cologne, Bochum, Düsseldorf. 1996-1997. Lang.: Ger. 1962
The work of director Einar Schleef. Germany: Düsseldorf. 1998. Lang.: Ger. 2026
Plays/librettos/scripts
Analysis of *Madschun al-Malik* by Michael Roes. Germany: Düsseldorf. 1998. Lang.: Ger. 3157
Dust
Performance/production
Collection of newspaper reviews by London theatre critics. UK-England: London. 1998. Lang.: Eng. 2440

Dust Off Vietnam
Plays/librettos/scripts
Australian plays about the war in Vietnam. Australia. 1990-1998. Lang.: Eng. 2776

DV8 Physical Theatre (London)
Institutions
Productions of Gothenburg's Dance and Theatre Festival. Sweden: Gothenburg. 1998. Lang.: Swe. 1253
Performance/production
Interview with Lloyd Newson of DV8 Physical Theatre. UK-England: London. 1995-1998. Lang.: Swe. 1313

Dybbuk, The
SEE
Dibuk.

Dyke and the Porn Star, The
Performance/production
Collection of newspaper reviews by London theatre critics. UK-England: London. 1998. Lang.: Eng. 2425

Dziady (Forefathers' Eve)
Performance/production
Analysis of productions of *Dziady (Forefather's Eve)* by Adam Mickiewicz. Poland. 1901-1995. Lang.: Pol. 2220
Plays/librettos/scripts
The current state of studies on playwright Adam Mickiewicz. Poland. 1843-1998. Lang.: Pol. 3302
The Polish national style in Romantic dramas. Poland. 1832-1835. Lang.: Pol. 3304

Džigarchanjan, Armen B.
Performance/production
Interview with actor Armen Džigarchanjan. Russia: Moscow. 1998. Lang.: Rus. 2232
Profile of stage and film actor Armen B. Džigarchanjan. Russia: Moscow. 1998. Lang.: Rus. 2290

Dživaev, A.
Institutions
A. Dživaev's equestrian theatre Konnyj Teat'r 'Narty'. Russia: Vladikavkaz. 1998. Lang.: Rus. 4272

Eady, Cornelius
Plays/librettos/scripts
Panel discussion on contemporary musical theatre. USA: New York, NY. 1998. Lang.: Eng. 4398

Eagles Auditorium (Seattle, WA)
Performance spaces
Seattle's new and renovated theatres. USA: Seattle, WA. 1998. Lang.: Eng. 475

Eagleton, Terry
Plays/librettos/scripts
Gender and nationalism in Northern Irish drama. UK-Ireland. 1902-1997. Lang.: Eng. 3511

Earl, Susan
Performance/production
Collection of newspaper reviews by London theatre critics. UK-England: London. 1998. Lang.: Eng. 2588

Early, Max
Performance/production
Collection of newspaper reviews by London theatre critics. UK-England: London. 1998. Lang.: Eng. 2470

East Bay Center for the Performing Arts (Richmond, CA)
Institutions
East Bay Center for the Performing Arts and the revival of a community. USA: Richmond, CA. 1958-1998. Lang.: Eng. 1764

East West Players (Los Angeles, CA)
Administration
Equity's new contract with East West Players. USA: Los Angeles, CA. 1998. Lang.: Eng. 62

East, Thomas
Performance/production
Collection of newspaper reviews by London theatre critics. UK-England: London. 1998. Lang.: Eng. 2574

Easter
SEE
Påsk.

Eastern Front Theatre (Dartmouth, NS)
Performance/production
Directing shows with three-week rehearsal time at Eastern Front Theatre. Canada: Dartmouth, NS. 1980-1998. Lang.: Eng. 1868

Eastward Ho
Plays/librettos/scripts
The politics of gender in the plays of John Marston. England. 1599-1634. Lang.: Eng. 3009

Easy Access (for the boys)
Performance/production
Collection of newspaper reviews by London theatre critics. UK-England: London. 1998. Lang.: Eng. 2581

Eaton, Dilys
Performance/production
Collection of newspaper reviews by London theatre critics. UK-England: London. 1998. Lang.: Eng. 2463

Eaton, Jonathan
Performance/production
Production history of *Die Bürgschaft* by Kurt Weill and Casper Neher. Germany: Berlin, Bielefeld. 1931-1998. Lang.: Eng. 4588

Eatough, Graham
Performance/production
Collection of newspaper reviews by London theatre critics. UK-England: London. 1998. Lang.: Eng. 2434

Ebb, Fred
Design/technology
Sound design for the London production of *Chicago.* UK-England: London. 1998. Lang.: Eng. 4326
Technical designs for Sam Mendes' production of *Cabaret.* USA: New York, NY. 1998. Lang.: Eng. 4343
Lighting design for Sam Mendes' production of *Cabaret.* USA: New York, NY. 1998. Lang.: Eng. 4344
Institutions
Profile of Watermill Theatre. UK-England: Newbury. 1998. Lang.: Eng. 1744
Performance spaces
The creation of a site-specific performance space for Sam Mendes' production of *Cabaret.* USA: New York, NY. 1998. Lang.: Eng. 4350
Performance/production
Collection of newspaper reviews by London theatre critics. UK-England: London. 1998. Lang.: Eng. 2500
Friends and colleagues recall singer Lotte Lenya. Germany. 1928-1981. Lang.: Eng. 4355

Ebeling, Robert
Design/technology
The work of costume designer Robert Ebeling. Germany. 1995-1998. Lang.: Ger. 185

Ebert, Carl
Performance/production
Production history of *Die Bürgschaft* by Kurt Weill and Casper Neher. Germany: Berlin, Bielefeld. 1931-1998. Lang.: Eng. 4588

Ecce Homo
Performance/production
Comparison of simple productions and visual shows. Canada: Montreal, PQ, Quebec, PQ, Toronto, ON. 1998. Lang.: Fre. 1861

Échantillon, Jacques
Basic theatrical documents
Text of *La Médée de Saint-Médard (The Medea of Saint-Medard)* by Anca Visdei. France. 1998. Lang.: Fre. 1436

Echegaray, José
Basic theatrical documents
Russian translations of plays by Nobel Prize winners. Italy. 1848-1998. Lang.: Rus. 1446
Plays/librettos/scripts
Critical re-examination of the theatre of José Echegaray. Spain. 1874-1904. Lang.: Eng. 3375

Eck, Imre
Institutions
Dance training at Pécs School of the Arts. Hungary: Pécs. 1975-1998. Lang.: Hun. 1043

Ecole de danse de l'Opéra de Paris
Training
Gala concert of the Paris Opera ballet school. France: Paris. 1998. Lang.: Hun. 1205

Economics
Administration
Economic forces and the Australian theatre industry. Australia. 1990-1998. Lang.: Eng. 2
Adelaide Festival Centre Trust's database for tracking economics and cultural impact of events. Australia: Adelaide. 1991-1998. Lang.: Eng. 3
Interview with Frank Baumbauer of Deutsches Schauspielhaus Hamburg. Germany: Hamburg. 1993-2000. Lang.: Ger. 11
Sarah Bernhardt's farewell tour and its revenues. USA. 1905-1906. Lang.: Eng. 28
The playbill as a reflection of social and economic forces. USA. 1875-1899. Lang.: Eng. 31

Economics — cont'd

Speculation on the future effects of technology and ethnic diversity on theatre. USA. 1990-1993. Lang.: Eng. 42

The publicizing of financial information about nonprofit arts organizations. USA. 1998. Lang.: Eng. 137

Various conditions affecting production, pricing, marketing and communication in German theatre. Germany. 1986-1998. Lang.: Ger. 4316

Pricing strategy for puppeteers. USA. 1998. Lang.: Eng. 4864

Audience

Gender-related social issues, theatre, and historiography. USA. 1830-1860. Lang.: Eng. 157

Institutions

Survey of drama graduates' financial and employment conditions. Canada: Toronto, ON. 1989-1997. Lang.: Eng. 341

Economics and the Federal Theatre Project. USA. 1935-1939. Lang.: Eng. 428

The growth of regional dance companies. USA. 1963-1998. Lang.: Eng. 908

Economic history of the Chamberlain's Men/King's Men. England. 1599-1642. Lang.: Eng. 1598

German theatres' responses to threatened closings and mergers. Germany: Esslingen, Tübingen. 1998. Lang.: Ger. 1665

Fiscal survey of not-for-profit theatre. USA. 1997. Lang.: Eng. 1754

The economic failure of the American Repertory Theatre. USA: New York, NY. 1946-1947. Lang.: Eng. 1790

Performance spaces

Speculations on the theatre of John Rastell. England: London. 1524-1530. Lang.: Eng. 1799

Performance/production

Contemporary Asian-Australian theatre. Australia. 1990-1998. Lang.: Eng. 488

Commercial theatre in early modern London. England: London. 1550-1680. Lang.: Eng. 518

Speculation on the future of Latvian theatre. Latvia. 1918-1998. Lang.: Swe, Eng, Ger. 558

The idea of Hollywood in theatre autobiographies. USA. 1950-1990. Lang.: Eng. 665

Boucicault's *The Octoroon* and the performance of race, gender, and power. USA. 1800-1860. Lang.: Eng. 669

Commercial theatre and the values of the Reagan era. USA. 1980-1990. Lang.: Eng. 685

Performance and the nineteenth-century economy. USA. 1850-1890. Lang.: Eng. 4134

Social concerns reflected in popular entertainment publications. USA. 1870-1910. Lang.: Eng. 4144

The decline of live entertainment at seaside resorts. UK-England. 1950-1998. Lang.: Eng. 4278

Roberto Paternostro, new music director at Staatstheater Kassel. Germany: Kassel. 1997-1998. Lang.: Ger. 4296

Review of opera productions. Germany: Stuttgart, Leipzig. 1998. Lang.: Ger. 4584

Plays/librettos/scripts

Social, economic, and political thought in Shakespeare's chronicle plays. England. 1590-1613. Lang.: Eng. 2869

Analysis of *The Witch of Edmonton* by Ford, Dekker, and Rowley. England. 1621. Lang.: Eng. 2928

Comparison of the Dutch *Elckerlijck* and the English *Everyman*. England. Netherlands. 1495-1525. Lang.: Eng. 2982

Analysis of *The Island Princess* by John Fletcher. England. 1621. Lang.: Eng. 2988

The diminishing importance of Bertolt Brecht in reunified Germany. Germany. 1989-1998. Lang.: Ger. 3170

Byron's heroes and the Byronic hero. UK-England. 1800-1824. Lang.: Eng. 3484

The comedies of manners of S.N. Behrman and Philip Barry. USA. 1920-1964. Lang.: Eng. 3648

Marxian analysis of dramatic parody and burlesque. USA. Europe. 1998. Lang.: Eng. 3664

Relation to other fields

Government and budget cuts in German theatres. Germany: Bochum, Cologne. 1991-1998. Lang.: Ger. 738

The effects of postwar monetary reform on theatres in East and West Germany. Germany. 1945-1949. Lang.: Ger. 739

The movement of performing artists between economic sectors. USA. 1998. Lang.: Eng. 793

Narrative strategy in the analysis of theatre economics. USA. 1960-1995. Lang.: Eng. 802

Tourism and the development of theatre districts. USA: New York, NY. Germany: Berlin. 1998. Lang.: Eng. 807

Fitzroy Davis's theatre novel *Quicksilver*. USA. 1930-1940. Lang.: Eng. 810

Václav Havel, the Czech Republic, and the European Union. Czech Republic. 1989-1998. Lang.: Eng. 3743

Using *Seinfeld* to contrast New York and Los Angeles. USA. 1998. Lang.: Eng. 4082

Economic forces and the Chester Whitsun plays. England: Chester. 1521-1678. Lang.: Eng. 4226

Research/historiography

Social and economic forces that shaped American theatre. USA. 1780-1995. Lang.: Eng. 827

Ecstasy

Performance/production

Collection of newspaper reviews by London theatre critics. UK-England: London. 1998. Lang.: Eng. 2537

Ecstasy of Rita Joe, The

Plays/librettos/scripts

Language and rhetoric in plays of George Ryga. Canada. 1967-1985. Lang.: Eng. 2792

Eda-Pierre, Christiane

Performance/production

Interpreters of the title role in Delibes' opera *Lakmé*. 1932-1995. Lang.: Fre. 4505

Éden cinéma, L'

Plays/librettos/scripts

Analysis of plays by Marguerite Duras and Marie Redonnet. France. 1977-1992. Lang.: Eng. 3071

Narrative and form as theatrical media in the plays of Marguerite Duras. France. 1914-1986. Lang.: Eng. 3101

Space and pre-verbal memory in later works of Marguerite Duras. France. 1970-1982. Lang.: Eng. 3106

Édes Anna (Anna Édes)

Performance/production

Review of *Édes Anna (Anna Édes)*, Madách Chamber Theatre. Hungary: Budapest. 1997. Lang.: Hun. 2136

Edgar, Alison

Performance/production

Collection of newspaper reviews by London theatre critics. UK-England: London. 1998. Lang.: Eng. 2463

Edgar, David

Performance/production

Collection of newspaper reviews by London theatre critics. UK-England: London. 1998. Lang.: Eng. 2414

Edinburgh Festival

Institutions

Theatre selections at the 1998 Edinburgh Festival and Edinburgh Fringe Festival. UK-England: London. 1998. Lang.: Eng. 1743

Report on the 1998 Edinburgh Fringe Festival. UK-Scotland: Edinburgh. 1998. Lang.: Eng. 1750

Report on the Edinburgh Festival. UK-Scotland: Edinburgh. 1998. Lang.: Rus. 1751

Performance spaces

Profile of Traverse Theatre. UK-Scotland: Edinburgh. 1998. Lang.: Eng. 462

Performance/production

London summer theatre and the Edinburgh Festival. UK-England: London. UK-Scotland: Edinburgh. 1998. Lang.: Eng. 2603

Shakespearean influence on the 1987 Edinburgh Festival. UK-Scotland: Edinburgh. 1997. Lang.: Eng. 2653

High-school students' production of *The Wiz* at the Edinburgh Fringe Festival. USA: Hattiesburg, MS. UK-Scotland: Edinburgh. 1996. Lang.: Eng. 4381

Edinburgh Playhouse

Performance/production

Collection of newspaper reviews by London theatre critics. UK-Scotland: Edinburgh. 1998. Lang.: Eng. 2650

Edipo Re

Performance/production

Opera director Katja Czellnik. Germany: Oldenburg, Kiel. 1996-1998. Lang.: Ger. 4583

Editions
Plays/librettos/scripts
Analysis of the frontispiece of Nicholas Rowe's edition of Shakespeare's *King Lear*. England. 1709-1714. Lang.: Eng. 2859
Analysis of an edition of William Percy's *Faery Pastorall*. England. 1603-1646. Lang.: Eng. 2916
Comparison of final scenes in quarto and folio versions of Shakespeare's plays. England. 1597-1601. Lang.: Eng. 3005
The first quarto of Shakespeare's *Henry V* and the anonymous *Famous Victories of Henrie the Fifth*. England. 1599-1600. Lang.: Eng. 3022
Comparison of second quarto and first folio versions of Shakespeare's *Hamlet*. England. 1600-1623. Lang.: Eng. 3043
Brecht's working methods as a playwright as documented in annotated editions of his plays. Germany. 1998. Lang.: Ger. 3144
Description of a Web site devoted to *Los espanñoles en Chile* by Francisco Ganzalez de Busto. Spain. 1665-1998. Lang.: Eng. 3366
The New Shakespeare Society's unfinished four-text edition of *Hamlet*. UK-England. 1882-1883. Lang.: Eng. 3497

Edmondson, James
Design/technology
Costume designs for Oregon Shakespeare Festival productions. USA: Ashland, OR. 1998. Lang.: Eng. 1543

Edmundson, Helen
Performance/production
Collection of newspaper reviews by London theatre critics. UK-England: London. 1998. Lang.: Eng. 2506
Plays/librettos/scripts
Shared Experience's stage adaptations of nineteenth-century novels. USA: New York, NY. UK-England: London. 1998. Lang.: Eng. 3518

Education
Administration
The effect of formal training on arts administrators. USA. 1998. Lang.: Eng. 45
External fundraising for theatre arts programs. USA. 1985-1987. Lang.: Eng. 133
Design/technology
Students' recreation of paintings on stage. USA: Huntington, WV. 1996-1997. Lang.: Eng. 313
Institutions
Survey of drama graduates' financial and employment conditions. Canada: Toronto, ON. 1989-1997. Lang.: Eng. 341
Theatre history course of study. Russia. 1998. Lang.: Rus. 381
Profile of TAXI Children's Theatre. USA: Louisville, KY. 1992-1998. Lang.: Eng. 390
Interdisciplinarity in post-secondary theatre studies programs. USA. 1998. Lang.: Eng. 407
Proposal to apply alternative pedagogy and cultural studies to university theatre education. Canada: Guelph, ON. 1998. Lang.: Eng. 1586
A program of study including playwriting and production. Russia: Moscow. 1998. Lang.: Rus. 1699
Performance/production
The current state of Australian theatre for youth. Australia. 1990-1998. Lang.: Eng. 489
Lithuanian theatre education and the visit of Tadashi Suzuki. Lithuania. 1998. Lang.: Fin. 559
Early work of Jerzy Grotowski. Poland: Cracow. 1951-1959. Lang.: Pol. 575
Auditioning for an Irene Ryan Scholarship. USA. 1998. Lang.: Eng. 635
Analysis of character development for acting degree. USA: Long Beach, CA. 1988. Lang.: Eng. 637
The student-created community theatre piece *Walk Together Children*. USA. 1996-1997. Lang.: Eng. 652
Theatre's educational power and socially relevant performance. USA. 1965-1997. Lang.: Eng. 681
Problems of post-secondary theatre training. Canada: Edmonton, AB. 1919-1998. Lang.: Eng. 1848
Acting analysis of character development. USA: Long Beach, CA. 1988. Lang.: Eng. 2662
Plays/librettos/scripts
Survey of major dramatists. Lang.: Rus. 2771
Marlowe's tragedies and peer evaluation in the composition classroom. USA. 1997-1998. Lang.: Eng. 3532
American College Theatre Festival's showcase of student plays. USA. 1998. Lang.: Eng. 3583
Relation to other fields
Evaluation of Ph.D. programs in theatre and drama. Canada. USA. UK-England. 1998. Lang.: Eng. 716
Theatre of the Oppressed and racism in high schools. Canada. 1991-1998. Lang.: Eng. 717
The role of the drama specialist in the classroom. France. 1997. Lang.: Eng. 736
Handbook of teachers of drama in secondary school. Netherlands. 1990-1998. Lang.: Dut. 753
The use of theatre to teach foreign languages. Russia: Moscow. Lang.: Rus. 761
The use of theatre rehearsal techniques for socially emotionally disturbed youth. USA. 1985-1987. Lang.: Eng. 774
Creative dramatics and the literature and language arts curriculum. USA. 1980-1987. Lang.: Eng. 776
Engaging the students in large introductory theatre courses. USA. 1996-1998. Lang.: Eng. 779
Teaching African-American performance and the meaning of race. USA. 1996-1997. Lang.: Eng. 783
The University of Louisville's African-American Theatre Program. USA: Louisville, KY. 1998. Lang.: Eng. 790
Creating interdisciplinary courses: the challenge for theatre educators. USA. 1994-1998. Lang.: Eng. 792
Student responses to the autobiography of actress Charlotte Cibber Charke. USA. 1998. Lang.: Eng. 800
Children's processing of live theatre. USA. 1985. Lang.: Eng. 801
Non-Western dance forms in the teaching of theatre arts. USA: Davis, CA. 1990-1997. Lang.: Eng. 809
Detroit's Black theatres and training opportunities for high school students. USA: Detroit, MI. 1984-1987. Lang.: Eng. 813
A dramatic perspective on teaching and learning. USA. 1997. Lang.: Eng. 814
Australian Shakespeare studies. Australia. 1998. Lang.: Eng. 3728
Process drama in secondary school drama education. Canada. 1970-1998. Lang.: Eng. 3736
The use of performance skills in the primary school classroom. Canada: Montreal, PQ. 1993-1998. Lang.: Fre. 3739
Account of teaching Shakespeare to Chinese students. China, People's Republic of: Changsha. 1987. Lang.: Eng. 3740
Chinese Shakespeare studies. China, People's Republic of. 1990-1998. Lang.: Eng. 3741
Use of theatre in Holocaust education. Germany: Essen. 1985-1998. Lang.: Ger. 3767
A joint project for teaching Shakespeare with professional actors. Sweden. 1988-1998. Lang.: Swe. 3776
The state of Shakespearean studies in public education. USA. UK-England. 1998. Lang.: Eng. 3786
Arts education as audience-building. USA. 1998. Lang.: Eng. 3790
Drama in cross-cultural literature courses for foreign students. USA. 1987. Lang.: Eng. 3791
Interdisciplinary appraoches to the teaching of music theatre. USA. 1987. Lang.: Eng. 4402
Puppeteer Ken McKay on puppetry in education. Canada. 1994-1998. Lang.: Eng. 4915
Research/historiography
The Shakespeare Interactive Research Group. USA: Cambridge, MA. 1991-1997. Lang.: Eng. 3799
Theory/criticism
Tools for analysis of improvisation. Canada: Montreal, PQ. 1998. Lang.: Fre. 834
Training
Proposal to diversify activities in graduate theatre programs. Canada. 1998. Lang.: Eng. 872
Standards for future directors and teachers of directing. Russia. 1998. Lang.: Rus. 877
Playwright Tony Kushner's address to the Association of Theatre in Higher Education. USA. 1997. Lang.: Eng. 3851
Details of a media acting curriculum. USA. 1994-1998. Lang.: Eng. 4041

Educational theatre
Relation to other fields
Theatre of the Oppressed and racism in high schools. Canada. 1991-1998. Lang.: Eng. 717

Edward I
Plays/librettos/scripts
Robin Hood and Elizabethan theatre. England. 1588-1601. Lang.: Eng. 2902

Edward II
Plays/librettos/scripts
Comic scenes and characters in the Elizabethan history play. England. 1590-1618. Lang.: Eng. 2955
Marlowe's *Edward II* and the medieval passion play. England. 1590-1592. Lang.: Eng. 3011

Edward IV
Plays/librettos/scripts
The depiction of Jane Shore in the anonymous *True Tragedy of Richard III*. England. 1540-1594. Lang.: Eng. 2885

Edward, Joseph
Plays/librettos/scripts
Playwright and actor Joseph Edward. USA: New York, NY. 1997. Lang.: Eng. 3564

Edwards, Barry
Performance/production
Barry Edwards on his theatrical movement work with OPTIK. UK-England: London. 1997-1998. Lang.: Eng. 609

Edwards, Dex
Design/technology
Dex Edwards' set design for *The Comedy of Errors*, Shakespeare Repertory Company. USA: Chicago, IL. 1998. Lang.: Eng. 1560

Edwards, Gale
Performance/production
Collection of newspaper reviews by London theatre critics. UK-England: London. 1998. Lang.: Eng. 2425
Michael Siberry on performing in an RSC production of *The Taming of the Shrew*. UK-England: London, Stratford. 1995-1996. Lang.:Eng. 2637

Edwards, Michael Donald
Design/technology
Costume designs for Oregon Shakespeare Festival productions. USA: Ashland, OR. 1998. Lang.: Eng. 1543

Edwards, Richard
Performance/production
Gaynor Macfarlane's production of Edwards' *Damon and Pythias* at Shakespeare's Globe. UK-England: London. 1996. Lang.: Eng. 2613

Eerie Entertainment (New York, NY)
Administration
Jekyll and Hyde restaurants sign Equity contract. USA: New York, NY. 1998. Lang.: Eng. 69

Eerste Bliscap van Maria, De (First Joy of Mary, The)
Plays/librettos/scripts
Analysis of *De Eerste Bliscap van Maria (The First Joy of Mary)*. Belgium: Brussels. 1440-1560. Lang.: Eng. 2790

Effi Briest
Institutions
New productions of Düsseldorfer Schauspielhaus. Germany: Dusseldorf. 1998. Lang.: Ger. 1654

Efremov, Oleg
SEE
Jéfremov, Oleg.

Efros, Anatolij
Performance/production
Director Anatolij Efros. Russia: Moscow. 1998. Lang.: Rus. 2251
Director Anatolij Efros. Russia: Moscow. 1998. Lang.: Rus. 2273

Efter orgiet (After the Orgy)
Plays/librettos/scripts
Female characters in plays by Scandinavian women. Norway. Sweden. Denmark. 1998. Lang.: Eng. 3299

Egea, Octavi
Basic theatrical documents
Text of *Davant l'Empire (Inside the Empire)* by Octavi Egea. Spain-Catalonia. 1999. Lang.: Cat. 1465

Egerházi, Attila
Performance/production
New work of Budapest Táncszínház. Hungary: Budapest. 1998. Lang.: Hun. 1294

Egmont
Performance/production
Television adaptations of works by Goethe. Germany. 1965-1997. Lang.: Eng. 4061

Egoyan, Atom
Plays/librettos/scripts
Homosexuality in Canadian opera. Canada. 1970-1998. Lang.: Eng. 4762

Egyetemi Színpad (Szeged)
Institutions
István Paál's Egyetemi Színpad. Hungary: Szeged. 1960-1998. Lang.: Hun. 361

Eh Joe
Plays/librettos/scripts
Analysis of filmscripts by Samuel Beckett. 1966-1970. Lang.: Eng. 3961

Eh, Joe
Plays/librettos/scripts
Analysis of television plays by Samuel Beckett. France. 1965-1989. Lang.: Eng. 4077

Ehepaar Schiller (Schillers, The)
Performance/production
Recent productions of Schauspiel Leipzig. Germany: Leipzig. 1997-1998. Lang.: Ger. 2011

Eichelberger, Ethyl
Performance/production
Analysis of pop performance. USA: New York, NY. 1980-1988. Lang.: Eng. 664

Eidt, Stephanie
Performance/production
Actress Stephanie Eidt. Germany. 1990-1998. Lang.: Ger. 1982

Eiko & Koma (New York, NY)
Performance/production
Performances by dance couple Eiko & Koma. USA: Washington, DC. 1998. Lang.: Hun. 1336

Einarsson, Svein
Performance/production
Collection of newspaper reviews by London theatre critics. UK-England: London. 1998. Lang.: Eng. 2464

Einen Jux will er sich machen
SEE
Jux will er sich machen, Einen.

Einsame Menschen (Lone Men)
Plays/librettos/scripts
Power, gender relations, and communication in German drama. Germany. 1776-1989. Lang.: Ger. 3138

Eisenberg, Alan
Administration
Report of Equity Executive Director on finance and organization. USA. 1998. Lang.: Eng. 51
Equity Executive Director's investigation into union issues. USA. 1998. Lang.: Eng. 55
Equity Executive Director Alan Eisenberg's experience with a touring production of *Cats*. USA: New York, NY. 1998. Lang.: Eng. 4318

Eisenhauer, Peggy
Design/technology
Lighting and projections for the musical *Ragtime*. USA: New York, NY. 1998. Lang.: Eng. 4328
Technical designs for Sam Mendes' production of *Cabaret*. USA: New York, NY. 1998. Lang.: Eng. 4343
Lighting design for Sam Mendes' production of *Cabaret*. USA: New York, NY. 1998. Lang.: Eng. 4344

Eisler, Hanns
Performance/production
Comparison of productions of Brecht's *Die Massnahme (The Measures Taken)*. Germany: Berlin, Wuppertal. 1995-1998. Lang.: Ger. 1950
Brecht and the vocal role. Germany. 1920-1998. Lang.: Swe. 4295
Composers and the work of Bertolt Brecht. Germany. 1928-1998. Lang.: Ger. 4297
Plays/librettos/scripts
Musicological perspective on *Die Massnahme (The Measures Taken)* by Brecht and Eisler. Germany: Berlin. 1929-1998. Lang.: Ger. 3125

Ejfman, Boris
Performance/production
Choreographer Boris Ejfman. Russia: St. Petersburg. 1972-1998. Lang.: Eng. 1126
Boris Ejfman's Teat'r Sovremennogo Baleta. Russia: St. Petersburg. 1998. Lang.: Rus. 1298

Ek, Harald
Training
Singer training at Teater- & Operahögskolan. Sweden: Gothenburg. 1960-1998. Lang.: Swe. 4848

Ek, Mats
Institutions
Report on biennial dance conference. Sweden: Stockholm. 1998. Lang.: Swe. 902

Ek, Mats — cont'd

Performance/production
Dancer Ana Laguna of Cullbergbaletten. Sweden: Stockholm. 1974-1998. Lang.: Swe. 1305

Ekberg, Kent
Performance/production
Interview with community theatre director Kent Ekberg. Sweden: Stockholm. 1973-1998. Lang.: Swe. 2385

Ekborg, Dan
Performance/production
Interview with actor Dan Ekborg. Sweden: Stockholm. 1998. Lang.: Swe. 2367

Ekborg, Lars
Performance/production
Interview with actor Dan Ekborg. Sweden: Stockholm. 1998. Lang.: Swe. 2367

Ekster, Alexandra
Design/technology
Avant-garde Russian women artist/designers. Russia. USSR. 1880-1949. Lang.: Eng. 214

El-hakim, Tewfik
SEE
al-Hakim, Tawfiq.

Elaborate Lives: The Legend of Aida
Performance/production
Elton John as musical theatre composer. UK-England. 1998. Lang.: Rus. 4371

The premiere of the musical *Elaborate Lives: The Legend of Aida.* USA: Atlanta, GA. 1998. Lang.: Eng. 4385

Elanskaja, Ekaterina
Institutions
Report on the Stockholm theatre festival. Sweden: Stockholm. 1998. Lang.: Eng. 1724

Elckerlijck (Everyman)
Plays/librettos/scripts
Comparison of the Dutch *Elckerlijck* and the English *Everyman.* England. Netherlands. 1495-1525. Lang.: Eng. 2982

Eldridge, David
Performance/production
Collection of newspaper reviews by London theatre critics. UK-England: London. 1998. Lang.: Eng. 2427

Election Night in the Yard
Performance/production
Collection of newspaper reviews by London theatre critics. UK-England: London. 1998. Lang.: Eng. 2427

Electra
Performance spaces
Michael Marmarinos' production of Sophocles' *Electra* at the Epidauros amphitheatre. Greece: Epidauros. 1938-1998. Lang.: Ger. 445

Performance/production
Massimo Castri's production of Euripides' *Electra.* Italy: Spoleto. 1993. Lang.: Ita. 2179

Plays/librettos/scripts
Electra and Orestes in plays of Aeschylus, Euripides, and Sophocles. Greece. 438-411 B.C. Lang.: Eng. 3184

Ellen McLaughlin's *Iphigenia and Other Daughters* at CSC Repertory. USA: New York, NY. 1995. Lang.: Eng. 3520

Elektra
Design/technology
Herbert Wernicke's set and costume designs for his own production of Strauss's *Elektra.* Germany: Munich. 1998. Lang.: Eng. 4429

Plays/librettos/scripts
The image of motherhood in German-language drama. Austria. Germany. 1890-1910. Lang.: Ger. 2787

Elevator
Basic theatrical documents
Texts of *WWW.chat* and *Elevator* by Chris Edwin Rose. USA. 1998. Lang.: Eng. 1506

Elgin Theatre (Toronto, ON)
Performance spaces
Toronto's theatres. Canada: Toronto, ON. 1998. Lang.: Eng. 434

Elija
Plays/librettos/scripts
Analysis of plays based on the Hebrew prophets. USA. Europe. 1919-1970. Lang.: Eng. 3659

Eliot, George (Evans, Mary Ann)
Performance/production
Collection of newspaper reviews by London theatre critics. UK-England: London. 1998. Lang.: Eng. 2459

Plays/librettos/scripts
Shared Experience's stage adaptations of nineteenth-century novels. USA: New York, NY. UK-England: London. 1998. Lang.: Eng. 3518

Eliot, Thomas Stearns
Performance/production
Collection of newspaper reviews by London theatre critics. UK-England: London. 1998. Lang.: Eng. 2474

Plays/librettos/scripts
The Orestes myth in twentieth-century drama. Europe. USA. 1914-1943. Lang.: Eng. 3052

The rebel in modern drama. Europe. 1950-1988. Lang.: Eng. 3053

Elisir d'Amore, L'
Performance/production
Background material on Metropolitan Opera radio broadcast performances. USA: New York, NY. 1998. Lang.: Eng. 4713

Elizabeth
Performance/production
The performance of *onnagata* Tamasaburō in *Elizabeth* by Francisco Ors. Japan: Tokyo. 1993-1995. Lang.: Eng. 1362

Elizabethan theatre
SEE ALSO
Geographical-Chronological Index under England 1558-1603.

Institutions
Economic history of the Chamberlain's Men/King's Men. England. 1599-1642. Lang.: Eng. 1598

Performance spaces
Analysis of a sketch of the Swan Theatre. England: London. 1596. Lang.: Eng. 1801

Performance/production
Shakespeare's *Titus Andronicus* and the political power of symbolic performance. England. 1590-1595. Lang.: Eng. 1893

Census of Renaissance drama productions and staged readings. UK-England. 1997. Lang.: Eng. 2635

Plays/librettos/scripts
Assessment of Marlowe's *Tamburlaine the Great.* England. 1587-1588. Lang.: Eng. 2866

Social, economic, and political thought in Shakespeare's chronicle plays. England. 1590-1613. Lang.: Eng. 2869

Wonder and recognition in medieval and Renaissance drama. England. 1400-1612. Lang.: Eng. 2874

Robin Hood and Elizabethan theatre. England. 1588-1601. Lang.: Eng. 2902

Crimes against property in plays of Henry Fielding and Elizabethan playwrights. England. 1590-1745. Lang.: Eng. 2912

The representation of historical female characters on the Renaissance stage. England. 1580-1615. Lang.: Eng. 2922

English national identity and the representation of foreigners on stage. England. 1560-1613. Lang.: Eng. 2946

Flemish immigrants in English Renaissance drama. England. 1515-1635. Lang.: Eng. 2976

Shakespeare, feminism, and his sources. England. 1590-1616. Lang.: Eng. 2977

The malcontent scholar in Elizabethan and Jacobean theatre. England. 1590-1642. Lang.: Eng. 3003

Analysis of *Downfall of Robert Earl of Huntingdon* by Anthony Munday. England. 1598-1599. Lang.: Eng. 3018

Space and measurement in *Tamburlaine the Great* by Christopher Marlowe. England. 1587-1588. Lang.: Eng. 3029

Authority in Elizabethan England as reflected in the plays of Shakespeare. England. 1501-1600. Lang.: Eng. 3042

Plays of Peter Barnes compared to those of Renaissance dramatists. UK-England. 1968-1974. Lang.: Eng. 3449

Relation to other fields
New-historicist analysis of Shakespeare and his time. England. 1580-1616. Lang.: Eng. 3745

Cross-dressing and gender struggle on the early modern English stage. England. 1580-1620. Lang.: Eng. 3749

Elka u Ivanovych (Christmas with the Ivanovs)
Design/technology
Costume design for *Christmas with the Ivanovs,* CSC Repertory. USA: New York, NY. 1998. Lang.: Eng. 1533

Elkunchwar, Mahesh
Plays/librettos/scripts
Diaspora and home in postcolonial Indian drama. India. 1978-1985. Lang.: Eng. 3193

Elle est là (It Is There)
Plays/librettos/scripts
Analysis of *Elle est là (It Is There)* by Nathalie Sarraute. France. 1967-1982. Lang.: Eng. 3107

Elliot, Stephan
Design/technology
Costumes for the film *Welcome to Woop Woop.* Australia. 1998. Lang.: Eng. 3899
Elliott, Michael
Performance/production
Analysis of Shakespeare's *King Lear* on television. UK-England. 1982-1983. Lang.: Eng. 4064
Elliott, Scott
Design/technology
Derek McLane's set designs for recent Off Broadway productions. USA: New York, NY. 1998. Lang.: Eng. 1538
Elliston, Grace
Plays/librettos/scripts
The development and casting of Booth Tarkington's *The Country Cousin.* USA. 1921. Lang.: Eng. 3699
Ellwood, Colin
Performance/production
Collection of newspaper reviews by London theatre critics. UK-England: London. 1998. Lang.: Eng. 2452
Elmhurst Ballet School (Camberley)
Institutions
Student's view of the Elmhurst Ballet School. UK-England: Camberley. 1997-1998. Lang.: Hun. 1055
Elsewhereness
Plays/librettos/scripts
Homosexuality in Canadian opera. Canada. 1970-1998. Lang.: Eng. 4762
Elsineur (Elsinore)
Performance/production
Modernist and postmodernist Shakespearean production. UK-England. Canada. 1966-1996. Lang.: Eng. 2618
Theory/criticism
Critical response to *Elsineur (Elsinore)*, Robert Lepage's multimedia adaptation of *Hamlet.* Canada. 1995-1996. Lang.: Eng. 3810
Elstroedt, Iris
Design/technology
Profiles of young theatrical designers. Netherlands. 1990-1998. Lang.: Dut. 207
Eltinge, Julian
Performance/production
Female impersonation and the construction of the female stereotype. USA. 1890-1930. Lang.: Eng. 651
Elton John's Glasses
Performance/production
Collection of newspaper reviews by London theatre critics. UK-England: London. 1998. Lang.: Eng. 2415
Elton, Ben
Basic theatrical documents
French translation of *Popcorn* by Ben Elton. UK-England. France. 1996-1998. Lang.: Fre. 1475
Performance/production
Collection of newspaper reviews by London theatre critics. UK-England: London. 1998. Lang.: Eng. 2437
Collection of newspaper reviews by London theatre critics. UK-England. 1998. Lang.: Eng. 2456
Elyot, Kevin
Performance/production
Collection of newspaper reviews by London theatre critics. UK-England: London. 1998. Lang.: Eng. 2567
Emanacije (Emanations)
Basic theatrical documents
Text of the musical play *Emanacije (Emanations)* by Tomaž Brenk and Mojca Kasjak. Slovenia. 1997. Lang.: Eng, Slo. 4288
Emanuel, Gabriel
Plays/librettos/scripts
Analysis of historical drama of the holocaust. USA. Canada. Germany. 1950-1980. Lang.: Eng. 3610
Ember tragédiája, Az (Tragedy of Man, The)
Performance/production
Review of Madách's *Tragedy of Man* at the Hungarian Theatre of Kolozsvár. Hungary. Romania: Cluj-Napoca. 1997. Lang.: Hun. 2065
Madách's *Tragedy of Man* directed by Sándor Beke. Hungary: Eger. 1998. Lang.: Hun. 2090
A puppet production of Madách's *Az ember tragédiája (The Tragedy of Man).* France: Colmar. 1998. Lang.: Hun. 4893
Emerson College Youtheatre (Cambridge, MA)
Relation to other fields
Developmental differences in adolescents' ability to enact character. USA. 1988. Lang.: Eng. 782
Emerson Majestic Theatre (Boston, MA)
Performance spaces
Community efforts to save the Emerson Majestic and Rialto theatres. USA: Boston, MA, Chicago, IL. 1988-1998. Lang.: Eng. 474
Performance/production
New England Marionettes' production of Mozart's *Die Zauberflöte.* USA: Boston, MA. 1998. Lang.: Eng. 4900
Emig-Könning, Christina
Performance/production
The performance of Shakespeare in the former East Germany. Germany: Rostock, Leipzig, Berlin, Dessau. 1996-1997. Lang.: Ger. 1974
Director Christina Emig-Könning. Germany: Rostock. 1995-1997. Lang.: Ger. 2000
Emigrantska tragedija (Émigré Tragedy, An)
Basic theatrical documents
Text of plays and other works by Ivan Mrak. Slovenia. 1930-1975. Lang.: Slo. 1459
Emilia Galotti
Plays/librettos/scripts
Lessing's *Emilia Galotti* and reader-response criticism. Germany. 1772. Lang.: Eng. 3166
Female sacrifice in eighteenth-century German drama. Germany. 1772-1781. Lang.: Eng. 3167
Representation of the virginal body on the German stage. Germany. 1600-1800. Lang.: Ger. 3171
Emmerich, Klaus
Performance/production
Comparison of productions of Brecht's *Die Massnahme (The Measures Taken).* Germany: Berlin, Wuppertal. 1995-1998. Lang.: Ger. 1950
Emmerich, Roland
Design/technology
Lighting design for Roland Emmerich's film *Godzilla.* USA. 1998. Lang.: Eng. 3917
Emmons, Beverly
Design/technology
Lighting design for *Jekyll & Hyde* directed by Robin Phillips. USA: New York, NY. 1998. Lang.: Eng. 4345
Emperor Jones, The
Plays/librettos/scripts
Themes of Eugene O'Neill's early plays. USA. 1915-1925. Lang.: Eng. 3668
African- and Irish-Americans in the plays of Eugene O'Neill. USA. 1916-1953. Lang.: Eng. 3687
Empson, William
Performance/production
William Empson's *The Masque of Steel* and its presentation before Queen Elizabeth II. UK-England: Sheffield. 1954. Lang.: Eng. 4199
Empty Plate in the Café du Grand, An
Performance/production
Collection of newspaper reviews by London theatre critics. UK-England: London. 1998. Lang.: Eng. 2585
En attendant Godot (Waiting for Godot)
Performance/production
Collection of newspaper reviews by London theatre critics. UK-England: London. 1998. Lang.: Eng. 2442
Possible castings for Beckett's *En attendant Godot (Waiting for Godot).* UK-England. 1998. Lang.: Eng. 2645
Plays/librettos/scripts
Beckett's influence on *Che zhan (The Bus Stop)* by Gao Xingjian. China, People's Republic of. 1983. Lang.: Eng. 2844
Analysis of *En attendant Godot (Waiting for Godot)* and *Rockaby* by Samuel Beckett. France. Ireland. 1953-1981. Lang.: Eng. 3087
Criticism of the creation of literary 'genealogies' for dramatic characters. Ireland. France. 1953-1998. Lang.: Swe. 3211
A method of analysis for the drama. USA. 1920-1975. Lang.: Eng. 3537
En prišparan tolar danes (One Tolar Saved Today)
Performance/production
Slovene puppet film. Slovenia. 1947-1997. Lang.: Slo. 4899
Enchanted Island, The
Plays/librettos/scripts
Analysis of Dryden and Davenant's *Enchanted Island.* England. 1674. Lang.: Eng. 2873
Encina, Juan del
Plays/librettos/scripts
Playwright Juan del Encina. Spain. 1468-1529. Lang.: Eng. 3406
Encyclopedias
Reference materials
Encyclopedia of Slovene folk dance. Slovenia. 1997. Lang.: Slo. 1243

endAusscheid
Performance/production
Recent productions of Schauspiel Leipzig. Germany: Leipzig. 1997-1998. Lang.: Ger. 2011
Endgame
SEE
Fin de partie.
Endre, Lena
Performance/production
Interviews with actresses of three generations on female roles. Sweden: Stockholm. 1945-1998. Lang.: Swe. 2380
Endymion
Plays/librettos/scripts
Tudor religious and social issues in John Lily's *Endymion* and *Midas.* England. 1587-1590. Lang.: Eng. 2871
Eneka
Plays/librettos/scripts
Analysis of unpublished plays by Ken Saro-Wiwa. Nigeria. 1971-1991. Lang.: Eng. 3282
Enemy of the People, An
SEE
Folkefiende, En.
Enfant-rat, L' (Rat Child, The)
Plays/librettos/scripts
The Holocaust in *L'Enfant-rat (The Rat Child)* by Armand Gatti. France. 1961-1970. Lang.: Eng. 3092
Enfants Terribles, Les
Performance/production
The theory of movement in *Les Enfants Terribles,* adapted to dance-opera by Philip Glass and Susan Marshall. North America. 1997. Lang.: Eng. 1353
Enge, Herbert
Institutions
Holocaust education and Thalia Treffpunkt. Germany: Hamburg. 1988-1998. Lang.: Ger. 1630
Engel, Aaron Lehman
Theory/criticism
Musical-theatre composer and critic Aaron Lehman Engel. USA. 1940-1982. Lang.: Eng. 4403
Engel, Wolfgang
Institutions
Schauspiel Leipzig under the direction of Wolfgang Engel. Germany: Leipzig. 1996-1998. Lang.: Ger. 1638
Performance/production
The performance of Shakespeare in the former East Germany. Germany: Rostock, Leipzig, Berlin, Dessau. 1996-1997. Lang.: Ger. 1974
Recent productions of Schauspiel Leipzig. Germany: Leipzig. 1997-1998. Lang.: Ger. 2011
German productions of Shakespeare. Germany: Leipzig, Hamburg, Berlin. 1998. Lang.: Ger. 2033
Engine House Theatre (Madrid, NM)
Institutions
Profile of Engine House Theatre. USA: Madrid, NM. 1982-1998. Lang.: Eng. 1760
English Journeys
Performance/production
Collection of newspaper reviews by London theatre critics. UK-England: London. 1998. Lang.: Eng. 2440
English National Opera (London)
Institutions
Paul Daniel, music director of the English National Opera. UK-England: London. 1997-1998. Lang.: Eng. 4475
The Royal Opera House, Covent Garden, and the English National Opera. UK-England: London. 1988-1998. Lang.: Eng. 4479
Performance/production
The current state of opera in England. UK-England. 1997. Lang.: Eng. 4705
English Stage Company (London)
SEE ALSO
Royal Court Theatre (London).
Performance/production
Correspondence of George Devine and Michel Saint-Denis. UK-England: London. 1939-1945. Lang.: Eng. 2630
Enquist, Per Olov
Performance/production
Reviews of two plays by Per Olov Enquist. Hungary: Budapest. 1998. Lang.: Hun. 2089
Enrico IV (Henry IV)
Performance/production
Seven critics on their favorite character or portrayal. Sweden. 1950. Lang.: Swe. 2369
Plays/librettos/scripts
Gender and madness in modern drama. Europe. 1880-1969. Lang.: Eng. 3061
Enrobantes, Les (Wrappers, The)
Performance/production
Derision in recent productions. Canada: Quebec, PQ. 1998. Lang.: Fre. 509
Ensaio sobre o Latão (Lessons On the Latão)
Performance/production
Review of Brazilian performances of plays by Brecht. Brazil: São Paulo. 1998. Lang.: Ger. 1832
Enter Achilles
Institutions
Productions of Gothenburg's Dance and Theatre Festival. Sweden: Gothenburg. 1998. Lang.: Swe. 1253
Performance/production
Interview with Lloyd Newson of DV8 Physical Theatre. UK-England: London. 1995-1998. Lang.: Swe. 1313
Enter the Night
Plays/librettos/scripts
Theatrical space in plays of Maria Irene Fornes. USA. 1977-1989. Lang.: Eng. 3571
Enter Women
Plays/librettos/scripts
Analysis of plays about the women's movement. USA. 1900-1940. Lang.: Eng. 3559
Enters, Angna
Performance/production
Dance-mime Angna Enters. USA. 1905-1923. Lang.: Eng. 1319
Entführung aus dem Serail, Die
Performance/production
Mozart's operas and contemporary Viennese performance spaces. Austria: Vienna. 1782-1791. Lang.: Eng. 4528
The work of opera director Barbara Beyer. Germany: Nuremberg. 1996-1998. Lang.: Ger. 4589
Interview with opera director Jossi Wieler. Germany: Stuttgart. Switzerland: Basel. 1998. Lang.: Ger. 4592
Reviews of recent opera productions. Switzerland: Basel. Germany: Stuttgart, Berlin, Hamburg. France: Strasbourg. 1997-1998. Lang.: Ger. 4702
Entre bobos anda el juego (Fool's Game, A)
Plays/librettos/scripts
Playwright Francisco de Rojas Zorrilla. Spain. 1607-1648. Lang.: Eng. 3396
Entremeses
Plays/librettos/scripts
Playwright Luis Quiñones de Benavente. Spain. 1600-1651. Lang.: Eng. 3376
Environmental theatre
SEE ALSO
Site-specific performance.
Design/technology
R. Murray Schaffer's environmental opera *The Princess of the Stars.* Canada. 1981-1997. Lang.: Eng. 4424
Performance/production
Role-playing in historical reconstructions as a form of environmental theatre. USA: Plymouth, MA. 1950-1987. Lang.: Eng. 4147
Eörsi, István
Plays/librettos/scripts
New Hungarian translations of Shakespeare. Hungary. 1990-1998. Lang.: Hun. 3187
Épel'baum, Ilja
Performance/production
Teat'r Ten's *Ten' opery (The Shadow of the Opera).* Russia: Moscow. 1998. Lang.: Rus. 4679
Ten' Puppet Theatre's production of Čajkovskij's opera *Iolanta.* Russia: Moscow. Lang.: Rus. 4680
Epic theatre
Plays/librettos/scripts
Brechtian epic devices in the theatre of Caryl Churchill. UK-England. 1976-1986. Lang.: Eng. 3477
Epicharis
Plays/librettos/scripts
Representation of the virginal body on the German stage. Germany. 1600-1800. Lang.: Ger. 3171

Epileptic Seizure Comparison
Audience
The prompting of epileptic seizures by film. 1960-1988. Lang.: Eng. 3876

Eppendorfer, Hans
Plays/librettos/scripts
Homosexuality on the German stage. Germany. 1920-1980. Lang.: Eng. 3147

Equestrian acts
Institutions
A. Dživaev's equestrian theatre Konnyj Teat'r 'Narty'. Russia: Vladikavkaz. 1998. Lang.: Rus. 4272

Equilibrists
Performance/production
Changes in the nature of circus performance. Finland. 1980-1998. Lang.: Fin. 4181

Équipe (Montreal, PQ)
Performance/production
Pierre Dagenais and his company L'Équipe. Canada: Montreal, PQ. 1933-1990. Lang.: Fre. 1846

Equipment
Design/technology
Technology and its use by artists. 1913-1988. Lang.: Eng. 166
Directory of manufacturers and distributors of lighting equipment. Canada. USA. 1998. Lang.: Eng. 169
Presentation of stage equipment by manufacturers. Germany. 1998. Lang.: Ger. 184
Survey of Light Fair. Germany: Hannover. 1998. Lang.: Eng. 186
Max Keller, lighting designer of Münchner Kammerspiele. Germany: Munich. 1997. Lang.: Ger. 188
New lighting equipment of Lithuanian Opera and Ballet Theatre. Lithuania: Vilnius. 1974-1998. Lang.: Swe, Eng, Ger. 205
Survey of lighting equipment, design, and information. North America. 1998. Lang.: Eng. 209
Seminar on flying on stage. Norway: Oslo. 1998. Lang.: Swe. 211
Locking and controlling stage rigging. Sweden: Stockholm. 1998. Lang.: Swe. 220
The restructuring of the lighting company AVAB Scandinavia. Sweden: Stockholm. 1998. Lang.: Swe. 221
Report on PLASA trade show. UK-England: London. 1998. Lang.: Eng. 230
Lighting technology manufacturer AC Lighting. UK-England. 1998. Lang.: Eng. 233
AC Lighting's North American operation. UK-England. USA. 1998. Lang.: Eng. 234
Report on sound and lighting equipment fair Live!. UK-England: London. 1998. Lang.: Eng. 235
New theatrical sound equiment. USA. 1997. Lang.: Eng. 238
New theatrical lighting equipment. USA. 1997. Lang.: Eng. 239
Guide to theatrical design manufacturers and equipment. USA. 1998. Lang.: Eng. 241
Guide to equipment and services for the theatre and film industries. USA. 1998. Lang.: Eng. 242
Survey of lighting-design software manufacturers. USA. 1998. Lang.: Eng. 245
Guide to lighting equipment and services. USA. 1998. Lang.: Eng. 246
Guide to lighting equipment. USA. 1998. Lang.: Eng. 247
Rigging a pneumatically activated curtain. USA. 1998. Lang.: Eng. 263
Samuel Resnick, cofounder of Barbizon, distributor of electrical and video equipment. USA. 1918-1998. Lang.: Eng. 264
Construction and operation of a trap unit. USA. 1998. Lang.: Eng. 269
Review of new lighting software. USA. 1998. Lang.: Eng. 273
Lighting expert Gary Whittington. USA. 1952-1998. Lang.: Eng. 275
Lighting design and equipment in various Las Vegas spaces. USA: Las Vegas, NV. 1998. Lang.: Eng. 276
Stage lighting at the War Memorial Opera House. USA: San Francisco, CA. 1998. Lang.: Eng. 280
Update on construction of tuffets for scene-shop use. USA. 1998. Lang.: Eng. 283
Sound system manufacturer Eastern Acoustic Works. USA: Whitinsville, MA. 1996-1998. Lang.: Eng. 286
Panel discussion of sound designers. USA. 1998. Lang.: Eng. 287
NSCA sound products and technology trade show. USA: Las Vegas, NV. 1998. Lang.: Eng. 288
Report on AES trade show. USA: San Francisco, CA. 1998. Lang.: Eng. 289
Constructing collapsible changing booths for actors. USA. 1998. Lang.: Eng. 295
A fly system for low-ceilinged theatres. USA. 1998. Lang.: Eng. 296
Building a two-scene sound controller. USA. 1998. Lang.: Eng. 297
Report on new technical gadgets. USA. 1998. Lang.: Eng. 299
The new sound system of the Frauenthal Theatre. USA: Muskegon, MI. 1998. Lang.: Eng. 300
Lighting designer Glen Cunningham. USA. 1956-1998. Lang.: Eng. 301
Report on annual USITT conference. USA: Long Beach, CA. 1998. Lang.: Eng. 302
Preview of LDI98 trade show. USA: Las Vegas, NV. 1998. Lang.: Eng. 303
The Datatron control system for visual projections. USA. 1998. Lang.: Eng. 304
Preview of LDI convention. USA: Phoenix, AZ. 1998. Lang.: Eng. 305
Stage, lighting, and sound design for Rolling Stones tour. USA. 1996-1997. Lang.: Eng. 308
Recommendation for inexpensive digital noise-reduction software. USA. 1998. Lang.: Eng. 319
Construction of nylon turntable rollers. USA. 1998. Lang.: Eng. 321
Stage automation and its effect on set design. USA. 1998. Lang.: Eng. 325
Suppliers of lighting equipment for the music industry. USA: Tualatin, OR. 1996-1998. Lang.: Eng. 328
Evaluation of Sound Score playback equipment. USA. 1998. Lang.: Eng. 329
A four sided steel-marking guide. USA. 1998. Lang.: Eng. 331
Low-voltage cue light system. USA. 1998. Lang.: Eng. 332
New stage technology and the dance performance. 1998. Lang.: Eng. 888
Mick O'Gorman's sound design and equipment for *Riverdance*. Ireland. 1998. Lang.: Eng. 1218
The original stage machinery designed by John White at Her Majesty's Theatre. UK-England: London. 1887-1986. Lang.: Eng. 1528
Virtual reality technology for set design. USA: Lawrence, KS. 1997. Lang.: Eng. 1562
Advances in motion picture lighting. USA. 1998. Lang.: Eng. 3918
Production design for rock group Genesis' European tour. Europe. 1998. Lang.: Eng. 4096
Peter Morse's lighting design for country music tour. USA. 1998. Lang.: Eng. 4108
Lighting and sound control for the Disneyland 'Light Magic' show. USA: Anaheim, CA. 1998. Lang.: Eng. 4109
Technical effects control system used in a production of *Joe—The Musical* at Koninklijk Theater Carré. Netherlands: Amsterdam. 1998. Lang.: Eng. 4324
Technical designs for the musical *Doctor Doolittle* directed by Steven Pimlott. UK-England: London. 1998. Lang.: Eng. 4325
Digital lighting control for *A Chorus Line*. USA: New York, NY. 1974-1975. Lang.: Eng. 4337
Sound design for the musical *The Capeman*. USA: New York, NY. 1998. Lang.: Eng. 4339
Technical designs for the Broadway production of *The Lion King*. USA: New York, NY. 1998. Lang.: Eng. 4342
Stage machinery in *Il Rapimento di Cefalo* staged by Bernardo Buontalenti. Italy: Florence. 1600. Lang.: Eng. 4436
Performance spaces
Stage technology and equipment of Trøndelag Teater. Norway: Trondheim. 1997. Lang.: Nor. 454
Excerpts from the diary of the builder of Drottningholms Slottsteater. Sweden: Stockholm. 1755-1766. Lang.: Swe. 458
New stage lighting of War Memorial Opera House. USA: San Francisco, CA. 1998. Lang.: Eng. 465
Profile of the New Jersey Performing Arts Center. USA: Newark, NJ. 1988-1998. Lang.: Eng. 467

Equipment — cont'd
Materials and finishes for the stage floor. USA. 1970-1998. Lang.: Eng. 472
The influence of the Salle le Peletier on French grand opera. France: Paris. 1823-1873. Lang.: Eng. 4494
Sante Fe Opera's newly renovated open-air theatre. USA: Santa Fe, NM. 1991-1998. Lang.: Eng. 4499
Performance/production
Renaissance ideas about classical Greek staging. Europe. 1400-1600. Lang.: Slo. 521
Plays/librettos/scripts
Description of a Web site devoted to *Los españoles en Chile* by Francisco Ganzalez de Busto. Spain. 1665-1998. Lang.: Eng. 3366

Equus
Performance/production
Director Armin Petras. Germany: Nordhausen. 1970-1998. Lang.: Ger. 2001
Plays/librettos/scripts
A method of analysis for the drama. USA. 1920-1975. Lang.: Eng. 3537
Theatrical ritual in plays of Peter Shaffer. USA. 1975-1985. Lang.: Eng. 3707

er nicht als er (he not as himself)
Institutions
Productions of the Salzburg Festival. Austria: Salzburg. 1998. Lang.: Ger. 1573

Er treibt einen Teufel aus (He Exorcizes a Devil)
Basic theatrical documents
Catalan translations of plays by Bertolt Brecht (volume 1). Germany. 1919-1954. Lang.: Cat. 1437

Erceg, Mirca
Performance/production
The performance of Shakespeare in the former East Germany. Germany: Rostock, Leipzig, Berlin, Dessau. 1996-1997. Lang.: Ger. 1974

Ergen, Mehmet
Performance/production
Collection of newspaper reviews by London theatre critics. UK-England: London. 1998. Lang.: Eng. 2515
Collection of newspaper reviews by London theatre critics. UK-England: London. 1998. Lang.: Eng. 2573
Collection of newspaper reviews by London theatre critics. UK-England: London. 1998. Lang.: Eng. 2576

ERIC
SEE
Educational Resources Information Center.

Erik XIV
Institutions
Report on the Stockholm theatre festival. Sweden: Stockholm. 1998. Lang.: Eng. 1724

Erkel Néptáncegyüttes (Budapest)
Institutions
History of the folk dance ensemble Erkel Néptáncegyüttes. Hungary. 1948-1998. Lang.: Hun. 1220

Erkel Színház (Budapest)
Performance/production
La Fille mal Gardée at Erkel Színház. Hungary: Budapest. 1997. Lang.: Hun. 1087
Reference materials
Yearbook of the Hungarian State Opera House. Hungary: Budapest. 1996-1997. Lang.: Hun. 4832

Erlanger, Abraham Lincoln
Institutions
The Shuberts vs. the Syndicate. USA: New York, NY. 1976-1998. Lang.: Eng. 427

Ermittlung, Die (Investigation, The)
Performance/production
Interview with director Jochen Gerz. Germany: Berlin. 1998. Lang.: Ger, Fre, Dut, Eng. 1967

Ernotte, Andre
Design/technology
Neil Patel's scene design for *Mirette*, Goodspeed Opera House. USA: East Haddam, CT. 1998. Lang.: Eng. 4334

Ernst-Busch-Schule (Berlin)
Institutions
Actor training at Hochschule der Künste and Ernst-Busch-Schule. Germany: Berlin. 1998. Lang.: Ger. 1622
Director training at Ernst-Busch-Schule and some of its graduates. Germany: Berlin. 1972-1998. Lang.: Ger. 1648

Eroberung des Südpols, Die (Conquest of the South Pole, The)
Performance/production
Director Angela Brodauf. Germany: Dortmund. 1984-1998. Lang.: Ger. 1989

Erofeev, Venedikt
Plays/librettos/scripts
Stephen Mulrine's translation and stage adaptation of *Moscow Stations* by Venedikt Erofeev. USSR. UK-England. 1973-1998. Lang.: Eng. 3718

Eros (Epidauros)
Performance spaces
Michael Marmarinos' production of Sophocles' *Electra* at the Epidauros amphitheatre. Greece: Epidauros. 1938-1998. Lang.: Ger. 445

Ertl, Fritz
Performance/production
The 'viewpoint theory' of actor training. USA. 1998. Lang.: Eng. 2677

Eschberg, Peter
Performance/production
Recent productions of plays by Bertolt Brecht. Germany. 1997-1998. Lang.: Ger. 2028

Escudero, Vicente
Performance/production
Dancer Antonia Merce, La Argentina. France. Spain. 1888-1936. Lang.: Eng. 922

Esdaile, Sarah
Performance/production
Collection of newspaper reviews by London theatre critics. UK-England: London. 1998. Lang.: Eng. 2574

Esenin, Sergej Aleksandrovič
Performance/production
Dancer Isadora Duncan's relationship with poet Sergej Esenin. Russia. 1919-1925. Lang.: Rus. 1297
Sergej Bezrukov's creation of the character of poet Sergej Esenin. Russia: Moscow. 1998. Lang.: Rus. 2278

Eskelinen, Päivi
Performance/production
Interview with dance notator Päivi Eskelinen. Finland. 1998. Lang.: Fin. 920

Espace GO (Montreal, PQ)
Performance/production
Productions of plays by Bernard-Marie Koltès. Canada: Montreal, PQ. 1991-1997. Lang.: Fre. 1862

Españoles en Chile, Los (Spanish in Chile, The)
Plays/librettos/scripts
Description of a Web site devoted to *Los españoles en Chile* by Francisco Ganzalez de Busto. Spain. 1665-1998. Lang.: Eng. 3366

Espert, Nuria
Performance/production
The performance of *onnagata* Tamasaburō in *Elizabeth* by Francisco Ors. Japan: Tokyo. 1993-1995. Lang.: Eng. 1362

Espina, Concha
Plays/librettos/scripts
The image of women on the Spanish stage. Spain. 1908-1936. Lang.: Eng. 3399

Essex House Masque, The
Plays/librettos/scripts
The design and authorship of *The Essex House Masque*. England. 1621. Lang.: Eng. 4209

Estrella de Sevilla, La (Star of Seville, The)
Plays/librettos/scripts
Playwright Andrés de Claramonte. Spain. 1580-1626. Lang.: Eng. 3404

Et les Chiens se taisaient (And the Dogs Were Silent)
Plays/librettos/scripts
Analysis and translation of *Et les Chiens se taisaient (And the Dogs Were Silent)* by Aimé Césaire. Martinique. 1946-1969. Lang.: Eng. 3269

Et soudain, des nuits d'éveil (And Suddenly, Sleepless Nights)
Performance/production
Reviews of productions by Wilson, Greenaway, and Mnouchkine. France: Paris. 1997-1998. Lang.: Eng. 1926
Survey of Parisian productions. France: Paris. 1997-1998. Lang.: Eng. 1937
Productions of international Čechov festival. Russia: Moscow. 1998. Lang.: Swe. 2306

Etcetera Theatre Club (London)
Performance/production
Collection of newspaper reviews by London theatre critics. UK-England: London. 1998. Lang.: Eng. 2429
Collection of newspaper reviews by London theatre critics. UK-England: London. 1998. Lang.: Eng. 2454

Etcetera Theatre Club (London) — cont'd

Collection of newspaper reviews by London theatre critics. UK-England: London. 1998. Lang.: Eng. 2459
Collection of newspaper reviews by London theatre critics. UK-England: London. 1998. Lang.: Eng. 2471
Collection of newspaper reviews by London theatre critics. UK-England: London. 1998. Lang.: Eng. 2481
Collection of newspaper reviews by London theatre critics. UK-England: London. 1998. Lang.: Eng. 2494
Collection of newspaper reviews by London theatre critics. UK-England: London. 1998. Lang.: Eng. 2517
Collection of newspaper reviews by London theatre critics. UK-England: London. 1998. Lang.: Eng. 2522
Collection of newspaper reviews by London theatre critics. UK-England: London. 1998. Lang.: Eng. 2532
Collection of newspaper reviews by London theatre critics. UK-England: London. 1998. Lang.: Eng. 2534
Collection of newspaper reviews by London theatre critics. UK-England: London. 1998. Lang.: Eng. 2550
Collection of newspaper reviews by London theatre critics. UK-England: London. 1998. Lang.: Eng. 2561
Collection of newspaper reviews by London theatre critics. UK-England: London. 1998. Lang.: Eng. 2576

Etchells, Tim
Performance/production
Collection of newspaper reviews by London theatre critics. UK-England: London. 1998. Lang.: Eng. 2572

Été, L' (Summer)
Performance/production
Collection of newspaper reviews by London theatre critics. UK-England: London. 1998. Lang.: Eng. 2514

Etherege, George
Plays/librettos/scripts
Motherhood in Restoration comedy. England. 1642-1729. Lang.: Eng. 2864

Ethics
Design/technology
Entertainment Services and Technology Association's guidelines on ethics. USA. 1998. Lang.: Eng. 256
Performance/production
Ethical guidelines for the social context performance. USA. 1987. Lang.: Eng. 632
Plays/librettos/scripts
Conscience in early modern literature including Shakespeare. England. 1590-1620. Lang.: Eng. 3020
Prejudice and law in Shakespeare's *The Merchant of Venice.* England. 1596. Lang.: Eng. 3027
Relation to other fields
The Rodney King beating and how a news event is shaped by the media. USA: Los Angeles, CA. 1992. Lang.: Eng. 4084

Ethnic dance
SEE ALSO
Classed Entries under DANCE—Ethnic dance.
Performance/production
Sanjukta Panigrahi, dancer, choreographer, and co-founder of ISTA. India. 1944-1997. Lang.: Eng. 952
Interview with choreographer Birgit Åkesson. Sweden. Africa. Asia. 1908. Lang.: Swe. 963
Interview with *butō* dancer Susanna Åkerlund. Sweden. Japan. 1990-1998. Lang.: Swe. 1300
Women in the *canboulay* ceremony. Trinidad and Tobago. 1998. Lang.: Eng. 4166
Relation to other fields
The 'bird-woman' folktale in Southeast Asian shamanic healing rituals. Ireland. Thailand. Malaysia. Lang.: Eng. 1358

Ethnic theatre
Institutions
HaBimah and colonialism. Israel. 1920-1998. Lang.: Eng. 1673
Performance/production
Aborigines in Australian theatre. Australia. 1990-1998. Lang.: Eng. 486
Historical, political, and aesthetic context of *madang* theatre. Korea. 1976-1998. Lang.: Ger. 557
Polish-Jewish cultural relations as reflected in theatre. Poland. 1850-1950. Lang.: Eng. 577
Theatrical rebellion and sociopolitical chaos. Zimbabwe. Kenya. 1990-1998. Lang.: Eng. 687
Autobiography of Yiddish theatre actress Moni Ovadia. Italy. Bulgaria. 1946-1998. Lang.: Ita. 2174
Indian theatre in South Africa. South Africa, Republic of. 1900-1998. Lang.: Eng. 2356
Theatrical activities of the Polynesian Cultural Center. USA: Laie, HI. 1963-1983. Lang.: Eng. 4221
Plays/librettos/scripts
Analysis of *Bandido!* by Luis Valdez. USA. 1982. Lang.: Eng. 3708
History of Hungarian-language theatre in the Voivodship region. Yugoslavia: Subotica, Novi Sad. 1837-1998. Lang.: Hun. 3720
Theory/criticism
Theory and Asian-American theatre. USA: Minneapolis, MN. 1994-1995. Lang.: Eng. 869

Eti Kal'a Quinat (Other War, The)
Plays/librettos/scripts
Theatre as cultural weapon and military education in the Eritrean war. Eritrea. 1980-1984. Lang.: Eng. 3048

Etienne, Treva
Performance/production
Collection of newspaper reviews by London theatre critics. UK-England: London. 1998. Lang.: Eng. 2475

Étranger, L' (Stranger, The)
Performance/production
Teater UNO's stage adaptation of *L'Étranger (The Stranger)* by Albert Camus. Sweden: Gothenburg. 1998. Lang.: Swe. 2395

Eugene Onegin
Institutions
The current state of Theater Bielefeld. Germany: Bielefeld. 1998. Lang.: Ger. 1621
The Bolšoj Ballet and the experimental company Gelikon. Russia: Moscow. 1997. Lang.: Swe. 4467
Performance/production
Bayerische Staatsballett's guest performances at Budapest Opera House. Hungary: Budapest. 1998. Lang.: Hun. 1092
Čajkovskij's *Eugene Onegin* directed by A. Stepanov. Russia: St. Petersburg. 1998. Lang.: Rus. 4671

Euripides
Performance/production
Comparison of fifteen productions of Euripides' *Medea.* Czech Republic. 1921-1998. Lang.: Cze. 1885
Péter Valló's production of *Iphigéneia he en Aulide (Iphigenia in Aulis)* by Euripides. Hungary: Budapest. 1998. Lang.: Hun. 2132
Massimo Castri's production of Euripides' *Electra.* Italy: Spoleto. 1993. Lang.: Ita. 2179
Collection of newspaper reviews by London theatre critics. UK-England: London. 1998. Lang.: Eng. 2468
Collection of newspaper reviews by London theatre critics. UK-England: London. 1998. Lang.: Eng. 2562
Twentieth-century productions of Euripidean tragedy. USA. 1915-1969. Lang.: Eng. 2678
Interview with actress Phylicia Rashad. USA: Atlanta, GA. 1998. Lang.: Eng. 2695
Plays/librettos/scripts
The character Medea in European drama. Europe. 450 B.C.-1998 A.D. Lang.: Ger. 3063
The playwright Euripides as a character in *Thesmophoriazusae* of Aristophanes. Greece. 438-411 B.C. Lang.: Eng. 3181
Electra and Orestes in plays of Aeschylus, Euripides, and Sophocles. Greece. 438-411 B.C. Lang.: Eng. 3184
Civic discourse and civil discord in Greek tragedy. Greece. 475-400 B.C. Lang.: Eng. 3185
Adaptations of Greek tragedy by contemporary Irish writers. Ireland. UK-Ireland. 1984-1998. Lang.: Eng. 3214
Ellen McLaughlin's *Iphigenia and Other Daughters* at CSC Repertory. USA: New York, NY. 1995. Lang.: Eng. 3520
Analysis of Countée Cullen's translation of Euripides' *Medea.* USA. 1936. Lang.: Eng. 3567
Training
Anne-Lise Gabold's use of the methods of Tadashi Suzuki in her production of Euripides' *Bákchai (The Bacchae).* Japan. Denmark: Copenhagen. 1960-1998. Lang.: Dan. 1359

Europeans Only
Performance/production
Collection of newspaper reviews by London theatre critics. UK-England: London. 1998. Lang.: Eng. 2411

Europeras 1 and 2
Performance/production
The police and John Cage's *Europeras 1 and 2* at Frankfurter Theater. Germany: Frankfurt. 1987. Lang.: Eng. 4586
Eurydice
Performance/production
Collection of newspaper reviews by London theatre critics. UK-England: London. 1998. Lang.: Eng. 2548
Eurythmics
Performance/production
Dancer and eurythmics teacher Klára Hajós. Hungary. 1911-1998. Lang.: Hun. 936
Evangeline
Plays/librettos/scripts
Dramatic adaptations of Henry Wadsworth Longfellow's poem *Evangeline*. USA. Canada. 1860-1976. Lang.: Eng. 3643
Evangeline Deusse (Evangeline the Second)
Plays/librettos/scripts
Dramatic adaptations of Henry Wadsworth Longfellow's poem *Evangeline*. USA. Canada. 1860-1976. Lang.: Eng. 3643
Evans Rees, David
Performance/production
Collection of newspaper reviews by London theatre critics. UK-England: London. 1998. Lang.: Eng. 2449
Collection of newspaper reviews by London theatre critics. UK-England: London. 1998. Lang.: Eng. 2482
Collection of newspaper reviews by London theatre critics. UK-England: London. 1998. Lang.: Eng. 2567
Evans, Albert
Performance/production
Dancer Albert Evans of New York City Ballet. USA: New York, NY. 1987-1998. Lang.: Eng. 1181
Evans, Lee
Performance/production
Collection of newspaper reviews by London theatre critics. UK-England: London. 1998. Lang.: Eng. 2508
Evans, Lissa
Performance/production
Collection of newspaper reviews by London theatre critics. UK-England: London. 1998. Lang.: Eng. 2475
Evarts, William Johnson
Basic theatrical documents
Text of *The Ballad of Sam Bass* by William Johnson Evarts. USA. 1988. Lang.: Eng. 1484
Eve's Bayou
Basic theatrical documents
Screenplay of *Eve's Bayou* by Kasi Lemmons. USA. 1994-1998. Lang.: Eng. 3892
Plays/librettos/scripts
Interview with screenwriter and director Kasi Lemmons. USA. 1994-1998. Lang.: Eng. 4000
Eve's Diary
Basic theatrical documents
Dutch translations of women's monologues by Dario Fo. Italy. 1998. Lang.: Dut. 1440
Evénements, Les
Performance/production
Collection of newspaper reviews by London theatre critics. UK-England: London. 1998. Lang.: Eng. 2427
Evening with Ira Aldridge, An
Basic theatrical documents
Texts of plays by Eddie Paul Bradley, Jr. USA. 1998. Lang.: Eng. 1482
Everding, August
Institutions
The curriculum at Bayerische Theaterakademie. Germany: Munich. 1985-1998. Lang.: Ger. 1659
Every Day Life in the Sixties
Performance/production
Collection of newspaper reviews by London theatre critics. UK-England. 1998. Lang.: Eng. 2489
Everybody's Ruby
Plays/librettos/scripts
Novelist and playwright Thulani Davis. USA. 1998. Lang.: Eng. 3689
Everyman
Performance/production
Collection of newspaper reviews by London theatre critics. UK-England: London. 1998. Lang.: Eng. 2587
Plays/librettos/scripts
Comparison of the Dutch *Elckerlijck* and the English *Everyman*. England. Netherlands. 1495-1525. Lang.: Eng. 2982
Everyman Theatre (Liverpool)
Plays/librettos/scripts
Interview with playwright Jonathan Harvey. UK-England. 1998. Lang.: Eng. 3472
Evreinov, Nikolaj Nikolajėvič
SEE
Jėvrejnov, Nikolaj Nikolajėvič.
Ex Machina (Montreal, PQ)
Design/technology
Set design for Robert Lepage's *Geometry of Miracles*. Canada: Quebec, PQ. 1998. Lang.: Eng. 1516
Institutions
Robert Lepage and his experimental company Ex Machina. Canada: Quebec, PQ. 1998. Lang.: Fre. 1587
Performance/production
Interview with director Robert Lepage. Sweden: Stockholm. Canada: Montreal, PQ. 1997. Lang.: Swe. 2397
Example: The Case of Craig and Bentley
Basic theatrical documents
Text of *Example: The Case of Craig and Bentley* adapted by Tom Barrie. UK-England. 1998. Lang.: Eng. 1472
Performance/production
Collection of newspaper reviews by London theatre critics. UK-England: London. 1998. Lang.: Eng. 2528
Exclusés ou Le Cabaret de la p'tite misère, Les (Excluded, or The Poverty Cabaret, The)
Basic theatrical documents
Text of *Les Exclusés*, poetry adapted for the stage by Isabelle Starkier. France. 1998. Lang.: Fre. 1423
Exécution de Pierre Laporte, les dessous de l'opération, L' (Laporte's Execution: The Hidden Story)
Plays/librettos/scripts
Quebecois plays about the crisis of October 1970. Canada. 1970-1990. Lang.: Fre, Eng. 2812
Exhibitions
Design/technology
A staged costume exhibition. 1998. Lang.: Swe. 167
An exhibition of sets and environments by Hungarian designers. Hungary: Budapest. 1998. Lang.: Hun. 196
Catalogue of an exhibition devoted to Hungarian theatre and film. Hungary: Budapest. 1998. Lang.: Hun. 197
Institutions
Display of objects related to guest performances of the Ballets Russes. Germany: Berlin. 1910-1914. Lang.: Hun. 1040
Exodus
Performance/production
Collection of newspaper reviews by London theatre critics. UK-England: London. 1998. Lang.: Eng. 2525
Experiment with an Airpump, An
Performance/production
Collection of newspaper reviews by London theatre critics. UK-England: Leeds, Manchester. 1998. Lang.: Eng. 2433
Collection of newspaper reviews by London theatre critics. UK-England: London. 1998. Lang.: Eng. 2523
Experimental theatre
SEE ALSO
Avant-garde theatre.
Alternative theatre.
Audience
Interview with performance artist Tim Brennan. Netherlands: Arnhem. 1989. Lang.: Eng. 4231
Design/technology
Design in contemporary opera performance. Canada: Toronto, ON. 1983-1998. Lang.: Eng. 4425
Institutions
Robert Lepage and his experimental company Ex Machina. Canada: Quebec, PQ. 1998. Lang.: Fre. 1587
Jacques Crête and Atelier de recherche théâtrale l'Eskabel. Canada: Montreal, PQ. 1971-1989. Lang.: Eng. 1590
Report on the Cairo festival and symposia on women's theatre. Egypt: Cairo. 1997. Lang.: Eng. 1597
Report on the Spielart '97 experimental theatre festival. Germany: Munich. 1997. Lang.: Eng. 1618
Italian experimental theatre at Spielart '97. Germany: Munich. Italy. 1997. Lang.: Eng. 1619
Polish experimental theatre training. Poland: Cracow, Wrocław, Warsaw. 1930-1998. Lang.: Pol. 1685

Experimental theatre — cont'd

Ellen Stewart and La MaMa Experimental Theatre Club. USA: New York, NY. 1961-1985. Lang.: Eng. 1762

Profile of Arbo Cyber, théâtre (?). Canada: Quebec, PQ. 1985-1998. Lang.: Fre. 4232

Experimental performances of Helena Waldmann and Showcase Beat le Mot. Germany: Franfurt. 1993-1998. Lang.: Ger. 4234

Performance spaces

Essays on experimental theatre world wide. Europe. North America. Asia. 1918-1998. Lang.: Pol. 438

Performance/production

Account of the theatre anthropology workshop. Austria: Vienna. 1989-1998. Lang.: Hun. 494

Social criticism and alternative theatre in Quebec and Newfoundland. Canada. 1970-1985. Lang.: Eng. 500

The influence of experimental performance on contemporary drama. Europe. USA. 1960-1987. Lang.: Eng. 526

Forced Entertainment and Berlin's Live Art Festival. UK-England, Sheffield. Germany: Berlin. 1984-1998. Lang.: Ger. 539

The integration of playwriting into the production process at Théâtre Niveau Parking. Canada: Quebec, PQ. 1990-1998. Lang.: Fre. 1857

Michel Laprise's *Masculin/Féminin (Male/Female)*, presented to audiences segregated by sex. Canada: Montreal, PQ. 1998. Lang.: Fre. 1867

Impressions from Podewil theatre workshop. Germany: Berlin. 1998. Lang.: Ger. 2024

The actor/clown team of Claudio Remondi and Riccardo Caporossi. Italy. 1971-1998. Lang.: Eng. 2176

Roman theatre, traditional and experimental. Italy: Rome. 1994-1998. Lang.: Eng. 2187

Productions of the festival of experimental theatre. Poland: Cracow. 1998. Lang.: Ger. 2225

Experimental Shakespeare production at the Gaiety Theatre. UK-England: Manchester. 1908-1915. Lang.: Eng. 2605

A production of Susan Glaspell's experimental play *The Verge*. UK-Scotland: Glasgow. 1996. Lang.: Eng. 2651

Avant-garde American women directors' productions of *Doctor Faustus Lights the Lights* by Gertrude Stein. USA. 1940-1995. Lang.:Eng. 2735

Plays/librettos/scripts

Insanity in nineteenth- and twentieth-century theatre. Europe. 1880-1970. Lang.: Eng. 3050

Playwrights Annibale Ruccello, Enzo Moscato, and Manlio Santanelli. Italy: Naples. 1980-1989. Lang.: Eng. 3261

Analysis of *Processional* by John Howard Lawson. USA. 1925. Lang.: Eng. 3535

Joseph Chaikin's adaptation of *Textes pour rien (Texts for Nothing)* by Samuel Beckett. USA: New York, NY. 1995. Lang.: Eng. 3563

Revolutionary Off Broadway playwriting. USA: New York, NY. 1959-1969. Lang.: Eng. 3604

Experimental theatre of Elmer Rice. USA. 1914-1963. Lang.: Eng. 3620

Experimental writing in Finnish radio drama. Finland. 1998. Lang.: Fin. 3866

Relation to other fields

Situational theory in counter-cultural theatre. UK-England. 1960-1969. Lang.: Eng. 771

Ritual in encounter groups and experimental theatre. USA. 1960-1970. Lang.: Eng. 788

Cultural trends of the younger generation. Europe. 1995-1998. Lang.: Swe. 4150

Theory/criticism

Artaud's theatre of cruelty and contemporary experimental theatre. France. 1945-1998. Lang.: Ger. 3818

The influence of Antonin Artaud on director Paul Pörtner. France. 1920-1973. Lang.: Ger. 3870

Expressionism

Performance/production

The nature of acting in German Expressionist production. Germany. 1916-1921. Lang.: Eng. 536

Plays/librettos/scripts

Social criticism in Viennese Expressionist drama. Austria: Vienna. 1907-1922. Lang.: Ger. 2779

Language and silence in German Expressionist drama. Germany. 1913-1923. Lang.: Eng. 3159

Comparison of characters in plays of Georg Kaiser and Tennessee Williams. USA. Germany. 1912-1945. Lang.: Eng. 3588

Eyam

Performance/production

Collection of newspaper reviews by London theatre critics. UK-England: London. 1998. Lang.: Eng. 2470

Eyen, Tom

Plays/librettos/scripts

Revolutionary Off Broadway playwriting. USA: New York, NY. 1959-1969. Lang.: Eng. 3604

Eyes for Consuela

Design/technology

Set designs by Santo Loquasto at Manhattan Theatre Club. USA: New York, NY. 1998. Lang.: Eng. 1536

Eyre, Richard

Performance/production

Collection of newspaper reviews by London theatre critics. UK-England: London. 1998. Lang.: Eng. 2444

Collection of newspaper reviews by London theatre critics. UK-England: London. 1998. Lang.: Eng. 2533

Collection of newspaper reviews by London theatre critics. UK-England: London. 1998. Lang.: Eng. 2569

F. Otto Haas Theatre (Philadelphia, PA)

Performance spaces

The renovation of Arden Theatre Company's F. Otto Haas Theatre. USA: Philadelphia, PA. 1998. Lang.: Eng. 469

F.M. Kirby Theatre (Madison, NJ)

Institutions

Bonnie Monte of New Jersey Shakespeare Festival. USA: Madison, NJ. 1996-1998. Lang.: Eng. 1772

Fabian, Jo

Performance/production

Recent dance performances in Berlin. Germany: Berlin. 1998. Lang.: Ger. 933

Fából faragott királyfi, A (Wooden Prince, The)

Performance/production

Bartók's *A fából faragott királyfi (The Wooden Prince)* choreographed by László Seregi. Hungary: Budapest. 1998. Lang.: Hun. 1103

Fabre, Jan

Theory/criticism

Artaud's theatre of cruelty and contemporary experimental theatre. France. 1945-1998. Lang.: Ger. 3818

Fábri, Péter

Administration

Round-table on author's rights. Hungary. 1990-1998. Lang.: Hun. 16

Plays/librettos/scripts

New Hungarian translations of Shakespeare. Hungary. 1990-1998. Lang.: Hun. 3187

Facer, Jamie

Performance/production

Collection of newspaper reviews by London theatre critics. UK-England: London. 1998. Lang.: Eng. 2475

Faces in the Rock

Performance/production

Beothuk Street Players' production of *Faces in the Rock* by Fred Hawksley. Canada: St. John's, NF. 1998. Lang.: Eng. 1863

Fadren (Father, The)

Performance/production

Recent productions of plays by Ibsen and Strindberg. Sweden: Stockholm. 1997. Lang.: Eng. 2393

Plays/librettos/scripts

Gender and madness in modern drama. Europe. 1880-1969. Lang.: Eng. 3061

Realism in plays of Strindberg. Sweden. 1872-1886. Lang.: Eng. 3416

Faery Pastorall

Plays/librettos/scripts

Analysis of an edition of William Percy's *Faery Pastorall*. England. 1603-1646. Lang.: Eng. 2916

Fair Quarrel, A

Plays/librettos/scripts

Male and female honor in *A Fair Quarrel* by Middleton and Rowley. England. 1615-1617. Lang.: Eng. 2993

Fairbanks, Douglas

Plays/librettos/scripts

Robin Hood on film. England. USA. 1920-1992. Lang.: Eng. 3969

Fairs, Nigel

Performance/production

Collection of newspaper reviews by London theatre critics. UK-England: London. 1998. Lang.: Eng. 2479

Fairytaleheart

Performance/production

Collection of newspaper reviews by London theatre critics. UK-England: London. 1998. Lang.: Eng. 2575

Faith and Dancing
Performance/production
Lois Weaver's *Faith and Dancing* and the CD-ROM in interactive performance. UK-England. USA. 1996. Lang.: Eng. 971
Fáklya Horvát Táncegyüttes (Budapest)
Performance/production
Fáklya Horvát Táncegyüttes' folk dance production *Napmadarak (Sunbirds).* Hungary. 1998. Lang.: Hun. 1227
Fala baixo senão eu grito (Speak Softly, Or I'll Scream)
Plays/librettos/scripts
Cruelty and the absurd in theatre of Latin American playwrights. Latin America. 1960-1980. Lang.: Eng. 3267
Falconer, Edmund
Performance/production
Irish and Irish-American characters on the stages of the Midwest. USA. 1875-1915. Lang.: Eng. 2696
Fall of Robespierre, The
Plays/librettos/scripts
The feminine ideal in the drama of English Romantic poets. England. 1794-1840. Lang.: Eng. 2886
Falling Man, The
Basic theatrical documents
Text of three monologues by Will Scheffer. USA. 1997. Lang.: Eng. 1509
Falls, Robert
Design/technology
Technical designs for *Griller* by Eric Bogosian. USA: Chicago, IL. 1998. Lang.: Eng. 1558
Performance/production
Recent productions in Ireland of plays by Eugene O'Neill. Ireland: Dublin. UK-Ireland: Belfast. 1989-1998. Lang.: Eng. 2154
Falso Movimento (Naples)
Performance/production
Interview with director Mario Martone. Italy: Naples. 1977-1997. Lang.: Eng. 2166
Falstaff
Performance/production
The current state of opera in England. UK-England. 1997. Lang.: Eng. 4705
Training
Singer training at Teater- & Operahögskolan. Sweden: Gothenburg. 1960-1998. Lang.: Swe. 4848
Falstaff **by Salieri**
Performance/production
Antonio Salieri and his opera *Falstaff*, recently revived. Italy: Milan. 1799-1998. Lang.: Eng. 4654
Fame
Performance/production
Collection of newspaper reviews by London theatre critics. UK-England: London. 1998. Lang.: Eng. 2525
Family Outing, A
Performance/production
Collection of newspaper reviews by London theatre critics. UK-England: London. 1998. Lang.: Eng. 2531
Family Reunion, The
Plays/librettos/scripts
The Orestes myth in twentieth-century drama. Europe. USA. 1914-1943. Lang.: Eng. 3052
Famous Victories of Henrie the Fifth, The
Plays/librettos/scripts
The first quarto of Shakespeare's *Henry V* and the anonymous *Famous Victories of Henrie the Fifth.* England. 1599-1600. Lang.: Eng. 3022
Fanciulla del West, La
Design/technology
Lighting and realism in opera and theatre: Belasco and Puccini. Italy. USA. 1890-1910. Lang.: Eng. 203
Fando et Lis (Fando and Lis)
Performance/production
Collection of newspaper reviews by London theatre critics. UK-England. 1998. Lang.: Eng. 2485
Fannin, Hilary
Performance/production
Collection of newspaper reviews by London theatre critics. UK-England: London. 1998. Lang.: Eng. 2434
Report on several English performances. UK-England: London, Stratford. 1998. Lang.: Swe. 2634
Fanshen
Institutions
The aesthetics of performances based on non-fiction texts at Lifeline Theatre. USA: Chicago, IL. 1996-1998. Lang.: Eng. 1788
Fär Vårt Högst Personliga Nöje (For Our Most Personal Pleasure)
Plays/librettos/scripts
Interview with playwright-director Kajsa Isakson. Sweden: Stockholm. 1997-1998. Lang.: Swe. 3414
Fára, Libor
Design/technology
The work of scene designer Libor Fára. Czech Republic: Prague. 1950-1981. Lang.: Cze. 1518
Faragó, Béla
Performance/production
Brecht's *Der Kaukasische Kreidkreis (The Caucasian Chalk Circle)* adapted and directed by János Mohácsi. Hungary: Nyíregyháza. 1998. Lang.: Hun. 2127
Faragoh, Francis Edwards
Institutions
The New Playwrights Theatre Company. USA: New York, NY. 1927-1929. Lang.: Eng. 410
Farce
Plays/librettos/scripts
Comedy and farce in Finnish theatre and film. Finland. 1950-1998. Lang.: Fin. 3070
Absurdism in children's theatre. North America. Europe. 1896-1970. Lang.: Eng. 3288
Fargearel, Jacques
Performance/production
Dance improvisation with children. France. 1998. Lang.: Fre. 1275
Farges, Brigitte
Performance/production
The body and personality of the dancer as the source of the physical vocabulary of dance. Europe. 1989. Lang.: Eng. 1269
Farinelli (Broschi, Carlo)
Plays/librettos/scripts
The *castrato*, the contralto, and the film *Farinelli.* France. Italy. 1994. Lang.: Eng. 4787
Farinelli, Il Castrato
Plays/librettos/scripts
The *castrato*, the contralto, and the film *Farinelli.* France. Italy. 1994. Lang.: Eng. 4787
Farjeon, Annabel
Performance/production
Annabel Farjeon on dancing for Ninette de Valois and Frederick Ashton. UK-England: London. 1930-1940. Lang.: Eng. 1158
Farmer, David
Performance/production
Collection of newspaper reviews by London theatre critics. UK-England: London. 1998. Lang.: Eng. 2556
Farr, David
Performance/production
Collection of newspaper reviews by London theatre critics. UK-England: London. 1998. Lang.: Eng. 2415
Farrelly, Bobby
Plays/librettos/scripts
The popularity of crude comedy in recent American films. USA. 1998. Lang.: Eng. 4004
Farrelly, Peter
Plays/librettos/scripts
The popularity of crude comedy in recent American films. USA. 1998. Lang.: Eng. 4004
Farrow, Graham
Performance/production
Collection of newspaper reviews by London theatre critics. UK-England: London. 1998. Lang.: Eng. 2502
Fascinations from the Crowd
Performance/production
Collection of newspaper reviews by London theatre critics. UK-England: London. 1998. Lang.: Eng. 2535
Fassbinder, Rainer Werner
Institutions
Gunnar Martin Aronsson of TeaterX2 recalls Action-Theater. Sweden: Stockholm. Germany: Munich. 1968-1998. Lang.: Swe. 1722
Performance/production
Interview with director Bernd Wilms. Germany: Berlin. 1998. Lang.: Swe. 2018
Theatrical influences on director Rainer Werner Fassbinder. East Germany: Berlin. 1969-1982. Lang.: Fre. 4058
Plays/librettos/scripts
Homosexuality on the German stage. Germany. 1920-1980. Lang.: Eng. 3147

Fassbinder, Rainer Werner — cont'd

Fassbinder's *Der Müll, die Stadt und der Tod (Garbage, the City and Death)*. Germany: Berlin. 1976-1998. Lang.: Ger. 3175

Fathers and Sons
Plays/librettos/scripts
Don Hannah's *Fathers and Sons* at Tarragon Theatre. Canada: Toronto, ON. 1998. Lang.: Eng. 2833

Faulkner, William
Performance/production
Collection of newspaper reviews by London theatre critics. UK-England: London. 1998. Lang.: Eng. 2413

Faun délelőttje, Egy (Morning of a Faun, The)
Performance/production
Visual dance productions by Cie, 2 in 1. Hungary: Budapest. 1998. Lang.: Hun. 942

Faust
Design/technology
Josef Svoboda's set design for Goethe's *Faust*. Czech Republic: Prague. 1997. Lang.: Eng. 1517
Performance/production
Otomar Krejča's production of *Faust* at Národní Divadlo. Czech Republic: Prague. 1997. Lang.: Eng, Fre. 1881
French productions of German plays. France. 1998. Lang.: Ger. 1935
Plays/librettos/scripts
The reciprocal influence of opera and film. Europe. North America. 1904-1994. Lang.: Eng. 4770

Favorite, La
Performance/production
Evaluation of video performances of Donizetti's operas. Europe. USA. 1980-1998. Lang.: Eng. 4557
Hector Berlioz's review of Donizetti's *La Favorite*. France: Paris. 1840. Lang.: Eng. 4565

Fawn, The
Plays/librettos/scripts
The politics of gender in the plays of John Marston. England. 1599-1634. Lang.: Eng. 3009

Fay, Jimmy
Performance/production
Collection of newspaper reviews by London theatre critics. UK-England: London. 1998. Lang.: Eng. 2445

Faye, Habib
Performance/production
Collection of newspaper reviews by London theatre critics. UK-England: London. 1998. Lang.: Eng. 2457

Faye, Joey
Performance/production
Burlesque comedian Joey Faye. USA. 1925-1960. Lang.: Eng. 4140

Fayette, James
Performance/production
New male dancers of New York City Ballet. USA: New York, NY. 1998. Lang.: Eng. 1177

Featherstone, Vicky
Performance/production
Collection of newspaper reviews by London theatre critics. UK-England: London. 1998. Lang.: Eng. 2434
Collection of newspaper reviews by London theatre critics. UK-England: London. 1998. Lang.: Eng. 2493

Featherstonehaughs (London)
Performance/production
Analysis of *The Featherstonehaughs Draw on the Sketchbooks of Egon Schiele* by choreographer Lea Anderson. UK-England: London. 1998. Lang.: Eng. 1315

Featherstonehaughs Draw on the Sketchbooks of Egon Schiele, The
Performance/production
Analysis of *The Featherstonehaughs Draw on the Sketchbooks of Egon Schiele* by choreographer Lea Anderson. UK-England: London. 1998. Lang.: Eng. 1315

Featuring Loretta
Performance/production
Collection of newspaper reviews by London theatre critics. UK-England: London. 1998. Lang.: Eng. 2578

Fedák-ügy, A (Fedák Case, The)
Performance/production
Denise Radó's *A Fedák-ügy (The Fedak Case)* at József Attila Theatre. Hungary: Budapest. 1998. Lang.: Hun. 2139

Federal Theatre Project (Washington, DC)
Institutions
State-wide tours of the Florida Federal Theatre Project. USA. 1937-1939. Lang.: Eng. 411
Economics and the Federal Theatre Project. USA. 1935-1939. Lang.: Eng. 428
Federal Theatre Project Shakespearean productions. USA. 1935-1939. Lang.: Eng. 1761
New plays and the Federal Theatre Project. USA. 1935-1939. Lang.: Eng. 1768
History of Mercury Theatre. USA: New York, NY. 1937-1942. Lang.: Eng. 1776
Performance/production
Productions of the Federal Theatre Project's Living Newspapers. USA: New York, NY. 1935-1939. Lang.: Eng. 643

Federico
Performance/production
Flamenco dancer and choreographer Carlota Santana. USA: New York, NY. 1998. Lang.: Eng. 1239

Feetgericht (Partywards)
Performance/production
Ballets of Hans van Manen. Netherlands. 1951-1998. Lang.: Eng. 1120

Fefu and Her Friends
Plays/librettos/scripts
Theatrical space in plays of Maria Irene Fornes. USA. 1977-1989. Lang.: Eng. 3571

Fehlandt, Tina
Performance/production
Dancers Tina Fehlandt and Ruth Davidson of Mark Morris Dance Group. USA: New York, NY. 1980-1998. Lang.: Eng. 1327

Feist, Gene
Plays/librettos/scripts
History of the Playwrights Unit. USA. 1963-1971. Lang.: Eng. 3570

Fekete, Hedvig
Performance/production
Interview with dancer and choreographer Hedvig Fekete. Hungary: Budapest. 1998. Lang.: Hun. 1291

Fekete, Veronika
Performance/production
Profile of soprano Veronika Fekete. Hungary. 1958-1998. Lang.: Hun. 4632

Feld, Marc
Performance/production
Productions of the Paris Festival d'Automne. France: Paris. 1998. Lang.: Fre. 1931

Feldenkrais, Moshe
Performance/production
History of movement training for the actor. USA. 1910-1985. Lang.: Eng. 675
Training
Feldenkreis movement theory. USA. 1905-1985. Lang.: Eng. 880

Feldman, Morton
Plays/librettos/scripts
Morton Feldman's musical setting for Samuel Beckett's radio play *Words and Music*. Europe. 1987. Lang.: Eng. 3865
The opera *Neither* by Morton Feldman and Samuel Beckett. Europe. 1976-1977. Lang.: Eng. 4772

Feldshuh, David
Performance/production
Collection of newspaper reviews by London theatre critics. UK-England: London. 1998. Lang.: Eng. 2506

Feldtenstein, C.J. von
Performance/production
The publication of a work by eighteenth-century dancing master C.J. von Feldtenstein. Germany: Braunschweig. 1767-1775. Lang.: Hun. 927

Feldtmann, Marie
Performance/production
Theatrical adaptations of children's stories by Astrid Lindgren. Sweden: Stockholm. 1998. Lang.: Eng. 2374
Interview with children's theatre director Marie Feldtmann. Sweden: Stockholm. 1996-1998. Lang.: Swe. 2388

Felix, Seymour
Performance/production
Dance director Seymour Felix. USA. 1918-1953. Lang.: Eng. 976

Feller, Pete
Design/technology
Stage technician Pete Feller. USA. 1920-1998. Lang.: Eng. 330

Fellini, Federico
Plays/librettos/scripts
The fool character in works of Handke, Fellini, and Singer. USA. Germany. Italy. 1960-1968. Lang.: Eng. 3667

Fellini, Federico — cont'd

Arthur Kopit's *Nine*, a musical adaptation of Fellini's *8 1/2*. USA. 1963-1982. Lang.: Eng. 4401
Relation to other fields
The influence of Fellini's *La Dolce Vita* on a novel of film critic Guillermo Cabrera Infante. Spain. Italy. 1960-1967. Lang.: Eng. 4035

Felsenstein, Walter
Training
Singer training at Teater- & Operahögskolan. Sweden: Gothenburg. 1960-1998. Lang.: Swe. 4848

Feluettes, Les (Lilies)
Plays/librettos/scripts
Interview with playwright and scriptwriter Michel Marc Bouchard. Canada: Montreal, PQ. 1987-1998. Lang.: Fre. 3963

Feminist criticism
Audience
Analysis of the teenage-girl audience. USA. UK-England. 1950-1970. Lang.: Ger. 161
Institutions
Feminist theatre of Ladies Against Women. USA: Berkeley, CA. 1979-1993. Lang.: Eng. 396
Performance/production
The dramaturg and feminist theory and practice. North America. 1998. Lang.: Eng. 568
Women and improvisation. USA. 1970-1997. Lang.: Eng. 672
Feminist analysis of female roles in *kabuki*. Japan. 1600-1900. Lang.: Eng. 1363
Feminist analysis of the life of actress Charlotte Cibber Charke. England. 1713-1760. Lang.: Eng. 1904
Actress Charlotte Cibber Charke and cross-dressing. England. 1713-1760. Lang.: Eng. 1906
Actresses and female managers in Spanish theatre. Spain. 1600-1700. Lang.: Eng. 2357
Screenwriter and producer June Mathis. USA. 1916-1927. Lang.: Eng. 3959
The kitchen in performance art of Bobby Baker and Jeanne Goosen. UK-England. South Africa, Republic of. 1990-1992. Lang.: Eng. 4243
Lucy Vestris in *Giovanni in London*. England: London. 1842. Lang.: Eng. 4546
Gendered readings of Bellini's *La Sonnambula* in performance. USA. 1835-1860. Lang.: Eng. 4748
Plays/librettos/scripts
Analysis of *Dead White Males* by David Williamson. Australia. 1995. Lang.: Eng. 2773
The representation of historical female characters on the Renaissance stage. England. 1580-1615. Lang.: Eng. 2922
Shakespeare, feminism, and his sources. England. 1590-1616. Lang.: Eng. 2977
'Demonic' women in Shakespeare's tragedies. England. 1590-1613. Lang.: Eng. 2999
Feminism and seventeenth-century city comedy. England. 1600-1700. Lang.: Eng. 3000
Feminist analysis of *The Tragedy of Mariam* by Elizabeth Cary. England. 1602-1612. Lang.: Eng. 3019
Food and alienation in plays of Chantal Chawaf and Denise Chalem. France. 1970-1989. Lang.: Eng. 3072
Analysis of *Les Nombres (The Numbers)* by Andrée Chedid. France. 1965. Lang.: Eng. 3090
Power, gender relations, and communication in German drama. Germany. 1776-1989. Lang.: Ger. 3138
Cruelty and the absurd in theatre of Latin American playwrights. Latin America. 1960-1980. Lang.: Eng. 3267
Ibsen, translation, and feminine discourse. Norway. 1888. Lang.: Eng. 3295
Feminist analysis of plays by Gabriela Zapolska. Poland. 1885-1998. Lang.: Pol. 3301
Feminist analysis of seventeenth-century plays by women. Spain. 1605-1675. Lang.: Eng. 3385
George Bernard Shaw: life, work, influences. UK-England. Ireland. 1886-1955. Lang.: Eng. 3437
Radio, television, and stage plays of Caryl Churchill. UK-England. 1959-1985. Lang.: Eng. 3464
Brechtian epic devices in the theatre of Caryl Churchill. UK-England. 1976-1986. Lang.: Eng. 3477
George Bernard Shaw and feminism. UK-England. 1856-1950. Lang.: Eng. 3481
Feminist analysis of plays for young people by women playwrights. USA. 1903-1983. Lang.: Eng. 3521
Female characters in Eugene O'Neill's plays. USA. 1920-1953. Lang.: Eng. 3525
Fairy-tale heroines in American drama and musical theatre. USA. 1945-1965. Lang.: Eng. 3617
The representation of true crime in modern drama. USA. France. 1955-1996. Lang.: Eng. 3673
John Stahl's film adaptation of *Imitation of Life* by Fannie Hurst. USA: Hollywood, CA. 1934. Lang.: Eng. 4029
The trivialization of feminism in librettos of W.S. Gilbert. UK-England. 1880-1890. Lang.: Eng. 4861
Theory/criticism
Feminism and children's theatre. North America. 1997-1998. Lang.: Eng. 852
JDTC's ongoing discussion of feminism and children's theatre. North America. 1997-1998. Lang.: Eng. 853
Theatrical dancing and the performance aesthetics of Wilde, Yeats, and Shaw. UK-England. Ireland. 1890-1950. Lang.: Eng. 1012
Analysis of Yoko Ono's performance work *Cut Piece*. USA. 1964-1998. Lang.: Eng. 4151

Feminist theatre
Institutions
Program of the 'City of Women' International Festival of Contemporary Arts. Slovenia: Ljubljana. 1998. Lang.: Slo. 384
Feminist theatre of Ladies Against Women. USA: Berkeley, CA. 1979-1993. Lang.: Eng. 396
Profile of Women's Circus. Australia: Melbourne. 1990-1998. Lang.: Eng. 1568
Profile of independent feminist theatre Kvinnliga Dramatiska Teatern. Sweden: Stockholm. 1997-1998. Lang.: Swe. 1725
Performance/production
The first wave of American feminist theatre. USA. 1890-1930. Lang.: Eng. 648
Analysis of two productions of Caryl Churchill's *Top Girls*. UK-England. 1982-1991. Lang.: Eng. 2608
A production of Susan Glaspell's experimental play *The Verge*. UK-Scotland: Glasgow. 1996. Lang.: Eng. 2651
Statements of women directors on their work. USA. 1996. Lang.: Eng. 2674
The language of costume in a video production of Caryl Churchill's *Top Girls*. UK-England. 1982-1991. Lang.: Eng. 4065
The feminist performance trend Angry Essentialism. USA. 1981-1998. Lang.: Eng. 4249
Plays/librettos/scripts
Australian women playwrights and their work. Australia. 1972-1998. Lang.: Eng. 2778
Analysis of *Queen Lear* by Beau Coleman. Canada: Edmonton, AB. 1995-1997. Lang.: Eng. 2800
Feminist theory and practice on the French stage. France. 1998. Lang.: Eng. 3075
Analysis of *Le Voyage sans fin (The Constant Journey)* by Monique Wittig. France. 1985. Lang.: Eng. 3100
Feminist questioning of language and authority in plays of Nathalie Sarraute. France. 1967-1995. Lang.: Eng. 3103
Response to the structures of male oppression in plays of Yourcenar, Sarraute, and Duras. France. 1975-1995. Lang.: Fre. 3119
Feminism and plays of Henrik Ibsen. Norway. 1879-1979. Lang.: Eng. 3293
Ecology and the plays of Caryl Churchill. UK-England. 1971-1989. Lang.: Eng. 3422
Gender and sexuality in Caryl Churchill's *Cloud Nine*. UK-England. 1979. Lang.: Eng. 3426
Caryl Churchill's *The Skriker* compared to her earlier plays. UK-England. 1994. Lang.: Eng. 3436
Shakespeare and the feminist theatre of Bryony Lavery and Jane Prendergast. UK-England. 1997. Lang.: Eng. 3439
Fragmentation and skepticism in Caryl Churchill's *Icecream*. UK-England. 1989. Lang.: Eng. 3451
A paradigm for analysis of works by Caryl Churchill. UK-England. 1975-1997. Lang.: Eng. 3458

Feminist theatre — cont'd

Systemic poisons in plays of Caryl Churchill. UK-England. 1990-1997. Lang.: Eng. 3463
Secrets in Caryl Churchill's *Top Girls*. UK-England. 1982. Lang.: Eng. 3466
Analysis of *Light Shining in Buckinghamshire* by Caryl Churchill. UK-England. 1970-1976. Lang.: Eng. 3483
Analysis of *The Skriker* by Caryl Churchill. UK-England. 1994. Lang.: Eng. 3489
The critical and popular failure of *The Skriker* by Caryl Churchill. UK-England. 1994. Lang.: Eng. 3504
Analysis of *Mad Forest* by Caryl Churchill. UK-England. 1990. Lang.: Eng. 3505
Analysis of plays about the women's movement. USA. 1900-1940. Lang.: Eng. 3559
Gendered political critique in *The Club* by Eve Merriam. USA. 1976. Lang.: Eng. 3572
Feminist theatre of Martha Boesing. USA: Minneapolis, MN. 1974-1984. Lang.: Eng. 3603
Politics and feminism in the plays of Maria Irene Fornes. USA. 1975-1995. Lang.: Eng. 3635

Theory/criticism
JDTC's ongoing discussion of feminism and children's theatre. North America. 1997-1998. Lang.: Eng. 853

Femmes savantes, Les (Learned Ladies, The)
Basic theatrical documents
Catalan translation of *Les Femmes savantes (The Learned Ladies)* by Molière. France. 1672. Lang.: Cat. 1433
Performance/production
Student production of *Les Femmes savantes (The Learned Ladies)* by Molière. Canada: Calgary, AB. 1997. Lang.: Eng. 1859
Productions by Toni Bertorelli and Alfiero Alfieri. Italy: Rome. 1997. Lang.: Eng. 2175

Fen
Plays/librettos/scripts
Brechtian epic devices in the theatre of Caryl Churchill. UK-England. 1976-1986. Lang.: Eng. 3477

Fences
Plays/librettos/scripts
Analysis of *Fences* by August Wilson. USA. 1987. Lang.: Eng. 3693

Feniksov let (Flight of the Phoenix, The)
Basic theatrical documents
Plays and screenplays by Vili Ravnjak. Slovenia. 1991-1997. Lang.: Slo. 1460

Fensham, Rachel
Performance/production
Directing the documentary-based performance project *The Worst Woman in the World*. Australia. 1994. Lang.: Eng. 1816

Fensterputzer, Der (Window-cleaner, The)
Performance/production
Reactions to guest performances of dancer/choreographer Pina Bausch. Sweden: Stockholm. 1998. Lang.: Swe. 1301

Fentiman, Alan
Performance/production
Collection of newspaper reviews by London theatre critics. UK-England: London. 1998. Lang.: Eng. 2478

Ferencvárosi ünnepi Játékok (Budapest)
Performance/production
Antal Fodor's ballet *A Próba (The Rehearsal)*. Hungary: Budapest. 1998. Lang.: Hun. 1111

Ferme du Garet, La (Garet Farm, The)
Performance/production
Productions of the Paris Festival d'Automne. France: Paris. 1998. Lang.: Fre. 1931

Fernández de Moratín, Leandro
Performance/production
Collection of newspaper reviews by London theatre critics. UK-England: London. 1998. Lang.: Eng. 2490

Fernandez, José
Performance/production
Collection of newspaper reviews by London theatre critics. UK-England: London. 1998. Lang.: Eng. 2525

Fernandez, Kristina
Performance/production
Ballerina Kristina Fernandez on working with choreographer Jerome Robbins. USA. 1998. Lang.: Eng. 1171

Ferrari, Paolo
Plays/librettos/scripts
Italian realist drama. Italy. 1860-1918. Lang.: Eng. 3260

Ferrers, George
Relation to other fields
George Ferrers' Christmas revels and the execution of the Duke of Somerset. England. 1551-1552. Lang.: Eng. 4211

Festival d'Avignon
Institutions
Report on the Avignon theatre festival. France: Avignon. 1998. Lang.: Eng. 1611
Impressions from the Avignon theatre festival. France: Avignon. 1998. Lang.: Ger. 1612
Reviews of some productions at the Avignon Festival. France: Avignon. 1998. Lang.: Hun. 1615
Performance/production
The Avignon Festival under the direction of Bernard Faivre D'Arcier. France: Avignon. 1998. Lang.: Ger. 1927

Festivals
Administration
Interview with Tankred Dorst and Hannah Hurtzig of the Bonner Biennale festival. Germany: Bonn. 1998. Lang.: Ger. 1379
History of the Brighton performance festival. UK-England: Brighton. 1967-1988. Lang.: Eng. 4229
Audience
Ten-year study of audience response to Dutch theatre festivals. Netherlands. 1987-1996. Lang.: Dut. 155
Design/technology
Scenic elements in *Titanic* by street theatre group Theater Titanick. Germany: Münster, Leipzig. Australia: Perth. 1998. Lang.: Eng. 191
Winners of American College Theatre Festival design competitions. USA. 1998. Lang.: Eng. 279
Set and costume design for *Patience and Sarah* at Lincoln Center. USA: New York, NY. 1998. Lang.: Eng. 4440
Institutions
Impressions from Australian theatre festivals. Australia: Perth, Adelaide. 1998. Lang.: Ger. 334
Peter Stein's last season as director at the Salzburg Festival. Austria: Salzburg. 1997. Lang.: Eng. 336
Account of children's theatre festival. Canada: Montreal, PQ. 1998. Lang.: Fre. 337
Czech theatre at the Plzeň festival. Czech Republic: Pilsen. 1997. Lang.: Hun. 344
Offerings at the Festival d'Automne. France: Paris. 1997. Lang.: Fre. 346
Festivals of theatre by and for youth. Germany: Dresden, Stuttgart. 1998. Lang.: Ger. 349
The avant-garde theatre festival Theaterformen. Germany: Braunschweig, Hannover. 1998. Lang.: Ger. 351
Profile of the Theaterformen festival. Germany: Braunschweig, Hannover. 1998. Lang.: Ger. 353
Festival of Hungarian-language theatres abroad. Hungary: Kisvárda. 1998. Lang.: Hun. 357
Interviews with the jury who selected the National Theatre Festival presentations. Hungary. 1996-1997. Lang.: Hun. 363
The Kontakt '98 theatre festival. Poland: Toruń. 1998. Lang.: Hun. 373
Profile of National Theatre Festival. Romania: Bucharest. 1998. Lang.: Hun. 377
Annual festival of theatre performed by children. Russia: Kaluga. 1998. Lang.: Rus. 382
The Nitra '98 theatre festival. Slovakia: Nitra. 1998. Lang.: Hun. 383
Program of the 'City of Women' International Festival of Contemporary Arts. Slovenia: Ljubljana. 1998. Lang.: Slo. 384
Report on the Standard Bank National Arts Festival. South Africa, Republic of: Grahamstown. 1998. Lang.: Eng. 385
Latin American guest performances at the Kuopio theatre festival. Finland: Kuopio. 1998. Lang.: Swe. 890
The work of young choreographers at the Councours de Bagnolet. France: Bagnolet. 1998. Lang.: Swe. 891
Profiles of dance festivals. Hungary: Győr, Veszprém. 1998. Lang.: Hun. 895
Notes on Interballet and Spring festivals. Hungary: Budapest. 1998. Lang.: Hun. 896
Report on the Altogether Different dance festival. USA: New York, NY. 1998. Lang.: Eng. 906
Dance festival commemorating 225th anniversary of the Royal Swedish Ballet. Sweden: Stockholm. 1998. Lang.: Eng. 1051

Festivals — cont'd

The Kongsberg Kappleiken festival of Norwegian folk music and dance. Norway: Kongsberg. 1923-1998. Lang.: Swe. 1221

Report on folk dance festival and competition. Russia: Voskresensk. 1998. Lang.: Rus. 1222

Profile of modern dance festival. Russia. 1998. Lang.: Rus. 1252

Productions of Gothenburg's Dance and Theatre Festival. Sweden: Gothenburg. 1998. Lang.: Swe. 1253

Directory of theatre festivals. 1998. Lang.: Eng. 1566

Interview with Ivan Nagel, drama manager of the Salzburg Festival. Austria: Salzburg. 1998. Lang.: Ger. 1572

Account of Slavic Theatre Meeting. Belorussia: Gomel'. 1998. Lang.: Rus. 1575

Shakespearean productions at the Carrefour international theatre festival. Canada: Quebec, PQ. 1998. Lang.: Fre. 1588

Criticism of the Carrefour international theatre festival. Canada: Quebec, PQ. 1998. Lang.: Fre. 1591

Taganka Theatre's performance at the Bogotá theatre festival. Colombia: Bogotá. 1998. Lang.: Rus. 1595

Report on the Cairo festival and symposia on women's theatre. Egypt: Cairo. 1997. Lang.: Eng. 1597

The evolution of Shakespeare festivals. Europe. USA. 1950-1997. Lang.: Eng. 1601

Survey of the fifty-second annual Avignon Festival. France: Avignon. 1998. Lang.: Eng. 1608

Report on the Spielart '97 experimental theatre festival. Germany: Munich. 1997. Lang.: Eng. 1618

Italian experimental theatre at Spielart '97. Germany: Munich. Italy. 1997. Lang.: Eng. 1619

English-language plays at Berlin Festwochen. Germany: Berlin. 1998. Lang.: Ger. 1623

Report on the fourth Bonner Biennale. Germany: Bonn. 1998. Lang.: Ger. 1627

Israeli theatre at the Kampnagel summer theatre festival. Germany: Hamburg. 1998. Lang.: Ger. 1635

Children's theatre festivals in Baden-Württemberg. Germany: Stuttgart. 1998. Lang.: Ger. 1641

German-Danish children's theatre festival. Germany. Denmark. 1998. Lang.: Ger. 1642

Report on theatre festival. Germany: Frankfurt/Oder. 1998. Lang.: Ger. 1646

Contemporary drama at Bonner Biennale. Germany: Bonn. 1998. Lang.: Ger. 1647

Survey of the Theatertreffen festival. Germany: Berlin. 1998. Lang.: Swe. 1651

Independent German-language theatre festival Impulse. Germany. 1998. Lang.: Ger. 1652

Report on the Bonner Biennale theatre festival. Germany: Bonn. 1998. Lang.: Ger. 1663

Report on festival of physical theatre. Germany: Munich. 1997. Lang.: Eng. 1664

Report on European theatre festival. Greece: Thessaloniki. 1997. Lang.: Eng. 1667

History of annual festival of Hungarian-language theatre. Hungary: Kisvárda. 1989-1998. Lang.: Hun. 1669

Report on Ibsen festival. Norway: Oslo. 1998. Lang.: Eng. 1681

Survey of the 1998 Ibsen Festival. Norway: Oslo. 1998. Lang.: Eng. 1682

Survey of annual Ibsen festival. Norway: Oslo. 1998. Lang.: Eng. 1683

Impressions from the 'Golden Mask' festival. Russia: Minusinsk. 1998. Lang.: Ger. 1701

Account of the Saratov stage festival. Russia: Saratov. 1998. Lang.: Rus. 1708

Ostrovskij Festival celebrating the 175th anniversary of Malyj Teat'r. Russia: Moscow. 1998. Lang.: Rus. 1709

The Grec '97 festival. Spain-Catalonia: Barcelona. 1997. Lang.: Eng. 1721

Report on the Stockholm theatre festival. Sweden: Stockholm. 1998. Lang.: Eng. 1724

Children's theatre festival Spilplätz. Switzerland: Basel. 1998. Lang.: Ger. 1736

Report on the 1998 Istanbul Theatre Festival. Turkey: Istanbul. Turkey: Istanbul. 1998. Lang.: Eng. 1738

Theatre selections at the 1998 Edinburgh Festival and Edinburgh Fringe Festival. UK-England: London. 1998. Lang.: Eng. 1743

Report on the 1998 Edinburgh Fringe Festival. UK-Scotland: Edinburgh. 1998. Lang.: Eng. 1750

Report on the National Black Theatre Festival. USA: Winston-Salem, NC. 1997. Lang.: Eng. 1763

Productions of Actors' Theatre Humana Festival. USA: Louisville, KY. 1998. Lang.: Eng. 1779

Plays of 1998 Oregon Shakespeare Festival. USA: Ashland, OR. 1998. Lang.: Eng. 1783

Report on the National Black Theatre Festival. USA: Winston-Salem, NC. 1997. Lang.: Eng. 1787

History of the Women's Project of the American Place Theatre. USA: New York, NY. 1978-1979. Lang.: Eng. 1791

Report on the 1997 Toronto Film Festival. Canada: Toronto, ON. 1997. Lang.: Eng. 3923

Report on Black film festival. Mexico: Acapulco. 1997. Lang.: Eng. 3924

The 'diskurs' festival of the 'Gressener school'. Germany: Giessen. 1982-1998. Lang.: Ger. 4111

Mass festivals of the newly formed Soviet Union. USSR. 1917-1920. Lang.: Eng. 4113

Baktinian analysis of Kingston Buskers Rendez-vous. Canada: Kingston, ON. 1998. Lang.: Fre. 4161

Edge 88 experimental festival. UK-England: London. 1988. Lang.: Eng. 4235

Interview with Peter Ruzicka of the Münchener Biennale festival. Germany: Munich. 1998. Lang.: Ger. 4291

Interview with singer Carla Henius, manager of musik-theater-werkstatt festival. Germany: Wiesbaden. 1986-1998. Lang.: Ger. 4347

Ernst August Klötzke, new manager of musik-theater-werkstatt festival. Germany: Wiesbaden. 1998. Lang.: Ger. 4348

Peter Brook's production of Mozart's *Don Giovanni* at the Aix festival. France: Aix-en-Provence. 1998. Lang.: Swe. 4450

Comparison of Salzburg and Bayreuth festival seasons. Germany: Bayreuth. Austria: Salzburg. 1998. Lang.: Eng. 4452

Report on Dresden opera festival. Germany: Dresden. 1998. Lang.: Eng. 4453

The Münchener Biennale theatre festival. Germany: Munich. 1998. Lang.: Ger. 4456

Survey of the opera festival season. Germany: Munich. 1998. Lang.: Eng. 4457

The opera festival in the birthplace of Rossini. Italy: Pesaro. 1792-1998. Lang.: Eng. 4462

The Boldina Opera and Ballet festival honoring Puškin. Russia: Nizhni Novgorod. 1998. Lang.: Rus. 4469

Survey of summer opera. UK-England. 1998. Lang.: Eng. 4476

Program of the Kisel Festival, including theatrical and puppet productions. Slovenia: Kranj. 1998. Lang.: Slo. 4875

Report on international puppet festival. USA: New York, NY. 1998. Lang.: Eng. 4882

Performance spaces

Profile of Traverse Theatre. UK-Scotland: Edinburgh. 1998. Lang.: Eng. 462

The Dame Blanche theatre. Canada: Quebec, PQ. 1982-1998. Lang.: Fre. 1796

Performance/production

Productions of children's theatre festival. Canada: Montreal, PQ. 1998. Lang.: Fre. 503

Report on festival of performing and visual arts. France: Paris. 1997. Lang.: Eng. 532

Forced Entertainment and Berlin's Live Art Festival. UK-England, Sheffield. Germany: Berlin. 1984-1998. Lang.: Ger. 539

The symposium on acting at Theaterfestival. Netherlands: Amsterdam. 1998. Lang.: Dut. 562

Profile of Grahamstown National Arts Festival. South Africa, Republic of: Grahamstown. 1998. Lang.: Swe. 597

The first wave of American feminist theatre. USA. 1890-1930. Lang.: Eng. 648

Some productions of Im Puls Tanz '98 festival. Austria: Vienna. 1998. Lang.: Hun. 914

Festivals — cont'd

Comparison of performances by Rosas and Ballet Gulbenkian. Hungary: Budapest. 1992-1994. Lang.: Hun. 939
Hungarian dance companies at Interbalett '98. Hungary. 1998. Lang.: Hun. 946
Report on children's dance festival. Sweden: Malmö. Denmark: Copenhagen. 1997. Lang.: Swe. 966
Report on festival of dance on film. UK-England: London. 1997. Lang.: Eng. 969
Choreography of Javier De Frutos at the Dance Umbrella Festival. UK-England: London. 1998. Lang.: Hun. 970
Dutch National Ballet production at the Holland Festival. Netherlands: Amsterdam. 1997. Lang.: Hun. 1121
Interview with dancer and choreographer Hedvig Fekete. Hungary: Budapest. 1998. Lang.: Hun. 1291
Report on Dance Umbrella festival. UK-England: London. 1997. Lang.: Eng. 1310
Seminar on auditions for choreographers for Resolution dance festival. UK-England: London. Belgium: Brussels. 1998. Lang.: Swe. 1314
Report on Chinese Shakespeare festival. China, People's Republic of: Beijing, Shanghai. 1986. Lang.: Eng. 1873
Productions of the Paris Festival d'Automne. France: Paris. 1998. Lang.: Fre. 1931
Productions of the Bad Hersfelder Festspiele. Germany: Bad Hersfeld. 1998. Lang.: Ger. 1991
Productions of the Kleist theatre festival. Germany: Frankfurt/Oder. 1998. Lang.: Ger. 1993
Impressions from Podewil theatre workshop. Germany: Berlin. 1998. Lang.: Ger. 2024
Events of the Zsámbék theatre festival. Hungary: Zsámbék. 1998. Lang.: Hun. 2126
Italian productions of plays by Harold Pinter. Italy. 1997. Lang.: Eng. 2165
Theatrical component of Japan's UK98 Festival. Japan: Tokyo. 1994-1998. Lang.: Eng. 2192
Interview with director Stein Winge. Norway: Oslo. 1988-1998. Lang.: Eng. 2210
Report from Ibsen festival. Norway: Oslo. 1998. Lang.: Swe. 2211
Productions of the festival of experimental theatre. Poland: Cracow. 1998. Lang.: Ger. 2225
Seinen-za's performance at the Čechov festival. Russia: Moscow. 1998. Lang.: Rus. 2237
The work of Russian directors at the Golden Mask festival. Russia: Moscow, St. Petersburg. 1998. Lang.: Swe. 2305
Productions of Shakespeare's *Twelfth Night* at the Madrid Theatre Festival. Spain: Madrid. 1996-1997. Lang.: Eng. 2359
Harold Pinter's production of his play *Ashes to Ashes* at the Pinter festival. Spain-Catalonia: Barcelona. 1996. Lang.: Eng. 2364
Collection of newspaper reviews by London theatre critics. UK-England. 1998. Lang.: Eng. 2527
Collection of newspaper reviews by London theatre critics. UK-England: London. 1998. Lang.: Eng. 2542
London summer theatre and the Edinburgh Festival. UK-England: London. UK-Scotland: Edinburgh. 1998. Lang.: Eng. 2603
Shakespearean influence on the 1987 Edinburgh Festival. UK-Scotland: Edinburgh. 1997. Lang.: Eng. 2653
The Tennessee Williams/New Orleans Literary Festival. USA: New Orleans, LA. 1998. Lang.: Eng. 2726
Reviews of productions of plays by Ibsen. USA: New York, NY. Norway: Oslo. 1998. Lang.: Eng. 2747
Report on biennial festival of mixed media. France: Lyon. 1997. Lang.: Eng. 4042
The Sicilian chivalric tradition. Italy. 1500-1985. Lang.: Ita. 4125
History of the steeldrum, used in carnival celebrations. Trinidad and Tobago: Port of Spain. 1777-1998. Lang.: Eng. 4169
Kodály's *Háry János* at Szeged's Open-Air Festival. Hungary: Szeged. 1998. Lang.: Hun. 4359
High-school students' production of *The Wiz* at the Edinburgh Fringe Festival. USA: Hattiesburg, MS. UK-Scotland: Edinburgh. 1996. Lang.: Eng. 4381
Montemezzi's *L'amore dei tre re*, directed and designed by Philippe Arlaud. Austria: Bregenz. 1998. Lang.: Eng. 4532
Report on opera festival. France: Aix-en-Provence. 1998. Lang.: Eng. 4563
Peter Brook's *Don Giovanni* at the Aix Festival. France: Aix-en-Provence. 1998. Lang.: Eng. 4569
Sechs-Tage-Oper, festival of independent music theatre. Germany. 1998. Lang.: Ger. 4579
Interview with Miklós Gábor Kerényi on directing Verdi's *Un Ballo in Maschera*. Hungary: Budapest. 1998. Lang.: Hun. 4619
Report on the Fourth Annual Jim Henson Festival. USA: New York, NY. 1998. Lang.: Eng. 4903
Preview of the Puppeteers of America Festival. USA: Seattle, WA. 1999. Lang.: Eng. 4905

Plays/librettos/scripts
Analysis of Cuban theatre in Miami. USA: Miami, FL. 1985-1986. Lang.: Eng. 3574
American College Theatre Festival's showcase of student plays. USA. 1998. Lang.: Eng. 3583
The underrepresentation of Hispanics in American arts. USA. 1998. Lang.: Eng. 3716

Reference materials
Yearbook of Slovene theatre. Slovenia. 1996-1997. Lang.: Slo. 708

Theory/criticism
Children's theatre and contemporary aesthetics. Canada: Montreal, PQ. 1998. Lang.: Fre. 833
Report on a seminar for young theatre critics. Canada: Quebec, PQ. 1998. Lang.: Swe. 3809

Feuchtwanger, Lion
Basic theatrical documents
Catalan translations of plays by Bertolt Brecht (volume 1). Germany. 1919-1954. Lang.: Cat. 1437

Feuer aus den Kesseln (Fire from the Pots)
Plays/librettos/scripts
Analysis of revisions of plays by Ernst Toller. Germany. 1920-1939. Lang.: Eng. 3172

Feuer, Donya
Relation to other fields
A joint project for teaching Shakespeare with professional actors. Sweden. 1988-1998. Lang.: Swe. 3776

Feuergesicht (Fire Face)
Performance/production
Productions of the Kleist theatre festival. Germany: Frankfurt/Oder. 1998. Lang.: Ger. 1993
Plays/librettos/scripts
Analysis of plays by Marius von Mayenburg. Germany. 1972-1998. Lang.: Ger. 3131

Feydeau, Georges
Design/technology
Costume design for Feydeau's *A Flea in Her Ear (La Puce à l'Oreille)*, Roundabout Theatre Company. USA: New York, NY. 1998. Lang.: Eng. 1537
Performance/production
Interview with actors in Feydeau's *La Puce à l'Oreille (A Flea in Her Ear)* at Dramaten. Sweden: Stockholm. 1998. Lang.: Swe. 2396

Fiadiero, João
Performance/production
Politics, culture, and Portuguese dance and choreography. Portugal. 1998. Lang.: Eng. 959

Fichandler, Zelda
Performance/production
Statements of women directors on their work. USA. 1996. Lang.: Eng. 2674
The multifaceted nature of early nonprofit regional theatre. USA. 1940-1960. Lang.: Eng. 2705

Fidelio
Performance/production
The work of opera director Barbara Beyer. Germany: Nuremberg. 1996-1998. Lang.: Ger. 4589
Analysis of a scene from Beethoven's *Fidelio*. Germany. 1814. Lang.: Eng. 4595
Reviews of recent opera productions. Switzerland: Basel. Germany: Stuttgart, Berlin, Hamburg. France: Strasbourg. 1997-1998. Lang.: Ger. 4702
Plays/librettos/scripts
Hero and anti-hero in contemporary opera production. Germany. 1998. Lang.: Ger. 4791

Fidler, Michael
Performance/production
Collection of newspaper reviews by London theatre critics. UK-England: London. 1998. Lang.: Eng. 2447

Fieber, Pavel
Institutions
Interview with Pavel Fieber, manager of Badisches Staatstheater Karlsruhe. Germany: Karlsruhe. 1997-1998. Lang.: Ger. 1649
Field Day Theatre Company (Derry)
Plays/librettos/scripts
Brian Friel's plays and the Field Day Theatre Company. UK-Ireland. 1980-1988. Lang.: Eng. 3512
Field, Eliza Riddle
Performance/production
The Field frontier acting family. USA. 1830-1860. Lang.: Eng. 641
Field, Joseph M.
Performance/production
The Field frontier acting family. USA. 1830-1860. Lang.: Eng. 641
Field, Matthew
Performance/production
The Field frontier acting family. USA. 1830-1860. Lang.: Eng. 641
Fielding, Henry
Plays/librettos/scripts
Crimes against property in plays of Henry Fielding and Elizabethan playwrights. England. 1590-1745. Lang.: Eng. 2912
Fielding, Ruth
Performance/production
Collection of newspaper reviews by London theatre critics. UK-England: London. 1998. Lang.: Eng. 2463
Fields, Dorothy
Performance/production
Collection of newspaper reviews by London theatre critics. UK-England: London. 1998. Lang.: Eng. 2410
Fields, Joseph
Performance/production
Collection of newspaper reviews by London theatre critics. UK-England: London. 1998. Lang.: Eng. 2480
Fields, Nathan
Plays/librettos/scripts
The treatment of single women in early Stuart drama. England. 1604-1608. Lang.: Eng. 2979
Fierrabras
Plays/librettos/scripts
Analysis of Schubert's unperformed opera *Fierrabras*. Austria. 1823. Lang.: Eng. 4759
Fierstein, Harvey
Plays/librettos/scripts
American gay drama and the impact of AIDS. USA. 1960-1987. Lang.: Eng. 3670
Fiesco
Performance/production
Productions of the Bad Hersfelder Festspiele. Germany: Bad Hersfeld. 1998. Lang.: Ger. 1991
Fifth of July
Performance/production
The collaboration of playwright Lanford Wilson and director Marshall W. Mason. USA: New York, NY. 1978-1986. Lang.: Eng. 2756
Plays/librettos/scripts
Comedy and humor in plays of Lanford Wilson. USA. 1961-1985. Lang.: Eng. 3595
American gay drama and the impact of AIDS. USA. 1960-1987. Lang.: Eng. 3670
Figaro lässt sich scheiden (Figaro Gets Divorced)
Performance/production
Luc Bondy's production of Horváth's *Figaro lässt sich scheiden (Figaro Gets Divorced)*. Austria: Vienna. 1998. Lang.: Ger. 1822
Fighting the Waves
Performance/production
Collaborative Symbolist dance/theatre projects. Europe. USA. 1916-1934. Lang.: Eng. 1268
Figurative arts
Audience
Interview with performance artist Tim Brennan. Netherlands: Arnhem. 1989. Lang.: Eng. 4231
Design/technology
Works of painter, sculptor, and scenographer Eugenio Guglielminetti. Italy. 1961-1997. Lang.: Ita. 204
Gerard de Lairesse, painter and stage designer. Netherlands. 1640-1711. Lang.: Eng. 208
Institutions
Display of objects related to guest performances of the Ballets Russes. Germany: Berlin. 1910-1914. Lang.: Hun. 1040
European activities of the Living Theatre. Europe. USA. 1964-1983. Lang.: Ita. 1602
Performance spaces
Analysis of a sketch of the Swan Theatre. England: London. 1596. Lang.: Eng. 1801
Performance/production
Report on festival of performing and visual arts. France: Paris. 1997. Lang.: Eng. 532
Sketches and caricatures of dialect actor Gilberto Govi. Italy: Genoa. 1885-1966. Lang.: Ita. 543
The interdisciplinary workshop of Teaterskollektivet Rex. Sweden: Stockholm. 1997. Lang.: Swe. 600
Performer, director, and artist Wolfgang Martin Schede. Germany. 1898-1975. Lang.: Ger. 929
The choreography of William Forsythe and the painting of Marcel Duchamp. Germany. France. 1915-1998. Lang.: Eng. 1280
Images associated with actress Charlotte Cibber Charke. England. 1713-1760. Lang.: Eng. 1896
Shakespearean production and the theatrical portrait collection of the Garrick Club. England: London. 1702-1814. Lang.: Eng. 1903
Evidence for performance of medieval religious drama. Sweden. 1140-1500. Lang.: Eng. 2392
The influence of collage on director Charles Marowitz. UK-England. USA. 1962-1979. Lang.: Eng. 2624
Report on biennial festival of mixed media. France: Lyon. 1997. Lang.: Eng. 4042
Performance in the work of mixed-media artist Tina Keane. UK-England. 1970-1988. Lang.: Eng. 4044
A painting of *commedia dell'arte* performer Tiberio Fiorilli. Italy. 1625-1700. Lang.: Eng. 4190
Performance artist Egon Schrick. Germany. 1976-1987. Lang.: Eng. 4241
Performance artist Rei Naito. Japan. 1996-1998. Lang.: Eng. 4242
The 'living paintings' of Steven Taylor Woodrow. UK-England. USA. 1987-1988. Lang.: Eng. 4247
The Chou dynasty in Chinese opera and theatrical paintings. China. 1027-771 B.C. Lang.: Rus. 4311
Plays/librettos/scripts
The character of Ivan the Terrible. USSR. 1800-1965. Lang.: Eng. 692
Quebecois drama and the influence of visual arts. Canada. 1980-1990. Lang.: Fre. 2816
Visual imagery in *El padre muerto (The Dead Father)* by Marco Antonio de la Parra. Chile. 1993. Lang.: Eng. 2839
The influence of the figurative arts on the plays of William Shakespeare. England. 1589-1613. Lang.: Ita. 2858
Analysis of the frontispiece of Nicholas Rowe's edition of Shakespeare's *King Lear*. England. 1709-1714. Lang.: Eng. 2859
An illustration of Queen Tamora of Shakespeare's *Titus Andronicus*. England. 1590-1594. Lang.: Eng. 2880
Nicholas Rowe's illustration of a scene from *Macbeth*. England. 1709. Lang.: Eng. 2953
Portraits of Shakespeare. England. 1623-1640. Lang.: Rus. 2963
Renaissance emblems of death and Shakespeare's *King John*. England. 1596-1599. Lang.: Eng. 2967
Painter Wassily Kandinsky and theatre. France. 1908-1944. Lang.: Eng. 3111
Pictorial and staged versions of the Passion. Savoy. 1435-1505. Lang.: Eng. 3342
Reference materials
Dictionary of history and the arts. Lang.: Ita. 695
Relation to other fields
The tasks of the theatre photographer. Germany: Nordhausen. 1998. Lang.: Ger. 737
Drama therapy, personal narrative, and performance. USA. 1998. Lang.: Eng. 797
Locating and defining the 'unincorporated' arts. USA. 1998. Lang.: Eng. 806
Dance photos by Jack Mitchell. USA. 1960-1995. Lang.: Eng. 1000
The impact of photography and cinema on theatre. Canada. 1998. Lang.: Fre. 3732
The relationship between the York Cycle and the Bolton Book of Hours. England: York. 1405-1500. Lang.: Eng. 3750
Depictions of Shakespeare's Othello. Europe. 1709-1804. Lang.: Eng. 3758

Figurative arts — cont'd

Fouquet's miniature of St. Apollonia and its relationship to the mystery play. France. 1452-1577. Lang.: Eng. 3761
Jean Fouquet's miniature of St. Apollonia and its relationship to performance. France: Tours. 1452-1577. Lang.: Eng. 3762
Fouquet's depiction of the martyrdom of St. Apollonia as a record of a performance. France. 1452-1577. Lang.: Eng. 3763
Analysis of illustrations of first editions of tragedies by Gryphius. Germany. 1635-1664. Lang.: Eng. 3765
The Arte Povera movement. Italy. 1967-1985. Lang.: Eng. 4264
The Fluxus movement. USA. Europe. 1961-1979. Lang.: Eng. 4265

Filatov, Leonid
Basic theatrical documents
Theatrical and other writings of actor Leonid Filatov. Russia: Moscow. 1998. Lang.: Rus. 163
Relation to other fields
The poetry of actors Leonid Filatov and Valentin Gaft. Russia: Moscow. 1998. Lang.: Rus. 758

Filiatrault, Denise
Performance/production
English and French-language productions of *Picasso at the Lapin Agile* by Steve Martin. Canada: Montreal, PQ. 1997. Lang.: Fre. 1836

Filipčič, Emil
Basic theatrical documents
Text of *Suženj akcije—Kralj Peter Šesti (A Slave of Action—King Peter the Sixth)* by Emil Filipčič. Slovenia. 1997. Lang.: Slo. 1455

Fill the Woods with Light
Performance/production
David Parsons Dance Company's *Fill the Woods with Light.* USA: Washington, DC. 1998. Lang.: Hun. 1195

Fille mal Gardée, La
Performance/production
La Fille mal Gardée at Erkel Színház. Hungary: Budapest. 1997. Lang.: Hun. 1087

Film
Plays/librettos/scripts
Analysis of filmscripts by Samuel Beckett. 1966-1970. Lang.: Eng. 3961

Film
SEE ALSO
Classed Entries under MEDIA—Film.
Administration
Theatre manager and entrepreneur Harry Davis. USA: Pittsburgh, PA. 1893-1927. Lang.: Eng. 134
Censorship and Russian and East European theatre and film. USSR. Europe. 1963-1980. Lang.: Eng. 145
Interviews with German theatre and film directors. Germany. 1998. Lang.: Ger. 1385
Producer Aida Young. UK-England. 1950-1998. Lang.: Eng. 3854
Marketing strategies for puppetry in film and TV. USA. 1998. Lang.: Eng. 4863
Audience
Theatrical production and reception. Canada. 1988. Lang.: Eng. 146
Design/technology
Catalogue of an exhibition devoted to Hungarian theatre and film. Hungary: Budapest. 1998. Lang.: Hun. 197
Memoirs of scenographer Jėvgenij Kumankov. Russia. 1998. Lang.: Rus. 215
Costumer Kermit Love. USA. 1935-1998. Lang.: Eng. 271
Lighting designer John Osborne. USA. 1998. Lang.: Eng. 310
TV and film make-up artists Tom Burman and Bari Dreiband-Burman. USA: Hollywood, CA. 1998. Lang.: Eng. 4050
Institutions
The Walker Arts Center's exhibition on dance. USA: Minneapolis, MN. 1998. Lang.: Eng. 905
Theatrical space in productions of Ariane Mnouchkine. France: Paris. 1970-1995. Lang.: Eng. 1607
Interview with playwright, director, and film-maker Xavier Durringer. France: Paris. 1988-1998. Lang.: Ger. 1609
Appealing to the youth audience at Theater Dresden. Germany: Dresden. 1997-1998. Lang.: Ger. 1631
Gunnar Martin Aronsson of TeaterX2 recalls Action-Theater. Sweden: Stockholm. Germany: Munich. 1968-1998. Lang.: Swe. 1722
History of Mercury Theatre. USA: New York, NY. 1937-1942. Lang.: Eng. 1776
Performance/production
Differences between nudity onstage and on screen. Canada: Montreal, PQ. 1995-1997. Lang.: Fre. 499
Opportunities for South Asian actors. Canada: Toronto, ON. 1997. Lang.: Eng. 508
The disappearance of the diva in the modern world. Europe. USA. 1890-1998. Lang.: Swe. 525
Ettore Giannini's film and stage work *Carosello Napoletano (Neapolitan Carousel).* Italy. 1950. Lang.: Ita. 546
Memoirs of actress Tatjana Okunevskaja. Russia. 1998. Lang.: Rus. 582
Interview with actor Jėvgenij Vesnik. Russia: Moscow. 1998. Lang.: Rus. 586
The interdisciplinary workshop of Teaterskollektivet Rex. Sweden: Stockholm. 1997. Lang.: Swe. 600
Excessive stage and screen melodrama. UK-England. USA. 1830-1970. Lang.: Eng. 608
Performer, writer, director Elsie Janis and the 'gay sensibility'. UK-England. 1889-1956. Lang.: Eng. 612
The mediation of theatre and film between immigrant and mainstream cultures. USA: New York, NY. 1890-1915. Lang.: Eng. 638
The idea of Hollywood in theatre autobiographies. USA. 1950-1990. Lang.: Eng. 665
Director Gerald Freedman on 'real' theatre. USA: Birmingham, AL. 1998. Lang.: Eng. 684
An exhibition devoted to dance and silent film star Lya de Putti. Hungary. Germany. 1898-1931. Lang.: Hun. 944
Report on festival of dance on film. UK-England: London. 1997. Lang.: Eng. 969
Dance director Seymour Felix. USA. 1918-1953. Lang.: Eng. 976
Analysis of the *Night and Day* dance sequence of *The Gay Divorcee.* USA: Hollywood, CA. 1934. Lang.: Eng. 977
Choreography in the musical film *The Bandwagon.* USA. 1953. Lang.: Eng. 982
Harlequin as a character in ballet. France. 1550-1965. Lang.: Eng. 1069
Dancer and choreographer Brygida Ochaim. Germany. France. 1970-1998. Lang.: Ger. 1283
Dancer/choreographer Rosemary Lee. UK-England: London. 1989-1998. Lang.: Eng. 1307
Interview with actor Gérard Poirier. Canada: Montreal, PQ. 1942-1998. Lang.: Fre. 1834
Actress Anne-Marie Cadieux on working in theatre and in film. Canada: Montreal, PQ. 1998. Lang.: Fre. 1838
Jean-Claude Coulbois on filming theatrical productions. Canada: Montreal, PQ. 1996-1998. Lang.: Fre. 1839
Interview with actress Fanny Ardant. France: Paris. 1990-1998. Lang.: Swe. 1944
The function of sound in productions of *India Song* by Marguerite Duras. France. UK-Wales: Mold. 1973-1993. Lang.: Eng. 1945
Interview with actor Vachtang Kikabidze. Georgia. 1998. Lang.: Rus. 1947
Articles on stage and film actors and other celebrities. Latvia. 1998. Lang.: Rus. 2197
Interview with actor Armen Džigarchanjan. Russia: Moscow. 1998. Lang.: Rus. 2232
Actor Vladislav Stržel'čik. Russia: St. Petersburg. 1998. Lang.: Rus. 2235
Memoirs of actor Georgij Burkov. Russia. 1933-1990. Lang.: Rus. 2241
Actress Elina Bystrickaja. Russia: Moscow. 1998. Lang.: Rus. 2242
Memoirs of actor Oleg Dal'. Russia: Moscow. 1998. Lang.: Rus. 2247
Actress Alla S. Demidova. Russia. 1998. Lang.: Rus. 2249
Actress Tatjana Doronina. Russia. 1998. Lang.: Rus. 2254
Actor Juri Nazarov. Russia. 1998. Lang.: Rus. 2275
Actress E. Majorova and her husband, scenographer S. Šerstjuk. Russia: Moscow. 1998. Lang.: Rus. 2283
Religion and actor Oleg Borisov. Russia: St. Petersburg. 1998. Lang.: Rus. 2287
Actor Nikolaj Simonov. Russia: St. Petersburg. 1998. Lang.: Rus. 2289
Profile of stage and film actor Armen B. Džigarchanjan. Russia: Moscow. 1998. Lang.: Rus. 2290
Memoirs of actress I.V. Makarova. Russia: Moscow. 1998. Lang.: Rus. 2294
Actor Sergej Makoveckij. Russia: Moscow. 1998. Lang.: Rus. 2295
Actress Farida Muminova. Russia: Magnitogorsk. 1998. Lang.: Rus. 2299

Film — cont'd

Actor Oleg Menšikov. Russia: Moscow. Russia. 1998. Lang.: Rus. 2304
Biography of actress Faina Ranevskaja. Russia. 1896-1984. Lang.: Rus. 2320
Memoirs of actor Innokentij Smoktunovskij. Russia: Moscow. 1998. Lang.: Rus. 2323
Memoirs of Malyj Theatre actor E. Ja. Vesnik. Russia: Moscow. 1998. Lang.: Rus. 2336
Actor Sergej Bezrukov. Russia: Moscow. Lang.: Rus. 2341
Actress Betty Marsden. UK-England: London. 1930-1998. Lang.: Eng. 2596
Career of actress Joan Hickson. UK-England: London. 1927-1998. Lang.: Eng. 2597
Career of actor Marius Goring. UK-England: London. 1930-1998. Lang.: Eng. 2598
Actor Leslie Howard. UK-England: London. USA: New York, NY. 1893-1943. Lang.: Eng. 2631
Actor Charles Laughton. UK-England: London. USA: Hollywood, CA. 1899-1962. Lang.: Eng. 2632
Actor Robert Donat. UK-England: London. 1905-1958. Lang.: Eng. 2633
Actor John Barrymore. USA: New York, NY. 1882-1942. Lang.: Eng. 2732
Actor Paul Muni. USA: New York, NY. 1895-1998. Lang.: Eng. 2733
Actress Marie Dressler. USA: New York, NY. 1869-1934. Lang.: Eng. 2734
Interview with film and television actor Jean-Louis Millette. Canada: Montreal, PQ. 1965-1998. Lang.: Fre. 3856
Interview with film and television actress Andrée Lachapelle. Canada: Montreal, PQ. 1964-1998. Lang.: Fre. 3857
Actress Ljudmila Gurčenko. Russia: Moscow. 1998. Lang.: Rus. 3859
Dance on screen. USA. Europe. 1920-1998. Lang.: Ger. 3860
Report on biennial festival of mixed media. France: Lyon. 1997. Lang.: Eng. 4042
Mixed media artist Ebon Fisher. USA. 1998. Lang.: Eng. 4045
Television adaptations of works by Goethe. Germany. 1965-1997. Lang.: Eng. 4061
Actors' interpretations of the title role in Oscar Wilde's *The Canterville Ghost*. UK-England. USA. 1943-1998. Lang.: Eng. 4066
Popular entertainer Elsie Janis. USA. 1896-1941. Lang.: Eng. 4145
Career of entertainer Al Jolson. USA. 1886-1950. Lang.: Eng. 4280
Interview with puppet animator Brian Duchscherer. Canada. 1980-1998. Lang.: Eng. 4886
Slovene puppet film. Slovenia. 1947-1997. Lang.: Slo. 4899

Plays/librettos/scripts
The representation of Vietnamese in film and stage depictions of the Vietnam war. USA. 1965-1993. Lang.: Eng. 690
Adoption narratives in novels, plays, and films. USA. 1960-1997. Lang.: Eng. 691
The character of Ivan the Terrible. USSR. 1800-1965. Lang.: Eng. 692
Interview with playwright Peter Asmussen. Denmark: Copenhagen. 1989-1998. Lang.: Swe. 2853
Shakespeare, Branagh, and the concept of the author. England. 1590-1998. Lang.: Eng. 2958
Comedy and farce in Finnish theatre and film. Finland. 1950-1998. Lang.: Fin. 3070
Director and playwright Pier Paolo Pasolini. Italy. 1922-1975. Lang.: Ita. 3227
Comparison between *Krísis (Crisis)* by Sabina Berman and Quentin Tarantino's film *Pulp Fiction*. Mexico. USA. 1993-1996. Lang.: Spa. 3276
Popular adaptations of the works of George Bernard Shaw. UK-England. 1890-1990. Lang.: Eng. 3445
Comparison of Harold Pinter's *Party Time* with his screenplay for *The Remains of the Day*. UK-England. 1991-1996. Lang.: Eng. 3490
Stage and screenwriter John Hopkins. UK-England: London. USA: Hollywood, CA. 1931-1998. Lang.: Eng. 3498
Interview with playwright and screenwriter Robert Anderson. USA. 1945-1998. Lang.: Eng. 3515
Interview with playwright Douglas Carter Beane. USA. 1980-1998. Lang.: Eng. 3516
Tennessee Williams's short story *Twenty-Seven Wagons Full of Cotton* and the plays based on it. USA. 1936-1979. Lang.: Eng. 3622
The fool character in works of Handke, Fellini, and Singer. USA. Germany. Italy. 1960-1968. Lang.: Eng. 3667
Film and video productions of plays by Eugene O'Neill. USA. 1935-1988. Lang.: Eng. 4078
Lyricist and librettist Betty Comden. USA. 1938-1998. Lang.: Eng. 4400
Arthur Kopit's *Nine*, a musical adaptation of Fellini's *8 1/2*. USA. 1963-1982. Lang.: Eng. 4401
The reciprocal influence of opera and film. Europe. North America. 1904-1994. Lang.: Eng. 4770
The *castrato*, the contralto, and the film *Farinelli*. France. Italy. 1994. Lang.: Eng. 4787
Derek Jarman's adaptation of works by Benjamin Britten and Wilfred Owen. UK-England. 1968-1988. Lang.: Eng. 4822

Reference materials
Dictionary of history and the arts. Lang.: Ita. 695
Index to performing arts articles in Bragaglia's *Chronache d'attualità*. Italy: Rome. 1916-1922. Lang.: Ita. 704

Relation to other fields
The culture of decadence in theatre and film. Finland. 1990-1998. Lang.: Fin. 732
Topics in post-apartheid South African literature and theatre. South Africa, Republic of. 1995-1998. Lang.: Eng. 764
European fears of American cultural hegemony. USA. Europe. 1998. Lang.: Eng. 773
The impact of photography and cinema on theatre. Canada. 1998. Lang.: Fre. 3732
References to film in theatre of Robert Lepage. Canada. 1990-1998. Lang.: Fre. 3734
Nigerian video films. Nigeria. 1992-1998. Lang.: Eng. 4081

Theory/criticism
The urge to make Shakespeare contemporary. USA. 1990-1998. Lang.: Eng. 3844

Filosofo, Il (Philosopher, The)
Plays/librettos/scripts
The comedies of Pietro Aretino. Italy. 1534-1556. Lang.: Eng. 3251

Filumena Marturano
Performance/production
Collection of newspaper reviews by London theatre critics. UK-England: London. 1998. Lang.: Eng. 2518

Fin de partie (Endgame)
Performance/production
Actors Gert Voss and Ignaz Kirchner on George Tabori's production of *Fin de partie (Endgame)*. Austria: Vienna. 1998. Lang.: Ger. 1821
Gert Voss and Ignaz Kirchner, *Theater Heute*'s actors of the year. Austria: Vienna. 1988-1998. Lang.: Ger. 1823
Plays/librettos/scripts
The influence Dryden and Johnson's theories on self-translated works of Samuel Beckett. France. Ireland. 1957-1976. Lang.: Eng. 3077

Final Call
Performance/production
Collection of newspaper reviews by London theatre critics. UK-England: London. 1998. Lang.: Eng. 2414

Financial operations
Administration
Economic forces and the Australian theatre industry. Australia. 1990-1998. Lang.: Eng. 2
On the history of arts patronage. Poland. 1998. Lang.: Rus. 19
New funding options for Romanian arts groups. Romania. 1989-1998. Lang.: Eng. 20
Interview with John Tusa, managing director of the Barbican Centre. UK-England: London. 1996-1998. Lang.: Eng. 24
The decline in corporate funding for the arts. USA. 1980-1988. Lang.: Eng. 32
Performance in fundraising. USA: New York, NY. 1998. Lang.: Eng. 34
Finding a reliable sample frame for potential audience data collection. USA. 1997. Lang.: Eng. 39
Fundraising on the World Wide Web. USA. 1998. Lang.: Eng. 41
History of circle stock touring. USA. 1907-1957. Lang.: Eng. 43
Report of Equity Executive Director on finance and organization. USA. 1998. Lang.: Eng. 51
Equity's support of air-rights proposal of Broadway Initiative. USA. 1998. Lang.: Eng. 53

Financial operations — cont'd

Changes to Equity's theatre bonding policy. USA. 1998. Lang.: Eng. 57
Effect on Actors Federal Credit Unions of a recent Supreme Court ruling. USA: New York, NY. 1998. Lang.: Eng. 67
Report on credit union legislation. USA: New York, NY. 1998. Lang.: Eng. 70
Annual report of the Equity pension fund. USA: New York, NY. 1998. Lang.: Eng. 81
Effect of recent legislation on the Actors Federal Credit Union. USA: New York, NY. 1998. Lang.: Eng. 83
Changes in Equity's bonding policy for regional theatres. USA: New York, NY. 1998. Lang.: Eng. 86
Survey of Equity membership and employment data. USA: New York, NY. 1998. Lang.: Eng. 115
In-kind contributions to non-profits and the organizations that solicit them. USA. 1998. Lang.: Eng. 119
'Arts incubator' organization Art's Bridge. USA: Chicago, IL. 1986-1998. Lang.: Eng. 120
The danger of a 'survival philosophy' to the mission of arts organizations. USA. 1998. Lang.: Eng. 121
Suggestions for fundraising events. USA. 1998. Lang.: Eng. 122
Workplace solicitation for contributions to the arts. USA. 1998. Lang.: Eng. 124
The commitment to arts funding by cities that sponsor major league sports. USA. 1989-1998. Lang.: Eng. 125
Dictionary of fundraising letters. USA. 1998. Lang.: Eng. 128
The importance of maintaining an up-to-date fundraising data base. USA. 1998. Lang.: Eng. 130
External fundraising for theatre arts programs. USA. 1985-1987. Lang.: Eng. 133
Current thinking on the impact of the arts. USA. 1998. Lang.: Eng. 142
Profile of management group National Arts Stabilization. USA. 1998. Lang.: Eng. 144
Riksteatern and Dansens Hus' Dansbiennal 98 meeting with government officials. Sweden. 1998. Lang.: Swe. 881
Sweden's new dance funding program. Sweden. 1998. Lang.: Swe. 883
Financially troubled Ohio ballet companies. USA: Cleveland, OH, Akron, OH. 1998. Lang.: Eng. 1027
The closing of Göteborgs Stadsteatern. Sweden. 1974-1997. Lang.: Dan. 1389
The Disney Corporation's Broadway musicals. USA: New York, NY. 1996-1998. Lang.: Eng. 4317
Pricing strategy for puppeteers. USA. 1998. Lang.: Eng. 4864

Institutions
The Vienna-based foundation for the development of Moscow's Bolšoj Theatre. Austria: Vienna. 1998. Lang.: Rus. 335
Profile of TAXI Children's Theatre. USA: Louisville, KY. 1992-1998. Lang.: Eng. 390
The management of the Shakespeare Festival of Dallas. USA: Dallas, TX. 1972-1988. Lang.: Eng. 393
Systems analysis of the Southwest Theatre Association. USA. 1988. Lang.: Eng. 418
Interview with Ingrid Dahlberg, manager of Dramaten. Sweden: Stockholm. 1996-1998. Lang.: Swe. 1730
Profile of Watermill Theatre. UK-England: Newbury. 1998. Lang.: Eng. 1744
Interview with Bjørn Simensen, director of Den Norske Opera. Norway: Oslo. 1998. Lang.: Swe. 4465
The cancellation of performances by the Royal Opera House, Covent Garden. UK-England: London. 1998. Lang.: Eng. 4478

Performance/production
Practical issues of cultural exchange: the Cry of Asia! tour. France. Philippines. 1988-1990. Lang.: Eng. 535

Plays/librettos/scripts
The playwright and the play development process. Canada. 1998. Lang.: Eng. 2811

Finborough Arms (London)
Performance/production
Collection of newspaper reviews by London theatre critics. UK-England: London. 1998. Lang.: Eng. 2411
Collection of newspaper reviews by London theatre critics. UK-England: London. 1998. Lang.: Eng. 2414
Collection of newspaper reviews by London theatre critics. UK-England: London. 1998. Lang.: Eng. 2418
Collection of newspaper reviews by London theatre critics. UK-England: London. 1998. Lang.: Eng. 2444
Collection of newspaper reviews by London theatre critics. UK-England: London. 1998. Lang.: Eng. 2457
Collection of newspaper reviews by London theatre critics. UK-England: London. 1998. Lang.: Eng. 2476
Collection of newspaper reviews by London theatre critics. UK-England: London. 1998. Lang.: Eng. 2479
Collection of newspaper reviews by London theatre critics. UK-England: London. 1998. Lang.: Eng. 2493
Collection of newspaper reviews by London theatre critics. UK-England: London. 1998. Lang.: Eng. 2506
Collection of newspaper reviews by London theatre critics. UK-England: London. 1998. Lang.: Eng. 2528
Collection of newspaper reviews by London theatre critics. UK-England: London. 1998. Lang.: Eng. 2537
Collection of newspaper reviews by London theatre critics. UK-England: London. 1998. Lang.: Eng. 2546
Collection of newspaper reviews by London theatre critics. UK-England: London. 1998. Lang.: Eng. 2566
Collection of newspaper reviews by London theatre critics. UK-England: London. 1998. Lang.: Eng. 2588

Finished
Basic theatrical documents
Screenplay of *Finished* by William E. Jones. USA. 1997. Lang.: Eng. 3889

Finlay, Leslie
Performance/production
Collection of newspaper reviews by London theatre critics. UK-England: London. 1998. Lang.: Eng. 2439

Finley, Karen
Performance/production
The feminist performance trend Angry Essentialism. USA. 1981-1998. Lang.: Eng. 4249

Finn, William
Performance/production
Collection of newspaper reviews by London theatre critics. UK-England: London. 1998. Lang.: Eng. 2498

Finnan, Kevin
Institutions
Profile of Motionhouse Dance Theatre. UK-England: London. 1988-1998. Lang.: Eng. 1254

Finnish National Opera
SEE
Suomen Kansallisoopera.

Finnish National Theatre
SEE
Suomen Kansallisteatteri.

Finnish Theatre Academy
SEE
Teatterikorkeakoulu (Helsinki).

Fiorentino, Imero
Design/technology
Imero Fiorentino, USITT's most distinguished lighting designer of 1997. USA. 1998. Lang.: Eng. 291

Fiorilli, Tiberio
Performance/production
A painting of *commedia dell'arte* performer Tiberio Fiorilli. Italy. 1625-1700. Lang.: Eng. 4190

Fire Station Theatre (London)
Performance/production
Collection of newspaper reviews by London theatre critics. UK-England. 1998. Lang.: Eng. 2504

Fires in the Mirror: Crown Heights, Brooklyn and Other Identities
Performance/production
Documentary theatre and the politics of representation. USA. 1966-1993. Lang.: Eng. 2728

Firesign Theatre (Los Angeles, CA)
Performance/production
The decline of radio comedy and the use of record albums by some comedians. USA. 1950-1998. Lang.: Eng. 3863

Fireworks
Performance/production
The pyrotechnic genre, the 'fort holding'. England. 1501-1600. Lang.: Eng. 4122

Firmeza en la ausencia, La (Constancy in Absence)
Plays/librettos/scripts
Feminist analysis of seventeenth-century plays by women. Spain. 1605-1675. Lang.: Eng. 3385
First Attempt, The
Plays/librettos/scripts
Analysis of letters between Lady Morgan and actor Richard Jones. UK-Ireland. 1807. Lang.: Eng. 4862
First One, The
Plays/librettos/scripts
Black dance in plays of Zora Neale Hurston. USA. 1925-1930. Lang.: Eng. 3633
First USA Riverfront Arts Center (Wilmington, DE)
Administration
The role of Riverfront Arts Center in revitalizing Wilmington's riverfront. USA: Wilmington, DE. 1998. Lang.: Eng. 123
First Wife, The
Basic theatrical documents
Screenplay for *The First Wife*, based on a story by Colette. USA. 1998. Lang.: Eng. 3888
Plays/librettos/scripts
Analysis of Douglas Heil's screenplay *The First Wife*. USA. 1998. Lang.: Eng. 4030
Firstborn, The
Plays/librettos/scripts
Analysis of plays based on the Hebrew prophets. USA. Europe. 1919-1970. Lang.: Eng. 3659
Fischzug, Der (Catch, The)
Basic theatrical documents
Catalan translations of plays by Bertolt Brecht (volume 1). Germany. 1919-1954. Lang.: Cat. 1437
Fish Story
Performance/production
Analysis of the Wooster Group's *Fish Story* directed by Elizabeth LeCompte. USA: New York, NY. 1990-1996. Lang.: Eng. 2667
Fisher, Caroline
Performance/production
Collection of newspaper reviews by London theatre critics. UK-England: London. 1998. Lang.: Eng. 2494
Fisher, Ebon
Performance/production
Mixed media artist Ebon Fisher. USA. 1998. Lang.: Eng. 4045
Fisher, Jules
Design/technology
Lighting and projections for the musical *Ragtime*. USA: New York, NY. 1998. Lang.: Eng. 4328
Fisher, Mark
Design/technology
Lighting design by Patrick Woodroffe and set design by Mark Fisher for Rolling Stones tour. USA. 1997-1998. Lang.: Eng. 4103
Fisher, Rick
Design/technology
Interview with lighting designer Rick Fisher. UK-England. 1998. Lang.: Eng. 1030
Technical designs for Matthew Bourne's productions of ballets by Čajkovskij and Prokofjėv. UK-England: London. 1998. Lang.: Eng. 1031
Fishermen of Beaudrais, The
Basic theatrical documents
Screenplay of *The Fishermen of Beaudrais* by Ring Lardner, Jr., and Dalton Trumbo. USA. 1943-1998. Lang.: Eng. 3891
Plays/librettos/scripts
Interview with screenwriter Ring Lardner, Jr. USA. 1943. Lang.: Eng. 3998
Background on *The Fishermen of Beaudrais* by Ring Lardner, Jr., and Dalton Trumbo. USA. 1943-1998. Lang.: Eng. 4025
Fiske, Minnie Maddern
Plays/librettos/scripts
Feminism and plays of Henrik Ibsen. Norway. 1879-1979. Lang.: Eng. 3293
Fitch, Clyde
Performance/production
Attempted censorship of productions. USA. 1900-1905. Lang.: Eng. 2698
New York City's attempt to impose censorship on theatre productions. USA: New York, NY. 1900-1927. Lang.: Eng. 2699
Fitzgerald, F. Scott
Performance/production
Collection of newspaper reviews by London theatre critics. UK-England: London. 1998. Lang.: Eng. 2410
Fitzgerald, Peter J.
Design/technology
Sound design for the musical *The Capeman*. USA: New York, NY. 1998. Lang.: Eng. 4339
Fitzgerald, Zelda
Performance/production
Collection of newspaper reviews by London theatre critics. UK-England: London. 1998. Lang.: Eng. 2512
Five Lesbian Brothers (New York, NY)
Performance/production
Profile of the satiric comedy troupe Five Lesbian Brothers. USA: New York, NY. 1989-1998. Lang.: Eng. 4282
Five or Six Characters in Search of Toronto
Basic theatrical documents
Text of *Five or Six Characters in Search of Toronto* by Rana Bose. Canada: Toronto, ON. 1993. Lang.: Eng. 1409
Flag Is Born, A
Performance/production
Ben Hecht's propaganda pageant *A Flag Is Born*. USA: New York, NY. 1946. Lang.: Eng. 4220
Flaherty, Stephen
Design/technology
Lighting and projections for the musical *Ragtime*. USA: New York, NY. 1998. Lang.: Eng. 4328
Technical designs for *Ragtime* at the Ford Center. USA: New York, NY. 1998. Lang.: Eng. 4338
Sound design for the Broadway premiere of the musical *Ragtime*. USA: New York, NY. 1998. Lang.: Eng. 4341
Flamenco
Performance/production
Flamenco variations worldwide. Spain. USA. 1901-1998. Lang.: Eng. 962
The Finnish enthusiasm for Flamenco dance. Spain. Finland. 1998. Lang.: Fin. 1234
Interview with Flamenco dancer Gabriela Gutarra. Spain: Seville. 1980-1998. Lang.: Swe. 1235
Interview with Flamenco dancer Eva Milich. Sweden: Gothenburg. Spain. 1990-1998. Lang.: Swe. 1236
Interview with Flamenco dancer Janni Berggren. Sweden. Spain. 1970. Lang.: Swe. 1237
Performances of Joaquím Cortez's flamenco troupe and the Ballets Africains of Guinea. UK-England: London. 1997. Lang.: Hun. 1238
Flamenco dancer and choreographer Carlota Santana. USA: New York, NY. 1998. Lang.: Eng. 1239
Flamenco Vivo Carlota Santana (New York, NY)
Performance/production
Flamenco dancer and choreographer Carlota Santana. USA: New York, NY. 1998. Lang.: Eng. 1239
Flatley, Michael
Performance/production
The success of dance extravaganzas and solo performance at the expense of traditional shows. USA: New York, NY. 1994-1998. Lang. :Eng. 645
Flea in Her Ear, A
SEE
Puce à l'Oreille, La.
Fledermaus, Die
Performance/production
Collection of newspaper reviews by London theatre critics. UK-England: London. 1998. Lang.: Eng. 2420
Frank Castorf's production of Strauss's *Die Fledermaus*. Germany: Hamburg. 1997-1998. Lang.: Ger. 4612
Reviews of recent opera productions. Switzerland: Basel. Germany: Stuttgart, Berlin, Hamburg. France: Strasbourg. 1997-1998. Lang.: Ger. 4702
Opera conductor Patrick Summers. USA. 1990-1998. Lang.: Eng. 4755
Flemr, Jan
Plays/librettos/scripts
New direction in Czech playwriting. Czech Republic. 1990-1997. Lang.: Cze. 2850
Flesh
Performance/production
Collection of newspaper reviews by London theatre critics. UK-England: London. 1998. Lang.: Eng. 2448
Fletcher, John
Institutions
The inaugural season of Shakespeare's Globe Theatre. UK-England: London. 1997-1998. Lang.: Eng. 1741

Fletcher, John — cont'd

Performance/production
The inaugural season of Shakespeare's Globe Theatre. UK-England: London. 1997. Lang.: Eng. 2601
Review of the opening season of Shakespeare's Globe Theatre. UK-England: London. 1997. Lang.: Eng. 2602
Plays/librettos/scripts
Playwriting and publishing for the London stage. England. 1590-1650. Lang.: Eng. 2881
Women's use of wit in response to men in English popular culture. England. 1590-1630. Lang.: Eng. 2884
Plague imagery in Jacobean tragedy. England. 1618-1642. Lang.: Eng. 2889
The murders of royal women in plays of Shakespeare and Beaumont and Fletcher. England. 1609-1610. Lang.: Eng. 2894
Casuistry and early modern English tragedy. England. 1600-1671. Lang.: Eng. 2980
Analysis of *The Island Princess* by John Fletcher. England. 1621. Lang.: Eng. 2988
Don Quixote, Lewis Theobald's *The Double Falsehood* and the lost *Cardenio* of Shakespeare and Fletcher. England. Spain. 1610-1727. Lang.: Eng. 3001

Flickan, Mamman och Soporna (Girl, the Mommy and the Garbage, The)
Performance/production
Interview with actress and director Anna Takanen. Sweden: Stockholm. 1994-1998. Lang.: Swe. 2372
Stockholm's children's theatre scene. Sweden: Stockholm. 1998. Lang.: Ger. 2389

Flicker, The
Audience
The prompting of epileptic seizures by film. 1960-1988. Lang.: Eng. 3876

Flimm, Jürgen
Performance/production
Interview with director Jürgen Flimm. Germany. 1998. Lang.: Ger. 2004

Flinck, Thorsten
Institutions
Report on the Stockholm theatre festival. Sweden: Stockholm. 1998. Lang.: Eng. 1724
Performance/production
Interview with actor Dan Ekborg. Sweden: Stockholm. 1998. Lang.: Swe. 2367
Seven critics on their favorite character or portrayal. Sweden. 1950. Lang.: Swe. 2369
Gerthi Kulle's role in Brecht's *Der Gute Mensch von Sezuan (The Good Person of Szechwan)* at Dramaten. Sweden: Stockholm. 1998. Lang.: Swe. 2384
Photos of rehearsals of O'Neill's *Long Day's Journey Into Night* at Dramaten. Sweden: Stockholm. 1998. Lang.: Swe. 2391

Flint, Diana
Performance/production
Collection of newspaper reviews by London theatre critics. UK-England: London. 1998. Lang.: Eng. 2506

Flipp Teatern (Helsinki)
Institutions
The proliferation of Swedish-language theatre groups in Helsinki. Finland: Helsinki. 1990-1998. Lang.: Eng, Fre. 1604

Flisar, Evald
Basic theatrical documents
Text of *Sončne pege (Sunspots)* by Evald Flisar. Slovenia. 1997. Lang.: Slo. 1456

Florence
Plays/librettos/scripts
Black self-determination in the plays of Alice Childress. USA. 1949-1969. Lang.: Eng. 3579

Florentine Tragedy, A
Basic theatrical documents
Max Meyerfeld's libretto for Zemlinsky's opera *Eine florentinische Tragödie*. Germany. 1917. Lang.: Ger, Fre. 4419
Plays/librettos/scripts
Max Meyerfeld's preface to the translation of *A Florentine Tragedy* by Oscar Wilde. Europe. 1895-1907. Lang.: Fre. 3057

Florentinische Tragödie, Eine
Basic theatrical documents
Max Meyerfeld's libretto for Zemlinsky's opera *Eine florentinische Tragödie*. Germany. 1917. Lang.: Ger, Fre. 4419
Performance/production
Recordings of Zemlinsky's *Eine florentinische Tragödie*. 1980-1997. Lang.: Fre. 4506
Productions of Zemlinsky's *Eine florentinische Tragödie*. 1917-1996. Lang.: Fre. 4515
A letter from composer Alexander Zemlinsky to Alma Mahler. Germany. 1917. Lang.: Fre. 4613
Plays/librettos/scripts
Max Meyerfeld's preface to the translation of *A Florentine Tragedy* by Oscar Wilde. Europe. 1895-1907. Lang.: Fre. 3057

Flower
Plays/librettos/scripts
Account of performances by Joan Dickinson. USA. 1997-1998. Lang.: Eng. 4263

Flower Drum Song
Design/technology
Costume designs by Irene Sharaff. USA. 1933-1976. Lang.: Eng. 277

Fluxus
Relation to other fields
The Fluxus movement. USA. Europe. 1961-1979. Lang.: Eng. 4265

Fly
Plays/librettos/scripts
Playwright and actor Joseph Edward. USA: New York, NY. 1997. Lang.: Eng. 3564

Flying Wallendas (USA)
Performance/production
Physical risk and its aesthetics in aerialist performance. USA. 1985-1997. Lang.: Eng. 4185

Fo, Dario
Basic theatrical documents
Dutch translations of women's monologues by Dario Fo. Italy. 1998. Lang.: Dut. 1440
Slovene translation of *Mistero Buffo* by Dario Fo. Italy. Slovenia. 1969-1997. Lang.: Slo. 1441
Russian translations of plays by Nobel Prize winners. Italy. 1848-1998. Lang.: Rus. 1446
Performance/production
Dario Fo and Giorgio Strehler honored at Venice Biennale. Italy: Venice. 1947-1998. Lang.: Eng. 2163
Collection of newspaper reviews by London theatre critics. UK-England: London. 1998. Lang.: Eng. 2430
Collection of newspaper reviews by London theatre critics. UK-England: London. 1998. Lang.: Eng. 2532
Collection of newspaper reviews by London theatre critics. UK-England: London. 1998. Lang.: Eng. 2565
Plays/librettos/scripts
Michel Tremblay's adaptation of *Mistero Buffo* by Dario Fo. Canada: Montreal, PQ. 1969-1973. Lang.: Fre. 2795
The clown as a character in modern drama. Europe. 1915-1995. Lang.: Eng. 3056
Profile of playwright, director, and actor Dario Fo. Italy. 1997-1998. Lang.: Ger. 3231
Dario Fo, translation, and authorial intent. Italy. 1978-1998. Lang.: Eng. 3238
Reactions to the awarding of the Nobel Prize to satirical playwright Dario Fo. Italy. 1998. Lang.: Eng. 3242
Playwright Dario Fo. Italy. 1998. Lang.: Eng. 3243
Techniques of opposition in the work of Dario Fo. Italy. 1950-1988. Lang.: Eng. 3265

Focus Theatre (Dublin)
Performance/production
Recent productions in Ireland of plays by Eugene O'Neill. Ireland: Dublin. UK-Ireland: Belfast. 1989-1998. Lang.: Eng. 2154

Född skyldig (Born Guilty)
Institutions
Interview with Ronnie Hallgren of Älvsborgsteatern about theatre for youth. Sweden: Borås. 1994-1998. Lang.: Swe. 1726

Fodor, Antal
Performance/production
Antal Fodor's ballet *A Próba (The Rehearsal)*. Hungary: Budapest. 1998. Lang.: Hun. 1111

Fodor, Tamás
Institutions
Tamás Fodor's Stúdió K. Hungary: Budapest. 1971-1997. 1971-1997. Lang.: Hun. 1671
Performance/production
Interviews with actors on Anatolij Vasiljév's guest direction at Szigligeti Theatre. Hungary: Szolnok. 1998. Lang.: Hun. 2061

Fodor, Tamás — cont'd

Sándor Lajos' *Szűrővizsgálat (Screen Test)* directed by Tamás Fodor. Hungary: Budapest. 1998. Lang.: Hun. 2103

Fogarty, Molly
Performance/production
Collection of newspaper reviews by London theatre critics. UK-England: London. 1998. Lang.: Eng. 2499

Fojtás (Tamping)
Performance/production
Ferenc Deák's *Fojtás (Tamping)* directed by László Babarczy. Hungary: Kaposvár. 1998. Lang.: Hun. 2117

Fokin, Michajl Michajlovič
Performance/production
Collaborative Symbolist dance/theatre projects. Europe. USA. 1916-1934. Lang.: Eng. 1268

Fokin, Valerij
Performance/production
The work of Russian directors at the Golden Mask festival. Russia: Moscow, St. Petersburg. 1998. Lang.: Swe. 2305

Foley, Sean
Performance/production
Collection of newspaper reviews by London theatre critics. UK-England: London. 1998. Lang.: Eng. 2564

Folger Library (Washington, DC)
Performance spaces
Evidence of theatre closings in a Folger Library manuscript. England: London. 1650. Lang.: Eng. 1798

Folger Shakespeare Theatre (Washington, DC)
SEE
Shakespeare Theatre.

Folk dance
Institutions
History of the folk dance ensemble Erkel Néptáncegyüttes. Hungary. 1948-1998. Lang.: Hun. 1220

Report on folk dance festival and competition. Russia: Voskresensk. 1998. Lang.: Rus. 1222

Performance/production
Danish guest performance of Honvéd Táncszínház. Denmark: Copenhagen. 1998. Lang.: Hun. 1224

Fáklya Horvát Táncegyüttes' folk dance production *Napmadarak (Sunbirds)*. Hungary. 1998. Lang.: Hun. 1227

Modern tendencies in Hungarian folk dance. Hungary. 1970-1977. Lang.: Hun. 1228

Folk dance program in honor of choreographer István Molnár. Hungary: Budapest. 1930-1998. Lang.: Hun. 1229

Tatar folk dance in Siberia. Russia. 1998. Lang.: Rus. 1232

Folk dancing in the Soviet Union during the 1930s. USSR. 1930-1939. Lang.: Rus. 1242

Folk theatre
Performance/production
Northern Brazilian folk theatre forms. Brazil. 1972-1997. Lang.: Eng. 497

Plays/librettos/scripts
Recovered ritual in seemingly non-ritualistic theatre. England. 1600-1779. Lang.: Eng. 2904

Relation to other fields
The 'bird-woman' folktale in Southeast Asian shamanic healing rituals. Ireland. Thailand. Malaysia. Lang.: Eng. 1358

Folkefiende, En (Enemy of the People, An)
Performance/production
Collection of newspaper reviews by London theatre critics. UK-England: London. 1998. Lang.: Eng. 2466

Trevor Nunn's production of *An Enemy of the People* by Ibsen. UK-England: London. 1998. Lang.: Eng. 2627

Plays/librettos/scripts
The rebel in modern drama. Europe. 1950-1988. Lang.: Eng. 3053

Henrik Ibsen and social criticism in *En Folkefiende (An Enemy of the People)*. Norway. 1882. Lang.: Swe. 3300

Folklore
Performance/production
The puppet nativity play of Eastern and Central Europe. Europe. 1700-1990. Lang.: Hun. 4891

Plays/librettos/scripts
Folklore and Shakespeare's *King Lear*. England. 1605-1606. Lang.: Eng. 3010

A folktale source of *The Playboy of the Western World*. Ireland. 1907. Lang.: Eng. 3202

Analysis of *The Swamp Dwellers* by Wole Soyinka. Nigeria. 1973. Lang.: Eng. 3283

Analysis of the 'Russian Robin Hood' Stepan Razin. Russia. 1620-1900. Lang.: Eng. 3327

Folklore and occultism in August Strindberg's *Lycko-Pers resa (Lucky Per's Journey)*. Sweden. 1912. Lang.: Swe. 3412

Irish folklore in plays of Eugene O'Neill. USA. 1942-1956. Lang.: Eng. 3522

Folkwang Hochschule (Essen)
Training
Dance training at Folkwang Hochschule. Germany: Essen. 1996-1998. Lang.: Hun. 1341

Follies
Design/technology
Lighting design for the musical *Follies*, Paper Mill Playhouse. USA: Millburn, NJ. 1998. Lang.: Eng. 4335

Plays/librettos/scripts
The disintegration of the American dream in works of Stephen Sondheim. USA. 1970-1984. Lang.: Eng. 4397

Follini, Charles
Plays/librettos/scripts
Playwright, actor, and director Charles Follini. Canada. 1972-1998. Lang.: Eng. 2818

Foltin, Jolán
Performance/production
Modern tendencies in Hungarian folk dance. Hungary. 1970-1977. Lang.: Hun. 1228

Fomenko, Pëtr
Performance/production
A friend's view of director Pëtr Fomenko. Russia: Moscow. 1998. Lang.: Rus. 2281

Pëtr Fomenko's theatrical adaptation of Gogol's *Dead Souls*. Russia: Moscow. 1998. Lang.: Rus. 2303

The work of Russian directors at the Golden Mask festival. Russia: Moscow, St. Petersburg. 1998. Lang.: Swe. 2305

Pëtr Fomenko's production of *V Čičikovskoj krugoverti (In Čičikov's Chaos)*. Russia: Moscow. 1998. Lang.: Rus. 2340

Fontane, Theodor
Institutions
New productions of Düsseldorfer Schauspielhaus. Germany: Dusseldorf. 1998. Lang.: Ger. 1654

Theory/criticism
How theatre criticism of Theodor Fontane influenced his novels. Germany: Berlin. 1870-1890. Lang.: Ger. 843

Fontanne, Lynn
Performance/production
Acting couple Alfred Lunt and Lynn Fontanne: 'idealized heterosexuality'. USA. 1887-1983. Lang.: Eng. 2656

Fonteyn, Margot
Performance/production
Recollections of ballerina Margot Fonteyn. USA. Panama. 1946-1998. Lang.: Eng. 1182

Fonvizin, Denis Ivanovič
Plays/librettos/scripts
Russian literature and theatre of the eighteenth century. Russia. 1701-1800. Lang.: Rus. 3322

Morality in plays of Fonvizin, Ostrovskij, and A.K. Tolstoj. Russia. 1764-1869. Lang.: Rus. 3325

Food
Performance/production
Collection of newspaper reviews by London theatre critics. UK-England: London. 1998. Lang.: Eng. 2463

Fool for Love
Plays/librettos/scripts
Analysis of Sam Shepard's *Fool for Love*. USA. 1979. Lang.: Dut. 3540

The screen adaptation of Sam Shepard's *Fool for Love*. USA. 1979. Lang.: Eng. 4008

Footballer's Wife, The
Performance/production
Collection of newspaper reviews by London theatre critics. UK-England: London. 1998. Lang.: Eng. 2469

Foote, Samuel
Plays/librettos/scripts
Caricature and satire in the plays of Samuel Foote. England. 1775-1800. Lang.: Eng. 2930

Footfalls
Plays/librettos/scripts
Recognition in plays of Čechov, Shakespeare, and Beckett. England. France. Russia. 1596-1980. Lang.: Eng. 2949

Footsbarn Travelling Theatre Company (Herisson)
Institutions
Margarethe Biereye and David Johnston of the touring company Ton und Kirschen. Germany: Glindow. 1992-1997. Lang.: Eng. 1624
for colored girls who have considered suicide/when the rainbow is enuf
Plays/librettos/scripts
Boal's 'joker system' in plays of Ntozake Shange. USA. 1977-1981. Lang.: Eng. 3692
For Jerry—Part I
Relation to other fields
Shelly Hirsch on her performance piece *For Jerry—Part I.* USA. Germany. 1997-1998. Lang.: Ger, Fre, Dut, Eng. 4266
Forbidden Dance
Performance/production
Collection of newspaper reviews by London theatre critics. UK-England: London. 1998. Lang.: Eng. 2524
Forced Entertainment Theatre Cooperative (Sheffield)
Institutions
Profile of the Forced Entertainment Theatre Cooperative. UK-England: Sheffield. 1996. Lang.: Dut. 1739
Performance/production
Derision in recent productions. Canada: Quebec, PQ. 1998. Lang.: Fre. 509
Forced Entertainment and Berlin's Live Art Festival. UK-England, Sheffield. Germany: Berlin. 1984-1998. Lang.: Ger. 539
Relation to other fields
Cultural trends of the younger generation. Europe. 1995-1998. Lang.: Swe. 4150
Forcier, André
Plays/librettos/scripts
Surrealism and metaphor in the films of André Forcier. Canada. 1998. Lang.: Fre. 3965
Ford Center for the Performing Arts (New York, NY)
Design/technology
Lighting and projections for the musical *Ragtime.* USA: New York, NY. 1998. Lang.: Eng. 4328
Technical designs for *Ragtime* at the Ford Center. USA: New York, NY. 1998. Lang.: Eng. 4338
Eugene Lee's set design for Frank Galati's production of *Ragtime.* USA. 1997-1998. Lang.: Eng. 4340
Sound design for the Broadway premiere of the musical *Ragtime.* USA: New York, NY. 1998. Lang.: Eng. 4341
Performance spaces
Architectural critique of the new Ford Center. USA: New York, NY. 1998. Lang.: Eng. 468
Ford, John
Performance/production
Student production of Ford's *'Tis Pity She's a Whore.* Canada. 1997. Lang.: Eng. 1849
Plays/librettos/scripts
Analysis of *The Witch of Edmonton* by Ford, Dekker, and Rowley. England. 1621. Lang.: Eng. 2928
Influences on *'Tis Pity She's a Whore* by John Ford. England. 1587-1631. Lang.: Eng. 2937
History and John Ford's *Perkin Warbeck.* England. 1634. Lang.: Eng. 2938
Foreman, Gill
Performance/production
Collection of newspaper reviews by London theatre critics. UK-England: London. 1998. Lang.: Eng. 2506
Foreman, Richard
Performance/production
The influence of experimental performance on contemporary drama. Europe. USA. 1960-1987. Lang.: Eng. 526
Richard Foreman's notes for a production of his *Pearls for Pigs.* USA: Hartford, CT. 1997. Lang.: Eng. 2681
Interview with director Richard Foreman. USA: New York, NY. 1975-1990. Lang.: Eng. 2700
Relation to other fields
Quantum theory in recent New York performances. USA: New York, NY. 1995-1996. Lang.: Eng. 794
Theory/criticism
The theatrical structure of autonomous theatre. USA. 1967-1979. Lang.: Eng. 867
Chaos theory and its application to theatre and drama theory. USA. 1998. Lang.: Eng. 3839
Foreskin's Lament
Plays/librettos/scripts
Women in plays about war and male contact sports. New Zealand. Europe. 1998. Lang.: Eng. 3281
Foresters, The
Plays/librettos/scripts
Analysis of *The Foresters* by Alfred, Lord Tennyson. England. USA. 1700-1910. Lang.: Eng. 2998
Forêt, La (Forest, The)
Plays/librettos/scripts
Analysis of plays by Gilles Maheu. Canada: Montreal, PQ. 1994-1998. Lang.: Fre. 1357
Forever After
Plays/librettos/scripts
The development of playwright Owen Davis. USA. 1905-1923. Lang.: Eng. 3526
Forever Plaid
Performance/production
Collection of newspaper reviews by London theatre critics. UK-England: London. 1998. Lang.: Eng. 2555
Forgách, András
Plays/librettos/scripts
Commentary on plays newly translated into Hungarian. Hungary. 1990-1998. Lang.: Hun. 3189
Forgách, Péter
Performance/production
Review of Péter Forgách's *Kaspar,* Győr National Theatre. Hungary: Győr. 1998. Lang.: Hun. 2106
Forjaz, Cibele
Performance/production
Review of Brazilian performances of plays by Brecht. Brazil: São Paulo. 1998. Lang.: Ger. 1832
Forkbeard Fantasy (London)
Performance/production
Collection of newspaper reviews by London theatre critics. UK-England: London. 1998. Lang.: Eng. 2436
Fornes, Maria Irene
Performance/production
Theatre Magazine's anniversary issue. USA. 1968-1998. Lang.: Eng. 617
Plays/librettos/scripts
Theatrical space in plays of Maria Irene Fornes. USA. 1977-1989. Lang.: Eng. 3571
Women playwrights' addresses to the Women's Project conference. USA. 1997. Lang.: Eng. 3589
Revolutionary Off Broadway playwriting. USA: New York, NY. 1959-1969. Lang.: Eng. 3604
Politics and feminism in the plays of Maria Irene Fornes. USA. 1975-1995. Lang.: Eng. 3635
Forrest, Edwin
Performance/production
Actor Edwin Forrest and the construction of masculinity. USA. 1806-1872. Lang.: Eng. 674
Forrest, Robin
Performance/production
Collection of newspaper reviews by London theatre critics. UK-England: London. 1998. Lang.: Eng. 2447
Forssell, Jonas
Institutions
Problems of administration at Norrlandsoperan. Sweden: Umeå. 1998. Lang.: Swe. 4473
Forster, Margaret
Performance/production
Collection of newspaper reviews by London theatre critics. UK-England: London. 1998. Lang.: Eng. 2468
Forsythe, William
Performance/production
Choreographer William Forsythe. Germany: Frankfurt. 1973-1998. Lang.: Eng. 1081
Choreographer William Forsythe, director of Ballett Frankfurt. Germany: Frankfurt. 1949-1998. Lang.: Eng. 1084
The choreography of William Forsythe and the painting of Marcel Duchamp. Germany. France. 1915-1998. Lang.: Eng. 1280
William Forsythe of Ballett Frankfurt. Germany: Frankfurt. 1984-1998. Lang.: Ger. 1284
The collaborative art installation *Tight Roaring Circle.* UK-England: London. 1993-1997. Lang.: Eng. 4133
Forth, Alison
Performance/production
Collection of newspaper reviews by London theatre critics. UK-England: London. 1998. Lang.: Eng. 2521

Fortner, Wolfgang
Plays/librettos/scripts
Composer Wolfgang Fortner's adaptation of *That Time* by Samuel Beckett. Europe. 1974-1977. Lang.: Eng. 4777
Fortune Heights
Performance/production
Aleksand'r Tairov's production of *Fortune Heights* by John Dos Passos. USA. 1930-1935. Lang.: Rus. 2739
Fortune Theatre (London)
Performance spaces
Evidence of theatre closings in a Folger Library manuscript. England: London. 1650. Lang.: Eng. 1798
Foss, Karen
Institutions
Profile of dance company Nye Carte Blanche. Norway: Bergen. 1990-1998. Lang.: Swe. 1251
Fosse, Bob
Performance/production
The development of Bob Fosse's choreographic style. USA. 1953-1987. Lang.: Eng. 4377
Fosse, Jon
Performance/production
Collection of newspaper reviews by London theatre critics. UK-England: London. 1998. Lang.: Eng. 2582
Fossil Woman
Performance/production
Collection of newspaper reviews by London theatre critics. UK-England: London. 1998. Lang.: Eng. 2570
Foster, Hannah
Performance/production
Theatre and gender in the novels of Hannah Foster. UK-England. 1759-1840. Lang.: Eng. 613
Foster, Norm
Performance spaces
Theatre SKAM's production of *Louis and Dave* in a Plymouth Volaré. Canada: Victoria, BC. 1996. Lang.: Eng. 1797
Plays/librettos/scripts
Playwright Norm Foster. Canada. 1980-1998. Lang.: Eng. 2798
Foster, Paul
Plays/librettos/scripts
Revolutionary Off Broadway playwriting. USA: New York, NY. 1959-1969. Lang.: Eng. 3604
Found spaces
Design/technology
Derek McLane's set designs for recent Off Broadway productions. USA: New York, NY. 1998. Lang.: Eng. 1538
R. Murray Schaffer's environmental opera *The Princess of the Stars.* Canada. 1981-1997. Lang.: Eng. 4424
Institutions
Experiential memory work and acting at Theater Jugend Club. Germany: Nordhausen. 1995-1998. Lang.: Ger. 1629
Performance spaces
The feasibility of a floating open-air theatre. Europe. 1998. Lang.: Swe. 436
Essays on experimental theatre world wide. Europe. North America. Asia. 1918-1998. Lang.: Pol. 438
History and nature of German open-air theatre. Germany. 1700-1994. Lang.: Eng. 442
Modern dance and site-specific performance. Denmark. 1970-1998. Lang.: Dan. 1257
Theatre SKAM's production of *Louis and Dave* in a Plymouth Volaré. Canada: Victoria, BC. 1996. Lang.: Eng. 1797
The building of an ideal operatic stage in a disused limestone quarry. Sweden: Rättvik. 1997. Lang.: Swe. 4497
Performance/production
Performance artist Leslie Hill's *Push the Boat Out.* UK-England: London. USA. 1995-1997. Lang.: Eng. 4245
Fountain, Tim
Performance/production
Collection of newspaper reviews by London theatre critics. UK-England: London. 1998. Lang.: Eng. 2475
Four
Performance/production
Collection of newspaper reviews by London theatre critics. UK-England: London. 1998. Lang.: Eng. 2549
Four Temperaments, The
Performance/production
Interviews with dancers about performance. UK-England. USA. Cuba. 1942-1989. Lang.: Eng. 1162
Theory/criticism
The use of different analytical strategies to obtain multiple readings of dance performance. USA. Europe. 1946-1982. Lang.: Eng. 1200
Fourberies de Scapin, Les (Tricks of Scapin, The)
Performance/production
Social context of French and Canadian productions of *Les Fourberies de Scapin* by Molière. Canada: Montreal, PQ. France: Paris. 1998. Lang.: Fre. 1842
Director Jacques Copeau and his theatrical aesthetic. France. 1913-1920. Lang.: Eng. 1941
Fourteen Songs, Two Weddings and a Funeral
Performance/production
Collection of newspaper reviews by London theatre critics. UK-England: London. 1998. Lang.: Eng. 2541
Fowles, John
Plays/librettos/scripts
The film adaptation by Harold Pinter and Karel Reisz of *The French Lieutenant's Woman* by John Fowles. UK-England. USA. 1982. Lang.: Eng. 3982
Fox, John
Institutions
Interview with John Fox of Welfare State International. UK-England: Ulverston. 1968-1988. Lang.: Eng. 4236
Foxhole
Performance/production
Collection of newspaper reviews by London theatre critics. UK-England: London. 1998. Lang.: Eng. 2478
Foy, Ken
Performance spaces
A modular stage used for touring by the Houston Grand Opera. USA: Houston, TX. 1998. Lang.: Eng. 4500
Foyer
Performance spaces
The architecture of the Bass Performance Hall. USA: Ft. Worth, TX. 1998. Lang.: Eng. 477
Fragmenting Red
Performance/production
Collection of newspaper reviews by London theatre critics. UK-England: London. 1998. Lang.: Eng. 2427
Fragments from a Language of Love
Performance/production
Collection of newspaper reviews by London theatre critics. UK-England: London. 1998. Lang.: Eng. 2572
Francis, Dominic
Performance/production
Collection of newspaper reviews by London theatre critics. UK-England: London. 1998. Lang.: Eng. 2411
Francis, Matthew
Performance/production
Collection of newspaper reviews by London theatre critics. UK-England: London. 1998. Lang.: Eng. 2475
Franck, Hans
Plays/librettos/scripts
The relationship between writers Hans Franck and Gerhart Hauptmann. Germany. 1910-1948. Lang.: Ger. 3127
Frandsen, Erik
Performance/production
Collection of newspaper reviews by London theatre critics. UK-England. 1998. Lang.: Eng. 2489
Frank and Stein
Institutions
Profile of Nordhessisches Landestheater Marburg. Germany: Marburg. 1997-1998. Lang.: Ger. 1653
Frank Productions (Brisbane)
Performance/production
The training of actors in Asian performance styles. Australia: Brisbane. 1992-1998. Lang.: Eng. 1817
Frank, Scott
Basic theatrical documents
Screenplay of *Out of Sight* by Scott Frank. USA. 1998. Lang.: Eng. 3884
Performance/production
Steven Soderbergh on directing *Out of Sight.* USA. 1998. Lang.: Eng. 3944
Plays/librettos/scripts
Interview with screenwriter Scott Frank. USA. 1998. Lang.: Eng. 3995
Frankel, Kenneth
Performance/production
Obituaries for Roger L. Stevens, Kenneth Frankel, Donald Davis, and Edith Oliver. USA. Canada. 1910-1998. Lang.: Eng. 2742

Franken, Rose
Plays/librettos/scripts
The Broadway success of women playwrights. USA. 1906-1944. Lang.: Eng. 3590
Frankenstein
Institutions
New productions of Düsseldorfer Schauspielhaus. Germany: Dusseldorf. 1998. Lang.: Ger. 1654
Frankfurter Schauspielhaus (Frankfurt)
Audience
The relationship between theatres and the youth audience. Germany. 1998. Lang.: Ger. 152
Institutions
Director training at Ernst-Busch-Schule and some of its graduates. Germany: Berlin. 1972-1998. Lang.: Ger. 1648
Performance/production
Productions directed by Christian Stückl, Tom Kühnel, and Robert Schuster. Germany: Frankfurt. 1997-1998. Lang.: Ger. 1969
Recent productions of plays by Bertolt Brecht. Germany. 1997-1998. Lang.: Ger. 2028
Productions of plays by Shakespeare, Brecht, and Camus. Germany. 1998. Lang.: Ger. 2032
Frankfurter Theater (Frankfurt)
Performance/production
The police and John Cage's *Europeras 1 and 2* at Frankfurter Theater. Germany: Frankfurt. 1987. Lang.: Eng. 4586
Franklin, Frederic
Performance/production
Tributes to ballerina Alexandra Danilova. USA: New York, NY. 1997. Lang.: Eng. 1165
Frantic Assembly (Swansea)
Performance/production
Collection of newspaper reviews by London theatre critics. UK-England: London. 1998. Lang.: Eng. 2448
Franzén, Ann Charlotte
Institutions
Profile of independent feminist theatre Kvinnliga Dramatiska Teatern. Sweden: Stockholm. 1997-1998. Lang.: Swe. 1725
Franziska
Performance/production
Collection of newspaper reviews by London theatre critics. UK-England: London. Lang.: Eng. 2408
Fraser-Munro, Ronald
Performance/production
Collection of newspaper reviews by London theatre critics. UK-England: London. 1998. Lang.: Eng. 2427
Fraser, Brad
Plays/librettos/scripts
Brad Fraser's direction of a film version of his *Poor Superman.* Canada. 1994-1998. Lang.: Eng. 3966
Fraser, Gilly
Performance/production
Collection of newspaper reviews by London theatre critics. UK-England: London. 1998. Lang.: Eng. 2581
Fraser, Mary
Performance/production
Theatrical component of Japan's UK98 Festival. Japan: Tokyo. 1994-1998. Lang.: Eng. 2192
Frau ohne Schatten, Die
Performance/production
Recordings of Strauss's *Die Frau ohne Schatten.* Europe. 1954. Lang.: Swe. 4554
Plays/librettos/scripts
Strauss's *Die Frau ohne Schatten* and a recent production by Giuseppe Sinopoli. Germany. 1917-1998. Lang.: Swe. 4795
Frauenthal Theatre (Muskegon, MI)
Design/technology
The new sound system of the Frauenthal Theatre. USA: Muskegon, MI. 1998. Lang.: Eng. 300
Fräulein Danzer (Miss Danzer)
Plays/librettos/scripts
Analysis of plays by Marius von Mayenburg. Germany. 1972-1998. Lang.: Ger. 3131
Frayn, Michael
Performance/production
Director Angela Brodauf. Germany: Dortmund. 1984-1998. Lang.: Ger. 1989
Collection of newspaper reviews by London theatre critics. UK-England: London. 1998. Lang.: Eng. 2501
Collection of newspaper reviews by London theatre critics. UK-England: London. 1998. Lang.: Eng. 2505
Fredén, Sofia
Plays/librettos/scripts
Interview with playwright Sofia Fredén. Sweden: Stockholm. Denmark: Copenhagen. 1995-1998. Lang.: Swe. 3409
Fredro, Aleksander
Performance/production
Actor/director Aleksander Zelwerowicz. Poland: Vilna. 1929-1931. Lang.: Pol. 2223
Free Southern Theatre (New Orleans, LA)
Administration
Obituary for Tom Dent, former chairman of the Free Southern Theatre board. USA: New Orleans, LA. 1998. Lang.: Eng. 1395
Institutions
The mission and management of the Free Southern Theatre. USA: New Orleans, LA. 1963-1980. Lang.: Eng. 1769
Free, Richard
Performance/production
Collection of newspaper reviews by London theatre critics. UK-England: London. 1998. Lang.: Eng. 2436
Freed, Amy
Design/technology
Design concept for Amy Freed's *The Psychic Life of Savages*, Wilma Theatre. USA: Philadelphia, PA. 1998. Lang.: Eng. 1555
Plays/librettos/scripts
Playwright Amy Freed. USA. 1998. Lang.: Eng. 3717
Freedman, Gerald
Performance/production
Director Gerald Freedman on 'real' theatre. USA: Birmingham, AL. 1998. Lang.: Eng. 684
Freedman, Harris W.
Performance/production
Collection of newspaper reviews by London theatre critics. UK-England: London. 1998. Lang.: Eng. 2516
Freedman, Sylvia
Performance/production
Collection of newspaper reviews by London theatre critics. UK-England: London. 1998. Lang.: Eng. 2552
Freedomland
Plays/librettos/scripts
Playwright Amy Freed. USA. 1998. Lang.: Eng. 3717
Freeman, David
Institutions
The inaugural season of Shakespeare's Globe Theatre. UK-England: London. 1997-1998. Lang.: Eng. 1741
Performance/production
Collection of newspaper reviews by London theatre critics. UK-England: London. 1998. Lang.: Eng. 2457
The inaugural season of Shakespeare's Globe Theatre. UK-England: London. 1997. Lang.: Eng. 2601
Freeman, Deborah
Performance/production
Collection of newspaper reviews by London theatre critics. UK-England: London. 1998. Lang.: Eng. 2480
Frei Luís de Sousa (Pilgrim, The)
Performance/production
Collection of newspaper reviews by London theatre critics. UK-England: London. 1998. Lang.: Eng. 2490
Freie Kammerspiele (Magdeburg)
Administration
Dramaturg Hans-Peter Frings on his role in the theatre. Germany: Magdeburg. 1990-1998. Lang.: Ger. 1382
Design/technology
Scenographer and now director Klaus Noack. Germany. 1953. Lang.: Ger. 190
Freie Volksbühne (Berlin)
SEE ALSO
Volksbühne.
Freihaus Theater (Vienna)
Performance/production
Mozart's operas and contemporary Viennese performance spaces. Austria: Vienna. 1782-1791. Lang.: Eng. 4528
Freiheit in Krähwinkel (Freedom in Krähwinkel)
Plays/librettos/scripts
Recent productions directed by Frank Castorf. Austria: Vienna. 1998. Lang.: Ger. 2788
Freischütz, Der
Performance/production
Weber's *Der Freischütz* and the Neues Schauspielhaus. Germany: Berlin. 1821. Lang.: Eng. 4581

Fremde Mädchen, Das (Foreign Girl, The)
Performance/production
Collaborative Symbolist dance/theatre projects. Europe. USA. 1916-1934. Lang.: Eng. 1268
Fremdes Haus (Stranger's House)
Institutions
New plays by Dea Loher at Staatsschauspiel Hannover. Germany: Hannover. 1992-1998. Lang.: Ger. 1643
Plays/librettos/scripts
Analysis of *Fremdes Haus (Strangers House)* by Dea Loher. Germany. 1998. Lang.: Ger. 3161
Marginal notes by Dea Loher on her plays. Germany. 1991-1998. Lang.: Ger. 3162
French Classicism
SEE
Neoclassicism.
French Lieutenant's Woman, The
Plays/librettos/scripts
The film adaptation by Harold Pinter and Karel Reisz of *The French Lieutenant's Woman* by John Fowles. UK-England. USA. 1982. Lang.: Eng. 3982
French, Arthur
Performance/production
Actor Arthur French. USA: New York, NY. 1962-1998. Lang.: Eng. 2671
French, Harold
Performance/production
Actor and director Harold French. UK-England: London. 1900-1998. Lang.: Eng. 2614
Frenkel, Vera
Performance/production
Brief biographies of performance artists. 1963-1988. Lang.: Eng. 4238
Fresh Blood—A Dream Morphology
Performance/production
Interview with performance artist Carolee Schneemann. USA. 1964-1989. Lang.: Eng. 4257
Freyer, Achim
Performance/production
Reviews of recent opera productions. Switzerland: Basel. Germany: Stuttgart, Berlin, Hamburg. France: Strasbourg. 1997-1998. Lang.: Ger. 4702
Freytag, Holk
Performance/production
Comparison of productions of Brecht's *Die Massnahme (The Measures Taken)*. Germany: Berlin, Wuppertal. 1995-1998. Lang.: Ger. 1950
Reviews of German Shakespearean productions. Germany: Wuppertal, Cologne, Oberhausen. 1998. Lang.: Ger. 2017
Relation to other fields
Revivals of Hanns Johst's national socialist play *Schlageter*. Germany: Uelzen, Wuppertal. 1977-1992. Lang.: Ger. 3770
Friar Bacon and Friar Bungay
Plays/librettos/scripts
Analysis of *Friar Bacon and Friar Bungay* by Robert Greene. England. 1594. Lang.: Eng. 2974
Fricke, Heinz
Performance/production
Heinz Fricke, music director of Washington Opera. USA: Washington, DC. 1993-1998. Lang.: Eng. 4734
Fricsay Kali Son, András
Performance/production
German productions of adaptations of *A Clockwork Orange* by Anthony Burgess. Germany: Dresden, Hamburg, Stendal. 1998. Lang.: Ger. 1972
Friday Night Theatre Group (Toronto, ON)
Plays/librettos/scripts
Political community theatre by South Indian emigrants. Canada: Toronto, ON, Montreal, PQ. India. 1984-1998. Lang.: Eng. 2821
Fridell, Lena
Performance/production
Conference on theatre for children ages 2-4. Sweden: Stockholm. 1998. Lang.: Swe. 2368
Friedland, Dahlia
Performance/production
Collection of newspaper reviews by London theatre critics. UK-England: London. 1998. Lang.: Eng. 2467
Friedman, Jane
Performance/production
Seven critics on their favorite character or portrayal. Sweden. 1950. Lang.: Swe. 2369
Friedman, Joel Phillip
Performance/production
Collection of newspaper reviews by London theatre critics. UK-England: London. 1998. Lang.: Eng. 2492
Friedman, Seth
Performance/production
Collection of newspaper reviews by London theatre critics. UK-England: London. 1998. Lang.: Eng. 2492
Friedrich, Götz
Design/technology
Lighting for Henze's opera *Der Prinz von Homburg* at Deutsche Oper Berlin. Germany: Berlin. 1997. Lang.: Ger. 4431
Friel, Brian
Performance/production
Collection of newspaper reviews by London theatre critics. UK-England: London. 1998. Lang.: Eng. 2451
Collection of newspaper reviews by London theatre critics. UK-England: London. 1998. Lang.: Eng. 2484
Collection of newspaper reviews by London theatre critics. UK-England: London. 1998. Lang.: Eng. 2530
Collection of newspaper reviews by London theatre critics. UK-England. 1998. Lang.: Eng. 2558
Plays/librettos/scripts
Analysis of *Translations* by Brian Friel. Ireland. 1980. Lang.: Eng. 3197
Brian Friel's plays and the Field Day Theatre Company. UK-Ireland. 1980-1988. Lang.: Eng. 3512
Friel, Judy
Performance/production
Recent productions in Ireland of plays by Eugene O'Neill. Ireland: Dublin. UK-Ireland: Belfast. 1989-1998. Lang.: Eng. 2154
Frindley, David
Performance/production
Collection of newspaper reviews by London theatre critics. UK-England: London. 1998. Lang.: Eng. 2482
Fringe theatre
SEE ALSO
Alternative theatre.
Frings, Hans-Peter
Administration
Dramaturg Hans-Peter Frings on his role in the theatre. Germany: Magdeburg. 1990-1998. Lang.: Ger. 1382
Frisch, Max
Performance/production
Collection of newspaper reviews by London theatre critics. UK-England: London. 1998. Lang.: Eng. 2442
Frisell, Karl-Gunnar
Design/technology
Obituary for Karl-Gunnar Frisell, who oversaw the technical restoration of Södra Teatern. Sweden: Solna. 1920-1998. Lang.: Swe. 226
Fritsch, Herbert
Performance/production
Actor Herbert Fritsch. Germany. 1992-1998. Lang.: Ger. 1985
Fritsch, Werner
Performance/production
Premieres of plays on the Nazi theme. Germany: Darmstadt. Austria: Vienna. 1998. Lang.: Ger. 2030
Fröding, Gustaf
Institutions
Profile of Svensk Symbolisk Teater. Sweden: Malmö. 1997. Lang.: Swe. 1728
Fröhliche Weinberg, Der (Happy Vineyard, The)
Audience
Audience response to Bronnen's *Der Vatermord (Parricide)* and German culture. Germany: Frankfurt. 1922. Lang.: Eng. 1403
Fröken Julie (Miss Julie)
Performance/production
Collection of newspaper reviews by London theatre critics. UK-England: London. 1998. Lang.: Eng. 2495
Fröman, Georg
Performance spaces
Excerpts from the diary of the builder of Drottningholms Slottsteater. Sweden: Stockholm. 1755-1766. Lang.: Swe. 458
Front, Jeremy
Performance/production
Collection of newspaper reviews by London theatre critics. UK-England: London. 1998. Lang.: Eng. 2475
Frontera Theatre (Austin, TX)
Institutions
Vicky Boone, artistic director of Frontera Theatre. USA: Austin, TX. 1998. Lang.: Eng. 1759

Froomkin, Joel
Performance/production
Collection of newspaper reviews by London theatre critics. UK-England: London. 1998. Lang.: Eng. 2483
Collection of newspaper reviews by London theatre critics. UK-England: London. 1998. Lang.: Eng. 2491
Froschkönigin, Die (Frog Princess, The)
Plays/librettos/scripts
Kerstin Specht's *Die Froschkönigin (The Frog Princess)* and its premiere at Staatstheater Stuttgart. Germany: Stuttgart. 1998. Lang.: Ger. 3174
Frost, Sue
Administration
Interviews with women in top management of theatres. USA: New Haven, CT, Seattle, WA, East Haddam, CT. 1998. Lang.: Eng. 1397
Frostensson, Katarina
Performance/production
Reactions to the opera *Staden* by Sven-David Sandström and Katarina Frostensson. Sweden: Stockholm. 1998. Lang.: Swe. 4699
Plays/librettos/scripts
Interview with opera composer Sven-David Sandström. Sweden: Stockholm. 1998. Lang.: Swe. 4821
Fruen fra havet (Lady from the Sea, The)
Plays/librettos/scripts
Ibsen, translation, and feminine discourse. Norway. 1888. Lang.: Eng. 3295
Andreas-Salomé's view of Ibsen's female characters. Norway. Germany. 1879-1906. Lang.: Eng. 3296
Trolls in the late plays of Ibsen. Norway. 1886-1894. Lang.: Eng. 3298
Fry, Christopher
Plays/librettos/scripts
Analysis of plays based on the Hebrew prophets. USA. Europe. 1919-1970. Lang.: Eng. 3659
Fry, Michael
Performance/production
Collection of newspaper reviews by London theatre critics. UK-England: London. 1998. Lang.: Eng. 2466
Collection of newspaper reviews by London theatre critics. UK-England: London. 1998. Lang.: Eng. 2541
Fuchs, Lívia
Performance/production
The importance of workshops in dance. Hungary: Budapest. 1960-1990. Lang.: Hun. 951
Fuente ovejuna (Sheep Well, The)
Plays/librettos/scripts
Playwright Lope de Vega. Spain. 1562-1635. Lang.: Eng. 3377
Fugard, Athol
Performance/production
Market Theatre productions of plays by Athol Fugard. South Africa, Republic of. 1993-1994. Lang.: Eng. 2351
Athol Fugard and the *Oresteia* of Aeschylus. South Africa, Republic of: Cape Town. 1978. Lang.: Eng. 2354
Plays/librettos/scripts
Rhetorical analysis of works by Athol Fugard and Nadine Gordimer. South Africa, Republic of. 1958-1988. Lang.: Eng. 3361
The influence of Albert Camus on playwright Athol Fugard. South Africa, Republic of. 1960-1985. Lang.: Eng. 3362
Post-apartheid analysis of plays by Athol Fugard. South Africa, Republic of. 1991-1998. Lang.: Eng. 3364
Független Színpad (Szeged)
Performance/production
Interview with director József Ruszt. Hungary. 1963-1997. Lang.: Hun. 2115
Fuhrmann Henschel (Drayman Henschel)
Performance/production
Hauptmann's *Fuhrmann Henschel (Drayman Henschel)* and realism. Germany. 1899-1933. Lang.: Eng. 1970
Hauptmann's *Fuhrmann Henschel (Drayman Henschel)* directed by Sándor Zsótér. Hungary: Budapest. 1997. Lang.: Hun. 2088
Fujimoto, Takayuki
Performance/production
Collection of newspaper reviews by London theatre critics. UK-England: London. 1998. Lang.: Eng. 2512
Fuld, Catherine Elina
Relation to other fields
The creation and use of ritual theatre for drama therapy. USA. 1997. Lang.: Eng. 3787
Fulgens and Lucrece
Performance/production
Music in Tudor drama. England. 1497-1569. Lang.: Eng. 1902
Full Gallop
Performance/production
Collection of newspaper reviews by London theatre critics. UK-England: London. 1998. Lang.: Eng. 2491
Full Monty, The
Basic theatrical documents
Text of Simon Beaufoy's screenplay *The Full Monty*. UK-England. 1997. Lang.: Eng. 3879
Plays/librettos/scripts
Interview with Simon Beaufoy, author of *The Full Monty*. UK-England. 1997. Lang.: Eng. 3979
Observations on screenwriting and Beaufoy's *The Full Monty*. UK-England. 1997. Lang.: Eng. 3989
Fuller, Charles
Plays/librettos/scripts
Afrocentricity in plays of Charles Fuller, Amiri Baraka, and Larry Neal. USA. 1960-1998. Lang.: Eng. 3519
Fuller, Loie
Performance spaces
Dancers and performance space. Europe. 1895-1937. Lang.: Ger. 909
Performance/production
Dancer and choreographer Brygida Ochaim. Germany. France. 1970-1998. Lang.: Ger. 1283
Modern dance and the female body. USA. Europe. 1900-1930. Lang.: Eng. 1321
Fuller, Marty
Design/technology
Profile of technicians for Grammy Awards television broadcast. USA: New York, NY. 1998. Lang.: Eng. 4056
Fuller, Samuel
Basic theatrical documents
Screenplay for *Pickup on South Street* by Sam Fuller. USA. 1953. Lang.: Eng. 3885
Screenplay for *Shock Corridor* by Sam Fuller. USA. 1963. Lang.: Eng. 3886
Performance/production
Excerpts from notes and diaries of film maker Sam Fuller. USA. 1937-1994. Lang.: Eng. 3942
Sam Fuller's career as a film maker. USA. 1912-1997. Lang.: Eng. 3943
Sam Fuller 'interviews' a canine actor from *White Dog*. USA. 1982. Lang.: Eng. 3945
The career of action film maker Sam Fuller. USA. 1937-1994. Lang.: Eng. 3951
Funding
Administration
Interview with John Tusa, managing director of the Barbican Centre. UK-England: London. 1996-1998. Lang.: Eng. 24
Report on the ARTNOW arts advocacy demonstration. USA: Washington, DC. 1997. Lang.: Eng. 29
The ARTNOW demonstration. USA: Washington, DC. 1997. Lang.: Eng. 132
External fundraising for theatre arts programs. USA. 1985-1987. Lang.: Eng. 133
Arts Minister on the current state of dance, training, and funding. UK-England. 1998. Lang.: Eng. 884
Financially troubled Ohio ballet companies. USA: Cleveland, OH, Akron, OH. 1998. Lang.: Eng. 1027
Institutions
Financial and artistic success of Kennedy Center and New Jersey Performing Arts Center. USA: Washington, DC, Newark, NJ. 1971-1998. Lang.: Eng. 424
The growth of regional dance companies. USA. 1963-1998. Lang.: Eng. 908
Profile of Pennsylvania Ballet. USA: Philadelphia, PA. 1970-1998. Lang.: Eng. 1058
Profile of Women's Circus. Australia: Melbourne. 1990-1998. Lang.: Eng. 1568
Profile of Watermill Theatre. UK-England: Newbury. 1998. Lang.: Eng. 1744
Funding status of London's fringe theatres. UK-England: London. 1998. Lang.: Eng. 1748
TCG annual report. USA. 1997-1998. Lang.: Eng. 1753
Fiscal survey of not-for-profit theatre. USA. 1997. Lang.: Eng. 1754
Bonnie Monte of New Jersey Shakespeare Festival. USA: Madison, NJ. 1996-1998. Lang.: Eng. 1772

Funding, corporate
Administration
New funding options for Romanian arts groups. Romania. 1989-1998. Lang.: Eng. 20
The decline in corporate funding for the arts. USA. 1980-1988. Lang.: Eng. 32
The role of Riverfront Arts Center in revitalizing Wilmington's riverfront. USA: Wilmington, DE. 1998. Lang.: Eng. 123
Institutions
The partnership between San Francisco Opera and Chase Manhattan Bank. USA: San Francisco, CA, New York, NY. 1998. Lang.: Eng. 423
Funding, government
Administration
The role of government in audience and marketing development for arts organizations. 1996. Lang.: Eng. 1
Economic forces and the Australian theatre industry. Australia. 1990-1998. Lang.: Eng. 2
Comparative analysis of national cultural policies. Canada. France. Germany. Norway. 1905-1998. Lang.: Eng. 4
The system of subsidized theatre in Germany, and suggestions for changing it. Germany. 1989-1998. Lang.: Ger. 13
New funding options for Romanian arts groups. Romania. 1989-1998. Lang.: Eng. 20
The nomination of William J. Ivey as head of NEA. USA. 1998. Lang.: Eng. 59
The commitment to arts funding by cities that sponsor major league sports. USA. 1989-1998. Lang.: Eng. 125
The cancellation of Kansas University's cultural exchange program with Eastern Europe. USA: Lawrence, KS. Europe. 1964-1969. Lang.: Eng. 131
The effect of outcome analysis and impact studies on cultural policy. USA. 1998. Lang.: Eng. 136
American and Japanese cultural policy. USA. Japan. 1949-1998. Lang.: Eng. 141
Riksteatern and Dansens Hus' Dansbiennal 98 meeting with government officials. Sweden. 1998. Lang.: Swe. 881
Sweden's new dance funding program. Sweden. 1998. Lang.: Swe. 883
Arts Minister on the current state of dance, training, and funding. UK-England. 1998. Lang.: Eng. 884
How Chisenhale Dance Space coped with loss of funding. UK-England: London. 1998. Lang.: Eng. 885
Alternative funding strategies for dance companies. USA. 1998. Lang.: Eng. 886
Interviews with theatre managers regarding the changing cultural landscape. Germany: Bruchsal, Esslingen, Tübingen. 1998. Lang.: Ger. 1381
The closing of Göteborgs Stadsteatern. Sweden. 1974-1997. Lang.: Dan. 1389
Theatre directors on the future of subsidized theatre. Switzerland: Zurich. Germany: Hannover, Berlin. 1998. Lang.: Ger. 1390
Institutions
The theatre program of the National Endowment for the Arts. USA. 1965-1988. Lang.: Eng. 391
Proposal for changes in the mission of the National Endowment for the Arts. USA. 1998. Lang.: Eng. 397
William J. Ivey, nominee for chair of NEA. USA: Washington, DC. 1998. Lang.: Eng. 420
The status of the National Endowment for the Arts. USA: Washington, DC. 1997-2000. Lang.: Eng. 422
American Ballet Theatre and diminishing government support. USA: New York, NY. 1998. Lang.: Eng. 1059
The Mummers' Troupe and the Canada Council. Canada: St. John's, NF. 1972-1982. Lang.: Eng. 1581
Profile of Landestheater Württemberg-Hohenzollern. Germany: Tübingen. 1996-1997. Lang.: Ger. 1634
Performance/production
Futurism, Fascism, and Italian theatre. Italy. 1919-1940. Lang.: Eng. 545
The prospects for Danish modern dance. Denmark. 1998. Lang.: Dan. 1267
Plays/librettos/scripts
Interview with playwright Rod Dungate. UK-England: Birmingham. 1998. Lang.: Eng. 3442
Analysis of performance art on *The Larry Sanders Show*. USA. 1995. Lang.: Eng. 4079
Relation to other fields
Theatre in Danish cultural policy. Denmark. 1990-1998. Lang.: Dan. 724
Government and budget cuts in German theatres. Germany: Bochum, Cologne. 1991-1998. Lang.: Ger. 738
The current status of English cultural policy. UK-England. 1997-1998. Lang.: Ger. 769
Cultural policy and French theatre structures. France. 1945-1998. Lang.: Ger. 3760
The upcoming Supreme Court hearing on the government's right to impose decency standards on arts grants. USA: Washington, DC. 1998. Lang.: Eng. 3793
Training
Playwright Tony Kushner's address to the Association of Theatre in Higher Education. USA. 1997. Lang.: Eng. 3851
Funding, private
Administration
On the history of arts patronage. Poland. 1998. Lang.: Rus. 19
New funding options for Romanian arts groups. Romania. 1989-1998. Lang.: Eng. 20
Workplace solicitation for contributions to the arts. USA. 1998. Lang.: Eng. 124
How Chisenhale Dance Space coped with loss of funding. UK-England: London. 1998. Lang.: Eng. 885
Alternative funding strategies for dance companies. USA. 1998. Lang.: Eng. 886
Relation to other fields
Cultural policy and French theatre structures. France. 1945-1998. Lang.: Ger. 3760
Fundraising
Administration
Performance in fundraising. USA: New York, NY. 1998. Lang.: Eng. 34
Fundraising on the World Wide Web. USA. 1998. Lang.: Eng. 41
Reports on the 10th Anniversary of Broadway Cares/Equity Fights AIDS. USA: New York, NY. 1998. Lang.: Eng. 52
Report on Easter Bonnet fundraiser for AIDS. USA: New York, NY. 1998. Lang.: Eng. 72
Flea Market fundraiser for AIDS. USA: New York, NY. 1998. Lang.: Eng. 109
Celebrities as spokespersons for non-profits. USA. 1998. Lang.: Eng. 117
Suggestions for fundraising events. USA. 1998. Lang.: Eng. 122
Workplace solicitation for contributions to the arts. USA. 1998. Lang.: Eng. 124
Dictionary of fundraising letters. USA. 1998. Lang.: Eng. 128
The importance of maintaining an up-to-date fundraising data base. USA. 1998. Lang.: Eng. 130
External fundraising for theatre arts programs. USA. 1985-1987. Lang.: Eng. 133
Institutions
The Vienna-based foundation for the development of Moscow's Bolšoj Theatre. Austria: Vienna. 1998. Lang.: Rus. 335
Funeral Games
Performance/production
Collection of newspaper reviews by London theatre critics. UK-England: London. 1998. Lang.: Eng. 2477
Funicello, Ralph
Design/technology
Creativity and beauty in theatrical design. USA. 1998. Lang.: Eng. 322
Funny Girl
Design/technology
Costume designs by Irene Sharaff. USA. 1933-1976. Lang.: Eng. 277
Funny Money
Basic theatrical documents
French translation of *Funny Money* by Ray Cooney. UK-England. France. 1995-1997. Lang.: Fre. 1473
Funnyhouse of a Negro
Plays/librettos/scripts
The dramaturgical evolution of playwright Adrienne Kennedy. USA. 1964-1990. Lang.: Eng. 3691
Funtek, Anton
Plays/librettos/scripts
Social roles and ideologies in plays of Anton Funtek and Ivo Šorli. Slovenia. 1897-1920. Lang.: Slo. 3353
Fura dels Baus, La (Barcelona)
Performance/production
Truth and authenticity in *M.T.M.* by La Fura dels Baus. Spain: Barcelona. 1983-1998. Lang.: Eng. 598

Fura dels Baus, La (Barcelona) — cont'd

Collection of newspaper reviews by London theatre critics. UK-England: London. 1998. Lang.: Eng. 2473

Furioso all'isola di San Domingo, Il
Plays/librettos/scripts
The use of the tenor in operas of Donizetti. Italy. 1816-1845. Lang.: Eng. 4802

Furnivall, Frederick
Plays/librettos/scripts
The New Shakespeare Society's unfinished four-text edition of *Hamlet*. UK-England. 1882-1883. Lang.: Eng. 3497

Furtwängler, Wilhelm
Performance/production
Historical overview of Wagnerian singing. Germany: Bayreuth. 1850-1998. Lang.: Eng. 4610

Furukawa, Anzu
Training
Dance teaching methods of Anzu Furukawa. Finland. 1998. Lang.: Fin. 1017

Fusco, Coco
Performance/production
Analysis of Guillermo Gómez-Peña and Coco Fusco's performance piece *The Couple in the Cage*. USA. 1995. Lang.: Eng. 4255
Background on *The Couple in the Cage* by Guillermo Gómez-Peña and Coco Fusco. USA. 1992-1995. Lang.: Eng. 4259

Futurism
Performance/production
Futurism, Fascism, and Italian theatre. Italy. 1919-1940. Lang.: Eng. 545
The early life and career of F.T. Marinetti, leader of the Futurist movement. Italy. 1876-1909. Lang.: Eng. 551
Performance culture in prerevolutionary Russia. Russia. 1910-1915. Lang.: Eng. 580

Fydrych, Waldemar
Institutions
The Orange Alternative, a street theatre opponent of martial law. Poland: Wroclaw. 1981-1988. Lang.: Eng. 375

Gaál, Erzsébet
Performance/production
Čechov's *Platonov* as adapted and directed by Erzsébet Gaál. Hungary: Budapest. 1997. Lang.: Hun. 2082
Tribute to the late actress and director Erzsébet Gaál. Hungary. 1951-1998. Lang.: Hun. 2141
Profile of actor-director Erzsébet Gaál. Hungary. 1951-1998. Lang.: Hun. 2147

Gabold, Anne-Lise
Training
Anne-Lise Gabold's use of the methods of Tadashi Suzuki in her production of Euripides' *Bákchai (The Bacchae)*. Japan. Denmark: Copenhagen. 1960-1998. Lang.: Dan. 1359

Gábor, László
Performance/production
Lilla Pártay's *Meztelen rózsa (Naked Rose)*, a ballet based on the life of Nižinskij. Hungary: Budapest. 1998. Lang.: Hun. 1110

Gábor, Miklós
Performance/production
Reviews and photos from the career of the late actor Miklós Gábor. Hungary. 1948-1998. Lang.: Hun. 2055
Excerpt from an illustrated novel by actor Miklós Gábor. Hungary. 1971. Lang.: Hun. 2076
Obituary for actor Miklós Gábor. Hungary. 1919-1998. Lang.: Hun. 2093
Director József Ruszt recalls actor Miklós Gábor. Hungary. 1919-1998. Lang.: Hun. 2120

Gaddes, James
Performance/production
Collection of newspaper reviews by London theatre critics. UK-England: London. 1998. Lang.: Eng. 2579

Gaft, Valentin
Relation to other fields
The poetry of actors Leonid Filatov and Valentin Gaft. Russia: Moscow. 1998. Lang.: Rus. 758

Gagliano, Lynne
Performance/production
Collection of newspaper reviews by London theatre critics. UK-England: London. 1998. Lang.: Eng. 2464

Gagnon, Denise
Performance/production
Interview with actress Denise Gagnon. Canada: Quebec, PQ. 1958-1998. Lang.: Fre. 1864

Gaiety Theatre (Budapest)
SEE
Vígszínház.

Gaiety Theatre (Manchester)
Performance/production
Experimental Shakespeare production at the Gaiety Theatre. UK-England: Manchester. 1908-1915. Lang.: Eng. 2605

Gaiety Theatre (Yokohama)
Performance/production
George Crichton Miln's touring Shakespearean company in Japan. USA: Chicago, IL. Japan: Yokohama. 1882. Lang.: Eng. 2702

Gaines, Barbara
Performance/production
Hamlet at Shakespeare Repertory Theatre, directed by Barbara Gaines. USA: Chicago, IL. 1996. Lang.: Eng. 2666

Gala, Antonio
Plays/librettos/scripts
Jewish characters in Spanish drama. Spain. 1400-1950. Lang.: Spa. 3402

Galambos, Tibor
Institutions
History of the folk dance ensemble Erkel Néptáncegyüttes. Hungary. 1948-1998. Lang.: Hun. 1220

Galas, Diamanda
Plays/librettos/scripts
Analysis of *Plague Mass* by Diamanda Galas. USA. 1991. Lang.: Eng. 4828

Galati, Frank
Design/technology
Lighting and projections for the musical *Ragtime*. USA: New York, NY. 1998. Lang.: Eng. 4328
Technical designs for *Ragtime* at the Ford Center. USA: New York, NY. 1998. Lang.: Eng. 4338
Eugene Lee's set design for Frank Galati's production of *Ragtime*. USA. 1997-1998. Lang.: Eng. 4340
Sound design for the Broadway premiere of the musical *Ragtime*. USA: New York, NY. 1998. Lang.: Eng. 4341

Gale, George A.
Design/technology
Costume design for revival of *As Thousands Cheer* by Drama Dept. USA: New York, NY. 1998. Lang.: Eng. 4333

Galgóczy, Judit
Performance/production
Mozart's *Le Nozze di Figaro* at the Hungarian State Opera House. Hungary: Budapest. 1998. Lang.: Hun. 4638

Gallagher, Richard
Performance/production
Collection of newspaper reviews by London theatre critics. UK-England: London. 1998. Lang.: Eng. 2487

Gallathea
Plays/librettos/scripts
Analysis of *Gallathea* by John Lyly. England. 1584. Lang.: Eng. 2888

Gallet, Louis
Basic theatrical documents
The libretto to Jules Massenet's *Le Roi de Lahore*. France. 1877. Lang.: Fre. 4417
Performance/production
Premieres of Massenet's *Le Roi de Lahore*. 1877-1923. Lang.: Fre. 4521
Vocal requirements and recording of Massenet's *Le Roi de Lahore*. 1979. Lang.: Fre. 4525
The creation of Massenet's opera *Le Roi de Lahore*. France. 1877. Lang.: Fre. 4568
Plays/librettos/scripts
Collaboration of composer Jules Massenet and librettist Louis Gallet. France. 1877-1894. Lang.: Fre. 4778

Galli-Bibiena, Carlo
Design/technology
Reconstruction of a performance of *A Midsummer Night's Dream* designed by Galli-Bibiena. Germany: Bayreuth. 1997-1998. Lang.: Ger. 1521

Galli-Bibiena, Giuseppe
Design/technology
Reconstruction of a performance of *A Midsummer Night's Dream* designed by Galli-Bibiena. Germany: Bayreuth. 1997-1998. Lang.: Ger. 1521

Gallo, David
Design/technology
Professional theatrical designers on design training. USA. 1998. Lang.: Eng. 252

Gallo, David — cont'd
Set designer David Gallo. USA. 1988-1998. Lang.: Eng. 255
Gallodiert, Louis
Institutions
Profile of the Royal Swedish Ballet. Sweden: Stockholm. 1773-1998. Lang.: Hun. 1053
Gambaro, Griselda
Plays/librettos/scripts
Cruelty and the absurd in theatre of Latin American playwrights. Latin America. 1960-1980. Lang.: Eng. 3267
Genocide, theatre, and the human body. North America. UK-England. Argentina. 1998. Lang.: Eng. 3290
Gammer Gurton's Needle
Performance/production
Music in Tudor drama. England. 1497-1569. Lang.: Eng. 1902
Gammie, Gordon
Performance spaces
Theatre SKAM's production of *Louis and Dave* in a Plymouth Volaré. Canada: Victoria, BC. 1996. Lang.: Eng. 1797
Ganzalez de Busto, Francisco
Plays/librettos/scripts
Description of a Web site devoted to *Los espanñoles en Chile* by Francisco Ganzalez de Busto. Spain. 1665-1998. Lang.: Eng. 3366
Gao, Xingjian
Basic theatrical documents
Anthology of contemporary Chinese drama. China, People's Republic of. 1979-1986. Lang.: Eng. 1414
Plays/librettos/scripts
Beckett's influence on *Che zhan (The Bus Stop)* by Gao Xingjian. China, People's Republic of. 1983. Lang.: Eng. 2844
García Lorca, Federico
Performance/production
Hanne Tierney's adaptation of *Bodas de sangre (Blood Wedding)* by García Lorca. USA. 1997. Lang.: Eng. 647
Flamenco dancer and choreographer Carlota Santana. USA: New York, NY. 1998. Lang.: Eng. 1239
Roberto Ciulli's production of *Doña Rosita la Soltera (Doña Rosita the Spinster)* by Federico García Lorca. Germany: Munich. 1998. Lang.: Ger. 2021
Lorca's *Doña Rosita* directed by Gergő Kaszás. Hungary: Budapest. 1998. Lang.: Hun. 2099
Collection of newspaper reviews by London theatre critics. UK-England: London. 1998. Lang.: Eng. 2499
Collection of newspaper reviews by London theatre critics. UK-England: London. 1998. Lang.: Eng. 2586
Plays/librettos/scripts
Profile of playwright Federico García Lorca. Spain. 1930-1998. Lang.: Dut. 3368
Imagery in the plays of Federico García Lorca. Spain. 1920-1936. Lang.: Eng. 3380
Power and authority in the plays of García Lorca. Spain. 1920-1936. Lang.: Eng. 3386
The life and work of Federico García Lorca. Spain. 1898-1936. Lang.: Swe. 3393
The image of women on the Spanish stage. Spain. 1908-1936. Lang.: Eng. 3399
The influence of Federico García Lorca on playwright Bernardo Santareno. Spain. Portugal. 1919-1965. Lang.: Eng. 3400
Background on Lorca's *El Público (The Public)*, about to have its New York premiere. USA: New York, NY. 1930-1998. Lang.: Eng. 3651
Gardiner, Lizzy
Design/technology
Costumes for the film *Welcome to Woop Woop.* Australia. 1998. Lang.: Eng. 3899
Gárdonyi Géza Színház (Eger)
Performance/production
Madách's *Tragedy of Man* directed by Sándor Beke. Hungary: Eger. 1998. Lang.: Hun. 2090
Gardyne, John
Performance/production
Collection of newspaper reviews by London theatre critics. UK-England: London. 1998. Lang.: Eng. 2500
Gardzienice Theatre Association (Poland)
SEE
Ośrodek Praktyk Teatralnych.
Garfield, Keely
Performance/production
Interview with choreographer Keely Garfield. UK-England. 1998. Lang.: Eng. 1308
Garin, Michael
Performance/production
Collection of newspaper reviews by London theatre critics. UK-England. 1998. Lang.: Eng. 2489
Garland, Patrick
Performance/production
Collection of newspaper reviews by London theatre critics. UK-England: London. 1998. Lang.: Eng. 2445
Collection of newspaper reviews by London theatre critics. UK-England. 1998. Lang.: Eng. 2485
Actor Michael Williams. UK-England: London. 1950-1998. Lang.: Eng. 2644
Garneau, Michel
Performance/production
French Canadian translations/adaptations of Shakespeare. Canada: Montreal, PQ. 1988. Lang.: Fre. 1855
Garrett-Groag, Lillian
Plays/librettos/scripts
Playwright Lillian Garrett-Groag. USA: Los Angeles, CA. 1998. Lang.: Eng. 3683
Garrett, Almeida
Performance/production
Collection of newspaper reviews by London theatre critics. UK-England: London. 1998. Lang.: Eng. 2490
Garrick Club (London)
Performance/production
Shakespearean production and the theatrical portrait collection of the Garrick Club. England: London. 1702-1814. Lang.: Eng. 1903
Garrick, David
Performance/production
History of movement training for the actor. USA. 1910-1985. Lang.: Eng. 675
The feud between David Garrick and Charles Macklin. England: London. 1743-1777. Lang.: Eng. 1897
Contemporary remarks on the styles and manners of actors. England: London. 1740-1779. Lang.: Eng. 1898
The cultural background of eighteenth-century British pantomime. England. 1700-1800. Lang.: Eng. 4093
Plays/librettos/scripts
Analysis of *The Clandestine Marriage* by David Garrick. England. 1766. Lang.: Eng. 2926
The obedient daughter in adaptations of Shakespeare's plays. England. 1701-1800. Lang.: Eng. 2969
Garrison, Lydia
Audience
George Pierce Baker's 47 Workshop and the construction of the audience. USA: Cambridge, MA. 1918-1924. Lang.: Eng. 159
Garro, Elena
Plays/librettos/scripts
Cruelty and the absurd in theatre of Latin American playwrights. Latin America. 1960-1980. Lang.: Eng. 3267
Gartman, V.
Design/technology
Scene designs for *Ruslan i Ljudmila* by V. Gartman. Russia: St. Petersburg. 1876. Lang.: Rus. 4438
Garwood, Norman
Design/technology
Production design for the film *Lost in Space.* USA: Hollywood, CA. 1998. Lang.: Eng. 3904
Gary Oldman Fanclub, The
Performance/production
Collection of newspaper reviews by London theatre critics. UK-England: London. 1998. Lang.: Eng. 2528
Gas Station Angel
Performance/production
Collection of newspaper reviews by London theatre critics. UK-England: London. 1998. Lang.: Eng. 2414
Gasbarra, Felix
Performance/production
Erwin Piscator and Brecht's *Schwejk im zweiten Weltkrieg (Schweik in the Second World War).* Germany: Berlin. 1928. Lang.: Ger. 1952
Gassman, Vittorio
Performance/production
The Italian premiere of *A Streetcar Named Desire* by Tennessee Williams. Italy: Rome. 1949. Lang.: Eng. 2172
Gate Theatre (Dublin)
Performance/production
Recent productions in Ireland of plays by Eugene O'Neill. Ireland: Dublin. UK-Ireland: Belfast. 1989-1998. Lang.: Eng. 2154

Gate Theatre (London)
Institutions
Funding status of London's fringe theatres. UK-England: London. 1998. Lang.: Eng. 1748
Performance/production
Collection of newspaper reviews by London theatre critics. UK-England: London. Lang.: Eng. 2408
Collection of newspaper reviews by London theatre critics. UK-England: London. 1998. Lang.: Eng. 2418
Collection of newspaper reviews by London theatre critics. UK-England: London. 1998. Lang.: Eng. 2438
Collection of newspaper reviews by London theatre critics. UK-England: London. 1998. Lang.: Eng. 2451
Collection of newspaper reviews by London theatre critics. UK-England: London. 1998. Lang.: Eng. 2462
Collection of newspaper reviews by London theatre critics. UK-England: London. 1998. Lang.: Eng. 2468
Collection of newspaper reviews by London theatre critics. UK-England: London. 1998. Lang.: Eng. 2481
Collection of newspaper reviews by London theatre critics. UK-England: London. 1998. Lang.: Eng. 2509
Collection of newspaper reviews by London theatre critics. UK-England: London. 1998. Lang.: Eng. 2530
Collection of newspaper reviews by London theatre critics. UK-England: London. 1998. Lang.: Eng. 2545
Collection of newspaper reviews by London theatre critics. UK-England: London. 1998. Lang.: Eng. 2553
Collection of newspaper reviews by London theatre critics. UK-England: London. 1998. Lang.: Eng. 2565
Collection of newspaper reviews by London theatre critics. UK-England: London. 1998. Lang.: Eng. 2582

Gáti, István
Performance/production
Interview with baritone István Gáti. Hungary. 1971-1998. Lang.: Hun. 4618

Gatti, Armand
Plays/librettos/scripts
The Holocaust in *L'Enfant-rat (The Rat Child)* by Armand Gatti. France. 1961-1970. Lang.: Eng. 3092
The Holocaust in environmental theatre of Armand Gatti. France. 1989-1993. Lang.: Eng. 3097

Gaulier, Philippe
Performance/production
Clown teachers Richard Pochinko and Philippe Gaulier. Canada. 1980-1998. Lang.: Eng. 4117

Gay Divorcee, The
Performance/production
Analysis of the *Night and Day* dance sequence of *The Gay Divorcee*. USA: Hollywood, CA. 1934. Lang.: Eng. 977

Gay Lord Quex, The
Plays/librettos/scripts
Analysis of plays by Arthur Wing Pinero. UK-England. 1890-1910. Lang.: Eng. 3440

Gay theatre
Administration
The lesbian relationship of agent Elisabeth Marbury and designer Elsie de Wolfe. USA. 1886-1933. Lang.: Eng. 44
Producer Cheryl Crawford, gender and sexuality. USA. 1902-1986. Lang.: Eng. 116
Institutions
Producer Joseph Cino and Off-off Broadway theatre. USA: New York, NY. 1931-1967. Lang.: Eng. 404
Performance/production
Actress/director Alla Nazimova. Russia. USA. 1878-1945. Lang.: Eng. 585
Performer, writer, director Elsie Janis and the 'gay sensibility'. UK-England. 1889-1956. Lang.: Eng. 612
Performativity in postmodern 'queer' works. USA. 1985-1995. Lang.: Eng. 616
Audience reaction to actress Adah Isaacs Menken. USA. 1835-1869. Lang.: Eng. 619
The marriage of theatre artists Katharine Cornell and Guthrie McClintic. USA. 1893-1974. Lang.: Eng. 634
Actor Edwin Forrest and the construction of masculinity. USA. 1806-1872. Lang.: Eng. 674
Gender and the career of actress Charlotte Cushman. USA. 1816-1876. Lang.: Eng. 680
Actor/director Margaret Webster, gender and sexuality. UK-England. USA. 1905-1972. Lang.: Eng. 2590
The career of gay actor Monty Woolley. USA. 1888-1963. Lang.: Eng. 2691
Contemporary queer politics and the production of gay and lesbian theatre. USA. 1970-1997. Lang.: Eng. 2710
Plays/librettos/scripts
The current state of Australian gay and lesbian theatre. Australia. 1990-1998. Lang.: Eng. 2775
Review of collections of plays with gay themes. Canada. 1996. Lang.: Eng. 2802
R.M. Vaughan's *Camera, Woman* at Buddies in Bad Times. Canada: Toronto, ON. 1998. Lang.: Eng. 2835
Homosexuality on the German stage. Germany. 1920-1980. Lang.: Eng. 3147
American gay drama and the impact of AIDS. USA. 1960-1987. Lang.: Eng. 3670
Analysis of performance art on *The Larry Sanders Show*. USA. 1995. Lang.: Eng. 4079
Homosexuality in Canadian opera. Canada. 1970-1998. Lang.: Eng. 4762
The AIDS epidemic in contemporary opera. Europe. North America. 1985-1995. Lang.: Eng. 4771
Analysis of *Plague Mass* by Diamanda Galas. USA. 1991. Lang.: Eng. 4828
Relation to other fields
Actress Nance O'Neil and her friendship with Lizzie Borden. USA. 1874-1965. Lang.: Eng. 799
American modern dance and gay culture. USA. 1933-1998. Lang.: Eng. 1337
Controversy over Terrence McNally's *Corpus Christi*, Manhattan Theatre Club. USA: New York, NY. 1998. Lang.: Eng. 3792

Gay, John
Plays/librettos/scripts
Music and the ballad opera in English popular theatre. England. 1728-1780. Lang.: Eng. 4390

Gayton, Howard
Performance/production
Ophaboom Theatre's experience in recreating *commedia dell'arte*. UK-England: London. 1991-1998. Lang.: Eng. 4193

Gazsó, György
Performance/production
Interview with actor György Gazsó. Hungary. 1980-1998. Lang.: Hun. 2072

GBS: Fighting to Live Again
Basic theatrical documents
Text of *GBS: Fighting to Live Again* by Beverly J. Robertson. USA. 1997. Lang.: Eng. 1504

Geal, Simon
Performance/production
Collection of newspaper reviews by London theatre critics. UK-England: London. 1998. Lang.: Eng. 2561

Gedda, Nicolai
Performance/production
Interview with singer Nicolai Gedda. UK-England: London. Germany, West: Munich. 1952-1984. Lang.: Swe. 4859

Gee, Shirley
Performance/production
Creating the role of Mrs. Scully in Shirley Gee's *Warrior*. USA: Long Beach, CA. 1997. Lang.: Eng. 2753
Creating the role of Billy Cuttle in Shirley Gee's *Warrior*. USA: Long Beach, CA. 1997. Lang.: Eng. 2758

Geise, Barbara
Institutions
Music theatre studies at the Hochschule für Musik und Theater. Germany: Hamburg. 1988-1998. Lang.: Ger. 4459

Gelbart, Larry
Performance/production
Collection of newspaper reviews by London theatre critics. UK-England: London. 1998. Lang.: Eng. 2516

Gélinas, Marc
Performance/production
Robert Gurik's adaptation of Shakespeare's *Hamlet*. Canada: Montreal, PQ, London, ON. 1968. Lang.: Fre. 1866

Gems, Pam
Performance/production
Collection of newspaper reviews by London theatre critics. UK-England: London. 1998. Lang.: Eng. 2548
Gender studies
Administration
Gender and the career advancement of arts managers. USA. 1996. Lang.: Eng. 35
Producer Cheryl Crawford, gender and sexuality. USA. 1902-1986. Lang.: Eng. 116
Nineteenth-century women theatre managers. USA. 1800-1900. Lang.: Eng. 129
Audience
Gender-related social issues, theatre, and historiography. USA. 1830-1860. Lang.: Eng. 157
Analysis of the teenage-girl audience. USA. UK-England. 1950-1970. Lang.: Ger. 161
Gender and social warfare at the Metropolitan Opera. USA. 1890-1910. Lang.: Eng. 4411
Institutions
Feminist theatre of Ladies Against Women. USA: Berkeley, CA. 1979-1993. Lang.: Eng. 396
The theatrical method of Joint Stock Theatre Group. UK-England: London. 1974-1989. Lang.: Eng. 1749
Performance/production
Recent developments in Australian 'physical theatre'. Australia. 1990-1998. Lang.: Eng. 492
Afro-Cuban identity in Cuban theatre and popular arts. Cuba. 1959-1996. Lang.: Spa. 513
The 'grande coquette' on the Parisian stage. France: Paris. 1885-1925. Lang.: Eng. 531
Early modern French and Italian actresses. Italy. France. 1550-1750. Lang.: Eng. 553
Performer, writer, director Elsie Janis and the 'gay sensibility'. UK-England. 1889-1956. Lang.: Eng. 612
Theatre and gender in the novels of Hannah Foster. UK-England. 1759-1840. Lang.: Eng. 613
Audience reaction to actress Adah Isaacs Menken. USA. 1835-1869. Lang.: Eng. 619
Sociolinguistics, gender, and the actor. USA. 1997-1998. Lang.: Eng. 642
The first wave of American feminist theatre. USA. 1890-1930. Lang.: Eng. 648
Race, gender, and oral life history narrative. USA. 1988-1997. Lang.: Eng. 649
Female impersonation and the construction of the female stereotype. USA. 1890-1930. Lang.: Eng. 651
Boucicault's *The Octoroon* and the performance of race, gender, and power. USA. 1800-1860. Lang.: Eng. 669
Women and improvisation. USA. 1970-1997. Lang.: Eng. 672
Actor Edwin Forrest and the construction of masculinity. USA. 1806-1872. Lang.: Eng. 674
Gender and the career of actress Charlotte Cushman. USA. 1816-1876. Lang.: Eng. 680
Gender and politics in German dance. Germany. 1930-1932. Lang.: Eng. 928
Dance, music video, and popular culture. USA. 1987-1997. Lang.: Eng. 978
Masculinity in ballet. France: Paris. 1908-1915. Lang.: Eng. 1070
Baroque ballet at the Jesuit College of Clermont/Louis le Grand. France: Paris. 1660-1761. Lang.: Eng. 1076
Female characters in male folk dance. England. Mexico. 1500-1900. Lang.: Eng. 1225
Men in modern dance. Europe. 1960-1998. Lang.: Dan. 1271
Sexuality and gender in modern dance. Finland. 1998. Lang.: Fin. 1274
Modern dance and the female body. USA. Europe. 1900-1930. Lang.: Eng. 1321
Female performers of the formerly all-male genre *randai*. Sumatra. 1980-1998. Lang.: Eng. 1354
Feminist analysis of female roles in *kabuki*. Japan. 1600-1900. Lang.: Eng. 1363
The role of the *onnagata* heroine in late eighteenth-century *kabuki*. Japan. 1770-1800. Lang.: Eng. 1364
Representations of the feminine in *kathakali*. India. 1700-1995. Lang.: Eng. 1370
Women's roles in Shakespeare. 1600-1998. Lang.: Ger. 1813
Canadian representations of Ophelia from Shakespeare's *Hamlet*. Canada. 1980-1997. Lang.: Eng. 1852
Michel Laprise's *Masculin/Féminin (Male/Female)*, presented to audiences segregated by sex. Canada: Montreal, PQ. 1998. Lang.: Fre. 1867
Feminist analysis of the life of actress Charlotte Cibber Charke. England. 1713-1760. Lang.: Eng. 1904
Actress Charlotte Cibber Charke and cross-dressing. England. 1713-1760. Lang.: Eng. 1906
Press responses to the autobiography of actress Charlotte Cibber Charke. England. 1713-1760. Lang.: Eng. 1908
The function of sound in productions of *India Song* by Marguerite Duras. France. UK-Wales: Mold. 1973-1993. Lang.: Eng. 1945
Martyrdom in the plays of Hrotsvitha. Germany. 900-1050. Lang.: Eng. 1960
Gender and Shakespearean production in the GDR. Germany, East. 1982-1990. Lang.: Eng. 2044
Market Theatre productions of plays by Athol Fugard. South Africa, Republic of. 1993-1994. Lang.: Eng. 2351
Actresses and female managers in Spanish theatre. Spain. 1600-1700. Lang.: Eng. 2357
Actor/director Margaret Webster, gender and sexuality. UK-England. USA. 1905-1972. Lang.: Eng. 2590
Acting couple Alfred Lunt and Lynn Fontanne: 'idealized heterosexuality'. USA. 1887-1983. Lang.: Eng. 2656
French cultural and intellectual history, including the work of Molière. USA. 1650-1950. Lang.: Eng. 2663
Statements of women directors on their work. USA. 1996. Lang.: Eng. 2674
The career of gay actor Monty Woolley. USA. 1888-1963. Lang.: Eng. 2691
Contemporary queer politics and the production of gay and lesbian theatre. USA. 1970-1997. Lang.: Eng. 2710
Avant-garde American women directors' productions of *Doctor Faustus Lights the Lights* by Gertrude Stein. USA. 1940-1995. Lang.:Eng. 2735
Lesbianism and performer Mary Martin. USA. 1913-1990. Lang.: Eng. 2757
The language of costume in a video production of Caryl Churchill's *Top Girls*. UK-England. 1982-1991. Lang.: Eng. 4065
Antitheatricalism in the Circuit Chautauqua. USA. 1913-1930. Lang.: Eng. 4135
Account of life in drag. USA: New Orleans, LA. 1995. Lang.: Eng. 4138
Women in the *canboulay* ceremony. Trinidad and Tobago. 1998. Lang.: Eng. 4166
The staging of the complete *York Cycle* by the University of Toronto. Canada: Toronto, ON. 1998. Lang.: Eng. 4214
Analysis of beauty pageants. USA. 1920-1968. Lang.: Eng. 4222
The kitchen in performance art of Bobby Baker and Jeanne Goosen. UK-England. South Africa, Republic of. 1990-1992. Lang.: Eng. 4243
Male impersonation in variety and vaudeville. USA. 1868-1930. Lang.: Eng. 4281
Profile of the satiric comedy troupe Five Lesbian Brothers. USA: New York, NY. 1989-1998. Lang.: Eng. 4282
Characterization of male and female roles in Chinese opera. China. 1500-1980. Lang.: Eng. 4312
Lucy Vestris in *Giovanni in London*. England: London. 1842. Lang.: Eng. 4546
Gender, nation, and sexuality in opera. Europe. North America. 1998. Lang.: Eng. 4552
Gendered readings of Bellini's *La Sonnambula* in performance. USA. 1835-1860. Lang.: Eng. 4748
Gender construction and aesthetics of Central Javanese *wayang*. Indonesia. 1650-1998. Lang.: Eng. 4925
Plays/librettos/scripts
Female role models in plays by Austrian women. Austria. 1776-1914. Lang.: Ger. 2786
Analysis of *Queen Lear* by Beau Coleman. Canada: Edmonton, AB. 1995-1997. Lang.: Eng. 2800

Gender studies — cont'd

R.M. Vaughan's *Camera, Woman* at Buddies in Bad Times. Canada: Toronto, ON. 1998. Lang.: Eng. 2835

Women and politics in Restoration heroic plays. England. 1660-1710. Lang.: Eng. 2872

Women's use of wit in response to men in English popular culture. England. 1590-1630. Lang.: Eng. 2884

The feminine ideal in the drama of English Romantic poets. England. 1794-1840. Lang.: Eng. 2886

The defense of prostitution in Lillo's *Marina*. England. 1738. Lang.: Eng. 2887

Cross-dressing in Shakespeare's *The Merchant of Venice* and in the autobiography of actress Charlotte Cibber Charke. England. 1713-1760. Lang.: Eng. 2891

Marriage and patriarchy in *The Tragedy of Mariam* by Elizabeth Cary. England. 1613. Lang.: Eng. 2893

The murders of royal women in plays of Shakespeare and Beaumont and Fletcher. England. 1609-1610. Lang.: Eng. 2894

Shakespeare's *King Lear* and the gender constructions of three daughters. England. 1605-1606. Lang.: Eng. 2898

The influence of Webster, Middleton, and Shakespeare on the poetry of Robert Browning. England. 1590-1889. Lang.: Eng. 2906

Female power and the emblem tradition in plays of Shakespeare and Middleton. England. 1604-1625. Lang.: Eng. 2913

The representation of historical female characters on the Renaissance stage. England. 1580-1615. Lang.: Eng. 2922

The 'unruly' speech of Ariana in Shakespeare's *Comedy of Errors*. England. 1590-1593. Lang.: Eng. 2924

Women in Shakespeare's *Richard III*. England. 1592-1593. Lang.: Eng. 2929

Feminist analysis of Webster's *The Duchess of Malfi*. England. 1613. Lang.: Eng. 2931

Analysis of *Marina*, George Lillo's adaptation of Shakespeare's *Pericles*. England. 1738. Lang.: Eng. 2971

The treatment of single women in early Stuart drama. England. 1604-1608. Lang.: Eng. 2979

Language, rank, and sexuality in the anonymous *Arden of Faversham*. England. 1592. Lang.: Eng. 2986

Male and female honor in *A Fair Quarrel* by Middleton and Rowley. England. 1615-1617. Lang.: Eng. 2993

Feminism and seventeenth-century city comedy. England. 1600-1700. Lang.: Eng. 3000

Restoration playwright Margaret Cavendish. England. 1645-1662. Lang.: Eng. 3002

The politics of consent in Shakespeare's *Titus Andronicus*. England. 1590-1594. Lang.: Eng. 3006

The politics of gender in the plays of John Marston. England. 1599-1634. Lang.: Eng. 3009

The subversion of male authority in Shakespeare's *Henry VI* and *Richard III*. England. 1590-1593. Lang.: Eng. 3015

Cross-dressing in Elizabethan Robin Hood plays. England. 1589-1598. Lang.: Eng. 3016

Feminist analysis of *The Tragedy of Mariam* by Elizabeth Cary. England. 1602-1612. Lang.: Eng. 3019

Gender and religion in Shakespeare's *Measure for Measure*. England. 1604. Lang.: Eng. 3021

Sexual politics in *The Rover* by Aphra Behn. England. 1677. Lang.: Eng. 3031

The women in Shakespeare's *Hamlet*. England. 1600-1601. Lang.: Eng. 3046

The devouring woman in plays of Racine, Kleist, Ibsen, and Beckett. Europe. 1760-1992. Lang.: Eng. 3058

Gender and madness in modern drama. Europe. 1880-1969. Lang.: Eng. 3061

Food and alienation in plays of Chantal Chawaf and Denise Chalem. France. 1970-1989. Lang.: Eng. 3072

Feminist theory and practice on the French stage. France. 1998. Lang.: Eng. 3075

Poetic identity in plays of Hélène Cixous. France. 1988-1994. Lang.: Eng. 3083

Bisexuality in *Le Nom d'Oedipe (The Name of Oedipus)* by Hélène Cixous. France. 1978. Lang.: Eng. 3089

Analysis of *Les Nombres (The Numbers)* by Andrée Chedid. France. 1965. Lang.: Eng. 3090

Analysis of *Le Voyage sans fin (The Constant Journey)* by Monique Wittig. France. 1985. Lang.: Eng. 3100

Feminist questioning of language and authority in plays of Nathalie Sarraute. France. 1967-1995. Lang.: Eng. 3103

Postcolonialism, ethnicity, and feminism in French and Caribbean plays. France. Martinique. Guadeloupe. 1960-1990. Lang.: Eng. 3104

Space and pre-verbal memory in later works of Marguerite Duras. France. 1970-1982. Lang.: Eng. 3106

Analysis of *Elle est là (It Is There)* by Nathalie Sarraute. France. 1967-1982. Lang.: Eng. 3107

Response to the structures of male oppression in plays of Yourcenar, Sarraute, and Duras. France. 1975-1995. Lang.: Fre. 3119

Power, gender relations, and communication in German drama. Germany. 1776-1989. Lang.: Ger. 3138

Women in German turn-of-the-century drama. Germany. 1890-1910. Lang.: Eng. 3158

Female sacrifice in eighteenth-century German drama. Germany. 1772-1781. Lang.: Eng. 3167

Colonial and postcolonial narrative and the politics of representation. India. 1900-1985. Lang.: Eng. 3192

Cruelty and the absurd in theatre of Latin American playwrights. Latin America. 1960-1980. Lang.: Eng. 3267

Celebration and the body in plays of Ina Césaire and Simone Schwarz-Bart. Martinique. Guadeloupe. 1975-1998. Lang.: Eng. 3270

Women in plays about war and male contact sports. New Zealand. Europe. 1998. Lang.: Eng. 3281

Ibsen, translation, and feminine discourse. Norway. 1888. Lang.: Eng. 3295

Andreas-Salomé's view of Ibsen's female characters. Norway. Germany. 1879-1906. Lang.: Eng. 3296

Female characters in plays by Scandinavian women. Norway. Sweden. Denmark. 1998. Lang.: Eng. 3299

Feminist analysis of plays by Gabriela Zapolska. Poland. 1885-1998. Lang.: Pol. 3301

Feminist analysis of seventeenth-century plays by women. Spain. 1605-1675. Lang.: Eng. 3385

Allegorical dramas of Sor Marcela de San Félix. Spain. 1595-1650. Lang.: Eng. 3395

The image of women on the Spanish stage. Spain. 1908-1936. Lang.: Eng. 3399

Ecology and the plays of Caryl Churchill. UK-England. 1971-1989. Lang.: Eng. 3422

Colonialism and misogyny in J.M. Barrie's *Peter Pan*. UK-England. 1908. Lang.: Eng. 3423

Gender and sexuality in Caryl Churchill's *Cloud Nine*. UK-England. 1979. Lang.: Eng. 3426

The censorship of the unpublished *Her Wedding Night* by Florence Bates. UK-England. 1917. Lang.: Eng. 3454

Rape in Middleton's *Women Beware Women* and its adaptation by Howard Barker. UK-England. 1625-1986. Lang.: Eng. 3468

Brechtian epic devices in the theatre of Caryl Churchill. UK-England. 1976-1986. Lang.: Eng. 3477

Byron's heroes and the Byronic hero. UK-England. 1800-1824. Lang.: Eng. 3484

George Bernard Shaw and the 'New Woman'. UK-England. 1890-1900. Lang.: Eng. 3486

Talk as performance in the life and work of Oscar Wilde. UK-England. 1890-1900. Lang.: Eng. 3492

Gender and nationalism in Northern Irish drama. UK-Ireland. 1902-1997. Lang.: Eng. 3511

The romantic nature of Tennessee Williams' *The Glass Menagerie*. USA. 1944. Lang.: Eng. 3558

Gendered political critique in *The Club* by Eve Merriam. USA. 1976. Lang.: Eng. 3572

Gender and politics in Romantic tragedies of Mercy Otis Warren. USA. 1783-1785. Lang.: Eng. 3575

Analysis of *Venus* by Suzan-Lori Parks. USA. 1996. Lang.: Eng. 3582

Women playwrights' addresses to the Women's Project conference. USA. 1997. Lang.: Eng. 3589

Gender studies — cont'd

The Broadway success of women playwrights. USA. 1906-1944. Lang.: Eng. 3590
Female presence/absence in plays of O'Neill, Pinter, and Shepard. USA. UK-England. 1936-1985. Lang.: Eng. 3607
Playwright Tina Howe on gender expectations on playwrights. USA: New York, NY. 1980-1997. Lang.: Eng. 3614
Fairy-tale heroines in American drama and musical theatre. USA. 1945-1965. Lang.: Eng. 3617
Gender-role reversal in plays of William Inge. USA. 1950-1958. Lang.: Eng. 3623
Analysis of *Bus Stop* by William Inge. USA. 1955. Lang.: Eng. 3624
Analysis of *Keely and Du* by Jane Martin. USA. 1993. Lang.: Eng. 3629
Politics and feminism in the plays of Maria Irene Fornes. USA. 1975-1995. Lang.: Eng. 3635
The social roles of women playwrights. USA. 1890-1910. Lang.: Eng. 3637
Analysis of *The Dining Room* by A.R. Gurney. USA. 1982-1984. Lang.: Eng. 3642
The representation of true crime in modern drama. USA. France. 1955-1996. Lang.: Eng. 3673
Playwrights Adrienne Kennedy, Ntozake Shange, and Suzan-Lori Parks. USA. 1970-1998. Lang.: Eng. 3714
Transvestism in contemporary film as the 'blackface' of the nineties. UK-England. USA. 1993-1996. Lang.: Eng. 3983
Marriage, divorce, and gender in the Hollywood comedy of remarriage. USA. 1935-1942. Lang.: Eng. 4010
Gender and politics in masques of Ben Jonson and Samuel Daniel. England. 1604-1605. Lang.: Eng. 4200
Power, gender, and race in *The Masque of Blackness* by Ben Jonson. England. 1605-1611. Lang.: Eng. 4208
Attacks on *castrati* in English pamphlets. England: London. 1710-1740. Lang.: Eng. 4766
The AIDS epidemic in contemporary opera. Europe. North America. 1985-1995. Lang.: Eng. 4771
Ambition and gender in Bizet's *Carmen*. France. 1870-1879. Lang.: Eng. 4786
The *castrato*, the contralto, and the film *Farinelli*. France. Italy. 1994. Lang.: Eng. 4787
Nationalism and sexuality in Wagner's *Ring* cycle. Germany. 1870-1880. Lang.: Eng. 4796
Gender, nationalism, and Orientalism in *Samson et Dalila* by Saint-Saëns. Germany. 1868-1877. Lang.: Eng. 4797
Analysis of Jesuit opera by Giovanni Girolamo Kapsberger and Orazio Grassi. Italy: Rome. 1622. Lang.: Eng. 4803
Virginal heroines in Alpine settings in operas of Bellini, Donizetti, and Verdi. Italy. 1800-1850. Lang.: Eng. 4812
Gender in Bellini's *Norma* and Verdi's *Aida*. Italy. 1831-1871. Lang.: Eng. 4813
Female operatic cross-dressing. Italy: Naples, Venice. 1601-1800. Lang.: Eng. 4814
Derek Jarman's adaptation of works by Benjamin Britten and Wilfred Owen. UK-England. 1968-1988. Lang.: Eng. 4822
Analysis of Benjamin Britten's opera *Death in Venice*. UK-England. 1912-1992. Lang.: Eng. 4823

Relation to other fields
Analysis of anti-theatricalism. England. 1579-1642. 726
Gender, class, nationality, and sanitary reform in nineteenth-century English theatre. UK-England. 1790-1890. Lang.: Eng. 768
Actress Nance O'Neil and her friendship with Lizzie Borden. USA. 1874-1965. Lang.: Eng. 799
Student responses to the autobiography of actress Charlotte Cibber Charke. USA. 1998. Lang.: Eng. 800
Cross-dressing and gender struggle on the early modern English stage. England. 1580-1620. Lang.: Eng. 3749
Psychoanalysis, the female body, and Shakespeare's *Henriad*. England. 1589-1597. Lang.: Eng. 3756
Analysis of striptease events. USA. 1992-1998. Lang.: Eng. 4285

Research/historiography
Alternative models of performance documentation. Europe. 1984-1997. Lang.: Eng. 818
Gender difference and theatricality. Germany. France. USA. 1959-1998. Lang.: Ger. 821

Theory/criticism
Gender and culture in dance analysis. Europe. North America. 1998. Lang.: Eng. 1006
Theatrical dancing and the performance aesthetics of Wilde, Yeats, and Shaw. UK-England. Ireland. 1890-1950. Lang.: Eng. 1012
The use of different analytical strategies to obtain multiple readings of dance performance. USA. Europe. 1946-1982. Lang.: Eng. 1200
Gender in Francesca Zambello's production of *Iphigénie en Tauride*. USA: Cooperstown, NY. 1997. Lang.: Eng. 4843

Training
Swedish attitudes toward Oriental female dance. Sweden. 1995. Lang.: Swe. 1245

General of Hot Desire, The
Performance/production
Collection of newspaper reviews by London theatre critics. UK-England: London. 1998. Lang.: Eng. 2498

Genet, Jean
Performance/production
Collection of newspaper reviews by London theatre critics. UK-England: London. 1998. Lang.: Eng. 2547
The change in Shakespearean production. UK-England. 1960-1980. Lang.: Eng. 2628
Plays/librettos/scripts
Analysis of Jean Genet's dance work *Adame Miroir*. France. 1949. Lang.: Ita. 993
Insanity in nineteenth- and twentieth-century theatre. Europe. 1880-1970. Lang.: Eng. 3050
Postcolonialism, ethnicity, and feminism in French and Caribbean plays. France. Martinique. Guadeloupe. 1960-1990. Lang.: Eng. 3104
The representation of true crime in modern drama. USA. France. 1955-1996. Lang.: Eng. 3673

Genetik Woyzeck (Genetics Woyzeck)
Performance/production
Impressions from Podewil theatre workshop. Germany: Berlin. 1998. Lang.: Ger. 2024

Gengangere (Ghosts)
Plays/librettos/scripts
Feminism and plays of Henrik Ibsen. Norway. 1879-1979. Lang.: Eng. 3293

Génie de la rue Drolet, Le (Genius of Drolet Street, The)
Plays/librettos/scripts
Analysis of works by Larry Tremblay. Canada: Montreal, PQ. 1995-1998. Lang.: Fre. 2804

Genres
Performance/production
Performance culture in prerevolutionary Russia. Russia. 1910-1915. Lang.: Eng. 580
The popular theatre genre *teatro por horas*. Spain. 1867-1922. Lang.: Eng. 2361
Spielberg's *Saving Private Ryan* and the war film. USA: Hollywood, CA. 1998. Lang.: Eng. 3948
G. Chazanov of Teat'r Estrady. Russia: Moscow. Lang.: Rus. 4277
Plays/librettos/scripts
Cross-dressing in Shakespeare's *The Merchant of Venice* and in the autobiography of actress Charlotte Cibber Charke. England. 1713-1760. Lang.: Eng. 2891
George Bernard Shaw and the history-play tradition. UK-England. 1899-1939. Lang.: Eng. 3503
George Bernard Shaw and science fiction. UK-England. Ireland. 1887-1998. Lang.: Eng. 3508

Gentlemen Prefer Blondes
Performance/production
Collection of newspaper reviews by London theatre critics. UK-England: London. 1998. Lang.: Eng. 2480

Genty, Philippe
Performance/production
The present state of French puppetry. France. 1970-1998. Lang.: Ger. 4892

Geography
Design/technology
Design concept for Ralph Lemon's dance piece *Geography* at BAM. USA: New York, NY. 1998. Lang.: Eng. 1248

Geography of a Horse Dreamer
Plays/librettos/scripts
National identity in plays of Sam Shepard. USA. 1965-1995. Lang.: Eng. 3545

Geometry of Miracles
Design/technology
Set design for Robert Lepage's *Geometry of Miracles*. Canada: Quebec, PQ. 1998. Lang.: Eng. 1516
Institutions
Productions of Salzburger Festspiele. Austria: Salzburg. 1998. Lang.: Ger. 1571
Performance/production
Robert Lepage's *Geometry of Miracles* at the Salzburg Festival. Austria: Salzburg. 1998. Lang.: Ger. 1824

Georg II, Duke of Saxe-Meiningen
Performance/production
The rise of the modern Shakespearean director. Europe. 1878-1995. Lang.: Eng. 1911

George a Greene, the Pinner of Wakefield
Plays/librettos/scripts
Robin Hood and Elizabethan theatre. England. 1588-1601. Lang.: Eng. 2902
The authorship of *George a Greene*. England. 1593-1599. Lang.: Eng. 2989

George, Jeannette Clift
Institutions
Jeannette Clift George and the A.D. Players. USA: Houston, TX. 1967-1997. Lang.: Eng. 1785

George, Meganne
Design/technology
Set design for Chain Lightning Theatre's production of *Beyond the Horizon* by Eugene O'Neill. USA: New York, NY. 1998. Lang.: Eng. 1551

Georges Dandin
Performance/production
Three Hungarian productions of plays by Molière. Hungary: Szentendre, Kapolcs, Kőszeg. 1998. Lang.: Hun. 2142

Georgian Academic Theatre (Tbilisi)
SEE
Gruzinskij Akademičeskij Teat'r im. Kote Mordžanišvili.

Gerard, Rose
Performance/production
Brief biographies of performance artists. 1963-1988. Lang.: Eng. 4238

Gerbaulet, Françoise
Basic theatrical documents
Text of *Le Roi Hâtif (King Hasty)* by Françoise Gerbaulet. France. 1993-1998. Lang.: Fre. 1425

Gerber, Regula
Institutions
The current state of Theater Bielefeld. Germany: Bielefeld. 1998. Lang.: Ger. 1621

Gergiev, Valerij
Institutions
The world tour of the Kirov Opera, headed by Valerij Gergiev. Russia: St. Petersburg. 1998. Lang.: Eng. 4471

Gerhart Hauptmann Theater (Zittau)
Institutions
Profiles of theatres in Saxony. Germany: Zittau, Bautzen, Görlitz. 1997-1998. Lang.: Ger. 1650

Gericke, Katharina
Performance/production
Productions of new plays by Peter Handke and Katharine Gericke at Niedersächsische Staatstheater. Germany: Hannover. 1998. Lang.: Ger. 1983

Gerima, Haile
Plays/librettos/scripts
Analysis of Haile Gerima's film *Sankofa*. Ghana. 1993. Lang.: Eng. 3973

German, Anna
Performance/production
Musical theatre performer Anna German. Poland. 1998. Lang.: Rus. 4365

Germania III
Performance/production
French productions of German plays. France. 1998. Lang.: Ger. 1935

Gershwin, George
Performance/production
The songs of George and Ira Gershwin. USA. 1896-1998. Lang.: Eng. 4376
The music of George Gershwin available on compact disc. USA. 1998. Lang.: Eng. 4382
Musical analysis of Gershwin's *Porgy and Bess*. USA. 1937. Lang.: Eng. 4753

Gershwin, Ira
Performance/production
The songs of George and Ira Gershwin. USA. 1896-1998. Lang.: Eng. 4376
Musical analysis of Gershwin's *Porgy and Bess*. USA. 1937. Lang.: Eng. 4753

Gertrude morte cet après-midi (Gertrude Dead This Afternoon)
Relation to other fields
Author Gertrude Stein, subject of *Gertrude morte cet après-midi (Gertrude Dead This Afternoon)* by Monique Lepeu. France: Paris. 1874-1997. Lang.: Fre. 3759

Gerz, Jochen
Performance/production
Interview with director Jochen Gerz. Germany: Berlin. 1998. Lang.: Ger, Fre, Dut, Eng. 1967
Relation to other fields
Die Berliner Ermittlung (The Berlin Investigation), an interactive theatre project by Jochen Gerz and Esther Shalev-Gerz. Germany: Berlin. 1998. Lang.: Ger. 3768

Geschichten aus dem Wienerwald (Tales from the Vienna Woods)
Performance/production
Productions of Horváth's *Geschichten aus dem Wienerwald (Tales from the Vienna Woods)*. Germany: Hamburg, Hannover. Austria: Vienna. 1998. Lang.: Ger. 2003

Gestrandet vor Guadeloupe (Stranded in Guadeloupe)
Plays/librettos/scripts
Playwright Hans Zimmer. Germany: Hannover. 1993-1998. Lang.: Ger. 3136

Getting Married
Plays/librettos/scripts
Shaw's 'theatre of ideas' and its influence. UK-England. 1890-1910. Lang.: Eng. 3457
Rhetorical analysis of plays by George Bernard Shaw. UK-England. 1896-1908. Lang.: Eng. 3480

Ghasel, En (Gazelle, A)
Institutions
Profile of Svensk Symbolisk Teater. Sweden: Malmö. 1997. Lang.: Swe. 1728

Ghelderode, Michel de
Performance/production
Collection of newspaper reviews by London theatre critics. UK-England: London. 1998. Lang.: Eng. 2581

Ghost Sonata
SEE
Spöksonaten.

Ghost Trio
Plays/librettos/scripts
Analysis of *Ghost Trio* by Samuel Beckett. France. Ireland. 1976. Lang.: Eng. 4076
Analysis of television plays by Samuel Beckett. France. 1965-1989. Lang.: Eng. 4077

Ghosts
SEE
Gengangere.

Ghosts of Versailles, The
Plays/librettos/scripts
Operatic realizations of Beaumarchais' character Rosina. Europe. North America. 1784-1991. Lang.: Eng. 4773

Giacometti, Paolo
Plays/librettos/scripts
Italian realist drama. Italy. 1860-1918. Lang.: Eng. 3260

Giacosa, Giuseppe
Plays/librettos/scripts
Analysis of plays by Giuseppe Giacosa. Italy. 1847-1906. Lang.: Ita. 3237
Italian realist drama. Italy. 1860-1918. Lang.: Eng. 3260

Giannini, Ettore
Performance/production
Ettore Giannini's film and stage work *Carosello Napoletano (Neapolitan Carousel)*. Italy. 1950. Lang.: Ita. 546

Giant Steps
Performance/production
Collection of newspaper reviews by London theatre critics. UK-England: London. 1998. Lang.: Eng. 2545

Giardini Pensili (Rimini)
Institutions
Italian experimental theatre at Spielart '97. Germany: Munich. Italy. 1997. Lang.: Eng. 1619

Gibson, Harry
Performance/production
Collection of newspaper reviews by London theatre critics. UK-England: London. 1998. Lang.: Eng. 2412
Gide, André
Performance/production
Mythology in theatre works of Stravinskij, especially *Perséphone*. Russia. 1934. Lang.: Eng. 4682
Plays/librettos/scripts
Wilde, Gide, and the censorship of Biblical drama. UK-England. France. 1892-1898. Lang.: Eng. 3441
Gielen, Michael
Performance/production
Director Ruth Berghaus. Germany. 1970-1996. Lang.: Ger. 4596
Gielgud Theatre (London)
Performance/production
Collection of newspaper reviews by London theatre critics. UK-England: London. 1998. Lang.: Eng. 2438
Collection of newspaper reviews by London theatre critics. UK-England: London. 1998. Lang.: Eng. 2505
Gielgud, John
Performance/production
Speaking styles of selected actors reading Shakespeare's *Henry V*. North America. UK-England. 1998. Lang.: Eng. 2208
Types of actors and their relationship with directors. UK-England. Sweden. 1950-1998. Lang.: Swe. 2648
Actors' interpretations of the title role in Oscar Wilde's *The Canterville Ghost*. UK-England. USA. 1943-1998. Lang.: Eng. 4066
Gielgud, Maina
Performance/production
Hungarian guest performances of world ballet stars. Hungary: Budapest. 1975-1978. Lang.: Hun. 1085
Gierow, Karl Ragnar
Performance/production
Collection of newspaper reviews by London theatre critics. UK-Scotland: Edinburgh. 1998. Lang.: Eng. 2650
Gift of the Gorgon, The
Plays/librettos/scripts
Recent history in Irish theatre and drama. Ireland: Dublin. UK-Ireland: Belfast. 1993-1996. Lang.: Eng. 3212
Gift, The
Performance/production
Collection of newspaper reviews by London theatre critics. UK-England: London. 1998. Lang.: Eng. 2421
Giganti della montagna, I (Mountain Giants, The)
Plays/librettos/scripts
Analysis of *I giganti della montagna (The Mountain Giants)* by Luigi Pirandello. Italy. 1936. Lang.: Eng. 3235
Gigli, Girolamo
Plays/librettos/scripts
The theatre of Girolamo Gigli. Italy. 1660-1722. Lang.: Eng. 4307
Giglio, Lisa
Performance/production
Collection of newspaper reviews by London theatre critics. UK-England: London. 1998. Lang.: Eng. 2427
Collection of newspaper reviews by London theatre critics. UK-England: London. 1998. Lang.: Eng. 2491
Gignac, Marie
Theory/criticism
Round-table discussion on theatre and impurity. Canada: Quebec, PQ. 1998. Lang.: Fre. 835
Gilbert, William Schwenck
Performance/production
Collection of newspaper reviews by London theatre critics. UK-England: London. 1998. Lang.: Eng. 2553
Plays/librettos/scripts
The trivialization of feminism in librettos of W.S. Gilbert. UK-England. 1880-1890. Lang.: Eng. 4861
Gilfert, Charles H.
Administration
Theatre manager Charles H. Gilfert. USA: Charleston, SC. 1817-1822. Lang.: Eng. 135
Gilfry, Rodney
Performance/production
Baritone Rodney Gilfry. USA. 1998. Lang.: Eng. 4736
Gilger, Paul
Performance/production
Collection of newspaper reviews by London theatre critics. UK-England: London. 1998. Lang.: Eng. 2483
Collection of newspaper reviews by London theatre critics. UK-England: London. 1998. Lang.: Eng. 2544
Gill, Claes
Performance/production
Seven critics on their favorite character or portrayal. Sweden. 1950. Lang.: Swe. 2369
Gill, James
Performance/production
Collection of newspaper reviews by London theatre critics. UK-England: London. 1998. Lang.: Eng. 2579
Gill, Janet
Performance/production
Collection of newspaper reviews by London theatre critics. UK-England: London. 1998. Lang.: Eng. 2452
Gille, Philippe
Audience
The negative influence of Wagnerianism on the reception of Delibes' opera *Lakmé*. 1900-1996. Lang.: Fre. 4409
Basic theatrical documents
Libretto of *Lakmé* by Léo Delibes, Edmond Gondinet, and Philippe Gille. France. 1883. Lang.: Fre. 4415
Plays/librettos/scripts
Analysis of Delibes' opera *Lakmé*. France. 1883. Lang.: Fre. 4782
The source of the libretto for Delibes' *Lakmé*. France. 1853-1883. Lang.: Fre. 4784
Gillman, Denise
Performance/production
Denise Gillman's production of Webster's *The Duchess of Malfi*, Theatre of NOTE. USA: Los Angeles, CA. 1998. Lang.: Eng. 2714
Gilmore, David
Performance/production
Collection of newspaper reviews by London theatre critics. UK-England: London. 1998. Lang.: Eng. 2539
Gilmour, Graeme
Performance/production
Collection of newspaper reviews by London theatre critics. UK-England: London. 1998. Lang.: Eng. 2465
Gilpin, Charles
Plays/librettos/scripts
African- and Irish-Americans in the plays of Eugene O'Neill. USA. 1916-1953. Lang.: Eng. 3687
Gilroy, Steve
Performance/production
Collection of newspaper reviews by London theatre critics. UK-England: London. 1998. Lang.: Eng. 2549
Ginkas, Kama
Performance/production
Director Kama Ginkas of Teat'r Junogo Zritelja. Russia. 1998. Lang.: Rus. 2265
Gint
Performance/production
Comparison of productions of Ibsen's *Peer Gynt*. USA: Providence, RI, New York, NY, Washington, DC, Nacogdoches, TX. 1998. Lang.: Eng. 2711
Reviews of productions of plays by Ibsen. USA: New York, NY. Norway: Oslo. 1998. Lang.: Eng. 2747
Giordano Bruno
Basic theatrical documents
Plays and screenplays by Vili Ravnjak. Slovenia. 1991-1997. Lang.: Slo. 1460
Giordano, Gus
Performance/production
Jazz dancer and choreographer Gus Giordano. USA: Chicago, IL. 1962-1998. Lang.: Eng. 988
Giovanni in London, or The Libertine Reclaimed
Performance/production
Lucy Vestris in *Giovanni in London*. England: London. 1842. Lang.: Eng. 4546
Giraudoux, Jean
Design/technology
A stage design for Jean Giraudoux's *Ondine*. USA. 1987. Lang.: Eng. 1529
Girl of the Golden West, The
Design/technology
Lighting and realism in opera and theatre: Belasco and Puccini. Italy. USA. 1890-1910. Lang.: Eng. 203
Girls Night Out
Performance/production
Collection of newspaper reviews by London theatre critics. UK-England: London. 1998. Lang.: Eng. 2435

Girlz, The
Performance/production
Collection of newspaper reviews by London theatre critics. UK-England: London. 1998. Lang.: Eng. 2446

Giselle
Performance/production
Premiere of Sylvie Guillem's new choreography for Adolphe Adam's *Giselle*. Finland: Helsinki. 1998. Lang.: Hun. 1068
The Budapest Opera House's new production of *Giselle*. Hungary: Budapest. 1998. Lang.: Hun. 1094
Interviews with dancers about performance. UK-England. USA. Cuba. 1942-1989. Lang.: Eng. 1162

GITIS (Moscow)
SEE
Gosudarstvénnyj Institut Teatral'nogo Iskusstva.

Giulietta degli Spiriti (Juliet of the Spirits)
Plays/librettos/scripts
The fool character in works of Handke, Fellini, and Singer. USA. Germany. Italy. 1960-1968. Lang.: Eng. 3667

Giulio Cesare
Institutions
Italian experimental theatre at Spielart '97. Germany: Munich. Italy. 1997. Lang.: Eng. 1619

Give Me Your Answer, Do!
Performance/production
Collection of newspaper reviews by London theatre critics. UK-England: London. 1998. Lang.: Eng. 2451

Gizzatulina-Volžskaja, S.
Performance/production
Profile of actress S. Gizzatulina-Volžskaja. Tatarstan. 1998. Lang.: Rus. 2405

Gladstone, Amiel
Performance spaces
Theatre SKAM's production of *Louis and Dave* in a Plymouth Volaré. Canada: Victoria, BC. 1996. Lang.: Eng. 1797

Glapthorne, Henry
Plays/librettos/scripts
Flemish immigrants in English Renaissance drama. England. 1515-1635. Lang.: Eng. 2976

Glaspell, Susan
Performance/production
The first wave of American feminist theatre. USA. 1890-1930. Lang.: Eng. 648
A production of Susan Glaspell's experimental play *The Verge*. UK-Scotland: Glasgow. 1996. Lang.: Eng. 2651

Glass
Performance/production
Collection of newspaper reviews by London theatre critics. UK-England: London. 1998. Lang.: Eng. 2464

Glass Menagerie, The
Performance/production
Collection of newspaper reviews by London theatre critics. UK-England: London. 1998. Lang.: Eng. 2424
Collection of newspaper reviews by London theatre critics. UK-England. 1998. Lang.: Eng. 2510
Plays/librettos/scripts
Analysis of plays by Tennessee Williams. USA. 1943-1970. Lang.: Eng. 3539
The romantic nature of Tennessee Williams' *The Glass Menagerie*. USA. 1944. Lang.: Eng. 3558
Comparison of characters in plays of Georg Kaiser and Tennessee Williams. USA. Germany. 1912-1945. Lang.: Eng. 3588
Fairy-tale heroines in American drama and musical theatre. USA. 1945-1965. Lang.: Eng. 3617
Realism and anti-realism in plays of Tennessee Williams. USA. 1945-1986. Lang.: Eng. 3626
Effeminacy on the American stage. USA. 1920-1998. Lang.: Eng. 3682
Metadrama in plays of Tennessee Williams. USA. 1944-1978. Lang.: Eng. 3686

Glass, David
Performance/production
Collection of newspaper reviews by London theatre critics. UK-England: London. 1998. Lang.: Eng. 2436

Glass, Philip
Performance/production
The theory of movement in *Les Enfants Terribles*, adapted to dance-opera by Philip Glass and Susan Marshall. North America. 1997. Lang.: Eng. 1353
Collection of newspaper reviews by London theatre critics. UK-England: London. 1998. Lang.: Eng. 2409
Reviews of recent London performances. UK-England: London. 1998. Lang.: Ger. 2591
Ópera Seca's *Mattogrosso*. Brazil: Rio de Janeiro. 1989. Lang.: Eng. 4537
Plays/librettos/scripts
Composer Philip Glass on Beckett's influence on his work. Ireland. France. USA. 1965-1995. Lang.: Eng. 3194
The reciprocal influence of opera and film. Europe. North America. 1904-1994. Lang.: Eng. 4770

Glazunov, Aleksand'r
Performance/production
The history of the ballet *Raymonda* by Glazunov and Petipa. Russia. 1898-1998. Lang.: Eng. 1133
Ballerina Alexandra Danilova on Balanchine's *Raymonda*. USA: New York, NY. 1946. Lang.: Eng. 1172

Glengarry Glen Ross
Plays/librettos/scripts
Analysis of *Glengarry Glen Ross*. USA. 1983. Lang.: Dut. 3556
Rites of passage in the plays of David Mamet. USA. 1975-1995. Lang.: Eng. 3680

Glimmerglass Opera (Cooperstown, NY)
Performance/production
Baritone Nathan Gunn. USA. 1971-1998. Lang.: Eng. 4723
Theory/criticism
Gender in Francesca Zambello's production of *Iphigénie en Tauride*. USA: Cooperstown, NY. 1997. Lang.: Eng. 4843

Glinka, Michajl Ivanovič
Design/technology
Scene designs for *Ruslan i Ljudmila* by V. Gartman. Russia: St. Petersburg. 1876. Lang.: Rus. 4438

Globe Teater (Eindhoven)
Plays/librettos/scripts
Dutch and Flemish Shakespearean productions. Belgium. Netherlands. 1980-1983. Lang.: Dut. 2789

Globe Theatre (London)
SEE ALSO
Shakespeare's Globe Theatre.
Performance spaces
Evidence of theatre closings in a Folger Library manuscript. England: London. 1650. Lang.: Eng. 1798
The remains of the original Globe Theatre. UK-England: London. 1989-1997. Lang.: Eng. 1808

Globe Theatre (Regina, SK)
Institutions
Ruth Smillie, artistic director of Regina's Globe Theatre. Canada: Regina, SK. 1998. Lang.: Eng. 338

Glossaries
Reference materials
Glossary of Trinidadian carnival terms. Trinidad and Tobago. 1998. Lang.: Eng. 4173

Glover, Julian
Performance/production
Julian Glover on his performance in *Romeo and Juliet* for RSC. UK-England: London, Stratford. 1995-1996. Lang.: Eng. 2606

Gluck, Christoph Willibald
Performance/production
Stockholm's year as Cultural Capital of Europe. Sweden: Stockholm. 1766-1998. Lang.: Eng. 2394
Theory/criticism
Gender in Francesca Zambello's production of *Iphigénie en Tauride*. USA: Cooperstown, NY. 1997. Lang.: Eng. 4843

Glyndebourne Opera (Lewes)
Institutions
Survey of summer opera. UK-England. 1998. Lang.: Eng. 4476

Glynn, Dianne
Performance/production
Collection of newspaper reviews by London theatre critics. UK-England: London. 1998. Lang.: Eng. 2588

Glynn, Martin
Performance/production
Collection of newspaper reviews by London theatre critics. UK-England: London. 1998. Lang.: Eng. 2515

Gneušev, V.
Performance/production
Circus producer V. Gneušev. Russia: Moscow. 1998. Lang.: Rus. 4183

Goat Island (Chicago, IL)
Institutions
The work of performance troupe Goat Island. USA: Chicago, IL. 1987-1998. Lang.: Eng. 395
Interview with Matthew Goulish and Lin Hixson of Goat Island. USA: Chicago, IL. 1990. Lang.: Eng. 4237
Goda, Gábor
Performance/production
Artus Táncegyüttes' new production *Csillagőrlő (Starmill)*. Hungary: Budapest. 1998. Lang.: Hun. 948
Godard, Jean-Luc
Performance/production
Postmodernism in Jean-Luc Godard's film adaptation of Shakespeare's *King Lear*. France. 1988. Lang.: Eng. 3931
Retrospectives of filmmakers Jean-Luc Godard and William Kentridge. USA: New York, NY. 1998. Lang.: Eng. 3958
Godfather III
Plays/librettos/scripts
Opera in American gangster films. USA. 1932-1990. Lang.: Eng. 4023
Godfather, The
Plays/librettos/scripts
Gangster film and Shakespearean tragedy. USA. 1971-1991. Lang.: Eng. 4009
Gods and Monsters
Basic theatrical documents
Screenplay of *Gods and Monsters* by Bill Condon. USA. 1998. Lang.: Eng. 3882
Design/technology
Production design for Bill Condon's film *Gods and Monsters*. USA: Hollywood, CA. 1998. Lang.: Eng. 3908
Plays/librettos/scripts
Interview with film-maker Bill Condon. USA. 1998. Lang.: Eng. 4021
Godwin, Simon
Performance/production
Collection of newspaper reviews by London theatre critics. UK-England: London. 1998. Lang.: Eng. 2548
Godzilla
Design/technology
Lighting design for Roland Emmerich's film *Godzilla*. USA. 1998. Lang.: Eng. 3917
Goebbels, Heiner
Performance/production
Composers and the work of Bertolt Brecht. Germany. 1928-1998. Lang.: Ger. 4297
Goerne, Matthias
Performance/production
Recordings of *Lieder* by Schumann. Germany. UK-England. 1998. Lang.: Eng. 4601
Goese, Mimi
Performance/production
Performance artist Mimi Goese. USA. 1982-1998. Lang.: Eng. 4252
Goethe, Johann Wolfgang von
Design/technology
Josef Svoboda's set design for Goethe's *Faust*. Czech Republic: Prague. 1997. Lang.: Eng. 1517
Performance/production
Otomar Krejča's production of *Faust* at Národní Divadlo. Czech Republic: Prague. 1997. Lang.: Eng, Fre. 1881
French productions of German plays. France. 1998. Lang.: Ger. 1935
Klaus Michael Grüber's production of Goethe's *Iphigenia auf Tauris*. Germany: Berlin. 1998. Lang.: Swe. 1997
Recent productions of Bochumer Schauspielhaus. Germany: Bochum. 1998. Lang.: Ger. 2009
Klaus Michael Grüber's production of Goethe's *Iphigenia auf Tauris*. Germany: Berlin. 1998. Lang.: Ger. 2031
Television adaptations of works by Goethe. Germany. 1965-1997. Lang.: Eng. 4061
Plays/librettos/scripts
Female sacrifice in eighteenth-century German drama. Germany. 1772-1781. Lang.: Eng. 3167
Relation to other fields
Shakespeare's Hamlet in novels of Goethe and Scott. England. Germany. 1776-1824. Lang.: Eng. 3757
Theory/criticism
Critical response to Klaus Michael Grüber's production of Goethe's *Iphigenia auf Tauris*. Germany. 1998. Lang.: Ger. 3821
Goetz, Curt
Plays/librettos/scripts
Actor and playwright Curt Goetz and Nazi attitudes toward theatre. Germany. 1933-1944. Lang.: Eng. 3139
Goetz, Rainald
Performance/production
Recent productions of Deutsches Schauspielhaus. Germany: Hamburg. 1998. Lang.: Ger. 2034
Gofton, Richard
Performance/production
Collection of newspaper reviews by London theatre critics. UK-England. 1998. Lang.: Eng. 2497
Gogol Theatre (Moscow)
SEE
Dramatičeskij Teat'r im. N. Gogolja.
Gogol, Nikolaj Vasiljévič
Basic theatrical documents
English translation of Mejerchol'd's adaptation of *Revizor (The Inspector General)* by Gogol. Russia. USSR. 1838-1926. Lang.: Eng. 1450
Performance/production
Gogol's *Revizor (The Inspector General)* directed by Árpád Jutocsa Hegyi. Hungary: Miskolc. 1998. Lang.: Hun. 2108
Pëtr Fomenko's theatrical adaptation of Gogol's *Dead Souls*. Russia: Moscow. 1998. Lang.: Rus. 2303
Pëtr Fomenko's production of *V Čičikovskoj krugoverti (In Čičikov's Chaos)*. Russia: Moscow. 1998. Lang.: Rus. 2340
Interview with composer Paul Schmidt. USA: New Haven, CT. 1998. Lang.: Eng. 2660
Interview with director Peter Sellars. USA: Cambridge, MA. 1980-1981. Lang.: Eng. 2661
Yale Drama Department's reconstruction of Gogol's *Revizor (The Inspector General)* as staged by Mejerchol'd. USA: New Haven, CT. 1997. Lang.: Eng. 2668
The development of the character Khlezstakov in Gogol's *Revizor (The Inspector General)* in productions by Mejerchol'd. USSR. 1926-1939. Lang.: Eng. 2762
Mejerchol'd's production of Gogol's *Revizor (The Inspector General)*. USSR: Moscow. 1926. Lang.: Eng. 2763
Director Harold Clurman's reaction to Mejerchol'd's *Revizor (The Inspector General)*. USSR: Moscow. 1935. Lang.: Eng. 2764
Gold, Michael
Institutions
The New Playwrights Theatre Company. USA: New York, NY. 1927-1929. Lang.: Eng. 410
Goldberg, Whoopi
Performance/production
Analysis of transformative comedy. USA. 1975-1988. Lang.: Eng. 666
Golden Child
Design/technology
Lighting design for Hwang's *Golden Child* at the Public Theatre. USA: New York, NY. 1996-1998. Lang.: Eng. 1540
Performance/production
Julyana Soelistyo and Sam Trammel, winners of the Derwent Award. USA: New York, NY. 1998. Lang.: Eng. 2719
Careeer of actress Tsai Chin. USA. 1959-1998. Lang.: Eng. 2754
Golden Door, The
Plays/librettos/scripts
Jean Randich's production of *The Golden Door* by Sylvia Regan, Tenement Museum. USA: New York, NY. 1940-1998. Lang.: Eng. 3606
Golden Girls, The
Plays/librettos/scripts
Analysis of plays by Dymphna Cusack. Australia. 1927-1959. Lang.: Eng. 2777
Golden Pippin, The
Plays/librettos/scripts
Music and the ballad opera in English popular theatre. England. 1728-1780. Lang.: Eng. 4390
Golden, Emily
Performance/production
Singers' approaches to the title role in Bizet's *Carmen*. 1875-1998. Lang.: Eng. 4502
Golder, Sid
Performance/production
Collection of newspaper reviews by London theatre critics. UK-England: London. 1998. Lang.: Eng. 2505
Goldfaden, Abraham
Plays/librettos/scripts
Enlightenment influences on modern Jewish theatre. Poland. 1500-1914. Lang.: Pol. 3307
Goldman, James
Design/technology
Lighting design for the musical *Follies*, Paper Mill Playhouse. USA: Millburn, NJ. 1998. Lang.: Eng. 4335

Goldman, Lisa
Performance/production
Collection of newspaper reviews by London theatre critics. UK-England: London. 1998. Lang.: Eng. 2427
Collection of newspaper reviews by London theatre critics. UK-England: London. 1998. Lang.: Eng. 2532
Goldoni, Carlo
Basic theatrical documents
Catalan translation of *Il Ventaglio (The Fan)* by Carlo Goldoni. Italy. 1765. Lang.: Cat. 1442
Catalan translation of *Gl'Innamorati (The Lovers)* by Carlo Goldoni. Italy. 1765. Lang.: Cat. 1443
Catalan translation of *La Bottega del caffè (The Coffee Shop)* by Carlo Goldoni. Italy. 1750. Lang.: Cat. 1444
Performance/production
Goldoni's *La Locandiera* directed by Lászlo Keszég. Hungary: Kaposvár. 1998. Lang.: Hun. 2092
Excerpts from the notebooks of director Massimo Castri. Italy: Prato. 1996. Lang.: Ita. 2162
Text of an address by director Giorgio Strehler at the University of Turin. Italy. 1997. Lang.: Ita. 2184
Collection of newspaper reviews by London theatre critics. UK-England: London. 1998. Lang.: Eng. 2474
Plays/librettos/scripts
The character Giacinta in Goldoni's *Trilogia della villeggiatura (Holiday Trilogy)*. Italy: Venice. 1761. Lang.: Ita. 3221
Analysis of *Trilogia della villeggiatura (Holiday Trilogy)* by Carlo Goldoni. Italy. 1751-1761. Lang.: Ita. 3236
Catalan translation of the memoirs of playwright Carlo Goldoni. Italy. 1707-1793. Lang.: Cat. 3241
Analysis of comedies by Goldoni. Italy: Venice. 1707-1793. Lang.: Ita. 3258
Carlo Goldoni's comic-opera libretti. Italy. 1748-1762. Lang.: Eng. 4807
Goldschmidt, Miriam
Plays/librettos/scripts
Playwright Volker Lüdecke. Germany: Kaiserslautern. 1992-1998. Lang.: Ger. 3141
Goldsmith, Oliver
Plays/librettos/scripts
The character Honeywood in Goldsmith's *The Good Natur'd Man*. England. 1767-1768. Lang.: Eng. 3045
Martial law and Renaissance drama and fiction. Europe. 1563-1753. Lang.: Eng. 3059
Goldstein, Jack
Administration
Jack Goldstein's departure from Equity to head Theatre Development Fund. USA: New York, NY. 1998. Lang.: Eng. 56
Golejzovskij, Kasjan
Performance/production
Interview with choreographer Kasjan Golejzovskij. Russia. 1892-1970. Lang.: Rus. 960
Golem, The
Performance/production
Collection of newspaper reviews by London theatre critics. UK-England: London. 1998. Lang.: Eng. 2584
Golove, Jonathan
Basic theatrical documents
Jonathan Golove's opera *Red Harvest*. USA. 1940-1950. Lang.: Eng. 4422
Golubovskij, Boris
Performance/production
Producer and director Boris Golubovskij. Russia. 1998. Lang.: Rus. 2271
Gombrowicz, Witold
Basic theatrical documents
English translation of *Historia (History)* by Witold Gombrowicz. Poland. 1998. Lang.: Eng. 1448
Performance/production
Review of Gombrowicz's *Princess Yvonne*, Katona József Theatre. Hungary: Budapest. 1997. Lang.: Hun. 2079
Jerzy Grzegorzewski's production of *Ślub (The Marriage)* by Witold Gombrowicz. Poland: Warsaw. 1998. Lang.: Pol. 2218
Plays/librettos/scripts
Translating the unfinished *Historia (History)* by Witold Gombrowicz. Poland. 1951-1998. Lang.: Eng. 3303
Gómez-Peña, Guillermo
Performance/production
Analysis of Guillermo Gómez-Peña and Coco Fusco's performance piece *The Couple in the Cage*. USA. 1995. Lang.: Eng. 4255
Background on *The Couple in the Cage* by Guillermo Gómez-Peña and Coco Fusco. USA. 1992-1995. Lang.: Eng. 4259
Gómez, Sara
Plays/librettos/scripts
Afrocuban religion in Cuban films. Cuba. 1974-1991. Lang.: Eng. 3968
Gončarov, Andrej Aleksandrovič
Performance/production
Interview with director Andrej Gončarov. Russia: Moscow. 1998. Lang.: Rus. 2272
Gončarova, Natalija
Design/technology
Avant-garde Russian women artist/designers. Russia. USSR. 1880-1949. Lang.: Eng. 214
Gondinet, Edmond
Audience
The negative influence of Wagnerianism on the reception of Delibes' opera *Lakmé*. 1900-1996. Lang.: Fre. 4409
Basic theatrical documents
Libretto of *Lakmé* by Léo Delibes, Edmond Gondinet, and Philippe Gille. France. 1883. Lang.: Fre. 4415
Plays/librettos/scripts
Analysis of Delibes' opera *Lakmé*. France. 1883. Lang.: Fre. 4782
The source of the libretto for Delibes' *Lakmé*. France. 1853-1883. Lang.: Fre. 4784
Gooch, Dan
Performance/production
Collection of newspaper reviews by London theatre critics. UK-England: London. 1998. Lang.: Eng. 2475
Good Natur'd Man, The
Plays/librettos/scripts
The character Honeywood in Goldsmith's *The Good Natur'd Man*. England. 1767-1768. Lang.: Eng. 3045
Good Person of Szechwan, The
SEE
Gute Mensch von Sezuan, Der.
Goodman Theatre (Chicago, IL)
Design/technology
Technical designs for *Griller* by Eric Bogosian. USA: Chicago, IL. 1998. Lang.: Eng. 1558
Goodnight Desdemona, Good Morning Juliet
Performance/production
Collection of newspaper reviews by London theatre critics. UK-England: London. 1998. Lang.: Eng. 2562
Goodrich, Frances
Performance/production
Student production of *The Diary of Anne Frank*. USA. 1955. Lang.: Eng. 2703
Plays/librettos/scripts
Reactions to the revised version of *The Diary of Anne Frank*. USA: New York, NY. 1998. Lang.: Eng. 3618
Goodspeed Opera House (East Haddam, CT)
Administration
Interviews with women in top management of theatres. USA: New Haven, CT, Seattle, WA, East Haddam, CT. 1998. Lang.: Eng. 1397
Design/technology
Neil Patel's scene design for *Mirette*, Goodspeed Opera House. USA: East Haddam, CT. 1998. Lang.: Eng. 4334
Goodwin, John
Plays/librettos/scripts
Dramatic adaptations of Henry Wadsworth Longfellow's poem *Evangeline*. USA. Canada. 1860-1976. Lang.: Eng. 3643
Goodwin, Nathan
Performance/production
Collection of newspaper reviews by London theatre critics. UK-England: London. 1998. Lang.: Eng. 2454
Goold, Rupert
Performance/production
Collection of newspaper reviews by London theatre critics. UK-England: London. 1998. Lang.: Eng. 2583
Goosen, Jeanne
Performance/production
The kitchen in performance art of Bobby Baker and Jeanne Goosen. UK-England. South Africa, Republic of. 1990-1992. Lang.: Eng. 4243
Gopal, Ram
Performance/production
Western ballet's influence on Indian classical dancer Ram Gopal. Europe. India. 1930-1960. Lang.: Ita. 915
Göranzon, Marie
Performance/production
Interviews with actresses of three generations on female roles. Sweden: Stockholm. 1945-1998. Lang.: Swe. 2380

Gorboduc
Performance/production
Music in Tudor drama. England. 1497-1569. Lang.: Eng. 1902
Gordon, Janet
Performance/production
Collection of newspaper reviews by London theatre critics. UK-England: London. 1998. Lang.: Eng. 2420
Gordon, Mel
Performance/production
Director Mel Gordon on Mejerchol'd's influence. USSR. 1920-1931. Lang.: Eng. 2765
Gordon, Mick
Performance/production
Collection of newspaper reviews by London theatre critics. UK-England: London. 1998. Lang.: Eng. 2509
Collection of newspaper reviews by London theatre critics. UK-England: London. 1998. Lang.: Eng. 2530
Collection of newspaper reviews by London theatre critics. UK-England: London. 1998. Lang.: Eng. 2547
Gordon, Ruth
Plays/librettos/scripts
Feminism and plays of Henrik Ibsen. Norway. 1879-1979. Lang.: Eng. 3293
Gore ot uma (Wit Works Woe)
Performance/production
Oleg Menšikov's production of *Gore ot uma (Wit Works Woe)* by Gribojédov. Russia: Moscow. 1998. Lang.: Rus. 2267
Gore-Booth, Eva
Plays/librettos/scripts
Gender and nationalism in Northern Irish drama. UK-Ireland. 1902-1997. Lang.: Eng. 3511
Gorey, Edward
Basic theatrical documents
Text of *The Black Doll* by Edward Gorey. USA. 1973. Lang.: Eng. 3887
Plays/librettos/scripts
Interview with Edward Gorey about his animated film *The Black Doll.* USA. 1973-1997. Lang.: Eng. 3994
Goring, Marius
Performance/production
Career of actor Marius Goring. UK-England: London. 1930-1998. Lang.: Eng. 2598
Gorkij, Maksim
Plays/librettos/scripts
Kazan in the life of Maksim Gorkij and Fëdor Šaljapin. Tatarstan: Kazan. 1868-1938. Lang.: Rus. 689
Analysis of *Voskresšij syn (Reincarnated Son)* by Maksim Gorkij. Russia. 1930-1932. Lang.: Rus. 3321
Translations of Čechov's *Three Sisters* and Gorkij's *The Lower Depths.* Russia. 1901-1902. Lang.: Rus. 3326
Gorkij and the 'new drama' of the turn of the century. Russia. 1890-1910. Lang.: Rus. 3341
Görne, Dieter
Institutions
Profile of Theater in der Fabrik. Germany: Dresden. 1993-1998. Lang.: Ger. 1644
Gorr, Rita
Performance/production
Mezzo soprano Rita Gorr. Belgium. 1998. Lang.: Eng. 4536
Goslar, Lotte
Performance/production
Lotte Goslar's Pantomime Circus. Germany: Dresden. USA: Los Angeles, CA. 1907-1997. Lang.: Eng. 4123
Comic dance performer Lotte Goslar. Germany. USA. 1907-1997. Lang.: Eng. 4124
Gossett, Philip
Performance/production
Musicological preparation for the Metropolitan Opera production of Rossini's *La Cenerentola.* USA: Chicago, IL. 1998. Lang.: Eng. 4737
Gosudarstvénnyj Akademičéskij Bolšoj Teat'r (Moscow)
Institutions
The Vienna-based foundation for the development of Moscow's Bolšoj Theatre. Austria: Vienna. 1998. Lang.: Rus. 335
Assessment of the Bolšoj Theatre season. Russia: Moscow. 1997-1998. Lang.: Rus. 1046
The Bolšoj Theatre's 222nd season. Russia: Moscow. 1997-1998. Lang.: Rus. 4466
Performance/production
Guest performances of dancers and ballet masters of the Kirov and Bolšoj ballets. Hungary. 1975-1978. Lang.: Hun. 1086
Obituary for ballerina Galina Ulanova. Russia. 1910-1998. Lang.: Eng. 1125
Collaboration of the Bolšoj and Mariinskij ballet troupes. Russia: Moscow, St. Petersburg. 1998. Lang.: Rus. 1135
Bolšoj Ballet director Jurij Grigorovič. Russia: Moscow. 1998. Lang.: Rus. 1141
Bolšoj ballet master and choreographer Vladimir Vasiljév. Russia: Moscow. 1998. Lang.: Rus. 1147
Bolšoj Opera star V. Bukin. Russia: Moscow. Lang.: Rus. 4683
Bolšoj Opera singer M. Mincaev. Russia: Moscow. 1998. Lang.: Rus. 4684
Bolšoj Opera singer V. Matorin. Russia: Moscow. 1998. Lang.: Rus. 4692
Premieres of the Bolšoj Theatre. Russia: Moscow. 1825-1997. Lang.: Rus. 4693
Gosudarstvénnyj Akademičéskij Teat'r Opery i Baleta im. N.A. Rimskogo-Korsakova (St. Petersburg)
Performance/production
Čajkovskij's *Eugene Onegin* directed by A. Stepanov. Russia: St. Petersburg. 1998. Lang.: Rus. 4671
Gosudarstvénnyj Akademičéskij Teat'r Opery i Baleta im. S.M. Kirova (St. Petersburg)
Performance/production
Collaboration of the Bolšoj and Mariinskij ballet troupes. Russia: Moscow, St. Petersburg. 1998. Lang.: Rus. 1135
Gosudarstvénnyj Central'nyj Teat'r Kukol (Moscow)
Institutions
Profile of the National Puppet Theatre. Russia: Moscow. 1998. Lang.: Rus. 4872
Gosudarstvénnyj Dramatičéskij Pjatyj Teat'r (Omsk)
Performance/production
Director Sergej Rudzinskij. Russia: Omsk. 1998. Lang.: Rus. 2325
Gosudarstvénnyj Institut Teatral'nogo Iskusstva im. A.V. Lunačarskogo (GITIS, Moscow)
SEE ALSO
Rossiskaja Akademija Teatral'nogo Iskusstva.
Gosudarstvénnyj Teat'r Družby Narodov (Moscow)
SEE ALSO
Gosudarstvénnyj Teat'r Nacij.
Teat'r Nacij.
Gosudarstvénnyj Teat'r Kukol (Kurgan)
Performance/production
History of Kurgan's puppet theatre. Russia: Kurgan. 1948-1998. Lang.: Rus. 4897
Gosudarstvénnyj teat'r kukol 'Ognivo' (Mytišči)
Institutions
Profile of 'Ognivo' puppet theatre. Russia: Mytišchi. 1998. Lang.: Rus. 4871
Gosudarstvényij Akademičéskij Bolšoj Teat'r (Moscow)
Institutions
The Bolšoj Ballet and the experimental company Gelikon. Russia: Moscow. 1997. Lang.: Swe. 4467
Göteborgs Stadsteatern (Gothenburg)
Administration
The closing of Göteborgs Stadsteatern. Sweden. 1974-1997. Lang.: Dan. 1389
GöteborgsOperan (Gothenburg)
Performance/production
Interview with opera singer Anne Bolstad. Norway. Sweden. 1980-1998. Lang.: Swe. 4665
Gothár, Péter
Plays/librettos/scripts
New Hungarian translations of Shakespeare. Hungary. 1990-1998. Lang.: Hun. 3187
Göthe, Staffan
Plays/librettos/scripts
Interview with Staffan Göthe, author, director, and one of the actors of *Ett Lysand elände (A Brilliant Misery).* Sweden: Stockholm. 1990-1998. Lang.: Swe. 3408
Gotscheff, Dimiter
Institutions
Productions of Bochumer Schauspielhaus. Germany: Bochum. 1998. Lang.: Ger. 1655
Performance/production
Shakespeare performance on the Rhine and the Ruhr. Germany: Cologne, Bochum, Düsseldorf. 1996-1997. Lang.: Ger. 1962

Gotscheff, Dimiter — cont'd

Recent productions of Bochumer Schauspielhaus. Germany: Bochum. 1998. Lang.: Ger. 2009

Recent productions of Deutsches Schauspielhaus. Germany: Hamburg. 1998. Lang.: Ger. 2034

Götterdämmerung
Plays/librettos/scripts
Outline of Wagner's *Götterdämmerung*. Hungary: Budapest. 1998. Lang.: Hun. 4800

Gottfridsson, Cristina
Performance/production
Interview with director Anders Paulin. Sweden: Malmö. 1997-1998. Lang.: Swe. 2377
Plays/librettos/scripts
Swedish theatres and young Swedish playwrights. Sweden: Malmö, Gothenburg, Stockholm. 1994-1998. Lang.: Swe. 3411

Gottlieb, Jon
Design/technology
Professional theatrical designers on design training. USA. 1998. Lang.: Eng. 252

Gottlieb, Michael
Design/technology
Lighting designer Michael Gottlieb. USA: New York, NY. 1998. Lang.: Eng. 281

Gottsched, Luise
Plays/librettos/scripts
Shakespeare translators Luise Gottsched and Dorothea Tieck. Germany. 1739-1833. Lang.: Ger. 3156

Gottschild, Hellmut
Performance/production
Dancer, choreographer, and teacher Hellmut Gottschild. Germany. USA. 1936-1998. Lang.: Ger. 1287

Götz von Berlichingen
Performance/production
Television adaptations of works by Goethe. Germany. 1965-1997. Lang.: Eng. 4061

Götz, Christian von
Performance/production
Music theatre production in northern Germany. Germany: Lübeck, Hamburg, Bremen, Kiel. 1998. Lang.: Ger. 4293

Gough, Andy
Performance/production
Collection of newspaper reviews by London theatre critics. UK-England: London. 1998. Lang.: Eng. 2506

Gould, David
Performance/production
Analysis of the *Night and Day* dance sequence of *The Gay Divorcee*. USA: Hollywood, CA. 1934. Lang.: Eng. 977

Goulish, Matthew
Institutions
Interview with Matthew Goulish and Lin Hixson of Goat Island. USA: Chicago, IL. 1990. Lang.: Eng. 4237

Goulue, La (Weber, Louise)
Performance spaces
Dancers and performance space. Europe. 1895-1937. Lang.: Ger. 909

Gounod, Charles
Performance/production
Background material on Metropolitan Opera radio broadcast performances. USA: New York, NY. 1998. Lang.: Eng. 4713

Verdi's *Stiffelio* and Gounod's *Roméo et Juliette* in New York. USA: New York, NY. 1850-1998. Lang.: Eng. 4730

Gourlay, Eileen
Performance/production
Collection of newspaper reviews by London theatre critics. UK-England: London. 1998. Lang.: Eng. 2516

Gourley, Matthew J.
Performance/production
Creating the role of Biagio Buonaccorsi in Robert Cohen's *The Prince*. USA. 1997. Lang.: Eng. 2686

Govekar, Fran
Plays/librettos/scripts
Social roles in plays by Fran Govekar and Anton Medved. Slovenia. 1897-1910. Lang.: Slo. 3352

Government Inspector, The
SEE
Revizor.

Government subsidies
SEE
Funding, government.

Govi, Gilberto
Performance/production
Sketches and caricatures of dialect actor Gilberto Govi. Italy: Genoa. 1885-1966. Lang.: Ita. 543

Gow, Ruth
Performance/production
Collection of newspaper reviews by London theatre critics. UK-England: London. 1998. Lang.: Eng. 2443

Grace Theatre (London)
SEE ALSO
Latchmere Theatre.
Performance/production
Collection of newspaper reviews by London theatre critics. UK-England: London. 1998. Lang.: Eng. 2418

Collection of newspaper reviews by London theatre critics. UK-England: London. 1998. Lang.: Eng. 2437

Collection of newspaper reviews by London theatre critics. UK-England: London. 1998. Lang.: Eng. 2464

Collection of newspaper reviews by London theatre critics. UK-England: London. 1998. Lang.: Eng. 2480

Collection of newspaper reviews by London theatre critics. UK-England: London. 1998. Lang.: Eng. 2483

Collection of newspaper reviews by London theatre critics. UK-England: London. 1998. Lang.: Eng. 2491

Collection of newspaper reviews by London theatre critics. UK-England: London. 1998. Lang.: Eng. 2517

Collection of newspaper reviews by London theatre critics. UK-England: London. 1998. Lang.: Eng. 2560

Collection of newspaper reviews by London theatre critics. UK-England: London. 1998. Lang.: Eng. 2574

Collection of newspaper reviews by London theatre critics. UK-England: London. 1998. Lang.: Eng. 2585

Grace, Nicholas
Performance/production
Collection of newspaper reviews by London theatre critics. UK-England: London. 1998. Lang.: Eng. 2499

Grade, Lew
Administration
Obituary for producer Lew Grade. UK-England. 1908-1998. Lang.: Eng. 3872

Graham, Martha
Performance/production
Dance-mime Angna Enters. USA. 1905-1923. Lang.: Eng. 1319

Modern dance and the female body. USA. Europe. 1900-1930. Lang.: Eng. 1321

Martha Graham on life devoted to choreography and dance. USA. 1930. Lang.: Eng. 1323

Graham, Philip
Performance/production
Collection of newspaper reviews by London theatre critics. UK-England: London. 1998. Lang.: Eng. 2416

Graham, Ranald
Performance/production
Collection of newspaper reviews by London theatre critics. UK-England: London. Lang.: Eng. 2408

Gran Scena, La (New York, NY)
Performance/production
Interview with Ira Siff of La Gran Scena. USA: New York, NY. 1998. Lang.: Eng. 4719

Gran Teatro del Liceu (Barcelona)
Performance spaces
The restoration of the opera houses Gran Teatro del Liceu and Teatro La Fenice. Spain: Barcelona. Italy: Venice. 1994-1998. Lang.: Eng. 4495

Granath, Björn
Performance/production
Interviews with actors Lil Terselius and Björn Granath. Sweden: Stockholm. 1998. Lang.: Swe. 2381

Grand Cirque Ordinaire, Le (Montreal, PQ)
Performance/production
Social criticism and alternative theatre in Quebec and Newfoundland. Canada. 1970-1985. Lang.: Eng. 500

Grand Macabre, Le
Performance/production
György Ligeti's *Le Grand Macabre* directed by Balázs Kovalik. Hungary: Budapest. 1998. Lang.: Hun. 4642

Grand Théâtre (Geneva)
Performance spaces
The construction of the Grand Théâtre de Genève. Switzerland: Geneva. 1984-1998. Lang.: Ger. 459

Grand Théâtre (Geneva) — cont'd

Performance/production
Press reactions to productions of Offenbach's *Orphée aux Enfers*. Belgium. Switzerland. France. 1997. Lang.: Fre. 4535

Grand Theatre (Shanghai)
Institutions
Opening of the Grand Theatre in Shanghai. China, People's Republic of: Shanghai. 1998. Lang.: Eng. 4448

Grandage, Michael
Performance/production
Collection of newspaper reviews by London theatre critics. UK-England. 1998. Lang.: Eng. 2504

Grande amor de nossas vidas, O (Great Love of Our Lives)
Plays/librettos/scripts
Cruelty and the absurd in theatre of Latin American playwrights. Latin America. 1960-1980. Lang.: Eng. 3267

Granlund, Victoria
Training
Singer training at Teater- & Operahögskolan. Sweden: Gothenburg. 1960-1998. Lang.: Swe. 4848

Granqvist, Tove
Plays/librettos/scripts
Recent drama and revue in Swedish. Finland. 1998. Lang.: Eng, Fre. 3069

Grant, Curry
Design/technology
Pop music lighting design of Steve Cohen and Curry Grant. USA. 1997. Lang.: Eng. 4102

Granville-Barker, Harley
Plays/librettos/scripts
George Bernard Shaw's involvement with the Court Theatre. UK-England. 1904-1909. Lang.: Eng. 3471
Comparison of plays by Harley Granville-Barker and Anton Čechov. UK-England. Russia. 1900-1946. Lang.: Eng. 3501

Grass and Wild Strawberries
Plays/librettos/scripts
Language and rhetoric in plays of George Ryga. Canada. 1967-1985. Lang.: Eng. 2792

Grassi, Orazio
Plays/librettos/scripts
Analysis of Jesuit opera by Giovanni Girolamo Kapsberger and Orazio Grassi. Italy: Rome. 1622. Lang.: Eng. 4803

Graves, Denyce
Performance/production
Singers' approaches to the title role in Bizet's *Carmen*. 1875-1998. Lang.: Eng. 4502

Gray, Ramin
Performance/production
Collection of newspaper reviews by London theatre critics. UK-England: London. 1998. Lang.: Eng. 2582

Grča (Knot, The)
Plays/librettos/scripts
Social roles in plays by Fran Govekar and Anton Medved. Slovenia. 1897-1910. Lang.: Slo. 3352

Great Gatsby, The
Performance/production
Collection of newspaper reviews by London theatre critics. UK-England: London. 1998. Lang.: Eng. 2410

Great God Brown, The
Institutions
Interview with Kricker James and Claire Higgins of Chain Lightning Theatre. USA: New York, NY. 1991-1998. Lang.: Eng. 1780
Plays/librettos/scripts
Race and gender in *The Great God Brown* by Eugene O'Neill. USA. 1926. Lang.: Eng. 3608
Analysis of Eugene O'Neill's 'middle period' plays. USA. 1925-1938. Lang.: Eng. 3675

Great White Hope, The
Plays/librettos/scripts
Miscegenation in American drama. USA. 1909-1969. Lang.: Eng. 3599

Grecs, Les (Greeks, The)
Plays/librettos/scripts
The use of collage in contemporary productions involving Greek myths. Canada: Montreal, PQ. 1998. Lang.: Fre. 2814

Greek Theatre (Los Angeles, CA)
Performance spaces
Profiles of Southern California theatres. USA. 1998. Lang.: Eng. 473

Green Helmet, The
Performance/production
Collection of newspaper reviews by London theatre critics. UK-England: London. 1998. Lang.: Eng. 2458

Green, Jeff
Performance/production
Collection of newspaper reviews by London theatre critics. UK-England: London. 1998. Lang.: Eng. 2546

Green, Mark R.
Basic theatrical documents
Text of *The Metropolitan*, formerly called *The Ten Minute Play* by Mark R. Green. USA. 1995. Lang.: Eng. 1485

Green, Nick
Performance/production
Collection of newspaper reviews by London theatre critics. UK-England: London. 1998. Lang.: Eng. 2522

Greenaway, Peter
Performance/production
Reviews of productions by Wilson, Greenaway, and Mnouchkine. France: Paris. 1997-1998. Lang.: Eng. 1926
Plays/librettos/scripts
Analysis of Peter Greenaway's film *Prospero's Books*. UK-England. 1991. Lang.: Fre. 3990

Greenberg, Gordon
Performance/production
Collection of newspaper reviews by London theatre critics. UK-England: London. 1998. Lang.: Eng. 2587

Greenberg, Neil
Performance/production
Analysis of dance trilogy by choreographer Neil Greenberg. USA. 1994-1998. Lang.: Eng. 1334

Greenberg, Richard
Basic theatrical documents
Text of *Three Days of Rain* by Richard Greenberg. USA. 1998. Lang.: Eng. 1486

Greene, Robert
Plays/librettos/scripts
Analysis of *Friar Bacon and Friar Bungay* by Robert Greene. England. 1594. Lang.: Eng. 2974
The authorship of *George a Greene*. England. 1593-1599. Lang.: Eng. 2989

Greenfield, William
Design/technology
TV lighting designer William Greenfield. USA. 1930-1998. Lang.: Eng. 4049

Greenhorn, Stephen
Performance/production
Collection of newspaper reviews by London theatre critics. UK-England: London. 1998. Lang.: Eng. 2434
Report on several English performances. UK-England: London, Stratford. 1998. Lang.: Swe. 2634

Greenman
Performance/production
Dancer/choreographer Rosemary Lee. UK-England: London. 1989-1998. Lang.: Eng. 1307

Greenspan, Hank
Plays/librettos/scripts
Survivors' testimony in Holocaust theatre. USA. 1975-1995. Lang.: Eng. 3605

Greenwich House Theatre (New York, NY)
Design/technology
Costume design for revival of *As Thousands Cheer* by Drama Dept. USA: New York, NY. 1998. Lang.: Eng. 4333

Greenwich Theatre (London)
Institutions
Funding status of London's fringe theatres. UK-England: London. 1998. Lang.: Eng. 1748
Performance/production
Collection of newspaper reviews by London theatre critics. UK-England: London. 1998. Lang.: Eng. 2473
Collection of newspaper reviews by London theatre critics. UK-England: London. 1998. Lang.: Eng. 2583

Greenwood, George
Theory/criticism
Marginalia in Sir George Greenwood's copy of *Is Shakespeare Dead?* by Mark Twain. USA. 1909. Lang.: Eng. 863

Greenwood, Jane
Design/technology
Technical designs for *The Scarlet Pimpernel* directed by Robert Longbottom. USA: New York, NY. 1998. Lang.: Eng. 4331

Greer, Bonnie
Performance/production
Collection of newspaper reviews by London theatre critics. UK-England: London. 1998. Lang.: Eng. 2584

Gregg, Jess
Performance/production
Playwright Jess Gregg's relationship with choreographer Agnes De Mille. USA: New York, NY. 1961-1998. Lang.: Eng. 1178
Gregory, Augusta Isabella, Lady
Plays/librettos/scripts
Gender and nationalism in Northern Irish drama. UK-Ireland. 1902-1997. Lang.: Eng. 3511
Gregory, Emma
Performance/production
Collection of newspaper reviews by London theatre critics. UK-England: London. 1998. Lang.: Eng. 2543
Gregory, Richard
Performance/production
Collection of newspaper reviews by London theatre critics. UK-England: London. 1998. Lang.: Eng. 2443
Gregs, Kevin
Plays/librettos/scripts
Review of collections of plays with gay themes. Canada. 1996. Lang.: Eng. 2802
Greif, Michael
Performance/production
Collection of newspaper reviews by London theatre critics. UK-England: London. 1998. Lang.: Eng. 2561
Greig, David
Performance/production
Collection of newspaper reviews by London theatre critics. UK-England: London. 1998. Lang.: Eng. 2434
Grémont, Henri
Plays/librettos/scripts
Massenet's opera *Hérodiade* and its literary sources. France. 1881. Lang.: Fre. 4779
Greville, Fulke
Plays/librettos/scripts
Analysis of a scene from *Mustapha* by Fulke Greville. England. 1609-1633. Lang.: Eng. 3044
Gribojédov, Aleksand'r Sergejévič
Performance/production
Oleg Menšikov's production of *Gore ot uma (Wit Works Woe)* by Gribojédov. Russia: Moscow. 1998. Lang.: Rus. 2267
Grieg, Noël
Performance/production
Collection of newspaper reviews by London theatre critics. UK-England: London. 1998. Lang.: Eng. 2477
Griffey, Anthony Dean
Performance/production
Tenor Anthony Dean Griffey's career and Metropolitan Opera debut. USA: New York, NY. 1998. Lang.: Eng. 4752
Griffin, Merv
Performance spaces
The supper and swing-music venue the Coconut Club. USA: Los Angeles, CA. 1998. Lang.: Eng. 4115
Griffin, Tamzin
Performance/production
Collection of newspaper reviews by London theatre critics. UK-England: London. 1998. Lang.: Eng. 2465
Griffiths, Linda
Plays/librettos/scripts
Playwright/actress Linda Griffiths on the creative process. Canada: Saskatoon, SK. 1970-1998. Lang.: Eng. 2806
Grigorovič, Jurij
Performance/production
Bolšoj Ballet director Jurij Grigorovič. Russia: Moscow. 1998. Lang.: Rus. 1141
Grill, David
Design/technology
Professional theatrical designers on design training. USA. 1998. Lang.: Eng. 252
Griller
Design/technology
Technical designs for *Griller* by Eric Bogosian. USA: Chicago, IL. 1998. Lang.: Eng. 1558
Grillparzer, Franz
Institutions
Peter Stein's last season as director at the Salzburg Festival. Austria: Salzburg. 1997. Lang.: Eng. 336
Plays/librettos/scripts
The image of motherhood in German-language drama. Austria. Germany. 1890-1910. Lang.: Ger. 2787
The character Medea in European drama. Europe. 450 B.C.-1998 A.D. Lang.: Ger. 3063
Grimaldi, Joey
Performance/production
Possible illustrations of Dibdin's *Harlequin and Mother Goose* at Covent Garden. UK-England: London. 1806-1808. Lang.: Eng. 2639
Grimké, Angelina Weld
Performance/production
The first wave of American feminist theatre. USA. 1890-1930. Lang.: Eng. 648
Plays/librettos/scripts
Lynching in plays of Angelina Weld Grimké and Lorraine Hansberry. USA. 1916-1958. Lang.: Eng. 3602
GRIPS Theater (Berlin)
Institutions
Children's theatres GRIPS and Carrousel. Germany: Berlin. 1998. Lang.: Ger. 347
Plays/librettos/scripts
Children's theatre at GRIPS. Germany: Berlin. 1966-1998. Lang.: Ger. 3152
Analysis of *Café Mitte (Café Center)* by Volker Ludwig. Germany: Berlin. 1997-1998. Lang.: Ger. 4393
Grizzard, George
Performance/production
Actor George Grizzard. UK-England: London. USA: New York, NY. 1954-1998. Lang.: Eng. 2646
Grmače
Plays/librettos/scripts
Analysis of *Grmače* by Dane Zajc. Slovenia. 1991. Lang.: Slo. 3356
Groke, George
Performance/production
Returned emigrant dancer George Groke. Germany. Poland. 1904-1972. Lang.: Ger. 925
Gromada, John
Design/technology
Panel discussion of sound designers. USA. 1998. Lang.: Eng. 287
Grootboom, Mpumelelo
Relation to other fields
Topics in post-apartheid South African literature and theatre. South Africa, Republic of. 1995-1998. Lang.: Eng. 764
Groovy Times
Performance/production
Collection of newspaper reviews by London theatre critics. UK-England: London. 1998. Lang.: Eng. 2494
Gropper, Wolfgang
Administration
Wolfgang Gropper, director of Staatstheater Braunschweig. Germany: Braunschweig. 1997-1998. Lang.: Ger. 8
Gross Indecency
Performance/production
Analysis of recent New York productions. USA: New York, NY. 1997-1998. Lang.: Eng. 2759
Grosse Fuge
Performance/production
Ballets of Hans van Manen. Netherlands. 1951-1998. Lang.: Eng. 1120
Grosse Kampf, Der (Great Struggle, The)
Plays/librettos/scripts
Social criticism in Viennese Expressionist drama. Austria: Vienna. 1907-1922. Lang.: Ger. 2779
Grosses Schauspielhaus (Berlin)
Performance/production
The performance of sacrifice on stage. France. Germany. 1900-1998. Lang.: Ger. 530
Grossman, Jan
Design/technology
The work of scene designer Libor Fára. Czech Republic: Prague. 1950-1981. Lang.: Cze. 1518
Grosso, Nick
Performance/production
Collection of newspaper reviews by London theatre critics. UK-England: London. 1998. Lang.: Eng. 2526
Groth, Joakim
Plays/librettos/scripts
Recent drama and revue in Swedish. Finland. 1998. Lang.: Eng, Fre. 3069
Grotowski, Jerzy
Institutions
Polish experimental theatre training. Poland: Cracow, Wrocław, Warsaw. 1930-1998. Lang.: Pol. 1685

Grotowski, Jerzy — cont'd

Performance/production
The influence of experimental performance on contemporary drama. Europe. USA. 1960-1987. Lang.: Eng. 526
Early work of Jerzy Grotowski. Poland: Cracow. 1951-1959. Lang.: Pol. 575
History of movement training for the actor. USA. 1910-1985. Lang.: Eng. 675
Acting and directing influences on Eugenio Barba. Denmark: Holstebro. 1997. Lang.: Eng. 1886
Ritual in the theatre of Jerzy Grotowski. Poland. 1960-1975. Lang.: Pol. 2221
Interview with director Andrzej Wajda. Poland. 1960-1998. Lang.: Fin. 2224
Spirituality and the theatre of Jerzy Grotowski. Poland. 1958-1998. Lang.: Ger, Fre, Dut, Eng. 2226
Russian reception and interpretation of the work of Jerzy Grotowski. Russia. 1913-1998. Lang.: Pol. 2236
Etienne Decroux's concept of actor-centered theatre. USA. France. 1920-1998. Lang.: Eng. 4091
Theory/criticism
Changes in the social and political situation of Polish fringe theatre. Poland. 1980-1995. Lang.: Pol. 3826
Training
Director Walter Pfaff on the influence of Jerzy Grotowski. Poland. Germany. 1998. Lang.: Eng. 876

Group Theatre (New York, NY)
Administration
Producer Cheryl Crawford and her contributions to the American stage. USA. 1930-1965. Lang.: Eng. 1396

Grout, Philip
Performance/production
Collection of newspaper reviews by London theatre critics. UK-England: London. 1998. Lang.: Eng. 2444

Groza (Storm, The)
Institutions
Reviews of some productions at the Avignon Festival. France: Avignon. 1998. Lang.: Hun. 1615
Impressions from the 'Golden Mask' festival. Russia: Minusinsk. 1998. Lang.: Ger. 1701
Performance/production
Collection of newspaper reviews by London theatre critics. UK-England: London. 1998. Lang.: Eng. 2543

Grüber, Klaus Michael
Performance/production
Klaus Michael Grüber's production of Goethe's *Iphigenia auf Tauris.* Germany: Berlin. 1998. Lang.: Swe. 1997
Klaus Michael Grüber's production of Goethe's *Iphigenia auf Tauris.* Germany: Berlin. 1998. Lang.: Ger. 2031
Theory/criticism
Critical response to Klaus Michael Grüber's production of Goethe's *Iphigenia auf Tauris.* Germany. 1998. Lang.: Ger. 3821

Gruberova, Edita
Performance/production
Interview with soprano Edita Gruberova. Slovakia. 1975-1998. Lang.: Eng. 4695

Grumberg, Jean-Claude
Plays/librettos/scripts
Analysis of Holocaust plays by Jean-Claude Grumberg. France. 1974-1991. Lang.: Eng. 3108

Grüne Tisch, Der (Green Table, The)
Performance/production
Gender and politics in German dance. Germany. 1930-1932. Lang.: Eng. 928

Gruner, Michael
Performance/production
Productions of Horváth's *Geschichten aus dem Wienerwald (Tales from the Vienna Woods).* Germany: Hamburg, Hannover. Austria: Vienna. 1998. Lang.: Ger. 2003

Grupo Corpo (Belo Horizonte)
Institutions
Profile of contemporary ballet company Grupo Corpo. Brazil: Belo Horizonte. 1998. Lang.: Rus. 1249

Grupp 98 (Stockholm)
Performance/production
Seven critics on their favorite character or portrayal. Sweden. 1950. Lang.: Swe. 2369

Gruszynski, Alexander
Design/technology
Lighting design for Mark Christopher's film *54.* USA. 1998. Lang.: Eng. 3913

Grynberg, Henryk
Performance/production
The Jewish Kabaret za murem and its treatment in Polish theatre. Poland: Warsaw. 1939-1988. Lang.: Pol. 4157

Gryphius, Andreas
Plays/librettos/scripts
Representation of the virginal body on the German stage. Germany. 1600-1800. Lang.: Ger. 3171
Relation to other fields
Analysis of illustrations of first editions of tragedies by Gryphius. Germany. 1635-1664. Lang.: Eng. 3765

Grzegorzewski, Jerzy
Performance/production
Jerzy Grzegorzewski's production of *Ślub (The Marriage)* by Witold Gombrowicz. Poland: Warsaw. 1998. Lang.: Pol. 2218
Analysis of productions of *Dziady (Forefather's Eve)* by Adam Mickiewicz. Poland. 1901-1995. Lang.: Pol. 2220

Guangdong Dance Company (Canton)
Performance/production
Performances of the Ballet Folklórico de México and the Guangdong Dance Company. USA: Washington, DC. 1997. Lang.: Hun. 1241

Guards! Guards!
Performance/production
Collection of newspaper reviews by London theatre critics. UK-England: London. 1998. Lang.: Eng. 2446

Guare, John
Performance/production
Collection of newspaper reviews by London theatre critics. UK-England: London. 1998. Lang.: Eng. 2498
Plays/librettos/scripts
Adoption narratives in novels, plays, and films. USA. 1960-1997. Lang.: Eng. 691
History of the Playwrights Unit. USA. 1963-1971. Lang.: Eng. 3570
Revolutionary Off Broadway playwriting. USA: New York, NY. 1959-1969. Lang.: Eng. 3604

Guay, Marie-Ginette
Performance/production
Marie-Ginette Guay's wordless performance in Franz Xaver Kroetz's *Wunschkonzert (Request Concert).* Canada: Quebec, PQ. 1995-1997. Lang.: Fre. 1847

Guenveur Smith, Roger
Performance/production
Collection of newspaper reviews by London theatre critics. UK-England: London. 1998. Lang.: Eng. 2515

Guests, The
Performance/production
Synopses of lost choreographies by Jerome Robbins. USA: New York, NY. 1949-1952. Lang.: Eng. 1166

Guglielminetti, Eugenio
Design/technology
Works of painter, sculptor, and scenographer Eugenio Guglielminetti. Italy. 1961-1997. Lang.: Ita. 204

Guid Sisters, The
SEE
Belles-soeurs, Les.

Guides
Reference materials
Guide to opera. 1998. Lang.: Rus. 4830

Guiding Star
Performance/production
Collection of newspaper reviews by London theatre critics. UK-England: London. 1998. Lang.: Eng. 2540
Plays/librettos/scripts
Interview with playwright Jonathan Harvey. UK-England. 1998. Lang.: Eng. 3472

Guillard, Nicolas-François
Theory/criticism
Gender in Francesca Zambello's production of *Iphigénie en Tauride.* USA: Cooperstown, NY. 1997. Lang.: Eng. 4843

Guillem, Sylvie
Performance/production
Premiere of Sylvie Guillem's new choreography for Adolphe Adam's *Giselle.* Finland: Helsinki. 1998. Lang.: Hun. 1068

Guitry, Sacha
Basic theatrical documents
Text of *Jean III (John III)* by Sacha Guitry. France. 1912-1998. Lang.: Fre. 1426

Gun Shy
Design/technology
Set design for *Gun Shy* by Richard Dresser at Playwrights Horizons. USA: New York, NY. 1998. Lang.: Eng. 1535

Gundersheimer, Lee
Performance/production
Reviews of productions of plays by Ibsen. USA: New York, NY. Norway: Oslo. 1998. Lang.: Eng. 2747
Gunn, Nathan
Performance/production
Baritone Nathan Gunn. USA. 1971-1998. Lang.: Eng. 4723
Guo, Shixing
Plays/librettos/scripts
The view of foreigners in *Niaoren (Bird Men)* by Guo Shixing. China, People's Republic of. 1991. Lang.: Eng. 2842
Gupta, Tanika
Performance/production
Collection of newspaper reviews by London theatre critics. UK-England: London. 1998. Lang.: Eng. 2427
Gurantz, Maya
Performance/production
Theatre Magazine's anniversary issue. USA. 1968-1998. Lang.: Eng. 617
Gurčenko, Ljudmila Michajlovna
Performance/production
Actress Ljudmila Gurčenko. Russia: Moscow. 1998. Lang.: Rus. 3859
Gurik, Robert
Performance/production
Robert Gurik's adaptation of Shakespeare's *Hamlet*. Canada: Montreal, PQ, London, ON. 1968. Lang.: Fre. 1866
Gurney, A.R.
Plays/librettos/scripts
History of the Playwrights Unit. USA. 1963-1971. Lang.: Eng. 3570
Revolutionary Off Broadway playwriting. USA: New York, NY. 1959-1969. Lang.: Eng. 3604
Analysis of *The Dining Room* by A.R. Gurney. USA. 1982-1984. Lang.: Eng. 3642
Gus Giordano Jazz Dance Chicago (Chicago, IL)
Performance/production
Jazz dancer and choreographer Gus Giordano. USA: Chicago, IL. 1962-1998. Lang.: Eng. 988
Gustafsson, Isabel
Performance/production
Interview with dancers who became doctors. Sweden: Stockholm. 1974. Lang.: Swe. 968
Gutarra, Gabriela
Performance/production
Interview with Flamenco dancer Gabriela Gutarra. Spain: Seville. 1980-1998. Lang.: Swe. 1235
Gute Mensch von Sezuan, Der (Good Person of Szechwan, The)
Performance/production
Recent productions of plays by Bertolt Brecht. Germany. 1997-1998. Lang.: Ger. 2028
Gerthi Kulle's role in Brecht's *Der Gute Mensch von Sezuan (The Good Person of Szechwan)* at Dramaten. Sweden: Stockholm. 1998. Lang.: Swe. 2384
Plays/librettos/scripts
Wonderbolt Circus's *Maid of Avalon*, a loose adaptation of *Der Gute Mensch von Sezuan (The Good Person of Szechwan)* by Brecht.Canada: St. John's, NF. 1950-1998. Lang.: Eng. 2825
Gender and madness in modern drama. Europe. 1880-1969. Lang.: Eng. 3061
Recent German productions of Brecht's plays. Germany. 1998. Lang.: Ger. 3150
Guthrie Theatre (Minneapolis, MN)
Performance/production
Director Garland Wright. USA. 1946-1998. Lang.: Eng. 2707
Guthrie, Tyrone
Administration
The 'Group of Four' at the Lyric Hammersmith and the concept of a national theatre. UK-England: London. 1945-1956. Lang.: Eng. 1392
Performance/production
Correspondence of George Devine and Michel Saint-Denis. UK-England: London. 1939-1945. Lang.: Eng. 2630
Gutierrez, Gerald
Plays/librettos/scripts
Recent productions of plays by Edward Albee. USA: New York, NY, Hartford, CT. 1959-1998. Lang.: Eng. 3578
Guyer, Murphy
Plays/librettos/scripts
Playwright Murphy Guyer and the Cleveland Playhouse. USA: Cleveland, OH. 1998. Lang.: Eng. 3598
Guzmán, Feliciana Enríquez de
Plays/librettos/scripts
Feminist analysis of seventeenth-century plays by women. Spain. 1605-1675. Lang.: Eng. 3385
Gvozdickij, Viktor
Performance/production
Moscow Art Theatre actor Viktor Gvozdickij. Russia: Moscow. 1998. Lang.: Rus. 2259
Gwiazda za murem (Star Behind the Wall, The)
Performance/production
The Jewish Kabaret za murem and its treatment in Polish theatre. Poland: Warsaw. 1939-1988. Lang.: Pol. 4157
Györgyfalvay, Katalin
Performance/production
Modern tendencies in Hungarian folk dance. Hungary. 1970-1977. Lang.: Hun. 1228
Győri Balett (Győr)
Performance/production
Hungarian dance companies at Interbalett '98. Hungary. 1998. Lang.: Hun. 946
New productions of Győri Balett. Hungary: Budapest. 1998. Lang.: Hun. 1095
Győri Nemzeti Színház (Győr)
Performance/production
Dostojévskij's *Crime and Punishment* directed by Géza Tordy. Hungary: Győr. 1998. Lang.: Hun. 2100
Two productions of Ernő Szép's *Vőlegény (The Fiancé)*. Hungary: Nyíregyháza. Hungary: Győr. 1998.Lang.: Hun. 2118
Győri Nemzeti Színház, Padlásszínház (Győr)
Performance/production
Performances at the new Bárka Színház. Hungary: Budapest. 1997. Lang.: Hun. 2097
Csaba Kiss's adaptation of Shakespeare's chronicle plays at Bárka Színház. Hungary: Győr. 1997. Lang.: Hun. 2101
Review of Péter Forgách's *Kaspar*, Győr National Theatre. Hungary: Győr. 1998. Lang.: Hun. 2106
Gypsy
Plays/librettos/scripts
The creation of the musical *Gypsy*. USA: New York, NY. 1956-1959. Lang.: Eng. 4399
Haarmann
Plays/librettos/scripts
Analysis of plays by Marius von Mayenburg. Germany. 1972-1998. Lang.: Ger. 3131
HaBimah (Tel Aviv)
Institutions
HaBimah and colonialism. Israel. 1920-1998. Lang.: Eng. 1673
Polish guest performances of HaBimah. Poland. 1926-1938. Lang.: Pol. 1689
Performance/production
Profile of the Hebrew Dramatic Studio. Poland: Vilna. 1927-1933. Lang.: Pol. 2222
Hackett, Albert
Performance/production
Student production of *The Diary of Anne Frank*. USA. 1955. Lang.: Eng. 2703
Plays/librettos/scripts
Reactions to the revised version of *The Diary of Anne Frank*. USA: New York, NY. 1998. Lang.: Eng. 3618
Hackney Empire Theatre (London)
Performance/production
Collection of newspaper reviews by London theatre critics. UK-England: London. 1998. Lang.: Eng. 2432
Collection of newspaper reviews by London theatre critics. UK-England: London. 1998. Lang.: Eng. 2446
Collection of newspaper reviews by London theatre critics. UK-England: London. 1998. Lang.: Eng. 2523
Collection of newspaper reviews by London theatre critics. UK-England. 1998. Lang.: Eng. 2558
Collection of newspaper reviews by London theatre critics. UK-England: London. 1998. Lang.: Eng. 2579
Hacks, Peter
Performance/production
A production of Offenbach's *Orphée aux Enfers* directed by Jens Mehrle and Stefan Nolte. Germany: Bitterfeld. 1998. Lang.: Ger. 4856
Hadari, Atar
Performance/production
Collection of newspaper reviews by London theatre critics. UK-England: London. 1998. Lang.: Eng. 2434
Hadley, Jerry
Theory/criticism
Performers and conductors complain about unfair reviews. USA. 1998. Lang.: Eng. 4844

Haentjens, Brigitte
Performance/production
Productions of plays by Bernard-Marie Koltès. Canada: Montreal, PQ. 1991-1997. Lang.: Fre. 1862
Hágai, Katalin
Performance/production
Interview with ballerina Katalin Hágai. Hungary. 1961-1998. Lang.: Hun. 1096
Interview with dancer Katalin Hágai. Hungary. 1998. Lang.: Hun. 1107
Hagen, Michael
Design/technology
Technical designs for Čajovskij's *Sneguročka*, Houston Ballet. USA: Houston, TX. 1998. Lang.: Eng. 1033
Hagen, Uta
Performance/production
Actress and teacher Uta Hagen. USA. 1998. Lang.: Eng. 2745
Hägglund, Kent
Performance/production
Kent Hägglund on his favorite role, Bottom in Shakespeare's *Midsummer Night's Dream.* Sweden. 1978-1998. Lang.: Swe. 2375
Hahoe pyolsin-kut
Performance/production
Analysis of Korean mask-dance theatre form *hahoe pyolsin-kut.* Korea. 1150-1928. Lang.: Eng. 1352
Haifa Municipal Theatre
SEE
Teatron HaIroni (Haifa).
Haïm, Victor
Basic theatrical documents
Text of *Le Vampire suce toujours deux fois (The Vampire Always Sucks Twice)* by Victor Haïm. France. 1998. Lang.: Fre. 1427
Haimsohn, George
Design/technology
Costume design for *Dames at Sea*, Marine Memorial Theatre. USA: San Francisco, CA. 1998. Lang.: Eng. 4332
Hairston, Jerome
Theory/criticism
Winning essay of Critics Institute Competition on *Carriage* by Jerome Hairston. USA. 1998. Lang.: Eng. 3838
Hairy Ape, The
Performance/production
Aleksand'r Tairov's productions of plays by Eugene O'Neill. USSR. 1926-1929. Lang.: Eng. 2769
Plays/librettos/scripts
Eugene O'Neill's *The Hairy Ape* and the belief in racial degeneration. USA. 1922. Lang.: Eng. 3657
Themes of Eugene O'Neill's early plays. USA. 1915-1925. Lang.: Eng. 3668
African- and Irish-Americans in the plays of Eugene O'Neill. USA. 1916-1953. Lang.: Eng. 3687
Hajós, Klára
Performance/production
Dancer and eurythmics teacher Klára Hajós. Hungary. 1911-1998. Lang.: Hun. 936
Hajzer, Gábor
Performance/production
Open-air dance performances. Hungary: Pécs. 1998. Lang.: Hun. 1292
Hakim, Elinor
Performance/production
Contemporary queer politics and the production of gay and lesbian theatre. USA. 1970-1997. Lang.: Eng. 2710
Halac, Ricardo
Plays/librettos/scripts
Playwright Ricardo Halac and Argentina's sociopolitical upheavals. Argentina. 1955-1991. Lang.: Eng. 2772
Halévy, Ludovic
Basic theatrical documents
Text of Offenbach's *Orphée aux Enfers.* France. 1874. Lang.: Fre. 4418
Plays/librettos/scripts
Contributions of Meilhac and Halévy to the development of the French libretto. France. 1800-1900. Lang.: Fre. 4781
Half Moon
Performance/production
Collection of newspaper reviews by London theatre critics. UK-England: London. 1998. Lang.: Eng. 2541
Hall, Adrian
Performance/production
Reviews of Actors' Theatre productions. USA: Louisville, KY. 1998. Lang.: Eng. 2727
Hall, Bob
Design/technology
Magical stage effects in 'vampire' plays. USA. 1820-1977. Lang.: Eng. 1548
Hall, Edward
Performance/production
Collection of newspaper reviews by London theatre critics. UK-England: London. 1998. Lang.: Eng. 2415
Collection of newspaper reviews by London theatre critics. UK-England: Stratford. 1998. Lang.: Eng. 2431
Collection of newspaper reviews by London theatre critics. UK-England: London. 1998. Lang.: Eng. 2551
Hall, Katie
Performance/production
Collection of newspaper reviews by London theatre critics. UK-England: London. 1998. Lang.: Eng. 2460
Hall, Lee
Performance/production
Collection of newspaper reviews by London theatre critics. UK-England: London. 1998. Lang.: Eng. 2522
Hall, Peter
Performance/production
Collection of newspaper reviews by London theatre critics. UK-England: London. 1998. Lang.: Eng. 2442
Collection of newspaper reviews by London theatre critics. UK-England: London. 1998. Lang.: Eng. 2450
Collection of newspaper reviews by London theatre critics. UK-England: London. 1998. Lang.: Eng. 2518
Collection of newspaper reviews by London theatre critics. UK-England: London. 1998. Lang.: Eng. 2528
Collection of newspaper reviews by London theatre critics. UK-England: London. 1998. Lang.: Eng. 2545
Collection of newspaper reviews by London theatre critics. UK-England: London. 1998. Lang.: Eng. 2562
John Nettles on his role in an RSC production of *Julius Caesar.* UK-England: London, Stratford. 1995. Lang.: Eng. 2625
Semiotic analysis of Peter Hall's National Theatre production of Shakespeare's *Coriolanus.* UK-England. 1985. Lang.: Eng. 2647
Hall, Willis
Performance/production
Collection of newspaper reviews by London theatre critics. UK-England: London. 1998. Lang.: Eng. 2425
Collection of newspaper reviews by London theatre critics. UK-England: London. 1998. Lang.: Eng. 2502
Hallgren, Ronnie
Institutions
Interview with Ronnie Hallgren of Älvsborgsteatern about theatre for youth. Sweden: Borås. 1994-1998. Lang.: Swe. 1726
Profile of children's and youth theatre Älvsborgsteatern. Sweden: Borås. 1995-1998. Lang.: Swe. 1731
Halligan, Liam
Performance/production
Recent productions in Ireland of plays by Eugene O'Neill. Ireland: Dublin. UK-Ireland: Belfast. 1989-1998. Lang.: Eng. 2154
Halliwell, David
Performance/production
Collection of newspaper reviews by London theatre critics. UK-England: London. 1998. Lang.: Eng. 2544
Halls
Institutions
Popular entertainment at the New Haven Assembly Hall and Columbian Museum and Gardens. USA: New Haven, CT. 1796-1820. Lang.: Eng. 394
Performance spaces
The architecture of the Bass Performance Hall. USA: Ft. Worth, TX. 1998. Lang.: Eng. 477
Dancers and performance space. Europe. 1895-1937. Lang.: Ger. 909
The supper and swing-music venue the Coconut Club. USA: Los Angeles, CA. 1998. Lang.: Eng. 4115
Naples and the *café chantant.* Italy: Naples. 1880-1915. Lang.: Ita. 4273
Halprin, Anna
Relation to other fields
Dancer, teacher, and healing facilitator Anna Halprin of Tamalpa Institute. USA: Kentfield, CA. 1978-1998. Lang.: Ger. 1338
Halsted, Ian
Performance/production
Collection of newspaper reviews by London theatre critics. UK-England: London. 1998. Lang.: Eng. 2553

Hamburg Ballet
Institutions
Guest performances of the ballet companies of Stuttgart and Hamburg. Hungary. 1980-1986. Lang.: Hun. 1041
Performance/production
Choreographer John Neumeier. Germany: Hamburg. USA: New York, NY. 1998. Lang.: Eng. 1082
Hamburger Schauspielhaus (Hamburg)
Performance/production
Recent German productions of plays by Bertolt Brecht. Germany: Hamburg, Berlin. 1997. Lang.: Swe. 1977
Hamilton, Patrick
Performance/production
Collection of newspaper reviews by London theatre critics. UK-England: London. 1998. Lang.: Eng. 2577
Hamilton, Robert
Performance/production
Collection of newspaper reviews by London theatre critics. UK-England: London. 1998. Lang.: Eng. 2481
Collection of newspaper reviews by London theatre critics. UK-England: London. 1998. Lang.: Eng. 2561
Hamilton, Scott
Performance/production
Collection of newspaper reviews by London theatre critics. UK-England: London. 1998. Lang.: Eng. 2439
Hamilton, Stuart
Performance/production
Vocal coach Stuart Hamilton on the Canadian operatic scene. Canada. 1998. Lang.: Eng. 4540
Hamlet
Basic theatrical documents
English translation of *Kanadehon Hamlet* by Harue Tsutsumi. Japan. 1997. Lang.: Eng. 1360
Design/technology
Lighting designer Hugh Vanstone. USA: New York, NY. 1998. Lang.: Eng. 1554
Institutions
Shakespearean productions at the Carrefour international theatre festival. Canada: Quebec, PQ. 1998. Lang.: Fre. 1588
Reviews of some productions at the Avignon Festival. France: Avignon. 1998. Lang.: Hun. 1615
Profile of Württembergische Landesbühne. Germany: Esslingen. 1996-1997. Lang.: Ger. 1639
Performance/production
Dance adaptations of Shakespeare's *Hamlet*. Germany: Bremen, Weimar. 1996-1997. Lang.: Ger. 930
Canadian representations of Ophelia from Shakespeare's *Hamlet*. Canada. 1980-1997. Lang.: Eng. 1852
Robert Gurik's adaptation of Shakespeare's *Hamlet*. Canada: Montreal, PQ, London, ON. 1968. Lang.: Fre. 1866
Performing the killing of Polonius in Shakespeare's *Hamlet*. England. 1600-1601. Lang.: Eng. 1892
Reviews of German Shakespearean productions. Germany: Wuppertal, Cologne, Oberhausen. 1998. Lang.: Ger. 2017
Interview with director Adolf Dresen. Germany, East. 1965-1985. Lang.: Eng. 2036
Interview with director Frank Castorf. Germany, East. 1980-1990. Lang.: Eng. 2041
Shakespearean production and the GDR's 'existential crisis'. Germany, East. 1976-1980. Lang.: Eng. 2051
The political and social climate of East German theatre in the sixties. Germany, East. 1960-1970. Lang.: Eng. 2052
István Verebes' production of Shakespeare's *Hamlet*. Hungary: Nyíregyháza. 1997. Lang.: Hun. 2116
Report from Ibsen festival. Norway: Oslo. 1998. Lang.: Swe. 2211
Contemporary Polish productions of Shakespeare. Poland. 1990-1998. Lang.: Pol. 2213
Recent Russian productions of Shakespeare's *Hamlet*. Russia: Moscow. 1998. Lang.: Rus. 2268
Shakespeare productions in German Switzerland. Switzerland: Basel, Zurich. 1996-1997. Lang.: Ger. 2398
Collection of newspaper reviews by London theatre critics. UK-England: London. 1998. Lang.: Eng. 2484
Hamlet at Shakespeare Repertory Theatre, directed by Barbara Gaines. USA: Chicago, IL. 1996. Lang.: Eng. 2666
Plays/librettos/scripts
French translations of Shakespeare by Antonine Maillet and Jean-Louis Roux. Canada: Montreal, PQ. 1988-1993. Lang.: Fre. 2793
Student casebook on Shakespeare's *Hamlet*. England. 1532-1608. Lang.: Eng. 2897
Recovered ritual in seemingly non-ritualistic theatre. England. 1600-1779. Lang.: Eng. 2904
Possible influence of Giordano Bruno on Shakespeare's *Hamlet*. England. 1600-1601. Lang.: Ita. 2921
Handwriting and character in Shakespeare's *Hamlet*. England. 1600-1601. Lang.: Eng. 2925
Annunciation motifs in Shakespeare's *Hamlet*. England. 1600-1601. Lang.: Eng. 2934
Corporeal imagery in Shakespeare's *Hamlet*. England. 1600-1601. Lang.: Eng. 2939
Recognition in plays of Čechov, Shakespeare, and Beckett. England. France. Russia. 1596-1980. Lang.: Eng. 2949
Shakespeare and the limitation of political and textual control. England. 1600-1611. Lang.: Eng. 2965
The concept of the self in Shakespearean tragedy. England. 1590-1612. Lang.: Eng. 2992
'Demonic' women in Shakespeare's tragedies. England. 1590-1613. Lang.: Eng. 2999
The malcontent scholar in Elizabethan and Jacobean theatre. England. 1590-1642. Lang.: Eng. 3003
Analysis of a speech by the Ghost in Shakespeare's *Hamlet*. England. 1600-1601. Lang.: Eng. 3004
Comparison of final scenes in quarto and folio versions of Shakespeare's plays. England. 1597-1601. Lang.: Eng. 3005
Conscience in early modern literature including Shakespeare. England. 1590-1620. Lang.: Eng. 3020
The skull in plays of Shakespeare, Dekker, and Tourneur. England. 1606. Lang.: Eng. 3026
The interaction of other characters with Shakespeare's tragic heroes. England. 1590-1613. Lang.: Eng. 3037
Comparison of second quarto and first folio versions of Shakespeare's *Hamlet*. England. 1600-1623. Lang.: Eng. 3043
The women in Shakespeare's *Hamlet*. England. 1600-1601. Lang.: Eng. 3046
Family conflict in *Was sollen wir tun (What Shall We Do)* by Tankred Dorst and *Die Hamletmaschine (Hamletmachine)* by Heiner Müller. Germany. 1997-1998. Lang.: Ger. 3148
Brecht's *Leben des Galilei (The Life of Galileo)* as an adaptation of Shakespeare's *Hamlet*. Germany. 1600-1932. Lang.: Eng. 3160
The New Shakespeare Society's unfinished four-text edition of *Hamlet*. UK-England. 1882-1883. Lang.: Eng. 3497
Film interpretations of Ophelia in Shakespeare's *Hamlet*. USA. UK-England. USSR. 1947-1990. Lang.: Eng. 4024
Relation to other fields
Shakespeare's Hamlet in novels of Goethe and Scott. England. Germany. 1776-1824. Lang.: Eng. 3757
Theory/criticism
Critical response to *Elsineur (Elsinore)*, Robert Lepage's multimedia adaptation of *Hamlet*. Canada. 1995-1996. Lang.: Eng. 3810
Hamlet I, II, III
Performance/production
Dance adaptations of Shakespeare's *Hamlet*. Germany: Bremen, Weimar. 1996-1997. Lang.: Ger. 930
Hamlet szenen (Scenes of Hamlet)
Performance/production
Dance adaptations of Shakespeare's *Hamlet*. Germany: Bremen, Weimar. 1996-1997. Lang.: Ger. 930
Hamlet, prince du Québec (Hamlet, Prince of Quebec)
Performance/production
Robert Gurik's adaptation of Shakespeare's *Hamlet*. Canada: Montreal, PQ, London, ON. 1968. Lang.: Fre. 1866
Hamletmaschine, Die (Hamletmachine)
Performance/production
Interview with playwright Heiner Müller about his adaptations of Shakespeare. Germany, East. 1965-1990. Lang.: Eng. 2039
Plays/librettos/scripts
Family conflict in *Was sollen wir tun (What Shall We Do)* by Tankred Dorst and *Die Hamletmaschine (Hamletmachine)* by Heiner Müller. Germany. 1997-1998. Lang.: Ger. 3148

Hamlisch, Marvin
Design/technology
Digital lighting control for *A Chorus Line*. USA: New York, NY. 1974-1975. Lang.: Eng. 4337
Hammerstein, Oscar, I
Performance spaces
Oscar Hammerstein I and the creation and development of Times Square. USA. 1895-1915. Lang.: Eng. 463
Hammerstein, Oscar, II
Design/technology
Costume designs by Irene Sharaff. USA. 1933-1976. Lang.: Eng. 277
Performance/production
Collection of newspaper reviews by London theatre critics. UK-England: London. 1998. Lang.: Eng. 2466
Collection of newspaper reviews by London theatre critics. UK-England: London. 1998. Lang.: Eng. 2474
Collection of newspaper reviews by London theatre critics. UK-England: London. 1998. Lang.: Eng. 2554
The success of a revival of *Oklahoma!* at the Olivier. UK-England: London. 1998. Lang.: Eng. 4373
Plays/librettos/scripts
Treatments of the Cinderella theme, with emphasis on *La Cenerentola* by Rossini. 1817-1998. Lang.: Eng. 4757
Hammond, Susan
Performance/production
New England Marionettes' production of Mozart's *Die Zauberflöte*. USA: Boston, MA. 1998. Lang.: Eng. 4900
Hampstead Theatre (London)
Performance/production
Collection of newspaper reviews by London theatre critics. UK-England: London. 1998. Lang.: Eng. 2410
Collection of newspaper reviews by London theatre critics. UK-England: London. 1998. Lang.: Eng. 2434
Collection of newspaper reviews by London theatre critics. UK-England: London. 1998. Lang.: Eng. 2440
Collection of newspaper reviews by London theatre critics. UK-England: London. 1998. Lang.: Eng. 2451
Collection of newspaper reviews by London theatre critics. UK-England: London. 1998. Lang.: Eng. 2470
Collection of newspaper reviews by London theatre critics. UK-England: London. 1998. Lang.: Eng. 2491
Collection of newspaper reviews by London theatre critics. UK-England: London. 1998. Lang.: Eng. 2523
Collection of newspaper reviews by London theatre critics. UK-England: London. 1998. Lang.: Eng. 2544
Collection of newspaper reviews by London theatre critics. UK-England: London. 1998. Lang.: Eng. 2574
Collection of newspaper reviews by London theatre critics. UK-England: London. 1998. Lang.: Eng. 2575
Collection of newspaper reviews by London theatre critics. UK-England: London. 1998. Lang.: Eng. 2578
Hampton, Christopher
Performance/production
Collection of newspaper reviews by London theatre critics. UK-England: London. 1998. Lang.: Eng. 2419
Collection of newspaper reviews by London theatre critics. UK-England: London. 1998. Lang.: Eng. 2461
Hampton, Mark
Performance/production
Collection of newspaper reviews by London theatre critics. UK-England: London. 1998. Lang.: Eng. 2491
Hancock, W. David
Plays/librettos/scripts
Playwright W. David Hancock. USA. 1998. Lang.: Eng. 3646
Handbag
Institutions
English-language plays at Berlin Festwochen. Germany: Berlin. 1998. Lang.: Ger. 1623
Performance/production
Collection of newspaper reviews by London theatre critics. UK-England: London. 1998. Lang.: Eng. 2503
Plays/librettos/scripts
German view of English and American drama. UK-England. USA. 1998. Lang.: Ger. 3455
Handel, George Frideric
Performance/production
The influence of the Haymarket Theatre on Handelian opera. England: London. 1710-1739. Lang.: Eng. 4549
Interview with opera director Jossi Wieler. Germany: Stuttgart. Switzerland: Basel. 1998. Lang.: Ger. 4592
Handicapped theatre
Performance/production
Directing and design to accommodate the disabled in performance. USA. 1988. Lang.: Eng. 623
Guest performance of Théâtre du Plantin, a company for developmentally disabled actors. Hungary: Budapest. 1983-1998. Lang.: Hun. 2081
Handke, Peter
Performance/production
Productions of new plays by Peter Handke and Katharine Gericke at Niedersächsische Staatstheater. Germany: Hannover. 1998. Lang.: Ger. 1983
Plays/librettos/scripts
Aggressive language in modern drama. Europe. USA. 1960-1985. Lang.: Eng. 3055
The fool character in works of Handke, Fellini, and Singer. USA. Germany. Italy. 1960-1968. Lang.: Eng. 3667
Handman, Wynn
Plays/librettos/scripts
Playwright and actor Joseph Edward. USA: New York, NY. 1997. Lang.: Eng. 3564
Handover, Elizabeth
Performance/production
Theatrical component of Japan's UK98 Festival. Japan: Tokyo. 1994-1998. Lang.: Eng. 2192
Hands, Terry
Performance/production
Three productions of Shakespeare's *Richard III*. UK-England. 1973-1984. Lang.: Eng. 2612
Hanke, Dirk Olaf
Administration
Dramaturg Dirk Olaf Hanke on the dramaturg's complex role. Germany: Konstanz. 1998. Lang.: Ger. 1383
Hanks, Tom
Performance/production
Profile of actor Tom Hanks. USA. 1983-1998. Lang.: Eng. 3950
Hannah, Don
Plays/librettos/scripts
Don Hannah's *Fathers and Sons* at Tarragon Theatre. Canada: Toronto, ON. 1998. Lang.: Eng. 2833
Hannah, Jane
Performance/production
Collection of newspaper reviews by London theatre critics. UK-England: London. 1998. Lang.: Eng. 2483
Hans Im Glück (Lucky Dog)
Performance/production
Reviews of productions of plays by Brecht. Germany. 1998. Lang.: Ger. 1986
Hansberry, Lorraine
Plays/librettos/scripts
Student casebook on *A Raisin in the Sun* by Lorraine Hansberry. USA. 1957-1997. Lang.: Eng. 3577
Analysis of *Les Blancs* by Lorraine Hansberry. USA. 1970. Lang.: Eng. 3581
Lynching in plays of Angelina Weld Grimké and Lorraine Hansberry. USA. 1916-1958. Lang.: Eng. 3602
Playwright Lorraine Hansberry. USA. 1950-1965. Lang.: Eng. 3615
Lorraine Hansberry and Black Americans in theatre. USA. 1769-1986. Lang.: Eng. 3640
Hansel and Gretel Machine, The
Performance/production
Collection of newspaper reviews by London theatre critics. UK-England: London. 1998. Lang.: Eng. 2436
Hänsel und Gretel
Design/technology
Maurice Sendak's set design for *Hänsel und Gretel*, Canadian Opera Company. Canada: Toronto, ON. 1998. Lang.: Eng. 4427
Happiness
Performance/production
Analysis of Todd Solondz' film *Happiness*. USA. 1998. Lang.: Eng. 3949
Happy Days
Performance/production
Seven critics on their favorite character or portrayal. Sweden. 1950. Lang.: Swe. 2369
Collection of newspaper reviews by London theatre critics. UK-England: London. 1998. Lang.: Eng. 2578

***Happy Days* — cont'd**

Plays/librettos/scripts
Beckett's *Happy Days* as a rewriting of *Lady Chatterley's Lover*. France. Ireland. UK-England. 1961. Lang.: Eng. 3120

Beckett's character Winnie in *Happy Days*. Ireland. France. 1960-1963. Lang.: Ita. 3200

Happy Savages
Performance/production
Collection of newspaper reviews by London theatre critics. UK-England: London. 1998. Lang.: Eng. 2482

Harag, György
Performance/production
Director György Harag. Romania. Hungary. 1925-1985. Lang.: Hun. 2229

Harangozó, Gyula
Performance/production
Bartók's *A csodálatos mandarin (The Miraculous Mandarin)* choreographed by Gyula Harangozó. Hungary: Budapest. 1998.Lang.: Hun. 1088

Choreographer Gyula Harangozó and the Hungarian National Ballet. Hungary. 1908-1998. Lang.: Hun. 1104

Harcourt, Thierry
Performance/production
Collection of newspaper reviews by London theatre critics. UK-England: London. 1998. Lang.: Eng. 2469

Hardy, Hugh
Design/technology
The 1998 TCI awards. USA. 1998. Lang.: Eng. 243

Hardy, Thomas
Performance/production
Collection of newspaper reviews by London theatre critics. UK-England: London. 1998. Lang.: Eng. 2541

Hare, David
Administration
Theatrical agent Margaret Ramsey. UK-England: London. 1908-1991. Lang.: Ger. 1394

Performance/production
Collection of newspaper reviews by London theatre critics. UK-England: London. 1998. Lang.: Eng. 2444

Collection of newspaper reviews by London theatre critics. UK-England: London. 1998. Lang.: Eng. 2495

Collection of newspaper reviews by London theatre critics. UK-England: London. 1998. Lang.: Eng. 2509

Collection of newspaper reviews by London theatre critics. UK-England: London. 1998. Lang.: Eng. 2569

Plays/librettos/scripts
Analysis of plays by David Hare and Caryl Churchill. UK-England. 1971-1997. Lang.: Dut. 3432

Social and political issues in the plays of David Hare. UK-England. 1969-1986. Lang.: Eng. 3479

Hargitai, Ákos
Performance/production
Visual dance productions by Cie, 2 in 1. Hungary: Budapest. 1998. Lang.: Hun. 942

Hargitai, Iván
Performance/production
Two productions of Csokonai Vitéz's *Karnyóné és a két szeleburdiak (Mrs. Karnyó and the Two Feather-Brains)*. Hungary: Budapest. 1998. Lang.: Hun. 2113

Three Hungarian productions of plays by Molière. Hungary: Szentendre, Kapolcs, Kőszeg. 1998. Lang.: Hun. 2142

Harlem Gospel Singers (New York, NY)
Performance/production
Collection of newspaper reviews by London theatre critics. UK-England: London. 1998. Lang.: Eng. 2432

Harlequin and Mother Goose
Performance/production
Possible illustrations of Dibdin's *Harlequin and Mother Goose* at Covent Garden. UK-England: London. 1806-1808. Lang.: Eng. 2639

Harlequin's Invasion
Performance/production
The cultural background of eighteenth-century British pantomime. England. 1700-1800. Lang.: Eng. 4093

Harlequinade
Performance/production
Collection of newspaper reviews by London theatre critics. UK-England: London. 1998. Lang.: Eng. 2452

Harmadik Színház (Pécs)
Performance/production
György Spiró's *Kvartett (Quartet)* directed by János Vincze. Hungary: Pécs. 1997. Lang.: Hun. 2067

Harmston, Joe
Performance/production
Collection of newspaper reviews by London theatre critics. UK-England: London. 1998. Lang.: Eng. 2511

Collection of newspaper reviews by London theatre critics. UK-England: London. 1998. Lang.: Eng. 2561

Collection of newspaper reviews by London theatre critics. UK-England: London. 1998. Lang.: Eng. 2581

Recent productions of plays by Harold Pinter at Donmar Warehouse. UK-England: London. 1998. Lang.: Eng. 2609

Haroun and the Sea of Stories
Performance/production
Collection of newspaper reviews by London theatre critics. UK-England: London. 1998. Lang.: Eng. 2514

Harrington, Wendall K.
Design/technology
Lighting and projections for the musical *Ragtime*. USA: New York, NY. 1998. Lang.: Eng. 4328

Harris, Aurand
Plays/librettos/scripts
Absurdism in children's theatre. North America. Europe. 1896-1970. Lang.: Eng. 3288

Harris, Greg
Performance/production
Collection of newspaper reviews by London theatre critics. UK-England: London. 1998. Lang.: Eng. 2436

Harris, Julie
Institutions
Arthur Penn and Actors Studio. USA: New York, NY. 1997. Lang.: Eng. 1767

Harrison, Ben
Performance/production
Collection of newspaper reviews by London theatre critics. UK-England: London. 1998. Lang.: Eng. 2437

Harrower, David
Plays/librettos/scripts
Analysis of plays by Sarah Kane and David Harrower, recently produced in Germany. UK-England. Germany: Cologne, Bonn. 1998. Lang.: Ger. 3487

Hart, Charles
Design/technology
The original stage machinery designed by John White at Her Majesty's Theatre. UK-England: London. 1887-1986. Lang.: Eng. 1528

Hart, Lorenz
Plays/librettos/scripts
The portrayal of Franklin Delano Roosevelt in the musical *I'd Rather Be Right*. USA. 1937. Lang.: Eng. 4396

Hart, Moss
Design/technology
Costume design for revival of *As Thousands Cheer* by Drama Dept. USA: New York, NY. 1998. Lang.: Eng. 4333

Performance/production
Collection of newspaper reviews by London theatre critics. UK-England: London. 1998. Lang.: Eng. 2476

Plays/librettos/scripts
The portrayal of Franklin Delano Roosevelt in the musical *I'd Rather Be Right*. USA. 1937. Lang.: Eng. 4396

Hart, Rosa
Institutions
History of Lake Charles Little Theatre. USA: Lake Charles, LA. 1927-1982. Lang.: Eng. 1770

Hart, Susannah
Performance/production
Collection of newspaper reviews by London theatre critics. UK-England. 1998. Lang.: Eng. 2504

Hartford Stage Company (Hartford, CT)
Performance/production
Richard Foreman's notes for a production of his *Pearls for Pigs*. USA: Hartford, CT. 1997. Lang.: Eng. 2681

José Rivera's production of *La Vida es sueño (Life Is a Dream)*, Hartford Stage. USA: Hartford, CT. 1998. Lang.: Eng. 2722

Plays/librettos/scripts
Recent productions of plays by Edward Albee. USA: New York, NY, Hartford, CT. 1959-1998. Lang.: Eng. 3578

Hartmann, Matthias
Performance/production
Comparison of two productions of Shakespeare's *Richard III*. Germany: Munich. 1996-1997. Lang.: Ger. 1976

Hartridge, Barbara
Performance/production
Collection of newspaper reviews by London theatre critics. UK-England: London. 1998. Lang.: Eng. 2568
Harue, Tsutsumi
Basic theatrical documents
English translation of *Kanadehon Hamlet* by Harue Tsutsumi. Japan. 1997. Lang.: Eng. 1360
Harut and Marut
Basic theatrical documents
English translation and analysis of two plays by Ali Ahmad Bakathir. Egypt. 1908-1969. Lang.: Eng. 1417
Harvey
Plays/librettos/scripts
Playwright Mary Chase, author of *Harvey*. USA. 1944. Lang.: Eng. 3711
Harvey, Jonathan
Performance/production
Collection of newspaper reviews by London theatre critics. UK-England: London. 1998. Lang.: Eng. 2540
Plays/librettos/scripts
Interview with playwright Jonathan Harvey. UK-England. 1998. Lang.: Eng. 3472
Háry János
Performance/production
Kodály's *Háry János* at Szeged's Open-Air Festival. Hungary: Szeged. 1998. Lang.: Hun. 4359
Harz, Claude
Performance/production
Collection of newspaper reviews by London theatre critics. UK-England: London. Lang.: Eng. 2408
Hašek, Jaroslav
Performance/production
Erwin Piscator and Brecht's *Schwejk im zweiten Weltkrieg (Schweik in the Second World War)*. Germany: Berlin. 1928. Lang.: Ger. 1952
Haselbeck, Olga
Performance/production
Soprano Olga Haselbeck. Hungary. 1884-1961. Lang.: Hun. 4626
Hastings, Baird
Performance/production
Tributes to ballerina Alexandra Danilova. USA: New York, NY. 1997. Lang.: Eng. 1165
Haughton, William
Plays/librettos/scripts
Women's use of wit in response to men in English popular culture. England. 1590-1630. Lang.: Eng. 2884
Hauptmann, Gerhart
Audience
Audience response to *Vor Sonnenaufgang (Before Sunrise)* by Gerhart Hauptmann. Germany: Berlin. 1889-1890. Lang.: Eng. 1402
Basic theatrical documents
Russian translations of plays by Nobel Prize winners. Italy. 1848-1998. Lang.: Rus. 1446
Performance/production
Hauptmann's *Fuhrmann Henschel (Drayman Henschel)* and realism. Germany. 1899-1933. Lang.: Eng. 1970
Hauptmann's *Fuhrmann Henschel (Drayman Henschel)* directed by Sándor Zsótér. Hungary: Budapest. 1997. Lang.: Hun. 2088
Plays/librettos/scripts
Robert Musil and the 'crisis of modern drama'. Europe. 1880-1930. Lang.: Eng. 3062
The relationship between writers Hans Franck and Gerhart Hauptmann. Germany. 1910-1948. Lang.: Ger. 3127
Power, gender relations, and communication in German drama. Germany. 1776-1989. Lang.: Ger. 3138
Women in German turn-of-the-century drama. Germany. 1890-1910. Lang.: Eng. 3158
Translating Hauptmann's *Die Weber (The Weavers)* into Scots dialect. UK-Scotland: Dundee, Glasgow. 1997. Lang.: Eng. 3513
Hausch, Mary
Performance/production
Director Mary Hausch of Hippodrome State Theatre. USA: Gainesville, FL. 1973-1998. Lang.: Eng. 2709
Haussmann, Leander
Performance/production
German directors about the meaning of Brecht today. Germany. 1998. Lang.: Ger. 1948
Shakespeare performance on the Rhine and the Ruhr. Germany: Cologne, Bochum, Düsseldorf. 1996-1997. Lang.: Ger. 1962
Recent productions of Bochumer Schauspielhaus. Germany: Bochum. 1998. Lang.: Ger. 2009
Haute Surveillance (Deathwatch)
Performance/production
Collection of newspaper reviews by London theatre critics. UK-England: London. 1998. Lang.: Eng. 2547
Have the Men Had Enough
Performance/production
Collection of newspaper reviews by London theatre critics. UK-England: London. 1998. Lang.: Eng. 2468
Havel, Václav
Plays/librettos/scripts
Aggressive language in modern drama. Europe. USA. 1960-1985. Lang.: Eng. 3055
Relation to other fields
Václav Havel, the Czech Republic, and the European Union. Czech Republic. 1989-1998. Lang.: Eng. 3743
Hawks, Howard
Plays/librettos/scripts
Opera in American gangster films. USA. 1932-1990. Lang.: Eng. 4023
Hawksley, Fred
Performance/production
Beothuk Street Players' production of *Faces in the Rock* by Fred Hawksley. Canada: St. John's, NF. 1998. Lang.: Eng. 1863
Hay, Rob
Performance/production
Collection of newspaper reviews by London theatre critics. UK-England: London. 1998. Lang.: Eng. 2533
Hayes, Catherine
Performance/production
Soprano Catherine Hayes. Ireland. Italy. 1839-1861. Lang.: Eng. 4645
Audience reaction to Irish opera singer Catherine Hayes. USA: New Orleans, LA. 1852. Lang.: Eng. 4745
Haymarket Theatre (London)
Performance/production
Excerpts from Johanna Schopenhauer's journal relating to London theatre. UK-England: London. Germany. 1803-1805. Lang.: Eng. 2615
The influence of the Haymarket Theatre on Handelian opera. England: London. 1710-1739. Lang.: Eng. 4549
Haynes, Elizabeth Sterling
Plays/librettos/scripts
Theatre artist Elizabeth Sterling Haynes and Alberta theatre. Canada. 1916-1957. Lang.: Eng. 2799
Hazel, Jean
Design/technology
Set designer Jean Hazel. Canada: Quebec, PQ. 1985-1998. Lang.: Fre. 1515
Hazel, Spencer
Performance/production
Collection of newspaper reviews by London theatre critics. UK-England: London. 1998. Lang.: Eng. 2448
Hazelwood Junior High
Design/technology
Derek McLane's set designs for recent Off Broadway productions. USA: New York, NY. 1998. Lang.: Eng. 1538
HB Thom Theatre (Capetown)
Performance/production
Chris Vorster's production of *Baal* by Bertolt Brecht. South Africa, Republic of: Capetown. 1998. Lang.: Eng. 2350
Head Invents, the Heart Discovers, The
Performance/production
Collection of newspaper reviews by London theatre critics. UK-England: London. 1998. Lang.: Eng. 2427
Healey, Aidan
Performance/production
Collection of newspaper reviews by London theatre critics. UK-England: London. 1998. Lang.: Eng. 2427
Healey, Desmond
Design/technology
Technical designs for Čajovskij's *Sneguročka*, Houston Ballet. USA: Houston, TX. 1998. Lang.: Eng. 1033
Healey, Michael
Basic theatrical documents
Text of Michael Healey's one-man show *Kicked*. Canada: Toronto, ON. 1993. Lang.: Eng. 1410
Performance/production
Actor/playwright Michael Healey on the purpose of theatre. Canada. 1998. Lang.: Eng. 501

Healing Theater (Cologne)
Performance/production
The Cologne theatre scene. Germany: Cologne. 1985-1997. Lang.: Ger. 1964

Health/safety
Administration
Reports on the 10th Anniversary of Broadway Cares/Equity Fights AIDS. USA: New York, NY. 1998. Lang.: Eng. 52
Changes in Equity's health insurance coverage. USA: New York, NY. 1998. Lang.: Eng. 65
Actors' Fund annual benefit for women's health. USA: New York, NY. 1998. Lang.: Eng. 68
Report on Easter Bonnet fundraiser for AIDS. USA: New York, NY. 1998. Lang.: Eng. 72
Report on 'Broadway Bares' benefit for AIDS. USA: New York, NY. 1998. Lang.: Eng. 76
Issues of concern to Equity members in current Broadway shows. USA: New York, NY. 1998. Lang.: Eng. 77
Annual report of the Equity pension fund. USA: New York, NY. 1998. Lang.: Eng. 81
The waiting period before Equity health benefits take effect. USA: New York, NY. 1998. Lang.: Eng. 91
Securing sick pay and worker's compensation for an on-the-job injury. USA: New York, NY. 1998. Lang.: Eng. 93
The Palm View residence for people with AIDS. USA: Hollywood, CA. 1998. Lang.: Eng. 95
Shubert Alley's breast cancer screening program. USA: New York, NY. 1998. Lang.: Eng. 101
The loss of medical coverage for Equity dependents over nineteen years of age. USA: New York, NY. 1998. Lang.: Eng. 105
Actress Helen Hunt's support of Equity's holiday basket program for people with AIDS. USA: New York, NY. 1986-1998. Lang.: Eng. 107
Flea Market fundraiser for AIDS. USA: New York, NY. 1998. Lang.: Eng. 109
Design/technology
Account of ACTSAFE conference on theatre safety. France: Paris. 1998. Lang.: Swe. 181
Seminar on flying on stage. Norway: Oslo. 1998. Lang.: Swe. 211
Locking and controlling stage rigging. Sweden: Stockholm. 1998. Lang.: Swe. 220
Index to *Technical Brief* volumes 11-17. USA. 1998. Lang.: Eng. 323
Performance/production
Actress Betty Buckley's performance in AIDS fundraiser. Switzerland: Geneva. 1998. Lang.: Eng. 603
Solutions to neck pain in dancers. Sweden. 1998. Lang.: Swe. 965
The trend of dancers continuing their careers after age forty. USA. 1998. Lang.: Eng. 991
Ballerina Zippora Karz on dancing while suffering from diabetes. USA: New York, NY. 1983-1998. Lang.: Eng. 1183
Actors' handling of a mishap on stage during a production of *The Phantom of the Opera*. UK-England: Basingstoke. 1998. Lang.: Eng. 4369
Relation to other fields
A warning to dancers not to become malnourished. Sweden. 1998. Lang.: Swe. 998
Medieval religious theatre and the public safety. Germany. 1234-1656. Lang.: Eng. 3771

Heaney, Seamus
Plays/librettos/scripts
Adaptations of Greek tragedy by contemporary Irish writers. Ireland. UK-Ireland. 1984-1998. Lang.: Eng. 3214
Gender and nationalism in Northern Irish drama. UK-Ireland. 1902-1997. Lang.: Eng. 3511

HeartBeat:mb
Performance/production
A performance by Mikhail Baryshnikov and the White Oak Dance Project. USA: Washington, DC. 1990-1998. Lang.: Hun. 1194

Heartbreak House
Plays/librettos/scripts
Analysis of *Heartbreak House* by George Bernard Shaw. UK-England. 1916-1919. Lang.: Eng. 3429
Colonialism in the plays of George Bernard Shaw. UK-England. 1895-1935. Lang.: Eng. 3438
Disillusionment in George Bernard Shaw's *Heartbreak House*. UK-England. 1920. Lang.: Eng. 3456
Linguistic style and action in plays of Wilde, Shaw, and Stoppard. UK-England. 1890-1985. Lang.: Eng. 3467
George Bernard Shaw and the 'New Woman'. UK-England. 1890-1900. Lang.: Eng. 3486

Heatstroke
Basic theatrical documents
Text of *Heatstroke* by James Purdy. USA. 1989. Lang.: Eng. 1502
Plays/librettos/scripts
Analysis of plays by James Purdy. USA. 1957-1998. Lang.: Eng. 3700

Hebanowski, Stanisław
Performance/production
History of Teatr Wybrzeże. Poland: Gdańsk, Warsaw, Cracow. 1952-1997. Lang.: Pol. 2215

Hebbel-Theater (Berlin)
Plays/librettos/scripts
New directions in the plays of Botho Strauss. Europe. 1971-1998. Lang.: Ger. 3067
Hero and anti-hero in contemporary opera production. Germany. 1998. Lang.: Ger. 4791
Relation to other fields
Die Berliner Ermittlung (The Berlin Investigation), an interactive theatre project by Jochen Gerz and Esther Shalev-Gerz. Germany: Berlin. 1998. Lang.: Ger. 3768

Hebbel, Friedrich
Administration
Theater Basel under the direction of Stefan Bachmann. Switzerland: Basel. 1996-1998. Lang.: Ger. 1391
Institutions
Stefan Bachmann of Basler Theater. Switzerland: Basel. 1998. Lang.: Ger. 1737

Hébert, Paul
Performance/production
Interview with actor/director Paul Hébert. Canada: Quebec, PQ. 1952-1998. Lang.: Fre. 1854

Hebrajskie Studium Dramatyczne (Vilna)
Performance/production
Profile of the Hebrew Dramatic Studio. Poland: Vilna. 1927-1933. Lang.: Pol. 2222

Hecht, Ben
Performance/production
Ben Hecht's propaganda pageant *A Flag Is Born*. USA: New York, NY. 1946. Lang.: Eng. 4220

Heckert, Matt
Performance/production
The work of some North American performance artists. USA. Canada. 1960-1988. Lang.: Eng. 4251

Hedda Gabler
Design/technology
Set design and lighting for a production of Ibsen's *Hedda Gabler*. USA: Louisville, KY. 1988. Lang.: Eng. 1564
Performance/production
Collection of newspaper reviews by London theatre critics. UK-England: London. 1998. Lang.: Eng. 2422
Reviews of productions of plays by Ibsen. USA: New York, NY. Norway: Oslo. 1998. Lang.: Eng. 2747
Plays/librettos/scripts
The devouring woman in plays of Racine, Kleist, Ibsen, and Beckett. Europe. 1760-1992. Lang.: Eng. 3058
Feminism and plays of Henrik Ibsen. Norway. 1879-1979. Lang.: Eng. 3293
Stage directions in Ibsen's *Hedda Gabler*. Norway. 1987. Lang.: Eng. 3294
Trolls in the late plays of Ibsen. Norway. 1886-1894. Lang.: Eng. 3298

Hedeland Amfiteater
Performance spaces
Malmö Musikteater's production of *Lucia di Lammermoor* at Hedeland Amfiteater. Denmark: Hedeland. 1997. Lang.: Swe. 4491

Hedwig and the Angry Inch
Performance/production
Musical performances on and off Broadway. USA: New York. 1998. Lang.: Ger. 4383

Hegarty, Judy
Performance/production
Collection of newspaper reviews by London theatre critics. UK-England: London. 1998. Lang.: Eng. 2547

Heggie, Jake
Institutions
The partnership between San Francisco Opera and Chase Manhattan Bank. USA: San Francisco, CA, New York, NY. 1998. Lang.: Eng. 423
Hegyi, Árpád Jutocsa
Performance/production
Gogol's *Revizor (The Inspector General)* directed by Árpád Jutocsa Hegyi. Hungary: Miskolc. 1998. Lang.: Hun. 2108
Heil, Douglas
Basic theatrical documents
Screenplay for *The First Wife*, based on a story by Colette. USA. 1998. Lang.: Eng. 3888
Plays/librettos/scripts
Analysis of Douglas Heil's screenplay *The First Wife*. USA. 1998. Lang.: Eng. 4030
Heilbronn, Marie
Performance/production
Massenet's revisions to *Manon* for performance by Sybil Sanderson. France. 1885-1903. Lang.: Eng. 4572
Heilige Johanna der Schlachthöfe, Die (Saint Joan of the Stockyards)
Performance/production
Recent productions of plays by Bertolt Brecht. Germany. 1997-1998. Lang.: Ger. 2028
Brecht's *Die Heilige Johanna der Schlachthöfe (Saint Joan of the Stockyards)* directed by Sándor Zsóter. Hungary: Miskolc. 1998. Lang.: Hun. 2084
Katharina Thalbach in Brecht's *Die heilige Johanna der Schlachthöfe (Saint Joan of the Stockyards)* directed by Benno Besson. Switzerland: Zurich. 1998. Lang.: Ger. 2400
Heise, Thomas
Administration
Interviews with German theatre and film directors. Germany. 1998. Lang.: Ger. 1385
Heldenplatz (Heroes' Square)
Plays/librettos/scripts
Thomas Bernhard's Holocaust play, *Heldenplatz (Heroes' Square)*. Austria. 1988. Lang.: Eng. 2784
Hellman, Lillian
Performance/production
The idea of Hollywood in theatre autobiographies. USA. 1950-1990. Lang.: Eng. 665
Hello and Goodbye
Performance/production
Market Theatre productions of plays by Athol Fugard. South Africa, Republic of. 1993-1994. Lang.: Eng. 2351
Plays/librettos/scripts
The influence of Albert Camus on playwright Athol Fugard. South Africa, Republic of. 1960-1985. Lang.: Eng. 3362
Helmholtz-Gamnasium (Essen)
Relation to other fields
Use of theatre in Holocaust education. Germany: Essen. 1985-1998. Lang.: Ger. 3767
Helper, Courtney
Performance/production
Collection of newspaper reviews by London theatre critics. UK-England: London. 1998. Lang.: Eng. 2487
Helsinki City Theatre
SEE
Helsingin Kaupunginteatteri.
Hen & Chickens Theatre (London)
Performance/production
Collection of newspaper reviews by London theatre critics. UK-England: London. 1998. Lang.: Eng. 2442
Collection of newspaper reviews by London theatre critics. UK-England: London. 1998. Lang.: Eng. 2451
Collection of newspaper reviews by London theatre critics. UK-England: London. 1998. Lang.: Eng. 2560
Collection of newspaper reviews by London theatre critics. UK-England: London. 1998. Lang.: Eng. 2579
Henderson, Gary
Performance/production
Collection of newspaper reviews by London theatre critics. UK-England: London. 1998. Lang.: Eng. 2503
Henderson, Gavin
Administration
History of the Brighton performance festival. UK-England: Brighton. 1967-1988. Lang.: Eng. 4229
Henius, Carla
Institutions
Interview with singer Carla Henius, manager of musik-theater-werkstatt festival. Germany: Wiesbaden. 1986-1998. Lang.: Ger. 4347
Henley, Beth
Performance/production
Collection of newspaper reviews by London theatre critics. UK-England: London. 1998. Lang.: Eng. 2539
An approach to playing Babe Botrelle in Beth Henley's *Crimes of the Heart*. USA. 1987. Lang.: Eng. 2690
Plays/librettos/scripts
Playwright Beth Henley. USA. 1998. Lang.: Eng. 3671
Hennekam, Sosthen
Performance/production
Collection of newspaper reviews by London theatre critics. UK-England: London. 1998. Lang.: Eng. 2533
Hennequin, Maurice
Performance/production
Collection of newspaper reviews by London theatre critics. UK-England: London. 1998. Lang.: Eng. 2552
Henning-Jensen, Gert
Performance/production
Tenor Gert Henning-Jensen. Denmark. 1992-1998. Lang.: Eng. 4544
Henrici, C.F.
Design/technology
Scenographic concept for the *dramma per musica, Aeolus Appeased*. USA. 1988. Lang.: Eng. 4442
Henriksson, Krister
Performance/production
Interviews with actors Börje Ahlstedt and Krister Henriksson. Sweden: Stockholm. 1962-1998. Lang.: Swe. 2383
Henry IV
Plays/librettos/scripts
The relationship between Falstaff and Prince Hal in Shakespeare's *Henry IV*. England. 1596-1597. Lang.: Eng. 2870
Analysis of Shakespeare's history plays. England. 1590-1599. Lang.: Eng. 2911
'Demonic' women in Shakespeare's tragedies. England. 1590-1613. Lang.: Eng. 2999
The subversion of male authority in Shakespeare's *Henry VI* and *Richard III*. England. 1590-1593. Lang.: Eng. 3015
The 'troubler' personality in Shakespeare's *Henry IV, Part One*. England. 1596-1597. Lang.: Eng. 3032
Gangster film and Shakespearean tragedy. USA. 1971-1991. Lang.: Eng. 4009
Relation to other fields
Psychoanalysis, the female body, and Shakespeare's *Henriad*. England. 1589-1597. Lang.: Eng. 3756
Henry IV by Pirandello
SEE
Enrico IV.
Henry IV, Part One
Design/technology
Costume designs for Oregon Shakespeare Festival productions. USA: Ashland, OR. 1998. Lang.: Eng. 1543
Plays/librettos/scripts
Girardian analysis of Shakespeare plays. England. 1590-1599. Lang.: Eng. 2935
Catholic and Protestant in Shakespeare's Second Henriad. England. 1596-1599. Lang.: Eng. 2940
Henry IV, Part Two
Plays/librettos/scripts
Girardian analysis of Shakespeare plays. England. 1590-1599. Lang.: Eng. 2935
Catholic and Protestant in Shakespeare's Second Henriad. England. 1596-1599. Lang.: Eng. 2940
Henry Miller Theatre (New York, NY)
Performance spaces
The creation of a site-specific performance space for Sam Mendes' production of *Cabaret*. USA: New York, NY. 1998. Lang.: Eng. 4350
Henry Street Settlement (New York, NY)
Administration
Christine Melton on the production of her play *Still Life Goes On*. USA: New York, NY. 1997. Lang.: Eng. 1398
Henry V
Design/technology
Set design for a University of Michigan production of *Henry V*. USA: Ann Arbor, MI. 1998. Lang.: Eng. 1557

***Henry V* — cont'd**

Institutions
The inaugural season of Shakespeare's Globe Theatre. UK-England: London. 1997-1998. Lang.: Eng. 1741
Performance/production
Speaking styles of selected actors reading Shakespeare's *Henry V*. North America. UK-England. 1998. Lang.: Eng. 2208
Collection of newspaper reviews by London theatre critics. UK-England: London. 1998. Lang.: Eng. 2415
The inaugural season of Shakespeare's Globe Theatre. UK-England: London. 1997. Lang.: Eng. 2601
Review of the opening season of Shakespeare's Globe Theatre. UK-England: London. 1997. Lang.: Eng. 2602
Postmodern staging and design: Matthew Warchus' *Henry V*. UK-England. 1970-1994. Lang.: Eng. 2636
Plays/librettos/scripts
Analysis of Shakespeare's history plays. England. 1590-1599. Lang.: Eng. 2911
Girardian analysis of Shakespeare plays. England. 1590-1599. Lang.: Eng. 2935
Catholic and Protestant in Shakespeare's Second Henriad. England. 1596-1599. Lang.: Eng. 2940
Comic scenes and characters in the Elizabethan history play. England. 1590-1618. Lang.: Eng. 2955
Comparison of final scenes in quarto and folio versions of Shakespeare's plays. England. 1597-1601. Lang.: Eng. 3005
The first quarto of Shakespeare's *Henry V* and the anonymous *Famous Victories of Henrie the Fifth*. England. 1599-1600. Lang.: Eng. 3022
Relation to other fields
Psychoanalysis, the female body, and Shakespeare's *Henriad*. England. 1589-1597. Lang.: Eng. 3756

Henry VI
Plays/librettos/scripts
Analysis of Shakespeare's history plays. England. 1590-1599. Lang.: Eng. 2911
Comic scenes and characters in the Elizabethan history play. England. 1590-1618. Lang.: Eng. 2955

Henry VI, Part Two
Plays/librettos/scripts
The Lacy family and the pretender to the throne in Shakespeare's *Henry VI, Part Two*. England. 1590-1592. Lang.: Eng. 2964

Henry VIII
Performance/production
Collection of newspaper reviews by London theatre critics. UK-England: London. 1998. Lang.: Eng. 2587
Paul Jesson's role in *Henry VIII* at RSC. UK-England: London, Stratford. 1996-1997. Lang.: Eng. 2617
Jane Lapotaire on her performance in *Henry VIII* at RSC. UK-England: London, Stratford. 1996-1997. Lang.: Eng. 2619
Plays/librettos/scripts
Queens Anne and Katherine in Shakespeare's *Henry VIII*. England. 1612-1613. Lang.: Eng. 2990

Henry, Martha
Performance/production
The performances of Frances Hyland, Kate Reid, and Martha Henry in *The Cherry Orchard*. Canada: Stratford, ON. 1965. Lang.: Eng. 1865

Henry, Stephen
Performance/production
Collection of newspaper reviews by London theatre critics. UK-England: London. 1998. Lang.: Eng. 2525

Henslowe, Philip
Performance spaces
The archaeological excavation of the Rose Theatre. UK-England: London. 1988-1989. Lang.: Eng. 1805
The excavation of the Rose Theatre's foundations. UK-England: London. 1988-1989. Lang.: Eng. 1807

Henson, Jim
Performance/production
The influence of *Sesame Street*. USA. 1968-1998. Lang.: Eng. 4923

Henze, Hans Werner
Design/technology
Lighting for Henze's opera *Der Prinz von Homburg* at Deutsche Oper Berlin. Germany: Berlin. 1997. Lang.: Ger. 4431
Plays/librettos/scripts
W.H. Auden as an opera librettist and translator. UK-England. 1907-1973. Lang.: Eng. 4825

Hepburn, Judy
Performance/production
Collection of newspaper reviews by London theatre critics. UK-England: London. 1998. Lang.: Eng. 2460

Heppner, Ben
Performance/production
Tenor Ben Heppner. Canada. 1998. Lang.: Eng. 4539

Her Alabaster Skin
Performance/production
Collection of newspaper reviews by London theatre critics. UK-England: London. 1998. Lang.: Eng. 2522

Her Majesty's Theatre (London)
Design/technology
The original stage machinery designed by John White at Her Majesty's Theatre. UK-England: London. 1887-1986. Lang.: Eng. 1528

Her Wedding Night
Plays/librettos/scripts
The censorship of the unpublished *Her Wedding Night* by Florence Bates. UK-England. 1917. Lang.: Eng. 3454

Héraclius
Plays/librettos/scripts
Analysis of plays by Pierre Corneille. France. 1643-1652. Lang.: Eng. 3112

Herakles
Performance/production
Collection of newspaper reviews by London theatre critics. UK-England: London. 1998. Lang.: Eng. 2468

Herberger Theatre Center (Phoenix, AZ)
Design/technology
Ethernet computer connections between lighting systems of two theatres at Herberger Theatre Center. USA: Phoenix, AZ. 1998. Lang.: Eng. 294

Hercules furens
Plays/librettos/scripts
Analysis of Seneca's *Oedipus* and *Hercules furens*. Roman Empire. 4 B. C.-65 A.D. Lang.: Eng. 3313

Herdemerten, Frank
Relation to other fields
Use of theatre in Holocaust education. Germany: Essen. 1985-1998. Lang.: Ger. 3767

Here
Performance/production
Director Angela Brodauf. Germany: Dortmund. 1984-1998. Lang.: Ger. 1989

Herhi, Mirja-Liisa
Training
Interview with dance teacher Mirja-Liisa Herhi. Finland. 1998. Lang.: Fin. 1016

Héritier, Jean-Philippe
Performance/production
Yvette Bozsik's *Nevess remegve (Emlék) (Laugh Tremble—Memory)* at Trafó. Hungary: Budapest. 1998. Lang.: Hun. 1293

Herman, Jerry
Performance/production
Collection of newspaper reviews by London theatre critics. UK-England: London. 1998. Lang.: Eng. 2544

Herman, Judi
Performance/production
Collection of newspaper reviews by London theatre critics. UK-England: London. 1998. Lang.: Eng. 2521

Herman, Mark
Performance/production
Collection of newspaper reviews by London theatre critics. UK-England: London. 1998. Lang.: Eng. 2414

Hermes in der Stadt (Hermes in Town)
Performance/production
Recent productions of Deutsches Schauspielhaus. Germany: Hamburg. 1998. Lang.: Ger. 2034

Hernan Cortez
Basic theatrical documents
Text of plays by Carlos Morton. USA. 1986. Lang.: Eng. 1499

Hernandez, Riccardo
Design/technology
Technical designs for Off Broadway Shakespearean productions. USA: New York, NY. 1998. Lang.: Eng. 1539

Hérodiade
Basic theatrical documents
Libretto to Massenet's opera *Hérodiade*. France. 1881. Lang.: Fre. 4416
Performance/production
Productions of Massenet's *Hérodiade*. 1881-1995. Lang.: Fre. 4520
Complete recordings of Massenet's opera *Hérodiade*. 1974-1994. Lang.: Fre. 4523
Plays/librettos/scripts
Massenet's opera *Hérodiade* and its literary sources. France. 1881. Lang.: Fre. 4779

Herodus Magnus
Basic theatrical documents
Text of plays and other works by Ivan Mrak. Slovenia. 1930-1975. Lang.: Slo. 1459
Herold, Ferdinand
Performance/production
La Fille mal Gardée at Erkel Színház. Hungary: Budapest. 1997. Lang.: Hun. 1087
Herr Puntila und sein Knecht Matti (Herr Puntila and His Man Matti)
Performance/production
Recent German productions of plays by Bertolt Brecht. Germany: Hamburg, Berlin. 1997. Lang.: Swe. 1977
Productions of plays by Shakespeare, Brecht, and Camus. Germany. 1998. Lang.: Ger. 2032
Collection of newspaper reviews by London theatre critics. UK-England: London. 1998. Lang.: Eng. 2522
Plays/librettos/scripts
Recent German productions of Brecht's plays. Germany. 1998. Lang.: Ger. 3150
Herriott, Chuck
Plays/librettos/scripts
Wonderbolt Circus's *Maid of Avalon*, a loose adaptation of *Der Gute Mensch von Sezuan (The Good Person of Szechwan)* by Brecht.Canada: St. John's, NF. 1950-1998. Lang.: Eng. 2825
Hersov, Gregory
Performance/production
Collection of newspaper reviews by London theatre critics. UK-England: London. 1998. Lang.: Eng. 2420
Herst, Beth
Performance/production
Collection of newspaper reviews by London theatre critics. UK-England: London. 1998. Lang.: Eng. 2458
Herzberg, Judith
Performance/production
Collection of newspaper reviews by London theatre critics. UK-England: London. 1998. Lang.: Eng. 2462
Herzog, Jens-Daniel
Institutions
The aesthetic perspectives of the ensemble at Münchner Kammerspiele. Germany: Munich. 1997-1998. Lang.: Ger. 1666
Herzog, Werner
Institutions
Gunnar Martin Aronsson of TeaterX2 recalls Action-Theater. Sweden: Stockholm. Germany: Munich. 1968-1998. Lang.: Swe. 1722
Herzschmerzen (Heartaches)
Plays/librettos/scripts
Recent productions directed by Frank Castorf. Austria: Vienna. 1998. Lang.: Ger. 2788
Hescott, Bob
Performance/production
Collection of newspaper reviews by London theatre critics. UK-England: London. 1998. Lang.: Eng. 2574
Hesketh-Harvey, Kit
Performance/production
Collection of newspaper reviews by London theatre critics. UK-England: London. 1998. Lang.: Eng. 2462
Collection of newspaper reviews by London theatre critics. UK-England: London. 1998. Lang.: Eng. 2549
Collection of newspaper reviews by London theatre critics. UK-England: London. 1998. Lang.: Eng. 2568
Hesse, Volker
Administration
Theatre directors on the future of subsidized theatre. Switzerland: Zurich. Germany: Hannover, Berlin. 1998. Lang.: Ger. 1390
Performance/production
Volker Hesse's production of *King Kongs Töchter (King Kong's Daughters)* by Theresia Walser. Switzerland: Zurich. 1998. Lang.: Ger. 2401
Volker Hesse's production of *Die schwarze Spinne (The Black Spider)* by Urs Widmer. Switzerland: Zurich. 1998. Lang.: Ger. 2402
Hessel, Tina
Training
Tina Hessel's relaxation and breathing techniques for dance training. Sweden: Stockholm. 1998. Lang.: Swe. 1211
Hessisches Staatstheater (Wiesbaden)
Institutions
Interview with singer Carla Henius, manager of musik-theater-werkstatt festival. Germany: Wiesbaden. 1986-1998. Lang.: Ger. 4347
Ernst August Klötzke, new manager of musik-theater-werkstatt festival. Germany: Wiesbaden. 1998. Lang.: Ger. 4348
Performance/production
Daniel Karasek, drama director at Hessisches Staatstheater. Germany: Wiesbaden. 1997-1998. Lang.: Ger. 1955
Hetz, Amos
Performance/production
Dancer, choreographer, and teacher Amos Hetz. Israel: Jerusalem. 1978-1998. Lang.: Ger. 953
Hewitson, Derek
Performance/production
Collection of newspaper reviews by London theatre critics. UK-England: London. 1998. Lang.: Eng. 2512
Hey, Mr. Producer
Performance/production
Collection of newspaper reviews by London theatre critics. UK-England: London, Scarborough. 1998. Lang.: Eng. 2426
Heywood, John
Performance/production
Music in Tudor drama. England. 1497-1569. Lang.: Eng. 1902
Plays/librettos/scripts
Lucian's *Icaromenippus* as a source for Heywood's *The Play of the Wether*. England. 1533. Lang.: Eng. 2920
Heywood, Thomas
Performance/production
Director Jacques Copeau and his theatrical aesthetic. France. 1913-1920. Lang.: Eng. 1941
Plays/librettos/scripts
Playwriting and publishing for the London stage. England. 1590-1650. Lang.: Eng. 2881
Casuistry and early modern English tragedy. England. 1600-1671. Lang.: Eng. 2980
Hibbert, Karl
Performance/production
Collection of newspaper reviews by London theatre critics. UK-England: London. 1998. Lang.: Eng. 2568
Hibbitt, Peyton
Institutions
Profile of Tri-Cities Opera. USA: Binghamton, NY. 1949-1998. Lang.: Eng. 4490
Hickson, Joan
Performance/production
Career of actress Joan Hickson. UK-England: London. 1927-1998. Lang.: Eng. 2597
Higgins, Claire
Institutions
Interview with Kricker James and Claire Higgins of Chain Lightning Theatre. USA: New York, NY. 1991-1998. Lang.: Eng. 1780
Higgins, Norman
Administration
The 'Group of Four' at the Lyric Hammersmith and the concept of a national theatre. UK-England: London. 1945-1956. Lang.: Eng. 1392
Highway, Tomson
Plays/librettos/scripts
Theatre and the creation of a new nationalism. Canada. Saint Lucia. 1980-1995. Lang.: Eng. 2808
Hikétides (Suppliant Women)
Performance/production
Collection of newspaper reviews by London theatre critics. UK-England: London. 1998. Lang.: Eng. 2545
Hiko, Kazuko
Performance/production
Collection of newspaper reviews by London theatre critics. UK-England: London. 1998. Lang.: Eng. 2535
Hildegard, Saint
Performance/production
Sequentia's new recording of *Ordo Virtutum* by Hildegard of Bingen. Germany. 1997. Lang.: Eng. 4294
Hill, Andrew
Design/technology
Lighting design for Basil Twist's puppet production *Symphonie Fantastique*. USA: New York, NY. 1998. Lang.: Eng. 4867
Hill, Dean
Performance/production
Collection of newspaper reviews by London theatre critics. UK-England: London. 1998. Lang.: Eng. 2575
Hill, Dominic
Performance/production
Collection of newspaper reviews by London theatre critics. UK-England: London. 1998. Lang.: Eng. 2490

Hill, Dominic — cont'd

Collection of newspaper reviews by London theatre critics. UK-England: London. 1998. Lang.: Eng. 2530

Hill, Gary
Performance/production
Interview with video and installation artist Gary Hill. USA. 1969-1998. Lang.: Eng. 4258

Hill, Leslie
Performance/production
Performance artist Leslie Hill's *Push the Boat Out.* UK-England: London. USA. 1995-1997. Lang.: Eng. 4245

Hiller, Wilfried
Performance/production
Opera director Katja Czellnik. Germany: Oldenburg, Kiel. 1996-1998. Lang.: Ger. 4583

Hilley, Seamus
Performance/production
Collection of newspaper reviews by London theatre critics. UK-England: London. 1998. Lang.: Eng. 2475

Hillje, Jens
Institutions
Profile of Deutsches Theater, Baracke. Germany: Berlin. 1996-1998. Lang.: Ger. 1637

Hills, Nancy
Design/technology
The 1998 USITT expo. USA: Long Beach, CA. 1998. Lang.: Eng. 251

Hilne, Astrid
Performance/production
Collection of newspaper reviews by London theatre critics. UK-England: London. 1998. Lang.: Eng. 2462

Hilton, Rebecca
Performance/production
Interview with dancer/choreographer Rebecca Hilton. Australia. USA. 1983-1995. Lang.: Eng. 913

Hime, Ed
Performance/production
Collection of newspaper reviews by London theatre critics. UK-England: London. 1998. Lang.: Eng. 2549

Hims, Katie
Performance/production
Collection of newspaper reviews by London theatre critics. UK-England: London. 1998. Lang.: Eng. 2411

Hindemith, Paul
Plays/librettos/scripts
Hero and anti-hero in contemporary opera production. Germany. 1998. Lang.: Ger. 4791

Hindle Wakes
Performance/production
Collection of newspaper reviews by London theatre critics. UK-England. 1998. Lang.: Eng. 2558

Hinkemann
Plays/librettos/scripts
Analysis of revisions of plays by Ernst Toller. Germany. 1920-1939. Lang.: Eng. 3172

Hinton, Spencer
Performance/production
Collection of newspaper reviews by London theatre critics. UK-England: London. 1998. Lang.: Eng. 2444

Collection of newspaper reviews by London theatre critics. UK-England: London. 1998. Lang.: Eng. 2566

Hintson, Martin
Performance/production
Collection of newspaper reviews by London theatre critics. UK-England: London. 1998. Lang.: Eng. 2421

Hipkens, Robert
Performance/production
Collection of newspaper reviews by London theatre critics. UK-England. 1998. Lang.: Eng. 2489

Hippodrome State Theatre (Gainesville, FL)
Performance/production
Director Mary Hausch of Hippodrome State Theatre. USA: Gainesville, FL. 1973-1998. Lang.: Eng. 2709

Hippolyte et Aricie
Plays/librettos/scripts
Politics and the unity of place in *Hippolyte et Aricie* by Rameau and Pelligrin. France. 1733. Lang.: Eng. 4780

Themes from Greek tragedy in opera. France. 1635-1774. Lang.: Eng. 4783

Racine's *Phèdre* as a source for *Hippolyte et Aricie* by Rameau and Pelligrin. France. 1660-1733. Lang.: Eng. 4788

The shaping influence of Pelligrin's libretto on Rameau's *Hippolyte et Aricie.* France. 1733. Lang.: Eng. 4790

Hirche, Knut
Administration
Interviews with German theatre and film directors. Germany. 1998. Lang.: Ger. 1385

Hirsch, John
Performance/production
The performances of Frances Hyland, Kate Reid, and Martha Henry in *The Cherry Orchard.* Canada: Stratford, ON. 1965. Lang.: Eng. 1865

Hirsch, Shelley
Relation to other fields
Shelly Hirsch on her performance piece *For Jerry—Part I.* USA. Germany. 1997-1998. Lang.: Ger, Fre, Dut, Eng. 4266

Hirson, Roger O.
Performance/production
Collection of newspaper reviews by London theatre critics. UK-England: London. 1998. Lang.: Eng. 2501

His House in Order
Plays/librettos/scripts
Analysis of plays by Arthur Wing Pinero. UK-England. 1890-1910. Lang.: Eng. 3440

Hiscock, Matthew
Performance/production
Collection of newspaper reviews by London theatre critics. UK-England: London. 1998. Lang.: Eng. 2474

Hispanic theatre
Performance/production
Afro-Cuban identity in Cuban theatre and popular arts. Cuba. 1959-1996. Lang.: Spa. 513

The performance of plays by Hispanic women. North America. 1993-1998. Lang.: Eng. 2209

Plays/librettos/scripts
Analysis of Cuban theatre in Miami. USA: Miami, FL. 1985-1986. Lang.: Eng. 3574

Analysis of *Bandido!* by Luis Valdez. USA. 1982. Lang.: Eng. 3708

The underrepresentation of Hispanics in American arts. USA. 1998. Lang.: Eng. 3716

Histoire (qu'on ne connaîtra jamais), L' (Story That Will Never Be Known, The)
Plays/librettos/scripts
Poetic identity in plays of Hélène Cixous. France. 1988-1994. Lang.: Eng. 3083

Histoire de l'Oie, L' (Tale of Teeka, The)
Plays/librettos/scripts
Interview with playwright and scriptwriter Michel Marc Bouchard. Canada: Montreal, PQ. 1987-1998. Lang.: Fre. 3963

Histoire des Atrides, L' (House of Atreus, The)
Plays/librettos/scripts
The use of collage in contemporary productions involving Greek myths. Canada: Montreal, PQ. 1998. Lang.: Fre. 2814

Historia (History)
Basic theatrical documents
English translation of *Historia (History)* by Witold Gombrowicz. Poland. 1998. Lang.: Eng. 1448

Plays/librettos/scripts
Translating the unfinished *Historia (History)* by Witold Gombrowicz. Poland. 1951-1998. Lang.: Eng. 3303

Historiography
SEE
Research/historiography.

Hitchcock, Alfred
Performance/production
Hitchcock's influence on *The Spanish Prisoner* by David Mamet. USA. 1998. Lang.: Eng. 3956

Hiver/Winterland, L'
Plays/librettos/scripts
Analysis of plays by Gilles Maheu. Canada: Montreal, PQ. 1994-1998. Lang.: Fre. 1357

Hixson, Lin
Institutions
Interview with Matthew Goulish and Lin Hixson of Goat Island. USA: Chicago, IL. 1990. Lang.: Eng. 4237

Hjelm, Keve
Performance/production
Keve Hjelm's production of *Ett Drömspel (A Dream Play)* by Strindberg. Sweden: Malmö. 1998. Lang.: Eng. 2373

Hlinka, Nichol
Performance/production
Dancer Nichol Hlinka of New York City Ballet. USA: New York, NY. 1975-1998. Lang.: Eng. 1173

Hoa Phuong Water Puppet Theatre (Vietnam)
Performance/production
Collection of newspaper reviews by London theatre critics. UK-England: London. 1998. Lang.: Eng. 2464
Hoch, Danny
Basic theatrical documents
Text of *Jails, Hospitals and Hip-Hop* by Danny Hoch. USA. 1998. Lang.: Eng. 1487
Hochschule der Künste (Berlin)
Institutions
Actor training at Hochschule der Künste and Ernst-Busch-Schule. Germany: Berlin. 1998. Lang.: Ger. 1622
Hochschule für Musik und Darstellende Kunst (Frankfurt am Main)
Institutions
Actor and director training at Hochschule für Musik and Darstellende Kunst. Germany: Frankfurt/Main. 1998. Lang.: Ger. 350
Hochschule für Musik und Theater (Hamburg)
Institutions
Music theatre studies at the Hochschule für Musik und Theater. Germany: Hamburg. 1988-1998. Lang.: Ger. 4459
Hochzeit (Wedding)
Basic theatrical documents
Catalan translations of plays by Bertolt Brecht (volume 1). Germany. 1919-1954. Lang.: Cat. 1437
Hochzeit von Haiti, Die (Marriage of Haiti, The)
Performance/production
Productions of the Kleist theatre festival. Germany: Frankfurt/Oder. 1998. Lang.: Ger. 1993
Hoctor, Danny
Performance/production
Tap dance team of Betty Byrd and Danny Hoctor. USA. 1959-1998. Lang.: Eng. 983
Hodgkinson, Greta
Performance/production
Ballerina Greta Hodgkinson of National Ballet of Canada. Canada: Toronto, ON. 1998. Lang.: Eng. 1067
Hodson, Millicent
Performance/production
The reconstruction of Jean Börlin's ballet *Dervisher*. Sweden: Stockholm. 1997. Lang.: Eng. 1150
Hoffman, Phillip
Performance/production
Collection of newspaper reviews by London theatre critics. UK-England: London. 1998. Lang.: Eng. 2441
Hoffman, William M.
Plays/librettos/scripts
Revolutionary Off Broadway playwriting. USA: New York, NY. 1959-1969. Lang.: Eng. 3604
Hofmannsthal, Hugo von
Performance/production
Collaborative Symbolist dance/theatre projects. Europe. USA. 1916-1934. Lang.: Eng. 1268
Plays/librettos/scripts
The image of motherhood in German-language drama. Austria. Germany. 1890-1910. Lang.: Ger. 2787
Strauss's *Die Frau ohne Schatten* and a recent production by Giuseppe Sinopoli. Germany. 1917-1998. Lang.: Swe. 4795
Hofsiss, Jack
Performance/production
Documentary theatre and the politics of representation. USA. 1966-1993. Lang.: Eng. 2728
Holberg, Ludvig
Performance/production
The influence of *commedia dell'arte* on eighteenth-century Danish theatre. Denmark: Copenhagen. 1700-1750. Lang.: Eng. 4186
Hold, The
Performance/production
Collection of newspaper reviews by London theatre critics. UK-England: London. 1998. Lang.: Eng. 2506
Holder, Donald
Design/technology
Technical designs for Off Broadway Shakespearean productions. USA: New York, NY. 1998. Lang.: Eng. 1539
Donald Holder's lighting design for *The Lion King*. USA: New York, NY. 1997-1998. Lang.: Eng. 4336
Technical designs for the Broadway production of *The Lion King*. USA: New York, NY. 1998. Lang.: Eng. 4342
Holl, István
Performance/production
Interview with actor István Holl. Hungary. 1960-1998. Lang.: Hun. 2059
Hollander, The
Plays/librettos/scripts
Flemish immigrants in English Renaissance drama. England. 1515-1635. Lang.: Eng. 2976
Hollandia (Amsterdam)
Plays/librettos/scripts
Johan Simons and the independent theatre group in Hollandia. Netherlands: Amsterdam. 1985-1998. Lang.: Ger. 3280
Holliger, Heinz
Plays/librettos/scripts
Heinz Holliger's operatic adaptation of Samuel Beckett's *What Where*. Europe. 1992. Lang.: Eng. 4768
Operatic adaptations of Beckett's plays by Heinz Holliger. Europe. 1976-1988. Lang.: Eng. 4776
Hollinger, Michael
Performance/production
Collection of newspaper reviews by London theatre critics. UK-England: London. 1998. Lang.: Eng. 2585
Holloway, Jonathan
Performance/production
Collection of newspaper reviews by London theatre critics. UK-England: London. 1998. Lang.: Eng. 2409
Holly, John
Administration
John Holly, Western Regional Director of Equity. USA: New York, NY. 1998. Lang.: Eng. 80
Hollywood Pantages Theatre (Hollywood, CA)
Performance spaces
Profiles of Southern California theatres. USA. 1998. Lang.: Eng. 473
Holm, Ian
Performance/production
Speaking styles of selected actors reading Shakespeare's *Henry V*. North America. UK-England. 1998. Lang.: Eng. 2208
Holm, Staffan Valdemar
Administration
Stockholm's debut as cultural capital of Europe. Sweden: Stockholm. 1998. Lang.: Dan. 22
Institutions
Investing in culture in Malmö, formerly an industrial city. Sweden: Malmö. 1995-1998. Lang.: Swe. 1723
Report on the Stockholm theatre festival. Sweden: Stockholm. 1998. Lang.: Eng. 1724
Performance/production
Recent productions of plays by Ibsen and Strindberg. Sweden: Stockholm. 1997. Lang.: Eng. 2393
Holman, Robert
Performance/production
Collection of newspaper reviews by London theatre critics. UK-England: London, Stratford, Derby. 1998. Lang.: Eng. 2417
Holmstedt, Janna
Training
Singer training at Teater- & Operahögskolan. Sweden: Gothenburg. 1960-1998. Lang.: Swe. 4848
Holocaust theatre
Performance/production
Alexander Stillmark's production of *Bruder Eichmann (Brother Eichmann)* by Heinar Kipphardt. Germany: Berlin. 1984-1992. Lang.: Eng. 2022
Gianfranco De Bosio's production of *Se questo è un uomo (If This Is a Man)* by Primo Levi. Italy: Turin. 1963-1966. Lang.: Eng. 2168
Cabaret performances at the Theresienstadt concentration camp. Czechoslovakia: Terezin. 1944. Lang.: Eng. 4153
Ben Hecht's propaganda pageant *A Flag Is Born*. USA: New York, NY. 1946. Lang.: Eng. 4220
Plays/librettos/scripts
Thomas Bernhard's Holocaust play, *Heldenplatz (Heroes' Square)*. Austria. 1988. Lang.: Eng. 2784
Bibliography of Holocaust drama. Europe. North America. 1933-1997. Lang.: Eng. 3054
Essay on Holocaust theatre. Europe. 1940-1997. Lang.: Eng. 3064
The Holocaust in *L'Enfant-rat (The Rat Child)* by Armand Gatti. France. 1961-1970. Lang.: Eng. 3092
The Holocaust in environmental theatre of Armand Gatti. France. 1989-1993. Lang.: Eng. 3097

Holocaust theatre — cont'd

Analysis of *Un opéra pour Terezin (An Opera for Terezin)* by Liliane Atlan. France. 1986. Lang.: Eng. 3105
The Holocaust in plays of Charlotte Delbo. France. 1913-1985. Lang.: Eng. 3115
Analysis of *Jubiläum* by George Tabori. Germany. 1983. Lang.: Eng. 3137
Israeli attitudes toward Holocaust theatre. Israel. 1944-1995. Lang.: Eng. 3217
Danny Horowitz's *Uncle Artur* and the limits of representation. Israel. 1980-1995. Lang.: Eng. 3218
Ida Kamińska's production of *Der Kheshbn (The Final Reckoning)* by Mikhl Mirsky. Poland: Warsaw. 1963. Lang.: Eng. 3310
The survivor character in contemporary American drama. USA. 1970-1997. Lang.: Eng. 3600
Survivors' testimony in Holocaust theatre. USA. 1975-1995. Lang.: Eng. 3605
Analysis of historical drama of the holocaust. USA. Canada. Germany. 1950-1980. Lang.: Eng. 3610
Shocking the audience in Holocaust theatre. USA. 1980-1995. Lang.: Eng. 3628

Holocauste
Performance/production
Recent Paris productions. France: Paris. 1997-1998. Lang.: Ger. 1933

Holoubek, Gustaw
Institutions
History of the Polish Theatre Association. Poland: Warsaw. 1918-1998. Lang.: Pol. 1692

Holt, Lori
Performance/production
Actress Lori Holt. USA: San Francisco, CA. 1978-1998. Lang.: Eng. 2740

Holzmair, Wolfgang
Performance/production
Reviews of *Lieder* recordings. USA. Slovenia. Austria. 1998. Lang.: Eng. 4720

Home Truths
Performance/production
Collection of newspaper reviews by London theatre critics. UK-England: Leeds, Manchester. 1998. Lang.: Eng. 2433

Homecoming, The
Basic theatrical documents
Typescript of the first draft of *The Homecoming* by Harold Pinter. UK-England. 1964. Lang.: Eng. 1477
Plays/librettos/scripts
Comparison of the first and final drafts of *The Homecoming* by Harold Pinter. UK-England. 1964. Lang.: Eng. 3447
Female presence/absence in plays of O'Neill, Pinter, and Shepard. USA. UK-England. 1936-1985. Lang.: Eng. 3607

Homme atlantique, L' (Atlantic Man)
Performance/production
Music in films of Marguerite Duras. France. 1974-1981. Lang.: Eng. 3932

Homme du hasard, L' (Unexpected Man, The)
Performance/production
Collection of newspaper reviews by London theatre critics. UK-England: London. 1998. Lang.: Eng. 2419
Collection of newspaper reviews by London theatre critics. UK-England: London. 1998. Lang.: Eng. 2461

Homme et son désir, L' (Man and His Desire)
Performance/production
Collaborative Symbolist dance/theatre projects. Europe. USA. 1916-1934. Lang.: Eng. 1268

Hommes, Les (Men, The)
Plays/librettos/scripts
The Holocaust in plays of Charlotte Delbo. France. 1913-1985. Lang.: Eng. 3115

Honest Whore, Part I, The
Plays/librettos/scripts
The skull in plays of Shakespeare, Dekker, and Tourneur. England. 1606. Lang.: Eng. 3026

Honest Whore, The
Performance/production
Collection of newspaper reviews by London theatre critics. UK-England: London. 1998. Lang.: Eng. 2486

Hong Kong Repertory Theatre
Relation to other fields
Theatre and politics in Hong Kong. Hong Kong. 1984-1996. Lang.: Eng. 3772

Honvéd Táncszínház (Budapest)
Institutions
Work of Honvéd Táncszínház under the direction of Ferenc Novák. Hungary. 1998. Lang.: Hun. 1219
Performance/production
Danish guest performance of Honvéd Táncszínház. Denmark: Copenhagen. 1998. Lang.: Hun. 1224

Hood, Kevin
Performance/production
Collection of newspaper reviews by London theatre critics. UK-England: Leeds, Manchester. 1998. Lang.: Eng. 2559

Hoover, Richard
Design/technology
Set design for Tennessee Williams' *Not About Nightingales* at the National. UK-England: London. 1998. Lang.: Eng. 1526

Hope Theatre (London)
Performance spaces
Evidence that Davies' bear-baiting ring may have been a restoration of the Hope Theatre. England: London. 1647-1682. Lang.: Eng. 435
Evidence of theatre closings in a Folger Library manuscript. England: London. 1650. Lang.: Eng. 1798

Hope, Frederic Paddock
Design/technology
Frederic Paddock Hope, planner of Walt Disney World. USA. 1930-1998. Lang.: Eng. 4098

Hope, Tim
Performance/production
Collection of newspaper reviews by London theatre critics. UK-England: London. 1998. Lang.: Eng. 2535

Hopgood, Alan
Plays/librettos/scripts
Australian plays about the war in Vietnam. Australia. 1990-1998. Lang.: Eng. 2776

Hopkins, John
Plays/librettos/scripts
Stage and screenwriter John Hopkins. UK-England: London. USA: Hollywood, CA. 1931-1998. Lang.: Eng. 3498

Hopkins, Stephen
Design/technology
Production design for the film *Lost in Space*. USA: Hollywood, CA. 1998. Lang.: Eng. 3904

Hopkinson, Claire
Institutions
Profile of Tapestry Music Theatre. Canada: Toronto, ON. 1985-1998. Lang.: Eng. 4346

Hoppe, Christine
Performance/production
Actress Christine Hoppe. Germany: Dresden. 1993-1998. Lang.: Ger. 1973

Hoppe, Gip
Performance/production
Collection of newspaper reviews by London theatre critics. UK-England: London. 1998. Lang.: Eng. 2530

Hoppla, wir leben! (Hoppla, We're Alive!)
Plays/librettos/scripts
Analysis of revisions of plays by Ernst Toller. Germany. 1920-1939. Lang.: Eng. 3172

Horestes
Plays/librettos/scripts
Protestant belief and English Reformation drama. England. 1535-1607. Lang.: Eng. 2972

Horgan, Barbara
Performance/production
Tributes to ballerina Alexandra Danilova. USA: New York, NY. 1997. Lang.: Eng. 1165

Horgas, Péter
Design/technology
Survey of an exhibition of Hungarian scene design. Hungary: Budapest. 1998. Lang.: Hun. 195
An exhibition of sets and environments by Hungarian designers. Hungary: Budapest. 1998. Lang.: Hun. 196
Catalogue of an exhibition devoted to Hungarian theatre and film. Hungary: Budapest. 1998. Lang.: Hun. 197

Hori, Akemi
Performance/production
Collection of newspaper reviews by London theatre critics. UK-England: London. 1998. Lang.: Eng. 2420

Horne, Marilyn
Performance/production
Singers' approaches to the title role in Bizet's *Carmen*. 1875-1998. Lang.: Eng. 4502

Hornimann, Annie
Performance/production
Experimental Shakespeare production at the Gaiety Theatre. UK-England: Manchester. 1908-1915. Lang.: Eng. 2605
Horovitz, Israel
Basic theatrical documents
French translation of *Lebensraum* by Israel Horovitz. USA. France. 1996-1997. Lang.: Fre. 1488
French translation of *The Primary English Class* by Israel Horovitz. USA. France. 1996. Lang.: Fre. 1489
Institutions
Arthur Penn and Actors Studio. USA: New York, NY. 1997. Lang.: Eng. 1767
Performance/production
Collection of newspaper reviews by London theatre critics. UK-England: London. 1998. Lang.: Eng. 2466
Horowitz, Danny
Plays/librettos/scripts
Danny Horowitz's *Uncle Artur* and the limits of representation. Israel. 1980-1995. Lang.: Eng. 3218
Horres, Bernarda
Performance/production
German directors about the meaning of Brecht today. Germany. 1998. Lang.: Ger. 1948
Horres, Gregor
Institutions
The current state of Theater Bielefeld. Germany: Bielefeld. 1998. Lang.: Ger. 1621
Horváth, Ödön von
Performance/production
Luc Bondy's production of Horváth's *Figaro lässt sich scheiden (Figaro Gets Divorced)*. Austria: Vienna. 1998. Lang.: Ger. 1822
Productions of Horváth's *Geschichten aus dem Wienerwald (Tales from the Vienna Woods)*. Germany: Hamburg, Hannover. Austria: Vienna. 1998. Lang.: Ger. 2003
Horváth, Tomáš
Plays/librettos/scripts
New direction in Czech playwriting. Czech Republic. 1990-1997. Lang.: Cze. 2850
Horwood, John
Performance/production
Collection of newspaper reviews by London theatre critics. UK-England: London. 1998. Lang.: Eng. 2411
Hostage, The
Plays/librettos/scripts
Music and song in plays of Brendan Behan. Ireland. 1954-1958. Lang.: Eng. 3206
Hot l Baltimore, The
Plays/librettos/scripts
Comedy and humor in plays of Lanford Wilson. USA. 1961-1985. Lang.: Eng. 3595
Hotel Lux
Performance/production
Recent dance performances in Berlin. Germany: Berlin. 1998. Lang.: Ger. 933
Hothouse, The
Performance/production
Survey of Parisian productions. France: Paris. 1997-1998. Lang.: Eng. 1937
Italian productions of plays by Harold Pinter. Italy. 1997. Lang.: Eng. 2165
Houben, Josef
Performance/production
Collection of newspaper reviews by London theatre critics. UK-England: London. 1998. Lang.: Eng. 2421
Collection of newspaper reviews by London theatre critics. UK-England: London. 1998. Lang.: Eng. 2556
Collection of newspaper reviews by London theatre critics. UK-England: London. 1998. Lang.: Eng. 2564
Houghton, Stanley
Performance/production
Collection of newspaper reviews by London theatre critics. UK-England. 1998. Lang.: Eng. 2558
Hourie, Troy
Design/technology
The 1998 USITT expo. USA: Long Beach, CA. 1998. Lang.: Eng. 251
House management
SEE
Management, house.
House of Martin Guerre, The
Plays/librettos/scripts
Leslie Arden's career in musical theatre. Canada. 1993-1998. Lang.: Eng. 4389
House/Lights
Performance/production
Interview with actress Kate Valk. USA: New York, NY. 1979-1998. Lang.: Eng. 2736
Analysis of recent New York productions. USA: New York, NY. 1997-1998. Lang.: Eng. 2759
House, The
Institutions
Effects of a TV documentary on the Royal Opera House. UK-England: London. 1993-1998. Lang.: Eng. 4474
Houseman, John
Institutions
History of Mercury Theatre. USA: New York, NY. 1937-1942. Lang.: Eng. 1776
Performance/production
The idea of Hollywood in theatre autobiographies. USA. 1950-1990. Lang.: Eng. 665
Houston Ballet (Houston, TX)
Design/technology
Technical designs for Čajovskij's *Snegur očka*, Houston Ballet. USA: Houston, TX. 1998. Lang.: Eng. 1033
Lighting design for Čajkovskij's *Snegur očka (The Snow Maiden)* at Houston Ballet. USA: Houston, TX. 1998. Lang.: Eng. 1035
Performance/production
Dancer Carlos Acosta of Royal Ballet and Houston Ballet. USA: Houston, TX. UK-England: London. 1993-1998. Lang.: Eng. 1190
Dancer Nina Ananiašvili. USA: Houston, TX. 1986-1998. Lang.: Eng. 1193
Houston Grand Opera (Houston, TX)
Performance spaces
A modular stage used for touring by the Houston Grand Opera. USA: Houston, TX. 1998. Lang.: Eng. 4500
Performance/production
Opera conductor Patrick Summers. USA. 1990-1998. Lang.: Eng. 4755
Houston Opera Studio (Houston, TX)
Institutions
Training practices of Houston Opera Studio. USA: Houston, TX. 1977-1998. Lang.: Eng. 4489
Houstoun, Wendy
Performance/production
Performer/choreographer Wendy Houstoun. UK-England. 1989-1998. Lang.: Eng. 1309
Hová lett a rózsa lelke? (What Has Become of the Spirit of the Rose?)
Performance/production
Miklós Hubay's *Hová lett a rózsa lelke? (What Has Become of the Spirit of the Rose?)* directed by György Lengyel. Hungary: Debrecen. 1998. Lang.: Hun. 2150
How Dear to Me the Hour When Daylight Dies
Institutions
The work of performance troupe Goat Island. USA: Chicago, IL. 1987-1998. Lang.: Eng. 395
How I Learned to Drive
Performance/production
Collection of newspaper reviews by London theatre critics. UK-England: London. 1998. Lang.: Eng. 2423
Plays/librettos/scripts
Interview with playwright Paula Vogel. USA: New York, NY. 1998. Lang.: Eng. 3679
Howard, David
Training
Interview with dancer and teacher David Howard. USA. 1966-1998. Lang.: Swe. 1216
Howard, Leslie
Performance/production
Actor Leslie Howard. UK-England: London. USA: New York, NY. 1893-1943. Lang.: Eng. 2631
Howard, Robert
Plays/librettos/scripts
Analysis of Restoration anti-Puritan comedies. England. 1661-1663. Lang.: Eng. 2907
Howe, Tina
Design/technology
Lighting designer Kenneth Posner. USA. 1998. Lang.: Eng. 1545

Howe, Tina — cont'd

Plays/librettos/scripts
Playwright Tina Howe on gender expectations on playwrights. USA: New York, NY. 1980-1997. Lang.: Eng. 3614

Howett, Mark
Design/technology
Lighting designer Mark Howett's work for Black Swan Theatre Company. Australia: Fremantle. 1998. Lang.: Eng. 1513

Hrotsvitha
Performance/production
Martyrdom in the plays of Hrotsvitha. Germany. 900-1050. Lang.: Eng. 1960

Hrubín, František
Performance/production
The adaptation of classic Czech works to the stage. Czech Republic: Prague, Brno. 1990-1998. Lang.: Cze. 1877

Hsi ch'ü
SEE
Classed Entries under MUSIC-DRAMA—Chinese opera.

Huaja
Plays/librettos/scripts
The West in Chinese spoken drama and the effacement of the individual author. China, People's Republic of. 1949-1976. Lang.: Eng. 2843

Hubay, Miklós
Performance/production
Miklós Hubay's *Hová lett a rózsa lelke? (What Has Become of the Spirit of the Rose?)* directed by György Lengyel. Hungary: Debrecen. 1998. Lang.: Hun. 2150

Huber, Anna
Performance/production
Avant-garde dancer Anna Huber. Germany: Berlin. 1994-1998. Lang.: Ger. 1286

Hübner, Jens
Design/technology
Reconstruction of a performance of *A Midsummer Night's Dream* designed by Galli-Bibiena. Germany: Bayreuth. 1997-1998. Lang.: Ger. 1521

Huch, Ricarda
Plays/librettos/scripts
Women in German turn-of-the-century drama. Germany. 1890-1910. Lang.: Eng. 3158

Hudeček, Václav
Design/technology
Josef Svoboda's set design for Goethe's *Faust*. Czech Republic: Prague. 1997. Lang.: Eng. 1517

Hudson, Richard
Design/technology
Scene designer Richard Hudson and his work on *Samson et Dalila* at the Metropolitan Opera. UK-England. USA. 1954-1998. Lang.: Eng. 4289

Huey P Newton Story, A
Performance/production
Collection of newspaper reviews by London theatre critics. UK-England: London. 1998. Lang.: Eng. 2515

Hughes, Adrian
Performance/production
Collection of newspaper reviews by London theatre critics. UK-England: London. 1998. Lang.: Eng. 2465

Hughes, Doug
Performance/production
Collection of newspaper reviews by London theatre critics. UK-England: London. 1998. Lang.: Eng. 2465

Hughes, Holly
Performance/production
The feminist performance trend Angry Essentialism. USA. 1981-1998. Lang.: Eng. 4249

Hughes, John Osborne
Performance/production
Collection of newspaper reviews by London theatre critics. UK-England: London. 1998. Lang.: Eng. 2447

Hughes, Langston
Plays/librettos/scripts
Poet Langston Hughes and the theatre. USA: New York, NY. 1926-1967. Lang.: Eng. 3585

Black dance in plays of Zora Neale Hurston. USA. 1925-1930. Lang.: Eng. 3633

Analysis of *Mulatto* by Langston Hughes. USA. 1935. Lang.: Eng. 3709

Hughes, Ted
Performance/production
Collection of newspaper reviews by London theatre critics. UK-England: London. 1998. Lang.: Eng. 2494

Hughes, Terry
Performance/production
Collection of newspaper reviews by London theatre critics. UK-England: London. 1998. Lang.: Eng. 2418

Hughie
Performance/production
Recent productions in Ireland of plays by Eugene O'Neill. Ireland: Dublin. UK-Ireland: Belfast. 1989-1998. Lang.: Eng. 2154

Notable productions of plays by Eugene O'Neill. USA. 1916-1996. Lang.: Eng. 2752

Plays/librettos/scripts
The late plays of Eugene O'Neill. USA. 1939-1943. Lang.: Eng. 3528

Analysis of *Hughie* by Eugene O'Neill. USA. 1959. Lang.: Eng. 3529

Hugo, François-Victor
Performance/production
French Canadian translations/adaptations of Shakespeare. Canada: Montreal, PQ. 1988. Lang.: Fre. 1855

Huibers, José
Design/technology
Profiles of young theatrical designers. Netherlands. 1990-1998. Lang.: Dut. 207

Huldt-Ramberg, Charlotta
Institutions
Opera and food at Regina. Sweden: Stockholm. 1997. Lang.: Swe. 4472

Hull, Bryan
Administration
Securing sick pay and worker's compensation for an on-the-job injury. USA: New York, NY. 1998. Lang.: Eng. 93

Human Being
Performance/production
Collection of newspaper reviews by London theatre critics. UK-England: London. 1998. Lang.: Eng. 2428

Humana Festival of New American Plays (Louisville, KY)
Institutions
Criticism of plays at Humana Festival. USA: Louisville, KY. 1998. Lang.: Eng. 1793

Humorous Day's Mirth, A
Plays/librettos/scripts
The malcontent scholar in Elizabethan and Jacobean theatre. England. 1590-1642. Lang.: Eng. 3003

Humperdinck, Englebert
Design/technology
Maurice Sendak's set design for *Hänsel und Gretel*, Canadian Opera Company. Canada: Toronto, ON. 1998. Lang.: Eng. 4427

Humphrey, Doris
Performance/production
Dance-mime Angna Enters. USA. 1905-1923. Lang.: Eng. 1319

Humphreys, Chris
Performance/production
Collection of newspaper reviews by London theatre critics. UK-England: London. 1998. Lang.: Eng. 2444

Humphries, Barry
Performance/production
Collection of newspaper reviews by London theatre critics. UK-England: London. 1998. Lang.: Eng. 2462

Hungarian National Theatre
SEE
Nemzeti Szinház.

Hungarian State Opera
SEE
Magyar Állami Operaház.

Hungarian State Puppet Theatre
SEE
Állami Bábszinház.

Hungarian State Theatre (Kolozsvár)
SEE
Állami Magyar Szinház (Cluj).

Hungarian Theatre Institute
SEE
Magyar Szinházi Intézet.

Hunt, David
Performance/production
Collection of newspaper reviews by London theatre critics. UK-England: London. 1998. Lang.: Eng. 2442

Hunt, Helen
Administration
Actress Helen Hunt's support of Equity's holiday basket program for people with AIDS. USA: New York, NY. 1986-1998. Lang.: Eng. 107

Hunt, Jerry
Relation to other fields
Shelly Hirsch on her performance piece *For Jerry—Part I.* USA. Germany. 1997-1998. Lang.: Ger, Fre, Dut, Eng. 4266

Hunt, Lorraine
Performance/production
Singers' approaches to the title role in Bizet's *Carmen.* 1875-1998. Lang.: Eng. 4502

Hunter, Kathryn
Performance/production
Collection of newspaper reviews by London theatre critics. UK-England: London. 1998. Lang.: Eng. 2522
Collection of newspaper reviews by London theatre critics. UK-England: London. 1998. Lang.: Eng. 2587

Hunter, Kim
Institutions
Arthur Penn and Actors Studio. USA: New York, NY. 1997. Lang.: Eng. 1767

Hunter's Moon
Plays/librettos/scripts
Account of performances by Joan Dickinson. USA. 1997-1998. Lang.: Eng. 4263

Hürlimann, Thomas
Plays/librettos/scripts
Thomas Hürlimann's *Das Lied der Heimat (The Song of the Homeland)* and its production by Werner Düggelin. Switzerland: Zurich. 1998. Lang.: Ger. 3417

Hurry, Leslie
Performance/production
The Stratford Festival production of Shakespeare's *King Lear.* Canada: Stratford, ON. 1964. Lang.: Eng. 506

Hurst, Fannie
Plays/librettos/scripts
John Stahl's film adaptation of *Imitation of Life* by Fannie Hurst. USA: Hollywood, CA. 1934. Lang.: Eng. 4029

Hurston, Zora Neale
Basic theatrical documents
Texts of plays about Zora Neale Hurston by Barbara Waddell Speisman. USA. 1988. Lang.: Eng. 1510
Plays/librettos/scripts
Blues music in the writings of Zora Neale Hurston. USA. 1920-1940. Lang.: Eng. 3625
Black dance in plays of Zora Neale Hurston. USA. 1925-1930. Lang.: Eng. 3633
The critical reception of Zora Neale Hurston's autobiography. USA. 1942. Lang.: Eng. 3704

Hurtzig, Hannah
Administration
Interview with Tankred Dorst and Hannah Hurtzig of the Bonner Biennale festival. Germany: Bonn. 1998. Lang.: Ger. 1379

Hutchinson, Ron
Performance/production
Collection of newspaper reviews by London theatre critics. UK-England: London. 1998. Lang.: Eng. 2586

Hutt, Rosamunde
Performance/production
Collection of newspaper reviews by London theatre critics. UK-England: London. 1998. Lang.: Eng. 2499

Hutt, William
Performance/production
Interview with actor William Hutt. Canada: Stratford, ON. 1962-1996. Lang.: Eng. 1844
Actor William Hutt. Canada: Stratford, ON. USA. 1953-1998. Lang.: Eng. 1858

Hwang, David Henry
Design/technology
Lighting design for Hwang's *Golden Child* at the Public Theatre. USA: New York, NY. 1996-1998. Lang.: Eng. 1540
Performance/production
Comparison of productions of Ibsen's *Peer Gynt.* USA: Providence, RI, New York, NY, Washington, DC, Nacogdoches, TX. 1998. Lang.: Eng. 2711
Julyana Soelistyo and Sam Trammel, winners of the Derwent Award. USA: New York, NY. 1998. Lang.: Eng. 2719
Careeer of actress Tsai Chin. USA. 1959-1998. Lang.: Eng. 2754
Plays/librettos/scripts
Interview with playwright David Henry Hwang. USA. 1980-1998. Lang.: Eng. 3530
Playwright David Henry Hwang. USA. 1980-1998. Lang.: Eng. 3573
Interview with playwright David Henry Hwang. USA. 1980-1998. Lang.: Eng. 3669

Hyatt, John
Performance/production
Collection of newspaper reviews by London theatre critics. UK-England: London. 1998. Lang.: Eng. 2575

Hydraulics Phat Like Mean
Performance/production
Collection of newspaper reviews by London theatre critics. UK-England: London. 1998. Lang.: Eng. 2498

Hyers, Anna Madah
Performance/production
The Hyers sisters and Black musical comedy. USA. 1870-1902. Lang.: Eng. 4384

Hyers, Emma Louise
Performance/production
The Hyers sisters and Black musical comedy. USA. 1870-1902. Lang.: Eng. 4384

Hyland, Frances
Performance/production
The performances of Frances Hyland, Kate Reid, and Martha Henry in *The Cherry Orchard.* Canada: Stratford, ON. 1965. Lang.: Eng. 1865

Hyland, James
Performance/production
Collection of newspaper reviews by London theatre critics. UK-England: London. 1998. Lang.: Eng. 2471

Hymn to Love
Performance/production
Collection of newspaper reviews by London theatre critics. UK-England: London. 1998. Lang.: Eng. 2511
Collection of newspaper reviews by London theatre critics. UK-England: London. 1998. Lang.: Eng. 2560

Hynes, Garry
Design/technology
Set designs of Francis O'Connor. USA: New York, NY. 1998. Lang.: Eng. 1541

Hyperion
Plays/librettos/scripts
Hero and anti-hero in contemporary opera production. Germany. 1998. Lang.: Ger. 4791

Hysell, Harvey
Training
Dance teacher Harvey Hysell. USA: New Orleans, LA. 1969-1998. Lang.: Eng. 1217

Hytner, Nicholas
Design/technology
Lighting design for Shakespeare's *Twelfth Night* at the Vivian Beaumont. USA: New York, NY. 1998. Lang.: Eng. 1546
The design concept for Nicholas Hytner's production of Shakespeare's *Twelfth Night.* USA: New York, NY. 1998. Lang.: Eng. 1556

I Am Yours
Performance/production
Collection of newspaper reviews by London theatre critics. UK-England: London. 1998. Lang.: Eng. 2432

I Can't Remember Anything
Design/technology
Set design for Joseph Chaikin's production of two one-acts by Arthur Miller. USA: New york, NY. 1998. Lang.: Eng. 1532

I Love You, I Love You Not
Plays/librettos/scripts
The survivor character in contemporary American drama. USA. 1970-1997. Lang.: Eng. 3600

I Shall Never Return
SEE
Nigdy tu już nie powrócę.

I, Hamlet
Plays/librettos/scripts
Shakespeare and the feminist theatre of Bryony Lavery and Jane Prendergast. UK-England. 1997. Lang.: Eng. 3439

I'd Rather Be Right
Plays/librettos/scripts
The portrayal of Franklin Delano Roosevelt in the musical *I'd Rather Be Right.* USA. 1937. Lang.: Eng. 4396

I'm Not Your Baby
Plays/librettos/scripts
AIDS and the work of performance artist Franko B. UK-England. 1996-1998. Lang.: Eng. 4261

Iacovelli, John
Design/technology
The 1998 USITT expo. USA: Long Beach, CA. 1998. Lang.: Eng. 251
Ianucci, Armando
Performance/production
Collection of newspaper reviews by London theatre critics. UK-England: London. 1998. Lang.: Eng. 2513
Ibrahim Sultan
Plays/librettos/scripts
Representation of the virginal body on the German stage. Germany. 1600-1800. Lang.: Ger. 3171
Ibsen, Henrik
Design/technology
Set design and lighting for a production of Ibsen's *Hedda Gabler*. USA: Louisville, KY. 1988. Lang.: Eng. 1564
Institutions
Director training at Ernst-Busch-Schule and some of its graduates. Germany: Berlin. 1972-1998. Lang.: Ger. 1648
Report on Ibsen festival. Norway: Oslo. 1998. Lang.: Eng. 1681
Survey of the 1998 Ibsen Festival. Norway: Oslo. 1998. Lang.: Eng. 1682
Survey of annual Ibsen festival. Norway: Oslo. 1998. Lang.: Eng. 1683
Ibsen Society of America's celebration of the centennial of *Når vi døde vågner (When We Dead Awaken)*. USA: New York, NY. 1998. Lang.: Eng. 1755
Performance/production
Productions directed by Christian Stückl, Tom Kühnel, and Robert Schuster. Germany: Frankfurt. 1997-1998. Lang.: Ger. 1969
Interview with director Stein Winge. Norway: Oslo. 1988-1998. Lang.: Eng. 2210
Report from Ibsen festival. Norway: Oslo. 1998. Lang.: Swe. 2211
Seven critics on their favorite character or portrayal. Sweden. 1950. Lang.: Swe. 2369
Recent productions of plays by Ibsen and Strindberg. Sweden: Stockholm. 1997. Lang.: Eng. 2393
Collection of newspaper reviews by London theatre critics. UK-England: London. 1998. Lang.: Eng. 2422
Collection of newspaper reviews by London theatre critics. UK-England: London. 1998. Lang.: Eng. 2466
Trevor Nunn's production of *An Enemy of the People* by Ibsen. UK-England: London. 1998. Lang.: Eng. 2627
Comparison of productions of Ibsen's *Peer Gynt*. USA: Providence, RI, New York, NY, Washington, DC, Nacogdoches, TX. 1998. Lang.: Eng. 2711
Reviews of productions of plays by Ibsen. USA: New York, NY. Norway: Oslo. 1998. Lang.: Eng. 2747
Plays/librettos/scripts
Analysis of Elfriede Jelinek's adaptation of *Et Dukkehjem (A Doll's House)* by Ibsen. Austria. 1979. Lang.: Eng. 2782
The rebel in modern drama. Europe. 1950-1988. Lang.: Eng. 3053
The devouring woman in plays of Racine, Kleist, Ibsen, and Beckett. Europe. 1760-1992. Lang.: Eng. 3058
Robert Musil and the 'crisis of modern drama'. Europe. 1880-1930. Lang.: Eng. 3062
Hegel's influence on the plays of Henrik Ibsen. Norway. Germany. 1870-1898. Lang.: Eng. 3292
Feminism and plays of Henrik Ibsen. Norway. 1879-1979. Lang.: Eng. 3293
Stage directions in Ibsen's *Hedda Gabler*. Norway. 1987. Lang.: Eng. 3294
Ibsen, translation, and feminine discourse. Norway. 1888. Lang.: Eng. 3295
Andreas-Salomé's view of Ibsen's female characters. Norway. Germany. 1879-1906. Lang.: Eng. 3296
The development of the character Dr. Rank in Ibsen's *Et Dukkehjem (A Doll's House)*. Norway. 1879. Lang.: Eng. 3297
Trolls in the late plays of Ibsen. Norway. 1886-1894. Lang.: Eng. 3298
Henrik Ibsen and social criticism in *En Folkefiende (An Enemy of the People)*. Norway. 1882. Lang.: Swe. 3300
Ibsen's *Peer Gynt* and its new Polish translation. Poland. Norway. 1867-1967. Lang.: Pol. 3308
Intellectual and artistic influences on playwright Eugene O'Neill. USA. 1888-1953. Lang.: Eng. 3697
Research/historiography
The Marvin Carlson collection of materials at the Ibsen Center. Norway: Oslo. 1998. Lang.: Eng. 3797
Theory/criticism
Theatrical theory and practice. 600 B.C.-1997 A.D. Lang.: Slo. 3804
Ibusár
Performance/production
Lajos Parti Nagy's *Ibusár* directed by János Mikuli. Hungary: Kecskemét, Pécs. 1998. Lang.: Hun. 2110
ICA Theatre (London)
Performance/production
Collection of newspaper reviews by London theatre critics. UK-England: London. 1998. Lang.: Eng. 2572
Collection of newspaper reviews by London theatre critics. UK-England: London. 1998. Lang.: Eng. 2580
Ice dancing
Performance/production
Interview with ice-dancing team Susanna Rahkamo and Petri Kokko. Finland. 1998. Lang.: Fin. 919
Report on touring ice show *Stars on Ice*. USA. 1998. Lang.: Eng. 990
Ice dancers Renee Roca and Gorsha Sur. USA. 1992-1998. Lang.: Eng. 992
Ice Station H.I.P.P.O.
Performance/production
Collection of newspaper reviews by London theatre critics. UK-England: London. 1998. Lang.: Eng. 2475
Icebound
Plays/librettos/scripts
The development of playwright Owen Davis. USA. 1905-1923. Lang.: Eng. 3526
Icecream
Plays/librettos/scripts
Ecology and the plays of Caryl Churchill. UK-England. 1971-1989. Lang.: Eng. 3422
Fragmentation and skepticism in Caryl Churchill's *Icecream*. UK-England. 1989. Lang.: Eng. 3451
Iced
Performance/production
Collection of newspaper reviews by London theatre critics. UK-England: London. 1998. Lang.: Eng. 2572
Iceman Cometh, The
Performance/production
Recent productions in Ireland of plays by Eugene O'Neill. Ireland: Dublin. UK-Ireland: Belfast. 1989-1998. Lang.: Eng. 2154
Collection of newspaper reviews by London theatre critics. UK-England: London. 1998. Lang.: Eng. 2459
Plays/librettos/scripts
Female characters in Eugene O'Neill's plays. USA. 1920-1953. Lang.: Eng. 3525
The late plays of Eugene O'Neill. USA. 1939-1943. Lang.: Eng. 3528
Female presence/absence in plays of O'Neill, Pinter, and Shepard. USA. UK-England. 1936-1985. Lang.: Eng. 3607
The Iceman Cometh by Eugene O'Neill compared to a short story by Ernest Hemingway. USA. 1939-1946. Lang.: Eng. 3609
African- and Irish-Americans in the plays of Eugene O'Neill. USA. 1916-1953. Lang.: Eng. 3687
Closure in plays of Eugene O'Neill. USA. 1918-1950. Lang.: Eng. 3703
Ich czworo (Four of Them, The)
Plays/librettos/scripts
Feminist analysis of plays by Gabriela Zapolska. Poland. 1885-1998. Lang.: Pol. 3301
Id
Performance/production
Collection of newspaper reviews by London theatre critics. UK-England: London. 1998. Lang.: Eng. 2554
Idomeneo
Performance/production
Background material on Lyric Opera of Chicago radio broadcast performances. USA: Chicago, IL. 1998. Lang.: Eng. 4709
If I Were Lifted Up from Earth
Performance/production
Collection of newspaper reviews by London theatre critics. UK-England: London. 1998. Lang.: Eng. 2554
If You Yams White
Performance/production
The use of English and Krio in theatre of Michael Yaarimeh Bangura. Sierra Leone: Freetown. 1960-1998. Lang.: Eng. 2343

Igin, I.
Performance/production
I. Igin's *Czars*, a biography of dancers Konstantin Sergejév and Natalija Dudinskaja. Russia: Leningrad. 1940. Lang.: Rus. 1138
Iglódi, István
Performance/production
Reviews of new Hungarian musicals. Hungary: Budapest. 1997. Lang.: Hun. 4360
Iizuka, Naomi
Plays/librettos/scripts
Playwright Naomi Iizuka. USA. 1998. Lang.: Eng. 3531
Ilbijeri (Melbourne)
Performance/production
Aborigines in Australian theatre. Australia. 1990-1998. Lang.: Eng. 486
Illés, István
Performance/production
Two productions of Ernő Szép's *Vőlegény (The Fiancé)*. Hungary: Nyíregyháza. Hungary: Győr. 1998.Lang.: Hun. 2118
Illusion Theatre (Minneapolis, MN)
Theory/criticism
Theory and Asian-American theatre. USA: Minneapolis, MN. 1994-1995. Lang.: Eng. 869
Illyés Gyula Magyar Nemzeti Színház (Beregovo)
Institutions
History of annual festival of Hungarian-language theatre. Hungary: Kisvárda. 1989-1998. Lang.: Hun. 1669
Performance/production
One-act plays of Čechov by the Illyés Gyula National Theatre. Hungary. Ukraine: Beregovo. 1997. Lang.: Hun. 2104
Im Dickicht der Städte (In the Jungle of Cities)
Basic theatrical documents
Catalan translations of plays by Bertolt Brecht (volume 1). Germany. 1919-1954. Lang.: Cat. 1437
Performance/production
Recent Paris productions. France: Paris. 1997-1998. Lang.: Ger. 1933
French production of *Im Dickicht der Städte (In the Jungle of Cities)* by Bertolt Brecht. France. 1997-1998. Lang.: Ger. 1946
Reviews of productions of plays by Brecht. Germany. 1998. Lang.: Ger. 1986
Plays/librettos/scripts
Brecht and the city as an expressionistic setting. Germany. USA. 1923-1926. Lang.: Eng. 3168
Imitation of Life
Plays/librettos/scripts
John Stahl's film adaptation of *Imitation of Life* by Fannie Hurst. USA: Hollywood, CA. 1934. Lang.: Eng. 4029
Immaterial Time
Performance/production
Collection of newspaper reviews by London theatre critics. UK-England: London. 1998. Lang.: Eng. 2469
Immigrant Song, The
Performance/production
Collection of newspaper reviews by London theatre critics. UK-England: London. 1998. Lang.: Eng. 2528
Imperceptible Mutabilities in the Third Kingdom
Plays/librettos/scripts
Analysis of *Imperceptible Mutabilities in the Third Kingdom* by Suzan-Lori Parks. USA. 1995. Lang.: Eng. 3592
Importance of Being Earnest, The
Basic theatrical documents
Catalan translation of *The Importance of Being Earnest* by Oscar Wilde. UK-England. 1895. Lang.: Cat. 1479
Performance/production
Collection of newspaper reviews by London theatre critics. UK-England: London. 1998. Lang.: Eng. 2566
Plays/librettos/scripts
Linguistic style and action in plays of Wilde, Shaw, and Stoppard. UK-England. 1890-1985. Lang.: Eng. 3467
The source of the name Bunbury in Wilde's *Importance of Being Earnest*. UK-England: Worthing. 1894. Lang.: Eng. 3469
Impostors, The
Design/technology
Technical designs for Stanley Tucci's film *The Impostors*. USA. 1998. Lang.: Eng. 3901
Impromptu de l'Alma ou Le Caméléon du berger, L' (Improvisation of the Shepherd's Chameleon)
Plays/librettos/scripts
Analysis of *L'Impromptu de l'Alma ou Le Caméléon du Berger (Improvisation of the Shepherd's Chameleon)* by Eugène Ionesco. France. 1970. Lang.: Fre. 3088
Improvisation
Institutions
History of the Ligue Nationale de l'Improvisation. Canada: Montreal, PQ. 1979-1997. Lang.: Fre. 339
Improvisations by Stockholms Improvisationsteater. Sweden: Stockholm. 1989-1998. Lang.: Swe. 1733
The theatrical method of Joint Stock Theatre Group. UK-England: London. 1974-1989. Lang.: Eng. 1749
Performance/production
Women and improvisation. USA. 1970-1997. Lang.: Eng. 672
Interview with dancer/choreographer Rebecca Hilton. Australia. USA. 1983-1995. Lang.: Eng. 913
Dance improvisation with children. France. 1998. Lang.: Fre. 1275
Actor/director Jaroslav Dušek of Divadlo Vizita. Czech Republic: Prague. 1987-1998. Lang.: Cze. 1884
Musical improvisation in Chinese opera. China, People's Republic of. 1920-1997. Lang.: Eng. 4313
Theory/criticism
Tools for analysis of improvisation. Canada: Montreal, PQ. 1998. Lang.: Fre. 834
Training
Ferruccio Di Cori's improvisational workshops for actors and directors. Italy: Rome. 1994-1996. Lang.: Ita. 874
Improvisational training and psychological resilience. USA. 1996-1998. Lang.: Eng. 879
In a Little World of Our Own
Performance/production
Collection of newspaper reviews by London theatre critics. UK-England: London. 1998. Lang.: Eng. 2443
In Close Relation
Performance/production
Collection of newspaper reviews by London theatre critics. UK-England: London. 1998. Lang.: Eng. 2548
In Dahomey
Performance/production
Musical theatre composer Will Marion Cook. USA. 1898-1950. Lang.: Eng. 4378
In der Löwengrube (In the Lions' Den)
Performance/production
Premieres of plays on the Nazi theme. Germany: Darmstadt. Austria: Vienna. 1998. Lang.: Ger. 2030
'In Good King Charles's Golden Days'
Plays/librettos/scripts
Analysis of the later plays of George Bernard Shaw. UK-England. 1923-1947. Lang.: Eng. 3444
George Bernard Shaw and the history-play tradition. UK-England. 1899-1939. Lang.: Eng. 3503
In the Family
Performance/production
Collection of newspaper reviews by London theatre critics. UK-England: London. 1998. Lang.: Eng. 2549
In the Jungle of the Cities
SEE
Im Dickicht der Städte.
In the Native State
Plays/librettos/scripts
Analysis of *In the Native State* and *Indian Ink* by Tom Stoppard. UK-England. 1991-1995. Lang.: Eng. 3459
In the Summer House
Plays/librettos/scripts
Analysis of Jane Bowles' play *In the Summer House*. USA. 1986. Lang.: Dut. 3555
In the Zone
Performance/production
Notable productions of plays by Eugene O'Neill. USA. 1916-1996. Lang.: Eng. 2752
In White America
Performance/production
Documentary theatre and the politics of representation. USA. 1966-1993. Lang.: Eng. 2728
Incoronazione di Poppea, L'
Design/technology
Set and costume design for San Francisco Opera productions. USA: San Francisco, CA. 1998. Lang.: Eng. 4443
Independent theatre
Administration
The effects of independent theatre in Berlin. Germany: Berlin. 1998. Lang.: Ger. 14

Independent theatre — cont'd

Audience
The importance of independent theatre for children. Germany: Hannover. 1998. Lang.: Ger. 151
Institutions
Independent children's theatre workshop. Germany: Hannover. 1998. Lang.: Ger. 352
Profile of Theater in der Fabrik. Germany: Dresden. 1993-1998. Lang.: Ger. 1644
Independent German-language theatre festival Impulse. Germany. 1998. Lang.: Ger. 1652
Profile of independent feminist theatre Kvinnliga Dramatiska Teatern. Sweden: Stockholm. 1997-1998. Lang.: Swe. 1725
Performance/production
The contribution of unaffiliated dancers and choreographers. Finland. 1998. Lang.: Fin. 917
Sechs-Tage-Oper, festival of independent music theatre. Germany. 1998. Lang.: Ger. 4579
Plays/librettos/scripts
Johan Simons and the independent theatre group in Hollandia. Netherlands: Amsterdam. 1985-1998. Lang.: Ger. 3280
Relation to other fields
The quality of Berlin's independent theatres. Germany: Berlin. 1998. Lang.: Ger. 748

Indexes
Reference materials
Index to the first twenty volumes of *Medieval English Theatre*. England. 1979-1998. Lang.: Eng. 696
Index to performing arts articles in Bragaglia's *Chronache d'attualità*. Italy: Rome. 1916-1922. Lang.: Ita. 704
Index of the first twenty volumes of *The Passing Show*. USA: New York, NY. 1976-1998. Lang.: Eng. 709
Index to *The Pinter Review*, 1992-1996. UK-England. 1992-1996. Lang.: Eng. 3727
Index to *Opera* volume 49. UK-England. Europe. USA. 1998. Lang.: Eng. 4834

India Song
Performance/production
The function of sound in productions of *India Song* by Marguerite Duras. France. UK-Wales: Mold. 1973-1993. Lang.: Eng. 1945
Music in films of Marguerite Duras. France. 1974-1981. Lang.: Eng. 3932
Plays/librettos/scripts
Narrative and form as theatrical media in the plays of Marguerite Duras. France. 1914-1986. Lang.: Eng. 3101
Space and pre-verbal memory in later works of Marguerite Duras. France. 1970-1982. Lang.: Eng. 3106

Indian Ink
Plays/librettos/scripts
The speaking subject in plays of Beckett and Stoppard. France. Ireland. UK-England. 1945-1998. Lang.: Ger. 3098
Analysis of *In the Native State* and *Indian Ink* by Tom Stoppard. UK-England. 1991-1995. Lang.: Eng. 3459

Indians
Performance/production
Documentary theatre and the politics of representation. USA. 1966-1993. Lang.: Eng. 2728
Plays/librettos/scripts
Genocide, theatre, and the human body. North America. UK-England. Argentina. 1998. Lang.: Eng. 3290

Indigenous theatre
Basic theatrical documents
English translation of *terukkūttu* piece *Pakaṭai Tuyil (The Dice Game and the Disrobing)*. India. 1998. Lang.: Eng. 1345
Performance/production
Aborigines in Australian theatre. Australia. 1990-1998. Lang.: Eng. 486
Northern Brazilian folk theatre forms. Brazil. 1972-1997. Lang.: Eng. 497
Indigenous Mexican theatre and colonialism. Mexico. 1975-1998. Lang.: Eng. 560
Female performers of the formerly all-male genre *randai*. Sumatra. 1980-1998. Lang.: Eng. 1354
Report from a symposium on traditional Korean theatre. Korea. Germany: Berlin. 1980-1998. Lang.: Ger, Fre, Dut, Eng. 2196
Cossack theatre of the Choper Valley. Russia. Lang.: Rus. 2332
Indian theatre in South Africa. South Africa, Republic of. 1900-1998. Lang.: Eng. 2356
Plays/librettos/scripts
Theatre and the creation of a new nationalism. Canada. Saint Lucia. 1980-1995. Lang.: Eng. 2808

Indiscretions
SEE
Parents Terribles, Les.

Inexpressible Island
Plays/librettos/scripts
David Young on his play *Inexpressible Island*. Canada: Toronto, ON. 1990-1997. Lang.: Eng. 2837

Infelice Dorotea, La (Unfortunate Dorotea, The)
Plays/librettos/scripts
Playwright Andrés de Claramonte. Spain. 1580-1626. Lang.: Eng. 3404

Inge, William
Plays/librettos/scripts
Gender-role reversal in plays of William Inge. USA. 1950-1958. Lang.: Eng. 3623
Analysis of *Bus Stop* by William Inge. USA. 1955. Lang.: Eng. 3624

Injunction Granted
Performance/production
Productions of the Federal Theatre Project's Living Newspapers. USA: New York, NY. 1935-1939. Lang.: Eng. 643

Innamorati, Gl' (Lovers, The)
Basic theatrical documents
Catalan translation of *Gl'Innamorati (The Lovers)* by Carlo Goldoni. Italy. 1765. Lang.: Cat. 1443

Innesto, L' (Grafting, The)
Plays/librettos/scripts
Yearbook of Pirandello studies. Italy. 1589-1926. Lang.: Eng. 3247

Innocente, L' (Innocent One, The)
Performance/production
Collection of newspaper reviews by London theatre critics. UK-England: London. 1998. Lang.: Eng. 2517

INRI
Performance/production
Review of András Bálint's one-man show *INRI*. Hungary: Budapest. 1997. Lang.: Hun. 2073

Insatiate Countess, The
Plays/librettos/scripts
The politics of gender in the plays of John Marston. England. 1599-1634. Lang.: Eng. 3009

Inspector Calls, An
Plays/librettos/scripts
The detective plays of Jardiel Poncela. Spain. 1940-1969. Lang.: Spa. 3392

Inspector General, The
SEE
Revizor.

Inspiration
Performance/production
Collection of newspaper reviews by London theatre critics. UK-England: London. 1998. Lang.: Eng. 2432

Installations
Audience
The prompting of epileptic seizures by film. 1960-1988. Lang.: Eng. 3876
Performance/production
'The Speaking Body' museum installation, site of theatre anthropology seminars. Austria: Vienna. Switzerland: Zurich. 1996-1998. Lang.: Eng. 493
Report on biennial festival of mixed media. France: Lyon. 1997. Lang.: Eng. 4042
Multimedia and the productions of Giorgio Barberio Corsetti. Italy: Rome, Milan. 1985-1998. Lang.: Eng. 4043
Performance in the work of mixed-media artist Tina Keane. UK-England. 1970-1988. Lang.: Eng. 4044
Video artist Bill Viola. USA: New York, NY. 1976-1998. Lang.: Eng. 4071
The performance installations *Santa Cruzan/Flores de Mayo* by DIWA Arts. USA: San Francisco, CA. 1994-1996. Lang.: Eng. 4256
Interview with video and installation artist Gary Hill. USA. 1969-1998. Lang.: Eng. 4258

Institut für Theater, Musik, und Film (Hamburg)
Institutions
Director training at Universität und Musikhochschule. Germany: Hamburg. 1988-1998. Lang.: Ger. 1658

Institute of Contemporary Arts (London)
Performance/production
Performance artist Leslie Hill's *Push the Boat Out*. UK-England: London. USA. 1995-1997. Lang.: Eng. 4245

Institutions
Administration
Profile of management group National Arts Stabilization. USA. 1998. Lang.: Eng. 144
Plays/librettos/scripts
Essays on Polish theatre. Poland. 1960-1990. Lang.: Hun. 3305
Institutions, associations
Institutions
History of the Polish Theatre Association. Poland: Warsaw. 1918-1998. Lang.: Pol. 1692
Institutions, service
Institutions
History of the Metropolitan Opera Guild. USA. 1935-1975. Lang.: Eng. 4486
Relation to other fields
The theatrical nature of Salvation Army activities. USA. 1865-1950. Lang.: Eng. 796
Institutions, special
Institutions
Working at the Shubert archive. USA: New York, NY. 1988-1998. Lang.: Eng. 426
Institutions, training
Institutions
Survey of drama graduates' financial and employment conditions. Canada: Toronto, ON. 1989-1997. Lang.: Eng. 341
Profile of Munich's theatre training institutions. Germany: Munich. 1998. Lang.: Ger. 348
Actor and director training at Hochschule für Musik and Darstellende Kunst. Germany: Frankfurt/Main. 1998. Lang.: Ger. 350
The eleventh session of the International School of Theatre Anthropology. Portugal: Lisbon. Denmark: Holstebro. 1998. Lang.: Eng. 376
Report on Vachtangov School conference. Russia: Moscow. 1990-1998. Lang.: Rus. 380
The work of training organization Metier in creating national standards for arts training. UK-England: Bradford. 1996-1998. Lang.: Eng. 388
Interdisciplinarity in post-secondary theatre studies programs. USA. 1998. Lang.: Eng. 407
The training program of the Clarence B. Hilberry Repertory Theatre. USA: Detroit, MI. 1963-1973. Lang.: Eng. 408
Interview with Imre Dózsa, managing director of Táncművészeti Főiskola. Hungary: Budapest. 1998. Lang.: Hun. 897
The performing arts curriculum of Skytteholmsgymnasiet. Sweden: Solna. 1990-1998. Lang.: Swe. 898
Interview with dance teacher Lia Schubert. Sweden: Stockholm, Gothenburg. 1935-1998. Lang.: Swe. 900
History of Ballettakademian, Lillemor Lundberg, artistic director. Sweden: Stockholm. 1957-1998. Lang.: Swe. 901
Appeal for more varied dance training. Sweden. 1998. Lang.: Swe. 903
The dance training program of Houston High School for the Performing and Visual Arts. USA: Houston, TX. 1998. Lang.: Eng. 907
Dance training at Pécs School of the Arts. Hungary: Pécs. 1975-1998. Lang.: Hun. 1043
Interview with ballet teacher Dóra Uhrik. Hungary: Pécs. 1978-1998. Lang.: Hun. 1045
Criticism of Svenska Bakettskolan. Sweden: Stockholm. 1984. Lang.: Swe. 1049
Defense of Svenska Balettskolan by a former student. Sweden: Stockholm. 1996. Lang.: Swe. 1052
Training methods of the Conservatoire d'art dramatique de Québec. Canada: Quebec, PQ. 1998. Lang.: Fre. 1578
Proposal to apply alternative pedagogy and cultural studies to university theatre education. Canada: Guelph, ON. 1998. Lang.: Eng. 1586
Profile of the Swedish Institute of Acting at the Finnish Theatre Academy. Finland: Helsinki. 1908-1998. Lang.: Eng, Fre. 1603
Actor training at Hochschule der Künste and Ernst-Busch-Schule. Germany: Berlin. 1998. Lang.: Ger. 1622
Director training at Ernst-Busch-Schule and some of its graduates. Germany: Berlin. 1972-1998. Lang.: Ger. 1648
Director training at Universität und Musikhochschule. Germany: Hamburg. 1988-1998. Lang.: Ger. 1658
The curriculum at Bayerische Theaterakademie. Germany: Munich. 1985-1998. Lang.: Ger. 1659
Carlo Quartucci's acting workshop on Shakespeare's *Macbeth*. Italy: Rome. 1991-1992. Lang.: Ita. 1674
Polish experimental theatre training. Poland: Cracow, Wrocław, Warsaw. 1930-1998. Lang.: Pol. 1685
A program of study including playwriting and production. Russia: Moscow. 1998. Lang.: Rus. 1699
Theatre schools: production of showcases for graduating students. UK-England: London. 1998. Lang.: Eng. 1746
The musical theatre program at Balettakademien. Sweden: Gothenburg. 1984-1998. Lang.: Swe. 4349
Profile of Opera Akademiet. Denmark. 1956-1998. Lang.: Dan. 4449
Music theatre studies at the Hochschule für Musik und Theater. Germany: Hamburg. 1988-1998. Lang.: Ger. 4459
Interviews with graduate students at Yale University School of Music. USA: New Haven, CT. 1998. Lang.: Eng. 4483
Training practices of Houston Opera Studio. USA: Houston, TX. 1977-1998. Lang.: Eng. 4489
Performance/production
The training of actors in Asian performance styles. Australia: Brisbane. 1992-1998. Lang.: Eng. 1817
Relation to other fields
Evaluation of Ph.D. programs in theatre and drama. Canada. USA. UK-England. 1998. Lang.: Eng. 716
Training
Guide to theatrical training. Italy: Rome. 1998. Lang.: Rus. 875
Instrumentalists
Performance/production
Popular entertainment in Uganda after Idi Amin. Uganda. 1979-1998. Lang.: Eng. 604
Flamenco variations worldwide. Spain. USA. 1901-1998. Lang.: Eng. 962
Music in German-language Prague productions. Austrian Empire: Prague. 1750-1800. Lang.: Cze. 1826
History of the steeldrum, used in carnival celebrations. Trinidad and Tobago: Port of Spain. 1777-1998. Lang.: Eng. 4169
Carnival performances of a *jouvay* band. Trinidad and Tobago: Port of Spain. 1996. Lang.: Eng. 4171
Insurrection: Holding History
Basic theatrical documents
Text of *Insurrection: Holding History* by Robert O'Hara. USA. 1998. Lang.: Eng. 1500
Interactive theatre
Performance/production
Interactive mystery theatre weekends in an old inn. Sweden: Mariefred. 1993-1998. Lang.: Swe. 602
Relation to other fields
Die Berliner Ermittlung (The Berlin Investigation), an interactive theatre project by Jochen Gerz and Esther Shalev-Gerz. Germany: Berlin. 1998. Lang.: Ger. 3768
Interbalett'98 (Budapest)
Institutions
Notes on Interballet and Spring festivals. Hungary: Budapest. 1998. Lang.: Hun. 896
Interfacing Joan
Relation to other fields
Quantum theory in recent New York performances. USA: New York, NY. 1995-1996. Lang.: Eng. 794
Interlude of the Four Elements, The
Performance/production
Music in Tudor drama. England. 1497-1569. Lang.: Eng. 1902
Interludes
Plays/librettos/scripts
Analysis of the interludes of Cervantes. Spain. 1600-1630. Lang.: Spa. 3391
International Centre for Theatre Research
SEE
Centre international de recherche théâtrale.
International Organization of Scenographers, Theatre Technicians, and Architects
SEE
Organisation Internationale de Scénographes, Techniciens et Architectes de Théâtre.
International School of Theatre Anthropology (ISTA, Holstebro)
SEE ALSO
Odin Teatret.
Institutions
The eleventh session of the International School of Theatre Anthropology. Portugal: Lisbon. Denmark: Holstebro. 1998. Lang.: Eng. 376

International School of Theatre Anthropology (ISTA, Holstebro) — cont'd

Performance/production
Sanjukta Panigrahi, dancer, choreographer, and co-founder of ISTA. India. 1944-1997. Lang.: Eng. 952

International Theatre Institute (ITI)
Institutions
On the fiftieth anniversary of the International Theatre Institute. 1994-1996. Lang.: Hun. 333

Interview, The
Performance/production
Collection of newspaper reviews by London theatre critics. UK-England: London. 1998. Lang.: Eng. 2561

Intima Teatern (Stockholm)
Performance/production
Shakespeare's influence on Strindberg's modernism. Sweden. 1907-1910. Lang.: Eng. 2370

Intiman Theatre (Seattle, WA)
Administration
Interviews with women in top management of theatres. USA: New Haven, CT, Seattle, WA, East Haddam, CT. 1998. Lang.: Eng. 1397

Into the Woods
Performance/production
Collection of newspaper reviews by London theatre critics. UK-England: London. 1998. Lang.: Eng. 2543

Invention of Love, The
Performance/production
Collection of newspaper reviews by London theatre critics. UK-England: London. 1998. Lang.: Eng. 2533

Investigation of the Murder in El Salvador, The
Basic theatrical documents
Collection of plays by Charles L. Mee. USA. 1986-1995. Lang.: Eng. 1496

Iolanta
Performance/production
Ten' Puppet Theatre's production of Čajkovskij's opera *Iolanta.* Russia: Moscow. Lang.: Rus. 4680

Iolanthe
Plays/librettos/scripts
The trivialization of feminism in librettos of W.S. Gilbert. UK-England. 1880-1890. Lang.: Eng. 4861

Ionesco, Eugène
Design/technology
Technical designs for *The Chairs (Les Chaises),* Théâtre de Complicité. UK-England: London. 1998. Lang.: Eng. 1524
Plays/librettos/scripts
The rebel in modern drama. Europe. 1950-1988. Lang.: Eng. 3053
Aggressive language in modern drama. Europe. USA. 1960-1985. Lang.: Eng. 3055
The theatre of Eugène Ionesco. France. 1912-1994. Lang.: Ita. 3079
Analysis of *Le Roi se meurt (Exit the King)* by Eugène Ionesco. France. 1962. Lang.: Eng. 3080
Analysis of *L'Impromptu de l'Alma ou Le Caméléon du Berger (Improvisation of the Shepherd's Chameleon)* by Eugène Ionesco. France. 1970. Lang.: Fre. 3088
Absurdism in children's theatre. North America. Europe. 1896-1970. Lang.: Eng. 3288

Iphigéneia he en Aulíde (Iphigenia in Aulis)
Performance/production
Péter Valló's production of *Iphigéneia he en Aulide (Iphigenia in Aulis)* by Euripides. Hungary: Budapest. 1998. Lang.: Hun. 2132
Plays/librettos/scripts
Ellen McLaughlin's *Iphigenia and Other Daughters* at CSC Repertory. USA: New York, NY. 1995. Lang.: Eng. 3520

Iphigéneia hé en Tauríde (Iphegenia in Tauris)
Plays/librettos/scripts
Ellen McLaughlin's *Iphigenia and Other Daughters* at CSC Repertory. USA: New York, NY. 1995. Lang.: Eng. 3520

Iphigenia
Performance/production
Collection of newspaper reviews by London theatre critics. UK-England: London. 1998. Lang.: Eng. 2562

Iphigenia and Other Daughters
Plays/librettos/scripts
Ellen McLaughlin's *Iphigenia and Other Daughters* at CSC Repertory. USA: New York, NY. 1995. Lang.: Eng. 3520

Iphigenia auf Tauris (Iphigenia in Tauris)
Performance/production
Klaus Michael Grüber's production of Goethe's *Iphigenia auf Tauris.* Germany: Berlin. 1998. Lang.: Swe. 1997
Klaus Michael Grüber's production of Goethe's *Iphigenia auf Tauris.* Germany: Berlin. 1998. Lang.: Ger. 2031
Theory/criticism
Critical response to Klaus Michael Grüber's production of Goethe's *Iphigenia auf Tauris.* Germany. 1998. Lang.: Ger. 3821

Iphigénie en Tauride
Theory/criticism
Gender in Francesca Zambello's production of *Iphigénie en Tauride.* USA: Cooperstown, NY. 1997. Lang.: Eng. 4843

Ipi Zombi?
Performance/production
African ritual in the work of director and playwright Brett Bailey. South Africa, Republic of. 1997-1998. Lang.: Eng. 2349

Ipocrito, Lo (Hypocrite, The)
Plays/librettos/scripts
The comedies of Pietro Aretino. Italy. 1534-1556. Lang.: Eng. 3251

Ipsen, Bodil
Administration
The star system and Danish theatre. Denmark. 1930-1997. Lang.: Dan. 1377

Irish National Theatre Society (Dublin)
SEE
Abbey Theatre.

Irondale Ensemble (Halifax, NS)
Performance/production
Irondale Ensemble's production of *Leben des Galilei (The Life of Galileo)* by Bertolt Brecht. Canada: Halifax, NS. 1998. Lang.: Eng. 1869

Irrläufer. Nach Paris (Stray Letter: To Paris)
Plays/librettos/scripts
Playwright Hans Zimmer. Germany: Hannover. 1993-1998. Lang.: Ger. 3136

Irvin, Polly
Performance/production
Collection of newspaper reviews by London theatre critics. UK-England: London. 1998. Lang.: Eng. 2419

Irving, Jules
Performance/production
The multifaceted nature of early nonprofit regional theatre. USA. 1940-1960. Lang.: Eng. 2705

Irwin, Bill
Design/technology
Costume design for Feydeau's *A Flea in Her Ear (La Puce à l'Oreille),* Roundabout Theatre Company. USA: New York, NY. 1998. Lang.: Eng. 1537
Performance/production
A photo session involving mimes Marcel Marceau and Bill Irwin. USA: New York, NY. 1998. Lang.: Eng. 4092

Isakson, Kajsa
Plays/librettos/scripts
Interview with playwright-director Kajsa Isakson. Sweden: Stockholm. 1997-1998. Lang.: Swe. 3414

Isangulova, G.
Performance/production
Actress G. Isangulova. Tatarstan: Kazan. 1998. Lang.: Rus. 2404

Isherwood, Christopher
Performance/production
Musical performances on and off Broadway. USA: New York. 1998. Lang.: Ger. 4383

Island Princess, The
Plays/librettos/scripts
Analysis of *The Island Princess* by John Fletcher. England. 1621. Lang.: Eng. 2988

Island, The
Plays/librettos/scripts
The influence of Albert Camus on playwright Athol Fugard. South Africa, Republic of. 1960-1985. Lang.: Eng. 3362

Israel, Robert
Design/technology
Creativity and beauty in theatrical design. USA. 1998. Lang.: Eng. 322

Israfilov, Rifkat
Performance/production
Rijfkat Israfilov's production of *Bibinur, ah, Bibinur!.* Bashkir: Ufa. 1998. Lang.: Rus. 1827

Issey Ogata no Toshiseikatsuno (Catalogue of Modern City Life, A)
Performance/production
Collection of newspaper reviews by London theatre critics. UK-England: London. 1998. Lang.: Eng. 2430

Istoriko-étnograficëskij Teat'r (Moscow)
Performance/production
Mikle Mizjukov's production of *Pesn' sud'by (The Song of Fate)* by Blok. Russia: Moscow. 1998. Lang.: Rus. 2276

It, Wit, Don't Give a Shit Girls
Performance/production
Collection of newspaper reviews by London theatre critics. UK-England: London. 1998. Lang.: Eng. 2568

It's Better with a Band
Performance/production
Collection of newspaper reviews by London theatre critics. UK-England: London. 1998. Lang.: Eng. 2421

It's Jackie
Performance/production
Collection of newspaper reviews by London theatre critics. UK-England: London. 1998. Lang.: Eng. 2508

Italian Opera House (London)
Performance/production
Excerpts from Johanna Schopenhauer's journal relating to London theatre. UK-England: London. Germany. 1803-1805. Lang.: Eng. 2615

Ithaka
Performance/production
Productions directed by Christian Stückl, Tom Kühnel, and Robert Schuster. Germany: Frankfurt. 1997-1998. Lang.: Ger. 1969

Ito, Michio
Performance/production
Collaborative Symbolist dance/theatre projects. Europe. USA. 1916-1934. Lang.: Eng. 1268

Iubilei (Jubilee, The)
Basic theatrical documents
Catalan translations of the complete plays of Anton Čechov. Russia. 1884-1904. Lang.: Cat. 1449

Ivan Vasiljėvič
Performance/production
Review of Bulgakov's *Ivan Vasiljėvič* directed by János Mohácsi. Hungary: Kaposvár. 1998. Lang.: Hun. 2095

Ivanov
Basic theatrical documents
Catalan translations of the complete plays of Anton Čechov. Russia. 1884-1904. Lang.: Cat. 1449
Performance/production
Actors Helen Carey and Max Wright, winners of Joe A. Callaway Award. USA. 1998. Lang.: Eng. 2716

Ivanova, L.
Performance/production
Musical theatre performer L. Ivanova. Bulgaria. 1998. Lang.: Rus. 4353

Ives, Philip
Performance/production
Collection of newspaper reviews by London theatre critics. UK-England: London. 1998. Lang.: Eng. 2451

Ivey, William J.
Administration
The nomination of William J. Ivey as head of NEA. USA. 1998. Lang.: Eng. 59
Institutions
William J. Ivey, nominee for chair of NEA. USA: Washington, DC. 1998. Lang.: Eng. 420

Ivgi, Uri
Performance/production
Productions of Szegedi Kortárs Balett. Hungary: Szeged. 1998. Lang.: Hun. 1102

Iwaszko, Danusia
Performance/production
Collection of newspaper reviews by London theatre critics. UK-England: London. 1998. Lang.: Eng. 2576

Iwona, Księżniczka Burgundia (Princess Yvonne)
Performance/production
Review of Gombrowicz's *Princess Yvonne*, Katona József Theatre. Hungary: Budapest. 1997. Lang.: Hun. 2079

Izutsu (Well-Stone, The)
Performance/production
Collection of newspaper reviews by London theatre critics. UK-England: London. 1998. Lang.: Eng. 2420

Izzard, Eddie
Performance/production
The North American tour of English comedian Eddie Izzard. North America. UK-England. 1998. Lang.: Eng. 4127

J'étais dans ma maison et j'attendais que la pluie vienne (I Was In My House and I Was Waiting for the Rain to Come)
Performance/production
Comparison of text-based and visual productions. France. 1998. Lang.: Fre. 1939

Jackie O
Plays/librettos/scripts
The American and Canadian premieres of *Jackie O.* Canada: Banff, AB. USA: Houston, TX. 1997. Lang.: Eng. 4761

Jackie: An American Life
Performance/production
Collection of newspaper reviews by London theatre critics. UK-England: London. 1998. Lang.: Eng. 2530

Jackness, Andrew
Design/technology
Technical designs for Stanley Tucci's film *The Impostors.* USA. 1998. Lang.: Eng. 3901
Technical designs for *The Scarlet Pimpernel* directed by Robert Longbottom. USA: New York, NY. 1998. Lang.: Eng. 4331

Jackson, Carrie
Administration
Interview with Carrie Jackson, executive director of AUDELCO. USA: New York, NY. 1998. Lang.: Eng. 1399

Jackson, Shannon
Basic theatrical documents
Text of *White Noises* by Shannon Jackson. USA. 1998. Lang.: Eng. 1490
Plays/librettos/scripts
Shannon Jackson on her solo piece *White Noises.* USA. 1998. Lang.: Eng. 3619

Jackson's Lane Theatre (London)
Performance/production
Collection of newspaper reviews by London theatre critics. UK-England: London. 1998. Lang.: Eng. 2533
Collection of newspaper reviews by London theatre critics. UK-England: London. 1998. Lang.: Eng. 2538

Jacobean theatre
SEE ALSO
Geographical-Chronological Index under: England, 1603-1625.
Performance/production
Analysis of a London theatre season. England: London. 1609-1610. Lang.: Eng. 515
Census of Renaissance drama productions and staged readings. UK-England. 1997. Lang.: Eng. 2635
Plays/librettos/scripts
Plague imagery in Jacobean tragedy. England. 1618-1642. Lang.: Eng. 2889
The influence of Webster, Middleton, and Shakespeare on the poetry of Robert Browning. England. 1590-1889. Lang.: Eng. 2906
Authority and medicine in Webster's *The Duchess of Malfi.* England. 1613. Lang.: Eng. 2947
The treatment of single women in early Stuart drama. England. 1604-1608. Lang.: Eng. 2979
Analysis of *The Island Princess* by John Fletcher. England. 1621. Lang.: Eng. 2988
The malcontent scholar in Elizabethan and Jacobean theatre. England. 1590-1642. Lang.: Eng. 3003
The influence of Jacobean theatre on contemporary plays and productions. UK-England. 1986-1998. Lang.: Eng. 3428
Theatricality and the printed texts of civic pageants. England. 1604-1637. Lang.: Eng. 4225
Relation to other fields
Cross-dressing and gender struggle on the early modern English stage. England. 1580-1620. Lang.: Eng. 3749

Jacobi, Derek
Performance/production
Speaking styles of selected actors reading Shakespeare's *Henry V.* North America. UK-England. 1998. Lang.: Eng. 2208
Derek Jacobi on playing Macbeth for the RSC. UK-England: London, Stratford. 1993-1994. Lang.: Eng. 2616

Jacquerello, Roland
Performance/production
Recent productions in Ireland of plays by Eugene O'Neill. Ireland: Dublin. UK-Ireland: Belfast. 1989-1998. Lang.: Eng. 2154

Jacques, Martyn
Performance/production
Collection of newspaper reviews by London theatre critics. UK-England: London. 1998. Lang.: Eng. 2465

Jaffe, Susan
Institutions
American Ballet Theatre and diminishing government support. USA: New York, NY. 1998. Lang.: Eng. 1059

Jaffrey, Saeed
Performance/production
Interview with actor Saeed Jaffrey. UK-England. USA. India. 1950-1998. Lang.: Eng. 2589

Jahn-Olsson, Yvonne
Training
Interview with children's dance teacher Yvonne Jahn-Olsson. Sweden: Stockholm. 1945-1998. Lang.: Swe. 1019
Jahn, Rolf
Plays/librettos/scripts
Letters of Pirandello, Moissiu, and Jahn. Italy. Austria: Vienna. 1934. Lang.: Ita. 3219
Jahnn, Hans Henny
Performance/production
Composer Matthias Pintscher and his opera *Thomas Chatterton*. Germany. 1990-2001. Lang.: Ger. 4607
Plays/librettos/scripts
The character Medea in European drama. Europe. 450 B.C.-1998 A.D. Lang.: Ger. 3063
Jails, Hospitals & Hip-Hop
Basic theatrical documents
Text of *Jails, Hospitals and Hip-Hop* by Danny Hoch. USA. 1998. Lang.: Eng. 1487
Jakub a jeho pán
SEE
Jacques et son maître.
Jamaica House
Performance/production
Collection of newspaper reviews by London theatre critics. UK-England: London. 1998. Lang.: Eng. 2473
Jámbor, József
Performance/production
One-act plays by Brecht directed by József Jámbor. Hungary: Debrecen. 1998. Lang.: Hun. 2131
James, Burton
Relation to other fields
The blacklisting of Burton and Florence Bean James, founders of Seattle Repertory Playhouse. USA: Seattle, WA. 1951. Lang.: Eng. 3784
James, Diqui
Institutions
Report on festival of physical theatre. Germany: Munich. 1997. Lang.: Eng. 1664
James, Edward
Plays/librettos/scripts
The search for a lost translation of *The Seven Deadly Sins* by Brecht and Weill. Germany. UK-England. 1933-1998. Lang.: Eng. 4392
James, Florence Bean
Relation to other fields
The blacklisting of Burton and Florence Bean James, founders of Seattle Repertory Playhouse. USA: Seattle, WA. 1951. Lang.: Eng. 3784
James, Henry
Performance/production
Collection of newspaper reviews by London theatre critics. UK-England: London. 1998. Lang.: Eng. 2409
James, Jack
Performance/production
Collection of newspaper reviews by London theatre critics. UK-England: London. 1998. Lang.: Eng. 2576
James, Kricker
Institutions
Interview with Kricker James and Claire Higgins of Chain Lightning Theatre. USA: New York, NY. 1991-1998. Lang.: Eng. 1780
James, Paul
Performance/production
Collection of newspaper reviews by London theatre critics. UK-England: London. 1998. Lang.: Eng. 2553
James, Sheila
Basic theatrical documents
Excerpt from *a canadian monsoon* by Sheila James. Canada: Toronto, ON. 1993-1996. Lang.: Eng. 1411
Plays/librettos/scripts
Interview with playwright/director Sheila James. Canada: Toronto, ON. 1990-1998. Lang.: Eng. 2809
Jamieson, Bruce
Performance/production
Collection of newspaper reviews by London theatre critics. UK-England: London. 1998. Lang.: Eng. 2490
Jamieson, Daniel
Performance/production
Collection of newspaper reviews by London theatre critics. UK-England: London. 1998. Lang.: Eng. 2438
Jamison, Sarah
Institutions
Profile of CoOPERAtive Opera Company of New York. USA: New York, NY. 1995-1998. Lang.: Eng. 4487
Janáček, Leoš
Performance/production
Review of Salzburger Festspiele performances. Austria: Salzburg. 1998. Lang.: Ger. 4527
Background material on Metropolitan Opera radio broadcast performances. USA: New York, NY. 1998. Lang.: Eng. 4713
Organizing two performances at the Metropolitan Opera on a single day. USA: New York, NY. 1997-1998. Lang.: Eng. 4741
Plays/librettos/scripts
Analysis of Janáček's *Věc Makropulos*. Czechoslovakia. 1922-1998. Lang.: Eng. 4765
Janis, Elsie
Performance/production
Performer, writer, director Elsie Janis and the 'gay sensibility'. UK-England. 1889-1956. Lang.: Eng. 612
Popular entertainer Elsie Janis. USA. 1896-1941. Lang.: Eng. 4145
Janovskaja, Genrietta
Institutions
Reviews of some productions at the Avignon Festival. France: Avignon. 1998. Lang.: Hun. 1615
Impressions from the 'Golden Mask' festival. Russia: Minusinsk. 1998. Lang.: Ger. 1701
Janszen, Sierk
Design/technology
Technical effects control system used in a production of *Joe—The Musical* at Koninklijk Theater Carré. Netherlands: Amsterdam. 1998. Lang.: Eng. 4324
Janus Egyetemi Színház (Pécs)
Performance/production
Lajos Parti Nagy's *Ibusár* directed by János Mikuli. Hungary: Kecskemét, Pécs. 1998. Lang.: Hun. 2110
Jaques-Dalcroze, Émile
Design/technology
The influence of Dalcroze's eurhythmics on designer Adolphe Appia. Switzerland. 1906-1915. Lang.: Eng. 228
Jarman, Derek
Plays/librettos/scripts
Derek Jarman's adaptation of works by Benjamin Britten and Wilfred Owen. UK-England. 1968-1988. Lang.: Eng. 4822
Jarocki, Jerzy
Performance/production
Productions of international Čechov festival. Russia: Moscow. 1998. Lang.: Swe. 2306
Jaroschinski, Ralf
Performance/production
Dancer/choreographer Ralf Jaroschinski. Germany: Hannover. 1966-1998. Lang.: Ger. 1288
Jarry, Alfred
Basic theatrical documents
Text of *Ubu déchaîné (Ubu Unchained)* by Richard Demarcy. Benin. France. 1998. Lang.: Fre. 4287
Design/technology
The work of scene designer Libor Fára. Czech Republic: Prague. 1950-1981. Lang.: Cze. 1518
Performance/production
Semiotic analysis of Jarry's *Ubu Roi* as staged by Vitez. France: Paris. 1985. Lang.: Eng. 528
Collection of newspaper reviews by London theatre critics. UK-England: London. 1998. Lang.: Eng. 2478
Plays/librettos/scripts
Absurdism in children's theatre. North America. Europe. 1896-1970. Lang.: Eng. 3288
Jarzyna, Grzegorz
Performance/production
The new generation of Polish directors. Poland. 1989-1998. Lang.: Pol. 2219
Játékszín (Budapest)
SEE
Magyar Játékszín.
Jaunais Rigas Teatris (Riga)
Institutions
Report on a visit to Riga's theatres. Latvia: Riga. 1997. Lang.: Swe, Eng, Ger. 369
Jaunimo Teatras (Vilnius)
Institutions
The theatres of Vilnius. Lithuania: Vilnius. 1993-1998. Lang.: Swe, Eng, Ger. 370
Javorskij, E.V.
Performance/production
Choreographers and theorists E.V. Javorskij and N.S. Poznjakov. Russia: Moscow. 1920-1939. Lang.: Rus. 961

Jazz dance
Performance/production
Jazz dancer and choreographer Mia Michaels. USA. 1998. Lang.: Eng. 987
Jazz dancer and choreographer Gus Giordano. USA: Chicago, IL. 1962-1998. Lang.: Eng. 988
Training
Illustrated history of jazz dance. USA. Slovenia. 1900-1997. Lang.: Slo. 1023
Je suis un phénomène (I Am a Phenomenon)
Performance/production
Peter Brook's *Je suis un phénomène (I Am a Phenomenon)* at Bouffes du Nord. France: Paris. 1998. Lang.: Hun. 1930
Peter Brook's *Je suis un phénomène (I Am a Phenomenon)*. France: Paris. 1998. Lang.: Ger. 1934
Jean Cocteau Repertory (New York, NY)
Performance/production
Reviews of productions of plays by Ibsen. USA: New York, NY. Norway: Oslo. 1998. Lang.: Eng. 2747
Jean III (John III)
Basic theatrical documents
Text of *Jean III (John III)* by Sacha Guitry. France. 1912-1998. Lang.: Fre. 1426
Jeffers Akt I & II (Jeffer's Act I and II)
Plays/librettos/scripts
New directions in the plays of Botho Strauss. Europe. 1971-1998. Lang.: Ger. 3067
Jeffers, Robinson
Performance/production
Twentieth-century productions of Euripidean tragedy. USA. 1915-1969. Lang.: Eng. 2678
Jéfremov, Oleg Nikolajévič
Institutions
Moscow Art Theatre's two theatres and their artistic directors. Russia: Moscow. 1998. Lang.: Rus. 1698
Jekyll & Hyde: The Musical
Administration
Performer Rebecca Spencer's experience as an Equity Deputy. USA: New York, NY. 1998. Lang.: Eng. 4320
Design/technology
Lighting design for *Jekyll & Hyde* directed by Robin Phillips. USA: New York, NY. 1998. Lang.: Eng. 4345
Jeles, András
Performance/production
Andrés Jeles's *Szenvedéstërténet (Passion Play)* directed by Gábor Máté. Hungary: Budapest. 1998. Lang.: Hun. 2145
Jelinek, Elfriede
Institutions
Interview with Ivan Nagel, drama manager of the Salzburg Festival. Austria: Salzburg. 1998. Lang.: Ger. 1572
Productions of the Salzburg Festival. Austria: Salzburg. 1998. Lang.: Ger. 1573
Survey of the Theatertreffen festival. Germany: Berlin. 1998. Lang.: Swe. 1651
Performance/production
Analysis of *Sportstück (Sport Play)* by Elfriede Jelinek. Austria: Vienna. 1998. Lang.: Ger. 1818
Premieres of plays on the Nazi theme. Germany: Darmstadt. Austria: Vienna. 1998. Lang.: Ger. 2030
Plays/librettos/scripts
Playwright Elfriede Jelinek on the relationship between author and play in rehearsal. Austria: Vienna. 1997. Lang.: Ger. 2780
Analysis of Elfriede Jelinek's adaptation of *Et Dukkehjem (A Doll's House)* by Ibsen. Austria. 1979. Lang.: Eng. 2782
Ivan Nagel's speech on awarding the Büchner Prize to playwright Elfriede Jelinek. Germany. 1998. Lang.: Ger. 3154
Relation to other fields
The artist and the world in recent productions. Austria: Vienna. Germany. 1997-1998. Lang.: Ger. 3729
Jellen, Scott Jason
Design/technology
Film and TV lighting man Scott Jason Jellen. USA. 1973-1998. Lang.: Eng. 3855
Jemmett, Dan
Performance/production
Collection of newspaper reviews by London theatre critics. UK-England: London. 1998. Lang.: Eng. 2478
Jenkin, Len
Plays/librettos/scripts
Strindberg's influence on playwrights Len Jenkin and Mac Wellman. USA. 1887-1998. Lang.: Eng. 3584
Jenkins, Mark
Performance/production
Collection of newspaper reviews by London theatre critics. UK-England: London. 1998. Lang.: Eng. 2522
Jennifer, Tipton
Performance/production
Profile of lighting designer Jennifer Tipton. USA. 1937-1998. Lang.: Eng. 4747
Jensen, Julie
Performance/production
Collection of newspaper reviews by London theatre critics. UK-England: London. 1998. Lang.: Eng. 2420
Jeremias (Jeremiah)
Plays/librettos/scripts
Analysis of plays based on the Hebrew prophets. USA. Europe. 1919-1970. Lang.: Eng. 3659
Jermyn Street Theatre (London)
Performance/production
New London venues and productions. UK-England: London. 1994-1998. Lang.: Eng. 605
Collection of newspaper reviews by London theatre critics. UK-England: London. 1998. Lang.: Eng. 2476
Collection of newspaper reviews by London theatre critics. UK-England. 1998. Lang.: Eng. 2489
Collection of newspaper reviews by London theatre critics. UK-England: London. 1998. Lang.: Eng. 2499
Collection of newspaper reviews by London theatre critics. UK-England: London. 1998. Lang.: Eng. 2507
Collection of newspaper reviews by London theatre critics. UK-England: London. 1998. Lang.: Eng. 2531
Collection of newspaper reviews by London theatre critics. UK-England: London. 1998. Lang.: Eng. 2553
Jero's Metamorphosis
Plays/librettos/scripts
Political satire in the plays of Wole Soyinka. Nigeria. 1960-1979. Lang.: Eng. 3284
Jerofejév, Venedikt
Performance/production
Productions of plays by Koljada and Jerofejév at Csiky Gergely Theatre. Hungary: Kaposvár. 1998. Lang.: Hun. 2149
Jerome, Ninon
Performance/production
Collection of newspaper reviews by London theatre critics. UK-England: London. 1998. Lang.: Eng. 2585
Jesson, Paul
Performance/production
Paul Jesson's role in *Henry VIII* at RSC. UK-England: London, Stratford. 1996-1997. Lang.: Eng. 2617
Jésus de Montréal (Jesus of Montreal)
Plays/librettos/scripts
Representations of theatre in the film *Jésus de Montréal*. Canada. 1990-1998. Lang.: Fre. 3964
Jesus, My Boy
Basic theatrical documents
Text of *Jesus, My Boy* by John Dowie. UK-England. 1998. Lang.: Eng. 1474
Performance/production
Collection of newspaper reviews by London theatre critics. UK-England: London. 1998. Lang.: Eng. 2552
Profile of actor Tom Conti. UK-England. 1998. Lang.: Eng. 2629
Jeu de l'amour et du hasard, Le (Play of Love and Chance, The)
Basic theatrical documents
Catalan translation of *Le Jeu de l'amour et du hasard (The Play of Love and Chance)* by Marivaux. France. 1730. Lang.: Cat. 1432
Jeune Ballet de France (Paris)
Performance/production
Hungarian student's training at Jeune Ballet de France. France: Paris. 1996-1998. Lang.: Hun. 1075
Jévrejnov, Nikolaj Nikolajévič
Institutions
Theatrical parodies of Krivoje zerkalo. Russia: St. Petersburg. 1908-1931. Lang.: Eng. 1705
Performance/production
Memoirs of director and playwright Nikolaj Jévrejnov. Russia. 1879-1953. Lang.: Rus. 2279
Jew of Malta, The
Plays/librettos/scripts
The figure of the Jew in Marlowe and Shakespeare. England. 1590-1600. Lang.: Eng. 2868

Jewels
Performance/production
Panel discussion on Balanchine's *Jewels*. USA: New York, NY. 1967. Lang.: Eng. 1188
Jewish Repertory Theatre (New York, NY)
Institutions
History of the Jewish Repertory Theatre. USA: New York, NY. 1974-1984. Lang.: Eng. 1757
Jewish theatre
SEE ALSO
Yiddish theatre.
Institutions
Jakub Rotbaum's leadership of Trupa Wileńska. Poland: Vilna. 1929-1938. Lang.: Pol. 1686
Polish guest performances of HaBimah. Poland. 1926-1938. Lang.: Pol. 1689
Performance/production
Collaboration of Jewish and Polish theatres in the interwar period. Poland: Warsaw. 1923-1937. Lang.: Pol. 574
Solomon Michoëls of Moscow's Jewish Theatre. Russia: Moscow. 1998. Lang.: Rus. 2264
The Jewish Kabaret za murem and its treatment in Polish theatre. Poland: Warsaw. 1939-1988. Lang.: Pol. 4157
Plays/librettos/scripts
Enlightenment influences on modern Jewish theatre. Poland. 1500-1914. Lang.: Pol. 3307
Jeyasingh, Shobana
Performance/production
National identity and the choreography of Shobana Jeyasingh. UK-England. 1991-1994. Lang.: Eng. 972
Jim & Wanda
Basic theatrical documents
Tod Lippy's unproduced screenplay *Jim & Wanda*. USA. 1996. Lang.: Eng. 3895
Jinx
Performance/production
Collection of newspaper reviews by London theatre critics. UK-England: London. 1998. Lang.: Eng. 2503
Jitney
Plays/librettos/scripts
Analysis of *Jitney* by August Wilson. USA. 1979. Lang.: Eng. 3611
Joan of Arc
Plays/librettos/scripts
The theory and practice of playwriting for different age groups. USA. 1988. Lang.: Eng. 3524
Job Stealer
Basic theatrical documents
Excerpt from *Job Stealer* by Rahul Varma, Helen Vlachos and Ian Lloyd George. Canada: Montreal, PQ. 1998. Lang.: Eng. 1412
Joe—The Musical
Design/technology
Technical effects control system used in a production of *Joe—The Musical* at Koninklijk Theater Carré. Netherlands: Amsterdam. 1998. Lang.: Eng. 4324
Joglars, Els (Barcelona)
Relation to other fields
Catalonian cultural politics and Els Joglars. Spain-Catalonia. 1962-1998. Lang.: Eng. 3775
Johan Padan o la scoperta dell'America (Johan Padan and the Discovery of America)
Plays/librettos/scripts
Playwright Dario Fo. Italy. 1998. Lang.: Eng. 3243
Johannessen, Ina Christel
Institutions
Profile of dance company Nye Carte Blanche. Norway: Bergen. 1990-1998. Lang.: Swe. 1251
Johannsmeier, Rolf
Institutions
Profile of Junges Theater. Germany: Göttingen. 1996-1998. Lang.: Ger. 1636
Johanson, Robert
Design/technology
Lighting design for the musical *Follies*, Paper Mill Playhouse. USA: Millburn, NJ. 1998. Lang.: Eng. 4335
John Anson Ford Amphitheatre (Los Angeles, CA)
Performance spaces
Profiles of Southern California theatres. USA. 1998. Lang.: Eng. 473
John Bull's Other Island
Plays/librettos/scripts
Colonialism in the plays of George Bernard Shaw. UK-England. 1895-1935. Lang.: Eng. 3438
John F. Kennedy Center for the Performing Arts (Washington, DC)
Institutions
Financial and artistic success of Kennedy Center and New Jersey Performing Arts Center. USA: Washington, DC, Newark, NJ. 1971-1998. Lang.: Eng. 424
Performance/production
Performances by dance couple Eiko & Koma. USA: Washington, DC. 1998. Lang.: Hun. 1336
John Gabriel Borkman
SEE
Johan Gabriel Borkman.
John Houseman Theatre (New York, NY)
Design/technology
Lighting design for *Never the Sinner* by John Logan, directed by Ethan McSweeney. USA: New York, NY. 1998. Lang.: Eng. 1534
John Lyman Center for the Performing Arts (New Haven, CT)
Design/technology
The new sound system of the Lyman Center, Southern Connecticut State University. USA: New Haven, CT. 1998. Lang.: Eng. 268
John, Elton
Administration
The Disney Corporation's Broadway musicals. USA: New York, NY. 1996-1998. Lang.: Eng. 4317
Design/technology
Donald Holder's lighting design for *The Lion King*. USA: New York, NY. 1997-1998. Lang.: Eng. 4336
Technical designs for the Broadway production of *The Lion King*. USA: New York, NY. 1998. Lang.: Eng. 4342
Performance/production
Elton John as musical theatre composer. UK-England. 1998. Lang.: Rus. 4371
The premiere of the musical *Elaborate Lives: The Legend of Aida*. USA: Atlanta, GA. 1998. Lang.: Eng. 4385
Johnny Song
Performance/production
Collection of newspaper reviews by London theatre critics. UK-England: London. 1998. Lang.: Eng. 2421
Johnny Tenorio
Basic theatrical documents
Text of plays by Carlos Morton. USA. 1986. Lang.: Eng. 1499
Johnson, Alan
Performance/production
Collection of newspaper reviews by London theatre critics. UK-England: London. 1998. Lang.: Eng. 2516
Johnson, Ben
Design/technology
Costume designer Isabelle Larivière. Canada: Quebec, PQ. 1994-1995. Lang.: Fre. 1514
Johnson, Catherine
Performance/production
Collection of newspaper reviews by London theatre critics. UK-England: London. 1998. Lang.: Eng. 2537
Johnson, Charles
Plays/librettos/scripts
Political context of Charles Johnson's *Love in a Forest*, an adaptation of *As You Like It*. England. 1723. Lang.: Eng. 3013
Johnson, James
Performance/production
Bass James Johnson. USA. 1998. Lang.: Eng. 4722
Johnson, Samuel
Plays/librettos/scripts
The influence Dryden and Johnson's theories on self-translated works of Samuel Beckett. France. Ireland. 1957-1976. Lang.: Eng. 3077
Johnson, Terry
Performance/production
Collection of newspaper reviews by London theatre critics. UK-England: London. 1998. Lang.: Eng. 2415
Collection of newspaper reviews by London theatre critics. UK-England: London. 1998. Lang.: Eng. 2448
Collection of newspaper reviews by London theatre critics. UK-England. 1998. Lang.: Eng. 2497
Collection of newspaper reviews by London theatre critics. UK-England: London. 1998. Lang.: Eng. 2508
Johnston, Alex
Performance/production
Collection of newspaper reviews by London theatre critics. UK-England: London. 1998. Lang.: Eng. 2445
Johnston, David
Institutions
Margarethe Biereye and David Johnston of the touring company Ton und Kirschen. Germany: Glindow. 1992-1997. Lang.: Eng. 1624

Johnstone, Keith
Institutions
Improvisations by Stockholms Improvisationsteater. Sweden: Stockholm. 1989-1998. Lang.: Swe. 1733
Performance/production
Collection of newspaper reviews by London theatre critics. UK-England: London. 1998. Lang.: Eng. 2421
Johst, Hanns
Relation to other fields
Revivals of Hanns Johst's national socialist play *Schlageter*. Germany: Uelzen, Wuppertal. 1977-1992. Lang.: Ger. 3770
Joint Stock Theatre Group (London)
Institutions
The theatrical method of Joint Stock Theatre Group. UK-England: London. 1974-1989. Lang.: Eng. 1749
Jókai Színház (Komarno)
Institutions
History of annual festival of Hungarian-language theatre. Hungary: Kisvárda. 1989-1998. Lang.: Hun. 1669
Jolson, Al
Performance/production
Career of entertainer Al Jolson. USA. 1886-1950. Lang.: Eng. 4280
Jones, Bill T.
Performance/production
Interview with choreographer Bill T. Jones. USA. 1990-1998. Lang.: Eng. 1316
Defense of Bill T. Jones' dance piece *Still/Here*. USA. 1994. Lang.: Eng. 1318
Jones, C.M.
Performance/production
Collection of newspaper reviews by London theatre critics. UK-England: London. 1998. Lang.: Eng. 2535
Jones, Christina
Performance/production
Collection of newspaper reviews by London theatre critics. UK-England: London. 1998. Lang.: Eng. 2535
Jones, Christine
Design/technology
Set and lighting designs for *The Taming of the Shrew*, American Repertory Theatre. USA: Cambridge, MA. 1998. Lang.: Eng. 1559
Jones, Gari
Performance/production
Collection of newspaper reviews by London theatre critics. UK-England: London. 1998. Lang.: Eng. 2469
Collection of newspaper reviews by London theatre critics. UK-England: London. 1998. Lang.: Eng. 2550
Jones, LeRoi
SEE
Baraka, Imamu Amiri.
Jones, Margo
Performance/production
The multifaceted nature of early nonprofit regional theatre. USA. 1940-1960. Lang.: Eng. 2705
Jones, Preston
Plays/librettos/scripts
Analysis of Preston Jones's plays about Texas. USA. 1977. Lang.: Eng. 3645
Jones, Rhodessa
Plays/librettos/scripts
The representation of true crime in modern drama. USA. France. 1955-1996. Lang.: Eng. 3673
Jones, Richard
Plays/librettos/scripts
Analysis of letters between Lady Morgan and actor Richard Jones. UK-Ireland. 1807. Lang.: Eng. 4862
Jones, Rosalie
Performance/production
Rosalie Jones of Native American dance company Daystar. USA: Santa Fe, NM. 1966-1998. Lang.: Eng. 1240
Jones, Tom
Design/technology
Neil Patel's scene design for *Mirette*, Goodspeed Opera House. USA: East Haddam, CT. 1998. Lang.: Eng. 4334
Jones, William E.
Basic theatrical documents
Screenplay of *Finished* by William E. Jones. USA. 1997. Lang.: Eng. 3889
Jonigk, Thomas
Plays/librettos/scripts
Playwright, dramaturg, and director Thomas Jonigk on contemporary theatre. Austria: Vienna. 1998. Lang.: Ger. 2781
Jonson, Ben
Plays/librettos/scripts
Playwriting and publishing for the London stage. England. 1590-1650. Lang.: Eng. 2881
The control of time in Renaissance English drama. England. 1590-1620. Lang.: Eng. 2883
Women's use of wit in response to men in English popular culture. England. 1590-1630. Lang.: Eng. 2884
Analysis of *The Masque of Blackness* by Ben Jonson. England. 1605. Lang.: Eng. 2919
Gender and politics in masques of Ben Jonson and Samuel Daniel. England. 1604-1605. Lang.: Eng. 4200
Political tensions reflected in Ben Jonson's masque *Oberon*. England. 1611. Lang.: Eng. 4203
Royal policy, subversion, and Ben Jonson's *Oberon*. England. 1611. Lang.: Eng. 4204
Ben Jonson's antimasques. England. 1612-1632. Lang.: Eng. 4205
Political and ideological struggles in Jacobean masques. England. 1604-1609. Lang.: Eng. 4206
Power, gender, and race in *The Masque of Blackness* by Ben Jonson. England. 1605-1611. Lang.: Eng. 4208
Research/historiography
Jonson's *The Alchemist* and source studies. England. USA. 1610-1998. Lang.: Eng. 3795
Jonsson, Christian
Institutions
Profile of Svensk Symbolisk Teater. Sweden: Malmö. 1997. Lang.: Swe. 1728
Jonsson, Ulrike
Performance/production
Collection of newspaper reviews by London theatre critics. UK-England: London. 1998. Lang.: Eng. 2573
Jooss, Kurt
Performance/production
Gender and politics in German dance. Germany. 1930-1932. Lang.: Eng. 928
Jordan, Chris
Performance/production
Collection of newspaper reviews by London theatre critics. UK-England: London. 1998. Lang.: Eng. 2420
Jordan, Neil
Plays/librettos/scripts
Transvestism in contemporary film as the 'blackface' of the nineties. UK-England. USA. 1993-1996. Lang.: Eng. 3983
Jordan, R. Kim
Administration
Interview with father and daughter serving on Equity council. USA: New York, NY. 1998. Lang.: Eng. 113
Jordan, S. Marc
Administration
Interview with father and daughter serving on Equity council. USA: New York, NY. 1998. Lang.: Eng. 113
Jorge, Donn
Performance/production
Hungarian guest performances of world ballet stars. Hungary: Budapest. 1975-1978. Lang.: Hun. 1085
Jorginho, o Machao (Jorginho, the Stud)
Plays/librettos/scripts
Cruelty and the absurd in theatre of Latin American playwrights. Latin America. 1960-1980. Lang.: Eng. 3267
Joris, Charles
Plays/librettos/scripts
Analysis of *Par-dessus bord (Overboard)* by Michel Vinaver. France. Switzerland: La Chaux-de-Fonds. 1960-1998. Lang.: Ger. 3118
Joseph Papp Public Theatre (New York, NY)
SEE
Public Theatre.
Josephson, Erland
Performance/production
Actor Erland Josephson on his profession. Sweden. 1945-1998. Lang.: Swe. 2379
Journey's End
Performance/production
Collection of newspaper reviews by London theatre critics. UK-England: London. 1998. Lang.: Eng. 2567
Jouvet, Louis
Performance/production
Types of actors and their relationship with directors. UK-England. Sweden. 1950-1998. Lang.: Swe. 2648

Jovanovič, Dušan
Theory/criticism
Theatrical theory and practice. 600 B.C.-1997 A.D. Lang.: Slo. 3804
Jovánovics, György
Design/technology
An exhibition of sets and environments by Hungarian designers. Hungary: Budapest. 1998. Lang.: Hun. 196
Joyce, Candice
Performance/production
Collection of newspaper reviews by London theatre critics. UK-England: London. 1998. Lang.: Eng. 2534
Joyce, Tom
Administration
Equity Council member Tom Joyce. USA: Chicago, IL. 1998. Lang.: Eng. 48
József Attila Színház (Budapest)
Administration
Interview with director Péter Léner of József Attila Theatre. Hungary: Budapest. 1960-1998. Lang.: Hun. 15
József Attila Színház, Aluljáró (Budapest)
Performance/production
Denise Radó's *A Fedák-ügy (The Fedak Case)* at József Attila Theatre. Hungary: Budapest. 1998. Lang.: Hun. 2139
József és testvérei (Joseph and His Brothers)
Performance/production
Interview with choreographer Iván Markó. Hungary: Budapest. 1998. Lang.: Hun. 1101
József Katona Theatre
SEE
Katona József Szinház.
Jroazanmo
Basic theatrical documents
Slovene translations of Tibetan plays. Tibet. 1400-1990. Lang.: Slo. 1470
Jubiläum
Plays/librettos/scripts
Analysis of *Jubiläum* by George Tabori. Germany. 1983. Lang.: Eng. 3137
Jubilej (Jubilee)
Performance/production
Čechov's one-act plays at Thália Színház. Hungary. Slovakia: Košice. 1998. Lang.: Hun. 2075
One-act comedies by Čechov directed by Péter Valló. Hungary: Dunaújváros. 1998. Lang.: Hun. 2080
Judas Kiss, The
Performance/production
Collection of newspaper reviews by London theatre critics. UK-England: London. 1998. Lang.: Eng. 2444
Judas Worm
Performance/production
Collection of newspaper reviews by London theatre critics. UK-England: London. 1998. Lang.: Eng. 2476
Judge, Ian
Performance/production
Christopher Luscombe on acting in RSC productions. UK-England: London, Stratford. 1993-1994. Lang.: Eng. 2620
Jugendclub Mo (Zurich)
Institutions
Swiss theatre clubs for children and youth. Switzerland. 1998. Lang.: Ger, Fre. 1735
Juggling
Performance/production
Profile of MacArthur fellow and juggler Michael Moschen. USA. 1955-1998. Lang.: Eng. 4141
Juicy Bits
Performance/production
Collection of newspaper reviews by London theatre critics. UK-England: London. 1998. Lang.: Eng. 2483
Juilliard Drama Theatre (New York, NY)
Performance spaces
Theatre space and performance. USA: New York, NY. 1925-1985. Lang.: Eng. 464
Julius Caesar
Design/technology
Karen TenEyck's projections for a site-specific production of Shakespeare's *Julius Caesar*. USA: Los Angeles, CA. 1998. Lang.: Eng. 1552
Performance/production
John Nettles on his role in an RSC production of *Julius Caesar*. UK-England: London, Stratford. 1995. Lang.: Eng. 2625
Brief productions of Shakespeare, Shaw, and Marlowe at the World's Fair. USA: Chicago, IL. 1934. Lang.: Eng. 2701
Plays/librettos/scripts
Analysis of Shakespeare's *Julius Caesar*. England. 1599. Lang.: Eng. 2948
'Demonic' women in Shakespeare's tragedies. England. 1590-1613. Lang.: Eng. 2999
Junges Theater (Basel)
Institutions
Swiss theatre clubs for children and youth. Switzerland. 1998. Lang.: Ger, Fre. 1735
Junges Theater (Frauenfeld)
Institutions
Swiss theatre clubs for children and youth. Switzerland. 1998. Lang.: Ger, Fre. 1735
Junges Theater (Göttingen)
Institutions
Profile of Junges Theater. Germany: Göttingen. 1996-1998. Lang.: Ger. 1636
Jungfräu von Orleans, Die (Maid of Orleans, The)
Plays/librettos/scripts
Representation of the virginal body on the German stage. Germany. 1600-1800. Lang.: Ger. 3171
Junk
Performance/production
Collection of newspaper reviews by London theatre critics. UK-England: London. 1998. Lang.: Eng. 2580
Juronics, Tamás
Performance/production
Round-table discussion on dance and movement. Hungary. 1998. Lang.: Hun. 938
Productions of Szegedi Kortárs Balett. Hungary: Szeged. 1998. Lang.: Hun. 1102
Jurskij, Sergej Ju.
Performance/production
Articles on stage and film actors and other celebrities. Latvia. 1998. Lang.: Rus. 2197
Jusits, Rudolf
Performance/production
Premieres of plays on the Nazi theme. Germany: Darmstadt. Austria: Vienna. 1998. Lang.: Ger. 2030
Justice Luck
Performance/production
Collection of newspaper reviews by London theatre critics. UK-England: London. 1998. Lang.: Eng. 2463
Justifikacija Execution, The)
Plays/librettos/scripts
The individual and his world in Slovene theatre. Slovenia. 1943-1985. Lang.: Slo. 3347
K
Performance/production
Performativity in postmodern 'queer' works. USA. 1985-1995. Lang.: Eng. 616
Kabaré (Cabaret)
Performance/production
The premiere of *Kabaré (Cabaret)* choreographed by Yvette Bozsik. Hungary: Budapest. 1998. Lang.: Hun. 945
Kabaret po tamtej stronie (Cabaret on the Other Side)
Performance/production
The Jewish Kabaret za murem and its treatment in Polish theatre. Poland: Warsaw. 1939-1988. Lang.: Pol. 4157
Kabuki
SEE ALSO
Classed Entries under DANCE-DRAMA—*Kabuki*.
Design/technology
Rapid on-stage costume changes in dance. Russia. Sweden. Japan. 1840-1998. Lang.: Swe. 889
Reference materials
History of Japanese theatre and drama. Japan. 350 B.C.-1998 A.D. Lang.: Ita. 705
Kačer, Jan
Design/technology
The work of scene designer Libor Fára. Czech Republic: Prague. 1950-1981. Lang.: Cze. 1518
Kadongo Kamu
Performance/production
Popular entertainment in Uganda after Idi Amin. Uganda. 1979-1998. Lang.: Eng. 604

Kafka's Dick
Performance/production
Collection of newspaper reviews by London theatre critics. UK-England: London. 1998. Lang.: Eng. 2545
Kahn, Michael
Performance/production
Comparison of productions of Ibsen's *Peer Gynt*. USA: Providence, RI, New York, NY, Washington, DC, Nacogdoches, TX. 1998. Lang.: Eng. 2711
Kahn, Otto
Institutions
The New Playwrights Theatre Company. USA: New York, NY. 1927-1929. Lang.: Eng. 410
Kai, Una
Training
Balanchine's ballet mistress on his training methods. USA. 1947-1998. Lang.: Eng. 1214
Kaiser, Georg
Plays/librettos/scripts
Mythological figures in late plays of Georg Kaiser. Germany. 1914-1940. Lang.: Ger. 3143
Language and silence in German Expressionist drama. Germany. 1913-1923. Lang.: Eng. 3159
Comparison of characters in plays of Georg Kaiser and Tennessee Williams. USA. Germany. 1912-1945. Lang.: Eng. 3588
Kaiser, Michael
Institutions
The present state of the Royal Ballet under Michael Kaiser. UK-England: London. 1998. Lang.: Hun. 1054
Kakko, Johan
Performance/production
Interview with dancers who became doctors. Sweden: Stockholm. 1974. Lang.: Swe. 968
Kalcheim, Lee
Plays/librettos/scripts
History of the Playwrights Unit. USA. 1963-1971. Lang.: Eng. 3570
Kaleidoscope of the American Dream
Administration
The cancellation of Kansas University's cultural exchange program with Eastern Europe. USA: Lawrence, KS. Europe. 1964-1969. Lang.: Eng. 131
Kaliningradskij Teat'r (Kaliningrad)
Institutions
History of the Kaliningrad Theatre. Russia: Kaliningrad. 1947-1997. Lang.: Rus. 1702
Kalinoski, Richard
Basic theatrical documents
French translation of *Beast on the Moon* by Richard Kalinoski. USA. France. 1995-1997. Lang.: Fre. 1491
Kalinovskaja, G.
Performance/production
Interview with Moscow Art Theatre actress G. Kalinovskaja. Russia: Moscow. 1998. Lang.: Rus. 2238
Moscow Art Theatre actress G. Kalinovskaja. Russia: Moscow. 1998. Lang.: Rus. 2280
Kalins, Tom
Relation to other fields
Symposium on fashion and film. USA: New York, NY. 1997. Lang.: Eng. 4037
Kallman, Chester
Plays/librettos/scripts
The libretto of *The Rake's Progress* by W.H. Auden and Chester Kallman. UK-England. 1971. Lang.: Eng. 4824
W.H. Auden as an opera librettist and translator. UK-England. 1907-1973. Lang.: Eng. 4825
Kalmar, Bert
Performance/production
Collection of newspaper reviews by London theatre critics. UK-England: London. 1998. Lang.: Eng. 2420
Kaltneker, Hans
Plays/librettos/scripts
Social criticism in Viennese Expressionist drama. Austria: Vienna. 1907-1922. Lang.: Ger. 2779
Kamal Theatre
SEE
Tatarskij Gosudarstvénnyj Akademičéskij Teat'r im. Kamala.
Kamennyj gost
Plays/librettos/scripts
Operas of Dargomyžskij and Rimskij-Korsakov on texts of Puškin. Russia. 1799-1869. Lang.: Rus. 4815
Kamernyj Muzykal'nyj Teat'r (Moscow)
Performance/production
Aleksand'r Tairov's production of *Fortune Heights* by John Dos Passos. USA. 1930-1935. Lang.: Rus. 2739
Kamińska, Ida
Plays/librettos/scripts
Ida Kamińska's production of *Der Kheshbn (The Final Reckoning)* by Mikhl Mirsky. Poland: Warsaw. 1963. Lang.: Eng. 3310
Kamiriithu Theatre (Kenya)
Performance/production
Theatrical rebellion and sociopolitical chaos. Zimbabwe. Kenya. 1990-1998. Lang.: Eng. 687
Kammerspiele (Munich)
Institutions
Survey of Munich's theatre scene. Germany: Munich. 1997. Lang.: Ger. 1626
Kammertheater (Neubrandenburg)
Administration
Interviews with German theatre and film directors. Germany. 1998. Lang.: Ger. 1385
Kamphuis, Marike
Design/technology
Profiles of young theatrical designers. Netherlands. 1990-1998. Lang.: Dut. 207
Kanadehon Hamlet
Basic theatrical documents
English translation of *Kanadehon Hamlet* by Harue Tsutsumi. Japan. 1997. Lang.: Eng. 1360
Kander, John
Design/technology
Sound design for the London production of *Chicago*. UK-England: London. 1998. Lang.: Eng. 4326
Technical designs for Sam Mendes' production of *Cabaret*. USA: New York, NY. 1998. Lang.: Eng. 4343
Lighting design for Sam Mendes' production of *Cabaret*. USA: New York, NY. 1998. Lang.: Eng. 4344
Institutions
Profile of Watermill Theatre. UK-England: Newbury. 1998. Lang.: Eng. 1744
Performance spaces
The creation of a site-specific performance space for Sam Mendes' production of *Cabaret*. USA: New York, NY. 1998. Lang.: Eng. 4350
Performance/production
Collection of newspaper reviews by London theatre critics. UK-England: London. 1998. Lang.: Eng. 2500
Friends and colleagues recall singer Lotte Lenya. Germany. 1928-1981. Lang.: Eng. 4355
Kandinsky, Wassily
Plays/librettos/scripts
Painter Wassily Kandinsky and theatre. France. 1908-1944. Lang.: Eng. 3111
Language and silence in German Expressionist drama. Germany. 1913-1923. Lang.: Eng. 3159
Kane, Richard
Performance/production
Collection of newspaper reviews by London theatre critics. UK-England: London. 1998. Lang.: Eng. 2577
Kane, Sarah
Performance/production
Collection of newspaper reviews by London theatre critics. UK-England: London. 1998. Lang.: Eng. 2467
Collection of newspaper reviews by London theatre critics. UK-England: London. 1998. Lang.: Eng. 2493
Reviews of recent London performances. UK-England: London. 1998. Lang.: Ger. 2591
Plays/librettos/scripts
German view of English and American drama. UK-England. USA. 1998. Lang.: Ger. 3455
Analysis of plays by Sarah Kane and David Harrower, recently produced in Germany. UK-England. Germany: Cologne, Bonn. 1998. Lang.: Ger. 3487
Sex, drugs, and violence in contemporary British drama. UK-England. 1991-1998. Lang.: Eng. 3494
Kanonhallen (Copenhagen)
Training
Anne-Lise Gabold's use of the methods of Tadashi Suzuki in her production of Euripides' *Bákchai (The Bacchae)*. Japan. Denmark: Copenhagen. 1960-1998. Lang.: Dan. 1359

Kanter, Shauna
Performance/production
Collection of newspaper reviews by London theatre critics. UK-England: London. 1998. Lang.: Eng. 2555
Collection of newspaper reviews by London theatre critics. UK-England: London. 1998. Lang.: Eng. 2570
Kantor, Tadeusz
Institutions
Polish experimental theatre training. Poland: Cracow, Wrocław, Warsaw. 1930-1998. Lang.: Pol. 1685
Performance/production
Tadeusz Kantor's directorial process. Poland: Cracow. 1987. Lang.: Eng. 2217
Ritual in the theatre of Jerzy Grotowski. Poland. 1960-1975. Lang.: Pol. 2221
Interview with director Andrzej Wajda. Poland. 1960-1998. Lang.: Fin. 2224
Theory/criticism
Performance art and the 'poetics of space'. USA. Poland. 1952-1984. Lang.: Eng. 4270
Kapás, Dezső
Performance/production
Dostojévskij's *Crime and Punishment* directed by Géza Tordy. Hungary: Győr. 1998. Lang.: Hun. 2100
Kaplan, Joel
Performance/production
Director Joel Kaplan on his production of the *York Cycle*. Canada: Toronto, ON. 1998. Lang.: Eng. 4213
Kapnist, Vasilij
Plays/librettos/scripts
Russian literature and theatre of the eighteenth century. Russia. 1701-1800. Lang.: Rus. 3322
Kaprow, Allan
Relation to other fields
Ritual in encounter groups and experimental theatre. USA. 1960-1970. Lang.: Eng. 788
Kapsberger, Giovanni Girolamo
Plays/librettos/scripts
Analysis of Jesuit opera by Giovanni Girolamo Kapsberger and Orazio Grassi. Italy: Rome. 1622. Lang.: Eng. 4803
Karahasan, Děvad
Relation to other fields
Manfred Weber on directing Děvad Karahasan's translation of *Leonce und Lena* by Büchner. Bosnia: Sarajevo. 1997-1998. Lang.: Ger. 3730
Karamazov Brothers, Flying
SEE
Flying Karamazov Brothers.
Karasek, Daniel
Performance/production
Daniel Karasek, drama director at Hessisches Staatstheater. Germany: Wiesbaden. 1997-1998. Lang.: Ger. 1955
Karcev, R.
Performance/production
Interview with actor R. Karcev. Russia. 1998. Lang.: Rus. 4276
Karge, Manfred
Performance/production
Director Angela Brodauf. Germany: Dortmund. 1984-1998. Lang.: Ger. 1989
Karina, Lilian
Performance/production
Interview with dancer, choreographer, and teacher Lilian Karina. Germany. 1911-1998. Lang.: Ger. 1289
Karkar, Waltraud
Training
Ballet teacher Waltraud Karkar. USA: Wausau, WI. 1998. Lang.: Eng. 1215
Karl Marx Theatre (Saratov)
SEE
Oblastnoj Dramatičeskij Teat'r im. K. Marksa.
Karnyóné és a két szeleburdiak (Mrs. Karnyó and the Two Feather-Brains)
Performance/production
Two productions of Csokonai Vitéz's *Karnyóné és a két szeleburdiak (Mrs. Karnyó and the Two Feather-Brains)*. Hungary: Budapest. 1998. Lang.: Hun. 2113
Karp, Jack Martin
Basic theatrical documents
Text of *Medicine Men* by Jack Martin Karp. USA. 1998. Lang.: Eng. 1492
Kárpáti, Péter
Performance/production
Péter Kárpáti's *Díszelőadás (Gala Performance)* directed by Balázs Simon. Hungary: Budapest. 1998. Lang.: Hun. 2057
Performances at the new Bárka Színház. Hungary: Budapest. 1997. Lang.: Hun. 2097
Karusseit, Ursula
Performance/production
Actor/director Ursula Karusseit. Germany, East. 1977-1995. Lang.: Eng. 2047
Karz, Zippora
Performance/production
Ballerina Zippora Karz on dancing while suffering from diabetes. USA: New York, NY. 1983-1998. Lang.: Eng. 1183
Kasjak, Mojca
Basic theatrical documents
Text of the musical play *Emanacije (Emanations)* by Tomaž Brenk and Mojca Kasjak. Slovenia. 1997. Lang.: Eng, Slo. 4288
Kaspar
Performance/production
Review of Péter Forgách's *Kaspar*, Győr National Theatre. Hungary: Győr. 1998. Lang.: Hun. 2106
Plays/librettos/scripts
Aggressive language in modern drama. Europe. USA. 1960-1985. Lang.: Eng. 3055
The fool character in works of Handke, Fellini, and Singer. USA. Germany. Italy. 1960-1968. Lang.: Eng. 3667
Kassai Thália Színház
SEE
Thália Színház (Kosiče).
Kastal'skaja, K.
Performance/production
Ballet dancer K. Kastal'skaja. France: Lyon. 1998. Lang.: Rus. 1073
Kasten, Kate
Performance/production
Contemporary queer politics and the production of gay and lesbian theatre. USA. 1970-1997. Lang.: Eng. 2710
Kaszás, Gergő
Performance/production
Interviews with actors on Anatolij Vasiljév's guest direction at Szigligeti Theatre. Hungary: Szolnok. 1998. Lang.: Hun. 2061
Lorca's *Doña Rosita* directed by Gergő Kaszás. Hungary: Budapest. 1998. Lang.: Hun. 2099
Kaszás, Mihály
Performance/production
Interviews with actors on Anatolij Vasiljév's guest direction at Szigligeti Theatre. Hungary: Szolnok. 1998. Lang.: Hun. 2061
Kasztner, Israel
Plays/librettos/scripts
Israeli attitudes toward Holocaust theatre. Israel. 1944-1995. Lang.: Eng. 3217
Kat and the Kings
Performance/production
Collection of newspaper reviews by London theatre critics. UK-England: London. 1998. Lang.: Eng. 2447
Kát'a Kabanová
Performance/production
Review of Salzburger Festspiele performances. Austria: Salzburg. 1998. Lang.: Ger. 4527
Katherine Howard
Performance/production
Collection of newspaper reviews by London theatre critics. UK-England. 1998. Lang.: Eng. 2510
Katona József Színház (Budapest)
Performance/production
Tom Stoppard's *Arcadia* as directed by Tamás Ascher. Hungary: Budapest. 1998. Lang.: Hun. 2058
Review of Gombrowicz's *Princess Yvonne*, Katona József Theatre. Hungary: Budapest. 1997. Lang.: Hun. 2079
Review of István Örkény's *Kulcskeresők (Searching for the Key)*, Katona József Theatre. Hungary: Budapest. 1998. Lang.: Hun. 2083
Interview with Péter Blaskó. Hungary. 1970-1998. Lang.: Hun. 2119
Review of Tom Stoppard's *Arcadia* directed by Tamás Ascher. Hungary: Budapest. 1998. Lang.: Hun. 2133
Katona József Színház (Kecskemét)
Performance/production
Two productions of Shakespeare's *Richard III* by József Ruszt. Hungary: Budapest. Hungary: Kecskemét. 1973-1997. Lang.: Hun. 2070

Katona József Színház (Kecskemét) — cont'd

Lajos Parti Nagy's *Ibusár* directed by János Mikuli. Hungary: Kecskemét, Pécs. 1998. Lang.: Hun. 2110

Turgenjév's *Mesjac v derevne (A Month in the Country)* directed by Zoltán Lendvar. Hungary: Kecskemét. 1998. Lang.: Hun. 2134

Katona József Színház, Kamra (Budapest)

Performance/production

The premiere of *Kabaré (Cabaret)* choreographed by Yvette Bozsik. Hungary: Budapest. 1998. Lang.: Hun. 945

Review of plays directed by Árpad Schilling. Hungary: Budapest. 1998. Lang.: Hun. 2085

Hauptmann's *Fuhrmann Henschel (Drayman Henschel)* directed by Sándor Zsótér. Hungary: Budapest. 1997. Lang.: Hun. 2088

Csaba Kiss's adaptation and direction of *Lady Macbeth of the Provinces* by Leskov. Hungary: Budapest. 1998. Lang.: Hun. 2138

Andrés Jeles's *Szenvedéstërténet (Passion Play)* directed by Gábor Máté. Hungary: Budapest. 1998. Lang.: Hun. 2145

Katona, Zs. József

Performance/production

A production of László Lajtha's comic opera *Le chapeau bleu*. Romania: Cluj-Napoca. Hungary. 1998. Lang.: Hun. 4666

Production of László Lajtha's comic opera *Le chapeau bleu*. Romania: Cluj-Napoca. Hungary. 1948-1998. Lang.: Hun. 4668

Katsura, Keiko

Performance/production

Theatrical component of Japan's UK98 Festival. Japan: Tokyo. 1994-1998. Lang.: Eng. 2192

Katz, Allan

Performance/production

Collection of newspaper reviews by London theatre critics. UK-England. 1998. Lang.: Eng. 2489

Katz, Natasha

Design/technology

Lighting design for Shakespeare's *Twelfth Night* at the Vivian Beaumont. USA: New York, NY. 1998. Lang.: Eng. 1546

The design concept for Nicholas Hytner's production of Shakespeare's *Twelfth Night*. USA: New York, NY. 1998. Lang.: Eng. 1556

Kauffman, Marta

Performance/production

Collection of newspaper reviews by London theatre critics. UK-England: London. 1998. Lang.: Eng. 2492

Kaufman, George S.

Performance/production

Collection of newspaper reviews by London theatre critics. UK-England: London. 1998. Lang.: Eng. 2420

Collection of newspaper reviews by London theatre critics. UK-England: London. 1998. Lang.: Eng. 2476

Plays/librettos/scripts

The portrayal of Franklin Delano Roosevelt in the musical *I'd Rather Be Right*. USA. 1937. Lang.: Eng. 4396

Kaufman, Hank

Performance/production

Friends and colleagues recall singer Lotte Lenya. Germany. 1928-1981. Lang.: Eng. 4355

Kaufman, Jonathan

Performance/production

Collection of newspaper reviews by London theatre critics. UK-England: London. 1998. Lang.: Eng. 2494

Kaufman, Millard

Plays/librettos/scripts

Screenwriter Millard Kaufman. USA. 1917-1998. Lang.: Eng. 4013

Kaufman, Moisés

Performance/production

The 'viewpoint theory' of actor training. USA. 1998. Lang.: Eng. 2677

Analysis of recent New York productions. USA: New York, NY. 1997-1998. Lang.: Eng. 2759

Kaukasische Kreidekreis, Der (Caucasian Chalk Circle, The)

Design/technology

Costume designer Isabelle Larivière. Canada: Quebec, PQ. 1994-1995. Lang.: Fre. 1514

Performance/production

Two productions of Brecht's *Der Kaukasische Kreidekreis (The Caucasian Chalk Circle)*. Germany: Berlin, Hamburg. 1998. Lang.: Ger. 1957

Thomas Langhoff's production of Brecht's *Der Kaukasische Kreidekreis (The Caucasian Chalk Circle)* at Deutsches Theater. Germany: Berlin. 1998. Lang.: Ger. 1965

Recent German productions of plays by Bertolt Brecht. Germany: Hamburg, Berlin. 1997. Lang.: Swe. 1977

Recent productions of plays by Bertolt Brecht. Germany. 1997-1998. Lang.: Ger. 2028

Brecht's *Der Kaukasische Kreidkreis (The Caucasian Chalk Circle)* adapted and directed by János Mohácsi. Hungary: Nyíregyháza. 1998. Lang.: Hun. 2127

Productions of plays by Brecht and Shakespeare at the Hungarian theatre of Satu Mare. Romania: Satu Mare. 1998. Lang.: Hun. 2228

Interview with director Simon McBurney. UK-England: London. 1997. Lang.: Swe. 2641

Kaupunginteatteri (Helsinki)

SEE

Helsingin Kaupunginteatteri.

Kaurismaki, Aki

Performance/production

Minimalist film director Aki Kaurismaki. Finland. 1988-1998. Lang.: Eng. 3930

Kaut-Howson, Helena

Performance/production

Collection of newspaper reviews by London theatre critics. UK-England. 1998. Lang.: Eng. 2558

Kavanaugh, Patrick

Performance/production

Collection of newspaper reviews by London theatre critics. UK-England. 1998. Lang.: Eng. 2489

Kavanaugh, Rachel

Performance/production

Collection of newspaper reviews by London theatre critics. UK-England: London. 1998. Lang.: Eng. 2498

Kavčič, Maks

Design/technology

Scenographic work of painter Maks Kavčič. Slovenia. 1945-1972. Lang.: Slo. 218

Kay, Nicolette

Performance/production

Collection of newspaper reviews by London theatre critics. UK-England: London. 1998. Lang.: Eng. 2463

Kaye, Nora

Performance/production

Interviews with dancers about performance. UK-England. USA. Cuba. 1942-1989. Lang.: Eng. 1162

Kazan, Elia

Performance/production

The idea of Hollywood in theatre autobiographies. USA. 1950-1990. Lang.: Eng. 665

Kdo je navil rumeno budilko? (Who Set the Yellow Alarm Clock?)

Basic theatrical documents

Text of Borut Combač's puppet play *Kdo je navil rumeno budilko? (Who Set the Yellow Alarm Clock)?*. Slovenia. 1997. Lang.: Slo. 4866

Kealey, Patrick

Performance/production

Collection of newspaper reviews by London theatre critics. UK-England: London. 1998. Lang.: Eng. 2454

Keane, Dillie

Performance/production

Collection of newspaper reviews by London theatre critics. UK-England: London. 1998. Lang.: Eng. 2568

Keane, Tina

Performance/production

Performance in the work of mixed-media artist Tina Keane. UK-England. 1970-1988. Lang.: Eng. 4044

Keates, John

Performance/production

Collection of newspaper reviews by London theatre critics. UK-England: London. 1998. Lang.: Eng. 2535

Keats, John

Plays/librettos/scripts

The feminine ideal in the drama of English Romantic poets. England. 1794-1840. Lang.: Eng. 2886

Keefe, Barrie

Performance/production

Collection of newspaper reviews by London theatre critics. UK-England: London. 1998. Lang.: Eng. 2528

Keely and Du

Plays/librettos/scripts

Analysis of *Keely and Du* by Jane Martin. USA. 1993. Lang.: Eng. 3629

Kegyelem (Mercy)

Performance/production

András Szigethy's *Kegyelem (Mercy)* directed by László Vándorfi. Hungary: Veszprém. 1998. Lang.: Hun. 2105

Kejser og Galilaeer (Emperor and the Galilean, The)
Plays/librettos/scripts
Hegel's influence on the plays of Henrik Ibsen. Norway. Germany. 1870-1898. Lang.: Eng. 3292
Kékszakállú herceg vára, A
Performance/production
Soprano Olga Haselbeck. Hungary. 1884-1961. Lang.: Hun. 4626
Kékszakállú két arca, A (Bluebeard's Two Faces)
Performance/production
Productions of the Magyar Fesztival Balett choreographed by Iván Markó. Hungary: Budapest. 1998. Lang.: Hun. 1097
Keleti, István
Institutions
History of Szkéné Színház. Hungary: Budapest. 1963-1995. Lang.: Hun. 1668
Kellard, Bill
Design/technology
Costume design for Feydeau's *A Flea in Her Ear (La Puce à l'Oreille)*, Roundabout Theatre Company. USA: New York, NY. 1998. Lang.: Eng. 1537
Keller, Max
Design/technology
Max Keller, lighting designer of Münchner Kammerspiele. Germany: Munich. 1997. Lang.: Ger. 188
Kelley, David E.
Design/technology
Lighting design for TV series *Ally MacBeal*. USA. 1998. Lang.: Eng. 4054
Kellner, Hans-Peter
Performance/production
Collection of newspaper reviews by London theatre critics. UK-England: London. 1998. Lang.: Eng. 2524
Collection of newspaper reviews by London theatre critics. UK-England: London. 1998. Lang.: Eng. 2582
Kelly, Dennis
Performance/production
Collection of newspaper reviews by London theatre critics. UK-England: London. 1998. Lang.: Eng. 2570
Kelly, Gene
Performance/production
Dance on screen. USA. Europe. 1920-1998. Lang.: Ger. 3860
Kelly, Helen
Performance/production
Collection of newspaper reviews by London theatre critics. UK-England: London. 1998. Lang.: Eng. 2427
Kelly, Jude
Performance/production
Collection of newspaper reviews by London theatre critics. UK-England. 1998. Lang.: Eng. 2456
Collection of newspaper reviews by London theatre critics. UK-England. 1998. Lang.: Eng. 2504
Collection of newspaper reviews by London theatre critics. UK-England: London. 1998. Lang.: Eng. 2542
Interview with actor Patrick Stewart. USA: Washington, DC. 1998. Lang.: Eng. 2760
Kemp, Edward
Performance/production
Collection of newspaper reviews by London theatre critics. UK-England: London. 1998. Lang.: Eng. 2413
Collection of newspaper reviews by London theatre critics. UK-England: London. 1998. Lang.: Eng. 2573
Kemp, Jan-Gregor
Performance/production
Comparison of two productions of Shakespeare's *Richard III*. Germany: Munich. 1996-1997. Lang.: Ger. 1976
Kemsie Ntezechrewn Nehru (If It Had Been Like This)
Plays/librettos/scripts
Theatre as cultural weapon and military education in the Eritrean war. Eritrea. 1980-1984. Lang.: Eng. 3048
Kennedy Center for the Performing Arts (Washington, DC)
SEE ALSO
John F. Kennedy Center for the Performing Arts.
Kennedy, Adrienne
Plays/librettos/scripts
History of the Playwrights Unit. USA. 1963-1971. Lang.: Eng. 3570
The dramaturgical evolution of playwright Adrienne Kennedy. USA. 1964-1990. Lang.: Eng. 3691
Playwrights Adrienne Kennedy, Ntozake Shange, and Suzan-Lori Parks. USA. 1970-1998. Lang.: Eng. 3714
Kennedy, R. Lee
Design/technology
The 1998 USITT expo. USA: Long Beach, CA. 1998. Lang.: Eng. 251
Kennelly, Brendan
Plays/librettos/scripts
Adaptations of Greek tragedy by contemporary Irish writers. Ireland. UK-Ireland. 1984-1998. Lang.: Eng. 3214
Kent, Jonathan
Performance/production
Collection of newspaper reviews by London theatre critics. UK-England: London. 1998. Lang.: Eng. 2494
Collection of newspaper reviews by London theatre critics. UK-England: London. 1998. Lang.: Eng. 2534
Collection of newspaper reviews by London theatre critics. UK-England: London. 1998. Lang.: Eng. 2588
Kent, Julie
Performance/production
Interview with dancer Julie Kent. USA. 1998. Lang.: Eng. 1184
Kent, Nicholas
Performance/production
Collection of newspaper reviews by London theatre critics. UK-England: London. 1998. Lang.: Eng. 2453
Kent, Steve
Plays/librettos/scripts
Joseph Chaikin's adaptation of *Textes pour rien (Texts for Nothing)* by Samuel Beckett. USA: New York, NY. 1995. Lang.: Eng. 3563
Kentaur
Design/technology
Survey of an exhibition of Hungarian scene design. Hungary: Budapest. 1998. Lang.: Hun. 195
An exhibition of sets and environments by Hungarian designers. Hungary: Budapest. 1998. Lang.: Hun. 196
Catalogue of an exhibition devoted to Hungarian theatre and film. Hungary: Budapest. 1998. Lang.: Hun. 197
Kentridge, William
Performance/production
Retrospectives of filmmakers Jean-Luc Godard and William Kentridge. USA: New York, NY. 1998. Lang.: Eng. 3958
Plays/librettos/scripts
Analysis of *Ubu & the Truth Commission*, a puppet play by William Kentridge. South Africa, Republic of. 1997. Lang.: Eng. 4913
Kentrup, Norbert
Performance spaces
Shakespeare's Globe and the staging of *The Merchant of Venice*. UK-England: London. 1998. Lang.: Ger. 1810
Kenworth, Jim
Performance/production
Collection of newspaper reviews by London theatre critics. UK-England: London. 1998. Lang.: Eng. 2421
Keogh, Nina
Performance/production
Interview with television puppeteer Nina Keogh. Canada: Toronto, ON. 1953-1998. Lang.: Eng. 4888
Kerényi, Imre
Performance/production
Kodály's *Székely fonó (The Székler Spinnery)*. Hungary: Budapest. 1998. Lang.: Hun. 4298
Interview with Imre Kerényi, director of Kodály's *Székely fonó (The Székler Spinnery)*. Hungary: Budapest. 1997. Lang.: Hun. 4299
Kerényi, Miklós Gábor
Performance/production
Interview with Miklós Gábor Kerényi on directing Verdi's *Un Ballo in Maschera*. Hungary: Budapest. 1998. Lang.: Hun. 4619
Verdi's *Un Ballo in Maschera* at the Hungarian State Opera House. Hungary: Budapest. 1998. Lang.: Hun. 4629
Interview with Miklós Gábor Kerényi on his production of *Un Ballo in maschera*. Hungary: Budapest, Szeged. 1998. Lang.: Hun. 4636
Wagner's *Ring* cycle at the Hungarian Opera House. Hungary: Budapest. 1998. Lang.: Hun. 4644
Kerley, William
Performance/production
Collection of newspaper reviews by London theatre critics. UK-England: London. 1998. Lang.: Eng. 2490
Kern, Jerome
Performance/production
Collection of newspaper reviews by London theatre critics. UK-England: London. 1998. Lang.: Eng. 2466

Kerr, James
Performance/production
Collection of newspaper reviews by London theatre critics. UK-England: London. 1998. Lang.: Eng. 2427
Collection of newspaper reviews by London theatre critics. UK-England: London. 1998. Lang.: Eng. 2545
Kesselman, Wendy
Design/technology
Recent work of lighting designer Brian MacDevitt. USA: New York, NY. 1997. Lang.: Eng. 1530
Sound design for *The Diary of Anne Frank* directed by James Lapine. USA: New York, NY. 1998. Lang.: Eng. 1553
Plays/librettos/scripts
The survivor character in contemporary American drama. USA. 1970-1997. Lang.: Eng. 3600
Reactions to the revised version of *The Diary of Anne Frank*. USA: New York, NY. 1998. Lang.: Eng. 3618
The representation of true crime in modern drama. USA. France. 1955-1996. Lang.: Eng. 3673
Kesselring, Joseph
Performance/production
Rehearsals of Christoph Marthaler's production of *Arsenic and Old Lace* by Joseph Kesselring. Germany: Hamburg. 1998. Lang.: Ger. 1953
Christoph Marthaler's approach to directing Joseph Kesselring's *Arsenic and Old Lace*. Germany: Hamburg. 1998. Lang.: Ger. 1956
Keszég, László
Performance/production
Goldoni's *La Locandiera* directed by Lászlo Keszég. Hungary: Kaposvár. 1998. Lang.: Hun. 2092
Productions of plays by Koljada and Jerofejév at Csiky Gergely Theatre. Hungary: Kaposvár. 1998. Lang.: Hun. 2149
Kézdy, György
Institutions
Interviews with the jury who selected the National Theatre Festival presentations. Hungary. 1996-1997. Lang.: Hun. 363
Khan Theatre (Jerusalem)
SEE
Teatron HaChan.
Khayaal Theatre Company (London)
Performance/production
Collection of newspaper reviews by London theatre critics. UK-England: London. 1998. Lang.: Eng. 2501
Khell, Zsolt
Design/technology
Survey of an exhibition of Hungarian scene design. Hungary: Budapest. 1998. Lang.: Hun. 195
Catalogue of an exhibition devoted to Hungarian theatre and film. Hungary: Budapest. 1998. Lang.: Hun. 197
Kheshbn, Der (Final Reckoning, The)
Plays/librettos/scripts
Ida Kamińska's production of *Der Kheshbn (The Final Reckoning)* by Mikhl Mirsky. Poland: Warsaw. 1963. Lang.: Eng. 3310
Khovanshchina
SEE
Chovanščina.
Khuon, Ulrich
Administration
Theatre directors on the future of subsidized theatre. Switzerland: Zurich. Germany: Hannover, Berlin. 1998. Lang.: Ger. 1390
Khutan, Ranjit
Performance/production
Collection of newspaper reviews by London theatre critics. UK-England: London. 1998. Lang.: Eng. 2549
Kiátkozott, A (Outcast, The)
Performance/production
Reviews of new Hungarian musicals. Hungary: Budapest. 1997. Lang.: Hun. 4360
Kicked
Basic theatrical documents
Text of Michael Healey's one-man show *Kicked*. Canada: Toronto, ON. 1993. Lang.: Eng. 1410
Kicsi (Little One, The)
Institutions
Theatre critics' awards 97-98. Hungary. 1997-1998. Lang.: Hun. 355
Performance/production
Review of plays directed by Árpad Schilling. Hungary: Budapest. 1998. Lang.: Hun. 2085
Kicsiny, Balázs
Design/technology
Survey of an exhibition of Hungarian scene design. Hungary: Budapest. 1998. Lang.: Hun. 195
Catalogue of an exhibition devoted to Hungarian theatre and film. Hungary: Budapest. 1998. Lang.: Hun. 197
Kierkegaard, Søren
Theory/criticism
Essay on the nature of talent. Denmark. Sweden. UK-England. 1847-1987. Lang.: Dan. 838
Kiernan, Pat
Performance/production
Collection of newspaper reviews by London theatre critics. UK-England: London. 1998. Lang.: Eng. 2416
Kikabidze, Vachtang
Performance/production
Interview with actor Vachtang Kikabidze. Georgia. 1998. Lang.: Rus. 1947
Killer Soprano, The
Performance/production
Collection of newspaper reviews by London theatre critics. UK-England: London. 1998. Lang.: Eng. 2517
Killing Rasputin
Performance/production
Collection of newspaper reviews by London theatre critics. UK-England: London. 1998. Lang.: Eng. 2549
Kilroy, Thomas
Plays/librettos/scripts
BBC radio plays with Anglo-Irish themes. UK-England. Ireland. 1973-1986. Lang.: Eng. 3868
Kilty, Jerome
Plays/librettos/scripts
Popular adaptations of the works of George Bernard Shaw. UK-England. 1890-1990. Lang.: Eng. 3445
Kim, Chong Ku
Performance/production
Historical, political, and aesthetic context of *madang* theatre. Korea. 1976-1998. Lang.: Ger. 557
Kim, Earl
Plays/librettos/scripts
Earl Kim's musical piece *Dead Calm*, based on a text by Samuel Beckett. 1945-1995. Lang.: Eng. 4306
Kim, Willa
Design/technology
Professional theatrical designers on design training. USA. 1998. Lang.: Eng. 252
Kimmig, Stephan
Performance/production
Productions of plays by Shakespeare, Brecht, and Camus. Germany. 1998. Lang.: Ger. 2032
Kimper, Paula M.
Design/technology
Set and costume design for *Patience and Sarah* at Lincoln Center. USA: New York, NY. 1998. Lang.: Eng. 4440
Kind of Alaska, A
Performance/production
Collection of newspaper reviews by London theatre critics. UK-England: London. 1998. Lang.: Eng. 2561
Recent productions of plays by Harold Pinter at Donmar Warehouse. UK-England: London. 1998. Lang.: Eng. 2609
Plays/librettos/scripts
Female presence/absence in plays of O'Neill, Pinter, and Shepard. USA. UK-England. 1936-1985. Lang.: Eng. 3607
Kind-Harts Dreame
Plays/librettos/scripts
Henry Chettle's supposed apology to Shakespeare. England: London. 1592-1607. Lang.: Eng. 2915
Kind, Johann Friedrich
Performance/production
Weber's *Der Freischütz* and the Neues Schauspielhaus. Germany: Berlin. 1821. Lang.: Eng. 4581
Kindertotenlieder (Songs on the Death of Children)
Performance/production
Collection of newspaper reviews by London theatre critics. UK-England: London. 1998. Lang.: Eng. 2409
Reviews of recent London performances. UK-England: London. 1998. Lang.: Ger. 2591
King and I, The
Design/technology
Costume designs by Irene Sharaff. USA. 1933-1976. Lang.: Eng. 277

***King and I, The* — cont'd**

Performance/production
Collection of newspaper reviews by London theatre critics. UK-England: London. 1998. Lang.: Eng. 2554

King Arthur
Plays/librettos/scripts
The relative absence of political allegory in English opera. England: London. 1620-1711. Lang.: Eng. 4767

King Goes Forth to France, The
SEE
Kuningas lähtee Ranskaan.

King Johan
Performance/production
Music in Tudor drama. England. 1497-1569. Lang.: Eng. 1902

King John
Institutions
Reviews of some productions at the Avignon Festival. France: Avignon. 1998. Lang.: Hun. 1615
Plays/librettos/scripts
Comic scenes and characters in the Elizabethan history play. England. 1590-1618. Lang.: Eng. 2955
Renaissance emblems of death and Shakespeare's *King John.* England. 1596-1599. Lang.: Eng. 2967

King Kongs Töchter (King Kong's Daughters)
Performance/production
Volker Hesse's production of *King Kongs Töchter (King Kong's Daughters)* by Theresia Walser. Switzerland: Zurich. 1998. Lang.: Ger. 2401

King Lear
Performance/production
The Stratford Festival production of Shakespeare's *King Lear.* Canada: Stratford, ON. 1964. Lang.: Eng. 506
Interview with actor William Hutt. Canada: Stratford, ON. 1962-1996. Lang.: Eng. 1844
German productions of Shakespeare. Germany: Leipzig, Hamburg, Berlin. 1998. Lang.: Ger. 2033
Productions of plays by Brecht and Shakespeare at the Hungarian theatre of Satu Mare. Romania: Satu Mare. 1998. Lang.: Hun. 2228
Interview with actress Fiona Shaw. UK-England. 1995-1997. Lang.: Eng. 2607
Brief productions of Shakespeare, Shaw, and Marlowe at the World's Fair. USA: Chicago, IL. 1934. Lang.: Eng. 2701
Postmodernism in Jean-Luc Godard's film adaptation of Shakespeare's *King Lear.* France. 1988. Lang.: Eng. 3931
Analysis of Shakespeare's *King Lear* on television. UK-England. 1982-1983. Lang.: Eng. 4064
Plays/librettos/scripts
French translations of Shakespeare by Antonine Maillet and Jean-Louis Roux. Canada: Montreal, PQ. 1988-1993. Lang.: Fre. 2793
Analysis of *Queen Lear* by Beau Coleman. Canada: Edmonton, AB. 1995-1997. Lang.: Eng. 2800
Delia Bacon's analysis of Shakespeare's *King Lear.* England. 1605. Lang.: Eng. 2860
The mad scenes in Shakespeare's *King Lear.* England. 1605-1606. Lang.: Eng. 2876
Shakespeare's *King Lear* and the gender constructions of three daughters. England. 1605-1606. Lang.: Eng. 2898
Feeling in Shakespeare's *King Lear.* England. 1605-1606. Lang.: Eng. 2952
The obedient daughter in adaptations of Shakespeare's plays. England. 1701-1800. Lang.: Eng. 2969
The concept of the self in Shakespearean tragedy. England. 1590-1612. Lang.: Eng. 2992
Historical background of the depiction of the Gloucesters in Shakespeare's *King Lear.* England. 1605-1606. Lang.: Eng. 2994
'Demonic' women in Shakespeare's tragedies. England. 1590-1613. Lang.: Eng. 2999
Folklore and Shakespeare's *King Lear.* England. 1605-1606. Lang.: Eng. 3010
The vagueness of locale in Shakespeare's *King Lear.* England. 1605-1606. Lang.: Eng. 3036
Gangster film and Shakespearean tragedy. USA. 1971-1991. Lang.: Eng. 4009

King of the Great Clock Tower, The
Performance/production
Collaborative Symbolist dance/theatre projects. Europe. USA. 1916-1934. Lang.: Eng. 1268

King's Head Theatre (London)
Institutions
History of the King's Head Theatre and pub. UK-England: London. 1970-1998. Lang.: Eng. 1747
Funding status of London's fringe theatres. UK-England: London. 1998. Lang.: Eng. 1748
Performance/production
Collection of newspaper reviews by London theatre critics. UK-England: London. 1998. Lang.: Eng. 2443
Collection of newspaper reviews by London theatre critics. UK-England: London. 1998. Lang.: Eng. 2452
Collection of newspaper reviews by London theatre critics. UK-England: London. 1998. Lang.: Eng. 2466
Collection of newspaper reviews by London theatre critics. UK-England: London. 1998. Lang.: Eng. 2477
Collection of newspaper reviews by London theatre critics. UK-England: London. 1998. Lang.: Eng. 2487
Collection of newspaper reviews by London theatre critics. UK-England: London. 1998. Lang.: Eng. 2488
Collection of newspaper reviews by London theatre critics. UK-England: London. 1998. Lang.: Eng. 2502
Collection of newspaper reviews by London theatre critics. UK-England: London. 1998. Lang.: Eng. 2513
Collection of newspaper reviews by London theatre critics. UK-England: London. 1998. Lang.: Eng. 2539
Collection of newspaper reviews by London theatre critics. UK-England: London. 1998. Lang.: Eng. 2567
Collection of newspaper reviews by London theatre critics. UK-England: London. 1998. Lang.: Eng. 2587

King's Men (London)
Institutions
Economic history of the Chamberlain's Men/King's Men. England. 1599-1642. Lang.: Eng. 1598

King's Theatre (Edinburgh)
Performance/production
Collection of newspaper reviews by London theatre critics. UK-Scotland: Edinburgh. 1998. Lang.: Eng. 2650

King's Threshold, The
Performance/production
The staging of *The King's Threshold* by W.B. Yeats. Ireland: Dublin. UK-England: London. 1903. Lang.: Eng. 2153

Kingdom of Earth
Plays/librettos/scripts
Effeminacy on the American stage. USA. 1920-1998. Lang.: Eng. 3682

Kingdom on Earth
Performance/production
Collection of newspaper reviews by London theatre critics. UK-England: London. 1998. Lang.: Eng. 2412

Kingshill, Sophia
Performance/production
Collection of newspaper reviews by London theatre critics. UK-England: London. 1998. Lang.: Eng. 2506

Kingsman, Philip
Performance/production
English actors in Kassel. Germany: Kassel. 1592-1620. Lang.: Eng. 2016

Kinninmont, Tom
Performance/production
Collection of newspaper reviews by London theatre critics. UK-England: London. 1998. Lang.: Eng. 2552

Kipp, Heidi
Performance/production
Shakespearean production and the GDR's 'existential crisis'. Germany, East. 1976-1980. Lang.: Eng. 2051

Kipphardt, Heinar
Performance/production
Alexander Stillmark's production of *Bruder Eichmann (Brother Eichmann)* by Heinar Kipphardt. Germany: Berlin. 1984-1992. Lang.: Eng. 2022

Kirby, Michael
Theory/criticism
The theatrical structure of autonomous theatre. USA. 1967-1979. Lang.: Eng. 867

Kirchmayer, Thomas
Plays/librettos/scripts
Protestant belief and English Reformation drama. England. 1535-1607. Lang.: Eng. 2972

Kirchner, Alfred
Institutions
Review of Wagner's *Ring* cycle at the Bayreuth Festival. Germany: Bayreuth. 1997-1998. Lang.: Hun. 4454

Kirchner, Ignaz
Performance/production
Actors Gert Voss and Ignaz Kirchner on George Tabori's production of *Fin de partie (Endgame)*. Austria: Vienna. 1998. Lang.: Ger. 1821
Gert Voss and Ignaz Kirchner, *Theater Heute*'s actors of the year. Austria: Vienna. 1988-1998. Lang.: Ger. 1823

Kirk, Peader
Performance/production
Collection of newspaper reviews by London theatre critics. UK-England: London. 1998. Lang.: Eng. 2548

Kirkkopelto, Esa
Theory/criticism
Director Esa Kirkkopelto on theatre as great art. Finland. 1998. Lang.: Fin. 3815

Kirkland, Sally
Institutions
Arthur Penn and Actors Studio. USA: New York, NY. 1997. Lang.: Eng. 1767

Kirkwood, James
Design/technology
Digital lighting control for *A Chorus Line*. USA: New York, NY. 1974-1975. Lang.: Eng. 4337

Kirov Opera and Ballet Theatre (Leningrad/St.Petersburg)
SEE
Akademičeskij Teat'r Opery i Baleta im. S.M. Kirova.

Kiss, Csaba
Administration
Round-table on author's rights. Hungary. 1990-1998. Lang.: Hun. 16
Performance/production
Performances at the new Bárka Színház. Hungary: Budapest. 1997. Lang.: Hun. 2097
Csaba Kiss's adaptation of Shakespeare's chronicle plays at Bárka Színház. Hungary: Győr. 1997. Lang.: Hun. 2101
Interview with director Csaba Kiss. Hungary. 1990-1998. Lang.: Hun. 2112
Csaba Kiss's adaptation and direction of *Lady Macbeth of the Provinces* by Leskov. Hungary: Budapest. 1998. Lang.: Hun. 2138

Kisvárdai Várszínház (Kisvárda)
Institutions
History of annual festival of Hungarian-language theatre. Hungary: Kisvárda. 1989-1998. Lang.: Hun. 1669

Kisvárosi Lady Macbeth (Lady Macbeth of the Provinces)
Performance/production
Csaba Kiss's adaptation and direction of *Lady Macbeth of the Provinces* by Leskov. Hungary: Budapest. 1998. Lang.: Hun. 2138

Kit Kat Klub (New York, NY)
Design/technology
Technical designs for Sam Mendes' production of *Cabaret*. USA: New York, NY. 1998. Lang.: Eng. 4343
Performance spaces
The creation of a site-specific performance space for Sam Mendes' production of *Cabaret*. USA: New York, NY. 1998. Lang.: Eng. 4350

Kitaev, Mart
Design/technology
Scene design and the plays of Ostrovskij. Russia. 1998. Lang.: Rus. 1523

Kitchen Blues
Performance/production
The kitchen in performance art of Bobby Baker and Jeanne Goosen. UK-England. South Africa, Republic of. 1990-1992. Lang.: Eng. 4243

Kitchen Show
Performance/production
The kitchen in performance art of Bobby Baker and Jeanne Goosen. UK-England. South Africa, Republic of. 1990-1992. Lang.: Eng. 4243

Kitchen, Heather
Institutions
Women in top management of American Conservatory Theatre. USA: San Francisco, CA. 1992-1998. Lang.: Eng. 1781

Kjellson, Ingvar
Performance/production
Interview with actors in Feydeau's *La Puce à l'Oreille (A Flea in Her Ear)* at Dramaten. Sweden: Stockholm. 1998. Lang.: Swe. 2396

Klabund
SEE
Henschke, Alfred.

Klarateatern (Stockholm)
Performance/production
Interview with actress and director Anna Takanen. Sweden: Stockholm. 1994-1998. Lang.: Swe. 2372

Klaren, Georg C.
Basic theatrical documents
Klaren's librettos for *Der Zwerg* by Alexander Zemlinsky. Germany. 1922. Lang.: Fre, Ger. 4420
Plays/librettos/scripts
Analysis of Alexander Zemlinsky's *Der Zwerg*. Germany. 1922. Lang.: Fre. 4793

Klass, Dieter
Performance/production
Productions of the Bad Hersfelder Festspiele. Germany: Bad Hersfeld. 1998. Lang.: Ger. 1991

Klaw & Erlanger (New York, NY)
Institutions
The Shuberts vs. the Syndicate. USA: New York, NY. 1976-1998. Lang.: Eng. 427

Klaw, Marc
Institutions
The Shuberts vs. the Syndicate. USA: New York, NY. 1976-1998. Lang.: Eng. 427

Kleinbürgerhochzeit, Die (Respectable Wedding, A)
Performance/production
French productions of German plays. France. 1998. Lang.: Ger. 1935

Kleist Theater (Franfurt/Oder)
Relation to other fields
Manfred Weber on directing Děvad Karahasan's translation of *Leonce und Lena* by Büchner. Bosnia: Sarajevo. 1997-1998. Lang.: Ger. 3730

Kleist, Heinrich von
Design/technology
Lighting for Henze's opera *Der Prinz von Homburg* at Deutsche Oper Berlin. Germany: Berlin. 1997. Lang.: Ger. 4431
Performance/production
Recent Paris productions. France: Paris. 1997-1998. Lang.: Ger. 1933
Productions of the Kleist theatre festival. Germany: Frankfurt/Oder. 1998. Lang.: Ger. 1993
Recent productions of Bochumer Schauspielhaus. Germany: Bochum. 1998. Lang.: Ger. 2009
Plays/librettos/scripts
The devouring woman in plays of Racine, Kleist, Ibsen, and Beckett. Europe. 1760-1992. Lang.: Eng. 3058
Relation to other fields
The context of Heinrich von Kleist's periodical *Berliner Abendblätter*. Germany: Berlin. 1810-1811. Lang.: Ger. 741

Kleiszter Ugrócsoport (Budapest)
Performance/production
Molière's *Misanthrope* directed by Andor Lukáts. Hungary: Budapest. 1998. Lang.: Hun. 2091

Klicperovo Divadlo (Hradec)
Performance/production
Interview with director Vladimír Morávek. Czech Republic: Hradec. 1985-1998. Lang.: Cze. 1880

Kliewer, Warren
Performance/production
Obituaries for Joseph Maher, Warren Kliewer, and E.G. Marshall. USA. 1912-1998. Lang.: Eng. 2655

Klim
Institutions
Impressions from the 'Golden Mask' festival. Russia: Minusinsk. 1998. Lang.: Ger. 1701

Klíma, Ladislav
Performance/production
Review of plays directed by Árpad Schilling. Hungary: Budapest. 1998. Lang.: Hun. 2085

Klimáček, Viliam
Plays/librettos/scripts
New direction in Czech playwriting. Czech Republic. 1990-1997. Lang.: Cze. 2850

Klimenko, Vladimir
Performance/production
The work of Russian directors at the Golden Mask festival. Russia: Moscow, St. Petersburg. 1998. Lang.: Swe. 2305

Klimper, Paula
Performance/production
Paula Klimper and Wende Persons' opera *Patience and Sarah*. USA. 1969-1998. Lang.: Eng. 4725

Klinga, Hans
Performance/production
Theatrical adaptations of children's stories by Astrid Lindgren. Sweden: Stockholm. 1998. Lang.: Eng. 2374

Klinga, Hans — cont'd

Hans Klinga's production of *Mio, Min Mio (Mio, My Mio)* at Dramaten. Sweden: Stockholm. 1997. Lang.: Swe. 2386

Klinger, Friedrich Maximilian
Plays/librettos/scripts
The character Medea in European drama. Europe. 450 B.C.-1998 A.D. Lang.: Ger. 3063

Klockrike (Helsinki)
Institutions
The proliferation of Swedish-language theatre groups in Helsinki. Finland: Helsinki. 1990-1998. Lang.: Eng, Fre. 1604

Kloepper, Louise
Training
Dance teacher Louise Kloepper. USA. 1910-1996. Lang.: Eng. 1213

Klotz, Volker
Theory/criticism
Hungarian translation of Volker Klotz on theatre aesthetics. Germany. 1995. Lang.: Hun. 842

Klötzke, Ernst August
Institutions
Ernst August Klötzke, new manager of musik-theater-werkstatt festival. Germany: Wiesbaden. 1998. Lang.: Ger. 4348

Klub
Performance/production
Collection of newspaper reviews by London theatre critics. UK-England: London. 1998. Lang.: Eng. 2448

Kmecl, Matjaž
Plays/librettos/scripts
The individual and his world in Slovene theatre. Slovenia. 1943-1985. Lang.: Slo. 3347

Knapp, Bob
Administration
Profiles of Equity council members. USA: New York, NY. 1998. Lang.: Eng. 82

Knebel', Marija Osipovna
Training
Actress, director, and teacher Marija Knebel'. Russia. 1898-1989. Lang.: Rus. 3850

Kniaz Igor (Prince Igor)
Institutions
The Bolšoj Ballet and the experimental company Gelikon. Russia: Moscow. 1997. Lang.: Swe. 4467

Kniefall in Warschau
Plays/librettos/scripts
Hero and anti-hero in contemporary opera production. Germany. 1998. Lang.: Ger. 4791

Knight, Stephen
Performance/production
Collection of newspaper reviews by London theatre critics. UK-England: London. 1998. Lang.: Eng. 2500

Knighton, Nan
Design/technology
Technical designs for *The Scarlet Pimpernel* directed by Robert Longbottom. USA: New York, NY. 1998. Lang.: Eng. 4331
Performance/production
Collection of newspaper reviews by London theatre critics. UK-England: London. 1998. Lang.: Eng. 2467

Knives in Hens
Plays/librettos/scripts
Analysis of plays by Sarah Kane and David Harrower, recently produced in Germany. UK-England. Germany: Cologne, Bonn. 1998. Lang.: Ger. 3487

Knop, Patricia
Performance/production
Collection of newspaper reviews by London theatre critics. UK-England: London. 1998. Lang.: Eng. 2425

Know Your Rights
Performance/production
Collection of newspaper reviews by London theatre critics. UK-England: London. 1998. Lang.: Eng. 2427

Knutton, Dominic
Performance/production
Collection of newspaper reviews by London theatre critics. UK-England: London. 1998. Lang.: Eng. 2476

Kocbek, Edvard
Plays/librettos/scripts
The individual and his world in Slovene theatre. Slovenia. 1943-1985. Lang.: Slo. 3347

Kočetova, E.
Performance/production
Opera singers E. Kočetova and A. Abdrazakov. Bashkir. 1998. Lang.: Rus. 4534

Koch, Kenneth
Plays/librettos/scripts
Revolutionary Off Broadway playwriting. USA: New York, NY. 1959-1969. Lang.: Eng. 3604

Kociper, Stanko
Plays/librettos/scripts
Fascism and the peasant in pre-War Slovene drama. Slovenia. 1940. Lang.: Slo. 3349

Kodály, Zoltán
Performance/production
Kodály's *Székely fonó (The Székler Spinnery)*. Hungary: Budapest. 1998. Lang.: Hun. 4298
Interview with Imre Kerényi, director of Kodály's *Székely fonó (The Székler Spinnery)*. Hungary: Budapest. 1997. Lang.: Hun. 4299
Kodály's *Háry János* at Szeged's Open-Air Festival. Hungary: Szeged. 1998. Lang.: Hun. 4359

Koestenbaum, Wayne
Plays/librettos/scripts
The American and Canadian premieres of *Jackie O.* Canada: Banff, AB. USA: Houston, TX. 1997. Lang.: Eng. 4761

Kōjiro, Kataoka
Performance/production
Onnagata performer Kataoka Kōjiro. Japan. 1603-1998. Lang.: Fre. 1365

Kok, Nicholas
Performance/production
Collection of newspaper reviews by London theatre critics. UK-England: London. 1998. Lang.: Eng. 2500

Kokko, Petri
Performance/production
Interview with ice-dancing team Susanna Rahkamo and Petri Kokko. Finland. 1998. Lang.: Fin. 919

Koko, Koffi
Performance/production
Choreographer Koffi Koko. France: Paris. Benin. 1990-1998. Lang.: Eng. 923

Kokoschka, Oskar
Plays/librettos/scripts
Social criticism in Viennese Expressionist drama. Austria: Vienna. 1907-1922. Lang.: Ger. 2779
Language and silence in German Expressionist drama. Germany. 1913-1923. Lang.: Eng. 3159

Kokotovic, Nada
Performance/production
Director and choreographer Nada Kokotovic. Europe. 1978-1998. Lang.: Ger. 1272

Kölcsey Művelődési Központ Kamaraszínháza (Debrecen)
Performance/production
Miklós Hubay's *Hová lett a rózsa lelke? (What Has Become of the Spirit of the Rose?)* directed by György Lengyel. Hungary: Debrecen. 1998. Lang.: Hun. 2150

Koljada, Nikolaj V.
Performance/production
Productions of plays by Koljada and Jerofejév at Csiky Gergely Theatre. Hungary: Kaposvár. 1998. Lang.: Hun. 2149

Koller, Karin
Institutions
Profile of Württembergische Landesbühne. Germany: Esslingen. 1996-1997. Lang.: Ger. 1639

Köllő, Miklós
Performance/production
Analysis of *Raszputyin (Rasputin)* by Közép-Európa Táncszínház. Hungary: Budapest. 1998. Lang.: Hun. 937

Kolos, István
Performance/production
Reviews of two plays by Per Olov Enquist. Hungary: Budapest. 1998. Lang.: Hun. 2089

Kolozsvár State Theatre
SEE
Állami Magyar Szinház (Cluj).

Kolozsvári Állami Színház
SEE
Állami Magyar Színház (Cluj-Napoca).

Koltai, Ralph
Design/technology
Scene designer Ralph Koltai. UK-England. 1944-1998. Lang.: Eng. 232

Koltès, Bernard-Marie
Basic theatrical documents
Catalan translation of *La Nuit juste avant les forêts (The Dark Just Before the Forests)* by Bernard-Marie Koltès. France. 1977. Lang.: Cat. 1428

Koltès, Bernard-Marie — cont'd

Performance/production
Productions of plays by Bernard-Marie Koltès. Canada: Montreal, PQ. 1991-1997. Lang.: Fre. 1862
Plays/librettos/scripts
Roberto Zucco and Bernard-Marie Koltès' idea of the tragic. France. 1835-1837. Lang.: Fre. 3076
Komische Oper (Berlin)
Performance/production
Opera director Christine Mielitz. Germany: Meiningen. 1991-1998. Lang.: Ger. 4597
Plays/librettos/scripts
Hero and anti-hero in contemporary opera production. Germany. 1998. Lang.: Ger. 4791
Komissarževskaja, Vera Fëdorovna
Performance/production
Major Russian actresses and ballerinas of the nineteenth and twentieth centuries. Russia. 1800-1998. Lang.: Rus. 2240
Komsomol Theatre (USSR)
SEE
Teat'r im. Leninskogo Komsomola.
Komuna Otwock
Performance/production
Productions of the festival of experimental theatre. Poland: Cracow. 1998. Lang.: Ger. 2225
Kondratjëv, Viačeslav
Performance/production
K. Dubinin's production of *Boi imeli mestnoe zančenie (The Battles Had Localized)* based on work of Viačeslav Kondratjëv. Russia: Volgograd. Lang.: Rus. 2331
Koner, Pauline
Training
Ballet teacher Pauline Koner. USA: New York, NY. 1920-1998. Lang.: Eng. 1212
Kong, Shangren
Plays/librettos/scripts
Personal identity in *Mudan ting (The Peony Pavilion)* by Tang Xianzu and *Taohua shan (The Peach Blossom Fan)* by Kong Shangren.China. 1575-1675. Lang.: Eng. 4315
Kongelige Teater (Copenhagen)
Performance/production
Interview with actress Tammi Øst. Denmark. 1982-1998. Lang.: Dan. 514
Kongi's Harvest
Plays/librettos/scripts
Political satire in the plays of Wole Soyinka. Nigeria. 1960-1979. Lang.: Eng. 3284
Kongres (Congress, The)
Plays/librettos/scripts
Analysis of plays by Primož Kozak. Slovenia. 1959-1969. Lang.: Slo. 3350
Koninklijk Ballet van Vlaanderen (Antwerp)
Performance/production
Premieres of choreographies by Danny Rosseel. Belgium: Antwerp. Netherlands: Amsterdam. 1998. Lang.: Hun. 1065
Koninklijk Theater Carré (Amsterdam)
Design/technology
Technical effects control system used in a production of *Joe—The Musical* at Koninklijk Theater Carré. Netherlands: Amsterdam. 1998. Lang.: Eng. 4324
Koninklijke Vlaamse Schouwburg (Brussels)
Plays/librettos/scripts
Dutch and Flemish Shakespearean productions. Belgium. Netherlands. 1980-1983. Lang.: Dut. 2789
Konnyj Teat'r 'Narty' (Vladikavkaz)
Institutions
A. Dživaev's equestrian theatre Konnyj Teat'r 'Narty'. Russia: Vladikavkaz. 1998. Lang.: Rus. 4272
Konopčuk, Pavlina
Performance/production
Actress Pavlina Konopčuk. Russia. 1998. Lang.: Rus. 2298
Konwitschny, Peter
Performance/production
Music theatre production in northern Germany. Germany: Lübeck, Hamburg, Bremen, Kiel. 1998. Lang.: Ger. 4293
Productions of Wagner's *Tristan und Isolde* by Peter Konwitschny and Werner Schroeter. Germany: Munich, Duisberg. 1998. Lang.: Ger. 4580
Kooemba Jdarra (Brisbane)
Performance/production
Aborigines in Australian theatre. Australia. 1990-1998. Lang.: Eng. 486
Kooris in Theatre (Sydney)
Performance/production
Aborigines in Australian theatre. Australia. 1990-1998. Lang.: Eng. 486
Kopit, Arthur
Design/technology
Virtual reality technology for set design. USA: Lawrence, KS. 1997. Lang.: Eng. 1562
Performance/production
Documentary theatre and the politics of representation. USA. 1966-1993. Lang.: Eng. 2728
Plays/librettos/scripts
Genocide, theatre, and the human body. North America. UK-England. Argentina. 1998. Lang.: Eng. 3290
Analysis of *Wings* by Arthur Kopit. USA. 1978. Lang.: Eng. 3616
Arthur Kopit's *Nine*, a musical adaptation of Fellini's *8 1/2*. USA. 1963-1982. Lang.: Eng. 4401
Korczak und die Kinder (Korczak and the Children)
Plays/librettos/scripts
Analysis of historical drama of the holocaust. USA. Canada. Germany. 1950-1980. Lang.: Eng. 3610
Korczak's Children
Plays/librettos/scripts
Analysis of historical drama of the holocaust. USA. Canada. Germany. 1950-1980. Lang.: Eng. 3610
Kordian (Knot, The)
Plays/librettos/scripts
The Polish national style in Romantic dramas. Poland. 1832-1835. Lang.: Pol. 3304
Koren, Tamás
Training
Interview with ballet master Tamás Koren. Hungary. 1959-1998. Lang.: Hun. 1207
Kornmüller, David
Plays/librettos/scripts
Analysis of plays by Sarah Kane and David Harrower, recently produced in Germany. UK-England. Germany: Cologne, Bonn. 1998. Lang.: Ger. 3487
Környey, Béla
Performance/production
Tenor Béla Környey. Hungary. 1875-1925. Lang.: Hun. 4616
Kosi, Tina
Institutions
The fiftieth anniversary of Ljubljana's puppet theatre. Slovenia: Ljubljana. 1968-1997. Lang.: Slo. 4873
Kőszegi Várszínház (Kőszeg)
Performance/production
Three Hungarian productions of plays by Molière. Hungary: Szentendre, Kapolcs, Kőszeg. 1998. Lang.: Hun. 2142
Kosztolányi, Dezső
Performance/production
Review of *Édes Anna (Anna Édes)*, Madách Chamber Theatre. Hungary: Budapest. 1997. Lang.: Hun. 2136
Kotlarczyk, Mieczyslaw
Performance/production
Postwar Polish theatre, culture, and politics. Poland. 1945-1950. Lang.: Eng. 573
Kott, Jan
Theory/criticism
Reviews of recent publications by Jan Kott. Poland. 1997-1998. Lang.: Hun. 854
Kovačevič, Dušan
Plays/librettos/scripts
Dissident playwright Dušan Kovačevič. Yugoslavia. 1972-1997. Lang.: Eng. 3719
Kovačevič, Sinisa
Plays/librettos/scripts
Contemporary drama of the former Yugoslavia in its political context. Yugoslavia. 1991-1998. Lang.: Ger. 3721
Kovalik, Balázs
Performance/production
György Ligeti's *Le Grand Macabre* directed by Balázs Kovalik. Hungary: Budapest. 1998. Lang.: Hun. 4642
Koyaanisqatsi (Madrid)
Plays/librettos/scripts
Playwright/director Alfonso Armada. Spain: Madrid. 1987-1998. Lang.: Eng. 3382
Koyamada, Toru
Performance/production
Collection of newspaper reviews by London theatre critics. UK-England: London. 1998. Lang.: Eng. 2512

Kozak, Primož
Plays/librettos/scripts
Analysis of plays by Primož Kozak. Slovenia. 1959-1969. Lang.: Slo. 3350
Kozel, Susan
Performance/production
Dancer Susan Kozel on performing in Paul Sermon's *Telematic Dreaming*. Netherlands: Amsterdam. 1997. Lang.: Eng. 956
Közép-Európa Táncszínház (Budapest)
Performance/production
Analysis of *Raszputyin (Rasputin)* by Közép-Európa Táncszínház. Hungary: Budapest. 1998. Lang.: Hun. 937
Kozincev, Grigorij
Plays/librettos/scripts
Film interpretations of Ophelia in Shakespeare's *Hamlet*. USA. UK-England. USSR. 1947-1990. Lang.: Eng. 4024
Kozlovskij, Ivan Semenovič
Performance/production
Opera singer Ivan Kozlovskij. Russia: Nizhni Novgorod. 1998. Lang.: Rus. 4301
Krähe, Die (Crow, The)
Performance/production
Recent dance performances in Berlin. Germany: Berlin. 1998. Lang.: Ger. 933
Krähwinkelfreiheit (Freedom of Krähwinkel)
Plays/librettos/scripts
Recent productions directed by Frank Castorf. Austria: Vienna. 1998. Lang.: Ger. 2788
Kramer, David
Performance/production
Collection of newspaper reviews by London theatre critics. UK-England: London. 1998. Lang.: Eng. 2447
Krämer, Günter
Institutions
Günter Krämer and children's opera. Germany: Cologne. 1996-1998. Lang.: Ger. 4458
Performance/production
The Cologne theatre scene. Germany: Cologne. 1985-1997. Lang.: Ger. 1964
Krámer, György
Performance/production
The ballet adaptation of the *Decameron* performed by Veszprém Dance Workshop. Hungary: Veszprém. 1998. Lang.: Hun. 1108
Kramer, Larry
Performance/production
Collection of newspaper reviews by London theatre critics. UK-England: London. 1998. Lang.: Eng. 2437
Plays/librettos/scripts
Effeminacy on the American stage. USA. 1920-1998. Lang.: Eng. 3682
Krankheit der Jugend (Malady of Youth)
Plays/librettos/scripts
Homosexuality on the German stage. Germany. 1920-1980. Lang.: Eng. 3147
Krankheit Tod, Die
SEE
Maladie de la Mort, La.
Krapp
Plays/librettos/scripts
Marcel Mihalovici's operatic adaptation of *Krapp's Last Tape* by Samuel Beckett. Europe. 1965. Lang.: Eng. 4769
Krapp's Last Tape
Performance/production
Collection of newspaper reviews by London theatre critics. UK-England: London. 1998. Lang.: Eng. 2442
Plays/librettos/scripts
Marcel Mihalovici's operatic adaptation of *Krapp's Last Tape* by Samuel Beckett. Europe. 1965. Lang.: Eng. 4769
Krasiński, Zygmunt
Plays/librettos/scripts
The Polish national style in Romantic dramas. Poland. 1832-1835. Lang.: Pol. 3304
Krasnopol'skaja, Maja
Performance/production
Teat'r Ten's *Ten' opery (The Shadow of the Opera)*. Russia: Moscow. 1998. Lang.: Rus. 4679
Ten' Puppet Theatre's production of Čajkovskij's opera *Iolanta*. Russia: Moscow. Lang.: Rus. 4680
Kraus, Duke
Performance/production
Obituary for puppeteer Duke Kraus. USA. 1937-1998. Lang.: Eng. 4902
Kraus, Karl
Plays/librettos/scripts
A private performance of *Die Büchse der Pandora (Pandora's Box)* by Frank Wedekind. Austria: Vienna. 1905. Lang.: Fre. 2783
Krauss, Clemens
Performance/production
Analysis of Richard Strauss's *Capriccio*. Germany. 1942. Lang.: Eng. 4606
Krausser, Helmut
Performance/production
Collection of newspaper reviews by London theatre critics. UK-England: London. 1998. Lang.: Eng. 2582
Kreczmar, Jan
Performance/production
Actor Jan Kreczmar. Poland: Warsaw, Lvov. 1939-1945. Lang.: Pol. 2216
Kreihsl, Michael
Performance/production
Premieres of new plays. Austria: Vienna. 1998. Lang.: Ger. 1820
Krejča, Otomar
Performance/production
Otomar Krejča's production of *Faust* at Národní Divadlo. Czech Republic: Prague. 1997. Lang.: Eng, Fre. 1881
Kremlevskij Balet (Moscow)
Performance/production
Guest performance of the Kremlevskij Balet. Russia. Hungary: Budapest. 1998. Lang.: Hun. 1137
Kresnigk, Johann
Performance/production
Recent dance performances in Berlin. Germany: Berlin. 1998. Lang.: Ger. 933
Nudity in dance theatre. Europe. 1970-1998. Lang.: Ger. 1270
Krétakör Színház (Budapest)
Performance/production
Review of plays directed by Árpad Schilling. Hungary: Budapest. 1998. Lang.: Hun. 2085
Kricskovics, Antal
Performance/production
Fáklya Horvát Táncegyüttes' folk dance production *Napmadarak (Sunbirds)*. Hungary. 1998. Lang.: Hun. 1227
Modern tendencies in Hungarian folk dance. Hungary. 1970-1977. Lang.: Hun. 1228
Krieg (War)
Performance/production
Recent productions of Deutsches Schauspielhaus. Germany: Hamburg. 1998. Lang.: Ger. 2034
Kriegenburg, Andreas
Administration
Theater Basel under the direction of Stefan Bachmann. Switzerland: Basel. 1996-1998. Lang.: Ger. 1391
Institutions
New plays by Dea Loher at Staatsschauspiel Hannover. Germany: Hannover. 1992-1998. Lang.: Ger. 1643
Stefan Bachmann of Basler Theater. Switzerland: Basel. 1998. Lang.: Ger. 1737
Performance/production
Natali Seelig, *Theater Heute*'s actress of the year. Germany: Munich. 1991-1998. Lang.: Ger. 1966
Interview with director Andreas Kriegenburg. Germany. 1992-1998. Lang.: Ger. 2010
Andreas Kriegenburg's production of Büchner's *Leonce und Lena*. Germany: Munich. 1998. Lang.: Ger. 2020
Plays/librettos/scripts
Analysis of plays by Dea Loher, directed by Andreas Kriegenburg. Germany: Hannover. 1998. Lang.: Ger. 3130
The collaboration of playwright Dea Loher and director Andreas Kriegenburg. Germany: Hannover, Munich. 1990-1998. Lang.: Ger. 3151
The development of *Blaubart—Hoffnung der Frauen (Bluebeard—Hope of Women)* by Dea Loher. Germany: Munich. 1998. Lang.: Ger. 3164
Krieger, Henry
Design/technology
Recent work of lighting designer Brian MacDevitt. USA: New York, NY. 1997. Lang.: Eng. 1530
Sound design for *Side Show* at Richard Rodgers Theatre. USA: New York, NY. 1998. Lang.: Eng. 4329
Krísis (Crisis)
Plays/librettos/scripts
Analysis of *Krísis (Crisis)* by Sabina Berman. Mexico. 1996. Lang.: Eng. 3273

***Krísis (Crisis)* — cont'd**

Comparison between *Krísis (Crisis)* by Sabina Berman and Quentin Tarantino's film *Pulp Fiction*. Mexico. USA. 1993-1996. Lang.: Spa. 3276

Kristalni Grad (Crystal Castle, The)
Plays/librettos/scripts
Social roles and ideologies in plays of Anton Funtek and Ivo Šorli. Slovenia. 1897-1920. Lang.: Slo. 3353

Kristan, Etbin
Plays/librettos/scripts
Analysis of *Zvestoba (Fidelity)* by Etbin Kristan. Slovenia. 1897-1910. Lang.: Slo. 3344

Kristina från Duvemåla (Kristina of Duvemåla)
Performance spaces
The rebuilding of the stage at Cirkus to accommodate a production of *Kristina från Duvemåla (Kristina of Duvemåla)*.Sweden: Stockholm. 1995. Lang.: Swe. 1804

Kristy-Brooks, Kathleen
Basic theatrical documents
Text of *Dreams* by Kathleen Kristy-Brooks. USA. 1988. Lang.: Eng. 1493

Křivánek, Rostislav
Plays/librettos/scripts
New direction in Czech playwriting. Czech Republic. 1990-1997. Lang.: Cze. 2850

Krivoje zerkalo (St. Petersburg)
Institutions
Theatrical parodies of Krivoje zerkalo. Russia: St. Petersburg. 1908-1931. Lang.: Eng. 1705

Krleža, Miroslav
Performance/production
Krleža's *U agoniji (In Agony)* directed by Péter Valló. Hungary: Budapest. 1998. Lang.: Hun. 2074

Krobot, Ivo
Performance/production
The adaptation of classic Czech works to the stage. Czech Republic: Prague, Brno. 1990-1998. Lang.: Cze. 1877

Krobot, Miroslav
Performance/production
The adaptation of classic Czech works to the stage. Czech Republic: Prague, Brno. 1990-1998. Lang.: Cze. 1877

Kroetz, Franz Xaver
Performance/production
Marie-Ginette Guay's wordless performance in Franz Xaver Kroetz's *Wunschkonzert (Request Concert)*. Canada: Quebec, PQ. 1995-1997. Lang.: Fre. 1847

Productions of plays by Shakespeare, Brecht, and Camus. Germany. 1998. Lang.: Ger. 2032

Interview with director Anders Paulin. Sweden: Malmö. 1997-1998. Lang.: Swe. 2377

Plays/librettos/scripts
Aggressive language in modern drama. Europe. USA. 1960-1985. Lang.: Eng. 3055

Analysis of plays by Franz Xaver Kroetz. Germany, West. 1970-1980. Lang.: Eng. 3178

Kroeze, Jan
Design/technology
Lighting design for fashion design awards ceremony at Lincoln Center. USA: New York, NY. 1995. Lang.: Eng. 312

Krofta, Jakub
Performance/production
Interview with director Jakub Krofta. Czech Republic. 1973-1998. Lang.: Cze. 1878

Krofta, Josef
Performance/production
Interview with director Josef Krofta of Divadlo Drak. Czech Republic: Hradec. 1990-1998. Lang.: Cze. 1879

Kron, Lisa
Performance/production
Collection of newspaper reviews by London theatre critics. UK-England: London. 1998. Lang.: Eng. 2471

Kronzer, James
Design/technology
Professional theatrical designers on design training. USA. 1998. Lang.: Eng. 252

Kroon, Barbara
Design/technology
Profiles of young theatrical designers. Netherlands. 1990-1998. Lang.: Dut. 207

Krupa, Thomas
Performance/production
Premieres of plays on the Nazi theme. Germany: Darmstadt. Austria: Vienna. 1998. Lang.: Ger. 2030

Kruse, Jürgen
Institutions
Productions of Bochumer Schauspielhaus. Germany: Bochum. 1998. Lang.: Ger. 1655

Performance/production
Recent productions of Bochumer Schauspielhaus. Germany: Bochum. 1998. Lang.: Ger. 2009

Kšesinskaja, Mathilde
Performance/production
Major Russian actresses and ballerinas of the nineteenth and twentieth centuries. Russia. 1800-1998. Lang.: Rus. 2240

Ktorov, Anatolij P.
Performance/production
Actor Anatolij Ktorov. Russia: Moscow. 1998. Lang.: Rus. 2286

Memoirs of actor A.P. Ktorov. Russia: Moscow. 1998. Lang.: Rus. 2292

Kubešová, Blanka
Plays/librettos/scripts
New direction in Czech playwriting. Czech Republic. 1990-1997. Lang.: Cze. 2850

Kubo, Koichi
Performance/production
Dancer Koichi Kubo of Colorado Ballet. USA: Denver, CO. 1991-1998. Lang.: Eng. 1174

Kuftinec, Sonja
Performance/production
The development of *Letters, or Where Does the Postman Go When All the Street Names Are Changed*, based on experiences of residents of Mostar. Bosnia-Herzegovina: Mostar. 1997. Lang.: Eng. 1831

Kuhle Wampe oder Wem gehört die Welt (Kuhle Wampe, or To Whom Does the World Belong?)
Plays/librettos/scripts
Bertolt Brecht and German cinema. Germany. 1919-1932. Lang.: Ita. 3972

Kuhlke, Kevin
Performance/production
The 'viewpoint theory' of actor training. USA. 1998. Lang.: Eng. 2677

Kuhn, Hans Peter
Plays/librettos/scripts
Hero and anti-hero in contemporary opera production. Germany. 1998. Lang.: Ger. 4791

Kühnel, Tom
Institutions
Director training at Ernst-Busch-Schule and some of its graduates. Germany: Berlin. 1972-1998. Lang.: Ger. 1648

Performance/production
Comparison of productions of Brecht's *Die Massnahme (The Measures Taken)*. Germany: Berlin, Wuppertal. 1995-1998. Lang.: Ger. 1950

Productions directed by Christian Stückl, Tom Kühnel, and Robert Schuster. Germany: Frankfurt. 1997-1998. Lang.: Ger. 1969

Productions of plays by Shakespeare, Brecht, and Camus. Germany. 1998. Lang.: Ger. 2032

Kujirano Bōyo (Epitaph for the Whales)
Performance/production
Collection of newspaper reviews by London theatre critics. UK-England: London. 1998. Lang.: Eng. 2438

Kukol'nyj Teat'r Ten' (Moscow)
Performance/production
Teat'r Ten's *Ten' opery (The Shadow of the Opera)*. Russia: Moscow. 1998. Lang.: Rus. 4679

Ten' Puppet Theatre's production of Čajkovskij's opera *Iolanta*. Russia: Moscow. Lang.: Rus. 4680

Kulcskeresők (Searching for the Key)
Performance/production
Review of István Örkény's *Kulcskeresők (Searching for the Key)*, Katona József Theatre. Hungary: Budapest. 1998. Lang.: Hun. 2083

Kulkla, Otto
Administration
Interviews with German theatre and film directors. Germany. 1998. Lang.: Ger. 1385

Kulle, Gerthi
Performance/production
Gerthi Kulle's role in Brecht's *Der Gute Mensch von Sezuan (The Good Person of Szechwan)* at Dramaten. Sweden: Stockholm. 1998. Lang.: Swe. 2384

Kulturamt (Eisleben)
Relation to other fields
The national movement, cultural policy, and German regional theatre. Germany: Eisleben. 1998. Lang.: Ger. 740
Kumankov, Jėvgenij
Design/technology
Memoirs of scenographer Jėvgenij Kumankov. Russia. 1998. Lang.: Rus. 215
Kumudini, Lakhiya
Performance/production
Kathak dancer Lakhiya Kumudini. India. 1998. Lang.: Rus. 1369
Kungliga Baletten (Stockholm)
Performance/production
Interview with ballerina Anneli Alhanko. Sweden: Stockholm. 1963. Lang.: Swe. 1151
Millicent Hodson and Kenneth Archer's revival of Jean Börlin's ballet *Dervisher*. UK-England: London. Sweden: Stockholm. 1920-1998. Lang.: Swe. 1311
Kungliga Dramatiska Teatern (Stockholm)
Audience
Reactions to Norén's *Personkrets 3:1 (Circle 3:1)* at Dramaten. Sweden: Stockholm. 1998. Lang.: Swe. 1405
Institutions
Report on the Stockholm theatre festival. Sweden: Stockholm. 1998. Lang.: Eng. 1724
Interview with Ingrid Dahlberg, manager of Dramaten. Sweden: Stockholm. 1996-1998. Lang.: Swe. 1730
Performance/production
Photographs of Dramaten actors. Sweden: Stockholm. 1998. Lang.: Swe. 2366
Interview with actor Dan Ekborg. Sweden: Stockholm. 1998. Lang.: Swe. 2367
Theatrical adaptations of children's stories by Astrid Lindgren. Sweden: Stockholm. 1998. Lang.: Eng. 2374
Interviews with actors Lil Terselius and Björn Granath. Sweden: Stockholm. 1998. Lang.: Swe. 2381
Gerthi Kulle's role in Brecht's *Der Gute Mensch von Sezuan (The Good Person of Szechwan)* at Dramaten. Sweden: Stockholm. 1998. Lang.: Swe. 2384
Hans Klinga's production of *Mio, Min Mio (Mio, My Mio)* at Dramaten. Sweden: Stockholm. 1997. Lang.: Swe. 2386
Interview with actor Jan-Olof Strandberg. Sweden: Stockholm, Gothenburg, Uppsala. 1948-1998. Lang.: Swe. 2390
Photos of rehearsals of O'Neill's *Long Day's Journey Into Night* at Dramaten. Sweden: Stockholm. 1998. Lang.: Swe. 2391
Interview with actors in Feydeau's *La Puce à l'Oreille (A Flea in Her Ear)* at Dramaten. Sweden: Stockholm. 1998. Lang.: Swe. 2396
Interview with director Robert Lepage. Sweden: Stockholm. Canada: Montreal, PQ. 1997. Lang.: Swe. 2397
Relation to other fields
A joint project for teaching Shakespeare with professional actors. Sweden. 1988-1998. Lang.: Swe. 3776
Kungliga Operan (Stockholm)
Performance spaces
The opening of Kungliga Operan. Sweden: Stockholm. 1898. Lang.: Swe. 4498
Performance/production
Interview with soprano Lena Nordin. Sweden: Stockholm. 1982-1998. Lang.: Swe. 4697
Reactions to the opera *Staden* by Sven-David Sandström and Katarina Frostensson. Sweden: Stockholm. 1998. Lang.: Swe. 4699
Johannes Schaaf's production of *Otello* at Kungliga Operan. Sweden: Stockholm. 1998. Lang.: Swe. 4701
Reactions to Offenbach operettas at Kungliga Operan. Sweden: Stockholm. 1860-1928. Lang.: Swe. 4858
Kungliga Teatern (Stockholm)
SEE
Kungliga Operan.
Kungliga Teaterns Balett (Stockholm)
Institutions
The 225th anniversary of the Royal Swedish Ballet. Sweden: Stockholm. 1773-1998. Lang.: Eng. 1048
The 225th anniversary season of the Royal Swedish Ballet. Sweden: Stockholm. 1998. Lang.: Eng. 1050
Dance festival commemorating 225th anniversary of the Royal Swedish Ballet. Sweden: Stockholm. 1998. Lang.: Eng. 1051
Profile of the Royal Swedish Ballet. Sweden: Stockholm. 1773-1998. Lang.: Hun. 1053
Performance/production
The reconstruction of Jean Börlin's ballet *Dervisher*. Sweden: Stockholm. 1997. Lang.: Eng. 1150
Kunikova, Elena
Performance/production
Interview with dancer/choreographer Elena Kunikova on her work with Les Ballets Trockadero. USA: New York, NY. 1997. Lang.: Eng. 1180
Kuntze, Kay
Institutions
Music theatre studies at the Hochschule für Musik und Theater. Germany: Hamburg. 1988-1998. Lang.: Ger. 4459
Kunze, Dieter
Institutions
Appealing to the youth audience at Theater Dresden. Germany: Dresden. 1997-1998. Lang.: Ger. 1631
Kuo, Yu-Chun
Basic theatrical documents
Score of Yu-Chun Kuo's concerto for dance and music, *Ring*. USA. 1988. Lang.: Eng. 887
Kupfer, Harry
Performance/production
Interview with opera director Christine Mielitz. Germany: Berlin. 1979-1997. Lang.: Eng. 4605
Plays/librettos/scripts
Hero and anti-hero in contemporary opera production. Germany. 1998. Lang.: Ger. 4791
Kupke, Peter
Performance/production
German directors about the meaning of Brecht today. Germany. 1998. Lang.: Ger. 1948
Plays/librettos/scripts
Recent German productions of Brecht's plays. Germany. 1998. Lang.: Ger. 3150
Kurbas, Les' Aleksand'r Stepanovič
Institutions
Les' Kurbas and Teat'r Berezil. USSR. 1922-1934. Lang.: Eng. 431
Performance/production
Analysis of Les' Kurbas' production of Shakespeare's *Macbeth*. USSR. 1924. Lang.: Eng. 2766
Kurlander, Gabrielle
Administration
Performance in fundraising. USA: New York, NY. 1998. Lang.: Eng. 34
Kurosawa, Akira
Performance/production
Obituary for film director Akira Kurosawa. Japan. 1910-1998. Lang.: Eng. 3937
Kurt, Aleš
Performance/production
Interview with director Aleš Kurt. Bosnia: Sarajevo. 1998. Lang.: Hun. 1830
Kušej, Martin
Design/technology
Scenographer Martin Zehetgruber. Austria: Graz. Germany: Stuttgart. 1979-1998. Lang.: Ger. 168
Performance/production
The performance of Shakespeare in the former East Germany. Germany: Rostock, Leipzig, Berlin, Dessau. 1996-1997. Lang.: Ger. 1974
Productions of Horváth's *Geschichten aus dem Wienerwald (Tales from the Vienna Woods)*. Germany: Hamburg, Hannover. Austria: Vienna. 1998. Lang.: Ger. 2003
Review of opera productions. Germany: Stuttgart, Leipzig. 1998. Lang.: Ger. 4584
Reviews of recent opera productions. Switzerland: Basel. Germany: Stuttgart, Berlin, Hamburg. France: Strasbourg. 1997-1998. Lang.: Ger. 4702
Kushida, Kazuyoshi
Performance/production
Collection of newspaper reviews by London theatre critics. UK-England: London. 1998. Lang.: Eng. 2438
Kushner, Tony
Performance/production
Collection of newspaper reviews by London theatre critics. UK-England: London. 1998. Lang.: Eng. 2498
Contemporary queer politics and the production of gay and lesbian theatre. USA. 1970-1997. Lang.: Eng. 2710

Kushner, Tony — cont'd

Plays/librettos/scripts
The medieval mystery play and Tony Kushner's *Angels in America.* USA. 1992-1994. Lang.: Eng. 3652
Training
Playwright Tony Kushner's address to the Association of Theatre in Higher Education. USA. 1997. Lang.: Eng. 3851

Kvartett (Quartet)
Institutions
Theatre critics' awards 97-98. Hungary. 1997-1998. Lang.: Hun. 355
Performance/production
György Spiró's *Kvartett (Quartet)* directed by János Vincze. Hungary: Pécs. 1997. Lang.: Hun. 2067

Kvinnliga Dramatiska Teatern (Stockholm)
Institutions
Profile of independent feminist theatre Kvinnliga Dramatiska Teatern. Sweden: Stockholm. 1997-1998. Lang.: Swe. 1725

Kyd, Thomas
Design/technology
Set and costume design for *The Spanish Tragedy* at RSC. UK-England: London. 1998. Lang.: Eng. 1525
Plays/librettos/scripts
Attitudes toward Spain in early modern English drama. England. 1492-1604. Lang.: Eng. 2927

Kyle, Barry
Performance/production
Three productions of Shakespeare's *Richard III.* UK-England. 1973-1984. Lang.: Eng. 2612

Kyōgen
Performance/production
Analysis of *kyōgen* performance. Japan. 1400-1700. Lang.: Eng. 1351

La Fenice (Venice)
SEE
Teatro La Fenice.

La MaMa Experimental Theatre Club (New York, NY)
Institutions
Ellen Stewart and La MaMa Experimental Theatre Club. USA: New York, NY. 1961-1985. Lang.: Eng. 1762

La Scala (Milan)
SEE
Teatro alla Scala.

Laban, Rudolf von
Performance/production
History of movement training for the actor. USA. 1910-1985. Lang.: Eng. 675
William Forsythe of Ballett Frankfurt. Germany: Frankfurt. 1984-1998. Lang.: Ger. 1284
Training
The development of Irmgard Bartenieff's corrective physical training methods. USA. 1925-1981. Lang.: Ger. 1024

Labatt's Apollo Theatre (London)
Performance/production
Collection of newspaper reviews by London theatre critics. UK-England: London. 1998. Lang.: Eng. 2472
Collection of newspaper reviews by London theatre critics. UK-England: London. 1998. Lang.: Eng. 2573

Laberge, Marc
Plays/librettos/scripts
Round-table discussion on story-telling and theatre. Canada: Montreal, PQ. 1998. Lang.: Fre. 688

Labey, Russell
Design/technology
Sound design for the musical *Bugsy Malone.* UK-England: London. 1997. Lang.: Eng. 4327

Labiche, Eugène
Institutions
Productions of Bochumer Schauspielhaus. Germany: Bochum. 1998. Lang.: Ger. 1655
Performance/production
Seven critics on their favorite character or portrayal. Sweden. 1950. Lang.: Swe. 2369

Labor relations
Administration
Interview with Frank Baumbauer of Deutsches Schauspielhaus Hamburg. Germany: Hamburg. 1993-2000. Lang.: Ger. 11
Equity agreement on New Orleans working conditions. USA: New Orleans, LA. 1998. Lang.: Eng. 63
Changes in Equity's health insurance coverage. USA: New York, NY. 1998. Lang.: Eng. 65
Equity agreement with Second City. USA: Chicago, IL, Detroit, MI. 1998. Lang.: Eng. 66
The campaign to ban child performers in New York City. USA: New York, NY. 1874-1919. Lang.: Eng. 139
Equity's contract with Resident Musical Theatre Association. USA. 1998. Lang.: Eng. 4319
Institutions
Women in top management of American Conservatory Theatre. USA: San Francisco, CA. 1992-1998. Lang.: Eng. 1781

Laboratory Theatre (Wroclaw)
SEE
Teatr Laboratorium.

Lachapelle, Andrée
Performance/production
Interview with actress Andrée Lachapelle. Canada: Montreal, PQ. 1950-1998. Lang.: Fre. 502
Interview with film and television actress Andrée Lachapelle. Canada: Montreal, PQ. 1964-1998. Lang.: Fre. 3857

LaChiusa, Michael John
Plays/librettos/scripts
Panel discussion on contemporary musical theatre. USA: New York, NY. 1998. Lang.: Eng. 4398

Laczó, István
Performance/production
Profile of tenor István Laczó. Hungary. 1904-1965. Lang.: Hun. 4625

Ladies Against Women (LAW, Berkeley, CA)
Institutions
Feminist theatre of Ladies Against Women. USA: Berkeley, CA. 1979-1993. Lang.: Eng. 396

Ladies of Castile, The
Plays/librettos/scripts
Gender and politics in Romantic tragedies of Mercy Otis Warren. USA. 1783-1785. Lang.: Eng. 3575

Ladipọ, Duro
Plays/librettos/scripts
Representation of character in plays by Duro Ladipọ. Nigeria. 1964-1970. Lang.: Eng. 3285

Lady Boys of Bangkok, The
Performance/production
Collection of newspaper reviews by London theatre critics. UK-England: London. 1998. Lang.: Eng. 2492

Lady for a Day
Performance/production
Analysis of Frank Capra's film *Lady for a Day.* USA. 1933. Lang.: Eng. 3952

Lady Macbeth of Mtsensk
SEE
Ledi Makbet Mtsenskogo Uezda.
Ledi Makbet Mtsenskogo Uezda.

Lafolie, Mattias
Institutions
Report on the Stockholm theatre festival. Sweden: Stockholm. 1998. Lang.: Eng. 1724

Lagarce, Jean-Luc
Performance/production
Comparison of text-based and visual productions. France. 1998. Lang.: Fre. 1939

Lagerlöf, Selma
Performance/production
Reviews of two plays by Per Olov Enquist. Hungary: Budapest. 1998. Lang.: Hun. 2089

LaGravenese, Richard
Basic theatrical documents
The screenplay of *Living Out Loud* by Richard LaGravenese. USA. 1998. Lang.: Eng. 3890
Plays/librettos/scripts
Interview with screenwriter and director Richard LaGravenese. USA. 1998. Lang.: Eng. 4019

Laguna, Ana
Performance/production
Dancer Ana Laguna of Cullbergbaletten. Sweden: Stockholm. 1974-1998. Lang.: Swe. 1305

Lahr, Bert
Performance/production
Actor Bert Lahr. USA. 1895-1967. Lang.: Eng. 3953

Lainé, Pascal
Basic theatrical documents
Text of *Capitaine Bringuier* by Pascal Lainé. France. 1998. Lang.: Fre. 1429

Laird, Fiona
Performance/production
Collection of newspaper reviews by London theatre critics. UK-England. 1998. Lang.: Eng. 2456
Collection of newspaper reviews by London theatre critics. UK-England: London. 1998. Lang.: Eng. 2461
Collection of newspaper reviews by London theatre critics. UK-England: London. 1998. Lang.: Eng. 2482
Collection of newspaper reviews by London theatre critics. UK-England: London. 1998. Lang.: Eng. 2555

Lairesse, Gerard de
Design/technology
Gerard de Lairesse, painter and stage designer. Netherlands. 1640-1711. Lang.: Eng. 208

Lajos, Sándor
Performance/production
Sándor Lajos' *Szűrővizsgálat (Screen Test)* directed by Tamás Fodor. Hungary: Budapest. 1998. Lang.: Hun. 2103

Lajtha, László
Performance/production
A production of László Lajtha's comic opera *Le chapeau bleu*. Romania: Cluj-Napoca. Hungary. 1998. Lang.: Hun. 4666
Production of László Lajtha's comic opera *Le chapeau bleu*. Romania: Cluj-Napoca. Hungary. 1948-1998. Lang.: Hun. 4668

Lake Charles Little Theatre (Lake Charles, LA)
Institutions
History of Lake Charles Little Theatre. USA: Lake Charles, LA. 1927-1982. Lang.: Eng. 1770

Lakeboat
Performance/production
Collection of newspaper reviews by London theatre critics. UK-England: London. 1998. Lang.: Eng. 2582

Lakmé
Audience
The negative influence of Wagnerianism on the reception of Delibes' opera *Lakmé*. 1900-1996. Lang.: Fre. 4409
Basic theatrical documents
Libretto of *Lakmé* by Léo Delibes, Edmond Gondinet, and Philippe Gille. France. 1883. Lang.: Fre. 4415
Performance/production
Interpreters of the title role in Delibes' opera *Lakmé*. 1932-1995. Lang.: Fre. 4505
Performances of Delibes' *Lakmé*. 1883-1997. Lang.: Fre. 4519
Recordings of Delibes' *Lakmé*. 1941-1998. Lang.: Fre. 4524
Natalie Dessay's role in Gilbert Blin's production of *Lakmé*. France: Paris. 1995. Lang.: Fre. 4570
Soprano Mady Mesplé on Delibes' *Lakmé*. France. 1961-1997. Lang.: Fre. 4573
Plays/librettos/scripts
Analysis of Delibes' opera *Lakmé*. France. 1883. Lang.: Fre. 4782
The source of the libretto for Delibes' *Lakmé*. France. 1853-1883. Lang.: Fre. 4784

Lallone, Ariana
Performance/production
Ballerina Ariana Lallone of Pacific Northwest Ballet. USA: Seattle, WA. 1984-1998. Lang.: Eng. 1168

Lamarche, Gustave
Relation to other fields
Amateur art theatre produced by Quebec priests. Canada: Montreal, PQ. 1930-1950. Lang.: Fre. 3733

Lambert, Gary
Institutions
Interview with members of dance group Creative Independent Artists. UK-Scotland: Glasgow. 1996-1998. Lang.: Eng. 904

Lamkey, Kathryn
Administration
Kathryn Lamkey, Director of Equity's Central Regional Office. USA: Chicago, IL. 1998. Lang.: Eng. 92

Lamont, Peter
Design/technology
Technical designs for the film *Titanic*. USA. 1997. Lang.: Eng. 3910

Lamos, Mark
Performance/production
Collection of newspaper reviews by London theatre critics. UK-England: London. 1998. Lang.: Eng. 2498
Plays/librettos/scripts
Recent productions of plays by Edward Albee. USA: New York, NY, Hartford, CT. 1959-1998. Lang.: Eng. 3578

Lanchbery, John
Design/technology
Lighting design for Čajkovskij's *Sneguročka (The Snow Maiden)* at Houston Ballet. USA: Houston, TX. 1998. Lang.: Eng. 1035

Landau, Tina
Performance/production
Steppenwolf Theatre Company's production of *Space* by Tina Landau. USA: Chicago, IL. 1998. Lang.: Eng. 2672
Plays/librettos/scripts
Interview with playwright and director Tina Landau. USA. 1998. Lang.: Eng. 3685

Lander, David
Design/technology
Lighting design for Hwang's *Golden Child* at the Public Theatre. USA: New York, NY. 1996-1998. Lang.: Eng. 1540

Lander, Thomas
Performance/production
Singer Thomas Lander. Germany. Austria. Sweden. 1981-1998. Lang.: Swe. 4591

Landesbühne Sachsen-Anhalt (Eisleben)
Relation to other fields
The national movement, cultural policy, and German regional theatre. Germany: Eisleben. 1998. Lang.: Ger. 740

Landestheater (Detmold)
Administration
Theatrical marketing in North Rhine-Westphalia. Germany. 1994-1998. Lang.: Ger. 6

Landestheater Württemberg-Hohenzollern (Tübingen)
Administration
Interviews with theatre managers regarding the changing cultural landscape. Germany: Bruchsal, Esslingen, Tübingen. 1998. Lang.: Ger. 1381
Institutions
Profile of Landestheater Württemberg-Hohenzollern. Germany: Tübingen. 1996-1997. Lang.: Ger. 1634
German theatres' responses to threatened closings and mergers. Germany: Esslingen, Tübingen. 1998. Lang.: Ger. 1665

Landon-Smith, Kristine
Performance/production
Collection of newspaper reviews by London theatre critics. UK-England: London. 1998. Lang.: Eng. 2413
Collection of newspaper reviews by London theatre critics. UK-England: London. 1998. Lang.: Eng. 2541

Landry, Pascale
Institutions
Émile Morin and Pascale Landry on their Productions Recto-Verso. Canada: Quebec, PQ. 1996. Lang.: Fre. 4233

Landsaat, Cees
Design/technology
Profiles of young theatrical designers. Netherlands. 1990-1998. Lang.: Dut. 207

Lang, Alexander
Performance/production
German productions of Shakespeare. Germany: Leipzig, Hamburg, Berlin. 1998. Lang.: Ger. 2033
Interview with director Alexander Lang. Germany, East. 1970-1990. Lang.: Eng. 2037
Shakespearean production and the GDR's 'existential crisis'. Germany, East. 1976-1980. Lang.: Eng. 2051

Lange, Irmgard
Performance/production
German productions of contemporary Russian drama. Germany. 1998. Lang.: Ger. 1984

Langham, Michael
Performance/production
The Stratford Festival production of Shakespeare's *King Lear*. Canada: Stratford, ON. 1964. Lang.: Eng. 506

Langhoff, Anna
Institutions
Schauspiel Leipzig under the direction of Wolfgang Engel. Germany: Leipzig. 1996-1998. Lang.: Ger. 1638

Langhoff, Lukas
Institutions
Schauspiel Leipzig under the direction of Wolfgang Engel. Germany: Leipzig. 1996-1998. Lang.: Ger. 1638

Langhoff, Matthias
Performance/production
Interview with director Matthias Langhoff. Germany: Berlin. 1945-1998. Lang.: Ger. 1987

Langhoff, Thomas
Performance/production
Two productions of Brecht's *Der Kaukasische Kreidekreis (The Caucasian Chalk Circle)*. Germany: Berlin, Hamburg. 1998. Lang.: Ger. 1957
Thomas Langhoff's production of Brecht's *Der Kaukasische Kreidekreis (The Caucasian Chalk Circle)* at Deutsches Theater. Germany: Berlin. 1998. Lang.: Ger. 1965
Interview with director Thomas Langhoff. Germany, East. 1970-1990. Lang.: Eng. 2038
Shakespearean production and the GDR's 'existential crisis'. Germany, East. 1976-1980. Lang.: Eng. 2051
Television adaptations of works by Goethe. Germany. 1965-1997. Lang.: Eng. 4061

Langkilde, Nicole Maria
Plays/librettos/scripts
Dramaturgs on recognizing talented new playwrights. Denmark. 1998. Lang.: Dan. 2854

Langlais, Jean-Louis
Performance/production
Guest performance of Théâtre du Plantin, a company for developmentally disabled actors. Hungary: Budapest. 1983-1998. Lang.: Hun. 2081

Language
Performance/production
Theatre as a phenomenon of language. Slovenia. 1997. Lang.: Slo. 590
Sociolinguistics, gender, and the actor. USA. 1997-1998. Lang.: Eng. 642
The use of English and Krio in theatre of Michael Yaarimeh Bangura. Sierra Leone: Freetown. 1960-1998. Lang.: Eng. 2343
Plays/librettos/scripts
The language used by devils in the *York Cycle*. England: York. 1400-1500. Lang.: Eng. 2933
Ibsen, translation, and feminine discourse. Norway. 1888. Lang.: Eng. 3295
Translating Hauptmann's *Die Weber (The Weavers)* into Scots dialect. UK-Scotland: Dundee, Glasgow. 1997. Lang.: Eng. 3513

Language of Their Own, A
Performance/production
Contemporary queer politics and the production of gay and lesbian theatre. USA. 1970-1997. Lang.: Eng. 2710

Lapine, James
Design/technology
Recent work of lighting designer Brian MacDevitt. USA: New York, NY. 1997. Lang.: Eng. 1530
Lighting design for Hwang's *Golden Child* at the Public Theatre. USA: New York, NY. 1996-1998. Lang.: Eng. 1540
Sound design for *The Diary of Anne Frank* directed by James Lapine. USA: New York, NY. 1998. Lang.: Eng. 1553
Performance/production
Collection of newspaper reviews by London theatre critics. UK-England: London. 1998. Lang.: Eng. 2543
Careeer of actress Tsai Chin. USA. 1959-1998. Lang.: Eng. 2754
Plays/librettos/scripts
Reactions to the revised version of *The Diary of Anne Frank*. USA: New York, NY. 1998. Lang.: Eng. 3618

Lapotaire, Jane
Performance/production
Jane Lapotaire on her performance in *Henry VIII* at RSC. UK-England: London, Stratford. 1996-1997. Lang.: Eng. 2619

Laprise, Michel
Performance/production
Michel Laprise's *Masculin/Féminin (Male/Female)*, presented to audiences segregated by sex. Canada: Montreal, PQ. 1998. Lang.: Fre. 1867

Lara Come Home
Performance/production
Collection of newspaper reviews by London theatre critics. UK-England: London. 1998. Lang.: Eng. 2475

Lara, Julia
Performance/production
Collection of newspaper reviews by London theatre critics. UK-England: London. 1998. Lang.: Eng. 2487

Lardner, Ring, Jr.
Basic theatrical documents
Screenplay of *The Fishermen of Beaudrais* by Ring Lardner, Jr., and Dalton Trumbo. USA. 1943-1998. Lang.: Eng. 3891
Plays/librettos/scripts
Interview with screenwriter Ring Lardner, Jr. USA. 1943. Lang.: Eng. 3998
Background on *The Fishermen of Beaudrais* by Ring Lardner, Jr., and Dalton Trumbo. USA. 1943-1998. Lang.: Eng. 4025

Larin, Sergej
Performance/production
Tenor Sergej Larin. Russia. 1959-1998. Lang.: Eng. 4674

Larivière, Isabelle
Design/technology
Costume designer Isabelle Larivière. Canada: Quebec, PQ. 1994-1995. Lang.: Fre. 1514

Larmore, Jennifer
Theory/criticism
Performers and conductors complain about unfair reviews. USA. 1998. Lang.: Eng. 4844

Laroche, Roland
Performance/production
Robert Gurik's adaptation of Shakespeare's *Hamlet*. Canada: Montreal, PQ, London, ON. 1968. Lang.: Fre. 1866

Laroque, Laurette
SEE
Despréz, Jean.

Larroche, Jean-Pierre
Performance/production
The present state of French puppetry. France. 1970-1998. Lang.: Ger. 4892

Larry Sanders Show, The
Plays/librettos/scripts
Analysis of performance art on *The Larry Sanders Show*. USA. 1995. Lang.: Eng. 4079

Larson, Jonathan
Administration
The legal battle over copyright of the musical *Rent*. USA: New York, NY. 1998. Lang.: Eng. 4321
The settlement of a copyright case regarding the musical *Rent*. USA: New York, NY. 1998. Lang.: Eng. 4322
Performance/production
Collection of newspaper reviews by London theatre critics. UK-England: London. 1998. Lang.: Eng. 2561
Review of Jonathan Larson's musical *Rent*. USA: New York, NY. 1990. Lang.: Hun. 4375
Relation to other fields
Quantum theory in recent New York performances. USA: New York, NY. 1995-1996. Lang.: Eng. 794

Larsson, Stefan
Performance/production
Interview with actor/director Stefan Larsson. Sweden: Stockholm. 1984-1998. Lang.: Swe. 2382

Lassalle, Jacques
Institutions
Impressions from the Avignon theatre festival. France: Avignon. 1998. Lang.: Ger. 1612

Last Flapper, The
Performance/production
Collection of newspaper reviews by London theatre critics. UK-England: London. 1998. Lang.: Eng. 2512

Last Meeting of the Knights of the White Magnolia, The
Plays/librettos/scripts
Analysis of Preston Jones's plays about Texas. USA. 1977. Lang.: Eng. 3645

Last Night of Ballyhoo, The
Design/technology
Lighting designer Kenneth Posner. USA. 1998. Lang.: Eng. 1545

Last Picture Show, The
Basic theatrical documents
Screenplay of *The Last Picture Show* by Larry McMurtry and Peter Bogdanovich. USA. 1971. Lang.: Eng. 3897
Plays/librettos/scripts
Larry McMurtry on *The Last Picture Show*. USA. 1971. Lang.: Eng. 4018
Interview with director Peter Bogdanovich. USA. 1971-1998. Lang.: Eng. 4020

Last Post, The
Performance/production
Collection of newspaper reviews by London theatre critics. UK-England: London. 1998. Lang.: Eng. 2463

Last Yankee, The
Design/technology
Set design for Joseph Chaikin's production of two one-acts by Arthur Miller. USA: New york, NY. 1998. Lang.: Eng. 1532

Latchmere Theatre (London)
SEE ALSO
Grace Theatre.
Late Nite Cathechism
Performance/production
Collection of newspaper reviews by London theatre critics. UK-England: London. 1998. Lang.: Eng. 2553
Latinovits Zoltán Játékszín (Veszprém)
Performance/production
András Szigethy's *Kegyelem (Mercy)* directed by László Vándorfi. Hungary: Veszprém. 1998. Lang.: Hun. 2105
Latvijas Dailes Teatris (Riga)
Institutions
Profile of Latvijas Dailes Teatris. Latvia: Riga. 1997. Lang.: Swe, Eng, Ger. 1676
Latvijas Nacionala Opera (Riga)
Institutions
Report on a visit to Riga's theatres. Latvia: Riga. 1997. Lang.: Swe, Eng, Ger. 369
Latvijas Nacionalais Teatris (Riga)
Institutions
Report on a visit to Riga's theatres. Latvia: Riga. 1997. Lang.: Swe, Eng, Ger. 369
Latvijas Valsio Lellu Teatris (Riga)
Institutions
Report on a visit to Riga's theatres. Latvia: Riga. 1997. Lang.: Swe, Eng, Ger. 369
Laufenberg, Uwe Eric
Performance/production
Premieres of new plays. Austria: Vienna. 1998. Lang.: Ger. 1820
Political changes reflected in Berlin theatre productions. Germany: Berlin. 1998. Lang.: Ger. 1958
Shakespeare productions in German Switzerland. Switzerland: Basel, Zurich. 1996-1997. Lang.: Ger. 2398
Laughton, Charles
Performance/production
Actor Charles Laughton. UK-England: London. USA: Hollywood, CA. 1899-1962. Lang.: Eng. 2632
Actors' interpretations of the title role in Oscar Wilde's *The Canterville Ghost*. UK-England. USA. 1943-1998. Lang.: Eng. 4066
Laurents, Arthur
Performance/production
Collection of newspaper reviews by London theatre critics. UK-England: London. 1998. Lang.: Eng. 2516
Plays/librettos/scripts
The creation of the musical *Gypsy*. USA: New York, NY. 1956-1959. Lang.: Eng. 4399
Lauten, Flora
Institutions
Profile of Teatro Buendía. Cuba: Havana. 1986-1998. Lang.: Ger. 1596
Performance/production
Collection of newspaper reviews by London theatre critics. UK-England: London. 1998. Lang.: Eng. 2477
Lauterbach, Konstanze
Performance/production
German directors about the meaning of Brecht today. Germany. 1998. Lang.: Ger. 1948
German productions of contemporary Russian drama. Germany. 1998. Lang.: Ger. 1984
Lauwers, Jan
Theory/criticism
Artaud's theatre of cruelty and contemporary experimental theatre. France. 1945-1998. Lang.: Ger. 3818
Lava
Performance/production
Interview with director Richard Foreman. USA: New York, NY. 1975-1990. Lang.: Eng. 2700
Lavaudant, Georges
Performance/production
French productions of German plays. France. 1998. Lang.: Ger. 1935
Lavelli, Jorge
Performance/production
Jorge Lavelli's production of *Sei personaggi in cerca d'autore (Six Characters in Search of an Author)* by Pirandello. France: Paris. 1925-1998. Lang.: Ita. 1921
Lavery, Bryony
Plays/librettos/scripts
Shakespeare and the feminist theatre of Bryony Lavery and Jane Prendergast. UK-England. 1997. Lang.: Eng. 3439
Lavia, Gabriele
Performance/production
Gabriele Lavia's production of *Non si sa come (How Is Unknown)* by Luigi Pirandello. Italy: Turin. 1982-1988. Lang.: Ita. 2157
Lavrík, Silvester
Plays/librettos/scripts
New direction in Czech playwriting. Czech Republic. 1990-1997. Lang.: Cze. 2850
Lavrovskij, Michajl
Performance/production
The Budapest Opera House's new production of *Giselle*. Hungary: Budapest. 1998. Lang.: Hun. 1094
Lawlor, Joe
Performance/production
Collection of newspaper reviews by London theatre critics. UK-England: London. 1998. Lang.: Eng. 2565
Lawrence, David Herbert
Plays/librettos/scripts
Beckett's *Happy Days* as a rewriting of *Lady Chatterley's Lover*. France. Ireland. UK-England. 1961. Lang.: Eng. 3120
Analysis of plays based on the Hebrew prophets. USA. Europe. 1919-1970. Lang.: Eng. 3659
Lawrence, William G.
Performance/production
Collection of newspaper reviews by London theatre critics. UK-England: London. 1998. Lang.: Eng. 2457
Lawson, Denis
Performance/production
Collection of newspaper reviews by London theatre critics. UK-England: London. 1998. Lang.: Eng. 2544
Lawson, John Howard
Institutions
The New Playwrights Theatre Company. USA: New York, NY. 1927-1929. Lang.: Eng. 410
Plays/librettos/scripts
Analysis of *Processional* by John Howard Lawson. USA. 1925. Lang.: Eng. 3535
Lawson, Sarah
Performance/production
Collection of newspaper reviews by London theatre critics. UK-England: London. 1998. Lang.: Eng. 2490
Lázár, Kati
Performance/production
Interview with actress Kati Lázár. Hungary. 1998. Lang.: Hun. 2062
Lazarjév, Aleksand'r
Institutions
The Bolšoj Ballet and the experimental company Gelikon. Russia: Moscow. 1997. Lang.: Swe. 4467
Lazarus Laughed
Performance/production
A rare production of Eugene O'Neill's *Lazarus Laughed*. USA: Detroit, MI. 1963. Lang.: Eng. 2673
Le Bonnieck, Yann
Basic theatrical documents
Text of *L'Ascenseur (The Elevator)* by Gérard Levoyer. France. 1984-1987. Lang.: Fre. 1431
Le Coz, André
Relation to other fields
Theatre photographer André Le Coz. Canada: Montreal, PQ. 1952-1998. Lang.: Fre. 3738
le Mar, Angie
Performance/production
Collection of newspaper reviews by London theatre critics. UK-England: London. 1998. Lang.: Eng. 2475
Le Valois d'Orville, Adrien-Joseph
Performance/production
Photographic essay of Rameau's *Platée* directed and choreographed by Mark Morris. USA: Berkeley, CA. 1998. Lang.: Eng. 4304
Leacock, George
Performance/production
Interview with *mas* music performer George Leacock. Trinidad and Tobago. 1923-1998. Lang.: Eng. 4167
League of Off Broadway Theatres and Producers (New York, NY)
Administration
Report on Equity's Off-Broadway contract agreement. USA. 1998. Lang.: Eng. 60
League of Resident Theatres (LORT, New York, NY)
Administration
Study of management in regional theatres. USA. 1987-1988. Lang.: Eng. 140

Leander, Harald
Institutions
Profile of Teater 23. Sweden: Malmö. 1959-1998. Lang.: Swe. 1727
Lebedinaja pesnija (Swan Song, The)
Basic theatrical documents
Catalan translations of the complete plays of Anton Čechov. Russia. 1884-1904. Lang.: Cat. 1449
Lebedinojė osero (Swan Lake)
Design/technology
Rapid on-stage costume changes in dance. Russia. Sweden. Japan. 1840-1998. Lang.: Swe. 889
Interview with lighting designer Rick Fisher. UK-England. 1998. Lang.: Eng. 1030
Technical designs for Matthew Bourne's productions of ballets by Čajkovskij and Prokofjėv. UK-England: London. 1998. Lang.: Eng. 1031
Performance/production
Nureyev's *Swan Lake* at Staatsoper. Austria: Vienna. 1998. Lang.: Hun. 1064
Analysis of choreographies of Matthew Bourne. UK-England: London. 1996-1997. Lang.: Eng. 1157
Matthew Bourne's choreography for *Swan Lake*. UK-England. 1998. Lang.: Eng. 1159
Leben des Galilei (Life of Galileo, The)
Performance/production
Review of Brazilian performances of plays by Brecht. Brazil: São Paulo. 1998. Lang.: Ger. 1832
Irondale Ensemble's production of *Leben des Galilei (The Life of Galileo)* by Bertolt Brecht. Canada: Halifax, NS. 1998. Lang.: Eng. 1869
Reviews of productions of plays by Brecht. Germany. 1998. Lang.: Ger. 1986
Recent productions of plays by Bertolt Brecht. Germany. 1997-1998. Lang.: Ger. 2028
Giorgio Strehler's productions of plays by Bertolt Brecht. Italy: Milan. 1956-1998. Lang.: Swe. 2171
Plays/librettos/scripts
The rebel in modern drama. Europe. 1950-1988. Lang.: Eng. 3053
Brecht's *Leben des Galilei (The Life of Galileo)* as an adaptation of Shakespeare's *Hamlet*. Germany. 1600-1932. Lang.: Eng. 3160
Leben Eduards des Zweiten von England (Edward the Second)
Basic theatrical documents
Catalan translations of plays by Bertolt Brecht (volume 1). Germany. 1919-1954. Lang.: Cat. 1437
Lebensraum
Basic theatrical documents
French translation of *Lebensraum* by Israel Horovitz. USA. France. 1996-1997. Lang.: Fre. 1488
Performance/production
Collection of newspaper reviews by London theatre critics. UK-England: London. 1998. Lang.: Eng. 2466
LeBlanc, Émilie
Plays/librettos/scripts
Women and Acadian theatre. Canada. 1870-1998. Lang.: Eng. 2810
Leblanc, Jacques
Performance/production
Interview with actor Jacques Leblanc. Canada: Quebec, PQ. 1980-1998. Lang.: Fre. 1853
Lebow, Barbara
Plays/librettos/scripts
The survivor character in contemporary American drama. USA. 1970-1997. Lang.: Eng. 3600
Lecat, Jean-Guy
Design/technology
Set designer Jean-Guy Lecat and his work with Peter Brook. France. Denmark. 1975-1998. Lang.: Dan. 182
Leclerc, Francis
Plays/librettos/scripts
Francis Leclerc's video adaptation of *Les Sept Branches de la Rivière Ota (The Seven Streams of the River Ota)* by Robert Lepage. Canada. 1998. Lang.: Fre. 4074
LeClercq, Tanaquil
Performance/production
Interviews with dancers about performance. UK-England. USA. Cuba. 1942-1989. Lang.: Eng. 1162
LeClerq, Tanaquil
Performance/production
Ballerina Tanaquil LeClerq on working with choreographer Jerome Robbins. USA. 1940-1998. Lang.: Eng. 1185
LeCompte, Elizabeth
Performance/production
Analysis of the Wooster Group's *Fish Story* directed by Elizabeth LeCompte. USA: New York, NY. 1990-1996. Lang.: Eng. 2667
Analysis of recent New York productions. USA: New York, NY. 1997-1998. Lang.: Eng. 2759
Lecouvreur, Adrienne
Performance/production
Letters of actress Adrienne Lecouvreur. France. 1720-1730. Lang.: Ita. 1940
Ledergeschicht (Leatherface)
Performance/production
Collection of newspaper reviews by London theatre critics. UK-England: London. 1998. Lang.: Eng. 2582
Ledermann spricht mit Hubert Fichte, Der (Tanner Is Speaking with Hubert Fichte, The)
Plays/librettos/scripts
Homosexuality on the German stage. Germany. 1920-1980. Lang.: Eng. 3147
Ledi Makbet Mtsenskogo Uezda
Plays/librettos/scripts
Analysis of Šostakovič's opera *Ledi Makbet Mtsenskogo Uezda*. USSR. 1930-1932. Lang.: Eng. 4829
Ledoux, Paul
Plays/librettos/scripts
Young People's Theatre's adaptation of *Anne of Green Gables*. Canada: Toronto, ON. 1911-1998. Lang.: Eng. 2832
Ledovskaja, Natalija
Performance/production
Ballerina Natalija Ledovskaja. Russia: Moscow. 1998. Lang.: Rus. 1136
Lee, Chris
Performance/production
Collection of newspaper reviews by London theatre critics. UK-England: London. 1998. Lang.: Eng. 2506
Lee, Don L.
SEE
Madhubuti, Haki R.
Lee, Eugene
Design/technology
Technical designs for *Ragtime* at the Ford Center. USA: New York, NY. 1998. Lang.: Eng. 4338
Eugene Lee's set design for Frank Galati's production of *Ragtime*. USA. 1997-1998. Lang.: Eng. 4340
Lee, Jenny
Performance/production
Collection of newspaper reviews by London theatre critics. UK-England: London. 1998. Lang.: Eng. 2577
Lee, John
Performance/production
Collection of newspaper reviews by London theatre critics. UK-England: London. 1998. Lang.: Eng. 2472
Lee, Lewis
Design/technology
The 1998 TCI awards. USA. 1998. Lang.: Eng. 243
Lee, Maryat
Performance/production
Maryat Lee and the creation of the street theatre piece *Dope!*. USA: New York, NY. 1949-1951. Lang.: Eng. 663
Lee, Ming Cho
Design/technology
Creativity and beauty in theatrical design. USA. 1998. Lang.: Eng. 322
Lee, Nathaniel
Plays/librettos/scripts
Recognition, repression, and ideology in Restoration drama. England: London. 1660-1680. Lang.: Eng. 2918
Lee, Ralph
Performance/production
Profile of master puppeteer Ralph Lee. USA. 1974-1998. Lang.: Eng. 4906
Lee, Rosemary
Performance/production
Dancer/choreographer Rosemary Lee. UK-England: London. 1989-1998. Lang.: Eng. 1307
Lee, Spike
Performance/production
Spike Lee's unsuccessful efforts to film parts of *Malcolm X* in Mecca. USA. 1992-1995. Lang.: Eng. 3954
Plays/librettos/scripts
Analysis of Spike Lee's film *Do the Right Thing*. USA. 1989. Lang.: Eng. 4017

Lee, Youn Taek
Performance/production
Report from a symposium on traditional Korean theatre. Korea. Germany: Berlin. 1980-1998. Lang.: Ger, Fre, Dut, Eng. 2196
Leech, Richard
Theory/criticism
Performers and conductors complain about unfair reviews. USA. 1998. Lang.: Eng. 4844
Lefevre, Robin
Performance/production
Collection of newspaper reviews by London theatre critics. UK-England: London. 1998. Lang.: Eng. 2451
Collection of newspaper reviews by London theatre critics. UK-England. 1998. Lang.: Eng. 2510
Collection of newspaper reviews by London theatre critics. UK-England: London. 1998. Lang.: Eng. 2578
Lefton, Sue
Performance/production
Collection of newspaper reviews by London theatre critics. UK-England: London. 1998. Lang.: Eng. 2486
Collection of newspaper reviews by London theatre critics. UK-England: London. 1998. Lang.: Eng. 2584
Legacy
Performance/production
Collection of newspaper reviews by London theatre critics. UK-England: London. 1998. Lang.: Eng. 2570
Legal aspects
Administration
Round-table on author's rights. Hungary. 1990-1998. Lang.: Hun. 16
Methods of organization-building in the arts. Netherlands. 1998. Lang.: Dut. 18
Early American anti-theatrical legislation. USA. 1770-1830. Lang.: Eng. 33
Gender and the career advancement of arts managers. USA. 1996. Lang.: Eng. 35
Equity's support of air-rights proposal of Broadway Initiative. USA. 1998. Lang.: Eng. 53
Effect on Actors Federal Credit Unions of a recent Supreme Court ruling. USA: New York, NY. 1998. Lang.: Eng. 67
Complaints against an Equity Councillor and the 1998 Council election. USA: New York, NY. 1998. Lang.: Eng. 87
The debate on organizing non-union tours of theatrical production. USA: New York, NY. 1998. Lang.: Eng. 88
City Council's approval of a plan to sell theatres' air rights to developers. USA: New York, NY. 1998. Lang.: Eng. 89
The cancellation of Kansas University's cultural exchange program with Eastern Europe. USA: Lawrence, KS. Europe. 1964-1969. Lang.: Eng. 131
Financially troubled Ohio ballet companies. USA: Cleveland, OH, Akron, OH. 1998. Lang.: Eng. 1027
The First Amendment and the striptease dancer. USA. 1998. Lang.: Eng. 4271
The legal battle over copyright of the musical *Rent*. USA: New York, NY. 1998. Lang.: Eng. 4321
The settlement of a copyright case regarding the musical *Rent*. USA: New York, NY. 1998. Lang.: Eng. 4322
Institutions
Popular entertainment at the New Haven Assembly Hall and Columbian Museum and Gardens. USA: New Haven, CT. 1796-1820. Lang.: Eng. 394
The Shuberts vs. the Syndicate. USA: New York, NY. 1976-1998. Lang.: Eng. 427
Performance/production
Analysis of Todd Solondz' film *Happiness*. USA. 1998. Lang.: Eng. 3949
The police and John Cage's *Europeras 1 and 2* at Frankfurter Theater. Germany: Frankfurt. 1987. Lang.: Eng. 4586
Plays/librettos/scripts
Analysis of *The Clandestine Marriage* by David Garrick. England. 1766. Lang.: Eng. 2926
Possible censorship of *The Tragedy of Philotas* by Samuel Daniel. England. 1605. Lang.: Eng. 2996
Political context of Charles Johnson's *Love in a Forest*, an adaptation of *As You Like It*. England. 1723. Lang.: Eng. 3013
Prejudice and law in Shakespeare's *The Merchant of Venice*. England. 1596. Lang.: Eng. 3027
Martial law and Renaissance drama and fiction. Europe. 1563-1753. Lang.: Eng. 3059
Relation to other fields
The changing face of Times Square and its effect on the local community. USA: New York, NY. 1998. Lang.: Eng. 812
Medieval religious theatre and the public safety. Germany. 1234-1656. Lang.: Eng. 3771
The upcoming Supreme Court hearing on the government's right to impose decency standards on arts grants. USA: Washington, DC. 1998. Lang.: Eng. 3793
LeGallienne, Eva
Plays/librettos/scripts
Feminism and plays of Henrik Ibsen. Norway. 1879-1979. Lang.: Eng. 3293
Legault, Émile
Institutions
Analysis of the bulletin of theatre company Les Compagnons du Saint-Laurent. Canada: Montreal, PQ. 1944-1947. Lang.: Fre. 1585
Relation to other fields
Amateur art theatre produced by Quebec priests. Canada: Montreal, PQ. 1930-1950. Lang.: Fre. 3733
Legend of the Invisible City of Kitezh, The
SEE
Skazanie o nevidimom grade Kiteže.
Legenda o svetem Che (Legend of Saint Che, The)
Plays/librettos/scripts
Analysis of plays by Primož Kozak. Slovenia. 1959-1969. Lang.: Slo. 3350
Legendary Golem, The
Performance/production
Collection of newspaper reviews by London theatre critics. UK-England: London. 1998. Lang.: Eng. 2552
Légende du manuel sacré, La (Legend of the Sacred Handbook, The)
Performance/production
Director and martial artist Huy-Phong Doàn's *La Légende du manuel sacré (The Legend of the Sacred Handbook)*. Canada: Montreal, PQ. 1992-1998. Lang.: Fre. 4118
Legge, Walter
Performance/production
Interview with singer Nicolai Gedda. UK-England: London. Germany, West: Munich. 1952-1984. Lang.: Swe. 4859
Lehár, Franz
Performance/production
Personal recollection of composer Franz Lehár. Austria: Vienna. 1936. Lang.: Swe. 4852
Lehmann, Lilli
Performance/production
Wagnerian soprano Lilli Lehmann. Germany. 1848-1929. Lang.: Eng. 4587
Lehr, Wendy
Design/technology
Costume design for a new version of *Peter Pan* at Children's Theatre Company. USA: Minneapolis, MN. 1998. Lang.: Eng. 4330
Lehrer, Scott
Design/technology
Professional theatrical designers on design training. USA. 1998. Lang.: Eng. 252
Leigh, Mike
Performance/production
Collection of newspaper reviews by London theatre critics. UK-England: London. 1998. Lang.: Eng. 2537
Leight, Warren
Basic theatrical documents
Text of *Side Man* by Warren Leight. USA. 1998. Lang.: Eng. 1494
Leimbach, Frank
Design/technology
Set and costume designer Frank Leimbach and his work with choreographers. Germany. 1991-1998. Lang.: Ger. 1247
Leka med elden (Playing with Fire)
Institutions
Report on the Stockholm theatre festival. Sweden: Stockholm. 1998. Lang.: Eng. 1724
Lekatompessy, Nels
Performance/production
The work of Theatergroep Delta. Netherlands: Amsterdam. 1983-1998. Lang.: Dut. 2200
Lemmons, Kasi
Basic theatrical documents
Screenplay of *Eve's Bayou* by Kasi Lemmons. USA. 1994-1998. Lang.: Eng. 3892

Lemmons, Kasi — cont'd
Plays/librettos/scripts
Interview with screenwriter and director Kasi Lemmons. USA. 1994-1998. Lang.: Eng. 4000
Lemon, Ralph
Design/technology
Design concept for Ralph Lemon's dance piece *Geography* at BAM. USA: New York, NY. 1998. Lang.: Eng. 1248
Lendvai, Zoltán
Performance/production
Turgenjév's *Mesjac v derevne (A Month in the Country)* directed by Zoltán Lendvar. Hungary: Kecskemét. 1998. Lang.: Hun. 2134
Léner, András
Performance/production
Review of *Édes Anna (Anna Édes)*, Madách Chamber Theatre. Hungary: Budapest. 1997. Lang.: Hun. 2136
Léner, Péter
Administration
Interview with director Péter Léner of József Attila Theatre. Hungary: Budapest. 1960-1998. Lang.: Hun. 15
Lengyel, György
Performance/production
Miklós Hubay's *Hová lett a rózsa lelke? (What Has Become of the Spirit of the Rose?)* directed by György Lengyel. Hungary: Debrecen. 1998. Lang.: Hun. 2150
Lenkeit, Antje
Institutions
New plays by Dea Loher at Staatsschauspiel Hannover. Germany: Hannover. 1992-1998. Lang.: Ger. 1643
Lenkom (Moscow)
SEE
Teat'r im. Leninskogo Komsomola.
Lennartz, Monika
Performance/production
Shakespearean production and the GDR's 'existential crisis'. Germany, East. 1976-1980. Lang.: Eng. 2051
Leno, Jay
Plays/librettos/scripts
Analysis of performance art on *The Larry Sanders Show*. USA. 1995. Lang.: Eng. 4079
Lenya, Lotte
Performance/production
Erwin Piscator and Brecht's *Schwejk im zweiten Weltkrieg (Schweik in the Second World War)*. Germany: Berlin. 1928. Lang.: Ger. 1952
Brecht and the vocal role. Germany. 1920-1998. Lang.: Swe. 4295
The career of soprano Lotte Lenya. Austria: Vienna. 1898-1981. Lang.: Eng. 4352
Excerpts from critical reviews of singer and actress Lotte Lenya. Germany. 1928-1966. Lang.: Eng. 4354
Friends and colleagues recall singer Lotte Lenya. Germany. 1928-1981. Lang.: Eng. 4355
Lotte Lenya's singing style. Germany. 1929-1965. Lang.: Eng. 4357
Lenz, Johann Michael Reinhold
Plays/librettos/scripts
Power, gender relations, and communication in German drama. Germany. 1776-1989. Lang.: Ger. 3138
Leo Kreielsheimer Theatre (Seattle, WA)
Performance spaces
Seattle's new and renovated theatres. USA: Seattle, WA. 1998. Lang.: Eng. 475
Leo, Trish
Performance/production
Collection of newspaper reviews by London theatre critics. UK-England: London. 1998. Lang.: Eng. 2568
Leon, Kenny
Performance/production
Interview with actress Phylicia Rashad. USA: Atlanta, GA. 1998. Lang.: Eng. 2695
Leonard, Elmore
Basic theatrical documents
Screenplay of *Out of Sight* by Scott Frank. USA. 1998. Lang.: Eng. 3884
Performance/production
Steven Soderbergh on directing *Out of Sight*. USA. 1998. Lang.: Eng. 3944
Plays/librettos/scripts
Interview with screenwriter Scott Frank. USA. 1998. Lang.: Eng. 3995
Leoncavallo, Ruggiero
Performance/production
Opera director Katja Czellnik. Germany: Oldenburg, Kiel. 1996-1998. Lang.: Ger. 4583
Leonce und Lena (Leonce and Lena)
Performance/production
Andreas Kriegenburg's production of Büchner's *Leonce und Lena*. Germany: Munich. 1998. Lang.: Ger. 2020
Relation to other fields
Manfred Weber on directing Děvad Karahasan's translation of *Leonce und Lena* by Büchner. Bosnia: Sarajevo. 1997-1998. Lang.: Ger. 3730
Leonidov, Lenid M.
Performance/production
Actor Lenid Leonidov. Russia: Moscow. 1873-1941. Lang.: Rus. 2312
Lepage, Robert
Design/technology
Costume designer Isabelle Larivière. Canada: Quebec, PQ. 1994-1995. Lang.: Fre. 1514
Set design for Robert Lepage's *Geometry of Miracles*. Canada: Quebec, PQ. 1998. Lang.: Eng. 1516
Institutions
Productions of Salzburger Festspiele. Austria: Salzburg. 1998. Lang.: Ger. 1571
Robert Lepage and his experimental company Ex Machina. Canada: Quebec, PQ. 1998. Lang.: Fre. 1587
Shakespearean productions at the Carrefour international theatre festival. Canada: Quebec, PQ. 1998. Lang.: Fre. 1588
Performance/production
Robert Lepage's *Geometry of Miracles* at the Salzburg Festival. Austria: Salzburg. 1998. Lang.: Ger. 1824
The methodology of director Robert Lepage. Canada: Toronto, ON. 1992. Lang.: Eng. 1845
French Canadian translations/adaptations of Shakespeare. Canada: Montreal, PQ. 1988. Lang.: Fre. 1855
Interviews with actors Lil Terselius and Björn Granath. Sweden: Stockholm. 1998. Lang.: Swe. 2381
Interview with director Robert Lepage. Sweden: Stockholm. Canada: Montreal, PQ. 1997. Lang.: Swe. 2397
Collection of newspaper reviews by London theatre critics. UK-England: London. 1998. Lang.: Eng. 2409
Reviews of recent London performances. UK-England: London. 1998. Lang.: Ger. 2591
Modernist and postmodernist Shakespearean production. UK-England. Canada. 1966-1996. Lang.: Eng. 2618
Cinematic work of director Robert Lepage. Canada. 1995-1998. Lang.: Fre. 3928
Plays/librettos/scripts
Francis Leclerc's video adaptation of *Les Sept Branches de la Rivière Ota (The Seven Streams of the River Ota)* by Robert Lepage. Canada. 1998. Lang.: Fre. 4074
Relation to other fields
References to film in theatre of Robert Lepage. Canada. 1990-1998. Lang.: Fre. 3734
Theory/criticism
Report on a seminar for young theatre critics. Canada: Quebec, PQ. 1998. Lang.: Swe. 3809
Critical response to *Elsineur (Elsinore)*, Robert Lepage's multimedia adaptation of *Hamlet*. Canada. 1995-1996. Lang.: Eng. 3810
Lepeu, Monique
Relation to other fields
Author Gertrude Stein, subject of *Gertrude morte cet après-midi (Gertrude Dead This Afternoon)* by Monique Lepeu. France: Paris. 1874-1997. Lang.: Fre. 3759
Leret, Xavier
Performance/production
Collection of newspaper reviews by London theatre critics. UK-England: London. 1998. Lang.: Eng. 2507
Collection of newspaper reviews by London theatre critics. UK-England: London. 1998. Lang.: Eng. 2566
Lerner, Alan Jay
Plays/librettos/scripts
Popular adaptations of the works of George Bernard Shaw. UK-England. 1890-1990. Lang.: Eng. 3445
Fairy-tale heroines in American drama and musical theatre. USA. 1945-1965. Lang.: Eng. 3617
Lerner, Avi
Administration
Profile of B-movie producer Avi Lerner. Israel. 1972-1998. Lang.: Eng. 3871
Lesage, Marie-Christine
Theory/criticism
Round-table discussion on theatre and impurity. Canada: Quebec, PQ. 1998. Lang.: Fre. 835

Lesbian Play for Lucy, A
Performance/production
Contemporary queer politics and the production of gay and lesbian theatre. USA. 1970-1997. Lang.: Eng. 2710

Lesbian theatre
Performance/production
Lois Weaver's *Faith and Dancing* and the CD-ROM in interactive performance. UK-England. USA. 1996. Lang.: Eng. 971
Contemporary queer politics and the production of gay and lesbian theatre. USA. 1970-1997. Lang.: Eng. 2710
Lesbianism and performer Mary Martin. USA. 1913-1990. Lang.: Eng. 2757
Profile of the satiric comedy troupe Five Lesbian Brothers. USA: New York, NY. 1989-1998. Lang.: Eng. 4282
Paula Klimper and Wende Persons' opera *Patience and Sarah*. USA. 1969-1998. Lang.: Eng. 4725
Plays/librettos/scripts
The current state of Australian gay and lesbian theatre. Australia. 1990-1998. Lang.: Eng. 2775

Lešji (Wood Demon, The)
Basic theatrical documents
Catalan translations of the complete plays of Anton Čechov. Russia. 1884-1904. Lang.: Cat. 1449
Performance/production
Analysis of Čechov's *Platonov* and *Lešji (The Wood Demon)*. Russia. 1878-1889. Lang.: Eng. 2297

Leskinen, Esa
Performance/production
Interview with director Esa Leskinen. Finland. 1998. Lang.: Fin. 1916

Leskov, Nikolaj
Performance/production
Csaba Kiss's adaptation and direction of *Lady Macbeth of the Provinces* by Leskov. Hungary: Budapest. 1998. Lang.: Hun. 2138

Leslie, Struan
Performance/production
Collection of newspaper reviews by London theatre critics. UK-England: London. 1998. Lang.: Eng. 2432

Lessing, Gotthold Ephraim
Institutions
The ninetieth anniversary of Staatstheater Cottbus. Germany: Cottbus. 1908-1998. Lang.: Ger. 1645
Slovene self-image and the national theatre. Slovenia. Germany. 1789-1867. Lang.: Slo. 1719
Plays/librettos/scripts
Lessing's *Emilia Galotti* and reader-response criticism. Germany. 1772. Lang.: Eng. 3166
Female sacrifice in eighteenth-century German drama. Germany. 1772-1781. Lang.: Eng. 3167
Representation of the virginal body on the German stage. Germany. 1600-1800. Lang.: Ger. 3171
Theory/criticism
Tragic theories of G.E. Lessing. Germany. 1760-1780. Lang.: Eng. 3822

Lesson from Aloes, A
Plays/librettos/scripts
The influence of Albert Camus on playwright Athol Fugard. South Africa, Republic of. 1960-1985. Lang.: Eng. 3362

Lester, Chuck
Design/technology
Lighting the 24-hour television event: QVC home shopping network. USA: West Chester, PA. 1998. Lang.: Eng. 4055

Let the Artists Die
SEE
Niech sczezną artyści.

Letters, or Where Does the Postman Go When All the Street Names Are Changed
Performance/production
The development of *Letters, or Where Does the Postman Go When All the Street Names Are Changed*, based on experiences of residents of Mostar. Bosnia-Herzegovina: Mostar. 1997. Lang.: Eng. 1831

Levant, Inge
Performance/production
Opera director Inge Levant. Germany: Stuttgart. 1959-1998. Lang.: Ger. 4611

Leveaux, David
Performance/production
Notable productions of plays by Eugene O'Neill. USA. 1916-1996. Lang.: Eng. 2752

Levi, Primo
Performance/production
Gianfranco De Bosio's production of *Se questo è un uomo (If This Is a Man)* by Primo Levi. Italy: Turin. 1963-1966. Lang.: Eng. 2168

Leviathan
Institutions
New plays by Dea Loher at Staatsschauspiel Hannover. Germany: Hannover. 1992-1998. Lang.: Ger. 1643
Plays/librettos/scripts
Marginal notes by Dea Loher on her plays. Germany. 1991-1998. Lang.: Ger. 3162

Levin, David
Performance/production
Productions of the Bad Hersfelder Festspiele. Germany: Bad Hersfeld. 1998. Lang.: Ger. 1991

Levin, Marc
Basic theatrical documents
Screenplay of the film *Slam*. USA. 1998. Lang.: Eng. 3893
Plays/librettos/scripts
Interview with creators of the film *Slam*. USA. 1998. Lang.: Eng. 4001

Levine, James
Design/technology
Lighting designer Jennifer Tipton. USA: New York, NY. 1998. Lang.: Eng. 4441

Levine, Michael
Design/technology
Opera scenographer Michael Levine. Canada: Toronto, ON. 1988-1998. Lang.: Eng. 4426

Levinson, Barry
Plays/librettos/scripts
David Mamet's success as a screenwriter and film director. USA. 1998. Lang.: Eng. 4003

Levitow, Roberta
Performance/production
Statements of women directors on their work. USA. 1996. Lang.: Eng. 2674

Levoyer, Gérard
Basic theatrical documents
Text of *Mendiants d'amour (Beggars of Love)* by Gérard Levoyer. France. 1998. Lang.: Fre. 1430
Text of *L'Ascenseur (The Elevator)* by Gérard Levoyer. France. 1984-1987. Lang.: Fre. 1431

Levy, Jacques
Performance/production
Collection of newspaper reviews by London theatre critics. UK-England: London. 1998. Lang.: Eng. 2525

Levy, Marvin David
Plays/librettos/scripts
Marvin David Levy's operatic adaptation of *Mourning Becomes Electra* by Eugene O'Neill. USA. 1931-1998. Lang.: Eng. 4827

Lewin, Alex
Basic theatrical documents
Screenplay for *Weeds* by Alex Lewin, winner of annual student screenplay competition. USA. 1998. Lang.: Eng. 3894

Lewis, Clive Staples
Performance/production
Collection of newspaper reviews by London theatre critics. UK-England: Stratford. 1998. Lang.: Eng. 2519

Lewis, David
Basic theatrical documents
Text of *Sperm Wars* by David Lewis. UK-England. 1998. Lang.: Eng. 1476
Performance/production
Collection of newspaper reviews by London theatre critics. UK-England: London. 1998. Lang.: Eng. 2505
Collection of newspaper reviews by London theatre critics. UK-England: London. 1998. Lang.: Eng. 2569

Lewis, Robert
Institutions
Interview with Robert Lewis on the founding of Actors Studio. USA: New York, NY. 1997. Lang.: Eng. 1766
Performance/production
The idea of Hollywood in theatre autobiographies. USA. 1950-1990. Lang.: Eng. 665

Lewis, Shari
Performance/production
Obituary for TV puppeteer Shari Lewis. USA. 1933-1998. Lang.: Eng. 4909

Leyador (Reader)
Performance/production
Collection of newspaper reviews by London theatre critics. UK-England: London. 1998. Lang.: Eng. 2577

Lézarde (Paris)
Institutions
Interview with playwright, director, and film-maker Xavier Durringer. France: Paris. 1988-1998. Lang.: Ger. 1609
Liabilities
Administration
Securing sick pay and worker's compensation for an on-the-job injury. USA: New York, NY. 1998. Lang.: Eng. 93
Liang, Edward
Performance/production
New male dancers of New York City Ballet. USA: New York, NY. 1998. Lang.: Eng. 1177
Liberovici, Andrea
Performance/production
Andrea Liberovici's production of *Sonetto. Un travestimento shakespeariano (Sonnet: A Shakespearean Travesty)* by Eduardo Sanguineti. Italy: Genoa. 1997. Lang.: Ita. 2159
Libraries
SEE
Archives/libraries.
Librettos
Basic theatrical documents
Complete libretto of Alban Berg's *Lulu.* Austria. 1935. Lang.: Fre, Ger. 4412
Text of libretto for *Beatrice Chancy.* Canada: Toronto, ON. 1998. Lang.: Eng. 4413
Libretto of *Lakmé* by Léo Delibes, Edmond Gondinet, and Philippe Gille. France. 1883. Lang.: Fre. 4415
Libretto to Massenet's opera *Hérodiade.* France. 1881. Lang.: Fre. 4416
The libretto to Jules Massenet's *Le Roi de Lahore.* France. 1877. Lang.: Fre. 4417
Text of Offenbach's *Orphée aux Enfers.* France. 1874. Lang.: Fre. 4418
Max Meyerfeld's libretto for Zemlinsky's opera *Eine florentinische Tragödie.* Germany. 1917. Lang.: Ger, Fre. 4419
Klaren's librettos for *Der Zwerg* by Alexander Zemlinsky. Germany. 1922. Lang.: Fre, Ger. 4420
Gaetano Rossini's libretto for Gioacchino Rossini's *Semiramide.* Italy. 1823. Lang.: Fre, Ita. 4421
Jonathan Golove's opera *Red Harvest.* USA. 1940-1950. Lang.: Eng. 4422
Libretto for *Christina, Queen of Sweden.* USA. 1988. Lang.: Eng. 4423
Libussa
Institutions
Peter Stein's last season as director at the Salzburg Festival. Austria: Salzburg. 1997. Lang.: Eng. 336
Plays/librettos/scripts
The image of motherhood in German-language drama. Austria. Germany. 1890-1910. Lang.: Ger. 2787
Lidská tragikomedie (Human Tragicomedy)
Performance/production
Review of plays directed by Árpad Schilling. Hungary: Budapest. 1998. Lang.: Hun. 2085
Lidström, Kerstin
Institutions
Criticism of Svenska Bakettskolan. Sweden: Stockholm. 1984. Lang.: Swe. 1049
Lie of the Mind, A
Plays/librettos/scripts
Female presence/absence in plays of O'Neill, Pinter, and Shepard. USA. UK-England. 1936-1985. Lang.: Eng. 3607
Language in the plays of Sam Shepard. USA. 1967-1985. Lang.: Eng. 3694
Liebeneiner, Wolfgang
Performance/production
Television adaptations of works by Goethe. Germany. 1965-1997. Lang.: Eng. 4061
Lieberman, Edith
Plays/librettos/scripts
Analysis of historical drama of the holocaust. USA. Canada. Germany. 1950-1980. Lang.: Eng. 3610
Lieberman, Harold
Plays/librettos/scripts
Analysis of historical drama of the holocaust. USA. Canada. Germany. 1950-1980. Lang.: Eng. 3610
Lied der Heimat, Das (Song of the Homeland, The)
Plays/librettos/scripts
Thomas Hürlimann's *Das Lied der Heimat (The Song of the Homeland)* and its production by Werner Düggelin. Switzerland: Zurich. 1998. Lang.: Ger. 3417
Lieder
Performance/production
Reviews of *Lieder* recordings. USA. Slovenia. Austria. 1998. Lang.: Eng. 4720
Lietuvos Nacionalinis Teatras (Vilnius)
Institutions
The theatres of Vilnius. Lithuania: Vilnius. 1993-1998. Lang.: Swe, Eng, Ger. 370
Lietuvos Valstybinis Operos ir Baleto Teatro (Vilnius)
Design/technology
New lighting equipment of Lithuanian Opera and Ballet Theatre. Lithuania: Vilnius. 1974-1998. Lang.: Swe, Eng, Ger. 205
Institutions
The theatres of Vilnius. Lithuania: Vilnius. 1993-1998. Lang.: Swe, Eng, Ger. 370
Life Is a Dream
SEE
Vida es sueño, La.
Life of Galileo, The
SEE
Leben des Galilei.
Life's a Gatecrash
Performance/production
Collection of newspaper reviews by London theatre critics. UK-England: London. 1998. Lang.: Eng. 2418
Lifegame
Performance/production
Collection of newspaper reviews by London theatre critics. UK-England: London. 1998. Lang.: Eng. 2421
Lifeline Theatre (Chicago, IL)
Institutions
The aesthetics of performances based on non-fiction texts at Lifeline Theatre. USA: Chicago, IL. 1996-1998. Lang.: Eng. 1788
Ligeti, György
Performance/production
György Ligeti's *Le Grand Macabre* directed by Balázs Kovalik. Hungary: Budapest. 1998. Lang.: Hun. 4642
Light Shining in Buckinghamshire
Plays/librettos/scripts
Brechtian epic devices in the theatre of Caryl Churchill. UK-England. 1976-1986. Lang.: Eng. 3477
Analysis of *Light Shining in Buckinghamshire* by Caryl Churchill. UK-England. 1970-1976. Lang.: Eng. 3483
Light, Tenebris
Performance/production
Collection of newspaper reviews by London theatre critics. UK-England: London. 1998. Lang.: Eng. 2432
Lighting
Design/technology
Technology and its use by artists. 1913-1988. Lang.: Eng. 166
Directory of manufacturers and distributors of lighting equipment. Canada. USA. 1998. Lang.: Eng. 169
Resignation of the founder of the Martin Group lighting equipment firm. Denmark: Copenhagen. 1998. Lang.: Eng. 174
Presentation of stage equipment by manufacturers. Germany. 1998. Lang.: Ger. 184
Survey of Light Fair. Germany: Hannover. 1998. Lang.: Eng. 186
Max Keller, lighting designer of Münchner Kammerspiele. Germany: Munich. 1997. Lang.: Ger. 188
Careers in technical theatre. Germany. Austria. 1998. Lang.: Ger. 189
Lighting in contemporary theatre. Germany. 1998. Lang.: Ger. 192
Combined video and lighting for U2 world tour. Ireland. 1997. Lang.: Eng. 198
Theatrical lighting design of Guido and Lucilla Baroni. Italy. 1946-1998. Lang.: Eng. 201
Lighting and realism in opera and theatre: Belasco and Puccini. Italy. USA. 1890-1910. Lang.: Eng. 203
New lighting equipment of Lithuanian Opera and Ballet Theatre. Lithuania: Vilnius. 1974-1998. Lang.: Swe, Eng, Ger. 205
Profiles of young theatrical designers. Netherlands. 1990-1998. Lang.: Dut. 207
Survey of lighting equipment, design, and information. North America. 1998. Lang.: Eng. 209
Locking and controlling stage rigging. Sweden: Stockholm. 1998. Lang.: Swe. 220

Lighting — cont'd

The restructuring of the lighting company AVAB Scandinavia. Sweden: Stockholm. 1998. Lang.: Swe. 221

Lighting operators' conference regarding controls at Dansens Hus. Sweden: Stockholm. 1998. Lang.: Swe. 223

Essay on lighting technology and the computer. Sweden. USA. 1992-1997. Lang.: Swe. 224

Exhibits at PLASA show. UK-England: London. 1998. Lang.: Eng. 229

Report on PLASA trade show. UK-England: London. 1998. Lang.: Eng. 230

The effect of lighting on the relationship between stage and audience. UK-England. 1820-1906. Lang.: Eng. 231

Lighting technology manufacturer AC Lighting. UK-England. 1998. Lang.: Eng. 233

AC Lighting's North American operation. UK-England. USA. 1998. Lang.: Eng. 234

Report on sound and lighting equipment fair Live!. UK-England: London. 1998. Lang.: Eng. 235

Report on PLASA light and sound equipment trade show. UK-England: London. 1998. Lang.: Swe. 236

New theatrical lighting equipment. USA. 1997. Lang.: Eng. 239

Calendar of events at LDI98 trade show. USA: Las Vegas, NV. 1998. Lang.: Eng. 240

Guide to theatrical design manufacturers and equipment. USA. 1998. Lang.: Eng. 241

The 1998 TCI awards. USA. 1998. Lang.: Eng. 243

List of exhibitors at LDI convention. USA: Phoenix, AZ. 1998. Lang.: Eng. 244

Survey of lighting-design software manufacturers. USA. 1998. Lang.: Eng. 245

Guide to lighting equipment and services. USA. 1998. Lang.: Eng. 246

Guide to lighting equipment. USA. 1998. Lang.: Eng. 247

Workshops of LDI expo. USA: Phoenix, AZ. 1998. Lang.: Eng. 248

Guidelines for a lighting design portfolio. USA. 1998. Lang.: Eng. 249

The 1998 USITT expo. USA: Long Beach, CA. 1998. Lang.: Eng. 251

Professional theatrical designers on design training. USA. 1998. Lang.: Eng. 252

Report on lighting designers' conference. USA: New York, NY. 1997. Lang.: Eng. 254

Lighting expert Francis P. De Verna. USA. 1928-1998. Lang.: Eng. 257

Lighting designer Kevin Adams. USA. 1979-1998. Lang.: Eng. 258

Sound design for Blue Man Group's Chicago production of *Tubes*. USA: Chicago, IL. 1996-1997. Lang.: Eng. 261

Set and lighting designer James Tilton. USA. 1938-1998. Lang.: Eng. 265

Review of new lighting software. USA. 1998. Lang.: Eng. 273

Lighting expert Gary Whittington. USA. 1952-1998. Lang.: Eng. 275

Lighting design and equipment in various Las Vegas spaces. USA: Las Vegas, NV. 1998. Lang.: Eng. 276

Preview of Lightfair seminar. USA: Las Vegas, NV. 1998. Lang.: Eng. 278

Stage lighting at the War Memorial Opera House. USA: San Francisco, CA. 1998. Lang.: Eng. 280

Lighting designer Michael Gottlieb. USA: New York, NY. 1998. Lang.: Eng. 281

Lighting designer Michael Brown. USA. 1998. Lang.: Eng. 282

Design for houses of worship, including their adaptation for performance and exhibitions. USA: Long Beach, CA. 1998. Lang.: Eng. 290

Imero Fiorentino, USITT's most distinguished lighting designer of 1997. USA. 1998. Lang.: Eng. 291

The use of entertainment technology beyond the entertainment industry. USA. 1998. Lang.: Eng. 293

Ethernet computer connections between lighting systems of two theatres at Herberger Theatre Center. USA: Phoenix, AZ. 1998. Lang.: Eng. 294

Lighting designer Glen Cunningham. USA. 1956-1998. Lang.: Eng. 301

Preview of LDI98 trade show. USA: Las Vegas, NV. 1998. Lang.: Eng. 303

Preview of LDI convention. USA: Phoenix, AZ. 1998. Lang.: Eng. 305

Lighting design for Mohegan Sun Casino. USA: Uncasville, CT. 1998. Lang.: Eng. 307

Stage, lighting, and sound design for Rolling Stones tour. USA. 1996-1997. Lang.: Eng. 308

Lighting technician Julian Winter. USA. 1971-1998. Lang.: Eng. 309

Lighting designer John Osborne. USA. 1998. Lang.: Eng. 310

Computer graphics as a lighting design tool. USA: Lawrence, KS. 1998. Lang.: Eng. 311

Lighting design for fashion design awards ceremony at Lincoln Center. USA: New York, NY. 1995. Lang.: Eng. 312

Students' recreation of paintings on stage. USA: Huntington, WV. 1996-1997. Lang.: Eng. 313

Former student on learning lighting design. USA: Las Vegas, NV. 1997. Lang.: Eng. 316

Lighting design for musical performance and sports at the Nashville arena. USA: Nashville, TN. 1998. Lang.: Eng. 317

Sound, lighting, and scenic elements of *Star Trek: The Next Generation* at the Las Vegas Hilton. USA: Las Vegas, NV. 1998. Lang.: Eng. 320

Creativity and beauty in theatrical design. USA. 1998. Lang.: Eng. 322

Index to *Technical Brief* volumes 11-17. USA. 1998. Lang.: Eng. 323

Comparison of computer-assisted and traditional scenery and lighting design. USA. 1980-1987. Lang.: Eng. 324

Lighting designer Tharon Musser. USA. 1965-1998. Lang.: Eng. 326

Suppliers of lighting equipment for the music industry. USA: Tualatin, OR. 1996-1998. Lang.: Eng. 328

Low-voltage cue light system. USA. 1998. Lang.: Eng. 332

Interview with lighting designer Rick Fisher. UK-England. 1998. Lang.: Eng. 1030

Technical designs for Matthew Bourne's productions of ballets by Čajkovskij and Prokofjėv. UK-England: London. 1998. Lang.: Eng. 1031

Marilyn Lowey's lighting design for Cleveland San Jose Ballet. USA: Cleveland, OH. 1997. Lang.: Eng. 1034

Lighting design for Čajkovskij's *Sneguročka (The Snow Maiden)* at Houston Ballet. USA: Houston, TX. 1998. Lang.: Eng. 1035

Design concept for Ralph Lemon's dance piece *Geography* at BAM. USA: New York, NY. 1998. Lang.: Eng. 1248

Lighting designer Mark Howett's work for Black Swan Theatre Company. Australia: Fremantle. 1998. Lang.: Eng. 1513

Technical designs for *The Chairs (Les Chaises)*, Théâtre de Complicité. UK-England: London. 1998. Lang.: Eng. 1524

Recent work of lighting designer Brian MacDevitt. USA: New York, NY. 1997. Lang.: Eng. 1530

Lighting design for *Never the Sinner* by John Logan, directed by Ethan McSweeney. USA: New York, NY. 1998. Lang.: Eng. 1534

Technical designs for Off Broadway Shakespearean productions. USA: New York, NY. 1998. Lang.: Eng. 1539

Lighting design for Hwang's *Golden Child* at the Public Theatre. USA: New York, NY. 1996-1998. Lang.: Eng. 1540

Lighting design for Donald Margulies' *Collected Stories*, directed by William Carden. USA: New York, NY. 1998. Lang.: Eng. 1544

Lighting designer Kenneth Posner. USA. 1998. Lang.: Eng. 1545

Lighting design for Shakespeare's *Twelfth Night* at the Vivian Beaumont. USA: New York, NY. 1998. Lang.: Eng. 1546

Lighting design for Mamet's *The Old Neighborhood* directed by Scott Zigler. USA: New York, NY. 1998. Lang.: Eng. 1547

Lighting designer Hugh Vanstone. USA: New York, NY. 1998. Lang.: Eng. 1554

Design concept for Amy Freed's *The Psychic Life of Savages*, Wilma Theatre. USA: Philadelphia, PA. 1998. Lang.: Eng. 1555

The design concept for Nicholas Hytner's production of Shakespeare's *Twelfth Night*. USA: New York, NY. 1998. Lang.: Eng. 1556

Technical designs for *Griller* by Eric Bogosian. USA: Chicago, IL. 1998. Lang.: Eng. 1558

Set and lighting designs for *The Taming of the Shrew*, American Repertory Theatre. USA: Cambridge, MA. 1998. Lang.: Eng. 1559

Set design and lighting for a production of Ibsen's *Hedda Gabler*. USA: Louisville, KY. 1988. Lang.: Eng. 1564

Film and TV lighting man Scott Jason Jellen. USA. 1973-1998. Lang.: Eng. 3855

Lighting — cont'd

Geoffrey Simpson's cinematography for Gillian Armstrong's *Oscar and Lucinda*. Australia. 1997. Lang.: Eng. 3900
Technical designs for the film *Titanic*. USA. 1997. Lang.: Eng. 3910
Introduction to an issue of *Lighting Dimensions* devoted to film lighting. USA. 1998. Lang.: Eng. 3911
Lighting design for Steven Soderbergh's film *Out of Sight*. USA. 1998. Lang.: Eng. 3912
Lighting design for Mark Christopher's film *54*. USA. 1998. Lang.: Eng. 3913
Lighting design for Joe Dante's film *Small Soldiers*. USA. 1998. Lang.: Eng. 3914
Matthews Studio Group, providing supplies for lighting design. USA: Hollywood, CA. 1970-1998. Lang.: Eng. 3915
Lighting design for Michael Bays' film *Armageddon*. USA. 1998. Lang.: Eng. 3916
Lighting design for Roland Emmerich's film *Godzilla*. USA. 1998. Lang.: Eng. 3917
Advances in motion picture lighting. USA. 1998. Lang.: Eng. 3918
Lighting design for Peter Weir's film *The Truman Show*. USA. 1998. Lang.: Eng. 3919
Lighting design for Rob Bowman's film *The X-Files*. USA. 1998. Lang.: Eng. 3922
TV lighting designer William Greenfield. USA. 1930-1998. Lang.: Eng. 4049
Design awards for the TV mini-series *Merlin*. USA: Pasadena, CA. 1998. Lang.: Eng. 4052
Lighting design for TV series *Ally MacBeal*. USA. 1998. Lang.: Eng. 4054
Lighting the 24-hour television event: QVC home shopping network. USA: West Chester, PA. 1998. Lang.: Eng. 4055
Profile of technicians for Grammy Awards television broadcast. USA: New York, NY. 1998. Lang.: Eng. 4056
Steve Cohen's lighting design for pop music tour. Australia. 1998. Lang.: Eng. 4095
Production design for rock group Genesis' European tour. Europe. 1998. Lang.: Eng. 4096
Sound design for The Spice Girls tour. UK-England. 1998. Lang.: Eng. 4097
Flexible lighting design for two-band tour by Norman Schwab and Alan Parker. USA. 1998. Lang.: Eng. 4099
Graeme Nicol's lighting design for pop music tours including *Lilith Fair*. USA. 1997-1998. Lang.: Eng. 4101
Pop music lighting design of Steve Cohen and Curry Grant. USA. 1997. Lang.: Eng. 4102
Lighting design by Patrick Woodroffe and set design by Mark Fisher for Rolling Stones tour. USA. 1997-1998. Lang.: Eng. 4103
Jim Chapman's lighting design for rock music tour. USA. 1998. Lang.: Eng. 4104
Howard Ungerleider's lighting design for Van Halen tour. USA. 1998. Lang.: Eng. 4105
Stan Crocker's lighting design for pop rock group tour. USA. 1998. Lang.: Eng. 4106
Graeme Nicol's lighting design for *Lilith Fair*. USA. 1998. Lang.: Eng. 4107
Peter Morse's lighting design for country music tour. USA. 1998. Lang.: Eng. 4108
Lighting and sound control for the Disneyland 'Light Magic' show. USA: Anaheim, CA. 1998. Lang.: Eng. 4109
Lighting for Washington Opera's production of *Doña Francisquita*. USA: Washington, DC. 1998. Lang.: Eng. 4290
Technical effects control system used in a production of *Joe—The Musical* at Koninklijk Theater Carré. Netherlands: Amsterdam. 1998. Lang.: Eng. 4324
Technical designs for the musical *Doctor Doolittle* directed by Steven Pimlott. UK-England: London. 1998. Lang.: Eng. 4325
Lighting and projections for the musical *Ragtime*. USA: New York, NY. 1998. Lang.: Eng. 4328
Lighting design for the musical *Follies*, Paper Mill Playhouse. USA: Millburn, NJ. 1998. Lang.: Eng. 4335
Donald Holder's lighting design for *The Lion King*. USA: New York, NY. 1997-1998. Lang.: Eng. 4336
Digital lighting control for *A Chorus Line*. USA: New York, NY. 1974-1975. Lang.: Eng. 4337
Technical designs for the Broadway production of *The Lion King*. USA: New York, NY. 1998. Lang.: Eng. 4342
Technical designs for Sam Mendes' production of *Cabaret*. USA: New York, NY. 1998. Lang.: Eng. 4343
Lighting design for Sam Mendes' production of *Cabaret*. USA: New York, NY. 1998. Lang.: Eng. 4344
Lighting design for *Jekyll & Hyde* directed by Robin Phillips. USA: New York, NY. 1998. Lang.: Eng. 4345
Geogre Tabori's production of Mozart's *Die Zauberflöte* in a circus ring. Germany: Berlin. 1998. Lang.: Ger. 4428
Lighting for Henze's opera *Der Prinz von Homburg* at Deutsche Oper Berlin. Germany: Berlin. 1997. Lang.: Ger. 4431
Sound system used in a soccer stadium for an operatic production. Italy: Rome. 1998. Lang.: Eng. 4434
Lighting design for Verdi's *Macbeth* at La Scala. Italy: Milan. 1998. Lang.: Eng. 4435
Lighting designer Jennifer Tipton. USA: New York, NY. 1998. Lang.: Eng. 4441
Technical designs for *Tristan und Isolde* at Seattle Opera. USA: Seattle, WA. 1998. Lang.: Eng. 4444
Lighting design for Basil Twist's puppet production *Symphonie Fantastique*. USA: New York, NY. 1998. Lang.: Eng. 4867

Institutions
Interview with members of dance group Creative Independent Artists. UK-Scotland: Glasgow. 1996-1998. Lang.: Eng. 904

Performance spaces
The construction of a theatre for *Beauty and the Beast*. Germany: Stuttgart. 1997. Lang.: Ger. 444
Profile of the New Jersey Performing Arts Center. USA: Newark, NJ. 1988-1998. Lang.: Eng. 467
Architectural critique of the new Ford Center. USA: New York, NY. 1998. Lang.: Eng. 468
The renovation of Arden Theatre Company's F. Otto Haas Theatre. USA: Philadelphia, PA. 1998. Lang.: Eng. 469
Architectural critique of the restored New Amsterdam Theatre. USA: New York, NY. 1998. Lang.: Eng. 476
The architecture of the Bass Performance Hall. USA: Ft. Worth, TX. 1998. Lang.: Eng. 477
The rebuilding of the stage at Cirkus to accommodate a production of *Kristina från Duvemåla (Kristina of Duvemåla)*.Sweden: Stockholm. 1995. Lang.: Swe. 1804
The supper and swing-music venue the Coconut Club. USA: Los Angeles, CA. 1998. Lang.: Eng. 4115
Sante Fe Opera's newly renovated open-air theatre. USA: Santa Fe, NM. 1991-1998. Lang.: Eng. 4499
The newly renovated Newberry Opera House. USA: Newberry, SC. 1998. Lang.: Eng. 4501

Performance/production
The 'scientific perspective' of director David Belasco. USA. 1882-1931. Lang.: Eng. 2741
Slovene translation of Adolphe Appia on staging Wagner. Europe. 1892. Lang.: Slo. 4550
Visual spectacle in Wagner's *Ring* cycle. Germany. 1869-1876. Lang.: Eng. 4585
Profile of lighting designer Jennifer Tipton. USA. 1937-1998. Lang.: Eng. 4747

Lights Twinkle Sometimes, The

Performance/production
Collection of newspaper reviews by London theatre critics. UK-England: London. 1998. Lang.: Eng. 2507

Ligue Nationale d'Improvisation (Montreal, PQ)

Institutions
History of the Ligue Nationale de l'Improvisation. Canada: Montreal, PQ. 1979-1997. Lang.: Fre. 339

Like a Dancer

Performance/production
Collection of newspaper reviews by London theatre critics. UK-England: London. 1998. Lang.: Eng. 2568

Like Father, Like Son

Basic theatrical documents
Text of *Like Father, Like Son* by Marc J. Aronin. USA. 1987. Lang.: Eng. 1481

Lill, Wendy
Plays/librettos/scripts
Analysis of *Corker* by Wendy Lill. Canada: Halifax, NS. 1994-1998. Lang.: Eng. 2836
Interview with playwright/MP Wendy Lill. USA: Halifax, NS. 1997-1998. Lang.: Eng. 3705
Lilla Teatern (Helsinki)
Performance/production
Finland's theatre offerings in Finnish and Swedish. Finland. 1998. Lang.: Eng, Fre. 1915
Lille Eyolf (Little Eyolf)
Performance/production
Report from Ibsen festival. Norway: Oslo. 1998. Lang.: Swe. 2211
Plays/librettos/scripts
Trolls in the late plays of Ibsen. Norway. 1886-1894. Lang.: Eng. 3298
Lille Grønnegade Teater (Copenhagen)
Performance/production
The influence of *commedia dell'arte* on eighteenth-century Danish theatre. Denmark: Copenhagen. 1700-1750. Lang.: Eng. 4186
Lillo, George
Plays/librettos/scripts
The defense of prostitution in Lillo's *Marina.* England. 1738. Lang.: Eng. 2887
The obedient daughter in adaptations of Shakespeare's plays. England. 1701-1800. Lang.: Eng. 2969
Analysis of *Marina,* George Lillo's adaptation of Shakespeare's *Pericles.* England. 1738. Lang.: Eng. 2971
Analysis of *The London Merchant* by George Lillo. England. 1731. Lang.: Eng. 2984
Limón Dance Company (New York, NY)
Performance/production
Guest performance of the Limón Dance Company. Hungary: Budapest. 1998. Lang.: Hun. 1089
Limón, José
Performance/production
Guest performance of the Limón Dance Company. Hungary: Budapest. 1998. Lang.: Hun. 1089
Lincoln Center for the Performing Arts (New York, NY)
Design/technology
Lighting design for fashion design awards ceremony at Lincoln Center. USA: New York, NY. 1995. Lang.: Eng. 312
Lighting design for Shakespeare's *Twelfth Night* at the Vivian Beaumont. USA: New York, NY. 1998. Lang.: Eng. 1546
Set and costume design for *Patience and Sarah* at Lincoln Center. USA: New York, NY. 1998. Lang.: Eng. 4440
Performance/production
Choreographer John Neumeier. Germany: Hamburg. USA: New York, NY. 1998. Lang.: Eng. 1082
Lincoln Center Theatre (New York, NY)
Design/technology
The design concept for Nicholas Hytner's production of Shakespeare's *Twelfth Night.* USA: New York, NY. 1998. Lang.: Eng. 1556
Plays/librettos/scripts
Recent productions of plays by Edward Albee. USA: New York, NY, Hartford, CT. 1959-1998. Lang.: Eng. 3578
Lincoln's Inn Fields (London)
Performance/production
Collection of newspaper reviews by London theatre critics. UK-England. 1998. Lang.: Eng. 2485
Collection of newspaper reviews by London theatre critics. UK-England: London. 1998. Lang.: Eng. 2554
Linda di Chamounix
Performance/production
Evaluation of video performances of Donizetti's operas. Europe. USA. 1980-1998. Lang.: Eng. 4557
Soprano Catherine Hayes. Ireland. Italy. 1839-1861. Lang.: Eng. 4645
Plays/librettos/scripts
Virginal heroines in Alpine settings in operas of Bellini, Donizetti, and Verdi. Italy. 1800-1850. Lang.: Eng. 4812
Lindgren, Astrid
Performance/production
Theatrical adaptations of children's stories by Astrid Lindgren. Sweden: Stockholm. 1998. Lang.: Eng. 2374
Hans Klinga's production of *Mio, Min Mio (Mio, My Mio)* at Dramaten. Sweden: Stockholm. 1997. Lang.: Swe. 2386
Interview with children's theatre director Marie Feldtmann. Sweden: Stockholm. 1996-1998. Lang.: Swe. 2388
Relation to other fields
Theatre and the psychological development of children. Sweden. 1988. Lang.: Swe. 3777
Lindgren, Robert
Performance/production
Tributes to ballerina Alexandra Danilova. USA: New York, NY. 1997. Lang.: Eng. 1165
Lindgren, Sonja
Performance/production
Tributes to ballerina Alexandra Danilova. USA: New York, NY. 1997. Lang.: Eng. 1165
Line 1
Plays/librettos/scripts
Comedy in the plays and musicals of Volker Ludwig. Germany: Berlin. 1968-1998. Lang.: Ger. 4391
Linke, Susanne
Design/technology
Set and costume designer Frank Leimbach and his work with choreographers. Germany. 1991-1998. Lang.: Ger. 1247
Performance/production
Dance adaptations of Shakespeare's *Hamlet.* Germany: Bremen, Weimar. 1996-1997. Lang.: Ger. 930
Linleys, Thomas
Plays/librettos/scripts
Music and the ballad opera in English popular theatre. England. 1728-1780. Lang.: Eng. 4390
Linney, Romulus
Institutions
Arthur Penn and Actors Studio. USA: New York, NY. 1997. Lang.: Eng. 1767
Performance/production
Comparison of productions of Ibsen's *Peer Gynt.* USA: Providence, RI, New York, NY, Washington, DC, Nacogdoches, TX. 1998. Lang.: Eng. 2711
Reviews of productions of plays by Ibsen. USA: New York, NY. Norway: Oslo. 1998. Lang.: Eng. 2747
Plays/librettos/scripts
Playwright Romulus Linney's address to SETC convention. USA: Birmingham, AL. 1998. Lang.: Eng. 3517
Lintern, Dawn
Performance/production
Collection of newspaper reviews by London theatre critics. UK-England: London. 1998. Lang.: Eng. 2420
Lion and Unicorn Theatre (London)
Performance/production
Collection of newspaper reviews by London theatre critics. UK-England: London. 1998. Lang.: Eng. 2449
Collection of newspaper reviews by London theatre critics. UK-England. 1998. Lang.: Eng. 2489
Lion King, The
Administration
The Disney Corporation's Broadway musicals. USA: New York, NY. 1996-1998. Lang.: Eng. 4317
Design/technology
Donald Holder's lighting design for *The Lion King.* USA: New York, NY. 1997-1998. Lang.: Eng. 4336
Technical designs for the Broadway production of *The Lion King.* USA: New York, NY. 1998. Lang.: Eng. 4342
Lion, the Witch, and the Wardrobe, The
Performance/production
Collection of newspaper reviews by London theatre critics. UK-England: Stratford. 1998. Lang.: Eng. 2519
Lipkin, Joan
Performance/production
Collection of newspaper reviews by London theatre critics. UK-England: London. 1998. Lang.: Eng. 2533
Lipovšek, Marjana
Performance/production
Reviews of *Lieder* recordings. USA. Slovenia. Austria. 1998. Lang.: Eng. 4720
Lippy, Tod
Basic theatrical documents
Tod Lippy's unproduced screenplay *Jim & Wanda.* USA. 1996. Lang.: Eng. 3895
Lips Together, Teeth Apart
Performance/production
Collection of newspaper reviews by London theatre critics. UK-England: London. 1998. Lang.: Eng. 2538
Lisbon Traviata, The
Performance/production
Comparison of productions of *The Lisbon Traviata* by Terrence McNally. Germany: Berlin, Essen. 1998. Lang.: Ger. 2005

Liška, Ivan
Administration
Interview with Ivan Liška, new director of Bayerische Staatsballett. Germany: Munich. 1998. Lang.: Hun. 1026

Lista Negra (Black List)
Performance/production
Eduardo Vasco's production of *Lista Negra (Black List)* by Yolanda Pallín. Spain. 1998. Lang.: Eng. 2360

Literature
Performance/production
Performance culture in prerevolutionary Russia. Russia. 1910-1915. Lang.: Eng. 580
Theatre and gender in the novels of Hannah Foster. UK-England. 1759-1840. Lang.: Eng. 613
Performance and the nineteenth-century economy. USA. 1850-1890. Lang.: Eng. 4134
Plays/librettos/scripts
The influence of Webster, Middleton, and Shakespeare on the poetry of Robert Browning. England. 1590-1889. Lang.: Eng. 2906
Don Quixote, Lewis Theobald's *The Double Falsehood* and the lost *Cardenio* of Shakespeare and Fletcher. England. Spain. 1610-1727. Lang.: Eng. 3001
Eighteenth-century editing and interpretation of Shakespeare. England. 1701-1800. Lang.: Eng. 3040
Music in Samuel Beckett's novel *Proust*. Ireland. France. 1931. Lang.: Eng. 3208
The adaptation of novels for the stage. UK-England. 1980-1995. Lang.: Eng. 3499
Blues music in the writings of Zora Neale Hurston. USA. 1920-1940. Lang.: Eng. 3625
Composer Gaetano Donizetti. Italy. Europe. 1835-1848. Lang.: Eng. 4805
Reference materials
Dictionary of history and the arts. Lang.: Ita. 695
Relation to other fields
Novelist Dmitri S. Merežkovskij and theatre. 1890-1909. Lang.: Rus. 712
Theatre and revolution in the English novel. England. 1790-1848. Lang.: Eng. 727
Modern fictional characters through the lens of Mejerchol'd's biomechanics and Oskar Schlemmer's puppets. Europe. 1913-1930. Lang.: Ger. 729
Literary influences of the characters Faust, Don Juan, Don Quixote, and Robinson Crusoe. Europe. 1587-1998. Lang.: Ita. 730
Analysis of Samuel Beckett's novel *Murphy*. France. Ireland. 1935. Lang.: Eng. 733
The context of Heinrich von Kleist's periodical *Berliner Abendblätter*. Germany: Berlin. 1810-1811. Lang.: Ger. 741
The poetry of actors Leonid Filatov and Valentin Gaft. Russia: Moscow. 1998. Lang.: Rus. 758
Memoirs of poet, journalist, and playwright A.B. Mariengof. Russia. 1897-1962. Lang.: Rus. 760
Topics in post-apartheid South African literature and theatre. South Africa, Republic of. 1995-1998. Lang.: Eng. 764
The performance style of poet Stevie Smith. UK-England. 1961-1970. Lang.: Eng. 770
Fitzroy Davis's theatre novel *Quicksilver*. USA. 1930-1940. Lang.: Eng. 810
The influence of Cervantes' *Don Quixote* on contemporary Quebec artists. Canada. 1967-1998. Lang.: Fre. 3737
The dramatic nature of the ancient Egyptian text *The Triumph of Horus*. Egypt. 2500 B.C. Lang.: Eng. 3744
A possible model for characters in Shakespeare's *Twelfth Night* and 'Venus and Adonis'. England. 1590-1593. Lang.: Eng. 3746
Theatre and drama in the life of Sir Thomas More. England. 1550-1590. Lang.: Eng. 3747
William Basse, author of the poem 'Epitaph for Shakespeare'. England. 1602-1653. Lang.: Eng. 3748
The publication of 'Venus and Adonis' by Shakespeare. England. 1589-1593. Lang.: Eng. 3751
Performance analysis of Shakespeare's sonnets. England. 1593-1599. Lang.: Eng. 3753
Novelist Samuel Richardson compared to Shakespeare. England. 1744-1747. Lang.: Eng. 3754
Shakespeare's Hamlet in novels of Goethe and Scott. England. Germany. 1776-1824. Lang.: Eng. 3757
Author Gertrude Stein, subject of *Gertrude morte cet après-midi (Gertrude Dead This Afternoon)* by Monique Lepeu. France: Paris. 1874-1997. Lang.: Fre. 3759
Shakespeare's influence on the novels of Virginia Woolf. UK-England. 1882-1941. Lang.: Eng. 3779
Interview with actor/writer Steven Berkoff, creator of actor character 'Harry'. UK-England: London. 1998. Lang.: Eng. 3780
The influence of Shakespeare's *Othello* on C.B. Brown's novel *Wieland*. USA. England. 1604-1798. Lang.: Eng. 3788
The influence of Fellini's *La Dolce Vita* on a novel of film critic Guillermo Cabrera Infante. Spain. Italy. 1960-1967. Lang.: Eng. 4035
Theory/criticism
How theatre criticism of Theodor Fontane influenced his novels. Germany: Berlin. 1870-1890. Lang.: Ger. 843
Texts of critical articles written by Pirandello under a psuedonym. Italy. 1898. Lang.: Ita. 3824

Littell, Philip
Performance/production
André Previn's opera *A Streetcar Named Desire*. USA: San Francisco. 1998. Lang.: Eng. 4742

Litter
Performance/production
Collection of newspaper reviews by London theatre critics. UK-England: London. 1998. Lang.: Eng. 2478

Little Clay Cart, The
SEE
Shākuntala.

Little Malcolm and His Struggle Against the Eunuchs
Performance/production
Collection of newspaper reviews by London theatre critics. UK-England: London. 1998. Lang.: Eng. 2544

Little Night Music, A
Plays/librettos/scripts
The disintegration of the American dream in works of Stephen Sondheim. USA. 1970-1984. Lang.: Eng. 4397

Little Princess, The
Performance/production
The influence of *The Little Princess* on popular theatre and culture. USA. 1903. Lang.: Eng. 2658
Plays/librettos/scripts
Feminist analysis of plays for young people by women playwrights. USA. 1903-1983. Lang.: Eng. 3521

Little Theatre (Chicago, IL)
Performance/production
Twentieth-century productions of Euripidean tragedy. USA. 1915-1969. Lang.: Eng. 2678

Little Theatre (Leningrad)
SEE
Malyj Dramatičeskij Teat'r.

Little Theatre (Moscow)
SEE
Malyj Teat'r.

Little theatre movement
Theory/criticism
Sociological influence on the little theatre movement. USA. 1890-1920. Lang.: Eng. 862

Littlewood, Joan
Performance/production
Collection of newspaper reviews by London theatre critics. UK-England. 1998. Lang.: Eng. 2456
Collection of newspaper reviews by London theatre critics. UK-England: London. 1998. Lang.: Eng. 2461
Collection of newspaper reviews by London theatre critics. UK-England: London. 1998. Lang.: Eng. 2482
Plays/librettos/scripts
The development of Theatre Workshop, founded by Ewan MacColl and Joan Littlewood. UK-England: London. 1945-1970. Lang.: Eng. 3491

Liturgical drama
Performance/production
Evidence for performance of medieval religious drama. Sweden. 1140-1500. Lang.: Eng. 2392

Lives of the Great Poisoners
Plays/librettos/scripts
Systemic poisons in plays of Caryl Churchill. UK-England. 1990-1997. Lang.: Eng. 3463

Living in the Mists
Relation to other fields
The creation and use of ritual theatre for drama therapy. USA. 1997. Lang.: Eng. 3787
Living Newspaper
Performance/production
Productions of the Federal Theatre Project's Living Newspapers. USA: New York, NY. 1935-1939. Lang.: Eng. 643
Living Out Loud
Basic theatrical documents
The screenplay of *Living Out Loud* by Richard LaGravenese. USA. 1998. Lang.: Eng. 3890
Plays/librettos/scripts
Interview with screenwriter and director Richard LaGravenese. USA. 1998. Lang.: Eng. 4019
Living Theatre (New York, NY)
Institutions
The present status of the Living Theatre. North America. 1991-1997. Lang.: Eng. 371
European activities of the Living Theatre. Europe. USA. 1964-1983. Lang.: Ita. 1602
Judith Malina's attempt to create an active mixed-media theatre. USA. 1968-1969. Lang.: Eng. 1765
Performance/production
Theatre Magazine's anniversary issue. USA. 1968-1998. Lang.: Eng. 617
The Living Theatre's *Paradise Now*—creation and production. USA. 1951-1968. Lang.: Eng. 667
Relation to other fields
Government response to Living Theatre's *Paradise Now*. USA. Europe. 1968. Lang.: Eng. 3789
Llerena, Maria
Training
Interview with dance teacher Maria Llerena. Sweden: Stockholm. 1966-1998. Lang.: Swe. 1018
Lloyd George, Ian
Basic theatrical documents
Excerpt from *Job Stealer* by Rahul Varma, Helen Vlachos and Ian Lloyd George. Canada: Montreal, PQ. 1998. Lang.: Eng. 1412
Lloyd Webber, Andrew
Administration
Equity Executive Director Alan Eisenberg's experience with a touring production of *Cats*. USA: New York, NY. 1998. Lang.: Eng. 4318
Design/technology
The original stage machinery designed by John White at Her Majesty's Theatre. UK-England: London. 1887-1986. Lang.: Eng. 1528
Performance/production
Collection of newspaper reviews by London theatre critics. UK-England: London. 1998. Lang.: Eng. 2425
Lloyd, George
Performance/production
Obituary for conductor/composer George Lloyd. UK-England. 1913-1998. Lang.: Eng. 4703
Lloyd, Jonathan
Performance/production
Collection of newspaper reviews by London theatre critics. UK-England: London. 1998. Lang.: Eng. 2550
Lloyd, Matthew
Performance/production
Collection of newspaper reviews by London theatre critics. UK-England: Leeds, Manchester. 1998. Lang.: Eng. 2433
Collection of newspaper reviews by London theatre critics. UK-England: London. 1998. Lang.: Eng. 2434
Collection of newspaper reviews by London theatre critics. UK-England: London. 1998. Lang.: Eng. 2523
Collection of newspaper reviews by London theatre critics. UK-England: Leeds, Manchester. 1998. Lang.: Eng. 2559
Lloyd, Phyllida
Performance/production
Collection of newspaper reviews by London theatre critics. UK-England: London. 1998. Lang.: Eng. 2423
Lobbes, Marcus
Performance/production
German productions of adaptations of *A Clockwork Orange* by Anthony Burgess. Germany: Dresden, Hamburg, Stendal. 1998. Lang.: Ger. 1972
Plays/librettos/scripts
Hero and anti-hero in contemporary opera production. Germany. 1998. Lang.: Ger. 4791
Locandiera, La (Mistress of the Inn, The)
Performance/production
Goldoni's *La Locandiera* directed by Lászlo Keszég. Hungary: Kaposvár. 1998. Lang.: Hun. 2092
Lockheart, Paula
Performance/production
Collection of newspaper reviews by London theatre critics. UK-England. 1998. Lang.: Eng. 2489
Lodge, David
Performance/production
Collection of newspaper reviews by London theatre critics. UK-England: Leeds, Manchester. 1998. Lang.: Eng. 2433
Lodwick, Keith
Performance/production
Collection of newspaper reviews by London theatre critics. UK-England: London. 1998. Lang.: Eng. 2437
Loewe, Frederick
Plays/librettos/scripts
Popular adaptations of the works of George Bernard Shaw. UK-England. 1890-1990. Lang.: Eng. 3445
Fairy-tale heroines in American drama and musical theatre. USA. 1945-1965. Lang.: Eng. 3617
Logan, John
Design/technology
Lighting design for *Never the Sinner* by John Logan, directed by Ethan McSweeney. USA: New York, NY. 1998. Lang.: Eng. 1534
Logeot, Vincent
Performance/production
Guest performance of Théâtre du Plantin, a company for developmentally disabled actors. Hungary: Budapest. 1983-1998. Lang.: Hun. 2081
Lohengrin
Performance/production
Historical overview of Wagnerian singing. Germany: Bayreuth. 1850-1998. Lang.: Eng. 4610
Background material on Metropolitan Opera radio broadcast performances. USA: New York, NY. 1998. Lang.: Eng. 4713
Robert Wilson's production of Wagner's *Lohengrin*. USA: New York, NY. 1998. Lang.: Eng. 4732
Robert Wilson's production of Wagner's *Lohengrin* at the Metropolitan Opera. USA: New York, NY. 1976-1998. Lang.: Eng. 4739
Plays/librettos/scripts
The brother-sister bond of Gottfried and Elsa in *Lohengrin* by Richard Wagner. Germany. 1850-1998. Lang.: Eng. 4794
Lohenstein, Daniel Casper von
Plays/librettos/scripts
Representation of the virginal body on the German stage. Germany. 1600-1800. Lang.: Ger. 3171
Loher, Dea
Institutions
New plays by Dea Loher at Staatsschauspiel Hannover. Germany: Hannover. 1992-1998. Lang.: Ger. 1643
Plays/librettos/scripts
German playwrights on the meaning of Brecht today. Germany. 1998. Lang.: Ger. 3123
The language of Dea Loher's *Tätowierung (Tattoo)*. Germany. 1995-1998. Lang.: Ger. 3126
Analysis of plays by Dea Loher, directed by Andreas Kriegenburg. Germany: Hannover. 1998. Lang.: Ger. 3130
The collaboration of playwright Dea Loher and director Andreas Kriegenburg. Germany: Hannover, Munich. 1990-1998. Lang.: Ger. 3151
Analysis of *Fremdes Haus (Strangers House)* by Dea Loher. Germany. 1998. Lang.: Ger. 3161
Marginal notes by Dea Loher on her plays. Germany. 1991-1998. Lang.: Ger. 3162
The development of *Blaubart—Hoffnung der Frauen (Bluebeard—Hope of Women)* by Dea Loher. Germany: Munich. 1998. Lang.: Ger. 3164
Interview with playwright Dea Loher. Germany. 1964-1998. Lang.: Ger. 3173
Lohner, Helmuth
Performance/production
Actor Helmuth Lohner's stint as administrative director of Theater in der Josefstadt. Austria: Vienna. 1960-1998. Lang.: Ger. 1819
Lommel, Daniel
Performance/production
Hungarian guest performances of world ballet stars. Hungary: Budapest. 1975-1978. Lang.: Hun. 1085
Loncraine, Richard
Performance/production
The body in stage-to-film versions of Shakespeare's *Richard III*. UK-England. USA. 1985-1998. Lang.: Eng. 3940

Loncraine, Richard — cont'd

Plays/librettos/scripts
Film adaptations of Shakespeare's *Richard III* by Richard Loncraine and Al Pacino. USA. UK-England. 1995-1996. Lang.: Fre. 4012

London Assurance
Performance/production
Actors Helen Carey and Max Wright, winners of Joe A. Callaway Award. USA. 1998. Lang.: Eng. 2716
Joe Dowling's production of *London Assurance* by Dion Boucicault. USA. 1997. Lang.: Eng. 2755

London Cuckolds, The
Performance/production
Collection of newspaper reviews by London theatre critics. UK-England: London. 1998. Lang.: Eng. 2448

London Dungeon
Performance/production
Collection of newspaper reviews by London theatre critics. UK-England: London. 1998. Lang.: Eng. 2437

London Merchant, The
Plays/librettos/scripts
Analysis of *The London Merchant* by George Lillo. England. 1731. Lang.: Eng. 2984

London Palladium
Performance/production
Collection of newspaper reviews by London theatre critics. UK-England: London. 1998. Lang.: Eng. 2467

London Theatre Studio
Performance/production
Correspondence of George Devine and Michel Saint-Denis. UK-England: London. 1939-1945. Lang.: Eng. 2630

Long Day's Journey Into Night
Institutions
Report on the Stockholm theatre festival. Sweden: Stockholm. 1998. Lang.: Eng. 1724
Performance/production
Recent productions in Ireland of plays by Eugene O'Neill. Ireland: Dublin. UK-Ireland: Belfast. 1989-1998. Lang.: Eng. 2154
Interview with actor Dan Ekborg. Sweden: Stockholm. 1998. Lang.: Swe. 2367
Photos of rehearsals of O'Neill's *Long Day's Journey Into Night* at Dramaten. Sweden: Stockholm. 1998. Lang.: Swe. 2391
An approach to playing Jamie in O'Neill's *Long Day's Journey Into Night*. USA. 1987. Lang.: Eng. 2697
Plays/librettos/scripts
Lars Norén's *Och ge oss skuggorna (And Give Us the Shadows)*. Sweden. 1980-1998. Lang.: Swe. 3413
Irish folklore in plays of Eugene O'Neill. USA. 1942-1956. Lang.: Eng. 3522
Female characters in Eugene O'Neill's plays. USA. 1920-1953. Lang.: Eng. 3525
The late plays of Eugene O'Neill. USA. 1939-1943. Lang.: Eng. 3528
Female presence/absence in plays of O'Neill, Pinter, and Shepard. USA. UK-England. 1936-1985. Lang.: Eng. 3607
The 'greatness' of *Long Day's Journey Into Night* by Eugene O'Neill. USA. 1956. Lang.: Eng. 3639
Effeminacy on the American stage. USA. 1920-1998. Lang.: Eng. 3682
African- and Irish-Americans in the plays of Eugene O'Neill. USA. 1916-1953. Lang.: Eng. 3687
Closure in plays of Eugene O'Neill. USA. 1918-1950. Lang.: Eng. 3703

Long, William Ivey
Design/technology
Technical designs for Sam Mendes' production of *Cabaret*. USA: New York, NY. 1998. Lang.: Eng. 4343

Longbottom, Robert
Design/technology
Recent work of lighting designer Brian MacDevitt. USA: New York, NY. 1997. Lang.: Eng. 1530
Sound design for *Side Show* at Richard Rodgers Theatre. USA: New York, NY. 1998. Lang.: Eng. 4329
Technical designs for *The Scarlet Pimpernel* directed by Robert Longbottom. USA: New York, NY. 1998. Lang.: Eng. 4331

Look About You
Plays/librettos/scripts
Cross-dressing in Elizabethan Robin Hood plays. England. 1589-1598. Lang.: Eng. 3016

Looking for a Bride
SEE
Ženitba.

Looking for Richard
Performance/production
The body in stage-to-film versions of Shakespeare's *Richard III*. UK-England. USA. 1985-1998. Lang.: Eng. 3940
Plays/librettos/scripts
Film adaptations of Shakespeare's *Richard III* by Richard Loncraine and Al Pacino. USA. UK-England. 1995-1996. Lang.: Fre. 4012
Theory/criticism
The urge to make Shakespeare contemporary. USA. 1990-1998. Lang.: Eng. 3844

Loos, Anita
Performance/production
Collection of newspaper reviews by London theatre critics. UK-England: London. 1998. Lang.: Eng. 2480

Loot
Institutions
Productions of Staatstheater Stuttgart. Germany: Stuttgart. 1998. Lang.: Ger. 1620
Performance/production
Collection of newspaper reviews by London theatre critics. UK-England: London. 1998. Lang.: Eng. 2482

Lopatkina, Uljana
Performance/production
Ballerina Uljana Lopatkina. Russia: St. Petersburg. 1998. Lang.: Rus. 1140
Ballet dancer Uljana Lopatkina. Russia: St. Petersburg. Lang.: Rus. 1146
Profile of ballerinas Uljana Lopatkina and Diana Višneva. Russia: St. Petersburg. 1998. Lang.: Rus. 1148

Lope de Vega
SEE
Vega Carpio, Lope Félix de.

López, Josefina
Plays/librettos/scripts
Analysis of plays by Josefina López. USA. 1988-1989. Lang.: Eng. 3650

Lopez, Sabatino
Plays/librettos/scripts
Italian realist drama. Italy. 1860-1918. Lang.: Eng. 3260

Loquasto, Santo
Design/technology
Set designs by Santo Loquasto at Manhattan Theatre Club. USA: New York, NY. 1998. Lang.: Eng. 1536
Technical designs for *Ragtime* at the Ford Center. USA: New York, NY. 1998. Lang.: Eng. 4338

Lorca, Federico García
SEE
García Lorca, Federico.

Lord Admiral's Men (London)
Performance/production
The activities of actor Edward Alleyn in retirement. England: London. 1597-1600. Lang.: Eng. 1894

Lord Chamberlain's Men (London)
Institutions
Economic history of the Chamberlain's Men/King's Men. England. 1599-1642. Lang.: Eng. 1598

Lord's Masque, The
Plays/librettos/scripts
Shakespeare's *The Tempest* and Thomas Campion's *The Lord's Masque*. England. 1613. Lang.: Eng. 4202

Lory, Andrea
Performance/production
Interview with soprano Andrea Lory. Romania: Iasi. Hungary. 1998. 19-1998. Lang.: Hun. 4667

Löscher, Peter
Performance/production
Shakespeare productions in German Switzerland. Switzerland: Basel, Zurich. 1996-1997. Lang.: Ger. 2398

Lost and Moated Land, The
Performance/production
Collection of newspaper reviews by London theatre critics. UK-England: London, Stratford, Derby. 1998. Lang.: Eng. 2417

Lost in a Mirror
SEE
Castigo sin venganza, El.

Lost in Space
Design/technology
Production design for the film *Lost in Space*. USA: Hollywood, CA. 1998. Lang.: Eng. 3904

***Lost in Space* — cont'd**
Performance/production
Collection of newspaper reviews by London theatre critics. UK-England: London. 1998. Lang.: Eng. 2506
Lost Vegas Series, The
Performance/production
Collection of newspaper reviews by London theatre critics. UK-England: London. 1998. Lang.: Eng. 2420
Loughborough Hotel (London)
Performance/production
Collection of newspaper reviews by London theatre critics. UK-England: London. 1998. Lang.: Eng. 2453
Louis and Dave
Performance spaces
Theatre SKAM's production of *Louis and Dave* in a Plymouth Volaré. Canada: Victoria, BC. 1996. Lang.: Eng. 1797
Louis, Murray
Performance/production
The Murray Louis/Alwin Nikolais dance archive. USA: Athens, OH. 1950-1998. Lang.: Eng. 1331
Love Bites
Performance/production
Collection of newspaper reviews by London theatre critics. UK-England: London. 1998. Lang.: Eng. 2546
Love Crazy
Plays/librettos/scripts
Marriage, divorce, and gender in the Hollywood comedy of remarriage. USA. 1935-1942. Lang.: Eng. 4010
Love in a Forest
Plays/librettos/scripts
Political context of Charles Johnson's *Love in a Forest*, an adaptation of *As You Like It*. England. 1723. Lang.: Eng. 3013
Love in a Village
Plays/librettos/scripts
Music and the ballad opera in English popular theatre. England. 1728-1780. Lang.: Eng. 4390
Love of a Good Man, The
Performance/production
Collection of newspaper reviews by London theatre critics. UK-England: London. 1998. Lang.: Eng. 2505
Love of Three Oranges by Prokofjév
SEE
Ljubov k Trem Apelsinam.
Love Upon the Throne
Performance/production
Collection of newspaper reviews by London theatre critics. UK-England: London. 1998. Lang.: Eng. 2495
Collection of newspaper reviews by London theatre critics. UK-England: London. 1998. Lang.: Eng. 2540
Love You, Too
Performance/production
Collection of newspaper reviews by London theatre critics. UK-England: London. 1998. Lang.: Eng. 2502
Love! Valour! Compassion!
Performance/production
Collection of newspaper reviews by London theatre critics. UK-England: London. 1998. Lang.: Eng. 2525
Plays/librettos/scripts
Effeminacy on the American stage. USA. 1920-1998. Lang.: Eng. 3682
Love, Kermit
Design/technology
Costumer Kermit Love. USA. 1935-1998. Lang.: Eng. 271
Love, Lust, and Sawdust
Performance/production
Collection of newspaper reviews by London theatre critics. UK-England: London. 1998. Lang.: Eng. 2560
Love's Labour's Lost
Basic theatrical documents
French translation of Shakespeare's *Love's Labour's Lost*. England. France. 1594-1998. Lang.: Fre. 1419
Performance/production
Reviews of German Shakespearean productions. Germany: Wuppertal, Cologne, Oberhausen. 1998. Lang.: Ger. 2017
Christopher Luscombe on acting in RSC productions. UK-England: London, Stratford. 1993-1994. Lang.: Eng. 2620
Plays/librettos/scripts
Regeneration in plays of Shakespeare. England. 1598-1613. Lang.: Eng. 2968
Loveid, Cecilie
Plays/librettos/scripts
Female characters in plays by Scandinavian women. Norway. Sweden. Denmark. 1998. Lang.: Eng. 3299
Lover, The
Performance/production
Italian productions of plays by Harold Pinter. Italy. 1997. Lang.: Eng. 2165
Collection of newspaper reviews by London theatre critics. UK-England: London. 1998. Lang.: Eng. 2561
Recent productions of plays by Harold Pinter at Donmar Warehouse. UK-England: London. 1998. Lang.: Eng. 2609
Lovers and Others of Eugene O'Neill, The
Plays/librettos/scripts
Marla del Collins on her play *The Lovers and Others of Eugene O'Neill*. USA. 1998. Lang.: Eng. 3565
Loves of Wayne Gretzky, The
Plays/librettos/scripts
Homosexuality in Canadian opera. Canada. 1970-1998. Lang.: Eng. 4762
Lovett, Jonathan
Performance/production
Collection of newspaper reviews by London theatre critics. UK-England: London. 1998. Lang.: Eng. 2495
Low, Betty
Performance/production
Tributes to ballerina Alexandra Danilova. USA: New York, NY. 1997. Lang.: Eng. 1165
Lowe, Lisa
Plays/librettos/scripts
Review of collections of plays with gay themes. Canada. 1996. Lang.: Eng. 2802
Lowey, Marilyn
Design/technology
Marilyn Lowey's lighting design for Cleveland San Jose Ballet. USA: Cleveland, OH. 1997. Lang.: Eng. 1034
Lu Ann Hampton Laverty Oberlander
Plays/librettos/scripts
Analysis of Preston Jones's plays about Texas. USA. 1977. Lang.: Eng. 3645
Lucas, Craig
Performance/production
Collection of newspaper reviews by London theatre critics. UK-England: London. 1998. Lang.: Eng. 2581
Luce, William
Performance/production
Collection of newspaper reviews by London theatre critics. UK-England: London. 1998. Lang.: Eng. 2512
Lucia di Lammermoor
Performance spaces
Malmö Musikteater's production of *Lucia di Lammermoor* at Hedeland Amfiteater. Denmark: Hedeland. 1997. Lang.: Swe. 4491
Performance/production
Maria Callas and Donizetti's *Lucia di Lammermoor*. Europe. 1953-1959. Lang.: Eng. 4553
Evaluation of video performances of Donizetti's operas. Europe. USA. 1980-1998. Lang.: Eng. 4557
Soprano Catherine Hayes. Ireland. Italy. 1839-1861. Lang.: Eng. 4645
Plays/librettos/scripts
The use of the tenor in operas of Donizetti. Italy. 1816-1845. Lang.: Eng. 4802
Lucian
Plays/librettos/scripts
Lucian's *Icaromenippus* as a source for Heywood's *The Play of the Wether*. England. 1533. Lang.: Eng. 2920
Lucie, Doug
Performance/production
Collection of newspaper reviews by London theatre critics. UK-England: London. 1998. Lang.: Eng. 2502
Lucille Lortel Theatre (New York, NY)
Design/technology
Lighting design for Donald Margulies' *Collected Stories*, directed by William Carden. USA: New York, NY. 1998. Lang.: Eng. 1544
Lucrezia Borgia
Performance/production
Evaluation of video performances of Donizetti's operas. Europe. USA. 1980-1998. Lang.: Eng. 4557
Analysis of Donizetti's opera *Lucrezia Borgia*. Italy. UK-England. 1797-1998. Lang.: Eng. 4649
Lucy Stone: A Chronicle Play
Plays/librettos/scripts
Analysis of plays about the women's movement. USA. 1900-1940. Lang.: Eng. 3559

Lüdecke, Volker
Plays/librettos/scripts
Playwright Volker Lüdecke. Germany: Kaiserslautern. 1992-1998. Lang.: Ger. 3141
Ludlam, Charles
Plays/librettos/scripts
Revolutionary Off Broadway playwriting. USA: New York, NY. 1959-1969. Lang.: Eng. 3604
Ludlow Fair
Plays/librettos/scripts
Comedy and humor in plays of Lanford Wilson. USA. 1961-1985. Lang.: Eng. 3595
Ludlow, Conrad
Performance/production
Panel discussion on Balanchine's *Jewels*. USA: New York, NY. 1967. Lang.: Eng. 1188
Ludwig, Volker
Plays/librettos/scripts
Children's theatre at GRIPS. Germany: Berlin. 1966-1998. Lang.: Ger. 3152
Comedy in the plays and musicals of Volker Ludwig. Germany: Berlin. 1968-1998. Lang.: Ger. 4391
Analysis of *Café Mitte (Café Center)* by Volker Ludwig. Germany: Berlin. 1997-1998. Lang.: Ger. 4393
Luft, Lorna
Performance/production
Singer Lorna Luft. USA. 1998. Lang.: Eng. 4158
Lugn, Kristina
Performance/production
Theatrical adaptations of children's stories by Astrid Lindgren. Sweden: Stockholm. 1998. Lang.: Eng. 2374
Plays/librettos/scripts
Female characters in plays by Scandinavian women. Norway. Sweden. Denmark. 1998. Lang.: Eng. 3299
Luhrmann, Baz
Plays/librettos/scripts
Baz Luhrmann's film adaptation of Shakespeare's *Romeo and Juliet*. USA. 1996. Lang.: Fre. 4016
Theory/criticism
The urge to make Shakespeare contemporary. USA. 1990-1998. Lang.: Eng. 3844
Luisa Miller
Plays/librettos/scripts
Virginal heroines in Alpine settings in operas of Bellini, Donizetti, and Verdi. Italy. 1800-1850. Lang.: Eng. 4812
Lukács, András
Institutions
Student's view of the Elmhurst Ballet School. UK-England: Camberley. 1997-1998. Lang.: Hun. 1055
Lukan, Blaž
Performance/production
Essays and reviews of contemporary theatre. Slovenia. 1980-1997. Lang.: Slo. 2346
Lukáts, Andor
Performance/production
Molière's *Misanthrope* directed by Andor Lukáts. Hungary: Budapest. 1998. Lang.: Hun. 2091
Lulu
Basic theatrical documents
Complete libretto of Alban Berg's *Lulu*. Austria. 1935. Lang.: Fre, Ger. 4412
Design/technology
Set and costume design for San Francisco Opera productions. USA: San Francisco, CA. 1998. Lang.: Eng. 4443
Performance/production
Discography of productions of Alban Berg's *Lulu*. 1935-1998. Lang.: Fre. 4508
Significant interpreters of the title role of Alban Berg's *Lulu*. 1937-1996. Lang.: Fre. 4509
Productions of Berg's *Lulu*. 1935-1998. Lang.: Fre. 4518
Arnold Schoenberg's refusal to complete Alban Berg's unfinished opera *Lulu*. Austria. 1935. Lang.: Fre. 4533
Conductor Pierre Boulez on Patrice Chéreau's production of *Lulu* by Alban Berg. France: Paris. 1979. Lang.: Fre. 4567
Plays/librettos/scripts
The image of motherhood in German-language drama. Austria. Germany. 1890-1910. Lang.: Ger. 2787
Dictionary of Alban Berg's *Lulu*. Austria. 1935. Lang.: Fre. 4760
Wedekind's Lulu plays and their adaptation by Berg. Germany. Austria. 1895-1935. Lang.: Fre. 4798
Luna, La
Performance/production
Analysis of films by Bernardo Bertolucci. 1979-1998. Lang.: Eng. 3927
Lunačarskij, Anatolij Vasiljévič
Performance/production
Mejerchol'd's production of Gogol's *Revizor (The Inspector General)*. USSR: Moscow. 1926. Lang.: Eng. 2763
Mejerchol'd's relationship with Lunačarskij. USSR. 1890-1931. Lang.: Eng. 2768
Lunacharsky Institute
SEE
Gosudarstvénnyj Institut Teatral'nogo Iskusstva im. A.V. Lunačarskogo.
Lunch Date, The
Basic theatrical documents
Screenplay of *The Lunch Date* by Adam Davidson. USA. 1998. Lang.: Eng. 3883
Lunchbox Theatre (Calgary, AB)
Institutions
Lunchbox Theatre's new play development program, Stage One. Canada: Calgary, AB. 1975-1998. Lang.: Eng. 1576
Lundberg, Lillemor
Institutions
History of Ballettakademian, Lillemor Lundberg, artistic director. Sweden: Stockholm. 1957-1998. Lang.: Swe. 901
Lunde, Robert Charles
Basic theatrical documents
Text of *The Country Mouse and the City Mouse* by Robert Charles Lunde. USA. 1986. Lang.: Eng. 1495
Lunt, Alfred
Performance/production
Acting couple Alfred Lunt and Lynn Fontanne: 'idealized heterosexuality'. USA. 1887-1983. Lang.: Eng. 2656
Luscombe, Christopher
Performance/production
Christopher Luscombe on acting in RSC productions. UK-England: London, Stratford. 1993-1994. Lang.: Eng. 2620
Luscombe, Tim
Plays/librettos/scripts
German view of English and American drama. UK-England. USA. 1998. Lang.: Ger. 3455
Luther
Plays/librettos/scripts
The rebel in modern drama. Europe. 1950-1988. Lang.: Eng. 3053
Lutkovno Gledališče Ljubljana (Ljubljana)
Institutions
The fiftieth anniversary of Ljubljana's puppet theatre. Slovenia: Ljubljana. 1968-1997. Lang.: Slo. 4873
Ljubljana's puppet theatre on its fiftieth anniversary. Slovenia: Ljubljana. 1948-1998. Lang.: Slo. 4874
Lux in Tenebris
Basic theatrical documents
Catalan translations of plays by Bertolt Brecht (volume 1). Germany. 1919-1954. Lang.: Cat. 1437
Performance/production
One-act plays by Brecht directed by József Jámbor. Hungary: Debrecen. 1998. Lang.: Hun. 2131
Lyceum Theatre (Edinburgh)
SEE
Royal Lyceum Theatre.
Lyceum Theatre (London)
Performance/production
Collection of newspaper reviews by London theatre critics. UK-England: London, Scarborough. 1998. Lang.: Eng. 2426
Collection of newspaper reviews by London theatre critics. UK-England: London. 1998. Lang.: Eng. 2513
Lycko-Pers resa (Lucky Per's Journey)
Plays/librettos/scripts
Folklore and occultism in August Strindberg's *Lycko-Pers resa (Lucky Per's Journey)*. Sweden. 1912. Lang.: Swe. 3412
Lyly, John
Plays/librettos/scripts
Tudor religious and social issues in John Lily's *Endymion* and *Midas*. England. 1587-1590. Lang.: Eng. 2871
Analysis of *Gallathea* by John Lyly. England. 1584. Lang.: Eng. 2888
Lyn, Eva
Performance/production
Collection of newspaper reviews by London theatre critics. UK-England: London. 1998. Lang.: Eng. 2479

Lynch, Kate
Performance/production
Voice teachers Alex Bulmer and Kate Lynch. Canada: Toronto, ON. UK-England: London. 1986-1998. Lang.: Eng. 1837
Lynne, Gillian
Performance/production
Gillian Lynne, director and choreographer. UK-England: London. USA: New York, NY. 1951-1998. Lang.: Eng. 4372
Lyric Hammersmith (London)
Administration
The 'Group of Four' at the Lyric Hammersmith and the concept of a national theatre. UK-England: London. 1945-1956. Lang.: Eng. 1392
Performance/production
Collection of newspaper reviews by London theatre critics. UK-England: London. 1998. Lang.: Eng. 2409
Collection of newspaper reviews by London theatre critics. UK-England: London. 1998. Lang.: Eng. 2421
Collection of newspaper reviews by London theatre critics. UK-England: London. 1998. Lang.: Eng. 2465
Collection of newspaper reviews by London theatre critics. UK-England: London. 1998. Lang.: Eng. 2469
Collection of newspaper reviews by London theatre critics. UK-England: London. 1998. Lang.: Eng. 2483
Collection of newspaper reviews by London theatre critics. UK-England: London. 1998. Lang.: Eng. 2506
Collection of newspaper reviews by London theatre critics. UK-England: London. 1998. Lang.: Eng. 2533
Collection of newspaper reviews by London theatre critics. UK-England: London. 1998. Lang.: Eng. 2556
Collection of newspaper reviews by London theatre critics. UK-England: London. 1998. Lang.: Eng. 2568
Collection of newspaper reviews by London theatre critics. UK-England: London. 1998. Lang.: Eng. 2584
Reviews of recent London performances. UK-England: London. 1998. Lang.: Ger. 2591
Report on several English performances. UK-England: London, Stratford. 1998. Lang.: Swe. 2634
Lyric Opera of Chicago (Chicago, IL)
Performance/production
Conductor Andrew Davis. UK-England. USA. 1998. Lang.: Eng. 4704
Background material on Lyric Opera of Chicago radio broadcast performances. USA: Chicago, IL. 1998. Lang.: Eng. 4709
Plays/librettos/scripts
Marvin David Levy's operatic adaptation of *Mourning Becomes Electra* by Eugene O'Neill. USA. 1931-1998. Lang.: Eng. 4827
Lyric Opera of Kansas City (Kansas City, MO)
Institutions
Retiring artistic directors of regional opera companies, Russell Patterson and Glyn Ross. USA. 1960-1998. Lang.: Eng. 4485
Lyric Studio (London)
Performance/production
Collection of newspaper reviews by London theatre critics. UK-England: London. 1998. Lang.: Eng. 2430
Collection of newspaper reviews by London theatre critics. UK-England: London. 1998. Lang.: Eng. 2436
Collection of newspaper reviews by London theatre critics. UK-England: London. 1998. Lang.: Eng. 2450
Collection of newspaper reviews by London theatre critics. UK-England: London. 1998. Lang.: Eng. 2452
Collection of newspaper reviews by London theatre critics. UK-England: London. 1998. Lang.: Eng. 2463
Collection of newspaper reviews by London theatre critics. UK-England: London. 1998. Lang.: Eng. 2472
Collection of newspaper reviews by London theatre critics. UK-England: London. 1998. Lang.: Eng. 2482
Collection of newspaper reviews by London theatre critics. UK-England: London. 1998. Lang.: Eng. 2500
Collection of newspaper reviews by London theatre critics. UK-England: London. 1998. Lang.: Eng. 2503
Collection of newspaper reviews by London theatre critics. UK-England: London. 1998. Lang.: Eng. 2541
Collection of newspaper reviews by London theatre critics. UK-England: London. 1998. Lang.: Eng. 2556
Collection of newspaper reviews by London theatre critics. UK-England: London. 1998. Lang.: Eng. 2570
Collection of newspaper reviews by London theatre critics. UK-England: London. 1998. Lang.: Eng. 2582
Lyric Theatre (Belfast)
Performance/production
Recent productions in Ireland of plays by Eugene O'Neill. Ireland: Dublin. UK-Ireland: Belfast. 1989-1998. Lang.: Eng. 2154
Lysande elände, Ett (Brilliant Misery, A)
Plays/librettos/scripts
Interview with Staffan Göthe, author, director, and one of the actors of *Ett Lysand elände (A Brilliant Misery)*. Sweden: Stockholm. 1990-1998. Lang.: Swe. 3408
Lysistrata
Basic theatrical documents
Catalan translation of Aristophanes' *Lysistrata*. Greece. 435 B.C. Lang.: Cat. 1438
Lyttelton Theatre (London)
SEE ALSO
National Theatre Company.
Performance/production
Collection of newspaper reviews by London theatre critics. UK-England: London. 1998. Lang.: Eng. 2423
Collection of newspaper reviews by London theatre critics. UK-England: London. 1998. Lang.: Eng. 2448
Collection of newspaper reviews by London theatre critics. UK-England: London. 1998. Lang.: Eng. 2466
Collection of newspaper reviews by London theatre critics. UK-England. 1998. Lang.: Eng. 2489
Collection of newspaper reviews by London theatre critics. UK-England: London. 1998. Lang.: Eng. 2508
Collection of newspaper reviews by London theatre critics. UK-England: London. 1998. Lang.: Eng. 2546
Plays/librettos/scripts
Theatrical activities of Harold Pinter. UK-England: London. 1996-1998. Lang.: Eng. 3462
M.T.M.
Performance/production
Truth and authenticity in *M.T.M.* by La Fura dels Baus. Spain: Barcelona. 1983-1998. Lang.: Eng. 598
Ma femme s'appelle Maurice (My Wife's Name Is Maurice)
Basic theatrical documents
Text of *Ma femme s'appelle Maurice (My Wife's Name Is Maurice)* by Raffy Shart. France. 1998. Lang.: Fre. 1435
Maan, Trudi
Design/technology
Profiles of young theatrical designers. Netherlands. 1990-1998. Lang.: Dut. 207
Mabou Mines (New York, NY)
Performance/production
The use of closed circuit television in avant-garde theatre performance. USA: New York, NY. 1978-1986. Lang.: Eng. 662
Ruth Maleczech of Mabou Mines. USA: New York, NY. 1970-1998. Lang.: Eng. 2694
Documentary theatre and the politics of representation. USA. 1966-1993. Lang.: Eng. 2728
Macartney, Syd
Performance/production
Actors' interpretations of the title role in Oscar Wilde's *The Canterville Ghost*. UK-England. USA. 1943-1998. Lang.: Eng. 4066
Macbeth
Design/technology
Technical designs for Off Broadway Shakespearean productions. USA: New York, NY. 1998. Lang.: Eng. 1539
Scenery in Orson Welles' film adaptation of Shakespeare's *Macbeth*. USA. 1948. Lang.: Fre. 3920
Lighting design for Verdi's *Macbeth* at La Scala. Italy: Milan. 1998. Lang.: Eng. 4435
Institutions
Carlo Quartucci's acting workshop on Shakespeare's *Macbeth*. Italy: Rome. 1991-1992. Lang.: Ita. 1674
Performance/production
The methodology of director Robert Lepage. Canada: Toronto, ON. 1992. Lang.: Eng. 1845
The performance of Shakespeare in the former East Germany. Germany: Rostock, Leipzig, Berlin, Dessau. 1996-1997. Lang.: Ger. 1974
Interview with playwright Heiner Müller about his adaptations of Shakespeare. Germany, East. 1965-1990. Lang.: Eng. 2039

Macbeth — cont'd

Collection of newspaper reviews by London theatre critics. UK-England: London. 1998. Lang.: Eng. 2471
Collection of newspaper reviews by London theatre critics. UK-England: London. 1998. Lang.: Eng. 2518
Collection of newspaper reviews by London theatre critics. UK-England: London. 1998. Lang.: Eng. 2585
Derek Jacobi on playing Macbeth for the RSC. UK-England: London, Stratford. 1993-1994. Lang.: Eng. 2616
Brief productions of Shakespeare, Shaw, and Marlowe at the World's Fair. USA: Chicago, IL. 1934. Lang.: Eng. 2701
Analysis of Les' Kurbas' production of Shakespeare's *Macbeth.* USSR. 1924. Lang.: Eng. 2766

Plays/librettos/scripts
Horace Walpole's *The Dear Witches* and Shakespeare's *Macbeth.* England. 1743. Lang.: Eng. 2857
Analysis of the frontispiece of Nicholas Rowe's edition of Shakespeare's *King Lear.* England. 1709-1714. Lang.: Eng. 2859
Christianity and Shakespeare's *Macbeth.* England. 1606. Lang.: Eng. 2890
Punishment and political power in plays of Shakespeare. England. 1604-1611. Lang.: Eng. 2944
Nicholas Rowe's illustration of a scene from *Macbeth.* England. 1709. Lang.: Eng. 2953
The nature of tyranny in plays of Shakespeare. England. 1595-1612. Lang.: Eng. 2978
Casuistry and early modern English tragedy. England. 1600-1671. Lang.: Eng. 2980
The concept of the self in Shakespearean tragedy. England. 1590-1612. Lang.: Eng. 2992
'Demonic' women in Shakespeare's tragedies. England. 1590-1613. Lang.: Eng. 2999
The interaction of other characters with Shakespeare's tragic heroes. England. 1590-1613. Lang.: Eng. 3037
Roman Polanski's film adaptation of Shakespeare's *Macbeth.* USA. 1971. Lang.: Fre. 4014

Theory/criticism
The urge to make Shakespeare contemporary. USA. 1990-1998. Lang.: Eng. 3844

MacColl, Ewan
Plays/librettos/scripts
The development of Theatre Workshop, founded by Ewan MacColl and Joan Littlewood. UK-England: London. 1945-1970. Lang.: Eng. 3491

MacDevitt, Brian
Design/technology
Recent work of lighting designer Brian MacDevitt. USA: New York, NY. 1997. Lang.: Eng. 1530

MacDonald, Anne-Marie
Performance/production
Collection of newspaper reviews by London theatre critics. UK-England: London. 1998. Lang.: Eng. 2562

Macdonald, Hettie
Performance/production
Collection of newspaper reviews by London theatre critics. UK-England: London. 1998. Lang.: Eng. 2543

Macdonald, James
Performance/production
Collection of newspaper reviews by London theatre critics. UK-England: London. 1998. Lang.: Eng. 2427
Collection of newspaper reviews by London theatre critics. UK-England: London. 1998. Lang.: Eng. 2467
Collection of newspaper reviews by London theatre critics. UK-England: London. 1998. Lang.: Eng. 2526
Reviews of recent London performances. UK-England: London. 1998. Lang.: Ger. 2591

Macfarlane, Gaynor
Performance/production
Gaynor Macfarlane's production of Edwards' *Damon and Pythias* at Shakespeare's Globe. UK-England: London. 1996. Lang.: Eng. 2613

Macgowan, Kenneth
Design/technology
Critic Kenneth Macgowan and the 'new stagecraft'. USA. 1912-1940. Lang.: Eng. 262

Machiavelli, Niccolò
Plays/librettos/scripts
Analysis of Machiavelli's *Clizia.* Italy. 1525. Lang.: Eng. 3257

Maciunas, George
Relation to other fields
The Fluxus movement. USA. Europe. 1961-1979. Lang.: Eng. 4265

MacIvor, Daniel
Plays/librettos/scripts
Analysis of Daniel MacIvor's *Monster* as directed by Daniel Brooks. Canada: Toronto, ON. 1998. Lang.: Eng. 2834

Mackie, Bob
Design/technology
Set and costume design for San Francisco Opera productions. USA: San Francisco, CA. 1998. Lang.: Eng. 4443

Mackintosh, Cameron
Performance/production
Collection of newspaper reviews by London theatre critics. UK-England: London, Scarborough. 1998. Lang.: Eng. 2426

Mackintosh, Robert
Design/technology
Costume designer Robert Mackintosh. USA. 1926-1998. Lang.: Eng. 284

Macklin, Charles
Performance/production
The feud between David Garrick and Charles Macklin. England: London. 1743-1777. Lang.: Eng. 1897

MacLeod, Wendy
Plays/librettos/scripts
Women playwrights' addresses to the Women's Project conference. USA. 1997. Lang.: Eng. 3589
Analysis of *The Water Children* by Wendy Macleod. USA. 1998. Lang.: Eng. 3613

Macor, Claudio
Performance/production
Collection of newspaper reviews by London theatre critics. UK-England: London. 1998. Lang.: Eng. 2517

Mad Forest
Plays/librettos/scripts
Systemic poisons in plays of Caryl Churchill. UK-England. 1990-1997. Lang.: Eng. 3463
Analysis of *Mad Forest* by Caryl Churchill. UK-England. 1990. Lang.: Eng. 3505

Mad World, My Masters, A
Performance/production
Collection of newspaper reviews by London theatre critics. UK-England: London. 1998. Lang.: Eng. 2486

Madách Kamaraszínház (Budapest)
Performance/production
Review of *Édes Anna (Anna Édes)*, Madách Chamber Theatre. Hungary: Budapest. 1997. Lang.: Hun. 2136

Madách Színház (Budapest)
Performance/production
Reviews of two plays by Per Olov Enquist. Hungary: Budapest. 1998. Lang.: Hun. 2089
Reviews of new Hungarian musicals. Hungary: Budapest. 1997. Lang.: Hun. 4360

Madách, Imre
Performance/production
Review of Madách's *Tragedy of Man* at the Hungarian Theatre of Kolozsvár. Hungary. Romania: Cluj-Napoca. 1997. Lang.: Hun. 2065
Madách's *Tragedy of Man* directed by Sándor Beke. Hungary: Eger. 1998. Lang.: Hun. 2090
A puppet production of Madách's *Az ember tragédiája (The Tragedy of Man).* France: Colmar. 1998. Lang.: Hun. 4893

Madama Butterfly
Performance/production
Background material on Lyric Opera of Chicago radio broadcast performances. USA: Chicago, IL. 1998. Lang.: Eng. 4709
Background material on Metropolitan Opera radio broadcast performances. USA: New York, NY. 1998. Lang.: Eng. 4713

Madame de Sade
SEE
Sado Koshaku fujin.

Madang
Performance/production
Historical, political, and aesthetic context of *madang* theatre. Korea. 1976-1998. Lang.: Ger. 557

Madariaga, Salvador de
Performance/production
A production of László Lajtha's comic opera *Le chapeau bleu.* Romania: Cluj-Napoca. Hungary. 1998. Lang.: Hun. 4666

Madariaga, Salvador de — cont'd

Production of László Lajtha's comic opera *Le chapeau bleu.* Romania: Cluj-Napoca. Hungary. 1948-1998. Lang.: Hun. 4668

Maddalena lasciva e penitente, La (Mary Magdalene, Lascivious and Penitent)
Performance/production
Analysis of religious theatre of Giambattista Andreini. Italy. 1576-1654. Lang.: Eng. 2190

Maddalena, La (Mary Magdalene)
Performance/production
Analysis of religious theatre of Giambattista Andreini. Italy. 1576-1654. Lang.: Eng. 2190

Madden, Aodhan
Performance/production
Collection of newspaper reviews by London theatre critics. UK-England: London. 1998. Lang.: Eng. 2483

Made in England
Performance/production
Collection of newspaper reviews by London theatre critics. UK-England: London. 1998. Lang.: Eng. 2427
Collection of newspaper reviews by London theatre critics. UK-England: London. 1998. Lang.: Eng. 2532

Mäde, Hans-Dieter
Performance/production
The political and social climate of East German theatre in the sixties. Germany, East. 1960-1970. Lang.: Eng. 2052

Maderna, Bruno
Plays/librettos/scripts
Hero and anti-hero in contemporary opera production. Germany. 1998. Lang.: Ger. 4791

Madmen and Specialists
Plays/librettos/scripts
Political satire in the plays of Wole Soyinka. Nigeria. 1960-1979. Lang.: Eng. 3284

Madness of George III, The
Plays/librettos/scripts
Playwright Alan Bennett. UK-England. 1994-1998. Lang.: Ger. 3488

Madness of Lady Bright, The
Plays/librettos/scripts
American gay drama and the impact of AIDS. USA. 1960-1987. Lang.: Eng. 3670

Madschun al-Malik. Der Narr des König (Madschun al-Malik, the King's Fool)
Plays/librettos/scripts
Analysis of *Madschun al-Malik* by Michael Roes. Germany: Düsseldorf. 1998. Lang.: Ger. 3157

Maerli, Terje
Performance/production
Report from Ibsen festival. Norway: Oslo. 1998. Lang.: Swe. 2211
Interview with actors in Feydeau's *La Puce à l'Oreille (A Flea in Her Ear)* at Dramaten. Sweden: Stockholm. 1998. Lang.: Swe. 2396

Maeterlinck, Maurice
Plays/librettos/scripts
The dramatic styles of Maurice Maeterlinck and Anton Čechov. Russia. Belgium. 1890-1949. Lang.: Rus. 3328

Maggie
Performance/production
Collection of newspaper reviews by London theatre critics. UK-England: London. Lang.: Eng. 2408

Maggio Musicale Fiorentino (Florence)
Performance/production
A production of Puccini's *Turandot* in Beijing. China, People's Republic of: Beijing. 1998. Lang.: Eng. 4542

Magic
Performance/production
Illusionist Dž. Mostoslavskij. Russia: Yaroslav. 1998. Lang.: Rus. 4129
Obituary for Bob McAllister, ventriloquist, magician, and former host of *Wonderama.* USA. 1935-1998. Lang.: Eng. 4149
The theory and practice of stage magic. 1998. Lang.: Rus. 4274

Magic Afternoon
Performance/production
Reviews of plays by Wolfgang Bauer and Thomas Bernhard. Switzerland: Basel. Austria: Vienna. 1998. Lang.: Ger. 2403

Magic Fire, The
Plays/librettos/scripts
Playwright Lillian Garrett-Groag. USA: Los Angeles, CA. 1998. Lang.: Eng. 3683

Magic Flute, The
SEE
Zauberflöte, Die.

Magill, Simon
Performance/production
Recent productions in Ireland of plays by Eugene O'Neill. Ireland: Dublin. UK-Ireland: Belfast. 1989-1998. Lang.: Eng. 2154

Magni, Marcello
Performance/production
Collection of newspaper reviews by London theatre critics. UK-England: London. 1998. Lang.: Eng. 2587

Magnus
Basic theatrical documents
Text of *Magnus* by Jordi Teixidor. Spain-Catalonia. 1994. Lang.: Cat. 1468

Magomaev, Muslim
Performance/production
Opera singers Tamara Sinjavskaja and Muslim Magomaev. Russia. 1998. Lang.: Rus. 4675

Maguire
Plays/librettos/scripts
BBC radio plays with Anglo-Irish themes. UK-England. Ireland. 1973-1986. Lang.: Eng. 3868

Magyar Állami Operaház (Budapest)
Design/technology
Profile of costume designer Tivadar Márk. Hungary. 1908-1998. Lang.: Hun. 4432
Performance/production
László Márkus, one-time director of the Budapest Opera House. Hungary. 1881-1948. Lang.: Hun. 540
Bartók's *A csodálatos mandarin (The Miraculous Mandarin)* choreographed by Gyula Harangozó. Hungary: Budapest. 1998.Lang.: Hun. 1088
Lilla Pártay's ballet adaptation of *Anna Karenina.* Hungary. 1991-1998. Lang.: Hun. 1090
Irma Nioradze in a performance of *Don Quixote* choreographed by Marius Petipa. Hungary: Budapest. 1998. Lang.: Hun. 1093
The Budapest Opera House's new production of *Giselle.* Hungary: Budapest. 1998. Lang.: Hun. 1094
A gala performance at the Magyar Állami Operaház. Hungary: Budapest. 1998. Lang.: Hun. 1099
Choreographer László Seregi. Hungary: Budapest. 1949-1998. Lang.: Hun. 1100
Bartók's *A fából faragott királyfi (The Wooden Prince)* choreographed by László Seregi. Hungary: Budapest. 1998. Lang.: Hun. 1103
Choreographer Gyula Harangozó and the Hungarian National Ballet. Hungary. 1908-1998. Lang.: Hun. 1104
Review of one-act ballets by Balanchine. Hungary: Budapest. 1997. Lang.: Hun. 1105
Interview with dancer Katalin Hágai. Hungary. 1998. Lang.: Hun. 1107
Interview with dancer Vera Szumrák. Hungary. 1950-1998. Lang.: Hun. 1114
The Nutcracker at the Budapest Opera House. Hungary: Budapest. 1998. Lang.: Hun. 1115
Interview with choreographer John Taras. USA: New York, NY. 1919-1998. Lang.: Hun. 1187
Kodály's *Székely fonó (The Székler Spinnery).* Hungary: Budapest. 1998. Lang.: Hun. 4298
Interview with Imre Kerényi, director of Kodály's *Székely fonó (The Székler Spinnery).* Hungary: Budapest. 1997. Lang.: Hun. 4299
Soprano Mária Németh. Hungary. Austria: Vienna. 1898-1967. Lang.: Hun. 4615
Interview with baritone István Gáti. Hungary. 1971-1998. Lang.: Hun. 4618
Interview with Miklós Gábor Kerényi on directing Verdi's *Un Ballo in Maschera.* Hungary: Budapest. 1998. Lang.: Hun. 4619
Interview with tenor Sándor Palcsó. Hungary. 1929-1998. Lang.: Hun. 4620
Tribute to the late soprano Júlia Orosz. Hungary. 1908-1997. Lang.: Hun. 4623
Profile of baritone György Radnai. Hungary. 1920-1977. Lang.: Hun. 4624
Obituary for baritone Zsolt Bende. Hungary. 1926-1998. Lang.: Hun. 4628
Verdi's *Un Ballo in Maschera* at the Hungarian State Opera House. Hungary: Budapest. 1998. Lang.: Hun. 4629

Magyar Állami Operaház (Budapest) — cont'd

Interview with director János Szikora. Hungary: Budapest. 1998. Lang.: Hun. 4630

Mozart's *Die Zauberflöte* directed by János Szikora. Hungary: Budapest. Hungary: Szeged. 1998. Lang.: Hun. 4631

Profile of soprano Veronika Fekete. Hungary. 1958-1998. Lang.: Hun. 4632

Baritone György Melis and the performance in celebration of his 75th birthday. Hungary. 1923-1998. Lang.: Hun. 4633

Interview with bass Albert Antalffy. Hungary. Austria: Mödling. 1924-1998. Lang.: Hun. 4634

Interview with director Viktor Nagy on Wagner's *Ring* cycle. Hungary: Budapest. 1998. Lang.: Hun. 4635

Interview with Miklós Gábor Kerényi on his production of *Un Ballo in maschera*. Hungary: Budapest, Szeged. 1998. Lang.: Hun. 4636

Interview with opera singer Judit Sándor on her male roles. Hungary. 1948-1998. Lang.: Hun. 4637

Mozart's *Le Nozze di Figaro* at the Hungarian State Opera House. Hungary: Budapest. 1998. Lang.: Hun. 4638

Album on the life and career of baritone György Melis. Hungary. 1923-1998. Lang.: Hun, Eng. 4639

Interview with bass László Polgár. Hungary. Switzerland: Zurich. 1947-1998. Lang.: Hun. 4640

Interview with soprano Mária Temesi. Hungary. 1977-1998. Lang.: Hun. 4643

Interview with soprano Andrea Lory. Romania: Iasi. Hungary. 1998. 19-1998. Lang.: Hun. 4667

Plays/librettos/scripts

Outline of Wagner's *Götterdämmerung*. Hungary: Budapest. 1998. Lang.: Hun. 4800

Reference materials

Yearbook of the Hungarian State Opera House. Hungary: Budapest. 1996-1997. Lang.: Hun. 4832

Training

Interview with ballet dancer and teacher Jacqueline Menyhárt. Hungary. 1954-1998. Lang.: Hun. 1206

Interview with ballet master Tamás Koren. Hungary. 1959-1998. Lang.: Hun. 1207

Magyar Állami Operaház Balettegyüttese (Budapest)

Performance/production

Interview with dancer and ballet mistress Márta Metzger. Budapest. 1968-1998. Lang.: Hun. 1066

La Fille mal Gardée at Erkel Színház. Hungary: Budapest. 1997. Lang.: Hun. 1087

Interview with ballerina Katalin Hágai. Hungary. 1961-1998. Lang.: Hun. 1096

Interview with ballerina Adél Orosz. Hungary. 1954-1998. Lang.: Hun. 1112

Critical reactions to the dance evening *Mokka*. Hungary: Budapest. 1998. Lang.: Hun. 1116

Magyar Elektra

Performance/production

István Somogyi's productions of *Magyar Elektra* by Péter Bornemisza. Hungary: Budapest. 1988-1998. Lang.: Hun. 2114

Two productions by István Somogyi of Bornemisza's *Magyar Elektra*. Hungary: Budapest. 1988-1998. Lang.: Hun. 2148

Magyar Fesztivál Balett (Budapest)

Performance/production

Iván Markó's choreography for Bayreuth Festival productions. Germany: Bayreuth. Hungary. 1998. Lang.: Hun. 1083

Productions of the Magyar Fesztival Balett choreographed by Iván Markó. Hungary: Budapest. 1998. Lang.: Hun. 1097

Interview with choreographer Iván Markó. Hungary: Budapest. 1998. Lang.: Hun. 1101

Magyar Királyi Operaház (Budapest)

Performance/production

Tenor Béla Környey. Hungary. 1875-1925. Lang.: Hun. 4616

Soprano Olga Haselbeck. Hungary. 1884-1961. Lang.: Hun. 4626

Profile of soprano Piroska Anday. Hungary: Budapest. Austria: Vienna. 1903-1977. Lang.: Hun. 4627

Magyar Színház (Budapest)

Performance/production

László Márkus, one-time director of the Budapest Opera House. Hungary. 1881-1948. Lang.: Hun. 540

Magyar Színház (New York, NY)

Institutions

History of annual festival of Hungarian-language theatre. Hungary: Kisvárda. 1989-1998. Lang.: Hun. 1669

Magyar Táncművészeti Főiskola (Budapest)

Institutions

Interview with Imre Dózsa, general director of Magyar Táncművészeti Főiskola. Hungary. 1998. Lang.: Hun. 894

Performance/production

Gala concert by students of the Hungarian Dance Academy. Hungary: Budapest. 1998. Lang.: Hun. 1091

Magyar, Attila

Institutions

Theatre critics' awards 97-98. Hungary. 1997-1998. Lang.: Hun. 355

Mahabharata, The

Performance/production

Peter Brook's *The Mahabharata*, and problems of intercultural performance. France. 1988-1992. Lang.: Eng. 1925

Maher, Joseph

Performance/production

Obituaries for Joseph Maher, Warren Kliewer, and E.G. Marshall. USA. 1912-1998. Lang.: Eng. 2655

Maheu, Gilles

Plays/librettos/scripts

Analysis of plays by Gilles Maheu. Canada: Montreal, PQ. 1994-1998. Lang.: Fre. 1357

Mahler, Gustav

Performance/production

Choreographer John Neumeier. Germany: Hamburg. USA: New York, NY. 1998. Lang.: Eng. 1082

Collection of newspaper reviews by London theatre critics. UK-England: London. 1998. Lang.: Eng. 2409

Reviews of recent London performances. UK-England: London. 1998. Lang.: Ger. 2591

Maid of Orleans, The

SEE

Orleanskaja Deva.

Maid of the Mill, The

Plays/librettos/scripts

Music and the ballad opera in English popular theatre. England. 1728-1780. Lang.: Eng. 4390

Maid's Tragedy, The

Institutions

The inaugural season of Shakespeare's Globe Theatre. UK-England: London. 1997-1998. Lang.: Eng. 1741

Performance/production

The inaugural season of Shakespeare's Globe Theatre. UK-England: London. 1997. Lang.: Eng. 2601

Review of the opening season of Shakespeare's Globe Theatre. UK-England: London. 1997. Lang.: Eng. 2602

Plays/librettos/scripts

Casuistry and early modern English tragedy. England. 1600-1671. Lang.: Eng. 2980

Maiden's Prayer, The

Design/technology

Derek McLane's set designs for recent Off Broadway productions. USA: New York, NY. 1998. Lang.: Eng. 1538

Maids, The

SEE

Bonnes, Les.

Maienschlager (May Pop-Song, A)

Performance/production

Productions of new plays by Peter Handke and Katharine Gericke at Niedersächsische Staatstheater. Germany: Hannover. 1998. Lang.: Ger. 1983

Maillet, Antonine

Plays/librettos/scripts

French translations of Shakespeare by Antonine Maillet and Jean-Louis Roux. Canada: Montreal, PQ. 1988-1993. Lang.: Fre. 2793

Women and Acadian theatre. Canada. 1870-1998. Lang.: Eng. 2810

Dramatic adaptations of Henry Wadsworth Longfellow's poem *Evangeline*. USA. Canada. 1860-1976. Lang.: Eng. 3643

Mains Sales, Les (Dirty Hands)

Performance/production

Political context of Frank Castorf's production of *Les Mains Sales (Dirty Hands)* by Sartre. Germany: Berlin. 1998. Lang.: Ger. 2002

Plays/librettos/scripts

Frank Castorf's production of Sartre's *Les Mains Sales (Dirty Hands)* and the civil war in Yugoslavia. Germany: Berlin. 1998. Lang.: Ger. 3129

Mairowitz, David Zaine
Performance/production
Collection of newspaper reviews by London theatre critics. UK-England: London. 1998. Lang.: Eng. 2524
Maison suspendue, La (House Among the Stars, The)
Performance/production
Collection of newspaper reviews by London theatre critics. UK-England: London. 1998. Lang.: Eng. 2530
Maitu Njugira
Plays/librettos/scripts
Playwright Ngugi wa Thiong'o and the Kamirithu theatre project. Kenya: Kamiriithu. 1979-1992. Lang.: Eng. 3266
Majakovskij, Vladimir Vladimirović
Plays/librettos/scripts
Drama and theatrical elements in the work of Vladimir Majakovskij. Russia. 1910-1930. Lang.: Eng. 3319
Majestic Theatre (New York, NY)
Design/technology
Design concept for Ralph Lemon's dance piece *Geography* at BAM. USA: New York, NY. 1998. Lang.: Eng. 1248
Plays/librettos/scripts
Shared Experience's stage adaptations of nineteenth-century novels. USA: New York, NY. UK-England: London. 1998. Lang.: Eng. 3518
Major Barbara
Performance/production
Shaw's *Major Barbara* at the People's Arts Theatre. China, People's Republic of: Beijing. 1991. Lang.: Eng. 1874
Collection of newspaper reviews by London theatre critics. UK-England: London. 1998. Lang.: Eng. 2562
Plays/librettos/scripts
Structure and philosophy in Shaw's *Major Barbara* and *Man and Superman*. UK-England. 1901-1905. Lang.: Eng. 3427
Linguistic style and action in plays of Wilde, Shaw, and Stoppard. UK-England. 1890-1985. Lang.: Eng. 3467
Majorova, E.
Performance/production
Actress E. Majorova and her husband, scenographer S. Šerstjuk. Russia: Moscow. 1998. Lang.: Rus. 2283
Makai, Péter
Design/technology
Set and costume designs of Péter Makai. Hungary. 1957-1991. Lang.: Hun. 194
Makarova, I.V.
Performance/production
Memoirs of actress I.V. Makarova. Russia: Moscow. 1998. Lang.: Rus. 2294
Makarova, Natalija
Performance/production
Russian émigré ballet dancers. Russia: St. Petersburg. Lang.: Rus. 1129
Make-up
Design/technology
Guide to theatrical design manufacturers and equipment. USA. 1998. Lang.: Eng. 241
TV and film make-up artists Tom Burman and Bari Dreiband-Burman. USA: Hollywood, CA. 1998. Lang.: Eng. 4050
Design awards for the TV mini-series *Merlin*. USA: Pasadena, CA. 1998. Lang.: Eng. 4052
Makoveckij, Sergej
Performance/production
Actor Sergej Makoveckij. Russia: Moscow. 1998. Lang.: Rus. 2295
Makovsky, Judianna
Design/technology
Production design for Gary Ross's film *Pleasantville*. USA: Hollywood, CA. 1998. Lang.: Eng. 3909
Makrancos Kata, A (Taming of the Shrew, The)
Performance/production
Interview with ballerina Katalin Hágai. Hungary. 1961-1998. Lang.: Hun. 1096
Maksimova, V.A.
Performance/production
Memoirs of actresses Olga Aroseva and V.A. Maksimova. Russia: Moscow. 1998. Lang.: Rus. 2234
Malade imaginaire, Le (Imaginary Invalid, The)
Performance/production
Three Hungarian productions of plays by Molière. Hungary: Szentendre, Kapolcs, Kőszeg. 1998. Lang.: Hun. 2142
Collection of newspaper reviews by London theatre critics. UK-England: London. 1998. Lang.: Eng. 2411
Plays/librettos/scripts
Analysis of medical plays by Molière. France. 1660-1722. Lang.: Eng. 3078
Maladie de la Mort, La (Sickness of Death, The)
Performance/production
Reviews of productions by Wilson, Greenaway, and Mnouchkine. France: Paris. 1997-1998. Lang.: Eng. 1926
The performances of Lucinda Childs and Michel Piccoli in *La Maladie de la Mort (The Sickness of Death)*, directed by Robert Wilson. France: Paris. 1997. Lang.: Eng. 1942
Interview with actress Lucinda Childs. France: Paris. 1976-1997. Lang.: Eng. 1943
The collaboration of choreographer Lucinda Childs and director Robert Wilson on *La Maladie de la Mort*. Germany. 1992-1997. Lang.: Eng. 2019
Malaparte, Curzio
Plays/librettos/scripts
The collaboration of playwright Curzio Malaparte and director Guido Salvini. Italy. 1905-1956. Lang.: Ita. 3239
Målarsalen (Stockholm)
Performance/production
Recent productions of plays by Ibsen and Strindberg. Sweden: Stockholm. 1997. Lang.: Eng. 2393
Malavika, Sarukkai
Performance/production
Classical Indian dance performer Malavika Sarukkai. India. 1998. Lang.: Rus. 1349
Malcolm X
Performance/production
Spike Lee's unsuccessful efforts to film parts of *Malcolm X* in Mecca. USA. 1992-1995. Lang.: Eng. 3954
Malcontent, The
Performance/production
Collection of newspaper reviews by London theatre critics. UK-England: London. 1998. Lang.: Eng. 2516
Plays/librettos/scripts
The politics of gender in the plays of John Marston. England. 1599-1634. Lang.: Eng. 3009
Maleczech, Ruth
Performance/production
Ruth Maleczech of Mabou Mines. USA: New York, NY. 1970-1998. Lang.: Eng. 2694
Malina, Judith
Institutions
The present status of the Living Theatre. North America. 1991-1997. Lang.: Eng. 371
Judith Malina's attempt to create an active mixed-media theatre. USA. 1968-1969. Lang.: Eng. 1765
Performance/production
Theatre Magazine's anniversary issue. USA. 1968-1998. Lang.: Eng. 617
The Living Theatre's *Paradise Now*—creation and production. USA. 1951-1968. Lang.: Eng. 667
Relation to other fields
Government response to Living Theatre's *Paradise Now*. USA. Europe. 1968. Lang.: Eng. 3789
Malinche
Basic theatrical documents
Text of plays by Carlos Morton. USA. 1986. Lang.: Eng. 1499
Malipiero, Gian Francesco
Performance/production
Music theatre production in northern Germany. Germany: Lübeck, Hamburg, Bremen, Kiel. 1998. Lang.: Ger. 4293
Malle, Louis
Plays/librettos/scripts
Analysis of Louis Malle's film *Vanya on 42nd Street*. USA. 1994. Lang.: Fre. 4031
Mallozzi, Dawn
Plays/librettos/scripts
Account of performances by Joan Dickinson. USA. 1997-1998. Lang.: Eng. 4263
Malmö Högskola
Design/technology
Theatre technician training at Malmö Högskola. Sweden: Malmö. 1998. Lang.: Swe. 225
Malmö Musikteater
Performance spaces
Malmö Musikteater's production of *Lucia di Lammermoor* at Hedeland Amfiteater. Denmark: Hedeland. 1997. Lang.: Swe. 4491

Malone, Beni
Plays/librettos/scripts
Wonderbolt Circus's *Maid of Avalon*, a loose adaptation of *Der Gute Mensch von Sezuan (The Good Person of Szechwan)* by Brecht.Canada: St. John's, NF. 1950-1998. Lang.: Eng. 2825
Malone, Bonz
Basic theatrical documents
Screenplay of the film *Slam.* USA. 1998. Lang.: Eng. 3893
Plays/librettos/scripts
Interview with creators of the film *Slam.* USA. 1998. Lang.: Eng. 4001
Malone, Greg
Plays/librettos/scripts
Wonderbolt Circus's *Maid of Avalon*, a loose adaptation of *Der Gute Mensch von Sezuan (The Good Person of Szechwan)* by Brecht.Canada: St. John's, NF. 1950-1998. Lang.: Eng. 2825
Malone, Michael
Performance/production
The 'viewpoint theory' of actor training. USA. 1998. Lang.: Eng. 2677
Malpertuis (Tielt)
Plays/librettos/scripts
Dutch and Flemish Shakespearean productions. Belgium. Netherlands. 1980-1983. Lang.: Dut. 2789
Maltby, Richard, Jr.
Performance/production
Collection of newspaper reviews by London theatre critics. UK-England: London. 1998. Lang.: Eng. 2476
Malter, Richard
Performance/production
Collection of newspaper reviews by London theatre critics. UK-England: London. 1998. Lang.: Eng. 2524
Malyj Dramatičeskij Teat'r (St. Petersburg)
Performance/production
Collection of newspaper reviews by London theatre critics. UK-England: London. 1998. Lang.: Eng. 2424
Malyj Teat'r (Moscow)
Institutions
Ostrovskij Festival celebrating the 175th anniversary of Malyj Teat'r. Russia: Moscow. 1998. Lang.: Rus. 1709
Performance/production
Director Jurij Solomin of Malyj Teat'r. Russia: Moscow. 1998. Lang.: Rus. 2326
Memoirs of Malyj Theatre actor E. Ja. Vesnik. Russia: Moscow. 1998. Lang.: Rus. 2336
Mama I Can't Sing
Plays/librettos/scripts
AIDS and the work of performance artist Franko B. UK-England. 1996-1998. Lang.: Eng. 4261
Mama je umria dvakrat (Mama Died Twice)
Basic theatrical documents
Texts of plays by Vinko Möderndorfer. Slovenia. 1997. Lang.: Slo. 1458
Mambachaka, Vincent
Basic theatrical documents
Text of *Ubu déchaîné (Ubu Unchained)* by Richard Demarcy. Benin. France. 1998. Lang.: Fre. 4287
Mambéty, Djibril Diop
Performance/production
Analysis of *Touki-Bouki (The Hyena's Travels)* by Djibril Diop Mambéty. Senegal. 1973. Lang.: Eng. 3938
Mamet, David
Basic theatrical documents
Text of *The Spanish Prisoner* by David Mamet. USA. 1998. Lang.: Eng. 3896
Design/technology
Lighting design for Mamet's *The Old Neighborhood* directed by Scott Zigler. USA: New York, NY. 1998. Lang.: Eng. 1547
Performance/production
Collection of newspaper reviews by London theatre critics. UK-England: London. 1998. Lang.: Eng. 2422
Collection of newspaper reviews by London theatre critics. UK-England: London. 1998. Lang.: Eng. 2430
Collection of newspaper reviews by London theatre critics. UK-England: London. 1998. Lang.: Eng. 2582
Interview with actor Peter Riegert. USA: New York, NY. 1998. Lang.: Eng. 2676
Hitchcock's influence on *The Spanish Prisoner* by David Mamet. USA. 1998. Lang.: Eng. 3956
Plays/librettos/scripts
Aggressive language in modern drama. Europe. USA. 1960-1985. Lang.: Eng. 3055
English-language plays on the Dutch and Flemish stage. Netherlands. 1920-1998. Lang.: Dut. 3278
Analysis of the plays of David Mamet. USA. 1970-1993. Lang.: Eng. 3541
Analysis of *Duck Variations* by David Mamet. USA. 1976. Lang.: Dut. 3554
Analysis of *Glengarry Glen Ross.* USA. 1983. Lang.: Dut. 3556
Language and aphasic speech patterns in the plays of David Mamet. USA. 1975-1987. Lang.: Eng. 3677
Rites of passage in the plays of David Mamet. USA. 1975-1995. Lang.: Eng. 3680
Mail interview with David Mamet about *The Spanish Prisoner.* USA. 1998. Lang.: Eng. 3993
David Mamet's success as a screenwriter and film director. USA. 1998. Lang.: Eng. 4003
Analysis of films of David Mamet. USA: Los Angeles, CA. 1980-1998. Lang.: Eng. 4006
Theory/criticism
Theatrical theory and practice. 600 B.C.-1997 A.D. Lang.: Slo. 3804
Mamontov, Savva Ivanovič
Design/technology
Scene designers of the Mamontovskaja Opera. Russia: Moscow. 1875-1925. Lang.: Rus. 4437
Mamontovskaja Opera (Moscow)
Design/technology
Scene designers of the Mamontovskaja Opera. Russia: Moscow. 1875-1925. Lang.: Rus. 4437
Mamulengo
Performance/production
Northern Brazilian folk theatre forms. Brazil. 1972-1997. Lang.: Eng. 497
Man Act
Performance/production
Interview with director Richard Schechner. USA. 1987. Lang.: Eng. 4260
Man and Superman
Performance/production
Seven critics on their favorite character or portrayal. Sweden. 1950. Lang.: Swe. 2369
Plays/librettos/scripts
Structure and philosophy in Shaw's *Major Barbara* and *Man and Superman.* UK-England. 1901-1905. Lang.: Eng. 3427
George Bernard Shaw: life, work, influences. UK-England. Ireland. 1886-1955. Lang.: Eng. 3437
Linguistic style and action in plays of Wilde, Shaw, and Stoppard. UK-England. 1890-1985. Lang.: Eng. 3467
George Bernard Shaw and the 'New Woman'. UK-England. 1890-1900. Lang.: Eng. 3486
Shaw's *Man and Superman* as a philosophical treatise. UK-England. 1905. Lang.: Eng. 3495
George Bernard Shaw and science fiction. UK-England. Ireland. 1887-1998. Lang.: Eng. 3508
Man in the Moon Theatre (London)
Performance/production
Collection of newspaper reviews by London theatre critics. UK-England: London. 1998. Lang.: Eng. 2412
Collection of newspaper reviews by London theatre critics. UK-England: London. 1998. Lang.: Eng. 2422
Collection of newspaper reviews by London theatre critics. UK-England: London. 1998. Lang.: Eng. 2437
Collection of newspaper reviews by London theatre critics. UK-England: London. 1998. Lang.: Eng. 2462
Collection of newspaper reviews by London theatre critics. UK-England: London. 1998. Lang.: Eng. 2477
Collection of newspaper reviews by London theatre critics. UK-England: London. 1998. Lang.: Eng. 2487
Collection of newspaper reviews by London theatre critics. UK-England: London. 1998. Lang.: Eng. 2495
Collection of newspaper reviews by London theatre critics. UK-England: London. 1998. Lang.: Eng. 2512
Collection of newspaper reviews by London theatre critics. UK-England: London. 1998. Lang.: Eng. 2524
Collection of newspaper reviews by London theatre critics. UK-England: London. 1998. Lang.: Eng. 2526

Man in the Moon Theatre (London) — cont'd

Collection of newspaper reviews by London theatre critics. UK-England: London. 1998. Lang.: Eng. 2528
Collection of newspaper reviews by London theatre critics. UK-England: London. 1998. Lang.: Eng. 2545
Collection of newspaper reviews by London theatre critics. UK-England: London. 1998. Lang.: Eng. 2549
Collection of newspaper reviews by London theatre critics. UK-England: London. 1998. Lang.: Eng. 2575

Man of Destiny, The
Plays/librettos/scripts
Rhetorical arguments in one-act plays of Shaw. UK-England. 1890-1945. Lang.: Eng. 3453

Man of La Mancha
Plays/librettos/scripts
W.H. Auden as an opera librettist and translator. UK-England. 1907-1973. Lang.: Eng. 4825

Man Who Came to Dinner, The
Performance/production
Collection of newspaper reviews by London theatre critics. UK-England: London. 1998. Lang.: Eng. 2476

Management
SEE ALSO
Administration.
Administration
Interview with director Péter Léner of József Attila Theatre. Hungary: Budapest. 1960-1998. Lang.: Hun. 15
Methods of organization-building in the arts. Netherlands. 1998. Lang.: Dut. 18
Operations manual for Taiwan's Cultural Center Theatres. Taiwan. 1985-1987. Lang.: Eng. 23
History of circle stock touring. USA. 1907-1957. Lang.: Eng. 43
Profile of management group National Arts Stabilization. USA. 1998. Lang.: Eng. 144
Institutions
The New Playwrights Theatre Company. USA: New York, NY. 1927-1929. Lang.: Eng. 410
The first decade of Ljubljana's municipal theatre, Mestno gledališče ljubljansko. Slovenia: Ljubljana. 1951-1961. Lang.: Slo. 1718
The mission and management of the Free Southern Theatre. USA: New Orleans, LA. 1963-1980. Lang.: Eng. 1769
Performance/production
László Márkus, one-time director of the Budapest Opera House. Hungary. 1881-1948. Lang.: Hun. 540
Acting in the private theatre of the Ming Dynasty. China. 1368-1644. Lang.: Eng. 1872

Management, stage
Administration
The work of an Equity Stage Manager. USA: New York, NY. 1998. Lang.: Eng. 84
Working conditions and requirements of stage managers. USA: New York, NY. 1998. Lang.: Eng. 96
Design/technology
Jason Barnes, production manager of the Royal National Theatre. UK-England: London. 1973-1998. Lang.: Eng. 1527

Management, top
Administration
Speculation on the future effects of technology and ethnic diversity on theatre. USA. 1990-1993. Lang.: Eng. 42
Nineteenth-century women theatre managers. USA. 1800-1900. Lang.: Eng. 129
Theatre manager and entrepreneur Harry Davis. USA: Pittsburgh, PA. 1893-1927. Lang.: Eng. 134
Theatre manager Charles H. Gilfert. USA: Charleston, SC. 1817-1822. Lang.: Eng. 135
Study of management in regional theatres. USA. 1987-1988. Lang.: Eng. 140
Interview with Jean-Pierre Miquel, managing director of the Comédie-Française. France. 1998. Lang.: Hun. 1378
Interview with Thomas Ostermeier, artistic director of Schaubühne. Germany: Berlin. 1996-1998. Lang.: Ger. 1386
Interviews with women in top management of theatres. USA: New Haven, CT, Seattle, WA, East Haddam, CT. 1998. Lang.: Eng. 1397
Interview with Carrie Jackson, executive director of AUDELCO. USA: New York, NY. 1998. Lang.: Eng. 1399
History of the Brighton performance festival. UK-England: Brighton. 1967-1988. Lang.: Eng. 4229
Institutions
The management of the Shakespeare Festival of Dallas. USA: Dallas, TX. 1972-1988. Lang.: Eng. 393
Systems analysis of the Southwest Theatre Association. USA. 1988. Lang.: Eng. 418
Profile of Universal Ballet Company. South Korea: Seoul. 1998. Lang.: Eng. 1047
Peter Martins, artistic director of New York City Ballet. USA: New York, NY. 1983-1998. Lang.: Eng. 1057
The fate of the Berliner Ensemble after the resignation of artistic director Manfred Wekwerth. Germany: Berlin. 1991-1998. Lang.:Ger. 1625
The future of Schaubühne after the resignation of artistic director Andrea Breth. Germany: Berlin. 1997. Lang.: Ger. 1633
Problems of management and repertory at Berliner Ensemble. Germany: Berlin. 1992-1998. Lang.: Ger. 1656
Caro Newling, executive producer of Donmar Warehouse. UK-England: London. 1998. Lang.: Eng. 1742
Vicky Boone, artistic director of Frontera Theatre. USA: Austin, TX. 1998. Lang.: Eng. 1759
Bonnie Monte of New Jersey Shakespeare Festival. USA: Madison, NJ. 1996-1998. Lang.: Eng. 1772
William Patton, executive director emeritus of Oregon Shakespeare Festival. USA: Ashland, OR. 1952-1998. Lang.: Eng. 1777
Women in top management of American Conservatory Theatre. USA: San Francisco, CA. 1992-1998. Lang.: Eng. 1781
Director Molly Smith, new artistic director of Arena Stage. USA: Washington, DC. 1998. Lang.: Eng. 1789
Effect of Wagner family memoirs on the Bayreuth Festival. Germany: Bayreuth. 1998. Lang.: Eng. 4451
Günter Krämer and children's opera. Germany: Cologne. 1996-1998. Lang.: Ger. 4458
Performance/production
Actresses and female managers in Spanish theatre. Spain. 1600-1700. Lang.: Eng. 2357
Managerial analysis of daytime serial TV industry. USA: New York, NY. 1950-1988. Lang.: Eng. 4072

Manaka, Matsemela
Plays/librettos/scripts
South African theatre after apartheid. South Africa, Republic of. 1976-1996. Lang.: Eng. 3365

Manbites Dog (Durham, NC)
Institutions
Profile of Manbites Dog and its topical and controversial productions. USA: Durham, NC. 1989-1998. Lang.: Eng. 1758

Mandelson Files, The
Performance/production
Collection of newspaper reviews by London theatre critics. UK-England: London. 1998. Lang.: Eng. 2427

Mandíbula afilada (Sharp Chin)
Basic theatrical documents
Text of *Mandibula afilada (Sharp Chin)* by Carles Alberola. Spain. 1997. Lang.: Eng. 1463

Mándy, Ildikó
Performance/production
Ildikó Mándy's *X.Y.Z.*, a film-dance theatre piece. Hungary: Budapest. 1998. Lang.: Hun. 947

Manen, Hans van
Performance/production
Gala concert by students of the Hungarian Dance Academy. Hungary: Budapest. 1998. Lang.: Hun. 1091
Ballets of Hans van Manen. Netherlands. 1951-1998. Lang.: Eng. 1120

Manes
Performance/production
Collection of newspaper reviews by London theatre critics. UK-England: London. 1998. Lang.: Eng. 2473

Manet, Eduardo
Performance/production
Collection of newspaper reviews by London theatre critics. UK-England: London. 1998. Lang.: Eng. 2524

Manhattan Theatre Club (New York, NY)
Design/technology
Set designs by Santo Loquasto at Manhattan Theatre Club. USA: New York, NY. 1998. Lang.: Eng. 1536

Manhattan Theatre Club (New York, NY) — cont'd

Relation to other fields
Controversy over Terrence McNally's *Corpus Christi*, Manhattan Theatre Club. USA: New York, NY. 1998. Lang.: Eng. 3792

Manitoba Theatre for Young People (Winnipeg, MB)
Performance/production
Productions of children's theatre festival. Canada: Montreal, PQ. 1998. Lang.: Fre. 503

Manker, Paulus
Performance/production
Comparison of two productions of Shakespeare's *Richard III*. Germany: Munich. 1996-1997. Lang.: Ger. 1976

Mankind
Plays/librettos/scripts
A new reading of *Mankind*. England. 1464-1470. Lang.: Eng. 3028

Mann ist Mann (Man's a Man, A)
Basic theatrical documents
Catalan translations of plays by Bertolt Brecht (volume 1). Germany. 1919-1954. Lang.: Cat. 1437
Performance/production
Recent German productions of plays by Bertolt Brecht. Germany: Hamburg, Berlin. 1997. Lang.: Swe. 1977
Plays/librettos/scripts
Analysis of *Mann ist Mann (A Man's a Man)* by Bertolt Brecht. Germany. 1926. Lang.: Swe. 3165

Mann, Charlotte
Performance/production
Collection of newspaper reviews by London theatre critics. UK-England: London. 1998. Lang.: Eng. 2447

Mann, Emily
Plays/librettos/scripts
Women playwrights' addresses to the Women's Project conference. USA. 1997. Lang.: Eng. 3589
The survivor character in contemporary American drama. USA. 1970-1997. Lang.: Eng. 3600

Mann, Thomas
Performance/production
Andrej Žitinkin directs *Confessions of Felix Krull, Confidence Man*, adapted from Thomas Mann. Russia: Moscow. 1998. Lang.: Rus. 2335
Plays/librettos/scripts
Analysis of Benjamin Britten's opera *Death in Venice*. UK-England. 1912-1992. Lang.: Eng. 4823

Mano que mece el pesebre, La (Hand that Rocks the Manger, The)
Plays/librettos/scripts
Playwright, director, and performer Jesusa Rodríguez. Mexico. 1970-1992. Lang.: Eng. 3275

Manon
Performance/production
Massenet's revisions to *Manon* for performance by Sybil Sanderson. France. 1885-1903. Lang.: Eng. 4572

Manon Lescaut
Performance/production
Productions of Puccini operas at La Scala. Italy: Milan. 1980-1998. Lang.: Swe. 4657

Månrenen (Moondeer, The)
Design/technology
Rapid on-stage costume changes in dance. Russia. Sweden. Japan. 1840-1998. Lang.: Swe. 889

Mansfield, Elizabeth
Performance/production
Collection of newspaper reviews by London theatre critics. UK-England: London. 1998. Lang.: Eng. 2511

Mant, Izzy
Performance/production
Collection of newspaper reviews by London theatre critics. UK-England: London. 1998. Lang.: Eng. 2457
Collection of newspaper reviews by London theatre critics. UK-England: London. 1998. Lang.: Eng. 2492

Mantell, Knight
Performance/production
Collection of newspaper reviews by London theatre critics. UK-England: London. 1998. Lang.: Eng. 2434

Mantello, Joe
Design/technology
Recent work of lighting designer Brian MacDevitt. USA: New York, NY. 1997. Lang.: Eng. 1530
Set designs by Santo Loquasto at Manhattan Theatre Club. USA: New York, NY. 1998. Lang.: Eng. 1536
Relation to other fields
Controversy over Terrence McNally's *Corpus Christi*, Manhattan Theatre Club. USA: New York, NY. 1998. Lang.: Eng. 3792

Mantero, Vera
Performance/production
Politics, culture, and Portuguese dance and choreography. Portugal. 1998. Lang.: Eng. 959

Mäntylä, Aarne
Training
Interview with dance teacher Aarne Mäntylä. Finland. 1998. Lang.: Fin. 1203

Manzoni, Giacomo
Plays/librettos/scripts
Composer Giacomo Manzoni and his work *Words by Beckett (Parole da Beckett)*. Italy. 1970-1971. Lang.: Eng. 3250

Maradudin, Peter
Design/technology
Professional theatrical designers on design training. USA. 1998. Lang.: Eng. 252
Creativity and beauty in theatrical design. USA. 1998. Lang.: Eng. 322

Maraffi, Matthew
Design/technology
Matthew Maraffi, production for the film *Pi*. USA. 1998. Lang.: Eng. 3906

Marat/Sade
Theory/criticism
Representation and delegation in theatre. 1998. Lang.: Eng. 3800

Marber, Patrick
Performance/production
Political changes reflected in Berlin theatre productions. Germany: Berlin. 1998. Lang.: Ger. 1958
Interview with actor/director Stefan Larsson. Sweden: Stockholm. 1984-1998. Lang.: Swe. 2382
Collection of newspaper reviews by London theatre critics. UK-England: London. 1998. Lang.: Eng. 2422
Collection of newspaper reviews by London theatre critics. UK-England: London. 1998. Lang.: Eng. 2452
Report on several English performances. UK-England: London, Stratford. 1998. Lang.: Swe. 2634
Plays/librettos/scripts
German view of English and American drama. UK-England. USA. 1998. Lang.: Ger. 3455

Marbury, Elisabeth
Administration
The lesbian relationship of agent Elisabeth Marbury and designer Elsie de Wolfe. USA. 1886-1933. Lang.: Eng. 44

Marc, Alessandra
Performance/production
Soprano Alessandra Marc. USA. 1998. Lang.: Eng. 4729
Theory/criticism
Performers and conductors complain about unfair reviews. USA. 1998. Lang.: Eng. 4844

Marc, Yves
Performance/production
Yves Marc on Etienne Decroux. France: Paris. 1998. Lang.: Eng. 4088

Marceau, Marcel
Performance/production
Collection of newspaper reviews by London theatre critics. UK-England: London. Lang.: Eng. 2408
A photo session involving mimes Marcel Marceau and Bill Irwin. USA: New York, NY. 1998. Lang.: Eng. 4092

Marcela de San Félix, Sor
Plays/librettos/scripts
Feminist analysis of seventeenth-century plays by women. Spain. 1605-1675. Lang.: Eng. 3385
Allegorical dramas of Sor Marcela de San Félix. Spain. 1595-1650. Lang.: Eng. 3395

Marčelli, Jėvgenij
Performance/production
Productions of international Čechov festival. Russia: Moscow. 1998. Lang.: Swe. 2306

Marchetto, Ennio
Performance/production
Collection of newspaper reviews by London theatre critics. UK-England: London. 1998. Lang.: Eng. 2533

Marcovici, Sébastien
Performance/production
New male dancers of New York City Ballet. USA: New York, NY. 1998. Lang.: Eng. 1177

Marcus, Neil
Performance/production
New London venues and productions. UK-England: London. 1994-1998. Lang.: Eng. 605

Marcus, Neil — cont'd

Collection of newspaper reviews by London theatre critics. UK-England: London. 1998. Lang.: Eng. 2479

Marescalco, Il (Stablemaster, The)
Plays/librettos/scripts
The comedies of Pietro Aretino. Italy. 1534-1556. Lang.: Eng. 3251

Margid, Elizabeth
Performance/production
Reviews of productions of plays by Ibsen. USA: New York, NY. Norway: Oslo. 1998. Lang.: Eng. 2747

Margison, Richard
Performance/production
Interview with Canadian tenor Richard Margison. Canada. 1998. Lang.: Eng. 4538

Margo Jones Theatre (Dallas, TX)
Performance/production
The multifaceted nature of early nonprofit regional theatre. USA. 1940-1960. Lang.: Eng. 2705

Margolin, Deb
Performance/production
Analysis of pop performance. USA: New York, NY. 1980-1988. Lang.: Eng. 664

Margoshes, Steve
Performance/production
Collection of newspaper reviews by London theatre critics. UK-England: London. 1998. Lang.: Eng. 2525

Margulies, David
Institutions
Arthur Penn and Actors Studio. USA: New York, NY. 1997. Lang.: Eng. 1767

Margulies, Donald
Design/technology
Lighting design for Donald Margulies' *Collected Stories*, directed by William Carden. USA: New York, NY. 1998. Lang.: Eng. 1544
Performance/production
Reviews of Actors' Theatre productions. USA: Louisville, KY. 1998. Lang.: Eng. 2727

Maria di Rohan
Performance/production
Soprano Catherine Hayes. Ireland. Italy. 1839-1861. Lang.: Eng. 4645

Maria Magdalene
Administration
Theater Basel under the direction of Stefan Bachmann. Switzerland: Basel. 1996-1998. Lang.: Ger. 1391
Institutions
Stefan Bachmann of Basler Theater. Switzerland: Basel. 1998. Lang.: Ger. 1737

Mariage Blanc
SEE
Białe małżeństwo.

Mariage de Figaro, Le (Marriage of Figaro, The)
Plays/librettos/scripts
Desire in *Le Mariage de Figaro (The Marriage of Figaro)* by Beaumarchais. France. 1784. Lang.: Eng. 3095

Operatic realizations of Beaumarchais' character Rosina. Europe. North America. 1784-1991. Lang.: Eng. 4773

Mariengof, A.B.
Relation to other fields
Memoirs of poet, journalist, and playwright A.B. Mariengof. Russia. 1897-1962. Lang.: Rus. 760

Mariinskij Teat'r (St. Petersburg)
SEE
Akademičeskij Teat'r Opery i Baleta im. S.M. Kirova.

Marija Tudor (Mary Tudor)
Basic theatrical documents
Text of plays and other works by Ivan Mrak. Slovenia. 1930-1975. Lang.: Slo. 1459

Marin, Cheech
Performance/production
The decline of radio comedy and the use of record albums by some comedians. USA. 1950-1998. Lang.: Eng. 3863

Marina
Plays/librettos/scripts
The defense of prostitution in Lillo's *Marina*. England. 1738. Lang.: Eng. 2887

The obedient daughter in adaptations of Shakespeare's plays. England. 1701-1800. Lang.: Eng. 2969

Analysis of *Marina*, George Lillo's adaptation of Shakespeare's *Pericles*. England. 1738. Lang.: Eng. 2971

Marine Memorial Theatre (San Francisco, CA)
Design/technology
Costume design for *Dames at Sea*, Marine Memorial Theatre. USA: San Francisco, CA. 1998. Lang.: Eng. 4332

Marinetti, Filippo Tommaso
Performance/production
The early life and career of F.T. Marinetti, leader of the Futurist movement. Italy. 1876-1909. Lang.: Eng. 551

Mario and the Magician
Plays/librettos/scripts
Homosexuality in Canadian opera. Canada. 1970-1998. Lang.: Eng. 4762

Mario Benzedrine's Pop-Up Apocalypse
Performance/production
Collection of newspaper reviews by London theatre critics. UK-England: London. 1998. Lang.: Eng. 2576

Mario the Magician
Plays/librettos/scripts
Analysis of the opera *Mario the Magician* by Harry Somers and Rod Anderson. Canada. 1965-1992. Lang.: Eng. 4763

Marionettes
SEE ALSO
Classed Entries under PUPPETRY—Marionettes.
Institutions
Puppetry exhibits at Chicago Children's Museum. USA: Chicago, IL. Mexico: Mexico City. 1998. Lang.: Eng. 4881
Performance/production
Preview of the Puppeteers of America Festival. USA: Seattle, WA. 1999. Lang.: Eng. 4905

Marisol
Performance/production
Collection of newspaper reviews by London theatre critics. UK-England: London. 1998. Lang.: Eng. 2454

Marivaux, Pierre Carlet de Chamblain de
Basic theatrical documents
Catalan translation of *Le Jeu de l'amour et du hasard (The Play of Love and Chance)* by Marivaux. France. 1730. Lang.: Cat. 1432

Marjanovic, Senada
Plays/librettos/scripts
Recent productions directed by Frank Castorf. Austria: Vienna. 1998. Lang.: Ger. 2788

Mark Hellinger Theatre (New York, NY)
Design/technology
The sound system at the Mark Hellinger Theatre, now a house of worship. USA: New York, NY. 1998. Lang.: Eng. 274

Mark Morris Dance Group (New York, NY)
Performance/production
Dancers Tina Fehlandt and Ruth Davidson of Mark Morris Dance Group. USA: New York, NY. 1980-1998. Lang.: Eng. 1327

Márk, Tivadar
Design/technology
Profile of costume designer Tivadar Márk. Hungary. 1908-1998. Lang.: Hun. 4432

Market Theatre (Johannesburg)
Performance/production
Market Theatre productions of plays by Athol Fugard. South Africa, Republic of. 1993-1994. Lang.: Eng. 2351

Marketing
Administration
The role of government in audience and marketing development for arts organizations. 1996. Lang.: Eng. 1

Marketing, advertising, and sponsorship of German theatre. Germany. 1998. Lang.: Ger. 7

Current conditions at Staatstheater Cottbus. Germany: Cottbus. 1992-1998. Lang.: Ger. 9

Cooperation of theatres and tourist organizations. Germany. 1993-1998. Lang.: Ger. 10

Audience questionnaire for use in theatrical marketing. Germany. 1998. Lang.: Ger. 12

Marketing strategies for the performing arts. Netherlands. 1990-1995. Lang.: Dut. 17

Ways to attract new young audiences to theatre. Sweden: Stockholm. 1995-1998. Lang.: Swe. 21

Target marketing and successful ticket sales. USA: Long Beach, CA. 1996-1998. Lang.: Eng. 37

Finding a reliable sample frame for potential audience data collection. USA. 1997. Lang.: Eng. 39

Marketing — cont'd

Marketing analysis and plan for Texas Tech University Theatre's subscription campaign. USA: Lubbock, TX. 1997-1998. Lang.: Eng. 46
Changes in arts marketing strategies. USA. 1977-1997. Lang.: Eng. 126
Alternative funding strategies for dance companies. USA. 1998. Lang.: Eng. 886
Financially troubled Ohio ballet companies. USA: Cleveland, OH, Akron, OH. 1998. Lang.: Eng. 1027
Oscar Micheaux's use of an interracial marriage case as a publicity tool for his films. USA. 1924. Lang.: Eng. 3874
Various conditions affecting production, pricing, marketing and communication in German theatre. Germany. 1986-1998. Lang.: Ger. 4316
Marketing practices of Deutsche Oper am Rhein. Germany: Duisburg. 1996-1998. Lang.: Ger. 4404
Bayerische Staatsoper's new marketing concept. Germany: Munich. 1993-1998. Lang.: Ger. 4405
Speculations on the future marketing of opera. USA. 1998. Lang.: Eng. 4406
Marketing strategies for puppetry in film and TV. USA. 1998. Lang.: Eng. 4863

Audience
The interpretation of audience research data to yield marketing strategies. Germany: Berlin. 1993-1998. Lang.: Ger. 153

Institutions
Graphic design and the theatrical evolution of Arena Stage. USA: Washington, DC. 1950-1987. Lang.: Eng. 414
Financial and artistic success of Kennedy Center and New Jersey Performing Arts Center. USA: Washington, DC, Newark, NJ. 1971-1998. Lang.: Eng. 424
Badische Landesbühne and the problem of declining audiences. Germany: Bruchsal. 1993-1998. Lang.: Ger. 1662
Investing in culture in Malmö, formerly an industrial city. Sweden: Malmö. 1995-1998. Lang.: Swe. 1723
Marketing techniques of Canadian Opera Company. Canada: Toronto, ON. 1996-1998. Lang.: Eng. 4447

Performance/production
Audience reaction to Irish opera singer Catherine Hayes. USA: New Orleans, LA. 1852. Lang.: Eng. 4745

Markgräfliches Opernhaus (Bayreuth)

Design/technology
Reconstruction of a performance of *A Midsummer Night's Dream* designed by Galli-Bibiena. Germany: Bayreuth. 1997-1998. Lang.: Ger. 1521

Markó, Iván

Performance/production
Iván Markó's choreography for Bayreuth Festival productions. Germany: Bayreuth. Hungary. 1998. Lang.: Hun. 1083
Productions of the Magyar Fesztival Balett choreographed by Iván Markó. Hungary: Budapest. 1998. Lang.: Hun. 1097
Interview with choreographer Iván Markó. Hungary: Budapest. 1998. Lang.: Hun. 1101

Markova, Alicia

Performance/production
Tributes to ballerina Alexandra Danilova. USA: New York, NY. 1997. Lang.: Eng. 1165

Markovič, Goran

Plays/librettos/scripts
Contemporary drama of the former Yugoslavia in its political context. Yugoslavia. 1991-1998. Lang.: Ger. 3721

Markovits, Ilka

Performance/production
Excerpts from the diary of singer and actress Ilka Markovits. Hungary. 1839-1915. Lang.: Hun. 2064

Marks, Bruce

Performance/production
Tributes to ballerina Alexandra Danilova. USA: New York, NY. 1997. Lang.: Eng. 1165

Márkus, László

Performance/production
László Márkus, one-time director of the Budapest Opera House. Hungary. 1881-1948. Lang.: Hun. 540

Marleau, Denis

Performance/production
Productions of plays by Bernard-Marie Koltès. Canada: Montreal, PQ. 1991-1997. Lang.: Fre. 1862

Marlowe, Christopher

Institutions
Profile of theatre company Teatr St I Witkiewicza. Poland: Zakopane. 1989. Lang.: Eng. 1684

Performance/production
Brief productions of Shakespeare, Shaw, and Marlowe at the World's Fair. USA: Chicago, IL. 1934. Lang.: Eng. 2701

Plays/librettos/scripts
Assessment of Marlowe's *Tamburlaine the Great.* England. 1587-1588. Lang.: Eng. 2866
The figure of the Jew in Marlowe and Shakespeare. England. 1590-1600. Lang.: Eng. 2868
The control of time in Renaissance English drama. England. 1590-1620. Lang.: Eng. 2883
Analysis of *The Massacre at Paris* by Christopher Marlowe. England. 1593. Lang.: Eng. 2917
The representation of historical female characters on the Renaissance stage. England. 1580-1615. Lang.: Eng. 2922
Influences on *'Tis Pity She's a Whore* by John Ford. England. 1587-1631. Lang.: Eng. 2937
Comic scenes and characters in the Elizabethan history play. England. 1590-1618. Lang.: Eng. 2955
Analysis of *The Massacre at Paris* by Christopher Marlowe. England. 1593. Lang.: Eng. 2997
Marlowe's *Edward II* and the medieval passion play. England. 1590-1592. Lang.: Eng. 3011
Analysis of *Tamburlaine the Great* by Christopher Marlowe. England. 1590-1998. Lang.: Eng. 3014
Space and measurement in *Tamburlaine the Great* by Christopher Marlowe. England. 1587-1588. Lang.: Eng. 3029
Marlowe's tragedies and peer evaluation in the composition classroom. USA. 1997-1998. Lang.: Eng. 3532

Marmarinos, Michael

Performance spaces
Michael Marmarinos' production of Sophocles' *Electra* at the Epidauros amphitheatre. Greece: Epidauros. 1938-1998. Lang.: Ger. 445

Maros, Máté

Performance/production
Visual dance productions by Cie, 2 in 1. Hungary: Budapest. 1998. Lang.: Hun. 942

Marosvásárhelyi Nemzeti Színház, Magyar Társulat (Târgu-Mureş)

Institutions
History of annual festival of Hungarian-language theatre. Hungary: Kisvárda. 1989-1998. Lang.: Hun. 1669
History of Hungarian-language theatre in Transylvania. Romania. Hungary. 1919-1992. Lang.: Hun, Rom. 1693

Performance/production
Director György Harag. Romania. Hungary. 1925-1985. Lang.: Hun. 2229

Marowitz, Charles

Performance/production
The influence of collage on director Charles Marowitz. UK-England. USA. 1962-1979. Lang.: Eng. 2624
Director Charles Marowitz on the actor's calling. USA. UK-England. 1958-1998. Lang.: Eng. 2706

Marquis Theatre (New York, NY)

Design/technology
Sound design for the musical *The Capeman.* USA: New York, NY. 1998. Lang.: Eng. 4339

Performance/production
Response to negative criticism of *The Capeman.* USA: New York, NY. 1998. Lang.: Eng. 4387

Marriage of Figaro, The by Mozart

SEE
Nozze di Figaro, Le.

Marriage, The

SEE ALSO
Ženitba.

Marrow, Queen Esther

Performance/production
Collection of newspaper reviews by London theatre critics. UK-England: London. 1998. Lang.: Eng. 2432

Mars Teatern (Helsinki)

Institutions
The proliferation of Swedish-language theatre groups in Helsinki. Finland: Helsinki. 1990-1998. Lang.: Eng, Fre. 1604

Marsan, Eddie
Performance/production
Interview with actor Eddie Marsan. UK-England: London. 1990-1998. Lang.: Eng. 2622
Marschall, Ken
Design/technology
Technical designs for the film *Titanic*. USA. 1997. Lang.: Eng. 3910
Marsden, Betty
Performance/production
Actress Betty Marsden. UK-England: London. 1930-1998. Lang.: Eng. 2596
Marsden, Roy
Performance/production
Collection of newspaper reviews by London theatre critics. UK-England: London. 1998. Lang.: Eng. 2477
Marsh, Richard
Performance/production
Collection of newspaper reviews by London theatre critics. UK-England: London. 1998. Lang.: Eng. 2412
Marshall, E.G.
Performance/production
Obituaries for Joseph Maher, Warren Kliewer, and E.G. Marshall. USA. 1912-1998. Lang.: Eng. 2655
Marshall, Rob
Performance/production
Musical performances on and off Broadway. USA: New York. 1998. Lang.: Ger. 4383
Marshall, Susan
Performance/production
The theory of movement in *Les Enfants Terribles*, adapted to dance-opera by Philip Glass and Susan Marshall. North America. 1997. Lang.: Eng. 1353
Marston, John
Performance/production
Collection of newspaper reviews by London theatre critics. UK-England: London. 1998. Lang.: Eng. 2516
Plays/librettos/scripts
The politics of gender in the plays of John Marston. England. 1599-1634. Lang.: Eng. 3009
Martha, István
Performance/production
Lilla Pártay's *Meztelen rózsa (Naked Rose)*, a ballet based on the life of Nižinskij. Hungary: Budapest. 1998. Lang.: Hun. 1110
Marthaler, Christoph
Performance/production
Rehearsals of Christoph Marthaler's production of *Arsenic and Old Lace* by Joseph Kesselring. Germany: Hamburg. 1998. Lang.: Ger. 1953
Christoph Marthaler's approach to directing Joseph Kesselring's *Arsenic and Old Lace*. Germany: Hamburg. 1998. Lang.: Ger. 1956
Kortner-award winners Anna Viebrock and Christoph Marthaler. Germany: Berlin. 1997. Lang.: Ger. 1968
Productions of international Čechov festival. Russia: Moscow. 1998. Lang.: Swe. 2306
Review of Salzburger Festspiele performances. Austria: Salzburg. 1998. Lang.: Ger. 4527
Reviews of recent opera productions. Switzerland: Basel. Germany: Stuttgart, Berlin, Hamburg. France: Strasbourg. 1997-1998. Lang.: Ger. 4702
Theory/criticism
The music-theatre concept of Christoph Marthaler. Germany: Berlin. 1993-1998. Lang.: Ger. 4310
Martial arts
Performance/production
Director and martial artist Huy-Phong Doàn's *La Légende du manuel sacré (The Legend of the Sacred Handbook)*. Canada: Montreal, PQ. 1992-1998. Lang.: Fre. 4118
Training
The use of martial arts in dance training. UK-England. 1998. Lang.: Eng. 1022
Martin and John
Performance/production
Collection of newspaper reviews by London theatre critics. UK-England: London. 1998. Lang.: Eng. 2566
Martin Guerre
Performance/production
Collection of newspaper reviews by London theatre critics. UK-England: Leeds, Manchester. 1998. Lang.: Eng. 2559
Martin, Jane
Performance/production
Analysis of transformative comedy. USA. 1975-1988. Lang.: Eng. 666
Plays/librettos/scripts
Analysis of *Keely and Du* by Jane Martin. USA. 1993. Lang.: Eng. 3629
Martin, Mary
Performance/production
Lesbianism and performer Mary Martin. USA. 1913-1990. Lang.: Eng. 2757
Martin, Mick
Performance/production
Collection of newspaper reviews by London theatre critics. UK-England: London. 1998. Lang.: Eng. 2528
Collection of newspaper reviews by London theatre critics. UK-England: London. 1998. Lang.: Eng. 2585
Martin, Nathan
Performance/production
Collection of newspaper reviews by London theatre critics. UK-England: London. 1998. Lang.: Eng. 2531
Martin, Nicholas
Performance/production
Collection of newspaper reviews by London theatre critics. UK-England: London. 1998. Lang.: Eng. 2491
Martin, Steve
Performance/production
English and French-language productions of *Picasso at the Lapin Agile* by Steve Martin. Canada: Montreal, PQ. 1997. Lang.: Fre. 1836
Martin, Thomas
Plays/librettos/scripts
Recent productions directed by Frank Castorf. Austria: Vienna. 1998. Lang.: Ger. 2788
Martin, Wayne
Performance/production
Puppeteer Wayne Martin. USA: Boston, MA. 1998. Lang.: Eng. 4070
Martinelli, Jean-Louis
Performance/production
French productions of German plays. France. 1998. Lang.: Ger. 1935
Martinez, Louis
Performance/production
Recollections of ballerina Margot Fonteyn. USA. Panama. 1946-1998. Lang.: Eng. 1182
Martinez, Ursula
Performance/production
Collection of newspaper reviews by London theatre critics. UK-England: London. 1998. Lang.: Eng. 2531
Martins, Peter
Institutions
Peter Martins, artistic director of New York City Ballet. USA: New York, NY. 1983-1998. Lang.: Eng. 1057
Performance/production
Interviews with dancers about performance. UK-England. USA. Cuba. 1942-1989. Lang.: Eng. 1162
Martinson Hall (New York, NY)
Design/technology
Technical designs for Off Broadway Shakespearean productions. USA: New York, NY. 1998. Lang.: Eng. 1539
Márton, László
Plays/librettos/scripts
New Hungarian translations of Shakespeare. Hungary. 1990-1998. Lang.: Hun. 3187
Martone, Mario
Performance/production
Interview with director Mario Martone. Italy: Naples. 1977-1997. Lang.: Eng. 2166
Martyre de Saint Sébastien, Le (Martyrdom of Saint Sebastian, The)
Performance/production
Robert Wilson's dance adaptation of *Le Martyre de Saint Sébastien* by D'Annunzio. France: Paris. 1988. Lang.: Ita. 1074
Collaborative Symbolist dance/theatre projects. Europe. USA. 1916-1934. Lang.: Eng. 1268
Marxist criticism
Plays/librettos/scripts
Marxian analysis of dramatic parody and burlesque. USA. Europe. 1998. Lang.: Eng. 3664
Mary and Martha
Plays/librettos/scripts
Mennonite drama of Veralyn Warkentin and Vern Thiessen. Canada. 1890-1997. Lang.: Eng. 2829
Mary and the Shaman
Performance/production
Collection of newspaper reviews by London theatre critics. UK-England: London. 1998. Lang.: Eng. 2535

Mary Play
Plays/librettos/scripts
The N-town Mary play and the Four Virtues of Psalm 84:11. England. 1120-1501. Lang.: Eng. 2983

Mary Stuart
Performance/production
Evaluation of video performances of Donizetti's operas. Europe. USA. 1980-1998. Lang.: Eng. 4557

Mas
Design/technology
Geraldo Andrew Vieira, carnival costumer and performer. Trinidad and Tobago. 1952-1996. Lang.: Eng. 4160
Plays/librettos/scripts
Interview with Peter Minshall, creator of theatre pieces and carnival performances. Trinidad and Tobago: Port of Spain. 1974-1997. Lang.: Eng. 4172

Máscara puertorriqueña (Puerto Rican Mask)
Plays/librettos/scripts
The mulatto in Puerto Rican drama. Puerto Rico. 1850-1985. Lang.: Spa. 3311

Maschinenstürmer, Die (Machine Wreckers, The)
Plays/librettos/scripts
Analysis of revisions of plays by Ernst Toller. Germany. 1920-1939. Lang.: Eng. 3172

Masculin/Féminin (Male/Female)
Performance/production
Michel Laprise's *Masculin/Féminin (Male/Female)*, presented to audiences segregated by sex. Canada: Montreal, PQ. 1998. Lang.: Fre. 1867

Masks
Design/technology
Masks in Venetian carnival. Italy: Venice. 1500-1650. Lang.: Ita. 4159
Technical designs for the Broadway production of *The Lion King*. USA: New York, NY. 1998. Lang.: Eng. 4342
Performance/production
History of Korean dance. Korea. 1600-1985. Lang.: Eng. 954
Analysis of Korean mask-dance theatre form *hahoe pyolsin-kut*. Korea. 1150-1928. Lang.: Eng. 1352
Director, costumer, and mask-maker Julie Taymor. USA. 1980-1998. Lang.: Eng. 2685
Interview with Marie-Hélène Dasté, daughter of Jacques Copeau. France: Paris. 1913-1992. Lang.: Eng. 4089
Characters and masks of the Genoese theatre tradition. Italy: Genoa. 1700-1998. Lang.: Ita. 4126
Amerindian influence on Trinidadian carnival. Trinidad and Tobago: San Fernando. 1700-1950. Lang.: Eng. 4164
The influence of *commedia dell'arte* on eighteenth-century Danish theatre. Denmark: Copenhagen. 1700-1750. Lang.: Eng. 4186
The Patum of Berga compared to sixteenth-century German festivities. Spain-Catalonia: Berga. Germany: Trent. 1549-1996. Lang.: Eng. 4218
The carnival parade of devils and imps. Trinidad and Tobago: Paramin. 1997. Lang.: Eng. 4219
Plays/librettos/scripts
Analysis of Eugene O'Neill's 'middle period' plays. USA. 1925-1938. Lang.: Eng. 3675
Relation to other fields
African and European influences on Trinidadian carnival. Trinidad and Tobago. 1501-1998. Lang.: Eng. 4175

Mason-John, Valerie
Performance/production
Collection of newspaper reviews by London theatre critics. UK-England: London. 1998. Lang.: Eng. 2575

Mason, Bob
Performance/production
Obituary for puppeteer Bob Mason. USA. 1924-1998. Lang.: Eng. 4908

Mason, Francis
Performance/production
Tributes to ballerina Alexandra Danilova. USA: New York, NY. 1997. Lang.: Eng. 1165

Mason, Jackie
Performance/production
Collection of newspaper reviews by London theatre critics. UK-England: London. 1998. Lang.: Eng. 2539

Mason, Marshall W.
Performance/production
The collaboration of playwright Lanford Wilson and director Marshall W. Mason. USA: New York, NY. 1978-1986. Lang.: Eng. 2756

Mason, Timothy
Design/technology
Costume design for a new version of *Peter Pan* at Children's Theatre Company. USA: Minneapolis, MN. 1998. Lang.: Eng. 4330

Masque
SEE ALSO
Classed Entries under MIXED ENTERTAINMENT—Court entertainment.
Performance/production
Accession Day masques and tensions between Queen Elizabeth I and the Earl of Essex. England. 1595. Lang.: Eng. 4196
Political aspects of music in the masque. England. 1620-1634. Lang.: Eng. 4197
Masque, movement, and social and political negotiations. England. 1610-1642. Lang.: Eng. 4198
William Empson's *The Masque of Steel* and its presentation before Queen Elizabeth II. UK-England: Sheffield. 1954. Lang.: Eng. 4199
Civic and court ceremonies in the Jacobean period. England. 1605-1610. Lang.: Eng. 4215
Plays/librettos/scripts
Analysis of *The Masque of Blackness* by Ben Jonson. England. 1605. Lang.: Eng. 2919
Gender and politics in masques of Ben Jonson and Samuel Daniel. England. 1604-1605. Lang.: Eng. 4200
Political aspects of Stuart court masques. England. 1610-1642. Lang.: Eng. 4201
Shakespeare's *The Tempest* and Thomas Campion's *The Lord's Masque*. England. 1613. Lang.: Eng. 4202
Political tensions reflected in Ben Jonson's masque *Oberon*. England. 1611. Lang.: Eng. 4203
Royal policy, subversion, and Ben Jonson's *Oberon*. England. 1611. Lang.: Eng. 4204
Ben Jonson's antimasques. England. 1612-1632. Lang.: Eng. 4205
Political and ideological struggles in Jacobean masques. England. 1604-1609. Lang.: Eng. 4206
Puritanism and Milton's *Comus*. England. 1634-1635. Lang.: Eng. 4207
Power, gender, and race in *The Masque of Blackness* by Ben Jonson. England. 1605-1611. Lang.: Eng. 4208
The design and authorship of *The Essex House Masque*. England. 1621. Lang.: Eng. 4209
Theory/criticism
Recent scholarship and popularity of the Stuart masque. UK-England. 1970-1995. Lang.: Eng. 4212

Masque of Blackness, The
Plays/librettos/scripts
Analysis of *The Masque of Blackness* by Ben Jonson. England. 1605. Lang.: Eng. 2919
Gender and politics in masques of Ben Jonson and Samuel Daniel. England. 1604-1605. Lang.: Eng. 4200
Power, gender, and race in *The Masque of Blackness* by Ben Jonson. England. 1605-1611. Lang.: Eng. 4208

Masque of Queens, The
Plays/librettos/scripts
Political and ideological struggles in Jacobean masques. England. 1604-1609. Lang.: Eng. 4206

Masque of Steel, The
Performance/production
William Empson's *The Masque of Steel* and its presentation before Queen Elizabeth II. UK-England: Sheffield. 1954. Lang.: Eng. 4199

Masquerade
SEE
Carnival.

Masquerade, The
Plays/librettos/scripts
Ritual in plays of John Bekederemo and Wole Soyinka. Nigeria. 1965-1998. Lang.: Eng. 3287

Massacre at Paris, The
Plays/librettos/scripts
Analysis of *The Massacre at Paris* by Christopher Marlowe. England. 1593. Lang.: Eng. 2917
Analysis of *The Massacre at Paris* by Christopher Marlowe. England. 1593. Lang.: Eng. 2997

Masse-Mensch (Masses and Man)
Plays/librettos/scripts
Analysis of revisions of plays by Ernst Toller. Germany. 1920-1939. Lang.: Eng. 3172

Massenet, Jules
Basic theatrical documents
Libretto to Massenet's opera *Hérodiade*. France. 1881. Lang.: Fre. 4416
The libretto to Jules Massenet's *Le Roi de Lahore*. France. 1877. Lang.: Fre. 4417
Performance/production
Productions of Massenet's *Hérodiade*. 1881-1995. Lang.: Fre. 4520
Premieres of Massenet's *Le Roi de Lahore*. 1877-1923. Lang.: Fre. 4521
Complete recordings of Massenet's opera *Hérodiade*. 1974-1994. Lang.: Fre. 4523
Vocal requirements and recording of Massenet's *Le Roi de Lahore*. 1979. Lang.: Fre. 4525
The creation of Massenet's opera *Le Roi de Lahore*. France. 1877. Lang.: Fre. 4568
Massenet's revisions to *Manon* for performance by Sybil Sanderson. France. 1885-1903. Lang.: Eng. 4572
Plays/librettos/scripts
Treatments of the Cinderella theme, with emphasis on *La Cenerentola* by Rossini. 1817-1998. Lang.: Eng. 4757
Collaboration of composer Jules Massenet and librettist Louis Gallet. France. 1877-1894. Lang.: Fre. 4778
Massenet's opera *Hérodiade* and its literary sources. France. 1881. Lang.: Fre. 4779

Massey, Daniel
Performance/production
Actor Daniel Massey. UK-England: London. 1968-1998. Lang.: Eng. 2595

Massinger, Philip
Plays/librettos/scripts
The malcontent scholar in Elizabethan and Jacobean theatre. England. 1590-1642. Lang.: Eng. 3003
Theory/criticism
Representation and delegation in theatre. 1998. Lang.: Eng. 3800

Massnahme, Die (Measures Taken, The)
Performance/production
Comparison of productions of Brecht's *Die Massnahme (The Measures Taken)*. Germany: Berlin, Wuppertal. 1995-1998. Lang.: Ger. 1950
Plays/librettos/scripts
Musicological perspective on *Die Massnahme (The Measures Taken)* by Brecht and Eisler. Germany: Berlin. 1929-1998. Lang.: Ger. 3125

Master Builder, The
SEE
Bygmester Solness.

Master Harold...and the boys
Plays/librettos/scripts
The influence of Albert Camus on playwright Athol Fugard. South Africa, Republic of. 1960-1985. Lang.: Eng. 3362
Post-apartheid analysis of plays by Athol Fugard. South Africa, Republic of. 1991-1998. Lang.: Eng. 3364

Master i Margarita (Master and Margarita, The)
Performance/production
Collection of newspaper reviews by London theatre critics. UK-England: London. 1998. Lang.: Eng. 2507

Mäster Olof (Master Olof)
Institutions
Report on the Stockholm theatre festival. Sweden: Stockholm. 1998. Lang.: Eng. 1724

Mäster Olog (Master Olof)
Plays/librettos/scripts
Realism in plays of Strindberg. Sweden. 1872-1886. Lang.: Eng. 3416

Masteroff, Joe
Performance/production
Friends and colleagues recall singer Lotte Lenya. Germany. 1928-1981. Lang.: Eng. 4355

Masters of Grace
Performance/production
Reviews of recent London performances. UK-England: London. 1998. Lang.: Ger. 2591

Masters, Christopher
Performance/production
Collection of newspaper reviews by London theatre critics. UK-England: London. 1998. Lang.: Eng. 2585

Masterskaja Petra Fomenko (Moscow)
Performance/production
Pëtr Fomenko's theatrical adaptation of Gogol's *Dead Souls*. Russia: Moscow. 1998. Lang.: Rus. 2303
Pëtr Fomenko's production of *V Čičikovskoj krugoverti (In Čičikov's Chaos)*. Russia: Moscow. 1998. Lang.: Rus. 2340

Masterson, Guy
Performance/production
Collection of newspaper reviews by London theatre critics. UK-England: London. 1998. Lang.: Eng. 2522

Mastrosimone, William
Performance/production
Collection of newspaper reviews by London theatre critics. UK-England: London. 1998. Lang.: Eng. 2574

Masuca Fogo
Performance/production
Analysis of Pina Bausch's dance work *Masuca Fogo*. Germany: Wuppertal. 1998. Lang.: Ger. 1282

Matchmaker, The
SEE ALSO
Jux will er sich machen, Einen.

Máté, Gábor
Performance/production
Review of István Örkény's *Kulcskeresők (Searching for the Key)*, Katona József Theatre. Hungary: Budapest. 1998. Lang.: Hun. 2083
Andrés Jeles's *Szenvedéstörténet (Passion Play)* directed by Gábor Máté. Hungary: Budapest. 1998. Lang.: Hun. 2145

Matera, Barbara
Design/technology
Technical designs for Čajovskij's *Sneguročka*, Houston Ballet. USA: Houston, TX. 1998. Lang.: Eng. 1033

Mathias, Sean
Performance/production
Collection of newspaper reviews by London theatre critics. UK-England: London. 1998. Lang.: Eng. 2523

Mathis, June
Performance/production
Screenwriter and producer June Mathis. USA. 1916-1927. Lang.: Eng. 3959

Mati na pogorišču (Mother In a Gutted Ruin)
Plays/librettos/scripts
The individual and his world in Slovene theatre. Slovenia. 1943-1985. Lang.: Slo. 3347

Matorin, V.
Performance/production
Bolšoj Opera singer V. Matorin. Russia: Moscow. 1998. Lang.: Rus. 4692

Matschke, Matthias
Performance/production
Matthias Matschke, *Theater Heute*'s young actor of the year. Germany: Berlin. 1985-1997. Lang.: Ger. 1963

Mattei, Peter
Performance/production
Interview with singer Peter Mattei. France: Aix-en-Provence. 1985-1998. Lang.: Swe. 4564

Mattogrosso
Performance/production
Ópera Seca's *Mattogrosso*. Brazil: Rio de Janeiro. 1989. Lang.: Eng. 4537

Maunder, Stuart
Performance/production
Collection of newspaper reviews by London theatre critics. UK-England: London. 1998. Lang.: Eng. 2553

Maxim Gorki Theater (Berlin)
Audience
The relationship between theatres and the youth audience. Germany. 1998. Lang.: Ger. 152
Institutions
Director training at Ernst-Busch-Schule and some of its graduates. Germany: Berlin. 1972-1998. Lang.: Ger. 1648
Performance/production
Political changes reflected in Berlin theatre productions. Germany: Berlin. 1998. Lang.: Ger. 1958
Interview with director Bernd Wilms. Germany: Berlin. 1998. Lang.: Swe. 2018
Shakespearean production and the GDR's 'existential crisis'. Germany, East. 1976-1980. Lang.: Eng. 2051
Plays/librettos/scripts
Fassbinder's *Der Müll, die Stadt und der Tod (Garbage, the City and Death)*. Germany: Berlin. 1976-1998. Lang.: Ger. 3175

May Day New
Performance/production
Collection of newspaper reviews by London theatre critics. UK-England: London. 1998. Lang.: Eng. 2479

May, Benjamin
Performance/production
Collection of newspaper reviews by London theatre critics. UK-England: London. 1998. Lang.: Eng. 2562
May, Elaine
Design/technology
Michael McGarty's set design for Elaine May and Alan Arkin's *Power Plays*. USA: New York, NY. 1998. Lang.: Eng. 1542
Mayakovsky Theatre (Moscow)
SEE
Teat'r im V. Majakovskogo.
Mayakovsky, Vladimir Vladimirovich
SEE
Majakovskij, Vladimir Vladimirovič.
Mayenburg, Marius von
Performance/production
Productions of the Kleist theatre festival. Germany: Frankfurt/Oder. 1998. Lang.: Ger. 1993
Plays/librettos/scripts
Analysis of plays by Marius von Mayenburg. Germany. 1972-1998. Lang.: Ger. 3131
Mayer, Michael
Performance/production
Director Michael Mayer. USA. 1998. Lang.: Eng. 2670
Maynard Smith, Julian
Performance/production
Collection of newspaper reviews by London theatre critics. UK-England. 1998. Lang.: Eng. 2504
Maynard, Trevor B.
Performance/production
Collection of newspaper reviews by London theatre critics. UK-England: London. 1998. Lang.: Eng. 2464
Maza, Mordechaj
Performance/production
Vilna's Yiddish theatre companies. Poland: Vilna, Cracow. 1918-1939. Lang.: Pol. 2212
Mazeppa
Performance/production
Guest performances of the Kirov Opera at the Metropolitan.. USA: New York, NY. 1998. Lang.: Eng. 4731
MC 93 Bobigny (Paris)
Basic theatrical documents
French translation of *Beast on the Moon* by Richard Kalinoski. USA. France. 1995-1997. Lang.: Fre. 1491
McAllister, Bob
Performance/production
Obituary for Bob McAllister, ventriloquist, magician, and former host of *Wonderama*. USA. 1935-1998. Lang.: Eng. 4149
McAnuff, Des
Design/technology
Des McAnuff's design concept for his film *Cousin Bette*. USA: Hollywood, CA. 1998. Lang.: Eng. 3905
McBurney, Simon
Design/technology
Technical designs for *The Chairs (Les Chaises)*, Théâtre de Complicité. UK-England: London. 1998. Lang.: Eng. 1524
Performance/production
The future of English repertory companies. UK-England: London. 1998. Lang.: Eng. 2563
Interview with director Simon McBurney. UK-England: London. 1997. Lang.: Swe. 2641
McCabe, Richard
Performance/production
Richard McCabe on his role in *The Winter's Tale* at RSC. UK-England: London, Stratford. 1992-1993. Lang.: Eng. 2623
McCaldon, Andrew
Performance/production
Collection of newspaper reviews by London theatre critics. UK-England: London. 1998. Lang.: Eng. 2463
McCarthy, Lillah
Plays/librettos/scripts
George Bernard Shaw's involvement with the Court Theatre. UK-England. 1904-1909. Lang.: Eng. 3471
McCarty, Nick
Performance/production
Collection of newspaper reviews by London theatre critics. UK-England: London. 1998. Lang.: Eng. 2553
McClintic, Guthrie
Performance/production
The marriage of theatre artists Katharine Cornell and Guthrie McClintic. USA. 1893-1974. Lang.: Eng. 634
McCloskey, Brian
Performance/production
Collection of newspaper reviews by London theatre critics. UK-England: London. 1998. Lang.: Eng. 2421
McClymont, Ken
Performance/production
Collection of newspaper reviews by London theatre critics. UK-England: London. 1998. Lang.: Eng. 2439
McColl, Hamish
Performance/production
Collection of newspaper reviews by London theatre critics. UK-England: London. 1998. Lang.: Eng. 2564
McConnel, James
Performance/production
Collection of newspaper reviews by London theatre critics. UK-England: London. 1998. Lang.: Eng. 2549
McCurrach, Ian
Performance/production
Collection of newspaper reviews by London theatre critics. UK-England: London. 1998. Lang.: Eng. 2554
McDermott, Phelim
Performance/production
Collection of newspaper reviews by London theatre critics. UK-England: London. 1998. Lang.: Eng. 2421
Collection of newspaper reviews by London theatre critics. UK-England: London. 1998. Lang.: Eng. 2465
Collection of newspaper reviews by London theatre critics. UK-England: London. 1998. Lang.: Eng. 2556
McDevitt, Roddy
Performance/production
Collection of newspaper reviews by London theatre critics. UK-England: London. 1998. Lang.: Eng. 2427
McDonagh, Martin
Design/technology
Set designs of Francis O'Connor. USA: New York, NY. 1998. Lang.: Eng. 1541
Performance/production
Productions of director Peter Wittenberg. Germany: Munich, Bonn. 1998. Lang.: Ger. 2013
Plays/librettos/scripts
Contemporary Irish playwrights. Ireland. 1998. Lang.: Eng. 3207
Playwright Martin McDonagh. Ireland. 1998. Lang.: Eng. 3216
McDonald, Audra
Performance/production
Actress Audra McDonald. USA. 1993-1998. Lang.: Eng. 2669
McDonald, Camden
Performance/production
Collection of newspaper reviews by London theatre critics. UK-England. 1998. Lang.: Eng. 2489
McDonnell, Eamon
Performance/production
Collection of newspaper reviews by London theatre critics. UK-England: London. 1998. Lang.: Eng. 2463
McElvany, Scot
Performance/production
The development of *Letters, or Where Does the Postman Go When All the Street Names Are Changed*, based on experiences of residents of Mostar. Bosnia-Herzegovina: Mostar. 1997. Lang.: Eng. 1831
McGarty, Michael
Design/technology
Michael McGarty's set design for Elaine May and Alan Arkin's *Power Plays*. USA: New York, NY. 1998. Lang.: Eng. 1542
McGee, Greg
Plays/librettos/scripts
Women in plays about war and male contact sports. New Zealand. Europe. 1998. Lang.: Eng. 3281
McGegan, Nicholas
Performance/production
Interview with conductor Nicholas McGegan. USA. UK-England. 1998. Lang.: Eng. 4740
McGregor, Wayne
Performance/production
Choreographer Wayne McGregor and his work with Swedish students. Sweden: Husby. 1998. Lang.: Swe. 1304
McGuinness, Frank
Performance/production
Collection of newspaper reviews by London theatre critics. UK-England: London. 1998. Lang.: Eng. 2543

McGuinness, Frank — cont'd

Plays/librettos/scripts
Contemporary Irish playwrights. Ireland. 1998. Lang.: Eng. 3207
Gender and nationalism in Northern Irish drama. UK-Ireland. 1902-1997. Lang.: Eng. 3511

McGurl, Mimi
Performance/production
Theatre Magazine's anniversary issue. USA. 1968-1998. Lang.: Eng. 617

McHale, Dominic
Performance/production
Collection of newspaper reviews by London theatre critics. UK-England: London. 1998. Lang.: Eng. 2521

McHugh, Dion
Performance/production
Collection of newspaper reviews by London theatre critics. UK-England: London. 1998. Lang.: Eng. 2492

McInerny, Nicholas
Performance/production
Collection of newspaper reviews by London theatre critics. UK-England: London. 1998. Lang.: Eng. 2455
Collection of newspaper reviews by London theatre critics. UK-England: London. 1998. Lang.: Eng. 2550

McKay, Ken
Relation to other fields
Puppeteer Ken McKay on puppetry in education. Canada. 1994-1998. Lang.: Eng. 4915

McKay, Malcolm
Performance/production
The inaugural season of Shakespeare's Globe Theatre. UK-England: London. 1997. Lang.: Eng. 2601

McKellen, Ian
Performance/production
Trevor Nunn's production of *An Enemy of the People* by Ibsen. UK-England: London. 1998. Lang.: Eng. 2627
The body in stage-to-film versions of Shakespeare's *Richard III*. UK-England. USA. 1985-1998. Lang.: Eng. 3940

McKenna, Siobhan
Plays/librettos/scripts
African- and Irish-Americans in the plays of Eugene O'Neill. USA. 1916-1953. Lang.: Eng. 3687

McKenna, Susie
Performance/production
Collection of newspaper reviews by London theatre critics. UK-England. 1998. Lang.: Eng. 2558

McKenzie, Julia
Performance/production
Collection of newspaper reviews by London theatre critics. UK-England: London, Scarborough. 1998. Lang.: Eng. 2426

McKenzie, Kevin
Institutions
Profile of the American Ballet Theatre. USA: New York, NY. 1998. Lang.: Hun. 1061

McKenzie, Paul
Performance/production
Collection of newspaper reviews by London theatre critics. UK-England: London. 1998. Lang.: Eng. 2475

McLaggan, Gavin
Performance/production
Collection of newspaper reviews by London theatre critics. UK-England: London. 1998. Lang.: Eng. 2418

McLane, Derek
Design/technology
Derek McLane's set designs for recent Off Broadway productions. USA: New York, NY. 1998. Lang.: Eng. 1538
Technical designs for *Griller* by Eric Bogosian. USA: Chicago, IL. 1998. Lang.: Eng. 1558

McLaughlin, Ellen
Plays/librettos/scripts
Ellen McLaughlin's *Iphigenia and Other Daughters* at CSC Repertory. USA: New York, NY. 1995. Lang.: Eng. 3520

McMurtry, Larry
Basic theatrical documents
Screenplay of *The Last Picture Show* by Larry McMurtry and Peter Bogdanovich. USA. 1971. Lang.: Eng. 3897
Plays/librettos/scripts
Larry McMurtry on *The Last Picture Show*. USA. 1971. Lang.: Eng. 4018
Interview with director Peter Bogdanovich. USA. 1971-1998. Lang.: Eng. 4020

McNally, Terrence
Design/technology
Lighting and projections for the musical *Ragtime*. USA: New York, NY. 1998. Lang.: Eng. 4328
Technical designs for *Ragtime* at the Ford Center. USA: New York, NY. 1998. Lang.: Eng. 4338
Sound design for the Broadway premiere of the musical *Ragtime*. USA: New York, NY. 1998. Lang.: Eng. 4341
Institutions
The partnership between San Francisco Opera and Chase Manhattan Bank. USA: San Francisco, CA, New York, NY. 1998. Lang.: Eng. 423
Performance/production
Comparison of productions of *The Lisbon Traviata* by Terrence McNally. Germany: Berlin, Essen. 1998. Lang.: Ger. 2005
Collection of newspaper reviews by London theatre critics. UK-England: London. 1998. Lang.: Eng. 2500
Collection of newspaper reviews by London theatre critics. UK-England: London. 1998. Lang.: Eng. 2525
Collection of newspaper reviews by London theatre critics. UK-England: London. 1998. Lang.: Eng. 2538
Plays/librettos/scripts
History of the Playwrights Unit. USA. 1963-1971. Lang.: Eng. 3570
Playwright Terrence McNally on his profession. USA. 1998. Lang.: Eng. 3644
Effeminacy on the American stage. USA. 1920-1998. Lang.: Eng. 3682
Relation to other fields
Controversy over Terrence McNally's *Corpus Christi*, Manhattan Theatre Club. USA: New York, NY. 1998. Lang.: Eng. 3792

McNamara, Brooks
Institutions
Brooks McNamara, founder and director of the Shubert archive. USA: New York, NY. 1976-1998. Lang.: Eng. 413
Brooks McNamara on the Shubert archive of which he is director. USA: New York, NY. 1976-1998. Lang.: Eng. 415

McNicholas, Steve
Performance/production
Collection of newspaper reviews by London theatre critics. UK-England: London. 1998. Lang.: Eng. 2544

McPherson, Conor
Performance/production
Collection of newspaper reviews by London theatre critics. UK-England: London. 1998. Lang.: Eng. 2416
Collection of newspaper reviews by London theatre critics. UK-England: London. 1998. Lang.: Eng. 2428
Collection of newspaper reviews by London theatre critics. UK-England: London. 1998. Lang.: Eng. 2520
Plays/librettos/scripts
Contemporary Irish playwrights. Ireland. 1998. Lang.: Eng. 3207
Playwright Conor McPherson. Ireland. 1998. Lang.: Eng. 3209

McPherson, Neil
Performance/production
Collection of newspaper reviews by London theatre critics. UK-England: London, Stratford, Derby. 1998. Lang.: Eng. 2417

McSweeney, Ethan
Design/technology
Lighting design for *Never the Sinner* by John Logan, directed by Ethan McSweeney. USA: New York, NY. 1998. Lang.: Eng. 1534

McSweeney, Sean
Performance/production
Collection of newspaper reviews by London theatre critics. UK-England: London. 1998. Lang.: Eng. 2514

Meacher, Harry
Performance/production
Collection of newspaper reviews by London theatre critics. UK-England: London. 1998. Lang.: Eng. 2422
Collection of newspaper reviews by London theatre critics. UK-England: London. 1998. Lang.: Eng. 2531

Meadow, Lynne
Performance/production
Career of director Lynne Meadow. USA: New York, NY. 1972-1985. Lang.: Eng. 2708

Measure for Measure
Basic theatrical documents
Catalan translation of Shakespeare's *Measure for Measure*. England. 1604. Lang.: Cat. 1420
Performance/production
German productions of Shakespeare. Germany: Leipzig, Hamburg, Berlin. 1998. Lang.: Ger. 2033

***Measure for Measure* — cont'd**

Collection of newspaper reviews by London theatre critics. UK. 1998. Lang.: Eng. 2407

Collection of newspaper reviews by London theatre critics. UK-England: London. 1998. Lang.: Eng. 2496

Experimental Shakespeare production at the Gaiety Theatre. UK-England: Manchester. 1908-1915. Lang.: Eng. 2605

Plays/librettos/scripts

Shakespeare's *Measure for Measure* and the King James Bible. England. 1604. Lang.: Eng. 2865

Hermeneutic analysis of Shakespearean comedies. England. 1590-1608. Lang.: Eng. 2877

Analysis of a speech in Shakespeare's *Measure for Measure*. England. 1604. Lang.: Eng. 2896

Cognitive analysis of Shakespeare's *Measure for Measure*. England. 1604. Lang.: Eng. 2900

Protestant aesthetics and Shakespeare's *Measure for Measure*. England. 1604. Lang.: Eng. 2908

Aspects of character in Shakespeare's *Measure for Measure*. England. 1604. Lang.: Eng. 2909

Punishment and political power in plays of Shakespeare. England. 1604-1611. Lang.: Eng. 2944

The theme of substitution in Shakespeare's *Measure for Measure*. England. 1604. Lang.: Eng. 2957

Psychological power and control in Shakespeare's *Measure for Measure*. England. 1604. Lang.: Eng. 2962

The psychology of punishment in Shakespeare's *Measure for Measure*. England. 1604. Lang.: Eng. 2975

Analysis of *Troilus and Cressida* and *Measure for Measure* by William Shakespeare. England. 1601-1604. Lang.: Ita. 3012

Gender and religion in Shakespeare's *Measure for Measure*. England. 1604. Lang.: Eng. 3021

The control of procreation and death in Shakespeare's *Measure for Measure*. England. 1604. Lang.: Eng. 3041

Theory/criticism

New historicism and Shakespeare's *Measure for Measure*. 1988. Lang.: Eng. 3801

Meat on the Bone

Performance/production

Collection of newspaper reviews by London theatre critics. UK-England: London. 1998. Lang.: Eng. 2568

Meckler, Nancy

Performance/production

Collection of newspaper reviews by London theatre critics. UK-England: London. 1998. Lang.: Eng. 2432

Collection of newspaper reviews by London theatre critics. UK-England: London. 1998. Lang.: Eng. 2506

Plays/librettos/scripts

Shared Experience's stage adaptations of nineteenth-century novels. USA: New York, NY. UK-England: London. 1998. Lang.: Eng. 3518

Medea

Performance/production

Comparison of fifteen productions of Euripides' *Medea*. Czech Republic. 1921-1998. Lang.: Cze. 1885

Twentieth-century productions of Euripidean tragedy. USA. 1915-1969. Lang.: Eng. 2678

Interview with actress Phylicia Rashad. USA: Atlanta, GA. 1998. Lang.: Eng. 2695

Plays/librettos/scripts

The character Medea in European drama. Europe. 450 B.C.-1998 A.D. Lang.: Ger. 3063

Adaptations of Greek tragedy by contemporary Irish writers. Ireland. UK-Ireland. 1984-1998. Lang.: Eng. 3214

Analysis of Countée Cullen's translation of Euripides' *Medea*. USA. 1936. Lang.: Eng. 3567

Médecin malgré lui, Le (Doctor in Spite of Himself, The)

Performance/production

Three Hungarian productions of plays by Molière. Hungary: Szentendre, Kapolcs, Kőszeg. 1998. Lang.: Hun. 2142

Plays/librettos/scripts

Analysis of medical plays by Molière. France. 1660-1722. Lang.: Eng. 3078

Médée de Saint-Médard, La (Medea of Saint-Medard, The)

Basic theatrical documents

Text of *La Médée de Saint-Médard (The Medea of Saint-Medard)* by Anca Visdei. France. 1998. Lang.: Fre. 1436

Medeja (Medea)

Plays/librettos/scripts

Analysis of *Medeja (Medea)* by Dane Zajc. Slovenia. 1988. Lang.: Slo. 3348

Media

SEE ALSO

Classed Entries under MEDIA.

Administration

Attempts to diversify offerings of the Barbican Centre. UK-England: London. 1998. Lang.: Eng. 25

Performance/production

Analysis of *1837: The Farmer's Revolt* directed by Bruce Barton of Carrefour Theatre. Canada: Charlottetown, PE. 1998. Lang.: Eng. 1856

Analysis of two productions of Caryl Churchill's *Top Girls*. UK-England. 1982-1991. Lang.: Eng. 2608

Relation to other fields

Changes in media and press coverage. Germany: Hamburg. 1996-1998. Lang.: Ger. 743

The impact of photography and cinema on theatre. Canada. 1998. Lang.: Fre. 3732

References to film in theatre of Robert Lepage. Canada. 1990-1998. Lang.: Fre. 3734

Theory/criticism

Theory and practice in realized performance. 1998. Lang.: Eng. 831

Medicine Men

Basic theatrical documents

Text of *Medicine Men* by Jack Martin Karp. USA. 1998. Lang.: Eng. 1492

Médico de su honra, El (Surgeon of Honor, The)

Performance/production

Collection of newspaper reviews by London theatre critics. UK-England: London. 1998. Lang.: Eng. 2441

Medieval theatre

Audience

Audience assumptions about the York *Resurrection*. England: York. 1275-1541. Lang.: Eng. 1400

The complex role of the audience in court entertainment. England: Greenwich. 1527. Lang.: Eng. 4194

Institutions

History of the Society for Old Music. USA: Kalamazoo, MI. 1968-1991. Lang.: Eng. 4292

Performance/production

Analysis of *Regularis Concordia* and *Quem quarteritis*. England. 1150-1228. Lang.: Eng. 516

Late medieval Savoy and theatre. Savoy. 1400-1600. Lang.: Eng. 589

Staging of the Cornish *Ordinalia*. England. 1375-1400. Lang.: Eng. 1890

Evidence for performance of medieval religious drama. Sweden. 1140-1500. Lang.: Eng. 2392

Census of productions of medieval plays. UK-England. 1997. Lang.: Eng. 2610

Katie Mitchell's production of mystery plays at RSC. UK-England: London. 1996-1998. Lang.: Eng. 2626

Director Joel Kaplan on his production of the *York Cycle*. Canada: Toronto, ON. 1998. Lang.: Eng. 4213

The staging of the complete *York Cycle* by the University of Toronto. Canada: Toronto, ON. 1998. Lang.: Eng. 4214

Sequentia's new recording of *Ordo Virtutum* by Hildegard of Bingen. Germany. 1997. Lang.: Eng. 4294

The survival of medieval English religious theatre on the puppet stage. England: London. 1500-1780. Lang.: Eng. 4890

Plays/librettos/scripts

Analysis of *De Eerste Bliscap van Maria (The First Joy of Mary)*. Belgium: Brussels. 1440-1560. Lang.: Eng. 2790

Wonder and recognition in medieval and Renaissance drama. England. 1400-1612. Lang.: Eng. 2874

The language used by devils in the *York Cycle*. England: York. 1400-1500. Lang.: Eng. 2933

Robin Hood in early English drama. England. 1425-1600. Lang.: Eng. 2941

The Easter play tradition. England. 1180-1557. Lang.: Eng. 2942

Comparison of the Dutch *Elckerlijck* and the English *Everyman*. England. Netherlands. 1495-1525. Lang.: Eng. 2982

The N-town Mary play and the Four Virtues of Psalm 84:11. England. 1120-1501. Lang.: Eng. 2983

The Expositor character of the Chester Cycle. England. 1400-1500. Lang.: Eng. 3033

Medieval theatre — cont'd

Analysis of post-medieval morality plays. Europe. Africa. 1400-1998. Lang.: Eng. 3051
A lost creed play from the twelfth century. Germany: Regensburg. 1184-1189. Lang.: Eng. 3176
Analysis of the Montecassino Passion Play. Italy. 1100-1200. Lang.: Eng. 3256
Dramatic devices in early Spanish drama. Spain. 1550-1722. Lang.: Eng. 3373
The medieval mystery play and Tony Kushner's *Angels in America*. USA. 1992-1994. Lang.: Eng. 3652
Roman 'saints' plays' at the Lille procession honoring the Virgin. Belgium: Lille. 1450-1499. Lang.: Eng. 4224
Reference materials
Index to the first twenty volumes of *Medieval English Theatre*. England. 1979-1998. Lang.: Eng. 696
Relation to other fields
The relationship between the York Cycle and the Bolton Book of Hours. England: York. 1405-1500. Lang.: Eng. 3750
Fouquet's miniature of St. Apollonia and its relationship to the mystery play. France. 1452-1577. Lang.: Eng. 3761
Jean Fouquet's miniature of St. Apollonia and its relationship to performance. France: Tours. 1452-1577. Lang.: Eng. 3762
Fouquet's depiction of the martyrdom of St. Apollonia as a record of a performance. France. 1452-1577. Lang.: Eng. 3763
Economic forces and the Chester Whitsun plays. England: Chester. 1521-1678. Lang.: Eng. 4226
Theory/criticism
Evaluation of scholarship on English cycle plays. 1998. Lang.: Eng. 3802
Cyberspace as performance site. North America. 1998. Lang.: Eng. 4048

Medina, Narciso
Institutions
Contemporary Cuban dance. Cuba: Havana. 1959-1998. Lang.: Swe. 1250

Mednick, Murray
Plays/librettos/scripts
Revolutionary Off Broadway playwriting. USA: New York, NY. 1959-1969. Lang.: Eng. 3604

Medved (Bear, The)
Basic theatrical documents
Catalan translations of the complete plays of Anton Čechov. Russia. 1884-1904. Lang.: Cat. 1449
Performance/production
Čechov's one-act plays at Thália Színház. Hungary. Slovakia: Košice. 1998. Lang.: Hun. 2075
One-act comedies by Čechov directed by Péter Valló. Hungary: Dunaújváros. 1998. Lang.: Hun. 2080
One-act plays of Čechov by the Illyés Gyula National Theatre. Hungary. Ukraine: Beregovo. 1997. Lang.: Hun. 2104

Medved, Anton
Plays/librettos/scripts
Social roles in plays by Fran Govekar and Anton Medved. Slovenia. 1897-1910. Lang.: Slo. 3352

Medvedev, Pavel M.
Performance/production
Actor/director Pavel Medvedev. Russia. 1851-1899. Lang.: Rus. 2330

Medwall, Henry
Performance/production
Music in Tudor drama. England. 1497-1569. Lang.: Eng. 1902

Mee, Charles L.
Basic theatrical documents
Collection of plays by Charles L. Mee. USA. 1986-1995. Lang.: Eng. 1496

Meech, Anthony
Performance/production
Collection of newspaper reviews by London theatre critics. UK-England: London. 1998. Lang.: Eng. 2582

Meehan, Thomas
Performance/production
Collection of newspaper reviews by London theatre critics. UK-England: London. 1998. Lang.: Eng. 2514

Mefistofole
Performance/production
Reconstruction of the premiere of Boito's *Mefistofele*. Italy. 1871-1881. Lang.: Ita. 4647

Mehrle, Jens
Performance/production
A production of Offenbach's *Orphée aux Enfers* directed by Jens Mehrle and Stefan Nolte. Germany: Bitterfeld. 1998. Lang.: Ger. 4856

Mehta, Zubin
Performance/production
A production of Puccini's *Turandot* in Beijing. China, People's Republic of: Beijing. 1998. Lang.: Eng. 4542

Mei, Lanfang
Performance/production
Mei Lanfang's influence on Bertolt Brecht. Germany. China. 1935. Lang.: Eng. 1951

Meilhac, Henri
Plays/librettos/scripts
Contributions of Meilhac and Halévy to the development of the French libretto. France. 1800-1900. Lang.: Fre. 4781

Meining, Peter
Performance/production
Impressions from Podewil theatre workshop. Germany: Berlin. 1998. Lang.: Ger. 2024

Meininger Theater (Meiningen)
Performance/production
Opera director Christine Mielitz. Germany: Meiningen. 1991-1998. Lang.: Ger. 4597

Meistersinger von Nürnberg, Die
Performance/production
Iván Markó's choreography for Bayreuth Festival productions. Germany: Bayreuth. Hungary. 1998. Lang.: Hun. 1083
Background material on Metropolitan Opera radio broadcast performances. USA: New York, NY. 1998. Lang.: Eng. 4713
Bass James Johnson. USA. 1998. Lang.: Eng. 4722
Organizing two performances at the Metropolitan Opera on a single day. USA: New York, NY. 1997-1998. Lang.: Eng. 4741
Plays/librettos/scripts
Comic and tragic elements in Wagner's *Die Meistersinger von Nürnberg*. Germany. 1868-1998. Lang.: Eng. 4792

Mejerchol'd, Vsevolod Emiljévič
Basic theatrical documents
English translation of Mejerchol'd's adaptation of *Revizor (The Inspector General)* by Gogol. Russia. USSR. 1838-1926. Lang.: Eng. 1450
Performance spaces
Non-traditional theatrical space. Germany. France. UK-England. 1898-1998. Lang.: Dan. 443
Performance/production
History of movement training for the actor. USA. 1910-1985. Lang.: Eng. 675
Collaborative Symbolist dance/theatre projects. Europe. USA. 1916-1934. Lang.: Eng. 1268
Acting and directing influences on Eugenio Barba. Denmark: Holstebro. 1997. Lang.: Eng. 1886
Director V.E. Mejerchol'd. Russia. 1900-1940. Lang.: Rus. 2230
Biography of director V.E. Mejerchol'd. Russia. 1874-1940. Lang.: Rus. 2258
Interview with director Lev Dodin. Russia. 1997. Lang.: Fre. 2260
The Russian-German theatrical relationship. Russia. Germany. 1920-1949. Lang.: Rus. 2285
Autobiographical writings by director V.E. Mejerchol'd. Russia. 1891-1903. Lang.: Rus. 2296
Interview with composer Paul Schmidt. USA: New Haven, CT. 1998. Lang.: Eng. 2660
Interview with director Peter Sellars. USA: Cambridge, MA. 1980-1981. Lang.: Eng. 2661
Yale Drama Department's reconstruction of Gogol's *Revizor (The Inspector General)* as staged by Mejerchol'd. USA: New Haven, CT. 1997. Lang.: Eng. 2668
The development of the character Khlezstakov in Gogol's *Revizor (The Inspector General)* in productions by Mejerchol'd. USSR. 1926-1939. Lang.: Eng. 2762
Mejerchol'd's production of Gogol's *Revizor (The Inspector General)*. USSR: Moscow. 1926. Lang.: Eng. 2763
Director Harold Clurman's reaction to Mejerchol'd's *Revizor (The Inspector General)*. USSR: Moscow. 1935. Lang.: Eng. 2764
Director Mel Gordon on Mejerchol'd's influence. USSR. 1920-1931. Lang.: Eng. 2765
Mejerchol'd's denial of charges that he was a counter-revolutionary. USSR: Moscow. 1940. Lang.: Eng. 2767
Mejerchol'd's relationship with Lunačarskij. USSR. 1890-1931. Lang.: Eng. 2768

Mejerchol'd, Vsevolod Emiljėvič — cont'd

Commedia dell'arte and twentieth-century theatre. Europe. 1860-1950. Lang.: Eng. 4187
Plays/librettos/scripts
The clown as a character in modern drama. Europe. 1915-1995. Lang.: Eng. 3056
Relation to other fields
Modern fictional characters through the lens of Mejerchol'd's biomechanics and Oskar Schlemmer's puppets. Europe. 1913-1930. Lang.: Ger. 729
Training
Mejerchol'd, actor training, and Trotsky. USSR. 1922-1929. Lang.: Eng. 3852

Meladze, Valerij
Performance/production
Singer Valerij Meladze. Russia. 1998. Lang.: Rus. 4130
Singer Valerij Meladze. Russia. 1998. Lang.: Rus. 4131

Melani, Jacopo
Performance/production
The evolution of comic opera. Italy: Florence, Rome. 1665-1700. Lang.: Eng. 4660

Melbourne Women's Theatre Group
Plays/librettos/scripts
Australian women playwrights and their work. Australia. 1972-1998. Lang.: Eng. 2778

Meldegg, Stephan
Basic theatrical documents
Text of *Pour la galerie (For the Gallery)* by Claude d'Anna and Laure Bonin. France. 1998. Lang.: Fre. 1424
French translation of *Popcorn* by Ben Elton. UK-England. France. 1996-1998. Lang.: Fre. 1475

Melfi, Leonard
Plays/librettos/scripts
History of the Playwrights Unit. USA. 1963-1971. Lang.: Eng. 3570

Méliès, Georges
Plays/librettos/scripts
The reciprocal influence of opera and film. Europe. North America. 1904-1994. Lang.: Eng. 4770

Melinkoff, Anthony
Performance/production
Collection of newspaper reviews by London theatre critics. UK-England: London, Stratford, Derby. 1998. Lang.: Eng. 2417

Melis, György
Performance/production
Baritone György Melis and the performance in celebration of his 75th birthday. Hungary. 1923-1998. Lang.: Hun. 4633
Album on the life and career of baritone György Melis. Hungary. 1923-1998. Lang.: Hun, Eng. 4639

Melodrama
Institutions
Profile of Engine House Theatre. USA: Madrid, NM. 1982-1998. Lang.: Eng. 1760
Performance/production
Excessive stage and screen melodrama. UK-England. USA. 1830-1970. Lang.: Eng. 608
Boucicault's *The Octoroon* and the performance of race, gender, and power. USA. 1800-1860. Lang.: Eng. 669
Directing the documentary-based performance project *The Worst Woman in the World.* Australia. 1994. Lang.: Eng. 1816
Actor and playwright George Dibdin Pitt. UK-England: London. 1806-1808. Lang.: Eng. 2592
Plays/librettos/scripts
The development of playwright Owen Davis. USA. 1905-1923. Lang.: Eng. 3526
Analysis of *Bandido!* by Luis Valdez. USA. 1986. Lang.: Eng. 3676

Melton, Christine
Administration
Christine Melton on the production of her play *Still Life Goes On.* USA: New York, NY. 1997. Lang.: Eng. 1398

Melwood, Mary
Plays/librettos/scripts
Absurdism in children's theatre. North America. Europe. 1896-1970. Lang.: Eng. 3288

Members Only
Performance/production
Collection of newspaper reviews by London theatre critics. UK-England: London. 1998. Lang.: Eng. 2475

Mémoires d'isles (Island Memories)
Plays/librettos/scripts
Postcolonialism, ethnicity, and feminism in French and Caribbean plays. France. Martinique. Guadeloupe. 1960-1990. Lang.: Eng. 3104

Menander
Plays/librettos/scripts
The subversion of tragic forms in comic plays of Menander. Greece. 342-291 B.C. Lang.: Eng. 3183

Menchell, Ivan
Performance/production
Collection of newspaper reviews by London theatre critics. UK-England: London. 1998. Lang.: Eng. 2491

Mencken, Alan
Performance spaces
The construction of a theatre for *Beauty and the Beast.* Germany: Stuttgart. 1997. Lang.: Ger. 444

Menczel, Róbert
Institutions
Theatre critics' awards 97-98. Hungary. 1997-1998. Lang.: Hun. 355

Mendes, Sam
Design/technology
Technical designs for Sam Mendes' production of *Cabaret.* USA: New York, NY. 1998. Lang.: Eng. 4343
Lighting design for Sam Mendes' production of *Cabaret.* USA: New York, NY. 1998. Lang.: Eng. 4344
Performance spaces
The creation of a site-specific performance space for Sam Mendes' production of *Cabaret.* USA: New York, NY. 1998. Lang.: Eng. 4350
Performance/production
Collection of newspaper reviews by London theatre critics. UK-England: London. 1998. Lang.: Eng. 2466
Collection of newspaper reviews by London theatre critics. UK-England: London. 1998. Lang.: Eng. 2509
Musical performances on and off Broadway. USA: New York. 1998. Lang.: Ger. 4383

Mendiants d'amour (Beggars of Love)
Basic theatrical documents
Text of *Mendiants d'amour (Beggars of Love)* by Gérard Levoyer. France. 1998. Lang.: Fre. 1430

Menken, Adah Isaacs
Performance/production
Audience reaction to actress Adah Isaacs Menken. USA. 1835-1869. Lang.: Eng. 619

Menken, Alan
Administration
The Disney Corporation's Broadway musicals. USA: New York, NY. 1996-1998. Lang.: Eng. 4317
Performance/production
Collection of newspaper reviews by London theatre critics. UK-England: London. 1998. Lang.: Eng. 2492

Mennyei híd, A (Heavenly Bridge, The)
Performance/production
János Acs' *A mennyei híd (The Heavenly Bridge)* directed by Gábor Cziezel. Hungary: Debrecen. 1998. Lang.: Hun. 2069

Menotti, Gian Carlo
Training
Actor training for the character tenor. USA. 1998. Lang.: Eng. 4849

Menšikov, Oleg
Performance/production
Oleg Menšikov's production of *Gore ot uma (Wit Works Woe)* by Gribojėdov. Russia: Moscow. 1998. Lang.: Rus. 2267
Actor Oleg Menšikov. Russia: Moscow. Russia. 1998. Lang.: Rus. 2304

Menyegző (Wedding)
Performance/production
Productions of the Magyar Fesztival Balett choreographed by Iván Markó. Hungary: Budapest. 1998. Lang.: Hun. 1097

Menyhárt, Jacqueline
Training
Interview with ballet dancer and teacher Jacqueline Menyhárt. Hungary. 1954-1998. Lang.: Hun. 1206

Meola, Tony
Design/technology
Panel discussion of sound designers. USA. 1998. Lang.: Eng. 287
Technical designs for the Broadway production of *The Lion King.* USA: New York, NY. 1998. Lang.: Eng. 4342

Mephisto
Institutions
Theatrical space in productions of Ariane Mnouchkine. France: Paris. 1970-1995. Lang.: Eng. 1607
Plays/librettos/scripts
Analysis of István Szabó's film *Mephisto.* Hungary. 1981. Lang.: Eng. 3974

Merce Cunningham Dance Company (New York, NY)
Performance/production
Interview with dancer/choreographer Merce Cunningham. USA. 1960-1998. Lang.: Eng. 1186
Theory/criticism
Critique of dance criticism. UK-England: London. 1989. Lang.: Eng. 1339

Merchant of Venice, The
Performance spaces
Shakespeare's Globe and the staging of *The Merchant of Venice*. UK-England: London. 1998. Lang.: Ger. 1810
Performance/production
Interview with director Thomas Langhoff. Germany, East. 1970-1990. Lang.: Eng. 2038
Interview with actor and director Róbert Alföldi. Hungary: Budapest. 1998. Lang.: Hun. 2056
Review of Shakespeare's *The Merchant of Venice*, Szigligeti Theatre. Hungary: Szolnok. 1997. Lang.: Hun. 2066
Round-table discussion on Tivoli Theatre's production of *The Merchant of Venice*. Hungary. 1986-1997. Lang.: Hun. 2109
Shakespeare's *The Merchant of Venice* directed by Róbert Alföldi. Hungary: Budapest. 1998. Lang.: Hun. 2111
Collection of newspaper reviews by London theatre critics. UK-England: London. 1998. Lang.: Eng. 2498
Collection of newspaper reviews by London theatre critics. UK-England: London. 1998. Lang.: Eng. 2551
Christopher Luscombe on acting in RSC productions. UK-England: London, Stratford. 1993-1994. Lang.: Eng. 2620
Richard Olivier's production of Shakespeare's *The Merchant of Venice*. UK-England: London. 1998. Lang.: Eng. 2621
Plays/librettos/scripts
Dutch and Flemish Shakespearean productions. Belgium. Netherlands. 1980-1983. Lang.: Dut. 2789
The figure of the Jew in Marlowe and Shakespeare. England. 1590-1600. Lang.: Eng. 2868
The control of time in Renaissance English drama. England. 1590-1620. Lang.: Eng. 2883
Cross-dressing in Shakespeare's *The Merchant of Venice* and in the autobiography of actress Charlotte Cibber Charke. England. 1713-1760. Lang.: Eng. 2891
The origin and meaning of the name Shylock in Shakespeare's *The Merchant of Venice*. England. 1596. Lang.: Eng. 2932
Prejudice and law in Shakespeare's *The Merchant of Venice*. England. 1596. Lang.: Eng. 3027
Two centuries' thought on Shakespeare's *The Merchant of Venice*. Europe. North America. 1788-1996. Lang.: Hun. 3066
Analysis of Imre Szabó Stein's new translation of Shakespeare's *The Merchant of Venice*. Hungary: Budapest. 1998. Lang.: Hun. 3188
Theory/criticism
Antisemitism and criticism of Shakespeare's *Merchant of Venice*. England. 1596-1986. Lang.: Eng. 3813

Merciful Coincidence, A
Plays/librettos/scripts
Roger Reynolds' musical settings of texts by Samuel Beckett. USA. 1968-1976. Lang.: Eng. 4309

Mercury Theatre (New York, NY)
Institutions
History of Mercury Theatre. USA: New York, NY. 1937-1942. Lang.: Eng. 1776
Performance/production
Popular American radio and the importance of the disembodied voice. USA. 1929-1940. Lang.: Eng. 3864

Mère Coupable, La (Guilty Mother, The)
Plays/librettos/scripts
Operatic realizations of Beaumarchais' character Rosina. Europe. North America. 1784-1991. Lang.: Eng. 4773

Mère Coupable, La **by Milhaud**
Plays/librettos/scripts
Operatic realizations of Beaumarchais' character Rosina. Europe. North America. 1784-1991. Lang.: Eng. 4773

Merežkovskij, Dmitri Sergejėvič
Relation to other fields
Novelist Dmitri S. Merežkovskij and theatre. 1890-1909. Lang.: Rus. 712

Merill, Scott
Performance/production
Friends and colleagues recall singer Lotte Lenya. Germany. 1928-1981. Lang.: Eng. 4355

Merkle, Matthias
Administration
Interviews with German theatre and film directors. Germany. 1998. Lang.: Ger. 1385

Merkuškin, G. Ja
Plays/librettos/scripts
Playwright and nationalist G. Ja. Merkuškin. Mordovia. Lang.: Rus. 3277

Merlin
Design/technology
Design awards for the TV mini-series *Merlin*. USA: Pasadena, CA. 1998. Lang.: Eng. 4052

Mermaid Theatre (Wolfville, NS)
Institutions
Puppetry at Mermaid Theatre. Canada: Wolfville, NS. 1972-1998. Lang.: Eng. 4870

Merő, Béla
Performance/production
Three Hungarian productions of plays by Molière. Hungary: Szentendre, Kapolcs, Kőszeg. 1998. Lang.: Hun. 2142

Merriam, Eve
Plays/librettos/scripts
Gendered political critique in *The Club* by Eve Merriam. USA. 1976. Lang.: Eng. 3572

Merrily We Roll Along
Plays/librettos/scripts
The disintegration of the American dream in works of Stephen Sondheim. USA. 1970-1984. Lang.: Eng. 4397

Merriman, Eve
Performance/production
Documentary theatre and the politics of representation. USA. 1966-1993. Lang.: Eng. 2728

Merritt, Chris
Theory/criticism
Performers and conductors complain about unfair reviews. USA. 1998. Lang.: Eng. 4844

Merritt, Theresa
Performance/production
Obituary for actress Theresa Merritt. USA: New York, NY. 1998. Lang.: Eng. 2749

Merry Wives of Windsor, The
Plays/librettos/scripts
Women's use of wit in response to men in English popular culture. England. 1590-1630. Lang.: Eng. 2884
Female power and the public sphere in Renaissance drama. England. 1597-1616. Lang.: Eng. 2943
Comparison of final scenes in quarto and folio versions of Shakespeare's plays. England. 1597-1601. Lang.: Eng. 3005

Merschmeier, Michael
Design/technology
Lighting in contemporary theatre. Germany. 1998. Lang.: Ger. 192

Mesjac v derevne (Month in the Country, A)
Performance/production
Turgenjėv's *Mesjac v derevne (A Month in the Country)* directed by Zoltán Lendvar. Hungary: Kecskemét. 1998. Lang.: Hun. 2134
Collection of newspaper reviews by London theatre critics. UK-England. 1998. Lang.: Eng. 2558

Mesplé, Mady
Performance/production
Interpreters of the title role in Delibes' opera *Lakmé*. 1932-1995. Lang.: Fre. 4505
Soprano Mady Mesplé on Delibes' *Lakmé*. France. 1961-1997. Lang.: Fre. 4573

Messer, Graeme
Performance/production
Collection of newspaper reviews by London theatre critics. UK-England: London. 1998. Lang.: Eng. 2560

Messiaen, Olivier
Performance/production
Opera productions of the Salzburg Festival. Austria: Salzburg. 1998. Lang.: Hun. 4531
Review of opera productions. Germany: Stuttgart, Leipzig. 1998. Lang.: Ger. 4584

Messier, Jean-Frédéric
Plays/librettos/scripts
Raymond Saint-Jean's film adaptation of *Cabaret neiges noires (Black Snow Cabaret)*. Canada. 1997. Lang.: Fre. 3967

Messingkauf (Messingkauf Dialogues, The)
Performance/production
Review of Brazilian performances of plays by Brecht. Brazil: São Paulo. 1998. Lang.: Ger. 1832

Mestno gledališče ljubljansko (Ljubljana)
Institutions
The first decade of Ljubljana's municipal theatre, Mestno gledališče ljubljansko. Slovenia: Ljubljana. 1951-1961. Lang.: Slo. 1718
Métaphore, La (Lille)
Performance/production
French production of *Im Dickicht der Städte (In the Jungle of Cities)* by Bertolt Brecht. France. 1997-1998. Lang.: Ger. 1946
Metastasio, Pietro
Plays/librettos/scripts
Playwright and poet Pietro Metastasio. Italy. 1698-1782. Lang.: Ita. 3252
Metatheatre
Plays/librettos/scripts
Dramatic devices in early Spanish drama. Spain. 1550-1722. Lang.: Eng. 3373
Metadrama in plays of Tennessee Williams. USA. 1944-1978. Lang.: Eng. 3686
Metcalfe, Carol
Performance/production
Collection of newspaper reviews by London theatre critics. UK-England: London. 1998. Lang.: Eng. 2410
Methodology
Research/historiography
Proposed ethnographic model for the study of rehearsal. 1985-1995. Lang.: Eng. 816
Alternative models of performance documentation. Europe. 1984-1997. Lang.: Eng. 818
Alternative forms of performance documentation. Europe. 1984-1997. Lang.: Eng. 819
The use of the term 'theatricality' in German theatre research. Germany. 1900-1998. Lang.: Ger. 820
Gender difference and theatricality. Germany. France. USA. 1959-1998. Lang.: Ger. 821
Critique of the biases of theatre history toward the exceptional. Poland. 1865-1998. Lang.: Pol. 822
The current state of research on Polish theatre in exile. UK-England: London. 1939-1998. Lang.: Pol. 824
New approaches to theatre studies and performance analysis. UK-England: Bristol. 1998. Lang.: Eng. 826
Problems of dance historiography. Europe. North America. 1997. Lang.: Eng. 1001
Research on dance and cultural studies. North America. Europe. 1998. Lang.: Eng. 1003
Theatre research and the analysis of plays and performance. 1998. Lang.: Eng. 3794
Problem of documentary performance art. 1950-1988. Lang.: Eng. 4267
Methodologies specific to the analysis of seventeenth-century Italian opera. Italy. 1601-1998. Lang.: Eng. 4835
Theory/criticism
The critical methodology of Giuseppe Bartolucci. Italy. 1982-1998. Lang.: Ita. 850
Synthetic account of Slovene theatre. Slovenia. 1997. Lang.: Slo. 858
The need for a critical vocabulary to evaluate operatic productions. Europe. 1987-1998. Lang.: Eng. 4836
Evaluating the work of opera directors. Europe. 1965-1998. Lang.: Eng. 4837
Metier (Bradford)
Institutions
The work of training organization Metier in creating national standards for arts training. UK-England: Bradford. 1996-1998. Lang.: Eng. 388
Metrodora
Institutions
Italian experimental theatre at Spielart '97. Germany: Munich. Italy. 1997. Lang.: Eng. 1619
Metropolitan Opera (New York, NY)
Administration
Standing-room-only practices at the Metropolitan Opera. USA: New York, NY. 1998. Lang.: Eng. 4407
Audience
Gender and social warfare at the Metropolitan Opera. USA. 1890-1910. Lang.: Eng. 4411
Design/technology
Scene designer Richard Hudson and his work on *Samson et Dalila* at the Metropolitan Opera. UK-England. USA. 1954-1998. Lang.: Eng. 4289
Lighting designer Jennifer Tipton. USA: New York, NY. 1998. Lang.: Eng. 4441
Institutions
Preview of the Kirov Opera's visit to the Metropolitan Opera. Russia: St. Petersburg. 1997. Lang.: Eng. 4470
History of the Metropolitan Opera Guild. USA. 1935-1975. Lang.: Eng. 4486
Annual report of the Metropolitan Opera Guild. USA: New York, NY. 1997-1998. Lang.: Eng. 4488
Performance/production
Tenor and artistic director of Washington Opera Plácido Domingo. 1941-1998. Lang.: Eng. 4512
Verdi's rarely performed opera *Stiffelio*. Italy. 1850-1998. Lang.: Hun. 4652
Conductor Andrew Davis. UK-England. USA. 1998. Lang.: Eng. 4704
Background material on Metropolitan Opera radio broadcast performances. USA: New York, NY. 1998. Lang.: Eng. 4713
Background material on telecast performance of Saint-Saëns' *Samson et Dalila* at the Metropolitan Opera. USA: New York, NY. 1998. Lang.: Eng. 4714
Novelist Joyce Carol Oates' reaction to Berg's *Wozzeck* at the Metropolitan Opera. USA: New York, NY. 1997. Lang.: Eng. 4718
Interview with Ira Siff of La Gran Scena. USA: New York, NY. 1998. Lang.: Eng. 4719
Baritone Nathan Gunn. USA. 1971-1998. Lang.: Eng. 4723
Soprano Marcella Sembrich's performances at the Metropolitan Opera. USA: New York, NY. 1883-1909. Lang.: Eng. 4724
Verdi's *Stiffelio* and Gounod's *Roméo et Juliette* in New York. USA: New York, NY. 1850-1998. Lang.: Eng. 4730
Guest performances of the Kirov Opera at the Metropolitan.. USA: New York, NY. 1998. Lang.: Eng. 4731
Robert Wilson's production of Wagner's *Lohengrin*. USA: New York, NY. 1998. Lang.: Eng. 4732
Jonathan Miller's production of *The Rake's Progress* at the Metropolitan Opera. USA: New York, NY. 1998. Lang.: Eng. 4733
Musicological preparation for the Metropolitan Opera production of Rossini's *La Cenerentola*. USA: Chicago, IL. 1998. Lang.: Eng. 4737
Robert Wilson's production of Wagner's *Lohengrin* at the Metropolitan Opera. USA: New York, NY. 1976-1998. Lang.: Eng. 4739
Organizing two performances at the Metropolitan Opera on a single day. USA: New York, NY. 1997-1998. Lang.: Eng. 4741
Major opera houses' proposals for productions to the end of the century. USA. Canada. 1998. Lang.: Eng. 4743
Bass Samuel Ramey. USA. 1940-1998. Lang.: Eng. 4744
Profile of lighting designer Jennifer Tipton. USA. 1937-1998. Lang.: Eng. 4747
Operas by Benjamin Britten in the repertory of the Metropolitan and the New York City Opera. USA: New York, NY. 1945-1998. Lang.:Eng. 4749
Baritone Dwayne Croft. USA: New York, NY. 1998. Lang.: Eng. 4751
Tenor Anthony Dean Griffey's career and Metropolitan Opera debut. USA: New York, NY. 1998. Lang.: Eng. 4752
Opera conductor Patrick Summers. USA. 1990-1998. Lang.: Eng. 4755
History of commercial TV opera broadcasts. USA: New York, NY. 1939-1980. Lang.: Eng. 4756
Plays/librettos/scripts
Marvin David Levy's operatic adaptation of *Mourning Becomes Electra* by Eugene O'Neill. USA. 1931-1998. Lang.: Eng. 4827
Metropolitan Opera Guild (New York, NY)
Institutions
History of the Metropolitan Opera Guild. USA. 1935-1975. Lang.: Eng. 4486
Annual report of the Metropolitan Opera Guild. USA: New York, NY. 1997-1998. Lang.: Eng. 4488
Metropolitan, The
Basic theatrical documents
Text of *The Metropolitan*, formerly called *The Ten Minute Play* by Mark R. Green. USA. 1995. Lang.: Eng. 1485
Metzger, Márta
Performance/production
Interview with dancer and ballet mistress Márta Metzger. Budapest. 1968-1998. Lang.: Hun. 1066

Metzler, Volker
Institutions
Profile of Theater in der Fabrik. Germany: Dresden. 1993-1998. Lang.: Ger. 1644
Meyer, John
Performance/production
Collection of newspaper reviews by London theatre critics. UK-England: London. 1998. Lang.: Eng. 2499
Meyer, Marlane
Basic theatrical documents
Text of *The Chemistry of Change* by Marlane Meyer. USA. 1998. Lang.: Eng. 1497
Meyerbeer, Giacomo
Performance/production
Hans Neuenfels's production of Meyerbeer's *Le Prophète*. Austria: Vienna. 1998. Lang.: Swe. 4530
Meyerfeld, Max
Basic theatrical documents
Max Meyerfeld's libretto for Zemlinsky's opera *Eine florentinische Tragödie*. Germany. 1917. Lang.: Ger, Fre. 4419
Plays/librettos/scripts
Max Meyerfeld's preface to the translation of *A Florentine Tragedy* by Oscar Wilde. Europe. 1895-1907. Lang.: Fre. 3057
Meyerhold, V.E.
SEE
Mejerchol'd, Vsevolod Emiljėvič.
Mężczyzna (Man, The)
Plays/librettos/scripts
Feminist analysis of plays by Gabriela Zapolska. Poland. 1885-1998. Lang.: Pol. 3301
Mezei, Mária
Performance/production
Actress Mária Mezei. Hungary. 1945-1983. Lang.: Hun. 2140
Meztelen rózsa (Naked Rose)
Performance/production
Lilla Pártay's *Meztelen rózsa (Naked Rose)*, a ballet based on the life of Nižinskij. Hungary: Budapest. 1998. Lang.: Hun. 1110
Mic, Constant
Performance/production
Commedia dell'arte and twentieth-century theatre. Europe. 1860-1950. Lang.: Eng. 4187
Michael, Kerry
Performance/production
Collection of newspaper reviews by London theatre critics. UK-England: London. 1998. Lang.: Eng. 2473
Collection of newspaper reviews by London theatre critics. UK-England: London. 1998. Lang.: Eng. 2557
Michael, Sebastian
Performance/production
Collection of newspaper reviews by London theatre critics. UK-England: London. 1998. Lang.: Eng. 2486
Michaelangelo's Slave
Performance/production
Collection of newspaper reviews by London theatre critics. UK-England: London. 1998. Lang.: Eng. 2434
Michaels, Mia
Performance/production
Jazz dancer and choreographer Mia Michaels. USA. 1998. Lang.: Eng. 987
Micheaux, Oscar
Administration
Oscar Micheaux's use of an interracial marriage case as a publicity tool for his films. USA. 1924. Lang.: Eng. 3874
Michoėls, Solomon Michajlovič
Performance/production
Solomon Michoėls of Moscow's Jewish Theatre. Russia: Moscow. 1998. Lang.: Rus. 2264
The murder of actor and director Solomon Michoėls. Russia: Moscow. 1948. Lang.: Rus. 2293
Mickiewicz, Adam
Performance/production
Analysis of productions of *Dziady (Forefather's Eve)* by Adam Mickiewicz. Poland. 1901-1995. Lang.: Pol. 2220
Plays/librettos/scripts
The current state of studies on playwright Adam Mickiewicz. Poland. 1843-1998. Lang.: Pol. 3302
The Polish national style in Romantic dramas. Poland. 1832-1835. Lang.: Pol. 3304
Microscope Stage (Budapest)
SEE
Mikroszkóp Szinpad.
Midas
Plays/librettos/scripts
Tudor religious and social issues in John Lily's *Endymion* and *Midas*. England. 1587-1590. Lang.: Eng. 2871
Music and the ballad opera in English popular theatre. England. 1728-1780. Lang.: Eng. 4390
Middleton, Thomas
Performance/production
Collection of newspaper reviews by London theatre critics. UK-England: London. 1998. Lang.: Eng. 2424
Collection of newspaper reviews by London theatre critics. UK-England: London. 1998. Lang.: Eng. 2455
Collection of newspaper reviews by London theatre critics. UK-England: London. 1998. Lang.: Eng. 2486
The inaugural season of Shakespeare's Globe Theatre. UK-England: London. 1997. Lang.: Eng. 2601
Review of the opening season of Shakespeare's Globe Theatre. UK-England: London. 1997. Lang.: Eng. 2602
Plays/librettos/scripts
The influence of Webster, Middleton, and Shakespeare on the poetry of Robert Browning. England. 1590-1889. Lang.: Eng. 2906
Female power and the emblem tradition in plays of Shakespeare and Middleton. England. 1604-1625. Lang.: Eng. 2913
The representation of historical female characters on the Renaissance stage. England. 1580-1615. Lang.: Eng. 2922
The Cardinal in Middleton's *Women Beware Women*. England. 1613-1621. Lang.: Eng. 2961
The treatment of single women in early Stuart drama. England. 1604-1608. Lang.: Eng. 2979
Male and female honor in *A Fair Quarrel* by Middleton and Rowley. England. 1615-1617. Lang.: Eng. 2993
Feminism and seventeenth-century city comedy. England. 1600-1700. Lang.: Eng. 3000
Rape in Middleton's *Women Beware Women* and its adaptation by Howard Barker. UK-England. 1625-1986. Lang.: Eng. 3468
The Bodyguard, Sam Shepard's screen adaptation of *The Changeling* by Middleton and Rowley. USA. 1970-1995. Lang.: Eng. 4007
Midsummer Night's Dream, A
Basic theatrical documents
Catalan translation of Shakespeare's *A Midsummer Night's Dream*. England. 1595. Lang.: Cat. 1422
Design/technology
Costume designer Isabelle Larivière. Canada: Quebec, PQ. 1994-1995. Lang.: Fre. 1514
Reconstruction of a performance of *A Midsummer Night's Dream* designed by Galli-Bibiena. Germany: Bayreuth. 1997-1998. Lang.: Ger. 1521
Design for Shakespeare's *A Midsummer Night's Dream*. USA. 1987. Lang.: Eng. 1563
Performance/production
French Canadian translations/adaptations of Shakespeare. Canada: Montreal, PQ. 1988. Lang.: Fre. 1855
Shakespeare performance on the Rhine and the Ruhr. Germany: Cologne, Bochum, Düsseldorf. 1996-1997. Lang.: Ger. 1962
Reviews of German Shakespearean productions. Germany: Wuppertal, Cologne, Oberhausen. 1998. Lang.: Ger. 2017
Interview with director Thomas Langhoff. Germany, East. 1970-1990. Lang.: Eng. 2038
Shakespearean production and the GDR's 'existential crisis'. Germany, East. 1976-1980. Lang.: Eng. 2051
Events of the Zsámbék theatre festival. Hungary: Zsámbék. 1998. Lang.: Hun. 2126
The evolution of the contemporary Shakespearean director. North America. Europe. 1967-1998. Lang.: Eng. 2207
Kent Hägglund on his favorite role, Bottom in Shakespeare's *Midsummer Night's Dream*. Sweden. 1978-1998. Lang.: Swe. 2375
Collection of newspaper reviews by London theatre critics. UK-England: London. 1998. Lang.: Eng. 2498
Modernist and postmodernist Shakespearean production. UK-England. Canada. 1966-1996. Lang.: Eng. 2618

***Midsummer Night's Dream, A* — cont'd**

Brief productions of Shakespeare, Shaw, and Marlowe at the World's Fair. USA: Chicago, IL. 1934. Lang.: Eng. 2701

Operas by Benjamin Britten in the repertory of the Metropolitan and the New York City Opera. USA: New York, NY. 1945-1998. Lang.:Eng. 4749

Plays/librettos/scripts

Women's use of wit in response to men in English popular culture. England. 1590-1630. Lang.: Eng. 2884

East and West in Shakepeare's *A Midsummer Night's Dream.* England. 1594-1595. Lang.: Eng. 2905

Shakespeare's *A Midsummer Night's Dream*, politics, and criticism. England. 1594-1595. Lang.: Eng. 2981

Miel est plus doux que le sang, Le (Honey Is Milder Than Blood)

Plays/librettos/scripts

Philippe Soldevila on his *Le miel est plus doux que sang (Honey Is Milder than Blood).* Canada: Quebec, PQ. 1995. Lang.: Fre. 2796

Mielitz, Christine

Performance/production

Opera director Christine Mielitz. Germany: Meiningen. 1991-1998. Lang.: Ger. 4597

Interview with opera director Christine Mielitz. Germany: Berlin. 1979-1997. Lang.: Eng. 4605

Mighton, John

Performance/production

Comparison of simple productions and visual shows. Canada: Montreal, PQ, Quebec, PQ, Toronto, ON. 1998. Lang.: Fre. 1861

Mihalovici, Marcel

Plays/librettos/scripts

Marcel Mihalovici's operatic adaptation of *Krapp's Last Tape* by Samuel Beckett. Europe. 1965. Lang.: Eng. 4769

Mikeln, Miloš

Basic theatrical documents

Text of *Miklavžev večer (St. Nicholas' Eve)* by Miloš Mikeln. Slovenia. 1997. Lang.: Slo. 1457

Miklavžev večer (St. Nicholas' Eve)

Basic theatrical documents

Text of *Miklavžev večer (St. Nicholas' Eve)* by Miloš Mikeln. Slovenia. 1997. Lang.: Slo. 1457

Mikuli, János

Performance/production

Lajos Parti Nagy's *Ibusár* directed by János Mikuli. Hungary: Kecskemét, Pécs. 1998. Lang.: Hun. 2110

Milenković, Radoslav

Performance/production

Productions of plays by Koljada and Jerofejév at Csiky Gergely Theatre. Hungary: Kaposvár. 1998. Lang.: Hun. 2149

Miles, Julia

Institutions

Brief history of the Women's Project and Productions. USA: New York, NY. 1978-1998. Lang.: Eng. 1774

History of the Women's Project of the American Place Theatre. USA: New York, NY. 1978-1979. Lang.: Eng. 1791

Milhaud, Darius

Performance/production

Collaborative Symbolist dance/theatre projects. Europe. USA. 1916-1934. Lang.: Eng. 1268

Plays/librettos/scripts

Operatic realizations of Beaumarchais' character Rosina. Europe. North America. 1784-1991. Lang.: Eng. 4773

Milich, Eva

Performance/production

Interview with Flamenco dancer Eva Milich. Sweden: Gothenburg. Spain. 1990-1998. Lang.: Swe. 1236

Military theatre

Institutions

Polish soldiers' theatre. USSR: Buzuluk. UK-England: London. 1941-1948. Lang.: Pol. 432

Performance/production

Polish soldiers' theatre as seen in the magazine *Parada.* Italy: Rome. Egypt: Cairo. 1942-1947. Lang.: Pol. 550

Polish soldiers' theatrical activities in the Comisani internment camp. Romania: Comisani. 1939-1940. Lang.: Pol. 578

Polish soldiers' theatre in London. UK-England: London. 1939-1998. Lang.: Pol. 610

Theatre for Polish soldiers. UK-England. France. Romania. 1939-1946. Lang.: Pol. 611

Mill on the Floss, The

Plays/librettos/scripts

Shared Experience's stage adaptations of nineteenth-century novels. USA: New York, NY. UK-England: London. 1998. Lang.: Eng. 3518

Millar, Mervyn

Performance/production

Collection of newspaper reviews by London theatre critics. UK-England: London. 1998. Lang.: Eng. 2414

Collection of newspaper reviews by London theatre critics. UK-England: London. 1998. Lang.: Eng. 2506

Millay, Edna St. Vincent

Performance/production

The first wave of American feminist theatre. USA. 1890-1930. Lang.: Eng. 648

Millepied, Benjamin

Performance/production

New male dancers of New York City Ballet. USA: New York, NY. 1998. Lang.: Eng. 1177

Miller, Amanda

Institutions

Amanda Miller and her ballet company Pretty Ugly. Germany: Freiburg. 1984-1998. Lang.: Ger. 1039

Miller, Arthur

Design/technology

Set design for Joseph Chaikin's production of two one-acts by Arthur Miller. USA: New york, NY. 1998. Lang.: Eng. 1532

Set designs of Francis O'Connor. USA: New York, NY. 1998. Lang.: Eng. 1541

Performance/production

The idea of Hollywood in theatre autobiographies. USA. 1950-1990. Lang.: Eng. 665

Review of Arthur Miller's *The Crucible* directed by Péter Rudolf. Hungary: Budapest. 1998. Lang.: Hun. 2068

Two Hungarian productions of Arthur Miller's *Death of a Salesman.* Hungary: Pécs, Szeged. 1998. Lang.: Hun. 2123

Seven critics on their favorite character or portrayal. Sweden. 1950. Lang.: Swe. 2369

Plays/librettos/scripts

Eugene O'Neill and the creation of autobiographical drama. USA. 1940-1995. Lang.: Eng. 3561

Autobiography of playwright Arthur Miller. USA. 1915-1998. Lang.: Rus. 3649

The return of the prodigal in American drama. USA. 1920-1985. Lang.: Eng. 3666

Miller, Isabel

Performance/production

Paula Klimper and Wende Persons' opera *Patience and Sarah.* USA. 1969-1998. Lang.: Eng. 4725

Miller, Jonathan

Performance/production

Analysis of Shakespeare's *King Lear* on television. UK-England. 1982-1983. Lang.: Eng. 4064

Jonathan Miller's production of *The Rake's Progress* at the Metropolitan Opera. USA: New York, NY. 1998. Lang.: Eng. 4733

Profile of lighting designer Jennifer Tipton. USA. 1937-1998. Lang.: Eng. 4747

Miller, Paul

Performance/production

Collection of newspaper reviews by London theatre critics. UK-England: London. 1998. Lang.: Eng. 2468

Miller, Robin

Design/technology

Costume design for *Dames at Sea*, Marine Memorial Theatre. USA: San Francisco, CA. 1998. Lang.: Eng. 4332

Miller, Susan

Basic theatrical documents

French translation of *My Left Breast* by Susan Miller. USA. France. 1994-1998. Lang.: Fre. 1498

Miller, Tim

Plays/librettos/scripts

Analysis of performance art on *The Larry Sanders Show.* USA. 1995. Lang.: Eng. 4079

Millette, Jean-Louis

Performance/production

Interview with film and television actor Jean-Louis Millette. Canada: Montreal, PQ. 1965-1998. Lang.: Fre. 3856

Milliet, Paul

Plays/librettos/scripts

Massenet's opera *Hérodiade* and its literary sources. France. 1881. Lang.: Fre. 4779

Millionairess, The

Plays/librettos/scripts

Analysis of the later plays of George Bernard Shaw. UK-England. 1923-1947. Lang.: Eng. 3444

Mills, Mary
Performance/production
Anecdotes about soprano Mary Mills. USA. 1998. Lang.: Eng. 4735
Miln Company (Chicago, IL)
Performance/production
George Crichton Miln's touring Shakespearean company in Japan. USA: Chicago, IL. Japan: Yokohama. 1882. Lang.: Eng. 2702
Miln, George Crichton
Performance/production
George Crichton Miln's touring Shakespearean company in Japan. USA: Chicago, IL. Japan: Yokohama. 1882. Lang.: Eng. 2702
Milner, Jack
Performance/production
Collection of newspaper reviews by London theatre critics. UK-England: London. 1998. Lang.: Eng. 2418
Milton, John
Plays/librettos/scripts
Puritanism and Milton's *Comus*. England. 1634-1635. Lang.: Eng. 4207
Mime
SEE ALSO
Classed Entries under MIME.
Pantomime.
Institutions
Report on a seminar on mime, illusionism, *commedia* and clowning in dance. Sweden: Stockholm. 1998. Lang.: Swe. 386
Performance/production
'The Speaking Body' museum installation, site of theatre anthropology seminars. Austria: Vienna. Switzerland: Zurich. 1996-1998. Lang.: Eng. 493
Interview with Bengt Andersson, artistic director of Teater Tre. Sweden. 1983-1998. Lang.: Swe. 601
Director Jacques Copeau and his theatrical aesthetic. France. 1913-1920. Lang.: Eng. 1941
Lotte Goslar's Pantomime Circus. Germany: Dresden. USA: Los Angeles, CA. 1907-1997. Lang.: Eng. 4123
Comic dance performer Lotte Goslar. Germany. USA. 1907-1997. Lang.: Eng. 4124
Mimmack, Peter
Performance/production
Collection of newspaper reviews by London theatre critics. UK-England: London. 1998. Lang.: Eng. 2442
Mincaev, M.
Performance/production
Bolšoj Opera singer M. Mincaev. Russia: Moscow. 1998. Lang.: Rus. 4684
Minerva Theatre (Chichester)
Performance/production
Collection of newspaper reviews by London theatre critics. UK-England. 1998. Lang.: Eng. 2489
Collection of newspaper reviews by London theatre critics. UK-England. 1998. Lang.: Eng. 2510
Minetta Lane Theatre (New York, NY)
Performance/production
Analysis of recent New York productions. USA: New York, NY. 1997-1998. Lang.: Eng. 2759
Minetti, Bernhard
Performance/production
The career of actor Bernhard Minetti. Germany. 1905-1998. Lang.: Ger. 1949
Tribute to the late actor Bernhard Minetti. Germany. 1905-1998. Lang.: Ger. 1992
Actor Bernhard Minetti. Germany. 1905-1998. Lang.: Ger. 2015
Miniature Theatre (Moscow)
SEE
Teat'r Minjatjur.
Minks, Wilfried
Institutions
Productions of Staatstheater Stuttgart. Germany: Stuttgart. 1998. Lang.: Ger. 1620
Minna von Barnhelm
Institutions
The ninetieth anniversary of Staatstheater Cottbus. Germany: Cottbus. 1908-1998. Lang.: Ger. 1645
Minnelli, Vincente
Performance/production
Choreography in the musical film *The Bandwagon*. USA. 1953. Lang.: Eng. 982
Minshall, Peter
Plays/librettos/scripts
Interview with Peter Minshall, creator of theatre pieces and carnival performances. Trinidad and Tobago: Port of Spain. 1974-1997. Lang.: Eng. 4172
Minskoff Theatre (New York, NY)
Design/technology
Technical designs for *The Scarlet Pimpernel* directed by Robert Longbottom. USA: New York, NY. 1998. Lang.: Eng. 4331
Minstrelsy
Performance/production
Norwich's unregulated entertainers. England: Norwich. 1530-1624. Lang.: Eng. 1907
Social concerns reflected in popular entertainment publications. USA. 1870-1910. Lang.: Eng. 4144
Minute of Silence, A
Performance/production
Collection of newspaper reviews by London theatre critics. UK-England: London. 1998. Lang.: Eng. 2516
Mio, Min Mio (Mio, My Mio)
Performance/production
Theatrical adaptations of children's stories by Astrid Lindgren. Sweden: Stockholm. 1998. Lang.: Eng. 2374
Hans Klinga's production of *Mio, Min Mio (Mio, My Mio)* at Dramaten. Sweden: Stockholm. 1997. Lang.: Swe. 2386
Relation to other fields
Theatre and the psychological development of children. Sweden. 1988. Lang.: Swe. 3777
Miquel, Jean-Pierre
Administration
Interview with Jean-Pierre Miquel, managing director of the Comédie-Française. France. 1998. Lang.: Hun. 1378
Institutions
Interview with Jean-Pierre Miquel, director of the Comédie-Française. France: Paris. 1993-1998. Lang.: Eng. 1613
Mira de Amescua, Antonio
Plays/librettos/scripts
Playwright Antonio Mira de Amescua. Spain. 1574-1644. Lang.: Eng. 3371
Miracle plays
Plays/librettos/scripts
Analysis of *De Eerste Bliscap van Maria (The First Joy of Mary)*. Belgium: Brussels. 1440-1560. Lang.: Eng. 2790
Miraculous Mandarin, The
SEE
Csodálatos mandarin, A.
Mirbt, Felix
Performance/production
Puppeteer Felix Mirbt. Canada. Germany: Berlin. 1945-1998. Lang.: Eng. 4887
Mirette
Design/technology
Neil Patel's scene design for *Mirette*, Goodspeed Opera House. USA: East Haddam, CT. 1998. Lang.: Eng. 4334
Mironov, Andrej A.
Performance/production
Actor Andrej Mironov. Russia: Moscow. 1998. Lang.: Rus. 2308
Mirrorman, The
Performance/production
Preparing a production of Brian Way's participatory *The Mirrorman*. USA. 1987. Lang.: Eng. 633
Mirsky, Mikhl
Plays/librettos/scripts
Ida Kamińska's production of *Der Kheshbn (The Final Reckoning)* by Mikhl Mirsky. Poland: Warsaw. 1963. Lang.: Eng. 3310
Mirvish, Edward
Administration
Interview with producer Ed Mirvish. UK-England: London. Canada: Toronto, ON. 1982-1998. Lang.: Eng. 1393
Misalliance
Plays/librettos/scripts
Shaw's 'theatre of ideas' and its influence. UK-England. 1890-1910. Lang.: Eng. 3457
Misanthrope, Le (Misanthrope, The)
Performance/production
Molière's *Misanthrope* directed by Andor Lukáts. Hungary: Budapest. 1998. Lang.: Hun. 2091
Collection of newspaper reviews by London theatre critics. UK-England: London. 1998. Lang.: Eng. 2450

Mise au Jeu Montréal (Montreal, PQ)
Relation to other fields
Performance ethnography of social action theatre Mise au Jeu Montréal. Canada: Montreal, PQ. 1995-1998. Lang.: Eng. 3735

Miser, The
SEE
Avare, L'.

Miskolci Nemzeti Színház (Miskolc)
Institutions
Miskolci National Theatre's new opera company. Hungary: Miskolc. 1998. Lang.: Hun. 4460
Performance spaces
Renovation of the Miskolc National Theatre. Hungary: Miskolc. 1823-1998. Lang.: Hun. 450
Performance/production
Gogol's *Revizor (The Inspector General)* directed by Árpád Jutocsa Hegyi. Hungary: Miskolc. 1998. Lang.: Hun. 2108
Interview with Péter Blaskó. Hungary. 1970-1998. Lang.: Hun. 2119

Miskolci Nemzeti Színház, Csarnok (Miskolc)
Performance/production
Brecht's *Die Heilige Johanna der Schlachthöfe (Saint Joan of the Stockyards)* directed by Sándor Zsóter. Hungary: Miskolc. 1998. Lang.: Hun. 2084

Miss Evers' Boys
Performance/production
Collection of newspaper reviews by London theatre critics. UK-England: London. 1998. Lang.: Eng. 2506

Miss Julie
SEE
Fröken Julie.

Miss Margarida's Way
SEE
Apareceu a Margarida.

Miss Roach's War
Performance/production
Collection of newspaper reviews by London theatre critics. UK-England: London. 1998. Lang.: Eng. 2577

Mission, The
SEE
Auftrag, Der.

Mistero Buffo
Basic theatrical documents
Slovene translation of *Mistero Buffo* by Dario Fo. Italy. Slovenia. 1969-1997. Lang.: Slo. 1441
Plays/librettos/scripts
Michel Tremblay's adaptation of *Mistero Buffo* by Dario Fo. Canada: Montreal, PQ. 1969-1973. Lang.: Fre. 2795

Mistress of the Inn
SEE
Locandiera, La.

Mistry, Cyrus
Plays/librettos/scripts
Diaspora and home in postcolonial Indian drama. India. 1978-1985. Lang.: Eng. 3193

Mitchell, Adrian
Performance/production
Collection of newspaper reviews by London theatre critics. UK-England: Stratford. 1998. Lang.: Eng. 2519
Collection of newspaper reviews by London theatre critics. UK-England: London. 1998. Lang.: Eng. 2567

Mitchell, Brian
Performance/production
Collection of newspaper reviews by London theatre critics. UK-England: London. 1998. Lang.: Eng. 2454
Collection of newspaper reviews by London theatre critics. UK-England. 1998. Lang.: Eng. 2497

Mitchell, Gary
Performance/production
Collection of newspaper reviews by London theatre critics. UK-England: London. 1998. Lang.: Eng. 2443

Mitchell, Jerry
Administration
Report on 'Broadway Bares' benefit for AIDS. USA: New York, NY. 1998. Lang.: Eng. 76

Mitchell, John Cameron
Performance/production
Musical performances on and off Broadway. USA: New York. 1998. Lang.: Ger. 4383

Mitchell, Katie
Performance/production
Collection of newspaper reviews by London theatre critics. UK-England: London. 1998. Lang.: Eng. 2453
Collection of newspaper reviews by London theatre critics. UK-England: London. 1998. Lang.: Eng. 2573
Interview with Katie Mitchell on directing plays of Beckett. UK-England. 1998. Lang.: Eng. 2594
Katie Mitchell's production of mystery plays at RSC. UK-England: London. 1996-1998. Lang.: Eng. 2626

Mitra, Śombhu
Performance/production
Obituary for actor and director Śombhu Mitra. India. 1914-1997. Lang.: Eng. 2151

Mitterer, Felix
Performance/production
Premieres of plays on the Nazi theme. Germany: Darmstadt. Austria: Vienna. 1998. Lang.: Ger. 2030

Mix, John
Institutions
Popular entertainment at the New Haven Assembly Hall and Columbian Museum and Gardens. USA: New Haven, CT. 1796-1820. Lang.: Eng. 394

Mixed entertainment
SEE ALSO
Classed Entries under MIXED ENTERTAINMENT.
Performance/production
The success of dance extravaganzas and solo performance at the expense of traditional shows. USA: New York, NY. 1994-1998. Lang. :Eng. 645
Adrian Pecknold and the Canadian Mime Theatre. Canada: Niagara-on-the-Lake, ON. 1940-1978. Lang.: Eng. 4085

Mixed media
SEE ALSO
Classed Entries under MEDIA.
Institutions
Judith Malina's attempt to create an active mixed-media theatre. USA. 1968-1969. Lang.: Eng. 1765
Performance/production
Lois Weaver's *Faith and Dancing* and the CD-ROM in interactive performance. UK-England. USA. 1996. Lang.: Eng. 971
The use of television in theatrical space. Netherlands. USA. 1970-1998. Lang.: Dut. 2206
Interview with actress Fiona Shaw. UK-England. 1995-1997. Lang.: Eng. 2607

Mizjukov, Mikle
Performance/production
Mikle Mizjukov's production of *Pesn' sud'by (The Song of Fate)* by Blok. Russia: Moscow. 1998. Lang.: Rus. 2276

Mizlansky/Zilinsky
Design/technology
Set designs by Santo Loquasto at Manhattan Theatre Club. USA: New York, NY. 1998. Lang.: Eng. 1536

Mjazinoj, E.
Performance/production
Actor E. Mjazinoj. Russia. 1998. Lang.: Rus. 2277

Mnouchkine, Ariane
Institutions
Theatrical space in productions of Ariane Mnouchkine. France: Paris. 1970-1995. Lang.: Eng. 1607
Ariane Mnouchkine and rehearsal techniques of Théâtre du Soleil. France: Paris. 1964-1997. Lang.: Eng. 1610
Performance/production
French political theatre: Boal and Mnouchkine. France. 1990-1996. Lang.: Eng. 529
The rise of the modern Shakespearean director. Europe. 1878-1995. Lang.: Eng. 1911
Reviews of productions by Wilson, Greenaway, and Mnouchkine. France: Paris. 1997-1998. Lang.: Eng. 1926
Survey of Parisian productions. France: Paris. 1997-1998. Lang.: Eng. 1937
Productions of international Čechov festival. Russia: Moscow. 1998. Lang.: Swe. 2306

Mobie-Diq (Moby Dick)
Plays/librettos/scripts
Analysis of plays by Marguerite Duras and Marie Redonnet. France. 1977-1992. Lang.: Eng. 3071

Mocedades del Cid, Las (Youthful Deeds of El Cid, The)
Plays/librettos/scripts
Life and career of playwright Guillén de Castro. Spain. 1569-1631. Lang.: Eng. 3384
Modern dance
SEE ALSO
Classed Entries under DANCE.
Institutions
Profile of Pina Bausch and her Tanztheater. Germany: Wuppertal. 1977-1998. Lang.: Eng. 893
Performance/production
Performativity in postmodern 'queer' works. USA. 1985-1995. Lang.: Eng. 616
Time aspects of video dance. Europe. 1970-1998. Lang.: Ger. 4059
Training
Illustrated history of jazz dance. USA. Slovenia. 1900-1997. Lang.: Slo. 1023
Experiences of a dancer at Jacob's Pillow. USA: Becket, MA. 1950. Lang.: Eng. 1025
Interview with dance teacher Aarne Mäntylä. Finland. 1998. Lang.: Fin. 1203
Modern Jazz Dans Ensemble (Stockholm)
Performance/production
Interview with dancer Jennie Widegren. Sweden: Stockholm. 1995-1998. Lang.: Swe. 1306
Möderndorfer, Vinko
Basic theatrical documents
Texts of plays by Vinko Möderndorfer. Slovenia. 1997. Lang.: Slo. 1458
Modrzejewska, Helena
SEE
Modjeska, Helena.
Moffat, Peter
Performance/production
Collection of newspaper reviews by London theatre critics. UK-England: London. 1998. Lang.: Eng. 2410
Mohácsi, István
Performance/production
Brecht's *Der Kaukasische Kreidkreis (The Caucasian Chalk Circle)* adapted and directed by János Mohácsi. Hungary: Nyíregyháza. 1998. Lang.: Hun. 2127
Mohácsi, János
Performance/production
Interview with director János Mohácsi. Hungary. 1998. Lang.: Hun. 2060
Review of Bulgakov's *Ivan Vasiljėvič* directed by János Mohácsi. Hungary: Kaposvár. 1998. Lang.: Hun. 2095
Brecht's *Der Kaukasische Kreidkreis (The Caucasian Chalk Circle)* adapted and directed by János Mohácsi. Hungary: Nyíregyháza. 1998. Lang.: Hun. 2127
Moisejėv, Igor Aleksandrovič
Performance/production
Choreographer Igor Moisejėv. Russia: Moscow. 1998. Lang.: Rus. 1231
Memoirs of choreographer Igor Moisejėv. Russia: Moscow. 1926-1998. 1920-1940. Lang.: Rus. 1233
Moissiu, Alexandër
Plays/librettos/scripts
Letters of Pirandello, Moissiu, and Jahn. Italy. Austria: Vienna. 1934. Lang.: Ita. 3219
Mojo
Plays/librettos/scripts
Sex, drugs, and violence in contemporary British drama. UK-England. 1991-1998. Lang.: Eng. 3494
Mokejėv, Michajl
Performance/production
Michajl Mokejėv's production of Shakespeare's *Romeo and Juliet*. Russia: Belgorod. 1998. Lang.: Rus. 2274
Mokka
Performance/production
Critical reactions to the dance evening *Mokka*. Hungary: Budapest. 1998. Lang.: Hun. 1116
Mokuami, Kawatake
Basic theatrical documents
English translation of *Takatoki* by Mokuami Kawatake. Japan. 1884-1998. Lang.: Eng. 1361
Molière
Institutions
Theatrical space in productions of Ariane Mnouchkine. France: Paris. 1970-1995. Lang.: Eng. 1607
Molière (Poquelin, Jean-Baptiste)
Basic theatrical documents
Catalan translation of *Les Femmes savantes (The Learned Ladies)* by Molière. France. 1672. Lang.: Cat. 1433
Institutions
Ariane Mnouchkine and rehearsal techniques of Théâtre du Soleil. France: Paris. 1964-1997. Lang.: Eng. 1610
Performance/production
The 'grande coquette' on the Parisian stage. France: Paris. 1885-1925. Lang.: Eng. 531
Social context of French and Canadian productions of *Les Fourberies de Scapin* by Molière. Canada: Montreal, PQ. France: Paris. 1998. Lang.: Fre. 1842
Student production of *Les Femmes savantes (The Learned Ladies)* by Molière. Canada: Calgary, AB. 1997. Lang.: Eng. 1859
Movement training for actors in plays of Molière. France. 1622-1673. Lang.: Eng. 1938
Director Jacques Copeau and his theatrical aesthetic. France. 1913-1920. Lang.: Eng. 1941
Molière's *Dom Juan* directed by Olga Barabás. Hungary. Romania: Sfântu-Gheorghe. 1998. Lang.: Hun. 2063
Molière's *Misanthrope* directed by Andor Lukáts. Hungary: Budapest. 1998. Lang.: Hun. 2091
Events of the Zsámbék theatre festival. Hungary: Zsámbék. 1998. Lang.: Hun. 2126
Three Hungarian productions of plays by Molière. Hungary: Szentendre, Kapolcs, Kőszeg. 1998. Lang.: Hun. 2142
Productions by Toni Bertorelli and Alfiero Alfieri. Italy: Rome. 1997. Lang.: Eng. 2175
Collection of newspaper reviews by London theatre critics. UK-England: London. 1998. Lang.: Eng. 2411
Collection of newspaper reviews by London theatre critics. UK-England: London. 1998. Lang.: Eng. 2450
Collection of newspaper reviews by London theatre critics. UK-England: London. 1998. Lang.: Eng. 2576
French cultural and intellectual history, including the work of Molière. USA. 1650-1950. Lang.: Eng. 2663
Plays/librettos/scripts
Analysis of medical plays by Molière. France. 1660-1722. Lang.: Eng. 3078
North American translations and adaptations of Molière. North America. 1998. Lang.: Eng. 3289
Food in the plays of Molière. USA. 1990-1998. Lang.: Ita. 3695
Molin, Eva
Institutions
Interview with Ronnie Hallgren of Älvsborgsteatern about theatre for youth. Sweden: Borås. 1994-1998. Lang.: Swe. 1726
Molina, Tirso de
Plays/librettos/scripts
Playwright Tirso de Molina. Spain. 1583-1648. Lang.: Eng. 3370
Playwright Andrés de Claramonte. Spain. 1580-1626. Lang.: Eng. 3404
Molinari, Nadia
Performance/production
Collection of newspaper reviews by London theatre critics. UK-England: London. 1998. Lang.: Eng. 2411
Molloy
Performance/production
Collection of newspaper reviews by London theatre critics. UK-England: London. 1998. Lang.: Eng. 2547
Molloy, Christine
Performance/production
Collection of newspaper reviews by London theatre critics. UK-England: London. 1998. Lang.: Eng. 2565
Molnár, Ferenc
Performance/production
Review of Molnár's *Az üvegcipő (The Glass Slipper)*, Új Színház. Hungary: Budapest. 1997. Lang.: Hun. 2094
Molnár, István
Performance/production
Folk dance program in honor of choreographer István Molnár. Hungary: Budapest. 1930-1998. Lang.: Hun. 1229
Molnár, Lajos
Performance/production
Modern tendencies in Hungarian folk dance. Hungary. 1970-1977. Lang.: Hun. 1228

Momolo
Plays/librettos/scripts
Analysis of comedies by Goldoni. Italy: Venice. 1707-1793. Lang.: Ita. 3258

Moncrieff, William Thomas
Performance/production
Lucy Vestris in *Giovanni in London.* England: London. 1842. Lang.: Eng. 4546

Monette, Richard
Performance/production
Interview with actor William Hutt. Canada: Stratford, ON. 1962-1996. Lang.: Eng. 1844

Moniglia, Giovanni Andrea
Performance/production
The evolution of comic opera. Italy: Florence, Rome. 1665-1700. Lang.: Eng. 4660

Monings, Edward
Performance/production
English actors in Kassel. Germany: Kassel. 1592-1620. Lang.: Eng. 2016

Monk, Meredith
Performance/production
Choreographer Meredith Monk. USA: New York, NY. 1964-1998. Lang.: Eng. 1325

Monodrama
Basic theatrical documents
Text of Evgen Car's monologue *Poredušov Janoš.* Slovenia. 1968-1998. Lang.: Slo. 1454

Monologteatern (Helsinki)
Institutions
The proliferation of Swedish-language theatre groups in Helsinki. Finland: Helsinki. 1990-1998. Lang.: Eng, Fre. 1604

Monsieur de Pourceaugnac
Plays/librettos/scripts
Analysis of medical plays by Molière. France. 1660-1722. Lang.: Eng. 3078

Monsieur l'inventeur (Mister Inventor)
Performance/production
Productions of children's theatre festival. Canada: Montreal, PQ. 1998. Lang.: Fre. 503

Monsieur Lovestar et son voisin de palier (Monsieur Lovestar and the Man Next Door)
Performance/production
Collection of newspaper reviews by London theatre critics. UK-England: London. 1998. Lang.: Eng. 2524

Monster
Plays/librettos/scripts
Analysis of Daniel MacIvor's *Monster* as directed by Daniel Brooks. Canada: Toronto, ON. 1998. Lang.: Eng. 2834

Monsterdämmerung (Monster Twilight)
Plays/librettos/scripts
Analysis of plays by Marius von Mayenburg. Germany. 1972-1998. Lang.: Ger. 3131

Monsters of Grace
Performance/production
Collection of newspaper reviews by London theatre critics. UK-England: London. 1998. Lang.: Eng. 2409

Montaigu, René Magnon de
Performance/production
The influence of *commedia dell'arte* on eighteenth-century Danish theatre. Denmark: Copenhagen. 1700-1750. Lang.: Eng. 4186

Montalbán, Juan Pérez de
Plays/librettos/scripts
Playwright Juan Pérez de Montalbán. Spain. 1601-1638. Lang.: Eng. 3379

Monte, Bonnie
Institutions
Bonnie Monte of New Jersey Shakespeare Festival. USA: Madison, NJ. 1996-1998. Lang.: Eng. 1772

Montemezzi, Italo
Performance/production
Montemezzi's *L'amore dei tre re,* directed and designed by Philippe Arlaud. Austria: Bregenz. 1998. Lang.: Eng. 4532

Monterey, Carlotta
SEE
O'Neill, Carlotta Monterey.

Monteverdi, Claudio
Design/technology
Set and costume design for San Francisco Opera productions. USA: San Francisco, CA. 1998. Lang.: Eng. 4443

Montresor, Beni
Performance/production
Antonio Salieri and his opera *Falstaff,* recently revived. Italy: Milan. 1799-1998. Lang.: Eng. 4654

Monty Python (England)
Plays/librettos/scripts
Analysis of *Monty Python and the Holy Grail.* UK-England. 1974. Lang.: Eng. 3987

Monty Python and the Holy Grail
Plays/librettos/scripts
Analysis of *Monty Python and the Holy Grail.* UK-England. 1974. Lang.: Eng. 3987

Monument National (Montreal, PQ)
Plays/librettos/scripts
On the text and staging of *La Cathédrale...* by Jean Depréz (Laurette Laroque). Canada: Montreal, PQ. 1949. Lang.: Fre. 2823

Moody, James
Design/technology
Creativity and beauty in theatrical design. USA. 1998. Lang.: Eng. 322

Moon for the Misbegotten, A
Institutions
Impressions from the 'Golden Mask' festival. Russia: Minusinsk. 1998. Lang.: Ger. 1701
Performance/production
Recent productions in Ireland of plays by Eugene O'Neill. Ireland: Dublin. UK-Ireland: Belfast. 1989-1998. Lang.: Eng. 2154
Plays/librettos/scripts
Irish folklore in plays of Eugene O'Neill. USA. 1942-1956. Lang.: Eng. 3522

The late plays of Eugene O'Neill. USA. 1939-1943. Lang.: Eng. 3528

A method of analysis for the drama. USA. 1920-1975. Lang.: Eng. 3537

Female presence/absence in plays of O'Neill, Pinter, and Shepard. USA. UK-England. 1936-1985. Lang.: Eng. 3607

African- and Irish-Americans in the plays of Eugene O'Neill. USA. 1916-1953. Lang.: Eng. 3687

Closure in plays of Eugene O'Neill. USA. 1918-1950. Lang.: Eng. 3703

Moon, Julia H.
Institutions
Profile of Universal Ballet Company. South Korea: Seoul. 1998. Lang.: Eng. 1047

Moon, The
Plays/librettos/scripts
Review of collections of plays with gay themes. Canada. 1996. Lang.: Eng. 2802

Moonlight
Plays/librettos/scripts
Analysis of *Moonlight* by Harold Pinter. UK-England. 1994. Lang.: Dut. 3433

Moonstompers
Performance/production
Collection of newspaper reviews by London theatre critics. UK-England: London. 1998. Lang.: Eng. 2475

Moore, Grace
Performance/production
Soprano Grace Moore. USA. 1901-1947. Lang.: Eng. 4715

Moore, Honor
Performance/production
Theatre Magazine's anniversary issue. USA. 1968-1998. Lang.: Eng. 617

Moore, Iris
Plays/librettos/scripts
Account of performances by Joan Dickinson. USA. 1997-1998. Lang.: Eng. 4263

Morahan, Christopher
Performance/production
Collection of newspaper reviews by London theatre critics. UK-England: London. 1998. Lang.: Eng. 2532

Morality plays
Plays/librettos/scripts
Comparison of the Dutch *Elckerlijck* and the English *Everyman.* England. Netherlands. 1495-1525. Lang.: Eng. 2982

Analysis of post-medieval morality plays. Europe. Africa. 1400-1998. Lang.: Eng. 3051

Moralność pani Dulskiej (Morality of Mrs. Dulska, The)
Plays/librettos/scripts
Feminist analysis of plays by Gabriela Zapolska. Poland. 1885-1998. Lang.: Pol. 3301

Moran, Bernadette
Performance/production
Collection of newspaper reviews by London theatre critics. UK-England: London. 1998. Lang.: Eng. 2427

Moran, Dylan
Performance/production
Collection of newspaper reviews by London theatre critics. UK-England: London. 1998. Lang.: Eng. 2475
Moravec, Dušan
Institutions
The first decade of Ljubljana's municipal theatre, Mestno gledališče ljubljansko. Slovenia: Ljubljana. 1951-1961. Lang.: Slo. 1718
Morávek, Vladimír
Performance/production
Interview with director Vladimír Morávek. Czech Republic: Hradec. 1985-1998. Lang.: Cze. 1880
Morcsányi, Géza
Administration
Round-table on author's rights. Hungary. 1990-1998. Lang.: Hun. 16
Mörder, Hoffnung der Frauen (Murderer, Hope of Women)
Plays/librettos/scripts
Social criticism in Viennese Expressionist drama. Austria: Vienna. 1907-1922. Lang.: Ger. 2779
Mordžanišvili Theatre (Tbilisi)
SEE
Gruzinskij Akademičėskij Teat'r im. Kote Mordžanišvili.
More Stately Mansions
Performance/production
Collection of newspaper reviews by London theatre critics. UK-Scotland: Edinburgh. 1998. Lang.: Eng. 2650
Plays/librettos/scripts
The posthumous publication of Eugene O'Neill's unfinished *More Stately Mansions.* USA. 1957-1964. Lang.: Eng. 3596
More, Thomas
Relation to other fields
Theatre and drama in the life of Sir Thomas More. England. 1550-1590. Lang.: Eng. 3747
Moreau, Jean-Luc
Basic theatrical documents
Text of *Ma femme s'appelle Maurice (My Wife's Name Is Maurice)* by Raffy Shart. France. 1998. Lang.: Fre. 1435
Morelli, Rina
Performance/production
The Italian premiere of *A Streetcar Named Desire* by Tennessee Williams. Italy: Rome. 1949. Lang.: Eng. 2172
Morgan, Abi
Performance/production
Collection of newspaper reviews by London theatre critics. UK-England: London. 1998. Lang.: Eng. 2434
Morgan, Lady (Owenson, Sydney)
Plays/librettos/scripts
Analysis of letters between Lady Morgan and actor Richard Jones. UK-Ireland. 1807. Lang.: Eng. 4862
Morgon, Abi
Performance/production
Report on several English performances. UK-England: London, Stratford. 1998. Lang.: Swe. 2634
Móricz Zsigmond Színház (Nyíregyháza)
Institutions
Theatre critics' awards 97-98. Hungary. 1997-1998. Lang.: Hun. 355
Performance/production
István Verebes' production of Shakespeare's *Hamlet.* Hungary: Nyíregyháza. 1997. Lang.: Hun. 2116
Two productions of Ernő Szép's *Vőlegény (The Fiancé).* Hungary: Nyíregyháza. Hungary: Győr. 1998.Lang.: Hun. 2118
Čechov's *Diadia Vania (Uncle Vanya)* directed by János Szász. Hungary: Nyíregyháza. 1998. Lang.: Hun. 2124
Brecht's *Der Kaukasische Kreidkreis (The Caucasian Chalk Circle)* adapted and directed by János Mohácsi. Hungary: Nyíregyháza. 1998. Lang.: Hun. 2127
Morin, Émile
Institutions
Émile Morin and Pascale Landry on their Productions Recto-Verso. Canada: Quebec, PQ. 1996. Lang.: Fre. 4233
Morir (Moment Before Dying, A)
Plays/librettos/scripts
Hasko Weber's production of *Morir (A Moment Before Dying)* by Sergi Belbel. Germany: Dresden. 1998. Lang.: Ger. 3132
Interview with playwright Sergi Belbel. Spain-Catalonia. 1963-1998. Lang.: Ger. 3407
Morita, Yuzo
Performance/production
Collection of newspaper reviews by London theatre critics. UK-England: London. 1998. Lang.: Eng. 2430
Mörk, Lennart
Design/technology
Interview with set designer Lennart Mörk. Sweden: Stockholm. France: Paris. 1958-1998. Lang.: Swe. 222
Scenographer Lennart Mörk. Sweden: Stockholm. France: Paris. 1957-1998. Lang.: Swe. 4439
Morning Star
Plays/librettos/scripts
Jean Randich's production of *The Golden Door* by Sylvia Regan, Tenement Museum. USA: New York, NY. 1940-1998. Lang.: Eng. 3606
Morris, Abigail
Performance/production
Collection of newspaper reviews by London theatre critics. UK-England: London. 1998. Lang.: Eng. 2550
Morris, Chris
Performance/production
Collection of newspaper reviews by London theatre critics. UK-England: London, Scarborough. 1998. Lang.: Eng. 2426
Morris, Mark
Design/technology
Sound design for the musical *The Capeman.* USA: New York, NY. 1998. Lang.: Eng. 4339
Performance/production
Analysis of the choreography of Mark Morris. USA. 1980-1997. Lang.: Eng. 1317
Dancers Tina Fehlandt and Ruth Davidson of Mark Morris Dance Group. USA: New York, NY. 1980-1998. Lang.: Eng. 1327
Photographic essay of Rameau's *Platée* directed and choreographed by Mark Morris. USA: Berkeley, CA. 1998. Lang.: Eng. 4304
Morris, Tom
Performance/production
Collection of newspaper reviews by London theatre critics. UK-England: London, Scarborough. 1998. Lang.: Eng. 2426
Morrison, Bill
Plays/librettos/scripts
Gender and nationalism in Northern Irish drama. UK-Ireland. 1902-1997. Lang.: Eng. 3511
BBC radio plays with Anglo-Irish themes. UK-England. Ireland. 1973-1986. Lang.: Eng. 3868
Morrison, Conall
Performance/production
Collection of newspaper reviews by London theatre critics. UK-England. 1998. Lang.: Eng. 2489
Collection of newspaper reviews by London theatre critics. UK-England: Leeds, Manchester. 1998. Lang.: Eng. 2559
Morrison, Terry
Performance/production
Collection of newspaper reviews by London theatre critics. UK-England: London. 1998. Lang.: Eng. 2526
Morrison, Toni
Audience
Jonathan Demme's film adaptation of *Beloved* by Toni Morrison. USA. 1998. Lang.: Eng. 3877
Morrow, Jim
Institutions
Puppetry at Mermaid Theatre. Canada: Wolfville, NS. 1972-1998. Lang.: Eng. 4870
Morse, Peter
Design/technology
Peter Morse's lighting design for country music tour. USA. 1998. Lang.: Eng. 4108
Morte accidentale di un anarchico (Accidental Death of an Anarchist)
Performance/production
Collection of newspaper reviews by London theatre critics. UK-England: London. 1998. Lang.: Eng. 2430
Collection of newspaper reviews by London theatre critics. UK-England: London. 1998. Lang.: Eng. 2532
Morticians in Love
Performance/production
Contemporary queer politics and the production of gay and lesbian theatre. USA. 1970-1997. Lang.: Eng. 2710
Mortier, Gérard
Performance/production
Director Ruth Berghaus. Germany. 1970-1996. Lang.: Ger. 4596
Mortimer, Bob
Performance/production
Collection of newspaper reviews by London theatre critics. UK-England: London. 1998. Lang.: Eng. 2573

Morton, Carlos
Basic theatrical documents
Text of plays by Carlos Morton. USA. 1986. Lang.: Eng. 1499
Morton, Charles
Performance/production
Irish and Irish-American characters on the stages of the Midwest. USA. 1875-1915. Lang.: Eng. 2696
Moscato, Enzo
Plays/librettos/scripts
Playwrights Annibale Ruccello, Enzo Moscato, and Manlio Santanelli. Italy: Naples. 1980-1989. Lang.: Eng. 3261
Moschen, Michael
Performance/production
Profile of MacArthur fellow and juggler Michael Moschen. USA. 1955-1998. Lang.: Eng. 4141
Moscow Art Theatre
SEE
Moskovskij Chudožestvénnyj Akademičeskij Teat'r.
Moscow Puppet Theatre
SEE
Gosudarstvénnyj Central'nyj Teat'r Kukol.
Moscow Stations
Plays/librettos/scripts
Stephen Mulrine's translation and stage adaptation of *Moscow Stations* by Venedikt Erofeev. USSR. UK-England. 1973-1998. Lang.: Eng. 3718
Moscow Theatre Institute, GITIS
SEE
Gosudarstvénnyj Institut Teatral'nogo Iskusstva.
Moser, Douglas
Design/technology
Set and costume design for *Patience and Sarah* at Lincoln Center. USA: New York, NY. 1998. Lang.: Eng. 4440
Moses, Daniel David
Plays/librettos/scripts
Review of collections of plays with gay themes. Canada. 1996. Lang.: Eng. 2802
Mosher, Gregory
Performance/production
Actors and directors on the late plays of Tennessee Williams. USA. 1966-1981. Lang.: Eng. 2675
Moshinsky, Elijah
Performance/production
Collection of newspaper reviews by London theatre critics. UK-England: Stratford, Birmingham. 1998. Lang.: Eng. 2536
Moskovskij Chudožestvénnyj Akademičeskij Teat'r (Moscow Art Theatre)
Institutions
The centennary of the Moscow Art Theatre. Russia: Moscow. 1898-1998. Lang.: Rus. 1694
Moscow Art Theatre's production of Čechov's *Tri sestry (Three Sisters)*. Russia: Moscow. 1901-1998. Lang.: Eng. 1713
History of Moscow Art Theatre, on the occasion of its centennial. Russia: Moscow. 1898-1998. Lang.: Rus. 1714
Performance/production
Seinen-za's performance at the Čechov festival. Russia: Moscow. 1998. Lang.: Rus. 2237
Moscow Art Theatre actor Viktor Gvozdickij. Russia: Moscow. 1998. Lang.: Rus. 2259
Memoirs of actor A.P. Ktorov. Russia: Moscow. 1998. Lang.: Rus. 2292
Productions of international Čechov festival. Russia: Moscow. 1998. Lang.: Swe. 2306
Actor Lenid Leonidov. Russia: Moscow. 1873-1941. Lang.: Rus. 2312
Relation to other fields
Postage stamps commemorating Russian theatre and opera. Russia: Moscow. 1998. Lang.: Rus. 762
Moskovskij Chudožestvénnyj Akademičeskij Teat'r im. A.M. Gor'kogo (Moscow)
Institutions
Moscow Art Theatre's tour in Minsk. Belorussia: Minsk. 1998. Lang.: Rus. 1574
Moscow Art Theatre's two theatres and their artistic directors. Russia: Moscow. 1998. Lang.: Rus. 1698
Description of the *Encyclopedia of the Moscow Art Theatre*. Russia: Moscow. 1898-1998. Lang.: Rus. 1703
The one-hundredth anniversary of the Moscow Art Theatre. Russia: Moscow. 1898-1998. Lang.: Rus. 1704
Centennial celebration of the Moscow Art Theatre. Russia: Moscow. 1898-1998. Lang.: Rus. 1710
Performance/production
Interview with Moscow Art Theatre actress G. Kalinovskaja. Russia: Moscow. 1998. Lang.: Rus. 2238
Journal of actress Tatjana Doronina. Russia: Moscow. 1998. Lang.: Rus. 2252
Actress and director Tatjana Doronina of Moscow Art Theatre. Russia: Moscow. Lang.: Rus. 2253
Memoirs of Moscow Art Theatre actress Tatjana Doronina. Russia: Moscow. 1998. Lang.: Rus. 2255
Moscow Art Theatre actress G. Kalinovskaja. Russia: Moscow. 1998. Lang.: Rus. 2280
A century of Čechov productions by the Moscow Art Theatre. Russia: Moscow. 1898-1998. Lang.: Rus. 2288
Actress Tatjana Doronina. Russia: Moscow. 1998. Lang.: Rus. 2302
Moskovskij Chudožestvénnyj Akademičeskij Teat'r im. A.P. Čechova (Moscow)
Institutions
Moscow Art Theatre's two theatres and their artistic directors. Russia: Moscow. 1998. Lang.: Rus. 1698
Performance/production
Director Leonid Truškin. Russia: Moscow. 1998. Lang.: Rus. 2233
Moskovskij Gosudarstvénnyj Cirk Nikulina na Cvetnom bul'vare (Moscow)
Performance/production
Circus producer V. Gneušev. Russia: Moscow. 1998. Lang.: Rus. 4183
Memoirs of film actor and clown Jurij Nikulin. Russia: Moscow. 1998. Lang.: Rus. 4184
Moskovskij Gosudarstvénnyj Evrejskij Teat'r (Moscow)
Performance/production
Solomon Michoėls of Moscow's Jewish Theatre. Russia: Moscow. 1998. Lang.: Rus. 2264
The murder of actor and director Solomon Michoėls. Russia: Moscow. 1948. Lang.: Rus. 2293
Moskovskij Muzykal'nyj Akademičeskij Teat'r im. K.S. Stanislavskogo i Vl.I. Nemiroviča-Dančenko (Moscow)
Performance/production
Ballet soloist T. Černobrivkina. Russia: Moscow. 1998. Lang.: Rus. 1130
Ballerina Natalija Ledovskaja. Russia: Moscow. 1998. Lang.: Rus. 1136
Moskovskij Muzykal'nyj Teat'r Gelikon (Moscow)
Institutions
The Bolšoj Ballet and the experimental company Gelikon. Russia: Moscow. 1997. Lang.: Swe. 4467
Portrait of Dmitrij Bertman, artistic director of Moskovskij Muzykal'nyj Teat'r Gelikon. Russia: Moscow. 1998. Lang.: Rus. 4468
Moss, Howard
Plays/librettos/scripts
History of the Playwrights Unit. USA. 1963-1971. Lang.: Eng. 3570
Moss, Robert
Performance/production
The 'viewpoint theory' of actor training. USA. 1998. Lang.: Eng. 2677
Mossovėt Theatre
SEE
Teat'r im. Mossovėta.
Mostoslavskij, Dž.
Performance/production
Illusionist Dž. Mostoslavskij. Russia: Yaroslav. 1998. Lang.: Rus. 4129
Mother Courage and Her Children
SEE
Mutter Courage und ihre Kinder.
Mother Hicks
Plays/librettos/scripts
Feminist analysis of plays for young people by women playwrights. USA. 1903-1983. Lang.: Eng. 3521
Motionhouse Dance Theatre (London)
Institutions
Profile of Motionhouse Dance Theatre. UK-England: London. 1988-1998. Lang.: Eng. 1254
Mots d'Amour, Les
Performance/production
Collection of newspaper reviews by London theatre critics. UK-England: London. 1998. Lang.: Eng. 2487
Mouawad, Wadji
Performance/production
Interview with director Dominic Champagne. Canada: Montreal, PQ. 1998. Lang.: Fre. 1860

Mouawad, Wadji — cont'd

Comparison of simple productions and visual shows. Canada: Montreal, PQ, Quebec, PQ, Toronto, ON. 1998. Lang.: Fre. 1861

Pierre Benoît's music for *Don Quichotte* at Théâtre du Nouveau Monde. Canada: Montreal, PQ. 1995-1998. Lang.: Fre. 1870

Plays/librettos/scripts

Cervantes' *Don Quixote* and Wadji Mouawad's adaptation, *Don Quichotte.* Canada: Montreal, PQ. 1998. Lang.: Fre. 2803

The character Sancho in Wadji Mouawad's *Don Quichotte (Don Quixote).* Canada: Montreal, PQ. 1998. Lang.: Fre. 2807

The contrast of form and content in Théâtre du Nouveau Monde's *Don Quichotte.* Canada: Montreal, PQ. 1998. Lang.: Fre. 2815

Don Quichotte, an adaptation of Cervantes' *Don Quixote* by Wadji Mouawad. Canada: Montreal, PQ. 1998. Lang.: Fre. 2830

Mouches, Les (Flies, The)

Plays/librettos/scripts

The Orestes myth in twentieth-century drama. Europe. USA. 1914-1943. Lang.: Eng. 3052

Moulin Rouge (Paris)

Performance spaces

Dancers and performance space. Europe. 1895-1937. Lang.: Ger. 909

Mound Builders, The

Plays/librettos/scripts

Analysis of *The Mound Builders* by Lanford Wilson. USA. 1976. Lang.: Eng. 3552

Mound, Vernon

Training

Singer training at Teater- & Operahögskolan. Sweden: Gothenburg. 1960-1998. Lang.: Swe. 4848

Mourning Becomes Electra

Performance/production

Luca Ronconi's production of *Mourning Becomes Electra* by Eugene O'Neill. Italy: Rome. 1996-1997. Lang.: Eng. 2183

Plays/librettos/scripts

The Orestes myth in twentieth-century drama. Europe. USA. 1914-1943. Lang.: Eng. 3052

Female characters in Eugene O'Neill's plays. USA. 1920-1953. Lang.: Eng. 3525

Analysis of Eugene O'Neill's 'middle period' plays. USA. 1925-1938. Lang.: Eng. 3675

Marvin David Levy's operatic adaptation of *Mourning Becomes Electra* by Eugene O'Neill. USA. 1931-1998. Lang.: Eng. 4827

Mousonturm (Frankfurt)

Performance spaces

Profile of the theatrical venue Mousonturm. Germany: Franfurt. 1978-1998. Lang.: Ger. 441

Moussorgsky, Modeste

SEE

Mussorgskij, Modest Pavlovič.

Mouthful of Birds, A

Plays/librettos/scripts

Brechtian epic devices in the theatre of Caryl Churchill. UK-England. 1976-1986. Lang.: Eng. 3477

Movement

Design/technology

The influence of Dalcroze's eurhythmics on designer Adolphe Appia. Switzerland. 1906-1915. Lang.: Eng. 228

Performance/production

The application of Laban Movement Studies to actor training. USA. 1997-1998. Lang.: Eng. 628

Sociolinguistics, gender, and the actor. USA. 1997-1998. Lang.: Eng. 642

History of movement training for the actor. USA. 1910-1985. Lang.: Eng. 675

Round-table discussion on dance and movement. Hungary. 1998. Lang.: Hun. 938

Interview with choreographer Birgit Åkesson. Sweden. Africa. Asia. 1908. Lang.: Swe. 963

Harlequin as a character in ballet. France. 1550-1965. Lang.: Eng. 1069

The theory of movement in *Les Enfants Terribles*, adapted to dance-opera by Philip Glass and Susan Marshall. North America. 1997. Lang.: Eng. 1353

Director Serge Ouaknine and his use of visual aids. Canada: Montreal, PQ. 1968-1998. Lang.: Fre. 1871

Movement training for actors in plays of Molière. France. 1622-1673. Lang.: Eng. 1938

Interview with Marie-Hélène Dasté, daughter of Jacques Copeau. France: Paris. 1913-1992. Lang.: Eng. 4089

Masque, movement, and social and political negotiations. England. 1610-1642. Lang.: Eng. 4198

Performance artist Rei Naito. Japan. 1996-1998. Lang.: Eng. 4242

Staging a musical without professional dancers. USA. 1998. Lang.: Eng. 4374

Relation to other fields

Non-Western dance forms in the teaching of theatre arts. USA: Davis, CA. 1990-1997. Lang.: Eng. 809

Research/historiography

Research on dance and cultural studies. North America. Europe. 1998. Lang.: Eng. 1003

Training

Feldenkreis movement theory. USA. 1905-1985. Lang.: Eng. 880

The use of martial arts in dance training. UK-England. 1998. Lang.: Eng. 1022

Interview with Steve Paxton, creator of contact improvisation. USA. 1973-1998. Lang.: Eng. 1343

Movida de Victor Campolo, La (Victor Campolo Scene, The)

Plays/librettos/scripts

The mulatto in Puerto Rican drama. Puerto Rico. 1850-1985. Lang.: Spa. 3311

Movie Man, The

Performance/production

Collection of newspaper reviews by London theatre critics. UK-England: London. 1998. Lang.: Eng. 2476

Movie Star Has to Star in Black and White, A

Plays/librettos/scripts

The dramaturgical evolution of playwright Adrienne Kennedy. USA. 1964-1990. Lang.: Eng. 3691

Mowat, John

Performance/production

Collection of newspaper reviews by London theatre critics. UK-England: London. 1998. Lang.: Eng. 2472

Moyer, Allen

Design/technology

Set design for *Gun Shy* by Richard Dresser at Playwrights Horizons. USA: New York, NY. 1998. Lang.: Eng. 1535

Mozart, Wolfgang Amadeus

Design/technology

Geogre Tabori's production of Mozart's *Die Zauberflöte* in a circus ring. Germany: Berlin. 1998. Lang.: Ger. 4428

Institutions

Peter Brook's production of Mozart's *Don Giovanni* at the Aix festival. France: Aix-en-Provence. 1998. Lang.: Swe. 4450

Performance/production

Mozart's operas and contemporary Viennese performance spaces. Austria: Vienna. 1782-1791. Lang.: Eng. 4528

The postwar Viennese Mozart style. Austria: Vienna. 1945-1955. Lang.: Eng. 4529

Opera productions of the Salzburg Festival. Austria: Salzburg. 1998. Lang.: Hun. 4531

Lucy Vestris in *Giovanni in London.* England: London. 1842. Lang.: Eng. 4546

Interview with singer Peter Mattei. France: Aix-en-Provence. 1985-1998. Lang.: Swe. 4564

Peter Brook's *Don Giovanni* at the Aix Festival. France: Aix-en-Provence. 1998. Lang.: Eng. 4569

The work of opera director Barbara Beyer. Germany: Nuremberg. 1996-1998. Lang.: Ger. 4589

Interview with opera director Jossi Wieler. Germany: Stuttgart. Switzerland: Basel. 1998. Lang.: Ger. 4592

Interview with Tamás Pál, conductor and musical director of Szeged National Theatre. Hungary: Szeged. 1998. Lang.: Hun. 4622

Interview with director János Szikora. Hungary: Budapest. 1998. Lang.: Hun. 4630

Mozart's *Die Zauberflöte* directed by János Szikora. Hungary: Budapest. Hungary: Szeged. 1998. Lang.: Hun. 4631

Baritone György Melis and the performance in celebration of his 75th birthday. Hungary. 1923-1998. Lang.: Hun. 4633

Mozart's *Le Nozze di Figaro* at the Hungarian State Opera House. Hungary: Budapest. 1998. Lang.: Hun. 4638

Reviews of recent opera productions. Switzerland: Basel. Germany: Stuttgart, Berlin, Hamburg. France: Strasbourg. 1997-1998. Lang.: Ger. 4702

Background material on Lyric Opera of Chicago radio broadcast performances. USA: Chicago, IL. 1998. Lang.: Eng. 4709

Mozart, Wolfgang Amadeus — cont'd

Background material on Metropolitan Opera radio broadcast performances. USA: New York, NY. 1998. Lang.: Eng. 4713

Background material on Metropolitan Opera radio broadcast performances. USA: New York, NY. 1998. Lang.: Eng. 4716

New England Marionettes' production of Mozart's *Die Zauberflöte*. USA: Boston, MA. 1998. Lang.: Eng. 4900

Plays/librettos/scripts

The reciprocal influence of opera and film. Europe. North America. 1904-1994. Lang.: Eng. 4770

Operatic realizations of Beaumarchais' character Rosina. Europe. North America. 1784-1991. Lang.: Eng. 4773

W.H. Auden as an opera librettist and translator. UK-England. 1907-1973. Lang.: Eng. 4825

Mr. Magoo

Design/technology

Costuming for the film *Mr. Magoo*. USA: Hollywood, CA. 1998. Lang.: Eng. 3903

Mr. Peter's Connections

Design/technology

Set designs of Francis O'Connor. USA: New York, NY. 1998. Lang.: Eng. 1541

Mrak, Ivan

Basic theatrical documents

Text of plays and other works by Ivan Mrak. Slovenia. 1930-1975. Lang.: Slo. 1459

Plays/librettos/scripts

Playwright Ivan Mrak. Slovenia. 1925-1986. Lang.: Slo. 3355

Religion and the individual in plays of Ivan Mrak. Slovenia. 1955. Lang.: Slo. 3358

Mrs. Warren's Profession

Performance/production

Attempted censorship of productions. USA. 1900-1905. Lang.: Eng. 2698

New York City's attempt to impose censorship on theatre productions. USA: New York, NY. 1900-1927. Lang.: Eng. 2699

Plays/librettos/scripts

Analysis of early plays by George Bernard Shaw. UK-England. 1892-1900. Lang.: Eng. 3470

Rhetorical analysis of plays by George Bernard Shaw. UK-England. 1896-1908. Lang.: Eng. 3480

George Bernard Shaw and the 'New Woman'. UK-England. 1890-1900. Lang.: Eng. 3486

Theory/criticism

Ibsen, 'new' theatre, and Shaw's *Plays Unpleasant*. UK-England. 1891-1898. Lang.: Eng. 3832

Mrštík, Alois

Performance/production

The adaptation of classic Czech works to the stage. Czech Republic: Prague, Brno. 1990-1998. Lang.: Cze. 1877

Mrštík, Vilém

Performance/production

The adaptation of classic Czech works to the stage. Czech Republic: Prague, Brno. 1990-1998. Lang.: Cze. 1877

MU Színház (Budapest)

Performance/production

Interview with dancer and choreographer Hedvig Fekete. Hungary: Budapest. 1998. Lang.: Hun. 1291

Much Ado About Everything

Performance/production

Collection of newspaper reviews by London theatre critics. UK-England: London. 1998. Lang.: Eng. 2539

Much Ado About Nothing

Performance/production

Review of Shakespeare's *Much Ado About Nothing*, Szeged National Theatre. Hungary: Szeged. 1997. Lang.: Hun. 2086

Collection of newspaper reviews by London theatre critics. UK-England: London. 1998. Lang.: Eng. 2413

Collection of newspaper reviews by London theatre critics. UK-England: London. 1998. Lang.: Eng. 2588

Report on several English performances. UK-England: London, Stratford. 1998. Lang.: Swe. 2634

Analysis of casting and acting in Kenneth Branagh's film adaptation of *Much Ado About Nothing*. UK. 1993. Lang.: Fre. 3939

Plays/librettos/scripts

Hermeneutic analysis of Shakespearean comedies. England. 1590-1608. Lang.: Eng. 2877

Muchamedov, Irek

Performance/production

Ballet dancer Irek Muchamedov. UK-England: London. 1998. Lang.: Rus. 1164

Mud

Plays/librettos/scripts

Theatrical space in plays of Maria Irene Fornes. USA. 1977-1989. Lang.: Eng. 3571

Mudan ting (Peony Pavilion, The)

Performance/production

Collection of newspaper reviews by London theatre critics. UK-England: London. 1998. Lang.: Eng. 2503

Preview of a guest performance of *The Peony Pavilion (Mudan ting)*. China, People's Republic of. 1998. Lang.: Eng. 4314

Plays/librettos/scripts

Personal identity in *Mudan ting (The Peony Pavilion)* by Tang Xianzu and *Taohua shan (The Peach Blossom Fan)* by Kong Shangren.China. 1575-1675. Lang.: Eng. 4315

Muerte del Apetito (Death of the Appetite)

Plays/librettos/scripts

Feminist analysis of seventeenth-century plays by women. Spain. 1605-1675. Lang.: Eng. 3385

Muizelaar, Titus

Performance/production

Collection of newspaper reviews by London theatre critics. UK-England: London. 1998. Lang.: Eng. 2422

Mujeres al borde de un ataque de nervios (Women on the Verge of a Nervous Breakdown)

Plays/librettos/scripts

The influence of Jean Cocteau on filmmaker Pedro Almodóvar. Spain. France. 1981. Lang.: Eng. 3978

Mulatto

Plays/librettos/scripts

Analysis of *Mulatto* by Langston Hughes. USA. 1935. Lang.: Eng. 3709

Mulder, Gert-Jan

Design/technology

Profiles of young theatrical designers. Netherlands. 1990-1998. Lang.: Dut. 207

Mule Bone

Plays/librettos/scripts

Black dance in plays of Zora Neale Hurston. USA. 1925-1930. Lang.: Eng. 3633

Müll, die Stadt und der Tod, Der (Garbage, the City and Death)

Performance/production

Interview with director Bernd Wilms. Germany: Berlin. 1998. Lang.: Swe. 2018

Plays/librettos/scripts

Fassbinder's *Der Müll, die Stadt und der Tod (Garbage, the City and Death)*. Germany: Berlin. 1976-1998. Lang.: Ger. 3175

Mullen, Aaron

Performance/production

Collection of newspaper reviews by London theatre critics. UK-England: London. 1998. Lang.: Eng. 2582

Mullen, Melissa

Plays/librettos/scripts

Analysis of Melissa Mullen's *Rough Waters* at Theatre PEI. Canada: Charlottetown, PE. 1990-1998. Lang.: Eng. 2817

Müller-Brandes, Holger

Institutions

Music theatre studies at the Hochschule für Musik und Theater. Germany: Hamburg. 1988-1998. Lang.: Ger. 4459

Müller, Heiner

Performance/production

French productions of German plays. France. 1998. Lang.: Ger. 1935

Shakespeare performance on the Rhine and the Ruhr. Germany: Cologne, Bochum, Düsseldorf. 1996-1997. Lang.: Ger. 1962

The performance of Shakespeare in the former East Germany. Germany: Rostock, Leipzig, Berlin, Dessau. 1996-1997. Lang.: Ger. 1974

Recent productions of Schauspiel Leipzig. Germany: Leipzig. 1997-1998. Lang.: Ger. 2011

Interview with playwright Heiner Müller about his adaptations of Shakespeare. Germany, East. 1965-1990. Lang.: Eng. 2039

Adaptations of Shakespeare in productions of Bertolt Brecht and Heiner Müller. Germany, East. 1945-1990. Lang.: Eng. 2049

Robert Wilson's production of Brecht's *Der Ozeanflug*. Germany: Berlin. 1998. Lang.: Ger. 4356

Plays/librettos/scripts

The character Medea in European drama. Europe. 450 B.C.-1998 A.D. Lang.: Ger. 3063

The meanings of the cigar in the appearance and works of Heiner Müller and Bertolt Brecht. Germany. 1930-1997. Lang.: Swe. 3134

Müller, Heiner — cont'd

Family conflict in *Was sollen wir tun (What Shall We Do)* by Tankred Dorst and *Die Hamletmaschine (Hamletmachine)* by Heiner Müller. Germany. 1997-1998. Lang.: Ger. 3148
Relation to other fields
Current attitudes toward socialism, individualism, and metaphysics in German culture, including theatre. Germany: Berlin. 1989-1998. Lang.: Ger. 3766
Theory/criticism
Representation and delegation in theatre. 1998. Lang.: Eng. 3800

Müller, Irene
Performance/production
Recent productions of Schauspiel Leipzig. Germany: Leipzig. 1997-1998. Lang.: Ger. 2011

Müller, Péter
Performance/production
Collection of newspaper reviews by London theatre critics. UK-England. 1998. Lang.: Eng. 2489

Müller, Stephan
Performance/production
The 'viewpoint theory' of actor training. USA. 1998. Lang.: Eng. 2677

Mulrine, Stephen
Plays/librettos/scripts
Stephen Mulrine's translation and stage adaptation of *Moscow Stations* by Venedikt Erofeev. USSR. UK-England. 1973-1998. Lang.: Eng. 3718

Multiculturalism
Institutions
Rahul Varma on his multicultural theatre company Teesri Duniya. Canada: Montreal, PQ. 1981-1998. Lang.: Eng. 1592
Interview with founders of Dutch multicultural group Cosmic Illusions. Netherlands: Amsterdam. Netherlands Antilles. 1988. Lang.:Eng. 1679
Performance/production
Multiculturalism and the site-specificity of theatre. Asia. North America. Europe. 1976-1997. Lang.: Eng. 485
Multiculturalism and Italo-Australian theatre. Australia. 1990-1998. Lang.: Eng. 490
Aboriginal arts on the Australian stage. Australia: Sydney. 1997. Lang.: Eng. 491
Opportunities for South Asian actors. Canada: Toronto, ON. 1997. Lang.: Eng. 508
Directing and intercultural theatre. Europe. 1930-1998. Lang.: Ger. 524
Sanjukta Panigrahi, dancer, choreographer, and co-founder of ISTA. India. 1944-1997. Lang.: Eng. 952
Swedish and bilingual Finnish-Swedish theatre. Finland: Turku, Vaasa. 1998. Lang.: Eng, Fre. 1913
Indian theatre in South Africa. South Africa, Republic of. 1900-1998. Lang.: Eng. 2356
Amerindian influence on Trinidadian carnival. Trinidad and Tobago: San Fernando. 1700-1950. Lang.: Eng. 4164
Carnival as a unifying force. Trinidad and Tobago. 1998. Lang.: Eng. 4170
Plays/librettos/scripts
Playwright Slobodan Šnajder. Croatia. 1982-1998. Lang.: Eng. 2848
The underrepresentation of Hispanics in American arts. USA. 1998. Lang.: Eng. 3716
The influence of Taliep Petersen's musical *District Six*. South Africa, Republic of. 1987. Lang.: Eng. 4394
Relation to other fields
Criticism of the American Assembly's approach to the arts sector. USA. 1997. Lang.: Eng. 780
Chinese influence on Trinidadian carnival. Trinidad and Tobago. China. 1808-1998. Lang.: Eng. 4174
Carnival, cultural identity, and assimilation. Trinidad and Tobago. 1889-1998. Lang.: Eng. 4177
Indian influence on Trinidadian carnival. Trinidad and Tobago. India. 1845-1998. Lang.: Eng. 4178
Theory/criticism
Multiculturalism and Australian theatre. Australia. 1990-1998. Lang.: Eng. 3807

Multimedia
Performance/production
Performance artist Leslie Hill's *Push the Boat Out*. UK-England: London. USA. 1995-1997. Lang.: Eng. 4245
Theory/criticism
Critical response to *Elsineur (Elsinore)*, Robert Lepage's multimedia adaptation of *Hamlet*. Canada. 1995-1996. Lang.: Eng. 3810

Mum
Performance/production
Collection of newspaper reviews by London theatre critics. UK-England: London. 1998. Lang.: Eng. 2513

¡Mumbo Jumbo
Performance/production
African ritual in the work of director and playwright Brett Bailey. South Africa, Republic of. 1997-1998. Lang.: Eng. 2349

Muminova, Farida
Performance/production
Actress Farida Muminova. Russia: Magnitogorsk. 1998. Lang.: Rus. 2299

Mummers' Troupe (St. John's, NF)
Institutions
The Mummers' Troupe and the Canada Council. Canada: St. John's, NF. 1972-1982. Lang.: Eng. 1581
Performance/production
Social criticism and alternative theatre in Quebec and Newfoundland. Canada. 1970-1985. Lang.: Eng. 500

Münchner Festspiele (Munich)
SEE
Bayerische Staatsoper im Nationaltheater.

Münchner Kammerspiele (Munich)
Design/technology
Max Keller, lighting designer of Münchner Kammerspiele. Germany: Munich. 1997. Lang.: Ger. 188
Institutions
The aesthetic perspectives of the ensemble at Münchner Kammerspiele. Germany: Munich. 1997-1998. Lang.: Ger. 1666
Performance/production
Comparison of two productions of Shakespeare's *Richard III*. Germany: Munich. 1996-1997. Lang.: Ger. 1976
Productions of director Peter Wittenberg. Germany: Munich, Bonn. 1998. Lang.: Ger. 2013
Productions of plays by Shakespeare, Brecht, and Camus. Germany. 1998. Lang.: Ger. 2032

Munday, Anthony
Plays/librettos/scripts
Analysis of *Downfall of Robert Earl of Huntingdon* by Anthony Munday. England. 1598-1599. Lang.: Eng. 3018

Muni, Nicholas
Plays/librettos/scripts
The American and Canadian premieres of *Jackie O*. Canada: Banff, AB. USA: Houston, TX. 1997. Lang.: Eng. 4761

Muni, Paul
Performance/production
Actor Paul Muni. USA: New York, NY. 1895-1998. Lang.: Eng. 2733

Munich Opera
SEE
Bayerische Staatsoper im Nationaltheater.

Municipal Theatre (Haifa)
SEE
Teatron HaIroni (Haifa).

Municipal Theatre (Helsinki)
SEE
Helsingin Kaupunginteatteri.

Munk, Kaj
Plays/librettos/scripts
Priest and playwright Kaj Munk. Denmark. 1898-1944. Lang.: Swe. 2855

Muñoz Pujol, Josep M.
Basic theatrical documents
Text of plays by Josep M. Muñoz Pujol. Spain-Catalonia. 1995. Lang.: Cat. 1466

Munrow, Julia
Performance/production
Collection of newspaper reviews by London theatre critics. UK-England: London. 1998. Lang.: Eng. 2468
Collection of newspaper reviews by London theatre critics. UK-England: London. 1998. Lang.: Eng. 2524

Muppets
Design/technology
Technical designs for the musical *Doctor Doolittle* directed by Steven Pimlott. UK-England: London. 1998. Lang.: Eng. 4325

Murder in the Cathedral
Plays/librettos/scripts
The rebel in modern drama. Europe. 1950-1988. Lang.: Eng. 3053

Murlin Murlo
Performance/production
Productions of plays by Koljada and Jerofejév at Csiky Gergely Theatre. Hungary: Kaposvár. 1998. Lang.: Hun. 2149

Murphy
Relation to other fields
Analysis of Samuel Beckett's novel *Murphy*. France. Ireland. 1935. Lang.: Eng. 733

Murphy, Mark
Performance/production
Narrative in choreographies of Matthew Bourne and Mark Murphy. UK-England. 1998. Lang.: Eng. 1156
Murray Brown, Nick
Performance/production
Collection of newspaper reviews by London theatre critics. UK-England: London. 1998. Lang.: Eng. 2460
Murray, Catriona
Performance/production
Collection of newspaper reviews by London theatre critics. UK-England: London. 1998. Lang.: Eng. 2459
Murray, Diedre
Plays/librettos/scripts
Panel discussion on contemporary musical theatre. USA: New York, NY. 1998. Lang.: Eng. 4398
Murray, Jacob
Performance/production
Collection of newspaper reviews by London theatre critics. UK-England. 1998. Lang.: Eng. 2510
Murray, Judith Sargent
Plays/librettos/scripts
Judith Sargent Murray's *Traveller Returned* and its source. USA. 1771-1796. Lang.: Eng. 3672
Murrin, Tom
Performance/production
Analysis of pop performance. USA: New York, NY. 1980-1988. Lang.: Eng. 664
Murx
Theory/criticism
The music-theatre concept of Christoph Marthaler. Germany: Berlin. 1993-1998. Lang.: Ger. 4310
Musco, Angelo
Performance/production
Actor Angelo Musco. Italy. 1872-1937. Lang.: Ita. 549
Muses
Performance/production
Contemporary queer politics and the production of gay and lesbian theatre. USA. 1970-1997. Lang.: Eng. 2710
Museums
Administration
Changes in arts marketing strategies. USA. 1977-1997. Lang.: Eng. 126
Design/technology
An exhibition of sets by Caspar Neher for the plays of Bertolt Brecht. Germany: Berlin. 1998. Lang.: Eng. 1522
Institutions
Popular entertainment at the New Haven Assembly Hall and Columbian Museum and Gardens. USA: New Haven, CT. 1796-1820. Lang.: Eng. 394
The Walker Arts Center's exhibition on dance. USA: Minneapolis, MN. 1998. Lang.: Eng. 905
The puppet collection of the Detroit Institute of the Arts. USA: Detroit, MI. 1998. Lang.: Eng. 4880
Puppetry exhibits at Chicago Children's Museum. USA: Chicago, IL. Mexico: Mexico City. 1998. Lang.: Eng. 4881
Performance/production
'The Speaking Body' museum installation, site of theatre anthropology seminars. Austria: Vienna. Switzerland: Zurich. 1996-1998. Lang.: Eng. 493
Performance at Hull House. USA: Chicago, IL. 1890-1997. Lang.: Eng. 644
Retrospectives of filmmakers Jean-Luc Godard and William Kentridge. USA: New York, NY. 1998. Lang.: Eng. 3958
Video artist Bill Viola. USA: New York, NY. 1976-1998. Lang.: Eng. 4071
A mock slave auction at Colonial Williamsburg. USA: Williamsburg, VA. 1994. Lang.: Eng. 4142
Theatrical activities of the Polynesian Cultural Center. USA: Laie, HI. 1963-1983. Lang.: Eng. 4221
Music
Administration
Stefan Soltesz's administration at Aalto-Musiktheater. Germany: Essen. 1997-1998. Lang.: Ger. 4286
Basic theatrical documents
Score of Yu-Chun Kuo's concerto for dance and music, *Ring*. USA. 1988. Lang.: Eng. 887
Design/technology
The influence of Dalcroze's eurhythmics on designer Adolphe Appia. Switzerland. 1906-1915. Lang.: Eng. 228
Suppliers of lighting equipment for the music industry. USA: Tualatin, OR. 1996-1998. Lang.: Eng. 328
Profile of technicians for Grammy Awards television broadcast. USA: New York, NY. 1998. Lang.: Eng. 4056
Peter Morse's lighting design for country music tour. USA. 1998. Lang.: Eng. 4108
Institutions
Popular entertainment at the New Haven Assembly Hall and Columbian Museum and Gardens. USA: New Haven, CT. 1796-1820. Lang.: Eng. 394
Public entertainments in Philadelphia's pleasure gardens. USA: Philadelphia, PA. 1723-1840. Lang.: Eng. 400
Popular entertainment at the Palace Garden. USA: New York, NY. 1858-1863. Lang.: Eng. 403
Performance spaces
The supper and swing-music venue the Coconut Club. USA: Los Angeles, CA. 1998. Lang.: Eng. 4115
Performance/production
Report on festival of performing and visual arts. France: Paris. 1997. Lang.: Eng. 532
History of Arabic theatre. Middle East. 225-1995. Lang.: Eng. 561
Popular entertainment in Uganda after Idi Amin. Uganda. 1979-1998. Lang.: Eng. 604
Hanne Tierney's adaptation of *Bodas de sangre (Blood Wedding)* by García Lorca. USA. 1997. Lang.: Eng. 647
History of Korean dance. Korea. 1600-1985. Lang.: Eng. 954
Flamenco variations worldwide. Spain. USA. 1901-1998. Lang.: Eng. 962
Music for ballet-pantomime at the Paris Opera. France. 1825-1850. Lang.: Eng. 1078
Interview with choreographer Merce Cunningham. USA. 1944-1998. Lang.: Eng. 1326
Shakespeare and traditional Asian theatrical forms. China, People's Republic of. India. Japan. 1981-1997. Lang.: Eng. 1346
Analysis of Korean mask-dance theatre form *hahoe pyolsin-kut*. Korea. 1150-1928. Lang.: Eng. 1352
Music in German-language Prague productions. Austrian Empire: Prague. 1750-1800. Lang.: Cze. 1826
Analysis of a student production of Caryl Churchill's *Cloud Nine*. Canada. 1997. Lang.: Eng. 1840
Pierre Benoît's music for *Don Quichotte* at Théâtre du Nouveau Monde. Canada: Montreal, PQ. 1995-1998. Lang.: Fre. 1870
Shakespeare's *The Tempest* on the eighteenth-century stage. England: London. 1701-1800. Lang.: Eng. 1895
Music for London Shakespearean productions. England: London. 1660-1830. Lang.: Eng. 1900
Music in Tudor drama. England. 1497-1569. Lang.: Eng. 1902
Interview with composer Paul Schmidt. USA: New Haven, CT. 1998. Lang.: Eng. 2660
Music in films of Marguerite Duras. France. 1974-1981. Lang.: Eng. 3932
The theory and practice of scoring a television production. USA. 1998. Lang.: Eng. 4069
Calypso music and carnival. Caribbean. 1933-1998. Lang.: Eng. 4119
Representations of regional identity in music hall. UK-England. 1880-1914. Lang.: Eng. 4132
The collaborative art installation *Tight Roaring Circle*. UK-England: London. 1993-1997. Lang.: Eng. 4133
Women in the *canboulay* ceremony. Trinidad and Tobago. 1998. Lang.: Eng. 4166
Interview with *mas* music performer George Leacock. Trinidad and Tobago. 1923-1998. Lang.: Eng. 4167
The figure of the Midnight Robber in Trinidadian carnival. Trinidad and Tobago. 1900-1998. Lang.: Eng. 4168
History of the steeldrum, used in carnival celebrations. Trinidad and Tobago: Port of Spain. 1777-1998. Lang.: Eng. 4169
Carnival as a unifying force. Trinidad and Tobago. 1998. Lang.: Eng. 4170
Carnival performances of a *jouvay* band. Trinidad and Tobago: Port of Spain. 1996. Lang.: Eng. 4171
Political aspects of music in the masque. England. 1620-1634. Lang.: Eng. 4197

Music — cont'd

Performance artist Mimi Goese. USA. 1982-1998. Lang.: Eng. 4252
Male impersonation in variety and vaudeville. USA. 1868-1930. Lang.: Eng. 4281
Sequentia's new recording of *Ordo Virtutum* by Hildegard of Bingen. Germany. 1997. Lang.: Eng. 4294
Composers and the work of Bertolt Brecht. Germany. 1928-1998. Lang.: Ger. 4297
Giovanni Tamborrino's opera without song. Italy. Lang.: Ita. 4300
Drama and spirituality in the music of Leonard Bernstein. USA. 1965-1990. Lang.: Eng. 4379
The use of the harpsichord in Stravinskij's opera *The Rake's Progress.* Europe. 1951. Lang.: Eng. 4559
The evolution of comic opera. Italy: Florence, Rome. 1665-1700. Lang.: Eng. 4660
Chinese street opera and nation-building. Singapore. 1965-1998. Lang.: Eng. 4694
Profile of composer Elliott Carter. USA. 1908-1998. Lang.: Eng. 4711
Basil Twist's puppetry interpretation of Berlioz's *Symphonie Fantastique.* USA: New York, NY. 1998. Lang.: Eng. 4904

Plays/librettos/scripts
Verbal and non-verbal communication in the theatre of Marguerite Duras. France. 1914-1985. Lang.: Eng. 3094
Musicological perspective on *Die Massnahme (The Measures Taken)* by Brecht and Eisler. Germany: Berlin. 1929-1998. Lang.: Ger. 3125
Composer Philip Glass on Beckett's influence on his work. Ireland. France. USA. 1965-1995. Lang.: Eng. 3194
Composer Luciano Berio on Beckett's influence on his work. Ireland. France. Italy. 1965-1985. Lang.: Eng. 3195
Music in the early life of Samuel Beckett. Ireland. 1912-1945. Lang.: Eng. 3196
Music and Samuel Beckett. Ireland. France. 1945-1990. Lang.: Eng. 3198
Melanie Daiken's musical settings of texts by Samuel Beckett. Ireland. France. 1945-1995. Lang.: Eng. 3201
Playwright Samuel Beckett's love of music. Ireland. France. 1955-1995. Lang.: Eng. 3204
Music and song in plays of Brendan Behan. Ireland. 1954-1958. Lang.: Eng. 3206
Music in Samuel Beckett's novel *Proust.* Ireland. France. 1931. Lang.: Eng. 3208
Beckett's work analyzed in terms of musical serialism. Ireland. France. 1945-1995. Lang.: Eng. 3215
Composer Giacomo Manzoni and his work *Words by Beckett (Parole da Beckett).* Italy. 1970-1971. Lang.: Eng. 3250
Analysis of the 'Russian Robin Hood' Stepan Razin. Russia. 1620-1900. Lang.: Eng. 3327
Music in the plays of George Bernard Shaw. UK-England. 1888-1950. Lang.: Eng. 3506
Samuel Beckett's influence on composer Humphrey Searle. UK-England. 1945-1995. Lang.: Eng. 3509
Blues music in the writings of Zora Neale Hurston. USA. 1920-1940. Lang.: Eng. 3625
Morton Feldman's musical setting for Samuel Beckett's radio play *Words and Music.* Europe. 1987. Lang.: Eng. 3865
Clarence Barlow's abstract musical setting of a prose text by Samuel Beckett. 1971-1972. Lang.: Eng. 4305
Earl Kim's musical piece *Dead Calm,* based on a text by Samuel Beckett. 1945-1995. Lang.: Eng. 4306
Samuel Beckett's short story *Bing* as adapted by Roger Reynolds and Jean-Yves Bosseur. USA. 1986. Lang.: Eng. 4308
Roger Reynolds' musical settings of texts by Samuel Beckett. USA. 1968-1976. Lang.: Eng. 4309
Heinz Holliger's operatic adaptation of Samuel Beckett's *What Where.* Europe. 1992. Lang.: Eng. 4768
Marcel Mihalovici's operatic adaptation of *Krapp's Last Tape* by Samuel Beckett. Europe. 1965. Lang.: Eng. 4769
The opera *Neither* by Morton Feldman and Samuel Beckett. Europe. 1976-1977. Lang.: Eng. 4772
Operatic adaptations of Beckett's plays by Heinz Holliger. Europe. 1976-1988. Lang.: Eng. 4776
Composer Wolfgang Fortner's adaptation of *That Time* by Samuel Beckett. Europe. 1974-1977. Lang.: Eng. 4777
Composer Sándor Szokolay on his opera *Szávitri.* Hungary: Budapest. 1998. Lang.: Hun. 4801

Reference materials
Dictionary of history and the arts. Lang.: Ita. 695
Index to performing arts articles in Bragaglia's *Chronache d'attualità.* Italy: Rome. 1916-1922. Lang.: Ita. 704
Encyclopedia of Slovene folk dance. Slovenia. 1997. Lang.: Slo. 1243

Relation to other fields
The theatrical nature of Salvation Army activities. USA. 1865-1950. Lang.: Eng. 796
Theatrical activities of the Mormon Church. USA. 1977-1986. Lang.: Eng. 811
Analysis of the jazz funeral. USA: New Orleans, LA. 1900-1990. Lang.: Eng. 4228

Theory/criticism
Performance art and the 'poetics of space'. USA. Poland. 1952-1984. Lang.: Eng. 4270
George Bernard Shaw as music critic. UK-England: London. 1887-1894. Lang.: Eng. 4838
Comments on the present state of music criticism. USA. Canada. 1998. Lang.: Eng. 4845

Music Box Theatre (New York, NY)

Design/technology
Recent work of lighting designer Brian MacDevitt. USA: New York, NY. 1997. Lang.: Eng. 1530
Sound design for *The Diary of Anne Frank* directed by James Lapine. USA: New York, NY. 1998. Lang.: Eng. 1553

Plays/librettos/scripts
Reactions to the revised version of *The Diary of Anne Frank.* USA: New York, NY. 1998. Lang.: Eng. 3618

Music Gallery (Toronto, ON)

Basic theatrical documents
Text of libretto for *Beatrice Chancy.* Canada: Toronto, ON. 1998. Lang.: Eng. 4413

Music hall

SEE ALSO
Classed Entries under MIXED ENTERTAINMENT—Variety acts.

Performance/production
Representations of regional identity in music hall. UK-England. 1880-1914. Lang.: Eng. 4132

Relation to other fields
'Up-to-dateness' on the music hall stage. UK-England: London. 1890-1914. Lang.: Eng. 4283
Brief history of London music hall. UK-England: London. 1843-1998. Lang.: Eng. 4284

Music-Drama

SEE ALSO
Classed Entries under MUSIC-DRAMA.

Musical theatre

SEE ALSO
Classed Entries under MUSIC-DRAMA—Musical theatre.

Design/technology
Recent work of lighting designer Brian MacDevitt. USA: New York, NY. 1997. Lang.: Eng. 1530

Performance/production
Dance director Seymour Felix. USA. 1918-1953. Lang.: Eng. 976
Choreography in the musical film *The Bandwagon.* USA. 1953. Lang.: Eng. 982
The influence of exhibition ballroom dance on theatrical entertainments. USA. 1910-1925. Lang.: Eng. 985
Choreographer Jerome Robbins. USA. 1918-1998. Lang.: Eng. 1167
Playwright Jess Gregg's relationship with choreographer Agnes De Mille. USA: New York, NY. 1961-1998. Lang.: Eng. 1178
The importance of Black performers in American musical films. USA. 1900-1957. Lang.: Swe. 3960
Popular entertainer Elsie Janis. USA. 1896-1941. Lang.: Eng. 4145
William Schuman on the differences between operatic and Broadway theatre singing. USA. 1998. Lang.: Eng. 4303
AIDS-benefit performance of the musical *Sweet Charity.* USA: New York, NY. 1998. Lang.: Eng. 4386
Obituaries of singers Randolph Symonette and Todd Duncan. USA. 1998. Lang.: Eng. 4708

Plays/librettos/scripts
Popular adaptations of the works of George Bernard Shaw. UK-England. 1890-1990. Lang.: Eng. 3445

Musical theatre — cont'd

Fairy-tale heroines in American drama and musical theatre. USA. 1945-1965. Lang.: Eng. 3617
The theatre of Girolamo Gigli. Italy. 1660-1722. Lang.: Eng. 4307
Reference materials
History of dance and ballet. 2000 B.C.-1990 A.D. Lang.: Slo. 995
Relation to other fields
Quantum theory in recent New York performances. USA: New York, NY. 1995-1996. Lang.: Eng. 794
The theatrical nature of Salvation Army activities. USA. 1865-1950. Lang.: Eng. 796

Musika!
Theory/criticism
Theory and Asian-American theatre. USA: Minneapolis, MN. 1994-1995. Lang.: Eng. 869

Musikteatern i Värmland (Karlstad)
Performance/production
Interview with opera singer Anne Bolstad. Norway. Sweden. 1980-1998. Lang.: Swe. 4665

Musil, Robert
Plays/librettos/scripts
Robert Musil and the 'crisis of modern drama'. Europe. 1880-1930. Lang.: Eng. 3062

Mussbach, Peter
Performance/production
Interview with opera composer Manfred Trojahn. Germany: Munich. 1998. Lang.: Ger. 4582

Musser, Tharon
Design/technology
Lighting designer Tharon Musser. USA. 1965-1998. Lang.: Eng. 326
Digital lighting control for *A Chorus Line*. USA: New York, NY. 1974-1975. Lang.: Eng. 4337

Musset, Alfred de
Plays/librettos/scripts
Fidelity in two plays of Musset. France. 1835-1837. Lang.: Eng. 3102

Mussorgskij, Modest Pavlovič
Performance/production
Opera director Inge Levant. Germany: Stuttgart. 1959-1998. Lang.: Ger. 4611
Personal recollections of Šaljapin singing on recordings of *Boris Godunov*. Russia. 1873-1938. Lang.: Eng. 4685
Background material on Metropolitan Opera radio broadcast performances. USA: New York, NY. 1998. Lang.: Eng. 4713
Bass Samuel Ramey. USA. 1940-1998. Lang.: Eng. 4744

Mustache, The
Basic theatrical documents
English translation of *The Mustache* by Sabine Berman. Mexico. 1992. Lang.: Eng. 1447

Mustapha
Plays/librettos/scripts
Analysis of a scene from *Mustapha* by Fulke Greville. England. 1609-1633. Lang.: Eng. 3044

Muti, Riccardo
Performance/production
Productions of Puccini operas at La Scala. Italy: Milan. 1980-1998. Lang.: Swe. 4657

Mutter Courage und ihre Kinder (Mother Courage and Her Children)
Performance/production
Bertolt Brecht's production of his *Mutter Courage (Mother Courage)*. Germany: Berlin. 1947-1956. Lang.: Ger. 1975

Művészetek Völgye '98 (Kapolcs)
Performance/production
Three Hungarian productions of plays by Molière. Hungary: Szentendre, Kapolcs, Kőszeg. 1998. Lang.: Hun. 2142

Muzio, Gloria
Design/technology
Set design for *Gun Shy* by Richard Dresser at Playwrights Horizons. USA: New York, NY. 1998. Lang.: Eng. 1535

My Children! My Africa!
Plays/librettos/scripts
Post-apartheid analysis of plays by Athol Fugard. South Africa, Republic of. 1991-1998. Lang.: Eng. 3364

My Fair Lady
Plays/librettos/scripts
Popular adaptations of the works of George Bernard Shaw. UK-England. 1890-1990. Lang.: Eng. 3445
Fairy-tale heroines in American drama and musical theatre. USA. 1945-1965. Lang.: Eng. 3617

My Left Breast
Basic theatrical documents
French translation of *My Left Breast* by Susan Miller. USA. France. 1994-1998. Lang.: Fre. 1498

My Life in Art
Performance/production
Collection of newspaper reviews by London theatre critics. UK-England: London. 1998. Lang.: Eng. 2534

My Lovely...Shayna Maidel
SEE
Shayna Maidel, A.

My Mother Was an Alien—Is That Why I'm Gay?
Performance/production
Collection of newspaper reviews by London theatre critics. UK-England: London. 1998. Lang.: Eng. 2479

My Queer Body
Plays/librettos/scripts
Analysis of performance art on *The Larry Sanders Show*. USA. 1995. Lang.: Eng. 4079

My Sister in This House
Plays/librettos/scripts
The representation of true crime in modern drama. USA. France. 1955-1996. Lang.: Eng. 3673

Myers, Keith
Performance/production
Collection of newspaper reviews by London theatre critics. UK-England: London. 1998. Lang.: Eng. 2474

Mysteries, The
Performance/production
Collection of newspaper reviews by London theatre critics. UK-England: London. 1998. Lang.: Eng. 2573
Katie Mitchell's production of mystery plays at RSC. UK-England: London. 1996-1998. Lang.: Eng. 2626

Mystery plays
SEE ALSO
Passion plays.
Performance/production
Staging of the Cornish *Ordinalia*. England. 1375-1400. Lang.: Eng. 1890
Katie Mitchell's production of mystery plays at RSC. UK-England: London. 1996-1998. Lang.: Eng. 2626
Plays/librettos/scripts
The language used by devils in the *York Cycle*. England: York. 1400-1500. Lang.: Eng. 2933
Biblical narrative and the order of the *York Cycle* episodes. England: York. 1401-1499. Lang.: Eng. 2950
Epiphany in the plays of Shakespeare. England. 1590-1613. Lang.: Eng. 3008
The Expositor character of the Chester Cycle. England. 1400-1500. Lang.: Eng. 3033
The medieval mystery play and Tony Kushner's *Angels in America*. USA. 1992-1994. Lang.: Eng. 3652
Relation to other fields
The relationship between the York Cycle and the Bolton Book of Hours. England: York. 1405-1500. Lang.: Eng. 3750
Fouquet's miniature of St. Apollonia and its relationship to the mystery play. France. 1452-1577. Lang.: Eng. 3761
Jean Fouquet's miniature of St. Apollonia and its relationship to performance. France: Tours. 1452-1577. Lang.: Eng. 3762
Fouquet's depiction of the martyrdom of St. Apollonia as a record of a performance. France. 1452-1577. Lang.: Eng. 3763

Mythology
Performance/production
Mythology in theatre works of Stravinskij, especially *Perséphone*. Russia. 1934. Lang.: Eng. 4682
Plays/librettos/scripts
The centaur in works of Shakespeare. England. 1590-1613. Lang.: Eng. 2882
The character Medea in European drama. Europe. 450 B.C.-1998 A.D. Lang.: Ger. 3063
Electra and Orestes in plays of Aeschylus, Euripides, and Sophocles. Greece. 438-411 B.C. Lang.: Eng. 3184
Analysis of *The Prodigal* by Jack Richardson. USA. 1960. Lang.: Eng. 3542
The Prodigal, Jack Richardson's adaptation of *The Oresteia*. USA. 1960. Lang.: Dut. 3547
Homeric influences on *The Prodigal* by Jack Richardson. USA. 1960. Lang.: Eng. 3549

Mythology — cont'd

Relation to other fields
Quantum theory in recent New York performances. USA: New York, NY. 1995-1996. Lang.: Eng. 794

N-town Plays
Plays/librettos/scripts
The Easter play tradition. England. 1180-1557. Lang.: Eng. 2942
The N-town Mary play and the Four Virtues of Psalm 84:11. England. 1120-1501. Lang.: Eng. 2983

Na bolšoj doroge (On the High Road)
Basic theatrical documents
Catalan translations of the complete plays of Anton Čechov. Russia. 1884-1904. Lang.: Cat. 1449

Na dnė (Lower Depths, The)
Plays/librettos/scripts
Translations of Čechov's *Three Sisters* and Gorkij's *The Lower Depths*. Russia. 1901-1902. Lang.: Rus. 3326

Na Gopaleen, Myles
SEE
O'Brien, Flann.

Nabokov's Gloves
Performance/production
Collection of newspaper reviews by London theatre critics. UK-England: London. 1998. Lang.: Eng. 2410

Nabucco
Performance/production
Background material on Lyric Opera of Chicago radio broadcast performances. USA: Chicago, IL. 1998. Lang.: Eng. 4709

Nacht und Träume
Plays/librettos/scripts
Analysis of television plays by Samuel Beckett. France. 1965-1989. Lang.: Eng. 4077

Nádasdy, Ádám
Plays/librettos/scripts
New Hungarian translations of Shakespeare. Hungary. 1990-1998. Lang.: Hun. 3187

Nadeau, Carole
Plays/librettos/scripts
Mixed media in theatre productions of Carole Nadeau. Canada: Quebec, PQ, Montreal, PQ. 1998. Lang.: Fre. 4047

Nadeau, Michel
Performance/production
The integration of playwriting into the production process at Théâtre Niveau Parking. Canada: Quebec, PQ. 1990-1998. Lang.: Fre. 1857
Comparison of simple productions and visual shows. Canada: Montreal, PQ, Quebec, PQ, Toronto, ON. 1998. Lang.: Fre. 1861
Theory/criticism
Round-table discussion on theatre and impurity. Canada: Quebec, PQ. 1998. Lang.: Fre. 835

Nadj, Josef
Institutions
Interview with Josef Nadj, choreographer. France. 1990-1998. Lang.: Hun. 892
Performance/production
Choreographer Josef Nadj and his company Théâtre du Signe. France. 1987-1998. Lang.: Hun. 924
Comparison of text-based and visual productions. France. 1998. Lang.: Fre. 1939

Nadolny, Hans
Performance/production
Adaptations and performances of *Alte Meister (Old Masters)* by Thomas Bernhard. Germany. 1997-1998. Lang.: Ger. 1996

Nagel, Ivan
Institutions
Productions of Salzburger Festspiele. Austria: Salzburg. 1998. Lang.: Ger. 1571
Interview with Ivan Nagel, drama manager of the Salzburg Festival. Austria: Salzburg. 1998. Lang.: Ger. 1572
Productions of the Salzburg Festival. Austria: Salzburg. 1998. Lang.: Ger. 1573
Plays/librettos/scripts
Ivan Nagel's speech on awarding the Büchner Prize to playwright Elfriede Jelinek. Germany. 1998. Lang.: Ger. 3154

Nagy, Phyllis
Performance/production
Collection of newspaper reviews by London theatre critics. UK-England: London. 1998. Lang.: Eng. 2569

Nagy, Viktor
Performance/production
Reviews of new Hungarian musicals. Hungary: Budapest. 1997. Lang.: Hun. 4360
Interview with director Viktor Nagy on Wagner's *Ring* cycle. Hungary: Budapest. 1998. Lang.: Hun. 4635
Wagner's *Ring* cycle at the Hungarian Opera House. Hungary: Budapest. 1998. Lang.: Hun. 4644
Plays/librettos/scripts
Outline of Wagner's *Götterdämmerung*. Hungary: Budapest. 1998. Lang.: Hun. 4800

Nagyszentpéteri, Miklós
Performance/production
Dancer Miklós Nagyszentpéteri. Hungary. 1989-1998. Lang.: Hun. 1113

Nagyváradi Állami Színház, Szigligeti Társulat (Oradea)
Institutions
Hungarian-language theatre in Transylvania. Hungary. Romania. 1798-1998. Lang.: Hun. 365
History of annual festival of Hungarian-language theatre. Hungary: Kisvárda. 1989-1998. Lang.: Hun. 1669
History of Hungarian-language theatre in Transylvania. Romania. Hungary. 1919-1992. Lang.: Hun, Rom. 1693

Naharin, Ohad
Performance/production
Contemporary Israeli dance. Israel. 1997. Lang.: Swe. 1117

Naito, Rei
Performance/production
Performance artist Rei Naito. Japan. 1996-1998. Lang.: Eng. 4242

Najmányi, László
Design/technology
Survey of an exhibition of Hungarian scene design. Hungary: Budapest. 1998. Lang.: Hun. 195
An exhibition of sets and environments by Hungarian designers. Hungary: Budapest. 1998. Lang.: Hun. 196
Catalogue of an exhibition devoted to Hungarian theatre and film. Hungary: Budapest. 1998. Lang.: Hun. 197

Nalen (Stockholm)
Performance spaces
The former dance palace Nalen, now restored as Nationalpalatset. Sweden: Stockholm. 1889-1998. Lang.: Swe. 4114

Nangsa Ohbum
Performance/production
Analysis of Tibetan Buddhist drama. Tibet. 1500-1984. Lang.: Eng. 1355

Nansal
Basic theatrical documents
Slovene translations of Tibetan plays. Tibet. 1400-1990. Lang.: Slo. 1470

Napmadarak (Sunbirds)
Performance/production
Fáklya Horvát Táncegyüttes' folk dance production *Napmadarak (Sunbirds)*. Hungary. 1998. Lang.: Hun. 1227

Napoli
Performance/production
Onstage costume changes. Japan. Russia. Denmark. 1752-1998. Lang.: Swe. 556

Når vi døde vågner (When We Dead Awaken)
Institutions
Ibsen Society of America's celebration of the centennial of *Når vi døde vågner (When We Dead Awaken)*. USA: New York, NY. 1998. Lang.: Eng. 1755

Národní Divadlo (Brno)
Performance/production
The adaptation of classic Czech works to the stage. Czech Republic: Prague, Brno. 1990-1998. Lang.: Cze. 1877

Národní Divadlo (Prague)
Design/technology
Josef Svoboda's set design for Goethe's *Faust*. Czech Republic: Prague. 1997. Lang.: Eng. 1517
Performance/production
The adaptation of classic Czech works to the stage. Czech Republic: Prague, Brno. 1990-1998. Lang.: Cze. 1877
Otomar Krejča's production of *Faust* at Národní Divadlo. Czech Republic: Prague. 1997. Lang.: Eng, Fre. 1881

Narodno gledališče (Ljubljana)
Theory/criticism
Reviews of performances at Ljubljana's National Theatre. Slovenia: Ljubljana. 1933-1939. Lang.: Slo. 3829

Narodno Pozorište (Novi Sad)
Performance/production
László Babarczy's production of *Pepe* by Andor Szilágy. Serbia: Novi Sad. 1998. Lang.: Hun. 2342

Nash, N. Richard
Plays/librettos/scripts
Fairy-tale heroines in American drama and musical theatre. USA. 1945-1965. Lang.: Eng. 3617

Nashe, Thomas
Plays/librettos/scripts
Recovered ritual in seemingly non-ritualistic theatre. England. 1600-1779. Lang.: Eng. 2904
Nashville Arena (Nashville, TN)
Design/technology
Lighting design for musical performance and sports at the Nashville arena. USA: Nashville, TN. 1998. Lang.: Eng. 317
National Arts Centre (Ottawa, ON)
Institutions
Backstage tours of the National Arts Centre. Canada: Ottawa, ON. 1997-1998. Lang.: Eng. 340
National Ballet (Amsterdam)
Performance/production
Dutch National Ballet production at the Holland Festival. Netherlands: Amsterdam. 1997. Lang.: Hun. 1121
National Ballet of Canada (Toronto, ON)
Performance/production
Ballerina Greta Hodgkinson of National Ballet of Canada. Canada: Toronto, ON. 1998. Lang.: Eng. 1067
National Endowment for the Arts (NEA, Washington, DC)
Administration
The nomination of William J. Ivey as head of NEA. USA. 1998. Lang.: Eng. 59
Alternative funding strategies for dance companies. USA. 1998. Lang.: Eng. 886
Institutions
The theatre program of the National Endowment for the Arts. USA. 1965-1988. Lang.: Eng. 391
Proposal for changes in the mission of the National Endowment for the Arts. USA. 1998. Lang.: Eng. 397
William J. Ivey, nominee for chair of NEA. USA: Washington, DC. 1998. Lang.: Eng. 420
The status of the National Endowment for the Arts. USA: Washington, DC. 1997-2000. Lang.: Eng. 422
Performance/production
Jane Alexander's return to acting after chairing the NEA. USA. 1998. Lang.: Eng. 2744
Plays/librettos/scripts
Analysis of performance art on *The Larry Sanders Show*. USA. 1995. Lang.: Eng. 4079
Relation to other fields
The upcoming Supreme Court hearing on the government's right to impose decency standards on arts grants. USA: Washington, DC. 1998. Lang.: Eng. 3793
National Theatre (Bratislava)
SEE
Slovenske Narodni Divadlo.
National Theatre (Budapest)
SEE
Nemzeti Szinház.
National Theatre (Dublin)
SEE
Abbey Theatre.
National Theatre (Helsinki)
SEE
Suomen Kansallisteatteri.
National Theatre (Ljubljana)
SEE
Narodno Gledališče.
National Theatre (Miskolc)
SEE
Miskolci Nemzeti Szinház.
National Theatre (Munich)
SEE
Bayerische Staatsoper.
National Theatre (Pécs)
SEE
Pécsi Nemzeti Szinház.
National Theatre (Prague)
SEE
Národní Divadlo.
National Theatre (Szeged)
SEE
Szegedi Nemzeti Szinház.
National Theatre (Tel Aviv)
SEE
HaBimah (Tel Aviv).
National Theatre Company (London)
SEE ALSO
Cottesloe Theatre (London).
Administration
The 'Group of Four' at the Lyric Hammersmith and the concept of a national theatre. UK-England: London. 1945-1956. Lang.: Eng. 1392
Design/technology
Technical designs for Matthew Bourne's productions of ballets by Čajkovskij and Prokofjév. UK-England: London. 1998. Lang.: Eng. 1031
Set design for Tennessee Williams' *Not About Nightingales* at the National. UK-England: London. 1998. Lang.: Eng. 1526
Jason Barnes, production manager of the Royal National Theatre. UK-England: London. 1973-1998. Lang.: Eng. 1527
Performance/production
Collection of newspaper reviews by London theatre critics. UK-England: London. 1998. Lang.: Eng. 2423
Collection of newspaper reviews by London theatre critics. UK-England: London. 1998. Lang.: Eng. 2435
Collection of newspaper reviews by London theatre critics. UK-England: London. 1998. Lang.: Eng. 2448
Collection of newspaper reviews by London theatre critics. UK-England. 1998. Lang.: Eng. 2456
Collection of newspaper reviews by London theatre critics. UK-England: London. 1998. Lang.: Eng. 2461
Collection of newspaper reviews by London theatre critics. UK-England: London. 1998. Lang.: Eng. 2466
Collection of newspaper reviews by London theatre critics. UK-England: London. 1998. Lang.: Eng. 2474
Collection of newspaper reviews by London theatre critics. UK-England: London. 1998. Lang.: Eng. 2482
Collection of newspaper reviews by London theatre critics. UK-England: London. 1998. Lang.: Eng. 2501
Collection of newspaper reviews by London theatre critics. UK-England: London. 1998. Lang.: Eng. 2508
Collection of newspaper reviews by London theatre critics. UK-England: London. 1998. Lang.: Eng. 2514
Collection of newspaper reviews by London theatre critics. UK-England: London. 1998. Lang.: Eng. 2523
Collection of newspaper reviews by London theatre critics. UK-England: London. 1998. Lang.: Eng. 2533
Collection of newspaper reviews by London theatre critics. UK-England: London. 1998. Lang.: Eng. 2540
Collection of newspaper reviews by London theatre critics. UK-England: London. 1998. Lang.: Eng. 2546
Collection of newspaper reviews by London theatre critics. UK-England: London. 1998. Lang.: Eng. 2555
Collection of newspaper reviews by London theatre critics. UK-England: London. 1998. Lang.: Eng. 2569
Collection of newspaper reviews by London theatre critics. UK-England: London. 1998. Lang.: Eng. 2586
Trevor Nunn's production of *Not About Nightingales* by Tennessee Williams, Royal National Theatre. UK-England: London. 1998. Lang.: Swe. 2604
Trevor Nunn's production of *An Enemy of the People* by Ibsen. UK-England: London. 1998. Lang.: Eng. 2627
Interview with director Simon McBurney. UK-England: London. 1997. Lang.: Swe. 2641
Semiotic analysis of Peter Hall's National Theatre production of Shakespeare's *Coriolanus*. UK-England. 1985. Lang.: Eng. 2647
The body in stage-to-film versions of Shakespeare's *Richard III*. UK-England. USA. 1985-1998. Lang.: Eng. 3940
Plays/librettos/scripts
Interview with playwright Jonathan Harvey. UK-England. 1998. Lang.: Eng. 3472
National Theatre of the Deaf (Chester, CT)
Performance/production
The failure of the Canadian Theatre of the Deaf. Canada. 1965-1998. Lang.: Eng. 507
Comparison of productions of Ibsen's *Peer Gynt*. USA: Providence, RI, New York, NY, Washington, DC, Nacogdoches, TX. 1998. Lang.: Eng. 2711
National Theatre, The
Performance/production
Collection of newspaper reviews by London theatre critics. UK-England: London. 1998. Lang.: Eng. 2414

Nationalist theatre
Institutions
Les' Kurbas and Teat'r Berezil. USSR. 1922-1934. Lang.: Eng. 431
Slovene self-image and the national theatre. Slovenia. Germany. 1789-1867. Lang.: Slo. 1719
European national theatres and their development. Slovenia. Germany. 1750-1910. Lang.: Slo. 1720
Performance/production
Theatrical events in Maribor during World War I. Slovenia: Maribor. 1914-1918. Lang.: Slo. 593
Theatre and Ukrainian national identity. Ukraine: Lviv, Kiev, Kharkiv. 1990-1995. Lang.: Eng. 615
Plays/librettos/scripts
Theatre and the creation of a new nationalism. Canada. Saint Lucia. 1980-1995. Lang.: Eng. 2808
History of Czech theatre. Czech Republic. 1800-1999. Lang.: Rus. 2849
Relation to other fields
Nationalism and Irish theatre. Ireland. UK-Ireland. 1890-1914. Lang.: Eng. 750

Nationalpalatset (Stockholm)
Performance spaces
The former dance palace Nalen, now restored as Nationalpalatset. Sweden: Stockholm. 1889-1998. Lang.: Swe. 4114

Nationaltheater (Weimar)
Design/technology
Lighting in contemporary theatre. Germany. 1998. Lang.: Ger. 192

Nationaltheatret (Oslo)
Institutions
Survey of annual Ibsen festival. Norway: Oslo. 1998. Lang.: Eng. 1683
Performance/production
Interview with director Stein Winge. Norway: Oslo. 1988-1998. Lang.: Eng. 2210
Report from Ibsen festival. Norway: Oslo. 1998. Lang.: Swe. 2211

Nazar, Krzysztof
Performance/production
Contemporary Polish productions of Shakespeare. Poland. 1990-1998. Lang.: Pol. 2213

Nazarov, Jurij
Performance/production
Actor Juri Nazarov. Russia. 1998. Lang.: Rus. 2275

Nazimova, Alla
Performance/production
Actress/director Alla Nazimova. Russia. USA. 1878-1945. Lang.: Eng. 585
Plays/librettos/scripts
Feminism and plays of Henrik Ibsen. Norway. 1879-1979. Lang.: Eng. 3293

Ndlovu, Duma
Performance/production
Collection of newspaper reviews by London theatre critics. UK-England: London. 1998. Lang.: Eng. 2511

Neal, Larry
Plays/librettos/scripts
Afrocentricity in plays of Charles Fuller, Amiri Baraka, and Larry Neal. USA. 1960-1998. Lang.: Eng. 3519

Near, Timothy
Performance/production
Statements of women directors on their work. USA. 1996. Lang.: Eng. 2674

Neary, Joanna
Performance/production
Collection of newspaper reviews by London theatre critics. UK-England: London. 1998. Lang.: Eng. 2454

Neath Opera Group (Brecon)
Institutions
The Neath Opera Group's festival and proposed music center at the former home of Adelina Patti. UK-Wales: Brecon. 1843-1919. Lang.: Eng. 4481

Nebeský, Jan
Performance/production
Actor Jan Nebeský. Czech Republic. 1982-1997. Lang.: Eng, Fre. 1883

Nederlands Dans Theater III (The Hague)
Performance/production
Argument in favor of lengthening dancers' careers. Netherlands: The Hague. Sweden. 1998. Lang.: Swe. 955

Nedorosl (Minor, The)
Plays/librettos/scripts
Morality in plays of Fonvizin, Ostrovskij, and A.K. Tolstoj. Russia. 1764-1869. Lang.: Rus. 3325

Needcompany (Brussels)
Theory/criticism
Artaud's theatre of cruelty and contemporary experimental theatre. France. 1945-1998. Lang.: Ger. 3818

Negro Ensemble Company (NEC, New York, NY)
Performance/production
Actor Arthur French. USA: New York, NY. 1962-1998. Lang.: Eng. 2671

Neher, Caspar
Design/technology
An exhibition of sets by Caspar Neher for the plays of Bertolt Brecht. Germany: Berlin. 1998. Lang.: Eng. 1522
Performance/production
Production history of *Die Bürgschaft* by Kurt Weill and Casper Neher. Germany: Berlin, Bielefeld. 1931-1998. Lang.: Eng. 4588

Neighborhood Playhouse (New York, NY)
Performance/production
The first wave of American feminist theatre. USA. 1890-1930. Lang.: Eng. 648

Neil, Andrew
Performance/production
Collection of newspaper reviews by London theatre critics. UK-England: London. 1998. Lang.: Eng. 2512

Neither
Plays/librettos/scripts
The opera *Neither* by Morton Feldman and Samuel Beckett. Europe. 1976-1977. Lang.: Eng. 4772

Nekrošius, Eimuntas
Institutions
Shakespearean productions at the Carrefour international theatre festival. Canada: Quebec, PQ. 1998. Lang.: Fre. 1588
Reviews of some productions at the Avignon Festival. France: Avignon. 1998. Lang.: Hun. 1615
Performance/production
Director Eimuntus Nekrošius. Lithuania. 1952-1998. Lang.: Pol. 2198
Report from Ibsen festival. Norway: Oslo. 1998. Lang.: Swe. 2211

Nel, Christof
Institutions
Director training at Universität und Musikhochschule. Germany: Hamburg. 1988-1998. Lang.: Ger. 1658
Performance/production
Adaptations and performances of *Alte Meister (Old Masters)* by Thomas Bernhard. Germany. 1997-1998. Lang.: Ger. 1996

Nelson, John
Theory/criticism
Performers and conductors complain about unfair reviews. USA. 1998. Lang.: Eng. 4844

Nelson, Richard
Design/technology
Lighting design for Hwang's *Golden Child* at the Public Theatre. USA: New York, NY. 1996-1998. Lang.: Eng. 1540

Němcová, Božena
Performance/production
The adaptation of classic Czech works to the stage. Czech Republic: Prague, Brno. 1990-1998. Lang.: Cze. 1877

Németh, Mária
Performance/production
Soprano Mária Németh. Hungary. Austria: Vienna. 1898-1967. Lang.: Hun. 4615

Nemzeti Színház (Budapest)
Institutions
History of a period of renewal at the National Theatre. Hungary: Budapest. 1978-1982. Lang.: Hun. 364
The National Theatre's experiment in artistic renewal. Hungary: Budapest. 1979-1982. Lang.: Hun. 1672
Performance spaces
Ferenc Bán's architectural design for Hungary's new National Theatre. Hungary: Budapest. 1998. Lang.: Hun. 446
Account of the competition for the design of the new National Theatre. Hungary: Budapest. 1996-1997. Lang.: Hun. 448
Interview with architect Miklós Ölveczky about Hungary's new National Theatre. Hungary. Norway. 1998. Lang.: Hun. 449
Performance/production
László Márkus, one-time director of the Budapest Opera House. Hungary. 1881-1948. Lang.: Hun. 540
Reviews of new Hungarian musicals. Hungary: Budapest. 1997. Lang.: Hun. 4360

Nemzeti Színház (Miskolc)
SEE
Miskolci Nemzeti Színház.

Nemzeti Színház (Pécs)
SEE
Pécsi Nemzeti Színház.
Nemzeti Színház (Pest)
SEE
Pesti Nemzeti Színház.
Nemzeti Színház (Szeged)
SEE
Szegedi Nemzeti Színház.
Neo-Futurists (Chicago, IL)
Performance/production
Review of *Too Much Light Makes the Baby Go Blind* by the Neo-Futurists. USA: Chicago, IL. 1997. Lang.: Eng. 620
Neoclassicism
SEE ALSO
Geographical-Chronological Index under Europe 1540-1660, France 1629-1660, Italy 1540-1576.
Neptune Theatre (Halifax, NS)
Performance spaces
The renovation of Neptune Theatre. Canada: Halifax, NS. 1963-1998. Lang.: Eng. 1794
Plays/librettos/scripts
Analysis of *Corker* by Wendy Lill. Canada: Halifax, NS. 1994-1998. Lang.: Eng. 2836
Nerve Bible
Performance/production
Theoretical implications of Laurie Anderson's use of media technology. USA. 1995. Lang.: Eng. 4046
Nesbitt, Caroline
Performance/production
Actress Caroline Nesbitt on giving up her theatrical career. USA: New York, NY. 1998. Lang.: Eng. 2723
Nestroy, Johann
Plays/librettos/scripts
Recent productions directed by Frank Castorf. Austria: Vienna. 1998. Lang.: Ger. 2788
Nethersole, Olga
Performance/production
Attempted censorship of productions. USA. 1900-1905. Lang.: Eng. 2698
New York City's attempt to impose censorship on theatre productions. USA: New York, NY. 1900-1927. Lang.: Eng. 2699
Nettles, John
Performance/production
John Nettles on his role in an RSC production of *Julius Caesar*. UK-England: London, Stratford. 1995. Lang.: Eng. 2625
Neuenfels, Hans
Performance/production
Actress Ilse Ritter. Germany. 1944-1998. Lang.: Ger. 1980
Hans Neuenfels's production of Meyerbeer's *Le Prophète*. Austria: Vienna. 1998. Lang.: Swe. 4530
Reviews of recent opera productions. Switzerland: Basel. Germany: Stuttgart, Berlin, Hamburg. France: Strasbourg. 1997-1998. Lang.: Ger. 4702
Neues Schauspielhaus (Berlin)
Performance/production
Weber's *Der Freischütz* and the Neues Schauspielhaus. Germany: Berlin. 1821. Lang.: Eng. 4581
Neues Theater (Munich)
Institutions
Survey of Munich's theatre scene. Germany: Munich. 1997. Lang.: Ger. 1626
Neufeldt, P.A.
Performance/production
Collection of newspaper reviews by London theatre critics. UK-England: London. 1998. Lang.: Eng. 2547
Neuköllner Oper (Berlin)
Administration
The effects of independent theatre in Berlin. Germany: Berlin. 1998. Lang.: Ger. 14
Neumeier, John
Performance/production
Choreographer John Neumeier. Germany: Hamburg. USA: New York, NY. 1998. Lang.: Eng. 1082
Neureiter, Barbara
Institutions
Profile of Württembergische Landesbühne. Germany: Esslingen. 1996-1997. Lang.: Ger. 1639
Never Land
Performance/production
Collection of newspaper reviews by London theatre critics. UK-England: London. 1998. Lang.: Eng. 2569
Never the Sinner
Design/technology
Lighting design for *Never the Sinner* by John Logan, directed by Ethan McSweeney. USA: New York, NY. 1998. Lang.: Eng. 1534
Nevess remegve (Emlék) (Laugh Tremble—Memory)
Performance/production
Yvette Bozsik's *Nevess remegve (Emlék) (Laugh Tremble—Memory)* at Trafó. Hungary: Budapest. 1998. Lang.: Hun. 1293
Neville-Andrews, John
Design/technology
Set design for a University of Michigan production of *Henry V*. USA: Ann Arbor, MI. 1998. Lang.: Eng. 1557
New Amsterdam Theatre (New York, NY)
Administration
The Disney Corporation's Broadway musicals. USA: New York, NY. 1996-1998. Lang.: Eng. 4317
Design/technology
Donald Holder's lighting design for *The Lion King*. USA: New York, NY. 1997-1998. Lang.: Eng. 4336
Technical designs for the Broadway production of *The Lion King*. USA: New York, NY. 1998. Lang.: Eng. 4342
Performance spaces
Architectural critique of the restored New Amsterdam Theatre. USA: New York, NY. 1998. Lang.: Eng. 476
New Edna—The Spectacle
Performance/production
Collection of newspaper reviews by London theatre critics. UK-England: London. 1998. Lang.: Eng. 2462
New End Theatre (London)
Performance/production
Collection of newspaper reviews by London theatre critics. UK-England: London. 1998. Lang.: Eng. 2410
Collection of newspaper reviews by London theatre critics. UK-England: London. 1998. Lang.: Eng. 2415
Collection of newspaper reviews by London theatre critics. UK-England: London. 1998. Lang.: Eng. 2440
Collection of newspaper reviews by London theatre critics. UK-England: London. 1998. Lang.: Eng. 2449
Collection of newspaper reviews by London theatre critics. UK-England: London. 1998. Lang.: Eng. 2467
Collection of newspaper reviews by London theatre critics. UK-England: London. 1998. Lang.: Eng. 2479
Collection of newspaper reviews by London theatre critics. UK-England: London. 1998. Lang.: Eng. 2492
Collection of newspaper reviews by London theatre critics. UK-England: London. 1998. Lang.: Eng. 2503
Collection of newspaper reviews by London theatre critics. UK-England: London. 1998. Lang.: Eng. 2522
Collection of newspaper reviews by London theatre critics. UK-England: London. 1998. Lang.: Eng. 2541
Collection of newspaper reviews by London theatre critics. UK-England: London. 1998. Lang.: Eng. 2552
Collection of newspaper reviews by London theatre critics. UK-England: London. 1998. Lang.: Eng. 2568
Collection of newspaper reviews by London theatre critics. UK-England: London. 1998. Lang.: Eng. 2585
New England Marionettes (Boston, MA)
Performance/production
New England Marionettes' production of Mozart's *Die Zauberflöte*. USA: Boston, MA. 1998. Lang.: Eng. 4900
New Group (New York, NY)
Design/technology
Derek McLane's set designs for recent Off Broadway productions. USA: New York, NY. 1998. Lang.: Eng. 1538
New Haven Assembly Hall (New Haven, CT)
Institutions
Popular entertainment at the New Haven Assembly Hall and Columbian Museum and Gardens. USA: New Haven, CT. 1796-1820. Lang.: Eng. 394
New historicism
Relation to other fields
New-historicist analysis of Shakespeare and his time. England. 1580-1616. Lang.: Eng. 3745
Theory/criticism
New historicism and Shakespeare's *Measure for Measure*. 1988. Lang.: Eng. 3801

New Jersey Performing Arts Center (Newark, NJ)
Institutions
Financial and artistic success of Kennedy Center and New Jersey Performing Arts Center. USA: Washington, DC, Newark, NJ. 1971-1998. Lang.: Eng. 424
Performance spaces
Profile of the New Jersey Performing Arts Center. USA: Newark, NJ. 1988-1998. Lang.: Eng. 467
New Jersey Shakespeare Festival (Madison, NJ)
Institutions
Bonnie Monte of New Jersey Shakespeare Festival. USA: Madison, NJ. 1996-1998. Lang.: Eng. 1772
New Playwrights Theatre Company (New York, NY)
Institutions
The New Playwrights Theatre Company. USA: New York, NY. 1927-1929. Lang.: Eng. 410
New Shakespeare Society (London)
Plays/librettos/scripts
The New Shakespeare Society's unfinished four-text edition of *Hamlet*. UK-England. 1882-1883. Lang.: Eng. 3497
New Street Theatre (Birmingham)
Performance spaces
Conjectural reconstruction of the New Street Theatre. England: Birmingham. 1772-1902. Lang.: Eng. 1800
New Year
Performance/production
Interview with singer Krister St. Hill. Germany. Sweden. 1988-1998. Lang.: Swe. 4590
New York City Ballet (New York, NY)
Institutions
Peter Martins, artistic director of New York City Ballet. USA: New York, NY. 1983-1998. Lang.: Eng. 1057
The founding of the New York City Ballet. USA: New York, NY. 1947-1948. Lang.: Eng. 1060
Performance/production
Dancer Nichol Hlinka of New York City Ballet. USA: New York, NY. 1975-1998. Lang.: Eng. 1173
New male dancers of New York City Ballet. USA: New York, NY. 1998. Lang.: Eng. 1177
Dancer Albert Evans of New York City Ballet. USA: New York, NY. 1987-1998. Lang.: Eng. 1181
Ballerina Zippora Karz on dancing while suffering from diabetes. USA: New York, NY. 1983-1998. Lang.: Eng. 1183
New York City Opera (New York, NY)
Performance/production
Background material on telecast performance of Britten's *Paul Bunyan* at New York City Opera. USA: New York, NY. 1998. Lang.: Eng. 4710
Verdi's *Stiffelio* and Gounod's *Roméo et Juliette* in New York. USA: New York, NY. 1850-1998. Lang.: Eng. 4730
Operas by Benjamin Britten in the repertory of the Metropolitan and the New York City Opera. USA: New York, NY. 1945-1998. Lang.:Eng. 4749
New York Shakespeare Festival
SEE
Public Theatre (New York, NY).
New York Theatre Workshop (New York, NY)
Administration
The legal battle over copyright of the musical *Rent*. USA: New York, NY. 1998. Lang.: Eng. 4321
Performance/production
Analysis of recent New York productions. USA: New York, NY. 1997-1998. Lang.: Eng. 2759
Review of Jonathan Larson's musical *Rent*. USA: New York, NY. 1990. Lang.: Hun. 4375
Newberry Opera House (Newberry, SC)
Performance spaces
The newly renovated Newberry Opera House. USA: Newberry, SC. 1998. Lang.: Eng. 4501
Newell, Charles
Institutions
Charles Newell, artistic director of the Court Theatre. USA: Chicago, IL. 1998. Lang.: Eng. 1792
Newling, Caro
Institutions
Caro Newling, executive producer of Donmar Warehouse. UK-England: London. 1998. Lang.: Eng. 1742
Newson, Lloyd
Performance/production
Interview with Lloyd Newson of DV8 Physical Theatre. UK-England: London. 1995-1998. Lang.: Swe. 1313
Neždanova, Antonina V.
Relation to other fields
Postage stamps commemorating Russian theatre and opera. Russia: Moscow. 1998. Lang.: Rus. 762
Ngaahika Ndeenda
Plays/librettos/scripts
Playwright Ngugi wa Thiong'o and the Kamirithu theatre project. Kenya: Kamiriithu. 1979-1992. Lang.: Eng. 3266
Ngugi wa Thiong'o
Performance/production
Theatrical rebellion and sociopolitical chaos. Zimbabwe. Kenya. 1990-1998. Lang.: Eng. 687
Plays/librettos/scripts
Playwright Ngugi wa Thiong'o and the Kamirithu theatre project. Kenya: Kamiriithu. 1979-1992. Lang.: Eng. 3266
Niaoren (Bird Men)
Plays/librettos/scripts
The view of foreigners in *Niaoren (Bird Men)* by Guo Shixing. China, People's Republic of. 1991. Lang.: Eng. 2842
Niblo's Garden (New York, NY)
Performance spaces
Popular entertainment at Niblo's Garden. USA: New York, NY. 1828-1846. Lang.: Eng. 470
Niccodemi, Dario
Plays/librettos/scripts
Italian realist drama. Italy. 1860-1918. Lang.: Eng. 3260
Nicholas, Paul
Performance/production
Collection of newspaper reviews by London theatre critics. UK-England: London. 1998. Lang.: Eng. 2467
Nichols, Mike
Plays/librettos/scripts
Transvestism in contemporary film as the 'blackface' of the nineties. UK-England. USA. 1993-1996. Lang.: Eng. 3983
Nicholson, Norman
Plays/librettos/scripts
Analysis of plays based on the Hebrew prophets. USA. Europe. 1919-1970. Lang.: Eng. 3659
Nicholson, William
Performance/production
Collection of newspaper reviews by London theatre critics. UK-England. 1998. Lang.: Eng. 2510
Collection of newspaper reviews by London theatre critics. UK-England: London. 1998. Lang.: Eng. 2586
Plays/librettos/scripts
Richard Attenborough's film adaptation of *Shadowlands* by William Nicholson. UK-England. 1993. Lang.: Eng. 3985
Nicol, Graeme B.
Design/technology
Graeme Nicol's lighting design for pop music tours including *Lilith Fair*. USA. 1997-1998. Lang.: Eng. 4101
Graeme Nicol's lighting design for *Lilith Fair*. USA. 1998. Lang.: Eng. 4107
Nie Wieder Friede! (Never Again Peace!)
Plays/librettos/scripts
Analysis of revisions of plays by Ernst Toller. Germany. 1920-1939. Lang.: Eng. 3172
Nie-boska komedia (Un-Divine Comedy, The)
Plays/librettos/scripts
The Polish national style in Romantic dramas. Poland. 1832-1835. Lang.: Pol. 3304
Niedersächsische Staatstheater (Hannover)
Administration
Theatre directors on the future of subsidized theatre. Switzerland: Zurich. Germany: Hannover, Berlin. 1998. Lang.: Ger. 1390
Performance/production
Productions of new plays by Peter Handke and Katharine Gericke at Niedersächsische Staatstheater. Germany: Hannover. 1998. Lang.: Ger. 1983
Productions of Horváth's *Geschichten aus dem Wienerwald (Tales from the Vienna Woods)*. Germany: Hamburg, Hannover. Austria: Vienna. 1998. Lang.: Ger. 2003
Plays/librettos/scripts
Analysis of plays by Dea Loher, directed by Andreas Kriegenburg. Germany: Hannover. 1998. Lang.: Ger. 3130
Niedersächsische Staatstheater, Schauspiel (Hannover)
Performance/production
Actress Maike Bollow. Germany: Hannover. 1991-1998. Lang.: Ger. 2006

Nielsen, Benedikte Hammershøye
Plays/librettos/scripts
Dramaturgs on recognizing talented new playwrights. Denmark. 1998. Lang.: Dan. 2854
Niepel, Ulrich
Design/technology
Lighting for Henze's opera *Der Prinz von Homburg* at Deutsche Oper Berlin. Germany: Berlin. 1997. Lang.: Ger. 4431
Nigger, The
Plays/librettos/scripts
Miscegenation in American drama. USA. 1909-1969. Lang.: Eng. 3599
Niggli, Josefina
Plays/librettos/scripts
Analysis of *Soldadera* by Josefina Niggli. Mexico. 1938. Lang.: Eng. 3272
Night Larry Kramer Kissed Me, The
Plays/librettos/scripts
Effeminacy on the American stage. USA. 1920-1998. Lang.: Eng. 3682
Night of the Iguana, The
Plays/librettos/scripts
Analysis of plays by Tennessee Williams. USA. 1943-1970. Lang.: Eng. 3539
Realism and anti-realism in plays of Tennessee Williams. USA. 1945-1986. Lang.: Eng. 3626
Shame, puritanism, and sexuality in plays of Tennessee Williams. USA. 1950-1970. Lang.: Eng. 3701
Nikitin, V.N.
Relation to other fields
Plastic-cognitive therapy and the actor. 1998. Lang.: Rus. 713
Nikitskij Gate Theatre (Moscow)
SEE
Teat'r-studija u Nikitskich Vorot.
Nikolais, Alwin
Performance/production
The Murray Louis/Alwin Nikolais dance archive. USA: Athens, OH. 1950-1998. Lang.: Eng. 1331
Nikulin, Jurij
Performance/production
Memoirs of film actor and clown Jurij Nikulin. Russia: Moscow. 1998. Lang.: Rus. 4184
Nilsson, Hans
Institutions
The 225th anniversary of the Royal Swedish Ballet. Sweden: Stockholm. 1773-1998. Lang.: Eng. 1048
Nilsson, Magnus Thure
Institutions
Investing in culture in Malmö, formerly an industrial city. Sweden: Malmö. 1995-1998. Lang.: Swe. 1723
Nin, Caroline
Performance/production
Collection of newspaper reviews by London theatre critics. UK-England: London. 1998. Lang.: Eng. 2487
Ninagawa, Yukio
Performance/production
Collection of newspaper reviews by London theatre critics. UK-England: London. 1998. Lang.: Eng. 2484
Nine
Plays/librettos/scripts
Arthur Kopit's *Nine*, a musical adaptation of Fellini's *8 1/2*. USA. 1963-1982. Lang.: Eng. 4401
Nine Lives, Ten Tales
Performance/production
Collection of newspaper reviews by London theatre critics. UK-England: London. 1998. Lang.: Eng. 2446
Niño, Jairo Aníbal
Plays/librettos/scripts
New Theatre of Buenaventura, Reyes, and Niño. Colombia. 1950-1985. Lang.: Spa. 2846
Nioradze, Irma
Performance/production
Irma Nioradze in a performance of *Don Quixote* choreographed by Marius Petipa. Hungary: Budapest. 1998. Lang.: Hun. 1093
Nisi, Giorgio
Design/technology
Sound system used in a soccer stadium for an operatic production. Italy: Rome. 1998. Lang.: Eng. 4434
Nitsch, Hermann
Performance/production
The performance of sacrifice on stage. France. Germany. 1900-1998. Lang.: Ger. 530
Performance artists Vito Acconci and Hermann Nitsch. Austria: Vienna. Italy. 1960-1977. Lang.: Eng. 4239
Nixon, David
Institutions
Profile of BalletMet. USA: Columbus, OH. 1978-1998. Lang.: Eng. 1062
Nižinskij, Vaclav Fomič
Performance/production
The performance of sacrifice on stage. France. Germany. 1900-1998. Lang.: Ger. 530
Masculinity in ballet. France: Paris. 1908-1915. Lang.: Eng. 1070
Lilla Pártay's *Meztelen rózsa (Naked Rose)*, a ballet based on the life of Nižinskij. Hungary: Budapest. 1998. Lang.: Hun. 1110
The artistic life of dancer Vaclav Nižinskij. Poland. Russia. France. 1881-1953. Lang.: Pol. 1123
Miklós Hubay's *Hová lett a rózsa lelke? (What Has Become of the Spirit of the Rose?)* directed by György Lengyel. Hungary: Debrecen. 1998. Lang.: Hun. 2150
Nō
SEE ALSO
Classed Entries under DANCE-DRAMA—*Nō*.
Performance/production
Cinematic work of director Robert Lepage. Canada. 1995-1998. Lang.: Fre. 3928
Plays/librettos/scripts
Yeats and the influence of *nō*. Ireland. 1914-1939. Lang.: Eng. 3213
William Butler Yeats, *japonisme*, and *nō*. UK-England. 1853-1939. Lang.: Eng. 3435
Reference materials
History of Japanese theatre and drama. Japan. 350 B.C.-1998 A.D. Lang.: Ita. 705
Relation to other fields
Therapeutic *nō* theatre for the mentally retarded. USA. 1998. Lang.: Eng. 798
No Man's Land
Plays/librettos/scripts
Female presence/absence in plays of O'Neill, Pinter, and Shepard. USA. UK-England. 1936-1985. Lang.: Eng. 3607
No Place Like Home
Plays/librettos/scripts
The development of playwright Owen Davis. USA. 1905-1923. Lang.: Eng. 3526
No Way to Treat a Lady
Performance/production
Collection of newspaper reviews by London theatre critics. UK-England: London. 1998. Lang.: Eng. 2479
Noack, Klaus
Design/technology
Scenographer and now director Klaus Noack. Germany. 1953. Lang.: Ger. 190
Noam Chomsky Lectures, The
Plays/librettos/scripts
Analysis of *The Noam Chomsky Lectures* by Daniel Brooks and Guillermo Verdecchio. Canada: Toronto, ON. 1990-1991. Lang.: Eng. 2797
Nobbs, David
Performance/production
Michael Birch's production of *Vanity Fair*. UK-England: Leeds. 1997. Lang.: Eng. 2600
Nobbs, John
Performance/production
The training of actors in Asian performance styles. Australia: Brisbane. 1992-1998. Lang.: Eng. 1817
Noble, Adrian
Design/technology
Lighting designer Hugh Vanstone. USA: New York, NY. 1998. Lang.: Eng. 1554
Performance/production
Collection of newspaper reviews by London theatre critics. UK-England: Stratford. 1998. Lang.: Eng. 2431
Collection of newspaper reviews by London theatre critics. UK-England: Stratford. 1998. Lang.: Eng. 2519
The future of English repertory companies. UK-England: London. 1998. Lang.: Eng. 2563
Collection of newspaper reviews by London theatre critics. UK-England: London. 1998. Lang.: Eng. 2571
Julian Glover on his performance in *Romeo and Juliet* for RSC. UK-England: London, Stratford. 1995-1996. Lang.: Eng. 2606

Noble, Adrian — cont'd

Derek Jacobi on playing Macbeth for the RSC. UK-England: London, Stratford. 1993-1994. Lang.: Eng. 2616

Richard McCabe on his role in *The Winter's Tale* at RSC. UK-England: London, Stratford. 1992-1993. Lang.: Eng. 2623

Nočs pered sudom (Night Before Trial, The)
Basic theatrical documents
Catalan translations of the complete plays of Anton Čechov. Russia. 1884-1904. Lang.: Cat. 1449

Noël, Philippe
Basic theatrical documents
French translation of *My Left Breast* by Susan Miller. USA. France. 1994-1998. Lang.: Fre. 1498

Noh, Caroline
Performance/production
Collection of newspaper reviews by London theatre critics. UK-England: London. 1998. Lang.: Eng. 2581

Nolan, Vicki
Administration
Interviews with women in top management of theatres. USA: New Haven, CT, Seattle, WA, East Haddam, CT. 1998. Lang.: Eng. 1397

Nolan, Yvette
Plays/librettos/scripts
Dramaturg's experience working on a play by Yvette Nolan. Canada. 1997-1998. Lang.: Eng. 2827

Nolte, Stefan
Performance/production
A production of Offenbach's *Orphée aux Enfers* directed by Jens Mehrle and Stefan Nolte. Germany: Bitterfeld. 1998. Lang.: Ger. 4856

Nom d'Oedipe, Le (Name of Oedipus, The)
Plays/librettos/scripts
Bisexuality in *Le Nom d'Oedipe (The Name of Oedipus)* by Hélène Cixous. France. 1978. Lang.: Eng. 3089

Nomai
Performance/production
Nomai dance drama. Japan. 1650-1985. Lang.: Eng. 1350

Nombres, Les (Numbers, The)
Plays/librettos/scripts
Analysis of *Les Nombres (The Numbers)* by Andrée Chedid. France. 1965. Lang.: Eng. 3090

Non si sa come (How Is Unknown)
Performance/production
Gabriele Lavia's production of *Non si sa come (How Is Unknown)* by Luigi Pirandello. Italy: Turin. 1982-1988. Lang.: Ita. 2157
Plays/librettos/scripts
Letters of Pirandello, Moissiu, and Jahn. Italy. Austria: Vienna. 1934. Lang.: Ita. 3219

Nono, Luigi
Performance/production
Review of opera productions. Germany: Stuttgart, Leipzig. 1998. Lang.: Ger. 4584

Noone, James
Design/technology
Scene designer James Noone's work at Playwrights Horizons. USA: New York, NY. 1986-1998. Lang.: Eng. 1531

Nørby, Ghita
Performance/production
Actress Ghita Nørby on adapting to various performance spaces. Denmark. 1970-1998. Lang.: Dan. 1889

Nordey, Stanislas
Institutions
Profile of Théâtre Gérard-Philippe. France: Paris. 1998. Lang.: Ger. 1617
Performance/production
Comparison of text-based and visual productions. France. 1998. Lang.: Fre. 1939

Nordhessisches Landestheater Marburg
Institutions
Profile of Nordhessisches Landestheater Marburg. Germany: Marburg. 1997-1998. Lang.: Ger. 1653

Nordin, Lena
Performance/production
Interview with soprano Lena Nordin. Sweden: Stockholm. 1982-1998. Lang.: Swe. 4697

Nordisk TeaterTeknik (NoTT)
Design/technology
Survey of NoTT98 at Oslo. Norway: Oslo. 1998. Lang.: Nor. 210

The combined conference and fair, Nordisk TeaterTeknik (NoTT). Sweden: Stockholm, Gothenburg. 1983-1998. Lang.: Swe. 227

Nordström, Anders
Institutions
The 225th anniversary of the Royal Swedish Ballet. Sweden: Stockholm. 1773-1998. Lang.: Eng. 1048

Nordström, Rolf
Performance/production
Seven critics on their favorite character or portrayal. Sweden. 1950. Lang.: Swe. 2369

Norén, Lars
Audience
Reactions to Norén's *Personkrets 3:1 (Circle 3:1)* at Dramaten. Sweden: Stockholm. 1998. Lang.: Swe. 1405
Performance/production
Interview with actress Anna Pettersson. Sweden: Stockholm. 1988-1998. Lang.: Swe. 2371

Dr. Kokos Kärlekslaboratorium (Dr. Koko's Laboratory of Love) at Backstage, Stockholms Stadsteater. Sweden: Stockholm. 1998. Lang.: Swe. 2378

Interview with actor/director Stefan Larsson. Sweden: Stockholm. 1984-1998. Lang.: Swe. 2382
Plays/librettos/scripts
Lars Norén's *Och ge oss skuggorna (And Give Us the Shadows)*. Sweden. 1980-1998. Lang.: Swe. 3413

Norma
Performance/production
Interview with soprano Lena Nordin. Sweden: Stockholm. 1982-1998. Lang.: Swe. 4697
Plays/librettos/scripts
Gender in Bellini's *Norma* and Verdi's *Aida*. Italy. 1831-1871. Lang.: Eng. 4813

Normal Heart, The
Performance/production
Collection of newspaper reviews by London theatre critics. UK-England: London. 1998. Lang.: Eng. 2437

Normal, Henry
Performance/production
Collection of newspaper reviews by London theatre critics. UK-England: London. 1998. Lang.: Eng. 2513

Norman, Marsha
Performance/production
Collection of newspaper reviews by London theatre critics. UK-England: London. 1998. Lang.: Eng. 2498

Norodom Sihanouk
Plays/librettos/scripts
Postcolonialism, ethnicity, and feminism in French and Caribbean plays. France. Martinique. Guadeloupe. 1960-1990. Lang.: Eng. 3104

Norris, Maggie
Performance/production
Collection of newspaper reviews by London theatre critics. UK-England: London. 1998. Lang.: Eng. 2440

Norris, Rufus
Performance/production
Collection of newspaper reviews by London theatre critics. UK-England: London. 1998. Lang.: Eng. 2549

Norrlandsoperan (Umeå)
Institutions
Problems of administration at Norrlandsoperan. Sweden: Umeå. 1998. Lang.: Swe. 4473

Norske Opera (Oslo)
Institutions
Interview with Bjørn Simensen, director of Den Norske Opera. Norway: Oslo. 1998. Lang.: Swe. 4465

North, Howard
Performance/production
Collection of newspaper reviews by London theatre critics. UK-England: London. 1998. Lang.: Eng. 2557

North, Robert
Performance/production
New productions of Győri Balett. Hungary: Budapest. 1998. Lang.: Hun. 1095

Norton, Thomas
Performance/production
Music in Tudor drama. England. 1497-1569. Lang.: Eng. 1902

Not About Nightingales
Design/technology
Set design for Tennessee Williams' *Not About Nightingales* at the National. UK-England: London. 1998. Lang.: Eng. 1526
Performance/production
Collection of newspaper reviews by London theatre critics. UK-England: London. 1998. Lang.: Eng. 2435

***Not About Nightingales* — cont'd**

Trevor Nunn's production of *Not About Nightingales* by Tennessee Williams, Royal National Theatre. UK-England: London. 1998. Lang.: Swe. 2604

Trevor Nunn's production of *Not About Nightingales* by Tennessee Williams, Alley Theatre. USA: Houston, TX. 1998. Lang.: Eng. 2729

Not I

Plays/librettos/scripts

The devouring woman in plays of Racine, Kleist, Ibsen, and Beckett. Europe. 1760-1992. Lang.: Eng. 3058

The influence Dryden and Johnson's theories on self-translated works of Samuel Beckett. France. Ireland. 1957-1976. Lang.: Eng. 3077

The speaking subject in plays of Beckett and Stoppard. France. Ireland. UK-England. 1945-1998. Lang.: Ger. 3098

Analysis of Samuel Beckett's later plays. Ireland. France. 1950-1989. Lang.: Eng. 3210

Not Not Not Not Enough Oxygen

Plays/librettos/scripts

Ecology and the plays of Caryl Churchill. UK-England. 1971-1989. Lang.: Eng. 3422

Not with My Gun

Relation to other fields

Topics in post-apartheid South African literature and theatre. South Africa, Republic of. 1995-1998. Lang.: Eng. 764

Not-About-AIDS-Dance

Performance/production

Analysis of dance trilogy by choreographer Neil Greenberg. USA. 1994-1998. Lang.: Eng. 1334

Notebooks of a Cameraman, Serafino Gubbio

SEE

Quaderni di Serafino Gubbio operatore.

Notorious Mrs. Ebbsmith, The

Plays/librettos/scripts

Analysis of plays by Arthur Wing Pinero. UK-England. 1890-1910. Lang.: Eng. 3440

Nouvelle Compagnie Théâtrale (Montreal, PQ)

Performance/production

Productions of plays by Bernard-Marie Koltès. Canada: Montreal, PQ. 1991-1997. Lang.: Fre. 1862

Novák, Eszter

Performance/production

Interview with directors Gábor Székely and Eszter Novák. Hungary: Budapest. 1998. Lang.: Hun. 2128

Two Hungarian productions of *Die Dreigroschenoper (The Three Penny Opera)*. Hungary: Budapest, Szeged. 1998. Lang.: Hun. 4362

Novák, Ferenc

Institutions

Work of Honvéd Táncszínház under the direction of Ferenc Novák. Hungary. 1998. Lang.: Hun. 1219

Performance/production

Modern tendencies in Hungarian folk dance. Hungary. 1970-1977. Lang.: Hun. 1228

Novarina, Valère

Plays/librettos/scripts

On translating into German the plays of Valère Novarina. France. Germany. 1947-1998. Lang.: Ger. 3122

Novosadsko Pozorište (Novi Sad)

SEE

Újvidéki Színház.

Nowra, Louis

Plays/librettos/scripts

Australian plays about the war in Vietnam. Australia. 1990-1998. Lang.: Eng. 2776

Nozze di Figaro, Le

Performance/production

Mozart's operas and contemporary Viennese performance spaces. Austria: Vienna. 1782-1791. Lang.: Eng. 4528

Opera productions of the Salzburg Festival. Austria: Salzburg. 1998. Lang.: Hun. 4531

Mozart's *Le Nozze di Figaro* at the Hungarian State Opera House. Hungary: Budapest. 1998. Lang.: Hun. 4638

Background material on Lyric Opera of Chicago radio broadcast performances. USA: Chicago, IL. 1998. Lang.: Eng. 4709

Background material on Metropolitan Opera radio broadcast performances. USA: New York, NY. 1998. Lang.: Eng. 4716

Plays/librettos/scripts

Operatic realizations of Beaumarchais' character Rosina. Europe. North America. 1784-1991. Lang.: Eng. 4773

Nuit de Valognes, La (Night of Valognes, The)

Theory/criticism

Analysis of plays by Eric-Emmanuel Schmitt. France. 1998. Lang.: Fin. 3819

Nuit juste avant les forêts, La (Dark Just Before the Forests, The)

Basic theatrical documents

Catalan translation of *La Nuit juste avant les forêts (The Dark Just Before the Forests)* by Bernard-Marie Koltès. France. 1977. Lang.: Cat. 1428

Nunn, Trevor

Design/technology

Set design for Tennessee Williams' *Not About Nightingales* at the National. UK-England: London. 1998. Lang.: Eng. 1526

Performance/production

Collection of newspaper reviews by London theatre critics. UK-England: London. 1998. Lang.: Eng. 2435

Collection of newspaper reviews by London theatre critics. UK-England: London. 1998. Lang.: Eng. 2466

Collection of newspaper reviews by London theatre critics. UK-England: London. 1998. Lang.: Eng. 2474

Collection of newspaper reviews by London theatre critics. UK-England: London. 1998. Lang.: Eng. 2546

Collection of newspaper reviews by London theatre critics. UK-England: London. 1998. Lang.: Eng. 2555

Trevor Nunn's production of *Not About Nightingales* by Tennessee Williams, Royal National Theatre. UK-England: London. 1998. Lang.: Swe. 2604

Trevor Nunn's production of *An Enemy of the People* by Ibsen. UK-England: London. 1998. Lang.: Eng. 2627

Trevor Nunn's production of *Not About Nightingales* by Tennessee Williams, Alley Theatre. USA: Houston, TX. 1998. Lang.: Eng. 2729

The success of a revival of *Oklahoma!* at the Olivier. UK-England: London. 1998. Lang.: Eng. 4373

Nuovo Piccolo (Milan)

Performance spaces

The opening of Nuovo Piccolo in honor of the late director Giorgio Strehler. Italy: Milan. 1998. Lang.: Eng. 1802

Nur du (Only You)

Performance/production

Analysis of *Nur du (Only You)* by choreographer Pina Bausch. Germany: Wuppertal. 1997. Lang.: Eng. 1278

Nureyev, Rudolf

Performance/production

Nureyev's *Swan Lake* at Staatsoper. Austria: Vienna. 1998. Lang.: Hun. 1064

Dancer Rudolf Nureyev. France. 1938-1993. Lang.: Rus. 1080

Russian émigré ballet dancers. Russia: St. Petersburg. Lang.: Rus. 1129

Autobiography of ballet dancer and choreographer Rudolf Nureyev. Russia. Lang.: Rus. 1144

Recollections of ballerina Margot Fonteyn. USA. Panama. 1946-1998. Lang.: Eng. 1182

Nutcracker, The

SEE

Ščelkunčik.

Nya vänner och älskare (New Friends and Lovers)

Plays/librettos/scripts

Interview with playwright Sofia Fredén. Sweden: Stockholm. Denmark: Copenhagen. 1995-1998. Lang.: Swe. 3409

Nye Carte Blanche (Bergen)

Institutions

Profile of dance company Nye Carte Blanche. Norway: Bergen. 1990-1998. Lang.: Swe. 1251

O vrede tabaka (On the Harmfulness of Tobacco)

Basic theatrical documents

Catalan translations of the complete plays of Anton Čechov. Russia. 1884-1904. Lang.: Cat. 1449

Performance/production

One-act plays of Čechov by the Illyés Gyula National Theatre. Hungary. Ukraine: Beregovo. 1997. Lang.: Hun. 2104

O'Brien, Jack

Design/technology

Lighting designer Kenneth Posner. USA. 1998. Lang.: Eng. 1545

O'Connor, Francis

Design/technology

Set designs of Francis O'Connor. USA: New York, NY. 1998. Lang.: Eng. 1541

O'Darkney, George
Performance/production
Premieres of new plays. Austria: Vienna. 1998. Lang.: Ger. 1820
O'Flaherty, V.C.
Plays/librettos/scripts
Rhetorical arguments in one-act plays of Shaw. UK-England. 1890-1945. Lang.: Eng. 3453
O'Gorman, Mick
Design/technology
Mick O'Gorman's sound design and equipment for *Riverdance*. Ireland. 1998. Lang.: Eng. 1218
O'Hara, Kane
Plays/librettos/scripts
Music and the ballad opera in English popular theatre. England. 1728-1780. Lang.: Eng. 4390
O'Hara, Robert
Basic theatrical documents
Text of *Insurrection: Holding History* by Robert O'Hara. USA. 1998. Lang.: Eng. 1500
O'Neil, Nance
Relation to other fields
Actress Nance O'Neil and her friendship with Lizzie Borden. USA. 1874-1965. Lang.: Eng. 799
O'Neil, Sean
Performance/production
Collection of newspaper reviews by London theatre critics. UK-England: London. 1998. Lang.: Eng. 2566
O'Neill, Eugene
Basic theatrical documents
Russian translations of plays by Nobel Prize winners. Italy. 1848-1998. Lang.: Rus. 1446
Design/technology
Set design for Chain Lightning Theatre's production of *Beyond the Horizon* by Eugene O'Neill. USA: New York, NY. 1998. Lang.: Eng. 1551
Institutions
Impressions from the 'Golden Mask' festival. Russia: Minusinsk. 1998. Lang.: Ger. 1701
Report on the Stockholm theatre festival. Sweden: Stockholm. 1998. Lang.: Eng. 1724
Interview with Kricker James and Claire Higgins of Chain Lightning Theatre. USA: New York, NY. 1991-1998. Lang.: Eng. 1780
Performance/production
Recent productions in Ireland of plays by Eugene O'Neill. Ireland: Dublin. UK-Ireland: Belfast. 1989-1998. Lang.: Eng. 2154
Luca Ronconi's production of *Mourning Becomes Electra* by Eugene O'Neill. Italy: Rome. 1996-1997. Lang.: Eng. 2183
Interview with actor Dan Ekborg. Sweden: Stockholm. 1998. Lang.: Swe. 2367
Photos of rehearsals of O'Neill's *Long Day's Journey Into Night* at Dramaten. Sweden: Stockholm. 1998. Lang.: Swe. 2391
Collection of newspaper reviews by London theatre critics. UK-England: London. 1998. Lang.: Eng. 2459
Collection of newspaper reviews by London theatre critics. UK-England: London. 1998. Lang.: Eng. 2476
Collection of newspaper reviews by London theatre critics. UK-Scotland: Edinburgh. 1998. Lang.: Eng. 2650
A rare production of Eugene O'Neill's *Lazarus Laughed*. USA: Detroit, MI. 1963. Lang.: Eng. 2673
Tribute to late director José Quintero. USA. 1924-1998. Lang.: Eng. 2683
Resistance to a Boston production of Eugene O'Neill's *Strange Interlude*. USA: Boston, MA. 1929. Lang.: Eng. 2693
An approach to playing Jamie in O'Neill's *Long Day's Journey Into Night*. USA. 1987. Lang.: Eng. 2697
Julyana Soelistyo and Sam Trammel, winners of the Derwent Award. USA: New York, NY. 1998. Lang.: Eng. 2719
Notable productions of plays by Eugene O'Neill. USA. 1916-1996. Lang.: Eng. 2752
Aleksand'r Tairov's productions of plays by Eugene O'Neill. USSR. 1926-1929. Lang.: Eng. 2769
Plays/librettos/scripts
The Orestes myth in twentieth-century drama. Europe. USA. 1914-1943. Lang.: Eng. 3052
English-language plays on the Dutch and Flemish stage. Netherlands. 1920-1998. Lang.: Dut. 3278
Lars Norén's *Och ge oss skuggorna (And Give Us the Shadows)*. Sweden. 1980-1998. Lang.: Swe. 3413
George Bernard Shaw: life, work, influences. UK-England. Ireland. 1886-1955. Lang.: Eng. 3437
Irish folklore in plays of Eugene O'Neill. USA. 1942-1956. Lang.: Eng. 3522
Female characters in Eugene O'Neill's plays. USA. 1920-1953. Lang.: Eng. 3525
The late plays of Eugene O'Neill. USA. 1939-1943. Lang.: Eng. 3528
Analysis of *Hughie* by Eugene O'Neill. USA. 1959. Lang.: Eng. 3529
Details of the personal life of playwright Eugene O'Neill. USA. 1911-1956. Lang.: Eng. 3533
The early life of playwright Eugene O'Neill. USA. 1888-1953. Lang.: Eng. 3534
A method of analysis for the drama. USA. 1920-1975. Lang.: Eng. 3537
The unseen character in plays of O'Neill, Albee, and Tennessee Williams. USA. 1915-1995. Lang.: Eng. 3538
Analysis of Eugene O'Neill's *Strange Interlude*. USA. 1926-1927. Lang.: Dut. 3551
Eugene O'Neill and the creation of autobiographical drama. USA. 1940-1995. Lang.: Eng. 3561
Existential analysis of Eugene O'Neill's *Anna Christie*. USA. 1921. Lang.: Eng. 3562
Reports of playwright Eugene O'Neill's ghost haunting a Boston University building. USA: Boston, MA. 1998. Lang.: Eng. 3587
Eugene O'Neill's unfinished *A Tale of Possessors Self-Dispossessed*. USA. 1945-1953. Lang.: Eng. 3594
The posthumous publication of Eugene O'Neill's unfinished *More Stately Mansions*. USA. 1957-1964. Lang.: Eng. 3596
Eugene O'Neill's biographer on some difficulties of her work. USA. 1954-1962. Lang.: Eng. 3597
Miscegenation in American drama. USA. 1909-1969. Lang.: Eng. 3599
Female presence/absence in plays of O'Neill, Pinter, and Shepard. USA. UK-England. 1936-1985. Lang.: Eng. 3607
Race and gender in *The Great God Brown* by Eugene O'Neill. USA. 1926. Lang.: Eng. 3608
The Iceman Cometh by Eugene O'Neill compared to a short story by Ernest Hemingway. USA. 1939-1946. Lang.: Eng. 3609
Analysis of *Days Without End* by Eugene O'Neill. USA. 1934. Lang.: Eng. 3636
Historical and cultural context of Eugene O'Neill. USA. 1888-1953. Lang.: Eng. 3638
The 'greatness' of *Long Day's Journey Into Night* by Eugene O'Neill. USA. 1956. Lang.: Eng. 3639
Influence of the novelistic monologues of Eugene O'Neill. USA. 1911-1998. Lang.: Eng. 3641
Eugene O'Neill's *Strange Interlude* and the interwar period. USA. 1917-1940. Lang.: Eng. 3654
Eugene O'Neill's *The Hairy Ape* and the belief in racial degeneration. USA. 1922. Lang.: Eng. 3657
Death in the plays of Eugene O'Neill. USA. 1914-1950. Lang.: Eng. 3663
The return of the prodigal in American drama. USA. 1920-1985. Lang.: Eng. 3666
Themes of Eugene O'Neill's early plays. USA. 1915-1925. Lang.: Eng. 3668
Analysis of Eugene O'Neill's 'middle period' plays. USA. 1925-1938. Lang.: Eng. 3675
Effeminacy on the American stage. USA. 1920-1998. Lang.: Eng. 3682
African- and Irish-Americans in the plays of Eugene O'Neill. USA. 1916-1953. Lang.: Eng. 3687
Intellectual and artistic influences on playwright Eugene O'Neill. USA. 1888-1953. Lang.: Eng. 3697
Closure in plays of Eugene O'Neill. USA. 1918-1950. Lang.: Eng. 3703
Playwright Eugene O'Neill's theatrical milieu. USA. 1888-1953. Lang.: Eng. 3706
Playwright Eugene O'Neill and the dramatic 'canon'. USA. 1997. Lang.: Eng. 3710
Film and video productions of plays by Eugene O'Neill. USA. 1935-1988. Lang.: Eng. 4078

O'Neill, Eugene — cont'd
Marvin David Levy's operatic adaptation of *Mourning Becomes Electra* by Eugene O'Neill. USA. 1931-1998. Lang.: Eng. 4827
Theory/criticism
Critical response to plays of Eugene O'Neill. USA. 1930-1997. Lang.: Eng. 3837
Summary of Eugene O'Neill criticism. USA. 1997. Lang.: Eng. 3845
O'Neill, James
Plays/librettos/scripts
Playwright Eugene O'Neill's theatrical milieu. USA. 1888-1953. Lang.: Eng. 3706
O'Neill, Kitt
Performance/production
Collection of newspaper reviews by London theatre critics. UK-England: London. 1998. Lang.: Eng. 2546
O'Reilly, Kaite
Performance/production
Collection of newspaper reviews by London theatre critics. UK-England: London. 1998. Lang.: Eng. 2515
O'Reilly, Mary
Plays/librettos/scripts
Dramatic adaptations of Henry Wadsworth Longfellow's poem *Evangeline.* USA. Canada. 1860-1976. Lang.: Eng. 3643
O'Sullivan, Maureen
Performance/production
Obituary for actress Maureen O'Sullivan. USA. 1911-1998. Lang.: Eng. 3947
Oates, Joyce Carol
Performance/production
Novelist Joyce Carol Oates' reaction to Berg's *Wozzeck* at the Metropolitan Opera. USA: New York, NY. 1997. Lang.: Eng. 4718
Ọba Kó So (King Did Not Hang, The)
Plays/librettos/scripts
Representation of character in plays by Duro Ladipọ. Nigeria. 1964-1970. Lang.: Eng. 3285
Ọbàtálá
Plays/librettos/scripts
Representation of character in plays by Duro Ladipọ. Nigeria. 1964-1970. Lang.: Eng. 3285
Oberg, Richard
Performance/production
Collection of newspaper reviews by London theatre critics. UK-England: London. 1998. Lang.: Eng. 2549
Oberon
Plays/librettos/scripts
Political tensions reflected in Ben Jonson's masque *Oberon.* England. 1611. Lang.: Eng. 4203
Royal policy, subversion, and Ben Jonson's *Oberon.* England. 1611. Lang.: Eng. 4204
Oblastnoj Dramatičeskij Teat'r im. M.S. Ščepkina (Belgorod)
Performance/production
Michajl Mokejév's production of Shakespeare's *Romeo and Juliet.* Russia: Belgorod. 1998. Lang.: Rus. 2274
Obraztsov Puppet Theatre
SEE
Gosudarstvénnyj Central'nyj Teat'r Kukol.
Obručinie v monastïre
Performance/production
Guest performances of the Kirov Opera at the Metropolitan.. USA: New York, NY. 1998. Lang.: Eng. 4731
Obsodili so Kristusa (They Condemned Christ)
Basic theatrical documents
Text of plays by Branko Rozman. Slovenia. 1990-1997. Lang.: Slo. 1461
Óbudai Kisfaludy Színház (Budapest)
Institutions
History of the Óbudai Kisfaludy Színház. Hungary: Budapest. 1892-1946. Lang.: Hun. 356
Och ge oss skuggorna (And Give Us the Shadows)
Plays/librettos/scripts
Lars Norén's *Och ge oss skuggorna (And Give Us the Shadows).* Sweden. 1980-1998. Lang.: Swe. 3413
Ochaim, Brygida
Performance/production
Dancer and choreographer Brygida Ochaim. Germany. France. 1970-1998. Lang.: Ger. 1283
Octoroon, The
Performance/production
Boucicault's *The Octoroon* and the performance of race, gender, and power. USA. 1800-1860. Lang.: Eng. 669
Ocvirk, Vasja
Plays/librettos/scripts
The individual and his world in Slovene theatre. Slovenia. 1943-1985. Lang.: Slo. 3347
Odd Couple, The
Performance/production
Collection of newspaper reviews by London theatre critics. UK-England: London. 1998. Lang.: Eng. 2491
Odéon (Paris)
SEE
Théâtre National de l'Odéon.
Odin Teatret (Holstebro)
Performance/production
Eugenio Barba's *Oxyrhyncus Evangeliet*, Odin Teatret. USA. 1988. Lang.: Eng. 646
Acting and directing influences on Eugenio Barba. Denmark: Holstebro. 1997. Lang.: Eng. 1886
Odissi
Performance/production
Obituary for dancer Sanjukta Panigrahi. India. 1944-1997. Lang.: Eng. 1230
Oedipus
Plays/librettos/scripts
Analysis of Seneca's *Oedipus* and *Hercules furens.* Roman Empire. 4 B. C.-65 A.D. Lang.: Eng. 3313
Oedipus the King by Sophocles
SEE
Oidípous Týrannos.
Oehme, Ralph
Institutions
Contemporary drama at Schauspiel Leipzig. Germany: Leipzig. 1998. Lang.: Ger. 1661
Oei, Angelike
Performance/production
The body and personality of the dancer as the source of the physical vocabulary of dance. Europe. 1989. Lang.: Eng. 1269
Of Blessed Memory
Performance/production
Collection of newspaper reviews by London theatre critics. UK-England: London. 1998. Lang.: Eng. 2587
Off Broadway theatre
Administration
Report on Equity's Off-Broadway contract agreement. USA. 1998. Lang.: Eng. 60
Design/technology
Lighting designer Kevin Adams. USA. 1979-1998. Lang.: Eng. 258
Costume designer Jeanne Button. USA. 1965-1998. Lang.: Eng. 260
Derek McLane's set designs for recent Off Broadway productions. USA: New York, NY. 1998. Lang.: Eng. 1538
Technical designs for Off Broadway Shakespearean productions. USA: New York, NY. 1998. Lang.: Eng. 1539
Lighting designer Kenneth Posner. USA. 1998. Lang.: Eng. 1545
Performance spaces
Theatre space and performance. USA: New York, NY. 1925-1985. Lang.: Eng. 464
Performance/production
German impressions of recent New York theatre. USA: New York, NY. 1998. Lang.: Ger. 655
Musical performances on and off Broadway. USA: New York. 1998. Lang.: Ger. 4383
Plays/librettos/scripts
Revolutionary Off Broadway playwriting. USA: New York, NY. 1959-1969. Lang.: Eng. 3604
Relation to other fields
Interactions between commercial and not-for-profit theatre. USA. 1998. Lang.: Eng. 3785
Theory/criticism
Obituary for critic Ross Wetzstoen, who inspired the Obie Awards. USA. 1932-1998. Lang.: Eng. 3847
Off the Road
Performance/production
Collection of newspaper reviews by London theatre critics. UK-England: London. 1998. Lang.: Eng. 2475
Off-off Broadway theatre
Design/technology
Set design for Chain Lightning Theatre's production of *Beyond the Horizon* by Eugene O'Neill. USA: New York, NY. 1998. Lang.: Eng. 1551

Off-off Broadway theatre — cont'd

Institutions
Producer Joseph Cino and Off-off Broadway theatre. USA: New York, NY. 1931-1967. Lang.: Eng. 404
Ellen Stewart and La MaMa Experimental Theatre Club. USA: New York, NY. 1961-1985. Lang.: Eng. 1762
Performance spaces
Theatre space and performance. USA: New York, NY. 1925-1985. Lang.: Eng. 464
Performance/production
German impressions of recent New York theatre. USA: New York, NY. 1998. Lang.: Ger. 655

Offenbach, Jacques
Basic theatrical documents
Text of Offenbach's *Orphée aux Enfers*. France. 1874. Lang.: Fre. 4418
Performance/production
Discography of Offenbach's *Orphée aux Enfers*. 1953-1997. Lang.: Fre. 4511
Productions of Offenbach's *Orphée aux Enfers*. 1858-1997. Lang.: Fre. 4516
Press reactions to productions of Offenbach's *Orphée aux Enfers*. Belgium. Switzerland. France. 1997. Lang.: Fre. 4535
Chronology of the life of composer Jacques Offenbach. France. 1819-1880. Lang.: Fre. 4561
Offenbach's *Orphée aux Enfers* from two acts to four. France. 1858-1874. Lang.: Fre. 4571
Reviews of recent opera productions. Switzerland: Basel. Germany: Stuttgart, Berlin, Hamburg. France: Strasbourg. 1997-1998. Lang.: Ger. 4702
Background material on Metropolitan Opera radio broadcast performances. USA: New York, NY. 1998. Lang.: Eng. 4713
Survey of recordings of the operettas by Offenbach. France. UK-England. 1950. Lang.: Swe. 4853
Opera composer Jacques Offenbach. France. 1819-1880. Lang.: Swe. 4854
A production of Offenbach's *Orphée aux Enfers* directed by Jens Mehrle and Stefan Nolte. Germany: Bitterfeld. 1998. Lang.: Ger. 4856
Reactions to Offenbach operettas at Kungliga Operan. Sweden: Stockholm. 1860-1928. Lang.: Swe. 4858
Plays/librettos/scripts
Opera and the myth of Orpheus. 1600-1986. Lang.: Fre. 4758
Humor and parody in Offenbach's opera *Orphée aux Enfers*. France. 1874. Lang.: Fre. 4785

Ogata, Issey
Performance/production
Collection of newspaper reviews by London theatre critics. UK-England: London. 1998. Lang.: Eng. 2430

Oggun
Plays/librettos/scripts
Afrocuban religion in Cuban films. Cuba. 1974-1991. Lang.: Eng. 3968

Ogre
Plays/librettos/scripts
Analysis of works by Larry Tremblay. Canada: Montreal, PQ. 1995-1998. Lang.: Fre. 2804

Oh, What a Lovely War!
Performance/production
Collection of newspaper reviews by London theatre critics. UK-England. 1998. Lang.: Eng. 2456
Collection of newspaper reviews by London theatre critics. UK-England: London. 1998. Lang.: Eng. 2461
Collection of newspaper reviews by London theatre critics. UK-England: London. 1998. Lang.: Eng. 2482

Ohio Ballet (Akron, OH)
Administration
Financially troubled Ohio ballet companies. USA: Cleveland, OH, Akron, OH. 1998. Lang.: Eng. 1027

Ohio Impromptu
Plays/librettos/scripts
Authority, truth, and the allegory of the cave in works of Samuel Beckett. France. Ireland. 1953-1986. Lang.: Eng. 3085

Ohio State Murders, The
Plays/librettos/scripts
The dramaturgical evolution of playwright Adrienne Kennedy. USA. 1964-1990. Lang.: Eng. 3691

Ohio Theatre (Cleveland, OH)
Institutions
Theatrical activity in Cleveland's Playhouse Square. USA: Cleveland, OH. 1998. Lang.: Eng. 416

Oidípous Týrannos (Oedipus the King)
Performance/production
The performance of sacrifice on stage. France. Germany. 1900-1998. Lang.: Ger. 530
Collection of newspaper reviews by London theatre critics. UK-England: London, Scarborough. 1998. Lang.: Eng. 2426
Collection of newspaper reviews by London theatre critics. UK-England: London. 1998. Lang.: Eng. 2490
Plays/librettos/scripts
Analysis of Sophocles' *Oidípous Týrannos (Oedipus the King)*. Greece. 420 B.C. Lang.: Dut. 3180

OISTAT
SEE
Organisation Internationale de Scénographes, Techniciens et Architectes de Théâtre.

Oklahoma!
Performance/production
Collection of newspaper reviews by London theatre critics. UK-England: London. 1998. Lang.: Eng. 2474
The success of a revival of *Oklahoma!* at the Olivier. UK-England: London. 1998. Lang.: Eng. 4373

Okunevskaja, Tatjana
Performance/production
Memoirs of actress Tatjana Okunevskaja. Russia. 1998. Lang.: Rus. 582

Old Friends
Performance/production
Productions of children's theatre festival. Canada: Montreal, PQ. 1998. Lang.: Fre. 503

Old Man of the Mountains, The
Plays/librettos/scripts
Analysis of plays based on the Hebrew prophets. USA. Europe. 1919-1970. Lang.: Eng. 3659

Old Neighborhood, The
Design/technology
Lighting design for Mamet's *The Old Neighborhood* directed by Scott Zigler. USA: New York, NY. 1998. Lang.: Eng. 1547
Performance/production
Collection of newspaper reviews by London theatre critics. UK-England: London. 1998. Lang.: Eng. 2422

Old Red Lion Theatre (London)
Performance/production
Collection of newspaper reviews by London theatre critics. UK-England: London. 1998. Lang.: Eng. 2439
Collection of newspaper reviews by London theatre critics. UK-England: London. 1998. Lang.: Eng. 2449
Collection of newspaper reviews by London theatre critics. UK-England: London. 1998. Lang.: Eng. 2460
Collection of newspaper reviews by London theatre critics. UK-England: London. 1998. Lang.: Eng. 2468
Collection of newspaper reviews by London theatre critics. UK-England: London. 1998. Lang.: Eng. 2478
Collection of newspaper reviews by London theatre critics. UK-England: London. 1998. Lang.: Eng. 2492
Collection of newspaper reviews by London theatre critics. UK-England: London. 1998. Lang.: Eng. 2511
Collection of newspaper reviews by London theatre critics. UK-England: London. 1998. Lang.: Eng. 2540
Collection of newspaper reviews by London theatre critics. UK-England: London. 1998. Lang.: Eng. 2547
Collection of newspaper reviews by London theatre critics. UK-England: London. 1998. Lang.: Eng. 2565
Collection of newspaper reviews by London theatre critics. UK-England: London. 1998. Lang.: Eng. 2581

Old Settler, The
Plays/librettos/scripts
Playwright John Henry Redwood. USA: Atlanta, GA. 1998. Lang.: Eng. 3656

Old Vic Theatre (Bristol)
SEE
Bristol Old Vic Theatre.

Old Vic Theatre (London)
Administration
Interview with producer Ed Mirvish. UK-England: London. Canada: Toronto, ON. 1982-1998. Lang.: Eng. 1393
Performance/production
Collection of newspaper reviews by London theatre critics. UK-England: London. Lang.: Eng. 2408

Old Vic Theatre (London) — cont'd

Collection of newspaper reviews by London theatre critics. UK-England: London. 1998. Lang.: Eng. 2528

Correspondence of George Devine and Michel Saint-Denis. UK-England: London. 1939-1945. Lang.: Eng. 2630

Oldenburgisches Staatstheater (Oldenburg)
Performance/production
Opera director Katja Czellnik. Germany: Oldenburg, Kiel. 1996-1998. Lang.: Ger. 4583

Oldest Living Graduate, The
Plays/librettos/scripts
Analysis of Preston Jones's plays about Texas. USA. 1977. Lang.: Eng. 3645

Oldfield, Kenny
Performance/production
Collection of newspaper reviews by London theatre critics. UK-England: London. 1998. Lang.: Eng. 2517

Oleanna
Plays/librettos/scripts
Rites of passage in the plays of David Mamet. USA. 1975-1995. Lang.: Eng. 3680

Olenius, Elsa
Institutions
Elsa Olenius and Vår Teater. Sweden: Stockholm. 1942-1980. Lang.: Swe. 1732

Olgas Raum (Olga's Room)
Institutions
New plays by Dea Loher at Staatsschauspiel Hannover. Germany: Hannover. 1992-1998. Lang.: Ger. 1643
Plays/librettos/scripts
Analysis of plays by Dea Loher, directed by Andreas Kriegenburg. Germany: Hannover. 1998. Lang.: Ger. 3130

The collaboration of playwright Dea Loher and director Andreas Kriegenburg. Germany: Hannover, Munich. 1990-1998. Lang.: Ger. 3151

Marginal notes by Dea Loher on her plays. Germany. 1991-1998. Lang.: Ger. 3162

Oliver, Clifford
Performance/production
Collection of newspaper reviews by London theatre critics. UK-England: London. 1998. Lang.: Eng. 2502

Oliver, Edith
Performance/production
Obituaries for Roger L. Stevens, Kenneth Frankel, Donald Davis, and Edith Oliver. USA. Canada. 1910-1998. Lang.: Eng. 2742

Olivetti
Performance/production
Laura Curano's solo piece *Olivetti*. Italy: Calabria. 1998. Lang.: Eng. 2156

Olivier Theatre (London)
SEE ALSO
National Theatre Company.
Performance/production
Collection of newspaper reviews by London theatre critics. UK-England: London. 1998. Lang.: Eng. 2414

Collection of newspaper reviews by London theatre critics. UK-England: London. 1998. Lang.: Eng. 2466

Collection of newspaper reviews by London theatre critics. UK-England: London. 1998. Lang.: Eng. 2474

Collection of newspaper reviews by London theatre critics. UK-England: London. 1998. Lang.: Eng. 2523

Collection of newspaper reviews by London theatre critics. UK-England: London. 1998. Lang.: Eng. 2555

Collection of newspaper reviews by London theatre critics. UK-England: London. 1998. Lang.: Eng. 2586

Trevor Nunn's production of *An Enemy of the People* by Ibsen. UK-England: London. 1998. Lang.: Eng. 2627

The success of a revival of *Oklahoma!* at the Olivier. UK-England: London. 1998. Lang.: Eng. 4373

Olivier, Laurence
Performance/production
Speaking styles of selected actors reading Shakespeare's *Henry V*. North America. UK-England. 1998. Lang.: Eng. 2208

Types of actors and their relationship with directors. UK-England. Sweden. 1950-1998. Lang.: Swe. 2648
Plays/librettos/scripts
Film interpretations of Ophelia in Shakespeare's *Hamlet*. USA. UK-England. USSR. 1947-1990. Lang.: Eng. 4024

Olivier, Richard
Institutions
The inaugural season of Shakespeare's Globe Theatre. UK-England: London. 1997-1998. Lang.: Eng. 1741
Performance spaces
Shakespeare's Globe and the staging of *The Merchant of Venice*. UK-England: London. 1998. Lang.: Ger. 1810
Performance/production
Collection of newspaper reviews by London theatre critics. UK-England: London. 1998. Lang.: Eng. 2498

The inaugural season of Shakespeare's Globe Theatre. UK-England: London. 1997. Lang.: Eng. 2601

Richard Olivier's production of Shakespeare's *The Merchant of Venice*. UK-England: London. 1998. Lang.: Eng. 2621

Olivo e Pasquale
Performance/production
Soprano Catherine Hayes. Ireland. Italy. 1839-1861. Lang.: Eng. 4645

Olmi, Véronique
Institutions
Impressions from the Avignon theatre festival. France: Avignon. 1998. Lang.: Ger. 1612

Olschok, Herbert
Performance/production
German directors about the meaning of Brecht today. Germany. 1998. Lang.: Ger. 1948

Olson, Charles
Theory/criticism
Performance art and the 'poetics of space'. USA. Poland. 1952-1984. Lang.: Eng. 4270

Ölveczky, Miklós
Performance spaces
Interview with architect Miklós Ölveczky about Hungary's new National Theatre. Hungary. Norway. 1998. Lang.: Hun. 449

Omskij Akademičeskij Teat'r Dramy (Omsk)
Institutions
Profile of the Omsk Drama Theatre. Russia: Omsk. 1998. Lang.: Rus. 1695

Profile of Omsk's Dramatic Theatre. Russia: Omsk. 1998. Lang.: Rus. 1707

Omskij Dramatičeskij Teat'r 'Galerka' (Omsk)
Institutions
Profile of the Omsk Dramatic Theatre, 'Galerka'. Russia: Omsk. 1998. Lang.: Rus. 1706

On Baile's Strand
Performance/production
Collection of newspaper reviews by London theatre critics. UK-England: London. 1998. Lang.: Eng. 2458

On the Couch with Enoch
Performance/production
Collection of newspaper reviews by London theatre critics. UK-England: London. 1998. Lang.: Eng. 2427

On the Razzle
SEE ALSO
Jux will er sich machen, Einen.

On the Rocks
Plays/librettos/scripts
Analysis of the later plays of George Bernard Shaw. UK-England. 1923-1947. Lang.: Eng. 3444

Once Is Never Enough
Performance/production
Collection of newspaper reviews by London theatre critics. UK-England: London. 1998. Lang.: Eng. 2539

Once Upon Four Robbers
Plays/librettos/scripts
Playwright Femi Osofisan on his political goals and strategies. Nigeria. 1978. Lang.: Eng. 3286

Ondine
Design/technology
A stage design for Jean Giraudoux's *Ondine*. USA. 1987. Lang.: Eng. 1529

One Hundred Objects to Represent the World
Performance/production
Reviews of productions by Wilson, Greenaway, and Mnouchkine. France: Paris. 1997-1998. Lang.: Eng. 1926

One You Love, The
Plays/librettos/scripts
German view of English and American drama. UK-England. USA. 1998. Lang.: Ger. 3455

One-Third of a Nation
Performance/production
Productions of the Federal Theatre Project's Living Newspapers. USA: New York, NY. 1935-1939. Lang.: Eng. 643
Onion Shed (London)
Performance/production
New London venues and productions. UK-England: London. 1994-1998. Lang.: Eng. 605
Collection of newspaper reviews by London theatre critics. UK-England: London. 1998. Lang.: Eng. 2505
Only Jealousy of Emer, The
Performance/production
Collection of newspaper reviews by London theatre critics. UK-England: London. 1998. Lang.: Eng. 2458
Plays/librettos/scripts
Yeats's *The Only Jealousy of Emer* and his anti-theatrical poetics. Ireland. 1916-1918. Lang.: Eng. 3203
Onnagata
Performance/production
The performance of *onnagata* Tamasaburō in *Elizabeth* by Francisco Ors. Japan: Tokyo. 1993-1995. Lang.: Eng. 1362
Onnagata performer Kataoka Kōjiro. Japan. 1603-1998. Lang.: Fre. 1365
Ono, Yoko
Theory/criticism
Analysis of Yoko Ono's performance work *Cut Piece*. USA. 1964-1998. Lang.: Eng. 4151
Ontological Hysteric Theatre (New York, NY)
Performance/production
Interview with director Richard Foreman. USA: New York, NY. 1975-1990. Lang.: Eng. 2700
Ooh Ah Showah Khan
Performance/production
Collection of newspaper reviews by London theatre critics. UK-England: London. 1998. Lang.: Eng. 2502
Open Air Theatre, Regent's Park (London)
Performance/production
Collection of newspaper reviews by London theatre critics. UK-England: London. 1998. Lang.: Eng. 2418
Collection of newspaper reviews by London theatre critics. UK-England: London. 1998. Lang.: Eng. 2472
Collection of newspaper reviews by London theatre critics. UK-England: London. 1998. Lang.: Eng. 2480
Collection of newspaper reviews by London theatre critics. UK-England: London. 1998. Lang.: Eng. 2498
Open Theatre (New York, NY)
Performance/production
Theatre Magazine's anniversary issue. USA. 1968-1998. Lang.: Eng. 617
Open-air theatre
Design/technology
Scenic elements in *Titanic* by street theatre group Theater Titanick. Germany: Münster, Leipzig. Australia: Perth. 1998. Lang.: Eng. 191
Institutions
Public entertainments in Philadelphia's pleasure gardens. USA: Philadelphia, PA. 1723-1840. Lang.: Eng. 400
Performance spaces
The feasibility of a floating open-air theatre. Europe. 1998. Lang.: Swe. 436
History and nature of German open-air theatre. Germany. 1700-1994. Lang.: Eng. 442
Profiles of Southern California theatres. USA. 1998. Lang.: Eng. 473
Malmö Musikteater's production of *Lucia di Lammermoor* at Hedeland Amfiteater. Denmark: Hedeland. 1997. Lang.: Swe. 4491
The building of an ideal operatic stage in a disused limestone quarry. Sweden: Rättvik. 1997. Lang.: Swe. 4497
Sante Fe Opera's newly renovated open-air theatre. USA: Santa Fe, NM. 1991-1998. Lang.: Eng. 4499
Performance/production
Antal Fodor's ballet *A Próba (The Rehearsal)*. Hungary: Budapest. 1998. Lang.: Hun. 1111
Open-air dance performances. Hungary: Pécs. 1998. Lang.: Hun. 1292
Laura Curano's solo piece *Olivetti*. Italy: Calabria. 1998. Lang.: Eng. 2156
Outdoor passion plays. USA. 1920-1995. Lang.: Eng. 2715
Commedia dell'arte and the street performances of charlatans. France. Italy. 1600-1700. Lang.: Eng. 4189
Kodály's *Háry János* at Szeged's Open-Air Festival. Hungary: Szeged. 1998. Lang.: Hun. 4359
An open-air production of *West Side Story* directed by László Vándorfi. Hungary: Veszprém. 1998. Lang.: Hun. 4361
Interview with Miklós Gábor Kerényi on directing Verdi's *Un Ballo in Maschera*. Hungary: Budapest. 1998. Lang.: Hun. 4619
Relation to other fields
The square in Italian pageants and open-air entertainment. Italy. 1933-1975. Lang.: Ita. 4227
Opening Night
Plays/librettos/scripts
Theatricality in John Cassavetes' film *Opening Night*. USA. 1978. Lang.: Fre. 4011
Oper (Frankfurt)
Relation to other fields
Political and cultural situation of Frankfurt theatres. Germany: Frankfurt. 1997-1999. Lang.: Ger. 744
Oper (Leipzig)
Performance/production
Review of opera productions. Germany: Stuttgart, Leipzig. 1998. Lang.: Ger. 4584
Opera
SEE ALSO
Classed Entries under MUSIC-DRAMA—Opera.
Administration
Theater Basel under the direction of Stefan Bachmann. Switzerland: Basel. 1996-1998. Lang.: Ger. 1391
Design/technology
Catalogue of an exhibition on scenography of Galileo Chini. Italy. 1908-1956. Lang.: Ita. 199
Lighting and realism in opera and theatre: Belasco and Puccini. Italy. USA. 1890-1910. Lang.: Eng. 203
New lighting equipment of Lithuanian Opera and Ballet Theatre. Lithuania: Vilnius. 1974-1998. Lang.: Swe, Eng, Ger. 205
Performance/production
The disappearance of the diva in the modern world. Europe. USA. 1890-1998. Lang.: Swe. 525
Survey of Berlin productions in the holiday season. Germany: Berlin. 1997-1998. Lang.: Eng. 538
Brief history of Slovene theatre. Slovenia. 1867-1997. Lang.: Slo. 595
Survey of London and Paris productions. UK-England: London. France: Paris. 1998. Lang.: Eng. 607
Music theatre production in northern Germany. Germany: Lübeck, Hamburg, Bremen, Kiel. 1998. Lang.: Ger. 4293
William Schuman on the differences between operatic and Broadway theatre singing. USA. 1998. Lang.: Eng. 4303
Plays/librettos/scripts
Kazan in the life of Maksim Gorkij and Fëdor Šaljapin. Tatarstan: Kazan. 1868-1938. Lang.: Rus. 689
The character of Ivan the Terrible. USSR. 1800-1965. Lang.: Eng. 692
Robin Hood and Restoration drama. England. 1660-1730. Lang.: Eng. 2954
Opera in American gangster films. USA. 1932-1990. Lang.: Eng. 4023
Operatic adaptations of Beckett's plays by Heinz Holliger. Europe. 1976-1988. Lang.: Eng. 4776
Reference materials
Yearbook of Slovene theatre. Slovenia. 1996-1997. Lang.: Slo. 708
Relation to other fields
Postage stamps commemorating Russian theatre and opera. Russia: Moscow. 1998. Lang.: Rus. 762
Opera Akademiet (Copenhagen)
Institutions
Profile of Opera Akademiet. Denmark. 1956-1998. Lang.: Dan. 4449
Opera Atelier (Toronto, ON)
Institutions
Profile of Opera Atelier. Canada: Toronto, ON. 1985-1998. Lang.: Eng. 4446
Opéra de Lyon
Performance/production
Ballet dancer K. Kastal'skaja. France: Lyon. 1998. Lang.: Rus. 1073
Press reactions to productions of Offenbach's *Orphée aux Enfers*. Belgium. Switzerland. France. 1997. Lang.: Fre. 4535
Review of Pierre Strosser's staging of Busoni's *Doktor Faust*. France: Lyons. 1997. Lang.: Eng. 4577
Opéra de Paris
Performance spaces
The influence of the Salle le Peletier on French grand opera. France: Paris. 1823-1873. Lang.: Eng. 4494

Opéra de Paris — cont'd
Performance/production
Music for ballet-pantomime at the Paris Opera. France. 1825-1850. Lang.: Eng. 1078
Hector Berlioz's review of Donizetti's *La Favorite*. France: Paris. 1840. Lang.: Eng. 4565
Opéra National du Rhin (Strasbourg)
Performance/production
Reviews of recent opera productions. Switzerland: Basel. Germany: Stuttgart, Berlin, Hamburg. France: Strasbourg. 1997-1998. Lang.: Ger. 4702
Opera North (Leeds)
Performance/production
The current state of opera in England. UK-England. 1997. Lang.: Eng. 4705
Opéra pour Terezin, Un (Opera for Terezin, An)
Plays/librettos/scripts
Analysis of *Un opéra pour Terezin (An Opera for Terezin)* by Liliane Atlan. France. 1986. Lang.: Eng. 3105
Opera San Jose (San Jose, CA)
Institutions
Mezzo soprano Irene Dalis, now in charge of Opera San Jose. USA: San José, CA. 1980-1998. Lang.: Eng. 4484
Ópera Seca (Rio de Janeiro)
Performance/production
Ópera Seca's *Mattogrosso*. Brazil: Rio de Janeiro. 1989. Lang.: Eng. 4537
Opera seria
Plays/librettos/scripts
Female operatic cross-dressing. Italy: Naples, Venice. 1601-1800. Lang.: Eng. 4814
Opera Wonyosi
Plays/librettos/scripts
Political satire in the plays of Wole Soyinka. Nigeria. 1960-1979. Lang.: Eng. 3284
Opéra-Bastille (Paris)
Design/technology
Interview with set designer Lennart Mörk. Sweden: Stockholm. France: Paris. 1958-1998. Lang.: Swe. 222
Scenographer Lennart Mörk. Sweden: Stockholm. France: Paris. 1957-1998. Lang.: Swe. 4439
Opéra-Comique (Paris)
Performance/production
Natalie Dessay's role in Gilbert Blin's production of *Lakmé*. France: Paris. 1995. Lang.: Fre. 4570
Plays/librettos/scripts
Contributions of Meilhac and Halévy to the development of the French libretto. France. 1800-1900. Lang.: Fre. 4781
Operation Sidewinder
Plays/librettos/scripts
Analysis of Sam Shepard's *Operation Sidewinder*. USA. 1970. Lang.: Eng. 3548
Operetta
SEE ALSO
Classed Entries under Music-Drama.
Performance/production
Vilna's Yiddish theatre companies. Poland: Vilna, Cracow. 1918-1939. Lang.: Pol. 2212
Opernhaus (Zurich)
Performance/production
Interview with bass László Polgár. Hungary. Switzerland: Zurich. 1947-1998. Lang.: Hun. 4640
Ophaboom Theatre (London)
Performance/production
Ophaboom Theatre's experience in recreating *commedia dell'arte*. UK-England: London. 1991-1998. Lang.: Eng. 4193
Ophelia
Plays/librettos/scripts
Shakespeare and the feminist theatre of Bryony Lavery and Jane Prendergast. UK-England. 1997. Lang.: Eng. 3439
Ophelia Speaks
Performance/production
Collection of newspaper reviews by London theatre critics. UK-England: London. 1998. Lang.: Eng. 2463
Oppenheimer, Joel
Plays/librettos/scripts
Revolutionary Off Broadway playwriting. USA: New York, NY. 1959-1969. Lang.: Eng. 3604
Oppewall, Jeannine
Design/technology
Production design for Gary Ross's film *Pleasantville*. USA: Hollywood, CA. 1998. Lang.: Eng. 3909
OPTIK (London)
Performance/production
Barry Edwards on his theatrical movement work with OPTIK. UK-England: London. 1997-1998. Lang.: Eng. 609
(OR)
Performance/production
Collection of newspaper reviews by London theatre critics. UK-England: London. 1998. Lang.: Eng. 2512
Ora der fregnone c'è pe 'tutti, L' (Hour of the Idiot Comes to Everyone, The)
Performance/production
Productions by Toni Bertorelli and Alfiero Alfieri. Italy: Rome. 1997. Lang.: Eng. 2175
Orange Tree Theatre (London)
Basic theatrical documents
Text of *Sperm Wars* by David Lewis. UK-England. 1998. Lang.: Eng. 1476
Performance/production
Collection of newspaper reviews by London theatre critics. UK-England: London. 1998. Lang.: Eng. 2419
Collection of newspaper reviews by London theatre critics. UK-England: London. 1998. Lang.: Eng. 2446
Collection of newspaper reviews by London theatre critics. UK-England: London. 1998. Lang.: Eng. 2455
Collection of newspaper reviews by London theatre critics. UK-England: London. 1998. Lang.: Eng. 2459
Collection of newspaper reviews by London theatre critics. UK-England: London. 1998. Lang.: Eng. 2490
Collection of newspaper reviews by London theatre critics. UK-England: London. 1998. Lang.: Eng. 2500
Collection of newspaper reviews by London theatre critics. UK-England: London. 1998. Lang.: Eng. 2503
Collection of newspaper reviews by London theatre critics. UK-England: London. 1998. Lang.: Eng. 2505
Collection of newspaper reviews by London theatre critics. UK-England: London. 1998. Lang.: Eng. 2530
Collection of newspaper reviews by London theatre critics. UK-England: London. 1998. Lang.: Eng. 2538
Collection of newspaper reviews by London theatre critics. UK-England: London. 1998. Lang.: Eng. 2543
Collection of newspaper reviews by London theatre critics. UK-England: London. 1998. Lang.: Eng. 2552
Collection of newspaper reviews by London theatre critics. UK-England: London. 1998. Lang.: Eng. 2569
Collection of newspaper reviews by London theatre critics. UK-England: London. 1998. Lang.: Eng. 2585
Orbakajte, Kristina
Performance/production
Singer Kristina Orbakajte. Russia: Moscow. 1998. Lang.: Rus. 4367
Orchestics
Performance/production
Interview with dancer Mária Tatai. Hungary. 1981-1998. Lang.: Hun. 935
Orchestre, L' (Ladies' Band, The)
Performance/production
Collection of newspaper reviews by London theatre critics. UK-England: London. 1998. Lang.: Eng. 2413
Ordinalia
Performance/production
Staging of the Cornish *Ordinalia*. England. 1375-1400. Lang.: Eng. 1890
Ordo Virtutum
Performance/production
Sequentia's new recording of *Ordo Virtutum* by Hildegard of Bingen. Germany. 1997. Lang.: Eng. 4294
Oregon Shakespeare Festival (Ashland, OR)
Design/technology
Costume designs for Oregon Shakespeare Festival productions. USA: Ashland, OR. 1998. Lang.: Eng. 1543
Institutions
William Patton, executive director emeritus of Oregon Shakespeare Festival. USA: Ashland, OR. 1952-1998. Lang.: Eng. 1777
Plays of 1998 Oregon Shakespeare Festival. USA: Ashland, OR. 1998. Lang.: Eng. 1783
Orestea (Una commedia organica?) (Oresteia: An Organic Comedy?)
Performance/production
Romeo Castellucci's adaptation of the *Oresteia* by Aeschylus. Italy: Cesena. 1997. Lang.: Eng. 2189

Oresteia
Performance/production
Athol Fugard and the *Oresteia* of Aeschylus. South Africa, Republic of: Cape Town. 1978. Lang.: Eng. 2354
Collection of newspaper reviews by London theatre critics. UK-England: London. 1998. Lang.: Eng. 2520
Plays/librettos/scripts
Ellen McLaughlin's *Iphigenia and Other Daughters* at CSC Repertory. USA: New York, NY. 1995. Lang.: Eng. 3520
Analysis of *The Prodigal* by Jack Richardson. USA. 1960. Lang.: Eng. 3542
The Prodigal, Jack Richardson's adaptation of *The Oresteia*. USA. 1960. Lang.: Dut. 3547
Homeric influences on *The Prodigal* by Jack Richardson. USA. 1960. Lang.: Eng. 3549

Orestes
Basic theatrical documents
Collection of plays by Charles L. Mee. USA. 1986-1995. Lang.: Eng. 1496
Performance/production
Athol Fugard and the *Oresteia* of Aeschylus. South Africa, Republic of: Cape Town. 1978. Lang.: Eng. 2354

Orff, Carl
Administration
Stockholm's debut as cultural capital of Europe. Sweden: Stockholm. 1998. Lang.: Dan. 22
Performance/production
Premieres of choreographies by Danny Rosseel. Belgium: Antwerp. Netherlands: Amsterdam. 1998. Lang.: Hun. 1065

Organisation Internationale de Scénographes, Techniciens et Architectes de Théâtre (OISTAT)
Design/technology
OISTAT meeting on technician training. Netherlands: Amsterdam. 1998. Lang.: Swe. 206
Institutions
Program of the Hungarian Centre of OISTAT's conference. USA: Pittsburgh, PA. 1997. Lang.: Hun. 392

Orgy
Plays/librettos/scripts
Theory and practice in the work of director Pier Paolo Pasolini. Italy. 1960-1970. Lang.: Eng. 3264

Örkény, István
Performance/production
Review of István Örkény's *Kulcskereső*k *(Searching for the Key)*, Katona József Theatre. Hungary: Budapest. 1998. Lang.: Hun. 2083

Orlowicz, Tadeusz
Design/technology
Scenographer Tadeusz Orlowicz. Poland: Cracow. Germany: Neubrandenburg. UK-England: London. 1907-1976. Lang.: Pol. 212

Ormond, George
Performance/production
Collection of newspaper reviews by London theatre critics. UK-England: London. 1998. Lang.: Eng. 2446
Collection of newspaper reviews by London theatre critics. UK-England: London. 1998. Lang.: Eng. 2569

Ornithes (Birds)
Performance/production
Culture Clash and their production of Aristophanes' *Birds*. USA: Berkeley, CA. 1984-1998. Lang.: Eng. 2713

Orosz, Adél
Performance/production
Interview with ballerina Adél Orosz. Hungary. 1954-1998. Lang.: Hun. 1112

Orosz, Júlia
Performance/production
Tribute to the late soprano Júlia Orosz. Hungary. 1908-1997. Lang.: Hun. 4623

Orphée aux Enfers
Basic theatrical documents
Text of Offenbach's *Orphée aux Enfers*. France. 1874. Lang.: Fre. 4418
Performance/production
Discography of Offenbach's *Orphée aux Enfers*. 1953-1997. Lang.: Fre. 4511
Productions of Offenbach's *Orphée aux Enfers*. 1858-1997. Lang.: Fre. 4516
Press reactions to productions of Offenbach's *Orphée aux Enfers*. Belgium. Switzerland. France. 1997. Lang.: Fre. 4535
Offenbach's *Orphée aux Enfers* from two acts to four. France. 1858-1874. Lang.: Fre. 4571
A production of Offenbach's *Orphée aux Enfers* directed by Jens Mehrle and Stefan Nolte. Germany: Bitterfeld. 1998. Lang.: Ger. 4856
Plays/librettos/scripts
Opera and the myth of Orpheus. 1600-1986. Lang.: Fre. 4758
Humor and parody in Offenbach's opera *Orphée aux Enfers*. France. 1874. Lang.: Fre. 4785

Orpheum Theatre (Phoenix, AZ)
Performance spaces
The restoration of the Orpheum Theatre. USA: Phoenix, AZ. 1929-1998. Lang.: Eng. 3926

Ors, Francisco
Performance/production
The performance of *onnagata* Tamasaburō in *Elizabeth* by Francisco Ors. Japan: Tokyo. 1993-1995. Lang.: Eng. 1362

Orsovszky, István
Performance/production
Utolsó kontrasztok (Last Contrasts) choreographed by István Orsovszky. Hungary: Zalaegerszeg. 1998. Lang.: Hun. 1295

Orton, Joe
Administration
Theatrical agent Margaret Ramsey. UK-England: London. 1908-1991. Lang.: Ger. 1394
Institutions
Productions of Staatstheater Stuttgart. Germany: Stuttgart. 1998. Lang.: Ger. 1620
Performance/production
Collection of newspaper reviews by London theatre critics. UK-England: London. 1998. Lang.: Eng. 2477
Collection of newspaper reviews by London theatre critics. UK-England: London. 1998. Lang.: Eng. 2482
Theory/criticism
Theatrical reviews and the nature of theatrical success. UK-England. 1950-1990. Lang.: Eng. 3836

Osato, Sono
Performance/production
Tributes to ballerina Alexandra Danilova. USA: New York, NY. 1997. Lang.: Eng. 1165

Osborne, John
Design/technology
Lighting designer John Osborne. USA. 1998. Lang.: Eng. 310
Plays/librettos/scripts
The rebel in modern drama. Europe. 1950-1988. Lang.: Eng. 3053

Oscar and Lucinda
Design/technology
Geoffrey Simpson's cinematography for Gillian Armstrong's *Oscar and Lucinda*. Australia. 1997. Lang.: Eng. 3900

Osgood, Nathan
Performance/production
Collection of newspaper reviews by London theatre critics. UK-England: London. 1998. Lang.: Eng. 2427

Osipenko, Alla
Performance/production
Ballerina Alla Osipenko. Russia. 1932-1998. Lang.: Eng. 1139

Oskam, Floor
Design/technology
Profiles of young theatrical designers. Netherlands. 1990-1998. Lang.: Dut. 207

Oskar Wilde: Sein Drama (Oscar Wilde: His Drama)
Plays/librettos/scripts
Homosexuality on the German stage. Germany. 1920-1980. Lang.: Eng. 3147

Oslund, Mary
Performance/production
Mary Oslund and Gregg Bielemeier of Conduit. USA: Portland, OR. 1995-1998. Lang.: Eng. 1333

Osofisan, Femi
Plays/librettos/scripts
Playwright Femi Osofisan on his political goals and strategies. Nigeria. 1978. Lang.: Eng. 3286

Ospice (Measles, The)
Performance/production
Collection of newspaper reviews by London theatre critics. UK-England: London. 1998. Lang.: Eng. 2451

Ośrodek Praktyk Teatralnych (Gardzienice)
Institutions
Interview with Wlodzimierz Staniewski of Gardzienice Theatre Association. Poland: Gardzienice. 1978-1998. Lang.: Ger, Fre, Dut, Eng. 1687

Øst, Tammi
Performance/production
Interview with actress Tammi Øst. Denmark. 1982-1998. Lang.: Dan. 514

Östberg, Jens
Institutions
Report on biennial dance conference. Sweden: Stockholm. 1998. Lang.: Swe. 902

Osten, Suzanne
Performance/production
Interview with actress and director Anna Takanen. Sweden: Stockholm. 1994-1998. Lang.: Swe. 2372
Stockholm's children's theatre scene. Sweden: Stockholm. 1998. Lang.: Ger. 2389

Ostermaier, Albert
Plays/librettos/scripts
German playwrights on the meaning of Brecht today. Germany. 1998. Lang.: Ger. 3123

Ostermeier, Thomas
Administration
Interview with Thomas Ostermeier, artistic director of Schaubühne. Germany: Berlin. 1996-1998. Lang.: Ger. 1386
Theatre directors on the future of subsidized theatre. Switzerland: Zurich. Germany: Hannover, Berlin. 1998. Lang.: Ger. 1390
Institutions
Profile of Deutsches Theater, Baracke. Germany: Berlin. 1996-1998. Lang.: Ger. 1637
Survey of the Theatertreffen festival. Germany: Berlin. 1998. Lang.: Swe. 1651
Performance/production
Political changes reflected in Berlin theatre productions. Germany: Berlin. 1998. Lang.: Ger. 1958
Profile of Thomas Ostermeier, *Theater Heute*'s young director of the year. Germany: Berlin. 1997-1998. Lang.: Ger. 1959
Recent German productions of plays by Bertolt Brecht. Germany: Hamburg, Berlin. 1997. Lang.: Swe. 1977
Director Thomas Ostermeier. Germany. 1997-1998. Lang.: Dan. 1979
Director Thomas Ostermeier. Germany: Berlin. 1996-1998. Lang.: Swe. 1998
Plays/librettos/scripts
Interview with director Thomas Ostermeier. Germany: Berlin. 1996-1998. Lang.: Ger. 3124
Mark Ravenhill's *Shopping and Fucking* and its production by Thomas Ostermeier. UK-England. Germany. 1998. Lang.: Ger. 3476

Osterwa, Juliusz
Institutions
Polish experimental theatre training. Poland: Cracow, Wrocław, Warsaw. 1930-1998. Lang.: Pol. 1685

Ostling, Daniel
Design/technology
Set designer Daniel Ostling. USA: Chicago, IL. 1998. Lang.: Eng. 314

Ostrovskij, Aleksand'r Nikolajėvič
Design/technology
Scene design and the plays of Ostrovskij. Russia. 1998. Lang.: Rus. 1523
Institutions
Reviews of some productions at the Avignon Festival. France: Avignon. 1998. Lang.: Hun. 1615
Impressions from the 'Golden Mask' festival. Russia: Minusinsk. 1998. Lang.: Ger. 1701
Ostrovskij Festival celebrating the 175th anniversary of Malyj Teat'r. Russia: Moscow. 1998. Lang.: Rus. 1709
Performance/production
A.A. Vasiljėv's production of *Bez viny vinovatjė (Guilty Though Innocent)* by Ostrovskij. Hungary: Szolnok. 1998. Lang.:Hun. 2096
Symbolism in Anatolij Vasiljėv's production of *Guilty Though Innocent* by Ostrovskij. Hungary: Szolnok. 1998. Lang.: Hun. 2098
Recent productions of plays by Ostrovskij. Russia. 1998. Lang.: Rus. 2314
Collection of newspaper reviews by London theatre critics. UK-England: London. 1998. Lang.: Eng. 2543
Plays/librettos/scripts
Articles on playwright A.N. Ostrovskij. Russia. Lang.: Rus. 3316
Morality in plays of Fonvizin, Ostrovskij, and A.K. Tolstoj. Russia. 1764-1869. Lang.: Rus. 3325

Òṣun
Plays/librettos/scripts
Representation of character in plays by Duro Ladipọ. Nigeria. 1964-1970. Lang.: Eng. 3285

Oswald, Peter
Performance/production
Collection of newspaper reviews by London theatre critics. UK-England: London. 1998. Lang.: Eng. 2583

Otello
Administration
Theater Basel under the direction of Stefan Bachmann. Switzerland: Basel. 1996-1998. Lang.: Ger. 1391
Performance/production
Music theatre production in northern Germany. Germany: Lübeck, Hamburg, Bremen, Kiel. 1998. Lang.: Ger. 4293
Johannes Schaaf's production of *Otello* at Kungliga Operan. Sweden: Stockholm. 1998. Lang.: Swe. 4701

Othello
Performance/production
Casting and performance in eighteenth-century productions of *Othello*. England. 1777-1800. Lang.: Eng. 1909
German productions of Shakespeare. Germany: Leipzig, Hamburg, Berlin. 1998. Lang.: Ger. 2033
Interview with director Frank Castorf. Germany, East. 1980-1990. Lang.: Eng. 2041
Collection of newspaper reviews by London theatre critics. UK-England: London. 1998. Lang.: Eng. 2466
Actor Tomasso Salvini. USA. Italy. 1856-1915. Lang.: Eng. 2731
Interview with actor Patrick Stewart. USA: Washington, DC. 1998. Lang.: Eng. 2760
Suzanne Cloutier's role in Shakespeare's *Othello*, directed by Orson Welles. Italy. 1952. Lang.: Fre. 3935
Plays/librettos/scripts
Women's use of wit in response to men in English popular culture. England. 1590-1630. Lang.: Eng. 2884
Patience and delay in Shakespeare's *Othello*. England. 1604. Lang.: Eng. 2903
Attitudes toward Spain in early modern English drama. England. 1492-1604. Lang.: Eng. 2927
Racial ambiguity, colonialism, and late twentieth-century criticism of Shakespeare's *Othello*. England. 1604-1998. Lang.: Eng. 2987
The concept of the self in Shakespearean tragedy. England. 1590-1612. Lang.: Eng. 2992
'Demonic' women in Shakespeare's tragedies. England. 1590-1613. Lang.: Eng. 2999
Race and imperialism in Shakespeare's *Othello*. England. 1604. Lang.: Eng. 3023
Relation to other fields
Depictions of Shakespeare's Othello. Europe. 1709-1804. Lang.: Eng. 3758
The influence of Shakespeare's *Othello* on C.B. Brown's novel *Wieland*. USA. England. 1604-1798. Lang.: Eng. 3788

Other Place, The (Stratford)
SEE ALSO
Royal Shakespeare Company.
Performance/production
Collection of newspaper reviews by London theatre critics. UK-England: London, Stratford, Derby. 1998. Lang.: Eng. 2417

Otho the Great
Plays/librettos/scripts
The feminine ideal in the drama of English Romantic poets. England. 1794-1840. Lang.: Eng. 2886

Otra Tempestad (Another Tempest)
Performance/production
Collection of newspaper reviews by London theatre critics. UK-England: London. 1998. Lang.: Eng. 2477

Ott, Sharon
Performance/production
Statements of women directors on their work. USA. 1996. Lang.: Eng. 2674

Otta Klasine, Ondina
Performance/production
Interview with soprano Ondina Otta Klasine. Slovenia. 1946-1998. Lang.: Slo. 4696

Otto e mezzo (8 1/2)
Plays/librettos/scripts
Arthur Kopit's *Nine*, a musical adaptation of Fellini's *8 1/2*. USA. 1963-1982. Lang.: Eng. 4401

Otto-Falckenberg-Schule (Munich)
Institutions
Profile of Munich's theatre training institutions. Germany: Munich. 1998. Lang.: Ger. 348

Ottwald, Ernst
Plays/librettos/scripts
Bertolt Brecht and German cinema. Germany. 1919-1932. Lang.: Ita. 3972
Ouaknine, Serge
Performance/production
Director Serge Ouaknine and his use of visual aids. Canada: Montreal, PQ. 1968-1998. Lang.: Fre. 1871
Our Country's Good
Performance/production
Collection of newspaper reviews by London theatre critics. UK-England: London. 1998. Lang.: Eng. 2507
Our Lady of Sligo
Performance/production
Collection of newspaper reviews by London theatre critics. UK-England: London. 1998. Lang.: Eng. 2461
Out of Our Father's House
Performance/production
Documentary theatre and the politics of representation. USA. 1966-1993. Lang.: Eng. 2728
Out of Sight
Basic theatrical documents
Screenplay of *Out of Sight* by Scott Frank. USA. 1998. Lang.: Eng. 3884
Design/technology
Lighting design for Steven Soderbergh's film *Out of Sight*. USA. 1998. Lang.: Eng. 3912
Performance/production
Steven Soderbergh on directing *Out of Sight*. USA. 1998. Lang.: Eng. 3944
Plays/librettos/scripts
Interview with screenwriter Scott Frank. USA. 1998. Lang.: Eng. 3995
Oval House Theatre (London)
Performance/production
Collection of newspaper reviews by London theatre critics. UK-England: London. 1998. Lang.: Eng. 2432
Collection of newspaper reviews by London theatre critics. UK-England: London. 1998. Lang.: Eng. 2450
Collection of newspaper reviews by London theatre critics. UK-England: London. 1998. Lang.: Eng. 2520
Collection of newspaper reviews by London theatre critics. UK-England: London. 1998. Lang.: Eng. 2535
Collection of newspaper reviews by London theatre critics. UK-England: London. 1998. Lang.: Eng. 2545
Collection of newspaper reviews by London theatre critics. UK-England: London. 1998. Lang.: Eng. 2566
Collection of newspaper reviews by London theatre critics. UK-England: London. 1998. Lang.: Eng. 2575
Collection of newspaper reviews by London theatre critics. UK-England: London. 1998. Lang.: Eng. 2577
Overlie, Mary
Performance/production
The 'viewpoint theory' of actor training. USA. 1998. Lang.: Eng. 2677
Overruled
Plays/librettos/scripts
Rhetorical arguments in one-act plays of Shaw. UK-England. 1890-1945. Lang.: Eng. 3453
Owen Wingrave
Plays/librettos/scripts
Derek Jarman's adaptation of works by Benjamin Britten and Wilfred Owen. UK-England. 1968-1988. Lang.: Eng. 4822
Owens, Rochelle
Performance/production
Theatre Magazine's anniversary issue. USA. 1968-1998. Lang.: Eng. 617
Plays/librettos/scripts
Revolutionary Off Broadway playwriting. USA: New York, NY. 1959-1969. Lang.: Eng. 3604
Oxford Playhouse
Performance/production
Collection of newspaper reviews by London theatre critics. UK-England: London. 1998. Lang.: Eng. 2580
Oxyrhyncus Evangeliet
Performance/production
Eugenio Barba's *Oxyrhyncus Evangeliet*, Odin Teatret. USA. 1988. Lang.: Eng. 646
Ozeanflug, Der
Design/technology
Robert Wilson and Vera Dobroschke's design for Brecht's *Ozeanflug*. Germany: Berlin. 1998. Lang.: Eng. 4430
Performance/production
Robert Wilson's production of Brecht's *Der Ozeanflug*. Germany: Berlin. 1998. Lang.: Ger. 4356
Interview with director Robert Wilson. Germany: Berlin. 1970-1998. Lang.: Swe. 4609
Plays/librettos/scripts
Recent German productions of Brecht's plays. Germany. 1998. Lang.: Ger. 3150
Hero and anti-hero in contemporary opera production. Germany. 1998. Lang.: Ger. 4791
P.S. 122 (New York, NY)
Performance/production
Analysis of recent New York productions. USA: New York, NY. 1997-1998. Lang.: Eng. 2759
P'ansori
Performance/production
The evolution of Korean *p'ansori* as modern Korean opera, *ch'angguk*. Korea. 1900-1998. Lang.: Eng. 4364
Paál, István
Institutions
István Paál's Egyetemi Színpad. Hungary: Szeged. 1960-1998. Lang.: Hun. 361
Performance/production
Obituary for director István Paál. Hungary: Szolnok. 1942-1998. Lang.: Hun. 2143
Pace, Guy
Administration
Profile of Equity administrator Guy Pace. USA: New York, NY. 1998. Lang.: Eng. 99
Pacific Northwest Ballet (Seattle, WA)
Performance/production
Ballerina Ariana Lallone of Pacific Northwest Ballet. USA: Seattle, WA. 1984-1998. Lang.: Eng. 1168
Dancer Manard Stewart of Pacific Northwest Ballet. USA: Seattle, WA. 1994-1998. Lang.: Eng. 1175
Pacific Overtures
Plays/librettos/scripts
The disintegration of the American dream in works of Stephen Sondheim. USA. 1970-1984. Lang.: Eng. 4397
Pacino, Al
Performance/production
Notable productions of plays by Eugene O'Neill. USA. 1916-1996. Lang.: Eng. 2752
The body in stage-to-film versions of Shakespeare's *Richard III*. UK-England. USA. 1985-1998. Lang.: Eng. 3940
Plays/librettos/scripts
Film adaptations of Shakespeare's *Richard III* by Richard Loncraine and Al Pacino. USA. UK-England. 1995-1996. Lang.: Fre. 4012
Theory/criticism
The urge to make Shakespeare contemporary. USA. 1990-1998. Lang.: Eng. 3844
Padre muerto, El (Dead Father, The)
Plays/librettos/scripts
Visual imagery in *El padre muerto (The Dead Father)* by Marco Antonio de la Parra. Chile. 1993. Lang.: Eng. 2839
Padve, E.
Performance/production
Children's theatre director E. Padve. Russia: St. Petersburg. 1998. Lang.: Rus. 2262
Pagan, Adrian
Performance/production
Collection of newspaper reviews by London theatre critics. UK-England: London. 1998. Lang.: Eng. 2550
Pageants/parades
SEE ALSO
Processional theatre.
Classed Entries under MIXED ENTERTAINMENT—Pageants/parades.
Institutions
Eighteenth-century amateur theatre in Vilna. Poland: Vilna. 1732-1798. Lang.: Pol. 1691
Mass festivals of the newly formed Soviet Union. USSR. 1917-1920. Lang.: Eng. 4113
Performance/production
The first wave of American feminist theatre. USA. 1890-1930. Lang.: Eng. 648
The Sicilian chivalric tradition. Italy. 1500-1985. Lang.: Ita. 4125
Amerindian influence on Trinidadian carnival. Trinidad and Tobago: San Fernando. 1700-1950. Lang.: Eng. 4164

Pageants/parades — cont'd

Plays/librettos/scripts
The Easter play tradition. England. 1180-1557. Lang.: Eng. 2942
Biblical narrative and the order of the *York Cycle* episodes. England: York. 1401-1499. Lang.: Eng. 2950
Relation to other fields
The theatrical nature of Salvation Army activities. USA. 1865-1950. Lang.: Eng. 796

Paget, Clive
Performance/production
Collection of newspaper reviews by London theatre critics. UK-England: London. 1998. Lang.: Eng. 2470

Pagliacci
Performance/production
Opera director Katja Czellnik. Germany: Oldenburg, Kiel. 1996-1998. Lang.: Ger. 4583

Paige, Deborah
Performance/production
Collection of newspaper reviews by London theatre critics. UK-England: London. 1998. Lang.: Eng. 2414

Paik, Nam June
Performance/production
The use of television in theatrical space. Netherlands. USA. 1970-1998. Lang.: Dut. 2206

Paines Plough Theatre Company (London)
Performance/production
Report on several English performances. UK-England: London, Stratford. 1998. Lang.: Swe. 2634

Painting You
Performance/production
Collection of newspaper reviews by London theatre critics. UK-England: London. 1998. Lang.: Eng. 2498

Paisiello, Giovanni
Plays/librettos/scripts
Operatic realizations of Beaumarchais' character Rosina. Europe. North America. 1784-1991. Lang.: Eng. 4773

Pakaṭai Tuyil (Dice Game and the Disrobing, The)
Basic theatrical documents
English translation of *terukkūttu* piece *Pakaṭai Tuyil (The Dice Game and the Disrobing)*. India. 1998. Lang.: Eng. 1345

Pál, Tamás
Performance/production
Interview with Tamás Pál, conductor and musical director of Szeged National Theatre. Hungary: Szeged. 1998. Lang.: Hun. 4622

Palace Garden (New York, NY)
Institutions
Popular entertainment at the Palace Garden. USA: New York, NY. 1858-1863. Lang.: Eng. 403

Palace Theatre (Cleveland, OH)
Institutions
Theatrical activity in Cleveland's Playhouse Square. USA: Cleveland, OH. 1998. Lang.: Eng. 416

Palace Theatre (New York, NY)
Administration
The Disney Corporation's Broadway musicals. USA: New York, NY. 1996-1998. Lang.: Eng. 4317

Palace Theatre (Watford)
Performance/production
Collection of newspaper reviews by London theatre critics. UK-England. 1998. Lang.: Eng. 2497

Palais Garnier (Paris)
Performance/production
Conductor James Conlon on his production of Zemlinsky's *Der Zwerg*. France: Paris. 1998. Lang.: Fre. 4562

Palais Royal (Paris)
Performance spaces
Baroque opera and ballet at the Salle des Machines and the Palais Royal. France: Paris. 1640-1690. Lang.: Eng. 4493

Palcsó, Sándor
Performance/production
Interview with tenor Sándor Palcsó. Hungary. 1929-1998. Lang.: Hun. 4620

Paliashvili Opera Theatre (Tbilisi)
SEE
Teat'r Opery i Baleta im. Z. Paliašvili.

Pallín, Yolanda
Performance/production
Eduardo Vasco's production of *Lista Negra (Black List)* by Yolanda Pallín. Spain. 1998. Lang.: Eng. 2360

Palme, Ulf
Performance/production
Types of actors and their relationship with directors. UK-England. Sweden. 1950-1998. Lang.: Swe. 2648

Palo Alto Children's Theatre (Palo Alto, CA)
Institutions
History of Palo Alto Children's Theatre. USA: Palo Alto, CA. 1932-1997. Lang.: Eng. 1778

Pammachius
Plays/librettos/scripts
Protestant belief and English Reformation drama. England. 1535-1607. Lang.: Eng. 2972

Pan Jinlian
Basic theatrical documents
Anthology of contemporary Chinese drama. China, People's Republic of. 1979-1986. Lang.: Eng. 1414

Panayiotis
Basic theatrical documents
Text of *Panayiotis* by Angela Costi. Australia. 1997. Lang.: Eng. 1406

Panigrahi, Sanjukta
Performance/production
Sanjukta Panigrahi, dancer, choreographer, and co-founder of ISTA. India. 1944-1997. Lang.: Eng. 952
Obituary for dancer Sanjukta Panigrahi. India. 1944-1997. Lang.: Eng. 1230

Panna Maliczewska (Miss Maliczewska)
Plays/librettos/scripts
Feminist analysis of plays by Gabriela Zapolska. Poland. 1885-1998. Lang.: Pol. 3301

Panova, N.
Design/technology
Scenographer N. Panova. Russia: Tver'. 1998. Lang.: Rus. 213

Pantages Theatre (Toronto, ON)
Performance spaces
Toronto's theatres. Canada: Toronto, ON. 1998. Lang.: Eng. 434

Pantera Imperial, La
Performance/production
Collection of newspaper reviews by London theatre critics. UK-Scotland: Edinburgh. 1998. Lang.: Eng. 2650

Pantomime
SEE ALSO
Mime.
Classed Entries under MIME—Pantomime. English Pantomime.
Performance/production
Working-class theatre and censorship. France: Paris. 1800-1862. Lang.: Eng. 533
New London venues and productions. UK-England: London. 1994-1998. Lang.: Eng. 605
Music for ballet-pantomime at the Paris Opera. France. 1825-1850. Lang.: Eng. 1078
Amedeo Amodio's new choreography for Čajkovskij's *The Nutcracker*. Italy: Rome. 1998. Lang.: Hun. 1118
Collaborative Symbolist dance/theatre projects. Europe. USA. 1916-1934. Lang.: Eng. 1268
Lotte Goslar's Pantomime Circus. Germany: Dresden. USA: Los Angeles, CA. 1907-1997. Lang.: Eng. 4123

Pantomime Circus (Los Angeles, CA)
Performance/production
Lotte Goslar's Pantomime Circus. Germany: Dresden. USA: Los Angeles, CA. 1907-1997. Lang.: Eng. 4123

Papa Mama
Institutions
Profile of Württembergische Landesbühne. Germany: Esslingen. 1996-1997. Lang.: Ger. 1639

Papaconstanou, Elli
Performance/production
Collection of newspaper reviews by London theatre critics. UK-England: London. 1998. Lang.: Eng. 2446

Papeles del infierno, Los (Leaflets from Hell)
Plays/librettos/scripts
Politics and violence in *Los papeles del infierno (Leaflets from Hell)* by Enrique Buenaventura. Colombia. 1970-1985. Lang.: Spa. 2847

Paper Mill Playhouse (Millburn, NJ)
Design/technology
Lighting design for the musical *Follies*, Paper Mill Playhouse. USA: Millburn, NJ. 1998. Lang.: Eng. 4335

Papinianus
Relation to other fields
Analysis of illustrations of first editions of tragedies by Gryphius. Germany. 1635-1664. Lang.: Eng. 3765

Papp, Tímea
Performance/production
Open-air dance performances. Hungary: Pécs. 1998. Lang.: Hun. 1292

Paquebot Tenacity, Le (S.S. Tenacity, The)
Performance/production
Director Jacques Copeau and his theatrical aesthetic. France. 1913-1920. Lang.: Eng. 1941
Par-dessus bord (Overboard)
Plays/librettos/scripts
Analysis of *Par-dessus bord (Overboard)* by Michel Vinaver. France. Switzerland: La Chaux-de-Fonds. 1960-1998. Lang.: Ger. 3118
Parades
SEE
Pageants/parades.
Paradise Now
Performance/production
Theatre Magazine's anniversary issue. USA. 1968-1998. Lang.: Eng. 617
The Living Theatre's *Paradise Now*—creation and production. USA. 1951-1968. Lang.: Eng. 667
Relation to other fields
Government response to Living Theatre's *Paradise Now*. USA. Europe. 1968. Lang.: Eng. 3789
Parameswaran, Uma
Plays/librettos/scripts
Analysis of *Rootless but Green Are the Boulevard Trees* by Uma Parameswaran. Canada: Winnipeg, MB. 1985. Lang.: Eng. 2819
Parászka, Miklós
Performance/production
Productions of plays by Brecht and Shakespeare at the Hungarian theatre of Satu Mare. Romania: Satu Mare. 1998. Lang.: Hun. 2228
Paravents, Les (Screens, The)
Plays/librettos/scripts
Postcolonialism, ethnicity, and feminism in French and Caribbean plays. France. Martinique. Guadeloupe. 1960-1990. Lang.: Eng. 3104
Párczen, Zsófia
Performance/production
Hungarian student's training at Jeune Ballet de France. France: Paris. 1996-1998. Lang.: Hun. 1075
Paridon, Egbert van
Performance/production
Memoirs of actor and director Egbert van Paridon. Netherlands. 1920-1990. Lang.: Dut. 2204
Parisian Center for the Theatre of the Oppressed (Paris)
Performance/production
French political theatre: Boal and Mnouchkine. France. 1990-1996. Lang.: Eng. 529
Park Theatre (London)
SEE
Battersea Park Theatre.
Park, Maud Wood
Plays/librettos/scripts
Analysis of plays about the women's movement. USA. 1900-1940. Lang.: Eng. 3559
Parker, Alan
Design/technology
Flexible lighting design for two-band tour by Norman Schwab and Alan Parker. USA. 1998. Lang.: Eng. 4099
Sound design for the musical *Bugsy Malone*. UK-England: London. 1997. Lang.: Eng. 4327
Parker, Gary
Performance/production
Collection of newspaper reviews by London theatre critics. UK-England: London. 1998. Lang.: Eng. 2517
Parker, Matt
Performance/production
Collection of newspaper reviews by London theatre critics. UK-England: London. 1998. Lang.: Eng. 2503
Parker, Stewart
Plays/librettos/scripts
Gender and nationalism in Northern Irish drama. UK-Ireland. 1902-1997. Lang.: Eng. 3511
Parks, Suzan-Lori
Basic theatrical documents
Text of *Venus* by Suzan Lori-Parks. USA. 1995. Lang.: Eng. 1501
Plays/librettos/scripts
Analysis of *Venus* by Suzan-Lori Parks. USA. 1996. Lang.: Eng. 3582
Women playwrights' addresses to the Women's Project conference. USA. 1997. Lang.: Eng. 3589
Analysis of *Imperceptible Mutabilities in the Third Kingdom* by Suzan-Lori Parks. USA. 1995. Lang.: Eng. 3592
Interview with playwright Suzan-Lori Parks. USA. 1996. Lang.: Eng. 3621
Playwrights Adrienne Kennedy, Ntozake Shange, and Suzan-Lori Parks. USA. 1970-1998. Lang.: Eng. 3714
Parody
Institutions
Theatrical parodies of Krivoje zerkalo. Russia: St. Petersburg. 1908-1931. Lang.: Eng. 1705
Plays/librettos/scripts
Horace Walpole's *The Dear Witches* and Shakespeare's *Macbeth*. England. 1743. Lang.: Eng. 2857
Marxian analysis of dramatic parody and burlesque. USA. Europe. 1998. Lang.: Eng. 3664
Contemporary parodies of nineteenth-century opera. Italy: Naples. 1813-1875. Lang.: Ita. 4811
Parole da Beckett (Words by Beckett)
Plays/librettos/scripts
Composer Giacomo Manzoni and his work *Words by Beckett (Parole da Beckett)*. Italy. 1970-1971. Lang.: Eng. 3250
Parsifal
Audience
Opera and the young audience. Germany. 1998. Lang.: Ger. 4410
Performance spaces
Opera composer Richard Wagner and performance space. Europe. 1835-1885. Lang.: Eng. 4492
Performance/production
Iván Markó's choreography for Bayreuth Festival productions. Germany: Bayreuth. Hungary. 1998. Lang.: Hun. 1083
Plays/librettos/scripts
The reciprocal influence of opera and film. Europe. North America. 1904-1994. Lang.: Eng. 4770
Wagner's *Parsifal* and the political aspirations of Catalonians. Spain-Catalonia: Barcelona. 1841-1914. Lang.: Eng. 4820
Parsons Dance Company (New York, NY)
Performance/production
Dancer/choreographer David Parsons. USA: New York, NY. 1998. Lang.: Eng. 1329
Parsons, David
Performance/production
David Parsons Dance Company's *Fill the Woods with Light*. USA: Washington, DC. 1998. Lang.: Hun. 1195
Dancer/choreographer David Parsons. USA: New York, NY. 1998. Lang.: Eng. 1329
Part Three
Performance/production
Analysis of dance trilogy by choreographer Neil Greenberg. USA. 1994-1998. Lang.: Eng. 1334
Pártay, Lilla
Performance/production
Lilla Pártay's ballet adaptation of *Anna Karenina*. Hungary. 1991-1998. Lang.: Hun. 1090
Lilla Pártay's *Meztelen rózsa (Naked Rose)*, a ballet based on the life of Nižinskij. Hungary: Budapest. 1998. Lang.: Hun. 1110
Parti Nagy, Lajos
Performance/production
Lajos Parti Nagy's *Ibusár* directed by János Mikuli. Hungary: Kecskemét, Pécs. 1998. Lang.: Hun. 2110
Partljič, Tone
Plays/librettos/scripts
The individual and his world in Slovene theatre. Slovenia. 1943-1985. Lang.: Slo. 3347
Party
Performance/production
Collection of newspaper reviews by London theatre critics. UK-England: London. 1998. Lang.: Eng. 2512
Party Time
Plays/librettos/scripts
Comparison of Harold Pinter's *Party Time* with his screenplay for *The Remains of the Day*. UK-England. 1991-1996. Lang.: Eng. 3490
Party, Die (Party, The)
Performance/production
Productions of the Bad Hersfelder Festspiele. Germany: Bad Hersfeld. 1998. Lang.: Ger. 1991
Paryla, Katja
Design/technology
Lighting in contemporary theatre. Germany. 1998. Lang.: Ger. 192
Performance/production
Actor/director Katja Paryla. Germany, East. 1975-1995. Lang.: Eng. 2046
Shakespearean production and the GDR's 'existential crisis'. Germany, East. 1976-1980. Lang.: Eng. 2051

Pasadena Civic Auditorium (Pasadena, CA)
Performance spaces
Profiles of Southern California theatres. USA. 1998. Lang.: Eng. 473

Pascoli, Anne-Marie
Performance/production
The collaboration of choreographers Claire Russ and Anne-Marie Pascoli. France. UK-England. 1994-1998. Lang.: Eng. 1276

Påsk (Easter)
Performance/production
Collection of newspaper reviews by London theatre critics. UK-England: London. 1998. Lang.: Eng. 2429

Pasolini, Pier Paolo
Plays/librettos/scripts
Director and playwright Pier Paolo Pasolini. Italy. 1922-1975. Lang.: Ita. 3227

Theory and practice in the work of director Pier Paolo Pasolini. Italy. 1960-1970. Lang.: Eng. 3264

Passion of Dracula, The
Design/technology
Magical stage effects in 'vampire' plays. USA. 1820-1977. Lang.: Eng. 1548

Passion plays
SEE ALSO
Mystery plays.
Audience
Audience assumptions about the York *Resurrection*. England: York. 1275-1541. Lang.: Eng. 1400
Performance/production
Outdoor passion plays. USA. 1920-1995. Lang.: Eng. 2715

Maltese Holy Week rituals. Malta. 1998. Lang.: Eng. 4217
Plays/librettos/scripts
The Easter play tradition. England. 1180-1557. Lang.: Eng. 2942

Marlowe's *Edward II* and the medieval passion play. England. 1590-1592. Lang.: Eng. 3011

Analysis of the Montecassino Passion Play. Italy. 1100-1200. Lang.: Eng. 3256

Pictorial and staged versions of the Passion. Savoy. 1435-1505. Lang.: Eng. 3342

Pastor Hall
Plays/librettos/scripts
Analysis of revisions of plays by Ernst Toller. Germany. 1920-1939. Lang.: Eng. 3172

Pastoril
Performance/production
Northern Brazilian folk theatre forms. Brazil. 1972-1997. Lang.: Eng. 497

Patel, Neil
Design/technology
Professional theatrical designers on design training. USA. 1998. Lang.: Eng. 252

Technical designs for Off Broadway Shakespearean productions. USA: New York, NY. 1998. Lang.: Eng. 1539

Neil Patel's scene design for *Mirette*, Goodspeed Opera House. USA: East Haddam, CT. 1998. Lang.: Eng. 4334

Paternostro, Roberto
Performance/production
Roberto Paternostro, new music director at Staatstheater Kassel. Germany: Kassel. 1997-1998. Lang.: Ger. 4296

Patience
Plays/librettos/scripts
The trivialization of feminism in librettos of W.S. Gilbert. UK-England. 1880-1890. Lang.: Eng. 4861

Patience and Sarah
Design/technology
Set and costume design for *Patience and Sarah* at Lincoln Center. USA: New York, NY. 1998. Lang.: Eng. 4440
Performance/production
Paula Klimper and Wende Persons' opera *Patience and Sarah*. USA. 1969-1998. Lang.: Eng. 4725

Patterson, Anne C.
Design/technology
Design concept for Amy Freed's *The Psychic Life of Savages*, Wilma Theatre. USA: Philadelphia, PA. 1998. Lang.: Eng. 1555

Patterson, Russell
Institutions
Retiring artistic directors of regional opera companies, Russell Patterson and Glyn Ross. USA. 1960-1998. Lang.: Eng. 4485

Patti, Adelina
Institutions
The Neath Opera Group's festival and proposed music center at the former home of Adelina Patti. UK-Wales: Brecon. 1843-1919. Lang.: Eng. 4481

Pattinson, Maria
Performance/production
Collection of newspaper reviews by London theatre critics. UK-England: London. 1998. Lang.: Eng. 2463

Patton, William
Institutions
William Patton, executive director emeritus of Oregon Shakespeare Festival. USA: Ashland, OR. 1952-1998. Lang.: Eng. 1777

Pauer, Gyula
Design/technology
Survey of an exhibition of Hungarian scene design. Hungary: Budapest. 1998. Lang.: Hun. 195

An exhibition of sets and environments by Hungarian designers. Hungary: Budapest. 1998. Lang.: Hun. 196

Catalogue of an exhibition devoted to Hungarian theatre and film. Hungary: Budapest. 1998. Lang.: Hun. 197

Paul Bunyan
Performance/production
Background material on telecast performance of Britten's *Paul Bunyan* at New York City Opera. USA: New York, NY. 1998. Lang.: Eng. 4710

Operas by Benjamin Britten in the repertory of the Metropolitan and the New York City Opera. USA: New York, NY. 1945-1998. Lang.:Eng. 4749
Plays/librettos/scripts
W.H. Auden as an opera librettist and translator. UK-England. 1907-1973. Lang.: Eng. 4825

Paulhofer, Christina
Administration
Interviews with German theatre and film directors. Germany. 1998. Lang.: Ger. 1385

Paulin, Anders
Performance/production
Interview with director Anders Paulin. Sweden: Malmö. 1997-1998. Lang.: Swe. 2377

Paulin, Tom
Plays/librettos/scripts
Adaptations of Greek tragedy by contemporary Irish writers. Ireland. UK-Ireland. 1984-1998. Lang.: Eng. 3214

Gender and nationalism in Northern Irish drama. UK-Ireland. 1902-1997. Lang.: Eng. 3511

Pauline, Mark
Performance/production
The work of some North American performance artists. USA. Canada. 1960-1988. Lang.: Eng. 4251

Pauls, Irina
Performance/production
Recent productions of Schauspiel Leipzig. Germany: Leipzig. 1997-1998. Lang.: Ger. 2011

Pavarotti, Luciano
Performance/production
Interview with tenor Luciano Pavarotti. Italy. 1935-1998. Lang.: Eng. 4662

Pavlova, Anna
Institutions
Display of objects related to guest performances of the Ballets Russes. Germany: Berlin. 1910-1914. Lang.: Hun. 1040

Paxton, Steve
Training
Interview with Steve Paxton, creator of contact improvisation. USA. 1973-1998. Lang.: Eng. 1343

Payne, Andrew
Performance/production
Collection of newspaper reviews by London theatre critics. UK-England: London. 1998. Lang.: Eng. 2565

Payne, Matthew
Performance spaces
Theatre SKAM's production of *Louis and Dave* in a Plymouth Volaré. Canada: Victoria, BC. 1996. Lang.: Eng. 1797

Payne, Tom
Performance/production
Collection of newspaper reviews by London theatre critics. UK-England: London. 1998. Lang.: Eng. 2576

Paysage/Eine Landschaft/A Landscape, Un
Institutions
Émile Morin and Pascale Landry on their Productions Recto-Verso. Canada: Quebec, PQ. 1996. Lang.: Fre. 4233

Peabody, Josephine Preston
Plays/librettos/scripts
Analysis of plays about the women's movement. USA. 1900-1940. Lang.: Eng. 3559
Peach Blossom Fan, The
SEE
Taohua shan.
Peacock Theatre (London)
Performance/production
Collection of newspaper reviews by London theatre critics. UK-England: London. 1998. Lang.: Eng. 2463
Collection of newspaper reviews by London theatre critics. UK-England. 1998. Lang.: Eng. 2497
Collection of newspaper reviews by London theatre critics. UK-England: London. 1998. Lang.: Eng. 2557
Peacock, Jo
Performance/production
Collection of newspaper reviews by London theatre critics. UK-England: London. 1998. Lang.: Eng. 2465
Pearl
Plays/librettos/scripts
BBC radio plays with Anglo-Irish themes. UK-England. Ireland. 1973-1986. Lang.: Eng. 3868
Pearls for Pigs
Performance/production
Richard Foreman's notes for a production of his *Pearls for Pigs.* USA: Hartford, CT. 1997. Lang.: Eng. 2681
Pearson, Sybille
Performance/production
Career of director Lynne Meadow. USA: New York, NY. 1972-1985. Lang.: Eng. 2708
Peaslee, Richard
Performance/production
Collection of newspaper reviews by London theatre critics. UK-England: London. 1998. Lang.: Eng. 2567
Peau des Yeux, La (Skin of the Eyes, The)
Plays/librettos/scripts
Mixed media in theatre productions of Carole Nadeau. Canada: Quebec, PQ, Montreal, PQ. 1998. Lang.: Fre. 4047
Pecha, Jiří
Performance/production
Interview with actor Jiří Pecha. Czech Republic. 1967-1998. Lang.: Cze. 1882
Pêchers de Perles, Les
Performance/production
Background material on Lyric Opera of Chicago radio broadcast performances. USA: Chicago, IL. 1998. Lang.: Eng. 4709
Peck, Dale
Performance/production
Collection of newspaper reviews by London theatre critics. UK-England: London. 1998. Lang.: Eng. 2566
Pecknold, Adrian
Performance/production
Adrian Pecknold and the Canadian Mime Theatre. Canada: Niagara-on-the-Lake, ON. 1940-1978. Lang.: Eng. 4085
Pečkovskij, N.K.
Performance/production
Opera singer N.K. Pečkovskij. Russia: Leningrad. 1998. Lang.: Rus. 4677
Pečnikov, Gennadij
Performance/production
Children's theatre actor Gennadij Pečnikov. Russia: Moscow. 1998. Lang.: Rus. 2310
Pécsi Balett (Pécs)
Institutions
Dance training at Pécs School of the Arts. Hungary: Pécs. 1975-1998. Lang.: Hun. 1043
Performance/production
Hungarian dance companies at Interbalett '98. Hungary. 1998. Lang.: Hun. 946
Pécsi Művészeti Szakközépiskola (Pécs)
Institutions
Dance training at Pécs School of the Arts. Hungary: Pécs. 1975-1998. Lang.: Hun. 1043
Interview with ballet teacher Dóra Uhrik. Hungary: Pécs. 1978-1998. Lang.: Hun. 1045
Pécsi Nemzeti Színház (Pécs)
Performance/production
Two Hungarian productions of Arthur Miller's *Death of a Salesman.* Hungary: Pécs, Szeged. 1998. Lang.: Hun. 2123
Peele, George
Plays/librettos/scripts
Robin Hood and Elizabethan theatre. England. 1588-1601. Lang.: Eng. 2902
Peer Gynt
Institutions
Director training at Ernst-Busch-Schule and some of its graduates. Germany: Berlin. 1972-1998. Lang.: Ger. 1648
Survey of annual Ibsen festival. Norway: Oslo. 1998. Lang.: Eng. 1683
Performance/production
Productions directed by Christian Stückl, Tom Kühnel, and Robert Schuster. Germany: Frankfurt. 1997-1998. Lang.: Ger. 1969
Seven critics on their favorite character or portrayal. Sweden. 1950. Lang.: Swe. 2369
Recent productions of plays by Ibsen and Strindberg. Sweden: Stockholm. 1997. Lang.: Eng. 2393
Comparison of productions of Ibsen's *Peer Gynt.* USA: Providence, RI, New York, NY, Washington, DC, Nacogdoches, TX. 1998. Lang.: Eng. 2711
Reviews of productions of plays by Ibsen. USA: New York, NY. Norway: Oslo. 1998. Lang.: Eng. 2747
Plays/librettos/scripts
Ibsen's *Peer Gynt* and its new Polish translation. Poland. Norway. 1867-1967. Lang.: Pol. 3308
Pegg, Simon
Performance/production
Collection of newspaper reviews by London theatre critics. UK-England: London. 1998. Lang.: Eng. 2513
Peggie, Andrew
Performance/production
Collection of newspaper reviews by London theatre critics. UK-England: London. 1998. Lang.: Eng. 2470
Pein, Michaela
Performance/production
Visual dance productions by Cie, 2 in 1. Hungary: Budapest. 1998. Lang.: Hun. 942
Pekkanen, Maija
Design/technology
Interview with costume designer Maija Pekkanen. Finland. 1998. Lang.: Fin. 179
Pelinčkov gospod in njegova hiša (Master Pelinček and His House)
Plays/librettos/scripts
Social roles and ideologies in plays of Anton Funtek and Ivo Šorli. Slovenia. 1897-1920. Lang.: Slo. 3353
Pelléas et Mélisande
Performance/production
Opera director Katja Czellnik. Germany: Oldenburg, Kiel. 1996-1998. Lang.: Ger. 4583
Pellegrina, La
Plays/librettos/scripts
Ludic aspects of Italian Renaissance theatre. Italy. 1500-1700. Lang.: Ita. 3240
Pelletier, Luce
Plays/librettos/scripts
The use of collage in contemporary productions involving Greek myths. Canada: Montreal, PQ. 1998. Lang.: Fre. 2814
Pelligrin, Simon-Joseph
Plays/librettos/scripts
Politics and the unity of place in *Hippolyte et Aricie* by Rameau and Pelligrin. France. 1733. Lang.: Eng. 4780
Themes from Greek tragedy in opera. France. 1635-1774. Lang.: Eng. 4783
Racine's *Phèdre* as a source for *Hippolyte et Aricie* by Rameau and Pelligrin. France. 1660-1733. Lang.: Eng. 4788
The shaping influence of Pelligrin's libretto on Rameau's *Hippolyte et Aricie.* France. 1733. Lang.: Eng. 4790
Pelly, Laurent
Institutions
Reviews of some productions at the Avignon Festival. France: Avignon. 1998. Lang.: Hun. 1615
Performance/production
Press reactions to productions of Offenbach's *Orphée aux Enfers.* Belgium. Switzerland. France. 1997. Lang.: Fre. 4535
Penhall, Joe
Performance/production
Collection of newspaper reviews by London theatre critics. UK-England: London. 1998. Lang.: Eng. 2454

Penn & Teller (New York, NY)
Performance/production
Profile of MacArthur fellow and juggler Michael Moschen. USA. 1955-1998. Lang.: Eng. 4141
Penn, Arthur
Institutions
Arthur Penn and Actors Studio. USA: New York, NY. 1997. Lang.: Eng. 1767
Penn, Laura
Administration
Interviews with women in top management of theatres. USA: New Haven, CT, Seattle, WA, East Haddam, CT. 1998. Lang.: Eng. 1397
Pennsylvania Ballet (Philadelphia, PA)
Institutions
Profile of Pennsylvania Ballet. USA: Philadelphia, PA. 1970-1998. Lang.: Eng. 1058
Penso, Dawn
Performance/production
Collection of newspaper reviews by London theatre critics. UK-England: London. 1998. Lang.: Eng. 2460
Pentameters Theatre (London)
Performance/production
Collection of newspaper reviews by London theatre critics. UK-England: London, Stratford, Derby. 1998. Lang.: Eng. 2417
Collection of newspaper reviews by London theatre critics. UK-England: London. 1998. Lang.: Eng. 2422
Collection of newspaper reviews by London theatre critics. UK-England: London. 1998. Lang.: Eng. 2476
Collection of newspaper reviews by London theatre critics. UK-England: London. 1998. Lang.: Eng. 2516
Collection of newspaper reviews by London theatre critics. UK-England: London. 1998. Lang.: Eng. 2586
Péntek, Kata
Performance/production
Dancer Kata Péntek. Hungary. 1987-1998. Lang.: Hun. 949
Penthesilea
Performance/production
Recent Paris productions. France: Paris. 1997-1998. Lang.: Ger. 1933
Plays/librettos/scripts
The devouring woman in plays of Racine, Kleist, Ibsen, and Beckett. Europe. 1760-1992. Lang.: Eng. 3058
Peony Pavilion, The
SEE ALSO
Mudan ting.
People's Arts Theatre (Beijing)
Performance/production
Shaw's *Major Barbara* at the People's Arts Theatre. China, People's Republic of: Beijing. 1991. Lang.: Eng. 1874
People's Theatre (Budapest)
SEE
Népszinház.
Pepe, avagy az angyalok lázadása (Pepe, or the Revolt of Angels)
Performance/production
László Babarczy's production of *Pepe* by Andor Szilágy. Serbia: Novi Sad. 1998. Lang.: Hun. 2342
Pepper, Robert
Performance/production
Collection of newspaper reviews by London theatre critics. UK-England: London. 1998. Lang.: Eng. 2412
Percy, William
Plays/librettos/scripts
Analysis of an edition of William Percy's *Faery Pastorall.* England. 1603-1646. Lang.: Eng. 2916
Perdziloa, Robert
Design/technology
Set and costume design for San Francisco Opera productions. USA: San Francisco, CA. 1998. Lang.: Eng. 4443
Pereira prétend (Pereira Claims)
Performance/production
Comparison of text-based and visual productions. France. 1998. Lang.: Fre. 1939
Peretz, Icchok Lejbo
Plays/librettos/scripts
Enlightenment influences on modern Jewish theatre. Poland. 1500-1914. Lang.: Pol. 3307
Pérez de la Fuente, Juan Carlos
Performance/production
Juan Carlos Pérez de la Fuente's production of *San Juan* by Max Aub. Spain: Madrid. 1998. Lang.: Eng. 2363
Perfect Words, The
Performance/production
Collection of newspaper reviews by London theatre critics. UK-England: London. 1998. Lang.: Eng. 2546
Performance art
SEE ALSO
Classed Entries under MIXED ENTERTAINMENT—Performance art.
Design/technology
Technology and its use by artists. 1913-1988. Lang.: Eng. 166
Performance spaces
Profile of the theatrical venue Mousonturm. Germany: Franfurt. 1978-1998. Lang.: Ger. 441
Performance/production
The performance of sacrifice on stage. France. Germany. 1900-1998. Lang.: Ger. 530
Hanne Tierney's adaptation of *Bodas de sangre (Blood Wedding)* by García Lorca. USA. 1997. Lang.: Eng. 647
Performer/choreographer Wendy Houstoun. UK-England. 1989-1998. Lang.: Eng. 1309
Dr. Kokos Kärlekslaboratorium (Dr. Koko's Laboratory of Love) at Backstage, Stockholms Stadsteater. Sweden: Stockholm. 1998. Lang.: Swe. 2378
Performance in the work of mixed-media artist Tina Keane. UK-England. 1970-1988. Lang.: Eng. 4044
Performance art and the reinvigoration of opera. Europe. 1964-1989. Lang.: Eng. 4556
Theory/criticism
Analysis of Yoko Ono's performance work *Cut Piece.* USA. 1964-1998. Lang.: Eng. 4151
Performance Group (New York, NY)
Performance/production
The influence of experimental performance on contemporary drama. Europe. USA. 1960-1987. Lang.: Eng. 526
Twentieth-century productions of Euripidean tragedy. USA. 1915-1969. Lang.: Eng. 2678
Relation to other fields
Ritual in encounter groups and experimental theatre. USA. 1960-1970. Lang.: Eng. 788
Performance spaces
SEE ALSO
Classed Entries.
Design/technology
Set designer Jean-Guy Lecat and his work with Peter Brook. France. Denmark. 1975-1998. Lang.: Dan. 182
Walther Unruh and German theatre technology. Germany. 1898-1998. Lang.: Ger. 187
New sound and video system in the performance space of Luxor Hotel and Casino. USA: Las Vegas, NV. 1998. Lang.: Eng. 285
Design for houses of worship, including their adaptation for performance and exhibitions. USA: Long Beach, CA. 1998. Lang.: Eng. 290
Institutions
Profile of TAXI Children's Theatre. USA: Louisville, KY. 1992-1998. Lang.: Eng. 390
Popular entertainment at the New Haven Assembly Hall and Columbian Museum and Gardens. USA: New Haven, CT. 1796-1820. Lang.: Eng. 394
Theatrical activity in Cleveland's Playhouse Square. USA: Cleveland, OH. 1998. Lang.: Eng. 416
The new home of Chicago Shakespeare Theatre, formerly Shakespeare Repertory Theatre. USA: Chicago, IL. 1998. Lang.: Eng. 1775
Performance/production
Mozart's operas and contemporary Viennese performance spaces. Austria: Vienna. 1782-1791. Lang.: Eng. 4528
English theatre architecture and the operas of Henry Purcell. England: London. 1659-1695. Lang.: Eng. 4548
The influence of the Haymarket Theatre on Handelian opera. England: London. 1710-1739. Lang.: Eng. 4549
Weber's *Der Freischütz* and the Neues Schauspielhaus. Germany: Berlin. 1821. Lang.: Eng. 4581
Relation to other fields
Tourism and the development of theatre districts. USA: New York, NY. Germany: Berlin. 1998. Lang.: Eng. 807
The social significance of the Disney Corporation's influence on Broadway theatre. USA: New York, NY. 1997. Lang.: Eng. 3782
The square in Italian pageants and open-air entertainment. Italy. 1933-1975. Lang.: Ita. 4227

Performance spaces — cont'd

Research/historiography
Problem of documentary performance art. 1950-1988. Lang.: Eng. 4267
Theory/criticism
Performance art and the 'poetics of space'. USA. Poland. 1952-1984. Lang.: Eng. 4270

Performance studies
Performance/production
Theatrical construction of Chilean national identity and history. Chile. 1990-1998. Lang.: Spa. 510
Theatre and gender in the novels of Hannah Foster. UK-England. 1759-1840. Lang.: Eng. 613
The semiotics of antebellum home tours. USA. 1985-1997. Lang.: Eng. 624
The performance of documentary theatre based on transcripts of a Lithuanian dissidence trial. USA. 1983-1997. Lang.: Eng. 627
Ethical guidelines for the social context performance. USA. 1987. Lang.: Eng. 632
Performance at Hull House. USA: Chicago, IL. 1890-1997. Lang.: Eng. 644
Race, gender, and oral life history narrative. USA. 1988-1997. Lang.: Eng. 649
Boucicault's *The Octoroon* and the performance of race, gender, and power. USA. 1800-1860. Lang.: Eng. 669
Performance and the nineteenth-century economy. USA. 1850-1890. Lang.: Eng. 4134
Account of life in drag. USA: New Orleans, LA. 1995. Lang.: Eng. 4138
Relation to other fields
Linguistic code-switching as a discourse strategy. Israel. 1950-1989. Lang.: Eng. 714
Gender, class, nationality, and sanitary reform in nineteenth-century English theatre. UK-England. 1790-1890. Lang.: Eng. 768
Story-telling as a way of knowing and communicating. UK-Scotland. 1985-1998. Lang.: Eng. 772
Performativity of informal story-telling in western Iowa. USA. 1998. Lang.: Eng. 785
Protest actions and the staging of claims to public space. USA: Trenton, NJ. 1936. Lang.: Eng. 791
Research/historiography
Alternative forms of performance documentation. Europe. 1984-1997. Lang.: Eng. 819

Perfumes de Tango
Performance/production
Collection of newspaper reviews by London theatre critics. UK-England: London. 1998. Lang.: Eng. 2463

Peri, Jacopo
Performance/production
Peri and Rinuccini's *Daphne*, the first opera. Italy: Florence. 1598. Lang.: Hun. 4651

Pericles
Plays/librettos/scripts
Dutch and Flemish Shakespearean productions. Belgium. Netherlands. 1980-1983. Lang.: Dut. 2789
Wonder and recognition in medieval and Renaissance drama. England. 1400-1612. Lang.: Eng. 2874
The defense of prostitution in Lillo's *Marina*. England. 1738. Lang.: Eng. 2887
The obedient daughter in adaptations of Shakespeare's plays. England. 1701-1800. Lang.: Eng. 2969
Analysis of *Marina*, George Lillo's adaptation of Shakespeare's *Pericles*. England. 1738. Lang.: Eng. 2971

Perkin Warbeck
Plays/librettos/scripts
History and John Ford's *Perkin Warbeck*. England. 1634. Lang.: Eng. 2938

Perloff, Carey
Institutions
Women in top management of American Conservatory Theatre. USA: San Francisco, CA. 1992-1998. Lang.: Eng. 1781

Perpetual Motion
Performance/production
Collection of newspaper reviews by London theatre critics. UK-England: London. 1998. Lang.: Eng. 2576

Perrin, Francis
Basic theatrical documents
Text of *Jean III (John III)* by Sacha Guitry. France. 1912-1998. Lang.: Fre. 1426

Perros, Los (Dogs, The)
Plays/librettos/scripts
Cruelty and the absurd in theatre of Latin American playwrights. Latin America. 1960-1980. Lang.: Eng. 3267

Perrot, Clive
Performance/production
Collection of newspaper reviews by London theatre critics. UK-England: London. 1998. Lang.: Eng. 2585

Perry, Antoinette
Administration
History of the Tony Awards. USA: New York, NY. 1950-1998. Lang.: Eng. 74

Perry, Elizabeth
Performance/production
Elizabeth Perry's one-woman show *Sun Flower* about Elizabeth Cady Stanton. USA: New York, NY. 1998. Lang.: Eng. 2718

Persefone
Performance/production
Productions of international Čechov festival. Russia: Moscow. 1998. Lang.: Swe. 2306

Perséphone
Performance/production
Mythology in theatre works of Stravinskij, especially *Perséphone*. Russia. 1934. Lang.: Eng. 4682

Personal Matters
Performance/production
Collection of newspaper reviews by London theatre critics. UK-England: London. 1998. Lang.: Eng. 2578

Personals
Performance/production
Collection of newspaper reviews by London theatre critics. UK-England: London. 1998. Lang.: Eng. 2492

Personkrets 3:1 (Circle 3:1)
Audience
Reactions to Norén's *Personkrets 3:1 (Circle 3:1)* at Dramaten. Sweden: Stockholm. 1998. Lang.: Swe. 1405
Performance/production
Interview with actress Anna Pettersson. Sweden: Stockholm. 1988-1998. Lang.: Swe. 2371
Dr. Kokos Kärlekslaboratorium (Dr. Koko's Laboratory of Love) at Backstage, Stockholms Stadsteater. Sweden: Stockholm. 1998. Lang.: Swe. 2378

Personnel
Administration
Interview with Malene Schwartz, manager of Aalborg Teater. Denmark: Aalborg. 1993-1998. Lang.: Dan. 5
The system of subsidized theatre in Germany, and suggestions for changing it. Germany. 1989-1998. Lang.: Ger. 13
Participants in rural community theatre. USA. 1986. Lang.: Eng. 30
Gender and the career advancement of arts managers. USA. 1996. Lang.: Eng. 35
The effect of formal training on arts administrators. USA. 1998. Lang.: Eng. 45
Carol Waaser, Eastern Region Equity Director. USA: New York, NY. 1998. Lang.: Eng. 47
Equity Council member Tom Joyce. USA: Chicago, IL. 1998. Lang.: Eng. 48
Negotiations between US and Canadian Equity. USA. Canada. 1998. Lang.: Eng. 54
Equity Executive Director's investigation into union issues. USA. 1998. Lang.: Eng. 55
Jack Goldstein's departure from Equity to head Theatre Development Fund. USA: New York, NY. 1998. Lang.: Eng. 56
Profiles of Equity council members. USA: New York, NY. 1998. Lang.: Eng. 82
Kathryn Lamkey, Director of Equity's Central Regional Office. USA: Chicago, IL. 1998. Lang.: Eng. 92
Profile of Equity administrator Guy Pace. USA: New York, NY. 1998. Lang.: Eng. 99
Equity's First Vice-President Patrick Quinn. USA: New York, NY. 1998. Lang.: Eng. 100
Interview with father and daughter serving on Equity council. USA: New York, NY. 1998. Lang.: Eng. 113
Equity seminar for young performers and their families. USA: New York, NY. 1998. Lang.: Eng. 114

Personnel — cont'd

Nineteenth-century women theatre managers. USA. 1800-1900. Lang.: Eng. 129
The campaign to ban child performers in New York City. USA: New York, NY. 1874-1919. Lang.: Eng. 139
The cooperative relationship between Czech and Slovak theatres. Czechoslovakia. Czech Republic. Slovakia. 1881-1998. Lang.: Ger. 1376
Dramaturg Hans-Peter Frings on his role in the theatre. Germany: Magdeburg. 1990-1998. Lang.: Ger. 1382
Dramaturg Dirk Olaf Hanke on the dramaturg's complex role. Germany: Konstanz. 1998. Lang.: Ger. 1383
Symposium on the position of young theatre professionals. Netherlands. 1998. Lang.: Dut. 1387
Interview with Tomas Bolme, director of the Swedish actors' union. Sweden: Stockholm. 1970-1998. Lang.: Swe. 1388
Interviews with women in top management of theatres. USA: New Haven, CT, Seattle, WA, East Haddam, CT. 1998. Lang.: Eng. 1397
Interview with Carrie Jackson, executive director of AUDELCO. USA: New York, NY. 1998. Lang.: Eng. 1399
Performer Rebecca Spencer's experience as an Equity Deputy. USA: New York, NY. 1998. Lang.: Eng. 4320

Institutions
The relationship between theatrical artists and theatrical institutions. USA: Tarrytown, NY. 1998. Lang.: Eng. 421
The fate of the Berliner Ensemble after the resignation of artistic director Manfred Wekwerth. Germany: Berlin. 1991-1998. Lang.:Ger. 1625
The future of Schaubühne after the resignation of artistic director Andrea Breth. Germany: Berlin. 1997. Lang.: Ger. 1633
Profile of Nordhessisches Landestheater Marburg. Germany: Marburg. 1997-1998. Lang.: Ger. 1653
Problems of management and repertory at Berliner Ensemble. Germany: Berlin. 1992-1998. Lang.: Ger. 1656
Effects of a TV documentary on the Royal Opera House. UK-England: London. 1993-1998. Lang.: Eng. 4474

Persons, Wende
Performance/production
Paula Klimper and Wende Persons' opera *Patience and Sarah*. USA. 1969-1998. Lang.: Eng. 4725

Persson, Bodil
Institutions
Report on biennial dance conference. Sweden: Stockholm. 1998. Lang.: Swe. 902

Pertharite
Plays/librettos/scripts
Analysis of plays by Pierre Corneille. France. 1643-1652. Lang.: Eng. 3112

Pervy Verse
Performance/production
Collection of newspaper reviews by London theatre critics. UK-England: London. 1998. Lang.: Eng. 2576

Pesel, Jens
Performance/production
Recent productions of plays by Bertolt Brecht. Germany. 1997-1998. Lang.: Ger. 2028
Plays/librettos/scripts
Recent German productions of Brecht's plays. Germany. 1998. Lang.: Ger. 3150

Pesn' sud'by (Song of Fate, The)
Performance/production
Mikle Mizjukov's production of *Pesn' sud'by (The Song of Fate)* by Blok. Russia: Moscow. 1998. Lang.: Rus. 2276

Pesti Nemzeti Színház (Pest)
Performance/production
Excerpts from the diary of singer and actress Ilka Markovits. Hungary. 1839-1915. Lang.: Hun. 2064

Pesti Színház (Budapest)
Performance/production
Review of Róbert Alföldi's *Phaedra-story*. Hungary: Budapest. 1997. Lang.: Hun. 2102

Peter Grimes
Performance/production
Interview with opera singer Anne Bolstad. Norway. Sweden. 1980-1998. Lang.: Swe. 4665
Background material on Lyric Opera of Chicago radio broadcast performances. USA: Chicago, IL. 1998. Lang.: Eng. 4709
Background material on Metropolitan Opera radio broadcast performances. USA: New York, NY. 1998. Lang.: Eng. 4713
Operas by Benjamin Britten in the repertory of the Metropolitan and the New York City Opera. USA: New York, NY. 1945-1998. Lang.:Eng. 4749

Peter Pan
Design/technology
Costume design for a new version of *Peter Pan* at Children's Theatre Company. USA: Minneapolis, MN. 1998. Lang.: Eng. 4330
Institutions
The curriculum at Bayerische Theaterakademie. Germany: Munich. 1985-1998. Lang.: Ger. 1659
Performance/production
Collection of newspaper reviews by London theatre critics. UK-England: London. 1998. Lang.: Eng. 2555
Plays/librettos/scripts
Colonialism and misogyny in J.M. Barrie's *Peter Pan*. UK-England. 1908. Lang.: Eng. 3423

Péter, Rudolf
Performance/production
Review of Arthur Miller's *The Crucible* directed by Péter Rudolf. Hungary: Budapest. 1998. Lang.: Hun. 2068

Petersen, Taliep
Performance/production
Collection of newspaper reviews by London theatre critics. UK-England: London. 1998. Lang.: Eng. 2447
Plays/librettos/scripts
The influence of Taliep Petersen's musical *District Six*. South Africa, Republic of. 1987. Lang.: Eng. 4394

Peterson, Lisa
Performance/production
The 'viewpoint theory' of actor training. USA. 1998. Lang.: Eng. 2677

Petherbridge, Edward
Performance/production
Collection of newspaper reviews by London theatre critics. UK-England: London. 1998. Lang.: Eng. 2442

Petherbridge, Jonathan
Performance/production
Collection of newspaper reviews by London theatre critics. UK-England: London. 1998. Lang.: Eng. 2557

Petipa, Marius
Performance/production
Irma Nioradze in a performance of *Don Quixote* choreographed by Marius Petipa. Hungary: Budapest. 1998. Lang.: Hun. 1093
Choreographer Marius Petipa and his wife, ballerina Marie Surovščikova. Russia. Lang.: Rus. 1128
The history of the ballet *Raymonda* by Glazunov and Petipa. Russia. 1898-1998. Lang.: Eng. 1133

Petit, Philippe
Performance/production
Physical risk and its aesthetics in aerialist performance. USA. 1985-1997. Lang.: Eng. 4185

Petőfi Színház (Veszprém)
Performance/production
The ballet adaptation of the *Decameron* performed by Veszprém Dance Workshop. Hungary: Veszprém. 1998. Lang.: Hun. 1108
Two Hungarian productions of Čechov's *Tri sestry (Three Sisters)*. Hungary: Veszprém, Szeged. 1998. Lang.: Hun. 2135
Brecht and Weill's *Die Dreigroschenoper (The Three Penny Opera)* directed by László Vándorfi. Hungary: Veszprém.1998. Lang.: Hun. 4358
An open-air production of *West Side Story* directed by László Vándorfi. Hungary: Veszprém. 1998. Lang.: Hun. 4361

Petras, Armin
Performance/production
Director Armin Petras. Germany: Nordhausen. 1970-1998. Lang.: Ger. 2001
Recent productions of Schauspiel Leipzig. Germany: Leipzig. 1997-1998. Lang.: Ger. 2011

Petruševskaja, Ljudmila
Performance/production
German productions of contemporary Russian drama. Germany. 1998. Lang.: Ger. 1984

Pettersson, Ann-Margret
Performance/production
Interview with soprano Lena Nordin. Sweden: Stockholm. 1982-1998. Lang.: Swe. 4697

Pettersson, Anna
Performance/production
Interview with actress Anna Pettersson. Sweden: Stockholm. 1988-1998. Lang.: Swe. 2371
Peymann, Claus
Performance/production
Actress Ilse Ritter. Germany. 1944-1998. Lang.: Ger. 1980
The career of director Claus Peymann. Germany. 1960-1984. Lang.: Eng. 2014
Peyret, Jean-François
Performance/production
French productions of German plays. France. 1998. Lang.: Ger. 1935
Pezzana, Giacinta
Performance/production
Actress Giacinta Pezzana. Italy. 1841-1919. Lang.: Ita. 2177
Pfaff, Walter
Performance/production
Account of the theatre anthropology workshop. Austria: Vienna. 1989-1998. Lang.: Hun. 494
Training
Director Walter Pfaff on the influence of Jerzy Grotowski. Poland. Germany. 1998. Lang.: Eng. 876
Pfalztheater (Kaiserslautern)
Plays/librettos/scripts
Playwright Volker Lüdecke. Germany: Kaiserslautern. 1992-1998. Lang.: Ger. 3141
Phaedra-story, A (Phaedra Story, The)
Performance/production
Review of Róbert Alföldi's *Phaedra-story*. Hungary: Budapest. 1997. Lang.: Hun. 2102
Phaedra's Love
Plays/librettos/scripts
Analysis of plays by Sarah Kane and David Harrower, recently produced in Germany. UK-England. Germany: Cologne, Bonn. 1998. Lang.: Ger. 3487
Phantom of the Opera, The
Design/technology
The original stage machinery designed by John White at Her Majesty's Theatre. UK-England: London. 1887-1986. Lang.: Eng. 1528
Performance/production
Actors' handling of a mishap on stage during a production of *The Phantom of the Opera*. UK-England: Basingstoke. 1998. Lang.: Eng. 4369
Phayre, Janice
Performance/production
Collection of newspaper reviews by London theatre critics. UK-England: London. 1998. Lang.: Eng. 2588
Phèdre
Performance/production
Collection of newspaper reviews by London theatre critics. UK-England: London. 1998. Lang.: Eng. 2494
Collection of newspaper reviews by London theatre critics. UK-England: London. 1998. Lang.: Eng. 2583
Collection of newspaper reviews by London theatre critics. UK-Scotland: Edinburgh. 1998. Lang.: Eng. 2650
Plays/librettos/scripts
The devouring woman in plays of Racine, Kleist, Ibsen, and Beckett. Europe. 1760-1992. Lang.: Eng. 3058
Social interactions in Racine's *Phèdre*. France. 1667. Lang.: Fre. 3074
Racine's *Phèdre* as a source for *Hippolyte et Aricie* by Rameau and Pelligrin. France. 1660-1733. Lang.: Eng. 4788
Phenomenology
Relation to other fields
Phenomenology and dance. 1997. Lang.: Eng. 996
Theory/criticism
Tools for analysis of improvisation. Canada: Montreal, PQ. 1998. Lang.: Fre. 834
Roman Ingarden, phenomenology, and theatre. Poland. 1998. Lang.: Pol. 855
Philanderer, The
Plays/librettos/scripts
Analysis of early plays by George Bernard Shaw. UK-England. 1892-1900. Lang.: Eng. 3470
George Bernard Shaw and the 'New Woman'. UK-England. 1890-1900. Lang.: Eng. 3486
Theory/criticism
Ibsen, 'new' theatre, and Shaw's *Plays Unpleasant*. UK-England. 1891-1898. Lang.: Eng. 3832
Philaster
Plays/librettos/scripts
The murders of royal women in plays of Shakespeare and Beaumont and Fletcher. England. 1609-1610. Lang.: Eng. 2894
Philippou, Nick
Performance/production
Collection of newspaper reviews by London theatre critics. UK-England: London. 1998. Lang.: Eng. 2468
Collection of newspaper reviews by London theatre critics. UK-England: London. 1998. Lang.: Eng. 2503
Phillips, Anton
Performance/production
Collection of newspaper reviews by London theatre critics. UK-England: London. 1998. Lang.: Eng. 2460
Phillips, Arlene
Performance/production
Collection of newspaper reviews by London theatre critics. UK-England: London. 1998. Lang.: Eng. 2467
Phillips, Robin
Design/technology
Lighting design for *Jekyll & Hyde* directed by Robin Phillips. USA: New York, NY. 1998. Lang.: Eng. 4345
Philoctetes
Plays/librettos/scripts
Adaptations of Greek tragedy by contemporary Irish writers. Ireland. UK-Ireland. 1984-1998. Lang.: Eng. 3214
Philosophaster
Basic theatrical documents
Critical edition and English translation of Robert Burton's *Philosophaster*. England. 1606-1618. Lang.: Eng. 1418
Philosophy
Plays/librettos/scripts
Possible influence of Giordano Bruno on Shakespeare's *Hamlet*. England. 1600-1601. Lang.: Ita. 2921
The influence of eighteenth-century philosophy on the work of Samuel Beckett. France. Ireland. 1935-1993. Lang.: Eng. 3084
Authority, truth, and the allegory of the cave in works of Samuel Beckett. France. Ireland. 1953-1986. Lang.: Eng. 3085
Analysis of *I giganti della montagna (The Mountain Giants)* by Luigi Pirandello. Italy. 1936. Lang.: Eng. 3235
Hegel's influence on the plays of Henrik Ibsen. Norway. Germany. 1870-1898. Lang.: Eng. 3292
Analysis of *Al-Mawik Huwa Al-Mawik (The King Is the King)* by Saadallah Wannus. Syria. 1977. Lang.: Eng. 3418
Structure and philosophy in Shaw's *Major Barbara* and *Man and Superman*. UK-England. 1901-1905. Lang.: Eng. 3427
Shaw's *Man and Superman* as a philosophical treatise. UK-England. 1905. Lang.: Eng. 3495
Intellectual and artistic influences on playwright Eugene O'Neill. USA. 1888-1953. Lang.: Eng. 3697
Relation to other fields
Humanist ideology and the imaginary stage. Europe. 1549-1629. Lang.: Eng. 731
Situational theory in counter-cultural theatre. UK-England. 1960-1969. Lang.: Eng. 771
Role playing in the Brook Farm transcendentalist community. USA: West Roxbury, MA. 1841-1847. Lang.: Eng. 777
Theatre and drama in the life of Sir Thomas More. England. 1550-1590. Lang.: Eng. 3747
Current attitudes toward socialism, individualism, and metaphysics in German culture, including theatre. Germany: Berlin. 1989-1998. Lang.: Ger. 3766
Phoenix Theatre (London)
Performance spaces
Evidence of theatre closings in a Folger Library manuscript. England: London. 1650. Lang.: Eng. 1798
Performance/production
Collection of newspaper reviews by London theatre critics. UK-England: London. 1998. Lang.: Eng. 2480
Photography
Institutions
Pictorial history of Teatr Ateneum. Poland: Warsaw. 1928-1998. Lang.: Pol. 1688
Performance/production
A pictorial history of dance in the Netherlands. Netherlands. 1917-1998. Lang.: Dut. 957

Photography — cont'd

Photographs of Dramaten actors. Sweden: Stockholm. 1998. Lang.: Swe. 2366

Photos of Trinidadian carnival. Trinidad and Tobago. 1997. Lang.: Eng. 4165

Relation to other fields

The tasks of the theatre photographer. Germany: Nordhausen. 1998. Lang.: Ger. 737

Catalogue of an exhibition of theatre photography by Pasquale De Antonis. Italy. 1908-1998. Lang.: Ita. 752

Dance photos by Jack Mitchell. USA. 1960-1995. Lang.: Eng. 1000

Interview with photographer and former ballerina Martha Swope. USA: New York, NY. 1950-1998. Lang.: Eng. 1198

The impact of photography and cinema on theatre. Canada. 1998. Lang.: Fre. 3732

Theatre photographer André Le Coz. Canada: Montreal, PQ. 1952-1998. Lang.: Fre. 3738

Pi

Basic theatrical documents

Screenplay of *Pi* by Darren Aronofsky. USA. 1998. Lang.: Eng. 3880

Design/technology

Matthew Maraffi, production for the film *Pi*. USA. 1998. Lang.: Eng. 3906

Plays/librettos/scripts

Interview with Darren Aronofsky, writer and director of the film *Pi*. USA. 1998. Lang.: Eng. 3996

Piaf, Edith

Performance/production

Collection of newspaper reviews by London theatre critics. UK-England: London. 1998. Lang.: Eng. 2487

Piano Lesson, The

Plays/librettos/scripts

Analysis of *The Piano Lesson* by August Wilson. USA. 1990. Lang.: Eng. 3536

Piave, Francesco Maria

Performance/production

The Hungarian premier of Verdi's *Stiffelio*. Hungary: Szeged. 1998. Lang.: Hun. 4621

Verdi's rarely performed opera *Stiffelio*. Italy. 1850-1998. Lang.: Hun. 4652

Picasso at the Lapin Agile

Performance/production

English and French-language productions of *Picasso at the Lapin Agile* by Steve Martin. Canada: Montreal, PQ. 1997. Lang.: Fre. 1836

Picasso: Art Is a Crime

Performance/production

Collection of newspaper reviews by London theatre critics. UK-England: London. 1998. Lang.: Eng. 2521

Piccadilly Theatre (London)

Design/technology

Technical designs for Matthew Bourne's productions of ballets by Čajkovskij and Prokofjév. UK-England: London. 1998. Lang.: Eng. 1031

Performance/production

Matthew Bourne's dance piece *Cinderella* to music of Prokofjév. UK-England: London. 1998. Lang.: Eng. 1161

Collection of newspaper reviews by London theatre critics. UK-England: London. 1998. Lang.: Eng. 2442

Collection of newspaper reviews by London theatre critics. UK-England: London. 1998. Lang.: Eng. 2450

Collection of newspaper reviews by London theatre critics. UK-England: London. 1998. Lang.: Eng. 2518

Collection of newspaper reviews by London theatre critics. UK-England: London. 1998. Lang.: Eng. 2545

Collection of newspaper reviews by London theatre critics. UK-England: London. 1998. Lang.: Eng. 2562

Piccoli, Michel

Performance/production

The performances of Lucinda Childs and Michel Piccoli in *La Maladie de la Mort (The Sickness of Death)*, directed by Robert Wilson. France: Paris. 1997. Lang.: Eng. 1942

Interview with actress Lucinda Childs. France: Paris. 1976-1997. Lang.: Eng. 1943

Piccolo Teatro (Milan)

Performance spaces

The opening of Nuovo Piccolo in honor of the late director Giorgio Strehler. Italy: Milan. 1998. Lang.: Eng. 1802

Performance/production

Survey of Milanese theatre. Italy: Milan. 1997-1998. Lang.: Eng. 2161

Dario Fo and Giorgio Strehler honored at Venice Biennale. Italy: Venice. 1947-1998. Lang.: Eng. 2163

Giorgio Strehler's productions of plays by Bertolt Brecht. Italy: Milan. 1956-1998. Lang.: Swe. 2171

The ideas and productions of director Giorgio Strehler. Italy. 1940-1998. Lang.: Swe. 2180

Giorgio Strehler of Piccolo Teatro. Italy: Milan. 1921-1997. Lang.: Ger. 2181

Interview with director Giorgio Strehler. Italy: Milan. 1993. Lang.: Hun. 2185

Piccolo Teatro after the death of director Giorgio Strehler. Italy: Milan. 1947-1998. Lang.: Hun. 2186

Piccolomini, Alessandro

Plays/librettos/scripts

Analysis of plays by Alessandro Piccolomini. Italy. 1508-1578. Lang.: Eng. 3244

Pickup on South Street

Basic theatrical documents

Screenplay for *Pickup on South Street* by Sam Fuller. USA. 1953. Lang.: Eng. 3885

Picnic

Plays/librettos/scripts

Gender-role reversal in plays of William Inge. USA. 1950-1958. Lang.: Eng. 3623

Pidgin Macbeth

Performance/production

Collection of newspaper reviews by London theatre critics. UK-England: London. 1998. Lang.: Eng. 2471

Collection of newspaper reviews by London theatre critics. UK-England: London. 1998. Lang.: Eng. 2518

Pied Piper, The

Performance/production

Synopses of lost choreographies by Jerome Robbins. USA: New York, NY. 1949-1952. Lang.: Eng. 1166

Piedra filosofal, La (Philosopher's Stone, The)

Plays/librettos/scripts

Life and career of playwright Francisco Antonio de Bances Candamo. Spain. 1662-1704. Lang.: Eng. 3374

Pierre, Lennox

Performance/production

Women in the *canboulay* ceremony. Trinidad and Tobago. 1998. Lang.: Eng. 4166

Pilade

Plays/librettos/scripts

Theory and practice in the work of director Pier Paolo Pasolini. Italy. 1960-1970. Lang.: Eng. 3264

Pillar of Fire

Performance/production

Interviews with dancers about performance. UK-England. USA. Cuba. 1942-1989. Lang.: Eng. 1162

Pilton, Nick

Performance/production

Collection of newspaper reviews by London theatre critics. UK-England: London. 1998. Lang.: Eng. 2460

Pilz, Gottfried

Performance/production

Review of opera productions. Germany: Stuttgart, Leipzig. 1998. Lang.: Ger. 4584

Pimlott, Steven

Design/technology

Technical designs for the musical *Doctor Doolittle* directed by Steven Pimlott. UK-England: London. 1998. Lang.: Eng. 4325

Performance/production

Collection of newspaper reviews by London theatre critics. UK-England: London, Stratford, Derby. 1998. Lang.: Eng. 2417

Collection of newspaper reviews by London theatre critics. UK-England: London. 1998. Lang.: Eng. 2435

Collection of newspaper reviews by London theatre critics. UK-England: London. 1998. Lang.: Eng. 2472

Collection of newspaper reviews by London theatre critics. UK-England: London. 1998. Lang.: Eng. 2569

Susan Brown on her role in *Richard III* at RSC. UK-England: London, Stratford. 1995-1996. Lang.: Eng. 2593

David Tennant on his performance in *As You Like It* at RSC. UK-England: London, Stratford. 1996-1997. Lang.: Eng. 2640

Pimlott, Steven — cont'd

David Troughton on playing Shakespeare's *Richard III*. UK-England: London, Stratford. 1995-1996. Lang.: Eng. 2642

Pincejáték (Cellar Play)

Performance/production

Pál Békés' *Pincejáték (Cellar Play)* directed by Zoltán Ternyák. Hungary: Budapest. 1997. Lang.: Hun. 2078

Pinceszínház (Budapest)

Performance/production

Pál Békés' *Pincejáték (Cellar Play)* directed by Zoltán Ternyák. Hungary: Budapest. 1997. Lang.: Hun. 2078

Pinero, Arthur Wing

Performance/production

Collection of newspaper reviews by London theatre critics. UK-England: London. 1998. Lang.: Eng. 2490

Plays/librettos/scripts

Analysis of plays by Arthur Wing Pinero. UK-England. 1890-1910. Lang.: Eng. 3440

Ping

Plays/librettos/scripts

Clarence Barlow's abstract musical setting of a prose text by Samuel Beckett. 1971-1972. Lang.: Eng. 4305

Samuel Beckett's short story *Bing* as adapted by Roger Reynolds and Jean-Yves Bosseur. USA. 1986. Lang.: Eng. 4308

Roger Reynolds' musical settings of texts by Samuel Beckett. USA. 1968-1976. Lang.: Eng. 4309

Pinter, Harold

Basic theatrical documents

Typescript of the first draft of *The Homecoming* by Harold Pinter. UK-England. 1964. Lang.: Eng. 1477

Institutions

Productions of Bochumer Schauspielhaus. Germany: Bochum. 1998. Lang.: Ger. 1655

Performance/production

Survey of Parisian productions. France: Paris. 1997-1998. Lang.: Eng. 1937

Italian productions of plays by Harold Pinter. Italy. 1997. Lang.: Eng. 2165

Harold Pinter's production of his play *Ashes to Ashes* at the Pinter festival. Spain-Catalonia: Barcelona. 1996. Lang.: Eng. 2364

Collection of newspaper reviews by London theatre critics. UK-England: London. 1998. Lang.: Eng. 2422

Collection of newspaper reviews by London theatre critics. UK-England: London. 1998. Lang.: Eng. 2546

Collection of newspaper reviews by London theatre critics. UK-England: London. 1998. Lang.: Eng. 2561

Recent productions of plays by Harold Pinter at Donmar Warehouse. UK-England: London. 1998. Lang.: Eng. 2609

Plays/librettos/scripts

Aggressive language in modern drama. Europe. USA. 1960-1985. Lang.: Eng. 3055

English-language plays on the Dutch and Flemish stage. Netherlands. 1920-1998. Lang.: Dut. 3278

Analysis of *Ashes to Ashes* by Harold Pinter. UK-England. 1996. Lang.: Eng. 3430

Analysis of *Moonlight* by Harold Pinter. UK-England. 1994. Lang.: Dut. 3433

Interview with biographer of playwright Harold Pinter. UK-England. 1961-1997. Lang.: Eng. 3446

Comparison of the first and final drafts of *The Homecoming* by Harold Pinter. UK-England. 1964. Lang.: Eng. 3447

Lacanian analysis of *The Birthday Party* by Harold Pinter. UK-England. 1958. Lang.: Eng. 3452

Transference in plays by Harold Pinter. UK-England. 1960-1985. Lang.: Eng. 3461

Theatrical activities of Harold Pinter. UK-England: London. 1996-1998. Lang.: Eng. 3462

Bibliography of works by or about Harold Pinter. UK-England. 1994-1996. Lang.: Eng. 3475

Comparison of Harold Pinter's *Party Time* with his screenplay for *The Remains of the Day*. UK-England. 1991-1996. Lang.: Eng. 3490

Analysis of *The Collection* by Harold Pinter. UK-England. 1975. Lang.: Eng. 3507

The nature and language of menace in the plays of John Whiting, Harold Pinter and Sam Shepard. USA. UK-England. 1960-1985. Lang. :Eng. 3576

Overview of the life and work of Harold Pinter. USA. 1997-1998. Lang.: Eng. 3593

Female presence/absence in plays of O'Neill, Pinter, and Shepard. USA. UK-England. 1936-1985. Lang.: Eng. 3607

The film adaptation by Harold Pinter and Karel Reisz of *The French Lieutenant's Woman* by John Fowles. UK-England. USA. 1982. Lang.: Eng. 3982

Harold Pinter's screenplay adaptation of *The Dreaming Child* by Isak Dinesen. UK-England. 1961-1997. Lang.: Eng. 3984

Reference materials

Index to *The Pinter Review*, 1992-1996. UK-England. 1992-1996. Lang.: Eng. 3727

Theory/criticism

Theatrical reviews and the nature of theatrical success. UK-England. 1950-1990. Lang.: Eng. 3836

Pinto, Ricardo

Performance/production

Collection of newspaper reviews by London theatre critics. UK-England: London. 1998. Lang.: Eng. 2530

Pintscher, Matthias

Performance/production

Composer Matthias Pintscher and his opera *Thomas Chatterton*. Germany. 1990-2001. Lang.: Ger. 4607

Piontek, Klaus

Performance/production

Interview with actor Klaus Piontek. Germany: Berlin. 1962-1998. Lang.: Ger. 2008

Piper, Tom

Design/technology

Set and costume design for *The Spanish Tragedy* at RSC. UK-England: London. 1998. Lang.: Eng. 1525

Pippin

Performance/production

Collection of newspaper reviews by London theatre critics. UK-England: London. 1998. Lang.: Eng. 2501

Pirandello, Luigi

Basic theatrical documents

Text of an unfinished verse drama by Pirandello. Italy. 1884-1887. Lang.: Ita. 1445

Performance/production

Actor Angelo Musco. Italy. 1872-1937. Lang.: Ita. 549

Pirandello's theatre on the Austrian stage. Austria. 1924-1989. Lang.: Ita. 1825

Jorge Lavelli's production of *Sei personaggi in cerca d'autore (Six Characters in Search of an Author)* by Pirandello. France: Paris. 1925-1998. Lang.: Ita. 1921

Pirandello on the French stage. France. 1950-1981. Lang.: Ita. 1932

Pirandello on the German-language stage. Germany. Austria. 1924-1986. Lang.: Ita. 1994

Pirandello on the Greek stage. Greece. 1914-1995. Lang.: Ita. 2054

Gabriele Lavia's production of *Non si sa come (How Is Unknown)* by Luigi Pirandello. Italy: Turin. 1982-1988. Lang.: Ita. 2157

Pirandello's Teatro d'Arte on tour in Trieste. Italy: Trieste. 1926. Lang.: Ita. 2178

Pirandello on the Russian stage. Russia. 1905-1989. Lang.: Ita. 2250

Pirandello on the Spanish stage. Spain. 1961-1986. Lang.: Ita. 2358

Seven critics on their favorite character or portrayal. Sweden. 1950. Lang.: Swe. 2369

Collection of newspaper reviews by London theatre critics. UK-England: London. 1998. Lang.: Eng. 2588

Plays/librettos/scripts

Gender and madness in modern drama. Europe. 1880-1969. Lang.: Eng. 3061

Robert Musil and the 'crisis of modern drama'. Europe. 1880-1930. Lang.: Eng. 3062

Letters of Pirandello, Moissiu, and Jahn. Italy. Austria: Vienna. 1934. Lang.: Ita. 3219

Analysis of correspondence between Pirandello and Marta Abba. Italy. 1925-1936. Lang.: Ita. 3222

Pirandello and his publishers. Italy. 1888-1936. Lang.: Ita. 3223

Pirandello's work as a translator. Italy. 1886-1936. Lang.: Ita. 3225

Pirandello's fictional characters and his relationship with actress Marta Abba. Italy. 1925-1936. Lang.: Ita. 3229

Luigi Pirandello's letters to Marta Abba. Italy. 1925-1936. Lang.: Ita. 3230

Pirandello, Luigi — cont'd

Marta Abba and Pirandellian dramaturgy. Italy. Lang.: Ita. 3232

An anecdote of Silvio D'Amico regarding Pirandello and Abba. Italy: Rome. 1933. Lang.: Ita. 3233

Analysis of *I giganti della montagna (The Mountain Giants)* by Luigi Pirandello. Italy. 1936. Lang.: Eng. 3235

Marta Abba and the characters of Pirandello's plays. Italy. 1925-1936. Lang.: Ita. 3245

Pirandello's influence on French theatre. Italy. France. 1998. Lang.: Ita. 3246

Yearbook of Pirandello studies. Italy. 1589-1926. Lang.: Eng. 3247

Pirandello, Abba, and the Teatro d'Arte. Italy: Rome. 1925-1927. Lang.: Ita. 3248

The life and work of playwright Luigi Pirandello. Italy. 1867-1936. Lang.: Ita. 3249

Correspondence of playwright Luigi Pirandello and actress Marta Abba. Italy. 1925-1936. Lang.: Ita. 3255

Luigi Pirandello and his great-uncle, a priest. Italy. 1784-1863. Lang.: Ita. 3259

Analysis of *Al-Mawik Huwa Al-Mawik (The King Is the King)* by Saadallah Wannus. Syria. 1977. Lang.: Eng. 3418

Pirandello, English theatre, and English scholarship. UK-England. 1924-1990. Lang.: Ita. 3473

Theory/criticism

Texts of critical articles written by Pirandello under a psuedonym. Italy. 1898. Lang.: Ita. 3824

Pirates of Penzance, The

Performance/production

Collection of newspaper reviews by London theatre critics. UK-England: London. 1998. Lang.: Eng. 2553

Pisanelle, ou la mort parfumée, La (Pisanelle, or Fragrant Death)

Performance/production

Collaborative Symbolist dance/theatre projects. Europe. USA. 1916-1934. Lang.: Eng. 1268

Pisano, Linda

Design/technology

The 1998 USITT expo. USA: Long Beach, CA. 1998. Lang.: Eng. 251

Piscator, Erwin

Performance/production

Erwin Piscator and Brecht's *Schwejk im zweiten Weltkrieg (Schweik in the Second World War)*. Germany: Berlin. 1928. Lang.: Ger. 1952

The Russian-German theatrical relationship. Russia. Germany. 1920-1949. Lang.: Rus. 2285

Pista del cabeceo, La (Land of Nod, The)

Performance/production

César Brie and *La pista del cabeceo (The Land of Nod)*. Bolivia. 1970-1985. Lang.: Ita. 1829

Pistoletto, Michelangelo

Relation to other fields

The Arte Povera movement. Italy. 1967-1985. Lang.: Eng. 4264

Pit, The (London)

SEE ALSO

Royal Shakespeare Company.

Design/technology

Set and costume design for *The Spanish Tragedy* at RSC. UK-England: London. 1998. Lang.: Eng. 1525

Performance/production

Collection of newspaper reviews by London theatre critics. UK-England: London. 1998. Lang.: Eng. 2421

Collection of newspaper reviews by London theatre critics. UK-England: London. 1998. Lang.: Eng. 2442

Collection of newspaper reviews by London theatre critics. UK-England: London. 1998. Lang.: Eng. 2461

Collection of newspaper reviews by London theatre critics. UK-England: London. 1998. Lang.: Eng. 2471

Collection of newspaper reviews by London theatre critics. UK-England: London. 1998. Lang.: Eng. 2498

Collection of newspaper reviews by London theatre critics. UK-England: London. 1998. Lang.: Eng. 2506

Collection of newspaper reviews by London theatre critics. UK-England: London. 1998. Lang.: Eng. 2515

Collection of newspaper reviews by London theatre critics. UK-England: London. 1998. Lang.: Eng. 2538

Collection of newspaper reviews by London theatre critics. UK-England: London. 1998. Lang.: Eng. 2551

Collection of newspaper reviews by London theatre critics. UK-England: London. 1998. Lang.: Eng. 2573

Collection of newspaper reviews by London theatre critics. UK-England: London. 1998. Lang.: Eng. 2587

PITA (Stockholm)

Administration

Ways to attract new young audiences to theatre. Sweden: Stockholm. 1995-1998. Lang.: Swe. 21

Pitarra, Serafí

SEE

Soler, Frederic.

Pithoiset, Dominique

Performance/production

French productions of German plays. France. 1998. Lang.: Ger. 1935

Pitínský, Jan Antonín (Petrželka, Zdeněk)

Performance/production

The adaptation of classic Czech works to the stage. Czech Republic: Prague, Brno. 1990-1998. Lang.: Cze. 1877

Plays/librettos/scripts

Playwright/director J.A. Pitínský (Zdeněk Petrželka). Czech Republic. 1995-1997. Lang.: Eng, Fre. 2851

Pitt, George Dibdin

Performance/production

Actor and playwright George Dibdin Pitt. UK-England: London. 1806-1808. Lang.: Eng. 2592

Pittman-Wallace, Lucy

Performance/production

Collection of newspaper reviews by London theatre critics. UK-England: London. 1998. Lang.: Eng. 2462

Collection of newspaper reviews by London theatre critics. UK-England: London. 1998. Lang.: Eng. 2511

Pity in History

Plays/librettos/scripts

Political thought in plays of Howard Barker. UK-England. 1960-1992. Lang.: Eng. 3502

Place, The (London)

SEE ALSO

Royal Shakespeare Company.

Performance/production

Collection of newspaper reviews by London theatre critics. UK-England: London. 1998. Lang.: Eng. 2420

Plague Mass

Plays/librettos/scripts

Analysis of *Plague Mass* by Diamanda Galas. USA. 1991. Lang.: Eng. 4828

Plague of the Gorgeous

Plays/librettos/scripts

Review of collections of plays with gay themes. Canada. 1996. Lang.: Eng. 2802

Plaice, Stephen

Performance/production

Collection of newspaper reviews by London theatre critics. UK-England: London. 1998. Lang.: Eng. 2463

Planchon, Roger

Plays/librettos/scripts

Analysis of *Par-dessus bord (Overboard)* by Michel Vinaver. France. Switzerland: La Chaux-de-Fonds. 1960-1998. Lang.: Ger. 3118

Planning/operation

Administration

Wolfgang Gropper, director of Staatstheater Braunschweig. Germany: Braunschweig. 1997-1998. Lang.: Ger. 8

Interview with Frank Baumbauer of Deutsches Schauspielhaus Hamburg. Germany: Hamburg. 1993-2000. Lang.: Ger. 11

The effects of independent theatre in Berlin. Germany: Berlin. 1998. Lang.: Ger. 14

Stockholm's debut as cultural capital of Europe. Sweden: Stockholm. 1998. Lang.: Dan. 22

Attempts to diversify offerings of the Barbican Centre. UK-England: London. 1998. Lang.: Eng. 25

London theatres' new summer productions. UK-England: London. 1998. Lang.: Eng. 26

Theatre manager and entrepreneur Harry Davis. USA: Pittsburgh, PA. 1893-1927. Lang.: Eng. 134

Theatre manager Charles H. Gilfert. USA: Charleston, SC. 1817-1822. Lang.: Eng. 135

Study of management in regional theatres. USA. 1987-1988. Lang.: Eng. 140

Planning/operation — cont'd

Survey of dance audition practices in Swedish schools and theatres. Sweden. 1990-1998. Lang.: Swe. 882

Alternative funding strategies for dance companies. USA. 1998. Lang.: Eng. 886

History of Quebec theatre. Canada: Montreal, PQ, Quebec, PQ. 1880-1950. Lang.: Fre. 1375

Interview with Tankred Dorst and Hannah Hurtzig of the Bonner Biennale festival. Germany: Bonn. 1998. Lang.: Ger. 1379

Ernö Weil, manager of Theater Pforzheim. Germany: Pforzheim. 1997-1998. Lang.: Ger. 1380

Interviews with theatre managers regarding the changing cultural landscape. Germany: Bruchsal, Esslingen, Tübingen. 1998. Lang.: Ger. 1381

Rüdiger Bloch, manager of West Pomeranian theatres. Germany: Greifswald, Straslund. 1997-1998. Lang.: Ger. 1384

Interviews with German theatre and film directors. Germany. 1998. Lang.: Ger. 1385

Interview with Thomas Ostermeier, artistic director of Schaubühne. Germany: Berlin. 1996-1998. Lang.: Ger. 1386

Theatre directors on the future of subsidized theatre. Switzerland: Zurich. Germany: Hannover, Berlin. 1998. Lang.: Ger. 1390

Theater Basel under the direction of Stefan Bachmann. Switzerland: Basel. 1996-1998. Lang.: Ger. 1391

The 'Group of Four' at the Lyric Hammersmith and the concept of a national theatre. UK-England: London. 1945-1956. Lang.: Eng. 1392

Interview with producer Ed Mirvish. UK-England: London. Canada: Toronto, ON. 1982-1998. Lang.: Eng. 1393

Producer Aida Young. UK-England. 1950-1998. Lang.: Eng. 3854

The influence of Walt Disney on the film industry. USA. 1968-1998. Lang.: Eng. 3873

Stefan Soltesz's administration at Aalto-Musiktheater. Germany: Essen. 1997-1998. Lang.: Ger. 4286

Institutions

The directorship of Ferdinand Rieser at Zürcher Schauspielhaus. Switzerland: Zurich. 1926-1938. Lang.: Ger. 387

Systems analysis of the Southwest Theatre Association. USA. 1988. Lang.: Eng. 418

Profile of Theater in der Fabrik. Germany: Dresden. 1993-1998. Lang.: Ger. 1644

Platée

Performance/production

Photographic essay of Rameau's *Platée* directed and choreographed by Mark Morris. USA: Berkeley, CA. 1998. Lang.: Eng. 4304

Platel, Alain

Performance/production

Interview with choreographer Alain Platel. Belgium: Ghent. 1984-1998. Lang.: Eng. 1261

Plato

Plays/librettos/scripts

Authority, truth, and the allegory of the cave in works of Samuel Beckett. France. Ireland. 1953-1986. Lang.: Eng. 3085

Platonov

Basic theatrical documents

Catalan translations of the complete plays of Anton Čechov. Russia. 1884-1904. Lang.: Cat. 1449

Performance/production

Čechov's *Platonov* as adapted and directed by Erzsébet Gaál. Hungary: Budapest. 1997. Lang.: Hun. 2082

Analysis of Čechov's *Platonov* and *Lešji (The Wood Demon)*. Russia. 1878-1889. Lang.: Eng. 2297

Productions of international Čechov festival. Russia: Moscow. 1998. Lang.: Swe. 2306

Platt, Martin L.

Performance/production

Collection of newspaper reviews by London theatre critics. UK-England: London. 1998. Lang.: Eng. 2506

Platter, Thomas

Performance/production

Mountebanks and the performance of *commedia dell'arte*. Italy. France: Avignon. 1550-1620. Lang.: Eng. 4191

Play

Performance/production

Collection of newspaper reviews by London theatre critics. UK-England: London. 1998. Lang.: Eng. 2511

Play About the Baby, The

Performance/production

Collection of newspaper reviews by London theatre critics. UK-England: London. 1998. Lang.: Eng. 2491

Plays/librettos/scripts

Recent productions of plays by Edward Albee. USA: New York, NY, Hartford, CT. 1959-1998. Lang.: Eng. 3578

Play of Love and Chance, The

SEE

Jeu de l'amour et du hasard, Le.

Play of the Wether, The

Performance/production

Music in Tudor drama. England. 1497-1569. Lang.: Eng. 1902

Plays/librettos/scripts

Lucian's *Icaromenippus* as a source for Heywood's *The Play of the Wether.* England. 1533. Lang.: Eng. 2920

Play's the Thing, The

SEE

Játek a kastélyban.

Playbills

Administration

The playbill as a reflection of social and economic forces. USA. 1875-1899. Lang.: Eng. 31

Playboy of the Western World, The

Audience

Nationalist response to the premiere of Synge's *Playboy of the Western World.* Ireland: Dublin. 1907. Lang.: Eng. 1404

Plays/librettos/scripts

A folktale source of *The Playboy of the Western World.* Ireland. 1907. Lang.: Eng. 3202

Players

SEE

Club, The.

Players Theatre (London)

Performance/production

Collection of newspaper reviews by London theatre critics. UK-England: London. 1998. Lang.: Eng. 2557

Playhouse Theatre (London)

Performance/production

Collection of newspaper reviews by London theatre critics. UK-England: London. 1998. Lang.: Eng. 2413

Collection of newspaper reviews by London theatre critics. UK-England: London. 1998. Lang.: Eng. 2444

Collection of newspaper reviews by London theatre critics. UK-England: London. 1998. Lang.: Eng. 2539

Playing Burton

Performance/production

Collection of newspaper reviews by London theatre critics. UK-England: London. 1998. Lang.: Eng. 2522

Plays Unpleasant

Theory/criticism

Ibsen, 'new' theatre, and Shaw's *Plays Unpleasant.* UK-England. 1891-1898. Lang.: Eng. 3832

Playtexts

Basic theatrical documents

Text of *The Wines of Tuscany* by Conrad Alexandrowicz. Canada: Vancouver, BC. 1996. Lang.: Eng. 1344

English translation of *terukkūttu* piece *Pakaṭai Tuyil (The Dice Game and the Disrobing).* India. 1998. Lang.: Eng. 1345

English translation of *Kanadehon Hamlet* by Harue Tsutsumi. Japan. 1997. Lang.: Eng. 1360

English translation of *Takatoki* by Mokuami Kawatake. Japan. 1884-1998. Lang.: Eng. 1361

Text of *Panayiotis* by Angela Costi. Australia. 1997. Lang.: Eng. 1406

Catalan translation of *Am Ziel (To the Goal)* by Thomas Bernhard. Austria. 1981. Lang.: Cat. 1407

Catalan translation of *Anatol* and *Anatols Grössenwahn (The Megalomania of Anatol)* by Arthur Schnitzler. Austria. 1889. Lang.: Cat. 1408

Text of *Five or Six Characters in Search of Toronto* by Rana Bose. Canada: Toronto, ON. 1993. Lang.: Eng. 1409

Text of Michael Healey's one-man show *Kicked.* Canada: Toronto, ON. 1993. Lang.: Eng. 1410

Excerpt from *a canadian monsoon* by Sheila James. Canada: Toronto, ON. 1993-1996. Lang.: Eng. 1411

Excerpt from *Job Stealer* by Rahul Varma, Helen Vlachos and Ian Lloyd George. Canada: Montreal, PQ. 1998. Lang.: Eng. 1412

Playtexts — cont'd

Text of *El príncipe desolado (The Desolate Prince)* by Juan Radrigán. Chile. 1998. Lang.: Spa. 1413

Anthology of contemporary Chinese drama. China, People's Republic of. 1979-1986. Lang.: Eng. 1414

English translation of *Zmijin svlak (Snake Skin)* by Slobodan Šnajder. Croatia. 1998. Lang.: Eng. 1415

English translations of plays by Tawfiq Al-Hakim. Egypt. 1930-1945. Lang.: Eng. 1416

English translation and analysis of two plays by Ali Ahmad Bakathir. Egypt. 1908-1969. Lang.: Eng. 1417

French translation of Shakespeare's *Love's Labour's Lost*. England. France. 1594-1998. Lang.: Fre. 1419

Catalan translation of Shakespeare's *Measure for Measure*. England. 1604. Lang.: Cat. 1420

Catalan translation of Shakespeare's *Romeo and Juliet*. England. 1591. Lang.: Cat. 1421

Catalan translation of Shakespeare's *A Midsummer Night's Dream*. England. 1595. Lang.: Cat. 1422

Text of *Les Exclusés*, poetry adapted for the stage by Isabelle Starkier. France. 1998. Lang.: Fre. 1423

Text of *Pour la galerie (For the Gallery)* by Claude d'Anna and Laure Bonin. France. 1998. Lang.: Fre. 1424

Text of *Le Roi Hâtif (King Hasty)* by Françoise Gerbaulet. France. 1993-1998. Lang.: Fre. 1425

Text of *Jean III (John III)* by Sacha Guitry. France. 1912-1998. Lang.: Fre. 1426

Text of *Le Vampire suce toujours deux fois (The Vampire Always Sucks Twice)* by Victor Haïm. France. 1998. Lang.: Fre. 1427

Catalan translation of *La Nuit juste avant les forêts (The Dark Just Before the Forests)* by Bernard-Marie Koltès. France. 1977. Lang.: Cat. 1428

Text of *Capitaine Bringuier* by Pascal Lainé. France. 1998. Lang.: Fre. 1429

Text of *Mendiants d'amour (Beggars of Love)* by Gérard Levoyer. France. 1998. Lang.: Fre. 1430

Text of *L'Ascenseur (The Elevator)* by Gérard Levoyer. France. 1984-1987. Lang.: Fre. 1431

Catalan translation of *Le Jeu de l'amour et du hasard (The Play of Love and Chance)* by Marivaux. France. 1730. Lang.: Cat. 1432

Catalan translation of *Les Femmes savantes (The Learned Ladies)* by Molière. France. 1672. Lang.: Cat. 1433

Text of *Soleil pour deux (Sun for Two)* by Pierre Sauvil. France. 1998. Lang.: Fre. 1434

Text of *Ma femme s'appelle Maurice (My Wife's Name Is Maurice)* by Raffy Shart. France. 1998. Lang.: Fre. 1435

Text of *La Médée de Saint-Médard (The Medea of Saint-Medard)* by Anca Visdei. France. 1998. Lang.: Fre. 1436

Catalan translations of plays by Bertolt Brecht (volume 1). Germany. 1919-1954. Lang.: Cat. 1437

Catalan translation of Aristophanes' *Lysistrata*. Greece. 435 B.C. Lang.: Cat. 1438

Dutch translations of women's monologues by Dario Fo. Italy. 1998. Lang.: Dut. 1440

Slovene translation of *Mistero Buffo* by Dario Fo. Italy. Slovenia. 1969-1997. Lang.: Slo. 1441

Catalan translation of *Il Ventaglio (The Fan)* by Carlo Goldoni. Italy. 1765. Lang.: Cat. 1442

Catalan translation of *Gl'Innamorati (The Lovers)* by Carlo Goldoni. Italy. 1765. Lang.: Cat. 1443

Catalan translation of *La Bottega del caffè (The Coffee Shop)* by Carlo Goldoni. Italy. 1750. Lang.: Cat. 1444

Text of an unfinished verse drama by Pirandello. Italy. 1884-1887. Lang.: Ita. 1445

Russian translations of plays by Nobel Prize winners. Italy. 1848-1998. Lang.: Rus. 1446

English translation of *The Mustache* by Sabine Berman. Mexico. 1992. Lang.: Eng. 1447

English translation of *Historia (History)* by Witold Gombrowicz. Poland. 1998. Lang.: Eng. 1448

Catalan translations of the complete plays of Anton Čechov. Russia. 1884-1904. Lang.: Cat. 1449

English translation of Mejerchol'd's adaptation of *Revizor (The Inspector General)* by Gogol. Russia. USSR. 1838-1926. Lang.: Eng. 1450

Anthology of literary texts including plays for use in school. Russia. 1998. Lang.: Rus. 1451

Text of Evgen Car's monologue *Poredušov Janoš*. Slovenia. 1968-1998. Lang.: Slo. 1454

Text of *Suženj akcije—Kralj Peter Šesti (A Slave of Action—King Peter the Sixth)* by Emil Filipčič. Slovenia. 1997. Lang.: Slo. 1455

Text of *Sončne pege (Sunspots)* by Evald Flisar. Slovenia. 1997. Lang.: Slo. 1456

Text of *Miklavžev večer (St. Nicholas' Eve)* by Miloš Mikeln. Slovenia. 1997. Lang.: Slo. 1457

Texts of plays by Vinko Möderndorfer. Slovenia. 1997. Lang.: Slo. 1458

Text of plays and other works by Ivan Mrak. Slovenia. 1930-1975. Lang.: Slo. 1459

Plays and screenplays by Vili Ravnjak. Slovenia. 1991-1997. Lang.: Slo. 1460

Text of plays by Branko Rozman. Slovenia. 1990-1997. Lang.: Slo. 1461

Texts of Slovene youth theatre plays. Slovenia. 1800-1988. Lang.: Slo. 1462

Text of *Mandíbula afilada (Sharp Chin)* by Carles Alberola. Spain. 1997. Lang.: Eng. 1463

French translation of *Tres diamantes y una mujer (Three Diamonds and One Woman)* by Alejandro Casona. Spain. France. 1959-1998. Lang.: Fre. 1464

Text of *Davant l'Empire (Inside the Empire)* by Octavi Egea. Spain-Catalonia. 1999. Lang.: Cat. 1465

Text of plays by Josep M. Muñoz Pujol. Spain-Catalonia. 1995. Lang.: Cat. 1466

Text of *Àfrica 30* by Mercè Sarrias Fornés. Spain-Catalonia. 1997. Lang.: Cat. 1467

Text of *Magnus* by Jordi Teixidor. Spain-Catalonia. 1994. Lang.: Cat. 1468

Text of *Arrête de rêver, l'Étrangère (Stop Dreaming, Stranger)*. Switzerland. 1998. Lang.: Fre. 1469

Slovene translations of Tibetan plays. Tibet. 1400-1990. Lang.: Slo. 1470

French translation of *Time of My Life* by Alan Ayckbourn. UK-England. France. 1993-1998. Lang.: Fre. 1471

Text of *Example: The Case of Craig and Bentley* adapted by Tom Barrie. UK-England. 1998. Lang.: Eng. 1472

French translation of *Funny Money* by Ray Cooney. UK-England. France. 1995-1997. Lang.: Fre. 1473

Text of *Jesus, My Boy* by John Dowie. UK-England. 1998. Lang.: Eng. 1474

French translation of *Popcorn* by Ben Elton. UK-England. France. 1996-1998. Lang.: Fre. 1475

Text of *Sperm Wars* by David Lewis. UK-England. 1998. Lang.: Eng. 1476

Typescript of the first draft of *The Homecoming* by Harold Pinter. UK-England. 1964. Lang.: Eng. 1477

Catalan translation of *Arms and the Man* by George Bernard Shaw. UK-England. 1894. Lang.: Cat. 1478

Catalan translation of *The Importance of Being Earnest* by Oscar Wilde. UK-England. 1895. Lang.: Cat. 1479

Excerpt from *Diva Studies* by Elizabeth Alexander. USA. 1996. Lang.: Eng. 1480

Text of *Like Father, Like Son* by Marc J. Aronin. USA. 1987. Lang.: Eng. 1481

Texts of plays by Eddie Paul Bradley, Jr. USA. 1998. Lang.: Eng. 1482

Text of *... Where Late the Sweet Birds Sang* by Sheryle Criswell. USA. 1998. Lang.: Eng. 1483

Text of *The Ballad of Sam Bass* by William Johnson Evarts. USA. 1988. Lang.: Eng. 1484

Text of *The Metropolitan*, formerly called *The Ten Minute Play* by Mark R. Green. USA. 1995. Lang.: Eng. 1485

Text of *Three Days of Rain* by Richard Greenberg. USA. 1998. Lang.: Eng. 1486

Text of *Jails, Hospitals and Hip-Hop* by Danny Hoch. USA. 1998. Lang.: Eng. 1487

Playtexts — cont'd

French translation of *Lebensraum* by Israel Horovitz. USA. France. 1996-1997. Lang.: Fre. 1488

French translation of *The Primary English Class* by Israel Horovitz. USA. France. 1996. Lang.: Fre. 1489

Text of *White Noises* by Shannon Jackson. USA. 1998. Lang.: Eng. 1490

French translation of *Beast on the Moon* by Richard Kalinoski. USA. France. 1995-1997. Lang.: Fre. 1491

Text of *Medicine Men* by Jack Martin Karp. USA. 1998. Lang.: Eng. 1492

Text of *Dreams* by Kathleen Kristy-Brooks. USA. 1988. Lang.: Eng. 1493

Text of *Side Man* by Warren Leight. USA. 1998. Lang.: Eng. 1494

Text of *The Country Mouse and the City Mouse* by Robert Charles Lunde. USA. 1986. Lang.: Eng. 1495

Collection of plays by Charles L. Mee. USA. 1986-1995. Lang.: Eng. 1496

Text of *The Chemistry of Change* by Marlane Meyer. USA. 1998. Lang.: Eng. 1497

French translation of *My Left Breast* by Susan Miller. USA. France. 1994-1998. Lang.: Fre. 1498

Text of plays by Carlos Morton. USA. 1986. Lang.: Eng. 1499

Text of *Insurrection: Holding History* by Robert O'Hara. USA. 1998. Lang.: Eng. 1500

Text of *Venus* by Suzan Lori-Parks. USA. 1995. Lang.: Eng. 1501

Text of *Heatstroke* by James Purdy. USA. 1989. Lang.: Eng. 1502

Text of *A Day at Musemeci's* by Scott R. Ritter. USA. 1987. Lang.: Eng. 1503

Text of *GBS: Fighting to Live Again* by Beverly J. Robertson. USA. 1997. Lang.: Eng. 1504

French translation of *Alfred Stieglitz Loves O'Keeffe* by Lanie Robertson. USA. France. 1987-1997. Lang.: Fre. 1505

Texts of *WWW.chat* and *Elevator* by Chris Edwin Rose. USA. 1998. Lang.: Eng. 1506

Original playtext dealing with conflict resolution by Catherine Louise Rowe. USA. 1997. Lang.: Eng. 1507

Text of *The Sisterhood of Dark Sanctuary* by Leslie Jean Sandberg. USA. 1986. Lang.: Eng. 1508

Text of three monologues by Will Scheffer. USA. 1997. Lang.: Eng. 1509

Texts of plays about Zora Neale Hurston by Barbara Waddell Speisman. USA. 1988. Lang.: Eng. 1510

Text of *Sound Check* by Dominick A. Taylor. USA. 1994. Lang.: Eng. 1511

Text of Sharon Gayle Tucker's *S.T.C.* USA. 1988. Lang.: Eng. 1512

Screenplay of *Pi* by Darren Aronofsky. USA. 1998. Lang.: Eng. 3880

Text of cabaret revue *Carnival Knowledge* by Philip D. Potak. USA. 1988. Lang.: Eng. 4152

Text of *Ubu déchaîné (Ubu Unchained)* by Richard Demarcy. Benin. France. 1998. Lang.: Fre. 4287

Text of the musical play *Emanacije (Emanations)* by Tomaž Brenk and Mojca Kasjak. Slovenia. 1997. Lang.: Eng, Slo. 4288

Text of *Raven's Song* by Angela Brannon Tarleton. USA. 1988. Lang.: Eng. 4323

Text of puppet play for children, *Pospravljica (Tidying Up)* by Irena Androjna. Slovenia. 1997. Lang.: Slo. 4865

Text of Borut Combač's puppet play *Kdo je navil rumeno budilko? (Who Set the Yellow Alarm Clock)?.* Slovenia. 1997. Lang.: Slo. 4866

Text of *Tinka's New Dress* by puppeteer Ronnie Burkett. Canada: Winnipeg, MB. 1994. Lang.: Eng. 4917

Plays/librettos/scripts

The inhuman and postmodernism in the creation of an original play. Canada. 1998. Lang.: Fre. 2822

Analysis and translation of *Et les Chiens se taisaient (And the Dogs Were Silent)* by Aimé Césaire. Martinique. 1946-1969. Lang.: Eng. 3269

Text of *Tangled Garden* by David Wright Crawford with documentation of the author's method. USA. 1987. Lang.: Eng. 3569

Playworks (Sydney)

Plays/librettos/scripts

Australian women playwrights and their work. Australia. 1972-1998. Lang.: Eng. 2778

Playwrights Horizons (New York, NY)

Design/technology

Scene designer James Noone's work at Playwrights Horizons. USA: New York, NY. 1986-1998. Lang.: Eng. 1531

Set design for *Gun Shy* by Richard Dresser at Playwrights Horizons. USA: New York, NY. 1998. Lang.: Eng. 1535

Playwrights Unit (New York, NY)

Plays/librettos/scripts

History of the Playwrights Unit. USA. 1963-1971. Lang.: Eng. 3570

Playwriting

Administration

Theatrical agent Margaret Ramsey. UK-England: London. 1908-1991. Lang.: Ger. 1394

Institutions

Contemporary drama at Bonner Biennale. Germany: Bonn. 1998. Lang.: Ger. 1647

A program of study including playwriting and production. Russia: Moscow. 1998. Lang.: Rus. 1699

Performance/production

The interdisciplinary workshop of Teaterskollektivet Rex. Sweden: Stockholm. 1997. Lang.: Swe. 600

The integration of playwriting into the production process at Théâtre Niveau Parking. Canada: Quebec, PQ. 1990-1998. Lang.: Fre. 1857

Rehearsal practices in British professional theatre. England. 1500-1700. Lang.: Eng. 1905

Playwright Nadežda Ptuškina on her plays in production. Russia. 1998. Lang.: Rus. 2309

Guide to home puppet theatre. 1998. Lang.: Rus. 4884

Plays/librettos/scripts

Playwright Elfriede Jelinek on the relationship between author and play in rehearsal. Austria: Vienna. 1997. Lang.: Ger. 2780

The West in Chinese spoken drama and the effacement of the individual author. China, People's Republic of. 1949-1976. Lang.: Eng. 2843

Collaborative drama in the English Renaissance theatre. England. 1598-1642. Lang.: Eng. 2936

Brecht's working methods as a playwright as documented in annotated editions of his plays. Germany. 1998. Lang.: Ger. 3144

Interview with playwright Thea Doelwijt. Netherlands. Suriname. 1988. Lang.: Eng. 3279

The adaptation of novels for the stage. UK-England. 1980-1995. Lang.: Eng. 3499

The theory and practice of playwriting for different age groups. USA. 1988. Lang.: Eng. 3524

Writing for both television and live theatre. USA. 1998. Lang.: Eng. 3560

Principles of artistry in playwriting manuals. USA. 1987. Lang.: Eng. 3568

Text of *Tangled Garden* by David Wright Crawford with documentation of the author's method. USA. 1987. Lang.: Eng. 3569

Women playwrights' addresses to the Women's Project conference. USA. 1997. Lang.: Eng. 3589

Playwright Tina Howe on gender expectations on playwrights. USA: New York, NY. 1980-1997. Lang.: Eng. 3614

Writing for the youth audience. USA. 1998. Lang.: Eng. 3630

Playwright Terrence McNally on his profession. USA. 1998. Lang.: Eng. 3644

Observations on screenwriting and Beaufoy's *The Full Monty.* UK-England. 1997. Lang.: Eng. 3989

Humorous account of screenwriting problems. USA. 1998. Lang.: Eng. 4015

Beginner's guide to playwriting for television. 1998. Lang.: Rus. 4073

The question of how to write a libretto. Europe. 1800-1998. Lang.: Ger. 4775

Pleasance Theatre (London)

Performance/production

Collection of newspaper reviews by London theatre critics. UK-England: London. 1998. Lang.: Eng. 2415

Collection of newspaper reviews by London theatre critics. UK-England: London. 1998. Lang.: Eng. 2439

Collection of newspaper reviews by London theatre critics. UK-England: London. 1998. Lang.: Eng. 2445

Collection of newspaper reviews by London theatre critics. UK-England: London. 1998. Lang.: Eng. 2464

Pleasance Theatre (London) — cont'd

Collection of newspaper reviews by London theatre critics. UK-England: London. 1998. Lang.: Eng. 2502
Collection of newspaper reviews by London theatre critics. UK-England: London. 1998. Lang.: Eng. 2517
Collection of newspaper reviews by London theatre critics. UK-England: London. 1998. Lang.: Eng. 2550
Collection of newspaper reviews by London theatre critics. UK-England: London. 1998. Lang.: Eng. 2553
Collection of newspaper reviews by London theatre critics. UK-England: London. 1998. Lang.: Eng. 2556
Collection of newspaper reviews by London theatre critics. UK-England: London. 1998. Lang.: Eng. 2579
Collection of newspaper reviews by London theatre critics. UK-England: London. 1998. Lang.: Eng. 2580

Pleasant Comodie of Patient Grissill, The
Plays/librettos/scripts
Women's use of wit in response to men in English popular culture. England. 1590-1630. Lang.: Eng. 2884

Pleasantville
Design/technology
Production design for Gary Ross's film *Pleasantville*. USA: Hollywood, CA. 1998. Lang.: Eng. 3909

Pleasure
Performance/production
Collection of newspaper reviews by London theatre critics. UK-England: London. 1998. Lang.: Eng. 2572

Plebs, Milena
Performance/production
Collection of newspaper reviews by London theatre critics. UK-England: London. 1998. Lang.: Eng. 2463

Pliseckaja, Maja M.
Performance/production
Biography of ballerina Maja Pliseckaja. Russia. 1925-1994. Lang.: Rus. 1131
Ballerina Maja Pliseckaja and her husband, composer Rodion Ščedrin. Russia: Moscow. 1998. Lang.: Rus. 1143
Memoirs of ballerina Maja Pliseckaja. Russia. 1998. Lang.: Rus. 1145
Training
Maja Pliseckaja on ballet training. Russia: Moscow. 1998. Lang.: Rus. 1208

Plishka, Paul
Theory/criticism
Performers and conductors complain about unfair reviews. USA. 1998. Lang.: Eng. 4844

Pluckrose, Carole
Performance/production
Collection of newspaper reviews by London theatre critics. UK-England: London. 1998. Lang.: Eng. 2502

Plummer, Christopher
Performance/production
Speaking styles of selected actors reading Shakespeare's *Henry V*. North America. UK-England. 1998. Lang.: Eng. 2208

Plutonium Players (Berkeley, CA)
Institutions
Feminist theatre of Ladies Against Women. USA: Berkeley, CA. 1979-1993. Lang.: Eng. 396

Plymouth Theatre (New York, NY)
Design/technology
Lighting design for *Jekyll & Hyde* directed by Robin Phillips. USA: New York, NY. 1998. Lang.: Eng. 4345

Pochinko, Richard
Performance/production
Clown teachers Richard Pochinko and Philippe Gaulier. Canada. 1980-1998. Lang.: Eng. 4117

Podewil (Berlin)
Performance/production
Impressions from Podewil theatre workshop. Germany: Berlin. 1998. Lang.: Ger. 2024

Podt, George
Institutions
Profile of the children's theatre Schauburg, George Podt, artistic director. Germany: Munich. 1993-1998. Lang.: Ger. 1640

Poel, William
Performance/production
The rise of the modern Shakespearean director. Europe. 1878-1995. Lang.: Eng. 1911
Experimental Shakespeare production at the Gaiety Theatre. UK-England: Manchester. 1908-1915. Lang.: Eng. 2605

Poetry
Performance/production
Performance culture in prerevolutionary Russia. Russia. 1910-1915. Lang.: Eng. 580
Plays/librettos/scripts
The influence of Webster, Middleton, and Shakespeare on the poetry of Robert Browning. England. 1590-1889. Lang.: Eng. 2906
Relation to other fields
The performance style of poet Stevie Smith. UK-England. 1961-1970. Lang.: Eng. 770
The publication of 'Venus and Adonis' by Shakespeare. England. 1589-1593. Lang.: Eng. 3751
Performance analysis of Shakespeare's sonnets. England. 1593-1599. Lang.: Eng. 3753

Poirier, Gérard
Performance/production
Interview with actor Gérard Poirier. Canada: Montreal, PQ. 1942-1998. Lang.: Fre. 1834

Pokorný, Jiří
Plays/librettos/scripts
New direction in Czech playwriting. Czech Republic. 1990-1997. Lang.: Cze. 2850

Polanski, Roman
Plays/librettos/scripts
Roman Polanski's film adaptation of Shakespeare's *Macbeth*. USA. 1971. Lang.: Fre. 4014

Polgár, László
Performance/production
Interview with bass László Polgár. Hungary. Switzerland: Zurich. 1947-1998. Lang.: Hun. 4640

Poliakoff, Stephen
Performance/production
Collection of newspaper reviews by London theatre critics. UK. 1998. Lang.: Eng. 2407

Political theatre
Basic theatrical documents
Slovene translation of *Mistero Buffo* by Dario Fo. Italy. Slovenia. 1969-1997. Lang.: Slo. 1441
Institutions
The Orange Alternative, a street theatre opponent of martial law. Poland: Wroclaw. 1981-1988. Lang.: Eng. 375
The New Playwrights Theatre Company. USA: New York, NY. 1927-1929. Lang.: Eng. 410
Sadhu Binning on his politically-oriented theatre group Vancouver Sath. Canada: Vancouver, BC. 1972-1989. Lang.: Eng. 1577
Bread and Puppet Theatre's postmodern puppetry. USA: Plainfield, VT. 1990-1997. Lang.: Eng. 4878
The political performance aesthetic of Bread and Puppet Theatre. USA: Plainfield, VT. 1991. Lang.: Eng. 4879
Performance/production
French political theatre: Boal and Mnouchkine. France. 1990-1996. Lang.: Eng. 529
Interview with director Augusto Boal. Brazil: Rio de Janeiro. 1992-1996. Lang.: Eng. 1833
Alexander Stillmark's production of *Bruder Eichmann (Brother Eichmann)* by Heinar Kipphardt. Germany: Berlin. 1984-1992. Lang.: Eng. 2022
Market Theatre productions of plays by Athol Fugard. South Africa, Republic of. 1993-1994. Lang.: Eng. 2351
Plays/librettos/scripts
Analysis of *The Noam Chomsky Lectures* by Daniel Brooks and Guillermo Verdecchio. Canada: Toronto, ON. 1990-1991. Lang.: Eng. 2797
Comparison of French and Canadian protest plays. Canada. France. 1980-1998. Lang.: Eng. 2801
Interview with playwright Rana Bose. Canada: Montreal, PQ. India: Calcutta. 1950-1998. Lang.: Eng. 2820
Political community theatre by South Indian emigrants. Canada: Toronto, ON, Montreal, PQ. India. 1984-1998. Lang.: Eng. 2821
New Theatre of Buenaventura, Reyes, and Niño. Colombia. 1950-1985. Lang.: Spa. 2846
Theatre as cultural weapon and military education in the Eritrean war. Eritrea. 1980-1984. Lang.: Eng. 3048
The diminishing importance of Bertolt Brecht in reunified Germany. Germany. 1989-1998. Lang.: Ger. 3170
Profile of playwright, director, and actor Dario Fo. Italy. 1997-1998. Lang.: Ger. 3231

Political theatre — cont'd

Dario Fo, translation, and authorial intent. Italy. 1978-1998. Lang.: Eng. 3238
Johan Simons and the independent theatre group in Hollandia. Netherlands: Amsterdam. 1985-1998. Lang.: Ger. 3280
Playwright Femi Osofisan on his political goals and strategies. Nigeria. 1978. Lang.: Eng. 3286
Ida Kamińska's production of *Der Kheshbn (The Final Reckoning)* by Mikhl Mirsky. Poland: Warsaw. 1963. Lang.: Eng. 3310
Plays of Peter Barnes compared to those of Renaissance dramatists. UK-England. 1968-1974. Lang.: Eng. 3449
Political thought in plays of Howard Barker. UK-England. 1960-1992. Lang.: Eng. 3502
Gendered political critique in *The Club* by Eve Merriam. USA. 1976. Lang.: Eng. 3572
Analysis of *Keely and Du* by Jane Martin. USA. 1993. Lang.: Eng. 3629
Politics and feminism in the plays of Maria Irene Fornes. USA. 1975-1995. Lang.: Eng. 3635
The musical *Sandhog* by blacklisted writers Earl Robinson and Waldo Salt. USA. 1954. Lang.: Eng. 4395

Relation to other fields
The rise and fall of German political theatre. Germany. 1928-1998. Lang.: Ger. 745
Contestatory playwriting under dictatorship. South Africa, Republic of. Spain. Chile. 1939-1994. Lang.: Eng. 765
Catalonian cultural politics and Els Joglars. Spain-Catalonia. 1962-1998. Lang.: Eng. 3775
The influence of Teatro Campesino on American politics. USA. 1965-1970. Lang.: Eng. 3783

Theory/criticism
Activist political theatre and Western democracy. USA. 1985-1997. Lang.: Eng. 870

Politics

Administration
The system of subsidized theatre in Germany, and suggestions for changing it. Germany. 1989-1998. Lang.: Ger. 13
New funding options for Romanian arts groups. Romania. 1989-1998. Lang.: Eng. 20
Early American anti-theatrical legislation. USA. 1770-1830. Lang.: Eng. 33
Preparations for the centennial of actor and singer Paul Robeson. USA. 1898-1998. Lang.: Eng. 61
The commitment to arts funding by cities that sponsor major league sports. USA. 1989-1998. Lang.: Eng. 125
Censorship and Russian and East European theatre and film. USSR. Europe. 1963-1980. Lang.: Eng. 145
How Chisenhale Dance Space coped with loss of funding. UK-England: London. 1998. Lang.: Eng. 885
Alternative funding strategies for dance companies. USA. 1998. Lang.: Eng. 886
The cooperative relationship between Czech and Slovak theatres. Czechoslovakia. Czech Republic. Slovakia. 1881-1998. Lang.: Ger. 1376
Interviews with theatre managers regarding the changing cultural landscape. Germany: Bruchsal, Esslingen, Tübingen. 1998. Lang.: Ger. 1381
The closing of Göteborgs Stadsteatern. Sweden. 1974-1997. Lang.: Dan. 1389
The First Amendment and the striptease dancer. USA. 1998. Lang.: Eng. 4271

Audience
Nationalist response to the premiere of Synge's *Playboy of the Western World*. Ireland: Dublin. 1907. Lang.: Eng. 1404
The complex role of the audience in court entertainment. England: Greenwich. 1527. Lang.: Eng. 4194
Gender and social warfare at the Metropolitan Opera. USA. 1890-1910. Lang.: Eng. 4411

Institutions
The proposed merger of Deutsches Nationaltheater Weimar and Theater Erfurt. Germany: Weimar, Erfurt. 1998. Lang.: Ger. 354
The quality of theatre for children and youth. Italy: Bologna. Sweden: Stockholm. Germany. 1998. Lang.: Ger. 367
Literary meetings in multiethnic Vilna. Poland: Vilna. 1927-1939. Lang.: Pol. 372
The directorship of Ferdinand Rieser at Zürcher Schauspielhaus. Switzerland: Zurich. 1926-1938. Lang.: Ger. 387
Anna Deavere Smith on the Institute on the Arts and Civic Dialogue. USA: Cambridge, MA. 1998. Lang.: Eng. 399
William J. Ivey, nominee for chair of NEA. USA: Washington, DC. 1998. Lang.: Eng. 420
The status of the National Endowment for the Arts. USA: Washington, DC. 1997-2000. Lang.: Eng. 422
The growth of regional dance companies. USA. 1963-1998. Lang.: Eng. 908
Sidetrack Performance Group, formerly Sidetrack Theatre Company. Australia: Sydney. 1990-1998. Lang.: Eng. 1567
Estonian theatre and actors before and after the end of Soviet rule. Estonia. 1985-1998. Lang.: Swe, Eng, Ger. 1600
Holocaust education and Thalia Treffpunkt. Germany: Hamburg. 1988-1998. Lang.: Ger. 1630
Report on the Bonner Biennale theatre festival. Germany: Bonn. 1998. Lang.: Ger. 1663
German theatres' responses to threatened closings and mergers. Germany: Esslingen, Tübingen. 1998. Lang.: Ger. 1665
HaBimah and colonialism. Israel. 1920-1998. Lang.: Eng. 1673
Polish guest performances of HaBimah. Poland. 1926-1938. Lang.: Pol. 1689
Theatrical parodies of Krivoje zerkalo. Russia: St. Petersburg. 1908-1931. Lang.: Eng. 1705
Slovene self-image and the national theatre. Slovenia. Germany. 1789-1867. Lang.: Slo. 1719
European national theatres and their development. Slovenia. Germany. 1750-1910. Lang.: Slo. 1720
Profile of Manbites Dog and its topical and controversial productions. USA: Durham, NC. 1989-1998. Lang.: Eng. 1758
Mass festivals of the newly formed Soviet Union. USSR. 1917-1920. Lang.: Eng. 4113
Interview with Matthew Goulish and Lin Hixson of Goat Island. USA: Chicago, IL. 1990. Lang.: Eng. 4237
Bread and Puppet Theatre's postmodern puppetry. USA: Plainfield, VT. 1990-1997. Lang.: Eng. 4878

Performance/production
Cultural identity and Brazilian theatre. Brazil. 1980-1995. Lang.: Eng. 496
Garrison and amateur theatricals during the British regime. Canada: Quebec, PQ, Kingston, ON. 1763-1867. Lang.: Eng. 505
Theatrical construction of Chilean national identity and history. Chile. 1990-1998. Lang.: Spa. 510
Commercial theatre in early modern London. England: London. 1550-1680. Lang.: Eng. 518
Estonian artists as war refugees in Sweden. Estonia. Sweden. 1939-1945. Lang.: Swe, Eng, Ger. 519
Practical issues of cultural exchange: the Cry of Asia! tour. France. Philippines. 1988-1990. Lang.: Eng. 535
Indian popular theatre as a vehicle for social protest. India. 1975-1995. Lang.: Eng. 541
Futurism, Fascism, and Italian theatre. Italy. 1919-1940. Lang.: Eng. 545
The dynamics and contradictions of avant-garde theatre. Italy. 1960-1985. Lang.: Ita. 554
Historical, political, and aesthetic context of *madang* theatre. Korea. 1976-1998. Lang.: Ger. 557
Speculation on the future of Latvian theatre. Latvia. 1918-1998. Lang.: Swe, Eng, Ger. 558
Indigenous Mexican theatre and colonialism. Mexico. 1975-1998. Lang.: Eng. 560
Theatrical representations of civil war and civil discord. North America. Europe. Africa. 1975-1998. Lang.: Eng. 567
Postwar Polish theatre, culture, and politics. Poland. 1945-1950. Lang.: Eng. 573
Spanish theatre after Franco. Spain. 1975-1985. Lang.: Eng. 599
Popular entertainment in Uganda after Idi Amin. Uganda. 1979-1998. Lang.: Eng. 604
Theatre Magazine's anniversary issue. USA. 1968-1998. Lang.: Eng. 617
The performance of documentary theatre based on transcripts of a Lithuanian dissidence trial. USA. 1983-1997. Lang.: Eng. 627

Politics — cont'd

The life and career of singer Paul Robeson. USA. 1998. Lang.: Eng. 631

Commercial theatre and the values of the Reagan era. USA. 1980-1990. Lang.: Eng. 685

Theatrical rebellion and sociopolitical chaos. Zimbabwe. Kenya. 1990-1998. Lang.: Eng. 687

Gender and politics in German dance. Germany. 1930-1932. Lang.: Eng. 928

History of Korean dance. Korea. 1600-1985. Lang.: Eng. 954

Politics, culture, and Portuguese dance and choreography. Portugal. 1998. Lang.: Eng. 959

National identity and the choreography of Shobana Jeyasingh. UK-England. 1991-1994. Lang.: Eng. 972

Marie Taglioni and French Romantic ballet. France. 1830-1875. Lang.: Eng. 1072

Contemporary Israeli dance. Israel. 1997. Lang.: Swe. 1117

Female characters in male folk dance. England. Mexico. 1500-1900. Lang.: Eng. 1225

Interview with dancer, choreographer, and teacher Lilian Karina. Germany. 1911-1998. Lang.: Ger. 1289

Dancer, choreographer, and teacher Ruth Abramowitsch-Sorel. Poland. 1907-1974. Lang.: Ger. 1296

Power relations in *nō* theatre. Japan. 1500-1998. Lang.: Eng. 1373

Analysis of performance pieces reacting to the Australian bicentenary. Australia: Darwin, Sydney. 1988. Lang.: Eng. 1815

The development of *Letters, or Where Does the Postman Go When All the Street Names Are Changed*, based on experiences of residents of Mostar. Bosnia-Herzegovina: Mostar. 1997. Lang.: Eng. 1831

Interview with director Augusto Boal. Brazil: Rio de Janeiro. 1992-1996. Lang.: Eng. 1833

Shaw's *Major Barbara* at the People's Arts Theatre. China, People's Republic of: Beijing. 1991. Lang.: Eng. 1874

Czech theatre after the end of Communist rule. Czech Republic. 1989-1998. Lang.: Eng, Fre. 1876

Actress/writer Charlotte Cibber Charke. England. 1713-1760. Lang.: Eng. 1891

Shakespeare's *Titus Andronicus* and the political power of symbolic performance. England. 1590-1595. Lang.: Eng. 1893

Peter Brook's *The Mahabharata*, and problems of intercultural performance. France. 1988-1992. Lang.: Eng. 1925

Political changes reflected in Berlin theatre productions. Germany: Berlin. 1998. Lang.: Ger. 1958

Interview with director Matthias Langhoff. Germany: Berlin. 1945-1998. Lang.: Ger. 1987

Political context of Frank Castorf's production of *Les Mains Sales (Dirty Hands)* by Sartre. Germany: Berlin. 1998. Lang.: Ger. 2002

Interview with director Jürgen Flimm. Germany. 1998. Lang.: Ger. 2004

Alexander Stillmark's production of *Bruder Eichmann (Brother Eichmann)* by Heinar Kipphardt. Germany: Berlin. 1984-1992. Lang.: Eng. 2022

Interview with director Christoph Schroth. Germany, East. 1970-1990. Lang.: Eng. 2035

Interview with director Adolf Dresen. Germany, East. 1965-1985. Lang.: Eng. 2036

Interview with director Alexander Lang. Germany, East. 1970-1990. Lang.: Eng. 2037

Interview with director Thomas Langhoff. Germany, East. 1970-1990. Lang.: Eng. 2038

Interview with playwright Heiner Müller about his adaptations of Shakespeare. Germany, East. 1965-1990. Lang.: Eng. 2039

Shakespeare in the GDR: producer and critic B.K. Tragelehn. Germany, East. 1950-1990. Lang.: Eng. 2040

Interview with director Frank Castorf. Germany, East. 1980-1990. Lang.: Eng. 2041

Interview with director Alexander Weigel. Germany, East. 1970-1990. Lang.: Eng. 2042

Directors Manfred Wekwerth and Robert Weimann on Brecht and Shakespeare. Germany, East. 1945-1990. Lang.: Eng. 2043

Gender and Shakespearean production in the GDR. Germany, East. 1982-1990. Lang.: Eng. 2044

Interview with actor/director Johanna Schall. Germany, East. 1980-1995. Lang.: Eng. 2045

Actor/director Katja Paryla. Germany, East. 1975-1995. Lang.: Eng. 2046

Actor/director Ursula Karusseit. Germany, East. 1977-1995. Lang.: Eng. 2047

Socialism and the use of Shakespeare in the German Democratic Republic. Germany, East. 1945-1990. Lang.: Eng. 2048

Adaptations of Shakespeare in productions of Bertolt Brecht and Heiner Müller. Germany, East. 1945-1990. Lang.: Eng. 2049

National identity and Shakespearean production. Germany, East. 1945-1990. Lang.: Eng. 2050

Shakespearean production and the GDR's 'existential crisis'. Germany, East. 1976-1980. Lang.: Eng. 2051

The political and social climate of East German theatre in the sixties. Germany, East. 1960-1970. Lang.: Eng. 2052

Market Theatre productions of plays by Athol Fugard. South Africa, Republic of. 1993-1994. Lang.: Eng. 2351

Twentieth-century productions of Euripidean tragedy. USA. 1915-1969. Lang.: Eng. 2678

Resistance to a Boston production of Eugene O'Neill's *Strange Interlude*. USA: Boston, MA. 1929. Lang.: Eng. 2693

Contemporary queer politics and the production of gay and lesbian theatre. USA. 1970-1997. Lang.: Eng. 2710

Documentary theatre and the politics of representation. USA. 1966-1993. Lang.: Eng. 2728

Jane Alexander's return to acting after chairing the NEA. USA. 1998. Lang.: Eng. 2744

Profile of performer and activist Paul Robeson. USA. 1898-1959. Lang.: Eng. 2750

The development of the character Khlezstakov in Gogol's *Revizor (The Inspector General)* in productions by Mejerchol'd. USSR. 1926-1939. Lang.: Eng. 2762

Mejerchol'd's production of Gogol's *Revizor (The Inspector General)*. USSR: Moscow. 1926. Lang.: Eng. 2763

Analysis of Les' Kurbas' production of Shakespeare's *Macbeth*. USSR. 1924. Lang.: Eng. 2766

Mejerchol'd's denial of charges that he was a counter-revolutionary. USSR: Moscow. 1940. Lang.: Eng. 2767

Mejerchol'd's relationship with Lunačarskij. USSR. 1890-1931. Lang.: Eng. 2768

Aleksand'r Tairov's productions of plays by Eugene O'Neill. USSR. 1926-1929. Lang.: Eng. 2769

Social commentary and *East Side/West Side*. USA. 1963-1964. Lang.: Eng. 4068

Calypso music and carnival. Caribbean. 1933-1998. Lang.: Eng. 4119

Comic dance performer Lotte Goslar. Germany. USA. 1907-1997. Lang.: Eng. 4124

A mock slave auction at Colonial Williamsburg. USA: Williamsburg, VA. 1994. Lang.: Eng. 4142

German refugee and emigrant performers in cabaret and revue. Netherlands. 1940-1944. Lang.: Ger. 4155

Accession Day masques and tensions between Queen Elizabeth I and the Earl of Essex. England. 1595. Lang.: Eng. 4196

Political aspects of music in the masque. England. 1620-1634. Lang.: Eng. 4197

Masque, movement, and social and political negotiations. England. 1610-1642. Lang.: Eng. 4198

William Empson's *The Masque of Steel* and its presentation before Queen Elizabeth II. UK-England: Sheffield. 1954. Lang.: Eng. 4199

Civic and court ceremonies in the Jacobean period. England. 1605-1610. Lang.: Eng. 4215

Ritual performance and the Third Reich. Germany. 1938-1945. Lang.: Eng. 4216

Analysis of beauty pageants. USA. 1920-1968. Lang.: Eng. 4222

The Scottish performance art scene. UK-Scotland. 1960-1988. Lang.: Eng. 4248

The postwar Viennese Mozart style. Austria: Vienna. 1945-1955. Lang.: Eng. 4529

Rural Chinese productions of Puccini's *Turandot*. China, People's Republic of: Beijing. 1998. Lang.: Eng. 4541

Lucy Vestris in *Giovanni in London*. England: London. 1842. Lang.: Eng. 4546

Politics — cont'd

Gender, nation, and sexuality in opera. Europe. North America. 1998. Lang.: Eng. 4552

Productions of Wagner's *Tristan und Isolde* by Peter Konwitschny and Werner Schroeter. Germany: Munich, Duisberg. 1998. Lang.: Ger. 4580

Account of shadow-puppet workshop for Bosnian refugee children. Slovenia: Ribnica. 1997. Lang.: Slo. 4926

Plays/librettos/scripts

Playwright Ricardo Halac and Argentina's sociopolitical upheavals. Argentina. 1955-1991. Lang.: Eng. 2772

Analysis of *The Noam Chomsky Lectures* by Daniel Brooks and Guillermo Verdecchio. Canada: Toronto, ON. 1990-1991. Lang.: Eng. 2797

Comparison of French and Canadian protest plays. Canada. France. 1980-1998. Lang.: Eng. 2801

Theatre and the creation of a new nationalism. Canada. Saint Lucia. 1980-1995. Lang.: Eng. 2808

Analysis of *Corker* by Wendy Lill. Canada: Halifax, NS. 1994-1998. Lang.: Eng. 2836

The view of foreigners in *Niaoren (Bird Men)* by Guo Shixing. China, People's Republic of. 1991. Lang.: Eng. 2842

The West in Chinese spoken drama and the effacement of the individual author. China, People's Republic of. 1949-1976. Lang.: Eng. 2843

'Underground realism' in contemporary Chinese drama. China, People's Republic of: Shanghai. 1993-1996. Lang.: Eng. 2845

New Theatre of Buenaventura, Reyes, and Niño. Colombia. 1950-1985. Lang.: Spa. 2846

Politics and violence in *Los papeles del infierno (Leaflets from Hell)* by Enrique Buenaventura. Colombia. 1970-1985. Lang.: Spa. 2847

Playwright Slobodan Šnajder. Croatia. 1982-1998. Lang.: Eng. 2848

Politics, censorship, and the 'authorial' studio theatre. Czechoslovakia. 1968-1989. Lang.: Eng. 2852

Priest and playwright Kaj Munk. Denmark. 1898-1944. Lang.: Swe. 2855

Horace Walpole's *The Dear Witches* and Shakespeare's *Macbeth*. England. 1743. Lang.: Eng. 2857

Shakespeare's *The Tempest* as an experiment in political control. England. 1611. Lang.: Eng. 2862

Shakespeare's *Measure for Measure* and the King James Bible. England. 1604. Lang.: Eng. 2865

Social, economic, and political thought in Shakespeare's chronicle plays. England. 1590-1613. Lang.: Eng. 2869

Plague imagery in Jacobean tragedy. England. 1618-1642. Lang.: Eng. 2889

Marriage and patriarchy in *The Tragedy of Mariam* by Elizabeth Cary. England. 1613. Lang.: Eng. 2893

Analysis of Restoration anti-Puritan comedies. England. 1661-1663. Lang.: Eng. 2907

Analysis of Shakespeare's history plays. England. 1590-1599. Lang.: Eng. 2911

Recognition, repression, and ideology in Restoration drama. England: London. 1660-1680. Lang.: Eng. 2918

The representation of historical female characters on the Renaissance stage. England. 1580-1615. Lang.: Eng. 2922

History and John Ford's *Perkin Warbeck*. England. 1634. Lang.: Eng. 2938

Punishment and political power in plays of Shakespeare. England. 1604-1611. Lang.: Eng. 2944

Authority and medicine in Webster's *The Duchess of Malfi*. England. 1613. Lang.: Eng. 2947

Shakespeare and the limitation of political and textual control. England. 1600-1611. Lang.: Eng. 2965

The obedient daughter in adaptations of Shakespeare's plays. England. 1701-1800. Lang.: Eng. 2969

Protestant belief and English Reformation drama. England. 1535-1607. Lang.: Eng. 2972

The nature of tyranny in plays of Shakespeare. England. 1595-1612. Lang.: Eng. 2978

Shakespeare's *A Midsummer Night's Dream*, politics, and criticism. England. 1594-1595. Lang.: Eng. 2981

Analysis of *The Island Princess* by John Fletcher. England. 1621. Lang.: Eng. 2988

Possible censorship of *The Tragedy of Philotas* by Samuel Daniel. England. 1605. Lang.: Eng. 2996

Analysis of *The Massacre at Paris* by Christopher Marlowe. England. 1593. Lang.: Eng. 2997

Restoration playwright Margaret Cavendish. England. 1645-1662. Lang.: Eng. 3002

The politics of consent in Shakespeare's *Titus Andronicus*. England. 1590-1594. Lang.: Eng. 3006

Political context of Charles Johnson's *Love in a Forest*, an adaptation of *As You Like It*. England. 1723. Lang.: Eng. 3013

Evil in Stuart tragedy. England. 1620-1642. Lang.: Eng. 3024

Sexual politics in *The Rover* by Aphra Behn. England. 1677. Lang.: Eng. 3031

Olympe de Gouges and the theatre of the French Revolution. France. 1789-1795. Lang.: Fre. 3109

Frank Castorf's production of Sartre's *Les Mains Sales (Dirty Hands)* and the civil war in Yugoslavia. Germany: Berlin. 1998. Lang.: Ger. 3129

The meanings of the cigar in the appearance and works of Heiner Müller and Bertolt Brecht. Germany. 1930-1997. Lang.: Swe. 3134

The relevance of Bertolt Brecht in reunified Germany. Germany. 1934-1998. Lang.: Ger. 3135

Actor and playwright Curt Goetz and Nazi attitudes toward theatre. Germany. 1933-1944. Lang.: Eng. 3139

The significance of Bertolt Brecht to theatre in the late twentieth century. Germany. USA. 1898-1998. Lang.: Eng. 3142

The diminishing importance of Bertolt Brecht in reunified Germany. Germany. 1989-1998. Lang.: Ger. 3170

Fassbinder's *Der Müll, die Stadt und der Tod (Garbage, the City and Death)*. Germany: Berlin. 1976-1998. Lang.: Ger. 3175

Analysis of plays by Franz Xaver Kroetz. Germany, West. 1970-1980. Lang.: Eng. 3178

Civic discourse and civil discord in Greek tragedy. Greece. 475-400 B.C. Lang.: Eng. 3185

The development of Western-style Bengali theatre. India: Calcutta. 1795-1900. Lang.: Eng. 3191

Recent history in Irish theatre and drama. Ireland: Dublin. UK-Ireland: Belfast. 1993-1996. Lang.: Eng. 3212

Profile of playwright, director, and actor Dario Fo. Italy. 1997-1998. Lang.: Ger. 3231

Reactions to the awarding of the Nobel Prize to satirical playwright Dario Fo. Italy. 1998. Lang.: Eng. 3242

Postwar Italian drama. Italy. 1945-1998. Lang.: Eng. 3253

Analysis of Machiavelli's *Clizia*. Italy. 1525. Lang.: Eng. 3257

Caribbean identity in plays of Daniel Boukman. Martinique. 1970-1995. Lang.: Eng. 3271

Analysis of *Soldadera* by Josefina Niggli. Mexico. 1938. Lang.: Eng. 3272

Analysis of *Krísis (Crisis)* by Sabina Berman. Mexico. 1996. Lang.: Eng. 3273

Analysis of *The Swamp Dwellers* by Wole Soyinka. Nigeria. 1973. Lang.: Eng. 3283

Playwright Femi Osofisan on his political goals and strategies. Nigeria. 1978. Lang.: Eng. 3286

Henrik Ibsen and social criticism in *En Folkefiende (An Enemy of the People)*. Norway. 1882. Lang.: Swe. 3300

Essays on Polish theatre. Poland. 1960-1990. Lang.: Hun. 3305

Ida Kamińska's production of *Der Kheshbn (The Final Reckoning)* by Mikhl Mirsky. Poland: Warsaw. 1963. Lang.: Eng. 3310

Analysis of *Zvestoba (Fidelity)* by Etbin Kristan. Slovenia. 1897-1910. Lang.: Slo. 3344

Analysis of plays by Primož Kozak. Slovenia. 1959-1969. Lang.: Slo. 3350

Analysis of *Zoran ali Kmetska vojna na Slovenskum (Zoran and the Peasant War in Slovenia)* by Ivan Vrhovec. Slovenia. 1870. Lang.: Slo. 3351

Social roles in plays by Fran Govekar and Anton Medved. Slovenia. 1897-1910. Lang.: Slo. 3352

Social roles and ideologies in plays of Anton Funtek and Ivo Šorli. Slovenia. 1897-1920. Lang.: Slo. 3353

Politics — cont'd

Post-apartheid analysis of plays by Athol Fugard. South Africa, Republic of. 1991-1998. Lang.: Eng. 3364
Thomas Hürlimann's *Das Lied der Heimat (The Song of the Homeland)* and its production by Werner Düggelin. Switzerland: Zurich. 1998. Lang.: Ger. 3417
Analysis of plays by David Hare and Caryl Churchill. UK-England. 1971-1997. Lang.: Dut. 3432
George Bernard Shaw: life, work, influences. UK-England. Ireland. 1886-1955. Lang.: Eng. 3437
Interview with biographer of playwright Harold Pinter. UK-England. 1961-1997. Lang.: Eng. 3446
The censorship of the unpublished *Her Wedding Night* by Florence Bates. UK-England. 1917. Lang.: Eng. 3454
Secrets in Caryl Churchill's *Top Girls*. UK-England. 1982. Lang.: Eng. 3466
Social and political issues in the plays of David Hare. UK-England. 1969-1986. Lang.: Eng. 3479
Analysis of *The Romans in Britain* by Howard Brenton. UK-England. 1980-1981. Lang.: Eng. 3482
Byron's heroes and the Byronic hero. UK-England. 1800-1824. Lang.: Eng. 3484
Account of National Black Theatre Summit. USA: Hanover, NH. 1998. Lang.: Eng. 3523
Analysis of plays about the women's movement. USA. 1900-1940. Lang.: Eng. 3559
Gendered political critique in *The Club* by Eve Merriam. USA. 1976. Lang.: Eng. 3572
Analysis of Cuban theatre in Miami. USA: Miami, FL. 1985-1986. Lang.: Eng. 3574
Gender and politics in Romantic tragedies of Mercy Otis Warren. USA. 1783-1785. Lang.: Eng. 3575
Analysis of *Les Blancs* by Lorraine Hansberry. USA. 1970. Lang.: Eng. 3581
Analysis of *Venus* by Suzan-Lori Parks. USA. 1996. Lang.: Eng. 3582
American drama and the war in Vietnam. USA. 1969-1987. Lang.: Eng. 3586
Analysis of *Keely and Du* by Jane Martin. USA. 1993. Lang.: Eng. 3629
Lorraine Hansberry and Black Americans in theatre. USA. 1769-1986. Lang.: Eng. 3640
The comedies of manners of S.N. Behrman and Philip Barry. USA. 1920-1964. Lang.: Eng. 3648
Marxian analysis of dramatic parody and burlesque. USA. Europe. 1998. Lang.: Eng. 3664
Interview with playwright/MP Wendy Lill. USA: Halifax, NS. 1997-1998. Lang.: Eng. 3705
The underrepresentation of Hispanics in American arts. USA. 1998. Lang.: Eng. 3716
Dissident playwright Dušan Kovačevič. Yugoslavia. 1972-1997. Lang.: Eng. 3719
Contemporary drama of the former Yugoslavia in its political context. Yugoslavia. 1991-1998. Lang.: Ger. 3721
BBC radio plays with Anglo-Irish themes. UK-England. Ireland. 1973-1986. Lang.: Eng. 3868
Harold Pinter's screenplay adaptation of *The Dreaming Child* by Isak Dinesen. UK-England. 1961-1997. Lang.: Eng. 3984
Screenwriting before the Motion Picture Production Code. USA. 1927-1934. Lang.: Eng. 4026
Analysis of performance art on *The Larry Sanders Show*. USA. 1995. Lang.: Eng. 4079
TV war series. USA. 1962-1975. Lang.: Eng. 4080
Gender and politics in masques of Ben Jonson and Samuel Daniel. England. 1604-1605. Lang.: Eng. 4200
Political aspects of Stuart court masques. England. 1610-1642. Lang.: Eng. 4201
Shakespeare's *The Tempest* and Thomas Campion's *The Lord's Masque*. England. 1613. Lang.: Eng. 4202
Political tensions reflected in Ben Jonson's masque *Oberon*. England. 1611. Lang.: Eng. 4203
Royal policy, subversion, and Ben Jonson's *Oberon*. England. 1611. Lang.: Eng. 4204
Ben Jonson's antimasques. England. 1612-1632. Lang.: Eng. 4205
Political and ideological struggles in Jacobean masques. England. 1604-1609. Lang.: Eng. 4206
Puritanism and Milton's *Comus*. England. 1634-1635. Lang.: Eng. 4207
Power, gender, and race in *The Masque of Blackness* by Ben Jonson. England. 1605-1611. Lang.: Eng. 4208
The musical *Sandhog* by blacklisted writers Earl Robinson and Waldo Salt. USA. 1954. Lang.: Eng. 4395
The portrayal of Franklin Delano Roosevelt in the musical *I'd Rather Be Right*. USA. 1937. Lang.: Eng. 4396
Analysis of the opera *Mario the Magician* by Harry Somers and Rod Anderson. Canada. 1965-1992. Lang.: Eng. 4763
National identity in new Canadian opera. Canada. 1967-1998. Lang.: Eng. 4764
The relative absence of political allegory in English opera. England: London. 1620-1711. Lang.: Eng. 4767
The AIDS epidemic in contemporary opera. Europe. North America. 1985-1995. Lang.: Eng. 4771
Politics and the unity of place in *Hippolyte et Aricie* by Rameau and Pelligrin. France. 1733. Lang.: Eng. 4780
Ambition and gender in Bizet's *Carmen*. France. 1870-1879. Lang.: Eng. 4786
Nationalism and sexuality in Wagner's *Ring* cycle. Germany. 1870-1880. Lang.: Eng. 4796
Gender, nationalism, and Orientalism in *Samson et Dalila* by Saint-Saëns. Germany. 1868-1877. Lang.: Eng. 4797
Analysis of Jesuit opera by Giovanni Girolamo Kapsberger and Orazio Grassi. Italy: Rome. 1622. Lang.: Eng. 4803
Virginal heroines in Alpine settings in operas of Bellini, Donizetti, and Verdi. Italy. 1800-1850. Lang.: Eng. 4812
Gender in Bellini's *Norma* and Verdi's *Aida*. Italy. 1831-1871. Lang.: Eng. 4813
Wagner's *Parsifal* and the political aspirations of Catalonians. Spain-Catalonia: Barcelona. 1841-1914. Lang.: Eng. 4820
Derek Jarman's adaptation of works by Benjamin Britten and Wilfred Owen. UK-England. 1968-1988. Lang.: Eng. 4822
Analysis of Benjamin Britten's opera *Death in Venice*. UK-England. 1912-1992. Lang.: Eng. 4823
Analysis of *Plague Mass* by Diamanda Galas. USA. 1991. Lang.: Eng. 4828
Antifascist puppet plays by Rafael Alberti. Spain. 1936-1939. Lang.: Eng. 4922

Relation to other fields

Postwar Austrian cultural and theatrical identity. Austria. 1945-1998. Lang.: Ger. 715
Secular ritual forms in early American political culture. Colonial America. 1650-1800. Lang.: Eng. 720
Survey of Czech avant-garde theatre and socialist realism. Czech Republic. 1925-1950. Lang.: Cze. 721
Jewish culture and the Prague theatre scene. Czechoslovakia: Prague. 1910-1939. Lang.: Ger. 722
Difficulties in evaluating the quality of theatre performances. Denmark. 1997-1998. Lang.: Dan. 723
Theatre in Danish cultural policy. Denmark. 1990-1998. Lang.: Dan. 724
The evaluation of theatrical quality in the Århus area. Denmark: Århus. 1993-1998. Lang.: Dan. 725
French theatre and the influence of the right wing. France. 1995-1998. Lang.: Ger. 734
The theatre of the French Revolution. France. 1780-1800. Lang.: Eng. 735
Government and budget cuts in German theatres. Germany: Bochum, Cologne. 1991-1998. Lang.: Ger. 738
The effects of postwar monetary reform on theatres in East and West Germany. Germany. 1945-1949. Lang.: Ger. 739
The national movement, cultural policy, and German regional theatre. Germany: Eisleben. 1998. Lang.: Ger. 740
Political-cultural influences on Berlin theatre. Germany: Berlin. 1989-1998. Lang.: Ger. 742
Political and cultural situation of Frankfurt theatres. Germany: Frankfurt. 1997-1999. Lang.: Ger. 744

Politics — cont'd

The rise and fall of German political theatre. Germany. 1928-1998. Lang.: Ger. 745

The debate over whether Germany needs a national cultural minister. Germany. 1998. Lang.: Ger. 746

Frank Castorf of Volksbühne and the object and possibilities of contemporary theatre. Germany: Berlin. 1998. Lang.: Ger. 747

The quality of Berlin's independent theatres. Germany: Berlin. 1998. Lang.: Ger. 748

German politicians interviewed on cultural policy. Germany. 1998. Lang.: Ger. 749

Nationalism and Irish theatre. Ireland. UK-Ireland. 1890-1914. Lang.: Eng. 750

Politics and the dramaturg. North America. 1990-1998. Lang.: Eng. 754

Theatre, the visual arts, and the debate on Puerto Rican cultural identity. Puerto Rico. 1998. Lang.: Eng. 755

Russian and American theatre and society of the twenties. Russia. USA. 1920-1929. Lang.: Rus. 756

The cultural atmosphere of the Russian Revolution. Russia. 1917-1920. Lang.: Rus. 757

The effect of social and political change on Slovakian theatre. Slovakia. 1989-1998. Lang.: Ger. 763

Topics in post-apartheid South African literature and theatre. South Africa, Republic of. 1995-1998. Lang.: Eng. 764

Contestatory playwriting under dictatorship. South Africa, Republic of. Spain. Chile. 1939-1994. Lang.: Eng. 765

Stockholm's cultural facilities. Sweden: Stockholm. 1998. Lang.: Eng. 766

Performative techniques in social and political movements. Taiwan. 1986-1997. Lang.: Eng. 767

The current status of English cultural policy. UK-England. 1997-1998. Lang.: Ger. 769

Situational theory in counter-cultural theatre. UK-England. 1960-1969. Lang.: Eng. 771

European fears of American cultural hegemony. USA. Europe. 1998. Lang.: Eng. 773

The arts as a sector in American life. USA. 1997-1998. Lang.: Eng. 775

Role playing in the Brook Farm transcendentalist community. USA: West Roxbury, MA. 1841-1847. Lang.: Eng. 777

Criticism of the American Assembly's approach to the arts sector. USA. 1997. Lang.: Eng. 780

Protest actions and the staging of claims to public space. USA: Trenton, NJ. 1936. Lang.: Eng. 791

The changing face of Times Square and its effect on the local community. USA: New York, NY. 1998. Lang.: Eng. 812

Theatricalization of court trials in post-revolutionary Russia. USSR. 1916-1935. Lang.: Eng. 815

Directory of emigrant and refugee dancers. Europe. North America. South America. 1933-1945. Lang.: Ger. 997

American modern dance and gay culture. USA. 1933-1998. Lang.: Eng. 1337

The artist and the world in recent productions. Austria: Vienna. Germany. 1997-1998. Lang.: Ger. 3729

Manfred Weber on directing Dževad Karahasan's translation of *Leonce und Lena* by Büchner. Bosnia: Sarajevo. 1997-1998. Lang.: Ger. 3730

Conditions of Bulgarian theatre and reform efforts. Bulgaria. 1997-1998. Lang.: Ger. 3731

Performance ethnography of social action theatre Mise au Jeu Montréal. Canada: Montreal, PQ. 1995-1998. Lang.: Eng. 3735

Chinese Shakespeare studies. China, People's Republic of. 1990-1998. Lang.: Eng. 3741

Playwright Sony Labou Tansi and Congolese politics. Congo. 1996. Lang.: Eng. 3742

Václav Havel, the Czech Republic, and the European Union. Czech Republic. 1989-1998. Lang.: Eng. 3743

The dramatic nature of the ancient Egyptian text *The Triumph of Horus*. Egypt. 2500 B.C. Lang.: Eng. 3744

New-historicist analysis of Shakespeare and his time. England. 1580-1616. Lang.: Eng. 3745

Theatre and drama in the life of Sir Thomas More. England. 1550-1590. Lang.: Eng. 3747

Cross-dressing and gender struggle on the early modern English stage. England. 1580-1620. Lang.: Eng. 3749

Drama and the English Reformation. England. 1530-1607. Lang.: Eng. 3755

Cultural policy and French theatre structures. France. 1945-1998. Lang.: Ger. 3760

The commemoration of Kristallnacht at Volksbühne. Germany: Berlin. 1998. Lang.: Ger. 3764

Current attitudes toward socialism, individualism, and metaphysics in German culture, including theatre. Germany: Berlin. 1989-1998. Lang.: Ger. 3766

Use of theatre in Holocaust education. Germany: Essen. 1985-1998. Lang.: Ger. 3767

Die Berliner Ermittlung (The Berlin Investigation), an interactive theatre project by Jochen Gerz and Esther Shalev-Gerz. Germany: Berlin. 1998. Lang.: Ger. 3768

Bertolt Brecht's working methods as described in recent books. Germany. 1926-1998. Lang.: Ger. 3769

Revivals of Hanns Johst's national socialist play *Schlageter*. Germany: Uelzen, Wuppertal. 1977-1992. Lang.: Ger. 3770

Theatre and politics in Hong Kong. Hong Kong. 1984-1996. Lang.: Eng. 3772

The arrest of playwright and activist Ratna Sarumpaet. Indonesia: Jakarta. 1998. Lang.: Eng. 3773

New Italian theatrical legislation. Italy. 1998. Lang.: Eng. 3774

Catalonian cultural politics and Els Joglars. Spain-Catalonia. 1962-1998. Lang.: Eng. 3775

Challenges facing Turkish theatre artists. Turkey: Istanbul. 1994-1997. Lang.: Eng. 3778

The influence of Teatro Campesino on American politics. USA. 1965-1970. Lang.: Eng. 3783

The blacklisting of Burton and Florence Bean James, founders of Seattle Repertory Playhouse. USA: Seattle, WA. 1951. Lang.: Eng. 3784

Government response to Living Theatre's *Paradise Now*. USA. Europe. 1968. Lang.: Eng. 3789

Controversy over Terrence McNally's *Corpus Christi*, Manhattan Theatre Club. USA: New York, NY. 1998. Lang.: Eng. 3792

The upcoming Supreme Court hearing on the government's right to impose decency standards on arts grants. USA: Washington, DC. 1998. Lang.: Eng. 3793

Political power and national identity in African cinema. Africa. 1990-1998. Lang.: Eng. 4034

Politics, knighthood, and actor Sean Connery. UK. 1998. Lang.: Eng. 4036

Depiction of Jews in Stalinist Russian film. USSR. 1924-1953. Lang.: Eng. 4039

Nigerian video films. Nigeria. 1992-1998. Lang.: Eng. 4081

TV westerns and their sociopolitical context. USA. 1957-1960. Lang.: Eng. 4083

The *jouvay* ceremony of Trinidadian carnival. Trinidad and Tobago: Port of Spain. 1838-1998. Lang.: Eng. 4176

Theatrical representation at the Austrian court. Austria: Vienna. 1650-1699. Lang.: Ger. 4210

George Ferrers' Christmas revels and the execution of the Duke of Somerset. England. 1551-1552. Lang.: Eng. 4211

The square in Italian pageants and open-air entertainment. Italy. 1933-1975. Lang.: Ita. 4227

Research/historiography

The current state of research on Polish theatre in exile. UK-England: London. 1939-1998. Lang.: Pol. 824

Theory/criticism

The importance to theatre of the politics of process and relationship of process to product. 1998. Lang.: Eng. 830

Terror in theatre. Europe. North America. 500 B.C.-1988 A.D. Lang.: Eng. 839

Political interpretations of Irish literary theatre. Ireland. 1897-1996. Lang.: Eng. 846

Politics, tradition, and avant-garde theatre. Italy. 1985. Lang.: Ita. 847

Survey of theatre studies as cultural studies. USA. UK-England. France. 1957-1998. Lang.: Ger. 865

Activist political theatre and Western democracy. USA. 1985-1997. Lang.: Eng. 870

Politics — cont'd

Analysis of choreography by Merce Cunningham. USA. 1998. Lang.: Eng. 1340
Representation and delegation in theatre. 1998. Lang.: Eng. 3800
Political criticism of early modern drama. Europe. North America. 1975-1997. Lang.: Eng. 3814
Changes in the social and political situation of Polish fringe theatre. Poland. 1980-1995. Lang.: Pol. 3826
The urge to make Shakespeare contemporary. USA. 1990-1998. Lang.: Eng. 3844
Recent scholarship and popularity of the Stuart masque. UK-England. 1970-1995. Lang.: Eng. 4212

Training
Playwright Tony Kushner's address to the Association of Theatre in Higher Education. USA. 1997. Lang.: Eng. 3851
Mejerchol'd, actor training, and Trotsky. USSR. 1922-1929. Lang.: Eng. 3852

Politz, Pierre-Walter
Performance/production
Recent productions of plays by Bertolt Brecht. Germany. 1997-1998. Lang.: Ger. 2028

Polka Theatre (London)
Performance/production
Collection of newspaper reviews by London theatre critics. UK-England: London. 1998. Lang.: Eng. 2550

Pollack, Mimi
Performance/production
Interview with actors in Feydeau's *La Puce à l'Oreille (A Flea in Her Ear)* at Dramaten. Sweden: Stockholm. 1998. Lang.: Swe. 2396

Pollock, Sharon
Plays/librettos/scripts
The representation of true crime in modern drama. USA. France. 1955-1996. Lang.: Eng. 3673

Polsca, Juliet
Design/technology
Technical designs for Stanley Tucci's film *The Impostors.* USA. 1998. Lang.: Eng. 3901

Polski Balet (Warsaw)
Performance/production
The European and American tour of the Polish National Ballet. Poland. France. USA. 1937-1939. Lang.: Pol. 1124

Polygraphe, Le (Polygraph, The)
Performance/production
Cinematic work of director Robert Lepage. Canada. 1995-1998. Lang.: Fre. 3928

Pomaranczowa Alternatywa (Wroclaw)
Institutions
The Orange Alternative, a street theatre opponent of martial law. Poland: Wroclaw. 1981-1988. Lang.: Eng. 375

Poncela, Jardiel
Plays/librettos/scripts
The detective plays of Jardiel Poncela. Spain. 1940-1969. Lang.: Spa. 3392

Pons, Amaryllis
Performance/production
The Tropicana night club show. Cuba: Havana. 1939. Lang.: Swe. 4120

Pons, Lily
Performance/production
Interpreters of the title role in Delibes' opera *Lakmé.* 1932-1995. Lang.: Fre. 4505

Poor Superman
Plays/librettos/scripts
Brad Fraser's direction of a film version of his *Poor Superman.* Canada. 1994-1998. Lang.: Eng. 3966

Popcorn
Basic theatrical documents
French translation of *Popcorn* by Ben Elton. UK-England. France. 1996-1998. Lang.: Fre. 1475

Popova, Ljubov
Design/technology
Avant-garde Russian women artist/designers. Russia. USSR. 1880-1949. Lang.: Eng. 214

Popular entertainment
SEE ALSO
Classed Entries under MIXED ENTERTAINMENT.
Institutions
Popular entertainment at the New Haven Assembly Hall and Columbian Museum and Gardens. USA: New Haven, CT. 1796-1820. Lang.: Eng. 394
Public entertainments in Philadelphia's pleasure gardens. USA: Philadelphia, PA. 1723-1840. Lang.: Eng. 400
Popular entertainment at the Palace Garden. USA: New York, NY. 1858-1863. Lang.: Eng. 403
Performance spaces
Popular entertainment at Niblo's Garden. USA: New York, NY. 1828-1846. Lang.: Eng. 470
Performance/production
Popular culture, entertainment, and performance in the United States. USA. 1990-1997. Lang.: Eng. 654
The Finnish enthusiasm for Flamenco dance. Spain. Finland. 1998. Lang.: Fin. 1234
Social concerns reflected in popular entertainment publications. USA. 1870-1910. Lang.: Eng. 4144
Reference materials
Bibliography of books on popular entertainment. USA. 1990-1997. Lang.: Eng. 710

Popular theatre
Performance/production
Interactive mystery theatre weekends in an old inn. Sweden: Mariefred. 1993-1998. Lang.: Swe. 602
Norwich's unregulated entertainers. England: Norwich. 1530-1624. Lang.: Eng. 1907
The popular theatre genre *teatro por horas.* Spain. 1867-1922. Lang.: Eng. 2361
Actor and playwright George Dibdin Pitt. UK-England: London. 1806-1808. Lang.: Eng. 2592
Plays/librettos/scripts
Analysis of *Gallathea* by John Lyly. England. 1584. Lang.: Eng. 2888

Poredušov Janoš
Basic theatrical documents
Text of Evgen Car's monologue *Poredušov Janoš.* Slovenia. 1968-1998. Lang.: Slo. 1454

Porgy and Bess
Performance/production
Musical analysis of Gershwin's *Porgy and Bess.* USA. 1937. Lang.: Eng. 4753

Pork Bellies
Performance/production
Collection of newspaper reviews by London theatre critics. UK-England: London. 1998. Lang.: Eng. 2499

Porno Boy Speaks, The
Performance/production
Performativity in postmodern 'queer' works. USA. 1985-1995. Lang.: Eng. 616

Pörtner, Paul
Theory/criticism
The influence of Antonin Artaud on director Paul Pörtner. France. 1920-1973. Lang.: Ger. 3870

Portrait of Mrs. W
Plays/librettos/scripts
Analysis of plays about the women's movement. USA. 1900-1940. Lang.: Eng. 3559

Portrait, The
Plays/librettos/scripts
Music and the ballad opera in English popular theatre. England. 1728-1780. Lang.: Eng. 4390

Posner, Geoff
Performance/production
Collection of newspaper reviews by London theatre critics. UK-England: London. 1998. Lang.: Eng. 2513

Posner, Kenneth
Design/technology
Lighting designer Kenneth Posner. USA. 1998. Lang.: Eng. 1545
Technical designs for *Griller* by Eric Bogosian. USA: Chicago, IL. 1998. Lang.: Eng. 1558

Posner, Lindsay
Performance/production
Collection of newspaper reviews by London theatre critics. UK-England: London. 1998. Lang.: Eng. 2470

Pospravljica (Tidying Up)
Basic theatrical documents
Text of puppet play for children, *Pospravljica (Tidying Up)* by Irena Androjna. Slovenia. 1997. Lang.: Slo. 4865

Possessed, The
SEE
Besy.

Possible Worlds
Performance/production
Comparison of simple productions and visual shows. Canada: Montreal, PQ, Quebec, PQ, Toronto, ON. 1998. Lang.: Fre. 1861
Post, Mike
Performance/production
The theory and practice of scoring a television production. USA. 1998. Lang.: Eng. 4069
Postmodernism
Performance/production
Postmodern acting theory. USA. 1988. Lang.: Eng. 622
Shakespeare and postmodern production. Europe. North America. 1950-1998. Lang.: Eng. 1912
Postmodern staging and design: Matthew Warchus' *Henry V*. UK-England. 1970-1994. Lang.: Eng. 2636
Postmodernism in Jean-Luc Godard's film adaptation of Shakespeare's *King Lear*. France. 1988. Lang.: Eng. 3931
Relation to other fields
Quantum theory in recent New York performances. USA: New York, NY. 1995-1996. Lang.: Eng. 794
Theory/criticism
Analysis of *Something Cloudy, Something Clear* by Tennessee Williams. USA. 1980-1981. Lang.: Eng. 3843
Potak, Philip D.
Basic theatrical documents
Text of cabaret revue *Carnival Knowledge* by Philip D. Potak. USA. 1988. Lang.: Eng. 4152
Potechin, A.
Plays/librettos/scripts
Playwright A. Potechin. Russia: Saratov. 1850-1899. Lang.: Rus. 3337
Potovanje v Rim (Journey to Rome, A)
Basic theatrical documents
Plays and screenplays by Vili Ravnjak. Slovenia. 1991-1997. Lang.: Slo. 1460
Potter, Miles
Performance/production
English and French-language productions of *Picasso at the Lapin Agile* by Steve Martin. Canada: Montreal, PQ. 1997. Lang.: Fre. 1836
Poulton, Michael
Performance/production
Collection of newspaper reviews by London theatre critics. UK-England: London. 1998. Lang.: Eng. 2575
Pour en finir avec le jugement de dieu (To Have Done with the Judgement of God)
Theory/criticism
The influence of Antonin Artaud on director Paul Pörtner. France. 1920-1973. Lang.: Ger. 3870
Pour la galerie (For the Gallery)
Basic theatrical documents
Text of *Pour la galerie (For the Gallery)* by Claude d'Anna and Laure Bonin. France. 1998. Lang.: Fre. 1424
Pour Louis de Funès (For Louis de Funès)
Plays/librettos/scripts
On translating into German the plays of Valère Novarina. France. Germany. 1947-1998. Lang.: Ger. 3122
Powell, Michael
Plays/librettos/scripts
The popularity and influence of the ballet film *The Red Shoes*. UK-England. 1948. Lang.: Eng. 3988
Powell, Nick
Performance/production
Collection of newspaper reviews by London theatre critics. UK-England: London. 1998. Lang.: Eng. 2434
Power
Performance/production
Productions of the Federal Theatre Project's Living Newspapers. USA: New York, NY. 1935-1939. Lang.: Eng. 643
Power of Love, The
Performance/production
Collection of newspaper reviews by London theatre critics. UK-England: London. 1998. Lang.: Eng. 2486
Power Plays
Design/technology
Michael McGarty's set design for Elaine May and Alan Arkin's *Power Plays*. USA: New York, NY. 1998. Lang.: Eng. 1542
Pöysti, Lasse
Performance/production
Actor Lasse Pöysti. Finland. 1944-1998. Lang.: Eng, Fre. 1917
Poznjakov, N.S.
Performance/production
Choreographers and theorists E.V. Javorskij and N.S. Poznjakov. Russia: Moscow. 1920-1939. Lang.: Rus. 961
Praga, Marco
Plays/librettos/scripts
Italian realist drama. Italy. 1860-1918. Lang.: Eng. 3260
Prärie (Prairie)
Basic theatrical documents
Catalan translations of plays by Bertolt Brecht (volume 1). Germany. 1919-1954. Lang.: Cat. 1437
Pratchett, Terry
Performance/production
Collection of newspaper reviews by London theatre critics. UK-England: London. 1998. Lang.: Eng. 2446
Pratt, Andrew
Performance/production
Collection of newspaper reviews by London theatre critics. UK-England: London. 1998. Lang.: Eng. 2499
Predloženijė (Proposal, The)
Basic theatrical documents
Catalan translations of the complete plays of Anton Čechov. Russia. 1884-1904. Lang.: Cat. 1449
Performance/production
Čechov's one-act plays at Thália Színház. Hungary. Slovakia: Košice. 1998. Lang.: Hun. 2075
One-act comedies by Čechov directed by Péter Valló. Hungary: Dunaújváros. 1998. Lang.: Hun. 2080
One-act plays of Čechov by the Illyés Gyula National Theatre. Hungary. Ukraine: Beregovo. 1997. Lang.: Hun. 2104
Prégardien, Christoph
Performance/production
Reviews of *Lieder* recordings. USA. Slovenia. Austria. 1998. Lang.: Eng. 4720
Prendergast, Jane
Plays/librettos/scripts
Shakespeare and the feminist theatre of Bryony Lavery and Jane Prendergast. UK-England. 1997. Lang.: Eng. 3439
Prendergast, Shaun
Performance/production
Collection of newspaper reviews by London theatre critics. UK-England: London, Scarborough. 1998. Lang.: Eng. 2426
Prescott, Paul
Performance/production
Collection of newspaper reviews by London theatre critics. UK-England: London. 1998. Lang.: Eng. 2507
Present Laughter
Performance/production
Collection of newspaper reviews by London theatre critics. UK-England: Leeds, Manchester. 1998. Lang.: Eng. 2559
Press
Administration
The practice of giving critics tickets for the second night of a show. UK-England: London. 1998. Lang.: Eng. 27
Institutions
Workshop of Association Internationale des Critiques de Théâtre. Canada: Quebec, PQ. 1998. Lang.: Fre. 342
Performance/production
Collection of theatre reviews by Roberto De Monticelli. Italy. 1974-1987. Lang.: Ita. 547
Polish soldiers' theatre as seen in the magazine *Parada*. Italy: Rome. Egypt: Cairo. 1942-1947. Lang.: Pol. 550
Press responses to the autobiography of actress Charlotte Cibber Charke. England. 1713-1760. Lang.: Eng. 1908
Collection of theatre reviews by Cesare Garboli. Italy. 1972-1977. Lang.: Ita. 2170
Vagant, a journal dedicated to the work of actor Vladimir Vysockij. Russia: Moscow. 1998. Lang.: Rus. 2339
Excerpts from critical reviews of singer and actress Lotte Lenya. Germany. 1928-1966. Lang.: Eng. 4354
Response to negative criticism of *The Capeman*. USA: New York, NY. 1998. Lang.: Eng. 4387
Press reactions to productions of Offenbach's *Orphée aux Enfers*. Belgium. Switzerland. France. 1997. Lang.: Fre. 4535
Plays/librettos/scripts
On the text and staging of *La Cathédrale...* by Jean Depréz (Laurette Laroque). Canada: Montreal, PQ. 1949. Lang.: Fre. 2823

Press — cont'd

Relation to other fields
The context of Heinrich von Kleist's periodical *Berliner Abendblätter*. Germany: Berlin. 1810-1811. Lang.: Ger. 741
Changes in media and press coverage. Germany: Hamburg. 1996-1998. Lang.: Ger. 743
The influence of Teatro Campesino on American politics. USA. 1965-1970. Lang.: Eng. 3783
Theory/criticism
On collected theatre reviews by Tamás Tarján. Hungary. 1993-1996. Lang.: Hun. 844
Excerpts from diary of theatre critic Andrej Inkret. Slovenia. 1992-1995. Lang.: Slo. 857
Collection of aphorisms on theatre criticism. Sweden. 1998. Lang.: Swe. 859
Theatre reviewers and popular entertainment. USA. 1975-1997. Lang.: Eng. 868
The nature of dance analysis. North America. Europe. 1998. Lang.: Eng. 1009
The nature of dance criticism. USA. Europe. 1997. Lang.: Eng. 1013
Dance critic on her profession. USA. Europe. 1990. Lang.: Eng. 1014
Contrasting reviews of Declan Donnellan's RSC production of *The School for Scandal*. UK-England: Stratford. 1998. Lang.: Eng. 3835
Changes in press coverage of opera and orchestras. UK-England. 1985-1999. Lang.: Eng. 4839
Music critic on his career. USA. 1965-1996. Lang.: Eng. 4840
Freelance music critic on her career. USA. 1998. Lang.: Eng. 4841
Newsweek's coverage of the arts. USA. 1942-1964. Lang.: Eng. 4842
Performers and conductors complain about unfair reviews. USA. 1998. Lang.: Eng. 4844
Advice to music critics. USA. 1940-1998. Lang.: Eng. 4846
Critique of press coverage of opera. USA. 1988-1999. Lang.: Eng. 4847

Pressburger, Emeric
Plays/librettos/scripts
The popularity and influence of the ballet film *The Red Shoes*. UK-England. 1948. Lang.: Eng. 3988

Presser, Gábor
Performance/production
Antal Fodor's ballet *A Próba (The Rehearsal)*. Hungary: Budapest. 1998. Lang.: Hun. 1111

Pressner, Stan
Design/technology
Design concept for Ralph Lemon's dance piece *Geography* at BAM. USA: New York, NY. 1998. Lang.: Eng. 1248

Preston, Thomas
Performance/production
Music in Tudor drama. England. 1497-1569. Lang.: Eng. 1902

Prestuplenijė i nakazanijė (Crime and Punishment)
Performance/production
Dostojėvskij's *Crime and Punishment* directed by Géza Tordy. Hungary: Győr. 1998. Lang.: Hun. 2100

Pretty Ugly (Freiburg)
Institutions
Amanda Miller and her ballet company Pretty Ugly. Germany: Freiburg. 1984-1998. Lang.: Ger. 1039

Previn, André
Performance/production
Baritone Rodney Gilfry. USA. 1998. Lang.: Eng. 4736
André Previn's opera *A Streetcar Named Desire*. USA: San Francisco. 1998. Lang.: Eng. 4742

Price, Jonathan
Performance/production
Theatre Magazine's anniversary issue. USA. 1968-1998. Lang.: Eng. 617

Price, Olive M.
Plays/librettos/scripts
Dramatic adaptations of Henry Wadsworth Longfellow's poem *Evangeline*. USA. Canada. 1860-1976. Lang.: Eng. 3643

Prichard, Andrew
Performance/production
Collection of newspaper reviews by London theatre critics. UK-England: London. 1998. Lang.: Eng. 2564

Prichard, Rebecca
Performance/production
Collection of newspaper reviews by London theatre critics. UK-England: London. 1998. Lang.: Eng. 2427
Collection of newspaper reviews by London theatre critics. UK-England: London. 1998. Lang.: Eng. 2560

Pride's Crossing
Design/technology
Lighting designer Kenneth Posner. USA. 1998. Lang.: Eng. 1545

Prideaux, Sophie
Performance/production
Collection of newspaper reviews by London theatre critics. UK-England: London. 1998. Lang.: Eng. 2550

Priestley, J.B.
Plays/librettos/scripts
The detective plays of Jardiel Poncela. Spain. 1940-1969. Lang.: Spa. 3392

Primary English Class, The
Basic theatrical documents
French translation of *The Primary English Class* by Israel Horovitz. USA. France. 1996. Lang.: Fre. 1489

Prime of Miss Jean Brodie, The
Performance/production
Collection of newspaper reviews by London theatre critics. UK-England: London. 1998. Lang.: Eng. 2423

Prince Edward Theatre (London)
Performance/production
Collection of newspaper reviews by London theatre critics. UK-England: London. 1998. Lang.: Eng. 2466
Collection of newspaper reviews by London theatre critics. UK-England: London. 1998. Lang.: Eng. 2516

Prince Igor
SEE
Kniaz Igor.

Prince of Wales Theatre (London)
Performance/production
Collection of newspaper reviews by London theatre critics. UK-England: London. 1998. Lang.: Eng. 2525

Prince on a White Bike
Performance/production
Collection of newspaper reviews by London theatre critics. UK-England: London. 1998. Lang.: Eng. 2573

Prince Theatre (London)
Performance/production
Collection of newspaper reviews by London theatre critics. UK-England: London. 1998. Lang.: Eng. 2444
Collection of newspaper reviews by London theatre critics. UK-England: London. 1998. Lang.: Eng. 2455
Collection of newspaper reviews by London theatre critics. UK-England: London. 1998. Lang.: Eng. 2474
Collection of newspaper reviews by London theatre critics. UK-England: London. 1998. Lang.: Eng. 2490

Prince, Harold
Design/technology
The original stage machinery designed by John White at Her Majesty's Theatre. UK-England: London. 1887-1986. Lang.: Eng. 1528
Performance/production
Collection of newspaper reviews by London theatre critics. UK-England: London. 1998. Lang.: Eng. 2466

Prince, Liz
Design/technology
Design concept for Ralph Lemon's dance piece *Geography* at BAM. USA: New York, NY. 1998. Lang.: Eng. 1248

Prince, The
Design/technology
Scenery by Yevgenia Nayberg for Robert Cohen's *The Prince*. USA: Long Beach, CA. 1997. Lang.: Eng. 1561
Performance/production
Creating the role of Biagio Buonaccorsi in Robert Cohen's *The Prince*. USA. 1997. Lang.: Eng. 2686

Princess Ida
Plays/librettos/scripts
The trivialization of feminism in librettos of W.S. Gilbert. UK-England. 1880-1890. Lang.: Eng. 4861

Princess of the Stars, The
Design/technology
R. Murray Schaffer's environmental opera *The Princess of the Stars*. Canada. 1981-1997. Lang.: Eng. 4424

Princess Yvonne
SEE
Iwona Księzniczka Burgundia.

Príncipe desolado, El (Desolate Prince, The)
Basic theatrical documents
Text of *El príncipe desolado (The Desolate Prince)* by Juan Radrigán. Chile. 1998. Lang.: Spa. 1413

***Príncipe desolado, El (Desolate Prince, The)* — cont'd**

Plays/librettos/scripts
Interview with playwright Juan Radrigán. Chile. 1998. Lang.: Spa. 2838

Prinz von Homburg, Der
Design/technology
Lighting for Henze's opera *Der Prinz von Homburg* at Deutsche Oper Berlin. Germany: Berlin. 1997. Lang.: Ger. 4431

Prinzregententheater (Munich)
Institutions
The curriculum at Bayerische Theaterakademie. Germany: Munich. 1985-1998. Lang.: Ger. 1659

Prison theatre
Performance/production
A production of Schiller's *Die Räuber (The Robbers)* performed by prisoners. Germany: Berlin. 1997. Lang.: Ger. 2025

Pritchard, Robin
Performance/production
Collection of newspaper reviews by London theatre critics. UK-England: London. 1998. Lang.: Eng. 2455

Private Life of the Master Race, The
SEE
Furcht und Elend des III. Reiches.

Private Lines
Performance/production
Collection of newspaper reviews by London theatre critics. UK-England: London. 1998. Lang.: Eng. 2566

Private Yuk Objects
Plays/librettos/scripts
Australian plays about the war in Vietnam. Australia. 1990-1998. Lang.: Eng. 2776

Priznanija avantjurista Feliksa Krulja (Confessions of Felix Krul, Confidence Man)
Performance/production
Andrej Žitinkin directs *Confessions of Felix Krull, Confidence Man*, adapted from Thomas Mann. Russia: Moscow. 1998. Lang.: Rus. 2335

Próba, A (Rehearsal, The)
Performance/production
Antal Fodor's ballet *A Próba (The Rehearsal)*. Hungary: Budapest. 1998. Lang.: Hun. 1111

Proces (Trial, The)
Plays/librettos/scripts
Religion and the individual in plays of Ivan Mrak. Slovenia. 1955. Lang.: Slo. 3358

Processional
Plays/librettos/scripts
Analysis of *Processional* by John Howard Lawson. USA. 1925. Lang.: Eng. 3535

Processional theatre
SEE ALSO
Pageants/parades.

Proclemer, Anna
Performance/production
Catalogue of an exhibition devoted to actress Anna Proclemer. Italy. 1923-1998. Lang.: Ita. 552

Prodigal, The
Plays/librettos/scripts
Analysis of *The Prodigal* by Jack Richardson. USA. 1960. Lang.: Eng. 3542

The Prodigal, Jack Richardson's adaptation of *The Oresteia*. USA. 1960. Lang.: Dut. 3547

Homeric influences on *The Prodigal* by Jack Richardson. USA. 1960. Lang.: Eng. 3549

Producing
Administration
Producer Cheryl Crawford, gender and sexuality. USA. 1902-1986. Lang.: Eng. 116

Theatre manager Charles H. Gilfert. USA: Charleston, SC. 1817-1822. Lang.: Eng. 135

Study of management in regional theatres. USA. 1987-1988. Lang.: Eng. 140

History of Quebec theatre. Canada: Montreal, PQ, Quebec, PQ. 1880-1950. Lang.: Fre. 1375

The 'Group of Four' at the Lyric Hammersmith and the concept of a national theatre. UK-England: London. 1945-1956. Lang.: Eng. 1392

Interview with producer Ed Mirvish. UK-England: London. Canada: Toronto, ON. 1982-1998. Lang.: Eng. 1393

Christine Melton on the production of her play *Still Life Goes On*. USA: New York, NY. 1997. Lang.: Eng. 1398

Producer Aida Young. UK-England. 1950-1998. Lang.: Eng. 3854

Obituary for producer Lew Grade. UK-England. 1908-1998. Lang.: Eng. 3872

Interviews about film producer Jack Warner. USA: Hollywood, CA. 1918-1978. Lang.: Eng. 3875

Various conditions affecting production, pricing, marketing and communication in German theatre. Germany. 1986-1998. Lang.: Ger. 4316

V. Vol'chovskij, puppet theatre producer. Russia. 1998. Lang.: Rus. 4916

Institutions
Producer Joseph Cino and Off-off Broadway theatre. USA: New York, NY. 1931-1967. Lang.: Eng. 404

Graphic design and the theatrical evolution of Arena Stage. USA: Washington, DC. 1950-1987. Lang.: Eng. 414

Systems analysis of the Southwest Theatre Association. USA. 1988. Lang.: Eng. 418

The Shuberts vs. the Syndicate. USA: New York, NY. 1976-1998. Lang.: Eng. 427

Caro Newling, executive producer of Donmar Warehouse. UK-England: London. 1998. Lang.: Eng. 1742

Performance spaces
Oscar Hammerstein I and the creation and development of Times Square. USA. 1895-1915. Lang.: Eng. 463

Performance/production
Performer, writer, director Elsie Janis and the 'gay sensibility'. UK-England. 1889-1956. Lang.: Eng. 612

Shakespearean production and the theatrical portrait collection of the Garrick Club. England: London. 1702-1814. Lang.: Eng. 1903

Shakespeare in the GDR: producer and critic B.K. Tragelehn. Germany, East. 1950-1990. Lang.: Eng. 2040

Interview with director Frank Castorf. Germany, East. 1980-1990. Lang.: Eng. 2041

Producer and director Boris Golubovskij. Russia. 1998. Lang.: Rus. 2271

Managerial analysis of daytime serial TV industry. USA: New York, NY. 1950-1988. Lang.: Eng. 4072

Theory/criticism
Theatre reviewers and popular entertainment. USA. 1975-1997. Lang.: Eng. 868

Productions Recto-Verso (Quebec, PQ)
Institutions
Émile Morin and Pascale Landry on their Productions Recto-Verso. Canada: Quebec, PQ. 1996. Lang.: Fre. 4233

Professional Lighting and Sound Associations (PLASA)
Design/technology
Report on PLASA light and sound equipment trade show. UK-England: London. 1998. Lang.: Swe. 236

Profligate, The
Plays/librettos/scripts
Analysis of plays by Arthur Wing Pinero. UK-England. 1890-1910. Lang.: Eng. 3440

Projections
Design/technology
Guide to theatrical design manufacturers and equipment. USA. 1998. Lang.: Eng. 241

The Datatron control system for visual projections. USA. 1998. Lang.: Eng. 304

New stage technology and the dance performance. 1998. Lang.: Eng. 888

Karen TenEyck's projections for a site-specific production of Shakespeare's *Julius Caesar*. USA: Los Angeles, CA. 1998. Lang.: Eng. 1552

Virtual reality technology for set design. USA: Lawrence, KS. 1997. Lang.: Eng. 1562

Production design for rock group Genesis' European tour. Europe. 1998. Lang.: Eng. 4096

Lighting and projections for the musical *Ragtime*. USA: New York, NY. 1998. Lang.: Eng. 4328

Prokofjev, Sergej Sergejevič
Design/technology
Technical designs for Matthew Bourne's productions of ballets by Čajkovskij and Prokofjev. UK-England: London. 1998. Lang.: Eng. 1031

Performance/production
Prokofjev's *Romeo and Juliet*, choreographed by Cranko, Wiener Staatsoper. Austria: Vienna. 1998. Lang.: Hun. 1063

Prokofjėv, Sergej Sergejėvič — cont'd

Analysis of choreographies of Matthew Bourne. UK-England: London. 1996-1997. Lang.: Eng. 1157

Matthew Bourne's dance piece *Cinderella* to music of Prokofjėv. UK-England: London. 1998. Lang.: Eng. 1161

Guest performances of the Kirov Opera at the Metropolitan.. USA: New York, NY. 1998. Lang.: Eng. 4731

Prokurator Poncij Pilat (Procurator Pontius Pilate)
Plays/librettos/scripts
Religion and the individual in plays of Ivan Mrak. Slovenia. 1955. Lang.: Slo. 3358

Promenade Theatre (New York, NY)
Design/technology
Michael McGarty's set design for Elaine May and Alan Arkin's *Power Plays.* USA: New York, NY. 1998. Lang.: Eng. 1542

Prometheus desmotes (Prometheus Bound)
Plays/librettos/scripts
Adaptations of Greek tragedy by contemporary Irish writers. Ireland. UK-Ireland. 1984-1998. Lang.: Eng. 3214

Promptbooks
Basic theatrical documents
Analysis of Smock Alley promptbook for Dryden's *Tyrannick Love.* Ireland: Dublin. 1669-1684. Lang.: Eng. 1439

Propaganda theatre
Performance/production
Ben Hecht's propaganda pageant *A Flag Is Born.* USA: New York, NY. 1946. Lang.: Eng. 4220

Properties
Design/technology
Handbook on stage spaces and physical elements. Slovenia. 1997. Lang.: Slo. 219

Treating muslin to look like Naugahyde. USA. 1998. Lang.: Eng. 267

Creating stage jewelry from polymer clays. USA. 1998. Lang.: Eng. 306

Index to *Technical Brief* volumes 11-17. USA. 1998. Lang.: Eng. 323

Performance/production
The Patum of Berga compared to sixteenth-century German festivities. Spain-Catalonia: Berga. Germany: Trent. 1549-1996. Lang.: Eng. 4218

Propfe, Michael
Institutions
Interview with director and dramaturg of Staatstheater Stuttgart. Germany: Stuttgart. 1993-1998. Lang.: Ger. 1632

Prophète, Le
Performance/production
Hans Neuenfels's production of Meyerbeer's *Le Prophète.* Austria: Vienna. 1998. Lang.: Swe. 4530

Proposals
Design/technology
Recent work of lighting designer Brian MacDevitt. USA: New York, NY. 1997. Lang.: Eng. 1530

Prosky, Robert
Performance/production
Excerpt from a speech by actor Robert Prosky. USA: Washington, DC. 1998. Lang.: Eng. 2720

Prospero's Books
Plays/librettos/scripts
Analysis of Peter Greenaway's film *Prospero's Books.* UK-England. 1991. Lang.: Fre. 3990

Protheroe, Brian
Performance/production
Collection of newspaper reviews by London theatre critics. UK-England: London. 1998. Lang.: Eng. 2557

Prova de fogo (Trial by Fire)
Plays/librettos/scripts
Cruelty and the absurd in theatre of Latin American playwrights. Latin America. 1960-1980. Lang.: Eng. 3267

Provincial theatre
SEE
Regional theatre.

Prowse, Philip
Performance/production
Collection of newspaper reviews by London theatre critics. UK-England: London. 1998. Lang.: Eng. 2488

Pryde, Bill
Performance/production
Collection of newspaper reviews by London theatre critics. UK-England: London. 1998. Lang.: Eng. 2565

Pryor, Richard
Performance/production
Analysis of transformative comedy. USA. 1975-1988. Lang.: Eng. 666

Przybyszewski, Stanisław
Plays/librettos/scripts
Russian reception of plays by Stanisław Przybyszewski. Russia: Moscow, St. Petersburg. 1901-1912. Lang.: Pol. 3330

Pskovskij Akademičeskij Teat'r Dramy im. A.S. Puškina (Pskov)
Institutions
Profile of the Pskov Pushkin Theatre. Russia: Pskov. Lang.: Rus. 1696

Psychic Life of Savages, The
Design/technology
Design concept for Amy Freed's *The Psychic Life of Savages*, Wilma Theatre. USA: Philadelphia, PA. 1998. Lang.: Eng. 1555

Psycho-Babble On!
Performance/production
Collection of newspaper reviews by London theatre critics. UK-England: London. 1998. Lang.: Eng. 2526

Psychology
Audience
Theatrical production and reception. Canada. 1988. Lang.: Eng. 146

The aesthetics of audience-performer interaction in the theatrical event. USA. 1970-1981. Lang.: Eng. 160

Performance/production
Coping with stage fright. Netherlands. 1998. Lang.: Dut. 566

Characteristics and development of ritual theatre. Slovenia. 1960-1998. Lang.: Slo. 592

The Creative Surges actor-training seminar. UK-England: Ipswich. 1998. Lang.: Eng. 606

Psychoanalytic study of the actor. USA. 1988. Lang.: Eng. 621

The effect of a heterogeneous audience on performance anxiety. USA. 1987. Lang.: Eng. 630

Actor training and psychotherapy-derived techniques. USA. 1988. Lang.: Eng. 639

A dancer's experience of and investigations into ecstasy. USA. Germany. 1969-1990. Lang.: Eng. 673

Creativity and ego identity in actors. USA. 1984-1987. Lang.: Eng. 678

The artistic life of dancer Vaclav Nižinskij. Poland. Russia. France. 1881-1953. Lang.: Pol. 1123

Psychotherapy and the actor. 1998. Lang.: Rus. 1812

The influence of psychotherapy on Finnish theatrical practices. Finland. 1998. Lang.: Fin. 1920

Actors and the psychology of identity. USA. 1959-1998. Lang.: Eng. 2724

Analysis of Todd Solondz' film *Happiness.* USA. 1998. Lang.: Eng. 3949

The absence of emotional impact on TV broadcasts of live theatre productions. 1998. Lang.: Rus. 4057

Stage fright and other psychological problems of singers and musicians. Germany: Berlin. 1998. Lang.: Swe. 4603

Plays/librettos/scripts
The mad scenes in Shakespeare's *King Lear.* England. 1605-1606. Lang.: Eng. 2876

The 'troubler' personality in Shakespeare's *Henry IV, Part One.* England. 1596-1597. Lang.: Eng. 3032

Insanity in nineteenth- and twentieth-century theatre. Europe. 1880-1970. Lang.: Eng. 3050

Social interactions in Racine's *Phèdre.* France. 1667. Lang.: Fre. 3074

Antonin Artaud's years in a mental hospital. France. 1896-1948. Lang.: Ita. 3113

Oscar Wilde biographer on his negative traits and addictive behaviors. UK-England. USA. 1998. Lang.: Eng. 3425

Transference in plays by Harold Pinter. UK-England. 1960-1985. Lang.: Eng. 3461

Psychology and the self in works of J.M. Barrie. UK-England. 1892-1937. Lang.: Eng. 3478

Feminist analysis of plays for young people by women playwrights. USA. 1903-1983. Lang.: Eng. 3521

Lorraine Hansberry and Black Americans in theatre. USA. 1769-1986. Lang.: Eng. 3640

The enneagram system applied to Albee's *Who's Afraid of Virginia Woolf?.* USA. 1998. Lang.: Eng. 3665

Analysis of Tennessee Williams' *Suddenly Last Summer* and 'Desire and the Black Masseur'. USA. 1946-1958. Lang.: Eng. 3678

Apocalyptic futures in science fiction films. USA. 1981-1990. Lang.: Eng. 4005

Psychology — cont'd

Relation to other fields
Plastic-cognitive therapy and the actor. 1998. Lang.: Rus. 713
Psychological aspects of the under-realized potential of the human voice. Europe. 1989. Lang.: Eng. 728
The use of theatre rehearsal techniques for socially emotionally disturbed youth. USA. 1985-1987. Lang.: Eng. 774
Drama therapy as a tool in the treatment of psychosis. USA. 1998. Lang.: Eng. 778
Developmental differences in adolescents' ability to enact character. USA. 1988. Lang.: Eng. 782
Factors influencing actors' ability to exit a role. USA. 1998. Lang.: Eng. 784
Spiritual practice and drama therapy. USA. 1998. Lang.: Eng. 786
Catharsis and contemporary theatre. USA. 1998. Lang.: Eng. 795
Drama therapy, personal narrative, and performance. USA. 1998. Lang.: Eng. 797
Therapeutic *nō* theatre for the mentally retarded. USA. 1998. Lang.: Eng. 798
Theatrical performance compared to multiple personality disorder. USA. 1998. Lang.: Eng. 803
Drama therapy and forgiveness. USA. 1998. Lang.: Eng. 804
The integration of Buddhism in drama therapy. USA. 1998. Lang.: Eng. 808
Phenomenology and dance. 1997. Lang.: Eng. 996
A warning to dancers not to become malnourished. Sweden. 1998. Lang.: Swe. 998
Dancer, teacher, and healing facilitator Anna Halprin of Tamalpa Institute. USA: Kentfield, CA. 1978-1998. Lang.: Ger. 1338
Psychoanalysis, the female body, and Shakespeare's *Henriad*. England. 1589-1597. Lang.: Eng. 3756
Theatre and the psychological development of children. Sweden. 1988. Lang.: Swe. 3777
The creation and use of ritual theatre for drama therapy. USA. 1997. Lang.: Eng. 3787
Using *Seinfeld* to contrast New York and Los Angeles. USA. 1998. Lang.: Eng. 4082

Training
Improvisational training and psychological resilience. USA. 1996-1998. Lang.: Eng. 879
Feldenkreis movement theory. USA. 1905-1985. Lang.: Eng. 880

Ptuškina, Nadežda

Performance/production
Playwright Nadežda Ptuškina on her plays in production. Russia. 1998. Lang.: Rus. 2309

Public relations

Administration
Theatrical marketing in North Rhine-Westphalia. Germany. 1994-1998. Lang.: Ger. 6
Marketing, advertising, and sponsorship of German theatre. Germany. 1998. Lang.: Ger. 7
Current conditions at Staatstheater Cottbus. Germany: Cottbus. 1992-1998. Lang.: Ger. 9
Cooperation of theatres and tourist organizations. Germany. 1993-1998. Lang.: Ger. 10
Interview with Frank Baumbauer of Deutsches Schauspielhaus Hamburg. Germany: Hamburg. 1993-2000. Lang.: Ger. 11
Audience questionnaire for use in theatrical marketing. Germany. 1998. Lang.: Ger. 12
Marketing strategies for the performing arts. Netherlands. 1990-1995. Lang.: Dut. 17
Methods of organization-building in the arts. Netherlands. 1998. Lang.: Dut. 18
Ways to attract new young audiences to theatre. Sweden: Stockholm. 1995-1998. Lang.: Swe. 21
The practice of giving critics tickets for the second night of a show. UK-England: London. 1998. Lang.: Eng. 27
The playbill as a reflection of social and economic forces. USA. 1875-1899. Lang.: Eng. 31
Target marketing and successful ticket sales. USA: Long Beach, CA. 1996-1998. Lang.: Eng. 37
Finding a reliable sample frame for potential audience data collection. USA. 1997. Lang.: Eng. 39
Marketing analysis and plan for Texas Tech University Theatre's subscription campaign. USA: Lubbock, TX. 1997-1998. Lang.: Eng. 46
Celebrities as spokespersons for non-profits. USA. 1998. Lang.: Eng. 117
The role of Riverfront Arts Center in revitalizing Wilmington's riverfront. USA: Wilmington, DE. 1998. Lang.: Eng. 123
The publicizing of financial information about nonprofit arts organizations. USA. 1998. Lang.: Eng. 137
How Chisenhale Dance Space coped with loss of funding. UK-England: London. 1998. Lang.: Eng. 885
Various conditions affecting production, pricing, marketing and communication in German theatre. Germany. 1986-1998. Lang.: Ger. 4316
Marketing practices of Deutsche Oper am Rhein. Germany: Duisburg. 1996-1998. Lang.: Ger. 4404
Bayerische Staatsoper's new marketing concept. Germany: Munich. 1993-1998. Lang.: Ger. 4405
Speculations on the future marketing of opera. USA. 1998. Lang.: Eng. 4406

Institutions
Institutional analysis of the Stratford Festival. Canada: Stratford, ON. 1953-1967. Lang.: Eng. 1584

Public Theatre (New York, NY)

Design/technology
Technical designs for Off Broadway Shakespearean productions. USA: New York, NY. 1998. Lang.: Eng. 1539
Lighting design for Hwang's *Golden Child* at the Public Theatre. USA: New York, NY. 1996-1998. Lang.: Eng. 1540

Performance spaces
Theatre space and performance. USA: New York, NY. 1925-1985. Lang.: Eng. 464

Plays/librettos/scripts
Joseph Chaikin's adaptation of *Textes pour rien (Texts for Nothing)* by Samuel Beckett. USA: New York, NY. 1995. Lang.: Eng. 3563

Público, El (Public, The)

Plays/librettos/scripts
Background on Lorca's *El Público (The Public)*, about to have its New York premiere. USA: New York, NY. 1930-1998. Lang.: Eng. 3651

Publishing

Plays/librettos/scripts
Playwriting and publishing for the London stage. England. 1590-1650. Lang.: Eng. 2881
Pirandello and his publishers. Italy. 1888-1936. Lang.: Ita. 3223
George Bernard Shaw and play publication. UK-England. 1883-1903. Lang.: Eng. 3460

Puccini, Giacomo

Design/technology
Lighting and realism in opera and theatre: Belasco and Puccini. Italy. USA. 1890-1910. Lang.: Eng. 203
Sound system used in a soccer stadium for an operatic production. Italy: Rome. 1998. Lang.: Eng. 4434

Institutions
The fourth international singing contest. Hungary: Budapest. 1998. Lang.: Hun. 4461

Performance/production
Rural Chinese productions of Puccini's *Turandot*. China, People's Republic of: Beijing. 1998. Lang.: Eng. 4541
A production of Puccini's *Turandot* in Beijing. China, People's Republic of: Beijing. 1998. Lang.: Eng. 4542
Productions of Puccini operas at La Scala. Italy: Milan. 1980-1998. Lang.: Swe. 4657
Background material on Lyric Opera of Chicago radio broadcast performances. USA: Chicago, IL. 1998. Lang.: Eng. 4709
Background material on Metropolitan Opera radio broadcast performances. USA: New York, NY. 1998. Lang.: Eng. 4713

Plays/librettos/scripts
Musical representation of death in Puccini's *Tosca*. Italy. 1900. Lang.: Eng. 4804

Puce à l'Oreille, La (Flea in Her Ear, A)

Design/technology
Costume design for Feydeau's *A Flea in Her Ear (La Puce à l'Oreille)*, Roundabout Theatre Company. USA: New York, NY. 1998. Lang.: Eng. 1537

Performance/production
Interview with actors in Feydeau's *La Puce à l'Oreille (A Flea in Her Ear)* at Dramaten. Sweden: Stockholm. 1998. Lang.: Swe. 2396

Pucher, Stefan
Performance/production
Interview with director Stefan Pucher. Germany. 1998. Lang.: Ger. 1999
Puckering, John
Plays/librettos/scripts
Protestant belief and English Reformation drama. England. 1535-1607. Lang.: Eng. 2972
Pula
Plays/librettos/scripts
South African theatre after apartheid. South Africa, Republic of. 1976-1996. Lang.: Eng. 3365
Pulling Together
Performance/production
Collection of newspaper reviews by London theatre critics. UK-England: London. 1998. Lang.: Eng. 2574
Pulp Fiction
Plays/librettos/scripts
Comparison between *Krisis (Crisis)* by Sabina Berman and Quentin Tarantino's film *Pulp Fiction.* Mexico. USA. 1993-1996. Lang.: Spa. 3276
Pulse
Performance/production
Performances by dance couple Eiko & Koma. USA: Washington, DC. 1998. Lang.: Hun. 1336
Punch and Judy
Plays/librettos/scripts
Absurdism in children's theatre. North America. Europe. 1896-1970. Lang.: Eng. 3288
Puppetry
SEE ALSO
Classed Entries.
Design/technology
Lighting design for Joe Dante's film *Small Soldiers.* USA. 1998. Lang.: Eng. 3914
Institutions
Report on a visit to Riga's theatres. Latvia: Riga. 1997. Lang.: Swe, Eng, Ger. 369
Appealing to the youth audience at Theater Dresden. Germany: Dresden. 1997-1998. Lang.: Ger. 1631
Performance/production
Brief history of Slovene theatre. Slovenia. 1867-1997. Lang.: Slo. 595
Hanne Tierney's adaptation of *Bodas de sangre (Blood Wedding)* by García Lorca. USA. 1997. Lang.: Eng. 647
Amedeo Amodio's new choreography for Čajkovskij's *The Nutcracker.* Italy: Rome. 1998. Lang.: Hun. 1118
Director, costumer, and mask-maker Julie Taymor. USA. 1980-1998. Lang.: Eng. 2685
Obituary for 'Buffalo Bob' Smith, former host of *The Howdy Doody Show.* USA. 1918-1998. Lang.: Eng. 4067
The Sicilian chivalric tradition. Italy. 1500-1985. Lang.: Ita. 4125
Teat'r Ten's *Ten' opery (The Shadow of the Opera).* Russia: Moscow. 1998. Lang.: Rus. 4679
Ten' Puppet Theatre's production of Čajkovskij's opera *Iolanta.* Russia: Moscow. Lang.: Rus. 4680
History of Sicilian 'teatro dei pupi'. Sicily. 1646-1996. Lang.: Hun. 4921
Plays/librettos/scripts
Absurdism in children's theatre. North America. Europe. 1896-1970. Lang.: Eng. 3288
Reference materials
Yearbook of Slovene theatre. Slovenia. 1996-1997. Lang.: Slo. 708
Puppets
Design/technology
Technical designs for the musical *Doctor Doolittle* directed by Steven Pimlott. UK-England: London. 1998. Lang.: Eng. 4325
How to make a puppet from a handle bag. USA. 1998. Lang.: Eng. 4868
Constructing miniature puppets from pipe cleaners and balsa wood. USA. 1998. Lang.: Eng. 4869
Use of a balance line in marionette construction. USA. 1998. Lang.: Eng. 4918
Institutions
The puppet collection of the Detroit Institute of the Arts. USA: Detroit, MI. 1998. Lang.: Eng. 4880
Puppetry exhibits at Chicago Children's Museum. USA: Chicago, IL. Mexico: Mexico City. 1998. Lang.: Eng. 4881
Report on Academy of String Puppetry Conference. USA: Storrs, CT. 1998. Lang.: Eng. 4883
Performance/production
Guide to home puppet theatre. 1998. Lang.: Rus. 4884
Children's puppet work. Austria. Slovenia. 1993-1997. Lang.: Slo. 4885
Interview with television puppeteer Nina Keogh. Canada: Toronto, ON. 1953-1998. Lang.: Eng. 4888
Relation to other fields
Modern fictional characters through the lens of Mejerchol'd's biomechanics and Oskar Schlemmer's puppets. Europe. 1913-1930. Lang.: Ger. 729
Puppeteer Ken McKay on puppetry in education. Canada. 1994-1998. Lang.: Eng. 4915
Purcarete, Silviu
Performance/production
Collection of newspaper reviews by London theatre critics. UK-England: London. 1998. Lang.: Eng. 2520
Purcell Room (London)
Performance/production
Collection of newspaper reviews by London theatre critics. UK-England: London. 1998. Lang.: Eng. 2436
Collection of newspaper reviews by London theatre critics. UK-England: London. 1998. Lang.: Eng. 2580
Purcell, Henry
Performance/production
English theatre architecture and the operas of Henry Purcell. England: London. 1659-1695. Lang.: Eng. 4548
Plays/librettos/scripts
The relative absence of political allegory in English opera. England: London. 1620-1711. Lang.: Eng. 4767
Purdy, James
Basic theatrical documents
Text of *Heatstroke* by James Purdy. USA. 1989. Lang.: Eng. 1502
Plays/librettos/scripts
Analysis of plays by James Purdy. USA. 1957-1998. Lang.: Eng. 3700
Purgatory
Performance/production
Collection of newspaper reviews by London theatre critics. UK-England: London. 1998. Lang.: Eng. 2551
Purple Flower, The
Plays/librettos/scripts
Analysis of *The Purple Flower* by Marita Bonner. USA. 1927. Lang.: Eng. 3527
Push the Boat Out
Performance/production
Performance artist Leslie Hill's *Push the Boat Out.* UK-England: London. USA. 1995-1997. Lang.: Eng. 4245
Pushkin Theatre (Leningrad)
SEE
Akademičeskij Teat'r Dramy im. A.S. Puškina.
Puškin, Aleksand'r Sergejėvič
Institutions
The Boldina Opera and Ballet festival honoring Puškin. Russia: Nizhni Novgorod. 1998. Lang.: Rus. 4469
Performance/production
Guest performances of the Kirov Opera at the Metropolitan.. USA: New York, NY. 1998. Lang.: Eng. 4731
Plays/librettos/scripts
Operas of Dargomyžskij and Rimskij-Korsakov on texts of Puškin. Russia. 1799-1869. Lang.: Rus. 4815
Putti, Lya de
Performance/production
An exhibition devoted to dance and silent film star Lya de Putti. Hungary. Germany. 1898-1931. Lang.: Hun. 944
Py, Olivier
Plays/librettos/scripts
Olivier Py, actor, playwright, director, and head of the Centre Dramatique d'Orléans. France: Orléans. 1966-1998. Lang.: Ger. 3073
Interview with playwright-director Olivier Py. France. 1988-1998. Lang.: Ger, Fre, Dut, Eng. 3117
Pygmalion
Basic theatrical documents
English translations of plays by Tawfiq Al-Hakim. Egypt. 1930-1945. Lang.: Eng. 1416
Plays/librettos/scripts
George Bernard Shaw: life, work, influences. UK-England. Ireland. 1886-1955. Lang.: Eng. 3437
Pyrotechnics
Performance/production
The pyrotechnic genre, the 'fort holding'. England. 1501-1600. Lang.: Eng. 4122

Pyschology
Plays/librettos/scripts
Food and alienation in plays of Chantal Chawaf and Denise Chalem. France. 1970-1989. Lang.: Eng. 3072
Qu'ils crèvent les artistes
SEE
Niech sczezną artyści.
Quad
Plays/librettos/scripts
Analysis of television plays by Samuel Beckett. France. 1965-1989. Lang.: Eng. 4077
Quai ouest (Key West)
Performance/production
Productions of plays by Bernard-Marie Koltès. Canada: Montreal, PQ. 1991-1997. Lang.: Fre. 1862
Quare Fellow, The
Plays/librettos/scripts
Music and song in plays of Brendan Behan. Ireland. 1954-1958. Lang.: Eng. 3206
Quare, Vicki
Performance/production
Collection of newspaper reviews by London theatre critics. UK-England: London. 1998. Lang.: Eng. 2553
Quarry Theatre (Leeds)
Performance/production
Collection of newspaper reviews by London theatre critics. UK-England: Leeds, Manchester. 1998. Lang.: Eng. 2559
Quarter Too Theatre Company (London)
Performance/production
Collection of newspaper reviews by London theatre critics. UK-England: London. 1998. Lang.: Eng. 2540
Quartucci, Carlo
Institutions
Carlo Quartucci's acting workshop on Shakespeare's *Macbeth.* Italy: Rome. 1991-1992. Lang.: Ita. 1674
Quatre Mains
Performance/production
Collection of newspaper reviews by London theatre critics. UK-England: London. 1998. Lang.: Eng. 2556
Quay, Stephen
Design/technology
Technical designs for *The Chairs (Les Chaises),* Théâtre de Complicité. UK-England: London. 1998. Lang.: Eng. 1524
Quay, Timothy
Design/technology
Technical designs for *The Chairs (Les Chaises),* Théâtre de Complicité. UK-England: London. 1998. Lang.: Eng. 1524
Queen Elizabeth Hall (London)
Performance/production
Collection of newspaper reviews by London theatre critics. UK-England: London. 1998. Lang.: Eng. 2448
Collection of newspaper reviews by London theatre critics. UK-England: London. 1998. Lang.: Eng. 2580
Queen Lear
Plays/librettos/scripts
Analysis of *Queen Lear* by Beau Coleman. Canada: Edmonton, AB. 1995-1997. Lang.: Eng. 2800
Queen of Puddings Theatre Company (Toronto, ON)
Basic theatrical documents
Text of libretto for *Beatrice Chancy.* Canada: Toronto, ON. 1998. Lang.: Eng. 4413
Queen of Spades (opera)
SEE
Pique Dame.
Queen of Spades by Puškin
SEE
Pikovaja Dama.
Queen's Theatre (London)
Design/technology
Sound design for the musical *Bugsy Malone.* UK-England: London. 1997. Lang.: Eng. 4327
Performance/production
Collection of newspaper reviews by London theatre critics. UK-England: London. 1998. Lang.: Eng. 2415
Collection of newspaper reviews by London theatre critics. UK-England: London. 1998. Lang.: Eng. 2447
Collection of newspaper reviews by London theatre critics. UK-England: London. 1998. Lang.: Eng. 2492
Collection of newspaper reviews by London theatre critics. UK-England: London. 1998. Lang.: Eng. 2530
Collection of newspaper reviews by London theatre critics. UK-England: London. 1998. Lang.: Eng. 2553
Collection of newspaper reviews by London theatre critics. UK-England: London. 1998. Lang.: Eng. 2571
Quel est ce sexe qu'ont les anges? (What Is This Sex that Angels Have?)
Performance/production
Comparison of text-based and visual productions. France. 1998. Lang.: Fre. 1939
Quem quaeritis
Performance/production
Analysis of *Regularis Concordia* and *Quem quarteritis.* England. 1150-1228. Lang.: Eng. 516
Quenouille de Barbérine, La (Distaff of Barberine, The)
Plays/librettos/scripts
Fidelity in two plays of Musset. France. 1835-1837. Lang.: Eng. 3102
Quentin, Caroline
Performance/production
Collection of newspaper reviews by London theatre critics. UK-England. 1998. Lang.: Eng. 2497
Question of Mercy, A
Performance/production
Collection of newspaper reviews by London theatre critics. UK-England: London. 1998. Lang.: Eng. 2465
Quigley, Patrick
Design/technology
Lighting design for musical performance and sports at the Nashville arena. USA: Nashville, TN. 1998. Lang.: Eng. 317
Quiles, Rosario
Plays/librettos/scripts
The mulatto in Puerto Rican drama. Puerto Rico. 1850-1985. Lang.: Spa. 3311
Quinn, Patrick
Administration
Equity's First Vice-President Patrick Quinn. USA: New York, NY. 1998. Lang.: Eng. 100
Quiñones de Benavente, Luis
Plays/librettos/scripts
Playwright Luis Quiñones de Benavente. Spain. 1600-1651. Lang.: Eng. 3376
Quintana, Alejandro
Performance/production
Recent productions of plays by Bertolt Brecht. Germany. 1997-1998. Lang.: Ger. 2028
Quintero, José
Performance/production
Tribute to late director José Quintero. USA. 1924-1998. Lang.: Eng. 2683
Quoi où
SEE
What Where.
R and J
Theory/criticism
The urge to make Shakespeare contemporary. USA. 1990-1998. Lang.: Eng. 3844
Rabb, Ellis
Performance/production
Obituaries for Ellis Rabb, Giorgio Strehler, and David Mark Cohen. USA. 1930-1997. Lang.: Eng. 2725
Rabe, David
Performance/production
Collection of newspaper reviews by London theatre critics. UK-England: London. 1998. Lang.: Eng. 2465
Rachel
Plays/librettos/scripts
Lynching in plays of Angelina Weld Grimké and Lorraine Hansberry. USA. 1916-1958. Lang.: Eng. 3602
Racine, Jean
Performance/production
Collection of newspaper reviews by London theatre critics. UK-England: London. 1998. Lang.: Eng. 2494
Collection of newspaper reviews by London theatre critics. UK-England: London. 1998. Lang.: Eng. 2534
Collection of newspaper reviews by London theatre critics. UK-England: London. 1998. Lang.: Eng. 2583

Racine, Jean — cont'd

Collection of newspaper reviews by London theatre critics. UK-Scotland: Edinburgh. 1998. Lang.: Eng. 2650
Plays/librettos/scripts
The devouring woman in plays of Racine, Kleist, Ibsen, and Beckett. Europe. 1760-1992. Lang.: Eng. 3058
Social interactions in Racine's *Phèdre*. France. 1667. Lang.: Fre. 3074
Statistical study of the theatre of Jean Racine. France. 1664-1691. Lang.: Eng. 3081
The ritual structure of Racine's *Athalie*. France. 1691. Lang.: Eng. 3099
Racine's *Phèdre* as a source for *Hippolyte et Aricie* by Rameau and Pelligrin. France. 1660-1733. Lang.: Eng. 4788

Radeke, Winfried
Administration
The effects of independent theatre in Berlin. Germany: Berlin. 1998. Lang.: Ger. 14

Radio
SEE
Audio forms.

Radio City Music Hall (New York, NY)
Design/technology
Profile of technicians for Grammy Awards television broadcast. USA: New York, NY. 1998. Lang.: Eng. 4056

Radio drama
Institutions
New Danish radio drama produced by Radioteatret. Denmark. 1989-1998. Lang.: Dan. 3862
Performance/production
Popular entertainment in Uganda after Idi Amin. Uganda. 1979-1998. Lang.: Eng. 604
Popular American radio and the importance of the disembodied voice. USA. 1929-1940. Lang.: Eng. 3864
Plays/librettos/scripts
Playwriting career of Carol Shields. Canada: Winnipeg, MB. 1972-1998. Lang.: Eng. 2794
Analysis of *In the Native State* and *Indian Ink* by Tom Stoppard. UK-England. 1991-1995. Lang.: Eng. 3459
Morton Feldman's musical setting for Samuel Beckett's radio play *Words and Music*. Europe. 1987. Lang.: Eng. 3865
Experimental writing in Finnish radio drama. Finland. 1998. Lang.: Fin. 3866
Analysis of Samuel Beckett's radio play *All That Fall*. Ireland. France. 1957. Lang.: Ita. 3867
BBC radio plays with Anglo-Irish themes. UK-England. Ireland. 1973-1986. Lang.: Eng. 3868
Relation to other fields
The influence of radio drama on professional theatre. Canada. 1922-1952. Lang.: Fre. 3869

Radio Sevilla (Radio Seville)
Plays/librettos/scripts
Antifascist puppet plays by Rafael Alberti. Spain. 1936-1939. Lang.: Eng. 4922

Radioteatret (Copenhagen)
Institutions
New Danish radio drama produced by Radioteatret. Denmark. 1989-1998. Lang.: Dan. 3862

Radnai, György
Performance/production
Profile of baritone György Radnai. Hungary. 1920-1977. Lang.: Hun. 4624

Radnóti Színház (Budapest)
Performance/production
Interview with actor Tibor Szervét. Hungary. 1988-1998. Lang.: Hun. 2071
Review of András Bálint's one-man show *INRI*. Hungary: Budapest. 1997. Lang.: Hun. 2073
Krleža's *U agoniji (In Agony)* directed by Péter Valló. Hungary: Budapest. 1998. Lang.: Hun. 2074
Péter Valló's production of *Iphigéneia he en Aulide (Iphigenia in Aulis)* by Euripides. Hungary: Budapest. 1998. Lang.: Hun. 2132
Calderón's *La cisma de Inglaterra (The Schism of England)* directed by Péter Telihay. Hungary: Budapest. 1997. Lang.: Hun. 2137

Radó, Denise
Performance/production
Denise Radó's *A Fedák-ügy (The Fedak Case)* at József Attila Theatre. Hungary: Budapest. 1998. Lang.: Hun. 2139

Radrigán, Juan
Basic theatrical documents
Text of *El príncipe desolado (The Desolate Prince)* by Juan Radrigán. Chile. 1998. Lang.: Spa. 1413
Plays/librettos/scripts
Interview with playwright Juan Radrigán. Chile. 1998. Lang.: Spa. 2838

Radykalna Frakcja Mazut (Znin)
Performance/production
Productions of the festival of experimental theatre. Poland: Cracow. 1998. Lang.: Ger. 2225

Rafie, Pascale
Plays/librettos/scripts
Raymond Saint-Jean's film adaptation of *Cabaret neiges noires (Black Snow Cabaret)*. Canada. 1997. Lang.: Fre. 3967

Ragtime
Design/technology
Lighting and projections for the musical *Ragtime*. USA: New York, NY. 1998. Lang.: Eng. 4328
Technical designs for *Ragtime* at the Ford Center. USA: New York, NY. 1998. Lang.: Eng. 4338
Eugene Lee's set design for Frank Galati's production of *Ragtime*. USA. 1997-1998. Lang.: Eng. 4340
Sound design for the Broadway premiere of the musical *Ragtime*. USA: New York, NY. 1998. Lang.: Eng. 4341

Rahimi, Chiman
Performance/production
Collection of newspaper reviews by London theatre critics. UK-England: London. 1998. Lang.: Eng. 2584

Rahkamo, Susanna
Performance/production
Interview with ice-dancing team Susanna Rahkamo and Petri Kokko. Finland. 1998. Lang.: Fin. 919

Rahmer, Hermann Schmidt
Institutions
Profile of Württembergische Landesbühne. Germany: Esslingen. 1996-1997. Lang.: Ger. 1639

Rahvusooper 'Estonia' (Tallin)
Design/technology
Scene designer Eldor Rentor. Estonia: Tallin. 1925-1998. Lang.: Swe, Eng, Ger. 175
Institutions
Profile of Estonian theatres. Estonia: Tallin, Tartu. 1997. Lang.: Swe, Eng, Ger. 345

Raimund, Ferdinand
Institutions
Peter Stein's last season as director at the Salzburg Festival. Austria: Salzburg. 1997. Lang.: Eng. 336

Rainer, Yvonne
Performance/production
Dancer Yvonne Rainer's rejection of spectacle. USA. 1965. Lang.: Eng. 989
Modern dance and the female body. USA. Europe. 1900-1930. Lang.: Eng. 1321

Rainmaker, The
Plays/librettos/scripts
Fairy-tale heroines in American drama and musical theatre. USA. 1945-1965. Lang.: Eng. 3617

Raisin in the Sun, A
Plays/librettos/scripts
Student casebook on *A Raisin in the Sun* by Lorraine Hansberry. USA. 1957-1997. Lang.: Eng. 3577
Lynching in plays of Angelina Weld Grimké and Lorraine Hansberry. USA. 1916-1958. Lang.: Eng. 3602

Raison, Jeremy
Performance/production
Collection of newspaper reviews by London theatre critics. UK-England: London. 1998. Lang.: Eng. 2475

Rajkin, Arkadij
Performance/production
Actor Arkadij Rajkin. Russia. 1998. Lang.: Rus. 579
Memoirs of actor Arkadij Rajkin. Russia. 1998. Lang.: Rus. 583

Rake's Progress, The
Design/technology
Lighting designer Jennifer Tipton. USA: New York, NY. 1998. Lang.: Eng. 4441
Performance/production
The use of the harpsichord in Stravinskij's opera *The Rake's Progress*. Europe. 1951. Lang.: Eng. 4559

***Rake's Progress, The* — cont'd**

Background material on Metropolitan Opera radio broadcast performances. USA: New York, NY. 1998. Lang.: Eng. 4713

Jonathan Miller's production of *The Rake's Progress* at the Metropolitan Opera. USA: New York, NY. 1998. Lang.: Eng. 4733

Bass Samuel Ramey. USA. 1940-1998. Lang.: Eng. 4744

Profile of lighting designer Jennifer Tipton. USA. 1937-1998. Lang.: Eng. 4747

Plays/librettos/scripts

The libretto of *The Rake's Progress* by W.H. Auden and Chester Kallman. UK-England. 1971. Lang.: Eng. 4824

Rakugo

Performance/production

The popular comic art-form *rakugo*. Japan. 1600-1980. Lang.: Eng. 2195

Ralph Royster Doyster

Performance/production

Music in Tudor drama. England. 1497-1569. Lang.: Eng. 1902

Ramberg, Hans

Institutions

Opera and food at Regina. Sweden: Stockholm. 1997. Lang.: Swe. 4472

Rambert Dance Company (London)

Institutions

Guest performance of the Rambert Dance Company in Budapest. Hungary: Budapest. 1998. Lang.: Hun. 1042

Performance/production

Guest performance of the Rambert Dance Company. Hungary: Budapest. 1998. Lang.: Hun. 1106

Interview with choreographer Christopher Bruce of the Rambert Dance Company. UK-England: London. 1998. Lang.: Hun. 1163

Rambert, Marie

Institutions

Guest performance of the Rambert Dance Company in Budapest. Hungary: Budapest. 1998. Lang.: Hun. 1042

Rameau, Jean-Philippe

Performance/production

Photographic essay of Rameau's *Platée* directed and choreographed by Mark Morris. USA: Berkeley, CA. 1998. Lang.: Eng. 4304

Plays/librettos/scripts

Politics and the unity of place in *Hippolyte et Aricie* by Rameau and Pelligrin. France. 1733. Lang.: Eng. 4780

Themes from Greek tragedy in opera. France. 1635-1774. Lang.: Eng. 4783

Racine's *Phèdre* as a source for *Hippolyte et Aricie* by Rameau and Pelligrin. France. 1660-1733. Lang.: Eng. 4788

The shaping influence of Pelligrin's libretto on Rameau's *Hippolyte et Aricie*. France. 1733. Lang.: Eng. 4790

Ramey, Samuel

Performance/production

Bass Samuel Ramey. USA. 1940-1998. Lang.: Eng. 4744

Ramm, John

Performance/production

Collection of newspaper reviews by London theatre critics. UK-England: London. 1998. Lang.: Eng. 2495

Collection of newspaper reviews by London theatre critics. UK-England: London. 1998. Lang.: Eng. 2540

Ramos-Perea, Roberto

Plays/librettos/scripts

Analysis of plays by Roberto Ramos-Perea. Puerto Rico. 1998. Lang.: Spa. 3312

Ramsey, Margaret

Administration

Theatrical agent Margaret Ramsey. UK-England: London. 1908-1991. Lang.: Ger. 1394

Ranae (Frogs, The)

Performance/production

Collection of newspaper reviews by London theatre critics. UK-England: London. 1998. Lang.: Eng. 2441

Randai

Performance/production

Female performers of the formerly all-male genre *randai*. Sumatra. 1980-1998. Lang.: Eng. 1354

Randall, Paulette

Performance/production

Collection of newspaper reviews by London theatre critics. UK-England: London. 1998. Lang.: Eng. 2475

Randall, Tony

Performance/production

Actor Tomasso Salvini. USA. Italy. 1856-1915. Lang.: Eng. 2731

Randich, Jean

Plays/librettos/scripts

Jean Randich's production of *The Golden Door* by Sylvia Regan, Tenement Museum. USA: New York, NY. 1940-1998. Lang.: Eng. 3606

Ranevskaja, Faina Grigorevna

Performance/production

Anecdotes by and about actress Faina Ranevskaja. Russia. 1896-1984. Lang.: Rus. 584

Singer and actress Faina Ranevskaja. Russia. 1896-1984. Lang.: Rus. 2319

Biography of actress Faina Ranevskaja. Russia. 1896-1984. Lang.: Rus. 2320

Ránki, György

Performance/production

Recalling the composer György Ránki. Hungary. 1907-1992. Lang.: Hun. 4617

Raper, Darren

Performance/production

Collection of newspaper reviews by London theatre critics. UK-England: London. 1998. Lang.: Eng. 2460

Rapimento di Cefalo, Il

Design/technology

Stage machinery in *Il Rapimento di Cefalo* staged by Bernardo Buontalenti. Italy: Florence. 1600. Lang.: Eng. 4436

Rashad, Phylicia

Performance/production

Interview with actress Phylicia Rashad. USA: Atlanta, GA. 1998. Lang.: Eng. 2695

Raslila

Performance/production

Analysis of the temple performance genre *raslila*. India. 1779-1985. Lang.: Eng. 1347

Rastell, John

Performance spaces

Speculations on the theatre of John Rastell. England: London. 1524-1530. Lang.: Eng. 1799

Performance/production

Music in Tudor drama. England. 1497-1569. Lang.: Eng. 1902

Rasumovskaja, Ljudmila

Performance/production

German productions of contemporary Russian drama. Germany. 1998. Lang.: Ger. 1984

Raszputyin (Rasputin)

Performance/production

Analysis of *Raszputyin (Rasputin)* by Közép-Európa Táncszínház. Hungary: Budapest. 1998. Lang.: Hun. 937

Rátóti, Zoltán

Institutions

Theatre critics' awards 97-98. Hungary. 1997-1998. Lang.: Hun. 355

Rattenfänger, Der

Performance/production

Opera director Katja Czellnik. Germany: Oldenburg, Kiel. 1996-1998. Lang.: Ger. 4583

Rattigan, Terence

Performance/production

Collection of newspaper reviews by London theatre critics. UK-England: London. 1998. Lang.: Eng. 2452

Collection of newspaper reviews by London theatre critics. UK-England: London. 1998. Lang.: Eng. 2584

Rattner, Gregory

Performance/production

Collection of newspaper reviews by London theatre critics. UK-England: London. 1998. Lang.: Eng. 2587

Räuber, Die (Robbers, The)

Institutions

Productions of Staatstheater Stuttgart. Germany: Stuttgart. 1998. Lang.: Ger. 1620

Performance/production

French productions of German plays. France. 1998. Lang.: Ger. 1935

A production of Schiller's *Die Räuber (The Robbers)* performed by prisoners. Germany: Berlin. 1997. Lang.: Ger. 2025

Collection of newspaper reviews by London theatre critics. UK-England: London. 1998. Lang.: Eng. 2488

Plays/librettos/scripts

Female sacrifice in eighteenth-century German drama. Germany. 1772-1781. Lang.: Eng. 3167

Rauber, Gérard

Basic theatrical documents

Text of *Le Roi Hâtif (King Hasty)* by Françoise Gerbaulet. France. 1993-1998. Lang.: Fre. 1425

Rauwald, Ute
Administration
Interviews with German theatre and film directors. Germany. 1998. Lang.: Ger. 1385
Raven's Song
Basic theatrical documents
Text of *Raven's Song* by Angela Brannon Tarleton. USA. 1988. Lang.: Eng. 4323
Ravenhill, Mark
Institutions
English-language plays at Berlin Festwochen. Germany: Berlin. 1998. Lang.: Ger. 1623
Survey of the Theatertreffen festival. Germany: Berlin. 1998. Lang.: Swe. 1651
Performance/production
Collection of newspaper reviews by London theatre critics. UK-England: London. 1998. Lang.: Eng. 2434
Collection of newspaper reviews by London theatre critics. UK-England: London. 1998. Lang.: Eng. 2503
Collection of newspaper reviews by London theatre critics. UK-England: London. 1998. Lang.: Eng. 2571
Report on several English performances. UK-England: London, Stratford. 1998. Lang.: Eng. 2634
Analysis of recent New York productions. USA: New York, NY. 1997-1998. Lang.: Eng. 2759
Plays/librettos/scripts
German view of English and American drama. UK-England. USA. 1998. Lang.: Ger. 3455
Mark Ravenhill's *Shopping and Fucking* and its production by Thomas Ostermeier. UK-England. Germany. 1998. Lang.: Ger. 3476
Sex, drugs, and violence in contemporary British drama. UK-England. 1991-1998. Lang.: Eng. 3494
Interview with playwright Mark Ravenhill. UK-England. 1998. Lang.: Ger. 3496
Ravenscroft, Edward
Performance/production
Collection of newspaper reviews by London theatre critics. UK-England: London. 1998. Lang.: Eng. 2448
Ravnjak, Vili
Basic theatrical documents
Plays and screenplays by Vili Ravnjak. Slovenia. 1991-1997. Lang.: Slo. 1460
Rawlins, Trevor
Performance/production
Collection of newspaper reviews by London theatre critics. UK-England: London. 1998. Lang.: Eng. 2481
Ray & Sons
Basic theatrical documents
Texts of plays by Eddie Paul Bradley, Jr. USA. 1998. Lang.: Eng. 1482
Raymond, Jennie
Plays/librettos/scripts
Young People's Theatre's adaptation of *Anne of Green Gables*. Canada: Toronto, ON. 1911-1998. Lang.: Eng. 2832
Raymonda
Performance/production
The history of the ballet *Raymonda* by Glazunov and Petipa. Russia. 1898-1998. Lang.: Eng. 1133
Ballerina Alexandra Danilova on Balanchine's *Raymonda*. USA: New York, NY. 1946. Lang.: Eng. 1172
Read, David
Performance/production
Collection of newspaper reviews by London theatre critics. UK-England: London. 1998. Lang.: Eng. 2463
Real Classy Affair
Performance/production
Collection of newspaper reviews by London theatre critics. UK-England: London. 1998. Lang.: Eng. 2526
Real Inspector Hound, The
Performance/production
Collection of newspaper reviews by London theatre critics. UK-England: London. 1998. Lang.: Eng. 2463
Real Women Have Curves
Plays/librettos/scripts
Analysis of plays by Josefina López. USA. 1988-1989. Lang.: Eng. 3650
Rebcová, Monika
Performance/production
Choreographers Monika Rebcová, Petr Tyc, and Petr Zuska. Czech Republic: Prague. 1997. Lang.: Eng, Fre. 1266
Reception theory
Theory/criticism
Analysis of Yoko Ono's performance work *Cut Piece*. USA. 1964-1998. Lang.: Eng. 4151
Reconstruction, dance
Theory/criticism
Gasparo Angiolini and eighteenth-century dance. Italy. 1761-1765. Lang.: Eng. 1199
Reconstruction, performance
Design/technology
Reconstruction of a performance of *A Midsummer Night's Dream* designed by Galli-Bibiena. Germany: Bayreuth. 1997-1998. Lang.: Ger. 1521
Performance/production
The reconstruction of Jean Börlin's ballet *Dervisher*. Sweden: Stockholm. 1997. Lang.: Eng. 1150
The possibilities for creativity in the reconstruction of dance choreographies. 1998. Lang.: Eng. 1258
Reconstruction, theatre
Performance spaces
Theatrical history of the building that houses Thália Színház. Hungary: Budapest. 1913-1996. Lang.: Hun. 447
The reconstruction of Drammens Teater after a fire. Norway: Drammen. 1993-1998. Lang.: Swe. 1803
Recordings
Performance/production
Sequentia's new recording of *Ordo Virtutum* by Hildegard of Bingen. Germany. 1997. Lang.: Eng. 4294
Lotte Lenya's singing style. Germany. 1929-1965. Lang.: Eng. 4357
Audio and video recordings of opera stars and complete operas. 1988-1998. Lang.: Eng. 4522
Recordings of *Lieder* by Schumann. Germany. UK-England. 1998. Lang.: Eng. 4601
Recordings of the different versions of Verdi's *Don Carlos*. Italy. Europe. 1866-1998. Lang.: Eng. 4650
Reviews of *Lieder* recordings. USA. Slovenia. Austria. 1998. Lang.: Eng. 4720
Operatic holdings of American and British record collectors. USA. UK-England. 1900-1998. Lang.: Eng. 4721
Reference materials
Discography of operas by Donizetti. Europe. North America. 1998. Lang.: Eng. 4831
Red Harvest
Basic theatrical documents
Jonathan Golove's opera *Red Harvest*. USA. 1940-1950. Lang.: Eng. 4422
Red Noses
Plays/librettos/scripts
Analysis of *Red Noses* by Peter Barnes. UK-Scotland. 1985. Lang.: Eng. 3514
Red Riding Hood and the Wolf
Performance/production
Collection of newspaper reviews by London theatre critics. UK-England: London. 1998. Lang.: Eng. 2557
Red Shoes, The
Plays/librettos/scripts
The popularity and influence of the ballet film *The Red Shoes*. UK-England. 1948. Lang.: Eng. 3988
Red Sky at Morning
Plays/librettos/scripts
Analysis of plays by Dymphna Cusack. Australia. 1927-1959. Lang.: Eng. 2777
Redeemer, The
Performance/production
Collection of newspaper reviews by London theatre critics. UK-England: London. 1998. Lang.: Eng. 2506
Redfarn, Roger
Performance/production
Collection of newspaper reviews by London theatre critics. UK-England. 1998. Lang.: Eng. 2489
Collection of newspaper reviews by London theatre critics. UK-England: London. 1998. Lang.: Eng. 2586
Redford, John
Performance/production
Music in Tudor drama. England. 1497-1569. Lang.: Eng. 1902
Redonnet, Marie
Plays/librettos/scripts
Analysis of plays by Marguerite Duras and Marie Redonnet. France. 1977-1992. Lang.: Eng. 3071

Redoutentheater (Vienna)
Performance spaces
The architectural and administrative history of Redoutentheater. Austria: Vienna. 1918-1992. Lang.: Ger. 433
Redwood, John Henry
Plays/librettos/scripts
Playwright John Henry Redwood. USA: Atlanta, GA. 1998. Lang.: Eng. 3656
Reece, Crispin
Performance/production
Actors' interpretations of the title role in Oscar Wilde's *The Canterville Ghost*. UK-England. USA. 1943-1998. Lang.: Eng. 4066
Reece, Robert
Performance/production
Collection of newspaper reviews by London theatre critics. UK-England: London. 1998. Lang.: Eng. 2557
Rees, Roger
Plays/librettos/scripts
Robin Hood on film. England. USA. 1920-1992. Lang.: Eng. 3969
Reeves, Vic
Performance/production
Collection of newspaper reviews by London theatre critics. UK-England: London. 1998. Lang.: Eng. 2573
Reference materials
SEE ALSO
Classed Entries.
Institutions
Description of the *Encyclopedia of the Moscow Art Theatre*. Russia: Moscow. 1898-1998. Lang.: Rus. 1703
Plays/librettos/scripts
Scenarios of Russian operas. Russia. 1998. Lang.: Rus. 4818
Reference materials
Overview of world theatre history. Lang.: Rus. 693
Regan, Sylvia
Plays/librettos/scripts
Jean Randich's production of *The Golden Door* by Sylvia Regan, Tenement Museum. USA: New York, NY. 1940-1998. Lang.: Eng. 3606
Regina, Stockholms Operamathus (Stockholm)
Institutions
Opera and food at Regina. Sweden: Stockholm. 1997. Lang.: Swe. 4472
Regional theatre
Administration
History of circle stock touring. USA. 1907-1957. Lang.: Eng. 43
Theatre and Equity business in the Atlanta area. USA: Atlanta, GA. 1998. Lang.: Eng. 49
Changes in Equity's bonding policy for regional theatres. USA: New York, NY. 1998. Lang.: Eng. 86
Theatre manager and entrepreneur Harry Davis. USA: Pittsburgh, PA. 1893-1927. Lang.: Eng. 134
Study of management in regional theatres. USA. 1987-1988. Lang.: Eng. 140
Design/technology
Lighting designer Kevin Adams. USA. 1979-1998. Lang.: Eng. 258
Lighting design for the musical *Follies*, Paper Mill Playhouse. USA: Millburn, NJ. 1998. Lang.: Eng. 4335
Institutions
Regional theatre in Mazovia. Poland: Płock. 1808-1975. Lang.: Pol. 374
History of Virginia Museum Theatre. USA: Richmond, VA. 1955-1987. Lang.: Eng. 406
The growth of regional dance companies. USA. 1963-1998. Lang.: Eng. 908
Profile of Nordhessisches Landestheater Marburg. Germany: Marburg. 1997-1998. Lang.: Ger. 1653
German theatres' responses to threatened closings and mergers. Germany: Esslingen, Tübingen. 1998. Lang.: Ger. 1665
Profile of the Omsk Dramatic Theatre, 'Galerka'. Russia: Omsk. 1998. Lang.: Rus. 1706
The mission and management of the Free Southern Theatre. USA: New Orleans, LA. 1963-1980. Lang.: Eng. 1769
History of Lake Charles Little Theatre. USA: Lake Charles, LA. 1927-1982. Lang.: Eng. 1770
The role of private community organizations in the restructuring of the Folger Shakespeare Theatre. USA: Washington, DC. 1985-1987. Lang.: Eng. 1771
William Patton, executive director emeritus of Oregon Shakespeare Festival. USA: Ashland, OR. 1952-1998. Lang.: Eng. 1777
Performance/production
Theatre in Vilna. Poland: Vilna. 1905-1915. Lang.: Pol. 576
Theatrical history of Nižnij Novgorod. Russia: Nižnij Novgorod. Lang.: Rus. 588
Saratov's theatrical life. Russia: Saratov. Lang.: Rus. 2245
Siberian theatre and culture. Russia. 1998. Lang.: Fin. 2311
The multifaceted nature of early nonprofit regional theatre. USA. 1940-1960. Lang.: Eng. 2705
The 'scientific perspective' of director David Belasco. USA. 1882-1931. Lang.: Eng. 2741
Antitheatricalism in the Circuit Chautauqua. USA. 1913-1930. Lang.: Eng. 4135
The Opera-in-English movement. USA. 1850-1985. Lang.: Eng. 4746
Plays/librettos/scripts
Women and Acadian theatre. Canada. 1870-1998. Lang.: Eng. 2810
Interview with playwright Rod Dungate. UK-England: Birmingham. 1998. Lang.: Eng. 3442
History of Hungarian-language theatre in the Voivodship region. Yugoslavia: Subotica, Novi Sad. 1837-1998. Lang.: Hun. 3720
Reference materials
Bibliography of prerevolutionary culture. Karachaevo-Cherkess. Lang.: Rus. 706
Relation to other fields
The national movement, cultural policy, and German regional theatre. Germany: Eisleben. 1998. Lang.: Ger. 740
Règlements de compte avec la mémoire (Settling Scores with Memory)
Plays/librettos/scripts
Quebecois plays about the crisis of October 1970. Canada. 1970-1990. Lang.: Fre, Eng. 2812
Regős, János
Institutions
Interview with director János Regős of Szkéné Színház. Hungary: Budapest. 1979-1998. Lang.: Hun. 362
History of Szkéné Színház. Hungary: Budapest. 1963-1995. Lang.: Hun. 1668
Regulations
Administation
American and French regulation of mass media. USA. France. 1912-1998. Lang.: Eng. 3853
Administration
Report on credit union legislation. USA: New York, NY. 1998. Lang.: Eng. 70
Issues of concern to Equity members in current Broadway shows. USA: New York, NY. 1998. Lang.: Eng. 77
Equity's Stage Reading Guidelines. USA: New York, NY. 1998. Lang.: Eng. 85
The waiting period before Equity health benefits take effect. USA: New York, NY. 1998. Lang.: Eng. 91
Securing sick pay and worker's compensation for an on-the-job injury. USA: New York, NY. 1998. Lang.: Eng. 93
The loss of medical coverage for Equity dependents over nineteen years of age. USA: New York, NY. 1998. Lang.: Eng. 105
Equity debate on member behavior when not under Equity contract. USA: New York, NY. 1998. Lang.: Eng. 106
The publicizing of financial information about nonprofit arts organizations. USA. 1998. Lang.: Eng. 137
Institutions
Popular entertainment at the New Haven Assembly Hall and Columbian Museum and Gardens. USA: New Haven, CT. 1796-1820. Lang.: Eng. 394
Performance/production
Norwich's unregulated entertainers. England: Norwich. 1530-1624. Lang.: Eng. 1907
The popular theatre genre *teatro por horas*. Spain. 1867-1922. Lang.: Eng. 2361
Relation to other fields
New Italian theatrical legislation. Italy. 1998. Lang.: Eng. 3774
Régy, Claude
Performance/production
Recent Paris productions. France: Paris. 1997-1998. Lang.: Ger. 1933
Rehan, Ada
Plays/librettos/scripts
Analysis of *The Foresters* by Alfred, Lord Tennyson. England. USA. 1700-1910. Lang.: Eng. 2998

Rehearsal process
Institutions
Ariane Mnouchkine and rehearsal techniques of Théâtre du Soleil. France: Paris. 1964-1997. Lang.: Eng. 1610
The theatrical method of Joint Stock Theatre Group. UK-England: London. 1974-1989. Lang.: Eng. 1749
Performance/production
Theory and the role of the dramaturg. North America. 1998. Lang.: Eng. 572
Analysis of a student production of Caryl Churchill's *Cloud Nine.* Canada. 1997. Lang.: Eng. 1840
The methodology of director Robert Lepage. Canada: Toronto, ON. 1992. Lang.: Eng. 1845
Directing shows with three-week rehearsal time at Eastern Front Theatre. Canada: Dartmouth, NS. 1980-1998. Lang.: Eng. 1868
Rehearsal practices in British professional theatre. England. 1500-1700. Lang.: Eng. 1905
Rehearsals of Christoph Marthaler's production of *Arsenic and Old Lace* by Joseph Kesselring. Germany: Hamburg. 1998. Lang.: Ger. 1953
Massimo Castri's production of Euripides' *Electra.* Italy: Spoleto. 1993. Lang.: Ita. 2179
Interviews with actors Lil Terselius and Björn Granath. Sweden: Stockholm. 1998. Lang.: Swe. 2381
Gerthi Kulle's role in Brecht's *Der Gute Mensch von Sezuan (The Good Person of Szechwan)* at Dramaten. Sweden: Stockholm. 1998. Lang.: Swe. 2384
Photos of rehearsals of O'Neill's *Long Day's Journey Into Night* at Dramaten. Sweden: Stockholm. 1998. Lang.: Swe. 2391
Hamlet at Shakespeare Repertory Theatre, directed by Barbara Gaines. USA: Chicago, IL. 1996. Lang.: Eng. 2666
Directors' nonverbal behavior in rehearsal. USA. 1987. Lang.: Eng. 2680
Robert Wilson's work with actors on a production of *Danton's Death (Dantons Tod).* USA: Houston, TX. 1997. Lang.: Eng. 2688
Plays/librettos/scripts
Playwright Elfriede Jelinek on the relationship between author and play in rehearsal. Austria: Vienna. 1997. Lang.: Ger. 2780
Relation to other fields
The use of theatre rehearsal techniques for socially emotionally disturbed youth. USA. 1985-1987. Lang.: Eng. 774
Research/historiography
Proposed ethnographic model for the study of rehearsal. 1985-1995. Lang.: Eng. 816
Reid, Christina
Plays/librettos/scripts
Gender and nationalism in Northern Irish drama. UK-Ireland. 1902-1997. Lang.: Eng. 3511
Reid, Kate
Performance/production
The performances of Frances Hyland, Kate Reid, and Martha Henry in *The Cherry Orchard.* Canada: Stratford, ON. 1965. Lang.: Eng. 1865
Reigen (Round)
Performance/production
Collection of newspaper reviews by London theatre critics. UK-England: London. 1998. Lang.: Eng. 2455
Reiher, Ulf
Performance/production
German directors about the meaning of Brecht today. Germany. 1998. Lang.: Ger. 1948
Reinhardt, Max
Performance spaces
Non-traditional theatrical space. Germany. France. UK-England. 1898-1998. Lang.: Dan. 443
Performance/production
The performance of sacrifice on stage. France. Germany. 1900-1998. Lang.: Ger. 530
Pirandello's theatre on the Austrian stage. Austria. 1924-1989. Lang.: Ita. 1825
Reinhardt, Paul
Design/technology
Costumer Paul Reinhardt. USA. 1998. Lang.: Eng. 253
Reinshagen, Gerlind
Performance/production
Collection of newspaper reviews by London theatre critics. UK-England: London. 1998. Lang.: Eng. 2481
Reise durch Jelineks Kopf (Journey through Jelinek's Head)
Institutions
Productions of the Salzburg Festival. Austria: Salzburg. 1998. Lang.: Ger. 1573
Reisman, Jane
Design/technology
Digital lighting control for *A Chorus Line.* USA: New York, NY. 1974-1975. Lang.: Eng. 4337
Reisz, Karel
Performance/production
Recent productions in Ireland of plays by Eugene O'Neill. Ireland: Dublin. UK-Ireland: Belfast. 1989-1998. Lang.: Eng. 2154
Collection of newspaper reviews by London theatre critics. UK-England: London. 1998. Lang.: Eng. 2561
Recent productions of plays by Harold Pinter at Donmar Warehouse. UK-England: London. 1998. Lang.: Eng. 2609
Plays/librettos/scripts
The film adaptation by Harold Pinter and Karel Reisz of *The French Lieutenant's Woman* by John Fowles. UK-England. USA. 1982. Lang.: Eng. 3982
Releasing Myra?
Performance/production
Collection of newspaper reviews by London theatre critics. UK-England: London. 1998. Lang.: Eng. 2442
Religion
Basic theatrical documents
Slovene translations of Tibetan plays. Tibet. 1400-1990. Lang.: Slo. 1470
Design/technology
Design for houses of worship, including their adaptation for performance and exhibitions. USA: Long Beach, CA. 1998. Lang.: Eng. 290
Institutions
Popular entertainment at the New Haven Assembly Hall and Columbian Museum and Gardens. USA: New Haven, CT. 1796-1820. Lang.: Eng. 394
History of Christian theatre company, the Covenant Players. USA: Camarillo, CA. 1988. Lang.: Eng. 429
Analysis of the bulletin of theatre company Les Compagnons du Saint-Laurent. Canada: Montreal, PQ. 1944-1947. Lang.: Fre. 1585
European national theatres and their development. Slovenia. Germany. 1750-1910. Lang.: Slo. 1720
Performance/production
Performance space in Aboriginal *corroboree.* Australia. 800 B.C.-1988 A.D. Lang.: Eng. 487
A dancer's experience of and investigations into ecstasy. USA. Germany. 1969-1990. Lang.: Eng. 673
The role of acting in preparing a homily. USA. 1997. Lang.: Eng. 679
Baroque ballet at the Jesuit College of Clermont/Louis le Grand. France: Paris. 1660-1761. Lang.: Eng. 1076
The creation of the religious ballet *A Dancer's Christmas.* USA: Boston, MA. 1980-1998. Lang.: Eng. 1192
Nomai dance drama. Japan. 1650-1985. Lang.: Eng. 1350
Analysis of Tibetan Buddhist drama. Tibet. 1500-1984. Lang.: Eng. 1355
Staging of the Cornish *Ordinalia.* England. 1375-1400. Lang.: Eng. 1890
Report from a symposium on traditional Korean theatre. Korea. Germany: Berlin. 1980-1998. Lang.: Ger, Fre, Dut, Eng. 2196
Religion and actor Oleg Borisov. Russia: St. Petersburg. 1998. Lang.: Rus. 2287
Homiletical drama in the free church tradition. USA: Chicago, IL. 1997. Lang.: Eng. 2721
Spike Lee's unsuccessful efforts to film parts of *Malcolm X* in Mecca. USA. 1992-1995. Lang.: Eng. 3954
Carnival as a unifying force. Trinidad and Tobago. 1998. Lang.: Eng. 4170
Maltese Holy Week rituals. Malta. 1998. Lang.: Eng. 4217
Reexamination of the performance art of Beuys, Abramovič, and Ulay. USA. Germany. Netherlands. 1964-1985. Lang.: Eng. 4254
Interview with director Peter Sellars. USA. 1990-1998. Lang.: Ger, Fre, Dut, Eng. 4727
Plays/librettos/scripts
Mennonite drama of Veralyn Warkentin and Vern Thiessen. Canada. 1890-1997. Lang.: Eng. 2829
Priest and playwright Kaj Munk. Denmark. 1898-1944. Lang.: Swe. 2855
Shakespeare's *Measure for Measure* and the King James Bible. England. 1604. Lang.: Eng. 2865
The figure of the Jew in Marlowe and Shakespeare. England. 1590-1600. Lang.: Eng. 2868

Religion — cont'd

Tudor religious and social issues in John Lily's *Endymion* and *Midas*. England. 1587-1590. Lang.: Eng. 2871

Plague imagery in Jacobean tragedy. England. 1618-1642. Lang.: Eng. 2889

Christianity and Shakespeare's *Macbeth*. England. 1606. Lang.: Eng. 2890

Stage devils in English Reformation plays. England. 1530-1583. Lang.: Eng. 2899

Analysis of Restoration anti-Puritan comedies. England. 1661-1663. Lang.: Eng. 2907

Protestant aesthetics and Shakespeare's *Measure for Measure*. England. 1604. Lang.: Eng. 2908

Analysis of Shakespeare's history plays. England. 1590-1599. Lang.: Eng. 2911

John Bale's characters Sodomy and Idolatry. England. 1536-1546. Lang.: Eng. 2914

Lucian's *Icaromenippus* as a source for Heywood's *The Play of the Wether*. England. 1533. Lang.: Eng. 2920

Analysis of *The Witch of Edmonton* by Ford, Dekker, and Rowley. England. 1621. Lang.: Eng. 2928

Annunciation motifs in Shakespeare's *Hamlet*. England. 1600-1601. Lang.: Eng. 2934

Catholic and Protestant in Shakespeare's Second Henriad. England. 1596-1599. Lang.: Eng. 2940

Religious controversy and the emerging print culture. England. 1590-1620. Lang.: Eng. 2956

God and man in Renaissance theatre. England. 1610-1625. Lang.: Eng. 2966

Protestant belief and English Reformation drama. England. 1535-1607. Lang.: Eng. 2972

Casuistry and early modern English tragedy. England. 1600-1671. Lang.: Eng. 2980

Analysis of *The Massacre at Paris* by Christopher Marlowe. England. 1593. Lang.: Eng. 2997

Epiphany in the plays of Shakespeare. England. 1590-1613. Lang.: Eng. 3008

Conscience in early modern literature including Shakespeare. England. 1590-1620. Lang.: Eng. 3020

Gender and religion in Shakespeare's *Measure for Measure*. England. 1604. Lang.: Eng. 3021

Prejudice and law in Shakespeare's *The Merchant of Venice*. England. 1596. Lang.: Eng. 3027

Analysis of *Bariona* by Jean-Paul Sartre. France. 1940-1945. Lang.: Eng. 3093

Analysis of Holocaust plays by Jean-Claude Grumberg. France. 1974-1991. Lang.: Eng. 3108

Interview with playwright-director Olivier Py. France. 1988-1998. Lang.: Ger, Fre, Dut, Eng. 3117

Morality plays of the Reformation. Germany. 1550-1584. Lang.: Eng. 3163

Hermes in the Greek theatre devoted to Dionysus. Greece. 600-411 B.C. Lang.: Eng. 3179

Hegel's influence on the plays of Henrik Ibsen. Norway. Germany. 1870-1898. Lang.: Eng. 3292

Analysis of *Zvestoba (Fidelity)* by Etbin Kristan. Slovenia. 1897-1910. Lang.: Slo. 3344

The priesthood in Slovene theatre. Slovenia. 1903-1994. Lang.: Slo. 3345

Analysis of *Zoran ali Kmetska vojna na Slovenskum (Zoran and the Peasant War in Slovenia)* by Ivan Vrhovec. Slovenia. 1870. Lang.: Slo. 3351

Social roles in plays by Fran Govekar and Anton Medved. Slovenia. 1897-1910. Lang.: Slo. 3352

Social roles and ideologies in plays of Anton Funtek and Ivo Šorli. Slovenia. 1897-1920. Lang.: Slo. 3353

Playwright Ivan Mrak. Slovenia. 1925-1986. Lang.: Slo. 3355

Religion and the individual in plays of Ivan Mrak. Slovenia. 1955. Lang.: Slo. 3358

Spanish Catholicism and the *autos sacramentales* of Calderón. Spain. 1637-1671. Lang.: Spa. 3405

William Butler Yeats, *japonisme*, and *nō*. UK-England. 1853-1939. Lang.: Eng. 3435

Wilde, Gide, and the censorship of Biblical drama. UK-England. France. 1892-1898. Lang.: Eng. 3441

Rhetorical analysis of plays by George Bernard Shaw. UK-England. 1896-1908. Lang.: Eng. 3480

Puritanism and predestination in *Suddenly Last Summer* by Tennessee Williams. USA. 1958. Lang.: Eng. 3631

Analysis of plays based on the Hebrew prophets. USA. Europe. 1919-1970. Lang.: Eng. 3659

Analysis of Eugene O'Neill's 'middle period' plays. USA. 1925-1938. Lang.: Eng. 3675

Afrocuban religion in Cuban films. Cuba. 1974-1991. Lang.: Eng. 3968

Puritanism and Milton's *Comus*. England. 1634-1635. Lang.: Eng. 4207

Wagner's *Parsifal* and the political aspirations of Catalonians. Spain-Catalonia: Barcelona. 1841-1914. Lang.: Eng. 4820

Relation to other fields

Jewish culture and the Prague theatre scene. Czechoslovakia: Prague. 1910-1939. Lang.: Ger. 722

Role playing in the Brook Farm transcendentalist community. USA: West Roxbury, MA. 1841-1847. Lang.: Eng. 777

Abilene Christian University Theatre and the role of theatre in the evangelical subculture. USA: Abilene, TX. 1995-1998. Lang.: Eng. 787

The theatrical nature of Salvation Army activities. USA. 1865-1950. Lang.: Eng. 796

The integration of Buddhism in drama therapy. USA. 1998. Lang.: Eng. 808

Theatrical activities of the Mormon Church. USA. 1977-1986. Lang.: Eng. 811

Religion and art in *nō*. Japan. 1300-1988. Lang.: Eng. 1374

Amateur art theatre produced by Quebec priests. Canada: Montreal, PQ. 1930-1950. Lang.: Fre. 3733

The dramatic nature of the ancient Egyptian text *The Triumph of Horus*. Egypt. 2500 B.C. Lang.: Eng. 3744

Cross-dressing and gender struggle on the early modern English stage. England. 1580-1620. Lang.: Eng. 3749

The relationship between the York Cycle and the Bolton Book of Hours. England: York. 1405-1500. Lang.: Eng. 3750

Drama and the English Reformation. England. 1530-1607. Lang.: Eng. 3755

Challenges facing Turkish theatre artists. Turkey: Istanbul. 1994-1997. Lang.: Eng. 3778

The use of original theatrical productions in the ministry. USA. 1998. Lang.: Eng. 3781

The influence of Shakespeare's *Othello* on C.B. Brown's novel *Wieland*. USA. England. 1604-1798. Lang.: Eng. 3788

Controversy over Terrence McNally's *Corpus Christi*, Manhattan Theatre Club. USA: New York, NY. 1998. Lang.: Eng. 3792

The gangster film and public concern about moral corruption. USA. 1931-1940. Lang.: Eng. 4038

Depiction of Jews in Stalinist Russian film. USSR. 1924-1953. Lang.: Eng. 4039

The square in Italian pageants and open-air entertainment. Italy. 1933-1975. Lang.: Ita. 4227

Shelly Hirsch on her performance piece *For Jerry—Part I*. USA. Germany. 1997-1998. Lang.: Ger, Fre, Dut, Eng. 4266

Theory/criticism

Antisemitism and criticism of Shakespeare's *Merchant of Venice*. England. 1596-1986. Lang.: Eng. 3813

Theatrical character development in Biblical texts. USA. 1998. Lang.: Eng. 3842

Religious theatre

Audience

Audience assumptions about the York *Resurrection*. England: York. 1275-1541. Lang.: Eng. 1400

Institutions

History of Christian theatre company, the Covenant Players. USA: Camarillo, CA. 1988. Lang.: Eng. 429

Jeannette Clift George and the A.D. Players. USA: Houston, TX. 1967-1997. Lang.: Eng. 1785

History of the Society for Old Music. USA: Kalamazoo, MI. 1968-1991. Lang.: Eng. 4292

Performance/production

Analysis of *Regularis Concordia* and *Quem quarteritis*. England. 1150-1228. Lang.: Eng. 516

Religious theatre — cont'd

Late medieval Savoy and theatre. Savoy. 1400-1600. Lang.: Eng. 589
Analysis of Tibetan Buddhist drama. Tibet. 1500-1984. Lang.: Eng. 1355
Analysis of religious theatre of Giambattista Andreini. Italy. 1576-1654. Lang.: Eng. 2190
Evidence for performance of medieval religious drama. Sweden. 1140-1500. Lang.: Eng. 2392
Katie Mitchell's production of mystery plays at RSC. UK-England: London. 1996-1998. Lang.: Eng. 2626
Homiletical drama in the free church tradition. USA: Chicago, IL. 1997. Lang.: Eng. 2721
Director Joel Kaplan on his production of the *York Cycle*. Canada: Toronto, ON. 1998. Lang.: Eng. 4213
The staging of the complete *York Cycle* by the University of Toronto. Canada: Toronto, ON. 1998. Lang.: Eng. 4214
Maltese Holy Week rituals. Malta. 1998. Lang.: Eng. 4217
The Patum of Berga compared to sixteenth-century German festivities. Spain-Catalonia: Berga. Germany: Trent. 1549-1996. Lang.: Eng. 4218
Sequentia's new recording of *Ordo Virtutum* by Hildegard of Bingen. Germany. 1997. Lang.: Eng. 4294
The survival of medieval English religious theatre on the puppet stage. England: London. 1500-1780. Lang.: Eng. 4890

Plays/librettos/scripts
Analysis of *De Eerste Bliscap van Maria (The First Joy of Mary)*. Belgium: Brussels. 1440-1560. Lang.: Eng. 2790
The language used by devils in the *York Cycle*. England: York. 1400-1500. Lang.: Eng. 2933
The Easter play tradition. England. 1180-1557. Lang.: Eng. 2942
Biblical narrative and the order of the *York Cycle* episodes. England: York. 1401-1499. Lang.: Eng. 2950
The N-town Mary play and the Four Virtues of Psalm 84:11. England. 1120-1501. Lang.: Eng. 2983
Morality plays of the Reformation. Germany. 1550-1584. Lang.: Eng. 3163
A lost creed play from the twelfth century. Germany: Regensburg. 1184-1189. Lang.: Eng. 3176
Analysis of the Montecassino Passion Play. Italy. 1100-1200. Lang.: Eng. 3256
Pictorial and staged versions of the Passion. Savoy. 1435-1505. Lang.: Eng. 3342
Religion and the individual in plays of Ivan Mrak. Slovenia. 1955. Lang.: Slo. 3358
Analysis of plays based on the Hebrew prophets. USA. Europe. 1919-1970. Lang.: Eng. 3659
Roman 'saints' plays' at the Lille procession honoring the Virgin. Belgium: Lille. 1450-1499. Lang.: Eng. 4224

Reference materials
Index to the first twenty volumes of *Medieval English Theatre*. England. 1979-1998. Lang.: Eng. 696

Relation to other fields
Abilene Christian University Theatre and the role of theatre in the evangelical subculture. USA: Abilene, TX. 1995-1998. Lang.: Eng. 787
Fouquet's miniature of St. Apollonia and its relationship to the mystery play. France. 1452-1577. Lang.: Eng. 3761
Jean Fouquet's miniature of St. Apollonia and its relationship to performance. France: Tours. 1452-1577. Lang.: Eng. 3762
Fouquet's depiction of the martyrdom of St. Apollonia as a record of a performance. France. 1452-1577. Lang.: Eng. 3763
Medieval religious theatre and the public safety. Germany. 1234-1656. Lang.: Eng. 3771
The use of original theatrical productions in the ministry. USA. 1998. Lang.: Eng. 3781
Economic forces and the Chester Whitsun plays. England: Chester. 1521-1678. Lang.: Eng. 4226

Theory/criticism
Evaluation of scholarship on English cycle plays. 1998. Lang.: Eng. 3802

Remains of the Day, The
Plays/librettos/scripts
Comparison of Harold Pinter's *Party Time* with his screenplay for *The Remains of the Day*. UK-England. 1991-1996. Lang.: Eng. 3490

Remembering Shanghai
Plays/librettos/scripts
Review of collections of plays with gay themes. Canada. 1996. Lang.: Eng. 2802

Remnants
Plays/librettos/scripts
Survivors' testimony in Holocaust theatre. USA. 1975-1995. Lang.: Eng. 3605

Remondi, Claudio
Performance/production
The theatre of Claudio Remondi and Riccardo Caporossi. Italy. 1970-1995. Lang.: Ita. 2169
The actor/clown team of Claudio Remondi and Riccardo Caporossi. Italy. 1971-1998. Lang.: Eng. 2176

Renaissance Theater (Berlin)
Performance/production
Comparison of productions of *The Lisbon Traviata* by Terrence McNally. Germany: Berlin, Essen. 1998. Lang.: Ger. 2005

Renaissance theatre
SEE ALSO
Geographical-Chronological Index under Europe 1400-1600, France 1500-1700, Italy 1400-1600, Spain 1400-1600.

Design/technology
Stage machinery in *Il Rapimento di Cefalo* staged by Bernardo Buontalenti. Italy: Florence. 1600. Lang.: Eng. 4436

Performance/production
Dance culture and the court of King Mátyás. Hungary. 1413-1485. Lang.: Hun. 943
Census of Renaissance drama productions and staged readings. UK-England. 1997. Lang.: Eng. 2635

Plays/librettos/scripts
Codes of politeness in Renaissance drama. England. 1500-1600. Lang.: Eng. 2878
Robin Hood in early English drama. England. 1425-1600. Lang.: Eng. 2941
Ludic aspects of Italian Renaissance theatre. Italy. 1500-1700. Lang.: Ita. 3240
Analysis of plays by Alessandro Piccolomini. Italy. 1508-1578. Lang.: Eng. 3244
The 'induction' in Renaissance Spanish drama. Spain. 1500-1600. Lang.: Eng. 3381

Renovation, theatre
Performance spaces
Renovation of the Miskolc National Theatre. Hungary: Miskolc. 1823-1998. Lang.: Hun. 450
History of Teatro Comunale. Italy: Ferrara. 1798-1998. Lang.: Ger. 453
The renovation of Arden Theatre Company's F. Otto Haas Theatre. USA: Philadelphia, PA. 1998. Lang.: Eng. 469
Community efforts to save the Emerson Majestic and Rialto theatres. USA: Boston, MA, Chicago, IL. 1988-1998. Lang.: Eng. 474
Architectural and technical renovations to the War Memorial Opera House. USA: San Francisco, CA. 1997. Lang.: Eng. 478
The renovation of Neptune Theatre. Canada: Halifax, NS. 1963-1998. Lang.: Eng. 1794
The influence of the Salle le Peletier on French grand opera. France: Paris. 1823-1873. Lang.: Eng. 4494

Rent
Administration
The legal battle over copyright of the musical *Rent*. USA: New York, NY. 1998. Lang.: Eng. 4321
The settlement of a copyright case regarding the musical *Rent*. USA: New York, NY. 1998. Lang.: Eng. 4322

Performance/production
Collection of newspaper reviews by London theatre critics. UK-England: London. 1998. Lang.: Eng. 2561
Review of Jonathan Larson's musical *Rent*. USA: New York, NY. 1990. Lang.: Hun. 4375

Relation to other fields
Quantum theory in recent New York performances. USA: New York, NY. 1995-1996. Lang.: Eng. 794

Rentor, Eldor
Design/technology
Scene designer Eldor Rentor. Estonia: Tallin. 1925-1998. Lang.: Swe, Eng, Ger. 175

Repertorio Español (New York, NY)
Plays/librettos/scripts
Background on Lorca's *El Público (The Public)*, about to have its New York premiere. USA: New York, NY. 1930-1998. Lang.: Eng. 3651

Research methods
Research/historiography
Recent developments in Australian theatre historiography. Australia. 1990-1997. Lang.: Eng. 817

Research methods — cont'd

Alternative forms of performance documentation. Europe. 1984-1997. Lang.: Eng. 819
Critique of the biases of theatre history toward the exceptional. Poland. 1865-1998. Lang.: Pol. 822

Research tools
Research/historiography
The use of 'Literature Online' for editing and attribution studies. UK-England. 1998. Lang.: Eng. 825
Problems of dance historiography. Europe. North America. 1997. Lang.: Eng. 1001
The THEATRON theatre history project. Europe. 1998. Lang.: Dut. 3796

Research/historiography
SEE ALSO
Classed Entries.
Audience
Gender-related social issues, theatre, and historiography. USA. 1830-1860. Lang.: Eng. 157
Institutions
The eleventh session of the International School of Theatre Anthropology. Portugal: Lisbon. Denmark: Holstebro. 1998. Lang.: Eng. 376
Theatre history course of study. Russia. 1998. Lang.: Rus. 381
Performance/production
The absence of research on South African directing. South Africa, Republic of. 1998. Lang.: Eng. 2355
Reference materials
Italian translation of *The Oxford Illustrated History of Theatre* (1995). Europe. North America. Asia. Africa. 500 B.C.-1995 A.D. Lang.: Ita. 697
Theory/criticism
Eighteenth-century approaches to Shakespearean criticism. England. 1701-1800. Lang.: Eng. 3811

Resident Musical Theatre Association (New York, NY)
Administration
Equity's contract with Resident Musical Theatre Association. USA. 1998. Lang.: Eng. 4319

Residenztheater (Munich)
SEE
Bayerisches Staatsschauspiel, Residenztheater.

Resistible Rise of Arturo Ui, The
SEE
Aufhaltsame Aufstieg des Arturo Ui, Der.

Resource Center for the Arts (St. John's, NF)
Plays/librettos/scripts
Wonderbolt Circus's *Maid of Avalon*, a loose adaptation of *Der Gute Mensch von Sezuan (The Good Person of Szechwan)* by Brecht.Canada: St. John's, NF. 1950-1998. Lang.: Eng. 2825

Restoration theatre
SEE ALSO
Geographical-Chronological Index under England 1660-1685.
Performance/production
Response to *castrato* performances. England: London. 1667-1737. Lang.: Eng. 4545
Plays/librettos/scripts
Motherhood in Restoration comedy. England. 1642-1729. Lang.: Eng. 2864
Women and politics in Restoration heroic plays. England. 1660-1710. Lang.: Eng. 2872
Analysis of Dryden and Davenant's *Enchanted Island.* England. 1674. Lang.: Eng. 2873
Analysis of Restoration anti-Puritan comedies. England. 1661-1663. Lang.: Eng. 2907
Recognition, repression, and ideology in Restoration drama. England: London. 1660-1680. Lang.: Eng. 2918
Robin Hood and Restoration drama. England. 1660-1730. Lang.: Eng. 2954
Confessional theatre in the Restoration period. England. 1690-1700. Lang.: Eng. 2991
Restoration playwright Margaret Cavendish. England. 1645-1662. Lang.: Eng. 3002

Restoration, theatre
Design/technology
Obituary for Karl-Gunnar Frisell, who oversaw the technical restoration of Södra Teatern. Sweden: Solna. 1920-1998. Lang.: Swe. 226
Institutions
Theatrical activity in Cleveland's Playhouse Square. USA: Cleveland, OH. 1998. Lang.: Eng. 416
Performance spaces
The newly reopened Shakespeare's Globe Theatre. UK-England: London. 1997. Lang.: Eng. 461
Architectural critique of the restored New Amsterdam Theatre. USA: New York, NY. 1998. Lang.: Eng. 476
The restoration of the opera houses Gran Teatro del Liceu and Teatro La Fenice. Spain: Barcelona. Italy: Venice. 1994-1998. Lang.: Eng. 4495

Résurrection de Lazare, La (Resurrection of Lazarus, The)
Plays/librettos/scripts
Michel Tremblay's adaptation of *Mistero Buffo* by Dario Fo. Canada: Montreal, PQ. 1969-1973. Lang.: Fre. 2795

Resurrection of John Frum, The
Plays/librettos/scripts
Mennonite drama of Veralyn Warkentin and Vern Thiessen. Canada. 1890-1997. Lang.: Eng. 2829

Resurrectionists, The
Performance/production
Collection of newspaper reviews by London theatre critics. UK-England: London. 1998. Lang.: Eng. 2521

Retallack, Guy
Performance/production
Collection of newspaper reviews by London theatre critics. UK-England: London. 1998. Lang.: Eng. 2579

Retallack, John
Performance/production
Collection of newspaper reviews by London theatre critics. UK-England: London. 1998. Lang.: Eng. 2580

Reunion
Plays/librettos/scripts
Rites of passage in the plays of David Mamet. USA. 1975-1995. Lang.: Eng. 3680

Reuss, Christian Gottlob
Performance spaces
Excerpts from the diary of the builder of Drottningholms Slottsteater. Sweden: Stockholm. 1755-1766. Lang.: Swe. 458

Revenger's Tragedy, The
Performance/production
Collection of newspaper reviews by London theatre critics. UK-England: London. 1998. Lang.: Eng. 2455
Plays/librettos/scripts
The skull in plays of Shakespeare, Dekker, and Tourneur. England. 1606. Lang.: Eng. 3026

Revenue, Petra
Plays/librettos/scripts
Interview with playwright-director Petra Revenue. Sweden: Gothenburg. 1980-1998. Lang.: Swe. 3415

Reverse Transcriptease
Plays/librettos/scripts
Review of collections of plays with gay themes. Canada. 1996. Lang.: Eng. 2802

Revizor (Inspector General, The)
Basic theatrical documents
English translation of Mejerchol'd's adaptation of *Revizor (The Inspector General)* by Gogol. Russia. USSR. 1838-1926. Lang.: Eng. 1450
Performance/production
Gogol's *Revizor (The Inspector General)* directed by Árpád Jutocsa Hegyi. Hungary: Miskolc. 1998. Lang.: Hun. 2108
Interview with composer Paul Schmidt. USA: New Haven, CT. 1998. Lang.: Eng. 2660
Interview with director Peter Sellars. USA: Cambridge, MA. 1980-1981. Lang.: Eng. 2661
Yale Drama Department's reconstruction of Gogol's *Revizor (The Inspector General)* as staged by Mejerchol'd. USA: New Haven, CT. 1997. Lang.: Eng. 2668
The development of the character Khlezstakov in Gogol's *Revizor (The Inspector General)* in productions by Mejerchol'd. USSR. 1926-1939. Lang.: Eng. 2762
Mejerchol'd's production of Gogol's *Revizor (The Inspector General).* USSR: Moscow. 1926. Lang.: Eng. 2763
Director Harold Clurman's reaction to Mejerchol'd's *Revizor (The Inspector General).* USSR: Moscow. 1935. Lang.: Eng. 2764

Revolution Theatre
SEE
Teat'r im. V. Majakovskogo.

Revue
Plays/librettos/scripts
Recent drama and revue in Swedish. Finland. 1998. Lang.: Eng, Fre. 3069

Reyes, Carlos José
Plays/librettos/scripts
New Theatre of Buenaventura, Reyes, and Niño. Colombia. 1950-1985. Lang.: Spa. 2846
Reynolds, Roger
Plays/librettos/scripts
Samuel Beckett's short story *Bing* as adapted by Roger Reynolds and Jean-Yves Bosseur. USA. 1986. Lang.: Eng. 4308
Roger Reynolds' musical settings of texts by Samuel Beckett. USA. 1968-1976. Lang.: Eng. 4309
Reza, Yasmina
Design/technology
Lighting designer Hugh Vanstone. USA: New York, NY. 1998. Lang.: Eng. 1554
Performance/production
Collection of newspaper reviews by London theatre critics. UK-England: London. 1998. Lang.: Eng. 2419
Collection of newspaper reviews by London theatre critics. UK-England: London. 1998. Lang.: Eng. 2461
Plays/librettos/scripts
Playwright Yasmina Reza. USA: New York, NY. France. 1998. Lang.: Eng. 3684
Reznikoff, Charles
Performance/production
Recent Paris productions. France: Paris. 1997-1998. Lang.: Ger. 1933
Rheinisches Landestheater (Neuss)
Administration
Theatrical marketing in North Rhine-Westphalia. Germany. 1994-1998. Lang.: Ger. 6
Rhinocéros
Plays/librettos/scripts
The rebel in modern drama. Europe. 1950-1988. Lang.: Eng. 3053
Rhys, Will
Performance/production
Comparison of productions of Ibsen's *Peer Gynt*. USA: Providence, RI, New York, NY, Washington, DC, Nacogdoches, TX. 1998. Lang.: Eng. 2711
Rialto Theatre (Chicago, IL)
Performance spaces
Community efforts to save the Emerson Majestic and Rialto theatres. USA: Boston, MA, Chicago, IL. 1988-1998. Lang.: Eng. 474
Rice, Edward Everett
Plays/librettos/scripts
Dramatic adaptations of Henry Wadsworth Longfellow's poem *Evangeline*. USA. Canada. 1860-1976. Lang.: Eng. 3643
Rice, Elmer
Plays/librettos/scripts
Experimental theatre of Elmer Rice. USA. 1914-1963. Lang.: Eng. 3620
Analysis of *Counsellor-at-Law* by Elmer Rice. USA. 1931. Lang.: Eng. 3712
Rice, Tim
Administration
The Disney Corporation's Broadway musicals. USA: New York, NY. 1996-1998. Lang.: Eng. 4317
Design/technology
Technical designs for the Broadway production of *The Lion King*. USA: New York, NY. 1998. Lang.: Eng. 4342
Performance spaces
The construction of a theatre for *Beauty and the Beast*. Germany: Stuttgart. 1997. Lang.: Ger. 444
Performance/production
The premiere of the musical *Elaborate Lives: The Legend of Aida*. USA: Atlanta, GA. 1998. Lang.: Eng. 4385
Richard II
Design/technology
Technical designs for Off Broadway Shakespearean productions. USA: New York, NY. 1998. Lang.: Eng. 1539
Performance/production
Three productions of Shakespeare's *Richard III*. UK-England. 1973-1984. Lang.: Eng. 2612
Plays/librettos/scripts
Analysis of Shakespeare's history plays. England. 1590-1599. Lang.: Eng. 2911
Girardian analysis of Shakespeare plays. England. 1590-1599. Lang.: Eng. 2935
Comic scenes and characters in the Elizabethan history play. England. 1590-1618. Lang.: Eng. 2955
Theory/criticism
The urge to make Shakespeare contemporary. USA. 1990-1998. Lang.: Eng. 3844
Richard III
Design/technology
Technical designs for Off Broadway Shakespearean productions. USA: New York, NY. 1998. Lang.: Eng. 1539
Performance/production
The performance of Shakespeare in the former East Germany. Germany: Rostock, Leipzig, Berlin, Dessau. 1996-1997. Lang.: Ger. 1974
Comparison of two productions of Shakespeare's *Richard III*. Germany: Munich. 1996-1997. Lang.: Ger. 1976
Productions of the Bad Hersfelder Festspiele. Germany: Bad Hersfeld. 1998. Lang.: Ger. 1991
Two productions of Shakespeare's *Richard III* by József Ruszt. Hungary: Budapest. Hungary: Kecskemét. 1973-1997. Lang.: Hun. 2070
Three Hungarian productions of Shakespeare's *Richard III*. Hungary: Budapest, Zsámbék, Szeged. 1997. Lang.: Hun. 2121
Shakespeare productions in German Switzerland. Switzerland: Basel, Zurich. 1996-1997. Lang.: Ger. 2398
Collection of newspaper reviews by London theatre critics. UK-England: London. 1998. Lang.: Eng. 2472
Collection of newspaper reviews by London theatre critics. UK-England: Stratford, Birmingham. 1998. Lang.: Eng. 2536
Collection of newspaper reviews by London theatre critics. UK-England: London. 1998. Lang.: Eng. 2579
Susan Brown on her role in *Richard III* at RSC. UK-England: London, Stratford. 1995-1996. Lang.: Eng. 2593
David Troughton on playing Shakespeare's *Richard III*. UK-England: London, Stratford. 1995-1996. Lang.: Eng. 2642
The body in stage-to-film versions of Shakespeare's *Richard III*. UK-England. USA. 1985-1998. Lang.: Eng. 3940
Plays/librettos/scripts
Dutch and Flemish Shakespearean productions. Belgium. Netherlands. 1980-1983. Lang.: Dut. 2789
French translations of Shakespeare by Antonine Maillet and Jean-Louis Roux. Canada: Montreal, PQ. 1988-1993. Lang.: Fre. 2793
Analysis of Shakespeare's history plays. England. 1590-1599. Lang.: Eng. 2911
Women in Shakespeare's *Richard III*. England. 1592-1593. Lang.: Eng. 2929
The nature of tyranny in plays of Shakespeare. England. 1595-1612. Lang.: Eng. 2978
The subversion of male authority in Shakespeare's *Henry VI* and *Richard III*. England. 1590-1593. Lang.: Eng. 3015
Conscience in early modern literature including Shakespeare. England. 1590-1620. Lang.: Eng. 3020
Film adaptations of Shakespeare's *Richard III* by Richard Loncraine and Al Pacino. USA. UK-England. 1995-1996. Lang.: Fre. 4012
Theory/criticism
The urge to make Shakespeare contemporary. USA. 1990-1998. Lang.: Eng. 3844
Richard Rodgers Theatre (New York, NY)
Design/technology
Recent work of lighting designer Brian MacDevitt. USA: New York, NY. 1997. Lang.: Eng. 1530
Sound design for *Side Show* at Richard Rodgers Theatre. USA: New York, NY. 1998. Lang.: Eng. 4329
Richards, Louise
Institutions
Profile of Motionhouse Dance Theatre. UK-England: London. 1988-1998. Lang.: Eng. 1254
Richardson, Ian
Performance/production
Actor Ian Richardson. UK-Scotland: Edinburgh. UK-England: London. 1945-1998. Lang.: Eng. 2652
Actors' interpretations of the title role in Oscar Wilde's *The Canterville Ghost*. UK-England. USA. 1943-1998. Lang.: Eng. 4066
Richardson, Jack
Plays/librettos/scripts
Analysis of *The Prodigal* by Jack Richardson. USA. 1960. Lang.: Eng. 3542
The Prodigal, Jack Richardson's adaptation of *The Oresteia*. USA. 1960. Lang.: Dut. 3547
Homeric influences on *The Prodigal* by Jack Richardson. USA. 1960. Lang.: Eng. 3549

Richardson, Natasha
Performance/production
Notable productions of plays by Eugene O'Neill. USA. 1916-1996. Lang.: Eng. 2752
Richardson, Samuel
Relation to other fields
Novelist Samuel Richardson compared to Shakespeare. England. 1744-1747. Lang.: Eng. 3754
Richie, Shane
Performance/production
Collection of newspaper reviews by London theatre critics. UK-England: London. 1998. Lang.: Eng. 2526
Richmond Theatre (London)
Performance/production
Collection of newspaper reviews by London theatre critics. UK-England: London. 1998. Lang.: Eng. 2423
Richmond, David
Design/technology
Magical stage effects in 'vampire' plays. USA. 1820-1977. Lang.: Eng. 1548
Richy, Pierre
Basic theatrical documents
French translation of *Tres diamantes y una mujer (Three Diamonds and One Woman)* by Alejandro Casona. Spain. France. 1959-1998. Lang.: Fre. 1464
Rickson, Ian
Performance/production
Collection of newspaper reviews by London theatre critics. UK-England: London. 1998. Lang.: Eng. 2428
Collection of newspaper reviews by London theatre critics. UK-England: London. 1998. Lang.: Eng. 2520
Collection of newspaper reviews by London theatre critics. UK-England: London. 1998. Lang.: Eng. 2549
Collection of newspaper reviews by London theatre critics. UK-England: London. 1998. Lang.: Eng. 2567
Riders to the Sea
Performance/production
Collection of newspaper reviews by London theatre critics. UK-England: London. 1998. Lang.: Eng. 2551
Ridley, Philip
Performance/production
Collection of newspaper reviews by London theatre critics. UK-England: London. 1998. Lang.: Eng. 2434
Collection of newspaper reviews by London theatre critics. UK-England: London. 1998. Lang.: Eng. 2575
Riegert, Peter
Performance/production
Interview with actor Peter Riegert. USA: New York, NY. 1998. Lang.: Eng. 2676
Rien ne va plus (Swindle, The)
Performance/production
Dancer and choreographer Brygida Ochaim. Germany. France. 1970-1998. Lang.: Ger. 1283
Rieser, Ferdinand
Institutions
The directorship of Ferdinand Rieser at Zürcher Schauspielhaus. Switzerland: Zurich. 1926-1938. Lang.: Ger. 387
Rieti, Vittorio
Performance/production
Review of one-act ballets by Balanchine. Hungary: Budapest. 1997. Lang.: Hun. 1105
Riga Russian Drama Theatre
SEE
Teat'r Russkoj Dramy.
Rigging
Design/technology
Locking and controlling stage rigging. Sweden: Stockholm. 1998. Lang.: Swe. 220
Right Size, The (London)
Performance/production
Collection of newspaper reviews by London theatre critics. UK-England: London. 1998. Lang.: Eng. 2564
Rigoletto
Performance/production
Director Anja Sündermann on her production of *Rigoletto*. Germany: Hamburg. 1991-1998. Lang.: Ger. 4608
Rijnders, Gerardjan
Performance/production
Collection of newspaper reviews by London theatre critics. UK-England: London. 1998. Lang.: Eng. 2422
Riksteatern (Norsborg)
Institutions
Joint project to promote dance throughout Sweden. Sweden. 1974-1998. Lang.: Swe. 899
Riksteatern (Stockholm)
Performance/production
Recent productions of plays by Ibsen and Strindberg. Sweden: Stockholm. 1997. Lang.: Eng. 2393
Riley, Peggy
Performance/production
Collection of newspaper reviews by London theatre critics. UK-England: London. 1998. Lang.: Eng. 2460
Rimskij-Korsakov, Nikolaj Andrejėvič
Performance/production
Correspondence of composer Nikolaj Rimskij-Korsakov and singer Nadežda Zabela-Vrubel'. Russia. 1868-1913. Lang.: Rus. 4670
Plays/librettos/scripts
Operas of Dargomyžskij and Rimskij-Korsakov on texts of Puškin. Russia. 1799-1869. Lang.: Rus. 4815
Rinaldo
Performance/production
The influence of the Haymarket Theatre on Handelian opera. England: London. 1710-1739. Lang.: Eng. 4549
Rinderknecht, Peter
Performance/production
Productions of children's theatre festival. Canada: Montreal, PQ. 1998. Lang.: Fre. 503
Ring
Basic theatrical documents
Score of Yu-Chun Kuo's concerto for dance and music, *Ring*. USA. 1988. Lang.: Eng. 887
Ring des Nibelungen, Der
Institutions
Review of Wagner's *Ring* cycle at the Bayreuth Festival. Germany: Bayreuth. 1997-1998. Lang.: Hun. 4454
Performance/production
Visual spectacle in Wagner's *Ring* cycle. Germany. 1869-1876. Lang.: Eng. 4585
Interview with director Viktor Nagy on Wagner's *Ring* cycle. Hungary: Budapest. 1998. Lang.: Hun. 4635
Wagner's *Ring* cycle at the Hungarian Opera House. Hungary: Budapest. 1998. Lang.: Hun. 4644
Plays/librettos/scripts
Nationalism and sexuality in Wagner's *Ring* cycle. Germany. 1870-1880. Lang.: Eng. 4796
Outline of Wagner's *Götterdämmerung*. Hungary: Budapest. 1998. Lang.: Hun. 4800
Ring Round the Moon
SEE
Invitation au château, L'.
Ringling Brothers and Barnum & Bailey Circus (Sarasota, FL)
SEE ALSO
Barnum and Bailey Circus.
Rink, The
Performance/production
Collection of newspaper reviews by London theatre critics. UK-England: London. 1998. Lang.: Eng. 2500
Rinuccini, Ottavio
Design/technology
Stage machinery in *Il Rapimento di Cefalo* staged by Bernardo Buontalenti. Italy: Florence. 1600. Lang.: Eng. 4436
Performance/production
Peri and Rinuccini's *Daphne*, the first opera. Italy: Florence. 1598. Lang.: Hun. 4651
Riot Act, The
Plays/librettos/scripts
Adaptations of Greek tragedy by contemporary Irish writers. Ireland. UK-Ireland. 1984-1998. Lang.: Eng. 3214
Rise and Fall of the City of Mahagonny
SEE
Aufstieg und Fall der Stadt Mahagonny.
Risorgimento
SEE
Geographical-Chronological Index under Italy 1815-1876.
Ritchie, Shane
Performance/production
Interview with Shane Ritchie and Jon Conway about the musical *Boogie Nights*. UK-England. 1998. Lang.: Eng. 4370

Rite of Spring, The
SEE
Vesna svjaščennaja.
Ritter, Dene, Voss
Performance/production
Thomas Bernhard's *Ritter, Dene, Voss* at Bárka Színház. Hungary: Budapest. 1997. Lang.: Hun. 2087
Performances at the new Bárka Színház. Hungary: Budapest. 1997. Lang.: Hun. 2097
Ritter, Ilse
Performance/production
Actress Ilse Ritter. Germany. 1944-1998. Lang.: Ger. 1980
Ritter, Scott R.
Basic theatrical documents
Text of *A Day at Musemeci's* by Scott R. Ritter. USA. 1987. Lang.: Eng. 1503
Ritual-ceremony
Institutions
Jacques Crête and Atelier de recherche théâtrale l'Eskabel. Canada: Montreal, PQ. 1971-1989. Lang.: Eng. 1590
Performance/production
Traditional and contemporary African drama. Africa. 1850-1987. Lang.: Eng. 483
Performance space in Aboriginal *corroboree*. Australia. 800 B.C.-1988 A.D. Lang.: Eng. 487
Theatrical construction of Chilean national identity and history. Chile. 1990-1998. Lang.: Spa. 510
Characteristics and development of ritual theatre. Slovenia. 1960-1998. Lang.: Slo. 592
The first wave of American feminist theatre. USA. 1890-1930. Lang.: Eng. 648
A dancer's experience of and investigations into ecstasy. USA. Germany. 1969-1990. Lang.: Eng. 673
The role of acting in preparing a homily. USA. 1997. Lang.: Eng. 679
Rosalie Jones of Native American dance company Daystar. USA: Santa Fe, NM. 1966-1998. Lang.: Eng. 1240
Analysis of Korean mask-dance theatre form *hahoe pyolsin-kut*. Korea. 1150-1928. Lang.: Eng. 1352
Report from a symposium on traditional Korean theatre. Korea. Germany: Berlin. 1980-1998. Lang.: Ger, Fre, Dut, Eng. 2196
Ritual in the theatre of Jerzy Grotowski. Poland. 1960-1975. Lang.: Pol. 2221
Spirituality and the theatre of Jerzy Grotowski. Poland. 1958-1998. Lang.: Ger, Fre, Dut, Eng. 2226
African ritual in the work of director and playwright Brett Bailey. South Africa, Republic of. 1997-1998. Lang.: Eng. 2349
Photos of Trinidadian carnival. Trinidad and Tobago. 1997. Lang.: Eng. 4165
Women in the *canboulay* ceremony. Trinidad and Tobago. 1998. Lang.: Eng. 4166
Carnival as a unifying force. Trinidad and Tobago. 1998. Lang.: Eng. 4170
Carnival performances of a *jouvay* band. Trinidad and Tobago: Port of Spain. 1996. Lang.: Eng. 4171
Civic and court ceremonies in the Jacobean period. England. 1605-1610. Lang.: Eng. 4215
Ritual performance and the Third Reich. Germany. 1938-1945. Lang.: Eng. 4216
Reexamination of the performance art of Beuys, Abramovič, and Ulay. USA. Germany. Netherlands. 1964-1985. Lang.: Eng. 4254
Plays/librettos/scripts
Recovered ritual in seemingly non-ritualistic theatre. England. 1600-1779. Lang.: Eng. 2904
Sociological analysis of *The Shoemaker's Holiday* by Thomas Dekker. England. 1600. Lang.: Eng. 2973
The ritual structure of Racine's *Athalie*. France. 1691. Lang.: Eng. 3099
Interview with Peter Minshall, creator of theatre pieces and carnival performances. Trinidad and Tobago: Port of Spain. 1974-1997. Lang.: Eng. 4172
Reference materials
History of Japanese theatre and drama. Japan. 350 B.C.-1998 A.D. Lang.: Ita. 705
Relation to other fields
The differences between theatre and ritual. 1998. Lang.: Ger. 711
Secular ritual forms in early American political culture. Colonial America. 1650-1800. Lang.: Eng. 720
Performative techniques in social and political movements. Taiwan. 1986-1997. Lang.: Eng. 767
Analysis of ritual fire-walking. USA. 1998. Lang.: Eng. 789
The theatrical nature of Salvation Army activities. USA. 1865-1950. Lang.: Eng. 796
Drama therapy and forgiveness. USA. 1998. Lang.: Eng. 804
The 'bird-woman' folktale in Southeast Asian shamanic healing rituals. Ireland. Thailand. Malaysia. Lang.: Eng. 1358
The dramatic nature of the ancient Egyptian text *The Triumph of Horus*. Egypt. 2500 B.C. Lang.: Eng. 3744
The creation and use of ritual theatre for drama therapy. USA. 1997. Lang.: Eng. 3787
African and European influences on Trinidadian carnival. Trinidad and Tobago. 1501-1998. Lang.: Eng. 4175
The *jouvay* ceremony of Trinidadian carnival. Trinidad and Tobago: Port of Spain. 1838-1998. Lang.: Eng. 4176
Carnival, cultural identity, and assimilation. Trinidad and Tobago. 1889-1998. Lang.: Eng. 4177
Analysis of the jazz funeral. USA: New Orleans, LA. 1900-1990. Lang.: Eng. 4228
Ritual, The
Performance/production
Collection of newspaper reviews by London theatre critics. UK-England: London. 1998. Lang.: Eng. 2511
River
Plays/librettos/scripts
Interview with Peter Minshall, creator of theatre pieces and carnival performances. Trinidad and Tobago: Port of Spain. 1974-1997. Lang.: Eng. 4172
River of Dreams
Theory/criticism
Theory and Asian-American theatre. USA: Minneapolis, MN. 1994-1995. Lang.: Eng. 869
Rivera, José
Performance/production
Collection of newspaper reviews by London theatre critics. UK-England: London. 1998. Lang.: Eng. 2454
José Rivera's production of *La Vida es sueño (Life Is a Dream)*, Hartford Stage. USA: Hartford, CT. 1998. Lang.: Eng. 2722
Riverdance
Design/technology
Mick O'Gorman's sound design and equipment for *Riverdance*. Ireland. 1998. Lang.: Eng. 1218
Performance/production
The success of dance extravaganzas and solo performance at the expense of traditional shows. USA: New York, NY. 1994-1998. Lang. :Eng. 645
Riverside Theatre (London)
Performance/production
Collection of newspaper reviews by London theatre critics. UK-England: London. 1998. Lang.: Eng. 2420
Collection of newspaper reviews by London theatre critics. UK-England: London. 1998. Lang.: Eng. 2422
Collection of newspaper reviews by London theatre critics. UK-England: London. 1998. Lang.: Eng. 2441
Collection of newspaper reviews by London theatre critics. UK-England: London. 1998. Lang.: Eng. 2455
Collection of newspaper reviews by London theatre critics. UK-England: London. 1998. Lang.: Eng. 2458
Collection of newspaper reviews by London theatre critics. UK-England: London. 1998. Lang.: Eng. 2464
Collection of newspaper reviews by London theatre critics. UK-England: London. 1998. Lang.: Eng. 2469
Collection of newspaper reviews by London theatre critics. UK-England: London. 1998. Lang.: Eng. 2475
Collection of newspaper reviews by London theatre critics. UK-England: London. 1998. Lang.: Eng. 2487
Collection of newspaper reviews by London theatre critics. UK-England. 1998. Lang.: Eng. 2504
Collection of newspaper reviews by London theatre critics. UK-England. 1998. Lang.: Eng. 2510

Riverside Theatre (London) — cont'd

Collection of newspaper reviews by London theatre critics. UK-England: London. 1998. Lang.: Eng. 2511
Collection of newspaper reviews by London theatre critics. UK-England: London. 1998. Lang.: Eng. 2520
Collection of newspaper reviews by London theatre critics. UK-England: London. 1998. Lang.: Eng. 2521
Collection of newspaper reviews by London theatre critics. UK-England: London. 1998. Lang.: Eng. 2547
Collection of newspaper reviews by London theatre critics. UK-England: London. 1998. Lang.: Eng. 2577
Collection of newspaper reviews by London theatre critics. UK-England: London. 1998. Lang.: Eng. 2582

RO-Theater (Rotterdam)
Performance/production
The use of television in theatrical space. Netherlands. USA. 1970-1998. Lang.: Dut. 2206
Plays/librettos/scripts
Dutch and Flemish Shakespearean productions. Belgium. Netherlands. 1980-1983. Lang.: Dut. 2789

Road to Graceland, The
Institutions
The aesthetics of performances based on non-fiction texts at Lifeline Theatre. USA: Chicago, IL. 1996-1998. Lang.: Eng. 1788

Road to Mecca, The
Plays/librettos/scripts
The influence of Albert Camus on playwright Athol Fugard. South Africa, Republic of. 1960-1985. Lang.: Eng. 3362
Post-apartheid analysis of plays by Athol Fugard. South Africa, Republic of. 1991-1998. Lang.: Eng. 3364

Roaring Girl, The
Plays/librettos/scripts
The treatment of single women in early Stuart drama. England. 1604-1608. Lang.: Eng. 2979

Röbbeling, Hermann
Plays/librettos/scripts
Analysis of plays by Carl Zuckmayer. Austria: Vienna. 1925-1938. Lang.: Ger. 2785

Robbins, Carrie
Design/technology
Professional theatrical designers on design training. USA. 1998. Lang.: Eng. 252

Robbins, Jerome
Performance/production
Director and choreographer Jerome Robbins. USA. 1919-1998. Lang.: Eng. 975
Tributes to ballerina Alexandra Danilova. USA: New York, NY. 1997. Lang.: Eng. 1165
Synopses of lost choreographies by Jerome Robbins. USA: New York, NY. 1949-1952. Lang.: Eng. 1166
Choreographer Jerome Robbins. USA. 1918-1998. Lang.: Eng. 1167
New York performances of the San Francisco Ballet. USA: New York, NY. 1998. Lang.: Eng. 1170
Ballerina Kristina Fernandez on working with choreographer Jerome Robbins. USA. 1998. Lang.: Eng. 1171
Ballerina Tanaquil LeClerq on working with choreographer Jerome Robbins. USA. 1940-1998. Lang.: Eng. 1185
Collection of newspaper reviews by London theatre critics. UK-England: London. 1998. Lang.: Eng. 2516

Roberto Devereux
Performance/production
Evaluation of video performances of Donizetti's operas. Europe. USA. 1980-1998. Lang.: Eng. 4557

Roberto Zucco
Performance/production
Productions of plays by Bernard-Marie Koltès. Canada: Montreal, PQ. 1991-1997. Lang.: Fre. 1862
Plays/librettos/scripts
Roberto Zucco and Bernard-Marie Koltès' idea of the tragic. France. 1835-1837. Lang.: Fre. 3076

Roberts, Cameron Lee
Design/technology
The 1998 USITT expo. USA: Long Beach, CA. 1998. Lang.: Eng. 251

Roberts, Judith
Performance/production
Collection of newspaper reviews by London theatre critics. UK-England: London. 1998. Lang.: Eng. 2441

Roberts, Rhoda
Performance/production
Aboriginal arts on the Australian stage. Australia: Sydney. 1997. Lang.: Eng. 491

Robertson, Beverly J.
Basic theatrical documents
Text of *GBS: Fighting to Live Again* by Beverly J. Robertson. USA. 1997. Lang.: Eng. 1504

Robertson, Cliff
Administration
Celebrities as spokespersons for non-profits. USA. 1998. Lang.: Eng. 117

Robertson, Hazel Glaister
Institutions
History of Palo Alto Children's Theatre. USA: Palo Alto, CA. 1932-1997. Lang.: Eng. 1778

Robertson, Lanie
Basic theatrical documents
French translation of *Alfred Stieglitz Loves O'Keeffe* by Lanie Robertson. USA. France. 1987-1997. Lang.: Fre. 1505

Robeson, Paul
Administration
Preparations for the centennial of actor and singer Paul Robeson. USA. 1898-1998. Lang.: Eng. 61
Performance/production
The life and career of singer Paul Robeson. USA. 1998. Lang.: Eng. 631
Photo essay on celebration of Paul Robeson. USA: New York, NY. 1998. Lang.: Eng. 660
Profile of performer and activist Paul Robeson. USA. 1898-1959. Lang.: Eng. 2750
Plays/librettos/scripts
African- and Irish-Americans in the plays of Eugene O'Neill. USA. 1916-1953. Lang.: Eng. 3687

Robin Hood
Plays/librettos/scripts
Robin Hood and Restoration drama. England. 1660-1730. Lang.: Eng. 2954

Robin Hood and His Crew of Souldiers
Plays/librettos/scripts
Robin Hood and Restoration drama. England. 1660-1730. Lang.: Eng. 2954

Robin Hood: Men in Tights
Plays/librettos/scripts
Robin Hood on film. England. USA. 1920-1992. Lang.: Eng. 3969

Robin, Leo
Performance/production
Collection of newspaper reviews by London theatre critics. UK-England: London. 1998. Lang.: Eng. 2480

Robin, Mado
Performance/production
Interpreters of the title role in Delibes' opera *Lakmé*. 1932-1995. Lang.: Fre. 4505

Robinette, Joseph
Performance/production
Collection of newspaper reviews by London theatre critics. UK-England: London. 1998. Lang.: Eng. 2550

Robins, Elizabeth
Plays/librettos/scripts
Feminism and plays of Henrik Ibsen. Norway. 1879-1979. Lang.: Eng. 3293

Robinson, Brian W.
Performance/production
Theatre Magazine's anniversary issue. USA. 1968-1998. Lang.: Eng. 617

Robinson, Earl
Plays/librettos/scripts
The musical *Sandhog* by blacklisted writers Earl Robinson and Waldo Salt. USA. 1954. Lang.: Eng. 4395

Robinson, Eloise
Institutions
Interview with members of dance group Creative Independent Artists. UK-Scotland: Glasgow. 1996-1998. Lang.: Eng. 904

Robinson, Julie-Anne
Performance/production
Collection of newspaper reviews by London theatre critics. UK-England: London. 1998. Lang.: Eng. 2515
Collection of newspaper reviews by London theatre critics. UK-England: London. 1998. Lang.: Eng. 2574

Robinson, Lenox
Performance/production
Collection of newspaper reviews by London theatre critics. UK-England: London. 1998. Lang.: Eng. 2473

Robitaille, Jack
Performance/production
Actor Jack Robitaille. Canada: Quebec, PQ. 1998. Lang.: Fre. 1835
Robson, Heather
Performance/production
Collection of newspaper reviews by London theatre critics. UK-England: London. 1998. Lang.: Eng. 2571
Roca, Renee
Performance/production
Ice dancers Renee Roca and Gorsha Sur. USA. 1992-1998. Lang.: Eng. 992
Rockaby
Plays/librettos/scripts
Analysis of *En attendant Godot (Waiting for Godot)* and *Rockaby* by Samuel Beckett. France. Ireland. 1953-1981. Lang.: Eng. 3087
Roda cor de roda
Plays/librettos/scripts
Cruelty and the absurd in theatre of Latin American playwrights. Latin America. 1960-1980. Lang.: Eng. 3267
Rodgers, Richard
Design/technology
Costume designs by Irene Sharaff. USA. 1933-1976. Lang.: Eng. 277
Performance/production
Collection of newspaper reviews by London theatre critics. UK-England: London. 1998. Lang.: Eng. 2474
Collection of newspaper reviews by London theatre critics. UK-England: London. 1998. Lang.: Eng. 2554
Plays/librettos/scripts
The portrayal of Franklin Delano Roosevelt in the musical *I'd Rather Be Right.* USA. 1937. Lang.: Eng. 4396
Treatments of the Cinderella theme, with emphasis on *La Cenerentola* by Rossini. 1817-1998. Lang.: Eng. 4757
Rodrigues, Nelson
Plays/librettos/scripts
Playwright Nelson Rodrigues. Brazil. 1912. Lang.: Rus. 2791
Rodríguez, Jesusa
Plays/librettos/scripts
Playwright, director, and performer Jesusa Rodríguez. Mexico. 1970-1992. Lang.: Eng. 3275
Roes, Michael
Plays/librettos/scripts
Analysis of *Madschun al-Malik* by Michael Roes. Germany: Düsseldorf. 1998. Lang.: Ger. 3157
Rogers, Ginger
Performance/production
Analysis of the *Night and Day* dance sequence of *The Gay Divorcee.* USA: Hollywood, CA. 1934. Lang.: Eng. 977
Rogers, Peter
Design/technology
Ethernet computer connections between lighting systems of two theatres at Herberger Theatre Center. USA: Phoenix, AZ. 1998. Lang.: Eng. 294
Rogers, Richard
Performance/production
The success of a revival of *Oklahoma!* at the Olivier. UK-England: London. 1998. Lang.: Eng. 4373
Rogers, Will
Performance/production
Entertainer Will Rogers. UK-England: London. 1879-1935. Lang.: Eng. 4279
Rogoff, Gordon
Performance/production
Theatre Magazine's anniversary issue. USA. 1968-1998. Lang.: Eng. 617
Rohweder, Heidemarie
Administration
Interviews with theatre managers regarding the changing cultural landscape. Germany: Bruchsal, Esslingen, Tübingen. 1998. Lang.: Ger. 1381
Roi de Lahore, Le
Basic theatrical documents
The libretto to Jules Massenet's *Le Roi de Lahore.* France. 1877. Lang.: Fre. 4417
Performance/production
Premieres of Massenet's *Le Roi de Lahore.* 1877-1923. Lang.: Fre. 4521
Vocal requirements and recording of Massenet's *Le Roi de Lahore.* 1979. Lang.: Fre. 4525
The creation of Massenet's opera *Le Roi de Lahore.* France. 1877. Lang.: Fre. 4568
Plays/librettos/scripts
Collaboration of composer Jules Massenet and librettist Louis Gallet. France. 1877-1894. Lang.: Fre. 4778
Roi Hâtif, Le (King Hasty)
Basic theatrical documents
Text of *Le Roi Hâtif (King Hasty)* by Françoise Gerbaulet. France. 1993-1998. Lang.: Fre. 1425
Roi se meurt, Le (Exit the King)
Plays/librettos/scripts
Analysis of *Le Roi se meurt (Exit the King)* by Eugène Ionesco. France. 1962. Lang.: Eng. 3080
Rojas Zorrilla, Francisco de
Plays/librettos/scripts
Playwright Francisco de Rojas Zorrilla. Spain. 1607-1648. Lang.: Eng. 3396
Rojas, Fernando de
Performance/production
Interviews with actors Lil Terselius and Björn Granath. Sweden: Stockholm. 1998. Lang.: Swe. 2381
Interview with director Robert Lepage. Sweden: Stockholm. Canada: Montreal, PQ. 1997. Lang.: Swe. 2397
Plays/librettos/scripts
Playwright Fernando de Rojas. Spain. 1476-1541. Lang.: Eng. 3388
Rok na vsi (Year in the Village, A)
Performance/production
The adaptation of classic Czech works to the stage. Czech Republic: Prague, Brno. 1990-1998. Lang.: Cze. 1877
Roka za steno (Hand Behind the Wall, The)
Basic theatrical documents
Text of plays by Branko Rozman. Slovenia. 1990-1997. Lang.: Slo. 1461
Rókás, László
Performance/production
Round-table discussion on dance and movement. Hungary. 1998. Lang.: Hun. 938
Rolando, Gloria
Plays/librettos/scripts
Afrocuban religion in Cuban films. Cuba. 1974-1991. Lang.: Eng. 3968
Roles
SEE
Characters/roles.
Rolfe, James
Basic theatrical documents
Text of libretto for *Beatrice Chancy.* Canada: Toronto, ON. 1998. Lang.: Eng. 4413
James Rolfe on his opera *Beatrice Chancy.* Canada: Toronto, ON. 1998. Lang.: Eng. 4414
Roman Actor, The
Theory/criticism
Representation and delegation in theatre. 1998. Lang.: Eng. 3800
Romance pro křídlovku (Romance for Flugelhorn)
Performance/production
The adaptation of classic Czech works to the stage. Czech Republic: Prague, Brno. 1990-1998. Lang.: Cze. 1877
Romani, Felice
Performance/production
Performance history of Rossini's *Aureliano in Palmira.* Italy. Europe. 1813-1996. Lang.: Eng. 4659
Plays/librettos/scripts
Analysis of the opera *Aureliano in Palmira* by Rossini and Romani. Italy. 1813. Lang.: Eng. 4806
Romans in Britain, The
Plays/librettos/scripts
Analysis of *The Romans in Britain* by Howard Brenton. UK-England. 1980-1981. Lang.: Eng. 3482
Romanticism
SEE ALSO
Geographical-Chronological Index under Europe 1800-1850, France 1810-1857, Germany 1798-1830, Italy 1815-1876, UK 1801-1850.
Romeo and Juliet
Basic theatrical documents
Catalan translation of Shakespeare's *Romeo and Juliet.* England. 1591. Lang.: Cat. 1421
Performance/production
Shakespearean productions in northern Germany. Germany: Hamburg. 1996-1997. Lang.: Ger. 1978
Michajl Mokejëv's production of Shakespeare's *Romeo and Juliet.* Russia: Belgorod. 1998. Lang.: Rus. 2274
Collection of newspaper reviews by London theatre critics. UK-England: London. 1998. Lang.: Eng. 2583
Julian Glover on his performance in *Romeo and Juliet* for RSC. UK-England: London, Stratford. 1995-1996. Lang.: Eng. 2606

***Romeo and Juliet* — cont'd**

Plays/librettos/scripts
Dutch and Flemish Shakespearean productions. Belgium. Netherlands. 1980-1983. Lang.: Dut. 2789
Symbolic action in Shakespeare's *Romeo and Juliet*. England. 1595-1596. Lang.: Eng. 3007
The interaction of other characters with Shakespeare's tragic heroes. England. 1590-1613. Lang.: Eng. 3037
Baz Luhrmann's film adaptation of Shakespeare's *Romeo and Juliet*. USA. 1996. Lang.: Fre. 4016
Theory/criticism
The urge to make Shakespeare contemporary. USA. 1990-1998. Lang.: Eng. 3844

Roméo et Juliette
Performance/production
Background material on Metropolitan Opera radio broadcast performances. USA: New York, NY. 1998. Lang.: Eng. 4713
Verdi's *Stiffelio* and Gounod's *Roméo et Juliette* in New York. USA: New York, NY. 1850-1998. Lang.: Eng. 4730

Romeo i Džuljetta (Romeo and Juliet)
Performance/production
Prokofjév's *Romeo and Juliet*, choreographed by Cranko, Wiener Staatsoper. Austria: Vienna. 1998. Lang.: Hun. 1063

Romitori (Hermits)
Performance/production
The actor/clown team of Claudio Remondi and Riccardo Caporossi. Italy. 1971-1998. Lang.: Eng. 2176

Rona, Frigyes
Performance/production
Production of László Lajtha's comic opera *Le chapeau bleu*. Romania: Cluj-Napoca. Hungary. 1948-1998. Lang.: Hun. 4668

Ronan, Brian
Design/technology
Panel discussion of sound designers. USA. 1998. Lang.: Eng. 287
Technical designs for Sam Mendes' production of *Cabaret*. USA: New York, NY. 1998. Lang.: Eng. 4343

Ronconi, Luca
Performance/production
Luca Ronconi's production of *Mourning Becomes Electra* by Eugene O'Neill. Italy: Rome. 1996-1997. Lang.: Eng. 2183
Luca Ronconi's stage adaptation of *The Brothers Karamazov*. Italy: Rome. 1997. Lang.: Eng. 2188
Luca Ronconi's stagings of opera. Italy. 1974-1992. Lang.: Ita. 4648

Ronde, La
SEE
Reigen.

Ronfard, Alice
Performance/production
French Canadian translations/adaptations of Shakespeare. Canada: Montreal, PQ. 1988. Lang.: Fre. 1855
Productions of plays by Bernard-Marie Koltès. Canada: Montreal, PQ. 1991-1997. Lang.: Fre. 1862

Ronfard, Jean-Pierre
Plays/librettos/scripts
Vie et mort du Roi Boiteux (Life and Death of the Lame King), Jean-Pierre Ronfard's adaptation of *Richard III*. Canada. 1981. Lang.: Fre. 2813
The use of collage in contemporary productions involving Greek myths. Canada: Montreal, PQ. 1998. Lang.: Fre. 2814

Ronnie Burkett Theatre of Marionettes (Calgary, AB)
Performance/production
Productions of children's theatre festival. Canada: Montreal, PQ. 1998. Lang.: Fre. 503

Room
Performance/production
Collection of newspaper reviews by London theatre critics. UK-England: London. 1998. Lang.: Eng. 2439

Room at the Top
Performance/production
Collection of newspaper reviews by London theatre critics. UK-England: London. 1998. Lang.: Eng. 2477

Room, The
Plays/librettos/scripts
Transference in plays by Harold Pinter. UK-England. 1960-1985. Lang.: Eng. 3461

Rootless but Green Are the Boulevard Trees
Plays/librettos/scripts
Analysis of *Rootless but Green Are the Boulevard Trees* by Uma Parameswaran. Canada: Winnipeg, MB. 1985. Lang.: Eng. 2819

Ros, Jan
Design/technology
Profiles of young theatrical designers. Netherlands. 1990-1998. Lang.: Dut. 207

Rosamunde Floris
Plays/librettos/scripts
Mythological figures in late plays of Georg Kaiser. Germany. 1914-1940. Lang.: Ger. 3143

Rosas (Brussels)
Performance/production
Comparison of performances by Rosas and Ballet Gulbenkian. Hungary: Budapest. 1992-1994. Lang.: Hun. 939
Dancer/choreographer Anne Teresa De Keersmaeker. Belgium: Brussels. 1981-1998. Lang.: Eng. 1260

Rose Tattoo, The
Plays/librettos/scripts
Shame, puritanism, and sexuality in plays of Tennessee Williams. USA. 1950-1970. Lang.: Eng. 3701

Rose Theatre (London)
Performance spaces
The archaeological excavation of the Rose Theatre. UK-England: London. 1988-1989. Lang.: Eng. 1805
The excavation of the Rose Theatre's foundations. UK-England: London. 1988-1989. Lang.: Eng. 1807

Rose, Chris Edwin
Basic theatrical documents
Texts of *WWW.chat* and *Elevator* by Chris Edwin Rose. USA. 1998. Lang.: Eng. 1506

Rose, Peter
Performance/production
Collection of newspaper reviews by London theatre critics. UK-England: London. 1998. Lang.: Eng. 2550

Rose, Reginald
Plays/librettos/scripts
Theatrical activities of Harold Pinter. UK-England: London. 1996-1998. Lang.: Eng. 3462

Rosemary Branch (London)
Performance/production
Collection of newspaper reviews by London theatre critics. UK-England: London. Lang.: Eng. 2408
Collection of newspaper reviews by London theatre critics. UK-England: London. 1998. Lang.: Eng. 2436
Collection of newspaper reviews by London theatre critics. UK-England: London. 1998. Lang.: Eng. 2581

Rosencrantz and Guildenstern Are Dead
Plays/librettos/scripts
Tom Stoppard's film adaptation of his own *Rosencrantz and Guildenstern Are Dead*. UK-England. 1967-1991. Lang.: Eng. 3980

Rosenfeld, Gerhard
Plays/librettos/scripts
Hero and anti-hero in contemporary opera production. Germany. 1998. Lang.: Ger. 4791

Rosina
Plays/librettos/scripts
Operatic realizations of Beaumarchais' character Rosina. Europe. North America. 1784-1991. Lang.: Eng. 4773

Rosmersholm
Performance/production
Report from Ibsen festival. Norway: Oslo. 1998. Lang.: Swe. 2211
Plays/librettos/scripts
Andreas-Salomé's view of Ibsen's female characters. Norway. Germany. 1879-1906. Lang.: Eng. 3296
Trolls in the late plays of Ibsen. Norway. 1886-1894. Lang.: Eng. 3298

Ross, Andrew
Design/technology
Lighting designer Mark Howett's work for Black Swan Theatre Company. Australia: Fremantle. 1998. Lang.: Eng. 1513

Ross, Gary
Design/technology
Production design for Gary Ross's film *Pleasantville*. USA: Hollywood, CA. 1998. Lang.: Eng. 3909

Ross, Glyn
Institutions
Retiring artistic directors of regional opera companies, Russell Patterson and Glyn Ross. USA. 1960-1998. Lang.: Eng. 4485

Ross, Stuart
Performance/production
Collection of newspaper reviews by London theatre critics. UK-England: London. 1998. Lang.: Eng. 2555

Rosseel, Danny
Performance/production
Premieres of choreographies by Danny Rosseel. Belgium: Antwerp. Netherlands: Amsterdam. 1998. Lang.: Hun. 1065
Rossi, Giacomo
Performance/production
The influence of the Haymarket Theatre on Handelian opera. England: London. 1710-1739. Lang.: Eng. 4549
Rossini, Gaetano
Basic theatrical documents
Gaetano Rossini's libretto for Gioacchino Rossini's *Semiramide*. Italy. 1823. Lang.: Fre, Ita. 4421
Rossini, Gioacchino
Basic theatrical documents
Gaetano Rossini's libretto for Gioacchino Rossini's *Semiramide*. Italy. 1823. Lang.: Fre, Ita. 4421
Institutions
The opera festival in the birthplace of Rossini. Italy: Pesaro. 1792-1998. Lang.: Eng. 4462
Performance/production
Video recordings of Rossini's *Semiramide*. 1980-1991. Lang.: Fre. 4503
Recordings of Rossini's *Semiramide*. 1962-1992. Lang.: Fre. 4504
Performances of Rossini's *Semiramide*. 1823-1998. Lang.: Fre. 4517
Performance history of Rossini's *Aureliano in Palmira*. Italy. Europe. 1813-1996. Lang.: Eng. 4659
Background material on Metropolitan Opera radio broadcast performances. USA: New York, NY. 1998. Lang.: Eng. 4713
Musicological preparation for the Metropolitan Opera production of Rossini's *La Cenerentola*. USA: Chicago, IL. 1998. Lang.: Eng. 4737
Bass Samuel Ramey. USA. 1940-1998. Lang.: Eng. 4744
Plays/librettos/scripts
Voltaire's *Sémiramis*, source of Rossini's *Semiramide*. France. 1748. Lang.: Fre. 3096
The writing and first performances of Voltaire's *Sémiramis*, the source of Rossini's opera *Semiramide*. France. 1746-1748. Lang.: Fre. 3114
Treatments of the Cinderella theme, with emphasis on *La Cenerentola* by Rossini. 1817-1998. Lang.: Eng. 4757
Operatic realizations of Beaumarchais' character Rosina. Europe. North America. 1784-1991. Lang.: Eng. 4773
Analysis of the opera *Aureliano in Palmira* by Rossini and Romani. Italy. 1813. Lang.: Eng. 4806
Background information on the title character of Rossini's opera *Semiramide*. Italy. 1823. Lang.: Fre. 4810
Rossiskaja Akademija Teatral'nogo Iskusstva (Moscow)
SEE ALSO
Gosudarstvénnyj Institut Teatral'nogo Iskusstva im. A.V. Lunačarskogo (Moscow).
Rosso di San Secondo, Pier Maria
Plays/librettos/scripts
Analysis of plays by Pier Maria Rosso di San Secondo. Italy. 1908-1956. Lang.: Ita. 3224
Rotbaum, Jakub
Institutions
Jakub Rotbaum's leadership of Trupa Wileńska. Poland: Vilna. 1929-1938. Lang.: Pol. 1686
Rote Strasse, Die (Red Road, The)
Plays/librettos/scripts
Social criticism in Viennese Expressionist drama. Austria: Vienna. 1907-1922. Lang.: Ger. 2779
Roth, Beatrice
Institutions
Arthur Penn and Actors Studio. USA: New York, NY. 1997. Lang.: Eng. 1767
Roth, Robert Jess
Administration
The Disney Corporation's Broadway musicals. USA: New York, NY. 1996-1998. Lang.: Eng. 4317
Performance/production
The premiere of the musical *Elaborate Lives: The Legend of Aida*. USA: Atlanta, GA. 1998. Lang.: Eng. 4385
Rotmanskij, A.
Performance/production
Ballerina Nina Ananiašvili. Russia. 1998. Lang.: Rus. 1142
Rouge (Red)
Plays/librettos/scripts
Mixed media in theatre productions of Carole Nadeau. Canada: Quebec, PQ, Montreal, PQ. 1998. Lang.: Fre. 4047
Rough Waters
Plays/librettos/scripts
Analysis of Melissa Mullen's *Rough Waters* at Theatre PEI. Canada: Charlottetown, PE. 1990-1998. Lang.: Eng. 2817
Round House Theatre (London)
Performance/production
Collection of newspaper reviews by London theatre critics. UK-England: London. 1998. Lang.: Eng. 2482
Collection of newspaper reviews by London theatre critics. UK-England: London. 1998. Lang.: Eng. 2544
The collaborative art installation *Tight Roaring Circle*. UK-England: London. 1993-1997. Lang.: Eng. 4133
Roundabout Theatre Company (New York, NY)
Design/technology
Costume design for Feydeau's *A Flea in Her Ear (La Puce à l'Oreille)*, Roundabout Theatre Company. USA: New York, NY. 1998. Lang.: Eng. 1537
Lighting design for Sam Mendes' production of *Cabaret*. USA: New York, NY. 1998. Lang.: Eng. 4344
Performance spaces
Theatre space and performance. USA: New York, NY. 1925-1985. Lang.: Eng. 464
Performance/production
Notable productions of plays by Eugene O'Neill. USA. 1916-1996. Lang.: Eng. 2752
Joe Dowling's production of *London Assurance* by Dion Boucicault. USA. 1997. Lang.: Eng. 2755
Roux, Jean-Louis
Plays/librettos/scripts
French translations of Shakespeare by Antonine Maillet and Jean-Louis Roux. Canada: Montreal, PQ. 1988-1993. Lang.: Fre. 2793
Rover, The
Plays/librettos/scripts
Sexual politics in *The Rover* by Aphra Behn. England. 1677. Lang.: Eng. 3031
Rovetta, Gerolamo
Plays/librettos/scripts
Italian realist drama. Italy. 1860-1918. Lang.: Eng. 3260
Rowe, Catherine Louise
Basic theatrical documents
Original playtext dealing with conflict resolution by Catherine Louise Rowe. USA. 1997. Lang.: Eng. 1507
Rowe, Nicholas
Performance/production
Rowe's Jane Shore as a major role for actresses. England. 1714. Lang.: Eng. 1899
Plays/librettos/scripts
Nicholas Rowe's illustration of a scene from *Macbeth*. England. 1709. Lang.: Eng. 2953
Rowley, William
Performance/production
Collection of newspaper reviews by London theatre critics. UK-England: London. 1998. Lang.: Eng. 2424
Plays/librettos/scripts
Analysis of *The Witch of Edmonton* by Ford, Dekker, and Rowley. England. 1621. Lang.: Eng. 2928
Male and female honor in *A Fair Quarrel* by Middleton and Rowley. England. 1615-1617. Lang.: Eng. 2993
The Bodyguard, Sam Shepard's screen adaptation of *The Changeling* by Middleton and Rowley. USA. 1970-1995. Lang.: Eng. 4007
Royal Albert Hall (London)
Performance/production
Collection of newspaper reviews by London theatre critics. UK-England: London. 1998. Lang.: Eng. 2429
Collection of newspaper reviews by London theatre critics. UK-England: London. 1998. Lang.: Eng. 2564
Royal Alexandra Theatre (Toronto, ON)
Performance spaces
Toronto's theatres. Canada: Toronto, ON. 1998. Lang.: Eng. 434
Royal Ballet (London)
Institutions
The present state of the Royal Ballet under Michael Kaiser. UK-England: London. 1998. Lang.: Hun. 1054
Performance/production
Dancer Carlos Acosta of Royal Ballet and Houston Ballet. USA: Houston, TX. UK-England: London. 1993-1998. Lang.: Eng. 1190
Recent work of choreographer Twyla Tharp. USA: New York, NY. 1988-1998. Lang.: Eng. 1328

Royal Court Theatre (London)
SEE ALSO
English Stage Company.
Design/technology
Technical designs for *The Chairs (Les Chaises)*, Théâtre de Complicité. UK-England: London. 1998. Lang.: Eng. 1524
Performance/production
Collection of newspaper reviews by London theatre critics. UK-England: London. 1998. Lang.: Eng. 2414
Collection of newspaper reviews by London theatre critics. UK-England: London. 1998. Lang.: Eng. 2422
Collection of newspaper reviews by London theatre critics. UK-England: London. 1998. Lang.: Eng. 2428
Collection of newspaper reviews by London theatre critics. UK-England: London. 1998. Lang.: Eng. 2467
Collection of newspaper reviews by London theatre critics. UK-England: London. 1998. Lang.: Eng. 2520
Collection of newspaper reviews by London theatre critics. UK-England: London. 1998. Lang.: Eng. 2526
Collection of newspaper reviews by London theatre critics. UK-England: London. 1998. Lang.: Eng. 2549
Collection of newspaper reviews by London theatre critics. UK-England: London. 1998. Lang.: Eng. 2560
Collection of newspaper reviews by London theatre critics. UK-England: London. 1998. Lang.: Eng. 2569
Correspondence of George Devine and Michel Saint-Denis. UK-England: London. 1939-1945. Lang.: Eng. 2630

Royal Court Upstairs Stage (London)
Performance/production
Collection of newspaper reviews by London theatre critics. UK-England: London. 1998. Lang.: Eng. 2432
Collection of newspaper reviews by London theatre critics. UK-England: London. 1998. Lang.: Eng. 2458
Collection of newspaper reviews by London theatre critics. UK-England: London. 1998. Lang.: Eng. 2493

Royal Dramatic Theatre (Stockholm)
SEE
Kungliga Dramatiska Teatern.

Royal Exchange Theatre (Manchester)
Performance/production
Collection of newspaper reviews by London theatre critics. UK-England. 1998. Lang.: Eng. 2558
Collection of newspaper reviews by London theatre critics. UK-England: Leeds, Manchester. 1998. Lang.: Eng. 2559

Royal Festival Hall (London)
Performance/production
Collection of newspaper reviews by London theatre critics. UK-England: London. 1998. Lang.: Eng. 2580

Royal Hunt of the Sun, The
Plays/librettos/scripts
Theatrical ritual in plays of Peter Shaffer. USA. 1975-1985. Lang.: Eng. 3707

Royal Lyceum Theatre (Edinburgh)
Performance/production
Collection of newspaper reviews by London theatre critics. UK-England: London. 1998. Lang.: Eng. 2488
Collection of newspaper reviews by London theatre critics. UK-Scotland: Edinburgh. 1998. Lang.: Eng. 2650

Royal National Theatre (London)
SEE
National Theatre Company.

Royal Opera House (Stockholm)
SEE
Kungliga Teatern.
Kungliga Operan.

Royal Opera House, Covent Garden (London)
Institutions
Effects of a TV documentary on the Royal Opera House. UK-England: London. 1993-1998. Lang.: Eng. 4474
Brief history of the Royal Opera House, Covent Garden. UK-England: London. 1732-1998. Lang.: Eng. 4477
The cancellation of performances by the Royal Opera House, Covent Garden. UK-England: London. 1998. Lang.: Eng. 4478
The Royal Opera House, Covent Garden, and the English National Opera. UK-England: London. 1988-1998. Lang.: Eng. 4479
Performance/production
The current state of opera in England. UK-England. 1997. Lang.: Eng. 4705

Royal Shakespeare Company (RSC, Stratford & London)
Design/technology
Set and costume design for *The Spanish Tragedy* at RSC. UK-England: London. 1998. Lang.: Eng. 1525
Lighting designer Hugh Vanstone. USA: New York, NY. 1998. Lang.: Eng. 1554
Performance/production
Collection of newspaper reviews by London theatre critics. UK. 1998. Lang.: Eng. 2407
Collection of newspaper reviews by London theatre critics. UK-England: London, Stratford, Derby. 1998. Lang.: Eng. 2417
Collection of newspaper reviews by London theatre critics. UK-England: London. 1998. Lang.: Eng. 2419
Collection of newspaper reviews by London theatre critics. UK-England: Stratford. 1998. Lang.: Eng. 2431
Collection of newspaper reviews by London theatre critics. UK-England: London. 1998. Lang.: Eng. 2435
Collection of newspaper reviews by London theatre critics. UK-England: London. 1998. Lang.: Eng. 2442
Collection of newspaper reviews by London theatre critics. UK-England: London. 1998. Lang.: Eng. 2453
Collection of newspaper reviews by London theatre critics. UK-England: London. 1998. Lang.: Eng. 2461
Collection of newspaper reviews by London theatre critics. UK-England: Stratford. 1998. Lang.: Eng. 2519
Collection of newspaper reviews by London theatre critics. UK-England: Stratford. 1998. Lang.: Eng. 2529
Collection of newspaper reviews by London theatre critics. UK-England: London. 1998. Lang.: Eng. 2531
Collection of newspaper reviews by London theatre critics. UK-England: Stratford, Birmingham. 1998. Lang.: Eng. 2536
Collection of newspaper reviews by London theatre critics. UK-England: London. 1998. Lang.: Eng. 2538
Collection of newspaper reviews by London theatre critics. UK-England: London. 1998. Lang.: Eng. 2551
Collection of newspaper reviews by London theatre critics. UK-England. 1998. Lang.: Eng. 2558
The future of English repertory companies. UK-England: London. 1998. Lang.: Eng. 2563
Collection of newspaper reviews by London theatre critics. UK-England: London. 1998. Lang.: Eng. 2571
Collection of newspaper reviews by London theatre critics. UK-England: London. 1998. Lang.: Eng. 2573
Collection of newspaper reviews by London theatre critics. UK-England: London. 1998. Lang.: Eng. 2587
Collection of newspaper reviews by London theatre critics. UK-England: London. 1998. Lang.: Eng. 2588
Susan Brown on her role in *Richard III* at RSC. UK-England: London, Stratford. 1995-1996. Lang.: Eng. 2593
Julian Glover on his performance in *Romeo and Juliet* for RSC. UK-England: London, Stratford. 1995-1996. Lang.: Eng. 2606
Three productions of Shakespeare's *Richard III*. UK-England. 1973-1984. Lang.: Eng. 2612
Derek Jacobi on playing Macbeth for the RSC. UK-England: London, Stratford. 1993-1994. Lang.: Eng. 2616
Paul Jesson's role in *Henry VIII* at RSC. UK-England: London, Stratford. 1996-1997. Lang.: Eng. 2617
Jane Lapotaire on her performance in *Henry VIII* at RSC. UK-England: London, Stratford. 1996-1997. Lang.: Eng. 2619
Christopher Luscombe on acting in RSC productions. UK-England: London, Stratford. 1993-1994. Lang.: Eng. 2620
Richard McCabe on his role in *The Winter's Tale* at RSC. UK-England: London, Stratford. 1992-1993. Lang.: Eng. 2623
John Nettles on his role in an RSC production of *Julius Caesar*. UK-England: London, Stratford. 1995. Lang.: Eng. 2625
Katie Mitchell's production of mystery plays at RSC. UK-England: London. 1996-1998. Lang.: Eng. 2626
Report on several English performances. UK-England: London, Stratford. 1998. Lang.: Swe. 2634

Royal Shakespeare Company (RSC, Stratford & London) — cont'd

Michael Siberry on performing in an RSC production of *The Taming of the Shrew*. UK-England: London, Stratford. 1995-1996. Lang.:Eng. 2637

Royal Shakespeare Company actors on their performances as Shakespearean characters. UK-England: London, Stratford. 1992-1997. Lang.: Eng. 2638

David Tennant on his performance in *As You Like It* at RSC. UK-England: London, Stratford. 1996-1997. Lang.: Eng. 2640

David Troughton on playing Shakespeare's *Richard III*. UK-England: London, Stratford. 1995-1996. Lang.: Eng. 2642

Philip Voss on his role in *Coriolanus* at RSC. UK-England: London, Stratford. 1994. Lang.: Eng. 2643

John Barton's workshop on Shakespearean performance. USA: New York, NY. 1998. Lang.: Eng. 2704

Theory/criticism

Contrasting reviews of Declan Donnellan's RSC production of *The School for Scandal*. UK-England: Stratford. 1998. Lang.: Eng. 3835

Royal Shakespeare Theatre (Stratford)

Performance/production

Collection of newspaper reviews by London theatre critics. UK. 1998. Lang.: Eng. 2407

Collection of newspaper reviews by London theatre critics. UK-England: Stratford. 1998. Lang.: Eng. 2431

Collection of newspaper reviews by London theatre critics. UK-England: Stratford. 1998. Lang.: Eng. 2519

Collection of newspaper reviews by London theatre critics. UK-England: Stratford. 1998. Lang.: Eng. 2529

Collection of newspaper reviews by London theatre critics. UK-England: Stratford, Birmingham. 1998. Lang.: Eng. 2536

Royal Swedish Ballet

SEE

Kungliga Teaterns Balett.

Royal Swedish Opera

SEE

Kungliga Teatern.

Kungliga Operan.

Różewicz, Tadeusz

Plays/librettos/scripts

Old age in plays of Różewicz. Poland. 1945-1998. Lang.: Pol. 3309

Rozman, Branko

Basic theatrical documents

Text of plays by Branko Rozman. Slovenia. 1990-1997. Lang.: Slo. 1461

Rozov, Viktor S.

Plays/librettos/scripts

Playwright Viktor Rozov. Russia. 1913-1998. Lang.: Rus. 3329

Rubasingham, Indhu

Performance/production

Collection of newspaper reviews by London theatre critics. UK-England: London. 1998. Lang.: Eng. 2509

Collection of newspaper reviews by London theatre critics. UK-England: London. 1998. Lang.: Eng. 2549

Rubidge, Sarah

Performance/production

Digital dance. UK-England. 1998. Lang.: Eng. 974

Rubinstein, Ida

Performance/production

Collaborative Symbolist dance/theatre projects. Europe. USA. 1916-1934. Lang.: Eng. 1268

Ruby, Harry

Performance/production

Collection of newspaper reviews by London theatre critics. UK-England: London. 1998. Lang.: Eng. 2420

Ruccello, Annibale

Plays/librettos/scripts

Playwrights Annibale Ruccello, Enzo Moscato, and Manlio Santanelli. Italy: Naples. 1980-1989. Lang.: Eng. 3261

Rückert, Friedrich

Performance/production

Collection of newspaper reviews by London theatre critics. UK-England: London. 1998. Lang.: Eng. 2409

Rudkin, David

Performance/production

Career of director Lynne Meadow. USA: New York, NY. 1972-1985. Lang.: Eng. 2708

Plays/librettos/scripts

Gender and nationalism in Northern Irish drama. UK-Ireland. 1902-1997. Lang.: Eng. 3511

BBC radio plays with Anglo-Irish themes. UK-England. Ireland. 1973-1986. Lang.: Eng. 3868

Rudolf, Teréz

Performance/production

Interviews with actors on Anatolij Vasiljév's guest direction at Szigligeti Theatre. Hungary: Szolnok. 1998. Lang.: Hun. 2061

Rudolfsson, Lars

Performance spaces

The rebuilding of the stage at Cirkus to accommodate a production of *Kristina från Duvemåla (Kristina of Duvemåla)*.Sweden: Stockholm. 1995. Lang.: Swe. 1804

Performance/production

Reactions to the opera *Staden* by Sven-David Sandström and Katarina Frostensson. Sweden: Stockholm. 1998. Lang.: Swe. 4699

Rudzinskij, Sergej

Performance/production

Director Sergej Rudzinskij. Russia: Omsk. 1998. Lang.: Rus. 2325

Rueda de la fortuna, La (Wheel of Fortune, The)

Plays/librettos/scripts

Playwright Antonio Mira de Amescua. Spain. 1574-1644. Lang.: Eng. 3371

Rueda, Lope de

Plays/librettos/scripts

Playwright Lope de Rueda. Spain. 1510-1565. Lang.: Eng. 3403

Ruf des Lebens (Call of Life)

Performance/production

Productions of director Peter Wittenberg. Germany: Munich, Bonn. 1998. Lang.: Ger. 2013

Rugg, Rebecca Ann

Performance/production

Theatre Magazine's anniversary issue. USA. 1968-1998. Lang.: Eng. 617

Ruiz de Alarcón y Mendoza, Juan

Plays/librettos/scripts

Life and career of playwright Juan Ruiz de Alarcón y Mendoza. Spain. 1580-1639. Lang.: Eng. 3389

Rules of the Game, The

SEE

Giuoco delle parti, Il.

Ruling Class, The

Plays/librettos/scripts

Gender and madness in modern drama. Europe. 1880-1969. Lang.: Eng. 3061

Plays of Peter Barnes compared to those of Renaissance dramatists. UK-England. 1968-1974. Lang.: Eng. 3449

Rum and Vodka

Performance/production

Collection of newspaper reviews by London theatre critics. UK-England: London. 1998. Lang.: Eng. 2416

Rumäner (Romanians)

Performance/production

Interview with actor/director Stefan Larsson. Sweden: Stockholm. 1984-1998. Lang.: Swe. 2382

Rumi, Jalaluddin

Performance/production

Collection of newspaper reviews by London theatre critics. UK-England: London. 1998. Lang.: Eng. 2409

Rundgång, Undergång och Demedon (Vicious Circle, Extinction and Demedon)

Plays/librettos/scripts

Interview with playwright-director Kajsa Isakson. Sweden: Stockholm. 1997-1998. Lang.: Swe. 3414

Rung/You Are Here

Performance/production

Collection of newspaper reviews by London theatre critics. UK-England: London. 1998. Lang.: Eng. 2540

Ruslan i Ljudmila

Design/technology

Scene designs for *Ruslan i Ljudmila* by V. Gartman. Russia: St. Petersburg. 1876. Lang.: Rus. 4438

Russ, Claire

Performance/production

The collaboration of choreographers Claire Russ and Anne-Marie Pascoli. France. UK-England. 1994-1998. Lang.: Eng. 1276

Russell, Bill

Design/technology

Recent work of lighting designer Brian MacDevitt. USA: New York, NY. 1997. Lang.: Eng. 1530

Sound design for *Side Show* at Richard Rodgers Theatre. USA: New York, NY. 1998. Lang.: Eng. 4329

Russell, Ward
Design/technology
Lighting design for Rob Bowman's film *The X-Files*. USA. 1998. Lang.: Eng. 3922
Russell, Willy
Performance/production
Collection of newspaper reviews by London theatre critics. UK-England: London. 1998. Lang.: Eng. 2480
Russkij Dramatičeskij Teat'r Ufy (Ufa)
Institutions
Profile of the Russian theatre in Ufa. Chuvashia: Ufa. 1922-1997. Lang.: Rus. 1594
Ruszt, József
Administration
Round-table on author's rights. Hungary. 1990-1998. Lang.: Hun. 16
Performance/production
Two productions of Shakespeare's *Richard III* by József Ruszt. Hungary: Budapest. Hungary: Kecskemét. 1973-1997. Lang.: Hun. 2070
Interview with director József Ruszt. Hungary. 1963-1997. Lang.: Hun. 2115
Director József Ruszt recalls actor Miklós Gábor. Hungary. 1919-1998. Lang.: Hun. 2120
Three Hungarian productions of Shakespeare's *Richard III*. Hungary: Budapest, Zsámbék, Szeged. 1997. Lang.: Hun. 2121
Ruta, Michael
Performance/production
Collection of newspaper reviews by London theatre critics. UK-England: London. 1998. Lang.: Eng. 2439
Ruttkai, Éva
Performance/production
Review of biographies of actors Ádám Szirtes and Éva Ruttkai. Hungary. 1998. Lang.: Hun. 2077
Ruzicka, Peter
Institutions
Interview with Peter Ruzicka of the Münchener Biennale festival. Germany: Munich. 1998. Lang.: Ger. 4291
Ruzika, Tom
Design/technology
Professional theatrical designers on design training. USA. 1998. Lang.: Eng. 252
Ruzzante
SEE
Beolco, Angelo.
Ryan, Joel
Performance/production
The collaborative art installation *Tight Roaring Circle*. UK-England: London. 1993-1997. Lang.: Eng. 4133
Ryan, Richard
Design/technology
Technical designs for the musical *Doctor Doolittle* directed by Steven Pimlott. UK-England: London. 1998. Lang.: Eng. 4325
Ryan, Sam
Performance/production
Irish and Irish-American characters on the stages of the Midwest. USA. 1875-1915. Lang.: Eng. 2696
Rychlík, Břetéslav
Performance/production
The adaptation of classic Czech works to the stage. Czech Republic: Prague, Brno. 1990-1998. Lang.: Cze. 1877
Ryga, George
Plays/librettos/scripts
Language and rhetoric in plays of George Ryga. Canada. 1967-1985. Lang.: Eng. 2792
Ryskind, Morrie
Performance/production
Collection of newspaper reviews by London theatre critics. UK-England: London. 1998. Lang.: Eng. 2420
S.T.C.
Basic theatrical documents
Text of Sharon Gayle Tucker's *S.T.C.* USA. 1988. Lang.: Eng. 1512
Saarinen, Juho
Performance/production
Interview with Deaf dancer Juho Saarinen. Finland. 1998. Lang.: Fin. 1273
Sabato, domenica, lunedì (Saturday, Sunday, Monday)
Performance/production
Collection of newspaper reviews by London theatre critics. UK-England. 1998. Lang.: Eng. 2504
Sabina!
Performance/production
Collection of newspaper reviews by London theatre critics. UK-England: London. 1998. Lang.: Eng. 2439
Collection of newspaper reviews by London theatre critics. UK-England: London. 1998. Lang.: Eng. 2583
Sabotage Baby
Institutions
Productions of Gothenburg's Dance and Theatre Festival. Sweden: Gothenburg. 1998. Lang.: Swe. 1253
Sabre's Edge, The
Performance/production
Collection of newspaper reviews by London theatre critics. UK-England: London. 1998. Lang.: Eng. 2457
Sachs, Alain
Basic theatrical documents
French translation of *Time of My Life* by Alan Ayckbourn. UK-England. France. 1993-1998. Lang.: Fre. 1471
Sack of Rome, The
Plays/librettos/scripts
Gender and politics in Romantic tragedies of Mercy Otis Warren. USA. 1783-1785. Lang.: Eng. 3575
Sackler, Howard
Plays/librettos/scripts
Miscegenation in American drama. USA. 1909-1969. Lang.: Eng. 3599
Sackville, Thomas
Performance/production
Music in Tudor drama. England. 1497-1569. Lang.: Eng. 1902
Sacramento Light Opera Association (Sacramento, CA)
Administration
Leland Ball of Sacramento Light Opera Association, winner of Rosetta LeNoire Award. USA: Sacramento, CA. 1998. Lang.: Eng. 4408
Sacre du printemps, Le
SEE
Vesna svjaščennaja.
Sacred Naked Nature Girls (Los Angeles, CA)
Plays/librettos/scripts
Analysis of *Untitled Flesh* by Sacred Naked Nature Girls. USA: Los Angeles, CA. 1994-1997. Lang.: Eng. 4262
Sada, Yacco
SEE
Kawakami, Sadayacco.
Saddler, Donald
Performance/production
Tributes to ballerina Alexandra Danilova. USA: New York, NY. 1997. Lang.: Eng. 1165
Saddumene, Bernardo
Plays/librettos/scripts
Female operatic cross-dressing. Italy: Naples, Venice. 1601-1800. Lang.: Eng. 4814
Sadler's Wells Ballet Company (London)
Performance/production
Annabel Farjeon on dancing for Ninette de Valois and Frederick Ashton. UK-England: London. 1930-1940. Lang.: Eng. 1158
Sadler's Wells Theatre (London)
Design/technology
Technical designs for Matthew Bourne's productions of ballets by Čajkovskij and Prokofjév. UK-England: London. 1998. Lang.: Eng. 1031
Institutions
The cancellation of performances by the Royal Opera House, Covent Garden. UK-England: London. 1998. Lang.: Eng. 4478
Performance/production
Excerpts from Johanna Schopenhauer's journal relating to London theatre. UK-England: London. Germany. 1803-1805. Lang.: Eng. 2615
Theory/criticism
Critique of dance criticism. UK-England: London. 1989. Lang.: Eng. 1339
Safe Sex
Plays/librettos/scripts
American gay drama and the impact of AIDS. USA. 1960-1987. Lang.: Eng. 3670
Safety
SEE
Health/safety.
Sagouine, La (Slattern The)
Plays/librettos/scripts
Women and Acadian theatre. Canada. 1870-1998. Lang.: Eng. 2810
Saint Joan
Plays/librettos/scripts
The rebel in modern drama. Europe. 1950-1988. Lang.: Eng. 3053

***Saint Joan* — cont'd**

Colonialism in the plays of George Bernard Shaw. UK-England. 1895-1935. Lang.: Eng. 3438

Analysis of the later plays of George Bernard Shaw. UK-England. 1923-1947. Lang.: Eng. 3444

George Bernard Shaw and the history-play tradition. UK-England. 1899-1939. Lang.: Eng. 3503

George Bernard Shaw and science fiction. UK-England. Ireland. 1887-1998. Lang.: Eng. 3508

Saint Joseph Ballet (Santa Ana, CA)

Institutions

Profile of Saint Joseph Ballet. USA: Santa Ana, CA. 1983-1998. Lang.: Eng. 1056

Saint-Denis, Michel

Performance/production

Correspondence of George Devine and Michel Saint-Denis. UK-England: London. 1939-1945. Lang.: Eng. 2630

Commedia dell'arte and twentieth-century theatre. Europe. 1860-1950. Lang.: Eng. 4187

Saint-François d'Assise

Performance/production

Opera productions of the Salzburg Festival. Austria: Salzburg. 1998. Lang.: Hun. 4531

Review of opera productions. Germany: Stuttgart, Leipzig. 1998. Lang.: Ger. 4584

Saint-Gelais, Joseph

Performance/production

Social context of French and Canadian productions of *Les Fourberies de Scapin* by Molière. Canada: Montreal, PQ. France: Paris. 1998. Lang.: Fre. 1842

Saint-Jean, Raymond

Plays/librettos/scripts

Raymond Saint-Jean's film adaptation of *Cabaret neiges noires (Black Snow Cabaret)*. Canada. 1997. Lang.: Fre. 3967

Saint-Saëns, Camille

Design/technology

Scene designer Richard Hudson and his work on *Samson et Dalila* at the Metropolitan Opera. UK-England. USA. 1954-1998. Lang.: Eng. 4289

Performance/production

The stage history of *Samson et Dalila* by Saint-Saëns. France. Germany. USA. 1877-1998. Lang.: Eng. 4566

Oriental themes in operas and instrumental works of Saint-Saëns. France. 1872-1911. Lang.: Eng. 4576

Background material on Metropolitan Opera radio broadcast performances. USA: New York, NY. 1998. Lang.: Eng. 4713

Background material on telecast performance of Saint-Saëns' *Samson et Dalila* at the Metropolitan Opera. USA: New York, NY. 1998. Lang.: Eng. 4714

Plays/librettos/scripts

Gender, nationalism, and Orientalism in *Samson et Dalila* by Saint-Saëns. Germany. 1868-1877. Lang.: Eng. 4797

Saints and Singing

Plays/librettos/scripts

Hero and anti-hero in contemporary opera production. Germany. 1998. Lang.: Ger. 4791

Saison au Congo, Une (Season in the Congo, A)

Plays/librettos/scripts

Analysis and translation of *Et les Chiens se taisaient (And the Dogs Were Silent)* by Aimé Césaire. Martinique. 1946-1969. Lang.: Eng. 3269

Sakate, Yoji

Performance/production

Collection of newspaper reviews by London theatre critics. UK-England: London. 1998. Lang.: Eng. 2438

Sal'nikov, G.I.

Performance/production

Actor G.I Sal'nikov. Russia: Saratov. 1998. Lang.: Rus. 2315

Sala Eugenio Montale (Genoa)

Performance/production

Andrea Liberovici's production of *Sonetto. Un travestimento shakespeariano (Sonnet: A Shakespearean Travesty)* by Eduardo Sanguineti. Italy: Genoa. 1997. Lang.: Ita. 2159

Sala Milloss (Rome)

Performance/production

Amedeo Amodio's new choreography for Čajkovskij's *The Nutcracker*. Italy: Rome. 1998. Lang.: Hun. 1118

Salieri, Antonio

Performance/production

Antonio Salieri and his opera *Falstaff*, recently revived. Italy: Milan. 1799-1998. Lang.: Eng. 4654

Salisbury Court Theatre (London)

Performance spaces

Evidence of theatre closings in a Folger Library manuscript. England: London. 1650. Lang.: Eng. 1798

Šaljapin, Fëdor Ivanovič

Performance/production

Opera singer Fëdor Šaljapin. Russia. 1873-1938. Lang.: Rus. 4669

Life and work of singer Fëdor Šaljapin. Russia. 1873-1938. Lang.: Rus. 4672

The early operatic career of Fëdor Šaljapin. Russia: Nizhni Novgorod. 1890-1899. Lang.: Rus. 4676

Analysis of the first book about opera singer Fëdor Šaljapin. Russia. 1916. Lang.: Rus. 4678

The life of the opera singer Fëdor Šaljapin. Russia. 1873-1938. Lang.: Rus. 4681

Personal recollections of Šaljapin singing on recordings of *Boris Godunov*. Russia. 1873-1938. Lang.: Eng. 4685

Opera singer Fëdor Šaljapin and his roots in Vjatka. Russia: Vjatka. 1873-1938. Lang.: Rus. 4687

Career of opera singer Fëdor Šaljapin. Russia. 1873-1938. Lang.: Rus. 4688

Books in the life of opera singer Fëdor Šaljapin. Russia. 1873-1938. Lang.: Rus. 4691

Plays/librettos/scripts

Kazan in the life of Maksim Gorkij and Fëdor Šaljapin. Tatarstan: Kazan. 1868-1938. Lang.: Rus. 689

Salle des Machines (Paris)

Performance spaces

Baroque opera and ballet at the Salle des Machines and the Palais Royal. France: Paris. 1640-1690. Lang.: Eng. 4493

Salle le Peletier (Paris)

Performance spaces

The influence of the Salle le Peletier on French grand opera. France: Paris. 1823-1873. Lang.: Eng. 4494

Sally and Marsha

Performance/production

Career of director Lynne Meadow. USA: New York, NY. 1972-1985. Lang.: Eng. 2708

Salomé

Performance/production

Roman Viktjuk's production of *Salomé* by Oscar Wilde. Russia: Moscow. 1998. Lang.: Rus. 2266

Collection of newspaper reviews by London theatre critics. UK-England: London. 1998. Lang.: Eng. 2547

Plays/librettos/scripts

Wilde, Gide, and the censorship of Biblical drama. UK-England. France. 1892-1898. Lang.: Eng. 3441

Salome

Institutions

Survey of the Theatertreffen festival. Germany: Berlin. 1998. Lang.: Swe. 1651

Performance/production

The work of director Einar Schleef. Germany: Düsseldorf. 1998. Lang.: Ger. 2026

Opera director Inge Levant. Germany: Stuttgart. 1959-1998. Lang.: Ger. 4611

Interview with opera singer Anne Bolstad. Norway. Sweden. 1980-1998. Lang.: Swe. 4665

Theory/criticism

Theatrical dancing and the performance aesthetics of Wilde, Yeats, and Shaw. UK-England. Ireland. 1890-1950. Lang.: Eng. 1012

Salonen, Esa-Pekka

Performance/production

Interview with conductor Esa-Pekka Salonen. Finland. 1998. Lang.: Eng. 4560

Salt, Waldo

Plays/librettos/scripts

The musical *Sandhog* by blacklisted writers Earl Robinson and Waldo Salt. USA. 1954. Lang.: Eng. 4395

Salutin, Rick

Performance/production

Analysis of *1837: The Farmer's Revolt* directed by Bruce Barton of Carrefour Theatre. Canada: Charlottetown, PE. 1998. Lang.: Eng. 1856

Salvadores de España, Los (Saviors of Spain, The)

Plays/librettos/scripts

Antifascist puppet plays by Rafael Alberti. Spain. 1936-1939. Lang.: Eng. 4922

Salvini, Guido
Plays/librettos/scripts
The collaboration of playwright Curzio Malaparte and director Guido Salvini. Italy. 1905-1956. Lang.: Ita. 3239
Salvini, Tomasso
Performance/production
Actor Tomasso Salvini. USA. Italy. 1856-1915. Lang.: Eng. 2731
Salzburger Festspiele (Salzburg)
Institutions
Peter Stein's last season as director at the Salzburg Festival. Austria: Salzburg. 1997. Lang.: Eng. 336
The program of the Salzburg Festival. Austria: Salzburg. 1997. Lang.: Hun. 1569
Productions by Stefan Bachmann and Robert Wilson at the Salzburg Festival. Austria: Salzburg. 1998. Lang.: Hun. 1570
Productions of Salzburger Festspiele. Austria: Salzburg. 1998. Lang.: Ger. 1571
Interview with Ivan Nagel, drama manager of the Salzburg Festival. Austria: Salzburg. 1998. Lang.: Ger. 1572
Productions of the Salzburg Festival. Austria: Salzburg. 1998. Lang.: Ger. 1573
Comparison of Salzburg and Bayreuth festival seasons. Germany: Bayreuth. Austria: Salzburg. 1998. Lang.: Eng. 4452
Performance/production
Robert Lepage's *Geometry of Miracles* at the Salzburg Festival. Austria: Salzburg. 1998. Lang.: Ger. 1824
Review of Salzburger Festspiele performances. Austria: Salzburg. 1998. Lang.: Ger. 4527
Opera productions of the Salzburg Festival. Austria: Salzburg. 1998. Lang.: Hun. 4531
Salzer, Beeb
Design/technology
Creativity and beauty in theatrical design. USA. 1998. Lang.: Eng. 322
Sambin, Michele
Performance/production
Directing and intercultural theatre. Europe. 1930-1998. Lang.: Ger. 524
Samson et Dalila
Design/technology
Scene designer Richard Hudson and his work on *Samson et Dalila* at the Metropolitan Opera. UK-England. USA. 1954-1998. Lang.: Eng. 4289
Performance/production
The stage history of *Samson et Dalila* by Saint-Saëns. France. Germany. USA. 1877-1998. Lang.: Eng. 4566
Oriental themes in operas and instrumental works of Saint-Saëns. France. 1872-1911. Lang.: Eng. 4576
Background material on Metropolitan Opera radio broadcast performances. USA: New York, NY. 1998. Lang.: Eng. 4713
Background material on telecast performance of Saint-Saëns' *Samson et Dalila* at the Metropolitan Opera. USA: New York, NY. 1998. Lang.: Eng. 4714
Plays/librettos/scripts
Gender, nationalism, and Orientalism in *Samson et Dalila* by Saint-Saëns. Germany. 1868-1877. Lang.: Eng. 4797
Samstagabend: Eine Liebesgeschichte (Saturday Evening: A Life History)
Plays/librettos/scripts
Homosexuality on the German stage. Germany. 1920-1980. Lang.: Eng. 3147
Samuelsson, Mikael
Performance/production
Interview with singer Mikael Samuelsson. Sweden. 1960-1998. Lang.: Swe. 4698
San Francisco Ballet (San Francisco, CA)
Performance/production
New York performances of the San Francisco Ballet. USA: New York, NY. 1998. Lang.: Eng. 1170
Dancer Christopher Stowell of San Francisco Ballet. USA: San Francisco, CA. 1998. Lang.: Eng. 1191
San Francisco Opera (San Francisco, CA)
Design/technology
Set and costume design for San Francisco Opera productions. USA: San Francisco, CA. 1998. Lang.: Eng. 4443
Institutions
The partnership between San Francisco Opera and Chase Manhattan Bank. USA: San Francisco, CA, New York, NY. 1998. Lang.: Eng. 423
Performance/production
Baritone Rodney Gilfry. USA. 1998. Lang.: Eng. 4736
Major opera houses' proposals for productions to the end of the century. USA. Canada. 1998. Lang.: Eng. 4743
Opera conductor Patrick Summers. USA. 1990-1998. Lang.: Eng. 4755
San Juan
Performance/production
Juan Carlos Pérez de la Fuente's production of *San Juan* by Max Aub. Spain: Madrid. 1998. Lang.: Eng. 2363
Sandberg, Leslie Jean
Basic theatrical documents
Text of *The Sisterhood of Dark Sanctuary* by Leslie Jean Sandberg. USA. 1986. Lang.: Eng. 1508
Sanderson, Sibyl
Performance/production
Massenet's revisions to *Manon* for performance by Sybil Sanderson. France. 1885-1903. Lang.: Eng. 4572
Sandhog
Plays/librettos/scripts
The musical *Sandhog* by blacklisted writers Earl Robinson and Waldo Salt. USA. 1954. Lang.: Eng. 4395
Sándor, Judit
Performance/production
Interview with opera singer Judit Sándor on her male roles. Hungary. 1948-1998. Lang.: Hun. 4637
Sandrich, Mark
Performance/production
Analysis of the *Night and Day* dance sequence of *The Gay Divorcee*. USA: Hollywood, CA. 1934. Lang.: Eng. 977
Sandström, Sven-David
Performance/production
Reactions to the opera *Staden* by Sven-David Sandström and Katarina Frostensson. Sweden: Stockholm. 1998. Lang.: Swe. 4699
Plays/librettos/scripts
Interview with opera composer Sven-David Sandström. Sweden: Stockholm. 1998. Lang.: Swe. 4821
Sangshuping Jishi (Tales of Mulberry Village)
Basic theatrical documents
Anthology of contemporary Chinese drama. China, People's Republic of. 1979-1986. Lang.: Eng. 1414
Sanguineti, Edoardo
Performance/production
Andrea Liberovici's production of *Sonetto. Un travestimento shakespeariano (Sonnet: A Shakespearean Travesty)* by Eduardo Sanguineti. Italy: Genoa. 1997. Lang.: Ita. 2159
Sankai Juku (Tokyo)
Performance/production
Guest performance of Sankai Juku *butō* company. Hungary: Budapest. 1998. Lang.: Hun. 941
Sankey, Tom
Plays/librettos/scripts
Revolutionary Off Broadway playwriting. USA: New York, NY. 1959-1969. Lang.: Eng. 3604
Sankofa
Plays/librettos/scripts
Analysis of Haile Gerima's film *Sankofa*. Ghana. 1993. Lang.: Eng. 3973
Santa Cruzan/Flores de Mayo
Performance/production
The performance installations *Santa Cruzan/Flores de Mayo* by DIWA Arts. USA: San Francisco, CA. 1994-1996. Lang.: Eng. 4256
Santa Fe Opera (Santa Fe, NM)
Performance spaces
Sante Fe Opera's newly renovated open-air theatre. USA: Santa Fe, NM. 1991-1998. Lang.: Eng. 4499
Santana, Carlota
Performance/production
Flamenco dancer and choreographer Carlota Santana. USA: New York, NY. 1998. Lang.: Eng. 1239
Santanelli, Manlio
Plays/librettos/scripts
Playwrights Annibale Ruccello, Enzo Moscato, and Manlio Santanelli. Italy: Naples. 1980-1989. Lang.: Eng. 3261
Santareno, Bernardo
Plays/librettos/scripts
The influence of Federico García Lorca on playwright Bernardo Santareno. Spain. Portugal. 1919-1965. Lang.: Eng. 3400
Santini, Pierre
Basic theatrical documents
Text of *Capitaine Bringuier* by Pascal Lainé. France. 1998. Lang.: Fre. 1429

Santo rey don Fernando, El (Holy King Don Fernando, The)
Plays/librettos/scripts
Spanish Catholicism and the *autos sacramentales* of Calderón. Spain. 1637-1671. Lang.: Spa. 3405
Santos, Carles
Performance/production
Collection of newspaper reviews by London theatre critics. UK-Scotland: Edinburgh. 1998. Lang.: Eng. 2650
Sapho
Performance/production
Attempted censorship of productions. USA. 1900-1905. Lang.: Eng. 2698
New York City's attempt to impose censorship on theatre productions. USA: New York, NY. 1900-1927. Lang.: Eng. 2699
Sarajevski Ratni Teater (Sarajevo)
Performance/production
Interview with director Aleš Kurt. Bosnia: Sarajevo. 1998. Lang.: Hun. 1830
Sárga csikó (Yellow Colt, The)
Institutions
Theatre critics' awards 97-98. Hungary. 1997-1998. Lang.: Hun. 355
Sarigakham, Gorsem
Performance/production
Collection of newspaper reviews by London theatre critics. UK-England: London. 1998. Lang.: Eng. 2492
Sarita
Plays/librettos/scripts
Theatrical space in plays of Maria Irene Fornes. USA. 1977-1989. Lang.: Eng. 3571
Saro-Wiwa, Ken
Plays/librettos/scripts
Analysis of unpublished plays by Ken Saro-Wiwa. Nigeria. 1971-1991. Lang.: Eng. 3282
Sarraute, Nathalie
Plays/librettos/scripts
Feminist questioning of language and authority in plays of Nathalie Sarraute. France. 1967-1995. Lang.: Eng. 3103
Analysis of *Elle est là (It Is There)* by Nathalie Sarraute. France. 1967-1982. Lang.: Eng. 3107
Response to the structures of male oppression in plays of Yourcenar, Sarraute, and Duras. France. 1975-1995. Lang.: Fre. 3119
Sarrias Fornés, Mercè
Basic theatrical documents
Text of *Àfrica 30* by Mercè Sarrias Fornés. Spain-Catalonia. 1997. Lang.: Cat. 1467
Sartre, Jean-Paul
Performance/production
Political context of Frank Castorf's production of *Les Mains Sales (Dirty Hands)* by Sartre. Germany: Berlin. 1998. Lang.: Ger. 2002
Plays/librettos/scripts
The Orestes myth in twentieth-century drama. Europe. USA. 1914-1943. Lang.: Eng. 3052
Analysis of *Bariona* by Jean-Paul Sartre. France. 1940-1945. Lang.: Eng. 3093
Frank Castorf's production of Sartre's *Les Mains Sales (Dirty Hands)* and the civil war in Yugoslavia. Germany: Berlin. 1998. Lang.: Ger. 3129
Existential analysis of Eugene O'Neill's *Anna Christie.* USA. 1921. Lang.: Eng. 3562
Sarumpaet, Ratna
Relation to other fields
The arrest of playwright and activist Ratna Sarumpaet. Indonesia: Jakarta. 1998. Lang.: Eng. 3773
Satire
Institutions
The student satirical company Teat'r Grotesk. Russia: Surgut. 1998. Lang.: Rus. 1712
Performance/production
Polish cabaret at the front and abroad. Europe. 1939-1998. Lang.: Pol. 4154
Plays/librettos/scripts
Analysis of *The Massacre at Paris* by Christopher Marlowe. England. 1593. Lang.: Eng. 2917
Lucian's *Icaromenippus* as a source for Heywood's *The Play of the Wether.* England. 1533. Lang.: Eng. 2920
Caricature and satire in the plays of Samuel Foote. England. 1775-1800. Lang.: Eng. 2930
Reactions to the awarding of the Nobel Prize to satirical playwright Dario Fo. Italy. 1998. Lang.: Eng. 3242
Satirikon (Moscow)
Performance/production
Recent Russian productions of Shakespeare's *Hamlet.* Russia: Moscow. 1998. Lang.: Rus. 2268
Saturday Night Fever
Performance/production
Collection of newspaper reviews by London theatre critics. UK-England: London. 1998. Lang.: Eng. 2467
Sauce for the Goose
SEE
Dindon, Le.
Saucy Jack and the Space Vixens
Performance/production
Collection of newspaper reviews by London theatre critics. UK-England: London. 1998. Lang.: Eng. 2447
Sauerbaum, Peter
Institutions
Problems of management and repertory at Berliner Ensemble. Germany: Berlin. 1992-1998. Lang.: Ger. 1656
Saül
Plays/librettos/scripts
Wilde, Gide, and the censorship of Biblical drama. UK-England. France. 1892-1898. Lang.: Eng. 3441
Saul
Performance/production
Collection of newspaper reviews by London theatre critics. UK-England. 1998. Lang.: Eng. 2497
Saunders, Mary
Performance/production
Collection of newspaper reviews by London theatre critics. UK-England: London. 1998. Lang.: Eng. 2576
Sauvil, Pierre
Basic theatrical documents
Text of *Soleil pour deux (Sun for Two)* by Pierre Sauvil. France. 1998. Lang.: Fre. 1434
Savage King, Chris
Performance/production
Collection of newspaper reviews by London theatre critics. UK-England: London. 1998. Lang.: Eng. 2517
Savage/Love
Plays/librettos/scripts
Analysis of *Savage/Love* by Joseph Chaikin and Sam Shepard. USA. 1991-1996. Lang.: Eng. 3543
Savannah Bay
Plays/librettos/scripts
Analysis of plays by Marguerite Duras and Marie Redonnet. France. 1977-1992. Lang.: Eng. 3071
Space and pre-verbal memory in later works of Marguerite Duras. France. 1970-1982. Lang.: Eng. 3106
Savary, Jérôme
Performance/production
Productions of the Bad Hersfelder Festspiele. Germany: Bad Hersfeld. 1998. Lang.: Ger. 1991
Savina, Marija Gavrilovna
Performance/production
Major Russian actresses and ballerinas of the nineteenth and twentieth centuries. Russia. 1800-1998. Lang.: Rus. 2240
Saving Charlotte
Performance/production
Collection of newspaper reviews by London theatre critics. UK-England: London. 1998. Lang.: Eng. 2521
Saving Private Ryan
Performance/production
Spielberg's *Saving Private Ryan* and the war film. USA: Hollywood, CA. 1998. Lang.: Eng. 3948
Saving Winnie
Performance/production
Collection of newspaper reviews by London theatre critics. UK-England: London. 1998. Lang.: Eng. 2418
Savinio, Alberto
SEE
De Chirico, Andrea.
Savoca, Carmen
Institutions
Profile of Tri-Cities Opera. USA: Binghamton, NY. 1949-1998. Lang.: Eng. 4490
Savoy Theatre (London)
Performance/production
Collection of newspaper reviews by London theatre critics. UK-England: London. 1998. Lang.: Eng. 2526

Savvina, I.S.
Performance/production
Actress I.S. Savvina. Russia: Moscow. 1998. Lang.: Rus. 2318
Scaffold Theatre Project (Hamilton, ON)
Institutions
Street theatre company Scaffold Theatre Project. Canada: Hamilton, ON. 1995-1998. Lang.: Eng. 1593
Scala, Flaminio
Performance/production
Dramatic writings of Flaminio Scala and Giambattista Andreini. Italy. 1600-1700. Lang.: Eng. 4192
Scapin's Tricks
SEE
Fourberies de Scapin, Les.
Scarface
Plays/librettos/scripts
Opera in American gangster films. USA. 1932-1990. Lang.: Eng. 4023
Scarlet Pimpernel, The
Design/technology
Technical designs for *The Scarlet Pimpernel* directed by Robert Longbottom. USA: New York, NY. 1998. Lang.: Eng. 4331
Ščedrin, Rodion Konstantinovič
Performance/production
Ballerina Maja Pliseckaja and her husband, composer Rodion Ščedrin. Russia: Moscow. 1998. Lang.: Rus. 1143
Ščelkunčik (Nutcracker, The)
Performance/production
The Nutcracker at the Budapest Opera House. Hungary: Budapest. 1998. Lang.: Hun. 1115
Amedeo Amodio's new choreography for Čajkovskij's *The Nutcracker*. Italy: Rome. 1998. Lang.: Hun. 1118
Scena Plasticzna Katolickiego Uniwersyteto Lubelskiego (Lublin)
Performance/production
Productions of the festival of experimental theatre. Poland: Cracow. 1998. Lang.: Ger. 2225
Scenery
SEE ALSO
Training, design.
Design/technology
Directions in present-day scenic design. 1998. Lang.: Rus. 165
Technology and its use by artists. 1913-1988. Lang.: Eng. 166
Scenographer Martin Zehetgruber. Austria: Graz. Germany: Stuttgart. 1979-1998. Lang.: Ger. 168
Action design scenographer Jan Dušek. Czech Republic: Prague. 1970-1998. Lang.: Eng. 173
Scene designer Eldor Rentor. Estonia: Tallin. 1925-1998. Lang.: Swe, Eng, Ger. 175
Criticism of methods used in design training. Finland. 1998. Lang.: Fin. 180
Set designer Jean-Guy Lecat and his work with Peter Brook. France. Denmark. 1975-1998. Lang.: Dan. 182
Impressions from the Salon de Théâtre. France: Paris. 1998. Lang.: Ger. 183
Presentation of stage equipment by manufacturers. Germany. 1998. Lang.: Ger. 184
Walther Unruh and German theatre technology. Germany. 1898-1998. Lang.: Ger. 187
Careers in technical theatre. Germany. Austria. 1998. Lang.: Ger. 189
Scenographer and now director Klaus Noack. Germany. 1953. Lang.: Ger. 190
Scenic elements in *Titanic* by street theatre group Theater Titanick. Germany: Münster, Leipzig. Australia: Perth. 1998. Lang.: Eng. 191
Lighting in contemporary theatre. Germany. 1998. Lang.: Ger. 192
Set and costume designs of Péter Makai. Hungary. 1957-1991. Lang.: Hun. 194
Survey of an exhibition of Hungarian scene design. Hungary: Budapest. 1998. Lang.: Hun. 195
An exhibition of sets and environments by Hungarian designers. Hungary: Budapest. 1998. Lang.: Hun. 196
Catalogue of an exhibition devoted to Hungarian theatre and film. Hungary: Budapest. 1998. Lang.: Hun. 197
Catalogue of an exhibition on scenography of Galileo Chini. Italy. 1908-1956. Lang.: Ita. 199
Set designer and builder Ado Cantin. Italy: Verona. 1967-1998. Lang.: Eng. 200
New edition of the autobiography of painter and scenographer Giorgio De Chirico. Italy. 1888-1978. Lang.: Ita. 202
Works of painter, sculptor, and scenographer Eugenio Guglielminetti. Italy. 1961-1997. Lang.: Ita. 204
Profiles of young theatrical designers. Netherlands. 1990-1998. Lang.: Dut. 207
Gerard de Lairesse, painter and stage designer. Netherlands. 1640-1711. Lang.: Eng. 208
Scenographer Tadeusz Orłowicz. Poland: Cracow. Germany: Neubrandenburg. UK-England: London. 1907-1976. Lang.: Pol. 212
Scenographer N. Panova. Russia: Tver'. 1998. Lang.: Rus. 213
Avant-garde Russian women artist/designers. Russia. USSR. 1880-1949. Lang.: Eng. 214
Memoirs of scenographer Jévgenij Kumankov. Russia. 1998. Lang.: Rus. 215
Scenographer Tatjana Sel'vinskaja. Russia. 1998. Lang.: Rus. 216
Two decades of St. Petersburg scene design. Russia: St. Petersburg. 1910-1929. Lang.: Rus. 217
Scenographic work of painter Maks Kavčič. Slovenia. 1945-1972. Lang.: Slo. 218
Handbook on stage spaces and physical elements. Slovenia. 1997. Lang.: Slo. 219
Interview with set designer Lennart Mörk. Sweden: Stockholm. France: Paris. 1958-1998. Lang.: Swe. 222
The influence of Dalcroze's eurhythmics on designer Adolphe Appia. Switzerland. 1906-1915. Lang.: Eng. 228
Scene designer Ralph Koltai. UK-England. 1944-1998. Lang.: Eng. 232
Dancer Isadora Duncan's influence on the designs of Edward Gordon Craig. UK-England. 1904-1905. Lang.: Eng. 237
Guide to theatrical design manufacturers and equipment. USA. 1998. Lang.: Eng. 241
The 1998 USITT expo. USA: Long Beach, CA. 1998. Lang.: Eng. 251
Professional theatrical designers on design training. USA. 1998. Lang.: Eng. 252
Set designer David Gallo. USA. 1988-1998. Lang.: Eng. 255
Critic Kenneth Macgowan and the 'new stagecraft'. USA. 1912-1940. Lang.: Eng. 262
Rigging a pneumatically activated curtain. USA. 1998. Lang.: Eng. 263
Set and lighting designer James Tilton. USA. 1938-1998. Lang.: Eng. 265
Simulating stained glass on stage. USA. 1998. Lang.: Eng. 266
Treating muslin to look like Naugahyde. USA. 1998. Lang.: Eng. 267
Construction and operation of a trap unit. USA. 1998. Lang.: Eng. 269
Tubular steel framing for large scenery flats. USA. 1998. Lang.: Eng. 270
Catalog of the Tobin scenography collection. USA. Europe. 1500-1900. Lang.: Eng. 272
Design for houses of worship, including their adaptation for performance and exhibitions. USA: Long Beach, CA. 1998. Lang.: Eng. 290
Set and costume designer Eduardo Sicangco, judge of SETC design competition. USA: Birmingham, AL. 1998. Lang.: Eng. 292
The use of entertainment technology beyond the entertainment industry. USA. 1998. Lang.: Eng. 293
A fly system for low-ceilinged theatres. USA. 1998. Lang.: Eng. 296
An ontological approach to the aesthetics of scenography. USA. 1987. Lang.: Eng. 298
Stage, lighting, and sound design for Rolling Stones tour. USA. 1996-1997. Lang.: Eng. 308
Students' recreation of paintings on stage. USA: Huntington, WV. 1996-1997. Lang.: Eng. 313
Set designer Daniel Ostling. USA: Chicago, IL. 1998. Lang.: Eng. 314
Sound, lighting, and scenic elements of *Star Trek: The Next Generation* at the Las Vegas Hilton. USA: Las Vegas, NV. 1998. Lang.: Eng. 320
Construction of nylon turntable rollers. USA. 1998. Lang.: Eng. 321
Creativity and beauty in theatrical design. USA. 1998. Lang.: Eng. 322
Index to *Technical Brief* volumes 11-17. USA. 1998. Lang.: Eng. 323
Comparison of computer-assisted and traditional scenery and lighting design. USA. 1980-1987. Lang.: Eng. 324

Scenery — cont'd

Stage automation and its effect on set design. USA. 1998. Lang.: Eng. 325

A four sided steel-marking guide. USA. 1998. Lang.: Eng. 331

New stage technology and the dance performance. 1998. Lang.: Eng. 888

Technical designs for Matthew Bourne's productions of ballets by Čajkovskij and Prokofjév. UK-England: London. 1998. Lang.: Eng. 1031

Technical designs for Čajovskij's *Sneguročka*, Houston Ballet. USA: Houston, TX. 1998. Lang.: Eng. 1033

Set and costume designer Frank Leimbach and his work with choreographers. Germany. 1991-1998. Lang.: Ger. 1247

Design concept for Ralph Lemon's dance piece *Geography* at BAM. USA: New York, NY. 1998. Lang.: Eng. 1248

Set designer Jean Hazel. Canada: Quebec, PQ. 1985-1998. Lang.: Fre. 1515

Set design for Robert Lepage's *Geometry of Miracles*. Canada: Quebec, PQ. 1998. Lang.: Eng. 1516

Josef Svoboda's set design for Goethe's *Faust*. Czech Republic: Prague. 1997. Lang.: Eng. 1517

The work of scene designer Libor Fára. Czech Republic: Prague. 1950-1981. Lang.: Cze. 1518

Reconstruction of a performance of *A Midsummer Night's Dream* designed by Galli-Bibiena. Germany: Bayreuth. 1997-1998. Lang.: Ger. 1521

An exhibition of sets by Caspar Neher for the plays of Bertolt Brecht. Germany: Berlin. 1998. Lang.: Eng. 1522

Scene design and the plays of Ostrovskij. Russia. 1998. Lang.: Rus. 1523

Technical designs for *The Chairs (Les Chaises)*, Théâtre de Complicité. UK-England: London. 1998. Lang.: Eng. 1524

Set and costume design for *The Spanish Tragedy* at RSC. UK-England: London. 1998. Lang.: Eng. 1525

Set design for Tennessee Williams' *Not About Nightingales* at the National. UK-England: London. 1998. Lang.: Eng. 1526

The original stage machinery designed by John White at Her Majesty's Theatre. UK-England: London. 1887-1986. Lang.: Eng. 1528

A stage design for Jean Giraudoux's *Ondine*. USA. 1987. Lang.: Eng. 1529

Scene designer James Noone's work at Playwrights Horizons. USA: New York, NY. 1986-1998. Lang.: Eng. 1531

Set design for Joseph Chaikin's production of two one-acts by Arthur Miller. USA: New york, NY. 1998. Lang.: Eng. 1532

Set design for *Gun Shy* by Richard Dresser at Playwrights Horizons. USA: New York, NY. 1998. Lang.: Eng. 1535

Set designs by Santo Loquasto at Manhattan Theatre Club. USA: New York, NY. 1998. Lang.: Eng. 1536

Derek McLane's set designs for recent Off Broadway productions. USA: New York, NY. 1998. Lang.: Eng. 1538

Technical designs for Off Broadway Shakespearean productions. USA: New York, NY. 1998. Lang.: Eng. 1539

Set designs of Francis O'Connor. USA: New York, NY. 1998. Lang.: Eng. 1541

Michael McGarty's set design for Elaine May and Alan Arkin's *Power Plays*. USA: New York, NY. 1998. Lang.: Eng. 1542

Set designer Karen TenEyck. USA. 1998. Lang.: Eng. 1550

Set design for Chain Lightning Theatre's production of *Beyond the Horizon* by Eugene O'Neill. USA: New York, NY. 1998. Lang.: Eng. 1551

Karen TenEyck's projections for a site-specific production of Shakespeare's *Julius Caesar*. USA: Los Angeles, CA. 1998. Lang.: Eng. 1552

Design concept for Amy Freed's *The Psychic Life of Savages*, Wilma Theatre. USA: Philadelphia, PA. 1998. Lang.: Eng. 1555

The design concept for Nicholas Hytner's production of Shakespeare's *Twelfth Night*. USA: New York, NY. 1998. Lang.: Eng. 1556

Set design for a University of Michigan production of *Henry V*. USA: Ann Arbor, MI. 1998. Lang.: Eng. 1557

Technical designs for *Griller* by Eric Bogosian. USA: Chicago, IL. 1998. Lang.: Eng. 1558

Set and lighting designs for *The Taming of the Shrew*, American Repertory Theatre. USA: Cambridge, MA. 1998. Lang.: Eng. 1559

Dex Edwards' set design for *The Comedy of Errors*, Shakespeare Repertory Company. USA: Chicago, IL. 1998. Lang.: Eng. 1560

Scenery by Yevgenia Nayberg for Robert Cohen's *The Prince*. USA: Long Beach, CA. 1997. Lang.: Eng. 1561

Virtual reality technology for set design. USA: Lawrence, KS. 1997. Lang.: Eng. 1562

Design for Shakespeare's *A Midsummer Night's Dream*. USA. 1987. Lang.: Eng. 1563

Set design and lighting for a production of Ibsen's *Hedda Gabler*. USA: Louisville, KY. 1988. Lang.: Eng. 1564

Contemporary design and stage-painting techniques of the early twentieth century. USA. 1900-1998. Lang.: Eng. 1565

Technical designs for Stanley Tucci's film *The Impostors*. USA. 1998. Lang.: Eng. 3901

Film design work of Tony Walton. USA. 1965-1998. Lang.: Eng. 3902

Production design for the film *Lost in Space*. USA: Hollywood, CA. 1998. Lang.: Eng. 3904

Des McAnuff's design concept for his film *Cousin Bette*. USA: Hollywood, CA. 1998. Lang.: Eng. 3905

Matthew Maraffi, production for the film *Pi*. USA. 1998. Lang.: Eng. 3906

Production design for the film *The Avengers*. USA: Hollywood, CA. 1998. Lang.: Eng. 3907

Production design for Bill Condon's film *Gods and Monsters*. USA: Hollywood, CA. 1998. Lang.: Eng. 3908

Production design for Gary Ross's film *Pleasantville*. USA: Hollywood, CA. 1998. Lang.: Eng. 3909

Technical designs for the film *Titanic*. USA. 1997. Lang.: Eng. 3910

Scenery in Orson Welles' film adaptation of Shakespeare's *Macbeth*. USA. 1948. Lang.: Fre. 3920

Computer-aided design in TV production. USA: Hollywood, CA. 1998. Lang.: Eng. 4051

Design awards for the TV mini-series *Merlin*. USA: Pasadena, CA. 1998. Lang.: Eng. 4052

Profile of technicians for Grammy Awards television broadcast. USA: New York, NY. 1998. Lang.: Eng. 4056

Production design for rock group Genesis' European tour. Europe. 1998. Lang.: Eng. 4096

Tom Strahan, scenic designer for rock concerts and corporate events. USA: San Francisco, CA. 1976-1998. Lang.: Eng. 4100

Landmark Entertainment Group, specializing in theme-park design. USA: Hollywood, CA. 1970-1998. Lang.: Eng. 4110

Geraldo Andrew Vieira, carnival costumer and performer. Trinidad and Tobago. 1952-1996. Lang.: Eng. 4160

Scene designer Richard Hudson and his work on *Samson et Dalila* at the Metropolitan Opera. UK-England. USA. 1954-1998. Lang.: Eng. 4289

Technical effects control system used in a production of *Joe—The Musical* at Koninklijk Theater Carré. Netherlands: Amsterdam. 1998. Lang.: Eng. 4324

Technical designs for the musical *Doctor Doolittle* directed by Steven Pimlott. UK-England: London. 1998. Lang.: Eng. 4325

Technical designs for *The Scarlet Pimpernel* directed by Robert Longbottom. USA: New York, NY. 1998. Lang.: Eng. 4331

Neil Patel's scene design for *Mirette*, Goodspeed Opera House. USA: East Haddam, CT. 1998. Lang.: Eng. 4334

Technical designs for *Ragtime* at the Ford Center. USA: New York, NY. 1998. Lang.: Eng. 4338

Eugene Lee's set design for Frank Galati's production of *Ragtime*. USA. 1997-1998. Lang.: Eng. 4340

Design in contemporary opera performance. Canada: Toronto, ON. 1983-1998. Lang.: Eng. 4425

Opera scenographer Michael Levine. Canada: Toronto, ON. 1988-1998. Lang.: Eng. 4426

Maurice Sendak's set design for *Hänsel und Gretel*, Canadian Opera Company. Canada: Toronto, ON. 1998. Lang.: Eng. 4427

Geogre Tabori's production of Mozart's *Die Zauberflöte* in a circus ring. Germany: Berlin. 1998. Lang.: Ger. 4428

Herbert Wernicke's set and costume designs for his own production of Strauss's *Elektra*. Germany: Munich. 1998. Lang.: Eng. 4429

Scenery — cont'd

Robert Wilson and Vera Dobroschke's design for Brecht's *Ozeanflug*. Germany: Berlin. 1998. Lang.: Eng. 4430
Verdi's operas and the influence of La Fenice scene designer Giuseppe Bertoja. Italy: Venice. 1840-1870. Lang.: Eng. 4433
Stage machinery in *Il Rapimento di Cefalo* staged by Bernardo Buontalenti. Italy: Florence. 1600. Lang.: Eng. 4436
Scene designers of the Mamontovskaja Opera. Russia: Moscow. 1875-1925. Lang.: Rus. 4437
Scene designs for *Ruslan i Ljudmila* by V. Gartman. Russia: St. Petersburg. 1876. Lang.: Rus. 4438
Scenographer Lennart Mörk. Sweden: Stockholm. France: Paris. 1957-1998. Lang.: Swe. 4439
Set and costume design for *Patience and Sarah* at Lincoln Center. USA: New York, NY. 1998. Lang.: Eng. 4440
Scenographic concept for the *dramma per musica, Aeolus Appeased*. USA. 1988. Lang.: Eng. 4442
Set and costume design for San Francisco Opera productions. USA: San Francisco, CA. 1998. Lang.: Eng. 4443
Technical designs for *Tristan und Isolde* at Seattle Opera. USA: Seattle, WA. 1998. Lang.: Eng. 4444

Institutions
Interview with members of dance group Creative Independent Artists. UK-Scotland: Glasgow. 1996-1998. Lang.: Eng. 904

Performance spaces
The construction of a theatre for *Beauty and the Beast*. Germany: Stuttgart. 1997. Lang.: Ger. 444
The creation of a site-specific performance space for Sam Mendes' production of *Cabaret*. USA: New York, NY. 1998. Lang.: Eng. 4350
The influence of the Salle le Peletier on French grand opera. France: Paris. 1823-1873. Lang.: Eng. 4494
A modular stage used for touring by the Houston Grand Opera. USA: Houston, TX. 1998. Lang.: Eng. 4500

Performance/production
Renaissance ideas about classical Greek staging. Europe. 1400-1600. Lang.: Slo. 521
László Márkus, one-time director of the Budapest Opera House. Hungary. 1881-1948. Lang.: Hun. 540
The staging of *The King's Threshold* by W.B. Yeats. Ireland: Dublin. UK-England: London. 1903. Lang.: Eng. 2153
Actress E. Majorova and her husband, scenographer S. Šerstjuk. Russia: Moscow. 1998. Lang.: Rus. 2283
The 'scientific perspective' of director David Belasco. USA. 1882-1931. Lang.: Eng. 2741
The cultural background of eighteenth-century British pantomime. England. 1700-1800. Lang.: Eng. 4093
Slovene translation of Adolphe Appia on staging Wagner. Europe. 1892. Lang.: Slo. 4550
Opera director Robert Carson. Europe. 1989-1998. Lang.: Ger. 4558

Plays/librettos/scripts
Description of a Web site devoted to *Los espanñoles en Chile* by Francisco Ganzalez de Busto. Spain. 1665-1998. Lang.: Eng. 3366
Interview with Peter Minshall, creator of theatre pieces and carnival performances. Trinidad and Tobago: Port of Spain. 1974-1997. Lang.: Eng. 4172
The design and authorship of *The Essex House Masque*. England. 1621. Lang.: Eng. 4209

Training
The use of computer animation techniques in design training. USA: Athens, GA. 1988-1998. Lang.: Eng. 878

Ščepkin, Michajl Semėnovič
Performance/production
Serf actor Michajl Ščepkin. Russia: Samara. 1788-1863. Lang.: Rus. 2300

Schaaf, Johannes
Performance/production
Johannes Schaaf's production of *Otello* at Kungliga Operan. Sweden: Stockholm. 1998. Lang.: Swe. 4701

Schaffer, R. Murray
Design/technology
R. Murray Schaffer's environmental opera *The Princess of the Stars*. Canada. 1981-1997. Lang.: Eng. 4424

Schall, Ekkehard
Performance/production
Interview with actor Ekkehard Schall. Germany: Berlin. 1959-1998. Lang.: Ger. 1990

Schall, Johanna
Performance/production
Reviews of productions of plays by Brecht. Germany. 1998. Lang.: Ger. 1986
Interview with actor/director Johanna Schall. Germany, East. 1980-1995. Lang.: Eng. 2045

Schaubühne (Berlin)
Administration
Interview with Thomas Ostermeier, artistic director of Schaubühne. Germany: Berlin. 1996-1998. Lang.: Ger. 1386
Design/technology
Lighting in contemporary theatre. Germany. 1998. Lang.: Ger. 192
Institutions
The future of Schaubühne after the resignation of artistic director Andrea Breth. Germany: Berlin. 1997. Lang.: Ger. 1633
Performance/production
Political changes reflected in Berlin theatre productions. Germany: Berlin. 1998. Lang.: Ger. 1958

Schaubühne am Lehniner Platz (Berlin)
Performance/production
Klaus Michael Grüber's production of Goethe's *Iphigenia auf Tauris*. Germany: Berlin. 1998. Lang.: Swe. 1997
Klaus Michael Grüber's production of Goethe's *Iphigenia auf Tauris*. Germany: Berlin. 1998. Lang.: Ger. 2031
Theory/criticism
Critical response to Klaus Michael Grüber's production of Goethe's *Iphigenia auf Tauris*. Germany. 1998. Lang.: Ger. 3821

Schauburg (Munich)
Institutions
Profile of the children's theatre Schauburg, George Podt, artistic director. Germany: Munich. 1993-1998. Lang.: Ger. 1640
The new children's theatre at Schauburg. Germany: Munich. 1998. Lang.: Ger. 1657

Schauspiel (Essen)
Performance/production
Comparison of productions of *The Lisbon Traviata* by Terrence McNally. Germany: Berlin, Essen. 1998. Lang.: Ger. 2005

Schauspiel (Leipzig)
Audience
The relationship between theatres and the youth audience. Germany. 1998. Lang.: Ger. 152
Institutions
Schauspiel Leipzig under the direction of Wolfgang Engel. Germany: Leipzig. 1996-1998. Lang.: Ger. 1638
Contemporary drama at Schauspiel Leipzig. Germany: Leipzig. 1998. Lang.: Ger. 1661
Performance/production
German productions of contemporary Russian drama. Germany. 1998. Lang.: Ger. 1984
Recent productions of Schauspiel Leipzig. Germany: Leipzig. 1997-1998. Lang.: Ger. 2011
German productions of Shakespeare. Germany: Leipzig, Hamburg, Berlin. 1998. Lang.: Ger. 2033

Schauspiel (Wuppertal)
Performance/production
Reviews of German Shakespearean productions. Germany: Wuppertal, Cologne, Oberhausen. 1998. Lang.: Ger. 2017
Relation to other fields
Revivals of Hanns Johst's national socialist play *Schlageter*. Germany: Uelzen, Wuppertal. 1977-1992. Lang.: Ger. 3770

Schauspielhaus (Bonn)
Performance/production
Productions of Tankred Dorst's *Was sollen wir tun (What Shall We Do)*. Germany: Dresden, Bonn. 1997-1998. Lang.: Ger. 1971
Productions of director Peter Wittenberg. Germany: Munich, Bonn. 1998. Lang.: Ger. 2013
Plays/librettos/scripts
Analysis of plays by Sarah Kane and David Harrower, recently produced in Germany. UK-England. Germany: Cologne, Bonn. 1998. Lang.: Ger. 3487

Schauspielhaus (Hannover)
Institutions
New plays by Dea Loher at Staatsschauspiel Hannover. Germany: Hannover. 1992-1998. Lang.: Ger. 1643
Plays/librettos/scripts
The language of Dea Loher's *Tätowierung (Tattoo)*. Germany. 1995-1998. Lang.: Ger. 3126
The collaboration of playwright Dea Loher and director Andreas Kriegenburg. Germany: Hannover, Munich. 1990-1998. Lang.: Ger. 3151

Schauspielhaus (Leipzig)
Performance/production
The performance of Shakespeare in the former East Germany. Germany: Rostock, Leipzig, Berlin, Dessau. 1996-1997. Lang.: Ger. 1974

Schauspielhaus Köln (Cologne)
Performance/production
Shakespeare performance on the Rhine and the Ruhr. Germany: Cologne, Bochum, Düsseldorf. 1996-1997. Lang.: Ger. 1962
Reviews of German Shakespearean productions. Germany: Wuppertal, Cologne, Oberhausen. 1998. Lang.: Ger. 2017
Plays/librettos/scripts
Analysis of plays by Sarah Kane and David Harrower, recently produced in Germany. UK-England. Germany: Cologne, Bonn. 1998. Lang.: Ger. 3487

Schechner, Richard
Performance/production
The influence of experimental performance on contemporary drama. Europe. USA. 1960-1987. Lang.: Eng. 526
The ideological system of theatre artist Richard Schechner. USA. 1965-1997. Lang.: Eng. 640
Interview with director Richard Schechner. USA. 1987. Lang.: Eng. 4260
Theory/criticism
The theatrical structure of autonomous theatre. USA. 1967-1979. Lang.: Eng. 867

Schede, Wolfgang Martin
Performance/production
Performer, director, and artist Wolfgang Martin Schede. Germany. 1898-1975. Lang.: Ger. 929

Scheffer, Will
Basic theatrical documents
Text of three monologues by Will Scheffer. USA. 1997. Lang.: Eng. 1509

Schéhadé, Georges
Plays/librettos/scripts
The journey in plays of Georges Schéhadé. Lebanon. 1940-1989. Lang.: Fre. 3268

Schein trügt, Der (Appearances Are Deceiving)
Institutions
The aesthetic perspectives of the ensemble at Münchner Kammerspiele. Germany: Munich. 1997-1998. Lang.: Ger. 1666

Schein, Hermann
Institutions
The current state of Theater Bielefeld. Germany: Bielefeld. 1998. Lang.: Ger. 1621

Schelm von Bergen, Der (Wag from Bergen, The)
Plays/librettos/scripts
Analysis of plays by Carl Zuckmayer. Austria: Vienna. 1925-1938. Lang.: Ger. 2785

Schenfeld, Rina
Performance/production
Contemporary Israeli dance. Israel. 1997. Lang.: Swe. 1117

Schenkar, Joan
Performance/production
Documentary theatre and the politics of representation. USA. 1966-1993. Lang.: Eng. 2728

Schiaccianoci, Lo (Nutcracker, The)
Performance/production
Amedeo Amodio's new choreography for Čajkovskij's *The Nutcracker*. Italy: Rome. 1998. Lang.: Hun. 1118

Schiemann, Helmut
Performance/production
Television adaptations of works by Goethe. Germany. 1965-1997. Lang.: Eng. 4061

Schiller, Friedrich von
Institutions
Productions of Staatstheater Stuttgart. Germany: Stuttgart. 1998. Lang.: Ger. 1620
Performance/production
French productions of German plays. France. 1998. Lang.: Ger. 1935
Productions of the Bad Hersfelder Festspiele. Germany: Bad Hersfeld. 1998. Lang.: Ger. 1991
A production of Schiller's *Die Räuber (The Robbers)* performed by prisoners. Germany: Berlin. 1997. Lang.: Ger. 2025
Collection of newspaper reviews by London theatre critics. UK-England: London. 1998. Lang.: Eng. 2488
Plays/librettos/scripts
Female sacrifice in eighteenth-century German drama. Germany. 1772-1781. Lang.: Eng. 3167
Representation of the virginal body on the German stage. Germany. 1600-1800. Lang.: Ger. 3171

Schiller, Leon
Institutions
History of the Polish Theatre Association. Poland: Warsaw. 1918-1998. Lang.: Pol. 1692

Schiller, Robert
Design/technology
Scenic elements in *Titanic* by street theatre group Theater Titanick. Germany: Münster, Leipzig. Australia: Perth. 1998. Lang.: Eng. 191

Schillertheater (Wuppertal)
Performance/production
Comparison of productions of Brecht's *Die Massnahme (The Measures Taken)*. Germany: Berlin, Wuppertal. 1995-1998. Lang.: Ger. 1950

Schilling, Árpád
Institutions
Theatre critics' awards 97-98. Hungary. 1997-1998. Lang.: Hun. 355
Performance/production
Review of plays directed by Árpad Schilling. Hungary: Budapest. 1998. Lang.: Hun. 2085
Interview with directors János Szász and Árpád Schilling. Hungary. 1998. Lang.: Hun. 2129

Schirmer, Friedrich
Institutions
Interview with director and dramaturg of Staatstheater Stuttgart. Germany: Stuttgart. 1993-1998. Lang.: Ger. 1632

Schlageter
Relation to other fields
Revivals of Hanns Johst's national socialist play *Schlageter*. Germany: Uelzen, Wuppertal. 1977-1992. Lang.: Ger. 3770

Schleef, Einar
Institutions
Survey of the Theatertreffen festival. Germany: Berlin. 1998. Lang.: Swe. 1651
Performance/production
Analysis of *Sportstück (Sport Play)* by Elfriede Jelinek. Austria: Vienna. 1998. Lang.: Ger. 1818
Productions of the Bad Hersfelder Festspiele. Germany: Bad Hersfeld. 1998. Lang.: Ger. 1991
The work of director Einar Schleef. Germany: Düsseldorf. 1998. Lang.: Ger. 2026
Theatre, society, and directors Frank Castorf, Peter Stein, and Einar Schleef. Germany. 1998. Lang.: Ger. 2029
Premieres of plays on the Nazi theme. Germany: Darmstadt. Austria: Vienna. 1998. Lang.: Ger. 2030
Relation to other fields
The artist and the world in recent productions. Austria: Vienna. Germany. 1997-1998. Lang.: Ger. 3729
Current attitudes toward socialism, individualism, and metaphysics in German culture, including theatre. Germany: Berlin. 1989-1998. Lang.: Ger. 3766

Schlemmer, Oskar
Relation to other fields
Modern fictional characters through the lens of Mejerchol'd's biomechanics and Oskar Schlemmer's puppets. Europe. 1913-1930. Lang.: Ger. 729

Schlesinger, Sarah
Plays/librettos/scripts
Panel discussion on contemporary musical theatre. USA: New York, NY. 1998. Lang.: Eng. 4398

Schlingensief, Christoph
Performance/production
Christoph Schlingensief's project with the homeless at Deutsches Schauspielhaus. Germany: Hamburg. 1998. Lang.: Ger. 1961
Director and actor Christoph Schlingensief. Germany. 1993-1998. Lang.: Ger. 1988
Relation to other fields
The artist and the world in recent productions. Austria: Vienna. Germany. 1997-1998. Lang.: Ger. 3729

Schlömer, Joachim
Design/technology
Set and costume designer Frank Leimbach and his work with choreographers. Germany. 1991-1998. Lang.: Ger. 1247
Performance/production
Dance adaptations of Shakespeare's *Hamlet*. Germany: Bremen, Weimar. 1996-1997. Lang.: Ger. 930

Schlöttke, Sven
Administration
Interviews with German theatre and film directors. Germany. 1998. Lang.: Ger. 1385

Schlüter, Christian
Performance/production
Reviews of productions of plays by Brecht. Germany. 1998. Lang.: Ger. 1986
Schmid, Daniel
Performance/production
Evaluation of video performances of Donizetti's operas. Europe. USA. 1980-1998. Lang.: Eng. 4557
Schmidt, Dagmar
Institutions
The new children's theatre at Schauburg. Germany: Munich. 1998. Lang.: Ger. 1657
Schmidt, Douglas W.
Design/technology
Creativity and beauty in theatrical design. USA. 1998. Lang.: Eng. 322
Schmidt, Harvey
Design/technology
Neil Patel's scene design for *Mirette*, Goodspeed Opera House. USA: East Haddam, CT. 1998. Lang.: Eng. 4334
Schmidt, Paul
Performance/production
Interview with composer Paul Schmidt. USA: New Haven, CT. 1998. Lang.: Eng. 2660
Schmitt, Eric-Emmanuel
Theory/criticism
Analysis of plays by Eric-Emmanuel Schmitt. France. 1998. Lang.: Fin. 3819
Schneemann, Carolee
Performance/production
The work of some North American performance artists. USA. Canada. 1960-1988. Lang.: Eng. 4251
Interview with performance artist Carolee Schneemann. USA. 1964-1989. Lang.: Eng. 4257
Schnitzler, Arthur
Basic theatrical documents
Catalan translation of *Anatol* and *Anatols Grössenwahn (The Megalomania of Anatol)* by Arthur Schnitzler. Austria. 1889. Lang.: Cat. 1408
Performance/production
Productions of director Peter Wittenberg. Germany: Munich, Bonn. 1998. Lang.: Ger. 2013
Collection of newspaper reviews by London theatre critics. UK-England: London. 1998. Lang.: Eng. 2455
Schöbel, Manuel
Institutions
History of Carrousel Theater, formerly Theater der Freundschaft. Germany: Berlin. 1950-1998. Lang.: Ger. 1628
Profile of Nordhessisches Landestheater Marburg. Germany: Marburg. 1997-1998. Lang.: Ger. 1653
Schoenberg, Arnold
Performance/production
Arnold Schoenberg's refusal to complete Alban Berg's unfinished opera *Lulu*. Austria. 1935. Lang.: Fre. 4533
Arnold Schoenberg on composer Alexander Zemlinsky. Germany. 1921. Lang.: Fre. 4604
Schoenfeld, Gerald
Institutions
The twentieth anniversary of the Shubert archive newsletter *The Passing Show*. USA: New York, NY. 1949-1998. Lang.: Eng. 425
Schönberg, Claude-Michel
Performance/production
Collection of newspaper reviews by London theatre critics. UK-England: Leeds, Manchester. 1998. Lang.: Eng. 2559
Schöne und das Biest Theater, Die (Stuttgart)
Performance spaces
The construction of a theatre for *Beauty and the Beast*. Germany: Stuttgart. 1997. Lang.: Ger. 444
School for Scandal, The
Performance/production
Collection of newspaper reviews by London theatre critics. UK-England: Stratford. 1998. Lang.: Eng. 2529
Collection of newspaper reviews by London theatre critics. UK-England: London. 1998. Lang.: Eng. 2531
Theory/criticism
Contrasting reviews of Declan Donnellan's RSC production of *The School for Scandal*. UK-England: Stratford. 1998. Lang.: Eng. 3835
Schorer, Suki
Performance/production
Panel discussion on Balanchine's *Jewels*. USA: New York, NY. 1967. Lang.: Eng. 1188
Schottelius, Renate
Performance/production
Interview with choreographer Renate Schottelius. Germany. 1936-1998. Lang.: Ger. 934
Schreier, Dan Moses
Design/technology
Panel discussion of sound designers. USA. 1998. Lang.: Eng. 287
Sound design for *The Diary of Anne Frank* directed by James Lapine. USA: New York, NY. 1998. Lang.: Eng. 1553
Schreker, Franz
Performance/production
Composer Franz Schreker and his connection with Zemlinsky's *Der Zwerg*. Germany. 1908-1923. Lang.: Fre. 4094
Schrick, Egon
Performance/production
Performance artist Egon Schrick. Germany. 1976-1987. Lang.: Eng. 4241
Schroeter, Werner
Performance/production
Productions of Wagner's *Tristan und Isolde* by Peter Konwitschny and Werner Schroeter. Germany: Munich, Duisberg. 1998. Lang.: Ger. 4580
Schroth, Christoph
Institutions
The ninetieth anniversary of Staatstheater Cottbus. Germany: Cottbus. 1908-1998. Lang.: Ger. 1645
Performance spaces
The ninetieth anniversary of the Cottbus theatre building. Germany: Cottbus. 1908-1998. Lang.: Ger. 440
Performance/production
Actor Oliver Bässler. Germany: Cottbus. 1985-1998. Lang.: Ger. 1995
Interview with director Christoph Schroth. Germany, East. 1970-1990. Lang.: Eng. 2035
Schroth, Peter
Performance/production
German directors about the meaning of Brecht today. Germany. 1998. Lang.: Ger. 1948
Plays/librettos/scripts
Recent German productions of Brecht's plays. Germany. 1998. Lang.: Ger. 3150
Schubert, Franz
Performance/production
Interview with singer Mikael Samuelsson. Sweden. 1960-1998. Lang.: Swe. 4698
Plays/librettos/scripts
Analysis of Schubert's unperformed opera *Fierrabras*. Austria. 1823. Lang.: Eng. 4759
Schubert, Lia
Institutions
Interview with dance teacher Lia Schubert. Sweden: Stockholm, Gothenburg. 1935-1998. Lang.: Swe. 900
Training
Memoirs of dance teacher Lia Schubert. Sweden: Malmö, Stockholm, Gothenburg. 1950-1998. Lang.: Swe. 1021
Schuler, Duane
Design/technology
Lighting design for Čajkovskij's *Sneguročka (The Snow Maiden)* at Houston Ballet. USA: Houston, TX. 1998. Lang.: Eng. 1035
Schulze, Ingo
Institutions
Schauspiel Leipzig under the direction of Wolfgang Engel. Germany: Leipzig. 1996-1998. Lang.: Ger. 1638
Schuman, William
Performance/production
William Schuman on the differences between operatic and Broadway theatre singing. USA. 1998. Lang.: Eng. 4303
Schumann, Cal
Performance/production
Obituary for TV puppeteer Cal Schumann. USA. 1930-1998. Lang.: Eng. 4907
Schumann, Peter
Institutions
Profile of the Bread and Puppet Theatre. USA: Plainfield, VT. 1963-1998. Lang.: Hun. 4877
Schumann, Robert
Performance/production
Recordings of *Lieder* by Schumann. Germany. UK-England. 1998. Lang.: Eng. 4601
Schuster, Robert
Institutions
Director training at Ernst-Busch-Schule and some of its graduates. Germany: Berlin. 1972-1998. Lang.: Ger. 1648

Schuster, Robert — cont'd

Performance/production
Comparison of productions of Brecht's *Die Massnahme (The Measures Taken)*. Germany: Berlin, Wuppertal. 1995-1998. Lang.: Ger. 1950
Productions directed by Christian Stückl, Tom Kühnel, and Robert Schuster. Germany: Frankfurt. 1997-1998. Lang.: Ger. 1969

Schwab, Norman
Design/technology
Flexible lighting design for two-band tour by Norman Schwab and Alan Parker. USA. 1998. Lang.: Eng. 4099

Schwajda, György
Performance/production
Review of Shakespeare's *The Merchant of Venice*, Szigligeti Theatre. Hungary: Szolnok. 1997. Lang.: Hun. 2066

Schwärmer, Die (Enthusiasts, The)
Plays/librettos/scripts
Robert Musil and the 'crisis of modern drama'. Europe. 1880-1930. Lang.: Eng. 3062

Schwartz, Arthur
Performance/production
Choreography in the musical film *The Bandwagon*. USA. 1953. Lang.: Eng. 982

Schwartz, Dorothy
Institutions
Profile of Birmingham Children's Theatre. USA: Birmingham, AL. 1947-1998. Lang.: Eng. 412

Schwartz, Malene
Administration
Interview with Malene Schwartz, manager of Aalborg Teater. Denmark: Aalborg. 1993-1998. Lang.: Dan. 5

Schwartz, Stephen
Performance/production
Collection of newspaper reviews by London theatre critics. UK-England: London. 1998. Lang.: Eng. 2492
Collection of newspaper reviews by London theatre critics. UK-England: London. 1998. Lang.: Eng. 2501

Schwartzman, John
Design/technology
Lighting design for Michael Bays' film *Armageddon*. USA. 1998. Lang.: Eng. 3916

Schwarz-Bart, Simone
Plays/librettos/scripts
Postcolonialism, ethnicity, and feminism in French and Caribbean plays. France. Martinique. Guadeloupe. 1960-1990. Lang.: Eng. 3104
Celebration and the body in plays of Ina Césaire and Simone Schwarz-Bart. Martinique. Guadeloupe. 1975-1998. Lang.: Eng. 3270

Schwarze Spinne, Die (Black Spider, The)
Performance/production
Volker Hesse's production of *Die schwarze Spinne (The Black Spider)* by Urs Widmer. Switzerland: Zurich. 1998. Lang.: Ger. 2402

Schwarzkopf, Elisabeth
Performance/production
Interview with singer Elisabeth Schwarzkopf. UK-England. Austria. 1950-1998. Lang.: Swe. 4860

Schweeger, Elisabeth
Institutions
Profile of new venue, Bayerisches Staatsschauspiel, Marstall. Germany: Munich. 1993-1998. Lang.: Ger. 1660

Schwejk im zweiten Weltkrieg (Schweik in the Second World War)
Performance/production
Erwin Piscator and Brecht's *Schwejk im zweiten Weltkrieg (Schweik in the Second World War)*. Germany: Berlin. 1928. Lang.: Ger. 1952

Scores
Basic theatrical documents
Score of Yu-Chun Kuo's concerto for dance and music, *Ring*. USA. 1988. Lang.: Eng. 887
James Rolfe on his opera *Beatrice Chancy*. Canada: Toronto, ON. 1998. Lang.: Eng. 4414

SCOT (Suzuki Company of Toga)
Performance/production
Tadashi Suzuki and Suzuki Company of Toga. Japan. 1939-1984. Lang.: Eng. 555

Scott, Michael
Performance/production
Collection of newspaper reviews by London theatre critics. UK-England: London. 1998. Lang.: Eng. 2458

Scottish National Players (Glasgow)
Institutions
History of the Scottish National Players. UK-Scotland. 1913-1934. Lang.: Eng. 1752

Scottish National Theatre Society (Glasgow)
Institutions
History of the Scottish National Players. UK-Scotland. 1913-1934. Lang.: Eng. 1752

Scottish Opera (Edinburgh)
Institutions
Brief history of the Scottish Opera. UK-Scotland: Edinburgh. 1963-1998. Lang.: Eng. 4480

Scraping the Surface
Performance/production
Productions of children's theatre festival. Canada: Montreal, PQ. 1998. Lang.: Fre. 503

Screen Actors Guild (USA)
Administration
The merger plan of the Screen Actors Guild and the American Federation of Television and Radio Artists. USA: New York, NY. 1998. Lang.: Eng. 102

Screenplays
Basic theatrical documents
Text of Simon Beaufoy's screenplay *The Full Monty*. UK-England. 1997. Lang.: Eng. 3879
Screenplay for *The Secret Cinema* by Paul Bartel. USA. 1966. Lang.: Eng. 3881
Screenplay of *Gods and Monsters* by Bill Condon. USA. 1998. Lang.: Eng. 3882
Screenplay of *The Lunch Date* by Adam Davidson. USA. 1998. Lang.: Eng. 3883
Screenplay of *Out of Sight* by Scott Frank. USA. 1998. Lang.: Eng. 3884
Screenplay for *Pickup on South Street* by Sam Fuller. USA. 1953. Lang.: Eng. 3885
Screenplay for *Shock Corridor* by Sam Fuller. USA. 1963. Lang.: Eng. 3886
Text of *The Black Doll* by Edward Gorey. USA. 1973. Lang.: Eng. 3887
Screenplay for *The First Wife*, based on a story by Colette. USA. 1998. Lang.: Eng. 3888
Screenplay of *Finished* by William E. Jones. USA. 1997. Lang.: Eng. 3889
The screenplay of *Living Out Loud* by Richard LaGravenese. USA. 1998. Lang.: Eng. 3890
Screenplay of *The Fishermen of Beaudrais* by Ring Lardner, Jr., and Dalton Trumbo. USA. 1943-1998. Lang.: Eng. 3891
Screenplay of *Eve's Bayou* by Kasi Lemmons. USA. 1994-1998. Lang.: Eng. 3892
Screenplay of the film *Slam*. USA. 1998. Lang.: Eng. 3893
Screenplay for *Weeds* by Alex Lewin, winner of annual student screenplay competition. USA. 1998. Lang.: Eng. 3894
Tod Lippy's unproduced screenplay *Jim & Wanda*. USA. 1996. Lang.: Eng. 3895
Text of *The Spanish Prisoner* by David Mamet. USA. 1998. Lang.: Eng. 3896
Screenplay of *The Last Picture Show* by Larry McMurtry and Peter Bogdanovich. USA. 1971. Lang.: Eng. 3897
Text of *Young Frankenstein* by Gene Wilder and Mel Brooks. USA. 1974. Lang.: Eng. 3898

Scrivenor, Alex
Performance/production
Collection of newspaper reviews by London theatre critics. UK-England: London. 1998. Lang.: Eng. 2566

Se questo è un uomo (If This Is a Man)
Performance/production
Gianfranco De Bosio's production of *Se questo è un uomo (If This Is a Man)* by Primo Levi. Italy: Turin. 1963-1966. Lang.: Eng. 2168

Sea Urchins
Performance/production
Collection of newspaper reviews by London theatre critics. UK-England: London. 1998. Lang.: Eng. 2483

Seagull, The
SEE
Čajka.

Sealey, Jenny
Performance/production
Collection of newspaper reviews by London theatre critics. UK-England: London. 1998. Lang.: Eng. 2450
Collection of newspaper reviews by London theatre critics. UK-England: London. 1998. Lang.: Eng. 2477

Searle, Humphrey
Plays/librettos/scripts
Samuel Beckett's influence on composer Humphrey Searle. UK-England. 1945-1995. Lang.: Eng. 3509
Sears, Djanet
Plays/librettos/scripts
Director Djanet Sears and actor Alison Sealy Smith on all-Black theatre. Canada: Toronto, ON. 1998. Lang.: Eng. 2826
Seaside
Plays/librettos/scripts
Analysis of plays by Marguerite Duras and Marie Redonnet. France. 1977-1992. Lang.: Eng. 3071
Seattle Opera (Seattle, WA)
Design/technology
Technical designs for *Tristan und Isolde* at Seattle Opera. USA: Seattle, WA. 1998. Lang.: Eng. 4444
Seattle Repertory Playhouse (Seattle, WA)
Relation to other fields
The blacklisting of Burton and Florence Bean James, founders of Seattle Repertory Playhouse. USA: Seattle, WA. 1951. Lang.: Eng. 3784
Seattle Repertory Theatre (Seattle, WA)
Performance spaces
Seattle's new and renovated theatres. USA: Seattle, WA. 1998. Lang.: Eng. 475
Sebastian, Mitch
Performance/production
Collection of newspaper reviews by London theatre critics. UK-England: London. 1998. Lang.: Eng. 2501
Second City (Chicago, IL)
Administration
Equity agreement with Second City. USA: Chicago, IL, Detroit, MI. 1998. Lang.: Eng. 66
Second City (Detroit, MI)
Administration
Equity agreement with Second City. USA: Chicago, IL, Detroit, MI. 1998. Lang.: Eng. 66
Second Cosmic Hair Gallery, The
Performance/production
Collection of newspaper reviews by London theatre critics. UK-England: London. 1998. Lang.: Eng. 2419
Second Maiden's Tragedy, The
Plays/librettos/scripts
Female power and the emblem tradition in plays of Shakespeare and Middleton. England. 1604-1625. Lang.: Eng. 2913
Second Mrs. Tanqueray, The
Plays/librettos/scripts
Analysis of plays by Arthur Wing Pinero. UK-England. 1890-1910. Lang.: Eng. 3440
Second Shepherd's Play
SEE
Secundum Pastorum.
Second Stage (New York, NY)
Performance spaces
Theatre space and performance. USA: New York, NY. 1925-1985. Lang.: Eng. 464
Secret Cinema, The
Basic theatrical documents
Screenplay for *The Secret Cinema* by Paul Bartel. USA. 1966. Lang.: Eng. 3881
Secret of Shahrazad, The
Basic theatrical documents
English translation and analysis of two plays by Ali Ahmad Bakathir. Egypt. 1908-1969. Lang.: Eng. 1417
Secreto en la mujer, El (Woman's Secret, The)
Plays/librettos/scripts
Playwright Andrés de Claramonte. Spain. 1580-1626. Lang.: Eng. 3404
Sedgwick, Toby
Performance/production
Collection of newspaper reviews by London theatre critics. UK-England: London. 1998. Lang.: Eng. 2471
Sedler, Erich
Administration
Interviews with German theatre and film directors. Germany. 1998. Lang.: Ger. 1385
Seducció (Seduction)
Basic theatrical documents
Text of plays by Josep M. Muñoz Pujol. Spain-Catalonia. 1995. Lang.: Cat. 1466
See-Saw
Performance/production
Collection of newspaper reviews by London theatre critics. UK-England: London. 1998. Lang.: Eng. 2568
Seeking the Genesis
Plays/librettos/scripts
Interview with playwright Kia Corthon. USA. 1998. Lang.: Eng. 3696
Seelig, Natali
Performance/production
Natali Seelig, *Theater Heute*'s actress of the year. Germany: Munich. 1991-1998. Lang.: Ger. 1966
Seen within a Square
Performance/production
Premieres of choreographies by Danny Rosseel. Belgium: Antwerp. Netherlands: Amsterdam. 1998. Lang.: Hun. 1065
Seepage
Performance/production
Collection of newspaper reviews by London theatre critics. UK-England: London. 1998. Lang.: Eng. 2459
Sei personaggi in cerca d'autore (Six Characters in Search of an Author)
Performance/production
Jorge Lavelli's production of *Sei personaggi in cerca d'autore (Six Characters in Search of an Author)* by Pirandello. France: Paris. 1925-1998. Lang.: Ita. 1921
Seifert, Ilka
Administration
The effects of independent theatre in Berlin. Germany: Berlin. 1998. Lang.: Ger. 14
Seinen-za (Tokyo)
Performance/production
Seinen-za's performance at the Čechov festival. Russia: Moscow. 1998. Lang.: Rus. 2237
Seinfeld
Relation to other fields
Using *Seinfeld* to contrast New York and Los Angeles. USA. 1998. Lang.: Eng. 4082
Seize the Fire
Plays/librettos/scripts
Adaptations of Greek tragedy by contemporary Irish writers. Ireland. UK-Ireland. 1984-1998. Lang.: Eng. 3214
Sekhabi, Aubrey
Relation to other fields
Topics in post-apartheid South African literature and theatre. South Africa, Republic of. 1995-1998. Lang.: Eng. 764
Sel'vinskaja, Tatjana
Design/technology
Scenographer Tatjana Sel'vinskaja. Russia. 1998. Lang.: Rus. 216
Self Meant to Govern
Performance/production
The choreography of William Forsythe and the painting of Marcel Duchamp. Germany. France. 1915-1998. Lang.: Eng. 1280
Sellars, Peter
Performance/production
Collection of newspaper reviews by London theatre critics. UK-England: London. 1998. Lang.: Eng. 2503
Interview with director Peter Sellars. USA: Cambridge, MA. 1980-1981. Lang.: Eng. 2661
Opera productions of the Salzburg Festival. Austria: Salzburg. 1998. Lang.: Hun. 4531
Interview with director Peter Sellars. USA. 1990-1998. Lang.: Ger, Fre, Dut, Eng. 4727
Sembéne, Ousmane
Plays/librettos/scripts
Ousmane Sembéne's film adaptation of his own novel *Xala*. Senegal. 1973-1974. Lang.: Eng. 3977
Sembrich, Marcella
Performance/production
Soprano Marcella Sembrich's performances at the Metropolitan Opera. USA: New York, NY. 1883-1909. Lang.: Eng. 4724
Semiotics
Audience
Theatrical production and reception. Canada. 1988. Lang.: Eng. 146
Performance/production
Empathy and distancing in theatre education. Europe. 1998. Lang.: Fin. 523
Representation of the historical past on the French stage. France. 1810-1820. Lang.: Eng. 527
Semiotic analysis of Jarry's *Ubu Roi* as staged by Vitez. France: Paris. 1985. Lang.: Eng. 528
The semiotics of antebellum home tours. USA. 1985-1997. Lang.: Eng. 624

Semiotics — cont'd

Semiotic analysis of the nature of theatrical directing. USA. 1988. Lang.: Eng. 650
Semiotic analysis of Peter Hall's National Theatre production of Shakespeare's *Coriolanus*. UK-England. 1985. Lang.: Eng. 2647
Semiotic analysis of ventriloquism. USA. 1998. Lang.: Eng. 4136
Research/historiography
Research on dance and cultural studies. North America. Europe. 1998. Lang.: Eng. 1003
Theory/criticism
Dramatic discourse as a speech act. 1998. Lang.: Eng. 832
Semiotic analysis of theatre by the Prague School. Czechoslovakia. 1925-1930. Lang.: Eng. 837
Transcript of a lecture on language and gesture. Hungary. 1997. Lang.: Hun. 845
Essay on theatre and reception theory. Poland. 1998. Lang.: Pol. 856
Hungarian translation of Pëtr Bogatyrëv's essay on the costume as sign. USSR. 1893-1971. Lang.: Hun. 871
The use of different analytical strategies to obtain multiple readings of dance performance. USA. Europe. 1946-1982. Lang.: Eng. 1200
Analysis of staging as the rhetorical elocution of directorial interpretation. 1998. Lang.: Fre. 3805
Method for the analysis of space. Canada. 1998. Lang.: Fre. 3808

Semiramide
Basic theatrical documents
Gaetano Rossini's libretto for Gioacchino Rossini's *Semiramide*. Italy. 1823. Lang.: Fre, Ita. 4421
Performance/production
Video recordings of Rossini's *Semiramide*. 1980-1991. Lang.: Fre. 4503
Recordings of Rossini's *Semiramide*. 1962-1992. Lang.: Fre. 4504
Performances of Rossini's *Semiramide*. 1823-1998. Lang.: Fre. 4517
Plays/librettos/scripts
Voltaire's *Sémiramis*, source of Rossini's *Semiramide*. France. 1748. Lang.: Fre. 3096
The writing and first performances of Voltaire's *Sémiramis*, the source of Rossini's opera *Semiramide*. France. 1746-1748. Lang.: Fre. 3114
Background information on the title character of Rossini's opera *Semiramide*. Italy. 1823. Lang.: Fre. 4810

Sémiramis
Plays/librettos/scripts
Voltaire's *Sémiramis*, source of Rossini's *Semiramide*. France. 1748. Lang.: Fre. 3096
The writing and first performances of Voltaire's *Sémiramis*, the source of Rossini's opera *Semiramide*. France. 1746-1748. Lang.: Fre. 3114

Semper Court Theatre
SEE
Dresdner Hoftheater.

Semper Opera
SEE
Dresdner Hoftheater.

Sempronio
SEE
Artis, Avelli.

Sendak, Maurice
Design/technology
Maurice Sendak's set design for *Hänsel und Gretel*, Canadian Opera Company. Canada: Toronto, ON. 1998. Lang.: Eng. 4427

Seneca, Lucius Annaeus
Performance/production
The performance of Senecan tragedy. Roman Empire. 4 B.C.-150 A.D. Lang.: Eng. 2227
Plays/librettos/scripts
The character Medea in European drama. Europe. 450 B.C.-1998 A.D. Lang.: Ger. 3063
Analysis of Seneca's *Oedipus* and *Hercules furens*. Roman Empire. 4 B. C.-65 A.D. Lang.: Eng. 3313

Señora Carrar's Rifles
SEE
Gewehre der Frau Carrar, Die.

Señora en su balcón, La (Lady on the Balcony, The)
Plays/librettos/scripts
Cruelty and the absurd in theatre of Latin American playwrights. Latin America. 1960-1980. Lang.: Eng. 3267

Sentence, La (Sentence, The)
Plays/librettos/scripts
The Holocaust in plays of Charlotte Delbo. France. 1913-1985. Lang.: Eng. 3115

Sept Branches de la rivière Ota, Les (Seven Streams of the River Ota, The)
Plays/librettos/scripts
Francis Leclerc's video adaptation of *Les Sept Branches de la Rivière Ota (The Seven Streams of the River Ota)* by Robert Lepage. Canada. 1998. Lang.: Fre. 4074

Sequentia (Cologne)
Performance/production
Sequentia's new recording of *Ordo Virtutum* by Hildegard of Bingen. Germany. 1997. Lang.: Eng. 4294

Serban, Andrei
Design/technology
Set and lighting designs for *The Taming of the Shrew*, American Repertory Theatre. USA: Cambridge, MA. 1998. Lang.: Eng. 1559
Performance/production
Musical performances on and off Broadway. USA: New York. 1998. Lang.: Ger. 4383

Seregi, László
Performance/production
Interview with ballerina Katalin Hágai. Hungary. 1961-1998. Lang.: Hun. 1096
Choreographer László Seregi. Hungary: Budapest. 1949-1998. Lang.: Hun. 1100
Bartók's *A fából faragott királyfi (The Wooden Prince)* choreographed by László Seregi. Hungary: Budapest. 1998. Lang.: Hun. 1103

Seren, Phil
Performance/production
Collection of newspaper reviews by London theatre critics. UK-England: London. 1998. Lang.: Eng. 2539

Serenade
Performance/production
Review of one-act ballets by Balanchine. Hungary: Budapest. 1997. Lang.: Hun. 1105

Sergejév, Konstantin M.
Performance/production
I. Igin's *Czars*, a biography of dancers Konstantin Sergejév and Natalija Dudinskaja. Russia: Leningrad. 1940. Lang.: Rus. 1138

Serious Money
Performance/production
Collection of newspaper reviews by London theatre critics. UK-England: London. 1998. Lang.: Eng. 2462

Sermon, Paul
Performance/production
Dancer Susan Kozel on performing in Paul Sermon's *Telematic Dreaming*. Netherlands: Amsterdam. 1997. Lang.: Eng. 956

Serov, Aleksand'r
Performance/production
Opera singer Aleksand'r Serov. Russia. 1820-1871. Lang.: Rus. 4673

Šerstjuk, S.
Performance/production
Actress E. Majorova and her husband, scenographer S. Šerstjuk. Russia: Moscow. 1998. Lang.: Rus. 2283

Sesame Street
Performance/production
The influence of *Sesame Street*. USA. 1968-1998. Lang.: Eng. 4923

Šestakov, Vladimir
Design/technology
Scene design and the plays of Ostrovskij. Russia. 1998. Lang.: Rus. 1523

Sete cabras (Seven Goats)
Plays/librettos/scripts
Playwright Nelson Rodrigues. Brazil. 1912. Lang.: Rus. 2791

Seven Sacraments
Performance/production
Collection of newspaper reviews by London theatre critics. UK-England: London. 1998. Lang.: Eng. 2500

Sévigné, Madame de
Performance/production
Parisian theatre in the letters of Mme. de Sévigné. France: Paris. 1671-1694. Lang.: Pol. 534

Sex Is My Religion
Plays/librettos/scripts
Review of collections of plays with gay themes. Canada. 1996. Lang.: Eng. 2802

sex, lies, and videotape
Plays/librettos/scripts
Analysis of Steven Soderbergh's film *sex, lies, and videotape*. USA. 1989. Lang.: Eng. 4028

Sexual Life of a Camel, The
Performance/production
Collection of newspaper reviews by London theatre critics. UK-England: London. 1998. Lang.: Eng. 2412

Sexual Perversity in Chicago
Performance/production
Collection of newspaper reviews by London theatre critics. UK-England: London. 1998. Lang.: Eng. 2430
Plays/librettos/scripts
Analysis of films of David Mamet. USA: Los Angeles, CA. 1980-1998. Lang.: Eng. 4006
Sexy Girls, The
Relation to other fields
Topics in post-apartheid South African literature and theatre. South Africa, Republic of. 1995-1998. Lang.: Eng. 764
Seyf, Mehrdad
Performance/production
Collection of newspaper reviews by London theatre critics. UK-England: London. 1998. Lang.: Eng. 2582
Sezon Gekijo (Tokyo)
Performance/production
The performance of *onnagata* Tamasaburō in *Elizabeth* by Francisco Ors. Japan: Tokyo. 1993-1995. Lang.: Eng. 1362
Sforim, Mendele Mojcher
Plays/librettos/scripts
Enlightenment influences on modern Jewish theatre. Poland. 1500-1914. Lang.: Pol. 3307
Shadow of the Glen, The
Performance/production
Collection of newspaper reviews by London theatre critics. UK-England: London. 1998. Lang.: Eng. 2551
Shadow puppets
SEE ALSO
Classed Entries under PUPPETRY—Shadow puppets.
Performance/production
Preview of the Puppeteers of America Festival. USA: Seattle, WA. 1999. Lang.: Eng. 4905
Shadowboxing
Performance/production
Collection of newspaper reviews by London theatre critics. UK-England: London. 1998. Lang.: Eng. 2579
Shadowlands
Performance/production
Collection of newspaper reviews by London theatre critics. UK-England: London. 1998. Lang.: Eng. 2586
Plays/librettos/scripts
Richard Attenborough's film adaptation of *Shadowlands* by William Nicholson. UK-England. 1993. Lang.: Eng. 3985
Shaffer, Peter
Performance/production
Director Armin Petras. Germany: Nordhausen. 1970-1998. Lang.: Ger. 2001
Collection of newspaper reviews by London theatre critics. UK-England: London. 1998. Lang.: Eng. 2463
Collection of newspaper reviews by London theatre critics. UK-England: London. 1998. Lang.: Eng. 2528
Plays/librettos/scripts
A method of analysis for the drama. USA. 1920-1975. Lang.: Eng. 3537
Theatrical ritual in plays of Peter Shaffer. USA. 1975-1985. Lang.: Eng. 3707
Shaftesbury Theatre (London)
Performance/production
Collection of newspaper reviews by London theatre critics. UK-England: London. 1998. Lang.: Eng. 2561
Shakespeare Festival of Dallas (Dallas, TX)
Institutions
The management of the Shakespeare Festival of Dallas. USA: Dallas, TX. 1972-1988. Lang.: Eng. 393
Shakespeare Repertory Company (Chicago, IL)
Design/technology
Dex Edwards' set design for *The Comedy of Errors*, Shakespeare Repertory Company. USA: Chicago, IL. 1998. Lang.: Eng. 1560
Shakespeare Repertory Theatre (Chicago, IL)
Performance/production
Hamlet at Shakespeare Repertory Theatre, directed by Barbara Gaines. USA: Chicago, IL. 1996. Lang.: Eng. 2666
Shakespeare Theatre (Washington, DC)
Institutions
The role of private community organizations in the restructuring of the Folger Shakespeare Theatre. USA: Washington, DC. 1985-1987. Lang.: Eng. 1771
Performance/production
Comparison of productions of Ibsen's *Peer Gynt*. USA: Providence, RI, New York, NY, Washington, DC, Nacogdoches, TX. 1998. Lang.: Eng. 2711
Interview with actor Patrick Stewart. USA: Washington, DC. 1998. Lang.: Eng. 2760
Shakespeare-királydrámák (Kings and Queens)
Performance/production
Performances at the new Bárka Színház. Hungary: Budapest. 1997. Lang.: Hun. 2097
Shakespeare, William
Administration
Theater Basel under the direction of Stefan Bachmann. Switzerland: Basel. 1996-1998. Lang.: Ger. 1391
Basic theatrical documents
English translation of *Kanadehon Hamlet* by Harue Tsutsumi. Japan. 1997. Lang.: Eng. 1360
French translation of Shakespeare's *Love's Labour's Lost*. England. France. 1594-1998. Lang.: Fre. 1419
Catalan translation of Shakespeare's *Measure for Measure*. England. 1604. Lang.: Cat. 1420
Catalan translation of Shakespeare's *Romeo and Juliet*. England. 1591. Lang.: Cat. 1421
Catalan translation of Shakespeare's *A Midsummer Night's Dream*. England. 1595. Lang.: Cat. 1422
Design/technology
Costume designer Isabelle Larivière. Canada: Quebec, PQ. 1994-1995. Lang.: Fre. 1514
Reconstruction of a performance of *A Midsummer Night's Dream* designed by Galli-Bibiena. Germany: Bayreuth. 1997-1998. Lang.: Ger. 1521
Technical designs for Off Broadway Shakespearean productions. USA: New York, NY. 1998. Lang.: Eng. 1539
Costume designs for Oregon Shakespeare Festival productions. USA: Ashland, OR. 1998. Lang.: Eng. 1543
Lighting design for Shakespeare's *Twelfth Night* at the Vivian Beaumont. USA: New York, NY. 1998. Lang.: Eng. 1546
Karen TenEyck's projections for a site-specific production of Shakespeare's *Julius Caesar*. USA: Los Angeles, CA. 1998. Lang.: Eng. 1552
Lighting designer Hugh Vanstone. USA: New York, NY. 1998. Lang.: Eng. 1554
The design concept for Nicholas Hytner's production of Shakespeare's *Twelfth Night*. USA: New York, NY. 1998. Lang.: Eng. 1556
Set design for a University of Michigan production of *Henry V*. USA: Ann Arbor, MI. 1998. Lang.: Eng. 1557
Set and lighting designs for *The Taming of the Shrew*, American Repertory Theatre. USA: Cambridge, MA. 1998. Lang.: Eng. 1559
Dex Edwards' set design for *The Comedy of Errors*, Shakespeare Repertory Company. USA: Chicago, IL. 1998. Lang.: Eng. 1560
Design for Shakespeare's *A Midsummer Night's Dream*. USA. 1987. Lang.: Eng. 1563
Scenery in Orson Welles' film adaptation of Shakespeare's *Macbeth*. USA. 1948. Lang.: Fre. 3920
Institutions
Productions by Stefan Bachmann and Robert Wilson at the Salzburg Festival. Austria: Salzburg. 1998. Lang.: Hun. 1570
Productions of Salzburger Festspiele. Austria: Salzburg. 1998. Lang.: Ger. 1571
Shakespearean productions at the Carrefour international theatre festival. Canada: Quebec, PQ. 1998. Lang.: Fre. 1588
Profile of Teatro Buendía. Cuba: Havana. 1986-1998. Lang.: Ger. 1596
Economic history of the Chamberlain's Men/King's Men. England. 1599-1642. Lang.: Eng. 1598
The evolution of Shakespeare festivals. Europe. USA. 1950-1997. Lang.: Eng. 1601
Reviews of some productions at the Avignon Festival. France: Avignon. 1998. Lang.: Hun. 1615
Profile of Württembergische Landesbühne. Germany: Esslingen. 1996-1997. Lang.: Ger. 1639
Carlo Quartucci's acting workshop on Shakespeare's *Macbeth*. Italy: Rome. 1991-1992. Lang.: Ita. 1674
The inaugural season of Shakespeare's Globe Theatre. UK-England: London. 1997-1998. Lang.: Eng. 1741
Federal Theatre Project Shakespearean productions. USA. 1935-1939. Lang.: Eng. 1761
Plays of 1998 Oregon Shakespeare Festival. USA: Ashland, OR. 1998. Lang.: Eng. 1783

Shakespeare, William — cont'd

Profile of Alabama Shakespeare Festival. USA: Montgomery, AL. 1972-1998. Lang.: Eng. 1784

Performance spaces

The newly reopened Shakespeare's Globe Theatre. UK-England: London. 1997. Lang.: Eng. 461

Shakespeare's Globe and the staging of *The Merchant of Venice*. UK-England: London. 1998. Lang.: Ger. 1810

Performance/production

The Stratford Festival production of Shakespeare's *King Lear*. Canada: Stratford, ON. 1964. Lang.: Eng. 506

Dance adaptations of Shakespeare's *Hamlet*. Germany: Bremen, Weimar. 1996-1997. Lang.: Ger. 930

Interview with ballerina Katalin Hágai. Hungary. 1961-1998. Lang.: Hun. 1096

Shakespeare and traditional Asian theatrical forms. China, People's Republic of. India. Japan. 1981-1997. Lang.: Eng. 1346

Women's roles in Shakespeare. 1600-1998. Lang.: Ger. 1813

List of French-language productions of Shakespeare. Canada: Montreal, PQ, Quebec, PQ. 1945-1998. Lang.: Fre. 1841

Interview with actor William Hutt. Canada: Stratford, ON. 1962-1996. Lang.: Eng. 1844

The methodology of director Robert Lepage. Canada: Toronto, ON. 1992. Lang.: Eng. 1845

Canadian representations of Ophelia from Shakespeare's *Hamlet*. Canada. 1980-1997. Lang.: Eng. 1852

French Canadian translations/adaptations of Shakespeare. Canada: Montreal, PQ. 1988. Lang.: Fre. 1855

Robert Gurik's adaptation of Shakespeare's *Hamlet*. Canada: Montreal, PQ, London, ON. 1968. Lang.: Fre. 1866

Report on Chinese Shakespeare festival. China, People's Republic of: Beijing, Shanghai. 1986. Lang.: Eng. 1873

Performing the killing of Polonius in Shakespeare's *Hamlet*. England. 1600-1601. Lang.: Eng. 1892

Shakespeare's *Titus Andronicus* and the political power of symbolic performance. England. 1590-1595. Lang.: Eng. 1893

Shakespeare's *The Tempest* on the eighteenth-century stage. England: London. 1701-1800. Lang.: Eng. 1895

Music for London Shakespearean productions. England: London. 1660-1830. Lang.: Eng. 1900

Shakespearean production and the theatrical portrait collection of the Garrick Club. England: London. 1702-1814. Lang.: Eng. 1903

Casting and performance in eighteenth-century productions of *Othello*. England. 1777-1800. Lang.: Eng. 1909

Shakespeare and postmodern production. Europe. North America. 1950-1998. Lang.: Eng. 1912

Director Jacques Copeau and his theatrical aesthetic. France. 1913-1920. Lang.: Eng. 1941

Shakespeare performance on the Rhine and the Ruhr. Germany: Cologne, Bochum, Düsseldorf. 1996-1997. Lang.: Ger. 1962

The performance of Shakespeare in the former East Germany. Germany: Rostock, Leipzig, Berlin, Dessau. 1996-1997. Lang.: Ger. 1974

Comparison of two productions of Shakespeare's *Richard III*. Germany: Munich. 1996-1997. Lang.: Ger. 1976

Shakespearean productions in northern Germany. Germany: Hamburg. 1996-1997. Lang.: Ger. 1978

Productions of the Bad Hersfelder Festspiele. Germany: Bad Hersfeld. 1998. Lang.: Ger. 1991

Reviews of German Shakespearean productions. Germany: Wuppertal, Cologne, Oberhausen. 1998. Lang.: Ger. 2017

Productions of plays by Shakespeare, Brecht, and Camus. Germany. 1998. Lang.: Ger. 2032

German productions of Shakespeare. Germany: Leipzig, Hamburg, Berlin. 1998. Lang.: Ger. 2033

Interview with director Christoph Schroth. Germany, East. 1970-1990. Lang.: Eng. 2035

Interview with director Adolf Dresen. Germany, East. 1965-1985. Lang.: Eng. 2036

Interview with director Alexander Lang. Germany, East. 1970-1990. Lang.: Eng. 2037

Interview with director Thomas Langhoff. Germany, East. 1970-1990. Lang.: Eng. 2038

Interview with playwright Heiner Müller about his adaptations of Shakespeare. Germany, East. 1965-1990. Lang.: Eng. 2039

Shakespeare in the GDR: producer and critic B.K. Tragelehn. Germany, East. 1950-1990. Lang.: Eng. 2040

Interview with director Frank Castorf. Germany, East. 1980-1990. Lang.: Eng. 2041

Interview with director Alexander Weigel. Germany, East. 1970-1990. Lang.: Eng. 2042

Directors Manfred Wekwerth and Robert Weimann on Brecht and Shakespeare. Germany, East. 1945-1990. Lang.: Eng. 2043

Gender and Shakespearean production in the GDR. Germany, East. 1982-1990. Lang.: Eng. 2044

Interview with actor/director Johanna Schall. Germany, East. 1980-1995. Lang.: Eng. 2045

Actor/director Katja Paryla. Germany, East. 1975-1995. Lang.: Eng. 2046

Actor/director Ursula Karusseit. Germany, East. 1977-1995. Lang.: Eng. 2047

Socialism and the use of Shakespeare in the German Democratic Republic. Germany, East. 1945-1990. Lang.: Eng. 2048

Adaptations of Shakespeare in productions of Bertolt Brecht and Heiner Müller. Germany, East. 1945-1990. Lang.: Eng. 2049

National identity and Shakespearean production. Germany, East. 1945-1990. Lang.: Eng. 2050

Shakespearean production and the GDR's 'existential crisis'. Germany, East. 1976-1980. Lang.: Eng. 2051

The political and social climate of East German theatre in the sixties. Germany, East. 1960-1970. Lang.: Eng. 2052

Director Robert Weimann on East German Shakespeare production. Germany, East. 1945-1995. Lang.: Eng. 2053

Review of Shakespeare's *The Merchant of Venice*, Szigligeti Theatre. Hungary: Szolnok. 1997. Lang.: Hun. 2066

Two productions of Shakespeare's *Richard III* by József Ruszt. Hungary: Budapest. Hungary: Kecskemét. 1973-1997. Lang.: Hun. 2070

Review of Shakespeare's *Much Ado About Nothing*, Szeged National Theatre. Hungary: Szeged. 1997. Lang.: Hun. 2086

Csaba Kiss's adaptation of Shakespeare's chronicle plays at Bárka Színház. Hungary: Győr. 1997. Lang.: Hun. 2101

Round-table discussion on Tivoli Theatre's production of *The Merchant of Venice*. Hungary. 1986-1997. Lang.: Hun. 2109

Shakespeare's *The Merchant of Venice* directed by Róbert Alföldi. Hungary: Budapest. 1998. Lang.: Hun. 2111

István Verebes' production of Shakespeare's *Hamlet*. Hungary: Nyíregyháza. 1997. Lang.: Hun. 2116

Three Hungarian productions of Shakespeare's *Richard III*. Hungary: Budapest, Zsámbék, Szeged. 1997. Lang.: Hun. 2121

Events of the Zsámbék theatre festival. Hungary: Zsámbék. 1998. Lang.: Hun. 2126

Iraqi productions of Shakespeare. Iraq. 1880-1988. Lang.: Eng. 2152

Andrea Liberovici's production of *Sonetto. Un travestimento shakespeariano (Sonnet: A Shakespearean Travesty)* by Eduardo Sanguineti. Italy: Genoa. 1997. Lang.: Ita. 2159

The evolution of the contemporary Shakespearean director. North America. Europe. 1967-1998. Lang.: Eng. 2207

Speaking styles of selected actors reading Shakespeare's *Henry V*. North America. UK-England. 1998. Lang.: Eng. 2208

Report from Ibsen festival. Norway: Oslo. 1998. Lang.: Swe. 2211

Contemporary Polish productions of Shakespeare. Poland. 1990-1998. Lang.: Pol. 2213

Productions of plays by Brecht and Shakespeare at the Hungarian theatre of Satu Mare. Romania: Satu Mare. 1998. Lang.: Hun. 2228

Recent Russian productions of Shakespeare's *Hamlet*. Russia: Moscow. 1998. Lang.: Rus. 2268

Michajl Mokejėv's production of Shakespeare's *Romeo and Juliet*. Russia: Belgorod. 1998. Lang.: Rus. 2274

Productions of Shakespeare's *Twelfth Night* at the Madrid Theatre Festival. Spain: Madrid. 1996-1997. Lang.: Eng. 2359

Shakespeare's influence on Strindberg's modernism. Sweden. 1907-1910. Lang.: Eng. 2370

Kent Hägglund on his favorite role, Bottom in Shakespeare's *Midsummer Night's Dream*. Sweden. 1978-1998. Lang.: Swe. 2375

Shakespeare, William — cont'd

Shakespeare productions in German Switzerland. Switzerland: Basel, Zurich. 1996-1997. Lang.: Ger. 2398

Stefan Bachmann's production of Shakespeare's *Troilus and Cressida*. Switzerland: Basle. 1998. Lang.: Ger. 2399

Collection of newspaper reviews by London theatre critics. UK. 1998. Lang.: Eng. 2407

Collection of newspaper reviews by London theatre critics. UK-England: London. 1998. Lang.: Eng. 2413

Collection of newspaper reviews by London theatre critics. UK-England: London. 1998. Lang.: Eng. 2415

Collection of newspaper reviews by London theatre critics. UK-England: London. 1998. Lang.: Eng. 2418

Collection of newspaper reviews by London theatre critics. UK-England: Stratford. 1998. Lang.: Eng. 2431

Collection of newspaper reviews by London theatre critics. UK-England: London. 1998. Lang.: Eng. 2444

Collection of newspaper reviews by London theatre critics. UK-England: London. 1998. Lang.: Eng. 2466

Collection of newspaper reviews by London theatre critics. UK-England: London. 1998. Lang.: Eng. 2471

Collection of newspaper reviews by London theatre critics. UK-England: London. 1998. Lang.: Eng. 2472

Collection of newspaper reviews by London theatre critics. UK-England: London. 1998. Lang.: Eng. 2484

Collection of newspaper reviews by London theatre critics. UK-England. 1998. Lang.: Eng. 2485

Collection of newspaper reviews by London theatre critics. UK-England: London. 1998. Lang.: Eng. 2496

Collection of newspaper reviews by London theatre critics. UK-England: London. 1998. Lang.: Eng. 2498

Collection of newspaper reviews by London theatre critics. UK-England: London. 1998. Lang.: Eng. 2518

Collection of newspaper reviews by London theatre critics. UK-England: London. 1998. Lang.: Eng. 2523

Collection of newspaper reviews by London theatre critics. UK-England: Stratford, Birmingham. 1998. Lang.: Eng. 2536

Collection of newspaper reviews by London theatre critics. UK-England: London. 1998. Lang.: Eng. 2538

Collection of newspaper reviews by London theatre critics. UK-England: London. 1998. Lang.: Eng. 2551

Collection of newspaper reviews by London theatre critics. UK-England: London. 1998. Lang.: Eng. 2571

Collection of newspaper reviews by London theatre critics. UK-England: London. 1998. Lang.: Eng. 2572

Collection of newspaper reviews by London theatre critics. UK-England: London. 1998. Lang.: Eng. 2579

Collection of newspaper reviews by London theatre critics. UK-England: London. 1998. Lang.: Eng. 2583

Collection of newspaper reviews by London theatre critics. UK-England: London. 1998. Lang.: Eng. 2585

Collection of newspaper reviews by London theatre critics. UK-England: London. 1998. Lang.: Eng. 2587

Collection of newspaper reviews by London theatre critics. UK-England: London. 1998. Lang.: Eng. 2588

Susan Brown on her role in *Richard III* at RSC. UK-England: London, Stratford. 1995-1996. Lang.: Eng. 2593

The inaugural season of Shakespeare's Globe Theatre. UK-England: London. 1997. Lang.: Eng. 2601

Review of the opening season of Shakespeare's Globe Theatre. UK-England: London. 1997. Lang.: Eng. 2602

Experimental Shakespeare production at the Gaiety Theatre. UK-England: Manchester. 1908-1915. Lang.: Eng. 2605

Julian Glover on his performance in *Romeo and Juliet* for RSC. UK-England: London, Stratford. 1995-1996. Lang.: Eng. 2606

Interview with actress Fiona Shaw. UK-England. 1995-1997. Lang.: Eng. 2607

The evolution of the character Feste in productions of Shakespeare's *Twelfth Night*. UK-England. 1773-1988. Lang.: Eng. 2611

Three productions of Shakespeare's *Richard III*. UK-England. 1973-1984. Lang.: Eng. 2612

Derek Jacobi on playing Macbeth for the RSC. UK-England: London, Stratford. 1993-1994. Lang.: Eng. 2616

Paul Jesson's role in *Henry VIII* at RSC. UK-England: London, Stratford. 1996-1997. Lang.: Eng. 2617

Modernist and postmodernist Shakespearean production. UK-England. Canada. 1966-1996. Lang.: Eng. 2618

Jane Lapotaire on her performance in *Henry VIII* at RSC. UK-England: London, Stratford. 1996-1997. Lang.: Eng. 2619

Christopher Luscombe on acting in RSC productions. UK-England: London, Stratford. 1993-1994. Lang.: Eng. 2620

Richard Olivier's production of Shakespeare's *The Merchant of Venice*. UK-England: London. 1998. Lang.: Eng. 2621

Richard McCabe on his role in *The Winter's Tale* at RSC. UK-England: London, Stratford. 1992-1993. Lang.: Eng. 2623

The influence of collage on director Charles Marowitz. UK-England. USA. 1962-1979. Lang.: Eng. 2624

John Nettles on his role in an RSC production of *Julius Caesar*. UK-England: London, Stratford. 1995. Lang.: Eng. 2625

The change in Shakespearean production. UK-England. 1960-1980. Lang.: Eng. 2628

Report on several English performances. UK-England: London, Stratford. 1998. Lang.: Swe. 2634

Postmodern staging and design: Matthew Warchus' *Henry V*. UK-England. 1970-1994. Lang.: Eng. 2636

Michael Siberry on performing in an RSC production of *The Taming of the Shrew*. UK-England: London, Stratford. 1995-1996. Lang.:Eng. 2637

Royal Shakespeare Company actors on their performances as Shakespearean characters. UK-England: London, Stratford. 1992-1997. Lang.: Eng. 2638

David Tennant on his performance in *As You Like It* at RSC. UK-England: London, Stratford. 1996-1997. Lang.: Eng. 2640

David Troughton on playing Shakespeare's *Richard III*. UK-England: London, Stratford. 1995-1996. Lang.: Eng. 2642

Philip Voss on his role in *Coriolanus* at RSC. UK-England: London, Stratford. 1994. Lang.: Eng. 2643

Semiotic analysis of Peter Hall's National Theatre production of Shakespeare's *Coriolanus*. UK-England. 1985. Lang.: Eng. 2647

Shakespearean influence on the 1987 Edinburgh Festival. UK-Scotland: Edinburgh. 1997. Lang.: Eng. 2653

An approach to playing Malvolio in Shakespeare's *Twelfth Night*. USA. 1987. Lang.: Eng. 2659

Hamlet at Shakespeare Repertory Theatre, directed by Barbara Gaines. USA: Chicago, IL. 1996. Lang.: Eng. 2666

Using Renaissance dance in Shakespearean productions. USA. 1998. Lang.: Eng. 2692

Brief productions of Shakespeare, Shaw, and Marlowe at the World's Fair. USA: Chicago, IL. 1934. Lang.: Eng. 2701

George Crichton Miln's touring Shakespearean company in Japan. USA: Chicago, IL. Japan: Yokohama. 1882. Lang.: Eng. 2702

John Barton's workshop on Shakespearean performance. USA: New York, NY. 1998. Lang.: Eng. 2704

Actor Tomasso Salvini. USA. Italy. 1856-1915. Lang.: Eng. 2731

Interview with actor Patrick Stewart. USA: Washington, DC. 1998. Lang.: Eng. 2760

Analysis of Les' Kurbas' production of Shakespeare's *Macbeth*. USSR. 1924. Lang.: Eng. 2766

Postmodernism in Jean-Luc Godard's film adaptation of Shakespeare's *King Lear*. France. 1988. Lang.: Eng. 3931

Suzanne Cloutier's role in Shakespeare's *Othello*, directed by Orson Welles. Italy. 1952. Lang.: Fre. 3935

Analysis of casting and acting in Kenneth Branagh's film adaptation of *Much Ado About Nothing*. UK. 1993. Lang.: Fre. 3939

The body in stage-to-film versions of Shakespeare's *Richard III*. UK-England. USA. 1985-1998. Lang.: Eng. 3940

Analysis of Shakespeare's *King Lear* on television. UK-England. 1982-1983. Lang.: Eng. 4064

Reviews of new Hungarian musicals. Hungary: Budapest. 1997. Lang.: Hun. 4360

Musical performances on and off Broadway. USA: New York. 1998. Lang.: Ger. 4383

Shakespeare, William — cont'd

Interview with opera composer Manfred Trojahn. Germany: Munich. 1998. Lang.: Ger. 4582

Plays/librettos/scripts

The popularity of Shakespearean drama on the contemporary stage. 1998. Lang.: Eng. 2770

Analysis of *Dead White Males* by David Williamson. Australia. 1995. Lang.: Eng. 2773

Dutch and Flemish Shakespearean productions. Belgium. Netherlands. 1980-1983. Lang.: Dut. 2789

French translations of Shakespeare by Antonine Maillet and Jean-Louis Roux. Canada: Montreal, PQ. 1988-1993. Lang.: Fre. 2793

Analysis of *Queen Lear* by Beau Coleman. Canada: Edmonton, AB. 1995-1997. Lang.: Eng. 2800

Normand Chaurette's translations of *As You Like It* by Shakespeare. Canada: Montreal, PQ. 1989-1994. Lang.: Fre. 2824

The debate over the authorship of the plays attributed to Shakespeare. England. 1590-1616. Lang.: Rus. 2856

Horace Walpole's *The Dear Witches* and Shakespeare's *Macbeth.* England. 1743. Lang.: Eng. 2857

The influence of the figurative arts on the plays of William Shakespeare. England. 1589-1613. Lang.: Ita. 2858

Analysis of the frontispiece of Nicholas Rowe's edition of Shakespeare's *King Lear.* England. 1709-1714. Lang.: Eng. 2859

Delia Bacon's analysis of Shakespeare's *King Lear.* England. 1605. Lang.: Eng. 2860

Shakespeare's identity and Shakespeare studies. England. 1564-1616. Lang.: Rus. 2861

Shakespeare's *The Tempest* as an experiment in political control. England. 1611. Lang.: Eng. 2862

Treachery and the language of the marketplace in Shakespeare's *Troilus and Cressida.* England. 1601-1602. Lang.: Eng. 2863

Shakespeare's *Measure for Measure* and the King James Bible. England. 1604. Lang.: Eng. 2865

The figure of the Jew in Marlowe and Shakespeare. England. 1590-1600. Lang.: Eng. 2868

Social, economic, and political thought in Shakespeare's chronicle plays. England. 1590-1613. Lang.: Eng. 2869

The relationship between Falstaff and Prince Hal in Shakespeare's *Henry IV.* England. 1596-1597. Lang.: Eng. 2870

Analysis of Dryden and Davenant's *Enchanted Island.* England. 1674. Lang.: Eng. 2873

Wonder and recognition in medieval and Renaissance drama. England. 1400-1612. Lang.: Eng. 2874

Analysis of scenic transitions in the plays of Shakespeare. England. 1590-1613. Lang.: Eng. 2875

The mad scenes in Shakespeare's *King Lear.* England. 1605-1606. Lang.: Eng. 2876

Hermeneutic analysis of Shakespearean comedies. England. 1590-1608. Lang.: Eng. 2877

Game theory analysis of Shakespeare's *Antony and Cleopatra.* England. 1607. Lang.: Eng. 2879

An illustration of Queen Tamora of Shakespeare's *Titus Andronicus.* England. 1590-1594. Lang.: Eng. 2880

Playwriting and publishing for the London stage. England. 1590-1650. Lang.: Eng. 2881

The centaur in works of Shakespeare. England. 1590-1613. Lang.: Eng. 2882

The control of time in Renaissance English drama. England. 1590-1620. Lang.: Eng. 2883

Women's use of wit in response to men in English popular culture. England. 1590-1630. Lang.: Eng. 2884

The defense of prostitution in Lillo's *Marina.* England. 1738. Lang.: Eng. 2887

Plague imagery in Jacobean tragedy. England. 1618-1642. Lang.: Eng. 2889

Christianity and Shakespeare's *Macbeth.* England. 1606. Lang.: Eng. 2890

Cross-dressing in Shakespeare's *The Merchant of Venice* and in the autobiography of actress Charlotte Cibber Charke. England. 1713-1760. Lang.: Eng. 2891

The perception of self in Shakespeare's *Troilus and Cressida.* England. 1601-1602. Lang.: Eng. 2892

The murders of royal women in plays of Shakespeare and Beaumont and Fletcher. England. 1609-1610. Lang.: Eng. 2894

Militarism and masculinity in the early modern period. England. 1590-1650. Lang.: Eng. 2895

Analysis of a speech in Shakespeare's *Measure for Measure.* England. 1604. Lang.: Eng. 2896

Student casebook on Shakespeare's *Hamlet.* England. 1532-1608. Lang.: Eng. 2897

Shakespeare's *King Lear* and the gender constructions of three daughters. England. 1605-1606. Lang.: Eng. 2898

Cognitive analysis of Shakespeare's *Measure for Measure.* England. 1604. Lang.: Eng. 2900

A possible source for the character Young Bertram in Shakespeare's *All's Well That Ends Well.* England. 1602-1603. Lang.: Eng. 2901

Patience and delay in Shakespeare's *Othello.* England. 1604. Lang.: Eng. 2903

Recovered ritual in seemingly non-ritualistic theatre. England. 1600-1779. Lang.: Eng. 2904

East and West in Shakepeare's *A Midsummer Night's Dream.* England. 1594-1595. Lang.: Eng. 2905

The influence of Webster, Middleton, and Shakespeare on the poetry of Robert Browning. England. 1590-1889. Lang.: Eng. 2906

Protestant aesthetics and Shakespeare's *Measure for Measure.* England. 1604. Lang.: Eng. 2908

Aspects of character in Shakespeare's *Measure for Measure.* England. 1604. Lang.: Eng. 2909

Sources of the wager scene in Shakespeare's *Cymbeline.* England. 1609-1610. Lang.: Eng. 2910

Analysis of Shakespeare's history plays. England. 1590-1599. Lang.: Eng. 2911

Female power and the emblem tradition in plays of Shakespeare and Middleton. England. 1604-1625. Lang.: Eng. 2913

Henry Chettle's supposed apology to Shakespeare. England: London. 1592-1607. Lang.: Eng. 2915

Possible influence of Giordano Bruno on Shakespeare's *Hamlet.* England. 1600-1601. Lang.: Ita. 2921

The representation of historical female characters on the Renaissance stage. England. 1580-1615. Lang.: Eng. 2922

The use of proverbs in Shakespeare's plays. England. 1568-1613. Lang.: Eng. 2923

The 'unruly' speech of Ariana in Shakespeare's *Comedy of Errors.* England. 1590-1593. Lang.: Eng. 2924

Handwriting and character in Shakespeare's *Hamlet.* England. 1600-1601. Lang.: Eng. 2925

Attitudes toward Spain in early modern English drama. England. 1492-1604. Lang.: Eng. 2927

Women in Shakespeare's *Richard III.* England. 1592-1593. Lang.: Eng. 2929

The origin and meaning of the name Shylock in Shakespeare's *The Merchant of Venice.* England. 1596. Lang.: Eng. 2932

Annunciation motifs in Shakespeare's *Hamlet.* England. 1600-1601. Lang.: Eng. 2934

Girardian analysis of Shakespeare plays. England. 1590-1599. Lang.: Eng. 2935

Corporeal imagery in Shakespeare's *Hamlet.* England. 1600-1601. Lang.: Eng. 2939

Catholic and Protestant in Shakespeare's Second Henriad. England. 1596-1599. Lang.: Eng. 2940

Female power and the public sphere in Renaissance drama. England. 1597-1616. Lang.: Eng. 2943

Punishment and political power in plays of Shakespeare. England. 1604-1611. Lang.: Eng. 2944

Analysis of plays by Shakespeare. England. 1589-1613. Lang.: Rus. 2945

Analysis of Shakespeare's *Julius Caesar.* England. 1599. Lang.: Eng. 2948

Recognition in plays of Čechov, Shakespeare, and Beckett. England. France. Russia. 1596-1980. Lang.: Eng. 2949

Characters named Rosalind in Shakespeare's *As You Like It* and elsewhere. England. 1579-1600. Lang.: Eng. 2951

Feeling in Shakespeare's *King Lear.* England. 1605-1606. Lang.: Eng. 2952

Shakespeare, William — cont'd

Nicholas Rowe's illustration of a scene from *Macbeth*. England. 1709. Lang.: Eng. 2953

Comic scenes and characters in the Elizabethan history play. England. 1590-1618. Lang.: Eng. 2955

The theme of substitution in Shakespeare's *Measure for Measure*. England. 1604. Lang.: Eng. 2957

Shakespeare, Branagh, and the concept of the author. England. 1590-1998. Lang.: Eng. 2958

Variant spellings of Shakespeare's name. England. 1564-1623. Lang.: Eng. 2959

Seventeenth-century allusions to Shakespeare in short verse pieces. England. 1676-1678. Lang.: Eng. 2960

Psychological power and control in Shakespeare's *Measure for Measure*. England. 1604. Lang.: Eng. 2962

Portraits of Shakespeare. England. 1623-1640. Lang.: Rus. 2963

The Lacy family and the pretender to the throne in Shakespeare's *Henry VI, Part Two*. England. 1590-1592. Lang.: Eng. 2964

Shakespeare and the limitation of political and textual control. England. 1600-1611. Lang.: Eng. 2965

God and man in Renaissance theatre. England. 1610-1625. Lang.: Eng. 2966

Renaissance emblems of death and Shakespeare's *King John*. England. 1596-1599. Lang.: Eng. 2967

Regeneration in plays of Shakespeare. England. 1598-1613. Lang.: Eng. 2968

The obedient daughter in adaptations of Shakespeare's plays. England. 1701-1800. Lang.: Eng. 2969

The two Jaques in Shakespeare's *As You Like It*. England. 1599-1600. Lang.: Eng. 2970

Analysis of *Marina*, George Lillo's adaptation of Shakespeare's *Pericles*. England. 1738. Lang.: Eng. 2971

The psychology of punishment in Shakespeare's *Measure for Measure*. England. 1604. Lang.: Eng. 2975

Shakespeare, feminism, and his sources. England. 1590-1616. Lang.: Eng. 2977

The nature of tyranny in plays of Shakespeare. England. 1595-1612. Lang.: Eng. 2978

Casuistry and early modern English tragedy. England. 1600-1671. Lang.: Eng. 2980

Shakespeare's *A Midsummer Night's Dream*, politics, and criticism. England. 1594-1595. Lang.: Eng. 2981

The urban crowd in early modern drama. England. 1590-1630. Lang.: Eng. 2985

Racial ambiguity, colonialism, and late twentieth-century criticism of Shakespeare's *Othello*. England. 1604-1998. Lang.: Eng. 2987

The authorship of *George a Greene*. England. 1593-1599. Lang.: Eng. 2989

Queens Anne and Katherine in Shakespeare's *Henry VIII*. England. 1612-1613. Lang.: Eng. 2990

The concept of the self in Shakespearean tragedy. England. 1590-1612. Lang.: Eng. 2992

Historical background of the depiction of the Gloucesters in Shakespeare's *King Lear*. England. 1605-1606. Lang.: Eng. 2994

'Demonic' women in Shakespeare's tragedies. England. 1590-1613. Lang.: Eng. 2999

Don Quixote, Lewis Theobald's *The Double Falsehood* and the lost *Cardenio* of Shakespeare and Fletcher. England. Spain. 1610-1727. Lang.: Eng. 3001

The malcontent scholar in Elizabethan and Jacobean theatre. England. 1590-1642. Lang.: Eng. 3003

Analysis of a speech by the Ghost in Shakespeare's *Hamlet*. England. 1600-1601. Lang.: Eng. 3004

Comparison of final scenes in quarto and folio versions of Shakespeare's plays. England. 1597-1601. Lang.: Eng. 3005

The politics of consent in Shakespeare's *Titus Andronicus*. England. 1590-1594. Lang.: Eng. 3006

Symbolic action in Shakespeare's *Romeo and Juliet*. England. 1595-1596. Lang.: Eng. 3007

Epiphany in the plays of Shakespeare. England. 1590-1613. Lang.: Eng. 3008

Folklore and Shakespeare's *King Lear*. England. 1605-1606. Lang.: Eng. 3010

Analysis of *Troilus and Cressida* and *Measure for Measure* by William Shakespeare. England. 1601-1604. Lang.: Ita. 3012

Political context of Charles Johnson's *Love in a Forest*, an adaptation of *As You Like It*. England. 1723. Lang.: Eng. 3013

The subversion of male authority in Shakespeare's *Henry VI* and *Richard III*. England. 1590-1593. Lang.: Eng. 3015

Shakespeare and the creation of a theatre audience. England. 1600-1616. Lang.: Eng. 3017

Conscience in early modern literature including Shakespeare. England. 1590-1620. Lang.: Eng. 3020

Gender and religion in Shakespeare's *Measure for Measure*. England. 1604. Lang.: Eng. 3021

The first quarto of Shakespeare's *Henry V* and the anonymous *Famous Victories of Henrie the Fifth*. England. 1599-1600. Lang.: Eng. 3022

Race and imperialism in Shakespeare's *Othello*. England. 1604. Lang.: Eng. 3023

Malvolio's riddle in Shakespeare's *Twelfth Night*, II.5. England. 1600-1601. Lang.: Eng. 3025

The skull in plays of Shakespeare, Dekker, and Tourneur. England. 1606. Lang.: Eng. 3026

Prejudice and law in Shakespeare's *The Merchant of Venice*. England. 1596. Lang.: Eng. 3027

Closure and the happy ending in Shakespeare's *All's Well That Ends Well*. England. 1602-1603. Lang.: Eng. 3030

The 'troubler' personality in Shakespeare's *Henry IV, Part One*. England. 1596-1597. Lang.: Eng. 3032

The dating of Shakespeare's early plays. England. 1586-1593. Lang.: Eng. 3034

The vagueness of locale in Shakespeare's *King Lear*. England. 1605-1606. Lang.: Eng. 3036

The interaction of other characters with Shakespeare's tragic heroes. England. 1590-1613. Lang.: Eng. 3037

Shakespeare's *The Tempest* as an allegory of colonial America. England. 1611. Lang.: Eng. 3038

Fantasy and history in the plays of Shakespeare. England. 1589-1616. Lang.: Rus. 3039

Eighteenth-century editing and interpretation of Shakespeare. England. 1701-1800. Lang.: Eng. 3040

The control of procreation and death in Shakespeare's *Measure for Measure*. England. 1604. Lang.: Eng. 3041

Authority in Elizabethan England as reflected in the plays of Shakespeare. England. 1501-1600. Lang.: Eng. 3042

Comparison of second quarto and first folio versions of Shakespeare's *Hamlet*. England. 1600-1623. Lang.: Eng. 3043

The women in Shakespeare's *Hamlet*. England. 1600-1601. Lang.: Eng. 3046

Shakespeare's plays and human nature. England. 1590-1613. Lang.: Slo. 3047

Martial law and Renaissance drama and fiction. Europe. 1563-1753. Lang.: Eng. 3059

Two centuries' thought on Shakespeare's *The Merchant of Venice*. Europe. North America. 1788-1996. Lang.: Hun. 3066

Essay on French translations of Shakespeare. France. 1974-1998. Lang.: Fre. 3082

Family conflict in *Was sollen wir tun (What Shall We Do)* by Tankred Dorst and *Die Hamletmaschine (Hamletmachine)* by Heiner Müller. Germany. 1997-1998. Lang.: Ger. 3148

Shakespeare translators Luise Gottsched and Dorothea Tieck. Germany. 1739-1833. Lang.: Ger. 3156

Brecht's *Leben des Galilei (The Life of Galileo)* as an adaptation of Shakespeare's *Hamlet*. Germany. 1600-1932. Lang.: Eng. 3160

Brecht and the translation of Shakespeare into German. Germany, East. 1945-1990. Lang.: Eng. 3177

New Hungarian translations of Shakespeare. Hungary. 1990-1998. Lang.: Hun. 3187

Analysis of Imre Szabó Stein's new translation of Shakespeare's *The Merchant of Venice*. Hungary: Budapest. 1998. Lang.: Hun. 3188

Analysis and translation of *Et les Chiens se taisaient (And the Dogs Were Silent)* by Aimé Césaire. Martinique. 1946-1969. Lang.: Eng. 3269

Shakespeare, William — cont'd

Women in plays about war and male contact sports. New Zealand. Europe. 1998. Lang.: Eng. 3281
The statesman on the modern stage. North America. 1950-1995. Lang.: Eng. 3291
Shakespeare and the feminist theatre of Bryony Lavery and Jane Prendergast. UK-England. 1997. Lang.: Eng. 3439
Envy in the plays of Shakespeare. UK-England. 1990. Lang.: Ita. 3448
Plays of Peter Barnes compared to those of Renaissance dramatists. UK-England. 1968-1974. Lang.: Eng. 3449
The New Shakespeare Society's unfinished four-text edition of *Hamlet*. UK-England. 1882-1883. Lang.: Eng. 3497
Shakespeare's *The Tempest* on film. UK-England. USA. 1905-1991. Lang.: Eng. 3981
Film adaptations of Shakespeare's plays. UK-England. 1900-1998. Lang.: Ita. 3986
Analysis of Peter Greenaway's film *Prospero's Books*. UK-England. 1991. Lang.: Fre. 3990
Gangster film and Shakespearean tragedy. USA. 1971-1991. Lang.: Eng. 4009
Film adaptations of Shakespeare's *Richard III* by Richard Loncraine and Al Pacino. USA. UK-England. 1995-1996. Lang.: Fre. 4012
Roman Polanski's film adaptation of Shakespeare's *Macbeth*. USA. 1971. Lang.: Fre. 4014
Baz Luhrmann's film adaptation of Shakespeare's *Romeo and Juliet*. USA. 1996. Lang.: Fre. 4016
Film interpretations of Ophelia in Shakespeare's *Hamlet*. USA. UK-England. USSR. 1947-1990. Lang.: Eng. 4024
Shakespeare's *The Tempest* and Thomas Campion's *The Lord's Masque*. England. 1613. Lang.: Eng. 4202

Reference materials
Annual bibliography of Shakespeare studies. 1997. Lang.: Eng. 3722
Annual Shakespeare bibliography. 1988. Lang.: Eng. 3723
Annual Shakespeare studies bibliography. 1987. Lang.: Eng. 3724

Relation to other fields
Australian Shakespeare studies. Australia. 1998. Lang.: Eng. 3728
Account of teaching Shakespeare to Chinese students. China, People's Republic of: Changsha. 1987. Lang.: Eng. 3740
Chinese Shakespeare studies. China, People's Republic of. 1990-1998. Lang.: Eng. 3741
New-historicist analysis of Shakespeare and his time. England. 1580-1616. Lang.: Eng. 3745
A possible model for characters in Shakespeare's *Twelfth Night* and 'Venus and Adonis'. England. 1590-1593. Lang.: Eng. 3746
William Basse, author of the poem 'Epitaph for Shakespeare'. England. 1602-1653. Lang.: Eng. 3748
The publication of 'Venus and Adonis' by Shakespeare. England. 1589-1593. Lang.: Eng. 3751
Performance analysis of Shakespeare's sonnets. England. 1593-1599. Lang.: Eng. 3753
Novelist Samuel Richardson compared to Shakespeare. England. 1744-1747. Lang.: Eng. 3754
Psychoanalysis, the female body, and Shakespeare's *Henriad*. England. 1589-1597. Lang.: Eng. 3756
Shakespeare's Hamlet in novels of Goethe and Scott. England. Germany. 1776-1824. Lang.: Eng. 3757
Depictions of Shakespeare's Othello. Europe. 1709-1804. Lang.: Eng. 3758
A joint project for teaching Shakespeare with professional actors. Sweden. 1988-1998. Lang.: Swe. 3776
Shakespeare's influence on the novels of Virginia Woolf. UK-England. 1882-1941. Lang.: Eng. 3779
The state of Shakespearean studies in public education. USA. UK-England. 1998. Lang.: Eng. 3786
The influence of Shakespeare's *Othello* on C.B. Brown's novel *Wieland*. USA. England. 1604-1798. Lang.: Eng. 3788

Research/historiography
The Shakespeare Interactive Research Group. USA: Cambridge, MA. 1991-1997. Lang.: Eng. 3799

Theory/criticism
Marginalia in Sir George Greenwood's copy of *Is Shakespeare Dead?* by Mark Twain. USA. 1909. Lang.: Eng. 863
New historicism and Shakespeare's *Measure for Measure*. 1988. Lang.: Eng. 3801
Call for imaginative critical readings of Shakespeare's plays. 1998. Lang.: Eng. 3803
Theatrical theory and practice. 600 B.C.-1997 A.D. Lang.: Slo. 3804
Shakespeare, Oxford and the Tudor Rose theory. 1591-1998. Lang.: Eng. 3806
Critical response to *Elsineur (Elsinore)*, Robert Lepage's multimedia adaptation of *Hamlet*. Canada. 1995-1996. Lang.: Eng. 3810
Eighteenth-century approaches to Shakespearean criticism. England. 1701-1800. Lang.: Eng. 3811
Evidence of Oxfordian authorship of plays attributed to Shakespeare. England. 1622-1623. Lang.: Eng. 3812
Antisemitism and criticism of Shakespeare's *Merchant of Venice*. England. 1596-1986. Lang.: Eng. 3813
Political criticism of early modern drama. Europe. North America. 1975-1997. Lang.: Eng. 3814
The urge to make Shakespeare contemporary. USA. 1990-1998. Lang.: Eng. 3844

Shakespeare's Globe Theatre (London)

Institutions
The inaugural season of Shakespeare's Globe Theatre. UK-England: London. 1997-1998. Lang.: Eng. 1741

Performance spaces
The newly reopened Shakespeare's Globe Theatre. UK-England: London. 1997. Lang.: Eng. 461
Stage doors of the Globe Theatre. UK-England: London. 1599-1998. Lang.: Eng. 1806
Critique of Shakespeare's Globe Theatre. UK-England: London. 1997. Lang.: Eng. 1809
Shakespeare's Globe and the staging of *The Merchant of Venice*. UK-England: London. 1998. Lang.: Ger. 1810

Performance/production
Collection of newspaper reviews by London theatre critics. UK-England: London. 1998. Lang.: Eng. 2477
Collection of newspaper reviews by London theatre critics. UK-England: London. 1998. Lang.: Eng. 2486
Collection of newspaper reviews by London theatre critics. UK-England: London. 1998. Lang.: Eng. 2496
Collection of newspaper reviews by London theatre critics. UK-England: London. 1998. Lang.: Eng. 2498
The inaugural season of Shakespeare's Globe Theatre. UK-England: London. 1997. Lang.: Eng. 2601
Review of the opening season of Shakespeare's Globe Theatre. UK-England: London. 1997. Lang.: Eng. 2602
Gaynor Macfarlane's production of Edwards' *Damon and Pythias* at Shakespeare's Globe. UK-England: London. 1996. Lang.: Eng. 2613
Richard Olivier's production of Shakespeare's *The Merchant of Venice*. UK-England: London. 1998. Lang.: Eng. 2621

Shakespeare's Villains

Performance/production
Collection of newspaper reviews by London theatre critics. UK-England: London. 1998. Lang.: Eng. 2524

Shalev-Gerz, Esther

Performance/production
Interview with director Jochen Gerz. Germany: Berlin. 1998. Lang.: Ger, Fre, Dut, Eng. 1967

Relation to other fields
Die Berliner Ermittlung (The Berlin Investigation), an interactive theatre project by Jochen Gerz and Esther Shalev-Gerz. Germany: Berlin. 1998. Lang.: Ger. 3768

Shallow Cups

Plays/librettos/scripts
Analysis of plays by Dymphna Cusack. Australia. 1927-1959. Lang.: Eng. 2777

Shamanism

Performance/production
Reexamination of the performance art of Beuys, Abramovič, and Ulay. USA. Germany. Netherlands. 1964-1985. Lang.: Eng. 4254

Relation to other fields
The 'bird-woman' folktale in Southeast Asian shamanic healing rituals. Ireland. Thailand. Malaysia. Lang.: Eng. 1358

Shammah, André Ruth

Performance/production
Italian productions of plays by Harold Pinter. Italy. 1997. Lang.: Eng. 2165

Shammas, Sam
Performance/production
Collection of newspaper reviews by London theatre critics. UK-England: London. 1998. Lang.: Eng. 2455
Shandling, Gary
Plays/librettos/scripts
Analysis of performance art on *The Larry Sanders Show.* USA. 1995. Lang.: Eng. 4079
Shang-a-Lang
Performance/production
Collection of newspaper reviews by London theatre critics. UK-England: London. 1998. Lang.: Eng. 2537
Shange, Ntozake
Performance/production
Analysis of transformative comedy. USA. 1975-1988. Lang.: Eng. 666
Collection of newspaper reviews by London theatre critics. UK-England: London. 1998. Lang.: Eng. 2498
Plays/librettos/scripts
Account of National Black Theatre Summit. USA: Hanover, NH. 1998. Lang.: Eng. 3523
Shannon Jackson on her solo piece *White Noises.* USA. 1998. Lang.: Eng. 3619
Boal's 'joker system' in plays of Ntozake Shange. USA. 1977-1981. Lang.: Eng. 3692
Playwrights Adrienne Kennedy, Ntozake Shange, and Suzan-Lori Parks. USA. 1970-1998. Lang.: Eng. 3714
Shanghai Theatre Academy
Performance/production
Producing Howard Burman's *Article XXIV* at the Shanghai Theatre Academy. China, People's Republic of: Shanghai. 1995. Lang.: Eng. 511
Shanti
Plays/librettos/scripts
South African theatre after apartheid. South Africa, Republic of. 1976-1996. Lang.: Eng. 3365
Shantz, Valerie
Plays/librettos/scripts
Dramaturg's experience working on a play by Yvette Nolan. Canada. 1997-1998. Lang.: Eng. 2827
Sharaff, Irene
Design/technology
Costume designs by Irene Sharaff. USA. 1933-1976. Lang.: Eng. 277
Shared Experience (London)
Plays/librettos/scripts
Shared Experience's stage adaptations of nineteenth-century novels. USA: New York, NY. UK-England: London. 1998. Lang.: Eng. 3518
Sharits, Paul
Audience
The prompting of epileptic seizures by film. 1960-1988. Lang.: Eng. 3876
Sharman, Rodney
Plays/librettos/scripts
Homosexuality in Canadian opera. Canada. 1970-1998. Lang.: Eng. 4762
Shart, Raffy
Basic theatrical documents
Text of *Ma femme s'appelle Maurice (My Wife's Name Is Maurice)* by Raffy Shart. France. 1998. Lang.: Fre. 1435
Shatner, William
Performance/production
Speaking styles of selected actors reading Shakespeare's *Henry V.* North America. UK-England. 1998. Lang.: Eng. 2208
Shaw Festival (Niagara-on-the-Lake, ON)
Institutions
Comments on productions of the Shaw Festival. Canada: Niagara-on-the-Lake, ON. 1997. Lang.: Eng. 1579
The 1997 Shaw and Stratford Festival seasons. Canada: Stratford, ON, Niagara-on-the-Lake, ON. 1997. Lang.: Eng. 1582
Performance/production
The Shaw Festival season. Canada: Niagara-on-the-Lake, ON. 1998. Lang.: Eng. 1843
Shaw, Fiona
Performance/production
Interview with actress Fiona Shaw. UK-England. 1995-1997. Lang.: Eng. 2607
Analysis of two productions of Caryl Churchill's *Top Girls.* UK-England. 1982-1991. Lang.: Eng. 2608
The language of costume in a video production of Caryl Churchill's *Top Girls.* UK-England. 1982-1991. Lang.: Eng. 4065
Shaw, George Bernard
Basic theatrical documents
Catalan translation of *Arms and the Man* by George Bernard Shaw. UK-England. 1894. Lang.: Cat. 1478
Performance/production
Shaw's *Major Barbara* at the People's Arts Theatre. China, People's Republic of: Beijing. 1991. Lang.: Eng. 1874
The performance of Shakespeare in the former East Germany. Germany: Rostock, Leipzig, Berlin, Dessau. 1996-1997. Lang.: Ger. 1974
Seven critics on their favorite character or portrayal. Sweden. 1950. Lang.: Swe. 2369
Collection of newspaper reviews by London theatre critics. UK-England: London. 1998. Lang.: Eng. 2449
Collection of newspaper reviews by London theatre critics. UK-England. 1998. Lang.: Eng. 2504
Collection of newspaper reviews by London theatre critics. UK-England: London. 1998. Lang.: Eng. 2524
Collection of newspaper reviews by London theatre critics. UK-England: London. 1998. Lang.: Eng. 2562
Attempted censorship of productions. USA. 1900-1905. Lang.: Eng. 2698
New York City's attempt to impose censorship on theatre productions. USA: New York, NY. 1900-1927. Lang.: Eng. 2699
Brief productions of Shakespeare, Shaw, and Marlowe at the World's Fair. USA: Chicago, IL. 1934. Lang.: Eng. 2701
Plays/librettos/scripts
The rebel in modern drama. Europe. 1950-1988. Lang.: Eng. 3053
Structure and philosophy in Shaw's *Major Barbara* and *Man and Superman.* UK-England. 1901-1905. Lang.: Eng. 3427
Analysis of *Heartbreak House* by George Bernard Shaw. UK-England. 1916-1919. Lang.: Eng. 3429
George Bernard Shaw: life, work, influences. UK-England. Ireland. 1886-1955. Lang.: Eng. 3437
Colonialism in the plays of George Bernard Shaw. UK-England. 1895-1935. Lang.: Eng. 3438
Analysis of the later plays of George Bernard Shaw. UK-England. 1923-1947. Lang.: Eng. 3444
Popular adaptations of the works of George Bernard Shaw. UK-England. 1890-1990. Lang.: Eng. 3445
The comedy of George Bernard Shaw and Oscar Wilde. UK-England. 1885-1900. Lang.: Eng. 3450
Rhetorical arguments in one-act plays of Shaw. UK-England. 1890-1945. Lang.: Eng. 3453
Disillusionment in George Bernard Shaw's *Heartbreak House.* UK-England. 1920. Lang.: Eng. 3456
Shaw's 'theatre of ideas' and its influence. UK-England. 1890-1910. Lang.: Eng. 3457
George Bernard Shaw and play publication. UK-England. 1883-1903. Lang.: Eng. 3460
Linguistic style and action in plays of Wilde, Shaw, and Stoppard. UK-England. 1890-1985. Lang.: Eng. 3467
Analysis of early plays by George Bernard Shaw. UK-England. 1892-1900. Lang.: Eng. 3470
George Bernard Shaw's involvement with the Court Theatre. UK-England. 1904-1909. Lang.: Eng. 3471
Rhetorical analysis of plays by George Bernard Shaw. UK-England. 1896-1908. Lang.: Eng. 3480
George Bernard Shaw and feminism. UK-England. 1856-1950. Lang.: Eng. 3481
George Bernard Shaw and the 'New Woman'. UK-England. 1890-1900. Lang.: Eng. 3486
Shaw's *Man and Superman* as a philosophical treatise. UK-England. 1905. Lang.: Eng. 3495
George Bernard Shaw and the history-play tradition. UK-England. 1899-1939. Lang.: Eng. 3503
Music in the plays of George Bernard Shaw. UK-England. 1888-1950. Lang.: Eng. 3506
George Bernard Shaw and science fiction. UK-England. Ireland. 1887-1998. Lang.: Eng. 3508
Theory/criticism
Theatrical dancing and the performance aesthetics of Wilde, Yeats, and Shaw. UK-England. Ireland. 1890-1950. Lang.: Eng. 1012

Shaw, George Bernard — cont'd

Ibsen, 'new' theatre, and Shaw's *Plays Unpleasant*. UK-England. 1891-1898. Lang.: Eng. 3832

George Bernard Shaw as music critic. UK-England: London. 1887-1894. Lang.: Eng. 4838

Shaw, Peggy

Performance/production

Analysis of pop performance. USA: New York, NY. 1980-1988. Lang.: Eng. 664

Shawl, The

Plays/librettos/scripts

Rites of passage in the plays of David Mamet. USA. 1975-1995. Lang.: Eng. 3680

Shawn, Ted

Relation to other fields

American modern dance and gay culture. USA. 1933-1998. Lang.: Eng. 1337

Shayna Maidel, A

Plays/librettos/scripts

The survivor character in contemporary American drama. USA. 1970-1997. Lang.: Eng. 3600

Shearer, Jill

Performance/production

Contemporary Asian-Australian theatre. Australia. 1990-1998. Lang.: Eng. 488

Sheehan, Mary

Administration

Interview with actors on Equity. USA: New York, NY. 1998. Lang.: Eng. 75

Sheffield, Graham

Administration

Attempts to diversify offerings of the Barbican Centre. UK-England: London. 1998. Lang.: Eng. 25

Sheffield, Neil

Performance/production

Collection of newspaper reviews by London theatre critics. UK-England: London. 1998. Lang.: Eng. 2476

Shell, Ray

Performance/production

Collection of newspaper reviews by London theatre critics. UK-England: London. 1998. Lang.: Eng. 2572

Shelley, Mary

Institutions

New productions of Düsseldorfer Schauspielhaus. Germany: Dusseldorf. 1998. Lang.: Ger. 1654

Shelley, Percy Bysshe

Plays/librettos/scripts

The feminine ideal in the drama of English Romantic poets. England. 1794-1840. Lang.: Eng. 2886

Sheltering Sky, The

Performance/production

Analysis of films by Bernardo Bertolucci. 1979-1998. Lang.: Eng. 3927

Shelton, Edward

Plays/librettos/scripts

Miscegenation in American drama. USA. 1909-1969. Lang.: Eng. 3599

Shepard, Sam

Design/technology

Set designs by Santo Loquasto at Manhattan Theatre Club. USA: New York, NY. 1998. Lang.: Eng. 1536

Performance/production

The influence of experimental performance on contemporary drama. Europe. USA. 1960-1987. Lang.: Eng. 526

De Zaak's production of *Action* by Sam Shepard. Netherlands: Rotterdam. 1988. Lang.: Dut. 2201

Plays/librettos/scripts

English-language plays on the Dutch and Flemish stage. Netherlands. 1920-1998. Lang.: Dut. 3278

Analysis of Sam Shepard's *Fool for Love*. USA. 1979. Lang.: Dut. 3540

Analysis of *Savage/Love* by Joseph Chaikin and Sam Shepard. USA. 1991-1996. Lang.: Eng. 3543

Analysis of *States of Shock* by Sam Shepard. USA. 1965-1997. Lang.: Eng. 3544

National identity in plays of Sam Shepard. USA. 1965-1995. Lang.: Eng. 3545

Analysis of Sam Shepard's *Operation Sidewinder*. USA. 1970. Lang.: Eng. 3548

Profile of playwright Sam Shepard. USA. 1965-1992. Lang.: Dut. 3550

Analysis of the plays of Sam Shepard. USA. 1965-1988. Lang.: Eng. 3553

Essays on the theatre of Sam Shepard. USA. 1965-1998. Lang.: Eng. 3557

Eugene O'Neill and the creation of autobiographical drama. USA. 1940-1995. Lang.: Eng. 3561

History of the Playwrights Unit. USA. 1963-1971. Lang.: Eng. 3570

The nature and language of menace in the plays of John Whiting, Harold Pinter and Sam Shepard. USA. UK-England. 1960-1985. Lang.:Eng. 3576

Revolutionary Off Broadway playwriting. USA: New York, NY. 1959-1969. Lang.: Eng. 3604

Female presence/absence in plays of O'Neill, Pinter, and Shepard. USA. UK-England. 1936-1985. Lang.: Eng. 3607

Influence of the novelistic monologues of Eugene O'Neill. USA. 1911-1998. Lang.: Eng. 3641

Language and other elements of expression in plays of Beckett and Shepard. USA. France. Ireland. 1950-1988. Lang.: Eng. 3655

The return of the prodigal in American drama. USA. 1920-1985. Lang.: Eng. 3666

Language in the plays of Sam Shepard. USA. 1967-1985. Lang.: Eng. 3694

Open-endedness in plays of Sam Shepard. USA. 1966-1996. Lang.: Eng. 3713

The Bodyguard, Sam Shepard's screen adaptation of *The Changeling* by Middleton and Rowley. USA. 1970-1995. Lang.: Eng. 4007

The screen adaptation of Sam Shepard's *Fool for Love*. USA. 1979. Lang.: Eng. 4008

Sheperd, Tom

Performance/production

Collection of newspaper reviews by London theatre critics. UK-England: London. 1998. Lang.: Eng. 2467

Shepherd, Jack

Performance/production

Collection of newspaper reviews by London theatre critics. UK-England: London. 1998. Lang.: Eng. 2486

Collection of newspaper reviews by London theatre critics. UK-England: London. 1998. Lang.: Eng. 2541

Shepherd, Mike

Performance/production

Collection of newspaper reviews by London theatre critics. UK-England: London. 1998. Lang.: Eng. 2472

Shepphard, Nona

Performance/production

Collection of newspaper reviews by London theatre critics. UK-England: London. 1998. Lang.: Eng. 2555

Sheridan, Richard Brinsley

Performance/production

Collection of newspaper reviews by London theatre critics. UK-England: Stratford. 1998. Lang.: Eng. 2529

Collection of newspaper reviews by London theatre critics. UK-England: London. 1998. Lang.: Eng. 2531

Guest performances of the Kirov Opera at the Metropolitan.. USA: New York, NY. 1998. Lang.: Eng. 4731

Theory/criticism

Contrasting reviews of Declan Donnellan's RSC production of *The School for Scandal*. UK-England: Stratford. 1998. Lang.: Eng. 3835

Sherin, Mimi Jordan

Design/technology

Technical designs for *Tristan und Isolde* at Seattle Opera. USA: Seattle, WA. 1998. Lang.: Eng. 4444

Sherman, Guy

Design/technology

Panel discussion of sound designers. USA. 1998. Lang.: Eng. 287

Sherman, Richard

Design/technology

Production design for Bill Condon's film *Gods and Monsters*. USA: Hollywood, CA. 1998. Lang.: Eng. 3908

Sherriff, R.C.

Performance/production

Collection of newspaper reviews by London theatre critics. UK-England: London. 1998. Lang.: Eng. 2567

Shewing-Up of Blanco Posnet, The

Plays/librettos/scripts

Rhetorical arguments in one-act plays of Shaw. UK-England. 1890-1945. Lang.: Eng. 3453

Shezi, Mthuli ka

Plays/librettos/scripts

South African theatre after apartheid. South Africa, Republic of. 1976-1996. Lang.: Eng. 3365

Shields, Carol
Plays/librettos/scripts
Playwriting career of Carol Shields. Canada: Winnipeg, MB. 1972-1998. Lang.: Eng. 2794
Shimada
Performance/production
Contemporary Asian-Australian theatre. Australia. 1990-1998. Lang.: Eng. 488
Shining, The
Performance/production
Collection of newspaper reviews by London theatre critics. UK-England: London. 1998. Lang.: Eng. 2549
Shinkokuritsu Gekyo (Tokyo)
Institutions
Tokyo's new opera house. Japan: Tokyo. 1998. Lang.: Rus. 4464
Shinn, Christopher
Performance/production
Collection of newspaper reviews by London theatre critics. UK-England: London. 1998. Lang.: Eng. 2549
Shire, David
Performance/production
Collection of newspaper reviews by London theatre critics. UK-England: London. 1998. Lang.: Eng. 2476
Shock Corridor
Basic theatrical documents
Screenplay for *Shock Corridor* by Sam Fuller. USA. 1963. Lang.: Eng. 3886
Shockheaded Peter
Performance/production
Collection of newspaper reviews by London theatre critics. UK-England: London. 1998. Lang.: Eng. 2465
Shoemaker's Holiday, The
Plays/librettos/scripts
Comic scenes and characters in the Elizabethan history play. England. 1590-1618. Lang.: Eng. 2955
Sociological analysis of *The Shoemaker's Holiday* by Thomas Dekker. England. 1600. Lang.: Eng. 2973
Flemish immigrants in English Renaissance drama. England. 1515-1635. Lang.: Eng. 2976
Shöier, Isa
Plays/librettos/scripts
Swedish theatres and young Swedish playwrights. Sweden: Malmö, Gothenburg, Stockholm. 1994-1998. Lang.: Swe. 3411
Shooting Magda
SEE
Ha-Palistinait.
Shooting Stars/The Fast Show
Performance/production
Collection of newspaper reviews by London theatre critics. UK-England: London. 1998. Lang.: Eng. 2573
Shopping and Fucking
Institutions
Survey of the Theatertreffen festival. Germany: Berlin. 1998. Lang.: Swe. 1651
Performance/production
Collection of newspaper reviews by London theatre critics. UK-England: London. 1998. Lang.: Eng. 2571
Analysis of recent New York productions. USA: New York, NY. 1997-1998. Lang.: Eng. 2759
Plays/librettos/scripts
Mark Ravenhill's *Shopping and Fucking* and its production by Thomas Ostermeier. UK-England. Germany. 1998. Lang.: Ger. 3476
Sex, drugs, and violence in contemporary British drama. UK-England. 1991-1998. Lang.: Eng. 3494
Interview with playwright Mark Ravenhill. UK-England. 1998. Lang.: Ger. 3496
Shostak, Cathy
Performance/production
Collection of newspaper reviews by London theatre critics. UK-England: London. 1998. Lang.: Eng. 2552
Collection of newspaper reviews by London theatre critics. UK-England: London. 1998. Lang.: Eng. 2553
Shostakovich, Dmitri
SEE
Šostakovič, Dmitrij.
Show
Performance/production
Contemporary performance art's ignorance of its avant-garde antecedents. USA. 1996-1998. Lang.: Eng. 4250
Show Boat
Performance/production
Collection of newspaper reviews by London theatre critics. UK-England: London. 1998. Lang.: Eng. 2466
Show boats
Performance spaces
The feasibility of a floating open-air theatre. Europe. 1998. Lang.: Swe. 436
The theatre of the cruise ship *Grand Princess*. Italy. 1998. Lang.: Eng. 451
Showcase Beat le Mot (Frankfurt/Main)
Institutions
Experimental performances of Helena Waldmann and Showcase Beat le Mot. Germany: Franfurt. 1993-1998. Lang.: Ger. 4234
Showtime
Performance/production
Derision in recent productions. Canada: Quebec, PQ. 1998. Lang.: Fre. 509
Shrine Auditorium (Los Angeles, CA)
Performance spaces
Profiles of Southern California theatres. USA. 1998. Lang.: Eng. 473
Shrubshall, Peter
Performance/production
Collection of newspaper reviews by London theatre critics. UK-England: London. 1998. Lang.: Eng. 2436
Shubert Foundation (New York, NY)
Institutions
The twentieth anniversary of the Shubert archive newsletter *The Passing Show*. USA: New York, NY. 1949-1998. Lang.: Eng. 425
Shubert Organization (New York, NY)
Administration
Sarah Bernhardt's farewell tour and its revenues. USA. 1905-1906. Lang.: Eng. 28
Shubert Alley's breast cancer screening program. USA: New York, NY. 1998. Lang.: Eng. 101
Institutions
Shubert archivist on her work. USA: New York, NY. 1987-1998. Lang.: Eng. 398
Assistant archivist on the Shubert archive. USA: New York, NY. 1984-1998. Lang.: Eng. 401
The early years of the Shubert archive. USA: New York, NY. 1976-1987. Lang.: Eng. 409
Brooks McNamara, founder and director of the Shubert archive. USA: New York, NY. 1976-1998. Lang.: Eng. 413
Brooks McNamara on the Shubert archive of which he is director. USA: New York, NY. 1976-1998. Lang.: Eng. 415
The twentieth anniversary of the Shubert archive newsletter *The Passing Show*. USA: New York, NY. 1949-1998. Lang.: Eng. 425
Working at the Shubert archive. USA: New York, NY. 1988-1998. Lang.: Eng. 426
The Shuberts vs. the Syndicate. USA: New York, NY. 1976-1998. Lang.: Eng. 427
Reference materials
Index of the first twenty volumes of *The Passing Show*. USA: New York, NY. 1976-1998. Lang.: Eng. 709
Shubert Theatre (New York, NY)
Administration
Actors' Fund annual benefit for women's health. USA: New York, NY. 1998. Lang.: Eng. 68
Shubert, J.J.
Institutions
The Shuberts vs. the Syndicate. USA: New York, NY. 1976-1998. Lang.: Eng. 427
Shubert, Lee
Institutions
The Shuberts vs. the Syndicate. USA: New York, NY. 1976-1998. Lang.: Eng. 427
Sí de las niñas, El (The Girls' Consent)
Performance/production
Collection of newspaper reviews by London theatre critics. UK-England: London. 1998. Lang.: Eng. 2490
Siameses, Los (Siamese Twins, The)
Plays/librettos/scripts
Cruelty and the absurd in theatre of Latin American playwrights. Latin America. 1960-1980. Lang.: Eng. 3267
Siberry, Michael
Performance/production
Michael Siberry on performing in an RSC production of *The Taming of the Shrew*. UK-England: London, Stratford. 1995-1996. Lang.:Eng. 2637

Sicangco, Eduardo
Design/technology
Set and costume designer Eduardo Sicangco, judge of SETC design competition. USA: Birmingham, AL. 1998. Lang.: Eng. 292
Side Man
Basic theatrical documents
Text of *Side Man* by Warren Leight. USA. 1998. Lang.: Eng. 1494
Side Show
Design/technology
Recent work of lighting designer Brian MacDevitt. USA: New York, NY. 1997. Lang.: Eng. 1530
Sound design for *Side Show* at Richard Rodgers Theatre. USA: New York, NY. 1998. Lang.: Eng. 4329
Sidetrack Performance Group (Sydney)
Institutions
Sidetrack Performance Group, formerly Sidetrack Theatre Company. Australia: Sydney. 1990-1998. Lang.: Eng. 1567
Performance/production
Analysis of performance pieces reacting to the Australian bicentenary. Australia: Darwin, Sydney. 1988. Lang.: Eng. 1815
Sidler, Erich
Performance/production
Productions of new plays by Peter Handke and Katharine Gericke at Niedersächsische Staatstheater. Germany: Hannover. 1998. Lang.: Ger. 1983
Sidney, Philip
Plays/librettos/scripts
Militarism and masculinity in the early modern period. England. 1590-1650. Lang.: Eng. 2895
Sieben Todsünden, Die (Seven Deadly Sins, The)
Plays/librettos/scripts
The search for a lost translation of *The Seven Deadly Sins* by Brecht and Weill. Germany. UK-England. 1933-1998. Lang.: Eng. 4392
Siff, Ira
Performance/production
Interview with Ira Siff of La Gran Scena. USA: New York, NY. 1998. Lang.: Eng. 4719
Siglo de oro
SEE ALSO
Geographical-Chronological Index under Spain 1580-1680.
Plays/librettos/scripts
Dramatic devices in early Spanish drama. Spain. 1550-1722. Lang.: Eng. 3373
Background on the Spanish 'golden age'. Spain. 1517-1681. Lang.: Eng. 3387
Signature Theatre (New York, NY)
Design/technology
Set design for Joseph Chaikin's production of two one-acts by Arthur Miller. USA: New york, NY. 1998. Lang.: Eng. 1532
Set designs of Francis O'Connor. USA: New York, NY. 1998. Lang.: Eng. 1541
Signing
Performance/production
Collection of newspaper reviews by London theatre critics. UK-England: London. 1998. Lang.: Eng. 2463
Signs of Life
Performance/production
Documentary theatre and the politics of representation. USA. 1966-1993. Lang.: Eng. 2728
Sikora, Roman
Plays/librettos/scripts
New direction in Czech playwriting. Czech Republic. 1990-1997. Lang.: Cze. 2850
Silas Marner
Performance/production
Collection of newspaper reviews by London theatre critics. UK-England: London. 1998. Lang.: Eng. 2459
Silbert, Roxana
Performance/production
Collection of newspaper reviews by London theatre critics. UK-England: London. 1998. Lang.: Eng. 2458
Collection of newspaper reviews by London theatre critics. UK-England: London. 1998. Lang.: Eng. 2475
Collection of newspaper reviews by London theatre critics. UK-England: London. 1998. Lang.: Eng. 2556
Silent Night
Performance/production
Collection of newspaper reviews by London theatre critics. UK-England: London. 1998. Lang.: Eng. 2550
Silja, Anja
Performance/production
Director Ruth Berghaus. Germany. 1970-1996. Lang.: Ger. 4596
Sills, Paul
Performance/production
Theatre Magazine's anniversary issue. USA. 1968-1998. Lang.: Eng. 617
Silly Cow
Performance/production
Collection of newspaper reviews by London theatre critics. UK-England: London. 1998. Lang.: Eng. 2437
Silver, Nicky
Design/technology
Derek McLane's set designs for recent Off Broadway productions. USA: New York, NY. 1998. Lang.: Eng. 1538
Simensen, Bjørn
Institutions
Interview with Bjørn Simensen, director of Den Norske Opera. Norway: Oslo. 1998. Lang.: Swe. 4465
Simmonds, Peter
Performance/production
Collection of newspaper reviews by London theatre critics. UK-England: London. 1998. Lang.: Eng. 2414
Collection of newspaper reviews by London theatre critics. UK-England: London. 1998. Lang.: Eng. 2506
Simms, Willard
Performance/production
Collection of newspaper reviews by London theatre critics. UK-England: London. 1998. Lang.: Eng. 2522
Simon, Balázs
Performance/production
Péter Kárpáti's *Díszelőadás (Gala Performance)* directed by Balázs Simon. Hungary: Budapest. 1998. Lang.: Hun. 2057
Performances at the new Bárka Színház. Hungary: Budapest. 1997. Lang.: Hun. 2097
Simon, Michael
Design/technology
Lighting in contemporary theatre. Germany. 1998. Lang.: Ger. 192
Simon, Neil
Design/technology
Recent work of lighting designer Brian MacDevitt. USA: New York, NY. 1997. Lang.: Eng. 1530
Performance/production
Collection of newspaper reviews by London theatre critics. UK-England: London. 1998. Lang.: Eng. 2410
Collection of newspaper reviews by London theatre critics. UK-England: London. 1998. Lang.: Eng. 2484
Collection of newspaper reviews by London theatre critics. UK-England: London. 1998. Lang.: Eng. 2491
Simon, Paul
Design/technology
Sound design for the musical *The Capeman*. USA: New York, NY. 1998. Lang.: Eng. 4339
Performance/production
Response to negative criticism of *The Capeman*. USA: New York, NY. 1998. Lang.: Eng. 4387
Simonnet, Michèle
Basic theatrical documents
French translation of *My Left Breast* by Susan Miller. USA. France. 1994-1998. Lang.: Fre. 1498
Simonov, Nikolaj Konstantinovič
Performance/production
Actor Nikolaj K. Simonov. Russia: St. Petersburg. 1998. Lang.: Rus. 2248
Actor Nikolaj Simonov. Russia: St. Petersburg. 1998. Lang.: Rus. 2289
Simons, Johan
Plays/librettos/scripts
Johan Simons and the independent theatre group in Hollandia. Netherlands: Amsterdam. 1985-1998. Lang.: Ger. 3280
Simple Storys
Institutions
Schauspiel Leipzig under the direction of Wolfgang Engel. Germany: Leipzig. 1996-1998. Lang.: Ger. 1638
Simply Barbra—The Wedding Tour
Performance/production
Collection of newspaper reviews by London theatre critics. UK-England: London. 1998. Lang.: Eng. 2531
Simply Maria, or the American Dream
Plays/librettos/scripts
Analysis of plays by Josefina López. USA. 1988-1989. Lang.: Eng. 3650

Simpson, Dave
Performance/production
Collection of newspaper reviews by London theatre critics. UK-England: London. 1998. Lang.: Eng. 2435
Simpson, Geoffrey
Design/technology
Geoffrey Simpson's cinematography for Gillian Armstrong's *Oscar and Lucinda*. Australia. 1997. Lang.: Eng. 3900
Simpson, Lee
Performance/production
Collection of newspaper reviews by London theatre critics. UK-England: London. 1998. Lang.: Eng. 2421
Collection of newspaper reviews by London theatre critics. UK-England: London. 1998. Lang.: Eng. 2556
Sin Dykes
Performance/production
Collection of newspaper reviews by London theatre critics. UK-England: London. 1998. Lang.: Eng. 2575
Sinakulo
Performance/production
Contemporary Asian-Australian theatre. Australia. 1990-1998. Lang.: Eng. 488
Sinatra, Frank
Performance/production
Obituary for singer and actor Frank Sinatra. USA. 1916-1998. Lang.: Eng. 3946
Sinfonieorchester GmbH (Straslund)
Administration
Rüdiger Bloch, manager of West Pomeranian theatres. Germany: Greifswald, Straslund. 1997-1998. Lang.: Ger. 1384
Singer, Isaac Bashevis
Performance/production
Collection of newspaper reviews by London theatre critics. UK-England: London. 1998. Lang.: Eng. 2423
Singh, Tony
Performance/production
Collection of newspaper reviews by London theatre critics. UK-England: London. 1998. Lang.: Eng. 2578
Singha, Runa
Performance/production
Interview with choreographer Runa Singha. Canada: Toronto, ON. 1970-1998. Lang.: Eng. 1368
Singing
Administration
Preparations for the centennial of actor and singer Paul Robeson. USA. 1898-1998. Lang.: Eng. 61
Institutions
Interview with singer Carla Henius, manager of musik-theater-werkstatt festival. Germany: Wiesbaden. 1986-1998. Lang.: Ger. 4347
The fourth international singing contest. Hungary: Budapest. 1998. Lang.: Hun. 4461
Alphabetical listing of opera festival performance timetables throughout the United States in summer 1998. USA. 5/1998-9/1998. Lang.: Eng. 4482
Training practices of Houston Opera Studio. USA: Houston, TX. 1977-1998. Lang.: Eng. 4489
Performance/production
Estonian artists as war refugees in Sweden. Estonia. Sweden. 1939-1945. Lang.: Swe, Eng, Ger. 519
Actress Betty Buckley's performance in AIDS fundraiser. Switzerland: Geneva. 1998. Lang.: Eng. 603
Popular entertainment in Uganda after Idi Amin. Uganda. 1979-1998. Lang.: Eng. 604
The application of Laban Movement Studies to actor training. USA. 1997-1998. Lang.: Eng. 628
The life and career of singer Paul Robeson. USA. 1998. Lang.: Eng. 631
Flamenco variations worldwide. Spain. USA. 1901-1998. Lang.: Eng. 962
Acting in the private theatre of the Ming Dynasty. China. 1368-1644. Lang.: Eng. 1872
Excerpts from the diary of singer and actress Ilka Markovits. Hungary. 1839-1915. Lang.: Hun. 2064
Actress Audra McDonald. USA. 1993-1998. Lang.: Eng. 2669
Profile of performer and activist Paul Robeson. USA. 1898-1959. Lang.: Eng. 2750
Life and film career of singer Maurice Chevalier. France: Paris. USA. 1888-1972. Lang.: Eng. 3933
Obituary for singer and actor Frank Sinatra. USA. 1916-1998. Lang.: Eng. 3946
The importance of Black performers in American musical films. USA. 1900-1957. Lang.: Swe. 3960
Calypso music and carnival. Caribbean. 1933-1998. Lang.: Eng. 4119
Singer Valerij Meladze. Russia. 1998. Lang.: Rus. 4130
Singer Valerij Meladze. Russia. 1998. Lang.: Rus. 4131
Singer Lorna Luft. USA. 1998. Lang.: Eng. 4158
Career of entertainer Al Jolson. USA. 1886-1950. Lang.: Eng. 4280
Sequentia's new recording of *Ordo Virtutum* by Hildegard of Bingen. Germany. 1997. Lang.: Eng. 4294
Brecht and the vocal role. Germany. 1920-1998. Lang.: Swe. 4295
Opera singer Ivan Kozlovskij. Russia: Nizhni Novgorod. 1998. Lang.: Rus. 4301
Singer Ljudmila Zykina. Russia. Lang.: Rus. 4302
William Schuman on the differences between operatic and Broadway theatre singing. USA. 1998. Lang.: Eng. 4303
Musical theatre actress M. Chlebnikova. 1998. Lang.: Rus. 4351
The career of soprano Lotte Lenya. Austria: Vienna. 1898-1981. Lang.: Eng. 4352
Musical theatre performer L. Ivanova. Bulgaria. 1998. Lang.: Rus. 4353
Excerpts from critical reviews of singer and actress Lotte Lenya. Germany. 1928-1966. Lang.: Eng. 4354
Friends and colleagues recall singer Lotte Lenya. Germany. 1928-1981. Lang.: Eng. 4355
Lotte Lenya's singing style. Germany. 1929-1965. Lang.: Eng. 4357
Singer Larisa Dolina. Russia: Moscow. Lang.: Rus. 4366
Singer Kristina Orbakajte. Russia: Moscow. 1998. Lang.: Rus. 4367
Singer I. Tal'kov. Russia. 1998. Lang.: Rus. 4368
Singers' approaches to the title role in Bizet's *Carmen*. 1875-1998. Lang.: Eng. 4502
Interpreters of the title role in Delibes' opera *Lakmé*. 1932-1995. Lang.: Fre. 4505
Significant interpreters of the title role of Alban Berg's *Lulu*. 1937-1996. Lang.: Fre. 4509
Present-day opera singing and the Italian operatic tradition. 1998. Lang.: Eng. 4510
Tenor and artistic director of Washington Opera Plácido Domingo. 1941-1998. Lang.: Eng. 4512
Audio and video recordings of opera stars and complete operas. 1988-1998. Lang.: Eng. 4522
Recordings of Delibes' *Lakmé*. 1941-1998. Lang.: Fre. 4524
Soprano Joan Sutherland. Australia. 1998. Lang.: Eng. 4526
Opera singers E. Kočetova and A. Abdrazakov. Bashkir. 1998. Lang.: Rus. 4534
Mezzo soprano Rita Gorr. Belgium. 1998. Lang.: Eng. 4536
Interview with Canadian tenor Richard Margison. Canada. 1998. Lang.: Eng. 4538
Tenor Ben Heppner. Canada. 1998. Lang.: Eng. 4539
Vocal coach Stuart Hamilton on the Canadian operatic scene. Canada. 1998. Lang.: Eng. 4540
Tenor Gert Henning-Jensen. Denmark. 1992-1998. Lang.: Eng. 4544
Response to *castrato* performances. England: London. 1667-1737. Lang.: Eng. 4545
Maria Callas and Donizetti's *Lucia di Lammermoor*. Europe. 1953-1959. Lang.: Eng. 4553
Great female opera soloists. Europe. North America. 1650-1950. Lang.: Rus. 4555
Interview with singer Peter Mattei. France: Aix-en-Provence. 1985-1998. Lang.: Swe. 4564
Natalie Dessay's role in Gilbert Blin's production of *Lakmé*. France: Paris. 1995. Lang.: Fre. 4570
Massenet's revisions to *Manon* for performance by Sybil Sanderson. France. 1885-1903. Lang.: Eng. 4572
Soprano Mady Mesplé on Delibes' *Lakmé*. France. 1961-1997. Lang.: Fre. 4573
Tenor George Thill. France. 1897-1984. Lang.: Eng. 4574
Soprano Natalie Dessay. France. 1998. Lang.: Eng. 4575

Singing — cont'd

Wagnerian soprano Lilli Lehmann. Germany. 1848-1929. Lang.: Eng. 4587
Production history of *Die Bürgschaft* by Kurt Weill and Casper Neher. Germany: Berlin, Bielefeld. 1931-1998. Lang.: Eng. 4588
Interview with singer Krister St. Hill. Germany. Sweden. 1988-1998. Lang.: Swe. 4590
Singer Thomas Lander. Germany. Austria. Sweden. 1981-1998. Lang.: Swe. 4591
Baritone Wolfgang Brendel. Germany. 1998. Lang.: Eng. 4593
Recordings of *Lieder* by Schumann. Germany. UK-England. 1998. Lang.: Eng. 4601
Stage fright and other psychological problems of singers and musicians. Germany: Berlin. 1998. Lang.: Swe. 4603
Historical overview of Wagnerian singing. Germany: Bayreuth. 1850-1998. Lang.: Eng. 4610
Soprano Mária Németh. Hungary. Austria: Vienna. 1898-1967. Lang.: Hun. 4615
Tenor Béla Környey. Hungary. 1875-1925. Lang.: Hun. 4616
Interview with baritone István Gáti. Hungary. 1971-1998. Lang.: Hun. 4618
Interview with tenor Sándor Palcsó. Hungary. 1929-1998. Lang.: Hun. 4620
Tribute to the late soprano Júlia Orosz. Hungary. 1908-1997. Lang.: Hun. 4623
Profile of baritone György Radnai. Hungary. 1920-1977. Lang.: Hun. 4624
Profile of tenor István Laczó. Hungary. 1904-1965. Lang.: Hun. 4625
Soprano Olga Haselbeck. Hungary. 1884-1961. Lang.: Hun. 4626
Profile of soprano Piroska Anday. Hungary: Budapest. Austria: Vienna. 1903-1977. Lang.: Hun. 4627
Obituary for baritone Zsolt Bende. Hungary. 1926-1998. Lang.: Hun. 4628
Profile of soprano Veronika Fekete. Hungary. 1958-1998. Lang.: Hun. 4632
Baritone György Melis and the performance in celebration of his 75th birthday. Hungary. 1923-1998. Lang.: Hun. 4633
Interview with bass Albert Antalffy. Hungary. Austria: Mödling. 1924-1998. Lang.: Hun. 4634
Album on the life and career of baritone György Melis. Hungary. 1923-1998. Lang.: Hun, Eng. 4639
Interview with bass László Polgár. Hungary. Switzerland: Zurich. 1947-1998. Lang.: Hun. 4640
Interview with bass György Tréfás. Hungary: Debrecen. 1931-1998. Lang.: Hun. 4641
Interview with soprano Mária Temesi. Hungary. 1977-1998. Lang.: Hun. 4643
Soprano Catherine Hayes. Ireland. Italy. 1839-1861. Lang.: Eng. 4645
Opera singer Luigi Cucci. Italy. 1998. Lang.: Rus. 4646
Recordings of the different versions of Verdi's *Don Carlos*. Italy. Europe. 1866-1998. Lang.: Eng. 4650
Profile of tenor Andrea Bocelli. Italy. 1985-1998. Lang.: Swe. 4653
Profile of opera star Cecilia Bartoli. Italy. 1995-1998. Lang.: Eng. 4658
Verdi's important mezzo soprano roles, including Azucena in *Il Trovatore*. Italy. 1853. Lang.: Eng. 4661
Interview with tenor Luciano Pavarotti. Italy. 1935-1998. Lang.: Eng. 4662
Interview with singer Cecilia Bartoli. Italy. 1997. Lang.: Swe. 4663
Interview with opera singer Anne Bolstad. Norway. Sweden. 1980-1998. Lang.: Swe. 4665
Interview with soprano Andrea Lory. Romania: Iasi. Hungary. 1998. 19-1998. Lang.: Hun. 4667
Opera singer Fëdor Šaljapin. Russia. 1873-1938. Lang.: Rus. 4669
Life and work of singer Fëdor Šaljapin. Russia. 1873-1938. Lang.: Rus. 4672
Opera singer Aleksand'r Serov. Russia. 1820-1871. Lang.: Rus. 4673
Tenor Sergej Larin. Russia. 1959-1998. Lang.: Eng. 4674
The early operatic career of Fëdor Šaljapin. Russia: Nizhni Novgorod. 1890-1899. Lang.: Rus. 4676
Analysis of the first book about opera singer Fëdor Šaljapin. Russia. 1916. Lang.: Rus. 4678
The life of the opera singer Fëdor Šaljapin. Russia. 1873-1938. Lang.: Rus. 4681
Bolšoj Opera star V. Bukin. Russia: Moscow. Lang.: Rus. 4683
Bolšoj Opera singer M. Mincaev. Russia: Moscow. 1998. Lang.: Rus. 4684
Personal recollections of Šaljapin singing on recordings of *Boris Godunov*. Russia. 1873-1938. Lang.: Eng. 4685
Opera singer Fëdor Šaljapin and his roots in Vjatka. Russia: Vjatka. 1873-1938. Lang.: Rus. 4687
Career of opera singer Fëdor Šaljapin. Russia. 1873-1938. Lang.: Rus. 4688
Opera singer D.A. Smirnov. Russia. 1998. Lang.: Rus. 4689
The tour of the Mariinskij Theatre. Russia: Moscow. 1997. Lang.: Rus. 4690
Books in the life of opera singer Fëdor Šaljapin. Russia. 1873-1938. Lang.: Rus. 4691
Bolšoj Opera singer V. Matorin. Russia: Moscow. 1998. Lang.: Rus. 4692
Interview with soprano Edita Gruberova. Slovakia. 1975-1998. Lang.: Eng. 4695
Interview with soprano Lena Nordin. Sweden: Stockholm. 1982-1998. Lang.: Swe. 4697
Interview with singer Mikael Samuelsson. Sweden. 1960-1998. Lang.: Swe. 4698
The singer, the voice, and the body. Sweden. 1997. Lang.: Swe. 4700
The biennial Singer of the World contest. UK-Wales: Cardiff. 1997. Lang.: Eng. 4706
Tenor Bryn Terfel. UK-Wales. 1965-1998. Lang.: Eng. 4707
Obituaries of singers Randolph Symonette and Todd Duncan. USA. 1998. Lang.: Eng. 4708
Coloratura soprano June Anderson. USA. 1998. Lang.: Eng. 4712
Soprano Grace Moore. USA. 1901-1947. Lang.: Eng. 4715
Dramatic soprano Deborah Voigt. USA. 1998. Lang.: Eng. 4717
Reviews of *Lieder* recordings. USA. Slovenia. Austria. 1998. Lang.: Eng. 4720
Bass James Johnson. USA. 1998. Lang.: Eng. 4722
Baritone Nathan Gunn. USA. 1971-1998. Lang.: Eng. 4723
Soprano Marcella Sembrich's performances at the Metropolitan Opera. USA: New York, NY. 1883-1909. Lang.: Eng. 4724
Interview with soprano Joan Sutherland about vocal technique. USA: New York, NY. 1998. Lang.: Eng. 4728
Soprano Alessandra Marc. USA. 1998. Lang.: Eng. 4729
Verdi's *Stiffelio* and Gounod's *Roméo et Juliette* in New York. USA: New York, NY. 1850-1998. Lang.: Eng. 4730
Anecdotes about soprano Mary Mills. USA. 1998. Lang.: Eng. 4735
Baritone Rodney Gilfry. USA. 1998. Lang.: Eng. 4736
Tenor Tracey Welborn. USA. 1962-1998. Lang.: Eng. 4738
Bass Samuel Ramey. USA. 1940-1998. Lang.: Eng. 4744
Audience reaction to Irish opera singer Catherine Hayes. USA: New Orleans, LA. 1852. Lang.: Eng. 4745
Baritone Dwayne Croft. USA: New York, NY. 1998. Lang.: Eng. 4751
Tenor Anthony Dean Griffey's career and Metropolitan Opera debut. USA: New York, NY. 1998. Lang.: Eng. 4752
Soprano Barbara Bonney. USA. 1998. Lang.: Eng. 4754
Interview with singer Nicolai Gedda. UK-England: London. Germany, West: Munich. 1952-1984. Lang.: Swe. 4859
Interview with singer Elisabeth Schwarzkopf. UK-England. Austria. 1950-1998. Lang.: Swe. 4860

Plays/librettos/scripts
Kazan in the life of Maksim Gorkij and Fëdor Šaljapin. Tatarstan: Kazan. 1868-1938. Lang.: Rus. 689

Training
Singer training at Teater- & Operahögskolan. Sweden: Gothenburg. 1960-1998. Lang.: Swe. 4848

Sinjavskaja, Tamara I.

Performance/production
Opera singers Tamara Sinjavskaja and Muslim Magomaev. Russia. 1998. Lang.: Rus. 4675

Sinners

Plays/librettos/scripts
The development of playwright Owen Davis. USA. 1905-1923. Lang.: Eng. 3526

Sinopoli, Giuseppe
Plays/librettos/scripts
Strauss's *Die Frau ohne Schatten* and a recent production by Giuseppe Sinopoli. Germany. 1917-1998. Lang.: Swe. 4795
Sirett, Paul
Performance/production
Collection of newspaper reviews by London theatre critics. UK-England: London. 1998. Lang.: Eng. 2427
Collection of newspaper reviews by London theatre critics. UK-England: London. 1998. Lang.: Eng. 2473
Sirius Teatern (Helsinki)
Institutions
The proliferation of Swedish-language theatre groups in Helsinki. Finland: Helsinki. 1990-1998. Lang.: Eng, Fre. 1604
Sisson, Richard
Performance/production
Collection of newspaper reviews by London theatre critics. UK-England: London. 1998. Lang.: Eng. 2568
Sissons, Narelle
Design/technology
Professional theatrical designers on design training. USA. 1998. Lang.: Eng. 252
Sisterhood of Dark Sanctuary, The
Basic theatrical documents
Text of *The Sisterhood of Dark Sanctuary* by Leslie Jean Sandberg. USA. 1986. Lang.: Eng. 1508
Sisters
Performance/production
Collection of newspaper reviews by London theatre critics. UK-England: London. 1998. Lang.: Eng. 2475
Sitar, Jelena
Performance/production
Account of shadow-puppet workshop for Bosnian refugee children. Slovenia: Ribnica. 1997. Lang.: Slo. 4926
Site-specific performance
Design/technology
Karen TenEyck's projections for a site-specific production of Shakespeare's *Julius Caesar*. USA: Los Angeles, CA. 1998. Lang.: Eng. 1552
Performance spaces
Modern dance and site-specific performance. Denmark. 1970-1998. Lang.: Dan. 1257
The creation of a site-specific performance space for Sam Mendes' production of *Cabaret*. USA: New York, NY. 1998. Lang.: Eng. 4350
Performance/production
Multiculturalism and the site-specificity of theatre. Asia. North America. Europe. 1976-1997. Lang.: Eng. 485
Eduardo Vasco's production of *Lista Negra (Black List)* by Yolanda Pallín. Spain. 1998. Lang.: Eng. 2360
Plays/librettos/scripts
The Holocaust in environmental theatre of Armand Gatti. France. 1989-1993. Lang.: Eng. 3097
Sitting in Limbo
Performance/production
Collection of newspaper reviews by London theatre critics. UK-England: London. 1998. Lang.: Eng. 2460
Six Characters in Search of an Author
SEE
Sei personaggi in cerca d'autore.
Six of Calais, The
Plays/librettos/scripts
Rhetorical arguments in one-act plays of Shaw. UK-England. 1890-1945. Lang.: Eng. 3453
Sixteen
Performance/production
Collection of newspaper reviews by London theatre critics. UK-England: London. 1998. Lang.: Eng. 2581
Sizwe Bansi Is Dead
Plays/librettos/scripts
The influence of Albert Camus on playwright Athol Fugard. South Africa, Republic of. 1960-1985. Lang.: Eng. 3362
Sjöberg, Alf
Design/technology
Interview with set designer Lennart Mörk. Sweden: Stockholm. France: Paris. 1958-1998. Lang.: Swe. 222
Sjölander, Ingemar
Institutions
Problems of administration at Norrlandsoperan. Sweden: Umeå. 1998. Lang.: Swe. 4473
Skin Deep
Performance/production
Collection of newspaper reviews by London theatre critics. UK-England: London. 1998. Lang.: Eng. 2588
Skin Tight
Performance/production
Collection of newspaper reviews by London theatre critics. UK-England: London. 1998. Lang.: Eng. 2503
Skloff, Michael
Performance/production
Collection of newspaper reviews by London theatre critics. UK-England: London. 1998. Lang.: Eng. 2492
Škola Dramatičeskogo Iskusstva (Moscow)
Institutions
A visit to Anatolij Vasiljév's School of Dramatic art. Russia: Moscow. 1998. Lang.: Hun. 1697
Skrabalak, Duane
Institutions
Profile of Tri-Cities Opera. USA: Binghamton, NY. 1949-1998. Lang.: Eng. 4490
Skriker, The
Plays/librettos/scripts
Caryl Churchill's *The Skriker* compared to her earlier plays. UK-England. 1994. Lang.: Eng. 3436
Systemic poisons in plays of Caryl Churchill. UK-England. 1990-1997. Lang.: Eng. 3463
Analysis of *The Skriker* by Caryl Churchill. UK-England. 1994. Lang.: Eng. 3489
The critical and popular failure of *The Skriker* by Caryl Churchill. UK-England. 1994. Lang.: Eng. 3504
Skytteholmsgymnasiet (Solna)
Institutions
The performing arts curriculum of Skytteholmsgymnasiet. Sweden: Solna. 1990-1998. Lang.: Swe. 898
Slam
Basic theatrical documents
Screenplay of the film *Slam*. USA. 1998. Lang.: Eng. 3893
Plays/librettos/scripts
Interview with Sonja Sohn on writing and acting in the film *Slam*. USA. 1998. Lang.: Eng. 3997
Interview with creators of the film *Slam*. USA. 1998. Lang.: Eng. 4001
Interview with Saul Williams on writing and acting in the film *Slam*. USA. 1998. Lang.: Eng. 4002
Sled
Plays/librettos/scripts
Analysis of *Sled* by Judith Thompson. Canada. 1997-1998. Lang.: Eng. 2805
Sleeping Around
Performance/production
Collection of newspaper reviews by London theatre critics. UK-England: London. 1998. Lang.: Eng. 2434
Report on several English performances. UK-England: London, Stratford. 1998. Lang.: Swe. 2634
Slight Ache, A
Plays/librettos/scripts
Transference in plays by Harold Pinter. UK-England. 1960-1985. Lang.: Eng. 3461
Slow Drift
Performance/production
Collection of newspaper reviews by London theatre critics. UK-England: London. 1998. Lang.: Eng. 2427
Słowacki, Juliusz
Plays/librettos/scripts
The Polish national style in Romantic dramas. Poland. 1832-1835. Lang.: Pol. 3304
Ślub (Marriage, The)
Performance/production
Jerzy Grzegorzewski's production of *Ślub (The Marriage)* by Witold Gombrowicz. Poland: Warsaw. 1998. Lang.: Pol. 2218
Small Craft Warnings
Plays/librettos/scripts
Dramaturgical analysis of late plays of Tennessee Williams. USA. 1969-1978. Lang.: Eng. 3661
Small Domestic Acts
Performance/production
Collection of newspaper reviews by London theatre critics. UK-England: London. 1998. Lang.: Eng. 2533

Small Soldiers
Design/technology
Lighting design for Joe Dante's film *Small Soldiers*. USA. 1998. Lang.: Eng. 3914

Smalls, Charlie
Performance/production
High-school students' production of *The Wiz* at the Edinburgh Fringe Festival. USA: Hattiesburg, MS. UK-Scotland: Edinburgh. 1996. Lang.: Eng. 4381

Smeds, Kristian
Performance/production
Interview with director Kristian Smeds. Finland. 1998. Lang.: Eng. 1919

Smert Ioanna Groznogo (Death of Ivan the Terrible, The)
Plays/librettos/scripts
Morality in plays of Fonvizin, Ostrovskij, and A.K. Tolstoj. Russia. 1764-1869. Lang.: Rus. 3325

Smillie, Ruth
Institutions
Ruth Smillie, artistic director of Regina's Globe Theatre. Canada: Regina, SK. 1998. Lang.: Eng. 338

Smirnov, D.A.
Performance/production
Opera singer D.A. Smirnov. Russia. 1998. Lang.: Rus. 4689

Smith, Alison Sealy
Plays/librettos/scripts
Director Djanet Sears and actor Alison Sealy Smith on all-Black theatre. Canada: Toronto, ON. 1998. Lang.: Eng. 2826

Smith, Anna Deavere
Institutions
Anna Deavere Smith on the Institute on the Arts and Civic Dialogue. USA: Cambridge, MA. 1998. Lang.: Eng. 399
Performance/production
Documentary theatre and the politics of representation. USA. 1966-1993. Lang.: Eng. 2728

Smith, Auriol
Performance/production
Collection of newspaper reviews by London theatre critics. UK-England: London. 1998. Lang.: Eng. 2538

Smith, Caroline
Performance/production
Collection of newspaper reviews by London theatre critics. UK-England: London. 1998. Lang.: Eng. 2578

Smith, Charles
Plays/librettos/scripts
Analysis of *Les Trois Dumas* by Charles Smith. USA. 1998. Lang.: Eng. 3715

Smith, Fern
Performance/production
Collection of newspaper reviews by London theatre critics. UK-England: London. 1998. Lang.: Eng. 2448

Smith, Jack
Performance/production
Analysis of pop performance. USA: New York, NY. 1980-1988. Lang.: Eng. 664

Smith, Janette
Performance/production
Collection of newspaper reviews by London theatre critics. UK-England: London. 1998. Lang.: Eng. 2549

Smith, Julian Maynard
Performance/production
Interview with performance artist Julian Maynard Smith. UK-England: London. 1980-1988. Lang.: Eng. 4246

Smith, Louise
Relation to other fields
Quantum theory in recent New York performances. USA: New York, NY. 1995-1996. Lang.: Eng. 794

Smith, Melissa
Institutions
Women in top management of American Conservatory Theatre. USA: San Francisco, CA. 1992-1998. Lang.: Eng. 1781

Smith, Molly
Institutions
Director Molly Smith, new artistic director of Arena Stage. USA: Washington, DC. 1998. Lang.: Eng. 1789

Smith, Oliver
Institutions
Profile of the American Ballet Theatre. USA: New York, NY. 1998. Lang.: Hun. 1061

Smith, Othniel
Performance/production
Collection of newspaper reviews by London theatre critics. UK-England: London. 1998. Lang.: Eng. 2545

Smith, Phil
Performance/production
Collection of newspaper reviews by London theatre critics. UK-England: London. 1998. Lang.: Eng. 2410

Smith, Robert (Buffalo Bob)
Performance/production
Obituary for 'Buffalo Bob' Smith, former host of *The Howdy Doody Show*. USA. 1918-1998. Lang.: Eng. 4067

Smith, Stevie
Relation to other fields
The performance style of poet Stevie Smith. UK-England. 1961-1970. Lang.: Eng. 770

Smith, Teena Rochfort
Plays/librettos/scripts
The New Shakespeare Society's unfinished four-text edition of *Hamlet*. UK-England. 1882-1883. Lang.: Eng. 3497

Smock Alley Theatre (Dublin)
Basic theatrical documents
Analysis of Smock Alley promptbook for Dryden's *Tyrannick Love*. Ireland: Dublin. 1669-1684. Lang.: Eng. 1439

Smoke
Performance/production
Collection of newspaper reviews by London theatre critics. UK-England: London. 1998. Lang.: Eng. 2460

Smoktunovskij, Innokentij
Performance/production
Memoirs of actor Innokentij Smoktunovskij. Russia: Moscow. 1998. Lang.: Rus. 2323

Smrt dolgo po umiranju ali Marjetica (Death a Long Time After Dying, or Marjetica)
Plays/librettos/scripts
The individual and his world in Slovene theatre. Slovenia. 1943-1985. Lang.: Slo. 3347

Smuin Ballets (San Francisco, CA)
Design/technology
Costume design for the ballet *Cyrano de Bergerac*. USA: San Francisco, CA. 1998. Lang.: Eng. 1032

Smuin, Michael
Design/technology
Costume design for the ballet *Cyrano de Bergerac*. USA: San Francisco, CA. 1998. Lang.: Eng. 1032

Šnajder, Slobodan
Basic theatrical documents
English translation of *Zmijin svlak (Snake Skin)* by Slobodan Šnajder. Croatia. 1998. Lang.: Eng. 1415
Plays/librettos/scripts
Playwright Slobodan Šnajder. Croatia. 1982-1998. Lang.: Eng. 2848

Snakes and Ladders
Performance/production
Collection of newspaper reviews by London theatre critics. UK-England. 1998. Lang.: Eng. 2504

Snatch
Performance/production
Collection of newspaper reviews by London theatre critics. UK-England: London. 1998. Lang.: Eng. 2550

Sneer
Performance/production
Collection of newspaper reviews by London theatre critics. UK-England: London. 1998. Lang.: Eng. 2506

Sneguročka (Snow Maiden, The)
Design/technology
Technical designs for Čajovskij's *Sneguročka*, Houston Ballet. USA: Houston, TX. 1998. Lang.: Eng. 1033
Lighting design for Čajkovskij's *Sneguročka (The Snow Maiden)* at Houston Ballet. USA: Houston, TX. 1998. Lang.: Eng. 1035
Performance/production
Dancer Nina Ananiašvili. USA: Houston, TX. 1986-1998. Lang.: Eng. 1193

Snow Palace, The
Performance/production
Collection of newspaper reviews by London theatre critics. UK-England: London. 1998. Lang.: Eng. 2548

Snow Queen, The
Performance/production
Collection of newspaper reviews by London theatre critics. UK-England: London. 1998. Lang.: Eng. 2567

Snowman, The
Performance/production
Collection of newspaper reviews by London theatre critics. UK-England: London. 1998. Lang.: Eng. 2557

So Special
Performance/production
Collection of newspaper reviews by London theatre critics. UK-England: Leeds, Manchester. 1998. Lang.: Eng. 2559
Sobelle, Geoff
Performance/production
The development of *Letters, or Where Does the Postman Go When All the Street Names Are Changed*, based on experiences of residents of Mostar. Bosnia-Herzegovina: Mostar. 1997. Lang.: Eng. 1831
Sobol'ščikov-Samarin, N.I.
Plays/librettos/scripts
Actor and playwright N.I. Sobol'ščikov-Samarin. Russia. 1868-1945. Lang.: Rus. 3339
Società dell'Opera Buffa (Milan)
Performance/production
Antonio Salieri and his opera *Falstaff*, recently revived. Italy: Milan. 1799-1998. Lang.: Eng. 4654
Societas Raffaello Sanzio (Cesena)
Institutions
Italian experimental theatre at Spielart '97. Germany: Munich. Italy. 1997. Lang.: Eng. 1619
Performance/production
Romeo Castellucci's adaptation of the *Oresteia* by Aeschylus. Italy: Cesena. 1997. Lang.: Eng. 2189
Society for Old Music (Kalamazoo, MI)
Institutions
History of the Society for Old Music. USA: Kalamazoo, MI. 1968-1991. Lang.: Eng. 4292
Sociology
Administration
Adelaide Festival Centre Trust's database for tracking economics and cultural impact of events. Australia: Adelaide. 1991-1998. Lang.: Eng. 3
Sarah Bernhardt's farewell tour and its revenues. USA. 1905-1906. Lang.: Eng. 28
The playbill as a reflection of social and economic forces. USA. 1875-1899. Lang.: Eng. 31
Early American anti-theatrical legislation. USA. 1770-1830. Lang.: Eng. 33
Arts and culture indicators in community building. USA. 1996-1998. Lang.: Eng. 38
Speculation on the future effects of technology and ethnic diversity on theatre. USA. 1990-1993. Lang.: Eng. 42
Nineteenth-century women theatre managers. USA. 1800-1900. Lang.: Eng. 129
The use of impact analysis in the arts. USA. 1998. Lang.: Eng. 138
Outcome analysis of cultural activities and organizations. USA. 1998. Lang.: Eng. 143
The cooperative relationship between Czech and Slovak theatres. Czechoslovakia. Czech Republic. Slovakia. 1881-1998. Lang.: Ger. 1376
Oscar Micheaux's use of an interracial marriage case as a publicity tool for his films. USA. 1924. Lang.: Eng. 3874
Audience
Analysis of audience composition at London theatres. England: London. 1835-1861. Lang.: Eng. 147
The fickleness of theatrical audiences. Finland. 1998. Lang.: Fin. 148
Seven theatre-goers on their reasons for attending a performance. Finland. 1998. Lang.: Fin. 149
Analysis of patterns of theatre attendance. Netherlands: Rotterdam. 1802-1853. Lang.: Eng. 154
The role of the audience in performance. North America. Europe. 1795-1997. Lang.: Eng. 156
Gender-related social issues, theatre, and historiography. USA. 1830-1860. Lang.: Eng. 157
Audience response to the structuring of its expectations. USA: Madison, WI. 1993-1997. Lang.: Eng. 162
The popularity of *nō* among all the classes during the Edo period. Japan. 1603-1868. Lang.: Eng. 1371
Popularity of *nō* plays among common audiences. Japan: Edo. 1603-1868. Lang.: Eng. 1372
Audience response to *Vor Sonnenaufgang (Before Sunrise)* by Gerhart Hauptmann. Germany: Berlin. 1889-1890. Lang.: Eng. 1402
Audience response to Bronnen's *Der Vatermord (Parricide)* and German culture. Germany: Frankfurt. 1922. Lang.: Eng. 1403
Nationalist response to the premiere of Synge's *Playboy of the Western World.* Ireland: Dublin. 1907. Lang.: Eng. 1404
The current state of film, film criticism, and the audience. USA. 1998. Lang.: Eng. 3878
Social uses of entertainment in Warwickshire. England. 1431-1635. Lang.: Eng. 4195
Gender and social warfare at the Metropolitan Opera. USA. 1890-1910. Lang.: Eng. 4411
Design/technology
Lighting design and equipment in various Las Vegas spaces. USA: Las Vegas, NV. 1998. Lang.: Eng. 276
Institutions
Popular entertainment at the Palace Garden. USA: New York, NY. 1858-1863. Lang.: Eng. 403
Economics and the Federal Theatre Project. USA. 1935-1939. Lang.: Eng. 428
Theatre and land use in midtown Manhattan. USA: New York, NY. 1925-1928. Lang.: Eng. 430
Profile of Saint Joseph Ballet. USA: Santa Ana, CA. 1983-1998. Lang.: Eng. 1056
Sidetrack Performance Group, formerly Sidetrack Theatre Company. Australia: Sydney. 1990-1998. Lang.: Eng. 1567
The new children's theatre at Schauburg. Germany: Munich. 1998. Lang.: Ger. 1657
HaBimah and colonialism. Israel. 1920-1998. Lang.: Eng. 1673
Swedish-Lithuanian theatrical exchange. Lithuania: Valmeira. Sweden: Falun. 1996. Lang.: Swe, Eng, Ger. 1677
Polish guest performances of HaBimah. Poland. 1926-1938. Lang.: Pol. 1689
History of the Scottish National Players. UK-Scotland. 1913-1934. Lang.: Eng. 1752
Federal Theatre Project Shakespearean productions. USA. 1935-1939. Lang.: Eng. 1761
East Bay Center for the Performing Arts and the revival of a community. USA: Richmond, CA. 1958-1998. Lang.: Eng. 1764
The economic failure of the American Repertory Theatre. USA: New York, NY. 1946-1947. Lang.: Eng. 1790
Respectability and museum theatre. USA: New York, NY. 1840-1880. Lang.: Eng. 4112
Performance spaces
History and nature of German open-air theatre. Germany. 1700-1994. Lang.: Eng. 442
The present status of dinner theatre. USA. 1998. Lang.: Eng. 471
Naples and the *café chantant*. Italy: Naples. 1880-1915. Lang.: Ita. 4273
Performance/production
Multiculturalism and Italo-Australian theatre. Australia. 1990-1998. Lang.: Eng. 490
Recent developments in Australian 'physical theatre'. Australia. 1990-1998. Lang.: Eng. 492
Cultural identity and Brazilian theatre. Brazil. 1980-1995. Lang.: Eng. 496
Theatrical construction of Chilean national identity and history. Chile. 1990-1998. Lang.: Spa. 510
Blackface stereotypes of colonial Cuban *teatro bufo*. Cuba: Havana. 1840-1868. Lang.: Eng. 512
Commercial theatre in early modern London. England: London. 1550-1680. Lang.: Eng. 518
Practical issues of cultural exchange: the Cry of Asia! tour. France. Philippines. 1988-1990. Lang.: Eng. 535
Indian popular theatre as a vehicle for social protest. India. 1975-1995. Lang.: Eng. 541
Mass theatre in postwar Italy. Italy. 1945-1958. Lang.: Ita. 548
Historical, political, and aesthetic context of *madang* theatre. Korea. 1976-1998. Lang.: Ger. 557
Speculation on the future of Latvian theatre. Latvia. 1918-1998. Lang.: Swe, Eng, Ger. 558
Indigenous Mexican theatre and colonialism. Mexico. 1975-1998. Lang.: Eng. 560
History of Arabic theatre. Middle East. 225-1995. Lang.: Eng. 561
Theatre in periods of exploration and discovery. North America. Europe. Asia. 500 B.C.-1980 A.D. Lang.: Eng. 569
Postwar Polish theatre, culture, and politics. Poland. 1945-1950. Lang.: Eng. 573

Sociology — cont'd

Polish-Jewish cultural relations as reflected in theatre. Poland. 1850-1950. Lang.: Eng. 577

Popular entertainment in Uganda after Idi Amin. Uganda. 1979-1998. Lang.: Eng. 604

Tara Arts and English Indian theatre. UK-England. 1965-1995. Lang.: Eng. 614

Theatre and Ukrainian national identity. Ukraine: Lviv, Kiev, Kharkiv. 1990-1995. Lang.: Eng. 615

Theatre Magazine's anniversary issue. USA. 1968-1998. Lang.: Eng. 617

Analysis of performances at Polynesian Cultural Center. USA: Laie, HI. 1963-1997. Lang.: Eng. 618

The semiotics of antebellum home tours. USA. 1985-1997. Lang.: Eng. 624

Culture and the opera house in Appalachia. USA. 1875-1925. Lang.: Eng. 629

Ethical guidelines for the social context performance. USA. 1987. Lang.: Eng. 632

The marriage of theatre artists Katharine Cornell and Guthrie McClintic. USA. 1893-1974. Lang.: Eng. 634

The mediation of theatre and film between immigrant and mainstream cultures. USA: New York, NY. 1890-1915. Lang.: Eng. 638

Performance at Hull House. USA: Chicago, IL. 1890-1997. Lang.: Eng. 644

Race, gender, and oral life history narrative. USA. 1988-1997. Lang.: Eng. 649

Early American theatre and social organization and control. USA. 1770-1830. Lang.: Eng. 653

The idea of Hollywood in theatre autobiographies. USA. 1950-1990. Lang.: Eng. 665

Boucicault's *The Octoroon* and the performance of race, gender, and power. USA. 1800-1860. Lang.: Eng. 669

Theatre's educational power and socially relevant performance. USA. 1965-1997. Lang.: Eng. 681

Commercial theatre and the values of the Reagan era. USA. 1980-1990. Lang.: Eng. 685

Children on dance. Finland. 1998. Lang.: Fin. 918

The wide diversity of Jewish choreographers. Germany: Munich. 1998. Lang.: Ger. 931

History of Korean dance. Korea. 1600-1985. Lang.: Eng. 954

Politics, culture, and Portuguese dance and choreography. Portugal. 1998. Lang.: Eng. 959

Flamenco variations worldwide. Spain. USA. 1901-1998. Lang.: Eng. 962

National identity and the choreography of Shobana Jeyasingh. UK-England. 1991-1994. Lang.: Eng. 972

The receding place of dance in American culture. USA: New York, NY. 1996-1997. Lang.: Eng. 981

The trend of dancers continuing their careers after age forty. USA. 1998. Lang.: Eng. 991

Masculinity in ballet. France: Paris. 1908-1915. Lang.: Eng. 1070

Marie Taglioni and French Romantic ballet. France. 1830-1875. Lang.: Eng. 1072

Rival styles in *bharata natyam* performance. India. 1930-1990. Lang.: Eng. 1348

Female performers of the formerly all-male genre *randai*. Sumatra. 1980-1998. Lang.: Eng. 1354

The role of the *onnagata* heroine in late eighteenth-century *kabuki*. Japan. 1770-1800. Lang.: Eng. 1364

Power relations in *nō* theatre. Japan. 1500-1998. Lang.: Eng. 1373

Analysis of performance pieces reacting to the Australian bicentenary. Australia: Darwin, Sydney. 1988. Lang.: Eng. 1815

The development of *Letters, or Where Does the Postman Go When All the Street Names Are Changed*, based on experiences of residents of Mostar. Bosnia-Herzegovina: Mostar. 1997. Lang.: Eng. 1831

Interview with director Augusto Boal. Brazil: Rio de Janeiro. 1992-1996. Lang.: Eng. 1833

English and French-language productions of *Picasso at the Lapin Agile* by Steve Martin. Canada: Montreal, PQ. 1997. Lang.: Fre. 1836

Social context of French and Canadian productions of *Les Fourberies de Scapin* by Molière. Canada: Montreal, PQ. France: Paris. 1998. Lang.: Fre. 1842

Czech theatre after the end of Communist rule. Czech Republic. 1989-1998. Lang.: Eng, Fre. 1876

Staging of the Cornish *Ordinalia*. England. 1375-1400. Lang.: Eng. 1890

Contemporary remarks on the styles and manners of actors. England: London. 1740-1779. Lang.: Eng. 1898

Actress Charlotte Cibber Charke and cross-dressing. England. 1713-1760. Lang.: Eng. 1906

Norwich's unregulated entertainers. England: Norwich. 1530-1624. Lang.: Eng. 1907

Casting and performance in eighteenth-century productions of *Othello*. England. 1777-1800. Lang.: Eng. 1909

Finland's theatre offerings in Finnish and Swedish. Finland. 1998. Lang.: Eng, Fre. 1915

Peter Brook's *The Mahabharata*, and problems of intercultural performance. France. 1988-1992. Lang.: Eng. 1925

Martyrdom in the plays of Hrotsvitha. Germany. 900-1050. Lang.: Eng. 1960

Deconstructionist analysis of acting in the theatre of Bertolt Brecht. Germany. 1922-1956. Lang.: Eng. 2007

Theatre, society, and directors Frank Castorf, Peter Stein, and Einar Schleef. Germany. 1998. Lang.: Ger. 2029

Interview with director Christoph Schroth. Germany, East. 1970-1990. Lang.: Eng. 2035

Interview with director Adolf Dresen. Germany, East. 1965-1985. Lang.: Eng. 2036

Interview with director Alexander Lang. Germany, East. 1970-1990. Lang.: Eng. 2037

Interview with director Thomas Langhoff. Germany, East. 1970-1990. Lang.: Eng. 2038

Interview with playwright Heiner Müller about his adaptations of Shakespeare. Germany, East. 1965-1990. Lang.: Eng. 2039

Shakespeare in the GDR: producer and critic B.K. Tragelehn. Germany, East. 1950-1990. Lang.: Eng. 2040

Interview with director Frank Castorf. Germany, East. 1980-1990. Lang.: Eng. 2041

Interview with director Alexander Weigel. Germany, East. 1970-1990. Lang.: Eng. 2042

Directors Manfred Wekwerth and Robert Weimann on Brecht and Shakespeare. Germany, East. 1945-1990. Lang.: Eng. 2043

Gender and Shakespearean production in the GDR. Germany, East. 1982-1990. Lang.: Eng. 2044

Interview with actor/director Johanna Schall. Germany, East. 1980-1995. Lang.: Eng. 2045

Actor/director Katja Paryla. Germany, East. 1975-1995. Lang.: Eng. 2046

Actor/director Ursula Karusseit. Germany, East. 1977-1995. Lang.: Eng. 2047

Socialism and the use of Shakespeare in the German Democratic Republic. Germany, East. 1945-1990. Lang.: Eng. 2048

National identity and Shakespearean production. Germany, East. 1945-1990. Lang.: Eng. 2050

Shakespearean production and the GDR's 'existential crisis'. Germany, East. 1976-1980. Lang.: Eng. 2051

The political and social climate of East German theatre in the sixties. Germany, East. 1960-1970. Lang.: Eng. 2052

Iraqi productions of Shakespeare. Iraq. 1880-1988. Lang.: Eng. 2152

The popular comic art-form *rakugo*. Japan. 1600-1980. Lang.: Eng. 2195

Russian reception and interpretation of the work of Jerzy Grotowski. Russia. 1913-1998. Lang.: Pol. 2236

Changing attitudes toward the acting profession. Sweden. 1800-1998. Lang.: Swe. 2387

Overview of Ugandan theatre. Uganda. 1998. Lang.: Rus. 2406

Analysis of Les' Kurbas' production of Shakespeare's *Macbeth*. USSR. 1924. Lang.: Eng. 2766

The decline of radio comedy and the use of record albums by some comedians. USA. 1950-1998. Lang.: Eng. 3863

Postmodernism in Jean-Luc Godard's film adaptation of Shakespeare's *King Lear*. France. 1988. Lang.: Eng. 3931

Television's impact on culture and social behavior. Italy. 1940-1998. Lang.: Ita. 4063

Sociology — cont'd

Social commentary and *East Side/West Side*. USA. 1963-1964. Lang.: Eng. 4068

The cultural background of eighteenth-century British pantomime. England. 1700-1800. Lang.: Eng. 4093

Account of life in drag. USA: New Orleans, LA. 1995. Lang.: Eng. 4138

A mock slave auction at Colonial Williamsburg. USA: Williamsburg, VA. 1994. Lang.: Eng. 4142

Social concerns reflected in popular entertainment publications. USA. 1870-1910. Lang.: Eng. 4144

History of Venetian carnival. Italy: Venice. Lang.: Rus. 4163

Carnival as a unifying force. Trinidad and Tobago. 1998. Lang.: Eng. 4170

A painting of *commedia dell'arte* performer Tiberio Fiorilli. Italy. 1625-1700. Lang.: Eng. 4190

Masque, movement, and social and political negotiations. England. 1610-1642. Lang.: Eng. 4198

Analysis of beauty pageants. USA. 1920-1968. Lang.: Eng. 4222

Portraying Mickey Mouse at Walt Disney World. USA: Orlando, FL. 1998. Lang.: Eng. 4223

Performance artists Vito Acconci and Hermann Nitsch. Austria: Vienna. Italy. 1960-1977. Lang.: Eng. 4239

The decline of live entertainment at seaside resorts. UK-England. 1950-1998. Lang.: Eng. 4278

American musicals on the Japanese stage. Japan: Tokyo. 1963-1998. Lang.: Eng. 4363

The Hyers sisters and Black musical comedy. USA. 1870-1902. Lang.: Eng. 4384

Gender, nation, and sexuality in opera. Europe. North America. 1998. Lang.: Eng. 4552

Opera in German culture. Germany. 1950-1998. Lang.: Rus. 4599

Chinese street opera and nation-building. Singapore. 1965-1998. Lang.: Eng. 4694

Audience reaction to Irish opera singer Catherine Hayes. USA: New Orleans, LA. 1852. Lang.: Eng. 4745

The survival of medieval English religious theatre on the puppet stage. England: London. 1500-1780. Lang.: Eng. 4890

Plays/librettos/scripts

Playwright Ricardo Halac and Argentina's sociopolitical upheavals. Argentina. 1955-1991. Lang.: Eng. 2772

Female role models in plays by Austrian women. Austria. 1776-1914. Lang.: Ger. 2786

Michel Tremblay's adaptation of *Mistero Buffo* by Dario Fo. Canada: Montreal, PQ. 1969-1973. Lang.: Fre. 2795

Theatre and the creation of a new nationalism. Canada. Saint Lucia. 1980-1995. Lang.: Eng. 2808

Quebecois plays about the crisis of October 1970. Canada. 1970-1990. Lang.: Fre, Eng. 2812

The view of foreigners in *Niaoren (Bird Men)* by Guo Shixing. China, People's Republic of. 1991. Lang.: Eng. 2842

The West in Chinese spoken drama and the effacement of the individual author. China, People's Republic of. 1949-1976. Lang.: Eng. 2843

'Underground realism' in contemporary Chinese drama. China, People's Republic of: Shanghai. 1993-1996. Lang.: Eng. 2845

Shakespeare's *The Tempest* as an experiment in political control. England. 1611. Lang.: Eng. 2862

The figure of the Jew in Marlowe and Shakespeare. England. 1590-1600. Lang.: Eng. 2868

Social, economic, and political thought in Shakespeare's chronicle plays. England. 1590-1613. Lang.: Eng. 2869

The defense of prostitution in Lillo's *Marina*. England. 1738. Lang.: Eng. 2887

Plague imagery in Jacobean tragedy. England. 1618-1642. Lang.: Eng. 2889

East and West in Shakepeare's *A Midsummer Night's Dream*. England. 1594-1595. Lang.: Eng. 2905

Crimes against property in plays of Henry Fielding and Elizabethan playwrights. England. 1590-1745. Lang.: Eng. 2912

John Bale's characters Sodomy and Idolatry. England. 1536-1546. Lang.: Eng. 2914

Recognition, repression, and ideology in Restoration drama. England: London. 1660-1680. Lang.: Eng. 2918

Analysis of *The Masque of Blackness* by Ben Jonson. England. 1605. Lang.: Eng. 2919

The representation of historical female characters on the Renaissance stage. England. 1580-1615. Lang.: Eng. 2922

Attitudes toward Spain in early modern English drama. England. 1492-1604. Lang.: Eng. 2927

Analysis of *The Witch of Edmonton* by Ford, Dekker, and Rowley. England. 1621. Lang.: Eng. 2928

Punishment and political power in plays of Shakespeare. England. 1604-1611. Lang.: Eng. 2944

Biblical narrative and the order of the *York Cycle* episodes. England: York. 1401-1499. Lang.: Eng. 2950

Religious controversy and the emerging print culture. England. 1590-1620. Lang.: Eng. 2956

Shakespeare, Branagh, and the concept of the author. England. 1590-1998. Lang.: Eng. 2958

Shakespeare and the limitation of political and textual control. England. 1600-1611. Lang.: Eng. 2965

The obedient daughter in adaptations of Shakespeare's plays. England. 1701-1800. Lang.: Eng. 2969

Analysis of *Marina*, George Lillo's adaptation of Shakespeare's *Pericles*. England. 1738. Lang.: Eng. 2971

Sociological analysis of *The Shoemaker's Holiday* by Thomas Dekker. England. 1600. Lang.: Eng. 2973

Flemish immigrants in English Renaissance drama. England. 1515-1635. Lang.: Eng. 2976

Shakespeare, feminism, and his sources. England. 1590-1616. Lang.: Eng. 2977

Comparison of the Dutch *Elckerlijck* and the English *Everyman*. England. Netherlands. 1495-1525. Lang.: Eng. 2982

Analysis of *The London Merchant* by George Lillo. England. 1731. Lang.: Eng. 2984

Language, rank, and sexuality in the anonymous *Arden of Faversham*. England. 1592. Lang.: Eng. 2986

The concept of the self in Shakespearean tragedy. England. 1590-1612. Lang.: Eng. 2992

Prostitution in and outside of the theatre. England: London. 1600-1610. Lang.: Eng. 2995

Feminist analysis of *The Tragedy of Mariam* by Elizabeth Cary. England. 1602-1612. Lang.: Eng. 3019

Conscience in early modern literature including Shakespeare. England. 1590-1620. Lang.: Eng. 3020

Evil in Stuart tragedy. England. 1620-1642. Lang.: Eng. 3024

Prejudice and law in Shakespeare's *The Merchant of Venice*. England. 1596. Lang.: Eng. 3027

Space and measurement in *Tamburlaine the Great* by Christopher Marlowe. England. 1587-1588. Lang.: Eng. 3029

Sexual politics in *The Rover* by Aphra Behn. England. 1677. Lang.: Eng. 3031

Authority in Elizabethan England as reflected in the plays of Shakespeare. England. 1501-1600. Lang.: Eng. 3042

Theatre as cultural weapon and military education in the Eritrean war. Eritrea. 1980-1984. Lang.: Eng. 3048

Martial law and Renaissance drama and fiction. Europe. 1563-1753. Lang.: Eng. 3059

Food and alienation in plays of Chantal Chawaf and Denise Chalem. France. 1970-1989. Lang.: Eng. 3072

Social interactions in Racine's *Phèdre*. France. 1667. Lang.: Fre. 3074

Olympe de Gouges and the theatre of the French Revolution. France. 1789-1795. Lang.: Fre. 3109

The development of Western-style Bengali theatre. India: Calcutta. 1795-1900. Lang.: Eng. 3191

Colonial and postcolonial narrative and the politics of representation. India. 1900-1985. Lang.: Eng. 3192

Diaspora and home in postcolonial Indian drama. India. 1978-1985. Lang.: Eng. 3193

Analysis of *Translations* by Brian Friel. Ireland. 1980. Lang.: Eng. 3197

A folktale source of *The Playboy of the Western World*. Ireland. 1907. Lang.: Eng. 3202

Sociology — cont'd

Recent history in Irish theatre and drama. Ireland: Dublin. UK-Ireland: Belfast. 1993-1996. Lang.: Eng. 3212

Caribbean identity in plays of Daniel Boukman. Martinique. 1970-1995. Lang.: Eng. 3271

Analysis of *Soldadera* by Josefina Niggli. Mexico. 1938. Lang.: Eng. 3272

Analysis of *The Swamp Dwellers* by Wole Soyinka. Nigeria. 1973. Lang.: Eng. 3283

Playwright Femi Osofisan on his political goals and strategies. Nigeria. 1978. Lang.: Eng. 3286

Absurdism in children's theatre. North America. Europe. 1896-1970. Lang.: Eng. 3288

Roman tragic theatre from literary origins to the Roman arena. Rome. 500 B.C.-476 A.D. Lang.: Eng. 3315

Analysis of the 'Russian Robin Hood' Stepan Razin. Russia. 1620-1900. Lang.: Eng. 3327

The influence of the war of 1812 on Russian drama. Russia. 1800-1825. Lang.: Rus. 3334

Čechov's character Treplev. Russia. 1890-1910. Lang.: Rus. 3336

Pictorial and staged versions of the Passion. Savoy. 1435-1505. Lang.: Eng. 3342

Analysis of *Zvestoba (Fidelity)* by Etbin Kristan. Slovenia. 1897-1910. Lang.: Slo. 3344

The priesthood in Slovene theatre. Slovenia. 1903-1994. Lang.: Slo. 3345

The individual and his world in Slovene theatre. Slovenia. 1943-1985. Lang.: Slo. 3347

Fascism and the peasant in pre-War Slovene drama. Slovenia. 1940. Lang.: Slo. 3349

Analysis of *Zoran ali Kmetska vojna na Slovenskum (Zoran and the Peasant War in Slovenia)* by Ivan Vrhovec. Slovenia. 1870. Lang.: Slo. 3351

Social roles in plays by Fran Govekar and Anton Medved. Slovenia. 1897-1910. Lang.: Slo. 3352

Social roles and ideologies in plays of Anton Funtek and Ivo Šorli. Slovenia. 1897-1920. Lang.: Slo. 3353

South African theatre after apartheid. South Africa, Republic of. 1976-1996. Lang.: Eng. 3365

Analysis of plays by David Hare and Caryl Churchill. UK-England. 1971-1997. Lang.: Dut. 3432

George Bernard Shaw: life, work, influences. UK-England. Ireland. 1886-1955. Lang.: Eng. 3437

The censorship of the unpublished *Her Wedding Night* by Florence Bates. UK-England. 1917. Lang.: Eng. 3454

Social and political issues in the plays of David Hare. UK-England. 1969-1986. Lang.: Eng. 3479

Byron's heroes and the Byronic hero. UK-England. 1800-1824. Lang.: Eng. 3484

Talk as performance in the life and work of Oscar Wilde. UK-England. 1890-1900. Lang.: Eng. 3492

Analysis of plays about the women's movement. USA. 1900-1940. Lang.: Eng. 3559

Analysis of Cuban theatre in Miami. USA: Miami, FL. 1985-1986. Lang.: Eng. 3574

Gender and politics in Romantic tragedies of Mercy Otis Warren. USA. 1783-1785. Lang.: Eng. 3575

Student casebook on *A Raisin in the Sun* by Lorraine Hansberry. USA. 1957-1997. Lang.: Eng. 3577

American drama and the war in Vietnam. USA. 1969-1987. Lang.: Eng. 3586

Miscegenation in American drama. USA. 1909-1969. Lang.: Eng. 3599

Playwright Tina Howe on gender expectations on playwrights. USA: New York, NY. 1980-1997. Lang.: Eng. 3614

The social roles of women playwrights. USA. 1890-1910. Lang.: Eng. 3637

The representation od social issues on the American stage. USA. 1850-1859. Lang.: Eng. 3647

The comedies of manners of S.N. Behrman and Philip Barry. USA. 1920-1964. Lang.: Eng. 3648

Eugene O'Neill's *The Hairy Ape* and the belief in racial degeneration. USA. 1922. Lang.: Eng. 3657

Analysis of *The White Slave* by Bartley Campbell. USA. 1882. Lang.: Eng. 3660

Analysis of *Bandido!* by Luis Valdez. USA. 1986. Lang.: Eng. 3676

African- and Irish-Americans in the plays of Eugene O'Neill. USA. 1916-1953. Lang.: Eng. 3687

Analysis of *Bandido!* by Luis Valdez. USA. 1982. Lang.: Eng. 3708

The underrepresentation of Hispanics in American arts. USA. 1998. Lang.: Eng. 3716

The popularity of crude comedy in recent American films. USA. 1998. Lang.: Eng. 4004

Apocalyptic futures in science fiction films. USA. 1981-1990. Lang.: Eng. 4005

Analysis of Spike Lee's film *Do the Right Thing*. USA. 1989. Lang.: Eng. 4017

Screenwriting before the Motion Picture Production Code. USA. 1927-1934. Lang.: Eng. 4026

The Roman Empire in postwar American cinema. USA. 1945-1998. Lang.: Eng. 4032

Puritanism and Milton's *Comus*. England. 1634-1635. Lang.: Eng. 4207

Power, gender, and race in *The Masque of Blackness* by Ben Jonson. England. 1605-1611. Lang.: Eng. 4208

Analysis of the opera *Mario the Magician* by Harry Somers and Rod Anderson. Canada. 1965-1992. Lang.: Eng. 4763

National identity in new Canadian opera. Canada. 1967-1998. Lang.: Eng. 4764

The AIDS epidemic in contemporary opera. Europe. North America. 1985-1995. Lang.: Eng. 4771

Ambition and gender in Bizet's *Carmen*. France. 1870-1879. Lang.: Eng. 4786

The *castrato*, the contralto, and the film *Farinelli*. France. Italy. 1994. Lang.: Eng. 4787

Nationalism and sexuality in Wagner's *Ring* cycle. Germany. 1870-1880. Lang.: Eng. 4796

Gender, nationalism, and Orientalism in *Samson et Dalila* by Saint-Saëns. Germany. 1868-1877. Lang.: Eng. 4797

Analysis of Jesuit opera by Giovanni Girolamo Kapsberger and Orazio Grassi. Italy: Rome. 1622. Lang.: Eng. 4803

Virginal heroines in Alpine settings in operas of Bellini, Donizetti, and Verdi. Italy. 1800-1850. Lang.: Eng. 4812

Gender in Bellini's *Norma* and Verdi's *Aida*. Italy. 1831-1871. Lang.: Eng. 4813

Female operatic cross-dressing. Italy: Naples, Venice. 1601-1800. Lang.: Eng. 4814

Derek Jarman's adaptation of works by Benjamin Britten and Wilfred Owen. UK-England. 1968-1988. Lang.: Eng. 4822

Analysis of Benjamin Britten's opera *Death in Venice*. UK-England. 1912-1992. Lang.: Eng. 4823

Analysis of *Plague Mass* by Diamanda Galas. USA. 1991. Lang.: Eng. 4828

Relation to other fields

The differences between theatre and ritual. 1998. Lang.: Ger. 711

Linguistic code-switching as a discourse strategy. Israel. 1950-1989. Lang.: Eng. 714

Postwar Austrian cultural and theatrical identity. Austria. 1945-1998. Lang.: Ger. 715

Theatre of the Oppressed and racism in high schools. Canada. 1991-1998. Lang.: Eng. 717

Antitheatricalism in early America. Colonial America. 1620-1750. Lang.: Eng. 719

Survey of Czech avant-garde theatre and socialist realism. Czech Republic. 1925-1950. Lang.: Cze. 721

Jewish culture and the Prague theatre scene. Czechoslovakia: Prague. 1910-1939. Lang.: Ger. 722

Analysis of anti-theatricalism. England. 1579-1642. 726

Theatre and revolution in the English novel. England. 1790-1848. Lang.: Eng. 727

Humanist ideology and the imaginary stage. Europe. 1549-1629. Lang.: Eng. 731

The culture of decadence in theatre and film. Finland. 1990-1998. Lang.: Fin. 732

Sociology — cont'd

Political-cultural influences on Berlin theatre. Germany: Berlin. 1989-1998. Lang.: Ger. 742

The rise and fall of German political theatre. Germany. 1928-1998. Lang.: Ger. 745

Nationalism and Irish theatre. Ireland. UK-Ireland. 1890-1914. Lang.: Eng. 750

Politics and the dramaturg. North America. 1990-1998. Lang.: Eng. 754

Theatre, the visual arts, and the debate on Puerto Rican cultural identity. Puerto Rico. 1998. Lang.: Eng. 755

Russian and American theatre and society of the twenties. Russia. USA. 1920-1929. Lang.: Rus. 756

The cultural atmosphere of the Russian Revolution. Russia. 1917-1920. Lang.: Rus. 757

Intellectual life in Nižni Novgorod. Russia: Nizhegorod. 1918-1998. Lang.: Rus. 759

The effect of social and political change on Slovakian theatre. Slovakia. 1989-1998. Lang.: Ger. 763

Topics in post-apartheid South African literature and theatre. South Africa, Republic of. 1995-1998. Lang.: Eng. 764

Contestatory playwriting under dictatorship. South Africa, Republic of. Spain. Chile. 1939-1994. Lang.: Eng. 765

Stockholm's cultural facilities. Sweden: Stockholm. 1998. Lang.: Eng. 766

Performative techniques in social and political movements. Taiwan. 1986-1997. Lang.: Eng. 767

Gender, class, nationality, and sanitary reform in nineteenth-century English theatre. UK-England. 1790-1890. Lang.: Eng. 768

Story-telling as a way of knowing and communicating. UK-Scotland. 1985-1998. Lang.: Eng. 772

European fears of American cultural hegemony. USA. Europe. 1998. Lang.: Eng. 773

The use of theatre rehearsal techniques for socially emotionally disturbed youth. USA. 1985-1987. Lang.: Eng. 774

The arts as a sector in American life. USA. 1997-1998. Lang.: Eng. 775

Role playing in the Brook Farm transcendentalist community. USA: West Roxbury, MA. 1841-1847. Lang.: Eng. 777

Criticism of the American Assembly's approach to the arts sector. USA. 1997. Lang.: Eng. 780

Redefining the 'arts sector'. USA. 1998. Lang.: Eng. 781

Performativity of informal story-telling in western Iowa. USA. 1998. Lang.: Eng. 785

Analysis of ritual fire-walking. USA. 1998. Lang.: Eng. 789

Quantum theory in recent New York performances. USA: New York, NY. 1995-1996. Lang.: Eng. 794

Actress Nance O'Neil and her friendship with Lizzie Borden. USA. 1874-1965. Lang.: Eng. 799

Narrative strategy in the analysis of theatre economics. USA. 1960-1995. Lang.: Eng. 802

Theatrical performance compared to multiple personality disorder. USA. 1998. Lang.: Eng. 803

Arts and the public purpose. USA. 1998. Lang.: Eng. 805

Locating and defining the 'unincorporated' arts. USA. 1998. Lang.: Eng. 806

Fitzroy Davis's theatre novel *Quicksilver*. USA. 1930-1940. Lang.: Eng. 810

The changing face of Times Square and its effect on the local community. USA: New York, NY. 1998. Lang.: Eng. 812

Theatricalization of court trials in post-revolutionary Russia. USSR. 1916-1935. Lang.: Eng. 815

The cultural stereotype of the dancer's body. UK-England. USA. 1998. Lang.: Eng. 999

The effect of emigration on Russian dance. Russia. Lang.: Rus. 1197

American modern dance and gay culture. USA. 1933-1998. Lang.: Eng. 1337

The 'bird-woman' folktale in Southeast Asian shamanic healing rituals. Ireland. Thailand. Malaysia. Lang.: Eng. 1358

Amateur art theatre produced by Quebec priests. Canada: Montreal, PQ. 1930-1950. Lang.: Fre. 3733

Performance ethnography of social action theatre Mise au Jeu Montréal. Canada: Montreal, PQ. 1995-1998. Lang.: Eng. 3735

Chinese Shakespeare studies. China, People's Republic of. 1990-1998. Lang.: Eng. 3741

New-historicist analysis of Shakespeare and his time. England. 1580-1616. Lang.: Eng. 3745

Cross-dressing and gender struggle on the early modern English stage. England. 1580-1620. Lang.: Eng. 3749

The idea of culture in the English Renaissance. England. 1575-1630. Lang.: Eng. 3752

Psychoanalysis, the female body, and Shakespeare's *Henriad*. England. 1589-1597. Lang.: Eng. 3756

Theatre and politics in Hong Kong. Hong Kong. 1984-1996. Lang.: Eng. 3772

Catalonian cultural politics and Els Joglars. Spain-Catalonia. 1962-1998. Lang.: Eng. 3775

The social significance of the Disney Corporation's influence on Broadway theatre. USA: New York, NY. 1997. Lang.: Eng. 3782

The influence of Teatro Campesino on American politics. USA. 1965-1970. Lang.: Eng. 3783

The blacklisting of Burton and Florence Bean James, founders of Seattle Repertory Playhouse. USA: Seattle, WA. 1951. Lang.: Eng. 3784

Interactions between commercial and not-for-profit theatre. USA. 1998. Lang.: Eng. 3785

Arts education as audience-building. USA. 1998. Lang.: Eng. 3790

The influence of radio drama on professional theatre. Canada. 1922-1952. Lang.: Fre. 3869

Political power and national identity in African cinema. Africa. 1990-1998. Lang.: Eng. 4034

Symposium on fashion and film. USA: New York, NY. 1997. Lang.: Eng. 4037

The gangster film and public concern about moral corruption. USA. 1931-1940. Lang.: Eng. 4038

Depiction of Jews in Stalinist Russian film. USSR. 1924-1953. Lang.: Eng. 4039

Nigerian video films. Nigeria. 1992-1998. Lang.: Eng. 4081

Using *Seinfeld* to contrast New York and Los Angeles. USA. 1998. Lang.: Eng. 4082

TV westerns and their sociopolitical context. USA. 1957-1960. Lang.: Eng. 4083

The Rodney King beating and how a news event is shaped by the media. USA: Los Angeles, CA. 1992. Lang.: Eng. 4084

Cultural trends of the younger generation. Europe. 1995-1998. Lang.: Swe. 4150

Chinese influence on Trinidadian carnival. Trinidad and Tobago. China. 1808-1998. Lang.: Eng. 4174

African and European influences on Trinidadian carnival. Trinidad and Tobago. 1501-1998. Lang.: Eng. 4175

The *jouvay* ceremony of Trinidadian carnival. Trinidad and Tobago: Port of Spain. 1838-1998. Lang.: Eng. 4176

Carnival, cultural identity, and assimilation. Trinidad and Tobago. 1889-1998. Lang.: Eng. 4177

Indian influence on Trinidadian carnival. Trinidad and Tobago. India. 1845-1998. Lang.: Eng. 4178

Theatrical representation at the Austrian court. Austria: Vienna. 1650-1699. Lang.: Ger. 4210

The square in Italian pageants and open-air entertainment. Italy. 1933-1975. Lang.: Ita. 4227

'Up-to-dateness' on the music hall stage. UK-England: London. 1890-1914. Lang.: Eng. 4283

Brief history of London music hall. UK-England: London. 1843-1998. Lang.: Eng. 4284

Analysis of striptease events. USA. 1992-1998. Lang.: Eng. 4285

Research/historiography

Social and economic forces that shaped American theatre. USA. 1780-1995. Lang.: Eng. 827

Research on dance and cultural studies. North America. Europe. 1998. Lang.: Eng. 1003

Theory/criticism

Terror in theatre. Europe. North America. 500 B.C.-1988 A.D. Lang.: Eng. 839

Society's fundamental need for theatre. Finland. 1998. Lang.: Fin. 840

Political interpretations of Irish literary theatre. Ireland. 1897-1996. Lang.: Eng. 846

Sociology — cont'd

Sociological influence on the little theatre movement. USA. 1890-1920. Lang.: Eng. 862
Survey of theatre studies as cultural studies. USA. UK-England. France. 1957-1998. Lang.: Ger. 865
Gender and culture in dance analysis. Europe. North America. 1998. Lang.: Eng. 1006
Origins of dance as an art form. North America. Europe. 1998. Lang.: Eng. 1011
Eighteenth-century approaches to Shakespearean criticism. England. 1701-1800. Lang.: Eng. 3811
Antisemitism and criticism of Shakespeare's *Merchant of Venice.* England. 1596-1986. Lang.: Eng. 3813
Changes in the social and political situation of Polish fringe theatre. Poland. 1980-1995. Lang.: Pol. 3826
The urge to make Shakespeare contemporary. USA. 1990-1998. Lang.: Eng. 3844

Soderbergh, Steven
Design/technology
Lighting design for Steven Soderbergh's film *Out of Sight.* USA. 1998. Lang.: Eng. 3912
Performance/production
Steven Soderbergh on directing *Out of Sight.* USA. 1998. Lang.: Eng. 3944
Plays/librettos/scripts
Analysis of Steven Soderbergh's film *sex, lies, and videotape.* USA. 1989. Lang.: Eng. 4028

Södra Teatern (Stockholm)
Design/technology
Obituary for Karl-Gunnar Frisell, who oversaw the technical restoration of Södra Teatern. Sweden: Solna. 1920-1998. Lang.: Swe. 226

Soelistyo, Julyana
Performance/production
Julyana Soelistyo and Sam Trammel, winners of the Derwent Award. USA: New York, NY. 1998. Lang.: Eng. 2719

Softcops
Performance/production
Collection of newspaper reviews by London theatre critics. UK-England: London. 1998. Lang.: Eng. 2537

Sohn, Sonja
Basic theatrical documents
Screenplay of the film *Slam.* USA. 1998. Lang.: Eng. 3893
Plays/librettos/scripts
Interview with Sonja Sohn on writing and acting in the film *Slam.* USA. 1998. Lang.: Eng. 3997

Soldadera
Plays/librettos/scripts
Analysis of *Soldadera* by Josefina Niggli. Mexico. 1938. Lang.: Eng. 3272

Soldaten, Die (Soldiers, The)
Plays/librettos/scripts
Power, gender relations, and communication in German drama. Germany. 1776-1989. Lang.: Ger. 3138

Soldevila, Philippe
Plays/librettos/scripts
Philippe Soldevila on his *Le miel est plus doux que sang (Honey Is Milder than Blood).* Canada: Quebec, PQ. 1995. Lang.: Fre. 2796

Soleil pour deux (Sun for Two)
Basic theatrical documents
Text of *Soleil pour deux (Sun for Two)* by Pierre Sauvil. France. 1998. Lang.: Fre. 1434

Solitaire
Plays/librettos/scripts
Science fiction drama since World War II. USA. 1945-1988. Lang.: Eng. 3591

Solo performance
SEE ALSO
Monodrama.
Basic theatrical documents
Text of Michael Healey's one-man show *Kicked.* Canada: Toronto, ON. 1993. Lang.: Eng. 1410
Dutch translations of women's monologues by Dario Fo. Italy. 1998. Lang.: Dut. 1440
Text of *Jesus, My Boy* by John Dowie. UK-England. 1998. Lang.: Eng. 1474
Text of *White Noises* by Shannon Jackson. USA. 1998. Lang.: Eng. 1490
Text of three monologues by Will Scheffer. USA. 1997. Lang.: Eng. 1509
Performance/production
The success of dance extravaganzas and solo performance at the expense of traditional shows. USA: New York, NY. 1994-1998. Lang. :Eng. 645
Hanne Tierney's adaptation of *Bodas de sangre (Blood Wedding)* by García Lorca. USA. 1997. Lang.: Eng. 647
Analysis of transformative comedy. USA. 1975-1988. Lang.: Eng. 666
Interview with dancer and choreographer Hedvig Fekete. Hungary: Budapest. 1998. Lang.: Hun. 1291
Dancer Frances Alenikoff. USA: New York, NY. 1960-1998. Lang.: Eng. 1324
Marie-Ginette Guay's wordless performance in Franz Xaver Kroetz's *Wunschkonzert (Request Concert).* Canada: Quebec, PQ. 1995-1997. Lang.: Fre. 1847
Review of András Bálint's one-man show *INRI.* Hungary: Budapest. 1997. Lang.: Hun. 2073
Laura Curano's solo piece *Olivetti.* Italy: Calabria. 1998. Lang.: Eng. 2156
Profile of actor Tom Conti. UK-England. 1998. Lang.: Eng. 2629
Actor Michael Williams. UK-England: London. 1950-1998. Lang.: Eng. 2644
Analysis of Rae C. Wright's solo performance piece *Animal Instincts.* USA: New York, NY. 1997. Lang.: Eng. 2684
Elizabeth Perry's one-woman show *Sun Flower* about Elizabeth Cady Stanton. USA: New York, NY. 1998. Lang.: Eng. 2718
Performance artist Mimi Goese. USA. 1982-1998. Lang.: Eng. 4252
Plays/librettos/scripts
Shannon Jackson on her solo piece *White Noises.* USA. 1998. Lang.: Eng. 3619
Relation to other fields
'Up-to-dateness' on the music hall stage. UK-England: London. 1890-1914. Lang.: Eng. 4283
Theory/criticism
Aesthetic criteria of critics evaluating monodrama. USA: New York, NY. 1952-1996. Lang.: Eng. 3841

Solodovnikov, Gavrila
Institutions
Gavrila Solodovnikov's Teat'r na Dmitrovke. Russia: Moscow. 1890-1899. Lang.: Rus. 1717

Solomin, Jurij
Performance/production
Director Jurij Solomin of Malyj Teat'r. Russia: Moscow. 1998. Lang.: Rus. 2326

Solondz, Todd
Performance/production
Analysis of Todd Solondz' film *Happiness.* USA. 1998. Lang.: Eng. 3949

Solórzano, Carlos
Plays/librettos/scripts
The postwar existentialist drama of Albert Camus and Carlos Solórzano. Mexico. France. 1948-1955. Lang.: Spa. 3274

Solter, Friedo
Performance/production
Adaptations and performances of *Alte Meister (Old Masters)* by Thomas Bernhard. Germany. 1997-1998. Lang.: Ger. 1996

Soltesz, Stefan
Administration
Stefan Soltesz's administration at Aalto-Musiktheater. Germany: Essen. 1997-1998. Lang.: Ger. 4286

Solženicin, Aleksand'r I.
Performance/production
Jurij Ljubimov's production of *The First Circle,* based on Solženicin's novel. Russia: Moscow. 1998. Lang.: Rus. 2270

Solzhenitsyn, Alexander
SEE
Solženicin, Aleksand'r I.

Some Like It Hot
Plays/librettos/scripts
Opera in American gangster films. USA. 1932-1990. Lang.: Eng. 4023

Somers, Harry
Plays/librettos/scripts
Homosexuality in Canadian opera. Canada. 1970-1998. Lang.: Eng. 4762
Analysis of the opera *Mario the Magician* by Harry Somers and Rod Anderson. Canada. 1965-1992. Lang.: Eng. 4763

Somerville, Jacqui
Performance/production
Collection of newspaper reviews by London theatre critics. UK-England: London. 1998. Lang.: Eng. 2521

Somes, Michael
Performance/production
Recollections of ballerina Margot Fonteyn. USA. Panama. 1946-1998. Lang.: Eng. 1182
Something Cloudy, Something Clear
Theory/criticism
Analysis of *Something Cloudy, Something Clear* by Tennessee Williams. USA. 1980-1981. Lang.: Eng. 3843
Somlyó, György
Plays/librettos/scripts
New Hungarian translations of Shakespeare. Hungary. 1990-1998. Lang.: Hun. 3187
Somogyi, István
Performance/production
István Somogyi's productions of *Magyar Elektra* by Péter Bornemisza. Hungary: Budapest. 1988-1998. Lang.: Hun. 2114
Two productions by István Somogyi of Bornemisza's *Magyar Elektra.* Hungary: Budapest. 1988-1998. Lang.: Hun. 2148
Sonata Belzebuba (Beelzebub's Sonata)
Institutions
Profile of theatre company Teatr St I Witkiewicza. Poland: Zakopane. 1989. Lang.: Eng. 1684
Sončne pege (Sunspots)
Basic theatrical documents
Text of *Sončne pege (Sunspots)* by Evald Flisar. Slovenia. 1997. Lang.: Slo. 1456
Sondheim, Stephen
Design/technology
Costume designs by Irene Sharaff. USA. 1933-1976. Lang.: Eng. 277
Lighting design for the musical *Follies*, Paper Mill Playhouse. USA: Millburn, NJ. 1998. Lang.: Eng. 4335
Performance/production
Collection of newspaper reviews by London theatre critics. UK-England: London. 1998. Lang.: Eng. 2516
Collection of newspaper reviews by London theatre critics. UK-England: London. 1998. Lang.: Eng. 2543
An open-air production of *West Side Story* directed by László Vándorfi. Hungary: Veszprém. 1998. Lang.: Hun. 4361
Plays/librettos/scripts
The disintegration of the American dream in works of Stephen Sondheim. USA. 1970-1984. Lang.: Eng. 4397
The creation of the musical *Gypsy.* USA: New York, NY. 1956-1959. Lang.: Eng. 4399
Sones, Duncan
Institutions
The work of training organization Metier in creating national standards for arts training. UK-England: Bradford. 1996-1998. Lang.: Eng. 388
Sonetto. Un travestimento shakespeariano (Sonnet: A Shakespearean Travesty)
Performance/production
Andrea Liberovici's production of *Sonetto. Un travestimento shakespeariano (Sonnet: A Shakespearean Travesty)* by Eduardo Sanguineti. Italy: Genoa. 1997. Lang.: Ita. 2159
Song of a Goat
Plays/librettos/scripts
Ritual in plays of John Bekederemo and Wole Soyinka. Nigeria. 1965-1998. Lang.: Eng. 3287
Song of Deborah, The
Performance/production
Collection of newspaper reviews by London theatre critics. UK-England: London. 1998. Lang.: Eng. 2480
Song of Singapore
Performance/production
Collection of newspaper reviews by London theatre critics. UK-England. 1998. Lang.: Eng. 2489
Songs for Sinners
Performance/production
The collaborative process at Catalyst Theatre. Canada: Edmonton, AB. 1986-1998. Lang.: Eng. 504
Songtsan Gampo
Performance/production
Analysis of Tibetan Buddhist drama. Tibet. 1500-1984. Lang.: Eng. 1355
Sonnambula, La
Performance/production
Review of one-act ballets by Balanchine. Hungary: Budapest. 1997. Lang.: Hun. 1105
Gendered readings of Bellini's *La Sonnambula* in performance. USA. 1835-1860. Lang.: Eng. 4748
Plays/librettos/scripts
Virginal heroines in Alpine settings in operas of Bellini, Donizetti, and Verdi. Italy. 1800-1850. Lang.: Eng. 4812
Sonny De Ree's Life Flashes Before His Eyes
Performance/production
Collection of newspaper reviews by London theatre critics. UK-England: London. 1998. Lang.: Eng. 2543
Sontag, Susan
Performance/production
Documentary theatre and the politics of representation. USA. 1966-1993. Lang.: Eng. 2728
Sophocles
Performance spaces
Michael Marmarinos' production of Sophocles' *Electra* at the Epidauros amphitheatre. Greece: Epidauros. 1938-1998. Lang.: Ger. 445
Performance/production
The performance of sacrifice on stage. France. Germany. 1900-1998. Lang.: Ger. 530
Collection of newspaper reviews by London theatre critics. UK-England: London, Scarborough. 1998. Lang.: Eng. 2426
Collection of newspaper reviews by London theatre critics. UK-England: London. 1998. Lang.: Eng. 2441
Collection of newspaper reviews by London theatre critics. UK-England: London. 1998. Lang.: Eng. 2490
Plays/librettos/scripts
Analysis of Sophocles' *Oidipous Týrannos (Oedipus the King).* Greece. 420 B.C. Lang.: Dut. 3180
Electra and Orestes in plays of Aeschylus, Euripides, and Sophocles. Greece. 438-411 B.C. Lang.: Eng. 3184
Civic discourse and civil discord in Greek tragedy. Greece. 475-400 B.C. Lang.: Eng. 3185
Adaptations of Greek tragedy by contemporary Irish writers. Ireland. UK-Ireland. 1984-1998. Lang.: Eng. 3214
Ellen McLaughlin's *Iphigenia and Other Daughters* at CSC Repertory. USA: New York, NY. 1995. Lang.: Eng. 3520
Theory/criticism
Theatrical theory and practice. 600 B.C.-1997 A.D. Lang.: Slo. 3804
Sorel, Cécile
Performance/production
The 'grande coquette' on the Parisian stage. France: Paris. 1885-1925. Lang.: Eng. 531
Sorellina di Don Pilone, La (Don Pilone's Little Sister)
Plays/librettos/scripts
The theatre of Girolamo Gigli. Italy. 1660-1722. Lang.: Eng. 4307
Sori-Kut Ahgu
Performance/production
Historical, political, and aesthetic context of *madang* theatre. Korea. 1976-1998. Lang.: Ger. 557
Šorli, Ivo
Plays/librettos/scripts
Social roles and ideologies in plays of Anton Funtek and Ivo Šorli. Slovenia. 1897-1920. Lang.: Slo. 3353
Sossna, Rolf
Institutions
Interview with Rolf Sossna of En Annan Teater. Sweden: Gothenburg. 1992-1998. Lang.: Swe. 1734
Šostakovič, Dmitrij
Plays/librettos/scripts
Analysis of Šostakovič's opera *Ledi Makbet Mtsenskogo Uezda.* USSR. 1930-1932. Lang.: Eng. 4829
Soto, Luis Alberto
Performance/production
Collection of newspaper reviews by London theatre critics. UK-England: London. 1998. Lang.: Eng. 2478
Soul of a Jew
SEE
Nefeš-Jehudi.
Soul of the Rice Fields, The
Performance/production
Collection of newspaper reviews by London theatre critics. UK-England: London. 1998. Lang.: Eng. 2464
Soum, Corinne
Performance/production
Corinne Soum, former assistant to Etienne Decroux. France: Paris. UK-England: London. 1968-1998. Lang.: Eng. 4090
Sound
Design/technology
Presentation of stage equipment by manufacturers. Germany. 1998. Lang.: Ger. 184

Sound — cont'd

Exhibits at PLASA show. UK-England: London. 1998. Lang.: Eng. 229
Report on PLASA trade show. UK-England: London. 1998. Lang.: Eng. 230
Report on sound and lighting equipment fair Live!. UK-England: London. 1998. Lang.: Eng. 235
Report on PLASA light and sound equipment trade show. UK-England: London. 1998. Lang.: Swe. 236
New theatrical sound equiment. USA. 1997. Lang.: Eng. 238
Guide to theatrical design manufacturers and equipment. USA. 1998. Lang.: Eng. 241
The 1998 TCI awards. USA. 1998. Lang.: Eng. 243
Professional theatrical designers on design training. USA. 1998. Lang.: Eng. 252
The new sound system of the Lyman Center, Southern Connecticut State University. USA: New Haven, CT. 1998. Lang.: Eng. 268
The sound system at the Mark Hellinger Theatre, now a house of worship. USA: New York, NY. 1998. Lang.: Eng. 274
New sound and video system in the performance space of Luxor Hotel and Casino. USA: Las Vegas, NV. 1998. Lang.: Eng. 285
Sound system manufacturer Eastern Acoustic Works. USA: Whitinsville, MA. 1996-1998. Lang.: Eng. 286
Panel discussion of sound designers. USA. 1998. Lang.: Eng. 287
NSCA sound products and technology trade show. USA: Las Vegas, NV. 1998. Lang.: Eng. 288
Report on AES trade show. USA: San Francisco, CA. 1998. Lang.: Eng. 289
Design for houses of worship, including their adaptation for performance and exhibitions. USA: Long Beach, CA. 1998. Lang.: Eng. 290
The use of entertainment technology beyond the entertainment industry. USA. 1998. Lang.: Eng. 293
Building a two-scene sound controller. USA. 1998. Lang.: Eng. 297
The new sound system of the Frauenthal Theatre. USA: Muskegon, MI. 1998. Lang.: Eng. 300
Preview of LDI convention. USA: Phoenix, AZ. 1998. Lang.: Eng. 305
Stage, lighting, and sound design for Rolling Stones tour. USA. 1996-1997. Lang.: Eng. 308
Loudspeaker directivity and theatrical sound systems. USA. 1987. Lang.: Eng. 318
Recommendation for inexpensive digital noise-reduction software. USA. 1998. Lang.: Eng. 319
Sound, lighting, and scenic elements of *Star Trek: The Next Generation* at the Las Vegas Hilton. USA: Las Vegas, NV. 1998. Lang.: Eng. 320
Index to *Technical Brief* volumes 11-17. USA. 1998. Lang.: Eng. 323
Evaluation of Sound Score playback equipment. USA. 1998. Lang.: Eng. 329
Mick O'Gorman's sound design and equipment for *Riverdance*. Ireland. 1998. Lang.: Eng. 1218
Technical designs for *The Chairs (Les Chaises)*, Théâtre de Complicité. UK-England: London. 1998. Lang.: Eng. 1524
Sound design for *The Diary of Anne Frank* directed by James Lapine. USA: New York, NY. 1998. Lang.: Eng. 1553
Design concept for Amy Freed's *The Psychic Life of Savages*, Wilma Theatre. USA: Philadelphia, PA. 1998. Lang.: Eng. 1555
The design concept for Nicholas Hytner's production of Shakespeare's *Twelfth Night*. USA: New York, NY. 1998. Lang.: Eng. 1556
Technical designs for the film *Titanic*. USA. 1997. Lang.: Eng. 3910
Model syllabus for a course or unit on sound in film. USA. 1998. Lang.: Eng. 3921
Production design for rock group Genesis' European tour. Europe. 1998. Lang.: Eng. 4096
Sound design for The Spice Girls tour. UK-England. 1998. Lang.: Eng. 4097
Lighting and sound control for the Disneyland 'Light Magic' show. USA: Anaheim, CA. 1998. Lang.: Eng. 4109
Technical effects control system used in a production of *Joe—The Musical* at Koninklijk Theater Carré. Netherlands: Amsterdam. 1998. Lang.: Eng. 4324
Technical designs for the musical *Doctor Doolittle* directed by Steven Pimlott. UK-England: London. 1998. Lang.: Eng. 4325
Sound design for the London production of *Chicago*. UK-England: London. 1998. Lang.: Eng. 4326
Sound design for the musical *Bugsy Malone*. UK-England: London. 1997. Lang.: Eng. 4327
Sound design for *Side Show* at Richard Rodgers Theatre. USA: New York, NY. 1998. Lang.: Eng. 4329
Sound design for the musical *The Capeman*. USA: New York, NY. 1998. Lang.: Eng. 4339
Sound design for the Broadway premiere of the musical *Ragtime*. USA: New York, NY. 1998. Lang.: Eng. 4341
Technical designs for the Broadway production of *The Lion King*. USA: New York, NY. 1998. Lang.: Eng. 4342
Technical designs for Sam Mendes' production of *Cabaret*. USA: New York, NY. 1998. Lang.: Eng. 4343
Sound system used in a soccer stadium for an operatic production. Italy: Rome. 1998. Lang.: Eng. 4434

Performance spaces
Brief history of theatre architecture. Europe. 340 B.C.-1998 A.D. Lang.: Dan. 437
Profile of the New Jersey Performing Arts Center. USA: Newark, NJ. 1988-1998. Lang.: Eng. 467
Architectural critique of the new Ford Center. USA: New York, NY. 1998. Lang.: Eng. 468
The renovation of Arden Theatre Company's F. Otto Haas Theatre. USA: Philadelphia, PA. 1998. Lang.: Eng. 469
Architectural critique of the restored New Amsterdam Theatre. USA: New York, NY. 1998. Lang.: Eng. 476
The architecture of the Bass Performance Hall. USA: Ft. Worth, TX. 1998. Lang.: Eng. 477
The supper and swing-music venue the Coconut Club. USA: Los Angeles, CA. 1998. Lang.: Eng. 4115
Sante Fe Opera's newly renovated open-air theatre. USA: Santa Fe, NM. 1991-1998. Lang.: Eng. 4499
The newly renovated Newberry Opera House. USA: Newberry, SC. 1998. Lang.: Eng. 4501

Performance/production
The theory and practice of scoring a television production. USA. 1998. Lang.: Eng. 4069

Sound Check

Basic theatrical documents
Text of *Sound Check* by Dominick A. Taylor. USA. 1994. Lang.: Eng. 1511

South Coast Repertory (Costa Mesa, CA)

Performance/production
Culture Clash and their production of Aristophanes' *Birds*. USA: Berkeley, CA. 1984-1998. Lang.: Eng. 2713

Southard, Michael

Design/technology
Production design for Gary Ross's film *Pleasantville*. USA: Hollywood, CA. 1998. Lang.: Eng. 3909

Southwark Cathedral (London)

Performance/production
Collection of newspaper reviews by London theatre critics. UK-England: London. 1998. Lang.: Eng. 2500

Southwark Playhouse (London)

Performance/production
Collection of newspaper reviews by London theatre critics. UK-England: London. 1998. Lang.: Eng. 2413
Collection of newspaper reviews by London theatre critics. UK-England: London. 1998. Lang.: Eng. 2441
Collection of newspaper reviews by London theatre critics. UK-England: London. 1998. Lang.: Eng. 2454
Collection of newspaper reviews by London theatre critics. UK-England: London. 1998. Lang.: Eng. 2474
Collection of newspaper reviews by London theatre critics. UK-England: London. 1998. Lang.: Eng. 2486
Collection of newspaper reviews by London theatre critics. UK-England. 1998. Lang.: Eng. 2497
Collection of newspaper reviews by London theatre critics. UK-England: London. 1998. Lang.: Eng. 2515
Collection of newspaper reviews by London theatre critics. UK-England: London. 1998. Lang.: Eng. 2541
Collection of newspaper reviews by London theatre critics. UK-England: London. 1998. Lang.: Eng. 2562

Southwark Playhouse (London) — cont'd

Collection of newspaper reviews by London theatre critics. UK-England: London. 1998. Lang.: Eng. 2573

Collection of newspaper reviews by London theatre critics. UK-England: London. 1998. Lang.: Eng. 2586

Souvenirs

Plays/librettos/scripts

Analysis of plays by James Purdy. USA. 1957-1998. Lang.: Eng. 3700

Soyinka, Wole

Basic theatrical documents

Russian translations of plays by Nobel Prize winners. Italy. 1848-1998. Lang.: Rus. 1446

Plays/librettos/scripts

Analysis of *The Swamp Dwellers* by Wole Soyinka. Nigeria. 1973. Lang.: Eng. 3283

Political satire in the plays of Wole Soyinka. Nigeria. 1960-1979. Lang.: Eng. 3284

Ritual in plays of John Bekederemo and Wole Soyinka. Nigeria. 1965-1998. Lang.: Eng. 3287

Space

Performance/production

Steppenwolf Theatre Company's production of *Space* by Tina Landau. USA: Chicago, IL. 1998. Lang.: Eng. 2672

Space Theatre (Cape Town)

Performance/production

Athol Fugard and the *Oresteia* of Aeschylus. South Africa, Republic of: Cape Town. 1978. Lang.: Eng. 2354

Spaducci, Giggi

Performance/production

Productions by Toni Bertorelli and Alfiero Alfieri. Italy: Rome. 1997. Lang.: Eng. 2175

Špalikov, Gennadij

Plays/librettos/scripts

Collected writings of filmmaker Gennadij Špalikov. Russia. Lang.: Rus. 3975

Letters and writings of film actor and writer Gennadij Špalikov. Russia. 1998. Lang.: Rus. 3976

Spanische Lunte, Die (Spanish Fuse, The)

Institutions

Contemporary drama at Schauspiel Leipzig. Germany: Leipzig. 1998. Lang.: Ger. 1661

Spanish Prisoner, The

Basic theatrical documents

Text of *The Spanish Prisoner* by David Mamet. USA. 1998. Lang.: Eng. 3896

Performance/production

Hitchcock's influence on *The Spanish Prisoner* by David Mamet. USA. 1998. Lang.: Eng. 3956

Plays/librettos/scripts

Mail interview with David Mamet about *The Spanish Prisoner*. USA. 1998. Lang.: Eng. 3993

Spanish Tragedy, The

Design/technology

Set and costume design for *The Spanish Tragedy* at RSC. UK-England: London. 1998. Lang.: Eng. 1525

Plays/librettos/scripts

Attitudes toward Spain in early modern English drama. England. 1492-1604. Lang.: Eng. 2927

Spark, Muriel

Performance/production

Collection of newspaper reviews by London theatre critics. UK-England: London. 1998. Lang.: Eng. 2423

Spassova, Jeanette

Performance/production

Impressions from Podewil theatre workshop. Germany: Berlin. 1998. Lang.: Ger. 2024

Specht, Kerstin

Plays/librettos/scripts

German playwrights on the meaning of Brecht today. Germany. 1998. Lang.: Ger. 3123

Kerstin Specht's *Die Froschkönigin (The Frog Princess)* and its premiere at Staatstheater Stuttgart. Germany: Stuttgart. 1998. Lang.: Ger. 3174

Special effects

Design/technology

Pyrotechnics and its use in theatre. Europe. 1200 B.C.-1998 A.D. Lang.: Ger. 178

Lighting and realism in opera and theatre: Belasco and Puccini. Italy. USA. 1890-1910. Lang.: Eng. 203

Seminar on flying on stage. Norway: Oslo. 1998. Lang.: Swe. 211

Guide to theatrical design manufacturers and equipment. USA. 1998. Lang.: Eng. 241

Lighting design and equipment in various Las Vegas spaces. USA: Las Vegas, NV. 1998. Lang.: Eng. 276

The use of entertainment technology beyond the entertainment industry. USA. 1998. Lang.: Eng. 293

The Datatron control system for visual projections. USA. 1998. Lang.: Eng. 304

Index to *Technical Brief* volumes 11-17. USA. 1998. Lang.: Eng. 323

Magical stage effects in 'vampire' plays. USA. 1820-1977. Lang.: Eng. 1548

Design concept for Amy Freed's *The Psychic Life of Savages*, Wilma Theatre. USA: Philadelphia, PA. 1998. Lang.: Eng. 1555

Production design for the film *Lost in Space*. USA: Hollywood, CA. 1998. Lang.: Eng. 3904

Production design for Gary Ross's film *Pleasantville*. USA: Hollywood, CA. 1998. Lang.: Eng. 3909

TV and film make-up artists Tom Burman and Bari Dreiband-Burman. USA: Hollywood, CA. 1998. Lang.: Eng. 4050

Design awards for the TV mini-series *Merlin*. USA: Pasadena, CA. 1998. Lang.: Eng. 4052

Landmark Entertainment Group, specializing in theme-park design. USA: Hollywood, CA. 1970-1998. Lang.: Eng. 4110

Technical effects control system used in a production of *Joe—The Musical* at Koninklijk Theater Carré. Netherlands: Amsterdam. 1998. Lang.: Eng. 4324

Performance/production

Time aspects of video dance. Europe. 1970-1998. Lang.: Ger. 4059

The Patum of Berga compared to sixteenth-century German festivities. Spain-Catalonia: Berga. Germany: Trent. 1549-1996. Lang.: Eng. 4218

Visual spectacle in Wagner's *Ring* cycle. Germany. 1869-1876. Lang.: Eng. 4585

Spector, Naomi

Performance/production

Tributes to ballerina Alexandra Danilova. USA: New York, NY. 1997. Lang.: Eng. 1165

Speed-the-Plow

Plays/librettos/scripts

Rites of passage in the plays of David Mamet. USA. 1975-1995. Lang.: Eng. 3680

Analysis of films of David Mamet. USA: Los Angeles, CA. 1980-1998. Lang.: Eng. 4006

Speisman, Barbara Waddell

Basic theatrical documents

Texts of plays about Zora Neale Hurston by Barbara Waddell Speisman. USA. 1988. Lang.: Eng. 1510

spell #7

Plays/librettos/scripts

Shannon Jackson on her solo piece *White Noises*. USA. 1998. Lang.: Eng. 3619

Boal's 'joker system' in plays of Ntozake Shange. USA. 1977-1981. Lang.: Eng. 3692

Spencer, James

Plays/librettos/scripts

Science fiction drama since World War II. USA. 1945-1988. Lang.: Eng. 3591

Spencer, Rebecca

Administration

Performer Rebecca Spencer's experience as an Equity Deputy. USA: New York, NY. 1998. Lang.: Eng. 4320

Sperm Wars

Basic theatrical documents

Text of *Sperm Wars* by David Lewis. UK-England. 1998. Lang.: Eng. 1476

Performance/production

Collection of newspaper reviews by London theatre critics. UK-England: London. 1998. Lang.: Eng. 2505

Spielberg, Steven

Performance/production

Spielberg's *Saving Private Ryan* and the war film. USA: Hollywood, CA. 1998. Lang.: Eng. 3948

Plays/librettos/scripts

Spielberg's *Amistad* and historical films. 1963-1997. Lang.: Eng. 3962

Spira, Elisabeth

Plays/librettos/scripts

Recent productions directed by Frank Castorf. Austria: Vienna. 1998. Lang.: Ger. 2788

Spirit Dance
Performance/production
The success of dance extravaganzas and solo performance at the expense of traditional shows. USA: New York, NY. 1994-1998. Lang. :Eng. 645
Spiró, György
Administration
Round-table on author's rights. Hungary. 1990-1998. Lang.: Hun. 16
Institutions
Theatre critics' awards 97-98. Hungary. 1997-1998. Lang.: Hun. 355
Performance/production
György Spiró's *Kvartett (Quartet)* directed by János Vincze. Hungary: Pécs. 1997. Lang.: Hun. 2067
Plays/librettos/scripts
New Hungarian translations of Shakespeare. Hungary. 1990-1998. Lang.: Hun. 3187
Spitz Theatre (London)
Performance/production
Collection of newspaper reviews by London theatre critics. UK-England: London. 1998. Lang.: Eng. 2580
Splash Hatch on the E Going Down
Plays/librettos/scripts
Interview with playwright Kia Corthon. USA. 1998. Lang.: Eng. 3696
Split Britches (New York, NY)
Performance/production
Analysis of pop performance. USA: New York, NY. 1980-1988. Lang.: Eng. 664
Plays/librettos/scripts
Effeminacy on the American stage. USA. 1920-1998. Lang.: Eng. 3682
Split Second Paradise
Performance/production
Interview with performance artist Julian Maynard Smith. UK-England: London. 1980-1988. Lang.: Eng. 4246
Spolarics, Andrea
Institutions
Theatre critics' awards 97-98. Hungary. 1997-1998. Lang.: Hun. 355
Sportstück (Sport Play)
Institutions
Survey of the Theatertreffen festival. Germany: Berlin. 1998. Lang.: Swe. 1651
Performance/production
Analysis of *Sportstück (Sport Play)* by Elfriede Jelinek. Austria: Vienna. 1998. Lang.: Ger. 1818
Premieres of plays on the Nazi theme. Germany: Darmstadt. Austria: Vienna. 1998. Lang.: Ger. 2030
Relation to other fields
The artist and the world in recent productions. Austria: Vienna. Germany. 1997-1998. Lang.: Ger. 3729
Sprechen-Schweigen (Speak-Be Silent)
Performance/production
Impressions from Podewil theatre workshop. Germany: Berlin. 1998. Lang.: Ger. 2024
Sprenger, Wolf-Dietrich
Performance/production
Productions of Horváth's *Geschichten aus dem Wienerwald (Tales from the Vienna Woods)*. Germany: Hamburg, Hannover. Austria: Vienna. 1998. Lang.: Ger. 2003
Spring Awakening
SEE
Frühlings Erwachen.
Square, Le (Square, The)
Plays/librettos/scripts
Narrative and form as theatrical media in the plays of Marguerite Duras. France. 1914-1986. Lang.: Eng. 3101
Squash
Performance/production
Collection of newspaper reviews by London theatre critics. UK-England: London. 1998. Lang.: Eng. 2565
Squat Theatre (New York, NY)
Institutions
History of Squat Theatre. Hungary. USA: New York, NY. 1969-1981. Lang.: Ita. 1670
Performance spaces
Theatre space and performance. USA: New York, NY. 1925-1985. Lang.: Eng. 464
Performance/production
The use of closed circuit television in avant-garde theatre performance. USA: New York, NY. 1978-1986. Lang.: Eng. 662
Squires, Richard
Performance/production
A dancer's experience of and investigations into ecstasy. USA. Germany. 1969-1990. Lang.: Eng. 673
Srba, Zbyněk
Performance/production
The adaptation of classic Czech works to the stage. Czech Republic: Prague, Brno. 1990-1998. Lang.: Cze. 1877
Sreče kolo (Wheel of Fortune)
Plays/librettos/scripts
Social roles in plays by Fran Govekar and Anton Medved. Slovenia. 1897-1910. Lang.: Slo. 3352
Sroka, Adam
Performance/production
The new generation of Polish directors. Poland. 1989-1998. Lang.: Pol. 2219
Srpska drama (Serbian Drama, A)
Plays/librettos/scripts
Contemporary drama of the former Yugoslavia in its political context. Yugoslavia. 1991-1998. Lang.: Ger. 3721
Ssekiryangko, Jackson
Performance/production
Collection of newspaper reviews by London theatre critics. UK-England: London. 1998. Lang.: Eng. 2549
St. Clements Theatre (New York, NY)
Design/technology
Technical designs for Off Broadway Shakespearean productions. USA: New York, NY. 1998. Lang.: Eng. 1539
St. Denis, Ruth
Performance/production
Modern dance and the female body. USA. Europe. 1900-1930. Lang.: Eng. 1321
St. Hill, Krister
Performance/production
Interview with singer Krister St. Hill. Germany. Sweden. 1988-1998. Lang.: Swe. 4590
St. John's Lodge (London)
Performance/production
Collection of newspaper reviews by London theatre critics. UK-England: London, Scarborough. 1998. Lang.: Eng. 2426
Staatsoper (Dresden)
SEE
Dresdner Hoftheater.
Staatsoper (Hamburg)
Performance/production
Music theatre production in northern Germany. Germany: Lübeck, Hamburg, Bremen, Kiel. 1998. Lang.: Ger. 4293
Staatsoper (Munich)
Design/technology
Herbert Wernicke's set and costume designs for his own production of Strauss's *Elektra*. Germany: Munich. 1998. Lang.: Eng. 4429
Staatsoper (Stuttgart)
Performance/production
Reviews of recent opera productions. Switzerland: Basel. Germany: Stuttgart, Berlin, Hamburg. France: Strasbourg. 1997-1998. Lang.: Ger. 4702
Staatsoper (Vienna)
Performance/production
Prokofjév's *Romeo and Juliet*, choreographed by Cranko, Wiener Staatsoper. Austria: Vienna. 1998. Lang.: Hun. 1063
Nureyev's *Swan Lake* at Staatsoper. Austria: Vienna. 1998. Lang.: Hun. 1064
Hans Neuenfels's production of Meyerbeer's *Le Prophète*. Austria: Vienna. 1998. Lang.: Swe. 4530
Soprano Mária Németh. Hungary. Austria: Vienna. 1898-1967. Lang.: Hun. 4615
Profile of soprano Piroska Anday. Hungary: Budapest. Austria: Vienna. 1903-1977. Lang.: Hun. 4627
Staatsschauspiel (Dresden)
Institutions
Festivals of theatre by and for youth. Germany: Dresden, Stuttgart. 1998. Lang.: Ger. 349
Profile of Theater in der Fabrik. Germany: Dresden. 1993-1998. Lang.: Ger. 1644
Performance/production
Productions of Tankred Dorst's *Was sollen wir tun (What Shall We Do)*. Germany: Dresden, Bonn. 1997-1998. Lang.: Ger. 1971
German productions of adaptations of *A Clockwork Orange* by Anthony Burgess. Germany: Dresden, Hamburg, Stendal. 1998. Lang.: Ger. 1972
Actress Christine Hoppe. Germany: Dresden. 1993-1998. Lang.: Ger. 1973

Staatsschauspiel (Dresden) — cont'd

German productions of contemporary Russian drama. Germany. 1998. Lang.: Ger. 1984

Plays/librettos/scripts

Hasko Weber's production of *Morir (A Moment Before Dying)* by Sergi Belbel. Germany: Dresden. 1998. Lang.: Ger. 3132

Family conflict in *Was sollen wir tun (What Shall We Do)* by Tankred Dorst and *Die Hamletmaschine (Hamletmachine)* by Heiner Müller. Germany. 1997-1998. Lang.: Ger. 3148

Staatstheater (Braunschweig)

Administration

Wolfgang Gropper, director of Staatstheater Braunschweig. Germany: Braunschweig. 1997-1998. Lang.: Ger. 8

Staatstheater (Cottbus)

Administration

Current conditions at Staatstheater Cottbus. Germany: Cottbus. 1992-1998. Lang.: Ger. 9

Institutions

The ninetieth anniversary of Staatstheater Cottbus. Germany: Cottbus. 1908-1998. Lang.: Ger. 1645

Performance spaces

The ninetieth anniversary of the Cottbus theatre building. Germany: Cottbus. 1908-1998. Lang.: Ger. 440

Performance/production

Actor Oliver Bässler. Germany: Cottbus. 1985-1998. Lang.: Ger. 1995

Recent productions of plays by Bertolt Brecht. Germany. 1997-1998. Lang.: Ger. 2028

Staatstheater (Darmstadt)

Performance/production

Premieres of plays on the Nazi theme. Germany: Darmstadt. Austria: Vienna. 1998. Lang.: Ger. 2030

Staatstheater (Kassel)

Performance/production

Roberto Paternostro, new music director at Staatstheater Kassel. Germany: Kassel. 1997-1998. Lang.: Ger. 4296

Staatstheater (Schwerin)

Audience

The relationship between theatres and the youth audience. Germany. 1998. Lang.: Ger. 152

Staatstheater (Stuttgart)

Design/technology

Scenographer Martin Zehetgruber. Austria: Graz. Germany: Stuttgart. 1979-1998. Lang.: Ger. 168

Institutions

Productions of Staatstheater Stuttgart. Germany: Stuttgart. 1998. Lang.: Ger. 1620

Interview with director and dramaturg of Staatstheater Stuttgart. Germany: Stuttgart. 1993-1998. Lang.: Ger. 1632

Performance/production

Productions of plays by Shakespeare, Brecht, and Camus. Germany. 1998. Lang.: Ger. 2032

Review of opera productions. Germany: Stuttgart, Leipzig. 1998. Lang.: Ger. 4584

Interview with opera director Jossi Wieler. Germany: Stuttgart. Switzerland: Basel. 1998. Lang.: Ger. 4592

Opera director Inge Levant. Germany: Stuttgart. 1959-1998. Lang.: Ger. 4611

Staatstheater Stuttgart, Schauspiel

Plays/librettos/scripts

Kerstin Specht's *Die Froschkönigin (The Frog Princess)* and its premiere at Staatstheater Stuttgart. Germany: Stuttgart. 1998. Lang.: Ger. 3174

Stabat Mater

Performance/production

New productions of Győri Balett. Hungary: Budapest. 1998. Lang.: Hun. 1095

Staden

Performance/production

Reactions to the opera *Staden* by Sven-David Sandström and Katarina Frostensson. Sweden: Stockholm. 1998. Lang.: Swe. 4699

Plays/librettos/scripts

Interview with opera composer Sven-David Sandström. Sweden: Stockholm. 1998. Lang.: Swe. 4821

Stadsschouwburg (Amsterdam)

Performance/production

Analysis of the ballet *Berthalda en Hildebrand (Berthalda and Hildebrand).* Netherlands: Amsterdam. 1849. Lang.: Ger. 1122

Stadsteater (Borås)

Performance/production

Seven critics on their favorite character or portrayal. Sweden. 1950. Lang.: Swe. 2369

Städtische Bühne (Cologne)

Performance/production

The Cologne theatre scene. Germany: Cologne. 1985-1997. Lang.: Ger. 1964

Städtische Bühnen (Bielefeld)

Performance/production

Interview with director Heiner Bruns of Städtische Bühnen Bielefeld. Germany: Bielefeld. 1975-1998. Lang.: Ger. 4598

Städtische Bühnen (Dortmund)

Plays/librettos/scripts

Hero and anti-hero in contemporary opera production. Germany. 1998. Lang.: Ger. 4791

Städtische Bühnen (Frankfurt)

Relation to other fields

Political and cultural situation of Frankfurt theatres. Germany: Frankfurt. 1997-1999. Lang.: Ger. 744

Städtische Bühnen (Nuremberg)

Performance/production

The work of opera director Barbara Beyer. Germany: Nuremberg. 1996-1998. Lang.: Ger. 4589

Städtische Bühnen Velodrome (Regensburg)

Performance spaces

Städtische Bühnen's alternative venue, a velodrome. Germany: Regensburg. 1898-1998. Lang.: Ger. 439

Städtische Oper (Berlin)

Performance/production

Production history of *Die Bürgschaft* by Kurt Weill and Casper Neher. Germany: Berlin, Bielefeld. 1931-1998. Lang.: Eng. 4588

Stadttheater (Basel)

Performance/production

Shakespeare productions in German Switzerland. Switzerland: Basel, Zurich. 1996-1997. Lang.: Ger. 2398

Stadttheater (Konstanz)

Administration

Dramaturg Dirk Olaf Hanke on the dramaturg's complex role. Germany: Konstanz. 1998. Lang.: Ger. 1383

Stadttheater (Nordhausen)

Performance/production

Director Armin Petras. Germany: Nordhausen. 1970-1998. Lang.: Ger. 2001

Stafford-Clark, Max

Performance/production

Collection of newspaper reviews by London theatre critics. UK-England: London. 1998. Lang.: Eng. 2461

Collection of newspaper reviews by London theatre critics. UK-England: London. 1998. Lang.: Eng. 2507

Collection of newspaper reviews by London theatre critics. UK-England: London. 1998. Lang.: Eng. 2571

Analysis of two productions of Caryl Churchill's *Top Girls.* UK-England. 1982-1991. Lang.: Eng. 2608

Analysis of recent New York productions. USA: New York, NY. 1997-1998. Lang.: Eng. 2759

The language of costume in a video production of Caryl Churchill's *Top Girls.* UK-England. 1982-1991. Lang.: Eng. 4065

Stage

Performance spaces

Materials and finishes for the stage floor. USA. 1970-1998. Lang.: Eng. 472

Quebec's performance spaces. Canada: Quebec, PQ. 1992-1998. Lang.: Fre. 1795

The rebuilding of the stage at Cirkus to accommodate a production of *Kristina från Duvemåla (Kristina of Duvemåla).*Sweden: Stockholm. 1995. Lang.: Swe. 1804

The supper and swing-music venue the Coconut Club. USA: Los Angeles, CA. 1998. Lang.: Eng. 4115

Opera composer Richard Wagner and performance space. Europe. 1835-1885. Lang.: Eng. 4492

Baroque opera and ballet at the Salle des Machines and the Palais Royal. France: Paris. 1640-1690. Lang.: Eng. 4493

The influence of the Salle le Peletier on French grand opera. France: Paris. 1823-1873. Lang.: Eng. 4494

A modular stage used for touring by the Houston Grand Opera. USA: Houston, TX. 1998. Lang.: Eng. 4500

Stage combat

Performance/production

Director and martial artist Huy-Phong Doàn's *La Légende du manuel sacré (The Legend of the Sacred Handbook).* Canada: Montreal, PQ. 1992-1998. Lang.: Fre. 4118

Stage management
SEE
Management, stage.
Stage One (Calgary, AB)
Institutions
Lunchbox Theatre's new play development program, Stage One. Canada: Calgary, AB. 1975-1998. Lang.: Eng. 1576
Staging
Audience
The negative reaction to performance art. Europe. 1960-1988. Lang.: Eng. 4230
Interview with performance artist Tim Brennan. Netherlands: Arnhem. 1989. Lang.: Eng. 4231
Basic theatrical documents
Analysis of Smock Alley promptbook for Dryden's *Tyrannick Love.* Ireland: Dublin. 1669-1684. Lang.: Eng. 1439
Design/technology
Handbook on stage spaces and physical elements. Slovenia. 1997. Lang.: Slo. 219
R. Murray Schaffer's environmental opera *The Princess of the Stars.* Canada. 1981-1997. Lang.: Eng. 4424
Stage machinery in *Il Rapimento di Cefalo* staged by Bernardo Buontalenti. Italy: Florence. 1600. Lang.: Eng. 4436
Institutions
Survey of Stratford Festival season. Canada: Stratford, ON. 1998. Lang.: Eng. 1580
Survey of the 1998 Ibsen Festival. Norway: Oslo. 1998. Lang.: Eng. 1682
Report on the National Black Theatre Festival. USA: Winston-Salem, NC. 1997. Lang.: Eng. 1787
Criticism of plays at Humana Festival. USA: Louisville, KY. 1998. Lang.: Eng. 1793
Émile Morin and Pascale Landry on their Productions Recto-Verso. Canada: Quebec, PQ. 1996. Lang.: Fre. 4233
History of the Society for Old Music. USA: Kalamazoo, MI. 1968-1991. Lang.: Eng. 4292
Performance spaces
The present status of dinner theatre. USA. 1998. Lang.: Eng. 471
Theatre SKAM's production of *Louis and Dave* in a Plymouth Volaré. Canada: Victoria, BC. 1996. Lang.: Eng. 1797
Analysis of a sketch of the Swan Theatre. England: London. 1596. Lang.: Eng. 1801
Stage doors of the Globe Theatre. UK-England: London. 1599-1998. Lang.: Eng. 1806
Shakespeare's Globe and the staging of *The Merchant of Venice.* UK-England: London. 1998. Lang.: Ger. 1810
Performance/production
Multiculturalism and the site-specificity of theatre. Asia. North America. Europe. 1976-1997. Lang.: Eng. 485
Northern Brazilian folk theatre forms. Brazil. 1972-1997. Lang.: Eng. 497
Differences between nudity onstage and on screen. Canada: Montreal, PQ. 1995-1997. Lang.: Fre. 499
The collaborative process at Catalyst Theatre. Canada: Edmonton, AB. 1986-1998. Lang.: Eng. 504
Derision in recent productions. Canada: Quebec, PQ. 1998. Lang.: Fre. 509
Renaissance ideas about classical Greek staging. Europe. 1400-1600. Lang.: Slo. 521
The performance of sacrifice on stage. France. Germany. 1900-1998. Lang.: Ger. 530
Survey of Berlin productions in the holiday season. Germany: Berlin. 1997-1998. Lang.: Eng. 538
Collection of theatre reviews by Roberto De Monticelli. Italy. 1974-1987. Lang.: Ita. 547
Mass theatre in postwar Italy. Italy. 1945-1958. Lang.: Ita. 548
Historical, political, and aesthetic context of *madang* theatre. Korea. 1976-1998. Lang.: Ger. 557
History of Arabic theatre. Middle East. 225-1995. Lang.: Eng. 561
Collaboration of Jewish and Polish theatres in the interwar period. Poland: Warsaw. 1923-1937. Lang.: Pol. 574
German theatre in Russia: a report to Czar Alexander I. Russia. 1806. Lang.: Rus. 581
Theatrical history of Nižnij Novgorod. Russia: Nižnij Novgorod. Lang.: Rus. 588
Profile of Grahamstown National Arts Festival. South Africa, Republic of: Grahamstown. 1998. Lang.: Swe. 597
New London venues and productions. UK-England: London. 1994-1998. Lang.: Eng. 605
Hanne Tierney's adaptation of *Bodas de sangre (Blood Wedding)* by García Lorca. USA. 1997. Lang.: Eng. 647
A Hungarian view of the New York theatre scene. USA: New York, NY. 1997-1998. Lang.: Hun. 677
A guest performance by Stomp. Germany: Munich. 1992-1998. Lang.: Hun. 926
Analysis of *Raszputyin (Rasputin)* by Közép-Európa Táncszínház. Hungary: Budapest. 1998. Lang.: Hun. 937
Artus Táncegyüttes' new production *Csillagőrlő (Starmill).* Hungary: Budapest. 1998. Lang.: Hun. 948
Report on children's dance festival. Sweden: Malmö. Denmark: Copenhagen. 1997. Lang.: Swe. 966
Lois Weaver's *Faith and Dancing* and the CD-ROM in interactive performance. UK-England. USA. 1996. Lang.: Eng. 971
Report on touring ice show *Stars on Ice.* USA. 1998. Lang.: Eng. 990
Nureyev's *Swan Lake* at Staatsoper. Austria: Vienna. 1998. Lang.: Hun. 1064
Robert Wilson's dance adaptation of *Le Martyre de Saint Sébastien* by D'Annunzio. France: Paris. 1988. Lang.: Ita. 1074
La Fille mal Gardée at Erkel Színház. Hungary: Budapest. 1997. Lang.: Hun. 1087
Bartók's *A csodálatos mandarin (The Miraculous Mandarin)* choreographed by Gyula Harangozó. Hungary: Budapest. 1998.Lang.: Hun. 1088
Guest performance of the Limón Dance Company. Hungary: Budapest. 1998. Lang.: Hun. 1089
The Budapest Opera House's new production of *Giselle.* Hungary: Budapest. 1998. Lang.: Hun. 1094
Productions of the Magyar Fesztival Balett choreographed by Iván Markó. Hungary: Budapest. 1998. Lang.: Hun. 1097
Bartók's *A fából faragott királyfi (The Wooden Prince)* choreographed by László Seregi. Hungary: Budapest. 1998. Lang.: Hun. 1103
Review of one-act ballets by Balanchine. Hungary: Budapest. 1997. Lang.: Hun. 1105
Guest performance of Oleg Danovski Dance Theatre. Hungary: Budapest. 1998. Lang.: Hun. 1109
Antal Fodor's ballet *A Próba (The Rehearsal).* Hungary: Budapest. 1998. Lang.: Hun. 1111
The Nutcracker at the Budapest Opera House. Hungary: Budapest. 1998. Lang.: Hun. 1115
Amedeo Amodio's new choreography for Čajkovskij's *The Nutcracker.* Italy: Rome. 1998. Lang.: Hun. 1118
Dutch National Ballet production at the Holland Festival. Netherlands: Amsterdam. 1997. Lang.: Hun. 1121
The European and American tour of the Polish National Ballet. Poland. France. USA. 1937-1939. Lang.: Pol. 1124
Guest performance of the Kremlevskij Balet. Russia. Hungary: Budapest. 1998. Lang.: Hun. 1137
Matthew Bourne's choreography for *Swan Lake.* UK-England. 1998. Lang.: Eng. 1159
The body and personality of the dancer as the source of the physical vocabulary of dance. Europe. 1989. Lang.: Eng. 1269
Director and choreographer Nada Kokotovic. Europe. 1978-1998. Lang.: Ger. 1272
Open-air dance performances. Hungary: Pécs. 1998. Lang.: Hun. 1292
Report on Dance Umbrella festival. UK-England: London. 1997. Lang.: Eng. 1310
Shakespeare and traditional Asian theatrical forms. China, People's Republic of. India. Japan. 1981-1997. Lang.: Eng. 1346
Stage adaptations of literary classics and the effect on audiences. 1998. Lang.: Rus. 1811
Analysis of *Sportstück (Sport Play)* by Elfriede Jelinek. Austria: Vienna. 1998. Lang.: Ger. 1818
Luc Bondy's production of Horváth's *Figaro lässt sich scheiden (Figaro Gets Divorced).* Austria: Vienna. 1998. Lang.: Ger. 1822

Staging — cont'd

Robert Lepage's *Geometry of Miracles* at the Salzburg Festival. Austria: Salzburg. 1998. Lang.: Ger. 1824

Music in German-language Prague productions. Austrian Empire: Prague. 1750-1800. Lang.: Cze. 1826

Rijfkat Israfilov's production of *Bibinur, ah, Bibinur!*. Bashkir: Ufa. 1998. Lang.: Rus. 1827

Review of Brazilian performances of plays by Brecht. Brazil: São Paulo. 1998. Lang.: Ger. 1832

English and French-language productions of *Picasso at the Lapin Agile* by Steve Martin. Canada: Montreal, PQ. 1997. Lang.: Fre. 1836

Analysis of a student production of Caryl Churchill's *Cloud Nine*. Canada. 1997. Lang.: Eng. 1840

The Shaw Festival season. Canada: Niagara-on-the-Lake, ON. 1998. Lang.: Eng. 1843

The methodology of director Robert Lepage. Canada: Toronto, ON. 1992. Lang.: Eng. 1845

Interview with director Dominic Champagne. Canada: Montreal, PQ. 1998. Lang.: Fre. 1860

Comparison of simple productions and visual shows. Canada: Montreal, PQ, Quebec, PQ, Toronto, ON. 1998. Lang.: Fre. 1861

Michel Laprise's *Masculin/Féminin (Male/Female)*, presented to audiences segregated by sex. Canada: Montreal, PQ. 1998. Lang.: Fre. 1867

Report on Chinese Shakespeare festival. China, People's Republic of: Beijing, Shanghai. 1986. Lang.: Eng. 1873

Shaw's *Major Barbara* at the People's Arts Theatre. China, People's Republic of: Beijing. 1991. Lang.: Eng. 1874

Czech theatre after the end of Communist rule. Czech Republic. 1989-1998. Lang.: Eng, Fre. 1876

Otomar Krejča's production of *Faust* at Národní Divadlo. Czech Republic: Prague. 1997. Lang.: Eng, Fre. 1881

Comparison of fifteen productions of Euripides' *Medea*. Czech Republic. 1921-1998. Lang.: Cze. 1885

Staging of the Cornish *Ordinalia*. England. 1375-1400. Lang.: Eng. 1890

Performing the killing of Polonius in Shakespeare's *Hamlet*. England. 1600-1601. Lang.: Eng. 1892

Shakespeare's *The Tempest* on the eighteenth-century stage. England: London. 1701-1800. Lang.: Eng. 1895

Shakespearean production and the theatrical portrait collection of the Garrick Club. England: London. 1702-1814. Lang.: Eng. 1903

Rehearsal practices in British professional theatre. England. 1500-1700. Lang.: Eng. 1905

Norwich's unregulated entertainers. England: Norwich. 1530-1624. Lang.: Eng. 1907

Approaches to staging Brecht's plays, based on compiled reviews. Europe. 1961-1997. Lang.: Ger. 1910

The role of the dramaturg in script development and production. Finland. 1998. Lang.: Fin. 1914

The influence of psychotherapy on Finnish theatrical practices. Finland. 1998. Lang.: Fin. 1920

Survey of Parisian theatre. France: Paris. 1998. Lang.: Eng. 1924

The Avignon Festival under the direction of Bernard Faivre D'Arcier. France: Avignon. 1998. Lang.: Ger. 1927

Report on the Parisian theatre season. France: Paris. 1996-1997. Lang.: Eng. 1928

Peter Brook's *Je suis un phénomène (I Am a Phenomenon)* at Bouffes du Nord. France: Paris. 1998. Lang.: Hun. 1930

Productions of the Paris Festival d'Automne. France: Paris. 1998. Lang.: Fre. 1931

Pirandello on the French stage. France. 1950-1981. Lang.: Ita. 1932

Recent Paris productions. France: Paris. 1997-1998. Lang.: Ger. 1933

Peter Brook's *Je suis un phénomène (I Am a Phenomenon)*. France: Paris. 1998. Lang.: Ger. 1934

French productions of German plays. France. 1998. Lang.: Ger. 1935

Survey of Parisian productions. France: Paris. 1997-1998. Lang.: Eng. 1937

Comparison of text-based and visual productions. France. 1998. Lang.: Fre. 1939

French production of *Im Dickicht der Städte (In the Jungle of Cities)* by Bertolt Brecht. France. 1997-1998. Lang.: Ger. 1946

Comparison of productions of Brecht's *Die Massnahme (The Measures Taken)*. Germany: Berlin, Wuppertal. 1995-1998. Lang.: Ger. 1950

Erwin Piscator and Brecht's *Schwejk im zweiten Weltkrieg (Schweik in the Second World War)*. Germany: Berlin. 1928. Lang.: Ger. 1952

Rehearsals of Christoph Marthaler's production of *Arsenic and Old Lace* by Joseph Kesselring. Germany: Hamburg. 1998. Lang.: Ger. 1953

Peter Zadek's production of Čechov's *Višnëvyj sad (The Cherry Orchard)*. Germany. Netherlands. 1998. Lang.: Dut. 1954

Two productions of Brecht's *Der Kaukasische Kreidekreis (The Caucasian Chalk Circle)*. Germany: Berlin, Hamburg. 1998. Lang.: Ger. 1957

Political changes reflected in Berlin theatre productions. Germany: Berlin. 1998. Lang.: Ger. 1958

Shakespeare performance on the Rhine and the Ruhr. Germany: Cologne, Bochum, Düsseldorf. 1996-1997. Lang.: Ger. 1962

Interview with director Jochen Gerz. Germany: Berlin. 1998. Lang.: Ger, Fre, Dut, Eng. 1967

Productions directed by Christian Stückl, Tom Kühnel, and Robert Schuster. Germany: Frankfurt. 1997-1998. Lang.: Ger. 1969

Productions of Tankred Dorst's *Was sollen wir tun (What Shall We Do)*. Germany: Dresden, Bonn. 1997-1998. Lang.: Ger. 1971

German productions of adaptations of *A Clockwork Orange* by Anthony Burgess. Germany: Dresden, Hamburg, Stendal. 1998. Lang.: Ger. 1972

The performance of Shakespeare in the former East Germany. Germany: Rostock, Leipzig, Berlin, Dessau. 1996-1997. Lang.: Ger. 1974

Shakespearean productions in northern Germany. Germany: Hamburg. 1996-1997. Lang.: Ger. 1978

Interview with director Benno Besson. Germany: Berlin. 1947-1998. Lang.: Ger. 1981

Productions of new plays by Peter Handke and Katharine Gericke at Niedersächsische Staatstheater. Germany: Hannover. 1998. Lang.: Ger. 1983

German productions of contemporary Russian drama. Germany. 1998. Lang.: Ger. 1984

Reviews of productions of plays by Brecht. Germany. 1998. Lang.: Ger. 1986

Director Angela Brodauf. Germany: Dortmund. 1984-1998. Lang.: Ger. 1989

Productions of the Bad Hersfelder Festspiele. Germany: Bad Hersfeld. 1998. Lang.: Ger. 1991

Productions of the Kleist theatre festival. Germany: Frankfurt/Oder. 1998. Lang.: Ger. 1993

Adaptations and performances of *Alte Meister (Old Masters)* by Thomas Bernhard. Germany. 1997-1998. Lang.: Ger. 1996

Klaus Michael Grüber's production of Goethe's *Iphigenia auf Tauris*. Germany: Berlin. 1998. Lang.: Swe. 1997

Director Armin Petras. Germany: Nordhausen. 1970-1998. Lang.: Ger. 2001

Political context of Frank Castorf's production of *Les Mains Sales (Dirty Hands)* by Sartre. Germany: Berlin. 1998. Lang.: Ger. 2002

Productions of Horváth's *Geschichten aus dem Wienerwald (Tales from the Vienna Woods)*. Germany: Hamburg, Hannover. Austria: Vienna. 1998. Lang.: Ger. 2003

Comparison of productions of *The Lisbon Traviata* by Terrence McNally. Germany: Berlin, Essen. 1998. Lang.: Ger. 2005

Recent productions of Schauspiel Leipzig. Germany: Leipzig. 1997-1998. Lang.: Ger. 2011

Reviews of German Shakespearean productions. Germany: Wuppertal, Cologne, Oberhausen. 1998. Lang.: Ger. 2017

Andreas Kriegenburg's production of Büchner's *Leonce und Lena*. Germany: Munich. 1998. Lang.: Ger. 2020

Roberto Ciulli's production of *Doña Rosita la Soltera (Doña Rosita the Spinster)* by Federico García Lorca. Germany: Munich. 1998. Lang.: Ger. 2021

Impressions from Podewil theatre workshop. Germany: Berlin. 1998. Lang.: Ger. 2024

A production of Schiller's *Die Räuber (The Robbers)* performed by prisoners. Germany: Berlin. 1997. Lang.: Ger. 2025

Playwright Theresia Walser on children's reactions to Christmas plays. Germany. Switzerland. 1997. Lang.: Ger. 2027

Staging – cont'd

Recent productions of plays by Bertolt Brecht. Germany. 1997-1998. Lang.: Ger. 2028

Premieres of plays on the Nazi theme. Germany: Darmstadt. Austria: Vienna. 1998. Lang.: Ger. 2030

Klaus Michael Grüber's production of Goethe's *Iphigenia auf Tauris*. Germany: Berlin. 1998. Lang.: Ger. 2031

Productions of plays by Shakespeare, Brecht, and Camus. Germany. 1998. Lang.: Ger. 2032

German productions of Shakespeare. Germany: Leipzig, Hamburg, Berlin. 1998. Lang.: Ger. 2033

Recent productions of Deutsches Schauspielhaus. Germany: Hamburg. 1998. Lang.: Ger. 2034

Pirandello on the Greek stage. Greece. 1914-1995. Lang.: Ita. 2054

Péter Kárpáti's *Díszelőadás (Gala Performance)* directed by Balázs Simon. Hungary: Budapest. 1998. Lang.: Hun. 2057

Tom Stoppard's *Arcadia* as directed by Tamás Ascher. Hungary: Budapest. 1998. Lang.: Hun. 2058

Interviews with actors on Anatolij Vasiljév's guest direction at Szigligeti Theatre. Hungary: Szolnok. 1998. Lang.: Hun. 2061

Molière's *Dom Juan* directed by Olga Barabás. Hungary. Romania: Sfântu-Gheorghe. 1998. Lang.: Hun. 2063

Review of Madách's *Tragedy of Man* at the Hungarian Theatre of Kolozsvár. Hungary. Romania: Cluj-Napoca. 1997. Lang.: Hun. 2065

Review of Shakespeare's *The Merchant of Venice*, Szigligeti Theatre. Hungary: Szolnok. 1997. Lang.: Hun. 2066

György Spiró's *Kvartett (Quartet)* directed by János Vincze. Hungary: Pécs. 1997. Lang.: Hun. 2067

Review of Arthur Miller's *The Crucible* directed by Péter Rudolf. Hungary: Budapest. 1998. Lang.: Hun. 2068

János Acs' *A mennyei híd (The Heavenly Bridge)* directed by Gábor Cziezel. Hungary: Debrecen. 1998. Lang.: Hun. 2069

Review of András Bálint's one-man show *INRI*. Hungary: Budapest. 1997. Lang.: Hun. 2073

Krleža's *U agoniji (In Agony)* directed by Péter Valló. Hungary: Budapest. 1998. Lang.: Hun. 2074

Čechov's one-act plays at Thália Színház. Hungary. Slovakia: Košice. 1998. Lang.: Hun. 2075

Pál Békés' *Pincejáték (Cellar Play)* directed by Zoltán Ternyák. Hungary: Budapest. 1997. Lang.: Hun. 2078

Review of Gombrowicz's *Princess Yvonne*, Katona József Theatre. Hungary: Budapest. 1997. Lang.: Hun. 2079

One-act comedies by Čechov directed by Péter Valló. Hungary: Dunaújváros. 1998. Lang.: Hun. 2080

Guest performance of Théâtre du Plantin, a company for developmentally disabled actors. Hungary: Budapest. 1983-1998. Lang.: Hun. 2081

Čechov's *Platonov* as adapted and directed by Erzsébet Gaál. Hungary: Budapest. 1997. Lang.: Hun. 2082

Review of István Örkény's *Kulcskeresők (Searching for the Key)*, Katona József Theatre. Hungary: Budapest. 1998. Lang.: Hun. 2083

Brecht's *Die Heilige Johanna der Schlachthöfe (Saint Joan of the Stockyards)* directed by Sándor Zsóter. Hungary: Miskolc. 1998. Lang.: Hun. 2084

Review of plays directed by Árpad Schilling. Hungary: Budapest. 1998. Lang.: Hun. 2085

Review of Shakespeare's *Much Ado About Nothing*, Szeged National Theatre. Hungary: Szeged. 1997. Lang.: Hun. 2086

Thomas Bernhard's *Ritter, Dene, Voss* at Bárka Színház. Hungary: Budapest. 1997. Lang.: Hun. 2087

Hauptmann's *Fuhrmann Henschel (Drayman Henschel)* directed by Sándor Zsótér. Hungary: Budapest. 1997. Lang.: Hun. 2088

Reviews of two plays by Per Olov Enquist. Hungary: Budapest. 1998. Lang.: Hun. 2089

Madách's *Tragedy of Man* directed by Sándor Beke. Hungary: Eger. 1998. Lang.: Hun. 2090

Molière's *Misanthrope* directed by Andor Lukáts. Hungary: Budapest. 1998. Lang.: Hun. 2091

Goldoni's *La Locandiera* directed by Lászlo Keszég. Hungary: Kaposvár. 1998. Lang.: Hun. 2092

Review of Molnár's *Az üvegcipő (The Glass Slipper)*, Új Színház. Hungary: Budapest. 1997. Lang.: Hun. 2094

Review of Bulgakov's *Ivan Vasiljėvič* directed by János Mohácsi. Hungary: Kaposvár. 1998. Lang.: Hun. 2095

A.A. Vasiljév's production of *Bez viny vinovatjė (Guilty Though Innocent)* by Ostrovskij. Hungary: Szolnok. 1998. Lang.:Hun. 2096

Performances at the new Bárka Színház. Hungary: Budapest. 1997. Lang.: Hun. 2097

Symbolism in Anatolij Vasiljév's production of *Guilty Though Innocent* by Ostrovskij. Hungary: Szolnok. 1998. Lang.: Hun. 2098

Lorca's *Doña Rosita* directed by Gergő Kaszás. Hungary: Budapest. 1998. Lang.: Hun. 2099

Dostojévskij's *Crime and Punishment* directed by Géza Tordy. Hungary: Győr. 1998. Lang.: Hun. 2100

Csaba Kiss's adaptation of Shakespeare's chronicle plays at Bárka Színház. Hungary: Győr. 1997. Lang.: Hun. 2101

Review of Róbert Alföldi's *Phaedra-story*. Hungary: Budapest. 1997. Lang.: Hun. 2102

Sándor Lajos' *Szűrővizsgálat (Screen Test)* directed by Tamás Fodor. Hungary: Budapest. 1998. Lang.: Hun. 2103

One-act plays of Čechov by the Illyés Gyula National Theatre. Hungary. Ukraine: Beregovo. 1997. Lang.: Hun. 2104

András Szigethy's *Kegyelem (Mercy)* directed by László Vándorfi. Hungary: Veszprém. 1998. Lang.: Hun. 2105

Review of Péter Forgách's *Kaspar*, Győr National Theatre. Hungary: Győr. 1998. Lang.: Hun. 2106

Gogol's *Revizor (The Inspector General)* directed by Árpád Jutocsa Hegyi. Hungary: Miskolc. 1998. Lang.: Hun. 2108

Round-table discussion on Tivoli Theatre's production of *The Merchant of Venice*. Hungary. 1986-1997. Lang.: Hun. 2109

Lajos Parti Nagy's *Ibusár* directed by János Mikuli. Hungary: Kecskemét, Pécs. 1998. Lang.: Hun. 2110

Shakespeare's *The Merchant of Venice* directed by Róbert Alföldi. Hungary: Budapest. 1998. Lang.: Hun. 2111

Two productions of Csokonai Vitéz's *Karnyóné és a két szeleburdiak (Mrs. Karnyó and the Two Feather-Brains)*. Hungary: Budapest. 1998. Lang.: Hun. 2113

István Somogyi's productions of *Magyar Elektra* by Péter Bornemisza. Hungary: Budapest. 1988-1998. Lang.: Hun. 2114

István Verebes' production of Shakespeare's *Hamlet*. Hungary: Nyíregyháza. 1997. Lang.: Hun. 2116

Ferenc Deák's *Fojtás (Tamping)* directed by László Babarczy. Hungary: Kaposvár. 1998. Lang.: Hun. 2117

Two productions of Ernő Szép's *Vőlegény (The Fiancé)*. Hungary: Nyíregyháza. Hungary: Győr. 1998.Lang.: Hun. 2118

Three Hungarian productions of Shakespeare's *Richard III*. Hungary: Budapest, Zsámbék, Szeged. 1997. Lang.: Hun. 2121

Review of Darvasi's *Bolond Helga (Foolish Helga)*, Csokonai Theatre. Hungary: Debrecen. 1997. Lang.: Hun. 2122

Two Hungarian productions of Arthur Miller's *Death of a Salesman*. Hungary: Pécs, Szeged. 1998. Lang.: Hun. 2123

Čechov's *Diadia Vania (Uncle Vanya)* directed by János Szász. Hungary: Nyíregyháza. 1998. Lang.: Hun. 2124

Events of the Zsámbék theatre festival. Hungary: Zsámbék. 1998. Lang.: Hun. 2126

Brecht's *Der Kaukasische Kreidkreis (The Caucasian Chalk Circle)* adapted and directed by János Mohácsi. Hungary: Nyíregyháza. 1998. Lang.: Hun. 2127

One-act plays by Brecht directed by József Jámbor. Hungary: Debrecen. 1998. Lang.: Hun. 2131

Péter Valló's production of *Iphigéneia he en Aulide (Iphigenia in Aulis)* by Euripides. Hungary: Budapest. 1998. Lang.: Hun. 2132

Review of Tom Stoppard's *Arcadia* directed by Tamás Ascher. Hungary: Budapest. 1998. Lang.: Hun. 2133

Turgenjév's *Mesjac v derevne (A Month in the Country)* directed by Zoltán Lendvar. Hungary: Kecskemét. 1998. Lang.: Hun. 2134

Two Hungarian productions of Čechov's *Tri sestry (Three Sisters)*. Hungary: Veszprém, Szeged. 1998. Lang.: Hun. 2135

Review of *Édes Anna (Anna Édes)*, Madách Chamber Theatre. Hungary: Budapest. 1997. Lang.: Hun. 2136

Calderón's *La cisma de Inglaterra (The Schism of England)* directed by Péter Telihay. Hungary: Budapest. 1997. Lang.: Hun. 2137

Csaba Kiss's adaptation and direction of *Lady Macbeth of the Provinces* by Leskov. Hungary: Budapest. 1998. Lang.: Hun. 2138

Staging — cont'd

Denise Radó's *A Fedák-ügy (The Fedak Case)* at József Attila Theatre. Hungary: Budapest. 1998. Lang.: Hun. 2139

Three Hungarian productions of plays by Molière. Hungary: Szentendre, Kapolcs, Kőszeg. 1998. Lang.: Hun. 2142

István Tasnádi's *Titanic vízirevü (Titanic Water Show)* at Bárka Színház. Hungary: Budapest. 1998. Lang.: Hun. 2144

Andrés Jeles's *Szenvedéstörténet (Passion Play)* directed by Gábor Máté. Hungary: Budapest. 1998. Lang.: Hun. 2145

Two productions by István Somogyi of Bornemisza's *Magyar Elektra.* Hungary: Budapest. 1988-1998. Lang.: Hun. 2148

Productions of plays by Koljada and Jerofejév at Csiky Gergely Theatre. Hungary: Kaposvár. 1998. Lang.: Hun. 2149

Miklós Hubay's *Hová lett a rózsa lelke? (What Has Become of the Spirit of the Rose?)* directed by György Lengyel. Hungary: Debrecen. 1998. Lang.: Hun. 2150

The staging of *The King's Threshold* by W.B. Yeats. Ireland: Dublin. UK-England: London. 1903. Lang.: Eng. 2153

Recent productions in Ireland of plays by Eugene O'Neill. Ireland: Dublin. UK-Ireland: Belfast. 1989-1998. Lang.: Eng. 2154

Survey of Neapolitan theatre. Italy: Naples. 1998. Lang.: Eng. 2158

Andrea Liberovici's production of *Sonetto. Un travestimento shakespeariano (Sonnet: A Shakespearean Travesty)* by Eduardo Sanguineti. Italy: Genoa. 1997. Lang.: Ita. 2159

Theatrical activity in Italy's northern provinces. Italy. 1997-1998. Lang.: Eng. 2160

Excerpts from the notebooks of director Massimo Castri. Italy: Prato. 1996. Lang.: Ita. 2162

Italian productions of plays by Harold Pinter. Italy. 1997. Lang.: Eng. 2165

Collection of theatre reviews by Cesare Garboli. Italy. 1972-1977. Lang.: Ita. 2170

Giorgio Strehler's productions of plays by Bertolt Brecht. Italy: Milan. 1956-1998. Lang.: Swe. 2171

Essays on director Giorgio Strehler. Italy. 1936-1996. Lang.: Ita. 2173

Autobiography of Yiddish theatre actress Moni Ovadia. Italy. Bulgaria. 1946-1998. Lang.: Ita. 2174

Productions by Toni Bertorelli and Alfiero Alfieri. Italy: Rome. 1997. Lang.: Eng. 2175

Pirandello's Teatro d'Arte on tour in Trieste. Italy: Trieste. 1926. Lang.: Ita. 2178

Massimo Castri's production of Euripides' *Electra.* Italy: Spoleto. 1993. Lang.: Ita. 2179

Luca Ronconi's stage adaptation of *The Brothers Karamazov.* Italy: Rome. 1997. Lang.: Eng. 2188

Romeo Castellucci's adaptation of the *Oresteia* by Aeschylus. Italy: Cesena. 1997. Lang.: Eng. 2189

Theatrical component of Japan's UK98 Festival. Japan: Tokyo. 1994-1998. Lang.: Eng. 2192

Survey of Japanese theatre. Japan. 1998. Lang.: Rus. 2193

Japanese-Russian theatrical relations. Japan. Russia. 1900-1950. Lang.: Rus. 2194

Report from a symposium on traditional Korean theatre. Korea. Germany: Berlin. 1980-1998. Lang.: Ger, Fre, Dut, Eng. 2196

De Zaak's production of *Action* by Sam Shepard. Netherlands: Rotterdam. 1988. Lang.: Dut. 2201

Report from Ibsen festival. Norway: Oslo. 1998. Lang.: Swe. 2211

Contemporary Polish productions of Shakespeare. Poland. 1990-1998. Lang.: Pol. 2213

Analysis of productions of *Dziady (Forefather's Eve)* by Adam Mickiewicz. Poland. 1901-1995. Lang.: Pol. 2220

Productions of the festival of experimental theatre. Poland: Cracow. 1998. Lang.: Ger. 2225

The performance of Senecan tragedy. Roman Empire. 4 B.C.-150 A.D. Lang.: Eng. 2227

Productions of plays by Brecht and Shakespeare at the Hungarian theatre of Satu Mare. Romania: Satu Mare. 1998. Lang.: Hun. 2228

Director Leonid Truškin. Russia: Moscow. 1998. Lang.: Rus. 2233

Seinen-za's performance at the Čechov festival. Russia: Moscow. 1998. Lang.: Rus. 2237

Recent Russian productions of Shakespeare's *Hamlet.* Russia: Moscow. 1998. Lang.: Rus. 2268

Guest performances in Moscow. Russia: Moscow. 1998. Lang.: Rus. 2269

Jurij Ljubimov's production of *The First Circle,* based on Solženicin's novel. Russia: Moscow. 1998. Lang.: Rus. 2270

Mikle Mizjukov's production of *Pesn' sud'by (The Song of Fate)* by Blok. Russia: Moscow. 1998. Lang.: Rus. 2276

A century of Čechov productions by the Moscow Art Theatre. Russia: Moscow. 1898-1998. Lang.: Rus. 2288

The murder of actor and director Solomon Michoéls. Russia: Moscow. 1948. Lang.: Rus. 2293

Pëtr Fomenko's theatrical adaptation of Gogol's *Dead Souls.* Russia: Moscow. 1998. Lang.: Rus. 2303

The work of Russian directors at the Golden Mask festival. Russia: Moscow, St. Petersburg. 1998. Lang.: Swe. 2305

Productions of international Čechov festival. Russia: Moscow. 1998. Lang.: Swe. 2306

Director Mark Zacharov at Lenkom. Russia: Moscow. Lang.: Rus. 2316

Reconstruction of Stanislavskij's early stagings for the Alekseev Group. Russia: Moscow. 1877-1888. Lang.: Rus. 2322

Reviews of the Russian theatre season. Russia: Moscow. Lang.: Rus. 2324

Theatre in the time of Czar Peter I. Russia. 1689-1725. Lang.: Rus. 2329

K. Dubinin's production of *Boi imeli mestnoe zančenie (The Battles Had Localized)* based on work of Viačeslav Kondratjév. Russia: Volgograd. Lang.: Rus. 2331

Cossack theatre of the Choper Valley. Russia. Lang.: Rus. 2332

Andrej Žitinkin directs *Confessions of Felix Krull, Confidence Man,* adapted from Thomas Mann. Russia: Moscow. 1998. Lang.: Rus. 2335

Pëtr Fomenko's production of *V Čičikovskoj krugoverti (In Čičikov's Chaos).* Russia: Moscow. 1998. Lang.: Rus. 2340

László Babarczy's production of *Pepe* by Andor Szilágy. Serbia: Novi Sad. 1998. Lang.: Hun. 2342

Essays and reviews of contemporary theatre. Slovenia. 1980-1997. Lang.: Slo. 2346

Chris Vorster's production of *Baal* by Bertolt Brecht. South Africa, Republic of: Capetown. 1998. Lang.: Eng. 2350

Athol Fugard and the *Oresteia* of Aeschylus. South Africa, Republic of: Cape Town. 1978. Lang.: Eng. 2354

Pirandello on the Spanish stage. Spain. 1961-1986. Lang.: Ita. 2358

Productions of Shakespeare's *Twelfth Night* at the Madrid Theatre Festival. Spain: Madrid. 1996-1997. Lang.: Eng. 2359

Eduardo Vasco's production of *Lista Negra (Black List)* by Yolanda Pallín. Spain. 1998. Lang.: Eng. 2360

Overview of the Spanish theatre. Spain. 1998. Lang.: Rus. 2362

Juan Carlos Pérez de la Fuente's production of *San Juan* by Max Aub. Spain: Madrid. 1998. Lang.: Eng. 2363

Harold Pinter's production of his play *Ashes to Ashes* at the Pinter festival. Spain-Catalonia: Barcelona. 1996. Lang.: Eng. 2364

Keve Hjelm's production of *Ett Drömspel (A Dream Play)* by Strindberg. Sweden: Malmö. 1998. Lang.: Eng. 2373

Theatrical adaptations of children's stories by Astrid Lindgren. Sweden: Stockholm. 1998. Lang.: Eng. 2374

Dr. Kokos Kärlekslaboratorium (Dr. Koko's Laboratory of Love) at Backstage, Stockholms Stadsteater. Sweden: Stockholm. 1998. Lang.: Swe. 2378

Hans Klinga's production of *Mio, Min Mio (Mio, My Mio)* at Dramaten. Sweden: Stockholm. 1997. Lang.: Swe. 2386

Photos of rehearsals of O'Neill's *Long Day's Journey Into Night* at Dramaten. Sweden: Stockholm. 1998. Lang.: Swe. 2391

Recent productions of plays by Ibsen and Strindberg. Sweden: Stockholm. 1997. Lang.: Eng. 2393

Stockholm's year as Cultural Capital of Europe. Sweden: Stockholm. 1766-1998. Lang.: Eng. 2394

Teater UNO's stage adaptation of *L'Étranger (The Stranger)* by Albert Camus. Sweden: Gothenburg. 1998. Lang.: Swe. 2395

Shakespeare productions in German Switzerland. Switzerland: Basel, Zurich. 1996-1997. Lang.: Ger. 2398

Stefan Bachmann's production of Shakespeare's *Troilus and Cressida.* Switzerland: Basle. 1998. Lang.: Ger. 2399

Volker Hesse's production of *King Kongs Töchter (King Kong's Daughters)* by Theresia Walser. Switzerland: Zurich. 1998. Lang.: Ger. 2401

Staging — cont'd

Volker Hesse's production of *Die schwarze Spinne (The Black Spider)* by Urs Widmer. Switzerland: Zurich. 1998. Lang.: Ger. 2402

Reviews of plays by Wolfgang Bauer and Thomas Bernhard. Switzerland: Basel. Austria: Vienna. 1998. Lang.: Ger. 2403

Reviews of recent London performances. UK-England: London. 1998. Lang.: Ger. 2591

The inaugural season of Shakespeare's Globe Theatre. UK-England: London. 1997. Lang.: Eng. 2601

Review of the opening season of Shakespeare's Globe Theatre. UK-England: London. 1997. Lang.: Eng. 2602

London summer theatre and the Edinburgh Festival. UK-England: London. UK-Scotland: Edinburgh. 1998. Lang.: Eng. 2603

Experimental Shakespeare production at the Gaiety Theatre. UK-England: Manchester. 1908-1915. Lang.: Eng. 2605

Interview with actress Fiona Shaw. UK-England. 1995-1997. Lang.: Eng. 2607

Census of productions of medieval plays. UK-England. 1997. Lang.: Eng. 2610

The evolution of the character Feste in productions of Shakespeare's *Twelfth Night*. UK-England. 1773-1988. Lang.: Eng. 2611

Gaynor Macfarlane's production of Edwards' *Damon and Pythias* at Shakespeare's Globe. UK-England: London. 1996. Lang.: Eng. 2613

Excerpts from Johanna Schopenhauer's journal relating to London theatre. UK-England: London. Germany. 1803-1805. Lang.: Eng. 2615

Katie Mitchell's production of mystery plays at RSC. UK-England: London. 1996-1998. Lang.: Eng. 2626

The change in Shakespearean production. UK-England. 1960-1980. Lang.: Eng. 2628

Census of Renaissance drama productions and staged readings. UK-England. 1997. Lang.: Eng. 2635

Postmodern staging and design: Matthew Warchus' *Henry V*. UK-England. 1970-1994. Lang.: Eng. 2636

Possible illustrations of Dibdin's *Harlequin and Mother Goose* at Covent Garden. UK-England: London. 1806-1808. Lang.: Eng. 2639

Shakespearean influence on the 1987 Edinburgh Festival. UK-Scotland: Edinburgh. 1997. Lang.: Eng. 2653

Yale Drama Department's reconstruction of Gogol's *Revizor (The Inspector General)* as staged by Mejerchol'd. USA: New Haven, CT. 1997. Lang.: Eng. 2668

A rare production of Eugene O'Neill's *Lazarus Laughed*. USA: Detroit, MI. 1963. Lang.: Eng. 2673

Resistance to a Boston production of Eugene O'Neill's *Strange Interlude*. USA: Boston, MA. 1929. Lang.: Eng. 2693

Brief productions of Shakespeare, Shaw, and Marlowe at the World's Fair. USA: Chicago, IL. 1934. Lang.: Eng. 2701

Comparison of productions of Ibsen's *Peer Gynt*. USA: Providence, RI, New York, NY, Washington, DC, Nacogdoches, TX. 1998. Lang.: Eng. 2711

José Rivera's production of *La Vida es sueño (Life Is a Dream)*, Hartford Stage. USA: Hartford, CT. 1998. Lang.: Eng. 2722

Trevor Nunn's production of *Not About Nightingales* by Tennessee Williams, Alley Theatre. USA: Houston, TX. 1998. Lang.: Eng. 2729

Aleksand'r Tairov's production of *Fortune Heights* by John Dos Passos. USA. 1930-1935. Lang.: Rus. 2739

The 'scientific perspective' of director David Belasco. USA. 1882-1931. Lang.: Eng. 2741

Reviews of productions of plays by Ibsen. USA: New York, NY. Norway: Oslo. 1998. Lang.: Eng. 2747

Joe Dowling's production of *London Assurance* by Dion Boucicault. USA. 1997. Lang.: Eng. 2755

Analysis of recent New York productions. USA: New York, NY. 1997-1998. Lang.: Eng. 2759

The Hong Kong theatre and film industries. China, People's Republic of: Hong Kong. 1941-1996. Lang.: Eng. 3929

Performance in the work of mixed-media artist Tina Keane. UK-England. 1970-1988. Lang.: Eng. 4044

The cultural background of eighteenth-century British pantomime. England. 1700-1800. Lang.: Eng. 4093

The collaborative art installation *Tight Roaring Circle*. UK-England: London. 1993-1997. Lang.: Eng. 4133

A mock slave auction at Colonial Williamsburg. USA: Williamsburg, VA. 1994. Lang.: Eng. 4142

Polish cabaret at the front and abroad. Europe. 1939-1998. Lang.: Pol. 4154

History of Venetian carnival. Italy: Venice. Lang.: Rus. 4163

Changes in the nature of circus performance. Finland. 1980-1998. Lang.: Fin. 4181

Circus producer V. Gneušev. Russia: Moscow. 1998. Lang.: Rus. 4183

William Empson's *The Masque of Steel* and its presentation before Queen Elizabeth II. UK-England: Sheffield. 1954. Lang.: Eng. 4199

The staging of the complete *York Cycle* by the University of Toronto. Canada: Toronto, ON. 1998. Lang.: Eng. 4214

Maltese Holy Week rituals. Malta. 1998. Lang.: Eng. 4217

Performance artist Egon Schrick. Germany. 1976-1987. Lang.: Eng. 4241

Interview with performance artist Julian Maynard Smith. UK-England: London. 1980-1988. Lang.: Eng. 4246

The 'living paintings' of Steven Taylor Woodrow. UK-England. USA. 1987-1988. Lang.: Eng. 4247

Contemporary performance art's ignorance of its avant-garde antecedents. USA. 1996-1998. Lang.: Eng. 4250

Excerpts from a pictorial history of performance art. USA. 1960-1998. Lang.: Eng. 4253

Analysis of Guillermo Gómez-Peña and Coco Fusco's performance piece *The Couple in the Cage*. USA. 1995. Lang.: Eng. 4255

The performance installations *Santa Cruzan/Flores de Mayo* by DIWA Arts. USA: San Francisco, CA. 1994-1996. Lang.: Eng. 4256

Interview with performance artist Carolee Schneemann. USA. 1964-1989. Lang.: Eng. 4257

Background on *The Couple in the Cage* by Guillermo Gómez-Peña and Coco Fusco. USA. 1992-1995. Lang.: Eng. 4259

Music theatre production in northern Germany. Germany: Lübeck, Hamburg, Bremen, Kiel. 1998. Lang.: Ger. 4293

Composers and the work of Bertolt Brecht. Germany. 1928-1998. Lang.: Ger. 4297

Kodály's *Székely fonó (The Székler Spinnery)*. Hungary: Budapest. 1998. Lang.: Hun. 4298

Interview with Imre Kerényi, director of Kodály's *Székely fonó (The Székler Spinnery)*. Hungary: Budapest. 1997. Lang.: Hun. 4299

Photographic essay of Rameau's *Platée* directed and choreographed by Mark Morris. USA: Berkeley, CA. 1998. Lang.: Eng. 4304

The Chou dynasty in Chinese opera and theatrical paintings. China. 1027-771 B.C. Lang.: Rus. 4311

Robert Wilson's production of Brecht's *Der Ozeanflug*. Germany: Berlin. 1998. Lang.: Ger. 4356

Brecht and Weill's *Die Dreigroschenoper (The Three Penny Opera)* directed by László Vándorfi. Hungary: Veszprém.1998. Lang.: Hun. 4358

Kodály's *Háry János* at Szeged's Open-Air Festival. Hungary: Szeged. 1998. Lang.: Hun. 4359

Reviews of new Hungarian musicals. Hungary: Budapest. 1997. Lang.: Hun. 4360

An open-air production of *West Side Story* directed by László Vándorfi. Hungary: Veszprém. 1998. Lang.: Hun. 4361

Two Hungarian productions of *Die Dreigroschenoper (The Three Penny Opera)*. Hungary: Budapest, Szeged. 1998. Lang.: Hun. 4362

Review of Jonathan Larson's musical *Rent*. USA: New York, NY. 1990. Lang.: Hun. 4375

Musical performances on and off Broadway. USA: New York. 1998. Lang.: Ger. 4383

List of opera productions worldwide for the 1998-99 season. 1998. Lang.: Eng. 4513

Review of Salzburger Festspiele performances. Austria: Salzburg. 1998. Lang.: Ger. 4527

Opera productions of the Salzburg Festival. Austria: Salzburg. 1998. Lang.: Hun. 4531

Rural Chinese productions of Puccini's *Turandot*. China, People's Republic of: Beijing. 1998. Lang.: Eng. 4541

Review of the 1997 Czech opera season. Czech Republic. 1997. Lang.: Eng, Fre. 4543

Slovene translation of Adolphe Appia on staging Wagner. Europe. 1892. Lang.: Slo. 4550

Performance art and the reinvigoration of opera. Europe. 1964-1989. Lang.: Eng. 4556

Staging — cont'd

Evaluation of video performances of Donizetti's operas. Europe. USA. 1980-1998. Lang.: Eng. 4557
Report on opera festival. France: Aix-en-Provence. 1998. Lang.: Eng. 4563
Hector Berlioz's review of Donizetti's *La Favorite.* France: Paris. 1840. Lang.: Eng. 4565
The stage history of *Samson et Dalila* by Saint-Saëns. France. Germany. USA. 1877-1998. Lang.: Eng. 4566
Review of Pierre Strosser's staging of Busoni's *Doktor Faust.* France: Lyons. 1997. Lang.: Eng. 4577
Productions of Wagner's *Tristan und Isolde* by Peter Konwitschny and Werner Schroeter. Germany: Munich, Duisberg. 1998. Lang.: Ger. 4580
Review of opera productions. Germany: Stuttgart, Leipzig. 1998. Lang.: Ger. 4584
Visual spectacle in Wagner's *Ring* cycle. Germany. 1869-1876. Lang.: Eng. 4585
The police and John Cage's *Europeras 1 and 2* at Frankfurter Theater. Germany: Frankfurt. 1987. Lang.: Eng. 4586
Opera in German culture. Germany. 1950-1998. Lang.: Rus. 4599
F.W. Beidler's ideas for a different Bayreuth Festival. Germany: Bayreuth. 1901-1981. Lang.: Ger. 4602
Director Anja Sündermann on her production of *Rigoletto.* Germany: Hamburg. 1991-1998. Lang.: Ger. 4608
Opera director Inge Levant. Germany: Stuttgart. 1959-1998. Lang.: Ger. 4611
Frank Castorf's production of Strauss's *Die Fledermaus.* Germany: Hamburg. 1997-1998. Lang.: Ger. 4612
The influence of Wieland Wagner's production of *Lohengrin.* Germany, West: Bayreuth. 1966. Lang.: Eng. 4614
Interview with Tamás Pál, conductor and musical director of Szeged National Theatre. Hungary: Szeged. 1998. Lang.: Hun. 4622
Verdi's *Un Ballo in Maschera* at the Hungarian State Opera House. Hungary: Budapest. 1998. Lang.: Hun. 4629
Interview with director János Szikora. Hungary: Budapest. 1998. Lang.: Hun. 4630
Mozart's *Die Zauberflöte* directed by János Szikora. Hungary: Budapest. Hungary: Szeged. 1998. Lang.: Hun. 4631
Interview with director Viktor Nagy on Wagner's *Ring* cycle. Hungary: Budapest. 1998. Lang.: Hun. 4635
Interview with Miklós Gábor Kerényi on his production of *Un Ballo in maschera.* Hungary: Budapest, Szeged. 1998. Lang.: Hun. 4636
Mozart's *Le Nozze di Figaro* at the Hungarian State Opera House. Hungary: Budapest. 1998. Lang.: Hun. 4638
György Ligeti's *Le Grand Macabre* directed by Balázs Kovalik. Hungary: Budapest. 1998. Lang.: Hun. 4642
Wagner's *Ring* cycle at the Hungarian Opera House. Hungary: Budapest. 1998. Lang.: Hun. 4644
Reconstruction of the premiere of Boito's *Mefistofele.* Italy. 1871-1881. Lang.: Ita. 4647
Luca Ronconi's stagings of opera. Italy. 1974-1992. Lang.: Ita. 4648
Peri and Rinuccini's *Daphne,* the first opera. Italy: Florence. 1598. Lang.: Hun. 4651
Verdi's rarely performed opera *Stiffelio.* Italy. 1850-1998. Lang.: Hun. 4652
Performance history of Rossini's *Aureliano in Palmira.* Italy. Europe. 1813-1996. Lang.: Eng. 4659
A production of László Lajtha's comic opera *Le chapeau bleu.* Romania: Cluj-Napoca. Hungary. 1998. Lang.: Hun. 4666
Production of László Lajtha's comic opera *Le chapeau bleu.* Romania: Cluj-Napoca. Hungary. 1948-1998. Lang.: Hun. 4668
Čajkovskij's *Eugene Onegin* directed by A. Stepanov. Russia: St. Petersburg. 1998. Lang.: Rus. 4671
Teat'r Ten's *Ten' opery (The Shadow of the Opera).* Russia: Moscow. 1998. Lang.: Rus. 4679
St. Petersburg opera performances. Russia: St. Petersburg. 1801-1840. Lang.: Rus. 4686
Premieres of the Bolšoj Theatre. Russia: Moscow. 1825-1997. Lang.: Rus. 4693
Reactions to the opera *Staden* by Sven-David Sandström and Katarina Frostensson. Sweden: Stockholm. 1998. Lang.: Swe. 4699
Johannes Schaaf's production of *Otello* at Kungliga Operan. Sweden: Stockholm. 1998. Lang.: Swe. 4701
Reviews of recent opera productions. Switzerland: Basel. Germany: Stuttgart, Berlin, Hamburg. France: Strasbourg. 1997-1998. Lang.: Ger. 4702
Background material on Lyric Opera of Chicago radio broadcast performances. USA: Chicago, IL. 1998. Lang.: Eng. 4709
Critique of current trends in opera production. USA. 1942-1998. Lang.: Eng. 4726
Interview with director Peter Sellars. USA. 1990-1998. Lang.: Ger, Fre, Dut, Eng. 4727
Jonathan Miller's production of *The Rake's Progress* at the Metropolitan Opera. USA: New York, NY. 1998. Lang.: Eng. 4733
Robert Wilson's production of Wagner's *Lohengrin* at the Metropolitan Opera. USA: New York, NY. 1976-1998. Lang.: Eng. 4739
A production of Offenbach's *Orphée aux Enfers* directed by Jens Mehrle and Stefan Nolte. Germany: Bitterfeld. 1998. Lang.: Ger. 4856
The problem of staging operettas on the contemporary stage. Sweden. Germany. Austria. 1960-1998. Lang.: Swe. 4857
Basil Twist's puppetry interpretation of Berlioz's *Symphonie Fantastique.* USA: New York, NY. 1998. Lang.: Eng. 4904

Plays/librettos/scripts

Conrad Alexandrowicz on his dance-theatre piece *The Wines of Tuscany.* Canada: Vancouver, BC. 1992-1996. Lang.: Eng. 1356
The popularity of Shakespearean drama on the contemporary stage. 1998. Lang.: Eng. 2770
On the text and staging of *La Cathédrale...* by Jean Depréz (Laurette Laroque). Canada: Montreal, PQ. 1949. Lang.: Fre. 2823
Analysis of the frontispiece of Nicholas Rowe's edition of Shakespeare's *King Lear.* England. 1709-1714. Lang.: Eng. 2859
Nicholas Rowe's illustration of a scene from *Macbeth.* England. 1709. Lang.: Eng. 2953
Analysis of plays by Dea Loher, directed by Andreas Kriegenburg. Germany: Hannover. 1998. Lang.: Ger. 3130
Techniques of opposition in the work of Dario Fo. Italy. 1950-1988. Lang.: Eng. 3265
Stage directions in Ibsen's *Hedda Gabler.* Norway. 1987. Lang.: Eng. 3294
Essays on Polish theatre. Poland. 1960-1990. Lang.: Hun. 3305
Bibliography relating to plays of Andrejév and their productions. Russia. 1900-1919. Lang.: Rus. 3320
Mark Ravenhill's *Shopping and Fucking* and its production by Thomas Ostermeier. UK-England. Germany. 1998. Lang.: Ger. 3476
Analysis of *The Purple Flower* by Marita Bonner. USA. 1927. Lang.: Eng. 3527
Opera and the myth of Orpheus. 1600-1986. Lang.: Fre. 4758
The American and Canadian premieres of *Jackie O.* Canada: Banff, AB. USA: Houston, TX. 1997. Lang.: Eng. 4761

Reference materials

Bibliography of prerevolutionary culture. Karachaevo-Cherkess. Lang.: Rus. 706

Relation to other fields

Humanist ideology and the imaginary stage. Europe. 1549-1629. Lang.: Eng. 731

Theory/criticism

New historicism and Shakespeare's *Measure for Measure.* 1988. Lang.: Eng. 3801
The urge to make Shakespeare contemporary. USA. 1990-1998. Lang.: Eng. 3844
Performance art and the 'poetics of space'. USA. Poland. 1952-1984. Lang.: Eng. 4270
The need for a critical vocabulary to evaluate operatic productions. Europe. 1987-1998. Lang.: Eng. 4836

Stahl, John

Plays/librettos/scripts

John Stahl's film adaptation of *Imitation of Life* by Fannie Hurst. USA: Hollywood, CA. 1934. Lang.: Eng. 4029

Stalking Realness

Performance/production

Collection of newspaper reviews by London theatre critics. UK-England: London. 1998. Lang.: Eng. 2565

Stan, Alain

Performance/production

Austrian street theatre. Austria. 1953-1998. Lang.: Ger. 4116

Standidge, Eric
Performance/production
Collection of newspaper reviews by London theatre critics. UK-England: London. 1998. Lang.: Eng. 2581
Stanev, Ivan
Performance/production
Impressions from Podewil theatre workshop. Germany: Berlin. 1998. Lang.: Ger. 2024
Staniewski, Włodzimierz
Institutions
Interview with Włodzimierz Staniewski of Gardzienice Theatre Association. Poland: Gardzienice. 1978-1998. Lang.: Ger, Fre, Dut, Eng. 1687
Stanislavskij, Konstantin Sergejėvič
Institutions
Polish experimental theatre training. Poland: Cracow, Wrocław, Warsaw. 1930-1998. Lang.: Pol. 1685
Performance/production
History of movement training for the actor. USA. 1910-1985. Lang.: Eng. 675
Acting and directing influences on Eugenio Barba. Denmark: Holstebro. 1997. Lang.: Eng. 1886
Russian reception and interpretation of the work of Jerzy Grotowski. Russia. 1913-1998. Lang.: Pol. 2236
Interview with director Lev Dodin. Russia. 1997. Lang.: Fre. 2260
Reconstruction of Stanislavskij's early stagings for the Alekseev Group. Russia: Moscow. 1877-1888. Lang.: Rus. 2322
Letters of K.S. Stanislavskij. Russia. 1906-1917. Lang.: Rus. 2327
Italian translation of letters written by K.S. Stanislavskij. Russia. 1919-1938. Lang.: Ita. 2328
Theory/criticism
Essay on the nature of talent. Denmark. Sweden. UK-England. 1847-1987. Lang.: Dan. 838
Stanley, Mark
Design/technology
Lighting design for the musical *Follies*, Paper Mill Playhouse. USA: Millburn, NJ. 1998. Lang.: Eng. 4335
Star Théâtre (Paris)
Basic theatrical documents
Text of *Les Exclusés*, poetry adapted for the stage by Isabelle Starkier. France. 1998. Lang.: Fre. 1423
Star Trek: The Next Generation
Design/technology
Sound, lighting, and scenic elements of *Star Trek: The Next Generation* at the Las Vegas Hilton. USA: Las Vegas, NV. 1998. Lang.: Eng. 320
Performance/production
Interview with actor Patrick Stewart. USA: Washington, DC. 1998. Lang.: Eng. 2760
Stara kobieta wysiaduje (Old Woman Breeds)
Plays/librettos/scripts
Old age in plays of Różewicz. Poland. 1945-1998. Lang.: Pol. 3309
Stark, Ulf
Performance/production
Interview with children's theatre director Marie Feldtmann. Sweden: Stockholm. 1996-1998. Lang.: Swe. 2388
Starkenberg, Håkan
Training
Singer training at Teater- & Operahögskolan. Sweden: Gothenburg. 1960-1998. Lang.: Swe. 4848
Starkier, Isabelle
Basic theatrical documents
Text of *Les Exclusés*, poetry adapted for the stage by Isabelle Starkier. France. 1998. Lang.: Fre. 1423
Starkweather, David
Plays/librettos/scripts
Revolutionary Off Broadway playwriting. USA: New York, NY. 1959-1969. Lang.: Eng. 3604
Starr, Bill
Performance/production
Collection of newspaper reviews by London theatre critics. UK-England: London. 1998. Lang.: Eng. 2483
Collection of newspaper reviews by London theatre critics. UK-England: London. 1998. Lang.: Eng. 2544
Stars on Ice
Performance/production
Report on touring ice show *Stars on Ice*. USA. 1998. Lang.: Eng. 990
Starstruck
Performance/production
Collection of newspaper reviews by London theatre critics. UK-England: London. 1998. Lang.: Eng. 2509
Staruska
SEE
Latino, Staruska.
State Puppet Theatre (Budapest)
SEE
Állami Bábszinház.
State Puppet Theatre (Moscow)
SEE
Gosudarstvėnnyj Centralnyj Teat'r Kukol.
State Theatre (Cleveland, OH)
Institutions
Theatrical activity in Cleveland's Playhouse Square. USA: Cleveland, OH. 1998. Lang.: Eng. 416
State Theatre Institute (Moscow)
SEE
Gosudarstvėnnyj Institut Teatral'nogo Iskusstva.
States of Shock
Plays/librettos/scripts
Analysis of *States of Shock* by Sam Shepard. USA. 1965-1997. Lang.: Eng. 3544
Station House Opera (London)
Performance/production
Interview with performance artist Julian Maynard Smith. UK-England: London. 1980-1988. Lang.: Eng. 4246
Stauffer, Scott
Design/technology
The design concept for Nicholas Hytner's production of Shakespeare's *Twelfth Night*. USA: New York, NY. 1998. Lang.: Eng. 1556
Stealing Beauty
Performance/production
Analysis of films by Bernardo Bertolucci. 1979-1998. Lang.: Eng. 3927
Steckel, Frank-Patrick
Performance/production
Reviews of German Shakespearean productions. Germany: Wuppertal, Cologne, Oberhausen. 1998. Lang.: Ger. 2017
Stefanski, Roman
Performance/production
Collection of newspaper reviews by London theatre critics. UK-England: London. 1998. Lang.: Eng. 2550
Štefková, Kateřina
Design/technology
Costume designs of Kateřina Štefková and Zuzana Štefunková. Czech Republic. 1990-1998. Lang.: Eng, Fre. 172
Štefunková, Zuzana
Design/technology
Costume designs of Kateřina Štefková and Zuzana Štefunková. Czech Republic. 1990-1998. Lang.: Eng, Fre. 172
Steiger, Ueli
Design/technology
Lighting design for Roland Emmerich's film *Godzilla*. USA. 1998. Lang.: Eng. 3917
Stein, Gertrude
Performance/production
Robert Wilson's production of *Doctor Faustus Lights the Lights* by Gertrude Stein. Belgium: Antwerp. 1992. Lang.: Fle. 1828
Avant-garde American women directors' productions of *Doctor Faustus Lights the Lights* by Gertrude Stein. USA. 1940-1995. Lang.:Eng. 2735
Interview with actress Kate Valk. USA: New York, NY. 1979-1998. Lang.: Eng. 2736
Analysis of recent New York productions. USA: New York, NY. 1997-1998. Lang.: Eng. 2759
Plays/librettos/scripts
English-language plays on the Dutch and Flemish stage. Netherlands. 1920-1998. Lang.: Dut. 3278
Hero and anti-hero in contemporary opera production. Germany. 1998. Lang.: Ger. 4791
Relation to other fields
Author Gertrude Stein, subject of *Gertrude morte cet après-midi (Gertrude Dead This Afternoon)* by Monique Lepeu. France: Paris. 1874-1997. Lang.: Fre. 3759
Stein, Peter
Institutions
Peter Stein's last season as director at the Salzburg Festival. Austria: Salzburg. 1997. Lang.: Eng. 336
Performance/production
The rise of the modern Shakespearean director. Europe. 1878-1995. Lang.: Eng. 1911
Theatre, society, and directors Frank Castorf, Peter Stein, and Einar Schleef. Germany. 1998. Lang.: Ger. 2029

Stein, Peter — cont'd

Recent Russian productions of Shakespeare's *Hamlet*. Russia: Moscow. 1998. Lang.: Rus. 2268
Collection of newspaper reviews by London theatre critics. UK-England: London. 1998. Lang.: Eng. 2488
Plays/librettos/scripts
New directions in the plays of Botho Strauss. Europe. 1971-1998. Lang.: Ger. 3067

Steinberg's Day of Atonement
Performance/production
Collection of newspaper reviews by London theatre critics. UK-England: London, Stratford, Derby. 1998. Lang.: Eng. 2417

Steinman, Jim
Performance/production
Collection of newspaper reviews by London theatre critics. UK-England: London. 1998. Lang.: Eng. 2425

Steivel, Bruce
Institutions
Profile of Universal Ballet Company. South Korea: Seoul. 1998. Lang.: Eng. 1047

Stella
Performance/production
Television adaptations of works by Goethe. Germany. 1965-1997. Lang.: Eng. 4061
Plays/librettos/scripts
Female sacrifice in eighteenth-century German drama. Germany. 1772-1781. Lang.: Eng. 3167

Stembridge, Gerard
Performance/production
Collection of newspaper reviews by London theatre critics. UK-England: London. 1998. Lang.: Eng. 2473

Stepanov, A.
Performance/production
Čajkovskij's *Eugene Onegin* directed by A. Stepanov. Russia: St. Petersburg. 1998. Lang.: Rus. 4671

Stepanova, Varvara
Design/technology
Avant-garde Russian women artist/designers. Russia. USSR. 1880-1949. Lang.: Eng. 214

Stephen Joseph Theatre (Scarborough)
Performance/production
Collection of newspaper reviews by London theatre critics. UK-England: London, Scarborough. 1998. Lang.: Eng. 2426

Stephens, Simon
Performance/production
Collection of newspaper reviews by London theatre critics. UK-England: London. 1998. Lang.: Eng. 2549

Stephenson, Shelagh
Performance/production
Collection of newspaper reviews by London theatre critics. UK-England: Leeds, Manchester. 1998. Lang.: Eng. 2433
Collection of newspaper reviews by London theatre critics. UK-England: London. 1998. Lang.: Eng. 2523

Steppenwolf Theatre Company (Chicago, IL)
Performance/production
Collection of newspaper reviews by London theatre critics. UK-England: London. 1998. Lang.: Eng. 2476
Steppenwolf Theatre Company's production of *Space* by Tina Landau. USA: Chicago, IL. 1998. Lang.: Eng. 2672

Sternhagen, Frances
Performance/production
Actress Frances Sternhagen. USA. 1998. Lang.: Eng. 2687

Sternheim, Carl
Plays/librettos/scripts
Homosexuality on the German stage. Germany. 1920-1980. Lang.: Eng. 3147

Steve Coogan: The Man Who Thinks He's It
Performance/production
Collection of newspaper reviews by London theatre critics. UK-England: London. 1998. Lang.: Eng. 2513

Stevens, Gary
Performance/production
Collection of newspaper reviews by London theatre critics. UK-England: London. 1998. Lang.: Eng. 2478

Stevens, Risë
Performance/production
Singers' approaches to the title role in Bizet's *Carmen*. 1875-1998. Lang.: Eng. 4502

Stevens, Roger L.
Performance/production
Obituaries for Roger L. Stevens, Kenneth Frankel, Donald Davis, and Edith Oliver. USA. Canada. 1910-1998. Lang.: Eng. 2742

Stevens, Tassos
Performance/production
Collection of newspaper reviews by London theatre critics. UK-England: London. 1998. Lang.: Eng. 2424
Collection of newspaper reviews by London theatre critics. UK-England: London. 1998. Lang.: Eng. 2564

Stevens, Thomas Wood
Performance/production
Brief productions of Shakespeare, Shaw, and Marlowe at the World's Fair. USA: Chicago, IL. 1934. Lang.: Eng. 2701

Stevenson, Ben
Design/technology
Lighting design for Čajkovskij's *Sneguročka (The Snow Maiden)* at Houston Ballet. USA: Houston, TX. 1998. Lang.: Eng. 1035
Performance/production
Dancer Nina Ananiašvili. USA: Houston, TX. 1986-1998. Lang.: Eng. 1193

Stewart-Brown, Christi
Performance/production
Contemporary queer politics and the production of gay and lesbian theatre. USA. 1970-1997. Lang.: Eng. 2710

Stewart, Ellen
Institutions
Ellen Stewart and La MaMa Experimental Theatre Club. USA: New York, NY. 1961-1985. Lang.: Eng. 1762

Stewart, Manard
Performance/production
Dancer Manard Stewart of Pacific Northwest Ballet. USA: Seattle, WA. 1994-1998. Lang.: Eng. 1175

Stewart, Patrick
Performance/production
Interview with actor Patrick Stewart. USA: Washington, DC. 1998. Lang.: Eng. 2760
Actors' interpretations of the title role in Oscar Wilde's *The Canterville Ghost*. UK-England. USA. 1943-1998. Lang.: Eng. 4066

Stick Stack Stock
Performance/production
Collection of newspaper reviews by London theatre critics. UK-England: London. 1998. Lang.: Eng. 2427

Stiefel, Ethan
Institutions
American Ballet Theatre and diminishing government support. USA: New York, NY. 1998. Lang.: Eng. 1059

Stiffelio
Performance/production
Verdi's rarely performed opera *Stiffelio*. Italy. 1850-1998. Lang.: Hun. 4652
Background material on Metropolitan Opera radio broadcast performances. USA: New York, NY. 1998. Lang.: Eng. 4713
Verdi's *Stiffelio* and Gounod's *Roméo et Juliette* in New York. USA: New York, NY. 1850-1998. Lang.: Eng. 4730

Stiffs
Performance/production
Collection of newspaper reviews by London theatre critics. UK-England: London. 1998. Lang.: Eng. 2451

Stigsdotter, Karin
Institutions
Profile of independent feminist theatre Kvinnliga Dramatiska Teatern. Sweden: Stockholm. 1997-1998. Lang.: Swe. 1725

Stigwood, Robert
Performance/production
Collection of newspaper reviews by London theatre critics. UK-England: London. 1998. Lang.: Eng. 2467

Stilgoe, Richard
Design/technology
The original stage machinery designed by John White at Her Majesty's Theatre. UK-England: London. 1887-1986. Lang.: Eng. 1528

Still Life
Performance/production
Collection of newspaper reviews by London theatre critics. UK-England: London. 1998. Lang.: Eng. 2463
Collection of newspaper reviews by London theatre critics. UK-England: London. 1998. Lang.: Eng. 2576

Still Life Goes On
Administration
Christine Melton on the production of her play *Still Life Goes On*. USA: New York, NY. 1997. Lang.: Eng. 1398

Still/Here
Performance/production
Interview with choreographer Bill T. Jones. USA. 1990-1998. Lang.: Eng. 1316

***Still/Here* — cont'd**

Defense of Bill T. Jones' dance piece *Still/Here*. USA. 1994. Lang.: Eng. 1318

Stillmark, Alexander
Performance/production
Alexander Stillmark's production of *Bruder Eichmann (Brother Eichmann)* by Heinar Kipphardt. Germany: Berlin. 1984-1992. Lang.: Eng. 2022

Stinton, Myles
Performance/production
Collection of newspaper reviews by London theatre critics. UK-England: London. 1998. Lang.: Eng. 2421

Stirring Still
Plays/librettos/scripts
Analysis of Samuel Beckett's later plays. Ireland. France. 1950-1989. Lang.: Eng. 3210

Stjärnfall (Helsinki)
Institutions
The proliferation of Swedish-language theatre groups in Helsinki. Finland: Helsinki. 1990-1998. Lang.: Eng, Fre. 1604

Stockholms Improvisationsteater (SIT, Stockholm)
Institutions
Improvisations by Stockholms Improvisationsteater. Sweden: Stockholm. 1989-1998. Lang.: Swe. 1733

Stockholms Stadsteatern (Stockholm)
Administration
Ways to attract new young audiences to theatre. Sweden: Stockholm. 1995-1998. Lang.: Swe. 21
Design/technology
The experience of a costumer from Suomen Kansallisteatteri at Stockholms Stadsteatern. Finland: Helsinki. Sweden: Stockholm. 1996-1998. Lang.: Swe. 1519

Stoker, Bram
Performance/production
Collection of newspaper reviews by London theatre critics. UK-England: London. 1998. Lang.: Eng. 2579

Stollár, Xénia
Performance/production
Ildikó Mándy's *X.Y.Z.*, a film-dance theatre piece. Hungary: Budapest. 1998. Lang.: Hun. 947

Stolzenberg, Peter
Administration
The effects of independent theatre in Berlin. Germany: Berlin. 1998. Lang.: Ger. 14
Relation to other fields
The quality of Berlin's independent theatres. Germany: Berlin. 1998. Lang.: Ger. 748

Stomp
Performance/production
Collection of newspaper reviews by London theatre critics. UK-England: London. 1998. Lang.: Eng. 2544

Stomp (UK-England)
Performance/production
A guest performance by Stomp. Germany: Munich. 1992-1998. Lang.: Hun. 926

Stone, Allen
Performance/production
Collection of newspaper reviews by London theatre critics. UK-England: London. 1998. Lang.: Eng. 2470

Stone, Jonathan
Performance/production
Collection of newspaper reviews by London theatre critics. UK-England: London. 1998. Lang.: Eng. 2445

Stop machina (Stop Machine)
Performance/production
Interview with director Aleš Kurt. Bosnia: Sarajevo. 1998. Lang.: Hun. 1830

Stoppa, Paolo
Performance/production
The Italian premiere of *A Streetcar Named Desire* by Tennessee Williams. Italy: Rome. 1949. Lang.: Eng. 2172

Stoppard, Tom
Performance/production
Tom Stoppard's *Arcadia* as directed by Tamás Ascher. Hungary: Budapest. 1998. Lang.: Hun. 2058

Review of Tom Stoppard's *Arcadia* directed by Tamás Ascher. Hungary: Budapest. 1998. Lang.: Hun. 2133

Collection of newspaper reviews by London theatre critics. UK-England: London. 1998. Lang.: Eng. 2463

Collection of newspaper reviews by London theatre critics. UK-England: London. 1998. Lang.: Eng. 2533

Collection of newspaper reviews by London theatre critics. UK-England: London. 1998. Lang.: Eng. 2542
Plays/librettos/scripts
The speaking subject in plays of Beckett and Stoppard. France. Ireland. UK-England. 1945-1998. Lang.: Ger. 3098

Analysis of *In the Native State* and *Indian Ink* by Tom Stoppard. UK-England. 1991-1995. Lang.: Eng. 3459

Linguistic style and action in plays of Wilde, Shaw, and Stoppard. UK-England. 1890-1985. Lang.: Eng. 3467

Analysis of Tom Stoppard's *Arcadia*. UK-England. 1993. Lang.: Eng. 3474

Tom Stoppard's film adaptation of his own *Rosencrantz and Guildenstern Are Dead*. UK-England. 1967-1991. Lang.: Eng. 3980
Theory/criticism
Theatrical reviews and the nature of theatrical success. UK-England. 1950-1990. Lang.: Eng. 3836

Storace, Stephen
Performance/production
The English operas of Stephen Storace. England: London. 1762-1796. Lang.: Eng. 4547

Storm, The
SEE
Oväder.

Story-telling
Performance/production
History of Arabic theatre. Middle East. 225-1995. Lang.: Eng. 561

The evolution of Korean *p'ansori* as modern Korean opera, *ch'angguk*. Korea. 1900-1998. Lang.: Eng. 4364
Plays/librettos/scripts
Round-table discussion on story-telling and theatre. Canada: Montreal, PQ. 1998. Lang.: Fre. 688
Relation to other fields
Story-telling as a way of knowing and communicating. UK-Scotland. 1985-1998. Lang.: Eng. 772

Performativity of informal story-telling in western Iowa. USA. 1998. Lang.: Eng. 785

Stovall, Count
Administration
Christine Melton on the production of her play *Still Life Goes On*. USA: New York, NY. 1997. Lang.: Eng. 1398

Stowell, Christopher
Performance/production
Dancer Christopher Stowell of San Francisco Ballet. USA: San Francisco, CA. 1998. Lang.: Eng. 1191

Strachan, Alan
Performance/production
Collection of newspaper reviews by London theatre critics. UK-England: London. 1998. Lang.: Eng. 2418

Collection of newspaper reviews by London theatre critics. UK-England: London. 1998. Lang.: Eng. 2462

Strachan, Keith
Performance/production
Collection of newspaper reviews by London theatre critics. UK-England: London. 1998. Lang.: Eng. 2447

Strahan, Tom
Design/technology
Tom Strahan, scenic designer for rock concerts and corporate events. USA: San Francisco, CA. 1976-1998. Lang.: Eng. 4100

Stramm, August
Plays/librettos/scripts
Language and silence in German Expressionist drama. Germany. 1913-1923. Lang.: Eng. 3159

Strandberg, Jan-Olof
Performance/production
Interview with actor Jan-Olof Strandberg. Sweden: Stockholm, Gothenburg, Uppsala. 1948-1998. Lang.: Swe. 2390

Stranded
Performance/production
Collection of newspaper reviews by London theatre critics. UK-England: London. 1998. Lang.: Eng. 2534

Stranden (Strand, The)
Plays/librettos/scripts
Interview with playwright Peter Asmussen. Denmark: Copenhagen. 1989-1998. Lang.: Swe. 2853

Strange Cargo
Performance/production
Collection of newspaper reviews by London theatre critics. UK-England: London. 1998. Lang.: Eng. 2472

Strange Interlude
Performance/production
Resistance to a Boston production of Eugene O'Neill's *Strange Interlude*. USA: Boston, MA. 1929. Lang.: Eng. 2693
Plays/librettos/scripts
Female characters in Eugene O'Neill's plays. USA. 1920-1953. Lang.: Eng. 3525
Analysis of Eugene O'Neill's *Strange Interlude*. USA. 1926-1927. Lang.: Dut. 3551
Eugene O'Neill's *Strange Interlude* and the interwar period. USA. 1917-1940. Lang.: Eng. 3654
Analysis of Eugene O'Neill's 'middle period' plays. USA. 1925-1938. Lang.: Eng. 3675
Effeminacy on the American stage. USA. 1920-1998. Lang.: Eng. 3682

Strasberg, Lee
Performance/production
The idea of Hollywood in theatre autobiographies. USA. 1950-1990. Lang.: Eng. 665

Stratford Festival (Stratford, ON)
Institutions
Survey of Stratford Festival season. Canada: Stratford, ON. 1998. Lang.: Eng. 1580
The 1997 Shaw and Stratford Festival seasons. Canada: Stratford, ON, Niagara-on-the-Lake, ON. 1997. Lang.: Eng. 1582
Institutional analysis of the Stratford Festival. Canada: Stratford, ON. 1953-1967. Lang.: Eng. 1584
Performance/production
The Stratford Festival production of Shakespeare's *King Lear*. Canada: Stratford, ON. 1964. Lang.: Eng. 506
Interview with actor William Hutt. Canada: Stratford, ON. 1962-1996. Lang.: Eng. 1844
Actor Mervyn Blake. Canada: Stratford, ON. 1933-1998. Lang.: Eng. 1851
Actor William Hutt. Canada: Stratford, ON. USA. 1953-1998. Lang.: Eng. 1858
The performances of Frances Hyland, Kate Reid, and Martha Henry in *The Cherry Orchard*. Canada: Stratford, ON. 1965. Lang.: Eng. 1865

Stratford, Jonathan
Performance/production
Collection of newspaper reviews by London theatre critics. UK-England: London. 1998. Lang.: Eng. 2528

Stratton, Richard
Basic theatrical documents
Screenplay of the film *Slam*. USA. 1998. Lang.: Eng. 3893
Plays/librettos/scripts
Interview with creators of the film *Slam*. USA. 1998. Lang.: Eng. 4001

Strauss, Botho
Performance/production
Productions directed by Christian Stückl, Tom Kühnel, and Robert Schuster. Germany: Frankfurt. 1997-1998. Lang.: Ger. 1969
Collection of newspaper reviews by London theatre critics. UK-England: London. 1998. Lang.: Eng. 2488
Plays/librettos/scripts
New directions in the plays of Botho Strauss. Europe. 1971-1998. Lang.: Ger. 3067

Strauss, Johann
Performance/production
Collection of newspaper reviews by London theatre critics. UK-England: London. 1998. Lang.: Eng. 2420
Frank Castorf's production of Strauss's *Die Fledermaus*. Germany: Hamburg. 1997-1998. Lang.: Ger. 4612
Reviews of recent opera productions. Switzerland: Basel. Germany: Stuttgart, Berlin, Hamburg. France: Strasbourg. 1997-1998. Lang.: Ger. 4702

Strauss, Richard
Design/technology
Herbert Wernicke's set and costume designs for his own production of Strauss's *Elektra*. Germany: Munich. 1998. Lang.: Eng. 4429
Performance/production
Recordings of Strauss's *Die Frau ohne Schatten*. Europe. 1954. Lang.: Swe. 4554
Analysis of Richard Strauss's opera *Capriccio*. Germany. 1942-1998. Lang.: Eng. 4578
Analysis of Richard Strauss's *Capriccio*. Germany. 1942. Lang.: Eng. 4606
Opera director Inge Levant. Germany: Stuttgart. 1959-1998. Lang.: Ger. 4611
Interview with opera singer Anne Bolstad. Norway. Sweden. 1980-1998. Lang.: Swe. 4665
Conductor Andrew Davis. UK-England. USA. 1998. Lang.: Eng. 4704
Background material on Metropolitan Opera radio broadcast performances. USA: New York, NY. 1998. Lang.: Eng. 4713
Critique of current trends in opera production. USA. 1942-1998. Lang.: Eng. 4726
Plays/librettos/scripts
Strauss's *Die Frau ohne Schatten* and a recent production by Giuseppe Sinopoli. Germany. 1917-1998. Lang.: Swe. 4795

Stravinskij, Igor F.
Design/technology
Lighting designer Jennifer Tipton. USA: New York, NY. 1998. Lang.: Eng. 4441
Performance/production
The performance of sacrifice on stage. France. Germany. 1900-1998. Lang.: Ger. 530
The use of the harpsichord in Stravinskij's opera *The Rake's Progress*. Europe. 1951. Lang.: Eng. 4559
Mythology in theatre works of Stravinskij, especially *Perséphone*. Russia. 1934. Lang.: Eng. 4682
Background material on Metropolitan Opera radio broadcast performances. USA: New York, NY. 1998. Lang.: Eng. 4713
Jonathan Miller's production of *The Rake's Progress* at the Metropolitan Opera. USA: New York, NY. 1998. Lang.: Eng. 4733
Bass Samuel Ramey. USA. 1940-1998. Lang.: Eng. 4744
Profile of lighting designer Jennifer Tipton. USA. 1937-1998. Lang.: Eng. 4747
Plays/librettos/scripts
The libretto of *The Rake's Progress* by W.H. Auden and Chester Kallman. UK-England. 1971. Lang.: Eng. 4824
W.H. Auden as an opera librettist and translator. UK-England. 1907-1973. Lang.: Eng. 4825

Streeruwitz, Marlene
Plays/librettos/scripts
Power, gender relations, and communication in German drama. Germany. 1776-1989. Lang.: Ger. 3138

Street opera
Performance/production
Chinese street opera and nation-building. Singapore. 1965-1998. Lang.: Eng. 4694

Street theatre
Design/technology
Scenic elements in *Titanic* by street theatre group Theater Titanick. Germany: Münster, Leipzig. Australia: Perth. 1998. Lang.: Eng. 191
Institutions
The Orange Alternative, a street theatre opponent of martial law. Poland: Wroclaw. 1981-1988. Lang.: Eng. 375
Street theatre company Scaffold Theatre Project. Canada: Hamilton, ON. 1995-1998. Lang.: Eng. 1593
Performance/production
Maryat Lee and the creation of the street theatre piece *Dope!*. USA: New York, NY. 1949-1951. Lang.: Eng. 663
Austrian street theatre. Austria. 1953-1998. Lang.: Ger. 4116
Street performance in Washington Square Park. USA: New York, NY. 1980-1984. Lang.: Eng. 4137
Study of street performers. USA. 1980-1987. Lang.: Eng. 4139
Commedia dell'arte and the street performances of charlatans. France. Italy. 1600-1700. Lang.: Eng. 4189
The performance installations *Santa Cruzan/Flores de Mayo* by DIWA Arts. USA: San Francisco, CA. 1994-1996. Lang.: Eng. 4256

Street, Brennan
Performance/production
Collection of newspaper reviews by London theatre critics. UK-England: London. 1998. Lang.: Eng. 2440
Collection of newspaper reviews by London theatre critics. UK-England: London. 1998. Lang.: Eng. 2513
Collection of newspaper reviews by London theatre critics. UK-England: London. 1998. Lang.: Eng. 2552

Streetcar Named Desire, A
Performance/production
The Italian premiere of *A Streetcar Named Desire* by Tennessee Williams. Italy: Rome. 1949. Lang.: Eng. 2172
Baritone Rodney Gilfry. USA. 1998. Lang.: Eng. 4736

***Streetcar Named Desire, A* — cont'd**

André Previn's opera *A Streetcar Named Desire*. USA: San Francisco. 1998. Lang.: Eng. 4742
Plays/librettos/scripts
Analysis of plays by Tennessee Williams. USA. 1943-1970. Lang.: Eng. 3539
Realism and anti-realism in plays of Tennessee Williams. USA. 1945-1986. Lang.: Eng. 3626
Shame, puritanism, and sexuality in plays of Tennessee Williams. USA. 1950-1970. Lang.: Eng. 3701

Strehler, Giorgio
Performance spaces
The opening of Nuovo Piccolo in honor of the late director Giorgio Strehler. Italy: Milan. 1998. Lang.: Eng. 1802
Performance/production
Pirandello's theatre on the Austrian stage. Austria. 1924-1989. Lang.: Ita. 1825
Survey of Milanese theatre. Italy: Milan. 1997-1998. Lang.: Eng. 2161
Dario Fo and Giorgio Strehler honored at Venice Biennale. Italy: Venice. 1947-1998. Lang.: Eng. 2163
Giorgio Strehler's productions of plays by Bertolt Brecht. Italy: Milan. 1956-1998. Lang.: Swe. 2171
Essays on director Giorgio Strehler. Italy. 1936-1996. Lang.: Ita. 2173
The ideas and productions of director Giorgio Strehler. Italy. 1940-1998. Lang.: Swe. 2180
Giorgio Strehler of Piccolo Teatro. Italy: Milan. 1921-1997. Lang.: Ger. 2181
Text of an address by director Giorgio Strehler at the University of Turin. Italy. 1997. Lang.: Ita. 2184
Interview with director Giorgio Strehler. Italy: Milan. 1993. Lang.: Hun. 2185
Piccolo Teatro after the death of director Giorgio Strehler. Italy: Milan. 1947-1998. Lang.: Hun. 2186
Obituaries for Ellis Rabb, Giorgio Strehler, and David Mark Cohen. USA. 1930-1997. Lang.: Eng. 2725
Plays/librettos/scripts
The clown as a character in modern drama. Europe. 1915-1995. Lang.: Eng. 3056

Stricker, Johannes
Plays/librettos/scripts
Morality plays of the Reformation. Germany. 1550-1584. Lang.: Eng. 3163

Strindberg, August
Institutions
Report on the Stockholm theatre festival. Sweden: Stockholm. 1998. Lang.: Eng. 1724
Interview with Rolf Sossna of En Annan Teater. Sweden: Gothenburg. 1992-1998. Lang.: Swe. 1734
Performance/production
Reviews of two plays by Per Olov Enquist. Hungary: Budapest. 1998. Lang.: Hun. 2089
Shakespeare's influence on Strindberg's modernism. Sweden. 1907-1910. Lang.: Eng. 2370
Keve Hjelm's production of *Ett Drömspel (A Dream Play)* by Strindberg. Sweden: Malmö. 1998. Lang.: Eng. 2373
Recent productions of plays by Ibsen and Strindberg. Sweden: Stockholm. 1997. Lang.: Eng. 2393
Collection of newspaper reviews by London theatre critics. UK-England: London. 1998. Lang.: Eng. 2429
Collection of newspaper reviews by London theatre critics. UK-England: London. 1998. Lang.: Eng. 2453
Collection of newspaper reviews by London theatre critics. UK-England: London. 1998. Lang.: Eng. 2495
Plays/librettos/scripts
Gender and madness in modern drama. Europe. 1880-1969. Lang.: Eng. 3061
Time and space in *Ett Drömspel (A Dream Play)* by August Strindberg. Sweden. 1901-1902. Lang.: Eng. 3410
Folklore and occultism in August Strindberg's *Lycko-Pers resa (Lucky Per's Journey)*. Sweden. 1912. Lang.: Swe. 3412
Realism in plays of Strindberg. Sweden. 1872-1886. Lang.: Eng. 3416
Strindberg's influence on playwrights Len Jenkin and Mac Wellman. USA. 1887-1998. Lang.: Eng. 3584
Intellectual and artistic influences on playwright Eugene O'Neill. USA. 1888-1953. Lang.: Eng. 3697

Stringless Marionette, The
Performance/production
Collection of newspaper reviews by London theatre critics. UK-England: London. 1998. Lang.: Eng. 2455

Stripped
Performance/production
Collection of newspaper reviews by London theatre critics. UK-England: London. 1998. Lang.: Eng. 2520

Striptease
Administration
The First Amendment and the striptease dancer. USA. 1998. Lang.: Eng. 4271
Relation to other fields
Analysis of striptease events. USA. 1992-1998. Lang.: Eng. 4285

Strong Breed, The
Plays/librettos/scripts
Ritual in plays of John Bekederemo and Wole Soyinka. Nigeria. 1965-1998. Lang.: Eng. 3287

Strongman, Wayne
Institutions
Profile of Tapestry Music Theatre. Canada: Toronto, ON. 1985-1998. Lang.: Eng. 4346

Strosser, Pierre
Performance/production
Review of Pierre Strosser's staging of Busoni's *Doktor Faust*. France: Lyons. 1997. Lang.: Eng. 4577

Strouse, Charles
Performance/production
Collection of newspaper reviews by London theatre critics. UK-England: London. 1998. Lang.: Eng. 2514
Collection of newspaper reviews by London theatre critics. UK-England: London. 1998. Lang.: Eng. 2550

Stržel'čik, Vladislav
Performance/production
Actor Vladislav Stržel'čik. Russia: St. Petersburg. 1998. Lang.: Rus. 2235

STS (Warsaw)
Performance/production
Profiles of student cabaret groups. Poland: Warsaw, Gdańsk. 1954-1959. Lang.: Pol. 4156

Stuart theatre
Plays/librettos/scripts
Evil in Stuart tragedy. England. 1620-1642. Lang.: Eng. 3024

Stückl, Christian
Performance/production
Productions directed by Christian Stückl, Tom Kühnel, and Robert Schuster. Germany: Frankfurt. 1997-1998. Lang.: Ger. 1969

Studenčeskij teat'r MGU (Moscow)
Performance/production
Student performances in the State University's theatre. Russia: Moscow. 1998. Lang.: Rus. 2284

Studijteatris (Riga)
Institutions
Report on a visit to Riga's theatres. Latvia: Riga. 1997. Lang.: Swe, Eng, Ger. 369

Stúdió K (Budapest)
Institutions
Tamás Fodor's Stúdió K. Hungary: Budapest. 1971-1997. 1971-1997. Lang.: Hun. 1671
Performance/production
Sándor Lajos' *Szűrővizsgálat (Screen Test)* directed by Tamás Fodor. Hungary: Budapest. 1998. Lang.: Hun. 2103

Studio 7 (Cologne)
Performance/production
The Cologne theatre scene. Germany: Cologne. 1985-1997. Lang.: Ger. 1964

Studiobühne (Dortmund)
Performance/production
Director Angela Brodauf. Germany: Dortmund. 1984-1998. Lang.: Ger. 1989

Studium Teatralne (Warsaw)
Performance/production
Productions of the festival of experimental theatre. Poland: Cracow. 1998. Lang.: Ger. 2225

Sturm und Drang
SEE
Geographical-Chronological Index under Germany 1767-1787.

Sturua, Robert
Performance/production
Recent Russian productions of Shakespeare's *Hamlet*. Russia: Moscow. 1998. Lang.: Rus. 2268

Stuttgart Ballet
Institutions
Guest performances of the ballet companies of Stuttgart and Hamburg. Hungary. 1980-1986. Lang.: Hun. 1041
Stvar Jurija Trajbasa (Case of Jurij Trabas, The)
Plays/librettos/scripts
Fascism and the peasant in pre-War Slovene drama. Slovenia. 1940. Lang.: Slo. 3349
Styne, Jule
Design/technology
Costume designs by Irene Sharaff. USA. 1933-1976. Lang.: Eng. 277
Performance/production
Collection of newspaper reviews by London theatre critics. UK-England: London. 1998. Lang.: Eng. 2480
Plays/librettos/scripts
The creation of the musical *Gypsy*. USA: New York, NY. 1956-1959. Lang.: Eng. 4399
Subsidies
SEE
Funding, government.
Substance of Fire, The
Plays/librettos/scripts
The survivor character in contemporary American drama. USA. 1970-1997. Lang.: Eng. 3600
Sudarčikov, Igor
Performance/production
Onstage costume changes. Japan. Russia. Denmark. 1752-1998. Lang.: Swe. 556
Sudarčikova, Svetlana
Performance/production
Onstage costume changes. Japan. Russia. Denmark. 1752-1998. Lang.: Swe. 556
Suddenly Last Summer
Plays/librettos/scripts
Analysis of plays by Tennessee Williams. USA. 1943-1970. Lang.: Eng. 3539
Puritanism and predestination in *Suddenly Last Summer* by Tennessee Williams. USA. 1958. Lang.: Eng. 3631
Draft and revisions of *Suddenly Last Summer* by Tennessee Williams. USA. 1958. Lang.: Eng. 3658
Analysis of Tennessee Williams' *Suddenly Last Summer* and 'Desire and the Black Masseur'. USA. 1946-1958. Lang.: Eng. 3678
Metadrama in plays of Tennessee Williams. USA. 1944-1978. Lang.: Eng. 3686
Suffer Little Children
Performance/production
Collection of newspaper reviews by London theatre critics. UK-England: London. 1998. Lang.: Eng. 2517
Sugar Sugar
Performance/production
Collection of newspaper reviews by London theatre critics. UK-England: London. 1998. Lang.: Eng. 2468
Suicide, The
SEE
Samoubijca.
Sujir, Leila
Plays/librettos/scripts
Leila Sujir's video *The Dreams of the Night Cleaners*. Canada. 1989-1995. Lang.: Eng. 4075
Sullivan, Arthur
Performance/production
Collection of newspaper reviews by London theatre critics. UK-England: London. 1998. Lang.: Eng. 2553
Plays/librettos/scripts
The trivialization of feminism in librettos of W.S. Gilbert. UK-England. 1880-1890. Lang.: Eng. 4861
Sullivan, Joan
Design/technology
Lighting for Washington Opera's production of *Doña Francisquita*. USA: Washington, DC. 1998. Lang.: Eng. 4290
Summer
Plays/librettos/scripts
Analysis of Edward Bond's *Summer*. UK-England. 1982. Lang.: Dut. 3434
Summer and Smoke
Performance/production
Creating the character Alma in Tennessee Williams' *Summer and Smoke*. USA. 1997. Lang.: Eng. 2665
Plays/librettos/scripts
Shame, puritanism, and sexuality in plays of Tennessee Williams. USA. 1950-1970. Lang.: Eng. 3701
Summer theatre
Administration
London theatres' new summer productions. UK-England: London. 1998. Lang.: Eng. 26
Institutions
Israeli theatre at the Kampnagel summer theatre festival. Germany: Hamburg. 1998. Lang.: Ger. 1635
Summer's Last Will and Testament
Plays/librettos/scripts
Recovered ritual in seemingly non-ritualistic theatre. England. 1600-1779. Lang.: Eng. 2904
Summers, Leverne
Performance/production
Obituary for actor Leverne Summers. USA: New York, NY. 1998. Lang.: Eng. 2748
Summers, Patrick
Performance/production
Opera conductor Patrick Summers. USA. 1990-1998. Lang.: Eng. 4755
Theory/criticism
Performers and conductors complain about unfair reviews. USA. 1998. Lang.: Eng. 4844
Summers, Peter
Performance/production
Collection of newspaper reviews by London theatre critics. UK-England: London. 1998. Lang.: Eng. 2560
Summerskill, Clare
Performance/production
Collection of newspaper reviews by London theatre critics. UK-England: London. 1998. Lang.: Eng. 2520
Sun Flower
Performance/production
Elizabeth Perry's one-woman show *Sun Flower* about Elizabeth Cady Stanton. USA: New York, NY. 1998. Lang.: Eng. 2718
Sun of the Sleepless
Plays/librettos/scripts
Analysis of plays by James Purdy. USA. 1957-1998. Lang.: Eng. 3700
Sundance Institute for Film and Video (Sundance, CO)
Institutions
History of the Sundance Institute for Film and Video. USA: Sundance, CO. 1981-1984. Lang.: Eng. 3925
Sunday in the Park with George
Plays/librettos/scripts
The disintegration of the American dream in works of Stephen Sondheim. USA. 1970-1984. Lang.: Eng. 4397
Sündermann, Anja
Performance/production
Director Anja Sündermann on her production of *Rigoletto*. Germany: Hamburg. 1991-1998. Lang.: Ger. 4608
Suomen Kansallisbaletti (Helsinki)
Institutions
New artistic goals of the Finnish National Ballet. Finland: Helsinki. 1992-1998. Lang.: Eng. 1037
Performance/production
Premiere of Sylvie Guillem's new choreography for Adolphe Adam's *Giselle*. Finland: Helsinki. 1998. Lang.: Hun. 1068
Suomen Kansallisteatteri (Helsinki)
Design/technology
The experience of a costumer from Suomen Kansallisteatteri at Stockholms Stadsteatern. Finland: Helsinki. Sweden: Stockholm. 1996-1998. Lang.: Swe. 1519
Supple, Tim
Performance/production
Collection of newspaper reviews by London theatre critics. UK-England: London. 1998. Lang.: Eng. 2413
Collection of newspaper reviews by London theatre critics. UK-England: London. 1998. Lang.: Eng. 2496
Collection of newspaper reviews by London theatre critics. UK-England: London. 1998. Lang.: Eng. 2514
Suppliants
Performance/production
Collection of newspaper reviews by London theatre critics. UK-England: London. 1998. Lang.: Eng. 2545
Support areas
Performance spaces
The construction of the Grand Théâtre de Genève. Switzerland: Geneva. 1984-1998. Lang.: Ger. 459

Supreme Commander, The
Plays/librettos/scripts
Analysis of unpublished plays by Ken Saro-Wiwa. Nigeria. 1971-1991. Lang.: Eng. 3282
Sur, Gorsha
Performance/production
Ice dancers Renee Roca and Gorsha Sur. USA. 1992-1998. Lang.: Eng. 992
Suréna
Plays/librettos/scripts
Analysis of plays by Pierre Corneille. France. 1643-1652. Lang.: Eng. 3112
Surfeurs (Surfers)
Institutions
Impressions from the Avignon theatre festival. France: Avignon. 1998. Lang.: Ger. 1612
Surovščikova, Marie S.
Performance/production
Choreographer Marius Petipa and his wife, ballerina Marie Surovščikova. Russia. Lang.: Rus. 1128
Surrealism
Plays/librettos/scripts
Analysis and translation of *Et les Chiens se taisaient (And the Dogs Were Silent)* by Aimé Césaire. Martinique. 1946-1969. Lang.: Eng. 3269
Surrey Theatre (London)
Audience
Analysis of audience composition at London theatres. England: London. 1835-1861. Lang.: Eng. 147
Suschke, Stephan
Institutions
Problems of management and repertory at Berliner Ensemble. Germany: Berlin. 1992-1998. Lang.: Ger. 1656
Susini, Pietro
Performance/production
The evolution of comic opera. Italy: Florence, Rome. 1665-1700. Lang.: Eng. 4660
Sutherland, Joan
Performance/production
Interpreters of the title role in Delibes' opera *Lakmé*. 1932-1995. Lang.: Fre. 4505
Soprano Joan Sutherland. Australia. 1998. Lang.: Eng. 4526
Interview with soprano Joan Sutherland about vocal technique. USA: New York, NY. 1998. Lang.: Eng. 4728
Sutherland, Malcolm
Performance/production
Collection of newspaper reviews by London theatre critics. UK-England: Leeds, Manchester. 1998. Lang.: Eng. 2559
Suthers, Trevor
Performance/production
Collection of newspaper reviews by London theatre critics. UK-England: London. 1998. Lang.: Eng. 2566
Sutton, Dolores
Performance/production
Friends and colleagues recall singer Lotte Lenya. Germany. 1928-1981. Lang.: Eng. 4355
Suženj akcije—Kralj Peter Šesti (Slave of Action—King Peter the Sixth, A)
Basic theatrical documents
Text of *Suženj akcije—Kralj Peter Šesti (A Slave of Action—King Peter the Sixth)* by Emil Filipčič. Slovenia. 1997. Lang.: Slo. 1455
Suzman, Janet
Performance/production
Collection of newspaper reviews by London theatre critics. UK-England: London. 1998. Lang.: Eng. 2548
Suzuki, Tadashi
Performance/production
Tadashi Suzuki and Suzuki Company of Toga. Japan. 1939-1984. Lang.: Eng. 555
Lithuanian theatre education and the visit of Tadashi Suzuki. Lithuania. 1998. Lang.: Fin. 559
The training of actors in Asian performance styles. Australia: Brisbane. 1992-1998. Lang.: Eng. 1817
Tadashi Suzuki's method of actor training. Japan. 1998. Lang.: Eng. 2191
Guest performances in Moscow. Russia: Moscow. 1998. Lang.: Rus. 2269
Training
Anne-Lise Gabold's use of the methods of Tadashi Suzuki in her production of Euripides' *Bákchai (The Bacchae)*. Japan. Denmark: Copenhagen. 1960-1998. Lang.: Dan. 1359
Svadba (Wedding, The)
Basic theatrical documents
Catalan translations of the complete plays of Anton Čechov. Russia. 1884-1904. Lang.: Cat. 1449
Performance/production
Čechov's one-act plays at Thália Színház. Hungary. Slovakia: Košice. 1998. Lang.: Hun. 2075
Svalberg, Göran
Institutions
The 225th anniversary of the Royal Swedish Ballet. Sweden: Stockholm. 1773-1998. Lang.: Eng. 1048
Performance/production
Interview with dancer Göran Svalberg. Sweden: Stockholm. 1975-1998. Lang.: Swe. 1152
Sved, Nikki
Performance/production
Collection of newspaper reviews by London theatre critics. UK-England: London. 1998. Lang.: Eng. 2438
Svedberg, Lars
Institutions
Profile of Swedish-language theatre company Svenska Teatern. Finland: Helsinki. 1919-1998. Lang.: Eng, Fre. 1606
Svensk Symbolisk Teater (Malmö)
Institutions
Profile of Svensk Symbolisk Teater. Sweden: Malmö. 1997. Lang.: Swe. 1728
Svensk Teaterteknisk Förening (STTF, Swedish Society for Theatre Technicians)
Design/technology
The combined conference and fair, Nordisk TeaterTeknik (NoTT). Sweden: Stockholm, Gothenburg. 1983-1998. Lang.: Swe. 227
Svenska Balettskolan (Stockholm)
Institutions
Criticism of Svenska Bakettskolan. Sweden: Stockholm. 1984. Lang.: Swe. 1049
Defense of Svenska Balettskolan by a former student. Sweden: Stockholm. 1996. Lang.: Swe. 1052
Svenska Riksteatern (Norsborg)
Administration
Riksteatern and Dansens Hus' Dansbiennal 98 meeting with government officials. Sweden. 1998. Lang.: Swe. 881
Svenska Teaterförbundet (Stockholm)
Administration
Interview with Tomas Bolme, director of the Swedish actors' union. Sweden: Stockholm. 1970-1998. Lang.: Swe. 1388
Svenska Teatern (Helsinki)
Institutions
Profile of Swedish-language theatre company Svenska Teatern. Finland: Helsinki. 1919-1998. Lang.: Eng, Fre. 1606
Svoboda, Josef
Design/technology
Josef Svoboda's set design for Goethe's *Faust*. Czech Republic: Prague. 1997. Lang.: Eng. 1517
Swamp Dwellers, The
Plays/librettos/scripts
Analysis of *The Swamp Dwellers* by Wole Soyinka. Nigeria. 1973. Lang.: Eng. 3283
Swan Lake
SEE ALSO
Lebedinoje osero.
Swan Theatre (London)
Performance spaces
Analysis of a sketch of the Swan Theatre. England: London. 1596. Lang.: Eng. 1801
Swan Theatre (Stratford)
Performance/production
Collection of newspaper reviews by London theatre critics. UK. 1998. Lang.: Eng. 2407
Collection of newspaper reviews by London theatre critics. UK-England: Stratford. 1998. Lang.: Eng. 2431
Collection of newspaper reviews by London theatre critics. UK-England. 1998. Lang.: Eng. 2558
Sweeney Todd
Plays/librettos/scripts
The disintegration of the American dream in works of Stephen Sondheim. USA. 1970-1984. Lang.: Eng. 4397
Sweet Charity
Performance/production
Collection of newspaper reviews by London theatre critics. UK-England: London. 1998. Lang.: Eng. 2410

***Sweet Charity* — cont'd**

AIDS-benefit performance of the musical *Sweet Charity*. USA: New York, NY. 1998. Lang.: Eng. 4386

Sweet, Sharon
Theory/criticism
Performers and conductors complain about unfair reviews. USA. 1998. Lang.: Eng. 4844

Swell, The
Performance/production
Collection of newspaper reviews by London theatre critics. UK-England: London. 1998. Lang.: Eng. 2438

Swetnam the Woman-Hater, Arraigned by Women
Plays/librettos/scripts
Female power and the public sphere in Renaissance drama. England. 1597-1616. Lang.: Eng. 2943

Swift, Amanda
Performance/production
Collection of newspaper reviews by London theatre critics. UK-England: London. 1998. Lang.: Eng. 2475

Swinarski, Konrad
Performance/production
History of Teatr Wybrzeże. Poland: Gdańsk, Warsaw, Cracow. 1952-1997. Lang.: Pol. 2215

Swiss Union of Theatre Makers
SEE
Vereinigte Theaterschaffenden der Schweiz.

Swope, Martha
Relation to other fields
Interview with photographer and former ballerina Martha Swope. USA: New York, NY. 1950-1998. Lang.: Eng. 1198

Syberberg, Hans-Jurgen
Plays/librettos/scripts
The reciprocal influence of opera and film. Europe. North America. 1904-1994. Lang.: Eng. 4770

Sycosch, Nicolai
Performance/production
Shakespeare performance on the Rhine and the Ruhr. Germany: Cologne, Bochum, Düsseldorf. 1996-1997. Lang.: Ger. 1962

Sylvanus, Erwin
Plays/librettos/scripts
Analysis of historical drama of the holocaust. USA. Canada. Germany. 1950-1980. Lang.: Eng. 3610

Symbolism
Performance/production
Collaborative Symbolist dance/theatre projects. Europe. USA. 1916-1934. Lang.: Eng. 1268
Theory/criticism
The influence of Symbolism on European dance. Europe. 1895-1939. Lang.: Eng. 1007

Symonette, Randolph
Performance/production
Obituaries of singers Randolph Symonette and Todd Duncan. USA. 1998. Lang.: Eng. 4708

Symphonic Variations
Theory/criticism
Comparison of critical reviews of dance performances. USA: New York, NY. 1992. Lang.: Eng. 1201

Symphonie Fantastique
Design/technology
Lighting design for Basil Twist's puppet production *Symphonie Fantastique*. USA: New York, NY. 1998. Lang.: Eng. 4867
Performance/production
Basil Twist's puppetry interpretation of Berlioz's *Symphonie Fantastique*. USA: New York, NY. 1998. Lang.: Eng. 4904

Symphony in C
Performance/production
Review of one-act ballets by Balanchine. Hungary: Budapest. 1997. Lang.: Hun. 1105

Syndrome de Cézanne, Le (Cézanne Syndrome, The)
Plays/librettos/scripts
Quebecois drama and the influence of visual arts. Canada. 1980-1990. Lang.: Fre. 2816

Synge, John Millington
Audience
Nationalist response to the premiere of Synge's *Playboy of the Western World*. Ireland: Dublin. 1907. Lang.: Eng. 1404
Performance/production
Collection of newspaper reviews by London theatre critics. UK-England: London. 1998. Lang.: Eng. 2551
Plays/librettos/scripts
A folktale source of *The Playboy of the Western World*. Ireland. 1907. Lang.: Eng. 3202

Szabadkai Népszínház (Subotica)
Institutions
History of annual festival of Hungarian-language theatre. Hungary: Kisvárda. 1989-1998. Lang.: Hun. 1669
Plays/librettos/scripts
History of Hungarian-language theatre in the Voivodship region. Yugoslavia: Subotica, Novi Sad. 1837-1998. Lang.: Hun. 3720

Szabó Stein, Imre
Plays/librettos/scripts
New Hungarian translations of Shakespeare. Hungary. 1990-1998. Lang.: Hun. 3187

Analysis of Imre Szabó Stein's new translation of Shakespeare's *The Merchant of Venice*. Hungary: Budapest. 1998. Lang.: Hun. 3188

Szabó, György
Institutions
Interview with György Szabó, director of Trafó. Hungary: Budapest. 1998. Lang.: Hun. 359

Szabó, István
Plays/librettos/scripts
Analysis of István Szabó's film *Mephisto*. Hungary. 1981. Lang.: Eng. 3974

Szakály, György
Performance/production
Lilla Pártay's *Meztelen rózsa (Naked Rose)*, a ballet based on the life of Nižinskij. Hungary: Budapest. 1998. Lang.: Hun. 1110

Szász, János
Institutions
Theatre critics' awards 97-98. Hungary. 1997-1998. Lang.: Hun. 355
Performance/production
Čechov's *Diadia Vania (Uncle Vanya)* directed by János Szász. Hungary: Nyíregyháza. 1998. Lang.: Hun. 2124

Interview with directors János Szász and Árpád Schilling. Hungary. 1998. Lang.: Hun. 2129

Szatmárnémeti Északi Színház, Harag György Társulat (Satu Mare)
Institutions
Hungarian dramatic art in Transylvania. Romania: Cluj-Napoca, Satu Mare. Hungary. 1965-1989. Lang.: Hun. 378

History of annual festival of Hungarian-language theatre. Hungary: Kisvárda. 1989-1998. Lang.: Hun. 1669

History of Hungarian-language theatre in Transylvania. Romania. Hungary. 1919-1992. Lang.: Hun, Rom. 1693
Performance/production
Productions of plays by Brecht and Shakespeare at the Hungarian theatre of Satu Mare. Romania: Satu Mare. 1998. Lang.: Hun. 2228

Szávitri
Plays/librettos/scripts
Composer Sándor Szokolay on his opera *Szávitri*. Hungary: Budapest. 1998. Lang.: Hun. 4801

Szczepkowski, Andrzej
Institutions
History of the Polish Theatre Association. Poland: Warsaw. 1918-1998. Lang.: Pol. 1692

Szegedi Kortárs Balett (Szeged)
Performance/production
Hungarian dance companies at Interbalett '98. Hungary. 1998. Lang.: Hun. 946

Productions of Szegedi Kortárs Balett. Hungary: Szeged. 1998. Lang.: Hun. 1102

Szegedi Nemzeti Színház (Szeged)
Performance/production
Two Hungarian productions of Arthur Miller's *Death of a Salesman*. Hungary: Pécs, Szeged. 1998. Lang.: Hun. 2123

Two Hungarian productions of *Die Dreigroschenoper (The Three Penny Opera)*. Hungary: Budapest, Szeged. 1998. Lang.: Hun. 4362

The Hungarian premier of Verdi's *Stiffelio*. Hungary: Szeged. 1998. Lang.: Hun. 4621

Interview with Tamás Pál, conductor and musical director of Szeged National Theatre. Hungary: Szeged. 1998. Lang.: Hun. 4622

Mozart's *Die Zauberflöte* directed by János Szikora. Hungary: Budapest. Hungary: Szeged. 1998. Lang.: Hun. 4631

Szegedi Nemzeti Színház Kamaraszínháza (Szeged)
Performance/production
Review of Shakespeare's *Much Ado About Nothing*, Szeged National Theatre. Hungary: Szeged. 1997. Lang.: Hun. 2086

Two Hungarian productions of Čechov's *Tri sestry (Three Sisters)*. Hungary: Veszprém, Szeged. 1998. Lang.: Hun. 2135

Szegedi Szabadtéri Játékok (Szeged)
Performance/production
Three Hungarian productions of Shakespeare's *Richard III*. Hungary: Budapest, Zsámbék, Szeged. 1997. Lang.: Hun. 2121
Kodály's *Háry János* at Szeged's Open-Air Festival. Hungary: Szeged. 1998. Lang.: Hun. 4359
Interview with Miklós Gábor Kerényi on directing Verdi's *Un Ballo in Maschera*. Hungary: Budapest. 1998. Lang.: Hun. 4619
Székely fonó (Székler Spinnery, The)
Performance/production
Kodály's *Székely fonó (The Székler Spinnery)*. Hungary: Budapest. 1998. Lang.: Hun. 4298
Interview with Imre Kerényi, director of Kodály's *Székely fonó (The Székler Spinnery)*. Hungary: Budapest. 1997. Lang.: Hun. 4299
Székely, Gábor
Institutions
Theatre critics' awards 97-98. Hungary. 1997-1998. Lang.: Hun. 355
The change of management at Új Színház. Hungary: Budapest. 1994-1998. Lang.: Hun. 358
The National Theatre's experiment in artistic renewal. Hungary: Budapest. 1979-1982. Lang.: Hun. 1672
Performance/production
Interview with directors Gábor Székely and Eszter Novák. Hungary: Budapest. 1998. Lang.: Hun. 2128
Székely, György
Plays/librettos/scripts
New Hungarian translations of Shakespeare. Hungary. 1990-1998. Lang.: Hun. 3187
Szemrebbenés (Twinkling)
Performance/production
Interview with dancer and choreographer Hedvig Fekete. Hungary: Budapest. 1998. Lang.: Hun. 1291
Szenes, Hannah
Plays/librettos/scripts
Israeli attitudes toward Holocaust theatre. Israel. 1944-1995. Lang.: Eng. 3217
Szentendrei Teátrum (Szentendre)
Performance/production
Three Hungarian productions of plays by Molière. Hungary: Szentendre, Kapolcs, Kőszeg. 1998. Lang.: Hun. 2142
Szentmihályi Szabó, Péter
Performance/production
Reviews of new Hungarian musicals. Hungary: Budapest. 1997. Lang.: Hun. 4360
Szenvedéstörténet (Passion Play)
Performance/production
Andrés Jeles's *Szenvedéstërtënet (Passion Play)* directed by Gábor Máté. Hungary: Budapest. 1998. Lang.: Hun. 2145
Szép, Ernő
Performance/production
Two productions of Ernő Szép's *Vőlegény (The Fiancé)*. Hungary: Nyíregyháza. Hungary: Győr. 1998.Lang.: Hun. 2118
Szervét, Tibor
Performance/production
Interview with actor Tibor Szervét. Hungary. 1988-1998. Lang.: Hun. 2071
Szigethy, András
Performance/production
András Szigethy's *Kegyelem (Mercy)* directed by László Vándorfi. Hungary: Veszprém. 1998. Lang.: Hun. 2105
Szigeti, Karoly
Performance/production
Modern tendencies in Hungarian folk dance. Hungary. 1970-1977. Lang.: Hun. 1228
Szigligeti Színház (Szolnok)
Performance/production
Interviews with actors on Anatolij Vasiljév's guest direction at Szigligeti Theatre. Hungary: Szolnok. 1998. Lang.: Hun. 2061
Review of Shakespeare's *The Merchant of Venice*, Szigligeti Theatre. Hungary: Szolnok. 1997. Lang.: Hun. 2066
A.A. Vasiljév's production of *Bez viny vinovatjė (Guilty Though Innocent)* by Ostrovskij. Hungary: Szolnok. 1998. Lang.:Hun. 2096
Symbolism in Anatolij Vasiljév's production of *Guilty Though Innocent* by Ostrovskij. Hungary: Szolnok. 1998. Lang.: Hun. 2098
Mari Törőcsik's performance in Ostrovskij's *Guilty Though Innocent* directed by Vasiljév. Hungary: Szolnok. 1997. Lang.: Hun. 2125
Obituary for director István Paál. Hungary: Szolnok. 1942-1998. Lang.: Hun. 2143
Szikora, János
Performance/production
Two Hungarian productions of *Die Dreigroschenoper (The Three Penny Opera)*. Hungary: Budapest, Szeged. 1998. Lang.: Hun. 4362
Interview with Tamás Pál, conductor and musical director of Szeged National Theatre. Hungary: Szeged. 1998. Lang.: Hun. 4622
Interview with director János Szikora. Hungary: Budapest. 1998. Lang.: Hun. 4630
Mozart's *Die Zauberflöte* directed by János Szikora. Hungary: Budapest. Hungary: Szeged. 1998. Lang.: Hun. 4631
Sziládi, János
Institutions
The National Theatre's experiment in artistic renewal. Hungary: Budapest. 1979-1982. Lang.: Hun. 1672
Szilágyi, Andor
Performance/production
László Babarczy's production of *Pepe* by Andor Szilágy. Serbia: Novi Sad. 1998. Lang.: Hun. 2342
Színház- és Filmművészeti Főiskola (Budapest)
Performance/production
Interview with director Tamás Ascher on director training. Hungary. 1960-1990. Lang.: Hun. 2146
Színművészeti Akadémia Szentgyörgyi István Tagozata (Târgu-Mureş)
Institutions
History of annual festival of Hungarian-language theatre. Hungary: Kisvárda. 1989-1998. Lang.: Hun. 1669
History of Hungarian-language theatre in Transylvania. Romania. Hungary. 1919-1992. Lang.: Hun, Rom. 1693
Szirtes, Ádám
Performance/production
Review of biographies of actors Ádám Szirtes and Éva Ruttkai. Hungary. 1998. Lang.: Hun. 2077
Szirtes, János
Design/technology
Survey of an exhibition of Hungarian scene design. Hungary: Budapest. 1998. Lang.: Hun. 195
An exhibition of sets and environments by Hungarian designers. Hungary: Budapest. 1998. Lang.: Hun. 196
Catalogue of an exhibition devoted to Hungarian theatre and film. Hungary: Budapest. 1998. Lang.: Hun. 197
Szkéné Színház (Budapest)
Institutions
Interview with director János Regős of Szkéné Színház. Hungary: Budapest. 1979-1998. Lang.: Hun. 362
History of Szkéné Színház. Hungary: Budapest. 1963-1995. Lang.: Hun. 1668
Performance/production
Program of *butō* festival, Szkéné Theatre. Hungary: Budapest. 1997. Lang.: Hun. 950
Guest performance of Théâtre du Plantin, a company for developmentally disabled actors. Hungary: Budapest. 1983-1998. Lang.: Hun. 2081
Szokolay, Sándor
Plays/librettos/scripts
Composer Sándor Szokolay on his opera *Szávitri*. Hungary: Budapest. 1998. Lang.: Hun. 4801
Szomorú vasárnap (Gloomy Sunday)
Performance/production
Collection of newspaper reviews by London theatre critics. UK-England. 1998. Lang.: Eng. 2489
Szörényi, Levente
Performance/production
Reviews of new Hungarian musicals. Hungary: Budapest. 1997. Lang.: Hun. 4360
Szűcs, Katalin
Institutions
Interviews with the jury who selected the National Theatre Festival presentations. Hungary. 1996-1997. Lang.: Hun. 363
Szumrák, Vera
Performance/production
Interview with dancer Vera Szumrák. Hungary. 1950-1998. Lang.: Hun. 1114
Szűrővizsgálat (Screen Test)
Performance/production
Sándor Lajos' *Szűrővizsgálat (Screen Test)* directed by Tamás Fodor. Hungary: Budapest. 1998. Lang.: Hun. 2103

Tabakov, Oleg Pavlovič
Institutions
Oleg Tabakov's Studio Theatre. Russia: Moscow. 1998. Lang.: Rus. 1715
Performance/production
Sergej Bezrukov's creation of the character of poet Sergej Esenin. Russia: Moscow. 1998. Lang.: Rus. 2278
Andrej Žitinkin directs *Confessions of Felix Krull, Confidence Man*, adapted from Thomas Mann. Russia: Moscow. 1998. Lang.: Rus. 2335
Actor Sergej Bezrukov. Russia: Moscow. Lang.: Rus. 2341
Tabard Theatre (London)
Performance/production
Collection of newspaper reviews by London theatre critics. UK-England: London. 1998. Lang.: Eng. 2494
Tabernacle Theatre (London)
Performance/production
Collection of newspaper reviews by London theatre critics. UK-England: London. 1998. Lang.: Eng. 2501
Table Number 7
Performance/production
Collection of newspaper reviews by London theatre critics. UK-England: London. 1998. Lang.: Eng. 2452
Tableaux vivants
Performance/production
Representation of the historical past on the French stage. France. 1810-1820. Lang.: Eng. 527
Tabori, George
Design/technology
Geogre Tabori's production of Mozart's *Die Zauberflöte* in a circus ring. Germany: Berlin. 1998. Lang.: Ger. 4428
Performance/production
Semiotic analysis of the nature of theatrical directing. USA. 1988. Lang.: Eng. 650
Actors Gert Voss and Ignaz Kirchner on George Tabori's production of *Fin de partie (Endgame)*. Austria: Vienna. 1998. Lang.: Ger. 1821
Gert Voss and Ignaz Kirchner, *Theater Heute*'s actors of the year. Austria: Vienna. 1988-1998. Lang.: Ger. 1823
Plays/librettos/scripts
Analysis of *Jubiläum* by George Tabori. Germany. 1983. Lang.: Eng. 3137
Tábori, György
SEE
Tabori, George.
Tabucchi, Antonio
Performance/production
Comparison of text-based and visual productions. France. 1998. Lang.: Fre. 1939
Taganka Theatre
SEE
Teat'r na Taganké.
Tagliarino, Sal
Design/technology
Professional theatrical designers on design training. USA. 1998. Lang.: Eng. 252
Taglioni, Filippo
Performance/production
Ballerina Marie Taglioni. France. 1804-1836. Lang.: Hun. 1071
Taglioni, Marie
Performance/production
Ballerina Marie Taglioni. France. 1804-1836. Lang.: Hun. 1071
Marie Taglioni and French Romantic ballet. France. 1830-1875. Lang.: Eng. 1072
Tairov, Aleksand'r Jakovlevič
Performance/production
The Russian-German theatrical relationship. Russia. Germany. 1920-1949. Lang.: Rus. 2285
Aleksand'r Tairov's production of *Fortune Heights* by John Dos Passos. USA. 1930-1935. Lang.: Rus. 2739
Aleksand'r Tairov's productions of plays by Eugene O'Neill. USSR. 1926-1929. Lang.: Eng. 2769
Takanen, Anna
Performance/production
Interview with actress and director Anna Takanen. Sweden: Stockholm. 1994-1998. Lang.: Swe. 2372
Takarazuka Kagekidan (Osaka)
Institutions
The all-female Takarazuka Revue Company. Japan. 1914-1988. Lang.: Eng. 368
Takatani, Shiro
Performance/production
Collection of newspaper reviews by London theatre critics. UK-England: London. 1998. Lang.: Eng. 2512
Takatoki
Basic theatrical documents
English translation of *Takatoki* by Mokuami Kawatake. Japan. 1884-1998. Lang.: Eng. 1361
Take Away
Performance/production
Collection of newspaper reviews by London theatre critics. UK-England: London. 1998. Lang.: Eng. 2500
Tal'kov, I.
Performance/production
Singer I. Tal'kov. Russia. 1998. Lang.: Rus. 4368
Talanta, La
Plays/librettos/scripts
The comedies of Pietro Aretino. Italy. 1534-1556. Lang.: Eng. 3251
Talawa Theatre Company (London)
Performance/production
Collection of newspaper reviews by London theatre critics. UK-England. 1998. Lang.: Eng. 2527
Talbot, Ian
Performance/production
Collection of newspaper reviews by London theatre critics. UK-England: London. 1998. Lang.: Eng. 2480
Tale of Possessors Self-Dispossessed, A
Plays/librettos/scripts
Eugene O'Neill's unfinished *A Tale of Possessors Self-Dispossessed*. USA. 1945-1953. Lang.: Eng. 3594
Tales of Hoffmann, The
SEE
Contes d'Hoffmann, Les.
Tales of the Lost Formicans
Performance/production
Collection of newspaper reviews by London theatre critics. UK-England: London. 1998. Lang.: Eng. 2566
Tales of the Walled City
Relation to other fields
Theatre and politics in Hong Kong. Hong Kong. 1984-1996. Lang.: Eng. 3772
Talk About the Passion
Performance/production
Collection of newspaper reviews by London theatre critics. UK-England: London. 1998. Lang.: Eng. 2502
Talk of the City
Performance/production
Collection of newspaper reviews by London theatre critics. UK. 1998. Lang.: Eng. 2407
Talke, Michael
Administration
Interviews with German theatre and film directors. Germany. 1998. Lang.: Ger. 1385
Talking AIDS to Death
Institutions
The aesthetics of performances based on non-fiction texts at Lifeline Theatre. USA: Chicago, IL. 1996-1998. Lang.: Eng. 1788
Talking Beans
Performance/production
Collection of newspaper reviews by London theatre critics. UK-England: London. 1998. Lang.: Eng. 2560
Talking Heads
Plays/librettos/scripts
Playwright Alan Bennett. UK-England. 1994-1998. Lang.: Ger. 3488
Talley and Son
Performance/production
The collaboration of playwright Lanford Wilson and director Marshall W. Mason. USA: New York, NY. 1978-1986. Lang.: Eng. 2756
Talley's Folly
Performance/production
The collaboration of playwright Lanford Wilson and director Marshall W. Mason. USA: New York, NY. 1978-1986. Lang.: Eng. 2756
Plays/librettos/scripts
Comedy and humor in plays of Lanford Wilson. USA. 1961-1985. Lang.: Eng. 3595
Tallinna Linnateater (Tallin)
Institutions
Profile of Estonian theatres. Estonia: Tallin, Tartu. 1997. Lang.: Swe, Eng, Ger. 345

Tamalpa Institute (Kentfield, CA)
Relation to other fields
Dancer, teacher, and healing facilitator Anna Halprin of Tamalpa Institute. USA: Kentfield, CA. 1978-1998. Lang.: Ger. 1338
Tamasaburō V, Bandō
Performance/production
The performance of *onnagata* Tamasaburō in *Elizabeth* by Francisco Ors. Japan: Tokyo. 1993-1995. Lang.: Eng. 1362
Tamási Áron Színház (Sfântu-Gheorghe)
Institutions
Hungarian-language theatre in Transylvania. Hungary. Romania. 1798-1998. Lang.: Hun. 365
History of Hungarian-language theatre in a Romanian city. Romania: Sfântu-Gheorghe. 1948-1992. Lang.: Hun. 379
History of annual festival of Hungarian-language theatre. Hungary: Kisvárda. 1989-1998. Lang.: Hun. 1669
History of Hungarian-language theatre in Transylvania. Romania. Hungary. 1919-1992. Lang.: Hun, Rom. 1693
Performance/production
Molière's *Dom Juan* directed by Olga Barabás. Hungary. Romania: Sfântu-Gheorghe. 1998. Lang.: Hun. 2063
Tamási, Áron
Plays/librettos/scripts
Essays on playwright Áron Tamási. Romania. 1907-1997. Lang.: Hun. 3314
Tamborrino, Giovanni
Performance/production
Giovanni Tamborrino's opera without song. Italy. Lang.: Ita. 4300
Tamburlaine the Great
Plays/librettos/scripts
Assessment of Marlowe's *Tamburlaine the Great*. England. 1587-1588. Lang.: Eng. 2866
Influences on *'Tis Pity She's a Whore* by John Ford. England. 1587-1631. Lang.: Eng. 2937
Analysis of *Tamburlaine the Great* by Christopher Marlowe. England. 1590-1998. Lang.: Eng. 3014
Space and measurement in *Tamburlaine the Great* by Christopher Marlowe. England. 1587-1588. Lang.: Eng. 3029
Tamburlaine The Great
Plays/librettos/scripts
Marlowe's tragedies and peer evaluation in the composition classroom. USA. 1997-1998. Lang.: Eng. 3532
Taming of the Shrew, The
Design/technology
Set and lighting designs for *The Taming of the Shrew*, American Repertory Theatre. USA: Cambridge, MA. 1998. Lang.: Eng. 1559
Performance/production
Interview with ballerina Katalin Hágai. Hungary. 1961-1998. Lang.: Hun. 1096
Shakespeare performance on the Rhine and the Ruhr. Germany: Cologne, Bochum, Düsseldorf. 1996-1997. Lang.: Ger. 1962
Contemporary Polish productions of Shakespeare. Poland. 1990-1998. Lang.: Pol. 2213
Michael Siberry on performing in an RSC production of *The Taming of the Shrew*. UK-England: London, Stratford. 1995-1996. Lang.:Eng. 2637
Brief productions of Shakespeare, Shaw, and Marlowe at the World's Fair. USA: Chicago, IL. 1934. Lang.: Eng. 2701
Plays/librettos/scripts
Women's use of wit in response to men in English popular culture. England. 1590-1630. Lang.: Eng. 2884
Tampereen Teatteri (Tampere)
Institutions
Competition and collaboration between Tampere's two resident theatres. Finland: Tampere. 1998. Lang.: Fin. 1605
Tampereen Työväen Teatteri (Tampere)
Institutions
Competition and collaboration between Tampere's two resident theatres. Finland: Tampere. 1998. Lang.: Fin. 1605
TamS (Munich)
Institutions
Survey of Munich's theatre scene. Germany: Munich. 1997. Lang.: Ger. 1626
Táncművészeti Főiskola (Budapest)
Institutions
Interview with Imre Dózsa, managing director of Táncművészeti Főiskola. Hungary: Budapest. 1998. Lang.: Hun. 897
Tandberg, Ole Anders
Performance/production
Report from Ibsen festival. Norway: Oslo. 1998. Lang.: Swe. 2211
Recent productions of plays by Ibsen and Strindberg. Sweden: Stockholm. 1997. Lang.: Eng. 2393
Tang, Xianzu
Performance/production
Collection of newspaper reviews by London theatre critics. UK-England: London. 1998. Lang.: Eng. 2503
Preview of a guest performance of *The Peony Pavilion (Mudan ting)*. China, People's Republic of. 1998. Lang.: Eng. 4314
Plays/librettos/scripts
Personal identity in *Mudan ting (The Peony Pavilion)* by Tang Xianzu and *Taohua shan (The Peach Blossom Fan)* by Kong Shangren.China. 1575-1675. Lang.: Eng. 4315
Tangled Garden
Plays/librettos/scripts
Text of *Tangled Garden* by David Wright Crawford with documentation of the author's method. USA. 1987. Lang.: Eng. 3569
Tango Room, The
Performance/production
Collection of newspaper reviews by London theatre critics. UK-England: London. 1998. Lang.: Eng. 2453
Tanguy, François
Institutions
Profile of Théâtre du Radeau. France: Le Mans. 1980-1998. Lang.: Ger. 1614
Tansi, Sony Labou
Relation to other fields
Playwright Sony Labou Tansi and Congolese politics. Congo. 1996. Lang.: Eng. 3742
Tant Blomma (Aunt Blomma)
Plays/librettos/scripts
Female characters in plays by Scandinavian women. Norway. Sweden. Denmark. 1998. Lang.: Eng. 3299
Tanztheater (Wuppertal)
Institutions
Profile of Pina Bausch and her Tanztheater. Germany: Wuppertal. 1977-1998. Lang.: Eng. 893
Performance/production
Dancer/choreographer Pina Bausch. Germany: Wuppertal. 1973-1997. Lang.: Eng. 932
A personal response to Pina Bausch's dance theatre. Germany: Wuppertal. 1982-1998. Lang.: Eng. 1277
Analysis of *Nur du (Only You)* by choreographer Pina Bausch. Germany: Wuppertal. 1997. Lang.: Eng. 1278
Interview with dancer and choreographer Pina Bausch. Germany: Wuppertal. 1973-1998. Lang.: Ger. 1279
Analysis of Pina Bausch's dance work *Masuca Fogo*. Germany: Wuppertal. 1998. Lang.: Ger. 1282
Taohua shan (Peach Blossom Fan, The)
Plays/librettos/scripts
Personal identity in *Mudan ting (The Peony Pavilion)* by Tang Xianzu and *Taohua shan (The Peach Blossom Fan)* by Kong Shangren.China. 1575-1675. Lang.: Eng. 4315
Tap dancing
Performance/production
Tap dance team of Betty Byrd and Danny Hoctor. USA. 1959-1998. Lang.: Eng. 983
Tapestry Music Theatre (Toronto, ON)
Institutions
Profile of Tapestry Music Theatre. Canada: Toronto, ON. 1985-1998. Lang.: Eng. 4346
Tapia y Rivera, Alejandro
Plays/librettos/scripts
The mulatto in Puerto Rican drama. Puerto Rico. 1850-1985. Lang.: Spa. 3311
Tara Arts Centre (London)
Performance/production
Tara Arts and English Indian theatre. UK-England. 1965-1995. Lang.: Eng. 614
Collection of newspaper reviews by London theatre critics. UK-England: London. 1998. Lang.: Eng. 2525
Tarantino, Quentin
Plays/librettos/scripts
Comparison between *Krísis (Crisis)* by Sabina Berman and Quentin Tarantino's film *Pulp Fiction*. Mexico. USA. 1993-1996. Lang.: Spa. 3276
Taras, John
Performance/production
Interview with choreographer John Taras. USA: New York, NY. 1919-1998. Lang.: Hun. 1187

Tarkington, Booth
Plays/librettos/scripts
The development and casting of Booth Tarkington's *The Country Cousin*. USA. 1921. Lang.: Eng. 3699
Tarleton, Angela Brannon
Basic theatrical documents
Text of *Raven's Song* by Angela Brannon Tarleton. USA. 1988. Lang.: Eng. 4323
Tarragon Theatre (Toronto, ON)
Plays/librettos/scripts
Don Hannah's *Fathers and Sons* at Tarragon Theatre. Canada: Toronto, ON. 1998. Lang.: Eng. 2833
Tarry Flynn
Performance/production
Collection of newspaper reviews by London theatre critics. UK-England. 1998. Lang.: Eng. 2489
Tartuffe
Institutions
Ariane Mnouchkine and rehearsal techniques of Théâtre du Soleil. France: Paris. 1964-1997. Lang.: Eng. 1610
Performance/production
Collection of newspaper reviews by London theatre critics. UK-England: London. 1998. Lang.: Eng. 2576
Tarzan
Performance/production
Obituary for actress Maureen O'Sullivan. USA. 1911-1998. Lang.: Eng. 3947
Tasnádi, István
Performance/production
Review of *Édes Anna (Anna Édes)*, Madách Chamber Theatre. Hungary: Budapest. 1997. Lang.: Hun. 2136
István Tasnádi's *Titanic vízirevü (Titanic Water Show)* at Bárka Színház. Hungary: Budapest. 1998. Lang.: Hun. 2144
TAT/Depot (Frankfurt)
Relation to other fields
Political and cultural situation of Frankfurt theatres. Germany: Frankfurt. 1997-1999. Lang.: Ger. 744
Tatai, Mária
Performance/production
Interview with dancer Mária Tatai. Hungary. 1981-1998. Lang.: Hun. 935
Tatarskij Gosudarstvėnnyj Akademičeskij Teat'r im. G. Kamala (Kazan)
Performance/production
Actress G. Isangulova. Tatarstan: Kazan. 1998. Lang.: Rus. 2404
Tate, Richard
Performance/production
Collection of newspaper reviews by London theatre critics. UK-England: London. 1998. Lang.: Eng. 2449
Tatiñá, Pera
Performance/production
Collection of newspaper reviews by London theatre critics. UK-England: London. 1998. Lang.: Eng. 2473
Tatjana Repina
Basic theatrical documents
Catalan translations of the complete plays of Anton Čechov. Russia. 1884-1904. Lang.: Cat. 1449
Tätowierung (Tattoo)
Institutions
New plays by Dea Loher at Staatsschauspiel Hannover. Germany: Hannover. 1992-1998. Lang.: Ger. 1643
Plays/librettos/scripts
The language of Dea Loher's *Tätowierung (Tattoo)*. Germany. 1995-1998. Lang.: Ger. 3126
Marginal notes by Dea Loher on her plays. Germany. 1991-1998. Lang.: Ger. 3162
Taube, Dietrich
Institutions
The proposed merger of Deutsches Nationaltheater Weimar and Theater Erfurt. Germany: Weimar, Erfurt. 1998. Lang.: Ger. 354
Tavel, Ronald
Plays/librettos/scripts
Revolutionary Off Broadway playwriting. USA: New York, NY. 1959-1969. Lang.: Eng. 3604
Taxes
Administration
Changes in income tax regulations and effect on theatre workers. USA. 1998. Lang.: Eng. 40
Benefits to performers of Taxpayer Relief Act. USA. 1998. Lang.: Eng. 58
'Arts incubator' organization Art's Bridge. USA: Chicago, IL. 1986-1998. Lang.: Eng. 120
The publicizing of financial information about nonprofit arts organizations. USA. 1998. Lang.: Eng. 137
Pricing strategy for puppeteers. USA. 1998. Lang.: Eng. 4864
TAXI Children's Theatre (Louisville, KY)
Institutions
Profile of TAXI Children's Theatre. USA: Louisville, KY. 1992-1998. Lang.: Eng. 390
Taylor, Andrew
Performance/production
Collection of newspaper reviews by London theatre critics. UK-England: London. 1998. Lang.: Eng. 2477
Taylor, Dominick A.
Basic theatrical documents
Text of *Sound Check* by Dominick A. Taylor. USA. 1994. Lang.: Eng. 1511
Taylor, Jeremy James
Design/technology
Sound design for the musical *Bugsy Malone*. UK-England: London. 1997. Lang.: Eng. 4327
Taylor, Paul
Performance/production
Choreographer Paul Taylor. USA. 1977-1998. Lang.: Eng. 1335
Taymor, Julie
Administration
The Disney Corporation's Broadway musicals. USA: New York, NY. 1996-1998. Lang.: Eng. 4317
Design/technology
The 1998 TCI awards. USA. 1998. Lang.: Eng. 243
Donald Holder's lighting design for *The Lion King*. USA: New York, NY. 1997-1998. Lang.: Eng. 4336
Technical designs for the Broadway production of *The Lion King*. USA: New York, NY. 1998. Lang.: Eng. 4342
Performance/production
Director, costumer, and mask-maker Julie Taymor. USA. 1980-1998. Lang.: Eng. 2685
Tchaikovsky, Peter Ilich
SEE
Čajkovskij, Pëtr Iljič.
Tea Party
Plays/librettos/scripts
Transference in plays by Harold Pinter. UK-England. 1960-1985. Lang.: Eng. 3461
Tea with Zora and Marjorie
Basic theatrical documents
Texts of plays about Zora Neale Hurston by Barbara Waddell Speisman. USA. 1988. Lang.: Eng. 1510
Teaching methods
Design/technology
Criticism of methods used in design training. Finland. 1998. Lang.: Fin. 180
Institutions
Report on Vachtangov School conference. Russia: Moscow. 1990-1998. Lang.: Rus. 380
Interdisciplinarity in post-secondary theatre studies programs. USA. 1998. Lang.: Eng. 407
Interview with dance teacher Lia Schubert. Sweden: Stockholm, Gothenburg. 1935-1998. Lang.: Swe. 900
Defense of Svenska Balettskolan by a former student. Sweden: Stockholm. 1996. Lang.: Swe. 1052
Training methods of the Conservatoire d'art dramatique de Québec. Canada: Quebec, PQ. 1998. Lang.: Fre. 1578
Proposal to apply alternative pedagogy and cultural studies to university theatre education. Canada: Guelph, ON. 1998. Lang.: Eng. 1586
Performance/production
Lithuanian theatre education and the visit of Tadashi Suzuki. Lithuania. 1998. Lang.: Fin. 559
The Creative Surges actor-training seminar. UK-England: Ipswich. 1998. Lang.: Eng. 606
The Alba Emoting system of actor training. USA. 1995-1998. Lang.: Eng. 668
Voice teachers Alex Bulmer and Kate Lynch. Canada: Toronto, ON. UK-England: London. 1986-1998. Lang.: Eng. 1837

Teaching methods — cont'd

Problems of post-secondary theatre training. Canada: Edmonton, AB. 1919-1998. Lang.: Eng. 1848
Tadashi Suzuki's method of actor training. Japan. 1998. Lang.: Eng. 2191

Relation to other fields
The role of the drama specialist in the classroom. France. 1997. Lang.: Eng. 736
Handbook of teachers of drama in secondary school. Netherlands. 1990-1998. Lang.: Dut. 753
The use of theatre to teach foreign languages. Russia: Moscow. Lang.: Rus. 761
Engaging the students in large introductory theatre courses. USA. 1996-1998. Lang.: Eng. 779
Children's processing of live theatre. USA. 1985. Lang.: Eng. 801
Non-Western dance forms in the teaching of theatre arts. USA: Davis, CA. 1990-1997. Lang.: Eng. 809
Process drama in secondary school drama education. Canada. 1970-1998. Lang.: Eng. 3736
Drama in cross-cultural literature courses for foreign students. USA. 1987. Lang.: Eng. 3791
Interdisciplinary appraoches to the teaching of music theatre. USA. 1987. Lang.: Eng. 4402

Research/historiography
The Shakespeare Interactive Research Group. USA: Cambridge, MA. 1991-1997. Lang.: Eng. 3799

Theory/criticism
Tools for analysis of improvisation. Canada: Montreal, PQ. 1998. Lang.: Fre. 834

Training
Proposal to diversify activities in graduate theatre programs. Canada. 1998. Lang.: Eng. 872
Actor/director Jean-Paul Denizon and his workshops on Peter Brook's approach to theatre. France. 1980-1998. Lang.: Ita. 873
Ferruccio Di Cori's improvisational workshops for actors and directors. Italy: Rome. 1994-1996. Lang.: Ita. 874
Director Walter Pfaff on the influence of Jerzy Grotowski. Poland. Germany. 1998. Lang.: Eng. 876
The use of computer animation techniques in design training. USA: Athens, GA. 1988-1998. Lang.: Eng. 878
Improvisational training and psychological resilience. USA. 1996-1998. Lang.: Eng. 879
Feldenkreis movement theory. USA. 1905-1985. Lang.: Eng. 880
Survey of twentieth-century dance styles and teaching methods. Europe. 1900-1998. Lang.: Ger. 1015
Interview with dance teacher Mirja-Liisa Herhi. Finland. 1998. Lang.: Fin. 1016
Dance teaching methods of Anzu Furukawa. Finland. 1998. Lang.: Fin. 1017
Interview with dance teacher Maria Llerena. Sweden: Stockholm. 1966-1998. Lang.: Swe. 1018
Interview with children's dance teacher Yvonne Jahn-Olsson. Sweden: Stockholm. 1945-1998. Lang.: Swe. 1019
Britt-Marie Berggren's dancing school for children. Sweden: Stockholm. 1946. Lang.: Swe. 1020
Memoirs of dance teacher Lia Schubert. Sweden: Malmö, Stockholm, Gothenburg. 1950-1998. Lang.: Swe. 1021
The use of martial arts in dance training. UK-England. 1998. Lang.: Eng. 1022
Illustrated history of jazz dance. USA. Slovenia. 1900-1997. Lang.: Slo. 1023
The development of Irmgard Bartenieff's corrective physical training methods. USA. 1925-1981. Lang.: Ger. 1024
Interview with dance teacher Aarne Mäntylä. Finland. 1998. Lang.: Fin. 1203
Classical dance training and its appeal to children. Finland. 1998. Lang.: Fin. 1204
Maja Pliseckaja on ballet training. Russia: Moscow. 1998. Lang.: Rus. 1208
Methodological manual for teaching ballet to children. Slovenia. 1998. Lang.: Slo. 1209
Traditional and contemporary approaches to ballet training. Sweden: Stockholm. 1998. Lang.: Swe. 1210
Tina Hessel's relaxation and breathing techniques for dance training. Sweden: Stockholm. 1998. Lang.: Swe. 1211
Ballet teacher Pauline Koner. USA: New York, NY. 1920-1998. Lang.: Eng. 1212
Dance teacher Louise Kloepper. USA. 1910-1996. Lang.: Eng. 1213
Balanchine's ballet mistress on his training methods. USA. 1947-1998. Lang.: Eng. 1214
Ballet teacher Waltraud Karkar. USA: Wausau, WI. 1998. Lang.: Eng. 1215
Interview with dancer and teacher David Howard. USA. 1966-1998. Lang.: Swe. 1216
Dance teacher Harvey Hysell. USA: New Orleans, LA. 1969-1998. Lang.: Eng. 1217
Barbro Thiel-Cramér, Swedish teacher of Spanish dance. Sweden: Stockholm. Spain. 1944-1997. Lang.: Swe. 1244
Dance training at Folkwang Hochschule. Germany: Essen. 1996-1998. Lang.: Hun. 1341
Modern dance teacher Elizabeth Waters. USA. 1920-1950. Lang.: Eng. 1342
Interview with Steve Paxton, creator of contact improvisation. USA. 1973-1998. Lang.: Eng. 1343
Anne-Lise Gabold's use of the methods of Tadashi Suzuki in her production of Euripides' *Bákchai (The Bacchae)*. Japan. Denmark: Copenhagen. 1960-1998. Lang.: Dan. 1359
Actress, director, and teacher Marija Knebel'. Russia. 1898-1989. Lang.: Rus. 3850
Playwright Tony Kushner's address to the Association of Theatre in Higher Education. USA. 1997. Lang.: Eng. 3851
Mejerchol'd, actor training, and Trotsky. USSR. 1922-1929. Lang.: Eng. 3852
Details of a media acting curriculum. USA. 1994-1998. Lang.: Eng. 4041
Actor training for the character tenor. USA. 1998. Lang.: Eng. 4849

Teague, Eileen
Design/technology
Design concept for Amy Freed's *The Psychic Life of Savages*, Wilma Theatre. USA: Philadelphia, PA. 1998. Lang.: Eng. 1555

Teale, Polly
Performance/production
Collection of newspaper reviews by London theatre critics. UK-England: London. 1998. Lang.: Eng. 2550

Teamtheater Tankstelle (Munich)
Institutions
Survey of Munich's theatre scene. Germany: Munich. 1997. Lang.: Ger. 1626

Teare, Jeff
Performance/production
Collection of newspaper reviews by London theatre critics. UK-England: London. 1998. Lang.: Eng. 2545

Teat'r A. Džigarchanjana (Moscow)
Performance/production
Interview with actor Armen Džigarchanjan. Russia: Moscow. 1998. Lang.: Rus. 2232
Profile of stage and film actor Armen B. Džigarchanjan. Russia: Moscow. 1998. Lang.: Rus. 2290

Teat'r Alekseeva (Moscow)
Performance/production
Reconstruction of Stanislavskij's early stagings for the Alekseev Group. Russia: Moscow. 1877-1888. Lang.: Rus. 2322

Teat'r Berezil (Kiev)
Institutions
Les' Kurbas and Teat'r Berezil. USSR. 1922-1934. Lang.: Eng. 431

Teat'r Dramy i Komedii (Moscow)
SEE
Teat'r na Tagankė.

Teat'r Estrady (Moscow)
Performance/production
G. Chazanov of Teat'r Estrady. Russia: Moscow. Lang.: Rus. 4277

Teat'r Grotesk (Surgut)
Institutions
The student satirical company Teat'r Grotesk. Russia: Surgut. 1998. Lang.: Rus. 1712

Teat'r im. A.A. Bachrušina (Moscow)
Performance/production
Mejerchol'd's production of Gogol's *Revizor (The Inspector General)*. USSR: Moscow. 1926. Lang.: Eng. 2763

Teat'r im. A.A. Bachrušina (Moscow) — cont'd

Director Harold Clurman's reaction to Mejerchol'd's *Revizor (The Inspector General)*. USSR: Moscow. 1935. Lang.: Eng. 2764

Teat'r im. Je. Vachtangova (Moscow)

Performance/production

Actress M. Vertinskaja on her father, singer Aleksand'r Vertinskij. Russia: Moscow. 1998. Lang.: Rus. 2334

Teat'r im. Kamala

SEE

Tatarskij Gosudarstvénnyj Akademičéskij Teat'r im. G. Kamala.

Teat'r im. Leninskogo Komsomola (Moscow)

Performance/production

Actress Inna Čurikova. Russia: Moscow. 1998. Lang.: Rus. 2301

Director Mark Zacharov at Lenkom. Russia: Moscow. Lang.: Rus. 2316

Teat'r im. Mossovéta (Moscow)

Performance/production

Roman Viktjuk's production of *Salomé* by Oscar Wilde. Russia: Moscow. 1998. Lang.: Rus. 2266

Oleg Menšikov's production of *Gore ot uma (Wit Works Woe)* by Gribojédov. Russia: Moscow. 1998. Lang.: Rus. 2267

Teat'r im. V. Majakovskogo (Moscow)

Institutions

The Majakovskij Theatre. Russia: Moscow. 1923-1998. Lang.: Rus. 1700

Performance/production

Interview with director Andrej Gončarov. Russia: Moscow. 1998. Lang.: Rus. 2272

Teat'r Junogo Zritelja (Moscow)

Performance/production

Director Kama Ginkas of Teat'r Junogo Zritelja. Russia. 1998. Lang.: Rus. 2265

Teat'r Krivoe Zerkalo (Russia)

Performance/production

Memoirs of director and playwright Nikolaj Jévrejnov. Russia. 1879-1953. Lang.: Rus. 2279

Teat'r na Dmitrovke (Moscow)

Institutions

Gavrila Solodovnikov's Teat'r na Dmitrovke. Russia: Moscow. 1890-1899. Lang.: Rus. 1717

Teat'r na Taganké (Moscow)

Basic theatrical documents

Selection of poems and songs by actor Vladimir Vysockij. Russia: Moscow. 1960-1970. Lang.: Rus. 164

Institutions

Taganka Theatre's performance at the Bogotá theatre festival. Colombia: Bogotá. 1998. Lang.: Rus. 1595

Performance/production

Jurij Ljubimov's production of *The First Circle*, based on Solženicin's novel. Russia: Moscow. 1998. Lang.: Rus. 2270

Biographical information on actor Vladimir Vysockij. Russia: Moscow. 1938-1980. Lang.: Rus. 2291

The final months of actor Vladimir Vysockij. Russia: Moscow. 1980. Lang.: Rus. 2307

Reviews of the Russian theatre season. Russia: Moscow. Lang.: Rus. 2324

The funeral of actor and playwright Vladimir Vysockij. Russia: Moscow. 1980. Lang.: Rus. 2333

Teat'r Rev'liucii

SEE

Teat'r im. V. Majakovskogo.

Teat'r Sfera (Moscow)

Institutions

Report on the Stockholm theatre festival. Sweden: Stockholm. 1998. Lang.: Eng. 1724

Teat'r Sovremennogo Baleta (St. Petersburg)

Performance/production

Boris Ejfman's Teat'r Sovremennogo Baleta. Russia: St. Petersburg. 1998. Lang.: Rus. 1298

Teat'r-studija (Moscow)

Institutions

Oleg Tabakov's Studio Theatre. Russia: Moscow. 1998. Lang.: Rus. 1715

Performance/production

Sergej Bezrukov's creation of the character of poet Sergej Esenin. Russia: Moscow. 1998. Lang.: Rus. 2278

Andrej Žitinkin directs *Confessions of Felix Krull, Confidence Man*, adapted from Thomas Mann. Russia: Moscow. 1998. Lang.: Rus. 2335

Actor Sergej Bezrukov. Russia: Moscow. Lang.: Rus. 2341

Teater NOR (Stamsund)

Institutions

Teater NOR and its relationship with the community. Norway: Stamsund. 1998. Lang.: Eng. 1680

Teater Salieri (Stockholm)

Plays/librettos/scripts

Interview with playwright-director Kajsa Isakson. Sweden: Stockholm. 1997-1998. Lang.: Swe. 3414

Teater Tre (Stockholm)

Performance/production

Interview with Bengt Andersson, artistic director of Teater Tre. Sweden. 1983-1998. Lang.: Swe. 601

Teater Trixter (Gothenburg)

Plays/librettos/scripts

Interview with playwright-director Petra Revenue. Sweden: Gothenburg. 1980-1998. Lang.: Swe. 3415

Teater UNO (Gothenburg)

Performance/production

Teater UNO's stage adaptation of *L'Étranger (The Stranger)* by Albert Camus. Sweden: Gothenburg. 1998. Lang.: Swe. 2395

Teater 23 (Malmö)

Institutions

Profile of Teater 23. Sweden: Malmö. 1959-1998. Lang.: Swe. 1727

Teater- & Operahögskolan (Gothenburg)

Training

Singer training at Teater- & Operahögskolan. Sweden: Gothenburg. 1960-1998. Lang.: Swe. 4848

Teaterkollektivet Rex (Stockholm)

Performance/production

The interdisciplinary workshop of Teaterskollektivet Rex. Sweden: Stockholm. 1997. Lang.: Swe. 600

Plays/librettos/scripts

Swedish theatres and young Swedish playwrights. Sweden: Malmö, Gothenburg, Stockholm. 1994-1998. Lang.: Swe. 3411

TeaterX2 (Stockholm)

Institutions

Gunnar Martin Aronsson of TeaterX2 recalls Action-Theater. Sweden: Stockholm. Germany: Munich. 1968-1998. Lang.: Swe. 1722

Teatr Ateneum (Warsaw)

Institutions

Pictorial history of Teatr Ateneum. Poland: Warsaw. 1928-1998. Lang.: Pol. 1688

Teatr Kameralny (Sopot)

SEE

Teatr Wybrzeże.

Teatr Narodowy (Warsaw)

Performance/production

Jerzy Grzegorzewski's production of *Ślub (The Marriage)* by Witold Gombrowicz. Poland: Warsaw. 1998. Lang.: Pol. 2218

Teatr Polski (Warsaw)

Plays/librettos/scripts

Ida Kamińska's production of *Der Kheshbn (The Final Reckoning)* by Mikhl Mirsky. Poland: Warsaw. 1963. Lang.: Eng. 3310

Teatr Rapsodyczny (Cracow)

Performance/production

Postwar Polish theatre, culture, and politics. Poland. 1945-1950. Lang.: Eng. 573

Teatr Śląski (Katowice)

Institutions

Wyspiański's Teatr Śląski. Poland: Katowice. 1949-1992. Lang.: Pol. 1690

Teatr St I Witkiewicza (Zakopane)

Institutions

Profile of theatre company Teatr St I Witkiewicza. Poland: Zakopane. 1989. Lang.: Eng. 1684

Teatr Wybrzeże (Gdańsk)

Performance/production

History of Teatr Wybrzeże. Poland: Gdańsk, Warsaw, Cracow. 1952-1997. Lang.: Pol. 2215

Teatri Uniti (Naples)

Performance/production

Interview with director Mario Martone. Italy: Naples. 1977-1997. Lang.: Eng. 2166

Teatridithalia (Milan)

Performance/production

Survey of Milanese theatre. Italy: Milan. 1997-1998. Lang.: Eng. 2161

Teatro alla Scala (Milan)

Design/technology

Lighting design for Verdi's *Macbeth* at La Scala. Italy: Milan. 1998. Lang.: Eng. 4435

Institutions

Profile of Teatro alla Scala. Italy: Milan. Lang.: Rus. 4463

Performance/production

Reconstruction of the premiere of Boito's *Mefistofele*. Italy. 1871-1881. Lang.: Ita. 4647

Teatro alla Scala (Milan) — cont'd

Productions of Puccini operas at La Scala. Italy: Milan. 1980-1998. Lang.: Swe. 4657

Teatro Argentina (Rome)
Performance/production
Luca Ronconi's stage adaptation of *The Brothers Karamazov*. Italy: Rome. 1997. Lang.: Eng. 2188

Teatro Ateneo (Rome)
Training
Ferruccio Di Cori's improvisational workshops for actors and directors. Italy: Rome. 1994-1996. Lang.: Ita. 874

Teatro Buendía (Havana)
Institutions
Profile of Teatro Buendía. Cuba: Havana. 1986-1998. Lang.: Ger. 1596

Teatro Campesino (San Juan Bautista, CA)
Relation to other fields
The influence of Teatro Campesino on American politics. USA. 1965-1970. Lang.: Eng. 3783

Teatro Carcano (Milan)
Performance/production
Survey of Milanese theatre. Italy: Milan. 1997-1998. Lang.: Eng. 2161

Teatro Carignano (Turin)
Performance/production
Gianfranco De Bosio's production of *Se questo è un uomo (If This Is a Man)* by Primo Levi. Italy: Turin. 1963-1966. Lang.: Eng. 2168

Teatro Carlo Felice (Genoa)
Performance/production
Andrea Liberovici's production of *Sonetto. Un travestimento shakespeariano (Sonnet: A Shakespearean Travesty)* by Eduardo Sanguineti. Italy: Genoa. 1997. Lang.: Ita. 2159

Teatro Comunale (Ferrara)
Performance spaces
History of Teatro Comunale. Italy: Ferrara. 1798-1998. Lang.: Ger. 453

Teatro d'Arte (Rome)
Performance/production
Pirandello's Teatro d'Arte on tour in Trieste. Italy: Trieste. 1926. Lang.: Ita. 2178
Plays/librettos/scripts
Pirandello, Abba, and the Teatro d'Arte. Italy: Rome. 1925-1927. Lang.: Ita. 3248

Teatro dell'Elfo (Milan)
Performance/production
Survey of Milanese theatre. Italy: Milan. 1997-1998. Lang.: Eng. 2161

Teatro di Portaromana (Milan)
Performance/production
Survey of Milanese theatre. Italy: Milan. 1997-1998. Lang.: Eng. 2161

Teatro di Roma (Rome)
Performance/production
Luca Ronconi's production of *Mourning Becomes Electra* by Eugene O'Neill. Italy: Rome. 1996-1997. Lang.: Eng. 2183

Teatro Eliseo (Rome)
Performance/production
The Italian premiere of *A Streetcar Named Desire* by Tennessee Williams. Italy: Rome. 1949. Lang.: Eng. 2172

Roman theatre, traditional and experimental. Italy: Rome. 1994-1998. Lang.: Eng. 2187

Teatro Filodrammatici (Milan)
Performance/production
Survey of Milanese theatre. Italy: Milan. 1997-1998. Lang.: Eng. 2161

Teatro Fondo (Naples)
Plays/librettos/scripts
Contemporary parodies of nineteenth-century opera. Italy: Naples. 1813-1875. Lang.: Ita. 4811

Teatro Ghione (Rome)
Performance/production
Productions by Toni Bertorelli and Alfiero Alfieri. Italy: Rome. 1997. Lang.: Eng. 2175

Teatro Instabile (Milan)
Performance/production
Survey of Milanese theatre. Italy: Milan. 1997-1998. Lang.: Eng. 2161

Teatro La Fenice (Venice)
Design/technology
Verdi's operas and the influence of La Fenice scene designer Giuseppe Bertoja. Italy: Venice. 1840-1870. Lang.: Eng. 4433
Performance spaces
The restoration of the opera houses Gran Teatro del Liceu and Teatro La Fenice. Spain: Barcelona. Italy: Venice. 1994-1998. Lang.: Eng. 4495

Teatro Litta (Milan)
Performance/production
Survey of Milanese theatre. Italy: Milan. 1997-1998. Lang.: Eng. 2161

Teatro Manzoni (Milan)
Performance/production
Survey of Milanese theatre. Italy: Milan. 1997-1998. Lang.: Eng. 2161

Teatro Massimo (Prato)
Performance/production
Excerpts from the notebooks of director Massimo Castri. Italy: Prato. 1996. Lang.: Ita. 2162

Teatro Nacional Chileno (Santiago)
Institutions
Report on the Stockholm theatre festival. Sweden: Stockholm. 1998. Lang.: Eng. 1724

Teatro Nacional María Guerrero (Madrid)
Performance/production
Juan Carlos Pérez de la Fuente's production of *San Juan* by Max Aub. Spain: Madrid. 1998. Lang.: Eng. 2363

Teatro Nuovo (Milan)
Performance/production
Survey of Milanese theatre. Italy: Milan. 1997-1998. Lang.: Eng. 2161

Teatro Quirino (Rome)
Performance/production
Italian productions of plays by Harold Pinter. Italy. 1997. Lang.: Eng. 2165

Roman theatre, traditional and experimental. Italy: Rome. 1994-1998. Lang.: Eng. 2187

Teatro Real (Madrid)
Performance spaces
The newly remodeled Teatro Real. Spain: Madrid. 1988-1997. Lang.: Eng. 4496

Teatro Regio (Parma)
Performance/production
Verdi's rarely performed opera *Stiffelio*. Italy. 1850-1998. Lang.: Hun. 4652

Teatro San Babila (Milan)
Performance/production
Survey of Milanese theatre. Italy: Milan. 1997-1998. Lang.: Eng. 2161

Teatro San Carlo (Naples)
Plays/librettos/scripts
Contemporary parodies of nineteenth-century opera. Italy: Naples. 1813-1875. Lang.: Ita. 4811

Teatro Stabile dell'Umbria (Spoleto)
Performance/production
Massimo Castri's production of Euripides' *Electra*. Italy: Spoleto. 1993. Lang.: Ita. 2179

Teatro Stabile di Torino (Turin)
Performance/production
Gabriele Lavia's production of *Non si sa come (How Is Unknown)* by Luigi Pirandello. Italy: Turin. 1982-1988. Lang.: Ita. 2157

Italian productions of plays by Harold Pinter. Italy. 1997. Lang.: Eng. 2165

Gianfranco De Bosio's production of *Se questo è un uomo (If This Is a Man)* by Primo Levi. Italy: Turin. 1963-1966. Lang.: Eng. 2168

Teatro Valle (Rome)
Performance spaces
History of Teatro Valle. Italy: Rome. 1726-1997. Lang.: Ita. 452
Performance/production
Roman theatre, traditional and experimental. Italy: Rome. 1994-1998. Lang.: Eng. 2187

Teatro Vascello (Rome)
Performance/production
Roman theatre, traditional and experimental. Italy: Rome. 1994-1998. Lang.: Eng. 2187

Teatrul de Nord Secţia Harag György (Satu-Mare)
SEE
Szatmärnémeti Északi Színház, Harag György Társulat.

Teatrul de Stat (Oradea)
SEE
Nagyváradi Állami Színház.

Teatrul de Stat Secţia Tamási Áron (Sfintu-Gheorghe)
SEE
Tamási Áron Színház.

Teatrul Maghiar de Stat (Cluj-Napoca)
SEE
Állami Magyar Színház (Cluj-Napoca).

Teatrul Naţional Târgu-Mureş secţia maghiara (Târgu-Mureş)
SEE
Marosvásárhelyi Nemzeti Színház, Magyar Társulat (Târgu-Mureş).

Teatterikorkeakoulu (Helsinki)
Institutions
Profile of the Swedish Institute of Acting at the Finnish Theatre Academy. Finland: Helsinki. 1908-1998. Lang.: Eng, Fre. 1603

Technicians/crews
Design/technology
Account of ACTSAFE conference on theatre safety. France: Paris. 1998. Lang.: Swe. 181
Careers in technical theatre. Germany. Austria. 1998. Lang.: Ger. 189
OISTAT meeting on technician training. Netherlands: Amsterdam. 1998. Lang.: Swe. 206
Theatre technician training at Malmö Högskola. Sweden: Malmö. 1998. Lang.: Swe. 225
Obituary for Karl-Gunnar Frisell, who oversaw the technical restoration of Södra Teatern. Sweden: Solna. 1920-1998. Lang.: Swe. 226
Professional theatrical designers on design training. USA. 1998. Lang.: Eng. 252
Lighting expert Francis P. De Verna. USA. 1928-1998. Lang.: Eng. 257
Lighting technician Julian Winter. USA. 1971-1998. Lang.: Eng. 309
American theatre designers and technicians' visit to China. USA. China, People's Republic of. 1998. Lang.: Eng. 327
Stage technician Pete Feller. USA. 1920-1998. Lang.: Eng. 330
Jason Barnes, production manager of the Royal National Theatre. UK-England: London. 1973-1998. Lang.: Eng. 1527
Film and TV lighting man Scott Jason Jellen. USA. 1973-1998. Lang.: Eng. 3855
Profile of technicians for Grammy Awards television broadcast. USA: New York, NY. 1998. Lang.: Eng. 4056
Technical designs for the musical *Doctor Doolittle* directed by Steven Pimlott. UK-England: London. 1998. Lang.: Eng. 4325

Technology
SEE
Design/technology.

Teesri Duniya (Montreal, PQ)
Institutions
Rahul Varma on his multicultural theatre company Teesri Duniya. Canada: Montreal, PQ. 1981-1998. Lang.: Eng. 1592

Teixidor, Jordi
Basic theatrical documents
Text of *Magnus* by Jordi Teixidor. Spain-Catalonia. 1994. Lang.: Cat. 1468

Teje, Tora
Performance/production
The disappearance of the diva in the modern world. Europe. USA. 1890-1998. Lang.: Swe. 525

Telematic Dreaming
Performance/production
Dancer Susan Kozel on performing in Paul Sermon's *Telematic Dreaming*. Netherlands: Amsterdam. 1997. Lang.: Eng. 956

Television
SEE
Video forms.

Telihay, Péter
Performance/production
Review of Shakespeare's *Much Ado About Nothing*, Szeged National Theatre. Hungary: Szeged. 1997. Lang.: Hun. 2086
Interview with director Péter Telihay. Hungary. 1993-1998. Lang.: Hun. 2130
Two Hungarian productions of Čechov's *Tri sestry (Three Sisters)*. Hungary: Veszprém, Szeged. 1998. Lang.: Hun. 2135
Calderón's *La cisma de Inglaterra (The Schism of England)* directed by Péter Telihay. Hungary: Budapest. 1997. Lang.: Hun. 2137

Teljakovskij, V.A.
Institutions
Diaries of theatre director V.A. Teljakovskij. Russia: St. Petersburg. 1898-1901. Lang.: Rus. 1716

Tell Me
Performance/production
Collection of newspaper reviews by London theatre critics. UK-England: London. 1998. Lang.: Eng. 2443

Tellet, John
Performance/production
Collection of newspaper reviews by London theatre critics. UK-England: London. 1998. Lang.: Eng. 2436

Temesi, Mária
Performance/production
Interview with soprano Mária Temesi. Hungary. 1977-1998. Lang.: Hun. 4643

Temesvári Csiky Gergely Színház
SEE
Csiky Gergely Színház (Timişoara).

Tempest, The
Institutions
Shakespearean productions at the Carrefour international theatre festival. Canada: Quebec, PQ. 1998. Lang.: Fre. 1588
Profile of Teatro Buendía. Cuba: Havana. 1986-1998. Lang.: Ger. 1596
Performance/production
French Canadian translations/adaptations of Shakespeare. Canada: Montreal, PQ. 1988. Lang.: Fre. 1855
Shakespeare's *The Tempest* on the eighteenth-century stage. England: London. 1701-1800. Lang.: Eng. 1895
Collection of newspaper reviews by London theatre critics. UK-England: Stratford. 1998. Lang.: Eng. 2431
Plays/librettos/scripts
Dutch and Flemish Shakespearean productions. Belgium. Netherlands. 1980-1983. Lang.: Dut. 2789
Shakespeare's *The Tempest* as an experiment in political control. England. 1611. Lang.: Eng. 2862
Analysis of Dryden and Davenant's *Enchanted Island*. England. 1674. Lang.: Eng. 2873
Shakespeare and the limitation of political and textual control. England. 1600-1611. Lang.: Eng. 2965
God and man in Renaissance theatre. England. 1610-1625. Lang.: Eng. 2966
Regeneration in plays of Shakespeare. England. 1598-1613. Lang.: Eng. 2968
The nature of tyranny in plays of Shakespeare. England. 1595-1612. Lang.: Eng. 2978
Shakespeare's *The Tempest* as an allegory of colonial America. England. 1611. Lang.: Eng. 3038
The statesman on the modern stage. North America. 1950-1995. Lang.: Eng. 3291
Shakespeare's *The Tempest* on film. UK-England. USA. 1905-1991. Lang.: Eng. 3981
Analysis of Peter Greenaway's film *Prospero's Books*. UK-England. 1991. Lang.: Fre. 3990
Shakespeare's *The Tempest* and Thomas Campion's *The Lord's Masque*. England. 1613. Lang.: Eng. 4202

Tempête, Une (Tempest, A)
Performance/production
Collection of newspaper reviews by London theatre critics. UK-England: London. 1998. Lang.: Eng. 2509
Plays/librettos/scripts
Analysis and translation of *Et les Chiens se taisaient (And the Dogs Were Silent)* by Aimé Césaire. Martinique. 1946-1969. Lang.: Eng. 3269

Ten Minute Play, The
Basic theatrical documents
Text of *The Metropolitan*, formerly called *The Ten Minute Play* by Mark R. Green. USA. 1995. Lang.: Eng. 1485

Ten' opery (Shadow of the Opera, The)
Performance/production
Teat'r Ten's *Ten' opery (The Shadow of the Opera)*. Russia: Moscow. 1998. Lang.: Rus. 4679

Tenement Museum (New York, NY)
Plays/librettos/scripts
Jean Randich's production of *The Golden Door* by Sylvia Regan, Tenement Museum. USA: New York, NY. 1940-1998. Lang.: Eng. 3606

TenEyck, Karen
Design/technology
Set designer Karen TenEyck. USA. 1998. Lang.: Eng. 1550
Karen TenEyck's projections for a site-specific production of Shakespeare's *Julius Caesar*. USA: Los Angeles, CA. 1998. Lang.: Eng. 1552

Tennant, David
Performance/production
David Tennant on his performance in *As You Like It* at RSC. UK-England: London, Stratford. 1996-1997. Lang.: Eng. 2640

Tennessee and Me
Basic theatrical documents
Text of three monologues by Will Scheffer. USA. 1997. Lang.: Eng. 1509

Tennyson, Alfred, Lord
Plays/librettos/scripts
Analysis of *The Foresters* by Alfred, Lord Tennyson. England. USA. 1700-1910. Lang.: Eng. 2998

Tent theatre
Performance/production
Antitheatricalism in the Circuit Chautauqua. USA. 1913-1930. Lang.: Eng. 4135

Terechova, Margarita
Performance/production
Actress Margarita Terechova. Russia. Spain. 1998. Lang.: Rus. 2261
Terence
SEE
Terentius Afer, Publius.
Terfel, Bryn
Performance/production
Tenor Bryn Terfel. UK-Wales. 1965-1998. Lang.: Eng. 4707
Terminating, or Lass Meine Schmertzen Nicht Verloren Sein, or Ambivalence
Performance/production
Collection of newspaper reviews by London theatre critics. UK-England: London. 1998. Lang.: Eng. 2498
Terms of Abuse
Performance/production
Collection of newspaper reviews by London theatre critics. UK-England: London. 1998. Lang.: Eng. 2574
Ternyák, Zoltán
Performance/production
Pál Békés' *Pincejáték (Cellar Play)* directed by Zoltán Ternyák. Hungary: Budapest. 1997. Lang.: Hun. 2078
Terry, Megan
Plays/librettos/scripts
History of the Playwrights Unit. USA. 1963-1971. Lang.: Eng. 3570
Revolutionary Off Broadway playwriting. USA: New York, NY. 1959-1969. Lang.: Eng. 3604
Terselius, Lil
Performance/production
Interviews with actors Lil Terselius and Björn Granath. Sweden: Stockholm. 1998. Lang.: Swe. 2381
Térszínház (Budapest)
Performance/production
Two productions of Csokonai Vitéz's *Karnyóné és a két szeleburdiak (Mrs. Karnyó and the Two Feather-Brains)*. Hungary: Budapest. 1998. Lang.: Hun. 2113
Terukkūttu
Basic theatrical documents
English translation of *terukkūttu* piece *Pakaṭai Tuyil (The Dice Game and the Disrobing)*. India. 1998. Lang.: Eng. 1345
Tesfai, Alemseged
Plays/librettos/scripts
Theatre as cultural weapon and military education in the Eritrean war. Eritrea. 1980-1984. Lang.: Eng. 3048
Tesori, Jeanine
Plays/librettos/scripts
Panel discussion on contemporary musical theatre. USA: New York, NY. 1998. Lang.: Eng. 4398
Tess of the D'Urbervilles
Performance/production
Collection of newspaper reviews by London theatre critics. UK-England: London. 1998. Lang.: Eng. 2541
Testori, Giovanni
Plays/librettos/scripts
The plays of Giovanni Testori and their production. Italy. 1923-1997. Lang.: Ita. 3262
Textes pour rien (Texts for Nothing)
Plays/librettos/scripts
Joseph Chaikin's adaptation of *Textes pour rien (Texts for Nothing)* by Samuel Beckett. USA: New York, NY. 1995. Lang.: Eng. 3563
Thacker, David
Performance/production
Christopher Luscombe on acting in RSC productions. UK-England: London, Stratford. 1993-1994. Lang.: Eng. 2620
Philip Voss on his role in *Coriolanus* at RSC. UK-England: London, Stratford. 1994. Lang.: Eng. 2643
Thackeray, William Makepeace
Performance/production
Michael Birch's production of *Vanity Fair*. UK-England: Leeds. 1997. Lang.: Eng. 2600
Thaïs
Plays/librettos/scripts
Collaboration of composer Jules Massenet and librettist Louis Gallet. France. 1877-1894. Lang.: Fre. 4778
Thalbach, Katharina
Performance/production
Katharina Thalbach in Brecht's *Die heilige Johanna der Schlachthöfe (Saint Joan of the Stockyards)* directed by Benno Besson. Switzerland: Zurich. 1998. Lang.: Ger. 2400
Thalheimer, Michael
Administration
Interviews with German theatre and film directors. Germany. 1998. Lang.: Ger. 1385
Thália Színház (Budapest)
Performance spaces
Theatrical history of the building that houses Thália Színház. Hungary: Budapest. 1913-1996. Lang.: Hun. 447
Performance/production
Mozart's *Die Zauberflöte* directed by János Szikora. Hungary: Budapest. Hungary: Szeged. 1998. Lang.: Hun. 4631
György Ligeti's *Le Grand Macabre* directed by Balázs Kovalik. Hungary: Budapest. 1998. Lang.: Hun. 4642
Thália Színház (Košice)
Institutions
History of annual festival of Hungarian-language theatre. Hungary: Kisvárda. 1989-1998. Lang.: Hun. 1669
Performance/production
Čechov's one-act plays at Thália Színház. Hungary. Slovakia: Košice. 1998. Lang.: Hun. 2075
Thália Társaság (Budapest)
Performance/production
László Márkus, one-time director of the Budapest Opera House. Hungary. 1881-1948. Lang.: Hun. 540
Reviews of two plays by Per Olov Enquist. Hungary: Budapest. 1998. Lang.: Hun. 2089
Thalia Theater (Hamburg)
Audience
The relationship between theatres and the youth audience. Germany. 1998. Lang.: Ger. 152
Performance/production
Shakespearean productions in northern Germany. Germany: Hamburg. 1996-1997. Lang.: Ger. 1978
Reviews of productions of plays by Brecht. Germany. 1998. Lang.: Ger. 1986
Productions of Horváth's *Geschichten aus dem Wienerwald (Tales from the Vienna Woods)*. Germany: Hamburg, Hannover. Austria: Vienna. 1998. Lang.: Ger. 2003
Thalia Treffpunkt (Hamburg)
Institutions
Holocaust education and Thalia Treffpunkt. Germany: Hamburg. 1988-1998. Lang.: Ger. 1630
Thanatos
Performance/production
Derision in recent productions. Canada: Quebec, PQ. 1998. Lang.: Fre. 509
Comparison of simple productions and visual shows. Canada: Montreal, PQ, Quebec, PQ, Toronto, ON. 1998. Lang.: Fre. 1861
Thanks Mum
Performance/production
Collection of newspaper reviews by London theatre critics. UK-England: London. 1998. Lang.: Eng. 2427
Tharp! (New York, NY)
Performance/production
Recent work of choreographer Twyla Tharp. USA: New York, NY. 1988-1998. Lang.: Eng. 1328
Tharp, Twyla
Performance/production
Critique of Twyla Tharp's *The Catherine Wheel*. USA: New York, NY. 1981. Lang.: Eng. 980
Recent work of choreographer Twyla Tharp. USA: New York, NY. 1988-1998. Lang.: Eng. 1328
That Man Bracken
Plays/librettos/scripts
BBC radio plays with Anglo-Irish themes. UK-England. Ireland. 1973-1986. Lang.: Eng. 3868
That Time
Plays/librettos/scripts
Analysis of Samuel Beckett's later plays. Ireland. France. 1950-1989. Lang.: Eng. 3210
Composer Wolfgang Fortner's adaptation of *That Time* by Samuel Beckett. Europe. 1974-1977. Lang.: Eng. 4777
Theater (Freiburg)
Institutions
Amanda Miller and her ballet company Pretty Ugly. Germany: Freiburg. 1984-1998. Lang.: Ger. 1039
Theater (Lübeck)
Performance/production
Music theatre production in northern Germany. Germany: Lübeck, Hamburg, Bremen, Kiel. 1998. Lang.: Ger. 4293

Theater (Oberhausen)
Performance/production
Reviews of German Shakespearean productions. Germany: Wuppertal, Cologne, Oberhausen. 1998. Lang.: Ger. 2017
Theater am Bauturm (Cologne)
Performance/production
The Cologne theatre scene. Germany: Cologne. 1985-1997. Lang.: Ger. 1964
Theater am Turm (Frankfurt)
Performance/production
Actor Herbert Fritsch. Germany. 1992-1998. Lang.: Ger. 1985
Theater Augsburg
Plays/librettos/scripts
Recent German productions of Brecht's plays. Germany. 1998. Lang.: Ger. 3150
Theater Bielefeld
Institutions
The current state of Theater Bielefeld. Germany: Bielefeld. 1998. Lang.: Ger. 1621
Theater der Altmark (Stendal)
Performance/production
German productions of adaptations of *A Clockwork Orange* by Anthony Burgess. Germany: Dresden, Hamburg, Stendal. 1998. Lang.: Ger. 1972
Theater der Freundschaft (Berlin)
Institutions
History of Carrousel Theater, formerly Theater der Freundschaft. Germany: Berlin. 1950-1998. Lang.: Ger. 1628
Theater Dresden
Institutions
Appealing to the youth audience at Theater Dresden. Germany: Dresden. 1997-1998. Lang.: Ger. 1631
Theater Erfeld
Performance/production
Recent productions of plays by Bertolt Brecht. Germany. 1997-1998. Lang.: Ger. 2028
Theater Erfurt
Institutions
The proposed merger of Deutsches Nationaltheater Weimar and Theater Erfurt. Germany: Weimar, Erfurt. 1998. Lang.: Ger. 354
Theater Görlitz
Institutions
Profiles of theatres in Saxony. Germany: Zittau, Bautzen, Görlitz. 1997-1998. Lang.: Ger. 1650
Theater in der Fabrik (Dresden)
Institutions
Profile of Theater in der Fabrik. Germany: Dresden. 1993-1998. Lang.: Ger. 1644
Theater in der Josefstadt (Vienna)
Performance/production
Actor Helmuth Lohner's stint as administrative director of Theater in der Josefstadt. Austria: Vienna. 1960-1998. Lang.: Ger. 1819
Luc Bondy's production of Horváth's *Figaro lässt sich scheiden (Figaro Gets Divorced)*. Austria: Vienna. 1998. Lang.: Ger. 1822
Plays/librettos/scripts
New directions in the plays of Botho Strauss. Europe. 1971-1998. Lang.: Ger. 3067
Theater Jugend Club (Nordhausen)
Institutions
Experiential memory work and acting at Theater Jugend Club. Germany: Nordhausen. 1995-1998. Lang.: Ger. 1629
Theater Junge Generation (Dresden)
Institutions
Festivals of theatre by and for youth. Germany: Dresden, Stuttgart. 1998. Lang.: Ger. 349
Theater Krefeld/Mönchengladbach (Krefeld)
Performance/production
Recent productions of plays by Bertolt Brecht. Germany. 1997-1998. Lang.: Ger. 2028
Plays/librettos/scripts
Recent German productions of Brecht's plays. Germany. 1998. Lang.: Ger. 3150
Theater Neumarkt (Zurich)
Administration
Theatre directors on the future of subsidized theatre. Switzerland: Zurich. Germany: Hannover, Berlin. 1998. Lang.: Ger. 1390
Performance/production
Volker Hesse's production of *King Kongs Töchter (King Kong's Daughters)* by Theresia Walser. Switzerland: Zurich. 1998. Lang.: Ger. 2401
Volker Hesse's production of *Die schwarze Spinne (The Black Spider)* by Urs Widmer. Switzerland: Zurich. 1998. Lang.: Ger. 2402
Theater Pforzheim
Administration
Ernö Weil, manager of Theater Pforzheim. Germany: Pforzheim. 1997-1998. Lang.: Ger. 1380
Theater Titanick (Münster/Leipzig)
Design/technology
Scenic elements in *Titanic* by street theatre group Theater Titanick. Germany: Münster, Leipzig. Australia: Perth. 1998. Lang.: Eng. 191
Theater 44 (Munich)
Institutions
Survey of Munich's theatre scene. Germany: Munich. 1997. Lang.: Ger. 1626
Theateragentur (Switzerland)
Performance/production
Productions of children's theatre festival. Canada: Montreal, PQ. 1998. Lang.: Fre. 503
Theatergroep Delta (Amsterdam)
Performance/production
The work of Theatergroep Delta. Netherlands: Amsterdam. 1983-1998. Lang.: Dut. 2200
Theaterhaus (Jena)
Administration
Interviews with German theatre and film directors. Germany. 1998. Lang.: Ger. 1385
Theaterjugendclub (Eisleben)
Relation to other fields
The national movement, cultural policy, and German regional theatre. Germany: Eisleben. 1998. Lang.: Ger. 740
Theaterschool (Amsterdam)
Design/technology
OISTAT meeting on technician training. Netherlands: Amsterdam. 1998. Lang.: Swe. 206
Theaterwerkstatt Pilkentafel (Flensburg)
Audience
Children's theatre and cultural exchange. Germany: Flensburg. 1998. Lang.: Ger. 1401
Theatr Clwyd (Mold)
Performance/production
The function of sound in productions of *India Song* by Marguerite Duras. France. UK-Wales: Mold. 1973-1993. Lang.: Eng. 1945
Théâtre aux Bouffes du Nord (Paris)
Design/technology
Set designer Jean-Guy Lecat and his work with Peter Brook. France. Denmark. 1975-1998. Lang.: Dan. 182
Performance/production
Peter Brook's *Je suis un phénomène (I Am a Phenomenon)* at Bouffes du Nord. France: Paris. 1998. Lang.: Hun. 1930
Peter Brook's *Je suis un phénomène (I Am a Phenomenon)*. France: Paris. 1998. Lang.: Ger. 1934
Théâtre Blanc (Quebec, PQ)
Design/technology
Set designer Jean Hazel. Canada: Quebec, PQ. 1985-1998. Lang.: Fre. 1515
Théâtre Bobigny (Paris)
Performance/production
Reviews of productions by Wilson, Greenaway, and Mnouchkine. France: Paris. 1997-1998. Lang.: Eng. 1926
The performances of Lucinda Childs and Michel Piccoli in *La Maladie de la Mort (The Sickness of Death)*, directed by Robert Wilson. France: Paris. 1997. Lang.: Eng. 1942
Interview with actress Lucinda Childs. France: Paris. 1976-1997. Lang.: Eng. 1943
Theatre Communications Group (TCG, New York, NY)
Institutions
TCG annual report. USA. 1997-1998. Lang.: Eng. 1753
Fiscal survey of not-for-profit theatre. USA. 1997. Lang.: Eng. 1754
Performance/production
Preview of TCG constituent theatre season. USA. 1998-1999. Lang.: Eng. 2654
Théâtre de Complicité (London)
Design/technology
Technical designs for *The Chairs (Les Chaises)*, Théâtre de Complicité. UK-England: London. 1998. Lang.: Eng. 1524
Performance/production
The future of English repertory companies. UK-England: London. 1998. Lang.: Eng. 2563

Théâtre de Dix-Heures (Paris)
Basic theatrical documents
Text of *L'Ascenseur (The Elevator)* by Gérard Levoyer. France. 1984-1987. Lang.: Fre. 1431
Théâtre de l'Ange Fou (London)
Performance/production
Corinne Soum, former assistant to Etienne Decroux. France: Paris. UK-England: London. 1968-1998. Lang.: Eng. 4090
Théâtre de l'Europe (Paris)
Performance/production
The ideas and productions of director Giorgio Strehler. Italy. 1940-1998. Lang.: Swe. 2180
Théâtre de l'Oeuvre (Paris)
Basic theatrical documents
Text of *Pour la galerie (For the Gallery)* by Claude d'Anna and Laure Bonin. France. 1998. Lang.: Fre. 1424
Théâtre de l'Opsis (Montreal, PQ)
Plays/librettos/scripts
The use of collage in contemporary productions involving Greek myths. Canada: Montreal, PQ. 1998. Lang.: Fre. 2814
Théâtre de la Bastille (Paris)
Performance/production
Recent Paris productions. France: Paris. 1997-1998. Lang.: Ger. 1933
Théâtre de la Colline (Paris)
Performance/production
Recent Paris productions. France: Paris. 1997-1998. Lang.: Ger. 1933
Survey of Parisian productions. France: Paris. 1997-1998. Lang.: Eng. 1937
French production of *Im Dickicht der Städte (In the Jungle of Cities)* by Bertolt Brecht. France. 1997-1998. Lang.: Ger. 1946
Théâtre de la Commune (Paris)
Performance/production
Comparison of text-based and visual productions. France. 1998. Lang.: Fre. 1939
Théâtre de la Michodière (Paris)
Basic theatrical documents
French translation of *Funny Money* by Ray Cooney. UK-England. France. 1995-1997. Lang.: Fre. 1473
Théâtre de la Monnaie (Brussels)
Performance/production
Press reactions to productions of Offenbach's *Orphée aux Enfers.* Belgium. Switzerland. France. 1997. Lang.: Fre. 4535
Théâtre de la Ville (Dijon)
Performance/production
French productions of German plays. France. 1998. Lang.: Ger. 1935
Théâtre de Madame Saqui (Paris)
Performance/production
Working-class theatre and censorship. France: Paris. 1800-1862. Lang.: Eng. 533
Théâtre Denise Pelletier (Montreal, PQ)
Performance/production
Social context of French and Canadian productions of *Les Fourberies de Scapin* by Molière. Canada: Montreal, PQ. France: Paris. 1998. Lang.: Fre. 1842
Théâtre des Auteurs Vivants (Paris)
Basic theatrical documents
Text of *Le Vampire suce toujours deux fois (The Vampire Always Sucks Twice)* by Victor Haïm. France. 1998. Lang.: Fre. 1427
Théâtre des Champs-Elysées (Paris)
Performance/production
The performance of sacrifice on stage. France. Germany. 1900-1998. Lang.: Ger. 530
Théâtre des Funambules (Paris)
Performance/production
Working-class theatre and censorship. France: Paris. 1800-1862. Lang.: Eng. 533
Théâtre des Millefontaines (Paris)
Basic theatrical documents
French translation of Shakespeare's *Love's Labour's Lost.* England. France. 1594-1998. Lang.: Fre. 1419
Théâtre des Moutons Noirs (Quebec, PQ)
Institutions
Quebec theatres specializing in new plays. Canada: Quebec, PQ. 1989-1998. Lang.: Fre. 1589
Performance/production
Derision in recent productions. Canada: Quebec, PQ. 1998. Lang.: Fre. 509
Comparison of simple productions and visual shows. Canada: Montreal, PQ, Quebec, PQ, Toronto, ON. 1998. Lang.: Fre. 1861
Théâtre des 2 Rives (Rouen)
Basic theatrical documents
French translation of *Alfred Stieglitz Loves O'Keeffe* by Lanie Robertson. USA. France. 1987-1997. Lang.: Fre. 1505
Theatre Development Fund (New York, NY)
Administration
Jack Goldstein's departure from Equity to head Theatre Development Fund. USA: New York, NY. 1998. Lang.: Eng. 56
Theatre Downstairs (London)
Performance/production
Reviews of recent London performances. UK-England: London. 1998. Lang.: Ger. 2591
Théâtre du Gymnase (Paris)
Basic theatrical documents
Text of *Ma femme s'appelle Maurice (My Wife's Name Is Maurice)* by Raffy Shart. France. 1998. Lang.: Fre. 1435
Théâtre du Mouvement (Paris)
Performance/production
Yves Marc on Etienne Decroux. France: Paris. 1998. Lang.: Eng. 4088
Théâtre du Nouveau Monde (Montreal, PQ)
Performance/production
French Canadian translations/adaptations of Shakespeare. Canada: Montreal, PQ. 1988. Lang.: Fre. 1855
Interview with director Dominic Champagne. Canada: Montreal, PQ. 1998. Lang.: Fre. 1860
Productions of plays by Bernard-Marie Koltès. Canada: Montreal, PQ. 1991-1997. Lang.: Fre. 1862
Pierre Benoît's music for *Don Quichotte* at Théâtre du Nouveau Monde. Canada: Montreal, PQ. 1995-1998. Lang.: Fre. 1870
Plays/librettos/scripts
Cervantes' *Don Quixote* and Wadji Mouawad's adaptation, *Don Quichotte.* Canada: Montreal, PQ. 1998. Lang.: Fre. 2803
The character Sancho in Wadji Mouawad's *Don Quichotte (Don Quixote).* Canada: Montreal, PQ. 1998. Lang.: Fre. 2807
The contrast of form and content in Théâtre du Nouveau Monde's *Don Quichotte.* Canada: Montreal, PQ. 1998. Lang.: Fre. 2815
Don Quichotte, an adaptation of Cervantes' *Don Quixote* by Wadji Mouawad. Canada: Montreal, PQ. 1998. Lang.: Fre. 2830
Théâtre du Palais-Royal (Paris)
Basic theatrical documents
French translation of *Time of My Life* by Alan Ayckbourn. UK-England. France. 1993-1998. Lang.: Fre. 1471
Théâtre du Paradox (Quebec, PQ)
Institutions
Quebec theatres specializing in new plays. Canada: Quebec, PQ. 1989-1998. Lang.: Fre. 1589
Théâtre du Petit Lazary (Paris)
Performance/production
Working-class theatre and censorship. France: Paris. 1800-1862. Lang.: Eng. 533
Théâtre du Plantin (Belgium)
Performance/production
Guest performance of Théâtre du Plantin, a company for developmentally disabled actors. Hungary: Budapest. 1983-1998. Lang.: Hun. 2081
Théâtre du Radeau (Le Mans)
Institutions
Profile of Théâtre du Radeau. France: Le Mans. 1980-1998. Lang.: Ger. 1614
Théâtre du Renard (Paris)
Basic theatrical documents
Text of *Le Roi Hâtif (King Hasty)* by Françoise Gerbaulet. France. 1993-1998. Lang.: Fre. 1425
Théâtre du Ricochet (Paris)
Basic theatrical documents
Text of *Mendiants d'amour (Beggars of Love)* by Gérard Levoyer. France. 1998. Lang.: Fre. 1430
Théâtre du Signe (Paris)
Institutions
Interview with Josef Nadj, choreographer. France. 1990-1998. Lang.: Hun. 892
Performance/production
Choreographer Josef Nadj and his company Théâtre du Signe. France. 1987-1998. Lang.: Hun. 924
Théâtre du Soleil (Paris)
Institutions
Theatrical space in productions of Ariane Mnouchkine. France: Paris. 1970-1995. Lang.: Eng. 1607

Théâtre du Soleil (Paris) — cont'd

Ariane Mnouchkine and rehearsal techniques of Théâtre du Soleil. France: Paris. 1964-1997. Lang.: Eng. 1610
Performance/production
French political theatre: Boal and Mnouchkine. France. 1990-1996. Lang.: Eng. 529
Reviews of productions by Wilson, Greenaway, and Mnouchkine. France: Paris. 1997-1998. Lang.: Eng. 1926
Survey of Parisian productions. France: Paris. 1997-1998. Lang.: Eng. 1937

Théâtre du Sous-Marin Jaune (Montreal, PQ)
Plays/librettos/scripts
Response to criticism of Théâtre du Sous-Marin Jaune's adaptation of Voltaire's *Candide*. Canada: Quebec, PQ. 1997. Lang.: Fre. 4912

Théâtre du Vieux Colombier (Paris)
Performance/production
Director Jacques Copeau and his theatrical aesthetic. France. 1913-1920. Lang.: Eng. 1941
Interview with Marie-Hélène Dasté, daughter of Jacques Copeau. France: Paris. 1913-1992. Lang.: Eng. 4089

Théâtre Eldorado (Paris)
Performance/production
Jorge Lavelli's production of *Sei personaggi in cerca d'autore (Six Characters in Search of an Author)* by Pirandello. France: Paris. 1925-1998. Lang.: Ita. 1921

Théâtre Euh! (Quebec, PQ)
Performance/production
Social criticism and alternative theatre in Quebec and Newfoundland. Canada. 1970-1985. Lang.: Eng. 500

Théâtre Expérimental des Femmes (Montreal, PQ)
Performance/production
French Canadian translations/adaptations of Shakespeare. Canada: Montreal, PQ. 1988. Lang.: Fre. 1855

Theatre for a New Audience (New York, NY)
Design/technology
Technical designs for Off Broadway Shakespearean productions. USA: New York, NY. 1998. Lang.: Eng. 1539

Theatre for the New City (New York, NY)
Performance/production
Comparison of productions of Ibsen's *Peer Gynt*. USA: Providence, RI, New York, NY, Washington, DC, Nacogdoches, TX. 1998. Lang.: Eng. 2711
Reviews of productions of plays by Ibsen. USA: New York, NY. Norway: Oslo. 1998. Lang.: Eng. 2747

Théâtre Gérard-Philippe (Suresnes)
Institutions
Profile of Théâtre Gérard-Philippe. France: Paris. 1998. Lang.: Ger. 1617

Theatre Guild (New York, NY)
Administration
Producer Cheryl Crawford and her contributions to the American stage. USA. 1930-1965. Lang.: Eng. 1396
Performance/production
Resistance to a Boston production of Eugene O'Neill's *Strange Interlude*. USA: Boston, MA. 1929. Lang.: Eng. 2693
Plays/librettos/scripts
Analysis of *Processional* by John Howard Lawson. USA. 1925. Lang.: Eng. 3535

Theatre in the Round (Budapest)
SEE
Körszinház.

Theatre Institute (Rome)
SEE
Accademia Nazionale d'Arte Drammatica.

Théâtre Jeune Public (Strasbourg)
Performance/production
A puppet production of Madách's *Az ember tragédiája (The Tragedy of Man)*. France: Colmar. 1998. Lang.: Hun. 4893

Théâtre Juste Pour Rire (Montreal, PQ)
Performance/production
English and French-language productions of *Picasso at the Lapin Agile* by Steve Martin. Canada: Montreal, PQ. 1997. Lang.: Fre. 1836

Théâtre La Bruyère (Paris)
Basic theatrical documents
Text of *Pour la galerie (For the Gallery)* by Claude d'Anna and Laure Bonin. France. 1998. Lang.: Fre. 1424
French translation of *Popcorn* by Ben Elton. UK-England. France. 1996-1998. Lang.: Fre. 1475

Théâtre les Enfants Terribles (Quebec, PQ)
Institutions
Quebec theatres specializing in new plays. Canada: Quebec, PQ. 1989-1998. Lang.: Fre. 1589

Théâtre Montansier (Paris)
Basic theatrical documents
Text of *Jean III (John III)* by Sacha Guitry. France. 1912-1998. Lang.: Fre. 1426

Théâtre Montparnasse (Paris)
Basic theatrical documents
Text of *Soleil pour deux (Sun for Two)* by Pierre Sauvil. France. 1998. Lang.: Fre. 1434

Theatre Mu (Minneapolis, MN)
Theory/criticism
Theory and Asian-American theatre. USA: Minneapolis, MN. 1994-1995. Lang.: Eng. 869

Théâtre National de l'Odéon (Paris)
Performance/production
French productions of German plays. France. 1998. Lang.: Ger. 1935

Théâtre National de Strasbourg
Performance/production
French productions of German plays. France. 1998. Lang.: Ger. 1935

Théâtre Niveau Parking (Quebec, PQ)
Performance/production
The integration of playwriting into the production process at Théâtre Niveau Parking. Canada: Quebec, PQ. 1990-1998. Lang.: Fre. 1857
Comparison of simple productions and visual shows. Canada: Montreal, PQ, Quebec, PQ, Toronto, ON. 1998. Lang.: Fre. 1861

Théâtre Ô Parleur (Montreal, PQ)
Performance/production
Comparison of simple productions and visual shows. Canada: Montreal, PQ, Quebec, PQ, Toronto, ON. 1998. Lang.: Fre. 1861

Theatre of Comedy (London)
Performance/production
Actor Michael Williams. UK-England: London. 1950-1998. Lang.: Eng. 2644

Theatre of NOTE (Los Angeles, CA)
Performance/production
Denise Gillman's production of Webster's *The Duchess of Malfi*, Theatre of NOTE. USA: Los Angeles, CA. 1998. Lang.: Eng. 2714

Theatre of the Eighth Day (Poznań)
SEE
Teatr Ósmego Dnia.

Theatre of the oppressed
Performance/production
Cultural identity and Brazilian theatre. Brazil. 1980-1995. Lang.: Eng. 496
French political theatre: Boal and Mnouchkine. France. 1990-1996. Lang.: Eng. 529
Interview with director Augusto Boal. Brazil: Rio de Janeiro. 1992-1996. Lang.: Eng. 1833

Theatre of the Revolution
SEE
Teat'r im. V. Majakovskogo.

Théâtre Omnibus (Montreal, PQ)
Performance/production
French Canadian translations/adaptations of Shakespeare. Canada: Montreal, PQ. 1988. Lang.: Fre. 1855

Théâtre Ouvert (Paris)
Performance/production
Comparison of text-based and visual productions. France. 1998. Lang.: Fre. 1939

Theatre Passe Muraille (Toronto, ON)
Performance/production
Comparison of simple productions and visual shows. Canada: Montreal, PQ, Quebec, PQ, Toronto, ON. 1998. Lang.: Fre. 1861
Plays/librettos/scripts
Analysis of *The Noam Chomsky Lectures* by Daniel Brooks and Guillermo Verdecchio. Canada: Toronto, ON. 1990-1991. Lang.: Eng. 2797

Theatre PEI (Charlottetown, PE)
Plays/librettos/scripts
Analysis of Melissa Mullen's *Rough Waters* at Theatre PEI. Canada: Charlottetown, PE. 1990-1998. Lang.: Eng. 2817

Théâtre Périscope (Quebec, PQ)
Performance/production
Marie-Ginette Guay's wordless performance in Franz Xaver Kroetz's *Wunschkonzert (Request Concert)*. Canada: Quebec, PQ. 1995-1997. Lang.: Fre. 1847

Théâtre Populaire Romand (La Chaux-de-Fonds)
Plays/librettos/scripts
Analysis of *Par-dessus bord (Overboard)* by Michel Vinaver. France. Switzerland: La Chaux-de-Fonds. 1960-1998. Lang.: Ger. 3118

Théâtre Populus Mordicus (Quebec, PQ)
Performance/production
Derision in recent productions. Canada: Quebec, PQ. 1998. Lang.: Fre. 509
Théâtre Richelieu (Paris)
Performance/production
Social context of French and Canadian productions of *Les Fourberies de Scapin* by Molière. Canada: Montreal, PQ. France: Paris. 1998. Lang.: Fre. 1842
Theatre Royal, Haymarket (London)
Performance/production
Collection of newspaper reviews by London theatre critics. UK-England: London. 1998. Lang.: Eng. 2462
Collection of newspaper reviews by London theatre critics. UK-England: London. 1998. Lang.: Eng. 2518
Collection of newspaper reviews by London theatre critics. UK-England: London. 1998. Lang.: Eng. 2524
Collection of newspaper reviews by London theatre critics. UK-England: London. 1998. Lang.: Eng. 2533
Theatre Royal, Margate (London)
Performance spaces
Anecdotes about old London theatres. UK-England: London. 1918-1998. Lang.: Eng. 460
Theatre Royal, Stratford East (London)
Performance/production
Collection of newspaper reviews by London theatre critics. UK-England: London. 1998. Lang.: Eng. 2557
Théâtre Sanza (Parakou)
Basic theatrical documents
Text of *Ubu déchaîné (Ubu Unchained)* by Richard Demarcy. Benin. France. 1998. Lang.: Fre. 4287
Théâtre Silvia Monfort (Paris)
Basic theatrical documents
French translation of *Alfred Stieglitz Loves O'Keeffe* by Lanie Robertson. USA. France. 1987-1997. Lang.: Fre. 1505
Theatre SKAM (Victoria, BC)
Performance spaces
Theatre SKAM's production of *Louis and Dave* in a Plymouth Volaré. Canada: Victoria, BC. 1996. Lang.: Eng. 1797
Théâtre Sortie de Secours (Quebec, PQ)
Institutions
Quebec theatres specializing in new plays. Canada: Quebec, PQ. 1989-1998. Lang.: Fre. 1589
Theatre Technicians Training Services (Dublin)
Design/technology
Account of ACTSAFE conference on theatre safety. France: Paris. 1998. Lang.: Swe. 181
Theatre Terrific (Vancouver, BC)
Performance/production
Productions of children's theatre festival. Canada: Montreal, PQ. 1998. Lang.: Fre. 503
Theatre Upstairs (London)
SEE ALSO
English Stage Company.
Théâtre Vidy (Lausanne)
Basic theatrical documents
French translation of *Beast on the Moon* by Richard Kalinoski. USA. France. 1995-1997. Lang.: Fre. 1491
Theatre Workshop (London)
Plays/librettos/scripts
The development of Theatre Workshop, founded by Ewan MacColl and Joan Littlewood. UK-England: London. 1945-1970. Lang.: Eng. 3491
Theatre-rites (London)
Performance/production
Collection of newspaper reviews by London theatre critics. UK-England: London, Stratford, Derby. 1998. Lang.: Eng. 2417
Theatres
Institutions
The directorship of Ferdinand Rieser at Zürcher Schauspielhaus. Switzerland: Zurich. 1926-1938. Lang.: Ger. 387
Interview with Bjørn Simensen, director of Den Norske Opera. Norway: Oslo. 1998. Lang.: Swe. 4465
Performance spaces
The architectural and administrative history of Redoutentheater. Austria: Vienna. 1918-1992. Lang.: Ger. 433
Toronto's theatres. Canada: Toronto, ON. 1998. Lang.: Eng. 434
Evidence that Davies' bear-baiting ring may have been a restoration of the Hope Theatre. England: London. 1647-1682. Lang.: Eng. 435
Brief history of theatre architecture. Europe. 340 B.C.-1998 A.D. Lang.: Dan. 437
The ninetieth anniversary of the Cottbus theatre building. Germany: Cottbus. 1908-1998. Lang.: Ger. 440
Profile of the theatrical venue Mousonturm. Germany: Franfurt. 1978-1998. Lang.: Ger. 441
The construction of a theatre for *Beauty and the Beast*. Germany: Stuttgart. 1997. Lang.: Ger. 444
Ferenc Bán's architectural design for Hungary's new National Theatre. Hungary: Budapest. 1998. Lang.: Hun. 446
Theatrical history of the building that houses Thália Színház. Hungary: Budapest. 1913-1996. Lang.: Hun. 447
Account of the competition for the design of the new National Theatre. Hungary: Budapest. 1996-1997. Lang.: Hun. 448
Interview with architect Miklós Ölveczky about Hungary's new National Theatre. Hungary. Norway. 1998. Lang.: Hun. 449
Renovation of the Miskolc National Theatre. Hungary: Miskolc. 1823-1998. Lang.: Hun. 450
The theatre of the cruise ship *Grand Princess*. Italy. 1998. Lang.: Eng. 451
History of Teatro Valle. Italy: Rome. 1726-1997. Lang.: Ita. 452
History of Teatro Comunale. Italy: Ferrara. 1798-1998. Lang.: Ger. 453
Stage technology and equipment of Trøndelag Teater. Norway: Trondheim. 1997. Lang.: Nor. 454
The new theatre building of Trøndelag Teater. Norway: Trondheim. 1994. Lang.: Swe. 455
Trøndelag Teater's new building. Norway: Trondheim. 1997. Lang.: Nor. 456
History of the Coliseo de la Cruz. Spain: Madrid. 1737-1859. Lang.: Eng. 457
Excerpts from the diary of the builder of Drottningholms Slottsteater. Sweden: Stockholm. 1755-1766. Lang.: Swe. 458
The construction of the Grand Théâtre de Genève. Switzerland: Geneva. 1984-1998. Lang.: Ger. 459
Anecdotes about old London theatres. UK-England: London. 1918-1998. Lang.: Eng. 460
The newly reopened Shakespeare's Globe Theatre. UK-England: London. 1997. Lang.: Eng. 461
Profile of Traverse Theatre. UK-Scotland: Edinburgh. 1998. Lang.: Eng. 462
Theatre space and performance. USA: New York, NY. 1925-1985. Lang.: Eng. 464
New stage lighting of War Memorial Opera House. USA: San Francisco, CA. 1998. Lang.: Eng. 465
Profile of the New Jersey Performing Arts Center. USA: Newark, NJ. 1988-1998. Lang.: Eng. 467
Architectural critique of the new Ford Center. USA: New York, NY. 1998. Lang.: Eng. 468
The renovation of Arden Theatre Company's F. Otto Haas Theatre. USA: Philadelphia, PA. 1998. Lang.: Eng. 469
The present status of dinner theatre. USA. 1998. Lang.: Eng. 471
Profiles of Southern California theatres. USA. 1998. Lang.: Eng. 473
Community efforts to save the Emerson Majestic and Rialto theatres. USA: Boston, MA, Chicago, IL. 1988-1998. Lang.: Eng. 474
Seattle's new and renovated theatres. USA: Seattle, WA. 1998. Lang.: Eng. 475
Architectural critique of the restored New Amsterdam Theatre. USA: New York, NY. 1998. Lang.: Eng. 476
Architectural and technical renovations to the War Memorial Opera House. USA: San Francisco, CA. 1997. Lang.: Eng. 478
The renovation of Times Square. USA: New York, NY. 1998. Lang.: Eng. 479
The renovation of Neptune Theatre. Canada: Halifax, NS. 1963-1998. Lang.: Eng. 1794
Quebec's performance spaces. Canada: Quebec, PQ. 1992-1998. Lang.: Fre. 1795
The Dame Blanche theatre. Canada: Quebec, PQ. 1982-1998. Lang.: Fre. 1796
Evidence of theatre closings in a Folger Library manuscript. England: London. 1650. Lang.: Eng. 1798

Theatres — cont'd

Speculations on the theatre of John Rastell. England: London. 1524-1530. Lang.: Eng. 1799
Conjectural reconstruction of the New Street Theatre. England: Birmingham. 1772-1902. Lang.: Eng. 1800
Analysis of a sketch of the Swan Theatre. England: London. 1596. Lang.: Eng. 1801
The opening of Nuovo Piccolo in honor of the late director Giorgio Strehler. Italy: Milan. 1998. Lang.: Eng. 1802
The reconstruction of Drammens Teater after a fire. Norway: Drammen. 1993-1998. Lang.: Swe. 1803
The rebuilding of the stage at Cirkus to accommodate a production of *Kristina från Duvemåla (Kristina of Duvemåla)*.Sweden: Stockholm. 1995. Lang.: Swe. 1804
The archaeological excavation of the Rose Theatre. UK-England: London. 1988-1989. Lang.: Eng. 1805
Stage doors of the Globe Theatre. UK-England: London. 1599-1998. Lang.: Eng. 1806
The excavation of the Rose Theatre's foundations. UK-England: London. 1988-1989. Lang.: Eng. 1807
The remains of the original Globe Theatre. UK-England: London. 1989-1997. Lang.: Eng. 1808
Critique of Shakespeare's Globe Theatre. UK-England: London. 1997. Lang.: Eng. 1809
Shakespeare's Globe and the staging of *The Merchant of Venice*. UK-England: London. 1998. Lang.: Ger. 1810
The restoration of the Orpheum Theatre. USA: Phoenix, AZ. 1929-1998. Lang.: Eng. 3926
The creation of a site-specific performance space for Sam Mendes' production of *Cabaret*. USA: New York, NY. 1998. Lang.: Eng. 4350
Opera composer Richard Wagner and performance space. Europe. 1835-1885. Lang.: Eng. 4492
Baroque opera and ballet at the Salle des Machines and the Palais Royal. France: Paris. 1640-1690. Lang.: Eng. 4493
The influence of the Salle le Peletier on French grand opera. France: Paris. 1823-1873. Lang.: Eng. 4494
The restoration of the opera houses Gran Teatro del Liceu and Teatro La Fenice. Spain: Barcelona. Italy: Venice. 1994-1998. Lang.: Eng. 4495
The newly remodeled Teatro Real. Spain: Madrid. 1988-1997. Lang.: Eng. 4496
The opening of Kungliga Operan. Sweden: Stockholm. 1898. Lang.: Swe. 4498
Sante Fe Opera's newly renovated open-air theatre. USA: Santa Fe, NM. 1991-1998. Lang.: Eng. 4499
The newly renovated Newberry Opera House. USA: Newberry, SC. 1998. Lang.: Eng. 4501

Performance/production
New London venues and productions. UK-England: London. 1994-1998. Lang.: Eng. 605
San Francisco's professional theatre. USA: San Francisco, CA. 1850-1860. Lang.: Eng. 682
Actress Ghita Nørby on adapting to various performance spaces. Denmark. 1970-1998. Lang.: Dan. 1889
Mozart's operas and contemporary Viennese performance spaces. Austria: Vienna. 1782-1791. Lang.: Eng. 4528
English theatre architecture and the operas of Henry Purcell. England: London. 1659-1695. Lang.: Eng. 4548
The influence of the Haymarket Theatre on Handelian opera. England: London. 1710-1739. Lang.: Eng. 4549
Weber's *Der Freischütz* and the Neues Schauspielhaus. Germany: Berlin. 1821. Lang.: Eng. 4581

Relation to other fields
The design firm Yabu Pushelberg. Canada: Toronto, ON. 1998. Lang.: Eng. 718

Theatrical Syndicate (New York, NY)

Administration
Sarah Bernhardt's farewell tour and its revenues. USA. 1905-1906. Lang.: Eng. 28

Theme parks

SEE
Amusement parks.

Themes and Variations

Performance/production
Balanchine's choreography to Čajkovskij's *Themes and Variations*. USA. 1960-1998. Lang.: Eng. 1179

Theory/criticism
Comparison of critical reviews of dance performances. USA: New York, NY. 1992. Lang.: Eng. 1201

Then What?

Performance/production
Collection of newspaper reviews by London theatre critics. UK-England: London. 1998. Lang.: Eng. 2565

Theobald, Lewis

Plays/librettos/scripts
Don Quixote, Lewis Theobald's *The Double Falsehood* and the lost *Cardenio* of Shakespeare and Fletcher. England. Spain. 1610-1727. Lang.: Eng. 3001

Theory/criticism

SEE ALSO
Classed Entries.

Audience
Theatrical production and reception. Canada. 1988. Lang.: Eng. 146
The current state of film, film criticism, and the audience. USA. 1998. Lang.: Eng. 3878

Design/technology
Critic Kenneth Macgowan and the 'new stagecraft'. USA. 1912-1940. Lang.: Eng. 262

Institutions
Workshop of Association Internationale des Critiques de Théâtre. Canada: Quebec, PQ. 1998. Lang.: Fre. 342
The curriculum at Bayerische Theaterakademie. Germany: Munich. 1985-1998. Lang.: Ger. 1659

Performance/production
Empathy and distancing in theatre education. Europe. 1998. Lang.: Fin. 523
Collection of theatre reviews by Roberto De Monticelli. Italy. 1974-1987. Lang.: Ita. 547
Dutch theatre and situationist theory. Netherlands. 1990-1997. Lang.: Eng. 565
Articles about integrating theory into theatrical practice. North America. 1997-1998. Lang.: Eng. 571
Theory and the role of the dramaturg. North America. 1998. Lang.: Eng. 572
Theatre Magazine's anniversary issue. USA. 1968-1998. Lang.: Eng. 617
Postmodern acting theory. USA. 1988. Lang.: Eng. 622
The ideological system of theatre artist Richard Schechner. USA. 1965-1997. Lang.: Eng. 640
The receding place of dance in American culture. USA: New York, NY. 1996-1997. Lang.: Eng. 981
Critical reactions to the dance evening *Mokka*. Hungary: Budapest. 1998. Lang.: Hun. 1116
Reactions to guest performances of dancer/choreographer Pina Bausch. Sweden: Stockholm. 1998. Lang.: Swe. 1301
Interview with choreographer Bill T. Jones. USA. 1990-1998. Lang.: Eng. 1316
Defense of Bill T. Jones' dance piece *Still/Here*. USA. 1994. Lang.: Eng. 1318
Power relations in *nō* theatre. Japan. 1500-1998. Lang.: Eng. 1373
Approaches to staging Brecht's plays, based on compiled reviews. Europe. 1961-1997. Lang.: Ger. 1910
Shakespeare and postmodern production. Europe. North America. 1950-1998. Lang.: Eng. 1912
Pirandello on the French stage. France. 1950-1981. Lang.: Ita. 1932
Shakespeare in the GDR: producer and critic B.K. Tragelehn. Germany, East. 1950-1990. Lang.: Eng. 2040
Socialism and the use of Shakespeare in the German Democratic Republic. Germany, East. 1945-1990. Lang.: Eng. 2048
Pirandello on the Greek stage. Greece. 1914-1995. Lang.: Ita. 2054
Collection of theatre reviews by Cesare Garboli. Italy. 1972-1977. Lang.: Ita. 2170
The present state of Italian theatre. Italy. 1998. Lang.: Eng. 2182
Pirandello on the Russian stage. Russia. 1905-1989. Lang.: Ita. 2250
The absence of research on South African directing. South Africa, Republic of. 1998. Lang.: Eng. 2355
Theoretical implications of Laurie Anderson's use of media technology. USA. 1995. Lang.: Eng. 4046
The feminist performance trend Angry Essentialism. USA. 1981-1998. Lang.: Eng. 4249

Theory/criticism — cont'd

Plays/librettos/scripts
The current state of Australian gay and lesbian theatre. Australia. 1990-1998. Lang.: Eng. 2775
Racial ambiguity, colonialism, and late twentieth-century criticism of Shakespeare's *Othello*. England. 1604-1998. Lang.: Eng. 2987
Confessional theatre in the Restoration period. England. 1690-1700. Lang.: Eng. 2991
A new reading of *Mankind*. England. 1464-1470. Lang.: Eng. 3028
Eighteenth-century editing and interpretation of Shakespeare. England. 1701-1800. Lang.: Eng. 3040
Insanity in nineteenth- and twentieth-century theatre. Europe. 1880-1970. Lang.: Eng. 3050
Two centuries' thought on Shakespeare's *The Merchant of Venice*. Europe. North America. 1788-1996. Lang.: Hun. 3066
Lessing's *Emilia Galotti* and reader-response criticism. Germany. 1772. Lang.: Eng. 3166
Analysis of plays of Enrico Bassano. Italy. 1899-1979. Lang.: Ita. 3226
Theory and practice in the work of director Pier Paolo Pasolini. Italy. 1960-1970. Lang.: Eng. 3264
Andreas-Salomé's view of Ibsen's female characters. Norway. Germany. 1879-1906. Lang.: Eng. 3296
Perceptions of Bertolt Brecht in the English-speaking world. UK-England. North America. 1933-1998. Lang.: Ger. 3443
The sacrifice of children in American drama. USA. 1910-1990. Lang.: Eng. 3566
Revolutionary elements in plays and theory of Baraka and Artaud. USA. France. 1920-1970. Lang.: Eng. 3580
Minority playwrights and mainstream theatres—theoretical implications. USA. 1980-1997. Lang.: Eng. 3612
The enneagram system applied to Albee's *Who's Afraid of Virginia Woolf?*. USA. 1998. Lang.: Eng. 3665
The critical reception of Zora Neale Hurston's autobiography. USA. 1942. Lang.: Eng. 3704
Playwrights Adrienne Kennedy, Ntozake Shange, and Suzan-Lori Parks. USA. 1970-1998. Lang.: Eng. 3714
Problems of adapting theatre to film. France. 1997. Lang.: Fre. 3971
Comedy in the plays and musicals of Volker Ludwig. Germany: Berlin. 1968-1998. Lang.: Ger. 4391
Analysis of Šostakovič's opera *Ledi Makbet Mtsenskogo Uezda*. USSR. 1930-1932. Lang.: Eng. 4829

Relation to other fields
Situational theory in counter-cultural theatre. UK-England. 1960-1969. Lang.: Eng. 771
The social significance of the Disney Corporation's influence on Broadway theatre. USA: New York, NY. 1997. Lang.: Eng. 3782

Research/historiography
The use of the term 'theatricality' in German theatre research. Germany. 1900-1998. Lang.: Ger. 820
Gender difference and theatricality. Germany. France. USA. 1959-1998. Lang.: Ger. 821
New approaches to theatre studies and performance analysis. UK-England: Bristol. 1998. Lang.: Eng. 826

Theory/criticism
The critical methodology of Giuseppe Bartolucci. Italy. 1982-1998. Lang.: Ita. 850
The present state of theatre criticism. USA. 1988. Lang.: Eng. 860

There's a J in Majorca
Performance/production
Collection of newspaper reviews by London theatre critics. UK-England: London. 1998. Lang.: Eng. 2483

There's Something About Mary
Plays/librettos/scripts
The popularity of crude comedy in recent American films. USA. 1998. Lang.: Eng. 4004

Thesmophoriazusae (Women Celebrating the Thesmophoria)
Plays/librettos/scripts
The playwright Euripides as a character in *Thesmophoriazusae* of Aristophanes. Greece. 438-411 B.C. Lang.: Eng. 3181

They Belong to God, Too!
Relation to other fields
The use of original theatrical productions in the ministry. USA. 1998. Lang.: Eng. 3781

Thiel-Cramér, Barbro
Training
Barbro Thiel-Cramér, Swedish teacher of Spanish dance. Sweden: Stockholm. Spain. 1944-1997. Lang.: Swe. 1244

Thiessen, Vern
Plays/librettos/scripts
Mennonite drama of Veralyn Warkentin and Vern Thiessen. Canada. 1890-1997. Lang.: Eng. 2829

Thieves Like Us
Performance/production
Collection of newspaper reviews by London theatre critics. UK-England: London. 1998. Lang.: Eng. 2515

Thill, Georges
Performance/production
Tenor George Thill. France. 1897-1984. Lang.: Eng. 4574

Things We Do for Love
Performance/production
Collection of newspaper reviews by London theatre critics. UK-England: London. 1998. Lang.: Eng. 2438
Plays/librettos/scripts
The comedies of Alan Ayckbourn. UK-England: London. 1998. Lang.: Eng. 3420

Think No Evil of Us: My Life with Kenneth Williams
Performance/production
Collection of newspaper reviews by London theatre critics. UK-England: London. 1998. Lang.: Eng. 2428

Thirteen Hands
Plays/librettos/scripts
Playwriting career of Carol Shields. Canada: Winnipeg, MB. 1972-1998. Lang.: Eng. 2794

Thirteenth Night
Performance/production
Collection of newspaper reviews by London theatre critics. UK. 1998. Lang.: Eng. 2407

Thomas and Sally
Plays/librettos/scripts
Music and the ballad opera in English popular theatre. England. 1728-1780. Lang.: Eng. 4390

Thomas Chatterton
Performance/production
Composer Matthias Pintscher and his opera *Thomas Chatterton*. Germany. 1990-2001. Lang.: Ger. 4607

Thomas, Charles
Performance/production
Collection of newspaper reviews by London theatre critics. UK-England: London. 1998. Lang.: Eng. 2573

Thomas, Colin
Plays/librettos/scripts
Review of collections of plays with gay themes. Canada. 1996. Lang.: Eng. 2802

Thomas, Daniela
Performance/production
Ópera Seca's *Mattogrosso*. Brazil: Rio de Janeiro. 1989. Lang.: Eng. 4537

Thomas, Ed
Performance/production
Collection of newspaper reviews by London theatre critics. UK-England: London. 1998. Lang.: Eng. 2414

Thomas, Gerald
Performance/production
Ópera Seca's *Mattogrosso*. Brazil: Rio de Janeiro. 1989. Lang.: Eng. 4537

Thomas, Rhys
Performance/production
Collection of newspaper reviews by London theatre critics. UK-England: London. 1998. Lang.: Eng. 2528

Thompson, Brian
Performance/production
Collection of newspaper reviews by London theatre critics. UK-England: London. 1998. Lang.: Eng. 2422

Thompson, Emma
Performance/production
Analysis of casting and acting in Kenneth Branagh's film adaptation of *Much Ado About Nothing*. UK. 1993. Lang.: Fre. 3939

Thompson, Garland Lee
Institutions
Playwright Garland Lee on the National Black Theatre Summit. USA: Dartmouth, NH. 1998. Lang.: Eng. 1786

Thompson, Gregory
Performance/production
Collection of newspaper reviews by London theatre critics. UK-England. 1998. Lang.: Eng. 2485
Collection of newspaper reviews by London theatre critics. UK-England: London. 1998. Lang.: Eng. 2554

Thompson, Judith
Performance/production
Collection of newspaper reviews by London theatre critics. UK-England: London. 1998. Lang.: Eng. 2432
Plays/librettos/scripts
Analysis of *Sled* by Judith Thompson. Canada. 1997-1998. Lang.: Eng. 2805
Thompson, Mark
Design/technology
Technical designs for the musical *Doctor Doolittle* directed by Steven Pimlott. UK-England: London. 1998. Lang.: Eng. 4325
Thompson, Russell
Relation to other fields
Topics in post-apartheid South African literature and theatre. South Africa, Republic of. 1995-1998. Lang.: Eng. 764
Thompson, Scott
Design/technology
Costume design for *Dames at Sea*, Marine Memorial Theatre. USA: San Francisco, CA. 1998. Lang.: Eng. 4332
Thomson, Lynn
Administration
The legal battle over copyright of the musical *Rent*. USA: New York, NY. 1998. Lang.: Eng. 4321
The settlement of a copyright case regarding the musical *Rent*. USA: New York, NY. 1998. Lang.: Eng. 4322
Thorogood, Robert
Performance/production
Collection of newspaper reviews by London theatre critics. UK-England: London. 1998. Lang.: Eng. 2565
Thoughts in the Margin
Performance/production
The performance of documentary theatre based on transcripts of a Lithuanian dissidence trial. USA. 1983-1997. Lang.: Eng. 627
Thousand Days, A
Performance/production
Collection of newspaper reviews by London theatre critics. UK-England: London. 1998. Lang.: Eng. 2511
Three Days of Rain
Basic theatrical documents
Text of *Three Days of Rain* by Richard Greenberg. USA. 1998. Lang.: Eng. 1486
Three Mills Island (London)
Performance/production
Collection of newspaper reviews by London theatre critics. UK-England: London. 1998. Lang.: Eng. 2473
Three Penny Opera, The
SEE
Dreigroschenoper, Die.
Three Short Breaths
Performance/production
Collection of newspaper reviews by London theatre critics. UK-England: London. 1998. Lang.: Eng. 2465
Three Sisters
SEE
Tri sestry.
Three Tall Women
Institutions
Profile of Württembergische Landesbühne. Germany: Esslingen. 1996-1997. Lang.: Ger. 1639
Throne of Straw
Plays/librettos/scripts
Analysis of historical drama of the holocaust. USA. Canada. Germany. 1950-1980. Lang.: Eng. 3610
Tieck, Dorothea
Plays/librettos/scripts
Shakespeare translators Luise Gottsched and Dorothea Tieck. Germany. 1739-1833. Lang.: Ger. 3156
Tiedemann, Philip
Performance/production
Premieres of new plays. Austria: Vienna. 1998. Lang.: Ger. 1820
Reviews of plays by Wolfgang Bauer and Thomas Bernhard. Switzerland: Basel. Austria: Vienna. 1998. Lang.: Ger. 2403
Tierney, Hanne
Performance/production
Hanne Tierney's adaptation of *Bodas de sangre (Blood Wedding)* by García Lorca. USA. 1997. Lang.: Eng. 647
Tiger Tail
Plays/librettos/scripts
Tennessee Williams's short story *Twenty-Seven Wagons Full of Cotton* and the plays based on it. USA. 1936-1979. Lang.: Eng. 3622
Tight Roaring Circle
Performance/production
The collaborative art installation *Tight Roaring Circle*. UK-England: London. 1993-1997. Lang.: Eng. 4133
Till, Lawrence
Performance/production
Collection of newspaper reviews by London theatre critics. UK-England: London. 1998. Lang.: Eng. 2521
Tiller, Ted
Design/technology
Magical stage effects in 'vampire' plays. USA. 1820-1977. Lang.: Eng. 1548
Tilley, Sam
Performance/production
Collection of newspaper reviews by London theatre critics. UK-England: London. 1998. Lang.: Eng. 2469
Tilton, James
Design/technology
Set and lighting designer James Tilton. USA. 1938-1998. Lang.: Eng. 265
Tímar, Sándor
Performance/production
Modern tendencies in Hungarian folk dance. Hungary. 1970-1977. Lang.: Hun. 1228
Time of My Life
Basic theatrical documents
French translation of *Time of My Life* by Alan Ayckbourn. UK-England. France. 1993-1998. Lang.: Fre. 1471
Time to Burn
Basic theatrical documents
Collection of plays by Charles L. Mee. USA. 1986-1995. Lang.: Eng. 1496
Time Vindicated
Plays/librettos/scripts
The control of time in Renaissance English drama. England. 1590-1620. Lang.: Eng. 2883
Ben Jonson's antimasques. England. 1612-1632. Lang.: Eng. 4205
Timeless
Performance/production
Collection of newspaper reviews by London theatre critics. UK-England: London. 1998. Lang.: Eng. 2434
Timon of Athens
Plays/librettos/scripts
The obedient daughter in adaptations of Shakespeare's plays. England. 1701-1800. Lang.: Eng. 2969
Tin Can Riots, The
Plays/librettos/scripts
Science fiction drama since World War II. USA. 1945-1988. Lang.: Eng. 3591
Tingalary Bird, The
Plays/librettos/scripts
Absurdism in children's theatre. North America. Europe. 1896-1970. Lang.: Eng. 3288
Tinline, Phil
Performance/production
Collection of newspaper reviews by London theatre critics. UK-England: London. 1998. Lang.: Eng. 2416
Tiny Alice
Plays/librettos/scripts
Recent productions of plays by Edward Albee. USA: New York, NY, Hartford, CT. 1959-1998. Lang.: Eng. 3578
Tippett, Michael
Performance/production
Interview with singer Krister St. Hill. Germany. Sweden. 1988-1998. Lang.: Swe. 4590
Tipton, Jennifer
Design/technology
Lighting designer Jennifer Tipton. USA: New York, NY. 1998. Lang.: Eng. 4441
'Tis Pity She's a Whore
Performance/production
Student production of Ford's *'Tis Pity She's a Whore*. Canada. 1997. Lang.: Eng. 1849
Plays/librettos/scripts
Influences on *'Tis Pity She's a Whore* by John Ford. England. 1587-1631. Lang.: Eng. 2937
Titanic
Design/technology
Scenic elements in *Titanic* by street theatre group Theater Titanick. Germany: Münster, Leipzig. Australia: Perth. 1998. Lang.: Eng. 191

***Titanic* — cont'd**

Technical designs for the film *Titanic*. USA. 1997. Lang.: Eng. 3910

Titanic vízirevü (Titanic Water Show, The)
Performance/production
István Tasnádi's *Titanic vízirevü (Titanic Water Show)* at Bárka Színház. Hungary: Budapest. 1998. Lang.: Hun. 2144

Titus Andronicus
Performance/production
Shakespeare's *Titus Andronicus* and the political power of symbolic performance. England. 1590-1595. Lang.: Eng. 1893
Productions of plays by Shakespeare, Brecht, and Camus. Germany. 1998. Lang.: Ger. 2032
Plays/librettos/scripts
An illustration of Queen Tamora of Shakespeare's *Titus Andronicus*. England. 1590-1594. Lang.: Eng. 2880
'Demonic' women in Shakespeare's tragedies. England. 1590-1613. Lang.: Eng. 2999
The politics of consent in Shakespeare's *Titus Andronicus*. England. 1590-1594. Lang.: Eng. 3006

Titus, Hiram
Design/technology
Costume design for a new version of *Peter Pan* at Children's Theatre Company. USA: Minneapolis, MN. 1998. Lang.: Eng. 4330
Plays/librettos/scripts
Operatic realizations of Beaumarchais' character Rosina. Europe. North America. 1784-1991. Lang.: Eng. 4773

Tivoli Színház (Budapest)
Performance/production
Interview with actor and director Róbert Alföldi. Hungary: Budapest. 1998. Lang.: Hun. 2056
Round-table discussion on Tivoli Theatre's production of *The Merchant of Venice*. Hungary. 1986-1997. Lang.: Hun. 2109
Shakespeare's *The Merchant of Venice* directed by Róbert Alföldi. Hungary: Budapest. 1998. Lang.: Hun. 2111
Plays/librettos/scripts
Analysis of Imre Szabó Stein's new translation of Shakespeare's *The Merchant of Venice*. Hungary: Budapest. 1998. Lang.: Hun. 3188

To the Chicago Abyss
Plays/librettos/scripts
Science fiction drama since World War II. USA. 1945-1988. Lang.: Eng. 3591

To Wong Foo, Thanks for Everything, Julie Newmar
Plays/librettos/scripts
Interview with playwright Douglas Carter Beane. USA. 1980-1998. Lang.: Eng. 3516

To, Raymond Kwak-wai
Relation to other fields
Theatre and politics in Hong Kong. Hong Kong. 1984-1996. Lang.: Eng. 3772

Tobin, David A.
Performance/production
Collection of newspaper reviews by London theatre critics. UK-England: London. 1998. Lang.: Eng. 2432

Today Is My Birthday
SEE
Dziś są moje urodziny.

Todd, Carole
Performance/production
Collection of newspaper reviews by London theatre critics. UK-England: London. 1998. Lang.: Eng. 2435

Tokyo Actors Repertory Company (Tokyo)
Performance/production
Theatrical component of Japan's UK98 Festival. Japan: Tokyo. 1994-1998. Lang.: Eng. 2192

Told by an Idiot (London)
Performance/production
Collection of newspaper reviews by London theatre critics. UK-England: London. 1998. Lang.: Eng. 2576

Toller, Ernst
Plays/librettos/scripts
Analysis of revisions of plays by Ernst Toller. Germany. 1920-1939. Lang.: Eng. 3172

Tolstoj, Aleksej Konstantinovič
Plays/librettos/scripts
Morality in plays of Fonvizin, Ostrovskij, and A.K. Tolstoj. Russia. 1764-1869. Lang.: Rus. 3325

Tolstoj, Lev Nikolajėvič
Performance/production
Collection of newspaper reviews by London theatre critics. UK-England: London. 1998. Lang.: Eng. 2506
Plays/librettos/scripts
Shared Experience's stage adaptations of nineteenth-century novels. USA: New York, NY. UK-England: London. 1998. Lang.: Eng. 3518

Tolstoy Regen, Sophie
Institutions
Profile of independent feminist theatre Kvinnliga Dramatiska Teatern. Sweden: Stockholm. 1997-1998. Lang.: Swe. 1725

Tomlin, Lily
Performance/production
Analysis of transformative comedy. USA. 1975-1988. Lang.: Eng. 666

Tomlinson, Robert
Performance/production
Collection of newspaper reviews by London theatre critics. UK-England: London. 1998. Lang.: Eng. 2429

Tommy
SEE ALSO
Who's Tommy, The.

Tompkins, Jon
Performance/production
Collection of newspaper reviews by London theatre critics. UK-England: London. 1998. Lang.: Eng. 2427

Tomson, Bob
Performance/production
Collection of newspaper reviews by London theatre critics. UK-England: London. 1998. Lang.: Eng. 2480

Ton beau capitaine (Your Handsome Captain)
Plays/librettos/scripts
Postcolonialism, ethnicity, and feminism in French and Caribbean plays. France. Martinique. Guadeloupe. 1960-1990. Lang.: Eng. 3104

Ton und Kirschen (Glindow)
Institutions
Margarethe Biereye and David Johnston of the touring company Ton und Kirschen. Germany: Glindow. 1992-1997. Lang.: Eng. 1624

Toneelgroep (Amsterdam)
Performance/production
Collection of newspaper reviews by London theatre critics. UK-England: London. 1998. Lang.: Eng. 2422

Tonight Show, The
Plays/librettos/scripts
Analysis of performance art on *The Larry Sanders Show*. USA. 1995. Lang.: Eng. 4079

Too Much Light Makes the Baby Go Blind
Performance/production
Review of *Too Much Light Makes the Baby Go Blind* by the Neo-Futurists. USA: Chicago, IL. 1997. Lang.: Eng. 620

Too True to Be Good
Plays/librettos/scripts
Colonialism in the plays of George Bernard Shaw. UK-England. 1895-1935. Lang.: Eng. 3438
Analysis of the later plays of George Bernard Shaw. UK-England. 1923-1947. Lang.: Eng. 3444

Toothless
Performance/production
Collection of newspaper reviews by London theatre critics. UK-England: London. 1998. Lang.: Eng. 2535

Top Dogs
Performance/production
Collection of newspaper reviews by London theatre critics. UK-England: London. 1998. Lang.: Eng. 2493

Top Girls
Performance/production
Analysis of two productions of Caryl Churchill's *Top Girls*. UK-England. 1982-1991. Lang.: Eng. 2608
Creating the character Marlene in Caryl Churchill's *Top Girls*. USA. 1997. Lang.: Eng. 2730
The language of costume in a video production of Caryl Churchill's *Top Girls*. UK-England. 1982-1991. Lang.: Eng. 4065
Plays/librettos/scripts
Secrets in Caryl Churchill's *Top Girls*. UK-England. 1982. Lang.: Eng. 3466
Brechtian epic devices in the theatre of Caryl Churchill. UK-England. 1976-1986. Lang.: Eng. 3477

Tor
Performance/production
Productions of Szegedi Kortárs Balett. Hungary: Szeged. 1998. Lang.: Hun. 1102

Tordy, Géza
Performance/production
Dostojėvskij's *Crime and Punishment* directed by Géza Tordy. Hungary: Győr. 1998. Lang.: Hun. 2100

Torelli, Achille
Plays/librettos/scripts
Italian realist drama. Italy. 1860-1918. Lang.: Eng. 3260
Torkar, Igor
Plays/librettos/scripts
Analysis of *Balada o taščici (Ballad of a Robin)* by Igor Torkar. Slovenia. 1946-1970. Lang.: Slo. 3346
Analysis of plays by Igor Torkar. Slovenia. 1946-1970. Lang.: Slo. 3354
Törőcsik, Mari
Institutions
Theatre critics' awards 97-98. Hungary. 1997-1998. Lang.: Hun. 355
Performance/production
Interviews with actors on Anatolij Vasiljév's guest direction at Szigligeti Theatre. Hungary: Szolnok. 1998. Lang.: Hun. 2061
Mari Törőcsik's performance in Ostrovskij's *Guilty Though Innocent* directed by Vasiljév. Hungary: Szolnok. 1997. Lang.: Hun. 2125
Torres Naharro, Bartolomé de
Plays/librettos/scripts
Playwright Bartolomé de Torres Naharro. Spain. 1480-1530. Lang.: Eng. 3383
Torse
Performance/production
Interview with dancer/choreographer Merce Cunningham. USA. 1960-1998. Lang.: Eng. 1186
Torshovteatret (Oslo)
Performance/production
Report from Ibsen festival. Norway: Oslo. 1998. Lang.: Swe. 2211
Tosca
Plays/librettos/scripts
Musical representation of death in Puccini's *Tosca.* Italy. 1900. Lang.: Eng. 4804
Totenmal (Call of the Dead)
Performance/production
Gender and politics in German dance. Germany. 1930-1932. Lang.: Eng. 928
Tóth, Géza M.
Performance/production
Ildikó Mándy's *X.Y.Z.*, a film-dance theatre piece. Hungary: Budapest. 1998. Lang.: Hun. 947
Tóth, Miklós
Performance/production
Productions of plays by Brecht and Shakespeare at the Hungarian theatre of Satu Mare. Romania: Satu Mare. 1998. Lang.: Hun. 2228
Totò (De Curtis, Antonio)
Performance/production
Catalogue of an exhibition on actor Totò. Italy: Naples. 1898-1998. Lang.: Ita. 542
The cult of actor Totò after his death. Italy: Naples. 1967-1997. Lang.: Ita. 2164
Touch of the Poet, A
Plays/librettos/scripts
African- and Irish-Americans in the plays of Eugene O'Neill. USA. 1916-1953. Lang.: Eng. 3687
Touki-Bouki (Hyena's Travels, The)
Performance/production
Analysis of *Touki-Bouki (The Hyena's Travels)* by Djibril Diop Mambéty. Senegal. 1973. Lang.: Eng. 3938
Touring companies
Administration
Sarah Bernhardt's farewell tour and its revenues. USA. 1905-1906. Lang.: Eng. 28
History of circle stock touring. USA. 1907-1957. Lang.: Eng. 43
The debate on organizing non-union tours of theatrical production. USA: New York, NY. 1998. Lang.: Eng. 88
Equity Executive Director Alan Eisenberg's experience with a touring production of *Cats.* USA: New York, NY. 1998. Lang.: Eng. 4318
Audience
Children's theatre and cultural exchange. Germany: Flensburg. 1998. Lang.: Ger. 1401
Design/technology
Mick O'Gorman's sound design and equipment for *Riverdance.* Ireland. 1998. Lang.: Eng. 1218
Institutions
State-wide tours of the Florida Federal Theatre Project. USA. 1937-1939. Lang.: Eng. 411
Moscow Art Theatre's tour in Minsk. Belorussia: Minsk. 1998. Lang.: Rus. 1574
Margarethe Biereye and David Johnston of the touring company Ton und Kirschen. Germany: Glindow. 1992-1997. Lang.: Eng. 1624
Profile of children's and youth theatre Älvsborgsteatern. Sweden: Borås. 1995-1998. Lang.: Swe. 1731
Performance spaces
A modular stage used for touring by the Houston Grand Opera. USA: Houston, TX. 1998. Lang.: Eng. 4500
Performance/production
The current state of Australian theatre for youth. Australia. 1990-1998. Lang.: Eng. 489
Practical issues of cultural exchange: the Cry of Asia! tour. France. Philippines. 1988-1990. Lang.: Eng. 535
Report on touring ice show *Stars on Ice.* USA. 1998. Lang.: Eng. 990
The European and American tour of the Polish National Ballet. Poland. France. USA. 1937-1939. Lang.: Pol. 1124
Collaboration of the Bolšoj and Mariinskij ballet troupes. Russia: Moscow, St. Petersburg. 1998. Lang.: Rus. 1135
Recent productions in Ireland of plays by Eugene O'Neill. Ireland: Dublin. UK-Ireland: Belfast. 1989-1998. Lang.: Eng. 2154
Pirandello's Teatro d'Arte on tour in Trieste. Italy: Trieste. 1926. Lang.: Ita. 2178
Irish and Irish-American characters on the stages of the Midwest. USA. 1875-1915. Lang.: Eng. 2696
George Crichton Miln's touring Shakespearean company in Japan. USA: Chicago, IL. Japan: Yokohama. 1882. Lang.: Eng. 2702
Antitheatricalism in the Circuit Chautauqua. USA. 1913-1930. Lang.: Eng. 4135
Ophaboom Theatre's experience in recreating *commedia dell'arte.* UK-England: London. 1991-1998. Lang.: Eng. 4193
Profile of baritone György Radnai. Hungary. 1920-1977. Lang.: Hun. 4624
Plays/librettos/scripts
Theatre as cultural weapon and military education in the Eritrean war. Eritrea. 1980-1984. Lang.: Eng. 3048
Relation to other fields
Government response to Living Theatre's *Paradise Now.* USA. Europe. 1968. Lang.: Eng. 3789
Tourneur, Cyril
Performance/production
Collection of newspaper reviews by London theatre critics. UK-England: London. 1998. Lang.: Eng. 2455
Plays/librettos/scripts
Plague imagery in Jacobean tragedy. England. 1618-1642. Lang.: Eng. 2889
The skull in plays of Shakespeare, Dekker, and Tourneur. England. 1606. Lang.: Eng. 3026
Towneley Cycle
Plays/librettos/scripts
The Easter play tradition. England. 1180-1557. Lang.: Eng. 2942
Townsend, Jessica
Performance/production
Collection of newspaper reviews by London theatre critics. UK-England: London. 1998. Lang.: Eng. 2550
Collection of newspaper reviews by London theatre critics. UK-England: London. 1998. Lang.: Eng. 2574
Trabusch, Markus
Plays/librettos/scripts
Kerstin Specht's *Die Froschkönigin (The Frog Princess)* and its premiere at Staatstheater Stuttgart. Germany: Stuttgart. 1998. Lang.: Ger. 3174
Trade
Performance/production
Collection of newspaper reviews by London theatre critics. UK-England: London. 1998. Lang.: Eng. 2549
Trafford, Steve
Performance/production
Collection of newspaper reviews by London theatre critics. UK-England: London. 1998. Lang.: Eng. 2511
Collection of newspaper reviews by London theatre critics. UK-England: London. 1998. Lang.: Eng. 2560
Trafó Kortárs Művészetek Háza (Budapest)
Institutions
Interview with György Szabó, director of Trafó. Hungary: Budapest. 1998. Lang.: Hun. 359
Performance/production
Ildikó Mándy's *X.Y.Z.*, a film-dance theatre piece. Hungary: Budapest. 1998. Lang.: Hun. 947

Trafó Kortárs Művészetek Háza (Budapest) — cont'd

Yvette Bozsik's *Nevess remegve (Emlék) (Laugh Tremble—Memory)* at Trafó. Hungary: Budapest. 1998. Lang.: Hun. 1293

Tragédie du roi Christophe, La (Tragedy of King Christopher, The)
Plays/librettos/scripts
Analysis and translation of *Et les Chiens se taisaient (And the Dogs Were Silent)* by Aimé Césaire. Martinique. 1946-1969. Lang.: Eng. 3269

Tragedy
Performance/production
A dancer's experience of and investigations into ecstasy. USA. Germany. 1969-1990. Lang.: Eng. 673
Massimo Castri's production of Euripides' *Electra.* Italy: Spoleto. 1993. Lang.: Ita. 2179
The performance of Senecan tragedy. Roman Empire. 4 B.C.-150 A.D. Lang.: Eng. 2227
Twentieth-century productions of Euripidean tragedy. USA. 1915-1969. Lang.: Eng. 2678
Plays/librettos/scripts
Plague imagery in Jacobean tragedy. England. 1618-1642. Lang.: Eng. 2889
Feminist analysis of Webster's *The Duchess of Malfi.* England. 1613. Lang.: Eng. 2931
Feeling in Shakespeare's *King Lear.* England. 1605-1606. Lang.: Eng. 2952
Casuistry and early modern English tragedy. England. 1600-1671. Lang.: Eng. 2980
Folklore and Shakespeare's *King Lear.* England. 1605-1606. Lang.: Eng. 3010
Evil in Stuart tragedy. England. 1620-1642. Lang.: Eng. 3024
Roberto Zucco and Bernard-Marie Koltès' idea of the tragic. France. 1835-1837. Lang.: Fre. 3076
Myth and technique in Greek tragedy. Greece. 490-406 B.C. Lang.: Ita. 3182
Civic discourse and civil discord in Greek tragedy. Greece. 475-400 B.C. Lang.: Eng. 3185
Adaptations of Greek tragedy by contemporary Irish writers. Ireland. UK-Ireland. 1984-1998. Lang.: Eng. 3214
Analysis and translation of *Et les Chiens se taisaient (And the Dogs Were Silent)* by Aimé Césaire. Martinique. 1946-1969. Lang.: Eng. 3269
Analysis of Seneca's *Oedipus* and *Hercules furens.* Roman Empire. 4 B. C.-65 A.D. Lang.: Eng. 3313
Roman tragic theatre from literary origins to the Roman arena. Rome. 500 B.C.-476 A.D. Lang.: Eng. 3315
Playwright Ivan Mrak. Slovenia. 1925-1986. Lang.: Slo. 3355
Analysis of Countée Cullen's translation of Euripides' *Medea.* USA. 1936. Lang.: Eng. 3567
Gender and politics in Romantic tragedies of Mercy Otis Warren. USA. 1783-1785. Lang.: Eng. 3575
Gangster film and Shakespearean tragedy. USA. 1971-1991. Lang.: Eng. 4009
Relation to other fields
Catharsis and contemporary theatre. USA. 1998. Lang.: Eng. 795
Novelist Samuel Richardson compared to Shakespeare. England. 1744-1747. Lang.: Eng. 3754
Analysis of illustrations of first editions of tragedies by Gryphius. Germany. 1635-1664. Lang.: Eng. 3765
Theory/criticism
The plays of Corneille and catharsis through admiration. France. 1651-1653. Lang.: Eng. 3820
Tragic theories of G.E. Lessing. Germany. 1760-1780. Lang.: Eng. 3822

Tragedy of Dido, The
Plays/librettos/scripts
Marlowe's tragedies and peer evaluation in the composition classroom. USA. 1997-1998. Lang.: Eng. 3532

Tragedy of Jane Shore, The
Performance/production
Rowe's Jane Shore as a major role for actresses. England. 1714. Lang.: Eng. 1899

Tragedy of Man, The
SEE
Ember tragédiája, Az.

Tragedy of Mariam, The
Plays/librettos/scripts
Women's use of wit in response to men in English popular culture. England. 1590-1630. Lang.: Eng. 2884
Marriage and patriarchy in *The Tragedy of Mariam* by Elizabeth Cary. England. 1613. Lang.: Eng. 2893
Feminist analysis of *The Tragedy of Mariam* by Elizabeth Cary. England. 1602-1612. Lang.: Eng. 3019

Tragedy of Philotas, The
Plays/librettos/scripts
Possible censorship of *The Tragedy of Philotas* by Samuel Daniel. England. 1605. Lang.: Eng. 2996

Tragelehn, B.K.
Performance/production
German directors about the meaning of Brecht today. Germany. 1998. Lang.: Ger. 1948
Reviews of productions of plays by Brecht. Germany. 1998. Lang.: Ger. 1986
Interview with playwright Heiner Müller about his adaptations of Shakespeare. Germany, East. 1965-1990. Lang.: Eng. 2039
Shakespeare in the GDR: producer and critic B.K. Tragelehn. Germany, East. 1950-1990. Lang.: Eng. 2040

Tragelehn, Christa
Performance/production
Interview with playwright Heiner Müller about his adaptations of Shakespeare. Germany, East. 1965-1990. Lang.: Eng. 2039

Tragic Life and Triumphant Death of Julia Pastrano, Ugliest Woman in the World, The
Performance/production
Collection of newspaper reviews by London theatre critics. UK-England: London, Scarborough. 1998. Lang.: Eng. 2426

Tragical History of Doctor Faustus
SEE
Doctor Faustus.

Tragicomedia jardines y campos sabeos (Tragicomedy Gardens and Fields of Saba)
Plays/librettos/scripts
Feminist analysis of seventeenth-century plays by women. Spain. 1605-1675. Lang.: Eng. 3385

Tragik ponevole (Tragedian in Spite of Himself, The)
Basic theatrical documents
Catalan translations of the complete plays of Anton Čechov. Russia. 1884-1904. Lang.: Cat. 1449

Trahern, Al
Administration
History of circle stock touring. USA. 1907-1957. Lang.: Eng. 43

Traición en la amistad (Treachery in Friendship)
Plays/librettos/scripts
Feminist analysis of seventeenth-century plays by women. Spain. 1605-1675. Lang.: Eng. 3385

Training
SEE ALSO
Classed Entries.

Training aids
Research/historiography
The Shakespeare Interactive Research Group. USA: Cambridge, MA. 1991-1997. Lang.: Eng. 3799

Training, actor
Institutions
Report on Vachtangov School conference. Russia: Moscow. 1990-1998. Lang.: Rus. 380
The work of training organization Metier in creating national standards for arts training. UK-England: Bradford. 1996-1998. Lang.: Eng. 388
The training program of the Clarence B. Hilberry Repertory Theatre. USA: Detroit, MI. 1963-1973. Lang.: Eng. 408
Training methods of the Conservatoire d'art dramatique de Québec. Canada: Quebec, PQ. 1998. Lang.: Fre. 1578
Profile of the Swedish Institute of Acting at the Finnish Theatre Academy. Finland: Helsinki. 1908-1998. Lang.: Eng, Fre. 1603
Actor training at Hochschule der Künste and Ernst-Busch-Schule. Germany: Berlin. 1998. Lang.: Ger. 1622
Carlo Quartucci's acting workshop on Shakespeare's *Macbeth.* Italy: Rome. 1991-1992. Lang.: Ita. 1674
Polish experimental theatre training. Poland: Cracow, Wrocław, Warsaw. 1930-1998. Lang.: Pol. 1685
Theatre schools: production of showcases for graduating students. UK-England: London. 1998. Lang.: Eng. 1746
Interview with Robert Lewis on the founding of Actors Studio. USA: New York, NY. 1997. Lang.: Eng. 1766

Training, actor — cont'd

Arthur Penn and Actors Studio. USA: New York, NY. 1997. Lang.: Eng. 1767

Performance/production

Handbook and training exercises for actors. Europe. 1998. Lang.: Ita. 520

Tadashi Suzuki and Suzuki Company of Toga. Japan. 1939-1984. Lang.: Eng. 555

Lithuanian theatre education and the visit of Tadashi Suzuki. Lithuania. 1998. Lang.: Fin. 559

Coping with stage fright. Netherlands. 1998. Lang.: Dut. 566

The Creative Surges actor-training seminar. UK-England: Ipswich. 1998. Lang.: Eng. 606

Actor-training project involving character development in drama and musical theatre. USA. 1987. Lang.: Eng. 625

Character development in drama and musical theatre: actor-training project. USA. 1987. Lang.: Eng. 626

The application of Laban Movement Studies to actor training. USA. 1997-1998. Lang.: Eng. 628

A model for systematic analysis of vocal performance. USA. 1988-1997. Lang.: Eng. 636

Actor training and psychotherapy-derived techniques. USA. 1988. Lang.: Eng. 639

The Alba Emoting system of actor training. USA. 1995-1998. Lang.: Eng. 668

Character development in dramas and musicals. USA. 1987. Lang.: Eng. 670

Actor-training project in character development. USA. 1987. Lang.: Eng. 671

Women and improvisation. USA. 1970-1997. Lang.: Eng. 672

History of movement training for the actor. USA. 1910-1985. Lang.: Eng. 675

Character development from the actor's point of view. USA. 1987. Lang.: Eng. 686

The training of actors in Asian performance styles. Australia: Brisbane. 1992-1998. Lang.: Eng. 1817

Voice teachers Alex Bulmer and Kate Lynch. Canada: Toronto, ON. UK-England: London. 1986-1998. Lang.: Eng. 1837

Problems of post-secondary theatre training. Canada: Edmonton, AB. 1919-1998. Lang.: Eng. 1848

Acting and directing influences on Eugenio Barba. Denmark: Holstebro. 1997. Lang.: Eng. 1886

The director's role in the development of good acting. Denmark. 1998. Lang.: Dan. 1887

Director Jonathan Paul Cook on developing talent in an ensemble. Denmark. 1997-1998. Lang.: Dan. 1888

Interview with acting teacher Kari Väänänen. Finland. 1998. Lang.: Fin. 1918

Movement training for actors in plays of Molière. France. 1622-1673. Lang.: Eng. 1938

Tadashi Suzuki's method of actor training. Japan. 1998. Lang.: Eng. 2191

Spirituality and the theatre of Jerzy Grotowski. Poland. 1958-1998. Lang.: Ger, Fre, Dut, Eng. 2226

Slovene translation of Cicely Berry's work on vocal training for the actor. Slovenia. UK-England. 1973-1993. Lang.: Slo. 2344

Research on the importance of vocal training for the actor. USA. 1986-1987. Lang.: Eng. 2657

An approach to playing Malvolio in Shakespeare's *Twelfth Night*. USA. 1987. Lang.: Eng. 2659

Account of an actor-training project focused on character development. USA. 1987. Lang.: Eng. 2664

The 'viewpoint theory' of actor training. USA. 1998. Lang.: Eng. 2677

Actor-training and character development. USA. 1987. Lang.: Eng. 2679

An approach to playing Babe Botrelle in Beth Henley's *Crimes of the Heart*. USA. 1987. Lang.: Eng. 2690

An approach to playing Jamie in O'Neill's *Long Day's Journey Into Night*. USA. 1987. Lang.: Eng. 2697

John Barton's workshop on Shakespearean performance. USA: New York, NY. 1998. Lang.: Eng. 2704

Character development in drama. USA. 1987. Lang.: Eng. 2743

Actress and teacher Uta Hagen. USA. 1998. Lang.: Eng. 2745

Actor's analysis of character development. USA. 1987. Lang.: Eng. 2746

The development of character in an actor training project. USA. 1987. Lang.: Eng. 2761

Director Mel Gordon on Mejerchol'd's influence. USSR. 1920-1931. Lang.: Eng. 2765

Yves Marc on Etienne Decroux. France: Paris. 1998. Lang.: Eng. 4088

Interview with Marie-Hélène Dasté, daughter of Jacques Copeau. France: Paris. 1913-1992. Lang.: Eng. 4089

Corinne Soum, former assistant to Etienne Decroux. France: Paris. UK-England: London. 1968-1998. Lang.: Eng. 4090

Etienne Decroux's concept of actor-centered theatre. USA. France. 1920-1998. Lang.: Eng. 4091

Theory/criticism

American acting theory. USA. 1923-1973. Lang.: Eng. 866

Training

Actor/director Jean-Paul Denizon and his workshops on Peter Brook's approach to theatre. France. 1980-1998. Lang.: Ita. 873

Ferruccio Di Cori's improvisational workshops for actors and directors. Italy: Rome. 1994-1996. Lang.: Ita. 874

Director Walter Pfaff on the influence of Jerzy Grotowski. Poland. Germany. 1998. Lang.: Eng. 876

Dance teaching methods of Anzu Furukawa. Finland. 1998. Lang.: Fin. 1017

Actress, director, and teacher Marija Knebel'. Russia. 1898-1989. Lang.: Rus. 3850

Mejerchol'd, actor training, and Trotsky. USSR. 1922-1929. Lang.: Eng. 3852

Details of a media acting curriculum. USA. 1994-1998. Lang.: Eng. 4041

Actor training for the character tenor. USA. 1998. Lang.: Eng. 4849

Training, ballet

Training

Methodological manual for teaching ballet to children. Slovenia. 1998. Lang.: Slo. 1209

Ballet teacher Pauline Koner. USA: New York, NY. 1920-1998. Lang.: Eng. 1212

Training, dance

Administration

Arts Minister on the current state of dance, training, and funding. UK-England. 1998. Lang.: Eng. 884

Institutions

Interview with Imre Dózsa, managing director of Táncművészeti Főiskola. Hungary: Budapest. 1998. Lang.: Hun. 897

The performing arts curriculum of Skytteholmsgymnasiet. Sweden: Solna. 1990-1998. Lang.: Swe. 898

Interview with dance teacher Lia Schubert. Sweden: Stockholm, Gothenburg. 1935-1998. Lang.: Swe. 900

Appeal for more varied dance training. Sweden. 1998. Lang.: Swe. 903

The dance training program of Houston High School for the Performing and Visual Arts. USA: Houston, TX. 1998. Lang.: Eng. 907

Criticism of Svenska Bakettskolan. Sweden: Stockholm. 1984. Lang.: Swe. 1049

Student's view of the Elmhurst Ballet School. UK-England: Camberley. 1997-1998. Lang.: Hun. 1055

Performance/production

Interview with dancer/choreographer Rebecca Hilton. Australia. USA. 1983-1995. Lang.: Eng. 913

Children on dance. Finland. 1998. Lang.: Fin. 918

Dancer, choreographer, and teacher Amos Hetz. Israel: Jerusalem. 1978-1998. Lang.: Ger. 953

Jazz dancer and choreographer Mia Michaels. USA. 1998. Lang.: Eng. 987

Hungarian student's training at Jeune Ballet de France. France: Paris. 1996-1998. Lang.: Hun. 1075

Modern tendencies in Hungarian folk dance. Hungary. 1970-1977. Lang.: Hun. 1228

Interview with Flamenco dancer Janni Berggren. Sweden. Spain. 1970. Lang.: Swe. 1237

William Forsythe of Ballett Frankfurt. Germany: Frankfurt. 1984-1998. Lang.: Ger. 1284

Dancer, choreographer, and teacher Hellmut Gottschild. Germany. USA. 1936-1998. Lang.: Ger. 1287

Training, dance — cont'd

Mary Wigman's summary of her work in choreography and dance training. Germany: Dresden. 1925. Lang.: Ger. 1290
Interview with choreographer Javier De Frutos. USA. 1990-1998. Lang.: Eng. 1332
Relation to other fields
Dancer, teacher, and healing facilitator Anna Halprin of Tamalpa Institute. USA: Kentfield, CA. 1978-1998. Lang.: Ger. 1338
Training
Survey of twentieth-century dance styles and teaching methods. Europe. 1900-1998. Lang.: Ger. 1015
Interview with children's dance teacher Yvonne Jahn-Olsson. Sweden: Stockholm. 1945-1998. Lang.: Swe. 1019
Britt-Marie Berggren's dancing school for children. Sweden: Stockholm. 1946. Lang.: Swe. 1020
The use of martial arts in dance training. UK-England. 1998. Lang.: Eng. 1022
Illustrated history of jazz dance. USA. Slovenia. 1900-1997. Lang.: Slo. 1023
The development of Irmgard Bartenieff's corrective physical training methods. USA. 1925-1981. Lang.: Ger. 1024
The place of the teacher in the world of classical dance. 1998. Lang.: Rus. 1202
Classical dance training and its appeal to children. Finland. 1998. Lang.: Fin. 1204
Interview with ballet dancer and teacher Jacqueline Menyhárt. Hungary. 1954-1998. Lang.: Hun. 1206
Interview with ballet master Tamás Koren. Hungary. 1959-1998. Lang.: Hun. 1207
Traditional and contemporary approaches to ballet training. Sweden: Stockholm. 1998. Lang.: Swe. 1210
Tina Hessel's relaxation and breathing techniques for dance training. Sweden: Stockholm. 1998. Lang.: Swe. 1211
Dance teacher Louise Kloepper. USA. 1910-1996. Lang.: Eng. 1213
Ballet teacher Waltraud Karkar. USA: Wausau, WI. 1998. Lang.: Eng. 1215
Interview with dancer and teacher David Howard. USA. 1966-1998. Lang.: Swe. 1216
Dance teacher Harvey Hysell. USA: New Orleans, LA. 1969-1998. Lang.: Eng. 1217
Dance training at Folkwang Hochschule. Germany: Essen. 1996-1998. Lang.: Hun. 1341
Modern dance teacher Elizabeth Waters. USA. 1920-1950. Lang.: Eng. 1342

Training, design
Design/technology
Pyrotechnics and its use in theatre. Europe. 1200 B.C.-1998 A.D. Lang.: Ger. 178
Criticism of methods used in design training. Finland. 1998. Lang.: Fin. 180
Impressions from the Salon de Théâtre. France: Paris. 1998. Lang.: Ger. 183
Walther Unruh and German theatre technology. Germany. 1898-1998. Lang.: Ger. 187
Professional theatrical designers on design training. USA. 1998. Lang.: Eng. 252
Students' recreation of paintings on stage. USA: Huntington, WV. 1996-1997. Lang.: Eng. 313
Former student on learning lighting design. USA: Las Vegas, NV. 1997. Lang.: Eng. 316
Loudspeaker directivity and theatrical sound systems. USA. 1987. Lang.: Eng. 318
A stage design for Jean Giraudoux's *Ondine*. USA. 1987. Lang.: Eng. 1529
Design for Shakespeare's *A Midsummer Night's Dream*. USA. 1987. Lang.: Eng. 1563
Set design and lighting for a production of Ibsen's *Hedda Gabler*. USA: Louisville, KY. 1988. Lang.: Eng. 1564
Training
The use of computer animation techniques in design training. USA: Athens, GA. 1988-1998. Lang.: Eng. 878

Training, director
Administration
Study of management in regional theatres. USA. 1987-1988. Lang.: Eng. 140
Institutions
Director training at Ernst-Busch-Schule and some of its graduates. Germany: Berlin. 1972-1998. Lang.: Ger. 1648
Director training at Universität und Musikhochschule. Germany: Hamburg. 1988-1998. Lang.: Ger. 1658
Performance/production
Preparing a production of Brian Way's participatory *The Mirrorman*. USA. 1987. Lang.: Eng. 633
Proposal for a college course in directing. USA: Brevard, NC. 1997-1998. Lang.: Eng. 683
Interview with director Tamás Ascher on director training. Hungary. 1960-1990. Lang.: Hun. 2146
Student production of *The Diary of Anne Frank*. USA. 1955. Lang.: Eng. 2703
Directing a student production of Yeats's *Deirdre*. USA: Louisville, KY. 1988. Lang.: Eng. 2738
Training
Actor/director Jean-Paul Denizon and his workshops on Peter Brook's approach to theatre. France. 1980-1998. Lang.: Ita. 873
Ferruccio Di Cori's improvisational workshops for actors and directors. Italy: Rome. 1994-1996. Lang.: Ita. 874
Standards for future directors and teachers of directing. Russia. 1998. Lang.: Rus. 877

Training, management
Administration
The effect of formal training on arts administrators. USA. 1998. Lang.: Eng. 45

Training, movement
Performance/production
Tadashi Suzuki and Suzuki Company of Toga. Japan. 1939-1984. Lang.: Eng. 555
The application of Laban Movement Studies to actor training. USA. 1997-1998. Lang.: Eng. 628

Training, singer
Institutions
Interviews with graduate students at Yale University School of Music. USA: New Haven, CT. 1998. Lang.: Eng. 4483
Training practices of Houston Opera Studio. USA: Houston, TX. 1977-1998. Lang.: Eng. 4489
Performance/production
Interview with soprano Joan Sutherland about vocal technique. USA: New York, NY. 1998. Lang.: Eng. 4728
Training
Singer training at Teater- & Operahögskolan. Sweden: Gothenburg. 1960-1998. Lang.: Swe. 4848
Actor training for the character tenor. USA. 1998. Lang.: Eng. 4849

Training, technician
Design/technology
Account of ACTSAFE conference on theatre safety. France: Paris. 1998. Lang.: Swe. 181
OISTAT meeting on technician training. Netherlands: Amsterdam. 1998. Lang.: Swe. 206
Theatre technician training at Malmö Högskola. Sweden: Malmö. 1998. Lang.: Swe. 225

Training, voice
Performance/production
The application of Laban Movement Studies to actor training. USA. 1997-1998. Lang.: Eng. 628
A model for systematic analysis of vocal performance. USA. 1988-1997. Lang.: Eng. 636
Voice teachers Alex Bulmer and Kate Lynch. Canada: Toronto, ON. UK-England: London. 1986-1998. Lang.: Eng. 1837
Slovene translation of Cicely Berry's work on vocal training for the actor. Slovenia. UK-England. 1973-1993. Lang.: Slo. 2344

Trainspotting
Performance/production
Collection of newspaper reviews by London theatre critics. UK-England: London. 1998. Lang.: Eng. 2412
Plays/librettos/scripts
Sex, drugs, and violence in contemporary British drama. UK-England. 1991-1998. Lang.: Eng. 3494

Trammell, Sam
Performance/production
Julyana Soelistyo and Sam Trammel, winners of the Derwent Award. USA: New York, NY. 1998. Lang.: Eng. 2719

Tramontani, Daniele
Design/technology
Sound system used in a soccer stadium for an operatic production. Italy: Rome. 1998. Lang.: Eng. 4434

Transatlantic
Performance/production
Opera composer George Antheil. USA. 1900-1959. Lang.: Eng. 4750
Translations
Plays/librettos/scripts
Analysis of *Translations* by Brian Friel. Ireland. 1980. Lang.: Eng. 3197
Translations
Basic theatrical documents
English translation of *terukkūttu* piece *Pakatai Tuyil (The Dice Game and the Disrobing)*. India. 1998. Lang.: Eng. 1345
English translation of *Kanadehon Hamlet* by Harue Tsutsumi. Japan. 1997. Lang.: Eng. 1360
English translation of *Takatoki* by Mokuami Kawatake. Japan. 1884-1998. Lang.: Eng. 1361
Catalan translation of *Am Ziel (To the Goal)* by Thomas Bernhard. Austria. 1981. Lang.: Cat. 1407
Catalan translation of *Anatol* and *Anatols Grössenwahn (The Megalomania of Anatol)* by Arthur Schnitzler. Austria. 1889. Lang.: Cat. 1408
English translation of *Zmijin svlak (Snake Skin)* by Slobodan Šnajder. Croatia. 1998. Lang.: Eng. 1415
English translations of plays by Tawfiq Al-Hakim. Egypt. 1930-1945. Lang.: Eng. 1416
English translation and analysis of two plays by Ali Ahmad Bakathir. Egypt. 1908-1969. Lang.: Eng. 1417
Critical edition and English translation of Robert Burton's *Philosophaster*. England. 1606-1618. Lang.: Eng. 1418
French translation of Shakespeare's *Love's Labour's Lost*. England. France. 1594-1998. Lang.: Fre. 1419
Catalan translation of Shakespeare's *Measure for Measure*. England. 1604. Lang.: Cat. 1420
Catalan translation of Shakespeare's *Romeo and Juliet*. England. 1591. Lang.: Cat. 1421
Catalan translation of Shakespeare's *A Midsummer Night's Dream*. England. 1595. Lang.: Cat. 1422
Catalan translation of *La Nuit juste avant les forêts (The Dark Just Before the Forests)* by Bernard-Marie Koltès. France. 1977. Lang.: Cat. 1428
Catalan translation of *Le Jeu de l'amour et du hasard (The Play of Love and Chance)* by Marivaux. France. 1730. Lang.: Cat. 1432
Catalan translation of *Les Femmes savantes (The Learned Ladies)* by Molière. France. 1672. Lang.: Cat. 1433
Catalan translations of plays by Bertolt Brecht (volume 1). Germany. 1919-1954. Lang.: Cat. 1437
Catalan translation of Aristophanes' *Lysistrata*. Greece. 435 B.C. Lang.: Cat. 1438
Dutch translations of women's monologues by Dario Fo. Italy. 1998. Lang.: Dut. 1440
Slovene translation of *Mistero Buffo* by Dario Fo. Italy. Slovenia. 1969-1997. Lang.: Slo. 1441
Catalan translation of *Il Ventaglio (The Fan)* by Carlo Goldoni. Italy. 1765. Lang.: Cat. 1442
Catalan translation of *Gl'Innamorati (The Lovers)* by Carlo Goldoni. Italy. 1765. Lang.: Cat. 1443
Catalan translation of *La Bottega del caffè (The Coffee Shop)* by Carlo Goldoni. Italy. 1750. Lang.: Cat. 1444
Russian translations of plays by Nobel Prize winners. Italy. 1848-1998. Lang.: Rus. 1446
English translation of *The Mustache* by Sabine Berman. Mexico. 1992. Lang.: Eng. 1447
English translation of *Historia (History)* by Witold Gombrowicz. Poland. 1998. Lang.: Eng. 1448
Catalan translations of the complete plays of Anton Čechov. Russia. 1884-1904. Lang.: Cat. 1449
English translation of Mejerchol'd's adaptation of *Revizor (The Inspector General)* by Gogol. Russia. USSR. 1838-1926. Lang.: Eng. 1450
French translation of *Tres diamantes y una mujer (Three Diamonds and One Woman)* by Alejandro Casona. Spain. France. 1959-1998. Lang.: Fre. 1464
Slovene translations of Tibetan plays. Tibet. 1400-1990. Lang.: Slo. 1470
French translation of *Time of My Life* by Alan Ayckbourn. UK-England. France. 1993-1998. Lang.: Fre. 1471
French translation of *Funny Money* by Ray Cooney. UK-England. France. 1995-1997. Lang.: Fre. 1473
French translation of *Popcorn* by Ben Elton. UK-England. France. 1996-1998. Lang.: Fre. 1475
Catalan translation of *Arms and the Man* by George Bernard Shaw. UK-England. 1894. Lang.: Cat. 1478
Catalan translation of *The Importance of Being Earnest* by Oscar Wilde. UK-England. 1895. Lang.: Cat. 1479
French translation of *Lebensraum* by Israel Horovitz. USA. France. 1996-1997. Lang.: Fre. 1488
French translation of *The Primary English Class* by Israel Horovitz. USA. France. 1996. Lang.: Fre. 1489
French translation of *Beast on the Moon* by Richard Kalinoski. USA. France. 1995-1997. Lang.: Fre. 1491
French translation of *My Left Breast* by Susan Miller. USA. France. 1994-1998. Lang.: Fre. 1498
French translation of *Alfred Stieglitz Loves O'Keeffe* by Lanie Robertson. USA. France. 1987-1997. Lang.: Fre. 1505
Performance/production
List of French-language productions of Shakespeare. Canada: Montreal, PQ, Quebec, PQ. 1945-1998. Lang.: Fre. 1841
French Canadian translations/adaptations of Shakespeare. Canada: Montreal, PQ. 1988. Lang.: Fre. 1855
Interview with director Alexander Weigel. Germany, East. 1970-1990. Lang.: Eng. 2042
Directors Manfred Wekwerth and Robert Weimann on Brecht and Shakespeare. Germany, East. 1945-1990. Lang.: Eng. 2043
Plays/librettos/scripts
French translations of Shakespeare by Antonine Maillet and Jean-Louis Roux. Canada: Montreal, PQ. 1988-1993. Lang.: Fre. 2793
Normand Chaurette's translations of *As You Like It* by Shakespeare. Canada: Montreal, PQ. 1989-1994. Lang.: Fre. 2824
Essays on play translation. Canada. 1998. Lang.: Eng. 2828
Don Quixote, Lewis Theobald's *The Double Falsehood* and the lost *Cardenio* of Shakespeare and Fletcher. England. Spain. 1610-1727. Lang.: Eng. 3001
Max Meyerfeld's preface to the translation of *A Florentine Tragedy* by Oscar Wilde. Europe. 1895-1907. Lang.: Fre. 3057
The influence Dryden and Johnson's theories on self-translated works of Samuel Beckett. France. Ireland. 1957-1976. Lang.: Eng. 3077
Essay on French translations of Shakespeare. France. 1974-1998. Lang.: Fre. 3082
On translating into German the plays of Valère Novarina. France. Germany. 1947-1998. Lang.: Ger. 3122
Shakespeare translators Luise Gottsched and Dorothea Tieck. Germany. 1739-1833. Lang.: Ger. 3156
Brecht and the translation of Shakespeare into German. Germany, East. 1945-1990. Lang.: Eng. 3177
New Hungarian translations of Shakespeare. Hungary. 1990-1998. Lang.: Hun. 3187
Analysis of Imre Szabó Stein's new translation of Shakespeare's *The Merchant of Venice*. Hungary: Budapest. 1998. Lang.: Hun. 3188
Commentary on plays newly translated into Hungarian. Hungary. 1990-1998. Lang.: Hun. 3189
Essay on the problem of translation. Hungary. 1990-1998. Lang.: Hun. 3190
Pirandello's work as a translator. Italy. 1886-1936. Lang.: Ita. 3225
Dario Fo, translation, and authorial intent. Italy. 1978-1998. Lang.: Eng. 3238
Catalan translation of the memoirs of playwright Carlo Goldoni. Italy. 1707-1793. Lang.: Cat. 3241
Analysis and translation of *Et les Chiens se taisaient (And the Dogs Were Silent)* by Aimé Césaire. Martinique. 1946-1969. Lang.: Eng. 3269
North American translations and adaptations of Molière. North America. 1998. Lang.: Eng. 3289
Ibsen, translation, and feminine discourse. Norway. 1888. Lang.: Eng. 3295
Translating the unfinished *Historia (History)* by Witold Gombrowicz. Poland. 1951-1998. Lang.: Eng. 3303
Ibsen's *Peer Gynt* and its new Polish translation. Poland. Norway. 1867-1967. Lang.: Pol. 3308

Translations — cont'd

Translations of Čechov's *Three Sisters* and Gorkij's *The Lower Depths*. Russia. 1901-1902. Lang.: Rus. 3326
Bibliography of Slovene writers and playwrights in translation. Slovenia. 1960-1997. Lang.: Eng. 3343
Translation work of playwright Oton Župančič. Slovenia. 1900-1954. Lang.: Slo. 3357
Translation and the plays of Valle-Inclán. Spain. 1936-1998. Lang.: Eng. 3378
Perceptions of Bertolt Brecht in the English-speaking world. UK-England. North America. 1933-1998. Lang.: Ger. 3443
The Break of Day, Timberlake Wertenbaker's adaptation of Čechov's *Three Sisters*. UK-England. Russia. 1901-1995. Lang.: Eng. 3510
Translating Hauptmann's *Die Weber (The Weavers)* into Scots dialect. UK-Scotland: Dundee, Glasgow. 1997. Lang.: Eng. 3513
Joseph Chaikin's adaptation of *Textes pour rien (Texts for Nothing)* by Samuel Beckett. USA: New York, NY. 1995. Lang.: Eng. 3563
Analysis of Countée Cullen's translation of Euripides' *Medea*. USA. 1936. Lang.: Eng. 3567
Stephen Mulrine's translation and stage adaptation of *Moscow Stations* by Venedikt Erofeev. USSR. UK-England. 1973-1998. Lang.: Eng. 3718
The search for a lost translation of *The Seven Deadly Sins* by Brecht and Weill. Germany. UK-England. 1933-1998. Lang.: Eng. 4392

Transvestism
Performance/production
Female impersonation and the construction of the female stereotype. USA. 1890-1930. Lang.: Eng. 651
Interview with dancer/choreographer Elena Kunikova on her work with Les Ballets Trockadero. USA: New York, NY. 1997. Lang.: Eng. 1180
Women's roles in Shakespeare. 1600-1998. Lang.: Ger. 1813
The resurgence of interest in actress Charlotte Cibber Charke. England. 1713-1760. Lang.: Eng. 1901
Actress Charlotte Cibber Charke and cross-dressing. England. 1713-1760. Lang.: Eng. 1906
Press responses to the autobiography of actress Charlotte Cibber Charke. England. 1713-1760. Lang.: Eng. 1908
Account of life in drag. USA: New Orleans, LA. 1995. Lang.: Eng. 4138
Lucy Vestris in *Giovanni in London*. England: London. 1842. Lang.: Eng. 4546
Plays/librettos/scripts
Cross-dressing in Shakespeare's *The Merchant of Venice* and in the autobiography of actress Charlotte Cibber Charke. England. 1713-1760. Lang.: Eng. 2891
Cross-dressing in Elizabethan Robin Hood plays. England. 1589-1598. Lang.: Eng. 3016
Transvestism in contemporary film as the 'blackface' of the nineties. UK-England. USA. 1993-1996. Lang.: Eng. 3983
Female operatic cross-dressing. Italy: Naples, Venice. 1601-1800. Lang.: Eng. 4814
Relation to other fields
Analysis of anti-theatricalism. England. 1579-1642. 726
Student responses to the autobiography of actress Charlotte Cibber Charke. USA. 1998. Lang.: Eng. 800
Cross-dressing and gender struggle on the early modern English stage. England. 1580-1620. Lang.: Eng. 3749

Transvestitska svatba (Transvestite Wedding)
Basic theatrical documents
Texts of plays by Vinko Möderndorfer. Slovenia. 1997. Lang.: Slo. 1458

Trap, The
SEE ALSO
Pułapka.
Audience
George Pierce Baker's 47 Workshop and the construction of the audience. USA: Cambridge, MA. 1918-1924. Lang.: Eng. 159

Trappa Ned, En (Gothenburg)
Performance/production
Conference on theatre for children ages 2-4. Sweden: Stockholm. 1998. Lang.: Swe. 2368

Trask, Stephen
Performance/production
Musical performances on and off Broadway. USA: New York. 1998. Lang.: Ger. 4383

Tratos de Argel, Los (Commerce in Algiers)
Plays/librettos/scripts
Life and career of dramatist Miguel de Cervantes. Spain. 1547-1616. Lang.: Eng. 3372

Traveller Returned, The
Plays/librettos/scripts
Judith Sargent Murray's *Traveller Returned* and its source. USA. 1771-1796. Lang.: Eng. 3672

Traverse Theatre (Edinburgh)
Performance spaces
Profile of Traverse Theatre. UK-Scotland: Edinburgh. 1998. Lang.: Eng. 462

Traviata, La
Performance/production
Background material on Metropolitan Opera radio broadcast performances. USA: New York, NY. 1998. Lang.: Eng. 4716
Plays/librettos/scripts
The inspiration for Dumas *fils*' Marguerite Gautier and Verdi's Violetta. France. Italy. 1848-1853. Lang.: Eng. 4789

Travis, Bayla
Performance/production
Collection of newspaper reviews by London theatre critics. UK-England: London. 1998. Lang.: Eng. 2425

Travis, David
Design/technology
Set design for Chain Lightning Theatre's production of *Beyond the Horizon* by Eugene O'Neill. USA: New York, NY. 1998. Lang.: Eng. 1551

Treadwell, Sophie
Plays/librettos/scripts
The Broadway success of women playwrights. USA. 1906-1944. Lang.: Eng. 3590

Tree, Herbert Beerbohm
Design/technology
The original stage machinery designed by John White at Her Majesty's Theatre. UK-England: London. 1887-1986. Lang.: Eng. 1528

Tréfás, György
Performance/production
Interview with bass György Tréfás. Hungary: Debrecen. 1931-1998. Lang.: Hun. 4641

Trelawny of the 'Wells'
Plays/librettos/scripts
Analysis of plays by Arthur Wing Pinero. UK-England. 1890-1910. Lang.: Eng. 3440

Tremblay, Larry
Plays/librettos/scripts
Analysis of works by Larry Tremblay. Canada: Montreal, PQ. 1995-1998. Lang.: Fre. 2804

Tremblay, Michel
Performance/production
Collection of newspaper reviews by London theatre critics. UK-England: London. 1998. Lang.: Eng. 2530
Plays/librettos/scripts
Michel Tremblay's adaptation of *Mistero Buffo* by Dario Fo. Canada: Montreal, PQ. 1969-1973. Lang.: Fre. 2795

Trembling Game, The
Performance/production
Collection of newspaper reviews by London theatre critics. UK-England: London. 1998. Lang.: Eng. 2481

Tres diamantes y una mujer (Three Diamonds and One Woman)
Basic theatrical documents
French translation of *Tres diamantes y una mujer (Three Diamonds and One Woman)* by Alejandro Casona. Spain. France. 1959-1998. Lang.: Fre. 1464

Trestle at Pope Lick Creek, The
Performance/production
Reviews of Actors' Theatre productions. USA: Louisville, KY. 1998. Lang.: Eng. 2727

Trettenero, Patrick
Performance/production
Collection of newspaper reviews by London theatre critics. UK-England: London. 1998. Lang.: Eng. 2553

Tri devuški v golubom (Three Girls in Blue)
Performance/production
German productions of contemporary Russian drama. Germany. 1998. Lang.: Ger. 1984

Tri sestry (Three Sisters)
Basic theatrical documents
Catalan translations of the complete plays of Anton Čechov. Russia. 1884-1904. Lang.: Cat. 1449
Institutions
Moscow Art Theatre's production of Čechov's *Tri sestry (Three Sisters)*. Russia: Moscow. 1901-1998. Lang.: Eng. 1713

***Tri sestry (Three Sisters)* — cont'd**

Performance/production
Two Hungarian productions of Čechov's *Tri sestry (Three Sisters).* Hungary: Veszprém, Szeged. 1998. Lang.: Hun. 2135
Productions of international Čechov festival. Russia: Moscow. 1998. Lang.: Swe. 2306
Collection of newspaper reviews by London theatre critics. UK-England: Stratford, Birmingham. 1998. Lang.: Eng. 2536
Career of director Lynne Meadow. USA: New York, NY. 1972-1985. Lang.: Eng. 2708
Plays/librettos/scripts
Recognition in plays of Čechov, Shakespeare, and Beckett. England. France. Russia. 1596-1980. Lang.: Eng. 2949
Translations of Čechov's *Three Sisters* and Gorkij's *The Lower Depths.* Russia. 1901-1902. Lang.: Rus. 3326
Linguistic questions in Čechov's *Tri sestry (Three Sisters).* Russia. 1901. Lang.: Rus. 3331
The Break of Day, Timberlake Wertenbaker's adaptation of Čechov's *Three Sisters.* UK-England. Russia. 1901-1995. Lang.: Eng. 3510

Tri-Cities Opera (Binghamton, NY)
Institutions
Profile of Tri-Cities Opera. USA: Binghamton, NY. 1949-1998. Lang.: Eng. 4490

Trial of Dedan Kimathi, The
Plays/librettos/scripts
Playwright Ngugi wa Thiong'o and the Kamirithu theatre project. Kenya: Kamiriithu. 1979-1992. Lang.: Eng. 3266

Trial of Ezra Pound, The
Performance/production
Creating the role of Julien Davis Cornell in *The Trial of Ezra Pound.* USA: Long Beach, CA. 1997. Lang.: Eng. 2712

Trial, The
Performance/production
Collection of newspaper reviews by London theatre critics. UK-England: London. 1998. Lang.: Eng. 2487

Trials of Brother Jero, The
Plays/librettos/scripts
Political satire in the plays of Wole Soyinka. Nigeria. 1960-1979. Lang.: Eng. 3284

Triana, José
Performance/production
Collection of newspaper reviews by London theatre critics. UK-England: London. 1998. Lang.: Eng. 2450

Trianon Theater (Vienna)
Plays/librettos/scripts
A private performance of *Die Büchse der Pandora (Pandora's Box)* by Frank Wedekind. Austria: Vienna. 1905. Lang.: Fre. 2783

Tribadernas natt (Night of the Tribades, The)
Performance/production
Reviews of two plays by Per Olov Enquist. Hungary: Budapest. 1998. Lang.: Hun. 2089

Trickster's Payback
Performance/production
Collection of newspaper reviews by London theatre critics. UK-England: London. 1998. Lang.: Eng. 2515

Tricycle Theatre (London)
Performance/production
Collection of newspaper reviews by London theatre critics. UK-England: London. 1998. Lang.: Eng. 2411
Collection of newspaper reviews by London theatre critics. UK-England: London. 1998. Lang.: Eng. 2419
Collection of newspaper reviews by London theatre critics. UK-England: London. 1998. Lang.: Eng. 2453
Collection of newspaper reviews by London theatre critics. UK-England: London. 1998. Lang.: Eng. 2460
Collection of newspaper reviews by London theatre critics. UK-England: London. 1998. Lang.: Eng. 2509
Collection of newspaper reviews by London theatre critics. UK-England: London. 1998. Lang.: Eng. 2532
Collection of newspaper reviews by London theatre critics. UK-England: London. 1998. Lang.: Eng. 2548
Collection of newspaper reviews by London theatre critics. UK-England: London. 1998. Lang.: Eng. 2572

Trier, Lars von
Plays/librettos/scripts
Interview with playwright Peter Asmussen. Denmark: Copenhagen. 1989-1998. Lang.: Swe. 2853

Trilogia della villeggiatura (Holiday Trilogy)
Performance/production
Excerpts from the notebooks of director Massimo Castri. Italy: Prato. 1996. Lang.: Ita. 2162
Plays/librettos/scripts
The character Giacinta in Goldoni's *Trilogia della villeggiatura (Holiday Trilogy).* Italy: Venice. 1761. Lang.: Ita. 3221
Analysis of *Trilogia della villeggiatura (Holiday Trilogy)* by Carlo Goldoni. Italy. 1751-1761. Lang.: Ita. 3236

Trinity Repertory Company (Providence, RI)
Performance/production
Comparison of productions of Ibsen's *Peer Gynt.* USA: Providence, RI, New York, NY, Washington, DC, Nacogdoches, TX. 1998. Lang.: Eng. 2711

Triple-A Plowed Under
Performance/production
Productions of the Federal Theatre Project's Living Newspapers. USA: New York, NY. 1935-1939. Lang.: Eng. 643

Tristan Bates Theatre (London)
Performance/production
Collection of newspaper reviews by London theatre critics. UK-England: London. 1998. Lang.: Eng. 2432
Collection of newspaper reviews by London theatre critics. UK-England: London. 1998. Lang.: Eng. 2491
Collection of newspaper reviews by London theatre critics. UK-England: London. 1998. Lang.: Eng. 2525

Tristan und Isolde
Design/technology
Interview with set designer Lennart Mörk. Sweden: Stockholm. France: Paris. 1958-1998. Lang.: Swe. 222
Scenographer Lennart Mörk. Sweden: Stockholm. France: Paris. 1957-1998. Lang.: Swe. 4439
Technical designs for *Tristan und Isolde* at Seattle Opera. USA: Seattle, WA. 1998. Lang.: Eng. 4444
Performance/production
Productions of Wagner's *Tristan und Isolde* by Peter Konwitschny and Werner Schroeter. Germany: Munich, Duisberg. 1998. Lang.: Ger. 4580

Triumph of Capitalism, The
Institutions
The political performance aesthetic of Bread and Puppet Theatre. USA: Plainfield, VT. 1991. Lang.: Eng. 4879

Troádes (Trojan Women, The)
Performance/production
Twentieth-century productions of Euripidean tragedy. USA. 1915-1969. Lang.: Eng. 2678
Plays/librettos/scripts
Adaptations of Greek tragedy by contemporary Irish writers. Ireland. UK-Ireland. 1984-1998. Lang.: Eng. 3214

Troilus and Cressida
Administration
Theater Basel under the direction of Stefan Bachmann. Switzerland: Basel. 1996-1998. Lang.: Ger. 1391
Institutions
Productions by Stefan Bachmann and Robert Wilson at the Salzburg Festival. Austria: Salzburg. 1998. Lang.: Hun. 1570
Productions of Salzburger Festspiele. Austria: Salzburg. 1998. Lang.: Ger. 1571
Performance/production
Stefan Bachmann's production of Shakespeare's *Troilus and Cressida.* Switzerland: Basle. 1998. Lang.: Ger. 2399
Collection of newspaper reviews by London theatre critics. UK-England: London. 1998. Lang.: Eng. 2418
Collection of newspaper reviews by London theatre critics. UK-England: London. 1998. Lang.: Eng. 2538
Plays/librettos/scripts
Treachery and the language of the marketplace in Shakespeare's *Troilus and Cressida.* England. 1601-1602. Lang.: Eng. 2863
The perception of self in Shakespeare's *Troilus and Cressida.* England. 1601-1602. Lang.: Eng. 2892
Analysis of *Troilus and Cressida* and *Measure for Measure* by William Shakespeare. England. 1601-1604. Lang.: Ita. 3012

Trois Dumas, Les
Plays/librettos/scripts
Analysis of *Les Trois Dumas* by Charles Smith. USA. 1998. Lang.: Eng. 3715

Troisi, Massimo
Performance/production
Humorous anecdotes by actor/director Massimo Troisi. Italy. 1953-1994. Lang.: Ita. 3858

Trojahn, Manfred
Performance/production
Interview with opera composer Manfred Trojahn. Germany: Munich. 1998. Lang.: Ger. 4582
Trojan Games
Performance/production
New productions of Győri Balett. Hungary: Budapest. 1998. Lang.: Hun. 1095
Trojan Women a Love Story, The
Basic theatrical documents
Collection of plays by Charles L. Mee. USA. 1986-1995. Lang.: Eng. 1496
Trojan Women, The by Euripides
SEE
Troádes.
Trolle, Lothar
Institutions
Profile of Württembergische Landesbühne. Germany: Esslingen. 1996-1997. Lang.: Ger. 1639
Performance/production
Recent productions of Deutsches Schauspielhaus. Germany: Hamburg. 1998. Lang.: Ger. 2034
Trollflöjten (Magic Flute, The)
Plays/librettos/scripts
The reciprocal influence of opera and film. Europe. North America. 1904-1994. Lang.: Eng. 4770
Trommeln in der Nacht (Drums in the Night)
Basic theatrical documents
Catalan translations of plays by Bertolt Brecht (volume 1). Germany. 1919-1954. Lang.: Cat. 1437
Performance/production
French productions of German plays. France. 1998. Lang.: Ger. 1935
Plays/librettos/scripts
Recent German productions of Brecht's plays. Germany. 1998. Lang.: Ger. 3150
Trøndelag Teater (Trondheim)
Performance spaces
Stage technology and equipment of Trøndelag Teater. Norway: Trondheim. 1997. Lang.: Nor. 454
The new theatre building of Trøndelag Teater. Norway: Trondheim. 1994. Lang.: Swe. 455
Trøndelag Teater's new building. Norway: Trondheim. 1997. Lang.: Nor. 456
Tropicana (Havana)
Performance/production
The Tropicana night club show. Cuba: Havana. 1939. Lang.: Swe. 4120
Trouble in Mind
Plays/librettos/scripts
Black self-determination in the plays of Alice Childress. USA. 1949-1969. Lang.: Eng. 3579
Troughton, David
Performance/production
David Troughton on playing Shakespeare's *Richard III*. UK-England: London, Stratford. 1995-1996. Lang.: Eng. 2642
Trovatore, Il
Performance/production
Verdi's important mezzo soprano roles, including Azucena in *Il Trovatore*. Italy. 1853. Lang.: Eng. 4661
Background material on Metropolitan Opera radio broadcast performances. USA: New York, NY. 1998. Lang.: Eng. 4713
Plays/librettos/scripts
The character Azucena in Verdi's *Il Trovatore*. Italy. 1853-1998. Lang.: Eng. 4808
True Tragedy of Richard III
Plays/librettos/scripts
The depiction of Jane Shore in the anonymous *True Tragedy of Richard III*. England. 1540-1594. Lang.: Eng. 2885
True West
Plays/librettos/scripts
Female presence/absence in plays of O'Neill, Pinter, and Shepard. USA. UK-England. 1936-1985. Lang.: Eng. 3607
Language in the plays of Sam Shepard. USA. 1967-1985. Lang.: Eng. 3694
Truman Building (London)
Performance/production
Collection of newspaper reviews by London theatre critics. UK-England: London. 1998. Lang.: Eng. 2493
Truman Show, The
Design/technology
Lighting design for Peter Weir's film *The Truman Show*. USA. 1998. Lang.: Eng. 3919
Trumbo, Dalton
Basic theatrical documents
Screenplay of *The Fishermen of Beaudrais* by Ring Lardner, Jr., and Dalton Trumbo. USA. 1943-1998. Lang.: Eng. 3891
Plays/librettos/scripts
Interview with screenwriter Ring Lardner, Jr. USA. 1943. Lang.: Eng. 3998
Profile of screenwriter Dalton Trumbo. USA. 1905-1976. Lang.: Eng. 3999
Background on *The Fishermen of Beaudrais* by Ring Lardner, Jr., and Dalton Trumbo. USA. 1943-1998. Lang.: Eng. 4025
Trupa Wileńska (Vilna)
Institutions
Jakub Rotbaum's leadership of Trupa Wileńska. Poland: Vilna. 1929-1938. Lang.: Pol. 1686
Truškin, Leonid
Performance/production
Director Leonid Truškin. Russia: Moscow. 1998. Lang.: Rus. 2233
Trust, De (Amsterdam)
Institutions
Profile of the young theatre company De Trust. Netherlands: Amsterdam. 1995-1998. Lang.: Dut. 1678
Tsao, Andrew
Design/technology
Karen TenEyck's projections for a site-specific production of Shakespeare's *Julius Caesar*. USA: Los Angeles, CA. 1998. Lang.: Eng. 1552
Tsoi, Hardy
Relation to other fields
Theatre and politics in Hong Kong. Hong Kong. 1984-1996. Lang.: Eng. 3772
Tsvetaeva, Marina
SEE
Cvetajeva, Marina.
Tsypin, George
Design/technology
Creativity and beauty in theatrical design. USA. 1998. Lang.: Eng. 322
Tu man hand (In Private)
Performance/production
Interview with Bengt Andersson, artistic director of Teater Tre. Sweden. 1983-1998. Lang.: Swe. 601
Tubes
Design/technology
Sound design for Blue Man Group's Chicago production of *Tubes*. USA: Chicago, IL. 1996-1997. Lang.: Eng. 261
Tucci, Stanley
Design/technology
Technical designs for Stanley Tucci's film *The Impostors*. USA. 1998. Lang.: Eng. 3901
Tucker, Sharon Gayle
Basic theatrical documents
Text of Sharon Gayle Tucker's *S.T.C.* USA. 1988. Lang.: Eng. 1512
Tudor theatre
Performance/production
Music in Tudor drama. England. 1497-1569. Lang.: Eng. 1902
Plays/librettos/scripts
Lucian's *Icaromenippus* as a source for Heywood's *The Play of the Wether*. England. 1533. Lang.: Eng. 2920
Tudor, Anthony
Performance/production
Interviews with dancers about performance. UK-England. USA. Cuba. 1942-1989. Lang.: Eng. 1162
Tugomer, ali tisti, ki meri žalost (Tugomer, or the One Who Measures Sadness)
Basic theatrical documents
Plays and screenplays by Vili Ravnjak. Slovenia. 1991-1997. Lang.: Slo. 1460
Tuminas, Rimas
Performance/production
Collection of newspaper reviews by London theatre critics. UK-England: London, Stratford, Derby. 1998. Lang.: Eng. 2417
Turandot
Design/technology
Sound system used in a soccer stadium for an operatic production. Italy: Rome. 1998. Lang.: Eng. 4434
Performance/production
Rural Chinese productions of Puccini's *Turandot*. China, People's Republic of: Beijing. 1998. Lang.: Eng. 4541

***Turandot* — cont'd**

A production of Puccini's *Turandot* in Beijing. China, People's Republic of: Beijing. 1998. Lang.: Eng. 4542

Turba, Ctibor

Performance/production

Ctibor Turba and his mime theatre Alfred ve dvoře. Czech Republic. 1966-1998. Lang.: Eng, Fre. 4086

Turgenjév, Ivan Sergejévič

Performance/production

Turgenjév's *Mesjac v derevne (A Month in the Country)* directed by Zoltán Lendvar. Hungary: Kecskemét. 1998. Lang.: Hun. 2134

Collection of newspaper reviews by London theatre critics. UK-England. 1998. Lang.: Eng. 2558

Turista, La

Plays/librettos/scripts

National identity in plays of Sam Shepard. USA. 1965-1995. Lang.: Eng. 3545

Turn of the Screw, The

Performance/production

The current state of opera in England. UK-England. 1997. Lang.: Eng. 4705

Operas by Benjamin Britten in the repertory of the Metropolitan and the New York City Opera. USA: New York, NY. 1945-1998. Lang.:Eng. 4749

Turneja (Journey, A)

Plays/librettos/scripts

Contemporary drama of the former Yugoslavia in its political context. Yugoslavia. 1991-1998. Lang.: Ger. 3721

Tusa, John

Administration

Interview with John Tusa, managing director of the Barbican Centre. UK-England: London. 1996-1998. Lang.: Eng. 24

Tusen och en Natt (Thousand and One Nights, A)

Institutions

Interview with Rolf Sossna of En Annan Teater. Sweden: Gothenburg. 1992-1998. Lang.: Swe. 1734

Tushingham, David

Performance/production

Collection of newspaper reviews by London theatre critics. UK-England: London. 1998. Lang.: Eng. 2514

Twain, Mark (Clemens, Samuel)

Theory/criticism

Marginalia in Sir George Greenwood's copy of *Is Shakespeare Dead?* by Mark Twain. USA. 1909. Lang.: Eng. 863

Twelfth Night

Design/technology

Lighting design for Shakespeare's *Twelfth Night* at the Vivian Beaumont. USA: New York, NY. 1998. Lang.: Eng. 1546

The design concept for Nicholas Hytner's production of Shakespeare's *Twelfth Night*. USA: New York, NY. 1998. Lang.: Eng. 1556

Performance/production

Director Jacques Copeau and his theatrical aesthetic. France. 1913-1920. Lang.: Eng. 1941

Shakespearean productions in northern Germany. Germany: Hamburg. 1996-1997. Lang.: Ger. 1978

Productions of Shakespeare's *Twelfth Night* at the Madrid Theatre Festival. Spain: Madrid. 1996-1997. Lang.: Eng. 2359

Collection of newspaper reviews by London theatre critics. UK-England. 1998. Lang.: Eng. 2485

Collection of newspaper reviews by London theatre critics. UK-England: London. 1998. Lang.: Eng. 2496

The evolution of the character Feste in productions of Shakespeare's *Twelfth Night*. UK-England. 1773-1988. Lang.: Eng. 2611

An approach to playing Malvolio in Shakespeare's *Twelfth Night*. USA. 1987. Lang.: Eng. 2659

Interview with opera composer Manfred Trojahn. Germany: Munich. 1998. Lang.: Ger. 4582

Plays/librettos/scripts

French translations of Shakespeare by Antonine Maillet and Jean-Louis Roux. Canada: Montreal, PQ. 1988-1993. Lang.: Fre. 2793

Hermeneutic analysis of Shakespearean comedies. England. 1590-1608. Lang.: Eng. 2877

Female power and the public sphere in Renaissance drama. England. 1597-1616. Lang.: Eng. 2943

Regeneration in plays of Shakespeare. England. 1598-1613. Lang.: Eng. 2968

Malvolio's riddle in Shakespeare's *Twelfth Night*, II.5. England. 1600-1601. Lang.: Eng. 3025

Relation to other fields

A possible model for characters in Shakespeare's *Twelfth Night* and 'Venus and Adonis'. England. 1590-1593. Lang.: Eng. 3746

Twelve Angry Men

Plays/librettos/scripts

Theatrical activities of Harold Pinter. UK-England: London. 1996-1998. Lang.: Eng. 3462

Twenty-Seven Wagons Full of Cotton

Plays/librettos/scripts

Tennessee Williams's short story *Twenty-Seven Wagons Full of Cotton* and the plays based on it. USA. 1936-1979. Lang.: Eng. 3622

Twilight of the Gods, The

SEE

Götterdämmerung.

Twist, Basil

Design/technology

Lighting design for Basil Twist's puppet production *Symphonie Fantastique*. USA: New York, NY. 1998. Lang.: Eng. 4867

Performance/production

Basil Twist's puppetry interpretation of Berlioz's *Symphonie Fantastique*. USA: New York, NY. 1998. Lang.: Eng. 4904

Two

Performance/production

Collection of newspaper reviews by London theatre critics. UK-England: London. 1998. Lang.: Eng. 2450

Two Gentlemen of Verona, The

Performance/production

Collection of newspaper reviews by London theatre critics. UK-England: Stratford. 1998. Lang.: Eng. 2431

Collection of newspaper reviews by London theatre critics. UK-England: London. 1998. Lang.: Eng. 2551

Two Way Mirror Theatre (London)

Performance/production

Collection of newspaper reviews by London theatre critics. UK-England: London. 1998. Lang.: Eng. 2530

Two-Character Play, The

Plays/librettos/scripts

Dramaturgical analysis of late plays of Tennessee Williams. USA. 1969-1978. Lang.: Eng. 3661

Metadrama in plays of Tennessee Williams. USA. 1944-1978. Lang.: Eng. 3686

Tyc, Petr

Performance/production

Choreographers Monika Rebcová, Petr Tyc, and Petr Zuska. Czech Republic: Prague. 1997. Lang.: Eng, Fre. 1266

Tyler, David

Performance/production

Collection of newspaper reviews by London theatre critics. UK-England: London. 1998. Lang.: Eng. 2513

Tyler, Royall

Performance/production

Collection of newspaper reviews by London theatre critics. UK-England: London. 1998. Lang.: Eng. 2507

Tyndale, William

Performance/production

Collection of newspaper reviews by London theatre critics. UK-England: London. 1998. Lang.: Eng. 2554

Tyrannick Love

Basic theatrical documents

Analysis of Smock Alley promptbook for Dryden's *Tyrannick Love*. Ireland: Dublin. 1669-1684. Lang.: Eng. 1439

U agoniji (In Agony)

Performance/production

Krleža's *U agoniji (In Agony)* directed by Péter Valló. Hungary: Budapest. 1998. Lang.: Hun. 2074

U potpalublju (In the Camp)

Plays/librettos/scripts

Contemporary drama of the former Yugoslavia in its political context. Yugoslavia. 1991-1998. Lang.: Ger. 3721

Ubu & the Truth Commission

Plays/librettos/scripts

Analysis of *Ubu & the Truth Commission*, a puppet play by William Kentridge. South Africa, Republic of. 1997. Lang.: Eng. 4913

Ubu déchaîné (Ubu Unchained)

Basic theatrical documents

Text of *Ubu déchaîné (Ubu Unchained)* by Richard Demarcy. Benin. France. 1998. Lang.: Fre. 4287

Ubu Kunst

Performance/production

Collection of newspaper reviews by London theatre critics. UK-England: London. 1998. Lang.: Eng. 2478

Ubu Roi (King Ubu)
Design/technology
The work of scene designer Libor Fára. Czech Republic: Prague. 1950-1981. Lang.: Cze. 1518
Performance/production
Semiotic analysis of Jarry's *Ubu Roi* as staged by Vitez. France: Paris. 1985. Lang.: Eng. 528
Collection of newspaper reviews by London theatre critics. UK-England: London. 1998. Lang.: Eng. 2478
Plays/librettos/scripts
Absurdism in children's theatre. North America. Europe. 1896-1970. Lang.: Eng. 3288
Udall, Nicholas
Performance/production
Music in Tudor drama. England. 1497-1569. Lang.: Eng. 1902
Uddenberg, Erik
Performance/production
Stockholm's children's theatre scene. Sweden: Stockholm. 1998. Lang.: Ger. 2389
Ugly Duckling, The
Performance/production
Collection of newspaper reviews by London theatre critics. UK-England: London. 1998. Lang.: Eng. 2556
Ugly Rumours
Performance/production
Collection of newspaper reviews by London theatre critics. UK-England: London. 1998. Lang.: Eng. 2532
Uhrik, Dóra
Institutions
Dance training at Pécs School of the Arts. Hungary: Pécs. 1975-1998. Lang.: Hun. 1043
Interview with ballet teacher Dóra Uhrik. Hungary: Pécs. 1978-1998. Lang.: Hun. 1045
Uhry, Alfred
Design/technology
Lighting designer Kenneth Posner. USA. 1998. Lang.: Eng. 1545
Uitdehaag, Antoine
Performance/production
Productions of Tankred Dorst's *Was sollen wir tun (What Shall We Do)*. Germany: Dresden, Bonn. 1997-1998. Lang.: Ger. 1971
Új Színház (Budapest)
Institutions
The change of management at Új Színház. Hungary: Budapest. 1994-1998. Lang.: Hun. 358
Performance/production
Review of Molnár's *Az üvegcipő (The Glass Slipper)*, Új Színház. Hungary: Budapest. 1997. Lang.: Hun. 2094
Two productions of Csokonai Vitéz's *Karnyóné és a két szeleburdiak (Mrs. Karnyó and the Two Feather-Brains)*. Hungary: Budapest. 1998. Lang.: Hun. 2113
Interview with directors Gábor Székely and Eszter Novák. Hungary: Budapest. 1998. Lang.: Hun. 2128
Two Hungarian productions of *Die Dreigroschenoper (The Three Penny Opera)*. Hungary: Budapest, Szeged. 1998. Lang.: Hun. 4362
Újvidéki Színház (Novi Sad)
Institutions
History of annual festival of Hungarian-language theatre. Hungary: Kisvárda. 1989-1998. Lang.: Hun. 1669
Plays/librettos/scripts
History of Hungarian-language theatre in the Voivodship region. Yugoslavia: Subotica, Novi Sad. 1837-1998. Lang.: Hun. 3720
Ulanova, Galina Sergejevna
Performance/production
Obituary for ballerina Galina Ulanova. Russia. 1910-1998. Lang.: Eng. 1125
Obituary for ballerina Galina Ulanova. Russia. 1910-1998. Lang.: Eng. 1127
Ballet in Sweden and the monument to Galina Ulanova. Sweden: Stockholm. 1998. 1984. Lang.: Rus. 1154
Ularu, Nic
Design/technology
The 1998 USITT expo. USA: Long Beach, CA. 1998. Lang.: Eng. 251
Ulay (Laysiepen, F. Uwe)
Performance/production
Recent collaboration of performance artists Marina Abramowič and Ulay. Europe. China, People's Republic of. 1970-1988. Lang.:Eng. 4240
Reexamination of the performance art of Beuys, Abramovič, and Ulay. USA. Germany. Netherlands. 1964-1985. Lang.: Eng. 4254
Unanswered Question, The
Performance/production
Reviews of recent opera productions. Switzerland: Basel. Germany: Stuttgart, Berlin, Hamburg. France: Strasbourg. 1997-1998. Lang.: Ger. 4702
Unblest, The
Performance/production
Collection of newspaper reviews by London theatre critics. UK-England: London. 1998. Lang.: Eng. 2443
Uncle Artur
Plays/librettos/scripts
Danny Horowitz's *Uncle Artur* and the limits of representation. Israel. 1980-1995. Lang.: Eng. 3218
Uncle Vanya
SEE
Diadia Vania.
Under the Influence
Performance/production
Collection of newspaper reviews by London theatre critics. UK-England. 1998. Lang.: Eng. 2510
Undesirable Elements
Theory/criticism
Theory and Asian-American theatre. USA: Minneapolis, MN. 1994-1995. Lang.: Eng. 869
Undine
Performance/production
Analysis of the ballet *Berthalda en Hildebrand (Berthalda and Hildebrand)*. Netherlands: Amsterdam. 1849. Lang.: Ger. 1122
Unga Klara (Stockholm)
Institutions
The quality of theatre for children and youth. Italy: Bologna. Sweden: Stockholm. Germany. 1998. Lang.: Ger. 367
Performance/production
Stockholm's children's theatre scene. Sweden: Stockholm. 1998. Lang.: Ger. 2389
Unga Teatern (Helsinki)
Institutions
The proliferation of Swedish-language theatre groups in Helsinki. Finland: Helsinki. 1990-1998. Lang.: Eng, Fre. 1604
Ungerleider, Howard
Design/technology
Howard Ungerleider's lighting design for Van Halen tour. USA. 1998. Lang.: Eng. 4105
Unicorn Theatre (London)
Performance/production
Collection of newspaper reviews by London theatre critics. UK-England: London. 1998. Lang.: Eng. 2567
Union Theatre (London)
Performance/production
Collection of newspaper reviews by London theatre critics. UK-England: London. 1998. Lang.: Eng. 2460
Collection of newspaper reviews by London theatre critics. UK-England: London. 1998. Lang.: Eng. 2524
Unions
Administration
Theatre and Equity business in the Atlanta area. USA: Atlanta, GA. 1998. Lang.: Eng. 49
Equity activity in central Texas. USA: Austin, TX, San Antonio, TX. 1998. Lang.: Eng. 50
Negotiations between US and Canadian Equity. USA. Canada. 1998. Lang.: Eng. 54
Equity agreement on New Orleans working conditions. USA: New Orleans, LA. 1998. Lang.: Eng. 63
Changes in Equity's health insurance coverage. USA: New York, NY. 1998. Lang.: Eng. 65
Effect on Actors Federal Credit Unions of a recent Supreme Court ruling. USA: New York, NY. 1998. Lang.: Eng. 67
Report on credit union legislation. USA: New York, NY. 1998. Lang.: Eng. 70
Record of Equity Council vote. USA: New York, NY. 1998. Lang.: Eng. 71
Interview with actors on Equity. USA: New York, NY. 1998. Lang.: Eng. 75
Annual report of the Equity pension fund. USA: New York, NY. 1998. Lang.: Eng. 81
Effect of recent legislation on the Actors Federal Credit Union. USA: New York, NY. 1998. Lang.: Eng. 83

Unions — cont'd

Equity's Stage Reading Guidelines. USA: New York, NY. 1998. Lang.: Eng. 85
Changes in Equity's bonding policy for regional theatres. USA: New York, NY. 1998. Lang.: Eng. 86
The debate on organizing non-union tours of theatrical production. USA: New York, NY. 1998. Lang.: Eng. 88
Current news on the theatre and Equity business. USA: New York, NY. 1998. Lang.: Eng. 90
The waiting period before Equity health benefits take effect. USA: New York, NY. 1998. Lang.: Eng. 91
Equity's National Council elections. USA: New York, NY. 1998. Lang.: Eng. 94
Equity's approval of a contract for the Chicago area. USA: Chicago, IL. 1998. Lang.: Eng. 98
The merger plan of the Screen Actors Guild and the American Federation of Television and Radio Artists. USA: New York, NY. 1998. Lang.: Eng. 102
Equity's casting website. USA: New York, NY. 1998. Lang.: Eng. 103
The loss of medical coverage for Equity dependents over nineteen years of age. USA: New York, NY. 1998. Lang.: Eng. 105
Equity debate on member behavior when not under Equity contract. USA: New York, NY. 1998. Lang.: Eng. 106
Equity's approval of Cabaret and Small Professional Theatre contracts. USA: New York, NY. 1998. Lang.: Eng. 108
Survey of Equity membership and employment data. USA: New York, NY. 1998. Lang.: Eng. 115
The creation of Actors' Equity in response to abusive working conditions. USA: New York, NY. 1913. Lang.: Eng. 127
Interview with Tomas Bolme, director of the Swedish actors' union. Sweden: Stockholm. 1970-1998. Lang.: Swe. 1388
Equity Executive Director Alan Eisenberg's experience with a touring production of *Cats*. USA: New York, NY. 1998. Lang.: Eng. 4318
Performer Rebecca Spencer's experience as an Equity Deputy. USA: New York, NY. 1998. Lang.: Eng. 4320
Marketing strategies for puppetry in film and TV. USA. 1998. Lang.: Eng. 4863

Performance/production
Equity's free seminar series for young performers and their families. USA: New York, NY. 1998. Lang.: Eng. 657

United States Institute for Theatre Technology (USITT)
Design/technology
Guidelines for a lighting design portfolio. USA. 1998. Lang.: Eng. 249
USITT membership directory. USA. 1998-1999. Lang.: Eng. 250
The 1998 USITT expo. USA: Long Beach, CA. 1998. Lang.: Eng. 251
Imero Fiorentino, USITT's most distinguished lighting designer of 1997. USA. 1998. Lang.: Eng. 291
Report on annual USITT conference. USA: Long Beach, CA. 1998. Lang.: Eng. 302

Universal Ballet (Seoul)
Institutions
Profile of Universal Ballet Company. South Korea: Seoul. 1998. Lang.: Eng. 1047

Universe (i.e., How It Works), The
Relation to other fields
Quantum theory in recent New York performances. USA: New York, NY. 1995-1996. Lang.: Eng. 794

Universitas (Budapest)
Performance/production
Interview with director József Ruszt. Hungary. 1963-1997. Lang.: Hun. 2115

Unruh, Walther
Design/technology
Walther Unruh and German theatre technology. Germany. 1898-1998. Lang.: Ger. 187

Untitled Flesh
Plays/librettos/scripts
Analysis of *Untitled Flesh* by Sacred Naked Nature Girls. USA: Los Angeles, CA. 1994-1997. Lang.: Eng. 4262

Untouchables, The
Plays/librettos/scripts
Opera in American gangster films. USA. 1932-1990. Lang.: Eng. 4023

Uotinen, Jorma
Institutions
New artistic goals of the Finnish National Ballet. Finland: Helsinki. 1992-1998. Lang.: Eng. 1037

Upor, László
Performance/production
A Hungarian view of the New York theatre scene. USA: New York, NY. 1997-1998. Lang.: Hun. 677

Upper Campfield Market Theatre (Manchester)
Performance/production
Collection of newspaper reviews by London theatre critics. UK-England: Leeds, Manchester. 1998. Lang.: Eng. 2433

Upstairs at the Gatehouse (London)
Performance/production
Collection of newspaper reviews by London theatre critics. UK-England: London. 1998. Lang.: Eng. 2481
Collection of newspaper reviews by London theatre critics. UK-England: London. 1998. Lang.: Eng. 2516
Collection of newspaper reviews by London theatre critics. UK-England: London. 1998. Lang.: Eng. 2531
Collection of newspaper reviews by London theatre critics. UK-England: London. 1998. Lang.: Eng. 2555

Upstairs at the Landor (London)
Performance/production
Collection of newspaper reviews by London theatre critics. UK-England: London. 1998. Lang.: Eng. 2412
Collection of newspaper reviews by London theatre critics. UK-England: London. 1998. Lang.: Eng. 2516

Upton, Judy
Performance/production
Collection of newspaper reviews by London theatre critics. UK-England: London. 1998. Lang.: Eng. 2427
Collection of newspaper reviews by London theatre critics. UK-England: London. 1998. Lang.: Eng. 2446

Urban Trauma
Performance/production
Collection of newspaper reviews by London theatre critics. UK-England: London. 1998. Lang.: Eng. 2429

Urbinati, Rob
Design/technology
Derek McLane's set designs for recent Off Broadway productions. USA: New York, NY. 1998. Lang.: Eng. 1538

Uren, Helena
Performance/production
Collection of newspaper reviews by London theatre critics. UK-England: London. 1998. Lang.: Eng. 2463
Collection of newspaper reviews by London theatre critics. UK-England: London. 1998. Lang.: Eng. 2570

Urfaust
Performance/production
Recent productions of Bochumer Schauspielhaus. Germany: Bochum. 1998. Lang.: Ger. 2009

Ursula: Fear of the Estuary
Performance/production
Collection of newspaper reviews by London theatre critics. UK-England. 1998. Lang.: Eng. 2504

Utolsó kontrasztok (Last Contrasts)
Performance/production
Utolsó kontrasztok (Last Contrasts) choreographed by István Orsovszky. Hungary: Zalaegerszeg. 1998. Lang.: Hun. 1295

Uvažaemyj tovarišč M.M. Zoščenko (Respected M.M. Zoščenko, The)
Plays/librettos/scripts
V.V. Zoščenko on his play, *Uvažaemyj tovarišč M.M. Zoščenko (The Respected M.M. Zoščenko)*. Russia. 1998. Lang.: Rus. 3340

Üvegcipő, Az (Glass Slipper, The)
Performance/production
Review of Molnár's *Az üvegcipő (The Glass Slipper)*, Új Színház. Hungary: Budapest. 1997. Lang.: Hun. 2094

Uys, Pieter-Dirk
Performance/production
Collection of newspaper reviews by London theatre critics. UK-England: London. 1998. Lang.: Eng. 2411

V Čičikovskoj krugoverti (In Čičikov's Chaos)
Performance/production
Pëtr Fomenko's theatrical adaptation of Gogol's *Dead Souls*. Russia: Moscow. 1998. Lang.: Rus. 2303
Pëtr Fomenko's production of *V Čičikovskoj krugoverti (In Čičikov's Chaos)*. Russia: Moscow. 1998. Lang.: Rus. 2340

V kruge pervom (First Circle, The)
Performance/production
Jurij Ljubimov's production of *The First Circle*, based on Solženicin's novel. Russia: Moscow. 1998. Lang.: Rus. 2270

Va-et-vient (Come and Go)
Plays/librettos/scripts
Operatic adaptations of Beckett's plays by Heinz Holliger. Europe. 1976-1988. Lang.: Eng. 4776

Väänänen, Kari
Performance/production
Interview with acting teacher Kari Väänänen. Finland. 1998. Lang.: Fin. 1918

Vachtangov, Jévgenij Bogrationovič
Institutions
Report on Vachtangov School conference. Russia: Moscow. 1990-1998. Lang.: Rus. 380
Performance/production
Acting and directing influences on Eugenio Barba. Denmark: Holstebro. 1997. Lang.: Eng. 1886

Vacis, Gabriele
Performance/production
Laura Curano's solo piece *Olivetti*. Italy: Calabria. 1998. Lang.: Eng. 2156

Vagabondage
Performance/production
Collection of newspaper reviews by London theatre critics. UK-England: London. 1998. Lang.: Eng. 2584

Vaja zbora (Choir Practice)
Basic theatrical documents
Texts of plays by Vinko Möderndorfer. Slovenia. 1997. Lang.: Slo. 1458

Vajnonen, Vasilij
Performance/production
The Nutcracker at the Budapest Opera House. Hungary: Budapest. 1998. Lang.: Hun. 1115

Vakhtangov Theatre
SEE
Teat'r im. Je. Vachtangova.

Valdez, Luis
Plays/librettos/scripts
Analysis of *Bandido!* by Luis Valdez. USA. 1986. Lang.: Eng. 3676
Analysis of *Bandido!* by Luis Valdez. USA. 1982. Lang.: Eng. 3708

Valdivielso, José de
Plays/librettos/scripts
Allegorical dramas of Sor Marcela de San Félix. Spain. 1595-1650. Lang.: Eng. 3395

Valentines
Performance/production
Collection of newspaper reviews by London theatre critics. UK-England: London. 1998. Lang.: Eng. 2421

Valk, Kate
Performance/production
Interview with actress Kate Valk. USA: New York, NY. 1979-1998. Lang.: Eng. 2736

Valle-Inclán, Ramón María del
Plays/librettos/scripts
Translation and the plays of Valle-Inclán. Spain. 1936-1998. Lang.: Eng. 3378
The image of women on the Spanish stage. Spain. 1908-1936. Lang.: Eng. 3399

Valley Song
Plays/librettos/scripts
Post-apartheid analysis of plays by Athol Fugard. South Africa, Republic of. 1991-1998. Lang.: Eng. 3364

Vallières, Pierre
Plays/librettos/scripts
Quebecois plays about the crisis of October 1970. Canada. 1970-1990. Lang.: Fre, Eng. 2812

Valló, Péter
Performance/production
Krleža's *U agoniji (In Agony)* directed by Péter Valló. Hungary: Budapest. 1998. Lang.: Hun. 2074
One-act comedies by Čechov directed by Péter Valló. Hungary: Dunaújváros. 1998. Lang.: Hun. 2080
Péter Valló's production of *Iphigéneia he en Aulide (Iphigenia in Aulis)* by Euripides. Hungary: Budapest. 1998. Lang.: Hun. 2132

Valpurzina noc (Walpurgis Night)
Performance/production
Productions of plays by Koljada and Jerofejév at Csiky Gergely Theatre. Hungary: Kaposvár. 1998. Lang.: Hun. 2149

Valverde, José
Basic theatrical documents
Text of *Le Vampire suce toujours deux fois (The Vampire Always Sucks Twice)* by Victor Haïm. France. 1998. Lang.: Fre. 1427

Vampilov, Aleksand'r Valentinovič
Plays/librettos/scripts
Analysis of plays by Aleksand'r Vampilov. Russia. 1998. Lang.: Rus. 3317

Vampire suce toujours deux fois, Le (Vampire Always Sucks Twice, The)
Basic theatrical documents
Text of *Le Vampire suce toujours deux fois (The Vampire Always Sucks Twice)* by Victor Haïm. France. 1998. Lang.: Fre. 1427

Vampire, The
Design/technology
Magical stage effects in 'vampire' plays. USA. 1820-1977. Lang.: Eng. 1548

van de Waterbeemd, Pieter
Design/technology
Technical effects control system used in a production of *Joe—The Musical* at Koninklijk Theater Carré. Netherlands: Amsterdam. 1998. Lang.: Eng. 4324

van Dijk, Ad
Design/technology
Technical effects control system used in a production of *Joe—The Musical* at Koninklijk Theater Carré. Netherlands: Amsterdam. 1998. Lang.: Eng. 4324

van Dijk, Koen
Design/technology
Technical effects control system used in a production of *Joe—The Musical* at Koninklijk Theater Carré. Netherlands: Amsterdam. 1998. Lang.: Eng. 4324

van Hamme, Andries Voitus
Performance/production
Analysis of the ballet *Berthalda en Hildebrand (Berthalda and Hildebrand)*. Netherlands: Amsterdam. 1849. Lang.: Ger. 1122

van Hove, Ivo
Performance/production
Collection of newspaper reviews by London theatre critics. UK-Scotland: Edinburgh. 1998. Lang.: Eng. 2650

Van Itallie, Jean-Claude
Plays/librettos/scripts
History of the Playwrights Unit. USA. 1963-1971. Lang.: Eng. 3570
Revolutionary Off Broadway playwriting. USA: New York, NY. 1959-1969. Lang.: Eng. 3604

van Lohuizen, Suzanne
Performance/production
Collection of newspaper reviews by London theatre critics. UK-England: London. 1998. Lang.: Eng. 2462

van Randwyck, Issy
Performance/production
Collection of newspaper reviews by London theatre critics. UK-England: London. 1998. Lang.: Eng. 2568

Van Tieghem, David
Design/technology
The 1998 TCI awards. USA. 1998. Lang.: Eng. 243

van Welie, Georgina
Performance/production
Collection of newspaper reviews by London theatre critics. UK-England: London. Lang.: Eng. 2408

Vance, Chris
Performance/production
Collection of newspaper reviews by London theatre critics. UK-England: London. 1998. Lang.: Eng. 2546

Vance, Nina
Performance/production
The multifaceted nature of early nonprofit regional theatre. USA. 1940-1960. Lang.: Eng. 2705

Vancouver Opera Company (Vancouver, BC)
Performance/production
Major opera houses' proposals for productions to the end of the century. USA. Canada. 1998. Lang.: Eng. 4743

Vancouver Sath (Vancouver, BC)
Institutions
Sadhu Binning on his politically-oriented theatre group Vancouver Sath. Canada: Vancouver, BC. 1972-1989. Lang.: Eng. 1577

Vándorfi, László
Performance/production
András Szigethy's *Kegyelem (Mercy)* directed by László Vándorfi. Hungary: Veszprém. 1998. Lang.: Hun. 2105
Brecht and Weill's *Die Dreigroschenoper (The Three Penny Opera)* directed by László Vándorfi. Hungary: Veszprém.1998. Lang.: Hun. 4358

Vándorfi, László — cont'd

An open-air production of *West Side Story* directed by László Vándorfi. Hungary: Veszprém. 1998. Lang.: Hun. 4361

Vanemuine (Tartu)
Institutions
Profile of Estonian theatres. Estonia: Tallin, Tartu. 1997. Lang.: Swe, Eng, Ger. 345

Vanity Fair
Performance/production
Michael Birch's production of *Vanity Fair*. UK-England: Leeds. 1997. Lang.: Eng. 2600

Vanstone, Hugh
Design/technology
Lighting designer Hugh Vanstone. USA: New York, NY. 1998. Lang.: Eng. 1554
Technical designs for the musical *Doctor Doolittle* directed by Steven Pimlott. UK-England: London. 1998. Lang.: Eng. 4325

Vanya on 42nd Street
Plays/librettos/scripts
Analysis of Louis Malle's film *Vanya on 42nd Street*. USA. 1994. Lang.: Fre. 4031

Vår Teater (Stockholm)
Institutions
Elsa Olenius and Vår Teater. Sweden: Stockholm. 1942-1980. Lang.: Swe. 1732

Variations Énigmatiques (Enigma Variations)
Theory/criticism
Analysis of plays by Eric-Emmanuel Schmitt. France. 1998. Lang.: Fin. 3819

Variety acts
Design/technology
Lighting design and equipment in various Las Vegas spaces. USA: Las Vegas, NV. 1998. Lang.: Eng. 276
Institutions
Report on a seminar on mime, illusionism, *commedia* and clowning in dance. Sweden: Stockholm. 1998. Lang.: Swe. 386
Popular entertainment at the New Haven Assembly Hall and Columbian Museum and Gardens. USA: New Haven, CT. 1796-1820. Lang.: Eng. 394
Reference materials
Index to performing arts articles in Bragaglia's *Chronache d'attualità*. Italy: Rome. 1916-1922. Lang.: Ita. 704

Várkonyi, Mátyás
Performance/production
Reviews of new Hungarian musicals. Hungary: Budapest. 1997. Lang.: Hun. 4360

Varma, Rahul
Basic theatrical documents
Excerpt from *Job Stealer* by Rahul Varma, Helen Vlachos and Ian Lloyd George. Canada: Montreal, PQ. 1998. Lang.: Eng. 1412
Institutions
Rahul Varma on his multicultural theatre company Teesri Duniya. Canada: Montreal, PQ. 1981-1998. Lang.: Eng. 1592
Plays/librettos/scripts
Political community theatre by South Indian emigrants. Canada: Toronto, ON, Montreal, PQ. India. 1984-1998. Lang.: Eng. 2821

Várszínház (Budapest)
Performance/production
Čechov's *Platonov* as adapted and directed by Erzsébet Gaál. Hungary: Budapest. 1997. Lang.: Hun. 2082
István Somogyi's productions of *Magyar Elektra* by Péter Bornemisza. Hungary: Budapest. 1988-1998. Lang.: Hun. 2114
Two productions by István Somogyi of Bornemisza's *Magyar Elektra*. Hungary: Budapest. 1988-1998. Lang.: Hun. 2148

Vasco, Eduardo
Performance/production
Eduardo Vasco's production of *Lista Negra (Black List)* by Yolanda Pallín. Spain. 1998. Lang.: Eng. 2360

Vasil'čikova, L.L.
Institutions
L.L. Vasil'čikova's amateur theatre group. France: Paris. 1930-1939. Lang.: Rus. 1616

Vasiljév, Anatolij Aleksandrovič
Design/technology
Scene design and the plays of Ostrovskij. Russia. 1998. Lang.: Rus. 1523
Institutions
A visit to Anatolij Vasiljév's School of Dramatic art. Russia: Moscow. 1998. Lang.: Hun. 1697
Performance/production
Interviews with actors on Anatolij Vasiljév's guest direction at Szigligeti Theatre. Hungary: Szolnok. 1998. Lang.: Hun. 2061
A.A. Vasiljév's production of *Bez viny vinovatjė (Guilty Though Innocent)* by Ostrovskij. Hungary: Szolnok. 1998. Lang.:Hun. 2096
Symbolism in Anatolij Vasiljév's production of *Guilty Though Innocent* by Ostrovskij. Hungary: Szolnok. 1998. Lang.: Hun. 2098
Mari Törőcsik's performance in Ostrovskij's *Guilty Though Innocent* directed by Vasiljév. Hungary: Szolnok. 1997. Lang.: Hun. 2125
Director Anatolij Vasiljév. Russia. 1942-1998. Lang.: Hun. 2282
Review of a Hungarian edition of writings by director A.A. Vasiljév. Russia: Moscow. 1998. Lang.: Hun. 2321

Vasiljév, Vladimir Viktorovič
Performance/production
Bolšoj ballet master and choreographer Vladimir Vasiljév. Russia: Moscow. 1998. Lang.: Rus. 1147

Vatermord, Der (Parricide)
Audience
Audience response to Bronnen's *Der Vatermord (Parricide)* and German culture. Germany: Frankfurt. 1922. Lang.: Eng. 1403
Plays/librettos/scripts
Social criticism in Viennese Expressionist drama. Austria: Vienna. 1907-1922. Lang.: Ger. 2779

Vaudeville
SEE ALSO
Classed Entries under MIXED ENTERTAINMENT—Variety acts.
Performance spaces
Oscar Hammerstein I and the creation and development of Times Square. USA. 1895-1915. Lang.: Eng. 463
Performance/production
Performer, writer, director Elsie Janis and the 'gay sensibility'. UK-England. 1889-1956. Lang.: Eng. 612
Female impersonation and the construction of the female stereotype. USA. 1890-1930. Lang.: Eng. 651
The influence of exhibition ballroom dance on theatrical entertainments. USA. 1910-1925. Lang.: Eng. 985
Popular entertainer Elsie Janis. USA. 1896-1941. Lang.: Eng. 4145
Vaudeville theatre on the West Coast. USA: Los Angeles, CA. 1850-1934. Lang.: Eng. 4146
Male impersonation in variety and vaudeville. USA. 1868-1930. Lang.: Eng. 4281
Plays/librettos/scripts
Analysis of *Processional* by John Howard Lawson. USA. 1925. Lang.: Eng. 3535

Vaudeville Theatre (London)
Performance/production
Collection of newspaper reviews by London theatre critics. UK-England: London. 1998. Lang.: Eng. 2428
Collection of newspaper reviews by London theatre critics. UK-England: London. 1998. Lang.: Eng. 2447
Collection of newspaper reviews by London theatre critics. UK-England: London. 1998. Lang.: Eng. 2482
Collection of newspaper reviews by London theatre critics. UK-England: London. 1998. Lang.: Eng. 2544
Collection of newspaper reviews by London theatre critics. UK-England: London. 1998. Lang.: Eng. 2564
Collection of newspaper reviews by London theatre critics. UK-England: London. 1998. Lang.: Eng. 2568

Vaughan, R.M.
Plays/librettos/scripts
R.M. Vaughan's *Camera, Woman* at Buddies in Bad Times. Canada: Toronto, ON. 1998. Lang.: Eng. 2835

Veber, Pierre
Performance/production
Collection of newspaper reviews by London theatre critics. UK-England: London. 1998. Lang.: Eng. 2552

Věc Makropulos
Performance/production
Background material on Metropolitan Opera radio broadcast performances. USA: New York, NY. 1998. Lang.: Eng. 4713
Organizing two performances at the Metropolitan Opera on a single day. USA: New York, NY. 1997-1998. Lang.: Eng. 4741
Plays/librettos/scripts
Analysis of Janáček's *Věc Makropulos*. Czechoslovakia. 1922-1998. Lang.: Eng. 4765

Večer pod Hmeljnikom (Evening Under Hmeljnik, An)
Plays/librettos/scripts
The individual and his world in Slovene theatre. Slovenia. 1943-1985. Lang.: Slo. 3347

Vedrenne, J.E.
Plays/librettos/scripts
George Bernard Shaw's involvement with the Court Theatre. UK-England. 1904-1909. Lang.: Eng. 3471
Vega Carpio, Lope Félix de
Plays/librettos/scripts
Classical allusion in the plays of Lope de Vega. Spain. 1562-1635. Lang.: Eng. 3367
Playwright Lope de Vega. Spain. 1562-1635. Lang.: Eng. 3377
Allegorical dramas of Sor Marcela de San Félix. Spain. 1595-1650. Lang.: Eng. 3395
Jewish characters in Spanish drama. Spain. 1400-1950. Lang.: Spa. 3402
Theory/criticism
Lope de Vega's defense of the 'new art' of theatre. Spain. 1600-1620. Lang.: Eng. 3830
Critical reception of the plays of Lope de Vega. Spain. 1609-1935. Lang.: Spa. 3831
Vega, Lope de
SEE
Vega Carpio, Lope Félix de.
Vélez de Guevara, Luis
Plays/librettos/scripts
Playwright Luis Vélez de Guevara. Spain. 1578-1644. Lang.: Eng. 3390
Veliki duhoven Kajfa (High Priest Caiaphas, The)
Plays/librettos/scripts
Religion and the individual in plays of Ivan Mrak. Slovenia. 1955. Lang.: Slo. 3358
Vene Draamateater (Tallin)
Institutions
Profile of Estonian theatres. Estonia: Tallin, Tartu. 1997. Lang.: Swe, Eng, Ger. 345
Venexiana
Plays/librettos/scripts
Ludic aspects of Italian Renaissance theatre. Italy. 1500-1700. Lang.: Ita. 3240
Ventaglio, Il (Fan, The)
Basic theatrical documents
Catalan translation of *Il Ventaglio (The Fan)* by Carlo Goldoni. Italy. 1765. Lang.: Cat. 1442
Ventriloquism
Performance/production
Semiotic analysis of ventriloquism. USA. 1998. Lang.: Eng. 4136
Report on ventriloquist's convention. USA: Las Vegas, NV. 1998. Lang.: Eng. 4143
Obituary for ventriloquist Stanley Burns. USA: New York, NY. 1919-1998. Lang.: Eng. 4148
Obituary for Bob McAllister, ventriloquist, magician, and former host of *Wonderama*. USA. 1935-1998. Lang.: Eng. 4149
Venus
Basic theatrical documents
Text of *Venus* by Suzan Lori-Parks. USA. 1995. Lang.: Eng. 1501
Plays/librettos/scripts
Analysis of *Venus* by Suzan-Lori Parks. USA. 1996. Lang.: Eng. 3582
Vera, Gerardo
Performance/production
Productions of Shakespeare's *Twelfth Night* at the Madrid Theatre Festival. Spain: Madrid. 1996-1997. Lang.: Eng. 2359
Verbrecher, Die (Perpetrator, The)
Plays/librettos/scripts
Homosexuality on the German stage. Germany. 1920-1980. Lang.: Eng. 3147
Verdecchia, Guillermo
Plays/librettos/scripts
Analysis of *The Noam Chomsky Lectures* by Daniel Brooks and Guillermo Verdecchio. Canada: Toronto, ON. 1990-1991. Lang.: Eng. 2797
Verdi, Giuseppe
Administration
Theater Basel under the direction of Stefan Bachmann. Switzerland: Basel. 1996-1998. Lang.: Ger. 1391
Design/technology
Verdi's operas and the influence of La Fenice scene designer Giuseppe Bertoja. Italy: Venice. 1840-1870. Lang.: Eng. 4433
Lighting design for Verdi's *Macbeth* at La Scala. Italy: Milan. 1998. Lang.: Eng. 4435
Performance/production
Music theatre production in northern Germany. Germany: Lübeck, Hamburg, Bremen, Kiel. 1998. Lang.: Ger. 4293
Review of Salzburger Festspiele performances. Austria: Salzburg. 1998. Lang.: Ger. 4527
Opera productions of the Salzburg Festival. Austria: Salzburg. 1998. Lang.: Hun. 4531
Director Anja Sündermann on her production of *Rigoletto*. Germany: Hamburg. 1991-1998. Lang.: Ger. 4608
Interview with Miklós Gábor Kerényi on directing Verdi's *Un Ballo in Maschera*. Hungary: Budapest. 1998. Lang.: Hun. 4619
The Hungarian premier of Verdi's *Stiffelio*. Hungary: Szeged. 1998. Lang.: Hun. 4621
Verdi's *Un Ballo in Maschera* at the Hungarian State Opera House. Hungary: Budapest. 1998. Lang.: Hun. 4629
Interview with Miklós Gábor Kerényi on his production of *Un Ballo in maschera*. Hungary: Budapest, Szeged. 1998. Lang.: Hun. 4636
Recordings of the different versions of Verdi's *Don Carlos*. Italy. Europe. 1866-1998. Lang.: Eng. 4650
Verdi's rarely performed opera *Stiffelio*. Italy. 1850-1998. Lang.: Hun. 4652
Verdi's metrics. Italy. 1813-1901. Lang.: Ita. 4655
Verdi's important mezzo soprano roles, including Azucena in *Il Trovatore*. Italy. 1853. Lang.: Eng. 4661
Johannes Schaaf's production of *Otello* at Kungliga Operan. Sweden: Stockholm. 1998. Lang.: Swe. 4701
The current state of opera in England. UK-England. 1997. Lang.: Eng. 4705
Background material on Lyric Opera of Chicago radio broadcast performances. USA: Chicago, IL. 1998. Lang.: Eng. 4709
Background material on Metropolitan Opera radio broadcast performances. USA: New York, NY. 1998. Lang.: Eng. 4713
Background material on Metropolitan Opera radio broadcast performances. USA: New York, NY. 1998. Lang.: Eng. 4716
Interview with Ira Siff of La Gran Scena. USA: New York, NY. 1998. Lang.: Eng. 4719
Verdi's *Stiffelio* and Gounod's *Roméo et Juliette* in New York. USA: New York, NY. 1850-1998. Lang.: Eng. 4730
Plays/librettos/scripts
The inspiration for Dumas *fils*' Marguerite Gautier and Verdi's Violetta. France. Italy. 1848-1853. Lang.: Eng. 4789
The character Azucena in Verdi's *Il Trovatore*. Italy. 1853-1998. Lang.: Eng. 4808
Virginal heroines in Alpine settings in operas of Bellini, Donizetti, and Verdi. Italy. 1800-1850. Lang.: Eng. 4812
Gender in Bellini's *Norma* and Verdi's *Aida*. Italy. 1831-1871. Lang.: Eng. 4813
Verdon, Gwen
Performance/production
AIDS-benefit performance of the musical *Sweet Charity*. USA: New York, NY. 1998. Lang.: Eng. 4386
Verebes, István
Performance/production
Čechov's one-act plays at Thália Színház. Hungary. Slovakia: Košice. 1998. Lang.: Hun. 2075
István Verebes' production of Shakespeare's *Hamlet*. Hungary: Nyíregyháza. 1997. Lang.: Hun. 2116
Vereecke, Robert
Performance/production
The creation of the religious ballet *A Dancer's Christmas*. USA: Boston, MA. 1980-1998. Lang.: Eng. 1192
Verenigung voor Podiumtechnologie (Amsterdam)
Design/technology
OISTAT meeting on technician training. Netherlands: Amsterdam. 1998. Lang.: Swe. 206
Verga, Giovanni
Plays/librettos/scripts
Italian realist drama. Italy. 1860-1918. Lang.: Eng. 3260
Verge, The
Performance/production
A production of Susan Glaspell's experimental play *The Verge*. UK-Scotland: Glasgow. 1996. Lang.: Eng. 2651
Verma, Jatinder
Performance/production
Collection of newspaper reviews by London theatre critics. UK-England: London. 1998. Lang.: Eng. 2525

Veronika Deseniška (Veronica of Desenice)
Plays/librettos/scripts
Analysis of *Veronika Deseniška (Veronica of Desenice)* by Oton Župančič. Slovenia. 1924. Lang.: Slo. 3360
Verse drama
Basic theatrical documents
Text of an unfinished verse drama by Pirandello. Italy. 1884-1887. Lang.: Ita. 1445
Excerpt from *Diva Studies* by Elizabeth Alexander. USA. 1996. Lang.: Eng. 1480
Vertinskaja, M.
Performance/production
Actress M. Vertinskaja on her father, singer Aleksand'r Vertinskij. Russia: Moscow. 1998. Lang.: Rus. 2334
Vertinskij, Aleksand'r N.
Performance/production
Actress M. Vertinskaja on her father, singer Aleksand'r Vertinskij. Russia: Moscow. 1998. Lang.: Rus. 2334
Very Important Postman, A
Performance/production
Collection of newspaper reviews by London theatre critics. UK-England: London. 1998. Lang.: Eng. 2454
Very Woman, A
Plays/librettos/scripts
The malcontent scholar in Elizabethan and Jacobean theatre. England. 1590-1642. Lang.: Eng. 3003
Vesna svjaščennaja (Rite of Spring, The)
Performance/production
The performance of sacrifice on stage. France. Germany. 1900-1998. Lang.: Ger. 530
Vesnik, E. Ja.
Performance/production
Memoirs of Malyj Theatre actor E. Ja. Vesnik. Russia: Moscow. 1998. Lang.: Rus. 2336
Vesnik, Jèvgenij
Performance/production
Interview with actor Jèvgenij Vesnik. Russia: Moscow. 1998. Lang.: Rus. 586
Vestire gli ignudi (Naked)
Performance/production
Collection of newspaper reviews by London theatre critics. UK-England: London. 1998. Lang.: Eng. 2588
Vestris, Lucy
Performance/production
Lucy Vestris in *Giovanni in London*. England: London. 1842. Lang.: Eng. 4546
Vevar, Rok
Institutions
The fiftieth anniversary of Ljubljana's puppet theatre. Slovenia: Ljubljana. 1968-1997. Lang.: Slo. 4873
Via Dolorosa
Performance/production
Collection of newspaper reviews by London theatre critics. UK-England: London. 1998. Lang.: Eng. 2495
Viaducs de la Seine-et-Oise, Les (Viaducts of the Seine, The)
Plays/librettos/scripts
The representation of true crime in modern drama. USA. France. 1955-1996. Lang.: Eng. 3673
Viardot, Pauline
Plays/librettos/scripts
The *castrato*, the contralto, and the film *Farinelli*. France. Italy. 1994. Lang.: Eng. 4787
Vick, Graham
Design/technology
Lighting design for Verdi's *Macbeth* at La Scala. Italy: Milan. 1998. Lang.: Eng. 4435
Victims of Duty
SEE
Victimes du devoir.
Victoria Palace (London)
Performance/production
Collection of newspaper reviews by London theatre critics. UK-England: London. 1998. Lang.: Eng. 2410
Collection of newspaper reviews by London theatre critics. UK-England: London. 1998. Lang.: Eng. 2435
Collection of newspaper reviews by London theatre critics. UK-England: London. 1998. Lang.: Eng. 2514
Victorian theatre
SEE
Geographical-Chronological Index under UK-England 1837-1901.

Victory: Choices in Reaction
Plays/librettos/scripts
Political thought in plays of Howard Barker. UK-England. 1960-1992. Lang.: Eng. 3502
Vida es sueño, La (Life Is a Dream)
Performance/production
Collection of newspaper reviews by London theatre critics. UK-England: London. 1998. Lang.: Eng. 2488
José Rivera's production of *La Vida es sueño (Life Is a Dream)*, Hartford Stage. USA: Hartford, CT. 1998. Lang.: Eng. 2722
Plays/librettos/scripts
Life and career of playwright Pedro Calderón de la Barca. Spain. 1600-1681. Lang.: Eng. 3397
Power relations in Calderón's *La Vida es Sueño (Life Is a Dream)*. Spain. 1635. Lang.: Spa. 3401
Video forms
SEE ALSO
Classed Entries under MEDIA—Video forms.
Administration
Producer Aida Young. UK-England. 1950-1998. Lang.: Eng. 3854
Marketing strategies for puppetry in film and TV. USA. 1998. Lang.: Eng. 4863
Audience
Interview with performance artist Tim Brennan. Netherlands: Arnhem. 1989. Lang.: Eng. 4231
Design/technology
Combined video and lighting for U2 world tour. Ireland. 1997. Lang.: Eng. 198
Costumer Kermit Love. USA. 1935-1998. Lang.: Eng. 271
Costume designer Robert Mackintosh. USA. 1926-1998. Lang.: Eng. 284
New sound and video system in the performance space of Luxor Hotel and Casino. USA: Las Vegas, NV. 1998. Lang.: Eng. 285
The use of entertainment technology beyond the entertainment industry. USA. 1998. Lang.: Eng. 293
Sound, lighting, and scenic elements of *Star Trek: The Next Generation* at the Las Vegas Hilton. USA: Las Vegas, NV. 1998. Lang.: Eng. 320
Production design for the film *Lost in Space*. USA: Hollywood, CA. 1998. Lang.: Eng. 3904
Production design for Gary Ross's film *Pleasantville*. USA: Hollywood, CA. 1998. Lang.: Eng. 3909
Institutions
The Walker Arts Center's exhibition on dance. USA: Minneapolis, MN. 1998. Lang.: Eng. 905
History of the Sundance Institute for Film and Video. USA: Sundance, CO. 1981-1984. Lang.: Eng. 3925
Effects of a TV documentary on the Royal Opera House. UK-England: London. 1993-1998. Lang.: Eng. 4474
Performance/production
Opportunities for South Asian actors. Canada: Toronto, ON. 1997. Lang.: Eng. 508
The use of closed circuit television in avant-garde theatre performance. USA: New York, NY. 1978-1986. Lang.: Eng. 662
Dance on Finnish television. Finland. 1998. Lang.: Fin. 921
Digital dance. UK-England. 1998. Lang.: Eng. 974
Dance, music video, and popular culture. USA. 1987-1997. Lang.: Eng. 978
Dancer/choreographer Rosemary Lee. UK-England: London. 1989-1998. Lang.: Eng. 1307
Director and actor Christoph Schlingensief. Germany. 1993-1998. Lang.: Ger. 1988
The use of television in theatrical space. Netherlands. USA. 1970-1998. Lang.: Dut. 2206
Actor Sergej Bezrukov. Russia: Moscow. Lang.: Rus. 2341
Actress Betty Marsden. UK-England: London. 1930-1998. Lang.: Eng. 2596
Career of actress Joan Hickson. UK-England: London. 1927-1998. Lang.: Eng. 2597
Career of actor Marius Goring. UK-England: London. 1930-1998. Lang.: Eng. 2598
Analysis of two productions of Caryl Churchill's *Top Girls*. UK-England. 1982-1991. Lang.: Eng. 2608
Interview with actor Patrick Stewart. USA: Washington, DC. 1998. Lang.: Eng. 2760

Video forms — cont'd

Interview with film and television actor Jean-Louis Millette. Canada: Montreal, PQ. 1965-1998. Lang.: Fre. 3856
Interview with film and television actress Andrée Lachapelle. Canada: Montreal, PQ. 1964-1998. Lang.: Fre. 3857
Dance on screen. USA. Europe. 1920-1998. Lang.: Ger. 3860
Report on biennial festival of mixed media. France: Lyon. 1997. Lang.: Eng. 4042
Multimedia and the productions of Giorgio Barberio Corsetti. Italy: Rome, Milan. 1985-1998. Lang.: Eng. 4043
Mixed media artist Ebon Fisher. USA. 1998. Lang.: Eng. 4045
Obituary for Bob McAllister, ventriloquist, magician, and former host of *Wonderama*. USA. 1935-1998. Lang.: Eng. 4149
Interview with video and installation artist Gary Hill. USA. 1969-1998. Lang.: Eng. 4258
Audio and video recordings of opera stars and complete operas. 1988-1998. Lang.: Eng. 4522
Evaluation of video performances of Donizetti's operas. Europe. USA. 1980-1998. Lang.: Eng. 4557
Background material on telecast performance of Britten's *Paul Bunyan* at New York City Opera. USA: New York, NY. 1998. Lang.: Eng. 4710
Background material on telecast performance of Saint-Saëns' *Samson et Dalila* at the Metropolitan Opera. USA: New York, NY. 1998. Lang.: Eng. 4714
The Opera-in-English movement. USA. 1850-1985. Lang.: Eng. 4746
History of commercial TV opera broadcasts. USA: New York, NY. 1939-1980. Lang.: Eng. 4756
Interview with television puppeteer Nina Keogh. Canada: Toronto, ON. 1953-1998. Lang.: Eng. 4888
Obituary for TV puppeteer Shari Lewis. USA. 1933-1998. Lang.: Eng. 4909

Plays/librettos/scripts
Description of a Web site devoted to *Los españoles en Chile* by Francisco Ganzalez de Busto. Spain. 1665-1998. Lang.: Eng. 3366
Radio, television, and stage plays of Caryl Churchill. UK-England. 1959-1985. Lang.: Eng. 3464
Stage and screenwriter John Hopkins. UK-England: London. USA: Hollywood, CA. 1931-1998. Lang.: Eng. 3498
Writing for both television and live theatre. USA. 1998. Lang.: Eng. 3560
Comparison of film and television versions of *Dances With Wolves*. USA. 1990-1993. Lang.: Eng. 4022
Mixed media in theatre productions of Carole Nadeau. Canada: Quebec, PQ, Montreal, PQ. 1998. Lang.: Fre. 4047
Account of performances by Joan Dickinson. USA. 1997-1998. Lang.: Eng. 4263

Relation to other fields
Therapeutic *nō* theatre for the mentally retarded. USA. 1998. Lang.: Eng. 798

Theory/criticism
Critique of dance criticism. UK-England: London. 1989. Lang.: Eng. 1339
Critique of the modernist tradition of defining each medium in its own terms. Europe. 1963-1997. Lang.: Eng. 3861
Critical approaches to science-fiction films. USA. 1960-1981. Lang.: Eng. 4040
Cyberspace as performance site. North America. 1998. Lang.: Eng. 4048

Training
Details of a media acting curriculum. USA. 1994-1998. Lang.: Eng. 4041

Videographies
Performance/production
Video recordings of Rossini's *Semiramide*. 1980-1991. Lang.: Fre. 4503

Vidić, Ivan
Performance/production
Collection of newspaper reviews by London theatre critics. UK-England: London. 1998. Lang.: Eng. 2451

Vidmar, Josip
Theory/criticism
Critical writing on theatre of Josip Vidmar. Slovenia. 1920-1941. Lang.: Slo. 3827

Vidnyánszky, Attila
Performance/production
One-act plays of Čechov by the Illyés Gyula National Theatre. Hungary. Ukraine: Beregovo. 1997. Lang.: Hun. 2104

Vie et mort du Roi Boiteux (Life and Death of the Lame King)
Plays/librettos/scripts
Vie et mort du Roi Boiteux (Life and Death of the Lame King), Jean-Pierre Ronfard's adaptation of *Richard III*. Canada. 1981. Lang.: Fre. 2813

Vie parisienne, La
Performance/production
Reviews of recent opera productions. Switzerland: Basel. Germany: Stuttgart, Berlin, Hamburg. France: Strasbourg. 1997-1998. Lang.: Ger. 4702

Viebrock, Anna
Performance/production
Kortner-award winners Anna Viebrock and Christoph Marthaler. Germany: Berlin. 1997. Lang.: Ger. 1968

Vieira, Geraldo Andrew
Design/technology
Geraldo Andrew Vieira, carnival costumer and performer. Trinidad and Tobago. 1952-1996. Lang.: Eng. 4160

Vienna: Lusthaus
Basic theatrical documents
Collection of plays by Charles L. Mee. USA. 1986-1995. Lang.: Eng. 1496

Vieux Carre
Plays/librettos/scripts
Dramaturgical analysis of late plays of Tennessee Williams. USA. 1969-1978. Lang.: Eng. 3661

Vígszínház (Budapest)
Performance/production
Review of Arthur Miller's *The Crucible* directed by Péter Rudolf. Hungary: Budapest. 1998. Lang.: Hun. 2068

Viirus (Helsinki)
Institutions
The proliferation of Swedish-language theatre groups in Helsinki. Finland: Helsinki. 1990-1998. Lang.: Eng, Fre. 1604

Viktjuk, Roman
Performance/production
Interview with director Roman Viktjuk. Russia: Moscow. 1998. Lang.: Rus. 2244
Roman Viktjuk's production of *Salomé* by Oscar Wilde. Russia: Moscow. 1998. Lang.: Rus. 2266

Vila i Casañas, Josep
Performance/production
Collection of newspaper reviews by London theatre critics. UK-Scotland: Edinburgh. 1998. Lang.: Eng. 2650

Vildanden (Wild Duck, The)
Performance/production
Reviews of productions of plays by Ibsen. USA: New York, NY. Norway: Oslo. 1998. Lang.: Eng. 2747

Vildrac, Charles
Performance/production
Director Jacques Copeau and his theatrical aesthetic. France. 1913-1920. Lang.: Eng. 1941

Villa, Villa
Institutions
Report on festival of physical theatre. Germany: Munich. 1997. Lang.: Eng. 1664

Ville parjure, La (Perjured City, The)
Plays/librettos/scripts
Poetic identity in plays of Hélène Cixous. France. 1988-1994. Lang.: Eng. 3083

Villella, Edward
Performance/production
Panel discussion on Balanchine's *Jewels*. USA: New York, NY. 1967. Lang.: Eng. 1188

Villifranchi, Giovanni Cosimo
Performance/production
The evolution of comic opera. Italy: Florence, Rome. 1665-1700. Lang.: Eng. 4660

Vinaver, Michel
Plays/librettos/scripts
Interview with playwright Michel Vinaver. Canada: Quebec, PQ. 1969-1998. Lang.: Fre. 2831
Interview with playwright Michel Vinaver. France. 1958-1998. Lang.: Ger. 3086
Analysis of *Par-dessus bord (Overboard)* by Michel Vinaver. France. Switzerland: La Chaux-de-Fonds. 1960-1998. Lang.: Ger. 3118

Vinci, Leonardo
Plays/librettos/scripts
Female operatic cross-dressing. Italy: Naples, Venice. 1601-1800. Lang.: Eng. 4814

Vincze, János
Performance/production
György Spiró's *Kvartett (Quartet)* directed by János Vincze. Hungary: Pécs. 1997. Lang.: Hun. 2067
Vinegar Tom
Plays/librettos/scripts
Brechtian epic devices in the theatre of Caryl Churchill. UK-England. 1976-1986. Lang.: Eng. 3477
Vineyard Theatre (New York, NY)
Design/technology
Derek McLane's set designs for recent Off Broadway productions. USA: New York, NY. 1998. Lang.: Eng. 1538
Vingoe, Mary
Performance/production
Directing shows with three-week rehearsal time at Eastern Front Theatre. Canada: Dartmouth, NS. 1980-1998. Lang.: Eng. 1868
Plays/librettos/scripts
Analysis of *Corker* by Wendy Lill. Canada: Halifax, NS. 1994-1998. Lang.: Eng. 2836
Vinokur, Vladimir
Performance/production
Actor Vladimir Vinokur. Russia. 1998. Lang.: Rus. 2337
Vinzenz und die Freundin bedeutender Manner (Vincent and the Lady Friend of Important Men)
Plays/librettos/scripts
Robert Musil and the 'crisis of modern drama'. Europe. 1880-1930. Lang.: Eng. 3062
Viola, Bill
Performance/production
Video artist Bill Viola. USA: New York, NY. 1976-1998. Lang.: Eng. 4071
Virginia Museum Theatre (Richmond, VA)
Institutions
History of Virginia Museum Theatre. USA: Richmond, VA. 1955-1987. Lang.: Eng. 406
vis plastica (Austria)
Performance/production
Austrian street theatre. Austria. 1953-1998. Lang.: Ger. 4116
Visage d'Orphée, Le (Face of Orpheus, The)
Plays/librettos/scripts
Interview with playwright-director Olivier Py. France. 1988-1998. Lang.: Ger, Fre, Dut, Eng. 3117
Visconti, Luchino
Performance/production
The Italian premiere of *A Streetcar Named Desire* by Tennessee Williams. Italy: Rome. 1949. Lang.: Eng. 2172
Visdei, Anca
Basic theatrical documents
Text of *La Médée de Saint-Médard (The Medea of Saint-Medard)* by Anca Visdei. France. 1998. Lang.: Fre. 1436
Vision of the Twelve Goddesses
Plays/librettos/scripts
Gender and politics in masques of Ben Jonson and Samuel Daniel. England. 1604-1605. Lang.: Eng. 4200
Political and ideological struggles in Jacobean masques. England. 1604-1609. Lang.: Eng. 4206
Visit, A
Plays/librettos/scripts
Theatrical space in plays of Maria Irene Fornes. USA. 1977-1989. Lang.: Eng. 3571
Visit, The
SEE
Besuch der alten Dame, Der.
Visiteuse, La (Visitor, The)
Theory/criticism
Analysis of plays by Eric-Emmanuel Schmitt. France. 1998. Lang.: Fin. 3819
Višneva, Diana
Performance/production
Profile of ballerinas Uljana Lopatkina and Diana Višneva. Russia: St. Petersburg. 1998. Lang.: Rus. 1148
Višnëvyj sad (Cherry Orchard, The)
Basic theatrical documents
Catalan translations of the complete plays of Anton Čechov. Russia. 1884-1904. Lang.: Cat. 1449
Design/technology
The work of scene designer Libor Fára. Czech Republic: Prague. 1950-1981. Lang.: Cze. 1518
Performance/production
The performances of Frances Hyland, Kate Reid, and Martha Henry in *The Cherry Orchard.* Canada: Stratford, ON. 1965. Lang.: Eng. 1865
Peter Zadek's production of Čechov's *Višnëvyj sad (The Cherry Orchard).* Germany. Netherlands. 1998. Lang.: Dut. 1954
Collection of newspaper reviews by London theatre critics. UK-England: London, Stratford, Derby. 1998. Lang.: Eng. 2417
Plays/librettos/scripts
Analysis of Čechov's *Višnëvyj sad (The Cherry Orchard).* Russia. 1904. Lang.: Rus. 3323
Visual Stage of the Catholic University
SEE
Scena Plastyczna Katolickiego Uniwersytetu Lubelskiego (Lublin).
Vitez, Antoine
Performance/production
Semiotic analysis of Jarry's *Ubu Roi* as staged by Vitez. France: Paris. 1985. Lang.: Eng. 528
Vitruvius
Performance spaces
The building of an ideal operatic stage in a disused limestone quarry. Sweden: Rättvik. 1997. Lang.: Swe. 4497
Vivaldi, Antonio
Performance/production
New productions of Győri Balett. Hungary: Budapest. 1998. Lang.: Hun. 1095
Vives, Amadeo
Design/technology
Lighting for Washington Opera's production of *Doña Francisquita.* USA: Washington, DC. 1998. Lang.: Eng. 4290
Vivian Beaumont Theatre (New York, NY)
Design/technology
Lighting design for Shakespeare's *Twelfth Night* at the Vivian Beaumont. USA: New York, NY. 1998. Lang.: Eng. 1546
Performance spaces
Theatre space and performance. USA: New York, NY. 1925-1985. Lang.: Eng. 464
Vlachos, Helen
Basic theatrical documents
Excerpt from *Job Stealer* by Rahul Varma, Helen Vlachos and Ian Lloyd George. Canada: Montreal, PQ. 1998. Lang.: Eng. 1412
Vodušek, Božo
Plays/librettos/scripts
The individual and his world in Slovene theatre. Slovenia. 1943-1985. Lang.: Slo. 3347
Voevoda
Plays/librettos/scripts
Morality in plays of Fonvizin, Ostrovskij, and A.K. Tolstoj. Russia. 1764-1869. Lang.: Rus. 3325
Vogel, Paula
Performance/production
Collection of newspaper reviews by London theatre critics. UK-England: London. 1998. Lang.: Eng. 2423
Plays/librettos/scripts
Interview with playwright Paula Vogel. USA: New York, NY. 1998. Lang.: Eng. 3679
Vogelnik, Eka
Performance/production
Slovene puppet film. Slovenia. 1947-1997. Lang.: Slo. 4899
Voice
Performance/production
The application of Laban Movement Studies to actor training. USA. 1997-1998. Lang.: Eng. 628
Sociolinguistics, gender, and the actor. USA. 1997-1998. Lang.: Eng. 642
The Alba Emoting system of actor training. USA. 1995-1998. Lang.: Eng. 668
Voice teachers Alex Bulmer and Kate Lynch. Canada: Toronto, ON. UK-England: London. 1986-1998. Lang.: Eng. 1837
Problems of post-secondary theatre training. Canada: Edmonton, AB. 1919-1998. Lang.: Eng. 1848
The classic French tradition of declaiming text. France. 1657-1749. Lang.: Fre. 1923
Speaking styles of selected actors reading Shakespeare's *Henry V.* North America. UK-England. 1998. Lang.: Eng. 2208
Research on the importance of vocal training for the actor. USA. 1986-1987. Lang.: Eng. 2657
Semiotic analysis of ventriloquism. USA. 1998. Lang.: Eng. 4136
The singer, the voice, and the body. Sweden. 1997. Lang.: Swe. 4700
Relation to other fields
Psychological aspects of the under-realized potential of the human voice. Europe. 1989. Lang.: Eng. 728

Voice — cont'd

Theory/criticism
The influence of Antonin Artaud on director Paul Pörtner. France. 1920-1973. Lang.: Ger. 3870

Voigt, Deborah
Performance/production
Dramatic soprano Deborah Voigt. USA. 1998. Lang.: Eng. 4717

Voile noire voile blanche (Black Sail White Sail)
Plays/librettos/scripts
Poetic identity in plays of Hélène Cixous. France. 1988-1994. Lang.: Eng. 3083

Voix humaine, La (Human Voice, The)
Plays/librettos/scripts
The influence of Jean Cocteau on filmmaker Pedro Almodóvar. Spain. France. 1981. Lang.: Eng. 3978

Vol'chovskij, V.
Administration
V. Vol'chovskij, puppet theatre producer. Russia. 1998. Lang.: Rus. 4916

Volcano Theatre (London)
Performance/production
Collection of newspaper reviews by London theatre critics. UK-England: London. 1998. Lang.: Eng. 2448

Vőlegény (Fiancé, The)
Performance/production
Two productions of Ernő Szép's *Vőlegény (The Fiancé)*. Hungary: Nyíregyháza. Hungary: Győr. 1998.Lang.: Hun. 2118

Volgogradskij Dramatičéskij Teat'r (Volgograd)
Performance/production
K. Dubinin's production of *Boi imeli mestnoe zančenie (The Battles Had Localized)* based on work of Viačeslav Kondratjév. Russia: Volgograd. Lang.: Rus. 2331

Volksbühne (Berlin)
Administration
Theatre directors on the future of subsidized theatre. Switzerland: Zurich. Germany: Hannover, Berlin. 1998. Lang.: Ger. 1390
Performance/production
Recent dance performances in Berlin. Germany: Berlin. 1998. Lang.: Ger. 933
Matthias Matschke, *Theater Heute*'s young actor of the year. Germany: Berlin. 1985-1997. Lang.: Ger. 1963
Kortner-award winners Anna Viebrock and Christoph Marthaler. Germany: Berlin. 1997. Lang.: Ger. 1968
The performance of Shakespeare in the former East Germany. Germany: Rostock, Leipzig, Berlin, Dessau. 1996-1997. Lang.: Ger. 1974
Actor Herbert Fritsch. Germany. 1992-1998. Lang.: Ger. 1985
Director and actor Christoph Schlingensief. Germany. 1993-1998. Lang.: Ger. 1988
Political context of Frank Castorf's production of *Les Mains Sales (Dirty Hands)* by Sartre. Germany: Berlin. 1998. Lang.: Ger. 2002
Swedish directors on recent Berlin productions. Germany: Berlin. 1998. Lang.: Swe. 2012
Shakespearean production and the GDR's 'existential crisis'. Germany, East. 1976-1980. Lang.: Eng. 2051
Reviews of recent opera productions. Switzerland: Basel. Germany: Stuttgart, Berlin, Hamburg. France: Strasbourg. 1997-1998. Lang.: Ger. 4702
Plays/librettos/scripts
Frank Castorf's production of Sartre's *Les Mains Sales (Dirty Hands)* and the civil war in Yugoslavia. Germany: Berlin. 1998. Lang.: Ger. 3129
Relation to other fields
Frank Castorf of Volksbühne and the object and possibilities of contemporary theatre. Germany: Berlin. 1998. Lang.: Ger. 747
The commemoration of Kristallnacht at Volksbühne. Germany: Berlin. 1998. Lang.: Ger. 3764
Die Berliner Ermittlung (The Berlin Investigation), an interactive theatre project by Jochen Gerz and Esther Shalev-Gerz. Germany: Berlin. 1998. Lang.: Ger. 3768

Volkstheater (Rostock)
Design/technology
Scenographer and now director Klaus Noack. Germany. 1953. Lang.: Ger. 190
Performance/production
The performance of Shakespeare in the former East Germany. Germany: Rostock, Leipzig, Berlin, Dessau. 1996-1997. Lang.: Ger. 1974
Director Christina Emig-Könning. Germany: Rostock. 1995-1997. Lang.: Ger. 2000
Director Anja Sündermann on her production of *Rigoletto*. Germany: Hamburg. 1991-1998. Lang.: Ger. 4608

Volkstheater (Vienna)
Performance/production
Productions of Horváth's *Geschichten aus dem Wienerwald (Tales from the Vienna Woods)*. Germany: Hamburg, Hannover. Austria: Vienna. 1998. Lang.: Ger. 2003
Premieres of plays on the Nazi theme. Germany: Darmstadt. Austria: Vienna. 1998. Lang.: Ger. 2030
Plays/librettos/scripts
Letters of Pirandello, Moissiu, and Jahn. Italy. Austria: Vienna. 1934. Lang.: Ita. 3219

Volonté, Gian Maria
Performance/production
Essays on actor Gian Maria Volonté. Italy. 1960-1994. Lang.: Ita. 3936

Volpone
Design/technology
Costume designer Isabelle Larivière. Canada: Quebec, PQ. 1994-1995. Lang.: Fre. 1514

Voltaire (Arouet, François-Marie)
Plays/librettos/scripts
Voltaire's *Sémiramis*, source of Rossini's *Semiramide*. France. 1748. Lang.: Fre. 3096
The writing and first performances of Voltaire's *Sémiramis*, the source of Rossini's opera *Semiramide*. France. 1746-1748. Lang.: Fre. 3114
Themes from Greek tragedy in opera. France. 1635-1774. Lang.: Eng. 4783
Response to criticism of Théâtre du Sous-Marin Jaune's adaptation of Voltaire's *Candide*. Canada: Quebec, PQ. 1997. Lang.: Fre. 4912

Volunteers
Performance/production
Collection of newspaper reviews by London theatre critics. UK-England: London. 1998. Lang.: Eng. 2530

Von Henning, Marc
Performance/production
Collection of newspaper reviews by London theatre critics. UK-England: London. 1998. Lang.: Eng. 2584

Von Morgens bis Mitternacht (From Morn to Midnight)
Plays/librettos/scripts
Comparison of characters in plays of Georg Kaiser and Tennessee Williams. USA. Germany. 1912-1945. Lang.: Eng. 3588

Vonj črnih vrtnic (Fragrance of Black Roses, The)
Basic theatrical documents
Plays and screenplays by Vili Ravnjak. Slovenia. 1991-1997. Lang.: Slo. 1460

Vor dem Ruhestand (Eve of Retirement)
Institutions
The current state of Theater Bielefeld. Germany: Bielefeld. 1998. Lang.: Ger. 1621

Vor Sonnenaufgang (Before Sunrise)
Audience
Audience response to *Vor Sonnenaufgang (Before Sunrise)* by Gerhart Hauptmann. Germany: Berlin. 1889-1890. Lang.: Eng. 1402

Vorbach, Eileen
Performance/production
Collection of newspaper reviews by London theatre critics. UK-England: London. 1998. Lang.: Eng. 2566

Vorpommersche Theater (Greifswald)
Administration
Rüdiger Bloch, manager of West Pomeranian theatres. Germany: Greifswald, Straslund. 1997-1998. Lang.: Ger. 1384

Vorster, Chris
Performance/production
Chris Vorster's production of *Baal* by Bertolt Brecht. South Africa, Republic of: Capetown. 1998. Lang.: Eng. 2350

Voskressij syn (Reincarnated Son)
Plays/librettos/scripts
Analysis of *Voskressij syn (Reincarnated Son)* by Maksim Gorkij. Russia. 1930-1932. Lang.: Rus. 3321

Voss, Gert
Performance/production
Actors Gert Voss and Ignaz Kirchner on George Tabori's production of *Fin de partie (Endgame)*. Austria: Vienna. 1998. Lang.: Ger. 1821
Gert Voss and Ignaz Kirchner, *Theater Heute*'s actors of the year. Austria: Vienna. 1988-1998. Lang.: Ger. 1823

Voss, Philip
Performance/production
Philip Voss on his role in *Coriolanus* at RSC. UK-England: London, Stratford. 1994. Lang.: Eng. 2643

Vous n'avez rien à déclarer? (Court in the Act)
Performance/production
Collection of newspaper reviews by London theatre critics. UK-England: London. 1998. Lang.: Eng. 2552

Voyage sans fin, Le (Constant Journey, The)
Plays/librettos/scripts
Analysis of *Le Voyage sans fin (The Constant Journey)* by Monique Wittig. France. 1985. Lang.: Eng. 3100

Vrhovec, Ivan
Plays/librettos/scripts
Analysis of *Zoran ali Kmetska vojna na Slovenskum (Zoran and the Peasant War in Slovenia)* by Ivan Vrhovec. Slovenia. 1870. Lang.: Slo. 3351

Vvedenskij, Aleksand'r Ivanovič
Design/technology
Costume design for *Christmas with the Ivanovs*, CSC Repertory. USA: New York, NY. 1998. Lang.: Eng. 1533

Vysockij, Vladimir
Basic theatrical documents
Selection of poems and songs by actor Vladimir Vysockij. Russia: Moscow. 1960-1970. Lang.: Rus. 164
Plays of Vladimir Vysockij. Russia: Moscow. 1998. Lang.: Rus. 1452
Songs and poems of Vladimir Vysockij. Russia: Moscow. 1938-1980. Lang.: Rus. 1453
Performance/production
Biographical information on actor Vladimir Vysockij. Russia: Moscow. 1938-1980. Lang.: Rus. 2291
The final months of actor Vladimir Vysockij. Russia: Moscow. 1980. Lang.: Rus. 2307
Report on international conference devoted to the work of Vladimir Vysockij. Russia: Moscow. 1998. Lang.: Rus. 2313
The funeral of actor and playwright Vladimir Vysockij. Russia: Moscow. 1980. Lang.: Rus. 2333
Vagant, a journal dedicated to the work of actor Vladimir Vysockij. Russia: Moscow. 1998. Lang.: Rus. 2339

Waaser, Carol
Administration
Carol Waaser, Eastern Region Equity Director. USA: New York, NY. 1998. Lang.: Eng. 47

Wada Chirebandi (Old Stone Mansion)
Plays/librettos/scripts
Diaspora and home in postcolonial Indian drama. India. 1978-1985. Lang.: Eng. 3193

Wag the Dog
Plays/librettos/scripts
David Mamet's success as a screenwriter and film director. USA. 1998. Lang.: Eng. 4003

Wager, Michael
Performance/production
Friends and colleagues recall singer Lotte Lenya. Germany. 1928-1981. Lang.: Eng. 4355

Wagner, Jane
Performance/production
Analysis of transformative comedy. USA. 1975-1988. Lang.: Eng. 666

Wagner, Kitte
Plays/librettos/scripts
Dramaturgs on recognizing talented new playwrights. Denmark. 1998. Lang.: Dan. 2854

Wagner, Paula
Performance/production
Documentary theatre and the politics of representation. USA. 1966-1993. Lang.: Eng. 2728

Wagner, Richard
Audience
Opera and the young audience. Germany. 1998. Lang.: Ger. 4410
Design/technology
Interview with set designer Lennart Mörk. Sweden: Stockholm. France: Paris. 1958-1998. Lang.: Swe. 222
Scenographer Lennart Mörk. Sweden: Stockholm. France: Paris. 1957-1998. Lang.: Swe. 4439
Technical designs for *Tristan und Isolde* at Seattle Opera. USA: Seattle, WA. 1998. Lang.: Eng. 4444
Institutions
Effect of Wagner family memoirs on the Bayreuth Festival. Germany: Bayreuth. 1998. Lang.: Eng. 4451
Review of Wagner's *Ring* cycle at the Bayreuth Festival. Germany: Bayreuth. 1997-1998. Lang.: Hun. 4454
Performance spaces
Opera composer Richard Wagner and performance space. Europe. 1835-1885. Lang.: Eng. 4492
Performance/production
Slovene translation of Adolphe Appia on staging Wagner. Europe. 1892. Lang.: Slo. 4550
Productions of Wagner's *Tristan und Isolde* by Peter Konwitschny and Werner Schroeter. Germany: Munich, Duisberg. 1998. Lang.: Ger. 4580
Visual spectacle in Wagner's *Ring* cycle. Germany. 1869-1876. Lang.: Eng. 4585
Wagnerian soprano Lilli Lehmann. Germany. 1848-1929. Lang.: Eng. 4587
F.W. Beidler's ideas for a different Bayreuth Festival. Germany: Bayreuth. 1901-1981. Lang.: Ger. 4602
Historical overview of Wagnerian singing. Germany: Bayreuth. 1850-1998. Lang.: Eng. 4610
The influence of Wieland Wagner's production of *Lohengrin*. Germany, West: Bayreuth. 1966. Lang.: Eng. 4614
Interview with director Viktor Nagy on Wagner's *Ring* cycle. Hungary: Budapest. 1998. Lang.: Hun. 4635
Wagner's *Ring* cycle at the Hungarian Opera House. Hungary: Budapest. 1998. Lang.: Hun. 4644
Background material on Metropolitan Opera radio broadcast performances. USA: New York, NY. 1998. Lang.: Eng. 4713
Bass James Johnson. USA. 1998. Lang.: Eng. 4722
Robert Wilson's production of Wagner's *Lohengrin*. USA: New York, NY. 1998. Lang.: Eng. 4732
Robert Wilson's production of Wagner's *Lohengrin* at the Metropolitan Opera. USA: New York, NY. 1976-1998. Lang.: Eng. 4739
Organizing two performances at the Metropolitan Opera on a single day. USA: New York, NY. 1997-1998. Lang.: Eng. 4741
Plays/librettos/scripts
The reciprocal influence of opera and film. Europe. North America. 1904-1994. Lang.: Eng. 4770
Comic and tragic elements in Wagner's *Die Meistersinger von Nürnberg*. Germany. 1868-1998. Lang.: Eng. 4792
The brother-sister bond of Gottfried and Elsa in *Lohengrin* by Richard Wagner. Germany. 1850-1998. Lang.: Eng. 4794
Nationalism and sexuality in Wagner's *Ring* cycle. Germany. 1870-1880. Lang.: Eng. 4796
Biography of composer Richard Wagner. Germany. 1923-1995. Lang.: Ita. 4799
Outline of Wagner's *Götterdämmerung*. Hungary: Budapest. 1998. Lang.: Hun. 4800
Wagner's *Parsifal* and the political aspirations of Catalonians. Spain-Catalonia: Barcelona. 1841-1914. Lang.: Eng. 4820
Daniel Barenboim and Edward Said on composer Richard Wagner. USA: New York, NY. Germany. 1995. Lang.: Eng. 4826
Theory/criticism
Evaluating the work of opera directors. Europe. 1965-1998. Lang.: Eng. 4837

Wagner, Wieland
Performance/production
The influence of Wieland Wagner's production of *Lohengrin*. Germany, West: Bayreuth. 1966. Lang.: Eng. 4614

Wagner, Wolfgang
Institutions
Effect of Wagner family memoirs on the Bayreuth Festival. Germany: Bayreuth. 1998. Lang.: Eng. 4451
Performance/production
Iván Markó's choreography for Bayreuth Festival productions. Germany: Bayreuth. Hungary. 1998. Lang.: Hun. 1083

Wague, Georges
Performance/production
Dancer Antonia Merce, La Argentina. France. Spain. 1888-1936. Lang.: Eng. 922

Waikiki Beach
Plays/librettos/scripts
Power, gender relations, and communication in German drama. Germany. 1776-1989. Lang.: Ger. 3138

Waiting for Godot
SEE
En attendant Godot.

Waiting for Philip Glass
Performance/production
Collection of newspaper reviews by London theatre critics. UK-England: London. 1998. Lang.: Eng. 2498

Waits, Tom
Performance/production
Music theatre production in northern Germany. Germany: Lübeck, Hamburg, Bremen, Kiel. 1998. Lang.: Ger. 4293

Wajda, Andrzej
Performance/production
History of Teatr Wybrzeże. Poland: Gdańsk, Warsaw, Cracow. 1952-1997. Lang.: Pol. 2215
Interview with director Andrzej Wajda. Poland. 1960-1998. Lang.: Fin. 2224

Walch, Eva
Performance/production
Gender and Shakespearean production in the GDR. Germany, East. 1982-1990. Lang.: Eng. 2044

Walcott, Derek
Design/technology
Sound design for the musical *The Capeman*. USA: New York, NY. 1998. Lang.: Eng. 4339
Performance/production
Response to negative criticism of *The Capeman*. USA: New York, NY. 1998. Lang.: Eng. 4387
Plays/librettos/scripts
Theatre and the creation of a new nationalism. Canada. Saint Lucia. 1980-1995. Lang.: Eng. 2808

Walczak, Barbara
Institutions
The founding of the New York City Ballet. USA: New York, NY. 1947-1948. Lang.: Eng. 1060

Waldmann, Helena
Institutions
Experimental performances of Helena Waldmann and Showcase Beat le Mot. Germany: Franfurt. 1993-1998. Lang.: Ger. 4234

Walk Together Children
Performance/production
The student-created community theatre piece *Walk Together Children*. USA. 1996-1997. Lang.: Eng. 652

Walker Arts Center (Minneapolis, MN)
Institutions
The Walker Arts Center's exhibition on dance. USA: Minneapolis, MN. 1998. Lang.: Eng. 905

Walker, Alex
Performance/production
Collection of newspaper reviews by London theatre critics. UK-England: London. 1998. Lang.: Eng. 2502

Walker, Che
Performance/production
Collection of newspaper reviews by London theatre critics. UK-England: London. 1998. Lang.: Eng. 2458
Collection of newspaper reviews by London theatre critics. UK-England: London. 1998. Lang.: Eng. 2562

Walker, George F.
Performance/production
Collection of newspaper reviews by London theatre critics. UK-England: London. 1998. Lang.: Eng. 2578
Musical theatre composer Will Marion Cook. USA. 1898-1950. Lang.: Eng. 4378

Walker, Leomi
Performance/production
Collection of newspaper reviews by London theatre critics. UK-England: London. 1998. Lang.: Eng. 2549

Wallace Brown, Gia
Performance/production
Obituary for puppeteer Gia Wallace Brown. USA. 1929-1998. Lang.: Eng. 4910

Wallace, Naomi
Performance/production
Reviews of Actors' Theatre productions. USA: Louisville, KY. 1998. Lang.: Eng. 2727

Wallach, Eli
Performance/production
Report on speech by actor Eli Wallach to Actors' Equity meeting. USA. 1998. Lang.: Eng. 2717

Wållgren, Gunn
Performance/production
Seven critics on their favorite character or portrayal. Sweden. 1950. Lang.: Swe. 2369

Wallis, D.A.
Performance/production
Collection of newspaper reviews by London theatre critics. UK-England: London. 1998. Lang.: Eng. 2478

Walpole, Horace
Plays/librettos/scripts
Horace Walpole's *The Dear Witches* and Shakespeare's *Macbeth*. England. 1743. Lang.: Eng. 2857

Walser, Theresia
Performance/production
Playwright Theresia Walser on children's reactions to Christmas plays. Germany. Switzerland. 1997. Lang.: Ger. 2027
Volker Hesse's production of *King Kongs Töchter (King Kong's Daughters)* by Theresia Walser. Switzerland: Zurich. 1998. Lang.: Ger. 2401

Walsh, Enda
Institutions
English-language plays at Berlin Festwochen. Germany: Berlin. 1998. Lang.: Ger. 1623
Performance/production
Political changes reflected in Berlin theatre productions. Germany: Berlin. 1998. Lang.: Ger. 1958
Collection of newspaper reviews by London theatre critics. UK-England: London. 1998. Lang.: Eng. 2416
Plays/librettos/scripts
German view of English and American drama. UK-England. USA. 1998. Lang.: Ger. 3455

Walter Kerr Theatre (New York, NY)
Design/technology
Set designs of Francis O'Connor. USA: New York, NY. 1998. Lang.: Eng. 1541

Walters, Sam
Basic theatrical documents
Text of *Sperm Wars* by David Lewis. UK-England. 1998. Lang.: Eng. 1476
Performance/production
Collection of newspaper reviews by London theatre critics. UK-England: London. 1998. Lang.: Eng. 2505
Collection of newspaper reviews by London theatre critics. UK-England: London. 1998. Lang.: Eng. 2552
Collection of newspaper reviews by London theatre critics. UK-England: London. 1998. Lang.: Eng. 2585

Walton, Dawn
Performance/production
Collection of newspaper reviews by London theatre critics. UK-England: London. 1998. Lang.: Eng. 2549

Walton, Tony
Design/technology
Creativity and beauty in theatrical design. USA. 1998. Lang.: Eng. 322
Stage technician Pete Feller. USA. 1920-1998. Lang.: Eng. 330
Film design work of Tony Walton. USA. 1965-1998. Lang.: Eng. 3902

Waltz, Sasha
Administration
Interviews with German theatre and film directors. Germany. 1998. Lang.: Ger. 1385
Performance/production
Interview with choreographer Sasha Waltz. Germany: Berlin. 1998. Lang.: Ger. 1285

Wandel, Rüdiger
Plays/librettos/scripts
Analysis of *Café Mitte (Café Center)* by Volker Ludwig. Germany: Berlin. 1997-1998. Lang.: Ger. 4393

Wandlung, Die (Transfiguration)
Plays/librettos/scripts
Analysis of revisions of plays by Ernst Toller. Germany. 1920-1939. Lang.: Eng. 3172

Wang, Gui
Basic theatrical documents
Anthology of contemporary Chinese drama. China, People's Republic of. 1979-1986. Lang.: Eng. 1414

Wang, Peigong
Basic theatrical documents
Anthology of contemporary Chinese drama. China, People's Republic of. 1979-1986. Lang.: Eng. 1414

Wannus, Saadallah
Plays/librettos/scripts
Analysis of *Al-Mawik Huwa Al-Mawik (The King Is the King)* by Saadallah Wannus. Syria. 1977. Lang.: Eng. 3418

War Memorial Opera House (San Francisco, CA)
Design/technology
Stage lighting at the War Memorial Opera House. USA: San Francisco, CA. 1998. Lang.: Eng. 280

War Memorial Opera House (San Francisco, CA) — cont'd

Performance spaces
New stage lighting of War Memorial Opera House. USA: San Francisco, CA. 1998. Lang.: Eng. 465
Architectural and technical renovations to the War Memorial Opera House. USA: San Francisco, CA. 1997. Lang.: Eng. 478

War of the Worlds
Performance/production
Popular American radio and the importance of the disembodied voice. USA. 1929-1940. Lang.: Eng. 3864

War Requiem
Plays/librettos/scripts
Derek Jarman's adaptation of works by Benjamin Britten and Wilfred Owen. UK-England. 1968-1988. Lang.: Eng. 4822

War to End War, The
Basic theatrical documents
Collection of plays by Charles L. Mee. USA. 1986-1995. Lang.: Eng. 1496

Warchus, Matthew
Design/technology
Lighting designer Hugh Vanstone. USA: New York, NY. 1998. Lang.: Eng. 1554
Performance/production
Collection of newspaper reviews by London theatre critics. UK-England: London. 1998. Lang.: Eng. 2419
Collection of newspaper reviews by London theatre critics. UK-England: London. 1998. Lang.: Eng. 2461
Postmodern staging and design: Matthew Warchus' *Henry V*. UK-England. 1970-1994. Lang.: Eng. 2636

Ward, Nira
Design/technology
Design concept for Ralph Lemon's dance piece *Geography* at BAM. USA: New York, NY. 1998. Lang.: Eng. 1248

Ward, Philip
Performance/production
Collection of newspaper reviews by London theatre critics. UK-England: London. Lang.: Eng. 2408

Wardle, Irving
Performance/production
Theatre Magazine's anniversary issue. USA. 1968-1998. Lang.: Eng. 617

Warenfalk, Wiveka
Performance/production
Seven critics on their favorite character or portrayal. Sweden. 1950. Lang.: Swe. 2369

Warfield, Jean Mae
Basic theatrical documents
Libretto for *Christina, Queen of Sweden*. USA. 1988. Lang.: Eng. 4423

Warkentin, Veralyn
Plays/librettos/scripts
Mennonite drama of Veralyn Warkentin and Vern Thiessen. Canada. 1890-1997. Lang.: Eng. 2829

Warlikowski, Krzysztof
Performance/production
Contemporary Polish productions of Shakespeare. Poland. 1990-1998. Lang.: Pol. 2213
The new generation of Polish directors. Poland. 1989-1998. Lang.: Pol. 2219

Warner, Chris
Performance/production
Collection of newspaper reviews by London theatre critics. UK-England: London. 1998. Lang.: Eng. 2421

Warner, Deborah
Performance/production
The current state of opera in England. UK-England. 1997. Lang.: Eng. 4705

Warner, Jack
Administration
Interviews about film producer Jack Warner. USA: Hollywood, CA. 1918-1978. Lang.: Eng. 3875

Warren, Lil
Performance/production
Collection of newspaper reviews by London theatre critics. UK-England: London. 1998. Lang.: Eng. 2446

Warren, Louise
Performance/production
Collection of newspaper reviews by London theatre critics. UK-England: London. 1998. Lang.: Eng. 2453
Collection of newspaper reviews by London theatre critics. UK-England: London. 1998. Lang.: Eng. 2570

Warren, Mercy Otis
Plays/librettos/scripts
Gender and politics in Romantic tragedies of Mercy Otis Warren. USA. 1783-1785. Lang.: Eng. 3575

Warrior
Performance/production
Creating the role of Mrs. Scully in Shirley Gee's *Warrior*. USA: Long Beach, CA. 1997. Lang.: Eng. 2753
Creating the role of Billy Cuttle in Shirley Gee's *Warrior*. USA: Long Beach, CA. 1997. Lang.: Eng. 2758

Was geschah, nachdem Nora ihren Mann verlassen hatte (What Happened After Nora Left Her Husband)
Plays/librettos/scripts
Analysis of Elfriede Jelinek's adaptation of *Et Dukkehjem (A Doll's House)* by Ibsen. Austria. 1979. Lang.: Eng. 2782

Was ihr wollt
Performance/production
Interview with opera composer Manfred Trojahn. Germany: Munich. 1998. Lang.: Ger. 4582

Was sollen wir tun (What Shall We Do)
Performance/production
Productions of Tankred Dorst's *Was sollen wir tun (What Shall We Do)*. Germany: Dresden, Bonn. 1997-1998. Lang.: Ger. 1971
Plays/librettos/scripts
Family conflict in *Was sollen wir tun (What Shall We Do)* by Tankred Dorst and *Die Hamletmaschine (Hamletmachine)* by Heiner Müller. Germany. 1997-1998. Lang.: Ger. 3148

Wasa Teater (Vaasa)
Performance/production
Swedish and bilingual Finnish-Swedish theatre. Finland: Turku, Vaasa. 1998. Lang.: Eng, Fre. 1913

Washington Opera (Washington, DC)
Design/technology
Lighting for Washington Opera's production of *Doña Francisquita*. USA: Washington, DC. 1998. Lang.: Eng. 4290
Performance/production
Tenor and artistic director of Washington Opera Plácido Domingo. 1941-1998. Lang.: Eng. 4512
Heinz Fricke, music director of Washington Opera. USA: Washington, DC. 1993-1998. Lang.: Eng. 4734

Washington Square Players (New York, NY)
Performance/production
Notable productions of plays by Eugene O'Neill. USA. 1916-1996. Lang.: Eng. 2752

Wasserstein, Wendy
Performance/production
Collection of newspaper reviews by London theatre critics. UK-England: London. 1998. Lang.: Eng. 2498
Plays/librettos/scripts
Women playwrights' addresses to the Women's Project conference. USA. 1997. Lang.: Eng. 3589

Wasted
Performance/production
Collection of newspaper reviews by London theatre critics. UK-England: London. 1998. Lang.: Eng. 2494

Waszerka, Ingo
Performance/production
Productions of the Bad Hersfelder Festspiele. Germany: Bad Hersfeld. 1998. Lang.: Ger. 1991

Watanabe, Kazuko
Institutions
New productions of Düsseldorfer Schauspielhaus. Germany: Dusseldorf. 1998. Lang.: Ger. 1654
Plays/librettos/scripts
Analysis of *Madschun al-Malik* by Michael Roes. Germany: Düsseldorf. 1998. Lang.: Ger. 3157

Water Children, The
Plays/librettos/scripts
Analysis of *The Water Children* by Wendy Macleod. USA. 1998. Lang.: Eng. 3613

Water Hen, The
SEE
Kurka vodna.

Water puppets
Performance/production
Collection of newspaper reviews by London theatre critics. UK-England: London. 1998. Lang.: Eng. 2464

Waterhouse, Keith
Performance/production
Collection of newspaper reviews by London theatre critics. UK-England: London. 1998. Lang.: Eng. 2425

Waterhouse, Keith — cont'd

Collection of newspaper reviews by London theatre critics. UK-England: London. 1998. Lang.: Eng. 2502

Watermans Theatre (London)

Performance/production

Collection of newspaper reviews by London theatre critics. UK-England: London. 1998. Lang.: Eng. 2409

Collection of newspaper reviews by London theatre critics. UK-England: London. 1998. Lang.: Eng. 2502

Watermill Theatre (Newbury)

Institutions

Profile of Watermill Theatre. UK-England: Newbury. 1998. Lang.: Eng. 1744

Waters, Elizabeth

Training

Modern dance teacher Elizabeth Waters. USA. 1920-1950. Lang.: Eng. 1342

Waters, Steve

Performance/production

Collection of newspaper reviews by London theatre critics. UK-England: London. 1998. Lang.: Eng. 2440

Watkeys, Colin

Performance/production

Collection of newspaper reviews by London theatre critics. UK-England: London. 1998. Lang.: Eng. 2546

Watson, Grant

Performance/production

Collection of newspaper reviews by London theatre critics. UK-England: London. 1998. Lang.: Eng. 2463

Way, Brian

Performance/production

Preparing a production of Brian Way's participatory *The Mirrorman.* USA. 1987. Lang.: Eng. 633

Wayang

Performance/production

Gender construction and aesthetics of Central Javanese *wayang.* Indonesia. 1650-1998. Lang.: Eng. 4925

Wayang kulit

Performance/production

Performative elements in *wayang kulit* puppet theatre. Indonesia. 1700-1998. Lang.: Eng. 4924

We're Hong Kong

Relation to other fields

Theatre and politics in Hong Kong. Hong Kong. 1984-1996. Lang.: Eng. 3772

Weaver, Lois

Performance/production

Analysis of pop performance. USA: New York, NY. 1980-1988. Lang.: Eng. 664

Lois Weaver's *Faith and Dancing* and the CD-ROM in interactive performance. UK-England. USA. 1996. Lang.: Eng. 971

Web, The

Performance/production

Collection of newspaper reviews by London theatre critics. UK-England: London. 1998. Lang.: Eng. 2476

Webb, Paul

Performance/production

Collection of newspaper reviews by London theatre critics. UK-England: London. 1998. Lang.: Eng. 2415

Weber, Anselm

Performance/production

Recent productions of Deutsches Schauspielhaus. Germany: Hamburg. 1998. Lang.: Ger. 2034

Weber, Carl Maria von

Performance/production

Weber's *Der Freischütz* and the Neues Schauspielhaus. Germany: Berlin. 1821. Lang.: Eng. 4581

Weber, Die (Weavers, The)

Plays/librettos/scripts

Translating Hauptmann's *Die Weber (The Weavers)* into Scots dialect. UK-Scotland: Dundee, Glasgow. 1997. Lang.: Eng. 3513

Weber, Hasko

Plays/librettos/scripts

Hasko Weber's production of *Morir (A Moment Before Dying)* by Sergi Belbel. Germany: Dresden. 1998. Lang.: Ger. 3132

Family conflict in *Was sollen wir tun (What Shall We Do)* by Tankred Dorst and *Die Hamletmaschine (Hamletmachine)* by Heiner Müller. Germany. 1997-1998. Lang.: Ger. 3148

Weber, Imre

Design/technology

Survey of an exhibition of Hungarian scene design. Hungary: Budapest. 1998. Lang.: Hun. 195

Catalogue of an exhibition devoted to Hungarian theatre and film. Hungary: Budapest. 1998. Lang.: Hun. 197

Weber, Knut

Administration

Interviews with theatre managers regarding the changing cultural landscape. Germany: Bruchsal, Esslingen, Tübingen. 1998. Lang.: Ger. 1381

Institutions

German theatres' responses to threatened closings and mergers. Germany: Esslingen, Tübingen. 1998. Lang.: Ger. 1665

Weber, Manfred

Performance/production

Productions of the Kleist theatre festival. Germany: Frankfurt/Oder. 1998. Lang.: Ger. 1993

Relation to other fields

Manfred Weber on directing Děvad Karahasan's translation of *Leonce und Lena* by Büchner. Bosnia: Sarajevo. 1997-1998. Lang.: Ger. 3730

Webster, George

Performance/production

English actors in Kassel. Germany: Kassel. 1592-1620. Lang.: Eng. 2016

Webster, John

Performance/production

Collection of newspaper reviews by London theatre critics. UK-England: London. 1998. Lang.: Eng. 2432

Denise Gillman's production of Webster's *The Duchess of Malfi,* Theatre of NOTE. USA: Los Angeles, CA. 1998. Lang.: Eng. 2714

Plays/librettos/scripts

Plague imagery in Jacobean tragedy. England. 1618-1642. Lang.: Eng. 2889

The influence of Webster, Middleton, and Shakespeare on the poetry of Robert Browning. England. 1590-1889. Lang.: Eng. 2906

The representation of historical female characters on the Renaissance stage. England. 1580-1615. Lang.: Eng. 2922

Feminist analysis of Webster's *The Duchess of Malfi.* England. 1613. Lang.: Eng. 2931

Authority and medicine in Webster's *The Duchess of Malfi.* England. 1613. Lang.: Eng. 2947

Martial law and Renaissance drama and fiction. Europe. 1563-1753. Lang.: Eng. 3059

Webster, Margaret

Performance/production

Actor/director Margaret Webster, gender and sexuality. UK-England. USA. 1905-1972. Lang.: Eng. 2590

Webster, Thomas

Design/technology

Lighting design for Verdi's *Macbeth* at La Scala. Italy: Milan. 1998. Lang.: Eng. 4435

Wedding Band

Plays/librettos/scripts

Black self-determination in the plays of Alice Childress. USA. 1949-1969. Lang.: Eng. 3579

Miscegenation in American drama. USA. 1909-1969. Lang.: Eng. 3599

Wedekind, Frank

Basic theatrical documents

Complete libretto of Alban Berg's *Lulu.* Austria. 1935. Lang.: Fre, Ger. 4412

Performance/production

Collection of newspaper reviews by London theatre critics. UK-England: London. Lang.: Eng. 2408

Significant interpreters of the title role of Alban Berg's *Lulu.* 1937-1996. Lang.: Fre. 4509

Arnold Schoenberg's refusal to complete Alban Berg's unfinished opera *Lulu.* Austria. 1935. Lang.: Fre. 4533

Plays/librettos/scripts

A private performance of *Die Büchse der Pandora (Pandora's Box)* by Frank Wedekind. Austria: Vienna. 1905. Lang.: Fre. 2783

The image of motherhood in German-language drama. Austria. Germany. 1890-1910. Lang.: Ger. 2787

Women in German turn-of-the-century drama. Germany. 1890-1910. Lang.: Eng. 3158

Excerpt of Frank Wedekind's preface to *Die Büchse der Pandora (Pandora's Box).* Germany. 1906. Lang.: Fre. 3169

Dictionary of Alban Berg's *Lulu.* Austria. 1935. Lang.: Fre. 4760

Wedekind's Lulu plays and their adaptation by Berg. Germany. Austria. 1895-1935. Lang.: Fre. 4798

Weeds

Basic theatrical documents

Screenplay for *Weeds* by Alex Lewin, winner of annual student screenplay competition. USA. 1998. Lang.: Eng. 3894

Weekenders
Performance/production
Collection of newspaper reviews by London theatre critics. UK-England: London. 1998. Lang.: Eng. 2454

Weel, Liva
Administration
The star system and Danish theatre. Denmark. 1930-1997. Lang.: Dan. 1377

Wehner, Ross
Performance/production
Collection of newspaper reviews by London theatre critics. UK-England: London. 1998. Lang.: Eng. 2442

Wei, Minglun
Basic theatrical documents
Anthology of contemporary Chinese drama. China, People's Republic of. 1979-1986. Lang.: Eng. 1414

Wei, Mingren
Performance/production
Rural Chinese productions of Puccini's *Turandot*. China, People's Republic of: Beijing. 1998. Lang.: Eng. 4541

Weiberkomödie (Women's Comedy)
Performance/production
Recent productions of Schauspiel Leipzig. Germany: Leipzig. 1997-1998. Lang.: Ger. 2011

Weidman, Charles
Performance/production
Dance-mime Angna Enters. USA. 1905-1923. Lang.: Eng. 1319

Weigel, Alexander
Performance/production
Interview with director Alexander Weigel. Germany, East. 1970-1990. Lang.: Eng. 2042

Weil, Ernö
Administration
Ernö Weil, manager of Theater Pforzheim. Germany: Pforzheim. 1997-1998. Lang.: Ger. 1380

Weill, Kurt
Performance/production
Interview with community theatre director Kent Ekberg. Sweden: Stockholm. 1973-1998. Lang.: Swe. 2385
Brecht and the vocal role. Germany. 1920-1998. Lang.: Swe. 4295
Composers and the work of Bertolt Brecht. Germany. 1928-1998. Lang.: Ger. 4297
The career of soprano Lotte Lenya. Austria: Vienna. 1898-1981. Lang.: Eng. 4352
Robert Wilson's production of Brecht's *Der Ozeanflug*. Germany: Berlin. 1998. Lang.: Ger. 4356
Brecht and Weill's *Die Dreigroschenoper (The Three Penny Opera)* directed by László Vándorfi. Hungary: Veszprém.1998. Lang.: Hun. 4358
Two Hungarian productions of *Die Dreigroschenoper (The Three Penny Opera)*. Hungary: Budapest, Szeged. 1998. Lang.: Hun. 4362
Review of Salzburger Festspiele performances. Austria: Salzburg. 1998. Lang.: Ger. 4527
Opera productions of the Salzburg Festival. Austria: Salzburg. 1998. Lang.: Hun. 4531
Production history of *Die Bürgschaft* by Kurt Weill and Casper Neher. Germany: Berlin, Bielefeld. 1931-1998. Lang.: Eng. 4588
Plays/librettos/scripts
The search for a lost translation of *The Seven Deadly Sins* by Brecht and Weill. Germany. UK-England. 1933-1998. Lang.: Eng. 4392
Hero and anti-hero in contemporary opera production. Germany. 1998. Lang.: Ger. 4791
W.H. Auden as an opera librettist and translator. UK-England. 1907-1973. Lang.: Eng. 4825

Weimann, Robert
Performance/production
Directors Manfred Wekwerth and Robert Weimann on Brecht and Shakespeare. Germany, East. 1945-1990. Lang.: Eng. 2043
Director Robert Weimann on East German Shakespeare production. Germany, East. 1945-1995. Lang.: Eng. 2053

Weingarten, Romain
Performance/production
Collection of newspaper reviews by London theatre critics. UK-England: London. 1998. Lang.: Eng. 2514

Weinstein, Arnold
Performance/production
Theatre Magazine's anniversary issue. USA. 1968-1998. Lang.: Eng. 617

Weir, Peter
Design/technology
Lighting design for Peter Weir's film *The Truman Show*. USA. 1998. Lang.: Eng. 3919

Weir, The
Performance/production
Collection of newspaper reviews by London theatre critics. UK-England: London. 1998. Lang.: Eng. 2428
Collection of newspaper reviews by London theatre critics. UK-England: London. 1998. Lang.: Eng. 2520
Plays/librettos/scripts
Playwright Conor McPherson. Ireland. 1998. Lang.: Eng. 3209

Weise, Klaus
Performance/production
Reviews of German Shakespearean productions. Germany: Wuppertal, Cologne, Oberhausen. 1998. Lang.: Ger. 2017

Weiss, Peter
Performance/production
Interview with director Jochen Gerz. Germany: Berlin. 1998. Lang.: Ger, Fre, Dut, Eng. 1967
Theory/criticism
Representation and delegation in theatre. 1998. Lang.: Eng. 3800

Weiss, Peter Eliot
Plays/librettos/scripts
Review of collections of plays with gay themes. Canada. 1996. Lang.: Eng. 2802

Weissberger, Augusta
Institutions
History of Mercury Theatre. USA: New York, NY. 1937-1942. Lang.: Eng. 1776

Wekwerth, Manfred
Institutions
The fate of the Berliner Ensemble after the resignation of artistic director Manfred Wekwerth. Germany: Berlin. 1991-1998. Lang.:Ger. 1625
Performance/production
German directors about the meaning of Brecht today. Germany. 1998. Lang.: Ger. 1948
Directors Manfred Wekwerth and Robert Weimann on Brecht and Shakespeare. Germany, East. 1945-1990. Lang.: Eng. 2043

Welborn, Tracey
Performance/production
Tenor Tracey Welborn. USA. 1962-1998. Lang.: Eng. 4738

Welch, Andrew
Institutions
Interview with Andrew Welch, new director of Chichester Festival. UK-England: Chichester. 1998. Lang.: Eng. 1745

Welcome to Woop Woop
Design/technology
Costumes for the film *Welcome to Woop Woop*. Australia. 1998. Lang.: Eng. 3899

Welfare State International (Ulverston)
Institutions
Interview with John Fox of Welfare State International. UK-England: Ulverston. 1968-1988. Lang.: Eng. 4236

Wellemeyer, Tobias
Performance/production
Productions of Tankred Dorst's *Was sollen wir tun (What Shall We Do)*. Germany: Dresden, Bonn. 1997-1998. Lang.: Ger. 1971
Plays/librettos/scripts
Family conflict in *Was sollen wir tun (What Shall We Do)* by Tankred Dorst and *Die Hamletmaschine (Hamletmachine)* by Heiner Müller. Germany. 1997-1998. Lang.: Ger. 3148

Welles, Orson
Design/technology
Scenery in Orson Welles' film adaptation of Shakespeare's *Macbeth*. USA. 1948. Lang.: Fre. 3920
Institutions
History of Mercury Theatre. USA: New York, NY. 1937-1942. Lang.: Eng. 1776
Performance/production
Collection of newspaper reviews by London theatre critics. UK-England. 1998. Lang.: Eng. 2485
Popular American radio and the importance of the disembodied voice. USA. 1929-1940. Lang.: Eng. 3864
Suzanne Cloutier's role in Shakespeare's *Othello*, directed by Orson Welles. Italy. 1952. Lang.: Fre. 3935

Wellman, Mac
Plays/librettos/scripts
Strindberg's influence on playwrights Len Jenkin and Mac Wellman. USA. 1887-1998. Lang.: Eng. 3584

Welsh, Irvine
Performance/production
Collection of newspaper reviews by London theatre critics. UK-England: London. 1998. Lang.: Eng. 2412
Collection of newspaper reviews by London theatre critics. UK-England: Leeds, Manchester. 1998. Lang.: Eng. 2433
Plays/librettos/scripts
Sex, drugs, and violence in contemporary British drama. UK-England. 1991-1998. Lang.: Eng. 3494
Werler, Georges
Basic theatrical documents
French translation of *Alfred Stieglitz Loves O'Keeffe* by Lanie Robertson. USA. France. 1987-1997. Lang.: Fre. 1505
Wernicke, Herbert
Design/technology
Herbert Wernicke's set and costume designs for his own production of Strauss's *Elektra*. Germany: Munich. 1998. Lang.: Eng. 4429
Performance/production
Review of Salzburger Festspiele performances. Austria: Salzburg. 1998. Lang.: Ger. 4527
Opera productions of the Salzburg Festival. Austria: Salzburg. 1998. Lang.: Hun. 4531
Press reactions to productions of Offenbach's *Orphée aux Enfers*. Belgium. Switzerland. France. 1997. Lang.: Fre. 4535
Opera director Herbert Wernicke. Germany. 1986-1998. Lang.: Ger. 4600
Wertenbaker, Timberlake
Performance/production
Collection of newspaper reviews by London theatre critics. UK-England: London. 1998. Lang.: Eng. 2470
Collection of newspaper reviews by London theatre critics. UK-England: London. 1998. Lang.: Eng. 2507
Collection of newspaper reviews by London theatre critics. UK-England: London. 1998. Lang.: Eng. 2518
Plays/librettos/scripts
The Break of Day, Timberlake Wertenbaker's adaptation of Čechov's *Three Sisters*. UK-England. Russia. 1901-1995. Lang.: Eng. 3510
West Indian, The
Plays/librettos/scripts
Judith Sargent Murray's *Traveller Returned* and its source. USA. 1771-1796. Lang.: Eng. 3672
West Side Story
Design/technology
Costume designs by Irene Sharaff. USA. 1933-1976. Lang.: Eng. 277
Performance/production
Collection of newspaper reviews by London theatre critics. UK-England: London. 1998. Lang.: Eng. 2516
An open-air production of *West Side Story* directed by László Vándorfi. Hungary: Veszprém. 1998. Lang.: Hun. 4361
West Yorkshire Playhouse (Leeds)
Performance/production
Collection of newspaper reviews by London theatre critics. UK-England. 1998. Lang.: Eng. 2456
Michael Birch's production of *Vanity Fair*. UK-England: Leeds. 1997. Lang.: Eng. 2600
Westfälisches Landestheater (Castrop-Rauxel)
Administration
Theatrical marketing in North Rhine-Westphalia. Germany. 1994-1998. Lang.: Ger. 6
Westphal, Gert
Performance/production
Television adaptations of works by Goethe. Germany. 1965-1997. Lang.: Eng. 4061
Wetterleuchten (Sheet Lightning)
Performance/production
Director Angela Brodauf. Germany: Dortmund. 1984-1998. Lang.: Ger. 1989
Wetzstoen, Ross
Theory/criticism
Obituary for critic Ross Wetzstoen, who inspired the Obie Awards. USA. 1932-1998. Lang.: Eng. 3847
Wexler, Norman
Performance/production
Collection of newspaper reviews by London theatre critics. UK-England: London. 1998. Lang.: Eng. 2467
Whale, James
Basic theatrical documents
Screenplay of *Gods and Monsters* by Bill Condon. USA. 1998. Lang.: Eng. 3882
Design/technology
Production design for Bill Condon's film *Gods and Monsters*. USA: Hollywood, CA. 1998. Lang.: Eng. 3908
Plays/librettos/scripts
Interview with film-maker Bill Condon. USA. 1998. Lang.: Eng. 4021
What Lesbians Do ... On Stage
Performance/production
Collection of newspaper reviews by London theatre critics. UK-England: London. 1998. Lang.: Eng. 2520
What Where
Plays/librettos/scripts
Authority, truth, and the allegory of the cave in works of Samuel Beckett. France. Ireland. 1953-1986. Lang.: Eng. 3085
Analysis of Samuel Beckett's later plays. Ireland. France. 1950-1989. Lang.: Eng. 3210
Heinz Holliger's operatic adaptation of Samuel Beckett's *What Where*. Europe. 1992. Lang.: Eng. 4768
Operatic adaptations of Beckett's plays by Heinz Holliger. Europe. 1976-1988. Lang.: Eng. 4776
What You Will
Plays/librettos/scripts
The politics of gender in the plays of John Marston. England. 1599-1634. Lang.: Eng. 3009
What? So What?
Performance/production
Collection of newspaper reviews by London theatre critics. UK-England: London. 1998. Lang.: Eng. 2517
Wheeldon, Christopher
Performance/production
New male dancers of New York City Ballet. USA: New York, NY. 1998. Lang.: Eng. 1177
Wheeler, Davis
Performance/production
Creating the role of Julien Davis Cornell in *The Trial of Ezra Pound*. USA: Long Beach, CA. 1997. Lang.: Eng. 2712
Wheeler, Trudy
Institutions
Profile of TAXI Children's Theatre. USA: Louisville, KY. 1992-1998. Lang.: Eng. 390
When Brains Don't Count
Performance/production
Collection of newspaper reviews by London theatre critics. UK-England: London. 1998. Lang.: Eng. 2549
When We Dead Awaken
SEE
Når vi døde vågner.
... Where Late the Sweet Birds Sang
Basic theatrical documents
Text of ... *Where Late the Sweet Birds Sang* by Sheryle Criswell. USA. 1998. Lang.: Eng. 1483
Plays/librettos/scripts
Interview with playwright Sheryle Criswell. USA. 1998. Lang.: Eng. 3681
Theory/criticism
Playwright Sheryle Criswell on criticism of her work. USA. 1998. Lang.: Eng. 3840
Whisper of a Leaf Falling, The
Performance/production
Collection of newspaper reviews by London theatre critics. UK-England: London. 1998. Lang.: Eng. 2538
Whispers in the Heart
Performance/production
Analysis of performance pieces reacting to the Australian bicentenary. Australia: Darwin, Sydney. 1988. Lang.: Eng. 1815
Whistle Down the Wind
Performance/production
Collection of newspaper reviews by London theatre critics. UK-England: London. 1998. Lang.: Eng. 2425
White Bear Theatre (London)
Performance/production
Collection of newspaper reviews by London theatre critics. UK-England: London. 1998. Lang.: Eng. 2416
Collection of newspaper reviews by London theatre critics. UK-England: London. 1998. Lang.: Eng. 2439
Collection of newspaper reviews by London theatre critics. UK-England: London. 1998. Lang.: Eng. 2452
Collection of newspaper reviews by London theatre critics. UK-England: London. 1998. Lang.: Eng. 2464

White Bear Theatre (London) — cont'd
Collection of newspaper reviews by London theatre critics. UK-England: London. 1998. Lang.: Eng. 2469
Collection of newspaper reviews by London theatre critics. UK-England: London. 1998. Lang.: Eng. 2478
Collection of newspaper reviews by London theatre critics. UK-England: London. 1998. Lang.: Eng. 2524
Collection of newspaper reviews by London theatre critics. UK-England: London. 1998. Lang.: Eng. 2550
Collection of newspaper reviews by London theatre critics. UK-England: London. 1998. Lang.: Eng. 2566

White Noises
Basic theatrical documents
Text of *White Noises* by Shannon Jackson. USA. 1998. Lang.: Eng. 1490
Plays/librettos/scripts
Shannon Jackson on her solo piece *White Noises.* USA. 1998. Lang.: Eng. 3619

White Oak Dance Project (New York, NY)
Performance/production
A performance by Mikhail Baryshnikov and the White Oak Dance Project. USA: Washington, DC. 1990-1998. Lang.: Hun. 1194

White Slave, The
Plays/librettos/scripts
Analysis of *The White Slave* by Bartley Campbell. USA. 1882. Lang.: Eng. 3660

White Wedding
SEE
Biale małżeństwo.

White, E.B.
Performance/production
Collection of newspaper reviews by London theatre critics. UK-England: London. 1998. Lang.: Eng. 2550

White, John
Design/technology
The original stage machinery designed by John White at Her Majesty's Theatre. UK-England: London. 1887-1986. Lang.: Eng. 1528

White, Matthew
Performance/production
Collection of newspaper reviews by London theatre critics. UK-England: London. 1998. Lang.: Eng. 2476
Collection of newspaper reviews by London theatre critics. UK-England: London. 1998. Lang.: Eng. 2553

White, Seta
Performance/production
Collection of newspaper reviews by London theatre critics. UK-England: London. 1998. Lang.: Eng. 2524

Whitefriars Company (London)
Institutions
History of the short-lived first Whitefriars Company. England: London. 1607-1608. Lang.: Eng. 1599

Whitehall Theatre (London)
Performance/production
Collection of newspaper reviews by London theatre critics. UK-England: London. 1998. Lang.: Eng. 2513

Whitehead, Simon
Performance/production
Dancer/choreographer Rosemary Lee. UK-England: London. 1989-1998. Lang.: Eng. 1307

Whiteheaded Boy, The
Performance/production
Collection of newspaper reviews by London theatre critics. UK-England: London. 1998. Lang.: Eng. 2473

Whitehouse, Paul
Performance/production
Collection of newspaper reviews by London theatre critics. UK-England: London. 1998. Lang.: Eng. 2573

Whiting, John
Plays/librettos/scripts
The nature and language of menace in the plays of John Whiting, Harold Pinter and Sam Shepard. USA. UK-England. 1960-1985. Lang. :Eng. 3576

Whittington Junior, and His Sensation Cat
Performance/production
Collection of newspaper reviews by London theatre critics. UK-England: London. 1998. Lang.: Eng. 2557

Whittington, Gary
Design/technology
Lighting expert Gary Whittington. USA. 1952-1998. Lang.: Eng. 275

Whittinton, Amanda
Performance/production
Collection of newspaper reviews by London theatre critics. UK-England: London. 1998. Lang.: Eng. 2550

Who's Afraid of Virginia Woolf?
Plays/librettos/scripts
Aggressive language in modern drama. Europe. USA. 1960-1985. Lang.: Eng. 3055
A method of analysis for the drama. USA. 1920-1975. Lang.: Eng. 3537
The enneagram system applied to Albee's *Who's Afraid of Virginia Woolf?.* USA. 1998. Lang.: Eng. 3665

Whore of Babylon, The
Plays/librettos/scripts
Protestant belief and English Reformation drama. England. 1535-1607. Lang.: Eng. 2972

Whoredom
Performance/production
Collection of newspaper reviews by London theatre critics. UK-England: London. 1998. Lang.: Eng. 2571

Wickert, Hartmut
Performance/production
Productions of new plays by Peter Handke and Katharine Gericke at Niedersächsische Staatstheater. Germany: Hannover. 1998. Lang.: Ger. 1983

Wickham House (London)
Performance/production
Collection of newspaper reviews by London theatre critics. UK-England: London. 1998. Lang.: Eng. 2473

Widegren, Jennie
Performance/production
Interview with dancer Jennie Widegren. Sweden: Stockholm. 1995-1998. Lang.: Swe. 1306

Widmer, Urs
Performance/production
Volker Hesse's production of *Die schwarze Spinne (The Black Spider)* by Urs Widmer. Switzerland: Zurich. 1998. Lang.: Ger. 2402
Collection of newspaper reviews by London theatre critics. UK-England: London. 1998. Lang.: Eng. 2493

Widow's Tears, The
Plays/librettos/scripts
Influences on *'Tis Pity She's a Whore* by John Ford. England. 1587-1631. Lang.: Eng. 2937

Widowers' Houses
Plays/librettos/scripts
Analysis of early plays by George Bernard Shaw. UK-England. 1892-1900. Lang.: Eng. 3470
Theory/criticism
Ibsen, 'new' theatre, and Shaw's *Plays Unpleasant.* UK-England. 1891-1898. Lang.: Eng. 3832

Wiederman, Katrine
Plays/librettos/scripts
Interview with playwright Sofia Fredén. Sweden: Stockholm. Denmark: Copenhagen. 1995-1998. Lang.: Swe. 3409

Wieler, Jossi
Institutions
Productions of the Salzburg Festival. Austria: Salzburg. 1998. Lang.: Ger. 1573
Performance/production
Interview with opera director Jossi Wieler. Germany: Stuttgart. Switzerland: Basel. 1998. Lang.: Ger. 4592

Wiener Schauspielhaus (Vienna)
Plays/librettos/scripts
Playwright, dramaturg, and director Thomas Jonigk on contemporary theatre. Austria: Vienna. 1998. Lang.: Ger. 2781

Wiesenthal, Grete
Performance/production
Collaborative Symbolist dance/theatre projects. Europe. USA. 1916-1934. Lang.: Eng. 1268

Wife Without a Smile, A
Performance/production
Collection of newspaper reviews by London theatre critics. UK-England: London. 1998. Lang.: Eng. 2490

Wigman, Mary
Performance/production
Gender and politics in German dance. Germany. 1930-1932. Lang.: Eng. 928
Mary Wigman's summary of her work in choreography and dance training. Germany: Dresden. 1925. Lang.: Ger. 1290

Wigman, Mary — cont'd

Training
Dance teacher Louise Kloepper. USA. 1910-1996. Lang.: Eng. 1213

Wikström, Jan-Erik
Institutions
The 225th anniversary of the Royal Swedish Ballet. Sweden: Stockholm. 1773-1998. Lang.: Eng. 1048

Wilby, Rebecca
Performance/production
Collection of newspaper reviews by London theatre critics. UK-England: London. 1998. Lang.: Eng. 2585

Wild Duck, The
SEE
Vildanden.

Wild Honey
SEE ALSO
Platonov.

Wild, Franz Joseph
Performance/production
Television adaptations of works by Goethe. Germany. 1965-1997. Lang.: Eng. 4061

Wilde, Oscar
Basic theatrical documents
Catalan translation of *The Importance of Being Earnest* by Oscar Wilde. UK-England. 1895. Lang.: Cat. 1479
Max Meyerfeld's libretto for Zemlinsky's opera *Eine florentinische Tragödie.* Germany. 1917. Lang.: Ger, Fre. 4419
Klaren's librettos for *Der Zwerg* by Alexander Zemlinsky. Germany. 1922. Lang.: Fre, Ger. 4420
Institutions
Survey of the Theatertreffen festival. Germany: Berlin. 1998. Lang.: Swe. 1651
Performance/production
The work of director Einar Schleef. Germany: Düsseldorf. 1998. Lang.: Ger. 2026
Roman Viktjuk's production of *Salomé* by Oscar Wilde. Russia: Moscow. 1998. Lang.: Rus. 2266
Collection of newspaper reviews by London theatre critics. UK-England: London. 1998. Lang.: Eng. 2547
Collection of newspaper reviews by London theatre critics. UK-England: London. 1998. Lang.: Eng. 2566
Actors' interpretations of the title role in Oscar Wilde's *The Canterville Ghost.* UK-England. USA. 1943-1998. Lang.: Eng. 4066
Composer Franz Schreker and his connection with Zemlinsky's *Der Zwerg.* Germany. 1908-1923. Lang.: Fre. 4094
Plays/librettos/scripts
Max Meyerfeld's preface to the translation of *A Florentine Tragedy* by Oscar Wilde. Europe. 1895-1907. Lang.: Fre. 3057
Erotics and aesthetics in the work of Oscar Wilde. UK-England. 1881-1898. Lang.: Eng. 3424
Oscar Wilde biographer on his negative traits and addictive behaviors. UK-England. USA. 1998. Lang.: Eng. 3425
Wilde, Gide, and the censorship of Biblical drama. UK-England. France. 1892-1898. Lang.: Eng. 3441
The comedy of George Bernard Shaw and Oscar Wilde. UK-England. 1885-1900. Lang.: Eng. 3450
Playwright and author Oscar Wilde. UK-England. France. 1854-1900. Lang.: Fre. 3465
Linguistic style and action in plays of Wilde, Shaw, and Stoppard. UK-England. 1890-1985. Lang.: Eng. 3467
The source of the name Bunbury in Wilde's *Importance of Being Earnest.* UK-England: Worthing. 1894. Lang.: Eng. 3469
Talk as performance in the life and work of Oscar Wilde. UK-England. 1890-1900. Lang.: Eng. 3492
Analysis of Alexander Zemlinsky's *Der Zwerg.* Germany. 1922. Lang.: Fre. 4793
Theory/criticism
Theatrical dancing and the performance aesthetics of Wilde, Yeats, and Shaw. UK-England. Ireland. 1890-1950. Lang.: Eng. 1012

Wilder, Billy
Plays/librettos/scripts
Opera in American gangster films. USA. 1932-1990. Lang.: Eng. 4023

Wilder, Clinton
Plays/librettos/scripts
History of the Playwrights Unit. USA. 1963-1971. Lang.: Eng. 3570

Wilder, Gene
Basic theatrical documents
Text of *Young Frankenstein* by Gene Wilder and Mel Brooks. USA. 1974. Lang.: Eng. 3898
Plays/librettos/scripts
Interview with actor and screenwriter Gene Wilder. USA. 1998. Lang.: Eng. 3991

Wilder, Thornton
Performance/production
János Acs' *A mennyei hid (The Heavenly Bridge)* directed by Gábor Cziezel. Hungary: Debrecen. 1998. Lang.: Hun. 2069

Wildhorn, Frank
Administration
Performer Rebecca Spencer's experience as an Equity Deputy. USA: New York, NY. 1998. Lang.: Eng. 4320
Design/technology
Technical designs for *The Scarlet Pimpernel* directed by Robert Longbottom. USA: New York, NY. 1998. Lang.: Eng. 4331
Lighting design for *Jekyll & Hyde* directed by Robin Phillips. USA: New York, NY. 1998. Lang.: Eng. 4345

Will Shakespeare avagy akit akartok (Will Shakespeare: or, Whom You Will)
Performance/production
Reviews of new Hungarian musicals. Hungary: Budapest. 1997. Lang.: Hun. 4360

Willert, Gerhard
Institutions
Profile of new venue, Bayerisches Staatsschauspiel, Marstall. Germany: Munich. 1993-1998. Lang.: Ger. 1660

Williams, Bert
Performance/production
Musical theatre composer Will Marion Cook. USA. 1898-1950. Lang.: Eng. 4378

Williams, Grace
Design/technology
The 1998 USITT expo. USA: Long Beach, CA. 1998. Lang.: Eng. 251

Williams, Michael
Performance/production
Actor Michael Williams. UK-England: London. 1950-1998. Lang.: Eng. 2644

Williams, Paul
Design/technology
Sound design for the musical *Bugsy Malone.* UK-England: London. 1997. Lang.: Eng. 4327

Williams, Robin
Performance/production
A model for systematic analysis of vocal performance. USA. 1988-1997. Lang.: Eng. 636

Williams, Roy
Performance/production
Collection of newspaper reviews by London theatre critics. UK-England: London. 1998. Lang.: Eng. 2509

Williams, Saul
Basic theatrical documents
Screenplay of the film *Slam.* USA. 1998. Lang.: Eng. 3893
Plays/librettos/scripts
Interview with Saul Williams on writing and acting in the film *Slam.* USA. 1998. Lang.: Eng. 4002

Williams, Tennessee
Design/technology
Set design for Tennessee Williams' *Not About Nightingales* at the National. UK-England: London. 1998. Lang.: Eng. 1526
Performance/production
The idea of Hollywood in theatre autobiographies. USA. 1950-1990. Lang.: Eng. 665
The Italian premiere of *A Streetcar Named Desire* by Tennessee Williams. Italy: Rome. 1949. Lang.: Eng. 2172
Collection of newspaper reviews by London theatre critics. UK-England: London. 1998. Lang.: Eng. 2424
Collection of newspaper reviews by London theatre critics. UK-England: London. 1998. Lang.: Eng. 2435
Collection of newspaper reviews by London theatre critics. UK-England. 1998. Lang.: Eng. 2510
Trevor Nunn's production of *Not About Nightingales* by Tennessee Williams, Royal National Theatre. UK-England: London. 1998. Lang.: Swe. 2604
Creating the character Alma in Tennessee Williams' *Summer and Smoke.* USA. 1997. Lang.: Eng. 2665
Actors and directors on the late plays of Tennessee Williams. USA. 1966-1981. Lang.: Eng. 2675
The Tennessee Williams/New Orleans Literary Festival. USA: New Orleans, LA. 1998. Lang.: Eng. 2726

Williams, Tennessee — cont'd

Trevor Nunn's production of *Not About Nightingales* by Tennessee Williams, Alley Theatre. USA: Houston, TX. 1998. Lang.: Eng. 2729
Baritone Rodney Gilfry. USA. 1998. Lang.: Eng. 4736
André Previn's opera *A Streetcar Named Desire*. USA: San Francisco. 1998. Lang.: Eng. 4742
Plays/librettos/scripts
The unseen character in plays of O'Neill, Albee, and Tennessee Williams. USA. 1915-1995. Lang.: Eng. 3538
Analysis of plays by Tennessee Williams. USA. 1943-1970. Lang.: Eng. 3539
The romantic nature of Tennessee Williams' *The Glass Menagerie*. USA. 1944. Lang.: Eng. 3558
Eugene O'Neill and the creation of autobiographical drama. USA. 1940-1995. Lang.: Eng. 3561
Comparison of characters in plays of Georg Kaiser and Tennessee Williams. USA. Germany. 1912-1945. Lang.: Eng. 3588
Analysis of short stories by playwright Tennessee Williams. USA. 1943-1955. Lang.: Eng. 3601
Fairy-tale heroines in American drama and musical theatre. USA. 1945-1965. Lang.: Eng. 3617
Tennessee Williams's short story *Twenty-Seven Wagons Full of Cotton* and the plays based on it. USA. 1936-1979. Lang.: Eng. 3622
Realism and anti-realism in plays of Tennessee Williams. USA. 1945-1986. Lang.: Eng. 3626
Puritanism and predestination in *Suddenly Last Summer* by Tennessee Williams. USA. 1958. Lang.: Eng. 3631
Individualism in plays of Tennessee Williams. USA. 1944-1980. Lang.: Eng. 3634
Influence of the novelistic monologues of Eugene O'Neill. USA. 1911-1998. Lang.: Eng. 3641
Draft and revisions of *Suddenly Last Summer* by Tennessee Williams. USA. 1958. Lang.: Eng. 3658
Dramaturgical analysis of late plays of Tennessee Williams. USA. 1969-1978. Lang.: Eng. 3661
The return of the prodigal in American drama. USA. 1920-1985. Lang.: Eng. 3666
The recent renewal of interest in the plays of Tennessee Williams. USA. 1996-1998. Lang.: Eng. 3674
Analysis of Tennessee Williams' *Suddenly Last Summer* and 'Desire and the Black Masseur'. USA. 1946-1958. Lang.: Eng. 3678
Effeminacy on the American stage. USA. 1920-1998. Lang.: Eng. 3682
Metadrama in plays of Tennessee Williams. USA. 1944-1978. Lang.: Eng. 3686
Shame, puritanism, and sexuality in plays of Tennessee Williams. USA. 1950-1970. Lang.: Eng. 3701
Theory/criticism
Analysis of *Something Cloudy, Something Clear* by Tennessee Williams. USA. 1980-1981. Lang.: Eng. 3843

Williams, Willie
Design/technology
Combined video and lighting for U2 world tour. Ireland. 1997. Lang.: Eng. 198

Williamson, David
Plays/librettos/scripts
Analysis of *Dead White Males* by David Williamson. Australia. 1995. Lang.: Eng. 2773

Willmott, Phil
Performance/production
Collection of newspaper reviews by London theatre critics. UK-England: London. 1998. Lang.: Eng. 2493
Collection of newspaper reviews by London theatre critics. UK-England: London. 1998. Lang.: Eng. 2554

Wills, Warren
Performance/production
Collection of newspaper reviews by London theatre critics. UK-England: London. 1998. Lang.: Eng. 2535

Willy Protagoras enfermé dans les toilettes (Willy Protagoras Holed Up in the Toilets)
Performance/production
Comparison of simple productions and visual shows. Canada: Montreal, PQ, Quebec, PQ, Toronto, ON. 1998. Lang.: Fre. 1861

Wilma Theatre (Philadelphia, PA)
Design/technology
Design concept for Amy Freed's *The Psychic Life of Savages*, Wilma Theatre. USA: Philadelphia, PA. 1998. Lang.: Eng. 1555

Wilms, Bernd
Performance/production
Interview with director Bernd Wilms. Germany: Berlin. 1998. Lang.: Swe. 2018

Wilner Trupe (Vilna)
Performance/production
Vilna's Yiddish theatre companies. Poland: Vilna, Cracow. 1918-1939. Lang.: Pol. 2212

Wilshire, Toby
Performance/production
Collection of newspaper reviews by London theatre critics. UK-England: London. 1998. Lang.: Eng. 2463

Wilson, Andy
Performance/production
Collection of newspaper reviews by London theatre critics. UK-England: London. 1998. Lang.: Eng. 2583

Wilson, August
Institutions
Report on National Black Theatre Summit. USA: Dartmouth, NH. 1998. Lang.: Eng. 1782
Playwright Garland Lee on the National Black Theatre Summit. USA: Dartmouth, NH. 1998. Lang.: Eng. 1786
Performance/production
Conference on African-American theatre convened by playwright August Wilson. USA: Hanover, NH. 1998. Lang.: Eng. 659
Plays/librettos/scripts
Account of National Black Theatre Summit. USA: Hanover, NH. 1998. Lang.: Eng. 3523
Analysis of *The Piano Lesson* by August Wilson. USA. 1990. Lang.: Eng. 3536
Analysis of *Jitney* by August Wilson. USA. 1979. Lang.: Eng. 3611
Minority playwrights and mainstream theatres—theoretical implications. USA. 1980-1997. Lang.: Eng. 3612
The return of the prodigal in American drama. USA. 1920-1985. Lang.: Eng. 3666
Analysis of *Fences* by August Wilson. USA. 1987. Lang.: Eng. 3693

Wilson, Doric
Plays/librettos/scripts
History of the Playwrights Unit. USA. 1963-1971. Lang.: Eng. 3570

Wilson, Edward
Performance/production
Collection of newspaper reviews by London theatre critics. UK-England: London. 1998. Lang.: Eng. 2484

Wilson, John
Plays/librettos/scripts
Analysis of Restoration anti-Puritan comedies. England. 1661-1663. Lang.: Eng. 2907

Wilson, John H.
Performance/production
Irish and Irish-American characters on the stages of the Midwest. USA. 1875-1915. Lang.: Eng. 2696

Wilson, Lanford
Performance/production
The collaboration of playwright Lanford Wilson and director Marshall W. Mason. USA: New York, NY. 1978-1986. Lang.: Eng. 2756
Plays/librettos/scripts
Analysis of the plays of Lanford Wilson. USA. 1960-1995. Lang.: Eng. 3546
Analysis of *The Mound Builders* by Lanford Wilson. USA. 1976. Lang.: Eng. 3552
History of the Playwrights Unit. USA. 1963-1971. Lang.: Eng. 3570
Comedy and humor in plays of Lanford Wilson. USA. 1961-1985. Lang.: Eng. 3595
Lanford Wilson's *Book of Days*. USA. 1998. Lang.: Eng. 3627
American gay drama and the impact of AIDS. USA. 1960-1987. Lang.: Eng. 3670

Wilson, Mary Louise
Performance/production
Collection of newspaper reviews by London theatre critics. UK-England: London. 1998. Lang.: Eng. 2491

Wilson, Richard
Performance/production
Collection of newspaper reviews by London theatre critics. UK-England: London. 1998. Lang.: Eng. 2549
Plays/librettos/scripts
Opera in American gangster films. USA. 1932-1990. Lang.: Eng. 4023

Wilson, Robert
Design/technology
Robert Wilson and Vera Dobroschke's design for Brecht's *Ozeanflug.* Germany: Berlin. 1998. Lang.: Eng. 4430
Institutions
Productions of Salzburger Festspiele. Austria: Salzburg. 1998. Lang.: Ger. 1571
Productions of the Salzburg Festival. Austria: Salzburg. 1998. Lang.: Ger. 1573
Performance/production
The influence of experimental performance on contemporary drama. Europe. USA. 1960-1987. Lang.: Eng. 526
Robert Wilson's dance adaptation of *Le Martyre de Saint Sébastien* by D'Annunzio. France: Paris. 1988. Lang.: Ita. 1074
Robert Wilson's production of *Doctor Faustus Lights the Lights* by Gertrude Stein. Belgium: Antwerp. 1992. Lang.: Fle. 1828
Reviews of productions by Wilson, Greenaway, and Mnouchkine. France: Paris. 1997-1998. Lang.: Eng. 1926
The performances of Lucinda Childs and Michel Piccoli in *La Maladie de la Mort (The Sickness of Death)*, directed by Robert Wilson. France: Paris. 1997. Lang.: Eng. 1942
Interview with actress Lucinda Childs. France: Paris. 1976-1997. Lang.: Eng. 1943
The collaboration of choreographer Lucinda Childs and director Robert Wilson on *La Maladie de la Mort.* Germany. 1992-1997. Lang.: Eng. 2019
Guest performances in Moscow. Russia: Moscow. 1998. Lang.: Rus. 2269
Productions of international Čechov festival. Russia: Moscow. 1998. Lang.: Swe. 2306
Collection of newspaper reviews by London theatre critics. UK-England: London. 1998. Lang.: Eng. 2409
Reviews of recent London performances. UK-England: London. 1998. Lang.: Ger. 2591
Robert Wilson's work with actors on a production of *Danton's Death (Dantons Tod).* USA: Houston, TX. 1997. Lang.: Eng. 2688
Music theatre production in northern Germany. Germany: Lübeck, Hamburg, Bremen, Kiel. 1998. Lang.: Ger. 4293
Robert Wilson's production of Brecht's *Der Ozeanflug.* Germany: Berlin. 1998. Lang.: Ger. 4356
Interview with director Robert Wilson. Germany: Berlin. 1970-1998. Lang.: Swe. 4609
Robert Wilson's production of Wagner's *Lohengrin.* USA: New York, NY. 1998. Lang.: Eng. 4732
Robert Wilson's production of Wagner's *Lohengrin* at the Metropolitan Opera. USA: New York, NY. 1976-1998. Lang.: Eng. 4739
Plays/librettos/scripts
Recent German productions of Brecht's plays. Germany. 1998. Lang.: Ger. 3150
Hero and anti-hero in contemporary opera production. Germany. 1998. Lang.: Ger. 4791
Theory/criticism
Artaud's theatre of cruelty and contemporary experimental theatre. France. 1945-1998. Lang.: Ger. 3818

Wilson, Snoo
Performance/production
Collection of newspaper reviews by London theatre critics. UK-England: London. 1998. Lang.: Eng. 2583

Wimbledon Studio Theatre (London)
Performance/production
Collection of newspaper reviews by London theatre critics. UK-England: London. 1998. Lang.: Eng. 2434
Collection of newspaper reviews by London theatre critics. UK-England: London. 1998. Lang.: Eng. 2458
Collection of newspaper reviews by London theatre critics. UK-England: London. 1998. Lang.: Eng. 2585

Wind
Performance/production
Performances by dance couple Eiko & Koma. USA: Washington, DC. 1998. Lang.: Hun. 1336

Wine in the Wilderness
Plays/librettos/scripts
Black self-determination in the plays of Alice Childress. USA. 1949-1969. Lang.: Eng. 3579

Wines of Tuscany, The
Basic theatrical documents
Text of *The Wines of Tuscany* by Conrad Alexandrowicz. Canada: Vancouver, BC. 1996. Lang.: Eng. 1344
Plays/librettos/scripts
Conrad Alexandrowicz on his dance-theatre piece *The Wines of Tuscany.* Canada: Vancouver, BC. 1992-1996. Lang.: Eng. 1356

Winge, Stein
Design/technology
Interview with set designer Lennart Mörk. Sweden: Stockholm. France: Paris. 1958-1998. Lang.: Swe. 222
Scenographer Lennart Mörk. Sweden: Stockholm. France: Paris. 1957-1998. Lang.: Swe. 4439
Performance/production
Interview with director Stein Winge. Norway: Oslo. 1988-1998. Lang.: Eng. 2210
Report from Ibsen festival. Norway: Oslo. 1998. Lang.: Swe. 2211

Wings
Design/technology
Virtual reality technology for set design. USA: Lawrence, KS. 1997. Lang.: Eng. 1562
Plays/librettos/scripts
Analysis of *Wings* by Arthur Kopit. USA. 1978. Lang.: Eng. 3616

Winter Garden Theatre (New York, NY)
Performance/production
Critique of Twyla Tharp's *The Catherine Wheel.* USA: New York, NY. 1981. Lang.: Eng. 980

Winter Garden Theatre (Toronto, ON)
Performance spaces
Toronto's theatres. Canada: Toronto, ON. 1998. Lang.: Eng. 434

Winter, Julian
Design/technology
Lighting technician Julian Winter. USA. 1971-1998. Lang.: Eng. 309

Winter's Tale, The
Institutions
The inaugural season of Shakespeare's Globe Theatre. UK-England: London. 1997-1998. Lang.: Eng. 1741
Performance/production
Contemporary Polish productions of Shakespeare. Poland. 1990-1998. Lang.: Pol. 2213
Collection of newspaper reviews by London theatre critics. UK-England: London. 1998. Lang.: Eng. 2444
The inaugural season of Shakespeare's Globe Theatre. UK-England: London. 1997. Lang.: Eng. 2601
Review of the opening season of Shakespeare's Globe Theatre. UK-England: London. 1997. Lang.: Eng. 2602
Richard McCabe on his role in *The Winter's Tale* at RSC. UK-England: London, Stratford. 1992-1993. Lang.: Eng. 2623
Plays/librettos/scripts
Women's use of wit in response to men in English popular culture. England. 1590-1630. Lang.: Eng. 2884
Female power and the emblem tradition in plays of Shakespeare and Middleton. England. 1604-1625. Lang.: Eng. 2913
Punishment and political power in plays of Shakespeare. England. 1604-1611. Lang.: Eng. 2944
Regeneration in plays of Shakespeare. England. 1598-1613. Lang.: Eng. 2968
The nature of tyranny in plays of Shakespeare. England. 1595-1612. Lang.: Eng. 2978

Winton, Tim
Design/technology
Lighting designer Mark Howett's work for Black Swan Theatre Company. Australia: Fremantle. 1998. Lang.: Eng. 1513

Wir Drei (We Three)
Plays/librettos/scripts
Power, gender relations, and communication in German drama. Germany. 1776-1989. Lang.: Ger. 3138

Wirth, Franz Peter
Performance/production
Television adaptations of works by Goethe. Germany. 1965-1997. Lang.: Eng. 4061

Wise, Jim
Design/technology
Costume design for *Dames at Sea*, Marine Memorial Theatre. USA: San Francisco, CA. 1998. Lang.: Eng. 4332

Wish, P.K.
Design/technology
Costume design for *Christmas with the Ivanovs*, CSC Repertory. USA: New York, NY. 1998. Lang.: Eng. 1533

Wishing Ring, The
Plays/librettos/scripts
The development of playwright Owen Davis. USA. 1905-1923. Lang.: Eng. 3526

Wisker, Stephen
Performance/production
Collection of newspaper reviews by London theatre critics. UK-England. 1998. Lang.: Eng. 2489

Wit Works Woe
SEE
Gore ot uma.

Witch of Edmonton, The
Plays/librettos/scripts
Analysis of *The Witch of Edmonton* by Ford, Dekker, and Rowley. England. 1621. Lang.: Eng. 2928

Witkacy
SEE
Witkiewicz, Stanisław Ignacy.

Witkiewicz, Stanisław Ignacy
Institutions
Profile of theatre company Teatr St I Witkiewicza. Poland: Zakopane. 1989. Lang.: Eng. 1684
Plays/librettos/scripts
George Bernard Shaw and science fiction. UK-England. Ireland. 1887-1998. Lang.: Eng. 3508

Witte Kraai, De (Antwerp)
Plays/librettos/scripts
Dutch and Flemish Shakespearean productions. Belgium. Netherlands. 1980-1983. Lang.: Dut. 2789

Wittenberg, Peter
Performance/production
Productions of director Peter Wittenberg. Germany: Munich, Bonn. 1998. Lang.: Ger. 2013

Wittig, Monique
Plays/librettos/scripts
Analysis of *Le Voyage sans fin (The Constant Journey)* by Monique Wittig. France. 1985. Lang.: Eng. 3100

Wiz, The
Performance/production
High-school students' production of *The Wiz* at the Edinburgh Fringe Festival. USA: Hattiesburg, MS. UK-Scotland: Edinburgh. 1996. Lang.: Eng. 4381

Wizard of Oz, The
Performance/production
Actor Bert Lahr. USA. 1895-1967. Lang.: Eng. 3953

Wm (We)
Basic theatrical documents
Anthology of contemporary Chinese drama. China, People's Republic of. 1979-1986. Lang.: Eng. 1414

Woe from Wit
SEE
Gore ot uma.

Wohnhaft (Resident)
Performance/production
German productions of contemporary Russian drama. Germany. 1998. Lang.: Ger. 1984

Wolf Road, The
Performance/production
Collection of newspaper reviews by London theatre critics. UK-England: London. 1998. Lang.: Eng. 2553

Wolf, Peter
Performance/production
Collection of newspaper reviews by London theatre critics. UK-England: London. 1998. Lang.: Eng. 2584

Wolfe, George C.
Design/technology
Technical designs for Off Broadway Shakespearean productions. USA: New York, NY. 1998. Lang.: Eng. 1539
Plays/librettos/scripts
Analysis of *The Colored Museum* by George C. Wolfe. USA. 1988. Lang.: Eng. 3690
Theory/criticism
The urge to make Shakespeare contemporary. USA. 1990-1998. Lang.: Eng. 3844

Wolk, Emil
Performance/production
Collection of newspaper reviews by London theatre critics. UK-England: London. 1998. Lang.: Eng. 2420

Woman Killed with Kindness, A
Performance/production
Director Jacques Copeau and his theatrical aesthetic. France. 1913-1920. Lang.: Eng. 1941
Plays/librettos/scripts
Casuistry and early modern English tragedy. England. 1600-1671. Lang.: Eng. 2980

Woman's Comedy, A
Performance/production
Collection of newspaper reviews by London theatre critics. UK-England: London. 1998. Lang.: Eng. 2458

Woman's Prize, The
Plays/librettos/scripts
Women's use of wit in response to men in English popular culture. England. 1590-1630. Lang.: Eng. 2884

Women Beware Women
Plays/librettos/scripts
The Cardinal in Middleton's *Women Beware Women.* England. 1613-1621. Lang.: Eng. 2961

Rape in Middleton's *Women Beware Women* and its adaptation by Howard Barker. UK-England. 1625-1986. Lang.: Eng. 3468

Women in theatre
Administration
The lesbian relationship of agent Elisabeth Marbury and designer Elsie de Wolfe. USA. 1886-1933. Lang.: Eng. 44

Actors' Fund annual benefit for women's health. USA: New York, NY. 1998. Lang.: Eng. 68

Nineteenth-century women theatre managers. USA. 1800-1900. Lang.: Eng. 129

Interviews with women in top management of theatres. USA: New Haven, CT, Seattle, WA, East Haddam, CT. 1998. Lang.: Eng. 1397
Basic theatrical documents
Dutch translations of women's monologues by Dario Fo. Italy. 1998. Lang.: Dut. 1440
Design/technology
Avant-garde Russian women artist/designers. Russia. USSR. 1880-1949. Lang.: Eng. 214
Institutions
Program of the 'City of Women' International Festival of Contemporary Arts. Slovenia: Ljubljana. 1998. Lang.: Slo. 384

Feminist theatre of Ladies Against Women. USA: Berkeley, CA. 1979-1993. Lang.: Eng. 396

Profile of Women's Circus. Australia: Melbourne. 1990-1998. Lang.: Eng. 1568

Report on the Cairo festival and symposia on women's theatre. Egypt: Cairo. 1997. Lang.: Eng. 1597

Profile of independent feminist theatre Kvinnliga Dramatiska Teatern. Sweden: Stockholm. 1997-1998. Lang.: Swe. 1725

Brief history of the Women's Project and Productions. USA: New York, NY. 1978-1998. Lang.: Eng. 1774

Women in top management of American Conservatory Theatre. USA: San Francisco, CA. 1992-1998. Lang.: Eng. 1781

Director Molly Smith, new artistic director of Arena Stage. USA: Washington, DC. 1998. Lang.: Eng. 1789

History of the Women's Project of the American Place Theatre. USA: New York, NY. 1978-1979. Lang.: Eng. 1791
Performance/production
The Cibber family: private life as public spectacle. England. 1713-1760. Lang.: Eng. 517

The 'grande coquette' on the Parisian stage. France: Paris. 1885-1925. Lang.: Eng. 531

Women in Dutch theatre. Netherlands. 1975-1998. Lang.: Dut. 563

Actress/director Alla Nazimova. Russia. USA. 1878-1945. Lang.: Eng. 585

Performer, writer, director Elsie Janis and the 'gay sensibility'. UK-England. 1889-1956. Lang.: Eng. 612

Audience reaction to actress Adah Isaacs Menken. USA. 1835-1869. Lang.: Eng. 619

The marriage of theatre artists Katharine Cornell and Guthrie McClintic. USA. 1893-1974. Lang.: Eng. 634

The first wave of American feminist theatre. USA. 1890-1930. Lang.: Eng. 648

Women and improvisation. USA. 1970-1997. Lang.: Eng. 672

Gender and the career of actress Charlotte Cushman. USA. 1816-1876. Lang.: Eng. 680

Sanjukta Panigrahi, dancer, choreographer, and co-founder of ISTA. India. 1944-1997. Lang.: Eng. 952

Survey of women's dance and choreography of the season. Canada: Montreal, PQ. 1998. Lang.: Fre. 1263

Women in theatre — cont'd

Modern dance and the female body. USA. Europe. 1900-1930. Lang.: Eng. 1321

Female performers of the formerly all-male genre *randai*. Sumatra. 1980-1998. Lang.: Eng. 1354

Actress/writer Charlotte Cibber Charke. England. 1713-1760. Lang.: Eng. 1891

Images associated with actress Charlotte Cibber Charke. England. 1713-1760. Lang.: Eng. 1896

The resurgence of interest in actress Charlotte Cibber Charke. England. 1713-1760. Lang.: Eng. 1901

Feminist analysis of the life of actress Charlotte Cibber Charke. England. 1713-1760. Lang.: Eng. 1904

Actress Charlotte Cibber Charke and cross-dressing. England. 1713-1760. Lang.: Eng. 1906

Press responses to the autobiography of actress Charlotte Cibber Charke. England. 1713-1760. Lang.: Eng. 1908

Gender and Shakespearean production in the GDR. Germany, East. 1982-1990. Lang.: Eng. 2044

Interview with actor/director Johanna Schall. Germany, East. 1980-1995. Lang.: Eng. 2045

Actor/director Katja Paryla. Germany, East. 1975-1995. Lang.: Eng. 2046

Actor/director Ursula Karusseit. Germany, East. 1977-1995. Lang.: Eng. 2047

The performance of plays by Hispanic women. North America. 1993-1998. Lang.: Eng. 2209

Actresses and female managers in Spanish theatre. Spain. 1600-1700. Lang.: Eng. 2357

Actor/director Margaret Webster, gender and sexuality. UK-England. USA. 1905-1972. Lang.: Eng. 2590

Analysis of two productions of Caryl Churchill's *Top Girls*. UK-England. 1982-1991. Lang.: Eng. 2608

Statements of women directors on their work. USA. 1996. Lang.: Eng. 2674

Elizabeth Perry's one-woman show *Sun Flower* about Elizabeth Cady Stanton. USA: New York, NY. 1998. Lang.: Eng. 2718

Avant-garde American women directors' productions of *Doctor Faustus Lights the Lights* by Gertrude Stein. USA. 1940-1995. Lang.:Eng. 2735

Jane Alexander's return to acting after chairing the NEA. USA. 1998. Lang.: Eng. 2744

Lesbianism and performer Mary Martin. USA. 1913-1990. Lang.: Eng. 2757

Screenwriter and producer June Mathis. USA. 1916-1927. Lang.: Eng. 3959

Performance in the work of mixed-media artist Tina Keane. UK-England. 1970-1988. Lang.: Eng. 4044

The language of costume in a video production of Caryl Churchill's *Top Girls*. UK-England. 1982-1991. Lang.: Eng. 4065

The staging of the complete *York Cycle* by the University of Toronto. Canada: Toronto, ON. 1998. Lang.: Eng. 4214

The Hyers sisters and Black musical comedy. USA. 1870-1902. Lang.: Eng. 4384

Plays/librettos/scripts

Analysis of plays by Dymphna Cusack. Australia. 1927-1959. Lang.: Eng. 2777

Australian women playwrights and their work. Australia. 1972-1998. Lang.: Eng. 2778

Female role models in plays by Austrian women. Austria. 1776-1914. Lang.: Ger. 2786

Theatre artist Elizabeth Sterling Haynes and Alberta theatre. Canada. 1916-1957. Lang.: Eng. 2799

Women and Acadian theatre. Canada. 1870-1998. Lang.: Eng. 2810

Women and politics in Restoration heroic plays. England. 1660-1710. Lang.: Eng. 2872

Cross-dressing in Shakespeare's *The Merchant of Venice* and in the autobiography of actress Charlotte Cibber Charke. England. 1713-1760. Lang.: Eng. 2891

Restoration playwright Margaret Cavendish. England. 1645-1662. Lang.: Eng. 3002

Analysis of plays by Marguerite Duras and Marie Redonnet. France. 1977-1992. Lang.: Eng. 3071

Postcolonialism, ethnicity, and feminism in French and Caribbean plays. France. Martinique. Guadeloupe. 1960-1990. Lang.: Eng. 3104

Cruelty and the absurd in theatre of Latin American playwrights. Latin America. 1960-1980. Lang.: Eng. 3267

Female characters in plays by Scandinavian women. Norway. Sweden. Denmark. 1998. Lang.: Eng. 3299

Feminist analysis of plays by Gabriela Zapolska. Poland. 1885-1998. Lang.: Pol. 3301

Feminist analysis of seventeenth-century plays by women. Spain. 1605-1675. Lang.: Eng. 3385

Allegorical dramas of Sor Marcela de San Félix. Spain. 1595-1650. Lang.: Eng. 3395

The image of women on the Spanish stage. Spain. 1908-1936. Lang.: Eng. 3399

Ecology and the plays of Caryl Churchill. UK-England. 1971-1989. Lang.: Eng. 3422

Gender and sexuality in Caryl Churchill's *Cloud Nine*. UK-England. 1979. Lang.: Eng. 3426

Caryl Churchill's *The Skriker* compared to her earlier plays. UK-England. 1994. Lang.: Eng. 3436

Fragmentation and skepticism in Caryl Churchill's *Icecream*. UK-England. 1989. Lang.: Eng. 3451

A paradigm for analysis of works by Caryl Churchill. UK-England. 1975-1997. Lang.: Eng. 3458

Systemic poisons in plays of Caryl Churchill. UK-England. 1990-1997. Lang.: Eng. 3463

Secrets in Caryl Churchill's *Top Girls*. UK-England. 1982. Lang.: Eng. 3466

Analysis of *Light Shining in Buckinghamshire* by Caryl Churchill. UK-England. 1970-1976. Lang.: Eng. 3483

George Bernard Shaw and the 'New Woman'. UK-England. 1890-1900. Lang.: Eng. 3486

Analysis of *The Skriker* by Caryl Churchill. UK-England. 1994. Lang.: Eng. 3489

The critical and popular failure of *The Skriker* by Caryl Churchill. UK-England. 1994. Lang.: Eng. 3504

Analysis of *Mad Forest* by Caryl Churchill. UK-England. 1990. Lang.: Eng. 3505

Gendered political critique in *The Club* by Eve Merriam. USA. 1976. Lang.: Eng. 3572

Gender and politics in Romantic tragedies of Mercy Otis Warren. USA. 1783-1785. Lang.: Eng. 3575

Student casebook on *A Raisin in the Sun* by Lorraine Hansberry. USA. 1957-1997. Lang.: Eng. 3577

Women playwrights' addresses to the Women's Project conference. USA. 1997. Lang.: Eng. 3589

The Broadway success of women playwrights. USA. 1906-1944. Lang.: Eng. 3590

Feminist theatre of Martha Boesing. USA: Minneapolis, MN. 1974-1984. Lang.: Eng. 3603

Playwright Tina Howe on gender expectations on playwrights. USA: New York, NY. 1980-1997. Lang.: Eng. 3614

Politics and feminism in the plays of Maria Irene Fornes. USA. 1975-1995. Lang.: Eng. 3635

The social roles of women playwrights. USA. 1890-1910. Lang.: Eng. 3637

Lorraine Hansberry and Black Americans in theatre. USA. 1769-1986. Lang.: Eng. 3640

Analysis of *Diva Studies* by Elizabeth Alexander. USA. 1996. Lang.: Eng. 3653

The dramaturgical evolution of playwright Adrienne Kennedy. USA. 1964-1990. Lang.: Eng. 3691

Playwrights Adrienne Kennedy, Ntozake Shange, and Suzan-Lori Parks. USA. 1970-1998. Lang.: Eng. 3714

Analysis of *Untitled Flesh* by Sacred Naked Nature Girls. USA: Los Angeles, CA. 1994-1997. Lang.: Eng. 4262

Analysis of letters between Lady Morgan and actor Richard Jones. UK-Ireland. 1807. Lang.: Eng. 4862

Relation to other fields

Actress Nance O'Neil and her friendship with Lizzie Borden. USA. 1874-1965. Lang.: Eng. 799

Women in theatre — cont'd

Student responses to the autobiography of actress Charlotte Cibber Charke. USA. 1998. Lang.: Eng. 800
Research/historiography
Alternative models of performance documentation. Europe. 1984-1997. Lang.: Eng. 818
Women's Circus (Melbourne)
Institutions
Profile of Women's Circus. Australia: Melbourne. 1990-1998. Lang.: Eng. 1568
Women's Project and Productions (New York, NY)
Institutions
Brief history of the Women's Project and Productions. USA: New York, NY. 1978-1998. Lang.: Eng. 1774
Plays/librettos/scripts
Women playwrights' addresses to the Women's Project conference. USA. 1997. Lang.: Eng. 3589
Playwright Tina Howe on gender expectations on playwrights. USA: New York, NY. 1980-1997. Lang.: Eng. 3614
Wonderama
Performance/production
Obituary for Bob McAllister, ventriloquist, magician, and former host of *Wonderama*. USA. 1935-1998. Lang.: Eng. 4149
Wonderbolt Circus (St. John's, NF)
Plays/librettos/scripts
Wonderbolt Circus's *Maid of Avalon*, a loose adaptation of *Der Gute Mensch von Sezuan (The Good Person of Szechwan)* by Brecht.Canada: St. John's, NF. 1950-1998. Lang.: Eng. 2825
Wondreber Totentanz (Wondreb Dance of Death)
Performance/production
Premieres of plays on the Nazi theme. Germany: Darmstadt. Austria: Vienna. 1998. Lang.: Ger. 2030
Wong, Paul
Performance/production
The work of some North American performance artists. USA. Canada. 1960-1988. Lang.: Eng. 4251
Wood-Jones, Nik
Performance/production
Collection of newspaper reviews by London theatre critics. UK-England: London. 1998. Lang.: Eng. 2550
Wood, Alice
Performance/production
Collection of newspaper reviews by London theatre critics. UK-England: London. 1998. Lang.: Eng. 2549
Wood, Jane Philbin
Institutions
The founding of the New York City Ballet. USA: New York, NY. 1947-1948. Lang.: Eng. 1060
Woodall, Ed
Performance/production
Collection of newspaper reviews by London theatre critics. UK-England: London. 1998. Lang.: Eng. 2478
Woodall, Sandra
Design/technology
Costume design for the ballet *Cyrano de Bergerac*. USA: San Francisco, CA. 1998. Lang.: Eng. 1032
Wooden Prince, The
SEE
Fából faragott királyfi, A.
Woodfield, Murray
Performance/production
Collection of newspaper reviews by London theatre critics. UK-England: London. 1998. Lang.: Eng. 2549
Woodroffe, Patrick
Design/technology
Lighting design by Patrick Woodroffe and set design by Mark Fisher for Rolling Stones tour. USA. 1997-1998. Lang.: Eng. 4103
Woodrow, Stephen Taylor
Performance/production
The 'living paintings' of Steven Taylor Woodrow. UK-England. USA. 1987-1988. Lang.: Eng. 4247
Woods, Phil
Performance/production
David Parsons Dance Company's *Fill the Woods with Light*. USA: Washington, DC. 1998. Lang.: Hun. 1195
Woods, Simon
Performance/production
The training of actors in Asian performance styles. Australia: Brisbane. 1992-1998. Lang.: Eng. 1817
Woods, The
Plays/librettos/scripts
Rites of passage in the plays of David Mamet. USA. 1975-1995. Lang.: Eng. 3680
Woodstock
Plays/librettos/scripts
Analysis of the anonymous *Woodstock*. England. 1592. Lang.: Eng. 3035
Woolard, David
Design/technology
Professional theatrical designers on design training. USA. 1998. Lang.: Eng. 252
Wooley, Sarah
Performance/production
Collection of newspaper reviews by London theatre critics. UK. 1998. Lang.: Eng. 2407
Woolf, Virginia
Relation to other fields
Shakespeare's influence on the novels of Virginia Woolf. UK-England. 1882-1941. Lang.: Eng. 3779
Woolgatherer, The
Performance/production
Collection of newspaper reviews by London theatre critics. UK-England: London. 1998. Lang.: Eng. 2574
Woolley, Monty (Montillion, Edgar)
Performance/production
The career of gay actor Monty Woolley. USA. 1888-1963. Lang.: Eng. 2691
Woolverton, Linda
Administration
The Disney Corporation's Broadway musicals. USA: New York, NY. 1996-1998. Lang.: Eng. 4317
Performance spaces
The construction of a theatre for *Beauty and the Beast*. Germany: Stuttgart. 1997. Lang.: Ger. 444
Performance/production
The premiere of the musical *Elaborate Lives: The Legend of Aida*. USA: Atlanta, GA. 1998. Lang.: Eng. 4385
Wooster Group (New York, NY)
Performance spaces
Theatre space and performance. USA: New York, NY. 1925-1985. Lang.: Eng. 464
Performance/production
The influence of experimental performance on contemporary drama. Europe. USA. 1960-1987. Lang.: Eng. 526
The use of closed circuit television in avant-garde theatre performance. USA: New York, NY. 1978-1986. Lang.: Eng. 662
The use of television in theatrical space. Netherlands. USA. 1970-1998. Lang.: Dut. 2206
Analysis of the Wooster Group's *Fish Story* directed by Elizabeth LeCompte. USA: New York, NY. 1990-1996. Lang.: Eng. 2667
Interview with actress Kate Valk. USA: New York, NY. 1979-1998. Lang.: Eng. 2736
Analysis of recent New York productions. USA: New York, NY. 1997-1998. Lang.: Eng. 2759
Wootton, Marc
Performance/production
Collection of newspaper reviews by London theatre critics. UK-England: London. 1998. Lang.: Eng. 2419
Collection of newspaper reviews by London theatre critics. UK-England: London. 1998. Lang.: Eng. 2455
Words and Music
Plays/librettos/scripts
Samuel Beckett's influence on composer Humphrey Searle. UK-England. 1945-1995. Lang.: Eng. 3509
Morton Feldman's musical setting for Samuel Beckett's radio play *Words and Music*. Europe. 1987. Lang.: Eng. 3865
Wordsworth, William
Plays/librettos/scripts
The feminine ideal in the drama of English Romantic poets. England. 1794-1840. Lang.: Eng. 2886
Worker's theatre
Plays/librettos/scripts
The musical *Sandhog* by blacklisted writers Earl Robinson and Waldo Salt. USA. 1954. Lang.: Eng. 4395
Workshops
Institutions
Carlo Quartucci's acting workshop on Shakespeare's *Macbeth*. Italy: Rome. 1991-1992. Lang.: Ita. 1674

Workshops — cont'd

Performance/production
The interdisciplinary workshop of Teaterskollektivet Rex. Sweden: Stockholm. 1997. Lang.: Swe. 600
Training
Actor/director Jean-Paul Denizon and his workshops on Peter Brook's approach to theatre. France. 1980-1998. Lang.: Ita. 873
Ferruccio Di Cori's improvisational workshops for actors and directors. Italy: Rome. 1994-1996. Lang.: Ita. 874
Woron, Andrej
Performance/production
Music theatre production in northern Germany. Germany: Lübeck, Hamburg, Bremen, Kiel. 1998. Lang.: Ger. 4293
Worst Woman in the World, The
Performance/production
Directing the documentary-based performance project *The Worst Woman in the World.* Australia. 1994. Lang.: Eng. 1816
WOW Café (New York, NY)
Performance/production
Profile of the satiric comedy troupe Five Lesbian Brothers. USA: New York, NY. 1989-1998. Lang.: Eng. 4282
Woyzeck
Plays/librettos/scripts
Gender and madness in modern drama. Europe. 1880-1969. Lang.: Eng. 3061
Wozzeck
Institutions
Peter Stein's last season as director at the Salzburg Festival. Austria: Salzburg. 1997. Lang.: Eng. 336
Performance/production
Music theatre production in northern Germany. Germany: Lübeck, Hamburg, Bremen, Kiel. 1998. Lang.: Ger. 4293
Novelist Joyce Carol Oates' reaction to Berg's *Wozzeck* at the Metropolitan Opera. USA: New York, NY. 1997. Lang.: Eng. 4718
Wren, James
Performance/production
Collection of newspaper reviews by London theatre critics. UK-England: London. 1998. Lang.: Eng. 2459
Wrentmore, Steven
Performance/production
Collection of newspaper reviews by London theatre critics. UK-England: London. 1998. Lang.: Eng. 2560
Wretched Splendour, The
Performance/production
Collection of newspaper reviews by London theatre critics. UK-England: London. 1998. Lang.: Eng. 2585
Wright, Garland
Performance/production
Director Garland Wright. USA. 1946-1998. Lang.: Eng. 2707
Wright, John
Performance/production
Collection of newspaper reviews by London theatre critics. UK-England: London. 1998. Lang.: Eng. 2576
Wright, Max
Performance/production
Actors Helen Carey and Max Wright, winners of Joe A. Callaway Award. USA. 1998. Lang.: Eng. 2716
Wright, Rae C.
Performance/production
Analysis of Rae C. Wright's solo performance piece *Animal Instincts.* USA: New York, NY. 1997. Lang.: Eng. 2684
Writing Home
Plays/librettos/scripts
Playwright Alan Bennett. UK-England. 1994-1998. Lang.: Ger. 3488
Wrobel, Martina
Institutions
Productions of Staatstheater Stuttgart. Germany: Stuttgart. 1998. Lang.: Ger. 1620
Współczesny Teatr (Szczecin)
Performance/production
Director Anna Augustynowicz. Poland: Szczecin. 1989-1998. Lang.: Pol. 2214
Wunschkonzert (Request Concert)
Performance/production
Marie-Ginette Guay's wordless performance in Franz Xaver Kroetz's *Wunschkonzert (Request Concert).* Canada: Quebec, PQ. 1995-1997. Lang.: Fre. 1847
Württembergische Landesbühne (Esslingen)
Administration
Interviews with theatre managers regarding the changing cultural landscape. Germany: Bruchsal, Esslingen, Tübingen. 1998. Lang.: Ger. 1381
Institutions
Profile of Württembergische Landesbühne. Germany: Esslingen. 1996-1997. Lang.: Ger. 1639
Württembergisches Landestheater (Esslingen)
Institutions
German theatres' responses to threatened closings and mergers. Germany: Esslingen, Tübingen. 1998. Lang.: Ger. 1665
WWW.chat
Basic theatrical documents
Texts of *WWW.chat* and *Elevator* by Chris Edwin Rose. USA. 1998. Lang.: Eng. 1506
Wycherley, William
Performance/production
Collection of newspaper reviews by London theatre critics. UK-England: London. 1998. Lang.: Eng. 2481
Plays/librettos/scripts
Motherhood in Restoration comedy. England. 1642-1729. Lang.: Eng. 2864
Wynyard, Melanie
Performance/production
Collection of newspaper reviews by London theatre critics. UK-England: London. 1998. Lang.: Eng. 2507
Wyspiański, Stanisław
Institutions
Wyspiański's Teatr Śląski. Poland: Katowice. 1949-1992. Lang.: Pol. 1690
Performance/production
Analysis of productions of *Dziady (Forefather's Eve)* by Adam Mickiewicz. Poland. 1901-1995. Lang.: Pol. 2220
Wyt and Science
Performance/production
Music in Tudor drama. England. 1497-1569. Lang.: Eng. 1902
X.Y.Z.
Performance/production
Ildikó Mándy's *X.Y.Z.*, a film-dance theatre piece. Hungary: Budapest. 1998. Lang.: Hun. 947
X-Files, The
Design/technology
Lighting design for Rob Bowman's film *The X-Files.* USA. 1998. Lang.: Eng. 3922
Xala
Plays/librettos/scripts
Ousmane Sembène's film adaptation of his own novel *Xala.* Senegal. 1973-1974. Lang.: Eng. 3977
Yaarimeh Bangura, Michael
Performance/production
The use of English and Krio in theatre of Michael Yaarimeh Bangura. Sierra Leone: Freetown. 1960-1998. Lang.: Eng. 2343
Yakult Halle (Cologne)
Institutions
Children's opera company Yakult Halle. Germany: Cologne. 1996-1998. Lang.: Ger. 4455
Yale Repertory Theatre (New Haven, CT)
Administration
Interviews with women in top management of theatres. USA: New Haven, CT, Seattle, WA, East Haddam, CT. 1998. Lang.: Eng. 1397
Yale University School of Music (New Haven, CT)
Institutions
Interviews with graduate students at Yale University School of Music. USA: New Haven, CT. 1998. Lang.: Eng. 4483
Yang, Daniel S.P.
Relation to other fields
Theatre and politics in Hong Kong. Hong Kong. 1984-1996. Lang.: Eng. 3772
Yankowitz, Susan
Performance/production
Theatre Magazine's anniversary issue. USA. 1968-1998. Lang.: Eng. 617
Plays/librettos/scripts
Women playwrights' addresses to the Women's Project conference. USA. 1997. Lang.: Eng. 3589
Yard
Performance/production
Collection of newspaper reviews by London theatre critics. UK-England: London. 1998. Lang.: Eng. 2515
Yard Gal
Performance/production
Collection of newspaper reviews by London theatre critics. UK-England: London. 1998. Lang.: Eng. 2560
Yearbooks
Reference materials
Yearbook of Hungarian theatre. Hungary. 1995-1996. Lang.: Hun. 698

Yearbooks — cont'd

Yearbook of Italian theatre. Italy. 1998. Lang.: Ita. 699
Yearbook of Italian children's theatre. Italy. 1998-1999. Lang.: Ita. 700
Yearbook of the arts and sciences. Russia. 1999. Lang.: Rus. 707
Yearbook of Slovene theatre. Slovenia. 1996-1997. Lang.: Slo. 708
Yearbook of the Hungarian State Opera House. Hungary: Budapest. 1996-1997. Lang.: Hun. 4832

Yeargen, Michael
Design/technology
Set and costume design for San Francisco Opera productions. USA: San Francisco, CA. 1998. Lang.: Eng. 4443

Yeats, William Butler
Performance/production
Collaborative Symbolist dance/theatre projects. Europe. USA. 1916-1934. Lang.: Eng. 1268
The staging of *The King's Threshold* by W.B. Yeats. Ireland: Dublin. UK-England: London. 1903. Lang.: Eng. 2153
Collection of newspaper reviews by London theatre critics. UK-England: London. 1998. Lang.: Eng. 2420
Collection of newspaper reviews by London theatre critics. UK-England: London. 1998. Lang.: Eng. 2458
Collection of newspaper reviews by London theatre critics. UK-England: London. 1998. Lang.: Eng. 2551
Directing a student production of Yeats's *Deirdre*. USA: Louisville, KY. 1988. Lang.: Eng. 2738
Plays/librettos/scripts
Yeats's *The Only Jealousy of Emer* and his anti-theatrical poetics. Ireland. 1916-1918. Lang.: Eng. 3203
Yeats and the influence of *nō*. Ireland. 1914-1939. Lang.: Eng. 3213
William Butler Yeats, *japonisme*, and *nō*. UK-England. 1853-1939. Lang.: Eng. 3435
Gender and nationalism in Northern Irish drama. UK-Ireland. 1902-1997. Lang.: Eng. 3511
Relation to other fields
The 'bird-woman' folktale in Southeast Asian shamanic healing rituals. Ireland. Thailand. Malaysia. Lang.: Eng. 1358
Theory/criticism
Political interpretations of Irish literary theatre. Ireland. 1897-1996. Lang.: Eng. 846
Theatrical dancing and the performance aesthetics of Wilde, Yeats, and Shaw. UK-England. Ireland. 1890-1950. Lang.: Eng. 1012

Yee-Haw!
Performance/production
Collection of newspaper reviews by London theatre critics. UK-England: London. 1998. Lang.: Eng. 2436

Yesterday Once More
Performance/production
Collection of newspaper reviews by London theatre critics. UK-England: London. 1998. Lang.: Eng. 2549

Yeston, Maury
Plays/librettos/scripts
Arthur Kopit's *Nine*, a musical adaptation of Fellini's *8 1/2*. USA. 1963-1982. Lang.: Eng. 4401

Yew, Chay
Performance/production
Contemporary queer politics and the production of gay and lesbian theatre. USA. 1970-1997. Lang.: Eng. 2710

Yiddish theatre
SEE ALSO
Ethnic theatre.
Jewish theatre.
Performance/production
Polish-Jewish cultural relations as reflected in theatre. Poland. 1850-1950. Lang.: Eng. 577
Autobiography of Yiddish theatre actress Moni Ovadia. Italy. Bulgaria. 1946-1998. Lang.: Ita. 2174
Vilna's Yiddish theatre companies. Poland: Vilna, Cracow. 1918-1939. Lang.: Pol. 2212
Plays/librettos/scripts
Enlightenment influences on modern Jewish theatre. Poland. 1500-1914. Lang.: Pol. 3307

Ying hsi
SEE
Shadow puppets.

Ying, Ruocheng
Performance/production
Shaw's *Major Barbara* at the People's Arts Theatre. China, People's Republic of: Beijing. 1991. Lang.: Eng. 1874

Yionoulis, Evan
Design/technology
Derek McLane's set designs for recent Off Broadway productions. USA: New York, NY. 1998. Lang.: Eng. 1538

Yirra Yaakin Youth Theatre (Western Australia)
Performance/production
Aborigines in Australian theatre. Australia. 1990-1998. Lang.: Eng. 486

Yong, Jin
Performance/production
Director and martial artist Huy-Phong Doàn's *La Légende du manuel sacré (The Legend of the Sacred Handbook)*. Canada: Montreal, PQ. 1992-1998. Lang.: Fre. 4118

York Cycle
Audience
Audience assumptions about the York *Resurrection*. England: York. 1275-1541. Lang.: Eng. 1400
Performance/production
Director Joel Kaplan on his production of the *York Cycle*. Canada: Toronto, ON. 1998. Lang.: Eng. 4213
The staging of the complete *York Cycle* by the University of Toronto. Canada: Toronto, ON. 1998. Lang.: Eng. 4214
Plays/librettos/scripts
The language used by devils in the *York Cycle*. England: York. 1400-1500. Lang.: Eng. 2933
The Easter play tradition. England. 1180-1557. Lang.: Eng. 2942
Biblical narrative and the order of the *York Cycle* episodes. England: York. 1401-1499. Lang.: Eng. 2950
Relation to other fields
The relationship between the York Cycle and the Bolton Book of Hours. England: York. 1405-1500. Lang.: Eng. 3750

You Never Can Tell
Plays/librettos/scripts
George Bernard Shaw: life, work, influences. UK-England. Ireland. 1886-1955. Lang.: Eng. 3437
George Bernard Shaw and the 'New Woman'. UK-England. 1890-1900. Lang.: Eng. 3486

You'll Have Had Your Hole
Performance/production
Collection of newspaper reviews by London theatre critics. UK-England: Leeds, Manchester. 1998. Lang.: Eng. 2433

Young Frankenstein
Basic theatrical documents
Text of *Young Frankenstein* by Gene Wilder and Mel Brooks. USA. 1974. Lang.: Eng. 3898
Plays/librettos/scripts
Interview with actor and screenwriter Gene Wilder. USA. 1998. Lang.: Eng. 3991
Interview with director and screenwriter Mel Brooks. USA. 1998. Lang.: Eng. 3992

Young People's Theatre (Toronto, ON)
Plays/librettos/scripts
Young People's Theatre's adaptation of *Anne of Green Gables*. Canada: Toronto, ON. 1911-1998. Lang.: Eng. 2832

Young Vic (London)
Performance/production
Collection of newspaper reviews by London theatre critics. UK-England: London. 1998. Lang.: Eng. 2413
Collection of newspaper reviews by London theatre critics. UK-England: London, Stratford, Derby. 1998. Lang.: Eng. 2417
Collection of newspaper reviews by London theatre critics. UK-England: London. 1998. Lang.: Eng. 2420
Collection of newspaper reviews by London theatre critics. UK-England: London. 1998. Lang.: Eng. 2435
Collection of newspaper reviews by London theatre critics. UK-England: London. 1998. Lang.: Eng. 2453
Collection of newspaper reviews by London theatre critics. UK-England: London. 1998. Lang.: Eng. 2478
Collection of newspaper reviews by London theatre critics. UK-England: London. 1998. Lang.: Eng. 2496
Collection of newspaper reviews by London theatre critics. UK-England: London. 1998. Lang.: Eng. 2507
Collection of newspaper reviews by London theatre critics. UK-England: London. 1998. Lang.: Eng. 2534
Collection of newspaper reviews by London theatre critics. UK-England: London. 1998. Lang.: Eng. 2548
Collection of newspaper reviews by London theatre critics. UK-England: London. 1998. Lang.: Eng. 2554

Young Vic (London) — cont'd
Collection of newspaper reviews by London theatre critics. UK-England: London. 1998. Lang.: Eng. 2555
Collection of newspaper reviews by London theatre critics. UK-England: London. 1998. Lang.: Eng. 2565
Collection of newspaper reviews by London theatre critics. UK-England: London. 1998. Lang.: Eng. 2584
Collection of newspaper reviews by London theatre critics. UK-England: London. 1998. Lang.: Eng. 2587
Young, Aida
Administration
Producer Aida Young. UK-England. 1950-1998. Lang.: Eng. 3854
Young, David
Plays/librettos/scripts
David Young on his play *Inexpressible Island.* Canada: Toronto, ON. 1990-1997. Lang.: Eng. 2837
Young, Phil
Performance/production
Collection of newspaper reviews by London theatre critics. UK-England: London. 1998. Lang.: Eng. 2464
Young, Sarah-Louise
Performance/production
Collection of newspaper reviews by London theatre critics. UK-England: London. 1998. Lang.: Eng. 2550
Yourcenar, Marguerite
Plays/librettos/scripts
Response to the structures of male oppression in plays of Yourcenar, Sarraute, and Duras. France. 1975-1995. Lang.: Fre. 3119
Youth theatre
SEE
Children's theatre.
Administration
Ways to attract new young audiences to theatre. Sweden: Stockholm. 1995-1998. Lang.: Swe. 21
Za koga naj še molim? (For Whom Shall I Still Pray?)
Plays/librettos/scripts
The individual and his world in Slovene theatre. Slovenia. 1943-1985. Lang.: Slo. 3347
Zaak, De (Rotterdam)
Performance/production
De Zaak's production of *Action* by Sam Shepard. Netherlands: Rotterdam. 1988. Lang.: Dut. 2201
Zabela-Vrubel', Nadežda I.
Performance/production
Correspondence of composer Nikolaj Rimskij-Korsakov and singer Nadežda Zabela-Vrubel'. Russia. 1868-1913. Lang.: Rus. 4670
Zacharov, Mark Analuljévič
Performance/production
Director Mark Zacharov at Lenkom. Russia: Moscow. Lang.: Rus. 2316
Zacharov, R.
Performance/production
Boris Asafjev's ballet *Bachčisarajskij fontan* directed by R. Zacharov at the Mariinskij. Russia: St. Petersburg. 1934. Lang.: Rus. 1134
Zadek, Peter
Performance/production
Peter Zadek's production of Čechov's *Višnëvyj sad (The Cherry Orchard).* Germany. Netherlands. 1998. Lang.: Dut. 1954
Comparison of two productions of Shakespeare's *Richard III.* Germany: Munich. 1996-1997. Lang.: Ger. 1976
Actress Ilse Ritter. Germany. 1944-1998. Lang.: Ger. 1980
Review of Salzburger Festspiele performances. Austria: Salzburg. 1998. Lang.: Ger. 4527
Opera productions of the Salzburg Festival. Austria: Salzburg. 1998. Lang.: Hun. 4531
Zajc, Dane
Plays/librettos/scripts
Analysis of *Medeja (Medea)* by Dane Zajc. Slovenia. 1988. Lang.: Slo. 3348
Analysis of *Grmače* by Dane Zajc. Slovenia. 1991. Lang.: Slo. 3356
Zajick, Dolora
Theory/criticism
Performers and conductors complain about unfair reviews. USA. 1998. Lang.: Eng. 4844
Zaks, Jerry
Performance/production
Response to negative criticism of *The Capeman.* USA: New York, NY. 1998. Lang.: Eng. 4387
Zambello, Francesca
Design/technology
Technical designs for *Tristan und Isolde* at Seattle Opera. USA: Seattle, WA. 1998. Lang.: Eng. 4444
Theory/criticism
Gender in Francesca Zambello's production of *Iphigénie en Tauride.* USA: Cooperstown, NY. 1997. Lang.: Eng. 4843
Zambuko/Izibuko Theatre (Zimbabwe)
Performance/production
Theatrical rebellion and sociopolitical chaos. Zimbabwe. Kenya. 1990-1998. Lang.: Eng. 687
Zanardini, Angelo
Plays/librettos/scripts
Massenet's opera *Hérodiade* and its literary sources. France. 1881. Lang.: Fre. 4779
Zanck & Zucker (Wettingen)
Institutions
Swiss theatre clubs for children and youth. Switzerland. 1998. Lang.: Ger, Fre. 1735
Žané, N.
Performance/production
Actors of the Adygeian Drama Theatre. Russia: Majkop. 1998. Lang.: Rus. 2239
Zanobia (Gothenburg)
Performance/production
Interview with dancer Farah Al-Bayaty. Sweden: Gothenburg. Iraq. 1983-1998. Lang.: Swe. 967
Zapatera prodigiosa, La (Shoemaker's Wonderful Wife, The)
Performance/production
Collection of newspaper reviews by London theatre critics. UK-England: London. 1998. Lang.: Eng. 2499
Zapolska, Gabriela
Plays/librettos/scripts
Feminist analysis of plays by Gabriela Zapolska. Poland. 1885-1998. Lang.: Pol. 3301
Zarzuela
Design/technology
Lighting for Washington Opera's production of *Doña Francisquita.* USA: Washington, DC. 1998. Lang.: Eng. 4290
Zasad
Plays/librettos/scripts
Fascism and the peasant in pre-War Slovene drama. Slovenia. 1940. Lang.: Slo. 3349
Zauberflöte, Die
Design/technology
Geogre Tabori's production of Mozart's *Die Zauberflöte* in a circus ring. Germany: Berlin. 1998. Lang.: Ger. 4428
Performance/production
Mozart's operas and contemporary Viennese performance spaces. Austria: Vienna. 1782-1791. Lang.: Eng. 4528
Interview with director János Szikora. Hungary: Budapest. 1998. Lang.: Hun. 4630
Mozart's *Die Zauberflöte* directed by János Szikora. Hungary: Budapest. Hungary: Szeged. 1998. Lang.: Hun. 4631
Background material on Metropolitan Opera radio broadcast performances. USA: New York, NY. 1998. Lang.: Eng. 4713
Background material on Metropolitan Opera radio broadcast performances. USA: New York, NY. 1998. Lang.: Eng. 4716
New England Marionettes' production of Mozart's *Die Zauberflöte.* USA: Boston, MA. 1998. Lang.: Eng. 4900
Plays/librettos/scripts
The reciprocal influence of opera and film. Europe. North America. 1904-1994. Lang.: Eng. 4770
Zayas y Sotomayor, María de
Plays/librettos/scripts
Feminist analysis of seventeenth-century plays by women. Spain. 1605-1675. Lang.: Eng. 3385
Zeami, Motokiyo
Performance/production
Collection of newspaper reviews by London theatre critics. UK-England: London. 1998. Lang.: Eng. 2420
Zedda, Alberto
Performance/production
Musicological preparation for the Metropolitan Opera production of Rossini's *La Cenerentola.* USA: Chicago, IL. 1998. Lang.: Eng. 4737
Zeder, Suzan
Plays/librettos/scripts
Feminist analysis of plays for young people by women playwrights. USA. 1903-1983. Lang.: Eng. 3521
Zeffirelli, Franco
Plays/librettos/scripts
Film interpretations of Ophelia in Shakespeare's *Hamlet.* USA. UK-England. USSR. 1947-1990. Lang.: Eng. 4024

Zehetgruber, Martin
Design/technology
Scenographer Martin Zehetgruber. Austria: Graz. Germany: Stuttgart. 1979-1998. Lang.: Ger. 168
Zeke, Edit
Institutions
Theatre critics' awards 97-98. Hungary. 1997-1998. Lang.: Hun. 355
Zelinda e Lindoro (Zelinda and Lindoro)
Plays/librettos/scripts
Analysis of comedies by Goldoni. Italy: Venice. 1707-1793. Lang.: Ita. 3258
Zelwerowicz, Aleksander
Performance/production
Actor/director Aleksander Zelwerowicz. Poland: Vilna. 1929-1931. Lang.: Pol. 2223
Zemlinsky, Alexander
Basic theatrical documents
Max Meyerfeld's libretto for Zemlinsky's opera *Eine florentinische Tragödie*. Germany. 1917. Lang.: Ger, Fre. 4419
Klaren's librettos for *Der Zwerg* by Alexander Zemlinsky. Germany. 1922. Lang.: Fre, Ger. 4420
Performance/production
Composer Franz Schreker and his connection with Zemlinsky's *Der Zwerg*. Germany. 1908-1923. Lang.: Fre. 4094
Recordings of Zemlinsky's *Eine florentinische Tragödie*. 1980-1997. Lang.: Fre. 4506
Recordings of Zemlinsky's *Der Zwerg*. 1983-1996. Lang.: Fre. 4507
Performances of Zemlinsky's *Der Zwerg*. 1922-1998. Lang.: Fre. 4514
Productions of Zemlinsky's *Eine florentinische Tragödie*. 1917-1996. Lang.: Fre. 4515
Conductor Riccardo Chailly on composer Alexander Zemlinsky. Europe. 1998. Lang.: Fre. 4551
Conductor James Conlon on his production of Zemlinsky's *Der Zwerg*. France: Paris. 1998. Lang.: Fre. 4562
Life of composer and conductor Alexander Zemlinsky. Germany. 1871-1942. Lang.: Fre. 4594
Arnold Schoenberg on composer Alexander Zemlinsky. Germany. 1921. Lang.: Fre. 4604
A letter from composer Alexander Zemlinsky to Alma Mahler. Germany. 1917. Lang.: Fre. 4613
Plays/librettos/scripts
Max Meyerfeld's preface to the translation of *A Florentine Tragedy* by Oscar Wilde. Europe. 1895-1907. Lang.: Fre. 3057
Playwright and author Oscar Wilde. UK-England. France. 1854-1900. Lang.: Fre. 3465
Analysis of Alexander Zemlinsky's *Der Zwerg*. Germany. 1922. Lang.: Fre. 4793
Zen Zen Zo (Brisbane)
Performance/production
The training of actors in Asian performance styles. Australia: Brisbane. 1992-1998. Lang.: Eng. 1817
Žene na grobu (Women at the Grave)
Plays/librettos/scripts
The individual and his world in Slovene theatre. Slovenia. 1943-1985. Lang.: Slo. 3347
Ženovač, Sergej
Performance/production
The work of Russian directors at the Golden Mask festival. Russia: Moscow, St. Petersburg. 1998. Lang.: Swe. 2305
Zerbrochene Krug, Der (Broken Jug, The)
Performance/production
Recent productions of Bochumer Schauspielhaus. Germany: Bochum. 1998. Lang.: Ger. 2009
Zero
Performance/production
Collection of newspaper reviews by London theatre critics. UK-England: London. 1998. Lang.: Eng. 2448
Zhang Xie Zhuangyuan (Top Graduate Zhang Xie)
Plays/librettos/scripts
Comic roles in the early Song play *Zhang Xie Zhuangyuan (Top Graduate Zhang Xie)*. China. 960-1127. Lang.: Eng. 2840
Zhang, Xian
Plays/librettos/scripts
'Underground realism' in contemporary Chinese drama. China, People's Republic of: Shanghai. 1993-1996. Lang.: Eng. 2845
Zhang, Yimou
Performance/production
Rural Chinese productions of Puccini's *Turandot*. China, People's Republic of: Beijing. 1998. Lang.: Eng. 4541
Ziegler, Alexander
Plays/librettos/scripts
Homosexuality on the German stage. Germany. 1920-1980. Lang.: Eng. 3147
Zielinski, Scott
Design/technology
Technical designs for Off Broadway Shakespearean productions. USA: New York, NY. 1998. Lang.: Eng. 1539
Zigler, Scott
Design/technology
Lighting design for Mamet's *The Old Neighborhood* directed by Scott Zigler. USA: New York, NY. 1998. Lang.: Eng. 1547
Zigong Sichuan Opera Company (Beijing)
Performance/production
Rural Chinese productions of Puccini's *Turandot*. China, People's Republic of: Beijing. 1998. Lang.: Eng. 4541
Zimmer, Hans
Plays/librettos/scripts
Playwright Hans Zimmer. Germany: Hannover. 1993-1998. Lang.: Ger. 3136
Zimmerman, Mary
Plays/librettos/scripts
Women playwrights' addresses to the Women's Project conference. USA. 1997. Lang.: Eng. 3589
Zindel, Paul
Plays/librettos/scripts
History of the Playwrights Unit. USA. 1963-1971. Lang.: Eng. 3570
Zingaro (Paris)
Performance/production
Analysis of the 'new circus'. France. Sweden. 1990-1998. Lang.: Swe. 4182
Zinn, David
Design/technology
Costume designs for Oregon Shakespeare Festival productions. USA: Ashland, OR. 1998. Lang.: Eng. 1543
Zinsou, Sénouvo Agbota
Plays/librettos/scripts
Playwright Sénouvo Agbota Zinsou. Togo. 1984-1998. Lang.: Eng. 3419
Zippel, David
Performance/production
Collection of newspaper reviews by London theatre critics. UK-England: London. 1998. Lang.: Eng. 2516
Zipprodt, Patricia
Design/technology
Creativity and beauty in theatrical design. USA. 1998. Lang.: Eng. 322
Zite 'n Galera, Li
Plays/librettos/scripts
Female operatic cross-dressing. Italy: Naples, Venice. 1601-1800. Lang.: Eng. 4814
Žitije Jurij Kuročkina i ego bližnich (Life of Jurij Kuročkin and His Neighbors, The)
Performance/production
German productions of contemporary Russian drama. Germany. 1998. Lang.: Ger. 1984
Žitinkin, Andrej
Performance/production
Andrej Žitinkin directs *Confessions of Felix Krull, Confidence Man*, adapted from Thomas Mann. Russia: Moscow. 1998. Lang.: Rus. 2335
Director Andrej Žitinkin. Russia: Moscow. 1998. Lang.: Rus. 2338
Zizka, Blanka
Design/technology
Design concept for Amy Freed's *The Psychic Life of Savages*, Wilma Theatre. USA: Philadelphia, PA. 1998. Lang.: Eng. 1555
Zloof, Fouad
Performance/production
Collection of newspaper reviews by London theatre critics. UK-England: London. 1998. Lang.: Eng. 2479
Zmijin svlak (Snake Skin)
Basic theatrical documents
English translation of *Zmijin svlak (Snake Skin)* by Slobodan Šnajder. Croatia. 1998. Lang.: Eng. 1415
Zoluška (Cinderella)
Design/technology
Technical designs for Matthew Bourne's productions of ballets by Čajkovskij and Prokofjėv. UK-England: London. 1998. Lang.: Eng. 1031
Performance/production
Analysis of choreographies of Matthew Bourne. UK-England: London. 1996-1997. Lang.: Eng. 1157

Zone libre (Free Zone)
Plays/librettos/scripts
Analysis of Holocaust plays by Jean-Claude Grumberg. France. 1974-1991. Lang.: Eng. 3108
Zonneville, Renée
Design/technology
Profiles of young theatrical designers. Netherlands. 1990-1998. Lang.: Dut. 207
Zora
Basic theatrical documents
Texts of plays about Zora Neale Hurston by Barbara Waddell Speisman. USA. 1988. Lang.: Eng. 1510
Zoran ali Kmetska vojna na Slovenskem (Zoran or the Peasant War in Slovenia)
Plays/librettos/scripts
Analysis of *Zoran ali Kmetska vojna na Slovenskum (Zoran and the Peasant War in Slovenia)* by Ivan Vrhovec. Slovenia. 1870. Lang.: Slo. 3351
Zoščenko, Michajl Michajlovič
Plays/librettos/scripts
V.V. Zoščenko on his play, *Uvažaemyj tovarišč M.M. Zoščenko (The Respected M.M. Zoščenko)*. Russia. 1998. Lang.: Rus. 3340
Zoščenko, V.V.
Plays/librettos/scripts
V.V. Zoščenko on his play, *Uvažaemyj tovarišč M.M. Zoščenko (The Respected M.M. Zoščenko)*. Russia. 1998. Lang.: Rus. 3340
Zotto, Miguel Angel
Performance/production
Collection of newspaper reviews by London theatre critics. UK-England: London. 1998. Lang.: Eng. 2463
Zsámbéki Nyári Színház (Zsámbék)
Performance/production
Three Hungarian productions of Shakespeare's *Richard III*. Hungary: Budapest, Zsámbék, Szeged. 1997. Lang.: Hun. 2121
Zsámbéki, Gábor
Institutions
The National Theatre's experiment in artistic renewal. Hungary: Budapest. 1979-1982. Lang.: Hun. 1672
Performance/production
Review of Gombrowicz's *Princess Yvonne*, Katona József Theatre. Hungary: Budapest. 1997. Lang.: Hun. 2079
Zsótér, Sándor
Performance/production
Brecht's *Die Heilige Johanna der Schlachthöfe (Saint Joan of the Stockyards)* directed by Sándor Zsóter. Hungary: Miskolc. 1998. Lang.: Hun. 2084
Hauptmann's *Fuhrmann Henschel (Drayman Henschel)* directed by Sándor Zsótér. Hungary: Budapest. 1997. Lang.: Hun. 2088
Three Hungarian productions of Shakespeare's *Richard III*. Hungary: Budapest, Zsámbék, Szeged. 1997. Lang.: Hun. 2121
Two Hungarian productions of Arthur Miller's *Death of a Salesman*. Hungary: Pécs, Szeged. 1998. Lang.: Hun. 2123
Zuber, Catherine
Design/technology
Costume designer Catherine Zuber. USA. 1998. Lang.: Eng. 315
Costume designer Catherine Zuber. USA. 1998. Lang.: Eng. 1549
The design concept for Nicholas Hytner's production of Shakespeare's *Twelfth Night*. USA: New York, NY. 1998. Lang.: Eng. 1556
Zuckmayer, Carl
Audience
Audience response to Bronnen's *Der Vatermord (Parricide)* and German culture. Germany: Frankfurt. 1922. Lang.: Eng. 1403
Plays/librettos/scripts
Analysis of plays by Carl Zuckmayer. Austria: Vienna. 1925-1938. Lang.: Ger. 2785
Zupan, Vitomil
Plays/librettos/scripts
Fascism and the peasant in pre-War Slovene drama. Slovenia. 1940. Lang.: Slo. 3349
Zupančič, Milena
Performance/production
Interview with actress Milena Zupančič. Slovenia. 1960-1997. Lang.: Slo. 596
Župančič, Oton
Performance/production
Oton Župančič and the Slovene stage language consultant. Slovenia. 1912-1927. Lang.: Slo. 2345
Plays/librettos/scripts
Translation work of playwright Oton Župančič. Slovenia. 1900-1954. Lang.: Slo. 3357
Analysis of *Veronika Deseniška (Veronica of Desenice)* by Oton Župančič. Slovenia. 1924. Lang.: Slo. 3360
Theory/criticism
Playwright Oton Župančič and the theatrical essay. Slovenia. 1905-1949. Lang.: Slo. 3828
Zürcher Schauspielhaus (Zurich)
Institutions
The directorship of Ferdinand Rieser at Zürcher Schauspielhaus. Switzerland: Zurich. 1926-1938. Lang.: Ger. 387
Performance/production
Shakespeare productions in German Switzerland. Switzerland: Basel, Zurich. 1996-1997. Lang.: Ger. 2398
Katharina Thalbach in Brecht's *Die heilige Johanna der Schlachthöfe (Saint Joan of the Stockyards)* directed by Benno Besson. Switzerland: Zurich. 1998. Lang.: Ger. 2400
Plays/librettos/scripts
Thomas Hürlimann's *Das Lied der Heimat (The Song of the Homeland)* and its production by Werner Düggelin. Switzerland: Zurich. 1998. Lang.: Ger. 3417
Zurüstungen für die Unsterblichkeit (Preparations for Immortality)
Performance/production
Productions of new plays by Peter Handke and Katharine Gericke at Niedersächsische Staatstheater. Germany: Hannover. 1998. Lang.: Ger. 1983
Zuska, Petr
Performance/production
Choreographers Monika Rebcová, Petr Tyc, and Petr Zuska. Czech Republic: Prague. 1997. Lang.: Eng, Fre. 1266
Zvestoba (Fidelity)
Plays/librettos/scripts
Analysis of *Zvestoba (Fidelity)* by Etbin Kristan. Slovenia. 1897-1910. Lang.: Slo. 3344
Zweig, Stefan
Performance/production
Analysis of Richard Strauss's *Capriccio*. Germany. 1942. Lang.: Eng. 4606
Plays/librettos/scripts
Analysis of plays based on the Hebrew prophets. USA. Europe. 1919-1970. Lang.: Eng. 3659
Zwerg, Der
Basic theatrical documents
Klaren's librettos for *Der Zwerg* by Alexander Zemlinsky. Germany. 1922. Lang.: Fre, Ger. 4420
Performance/production
Composer Franz Schreker and his connection with Zemlinsky's *Der Zwerg*. Germany. 1908-1923. Lang.: Fre. 4094
Recordings of Zemlinsky's *Der Zwerg*. 1983-1996. Lang.: Fre. 4507
Performances of Zemlinsky's *Der Zwerg*. 1922-1998. Lang.: Fre. 4514
Conductor James Conlon on his production of Zemlinsky's *Der Zwerg*. France: Paris. 1998. Lang.: Fre. 4562
Plays/librettos/scripts
Playwright and author Oscar Wilde. UK-England. France. 1854-1900. Lang.: Fre. 3465
Analysis of Alexander Zemlinsky's *Der Zwerg*. Germany. 1922. Lang.: Fre. 4793
Związek Artystów Scen Polskich (Warsaw)
Institutions
History of the Polish Theatre Association. Poland: Warsaw. 1918-1998. Lang.: Pol. 1692
Zykina, Ljudmila
Performance/production
Singer Ljudmila Zykina. Russia. Lang.: Rus. 4302
10,000 Broken Mirrors
Performance/production
Collection of newspaper reviews by London theatre critics. UK-England: London. 1998. Lang.: Eng. 2432
140
Performance/production
Collection of newspaper reviews by London theatre critics. UK-England: London. 1998. Lang.: Eng. 2498
1789
Institutions
Theatrical space in productions of Ariane Mnouchkine. France: Paris. 1970-1995. Lang.: Eng. 1607
1837: The Farmer's Revolt
Performance/production
Analysis of *1837: The Farmer's Revolt* directed by Bruce Barton of Carrefour Theatre. Canada: Charlottetown, PE. 1998. Lang.: Eng. 1856

1935
Performance/production
Productions of the Federal Theatre Project's Living Newspapers. USA: New York, NY. 1935-1939. Lang.: Eng. 643
1969 Terminal 1996
Performance/production
Theatre Magazine's anniversary issue. USA. 1968-1998. Lang.: Eng. 617
2.5 Minute Ride
Performance/production
Collection of newspaper reviews by London theatre critics. UK-England: London. 1998. Lang.: Eng. 2471
31 Days
Performance/production
Collection of newspaper reviews by London theatre critics. UK-England: London. 1998. Lang.: Eng. 2506
47 Workshop (Cambridge, MA)
Audience
George Pierce Baker's 47 Workshop and the construction of the audience. USA: Cambridge, MA. 1918-1924. Lang.: Eng. 159
54
Design/technology
Lighting design for Mark Christopher's film *54*. USA. 1998. Lang.: Eng. 3913

GEOGRAPHICAL - CHRONOLOGICAL INDEX

Africa

500 B.C.-1995 A.D. Reference materials.
Italian translation of *The Oxford Illustrated History of Theatre* (1995). Europe. North America. Asia. Lang.: Ita. 697

1400-1998. Plays/librettos/scripts.
Analysis of post-medieval morality plays. Europe. Lang.: Eng. 3051

1850-1987. Performance/production.
Traditional and contemporary African drama. Lang.: Eng. 483

1908. Performance/production.
Interview with choreographer Birgit Åkesson. Sweden. Asia. Lang.: Swe. 963

1975-1998. Performance/production.
Theatrical representations of civil war and civil discord. North America. Europe. Lang.: Eng. 567

1990-1998. Relation to other fields.
Political power and national identity in African cinema. Lang.: Eng. 4034

Algeria

1962-1998. Performance/production.
Survey of contemporary Algerian theatre. Lang.: Swe. 1814

Ancient Greece

Performance/production.
Early theatre. Roman Empire. India. Egypt. Lang.: Rus. 484

Argentina

Performance/production.
The influence of tango on world dance. Lang.: Rus. 1223

1600-1900. Plays/librettos/scripts.
Dramatic traditions in North and South America. USA. Lang.: Eng. 3698

1955-1991. Plays/librettos/scripts.
Playwright Ricardo Halac and Argentina's sociopolitical upheavals. Lang.: Eng. 2772

1998. Plays/librettos/scripts.
Genocide, theatre, and the human body. North America. UK-England. Lang.: Eng. 3290

Aruba

1998. Reference materials.
Bibliography of Dutch-language Caribbean literature. Suriname. Netherlands Antilles. Netherlands. Lang.: Eng. 3725

Asia

500 B.C.-1980 A.D. Performance/production.
Theatre in periods of exploration and discovery. North America. Europe. Lang.: Eng. 569

500 B.C.-1995 A.D. Reference materials.
Italian translation of *The Oxford Illustrated History of Theatre* (1995). Europe. North America. Africa. Lang.: Ita. 697

1908. Performance/production.
Interview with choreographer Birgit Åkesson. Sweden. Africa. Lang.: Swe. 963

1918-1998. Performance spaces.
Essays on experimental theatre world wide. Europe. North America. Lang.: Pol. 438

1976-1997. Performance/production.
Multiculturalism and the site-specificity of theatre. North America. Europe. Lang.: Eng. 485

1990-1998. Performance/production.
The dramaturg in the community theatre. North America. South America. Lang.: Eng. 570

Australia

800 B.C.-1988 A.D. Performance/production.
Performance space in Aboriginal *corroboree*. Lang.: Eng. 487

1910-1998. Performance/production.
Australian theatre in South Africa. South Africa, Republic of. Lang.: Eng. 2353

1927-1959. Plays/librettos/scripts.
Analysis of plays by Dymphna Cusack. Lang.: Eng. 2777

1972-1998. Plays/librettos/scripts.
Australian women playwrights and their work. Lang.: Eng. 2778

1983-1995. Performance/production.
Interview with dancer/choreographer Rebecca Hilton. USA. Lang.: Eng. 913

1988. Performance/production.
Analysis of performance pieces reacting to the Australian bicentenary. Darwin. Sydney. Lang.: Eng. 1815

1990-1997. Research/historiography.
Recent developments in Australian theatre historiography. Lang.: Eng. 817

1990-1998. Administration.
Economic forces and the Australian theatre industry. Lang.: Eng. 2

1990-1998. Institutions.
Sidetrack Performance Group, formerly Sidetrack Theatre Company. Sydney. Lang.: Eng. 1567
Profile of Women's Circus. Melbourne. Lang.: Eng. 1568

1990-1998. Performance/production.
Aborigines in Australian theatre. Lang.: Eng. 486
Contemporary Asian-Australian theatre. Lang.: Eng. 488
The current state of Australian theatre for youth. Lang.: Eng. 489
Multiculturalism and Italo-Australian theatre. Lang.: Eng. 490
Recent developments in Australian 'physical theatre'. Lang.: Eng. 492

1990-1998. Plays/librettos/scripts.
The community play *Aftershocks*. Newcastle, NSW. Lang.: Eng. 2774
The current state of Australian gay and lesbian theatre. Lang.: Eng. 2775
Australian plays about the war in Vietnam. Lang.: Eng. 2776

1990-1998. Theory/criticism.
Multiculturalism and Australian theatre. Lang.: Eng. 3807

1991-1998. Administration.
Adelaide Festival Centre Trust's database for tracking economics and cultural impact of events. Adelaide. Lang.: Eng. 3

1992-1998. Performance/production.
The training of actors in Asian performance styles. Brisbane. Lang.: Eng. 1817

1994. Performance/production.
Directing the documentary-based performance project *The Worst Woman in the World*. Lang.: Eng. 1816

1995. Plays/librettos/scripts.
Analysis of *Dead White Males* by David Williamson. Lang.: Eng. 2773

1997. Basic theatrical documents.
Text of *Panayiotis* by Angela Costi. Lang.: Eng. 1406

Australia — cont'd

1997. Design/technology.
Geoffrey Simpson's cinematography for Gillian Armstrong's *Oscar and Lucinda.* Lang.: Eng. 3900
1997. Performance/production.
Aboriginal arts on the Australian stage. Sydney. Lang.: Eng. 491
1998. Design/technology.
Scenic elements in *Titanic* by street theatre group Theater Titanick. Münster. Leipzig. Perth. Lang.: Eng. 191
Lighting designer Mark Howett's work for Black Swan Theatre Company. Fremantle. Lang.: Eng. 1513
Costumes for the film *Welcome to Woop Woop.* Lang.: Eng. 3899
Steve Cohen's lighting design for pop music tour. Lang.: Eng. 4095
1998. Institutions.
Impressions from Australian theatre festivals. Perth. Adelaide. Lang.: Ger. 334
1998. Performance/production.
Soprano Joan Sutherland. Lang.: Eng. 4526
1998. Relation to other fields.
Australian Shakespeare studies. Lang.: Eng. 3728

Austria

1650-1699. Relation to other fields.
Theatrical representation at the Austrian court. Vienna. Lang.: Ger. 4210
1776-1914. Plays/librettos/scripts.
Female role models in plays by Austrian women. Lang.: Ger. 2786
1782-1791. Performance/production.
Mozart's operas and contemporary Viennese performance spaces. Vienna. Lang.: Eng. 4528
1823. Plays/librettos/scripts.
Analysis of Schubert's unperformed opera *Fierrabras.* Lang.: Eng. 4759
1867-1997. Performance/production.
Slovenian reception of Austrian drama. Slovenia. Lang.: Ger. 2347
1889. Basic theatrical documents.
Catalan translation of *Anatol* and *Anatols Grössenwahn (The Megalomania of Anatol)* by Arthur Schnitzler. Lang.: Cat. 1408
1890-1910. Plays/librettos/scripts.
The image of motherhood in German-language drama. Germany. Lang.: Ger. 2787
1895-1935. Plays/librettos/scripts.
Wedekind's Lulu plays and their adaptation by Berg. Germany. Lang.: Fre. 4798
1898-1967. Performance/production.
Soprano Mária Németh. Hungary. Vienna. Lang.: Hun. 4615
1898-1981. Performance/production.
The career of soprano Lotte Lenya. Vienna. Lang.: Eng. 4352
1898-1998. Audience.
The decline in popularity of operetta. Vienna. Lang.: Eng. 4850
1903-1977. Performance/production.
Profile of soprano Piroska Anday. Budapest. Vienna. Lang.: Hun. 4627
1905. Plays/librettos/scripts.
A private performance of *Die Büchse der Pandora (Pandora's Box)* by Frank Wedekind. Vienna. Lang.: Fre. 2783
1907-1922. Plays/librettos/scripts.
Social criticism in Viennese Expressionist drama. Vienna. Lang.: Ger. 2779
1918-1992. Performance spaces.
The architectural and administrative history of Redoutentheater. Vienna. Lang.: Ger. 433
1924-1986. Performance/production.
Pirandello on the German-language stage. Germany. Lang.: Ita. 1994
1924-1989. Performance/production.
Pirandello's theatre on the Austrian stage. Lang.: Ita. 1825
1924-1998. Performance/production.
Interview with bass Albert Antalffy. Hungary. Mödling. Lang.: Hun. 4634
1925-1938. Plays/librettos/scripts.
Analysis of plays by Carl Zuckmayer. Vienna. Lang.: Ger. 2785
1934. Plays/librettos/scripts.
Letters of Pirandello, Moissiu, and Jahn. Italy. Vienna. Lang.: Ita. 3219
1935. Basic theatrical documents.
Complete libretto of Alban Berg's *Lulu.* Lang.: Fre, Ger. 4412
1935. Performance/production.
Arnold Schoenberg's refusal to complete Alban Berg's unfinished opera *Lulu.* Lang.: Fre. 4533
1935. Plays/librettos/scripts.
Dictionary of Alban Berg's *Lulu.* Lang.: Fre. 4760
1936. Performance/production.
Personal recollection of composer Franz Lehár. Vienna. Lang.: Swe. 4852
1945-1955. Performance/production.
The postwar Viennese Mozart style. Vienna. Lang.: Eng. 4529
1945-1998. Relation to other fields.
Postwar Austrian cultural and theatrical identity. Lang.: Ger. 715
1950-1998. Performance/production.
Interview with singer Elisabeth Schwarzkopf. UK-England. Lang.: Swe. 4860
1953-1998. Performance/production.
Austrian street theatre. Lang.: Ger. 4116
1960-1977. Performance/production.
Performance artists Vito Acconci and Hermann Nitsch. Vienna. Italy. Lang.: Eng. 4239
1960-1998. Performance/production.
Actor Helmuth Lohner's stint as administrative director of Theater in der Josefstadt. Vienna. Lang.: Ger. 1819
The problem of staging operettas on the contemporary stage. Sweden. Germany. Lang.: Swe. 4857
1979. Plays/librettos/scripts.
Analysis of Elfriede Jelinek's adaptation of *Et Dukkehjem (A Doll's House)* by Ibsen. Lang.: Eng. 2782
1979-1998. Design/technology.
Scenographer Martin Zehetgruber. Graz. Stuttgart. Lang.: Ger. 168
1981. Basic theatrical documents.
Catalan translation of *Am Ziel (To the Goal)* by Thomas Bernhard. Lang.: Cat. 1407
1981-1998. Performance/production.
Singer Thomas Lander. Germany. Sweden. Lang.: Swe. 4591
1988. Plays/librettos/scripts.
Thomas Bernhard's Holocaust play, *Heldenplatz (Heroes' Square).* Lang.: Eng. 2784
1988-1998. Performance/production.
Gert Voss and Ignaz Kirchner, *Theater Heute*'s actors of the year. Vienna. Lang.: Ger. 1823
1989-1998. Performance/production.
Account of the theatre anthropology workshop. Vienna. Lang.: Hun. 494
1993-1997. Performance/production.
Children's puppet work. Slovenia. Lang.: Slo. 4885
1996-1998. Performance/production.
'The Speaking Body' museum installation, site of theatre anthropology seminars. Vienna. Zurich. Lang.: Eng. 493
1997. Institutions.
Peter Stein's last season as director at the Salzburg Festival. Salzburg. Lang.: Eng. 336
The program of the Salzburg Festival. Salzburg. Lang.: Hun. 1569
1997. Plays/librettos/scripts.
Playwright Elfriede Jelinek on the relationship between author and play in rehearsal. Vienna. Lang.: Ger. 2780
1997-1998. Relation to other fields.
The artist and the world in recent productions. Vienna. Germany. Lang.: Ger. 3729
1998. Design/technology.
Careers in technical theatre. Germany. Lang.: Ger. 189
1998. Institutions.
The Vienna-based foundation for the development of Moscow's Bolšoj Theatre. Vienna. Lang.: Rus. 335
Productions by Stefan Bachmann and Robert Wilson at the Salzburg Festival. Salzburg. Lang.: Hun. 1570
Productions of Salzburger Festspiele. Salzburg. Lang.: Ger. 1571
Interview with Ivan Nagel, drama manager of the Salzburg Festival. Salzburg. Lang.: Ger. 1572
Productions of the Salzburg Festival. Salzburg. Lang.: Ger. 1573

Austria — cont'd

Comparison of Salzburg and Bayreuth festival seasons. Bayreuth. Salzburg. Lang.: Eng. 4452

1998. Performance/production.
Some productions of Im Puls Tanz '98 festival. Vienna. Lang.: Hun. 914
Prokofjév's *Romeo and Juliet*, choreographed by Cranko, Wiener Staatsoper. Vienna. Lang.: Hun. 1063
Nureyev's *Swan Lake* at Staatsoper. Vienna. Lang.: Hun. 1064
Analysis of *Sportstück (Sport Play)* by Elfriede Jelinek. Vienna. Lang.: Ger. 1818
Premieres of new plays. Vienna. Lang.: Ger. 1820
Actors Gert Voss and Ignaz Kirchner on George Tabori's production of *Fin de partie (Endgame)*. Vienna. Lang.: Ger. 1821
Luc Bondy's production of Horváth's *Figaro lässt sich scheiden (Figaro Gets Divorced)*. Vienna. Lang.: Ger. 1822
Robert Lepage's *Geometry of Miracles* at the Salzburg Festival. Salzburg. Lang.: Ger. 1824
Productions of Horváth's *Geschichten aus dem Wienerwald (Tales from the Vienna Woods)*. Hamburg. Hannover. Vienna. Lang.: Ger. 2003
Premieres of plays on the Nazi theme. Darmstadt. Vienna. Lang.: Ger. 2030
Reviews of plays by Wolfgang Bauer and Thomas Bernhard. Basel. Vienna. Lang.: Ger. 2403
Review of Salzburger Festspiele performances. Salzburg. Lang.: Ger. 4527
Hans Neuenfels's production of Meyerbeer's *Le Prophète*. Vienna. Lang.: Swe. 4530
Opera productions of the Salzburg Festival. Salzburg. Lang.: Hun. 4531
Montemezzi's *L'amore dei tre re*, directed and designed by Philippe Arlaud. Bregenz. Lang.: Eng. 4532
Reviews of *Lieder* recordings. USA. Slovenia. Lang.: Eng. 4720

1998. Plays/librettos/scripts.
Playwright, dramaturg, and director Thomas Jonigk on contemporary theatre. Vienna. Lang.: Ger. 2781
Recent productions directed by Frank Castorf. Vienna. Lang.: Ger. 2788

Austrian Empire

1750-1800. Performance/production.
Music in German-language Prague productions. Prague. Lang.: Cze. 1826

Bashkir

1998. Performance/production.
Rijfkat Israfilov's production of *Bibinur, ah, Bibinur!*. Ufa. Lang.: Rus. 1827
Opera singers E. Kočetova and A. Abdrazakov. Lang.: Rus. 4534

Belgium

1440-1560. Plays/librettos/scripts.
Analysis of *De Eerste Bliscap van Maria (The First Joy of Mary)*. Brussels. Lang.: Eng. 2790

1450-1499. Plays/librettos/scripts.
Roman 'saints' plays' at the Lille procession honoring the Virgin. Lille. Lang.: Eng. 4224

1890-1949. Plays/librettos/scripts.
The dramatic styles of Maurice Maeterlinck and Anton Čechov. Russia. Lang.: Rus. 3328

1980-1983. Plays/librettos/scripts.
Dutch and Flemish Shakespearean productions. Netherlands. Lang.: Dut. 2789

1981-1998. Performance/production.
Dancer/choreographer Anne Teresa De Keersmaeker. Brussels. Lang.: Eng. 1260

1984-1998. Performance/production.
Interview with choreographer Alain Platel. Ghent. Lang.: Eng. 1261

1992. Performance/production.
Robert Wilson's production of *Doctor Faustus Lights the Lights* by Gertrude Stein. Antwerp. Lang.: Fle. 1828

1997. Performance/production.
Press reactions to productions of Offenbach's *Orphée aux Enfers*. Switzerland. France. Lang.: Fre. 4535

1998. Performance/production.
Premieres of choreographies by Danny Rosseel. Antwerp. Amsterdam. Lang.: Hun. 1065
Seminar on auditions for choreographers for Resolution dance festival. London. Brussels. Lang.: Swe. 1314
Mezzo soprano Rita Gorr. Lang.: Eng. 4536

Belorussia

1998. Institutions.
Moscow Art Theatre's tour in Minsk. Minsk. Lang.: Rus. 1574
Account of Slavic Theatre Meeting. Gomel'. Lang.: Rus. 1575

Benin

1990-1998. Performance/production.
Choreographer Koffi Koko. Paris. Lang.: Eng. 923

1998. Basic theatrical documents.
Text of *Ubu déchaîné (Ubu Unchained)* by Richard Demarcy. France. Lang.: Fre. 4287

Bolivia

1970-1985. Performance/production.
César Brie and *La pista del cabeceo (The Land of Nod)*. Lang.: Ita. 1829

Bosnia

1996-1998. Performance/production.
Ethnicity, community youth theatre, and the dramaturg. Lang.: Eng. 495

1997-1998. Relation to other fields.
Manfred Weber on directing Děvad Karahasan's translation of *Leonce und Lena* by Büchner. Sarajevo. Lang.: Ger. 3730

1998. Performance/production.
Interview with director Aleš Kurt. Sarajevo. Lang.: Hun. 1830

Bosnia-Herzegovina

1997. Performance/production.
The development of *Letters, or Where Does the Postman Go When All the Street Names Are Changed*, based on experiences of residents of Mostar. Mostar. Lang.: Eng. 1831

Brazil

1912. Plays/librettos/scripts.
Playwright Nelson Rodrigues. Lang.: Rus. 2791

1972-1997. Performance/production.
Northern Brazilian folk theatre forms. Lang.: Eng. 497

1980-1995. Performance/production.
Cultural identity and Brazilian theatre. Lang.: Eng. 496

1989. Performance/production.
Ópera Seca's *Mattogrosso*. Rio de Janeiro. Lang.: Eng. 4537

1992-1996. Performance/production.
Interview with director Augusto Boal. Rio de Janeiro. Lang.: Eng. 1833

1998. Institutions.
Profile of contemporary ballet company Grupo Corpo. Belo Horizonte. Lang.: Rus. 1249

1998. Performance/production.
Review of Brazilian performances of plays by Brecht. São Paulo. Lang.: Ger. 1832

Bulgaria

1946-1998. Performance/production.
Autobiography of Yiddish theatre actress Moni Ovadia. Italy. Lang.: Ita. 2174

1997-1998. Relation to other fields.
Conditions of Bulgarian theatre and reform efforts. Lang.: Ger. 3731

1998. Performance/production.
Profile of choreographer Galina Borissova. Lang.: Dut. 1262
Musical theatre performer L. Ivanova. Lang.: Rus. 4353

Canada

1763-1867. Performance/production.
Garrison and amateur theatricals during the British regime. Quebec, PQ. Kingston, ON. Lang.: Eng. 505

1860-1976. Plays/librettos/scripts.
Dramatic adaptations of Henry Wadsworth Longfellow's poem *Evangeline*. USA. Lang.: Eng. 3643

1870-1998. Plays/librettos/scripts.
Women and Acadian theatre. Lang.: Eng. 2810

1880-1950. Administration.
History of Quebec theatre. Montreal, PQ. Quebec, PQ. Lang.: Fre. 1375

Canada — cont'd

1890-1997. **Plays/librettos/scripts.**
Mennonite drama of Veralyn Warkentin and Vern Thiessen. Lang.: Eng. 2829

1905-1998. **Administration.**
Comparative analysis of national cultural policies. France. Germany. Norway. Lang.: Eng. 4

1910-1998. **Performance/production.**
Obituaries for Roger L. Stevens, Kenneth Frankel, Donald Davis, and Edith Oliver. USA. Lang.: Eng. 2742

1911-1998. **Plays/librettos/scripts.**
Young People's Theatre's adaptation of *Anne of Green Gables.* Toronto, ON. Lang.: Eng. 2832

1916-1957. **Plays/librettos/scripts.**
Theatre artist Elizabeth Sterling Haynes and Alberta theatre. Lang.: Eng. 2799

1919-1998. **Performance/production.**
Problems of post-secondary theatre training. Edmonton, AB. Lang.: Eng. 1848

1922-1952. **Relation to other fields.**
The influence of radio drama on professional theatre. Lang.: Fre. 3869

1930-1950. **Relation to other fields.**
Amateur art theatre produced by Quebec priests. Montreal, PQ. Lang.: Fre. 3733

1933-1990. **Performance/production.**
Pierre Dagenais and his company L'Équipe. Montreal, PQ. Lang.: Fre. 1846

1933-1998. **Performance/production.**
Actor Mervyn Blake. Stratford, ON. Lang.: Eng. 1851

1940-1978. **Performance/production.**
Adrian Pecknold and the Canadian Mime Theatre. Niagara-on-the-Lake, ON. Lang.: Eng. 4085

1942-1998. **Performance/production.**
Interview with actor Gérard Poirier. Montreal, PQ. Lang.: Fre. 1834

1944-1947. **Institutions.**
Analysis of the bulletin of theatre company Les Compagnons du Saint-Laurent. Montreal, PQ. Lang.: Fre. 1585

1945-1998. **Performance/production.**
List of French-language productions of Shakespeare. Montreal, PQ. Quebec, PQ. Lang.: Fre. 1841

Puppeteer Felix Mirbt. Berlin. Lang.: Eng. 4887

1949. **Plays/librettos/scripts.**
On the text and staging of *La Cathédrale...* by Jean Depréz (Laurette Laroque). Montreal, PQ. Lang.: Fre. 2823

1950-1980. **Plays/librettos/scripts.**
Analysis of historical drama of the holocaust. USA. Germany. Lang.: Eng. 3610

1950-1998. **Performance/production.**
Interview with actress Andrée Lachapelle. Montreal, PQ. Lang.: Fre. 502

1950-1998. **Plays/librettos/scripts.**
Interview with playwright Rana Bose. Montreal, PQ. Calcutta. Lang.: Eng. 2820

Wonderbolt Circus's *Maid of Avalon,* a loose adaptation of *Der Gute Mensch von Sezuan (The Good Person of Szechwan)* by Brecht.St. John's, NF. Lang.: Eng. 2825

1952-1998. **Performance/production.**
Interview with actor/director Paul Hébert. Quebec, PQ. Lang.: Fre. 1854

1952-1998. **Relation to other fields.**
Theatre photographer André Le Coz. Montreal, PQ. Lang.: Fre. 3738

1953-1967. **Institutions.**
Institutional analysis of the Stratford Festival. Stratford, ON. Lang.: Eng. 1584

1953-1998. **Performance/production.**
Actor William Hutt. Stratford, ON. USA. Lang.: Eng. 1858

Interview with television puppeteer Nina Keogh. Toronto, ON. Lang.: Eng. 4888

1958-1998. **Performance/production.**
Interview with actress Denise Gagnon. Quebec, PQ. Lang.: Fre. 1864

1959-1998. **Performance/production.**
Playwright Rana Bose on memorable performances. Montreal, PQ. Lang.: Eng. 498

1960-1988. **Performance/production.**
The work of some North American performance artists. USA. Lang.: Eng. 4251

1962-1996. **Performance/production.**
Interview with actor William Hutt. Stratford, ON. Lang.: Eng. 1844

1963-1998. **Performance spaces.**
The renovation of Neptune Theatre. Halifax, NS. Lang.: Eng. 1794

1964. **Performance/production.**
The Stratford Festival production of Shakespeare's *King Lear.* Stratford, ON. Lang.: Eng. 506

1964-1998. **Performance/production.**
Interview with film and television actress Andrée Lachapelle. Montreal, PQ. Lang.: Fre. 3857

1965. **Performance/production.**
The performances of Frances Hyland, Kate Reid, and Martha Henry in *The Cherry Orchard.* Stratford, ON. Lang.: Eng. 1865

1965-1992. **Plays/librettos/scripts.**
Analysis of the opera *Mario the Magician* by Harry Somers and Rod Anderson. Lang.: Eng. 4763

1965-1998. **Performance/production.**
The failure of the Canadian Theatre of the Deaf. Lang.: Eng. 507

Interview with film and television actor Jean-Louis Millette. Montreal, PQ. Lang.: Fre. 3856

1966-1996. **Performance/production.**
Modernist and postmodernist Shakespearean production. UK-England. Lang.: Eng. 2618

1966-1998. **Institutions.**
Luman Coad on the work of Coad Canada Puppets. Vancouver, BC. Lang.: Eng. 4919

1967-1985. **Plays/librettos/scripts.**
Language and rhetoric in plays of George Ryga. Lang.: Eng. 2792

1967-1998. **Plays/librettos/scripts.**
National identity in new Canadian opera. Lang.: Eng. 4764

1967-1998. **Relation to other fields.**
The influence of Cervantes' *Don Quixote* on contemporary Quebec artists. Lang.: Fre. 3737

1968. **Performance/production.**
Robert Gurik's adaptation of Shakespeare's *Hamlet.* Montreal, PQ. London, ON. Lang.: Fre. 1866

1968-1975. **Performance/production.**
The development of Toronto's alternative theatres. Toronto, ON. Lang.: Eng. 1850

1968-1998. **Performance/production.**
Director Serge Ouaknine and his use of visual aids. Montreal, PQ. Lang.: Fre. 1871

1969-1973. **Plays/librettos/scripts.**
Michel Tremblay's adaptation of *Mistero Buffo* by Dario Fo. Montreal, PQ. Lang.: Fre. 2795

1969-1998. **Plays/librettos/scripts.**
Interview with playwright Michel Vinaver. Quebec, PQ. Lang.: Fre. 2831

1970-1985. **Performance/production.**
Social criticism and alternative theatre in Quebec and Newfoundland. Lang.: Eng. 500

1970-1990. **Plays/librettos/scripts.**
Quebecois plays about the crisis of October 1970. Lang.: Fre, Eng. 2812

1970-1998. **Performance/production.**
Interview with choreographer Runa Singha. Toronto, ON. Lang.: Eng. 1368

Puppeteer Ronnie Burkett. Calgary, AB. Winnipeg, MB. Lang.: Eng. 4920

1970-1998. **Plays/librettos/scripts.**
Playwright/actress Linda Griffiths on the creative process. Saskatoon, SK. Lang.: Eng. 2806

Homosexuality in Canadian opera. Lang.: Eng. 4762

1970-1998. **Relation to other fields.**
Process drama in secondary school drama education. Lang.: Eng. 3736

1971-1989. **Institutions.**
Jacques Crête and Atelier de recherche théâtrale l'Eskabel. Montreal, PQ. Lang.: Eng. 1590

1972-1982. **Institutions.**
The Mummers' Troupe and the Canada Council. St. John's, NF. Lang.: Eng. 1581

1972-1989. **Institutions.**
Sadhu Binning on his politically-oriented theatre group Vancouver Sath. Vancouver, BC. Lang.: Eng. 1577

Canada — cont'd

1972-1998. **Institutions.**
Puppetry at Mermaid Theatre. Wolfville, NS. Lang.: Eng. 4870
1972-1998. **Plays/librettos/scripts.**
Playwriting career of Carol Shields. Winnipeg, MB. Lang.: Eng. 2794
Playwright, actor, and director Charles Follini. Lang.: Eng. 2818
1974-1998. **Institutions.**
Profile of Belfry Theatre Company. Victoria, BC. Lang.: Eng. 1583
1975-1998. **Institutions.**
Lunchbox Theatre's new play development program, Stage One. Calgary, AB. Lang.: Eng. 1576
1979-1997. **Institutions.**
History of the Ligue Nationale de l'Improvisation. Montreal, PQ. Lang.: Fre. 339
1980-1990. **Plays/librettos/scripts.**
Quebecois drama and the influence of visual arts. Lang.: Fre. 2816
1980-1995. **Plays/librettos/scripts.**
Theatre and the creation of a new nationalism. Saint Lucia. Lang.: Eng. 2808
1980-1997. **Performance/production.**
Canadian representations of Ophelia from Shakespeare's *Hamlet*. Lang.: Eng. 1852
1980-1998. **Performance/production.**
Interview with actor Jacques Leblanc. Quebec, PQ. Lang.: Fre. 1853
Directing shows with three-week rehearsal time at Eastern Front Theatre. Dartmouth, NS. Lang.: Eng. 1868
Clown teachers Richard Pochinko and Philippe Gaulier. Lang.: Eng. 4117
Interview with puppet animator Brian Duchscherer. Lang.: Eng. 4886
1980-1998. **Plays/librettos/scripts.**
Playwright Norm Foster. Lang.: Eng. 2798
Comparison of French and Canadian protest plays. France. Lang.: Eng. 2801
1981. **Plays/librettos/scripts.**
Vie et mort du Roi Boiteux (Life and Death of the Lame King), Jean-Pierre Ronfard's adaptation of *Richard III*. Lang.: Fre. 2813
1981-1997. **Design/technology.**
R. Murray Schaffer's environmental opera *The Princess of the Stars*. Lang.: Eng. 4424
1981-1998. **Institutions.**
Rahul Varma on his multicultural theatre company Teesri Duniya. Montreal, PQ. Lang.: Eng. 1592
1982-1998. **Administration.**
Interview with producer Ed Mirvish. London. Toronto, ON. Lang.: Eng. 1393
1982-1998. **Performance spaces.**
The Dame Blanche theatre. Quebec, PQ. Lang.: Fre. 1796
1983-1998. **Design/technology.**
Design in contemporary opera performance. Toronto, ON. Lang.: Eng. 4425
1984-1998. **Plays/librettos/scripts.**
Political community theatre by South Indian emigrants. Toronto, ON. Montreal, PQ. India. Lang.: Eng. 2821
1985. **Plays/librettos/scripts.**
Analysis of *Rootless but Green Are the Boulevard Trees* by Uma Parameswaran. Winnipeg, MB. Lang.: Eng. 2819
1985-1998. **Design/technology.**
Set designer Jean Hazel. Quebec, PQ. Lang.: Fre. 1515
1985-1998. **Institutions.**
Profile of Arbo Cyber, théâtre (?). Quebec, PQ. Lang.: Fre. 4232
Profile of Tapestry Music Theatre. Toronto, ON. Lang.: Eng. 4346
Profile of Opera Atelier. Toronto, ON. Lang.: Eng. 4446
1986-1998. **Performance/production.**
The collaborative process at Catalyst Theatre. Edmonton, AB. Lang.: Eng. 504
Voice teachers Alex Bulmer and Kate Lynch. Toronto, ON. London. Lang.: Eng. 1837
1987-1998. **Performance/production.**
Choreographer Debra Brown of Cirque du Soleil. Montreal, PQ. Lang.: Eng. 4179
1987-1998. **Plays/librettos/scripts.**
Interview with playwright and scriptwriter Michel Marc Bouchard. Montreal, PQ. Lang.: Fre. 3963
1988. **Audience.**
Theatrical production and reception. Lang.: Eng. 146
1988. **Performance/production.**
French Canadian translations/adaptations of Shakespeare. Montreal, PQ. Lang.: Fre. 1855
1988-1993. **Plays/librettos/scripts.**
French translations of Shakespeare by Antonine Maillet and Jean-Louis Roux. Montreal, PQ. Lang.: Fre. 2793
1988-1998. **Design/technology.**
Opera scenographer Michael Levine. Toronto, ON. Lang.: Eng. 4426
1989-1994. **Plays/librettos/scripts.**
Normand Chaurette's translations of *As You Like It* by Shakespeare. Montreal, PQ. Lang.: Fre. 2824
1989-1995. **Plays/librettos/scripts.**
Leila Sujir's video *The Dreams of the Night Cleaners*. Lang.: Eng. 4075
1989-1997. **Institutions.**
Survey of drama graduates' financial and employment conditions. Toronto, ON. Lang.: Eng. 341
1989-1998. **Institutions.**
Quebec theatres specializing in new plays. Quebec, PQ. Lang.: Fre. 1589
1990-1991. **Plays/librettos/scripts.**
Analysis of *The Noam Chomsky Lectures* by Daniel Brooks and Guillermo Verdecchio. Toronto, ON. Lang.: Eng. 2797
1990-1997. **Plays/librettos/scripts.**
David Young on his play *Inexpressible Island*. Toronto, ON. Lang.: Eng. 2837
1990-1998. **Performance/production.**
The integration of playwriting into the production process at Théâtre Niveau Parking. Quebec, PQ. Lang.: Fre. 1857
1990-1998. **Plays/librettos/scripts.**
Interview with playwright/director Sheila James. Toronto, ON. Lang.: Eng. 2809
Analysis of Melissa Mullen's *Rough Waters* at Theatre PEI. Charlottetown, PE. Lang.: Eng. 2817
Representations of theatre in the film *Jésus de Montréal*. Lang.: Fre. 3964
1990-1998. **Relation to other fields.**
References to film in theatre of Robert Lepage. Lang.: Fre. 3734
1991-1997. **Performance/production.**
Productions of plays by Bernard-Marie Koltès. Montreal, PQ. Lang.: Fre. 1862
1991-1998. **Relation to other fields.**
Theatre of the Oppressed and racism in high schools. Lang.: Eng. 717
1992. **Performance/production.**
The methodology of director Robert Lepage. Toronto, ON. Lang.: Eng. 1845
1992-1996. **Plays/librettos/scripts.**
Conrad Alexandrowicz on his dance-theatre piece *The Wines of Tuscany*. Vancouver, BC. Lang.: Eng. 1356
1992-1998. **Design/technology.**
Costume designer Mara Blumenthal. Lang.: Eng. 170
1992-1998. **Performance spaces.**
Quebec's performance spaces. Quebec, PQ. Lang.: Fre. 1795
1992-1998. **Performance/production.**
Director and martial artist Huy-Phong Doàn's *La Légende du manuel sacré (The Legend of the Sacred Handbook)*. Montreal, PQ. Lang.: Fre. 4118
1993. **Basic theatrical documents.**
Text of *Five or Six Characters in Search of Toronto* by Rana Bose. Toronto, ON. Lang.: Eng. 1409
Text of Michael Healey's one-man show *Kicked*. Toronto, ON. Lang.: Eng. 1410
1993-1996. **Basic theatrical documents.**
Excerpt from *a canadian monsoon* by Sheila James. Toronto, ON. Lang.: Eng. 1411
1993-1998. **Plays/librettos/scripts.**
Leslie Arden's career in musical theatre. Lang.: Eng. 4389
1993-1998. **Relation to other fields.**
The use of performance skills in the primary school classroom. Montreal, PQ. Lang.: Fre. 3739

Canada — cont'd

1994. Basic theatrical documents.
Text of *Tinka's New Dress* by puppeteer Ronnie Burkett. Winnipeg, MB. Lang.: Eng. 4917

1994-1995. Design/technology.
Costume designer Isabelle Larivière. Quebec, PQ. Lang.: Fre. 1514

1994-1998. Plays/librettos/scripts.
Analysis of plays by Gilles Maheu. Montreal, PQ. Lang.: Fre. 1357

Analysis of *Corker* by Wendy Lill. Halifax, NS. Lang.: Eng. 2836

Brad Fraser's direction of a film version of his *Poor Superman*. Lang.: Eng. 3966

1994-1998. Relation to other fields.
Puppeteer Ken McKay on puppetry in education. Lang.: Eng. 4915

1995. Plays/librettos/scripts.
Philippe Soldevila on his *Le miel est plus doux que sang (Honey Is Milder than Blood)*. Quebec, PQ. Lang.: Fre. 2796

1995-1996. Theory/criticism.
Critical response to *Elsineur (Elsinore)*, Robert Lepage's multimedia adaptation of *Hamlet*. Lang.: Eng. 3810

1995-1997. Performance/production.
Differences between nudity onstage and on screen. Montreal, PQ. Lang.: Fre. 499

Marie-Ginette Guay's wordless performance in Franz Xaver Kroetz's *Wunschkonzert (Request Concert)*. Quebec, PQ. Lang.: Fre. 1847

1995-1997. Plays/librettos/scripts.
Analysis of *Queen Lear* by Beau Coleman. Edmonton, AB. Lang.: Eng. 2800

1995-1998. Institutions.
Profile of Acteurs Associés, an alternative to agencies. Lang.: Fre. 343

Street theatre company Scaffold Theatre Project. Hamilton, ON. Lang.: Eng. 1593

1995-1998. Performance/production.
Pierre Benoît's music for *Don Quichotte* at Théâtre du Nouveau Monde. Montreal, PQ. Lang.: Fre. 1870

Cinematic work of director Robert Lepage. Lang.: Fre. 3928

1995-1998. Plays/librettos/scripts.
Analysis of works by Larry Tremblay. Montreal, PQ. Lang.: Fre. 2804

1995-1998. Relation to other fields.
Performance ethnography of social action theatre Mise au Jeu Montréal. Montreal, PQ. Lang.: Eng. 3735

1996. Basic theatrical documents.
Text of *The Wines of Tuscany* by Conrad Alexandrowicz. Vancouver, BC. Lang.: Eng. 1344

1996. Institutions.
Émile Morin and Pascale Landry on their Productions Recto-Verso. Quebec, PQ. Lang.: Fre. 4233

1996. Performance spaces.
Theatre SKAM's production of *Louis and Dave* in a Plymouth Volaré. Victoria, BC. Lang.: Eng. 1797

1996. Plays/librettos/scripts.
Review of collections of plays with gay themes. Lang.: Eng. 2802

1996-1998. Institutions.
Marketing techniques of Canadian Opera Company. Toronto, ON. Lang.: Eng. 4447

1996-1998. Performance/production.
Jean-Claude Coulbois on filming theatrical productions. Montreal, PQ. Lang.: Fre. 1839

1997. Institutions.
Comments on productions of the Shaw Festival. Niagara-on-the-Lake, ON. Lang.: Eng. 1579

The 1997 Shaw and Stratford Festival seasons. Stratford, ON. Niagara-on-the-Lake, ON. Lang.: Eng. 1582

Report on the 1997 Toronto Film Festival. Toronto, ON. Lang.: Eng. 3923

1997. Performance/production.
Opportunities for South Asian actors. Toronto, ON. Lang.: Eng. 508

Profile of the Festival international de nouvelle danse. Montreal, PQ. Lang.: Fre. 1264

English and French-language productions of *Picasso at the Lapin Agile* by Steve Martin. Montreal, PQ. Lang.: Fre. 1836

Analysis of a student production of Caryl Churchill's *Cloud Nine*. Lang.: Eng. 1840

Student production of Ford's *'Tis Pity She's a Whore*. Lang.: Eng. 1849

Student production of *Les Femmes savantes (The Learned Ladies)* by Molière. Calgary, AB. Lang.: Eng. 1859

Interview with director Robert Lepage. Stockholm. Montreal, PQ. Lang.: Swe. 2397

1997. Plays/librettos/scripts.
Raymond Saint-Jean's film adaptation of *Cabaret neiges noires (Black Snow Cabaret)*. Lang.: Fre. 3967

The American and Canadian premieres of *Jackie O.* Banff, AB. Houston, TX. Lang.: Eng. 4761

Response to criticism of Théâtre du Sous-Marin Jaune's adaptation of Voltaire's *Candide*. Quebec, PQ. Lang.: Fre. 4912

1997-1998. Institutions.
Backstage tours of the National Arts Centre. Ottawa, ON. Lang.: Eng. 340

1997-1998. Plays/librettos/scripts.
Analysis of *Sled* by Judith Thompson. Lang.: Eng. 2805

Dramaturg's experience working on a play by Yvette Nolan. Lang.: Eng. 2827

1998. Administration.
Negotiations between US and Canadian Equity. USA. Lang.: Eng. 54

1998. Basic theatrical documents.
Excerpt from *Job Stealer* by Rahul Varma, Helen Vlachos and Ian Lloyd George. Montreal, PQ. Lang.: Eng. 1412

Text of libretto for *Beatrice Chancy*. Toronto, ON. Lang.: Eng. 4413

James Rolfe on his opera *Beatrice Chancy*. Toronto, ON. Lang.: Eng. 4414

1998. Design/technology.
Directory of manufacturers and distributors of lighting equipment. USA. Lang.: Eng. 169

Set design for Robert Lepage's *Geometry of Miracles*. Quebec, PQ. Lang.: Eng. 1516

Maurice Sendak's set design for *Hänsel und Gretel*, Canadian Opera Company. Toronto, ON. Lang.: Eng. 4427

1998. Institutions.
Account of children's theatre festival. Montreal, PQ. Lang.: Fre. 337

Ruth Smillie, artistic director of Regina's Globe Theatre. Regina, SK. Lang.: Eng. 338

Workshop of Association Internationale des Critiques de Théâtre. Quebec, PQ. Lang.: Fre. 342

Training methods of the Conservatoire d'art dramatique de Québec. Quebec, PQ. Lang.: Fre. 1578

Survey of Stratford Festival season. Stratford, ON. Lang.: Eng. 1580

Proposal to apply alternative pedagogy and cultural studies to university theatre education. Guelph, ON. Lang.: Eng. 1586

Robert Lepage and his experimental company Ex Machina. Quebec, PQ. Lang.: Fre. 1587

Shakespearean productions at the Carrefour international theatre festival. Quebec, PQ. Lang.: Fre. 1588

Criticism of the Carrefour international theatre festival. Quebec, PQ. Lang.: Fre. 1591

Baktinian analysis of Kingston Buskers Rendez-vous. Kingston, ON. Lang.: Fre. 4161

1998. Performance spaces.
Toronto's theatres. Toronto, ON. Lang.: Eng. 434

1998. Performance/production.
Actor/playwright Michael Healey on the purpose of theatre. Lang.: Eng. 501

Productions of children's theatre festival. Montreal, PQ. Lang.: Fre. 503

Derision in recent productions. Quebec, PQ. Lang.: Fre. 509

Ballerina Greta Hodgkinson of National Ballet of Canada. Toronto, ON. Lang.: Eng. 1067

Survey of women's dance and choreography of the season. Montreal, PQ. Lang.: Fre. 1263

Canada — cont'd

Actor Jack Robitaille. Quebec, PQ. Lang.: Fre. 1835
Actress Anne-Marie Cadieux on working in theatre and in film. Montreal, PQ. Lang.: Fre. 1838
Social context of French and Canadian productions of *Les Fourberies de Scapin* by Molière. Montreal, PQ. Paris. Lang.: Fre. 1842
The Shaw Festival season. Niagara-on-the-Lake, ON. Lang.: Eng. 1843
Analysis of *1837: The Farmer's Revolt* directed by Bruce Barton of Carrefour Theatre. Charlottetown, PE. Lang.: Eng. 1856
Interview with director Dominic Champagne. Montreal, PQ. Lang.: Fre. 1860
Comparison of simple productions and visual shows. Montreal, PQ. Quebec, PQ. Toronto, ON. Lang.: Fre. 1861
Beothuk Street Players' production of *Faces in the Rock* by Fred Hawksley. St. John's, NF. Lang.: Eng. 1863
Michel Laprise's *Masculin/Féminin (Male/Female)*, presented to audiences segregated by sex. Montreal, PQ. Lang.: Fre. 1867
Irondale Ensemble's production of *Leben des Galilei (The Life of Galileo)* by Bertolt Brecht. Halifax, NS. Lang.: Eng. 1869
Director Joel Kaplan on his production of the *York Cycle*. Toronto, ON. Lang.: Eng. 4213
The staging of the complete *York Cycle* by the University of Toronto. Toronto, ON. Lang.: Eng. 4214
Interview with Canadian tenor Richard Margison. Lang.: Eng. 4538
Tenor Ben Heppner. Lang.: Eng. 4539
Vocal coach Stuart Hamilton on the Canadian operatic scene. Lang.: Eng. 4540
Major opera houses' proposals for productions to the end of the century. USA. Lang.: Eng. 4743

1998. Plays/librettos/scripts.
Round-table discussion on story-telling and theatre. Montreal, PQ. Lang.: Fre. 688
Cervantes' *Don Quixote* and Wadji Mouawad's adaptation, *Don Quichotte*. Montreal, PQ. Lang.: Fre. 2803
The character Sancho in Wadji Mouawad's *Don Quichotte (Don Quixote)*. Montreal, PQ. Lang.: Fre. 2807
The playwright and the play development process. Lang.: Eng. 2811
The use of collage in contemporary productions involving Greek myths. Montreal, PQ. Lang.: Fre. 2814
The contrast of form and content in Théâtre du Nouveau Monde's *Don Quichotte*. Montreal, PQ. Lang.: Fre. 2815
The inhuman and postmodernism in the creation of an original play. Lang.: Fre. 2822
Director Djanet Sears and actor Alison Sealy Smith on all-Black theatre. Toronto, ON. Lang.: Eng. 2826
Essays on play translation. Lang.: Eng. 2828
Don Quichotte, an adaptation of Cervantes' *Don Quixote* by Wadji Mouawad. Montreal, PQ. Lang.: Fre. 2830
Don Hannah's *Fathers and Sons* at Tarragon Theatre. Toronto, ON. Lang.: Eng. 2833
Analysis of Daniel MacIvor's *Monster* as directed by Daniel Brooks. Toronto, ON. Lang.: Eng. 2834
R.M. Vaughan's *Camera, Woman* at Buddies in Bad Times. Toronto, ON. Lang.: Eng. 2835
Surrealism and metaphor in the films of André Forcier. Lang.: Fre. 3965
Mixed media in theatre productions of Carole Nadeau. Quebec, PQ. Montreal, PQ. Lang.: Fre. 4047
Francis Leclerc's video adaptation of *Les Sept Branches de la Rivière Ota (The Seven Streams of the River Ota)* by Robert Lepage. Lang.: Fre. 4074

1998. Relation to other fields.
Evaluation of Ph.D. programs in theatre and drama. USA. UK-England. Lang.: Eng. 716
The design firm Yabu Pushelberg. Toronto, ON. Lang.: Eng. 718
The impact of photography and cinema on theatre. Lang.: Fre. 3732

1998. Theory/criticism.
Children's theatre and contemporary aesthetics. Montreal, PQ. Lang.: Fre. 833
Tools for analysis of improvisation. Montreal, PQ. Lang.: Fre. 834
Round-table discussion on theatre and impurity. Quebec, PQ. Lang.: Fre. 835
Method for the analysis of space. Lang.: Fre. 3808
Report on a seminar for young theatre critics. Quebec, PQ. Lang.: Swe. 3809
Comments on the present state of music criticism. USA. Lang.: Eng. 4845

1998. Training.
Proposal to diversify activities in graduate theatre programs. Lang.: Eng. 872

Caribbean

1933-1998. Performance/production.
Calypso music and carnival. Lang.: Eng. 4119

Catalonia

SEE
Spain-Catalonia.

Chile

1939-1994. Relation to other fields.
Contestatory playwriting under dictatorship. South Africa, Republic of. Spain. Lang.: Eng. 765

1990-1998. Performance/production.
Theatrical construction of Chilean national identity and history. Lang.: Spa. 510

1993. Plays/librettos/scripts.
Visual imagery in *El padre muerto (The Dead Father)* by Marco Antonio de la Parra. Lang.: Eng. 2839

1998. Basic theatrical documents.
Text of *El principe desolado (The Desolate Prince)* by Juan Radrigán. Lang.: Spa. 1413

1998. Plays/librettos/scripts.
Interview with playwright Juan Radrigán. Lang.: Spa. 2838

China

1027-771 B.C. Performance/production.
The Chou dynasty in Chinese opera and theatrical paintings. Lang.: Rus. 4311

960-1127. Plays/librettos/scripts.
Comic roles in the early Song play *Zhang Xie Zhuangyuan (Top Graduate Zhang Xie)*. Lang.: Eng. 2840

1260-1368. Plays/librettos/scripts.
Ghosts and demons in northern Chinese drama. Lang.: Eng. 2841

1368-1644. Performance/production.
Acting in the private theatre of the Ming Dynasty. Lang.: Eng. 1872

1500-1980. Performance/production.
Characterization of male and female roles in Chinese opera. Lang.: Eng. 4312

1575-1675. Plays/librettos/scripts.
Personal identity in *Mudan ting (The Peony Pavilion)* by Tang Xianzu and *Taohua shan (The Peach Blossom Fan)* by Kong Shangren.Lang.: Eng. 4315

1808-1998. Relation to other fields.
Chinese influence on Trinidadian carnival. Trinidad and Tobago. Lang.: Eng. 4174

1910-1950. Theory/criticism.
Hungarian translation of Brecht's article on the alienation effect in Chinese theatre. Lang.: Hun. 836

1935. Performance/production.
Mei Lanfang's influence on Bertolt Brecht. Germany. Lang.: Eng. 1951

China, People's Republic of

1920-1997. Performance/production.
Musical improvisation in Chinese opera. Lang.: Eng. 4313

1941-1996. Performance/production.
The Hong Kong theatre and film industries. Hong Kong. Lang.: Eng. 3929

1949-1976. Plays/librettos/scripts.
The West in Chinese spoken drama and the effacement of the individual author. Lang.: Eng. 2843

1970-1988. Performance/production.
Recent collaboration of performance artists Marina Abramowič and Ulay. Europe. Lang.: Eng. 4240

China, People's Republic of — cont'd

1979-1986. **Basic theatrical documents.**
Anthology of contemporary Chinese drama. Lang.: Eng. 1414
1981-1997. **Performance/production.**
Shakespeare and traditional Asian theatrical forms. India. Japan. Lang.: Eng. 1346
1983. **Plays/librettos/scripts.**
Beckett's influence on *Che zhan (The Bus Stop)* by Gao Xingjian. Lang.: Eng. 2844
1986. **Performance/production.**
Report on Chinese Shakespeare festival. Beijing. Shanghai. Lang.: Eng. 1873
1987. **Relation to other fields.**
Account of teaching Shakespeare to Chinese students. Changsha. Lang.: Eng. 3740
1990-1998. **Relation to other fields.**
Chinese Shakespeare studies. Lang.: Eng. 3741
1991. **Performance/production.**
Shaw's *Major Barbara* at the People's Arts Theatre. Beijing. Lang.: Eng. 1874
1991. **Plays/librettos/scripts.**
The view of foreigners in *Niaoren (Bird Men)* by Guo Shixing. Lang.: Eng. 2842
1993-1996. **Plays/librettos/scripts.**
'Underground realism' in contemporary Chinese drama. Shanghai. Lang.: Eng. 2845
1995. **Performance/production.**
Producing Howard Burman's *Article XXIV* at the Shanghai Theatre Academy. Shanghai. Lang.: Eng. 511
1998. **Design/technology.**
American theatre designers and technicians' visit to China. USA. Lang.: Eng. 327
1998. **Institutions.**
Opening of the Grand Theatre in Shanghai. Shanghai. Lang.: Eng. 4448
1998. **Performance/production.**
Preview of a guest performance of *The Peony Pavilion (Mudan ting)*. Lang.: Eng. 4314
Rural Chinese productions of Puccini's *Turandot*. Beijing. Lang.: Eng. 4541
A production of Puccini's *Turandot* in Beijing. Beijing. Lang.: Eng. 4542

Chuvashia
1922-1997. **Institutions.**
Profile of the Russian theatre in Ufa. Ufa. Lang.: Rus. 1594

Colombia
1950-1985. **Plays/librettos/scripts.**
New Theatre of Buenaventura, Reyes, and Niño. Lang.: Spa. 2846
1970-1985. **Plays/librettos/scripts.**
Politics and violence in *Los papeles del infierno (Leaflets from Hell)* by Enrique Buenaventura. Lang.: Spa. 2847
1998. **Institutions.**
Taganka Theatre's performance at the Bogotá theatre festival. Bogotá. Lang.: Rus. 1595

Colonial America
1620-1750. **Relation to other fields.**
Antitheatricalism in early America. Lang.: Eng. 719
1650-1800. **Relation to other fields.**
Secular ritual forms in early American political culture. Lang.: Eng. 720

Congo
1996. **Relation to other fields.**
Playwright Sony Labou Tansi and Congolese politics. Lang.: Eng. 3742

Croatia
1800-1998. **Performance/production.**
The director in Slovene and Croatian theatre. Slovenia. Lang.: Rus. 1875
1982-1998. **Plays/librettos/scripts.**
Playwright Slobodan Šnajder. Lang.: Eng. 2848
1998. **Basic theatrical documents.**
English translation of *Zmijin svlak (Snake Skin)* by Slobodan Šnajder. Lang.: Eng. 1415

Cuba
1840-1868. **Performance/production.**
Blackface stereotypes of colonial Cuban *teatro bufo*. Havana. Lang.: Eng. 512
1939. **Performance/production.**
The Tropicana night club show. Havana. Lang.: Swe. 4120
1942-1989. **Performance/production.**
Interviews with dancers about performance. UK-England. USA. Lang.: Eng. 1162
1948-1998. **Institutions.**
Interview with Alicia Alonso of Ballet Nacional de Cuba. Havana. Lang.: Swe. 1036
1959-1996. **Performance/production.**
Afro-Cuban identity in Cuban theatre and popular arts. Lang.: Spa. 513
1959-1998. **Institutions.**
Contemporary Cuban dance. Havana. Lang.: Swe. 1250
1974-1991. **Plays/librettos/scripts.**
Afrocuban religion in Cuban films. Lang.: Eng. 3968
1986-1998. **Institutions.**
Profile of Teatro Buendía. Havana. Lang.: Ger. 1596
1998. **Design/technology.**
Report from the meeting of Asociación Cubana de Ingenieros y Técnicos de los Artes Escénicas (ACITAE). Havana. Lang.:Swe. 171

Czech Republic
1800-1999. **Plays/librettos/scripts.**
History of Czech theatre. Lang.: Rus. 2849
1881-1998. **Administration.**
The cooperative relationship between Czech and Slovak theatres. Czechoslovakia. Slovakia. Lang.: Ger. 1376
1921-1998. **Performance/production.**
Comparison of fifteen productions of Euripides' *Medea*. Lang.: Cze. 1885
1925-1950. **Relation to other fields.**
Survey of Czech avant-garde theatre and socialist realism. Lang.: Cze. 721
1950-1981. **Design/technology.**
The work of scene designer Libor Fára. Prague. Lang.: Cze. 1518
1953-1998. **Performance/production.**
Profile of puppet theatre Divadlo loutek Ostrava. Ostrava. Lang.: Cze. 4889
1966-1998. **Performance/production.**
Ctibor Turba and his mime theatre Alfred ve dvoře. Lang.: Eng, Fre. 4086
1967-1998. **Performance/production.**
Interview with actor Jiří Pecha. Lang.: Cze. 1882
1970-1998. **Design/technology.**
Action design scenographer Jan Dušek. Prague. Lang.: Eng. 173
1973-1998. **Performance/production.**
Interview with director Jakub Krofta. Lang.: Cze. 1878
1982-1997. **Performance/production.**
Actor Jan Nebeský. Lang.: Eng, Fre. 1883
1985-1998. **Performance/production.**
Interview with director Vladimír Morávek. Hradec. Lang.: Cze. 1880
1987-1998. **Performance/production.**
Actor/director Jaroslav Dušek of Divadlo Vizita. Prague. Lang.: Cze. 1884
1989-1998. **Performance/production.**
Czech theatre after the end of Communist rule. Lang.: Eng, Fre. 1876
1989-1998. **Relation to other fields.**
Václav Havel, the Czech Republic, and the European Union. Lang.: Eng. 3743
1990-1997. **Plays/librettos/scripts.**
New direction in Czech playwriting. Lang.: Cze. 2850
1990-1998. **Design/technology.**
Costume designs of Kateřina Štefková and Zuzana Štefunková. Lang.: Eng, Fre. 172
1990-1998. **Performance/production.**
The adaptation of classic Czech works to the stage. Prague. Brno. Lang.: Cze. 1877
Interview with director Josef Krofta of Divadlo Drak. Hradec. Lang.: Cze. 1879
1995-1997. **Plays/librettos/scripts.**
Playwright/director J.A. Pitínský (Zdeněk Petrželka). Lang.: Eng, Fre. 2851
1997. **Design/technology.**
Josef Svoboda's set design for Goethe's *Faust*. Prague. Lang.: Eng. 1517
1997. **Institutions.**
Czech theatre at the Plzeň festival. Pilsen. Lang.: Hun. 344
1997. **Performance/production.**
Choreographers Monika Rebcová, Petr Tyc, and Petr Zuska. Prague. Lang.: Eng, Fre. 1266

Czech Republic — cont'd

Otomar Krejča's production of *Faust* at Národní Divadlo. Prague. Lang.: Eng, Fre. 1881

Review of the 1997 Czech opera season. Lang.: Eng, Fre. 4543

1998. Performance/production.
The current status of Czech dance and choreography. Lang.: Cze. 1265

Czechoslovakia

1881-1998. Administration.
The cooperative relationship between Czech and Slovak theatres. Czech Republic. Slovakia. Lang.: Ger. 1376

1910-1939. Relation to other fields.
Jewish culture and the Prague theatre scene. Prague. Lang.: Ger. 722

1922-1998. Plays/librettos/scripts.
Analysis of Janáček's *Věc Makropulos*. Lang.: Eng. 4765

1925-1930. Theory/criticism.
Semiotic analysis of theatre by the Prague School. Lang.: Eng. 837

1944. Performance/production.
Cabaret performances at the Theresienstadt concentration camp. Terezin. Lang.: Eng. 4153

1968-1989. Plays/librettos/scripts.
Politics, censorship, and the 'authorial' studio theatre. Lang.: Eng. 2852

Denmark

1700-1750. Performance/production.
The influence of *commedia dell'arte* on eighteenth-century Danish theatre. Copenhagen. Lang.: Eng. 4186

1752-1998. Performance/production.
Onstage costume changes. Japan. Russia. Lang.: Swe. 556

1847-1987. Theory/criticism.
Essay on the nature of talent. Sweden. UK-England. Lang.: Dan. 838

1898-1944. Plays/librettos/scripts.
Priest and playwright Kaj Munk. Lang.: Swe. 2855

1930-1997. Administration.
The star system and Danish theatre. Lang.: Dan. 1377

1956-1998. Institutions.
Profile of Opera Akademiet. Lang.: Dan. 4449

1960-1998. Training.
Anne-Lise Gabold's use of the methods of Tadashi Suzuki in her production of Euripides' *Bákchai (The Bacchae)*. Japan. Copenhagen. Lang.: Dan. 1359

1970-1998. Performance spaces.
Modern dance and site-specific performance. Lang.: Dan. 1257

1970-1998. Performance/production.
Actress Ghita Nørby on adapting to various performance spaces. Lang.: Dan. 1889

1975-1998. Design/technology.
Set designer Jean-Guy Lecat and his work with Peter Brook. France. Lang.: Dan. 182

1982-1998. Performance/production.
Interview with actress Tammi Øst. Lang.: Dan. 514

1989-1998. Institutions.
New Danish radio drama produced by Radioteatret. Lang.: Dan. 3862

1989-1998. Plays/librettos/scripts.
Interview with playwright Peter Asmussen. Copenhagen. Lang.: Swe. 2853

1990-1998. Relation to other fields.
Theatre in Danish cultural policy. Lang.: Dan. 724

1992-1998. Performance/production.
Tenor Gert Henning-Jensen. Lang.: Eng. 4544

1993-1998. Administration.
Interview with Malene Schwartz, manager of Aalborg Teater. Aalborg. Lang.: Dan. 5

1993-1998. Relation to other fields.
The evaluation of theatrical quality in the Århus area. Århus. Lang.: Dan. 725

1995-1998. Plays/librettos/scripts.
Interview with playwright Sofia Fredén. Stockholm. Copenhagen. Lang.: Swe. 3409

1997. Performance spaces.
Malmö Musikteater's production of *Lucia di Lammermoor* at Hedeland Amfiteater. Hedeland. Lang.: Swe. 4491

1997. Performance/production.
Report on children's dance festival. Malmö. Copenhagen. Lang.: Swe. 966

Acting and directing influences on Eugenio Barba. Holstebro. Lang.: Eng. 1886

1997-1998. Performance/production.
Director Jonathan Paul Cook on developing talent in an ensemble. Lang.: Dan. 1888

1997-1998. Relation to other fields.
Difficulties in evaluating the quality of theatre performances. Lang.: Dan. 723

1998. Design/technology.
Resignation of the founder of the Martin Group lighting equipment firm. Copenhagen. Lang.: Eng. 174

1998. Institutions.
The eleventh session of the International School of Theatre Anthropology. Lisbon. Holstebro. Lang.: Eng. 376

German-Danish children's theatre festival. Germany. Lang.: Ger. 1642

1998. Performance/production.
Danish guest performance of Honvéd Táncszínház. Copenhagen. Lang.: Hun. 1224

The prospects for Danish modern dance. Lang.: Dan. 1267

The director's role in the development of good acting. Lang.: Dan. 1887

1998. Plays/librettos/scripts.
Dramaturgs on recognizing talented new playwrights. Lang.: Dan. 2854

Female characters in plays by Scandinavian women. Norway. Sweden. Lang.: Eng. 3299

East Germany

1969-1982. Performance/production.
Theatrical influences on director Rainer Werner Fassbinder. Berlin. Lang.: Fre. 4058

Egypt

Performance/production.
Early theatre. Ancient Greece. Roman Empire. India. Lang.: Rus. 484

2500 B.C. Relation to other fields.
The dramatic nature of the ancient Egyptian text *The Triumph of Horus*. Lang.: Eng. 3744

1908-1969. Basic theatrical documents.
English translation and analysis of two plays by Ali Ahmad Bakathir. Lang.: Eng. 1417

1930-1945. Basic theatrical documents.
English translations of plays by Tawfiq Al-Hakim. Lang.: Eng. 1416

1942-1947. Performance/production.
Polish soldiers' theatre as seen in the magazine *Parada*. Rome. Cairo. Lang.: Pol. 550

1997. Institutions.
Report on the Cairo festival and symposia on women's theatre. Cairo. Lang.: Eng. 1597

England

1120-1501. Plays/librettos/scripts.
The N-town Mary play and the Four Virtues of Psalm 84:11. Lang.: Eng. 2983

1150-1228. Performance/production.
Analysis of *Regularis Concordia* and *Quem quaeritis*. Lang.: Eng. 516

1180-1557. Plays/librettos/scripts.
The Easter play tradition. Lang.: Eng. 2942

1275-1541. Audience.
Audience assumptions about the York *Resurrection*. York. Lang.: Eng. 1400

1375-1400. Performance/production.
Staging of the Cornish *Ordinalia*. Lang.: Eng. 1890

1400-1500. Plays/librettos/scripts.
The language used by devils in the *York Cycle*. York. Lang.: Eng. 2933

The Expositor character of the Chester Cycle. Lang.: Eng. 3033

1400-1612. Plays/librettos/scripts.
Wonder and recognition in medieval and Renaissance drama. Lang.: Eng. 2874

1401-1499. Plays/librettos/scripts.
Biblical narrative and the order of the *York Cycle* episodes. York. Lang.: Eng. 2950

1405-1500. Relation to other fields.
The relationship between the York Cycle and the Bolton Book of Hours. York. Lang.: Eng. 3750

1425-1600. Plays/librettos/scripts.
Robin Hood in early English drama. Lang.: Eng. 2941

1431-1635. Audience.
Social uses of entertainment in Warwickshire. Lang.: Eng. 4195

England — cont'd

1464-1470. **Plays/librettos/scripts.**
A new reading of *Mankind*. Lang.: Eng. 3028
1492-1604. **Plays/librettos/scripts.**
Attitudes toward Spain in early modern English drama. Lang.: Eng. 2927
1495-1525. **Plays/librettos/scripts.**
Comparison of the Dutch *Elckerlijck* and the English *Everyman*. Netherlands. Lang.: Eng. 2982
1497-1569. **Performance/production.**
Music in Tudor drama. Lang.: Eng. 1902
1500-1600. **Plays/librettos/scripts.**
Codes of politeness in Renaissance drama. Lang.: Eng. 2878
1500-1700. **Performance/production.**
Rehearsal practices in British professional theatre. Lang.: Eng. 1905
1500-1780. **Performance/production.**
The survival of medieval English religious theatre on the puppet stage. London. Lang.: Eng. 4890
1500-1900. **Performance/production.**
Female characters in male folk dance. Mexico. Lang.: Eng. 1225
1501-1600. **Performance/production.**
The pyrotechnic genre, the 'fort holding'. Lang.: Eng. 4122
1501-1600. **Plays/librettos/scripts.**
Authority in Elizabethan England as reflected in the plays of Shakespeare. Lang.: Eng. 3042
1515-1635. **Plays/librettos/scripts.**
Flemish immigrants in English Renaissance drama. Lang.: Eng. 2976
1517-1616. **Performance/production.**
Analysis of records relating to the Earl of Derby's 'bearward'. Lang.: Eng. 4121
1521-1678. **Relation to other fields.**
Economic forces and the Chester Whitsun plays. Chester. Lang.: Eng. 4226
1524-1530. **Performance spaces.**
Speculations on the theatre of John Rastell. London. Lang.: Eng. 1799
1527. **Audience.**
The complex role of the audience in court entertainment. Greenwich. Lang.: Eng. 4194
1530-1583. **Plays/librettos/scripts.**
Stage devils in English Reformation plays. Lang.: Eng. 2899
1530-1607. **Relation to other fields.**
Drama and the English Reformation. Lang.: Eng. 3755
1530-1624. **Performance/production.**
Norwich's unregulated entertainers. Norwich. Lang.: Eng. 1907
1532-1608. **Plays/librettos/scripts.**
Student casebook on Shakespeare's *Hamlet*. Lang.: Eng. 2897
1533. **Plays/librettos/scripts.**
Lucian's *Icaromenippus* as a source for Heywood's *The Play of the Wether*. Lang.: Eng. 2920
1535-1607. **Plays/librettos/scripts.**
Protestant belief and English Reformation drama. Lang.: Eng. 2972
1536-1546. **Plays/librettos/scripts.**
John Bale's characters Sodomy and Idolatry. Lang.: Eng. 2914
1540-1594. **Plays/librettos/scripts.**
The depiction of Jane Shore in the anonymous *True Tragedy of Richard III*. Lang.: Eng. 2885
1550-1590. **Relation to other fields.**
Theatre and drama in the life of Sir Thomas More. Lang.: Eng. 3747
1550-1680. **Performance/production.**
Commercial theatre in early modern London. London. Lang.: Eng. 518
1551-1552. **Relation to other fields.**
George Ferrers' Christmas revels and the execution of the Duke of Somerset. Lang.: Eng. 4211
1560-1613. **Plays/librettos/scripts.**
English national identity and the representation of foreigners on stage. Lang.: Eng. 2946
1564-1616. **Plays/librettos/scripts.**
Shakespeare's identity and Shakespeare studies. Lang.: Rus. 2861
1564-1623. **Plays/librettos/scripts.**
Variant spellings of Shakespeare's name. Lang.: Eng. 2959
1568-1613. **Plays/librettos/scripts.**
The use of proverbs in Shakespeare's plays. Lang.: Eng. 2923
1575-1630. **Relation to other fields.**
The idea of culture in the English Renaissance. Lang.: Eng. 3752
1579-1600. **Plays/librettos/scripts.**
Characters named Rosalind in Shakespeare's *As You Like It* and elsewhere. Lang.: Eng. 2951
1579-1642. **Relation to other fields.**
Analysis of anti-theatricalism. 726
1580-1615. **Plays/librettos/scripts.**
The representation of historical female characters on the Renaissance stage. Lang.: Eng. 2922
1580-1616. **Relation to other fields.**
New-historicist analysis of Shakespeare and his time. Lang.: Eng. 3745
1580-1620. **Relation to other fields.**
Cross-dressing and gender struggle on the early modern English stage. Lang.: Eng. 3749
1584. **Plays/librettos/scripts.**
Analysis of *Gallathea* by John Lyly. Lang.: Eng. 2888
1586-1593. **Plays/librettos/scripts.**
The dating of Shakespeare's early plays. Lang.: Eng. 3034
1587-1588. **Plays/librettos/scripts.**
Assessment of Marlowe's *Tamburlaine the Great*. Lang.: Eng. 2866
Space and measurement in *Tamburlaine the Great* by Christopher Marlowe. Lang.: Eng. 3029
1587-1590. **Plays/librettos/scripts.**
Tudor religious and social issues in John Lily's *Endymion* and *Midas*. Lang.: Eng. 2871
1587-1631. **Plays/librettos/scripts.**
Influences on *'Tis Pity She's a Whore* by John Ford. Lang.: Eng. 2937
1588-1601. **Plays/librettos/scripts.**
Robin Hood and Elizabethan theatre. Lang.: Eng. 2902
1589-1593. **Relation to other fields.**
The publication of 'Venus and Adonis' by Shakespeare. Lang.: Eng. 3751
1589-1597. **Relation to other fields.**
Psychoanalysis, the female body, and Shakespeare's *Henriad*. Lang.: Eng. 3756
1589-1598. **Plays/librettos/scripts.**
Cross-dressing in Elizabethan Robin Hood plays. Lang.: Eng. 3016
1589-1613. **Plays/librettos/scripts.**
The influence of the figurative arts on the plays of William Shakespeare. Lang.: Ita. 2858
Analysis of plays by Shakespeare. Lang.: Rus. 2945
1589-1616. **Plays/librettos/scripts.**
Fantasy and history in the plays of Shakespeare. Lang.: Rus. 3039
1590-1592. **Plays/librettos/scripts.**
The Lacy family and the pretender to the throne in Shakespeare's *Henry VI, Part Two*. Lang.: Eng. 2964
Marlowe's *Edward II* and the medieval passion play. Lang.: Eng. 3011
1590-1593. **Plays/librettos/scripts.**
The 'unruly' speech of Ariana in Shakespeare's *Comedy of Errors*. Lang.: Eng. 2924
The subversion of male authority in Shakespeare's *Henry VI* and *Richard III*. Lang.: Eng. 3015
1590-1593. **Relation to other fields.**
A possible model for characters in Shakespeare's *Twelfth Night* and 'Venus and Adonis'. Lang.: Eng. 3746
1590-1594. **Plays/librettos/scripts.**
An illustration of Queen Tamora of Shakespeare's *Titus Andronicus*. Lang.: Eng. 2880
The politics of consent in Shakespeare's *Titus Andronicus*. Lang.: Eng. 3006
1590-1595. **Performance/production.**
Shakespeare's *Titus Andronicus* and the political power of symbolic performance. Lang.: Eng. 1893
1590-1599. **Plays/librettos/scripts.**
Analysis of Shakespeare's history plays. Lang.: Eng. 2911
Girardian analysis of Shakespeare plays. Lang.: Eng. 2935
1590-1600. **Plays/librettos/scripts.**
The figure of the Jew in Marlowe and Shakespeare. Lang.: Eng. 2868

England — cont'd

1590-1608. **Plays/librettos/scripts.**
Hermeneutic analysis of Shakespearean comedies. Lang.: Eng. 2877

1590-1612. **Plays/librettos/scripts.**
The concept of the self in Shakespearean tragedy. Lang.: Eng. 2992

1590-1613. **Plays/librettos/scripts.**
Social, economic, and political thought in Shakespeare's chronicle plays. Lang.: Eng. 2869

Analysis of scenic transitions in the plays of Shakespeare. Lang.: Eng. 2875

The centaur in works of Shakespeare. Lang.: Eng. 2882

'Demonic' women in Shakespeare's tragedies. Lang.: Eng. 2999

Epiphany in the plays of Shakespeare. Lang.: Eng. 3008

The interaction of other characters with Shakespeare's tragic heroes. Lang.: Eng. 3037

Shakespeare's plays and human nature. Lang.: Slo. 3047

1590-1616. **Plays/librettos/scripts.**
The debate over the authorship of the plays attributed to Shakespeare. Lang.: Rus. 2856

Shakespeare, feminism, and his sources. Lang.: Eng. 2977

1590-1618. **Plays/librettos/scripts.**
Comic scenes and characters in the Elizabethan history play. Lang.: Eng. 2955

1590-1620. **Plays/librettos/scripts.**
The control of time in Renaissance English drama. Lang.: Eng. 2883

Religious controversy and the emerging print culture. Lang.: Eng. 2956

Conscience in early modern literature including Shakespeare. Lang.: Eng. 3020

1590-1630. **Plays/librettos/scripts.**
Women's use of wit in response to men in English popular culture. Lang.: Eng. 2884

The urban crowd in early modern drama. Lang.: Eng. 2985

1590-1642. **Plays/librettos/scripts.**
The malcontent scholar in Elizabethan and Jacobean theatre. Lang.: Eng. 3003

1590-1650. **Plays/librettos/scripts.**
Playwriting and publishing for the London stage. Lang.: Eng. 2881

Militarism and masculinity in the early modern period. Lang.: Eng. 2895

1590-1745. **Plays/librettos/scripts.**
Crimes against property in plays of Henry Fielding and Elizabethan playwrights. Lang.: Eng. 2912

1590-1889. **Plays/librettos/scripts.**
The influence of Webster, Middleton, and Shakespeare on the poetry of Robert Browning. Lang.: Eng. 2906

1590-1998. **Plays/librettos/scripts.**
Shakespeare, Branagh, and the concept of the author. Lang.: Eng. 2958

Analysis of *Tamburlaine the Great* by Christopher Marlowe. Lang.: Eng. 3014

1591. **Basic theatrical documents.**
Catalan translation of Shakespeare's *Romeo and Juliet.* Lang.: Cat. 1421

1592. **Plays/librettos/scripts.**
Language, rank, and sexuality in the anonymous *Arden of Faversham.* Lang.: Eng. 2986

Analysis of the anonymous *Woodstock.* Lang.: Eng. 3035

1592-1593. **Plays/librettos/scripts.**
Women in Shakespeare's *Richard III.* Lang.: Eng. 2929

1592-1607. **Plays/librettos/scripts.**
Henry Chettle's supposed apology to Shakespeare. London. Lang.: Eng. 2915

1593. **Plays/librettos/scripts.**
Analysis of *The Massacre at Paris* by Christopher Marlowe. Lang.: Eng. 2917

Analysis of *The Massacre at Paris* by Christopher Marlowe. Lang.: Eng. 2997

1593-1599. **Plays/librettos/scripts.**
The authorship of *George a Greene.* Lang.: Eng. 2989

1593-1599. **Relation to other fields.**
Performance analysis of Shakespeare's sonnets. Lang.: Eng. 3753

1594. **Plays/librettos/scripts.**
Analysis of *Friar Bacon and Friar Bungay* by Robert Greene. Lang.: Eng. 2974

1594-1595. **Plays/librettos/scripts.**
East and West in Shakepeare's *A Midsummer Night's Dream.* Lang.: Eng. 2905

Shakespeare's *A Midsummer Night's Dream,* politics, and criticism. Lang.: Eng. 2981

1594-1998. **Basic theatrical documents.**
French translation of Shakespeare's *Love's Labour's Lost.* France. Lang.: Fre. 1419

1595. **Basic theatrical documents.**
Catalan translation of Shakespeare's *A Midsummer Night's Dream.* Lang.: Cat. 1422

1595. **Performance/production.**
Accession Day masques and tensions between Queen Elizabeth I and the Earl of Essex. Lang.: Eng. 4196

1595-1596. **Plays/librettos/scripts.**
Symbolic action in Shakespeare's *Romeo and Juliet.* Lang.: Eng. 3007

1595-1612. **Plays/librettos/scripts.**
The nature of tyranny in plays of Shakespeare. Lang.: Eng. 2978

1596. **Performance spaces.**
Analysis of a sketch of the Swan Theatre. London. Lang.: Eng. 1801

1596. **Plays/librettos/scripts.**
The origin and meaning of the name Shylock in Shakespeare's *The Merchant of Venice.* Lang.: Eng. 2932

Prejudice and law in Shakespeare's *The Merchant of Venice.* Lang.: Eng. 3027

1596-1597. **Plays/librettos/scripts.**
The relationship between Falstaff and Prince Hal in Shakespeare's *Henry IV.* Lang.: Eng. 2870

The 'troubler' personality in Shakespeare's *Henry IV, Part One.* Lang.: Eng. 3032

1596-1599. **Plays/librettos/scripts.**
Catholic and Protestant in Shakespeare's Second Henriad. Lang.: Eng. 2940

Renaissance emblems of death and Shakespeare's *King John.* Lang.: Eng. 2967

1596-1980. **Plays/librettos/scripts.**
Recognition in plays of Čechov, Shakespeare, and Beckett. France. Russia. Lang.: Eng. 2949

1596-1986. **Theory/criticism.**
Antisemitism and criticism of Shakespeare's *Merchant of Venice.* Lang.: Eng. 3813

1597-1600. **Performance/production.**
The activities of actor Edward Alleyn in retirement. London. Lang.: Eng. 1894

1597-1601. **Plays/librettos/scripts.**
Comparison of final scenes in quarto and folio versions of Shakespeare's plays. Lang.: Eng. 3005

1597-1616. **Plays/librettos/scripts.**
Female power and the public sphere in Renaissance drama. Lang.: Eng. 2943

1598-1599. **Plays/librettos/scripts.**
Analysis of *Downfall of Robert Earl of Huntingdon* by Anthony Munday. Lang.: Eng. 3018

1598-1613. **Plays/librettos/scripts.**
Regeneration in plays of Shakespeare. Lang.: Eng. 2968

1598-1642. **Plays/librettos/scripts.**
Collaborative drama in the English Renaissance theatre. Lang.: Eng. 2936

1599. **Plays/librettos/scripts.**
Analysis of Shakespeare's *Julius Caesar.* Lang.: Eng. 2948

1599-1600. **Plays/librettos/scripts.**
The two Jaques in Shakespeare's *As You Like It.* Lang.: Eng. 2970

The first quarto of Shakespeare's *Henry V* and the anonymous *Famous Victories of Henrie the Fifth.* Lang.: Eng. 3022

1599-1634. **Plays/librettos/scripts.**
The politics of gender in the plays of John Marston. Lang.: Eng. 3009

1599-1642. **Institutions.**
Economic history of the Chamberlain's Men/King's Men. Lang.: Eng. 1598

1600. **Plays/librettos/scripts.**
Sociological analysis of *The Shoemaker's Holiday* by Thomas Dekker. Lang.: Eng. 2973

England — cont'd

1600-1601. Performance/production.
Performing the killing of Polonius in Shakespeare's *Hamlet*. Lang.: Eng. 1892

1600-1601. Plays/librettos/scripts.
Possible influence of Giordano Bruno on Shakespeare's *Hamlet*. Lang.: Ita. 2921
Handwriting and character in Shakespeare's *Hamlet*. Lang.: Eng. 2925
Annunciation motifs in Shakespeare's *Hamlet*. Lang.: Eng. 2934
Corporeal imagery in Shakespeare's *Hamlet*. Lang.: Eng. 2939
Analysis of a speech by the Ghost in Shakespeare's *Hamlet*. Lang.: Eng. 3004
Malvolio's riddle in Shakespeare's *Twelfth Night*, II.5. Lang.: Eng. 3025
The women in Shakespeare's *Hamlet*. Lang.: Eng. 3046

1600-1610. Plays/librettos/scripts.
Prostitution in and outside of the theatre. London. Lang.: Eng. 2995

1600-1611. Plays/librettos/scripts.
Shakespeare and the limitation of political and textual control. Lang.: Eng. 2965

1600-1616. Plays/librettos/scripts.
Shakespeare and the creation of a theatre audience. Lang.: Eng. 3017

1600-1623. Plays/librettos/scripts.
Comparison of second quarto and first folio versions of Shakespeare's *Hamlet*. Lang.: Eng. 3043

1600-1671. Plays/librettos/scripts.
Casuistry and early modern English tragedy. Lang.: Eng. 2980

1600-1700. Plays/librettos/scripts.
Feminism and seventeenth-century city comedy. Lang.: Eng. 3000

1600-1779. Plays/librettos/scripts.
Recovered ritual in seemingly non-ritualistic theatre. Lang.: Eng. 2904

1601-1602. Plays/librettos/scripts.
Treachery and the language of the marketplace in Shakespeare's *Troilus and Cressida*. Lang.: Eng. 2863
The perception of self in Shakespeare's *Troilus and Cressida*. Lang.: Eng. 2892

1601-1604. Plays/librettos/scripts.
Analysis of *Troilus and Cressida* and *Measure for Measure* by William Shakespeare. Lang.: Ita. 3012

1602-1603. Plays/librettos/scripts.
A possible source for the character Young Bertram in Shakespeare's *All's Well That Ends Well*. Lang.: Eng. 2901
Closure and the happy ending in Shakespeare's *All's Well That Ends Well*. Lang.: Eng. 3030

1602-1612. Plays/librettos/scripts.
Feminist analysis of *The Tragedy of Mariam* by Elizabeth Cary. Lang.: Eng. 3019

1602-1653. Relation to other fields.
William Basse, author of the poem 'Epitaph for Shakespeare'. Lang.: Eng. 3748

1603-1646. Plays/librettos/scripts.
Analysis of an edition of William Percy's *Faery Pastorall*. Lang.: Eng. 2916

1604. Basic theatrical documents.
Catalan translation of Shakespeare's *Measure for Measure*. Lang.: Cat. 1420

1604. Plays/librettos/scripts.
Shakespeare's *Measure for Measure* and the King James Bible. Lang.: Eng. 2865
Historical allusion in Chapman's *Bussy d'Ambois*. Lang.: Eng. 2867
Analysis of a speech in Shakespeare's *Measure for Measure*. Lang.: Eng. 2896
Cognitive analysis of Shakespeare's *Measure for Measure*. Lang.: Eng. 2900
Patience and delay in Shakespeare's *Othello*. Lang.: Eng. 2903
Protestant aesthetics and Shakespeare's *Measure for Measure*. Lang.: Eng. 2908
Aspects of character in Shakespeare's *Measure for Measure*. Lang.: Eng. 2909
The theme of substitution in Shakespeare's *Measure for Measure*. Lang.: Eng. 2957
Psychological power and control in Shakespeare's *Measure for Measure*. Lang.: Eng. 2962
The psychology of punishment in Shakespeare's *Measure for Measure*. Lang.: Eng. 2975
Gender and religion in Shakespeare's *Measure for Measure*. Lang.: Eng. 3021
Race and imperialism in Shakespeare's *Othello*. Lang.: Eng. 3023
The control of procreation and death in Shakespeare's *Measure for Measure*. Lang.: Eng. 3041

1604-1605. Plays/librettos/scripts.
Gender and politics in masques of Ben Jonson and Samuel Daniel. Lang.: Eng. 4200

1604-1608. Plays/librettos/scripts.
The treatment of single women in early Stuart drama. Lang.: Eng. 2979

1604-1609. Plays/librettos/scripts.
Political and ideological struggles in Jacobean masques. Lang.: Eng. 4206

1604-1611. Plays/librettos/scripts.
Punishment and political power in plays of Shakespeare. Lang.: Eng. 2944

1604-1625. Plays/librettos/scripts.
Female power and the emblem tradition in plays of Shakespeare and Middleton. Lang.: Eng. 2913

1604-1637. Plays/librettos/scripts.
Theatricality and the printed texts of civic pageants. Lang.: Eng. 4225

1604-1798. Relation to other fields.
The influence of Shakespeare's *Othello* on C.B. Brown's novel *Wieland*. USA. Lang.: Eng. 3788

1604-1998. Plays/librettos/scripts.
Racial ambiguity, colonialism, and late twentieth-century criticism of Shakespeare's *Othello*. Lang.: Eng. 2987

1605. Plays/librettos/scripts.
Delia Bacon's analysis of Shakespeare's *King Lear*. Lang.: Eng. 2860
Analysis of *The Masque of Blackness* by Ben Jonson. Lang.: Eng. 2919
Possible censorship of *The Tragedy of Philotas* by Samuel Daniel. Lang.: Eng. 2996

1605-1606. Plays/librettos/scripts.
The mad scenes in Shakespeare's *King Lear*. Lang.: Eng. 2876
Shakespeare's *King Lear* and the gender constructions of three daughters. Lang.: Eng. 2898
Feeling in Shakespeare's *King Lear*. Lang.: Eng. 2952
Historical background of the depiction of the Gloucesters in Shakespeare's *King Lear*. Lang.: Eng. 2994
Folklore and Shakespeare's *King Lear*. Lang.: Eng. 3010
The vagueness of locale in Shakespeare's *King Lear*. Lang.: Eng. 3036

1605-1610. Performance/production.
Civic and court ceremonies in the Jacobean period. Lang.: Eng. 4215

1605-1611. Plays/librettos/scripts.
Power, gender, and race in *The Masque of Blackness* by Ben Jonson. Lang.: Eng. 4208

1606. Plays/librettos/scripts.
Christianity and Shakespeare's *Macbeth*. Lang.: Eng. 2890
The skull in plays of Shakespeare, Dekker, and Tourneur. Lang.: Eng. 3026

1606-1618. Basic theatrical documents.
Critical edition and English translation of Robert Burton's *Philosophaster*. Lang.: Eng. 1418

1607. Plays/librettos/scripts.
Game theory analysis of Shakespeare's *Antony and Cleopatra*. Lang.: Eng. 2879

1607-1608. Institutions.
History of the short-lived first Whitefriars Company. London. Lang.: Eng. 1599

1609-1610. Performance/production.
Analysis of a London theatre season. London. Lang.: Eng. 515

1609-1610. Plays/librettos/scripts.
The murders of royal women in plays of Shakespeare and Beaumont and Fletcher. Lang.: Eng. 2894

England — cont'd

Sources of the wager scene in Shakespeare's *Cymbeline*. Lang.: Eng. 2910

1609-1633. Plays/librettos/scripts.
Analysis of a scene from *Mustapha* by Fulke Greville. Lang.: Eng. 3044

1610-1625. Plays/librettos/scripts.
God and man in Renaissance theatre. Lang.: Eng. 2966

1610-1642. Performance/production.
Masque, movement, and social and political negotiations. Lang.: Eng. 4198

1610-1642. Plays/librettos/scripts.
Political aspects of Stuart court masques. Lang.: Eng. 4201

1610-1727. Plays/librettos/scripts.
Don Quixote, Lewis Theobald's *The Double Falsehood* and the lost *Cardenio* of Shakespeare and Fletcher. Spain. Lang.: Eng. 3001

1610-1998. Research/historiography.
Jonson's *The Alchemist* and source studies. USA. Lang.: Eng. 3795

1611. Plays/librettos/scripts.
Shakespeare's *The Tempest* as an experiment in political control. Lang.: Eng. 2862

Shakespeare's *The Tempest* as an allegory of colonial America. Lang.: Eng. 3038

Political tensions reflected in Ben Jonson's masque *Oberon*. Lang.: Eng. 4203

Royal policy, subversion, and Ben Jonson's *Oberon*. Lang.: Eng. 4204

1612-1613. Plays/librettos/scripts.
Queens Anne and Katherine in Shakespeare's *Henry VIII*. Lang.: Eng. 2990

1612-1632. Plays/librettos/scripts.
Ben Jonson's antimasques. Lang.: Eng. 4205

1613. Plays/librettos/scripts.
Marriage and patriarchy in *The Tragedy of Mariam* by Elizabeth Cary. Lang.: Eng. 2893

Feminist analysis of Webster's *The Duchess of Malfi*. Lang.: Eng. 2931

Authority and medicine in Webster's *The Duchess of Malfi*. Lang.: Eng. 2947

Shakespeare's *The Tempest* and Thomas Campion's *The Lord's Masque*. Lang.: Eng. 4202

1613-1621. Plays/librettos/scripts.
The Cardinal in Middleton's *Women Beware Women*. Lang.: Eng. 2961

1615-1617. Plays/librettos/scripts.
Male and female honor in *A Fair Quarrel* by Middleton and Rowley. Lang.: Eng. 2993

1618-1642. Plays/librettos/scripts.
Plague imagery in Jacobean tragedy. Lang.: Eng. 2889

1620-1634. Performance/production.
Political aspects of music in the masque. Lang.: Eng. 4197

1620-1642. Plays/librettos/scripts.
Evil in Stuart tragedy. Lang.: Eng. 3024

1620-1711. Plays/librettos/scripts.
The relative absence of political allegory in English opera. London. Lang.: Eng. 4767

1621. Plays/librettos/scripts.
Analysis of *The Witch of Edmonton* by Ford, Dekker, and Rowley. Lang.: Eng. 2928

Analysis of *The Island Princess* by John Fletcher. Lang.: Eng. 2988

The design and authorship of *The Essex House Masque*. Lang.: Eng. 4209

1622-1623. Theory/criticism.
Evidence of Oxfordian authorship of plays attributed to Shakespeare. Lang.: Eng. 3812

1623-1640. Plays/librettos/scripts.
Portraits of Shakespeare. Lang.: Rus. 2963

1634. Plays/librettos/scripts.
History and John Ford's *Perkin Warbeck*. Lang.: Eng. 2938

1634-1635. Plays/librettos/scripts.
Puritanism and Milton's *Comus*. Lang.: Eng. 4207

1642-1729. Plays/librettos/scripts.
Motherhood in Restoration comedy. Lang.: Eng. 2864

1645-1662. Plays/librettos/scripts.
Restoration playwright Margaret Cavendish. Lang.: Eng. 3002

1647-1682. Performance spaces.
Evidence that Davies' bear-baiting ring may have been a restoration of the Hope Theatre. London. Lang.: Eng. 435

1650. Performance spaces.
Evidence of theatre closings in a Folger Library manuscript. London. Lang.: Eng. 1798

1659-1695. Performance/production.
English theatre architecture and the operas of Henry Purcell. London. Lang.: Eng. 4548

1660-1680. Plays/librettos/scripts.
Recognition, repression, and ideology in Restoration drama. London. Lang.: Eng. 2918

1660-1710. Plays/librettos/scripts.
Women and politics in Restoration heroic plays. Lang.: Eng. 2872

1660-1730. Plays/librettos/scripts.
Robin Hood and Restoration drama. Lang.: Eng. 2954

1660-1830. Performance/production.
Music for London Shakespearean productions. London. Lang.: Eng. 1900

1661-1663. Plays/librettos/scripts.
Analysis of Restoration anti-Puritan comedies. Lang.: Eng. 2907

1667-1737. Performance/production.
Response to *castrato* performances. London. Lang.: Eng. 4545

1674. Plays/librettos/scripts.
Analysis of Dryden and Davenant's *Enchanted Island*. Lang.: Eng. 2873

1676-1678. Plays/librettos/scripts.
Seventeenth-century allusions to Shakespeare in short verse pieces. Lang.: Eng. 2960

1677. Plays/librettos/scripts.
Sexual politics in *The Rover* by Aphra Behn. Lang.: Eng. 3031

1690-1700. Plays/librettos/scripts.
Confessional theatre in the Restoration period. Lang.: Eng. 2991

1700-1800. Performance/production.
The cultural background of eighteenth-century British pantomime. Lang.: Eng. 4093

1700-1910. Plays/librettos/scripts.
Analysis of *The Foresters* by Alfred, Lord Tennyson. USA. Lang.: Eng. 2998

1701-1800. Performance/production.
Shakespeare's *The Tempest* on the eighteenth-century stage. London. Lang.: Eng. 1895

1701-1800. Plays/librettos/scripts.
The obedient daughter in adaptations of Shakespeare's plays. Lang.: Eng. 2969

Eighteenth-century editing and interpretation of Shakespeare. Lang.: Eng. 3040

1701-1800. Theory/criticism.
Eighteenth-century approaches to Shakespearean criticism. Lang.: Eng. 3811

1702-1814. Performance/production.
Shakespearean production and the theatrical portrait collection of the Garrick Club. London. Lang.: Eng. 1903

1709. Plays/librettos/scripts.
Nicholas Rowe's illustration of a scene from *Macbeth*. Lang.: Eng. 2953

1709-1714. Plays/librettos/scripts.
Analysis of the frontispiece of Nicholas Rowe's edition of Shakespeare's *King Lear*. Lang.: Eng. 2859

1710-1739. Performance/production.
The influence of the Haymarket Theatre on Handelian opera. London. Lang.: Eng. 4549

1710-1740. Plays/librettos/scripts.
Attacks on *castrati* in English pamphlets. London. Lang.: Eng. 4766

1713-1760. Performance/production.
The Cibber family: private life as public spectacle. Lang.: Eng. 517

Actress/writer Charlotte Cibber Charke. Lang.: Eng. 1891

Images associated with actress Charlotte Cibber Charke. Lang.: Eng. 1896

The resurgence of interest in actress Charlotte Cibber Charke. Lang.: Eng. 1901

Feminist analysis of the life of actress Charlotte Cibber Charke. Lang.: Eng. 1904

Actress Charlotte Cibber Charke and cross-dressing. Lang.: Eng. 1906

England — cont'd

Press responses to the autobiography of actress Charlotte Cibber Charke. Lang.: Eng. 1908
1713-1760. Plays/librettos/scripts.
Cross-dressing in Shakespeare's *The Merchant of Venice* and in the autobiography of actress Charlotte Cibber Charke. Lang.: Eng. 2891
1714. Performance/production.
Rowe's Jane Shore as a major role for actresses. Lang.: Eng. 1899
1723. Plays/librettos/scripts.
Political context of Charles Johnson's *Love in a Forest*, an adaptation of *As You Like It*. Lang.: Eng. 3013
1728-1780. Plays/librettos/scripts.
Music and the ballad opera in English popular theatre. Lang.: Eng. 4390
1731. Plays/librettos/scripts.
Analysis of *The London Merchant* by George Lillo. Lang.: Eng. 2984
1738. Plays/librettos/scripts.
The defense of prostitution in Lillo's *Marina*. Lang.: Eng. 2887
Analysis of *Marina*, George Lillo's adaptation of Shakespeare's *Pericles*. Lang.: Eng. 2971
1740-1779. Performance/production.
Contemporary remarks on the styles and manners of actors. London. Lang.: Eng. 1898
1743. Plays/librettos/scripts.
Horace Walpole's *The Dear Witches* and Shakespeare's *Macbeth*. Lang.: Eng. 2857
1743-1777. Performance/production.
The feud between David Garrick and Charles Macklin. London. Lang.: Eng. 1897
1744-1747. Relation to other fields.
Novelist Samuel Richardson compared to Shakespeare. Lang.: Eng. 3754
1762-1796. Performance/production.
The English operas of Stephen Storace. London. Lang.: Eng. 4547
1766. Plays/librettos/scripts.
Analysis of *The Clandestine Marriage* by David Garrick. Lang.: Eng. 2926
1767-1768. Plays/librettos/scripts.
The character Honeywood in Goldsmith's *The Good Natur'd Man*. Lang.: Eng. 3045
1772-1902. Performance spaces.
Conjectural reconstruction of the New Street Theatre. Birmingham. Lang.: Eng. 1800
1775-1800. Plays/librettos/scripts.
Caricature and satire in the plays of Samuel Foote. Lang.: Eng. 2930
1776-1824. Relation to other fields.
Shakespeare's Hamlet in novels of Goethe and Scott. Germany. Lang.: Eng. 3757
1777-1800. Performance/production.
Casting and performance in eighteenth-century productions of *Othello*. Lang.: Eng. 1909
1790-1848. Relation to other fields.
Theatre and revolution in the English novel. Lang.: Eng. 727
1794-1840. Plays/librettos/scripts.
The feminine ideal in the drama of English Romantic poets. Lang.: Eng. 2886
1800-1940. Plays/librettos/scripts.
Robin Hood and the bandit hero of the *kabuki*. Lang.: Eng. 1366
1835-1861. Audience.
Analysis of audience composition at London theatres. London. Lang.: Eng. 147
1842. Performance/production.
Lucy Vestris in *Giovanni in London*. London. Lang.: Eng. 4546
1920-1992. Plays/librettos/scripts.
Robin Hood on film. USA. Lang.: Eng. 3969
1979-1998. Reference materials.
Index to the first twenty volumes of *Medieval English Theatre*. Lang.: Eng. 696

Eritrea

1980-1984. Plays/librettos/scripts.
Theatre as cultural weapon and military education in the Eritrean war. Lang.: Eng. 3048

Estonia

1925-1998. Design/technology.
Scene designer Eldor Rentor. Tallin. Lang.: Swe, Eng, Ger. 175
1939-1945. Performance/production.
Estonian artists as war refugees in Sweden. Sweden. Lang.: Swe, Eng, Ger. 519
1985-1998. Institutions.
Estonian theatre and actors before and after the end of Soviet rule. Lang.: Swe, Eng, Ger. 1600
1997. Institutions.
Profile of Estonian theatres. Tallin. Tartu. Lang.: Swe, Eng, Ger. 345

Europe

1200 B.C.-1998 A.D. Design/technology.
Pyrotechnics and its use in theatre. Lang.: Ger. 178
500 B.C.-1980 A.D. Performance/production.
Theatre in periods of exploration and discovery. North America. Asia. Lang.: Eng. 569
500 B.C.-1988 A.D. Theory/criticism.
Terror in theatre. North America. Lang.: Eng. 839
500 B.C.-1995 A.D. Reference materials.
Italian translation of *The Oxford Illustrated History of Theatre* (1995). North America. Asia. Africa. Lang.: Ita. 697
450 B.C.-1998 A.D. Plays/librettos/scripts.
The character Medea in European drama. Lang.: Ger. 3063
340 B.C.-1998 A.D. Performance spaces.
Brief history of theatre architecture. Lang.: Dan. 437
1400-1600. Performance/production.
Renaissance ideas about classical Greek staging. Lang.: Slo. 521
1400-1998. Plays/librettos/scripts.
Analysis of post-medieval morality plays. Africa. Lang.: Eng. 3051
1500-1900. Design/technology.
Catalog of the Tobin scenography collection. USA. Lang.: Eng. 272
1549-1629. Relation to other fields.
Humanist ideology and the imaginary stage. Lang.: Eng. 731
1550-1950. Performance/production.
Brief history of *commedia dell'arte*. North America. Lang.: Eng. 4188
1563-1753. Plays/librettos/scripts.
Martial law and Renaissance drama and fiction. Lang.: Eng. 3059
1587-1998. Relation to other fields.
Literary influences of the characters Faust, Don Juan, Don Quixote, and Robinson Crusoe. Lang.: Ita. 730
1650-1950. Performance/production.
Great female opera soloists. North America. Lang.: Rus. 4555
1700-1990. Performance/production.
The puppet nativity play of Eastern and Central Europe. Lang.: Hun. 4891
1709-1804. Relation to other fields.
Depictions of Shakespeare's Othello. Lang.: Eng. 3758
1760-1992. Plays/librettos/scripts.
The devouring woman in plays of Racine, Kleist, Ibsen, and Beckett. Lang.: Eng. 3058
1784-1991. Plays/librettos/scripts.
Operatic realizations of Beaumarchais' character Rosina. North America. Lang.: Eng. 4773
1788-1996. Plays/librettos/scripts.
Two centuries' thought on Shakespeare's *The Merchant of Venice*. North America. Lang.: Hun. 3066
1795-1997. Audience.
The role of the audience in performance. North America. Lang.: Eng. 156
1800-1998. Plays/librettos/scripts.
The question of how to write a libretto. Lang.: Ger. 4775
1813-1996. Performance/production.
Performance history of Rossini's *Aureliano in Palmira*. Italy. Lang.: Eng. 4659
1816-1845. Reference materials.
Catalogue of the work of Donizetti. Italy. Lang.: Eng. 4833
1835-1848. Plays/librettos/scripts.
Composer Gaetano Donizetti. Italy. Lang.: Eng. 4805
1835-1885. Performance spaces.
Opera composer Richard Wagner and performance space. Lang.: Eng. 4492
1860-1950. Performance/production.
Commedia dell'arte and twentieth-century theatre. Lang.: Eng. 4187
1866-1998. Performance/production.
Recordings of the different versions of Verdi's *Don Carlos*. Italy. Lang.: Eng. 4650

Europe — cont'd

1878-1995. **Performance/production.**
The rise of the modern Shakespearean director. Lang.: Eng. 1911
1880-1930. **Plays/librettos/scripts.**
Robert Musil and the 'crisis of modern drama'. Lang.: Eng. 3062
1880-1969. **Plays/librettos/scripts.**
Gender and madness in modern drama. Lang.: Eng. 3061
1880-1970. **Plays/librettos/scripts.**
Insanity in nineteenth- and twentieth-century theatre. Lang.: Eng. 3050
1890-1998. **Performance/production.**
The disappearance of the diva in the modern world. USA. Lang.: Swe. 525
1892. **Performance/production.**
Slovene translation of Adolphe Appia on staging Wagner. Lang.: Slo. 4550
1895-1907. **Plays/librettos/scripts.**
Max Meyerfeld's preface to the translation of *A Florentine Tragedy* by Oscar Wilde. Lang.: Fre. 3057
1895-1937. **Performance spaces.**
Dancers and performance space. Lang.: Ger. 909
1895-1939. **Theory/criticism.**
The influence of Symbolism on European dance. Lang.: Eng. 1007
1896-1970. **Plays/librettos/scripts.**
Absurdism in children's theatre. North America. Lang.: Eng. 3288
1898-1998. **Plays/librettos/scripts.**
The influence of Bertolt's Brecht. Lang.: Swe. 3068
1899-1998. **Plays/librettos/scripts.**
Annual bibliography of modern drama studies. North America. Lang.: Eng. 3060
1900-1930. **Performance/production.**
Modern dance and the female body. USA. Lang.: Eng. 1321
1900-1996. **Plays/librettos/scripts.**
Representations of Joan of Arc in film and theatre. USA. Lang.: Eng. 3970
1900-1998. **Training.**
Survey of twentieth-century dance styles and teaching methods. Lang.: Ger. 1015
1904-1994. **Plays/librettos/scripts.**
The reciprocal influence of opera and film. North America. Lang.: Eng. 4770
1912-1998. **Plays/librettos/scripts.**
Text and story-line in twentieth-century opera. Lang.: Swe. 4774
1913-1930. **Relation to other fields.**
Modern fictional characters through the lens of Mejerchol'd's biomechanics and Oskar Schlemmer's puppets. Lang.: Ger. 729
1914-1943. **Plays/librettos/scripts.**
The Orestes myth in twentieth-century drama. USA. Lang.: Eng. 3052
1915-1995. **Plays/librettos/scripts.**
The clown as a character in modern drama. Lang.: Eng. 3056
1916-1934. **Performance/production.**
Collaborative Symbolist dance/theatre projects. USA. Lang.: Eng. 1268
1918-1998. **Performance spaces.**
Essays on experimental theatre world wide. North America. Asia. Lang.: Pol. 438
1919-1970. **Plays/librettos/scripts.**
Analysis of plays based on the Hebrew prophets. USA. Lang.: Eng. 3659
1920-1998. **Performance/production.**
Dance on screen. USA. Lang.: Ger. 3860
1930-1960. **Performance/production.**
Western ballet's influence on Indian classical dancer Ram Gopal. India. Lang.: Ita. 915
1930-1998. **Performance/production.**
Directing and intercultural theatre. Lang.: Ger. 524
1933-1945. **Relation to other fields.**
Directory of emigrant and refugee dancers. North America. South America. Lang.: Ger. 997
1933-1997. **Plays/librettos/scripts.**
Bibliography of Holocaust drama. North America. Lang.: Eng. 3054
1939-1998. **Performance/production.**
Polish cabaret at the front and abroad. Lang.: Pol. 4154
1940-1997. **Plays/librettos/scripts.**
Essay on Holocaust theatre. Lang.: Eng. 3064
1945-1998. **Design/technology.**
Costume practice and training in the U.S. and eastern Europe. USA. Lang.: Ger. 177
1946-1982. **Theory/criticism.**
The use of different analytical strategies to obtain multiple readings of dance performance. USA. Lang.: Eng. 1200
1950-1987. **Performance/production.**
The clown and the modern variety circus. Lang.: Eng. 4180
1950-1988. **Plays/librettos/scripts.**
The rebel in modern drama. Lang.: Eng. 3053
1950-1997. **Institutions.**
The evolution of Shakespeare festivals. USA. Lang.: Eng. 1601
1950-1998. **Performance/production.**
Shakespeare and postmodern production. North America. Lang.: Eng. 1912
1951. **Performance/production.**
The use of the harpsichord in Stravinskij's opera *The Rake's Progress*. Lang.: Eng. 4559
1953-1959. **Performance/production.**
Maria Callas and Donizetti's *Lucia di Lammermoor*. Lang.: Eng. 4553
1954. **Performance/production.**
Recordings of Strauss's *Die Frau ohne Schatten*. Lang.: Swe. 4554
1960-1985. **Plays/librettos/scripts.**
Aggressive language in modern drama. USA. Lang.: Eng. 3055
1960-1987. **Performance/production.**
The influence of experimental performance on contemporary drama. USA. Lang.: Eng. 526
1960-1988. **Audience.**
The negative reaction to performance art. Lang.: Eng. 4230
1960-1998. **Performance/production.**
Men in modern dance. Lang.: Dan. 1271
1961-1979. **Relation to other fields.**
The Fluxus movement. USA. Lang.: Eng. 4265
1961-1997. **Performance/production.**
Approaches to staging Brecht's plays, based on compiled reviews. Lang.: Ger. 1910
1963-1980. **Administration.**
Censorship and Russian and East European theatre and film. USSR. Lang.: Eng. 145
1963-1997. **Theory/criticism.**
Critique of the modernist tradition of defining each medium in its own terms. Lang.: Eng. 3861
1964-1969. **Administration.**
The cancellation of Kansas University's cultural exchange program with Eastern Europe. Lawrence, KS. Lang.: Eng. 131
1964-1983. **Institutions.**
European activities of the Living Theatre. USA. Lang.: Ita. 1602
1964-1989. **Performance/production.**
Performance art and the reinvigoration of opera. Lang.: Eng. 4556
1965. **Plays/librettos/scripts.**
Marcel Mihalovici's operatic adaptation of *Krapp's Last Tape* by Samuel Beckett. Lang.: Eng. 4769
1965-1998. **Theory/criticism.**
Evaluating the work of opera directors. Lang.: Eng. 4837
1967-1998. **Performance/production.**
The evolution of the contemporary Shakespearean director. North America. Lang.: Eng. 2207
1968. **Relation to other fields.**
Government response to Living Theatre's *Paradise Now*. USA. Lang.: Eng. 3789
1970-1988. **Performance/production.**
Recent collaboration of performance artists Marina Abramovič and Ulay. China, People's Republic of. Lang.: Eng. 4240
1970-1998. **Performance/production.**
Nudity in dance theatre. Lang.: Ger. 1270
Time aspects of video dance. Lang.: Ger. 4059
1971-1998. **Plays/librettos/scripts.**
New directions in the plays of Botho Strauss. Lang.: Ger. 3067
1974-1977. **Plays/librettos/scripts.**
Composer Wolfgang Fortner's adaptation of *That Time* by Samuel Beckett. Lang.: Eng. 4777
1975-1997. **Theory/criticism.**
Political criticism of early modern drama. North America. Lang.: Eng. 3814

Europe — cont'd

1975-1998. **Performance/production.**
Theatrical representations of civil war and civil discord. North America. Africa. Lang.: Eng. 567
1976-1977. **Plays/librettos/scripts.**
The opera *Neither* by Morton Feldman and Samuel Beckett. Lang.: Eng. 4772
1976-1988. **Plays/librettos/scripts.**
Operatic adaptations of Beckett's plays by Heinz Holliger. Lang.: Eng. 4776
1976-1997. **Performance/production.**
Multiculturalism and the site-specificity of theatre. Asia. North America. Lang.: Eng. 485
1978-1998. **Performance/production.**
Director and choreographer Nada Kokotovic. Lang.: Ger. 1272
1980-1998. **Performance/production.**
Evaluation of video performances of Donizetti's operas. USA. Lang.: Eng. 4557
1984-1997. **Research/historiography.**
Alternative models of performance documentation. Lang.: Eng. 818
Alternative forms of performance documentation. Lang.: Eng. 819
1985-1995. **Plays/librettos/scripts.**
The AIDS epidemic in contemporary opera. North America. Lang.: Eng. 4771
1987. **Plays/librettos/scripts.**
Morton Feldman's musical setting for Samuel Beckett's radio play *Words and Music*. Lang.: Eng. 3865
1987-1998. **Theory/criticism.**
The need for a critical vocabulary to evaluate operatic productions. Lang.: Eng. 4836
1989. **Performance/production.**
The body and personality of the dancer as the source of the physical vocabulary of dance. Lang.: Eng. 1269
1989. **Relation to other fields.**
Psychological aspects of the under-realized potential of the human voice. Lang.: Eng. 728
1989-1998. **Performance/production.**
Opera director Robert Carson. Lang.: Ger. 4558
1990. **Theory/criticism.**
Dance critic on her profession. USA. Lang.: Eng. 1014
1990-1998. **Performance/production.**
Account of the 1998 International European Theatre Meeting. Lang.: Eng. 522
1992. **Plays/librettos/scripts.**
Heinz Holliger's operatic adaptation of Samuel Beckett's *What Where*. Lang.: Eng. 4768
1995-1998. **Relation to other fields.**
Cultural trends of the younger generation. Lang.: Swe. 4150
1997. **Research/historiography.**
Problems of dance historiography. North America. Lang.: Eng. 1001
1997. **Theory/criticism.**
The nature of dance criticism. USA. Lang.: Eng. 1013
1998. **Design/technology.**
The application of new media for theatrical use. Lang.: Ger. 176
Production design for rock group Genesis' European tour. Lang.: Eng. 4096
1998. **Performance spaces.**
The feasibility of a floating open-air theatre. Lang.: Swe. 436
1998. **Performance/production.**
Handbook and training exercises for actors. Lang.: Ita. 520
Empathy and distancing in theatre education. Lang.: Fin. 523
Conductor Riccardo Chailly on composer Alexander Zemlinsky. Lang.: Fre. 4551
Gender, nation, and sexuality in opera. North America. Lang.: Eng. 4552
1998. **Plays/librettos/scripts.**
The recent revival of interest in works of Bertolt Brecht. Lang.: Eng. 3049
Survey of recent studies on closet drama. North America. Lang.: Eng. 3065
Women in plays about war and male contact sports. New Zealand. Lang.: Eng. 3281
Marxian analysis of dramatic parody and burlesque. USA. Lang.: Eng. 3664
1998. **Reference materials.**
Discography of operas by Donizetti. North America. Lang.: Eng. 4831
Index to *Opera* volume 49. UK-England. USA. Lang.: Eng. 4834
1998. **Relation to other fields.**
European fears of American cultural hegemony. USA. Lang.: Eng. 773
1998. **Research/historiography.**
Research on dance and cultural studies. North America. Lang.: Eng. 1003
The THEATRON theatre history project. Lang.: Dut. 3796
1998. **Theory/criticism.**
Gender and culture in dance analysis. North America. Lang.: Eng. 1006
The nature of dance analysis. North America. Lang.: Eng. 1009
The nature of the body in dance. North America. Lang.: Eng. 1010
Origins of dance as an art form. North America. Lang.: Eng. 1011

Federal Republic of Germany
SEE
Germany, West.

Finland
1908-1998. **Institutions.**
Profile of the Swedish Institute of Acting at the Finnish Theatre Academy. Helsinki. Lang.: Eng, Fre. 1603
1919-1998. **Institutions.**
Profile of Swedish-language theatre company Svenska Teatern. Helsinki. Lang.: Eng, Fre. 1606
1944-1998. **Performance/production.**
Actor Lasse Pöysti. Lang.: Eng, Fre. 1917
1950-1998. **Plays/librettos/scripts.**
Comedy and farce in Finnish theatre and film. Lang.: Fin. 3070
1980-1998. **Performance/production.**
Changes in the nature of circus performance. Lang.: Fin. 4181
1988-1998. **Performance/production.**
Minimalist film director Aki Kaurismaki. Lang.: Eng. 3930
1990-1998. **Institutions.**
The proliferation of Swedish-language theatre groups in Helsinki. Helsinki. Lang.: Eng, Fre. 1604
1990-1998. **Relation to other fields.**
The culture of decadence in theatre and film. Lang.: Fin. 732
1992-1998. **Institutions.**
New artistic goals of the Finnish National Ballet. Helsinki. Lang.: Eng. 1037
1996. **Theory/criticism.**
Report on congress of International Association of Theatre Critics. Helsinki. Lang.: Eng. 3816
1996-1998. **Design/technology.**
The experience of a costumer from Suomen Kansallisteatteri at Stockholms Stadsteatern. Helsinki. Stockholm. Lang.: Swe. 1519
1998. **Audience.**
The fickleness of theatrical audiences. Lang.: Fin. 148
Seven theatre-goers on their reasons for attending a performance. Lang.: Fin. 149
The role of the audience in performance. Lang.: Fin. 150
1998. **Design/technology.**
Interview with costume designer Maija Pekkanen. Lang.: Fin. 179
Criticism of methods used in design training. Lang.: Fin. 180
1998. **Institutions.**
Latin American guest performances at the Kuopio theatre festival. Kuopio. Lang.: Swe. 890
Competition and collaboration between Tampere's two resident theatres. Tampere. Lang.: Fin. 1605
1998. **Performance/production.**
The dancer-choreographer relationship. Lang.: Fin. 916
The contribution of unaffiliated dancers and choreographers. Lang.: Fin. 917
Children on dance. Lang.: Fin. 918
Interview with ice-dancing team Susanna Rahkamo and Petri Kokko. Lang.: Fin. 919
Interview with dance notator Päivi Eskelinen. Lang.: Fin. 920
Dance on Finnish television. Lang.: Fin. 921

Finland — cont'd

Premiere of Sylvie Guillem's new choreography for Adolphe Adam's *Giselle*. Helsinki. Lang.: Hun. 1068
The Finnish enthusiasm for Flamenco dance. Spain. Lang.: Fin. 1234
Interview with Deaf dancer Juho Saarinen. Lang.: Fin. 1273
Sexuality and gender in modern dance. Lang.: Fin. 1274
Swedish and bilingual Finnish-Swedish theatre. Turku. Vaasa. Lang.: Eng, Fre. 1913
The role of the dramaturg in script development and production. Lang.: Fin. 1914
Finland's theatre offerings in Finnish and Swedish. Lang.: Eng, Fre. 1915
Interview with director Esa Leskinen. Lang.: Fin. 1916
Interview with acting teacher Kari Väänänen. Lang.: Fin. 1918
Interview with director Kristian Smeds. Lang.: Eng. 1919
The influence of psychotherapy on Finnish theatrical practices. Lang.: Fin. 1920
Interview with conductor Esa-Pekka Salonen. Lang.: Eng. 4560

1998. Plays/librettos/scripts.
Recent drama and revue in Swedish. Lang.: Eng, Fre. 3069
Experimental writing in Finnish radio drama. Lang.: Fin. 3866

1998. Theory/criticism.
Society's fundamental need for theatre. Lang.: Fin. 840
The connection between dance and aerobics. Lang.: Fin. 1008
Director Esa Kirkkopelto on theatre as great art. Lang.: Fin. 3815

1998. Training.
Interview with dance teacher Mirja-Liisa Herhi. Lang.: Fin. 1016
Dance teaching methods of Anzu Furukawa. Lang.: Fin. 1017
Interview with dance teacher Aarne Mäntylä. Lang.: Fin. 1203
Classical dance training and its appeal to children. Lang.: Fin. 1204

France

1452-1577. Relation to other fields.
Fouquet's miniature of St. Apollonia and its relationship to the mystery play. Lang.: Eng. 3761
Jean Fouquet's miniature of St. Apollonia and its relationship to performance. Tours. Lang.: Eng. 3762
Fouquet's depiction of the martyrdom of St. Apollonia as a record of a performance. Lang.: Eng. 3763

1550-1620. Performance/production.
Mountebanks and the performance of *commedia dell'arte*. Italy. Avignon. Lang.: Eng. 4191

1550-1750. Performance/production.
Early modern French and Italian actresses. Italy. Lang.: Eng. 553

1550-1965. Performance/production.
Harlequin as a character in ballet. Lang.: Eng. 1069

1594-1998. Basic theatrical documents.
French translation of Shakespeare's *Love's Labour's Lost*. England. Lang.: Fre. 1419

1596-1980. Plays/librettos/scripts.
Recognition in plays of Čechov, Shakespeare, and Beckett. England. Russia. Lang.: Eng. 2949

1600-1700. Performance/production.
Commedia dell'arte and the street performances of charlatans. Italy. Lang.: Eng. 4189

1622-1673. Performance/production.
Movement training for actors in plays of Molière. Lang.: Eng. 1938

1635-1774. Plays/librettos/scripts.
Themes from Greek tragedy in opera. Lang.: Eng. 4783

1640-1690. Performance spaces.
Baroque opera and ballet at the Salle des Machines and the Palais Royal. Paris. Lang.: Eng. 4493

1643-1652. Plays/librettos/scripts.
Analysis of plays by Pierre Corneille. Lang.: Eng. 3112

1651-1653. Theory/criticism.
The plays of Corneille and catharsis through admiration. Lang.: Eng. 3820

1657-1749. Performance/production.
The classic French tradition of declaiming text. Lang.: Fre. 1923

1660-1722. Plays/librettos/scripts.
Analysis of medical plays by Molière. Lang.: Eng. 3078

1660-1733. Plays/librettos/scripts.
Racine's *Phèdre* as a source for *Hippolyte et Aricie* by Rameau and Pelligrin. Lang.: Eng. 4788

1660-1761. Performance/production.
Baroque ballet at the Jesuit College of Clermont/Louis le Grand. Paris. Lang.: Eng. 1076

1664-1691. Plays/librettos/scripts.
Statistical study of the theatre of Jean Racine. Lang.: Eng. 3081

1667. Plays/librettos/scripts.
Social interactions in Racine's *Phèdre*. Lang.: Fre. 3074

1671-1694. Performance/production.
Parisian theatre in the letters of Mme. de Sévigné. Paris. Lang.: Pol. 534

1672. Basic theatrical documents.
Catalan translation of *Les Femmes savantes (The Learned Ladies)* by Molière. Lang.: Cat. 1433

1691. Plays/librettos/scripts.
The ritual structure of Racine's *Athalie*. Lang.: Eng. 3099

1700-1998. Performance/production.
Mime, pantomime, and the work of Jean-Gaspard Deburau. Lang.: Swe. 4087

1720-1730. Performance/production.
Letters of actress Adrienne Lecouvreur. Lang.: Ita. 1940

1730. Basic theatrical documents.
Catalan translation of *Le Jeu de l'amour et du hasard (The Play of Love and Chance)* by Marivaux. Lang.: Cat. 1432

1733. Plays/librettos/scripts.
Politics and the unity of place in *Hippolyte et Aricie* by Rameau and Pelligrin. Lang.: Eng. 4780
The shaping influence of Pelligrin's libretto on Rameau's *Hippolyte et Aricie*. Lang.: Eng. 4790

1746-1748. Plays/librettos/scripts.
The writing and first performances of Voltaire's *Sémiramis*, the source of Rossini's opera *Semiramide*. Lang.: Fre. 3114

1748. Plays/librettos/scripts.
Voltaire's *Sémiramis*, source of Rossini's *Semiramide*. Lang.: Fre. 3096

1780-1800. Relation to other fields.
The theatre of the French Revolution. Lang.: Eng. 735

1784. Plays/librettos/scripts.
Desire in *Le Mariage de Figaro (The Marriage of Figaro)* by Beaumarchais. Lang.: Eng. 3095

1789-1795. Plays/librettos/scripts.
Olympe de Gouges and the theatre of the French Revolution. Lang.: Fre. 3109

1800-1862. Performance/production.
Working-class theatre and censorship. Paris. Lang.: Eng. 533

1800-1900. Plays/librettos/scripts.
Contributions of Meilhac and Halévy to the development of the French libretto. Lang.: Fre. 4781

1804-1836. Performance/production.
Ballerina Marie Taglioni. Lang.: Hun. 1071

1810-1820. Performance/production.
Representation of the historical past on the French stage. Lang.: Eng. 527

1815-1830. Design/technology.
The representation of history through costume in productions of the Comédie-Française. Paris. Lang.: Eng. 1520

1819-1880. Performance/production.
Chronology of the life of composer Jacques Offenbach. Lang.: Fre. 4561
Opera composer Jacques Offenbach. Lang.: Swe. 4854

1823-1873. Performance spaces.
The influence of the Salle le Peletier on French grand opera. Paris. Lang.: Eng. 4494

1825-1850. Performance/production.
Music for ballet-pantomime at the Paris Opera. Lang.: Eng. 1078

1830-1875. Performance/production.
Marie Taglioni and French Romantic ballet. Lang.: Eng. 1072

1835-1837. Plays/librettos/scripts.
Roberto Zucco and Bernard-Marie Koltès' idea of the tragic. Lang.: Fre. 3076
Fidelity in two plays of Musset. Lang.: Eng. 3102

1840. Performance/production.
Hector Berlioz's review of Donizetti's *La Favorite*. Paris. Lang.: Eng. 4565

France — cont'd

1845. **Plays/librettos/scripts.**
Spain as an exotic locale in Bizet's *Carmen* and its source. Spain. Lang.: Eng. 4819
1848-1853. **Plays/librettos/scripts.**
The inspiration for Dumas *fils*' Marguerite Gautier and Verdi's Violetta. Italy. Lang.: Eng. 4789
1853-1883. **Plays/librettos/scripts.**
The source of the libretto for Delibes' *Lakmé*. Lang.: Fre. 4784
1854-1900. **Plays/librettos/scripts.**
Playwright and author Oscar Wilde. UK-England. Lang.: Fre. 3465
1856-1883. **Performance/production.**
Léo Delibes as a composer of operetta. Lang.: Fre. 4855
1858-1874. **Performance/production.**
Offenbach's *Orphée aux Enfers* from two acts to four. Lang.: Fre. 4571
1860-1998. **Audience.**
Operetta and the contemporary audience. Germany. USA. Lang.: Swe. 4851
1870-1879. **Plays/librettos/scripts.**
Ambition and gender in Bizet's *Carmen*. Lang.: Eng. 4786
1872-1911. **Performance/production.**
Oriental themes in operas and instrumental works of Saint-Saëns. Lang.: Eng. 4576
1874. **Basic theatrical documents.**
Text of Offenbach's *Orphée aux Enfers*. Lang.: Fre. 4418
1874. **Plays/librettos/scripts.**
Humor and parody in Offenbach's opera *Orphée aux Enfers*. Lang.: Fre. 4785
1874-1997. **Relation to other fields.**
Author Gertrude Stein, subject of *Gertrude morte cet après-midi (Gertrude Dead This Afternoon)* by Monique Lepeu. Paris. Lang.: Fre. 3759
1877. **Basic theatrical documents.**
The libretto to Jules Massenet's *Le Roi de Lahore*. Lang.: Fre. 4417
1877. **Performance/production.**
The creation of Massenet's opera *Le Roi de Lahore*. Lang.: Fre. 4568
1877-1894. **Plays/librettos/scripts.**
Collaboration of composer Jules Massenet and librettist Louis Gallet. Lang.: Fre. 4778
1877-1998. **Performance/production.**
The stage history of *Samson et Dalila* by Saint-Saëns. Germany. USA. Lang.: Eng. 4566
1881. **Basic theatrical documents.**
Libretto to Massenet's opera *Hérodiade*. Lang.: Fre. 4416
1881. **Plays/librettos/scripts.**
Massenet's opera *Hérodiade* and its literary sources. Lang.: Fre. 4779
1881-1953. **Performance/production.**
The artistic life of dancer Vaclav Nižinskij. Poland. Russia. Lang.: Pol. 1123
1883. **Basic theatrical documents.**
Libretto of *Lakmé* by Léo Delibes, Edmond Gondinet, and Philippe Gille. Lang.: Fre. 4415
1883. **Plays/librettos/scripts.**
Analysis of Delibes' opera *Lakmé*. Lang.: Fre. 4782
1885-1903. **Performance/production.**
Massenet's revisions to *Manon* for performance by Sybil Sanderson. Lang.: Eng. 4572
1885-1925. **Performance/production.**
The 'grande coquette' on the Parisian stage. Paris. Lang.: Eng. 531
1888-1936. **Performance/production.**
Dancer Antonia Merce, La Argentina. Spain. Lang.: Eng. 922
1888-1972. **Performance/production.**
Life and film career of singer Maurice Chevalier. Paris. USA. Lang.: Eng. 3933
1892-1898. **Plays/librettos/scripts.**
Wilde, Gide, and the censorship of Biblical drama. UK-England. Lang.: Eng. 3441
1896-1948. **Plays/librettos/scripts.**
Antonin Artaud's years in a mental hospital. Lang.: Ita. 3113
1897-1984. **Performance/production.**
Tenor George Thill. Lang.: Eng. 4574
1898-1998. **Performance spaces.**
Non-traditional theatrical space. Germany. UK-England. Lang.: Dan. 443
1900-1998. **Performance/production.**
The performance of sacrifice on stage. Germany. Lang.: Ger. 530
1905-1998. **Administration.**
Comparative analysis of national cultural policies. Canada. Germany. Norway. Lang.: Eng. 4
1906-1914. **Audience.**
Diaghilev's strategies of audience development. Paris. Lang.: Eng. 1028
1906-1989. **Plays/librettos/scripts.**
Obituary for playwright Samuel Beckett. Ireland. Lang.: Dut. 3199
1908-1915. **Performance/production.**
Masculinity in ballet. Paris. Lang.: Eng. 1070
1908-1944. **Plays/librettos/scripts.**
Painter Wassily Kandinsky and theatre. Lang.: Eng. 3111
1912-1994. **Plays/librettos/scripts.**
The theatre of Eugène Ionesco. Lang.: Ita. 3079
1912-1998. **Administation.**
American and French regulation of mass media. USA. Lang.: Eng. 3853
1912-1998. **Basic theatrical documents.**
Text of *Jean III (John III)* by Sacha Guitry. Lang.: Fre. 1426
1913-1920. **Performance/production.**
Director Jacques Copeau and his theatrical aesthetic. Lang.: Eng. 1941
1913-1985. **Plays/librettos/scripts.**
The Holocaust in plays of Charlotte Delbo. Lang.: Eng. 3115
1913-1992. **Performance/production.**
Interview with Marie-Hélène Dasté, daughter of Jacques Copeau. Paris. Lang.: Eng. 4089
1914-1985. **Plays/librettos/scripts.**
Verbal and non-verbal communication in the theatre of Marguerite Duras. Lang.: Eng. 3094
1914-1986. **Plays/librettos/scripts.**
Narrative and form as theatrical media in the plays of Marguerite Duras. Lang.: Eng. 3101
1915-1998. **Performance/production.**
The choreography of William Forsythe and the painting of Marcel Duchamp. Germany. Lang.: Eng. 1280
1920-1970. **Plays/librettos/scripts.**
Revolutionary elements in plays and theory of Baraka and Artaud. USA. Lang.: Eng. 3580
1920-1973. **Theory/criticism.**
The influence of Antonin Artaud on director Paul Pörtner. Lang.: Ger. 3870
1920-1998. **Performance/production.**
Etienne Decroux's concept of actor-centered theatre. USA. Lang.: Eng. 4091
1925-1998. **Performance/production.**
Jorge Lavelli's production of *Sei personaggi in cerca d'autore (Six Characters in Search of an Author)* by Pirandello. Paris. Lang.: Ita. 1921
1927-1998. **Performance/production.**
Choreographer Maurice Béjart. Lang.: Rus. 1077
1930-1939. **Institutions.**
L.L. Vasil'čikova's amateur theatre group. Paris. Lang.: Rus. 1616
1931. **Plays/librettos/scripts.**
Music in Samuel Beckett's novel *Proust*. Ireland. Lang.: Eng. 3208
1935. **Relation to other fields.**
Analysis of Samuel Beckett's novel *Murphy*. Ireland. Lang.: Eng. 733
1935-1993. **Plays/librettos/scripts.**
The influence of eighteenth-century philosophy on the work of Samuel Beckett. Ireland. Lang.: Eng. 3084
1936-1937. **Performance/production.**
Antonin Artaud's journey to Mexico. Mexico. Lang.: Eng. 1922
1937-1939. **Performance/production.**
The European and American tour of the Polish National Ballet. Poland. USA. Lang.: Pol. 1124
1937-1958. **Plays/librettos/scripts.**
The sources of Camus's *Caligula*. Lang.: Ita. 3116
1938-1993. **Performance/production.**
Dancer Rudolf Nureyev. Lang.: Rus. 1080
1939-1946. **Performance/production.**
Theatre for Polish soldiers. UK-England. Romania. Lang.: Pol. 611

France — cont'd

1940-1945. **Plays/librettos/scripts.**
Analysis of *Bariona* by Jean-Paul Sartre. Lang.: Eng. 3093
1945-1990. **Plays/librettos/scripts.**
Music and Samuel Beckett. Ireland. Lang.: Eng. 3198
1945-1995. **Plays/librettos/scripts.**
Melanie Daiken's musical settings of texts by Samuel Beckett. Ireland. Lang.: Eng. 3201
Beckett's work analyzed in terms of musical serialism. Ireland. Lang.: Eng. 3215
1945-1998. **Plays/librettos/scripts.**
The speaking subject in plays of Beckett and Stoppard. Ireland. UK-England. Lang.: Ger. 3098
1945-1998. **Relation to other fields.**
Cultural policy and French theatre structures. Lang.: Ger. 3760
1945-1998. **Theory/criticism.**
Artaud's theatre of cruelty and contemporary experimental theatre. Lang.: Ger. 3818
1947-1948. **Performance/production.**
Balanchine's choreography for Bizet's *Symphony in C.* Paris. Lang.: Eng. 1079
1947-1998. **Plays/librettos/scripts.**
On translating into German the plays of Valère Novarina. Germany. Lang.: Ger. 3122
1948-1955. **Plays/librettos/scripts.**
The postwar existentialist drama of Albert Camus and Carlos Solórzano. Mexico. Lang.: Spa. 3274
1949. **Plays/librettos/scripts.**
Analysis of Jean Genet's dance work *Adame Miroir.* Lang.: Ita. 993
1950. **Performance/production.**
Survey of recordings of the operettas by Offenbach. UK-England. Lang.: Swe. 4853
1950-1980. **Performance/production.**
Samuel Beckett's plays in production. Lang.: Eng. 1936
1950-1981. **Performance/production.**
Pirandello on the French stage. Lang.: Ita. 1932
1950-1988. **Plays/librettos/scripts.**
The nature of conflict in the plays of Hugo Claus. Lang.: Eng. 3121
Language and other elements of expression in plays of Beckett and Shepard. USA. Ireland. Lang.: Eng. 3655
1950-1989. **Plays/librettos/scripts.**
Analysis of Samuel Beckett's later plays. Ireland. Lang.: Eng. 3210
1953-1981. **Plays/librettos/scripts.**
Analysis of *En attendant Godot (Waiting for Godot)* and *Rockaby* by Samuel Beckett. Ireland. Lang.: Eng. 3087
1953-1986. **Plays/librettos/scripts.**
Authority, truth, and the allegory of the cave in works of Samuel Beckett. Ireland. Lang.: Eng. 3085
Humor in the works of Samuel Beckett. Ireland. Lang.: Eng. 3110
1953-1998. **Plays/librettos/scripts.**
Criticism of the creation of literary 'genealogies' for dramatic characters. Ireland. Lang.: Swe. 3211
1955-1995. **Plays/librettos/scripts.**
Playwright Samuel Beckett's love of music. Ireland. Lang.: Eng. 3204
1955-1996. **Plays/librettos/scripts.**
The representation of true crime in modern drama. USA. Lang.: Eng. 3673
1957. **Plays/librettos/scripts.**
Analysis of Samuel Beckett's radio play *All That Fall.* Ireland. Lang.: Ita. 3867
1957-1976. **Plays/librettos/scripts.**
The influence Dryden and Johnson's theories on self-translated works of Samuel Beckett. Ireland. Lang.: Eng. 3077
1957-1998. **Design/technology.**
Scenographer Lennart Mörk. Stockholm. Paris. Lang.: Swe. 4439
1957-1998. **Theory/criticism.**
Survey of theatre studies as cultural studies. USA. UK-England. Lang.: Ger. 865
1958-1998. **Design/technology.**
Interview with set designer Lennart Mörk. Stockholm. Paris. Lang.: Swe. 222
1958-1998. **Plays/librettos/scripts.**
Interview with playwright Michel Vinaver. Lang.: Ger. 3086
1959-1998. **Basic theatrical documents.**
French translation of *Tres diamantes y una mujer (Three Diamonds and One Woman)* by Alejandro Casona. Spain. Lang.: Fre. 1464
1959-1998. **Research/historiography.**
Gender difference and theatricality. Germany. USA. Lang.: Ger. 821
1960-1963. **Plays/librettos/scripts.**
Beckett's character Winnie in *Happy Days.* Ireland. Lang.: Ita. 3200
1960-1990. **Plays/librettos/scripts.**
Postcolonialism, ethnicity, and feminism in French and Caribbean plays. Martinique. Guadeloupe. Lang.: Eng. 3104
1960-1998. **Plays/librettos/scripts.**
Analysis of *Par-dessus bord (Overboard)* by Michel Vinaver. La Chaux-de-Fonds. Lang.: Ger. 3118
1960-1998. **Theory/criticism.**
The persistent influence of generations of theory on French theatre. Lang.: Ger. 3817
1961. **Plays/librettos/scripts.**
Beckett's *Happy Days* as a rewriting of *Lady Chatterley's Lover.* Ireland. UK-England. Lang.: Eng. 3120
1961-1970. **Plays/librettos/scripts.**
The Holocaust in *L'Enfant-rat (The Rat Child)* by Armand Gatti. Lang.: Eng. 3092
1961-1997. **Performance/production.**
Soprano Mady Mesplé on Delibes' *Lakmé.* Lang.: Fre. 4573
1962. **Plays/librettos/scripts.**
Analysis of *Le Roi se meurt (Exit the King)* by Eugène Ionesco. Lang.: Eng. 3080
1964-1997. **Institutions.**
Ariane Mnouchkine and rehearsal techniques of Théâtre du Soleil. Paris. Lang.: Eng. 1610
1965. **Plays/librettos/scripts.**
Analysis of *Les Nombres (The Numbers)* by Andrée Chedid. Lang.: Eng. 3090
1965-1985. **Plays/librettos/scripts.**
Composer Luciano Berio on Beckett's influence on his work. Ireland. Italy. Lang.: Eng. 3195
1965-1989. **Plays/librettos/scripts.**
Analysis of television plays by Samuel Beckett. Lang.: Eng. 4077
1965-1995. **Plays/librettos/scripts.**
Composer Philip Glass on Beckett's influence on his work. Ireland. USA. Lang.: Eng. 3194
1966-1998. **Plays/librettos/scripts.**
Olivier Py, actor, playwright, director, and head of the Centre Dramatique d'Orléans. Orléans. Lang.: Ger. 3073
1967-1982. **Plays/librettos/scripts.**
Analysis of *Elle est là (It Is There)* by Nathalie Sarraute. Lang.: Eng. 3107
1967-1995. **Plays/librettos/scripts.**
Feminist questioning of language and authority in plays of Nathalie Sarraute. Lang.: Eng. 3103
1968-1988. **Plays/librettos/scripts.**
Anomie in French theatre. Lang.: Eng. 3091
1968-1998. **Performance/production.**
Corinne Soum, former assistant to Etienne Decroux. Paris. London. Lang.: Eng. 4090
1970. **Plays/librettos/scripts.**
Analysis of *L'Impromptu de l'Alma ou Le Caméléon du Berger (Improvisation of the Shepherd's Chameleon)* by Eugène Ionesco. Lang.: Fre. 3088
1970-1982. **Plays/librettos/scripts.**
Space and pre-verbal memory in later works of Marguerite Duras. Lang.: Eng. 3106
1970-1989. **Plays/librettos/scripts.**
Food and alienation in plays of Chantal Chawaf and Denise Chalem. Lang.: Eng. 3072
1970-1995. **Institutions.**
Theatrical space in productions of Ariane Mnouchkine. Paris. Lang.: Eng. 1607
1970-1998. **Performance/production.**
Dancer and choreographer Brygida Ochaim. Germany. Lang.: Ger. 1283
The present state of French puppetry. Lang.: Ger. 4892
1973-1993. **Performance/production.**
The function of sound in productions of *India Song* by Marguerite Duras. Mold. Lang.: Eng. 1945

France — cont'd

1974-1981. Performance/production.
Music in films of Marguerite Duras. Lang.: Eng. 3932
1974-1991. Plays/librettos/scripts.
Analysis of Holocaust plays by Jean-Claude Grumberg. Lang.: Eng. 3108
1974-1998. Plays/librettos/scripts.
Essay on French translations of Shakespeare. Lang.: Fre. 3082
1975-1995. Plays/librettos/scripts.
Response to the structures of male oppression in plays of Yourcenar, Sarraute, and Duras. Lang.: Fre. 3119
1975-1998. Design/technology.
Set designer Jean-Guy Lecat and his work with Peter Brook. Denmark. Lang.: Dan. 182
1976. Plays/librettos/scripts.
Analysis of *Ghost Trio* by Samuel Beckett. Ireland. Lang.: Eng. 4076
1976-1997. Performance/production.
Interview with actress Lucinda Childs. Paris. Lang.: Eng. 1943
1977. Basic theatrical documents.
Catalan translation of *La Nuit juste avant les forêts (The Dark Just Before the Forests)* by Bernard-Marie Koltès. Lang.: Cat. 1428
1977-1992. Plays/librettos/scripts.
Analysis of plays by Marguerite Duras and Marie Redonnet. Lang.: Eng. 3071
1978. Plays/librettos/scripts.
Bisexuality in *Le Nom d'Oedipe (The Name of Oedipus)* by Hélène Cixous. Lang.: Eng. 3089
1979. Performance/production.
Conductor Pierre Boulez on Patrice Chéreau's production of *Lulu* by Alban Berg. Paris. Lang.: Fre. 4567
1980-1998. Institutions.
Profile of Théâtre du Radeau. Le Mans. Lang.: Ger. 1614
1980-1998. Plays/librettos/scripts.
Comparison of French and Canadian protest plays. Canada. Lang.: Eng. 2801
1980-1998. Training.
Actor/director Jean-Paul Denizon and his workshops on Peter Brook's approach to theatre. Lang.: Ita. 873
1981. Plays/librettos/scripts.
The influence of Jean Cocteau on filmmaker Pedro Almodóvar. Spain. Lang.: Eng. 3978
1984-1987. Basic theatrical documents.
Text of *L'Ascenseur (The Elevator)* by Gérard Levoyer. Lang.: Fre. 1431
1985. Performance/production.
Semiotic analysis of Jarry's *Ubu Roi* as staged by Vitez. Paris. Lang.: Eng. 528
1985. Plays/librettos/scripts.
Analysis of *Le Voyage sans fin (The Constant Journey)* by Monique Wittig. Lang.: Eng. 3100
1985-1998. Performance/production.
Interview with singer Peter Mattei. Aix-en-Provence. Lang.: Swe. 4564
1986. Plays/librettos/scripts.
Analysis of *Un opéra pour Terezin (An Opera for Terezin)* by Liliane Atlan. Lang.: Eng. 3105
1987-1997. Basic theatrical documents.
French translation of *Alfred Stieglitz Loves O'Keeffe* by Lanie Robertson. USA. Lang.: Fre. 1505
1987-1998. Performance/production.
Choreographer Josef Nadj and his company Théâtre du Signe. Lang.: Hun. 924
1988. Performance/production.
Robert Wilson's dance adaptation of *Le Martyre de Saint Sébastien* by D'Annunzio. Paris. Lang.: Ita. 1074
Postmodernism in Jean-Luc Godard's film adaptation of Shakespeare's *King Lear*. Lang.: Eng. 3931
1988-1990. Performance/production.
Practical issues of cultural exchange: the Cry of Asia! tour. Philippines. Lang.: Eng. 535
1988-1992. Performance/production.
Peter Brook's *The Mahabharata*, and problems of intercultural performance. Lang.: Eng. 1925
1988-1994. Plays/librettos/scripts.
Poetic identity in plays of Hélène Cixous. Lang.: Eng. 3083
1988-1998. Institutions.
Interview with playwright, director, and film-maker Xavier Durringer. Paris. Lang.: Ger. 1609
1988-1998. Plays/librettos/scripts.
Interview with playwright-director Olivier Py. Lang.: Ger, Fre, Dut, Eng. 3117
1989-1993. Plays/librettos/scripts.
The Holocaust in environmental theatre of Armand Gatti. Lang.: Eng. 3097
1990-1996. Performance/production.
French political theatre: Boal and Mnouchkine. Lang.: Eng. 529
1990-1998. Institutions.
Interview with Josef Nadj, choreographer. Lang.: Hun. 892
1990-1998. Performance/production.
Choreographer Koffi Koko. Paris. Benin. Lang.: Eng. 923
Interview with actress Fanny Ardant. Paris. Lang.: Swe. 1944
Analysis of the 'new circus'. Sweden. Lang.: Swe. 4182
1993-1998. Basic theatrical documents.
Text of *Le Roi Hâtif (King Hasty)* by Françoise Gerbaulet. Lang.: Fre. 1425
French translation of *Time of My Life* by Alan Ayckbourn. UK-England. Lang.: Fre. 1471
1993-1998. Institutions.
Interview with Jean-Pierre Miquel, director of the Comédie-Française. Paris. Lang.: Eng. 1613
1994. Plays/librettos/scripts.
The *castrato*, the contralto, and the film *Farinelli*. Italy. Lang.: Eng. 4787
1994-1998. Basic theatrical documents.
French translation of *My Left Breast* by Susan Miller. USA. Lang.: Fre. 1498
1994-1998. Performance/production.
The collaboration of choreographers Claire Russ and Anne-Marie Pascoli. UK-England. Lang.: Eng. 1276
1995. Performance/production.
Natalie Dessay's role in Gilbert Blin's production of *Lakmé*. Paris. Lang.: Fre. 4570
1995-1997. Basic theatrical documents.
French translation of *Funny Money* by Ray Cooney. UK-England. Lang.: Fre. 1473
French translation of *Beast on the Moon* by Richard Kalinoski. USA. Lang.: Fre. 1491
1995-1998. Relation to other fields.
French theatre and the influence of the right wing. Lang.: Ger. 734
1996. Basic theatrical documents.
French translation of *The Primary English Class* by Israel Horovitz. USA. Lang.: Fre. 1489
1996-1997. Basic theatrical documents.
French translation of *Lebensraum* by Israel Horovitz. USA. Lang.: Fre. 1488
1996-1997. Performance/production.
Report on the Parisian theatre season. Paris. Lang.: Eng. 1928
Overview of the Paris theatre season. Paris. Lang.: Fre. 1929
1996-1998. Basic theatrical documents.
French translation of *Popcorn* by Ben Elton. UK-England. Lang.: Fre. 1475
1996-1998. Performance/production.
Hungarian student's training at Jeune Ballet de France. Paris. Lang.: Hun. 1075
1997. Institutions.
Offerings at the Festival d'Automne. Paris. Lang.: Fre. 346
1997. Performance/production.
Report on festival of performing and visual arts. Paris. Lang.: Eng. 532
The performances of Lucinda Childs and Michel Piccoli in *La Maladie de la Mort (The Sickness of Death)*, directed by Robert Wilson. Paris. Lang.: Eng. 1942
Report on biennial festival of mixed media. Lyon. Lang.: Eng. 4042
Press reactions to productions of Offenbach's *Orphée aux Enfers*. Belgium. Switzerland. Lang.: Fre. 4535
Review of Pierre Strosser's staging of Busoni's *Doktor Faust*. Lyons. Lang.: Eng. 4577
1997. Plays/librettos/scripts.
Problems of adapting theatre to film. Lang.: Fre. 3971
1997. Relation to other fields.
The role of the drama specialist in the classroom. Lang.: Eng. 736

France — cont'd

1997-1998. Performance/production.
Reviews of productions by Wilson, Greenaway, and Mnouchkine. Paris. Lang.: Eng. 1926
Recent Paris productions. Paris. Lang.: Ger. 1933
Survey of Parisian productions. Paris. Lang.: Eng. 1937
French production of *Im Dickicht der Städte (In the Jungle of Cities)* by Bertolt Brecht. Lang.: Ger. 1946
Reviews of recent opera productions. Basel. Stuttgart. Berlin. Hamburg. Strasbourg. Lang.: Ger. 4702

1998. Administration.
Interview with Jean-Pierre Miquel, managing director of the Comédie-Française. Lang.: Hun. 1378

1998. Basic theatrical documents.
Text of *Les Exclusés*, poetry adapted for the stage by Isabelle Starkier. Lang.: Fre. 1423
Text of *Pour la galerie (For the Gallery)* by Claude d'Anna and Laure Bonin. Lang.: Fre. 1424
Text of *Le Vampire suce toujours deux fois (The Vampire Always Sucks Twice)* by Victor Haïm. Lang.: Fre. 1427
Text of *Capitaine Bringuier* by Pascal Lainé. Lang.: Fre. 1429
Text of *Mendiants d'amour (Beggars of Love)* by Gérard Levoyer. Lang.: Fre. 1430
Text of *Soleil pour deux (Sun for Two)* by Pierre Sauvil. Lang.: Fre. 1434
Text of *Ma femme s'appelle Maurice (My Wife's Name Is Maurice)* by Raffy Shart. Lang.: Fre. 1435
Text of *La Médée de Saint-Médard (The Medea of Saint-Medard)* by Anca Visdei. Lang.: Fre. 1436
Text of *Ubu déchaîné (Ubu Unchained)* by Richard Demarcy. Benin. Lang.: Fre. 4287

1998. Design/technology.
Account of ACTSAFE conference on theatre safety. Paris. Lang.: Swe. 181
Impressions from the Salon de Théâtre. Paris. Lang.: Ger. 183

1998. Institutions.
The work of young choreographers at the Councours de Bagnolet. Bagnolet. Lang.: Swe. 891
Account of the eighth international ballet competition. Paris. Lang.: Hun. 1038
Survey of the fifty-second annual Avignon Festival. Avignon. Lang.: Eng. 1608
Report on the Avignon theatre festival. Avignon. Lang.: Eng. 1611
Impressions from the Avignon theatre festival. Avignon. Lang.: Ger. 1612
Reviews of some productions at the Avignon Festival. Avignon. Lang.: Hun. 1615
Profile of Théâtre Gérard-Philippe. Paris. Lang.: Ger. 1617
Peter Brook's production of Mozart's *Don Giovanni* at the Aix festival. Aix-en-Provence. Lang.: Swe. 4450

1998. Performance/production.
Survey of London and Paris productions. London. Paris. Lang.: Eng. 607
Ballet dancer K. Kastal'skaja. Lyon. Lang.: Rus. 1073
Dance improvisation with children. Lang.: Fre. 1275
Social context of French and Canadian productions of *Les Fourberies de Scapin* by Molière. Montreal, PQ. Paris. Lang.: Fre. 1842
Survey of Parisian theatre. Paris. Lang.: Eng. 1924
The Avignon Festival under the direction of Bernard Faivre D'Arcier. Avignon. Lang.: Ger. 1927
Peter Brook's *Je suis un phénomène (I Am a Phenomenon)* at Bouffes du Nord. Paris. Lang.: Hun. 1930
Productions of the Paris Festival d'Automne. Paris. Lang.: Fre. 1931
Peter Brook's *Je suis un phénomène (I Am a Phenomenon)*. Paris. Lang.: Ger. 1934
French productions of German plays. Lang.: Ger. 1935
Comparison of text-based and visual productions. Lang.: Fre. 1939
Yves Marc on Etienne Decroux. Paris. Lang.: Eng. 4088
Conductor James Conlon on his production of Zemlinsky's *Der Zwerg*. Paris. Lang.: Fre. 4562
Report on opera festival. Aix-en-Provence. Lang.: Eng. 4563
Peter Brook's *Don Giovanni* at the Aix Festival. Aix-en-Provence. Lang.: Eng. 4569
Soprano Natalie Dessay. Lang.: Eng. 4575
A puppet production of Madách's *Az ember tragédiája (The Tragedy of Man)*. Colmar. Lang.: Hun. 4893

1998. Plays/librettos/scripts.
Feminist theory and practice on the French stage. Lang.: Eng. 3075
Conversations with playwright Samuel Beckett. Ireland. Lang.: Ita. 3205
Pirandello's influence on French theatre. Italy. Lang.: Ita. 3246
Playwright Yasmina Reza. New York, NY. Lang.: Eng. 3684

1998. Theory/criticism.
Analysis of plays by Eric-Emmanuel Schmitt. Lang.: Fin. 3819

1998. Training.
Gala concert of the Paris Opera ballet school. Paris. Lang.: Hun. 1205

Georgia

1998. Performance/production.
Interview with actor Vachtang Kikabidze. Lang.: Rus. 1947

German Democratic Republic
SEE
Germany, East.

Germany

900-1050. Performance/production.
Martyrdom in the plays of Hrotsvitha. Lang.: Eng. 1960

1184-1189. Plays/librettos/scripts.
A lost creed play from the twelfth century. Regensburg. Lang.: Eng. 3176

1234-1656. Relation to other fields.
Medieval religious theatre and the public safety. Lang.: Eng. 3771

1549-1996. Performance/production.
The Patum of Berga compared to sixteenth-century German festivities. Berga. Trent. Lang.: Eng. 4218

1550-1584. Plays/librettos/scripts.
Morality plays of the Reformation. Lang.: Eng. 3163

1579-1998. Performance/production.
Review of recent works on children's and youth theatre. Lang.: Ger. 537

1592-1620. Performance/production.
English actors in Kassel. Kassel. Lang.: Eng. 2016

1600-1800. Plays/librettos/scripts.
Representation of the virginal body on the German stage. Lang.: Ger. 3171

1600-1932. Plays/librettos/scripts.
Brecht's *Leben des Galilei (The Life of Galileo)* as an adaptation of Shakespeare's *Hamlet*. Lang.: Eng. 3160

1635-1664. Relation to other fields.
Analysis of illustrations of first editions of tragedies by Gryphius. Lang.: Eng. 3765

1700-1994. Performance spaces.
History and nature of German open-air theatre. Lang.: Eng. 442

1727-1767. Performance/production.
Realism in acting death scenes. Lang.: Ger. 2023

1739-1833. Plays/librettos/scripts.
Shakespeare translators Luise Gottsched and Dorothea Tieck. Lang.: Ger. 3156

1750-1910. Institutions.
European national theatres and their development. Slovenia. Lang.: Slo. 1720

1760-1780. Theory/criticism.
Tragic theories of G.E. Lessing. Lang.: Eng. 3822

1767-1775. Performance/production.
The publication of a work by eighteenth-century dancing master C.J. von Feldtenstein. Braunschweig. Lang.: Hun. 927

1772. Plays/librettos/scripts.
Lessing's *Emilia Galotti* and reader-response criticism. Lang.: Eng. 3166

1772-1781. Plays/librettos/scripts.
Female sacrifice in eighteenth-century German drama. Lang.: Eng. 3167

Germany — cont'd

1776-1824. **Relation to other fields.**
Shakespeare's Hamlet in novels of Goethe and Scott. England. Lang.: Eng. 3757

1776-1989. **Plays/librettos/scripts.**
Power, gender relations, and communication in German drama. Lang.: Ger. 3138

1789-1867. **Institutions.**
Slovene self-image and the national theatre. Slovenia. Lang.: Slo. 1719

1803-1805. **Performance/production.**
Excerpts from Johanna Schopenhauer's journal relating to London theatre. London. Lang.: Eng. 2615

1810-1811. **Relation to other fields.**
The context of Heinrich von Kleist's periodical *Berliner Abendblätter*. Berlin. Lang.: Ger. 741

1814. **Performance/production.**
Analysis of a scene from Beethoven's *Fidelio*. Lang.: Eng. 4595

1821. **Performance/production.**
Weber's *Der Freischütz* and the Neues Schauspielhaus. Berlin. Lang.: Eng. 4581

1848-1929. **Performance/production.**
Wagnerian soprano Lilli Lehmann. Lang.: Eng. 4587

1850-1998. **Performance/production.**
Historical overview of Wagnerian singing. Bayreuth. Lang.: Eng. 4610

1850-1998. **Plays/librettos/scripts.**
The brother-sister bond of Gottfried and Elsa in *Lohengrin* by Richard Wagner. Lang.: Eng. 4794

1860-1998. **Audience.**
Operetta and the contemporary audience. France. USA. Lang.: Swe. 4851

1868-1877. **Plays/librettos/scripts.**
Gender, nationalism, and Orientalism in *Samson et Dalila* by Saint-Saëns. Lang.: Eng. 4797

1868-1998. **Plays/librettos/scripts.**
Comic and tragic elements in Wagner's *Die Meistersinger von Nürnberg*. Lang.: Eng. 4792

1869-1876. **Performance/production.**
Visual spectacle in Wagner's *Ring* cycle. Lang.: Eng. 4585

1870-1880. **Plays/librettos/scripts.**
Nationalism and sexuality in Wagner's *Ring* cycle. Lang.: Eng. 4796

1870-1890. **Theory/criticism.**
How theatre criticism of Theodor Fontane influenced his novels. Berlin. Lang.: Ger. 843

1870-1898. **Plays/librettos/scripts.**
Hegel's influence on the plays of Henrik Ibsen. Norway. Lang.: Eng. 3292

1871-1942. **Performance/production.**
Life of composer and conductor Alexander Zemlinsky. Lang.: Fre. 4594

1877-1998. **Performance/production.**
The stage history of *Samson et Dalila* by Saint-Saëns. France. USA. Lang.: Eng. 4566

1879-1906. **Plays/librettos/scripts.**
Andreas-Salomé's view of Ibsen's female characters. Norway. Lang.: Eng. 3296

1889-1890. **Audience.**
Audience response to *Vor Sonnenaufgang (Before Sunrise)* by Gerhart Hauptmann. Berlin. Lang.: Eng. 1402

1890-1910. **Plays/librettos/scripts.**
The image of motherhood in German-language drama. Austria. Lang.: Ger. 2787

Women in German turn-of-the-century drama. Lang.: Eng. 3158

1895-1935. **Plays/librettos/scripts.**
Wedekind's Lulu plays and their adaptation by Berg. Austria. Lang.: Fre. 4798

1898-1931. **Performance/production.**
An exhibition devoted to dance and silent film star Lya de Putti. Hungary. Lang.: Hun. 944

1898-1956. **Plays/librettos/scripts.**
Playwright Bertolt Brecht. Lang.: Rus. 3140

Late twentieth-century view of playwright Bertolt Brecht. Lang.: Fin. 3155

1898-1975. **Performance/production.**
Performer, director, and artist Wolfgang Martin Schede. Lang.: Ger. 929

1898-1998. **Design/technology.**
Walther Unruh and German theatre technology. Lang.: Ger. 187

1898-1998. **Performance spaces.**
Städtische Bühnen's alternative venue, a velodrome. Regensburg. Lang.: Ger. 439

Non-traditional theatrical space. France. UK-England. Lang.: Dan. 443

1898-1998. **Plays/librettos/scripts.**
The significance of Bertolt Brecht to theatre in the late twentieth century. USA. Lang.: Eng. 3142

Reevaluation of the legacy of Bertolt Brecht. Lang.: Swe. 3149

Brecht, copyright, and contemporary perceptions. Berlin. Lang.: Ger. 3153

1899-1933. **Performance/production.**
Hauptmann's *Fuhrmann Henschel (Drayman Henschel)* and realism. Lang.: Eng. 1970

1900-1998. **Performance/production.**
The performance of sacrifice on stage. France. Lang.: Ger. 530

1900-1998. **Research/historiography.**
The use of the term 'theatricality' in German theatre research. Lang.: Ger. 820

1901-1981. **Performance/production.**
F.W. Beidler's ideas for a different Bayreuth Festival. Bayreuth. Lang.: Ger. 4602

1904-1972. **Performance/production.**
Returned emigrant dancer George Groke. Poland. Lang.: Ger. 925

1905-1998. **Administration.**
Comparative analysis of national cultural policies. Canada. France. Norway. Lang.: Eng. 4

1905-1998. **Performance/production.**
The career of actor Bernhard Minetti. Lang.: Ger. 1949

Tribute to the late actor Bernhard Minetti. Lang.: Ger. 1992

Actor Bernhard Minetti. Lang.: Ger. 2015

1906. **Plays/librettos/scripts.**
Excerpt of Frank Wedekind's preface to *Die Büchse der Pandora (Pandora's Box)*. Lang.: Fre. 3169

1907-1976. **Design/technology.**
Scenographer Tadeusz Orlowicz. Cracow. Neubrandenburg. London. Lang.: Pol. 212

1907-1997. **Performance/production.**
Lotte Goslar's Pantomime Circus. Dresden. Los Angeles, CA. Lang.: Eng. 4123

Comic dance performer Lotte Goslar. USA. Lang.: Eng. 4124

1908-1923. **Performance/production.**
Composer Franz Schreker and his connection with Zemlinsky's *Der Zwerg*. Lang.: Fre. 4094

1908-1998. **Institutions.**
The ninetieth anniversary of Staatstheater Cottbus. Cottbus. Lang.: Ger. 1645

1908-1998. **Performance spaces.**
The ninetieth anniversary of the Cottbus theatre building. Cottbus. Lang.: Ger. 440

1910-1914. **Institutions.**
Display of objects related to guest performances of the Ballets Russes. Berlin. Lang.: Hun. 1040

1910-1948. **Plays/librettos/scripts.**
The relationship between writers Hans Franck and Gerhart Hauptmann. Lang.: Ger. 3127

1911-1998. **Performance/production.**
Interview with dancer, choreographer, and teacher Lilian Karina. Lang.: Ger. 1289

1912-1945. **Plays/librettos/scripts.**
Comparison of characters in plays of Georg Kaiser and Tennessee Williams. USA. Lang.: Eng. 3588

1913-1923. **Plays/librettos/scripts.**
Language and silence in German Expressionist drama. Lang.: Eng. 3159

1914-1940. **Plays/librettos/scripts.**
Mythological figures in late plays of Georg Kaiser. Lang.: Ger. 3143

1915-1998. **Performance/production.**
The choreography of William Forsythe and the painting of Marcel Duchamp. France. Lang.: Eng. 1280

1916-1921. **Performance/production.**
The nature of acting in German Expressionist production. Lang.: Eng. 536

1917. **Basic theatrical documents.**
Max Meyerfeld's libretto for Zemlinsky's opera *Eine florentinische Tragödie*. Lang.: Ger, Fre. 4419

Germany — cont'd

1917. Performance/production.
A letter from composer Alexander Zemlinsky to Alma Mahler. Lang.: Fre. 4613
1917-1998. Plays/librettos/scripts.
Strauss's *Die Frau ohne Schatten* and a recent production by Giuseppe Sinopoli. Lang.: Swe. 4795
1918-1922. Plays/librettos/scripts.
Aesthetic peculiarities of *Baal* by Bertolt Brecht. Lang.: Hun. 3146
1919-1932. Plays/librettos/scripts.
Bertolt Brecht and German cinema. Lang.: Ita. 3972
1919-1954. Basic theatrical documents.
Catalan translations of plays by Bertolt Brecht (volume 1). Lang.: Cat. 1437
1920-1939. Plays/librettos/scripts.
Analysis of revisions of plays by Ernst Toller. Lang.: Eng. 3172
1920-1949. Performance/production.
The Russian-German theatrical relationship. Russia. Lang.: Rus. 2285
1920-1980. Plays/librettos/scripts.
Homosexuality on the German stage. Lang.: Eng. 3147
1920-1998. Performance/production.
Brecht and the vocal role. Lang.: Swe. 4295
1921. Performance/production.
Arnold Schoenberg on composer Alexander Zemlinsky. Lang.: Fre. 4604
1922. Audience.
Audience response to Bronnen's *Der Vatermord (Parricide)* and German culture. Frankfurt. Lang.: Eng. 1403
1922. Basic theatrical documents.
Klaren's librettos for *Der Zwerg* by Alexander Zemlinsky. Lang.: Fre, Ger. 4420
1922. Plays/librettos/scripts.
Analysis of Alexander Zemlinsky's *Der Zwerg*. Lang.: Fre. 4793
1922-1956. Performance/production.
Deconstructionist analysis of acting in the theatre of Bertolt Brecht. Lang.: Eng. 2007
1923-1926. Plays/librettos/scripts.
Brecht and the city as an expressionistic setting. USA. Lang.: Eng. 3168
1923-1995. Plays/librettos/scripts.
Biography of composer Richard Wagner. Lang.: Ita. 4799
1924-1986. Performance/production.
Pirandello on the German-language stage. Austria. Lang.: Ita. 1994
1925. Performance/production.
Mary Wigman's summary of her work in choreography and dance training. Dresden. Lang.: Ger. 1290
1926. Plays/librettos/scripts.
Analysis of *Mann ist Mann (A Man's a Man)* by Bertolt Brecht. Lang.: Swe. 3165
1926-1998. Relation to other fields.
Bertolt Brecht's working methods as described in recent books. Lang.: Ger. 3769
1928. Performance/production.
Erwin Piscator and Brecht's *Schwejk im zweiten Weltkrieg (Schweik in the Second World War)*. Berlin. Lang.: Ger. 1952
1928-1966. Performance/production.
Excerpts from critical reviews of singer and actress Lotte Lenya. Lang.: Eng. 4354
1928-1981. Performance/production.
Friends and colleagues recall singer Lotte Lenya. Lang.: Eng. 4355
1928-1998. Performance/production.
Composers and the work of Bertolt Brecht. Lang.: Ger. 4297
1928-1998. Relation to other fields.
The rise and fall of German political theatre. Lang.: Ger. 745
1929-1965. Performance/production.
Lotte Lenya's singing style. Lang.: Eng. 4357
1929-1997. Design/technology.
Costume designer Margit Bárdy. Hungary. Munich. Lang.: Hun. 193
1929-1998. Plays/librettos/scripts.
Musicological perspective on *Die Massnahme (The Measures Taken)* by Brecht and Eisler. Berlin. Lang.: Ger. 3125
1930-1932. Performance/production.
Gender and politics in German dance. Lang.: Eng. 928
1930-1997. Plays/librettos/scripts.
The meanings of the cigar in the appearance and works of Heiner Müller and Bertolt Brecht. Lang.: Swe. 3134
1931-1998. Performance/production.
Production history of *Die Bürgschaft* by Kurt Weill and Casper Neher. Berlin. Bielefeld. Lang.: Eng. 4588
1933-1944. Plays/librettos/scripts.
Actor and playwright Curt Goetz and Nazi attitudes toward theatre. Lang.: Eng. 3139
1933-1998. Plays/librettos/scripts.
The search for a lost translation of *The Seven Deadly Sins* by Brecht and Weill. UK-England. Lang.: Eng. 4392
1934-1998. Plays/librettos/scripts.
The relevance of Bertolt Brecht in reunified Germany. Lang.: Ger. 3135
1935. Performance/production.
Mei Lanfang's influence on Bertolt Brecht. China. Lang.: Eng. 1951
1936-1998. Performance/production.
Interview with choreographer Renate Schottelius. Lang.: Ger. 934

Dancer, choreographer, and teacher Hellmut Gottschild. USA. Lang.: Ger. 1287
1938. Plays/librettos/scripts.
Analysis of *Die Ausnahme und die Regel (The Exception and the Rule)* by Bertolt Brecht. Lang.: Swe. 3133
1938-1945. Performance/production.
Ritual performance and the Third Reich. Lang.: Eng. 4216
1942. Performance/production.
Analysis of Richard Strauss's *Capriccio*. Lang.: Eng. 4606
1942-1998. Performance/production.
Analysis of Richard Strauss's opera *Capriccio*. Lang.: Eng. 4578
1944-1998. Performance/production.
Actress Ilse Ritter. Lang.: Ger. 1980
1945-1949. Relation to other fields.
The effects of postwar monetary reform on theatres in East and West Germany. Lang.: Ger. 739
1945-1998. Performance/production.
Interview with director Matthias Langhoff. Berlin. Lang.: Ger. 1987

Puppeteer Felix Mirbt. Canada. Berlin. Lang.: Eng. 4887
1947-1956. Performance/production.
Bertolt Brecht's production of his *Mutter Courage (Mother Courage)*. Berlin. Lang.: Ger. 1975
1947-1998. Performance/production.
Interview with director Benno Besson. Berlin. Lang.: Ger. 1981
1947-1998. Plays/librettos/scripts.
On translating into German the plays of Valère Novarina. France. Lang.: Ger. 3122
1949-1998. Performance/production.
Choreographer William Forsythe, director of Ballett Frankfurt. Frankfurt. Lang.: Eng. 1084
1950-1980. Plays/librettos/scripts.
Analysis of historical drama of the holocaust. USA. Canada. Lang.: Eng. 3610
1950-1998. Institutions.
History of Carrousel Theater, formerly Theater der Freundschaft. Berlin. Lang.: Ger. 1628
1950-1998. Performance/production.
Opera in German culture. Lang.: Rus. 4599
1953. Design/technology.
Scenographer and now director Klaus Noack. Lang.: Ger. 190
1959-1998. Performance/production.
Interview with actor Ekkehard Schall. Berlin. Lang.: Ger. 1990

Opera director Inge Levant. Stuttgart. Lang.: Ger. 4611
1959-1998. Research/historiography.
Gender difference and theatricality. France. USA. Lang.: Ger. 821
1960-1968. Plays/librettos/scripts.
The fool character in works of Handke, Fellini, and Singer. USA. Italy. Lang.: Eng. 3667
1960-1984. Performance/production.
The career of director Claus Peymann. Lang.: Eng. 2014
1960-1998. Performance/production.
The problem of staging operettas on the contemporary stage. Sweden. Austria. Lang.: Swe. 4857
1962-1998. Performance/production.
Interview with actor Klaus Piontek. Berlin. Lang.: Ger. 2008
1964-1985. Performance/production.
Reexamination of the performance art of Beuys, Abramovič, and Ulay. USA. Netherlands. Lang.: Eng. 4254

Germany — cont'd

1964-1998. **Plays/librettos/scripts.**
Interview with playwright Dea Loher. Lang.: Ger. 3173
1965-1997. **Performance/production.**
Television adaptations of works by Goethe. Lang.: Eng. 4061
1966-1998. **Performance/production.**
Dancer/choreographer Ralf Jaroschinski. Hannover. Lang.: Ger. 1288
1966-1998. **Plays/librettos/scripts.**
Children's theatre at GRIPS. Berlin. Lang.: Ger. 3152
1968-1998. **Institutions.**
Gunnar Martin Aronsson of TeaterX2 recalls Action-Theater. Stockholm. Munich. Lang.: Swe. 1722
1968-1998. **Plays/librettos/scripts.**
Comedy in the plays and musicals of Volker Ludwig. Berlin. Lang.: Ger. 4391
1969-1990. **Performance/production.**
A dancer's experience of and investigations into ecstasy. USA. Lang.: Eng. 673
1970-1996. **Performance/production.**
Director Ruth Berghaus. Lang.: Ger. 4596
1970-1998. **Performance/production.**
Dancer and choreographer Brygida Ochaim. France. Lang.: Ger. 1283
Director Armin Petras. Nordhausen. Lang.: Ger. 2001
Interview with director Robert Wilson. Berlin. Lang.: Swe. 4609
1972-1998. **Institutions.**
Director training at Ernst-Busch-Schule and some of its graduates. Berlin. Lang.: Ger. 1648
1972-1998. **Plays/librettos/scripts.**
Analysis of plays by Marius von Mayenburg. Lang.: Ger. 3131
1973-1997. **Performance/production.**
Dancer/choreographer Pina Bausch. Wuppertal. Lang.: Eng. 932
1973-1998. **Performance/production.**
Choreographer William Forsythe. Frankfurt. Lang.: Eng. 1081
Interview with dancer and choreographer Pina Bausch. Wuppertal. Lang.: Ger. 1279
Portrait of choreographer/director Pina Bausch. Wuppertal. Lang.: Ger. 1281
1975-1998. **Performance/production.**
Interview with director Heiner Bruns of Städtische Bühnen Bielefeld. Bielefeld. Lang.: Ger. 4598
1976-1987. **Performance/production.**
Performance artist Egon Schrick. Lang.: Eng. 4241
1976-1998. **Plays/librettos/scripts.**
Fassbinder's *Der Müll, die Stadt und der Tod (Garbage, the City and Death)*. Berlin. Lang.: Ger. 3175
1977-1992. **Relation to other fields.**
Revivals of Hanns Johst's national socialist play *Schlageter*. Uelzen. Wuppertal. Lang.: Ger. 3770
1977-1998. **Institutions.**
Profile of Pina Bausch and her Tanztheater. Wuppertal. Lang.: Eng. 893
1978-1998. **Performance spaces.**
Profile of the theatrical venue Mousonturm. Franfurt. Lang.: Ger. 441
1979-1997. **Performance/production.**
Interview with opera director Christine Mielitz. Berlin. Lang.: Eng. 4605
1979-1998. **Design/technology.**
Scenographer Martin Zehetgruber. Graz. Stuttgart. Lang.: Ger. 168
1980-1998. **Performance/production.**
Report from a symposium on traditional Korean theatre. Korea. Berlin. Lang.: Ger, Fre, Dut, Eng. 2196
1981-1998. **Performance/production.**
Singer Thomas Lander. Austria. Sweden. Lang.: Swe. 4591
1982-1998. **Institutions.**
The 'diskurs' festival of the 'Gressener school'. Giessen. Lang.: Ger. 4111
1982-1998. **Performance/production.**
A personal response to Pina Bausch's dance theatre. Wuppertal. Lang.: Eng. 1277
1983. **Plays/librettos/scripts.**
Analysis of *Jubiläum* by George Tabori. Lang.: Eng. 3137
1984-1992. **Performance/production.**
Alexander Stillmark's production of *Bruder Eichmann (Brother Eichmann)* by Heinar Kipphardt. Berlin. Lang.: Eng. 2022
1984-1998. **Institutions.**
Amanda Miller and her ballet company Pretty Ugly. Freiburg. Lang.: Ger. 1039
1984-1998. **Performance/production.**
Forced Entertainment and Berlin's Live Art Festival. UK-England. Sheffield. Berlin. Lang.: Ger. 539
William Forsythe of Ballett Frankfurt. Frankfurt. Lang.: Ger. 1284
Director Angela Brodauf. Dortmund. Lang.: Ger. 1989
1985-1997. **Performance/production.**
Matthias Matschke, *Theater Heute*'s young actor of the year. Berlin. Lang.: Ger. 1963
The Cologne theatre scene. Cologne. Lang.: Ger. 1964
1985-1998. **Institutions.**
The curriculum at Bayerische Theaterakademie. Munich. Lang.: Ger. 1659
1985-1998. **Performance/production.**
Actor Oliver Bässler. Cottbus. Lang.: Ger. 1995
1985-1998. **Relation to other fields.**
Use of theatre in Holocaust education. Essen. Lang.: Ger. 3767
1986-1998. **Administration.**
Various conditions affecting production, pricing, marketing and communication in German theatre. Lang.: Ger. 4316
1986-1998. **Institutions.**
Interview with singer Carla Henius, manager of musik-theater-werkstatt festival. Wiesbaden. Lang.: Ger. 4347
1986-1998. **Performance/production.**
Opera director Herbert Wernicke. Lang.: Ger. 4600
1987. **Performance/production.**
The police and John Cage's *Europeras 1 and 2* at Frankfurter Theater. Frankfurt. Lang.: Eng. 4586
1988-1998. **Institutions.**
Holocaust education and Thalia Treffpunkt. Hamburg. Lang.: Ger. 1630
Director training at Universität und Musikhochschule. Hamburg. Lang.: Ger. 1658
Music theatre studies at the Hochschule für Musik und Theater. Hamburg. Lang.: Ger. 4459
1988-1998. **Performance/production.**
Interview with singer Krister St. Hill. Sweden. Lang.: Swe. 4590
1989-1998. **Administration.**
The system of subsidized theatre in Germany, and suggestions for changing it. Lang.: Ger. 13
1989-1998. **Plays/librettos/scripts.**
The diminishing importance of Bertolt Brecht in reunified Germany. Lang.: Ger. 3170
1989-1998. **Relation to other fields.**
Political-cultural influences on Berlin theatre. Berlin. Lang.: Ger. 742
Current attitudes toward socialism, individualism, and metaphysics in German culture, including theatre. Berlin. Lang.: Ger. 3766
1990-1998. **Administration.**
Dramaturg Hans-Peter Frings on his role in the theatre. Magdeburg. Lang.: Ger. 1382
1990-1998. **Performance/production.**
Actress Stephanie Eidt. Lang.: Ger. 1982
1990-1998. **Plays/librettos/scripts.**
The collaboration of playwright Dea Loher and director Andreas Kriegenburg. Hannover. Munich. Lang.: Ger. 3151
1990-2001. **Performance/production.**
Composer Matthias Pintscher and his opera *Thomas Chatterton*. Lang.: Ger. 4607
1991-1998. **Design/technology.**
Set and costume designer Frank Leimbach and his work with choreographers. Lang.: Ger. 1247
1991-1998. **Institutions.**
The fate of the Berliner Ensemble after the resignation of artistic director Manfred Wekwerth. Berlin. Lang.: Ger. 1625
1991-1998. **Performance/production.**
Natali Seelig, *Theater Heute*'s actress of the year. Munich. Lang.: Ger. 1966
Actress Maike Bollow. Hannover. Lang.: Ger. 2006
Opera director Christine Mielitz. Meiningen. Lang.: Ger. 4597
Director Anja Sündermann on her production of *Rigoletto*. Hamburg. Lang.: Ger. 4608

Germany — cont'd

1991-1998. Plays/librettos/scripts.
Marginal notes by Dea Loher on her plays. Lang.: Ger. 3162
1991-1998. Relation to other fields.
Government and budget cuts in German theatres. Bochum. Cologne. Lang.: Ger. 738
1992. Theory/criticism.
A theory of authenticity in the theatre. Lang.: Hun. 841
1992-1997. Institutions.
Margarethe Biereye and David Johnston of the touring company Ton und Kirschen. Glindow. Lang.: Eng. 1624
1992-1997. Performance/production.
The collaboration of choreographer Lucinda Childs and director Robert Wilson on *La Maladie de la Mort.* Lang.: Eng. 2019
1992-1998. Administration.
Current conditions at Staatstheater Cottbus. Cottbus. Lang.: Ger. 9
1992-1998. Institutions.
New plays by Dea Loher at Staatsschauspiel Hannover. Hannover. Lang.: Ger. 1643

Problems of management and repertory at Berliner Ensemble. Berlin. Lang.: Ger. 1656
1992-1998. Performance/production.
A guest performance by Stomp. Munich. Lang.: Hun. 926

Actor Herbert Fritsch. Lang.: Ger. 1985

Interview with director Andreas Kriegenburg. Lang.: Ger. 2010
1992-1998. Plays/librettos/scripts.
Playwright Volker Lüdecke. Kaiserslautern. Lang.: Ger. 3141
1993-1998. Administration.
Cooperation of theatres and tourist organizations. Lang.: Ger. 10

Bayerische Staatsoper's new marketing concept. Munich. Lang.: Ger. 4405
1993-1998. Audience.
The interpretation of audience research data to yield marketing strategies. Berlin. Lang.: Ger. 153
1993-1998. Institutions.
Interview with director and dramaturg of Staatstheater Stuttgart. Stuttgart. Lang.: Ger. 1632

Profile of the children's theatre Schauburg, George Podt, artistic director. Munich. Lang.: Ger. 1640

Profile of Theater in der Fabrik. Dresden. Lang.: Ger. 1644

Profile of new venue, Bayerisches Staatsschauspiel, Marstall. Munich. Lang.: Ger. 1660

Badische Landesbühne and the problem of declining audiences. Bruchsal. Lang.: Ger. 1662

Experimental performances of Helena Waldmann and Showcase Beat le Mot. Franfurt. Lang.: Ger. 4234
1993-1998. Performance/production.
Actress Christine Hoppe. Dresden. Lang.: Ger. 1973

Director and actor Christoph Schlingensief. Lang.: Ger. 1988
1993-1998. Plays/librettos/scripts.
Playwright Hans Zimmer. Hannover. Lang.: Ger. 3136
1993-1998. Theory/criticism.
The music-theatre concept of Christoph Marthaler. Berlin. Lang.: Ger. 4310
1993-2000. Administration.
Interview with Frank Baumbauer of Deutsches Schauspielhaus Hamburg. Hamburg. Lang.: Ger. 11
1994-1998. Administration.
Theatrical marketing in North Rhine-Westphalia. Lang.: Ger. 6
1994-1998. Performance/production.
Avant-garde dancer Anna Huber. Berlin. Lang.: Ger. 1286
1995. Plays/librettos/scripts.
Daniel Barenboim and Edward Said on composer Richard Wagner. New York, NY. Lang.: Eng. 4826
1995. Theory/criticism.
Hungarian translation of Volker Klotz on theatre aesthetics. Lang.: Hun. 842
1995-1997. Performance/production.
Director Christina Emig-Könning. Rostock. Lang.: Ger. 2000
1995-1998. Design/technology.
The work of costume designer Robert Ebeling. Lang.: Ger. 185
1995-1998. Institutions.
Experiential memory work and acting at Theater Jugend Club. Nordhausen. Lang.: Ger. 1629
1995-1998. Performance/production.
Comparison of productions of Brecht's *Die Massnahme (The Measures Taken).* Berlin. Wuppertal. Lang.: Ger. 1950
1995-1998. Plays/librettos/scripts.
The language of Dea Loher's *Tätowierung (Tattoo).* Lang.: Ger. 3126
1996-1997. Institutions.
Profile of Landestheater Württemberg-Hohenzollern. Tübingen. Lang.: Ger. 1634

Profile of Württembergische Landesbühne. Esslingen. Lang.: Ger. 1639
1996-1997. Performance/production.
Dance adaptations of Shakespeare's *Hamlet.* Bremen. Weimar. Lang.: Ger. 930

Shakespeare performance on the Rhine and the Ruhr. Cologne. Bochum. Düsseldorf. Lang.: Ger. 1962

The performance of Shakespeare in the former East Germany. Rostock. Leipzig. Berlin. Dessau. Lang.: Ger. 1974

Comparison of two productions of Shakespeare's *Richard III.* Munich. Lang.: Ger. 1976

Shakespearean productions in northern Germany. Hamburg. Lang.: Ger. 1978
1996-1998. Administration.
Interview with Thomas Ostermeier, artistic director of Schaubühne. Berlin. Lang.: Ger. 1386

Marketing practices of Deutsche Oper am Rhein. Duisburg. Lang.: Ger. 4404
1996-1998. Institutions.
Profile of Junges Theater. Göttingen. Lang.: Ger. 1636

Profile of Deutsches Theater, Baracke. Berlin. Lang.: Ger. 1637

Schauspiel Leipzig under the direction of Wolfgang Engel. Leipzig. Lang.: Ger. 1638

Children's opera company Yakult Halle. Cologne. Lang.: Ger. 4455

Günter Krämer and children's opera. Cologne. Lang.: Ger. 4458
1996-1998. Performance/production.
Director Thomas Ostermeier. Berlin. Lang.: Swe. 1998

Opera director Katja Czellnik. Oldenburg. Kiel. Lang.: Ger. 4583

The work of opera director Barbara Beyer. Nuremberg. Lang.: Ger. 4589
1996-1998. Plays/librettos/scripts.
Interview with director Thomas Ostermeier. Berlin. Lang.: Ger. 3124
1996-1998. Relation to other fields.
Changes in media and press coverage. Hamburg. Lang.: Ger. 743
1996-1998. Training.
Dance training at Folkwang Hochschule. Essen. Lang.: Hun. 1341
1997. Design/technology.
Max Keller, lighting designer of Münchner Kammerspiele. Munich. Lang.: Ger. 188

Lighting for Henze's opera *Der Prinz von Homburg* at Deutsche Oper Berlin. Berlin. Lang.: Ger. 4431
1997. Institutions.
Report on the Spielart '97 experimental theatre festival. Munich. Lang.: Eng. 1618

Italian experimental theatre at Spielart '97. Munich. Italy. Lang.: Eng. 1619

Survey of Munich's theatre scene. Munich. Lang.: Ger. 1626

The future of Schaubühne after the resignation of artistic director Andrea Breth. Berlin. Lang.: Ger. 1633

Report on festival of physical theatre. Munich. Lang.: Eng. 1664
1997. Performance spaces.
The construction of a theatre for *Beauty and the Beast.* Stuttgart. Lang.: Ger. 444
1997. Performance/production.
Analysis of *Nur du (Only You)* by choreographer Pina Bausch. Wuppertal. Lang.: Eng. 1278

Kortner-award winners Anna Viebrock and Christoph Marthaler. Berlin. Lang.: Ger. 1968

Recent German productions of plays by Bertolt Brecht. Hamburg. Berlin. Lang.: Swe. 1977

Germany — cont'd

A production of Schiller's *Die Räuber (The Robbers)* performed by prisoners. Berlin. Lang.: Ger. 2025

Playwright Theresia Walser on children's reactions to Christmas plays. Switzerland. Lang.: Ger. 2027

Sequentia's new recording of *Ordo Virtutum* by Hildegard of Bingen. Lang.: Eng. 4294

1997-1998. Administration.

Wolfgang Gropper, director of Staatstheater Braunschweig. Braunschweig. Lang.: Ger. 8

Ernö Weil, manager of Theater Pforzheim. Pforzheim. Lang.: Ger. 1380

Rüdiger Bloch, manager of West Pomeranian theatres. Greifswald. Straslund. Lang.: Ger. 1384

Stefan Soltesz's administration at Aalto-Musiktheater. Essen. Lang.: Ger. 4286

1997-1998. Design/technology.

Reconstruction of a performance of *A Midsummer Night's Dream* designed by Galli-Bibiena. Bayreuth. Lang.: Ger. 1521

1997-1998. Institutions.

Appealing to the youth audience at Theater Dresden. Dresden. Lang.: Ger. 1631

Interview with Pavel Fieber, manager of Badisches Staatstheater Karlsruhe. Karlsruhe. Lang.: Ger. 1649

Profiles of theatres in Saxony. Zittau. Bautzen. Görlitz. Lang.: Ger. 1650

Profile of Nordhessisches Landestheater Marburg. Marburg. Lang.: Ger. 1653

The aesthetic perspectives of the ensemble at Münchner Kammerspiele. Munich. Lang.: Ger. 1666

Review of Wagner's *Ring* cycle at the Bayreuth Festival. Bayreuth. Lang.: Hun. 4454

1997-1998. Performance/production.

Survey of Berlin productions in the holiday season. Berlin. Lang.: Eng. 538

Daniel Karasek, drama director at Hessisches Staatstheater. Wiesbaden. Lang.: Ger. 1955

Profile of Thomas Ostermeier, *Theater Heute*'s young director of the year. Berlin. Lang.: Ger. 1959

Productions directed by Christian Stückl, Tom Kühnel, and Robert Schuster. Frankfurt. Lang.: Ger. 1969

Productions of Tankred Dorst's *Was sollen wir tun (What Shall We Do)*. Dresden. Bonn. Lang.: Ger. 1971

Director Thomas Ostermeier. Lang.: Dan. 1979

Adaptations and performances of *Alte Meister (Old Masters)* by Thomas Bernhard. Lang.: Ger. 1996

Recent productions of Schauspiel Leipzig. Leipzig. Lang.: Ger. 2011

Recent productions of plays by Bertolt Brecht. Lang.: Ger. 2028

Roberto Paternostro, new music director at Staatstheater Kassel. Kassel. Lang.: Ger. 4296

Frank Castorf's production of Strauss's *Die Fledermaus*. Hamburg. Lang.: Ger. 4612

Reviews of recent opera productions. Basel. Stuttgart. Berlin. Hamburg. Strasbourg. Lang.: Ger. 4702

1997-1998. Plays/librettos/scripts.

Family conflict in *Was sollen wir tun (What Shall We Do)* by Tankred Dorst and *Die Hamletmaschine (Hamletmachine)* by Heiner Müller. Lang.: Ger. 3148

Analysis of *Café Mitte (Café Center)* by Volker Ludwig. Berlin. Lang.: Ger. 4393

1997-1998. Relation to other fields.

The artist and the world in recent productions. Vienna. Lang.: Ger. 3729

Shelly Hirsch on her performance piece *For Jerry—Part I*. USA. Lang.: Ger, Fre, Dut, Eng. 4266

1997-1999. Relation to other fields.

Political and cultural situation of Frankfurt theatres. Frankfurt. Lang.: Ger. 744

1998. Administration.

Marketing, advertising, and sponsorship of German theatre. Lang.: Ger. 7

Audience questionnaire for use in theatrical marketing. Lang.: Ger. 12

The effects of independent theatre in Berlin. Berlin. Lang.: Ger. 14

Interview with Ivan Liška, new director of Bayerische Staatsballett. Munich. Lang.: Hun. 1026

Interview with Tankred Dorst and Hannah Hurtzig of the Bonner Biennale festival. Bonn. Lang.: Ger. 1379

Interviews with theatre managers regarding the changing cultural landscape. Bruchsal. Esslingen. Tübingen. Lang.: Ger. 1381

Dramaturg Dirk Olaf Hanke on the dramaturg's complex role. Konstanz. Lang.: Ger. 1383

Interviews with German theatre and film directors. Lang.: Ger. 1385

Theatre directors on the future of subsidized theatre. Zurich. Hannover. Berlin. Lang.: Ger. 1390

1998. Audience.

The importance of independent theatre for children. Hannover. Lang.: Ger. 151

The relationship between theatres and the youth audience. Lang.: Ger. 152

Children's theatre and cultural exchange. Flensburg. Lang.: Ger. 1401

Opera and the young audience. Lang.: Ger. 4410

1998. Design/technology.

Presentation of stage equipment by manufacturers. Lang.: Ger. 184

Survey of Light Fair. Hannover. Lang.: Eng. 186

Careers in technical theatre. Austria. Lang.: Ger. 189

Scenic elements in *Titanic* by street theatre group Theater Titanick. Münster. Leipzig. Perth. Lang.: Eng. 191

Lighting in contemporary theatre. Lang.: Ger. 192

An exhibition of sets by Caspar Neher for the plays of Bertolt Brecht. Berlin. Lang.: Eng. 1522

Geogre Tabori's production of Mozart's *Die Zauberflöte* in a circus ring. Berlin. Lang.: Ger. 4428

Herbert Wernicke's set and costume designs for his own production of Strauss's *Elektra*. Munich. Lang.: Eng. 4429

Robert Wilson and Vera Dobroschke's design for Brecht's *Ozeanflug*. Berlin. Lang.: Eng. 4430

1998. Institutions.

Children's theatres GRIPS and Carrousel. Berlin. Lang.: Ger. 347

Profile of Munich's theatre training institutions. Munich. Lang.: Ger. 348

Festivals of theatre by and for youth. Dresden. Stuttgart. Lang.: Ger. 349

Actor and director training at Hochschule für Musik and Darstellende Kunst. Frankfurt/Main. Lang.: Ger. 350

The avant-garde theatre festival Theaterformen. Braunschweig. Hannover. Lang.: Ger. 351

Independent children's theatre workshop. Hannover. Lang.: Ger. 352

Profile of the Theaterformen festival. Braunschweig. Hannover. Lang.: Ger. 353

The proposed merger of Deutsches Nationaltheater Weimar and Theater Erfurt. Weimar. Erfurt. Lang.: Ger. 354

The quality of theatre for children and youth. Bologna. Stockholm. Lang.: Ger. 367

Productions of Staatstheater Stuttgart. Stuttgart. Lang.: Ger. 1620

The current state of Theater Bielefeld. Bielefeld. Lang.: Ger. 1621

Actor training at Hochschule der Künste and Ernst-Busch-Schule. Berlin. Lang.: Ger. 1622

English-language plays at Berlin Festwochen. Berlin. Lang.: Ger. 1623

Report on the fourth Bonner Biennale. Bonn. Lang.: Ger. 1627

Israeli theatre at the Kampnagel summer theatre festival. Hamburg. Lang.: Ger. 1635

Germany — cont'd

Children's theatre festivals in Baden-Württemberg. Stuttgart. Lang.: Ger. 1641
German-Danish children's theatre festival. Denmark. Lang.: Ger. 1642
Report on theatre festival. Frankfurt/Oder. Lang.: Ger. 1646
Contemporary drama at Bonner Biennale. Bonn. Lang.: Ger. 1647
Survey of the Theatertreffen festival. Berlin. Lang.: Swe. 1651
Independent German-language theatre festival Impulse. Lang.: Ger. 1652
New productions of Düsseldorfer Schauspielhaus. Dusseldorf. Lang.: Ger. 1654
Productions of Bochumer Schauspielhaus. Bochum. Lang.: Ger. 1655
The new children's theatre at Schauburg. Munich. Lang.: Ger. 1657
Contemporary drama at Schauspiel Leipzig. Leipzig. Lang.: Ger. 1661
Report on the Bonner Biennale theatre festival. Bonn. Lang.: Ger. 1663
German theatres' responses to threatened closings and mergers. Esslingen. Tübingen. Lang.: Ger. 1665
Interview with Peter Ruzicka of the Münchener Biennale festival. Munich. Lang.: Ger. 4291
Ernst August Klötzke, new manager of musik-theater-werkstatt festival. Wiesbaden. Lang.: Ger. 4348
Effect of Wagner family memoirs on the Bayreuth Festival. Bayreuth. Lang.: Eng. 4451
Comparison of Salzburg and Bayreuth festival seasons. Bayreuth. Salzburg. Lang.: Eng. 4452
Report on Dresden opera festival. Dresden. Lang.: Eng. 4453
The Münchener Biennale theatre festival. Munich. Lang.: Ger. 4456
Survey of the opera festival season. Munich. Lang.: Eng. 4457

1998. Performance/production.

The wide diversity of Jewish choreographers. Munich. Lang.: Ger. 931
Recent dance performances in Berlin. Berlin. Lang.: Ger. 933
Choreographer John Neumeier. Hamburg. New York, NY. Lang.: Eng. 1082
Iván Markó's choreography for Bayreuth Festival productions. Bayreuth. Hungary. Lang.: Hun. 1083
Analysis of Pina Bausch's dance work *Masuca Fogo*. Wuppertal. Lang.: Ger. 1282
Interview with choreographer Sasha Waltz. Berlin. Lang.: Ger. 1285
German directors about the meaning of Brecht today. Lang.: Ger. 1948
Rehearsals of Christoph Marthaler's production of *Arsenic and Old Lace* by Joseph Kesselring. Hamburg. Lang.: Ger. 1953
Peter Zadek's production of Čechov's *Višnëvyj sad (The Cherry Orchard)*. Netherlands. Lang.: Dut. 1954
Christoph Marthaler's approach to directing Joseph Kesselring's *Arsenic and Old Lace*. Hamburg. Lang.: Ger. 1956
Two productions of Brecht's *Der Kaukasische Kreidekreis (The Caucasian Chalk Circle)*. Berlin. Hamburg. Lang.: Ger. 1957
Political changes reflected in Berlin theatre productions. Berlin. Lang.: Ger. 1958
Christoph Schlingensief's project with the homeless at Deutsches Schauspielhaus. Hamburg. Lang.: Ger. 1961
Thomas Langhoff's production of Brecht's *Der Kaukasische Kreidekreis (The Caucasian Chalk Circle)* at Deutsches Theater. Berlin.Lang.: Ger. 1965
Interview with director Jochen Gerz. Berlin. Lang.: Ger, Fre, Dut, Eng. 1967
German productions of adaptations of *A Clockwork Orange* by Anthony Burgess. Dresden. Hamburg. Stendal. Lang.: Ger. 1972
Productions of new plays by Peter Handke and Katharine Gericke at Niedersächsische Staatstheater. Hannover. Lang.: Ger. 1983
German productions of contemporary Russian drama. Lang.: Ger. 1984
Reviews of productions of plays by Brecht. Lang.: Ger. 1986
Productions of the Bad Hersfelder Festspiele. Bad Hersfeld. Lang.: Ger. 1991
Productions of the Kleist theatre festival. Frankfurt/Oder. Lang.: Ger. 1993
Klaus Michael Grüber's production of Goethe's *Iphigenia auf Tauris*. Berlin. Lang.: Swe. 1997
Interview with director Stefan Pucher. Lang.: Ger. 1999
Political context of Frank Castorf's production of *Les Mains Sales (Dirty Hands)* by Sartre. Berlin. Lang.: Ger. 2002
Productions of Horváth's *Geschichten aus dem Wienerwald (Tales from the Vienna Woods)*. Hamburg. Hannover. Vienna. Lang.: Ger. 2003
Interview with director Jürgen Flimm. Lang.: Ger. 2004
Comparison of productions of *The Lisbon Traviata* by Terrence McNally. Berlin. Essen. Lang.: Ger. 2005
Recent productions of Bochumer Schauspielhaus. Bochum. Lang.: Ger. 2009
Swedish directors on recent Berlin productions. Berlin. Lang.: Swe. 2012
Productions of director Peter Wittenberg. Munich. Bonn. Lang.: Ger. 2013
Reviews of German Shakespearean productions. Wuppertal. Cologne. Oberhausen. Lang.: Ger. 2017
Interview with director Bernd Wilms. Berlin. Lang.: Swe. 2018
Andreas Kriegenburg's production of Büchner's *Leonce und Lena*. Munich. Lang.: Ger. 2020
Roberto Ciulli's production of *Doña Rosita la Soltera (Doña Rosita the Spinster)* by Federico García Lorca. Munich. Lang.: Ger. 2021
Impressions from Podewil theatre workshop. Berlin. Lang.: Ger. 2024
The work of director Einar Schleef. Düsseldorf. Lang.: Ger. 2026
Theatre, society, and directors Frank Castorf, Peter Stein, and Einar Schleef. Lang.: Ger. 2029
Premieres of plays on the Nazi theme. Darmstadt. Vienna. Lang.: Ger. 2030
Klaus Michael Grüber's production of Goethe's *Iphigenia auf Tauris*. Berlin. Lang.: Ger. 2031
Productions of plays by Shakespeare, Brecht, and Camus. Lang.: Ger. 2032
German productions of Shakespeare. Leipzig. Hamburg. Berlin. Lang.: Ger. 2033
Recent productions of Deutsches Schauspielhaus. Hamburg. Lang.: Ger. 2034
The popular German TV show *Derrick*. Lang.: Eng. 4060
Music theatre production in northern Germany. Lübeck. Hamburg. Bremen. Kiel. Lang.: Ger. 4293
Robert Wilson's production of Brecht's *Der Ozeanflug*. Berlin. Lang.: Ger. 4356
Sechs-Tage-Oper, festival of independent music theatre. Lang.: Ger. 4579
Productions of Wagner's *Tristan und Isolde* by Peter Konwitschny and Werner Schroeter. Munich. Duisberg. Lang.: Ger. 4580
Interview with opera composer Manfred Trojahn. Munich. Lang.: Ger. 4582
Review of opera productions. Stuttgart. Leipzig. Lang.: Ger. 4584
Interview with opera director Jossi Wieler. Stuttgart. Basel. Lang.: Ger. 4592
Baritone Wolfgang Brendel. Lang.: Eng. 4593
Recordings of *Lieder* by Schumann. UK-England. Lang.: Eng. 4601
Stage fright and other psychological problems of singers and musicians. Berlin. Lang.: Swe. 4603

Germany — cont'd

A production of Offenbach's *Orphée aux Enfers* directed by Jens Mehrle and Stefan Nolte. Bitterfeld. Lang.: Ger. 4856

Profile of the Fidena puppet festival. Bochum. Lang.: Ger. 4894

1998. Plays/librettos/scripts.

German playwrights on the meaning of Brecht today. Lang.: Ger. 3123

The relevance of Bertolt Brecht in his centennial year. Lang.: Eng. 3128

Frank Castorf's production of Sartre's *Les Mains Sales (Dirty Hands)* and the civil war in Yugoslavia. Berlin. Lang.: Ger. 3129

Analysis of plays by Dea Loher, directed by Andreas Kriegenburg. Hannover. Lang.: Ger. 3130

Hasko Weber's production of *Morir (A Moment Before Dying)* by Sergi Belbel. Dresden. Lang.: Ger. 3132

Brecht's working methods as a playwright as documented in annotated editions of his plays. Lang.: Ger. 3144

Plays and performance, playwrights and directors. Hannover. Lang.: Ger. 3145

Recent German productions of Brecht's plays. Lang.: Ger. 3150

Ivan Nagel's speech on awarding the Büchner Prize to playwright Elfriede Jelinek. Lang.: Ger. 3154

Analysis of *Madschun al-Malik* by Michael Roes. Düsseldorf. Lang.: Ger. 3157

Analysis of *Fremdes Haus (Strangers House)* by Dea Loher. Lang.: Ger. 3161

The development of *Blaubart—Hoffnung der Frauen (Bluebeard—Hope of Women)* by Dea Loher. Munich. Lang.: Ger. 3164

Kerstin Specht's *Die Froschkönigin (The Frog Princess)* and its premiere at Staatstheater Stuttgart. Stuttgart. Lang.: Ger. 3174

Mark Ravenhill's *Shopping and Fucking* and its production by Thomas Ostermeier. UK-England. Lang.: Ger. 3476

Analysis of plays by Sarah Kane and David Harrower, recently produced in Germany. UK-England. Cologne. Bonn. Lang.: Ger. 3487

Hero and anti-hero in contemporary opera production. Lang.: Ger. 4791

1998. Relation to other fields.

The tasks of the theatre photographer. Nordhausen. Lang.: Ger. 737

The national movement, cultural policy, and German regional theatre. Eisleben. Lang.: Ger. 740

The debate over whether Germany needs a national cultural minister. Lang.: Ger. 746

Frank Castorf of Volksbühne and the object and possibilities of contemporary theatre. Berlin. Lang.: Ger. 747

The quality of Berlin's independent theatres. Berlin. Lang.: Ger. 748

German politicians interviewed on cultural policy. Lang.: Ger. 749

Tourism and the development of theatre districts. New York, NY. Berlin. Lang.: Eng. 807

The commemoration of Kristallnacht at Volksbühne. Berlin. Lang.: Ger. 3764

Die Berliner Ermittlung (The Berlin Investigation), an interactive theatre project by Jochen Gerz and Esther Shalev-Gerz. Berlin. Lang.: Ger. 3768

1998. Theory/criticism.

Critical response to Klaus Michael Grüber's production of Goethe's *Iphigenia auf Tauris.* Lang.: Ger. 3821

1998. Training.

Director Walter Pfaff on the influence of Jerzy Grotowski. Poland. Lang.: Eng. 876

Germany, East

1945-1990. Performance/production.

Directors Manfred Wekwerth and Robert Weimann on Brecht and Shakespeare. Lang.: Eng. 2043

Socialism and the use of Shakespeare in the German Democratic Republic. Lang.: Eng. 2048

Adaptations of Shakespeare in productions of Bertolt Brecht and Heiner Müller. Lang.: Eng. 2049

National identity and Shakespearean production. Lang.: Eng. 2050

1945-1990. Plays/librettos/scripts.

Brecht and the translation of Shakespeare into German. Lang.: Eng. 3177

1945-1995. Performance/production.

Director Robert Weimann on East German Shakespeare production. Lang.: Eng. 2053

1950-1990. Performance/production.

Shakespeare in the GDR: producer and critic B.K. Tragelehn. Lang.: Eng. 2040

1960-1970. Performance/production.

The political and social climate of East German theatre in the sixties. Lang.: Eng. 2052

1965-1985. Performance/production.

Interview with director Adolf Dresen. Lang.: Eng. 2036

1965-1990. Performance/production.

Interview with playwright Heiner Müller about his adaptations of Shakespeare. Lang.: Eng. 2039

1970-1990. Performance/production.

Interview with director Christoph Schroth. Lang.: Eng. 2035

Interview with director Alexander Lang. Lang.: Eng. 2037

Interview with director Thomas Langhoff. Lang.: Eng. 2038

Interview with director Alexander Weigel. Lang.: Eng. 2042

1975-1995. Performance/production.

Actor/director Katja Paryla. Lang.: Eng. 2046

1976-1980. Performance/production.

Shakespearean production and the GDR's 'existential crisis'. Lang.: Eng. 2051

1977-1995. Performance/production.

Actor/director Ursula Karusseit. Lang.: Eng. 2047

1980-1990. Performance/production.

Interview with director Frank Castorf. Lang.: Eng. 2041

1980-1995. Performance/production.

Interview with actor/director Johanna Schall. Lang.: Eng. 2045

1982-1990. Performance/production.

Gender and Shakespearean production in the GDR. Lang.: Eng. 2044

Germany, West

1952-1984. Performance/production.

Interview with singer Nicolai Gedda. London. Munich. Lang.: Swe. 4859

1966. Performance/production.

The influence of Wieland Wagner's production of *Lohengrin.* Bayreuth. Lang.: Eng. 4614

1970-1980. Plays/librettos/scripts.

Analysis of plays by Franz Xaver Kroetz. Lang.: Eng. 3178

Ghana

1993. Plays/librettos/scripts.

Analysis of Haile Gerima's film *Sankofa.* Lang.: Eng. 3973

Greece

600-411 B.C. Plays/librettos/scripts.

Hermes in the Greek theatre devoted to Dionysus. Lang.: Eng. 3179

438-411 B.C. Plays/librettos/scripts.

The playwright Euripides as a character in *Thesmophoriazusae* of Aristophanes. Lang.: Eng. 3181

Electra and Orestes in plays of Aeschylus, Euripides, and Sophocles. Lang.: Eng. 3184

435 B.C. Basic theatrical documents.

Catalan translation of Aristophanes' *Lysistrata.* Lang.: Cat. 1438

420 B.C. Plays/librettos/scripts.

Analysis of Sophocles' *Oidípous Týrannos (Oedipus the King).* Lang.: Dut. 3180

342-291 B.C. Plays/librettos/scripts.

The subversion of tragic forms in comic plays of Menander. Lang.: Eng. 3183

475-400 B.C. Plays/librettos/scripts.

Civic discourse and civil discord in Greek tragedy. Lang.: Eng. 3185

490-406 B.C. Plays/librettos/scripts.

Myth and technique in Greek tragedy. Lang.: Ita. 3182

1914-1995. Performance/production.

Pirandello on the Greek stage. Lang.: Ita. 2054

1938-1998. Performance spaces.

Michael Marmarinos' production of Sophocles' *Electra* at the Epidauros amphitheatre. Epidauros. Lang.: Ger. 445

Greece — cont'd

1997. **Institutions.**
Report on European theatre festival. Thessaloniki. Lang.: Eng. 1667
1998. **Performance/production.**
The ethnic dances of Crete. Sitia. Lang.: Swe. 1226

Guadeloupe
1960-1990. **Plays/librettos/scripts.**
Postcolonialism, ethnicity, and feminism in French and Caribbean plays. France. Martinique. Lang.: Eng. 3104
1965-1996. **Plays/librettos/scripts.**
Analysis of plays by Maryse Condé. Lang.: Eng. 3186
1975-1998. **Plays/librettos/scripts.**
Celebration and the body in plays of Ina Césaire and Simone Schwarz-Bart. Martinique. Lang.: Eng. 3270

Hong Kong
1984-1996. **Relation to other fields.**
Theatre and politics in Hong Kong. Lang.: Eng. 3772

Hungary
1413-1485. **Performance/production.**
Dance culture and the court of King Mátyás. Lang.: Hun. 943
1667-1848. **Performance/production.**
The ancient city of Pécs and its theatre history. Pécs. Lang.: Hun. 2107
1798-1998. **Institutions.**
Hungarian-language theatre in Transylvania. Romania. Lang.: Hun. 365
1823-1998. **Performance spaces.**
Renovation of the Miskolc National Theatre. Miskolc. Lang.: Hun. 450
1839-1915. **Performance/production.**
Excerpts from the diary of singer and actress Ilka Markovits. Lang.: Hun. 2064
1875-1925. **Performance/production.**
Tenor Béla Környey. Lang.: Hun. 4616
1881-1948. **Performance/production.**
László Márkus, one-time director of the Budapest Opera House. Lang.: Hun. 540
1884-1961. **Performance/production.**
Soprano Olga Haselbeck. Lang.: Hun. 4626
1892-1946. **Institutions.**
History of the Óbudai Kisfaludy Színház. Budapest. Lang.: Hun. 356
1898-1931. **Performance/production.**
An exhibition devoted to dance and silent film star Lya de Putti. Germany. Lang.: Hun. 944
1898-1967. **Performance/production.**
Soprano Mária Németh. Vienna. Lang.: Hun. 4615
1903-1977. **Performance/production.**
Profile of soprano Piroska Anday. Budapest. Vienna. Lang.: Hun. 4627
1904-1965. **Performance/production.**
Profile of tenor István Laczó. Lang.: Hun. 4625
1907-1992. **Performance/production.**
Recalling the composer György Ránki. Lang.: Hun. 4617
1908-1997. **Performance/production.**
Tribute to the late soprano Júlia Orosz. Lang.: Hun. 4623
1908-1998. **Design/technology.**
Profile of costume designer Tivadar Márk. Lang.: Hun. 4432
1908-1998. **Performance/production.**
Choreographer Gyula Harangozó and the Hungarian National Ballet. Lang.: Hun. 1104
1911-1998. **Performance/production.**
Dancer and eurythmics teacher Klára Hajós. Lang.: Hun. 936
1913-1996. **Performance spaces.**
Theatrical history of the building that houses Thália Színház. Budapest. Lang.: Hun. 447
1919-1992. **Institutions.**
History of Hungarian-language theatre in Transylvania. Romania. Lang.: Hun, Rom. 1693
1919-1998. **Performance/production.**
Obituary for actor Miklós Gábor. Lang.: Hun. 2093
Director József Ruszt recalls actor Miklós Gábor. Lang.: Hun. 2120
1920-1977. **Performance/production.**
Profile of baritone György Radnai. Lang.: Hun. 4624
1923-1998. **Performance/production.**
Baritone György Melis and the performance in celebration of his 75th birthday. Lang.: Hun. 4633
Album on the life and career of baritone György Melis. Lang.: Hun, Eng. 4639
1924-1998. **Performance/production.**
Interview with bass Albert Antalffy. Mödling. Lang.: Hun. 4634
1925-1985. **Performance/production.**
Director György Harag. Romania. Lang.: Hun. 2229
1926-1998. **Performance/production.**
Obituary for baritone Zsolt Bende. Lang.: Hun. 4628
1929-1997. **Design/technology.**
Costume designer Margit Bárdy. Munich. Lang.: Hun. 193
1929-1998. **Performance/production.**
Interview with tenor Sándor Palcsó. Lang.: Hun. 4620
1930-1998. **Performance/production.**
Folk dance program in honor of choreographer István Molnár. Budapest. Lang.: Hun. 1229
1931-1998. **Performance/production.**
Interview with bass György Tréfás. Debrecen. Lang.: Hun. 4641
1942-1998. **Performance/production.**
Obituary for director István Paál. Szolnok. Lang.: Hun. 2143
1945-1983. **Performance/production.**
Actress Mária Mezei. Lang.: Hun. 2140
1947-1998. **Performance/production.**
Interview with bass László Polgár. Zurich. Lang.: Hun. 4640
1948-1998. **Institutions.**
History of the folk dance ensemble Erkel Néptáncegyüttes. Lang.: Hun. 1220
1948-1998. **Performance/production.**
Reviews and photos from the career of the late actor Miklós Gábor. Lang.: Hun. 2055
Interview with opera singer Judit Sándor on her male roles. Lang.: Hun. 4637
Production of László Lajtha's comic opera *Le chapeau bleu.* Cluj-Napoca. Lang.: Hun. 4668
1949-1998. **Performance/production.**
Choreographer László Seregi. Budapest. Lang.: Hun. 1100
1950-1998. **Performance/production.**
Interview with dancer Vera Szumrák. Lang.: Hun. 1114
1951-1998. **Performance/production.**
Tribute to the late actress and director Erzsébet Gaál. Lang.: Hun. 2141
Profile of actor-director Erzsébet Gaál. Lang.: Hun. 2147
1954-1998. **Performance/production.**
Interview with ballerina Adél Orosz. Lang.: Hun. 1112
1954-1998. **Training.**
Interview with ballet dancer and teacher Jacqueline Menyhárt. Lang.: Hun. 1206
1957-1991. **Design/technology.**
Set and costume designs of Péter Makai. Lang.: Hun. 194
1958-1998. **Performance/production.**
Profile of soprano Veronika Fekete. Lang.: Hun. 4632
1959-1998. **Training.**
Interview with ballet master Tamás Koren. Lang.: Hun. 1207
1960-1990. **Institutions.**
The importance of theatre workshops. Lang.: Hun. 360
1960-1990. **Performance/production.**
The importance of workshops in dance. Budapest. Lang.: Hun. 951
Interview with director Tamás Ascher on director training. Lang.: Hun. 2146
1960-1998. **Administration.**
Interview with director Péter Léner of József Attila Theatre. Budapest. Lang.: Hun. 15
1960-1998. **Institutions.**
István Paál's Egyetemi Színpad. Szeged. Lang.: Hun. 361
1960-1998. **Performance/production.**
Interview with actor István Holl. Lang.: Hun. 2059
1961-1998. **Performance/production.**
Interview with ballerina Katalin Hágai. Lang.: Hun. 1096
1963-1995. **Institutions.**
History of Szkéné Színház. Budapest. Lang.: Hun. 1668
1963-1997. **Performance/production.**
Interview with director József Ruszt. Lang.: Hun. 2115
1965-1989. **Institutions.**
Hungarian dramatic art in Transylvania. Cluj-Napoca. Satu Mare. Lang.: Hun. 378
1969-1981. **Institutions.**
History of Squat Theatre. New York, NY. Lang.: Ita. 1670
1970-1977. **Performance/production.**
Modern tendencies in Hungarian folk dance. Lang.: Hun. 1228

Hungary — cont'd

1970-1998. Performance/production.
Interview with Péter Blaskó. Lang.: Hun. 2119
1971. Performance/production.
Excerpt from an illustrated novel by actor Miklós Gábor. Lang.: Hun. 2076
1971-1997. Institutions.
Tamás Fodor's Stúdió K. Budapest. Lang.: Hun. 1671
1971-1998. Performance/production.
Interview with baritone István Gáti. Lang.: Hun. 4618
1973-1997. Performance/production.
Two productions of Shakespeare's *Richard III* by József Ruszt. Budapest. Kecskemét. Lang.: Hun. 2070
1975-1978. Performance/production.
Hungarian guest performances of world ballet stars. Budapest. Lang.: Hun. 1085
Guest performances of dancers and ballet masters of the Kirov and Bolšoj ballets. Lang.: Hun. 1086
1975-1998. Institutions.
Dance training at Pécs School of the Arts. Pécs. Lang.: Hun. 1043
1977-1998. Performance/production.
Interview with soprano Mária Temesi. Lang.: Hun. 4643
1978-1982. Institutions.
History of a period of renewal at the National Theatre. Budapest. Lang.: Hun. 364
1978-1998. Institutions.
Interview with ballet teacher Dóra Uhrik. Pécs. Lang.: Hun. 1045
1979-1982. Institutions.
The National Theatre's experiment in artistic renewal. Budapest. Lang.: Hun. 1672
1979-1998. Institutions.
Interview with director János Regős of Szkéné Színház. Budapest. Lang.: Hun. 362
1980-1986. Institutions.
Guest performances of the ballet companies of Stuttgart and Hamburg. Lang.: Hun. 1041
1980-1998. Performance/production.
Interview with actor György Gazsó. Lang.: Hun. 2072
1981. Plays/librettos/scripts.
Analysis of István Szabó's film *Mephisto*. Lang.: Eng. 3974
1981-1998. Performance/production.
Interview with dancer Mária Tatai. Lang.: Hun. 935
1983-1998. Performance/production.
Guest performance of Théâtre du Plantin, a company for developmentally disabled actors. Budapest. Lang.: Hun. 2081
1984-1998. Performance/production.
Interview with ballet dancer Johanna Bodor. Lang.: Hun. 1098
1986-1997. Performance/production.
Round-table discussion on Tivoli Theatre's production of *The Merchant of Venice*. Lang.: Hun. 2109
1987-1998. Performance/production.
Dancer Kata Péntek. Lang.: Hun. 949
1988-1998. Performance/production.
Interview with actor Tibor Szervét. Lang.: Hun. 2071
István Somogyi's productions of *Magyar Elektra* by Péter Bornemisza. Budapest. Lang.: Hun. 2114
Two productions by István Somogyi of Bornemisza's *Magyar Elektra*. Budapest. Lang.: Hun. 2148
1989-1998. Institutions.
History of annual festival of Hungarian-language theatre. Kisvárda. Lang.: Hun. 1669
1989-1998. Performance/production.
Dancer Miklós Nagyszentpéteri. Lang.: Hun. 1113
1990-1998. Administration.
Round-table on author's rights. Lang.: Hun. 16
1990-1998. Performance/production.
Interview with director Csaba Kiss. Lang.: Hun. 2112
1990-1998. Plays/librettos/scripts.
New Hungarian translations of Shakespeare. Lang.: Hun. 3187
Commentary on plays newly translated into Hungarian. Lang.: Hun. 3189
Essay on the problem of translation. Lang.: Hun. 3190
1991-1998. Performance/production.
Lilla Pártay's ballet adaptation of *Anna Karenina*. Lang.: Hun. 1090
1992-1994. Performance/production.
Comparison of performances by Rosas and Ballet Gulbenkian. Budapest. Lang.: Hun. 939
1993-1996. Theory/criticism.
On collected theatre reviews by Tamás Tarján. Lang.: Hun. 844
1993-1998. Performance/production.
Interview with director Péter Telihay. Lang.: Hun. 2130
1994-1998. Institutions.
The change of management at Új Színház. Budapest. Lang.: Hun. 358
1995-1996. Reference materials.
Yearbook of Hungarian theatre. Lang.: Hun. 698
1996-1997. Institutions.
Interviews with the jury who selected the National Theatre Festival presentations. Lang.: Hun. 363
1996-1997. Performance spaces.
Account of the competition for the design of the new National Theatre. Budapest. Lang.: Hun. 448
1996-1997. Reference materials.
Yearbook of the Hungarian State Opera House. Budapest. Lang.: Hun. 4832
1997. Performance/production.
Yvette Bozsik's new choreography for Debussy's *L'après-midi d'un faune*. Budapest. Lang.: Hun. 940
Program of *butō* festival, Szkéné Theatre. Budapest. Lang.: Hun. 950
La Fille mal Gardée at Erkel Színház. Budapest. Lang.: Hun. 1087
Review of one-act ballets by Balanchine. Budapest. Lang.: Hun. 1105
Review of Madách's *Tragedy of Man* at the Hungarian Theatre of Kolozsvár. Cluj-Napoca. Lang.: Hun. 2065
Review of Shakespeare's *The Merchant of Venice*, Szigligeti Theatre. Szolnok. Lang.: Hun. 2066
György Spiró's *Kvartett (Quartet)* directed by János Vincze. Pécs. Lang.: Hun. 2067
Review of András Bálint's one-man show *INRI*. Budapest. Lang.: Hun. 2073
Pál Békés' *Pincejáték (Cellar Play)* directed by Zoltán Ternyák. Budapest. Lang.: Hun. 2078
Review of Gombrowicz's *Princess Yvonne*, Katona József Theatre. Budapest. Lang.: Hun. 2079
Čechov's *Platonov* as adapted and directed by Erzsébet Gaál. Budapest. Lang.: Hun. 2082
Review of Shakespeare's *Much Ado About Nothing*, Szeged National Theatre. Szeged. Lang.: Hun. 2086
Thomas Bernhard's *Ritter, Dene, Voss* at Bárka Színház. Budapest. Lang.: Hun. 2087
Hauptmann's *Fuhrmann Henschel (Drayman Henschel)* directed by Sándor Zsótér. Budapest. Lang.: Hun. 2088
Review of Molnár's *Az üvegcipő (The Glass Slipper)*, Új Színház. Budapest. Lang.: Hun. 2094
Performances at the new Bárka Színház. Budapest. Lang.: Hun. 2097
Csaba Kiss's adaptation of Shakespeare's chronicle plays at Bárka Színház. Győr. Lang.: Hun. 2101
Review of Róbert Alföldi's *Phaedra-story*. Budapest. Lang.: Hun. 2102
One-act plays of Čechov by the Illyés Gyula National Theatre. Beregovo. Lang.: Hun. 2104
István Verebes' production of Shakespeare's *Hamlet*. Nyíregyháza. Lang.: Hun. 2116
Three Hungarian productions of Shakespeare's *Richard III*. Budapest. Zsámbék. Szeged. Lang.: Hun. 2121
Review of Darvasi's *Bolond Helga (Foolish Helga)*, Csokonai Theatre. Debrecen. Lang.: Hun. 2122
Mari Törőcsik's performance in Ostrovskij's *Guilty Though Innocent* directed by Vasiljév. Szolnok. Lang.: Hun. 2125
Review of *Édes Anna (Anna Édes)*, Madách Chamber Theatre. Budapest. Lang.: Hun. 2136
Calderón's *La cisma de Inglaterra (The Schism of England)* directed by Péter Telihay. Budapest. Lang.: Hun. 2137
Interview with Imre Kerényi, director of Kodály's *Székely fonó (The Székler Spinnery)*. Budapest. Lang.: Hun. 4299

Hungary — cont'd

Reviews of new Hungarian musicals. Budapest. Lang.: Hun. 4360

1997. Theory/criticism.
Transcript of a lecture on language and gesture. Lang.: Hun. 845

1997-1998. Institutions.
Theatre critics' awards 97-98. Lang.: Hun. 355

1998. Design/technology.
Survey of an exhibition of Hungarian scene design. Budapest. Lang.: Hun. 195
An exhibition of sets and environments by Hungarian designers. Budapest. Lang.: Hun. 196
Catalogue of an exhibition devoted to Hungarian theatre and film. Budapest. Lang.: Hun. 197

1998. Institutions.
Festival of Hungarian-language theatres abroad. Kisvárda. Lang.: Hun. 357
Interview with György Szabó, director of Trafó. Budapest. Lang.: Hun. 359
Interview with Imre Dózsa, general director of Magyar Táncművészeti Főiskola. Lang.: Hun. 894
Profiles of dance festivals. Győr. Veszprém. Lang.: Hun. 895
Notes on Interballet and Spring festivals. Budapest. Lang.: Hun. 896
Interview with Imre Dózsa, managing director of Táncművészeti Főiskola. Budapest. Lang.: Hun. 897
Guest performance of the Rambert Dance Company in Budapest. Budapest. Lang.: Hun. 1042
The third international Nureyev ballet competition. Budapest. Lang.: Hun. 1044
Work of Honvéd Táncszínház under the direction of Ferenc Novák. Lang.: Hun. 1219
Miskolci National Theatre's new opera company. Miskolc. Lang.: Hun. 4460
The fourth international singing contest. Budapest. Lang.: Hun. 4461

1998. Performance spaces.
Ferenc Bán's architectural design for Hungary's new National Theatre. Budapest. Lang.: Hun. 446
Interview with architect Miklós Ölveczky about Hungary's new National Theatre. Norway. Lang.: Hun. 449

1998. Performance/production.
Analysis of *Raszputyin (Rasputin)* by Közép-Európa Táncszínház. Budapest. Lang.: Hun. 937
Round-table discussion on dance and movement. Lang.: Hun. 938
Guest performance of Sankai Juku *butō* company. Budapest. Lang.: Hun. 941
Visual dance productions by Cie, 2 in 1. Budapest. Lang.: Hun. 942
The premiere of *Kabaré (Cabaret)* choreographed by Yvette Bozsik. Budapest. Lang.: Hun. 945
Hungarian dance companies at Interbalett '98. Lang.: Hun. 946
Ildikó Mándy's *X.Y.Z.*, a film-dance theatre piece. Budapest. Lang.: Hun. 947
Artus Táncegyüttes' new production *Csillagőrlő (Starmill)*. Budapest. Lang.: Hun. 948
Iván Markó's choreography for Bayreuth Festival productions. Bayreuth. Lang.: Hun. 1083
Bartók's *A csodálatos mandarin (The Miraculous Mandarin)* choreographed by Gyula Harangozó. Budapest. Lang.: Hun. 1088
Guest performance of the Limón Dance Company. Budapest. Lang.: Hun. 1089
Gala concert by students of the Hungarian Dance Academy. Budapest. Lang.: Hun. 1091
Bayerische Staatsballett's guest performances at Budapest Opera House. Budapest. Lang.: Hun. 1092
Irma Nioradze in a performance of *Don Quixote* choreographed by Marius Petipa. Budapest. Lang.: Hun. 1093
The Budapest Opera House's new production of *Giselle*. Budapest. Lang.: Hun. 1094
New productions of Győri Balett. Budapest. Lang.: Hun. 1095
Productions of the Magyar Fesztival Balett choreographed by Iván Markó. Budapest. Lang.: Hun. 1097
A gala performance at the Magyar Állami Operaház. Budapest. Lang.: Hun. 1099
Interview with choreographer Iván Markó. Budapest. Lang.: Hun. 1101
Productions of Szegedi Kortárs Balett. Szeged. Lang.: Hun. 1102
Bartók's *A fából faragott királyfi (The Wooden Prince)* choreographed by László Seregi. Budapest. Lang.:Hun. 1103
Guest performance of the Rambert Dance Company. Budapest. Lang.: Hun. 1106
Interview with dancer Katalin Hágai. Lang.: Hun. 1107
The ballet adaptation of the *Decameron* performed by Veszprém Dance Workshop. Veszprém. Lang.: Hun. 1108
Guest performance of Oleg Danovski Dance Theatre. Budapest. Lang.: Hun. 1109
Lilla Pártay's *Meztelen rózsa (Naked Rose)*, a ballet based on the life of Nižinskij. Budapest. Lang.: Hun. 1110
Antal Fodor's ballet *A Próba (The Rehearsal)*. Budapest. Lang.: Hun. 1111
The Nutcracker at the Budapest Opera House. Budapest. Lang.: Hun. 1115
Critical reactions to the dance evening *Mokka*. Budapest. Lang.: Hun. 1116
Guest performance of the Kremlevskij Balet. Russia. Budapest. Lang.: Hun. 1137
Fáklya Horvát Táncegyüttes' folk dance production *Napmadarak (Sunbirds)*. Lang.: Hun. 1227
Interview with dancer and choreographer Hedvig Fekete. Budapest. Lang.: Hun. 1291
Open-air dance performances. Pécs. Lang.: Hun. 1292
Yvette Bozsik's *Nevess remegve (Emlék) (Laugh Tremble—Memory)* at Trafó. Budapest. Lang.: Hun. 1293
New work of Budapest Táncszínház. Budapest. Lang.: Hun. 1294
Utolsó kontrasztok (Last Contrasts) choreographed by István Orsovszky. Zalaegerszeg. Lang.: Hun. 1295
Interview with actor and director Róbert Alföldi. Budapest. Lang.: Hun. 2056
Péter Kárpáti's *Díszelőadás (Gala Performance)* directed by Balázs Simon. Budapest. Lang.: Hun. 2057
Tom Stoppard's *Arcadia* as directed by Tamás Ascher. Budapest. Lang.: Hun. 2058
Interview with director János Mohácsi. Lang.: Hun. 2060
Interviews with actors on Anatolij Vasiljév's guest direction at Szigligeti Theatre. Szolnok. Lang.: Hun. 2061
Interview with actress Kati Lázár. Lang.: Hun. 2062
Molière's *Dom Juan* directed by Olga Barabás. Sfântu-Gheorghe. Lang.: Hun. 2063
Review of Arthur Miller's *The Crucible* directed by Péter Rudolf. Budapest. Lang.: Hun. 2068
János Acs' *A mennyei hid (The Heavenly Bridge)* directed by Gábor Cziezel. Debrecen. Lang.: Hun. 2069
Krleža's *U agoniji (In Agony)* directed by Péter Valló. Budapest. Lang.: Hun. 2074
Čechov's one-act plays at Thália Színház. Košice. Lang.: Hun. 2075
Review of biographies of actors Ádám Szirtes and Éva Ruttkai. Lang.: Hun. 2077
One-act comedies by Čechov directed by Péter Valló. Dunaújváros. Lang.: Hun. 2080
Review of István Örkény's *Kulcskeresők (Searching for the Key)*, Katona József Theatre. Budapest. Lang.: Hun. 2083
Brecht's *Die Heilige Johanna der Schlachthöfe (Saint Joan of the Stockyards)* directed by Sándor Zsóter. Miskolc. Lang.: Hun. 2084

Hungary — cont'd

Review of plays directed by Árpad Schilling. Budapest. Lang.: Hun. 2085

Reviews of two plays by Per Olov Enquist. Budapest. Lang.: Hun. 2089

Madách's *Tragedy of Man* directed by Sándor Beke. Eger. Lang.: Hun. 2090

Molière's *Misanthrope* directed by Andor Lukáts. Budapest. Lang.: Hun. 2091

Goldoni's *La Locandiera* directed by Lászlo Keszég. Kaposvár. Lang.: Hun. 2092

Review of Bulgakov's *Ivan Vasiljėvič* directed by János Mohácsi. Kaposvár. Lang.: Hun. 2095

A.A. Vasiljév's production of *Bez viny vinovatjė (Guilty Though Innocent)* by Ostrovskij. Szolnok. Lang.: Hun. 2096

Symbolism in Anatolij Vasiljév's production of *Guilty Though Innocent* by Ostrovskij. Szolnok. Lang.: Hun. 2098

Lorca's *Doña Rosita* directed by Gergő Kaszás. Budapest. Lang.: Hun. 2099

Dostojévskij's *Crime and Punishment* directed by Géza Tordy. Győr. Lang.: Hun. 2100

Sándor Lajos' *Szűrővizsgálat (Screen Test)* directed by Tamás Fodor. Budapest. Lang.: Hun. 2103

András Szigethy's *Kegyelem (Mercy)* directed by László Vándorfi. Veszprém. Lang.: Hun. 2105

Review of Péter Forgách's *Kaspar*, Győr National Theatre. Győr. Lang.: Hun. 2106

Gogol's *Revizor (The Inspector General)* directed by Árpád Jutocsa Hegyi. Miskolc. Lang.: Hun. 2108

Lajos Parti Nagy's *Ibusár* directed by János Mikuli. Kecskemét. Pécs. Lang.: Hun. 2110

Shakespeare's *The Merchant of Venice* directed by Róbert Alföldi. Budapest. Lang.: Hun. 2111

Two productions of Csokonai Vitéz's *Karnyóné és a két szeleburdiak (Mrs. Karnyó and the Two Feather-Brains)*. Budapest. Lang.: Hun. 2113

Ferenc Deák's *Fojtás (Tamping)* directed by László Babarczy. Kaposvár. Lang.: Hun. 2117

Two productions of Ernő Szép's *Vőlegény (The Fiancé)*. Nyíregyháza. Győr. Lang.: Hun. 2118

Two Hungarian productions of Arthur Miller's *Death of a Salesman*. Pécs. Szeged. Lang.: Hun. 2123

Čechov's *Diadia Vania (Uncle Vanya)* directed by János Szász. Nyíregyháza. Lang.: Hun. 2124

Events of the Zsámbék theatre festival. Zsámbék. Lang.: Hun. 2126

Brecht's *Der Kaukasische Kreidkreis (The Caucasian Chalk Circle)* adapted and directed by János Mohácsi. Nyíregyháza. Lang.: Hun. 2127

Interview with directors Gábor Székely and Eszter Novák. Budapest. Lang.: Hun. 2128

Interview with directors János Szász and Árpád Schilling. Lang.: Hun. 2129

One-act plays by Brecht directed by József Jámbor. Debrecen. Lang.: Hun. 2131

Péter Valló's production of *Iphigéneia he en Aulide (Iphigenia in Aulis)* by Euripides. Budapest. Lang.: Hun. 2132

Review of Tom Stoppard's *Arcadia* directed by Tamás Ascher. Budapest. Lang.: Hun. 2133

Turgenjév's *Mesjac v derevne (A Month in the Country)* directed by Zoltán Lendvar. Kecskemét. Lang.: Hun. 2134

Two Hungarian productions of Čechov's *Tri sestry (Three Sisters)*. Veszprém. Szeged. Lang.: Hun. 2135

Csaba Kiss's adaptation and direction of *Lady Macbeth of the Provinces* by Leskov. Budapest. Lang.: Hun. 2138

Denise Radó's *A Fedák-ügy (The Fedak Case)* at József Attila Theatre. Budapest. Lang.: Hun. 2139

Three Hungarian productions of plays by Molière. Szentendre. Kapolcs. Kőszeg. Lang.: Hun. 2142

István Tasnádi's *Titanic vízirevü (Titanic Water Show)* at Bárka Színház. Budapest. Lang.: Hun. 2144

Andrés Jeles's *Szenvedéstërténet (Passion Play)* directed by Gábor Máté. Budapest. Lang.: Hun. 2145

Productions of plays by Koljada and Jerofejév at Csiky Gergely Theatre. Kaposvár. Lang.: Hun. 2149

Miklós Hubay's *Hová lett a rózsa lelke? (What Has Become of the Spirit of the Rose?)* directed by György Lengyel. Debrecen. Lang.: Hun. 2150

The death of actress Eva Bartok. London. Lang.: Eng. 3934

Kodály's *Székely fonó (The Székler Spinnery)*. Budapest. Lang.: Hun. 4298

Brecht and Weill's *Die Dreigroschenoper (The Three Penny Opera)* directed by László Vándorfi. Veszprém. Lang.: Hun. 4358

Kodály's *Háry János* at Szeged's Open-Air Festival. Szeged. Lang.: Hun. 4359

An open-air production of *West Side Story* directed by László Vándorfi. Veszprém. Lang.: Hun. 4361

Two Hungarian productions of *Die Dreigroschenoper (The Three Penny Opera)*. Budapest. Szeged. Lang.: Hun. 4362

Interview with Miklós Gábor Kerényi on directing Verdi's *Un Ballo in Maschera*. Budapest. Lang.: Hun. 4619

The Hungarian premier of Verdi's *Stiffelio*. Szeged. Lang.: Hun. 4621

Interview with Tamás Pál, conductor and musical director of Szeged National Theatre. Szeged. Lang.: Hun. 4622

Verdi's *Un Ballo in Maschera* at the Hungarian State Opera House. Budapest. Lang.: Hun. 4629

Interview with director János Szikora. Budapest. Lang.: Hun. 4630

Mozart's *Die Zauberflöte* directed by János Szikora. Budapest. Szeged. Lang.: Hun. 4631

Interview with director Viktor Nagy on Wagner's *Ring* cycle. Budapest. Lang.: Hun. 4635

Interview with Miklós Gábor Kerényi on his production of *Un Ballo in maschera*. Budapest. Szeged. Lang.: Hun. 4636

Mozart's *Le Nozze di Figaro* at the Hungarian State Opera House. Budapest. Lang.: Hun. 4638

György Ligeti's *Le Grand Macabre* directed by Balázs Kovalik. Budapest. Lang.: Hun. 4642

Wagner's *Ring* cycle at the Hungarian Opera House. Budapest. Lang.: Hun. 4644

A production of László Lajtha's comic opera *Le chapeau bleu*. Cluj-Napoca. Lang.: Hun. 4666

1998. Plays/librettos/scripts.

Analysis of Imre Szabó Stein's new translation of Shakespeare's *The Merchant of Venice*. Budapest. Lang.: Hun. 3188

Outline of Wagner's *Götterdämmerung*. Budapest. Lang.: Hun. 4800

Composer Sándor Szokolay on his opera *Szávitri*. Budapest. Lang.: Hun. 4801

1998. Performance/production.

Interview with soprano Andrea Lory. Iasi. Lang.: Hun. 4667

India

Performance/production.

Early theatre. Ancient Greece. Roman Empire. Egypt. Lang.: Rus. 484

1700-1995. Performance/production.

Representations of the feminine in *kathakali*. Lang.: Eng. 1370

1779-1985. Performance/production.

Analysis of the temple performance genre *raslila*. Lang.: Eng. 1347

1795-1900. Plays/librettos/scripts.

The development of Western-style Bengali theatre. Calcutta. Lang.: Eng. 3191

1845-1998. Relation to other fields.

Indian influence on Trinidadian carnival. Trinidad and Tobago. Lang.: Eng. 4178

1900-1985. Plays/librettos/scripts.

Colonial and postcolonial narrative and the politics of representation. Lang.: Eng. 3192

1914-1997. Performance/production.

Obituary for actor and director Sombhu Mitra. Lang.: Eng. 2151

India — cont'd

1930-1960. **Performance/production.**
Western ballet's influence on Indian classical dancer Ram Gopal. Europe. Lang.: Ita. 915
1930-1990. **Performance/production.**
Rival styles in *bharata natyam* performance. Lang.: Eng. 1348
1944-1997. **Performance/production.**
Sanjukta Panigrahi, dancer, choreographer, and co-founder of ISTA. Lang.: Eng. 952
Obituary for dancer Sanjukta Panigrahi. Lang.: Eng. 1230
1950-1998. **Performance/production.**
Interview with actor Saeed Jaffrey. UK-England. USA. Lang.: Eng. 2589
1950-1998. **Plays/librettos/scripts.**
Interview with playwright Rana Bose. Montreal, PQ. Calcutta. Lang.: Eng. 2820
1975-1995. **Performance/production.**
Indian popular theatre as a vehicle for social protest. Lang.: Eng. 541
1978-1985. **Plays/librettos/scripts.**
Diaspora and home in postcolonial Indian drama. Lang.: Eng. 3193
1981-1997. **Performance/production.**
Shakespeare and traditional Asian theatrical forms. China, People's Republic of. Japan. Lang.: Eng. 1346
1984-1998. **Plays/librettos/scripts.**
Political community theatre by South Indian emigrants. Toronto, ON. Montreal, PQ. Lang.: Eng. 2821
1998. **Basic theatrical documents.**
English translation of *terukkūttu* piece *Pakaṭai Tuyil (The Dice Game and the Disrobing)*. Lang.: Eng. 1345
1998. **Performance/production.**
Classical Indian dance performer Malavika Sarukkai. Lang.: Rus. 1349
Kathak dancer Lakhiya Kumudini. Lang.: Rus. 1369

Indonesia
1650-1998. **Performance/production.**
Gender construction and aesthetics of Central Javanese *wayang*. Lang.: Eng. 4925
1700-1998. **Performance/production.**
Performative elements in *wayang kulit* puppet theatre. Lang.: Eng. 4924
1998. **Relation to other fields.**
The arrest of playwright and activist Ratna Sarumpaet. Jakarta. Lang.: Eng. 3773

Iraq
1880-1988. **Performance/production.**
Iraqi productions of Shakespeare. Lang.: Eng. 2152
1983-1998. **Performance/production.**
Interview with dancer Farah Al-Bayaty. Gothenburg. Lang.: Swe. 967

Ireland
Relation to other fields.
The 'bird-woman' folktale in Southeast Asian shamanic healing rituals. Thailand. Malaysia. Lang.: Eng. 1358
1669-1684. **Basic theatrical documents.**
Analysis of Smock Alley promptbook for Dryden's *Tyrannick Love*. Dublin. Lang.: Eng. 1439
1839-1861. **Performance/production.**
Soprano Catherine Hayes. Italy. Lang.: Eng. 4645
1886-1955. **Plays/librettos/scripts.**
George Bernard Shaw: life, work, influences. UK-England. Lang.: Eng. 3437
1887-1998. **Plays/librettos/scripts.**
George Bernard Shaw and science fiction. UK-England. Lang.: Eng. 3508
1890-1914. **Relation to other fields.**
Nationalism and Irish theatre. UK-Ireland. Lang.: Eng. 750
1890-1950. **Theory/criticism.**
Theatrical dancing and the performance aesthetics of Wilde, Yeats, and Shaw. UK-England. Lang.: Eng. 1012
1897-1996. **Theory/criticism.**
Political interpretations of Irish literary theatre. Lang.: Eng. 846
1903. **Performance/production.**
The staging of *The King's Threshold* by W.B. Yeats. Dublin. London. Lang.: Eng. 2153
1906-1989. **Plays/librettos/scripts.**
Obituary for playwright Samuel Beckett. France. Lang.: Dut. 3199
1907. **Audience.**
Nationalist response to the premiere of Synge's *Playboy of the Western World*. Dublin. Lang.: Eng. 1404
1907. **Plays/librettos/scripts.**
A folktale source of *The Playboy of the Western World*. Lang.: Eng. 3202
1912-1945. **Plays/librettos/scripts.**
Music in the early life of Samuel Beckett. Lang.: Eng. 3196
1914-1939. **Plays/librettos/scripts.**
Yeats and the influence of *nō*. Lang.: Eng. 3213
1916-1918. **Plays/librettos/scripts.**
Yeats's *The Only Jealousy of Emer* and his anti-theatrical poetics. Lang.: Eng. 3203
1931. **Plays/librettos/scripts.**
Music in Samuel Beckett's novel *Proust*. France. Lang.: Eng. 3208
1935. **Relation to other fields.**
Analysis of Samuel Beckett's novel *Murphy*. France. Lang.: Eng. 733
1935-1993. **Plays/librettos/scripts.**
The influence of eighteenth-century philosophy on the work of Samuel Beckett. France. Lang.: Eng. 3084
1945-1990. **Plays/librettos/scripts.**
Music and Samuel Beckett. France. Lang.: Eng. 3198
1945-1995. **Plays/librettos/scripts.**
Melanie Daiken's musical settings of texts by Samuel Beckett. France. Lang.: Eng. 3201
Beckett's work analyzed in terms of musical serialism. France. Lang.: Eng. 3215
1945-1998. **Plays/librettos/scripts.**
The speaking subject in plays of Beckett and Stoppard. France. UK-England. Lang.: Ger. 3098
1950-1988. **Plays/librettos/scripts.**
Language and other elements of expression in plays of Beckett and Shepard. USA. France. Lang.: Eng. 3655
1950-1989. **Plays/librettos/scripts.**
Analysis of Samuel Beckett's later plays. France. Lang.: Eng. 3210
1953-1981. **Plays/librettos/scripts.**
Analysis of *En attendant Godot (Waiting for Godot)* and *Rockaby* by Samuel Beckett. France. Lang.: Eng. 3087
1953-1986. **Plays/librettos/scripts.**
Authority, truth, and the allegory of the cave in works of Samuel Beckett. France. Lang.: Eng. 3085
Humor in the works of Samuel Beckett. France. Lang.: Eng. 3110
1953-1998. **Plays/librettos/scripts.**
Criticism of the creation of literary 'genealogies' for dramatic characters. France. Lang.: Swe. 3211
1954-1958. **Plays/librettos/scripts.**
Music and song in plays of Brendan Behan. Lang.: Eng. 3206
1955-1995. **Plays/librettos/scripts.**
Playwright Samuel Beckett's love of music. France. Lang.: Eng. 3204
1957. **Plays/librettos/scripts.**
Analysis of Samuel Beckett's radio play *All That Fall*. France. Lang.: Ita. 3867
1957-1976. **Plays/librettos/scripts.**
The influence Dryden and Johnson's theories on self-translated works of Samuel Beckett. France. Lang.: Eng. 3077
1960-1963. **Plays/librettos/scripts.**
Beckett's character Winnie in *Happy Days*. France. Lang.: Ita. 3200
1961. **Plays/librettos/scripts.**
Beckett's *Happy Days* as a rewriting of *Lady Chatterley's Lover*. France. UK-England. Lang.: Eng. 3120
1965-1985. **Plays/librettos/scripts.**
Composer Luciano Berio on Beckett's influence on his work. France. Italy. Lang.: Eng. 3195
1965-1995. **Plays/librettos/scripts.**
Composer Philip Glass on Beckett's influence on his work. France. USA. Lang.: Eng. 3194
1973-1986. **Plays/librettos/scripts.**
BBC radio plays with Anglo-Irish themes. UK-England. Lang.: Eng. 3868
1976. **Plays/librettos/scripts.**
Analysis of *Ghost Trio* by Samuel Beckett. France. Lang.: Eng. 4076
1980. **Plays/librettos/scripts.**
Analysis of *Translations* by Brian Friel. Lang.: Eng. 3197
1984-1998. **Plays/librettos/scripts.**
Adaptations of Greek tragedy by contemporary Irish writers. UK-Ireland. Lang.: Eng. 3214

Ireland — cont'd

1989-1998. Performance/production.
Recent productions in Ireland of plays by Eugene O'Neill. Dublin. Belfast. Lang.: Eng. 2154
1993-1996. Plays/librettos/scripts.
Recent history in Irish theatre and drama. Dublin. Belfast. Lang.: Eng. 3212
1997. Design/technology.
Combined video and lighting for U2 world tour. Lang.: Eng. 198
1998. Design/technology.
Mick O'Gorman's sound design and equipment for *Riverdance*. Lang.: Eng. 1218
1998. Plays/librettos/scripts.
Conversations with playwright Samuel Beckett. France. Lang.: Ita. 3205
Contemporary Irish playwrights. Lang.: Eng. 3207
Playwright Conor McPherson. Lang.: Eng. 3209
Playwright Martin McDonagh. Lang.: Eng. 3216

Israel

1920-1998. Institutions.
HaBimah and colonialism. Lang.: Eng. 1673
1944-1995. Plays/librettos/scripts.
Israeli attitudes toward Holocaust theatre. Lang.: Eng. 3217
1972-1998. Administration.
Profile of B-movie producer Avi Lerner. Lang.: Eng. 3871
1978-1998. Performance/production.
Dancer, choreographer, and teacher Amos Hetz. Jerusalem. Lang.: Ger. 953
1980-1995. Plays/librettos/scripts.
Danny Horowitz's *Uncle Artur* and the limits of representation. Lang.: Eng. 3218
1993-1998. Performance/production.
Israeli children's theatre. Lang.: Ger. 2155
1997. Performance/production.
Contemporary Israeli dance. Lang.: Swe. 1117

Italy

Institutions.
Profile of Teatro alla Scala. Milan. Lang.: Rus. 4463
Performance/production.
History of Venetian carnival. Venice. Lang.: Rus. 4163
Giovanni Tamborrino's opera without song. Lang.: Ita. 4300
Plays/librettos/scripts.
Marta Abba and Pirandellian dramaturgy. Lang.: Ita. 3232
1100-1200. Plays/librettos/scripts.
Analysis of the Montecassino Passion Play. Lang.: Eng. 3256
1440-1470. Relation to other fields.
Renaissance architect Leone Battista Alberti and theatre design. Lang.: Eng. 751
1500-1650. Design/technology.
Masks in Venetian carnival. Venice. Lang.: Ita. 4159
1500-1700. Plays/librettos/scripts.
Ludic aspects of Italian Renaissance theatre. Lang.: Ita. 3240
1500-1700. Reference materials.
Catalogue of early theatre manuscripts of the Riccardi Library. Florence. Lang.: Ita. 3726
1500-1985. Performance/production.
The Sicilian chivalric tradition. Lang.: Ita. 4125
1508-1578. Plays/librettos/scripts.
Analysis of plays by Alessandro Piccolomini. Lang.: Eng. 3244
1525. Plays/librettos/scripts.
Analysis of Machiavelli's *Clizia*. Lang.: Eng. 3257
1534-1556. Plays/librettos/scripts.
The comedies of Pietro Aretino. Lang.: Eng. 3251
1550-1620. Performance/production.
Mountebanks and the performance of *commedia dell'arte*. Avignon. Lang.: Eng. 4191
1550-1750. Performance/production.
Early modern French and Italian actresses. France. Lang.: Eng. 553
1576-1654. Performance/production.
Analysis of religious theatre of Giambattista Andreini. Lang.: Eng. 2190
1589-1926. Plays/librettos/scripts.
Yearbook of Pirandello studies. Lang.: Eng. 3247
1598. Performance/production.
Peri and Rinuccini's *Daphne*, the first opera. Florence. Lang.: Hun. 4651
1600. Design/technology.
Stage machinery in *Il Rapimento di Cefalo* staged by Bernardo Buontalenti. Florence. Lang.: Eng. 4436
1600-1700. Performance/production.
Commedia dell'arte and the street performances of charlatans. France. Lang.: Eng. 4189
Dramatic writings of Flaminio Scala and Giambattista Andreini. Lang.: Eng. 4192
1600-1985. Performance/production.
History and interpretation of Venetian carnival. Venice. Lang.: Eng. 4162
1601-1800. Plays/librettos/scripts.
Female operatic cross-dressing. Naples. Venice. Lang.: Eng. 4814
1601-1998. Research/historiography.
Methodologies specific to the analysis of seventeenth-century Italian opera. Lang.: Eng. 4835
1622. Plays/librettos/scripts.
Analysis of Jesuit opera by Giovanni Girolamo Kapsberger and Orazio Grassi. Rome. Lang.: Eng. 4803
1625-1700. Performance/production.
A painting of *commedia dell'arte* performer Tiberio Fiorilli. Lang.: Eng. 4190
1660-1722. Plays/librettos/scripts.
The theatre of Girolamo Gigli. Lang.: Eng. 4307
1665-1700. Performance/production.
The evolution of comic opera. Florence. Rome. Lang.: Eng. 4660
1698-1782. Plays/librettos/scripts.
Playwright and poet Pietro Metastasio. Lang.: Ita. 3252
1700-1998. Performance/production.
Characters and masks of the Genoese theatre tradition. Genoa. Lang.: Ita. 4126
1707-1793. Plays/librettos/scripts.
Catalan translation of the memoirs of playwright Carlo Goldoni. Lang.: Cat. 3241
Analysis of comedies by Goldoni. Venice. Lang.: Ita. 3258
1725-1798. Reference materials.
Catalog of an exhibition devoted to dramatist Giacomo Casanova. Venice. Lang.: Ita. 701
1726-1997. Performance spaces.
History of Teatro Valle. Rome. Lang.: Ita. 452
1748-1762. Plays/librettos/scripts.
Carlo Goldoni's comic-opera libretti. Lang.: Eng. 4807
1750. Basic theatrical documents.
Catalan translation of *La Bottega del caffè (The Coffee Shop)* by Carlo Goldoni. Lang.: Cat. 1444
1751-1761. Plays/librettos/scripts.
Analysis of *Trilogia della villeggiatura (Holiday Trilogy)* by Carlo Goldoni. Lang.: Ita. 3236
1761. Plays/librettos/scripts.
The character Giacinta in Goldoni's *Trilogia della villeggiatura (Holiday Trilogy)*. Venice. Lang.: Ita. 3221
1761-1765. Theory/criticism.
Gasparo Angiolini and eighteenth-century dance. Lang.: Eng. 1199
1765. Basic theatrical documents.
Catalan translation of *Il Ventaglio (The Fan)* by Carlo Goldoni. Lang.: Cat. 1442
Catalan translation of *Gl'Innamorati (The Lovers)* by Carlo Goldoni. Lang.: Cat. 1443
1784-1863. Plays/librettos/scripts.
Luigi Pirandello and his great-uncle, a priest. Lang.: Ita. 3259
1792-1998. Institutions.
The opera festival in the birthplace of Rossini. Pesaro. Lang.: Eng. 4462
1797-1848. Performance/production.
The life and work of composer Gaetano Donizetti. Lang.: Eng. 4656
1797-1998. Performance/production.
Analysis of Donizetti's opera *Lucrezia Borgia*. UK-England. Lang.: Eng. 4649
1798-1998. Performance spaces.
History of Teatro Comunale. Ferrara. Lang.: Ger. 453
1799-1998. Performance/production.
Antonio Salieri and his opera *Falstaff*, recently revived. Milan. Lang.: Eng. 4654
1800-1850. Plays/librettos/scripts.
Virginal heroines in Alpine settings in operas of Bellini, Donizetti, and Verdi. Lang.: Eng. 4812
1813. Plays/librettos/scripts.
Analysis of the opera *Aureliano in Palmira* by Rossini and Romani. Lang.: Eng. 4806

Italy — cont'd

1813-1875. **Plays/librettos/scripts.**
Contemporary parodies of nineteenth-century opera. Naples. Lang.: Ita. 4811
1813-1901. **Performance/production.**
Verdi's metrics. Lang.: Ita. 4655
1813-1996. **Performance/production.**
Performance history of Rossini's *Aureliano in Palmira.* Europe. Lang.: Eng. 4659
1816-1845. **Plays/librettos/scripts.**
The use of the tenor in operas of Donizetti. Lang.: Eng. 4802
1816-1845. **Reference materials.**
Catalogue of the work of Donizetti. Europe. Lang.: Eng. 4833
1823. **Basic theatrical documents.**
Gaetano Rossini's libretto for Gioacchino Rossini's *Semiramide.* Lang.: Fre, Ita. 4421
1823. **Plays/librettos/scripts.**
Background information on the title character of Rossini's opera *Semiramide.* Lang.: Fre. 4810
1831-1871. **Plays/librettos/scripts.**
Gender in Bellini's *Norma* and Verdi's *Aida.* Lang.: Eng. 4813
1835-1848. **Plays/librettos/scripts.**
Composer Gaetano Donizetti. Europe. Lang.: Eng. 4805
1839-1861. **Performance/production.**
Soprano Catherine Hayes. Ireland. Lang.: Eng. 4645
1840-1870. **Design/technology.**
Verdi's operas and the influence of La Fenice scene designer Giuseppe Bertoja. Venice. Lang.: Eng. 4433
1841-1919. **Performance/production.**
Actress Giacinta Pezzana. Lang.: Ita. 2177
1845-1848. **Plays/librettos/scripts.**
Contemporary account of the last years of composer Gaetano Donizetti. Lang.: Eng. 4809
1847-1906. **Plays/librettos/scripts.**
Analysis of plays by Giuseppe Giacosa. Lang.: Ita. 3237
1848-1853. **Plays/librettos/scripts.**
The inspiration for Dumas *fils'* Marguerite Gautier and Verdi's Violetta. France. Lang.: Eng. 4789
1848-1998. **Basic theatrical documents.**
Russian translations of plays by Nobel Prize winners. Lang.: Rus. 1446
1850-1998. **Performance/production.**
Verdi's rarely performed opera *Stiffelio.* Lang.: Hun. 4652
1853. **Performance/production.**
Verdi's important mezzo soprano roles, including Azucena in *Il Trovatore.* Lang.: Eng. 4661
1853-1998. **Plays/librettos/scripts.**
The character Azucena in Verdi's *Il Trovatore.* Lang.: Eng. 4808
1856-1915. **Performance/production.**
Actor Tomasso Salvini. USA. Lang.: Eng. 2731
1858-1924. **Plays/librettos/scripts.**
Analysis of scripts by Eleanora Duse. Lang.: Ita. 3228
1860-1918. **Plays/librettos/scripts.**
Italian realist drama. Lang.: Eng. 3260
1863-1938. **Plays/librettos/scripts.**
Analysis of plays by Gabriele D'Annunzio. Lang.: Ita. 3263
1866-1998. **Performance/production.**
Recordings of the different versions of Verdi's *Don Carlos.* Europe. Lang.: Eng. 4650
1867-1936. **Plays/librettos/scripts.**
The life and work of playwright Luigi Pirandello. Lang.: Ita. 3249
1869-1876. **Plays/librettos/scripts.**
Playwright Cletto Arrighi and Milanese theatrical life. Milan. Lang.: Ita. 3220
1871-1881. **Performance/production.**
Reconstruction of the premiere of Boito's *Mefistofele.* Lang.: Ita. 4647
1872-1937. **Performance/production.**
Actor Angelo Musco. Lang.: Ita. 549
1876-1909. **Performance/production.**
The early life and career of F.T. Marinetti, leader of the Futurist movement. Lang.: Eng. 551
1880-1915. **Performance spaces.**
Naples and the *café chantant.* Naples. Lang.: Ita. 4273
1884-1887. **Basic theatrical documents.**
Text of an unfinished verse drama by Pirandello. Lang.: Ita. 1445
1885-1966. **Performance/production.**
Sketches and caricatures of dialect actor Gilberto Govi. Genoa. Lang.: Ita. 543
1886-1936. **Plays/librettos/scripts.**
Pirandello's work as a translator. Lang.: Ita. 3225
1888-1892. **Plays/librettos/scripts.**
Sketches and drafts of works by Gabriele D'Annunzio. Lang.: Ita. 3234
1888-1936. **Plays/librettos/scripts.**
Pirandello and his publishers. Lang.: Ita. 3223
1888-1978. **Design/technology.**
New edition of the autobiography of painter and scenographer Giorgio De Chirico. Lang.: Ita. 202
1890-1910. **Design/technology.**
Lighting and realism in opera and theatre: Belasco and Puccini. USA. Lang.: Eng. 203
1891-1948. **Performance/production.**
Variety actors Guido and Giorgio De Rege. Lang.: Ita. 4275
1898. **Theory/criticism.**
Texts of critical articles written by Pirandello under a psuedonym. Lang.: Ita. 3824
1898-1998. **Performance/production.**
Catalogue of an exhibition on actor Totò. Naples. Lang.: Ita. 542
1899-1979. **Plays/librettos/scripts.**
Analysis of plays of Enrico Bassano. Lang.: Ita. 3226
1900. **Plays/librettos/scripts.**
Musical representation of death in Puccini's *Tosca.* Lang.: Eng. 4804
1900-1984. **Plays/librettos/scripts.**
Essays on actor, director, and playwright Eduardo De Filippo. Lang.: Ita. 3254
1900-1998. **Reference materials.**
Performing arts dictionary. Lang.: Ita. 702
1905-1956. **Plays/librettos/scripts.**
The collaboration of playwright Curzio Malaparte and director Guido Salvini. Lang.: Ita. 3239
1908-1956. **Design/technology.**
Catalogue of an exhibition on scenography of Galileo Chini. Lang.: Ita. 199
1908-1956. **Plays/librettos/scripts.**
Analysis of plays by Pier Maria Rosso di San Secondo. Lang.: Ita. 3224
1908-1998. **Relation to other fields.**
Catalogue of an exhibition of theatre photography by Pasquale De Antonis. Lang.: Ita. 752
1916-1922. **Reference materials.**
Index to performing arts articles in Bragaglia's *Chronache d'attualità.* Rome. Lang.: Ita. 704
1919-1940. **Performance/production.**
Futurism, Fascism, and Italian theatre. Lang.: Eng. 545
1921-1997. **Performance/production.**
Giorgio Strehler of Piccolo Teatro. Milan. Lang.: Ger. 2181
1922-1975. **Plays/librettos/scripts.**
Director and playwright Pier Paolo Pasolini. Lang.: Ita. 3227
1923-1997. **Plays/librettos/scripts.**
The plays of Giovanni Testori and their production. Lang.: Ita. 3262
1923-1998. **Performance/production.**
Catalogue of an exhibition devoted to actress Anna Proclemer. Lang.: Ita. 552
1925-1927. **Plays/librettos/scripts.**
Pirandello, Abba, and the Teatro d'Arte. Rome. Lang.: Ita. 3248
1925-1936. **Plays/librettos/scripts.**
Analysis of correspondence between Pirandello and Marta Abba. Lang.: Ita. 3222
Pirandello's fictional characters and his relationship with actress Marta Abba. Lang.: Ita. 3229
Luigi Pirandello's letters to Marta Abba. Lang.: Ita. 3230
Marta Abba and the characters of Pirandello's plays. Lang.: Ita. 3245
Correspondence of playwright Luigi Pirandello and actress Marta Abba. Lang.: Ita. 3255
1926. **Performance/production.**
Pirandello's Teatro d'Arte on tour in Trieste. Trieste. Lang.: Ita. 2178
1933. **Plays/librettos/scripts.**
An anecdote of Silvio D'Amico regarding Pirandello and Abba. Rome. Lang.: Ita. 3233
1933-1975. **Relation to other fields.**
The square in Italian pageants and open-air entertainment. Lang.: Ita. 4227

Italy — cont'd

1934. **Plays/librettos/scripts.**
Letters of Pirandello, Moissiu, and Jahn. Vienna. Lang.: Ita. 3219
1935-1998. **Performance/production.**
Interview with tenor Luciano Pavarotti. Lang.: Eng. 4662
1936. **Plays/librettos/scripts.**
Analysis of *I giganti della montagna (The Mountain Giants)* by Luigi Pirandello. Lang.: Eng. 3235
1936-1996. **Performance/production.**
Essays on director Giorgio Strehler. Lang.: Ita. 2173
1937-1998. **Performance/production.**
Book-length interview with director Carmelo Bene. Lang.: Ita. 2167
1940-1998. **Performance/production.**
The ideas and productions of director Giorgio Strehler. Lang.: Swe. 2180
Television's impact on culture and social behavior. Lang.: Ita. 4063
1942-1947. **Performance/production.**
Polish soldiers' theatre as seen in the magazine *Parada*. Rome. Cairo. Lang.: Pol. 550
1945-1958. **Performance/production.**
Mass theatre in postwar Italy. Lang.: Ita. 548
1945-1998. **Plays/librettos/scripts.**
Postwar Italian drama. Lang.: Eng. 3253
1946-1998. **Design/technology.**
Theatrical lighting design of Guido and Lucilla Baroni. Lang.: Eng. 201
1946-1998. **Performance/production.**
Autobiography of Yiddish theatre actress Moni Ovadia. Bulgaria. Lang.: Ita. 2174
1947-1998. **Performance/production.**
Dario Fo and Giorgio Strehler honored at Venice Biennale. Venice. Lang.: Eng. 2163
Piccolo Teatro after the death of director Giorgio Strehler. Milan. Lang.: Hun. 2186
1949. **Performance/production.**
The Italian premiere of *A Streetcar Named Desire* by Tennessee Williams. Rome. Lang.: Eng. 2172
1950. **Performance/production.**
Ettore Giannini's film and stage work *Carosello Napoletano (Neapolitan Carousel)*. Lang.: Ita. 546
1950-1988. **Plays/librettos/scripts.**
Techniques of opposition in the work of Dario Fo. Lang.: Eng. 3265
1952. **Performance/production.**
Suzanne Cloutier's role in Shakespeare's *Othello*, directed by Orson Welles. Lang.: Fre. 3935
1953-1994. **Performance/production.**
Humorous anecdotes by actor/director Massimo Troisi. Lang.: Ita. 3858
1956-1998. **Performance/production.**
Giorgio Strehler's productions of plays by Bertolt Brecht. Milan. Lang.: Swe. 2171
1960-1967. **Relation to other fields.**
The influence of Fellini's *La Dolce Vita* on a novel of film critic Guillermo Cabrera Infante. Spain. Lang.: Eng. 4035
1960-1968. **Plays/librettos/scripts.**
The fool character in works of Handke, Fellini, and Singer. USA. Germany. Lang.: Eng. 3667
1960-1970. **Plays/librettos/scripts.**
Theory and practice in the work of director Pier Paolo Pasolini. Lang.: Eng. 3264
1960-1977. **Performance/production.**
Performance artists Vito Acconci and Hermann Nitsch. Vienna. Lang.: Eng. 4239
1960-1985. **Performance/production.**
The dynamics and contradictions of avant-garde theatre. Lang.: Ita. 554
1960-1994. **Performance/production.**
Essays on actor Gian Maria Volonté. Lang.: Ita. 3936
1960-1995. **Theory/criticism.**
Critical discourse and its adaptation to theatrical change. Lang.: Ita. 849
1961-1997. **Design/technology.**
Works of painter, sculptor, and scenographer Eugenio Guglielminetti. Lang.: Ita. 204
1963-1966. **Performance/production.**
Gianfranco De Bosio's production of *Se questo è un uomo (If This Is a Man)* by Primo Levi. Turin. Lang.: Eng. 2168
1965-1980. **Theory/criticism.**
The work of theatre critic Giuseppe Bartolucci. Lang.: Ita. 3823
1965-1985. **Plays/librettos/scripts.**
Composer Luciano Berio on Beckett's influence on his work. Ireland. France. Lang.: Eng. 3195
1967-1985. **Relation to other fields.**
The Arte Povera movement. Lang.: Eng. 4264
1967-1997. **Performance/production.**
The cult of actor Totò after his death. Naples. Lang.: Ita. 2164
1967-1998. **Design/technology.**
Set designer and builder Ado Cantin. Verona. Lang.: Eng. 200
1969-1997. **Basic theatrical documents.**
Slovene translation of *Mistero Buffo* by Dario Fo. Slovenia. Lang.: Slo. 1441
1970-1971. **Plays/librettos/scripts.**
Composer Giacomo Manzoni and his work *Words by Beckett (Parole da Beckett)*. Lang.: Eng. 3250
1970-1995. **Performance/production.**
The theatre of Claudio Remondi and Riccardo Caporossi. Lang.: Ita. 2169
1971-1998. **Performance/production.**
The actor/clown team of Claudio Remondi and Riccardo Caporossi. Lang.: Eng. 2176
1972-1977. **Performance/production.**
Collection of theatre reviews by Cesare Garboli. Lang.: Ita. 2170
1974-1987. **Performance/production.**
Collection of theatre reviews by Roberto De Monticelli. Lang.: Ita. 547
1974-1992. **Performance/production.**
Luca Ronconi's stagings of opera. Lang.: Ita. 4648
1977-1997. **Performance/production.**
Interview with director Mario Martone. Naples. Lang.: Eng. 2166
1978-1998. **Plays/librettos/scripts.**
Dario Fo, translation, and authorial intent. Lang.: Eng. 3238
1980-1989. **Plays/librettos/scripts.**
Playwrights Annibale Ruccello, Enzo Moscato, and Manlio Santanelli. Naples. Lang.: Eng. 3261
1980-1998. **Performance/production.**
Productions of Puccini operas at La Scala. Milan. Lang.: Swe. 4657
1982-1988. **Performance/production.**
Gabriele Lavia's production of *Non si sa come (How Is Unknown)* by Luigi Pirandello. Turin. Lang.: Ita. 2157
1982-1998. **Theory/criticism.**
The critical methodology of Giuseppe Bartolucci. Lang.: Ita. 850
1985. **Theory/criticism.**
Politics, tradition, and avant-garde theatre. Lang.: Ita. 847
1985-1998. **Performance/production.**
Multimedia and the productions of Giorgio Barberio Corsetti. Rome. Milan. Lang.: Eng. 4043
Profile of tenor Andrea Bocelli. Lang.: Swe. 4653
1991-1992. **Institutions.**
Carlo Quartucci's acting workshop on Shakespeare's *Macbeth*. Rome. Lang.: Ita. 1674
1993. **Performance/production.**
Massimo Castri's production of Euripides' *Electra*. Spoleto. Lang.: Ita. 2179
Interview with director Giorgio Strehler. Milan. Lang.: Hun. 2185
1994. **Plays/librettos/scripts.**
The *castrato*, the contralto, and the film *Farinelli*. France. Lang.: Eng. 4787
1994-1996. **Training.**
Ferruccio Di Cori's improvisational workshops for actors and directors. Rome. Lang.: Ita. 874
1994-1998. **Performance spaces.**
The restoration of the opera houses Gran Teatro del Liceu and Teatro La Fenice. Barcelona. Venice. Lang.: Eng. 4495
1994-1998. **Performance/production.**
Roman theatre, traditional and experimental. Rome. Lang.: Eng. 2187
1995-1998. **Performance/production.**
Profile of opera star Cecilia Bartoli. Lang.: Eng. 4658
1996. **Performance/production.**
Excerpts from the notebooks of director Massimo Castri. Prato. Lang.: Ita. 2162

Italy — cont'd

1996-1997. **Performance/production.**
Luca Ronconi's production of *Mourning Becomes Electra* by Eugene O'Neill. Rome. Lang.: Eng. 2183

1997. **Institutions.**
Italian experimental theatre at Spielart '97. Munich. Lang.: Eng. 1619

1997. **Performance/production.**
Andrea Liberovici's production of *Sonetto. Un travestimento shakespeariano (Sonnet: A Shakespearean Travesty)* by Eduardo Sanguineti. Genoa. Lang.: Ita. 2159
Italian productions of plays by Harold Pinter. Lang.: Eng. 2165
Productions by Toni Bertorelli and Alfiero Alfieri. Rome. Lang.: Eng. 2175
Text of an address by director Giorgio Strehler at the University of Turin. Lang.: Ita. 2184
Luca Ronconi's stage adaptation of *The Brothers Karamazov*. Rome. Lang.: Eng. 2188
Romeo Castellucci's adaptation of the *Oresteia* by Aeschylus. Cesena. Lang.: Eng. 2189
Interview with singer Cecilia Bartoli. Lang.: Swe. 4663

1997-1998. **Performance/production.**
Theatrical activity in Italy's northern provinces. Lang.: Eng. 2160
Survey of Milanese theatre. Milan. Lang.: Eng. 2161

1997-1998. **Plays/librettos/scripts.**
Profile of playwright, director, and actor Dario Fo. Lang.: Ger. 3231

1998. **Basic theatrical documents.**
Dutch translations of women's monologues by Dario Fo. Lang.: Dut. 1440

1998. **Design/technology.**
Sound system used in a soccer stadium for an operatic production. Rome. Lang.: Eng. 4434
Lighting design for Verdi's *Macbeth* at La Scala. Milan. Lang.: Eng. 4435

1998. **Institutions.**
Restoration of the Burcardo Palace, which includes a theatrical museum. Rome. Lang.: Ita. 366
The quality of theatre for children and youth. Bologna. Stockholm. Germany. Lang.: Ger. 367
Directory of Italian theatre websites. Lang.: Eng. 1675

1998. **Performance spaces.**
The theatre of the cruise ship *Grand Princess*. Lang.: Eng. 451
The opening of Nuovo Piccolo in honor of the late director Giorgio Strehler. Milan. Lang.: Eng. 1802

1998. **Performance/production.**
A conversation with actor and director Carmelo Bene. Lang.: Ita. 544
Amedeo Amodio's new choreography for Čajkovskij's *The Nutcracker*. Rome. Lang.: Hun. 1118
Laura Curano's solo piece *Olivetti*. Calabria. Lang.: Eng. 2156
Survey of Neapolitan theatre. Naples. Lang.: Eng. 2158
The present state of Italian theatre. Lang.: Eng. 2182
Interviews with Italian actresses. Lang.: Ita. 4062
Opera singer Luigi Cucci. Lang.: Rus. 4646

1998. **Plays/librettos/scripts.**
Reactions to the awarding of the Nobel Prize to satirical playwright Dario Fo. Lang.: Eng. 3242
Playwright Dario Fo. Lang.: Eng. 3243
Pirandello's influence on French theatre. France. Lang.: Ita. 3246

1998. **Reference materials.**
Yearbook of Italian theatre. Lang.: Ita. 699

1998. **Relation to other fields.**
New Italian theatrical legislation. Lang.: Eng. 3774

1998. **Theory/criticism.**
Avant-garde theatre and technology. Lang.: Ita. 848

1998. **Training.**
Guide to theatrical training. Rome. Lang.: Rus. 875

1998-1999. **Reference materials.**
Yearbook of Italian children's theatre. Lang.: Ita. 700
Catalogue of a Riccardi Library exhibition of theatrical manuscripts. Lang.: Ita. 703

Japan

350 B.C.-1998 A.D. **Reference materials.**
History of Japanese theatre and drama. Lang.: Ita. 705

1300-1988. **Relation to other fields.**
Religion and art in *nō*. Lang.: Eng. 1374

1400-1700. **Performance/production.**
Analysis of *kyōgen* performance. Lang.: Eng. 1351

1500-1998. **Performance/production.**
Power relations in *nō* theatre. Lang.: Eng. 1373

1600-1900. **Performance/production.**
Feminist analysis of female roles in *kabuki*. Lang.: Eng. 1363

1600-1980. **Performance/production.**
The popular comic art-form *rakugo*. Lang.: Eng. 2195

1603-1868. **Audience.**
The popularity of *nō* among all the classes during the Edo period. Lang.: Eng. 1371
Popularity of *nō* plays among common audiences. Edo. Lang.: Eng. 1372

1603-1998. **Performance/production.**
Onnagata performer Kataoka Kōjiro. Lang.: Fre. 1365

1650-1985. **Performance/production.**
Nomai dance drama. Lang.: Eng. 1350

1752-1998. **Performance/production.**
Onstage costume changes. Russia. Denmark. Lang.: Swe. 556

1770-1800. **Performance/production.**
The role of the *onnagata* heroine in late eighteenth-century *kabuki*. Lang.: Eng. 1364

1840-1998. **Design/technology.**
Rapid on-stage costume changes in dance. Russia. Sweden. Lang.: Swe. 889

1882. **Performance/production.**
George Crichton Miln's touring Shakespearean company in Japan. Chicago, IL. Yokohama. Lang.: Eng. 2702

1884-1998. **Basic theatrical documents.**
English translation of *Takatoki* by Mokuami Kawatake. Lang.: Eng. 1361

1900-1950. **Performance/production.**
Japanese-Russian theatrical relations. Russia. Lang.: Rus. 2194

1910-1998. **Performance/production.**
Obituary for film director Akira Kurosawa. Lang.: Eng. 3937

1914-1988. **Institutions.**
The all-female Takarazuka Revue Company. Lang.: Eng. 368

1939-1984. **Performance/production.**
Tadashi Suzuki and Suzuki Company of Toga. Lang.: Eng. 555

1949-1998. **Administration.**
American and Japanese cultural policy. USA. Lang.: Eng. 141

1960-1998. **Training.**
Anne-Lise Gabold's use of the methods of Tadashi Suzuki in her production of Euripides' *Bákchai (The Bacchae)*. Copenhagen. Lang.: Dan. 1359

1963-1998. **Performance/production.**
American musicals on the Japanese stage. Tokyo. Lang.: Eng. 4363

1981-1997. **Performance/production.**
Shakespeare and traditional Asian theatrical forms. China, People's Republic of. India. Lang.: Eng. 1346

1990-1998. **Performance/production.**
Interview with *butō* dancer Susanna Åkerlund. Sweden. Lang.: Swe. 1300

1993-1995. **Performance/production.**
The performance of *onnagata* Tamasaburō in *Elizabeth* by Francisco Ors. Tokyo. Lang.: Eng. 1362

1994-1998. **Performance/production.**
Theatrical component of Japan's UK98 Festival. Tokyo. Lang.: Eng. 2192

1996. **Theory/criticism.**
Report on *kabuki* conference. Tokyo. Lang.: Eng. 1367

1996-1998. **Performance/production.**
Performance artist Rei Naito. Lang.: Eng. 4242

1997. **Basic theatrical documents.**
English translation of *Kanadehon Hamlet* by Harue Tsutsumi. Lang.: Eng. 1360

1998. **Institutions.**
Tokyo's new opera house. Tokyo. Lang.: Rus. 4464

1998. **Performance/production.**
Tadashi Suzuki's method of actor training. Lang.: Eng. 2191
Survey of Japanese theatre. Lang.: Rus. 2193

Karachaevo-Cherkess

Reference materials.
Bibliography of prerevolutionary culture. Lang.: Rus. 706

Kenya
1979-1992. **Plays/librettos/scripts.**
Playwright Ngugi wa Thiong'o and the Kamirithu theatre project. Kamiriithu. Lang.: Eng. 3266
1990-1998. **Performance/production.**
Theatrical rebellion and sociopolitical chaos. Zimbabwe. Lang.: Eng. 687
Korea
1150-1928. **Performance/production.**
Analysis of Korean mask-dance theatre form *hahoe pyolsin-kut*. Lang.: Eng. 1352
1600-1985. **Performance/production.**
History of Korean dance. Lang.: Eng. 954
1900-1998. **Performance/production.**
The evolution of Korean *p'ansori* as modern Korean opera, *ch'angguk*. Lang.: Eng. 4364
1948-1998. **Performance/production.**
Traditional and Western elements in Korean opera. Lang.: Eng. 4664
1976-1998. **Performance/production.**
Historical, political, and aesthetic context of *madang* theatre. Lang.: Ger. 557
1980-1998. **Performance/production.**
Report from a symposium on traditional Korean theatre. Berlin. Lang.: Ger, Fre, Dut, Eng. 2196
Latin America
1960-1980. **Plays/librettos/scripts.**
Cruelty and the absurd in theatre of Latin American playwrights. Lang.: Eng. 3267
Latvia
1918-1998. **Performance/production.**
Speculation on the future of Latvian theatre. Lang.: Swe, Eng, Ger. 558
1948-1997. **Performance/production.**
Ballet soloist Mikhail Baryshnikov. USA. Lang.: Eng. 1119
1997. **Institutions.**
Report on a visit to Riga's theatres. Riga. Lang.: Swe, Eng, Ger. 369
Profile of Latvijas Dailes Teatris. Riga. Lang.: Swe, Eng, Ger. 1676
1998. **Performance/production.**
Articles on stage and film actors and other celebrities. Lang.: Rus. 2197
Lebanon
1940-1989. **Plays/librettos/scripts.**
The journey in plays of Georges Schéhadé. Lang.: Fre. 3268
Lithuania
1952-1998. **Performance/production.**
Director Eimuntus Nekrošius. Lang.: Pol. 2198
1974-1998. **Design/technology.**
New lighting equipment of Lithuanian Opera and Ballet Theatre. Vilnius. Lang.: Swe, Eng, Ger. 205
1993-1998. **Institutions.**
The theatres of Vilnius. Vilnius. Lang.: Swe, Eng, Ger. 370
1996. **Institutions.**
Swedish-Lithuanian theatrical exchange. Valmeira. Falun. Lang.: Swe, Eng, Ger. 1677
1998. **Performance/production.**
Lithuanian theatre education and the visit of Tadashi Suzuki. Lang.: Fin. 559
Malaysia
Relation to other fields.
The 'bird-woman' folktale in Southeast Asian shamanic healing rituals. Ireland. Thailand. Lang.: Eng. 1358
Malta
1998. **Performance/production.**
Maltese Holy Week rituals. Lang.: Eng. 4217
Martinique
1946-1969. **Plays/librettos/scripts.**
Analysis and translation of *Et les Chiens se taisaient (And the Dogs Were Silent)* by Aimé Césaire. Lang.: Eng. 3269
1960-1990. **Plays/librettos/scripts.**
Postcolonialism, ethnicity, and feminism in French and Caribbean plays. France. Guadeloupe. Lang.: Eng. 3104
1970-1995. **Plays/librettos/scripts.**
Caribbean identity in plays of Daniel Boukman. Lang.: Eng. 3271
1975-1998. **Plays/librettos/scripts.**
Celebration and the body in plays of Ina Césaire and Simone Schwarz-Bart. Guadeloupe. Lang.: Eng. 3270
Mexico
1500-1900. **Performance/production.**
Female characters in male folk dance. England. Lang.: Eng. 1225
1936-1937. **Performance/production.**
Antonin Artaud's journey to Mexico. France. Lang.: Eng. 1922
1938. **Plays/librettos/scripts.**
Analysis of *Soldadera* by Josefina Niggli. Lang.: Eng. 3272
1948-1955. **Plays/librettos/scripts.**
The postwar existentialist drama of Albert Camus and Carlos Solórzano. France. Lang.: Spa. 3274
1970-1992. **Plays/librettos/scripts.**
Playwright, director, and performer Jesusa Rodríguez. Lang.: Eng. 3275
1975-1998. **Performance/production.**
Indigenous Mexican theatre and colonialism. Lang.: Eng. 560
1992. **Basic theatrical documents.**
English translation of *The Mustache* by Sabine Berman. Lang.: Eng. 1447
1993-1996. **Plays/librettos/scripts.**
Comparison between *Krísis (Crisis)* by Sabina Berman and Quentin Tarantino's film *Pulp Fiction*. USA. Lang.: Spa. 3276
1996. **Plays/librettos/scripts.**
Analysis of *Krísis (Crisis)* by Sabina Berman. Lang.: Eng. 3273
1997. **Institutions.**
Report on Black film festival. Acapulco. Lang.: Eng. 3924
1998. **Institutions.**
Puppetry exhibits at Chicago Children's Museum. Chicago, IL. Mexico City. Lang.: Eng. 4881
1998. **Performance/production.**
Report on the state of the theatre in Mexico City. Mexico City. Lang.: Eng. 2199
Middle East
225-1995. **Performance/production.**
History of Arabic theatre. Lang.: Eng. 561
Mordovia
Plays/librettos/scripts.
Playwright and nationalist G. Ja. Merkuškin. Lang.: Rus. 3277
Netherlands
1495-1525. **Plays/librettos/scripts.**
Comparison of the Dutch *Elckerlijck* and the English *Everyman*. England. Lang.: Eng. 2982
1640-1711. **Design/technology.**
Gerard de Lairesse, painter and stage designer. Lang.: Eng. 208
1700-1772. **Performance/production.**
Eighteenth-century Dutch theatre. Lang.: Dut. 2202
1800-1995. **Performance/production.**
The development of Dutch theatre for children. Lang.: Dut. 2203
1802-1853. **Audience.**
Analysis of patterns of theatre attendance. Rotterdam. Lang.: Eng. 154
1849. **Performance/production.**
Analysis of the ballet *Berthalda en Hildebrand (Berthalda and Hildebrand)*. Amsterdam. Lang.: Ger. 1122
1917-1998. **Performance/production.**
A pictorial history of dance in the Netherlands. Lang.: Dut. 957
1920-1990. **Performance/production.**
Memoirs of actor and director Egbert van Paridon. Lang.: Dut. 2204
1920-1998. **Plays/librettos/scripts.**
English-language plays on the Dutch and Flemish stage. Lang.: Dut. 3278
1940-1944. **Performance/production.**
German refugee and emigrant performers in cabaret and revue. Lang.: Ger. 4155
1940-1998. **Performance/production.**
Dutch reception of the work of Bertolt Brecht. Lang.: Dut. 564
1951-1998. **Performance/production.**
Ballets of Hans van Manen. Lang.: Eng. 1120
1964-1985. **Performance/production.**
Reexamination of the performance art of Beuys, Abramovič, and Ulay. USA. Germany. Lang.: Eng. 4254
1970-1998. **Performance/production.**
The use of television in theatrical space. USA. Lang.: Dut. 2206
1975-1998. **Performance/production.**
Women in Dutch theatre. Lang.: Dut. 563
1980-1983. **Plays/librettos/scripts.**
Dutch and Flemish Shakespearean productions. Belgium. Lang.: Dut. 2789

Netherlands — cont'd

1983-1998. **Performance/production.**
The work of Theatergroep Delta. Amsterdam. Lang.: Dut. 2200
1985-1998. **Plays/librettos/scripts.**
Johan Simons and the independent theatre group in Hollandia. Amsterdam. Lang.: Ger. 3280
1987-1996. **Audience.**
Ten-year study of audience response to Dutch theatre festivals. Lang.: Dut. 155
1988. **Institutions.**
Interview with founders of Dutch multicultural group Cosmic Illusions. Amsterdam. Netherlands Antilles. Lang.: Eng. 1679
1988. **Performance/production.**
De Zaak's production of *Action* by Sam Shepard. Rotterdam. Lang.: Dut. 2201
1988. **Plays/librettos/scripts.**
Interview with playwright Thea Doelwijt. Suriname. Lang.: Eng. 3279
1989. **Audience.**
Interview with performance artist Tim Brennan. Arnhem. Lang.: Eng. 4231
1990-1995. **Administration.**
Marketing strategies for the performing arts. Lang.: Dut. 17
1990-1997. **Performance/production.**
Dutch theatre and situationist theory. Lang.: Eng. 565
1990-1998. **Design/technology.**
Profiles of young theatrical designers. Lang.: Dut. 207
1990-1998. **Performance/production.**
Contemporary Dutch theatre. Lang.: Dut. 2205
1990-1998. **Relation to other fields.**
Handbook of teachers of drama in secondary school. Lang.: Dut. 753
1990-1998. **Research/historiography.**
Symposium on Dutch dance history and historiography. Lang.: Dut. 1002
1995-1998. **Institutions.**
Profile of the young theatre company De Trust. Amsterdam. Lang.: Dut. 1678
1997. **Performance/production.**
Dancer Susan Kozel on performing in Paul Sermon's *Telematic Dreaming*. Amsterdam. Lang.: Eng. 956
Dutch National Ballet production at the Holland Festival. Amsterdam. Lang.: Hun. 1121
1998. **Administration.**
Methods of organization-building in the arts. Lang.: Dut. 18
Symposium on the position of young theatre professionals. Lang.: Dut. 1387
1998. **Design/technology.**
OISTAT meeting on technician training. Amsterdam. Lang.: Swe. 206
Technical effects control system used in a production of *Joe—The Musical* at Koninklijk Theater Carré. Amsterdam. Lang.: Eng. 4324
1998. **Performance/production.**
The symposium on acting at Theaterfestival. Amsterdam. Lang.: Dut. 562
Coping with stage fright. Lang.: Dut. 566
Argument in favor of lengthening dancers' careers. The Hague. Sweden. Lang.: Swe. 955
Premieres of choreographies by Danny Rosseel. Antwerp. Amsterdam. Lang.: Hun. 1065
Peter Zadek's production of Čechov's *Višnëvyj sad (The Cherry Orchard)*. Germany. Lang.: Dut. 1954
1998. **Reference materials.**
Bibliography of Dutch-language Caribbean literature. Aruba. Suriname. Netherlands Antilles. Lang.: Eng. 3725
1998. **Theory/criticism.**
Dutch theatre criticism. Lang.: Dut. 3825

Netherlands Antilles
1988. **Institutions.**
Interview with founders of Dutch multicultural group Cosmic Illusions. Amsterdam. Lang.: Eng. 1679
1998. **Reference materials.**
Bibliography of Dutch-language Caribbean literature. Aruba. Suriname. Netherlands. Lang.: Eng. 3725

New Zealand
1998. **Plays/librettos/scripts.**
Women in plays about war and male contact sports. Europe. Lang.: Eng. 3281

Nicaragua
1979-1998. **Performance/production.**
Interview with dancer and choreographer Gloria Bacon. Lang.: Swe. 958

Nigeria
1960-1979. **Plays/librettos/scripts.**
Political satire in the plays of Wole Soyinka. Lang.: Eng. 3284
1964-1970. **Plays/librettos/scripts.**
Representation of character in plays by Duro Ladipọ. Lang.: Eng. 3285
1965-1998. **Plays/librettos/scripts.**
Ritual in plays of John Bekederemo and Wole Soyinka. Lang.: Eng. 3287
1971-1991. **Plays/librettos/scripts.**
Analysis of unpublished plays by Ken Saro-Wiwa. Lang.: Eng. 3282
1973. **Plays/librettos/scripts.**
Analysis of *The Swamp Dwellers* by Wole Soyinka. Lang.: Eng. 3283
1978. **Plays/librettos/scripts.**
Playwright Femi Osofisan on his political goals and strategies. Lang.: Eng. 3286
1992-1998. **Relation to other fields.**
Nigerian video films. Lang.: Eng. 4081

North America
500 B.C.-1980 A.D. **Performance/production.**
Theatre in periods of exploration and discovery. Europe. Asia. Lang.: Eng. 569
500 B.C.-1988 A.D. **Theory/criticism.**
Terror in theatre. Europe. Lang.: Eng. 839
500 B.C.-1995 A.D. **Reference materials.**
Italian translation of *The Oxford Illustrated History of Theatre* (1995). Europe. Asia. Africa. Lang.: Ita. 697
1550-1950. **Performance/production.**
Brief history of *commedia dell'arte*. Europe. Lang.: Eng. 4188
1650-1950. **Performance/production.**
Great female opera soloists. Europe. Lang.: Rus. 4555
1784-1991. **Plays/librettos/scripts.**
Operatic realizations of Beaumarchais' character Rosina. Europe. Lang.: Eng. 4773
1788-1996. **Plays/librettos/scripts.**
Two centuries' thought on Shakespeare's *The Merchant of Venice*. Europe. Lang.: Hun. 3066
1795-1997. **Audience.**
The role of the audience in performance. Europe. Lang.: Eng. 156
1896-1970. **Plays/librettos/scripts.**
Absurdism in children's theatre. Europe. Lang.: Eng. 3288
1899-1998. **Plays/librettos/scripts.**
Annual bibliography of modern drama studies. Europe. Lang.: Eng. 3060
1904-1994. **Plays/librettos/scripts.**
The reciprocal influence of opera and film. Europe. Lang.: Eng. 4770
1918-1998. **Performance spaces.**
Essays on experimental theatre world wide. Europe. Asia. Lang.: Pol. 438
1933-1945. **Relation to other fields.**
Directory of emigrant and refugee dancers. Europe. South America. Lang.: Ger. 997
1933-1997. **Plays/librettos/scripts.**
Bibliography of Holocaust drama. Europe. Lang.: Eng. 3054
1933-1998. **Plays/librettos/scripts.**
Perceptions of Bertolt Brecht in the English-speaking world. UK-England. Lang.: Ger. 3443
1950-1995. **Plays/librettos/scripts.**
The statesman on the modern stage. Lang.: Eng. 3291
1950-1998. **Performance/production.**
Shakespeare and postmodern production. Europe. Lang.: Eng. 1912
1967-1998. **Performance/production.**
The evolution of the contemporary Shakespearean director. Europe. Lang.: Eng. 2207
1975-1997. **Theory/criticism.**
Political criticism of early modern drama. Europe. Lang.: Eng. 3814
1975-1998. **Performance/production.**
Theatrical representations of civil war and civil discord. Europe. Africa. Lang.: Eng. 567

North America — cont'd

1976-1997. **Performance/production.**
Multiculturalism and the site-specificity of theatre. Asia. Europe. Lang.: Eng. 485
1985-1995. **Plays/librettos/scripts.**
The AIDS epidemic in contemporary opera. Europe. Lang.: Eng. 4771
1990-1998. **Performance/production.**
The dramaturg in the community theatre. Asia. South America. Lang.: Eng. 570
1990-1998. **Relation to other fields.**
Politics and the dramaturg. Lang.: Eng. 754
1991-1997. **Institutions.**
The present status of the Living Theatre. Lang.: Eng. 371
1993-1998. **Performance/production.**
The performance of plays by Hispanic women. Lang.: Eng. 2209
1997. **Performance/production.**
The theory of movement in *Les Enfants Terribles*, adapted to dance-opera by Philip Glass and Susan Marshall. Lang.: Eng. 1353
1997. **Research/historiography.**
Problems of dance historiography. Europe. Lang.: Eng. 1001
1997-1998. **Performance/production.**
Articles about integrating theory into theatrical practice. Lang.: Eng. 571
1997-1998. **Theory/criticism.**
Feminism and children's theatre. Lang.: Eng. 852
JDTC's ongoing discussion of feminism and children's theatre. Lang.: Eng. 853
1998. **Design/technology.**
Survey of lighting equipment, design, and information. Lang.: Eng. 209
1998. **Performance/production.**
The dramaturg and feminist theory and practice. Lang.: Eng. 568
Theory and the role of the dramaturg. Lang.: Eng. 572
Speaking styles of selected actors reading Shakespeare's *Henry V*. UK-England. Lang.: Eng. 2208
The North American tour of English comedian Eddie Izzard. UK-England. Lang.: Eng. 4127
Gender, nation, and sexuality in opera. Europe. Lang.: Eng. 4552
1998. **Plays/librettos/scripts.**
Survey of recent studies on closet drama. Europe. Lang.: Eng. 3065
North American translations and adaptations of Molière. Lang.: Eng. 3289
Genocide, theatre, and the human body. UK-England. Argentina. Lang.: Eng. 3290
1998. **Reference materials.**
Discography of operas by Donizetti. Europe. Lang.: Eng. 4831
1998. **Research/historiography.**
Research on dance and cultural studies. Europe. Lang.: Eng. 1003
1998. **Theory/criticism.**
Theatre and 'a theory of looking'. Lang.: Eng. 851
Gender and culture in dance analysis. Europe. Lang.: Eng. 1006
The nature of dance analysis. Europe. Lang.: Eng. 1009
The nature of the body in dance. Europe. Lang.: Eng. 1010
Origins of dance as an art form. Europe. Lang.: Eng. 1011
Cyberspace as performance site. Lang.: Eng. 4048

Norway
1867-1967. **Plays/librettos/scripts.**
Ibsen's *Peer Gynt* and its new Polish translation. Poland. Lang.: Pol. 3308
1870-1898. **Plays/librettos/scripts.**
Hegel's influence on the plays of Henrik Ibsen. Germany. Lang.: Eng. 3292
1879. **Plays/librettos/scripts.**
The development of the character Dr. Rank in Ibsen's *Et Dukkehjem (A Doll's House)*. Lang.: Eng. 3297
1879-1906. **Plays/librettos/scripts.**
Andreas-Salomé's view of Ibsen's female characters. Germany. Lang.: Eng. 3296
1879-1979. **Plays/librettos/scripts.**
Feminism and plays of Henrik Ibsen. Lang.: Eng. 3293
1882. **Plays/librettos/scripts.**
Henrik Ibsen and social criticism in *En Folkefiende (An Enemy of the People)*. Lang.: Swe. 3300
1886-1894. **Plays/librettos/scripts.**
Trolls in the late plays of Ibsen. Lang.: Eng. 3298
1888. **Plays/librettos/scripts.**
Ibsen, translation, and feminine discourse. Lang.: Eng. 3295
1905-1998. **Administration.**
Comparative analysis of national cultural policies. Canada. France. Germany. Lang.: Eng. 4
1923-1998. **Institutions.**
The Kongsberg Kappleiken festival of Norwegian folk music and dance. Kongsberg. Lang.: Swe. 1221
1980-1998. **Performance/production.**
Interview with opera singer Anne Bolstad. Sweden. Lang.: Swe. 4665
1987. **Plays/librettos/scripts.**
Stage directions in Ibsen's *Hedda Gabler*. Lang.: Eng. 3294
1988-1998. **Performance/production.**
Interview with director Stein Winge. Oslo. Lang.: Eng. 2210
1990-1998. **Institutions.**
Profile of dance company Nye Carte Blanche. Bergen. Lang.: Swe. 1251
1993-1998. **Performance spaces.**
The reconstruction of Drammens Teater after a fire. Drammen. Lang.: Swe. 1803
1994. **Performance spaces.**
The new theatre building of Trøndelag Teater. Trondheim. Lang.: Swe. 455
1997. **Performance spaces.**
Stage technology and equipment of Trøndelag Teater. Trondheim. Lang.: Nor. 454
Trøndelag Teater's new building. Trondheim. Lang.: Nor. 456
1998. **Design/technology.**
Survey of NoTT98 at Oslo. Oslo. Lang.: Nor. 210
Seminar on flying on stage. Oslo. Lang.: Swe. 211
1998. **Institutions.**
Teater NOR and its relationship with the community. Stamsund. Lang.: Eng. 1680
Report on Ibsen festival. Oslo. Lang.: Eng. 1681
Survey of the 1998 Ibsen Festival. Oslo. Lang.: Eng. 1682
Survey of annual Ibsen festival. Oslo. Lang.: Eng. 1683
Interview with Bjørn Simensen, director of Den Norske Opera. Oslo. Lang.: Swe. 4465
1998. **Performance spaces.**
Interview with architect Miklós Ölveczky about Hungary's new National Theatre. Hungary. Lang.: Hun. 449
1998. **Performance/production.**
Report from Ibsen festival. Oslo. Lang.: Swe. 2211
Reviews of productions of plays by Ibsen. New York, NY. Oslo. Lang.: Eng. 2747
1998. **Plays/librettos/scripts.**
Female characters in plays by Scandinavian women. Sweden. Denmark. Lang.: Eng. 3299
1998. **Research/historiography.**
The Marvin Carlson collection of materials at the Ibsen Center. Oslo. Lang.: Eng. 3797

Ottoman Empire
SEE
Turkey.

Panama
1946-1998. **Performance/production.**
Recollections of ballerina Margot Fonteyn. USA. Lang.: Eng. 1182

Philippines
1988-1990. **Performance/production.**
Practical issues of cultural exchange: the Cry of Asia! tour. France. Lang.: Eng. 535

Poland
1500-1914. **Plays/librettos/scripts.**
Enlightenment influences on modern Jewish theatre. Lang.: Pol. 3307
1732-1798. **Institutions.**
Eighteenth-century amateur theatre in Vilna. Vilna. Lang.: Pol. 1691
1808-1975. **Institutions.**
Regional theatre in Mazovia. Płock. Lang.: Pol. 374

Poland — cont'd

1832-1835. **Plays/librettos/scripts.**
The Polish national style in Romantic dramas. Lang.: Pol. 3304
1843-1998. **Plays/librettos/scripts.**
The current state of studies on playwright Adam Mickiewicz. Lang.: Pol. 3302
1850-1950. **Performance/production.**
Polish-Jewish cultural relations as reflected in theatre. Lang.: Eng. 577
1865-1998. **Research/historiography.**
Critique of the biases of theatre history toward the exceptional. Lang.: Pol. 822
1867-1967. **Plays/librettos/scripts.**
Ibsen's *Peer Gynt* and its new Polish translation. Norway. Lang.: Pol. 3308
1881-1953. **Performance/production.**
The artistic life of dancer Vaclav Nižinskij. Russia. France. Lang.: Pol. 1123
1885-1998. **Plays/librettos/scripts.**
Feminist analysis of plays by Gabriela Zapolska. Lang.: Pol. 3301
1901-1995. **Performance/production.**
Analysis of productions of *Dziady (Forefather's Eve)* by Adam Mickiewicz. Lang.: Pol. 2220
1904-1972. **Performance/production.**
Returned emigrant dancer George Groke. Germany. Lang.: Ger. 925
1905-1915. **Performance/production.**
Theatre in Vilna. Vilna. Lang.: Pol. 576
1907-1974. **Performance/production.**
Dancer, choreographer, and teacher Ruth Abramowitsch-Sorel. Lang.: Ger. 1296
1907-1976. **Design/technology.**
Scenographer Tadeusz Orlowicz. Cracow. Neubrandenburg. London. Lang.: Pol. 212
1918-1939. **Performance/production.**
Vilna's Yiddish theatre companies. Vilna. Cracow. Lang.: Pol. 2212
1918-1998. **Institutions.**
History of the Polish Theatre Association. Warsaw. Lang.: Pol. 1692
1921-1933. **Performance/production.**
Nativity puppet plays as a form of cabaret. Vilna. Lang.: Pol. 4896
1923-1937. **Performance/production.**
Collaboration of Jewish and Polish theatres in the interwar period. Warsaw. Lang.: Pol. 574
1926-1938. **Institutions.**
Polish guest performances of HaBimah. Lang.: Pol. 1689
1927-1933. **Performance/production.**
Profile of the Hebrew Dramatic Studio. Vilna. Lang.: Pol. 2222
1927-1939. **Institutions.**
Literary meetings in multiethnic Vilna. Vilna. Lang.: Pol. 372
1928-1998. **Institutions.**
Pictorial history of Teatr Ateneum. Warsaw. Lang.: Pol. 1688
1929-1931. **Performance/production.**
Actor/director Aleksander Zelwerowicz. Vilna. Lang.: Pol. 2223
1929-1938. **Institutions.**
Jakub Rotbaum's leadership of Trupa Wileńska. Vilna. Lang.: Pol. 1686
1930-1998. **Institutions.**
Polish experimental theatre training. Cracow. Wroclaw. Warsaw. Lang.: Pol. 1685
1937-1939. **Performance/production.**
The European and American tour of the Polish National Ballet. France. USA. Lang.: Pol. 1124
1939-1945. **Performance/production.**
Actor Jan Kreczmar. Warsaw. Lvov. Lang.: Pol. 2216
1939-1984. **Plays/librettos/scripts.**
Home in Polish emigrant drama. UK-England. Lang.: Pol. 3306
1939-1988. **Performance/production.**
The Jewish Kabaret za murem and its treatment in Polish theatre. Warsaw. Lang.: Pol. 4157
1945-1950. **Performance/production.**
Postwar Polish theatre, culture, and politics. Lang.: Eng. 573
1945-1996. **Performance/production.**
Collection of reviews of puppet performances. Lang.: Pol. 4895
1945-1998. **Plays/librettos/scripts.**
Old age in plays of Różewicz. Lang.: Pol. 3309
1949-1992. **Institutions.**
Wyspiański's Teatr Śląski. Katowice. Lang.: Pol. 1690
1951-1959. **Performance/production.**
Early work of Jerzy Grotowski. Cracow. Lang.: Pol. 575
1951-1998. **Plays/librettos/scripts.**
Translating the unfinished *Historia (History)* by Witold Gombrowicz. Lang.: Eng. 3303
1952-1984. **Theory/criticism.**
Performance art and the 'poetics of space'. USA. Lang.: Eng. 4270
1952-1997. **Performance/production.**
History of Teatr Wybrzeże. Gdańsk. Warsaw. Cracow. Lang.: Pol. 2215
1954-1959. **Performance/production.**
Profiles of student cabaret groups. Warsaw. Gdańsk. Lang.: Pol. 4156
1958-1998. **Performance/production.**
Spirituality and the theatre of Jerzy Grotowski. Lang.: Ger, Fre, Dut, Eng. 2226
1960-1975. **Performance/production.**
Ritual in the theatre of Jerzy Grotowski. Lang.: Pol. 2221
1960-1990. **Plays/librettos/scripts.**
Essays on Polish theatre. Lang.: Hun. 3305
1960-1998. **Performance/production.**
Interview with director Andrzej Wajda. Lang.: Fin. 2224
1963. **Plays/librettos/scripts.**
Ida Kamińska's production of *Der Kheshbn (The Final Reckoning)* by Mikhl Mirsky. Warsaw. Lang.: Eng. 3310
1978-1998. **Institutions.**
Interview with Wlodzimierz Staniewski of Gardzienice Theatre Association. Gardzienice. Lang.: Ger, Fre, Dut, Eng. 1687
1980-1995. **Theory/criticism.**
Changes in the social and political situation of Polish fringe theatre. Lang.: Pol. 3826
1981-1988. **Institutions.**
The Orange Alternative, a street theatre opponent of martial law. Wroclaw. Lang.: Eng. 375
1987. **Performance/production.**
Tadeusz Kantor's directorial process. Cracow. Lang.: Eng. 2217
1989. **Institutions.**
Profile of theatre company Teatr St I Witkiewicza. Zakopane. Lang.: Eng. 1684
1989-1998. **Performance/production.**
Director Anna Augustynowicz. Szczecin. Lang.: Pol. 2214
The new generation of Polish directors. Lang.: Pol. 2219
1990-1998. **Performance/production.**
Contemporary Polish productions of Shakespeare. Lang.: Pol. 2213
1997-1998. **Theory/criticism.**
Reviews of recent publications by Jan Kott. Lang.: Hun. 854
1998. **Administration.**
On the history of arts patronage. Lang.: Rus. 19
1998. **Basic theatrical documents.**
English translation of *Historia (History)* by Witold Gombrowicz. Lang.: Eng. 1448
1998. **Institutions.**
The Kontakt '98 theatre festival. Toruń. Lang.: Hun. 373
1998. **Performance/production.**
Jerzy Grzegorzewski's production of *Ślub (The Marriage)* by Witold Gombrowicz. Warsaw. Lang.: Pol. 2218
Productions of the festival of experimental theatre. Cracow. Lang.: Ger. 2225
Musical theatre performer Anna German. Lang.: Rus. 4365
1998. **Theory/criticism.**
Roman Ingarden, phenomenology, and theatre. Lang.: Pol. 855
Essay on theatre and reception theory. Lang.: Pol. 856
1998. **Training.**
Director Walter Pfaff on the influence of Jerzy Grotowski. Germany. Lang.: Eng. 876

Portugal

1919-1965. **Plays/librettos/scripts.**
The influence of Federico García Lorca on playwright Bernardo Santareno. Spain. Lang.: Eng. 3400
1998. **Institutions.**
The eleventh session of the International School of Theatre Anthropology. Lisbon. Holstebro. Lang.: Eng. 376
1998. **Performance/production.**
Politics, culture, and Portuguese dance and choreography. Lang.: Eng. 959

Puerto Rico
1850-1985. **Plays/librettos/scripts.**
The mulatto in Puerto Rican drama. Lang.: Spa. 3311
1998. **Plays/librettos/scripts.**
Analysis of plays by Roberto Ramos-Perea. Lang.: Spa. 3312
1998. **Relation to other fields.**
Theatre, the visual arts, and the debate on Puerto Rican cultural identity. Lang.: Eng. 755
Roman Empire
Performance/production.
Early theatre. Ancient Greece. India. Egypt. Lang.: Rus. 484
Aesthetic analysis of ancient Roman 'blood spectacles'. Lang.: Eng. 4128
4 B.C.-65 A.D. **Plays/librettos/scripts.**
Analysis of Seneca's *Oedipus* and *Hercules furens*. Lang.: Eng. 3313
4 B.C.-150 A.D. **Performance/production.**
The performance of Senecan tragedy. Lang.: Eng. 2227
Romania
1798-1998. **Institutions.**
Hungarian-language theatre in Transylvania. Hungary. Lang.: Hun. 365
1907-1997. **Plays/librettos/scripts.**
Essays on playwright Áron Tamási. Lang.: Hun. 3314
1919-1992. **Institutions.**
History of Hungarian-language theatre in Transylvania. Hungary. Lang.: Hun, Rom. 1693
1925-1985. **Performance/production.**
Director György Harag. Hungary. Lang.: Hun. 2229
1939-1940. **Performance/production.**
Polish soldiers' theatrical activities in the Comisani internment camp. Comisani. Lang.: Pol. 578
1939-1946. **Performance/production.**
Theatre for Polish soldiers. UK-England. France. Lang.: Pol. 611
1948-1992. **Institutions.**
History of Hungarian-language theatre in a Romanian city. Sfântu-Gheorghe. Lang.: Hun. 379
1948-1998. **Performance/production.**
Production of László Lajtha's comic opera *Le chapeau bleu*. Cluj-Napoca. Hungary. Lang.: Hun. 4668
1965-1989. **Institutions.**
Hungarian dramatic art in Transylvania. Cluj-Napoca. Satu Mare. Hungary. Lang.: Hun. 378
1989-1998. **Administration.**
New funding options for Romanian arts groups. Lang.: Eng. 20
1997. **Performance/production.**
Review of Madách's *Tragedy of Man* at the Hungarian Theatre of Kolozsvár. Hungary. Cluj-Napoca. Lang.: Hun. 2065
1998. **Institutions.**
Profile of National Theatre Festival. Bucharest. Lang.: Hun. 377
1998. **Performance/production.**
Molière's *Dom Juan* directed by Olga Barabás. Hungary. Sfântu-Gheorghe. Lang.: Hun. 2063
Productions of plays by Brecht and Shakespeare at the Hungarian theatre of Satu Mare. Satu Mare. Lang.: Hun. 2228
A production of László Lajtha's comic opera *Le chapeau bleu*. Cluj-Napoca. Hungary. Lang.: Hun. 4666
Interview with soprano Andrea Lory. Iasi. Hungary. Lang.: Hun. 4667
Rome
500 B.C.-476 A.D. **Plays/librettos/scripts.**
Roman tragic theatre from literary origins to the Roman arena. Lang.: Eng. 3315
Russia
Institutions.
Profile of the Pskov Pushkin Theatre. Pskov. Lang.: Rus. 1696
Performance/production.
Theatrical history of Nižnij Novgorod. Nižnij Novgorod. Lang.: Rus. 588
Choreographer Marius Petipa and his wife, ballerina Marie Surovščikova. Lang.: Rus. 1128
Russian émigré ballet dancers. St. Petersburg. Lang.: Rus. 1129
Autobiography of ballet dancer and choreographer Rudolf Nureyev. Lang.: Rus. 1144
Ballet dancer Uljana Lopatkina. St. Petersburg. Lang.: Rus. 1146
Saratov's theatrical life. Saratov. Lang.: Rus. 2245
Actress and director Tatjana Doronina of Moscow Art Theatre. Moscow. Lang.: Rus. 2253
Director Mark Zacharov at Lenkom. Moscow. Lang.: Rus. 2316
Reviews of the Russian theatre season. Moscow. Lang.: Rus. 2324
K. Dubinin's production of *Boi imeli mestnoe zančenie (The Battles Had Localized)* based on work of Viačeslav Kondratjév. Volgograd. Lang.: Rus. 2331
Cossack theatre of the Choper Valley. Lang.: Rus. 2332
Actor Sergej Bezrukov. Moscow. Lang.: Rus. 2341
G. Chazanov of Teat'r Estrady. Moscow. Lang.: Rus. 4277
Singer Ljudmila Zykina. Lang.: Rus. 4302
Singer Larisa Dolina. Moscow. Lang.: Rus. 4366
Ten' Puppet Theatre's production of Čajkovskij's opera *Iolanta*. Moscow. Lang.: Rus. 4680
Bolšoj Opera star V. Bukin. Moscow. Lang.: Rus. 4683
Plays/librettos/scripts.
Articles on playwright A.N. Ostrovskij. Lang.: Rus. 3316
Collected writings of filmmaker Gennadij Špalikov. Lang.: Rus. 3975
Opera librettos of playwright Michajl Bulgakov. Lang.: Rus. 4817
Relation to other fields.
The use of theatre to teach foreign languages. Moscow. Lang.: Rus. 761
The effect of emigration on Russian dance. Lang.: Rus. 1197
1596-1980. **Plays/librettos/scripts.**
Recognition in plays of Čechov, Shakespeare, and Beckett. England. France. Lang.: Eng. 2949
1620-1900. **Plays/librettos/scripts.**
Analysis of the 'Russian Robin Hood' Stepan Razin. Lang.: Eng. 3327
1689-1725. **Performance/production.**
Theatre in the time of Czar Peter I. Lang.: Rus. 2329
1701-1800. **Plays/librettos/scripts.**
Russian literature and theatre of the eighteenth century. Lang.: Rus. 3322
1751-1799. **Plays/librettos/scripts.**
Playwright Michajl Cheraskov and late eighteenth-century drama. Lang.: Rus. 3332
1752-1998. **Performance/production.**
Onstage costume changes. Japan. Denmark. Lang.: Swe. 556
1764-1869. **Plays/librettos/scripts.**
Morality in plays of Fonvizin, Ostrovskij, and A.K. Tolstoj. Lang.: Rus. 3325
1768-1794. **Plays/librettos/scripts.**
Analysis of Catherine the Great's opera *The Beginning of Oleg's Reign*. Lang.: Eng. 4816
1785-1917. **Performance/production.**
Account of an exhibition devoted to Russian actors. St. Petersburg. Lang.: Rus. 2231
1788-1863. **Performance/production.**
Serf actor Michajl Ščepkin. Samara. Lang.: Rus. 2300
1799-1869. **Plays/librettos/scripts.**
Operas of Dargomyžskij and Rimskij-Korsakov on texts of Puškin. Lang.: Rus. 4815
1800-1825. **Plays/librettos/scripts.**
The influence of the war of 1812 on Russian drama. Lang.: Rus. 3334
1800-1998. **Performance/production.**
Major Russian actresses and ballerinas of the nineteenth and twentieth centuries. Lang.: Rus. 2240
1801-1840. **Performance/production.**
St. Petersburg opera performances. St. Petersburg. Lang.: Rus. 4686
1805. **Performance/production.**
Serf actors from Saratov in the theatre of Czar Alexander I. St. Petersburg. Lang.: Rus. 2246
1806. **Performance/production.**
German theatre in Russia: a report to Czar Alexander I. Lang.: Rus. 581
1820-1871. **Performance/production.**
Opera singer Aleksand'r Serov. Lang.: Rus. 4673
1825-1997. **Performance/production.**
Premieres of the Bolšoj Theatre. Moscow. Lang.: Rus. 4693

Russia — cont'd

1838-1926. **Basic theatrical documents.**
English translation of Mejerchol'd's adaptation of *Revizor (The Inspector General)* by Gogol. USSR. Lang.: Eng. 1450
1840-1998. **Design/technology.**
Rapid on-stage costume changes in dance. Sweden. Japan. Lang.: Swe. 889
1850-1899. **Plays/librettos/scripts.**
Playwright A. Potechin. Saratov. Lang.: Rus. 3337
1851-1899. **Performance/production.**
Actor/director Pavel Medvedev. Lang.: Rus. 2330
1868-1913. **Performance/production.**
Correspondence of composer Nikolaj Rimskij-Korsakov and singer Nadežda Zabela-Vrubel'. Lang.: Rus. 4670
1868-1945. **Plays/librettos/scripts.**
Actor and playwright N.I. Sobol'ščikov-Samarin. Lang.: Rus. 3339
1872-1929. **Performance/production.**
Diaghilev recalled by his stepmother. Lang.: Rus. 1132
1873-1938. **Performance/production.**
Opera singer Fëdor Šaljapin. Lang.: Rus. 4669
Life and work of singer Fëdor Šaljapin. Lang.: Rus. 4672
The life of the opera singer Fëdor Šaljapin. Lang.: Rus. 4681
Personal recollections of Šaljapin singing on recordings of *Boris Godunov*. Lang.: Eng. 4685
Opera singer Fëdor Šaljapin and his roots in Vjatka. Vjatka. Lang.: Rus. 4687
Career of opera singer Fëdor Šaljapin. Lang.: Rus. 4688
Books in the life of opera singer Fëdor Šaljapin. Lang.: Rus. 4691
1873-1941. **Performance/production.**
Actor Lenid Leonidov. Moscow. Lang.: Rus. 2312
1874-1940. **Performance/production.**
Biography of director V.E. Mejerchol'd. Lang.: Rus. 2258
1875-1925. **Design/technology.**
Scene designers of the Mamontovskaja Opera. Moscow. Lang.: Rus. 4437
1876. **Design/technology.**
Scene designs for *Ruslan i Ljudmila* by V. Gartman. St. Petersburg. Lang.: Rus. 4438
1877-1888. **Performance/production.**
Reconstruction of Stanislavskij's early stagings for the Alekseev Group. Moscow. Lang.: Rus. 2322
1878-1889. **Performance/production.**
Analysis of Čechov's *Platonov* and *Lešji (The Wood Demon)*. Lang.: Eng. 2297
1878-1945. **Performance/production.**
Actress/director Alla Nazimova. USA. Lang.: Eng. 585
1879-1953. **Performance/production.**
Memoirs of director and playwright Nikolaj Jévrejnov. Lang.: Rus. 2279
1880-1949. **Design/technology.**
Avant-garde Russian women artist/designers. USSR. Lang.: Eng. 214
1881-1953. **Performance/production.**
The artistic life of dancer Vaclav Nižinskij. Poland. France. Lang.: Pol. 1123
1884-1904. **Basic theatrical documents.**
Catalan translations of the complete plays of Anton Čechov. Lang.: Cat. 1449
1890-1899. **Institutions.**
Gavrila Solodovnikov's Teat'r na Dmitrovke. Moscow. Lang.: Rus. 1717
1890-1899. **Performance/production.**
The early operatic career of Fëdor Šaljapin. Nizhni Novgorod. Lang.: Rus. 4676
1890-1910. **Plays/librettos/scripts.**
Čechov's character Treplev. Lang.: Rus. 3336
Gorkij and the 'new drama' of the turn of the century. Lang.: Rus. 3341
1890-1936. **Plays/librettos/scripts.**
Comparison of the plays of Čechov and Bulgakov. Lang.: Rus. 3338
1890-1949. **Plays/librettos/scripts.**
The dramatic styles of Maurice Maeterlinck and Anton Čechov. Belgium. Lang.: Rus. 3328
1891-1903. **Performance/production.**
Autobiographical writings by director V.E. Mejerchol'd. Lang.: Rus. 2296
1892-1970. **Performance/production.**
Interview with choreographer Kasjan Golejzovskij. Lang.: Rus. 960
1896. **Plays/librettos/scripts.**
Analysis of *Čajka (The Seagull)* by Anton Čechov. Lang.: Eng. 3335
1896-1984. **Performance/production.**
Anecdotes by and about actress Faina Ranevskaja. Lang.: Rus. 584
Singer and actress Faina Ranevskaja. Lang.: Rus. 2319
Biography of actress Faina Ranevskaja. Lang.: Rus. 2320
1897-1962. **Relation to other fields.**
Memoirs of poet, journalist, and playwright A.B. Mariengof. Lang.: Rus. 760
1898-1901. **Institutions.**
Diaries of theatre director V.A. Teljakovskij. St. Petersburg. Lang.: Rus. 1716
1898-1989. **Training.**
Actress, director, and teacher Marija Knebel'. Lang.: Rus. 3850
1898-1998. **Institutions.**
The centennary of the Moscow Art Theatre. Moscow. Lang.: Rus. 1694
Description of the *Encyclopedia of the Moscow Art Theatre*. Moscow. Lang.: Rus. 1703
The one-hundredth anniversary of the Moscow Art Theatre. Moscow. Lang.: Rus. 1704
Centennial celebration of the Moscow Art Theatre. Moscow. Lang.: Rus. 1710
History of Moscow Art Theatre, on the occasion of its centennial. Moscow. Lang.: Rus. 1714
1898-1998. **Performance/production.**
The history of the ballet *Raymonda* by Glazunov and Petipa. Lang.: Eng. 1133
A century of Čechov productions by the Moscow Art Theatre. Moscow. Lang.: Rus. 2288
1899. **Plays/librettos/scripts.**
The character Sonya in Čechov's *Diadia Vania (Uncle Vanya)*. Lang.: Rus. 3333
1900-1919. **Plays/librettos/scripts.**
Bibliography relating to plays of Andrejëv and their productions. Lang.: Rus. 3320
1900-1940. **Performance/production.**
Director V.E. Mejerchol'd. Lang.: Rus. 2230
1900-1946. **Plays/librettos/scripts.**
Comparison of plays by Harley Granville-Barker and Anton Čechov. UK-England. Lang.: Eng. 3501
1900-1950. **Performance/production.**
Japanese-Russian theatrical relations. Japan. Lang.: Rus. 2194
1901. **Plays/librettos/scripts.**
Analysis of Čechov's *Drame na ochote (Drama of the Hunting Trip)*. Lang.: Rus. 3318
Linguistic questions in Čechov's *Tri sestry (Three Sisters)*. Lang.: Rus. 3331
1901-1902. **Plays/librettos/scripts.**
Translations of Čechov's *Three Sisters* and Gorkij's *The Lower Depths*. Lang.: Rus. 3326
1901-1912. **Plays/librettos/scripts.**
Russian reception of plays by Stanisław Przybyszewski. Moscow. St. Petersburg. Lang.: Pol. 3330
1901-1995. **Plays/librettos/scripts.**
The Break of Day, Timberlake Wertenbaker's adaptation of Čechov's *Three Sisters*. UK-England. Lang.: Eng. 3510
1901-1998. **Institutions.**
Moscow Art Theatre's production of Čechov's *Tri sestry (Three Sisters)*. Moscow. Lang.: Eng. 1713
1901-1998. **Performance/production.**
The influence of Russian dancers and choreographers on world ballet. Lang.: Eng. 1149
1904. **Plays/librettos/scripts.**
Analysis of Čechov's *Višnëvyj sad (The Cherry Orchard)*. Lang.: Rus. 3323
1905-1989. **Performance/production.**
Pirandello on the Russian stage. Lang.: Ita. 2250
1906-1917. **Performance/production.**
Letters of K.S. Stanislavskij. Lang.: Rus. 2327
1908-1931. **Institutions.**
Theatrical parodies of Krivoje zerkalo. St. Petersburg. Lang.: Eng. 1705

Russia — cont'd

1910-1915. **Performance/production.**
Performance culture in prerevolutionary Russia. Lang.: Eng. 580
1910-1929. **Design/technology.**
Two decades of St. Petersburg scene design. St. Petersburg. Lang.: Rus. 217
1910-1930. **Plays/librettos/scripts.**
Drama and theatrical elements in the work of Vladimir Majakovskij. Lang.: Eng. 3319
1910-1998. **Performance/production.**
Obituary for ballerina Galina Ulanova. Lang.: Eng. 1125
Obituary for ballerina Galina Ulanova. Lang.: Eng. 1127
1913-1998. **Performance/production.**
Russian reception and interpretation of the work of Jerzy Grotowski. Lang.: Pol. 2236
1913-1998. **Plays/librettos/scripts.**
Playwright Viktor Rozov. Lang.: Rus. 3329
1916. **Performance/production.**
Analysis of the first book about opera singer Fëdor Šaljapin. Lang.: Rus. 4678
1917-1920. **Relation to other fields.**
The cultural atmosphere of the Russian Revolution. Lang.: Rus. 757
1917-1980. **Performance/production.**
Memoirs of actress Ol'ga Čechova. Lang.: Rus. 2243
1918-1998. **Relation to other fields.**
Intellectual life in Nižni Novgorod. Nizhegorod. Lang.: Rus. 759
1919-1925. **Performance/production.**
Dancer Isadora Duncan's relationship with poet Sergej Esenin. Lang.: Rus. 1297
1919-1938. **Performance/production.**
Italian translation of letters written by K.S. Stanislavskij. Lang.: Ita. 2328
1920-1929. **Relation to other fields.**
Russian and American theatre and society of the twenties. USA. Lang.: Rus. 756
1920-1939. **Performance/production.**
Choreographers and theorists E.V. Javorskij and N.S. Poznjakov. Moscow. Lang.: Rus. 961
1920-1949. **Performance/production.**
The Russian-German theatrical relationship. Germany. Lang.: Rus. 2285
1923-1998. **Institutions.**
The Majakovskij Theatre. Moscow. Lang.: Rus. 1700
1925-1994. **Performance/production.**
Biography of ballerina Maja Pliseckaja. Lang.: Rus. 1131
1926-1998. **Performance/production.**
Memoirs of choreographer Igor Moisejèv. Moscow. Lang.: Rus. 1233
1930-1932. **Plays/librettos/scripts.**
Analysis of *Voskresšij syn (Reincarnated Son)* by Maksim Gorkij. Lang.: Rus. 3321
1932-1998. **Performance/production.**
Ballerina Alla Osipenko. Lang.: Eng. 1139
1933-1990. **Performance/production.**
Memoirs of actor Georgij Burkov. Lang.: Rus. 2241
1934. **Performance/production.**
Boris Asafjev's ballet *Bachčisarajskij fontan* directed by R. Zacharov at the Mariinskij. St. Petersburg. Lang.: Rus. 1134
Mythology in theatre works of Stravinskij, especially *Perséphone*. Lang.: Eng. 4682
1938-1980. **Basic theatrical documents.**
Songs and poems of Vladimir Vysockij. Moscow. Lang.: Rus. 1453
1938-1980. **Performance/production.**
Biographical information on actor Vladimir Vysockij. Moscow. Lang.: Rus. 2291
1940. **Performance/production.**
I. Igin's *Czars*, a biography of dancers Konstantin Sergejèv and Natalija Dudinskaja. Leningrad. Lang.: Rus. 1138
1940-1998. **Plays/librettos/scripts.**
Playwright Emil Braginskij. Lang.: Rus. 3324
1942-1998. **Performance/production.**
Director Anatolij Vasiljèv. Lang.: Hun. 2282
1947-1997. **Institutions.**
History of the Kaliningrad Theatre. Kaliningrad. Lang.: Rus. 1702
1948. **Performance/production.**
The murder of actor and director Solomon Michoéls. Moscow. Lang.: Rus. 2293
1948-1998. **Performance/production.**
History of Kurgan's puppet theatre. Kurgan. Lang.: Rus. 4897
1950-1998. **Performance/production.**
Profiles of major theatrical figures. Lang.: Rus. 2263
1959-1998. **Performance/production.**
Tenor Sergej Larin. Lang.: Eng. 4674
1960-1970. **Basic theatrical documents.**
Selection of poems and songs by actor Vladimir Vysockij. Moscow. Lang.: Rus. 164
1972-1998. **Performance/production.**
Choreographer Boris Ejfman. St. Petersburg. Lang.: Eng. 1126
1980. **Performance/production.**
The final months of actor Vladimir Vysockij. Moscow. Lang.: Rus. 2307
The funeral of actor and playwright Vladimir Vysockij. Moscow. Lang.: Rus. 2333
1990-1998. **Institutions.**
Report on Vachtangov School conference. Moscow. Lang.: Rus. 380
1995-1999. **Performance/production.**
Notes and essays on dancers and actors of the nineties. Lang.: Rus. 587
1997. **Institutions.**
The Bolšoj Ballet and the experimental company Gelikon. Moscow. Lang.: Swe. 4467
Preview of the Kirov Opera's visit to the Metropolitan Opera. St. Petersburg. Lang.: Eng. 4470
1997. **Performance/production.**
Interview with director Lev Dodin. Lang.: Fre. 2260
The tour of the Mariinskij Theatre. Moscow. Lang.: Rus. 4690
1997-1998. **Institutions.**
Assessment of the Bolšoj Theatre season. Moscow. Lang.: Rus. 1046
The Bolšoj Theatre's 222nd season. Moscow. Lang.: Rus. 4466
1998. **Administration.**
V. Vol'chovskij, puppet theatre producer. Lang.: Rus. 4916
1998. **Basic theatrical documents.**
Theatrical and other writings of actor Leonid Filatov. Moscow. Lang.: Rus. 163
Anthology of literary texts including plays for use in school. Lang.: Rus. 1451
Plays of Vladimir Vysockij. Moscow. Lang.: Rus. 1452
1998. **Design/technology.**
Scenographer N. Panova. Tver'. Lang.: Rus. 213
Memoirs of scenographer Jèvgenij Kumankov. Lang.: Rus. 215
Scenographer Tatjana Sel'vinskaja. Lang.: Rus. 216
Catalogue of an exhibition devoted to choreography of Diaghilev. St. Petersburg. Lang.: Rus. 1029
Scene design and the plays of Ostrovskij. Lang.: Rus. 1523
1998. **Institutions.**
Theatre history course of study. Lang.: Rus. 381
Annual festival of theatre performed by children. Kaluga. Lang.: Rus. 382
Report on folk dance festival and competition. Voskresensk. Lang.: Rus. 1222
Profile of modern dance festival. Lang.: Rus. 1252
Profile of the Omsk Drama Theatre. Omsk. Lang.: Rus. 1695
A visit to Anatolij Vasiljèv's School of Dramatic art. Moscow. Lang.: Hun. 1697
Moscow Art Theatre's two theatres and their artistic directors. Moscow. Lang.: Rus. 1698
A program of study including playwriting and production. Moscow. Lang.: Rus. 1699
Impressions from the 'Golden Mask' festival. Minusinsk. Lang.: Ger. 1701
Profile of the Omsk Dramatic Theatre, 'Galerka'. Omsk. Lang.: Rus. 1706
Profile of Omsk's Dramatic Theatre. Omsk. Lang.: Rus. 1707
Account of the Saratov stage festival. Saratov. Lang.: Rus. 1708
Ostrovskij Festival celebrating the 175th anniversary of Malyj Teat'r. Moscow. Lang.: Rus. 1709
Profile of the Kiselev Youth Theatre. Saratov. Lang.: Rus. 1711

Russia — cont'd

The student satirical company Teat'r Grotesk. Surgut. Lang.: Rus. 1712

Oleg Tabakov's Studio Theatre. Moscow. Lang.: Rus. 1715

A. Dživaev's equestrian theatre Konnyj Teat'r 'Narty'. Vladikavkaz. Lang.: Rus. 4272

Portrait of Dmitrij Bertman, artistic director of Moskovskij Muzykal'nyj Teat'r Gelikon. Moscow. Lang.: Rus. 4468

The Boldina Opera and Ballet festival honoring Puškin. Nizhni Novgorod. Lang.: Rus. 4469

The world tour of the Kirov Opera, headed by Valerij Gergiev. St. Petersburg. Lang.: Eng. 4471

Profile of 'Ognivo' puppet theatre. Mytišchi. Lang.: Rus. 4871

Profile of the National Puppet Theatre. Moscow. Lang.: Rus. 4872

1998. Performance/production.

Actor Arkadij Rajkin. Lang.: Rus. 579

Memoirs of actress Tatjana Okunevskaja. Lang.: Rus. 582

Memoirs of actor Arkadij Rajkin. Lang.: Rus. 583

Interview with actor Jėvgenij Vesnik. Moscow. Lang.: Rus. 586

Ballet soloist T. Černobrivkina. Moscow. Lang.: Rus. 1130

Collaboration of the Bolšoj and Mariinskij ballet troupes. Moscow. St. Petersburg. Lang.: Rus. 1135

Ballerina Natalija Ledovskaja. Moscow. Lang.: Rus. 1136

Guest performance of the Kremlevskij Balet. Budapest. Lang.: Hun. 1137

Ballerina Uljana Lopatkina. St. Petersburg. Lang.: Rus. 1140

Bolšoj Ballet director Jurij Grigorovič. Moscow. Lang.: Rus. 1141

Ballerina Nina Ananiašvili. Lang.: Rus. 1142

Ballerina Maja Pliseckaja and her husband, composer Rodion Ščedrin. Moscow. Lang.: Rus. 1143

Memoirs of ballerina Maja Pliseckaja. Lang.: Rus. 1145

Bolšoj ballet master and choreographer Vladimir Vasiljėv. Moscow. Lang.: Rus. 1147

Profile of ballerinas Uljana Lopatkina and Diana Višneva. St. Petersburg. Lang.: Rus. 1148

Choreographer Igor Moisejėv. Moscow. Lang.: Rus. 1231

Tatar folk dance in Siberia. Lang.: Rus. 1232

Boris Ejfman's Teat'r Sovremennogo Baleta. St. Petersburg. Lang.: Rus. 1298

Interview with actor Armen Džigarchanjan. Moscow. Lang.: Rus. 2232

Director Leonid Truškin. Moscow. Lang.: Rus. 2233

Memoirs of actresses Olga Aroseva and V.A. Maksimova. Moscow. Lang.: Rus. 2234

Actor Vladislav Stržel'čik. St. Petersburg. Lang.: Rus. 2235

Seinen-za's performance at the Čechov festival. Moscow. Lang.: Rus. 2237

Interview with Moscow Art Theatre actress G. Kalinovskaja. Moscow. Lang.: Rus. 2238

Actors of the Adygeian Drama Theatre. Majkop. Lang.: Rus. 2239

Actress Elina Bystrickaja. Moscow. Lang.: Rus. 2242

Interview with director Roman Viktjuk. Moscow. Lang.: Rus. 2244

Memoirs of actor Oleg Dal'. Moscow. Lang.: Rus. 2247

Actor Nikolaj K. Simonov. St. Petersburg. Lang.: Rus. 2248

Actress Alla S. Demidova. Lang.: Rus. 2249

Director Anatolij Efros. Moscow. Lang.: Rus. 2251

Journal of actress Tatjana Doronina. Moscow. Lang.: Rus. 2252

Actress Tatjana Doronina. Lang.: Rus. 2254

Memoirs of Moscow Art Theatre actress Tatjana Doronina. Moscow. Lang.: Rus. 2255

Mother and daughter actresses Nina and E. Dobyševa. Moscow. Lang.: Rus. 2256

Memoirs of actor Lev Durov. Moscow. Lang.: Rus. 2257

Moscow Art Theatre actor Viktor Gvozdickij. Moscow. Lang.: Rus. 2259

Actress Margarita Terechova. Spain. Lang.: Rus. 2261

Children's theatre director E. Padve. St. Petersburg. Lang.: Rus. 2262

Solomon Michoėls of Moscow's Jewish Theatre. Moscow. Lang.: Rus. 2264

Director Kama Ginkas of Teat'r Junogo Zritelja. Lang.: Rus. 2265

Roman Viktjuk's production of *Salomé* by Oscar Wilde. Moscow. Lang.: Rus. 2266

Oleg Menšikov's production of *Gore ot uma (Wit Works Woe)* by Gribojėdov. Moscow. Lang.: Rus. 2267

Recent Russian productions of Shakespeare's *Hamlet*. Moscow. Lang.: Rus. 2268

Guest performances in Moscow. Moscow. Lang.: Rus. 2269

Jurij Ljubimov's production of *The First Circle*, based on Solženicin's novel. Moscow. Lang.: Rus. 2270

Producer and director Boris Golubovskij. Lang.: Rus. 2271

Interview with director Andrej Gončarov. Moscow. Lang.: Rus. 2272

Director Anatolij Efros. Moscow. Lang.: Rus. 2273

Michajl Mokejėv's production of Shakespeare's *Romeo and Juliet*. Belgorod. Lang.: Rus. 2274

Actor Juri Nazarov. Lang.: Rus. 2275

Mikle Mizjukov's production of *Pesn' sud'by (The Song of Fate)* by Blok. Moscow. Lang.: Rus. 2276

Actor E. Mjazinoj. Lang.: Rus. 2277

Sergej Bezrukov's creation of the character of poet Sergej Esenin. Moscow. Lang.: Rus. 2278

Moscow Art Theatre actress G. Kalinovskaja. Moscow. Lang.: Rus. 2280

A friend's view of director Pëtr Fomenko. Moscow. Lang.: Rus. 2281

Actress E. Majorova and her husband, scenographer S. Šerstjuk. Moscow. Lang.: Rus. 2283

Student performances in the State University's theatre. Moscow. Lang.: Rus. 2284

Actor Anatolij Ktorov. Moscow. Lang.: Rus. 2286

Religion and actor Oleg Borisov. St. Petersburg. Lang.: Rus. 2287

Actor Nikolaj Simonov. St. Petersburg. Lang.: Rus. 2289

Profile of stage and film actor Armen B. Džigarchanjan. Moscow. Lang.: Rus. 2290

Memoirs of actor A.P. Ktorov. Moscow. Lang.: Rus. 2292

Memoirs of actress I.V. Makarova. Moscow. Lang.: Rus. 2294

Actor Sergej Makoveckij. Moscow. Lang.: Rus. 2295

Actress Pavlina Konopčuk. Lang.: Rus. 2298

Actress Farida Muminova. Magnitogorsk. Lang.: Rus. 2299

Actress Inna Čurikova. Moscow. Lang.: Rus. 2301

Actress Tatjana Doronina. Moscow. Lang.: Rus. 2302

Pëtr Fomenko's theatrical adaptation of Gogol's *Dead Souls*. Moscow. Lang.: Rus. 2303

Actor Oleg Menšikov. Moscow. Lang.: Rus. 2304

The work of Russian directors at the Golden Mask festival. Moscow. St. Petersburg. Lang.: Swe. 2305

Productions of international Čechov festival. Moscow. Lang.: Swe. 2306

Actor Andrej Mironov. Moscow. Lang.: Rus. 2308

Playwright Nadežda Ptuškina on her plays in production. Lang.: Rus. 2309

Children's theatre actor Gennadij Pečnikov. Moscow. Lang.: Rus. 2310

Siberian theatre and culture. Lang.: Fin. 2311

Report on international conference devoted to the work of Vladimir Vysockij. Moscow. Lang.: Rus. 2313

Russia — cont'd

Recent productions of plays by Ostrovskij. Lang.: Rus. 2314
Actor G.I Sal'nikov. Saratov. Lang.: Rus. 2315
Dictionary of Russian stage actors. Lang.: Rus. 2317
Actress I.S. Savvina. Moscow. Lang.: Rus. 2318
Review of a Hungarian edition of writings by director A.A. Vasiljév. Moscow. Lang.: Hun. 2321
Memoirs of actor Innokentij Smoktunovskij. Moscow. Lang.: Rus. 2323
Director Sergej Rudzinskij. Omsk. Lang.: Rus. 2325
Director Jurij Solomin of Malyj Teat'r. Moscow. Lang.: Rus. 2326
Actress M. Vertinskaja on her father, singer Aleksand'r Vertinskij. Moscow. Lang.: Rus. 2334
Andrej Žitinkin directs *Confessions of Felix Krull, Confidence Man*, adapted from Thomas Mann. Moscow. Lang.: Rus. 2335
Memoirs of Malyj Theatre actor E. Ja. Vesnik. Moscow. Lang.: Rus. 2336
Actor Vladimir Vinokur. Lang.: Rus. 2337
Director Andrej Žitinkin. Moscow. Lang.: Rus. 2338
Vagant, a journal dedicated to the work of actor Vladimir Vysockij. Moscow. Lang.: Rus. 2339
Pëtr Fomenko's production of *V Čičikovskoj krugoverti (In Čičikov's Chaos)*. Moscow. Lang.: Rus. 2340
Actress Ljudmila Gurčenko. Moscow. Lang.: Rus. 3859
Illusionist Dž. Mostoslavskij. Yaroslav. Lang.: Rus. 4129
Singer Valerij Meladze. Lang.: Rus. 4130
Singer Valerij Meladze. Lang.: Rus. 4131
Circus producer V. Gneušev. Moscow. Lang.: Rus. 4183
Memoirs of film actor and clown Jurij Nikulin. Moscow. Lang.: Rus. 4184
Interview with actor R. Karcev. Lang.: Rus. 4276
Opera singer Ivan Kozlovskij. Nizhni Novgorod. Lang.: Rus. 4301
Singer Kristina Orbakajte. Moscow. Lang.: Rus. 4367
Singer I. Tal'kov. Lang.: Rus. 4368
Čajkovskij's *Eugene Onegin* directed by A. Stepanov. St. Petersburg. Lang.: Rus. 4671
Opera singers Tamara Sinjavskaja and Muslim Magomaev. Lang.: Rus. 4675
Opera singer N.K. Pečkovskij. Leningrad. Lang.: Rus. 4677
Teat'r Ten's *Ten' opery (The Shadow of the Opera)*. Moscow. Lang.: Rus. 4679
Bolšoj Opera singer M. Mincaev. Moscow. Lang.: Rus. 4684
Opera singer D.A. Smirnov. Lang.: Rus. 4689
Bolšoj Opera singer V. Matorin. Moscow. Lang.: Rus. 4692

1998. Plays/librettos/scripts.
Analysis of plays by Aleksand'r Vampilov. Lang.: Rus. 3317
V.V. Zoščenko on his play, *Uvažaemyj tovarišč M.M. Zoščenko (The Respected M.M. Zoščenko)*. Lang.: Rus. 3340
Letters and writings of film actor and writer Gennadij Špalikov. Lang.: Rus. 3976
Scenarios of Russian operas. Lang.: Rus. 4818

1998. Reference materials.
Russian actors and film stars. Lang.: Rus. 4033

1998. Relation to other fields.
The poetry of actors Leonid Filatov and Valentin Gaft. Moscow. Lang.: Rus. 758
Postage stamps commemorating Russian theatre and opera. Moscow. Lang.: Rus. 762

1998. Research/historiography.
German holdings of St. Petersburg's National Theatre Library. St. Petersburg. Lang.: Rus. 823

1998. Training.
Standards for future directors and teachers of directing. Lang.: Rus. 877
Maja Pliseckaja on ballet training. Moscow. Lang.: Rus. 1208

1999. Reference materials.
Yearbook of the arts and sciences. Lang.: Rus. 707

Saint Lucia

1980-1995. Plays/librettos/scripts.
Theatre and the creation of a new nationalism. Canada. Lang.: Eng. 2808

Savoy

1400-1600. Performance/production.
Late medieval Savoy and theatre. Lang.: Eng. 589

1435-1505. Plays/librettos/scripts.
Pictorial and staged versions of the Passion. Lang.: Eng. 3342

Senegal

1973. Performance/production.
Analysis of *Touki-Bouki (The Hyena's Travels)* by Djibril Diop Mambéty. Lang.: Eng. 3938

1973-1974. Plays/librettos/scripts.
Ousmane Sembéne's film adaptation of his own novel *Xala*. Lang.: Eng. 3977

Serbia

1998. Performance/production.
László Babarczy's production of *Pepe* by Andor Szilágy. Novi Sad. Lang.: Hun. 2342

Sicily

1646-1996. Performance/production.
History of Sicilian 'teatro dei pupi'. Lang.: Hun. 4921

Sierra Leone

1960-1998. Performance/production.
The use of English and Krio in theatre of Michael Yaarimeh Bangura. Freetown. Lang.: Eng. 2343

Singapore

1965-1998. Performance/production.
Chinese street opera and nation-building. Lang.: Eng. 4694

Slovakia

1881-1998. Administration.
The cooperative relationship between Czech and Slovak theatres. Czechoslovakia. Czech Republic. Lang.: Ger. 1376

1975-1998. Performance/production.
Interview with soprano Edita Gruberova. Lang.: Eng. 4695

1989-1998. Relation to other fields.
The effect of social and political change on Slovakian theatre. Lang.: Ger. 763

1998. Institutions.
The Nitra '98 theatre festival. Nitra. Lang.: Hun. 383

1998. Performance/production.
Čechov's one-act plays at Thália Színház. Hungary. Košice. Lang.: Hun. 2075

Slovenia

600 B.C.-1890 A.D. Performance/production.
World history of puppet theatre. Lang.: Slo. 4898

1750-1910. Institutions.
European national theatres and their development. Germany. Lang.: Slo. 1720

1789-1867. Institutions.
Slovene self-image and the national theatre. Germany. Lang.: Slo. 1719

1800-1988. Basic theatrical documents.
Texts of Slovene youth theatre plays. Lang.: Slo. 1462

1800-1997. Plays/librettos/scripts.
History and analysis of Slovene youth drama. Lang.: Slo. 3359

1800-1998. Performance/production.
The director in Slovene and Croatian theatre. Croatia. Lang.: Rus. 1875

1867-1997. Performance/production.
Brief history of Slovene theatre. Lang.: Slo. 595
Slovenian reception of Austrian drama. Austria. Lang.: Ger. 2347

1870. Plays/librettos/scripts.
Analysis of *Zoran ali Kmetska vojna na Slovenskum (Zoran and the Peasant War in Slovenia)* by Ivan Vrhovec. Lang.: Slo. 3351

1897-1910. Plays/librettos/scripts.
Analysis of *Zvestoba (Fidelity)* by Etbin Kristan. Lang.: Slo. 3344
Social roles in plays by Fran Govekar and Anton Medved. Lang.: Slo. 3352

1897-1920. Plays/librettos/scripts.
Social roles and ideologies in plays of Anton Funtek and Ivo Šorli. Lang.: Slo. 3353

1900-1954. Plays/librettos/scripts.
Translation work of playwright Oton Župančič. Lang.: Slo. 3357

1900-1997. Training.
Illustrated history of jazz dance. USA. Lang.: Slo. 1023

Slovenia — cont'd

1903-1994. **Plays/librettos/scripts.**
The priesthood in Slovene theatre. Lang.: Slo. 3345
1905-1949. **Theory/criticism.**
Playwright Oton Župančič and the theatrical essay. Lang.: Slo. 3828
1912-1927. **Performance/production.**
Oton Župančič and the Slovene stage language consultant. Lang.: Slo. 2345
1914-1918. **Performance/production.**
Theatrical events in Maribor during World War I. Maribor. Lang.: Slo. 593
1920-1941. **Theory/criticism.**
Critical writing on theatre of Josip Vidmar. Lang.: Slo. 3827
1924. **Plays/librettos/scripts.**
Analysis of *Veronika Deseniška (Veronica of Desenice)* by Oton Župančič. Lang.: Slo. 3360
1925-1986. **Plays/librettos/scripts.**
Playwright Ivan Mrak. Lang.: Slo. 3355
1930-1975. **Basic theatrical documents.**
Text of plays and other works by Ivan Mrak. Lang.: Slo. 1459
1933-1939. **Theory/criticism.**
Reviews of performances at Ljubljana's National Theatre. Ljubljana. Lang.: Slo. 3829
1940. **Plays/librettos/scripts.**
Fascism and the peasant in pre-War Slovene drama. Lang.: Slo. 3349
1942-1997. **Reference materials.**
Bibliography of scripts for Slovene puppet theatre. Lang.: Slo. 4914
1943-1985. **Plays/librettos/scripts.**
The individual and his world in Slovene theatre. Lang.: Slo. 3347
1945-1972. **Design/technology.**
Scenographic work of painter Maks Kavčič. Lang.: Slo. 218
1945-1997. **Performance/production.**
Polde Bibič on other Slovene actors. Lang.: Slo. 591
1946-1970. **Plays/librettos/scripts.**
Analysis of *Balada o taščici (Ballad of a Robin)* by Igor Torkar. Lang.: Slo. 3346
Analysis of plays by Igor Torkar. Lang.: Slo. 3354
1946-1998. **Performance/production.**
Interview with soprano Ondina Otta Klasine. Lang.: Slo. 4696
1947-1997. **Performance/production.**
Slovene puppet film. Lang.: Slo. 4899
1948-1998. **Institutions.**
Ljubljana's puppet theatre on its fiftieth anniversary. Ljubljana. Lang.: Slo. 4874
1951-1961. **Institutions.**
The first decade of Ljubljana's municipal theatre, Mestno gledališče ljubljansko. Ljubljana. Lang.: Slo. 1718
1955. **Plays/librettos/scripts.**
Religion and the individual in plays of Ivan Mrak. Lang.: Slo. 3358
1959-1969. **Plays/librettos/scripts.**
Analysis of plays by Primož Kozak. Lang.: Slo. 3350
1960-1997. **Performance/production.**
Interview with actress Milena Zupančič. Lang.: Slo. 596
1960-1997. **Plays/librettos/scripts.**
Bibliography of Slovene writers and playwrights in translation. Lang.: Eng. 3343
1960-1998. **Performance/production.**
Characteristics and development of ritual theatre. Lang.: Slo. 592
1968-1997. **Institutions.**
The fiftieth anniversary of Ljubljana's puppet theatre. Ljubljana. Lang.: Slo. 4873
1968-1998. **Basic theatrical documents.**
Text of Evgen Car's monologue *Poredušov Janoš.* Lang.: Slo. 1454
1969-1997. **Basic theatrical documents.**
Slovene translation of *Mistero Buffo* by Dario Fo. Italy. Lang.: Slo. 1441
1973-1993. **Performance/production.**
Slovene translation of Cicely Berry's work on vocal training for the actor. UK-England. Lang.: Slo. 2344
1980-1997. **Performance/production.**
Essays and reviews of contemporary theatre. Lang.: Slo. 2346
1988. **Plays/librettos/scripts.**
Analysis of *Medeja (Medea)* by Dane Zajc. Lang.: Slo. 3348
1990-1997. **Basic theatrical documents.**
Text of plays by Branko Rozman. Lang.: Slo. 1461
1991. **Plays/librettos/scripts.**
Analysis of *Grmače* by Dane Zajc. Lang.: Slo. 3356
1991-1997. **Basic theatrical documents.**
Plays and screenplays by Vili Ravnjak. Lang.: Slo. 1460
1992-1995. **Theory/criticism.**
Excerpts from diary of theatre critic Andrej Inkret. Lang.: Slo. 857
1993-1997. **Performance/production.**
Children's puppet work. Austria. Lang.: Slo. 4885
1994-1997. **Performance/production.**
European influences on Slovene performance. Lang.: Slo. 594
1995-1997. **Performance/production.**
The Slovene language consultant (*lektor*). Lang.: Slo. 2348
1996-1997. **Reference materials.**
Yearbook of Slovene theatre. Lang.: Slo. 708
1997. **Basic theatrical documents.**
Text of *Suženj akcije—Kralj Peter Šesti (A Slave of Action—King Peter the Sixth)* by Emil Filipčič. Lang.: Slo. 1455
Text of *Sončne pege (Sunspots)* by Evald Flisar. Lang.: Slo. 1456
Text of *Miklavžev večer (St. Nicholas' Eve)* by Miloš Mikeln. Lang.: Slo. 1457
Texts of plays by Vinko Möderndorfer. Lang.: Slo. 1458
Text of the musical play *Emanacije (Emanations)* by Tomaž Brenk and Mojca Kasjak. Lang.: Eng, Slo. 4288
Text of puppet play for children, *Pospravljica (Tidying Up)* by Irena Androjna. Lang.: Slo. 4865
Text of Borut Combač's puppet play *Kdo je navil rumeno budilko? (Who Set the Yellow Alarm Clock)?.* Lang.: Slo. 4866
1997. **Design/technology.**
Handbook on stage spaces and physical elements. Lang.: Slo. 219
1997. **Performance/production.**
Theatre as a phenomenon of language. Lang.: Slo. 590
Account of shadow-puppet workshop for Bosnian refugee children. Ribnica. Lang.: Slo. 4926
1997. **Reference materials.**
Encyclopedia of Slovene folk dance. Lang.: Slo. 1243
1997. **Theory/criticism.**
Synthetic account of Slovene theatre. Lang.: Slo. 858
1998. **Institutions.**
Program of the 'City of Women' International Festival of Contemporary Arts. Ljubljana. Lang.: Slo. 384
Program of the Kisel Festival, including theatrical and puppet productions. Kranj. Lang.: Slo. 4875
1998. **Performance/production.**
Reviews of *Lieder* recordings. USA. Austria. Lang.: Eng. 4720
1998. **Training.**
Methodological manual for teaching ballet to children. Lang.: Slo. 1209

South Africa, Republic of
1861-1982. **Performance/production.**
South African amateur theatre. Lang.: Afr. 2352
1900-1998. **Performance/production.**
Indian theatre in South Africa. Lang.: Eng. 2356
1910-1998. **Performance/production.**
Australian theatre in South Africa. Australia. Lang.: Eng. 2353
1939-1994. **Relation to other fields.**
Contestatory playwriting under dictatorship. Spain. Chile. Lang.: Eng. 765
1950-1988. **Plays/librettos/scripts.**
The South African one-act play in English. Lang.: Eng. 3363
1958-1988. **Plays/librettos/scripts.**
Rhetorical analysis of works by Athol Fugard and Nadine Gordimer. Lang.: Eng. 3361
1960-1985. **Plays/librettos/scripts.**
The influence of Albert Camus on playwright Athol Fugard. Lang.: Eng. 3362
1976-1996. **Plays/librettos/scripts.**
South African theatre after apartheid. Lang.: Eng. 3365
1978. **Performance/production.**
Athol Fugard and the *Oresteia* of Aeschylus. Cape Town. Lang.: Eng. 2354
1987. **Plays/librettos/scripts.**
The influence of Taliep Petersen's musical *District Six.* Lang.: Eng. 4394

South Africa, Republic of — cont'd

1990-1992. **Performance/production.**
The kitchen in performance art of Bobby Baker and Jeanne Goosen. UK-England. Lang.: Eng. 4243
1991-1998. **Plays/librettos/scripts.**
Post-apartheid analysis of plays by Athol Fugard. Lang.: Eng. 3364
1993-1994. **Performance/production.**
Market Theatre productions of plays by Athol Fugard. Lang.: Eng. 2351
1995-1998. **Relation to other fields.**
Topics in post-apartheid South African literature and theatre. Lang.: Eng. 764
1997. **Plays/librettos/scripts.**
Analysis of *Ubu & the Truth Commission*, a puppet play by William Kentridge. Lang.: Eng. 4913
1997-1998. **Performance/production.**
African ritual in the work of director and playwright Brett Bailey. Lang.: Eng. 2349
1998. **Institutions.**
Report on the Standard Bank National Arts Festival. Grahamstown. Lang.: Eng. 385
1998. **Performance/production.**
Profile of Grahamstown National Arts Festival. Grahamstown. Lang.: Swe. 597
Chris Vorster's production of *Baal* by Bertolt Brecht. Capetown. Lang.: Eng. 2350
The absence of research on South African directing. Lang.: Eng. 2355

South America
1933-1945. **Relation to other fields.**
Directory of emigrant and refugee dancers. Europe. North America. Lang.: Ger. 997
1990-1998. **Performance/production.**
The dramaturg in the community theatre. North America. Asia. Lang.: Eng. 570

South Korea
1998. **Institutions.**
Profile of Universal Ballet Company. Seoul. Lang.: Eng. 1047

Spain
1400-1950. **Plays/librettos/scripts.**
Jewish characters in Spanish drama. Lang.: Spa. 3402
1468-1529. **Plays/librettos/scripts.**
Playwright Juan del Encina. Lang.: Eng. 3406
1476-1541. **Plays/librettos/scripts.**
Playwright Fernando de Rojas. Lang.: Eng. 3388
1480-1530. **Plays/librettos/scripts.**
Playwright Bartolomé de Torres Naharro. Lang.: Eng. 3383
1500-1600. **Plays/librettos/scripts.**
The 'induction' in Renaissance Spanish drama. Lang.: Eng. 3381
1510-1565. **Plays/librettos/scripts.**
Playwright Lope de Rueda. Lang.: Eng. 3403
1517-1681. **Plays/librettos/scripts.**
Background on the Spanish 'golden age'. Lang.: Eng. 3387
1543-1612. **Plays/librettos/scripts.**
Playwright Juan de la Cueva. Lang.: Eng. 3369
1547-1616. **Plays/librettos/scripts.**
Life and career of dramatist Miguel de Cervantes. Lang.: Eng. 3372
1550-1722. **Plays/librettos/scripts.**
Dramatic devices in early Spanish drama. Lang.: Eng. 3373
1562-1635. **Plays/librettos/scripts.**
Classical allusion in the plays of Lope de Vega. Lang.: Eng. 3367
Playwright Lope de Vega. Lang.: Eng. 3377
1569-1631. **Plays/librettos/scripts.**
Life and career of playwright Guillén de Castro. Lang.: Eng. 3384
1574-1644. **Plays/librettos/scripts.**
Playwright Antonio Mira de Amescua. Lang.: Eng. 3371
1578-1644. **Plays/librettos/scripts.**
Playwright Luis Vélez de Guevara. Lang.: Eng. 3390
1580-1626. **Plays/librettos/scripts.**
Playwright Andrés de Claramonte. Lang.: Eng. 3404
1580-1639. **Plays/librettos/scripts.**
Life and career of playwright Juan Ruiz de Alarcón y Mendoza. Lang.: Eng. 3389
1583-1648. **Plays/librettos/scripts.**
Playwright Tirso de Molina. Lang.: Eng. 3370
1595-1650. **Plays/librettos/scripts.**
Allegorical dramas of Sor Marcela de San Félix. Lang.: Eng. 3395
1600-1601. **Plays/librettos/scripts.**
Light/dark imagery in Calderón's plays. Lang.: Spa. 3394
1600-1620. **Theory/criticism.**
Lope de Vega's defense of the 'new art' of theatre. Lang.: Eng. 3830
1600-1630. **Plays/librettos/scripts.**
Analysis of the interludes of Cervantes. Lang.: Spa. 3391
1600-1651. **Plays/librettos/scripts.**
Playwright Luis Quiñones de Benavente. Lang.: Eng. 3376
1600-1681. **Plays/librettos/scripts.**
Life and career of playwright Pedro Calderón de la Barca. Lang.: Eng. 3397
1600-1700. **Performance/production.**
Actresses and female managers in Spanish theatre. Lang.: Eng. 2357
1601-1638. **Plays/librettos/scripts.**
Playwright Juan Pérez de Montalbán. Lang.: Eng. 3379
1605-1675. **Plays/librettos/scripts.**
Feminist analysis of seventeenth-century plays by women. Lang.: Eng. 3385
1607-1648. **Plays/librettos/scripts.**
Playwright Francisco de Rojas Zorrilla. Lang.: Eng. 3396
1609-1935. **Theory/criticism.**
Critical reception of the plays of Lope de Vega. Lang.: Spa. 3831
1610-1727. **Plays/librettos/scripts.**
Don Quixote, Lewis Theobald's *The Double Falsehood* and the lost *Cardenio* of Shakespeare and Fletcher. England. Lang.: Eng. 3001
1635. **Plays/librettos/scripts.**
Power relations in Calderón's *La Vida es Sueño (Life Is a Dream)*. Lang.: Spa. 3401
1637-1671. **Plays/librettos/scripts.**
Spanish Catholicism and the *autos sacramentales* of Calderón. Lang.: Spa. 3405
1660-1722. **Plays/librettos/scripts.**
Analysis of sonnets in the plays of Calderón. Lang.: Eng. 3398
1662-1704. **Plays/librettos/scripts.**
Life and career of playwright Francisco Antonio de Bances Candamo. Lang.: Eng. 3374
1665-1998. **Plays/librettos/scripts.**
Description of a Web site devoted to *Los españoles en Chile* by Francisco Ganzalez de Busto. Lang.: Eng. 3366
1737-1859. **Performance spaces.**
History of the Coliseo de la Cruz. Madrid. Lang.: Eng. 457
1845. **Plays/librettos/scripts.**
Spain as an exotic locale in Bizet's *Carmen* and its source. France. Lang.: Eng. 4819
1867-1922. **Performance/production.**
The popular theatre genre *teatro por horas*. Lang.: Eng. 2361
1874-1904. **Plays/librettos/scripts.**
Critical re-examination of the theatre of José Echegaray. Lang.: Eng. 3375
1888-1936. **Performance/production.**
Dancer Antonia Merce, La Argentina. France. Lang.: Eng. 922
1898-1936. **Plays/librettos/scripts.**
The life and work of Federico García Lorca. Lang.: Swe. 3393
1901-1998. **Performance/production.**
Flamenco variations worldwide. USA. Lang.: Eng. 962
1908-1936. **Plays/librettos/scripts.**
The image of women on the Spanish stage. Lang.: Eng. 3399
1919-1965. **Plays/librettos/scripts.**
The influence of Federico García Lorca on playwright Bernardo Santareno. Portugal. Lang.: Eng. 3400
1920-1936. **Plays/librettos/scripts.**
Imagery in the plays of Federico García Lorca. Lang.: Eng. 3380
Power and authority in the plays of García Lorca. Lang.: Eng. 3386
1930-1998. **Plays/librettos/scripts.**
Profile of playwright Federico García Lorca. Lang.: Dut. 3368
1936-1939. **Plays/librettos/scripts.**
Antifascist puppet plays by Rafael Alberti. Lang.: Eng. 4922
1936-1998. **Plays/librettos/scripts.**
Translation and the plays of Valle-Inclán. Lang.: Eng. 3378
1939-1994. **Relation to other fields.**
Contestatory playwriting under dictatorship. South Africa, Republic of. Chile. Lang.: Eng. 765

Spain — cont'd

1940-1969. **Plays/librettos/scripts.**
The detective plays of Jardiel Poncela. Lang.: Spa. 3392
1944-1997. **Training.**
Barbro Thiel-Cramér, Swedish teacher of Spanish dance. Stockholm. Lang.: Swe. 1244
1959-1998. **Basic theatrical documents.**
French translation of *Tres diamantes y una mujer (Three Diamonds and One Woman)* by Alejandro Casona. France. Lang.: Fre. 1464
1960-1967. **Relation to other fields.**
The influence of Fellini's *La Dolce Vita* on a novel of film critic Guillermo Cabrera Infante. Italy. Lang.: Eng. 4035
1961-1986. **Performance/production.**
Pirandello on the Spanish stage. Lang.: Ita. 2358
1970. **Performance/production.**
Interview with Flamenco dancer Janni Berggren. Sweden. Lang.: Swe. 1237
1975-1985. **Performance/production.**
Spanish theatre after Franco. Lang.: Eng. 599
1980-1998. **Performance/production.**
Interview with Flamenco dancer Gabriela Gutarra. Seville. Lang.: Swe. 1235
1981. **Plays/librettos/scripts.**
The influence of Jean Cocteau on filmmaker Pedro Almodóvar. France. Lang.: Eng. 3978
1983-1998. **Performance/production.**
Truth and authenticity in *M.T.M.* by La Fura dels Baus. Barcelona. Lang.: Eng. 598
1987-1998. **Plays/librettos/scripts.**
Playwright/director Alfonso Armada. Madrid. Lang.: Eng. 3382
1988-1997. **Performance spaces.**
The newly remodeled Teatro Real. Madrid. Lang.: Eng. 4496
1990-1998. **Performance/production.**
Interview with Flamenco dancer Eva Milich. Gothenburg. Lang.: Swe. 1236
1994-1998. **Performance spaces.**
The restoration of the opera houses Gran Teatro del Liceu and Teatro La Fenice. Barcelona. Venice. Lang.: Eng. 4495
1996-1997. **Performance/production.**
Productions of Shakespeare's *Twelfth Night* at the Madrid Theatre Festival. Madrid. Lang.: Eng. 2359
1997. **Basic theatrical documents.**
Text of *Mandíbula afilada (Sharp Chin)* by Carles Alberola. Lang.: Eng. 1463
1998. **Performance/production.**
The Finnish enthusiasm for Flamenco dance. Finland. Lang.: Fin. 1234
Actress Margarita Terechova. Russia. Lang.: Rus. 2261
Eduardo Vasco's production of *Lista Negra (Black List)* by Yolanda Pallín. Lang.: Eng. 2360
Overview of the Spanish theatre. Lang.: Rus. 2362
Juan Carlos Pérez de la Fuente's production of *San Juan* by Max Aub. Madrid. Lang.: Eng. 2363

Spain-Catalonia
1549-1996. **Performance/production.**
The Patum of Berga compared to sixteenth-century German festivities. Berga. Trent. Lang.: Eng. 4218
1841-1914. **Plays/librettos/scripts.**
Wagner's *Parsifal* and the political aspirations of Catalonians. Barcelona. Lang.: Eng. 4820
1962-1998. **Relation to other fields.**
Catalonian cultural politics and Els Joglars. Lang.: Eng. 3775
1963-1998. **Plays/librettos/scripts.**
Interview with playwright Sergi Belbel. Lang.: Ger. 3407
1994. **Basic theatrical documents.**
Text of *Magnus* by Jordi Teixidor. Lang.: Cat. 1468
1995. **Basic theatrical documents.**
Text of plays by Josep M. Muñoz Pujol. Lang.: Cat. 1466
1996. **Performance/production.**
Harold Pinter's production of his play *Ashes to Ashes* at the Pinter festival. Barcelona. Lang.: Eng. 2364
1997. **Basic theatrical documents.**
Text of *Àfrica 30* by Mercè Sarrias Fornés. Lang.: Cat. 1467
1997. **Institutions.**
The Grec '97 festival. Barcelona. Lang.: Eng. 1721
1999. **Basic theatrical documents.**
Text of *Davant l'Empire (Inside the Empire)* by Octavi Egea. Lang.: Cat. 1465

Sumatra
1980-1998. **Performance/production.**
Female performers of the formerly all-male genre *randai*. Lang.: Eng. 1354

Suriname
1988. **Plays/librettos/scripts.**
Interview with playwright Thea Doelwijt. Netherlands. Lang.: Eng. 3279
1998. **Reference materials.**
Bibliography of Dutch-language Caribbean literature. Aruba. Netherlands Antilles. Netherlands. Lang.: Eng. 3725

Sweden
1140-1500. **Performance/production.**
Evidence for performance of medieval religious drama. Lang.: Eng. 2392
1755-1766. **Performance spaces.**
Excerpts from the diary of the builder of Drottningholms Slottsteater. Stockholm. Lang.: Swe. 458
1766-1998. **Performance/production.**
Stockholm's year as Cultural Capital of Europe. Stockholm. Lang.: Eng. 2394
1773-1998. **Institutions.**
The 225th anniversary of the Royal Swedish Ballet. Stockholm. Lang.: Eng. 1048
Profile of the Royal Swedish Ballet. Stockholm. Lang.: Hun. 1053
1800-1998. **Performance/production.**
Changing attitudes toward the acting profession. Lang.: Swe. 2387
1840-1998. **Design/technology.**
Rapid on-stage costume changes in dance. Russia. Japan. Lang.: Swe. 889
1847-1987. **Theory/criticism.**
Essay on the nature of talent. Denmark. UK-England. Lang.: Dan. 838
1860-1928. **Performance/production.**
Reactions to Offenbach operettas at Kungliga Operan. Stockholm. Lang.: Swe. 4858
1872-1886. **Plays/librettos/scripts.**
Realism in plays of Strindberg. Lang.: Eng. 3416
1889-1998. **Performance spaces.**
The former dance palace Nalen, now restored as Nationalpalatset. Stockholm. Lang.: Swe. 4114
1898. **Performance spaces.**
The opening of Kungliga Operan. Stockholm. Lang.: Swe. 4498
1901-1902. **Plays/librettos/scripts.**
Time and space in *Ett Drömspel (A Dream Play)* by August Strindberg. Lang.: Eng. 3410
1907-1910. **Performance/production.**
Shakespeare's influence on Strindberg's modernism. Lang.: Eng. 2370
1908. **Performance/production.**
Interview with choreographer Birgit Åkesson. Africa. Asia. Lang.: Swe. 963
1908-1998. **Performance/production.**
Dancer/choreographer Birgit Cullberg. Stockholm. Lang.: Ger. 1302
Dancer Birgit Åkesson. Stockholm. Lang.: Ger. 1303
1912. **Plays/librettos/scripts.**
Folklore and occultism in August Strindberg's *Lycko-Pers resa (Lucky Per's Journey)*. Lang.: Swe. 3412
1920-1998. **Design/technology.**
Obituary for Karl-Gunnar Frisell, who oversaw the technical restoration of Södra Teatern. Solna. Lang.: Swe. 226
1920-1998. **Performance/production.**
Millicent Hodson and Kenneth Archer's revival of Jean Börlin's ballet *Dervisher*. London. Stockholm. Lang.: Swe. 1311
1935-1998. **Institutions.**
Interview with dance teacher Lia Schubert. Stockholm. Gothenburg. Lang.: Swe. 900
1939-1945. **Performance/production.**
Estonian artists as war refugees in Sweden. Estonia. Lang.: Swe, Eng, Ger. 519
1942-1980. **Institutions.**
Elsa Olenius and Vår Teater. Stockholm. Lang.: Swe. 1732
1944-1997. **Training.**
Barbro Thiel-Cramér, Swedish teacher of Spanish dance. Stockholm. Spain. Lang.: Swe. 1244
1945-1998. **Performance/production.**
Actor Erland Josephson on his profession. Lang.: Swe. 2379

Sweden — cont'd

Interviews with actresses of three generations on female roles. Stockholm. Lang.: Swe. 2380

1945-1998. Training.
Interview with children's dance teacher Yvonne Jahn-Olsson. Stockholm. Lang.: Swe. 1019

1946. Training.
Britt-Marie Berggren's dancing school for children. Stockholm. Lang.: Swe. 1020

1948-1998. Performance/production.
Interview with actor Jan-Olof Strandberg. Stockholm. Gothenburg. Uppsala. Lang.: Swe. 2390

1950. Performance/production.
Seven critics on their favorite character or portrayal. Lang.: Swe. 2369

1950-1998. Performance/production.
Types of actors and their relationship with directors. UK-England. Lang.: Swe. 2648

1950-1998. Training.
Memoirs of dance teacher Lia Schubert. Malmö. Stockholm. Gothenburg. Lang.: Swe. 1021

1956-1998. Performance/production.
Swedish actors who have won the O'Neill Prize. Stockholm. Lang.: Swe. 2365

1957-1998. Design/technology.
Scenographer Lennart Mörk. Stockholm. Paris. Lang.: Swe. 4439

1957-1998. Institutions.
History of Ballettakademian, Lillemor Lundberg, artistic director. Stockholm. Lang.: Swe. 901

1958-1998. Design/technology.
Interview with set designer Lennart Mörk. Stockholm. Paris. Lang.: Swe. 222

1959-1998. Institutions.
Profile of Teater 23. Malmö. Lang.: Swe. 1727

1960-1969. Institutions.
Swedish theatre of the sixties. Lang.: Swe. 1729

1960-1998. Performance/production.
Interview with singer Mikael Samuelsson. Lang.: Swe. 4698

The problem of staging operettas on the contemporary stage. Germany. Austria. Lang.: Swe. 4857

1960-1998. Training.
Singer training at Teater- & Operahögskolan. Gothenburg. Lang.: Swe. 4848

1962-1998. Performance/production.
Interviews with actors Börje Ahlstedt and Krister Henriksson. Stockholm. Lang.: Swe. 2383

1963. Performance/production.
Interview with ballerina Anneli Alhanko. Stockholm. Lang.: Swe. 1151

1966-1998. Training.
Interview with dance teacher Maria Llerena. Stockholm. Lang.: Swe. 1018

1968-1998. Institutions.
Gunnar Martin Aronsson of TeaterX2 recalls Action-Theater. Stockholm. Munich. Lang.: Swe. 1722

1970. Performance/production.
Interview with Flamenco dancer Janni Berggren. Spain. Lang.: Swe. 1237

1970-1998. Administration.
Interview with Tomas Bolme, director of the Swedish actors' union. Stockholm. Lang.: Swe. 1388

1970-1998. Performance/production.
The popularity of salsa dancing among Swedes. Lang.: Swe. 964

1973-1998. Performance/production.
Interview with community theatre director Kent Ekberg. Stockholm. Lang.: Swe. 2385

1974. Performance/production.
Interview with dancers who became doctors. Stockholm. Lang.: Swe. 968

1974-1997. Administration.
The closing of Göteborgs Stadsteatern. Lang.: Dan. 1389

1974-1998. Institutions.
Joint project to promote dance throughout Sweden. Lang.: Swe. 899

1974-1998. Performance/production.
Dancer Ana Laguna of Cullbergbaletten. Stockholm. Lang.: Swe. 1305

1975-1998. Performance/production.
Interview with dancer Göran Svalberg. Stockholm. Lang.: Swe. 1152

1978-1998. Performance/production.
Kent Hägglund on his favorite role, Bottom in Shakespeare's *Midsummer Night's Dream.* Lang.: Swe. 2375

1980-1998. Performance/production.
Interview with opera singer Anne Bolstad. Norway. Lang.: Swe. 4665

1980-1998. Plays/librettos/scripts.
Lars Norén's *Och ge oss skuggorna (And Give Us the Shadows).* Lang.: Swe. 3413

Interview with playwright-director Petra Revenue. Gothenburg. Lang.: Swe. 3415

1981-1998. Performance/production.
Singer Thomas Lander. Germany. Austria. Lang.: Swe. 4591

1982-1998. Performance/production.
Interview with soprano Lena Nordin. Stockholm. Lang.: Swe. 4697

1983-1998. Design/technology.
The combined conference and fair, Nordisk TeaterTeknik (NoTT). Stockholm. Gothenburg. Lang.: Swe. 227

1983-1998. Performance/production.
Interview with Bengt Andersson, artistic director of Teater Tre. Lang.: Swe. 601

Interview with dancer Farah Al-Bayaty. Gothenburg. Iraq. Lang.: Swe. 967

1984. Institutions.
Criticism of Svenska Bakettskolan. Stockholm. Lang.: Swe. 1049

1984-1998. Institutions.
The musical theatre program at Balettakademien. Gothenburg. Lang.: Swe. 4349

1984-1998. Performance/production.
Dancer Anja Birnbaum. Stockholm. Lang.: Swe. 1299

Interview with actor/director Stefan Larsson. Stockholm. Lang.: Swe. 2382

1988. Relation to other fields.
Theatre and the psychological development of children. Lang.: Swe. 3777

1988-1998. Performance/production.
Interview with actress Anna Pettersson. Stockholm. Lang.: Swe. 2371

Interview with singer Krister St. Hill. Germany. Lang.: Swe. 4590

1988-1998. Relation to other fields.
A joint project for teaching Shakespeare with professional actors. Lang.: Swe. 3776

1989-1998. Institutions.
Improvisations by Stockholms Improvisationsteater. Stockholm. Lang.: Swe. 1733

1990-1998. Administration.
Survey of dance audition practices in Swedish schools and theatres. Lang.: Swe. 882

1990-1998. Institutions.
The performing arts curriculum of Skytteholmsgymnasiet. Solna. Lang.: Swe. 898

1990-1998. Performance/production.
Interview with Flamenco dancer Eva Milich. Gothenburg. Spain. Lang.: Swe. 1236

Interview with *butō* dancer Susanna Åkerlund. Japan. Lang.: Swe. 1300

Analysis of the 'new circus'. France. Lang.: Swe. 4182

1990-1998. Plays/librettos/scripts.
Interview with Staffan Göthe, author, director, and one of the actors of *Ett Lysand elände (A Brilliant Misery).* Stockholm. Lang.: Swe. 3408

1992-1997. Design/technology.
Essay on lighting technology and the computer. USA. Lang.: Swe. 224

1992-1998. Institutions.
Interview with Rolf Sossna of En Annan Teater. Gothenburg. Lang.: Swe. 1734

1993-1998. Performance/production.
Interactive mystery theatre weekends in an old inn. Mariefred. Lang.: Swe. 602

1994-1998. Institutions.
Interview with Ronnie Hallgren of Älvsborgsteatern about theatre for youth. Borås. Lang.: Swe. 1726

1994-1998. Performance/production.
Interview with actress and director Anna Takanen. Stockholm. Lang.: Swe. 2372

Sweden — cont'd

1994-1998. **Plays/librettos/scripts.**
Swedish theatres and young Swedish playwrights. Malmö. Gothenburg. Stockholm. Lang.: Swe. 3411

1995. **Performance spaces.**
The rebuilding of the stage at Cirkus to accommodate a production of *Kristina från Duvemåla (Kristina of Duvemåla)*.Stockholm. Lang.: Swe. 1804

1995. **Training.**
Swedish attitudes toward Oriental female dance. Lang.: Swe. 1245

1995-1998. **Administration.**
Ways to attract new young audiences to theatre. Stockholm. Lang.: Swe. 21

1995-1998. **Institutions.**
Investing in culture in Malmö, formerly an industrial city. Malmö. Lang.: Swe. 1723

Profile of children's and youth theatre Älvsborgsteatern. Borås. Lang.: Swe. 1731

1995-1998. **Performance/production.**
Interview with dancer Jennie Widegren. Stockholm. Lang.: Swe. 1306

1995-1998. **Plays/librettos/scripts.**
Interview with playwright Sofia Fredén. Stockholm. Copenhagen. Lang.: Swe. 3409

1996. **Institutions.**
Defense of Svenska Balettskolan by a former student. Stockholm. Lang.: Swe. 1052

Swedish-Lithuanian theatrical exchange. Valmeira. Falun. Lang.: Swe, Eng, Ger. 1677

1996-1998. **Design/technology.**
The experience of a costumer from Suomen Kansallisteatteri at Stockholms Stadsteatern. Helsinki. Stockholm. Lang.: Swe. 1519

1996-1998. **Institutions.**
Interview with Ingrid Dahlberg, manager of Dramaten. Stockholm. Lang.: Swe. 1730

1996-1998. **Performance/production.**
Interview with children's theatre director Marie Feldtmann. Stockholm. Lang.: Swe. 2388

1997. **Institutions.**
Profile of Svensk Symbolisk Teater. Malmö. Lang.: Swe. 1728

Opera and food at Regina. Stockholm. Lang.: Swe. 4472

1997. **Performance spaces.**
The building of an ideal operatic stage in a disused limestone quarry. Rättvik. Lang.: Swe. 4497

1997. **Performance/production.**
The interdisciplinary workshop of Teaterskollektivet Rex. Stockholm. Lang.: Swe. 600

Report on children's dance festival. Malmö. Copenhagen. Lang.: Swe. 966

The reconstruction of Jean Börlin's ballet *Dervisher*. Stockholm. Lang.: Eng. 1150

Hans Klinga's production of *Mio, Min Mio (Mio, My Mio)* at Dramaten. Stockholm. Lang.: Swe. 2386

Recent productions of plays by Ibsen and Strindberg. Stockholm. Lang.: Eng. 2393

Interview with director Robert Lepage. Stockholm. Montreal, PQ. Lang.: Swe. 2397

The singer, the voice, and the body. Lang.: Swe. 4700

1997-1998. **Institutions.**
Profile of independent feminist theatre Kvinnliga Dramatiska Teatern. Stockholm. Lang.: Swe. 1725

1997-1998. **Performance/production.**
Interview with director Anders Paulin. Malmö. Lang.: Swe. 2377

1997-1998. **Plays/librettos/scripts.**
Interview with playwright-director Kajsa Isakson. Stockholm. Lang.: Swe. 3414

1998. **Administration.**
Stockholm's debut as cultural capital of Europe. Stockholm. Lang.: Dan. 22

Riksteatern and Dansens Hus' Dansbiennal 98 meeting with government officials. Lang.: Swe. 881

Sweden's new dance funding program. Lang.: Swe. 883

1998. **Audience.**
Reactions to Norén's *Personkrets 3:1 (Circle 3:1)* at Dramaten. Stockholm. Lang.: Swe. 1405

1998. **Design/technology.**
Locking and controlling stage rigging. Stockholm. Lang.: Swe. 220

The restructuring of the lighting company AVAB Scandinavia. Stockholm. Lang.: Swe. 221

Lighting operators' conference regarding controls at Dansens Hus. Stockholm. Lang.: Swe. 223

Theatre technician training at Malmö Högskola. Malmö. Lang.: Swe. 225

1998. **Institutions.**
The quality of theatre for children and youth. Bologna. Stockholm. Germany. Lang.: Ger. 367

Report on a seminar on mime, illusionism, *commedia* and clowning in dance. Stockholm. Lang.: Swe. 386

Report on biennial dance conference. Stockholm. Lang.: Swe. 902

Appeal for more varied dance training. Lang.: Swe. 903

The 225th anniversary season of the Royal Swedish Ballet. Stockholm. Lang.: Eng. 1050

Dance festival commemorating 225th anniversary of the Royal Swedish Ballet. Stockholm. Lang.: Eng. 1051

Productions of Gothenburg's Dance and Theatre Festival. Gothenburg. Lang.: Swe. 1253

Report on the Stockholm theatre festival. Stockholm. Lang.: Eng. 1724

Problems of administration at Norrlandsoperan. Umeå. Lang.: Swe. 4473

1998. **Performance/production.**
Argument in favor of lengthening dancers' careers. The Hague. Lang.: Swe. 955

Solutions to neck pain in dancers. Lang.: Swe. 965

Dance events during Stockholm's year as Cultural Capital. Stockholm. Lang.: Swe. 1153

Ballet in Sweden and the monument to Galina Ulanova. Stockholm. Lang.: Rus. 1154

Reactions to guest performances of dancer/choreographer Pina Bausch. Stockholm. Lang.: Swe. 1301

Choreographer Wayne McGregor and his work with Swedish students. Husby. Lang.: Swe. 1304

Photographs of Dramaten actors. Stockholm. Lang.: Swe. 2366

Interview with actor Dan Ekborg. Stockholm. Lang.: Swe. 2367

Conference on theatre for children ages 2-4. Stockholm. Lang.: Swe. 2368

Keve Hjelm's production of *Ett Drömspel (A Dream Play)* by Strindberg. Malmö. Lang.: Eng. 2373

Theatrical adaptations of children's stories by Astrid Lindgren. Stockholm. Lang.: Eng. 2374

Overview of children's theatre performances. Lang.: Swe. 2376

Dr. Kokos Kärlekslaboratorium (Dr. Koko's Laboratory of Love) at Backstage, Stockholms Stadsteater. Stockholm. Lang.: Swe. 2378

Interviews with actors Lil Terselius and Björn Granath. Stockholm. Lang.: Swe. 2381

Gerthi Kulle's role in Brecht's *Der Gute Mensch von Sezuan (The Good Person of Szechwan)* at Dramaten. Stockholm. Lang.: Swe. 2384

Stockholm's children's theatre scene. Stockholm. Lang.: Ger. 2389

Photos of rehearsals of O'Neill's *Long Day's Journey Into Night* at Dramaten. Stockholm. Lang.: Swe. 2391

Teater UNO's stage adaptation of *L'Étranger (The Stranger)* by Albert Camus. Gothenburg. Lang.: Swe. 2395

Interview with actors in Feydeau's *La Puce à l'Oreille (A Flea in Her Ear)* at Dramaten. Stockholm. Lang.: Swe. 2396

Reactions to the opera *Staden* by Sven-David Sandström and Katarina Frostensson. Stockholm. Lang.: Swe. 4699

Johannes Schaaf's production of *Otello* at Kungliga Operan. Stockholm. Lang.: Swe. 4701

1998. **Plays/librettos/scripts.**
Female characters in plays by Scandinavian women. Norway. Denmark. Lang.: Eng. 3299

Sweden — cont'd

Interview with opera composer Sven-David Sandström. Stockholm. Lang.: Swe. 4821
1998. Relation to other fields.
Stockholm's cultural facilities. Stockholm. Lang.: Eng. 766
A warning to dancers not to become malnourished. Lang.: Swe. 998
1998. Theory/criticism.
Collection of aphorisms on theatre criticism. Lang.: Swe. 859
1998. Training.
Traditional and contemporary approaches to ballet training. Stockholm. Lang.: Swe. 1210
Tina Hessel's relaxation and breathing techniques for dance training. Stockholm. Lang.: Swe. 1211

Switzerland
1906-1915. Design/technology.
The influence of Dalcroze's eurhythmics on designer Adolphe Appia. Lang.: Eng. 228
1926-1938. Institutions.
The directorship of Ferdinand Rieser at Zürcher Schauspielhaus. Zurich. Lang.: Ger. 387
1947-1998. Performance/production.
Interview with bass László Polgár. Hungary. Zurich. Lang.: Hun. 4640
1960-1998. Plays/librettos/scripts.
Analysis of *Par-dessus bord (Overboard)* by Michel Vinaver. France. La Chaux-de-Fonds. Lang.: Ger. 3118
1984-1998. Performance spaces.
The construction of the Grand Théâtre de Genève. Geneva. Lang.: Ger. 459
1996-1997. Performance/production.
Shakespeare productions in German Switzerland. Basel. Zurich. Lang.: Ger. 2398
1996-1998. Administration.
Theater Basel under the direction of Stefan Bachmann. Basel. Lang.: Ger. 1391
1996-1998. Performance/production.
'The Speaking Body' museum installation, site of theatre anthropology seminars. Vienna. Zurich. Lang.: Eng. 493
1997. Performance/production.
Playwright Theresia Walser on children's reactions to Christmas plays. Germany. Lang.: Ger. 2027
Press reactions to productions of Offenbach's *Orphée aux Enfers.* Belgium. France. Lang.: Fre. 4535
1997-1998. Performance/production.
Reviews of recent opera productions. Basel. Stuttgart. Berlin. Hamburg. Strasbourg. Lang.: Ger. 4702
1998. Administration.
Theatre directors on the future of subsidized theatre. Zurich. Hannover. Berlin. Lang.: Ger. 1390
1998. Basic theatrical documents.
Text of *Arrête de rêver, l'Étrangère (Stop Dreaming, Stranger).* Lang.: Fre. 1469
1998. Institutions.
Swiss theatre clubs for children and youth. Lang.: Ger, Fre. 1735
Children's theatre festival Spilplätz. Basel. Lang.: Ger. 1736
Stefan Bachmann of Basler Theater. Basel. Lang.: Ger. 1737
1998. Performance/production.
Actress Betty Buckley's performance in AIDS fundraiser. Geneva. Lang.: Eng. 603
Stefan Bachmann's production of Shakespeare's *Troilus and Cressida.* Basle. Lang.: Ger. 2399
Katharina Thalbach in Brecht's *Die heilige Johanna der Schlachthöfe (Saint Joan of the Stockyards)* directed by Benno Besson. Zurich. Lang.: Ger. 2400
Volker Hesse's production of *King Kongs Töchter (King Kong's Daughters)* by Theresia Walser. Zurich. Lang.: Ger. 2401
Volker Hesse's production of *Die schwarze Spinne (The Black Spider)* by Urs Widmer. Zurich. Lang.: Ger. 2402
Reviews of plays by Wolfgang Bauer and Thomas Bernhard. Basel. Vienna. Lang.: Ger. 2403
Interview with opera director Jossi Wieler. Stuttgart. Basel. Lang.: Ger. 4592
1998. Plays/librettos/scripts.
Thomas Hürlimann's *Das Lied der Heimat (The Song of the Homeland)* and its production by Werner Düggelin. Zurich. Lang.:Ger. 3417

Syria
1977. Plays/librettos/scripts.
Analysis of *Al-Mawik Huwa Al-Mawik (The King Is the King)* by Saadallah Wannus. Lang.: Eng. 3418

Taiwan
1985-1987. Administration.
Operations manual for Taiwan's Cultural Center Theatres. Lang.: Eng. 23
1986-1997. Relation to other fields.
Performative techniques in social and political movements. Lang.: Eng. 767

Tatarstan
1868-1938. Plays/librettos/scripts.
Kazan in the life of Maksim Gorkij and Fëdor Šaljapin. Kazan. Lang.: Rus. 689
1998. Performance/production.
Actress G. Isangulova. Kazan. Lang.: Rus. 2404
Profile of actress S. Gizzatulina-Volžskaja. Lang.: Rus. 2405

Thailand
Relation to other fields.
The 'bird-woman' folktale in Southeast Asian shamanic healing rituals. Ireland. Malaysia. Lang.: Eng. 1358

Tibet
1400-1990. Basic theatrical documents.
Slovene translations of Tibetan plays. Lang.: Slo. 1470
1500-1984. Performance/production.
Analysis of Tibetan Buddhist drama. Lang.: Eng. 1355

Togo
1984-1998. Plays/librettos/scripts.
Playwright Sénouvo Agbota Zinsou. Lang.: Eng. 3419

Trinidad and Tobago
1501-1998. Relation to other fields.
African and European influences on Trinidadian carnival. Lang.: Eng. 4175
1700-1950. Performance/production.
Amerindian influence on Trinidadian carnival. San Fernando. Lang.: Eng. 4164
1777-1998. Performance/production.
History of the steeldrum, used in carnival celebrations. Port of Spain. Lang.: Eng. 4169
1808-1998. Relation to other fields.
Chinese influence on Trinidadian carnival. China. Lang.: Eng. 4174
1838-1998. Relation to other fields.
The *jouvay* ceremony of Trinidadian carnival. Port of Spain. Lang.: Eng. 4176
1845-1998. Relation to other fields.
Indian influence on Trinidadian carnival. India. Lang.: Eng. 4178
1889-1998. Relation to other fields.
Carnival, cultural identity, and assimilation. Lang.: Eng. 4177
1900-1998. Performance/production.
The figure of the Midnight Robber in Trinidadian carnival. Lang.: Eng. 4168
1923-1998. Performance/production.
Interview with *mas* music performer George Leacock. Lang.: Eng. 4167
1952-1996. Design/technology.
Geraldo Andrew Vieira, carnival costumer and performer. Lang.: Eng. 4160
1974-1997. Plays/librettos/scripts.
Interview with Peter Minshall, creator of theatre pieces and carnival performances. Port of Spain. Lang.: Eng. 4172
1996. Performance/production.
Carnival performances of a *jouvay* band. Port of Spain. Lang.: Eng. 4171
1997. Performance/production.
Photos of Trinidadian carnival. Lang.: Eng. 4165
The carnival parade of devils and imps. Paramin. Lang.: Eng. 4219
1998. Performance/production.
Women in the *canboulay* ceremony. Lang.: Eng. 4166
Carnival as a unifying force. Lang.: Eng. 4170
1998. Reference materials.
Glossary of Trinidadian carnival terms. Lang.: Eng. 4173

Turkey
1994-1997. Relation to other fields.
Challenges facing Turkish theatre artists. Istanbul. Lang.: Eng. 3778

Turkey — cont'd

1998. Institutions.
Report on the 1998 Istanbul Theatre Festival. Istanbul. Istanbul. Lang.: Eng. 1738

Uganda

1979-1998. Performance/production.
Popular entertainment in Uganda after Idi Amin. Lang.: Eng. 604

1998. Performance/production.
Overview of Ugandan theatre. Lang.: Rus. 2406

Ukraine

1990-1995. Performance/production.
Theatre and Ukrainian national identity. Lviv. Kiev. Kharkiv. Lang.: Eng. 615

1997. Performance/production.
One-act plays of Čechov by the Illyés Gyula National Theatre. Hungary. Beregovo. Lang.: Hun. 2104

UK

1993. Performance/production.
Analysis of casting and acting in Kenneth Branagh's film adaptation of *Much Ado About Nothing*. Lang.: Fre. 3939

1998. Performance/production.
Collection of newspaper reviews by London theatre critics. Lang.: Eng. 2407

1998. Relation to other fields.
Politics, knighthood, and actor Sean Connery. Lang.: Eng. 4036

UK-England Part 1

Performance/production.
Collection of newspaper reviews by London theatre critics. London. Lang.: Eng. 2408

Research/historiography.
Theatricality on the contemporary British stage. Lang.: Eng. 3798

1625-1986. Plays/librettos/scripts.
Rape in Middleton's *Women Beware Women* and its adaptation by Howard Barker. Lang.: Eng. 3468

1732-1998. Institutions.
Brief history of the Royal Opera House, Covent Garden. London. Lang.: Eng. 4477

1759-1840. Performance/production.
Theatre and gender in the novels of Hannah Foster. Lang.: Eng. 613

1790-1890. Relation to other fields.
Gender, class, nationality, and sanitary reform in nineteenth-century English theatre. Lang.: Eng. 768

1797-1998. Performance/production.
Analysis of Donizetti's opera *Lucrezia Borgia*. Italy. Lang.: Eng. 4649

1800-1824. Plays/librettos/scripts.
Byron's heroes and the Byronic hero. Lang.: Eng. 3484

1820-1906. Design/technology.
The effect of lighting on the relationship between stage and audience. Lang.: Eng. 231

1847-1987. Theory/criticism.
Essay on the nature of talent. Denmark. Sweden. Lang.: Dan. 838

1853-1939. Plays/librettos/scripts.
William Butler Yeats, *japonisme*, and *nō*. Lang.: Eng. 3435

1854-1900. Plays/librettos/scripts.
Playwright and author Oscar Wilde. France. Lang.: Fre. 3465

1856-1950. Plays/librettos/scripts.
George Bernard Shaw and feminism. Lang.: Eng. 3481

1880-1890. Plays/librettos/scripts.
The trivialization of feminism in librettos of W.S. Gilbert. Lang.: Eng. 4861

1880-1914. Performance/production.
Representations of regional identity in music hall. Lang.: Eng. 4132

1881-1898. Plays/librettos/scripts.
Erotics and aesthetics in the work of Oscar Wilde. Lang.: Eng. 3424

1882-1883. Plays/librettos/scripts.
The New Shakespeare Society's unfinished four-text edition of *Hamlet*. Lang.: Eng. 3497

1883-1903. Plays/librettos/scripts.
George Bernard Shaw and play publication. Lang.: Eng. 3460

1885-1900. Plays/librettos/scripts.
The comedy of George Bernard Shaw and Oscar Wilde. Lang.: Eng. 3450

1886-1955. Plays/librettos/scripts.
George Bernard Shaw: life, work, influences. Ireland. Lang.: Eng. 3437

1887-1894. Theory/criticism.
George Bernard Shaw as music critic. London. Lang.: Eng. 4838

1887-1998. Plays/librettos/scripts.
George Bernard Shaw and science fiction. Ireland. Lang.: Eng. 3508

1888-1950. Plays/librettos/scripts.
Music in the plays of George Bernard Shaw. Lang.: Eng. 3506

1889-1956. Performance/production.
Performer, writer, director Elsie Janis and the 'gay sensibility'. Lang.: Eng. 612

1890-1900. Plays/librettos/scripts.
George Bernard Shaw and the 'New Woman'. Lang.: Eng. 3486

Talk as performance in the life and work of Oscar Wilde. Lang.: Eng. 3492

1890-1910. Plays/librettos/scripts.
Shaw's 'theatre of ideas' and its influence. Lang.: Eng. 3457

1890-1914. Relation to other fields.
'Up-to-dateness' on the music hall stage. London. Lang.: Eng. 4283

1890-1945. Plays/librettos/scripts.
Rhetorical arguments in one-act plays of Shaw. Lang.: Eng. 3453

1890-1950. Theory/criticism.
Theatrical dancing and the performance aesthetics of Wilde, Yeats, and Shaw. Ireland. Lang.: Eng. 1012

1890-1990. Plays/librettos/scripts.
Popular adaptations of the works of George Bernard Shaw. Lang.: Eng. 3445

1891-1898. Theory/criticism.
Ibsen, 'new' theatre, and Shaw's *Plays Unpleasant*. Lang.: Eng. 3832

1892-1898. Plays/librettos/scripts.
Wilde, Gide, and the censorship of Biblical drama. France. Lang.: Eng. 3441

1892-1900. Plays/librettos/scripts.
Analysis of early plays by George Bernard Shaw. Lang.: Eng. 3470

1892-1937. Plays/librettos/scripts.
Psychology and the self in works of J.M. Barrie. Lang.: Eng. 3478

1893-1943. Performance/production.
Actor Leslie Howard. London. New York, NY. Lang.: Eng. 2631

1894. Basic theatrical documents.
Catalan translation of *Arms and the Man* by George Bernard Shaw. Lang.: Cat. 1478

1894. Plays/librettos/scripts.
The source of the name Bunbury in Wilde's *Importance of Being Earnest*. Worthing. Lang.: Eng. 3469

1895. Basic theatrical documents.
Catalan translation of *The Importance of Being Earnest* by Oscar Wilde. Lang.: Cat. 1479

1895-1935. Plays/librettos/scripts.
Colonialism in the plays of George Bernard Shaw. Lang.: Eng. 3438

1896-1908. Plays/librettos/scripts.
Rhetorical analysis of plays by George Bernard Shaw. Lang.: Eng. 3480

1898-1998. Performance spaces.
Non-traditional theatrical space. Germany. France. Lang.: Dan. 443

1899-1939. Plays/librettos/scripts.
George Bernard Shaw and the history-play tradition. Lang.: Eng. 3503

1899-1962. Performance/production.
Actor Charles Laughton. London. Hollywood, CA. Lang.: Eng. 2632

1900-1998. Performance/production.
Operatic holdings of American and British record collectors. USA. Lang.: Eng. 4721

1900-1998. Plays/librettos/scripts.
Film adaptations of Shakespeare's plays. Lang.: Ita. 3986

1901-1905. Plays/librettos/scripts.
Structure and philosophy in Shaw's *Major Barbara* and *Man and Superman*. Lang.: Eng. 3427

1901-1995. Plays/librettos/scripts.
The Break of Day, Timberlake Wertenbaker's adaptation of Čechov's *Three Sisters*. Russia. Lang.: Eng. 3510

UK-England Part 1 — cont'd

1903. **Performance/production.**
The staging of *The King's Threshold* by W.B. Yeats. Dublin. London. Lang.: Eng. 2153
1904-1905. **Design/technology.**
Dancer Isadora Duncan's influence on the designs of Edward Gordon Craig. Lang.: Eng. 237
1904-1909. **Plays/librettos/scripts.**
George Bernard Shaw's involvement with the Court Theatre. Lang.: Eng. 3471
1905-1958. **Performance/production.**
Actor Robert Donat. London. Lang.: Eng. 2633
1905-1972. **Performance/production.**
Actor/director Margaret Webster, gender and sexuality. USA. Lang.: Eng. 2590
1905-1991. **Plays/librettos/scripts.**
Shakespeare's *The Tempest* on film. USA. Lang.: Eng. 3981
1907-1973. **Plays/librettos/scripts.**
W.H. Auden as an opera librettist and translator. Lang.: Eng. 4825
1907-1976. **Design/technology.**
Scenographer Tadeusz Orłowicz. Cracow. Neubrandenburg. London. Lang.: Pol. 212
1908. **Plays/librettos/scripts.**
Colonialism and misogyny in J.M. Barrie's *Peter Pan.* Lang.: Eng. 3423
1908-1991. **Administration.**
Theatrical agent Margaret Ramsey. London. Lang.: Ger. 1394
1908-1998. **Administration.**
Obituary for producer Lew Grade. Lang.: Eng. 3872
1912-1992. **Plays/librettos/scripts.**
Analysis of Benjamin Britten's opera *Death in Venice.* Lang.: Eng. 4823
1913-1998. **Performance/production.**
Obituary for conductor/composer George Lloyd. Lang.: Eng. 4703
1916-1919. **Plays/librettos/scripts.**
Analysis of *Heartbreak House* by George Bernard Shaw. Lang.: Eng. 3429
1917. **Plays/librettos/scripts.**
The censorship of the unpublished *Her Wedding Night* by Florence Bates. Lang.: Eng. 3454
1920. **Plays/librettos/scripts.**
Disillusionment in George Bernard Shaw's *Heartbreak House.* Lang.: Eng. 3456
1920-1998. **Performance/production.**
Millicent Hodson and Kenneth Archer's revival of Jean Börlin's ballet *Dervisher.* London. Stockholm. Lang.: Swe. 1311
1923-1947. **Plays/librettos/scripts.**
Analysis of the later plays of George Bernard Shaw. Lang.: Eng. 3444
1924-1990. **Plays/librettos/scripts.**
Pirandello, English theatre, and English scholarship. Lang.: Ita. 3473
1924-1998. **Plays/librettos/scripts.**
The renewed popularity of works by Noël Coward. Lang.: Eng. 3421
1927-1998. **Performance/production.**
Career of actress Joan Hickson. London. Lang.: Eng. 2597
1930-1940. **Performance/production.**
Annabel Farjeon on dancing for Ninette de Valois and Frederick Ashton. London. Lang.: Eng. 1158
1930-1998. **Performance/production.**
Actress Betty Marsden. London. Lang.: Eng. 2596
Career of actor Marius Goring. London. Lang.: Eng. 2598
1931-1998. **Plays/librettos/scripts.**
Stage and screenwriter John Hopkins. London. Hollywood, CA. Lang.: Eng. 3498
1933-1998. **Plays/librettos/scripts.**
Perceptions of Bertolt Brecht in the English-speaking world. North America. Lang.: Ger. 3443
The search for a lost translation of *The Seven Deadly Sins* by Brecht and Weill. Germany. Lang.: Eng. 4392
1936-1985. **Plays/librettos/scripts.**
Female presence/absence in plays of O'Neill, Pinter, and Shepard. USA. Lang.: Eng. 3607
1936-1998. **Performance/production.**
Acting career of Michael Denison. London. Lang.: Eng. 2599
1939-1946. **Performance/production.**
Theatre for Polish soldiers. France. Romania. Lang.: Pol. 611
1939-1984. **Plays/librettos/scripts.**
Home in Polish emigrant drama. Poland. Lang.: Pol. 3306
1939-1998. **Performance/production.**
Polish soldiers' theatre in London. London. Lang.: Pol. 610
1939-1998. **Research/historiography.**
The current state of research on Polish theatre in exile. London. Lang.: Pol. 824
1941-1948. **Institutions.**
Polish soldiers' theatre. Buzuluk. London. Lang.: Pol. 432
1942-1989. **Performance/production.**
Interviews with dancers about performance. USA. Cuba. Lang.: Eng. 1162
1944-1998. **Design/technology.**
Scene designer Ralph Koltai. Lang.: Eng. 232
1945-1956. **Administration.**
The 'Group of Four' at the Lyric Hammersmith and the concept of a national theatre. London. Lang.: Eng. 1392
1945-1995. **Plays/librettos/scripts.**
Samuel Beckett's influence on composer Humphrey Searle. Lang.: Eng. 3509
1945-1998. **Plays/librettos/scripts.**
The speaking subject in plays of Beckett and Stoppard. France. Ireland. Lang.: Ger. 3098
1947-1990. **Plays/librettos/scripts.**
Film interpretations of Ophelia in Shakespeare's *Hamlet.* USA. USSR. Lang.: Eng. 4024
1948. **Plays/librettos/scripts.**
The popularity and influence of the ballet film *The Red Shoes.* Lang.: Eng. 3988
1950. **Performance/production.**
Survey of recordings of the operettas by Offenbach. France. Lang.: Swe. 4853
1950-1970. **Audience.**
Analysis of the teenage-girl audience. USA. Lang.: Ger. 161
1950-1990. **Theory/criticism.**
Theatrical reviews and the nature of theatrical success. Lang.: Eng. 3836
1950-1998. **Administration.**
Producer Aida Young. Lang.: Eng. 3854
1950-1998. **Performance/production.**
Types of actors and their relationship with directors. Sweden. Lang.: Swe. 2648
Interview with singer Elisabeth Schwarzkopf. Austria. Lang.: Swe. 4860
1952-1984. **Performance/production.**
Interview with singer Nicolai Gedda. London. Munich. Lang.: Swe. 4859
1954. **Performance/production.**
William Empson's *The Masque of Steel* and its presentation before Queen Elizabeth II. Sheffield. Lang.: Eng. 4199
1954-1998. **Design/technology.**
Scene designer Richard Hudson and his work on *Samson et Dalila* at the Metropolitan Opera. USA. Lang.: Eng. 4289
1954-1998. **Performance/production.**
Actor George Grizzard. London. New York, NY. Lang.: Eng. 2646
1956-1988. **Plays/librettos/scripts.**
British historical drama. Lang.: Eng. 3500
1957-1998. **Theory/criticism.**
Survey of theatre studies as cultural studies. USA. France. Lang.: Ger. 865
1958. **Plays/librettos/scripts.**
Lacanian analysis of *The Birthday Party* by Harold Pinter. Lang.: Eng. 3452
1959-1985. **Plays/librettos/scripts.**
Radio, television, and stage plays of Caryl Churchill. Lang.: Eng. 3464
1959-1987. **Plays/librettos/scripts.**
The plays of Caryl Churchill. Lang.: Eng. 3493
1960-1969. **Relation to other fields.**
Situational theory in counter-cultural theatre. Lang.: Eng. 771
1960-1980. **Performance/production.**
The change in Shakespearean production. Lang.: Eng. 2628
1960-1985. **Plays/librettos/scripts.**
The nature and language of menace in the plays of John Whiting, Harold Pinter and Sam Shepard. USA. Lang.: Eng. 3576
1960-1992. **Plays/librettos/scripts.**
Political thought in plays of Howard Barker. Lang.: Eng. 3502

UK-England Part 1 — cont'd

1961. **Plays/librettos/scripts.**
Beckett's *Happy Days* as a rewriting of *Lady Chatterley's Lover.* France. Ireland. Lang.: Eng. 3120
1961-1970. **Relation to other fields.**
The performance style of poet Stevie Smith. Lang.: Eng. 770
1961-1997. **Plays/librettos/scripts.**
Interview with biographer of playwright Harold Pinter. Lang.: Eng. 3446
Harold Pinter's screenplay adaptation of *The Dreaming Child* by Isak Dinesen. Lang.: Eng. 3984
1962-1979. **Performance/production.**
The influence of collage on director Charles Marowitz. USA. Lang.: Eng. 2624
1964. **Basic theatrical documents.**
Typescript of the first draft of *The Homecoming* by Harold Pinter. Lang.: Eng. 1477
1964. **Plays/librettos/scripts.**
Comparison of the first and final drafts of *The Homecoming* by Harold Pinter. Lang.: Eng. 3447
1965-1995. **Performance/production.**
Tara Arts and English Indian theatre. Lang.: Eng. 614
1966-1996. **Performance/production.**
Modernist and postmodernist Shakespearean production. Canada. Lang.: Eng. 2618
1968-1974. **Plays/librettos/scripts.**
Plays of Peter Barnes compared to those of Renaissance dramatists. Lang.: Eng. 3449
1968-1988. **Plays/librettos/scripts.**
Derek Jarman's adaptation of works by Benjamin Britten and Wilfred Owen. Lang.: Eng. 4822
1968-1998. **Performance/production.**
Corinne Soum, former assistant to Etienne Decroux. Paris. London. Lang.: Eng. 4090
1969-1986. **Plays/librettos/scripts.**
Social and political issues in the plays of David Hare. Lang.: Eng. 3479
1970-1976. **Plays/librettos/scripts.**
Analysis of *Light Shining in Buckinghamshire* by Caryl Churchill. Lang.: Eng. 3483
1970-1994. **Performance/production.**
Postmodern staging and design: Matthew Warchus' *Henry V.* Lang.: Eng. 2636
1970-1995. **Theory/criticism.**
Recent scholarship and popularity of the Stuart masque. Lang.: Eng. 4212
1971. **Plays/librettos/scripts.**
The libretto of *The Rake's Progress* by W.H. Auden and Chester Kallman. Lang.: Eng. 4824
1971-1989. **Plays/librettos/scripts.**
Ecology and the plays of Caryl Churchill. Lang.: Eng. 3422
1971-1997. **Plays/librettos/scripts.**
Analysis of plays by David Hare and Caryl Churchill. Lang.: Dut. 3432
1973-1984. **Performance/production.**
Three productions of Shakespeare's *Richard III.* Lang.: Eng. 2612
1973-1986. **Plays/librettos/scripts.**
BBC radio plays with Anglo-Irish themes. Ireland. Lang.: Eng. 3868
1973-1993. **Performance/production.**
Slovene translation of Cicely Berry's work on vocal training for the actor. Slovenia. Lang.: Slo. 2344
1973-1998. **Design/technology.**
Jason Barnes, production manager of the Royal National Theatre. London. Lang.: Eng. 1527
1973-1998. **Plays/librettos/scripts.**
Stephen Mulrine's translation and stage adaptation of *Moscow Stations* by Venedikt Erofeev. USSR. Lang.: Eng. 3718
1974. **Plays/librettos/scripts.**
Analysis of *Monty Python and the Holy Grail.* Lang.: Eng. 3987
1974-1989. **Institutions.**
The theatrical method of Joint Stock Theatre Group. London. Lang.: Eng. 1749
1975. **Plays/librettos/scripts.**
Analysis of *The Collection* by Harold Pinter. Lang.: Eng. 3507
1975-1997. **Plays/librettos/scripts.**
A paradigm for analysis of works by Caryl Churchill. Lang.: Eng. 3458
1976-1986. **Plays/librettos/scripts.**
Brechtian epic devices in the theatre of Caryl Churchill. Lang.: Eng. 3477
1979. **Plays/librettos/scripts.**
Gender and sexuality in Caryl Churchill's *Cloud Nine.* Lang.: Eng. 3426
1980-1981. **Plays/librettos/scripts.**
Analysis of *The Romans in Britain* by Howard Brenton. Lang.: Eng. 3482
1980-1988. **Performance/production.**
Interview with performance artist Julian Maynard Smith. London. Lang.: Eng. 4246
1980-1995. **Plays/librettos/scripts.**
The adaptation of novels for the stage. Lang.: Eng. 3499
1981. **Plays/librettos/scripts.**
Analysis of *Decadence* by Steven Berkoff. Lang.: Dut. 3431
1982. **Plays/librettos/scripts.**
Analysis of Edward Bond's *Summer.* Lang.: Dut. 3434
Secrets in Caryl Churchill's *Top Girls.* Lang.: Eng. 3466
The film adaptation by Harold Pinter and Karel Reisz of *The French Lieutenant's Woman* by John Fowles. USA. Lang.: Eng. 3982
1982-1983. **Performance/production.**
Analysis of Shakespeare's *King Lear* on television. Lang.: Eng. 4064
1982-1991. **Performance/production.**
Analysis of two productions of Caryl Churchill's *Top Girls.* Lang.: Eng. 2608
The language of costume in a video production of Caryl Churchill's *Top Girls.* Lang.: Eng. 4065
1982-1998. **Administration.**
Interview with producer Ed Mirvish. London. Toronto, ON. Lang.: Eng. 1393
1985-1998. **Performance/production.**
The body in stage-to-film versions of Shakespeare's *Richard III.* USA. Lang.: Eng. 3940
1985-1999. **Theory/criticism.**
Changes in press coverage of opera and orchestras. Lang.: Eng. 4839
1986-1998. **Plays/librettos/scripts.**
The influence of Jacobean theatre on contemporary plays and productions. Lang.: Eng. 3428
1988-1998. **Institutions.**
Profile of Motionhouse Dance Theatre. London. Lang.: Eng. 1254
The Royal Opera House, Covent Garden, and the English National Opera. London. Lang.: Eng. 4479
1989. **Plays/librettos/scripts.**
Fragmentation and skepticism in Caryl Churchill's *Icecream.* Lang.: Eng. 3451
1989-1997. **Performance spaces.**
The remains of the original Globe Theatre. London. Lang.: Eng. 1808
1989-1998. **Performance/production.**
Dancer/choreographer Rosemary Lee. London. Lang.: Eng. 1307
Performer/choreographer Wendy Houstoun. Lang.: Eng. 1309
1990. **Plays/librettos/scripts.**
Envy in the plays of Shakespeare. Lang.: Ita. 3448
Analysis of *Mad Forest* by Caryl Churchill. Lang.: Eng. 3505
1990-1997. **Plays/librettos/scripts.**
Systemic poisons in plays of Caryl Churchill. Lang.: Eng. 3463
1991-1994. **Performance/production.**
National identity and the choreography of Shobana Jeyasingh. Lang.: Eng. 972
1991-1995. **Plays/librettos/scripts.**
Analysis of *In the Native State* and *Indian Ink* by Tom Stoppard. Lang.: Eng. 3459
1991-1996. **Plays/librettos/scripts.**
Comparison of Harold Pinter's *Party Time* with his screenplay for *The Remains of the Day.* Lang.: Eng. 3490
1991-1998. **Performance/production.**
Ophaboom Theatre's experience in recreating *commedia dell'arte.* London. Lang.: Eng. 4193
1992-1993. **Performance/production.**
Richard McCabe on his role in *The Winter's Tale* at RSC. London. Stratford. Lang.: Eng. 2623
1992-1996. **Reference materials.**
Index to *The Pinter Review*, 1992-1996. Lang.: Eng. 3727
1992-1997. **Performance/production.**
Royal Shakespeare Company actors on their performances as Shakespearean characters. London. Stratford. Lang.: Eng. 2638

UK-England Part 1 — cont'd

1993. Plays/librettos/scripts.
Analysis of Tom Stoppard's *Arcadia*. Lang.: Eng. 3474
Richard Attenborough's film adaptation of *Shadowlands* by William Nicholson. Lang.: Eng. 3985
1993-1994. Performance/production.
Derek Jacobi on playing Macbeth for the RSC. London. Stratford. Lang.: Eng. 2616
Christopher Luscombe on acting in RSC productions. London. Stratford. Lang.: Eng. 2620
1993-1996. Plays/librettos/scripts.
Transvestism in contemporary film as the 'blackface' of the nineties. USA. Lang.: Eng. 3983
1993-1998. Basic theatrical documents.
French translation of *Time of My Life* by Alan Ayckbourn. France. Lang.: Fre. 1471
1993-1998. Institutions.
Effects of a TV documentary on the Royal Opera House. London. Lang.: Eng. 4474
1993-1998. Performance/production.
Dancer Carlos Acosta of Royal Ballet and Houston Ballet. Houston, TX. London. Lang.: Eng. 1190
1994. Performance/production.
Philip Voss on his role in *Coriolanus* at RSC. London. Stratford. Lang.: Eng. 2643
1994. Plays/librettos/scripts.
Analysis of *Moonlight* by Harold Pinter. Lang.: Dut. 3433
Caryl Churchill's *The Skriker* compared to her earlier plays. Lang.: Eng. 3436
Analysis of *The Skriker* by Caryl Churchill. Lang.: Eng. 3489
The critical and popular failure of *The Skriker* by Caryl Churchill. Lang.: Eng. 3504
1994-1996. Plays/librettos/scripts.
Bibliography of works by or about Harold Pinter. Lang.: Eng. 3475
1994-1998. Performance/production.
The collaboration of choreographers Claire Russ and Anne-Marie Pascoli. France. Lang.: Eng. 1276
1994-1998. Plays/librettos/scripts.
Playwright Alan Bennett. Lang.: Ger. 3488
1995. Performance/production.
John Nettles on his role in an RSC production of *Julius Caesar*. London. Stratford. Lang.: Eng. 2625
1995-1996. Performance/production.
Susan Brown on her role in *Richard III* at RSC. London. Stratford. Lang.: Eng. 2593
Julian Glover on his performance in *Romeo and Juliet* for RSC. London. Stratford. Lang.: Eng. 2606
Michael Siberry on performing in an RSC production of *The Taming of the Shrew*. London. Stratford. Lang.: Eng. 2637
David Troughton on playing Shakespeare's *Richard III*. London. Stratford. Lang.: Eng. 2642
1995-1997. Basic theatrical documents.
French translation of *Funny Money* by Ray Cooney. France. Lang.: Fre. 1473
1995-1998. Performance/production.
Interview with dancer and choreographer Michael Clark. Lang.: Eng. 1312
Interview with Lloyd Newson of DV8 Physical Theatre. London. Lang.: Swe. 1313
1996. Institutions.
Profile of the Forced Entertainment Theatre Cooperative. Sheffield. Lang.: Dut. 1739
1996. Plays/librettos/scripts.
Analysis of *Ashes to Ashes* by Harold Pinter. Lang.: Eng. 3430
1996-1997. Performance/production.
Analysis of choreographies of Matthew Bourne. London. Lang.: Eng. 1157
Paul Jesson's role in *Henry VIII* at RSC. London. Stratford. Lang.: Eng. 2617
Jane Lapotaire on her performance in *Henry VIII* at RSC. London. Stratford. Lang.: Eng. 2619
David Tennant on his performance in *As You Like It* at RSC. London. Stratford. Lang.: Eng. 2640
1996-1998. Basic theatrical documents.
French translation of *Popcorn* by Ben Elton. France. Lang.: Fre. 1475
1996-1998. Institutions.
The work of training organization Metier in creating national standards for arts training. Bradford. Lang.: Eng. 388
1996-1998. Plays/librettos/scripts.
Theatrical activities of Harold Pinter. London. Lang.: Eng. 3462
AIDS and the work of performance artist Franko B. Lang.: Eng. 4261
1996-1998. Theory/criticism.
Interview with playwright Edward Bond. Lang.: Eng. 3834
1997. Basic theatrical documents.
Text of Simon Beaufoy's screenplay *The Full Monty*. Lang.: Eng. 3879
1997. Design/technology.
Sound design for the musical *Bugsy Malone*. London. Lang.: Eng. 4327
1997. Performance spaces.
The newly reopened Shakespeare's Globe Theatre. London. Lang.: Eng. 461
Critique of Shakespeare's Globe Theatre. London. Lang.: Eng. 1809
1997. Performance/production.
Report on festival of dance on film. London. Lang.: Eng. 969
Performances of Joaquím Cortez's flamenco troupe and the Ballets Africains of Guinea. London. Lang.: Hun. 1238
Report on Dance Umbrella festival. London. Lang.: Eng. 1310
The inaugural season of Shakespeare's Globe Theatre. London. Lang.: Eng. 2601
Review of the opening season of Shakespeare's Globe Theatre. London. Lang.: Eng. 2602
Census of productions of medieval plays. Lang.: Eng. 2610
Census of Renaissance drama productions and staged readings. Lang.: Eng. 2635
Interview with director Simon McBurney. London. Lang.: Swe. 2641
The current state of opera in England. Lang.: Eng. 4705
1997. Plays/librettos/scripts.
Interview with Simon Beaufoy, author of *The Full Monty*. Lang.: Eng. 3979
Observations on screenwriting and Beaufoy's *The Full Monty*. Lang.: Eng. 3989
1997-1998. Institutions.
Student's view of the Elmhurst Ballet School. Camberley. Lang.: Hun. 1055
The inaugural season of Shakespeare's Globe Theatre. London. Lang.: Eng. 1741
Paul Daniel, music director of the English National Opera. London. Lang.: Eng. 4475
1997-1998. Performance/production.
Barry Edwards on his theatrical movement work with OPTIK. London. Lang.: Eng. 609
1997-1998. Relation to other fields.
The current status of English cultural policy. Lang.: Ger. 769
1998. Administration.
London theatres' new summer productions. London. Lang.: Eng. 26
Arts Minister on the current state of dance, training, and funding. Lang.: Eng. 884
How Chisenhale Dance Space coped with loss of funding. London. Lang.: Eng. 885
1998. Basic theatrical documents.
Text of *Example: The Case of Craig and Bentley* adapted by Tom Barrie. Lang.: Eng. 1472
Text of *Jesus, My Boy* by John Dowie. Lang.: Eng. 1474
Text of *Sperm Wars* by David Lewis. Lang.: Eng. 1476
1998. Design/technology.
Exhibits at PLASA show. London. Lang.: Eng. 229
Report on PLASA trade show. London. Lang.: Eng. 230
Lighting technology manufacturer AC Lighting. Lang.: Eng. 233
AC Lighting's North American operation. USA. Lang.: Eng. 234
Report on sound and lighting equipment fair Live!. London. Lang.: Eng. 235

UK-England Part 1 — cont'd

Report on PLASA light and sound equipment trade show. London. Lang.: Swe. 236

Interview with lighting designer Rick Fisher. Lang.: Eng. 1030

Technical designs for Matthew Bourne's productions of ballets by Čajkovskij and Prokofjév. London. Lang.: Eng. 1031

Technical designs for *The Chairs (Les Chaises)*, Théâtre de Complicité. London. Lang.: Eng. 1524

Set and costume design for *The Spanish Tragedy* at RSC. London. Lang.: Eng. 1525

Set design for Tennessee Williams' *Not About Nightingales* at the National. London. Lang.: Eng. 1526

Sound design for The Spice Girls tour. Lang.: Eng. 4097

Technical designs for the musical *Doctor Doolittle* directed by Steven Pimlott. London. Lang.: Eng. 4325

Sound design for the London production of *Chicago*. London. Lang.: Eng. 4326

1998. Institutions.

The present state of the Royal Ballet under Michael Kaiser. London. Lang.: Hun. 1054

Interview with Bill Alexander, artistic director of Birmingham Repertory Theatre. Birmingham. Lang.: Eng. 1740

Theatre selections at the 1998 Edinburgh Festival and Edinburgh Fringe Festival. London. Lang.: Eng. 1743

Profile of Watermill Theatre. Newbury. Lang.: Eng. 1744

Interview with Andrew Welch, new director of Chichester Festival. Chichester. Lang.: Eng. 1745

Theatre schools: production of showcases for graduating students. London. Lang.: Eng. 1746

Survey of summer opera. Lang.: Eng. 4476

The cancellation of performances by the Royal Opera House, Covent Garden. London. Lang.: Eng. 4478

1998. Performance spaces.

Shakespeare's Globe and the staging of *The Merchant of Venice*. London. Lang.: Ger. 1810

1998. Performance/production.

Survey of London and Paris productions. London. Paris. Lang.: Eng. 607

Choreography of Javier De Frutos at the Dance Umbrella Festival. London. Lang.: Hun. 970

Hip-hop choreographer Jonzi D. London. Lang.: Eng. 973

Digital dance. Lang.: Eng. 974

The lack of new ballets. Lang.: Eng. 1155

Narrative in choreographies of Matthew Bourne and Mark Murphy. Lang.: Eng. 1156

Matthew Bourne's choreography for *Swan Lake*. Lang.: Eng. 1159

Interview with choreographer Matthew Bourne. Lang.: Eng. 1160

Matthew Bourne's dance piece *Cinderella* to music of Prokofjév. London. Lang.: Eng. 1161

Interview with choreographer Christopher Bruce of the Rambert Dance Company. London. Lang.: Hun. 1163

Ballet dancer Irek Muchamedov. London. Lang.: Rus. 1164

Interview with choreographer Keely Garfield. Lang.: Eng. 1308

Seminar on auditions for choreographers for Resolution dance festival. London. Brussels. Lang.: Swe. 1314

Analysis of *The Featherstonehaughs Draw on the Sketchbooks of Egon Schiele* by choreographer Lea Anderson. London. Lang.: Eng. 1315

Speaking styles of selected actors reading Shakespeare's *Henry V*. North America. Lang.: Eng. 2208

Collection of newspaper reviews by London theatre critics. London. Lang.: Eng. 2409

Collection of newspaper reviews by London theatre critics. London. Lang.: Eng. 2410

Collection of newspaper reviews by London theatre critics. London. Lang.: Eng. 2411

Collection of newspaper reviews by London theatre critics. London. Lang.: Eng. 2412

Collection of newspaper reviews by London theatre critics. London. Lang.: Eng. 2413

Collection of newspaper reviews by London theatre critics. London. Lang.: Eng. 2414

Collection of newspaper reviews by London theatre critics. London. Lang.: Eng. 2415

Collection of newspaper reviews by London theatre critics. London. Lang.: Eng. 2416

Collection of newspaper reviews by London theatre critics. London. Stratford. Derby. Lang.: Eng. 2417

Collection of newspaper reviews by London theatre critics. London. Lang.: Eng. 2418

Collection of newspaper reviews by London theatre critics. London. Lang.: Eng. 2419

Collection of newspaper reviews by London theatre critics. London. Lang.: Eng. 2420

Collection of newspaper reviews by London theatre critics. London. Lang.: Eng. 2421

Collection of newspaper reviews by London theatre critics. London. Lang.: Eng. 2422

Collection of newspaper reviews by London theatre critics. London. Lang.: Eng. 2423

Collection of newspaper reviews by London theatre critics. London. Lang.: Eng. 2424

Collection of newspaper reviews by London theatre critics. London. Lang.: Eng. 2425

Collection of newspaper reviews by London theatre critics. London. Scarborough. Lang.: Eng. 2426

Collection of newspaper reviews by London theatre critics. London. Lang.: Eng. 2427

Collection of newspaper reviews by London theatre critics. London. Lang.: Eng. 2428

Collection of newspaper reviews by London theatre critics. London. Lang.: Eng. 2429

Collection of newspaper reviews by London theatre critics. London. Lang.: Eng. 2430

Collection of newspaper reviews by London theatre critics. Stratford. Lang.: Eng. 2431

Collection of newspaper reviews by London theatre critics. London. Lang.: Eng. 2432

Collection of newspaper reviews by London theatre critics. Leeds. Manchester. Lang.: Eng. 2433

Collection of newspaper reviews by London theatre critics. London. Lang.: Eng. 2434

Collection of newspaper reviews by London theatre critics. London. Lang.: Eng. 2435

Collection of newspaper reviews by London theatre critics. London. Lang.: Eng. 2436

Collection of newspaper reviews by London theatre critics. London. Lang.: Eng. 2437

Collection of newspaper reviews by London theatre critics. London. Lang.: Eng. 2438

Collection of newspaper reviews by London theatre critics. London. Lang.: Eng. 2439

Collection of newspaper reviews by London theatre critics. London. Lang.: Eng. 2440

Collection of newspaper reviews by London theatre critics. London. Lang.: Eng. 2441

Collection of newspaper reviews by London theatre critics. London. Lang.: Eng. 2442

Collection of newspaper reviews by London theatre critics. London. Lang.: Eng. 2443

Collection of newspaper reviews by London theatre critics. London. Lang.: Eng. 2444

Collection of newspaper reviews by London theatre critics. London. Lang.: Eng. 2445

Collection of newspaper reviews by London theatre critics. London. Lang.: Eng. 2446

Collection of newspaper reviews by London theatre critics. London. Lang.: Eng. 2447

UK-England Part 1 — cont'd

Collection of newspaper reviews by London theatre critics. London. Lang.: Eng. 2448
Collection of newspaper reviews by London theatre critics. London. Lang.: Eng. 2449
Collection of newspaper reviews by London theatre critics. London. Lang.: Eng. 2450
Collection of newspaper reviews by London theatre critics. London. Lang.: Eng. 2451
Collection of newspaper reviews by London theatre critics. London. Lang.: Eng. 2452
Collection of newspaper reviews by London theatre critics. London. Lang.: Eng. 2453
Collection of newspaper reviews by London theatre critics. London. Lang.: Eng. 2454
Collection of newspaper reviews by London theatre critics. London. Lang.: Eng. 2455
Collection of newspaper reviews by London theatre critics. Lang.: Eng. 2456
Collection of newspaper reviews by London theatre critics. London. Lang.: Eng. 2457
Collection of newspaper reviews by London theatre critics. London. Lang.: Eng. 2458
Collection of newspaper reviews by London theatre critics. London. Lang.: Eng. 2459
Collection of newspaper reviews by London theatre critics. London. Lang.: Eng. 2460
Collection of newspaper reviews by London theatre critics. London. Lang.: Eng. 2461
Collection of newspaper reviews by London theatre critics. London. Lang.: Eng. 2462
Collection of newspaper reviews by London theatre critics. London. Lang.: Eng. 2463
Collection of newspaper reviews by London theatre critics. London. Lang.: Eng. 2464
Collection of newspaper reviews by London theatre critics. London. Lang.: Eng. 2465
Collection of newspaper reviews by London theatre critics. London. Lang.: Eng. 2466
Collection of newspaper reviews by London theatre critics. London. Lang.: Eng. 2467
Collection of newspaper reviews by London theatre critics. London. Lang.: Eng. 2468
Collection of newspaper reviews by London theatre critics. London. Lang.: Eng. 2469
Collection of newspaper reviews by London theatre critics. London. Lang.: Eng. 2470
Collection of newspaper reviews by London theatre critics. London. Lang.: Eng. 2471
Collection of newspaper reviews by London theatre critics. London. Lang.: Eng. 2472
Collection of newspaper reviews by London theatre critics. London. Lang.: Eng. 2473
Collection of newspaper reviews by London theatre critics. London. Lang.: Eng. 2474
Collection of newspaper reviews by London theatre critics. London. Lang.: Eng. 2475
Collection of newspaper reviews by London theatre critics. London. Lang.: Eng. 2476
Collection of newspaper reviews by London theatre critics. London. Lang.: Eng. 2477
Collection of newspaper reviews by London theatre critics. London. Lang.: Eng. 2478
Collection of newspaper reviews by London theatre critics. London. Lang.: Eng. 2479
Collection of newspaper reviews by London theatre critics. London. Lang.: Eng. 2480
Collection of newspaper reviews by London theatre critics. London. Lang.: Eng. 2481
Collection of newspaper reviews by London theatre critics. London. Lang.: Eng. 2482
Collection of newspaper reviews by London theatre critics. London. Lang.: Eng. 2483
Collection of newspaper reviews by London theatre critics. London. Lang.: Eng. 2484
Collection of newspaper reviews by London theatre critics. Lang.: Eng. 2485
Collection of newspaper reviews by London theatre critics. London. Lang.: Eng. 2486
Collection of newspaper reviews by London theatre critics. London. Lang.: Eng. 2487
Collection of newspaper reviews by London theatre critics. London. Lang.: Eng. 2488
Collection of newspaper reviews by London theatre critics. Lang.: Eng. 2489
Collection of newspaper reviews by London theatre critics. London. Lang.: Eng. 2490
Collection of newspaper reviews by London theatre critics. London. Lang.: Eng. 2491
Collection of newspaper reviews by London theatre critics. London. Lang.: Eng. 2492
Collection of newspaper reviews by London theatre critics. London. Lang.: Eng. 2493
Collection of newspaper reviews by London theatre critics. London. Lang.: Eng. 2494
Collection of newspaper reviews by London theatre critics. London. Lang.: Eng. 2495
Collection of newspaper reviews by London theatre critics. London. Lang.: Eng. 2496
Collection of newspaper reviews by London theatre critics. Lang.: Eng. 2497
Collection of newspaper reviews by London theatre critics. London. Lang.: Eng. 2498
Collection of newspaper reviews by London theatre critics. London. Lang.: Eng. 2499
Collection of newspaper reviews by London theatre critics. London. Lang.: Eng. 2500
Collection of newspaper reviews by London theatre critics. London. Lang.: Eng. 2501
Collection of newspaper reviews by London theatre critics. London. Lang.: Eng. 2502
Collection of newspaper reviews by London theatre critics. London. Lang.: Eng. 2503
Collection of newspaper reviews by London theatre critics. Lang.: Eng. 2504
Collection of newspaper reviews by London theatre critics. London. Lang.: Eng. 2505
Collection of newspaper reviews by London theatre critics. London. Lang.: Eng. 2506
Collection of newspaper reviews by London theatre critics. London. Lang.: Eng. 2507
Collection of newspaper reviews by London theatre critics. London. Lang.: Eng. 2508
Collection of newspaper reviews by London theatre critics. London. Lang.: Eng. 2509
Collection of newspaper reviews by London theatre critics. Lang.: Eng. 2510
Collection of newspaper reviews by London theatre critics. London. Lang.: Eng. 2511
Collection of newspaper reviews by London theatre critics. London. Lang.: Eng. 2512
Collection of newspaper reviews by London theatre critics. London. Lang.: Eng. 2513
Collection of newspaper reviews by London theatre critics. London. Lang.: Eng. 2514
Collection of newspaper reviews by London theatre critics. London. Lang.: Eng. 2515
Collection of newspaper reviews by London theatre critics. London. Lang.: Eng. 2516
Collection of newspaper reviews by London theatre critics. London. Lang.: Eng. 2517

UK-England Part 1 — cont'd

Collection of newspaper reviews by London theatre critics. London. Lang.: Eng. 2518

Collection of newspaper reviews by London theatre critics. Stratford. Lang.: Eng. 2519

Collection of newspaper reviews by London theatre critics. London. Lang.: Eng. 2520

Collection of newspaper reviews by London theatre critics. London. Lang.: Eng. 2521

Collection of newspaper reviews by London theatre critics. London. Lang.: Eng. 2522

Collection of newspaper reviews by London theatre critics. London. Lang.: Eng. 2523

Collection of newspaper reviews by London theatre critics. London. Lang.: Eng. 2524

Collection of newspaper reviews by London theatre critics. London. Lang.: Eng. 2525

Collection of newspaper reviews by London theatre critics. London. Lang.: Eng. 2526

Collection of newspaper reviews by London theatre critics. Lang.: Eng. 2527

Collection of newspaper reviews by London theatre critics. London. Lang.: Eng. 2528

Collection of newspaper reviews by London theatre critics. Stratford. Lang.: Eng. 2529

Collection of newspaper reviews by London theatre critics. London. Lang.: Eng. 2530

Collection of newspaper reviews by London theatre critics. London. Lang.: Eng. 2531

Collection of newspaper reviews by London theatre critics. London. Lang.: Eng. 2532

Collection of newspaper reviews by London theatre critics. London. Lang.: Eng. 2533

Collection of newspaper reviews by London theatre critics. London. Lang.: Eng. 2534

Collection of newspaper reviews by London theatre critics. London. Lang.: Eng. 2535

Collection of newspaper reviews by London theatre critics. Stratford. Birmingham. Lang.: Eng. 2536

Collection of newspaper reviews by London theatre critics. London. Lang.: Eng. 2537

Collection of newspaper reviews by London theatre critics. London. Lang.: Eng. 2538

Collection of newspaper reviews by London theatre critics. London. Lang.: Eng. 2539

Collection of newspaper reviews by London theatre critics. London. Lang.: Eng. 2540

Collection of newspaper reviews by London theatre critics. London. Lang.: Eng. 2541

Collection of newspaper reviews by London theatre critics. London. Lang.: Eng. 2542

Collection of newspaper reviews by London theatre critics. London. Lang.: Eng. 2543

Collection of newspaper reviews by London theatre critics. London. Lang.: Eng. 2544

Collection of newspaper reviews by London theatre critics. London. Lang.: Eng. 2545

Collection of newspaper reviews by London theatre critics. London. Lang.: Eng. 2546

Collection of newspaper reviews by London theatre critics. London. Lang.: Eng. 2547

Collection of newspaper reviews by London theatre critics. London. Lang.: Eng. 2548

Collection of newspaper reviews by London theatre critics. London. Lang.: Eng. 2549

Collection of newspaper reviews by London theatre critics. London. Lang.: Eng. 2550

Collection of newspaper reviews by London theatre critics. London. Lang.: Eng. 2551

Collection of newspaper reviews by London theatre critics. London. Lang.: Eng. 2552

Collection of newspaper reviews by London theatre critics. London. Lang.: Eng. 2553

Collection of newspaper reviews by London theatre critics. London. Lang.: Eng. 2554

Collection of newspaper reviews by London theatre critics. London. Lang.: Eng. 2555

Collection of newspaper reviews by London theatre critics. London. Lang.: Eng. 2556

Collection of newspaper reviews by London theatre critics. London. Lang.: Eng. 2557

Collection of newspaper reviews by London theatre critics. Lang.: Eng. 2558

Collection of newspaper reviews by London theatre critics. Leeds. Manchester. Lang.: Eng. 2559

Collection of newspaper reviews by London theatre critics. London. Lang.: Eng. 2560

Collection of newspaper reviews by London theatre critics. London. Lang.: Eng. 2561

Collection of newspaper reviews by London theatre critics. London. Lang.: Eng. 2562

The future of English repertory companies. London. Lang.: Eng. 2563

Collection of newspaper reviews by London theatre critics. London. Lang.: Eng. 2564

Collection of newspaper reviews by London theatre critics. London. Lang.: Eng. 2565

Collection of newspaper reviews by London theatre critics. London. Lang.: Eng. 2566

Collection of newspaper reviews by London theatre critics. London. Lang.: Eng. 2567

Collection of newspaper reviews by London theatre critics. London. Lang.: Eng. 2568

Collection of newspaper reviews by London theatre critics. London. Lang.: Eng. 2569

Collection of newspaper reviews by London theatre critics. London. Lang.: Eng. 2570

Collection of newspaper reviews by London theatre critics. London. Lang.: Eng. 2571

Collection of newspaper reviews by London theatre critics. London. Lang.: Eng. 2572

Collection of newspaper reviews by London theatre critics. London. Lang.: Eng. 2573

Collection of newspaper reviews by London theatre critics. London. Lang.: Eng. 2574

Collection of newspaper reviews by London theatre critics. London. Lang.: Eng. 2575

Collection of newspaper reviews by London theatre critics. London. Lang.: Eng. 2576

Collection of newspaper reviews by London theatre critics. London. Lang.: Eng. 2577

Collection of newspaper reviews by London theatre critics. London. Lang.: Eng. 2578

Collection of newspaper reviews by London theatre critics. London. Lang.: Eng. 2579

Collection of newspaper reviews by London theatre critics. London. Lang.: Eng. 2580

Collection of newspaper reviews by London theatre critics. London. Lang.: Eng. 2581

Collection of newspaper reviews by London theatre critics. London. Lang.: Eng. 2582

Collection of newspaper reviews by London theatre critics. London. Lang.: Eng. 2583

Collection of newspaper reviews by London theatre critics. London. Lang.: Eng. 2584

Collection of newspaper reviews by London theatre critics. London. Lang.: Eng. 2585

Collection of newspaper reviews by London theatre critics. London. Lang.: Eng. 2586

Collection of newspaper reviews by London theatre critics. London. Lang.: Eng. 2587

UK-England Part 1 — cont'd

Collection of newspaper reviews by London theatre critics. London. Lang.: Eng. 2588
Reviews of recent London performances. London. Lang.: Ger. 2591
Interview with Katie Mitchell on directing plays of Beckett. Lang.: Eng. 2594
London summer theatre and the Edinburgh Festival. London. Edinburgh. Lang.: Eng. 2603
Trevor Nunn's production of *Not About Nightingales* by Tennessee Williams, Royal National Theatre. London. Lang.: Swe. 2604
Recent productions of plays by Harold Pinter at Donmar Warehouse. London. Lang.: Eng. 2609
Richard Olivier's production of Shakespeare's *The Merchant of Venice.* London. Lang.: Eng. 2621
Trevor Nunn's production of *An Enemy of the People* by Ibsen. London. Lang.: Eng. 2627
Profile of actor Tom Conti. Lang.: Eng. 2629
Report on several English performances. London. Stratford. Lang.: Swe. 2634
The death of actress Eva Bartok. Hungary. London. Lang.: Eng. 3934
The North American tour of English comedian Eddie Izzard. North America. Lang.: Eng. 4127
Interview with performance artist Franko B. Lang.: Eng. 4244
Actors' handling of a mishap on stage during a production of *The Phantom of the Opera.* Basingstoke. Lang.: Eng. 4369
Interview with Shane Ritchie and Jon Conway about the musical *Boogie Nights.* Lang.: Eng. 4370
Elton John as musical theatre composer. Lang.: Rus. 4371
Recordings of *Lieder* by Schumann. Germany. Lang.: Eng. 4601
Conductor Andrew Davis. USA. Lang.: Eng. 4704
Interview with conductor Nicholas McGegan. USA. Lang.: Eng. 4740

1998. Plays/librettos/scripts.
Genocide, theatre, and the human body. North America. Argentina. Lang.: Eng. 3290
The comedies of Alan Ayckbourn. London. Lang.: Eng. 3420
Oscar Wilde biographer on his negative traits and addictive behaviors. USA. Lang.: Eng. 3425
German view of English and American drama. USA. Lang.: Ger. 3455
Interview with playwright Jonathan Harvey. Lang.: Eng. 3472
Mark Ravenhill's *Shopping and Fucking* and its production by Thomas Ostermeier. Germany. Lang.: Ger. 3476
Analysis of plays by Sarah Kane and David Harrower, recently produced in Germany. Cologne. Bonn. Lang.: Ger. 3487
Interview with playwright Mark Ravenhill. Lang.: Ger. 3496
Shared Experience's stage adaptations of nineteenth-century novels. New York, NY. London. Lang.: Eng. 3518

1998. Relation to other fields.
The cultural stereotype of the dancer's body. USA. Lang.: Eng. 999
Interview with actor/writer Steven Berkoff, creator of actor character 'Harry'. London. Lang.: Eng. 3780
The state of Shakespearean studies in public education. USA. Lang.: Eng. 3786

1998. Research/historiography.
The use of 'Literature Online' for editing and attribution studies. Lang.: Eng. 825
New approaches to theatre studies and performance analysis. Bristol. Lang.: Eng. 826

1998. Theory/criticism.
Italian translation of *The Empty Space* by Peter Brook. Lang.: Ita. 3833
Contrasting reviews of Declan Donnellan's RSC production of *The School for Scandal.* Stratford. Lang.: Eng. 3835

1998. Training.
The use of martial arts in dance training. Lang.: Eng. 1022

UK-England Part2

1599-1998. Performance spaces.
Stage doors of the Globe Theatre. London. Lang.: Eng. 1806

1773-1988. Performance/production.
The evolution of the character Feste in productions of Shakespeare's *Twelfth Night.* Lang.: Eng. 2611

1803-1805. Performance/production.
Excerpts from Johanna Schopenhauer's journal relating to London theatre. London. Germany. Lang.: Eng. 2615

1806-1808. Performance/production.
Actor and playwright George Dibdin Pitt. London. Lang.: Eng. 2592
Possible illustrations of Dibdin's *Harlequin and Mother Goose* at Covent Garden. London. Lang.: Eng. 2639

1830-1970. Performance/production.
Excessive stage and screen melodrama. USA. Lang.: Eng. 608

1843-1998. Relation to other fields.
Brief history of London music hall. London. Lang.: Eng. 4284

1868-1946. Performance/production.
Actor George Arliss. London. Lang.: Eng. 3941

1879-1935. Performance/production.
Entertainer Will Rogers. London. Lang.: Eng. 4279

1882-1941. Relation to other fields.
Shakespeare's influence on the novels of Virginia Woolf. Lang.: Eng. 3779

1887-1986. Design/technology.
The original stage machinery designed by John White at Her Majesty's Theatre. London. Lang.: Eng. 1528

1890-1910. Plays/librettos/scripts.
Analysis of plays by Arthur Wing Pinero. Lang.: Eng. 3440

1890-1985. Plays/librettos/scripts.
Linguistic style and action in plays of Wilde, Shaw, and Stoppard. Lang.: Eng. 3467

1900-1946. Plays/librettos/scripts.
Comparison of plays by Harley Granville-Barker and Anton Čechov. Russia. Lang.: Eng. 3501

1900-1998. Performance/production.
Actor and director Harold French. London. Lang.: Eng. 2614

1905. Plays/librettos/scripts.
Shaw's *Man and Superman* as a philosophical treatise. Lang.: Eng. 3495

1908-1915. Performance/production.
Experimental Shakespeare production at the Gaiety Theatre. Manchester. Lang.: Eng. 2605

1918-1998. Performance spaces.
Anecdotes about old London theatres. London. Lang.: Eng. 460

1939-1945. Performance/production.
Correspondence of George Devine and Michel Saint-Denis. London. Lang.: Eng. 2630

1943-1998. Performance/production.
Actors' interpretations of the title role in Oscar Wilde's *The Canterville Ghost.* USA. Lang.: Eng. 4066

1945-1970. Plays/librettos/scripts.
The development of Theatre Workshop, founded by Ewan MacColl and Joan Littlewood. London. Lang.: Eng. 3491

1945-1998. Performance/production.
Actor Ian Richardson. Edinburgh. London. Lang.: Eng. 2652

1950-1998. Performance/production.
Interview with actor Saeed Jaffrey. USA. India. Lang.: Eng. 2589
Actor Michael Williams. London. Lang.: Eng. 2644
The decline of live entertainment at seaside resorts. Lang.: Eng. 4278

1951-1998. Performance/production.
Gillian Lynne, director and choreographer. London. New York, NY. Lang.: Eng. 4372

1958-1998. Performance/production.
Director Charles Marowitz on the actor's calling. USA. Lang.: Eng. 2706

1960-1985. Plays/librettos/scripts.
Transference in plays by Harold Pinter. Lang.: Eng. 3461

1960-1988. Theory/criticism.
Criticism of performance art as no longer truly experimental. Lang.: Eng. 4269

1962-1987. Plays/librettos/scripts.
Contradiction in the plays of Edward Bond. Lang.: Eng. 3485

1967-1988. Administration.
History of the Brighton performance festival. Brighton. Lang.: Eng. 4229

UK-England Part2 — cont'd

1967-1991. **Plays/librettos/scripts.**
Tom Stoppard's film adaptation of his own *Rosencrantz and Guildenstern Are Dead.* Lang.: Eng. 3980
1968-1988. **Institutions.**
Interview with John Fox of Welfare State International. Ulverston. Lang.: Eng. 4236
1968-1998. **Performance/production.**
Actor Daniel Massey. London. Lang.: Eng. 2595
1970-1988. **Performance/production.**
Performance in the work of mixed-media artist Tina Keane. Lang.: Eng. 4044
1970-1998. **Institutions.**
History of the King's Head Theatre and pub. London. Lang.: Eng. 1747
1985. **Performance/production.**
Semiotic analysis of Peter Hall's National Theatre production of Shakespeare's *Coriolanus.* Lang.: Eng. 2647
1986-1998. **Performance/production.**
Voice teachers Alex Bulmer and Kate Lynch. Toronto, ON. London. Lang.: Eng. 1837
1987-1988. **Performance/production.**
The 'living paintings' of Steven Taylor Woodrow. USA. Lang.: Eng. 4247
1988. **Institutions.**
Edge 88 experimental festival. London. Lang.: Eng. 4235
1988. **Theory/criticism.**
Report on the Eighth National Review of Live Art. Lang.: Eng. 4268
1988-1989. **Performance spaces.**
The archaeological excavation of the Rose Theatre. London. Lang.: Eng. 1805
The excavation of the Rose Theatre's foundations. London. Lang.: Eng. 1807
1989. **Theory/criticism.**
Critique of dance criticism. London. Lang.: Eng. 1339
1990-1992. **Performance/production.**
The kitchen in performance art of Bobby Baker and Jeanne Goosen. South Africa, Republic of. Lang.: Eng. 4243
1990-1998. **Performance/production.**
Interview with actor Eddie Marsan. London. Lang.: Eng. 2622
1991. **Plays/librettos/scripts.**
Analysis of Peter Greenaway's film *Prospero's Books.* Lang.: Fre. 3990
1991-1998. **Plays/librettos/scripts.**
Sex, drugs, and violence in contemporary British drama. Lang.: Eng. 3494
1993-1997. **Performance/production.**
The collaborative art installation *Tight Roaring Circle.* London. Lang.: Eng. 4133
1994-1998. **Performance/production.**
New London venues and productions. London. Lang.: Eng. 605
1995-1996. **Plays/librettos/scripts.**
Film adaptations of Shakespeare's *Richard III* by Richard Loncraine and Al Pacino. USA. Lang.: Fre. 4012
1995-1997. **Performance/production.**
Interview with actress Fiona Shaw. Lang.: Eng. 2607
Performance artist Leslie Hill's *Push the Boat Out.* London. USA. Lang.: Eng. 4245
1996. **Performance/production.**
Lois Weaver's *Faith and Dancing* and the CD-ROM in interactive performance. USA. Lang.: Eng. 971
Gaynor Macfarlane's production of Edwards' *Damon and Pythias* at Shakespeare's Globe. London. Lang.: Eng. 2613
1996-1998. **Administration.**
Interview with John Tusa, managing director of the Barbican Centre. London. Lang.: Eng. 24
1996-1998. **Performance/production.**
Katie Mitchell's production of mystery plays at RSC. London. Lang.: Eng. 2626
1997. **Performance/production.**
Michael Birch's production of *Vanity Fair.* Leeds. Lang.: Eng. 2600
1997. **Plays/librettos/scripts.**
Shakespeare and the feminist theatre of Bryony Lavery and Jane Prendergast. Lang.: Eng. 3439
1998. **Administration.**
Attempts to diversify offerings of the Barbican Centre. London. Lang.: Eng. 25
The practice of giving critics tickets for the second night of a show. London. Lang.: Eng. 27
1998. **Institutions.**
Caro Newling, executive producer of Donmar Warehouse. London. Lang.: Eng. 1742
Funding status of London's fringe theatres. London. Lang.: Eng. 1748
1998. **Performance/production.**
The Creative Surges actor-training seminar. Ipswich. Lang.: Eng. 606
Possible castings for Beckett's *En attendant Godot (Waiting for Godot).* Lang.: Eng. 2645
The success of a revival of *Oklahoma!* at the Olivier. London. Lang.: Eng. 4373
1998. **Plays/librettos/scripts.**
Interview with playwright Rod Dungate. Birmingham. Lang.: Eng. 3442
1998. **Reference materials.**
Index to *Opera* volume 49. Europe. USA. Lang.: Eng. 4834
1998. **Relation to other fields.**
Evaluation of Ph.D. programs in theatre and drama. Canada. USA. Lang.: Eng. 716

UK-Ireland

1807. **Plays/librettos/scripts.**
Analysis of letters between Lady Morgan and actor Richard Jones. Lang.: Eng. 4862
1890-1914. **Relation to other fields.**
Nationalism and Irish theatre. Ireland. Lang.: Eng. 750
1902-1997. **Plays/librettos/scripts.**
Gender and nationalism in Northern Irish drama. Lang.: Eng. 3511
1980-1988. **Plays/librettos/scripts.**
Brian Friel's plays and the Field Day Theatre Company. Lang.: Eng. 3512
1984-1998. **Plays/librettos/scripts.**
Adaptations of Greek tragedy by contemporary Irish writers. Ireland. Lang.: Eng. 3214
1989-1998. **Performance/production.**
Recent productions in Ireland of plays by Eugene O'Neill. Dublin. Belfast. Lang.: Eng. 2154
1993-1996. **Plays/librettos/scripts.**
Recent history in Irish theatre and drama. Dublin. Belfast. Lang.: Eng. 3212

UK-Scotland

1913-1934. **Institutions.**
History of the Scottish National Players. Lang.: Eng. 1752
1945-1998. **Performance/production.**
Actor Ian Richardson. Edinburgh. London. Lang.: Eng. 2652
1960-1988. **Performance/production.**
The Scottish performance art scene. Lang.: Eng. 4248
1963-1998. **Institutions.**
Brief history of the Scottish Opera. Edinburgh. Lang.: Eng. 4480
1985. **Plays/librettos/scripts.**
Analysis of *Red Noses* by Peter Barnes. Lang.: Eng. 3514
1985-1998. **Relation to other fields.**
Story-telling as a way of knowing and communicating. Lang.: Eng. 772
1996. **Performance/production.**
A production of Susan Glaspell's experimental play *The Verge.* Glasgow. Lang.: Eng. 2651
High-school students' production of *The Wiz* at the Edinburgh Fringe Festival. Hattiesburg, MS. Edinburgh. Lang.: Eng. 4381
1996-1998. **Institutions.**
Interview with members of dance group Creative Independent Artists. Glasgow. Lang.: Eng. 904
1997. **Performance/production.**
Shakespearean influence on the 1987 Edinburgh Festival. Edinburgh. Lang.: Eng. 2653
1997. **Plays/librettos/scripts.**
Translating Hauptmann's *Die Weber (The Weavers)* into Scots dialect. Dundee. Glasgow. Lang.: Eng. 3513
1998. **Institutions.**
Report on the 1998 Edinburgh Fringe Festival. Edinburgh. Lang.: Eng. 1750
Report on the Edinburgh Festival. Edinburgh. Lang.: Rus. 1751
1998. **Performance spaces.**
Profile of Traverse Theatre. Edinburgh. Lang.: Eng. 462

UK-Scotland — cont'd

Conference on the need for new dance performance space. Glasgow. Lang.: Eng. 910
1998. Performance/production.
London summer theatre and the Edinburgh Festival. London. Edinburgh. Lang.: Eng. 2603
Collection of newspaper reviews by London theatre critics. Edinburgh. Lang.: Eng. 2649
Collection of newspaper reviews by London theatre critics. Edinburgh. Lang.: Eng. 2650

UK-Wales
1843-1919. Institutions.
The Neath Opera Group's festival and proposed music center at the former home of Adelina Patti. Brecon. Lang.: Eng. 4481
1965-1998. Performance/production.
Tenor Bryn Terfel. Lang.: Eng. 4707
1973-1993. Performance/production.
The function of sound in productions of *India Song* by Marguerite Duras. France. Mold. Lang.: Eng. 1945
1997. Performance/production.
The biennial Singer of the World contest. Cardiff. Lang.: Eng. 4706

USA
1500-1900. Design/technology.
Catalog of the Tobin scenography collection. Europe. Lang.: Eng. 272
1600-1900. Plays/librettos/scripts.
Dramatic traditions in North and South America. Argentina. Lang.: Eng. 3698
1604-1798. Relation to other fields.
The influence of Shakespeare's *Othello* on C.B. Brown's novel *Wieland.* England. Lang.: Eng. 3788
1610-1998. Research/historiography.
Jonson's *The Alchemist* and source studies. England. Lang.: Eng. 3795
1650-1950. Performance/production.
French cultural and intellectual history, including the work of Molière. Lang.: Eng. 2663
1700-1910. Plays/librettos/scripts.
Analysis of *The Foresters* by Alfred, Lord Tennyson. England. Lang.: Eng. 2998
1723-1840. Institutions.
Public entertainments in Philadelphia's pleasure gardens. Philadelphia, PA. Lang.: Eng. 400
1769-1986. Plays/librettos/scripts.
Lorraine Hansberry and Black Americans in theatre. Lang.: Eng. 3640
1770-1830. Administration.
Early American anti-theatrical legislation. Lang.: Eng. 33
1770-1830. Performance/production.
Early American theatre and social organization and control. Lang.: Eng. 653
1771-1796. Plays/librettos/scripts.
Judith Sargent Murray's *Traveller Returned* and its source. Lang.: Eng. 3672
1780-1995. Research/historiography.
Social and economic forces that shaped American theatre. Lang.: Eng. 827
1783-1785. Plays/librettos/scripts.
Gender and politics in Romantic tragedies of Mercy Otis Warren. Lang.: Eng. 3575
1796-1820. Institutions.
Popular entertainment at the New Haven Assembly Hall and Columbian Museum and Gardens. New Haven, CT. Lang.: Eng. 394
1800-1860. Performance/production.
Boucicault's *The Octoroon* and the performance of race, gender, and power. Lang.: Eng. 669
1800-1900. Administration.
Nineteenth-century women theatre managers. Lang.: Eng. 129
1800-1960. Performance spaces.
The history of theatre structures and producing organizations in a small city. Lancaster, PA. Lang.: Eng. 466
1806-1872. Performance/production.
Actor Edwin Forrest and the construction of masculinity. Lang.: Eng. 674
1816-1876. Performance/production.
Gender and the career of actress Charlotte Cushman. Lang.: Eng. 680
1817-1822. Administration.
Theatre manager Charles H. Gilfert. Charleston, SC. Lang.: Eng. 135
1820-1977. Design/technology.
Magical stage effects in 'vampire' plays. Lang.: Eng. 1548
1828-1846. Performance spaces.
Popular entertainment at Niblo's Garden. New York, NY. Lang.: Eng. 470
1830-1860. Audience.
Gender-related social issues, theatre, and historiography. Lang.: Eng. 157
1830-1860. Performance/production.
The Field frontier acting family. Lang.: Eng. 641
1830-1970. Performance/production.
Excessive stage and screen melodrama. UK-England. Lang.: Eng. 608
1835-1860. Performance/production.
Gendered readings of Bellini's *La Sonnambula* in performance. Lang.: Eng. 4748
1835-1869. Performance/production.
Audience reaction to actress Adah Isaacs Menken. Lang.: Eng. 619
1840-1880. Institutions.
Respectability and museum theatre. New York, NY. Lang.: Eng. 4112
1841-1847. Relation to other fields.
Role playing in the Brook Farm transcendentalist community. West Roxbury, MA. Lang.: Eng. 777
1850-1859. Plays/librettos/scripts.
The representation od social issues on the American stage. Lang.: Eng. 3647
1850-1860. Performance/production.
San Francisco's professional theatre. San Francisco, CA. Lang.: Eng. 682
1850-1890. Performance/production.
Performance and the nineteenth-century economy. Lang.: Eng. 4134
1850-1934. Performance/production.
Vaudeville theatre on the West Coast. Los Angeles, CA. Lang.: Eng. 4146
1850-1985. Performance/production.
The Opera-in-English movement. Lang.: Eng. 4746
1850-1998. Performance/production.
Verdi's *Stiffelio* and Gounod's *Roméo et Juliette* in New York. New York, NY. Lang.: Eng. 4730
1852. Performance/production.
Audience reaction to Irish opera singer Catherine Hayes. New Orleans, LA. Lang.: Eng. 4745
1856-1915. Performance/production.
Actor Tomasso Salvini. Italy. Lang.: Eng. 2731
1857-1927. Performance/production.
History of legitimate theatre in Omaha. Omaha, NB. Lang.: Eng. 676
1858-1863. Institutions.
Popular entertainment at the Palace Garden. New York, NY. Lang.: Eng. 403
1860-1976. Plays/librettos/scripts.
Dramatic adaptations of Henry Wadsworth Longfellow's poem *Evangeline.* Canada. Lang.: Eng. 3643
1860-1998. Audience.
Operetta and the contemporary audience. France. Germany. Lang.: Swe. 4851
1865-1950. Relation to other fields.
The theatrical nature of Salvation Army activities. Lang.: Eng. 796
1868-1930. Performance/production.
Male impersonation in variety and vaudeville. Lang.: Eng. 4281
1869-1934. Performance/production.
Actress Marie Dressler. New York, NY. Lang.: Eng. 2734
1870-1902. Performance/production.
The Hyers sisters and Black musical comedy. Lang.: Eng. 4384
1870-1910. Performance/production.
Social concerns reflected in popular entertainment publications. Lang.: Eng. 4144
1874-1919. Administration.
The campaign to ban child performers in New York City. New York, NY. Lang.: Eng. 139
1874-1965. Relation to other fields.
Actress Nance O'Neil and her friendship with Lizzie Borden. Lang.: Eng. 799

USA — cont'd

1875-1899. Administration.
The playbill as a reflection of social and economic forces. Lang.: Eng. 31
1875-1915. Performance/production.
Irish and Irish-American characters on the stages of the Midwest. Lang.: Eng. 2696
1875-1925. Performance/production.
Culture and the opera house in Appalachia. Lang.: Eng. 629
1877-1998. Performance/production.
The stage history of *Samson et Dalila* by Saint-Saëns. France. Germany. Lang.: Eng. 4566
1878-1945. Performance/production.
Actress/director Alla Nazimova. Russia. Lang.: Eng. 585
1882. Performance/production.
George Crichton Miln's touring Shakespearean company in Japan. Chicago, IL. Yokohama. Lang.: Eng. 2702
1882. Plays/librettos/scripts.
Analysis of *The White Slave* by Bartley Campbell. Lang.: Eng. 3660
1882-1931. Performance/production.
The 'scientific perspective' of director David Belasco. Lang.: Eng. 2741
1882-1942. Performance/production.
Actor John Barrymore. New York, NY. Lang.: Eng. 2732
1883-1909. Performance/production.
Soprano Marcella Sembrich's performances at the Metropolitan Opera. New York, NY. Lang.: Eng. 4724
1884-1983. Plays/librettos/scripts.
Stage adaptations of Mark Twain's *Adventures of Tom Sawyer*. Lang.: Eng. 3702
1886-1933. Administration.
The lesbian relationship of agent Elisabeth Marbury and designer Elsie de Wolfe. Lang.: Eng. 44
1886-1950. Performance/production.
Career of entertainer Al Jolson. Lang.: Eng. 4280
1887-1983. Performance/production.
Acting couple Alfred Lunt and Lynn Fontanne: 'idealized heterosexuality'. Lang.: Eng. 2656
1887-1998. Plays/librettos/scripts.
Strindberg's influence on playwrights Len Jenkin and Mac Wellman. Lang.: Eng. 3584
1888-1953. Plays/librettos/scripts.
The early life of playwright Eugene O'Neill. Lang.: Eng. 3534
Historical and cultural context of Eugene O'Neill. Lang.: Eng. 3638
Intellectual and artistic influences on playwright Eugene O'Neill. Lang.: Eng. 3697
Playwright Eugene O'Neill's theatrical milieu. Lang.: Eng. 3706
1888-1963. Performance/production.
The career of gay actor Monty Woolley. Lang.: Eng. 2691
1888-1972. Performance/production.
Life and film career of singer Maurice Chevalier. Paris. Lang.: Eng. 3933
1890-1910. Audience.
Gender and social warfare at the Metropolitan Opera. Lang.: Eng. 4411
1890-1910. Design/technology.
Lighting and realism in opera and theatre: Belasco and Puccini. Italy. Lang.: Eng. 203
1890-1910. Plays/librettos/scripts.
The social roles of women playwrights. Lang.: Eng. 3637
1890-1915. Performance/production.
The mediation of theatre and film between immigrant and mainstream cultures. New York, NY. Lang.: Eng. 638
1890-1920. Theory/criticism.
Sociological influence on the little theatre movement. Lang.: Eng. 862
1890-1930. Performance/production.
The first wave of American feminist theatre. Lang.: Eng. 648
Female impersonation and the construction of the female stereotype. Lang.: Eng. 651
1890-1997. Performance/production.
Performance at Hull House. Chicago, IL. Lang.: Eng. 644
1890-1998. Performance/production.
The disappearance of the diva in the modern world. Europe. Lang.: Swe. 525
1893-1927. Administration.
Theatre manager and entrepreneur Harry Davis. Pittsburgh, PA. Lang.: Eng. 134
1893-1943. Performance/production.
Actor Leslie Howard. London. New York, NY. Lang.: Eng. 2631
1893-1974. Performance/production.
The marriage of theatre artists Katharine Cornell and Guthrie McClintic. Lang.: Eng. 634
1895-1915. Performance spaces.
Oscar Hammerstein I and the creation and development of Times Square. Lang.: Eng. 463
1895-1967. Performance/production.
Actor Bert Lahr. Lang.: Eng. 3953
1895-1998. Performance/production.
Actor Paul Muni. New York, NY. Lang.: Eng. 2733
1896-1941. Performance/production.
Popular entertainer Elsie Janis. Lang.: Eng. 4145
1896-1998. Performance/production.
The songs of George and Ira Gershwin. Lang.: Eng. 4376
1898-1950. Performance/production.
Musical theatre composer Will Marion Cook. Lang.: Eng. 4378
1898-1959. Performance/production.
Profile of performer and activist Paul Robeson. Lang.: Eng. 2750
1898-1998. Administration.
Preparations for the centennial of actor and singer Paul Robeson. Lang.: Eng. 61
1898-1998. Plays/librettos/scripts.
The significance of Bertolt Brecht to theatre in the late twentieth century. Germany. Lang.: Eng. 3142
1899-1962. Performance/production.
Actor Charles Laughton. London. Hollywood, CA. Lang.: Eng. 2632
1900-1905. Performance/production.
Attempted censorship of productions. Lang.: Eng. 2698
1900-1927. Performance/production.
New York City's attempt to impose censorship on theatre productions. New York, NY. Lang.: Eng. 2699
1900-1930. Performance/production.
Modern dance and the female body. Europe. Lang.: Eng. 1321
1900-1940. Plays/librettos/scripts.
Analysis of plays about the women's movement. Lang.: Eng. 3559
1900-1950. Performance/production.
The Broadway directing career of George M. Cohan. Lang.: Eng. 2751
1900-1957. Performance/production.
The importance of Black performers in American musical films. Lang.: Swe. 3960
1900-1959. Performance/production.
Opera composer George Antheil. Lang.: Eng. 4750
1900-1969. Theory/criticism.
Theatre critic John Mason Brown. Lang.: Eng. 3846
1900-1990. Relation to other fields.
Analysis of the jazz funeral. New Orleans, LA. Lang.: Eng. 4228
1900-1996. Plays/librettos/scripts.
Representations of Joan of Arc in film and theatre. Europe. Lang.: Eng. 3970
1900-1997. Training.
Illustrated history of jazz dance. Slovenia. Lang.: Slo. 1023
1900-1998. Design/technology.
Contemporary design and stage-painting techniques of the early twentieth century. Lang.: Eng. 1565
1900-1998. Performance/production.
Operatic holdings of American and British record collectors. UK-England. Lang.: Eng. 4721
1901-1947. Performance/production.
Soprano Grace Moore. Lang.: Eng. 4715
1901-1992. Performance/production.
Biography of film star Marlene Dietrich by her daughter. Lang.: Rus. 3955
1901-1998. Performance/production.
Flamenco variations worldwide. Spain. Lang.: Eng. 962
1902-1986. Administration.
Producer Cheryl Crawford, gender and sexuality. Lang.: Eng. 116
1903. Performance/production.
The influence of *The Little Princess* on popular theatre and culture. Lang.: Eng. 2658
1903-1983. Plays/librettos/scripts.
Feminist analysis of plays for young people by women playwrights. Lang.: Eng. 3521

USA — cont'd

1905-1906. Administration.
Sarah Bernhardt's farewell tour and its revenues. Lang.: Eng. 28
1905-1923. Performance/production.
Dance-mime Angna Enters. Lang.: Eng. 1319
1905-1923. Plays/librettos/scripts.
The development of playwright Owen Davis. Lang.: Eng. 3526
1905-1972. Performance/production.
Actor/director Margaret Webster, gender and sexuality. UK-England. Lang.: Eng. 2590
1905-1976. Plays/librettos/scripts.
Profile of screenwriter Dalton Trumbo. Lang.: Eng. 3999
1905-1985. Training.
Feldenkreis movement theory. Lang.: Eng. 880
1905-1991. Plays/librettos/scripts.
Shakespeare's *The Tempest* on film. UK-England. Lang.: Eng. 3981
1906-1944. Plays/librettos/scripts.
The Broadway success of women playwrights. Lang.: Eng. 3590
1907-1957. Administration.
History of circle stock touring. Lang.: Eng. 43
1907-1997. Performance/production.
Lotte Goslar's Pantomime Circus. Dresden. Los Angeles, CA. Lang.: Eng. 4123
Comic dance performer Lotte Goslar. Germany. Lang.: Eng. 4124
1908-1998. Performance/production.
Composers of Hollywood film scores. Lang.: Eng. 3957
Profile of composer Elliott Carter. Lang.: Eng. 4711
1909. Theory/criticism.
Marginalia in Sir George Greenwood's copy of *Is Shakespeare Dead?* by Mark Twain. Lang.: Eng. 863
1909-1969. Plays/librettos/scripts.
Miscegenation in American drama. Lang.: Eng. 3599
1910-1925. Performance/production.
The influence of exhibition ballroom dance on theatrical entertainments. Lang.: Eng. 985
1910-1985. Performance/production.
History of movement training for the actor. Lang.: Eng. 675
1910-1990. Plays/librettos/scripts.
The sacrifice of children in American drama. Lang.: Eng. 3566
1910-1996. Training.
Dance teacher Louise Kloepper. Lang.: Eng. 1213
1910-1998. Administration.
Conductor Leonard dePaur, winner of the Paul Robeson Award. New York, NY. Lang.: Eng. 104
1910-1998. Performance/production.
Obituaries for Roger L. Stevens, Kenneth Frankel, Donald Davis, and Edith Oliver. Canada. Lang.: Eng. 2742
1911-1956. Plays/librettos/scripts.
Details of the personal life of playwright Eugene O'Neill. Lang.: Eng. 3533
1911-1998. Performance/production.
Obituary for actress Maureen O'Sullivan. Lang.: Eng. 3947
1911-1998. Plays/librettos/scripts.
Influence of the novelistic monologues of Eugene O'Neill. Lang.: Eng. 3641
1912-1940. Design/technology.
Critic Kenneth Macgowan and the 'new stagecraft'. Lang.: Eng. 262
1912-1945. Plays/librettos/scripts.
Comparison of characters in plays of Georg Kaiser and Tennessee Williams. Germany. Lang.: Eng. 3588
1912-1997. Performance/production.
Sam Fuller's career as a film maker. Lang.: Eng. 3943
1912-1998. Administation.
American and French regulation of mass media. France. Lang.: Eng. 3853
1912-1998. Performance/production.
Obituaries for Joseph Maher, Warren Kliewer, and E.G. Marshall. Lang.: Eng. 2655
1913. Administration.
The creation of Actors' Equity in response to abusive working conditions. New York, NY. Lang.: Eng. 127
1913-1930. Performance/production.
Antitheatricalism in the Circuit Chautauqua. Lang.: Eng. 4135
1913-1990. Performance/production.
Lesbianism and performer Mary Martin. Lang.: Eng. 2757
1914-1943. Plays/librettos/scripts.
The Orestes myth in twentieth-century drama. Europe. Lang.: Eng. 3052
1914-1950. Plays/librettos/scripts.
Death in the plays of Eugene O'Neill. Lang.: Eng. 3663
1914-1963. Plays/librettos/scripts.
Experimental theatre of Elmer Rice. Lang.: Eng. 3620
1915-1925. Plays/librettos/scripts.
Themes of Eugene O'Neill's early plays. Lang.: Eng. 3668
1915-1969. Performance/production.
Twentieth-century productions of Euripidean tragedy. Lang.: Eng. 2678
1915-1995. Plays/librettos/scripts.
The unseen character in plays of O'Neill, Albee, and Tennessee Williams. Lang.: Eng. 3538
1915-1998. Plays/librettos/scripts.
Autobiography of playwright Arthur Miller. Lang.: Rus. 3649
1916-1927. Performance/production.
Screenwriter and producer June Mathis. Lang.: Eng. 3959
1916-1934. Performance/production.
Collaborative Symbolist dance/theatre projects. Europe. Lang.: Eng. 1268
1916-1940. Audience.
The role of *Theatre Arts Monthly* in the development of the American audience. Lang.: Eng. 158
1916-1953. Plays/librettos/scripts.
African- and Irish-Americans in the plays of Eugene O'Neill. Lang.: Eng. 3687
1916-1958. Plays/librettos/scripts.
Lynching in plays of Angelina Weld Grimké and Lorraine Hansberry. Lang.: Eng. 3602
1916-1996. Performance/production.
Notable productions of plays by Eugene O'Neill. Lang.: Eng. 2752
1916-1998. Performance/production.
Obituary for singer and actor Frank Sinatra. Lang.: Eng. 3946
1917-1940. Plays/librettos/scripts.
Eugene O'Neill's *Strange Interlude* and the interwar period. Lang.: Eng. 3654
1917-1998. Plays/librettos/scripts.
Screenwriter Millard Kaufman. Lang.: Eng. 4013
1918-1924. Audience.
George Pierce Baker's 47 Workshop and the construction of the audience. Cambridge, MA. Lang.: Eng. 159
1918-1950. Plays/librettos/scripts.
Closure in plays of Eugene O'Neill. Lang.: Eng. 3703
1918-1953. Performance/production.
Dance director Seymour Felix. Lang.: Eng. 976
1918-1978. Administration.
Interviews about film producer Jack Warner. Hollywood, CA. Lang.: Eng. 3875
1918-1998. Design/technology.
Samuel Resnick, cofounder of Barbizon, distributor of electrical and video equipment. Lang.: Eng. 264
1918-1998. Performance/production.
Choreographer Jerome Robbins. Lang.: Eng. 1167
Obituary for 'Buffalo Bob' Smith, former host of *The Howdy Doody Show*. Lang.: Eng. 4067
1919-1970. Plays/librettos/scripts.
Analysis of plays based on the Hebrew prophets. Europe. Lang.: Eng. 3659
1919-1998. Performance/production.
Director and choreographer Jerome Robbins. Lang.: Eng. 975
Interview with choreographer John Taras. New York, NY. Lang.: Hun. 1187
Obituary for ventriloquist Stanley Burns. New York, NY. Lang.: Eng. 4148
1920-1929. Relation to other fields.
Russian and American theatre and society of the twenties. Russia. Lang.: Rus. 756
1920-1940. Plays/librettos/scripts.
Blues music in the writings of Zora Neale Hurston. Lang.: Eng. 3625
1920-1950. Training.
Modern dance teacher Elizabeth Waters. Lang.: Eng. 1342
1920-1953. Plays/librettos/scripts.
Female characters in Eugene O'Neill's plays. Lang.: Eng. 3525
1920-1964. Plays/librettos/scripts.
The comedies of manners of S.N. Behrman and Philip Barry. Lang.: Eng. 3648
1920-1968. Performance/production.
Analysis of beauty pageants. Lang.: Eng. 4222

USA — cont'd

1920-1970. **Plays/librettos/scripts.**
Revolutionary elements in plays and theory of Baraka and Artaud. France. Lang.: Eng. 3580
1920-1975. **Plays/librettos/scripts.**
A method of analysis for the drama. Lang.: Eng. 3537
1920-1985. **Plays/librettos/scripts.**
The return of the prodigal in American drama. Lang.: Eng. 3666
1920-1992. **Plays/librettos/scripts.**
Robin Hood on film. England. Lang.: Eng. 3969
1920-1995. **Performance/production.**
Outdoor passion plays. Lang.: Eng. 2715
1920-1998. **Design/technology.**
Stage technician Pete Feller. Lang.: Eng. 330
1920-1998. **Performance/production.**
Dance on screen. Europe. Lang.: Ger. 3860
Etienne Decroux's concept of actor-centered theatre. France. Lang.: Eng. 4091
1920-1998. **Plays/librettos/scripts.**
Effeminacy on the American stage. Lang.: Eng. 3682
1920-1998. **Training.**
Ballet teacher Pauline Koner. New York, NY. Lang.: Eng. 1212
1921. **Plays/librettos/scripts.**
Existential analysis of Eugene O'Neill's *Anna Christie*. Lang.: Eng. 3562
The development and casting of Booth Tarkington's *The Country Cousin*. Lang.: Eng. 3699
1922. **Plays/librettos/scripts.**
Eugene O'Neill's *The Hairy Ape* and the belief in racial degeneration. Lang.: Eng. 3657
1923-1926. **Plays/librettos/scripts.**
Brecht and the city as an expressionistic setting. Germany. Lang.: Eng. 3168
1923-1973. **Theory/criticism.**
American acting theory. Lang.: Eng. 866
1924. **Administration.**
Oscar Micheaux's use of an interracial marriage case as a publicity tool for his films. Lang.: Eng. 3874
1924-1998. **Performance/production.**
Tribute to late director José Quintero. Lang.: Eng. 2683
Obituary for puppeteer Bob Mason. Lang.: Eng. 4908
1925. **Plays/librettos/scripts.**
Analysis of *Processional* by John Howard Lawson. Lang.: Eng. 3535
1925-1928. **Institutions.**
Theatre and land use in midtown Manhattan. New York, NY. Lang.: Eng. 430
1925-1930. **Plays/librettos/scripts.**
Black dance in plays of Zora Neale Hurston. Lang.: Eng. 3633
1925-1938. **Plays/librettos/scripts.**
Analysis of Eugene O'Neill's 'middle period' plays. Lang.: Eng. 3675
1925-1960. **Performance/production.**
Burlesque comedian Joey Faye. Lang.: Eng. 4140
1925-1981. **Training.**
The development of Irmgard Bartenieff's corrective physical training methods. Lang.: Ger. 1024
1925-1985. **Performance spaces.**
Theatre space and performance. New York, NY. Lang.: Eng. 464
1926. **Plays/librettos/scripts.**
Race and gender in *The Great God Brown* by Eugene O'Neill. Lang.: Eng. 3608
1926-1927. **Plays/librettos/scripts.**
Analysis of Eugene O'Neill's *Strange Interlude*. Lang.: Dut. 3551
1926-1967. **Plays/librettos/scripts.**
Poet Langston Hughes and the theatre. New York, NY. Lang.: Eng. 3585
1926-1998. **Design/technology.**
Costume designer Robert Mackintosh. Lang.: Eng. 284
1927. **Plays/librettos/scripts.**
Analysis of *The Purple Flower* by Marita Bonner. Lang.: Eng. 3527
1927-1929. **Institutions.**
The New Playwrights Theatre Company. New York, NY. Lang.: Eng. 410
1927-1934. **Plays/librettos/scripts.**
Screenwriting before the Motion Picture Production Code. Lang.: Eng. 4026
1927-1982. **Institutions.**
History of Lake Charles Little Theatre. Lake Charles, LA. Lang.: Eng. 1770
1928-1998. **Design/technology.**
Lighting expert Francis P. De Verna. Lang.: Eng. 257
1929. **Performance/production.**
Resistance to a Boston production of Eugene O'Neill's *Strange Interlude*. Boston, MA. Lang.: Eng. 2693
1929-1940. **Performance/production.**
Popular American radio and the importance of the disembodied voice. Lang.: Eng. 3864
1929-1998. **Performance spaces.**
The restoration of the Orpheum Theatre. Phoenix, AZ. Lang.: Eng. 3926
1929-1998. **Performance/production.**
Obituary for puppeteer Gia Wallace Brown. Lang.: Eng. 4910
1930. **Performance/production.**
Martha Graham on life devoted to choreography and dance. Lang.: Eng. 1323
1930-1935. **Performance/production.**
Aleksand'r Tairov's production of *Fortune Heights* by John Dos Passos. Lang.: Rus. 2739
1930-1940. **Relation to other fields.**
Fitzroy Davis's theatre novel *Quicksilver*. Lang.: Eng. 810
1930-1965. **Administration.**
Producer Cheryl Crawford and her contributions to the American stage. Lang.: Eng. 1396
1930-1997. **Performance/production.**
Obituaries for Ellis Rabb, Giorgio Strehler, and David Mark Cohen. Lang.: Eng. 2725
Obituary for puppeteer Mary Churchill. Lang.: Eng. 4901
1930-1997. **Theory/criticism.**
Critical response to plays of Eugene O'Neill. Lang.: Eng. 3837
1930-1998. **Design/technology.**
TV lighting designer William Greenfield. Lang.: Eng. 4049
Frederic Paddock Hope, planner of Walt Disney World. Lang.: Eng. 4098
1930-1998. **Performance/production.**
Obituary for TV puppeteer Cal Schumann. Lang.: Eng. 4907
1930-1998. **Plays/librettos/scripts.**
Background on Lorca's *El Público (The Public)*, about to have its New York premiere. New York, NY. Lang.: Eng. 3651
1931. **Plays/librettos/scripts.**
Analysis of *Counsellor-at-Law* by Elmer Rice. Lang.: Eng. 3712
1931-1940. **Relation to other fields.**
The gangster film and public concern about moral corruption. Lang.: Eng. 4038
1931-1967. **Institutions.**
Producer Joseph Cino and Off-off Broadway theatre. New York, NY. Lang.: Eng. 404
1931-1998. **Plays/librettos/scripts.**
Stage and screenwriter John Hopkins. London. Hollywood, CA. Lang.: Eng. 3498
Marvin David Levy's operatic adaptation of *Mourning Becomes Electra* by Eugene O'Neill. Lang.: Eng. 4827
1932-1990. **Plays/librettos/scripts.**
Opera in American gangster films. Lang.: Eng. 4023
1932-1997. **Institutions.**
History of Palo Alto Children's Theatre. Palo Alto, CA. Lang.: Eng. 1778
1932-1998. **Theory/criticism.**
Obituary for critic Ross Wetzstoen, who inspired the Obie Awards. Lang.: Eng. 3847
1933. **Performance/production.**
Analysis of Frank Capra's film *Lady for a Day*. Lang.: Eng. 3952
1933-1976. **Design/technology.**
Costume designs by Irene Sharaff. Lang.: Eng. 277
1933-1998. **Performance/production.**
Obituary for TV puppeteer Shari Lewis. Lang.: Eng. 4909
1933-1998. **Relation to other fields.**
American modern dance and gay culture. Lang.: Eng. 1337
1934. **Performance/production.**
Analysis of the *Night and Day* dance sequence of *The Gay Divorcee*. Hollywood, CA. Lang.: Eng. 977
Brief productions of Shakespeare, Shaw, and Marlowe at the World's Fair. Chicago, IL. Lang.: Eng. 2701
1934. **Plays/librettos/scripts.**
Analysis of *Days Without End* by Eugene O'Neill. Lang.: Eng. 3636

USA — cont'd

John Stahl's film adaptation of *Imitation of Life* by Fannie Hurst. Hollywood, CA. Lang.: Eng. 4029
1935. Plays/librettos/scripts.
Analysis of *Mulatto* by Langston Hughes. Lang.: Eng. 3709
1935-1939. Institutions.
Economics and the Federal Theatre Project. Lang.: Eng. 428
Federal Theatre Project Shakespearean productions. Lang.: Eng. 1761
New plays and the Federal Theatre Project. Lang.: Eng. 1768
1935-1939. Performance/production.
Productions of the Federal Theatre Project's Living Newspapers. New York, NY. Lang.: Eng. 643
1935-1942. Plays/librettos/scripts.
Marriage, divorce, and gender in the Hollywood comedy of remarriage. Lang.: Eng. 4010
1935-1975. Institutions.
History of the Metropolitan Opera Guild. Lang.: Eng. 4486
1935-1988. Plays/librettos/scripts.
Film and video productions of plays by Eugene O'Neill. Lang.: Eng. 4078
1935-1998. Design/technology.
Costumer Kermit Love. Lang.: Eng. 271
1935-1998. Performance/production.
Obituary for Bob McAllister, ventriloquist, magician, and former host of *Wonderama*. Lang.: Eng. 4149
1936. Plays/librettos/scripts.
Analysis of Countée Cullen's translation of Euripides' *Medea*. Lang.: Eng. 3567
1936. Relation to other fields.
Protest actions and the staging of claims to public space. Trenton, NJ. Lang.: Eng. 791
1936-1979. Plays/librettos/scripts.
Tennessee Williams's short story *Twenty-Seven Wagons Full of Cotton* and the plays based on it. Lang.: Eng. 3622
1936-1980. Performance/production.
Gower Champion's work in musical theatre. New York, NY. Lang.: Eng. 4388
1936-1985. Plays/librettos/scripts.
Female presence/absence in plays of O'Neill, Pinter, and Shepard. UK-England. Lang.: Eng. 3607
1936-1998. Performance/production.
Dancer, choreographer, and teacher Hellmut Gottschild. Germany. Lang.: Ger. 1287
1937. Performance/production.
Musical analysis of Gershwin's *Porgy and Bess*. Lang.: Eng. 4753
1937. Plays/librettos/scripts.
The portrayal of Franklin Delano Roosevelt in the musical *I'd Rather Be Right*. Lang.: Eng. 4396
1937-1939. Institutions.
State-wide tours of the Florida Federal Theatre Project. Lang.: Eng. 411
1937-1939. Performance/production.
The European and American tour of the Polish National Ballet. Poland. France. Lang.: Pol. 1124
1937-1942. Institutions.
History of Mercury Theatre. New York, NY. Lang.: Eng. 1776
1937-1994. Performance/production.
Excerpts from notes and diaries of film maker Sam Fuller. Lang.: Eng. 3942
The career of action film maker Sam Fuller. Lang.: Eng. 3951
1937-1998. Performance/production.
Profile of lighting designer Jennifer Tipton. Lang.: Eng. 4747
Obituary for puppeteer Duke Kraus. Lang.: Eng. 4902
1938-1998. Design/technology.
Set and lighting designer James Tilton. Lang.: Eng. 265
1938-1998. Plays/librettos/scripts.
Lyricist and librettist Betty Comden. Lang.: Eng. 4400
1939-1943. Plays/librettos/scripts.
The late plays of Eugene O'Neill. Lang.: Eng. 3528
1939-1946. Plays/librettos/scripts.
The Iceman Cometh by Eugene O'Neill compared to a short story by Ernest Hemingway. Lang.: Eng. 3609
1939-1980. Performance/production.
History of commercial TV opera broadcasts. New York, NY. Lang.: Eng. 4756
1940-1950. Basic theatrical documents.
Jonathan Golove's opera *Red Harvest*. Lang.: Eng. 4422
1940-1960. Performance/production.
The multifaceted nature of early nonprofit regional theatre. Lang.: Eng. 2705
1940-1982. Theory/criticism.
Musical-theatre composer and critic Aaron Lehman Engel. Lang.: Eng. 4403
1940-1995. Performance/production.
Avant-garde American women directors' productions of *Doctor Faustus Lights the Lights* by Gertrude Stein. Lang.: Eng. 2735
1940-1995. Plays/librettos/scripts.
Eugene O'Neill and the creation of autobiographical drama. Lang.: Eng. 3561
1940-1998. Performance/production.
Ballerina Tanaquil LeClerq on working with choreographer Jerome Robbins. Lang.: Eng. 1185
Bass Samuel Ramey. Lang.: Eng. 4744
1940-1998. Plays/librettos/scripts.
Jean Randich's production of *The Golden Door* by Sylvia Regan, Tenement Museum. New York, NY. Lang.: Eng. 3606
1940-1998. Theory/criticism.
Advice to music critics. Lang.: Eng. 4846
1942. Plays/librettos/scripts.
The critical reception of Zora Neale Hurston's autobiography. Lang.: Eng. 3704
1942-1956. Plays/librettos/scripts.
Irish folklore in plays of Eugene O'Neill. Lang.: Eng. 3522
1942-1964. Theory/criticism.
Newsweek's coverage of the arts. Lang.: Eng. 4842
1942-1989. Performance/production.
Interviews with dancers about performance. UK-England. Cuba. Lang.: Eng. 1162
1942-1998. Performance/production.
Critique of current trends in opera production. Lang.: Eng. 4726
1943. Plays/librettos/scripts.
Interview with screenwriter Ring Lardner, Jr. Lang.: Eng. 3998
1943-1955. Plays/librettos/scripts.
Analysis of short stories by playwright Tennessee Williams. Lang.: Eng. 3601
1943-1970. Plays/librettos/scripts.
Analysis of plays by Tennessee Williams. Lang.: Eng. 3539
1943-1998. Basic theatrical documents.
Screenplay of *The Fishermen of Beaudrais* by Ring Lardner, Jr., and Dalton Trumbo. Lang.: Eng. 3891
1943-1998. Performance/production.
Actors' interpretations of the title role in Oscar Wilde's *The Canterville Ghost*. UK-England. Lang.: Eng. 4066
Dancer Gemze de Lappe's work with choreographer Agnes De Mille. New York, NY. Lang.: Eng. 4380
1943-1998. Plays/librettos/scripts.
Background on *The Fishermen of Beaudrais* by Ring Lardner, Jr., and Dalton Trumbo. Lang.: Eng. 4025
1944. Plays/librettos/scripts.
The romantic nature of Tennessee Williams' *The Glass Menagerie*. Lang.: Eng. 3558
Playwright Mary Chase, author of *Harvey*. Lang.: Eng. 3711
1944-1978. Plays/librettos/scripts.
Metadrama in plays of Tennessee Williams. Lang.: Eng. 3686
1944-1980. Plays/librettos/scripts.
Individualism in plays of Tennessee Williams. Lang.: Eng. 3634
1944-1998. Performance/production.
Interview with choreographer Merce Cunningham. Lang.: Eng. 1326
1945-1953. Plays/librettos/scripts.
Eugene O'Neill's unfinished *A Tale of Possessors Self-Dispossessed*. Lang.: Eng. 3594
1945-1965. Plays/librettos/scripts.
Fairy-tale heroines in American drama and musical theatre. Lang.: Eng. 3617
1945-1986. Plays/librettos/scripts.
Realism and anti-realism in plays of Tennessee Williams. Lang.: Eng. 3626
1945-1988. Plays/librettos/scripts.
Science fiction drama since World War II. Lang.: Eng. 3591
1945-1998. Design/technology.
Costume practice and training in the U.S. and eastern Europe. Europe. Lang.: Ger. 177
1945-1998. Performance/production.
Operas by Benjamin Britten in the repertory of the Metropolitan and the New York City Opera. New York, NY. Lang.: Eng. 4749

USA — cont'd

1945-1998. **Plays/librettos/scripts.**
Interview with playwright and screenwriter Robert Anderson. Lang.: Eng. 3515
The Roman Empire in postwar American cinema. Lang.: Eng. 4032

1946. **Performance/production.**
Ballerina Alexandra Danilova on Balanchine's *Raymonda*. New York, NY. Lang.: Eng. 1172
Ben Hecht's propaganda pageant *A Flag Is Born*. New York, NY. Lang.: Eng. 4220

1946-1947. **Institutions.**
The economic failure of the American Repertory Theatre. New York, NY. Lang.: Eng. 1790

1946-1958. **Plays/librettos/scripts.**
Analysis of Tennessee Williams' *Suddenly Last Summer* and 'Desire and the Black Masseur'. Lang.: Eng. 3678

1946-1982. **Theory/criticism.**
The use of different analytical strategies to obtain multiple readings of dance performance. Europe. Lang.: Eng. 1200

1946-1998. **Performance/production.**
Recollections of ballerina Margot Fonteyn. Panama. Lang.: Eng. 1182
Director Garland Wright. Lang.: Eng. 2707

1947-1948. **Institutions.**
The founding of the New York City Ballet. New York, NY. Lang.: Eng. 1060

1947-1990. **Plays/librettos/scripts.**
Film interpretations of Ophelia in Shakespeare's *Hamlet*. UK-England. USSR. Lang.: Eng. 4024

1947-1998. **Institutions.**
Profile of Birmingham Children's Theatre. Birmingham, AL. Lang.: Eng. 412

1947-1998. **Training.**
Balanchine's ballet mistress on his training methods. Lang.: Eng. 1214

1948. **Design/technology.**
Scenery in Orson Welles' film adaptation of Shakespeare's *Macbeth*. Lang.: Fre. 3920

1948-1997. **Performance/production.**
Ballet soloist Mikhail Baryshnikov. Latvia. Lang.: Eng. 1119

1948-1998. **Institutions.**
The fiftieth anniversary of *Puppetry Journal*. Lang.: Eng. 4876

1949-1951. **Performance/production.**
Maryat Lee and the creation of the street theatre piece *Dope!*. New York, NY. Lang.: Eng. 663

1949-1952. **Performance/production.**
Synopses of lost choreographies by Jerome Robbins. New York, NY. Lang.: Eng. 1166

1949-1969. **Plays/librettos/scripts.**
Black self-determination in the plays of Alice Childress. Lang.: Eng. 3579

1949-1998. **Administration.**
American and Japanese cultural policy. Japan. Lang.: Eng. 141

1949-1998. **Institutions.**
The twentieth anniversary of the Shubert archive newsletter *The Passing Show*. New York, NY. Lang.: Eng. 425
Profile of Tri-Cities Opera. Binghamton, NY. Lang.: Eng. 4490

1950. **Training.**
Experiences of a dancer at Jacob's Pillow. Becket, MA. Lang.: Eng. 1025

1950-1958. **Plays/librettos/scripts.**
Gender-role reversal in plays of William Inge. Lang.: Eng. 3623

1950-1965. **Plays/librettos/scripts.**
Playwright Lorraine Hansberry. Lang.: Eng. 3615

1950-1970. **Audience.**
Analysis of the teenage-girl audience. UK-England. Lang.: Ger. 161

1950-1970. **Plays/librettos/scripts.**
Shame, puritanism, and sexuality in plays of Tennessee Williams. Lang.: Eng. 3701

1950-1980. **Plays/librettos/scripts.**
Analysis of historical drama of the holocaust. Canada. Germany. Lang.: Eng. 3610

1950-1987. **Institutions.**
Graphic design and the theatrical evolution of Arena Stage. Washington, DC. Lang.: Eng. 414

1950-1987. **Performance/production.**
Role-playing in historical reconstructions as a form of environmental theatre. Plymouth, MA. Lang.: Eng. 4147

1950-1988. **Performance/production.**
Managerial analysis of daytime serial TV industry. New York, NY. Lang.: Eng. 4072

1950-1988. **Plays/librettos/scripts.**
Language and other elements of expression in plays of Beckett and Shepard. France. Ireland. Lang.: Eng. 3655

1950-1990. **Performance/production.**
The idea of Hollywood in theatre autobiographies. Lang.: Eng. 665

1950-1997. **Institutions.**
The evolution of Shakespeare festivals. Europe. Lang.: Eng. 1601

1950-1998. **Administration.**
History of the Tony Awards. New York, NY. Lang.: Eng. 74

1950-1998. **Performance/production.**
The Murray Louis/Alwin Nikolais dance archive. Athens, OH. Lang.: Eng. 1331
Interview with actor Saeed Jaffrey. UK-England. India. Lang.: Eng. 2589
The decline of radio comedy and the use of record albums by some comedians. Lang.: Eng. 3863

1950-1998. **Relation to other fields.**
Interview with photographer and former ballerina Martha Swope. New York, NY. Lang.: Eng. 1198

1951. **Relation to other fields.**
The blacklisting of Burton and Florence Bean James, founders of Seattle Repertory Playhouse. Seattle, WA. Lang.: Eng. 3784

1951-1968. **Performance/production.**
The Living Theatre's *Paradise Now*—creation and production. Lang.: Eng. 667

1951-1998. **Performance/production.**
Gillian Lynne, director and choreographer. London. New York, NY. Lang.: Eng. 4372

1952-1984. **Theory/criticism.**
Performance art and the 'poetics of space'. Poland. Lang.: Eng. 4270

1952-1996. **Theory/criticism.**
Aesthetic criteria of critics evaluating monodrama. New York, NY. Lang.: Eng. 3841

1952-1998. **Design/technology.**
Lighting expert Gary Whittington. Lang.: Eng. 275

1952-1998. **Institutions.**
William Patton, executive director emeritus of Oregon Shakespeare Festival. Ashland, OR. Lang.: Eng. 1777

1953. **Basic theatrical documents.**
Screenplay for *Pickup on South Street* by Sam Fuller. Lang.: Eng. 3885

1953. **Performance/production.**
Choreography in the musical film *The Bandwagon*. Lang.: Eng. 982

1953-1987. **Performance/production.**
The development of Bob Fosse's choreographic style. Lang.: Eng. 4377

1953-1998. **Performance/production.**
Actor William Hutt. Stratford, ON. Lang.: Eng. 1858

1954. **Plays/librettos/scripts.**
The musical *Sandhog* by blacklisted writers Earl Robinson and Waldo Salt. Lang.: Eng. 4395

1954-1962. **Plays/librettos/scripts.**
Eugene O'Neill's biographer on some difficulties of her work. Lang.: Eng. 3597

1954-1998. **Design/technology.**
Scene designer Richard Hudson and his work on *Samson et Dalila* at the Metropolitan Opera. UK-England. Lang.: Eng. 4289

1954-1998. **Performance/production.**
Actor George Grizzard. London. New York, NY. Lang.: Eng. 2646

1955. **Performance/production.**
Student production of *The Diary of Anne Frank*. Lang.: Eng. 2703

1955. **Plays/librettos/scripts.**
Analysis of *Bus Stop* by William Inge. Lang.: Eng. 3624

1955-1987. **Institutions.**
History of Virginia Museum Theatre. Richmond, VA. Lang.: Eng. 406

1955-1996. **Plays/librettos/scripts.**
The representation of true crime in modern drama. France. Lang.: Eng. 3673

USA — cont'd

1955-1998. **Performance/production.**
Profile of MacArthur fellow and juggler Michael Moschen. Lang.: Eng. 4141
1956. **Plays/librettos/scripts.**
The 'greatness' of *Long Day's Journey Into Night* by Eugene O'Neill. Lang.: Eng. 3639
1956-1959. **Plays/librettos/scripts.**
The creation of the musical *Gypsy*. New York, NY. Lang.: Eng. 4399
1956-1998. **Design/technology.**
Lighting designer Glen Cunningham. Lang.: Eng. 301
1957-1960. **Relation to other fields.**
TV westerns and their sociopolitical context. Lang.: Eng. 4083
1957-1964. **Plays/librettos/scripts.**
The posthumous publication of Eugene O'Neill's unfinished *More Stately Mansions*. Lang.: Eng. 3596
1957-1997. **Plays/librettos/scripts.**
Student casebook on *A Raisin in the Sun* by Lorraine Hansberry. Lang.: Eng. 3577
1957-1998. **Plays/librettos/scripts.**
Analysis of plays by James Purdy. Lang.: Eng. 3700
1957-1998. **Theory/criticism.**
Survey of theatre studies as cultural studies. UK-England. France. Lang.: Ger. 865
1958. **Plays/librettos/scripts.**
Puritanism and predestination in *Suddenly Last Summer* by Tennessee Williams. Lang.: Eng. 3631
Draft and revisions of *Suddenly Last Summer* by Tennessee Williams. Lang.: Eng. 3658
1958-1998. **Institutions.**
The fortieth anniversary of Alvin Ailey American Dance Company. New York, NY. Lang.: Eng. 1255
East Bay Center for the Performing Arts and the revival of a community. Richmond, CA. Lang.: Eng. 1764
1958-1998. **Performance/production.**
Director Charles Marowitz on the actor's calling. UK-England. Lang.: Eng. 2706
1959. **Plays/librettos/scripts.**
Analysis of *Hughie* by Eugene O'Neill. Lang.: Eng. 3529
1959-1969. **Plays/librettos/scripts.**
Revolutionary Off Broadway playwriting. New York, NY. Lang.: Eng. 3604
1959-1998. **Performance/production.**
Tap dance team of Betty Byrd and Danny Hoctor. Lang.: Eng. 983
Actors and the psychology of identity. Lang.: Eng. 2724
Careeer of actress Tsai Chin. Lang.: Eng. 2754
1959-1998. **Plays/librettos/scripts.**
Recent productions of plays by Edward Albee. New York, NY. Hartford, CT. Lang.: Eng. 3578
1959-1998. **Research/historiography.**
Gender difference and theatricality. Germany. France. Lang.: Ger. 821
1960. **Plays/librettos/scripts.**
Analysis of *The Prodigal* by Jack Richardson. Lang.: Eng. 3542
The Prodigal, Jack Richardson's adaptation of *The Oresteia*. Lang.: Dut. 3547
Homeric influences on *The Prodigal* by Jack Richardson. Lang.: Eng. 3549
1960-1968. **Plays/librettos/scripts.**
The fool character in works of Handke, Fellini, and Singer. Germany. Italy. Lang.: Eng. 3667
1960-1970. **Relation to other fields.**
Ritual in encounter groups and experimental theatre. Lang.: Eng. 788
1960-1981. **Theory/criticism.**
Critical approaches to science-fiction films. Lang.: Eng. 4040
1960-1985. **Plays/librettos/scripts.**
Aggressive language in modern drama. Europe. Lang.: Eng. 3055
The nature and language of menace in the plays of John Whiting, Harold Pinter and Sam Shepard. UK-England. Lang.: Eng. 3576
1960-1987. **Performance/production.**
The influence of experimental performance on contemporary drama. Europe. Lang.: Eng. 526
1960-1987. **Plays/librettos/scripts.**
American gay drama and the impact of AIDS. Lang.: Eng. 3670
1960-1988. **Performance/production.**
The work of some North American performance artists. Canada. Lang.: Eng. 4251
1960-1990. **Research/historiography.**
Bibliography of important works on American theatre. Lang.: Eng. 829
1960-1995. **Plays/librettos/scripts.**
Analysis of the plays of Lanford Wilson. Lang.: Eng. 3546
1960-1995. **Relation to other fields.**
Narrative strategy in the analysis of theatre economics. Lang.: Eng. 802
Dance photos by Jack Mitchell. Lang.: Eng. 1000
1960-1997. **Performance/production.**
African-American dance. Lang.: Eng. 986
1960-1997. **Plays/librettos/scripts.**
Adoption narratives in novels, plays, and films. Lang.: Eng. 691
1960-1997. **Theory/criticism.**
The influence of Lionel Trilling on criticism of Robert Brustein. Lang.: Eng. 3848
1960-1998. **Institutions.**
Retiring artistic directors of regional opera companies, Russell Patterson and Glyn Ross. Lang.: Eng. 4485
1960-1998. **Performance/production.**
Balanchine's choreography to Čajkovskij's *Themes and Variations*. Lang.: Eng. 1179
Interview with dancer/choreographer Merce Cunningham. Lang.: Eng. 1186
Dancer Frances Alenikoff. New York, NY. Lang.: Eng. 1324
Excerpts from a pictorial history of performance art. Lang.: Eng. 4253
1960-1998. **Plays/librettos/scripts.**
Afrocentricity in plays of Charles Fuller, Amiri Baraka, and Larry Neal. Lang.: Eng. 3519
1961-1979. **Relation to other fields.**
The Fluxus movement. Europe. Lang.: Eng. 4265
1961-1985. **Institutions.**
Ellen Stewart and La MaMa Experimental Theatre Club. New York, NY. Lang.: Eng. 1762
1961-1985. **Plays/librettos/scripts.**
Comedy and humor in plays of Lanford Wilson. Lang.: Eng. 3595
1961-1998. **Performance/production.**
Playwright Jess Gregg's relationship with choreographer Agnes De Mille. New York, NY. Lang.: Eng. 1178
1962-1975. **Plays/librettos/scripts.**
TV war series. Lang.: Eng. 4080
1962-1979. **Performance/production.**
The influence of collage on director Charles Marowitz. UK-England. Lang.: Eng. 2624
1962-1998. **Performance/production.**
Jazz dancer and choreographer Gus Giordano. Chicago, IL. Lang.: Eng. 988
Actor Arthur French. New York, NY. Lang.: Eng. 2671
Tenor Tracey Welborn. Lang.: Eng. 4738
1963. **Basic theatrical documents.**
Screenplay for *Shock Corridor* by Sam Fuller. Lang.: Eng. 3886
1963. **Performance/production.**
A rare production of Eugene O'Neill's *Lazarus Laughed*. Detroit, MI. Lang.: Eng. 2673
1963-1964. **Performance/production.**
Social commentary and *East Side/West Side*. Lang.: Eng. 4068
1963-1971. **Plays/librettos/scripts.**
History of the Playwrights Unit. Lang.: Eng. 3570
1963-1973. **Institutions.**
The training program of the Clarence B. Hilberry Repertory Theatre. Detroit, MI. Lang.: Eng. 408
1963-1980. **Institutions.**
The mission and management of the Free Southern Theatre. New Orleans, LA. Lang.: Eng. 1769
1963-1982. **Plays/librettos/scripts.**
Arthur Kopit's *Nine*, a musical adaptation of Fellini's *8 1/2*. Lang.: Eng. 4401
1963-1983. **Performance/production.**
Theatrical activities of the Polynesian Cultural Center. Laie, HI. Lang.: Eng. 4221
1963-1997. **Performance/production.**
Analysis of performances at Polynesian Cultural Center. Laie, HI. Lang.: Eng. 618

USA — cont'd

1963-1998. **Institutions.**
The growth of regional dance companies. Lang.: Eng. 908
Profile of the Bread and Puppet Theatre. Plainfield, VT. Lang.: Hun. 4877
1964-1969. **Administration.**
The cancellation of Kansas University's cultural exchange program with Eastern Europe. Lawrence, KS. Europe. Lang.: Eng. 131
1964-1983. **Institutions.**
European activities of the Living Theatre. Europe. Lang.: Ita. 1602
1964-1985. **Performance/production.**
Reexamination of the performance art of Beuys, Abramovič, and Ulay. Germany. Netherlands. Lang.: Eng. 4254
1964-1989. **Performance/production.**
Interview with performance artist Carolee Schneemann. Lang.: Eng. 4257
1964-1990. **Plays/librettos/scripts.**
The dramaturgical evolution of playwright Adrienne Kennedy. Lang.: Eng. 3691
1964-1998. **Performance/production.**
Choreographer Meredith Monk. New York, NY. Lang.: Eng. 1325
1964-1998. **Theory/criticism.**
Analysis of Yoko Ono's performance work *Cut Piece*. Lang.: Eng. 4151
1965. **Performance/production.**
Dancer Yvonne Rainer's rejection of spectacle. Lang.: Eng. 989
1965-1970. **Relation to other fields.**
The influence of Teatro Campesino on American politics. Lang.: Eng. 3783
1965-1988. **Institutions.**
The theatre program of the National Endowment for the Arts. Lang.: Eng. 391
History of the Chelsea Theatre Center. New York, NY. Lang.: Eng. 417
1965-1988. **Plays/librettos/scripts.**
Analysis of the plays of Sam Shepard. Lang.: Eng. 3553
1965-1990. **Performance/production.**
Drama and spirituality in the music of Leonard Bernstein. Lang.: Eng. 4379
1965-1992. **Plays/librettos/scripts.**
Profile of playwright Sam Shepard. Lang.: Dut. 3550
1965-1993. **Plays/librettos/scripts.**
The representation of Vietnamese in film and stage depictions of the Vietnam war. Lang.: Eng. 690
1965-1995. **Plays/librettos/scripts.**
Composer Philip Glass on Beckett's influence on his work. Ireland. France. Lang.: Eng. 3194
National identity in plays of Sam Shepard. Lang.: Eng. 3545
1965-1996. **Theory/criticism.**
Music critic on his career. Lang.: Eng. 4840
1965-1997. **Performance/production.**
The ideological system of theatre artist Richard Schechner. Lang.: Eng. 640
Theatre's educational power and socially relevant performance. Lang.: Eng. 681
1965-1997. **Plays/librettos/scripts.**
Analysis of *States of Shock* by Sam Shepard. Lang.: Eng. 3544
1965-1998. **Design/technology.**
Costume designer Jeanne Button. Lang.: Eng. 260
Lighting designer Tharon Musser. Lang.: Eng. 326
Film design work of Tony Walton. Lang.: Eng. 3902
1965-1998. **Plays/librettos/scripts.**
Essays on the theatre of Sam Shepard. Lang.: Eng. 3557
1966. **Basic theatrical documents.**
Screenplay for *The Secret Cinema* by Paul Bartel. Lang.: Eng. 3881
1966-1981. **Performance/production.**
Actors and directors on the late plays of Tennessee Williams. Lang.: Eng. 2675
1966-1993. **Performance/production.**
Documentary theatre and the politics of representation. Lang.: Eng. 2728
1966-1996. **Plays/librettos/scripts.**
Open-endedness in plays of Sam Shepard. Lang.: Eng. 3713
1966-1998. **Performance/production.**
Dancer/choreographer Mikhail Baryshnikov. USSR. Lang.: Eng. 1189
Rosalie Jones of Native American dance company Daystar. Santa Fe, NM. Lang.: Eng. 1240
1966-1998. **Training.**
Interview with dancer and teacher David Howard. Lang.: Swe. 1216
1967. **Performance/production.**
Panel discussion on Balanchine's *Jewels*. New York, NY. Lang.: Eng. 1188
1967-1979. **Theory/criticism.**
The theatrical structure of autonomous theatre. Lang.: Eng. 867
1967-1985. **Plays/librettos/scripts.**
Language in the plays of Sam Shepard. Lang.: Eng. 3694
1967-1997. **Institutions.**
Jeannette Clift George and the A.D. Players. Houston, TX. Lang.: Eng. 1785
1968. **Relation to other fields.**
Government response to Living Theatre's *Paradise Now*. Europe. Lang.: Eng. 3789
1968-1969. **Institutions.**
Judith Malina's attempt to create an active mixed-media theatre. Lang.: Eng. 1765
1968-1976. **Plays/librettos/scripts.**
Roger Reynolds' musical settings of texts by Samuel Beckett. Lang.: Eng. 4309
1968-1991. **Institutions.**
History of the Society for Old Music. Kalamazoo, MI. Lang.: Eng. 4292
1968-1998. **Administration.**
The influence of Walt Disney on the film industry. Lang.: Eng. 3873
1968-1998. **Performance/production.**
Theatre Magazine's anniversary issue. Lang.: Eng. 617
The influence of *Sesame Street*. Lang.: Eng. 4923
1969-1978. **Plays/librettos/scripts.**
Dramaturgical analysis of late plays of Tennessee Williams. Lang.: Eng. 3661
1969-1981. **Institutions.**
History of Squat Theatre. Hungary. New York, NY. Lang.: Ita. 1670
1969-1987. **Plays/librettos/scripts.**
American drama and the war in Vietnam. Lang.: Eng. 3586
1969-1990. **Performance/production.**
A dancer's experience of and investigations into ecstasy. Germany. Lang.: Eng. 673
1969-1998. **Performance/production.**
Choreographer Rosemary Butcher on her return to New York. New York, NY. Lang.: Eng. 979
Dancer/choreographer Mikhail Baryshnikov. USSR. Lang.: Eng. 1196
Interview with video and installation artist Gary Hill. Lang.: Eng. 4258
Paula Klimper and Wende Persons' opera *Patience and Sarah*. Lang.: Eng. 4725
1969-1998. **Training.**
Dance teacher Harvey Hysell. New Orleans, LA. Lang.: Eng. 1217
1970. **Plays/librettos/scripts.**
Analysis of Sam Shepard's *Operation Sidewinder*. Lang.: Eng. 3548
Analysis of *Les Blancs* by Lorraine Hansberry. Lang.: Eng. 3581
1970-1981. **Audience.**
The aesthetics of audience-performer interaction in the theatrical event. Lang.: Eng. 160
1970-1984. **Plays/librettos/scripts.**
The disintegration of the American dream in works of Stephen Sondheim. Lang.: Eng. 4397
1970-1993. **Plays/librettos/scripts.**
Analysis of the plays of David Mamet. Lang.: Eng. 3541
1970-1995. **Plays/librettos/scripts.**
The Bodyguard, Sam Shepard's screen adaptation of *The Changeling* by Middleton and Rowley. Lang.: Eng. 4007
1970-1997. **Performance/production.**
Women and improvisation. Lang.: Eng. 672
Contemporary queer politics and the production of gay and lesbian theatre. Lang.: Eng. 2710
1970-1997. **Plays/librettos/scripts.**
The survivor character in contemporary American drama. Lang.: Eng. 3600

USA — cont'd

1970-1998. Design/technology.
Matthews Studio Group, providing supplies for lighting design. Hollywood, CA. Lang.: Eng. 3915
Landmark Entertainment Group, specializing in theme-park design. Hollywood, CA. Lang.: Eng. 4110
1970-1998. Institutions.
Profile of Pennsylvania Ballet. Philadelphia, PA. Lang.: Eng. 1058
1970-1998. Performance spaces.
Materials and finishes for the stage floor. Lang.: Eng. 472
1970-1998. Performance/production.
The use of television in theatrical space. Netherlands. Lang.: Dut. 2206
Ruth Maleczech of Mabou Mines. New York, NY. Lang.: Eng. 2694
1970-1998. Plays/librettos/scripts.
Playwrights Adrienne Kennedy, Ntozake Shange, and Suzan-Lori Parks. Lang.: Eng. 3714
1971. Basic theatrical documents.
Screenplay of *The Last Picture Show* by Larry McMurtry and Peter Bogdanovich. Lang.: Eng. 3897
1971. Plays/librettos/scripts.
Roman Polanski's film adaptation of Shakespeare's *Macbeth*. Lang.: Fre. 4014
Larry McMurtry on *The Last Picture Show*. Lang.: Eng. 4018
1971-1991. Plays/librettos/scripts.
Gangster film and Shakespearean tragedy. Lang.: Eng. 4009
1971-1998. Design/technology.
Lighting technician Julian Winter. Lang.: Eng. 309
1971-1998. Institutions.
Financial and artistic success of Kennedy Center and New Jersey Performing Arts Center. Washington, DC. Newark, NJ. Lang.: Eng. 424
1971-1998. Performance/production.
Baritone Nathan Gunn. Lang.: Eng. 4723
1971-1998. Plays/librettos/scripts.
Interview with director Peter Bogdanovich. Lang.: Eng. 4020
1972-1985. Performance/production.
Career of director Lynne Meadow. New York, NY. Lang.: Eng. 2708
1972-1988. Institutions.
The management of the Shakespeare Festival of Dallas. Dallas, TX. Lang.: Eng. 393
1972-1998. Institutions.
Profile of Alabama Shakespeare Festival. Montgomery, AL. Lang.: Eng. 1784
1973. Basic theatrical documents.
Text of *The Black Doll* by Edward Gorey. Lang.: Eng. 3887
1973-1997. Plays/librettos/scripts.
Interview with Edward Gorey about his animated film *The Black Doll*. Lang.: Eng. 3994
1973-1998. Design/technology.
Film and TV lighting man Scott Jason Jellen. Lang.: Eng. 3855
1973-1998. Performance/production.
Director Mary Hausch of Hippodrome State Theatre. Gainesville, FL. Lang.: Eng. 2709
1973-1998. Training.
Interview with Steve Paxton, creator of contact improvisation. Lang.: Eng. 1343
1974. Basic theatrical documents.
Text of *Young Frankenstein* by Gene Wilder and Mel Brooks. Lang.: Eng. 3898
1974-1975. Design/technology.
Digital lighting control for *A Chorus Line*. New York, NY. Lang.: Eng. 4337
1974-1984. Institutions.
History of the Jewish Repertory Theatre. New York, NY. Lang.: Eng. 1757
1974-1984. Plays/librettos/scripts.
Feminist theatre of Martha Boesing. Minneapolis, MN. Lang.: Eng. 3603
1974-1998. Performance/production.
Choreographer Bill Cratty. Lang.: Eng. 1320
Profile of master puppeteer Ralph Lee. Lang.: Eng. 4906
1975-1985. Plays/librettos/scripts.
Theatrical ritual in plays of Peter Shaffer. Lang.: Eng. 3707
1975-1987. Plays/librettos/scripts.
Language and aphasic speech patterns in the plays of David Mamet. Lang.: Eng. 3677
1975-1988. Performance/production.
Analysis of transformative comedy. Lang.: Eng. 666
1975-1990. Performance/production.
Interview with director Richard Foreman. New York, NY. Lang.: Eng. 2700
1975-1995. Plays/librettos/scripts.
Survivors' testimony in Holocaust theatre. Lang.: Eng. 3605
Politics and feminism in the plays of Maria Irene Fornes. Lang.: Eng. 3635
Rites of passage in the plays of David Mamet. Lang.: Eng. 3680
1975-1997. Theory/criticism.
Theatre reviewers and popular entertainment. Lang.: Eng. 868
1975-1998. Performance/production.
Dancer Nichol Hlinka of New York City Ballet. New York, NY. Lang.: Eng. 1173
1976. Plays/librettos/scripts.
Analysis of *The Mound Builders* by Lanford Wilson. Lang.: Eng. 3552
Analysis of *Duck Variations* by David Mamet. Lang.: Dut. 3554
Gendered political critique in *The Club* by Eve Merriam. Lang.: Eng. 3572
1976-1987. Institutions.
The early years of the Shubert archive. New York, NY. Lang.: Eng. 409
1976-1998. Design/technology.
Tom Strahan, scenic designer for rock concerts and corporate events. San Francisco, CA. Lang.: Eng. 4100
1976-1998. Institutions.
Brooks McNamara, founder and director of the Shubert archive. New York, NY. Lang.: Eng. 413
Brooks McNamara on the Shubert archive of which he is director. New York, NY. Lang.: Eng. 415
The Shuberts vs. the Syndicate. New York, NY. Lang.: Eng. 427
1976-1998. Performance/production.
Video artist Bill Viola. New York, NY. Lang.: Eng. 4071
Robert Wilson's production of Wagner's *Lohengrin* at the Metropolitan Opera. New York, NY. Lang.: Eng. 4739
1976-1998. Reference materials.
Index of the first twenty volumes of *The Passing Show*. New York, NY. Lang.: Eng. 709
1977. Plays/librettos/scripts.
Analysis of Preston Jones's plays about Texas. Lang.: Eng. 3645
1977-1981. Plays/librettos/scripts.
Boal's 'joker system' in plays of Ntozake Shange. Lang.: Eng. 3692
1977-1986. Relation to other fields.
Theatrical activities of the Mormon Church. Lang.: Eng. 811
1977-1989. Plays/librettos/scripts.
Theatrical space in plays of Maria Irene Fornes. Lang.: Eng. 3571
1977-1997. Administration.
Changes in arts marketing strategies. Lang.: Eng. 126
1977-1998. Institutions.
Training practices of Houston Opera Studio. Houston, TX. Lang.: Eng. 4489
1977-1998. Performance/production.
Choreographer Paul Taylor. Lang.: Eng. 1335
1978. Plays/librettos/scripts.
Analysis of *Wings* by Arthur Kopit. Lang.: Eng. 3616
Theatricality in John Cassavetes' film *Opening Night*. Lang.: Fre. 4011
1978-1979. Institutions.
History of the Women's Project of the American Place Theatre. New York, NY. Lang.: Eng. 1791
1978-1986. Performance/production.
The use of closed circuit television in avant-garde theatre performance. New York, NY. Lang.: Eng. 662
The collaboration of playwright Lanford Wilson and director Marshall W. Mason. New York, NY. Lang.: Eng. 2756
1978-1998. Institutions.
Profile of BalletMet. Columbus, OH. Lang.: Eng. 1062
Brief history of the Women's Project and Productions. New York, NY. Lang.: Eng. 1774
1978-1998. Performance/production.
Actress Lori Holt. San Francisco, CA. Lang.: Eng. 2740

USA — cont'd

1978-1998. **Relation to other fields.**
Dancer, teacher, and healing facilitator Anna Halprin of Tamalpa Institute. Kentfield, CA. Lang.: Ger. 1338

1979. **Plays/librettos/scripts.**
Analysis of Sam Shepard's *Fool for Love*. Lang.: Dut. 3540
Analysis of *Jitney* by August Wilson. Lang.: Eng. 3611
The screen adaptation of Sam Shepard's *Fool for Love*. Lang.: Eng. 4008

1979-1993. **Institutions.**
Feminist theatre of Ladies Against Women. Berkeley, CA. Lang.: Eng. 396

1979-1998. **Design/technology.**
Lighting designer Kevin Adams. Lang.: Eng. 258

1979-1998. **Performance/production.**
Interview with actress Kate Valk. New York, NY. Lang.: Eng. 2736

1980-1981. **Performance/production.**
Interview with director Peter Sellars. Cambridge, MA. Lang.: Eng. 2661

1980-1981. **Theory/criticism.**
Analysis of *Something Cloudy, Something Clear* by Tennessee Williams. Lang.: Eng. 3843

1980-1984. **Performance/production.**
Street performance in Washington Square Park. New York, NY. Lang.: Eng. 4137

1980-1987. **Design/technology.**
Comparison of computer-assisted and traditional scenery and lighting design. Lang.: Eng. 324

1980-1987. **Performance/production.**
Study of street performers. Lang.: Eng. 4139

1980-1987. **Relation to other fields.**
Creative dramatics and the literature and language arts curriculum. Lang.: Eng. 776

1980-1988. **Administration.**
The decline in corporate funding for the arts. Lang.: Eng. 32

1980-1988. **Performance/production.**
Analysis of pop performance. New York, NY. Lang.: Eng. 664

1980-1989. **Plays/librettos/scripts.**
Drama and melodrama in American theatre of the eighties. Lang.: Rus. 3632

1980-1990. **Performance/production.**
Commercial theatre and the values of the Reagan era. Lang.: Eng. 685

1980-1995. **Plays/librettos/scripts.**
Shocking the audience in Holocaust theatre. Lang.: Eng. 3628

1980-1997. **Performance/production.**
Analysis of the choreography of Mark Morris. Lang.: Eng. 1317

1980-1997. **Plays/librettos/scripts.**
Minority playwrights and mainstream theatres—theoretical implications. Lang.: Eng. 3612
Playwright Tina Howe on gender expectations on playwrights. New York, NY. Lang.: Eng. 3614

1980-1998. **Institutions.**
Mezzo soprano Irene Dalis, now in charge of Opera San Jose. San José, CA. Lang.: Eng. 4484

1980-1998. **Performance/production.**
The creation of the religious ballet *A Dancer's Christmas*. Boston, MA. Lang.: Eng. 1192
Dancers Tina Fehlandt and Ruth Davidson of Mark Morris Dance Group. New York, NY. Lang.: Eng. 1327
Choreographer Mark Dendy. New York, NY. Lang.: Eng. 1330
Director, costumer, and mask-maker Julie Taymor. Lang.: Eng. 2685
Evaluation of video performances of Donizetti's operas. Europe. Lang.: Eng. 4557

1980-1998. **Plays/librettos/scripts.**
Interview with playwright Douglas Carter Beane. Lang.: Eng. 3516
Interview with playwright David Henry Hwang. Lang.: Eng. 3530
Playwright David Henry Hwang. Lang.: Eng. 3573
Interview with playwright David Henry Hwang. Lang.: Eng. 3669
Analysis of films of David Mamet. Los Angeles, CA. Lang.: Eng. 4006

1981. **Performance/production.**
Critique of Twyla Tharp's *The Catherine Wheel*. New York, NY. Lang.: Eng. 980

1981-1984. **Institutions.**
History of the Sundance Institute for Film and Video. Sundance, CO. Lang.: Eng. 3925

1981-1990. **Plays/librettos/scripts.**
Apocalyptic futures in science fiction films. Lang.: Eng. 4005

1981-1998. **Performance/production.**
Dancer Yan Chen of American Ballet Theatre. New York, NY. Lang.: Eng. 1176
The feminist performance trend Angry Essentialism. Lang.: Eng. 4249

1982. **Performance/production.**
Sam Fuller 'interviews' a canine actor from *White Dog*. Lang.: Eng. 3945

1982. **Plays/librettos/scripts.**
Analysis of *Bandido!* by Luis Valdez. Lang.: Eng. 3708
The film adaptation by Harold Pinter and Karel Reisz of *The French Lieutenant's Woman* by John Fowles. UK-England. Lang.: Eng. 3982

1982-1984. **Plays/librettos/scripts.**
Analysis of *The Dining Room* by A.R. Gurney. Lang.: Eng. 3642

1982-1998. **Institutions.**
Profile of Engine House Theatre. Madrid, NM. Lang.: Eng. 1760

1982-1998. **Performance/production.**
Directorial style of JoAnne Akalaitis. Lang.: Eng. 2737
Performance artist Mimi Goese. Lang.: Eng. 4252

1983. **Plays/librettos/scripts.**
Analysis of *Glengarry Glen Ross*. Lang.: Dut. 3556

1983-1995. **Performance/production.**
Interview with dancer/choreographer Rebecca Hilton. Australia. Lang.: Eng. 913

1983-1997. **Performance/production.**
The performance of documentary theatre based on transcripts of a Lithuanian dissidence trial. Lang.: Eng. 627

1983-1998. **Institutions.**
Profile of Saint Joseph Ballet. Santa Ana, CA. Lang.: Eng. 1056
Peter Martins, artistic director of New York City Ballet. New York, NY. Lang.: Eng. 1057

1983-1998. **Performance/production.**
Ballerina Zippora Karz on dancing while suffering from diabetes. New York, NY. Lang.: Eng. 1183
Profile of actor Tom Hanks. Lang.: Eng. 3950

1984-1987. **Performance/production.**
Creativity and ego identity in actors. Lang.: Eng. 678

1984-1987. **Relation to other fields.**
Detroit's Black theatres and training opportunities for high school students. Detroit, MI. Lang.: Eng. 813

1984-1998. **Institutions.**
Assistant archivist on the Shubert archive. New York, NY. Lang.: Eng. 401

1984-1998. **Performance/production.**
Ballerina Ariana Lallone of Pacific Northwest Ballet. Seattle, WA. Lang.: Eng. 1168
Culture Clash and their production of Aristophanes' *Birds*. Berkeley, CA. Lang.: Eng. 2713

1985. **Relation to other fields.**
Children's processing of live theatre. Lang.: Eng. 801

1985-1986. **Plays/librettos/scripts.**
Analysis of Cuban theatre in Miami. Miami, FL. Lang.: Eng. 3574

1985-1987. **Administration.**
External fundraising for theatre arts programs. Lang.: Eng. 133

1985-1987. **Institutions.**
The role of private community organizations in the restructuring of the Folger Shakespeare Theatre. Washington, DC. Lang.: Eng. 1771

1985-1987. **Relation to other fields.**
The use of theatre rehearsal techniques for socially emotionally disturbed youth. Lang.: Eng. 774

1985-1995. **Performance/production.**
Performativity in postmodern 'queer' works. Lang.: Eng. 616

1985-1997. **Performance/production.**
The semiotics of antebellum home tours. Lang.: Eng. 624
Physical risk and its aesthetics in aerialist performance. Lang.: Eng. 4185

1985-1997. **Theory/criticism.**
Activist political theatre and Western democracy. Lang.: Eng. 870

USA — cont'd

1985-1998. Performance/production.
The body in stage-to-film versions of Shakespeare's *Richard III*. UK-England. Lang.: Eng. 3940
1986. Administration.
Participants in rural community theatre. Lang.: Eng. 30
1986. Basic theatrical documents.
Text of *The Country Mouse and the City Mouse* by Robert Charles Lunde. Lang.: Eng. 1495
Text of plays by Carlos Morton. Lang.: Eng. 1499
Text of *The Sisterhood of Dark Sanctuary* by Leslie Jean Sandberg. Lang.: Eng. 1508
1986. Plays/librettos/scripts.
Analysis of Jane Bowles' play *In the Summer House*. Lang.: Dut. 3555
Analysis of *Bandido!* by Luis Valdez. Lang.: Eng. 3676
Samuel Beckett's short story *Bing* as adapted by Roger Reynolds and Jean-Yves Bosseur. Lang.: Eng. 4308
1986-1987. Performance/production.
Research on the importance of vocal training for the actor. Lang.: Eng. 2657
1986-1995. Basic theatrical documents.
Collection of plays by Charles L. Mee. Lang.: Eng. 1496
1986-1998. Administration.
Actress Helen Hunt's support of Equity's holiday basket program for people with AIDS. New York, NY. Lang.: Eng. 107
'Arts incubator' organization Art's Bridge. Chicago, IL. Lang.: Eng. 120
1986-1998. Design/technology.
Scene designer James Noone's work at Playwrights Horizons. New York, NY. Lang.: Eng. 1531
1986-1998. Performance/production.
Dancer Nina Ananiašvili. Houston, TX. Lang.: Eng. 1193
1987. Basic theatrical documents.
Text of *Like Father, Like Son* by Marc J. Aronin. Lang.: Eng. 1481
Text of *A Day at Musemeci's* by Scott R. Ritter. Lang.: Eng. 1503
1987. Design/technology.
An ontological approach to the aesthetics of scenography. Lang.: Eng. 298
Loudspeaker directivity and theatrical sound systems. Lang.: Eng. 318
A stage design for Jean Giraudoux's *Ondine*. Lang.: Eng. 1529
Design for Shakespeare's *A Midsummer Night's Dream*. Lang.: Eng. 1563
1987. Performance/production.
Actor-training project involving character development in drama and musical theatre. Lang.: Eng. 625
Character development in drama and musical theatre: actor-training project. Lang.: Eng. 626
The effect of a heterogeneous audience on performance anxiety. Lang.: Eng. 630
Ethical guidelines for the social context performance. Lang.: Eng. 632
Preparing a production of Brian Way's participatory *The Mirrorman*. Lang.: Eng. 633
Character development in dramas and musicals. Lang.: Eng. 670
Actor-training project in character development. Lang.: Eng. 671
Character development from the actor's point of view. Lang.: Eng. 686
An approach to playing Malvolio in Shakespeare's *Twelfth Night*. Lang.: Eng. 2659
Account of an actor-training project focused on character development. Lang.: Eng. 2664
Actor-training and character development. Lang.: Eng. 2679
Directors' nonverbal behavior in rehearsal. Lang.: Eng. 2680
An approach to playing Babe Botrelle in Beth Henley's *Crimes of the Heart*. Lang.: Eng. 2690
An approach to playing Jamie in O'Neill's *Long Day's Journey Into Night*. Lang.: Eng. 2697
Character development in drama. Lang.: Eng. 2743
Actor's analysis of character development. Lang.: Eng. 2746
The development of character in an actor training project. Lang.: Eng. 2761
Interview with director Richard Schechner. Lang.: Eng. 4260
1987. Plays/librettos/scripts.
Principles of artistry in playwriting manuals. Lang.: Eng. 3568
Text of *Tangled Garden* by David Wright Crawford with documentation of the author's method. Lang.: Eng. 3569
Analysis of *Fences* by August Wilson. Lang.: Eng. 3693
1987. Relation to other fields.
Drama in cross-cultural literature courses for foreign students. Lang.: Eng. 3791
Interdisciplinary appraoches to the teaching of music theatre. Lang.: Eng. 4402
1987-1988. Administration.
Study of management in regional theatres. Lang.: Eng. 140
1987-1988. Performance/production.
The 'living paintings' of Steven Taylor Woodrow. UK-England. Lang.: Eng. 4247
1987-1997. Basic theatrical documents.
French translation of *Alfred Stieglitz Loves O'Keeffe* by Lanie Robertson. France. Lang.: Fre. 1505
1987-1997. Performance/production.
Dance, music video, and popular culture. Lang.: Eng. 978
1987-1998. Institutions.
The work of performance troupe Goat Island. Chicago, IL. Lang.: Eng. 395
Shubert archivist on her work. New York, NY. Lang.: Eng. 398
1987-1998. Performance/production.
Dancer Albert Evans of New York City Ballet. New York, NY. Lang.: Eng. 1181
1988. Basic theatrical documents.
Score of Yu-Chun Kuo's concerto for dance and music, *Ring*. Lang.: Eng. 887
Text of *The Ballad of Sam Bass* by William Johnson Evarts. Lang.: Eng. 1484
Text of *Dreams* by Kathleen Kristy-Brooks. Lang.: Eng. 1493
Texts of plays about Zora Neale Hurston by Barbara Waddell Speisman. Lang.: Eng. 1510
Text of Sharon Gayle Tucker's *S.T.C.* Lang.: Eng. 1512
Text of cabaret revue *Carnival Knowledge* by Philip D. Potak. Lang.: Eng. 4152
Text of *Raven's Song* by Angela Brannon Tarleton. Lang.: Eng. 4323
Libretto for *Christina, Queen of Sweden*. Lang.: Eng. 4423
1988. Design/technology.
Set design and lighting for a production of Ibsen's *Hedda Gabler*. Louisville, KY. Lang.: Eng. 1564
Scenographic concept for the *dramma per musica*, *Aeolus Appeased*. Lang.: Eng. 4442
1988. Institutions.
Systems analysis of the Southwest Theatre Association. Lang.: Eng. 418
History of Christian theatre company, the Covenant Players. Camarillo, CA. Lang.: Eng. 429
1988. Performance/production.
Psychoanalytic study of the actor. Lang.: Eng. 621
Postmodern acting theory. Lang.: Eng. 622
Directing and design to accommodate the disabled in performance. Lang.: Eng. 623
Analysis of character development for acting degree. Long Beach, CA. Lang.: Eng. 637
Actor training and psychotherapy-derived techniques. Lang.: Eng. 639
Eugenio Barba's *Oxyrhyncus Evangeliet*, Odin Teatret. Lang.: Eng. 646
Semiotic analysis of the nature of theatrical directing. Lang.: Eng. 650
Acting analysis of character development. Long Beach, CA. Lang.: Eng. 2662
Directing a student production of Yeats's *Deirdre*. Louisville, KY. Lang.: Eng. 2738

USA — cont'd

1988. Plays/librettos/scripts.
The theory and practice of playwriting for different age groups. Lang.: Eng. 3524
Analysis of *The Colored Museum* by George C. Wolfe. Lang.: Eng. 3690
1988. Relation to other fields.
Developmental differences in adolescents' ability to enact character. Lang.: Eng. 782
1988. Theory/criticism.
The present state of theatre criticism. Lang.: Eng. 860
Aristotelian approach to Deaf performance. Lang.: Eng. 861
1988-1989. Plays/librettos/scripts.
Analysis of plays by Josefina López. Lang.: Eng. 3650
1988-1997. Performance/production.
A model for systematic analysis of vocal performance. Lang.: Eng. 636
Race, gender, and oral life history narrative. Lang.: Eng. 649
1988-1998. Design/technology.
Set designer David Gallo. Lang.: Eng. 255
1988-1998. Institutions.
Working at the Shubert archive. New York, NY. Lang.: Eng. 426
1988-1998. Performance spaces.
Profile of the New Jersey Performing Arts Center. Newark, NJ. Lang.: Eng. 467
Community efforts to save the Emerson Majestic and Rialto theatres. Boston, MA. Chicago, IL. Lang.: Eng. 474
1988-1998. Performance/production.
The influence of Merce Cunningham on choreographer Emma Diamond. Lang.: Eng. 1322
Recent work of choreographer Twyla Tharp. New York, NY. Lang.: Eng. 1328
1988-1998. Training.
The use of computer animation techniques in design training. Athens, GA. Lang.: Eng. 878
1988-1999. Theory/criticism.
Critique of press coverage of opera. Lang.: Eng. 4847
1989. Basic theatrical documents.
Text of *Heatstroke* by James Purdy. Lang.: Eng. 1502
1989. Plays/librettos/scripts.
Analysis of Spike Lee's film *Do the Right Thing.* Lang.: Eng. 4017
Analysis of Steven Soderbergh's film *sex, lies, and videotape.* Lang.: Eng. 4028
1989. Theory/criticism.
Text and performance in drama criticism. Lang.: Eng. 3849
1989-1998. Administration.
The commitment to arts funding by cities that sponsor major league sports. Lang.: Eng. 125
1989-1998. Institutions.
Profile of Manbites Dog and its topical and controversial productions. Durham, NC. Lang.: Eng. 1758
1989-1998. Performance/production.
Profile of the satiric comedy troupe Five Lesbian Brothers. New York, NY. Lang.: Eng. 4282
1990. Institutions.
Interview with Matthew Goulish and Lin Hixson of Goat Island. Chicago, IL. Lang.: Eng. 4237
1990. Performance/production.
Review of Jonathan Larson's musical *Rent.* New York, NY. Lang.: Hun. 4375
1990. Plays/librettos/scripts.
Analysis of *The Piano Lesson* by August Wilson. Lang.: Eng. 3536
1990. Theory/criticism.
Dance critic on her profession. Europe. Lang.: Eng. 1014
1990-1993. Administration.
Speculation on the future effects of technology and ethnic diversity on theatre. Lang.: Eng. 42
1990-1993. Plays/librettos/scripts.
Comparison of film and television versions of *Dances With Wolves.* Lang.: Eng. 4022
1990-1996. Performance/production.
Analysis of the Wooster Group's *Fish Story* directed by Elizabeth LeCompte. New York, NY. Lang.: Eng. 2667
1990-1997. Institutions.
Bread and Puppet Theatre's postmodern puppetry. Plainfield, VT. Lang.: Eng. 4878
1990-1997. Performance/production.
Popular culture, entertainment, and performance in the United States. Lang.: Eng. 654
1990-1997. Reference materials.
Bibliography of books on popular entertainment. Lang.: Eng. 710
1990-1997. Relation to other fields.
Non-Western dance forms in the teaching of theatre arts. Davis, CA. Lang.: Eng. 809
1990-1998. Performance/production.
A performance by Mikhail Baryshnikov and the White Oak Dance Project. Washington, DC. Lang.: Hun. 1194
Interview with choreographer Bill T. Jones. Lang.: Eng. 1316
Interview with choreographer Javier De Frutos. Lang.: Eng. 1332
Interview with director Peter Sellars. Lang.: Ger, Fre, Dut, Eng. 4727
Opera conductor Patrick Summers. Lang.: Eng. 4755
1990-1998. Plays/librettos/scripts.
Food in the plays of Molière. Lang.: Ita. 3695
1990-1998. Theory/criticism.
The urge to make Shakespeare contemporary. Lang.: Eng. 3844
1991. Institutions.
The political performance aesthetic of Bread and Puppet Theatre. Plainfield, VT. Lang.: Eng. 4879
1991. Plays/librettos/scripts.
Analysis of *Plague Mass* by Diamanda Galas. Lang.: Eng. 4828
1991-1996. Plays/librettos/scripts.
Analysis of *Savage/Love* by Joseph Chaikin and Sam Shepard. Lang.: Eng. 3543
1991-1997. Research/historiography.
The Shakespeare Interactive Research Group. Cambridge, MA. Lang.: Eng. 3799
1991-1998. Institutions.
Interview with Kricker James and Claire Higgins of Chain Lightning Theatre. New York, NY. Lang.: Eng. 1780
1991-1998. Performance spaces.
Sante Fe Opera's newly renovated open-air theatre. Santa Fe, NM. Lang.: Eng. 4499
1991-1998. Performance/production.
Dancer Koichi Kubo of Colorado Ballet. Denver, CO. Lang.: Eng. 1174
1992. Relation to other fields.
The Rodney King beating and how a news event is shaped by the media. Los Angeles, CA. Lang.: Eng. 4084
1992. Theory/criticism.
Comparison of critical reviews of dance performances. New York, NY. Lang.: Eng. 1201
1992-1994. Plays/librettos/scripts.
The medieval mystery play and Tony Kushner's *Angels in America.* Lang.: Eng. 3652
1992-1995. Performance/production.
Spike Lee's unsuccessful efforts to film parts of *Malcolm X* in Mecca. Lang.: Eng. 3954
Background on *The Couple in the Cage* by Guillermo Gómez-Peña and Coco Fusco. Lang.: Eng. 4259
1992-1997. Design/technology.
Essay on lighting technology and the computer. Sweden. Lang.: Swe. 224
1992-1998. Institutions.
Profile of TAXI Children's Theatre. Louisville, KY. Lang.: Eng. 390
Women in top management of American Conservatory Theatre. San Francisco, CA. Lang.: Eng. 1781
1992-1998. Performance/production.
Ice dancers Renee Roca and Gorsha Sur. Lang.: Eng. 992
1992-1998. Relation to other fields.
Analysis of striptease events. Lang.: Eng. 4285
1993. Plays/librettos/scripts.
Analysis of *Keely and Du* by Jane Martin. Lang.: Eng. 3629
1993-1996. Plays/librettos/scripts.
Comparison between *Krísis (Crisis)* by Sabina Berman and Quentin Tarantino's film *Pulp Fiction.* Mexico. Lang.: Spa. 3276
Transvestism in contemporary film as the 'blackface' of the nineties. UK-England. Lang.: Eng. 3983
1993-1997. Audience.
Audience response to the structuring of its expectations. Madison, WI. Lang.: Eng. 162

USA — cont'd

1993-1998. Performance/production.
Dancer Carlos Acosta of Royal Ballet and Houston Ballet. Houston, TX. London. Lang.: Eng. 1190
Actress Audra McDonald. Lang.: Eng. 2669
Heinz Fricke, music director of Washington Opera. Washington, DC. Lang.: Eng. 4734
1994. Basic theatrical documents.
Text of *Sound Check* by Dominick A. Taylor. Lang.: Eng. 1511
1994. Performance/production.
Defense of Bill T. Jones' dance piece *Still/Here*. Lang.: Eng. 1318
A mock slave auction at Colonial Williamsburg. Williamsburg, VA. Lang.: Eng. 4142
1994. Plays/librettos/scripts.
Čechov's influence on Woody Allen's film *Bullets Over Broadway*. Lang.: Eng. 4027
Analysis of Louis Malle's film *Vanya on 42nd Street*. Lang.: Fre. 4031
1994-1995. Theory/criticism.
Theory and Asian-American theatre. Minneapolis, MN. Lang.: Eng. 869
1994-1996. Performance/production.
The performance installations *Santa Cruzan/Flores de Mayo* by DIWA Arts. San Francisco, CA. Lang.: Eng. 4256
1994-1997. Plays/librettos/scripts.
Analysis of *Untitled Flesh* by Sacred Naked Nature Girls. Los Angeles, CA. Lang.: Eng. 4262
1994-1998. Basic theatrical documents.
French translation of *My Left Breast* by Susan Miller. France. Lang.: Fre. 1498
Screenplay of *Eve's Bayou* by Kasi Lemmons. Lang.: Eng. 3892
1994-1998. Institutions.
Profile of American Repertory Dance Company. Los Angeles, CA. Lang.: Eng. 1256
1994-1998. Performance/production.
The success of dance extravaganzas and solo performance at the expense of traditional shows. New York, NY. Lang.: Eng. 645
Dancer Manard Stewart of Pacific Northwest Ballet. Seattle, WA. Lang.: Eng. 1175
Analysis of dance trilogy by choreographer Neil Greenberg. Lang.: Eng. 1334
1994-1998. Plays/librettos/scripts.
Interview with screenwriter and director Kasi Lemmons. Lang.: Eng. 4000
1994-1998. Relation to other fields.
Creating interdisciplinary courses: the challenge for theatre educators. Lang.: Eng. 792
1994-1998. Training.
Details of a media acting curriculum. Lang.: Eng. 4041
1995. Basic theatrical documents.
Text of *The Metropolitan*, formerly called *The Ten Minute Play* by Mark R. Green. Lang.: Eng. 1485
Text of *Venus* by Suzan Lori-Parks. Lang.: Eng. 1501
1995. Design/technology.
Lighting design for fashion design awards ceremony at Lincoln Center. New York, NY. Lang.: Eng. 312
1995. Performance/production.
Theoretical implications of Laurie Anderson's use of media technology. Lang.: Eng. 4046
Account of life in drag. New Orleans, LA. Lang.: Eng. 4138
Analysis of Guillermo Gómez-Peña and Coco Fusco's performance piece *The Couple in the Cage*. Lang.: Eng. 4255
1995. Plays/librettos/scripts.
Ellen McLaughlin's *Iphigenia and Other Daughters* at CSC Repertory. New York, NY. Lang.: Eng. 3520
Joseph Chaikin's adaptation of *Textes pour rien (Texts for Nothing)* by Samuel Beckett. New York, NY. Lang.: Eng. 3563
Analysis of *Imperceptible Mutabilities in the Third Kingdom* by Suzan-Lori Parks. Lang.: Eng. 3592
Analysis of performance art on *The Larry Sanders Show*. Lang.: Eng. 4079
Daniel Barenboim and Edward Said on composer Richard Wagner. New York, NY. Germany. Lang.: Eng. 4826
1995-1996. Plays/librettos/scripts.
Film adaptations of Shakespeare's *Richard III* by Richard Loncraine and Al Pacino. UK-England. Lang.: Fre. 4012
1995-1996. Relation to other fields.
Quantum theory in recent New York performances. New York, NY. Lang.: Eng. 794
1995-1997. Basic theatrical documents.
French translation of *Beast on the Moon* by Richard Kalinoski. France. Lang.: Fre. 1491
1995-1997. Performance/production.
Performance artist Leslie Hill's *Push the Boat Out*. London. Lang.: Eng. 4245
1995-1998. Institutions.
Cooperation between Childsplay and the Arizona Theatre Company. Tempe, AZ. Tucson, AZ. Phoenix, AZ. Lang.: Eng. 1756
Profile of CoOPERAtive Opera Company of New York. New York, NY. Lang.: Eng. 4487
1995-1998. Performance/production.
The Alba Emoting system of actor training. Lang.: Eng. 668
Mary Oslund and Gregg Bielemeier of Conduit. Portland, OR. Lang.: Eng. 1333
1995-1998. Relation to other fields.
Abilene Christian University Theatre and the role of theatre in the evangelical subculture. Abilene, TX. Lang.: Eng. 787
1996. Administration.
Gender and the career advancement of arts managers. Lang.: Eng. 35
1996. Basic theatrical documents.
Excerpt from *Diva Studies* by Elizabeth Alexander. Lang.: Eng. 1480
French translation of *The Primary English Class* by Israel Horovitz. France. Lang.: Fre. 1489
Tod Lippy's unproduced screenplay *Jim & Wanda*. Lang.: Eng. 3895
1996. Performance/production.
Lois Weaver's *Faith and Dancing* and the CD-ROM in interactive performance. UK-England. Lang.: Eng. 971
Hamlet at Shakespeare Repertory Theatre, directed by Barbara Gaines. Chicago, IL. Lang.: Eng. 2666
Statements of women directors on their work. Lang.: Eng. 2674
High-school students' production of *The Wiz* at the Edinburgh Fringe Festival. Hattiesburg, MS. Edinburgh. Lang.: Eng. 4381
1996. Plays/librettos/scripts.
Analysis of *Venus* by Suzan-Lori Parks. Lang.: Eng. 3582
Interview with playwright Suzan-Lori Parks. Lang.: Eng. 3621
Analysis of *Diva Studies* by Elizabeth Alexander. Lang.: Eng. 3653
Interview with playwright Elizabeth Alexander. Lang.: Eng. 3662
Baz Luhrmann's film adaptation of Shakespeare's *Romeo and Juliet*. Lang.: Fre. 4016
1996-1997. Basic theatrical documents.
French translation of *Lebensraum* by Israel Horovitz. France. Lang.: Fre. 1488
1996-1997. Design/technology.
Sound design for Blue Man Group's Chicago production of *Tubes*. Chicago, IL. Lang.: Eng. 261
Stage, lighting, and sound design for Rolling Stones tour. Lang.: Eng. 308
Students' recreation of paintings on stage. Huntington, WV. Lang.: Eng. 313
1996-1997. Performance/production.
The student-created community theatre piece *Walk Together Children*. Lang.: Eng. 652
The receding place of dance in American culture. New York, NY. Lang.: Eng. 981
1996-1997. Relation to other fields.
Teaching African-American performance and the meaning of race. Lang.: Eng. 783
1996-1998. Administration.
Target marketing and successful ticket sales. Long Beach, CA. Lang.: Eng. 37
Arts and culture indicators in community building. Lang.: Eng. 38
The Disney Corporation's Broadway musicals. New York, NY. Lang.: Eng. 4317

USA — cont'd

1996-1998. Design/technology.
Sound system manufacturer Eastern Acoustic Works. Whitinsville, MA. Lang.: Eng. 286
Suppliers of lighting equipment for the music industry. Tualatin, OR. Lang.: Eng. 328
Lighting design for Hwang's *Golden Child* at the Public Theatre. New York, NY. Lang.: Eng. 1540

1996-1998. Institutions.
Bonnie Monte of New Jersey Shakespeare Festival. Madison, NJ. Lang.: Eng. 1772
The aesthetics of performances based on non-fiction texts at Lifeline Theatre. Chicago, IL. Lang.: Eng. 1788

1996-1998. Performance/production.
Contemporary performance art's ignorance of its avant-garde antecedents. Lang.: Eng. 4250

1996-1998. Plays/librettos/scripts.
The recent renewal of interest in the plays of Tennessee Williams. Lang.: Eng. 3674

1996-1998. Relation to other fields.
Engaging the students in large introductory theatre courses. Lang.: Eng. 779

1996-1998. Training.
Improvisational training and psychological resilience. Lang.: Eng. 879

1997. Administration.
Report on the ARTNOW arts advocacy demonstration. Washington, DC. Lang.: Eng. 29
Finding a reliable sample frame for potential audience data collection. Lang.: Eng. 39
The ARTNOW demonstration. Washington, DC. Lang.: Eng. 132
Christine Melton on the production of her play *Still Life Goes On*. New York, NY. Lang.: Eng. 1398

1997. Basic theatrical documents.
Text of *GBS: Fighting to Live Again* by Beverly J. Robertson. Lang.: Eng. 1504
Original playtext dealing with conflict resolution by Catherine Louise Rowe. Lang.: Eng. 1507
Text of three monologues by Will Scheffer. Lang.: Eng. 1509
Screenplay of *Finished* by William E. Jones. Lang.: Eng. 3889

1997. Design/technology.
New theatrical sound equiment. Lang.: Eng. 238
New theatrical lighting equipment. Lang.: Eng. 239
Report on lighting designers' conference. New York, NY. Lang.: Eng. 254
Former student on learning lighting design. Las Vegas, NV. Lang.: Eng. 316
Marilyn Lowey's lighting design for Cleveland San Jose Ballet. Cleveland, OH. Lang.: Eng. 1034
Recent work of lighting designer Brian MacDevitt. New York, NY. Lang.: Eng. 1530
Scenery by Yevgenia Nayberg for Robert Cohen's *The Prince*. Long Beach, CA. Lang.: Eng. 1561
Virtual reality technology for set design. Lawrence, KS. Lang.: Eng. 1562
Technical designs for the film *Titanic*. Lang.: Eng. 3910
Pop music lighting design of Steve Cohen and Curry Grant. Lang.: Eng. 4102

1997. Institutions.
Program of the Hungarian Centre of OISTAT's conference. Pittsburgh, PA. Lang.: Hun. 392
Fiscal survey of not-for-profit theatre. Lang.: Eng. 1754
Report on the National Black Theatre Festival. Winston-Salem, NC. Lang.: Eng. 1763
Interview with Robert Lewis on the founding of Actors Studio. New York, NY. Lang.: Eng. 1766
Arthur Penn and Actors Studio. New York, NY. Lang.: Eng. 1767
Report on the National Black Theatre Festival. Winston-Salem, NC. Lang.: Eng. 1787

1997. Performance spaces.
Architectural and technical renovations to the War Memorial Opera House. San Francisco, CA. Lang.: Eng. 478

1997. Performance/production.
Review of *Too Much Light Makes the Baby Go Blind* by the Neo-Futurists. Chicago, IL. Lang.: Eng. 620
Hanne Tierney's adaptation of *Bodas de sangre (Blood Wedding)* by García Lorca. Lang.: Eng. 647
The role of acting in preparing a homily. Lang.: Eng. 679
Tributes to ballerina Alexandra Danilova. New York, NY. Lang.: Eng. 1165
Interview with dancer/choreographer Elena Kunikova on her work with Les Ballets Trockadero. New York, NY. Lang.: Eng. 1180
Performances of the Ballet Folklórico de México and the Guangdong Dance Company. Washington, DC. Lang.: Hun. 1241
Creating the character Alma in Tennessee Williams' *Summer and Smoke*. Lang.: Eng. 2665
Yale Drama Department's reconstruction of Gogol's *Revizor (The Inspector General)* as staged by Mejerchol'd. New Haven, CT. Lang.: Eng. 2668
Richard Foreman's notes for a production of his *Pearls for Pigs*. Hartford, CT. Lang.: Eng. 2681
Analysis of Rae C. Wright's solo performance piece *Animal Instincts*. New York, NY. Lang.: Eng. 2684
Creating the role of Biagio Buonaccorsi in Robert Cohen's *The Prince*. Lang.: Eng. 2686
Robert Wilson's work with actors on a production of *Danton's Death (Dantons Tod)*. Houston, TX. Lang.: Eng. 2688
Creating the role of Julien Davis Cornell in *The Trial of Ezra Pound*. Long Beach, CA. Lang.: Eng. 2712
Homiletical drama in the free church tradition. Chicago, IL. Lang.: Eng. 2721
Creating the character Marlene in Caryl Churchill's *Top Girls*. Lang.: Eng. 2730
Creating the role of Mrs. Scully in Shirley Gee's *Warrior*. Long Beach, CA. Lang.: Eng. 2753
Joe Dowling's production of *London Assurance* by Dion Boucicault. Lang.: Eng. 2755
Creating the role of Billy Cuttle in Shirley Gee's *Warrior*. Long Beach, CA. Lang.: Eng. 2758
Novelist Joyce Carol Oates' reaction to Berg's *Wozzeck* at the Metropolitan Opera. New York, NY. Lang.: Eng. 4718

1997. Plays/librettos/scripts.
Playwright and actor Joseph Edward. New York, NY. Lang.: Eng. 3564
Women playwrights' addresses to the Women's Project conference. Lang.: Eng. 3589
Playwright Eugene O'Neill and the dramatic 'canon'. Lang.: Eng. 3710
The American and Canadian premieres of *Jackie O*. Banff, AB. Houston, TX. Lang.: Eng. 4761

1997. Relation to other fields.
Criticism of the American Assembly's approach to the arts sector. Lang.: Eng. 780
A dramatic perspective on teaching and learning. Lang.: Eng. 814
The social significance of the Disney Corporation's influence on Broadway theatre. New York, NY. Lang.: Eng. 3782
The creation and use of ritual theatre for drama therapy. Lang.: Eng. 3787
Symposium on fashion and film. New York, NY. Lang.: Eng. 4037

1997. Theory/criticism.
The nature of dance criticism. Europe. Lang.: Eng. 1013
Summary of Eugene O'Neill criticism. Lang.: Eng. 3845
Gender in Francesca Zambello's production of *Iphigénie en Tauride*. Cooperstown, NY. Lang.: Eng. 4843

1997. Training.
Playwright Tony Kushner's address to the Association of Theatre in Higher Education. Lang.: Eng. 3851

1997-1998. Administration.
Marketing analysis and plan for Texas Tech University Theatre's subscription campaign. Lubbock, TX. Lang.: Eng. 46

USA – cont'd

1997-1998. Audience.
New York reaction to visiting British dance companies. New York, NY. Lang.: Eng. 1246
1997-1998. Design/technology.
Graeme Nicol's lighting design for pop music tours including *Lilith Fair.* Lang.: Eng. 4101
Lighting design by Patrick Woodroffe and set design by Mark Fisher for Rolling Stones tour. Lang.: Eng. 4103
Donald Holder's lighting design for *The Lion King.* New York, NY. Lang.: Eng. 4336
Eugene Lee's set design for Frank Galati's production of *Ragtime.* Lang.: Eng. 4340
1997-1998. Institutions.
TCG annual report. Lang.: Eng. 1753
Annual report of the Metropolitan Opera Guild. New York, NY. Lang.: Eng. 4488
1997-1998. Performance/production.
The application of Laban Movement Studies to actor training. Lang.: Eng. 628
Sociolinguistics, gender, and the actor. Lang.: Eng. 642
A Hungarian view of the New York theatre scene. New York, NY. Lang.: Hun. 677
Proposal for a college course in directing. Brevard, NC. Lang.: Eng. 683
Analysis of recent New York productions. New York, NY. Lang.: Eng. 2759
Organizing two performances at the Metropolitan Opera on a single day. New York, NY. Lang.: Eng. 4741
1997-1998. Plays/librettos/scripts.
Marlowe's tragedies and peer evaluation in the composition classroom. Lang.: Eng. 3532
Overview of the life and work of Harold Pinter. Lang.: Eng. 3593
Interview with playwright/MP Wendy Lill. Halifax, NS. Lang.: Eng. 3705
Account of performances by Joan Dickinson. Lang.: Eng. 4263
1997-1998. Relation to other fields.
The arts as a sector in American life. Lang.: Eng. 775
Shelly Hirsch on her performance piece *For Jerry—Part I.* Germany. Lang.: Ger, Fre, Dut, Eng. 4266
1997-2000. Institutions.
The status of the National Endowment for the Arts. Washington, DC. Lang.: Eng. 422
1998. Administration.
Performance in fundraising. New York, NY. Lang.: Eng. 34
Alternative methods of measuring the success and failure of cultural institutions. Lang.: Eng. 36
Changes in income tax regulations and effect on theatre workers. Lang.: Eng. 40
Fundraising on the World Wide Web. Lang.: Eng. 41
The effect of formal training on arts administrators. Lang.: Eng. 45
Carol Waaser, Eastern Region Equity Director. New York, NY. Lang.: Eng. 47
Equity Council member Tom Joyce. Chicago, IL. Lang.: Eng. 48
Theatre and Equity business in the Atlanta area. Atlanta, GA. Lang.: Eng. 49
Equity activity in central Texas. Austin, TX. San Antonio, TX. Lang.: Eng. 50
Report of Equity Executive Director on finance and organization. Lang.: Eng. 51
Reports on the 10th Anniversary of Broadway Cares/Equity Fights AIDS. New York, NY. Lang.: Eng. 52
Equity's support of air-rights proposal of Broadway Initiative. Lang.: Eng. 53
Negotiations between US and Canadian Equity. Canada. Lang.: Eng. 54
Equity Executive Director's investigation into union issues. Lang.: Eng. 55
Jack Goldstein's departure from Equity to head Theatre Development Fund. New York, NY. Lang.: Eng. 56
Changes to Equity's theatre bonding policy. Lang.: Eng. 57
Benefits to performers of Taxpayer Relief Act. Lang.: Eng. 58
The nomination of William J. Ivey as head of NEA. Lang.: Eng. 59
Report on Equity's Off-Broadway contract agreement. Lang.: Eng. 60
Equity's new contract with East West Players. Los Angeles, CA. Lang.: Eng. 62
Equity agreement on New Orleans working conditions. New Orleans, LA. Lang.: Eng. 63
Equity's business theatre contract. New York, NY. Lang.: Eng. 64
Changes in Equity's health insurance coverage. New York, NY. Lang.: Eng. 65
Equity agreement with Second City. Chicago, IL. Detroit, MI. Lang.: Eng. 66
Effect on Actors Federal Credit Unions of a recent Supreme Court ruling. New York, NY. Lang.: Eng. 67
Actors' Fund annual benefit for women's health. New York, NY. Lang.: Eng. 68
Jekyll and Hyde restaurants sign Equity contract. New York, NY. Lang.: Eng. 69
Report on credit union legislation. New York, NY. Lang.: Eng. 70
Record of Equity Council vote. New York, NY. Lang.: Eng. 71
Report on Easter Bonnet fundraiser for AIDS. New York, NY. Lang.: Eng. 72
The debate on the rezoning of the New York theatre district. New York, NY. Lang.: Eng. 73
Interview with actors on Equity. New York, NY. Lang.: Eng. 75
Report on 'Broadway Bares' benefit for AIDS. New York, NY. Lang.: Eng. 76
Issues of concern to Equity members in current Broadway shows. New York, NY. Lang.: Eng. 77
The launch of the Equity website. New York, NY. Lang.: Eng. 78
Negotiations with Equity dinner theatres. New York, NY. Lang.: Eng. 79
John Holly, Western Regional Director of Equity. New York, NY. Lang.: Eng. 80
Annual report of the Equity pension fund. New York, NY. Lang.: Eng. 81
Profiles of Equity council members. New York, NY. Lang.: Eng. 82
Effect of recent legislation on the Actors Federal Credit Union. New York, NY. Lang.: Eng. 83
The work of an Equity Stage Manager. New York, NY. Lang.: Eng. 84
Equity's Stage Reading Guidelines. New York, NY. Lang.: Eng. 85
Changes in Equity's bonding policy for regional theatres. New York, NY. Lang.: Eng. 86
Complaints against an Equity Councillor and the 1998 Council election. New York, NY. Lang.: Eng. 87
The debate on organizing non-union tours of theatrical production. New York, NY. Lang.: Eng. 88
City Council's approval of a plan to sell theatres' air rights to developers. New York, NY. Lang.: Eng. 89
Current news on the theatre and Equity business. New York, NY. Lang.: Eng. 90
The waiting period before Equity health benefits take effect. New York, NY. Lang.: Eng. 91
Kathryn Lamkey, Director of Equity's Central Regional Office. Chicago, IL. Lang.: Eng. 92
Securing sick pay and worker's compensation for an on-the-job injury. New York, NY. Lang.: Eng. 93
Equity's National Council elections. New York, NY. Lang.: Eng. 94

USA — cont'd

The Palm View residence for people with AIDS. Hollywood, CA. Lang.: Eng. 95
Working conditions and requirements of stage managers. New York, NY. Lang.: Eng. 96
Summary of Equity's accomplishments in 1998. New York, NY. Lang.: Eng. 97
Equity's approval of a contract for the Chicago area. Chicago, IL. Lang.: Eng. 98
Profile of Equity administrator Guy Pace. New York, NY. Lang.: Eng. 99
Equity's First Vice-President Patrick Quinn. New York, NY. Lang.: Eng. 100
Shubert Alley's breast cancer screening program. New York, NY. Lang.: Eng. 101
The merger plan of the Screen Actors Guild and the American Federation of Television and Radio Artists. New York, NY. Lang.: Eng. 102
Equity's casting website. New York, NY. Lang.: Eng. 103
The loss of medical coverage for Equity dependents over nineteen years of age. New York, NY. Lang.: Eng. 105
Equity debate on member behavior when not under Equity contract. New York, NY. Lang.: Eng. 106
Equity's approval of Cabaret and Small Professional Theatre contracts. New York, NY. Lang.: Eng. 108
Flea Market fundraiser for AIDS. New York, NY. Lang.: Eng. 109
Record-breaking Equity membership in LA area. Los Angeles, CA. Lang.: Eng. 110
Equity seminar on finding an agent. New York, NY. Lang.: Eng. 111
Report on Equity deputy meetings. Lang.: Eng. 112
Interview with father and daughter serving on Equity council. New York, NY. Lang.: Eng. 113
Equity seminar for young performers and their families. New York, NY. Lang.: Eng. 114
Survey of Equity membership and employment data. New York, NY. Lang.: Eng. 115
Celebrities as spokespersons for non-profits. Lang.: Eng. 117
Guide to software for nonprofits. Lang.: Eng. 118
In-kind contributions to non-profits and the organizations that solicit them. Lang.: Eng. 119
The danger of a 'survival philosophy' to the mission of arts organizations. Lang.: Eng. 121
Suggestions for fundraising events. Lang.: Eng. 122
The role of Riverfront Arts Center in revitalizing Wilmington's riverfront. Wilmington, DE. Lang.: Eng. 123
Workplace solicitation for contributions to the arts. Lang.: Eng. 124
Dictionary of fundraising letters. Lang.: Eng. 128
The importance of maintaining an up-to-date fundraising data base. Lang.: Eng. 130
The effect of outcome analysis and impact studies on cultural policy. Lang.: Eng. 136
The publicizing of financial information about nonprofit arts organizations. Lang.: Eng. 137
The use of impact analysis in the arts. Lang.: Eng. 138
Current thinking on the impact of the arts. Lang.: Eng. 142
Outcome analysis of cultural activities and organizations. Lang.: Eng. 143
Profile of management group National Arts Stabilization. Lang.: Eng. 144
Alternative funding strategies for dance companies. Lang.: Eng. 886
Financially troubled Ohio ballet companies. Cleveland, OH. Akron, OH. Lang.: Eng. 1027
Obituary for Tom Dent, former chairman of the Free Southern Theatre board. New Orleans, LA. Lang.: Eng. 1395
Interviews with women in top management of theatres. New Haven, CT. Seattle, WA. East Haddam, CT. Lang.: Eng. 1397
Interview with Carrie Jackson, executive director of AUDELCO. New York, NY. Lang.: Eng. 1399
The First Amendment and the striptease dancer. Lang.: Eng. 4271
Equity Executive Director Alan Eisenberg's experience with a touring production of *Cats*. New York, NY. Lang.: Eng. 4318
Equity's contract with Resident Musical Theatre Association. Lang.: Eng. 4319
Performer Rebecca Spencer's experience as an Equity Deputy. New York, NY. Lang.: Eng. 4320
The legal battle over copyright of the musical *Rent*. New York, NY. Lang.: Eng. 4321
The settlement of a copyright case regarding the musical *Rent*. New York, NY. Lang.: Eng. 4322
Speculations on the future marketing of opera. Lang.: Eng. 4406
Standing-room-only practices at the Metropolitan Opera. New York, NY. Lang.: Eng. 4407
Leland Ball of Sacramento Light Opera Association, winner of Rosetta LeNoire Award. Sacramento, CA. Lang.: Eng. 4408
Marketing strategies for puppetry in film and TV. Lang.: Eng. 4863
Pricing strategy for puppeteers. Lang.: Eng. 4864

1998. Audience.
Jonathan Demme's film adaptation of *Beloved* by Toni Morrison. Lang.: Eng. 3877
The current state of film, film criticism, and the audience. Lang.: Eng. 3878

1998. Basic theatrical documents.
Texts of plays by Eddie Paul Bradley, Jr. Lang.: Eng. 1482
Text of ... *Where Late the Sweet Birds Sang* by Sheryle Criswell. Lang.: Eng. 1483
Text of *Three Days of Rain* by Richard Greenberg. Lang.: Eng. 1486
Text of *Jails, Hospitals and Hip-Hop* by Danny Hoch. Lang.: Eng. 1487
Text of *White Noises* by Shannon Jackson. Lang.: Eng. 1490
Text of *Medicine Men* by Jack Martin Karp. Lang.: Eng. 1492
Text of *Side Man* by Warren Leight. Lang.: Eng. 1494
Text of *The Chemistry of Change* by Marlane Meyer. Lang.: Eng. 1497
Text of *Insurrection: Holding History* by Robert O'Hara. Lang.: Eng. 1500
Texts of *WWW.chat* and *Elevator* by Chris Edwin Rose. Lang.: Eng. 1506
Screenplay of *Pi* by Darren Aronofsky. Lang.: Eng. 3880
Screenplay of *Gods and Monsters* by Bill Condon. Lang.: Eng. 3882
Screenplay of *The Lunch Date* by Adam Davidson. Lang.: Eng. 3883
Screenplay of *Out of Sight* by Scott Frank. Lang.: Eng. 3884
Screenplay for *The First Wife*, based on a story by Colette. Lang.: Eng. 3888
The screenplay of *Living Out Loud* by Richard LaGravenese. Lang.: Eng. 3890
Screenplay of the film *Slam*. Lang.: Eng. 3893
Screenplay for *Weeds* by Alex Lewin, winner of annual student screenplay competition. Lang.: Eng. 3894
Text of *The Spanish Prisoner* by David Mamet. Lang.: Eng. 3896

1998. Design/technology.
Directory of manufacturers and distributors of lighting equipment. Canada. Lang.: Eng. 169
AC Lighting's North American operation. UK-England. Lang.: Eng. 234
Calendar of events at LDI98 trade show. Las Vegas, NV. Lang.: Eng. 240
Guide to theatrical design manufacturers and equipment. Lang.: Eng. 241

USA – cont'd

Guide to equipment and services for the theatre and film industries. Lang.: Eng. 242
The 1998 TCI awards. Lang.: Eng. 243
List of exhibitors at LDI convention. Phoenix, AZ. Lang.: Eng. 244
Survey of lighting-design software manufacturers. Lang.: Eng. 245
Guide to lighting equipment and services. Lang.: Eng. 246
Guide to lighting equipment. Lang.: Eng. 247
Workshops of LDI expo. Phoenix, AZ. Lang.: Eng. 248
Guidelines for a lighting design portfolio. Lang.: Eng. 249
The 1998 USITT expo. Long Beach, CA. Lang.: Eng. 251
Professional theatrical designers on design training. Lang.: Eng. 252
Costumer Paul Reinhardt. Lang.: Eng. 253
Entertainment Services and Technology Association's guidelines on ethics. Lang.: Eng. 256
Job-hunting advice for costumers and theatrical professionals. Lang.: Eng. 259
Rigging a pneumatically activated curtain. Lang.: Eng. 263
Simulating stained glass on stage. Lang.: Eng. 266
Treating muslin to look like Naugahyde. Lang.: Eng. 267
The new sound system of the Lyman Center, Southern Connecticut State University. New Haven, CT. Lang.: Eng. 268
Construction and operation of a trap unit. Lang.: Eng. 269
Tubular steel framing for large scenery flats. Lang.: Eng. 270
Review of new lighting software. Lang.: Eng. 273
The sound system at the Mark Hellinger Theatre, now a house of worship. New York, NY. Lang.: Eng. 274
Lighting design and equipment in various Las Vegas spaces. Las Vegas, NV. Lang.: Eng. 276
Preview of Lightfair seminar. Las Vegas, NV. Lang.: Eng. 278
Winners of American College Theatre Festival design competitions. Lang.: Eng. 279
Stage lighting at the War Memorial Opera House. San Francisco, CA. Lang.: Eng. 280
Lighting designer Michael Gottlieb. New York, NY. Lang.: Eng. 281
Lighting designer Michael Brown. Lang.: Eng. 282
Update on construction of tuffets for scene-shop use. Lang.: Eng. 283
New sound and video system in the performance space of Luxor Hotel and Casino. Las Vegas, NV. Lang.: Eng. 285
Panel discussion of sound designers. Lang.: Eng. 287
NSCA sound products and technology trade show. Las Vegas, NV. Lang.: Eng. 288
Report on AES trade show. San Francisco, CA. Lang.: Eng. 289
Design for houses of worship, including their adaptation for performance and exhibitions. Long Beach, CA. Lang.: Eng. 290
Imero Fiorentino, USITT's most distinguished lighting designer of 1997. Lang.: Eng. 291
Set and costume designer Eduardo Sicangco, judge of SETC design competition. Birmingham, AL. Lang.: Eng. 292
The use of entertainment technology beyond the entertainment industry. Lang.: Eng. 293
Ethernet computer connections between lighting systems of two theatres at Herberger Theatre Center. Phoenix, AZ. Lang.: Eng. 294
Constructing collapsible changing booths for actors. Lang.: Eng. 295
A fly system for low-ceilinged theatres. Lang.: Eng. 296
Building a two-scene sound controller. Lang.: Eng. 297
Report on new technical gadgets. Lang.: Eng. 299
The new sound system of the Frauenthal Theatre. Muskegon, MI. Lang.: Eng. 300
Report on annual USITT conference. Long Beach, CA. Lang.: Eng. 302
Preview of LDI98 trade show. Las Vegas, NV. Lang.: Eng. 303
The Datatron control system for visual projections. Lang.: Eng. 304
Preview of LDI convention. Phoenix, AZ. Lang.: Eng. 305
Creating stage jewelry from polymer clays. Lang.: Eng. 306
Lighting design for Mohegan Sun Casino. Uncasville, CT. Lang.: Eng. 307
Lighting designer John Osborne. Lang.: Eng. 310
Computer graphics as a lighting design tool. Lawrence, KS. Lang.: Eng. 311
Set designer Daniel Ostling. Chicago, IL. Lang.: Eng. 314
Costume designer Catherine Zuber. Lang.: Eng. 315
Lighting design for musical performance and sports at the Nashville arena. Nashville, TN. Lang.: Eng. 317
Recommendation for inexpensive digital noise-reduction software. Lang.: Eng. 319
Sound, lighting, and scenic elements of *Star Trek: The Next Generation* at the Las Vegas Hilton. Las Vegas, NV. Lang.: Eng. 320
Construction of nylon turntable rollers. Lang.: Eng. 321
Creativity and beauty in theatrical design. Lang.: Eng. 322
Index to *Technical Brief* volumes 11-17. Lang.: Eng. 323
Stage automation and its effect on set design. Lang.: Eng. 325
American theatre designers and technicians' visit to China. China, People's Republic of. Lang.: Eng. 327
Evaluation of Sound Score playback equipment. Lang.: Eng. 329
A four sided steel-marking guide. Lang.: Eng. 331
Low-voltage cue light system. Lang.: Eng. 332
Costume design for the ballet *Cyrano de Bergerac*. San Francisco, CA. Lang.: Eng. 1032
Technical designs for Čajovskij's *Sneguročka*, Houston Ballet. Houston, TX. Lang.: Eng. 1033
Lighting design for Čajkovskij's *Sneguročka (The Snow Maiden)* at Houston Ballet. Houston, TX. Lang.: Eng. 1035
Design concept for Ralph Lemon's dance piece *Geography* at BAM. New York, NY. Lang.: Eng. 1248
Set design for Joseph Chaikin's production of two one-acts by Arthur Miller. New york, NY. Lang.: Eng. 1532
Costume design for *Christmas with the Ivanovs*, CSC Repertory. New York, NY. Lang.: Eng. 1533
Lighting design for *Never the Sinner* by John Logan, directed by Ethan McSweeney. New York, NY. Lang.: Eng. 1534
Set design for *Gun Shy* by Richard Dresser at Playwrights Horizons. New York, NY. Lang.: Eng. 1535
Set designs by Santo Loquasto at Manhattan Theatre Club. New York, NY. Lang.: Eng. 1536
Costume design for Feydeau's *A Flea in Her Ear (La Puce à l'Oreille)*, Roundabout Theatre Company. New York, NY. Lang.: Eng. 1537
Derek McLane's set designs for recent Off Broadway productions. New York, NY. Lang.: Eng. 1538
Technical designs for Off Broadway Shakespearean productions. New York, NY. Lang.: Eng. 1539
Set designs of Francis O'Connor. New York, NY. Lang.: Eng. 1541
Michael McGarty's set design for Elaine May and Alan Arkin's *Power Plays*. New York, NY. Lang.: Eng. 1542
Costume designs for Oregon Shakespeare Festival productions. Ashland, OR. Lang.: Eng. 1543
Lighting design for Donald Margulies' *Collected Stories*, directed by William Carden. New York, NY. Lang.: Eng. 1544
Lighting designer Kenneth Posner. Lang.: Eng. 1545
Lighting design for Shakespeare's *Twelfth Night* at the Vivian Beaumont. New York, NY. Lang.: Eng. 1546
Lighting design for Mamet's *The Old Neighborhood* directed by Scott Zigler. New York, NY. Lang.: Eng. 1547

USA — cont'd

Costume designer Catherine Zuber. Lang.: Eng. 1549

Set designer Karen TenEyck. Lang.: Eng. 1550

Set design for Chain Lightning Theatre's production of *Beyond the Horizon* by Eugene O'Neill. New York, NY. Lang.: Eng. 1551

Karen TenEyck's projections for a site-specific production of Shakespeare's *Julius Caesar*. Los Angeles, CA. Lang.: Eng. 1552

Sound design for *The Diary of Anne Frank* directed by James Lapine. New York, NY. Lang.: Eng. 1553

Lighting designer Hugh Vanstone. New York, NY. Lang.: Eng. 1554

Design concept for Amy Freed's *The Psychic Life of Savages*, Wilma Theatre. Philadelphia, PA. Lang.: Eng. 1555

The design concept for Nicholas Hytner's production of Shakespeare's *Twelfth Night*. New York, NY. Lang.: Eng. 1556

Set design for a University of Michigan production of *Henry V*. Ann Arbor, MI. Lang.: Eng. 1557

Technical designs for *Griller* by Eric Bogosian. Chicago, IL. Lang.: Eng. 1558

Set and lighting designs for *The Taming of the Shrew*, American Repertory Theatre. Cambridge, MA. Lang.: Eng. 1559

Dex Edwards' set design for *The Comedy of Errors*, Shakespeare Repertory Company. Chicago, IL. Lang.: Eng. 1560

Technical designs for Stanley Tucci's film *The Impostors*. Lang.: Eng. 3901

Costuming for the film *Mr. Magoo*. Hollywood, CA. Lang.: Eng. 3903

Production design for the film *Lost in Space*. Hollywood, CA. Lang.: Eng. 3904

Des McAnuff's design concept for his film *Cousin Bette*. Hollywood, CA. Lang.: Eng. 3905

Matthew Maraffi, production for the film *Pi*. Lang.: Eng. 3906

Production design for the film *The Avengers*. Hollywood, CA. Lang.: Eng. 3907

Production design for Bill Condon's film *Gods and Monsters*. Hollywood, CA. Lang.: Eng. 3908

Production design for Gary Ross's film *Pleasantville*. Hollywood, CA. Lang.: Eng. 3909

Introduction to an issue of *Lighting Dimensions* devoted to film lighting. Lang.: Eng. 3911

Lighting design for Steven Soderbergh's film *Out of Sight*. Lang.: Eng. 3912

Lighting design for Mark Christopher's film *54*. Lang.: Eng. 3913

Lighting design for Joe Dante's film *Small Soldiers*. Lang.: Eng. 3914

Lighting design for Michael Bays' film *Armageddon*. Lang.: Eng. 3916

Lighting design for Roland Emmerich's film *Godzilla*. Lang.: Eng. 3917

Advances in motion picture lighting. Lang.: Eng. 3918

Lighting design for Peter Weir's film *The Truman Show*. Lang.: Eng. 3919

Model syllabus for a course or unit on sound in film. Lang.: Eng. 3921

Lighting design for Rob Bowman's film *The X-Files*. Lang.: Eng. 3922

TV and film make-up artists Tom Burman and Bari Dreiband-Burman. Hollywood, CA. Lang.: Eng. 4050

Computer-aided design in TV production. Hollywood, CA. Lang.: Eng. 4051

Design awards for the TV mini-series *Merlin*. Pasadena, CA. Lang.: Eng. 4052

Costumes for a masked ball scene in the TV series *Another World*. Lang.: Eng. 4053

Lighting design for TV series *Ally MacBeal*. Lang.: Eng. 4054

Lighting the 24-hour television event: QVC home shopping network. West Chester, PA. Lang.: Eng. 4055

Profile of technicians for Grammy Awards television broadcast. New York, NY. Lang.: Eng. 4056

Flexible lighting design for two-band tour by Norman Schwab and Alan Parker. Lang.: Eng. 4099

Jim Chapman's lighting design for rock music tour. Lang.: Eng. 4104

Howard Ungerleider's lighting design for Van Halen tour. Lang.: Eng. 4105

Stan Crocker's lighting design for pop rock group tour. Lang.: Eng. 4106

Graeme Nicol's lighting design for *Lilith Fair*. Lang.: Eng. 4107

Peter Morse's lighting design for country music tour. Lang.: Eng. 4108

Lighting and sound control for the Disneyland 'Light Magic' show. Anaheim, CA. Lang.: Eng. 4109

Lighting for Washington Opera's production of *Doña Francisquita*. Washington, DC. Lang.: Eng. 4290

Lighting and projections for the musical *Ragtime*. New York, NY. Lang.: Eng. 4328

Sound design for *Side Show* at Richard Rodgers Theatre. New York, NY. Lang.: Eng. 4329

Costume design for a new version of *Peter Pan* at Children's Theatre Company. Minneapolis, MN. Lang.: Eng. 4330

Technical designs for *The Scarlet Pimpernel* directed by Robert Longbottom. New York, NY. Lang.: Eng. 4331

Costume design for *Dames at Sea*, Marine Memorial Theatre. San Francisco, CA. Lang.: Eng. 4332

Costume design for revival of *As Thousands Cheer* by Drama Dept. New York, NY. Lang.: Eng. 4333

Neil Patel's scene design for *Mirette*, Goodspeed Opera House. East Haddam, CT. Lang.: Eng. 4334

Lighting design for the musical *Follies*, Paper Mill Playhouse. Millburn, NJ. Lang.: Eng. 4335

Technical designs for *Ragtime* at the Ford Center. New York, NY. Lang.: Eng. 4338

Sound design for the musical *The Capeman*. New York, NY. Lang.: Eng. 4339

Sound design for the Broadway premiere of the musical *Ragtime*. New York, NY. Lang.: Eng. 4341

Technical designs for the Broadway production of *The Lion King*. New York, NY. Lang.: Eng. 4342

Technical designs for Sam Mendes' production of *Cabaret*. New York, NY. Lang.: Eng. 4343

Lighting design for Sam Mendes' production of *Cabaret*. New York, NY. Lang.: Eng. 4344

Lighting design for *Jekyll & Hyde* directed by Robin Phillips. New York, NY. Lang.: Eng. 4345

Set and costume design for *Patience and Sarah* at Lincoln Center. New York, NY. Lang.: Eng. 4440

Lighting designer Jennifer Tipton. New York, NY. Lang.: Eng. 4441

Set and costume design for San Francisco Opera productions. San Francisco, CA. Lang.: Eng. 4443

Technical designs for *Tristan und Isolde* at Seattle Opera. Seattle, WA. Lang.: Eng. 4444

Lighting design for Basil Twist's puppet production *Symphonie Fantastique*. New York, NY. Lang.: Eng. 4867

How to make a puppet from a handle bag. Lang.: Eng. 4868

Constructing miniature puppets from pipe cleaners and balsa wood. Lang.: Eng. 4869

Use of a balance line in marionette construction. Lang.: Eng. 4918

1998. Institutions.

Photographic essay on SETC convention. Birmingham, AL. Lang.: Eng. 389

Proposal for changes in the mission of the National Endowment for the Arts. Lang.: Eng. 397

USA – cont'd

Anna Deavere Smith on the Institute on the Arts and Civic Dialogue. Cambridge, MA. Lang.: Eng. 399

Convention of the Southeastern Theatre Conference. Birmingham, AL. Lang.: Eng. 402

Preview of SETC convention. Birmingham, AL. Lang.: Eng. 405

Interdisciplinarity in post-secondary theatre studies programs. Lang.: Eng. 407

Theatrical activity in Cleveland's Playhouse Square. Cleveland, OH. Lang.: Eng. 416

The temporary relocation of the New York Public Library for the Performing Arts. New York, NY. Lang.: Eng. 419

William J. Ivey, nominee for chair of NEA. Washington, DC. Lang.: Eng. 420

The relationship between theatrical artists and theatrical institutions. Tarrytown, NY. Lang.: Eng. 421

The partnership between San Francisco Opera and Chase Manhattan Bank. San Francisco, CA. New York, NY. Lang.: Eng. 423

The Walker Arts Center's exhibition on dance. Minneapolis, MN. Lang.: Eng. 905

Report on the Altogether Different dance festival. New York, NY. Lang.: Eng. 906

The dance training program of Houston High School for the Performing and Visual Arts. Houston, TX. Lang.: Eng. 907

American Ballet Theatre and diminishing government support. New York, NY. Lang.: Eng. 1059

Profile of the American Ballet Theatre. New York, NY. Lang.: Hun. 1061

Ibsen Society of America's celebration of the centennial of *Når vi døde vågner (When We Dead Awaken)*. New York, NY.Lang.: Eng. 1755

Vicky Boone, artistic director of Frontera Theatre. Austin, TX. Lang.: Eng. 1759

Report on the second National Black Theatre Summit. Atlanta, GA. Lang.: Eng. 1773

The new home of Chicago Shakespeare Theatre, formerly Shakespeare Repertory Theatre. Chicago, IL. Lang.: Eng. 1775

Productions of Actors' Theatre Humana Festival. Louisville, KY. Lang.: Eng. 1779

Report on National Black Theatre Summit. Dartmouth, NH. Lang.: Eng. 1782

Plays of 1998 Oregon Shakespeare Festival. Ashland, OR. Lang.: Eng. 1783

Playwright Garland Lee on the National Black Theatre Summit. Dartmouth, NH. Lang.: Eng. 1786

Director Molly Smith, new artistic director of Arena Stage. Washington, DC. Lang.: Eng. 1789

Charles Newell, artistic director of the Court Theatre. Chicago, IL. Lang.: Eng. 1792

Criticism of plays at Humana Festival. Louisville, KY. Lang.: Eng. 1793

Interviews with graduate students at Yale University School of Music. New Haven, CT. Lang.: Eng. 4483

The puppet collection of the Detroit Institute of the Arts. Detroit, MI. Lang.: Eng. 4880

Puppetry exhibits at Chicago Children's Museum. Chicago, IL. Mexico City. Lang.: Eng. 4881

Report on international puppet festival. New York, NY. Lang.: Eng. 4882

Report on Academy of String Puppetry Conference. Storrs, CT. Lang.: Eng. 4883

1998. Performance spaces.

New stage lighting of War Memorial Opera House. San Francisco, CA. Lang.: Eng. 465

Architectural critique of the new Ford Center. New York, NY. Lang.: Eng. 468

The renovation of Arden Theatre Company's F. Otto Haas Theatre. Philadelphia, PA. Lang.: Eng. 469

The present status of dinner theatre. Lang.: Eng. 471

Profiles of Southern California theatres. Lang.: Eng. 473

Seattle's new and renovated theatres. Seattle, WA. Lang.: Eng. 475

Architectural critique of the restored New Amsterdam Theatre. New York, NY. Lang.: Eng. 476

The architecture of the Bass Performance Hall. Ft. Worth, TX. Lang.: Eng. 477

The renovation of Times Square. New York, NY. Lang.: Eng. 479

The supper and swing-music venue the Coconut Club. Los Angeles, CA. Lang.: Eng. 4115

The creation of a site-specific performance space for Sam Mendes' production of *Cabaret*. New York, NY. Lang.: Eng. 4350

A modular stage used for touring by the Houston Grand Opera. Houston, TX. Lang.: Eng. 4500

The newly renovated Newberry Opera House. Newberry, SC. Lang.: Eng. 4501

1998. Performance/production.

The life and career of singer Paul Robeson. Lang.: Eng. 631

Auditioning for an Irene Ryan Scholarship. Lang.: Eng. 635

German impressions of recent New York theatre. New York, NY. Lang.: Ger. 655

Announcement of Equity's young performers seminar series. New York, NY. Lang.: Eng. 656

Equity's free seminar series for young performers and their families. New York, NY. Lang.: Eng. 657

Current news about the theatre and its people. New York, NY. Lang.: Eng. 658

Conference on African-American theatre convened by playwright August Wilson. Hanover, NH. Lang.: Eng. 659

Photo essay on celebration of Paul Robeson. New York, NY. Lang.: Eng. 660

Short news takes on current theatre events. New York, NY. Lang.: Eng. 661

Director Gerald Freedman on 'real' theatre. Birmingham, AL. Lang.: Eng. 684

Software for choreography. Lang.: Eng. 984

Jazz dancer and choreographer Mia Michaels. Lang.: Eng. 987

Report on touring ice show *Stars on Ice*. Lang.: Eng. 990

The trend of dancers continuing their careers after age forty. Lang.: Eng. 991

Choreographer John Neumeier. Hamburg. New York, NY. Lang.: Eng. 1082

Russsian-born dancer Mikhail Baryshnikov. Lang.: Rus. 1169

New York performances of the San Francisco Ballet. New York, NY. Lang.: Eng. 1170

Ballerina Kristina Fernandez on working with choreographer Jerome Robbins. Lang.: Eng. 1171

New male dancers of New York City Ballet. New York, NY. Lang.: Eng. 1177

Interview with dancer Julie Kent. Lang.: Eng. 1184

Dancer Christopher Stowell of San Francisco Ballet. San Francisco, CA. Lang.: Eng. 1191

David Parsons Dance Company's *Fill the Woods with Light*. Washington, DC. Lang.: Hun. 1195

Flamenco dancer and choreographer Carlota Santana. New York, NY. Lang.: Eng. 1239

Dancer/choreographer David Parsons. New York, NY. Lang.: Eng. 1329

Performances by dance couple Eiko & Koma. Washington, DC. Lang.: Hun. 1336

Interview with composer Paul Schmidt. New Haven, CT. Lang.: Eng. 2660

Director Michael Mayer. Lang.: Eng. 2670

Steppenwolf Theatre Company's production of *Space* by Tina Landau. Chicago, IL. Lang.: Eng. 2672

USA — cont'd

Interview with actor Peter Riegert. New York, NY. Lang.: Eng. 2676
The 'viewpoint theory' of actor training. Lang.: Eng. 2677
Alternative theatre and the Black audience. Lang.: Eng. 2682
Actress Frances Sternhagen. Lang.: Eng. 2687
Actress Ruby Dee. Lang.: Eng. 2689
Using Renaissance dance in Shakespearean productions. Lang.: Eng. 2692
Interview with actress Phylicia Rashad. Atlanta, GA. Lang.: Eng. 2695
John Barton's workshop on Shakespearean performance. New York, NY. Lang.: Eng. 2704
Comparison of productions of Ibsen's *Peer Gynt*. Providence, RI. New York, NY. Washington, DC. Nacogdoches, TX. Lang.: Eng. 2711
Denise Gillman's production of Webster's *The Duchess of Malfi*, Theatre of NOTE. Los Angeles, CA. Lang.: Eng. 2714
Actors Helen Carey and Max Wright, winners of Joe A. Callaway Award. Lang.: Eng. 2716
Report on speech by actor Eli Wallach to Actors' Equity meeting. Lang.: Eng. 2717
Elizabeth Perry's one-woman show *Sun Flower* about Elizabeth Cady Stanton. New York, NY. Lang.: Eng. 2718
Julyana Soelistyo and Sam Trammel, winners of the Derwent Award. New York, NY. Lang.: Eng. 2719
Excerpt from a speech by actor Robert Prosky. Washington, DC. Lang.: Eng. 2720
José Rivera's production of *La Vida es sueño (Life Is a Dream)*, Hartford Stage. Hartford, CT. Lang.: Eng. 2722
Actress Caroline Nesbitt on giving up her theatrical career. New York, NY. Lang.: Eng. 2723
The Tennessee Williams/New Orleans Literary Festival. New Orleans, LA. Lang.: Eng. 2726
Reviews of Actors' Theatre productions. Louisville, KY. Lang.: Eng. 2727
Trevor Nunn's production of *Not About Nightingales* by Tennessee Williams, Alley Theatre. Houston, TX. Lang.: Eng. 2729
Jane Alexander's return to acting after chairing the NEA. Lang.: Eng. 2744
Actress and teacher Uta Hagen. Lang.: Eng. 2745
Reviews of productions of plays by Ibsen. New York, NY. Oslo. Lang.: Eng. 2747
Obituary for actor Leverne Summers. New York, NY. Lang.: Eng. 2748
Obituary for actress Theresa Merritt. New York, NY. Lang.: Eng. 2749
Interview with actor Patrick Stewart. Washington, DC. Lang.: Eng. 2760
Steven Soderbergh on directing *Out of Sight*. Lang.: Eng. 3944
Spielberg's *Saving Private Ryan* and the war film. Hollywood, CA. Lang.: Eng. 3948
Analysis of Todd Solondz' film *Happiness*. Lang.: Eng. 3949
Hitchcock's influence on *The Spanish Prisoner* by David Mamet. Lang.: Eng. 3956
Retrospectives of filmmakers Jean-Luc Godard and William Kentridge. New York, NY. Lang.: Eng. 3958
Mixed media artist Ebon Fisher. Lang.: Eng. 4045
The theory and practice of scoring a television production. Lang.: Eng. 4069
Puppeteer Wayne Martin. Boston, MA. Lang.: Eng. 4070
A photo session involving mimes Marcel Marceau and Bill Irwin. New York, NY. Lang.: Eng. 4092
Semiotic analysis of ventriloquism. Lang.: Eng. 4136
Report on ventriloquist's convention. Las Vegas, NV. Lang.: Eng. 4143
Singer Lorna Luft. Lang.: Eng. 4158
Portraying Mickey Mouse at Walt Disney World. Orlando, FL. Lang.: Eng. 4223
William Schuman on the differences between operatic and Broadway theatre singing. Lang.: Eng. 4303
Photographic essay of Rameau's *Platée* directed and choreographed by Mark Morris. Berkeley, CA. Lang.: Eng. 4304
Staging a musical without professional dancers. Lang.: Eng. 4374
The music of George Gershwin available on compact disc. Lang.: Eng. 4382
Musical performances on and off Broadway. New York. Lang.: Ger. 4383
The premiere of the musical *Elaborate Lives: The Legend of Aida*. Atlanta, GA. Lang.: Eng. 4385
AIDS-benefit performance of the musical *Sweet Charity*. New York, NY. Lang.: Eng. 4386
Response to negative criticism of *The Capeman*. New York, NY. Lang.: Eng. 4387
Conductor Andrew Davis. UK-England. Lang.: Eng. 4704
Obituaries of singers Randolph Symonette and Todd Duncan. Lang.: Eng. 4708
Background material on Lyric Opera of Chicago radio broadcast performances. Chicago, IL. Lang.: Eng. 4709
Background material on telecast performance of Britten's *Paul Bunyan* at New York City Opera. New York, NY. Lang.: Eng. 4710
Coloratura soprano June Anderson. Lang.: Eng. 4712
Background material on Metropolitan Opera radio broadcast performances. New York, NY. Lang.: Eng. 4713
Background material on telecast performance of Saint-Saëns' *Samson et Dalila* at the Metropolitan Opera. New York, NY. Lang.: Eng. 4714
Background material on Metropolitan Opera radio broadcast performances. New York, NY. Lang.: Eng. 4716
Dramatic soprano Deborah Voigt. Lang.: Eng. 4717
Interview with Ira Siff of La Gran Scena. New York, NY. Lang.: Eng. 4719
Reviews of *Lieder* recordings. Slovenia. Austria. Lang.: Eng. 4720
Bass James Johnson. Lang.: Eng. 4722
Interview with soprano Joan Sutherland about vocal technique. New York, NY. Lang.: Eng. 4728
Soprano Alessandra Marc. Lang.: Eng. 4729
Guest performances of the Kirov Opera at the Metropolitan. New York, NY. Lang.: Eng. 4731
Robert Wilson's production of Wagner's *Lohengrin*. New York, NY. Lang.: Eng. 4732
Jonathan Miller's production of *The Rake's Progress* at the Metropolitan Opera. New York, NY. Lang.: Eng. 4733
Anecdotes about soprano Mary Mills. Lang.: Eng. 4735
Baritone Rodney Gilfry. Lang.: Eng. 4736
Musicological preparation for the Metropolitan Opera production of Rossini's *La Cenerentola*. Chicago, IL. Lang.: Eng. 4737
Interview with conductor Nicholas McGegan. UK-England. Lang.: Eng. 4740
André Previn's opera *A Streetcar Named Desire*. San Francisco. Lang.: Eng. 4742
Major opera houses' proposals for productions to the end of the century. Canada. Lang.: Eng. 4743
Baritone Dwayne Croft. New York, NY. Lang.: Eng. 4751
Tenor Anthony Dean Griffey's career and Metropolitan Opera debut. New York, NY. Lang.: Eng. 4752
Soprano Barbara Bonney. Lang.: Eng. 4754
New England Marionettes' production of Mozart's *Die Zauberflöte*. Boston, MA. Lang.: Eng. 4900
Report on the Fourth Annual Jim Henson Festival. New York, NY. Lang.: Eng. 4903

USA — cont'd

Basil Twist's puppetry interpretation of Berlioz's *Symphonie Fantastique*. New York, NY. Lang.: Eng. 4904

1998. Plays/librettos/scripts.

Oscar Wilde biographer on his negative traits and addictive behaviors. UK-England. Lang.: Eng. 3425

German view of English and American drama. UK-England. Lang.: Ger. 3455

Playwright Romulus Linney's address to SETC convention. Birmingham, AL. Lang.: Eng. 3517

Shared Experience's stage adaptations of nineteenth-century novels. New York, NY. London. Lang.: Eng. 3518

Account of National Black Theatre Summit. Hanover, NH. Lang.: Eng. 3523

Playwright Naomi Iizuka. Lang.: Eng. 3531

Writing for both television and live theatre. Lang.: Eng. 3560

Marla del Collins on her play *The Lovers and Others of Eugene O'Neill*. Lang.: Eng. 3565

American College Theatre Festival's showcase of student plays. Lang.: Eng. 3583

Reports of playwright Eugene O'Neill's ghost haunting a Boston University building. Boston, MA. Lang.: Eng. 3587

Playwright Murphy Guyer and the Cleveland Playhouse. Cleveland, OH. Lang.: Eng. 3598

Analysis of *The Water Children* by Wendy Macleod. Lang.: Eng. 3613

Reactions to the revised version of *The Diary of Anne Frank*. New York, NY. Lang.: Eng. 3618

Shannon Jackson on her solo piece *White Noises*. Lang.: Eng. 3619

Lanford Wilson's *Book of Days*. Lang.: Eng. 3627

Writing for the youth audience. Lang.: Eng. 3630

Playwright Terrence McNally on his profession. Lang.: Eng. 3644

Playwright W. David Hancock. Lang.: Eng. 3646

Playwright John Henry Redwood. Atlanta, GA. Lang.: Eng. 3656

Marxian analysis of dramatic parody and burlesque. Europe. Lang.: Eng. 3664

The enneagram system applied to Albee's *Who's Afraid of Virginia Woolf?*. Lang.: Eng. 3665

Playwright Beth Henley. Lang.: Eng. 3671

Interview with playwright Paula Vogel. New York, NY. Lang.: Eng. 3679

Interview with playwright Sheryle Criswell. Lang.: Eng. 3681

Playwright Lillian Garrett-Groag. Los Angeles, CA. Lang.: Eng. 3683

Playwright Yasmina Reza. New York, NY. France. Lang.: Eng. 3684

Interview with playwright and director Tina Landau. Lang.: Eng. 3685

Playwright Douglas Carter Beane. Lang.: Eng. 3688

Novelist and playwright Thulani Davis. Lang.: Eng. 3689

Interview with playwright Kia Corthon. Lang.: Eng. 3696

Analysis of *Les Trois Dumas* by Charles Smith. Lang.: Eng. 3715

The underrepresentation of Hispanics in American arts. Lang.: Eng. 3716

Playwright Amy Freed. Lang.: Eng. 3717

Interview with actor and screenwriter Gene Wilder. Lang.: Eng. 3991

Interview with director and screenwriter Mel Brooks. Lang.: Eng. 3992

Mail interview with David Mamet about *The Spanish Prisoner*. Lang.: Eng. 3993

Interview with screenwriter Scott Frank. Lang.: Eng. 3995

Interview with Darren Aronofsky, writer and director of the film *Pi*. Lang.: Eng. 3996

Interview with Sonja Sohn on writing and acting in the film *Slam*. Lang.: Eng. 3997

Interview with creators of the film *Slam*. Lang.: Eng. 4001

Interview with Saul Williams on writing and acting in the film *Slam*. Lang.: Eng. 4002

David Mamet's success as a screenwriter and film director. Lang.: Eng. 4003

The popularity of crude comedy in recent American films. Lang.: Eng. 4004

Humorous account of screenwriting problems. Lang.: Eng. 4015

Interview with screenwriter and director Richard LaGravenese. Lang.: Eng. 4019

Interview with film-maker Bill Condon. Lang.: Eng. 4021

Analysis of Douglas Heil's screenplay *The First Wife*. Lang.: Eng. 4030

Panel discussion on contemporary musical theatre. New York, NY. Lang.: Eng. 4398

1998. Reference materials.

Index to *Opera* volume 49. UK-England. Europe. Lang.: Eng. 4834

1998. Relation to other fields.

Evaluation of Ph.D. programs in theatre and drama. Canada. UK-England. Lang.: Eng. 716

European fears of American cultural hegemony. Europe. Lang.: Eng. 773

Drama therapy as a tool in the treatment of psychosis. Lang.: Eng. 778

Redefining the 'arts sector'. Lang.: Eng. 781

Factors influencing actors' ability to exit a role. Lang.: Eng. 784

Performativity of informal story-telling in western Iowa. Lang.: Eng. 785

Spiritual practice and drama therapy. Lang.: Eng. 786

Analysis of ritual fire-walking. Lang.: Eng. 789

The University of Louisville's African-American Theatre Program. Louisville, KY. Lang.: Eng. 790

The movement of performing artists between economic sectors. Lang.: Eng. 793

Catharsis and contemporary theatre. Lang.: Eng. 795

Drama therapy, personal narrative, and performance. Lang.: Eng. 797

Therapeutic *nō* theatre for the mentally retarded. Lang.: Eng. 798

Student responses to the autobiography of actress Charlotte Cibber Charke. Lang.: Eng. 800

Theatrical performance compared to multiple personality disorder. Lang.: Eng. 803

Drama therapy and forgiveness. Lang.: Eng. 804

Arts and the public purpose. Lang.: Eng. 805

Locating and defining the 'unincorporated' arts. Lang.: Eng. 806

Tourism and the development of theatre districts. New York, NY. Berlin. Lang.: Eng. 807

The integration of Buddhism in drama therapy. Lang.: Eng. 808

The changing face of Times Square and its effect on the local community. New York, NY. Lang.: Eng. 812

The cultural stereotype of the dancer's body. UK-England. Lang.: Eng. 999

The use of original theatrical productions in the ministry. Lang.: Eng. 3781

Interactions between commercial and not-for-profit theatre. Lang.: Eng. 3785

The state of Shakespearean studies in public education. UK-England. Lang.: Eng. 3786

Arts education as audience-building. Lang.: Eng. 3790

Controversy over Terrence McNally's *Corpus Christi*, Manhattan Theatre Club. New York, NY. Lang.: Eng. 3792

The upcoming Supreme Court hearing on the government's right to impose decency standards on arts grants. Washington, DC. Lang.: Eng. 3793

USA — cont'd

Using *Seinfeld* to contrast New York and Los Angeles. Lang.: Eng. 4082

1998. Research/historiography.
List of current doctoral dissertations in progress. Lang.: Eng. 828
Interview with dance historian Ann Hutchinson Guest on dance notation. Lang.: Eng. 1004

1998. Theory/criticism.
Theatre criticism as it is taught to students. Birmingham, AL. Lang.: Eng. 864
Analysis of choreography by Merce Cunningham. Lang.: Eng. 1340
Winning essay of Critics Institute Competition on *Carriage* by Jerome Hairston. Lang.: Eng. 3838
Chaos theory and its application to theatre and drama theory. Lang.: Eng. 3839
Playwright Sheryle Criswell on criticism of her work. Lang.: Eng. 3840
Theatrical character development in Biblical texts. Lang.: Eng. 3842
Freelance music critic on her career. Lang.: Eng. 4841
Performers and conductors complain about unfair reviews. Lang.: Eng. 4844
Comments on the present state of music criticism. Canada. Lang.: Eng. 4845

1998. Training.
Ballet teacher Waltraud Karkar. Wausau, WI. Lang.: Eng. 1215
Actor training for the character tenor. Lang.: Eng. 4849

1998-1999. Design/technology.
USITT membership directory. Lang.: Eng. 250

1998-1999. Performance/production.
Preview of TCG constituent theatre season. Lang.: Eng. 2654

1998-1998. Institutions.
Alphabetical listing of opera festival performance timetables throughout the United States in summer 1998. Lang.: Eng. 4482

1999. Performance/production.
Preview of the Puppeteers of America Festival. Seattle, WA. Lang.: Eng. 4905

USSR

1800-1965. Plays/librettos/scripts.
The character of Ivan the Terrible. Lang.: Eng. 692

1838-1926. Basic theatrical documents.
English translation of Mejerchol'd's adaptation of *Revizor (The Inspector General)* by Gogol. Russia. Lang.: Eng. 1450

1880-1949. Design/technology.
Avant-garde Russian women artist/designers. Russia. Lang.: Eng. 214

1890-1931. Performance/production.
Mejerchol'd's relationship with Lunačarskij. Lang.: Eng. 2768

1893-1971. Theory/criticism.
Hungarian translation of Pëtr Bogatyrëv's essay on the costume as sign. Lang.: Hun. 871

1916-1935. Relation to other fields.
Theatricalization of court trials in post-revolutionary Russia. Lang.: Eng. 815

1917-1920. Institutions.
Mass festivals of the newly formed Soviet Union. Lang.: Eng. 4113

1920-1931. Performance/production.
Director Mel Gordon on Mejerchol'd's influence. Lang.: Eng. 2765

1922-1929. Training.
Mejerchol'd, actor training, and Trotsky. Lang.: Eng. 3852

1922-1934. Institutions.
Les' Kurbas and Teat'r Berezil. Lang.: Eng. 431

1924. Performance/production.
Analysis of Les' Kurbas' production of Shakespeare's *Macbeth.* Lang.: Eng. 2766

1924-1953. Relation to other fields.
Depiction of Jews in Stalinist Russian film. Lang.: Eng. 4039

1926. Performance/production.
Mejerchol'd's production of Gogol's *Revizor (The Inspector General).* Moscow. Lang.: Eng. 2763

1926-1929. Performance/production.
Aleksand'r Tairov's productions of plays by Eugene O'Neill. Lang.: Eng. 2769

1926-1939. Performance/production.
The development of the character Khlezstakov in Gogol's *Revizor (The Inspector General)* in productions by Mejerchol'd. Lang.: Eng. 2762

1930-1932. Plays/librettos/scripts.
Analysis of Šostakovič's opera *Ledi Makbet Mtsenskogo Uezda.* Lang.: Eng. 4829

1930-1939. Performance/production.
Folk dancing in the Soviet Union during the 1930s. Lang.: Rus. 1242

1935. Performance/production.
Director Harold Clurman's reaction to Mejerchol'd's *Revizor (The Inspector General).* Moscow. Lang.: Eng. 2764

1940. Performance/production.
Mejerchol'd's denial of charges that he was a counter-revolutionary. Moscow. Lang.: Eng. 2767

1941-1948. Institutions.
Polish soldiers' theatre. Buzuluk. London. Lang.: Pol. 432

1947-1990. Plays/librettos/scripts.
Film interpretations of Ophelia in Shakespeare's *Hamlet.* USA. UK-England. Lang.: Eng. 4024

1963-1980. Administration.
Censorship and Russian and East European theatre and film. Europe. Lang.: Eng. 145

1966-1998. Performance/production.
Dancer/choreographer Mikhail Baryshnikov. USA. Lang.: Eng. 1189

1969-1998. Performance/production.
Dancer/choreographer Mikhail Baryshnikov. USA. Lang.: Eng. 1196

1973-1998. Plays/librettos/scripts.
Stephen Mulrine's translation and stage adaptation of *Moscow Stations* by Venedikt Erofeev. UK-England. Lang.: Eng. 3718

Wales

SEE
UK-Wales.

Yugoslavia

1837-1998. Plays/librettos/scripts.
History of Hungarian-language theatre in the Voivodship region. Subotica. Novi Sad. Lang.: Hun. 3720

1972-1997. Plays/librettos/scripts.
Dissident playwright Dušan Kovačevič. Lang.: Eng. 3719

1991-1998. Plays/librettos/scripts.
Contemporary drama of the former Yugoslavia in its political context. Lang.: Ger. 3721

Zimbabwe

1990-1998. Performance/production.
Theatrical rebellion and sociopolitical chaos. Kenya. Lang.: Eng. 687

DOCUMENT AUTHORS INDEX

Aaron, Melissa Diehl. 1598
Abaulin, D. 335
Abbotson, Susan C.W. 3980
Abdel-Latif, Mahmoud Hammam. 228
Abel, Iris. 4428
Abel, Sam. 2656
Abenius, Folke. 4857
Åberg, Tommy. 1226
Abraham, James Thorp. 3366
Abrahamson, Moa. 1048
Abramovskij, G. 4673
Abrams, Steve. 4902, 4903
Abu-Swailem, Abder-Rahim Elayan Moh'd. 1416
Acerboni, Giovanni. 3220
Acheson, James. 4716
Acker, Barbara Frances. 2657
Ackerley, C.J., ed. 733
Acocella, Joan. 1119, 1317
Ács, János. 3187
Adams, Stephen. 4424
Adams, William Jenkins. 4849
Adler-Friess, Aanya. 1342
Adler, Reba Ann. 976
Adshead, Janet. 1009
Aguigah, René. 4894
Ahačič, Draga. 590
Ahlfors, Bengt. 1913
Ahmad, Shafiuddin. 2792
Ahonen, Piia. 916
Åkesson, Birgit. 4087
Al-Sheddi, B. 561
Alarcón, Justo. 2838
Albèra, Philippe. 4768
Alberola, Carles. 1463
Albert, István. 4615, 4616
Albert, Mária. 1224
Aleksandrov, S. 1696
Alexander, Catherine M.S. 2857, 3811
Alexander, Elizabeth. 1480
Alexandrowicz, Conrad. 1344, 1356
Alfred Strasser, transl. 3126
Algra, Jacqueline. 1262
Ali, Mohamed El Shirbini Ahmed. 3837
Alipio, Amy. 4481
Aliverti, Maria Ines. 4190
Aljanskij, Ju.A. 693
Alkema, Hanny. 2200
Allain, Paul. 1684, 2191
Allan, Arlene Leslie. 3179
Allcott, A.M. 616
Allen-Barbour, Kristin. 527
Allen, Howard. 1756
Allis, Peter. 460
Allison, C. 1890
Allison, John. 4475, 4674
Allthorpe-Guyton, Marjorie. 4238, 4264
Alonge, Roberto. 1921, 2157, 3221
Alovert, Nina. 1126, 1127, 1196
Alpár, Ágnes. 356
Alper, Neil O. 793
Alschitz, Jurij. 520
Alsenad, Abedalmutalab Abood. 2152
Altena, Peter. 695
Amble, Lolo. 2367, 3408
Ames, Debra Collins. 3367
Amorosi, Matilde, ed. 2164
Amzoll, Stefan. 1950, 3125, 4791
An, Ben En. 3317
Anadolu-Okur, Nilgun. 3519
Anašina, T. 3318
Andersen, Kurt. 3950
Anderson, David James. 860
Anderson, Jack. 1212
Anderson, Mary Gresham. 774
Anderson, Michael. 4187
Anderson, Simon. 4265
Andreach, Robert J. 3520
Andreeva, T.P. 4897
Andreoli, Annamaria, ed. 3234
Andrews, Rusalyn Herma. 861
Androjna, Irena. 4865
Angelilli, Marco. 873
Angiolillo, Mary Carmel. 528
Ångström, Anna. 963, 4349
Anthony, Elizabeth Mazza. 3071
Anthony, Eugene. 4374
Anzi, Anna. 2858
Appia, Adolphe. 4550
Applebaum, Susan Rae. 2658, 3521
Archer, Kenneth. 1150, 1311
Archer, Stephen M. 28
Arciero, Pam. 4863
Ardolino, Frank. 3522
Ards, Angela. 3523
Arenhill, Jan. 181
Arifdžanov, R. 2233, 4675
Aristophanes. 1438
Arkad'ev, L. 579
Arko, Andrej, transl. 2344
Armati, Angela. 2054
Armstrong, Gordon. 567
Arndt, Roman. 925, 1296
Aronin, Marc J. 1481
Aronofsky, Darren. 3880
Aronov, L.M. 1811
Aronsson, Gunnar Martin. 1722
Aronsson, Katarina. 4467
Aroseva, Olga. 2234
Arrizón, Alicia. 3272
Artamonova, L. 1222
Arthur, Thomas H. 253
Arthurs, Alberta. 775
Artioli, Umberto. 3222
Asai, Susan Miyo. 1350
Ashbrook, William. 4647, 4802
Asselin, Olivier. 3732
Astington, John H. 2859
Atkins, Madeline Smith. 4390
Attisani, Antonio. 847
Atzpodien, Uta. 1832
Auerbach, Leslie Ann. 145
Auletta, Robert. 617
Ault, C. Thomas. 751
Austin, Gayle. 568
Austin, John Lewis. 2659
Avila, Roxana, transl. 952
Avrova, Nina, transl. 1449
Ayckbourn, Alan. 1471
Ayers, Robert. 910
Ayers, Stephen Michael. 391
Aza. 998
Bach, Faith, transl. 1361
Bachrevskij, V. 4676
Backalenick, Irene. 1757
Bäcker, Mats, photo. 1048, 1050, 1053
Backstrom, Ellen Lees. 776
Bacon, Delia. 2860
Baffi, Giulio. 2158
Bai, Ronnie. 1951
Baiardo, Enrico. 2159
Bailey, Brett. 2349
Bain, Keith. 385, 2350
Baisch, Axel. 4404
Bajama Griga, Stefano. 3867
Bajbekov, A. 2235
Baker-White, Robert. 3422
Baker, David J. 4483, 4578, 4712, 4792
Baker, Elliott, ed. 2860
Baker, Evan. 4433, 4453, 4492
Balagna, Olivier. 3126
Balanchine, George. 1166
Balašov, N.I. 2861
Baldwin, Elizabeth. 4121
Balme, Christopher. 618, 1618, 1619
Balogh, A. Fruzsina. 2056
Balogh, Anikó. 4454
Balsamico, Karen K. 1529
Bán, Ferenc, illus. 446, 449
Bán, Zoltán András. 2057, 2058
Bank, Rosemarie. 777
Bank, Rosemarie K. 157
Banks, Carol P. 3524
Bannerman, Eugen. 4085
Banoun, Bernard, transl. 4412, 4419

Banu, Georges. 3817
Baranova, T.V. 756
Barba, Eugenio. 376, 1230
Barbina, Alfred, ed. 3824
Barbina, Alfredo. 3223, 3224, 3225
Barbina, Alfredo, ed. 1445
Barbour, David. 229, 230, 254, 255, 256, 257, 258, 1530, 1531, 1532, 1533, 1534, 1535, 1536, 1537, 1538, 1539, 1540, 1541, 1542, 1543, 1544, 1545, 1546, 1556, 4328, 4329, 4330, 4331, 4332, 4333, 4334, 4335, 4350, 4440
Barbour, Kathryn. 2862
Barbour, Kristin Allen. 1520
Barda, Clive. 4713
Barfoot, C.C. 2863
Barhour, David. 1547
Barilier, Etienne. 4793
Barker, Peter. 4235
Barkman, Iris G. 2864
Barlow, Clarence. 4305
Barlow, Judith E. 3525
Barnaby, Andrew. 2865
Barnes-McLain, Noreen. 619
Barnes, Clive. 1167
Barnett, Dennis Carl. 3719
Barranger, Milly S. 2590
Barrie, Tom, adapt. 1472
Barroll, Leeds. 3745, 4200
Bartalini, Paola. 3226
Bartel, Paul. 3881
Bartha, Anikó. 4877
Bartlett, Neil. 1277
Barto, Dan. 3526
Bartolovich, Crystal. 2866
Baruth, Philip E. 1891
Baruth, Philip E., ed. 517, 800, 1891, 1896, 1901, 1904, 1906, 1908, 2891
Barzantny, Tamara. 1952
Bashynzhagian, Natella. 2236
Bassano, Serena. 543
Batasova, M. 213
Bates, Mark. 2660, 2661
Bauer, Gerald M. 4210
Baum, Rob K. 3423
Baumrin, Seth. 1886
Baxter, Paul Sandvold. 3292
Bazzocchi, Marco Antonio. 3227
Beach, Cecilia. 3072
Beach, Vincent Woodrow, Jr. 2867
Beachum, Richard. 617
Beale, Geoff. 4193
Beard, John. 4005
Beaufort, Philippe. 1835
Beaufoy, Simon. 3879
Beck, Dennis Charles. 2852
Becker, Becky K. 620
Beckett, Samuel. 733
Beckett, Walter. 3196
Beddows, Joël. 2793
Bednjakova, M. 2237
Beene, Geoffrey. 4037
Beer, Joseph Michael. 3781
Begley, Varun. 4006
Béhague, Emmanuel. 734
Behrendt, Eva. 4111
Behrendt, Patricia Flanagan. 3424
Békés, Pál. 4375
Belbel, Sergi, transl. 1428
Belford, Barbara. 3425
Belitska-Scholtz, Hedvig. 392
Bell, Deborah. 259, 260
Bell, John. 3782, 4878
Bell, Karen. 1576, 2794, 4389
Bellour, Helene. 4164
Belokopytov, A.A. 2238
Belzil, Patricia. 1836, 1867, 3939, 3963
Ben-Itzak, Paul. 1168
Ben'jaš, R., ed. 2255
Bénard, Johanne. 4161
Benardo, Margot L. 3783
Benda, Iván. 2101
Benda, Iván, photo. 2097, 2100, 2106, 2112, 2118
Bene, Carmelo. 544
Benecke, Patricia. 1953, 2591
Benn, Danielle. 4278
Bennahum, Ninotchka Devorah. 922
Bennett, Susan. 146, 3426, 3931, 4761
Bentley, Eric. 3142
Bentoglio, Alberto, ed. 2173
Bérczes, László. 377, 1697, 2059, 2060, 2061, 2062
Berek, Peter. 2868
Berezin, Mabel. 545
Berezkin, V. 1523
Berg, Alban. 4412
Berg, Allison. 3527
Berg, Eliana Goulart. 3267
Berg, Fredric. 3427
Berg, James Emmanuel. 2869
Bergel, Ralph. 737
Bergen, Jim van. 261
Berger, Harry, Jr. 2870
Berger, Jürgen. 1620
Bergeron, David M. 4225
Bergeron, Serge. 2795, 3808
Berggren, Klara. 898
Berglund, Kia. 2012
Bergman, Beth. 4714, 4741
Bergman, Beth, photo. 4407
Bergmane, Astra. 558
Bergmann, Beth. 4713
Bergmann, Ursula A. 2662
Bergström, Gunnel. 4564, 4697, 4698
Berlin, Normand. 3528
Berlin, Zeke. 368
Berlioz, Hector. 4565
Berman, Sabina. 1447
Bernard, Lauren S. 2663
Bernhard, Thomas. 1407
Bernhardt, Rüdiger. 3127
Bernheimer, Martin. 4840
Bernstein, Samuel J. 3529
Bernstein, Seymour. 1892
Berry, Cicely. 2344
Berry, Edward. 3740
Berry, Herbert. 1798
Bershatsky, Charles. 621
Berson, Misha. 3530, 3531, 3784
Berst, Charles A. 3832
Bertman, D. 4468
Bertolone, Paola. 3228
Besidžev, M. 2239
Bevan, Anthony. 4369
Bevington, David. 2871, 4201, 4202
Bevington, David, ed. 4196, 4197, 4198, 4200, 4201, 4202, 4203, 4204, 4205, 4206, 4207, 4208, 4212, 4215
Bezeljanskij, Ju. 2240
Bezencon, Hélène. 1469
Bibič, Polde. 591
Bierke, Astrid. 210
Bilby, Monika. 2872
Bílková, Marie. 172
Bindig, Susan Frances. 1069
Bini, Daniela. 3229
Binning, Sadhu. 1577
Bird, Robert R. 3532
Bíró, Béla. 2063
Bíró, Yvette. 1278
Bishop, Cynthia Ann. 622
Bishop, John. 2873
Bishop, Thomas Geoffrey. 2874
Bishop, Tom. 4203
Bixler, Jacqueline E. 3273
Bjarke, Kim. 1887
Bjerre, Ole. 1257
Björkstén, Ingmar. 2369
Black, Leo. 4759
Black, Stephen A. 3533, 3534
Blackadder, Neil. 1402, 1758
Blain, Lynda Carol. 393
Blair, Steven. 4502
Blake, Leslie (Hoban). 3901
Blanc, Michel, adapt. 1473
Blankemeyer, Silke. 6, 1279, 4286, 4455, 4579, 4580
Blaskó, Borbála. 1341
Blend, A., ed. 1144
Bleu, Loup. 4912
Blier, Steven. 4376, 4566
Blim, John Miles. 2875
Bloch, Beverle Rochelle. 3535
Blokdijk, Tom. 562
Blomquist, Kurt. 1676
Bloom, Arthur W. 394
Bloom, J. 3868
Bloom, Thomas Alan. 262
Bloomquist, Jane McCarthy. 623
Blumberg, Marcia. 2351, 4243
Blumenthal, Eileen. 1680
Blumer, Arnold. 3128
Bly, Mary. 1599
Blythe, Keith. 263
Boan, Devon. 3536
Bobkova, Hana. 1954, 3825
Bódis, Mária. 2064
Bodó, A. Ottó. 2065
Boecking, Ulrike. 3860
Boepple, Leanne. 264, 265, 293, 330, 451, 4049, 4336, 4342
Bogatirjov, Pjotr. 871
Bogatyreva, M. 1698
Bogdanov, G. 1242
Bogdanovich, Peter. 3897
Bőgel, József. 193, 357
Boglačev, S. 1128
Bohlin, Peter. 899
Böhnisch, Siemke. 841
Boiron, Chantal. 3073
Boldt-Irons, Leslie Anne. 1922
Boling, Ronald Jackson. 2876
Boltwood, Scott. 3197
Bomberger, E. Douglas. 4581
Bonin, Laure. 1424
Bónis, Ferenc. 4617
Boon, Richard. 541, 3428
Boon, Richard, ed. 496, 541, 614, 2772, 2808, 3048, 3271, 3286, 3365
Boorsma, Miranda. 17
Bordelon, Suzanne. 862
Bordwell, Marilyn. 1318
Borello, Christine. 2796, 4232
Borg, Dominica Mary. 2877
Borgstrom, Henrik Carl. 3050
Bornhofen, Patricia. 276
Boros, Attila. 4618
Boschán, Daisy, et al., ed. 194
Bose, Rana. 498, 1409
Bosisio, Paolo, ed. 694
Bosseur, Jean-Yves. 4308
Bóta, Gábor. 1668
Bots, Pieter. 1678
Bott, Robin Luana. 2878
Bottoms, Stephen J. 395, 2651
Bou, d'Eugeni, transl. 1407
Boudreault, Eric. 3074
Bouet, Jeanne. 1923
Boulez, Pierre. 4567
Boutorabi, Afsaneh. 2664

Bowen, Christopher. 1120
Bowers, Faubion. 1362
Bowers, Faubion, transl. 1360
Bowers, Rick. 2879
Bowman, Michael S. 624
Bowman, Ruth Laurion. 4134
Boyle, Eloise M. 3319
Bradby, David. 3075
Bradley, Eddie Paul, Jr. 1482
Bradshaw, Charles Randall. 625
Braibish Scott, Laura Christine. 2665
Braid, Donald. 772
Brailow, David G. 2666
Bramley, Ian. 1156, 4377
Brandenburg, Detlef. 1621, 1818, 1955, 4291, 4293, 4347, 4456, 4527, 4582, 4583, 4584
Brandon, James R. 1367
Brandstetter, Gabrielle. 1280
Brandt, Ellen. 347, 1986
Brandtner, Andreas, ed. 2347
Branger, Jean-Christophe. 4778
Brault, Pascale-Anne. 3076
Brazil, Tom, photo. 1327, 1336, 4304
Brecht, Bertolt. 836, 1437
Breier, René. 2880
Breight, Curtis Charles. 1893
Bren, Frank. 3929
Brenk, Tomaž. 4288
Brenna, Dwayne. 2592
Brèque, Jean-Michel. 4779
Breznik, Maja. 521
Brise, Eva. 600
Bristol, Michael D. 863
Brizzell, Cindy. 29, 617
Brock, David Carl. 30
Brockbank, J. Philip. 1873
Brockett, Oscar G. 827
Brody, Jeb. 3902
Broh, Michael. 266
Bromels, John E. 3838
Brook, Peter. 3833
Brook, Vincent. 4068
Brooks, Douglas Alan. 2881
Brooks, Mel. 3898
Brooks, Robert E. 3839
Brousseau, Elaine. 2797
Brovik, Ingela. 1723
Brown, Carol. 999
Brown, Eric C. 2882, 2883
Brown, John Russell. 485, 2770
Brown, John Russell, ed. 697
Brown, Kenneth. 617
Brown, Pamela Allen. 2884
Brown, Richard Danson. 2885
Brown, Susan. 2593
Brownell, Catherine. 1339
Browning, Nadine. 778
Bruch, Debra Lynn. 3537
Bruls, Willem. 3368
Brun, Fritz Constantin. 692
Bryden, Mary. 3077, 3198
Bryden, Mary, ed. 3194, 3195, 3196, 3198, 3201, 3204, 3208, 3215, 3250, 3509, 3865, 4305, 4306, 4308, 4309, 4768, 4769, 4772, 4776, 4777
Bryden, Mary, transl. 4308, 4768, 4769
Bryden, Ronald. 3429
Bucci, Moreno. 199
Buchanan, J.R. 3981
Buchau, Stephanie von. 4406, 4538, 4841
Bucher, John Joseph. 977
Buckland, Theresa. 978
Buckridge, Patrick. 3746
Budor, Dominique. 3230
Buedel, Barbara. 2360
Bukin, A. 1231
Bukowski, Dariusz, transl. 1448
Bułat, Mirosława. 2212
Buller, Jeffrey L. 4585
Bulmer, Alex. 1837
Burbank, Carol Elizabeth. 396
Burckhardt, Barbara. 738, 1379, 1390, 1622, 1623, 1956, 1957, 1958, 1959, 3129, 3130, 3131, 3132, 4356
Burgess, Geoffrey. 4780
Burgoyne, Lynda. 833, 3759
Burian, Jarka M. 1517
Burkett, Ronnie. 4917
Burkhardt, Peter. 176
Burkman, Katherine H. 3430
Burkov, G. 2241
Burningham, Bruce. 3830
Burroughs, Catherine Beauregard. 2886
Burt, Ramsay. 1070, 1258
Burtner, Dave. 278
Burton, David G. 3369
Burvill, Tom. 1567, 1815
Busch, April. 267
Busk, Yvonne. 2368
Butcher, Rosemary. 979
Butler, Martin. 4204
Butterworth, Philip. 4122
Bykov, L.,. 163
Byrd, Robert E., Jr. 3538
Bystrickaja, É. 2242
Byun, Chang-Ku. 3539
Cade, Francis. 605
Cadieux, Anne-Marie. 1838
Cady, Pamela. 626
Calderón, Luis Antonio. 3274
Caldwell, Carolyn E. 1396
Calhoun, John. 3899, 3900, 3903, 3904, 3905, 3906, 3907, 3908, 3909, 3910, 3911, 3912, 3913, 3914, 3915, 4050, 4051, 4052, 4053, 4054
Callaghan, David. 371
Callaghan, David Scott. 690
Callens, Johan. 1739, 1828, 2201, 2667, 2789, 3180, 3199, 3278, 3431, 3432, 3433, 3434, 3540, 3541, 3542, 3543, 3544, 3545, 3546, 3547, 3548, 3549, 3550, 3551, 3552, 3553, 3554, 3555, 3556, 3798, 4007, 4008
Callens, Johan, ed. 3542, 3557
Calobanova, V. 1129, 4677
Cameron, Rebecca, ed. 3060
Camilo, Juan. 2838
Camp, André, transl. 1464
Campbell, Julie. 2594
Campbell, Mary Schmidt. 397
Campbell, Patrick. 4244, 4261
Campos, Rémy. 4409
Campos, Rémy, ed. 4415, 4418
Canepa, Alessandro. 993
Canfield, J. Douglas. 2887
Canning, Charlotte. 4135
Canning, Hugh. 4706
Cantara, Jamie Smith. 1759
Capo, Kay Ellen. 627
Cappa, Felice, ed. 702
Caprara, Valerio. 546
Car, Evgen. 1454
Carandell, Christían, transl. 1438
Caras, Steven, photo. 987
Caravaglia, Tom, photo. 1331, 4092
Cardullo, Bert. 3558
Carlberg Kriig, Anne. 1221
Carlson, Harry G. 1724
Carlson, Marla. 1960
Carlson, Marvin. 31, 1924, 2160, 2161, 2210, 3774, 4586
Carlson, Marvin, transl. 1928, 2182, 2187, 2188
Carlsson, Hasse. 3133
Carlsson, Lars-Åke. 171
Carlyon, David. 779
Carp, Stefanie. 1961
Carpenter, Mark Peter. 4009
Carpenter, Sarah. 4194
Carroll, John F. 463
Carson, Rebecca. 3559
Carter, Alexandra. 1259
Carter, Alexandra, ed. 913, 928, 932, 956, 972, 978, 980, 982, 986, 989, 996, 1001, 1003, 1005, 1006, 1009, 1010, 1011, 1013, 1014, 1028, 1070, 1072, 1158, 1162, 1186, 1200, 1201, 1317, 1321, 1323
Carter, Cassie Elaine. 4249
Carter, Gary. 1307
Carter, Marva Griffin. 4378
Cartwright, John. 2790, 3051
Cartwright, Kent. 2888
Casas, Joan, transl. 1449, 3241
Cascetta, Annamaria. 3200
Casciero, Thomas. 628
Case, Sue-Ellen. 3134
Casey, Kevin, photo. 1056
Cashill, Robert. 3855, 3916, 3917, 4055
Cashman, Cheryl. 4117
Casona, Alejandro. 1464
Castelli, Silvia. 3726
Castiglioni, Elisabetta. 4648
Castri, Massimo. 2162
Caton, Shaun. 4241
Caudill, Helen Sue. 2889
Cavander, Kenneth. 3560
Cave, Richard Allen. 2153
Cavnar, Matt. 268
Čečetin, A. 1699
Čečetin, A.I. 381
Čechov, Anton Pavlovič. 1449
Čechova, O. 2243
Cederberg, Jörgen. 2012
Čegodar', N.I. 2193
Cenner, Mihály. 4432
Cerasano, S.P. 1805, 1894
Černobrivkina, T. 1130
Cervantes, Xavier. 4545
Chach, Maryann. 398
Chailly, Riccardo. 4551
Chałupnik, Agata. 3301
Chamberlain, Frank. 606
Chambers, David. 2668, 2762
Chambers, David, transl. 1450
Chan, Sau Y. 4313
Chandler, David. 2890
Chaney, Joseph. 2891
Chang, Carlisle. 4174
Chang, Ivy I-Chu. 767
Channer, Lisa. 617
Chansky, Dorothy. 158, 159
Charles, Peter. 2595, 2596, 2597, 2598, 2599
Charnes, Linda. 2892
Charney, Mark. 864
Chartrand, Harry Hillman. 780
Chatterjee, Sudipto. 1833, 2151, 3191
Chaudhary, Sheela Devi. 3192
Chaudhuri, Una. 1925
Chazanov, G. 4277
Cheatle, Esther. 4918
Chen, Wendi. 1874
Chen, Zidu. 511
Cheng, Kipp. 2669
Cheng, Meiling. 4262
Cherbo, Joni Maya. 781, 806, 3785
Chiba, Yoko. 3435
Chin, Daryl. 3923, 4250
Chirico, Miriam Madeleine. 3052
Chitrik, A.A. 823
Chitrik, A.A., ed. 1029

Chlebnikova, M. 4351
Chmeleva, N. 4437
Chojka, Joanna. 2213, 2214, 4156
Cholij, Irena. 1895
Cholodova, G. 2244
Chothia, Jean. 3561
Chotjewitz-Häfner, Renate. 3231
Christopher, Tracy Elizabeth. 3078
Chrustaleva, O. 1169
Ciechowicz, Jan. 3302
Ciechowicz, Jan, ed. 2215
Cindrič, Alojz, ed. 521
Cipollone, Pierpaola. 1674
Cirella, Anne Violette. 3288
Cisarž, Ja. 2771
Ciszkewycz, Ihor. 431
Citroen, Liesbeth. 566
Citron, Atay. 4220
Citron, Paula. 1067
Claesson, Christina. 2369
Clark, Amy C. 3181
Clark, Caryl. 4446
Clark, Danielle. 2893
Clark, Katerina. 2763
Clark, Mike. 200, 201, 1802, 4434, 4435
Clark, Phyllis. 3742
Clarke, George Elliot. 4413
Clarke, Sue. 2600
Clason, Mathias. 4851, 4853
Clay, Simone Monnier. 4781
Cleary, Beth. 4879
Clemens, Claus. 1962
Clurman, Harold. 2764
Coad, Luman. 4919
Cocuzza, Ginnine. 1319
Codde, Philippe. 3562
Cody, Gabrielle. 893, 1926
Coe, Tony. 2607
Coelho, Victor Anand. 4803
Coen, Stephanie. 2670
Coetzee, Yvette. 4913
Coeyman, Barbara. 4493
Coggan, Catherine. 1760
Cohn, Ruby. 3563
Colas, Damien, ed. 4421
Colby, Robert William. 782
Cole, Malcolm S. 4528
Coleman, Emily. 4715, 4842
Coleman, Stephen DuBois. 2671, 3564
Coleman, Wendy. 783
Colleran, Jeanne Marie. 3361
Colleran, Jeanne, ed. 529, 535, 846, 870, 1815, 1925, 2351, 2797, 3212, 3572, 3582, 3629, 3635, 4878
Collier, Susanne. 2894
Collins, Marla del. 3565
Colwin, Thomas Leonard. 1548
Combač, Borut. 4866
Cometta, Sandro. 4503, 4504
Concannon, Kevin Christopher. 4151
Conceison, Claire. 2842
Condé, Gérard. 4568, 4782
Condé, Gérard, ed. 4412, 4416, 4417
Condee, William F. 629
Condee, William Faricy. 464
Condon, Bill. 3882
Conley, Francine Heather. 1607
Connelly, Christopher Brian. 3566
Connolly, Jon Jerome. 2895
Connors, Thomas. 2672
Consoli, Virginia. 3079
Cook, Hardy Merrill, III. 4064
Cook, Jonathan Paul. 1888
Cooney, Ray. 1473
Cooper, Susan. 1320
Copeland, Philip Larue. 4379
Copeland, Roger. 1013, 1340
Copelin, David. 617
Copp, Karen Hadley. 32
Cordner, Michael. 2601
Cornell, Christine. 2896
Corti, Lillian. 3567
Corum, Richard. 2897
Cosgrove, James Daniel. 3053
Costas, photo. 1177
Costaz, Gilles. 3760
Costello, Charles, ed. 3060
Costi, Angela. 1406
Cote, John Louis. 3568
Coulbois, Jean-Claude. 1839
Court, Paul. 434
Cousin, Geraldine. 1624, 3436
Cowgill, Rachel. 4546
Cox, Catherine S. 2898
Cox, John D. 2899
Craig, Alexander. 2798
Craig, Hugh. 4205
Craik, Kevin Jay. 3080
Crane, Mary Thomas. 2900
Crawford, David Wright. 3569
Crawford, Fred D., ed. 3437
Creed, Victoria Schanck. 3081
Crémieux, Hector. 4418
Cremona, Vicki Ann. 4217
Crespy, David Allison. 3570
Crisson, James Edward. 630
Cristiano, Michael. 784
Criswell, Sheryle. 1483, 3840
Croce, Arlene. 980
Croce, Marcella. 4125
Crocker, Nicole Amanda. 4132
Croner, Claes. 964
Croydon, Margaret. 4569
Crutchfield, Will. 4587, 4649
Csák, P. Judit. 4619, 4666
Csáki, Judit. 358, 2066, 2067, 2068, 2069, 4358
Csalló, Erzsébet, biblio. 698
Cserje, Zsuzsa. 2070
Csillag, Pál, photo. 1075
Csutkai, Csaba, photo. 2116, 2118, 2124, 2141
Cummings, Scott T. 399, 3571, 3799
Cunningham, Frank R. 2673
Cunningham, Karen. 3786
Cunningham, Rebecca. 214
Cupid, John, intro. 4160
Custer, Marianne. 177
Cutler, Anna. 818
Čuvakov, V.N.,. 3320
Cyphert, Dale. 785
Cyr, Douglas Philip. 786
D'Ambrosio, Carla. 1829
D'Amico, Alessandro. 452, 3232
D'Amico, Sivio. 3233
d'Anna, Claude. 1424
D'Annunzio, Gabriele. 3234
D'Aponte, Mimi Gisolfi, transl. 3261
D'jakonov, V. 2245, 2246
D'jakonov, V., ed. 2315
D'Orazi, Maria Pia. 874
D'Orazi, Maria Pia, transl. 705
Da Costa Holton, Kimberly. 962
da Vinci Nichols, Nina. 2901, 3235
Daiber, Hans. 739
Daiken, Melanie. 3201
Dajnjak, A.A. 1131
Dal', E., ed. 2247
Dal', O. 2247
Dallet, Athenaide. 3800
Dalos, László. 4620
Dalton, Jennifer. 4045
Daly, Ann. 981
Damiani, Bruno M. 3370
Damm, Anja. 838, 1889
Daniels, Don. 1030, 1170, 1308
Daniels, Kelly Dawn. 1840
Daniels, Mary Blythe. 2357
Daniels, Rebecca. 2674
Danielsen, Allan. 3862
Danilova, L.S. 2248
Dannenhauer, Mark. 4864
Darvay Nagy, Adrienne. 333, 378, 1669
Dasgupta, Gautam. 2163
Daugenti, Carl. 1199
Davenport, Edwin. 2902
David, Gilbert. 1841, 1842, 2823, 3733
Davidsen, Mette Hvid. 723
Davidson, Adam. 3883
Davidson, Audrey Ekdahl. 4292, 4294
Davidson, Clifford. 4292
Davidson, Erika. 4713
Davis, C.B. 4136
Davis, Jim. 147
Davis, Peter A. 33
Davis, Tracy C. 156, 768, 3438, 3572
Davison, Peter. 4716
Dawson, Anthony B. 3801
Day, Moira Jean. 2799
De Backer, Paul, photo. 1065
de Blois, Marco. 499
De Chirico, Giorgio. 202
De Curtis, Liliana, ed. 2164
De Fino, Dean. 2903
de Gay, Jane. 3439, 4065
De Gruchy Cook, Patricia Margaret Anne. 500
de Haan, Christopher. 617, 2765
de Lappe, Gemze. 4380
De Lucis, Fulvio. 2159
De Monticelli, Roberto. 547
de Sagarra, Josep M., transl. 1420, 1421, 1422
De Shields, André. 631
de Stains, Ian. 2192
De, Esha Niyogi. 2904
Deans, Jill R. 691
DeBaun, Linda Louise. 3573
Debusscher, Gilbert. 3552
DeCarlo, Tessa. 4484
DeCock, Jean. 1608
Decroisette, Françoise. 3236
Del Campo, Carmen Alicia. 510
Del Cielo, Barbara, ed . 548
Del Corno, Dario. 3182
Delaney, Kate, ed. 3544
Delano, Pablo. 4165
Delgado, Manuel. 3371
Delibes, Léo. 4415
Della Seta, Fabrizio. 4835
Dellamora, Richard. 4552
Dellamora, Richard, ed. 4411, 4552, 4763, 4766, 4771, 4786, 4787, 4796, 4797, 4803, 4813, 4822, 4823, 4828
Demarcy, Richard. 4287
Demidova, A. 2249
Dempster, Elizabeth. 1321
Denby, David. 3878
Denisenko, G. 2325
Denison, Patricia Doreen. 3440
Denman, Stan C. 787
Dennis, Robert J. 4650
DePaula, Paulo Spurgeon. 3574
Déprats, Jean-Michel. 3082
Desai, R.W. 2905
Desclot, Miquel, transl. 1442
Desjatov, V.V. 3321
Desmond, Jane C. 1003
Dessay, Natalie. 4570
Dessen, Alan C. 2602
Detje, Robin. 1625, 1963, 3729
Detmer, Anne Elizabeth. 2906
Detsi, Zoe. 3575
Deuter, Ulrich. 1626, 1627, 1964

Devlin-Glass, Frances. 2773
Devlin, Joseph. 3202
Dharwadker, Aparna. 2907, 3193
Di Bernardi, Vito. 549, 915
Di Gaetani, John Louis. 607, 2603
Di Giulio, Maria. 2250
Di Nocera, Antonella. 2165, 2166
Diamond, Catherine. 3778
Diamond, Emma. 1322
Diamond, Pamela Hurley. 1056
Dickey, Jerry Richard. 3362
Dickey, Johanna Susan. 3576
Dickinson, Joan. 4263
Dickson, Malcolm. 4248
Dickson, Peter W. 3812
Dieckmann, Friedrich. 1965
Diehl, Huston. 2908
Dienes, Gedeon. 935
Dierks, Lynn. 1403
Dietschreit, Frank. 1628
Diggans, Elizabeth, illus. 4376
Dill, Charles. 4783
Dillon, Janette. 1799
DiMaggio, Paul. 39
Dineen, Jennifer L. 1397
Díner, Tamás, photo. 1101
Diner, Tamás, photo. 1097
Diop, Oumar Cherif. 3977
Diprima, Jay T. 3841
Disch, Matthias. 1629
Djagileva, E.V. 1132
Dmitriev, L.A. 4073
Dmitrieva, A. 2251
Dobrochotov, A.A. 164
Dobson, Julia. 3083
Dobson, Teresa. 2800
Dodd, William. 2909
Dodds, Sherril. 969, 1309
Dodson, Mary Lynn. 3982
Doherty, Mary Louise. 788
Dokučaeva, A. 4534
Dolina, Larisa. 4366
Doloff, Steven. 2910
Domina, Lynn. 3577
Dömötör, Adrienne. 2071, 2072
Doré, Marc. 1578
Dorff, Linda. 2675
Dorfmüller, Ingo. 1380
Dorogi, Katalin. 936
Doroni, Stefano. 3237
Doronina, T. 2252, 2253, 2254
Doronina, T.V. 2255
Dörr, Fritz. 3764
Dössel, Christine. 348, 1966
Dotto, Giancarlo. 2167
Douglas, James B. 1579, 1580, 1843
Douglas, Paul. 1022
Dowd, Garin V. 3084
Dowie, John. 1474
Downey, Katherine Brown. 3441
Downward, Lisa, transl. 3253
Doyle, Dennis Michael. 632
Doyle, Maria-Elena. 3511
Draper, Ellen Piper Myer. 608
Dresen, Adolf. 3135
Drewniak, Łukasz. 2198
Driscoll, F. Paul. 4704, 4717, 4718, 4719, 4720
Driver, Senta. 1157
Drobyševa, E. 2256
Drobyševa, N. 2256
Drukman, Steven. 2676, 2677, 3578
Druskin, M., ed. 4830
Du Toit, Petrus Jacobus. 2352
Duany, Jorge. 755
Dubrovskij, V. 1700
Duchscherer, Brian. 4886
Duckett, Josie W. 3924
Duclow, Geraldine. 400
Duffy, Brian. 3085
Dufva, Annelie. 3809
Dugan, Olga. 3579
Duggan, Robert. 269, 270
Dungate, Rod. 388, 3442
Dunham, Richard E. 4441
Duniec, Krystyna. 2216
Dunning, Jennifer. 1246
Dunton, Chris. 3282
Durland, Steven. 4251
Durov, L. 2257
Dürr, Carola. 1701
Dusa, Gábor, photo. 948
Dutronc, Jean-Louis. 4505
Dutton, Richard. 2911
Duval, Elaine Isolyn. 3580
Duvall, Matthew Evan. 2912
Dyer, Richard. 982
Dženikaeva, L. 4272
Eagleton, Julie. 766
Earnest, Steve. 1353
Eaton, Jonathan. 4588
Eaton, Sara. 2913
Eaves, Gregory N. 3203
Ebeling, Robert. 185
Eberhart, Christine. 2779
Ebrahim, Haseenah. 3968
Eccles, Christine. 4370
Eckert, Nora. 4589
Edney, David. 3289
Edström, Per Simon. 436, 458, 1803, 4497
Edwards, Barry. 609
Edwards, Emily D. 789
Edwards, Paul. 4829
Edwards, Paul A. 2678
Effiong, Philip Uko. 3581
Egan, Gabriel. 1806
Egea, Octavi. 1465
Ehrnrooth, Albert. 2604
Eidsvik, Charles. 878
Eifert, János, photo. 937
Eisen, Kurt. 4078
Eisenberg, Alan. 4318
Ekberg, Emil. 597
Elagin, Ju. 2258
Elam, Harry, Jr. 3582
Elbers, Johan. 4713
Elder, J.D. 4166
Elia, Susan. 271
Elliott, Beverly Fritsch. 3293
Ellis, Jim. 4822
Ellis, Kathi E.B. 790
Ellis, Morris Ray. 272
Elton, Ben. 1475
Elwell, Jeffery Scott. 4381
Emeljanow, Victor. 147, 231
Engdahl, Horace. 1299
Enge, Herbert. 1630
Engel, Gert. 4892
Engelander, Rudy. 522
Engelhardt, Barbara. 1381, 1385, 1609, 1631, 1632, 1927, 3086
Engle, Ron, ed. 28, 31, 33, 42, 129, 157, 428, 653, 665, 685, 802, 810, 827, 829, 1790, 3637, 3647, 4112, 4144, 4384
English, Cheryl. 278
Englund, Claes. 2369
Ente Teatrale Italiano. 700
Eörsi, István. 3187
Eősze, László. 4298, 4651, 4652
Epifanova, S. 2259
Epp, Garrett P.J. 2914
Epperson, Jim. 3583
Epstein, Lisa Jo. 529, 1610
Erdély, Mátyás, photo. 2085
Eremeeva, A.N. 757
Erickson, Jon. 3584
Eriksson, Torbjörn. 4472, 4590, 4591, 4653, 4699, 4821
Erne, Lukas. 2915
Espinosa Carbonel, Joaquín. 2358
Essif, Les. 3087
Essig, Linda. 4337
Esslin, Martin. 3443
Eström, Per Simon. 519
Evans, Don. 3585
Evans, Nicola. 3983
Evans, T.F. 3444
Evans, Tracy Ann. 633
Evarts, William Johnson. 1484
Everding, Robert G. 3445
Everett, Wendy. 3932
Evola, Dario. 3823
Ewbank, Inga-Stina. 2370
Ewerbeck, Niels. 1967
Exinger, Peter. 387
Eyoh, Dickson. 4034
Fábián, József, photo. 4360
Fábry, Péter, photo. 2103
Fadeeva, I.N. 1702
Faganel, Jože. 2345
Fajnštejn, F. 4872
Fajt, Ju.A., ed. 3976
Falvay, Károly. 937
Fangauf, Henning. 3136
Fano, Nicola. 4275
Farjeon, Annabel. 1158
Farkas, Virág. 2147
Farrell, John Edward. 2679
Farrell, Joseph. 3238
Farrelly, Mark. 4395
Feeley, Bruce R., photo. 1195
Fei, Faye C. 2843
Feigenbaum, Harvey B. 3853
Feinberg, Anat. 3137
Fel'dman, O.M., ed. 2296
Feldman, Sharon. 598, 3775
Feliciana, Rita. 1260
Feller, Elisabeth. 1391, 4592
Fenn, Jeffrey William. 3586
Fenn, Robert Denzel. 2916
Fensham, Rachel. 1816
Feola, Maryann. 2917
Féral, Josette. 1928, 1929, 2260
Fernandez, Kristina. 1171
Ferre, Craig. 4221
Ferris, Lesley. 634
Fiebach, Joachim. 865, 1633
Fiebach, Joachim, ed. 865
Fiedler, Manfred. 453
Filatov, L. 163
Filatov, L.A. 758
Filewod, Alan. 1581
Filipčič, Emil. 1455
Filippov, G.V., ed. 3340
Findlay, Bill. 3513
Findlay, J.M. 2217
Finger, Evelyn. 740
Fink, Edward J. 4069
Finlayson, Rebecca Scott. 3814
Finney, James Reed. 2680
Finter, Helga. 2168, 3818
Fischer-Lichte, Erika. 530
Fischer, Gerhard. 4391
Fischlin, Daniel. 4552, 4823
Fischlin, Daniel, ed. 4411, 4552, 4763, 4766, 4771, 4786, 4787, 4796, 4797, 4803, 4813, 4822, 4823, 4828
Fisher, Mark. 884
Fishkin, Amy Lynne. 3842
Fiske, Jeffrey Thomas. 569
Fitzgerald, Brian. 3587
Flaszen, Ludwik. 1685

Flatow, Sheryl. 4382
Fleischer, Mary Rita. 1268
Fleissner, Robert F. 3728
Fleming, Brent Leonard. 23
Fleming, Bruce. 1159
Flenga, Vassiliki. 3088
Fletcher, Reagan. 401
Flimm, Jürgen. 1968
Flinois, Pierre. 4506, 4507, 4508, 4509
Flisar, Evald. 1456
Flores, Stephan Paul. 2918
Floyd-Wilson, Mary. 2919
Flügel, J., photo. 1026
Fo, Dario. 1440, 1441
Fodor, Géza, intro. 836, 841, 842, 871
Foht, N. 2261
Földi, Imre, photo. 4638
Folkenflik, Robert. 1896
Fontcuberta, Joan, transl. 1437
Forbes, Jeff. 273
Fordyce, William. 3588
Foreman, Richard. 2681
Forest-Hill, Lynn. 2920
Forgách, András. 1930, 2073, 2074, 3188, 3189
Forgács, Miklós. 2075
Formasa, Felio, transl. 1449
Formosa, Clara, transl. 1437
Formosa, Feliu, transl. 1408, 1437
Fornes, Maria Irene. 617, 3589
Forrai, Éva. 970, 1238
Forsberg, Sofia, photo. 602
Fortier, Mark. 830
Fortner, Michael. 402
Foster, Susan Leigh. 1010
Fotheringham, Richard. 2
Fouquet, Ludovic. 346, 1931, 3734
Fournier, Edith. 4769
Fox, Ann Margaret. 3590
Fradkina, E. 2262
Fraison, Laurent. 4571
Fraleigh, Sondra. 996
Francis, Penny. 4898
Frank, Scott. 3884
Franke, Eckhard. 1969
Franses, Philip Hans. 154
Fransson, Emma. 2371, 2372, 3409
Frasca, Richard A., transl. 1345
Frazier, Paul M. 3591
Fredricks, Daniel David. 3747
Free, Rebecca. 531
Freeberg, Debra L. 2373, 2374
Freed, Donald. 3446
Freeman, John. 851
Freeman, John W. 4654
Freeman, Sandra. 3089
Freeman, Sara. 3090
French, Larry. 465
French, Liz. 274, 275, 4098, 4115
Frenquellucci, Chiara. 4307
Freund, Peter. 3961
Frick, John W. 403
Friedman, Edward H. 3372
Friedman, Martin Edward. 1761
Friedman, Michael Brian. 866
Friedmann, Gary, photo. 1194
Frielinghaus, Helmut. 4383
Frieze, James. 3592, 4252
Frings, Hans-Peter. 1382
Fritsch, Sibylle. 1819
Frost, Derek Trowbridge. 4035
Frost, Everett. 3865
Frye, Ellen Cressman. 3373
Fuchs, Elinor. 1611
Fuchs, Lívia. 359, 938
Fuld, Catherine Elina. 3787
Fuller, Sam. 3885
Fuller, Samuel. 3886
Fullington, Doug. 1133, 1172
Fuoss, Kirk. 791
Furmanov, R. 2263
Gable, Harvey L. 3788
Gábor, Miklós. 2076
Gabršek-Prosenc, Meta. 218
Gademan, Göran. 4498, 4854, 4858
Gaevskij, V. 1134
Gaevskij, V., ed. 1144
Gaft, V.O. 758
Gaganova, A. 4129
Gagnon, Pauline D. 792, 1762
Gaida, Maria Nicoletta, transl. 1415
Gaines, Robert D. 1844
Gajdó, Tamás. 447, 2077
Galadževa, N., ed. 2247
Galántai, Csaba. 540
Galasso, Sabrina. 2169
Galasso, Sabrina, ed. 1670
Gale, Shannon E. 3727
Gale, Steven H. 3593
Gallet, Louis. 4417
Galligan, Ann M. 793
Gallup, Donald. 3594
Galvez, Florante P. 2682
Gampert, Christian. 1634
Ganapathy-Dore, Geetha. 2801
Garafola, Lynn. 1028, 1048, 1173
Garanina, S. 4678
Garboli, Cesare. 2170
García Santo-Tomás, Enrique. 3831
García-Castañón, Santiago. 3374
Gardner, Carl. 186
Gardner, Richard Alvin. 1374
Gardner, Viv. 2605
Garebian, Keith. 1582, 2802
Garforth, Julian, transl. 4777
Gargano, Cara. 794
Garlato, Rita. 4655
Garlick, Görel. 1800
Garrett, Michael. 3918
Garrick, David A. 795
Garrison, Gary Wayne. 3595
Gaskell, Ivan. 4231
Gáspár, Ildikó. 854
Gáspár, Máté. 1378, 2078, 2079, 2080, 2081
Gasparro, Rosalba. 1932
Gastineau, Janine. 1174
Gatti, Hilary. 2921
Gau, Tracey Marianne. 2922
Gay, Derek. 4169
Gaynor, Mark. 4268
Gayton, Howard. 4193
Gbanou, Sélom-Komlan. 3419
Geary, Angela. 1007
Gee, Elwyn. 276
Geerts, Ronald, ed. 3543
Gejzer, M. 2264
Gelb, Arthur. 3596
Gelb, Barbara. 2683, 3596, 3597
Gelencsér, Ágnes. 939, 1041, 1042, 1085, 1086, 1087, 1088, 1089, 1090, 1091, 1092, 1093, 1094, 1095
Gelli, Piero, ed. 702
Gener, Randy. 3598
Gentry, Theodore L. 4804
George, David. 2923
George, David S. 4537
George, Ian Lloyd. 1412
Gerasimova, I.A. 911
Gerbaulet, Françoise. 1425
Gerdt, O. 1135
Gerold, László. 2342, 3720
Gesmer, Daniel. 4179
Gesquière, Jean-Charles, photo. 1038
Giani, Roberta. 3239
Giannetti, Laura. 3240
Gibson, K. Jane. 1845
Gibson, Rachel. 904
Gilbert, Bernard. 1795
Gilbert, Helen. 486
Gilbert, Reid. 1583
Gilbey, Liz. 1740
Giles, Freda Scott. 1763
Giles, Jane. 3876
Giles, Patrick. 4721
Gill, Glenda. 3599
Gille, Philippe. 4415
Gillen, Francis. 3447, 3984
Gilliam, Jobie. 796
Gilman, Todd S. 4766
Gilmore, Elsa M. 2839
Gilmour, Heather. 4010
Gingrich-Philbrook, Craig. 2684
Ginkas, K. 2265
Giorcelli, Christina, ed. 3544
Girard, René. 3448
Girdham, Jane Catherine. 4547
Gitelman, Claudia. 1213
Giurgea, Adrian. 4162
Gjestvang, Ingrid Leiser. 3138
Gladstone, Valerie. 1057, 1175, 1239
Glasow, E. Thomas. 4557, 4656
Glasow, E. Thomas, ed. 4831
Glasow, E. Thomas, transl. 4565, 4805
Glenzer, Allison. 635
Glover, Julian. 2606
Gluck, David. 1764
Gneušev, V. 4183
Goder, D. 1703, 1751, 2266, 2267, 2268, 2269, 2270, 4679, 4680
Godin, Diane. 2803, 2804, 4011, 4012
Godin, Jean Cléo. 1846
Godina, Rosemarie. 2924
Gogol, Nikolaj. 1450
Gohar, Kourosh. 3834
Gold, Sylviane. 2685
Goldberg, Jonathan. 2925
Goldberg, Phyllis. 34
Goldberg, RoseLee. 4253
Goldfarb, Alvin. 3054, 3600
Goldoni, Carlo. 1442, 1443, 1444, 3241
Golikova, N. 1297
Golomb, Liorah Anne. 3449
Golove, Jonathan. 4422
Golubovskij, A. 1704
Golubovskij, B.G. 2271
Gombrowicz, Witold. 1448
Gompes, Loes. 1387
Gončarov, A.A. 2272
Gondinet, Edmond. 4415
Goodfarb, Rowena Davis. 3601
Goodman, Lizbeth. 2607, 2608
Gordeeva, A. 1046
Gordon, David J. 3450
Gordon, Robert. 2609
Gordy, Douglas W. 404, 2747
Gorey, Edward. 3887
Gornall, Nick. 4324
Gosher, Sydney Paul. 3363
Goslar, Lotte. 4123
Gosset, Philip. 4805
Gothár, Péter, et al. 3187
Goto, Yukihiro. 555
Gotschall, Jeff, photo. 1062
Gottschild, Brenda Nixon. 1058
Götz, Eszter. 494
Gould, Evlyn. 532
Goulden, Jan. 971
Gounaridou, Kiki. 1667
Gourdine, Angeletta KM. 3602
Gourley, Matthew J. 2686
Goźliński, Paweł. 2218

Grace, Sherrill. 2805
Graham, Duncan W. 636
Graham, Martha. 1323
Grange, William. 3139
Grant, James. 4485, 4542
Gras, Henk. 154
Grau, Andrée. 1011
Grauch, Arlene Evangelista. 277
Graune, Erik. 4657
Gray, Stephen. 2353
Grečucha, Ž. 2273
Greeley, Lynne. 3603
Green, Harris. 1176, 1177
Green, Katherine S. 2926
Green, London. 4553, 4557
Green, Mark R. 1485
Greenberg, Richard. 1486
Greene, Alexis. 2687, 3604
Greene, Shannon Keenan. 3765
Greenfield, Lois, photo. 1195
Greenfield, Peter. 2610
Greenhouse, Richard N., photo. 1061
Greenspan, Hank. 3605
Greenwald, Helen M. 203
Greffard, Madeleine. 3869
Gregg, Jess. 1178
Gregor, Graham Keith. 2359
Gregory, Paul. 278
Greif, Karen. 2611
Grémont, Henri. 4416
Grezzi, Enrico. 544
Griffin, Eric John. 2927
Griffith, David W., transl. 1360
Griffith, Isela Angelica. 1765
Griffiths, Linda. 2806
Grigor'ev, A. 3140
Grindea, Miron. 3204
Grinnell, Richard W. 2928
Griščenko, N. 2274
Griševa, L.D. 2193
Groemer, Gerald. 1371, 1372
Grojsman, A.G. 1812
Groome, Margaret Estelle. 1584
Groševa, N. 2275
Gross, Jens. 1643, 3126, 3161, 3162, 3164
Gross, Robert. 3451, 4843
Gross, Robert F. 1970
Grosser, Helmut. 187, 448
Grubb, Shirley Carr. 2929
Grund, Stefan. 1635
Grundmann, Ute. 1971, 1972, 1973
Gruszczyński, Piotr. 2219
Guay, Marie-Ginette. 1847
Guccini, Gerardo. 4647
Guccini, Gerardo, ed. 4300
Guderian-Czaplińska, Ewa. 212, 824
Guedj, Attica, transl. 1475
Guess, Ann H. 2930
Guevara Salazar, Alberto José. 3735
Gugler, Josef. 3977
Guinther, Louise. 4716
Guinther, Louise T. 4476, 4593, 4722, 4723
Guitry, Sacha. 1426
Gukovskij, G.A. 3322
Gunne, Nina. 1300
Günter, Bernd. 7
Guntner, J. Lawrence. 2048
Guntner, J. Lawrence, ed. 2035, 2036, 2037, 2038, 2039, 2040, 2041, 2042, 2043, 2044, 2045, 2046, 2047, 2048, 2049, 2050, 2051, 2052, 2053, 3177
Gurantz, Maya. 617
Gurewitsch, Matthew. 4539, 4794
Gurkweitz, Dmitri Eugene. 637
Gussow, Mel. 1766, 3205
Gyarmati, Zsófia. 1068
Györffy, Anna, photo. 845, 2104
Haarbauer, Martha. 405
Haarbauer, Ward. 405
Haarer, Klaus. 439
Haas, Anna de. 2202
Haber, Judith. 2931
Haedicke, Susan Chandler. 570
Haenni, Sabine. 638
Haeong, Shik Kim. 557
Haff, Stephen. 3606
Hagedorn, Volker. 8, 1636
Hagen, Eric. 3410
Hagen, W.S. 3985
Hägglund, Kent. 2375
Haglund, Birgitta. 601, 1725
Hagman, Bertil. 4852
Hagoort, Giep. 18
Haïm, Victor. 1427
Hakli, Kari, photo. 1037
Hakola, Liisa. 2612
Halász, Tamás. 940
Halbach, Denise. 402
Halbreich, Harry. 4594
Hale, John K. 2932
Halévy, Ludovic. 4418
Hall, Ann C. 3452
Hall, Ann Christine. 3607
Hall, Ardencie. 4228
Hall, George. 4477, 4478
Hall, Tony. 4166, 4167
Halley, Richard. 4070
Hallin, Ulrika. 21, 3411
Halperin-Royer, Ellen. 2688
Halperin, Ellen Irene. 639
Halstead, John S. 867
Ham, Roderick. 448
Hamburger, Maik. 1974, 3177
Hamid, Mohamed Abubakr. 1417
Hamilton, David. 4357, 4529, 4716, 4824
Hamilton, Lonnée. 2689
Hamilton, Stuart. 4540
Hammarlund, Jan. 4295
Hammer, Paul E.J. 4196
Hammerstein, Dorothee. 1612, 1933, 1934, 1935
Hammett, Charlotte Kaye. 2690
Handel, Edit. 1205
Hanke, Dirk Olaf. 1383
Hanna, Judith Lynne. 4271
Hannowa, Anna. 1686
Hansell, Sven. 2211
Hansen, Jack Winsor. 4572
Hansen, Sophie. 888, 1310
Happé, Peter. 2613, 2933, 3802
Harbeck, James Christopher. 640
Harbin, Billy J. 2691
Hardin, Michael. 3608
Harless, Winston Neely. 3453
Harley, James. 3789, 4128
Harner, James L., ed. 3722
Harpe, Bill. 1254
Harri, Minna. 1016, 1203
Harris, Charlotte Daniels. 4486
Harris, Max. 1225, 4218, 4219
Harrison-Pepper, Sally. 4137
Harryson, Lotta. 386, 1301
Hartigan, Patti. 1549
Hartmann, David. 279
Hartog, Joh. 3
Hartung, Bernd, photo. 1281
Harue, Tsutsumi. 1360
Harvey, Don, ed. 323
Harvie, Jennifer. 716
Hassal, R. Chris, Jr. 2934
Hastings, Stephen. 4462, 4510
Hatch, Christopher. 4595
Hauck, Christina. 3454
Hauptfleisch, Gaerin, photo. 2350
Hausmann, Vincent. 3927
Hawkes, Sophie. 3269
Hawkins, Barrie. 3294
Hawkins, John A. 1848
Haynes, Jonathan. 4081
Haynes, Wendy Lynne. 797
Hays, Peter L. 3609
Head, Hayden Maxwell. 2935
Healey, Michael. 501, 1410
Heath, Veronica, transl. 4776
Heaton, Daniel W. 4138
Hecht, Werner. 1975
Heed, Sven Åke. 2171, 4450
Heidger, John Michael. 641
Heil, Douglas. 3888
Heil, LeighAnn. 2692
Heine, Beate. 1637, 3141, 3455
Heisserer, Gary Lawrence. 3610
Helander, Karin. 2376
Helavuori, Hanna-Leena. 179
Heliotis, Harry, photo. 4738
Hellemans, Dina, ed. 3543
Hellot, Marie-Christiane. 2807
Hellström Sveningson, Lis. 881, 900, 1049
Henderson, Heather. 3456
Henderson, Stephen. 3142, 3790, 4363
Hendrick, Pamela R. 642
Henk, Nancy B. 4880
Henke, James Scott. 466
Henne, Claudia. 1282
Hennessey, James Todd. 1849
Henry, B.J. 1705
Hepburn, Allan. 4762
Herbert, Simon. 4269
Hering, Doris. 1179
Heritage, Paul. 496
Herman, Josef. 721, 4543
Hermansson, Jan. 4554, 4795
Hermansson, Kristina. 1726
Hernandez, Librada. 3375
Hernik-Spalińska, Jagoda. 372
Herren, Graley V. 4076, 4077
Herrington, Joan. 3611, 3612
Herron, Donna G. 35
Herx, Stephen. 4724
Herzinger, Richard. 741, 3766
Hesse, Ulrich. 3767
Hessel, Tina. 965
Hessler, Ulrike. 4405
Heteren, Lucia van. 155
Heym, Anne. 9
Hézső, István. 1054, 1065, 1071
Highsaw, Carol Anne. 643
Hilferty, Robert. 4725, 4765
Hill, Ann. 280
Hill, Errol. 4384
Hill, Leslie. 4245
Hill, Philip G. 828
Hiltunen, Sirkku M. Sky. 798
Hinkel, Roland. 10
Hirche, Knut. 1385
Hirsch, Foster. 1767
Hirschfeld, Heather Anne. 2936
Hiss, Guido. 4310
Hoberman, J. 3951
Hočevar, Meta. 219
Hoch, Danny. 1487
Hodgdon, Barbara. 3940
Hodges, C. Walter. 1801
Hodsoll, Frank. 36, 775
Hodson, Millicent. 1150, 1311
Hoelterhoff, Manuela. 4658
Höfele, Andreas. 1976
Hoffman, Cheryl Conover. 4861
Hogan, Jane. 281, 282, 1550, 1551, 1552, 4867
Hogan, Patrick Colm. 3283
Högberg, Helena. 1301

Höglund, Christina. 1018, 1019
Hohenleitner, Kathleen. 3512
Holbrook, Peter. 4201, 4206
Holbrook, Peter, ed. 4196, 4197, 4198, 4200, 4201, 4202, 4203, 4204, 4205, 4206, 4207, 4208, 4212, 4215
Holden, Joan. 3242
Hollingsworth, Anthony Lee. 2227
Hollósi, Zsolt. 4359, 4621, 4622
Holm, Bent. 4186
Holmes, Michael Morgan. 3021
Honig, Joel. 4726, 4827
Honolka, K. 4555
Honoré, Brian. 4168
Hood, Woodrow. 4046
Hoogland, Rikard. 1727, 1728, 1977, 2377
Hope, Warren. 3748
Hopkins, Lisa. 2937, 2938
Hopkinson, Claire. 4346
Horner, Olga. 1400
Horosko, Marian. 983
Horovitz, Israel. 1488, 1489
Horrall, A.J. 4283
Horvat, Mojca. 1023
Horwitz, Dawn Lille. 1160, 1180
Hotinen, Juha-Pekka. 1914
Houchin, John H. 2693
Houppert, Karen. 2694, 3613
House, Jane E. 3091
Houser, Patricia G. 406
Howard, Jean E. 3749
Howard, Pamela. 232
Howe, Tina. 3614
Howell-Meri, Mark A. 435
Howley, Michael P. 461
Hrycak, Alexandra Martha. 615
Hubbard, Tamara S. 35
Huber, Werner, ed. 2667
Hughes, David. 1269, 4237, 4270
Hughes, Howard. 4278
Hulbert, Dan. 2695, 4385
Hulec, Vladimír, ed. 1882
Hulton-Baker, Robert. 1355
Hume, Robert D. 4767
Humfeld, Nancy Jo. 4402
Hummig, Wolfgang. 178
Humphries, Eugenia. 3615
Hunt, John. 2939
Hunt, Marilyn. 1050, 1181
Hunt, Maurice. 2940
Hunter, Kurt, photo. 4883
Hunter, Robin. 2614
Hurley, Erin. 407, 1675
Hurt, James. 3616
Huslarová, Iva. 1877
Huss, Pia. 2369, 3776
Hussey, Michael. 878
Hussey, Michael J. 4048
Hüster, Wiebke. 1039, 1247
Huston-Findley, Shirley Annette. 3617
Huszár, Klára. 4623, 4624
Hutcheon, Linda. 4763, 4764
Hutcheon, Michael. 4763, 4764
Hutera, Donald. 905
Hütter, Martina. 1978
Hüttler, Michael. 711
Iglesias, Diane. 3376
Ignatjuk, O. 1706, 2276
Ikládi, László, photo. 845, 2089, 3190
Il'in, I.A. 4681
Iles, Charles. 4240
Iljušin, A. 2277
Illo, John, ed. 4809
Ilovszky, Béla, photo. 1108, 2105, 2120, 2135, 2139, 2142, 3188, 3190, 4358, 4360
Immerwahr, Michael. 283
Infante, Andrea Elizabeth. 37
Ingber, Alix. 3377
Inkret, Andrej. 857
Innes, Christopher. 2808, 3457
Innes, Christopher, ed. 3427, 3429, 3438, 3444, 3445, 3450, 3457, 3460, 3470, 3471, 3481, 3486, 3503, 3506, 3832
Ireland, John. 3092, 3093
Ireland, Patricia L. 2696
Irmer, Thomas. 1638, 3768
Ismagulova, T.D. 2248
Israel, Chip. 276
Isza, Ferenc, photo. 2081
Ivanova, S. 2278
Iversen, Paul Andrew. 3183
Ivleva, T. 3323
Ivry, Benjamin. 3618
Jack, George Francis, Jr. 2697
Jackson, Mac D.P. 825
Jackson, Maria-Rosario. 38
Jackson, Russell. 2615
Jackson, Shannon. 644, 1490, 3619
Jacobi, Derek. 2616
Jacobs, Alfred Voris, Jr. 515
Jacobson, Daniel. 906
Jacobsson, Rigg-Olle. 211, 220
Jaeger, Ernest. 4139
Jaffer, Kay. 4394
Jahnke, Manfred. 349, 1639, 1640, 1641, 1642
Jakubcová, Alena. 1826
Jálics, Kinga. 1066, 1096, 1097, 1098
James, Sheila. 1411, 2809
Jameux, Dominique. 4760
Jamieson, Nigel. 4495
Jankowiak, Günter. 151
Jánosi, Ildikó. 4667
Janssens, Lidwine. 753
Jansson, Tomas. 1915, 3069
Janzon, Leif. 1729
Janzon, Leif, transl. 4150
Janzon, Mary Ulla-Britt. 3777
Jauslin, Christian. 2398
Jelinek, Elfriede. 2780
Jenkins, Anthony. 3458
Jenkins, Ron. 3243
Jesson, Paul. 2617
Jévrejenov, Nikolaj. 2279
Jew, Kimberly May. 3620
Jeyasingh, Shobana. 972
Jhaveri, Angana. 1347
Jiggetts, Shelby. 3621
Joe, Jeongwon. 4770
Johansen, Karsten. 1979
Johansson, Kerstin. 890, 1036, 4120
Johansson, Ola. 2378
Johansson, Ove. 221
Johansson, Pernilla. 891
Johnson, Anita Louise. 599
Johnson, Carla Jean. 3622
Johnson, Chelsey. 4844
Johnson, David. 174, 284, 285, 286, 287, 288, 289, 293, 1218, 1524, 1553, 1556, 3919, 4325, 4338, 4339, 4342
Johnson, David, ed. 290
Johnson, Jeff. 3623, 3624
Johnson, Jennifer Anne. 2207
Johnson, Kim. 4169
Johnson, Marcia V. 3625
Johnson, Mary Greenwood. 3094
Johnson, Rolfe. 4713
Johnson, Warren. 4819
Johnston, Alexandra F. 2941, 2942
Johnston, Carolyn Jane. 533
Johnston, David. 3378
Johnston, Denis William. 1850
Johnstone, Monica Carolyn. 3626
Jones, Ann Rosalind. 2943
Jones, Chris. 645, 3627
Jones, Ellen E. 291
Jones, Jennifer. 799, 4222
Jones, Kenneth Lee. 4903
Jones, S.G. 3970
Jones, William E. 3889
Jonigk, Thomas. 2781
Joób, Sándor. 2082, 2083, 2084
Jordan, Stephanie. 1182, 1200
Josephson, Erland. 2379
Jovičevič, Aleksandra. 3721
Jowitt, Deborah. 1072
Jubinville, Yves. 1585
Jugnot, Gérard, adapt. 1473
Julian, Patrick. 4396
Junion, David, photo. 1215
Jürgensen, Knud Arne. 4530
Jurkowski, Henryk. 4898
Justen, Wolfgang Heinrich. 3143
Jyrkkä, Hannele. 1234
Kaán, Zsuzsa. 894, 926, 941, 942, 1026, 1038, 1063, 1064, 1099, 1100, 1101, 1102, 1118, 1121, 1227
Kádár, Kata, photo. 896, 1219
Kahle, Ulrike. 1980
Kahn, Madeleine. 800
Kai, Una. 1214
Kaiku, Jan-Peter. 1017, 1603
Kalb, Jonathan. 1936
Kalemba-Kasprzak, Elżbieta. 610
Kalemba-Kasprzak, Elżbieta, ed. 610, 824, 3306, 4154
Kalin, Tom. 4037
Kalinoski, Richard. 1491
Kalinovskaja, G. 2280
Kalinowski, Daniel. 3826
Kallus, György, photo. 4629, 4631, 4642
Kálmán, Tamás, transl. 1053
Kandé, Sylvie. 3973
Kandell, Jonathan. 4495
Kántor, Lajos. 1693
Kanyó, Béla, photo. 894, 896, 1044, 1087, 1088, 1091, 1092, 1095, 1099, 1100, 1105, 1107, 1111, 1137, 1207, 1227
Kaough, Judith Elaine Bishop. 3791
Kapelke, Randy. 2698
Kapelke, Randy B. 2699
Kaplan, Joel. 4213
Kaplan, Laurie. 3459
Kaplan, Paul H.D. 3758
Kaplan, Philip Benjamin. 3813
Kaple, Deborah. 39
Kaposi, Edit. 927, 943
Kapusta, Janusz, illus. 4845
Karam, Edward. 1525, 1526
Karas, Sandra. 40
Karner, Doris. 722
Karp, Jack Martin. 1492
Karsai, György. 2085, 4360
Karz, Zippora. 1183
Kasjak, Mojca. 4288
Kassai, Róbert, photo. 2113
Kastal'skij, S. 1073
Kasule, Samuel. 604
Katkó, Tamás, photo. 2148
Katritzky, M.A. 4188, 4191
Katz, Genevieve. 984
Katz, Robert Scott. 4682
Kaufman, Millard. 4013
Kaufman, Tom. 4659
Kaup-Hasler, Veronica. 4727
Kaye, Ed. 276
Kaye, Nick. 2700, 4239, 4254, 4267
Kaynar, Gad. 1673, 3628
Kazacoff, George. 1768
Kearns, Gail. 4923
Kegl, Rosemary. 2701
Kehler, Grace. 4540

Kékesi Kun, Árpád. 1569, 2086, 2087
Keller, James M. 4728, 4845
Keller, Max. 188
Keller, Ron. 292
Kellow, Brian. 4526, 4707, 4729
Kelly, Katherine E. 3460
Kelly, Veronica. 817
Kelly, Veronica, ed. 2, 486, 488, 489, 490, 492, 817, 1567, 1568, 2774, 2775, 2776, 2778, 3807
Kelty, Mark James. 3275
Kemp, Gerard. 1851
Kendall, Elizabeth. 1037
Kendall, G.M. 2944
Kendall, Gillian Murray, ed. 2862, 2894, 2913, 2943, 2944, 2962, 2965, 2975, 3041
Kenez, Peter. 4039
Kennedy, Anja. 1024
Kennedy, Dennis. 1601
Kennedy, Paul. 1215
Kennedy, Stephen Mark. 3095
Kennedy, William Bruce. 4403
Kénnel, P. 2945
Kenney, Janet Rose. 1769
Kenworthy, Patricia. 3379
Kermauner, Taras. 858, 3344, 3345, 3346, 3347, 3348, 3349, 3350, 3351, 3352, 3353, 3354
Kermode, Frank. 3803
Kermode, Lloyd Edward. 2946
Kern, Barbara Ellen Goldstein. 3461
Kerner, Leighton. 4730
Kershaw, Baz. 4236
Kertész, Iván. 4625, 4626, 4627, 4628
Kerwin, William. 2947
Kevin, Jonna. 1250
Key, Nancy Martin. 1770
Kezar, Dennis. 2948
Khuon, Ulrich. 1643, 3126, 3161, 3162, 3164
Kičin, V. 3324
Kiebuzinska, Christine. 2782
Kiec, Izolda. 550, 4154
Kiepels, Caroline. 958
Kieser, Klaus, transl. 1302
Kieth, Chris. 4071
Kift, Roy. 4153
Killick, Andrew Peter. 4364
Kim, A., ed. 2323
Kim, Deukshin. 1352
Kim, Earl. 4306
Kim, Jin-A. 2949
Kim, Ju. 2281
Kim, Suzanne. 3834
Kimber, Robert James. 487
King, Kenneth. 1324
King, Kevin H. 41
King, Pamela M. 2950, 3750
Kinney, Clare R. 2951
Kinser, Samuel. 4164
Kintz, Linda. 3629
Kintzler, Catherine. 3096
Kiosses, James T. 3380
Kipling, Gordon. 3761, 3762
Király, Nina. 373
Király, Nina, ed. 2282
Kirdjašov, V.F. 3277
Kirkkopelto, Esa. 3815
Kirner, Amy E. 35
Kirsch, Arthur. 2952
Kirshenblatt-Gimblett, Barbara. 4255
Kiss, Csaba. 16
Kiss, Gabriella. 2088
Kiss, Krisztina. 195
Kiss, László. 379
Kitagava, T. 4464
Klančnik Kocutar, Katarina. 4696
Klaren, Georg C. 4420
Klautsch, Richard Joseph. 408
Klein, Jeanne Marie. 801
Klein, Richard Alan. 3381
Klein, Stacy A. 646
Kleinas, Levas. 205
Klemsdal, Ole. 1251
Klep, Mihael, transl. 4898
Klepac, Richard L. 1897
Klett, Renate. 334
Kliman, Bernice W. 2953
Klimontovič, N. 2283
Klimova, K. 2284
Klingan, Katrin. 4727
Kljavina, T.A. 1080
Ključevskij, V.O. 3325
Klotz, Günther. 2049
Klotz, Volker. 842
Kluetmeier, Heinz, photo. 990
Knapp, Margaret M. 802
Knight, Alan E. 4224
Knight, Stephen. 2954
Knopf, Jan. 3144
Knowles, Dorothy. 3097
Knowles, Richard Paul. 1586, 1852, 2618, 4447
Knowles, Ronald. 3462
Knox, Dianna Lynn Welch. 879
Knox, Robert Erskine, Jr. 4442
Knutson, Susan. 2810
Kobayashi, Kaori. 2702
Kobialka, Michal Andrzej. 516
Kočetkov, A.N. 3326
Kocijančič, Katarina, bibliog. 708
Koegler, Horst. 4124
Koek, Ariane. 4556
Kohler, Richard C. 1807
Kohn, Rita. 3630
Kohse, Petra. 1385, 1644, 3145
Kokich, Kim. 1184
Kolesnikova, E.D. 1249
Kolesova, N. 1136
Koli, Raija. 1604
Kolin, Philip. 2172
Kolin, Philip C. 3843
Koljazin, V. 2285
Kolk, Mieke. 563
Kolnik, Paul, photo. 1061
Kolnik, Paul, photo. 1058, 1181
Kolobov, O.A. 759
Kolobrodov, I.A. 2286
Koloski, Laurie S. 573
Koltai, Gábor. 3146
Koltai, Tamás. 1570, 2089, 2090, 2091, 2092, 2093, 4531, 4629, 4630
Koltès, Bernard-Marie. 1428
Konaev, S. 2251
Konarska-Pabiniak, Barbara. 374
Koncut, Suzana, transl. 4550
Koncz, Zsuzsa. 2088
Koncz, Zsuzsa, photo. 15, 358, 377, 845, 940, 2057, 2058, 2059, 2060, 2062, 2068, 2071, 2072, 2073, 2074, 2083, 2085, 2087, 2094, 2097, 2099, 2102, 2120, 2121, 2126, 2132, 2133, 2137, 2138, 2142, 2143, 2144, 2145, 2282, 2321, 4362, 4630
Kondorosi, Zoltán. 360
Konecny, Mark Clarence. 580
Kong, Eunah. 4664
Königer, Miklós. 944, 1040
Konjuškov, E. 2287
Konkle, Lincoln. 3631
Kononenko, Natalie O. 3327
Konovalova, T. 2277
Kopelson, Kevin. 4771
Korb, Richard Alan. 3147
Korish, David, transl. 952
Koritz, Amy E. 1012
Kornas, Tadeusz. 1687
Korniss, Péter, photo. 358, 447, 1219, 1220, 1224, 2125, 4644
Körtvélyes, Géza. 912, 1103, 1104, 1137, 1228
Kosi, Tina. 4873
Koski, Pirkko. 148
Kostalanetz, Richard. 3863
Kötő, József. 1693
Kotovič, T.V. 165
Kotte, Andreas. 820
Kourlas, Gia. 1325
Kovačič Peršin, Peter, ed. 3358
Kovács, Dezső. 196, 2094, 2095, 2096, 2097
Kovács, Zita, photo. 2056, 2111, 3188
Kovalenko, G.V. 2849, 3632
Kovrov, M. 2288
Kozak, Krištof Jacek. 3827
Kozel, Susan. 956
Kozień, Lucyna, ed. 4895
Kozłowska, Mirosława, ed. 1686, 1691, 2212, 2223, 4896
Kozma, András. 2098
Kozyreva, M. 4884
Král, Karel. 1878, 1879, 2850, 4086
Kralicek, Wolfgang. 1820
Kralj, Lado. 3804
Kramer, Lawrence. 4796
Kramer, Richard E. 868
Krämer, Timm. 4410
Kranz, Dieter. 1981, 4596, 4597
Krapivina, E. 1138
Krasil'nikova, T. 1231
Krasiński, Edward. 432, 574
Kraus, Karl. 2783
Kraut, Anthea. 3633
Kravcov, A. 2289
Kravos, Bogomila, transl. 1441
Kreis-Schinck, Annette. 3098
Krexner, Alice. 433
Kristoffersson, Birgitta. 222
Kristy-Brooks, Kathleen. 1493
Kritzer, Amelia Howe. 3463, 3464
Križanskaja, Daria, transl. 1450
Kroes, Rob, ed. 3544
Krogerus, Anna. 559
Krošin, G. 2290
Krotov, V. 1947
Krug, Hartmut. 1384, 1645
Krumbholz, Martin. 350, 1982
Krusche, Friedemann. 1646, 1983, 1984, 3148
Krylov, A.E. 2291
Krymov, V. 1197
Ktorov, A. 2292
Kubek, Elizabeth. 3952
Kubiak, Anthony. 719, 803
Kubiak, Anthony James. 839
Kubikowski, Tomasz. 1688
Kubler, John Albert. 160
Kuckhoff, Armin-Gerd. 2050
Kueppers, Brigitte. 409
Kuftinec, Sonja. 495, 1831
Kugler, D.D. 2811
Kuharski, Allen. 3303
Kuharski, Allen, transl. 1448
Kuhn, Laura. 1326
Kuhns, David Frederick. 536
Kulesza, Monika. 534
Kuligowska-Korzeniewska, Anna. 4157
Kuligowska-Korzeniewska, Anna, ed. 574, 1689, 2222, 3307
Kulikova, E. 3328
Kull, Gustaf. 206
Kumankov, Jévgenij. 215
Kumar, Pranab. 3634
Kumysnikov, H. 2404, 2405
Kúnos, László. 3190

Kuo, Yu-Chun. 887
Kuoshu, Harry H. 2844
Kuraś, Marzena. 578
Kurten, Allelu. 4903, 4904
Kurtz, Martha Anne. 2955
Kushner, Tony. 3851
Kútszegi, Csaba. 1105
Kuvakin, A.G., ed. 707
Kuz'mina, N.I.,. 4815
Kuz'mina, S. 1707
Kuźnicka, Danuta. 855
Kuźnicka, Danuta, ed. 822, 855, 856
Kvaløy, Pål. 454
Kyzer, Stanley Winford. 2703
Laages, Michael. 351, 1985, 1986
Laakkonen, Johanna. 917
Läänesaar, Monika. 1600
Laatto, Ritva. 3819
Labre, Jean-François. 3465
Lach, Elizabeth. 4881
Lacombe, Hervé. 4784
Ladouceur, Louise, transl. 1855
Lafon, Dominique. 1587, 2812, 2813
Lagercrantz, Ylva. 2380
Lagerlöf, Malin. 2853
LaGravenese, Richard. 3890
Lahger, Håkan. 1730, 2381, 2382, 2383
Lahr, John. 2704, 3953, 4127, 4340
Lahtinen, Outi. 180
Lainé, Pascal. 1429
Lajos, Sándor. 344, 2099, 2100
Lakos, Anna, comp. 4893
Laliberté, Hélène. 1853
Lamont, Rosette C. 647, 1937
Lampert-Gréaux, Ellen. 229, 230, 233, 293, 294, 467, 468, 469, 479, 1031, 1248, 1527, 1554, 1555, 1556, 3926, 4290, 4325, 4341, 4342, 4343, 4344, 4499
Lampič, Miha. 1023
Lander, Jesse Macliesh. 2956
Landro, Vincent. 2705
Landry, Pascale. 4233
Lane, Harry. 3466, 4346
Lane, Jill. 512
Långbacka, Ralf. 3149
Langhoff, Anna. 1987
Langkilde, Nicole Maria. 723
Langley, Stephen. 42
Langsted, Jørn. 724
Langston, Ann Lizbeth. 3244
Laor, Dan. 3217
Lapointe-Cloutier, Marie-Michèle. 2796
Lapotaire, Jane. 2619
Larabee, Ann E. 648
Lardner, Ring, Jr. 3891
Larina, S. 4469
Larrue, Jean-Marc. 1375
Larsson, Stellan. 3412
Lasky, Roberta Lynne. 410
Latshaw, George. 4868
Lau, Mariam. 1988
Laurendeau, Francine. 3856, 3857
Lauretta, Enzo. 3245
Lauzier, Gérard, transl. 1471
Lavoie, André. 3964
Lavoie, Pierre. 1588, 3920, 4014
Lawrence, Happy James. 411
Laws, Catherine. 4772
Layson, June. 1001
Lazar, Wanda. 3921
Lazaridès, Alexandre. 2814, 3971
Lazzarini-Dossin, Muriel. 3246
Lazzi, Giovanna, ed. 703
Leabhart, Sally, transl. 4088, 4089, 4090
Leabhart, Thomas. 4091
Leabhart, Thomas, transl. 4090
Leask, Josephine. 885, 923, 973
Lecat, Jean-Guy. 182
Lechuga, Myriam. 1771
LeClerq, Tanaquil. 1185
Lecure, Bruce. 1938
Lee, Cheng Heng. 295
Lee, Chester. 412
Lee, Eric, ed. 2201
Lee, Josephine. 869, 3635
Lee, Josephine D. 3467
Lee, Teresa. 402
Lee, Tong Soon. 4694
Leeuwen, Ger van. 957
Leggatt, Alexander. 2957
Lehmann, Courtney. 2958
Leigh, James. 3295
Leight, Warren. 1494, 4015
Lemmerman, Hans, ed. 207
Lemmons, Kasi. 3892
Lenčevskij, Ju. 3329
Lennartz, Knut. 445, 1571, 1647, 1648, 1649, 1989, 1990, 1991, 1992, 1993, 3150, 3151, 4598
Leon, Barbara A. 513
Leonard, Candyce. 2360, 3382
Leonardi, Susan J. 4828
Lepage, Robert. 1301
Lepine, Jacques Andre. 3099
Lepschy, Anna Laura, ed. 3247
Leroux, Élizabeth. 2815
Lesage, Marie-Christine. 1514, 1515, 1939, 2816, 4016
Leslie, Michael. 4199
Leslie, Russell. 278
Lesschaeve, Jacqueline. 1186
Lesser, Joseph Leroy. 4140
Lester, Richard. 2959, 3751
Levanen, Leo Johannes. 523
Levašov, V. 2293
Leve, James Samuel. 4660
Levene, Louise. 1161
Lévesque, Solange. 502, 1796, 1854, 3935, 4058, 4074
Levi, Paolo. 204
Levin, David J. 4836
Levin, M. 480
Levin, Marc. 3893
Levin, Richard. 2960, 3795
Levin, Richard A. 2961
Levine, Eric M. 3636
Levine, Laura Ellen. 726
Levine, Mark. 4141
Levitas, J.B.A. 750
Levith, Murray J. 3741
Levitt, John. 1898
Levočkina, N.A. 1232
Levoyer, Gérard. 1430, 1431
Lewalski, Barbara K. 4207
Lewin, Alex. 3894
Lewin, Jan. 1388, 1731
Lewis, David. 1476
Lewis, Valerie Hannagan. 3100
Ley, Graham. 481
Leyko, Małgorzata. 574
Leyko, Małgorzata, ed. 1689, 2222, 3307
Leżeńska, Katarzyna. 1689
Licher, Edmund. 564
Lieblein, Leanore. 1855
Liepe-Levinson, Katherine. 4285
Lihani, John. 3383
Lile, Jim. 296
Lindblad, Katarina. 4473
Linden, Mirjam van der. 1002
Linder, Jutta. 1994
Lindley, David. 4197
Lindman, Magnus, transl. 4609
Lindner, Thomas. 4806, 4833
Linds, Warren. 717
Lindvag, Anita Lydia. 1732
Linert, Andrzej. 1690
Linzer, Martin. 440, 1385, 1650, 1995
Lippy, Tod. 3895
Lister, Linda Joanne. 4773
Liszka, Tamás. 1830, 2101, 2102, 2103, 2104, 2105, 2106
Lisztes, Edina, photo. 935
Little, Arthur L., Jr. 2962
Little, William Kenneth. 4180
Litvinceva, G. 1708
Litvinova, M. 2963
Liverpool, Hollis Urban. 4175
Livio, Gigi, ed. 3233
Ljadov, V.I. 3850
Llamas, Regina Sofia. 2840
Lo Russo, Rosaria. 3248
Lo, Jacqueline. 488
Loayza, Daniel, transl. 1491
Lobenthal, Joel. 1059, 1139
Loboda, Matjaž. 4874
Locke, Ralph P. 4797
Löffler, Sigrid. 1996
Loffree, Carrie. 872
Lőkös, Ildikó. 361
Lomax, Sandra. 907
LoMonaco, Marti. 413
London, Todd. 3844
Londré, Felicia Hardison. 3637
Loney, Glenn. 336, 462, 4429, 4443, 4457, 4532
Longstaffe, Stephen. 2964
Lonink, Miranda, ed. 207
Loomis, George W. 4470, 4731
Lopez, A. Grace. 414
Lőrinc, Katalin. 895, 914, 945, 946, 947, 948, 1106, 1107, 1108, 1187, 1206, 1291, 1292, 1293, 1294
Lorincz, Chester Joseph. 2208
Louch, Hugh. 39
Lovelace, Earl. 4176
Loyd, Melissa. 804
Lu, Tina. 4315
Lucas, Scott. 4211
Luciani, Giovanni, transl. 3448
Ludwig, Volker. 3152
Luk, Yun Tong. 3772
Lukács, András. 1055
Lukan, Blaž. 2346
Lukan, Blaž, ed. 1458
Lunde, Robert Charles. 1495
Lundin, Bo. 2369
Luscombe, Christopher. 2620
Lutterbie, John. 754
Lynge, Claus. 966
Lysell, Roland. 1651, 1997
Määttänen, Markus. 1605
Macaulay, Alastair. 1201
Macdonald, Robert. 1808
Macdonald, Ronald R. 2965
Macedo, Catherine. 4820
MacGregor, Catherine. 3468
Machrova, É.V. 4599
Mack, Michael. 2966
Mäcken, Walter. 189
Mackenzie, Clayton G. 2967
Mackenzie, Phillip. 4260
Mackie, W. Craven. 3469
Mackrell, Judith. 1312
MacLennan, Karin. 967, 1236
MacLeod, Wendy. 3589
MacQueen, Brian. 297
Madison, D. Soyini. 649
Magill, Gordon L. 1240
Magnuson, Landis Kelly. 43
Magnusson, Anna. 1405, 2384
Mahfouz, Nazih Habib. 298

Mahon, John W. 2621
Maiman, William L. 234, 299, 300, 301, 302, 303, 304, 305, 4500
Majchrowski, Zbigniew. 2220
Majniece, V. 1140, 1298
Majoros, Tamás, photo. 2090
Makarova, I.V. 2294
Makaryk, Irena. 2766
Makeev, M. 1595
Makeham, Paul. 2774
Mäkinen, Eija. 149, 1916
Makoveckij, S. 2295
Maksimova, V.A. 2234
Mälhammar, Åsa. 1998
Malkin, Jeanette R. 2784
Malkin, Jeanette Rosenzweig. 3055
Mallard, Sidney. 4905
Mallett, Mark Edmund. 720
Mallory, Anne Boyd. 727
Mallozzi, Dawn. 4263
Malm, Anna Stina. 4774
Malnig, Julie M. 985
Malone, Bonz. 3893
Malone, Jacqui. 986
Malpede, Karen. 1597
Mamet, David. 3896
Manetta, Marco. 3249
Mango, Achille. 848
Mango, Lorenzo. 849
Manheim, Michael. 3638, 3639, 3845
Manheim, Michael, ed. 2752, 3525, 3528, 3534, 3561, 3594, 3638, 3639, 3654, 3668, 3675, 3687, 3697, 3706, 3710, 3845, 4078
Mann, Emily. 3589
Mannelli, Valeria, ed. 3936
Manning, Susan. 928, 1337
Manthei, Fred. 1978
Manuel, Alexis, transl. 1498
Manzoni, Giacomo. 3250
Marc, Yves. 4088
Marčac Mirčeta, Mimi. 1023
Marciano, Lisa Caughlin. 2968
Marcus, Leah S. 4212
Maree, Cathy. 765
Márfi, Attila. 2107
Margitházi, Beja. 844, 2228
Mariengof, A.B. 760
Marik, Noémi. 2108
Mariko, Hori, transl. 1360
Marinelli, David Newton. 4807
Marinelli, Donald. 551
Marivaux, Pierre Carlet de Chamblain de. 1432
Marker, Frederick J. 3470
Markina, I. 4683
Marking, Martha A. 306
Markotic, Lorraine. 3296
Marks, Jonathan. 4189
Marlow, Jane. 2622
Márok, Tamás. 4631
Marowitz, Charles. 2706
Marra, Kim. 44
Marra, Kim, ed. 44, 116, 404, 585, 612, 619, 634, 674, 680, 799, 2590, 2656, 2691, 2757
Marre, Diana Katherine. 3640
Marsden, Jean. 517
Marsden, Jean I. 2969
Marshall, Brenda K. Devore. 650
Marshall, Cynthia. 2970
Marshalsay, K.A. 1752
Martenson, Ed. 2707
Martin, Carol. 4173
Martin, Christopher, transl. 3721
Martin, Dan J. 45
Martin, Deborah Gail. 46
Martin, Mary Kathryn. 3101
Martini, Emanuela. 3986
Martinoty, Jean-Louis. 4785
Martinuzzi, Paola. 1074
Marx, Robert. 4732, 4825
Marzullo, Gigi. 4062
Maschio, Geraldine. 651
Masi, Alessandro. 366
Maslan, Susan Amy. 735
Masłowski, Michał. 3304
Mason, Francis. 1004, 1030, 1166, 1188, 1198
Massai, Sonia. 2971
Massenet, Jules. 4416, 4417
Massey, Dawn. 2972
Masson, Linda Joyce Krasnow. 2708
Massoth, Anja. 2785
Massoutre, Guylaine. 337, 1263, 1264, 1275, 1357
Masuch, Bettina. 1999
Mátai, Györgyi. 1109, 1110, 1111, 1207, 4361, 4632, 4633
Máthé, András, photo. 2069, 2122, 2131, 2150
Matheson, Katy. 470
Matschulatt, Kay. 1772
Matt, Wolff. 4733
Matthews, Lydia. 4256
Mátyus, Zsuzsa, comp., ed. 4832
Maufort, Marc. 3552, 3641
Maufort, Marc, ed. 3545
Maupin, Elizabeth. 2709
Maurer-Haas, Andrea. 2786
Maurer, Katherine. 307
Maver, Aleš. 3355, 3356
Mavrinskaja, L. 4916
Mawdsley, Alice Lorraine Shoger. 3744
Maxim, Nanette. 1327
May, Thomas. 4734
Mayer, Verena. 715
Maynard, Stephen. 2973
Mazanec, Brigitta. 441, 4296, 4348, 4600
Mazzocchi, Federica, ed. 2173
McAdam, Ian. 2974
McAuley, Guy. 816
McCabe, Richard. 2623
McCandless, David. 2975
McCarthy, James. 4922
McClary, Susan. 4786
McCluskey, Peter Matthew. 2976
McConachie, Brian. 4142
McConachie, Bruce. 156, 652
McConachie, Bruce A. 3642, 4112
McCready, Susan. 3102
McCully, Susan Beth. 2710
McDermott, Douglas. 653
McDonagh, Don. 987, 1255
McDonald, Jan. 3471
McEachern, Claire. 2977
McFarland, Ron. 3643
McGee, Randall. 4143
McGill, Rachael. 3472
McGrail, Mary Ann. 2978
McGurl, Mimi. 617
McHugh, Catherine. 230, 293, 308, 309, 310, 4056, 4095, 4097, 4099, 4100, 4101, 4102, 4103, 4104, 4105, 4106, 4107
McKay, Melissa Lynn. 3186
McKee, David. 4557, 4614, 4735
McKelly, James C. 4017
McKinley, Jesse. 2711
McLaughlin, William J. 3514
McLean, Andrew M., ed. 2035, 2036, 2037, 2038, 2039, 2040, 2041, 2042, 2043, 2044, 2045, 2046, 2047, 2048, 2049, 2050, 2051, 2052, 2053, 3177
McManus, Donald Cameron. 3056
McMurtry, Larry. 3897, 4018
McMurtry, Mervyn. 2354
McNally, Terrence. 3644
McNamara, Brooks. 415, 654, 4144
McNamara, Brooks, ed. 709
McNeill, Fiona. 2979
McNerney, Sheila. 1797, 3645
McNicholas, Steve, photo. 926
McNulty, Charles. 3646, 3792
McQuade, Paula. 2980
McQuaid, Sean. 1856, 2817
McQuillen, Connie H. 1418
McWilliam, G.H. 3473
Med, Milan, illus. 1265
‚Medieval English Theatre%. 696
Medina, Georgie. 3311
Medvedeva, I. 1709
Mee, Charles L. 1496
Meisner, Nadine. 1328
Mejerchol'd, Vsevolod. 1450, 2296, 2767
Mejia, Davis. 2712
Mel'nikova, S.I., ed. 581
Melbourne, Lucy. 3474
Melchiori, Angiolina. 3251
Meldegg, Stephan, transl. 1475
Melendres, Jaume, transl. 1443, 1478, 1479
Melick, Jennifer. 4736
Mellen, Peter J. 4216
Melrose, Susan. 819
Melton, Christine. 1398
Membrez, Nancy Jane Hartley. 2361
Mendenhall, Marie. 338
Menduni, Enrico. 4063
Ménes, Aranka. 4634
Mercado, Mario R. 4352
Mercier, Martin. 1589, 3805
Merck, Nikolaus. 2000, 2001, 2002
Merkuškina, L.G. 3277
Merlin, Christian. 4798
Mermelstein, David. 4737, 4738
Merritt, Susan Hollis. 3475
Merschmeier, Michael. 11, 655, 742, 743, 1386, 1390, 1572, 1821, 1822, 1823, 2003, 2004, 2005, 2399, 3142, 3153, 3476
Meserole, Harrison T., ed. 3723, 3724
Meserve, Walter J. 3647
Mesplé, Mady. 4573
Messmore, Francis B. 4072
Mészáros, Tamás. 2109
Metz, Katalin. 2229
Meyer-Arlt, Ronald. 2006
Meyer, Marlane. 1497
Meyer, Petra Maria. 3870
Meyerfeld, Max. 3057, 4419
Mezey, Béla, photo. 1107, 1187, 4298, 4832
Mezur, Katherine Marie. 1363
Michalik, Jan. 822
Michel, Pierre, ed. 2201
Micheli, Sergio. 3972
Michler, Werner, ed. 2347
Middeke, Martin, ed. 2667
Midgette, Anne. 4303, 4661, 4662, 4720, 4739
Midyett, Judith Ann. 3648
Mieszkowska, Anna. 611
Mihan, Jörg. 190
Mihurko Poniž, Katja. 2347
Mikeln, Miloš. 1457
Mikics, David. 2981
Miles, Shanda. 1773
Militz, Klaus Ulrich. 3861
Miller, Arthur. 3649
Miller, Edith Hoisington. 2818
Miller, Edward D. 3864
Miller, Felicia. 4787
Miller, Judith G. 3270
Miller, Susan. 1498
Miller, Tice L., ed. 28, 31, 33, 42, 129, 157, 428, 653, 665, 685, 802, 810, 827, 829, 1790, 3637, 3647, 4112, 4144, 4384

Milleret, Margo. 3650
Milliet, Paul. 4416
Mills, David. 2982, 2983, 4226
Milne, Geoffrey. 489
Milnes, Rodney, ed. 4834
Mincaev, M. 4684
Mingalon, Jean-Louis. 4089
Minogue, Valerie. 3103
Minter, Drew. 4740
Mirabella, Grace. 4037
Mirbt, Felix. 4887
Mireckaja, E.V. 875
Mireckaja, N.V. 875
Mišarin, A. 2272
Mitchell, Emily. 4407, 4741
Mitchell, Jack, photo. 1000
Mitchell, Tony. 490
Mittal, Bina. 2819
Miyasaki, June. 3104
Mize, Roberta Rae. 3058
Moder, Janko. 3357
Möderndorfer, Vinko. 1458
Modestov, V. 1141
Moeck, Martin. 311
Moen, Debi. 198, 276, 312, 4108
Mohamed, M.M.S. 2624
Moisejėv, Igor. 1233
Mokuami, Kawatake. 1361
Molarsky, Mona. 3651, 4882, 4906
Moles, Steve. 235, 4096
Moles, Steven. 4326, 4327
Molière (Poquelin, Jean-Baptiste). 1433
Molinari, Cesare. 4192
Møller, Søren Friis. 1267
Molloy, Jacqueline. 191, 1513
Molnár, Kata, photo. 359, 362, 947, 950, 1163
Molnár, Klára, comp., ed. 698
Monaghan, Constance. 2713, 2714
Monk, Charlene Faye. 2715
Monro, Mia, transl. 2641, 3134
Montee, David Duane. 2297
Montgomery, Benilde. 3652
Monton, Ramon, transl. 1437
Moore, Dick. 47, 48, 49, 50, 51, 52, 53, 54, 55, 56, 57, 58, 59, 60, 61, 62, 63, 64, 65, 66, 67, 68, 69, 70, 71, 72, 73, 74, 75, 76, 77, 78, 79, 80, 81, 82, 83, 84, 85, 86, 87, 88, 89, 90, 91, 92, 93, 94, 95, 96, 97, 98, 99, 100, 101, 102, 103, 104, 105, 106, 107, 108, 109, 110, 111, 112, 113, 114, 416, 482, 603, 656, 657, 658, 659, 660, 661, 1774, 1775, 2716, 2717, 2718, 2719, 2720, 4319, 4320, 4386, 4408
Moore, Frederick Timothy. 2721
Moore, Honor. 617
Moore, Iris. 4263
Moore, Opal J. 3653
Morales, Ed. 2722
Moraly, Yehuda. 3105
Moranti, Sandra, ed. 1940
Moravec, Dušan. 1718, 3828
Morávek, Vladimír. 1880
Morelli, Giovanni. 3252
Morelli, Henriette Marguerite. 3477
Moreno, Iani del Rosario. 3276
Moretti, Mario. 3253
Morgan, Kenneth. 4574
Morgan, Robert C. 4042
Morgensen-Lindsay, Annissa Marie. 3364
Morin, Émile. 4233
Morley, Carolyn Anne. 1351
Morozov, A. 2197, 2298
Morris, Lori. 39
Morris, Mark. 4304
Morrissey, Lee. 2984
Morrow, Jim. 4870
Morrow, Lee Alan. 612, 4145
Morsberger, Katharine M. 3969
Morsberger, Robert E. 3969
Mortensen, Bo. 437
Morton, Carlos. 1499
Moscati, Italo, ed. 3254
Moskwin, Andrej. 3330
Mosolova, L.M., ed. 4599
Most, Henrik. 22
Motýlová, Hermína. 4889
Mozgovoj, V. 2299
Mrak, Ivan. 1459
Mrazek, Jan. 4924
Mrzel, Ludvik. 3829
Mueller, John. 982
Mühl-Benninghaus, Wolfgang, ed. 865
Muinzer, Louis. 1681, 1682, 1683, 1741
Mujica, Barbara. 3384
Mulcahy, Kevin V. 4
Müller, Péter, P. 2110
Mulrine, Stephen. 3718
Mulroney, Diane Jean. 3385
Mulvad, Ninette. 5, 725
Mumford, M. 2007
Mumm, Robert C. 4109
Munk, Erika. 1738
Munk, Erika, ed. 617
Muñoz Pujol, Josep M. 1466
Munro, Ian Andrew. 2985
Murav'ëva, I.N. 712
Murphy, Brenda. 3654
Murphy, Deirdre Ann. 3206
Murphy, Hugh Mack, Jr. 1392
Murphy, Mike. 313
Murphy, Sarah. 4075
Murray, Elizabeth. 736
Murray, Frank J., Jr. 3655
Murray, Thomas J. 3478
Murrell, Elizabeth. 3987
Müry, Andres. 1824
Muse, Amy M. 1899
Mut'ja, N.N. 4438
Myers, Eric. 4575, 4742
Myhre, Karin Elizabeth. 2841
Myrvold, Paul. 4185
Myung, Inn Seo. 3846
Nadeau, Michel. 1857
Nadel, Alan. 4083
Nagel, Ivan. 3154
Nagy, András. 2111
Nánay, István. 449, 2112, 2113
Napoleon, Davi. 170, 314, 315, 1557, 1558, 1559, 1560
Napoleon, Davida S. 417
Nasierowski, Tadeusz. 1123
Näslund, Erik. 1302
Natanblut, Erez. 3184
Naude, Alice. 1329
Naumann, Anna. 2051
Nayberg, Yevgenia. 1561
Ndigirigi, Josphat Gichingiri. 3266
Needham, Mark, photo. 4407
Neely, Kent. 571, 831
Negre, Isabel, transl. 1437
Neighbarger, Randy Lyn. 1900
Neill, Michael. 2986, 2987, 2988
Nelson, Alan, H. 2989
Nelson, Brad. 316
Nelson, T.G.A. 3059
Németh, Juli, photo. 2089
Nesbitt, Caroline. 2723
Nesmith, N. Graham. 3656
Nestvogel, Claudius. 953
Nettl, Bruno, ed. 4313
Nettles, John. 2625
Neubauer, Henrik. 994, 1209
Neubert-Herwig, Christa. 2008, 2400
Newcomb, Lynn. 35
Newham, Paul. 728
Newhouse, John William. 662
Newman, Barbara. 1162
Newman, Mark A. 4345
Newson, Lloyd. 1301
Nicholls, Liz. 4920
Nickel, John. 3657
Nielsen, Ulf. 223, 1804, 4491
Niemi, Irmeli. 1917
Nikitin, V.N. 713
Nikolaevič, S. 1142
Nikulin, Ju. V. 4184
Niquille, Marie-Claire. 1736
Nobile, Philip. 3954
Nobling, Torsten. 236, 345, 455, 4114
Nocenti, Annie. 4019, 4020, 4021
Noling, Kim H. 2990
Noller, Joachim. 729
Noonan, Mary. 3075, 3106
Nordlund, David Earl. 3386
Noriko, Agati. 3331
Norman, Buford. 4788
Norman, Stanley Sain. 418
Normington, Kate. 2626
Norris, James. 24, 25, 1393, 2652, 4158
Norseng, Mary Kay. 2627
Norton, James. 2991
Noskov, A.I. 2300
Nouryeh, Andrea Janet. 1776
Novick, Julius. 2724
Novikova, L. 1143, 2301
Nugent, Ann. 1081, 1343
Nunns, Stephen. 419, 420, 1858, 3773, 3793, 4321, 4322
Nureyev, Rudolf. 1144
Nussbaum, Felicity A. 1901
Nwankwo, Nkeonye Caroline. 3284
Nyberg, Lennart Jan. 2628
Nygren, Per. 4439
Nyhn, Jaqueline. 1313
Nyytäjä, Outi. 3070, 3155, 3866
O'Brien, Jack. 2725
O'Brien, John. 4093
O'Connor, Patrick. 4601
O'Dair, Sharon Kay. 2992
O'Farrell, Lawrence. 3736
O'Flaherty, Margo Regan. 1859
O'Hara, Robert. 1500
O'Malley, Lurana Donnels. 4816
O'Pray, Michael. 4044
O'Quinn, Jim. 421, 1721, 2726, 3847
O'Shea, Janet. 1348
O'Toole, Fintan. 3207
Oberander, Thomas. 4150
Obernauer, Gréta. 4891
Ochaim, Brygida. 909
Odenthal, Johannes. 2196
Offenbach, Jacques. 4418
Ogúndèjì, Philip Adédọ́tun. 3285
Okunevskaja, T.K. 582
Olenin, A. 4371
Olesiewicz, Marek. 4896
Oliva, Judy Lee. 3479
Oliver, Michael. 663
Oller, Victor. 3407
Ollikainen, Anneli. 1918
Olsen, Jakob Steen. 1377, 2854
Olsen, Trygve. 456
Olsson, Irène. 882, 1020, 1151, 1152, 1216
Olzon, Janna. 2385
Omodele, Oluremi. 483
Onookome, Okome. 4081
Oppered, Inger Marie. 2386
Orbakajte, Kristina. 4367
Orchard, Lee Frederick. 4397
Orechanova, G. 1574, 1710
Orechanova, G.A. 2302

Orgel, Stephen. 1809, 4208
Ortolani, Benito. 705, 3255
Oseland, James. 471, 2199, 2727, 4387
Osiński, Zbigniew. 575, 2221, 2222
Osipova, L. 2303
Osofisan, Femi. 3286
Ossi, Massimo. 4436
Osterloff, Barbara. 2223
Ostlere, Hilary. 1047, 1189, 1330, 1331
Otrin, Iko. 995
Otten, Terry. 3297
Ovadia, Moni. 2174
Ovčinnikov, I. 2304
Ovčinnikova, S. 2304, 4057
Owens, Melody Sue. 3256
Owens, Rochelle. 617
Pace, Guy. 115
Pacelli, Martha. 2728
Pacheco, Anita. 2993
Page, Tim. 4846
Pakkanen, Päivi. 918
Paller, Rebecca. 4487, 4743
Pályi, András. 3305
Panken, Ton. 2203
Pankratz, David B. 805
Panovski, Naum. 2848
Papp, Dezső, photo. 945, 1088, 1090, 1093, 1094, 1096, 1098, 1100, 1102, 1103, 1110, 1293, 1294, 1341
Parameswaran, Uma. 1368, 2820
Paran, Janice. 1742, 2729
Parandovskij, Ja. 19
Párczen, Zsófia. 1075
Paridon, Egbert van. 2204
Paris, Barry. 4744
Parisious, Roger Nyle. 3806
Parker, Brian. 3658
Parker, Charles Leslie. 3659
Parker, Mary. 3387, 3388
Parker, Mary, ed. 3369, 3370, 3371, 3372, 3374, 3376, 3377, 3379, 3383, 3384, 3387, 3388, 3389, 3390, 3396, 3397, 3403, 3404, 3406
Parks, Barbara Louise. 3480
Parks, Suzan-Lori. 1501, 3589
Parnes, Uzi. 664
Parr, Bruce. 2775
Parr, James A. 3389
Parviainen, Jaana. 919
Pasero, Nicolò, ed. 4227
Pastušenko, L.M. 3332
Patapan, Haig. 3257
Patlakh, Irina Fjellner. 2305, 2306
Patočková, Jana. 1881
Patrick, K.C. 988
Patterson Nahas, Heather Ann. 2730
Patton, Harry J., photo. 4869
Patton, Roy. 4869
Pauka, Kirstin. 1354
Paulin, Diana R. 3660
Paulin, Roger. 3156
Paventi, Eva. 4047
Paventi, Eza. 339, 503, 1860, 1861, 3965
Pavis, Patrice. 694
Payne-Carter, David. 4388
Peale, George. 3390
Pearce, Brian Michael. 2355
Pecha, Jiří. 1882
Pecknold, Adrian. 4085
Pederson, Nadine. 2175
Peel, William Thomas. 1941
Peerbaye, Soraya. 2821
Peiseler, Christian. 1652
Pen, Polly, ed. 4398
Pendleton, Thomas A. 2731
Penny, Simon. 166
Perényi, Balázs. 362, 1671, 2114
Perevozčikov, V. 2307
Perez de Leon, Vicente. 3391
Perez-Rasilla Bayo, Eduardo. 3392
Perkins, Don. 504
Perkins, Elizabeth. 2776
Perlman, Doris. 1025, 3988
Perrello, Tony. 2994
Perroux, Alain. 4094, 4511
Perroux, Alain, ed. 4419, 4420
Perry, Maria. 3934
Peršak, Tone. 1719
Persson, Sven Hugo. 2387
Pesochinsky, Nikolai. 2768
Peter, Frank-Manuel. 929, 1303
Peter, Wolf-Dieter. 4602
Peters, Alton E. 4488
Peters, Margot. 4685
Peters, Monnie. 806
Peters, Sally. 3481
Peterson, Willam. 4257
Petrie, David Terry. 3925
Petrovskaja, I.F. 4686
Pettinelli, Frances. 3661
Petzold, Hans-Jörg. 1521
Pfaff, Walter. 876
Pfeiffer, Gabriele. 524
Pfister, Eva. 3157, 3769
Philips, Magda. 340
Phillip, Christine. 3662
Phillips-Matz, Mary Jane. 4789, 4808
Phillips, Diana, ed. 2201
Phillips, John. 3107
Phipps, A.M. 442
Pičugin, P.A. 1223
Pierce, Nancy Jean Frankian. 3158
Pieri, Marzia. 3258
Piette, Alain. 3974
Pietzsch, Ingeborg. 1653
Pilkington, Lionel. 846
Pillay, Kriben. 826, 2356
Pilling, John. 3208
Pinter, Harold. 1477
Pippen, Judy. 1817
Pirandello, Luigi. 1445, 3824
Pirnie, Karen Worley. 2995
Pitcher, John. 2996
Pitei, Bebe, photo. 1109
Pitkow, Marlene Beth. 1370
Pizzo, Antonio. 2176
Plastow, Jane. 3048
Plastow, Jane, ed. 496, 541, 614, 2772, 2808, 3048, 3271, 3286, 3365
Plesch, Véronique. 589, 3342
Pliberšek, Marjan, illustr. 1209
Pliseckaja, M. 1145, 1208
Plowright, Poh Sim. 1358
Plum, Jay. 116
Pochhammer, Sabine, ed. 1687, 1967, 2196, 2226, 3117, 4266, 4727
Pocknell, Brian. 3108
Podbevšek, Katja. 2348
Podmakovič, Dagmar. 763
Podol'skaja, O. 3333
Poisson, Gary Arthur. 3663
Pojurovskij, B.M.,. 2308
Polgár, Géza. 2115
Polhemus, Ted. 1006
Poljakov, O.E. 3277
Poljakova, O. 4872
Pollack, Steve. 472
Pollock, Adam. 4392
Pollock, Della, ed. 613, 624, 627, 644, 649, 669, 768, 791, 4134
Poniž, Denis. 3358
Poniž, Denis, ed. 1461
Ponnuswami, Meenakshi. 3482, 3483
Poole, Gabrielle. 3484
Poole, Kristen Elizabeth. 2997
Poole, Mary Margaret. 3485
Pope, Rebecca A. 4828
Popescu-Judetz, Eugenia E. 3159
Popovič, I. 1146
Popovich, George Lee. 4040
Pór, Anna. 896, 1229
Portnova, T. 960
Porubjak, Martin. 1376
Postlewait, Thomas. 665
Potak, Philip D. 4152
Potter, Bob. 4214
Potter, Lois. 2998
Potter, Lois, ed. 1225, 1366, 2902, 2941, 2954, 2998, 3016, 3018, 3327, 3969
Pottie, Lisa M., ed. 3060
Powell, Kerry. 3486
Powell, Susana. 2999
Pozdnjakova, A.P. 2406
Prats, Armando José. 4022
Pressler, Terra Daugirda. 666
Prestenskaja, Ju.L. 1029
Preston-Dunlop, Valerie. 1007
Preston, Deborah Elaine. 3664
Preusser, Gerhard. 1654, 1655, 2009, 3487
Price-Hendricks, Margo Jennett. 3000
Price, Amanda. 3428
Price, Jonathan. 617
Prien, Helen Elizabeth. 3665
Proehl, Geoff. 572
Proehl, Geoffrey Scott. 3666
Proiou, Alkistis. 2054
Prokof'eva, N.N. 3334
Pronko, Leonard. 2747
Proulx, Isabelle. 2822
Providenti, Elio. 3259
Prozorova, N., ed. 1711
Ptuškina, N. 2309
Pudełek, Janina. 1124
Puértolas, Pere, transl. 1444
Pujante, A. Luis. 3001
Pulvirenti, Grazia. 1825
Puppa, Paolo. 2177
Purdy, James. 1502
Purkhardt, Brigitte. 1862
Pusič, Barbara. 1720
Putnam, Margaret. 1190
Puukko, Martti. 2224
Qualls, Larry. 3923
Quasha, George. 4258
Quazzolo, Paolo. 2178
Quigley, Patrick. 317
Quinn, Michael Lowell. 837
Raab, Michael. 769, 1394, 3488
Raber, Karen L. 3002
Rabillard, Sheila, ed. 2608, 3422, 3426, 3436, 3451, 3458, 3463, 3466, 3483, 3489, 3504, 3505, 4065
Radbourne, Jennifer. 1
Raddatz, Frank. 2010
Radeščel, Borko. 4899
Radice, Mark A. 4548
Radice, Mark A., ed. 203, 4433, 4436, 4492, 4493, 4494, 4528, 4548, 4549, 4581
Radics, Viktória. 2116, 2117, 2118
Radrigán, Juan. 1413
Radvan, Florian. 3770
Ragni, Biancamaria. 2179
Rainer, Cosima. 161
Rainer, Yvonne. 989
Rainio, Elina. 150, 840
Rajk, András. 1112
Rajkin, A.I. 583
Ram, Jane. 4314, 4448
Ramanathan, Geetha. 3061
Ramírez, Elizabeth. 2209
Ramondetta, Joseph Thomas. 3003

Ramovš, Mirko. 1243
Ramsden, Timothy. 26, 1743, 1744
Ran, Faye. 3667
Ranald, Margaret Loftus. 3281, 3668
Rand, Herbert Carleton, II. 318
Ranevskaja, Faina G. 584
Ranieri, David. 278
Raphael, Mitchel. 3966
Raskina, Raissa, ed. 2328
Raskova, L. 2310
Ratajczak, Dobrochna. 3306
Ratajczak, Dobrochna, ed. 610, 824, 3306, 4154
Ratcliffe, Stephen. 3004
Rath, Eric Clemence. 1373
Ratsaby, Michele. 3109
Rauch, Rudolph S. 4512
Rauen, Margarida Gandara. 3005
Raugul, E. 4884
Raulo, Hanna. 2311
Ravelhofer, Barbara. 4198
Ravnjak, Vili. 1460
Ray, Douglass. 117
Ray, Sid. 3006
Raylor, Timothy. 4209
Raymond, Gerard. 3669
Raymond, Yves. 2823
Rayner, Alice. 3489, 3582
Razzakov, F. 4033
Reaney, Mark. 1562
Réblová, Kateřina. 1265
Redfern, Betty. 1005
Redfern, Walter. 3110
Redfern, Walter, transl. 3250
Reed, Melissa Ann. 3007
Rees, Charles A. 3670
Réfi, Zsuzsanna. 897, 949, 1113, 4460, 4635, 4636
Regester, Charlene. 3874
Regnault, François, transl. 1419
Rehm, Stefan Gerhard. 3822
Reid, John. 3335
Reid, Robert L. 3008
Reid, William Nicholas. 1563
Reilly, John. 4713
Reinelt, Janelle. 870
Reinhard, Sabine. 2011
Reininghaus, Frieder. 4297, 4558
Reis, George R. 118
Reiser-Memmer, Michelle. 35
Reiss, Alvin H. 20, 119, 120, 121, 122, 123, 124, 125, 422, 423, 424, 1777
Reiter, Susan. 990
Remnant, Mary. 1902
Renaud, Lissa Tyler. 3111
Renner, Pamela. 3209, 3671
Renton, Andrew. 3210
Renton, Linda. 3490
Rentschler, Ruth. 126
Reslová, Marie. 1883, 2851
Reslová, Marie, ed. 1880
Retallack, John. 2205
Rettig, Claes von. 2180, 3393
Rettig, Shane. 319
Rewa, Natalie. 505, 4425, 4426
Reynolds, Nancy. 1051
Reynolds, Roger. 4309
Rice, Annabelle. 2012
Rice, Raymond Joseph. 3009
Rich, J. Dennis. 45
Richard, Jean-Paul. 127
Richards, Alison. 1568
Richards, Jeffrey H. 613, 3672
Rickerd, Julie Rekai. 718, 1516, 4427, 4430
Ridden, Geoffrey M. 3010
Rieck, Dean. 128
Rieger, Maren. 1385
Riendeau, Pascal. 2824
Rifkind, Bryna Beth. 1778
Riggio, Milla C. 4160, 4172, 4177
Riggs, Mike. 667
Rigó, Béla. 4461
Riise, Michael. 2012
Ring, Lars. 2369
Risán, Anton. 1052
Rischbieter, Henning. 2013
Rischbieter, Henning, comp. 1910
Risdon, Michelle Elaine. 3673
Rishoi, Niel. 4557, 4695
Rislund, Staffan. 602, 1733
Risum, Janne. 443
Ritter, Scott R. 1503
Riva, M. 3955
Rivkin-Fish, Ziggy. 39
Rix, Roxane. 668
Rizzo, Frank. 3674
Roach, Joseph. 3852, 4745
Roach, Joseph R. 669
Roberts, Peter. 2629
Roberts, Philip. 2630
Roberts, Rhoda. 491
Roberts, Vera Mowry. 129
Robertson, Beverly J. 1504
Robertson, Lanie. 1505
Robertson, Michael E., II. 35
Robins, Daina Ilze. 2014
Robinson, Brian W. 617
Robinson, James A. 3675
Robson, Christopher. 1745, 2631, 2632, 2633, 2732, 2733, 2734, 3854, 3933, 3941, 4279, 4280
Rock, Judith. 1076
Rockwell, John. 4847
Rodenhuis, Willem. 3796
Rodger, Gillian Margaret. 4281
Rogačevskij, M.L. 2312
Rogers, Peter. 465
Rogers, Steve. 4229, 4246, 4247
Rogerson, Margaret. 4890
Rogoff, Gordon. 617
Rogowski, Christian Uwe. 3062
Rohde, Frank. 4458
Rohlehr, Gordon. 4119
Rojtman, Ju. 1575
Rókás, László. 1163
Rokem, Freddie. 3218
Roldan Rodriguez, Janet. 3312
Rolfe, James. 4414
Rolin, Christina. 1519
Romanowski, Andrzej. 576
Romanuško, M. 1947
Róna, Katalin. 15, 1043, 1114, 2119
Rönnberg, Ingergerd. 2388
Rosa, Marco Camarotti. 497
Rose, Chris Edwin. 1506
Rosenbaum, Jonathan. 3956
Rosenberg, Charles George. 4809
Rosenfeld, Lorraine. 4513
Rosetti Wagner, Teresina, transl. 4799
Rosiny, Claudia. 4059
Rosow, Lois. 4790
Ross, Alex. 3957, 4471
Rossi, Doc. 3160
Rossi, Roberto. 807
Rossini, Gaetano. 4421
Rossini, Gioacchino. 4421
Rossini, John. 3676
Rosten, Bevya. 2735, 2736
Roth, Frans, transl. 1440
Roth, Thomas. 1596
Roth, Wilhelm. 152, 744
Rothwell, Angela Downing, ed. 3798
Rotté, Joanna. 880
Rottensten, Rikke. 514
Röttger, Kati. 821
Roulston, Helen H. 4023
Routti, Laura. 920
Roux, Georges. 4810
Rowe, Catherine Louise. 1507
Rowe, Paul. 1863, 2825
Rowell, Charles H. 1679, 3279
Roy, Irène. 1864
Rozik, Eli. 832, 3794
Rozman, Branko. 1461
Rubidge, Bradley. 3112, 3820
Rubidge, Sarah. 974
Rubin, Judith. 320, 4110
Rubio, José Luis. 4496
Rudnik, N. 2313
Ruffini, Franco. 850
Rugg, Rebecca Ann. 617
Rühle, Günther. 2015, 2181
Runkel, Richard. 3491
Runnalls, Graham. 3763
Ruprecht, Alvina. 1590
Rush, Michael. 3958
Russ, Claire. 1261, 1276
Russell, Melinda, ed. 4313
Russo, Peggy Anne. 506
Rustan, John. 4041
Ruszt, József. 16, 2120
Rutter, Carol Chillington. 4024
Ruuskanen, Annukka. 1919
Rux, Paul. 130
Ruzika, Donna. 473
Ryan, Jim. 321
Ryan, Patrick. 3011
Ryan, Steven Daniel. 3677
Ryen, Dag. 1779
Saag, Kristjan. 859, 2369, 2634, 3211
Sabbadini, Silvano. 3012
Sabrey-Saperstein, Sheila. 4746
Sacks, David Harris. 3752
Saddik, Annette J. 3678
Sadyrin, B.V. 4687
Šafer, N. 4817
Šah-Azizova, T. 2314
Said, Aleya A. 3418
Saint-Jacques, Diane. 834
Saivetz, Deborah. 2737
Sajmon, G.U. 4818
Šakirzjanov, M. 1164
Saksida, Igor. 3359
Saksida, Igor, ed. 1462
Sal'nikov, G.I. 2315
Sal'tina, M. 761
Salamensky, Shelley Ilene. 3492
Salerno, Patricia Joan. 2738
Salisburgy, Wilma. 1027
Salmanova, E.M. 2739
Salzer, Beeb. 322
Sammler, Ben, ed. 323
Samsonowicz, Hanna, ed. 822, 855, 856
Sandberg, Leslie Jean. 1508
Sandgren, Maria. 4603, 4700
Sandla, Robert. 4747
Sándor, Erzsi. 363
Sándor, Judit. 4637
Sándor, L. István. 2121, 2122, 2123, 2124, 2125, 2126, 2127, 2128, 2129, 2130, 4362
Sandström, Ulf. 224
Sankeralli, Burton. 4178
Šaparova, O. 2316
Sapienza, Annamaria. 4043, 4811
Saraeva, L.M. 877
Sarrias Fornés, Mercè. 1467
Sarris, Andrew. 3989
Sarver, Susan. 1217
Sassine, Antoun S. 3268
Satake, Kenichi. 3394

Satanikovič, Juliana. 763
Sauvil, Pierre. 1434
Šav, Vlado. 592
Savant, Anthony Louis. 670
Savarese, Nicole, ed. 697
Savarino, Ida. 3113
Savčenko, B. 2317
Savran, David. 3679
Savvina, I.S. 2318
Scala, Alexander. 1439
Scarlini, Luca, ed. 552
Scarnati, Blase Samuel, Jr. 4748
Scarsella, Alessandro. 4159
Ščeglov, A. 2319
Ščeglov, D. 2320
Schabert, Ina. 1813
Schaeffer, Ira. 3680
Schafer, Elizabeth. 2635
Schalk, Axel. 1656
Schalkwyk, David. 3753
Schama, Simon. 3962
Schanke, Robert A. 585
Schanke, Robert A., ed. 44, 116, 404, 585, 612, 619, 634, 674, 680, 799, 2590, 2656, 2691, 2757
Scharbau, Puk. 1359
Scharine, Richard. 131
Schatz, Howard, photo. 1168, 1174, 1183, 1189, 1329, 1330
Schechner, Richard. 132, 1833, 4172
Scheffer, Will. 1509
Schely-Newman, Esther. 714, 4079
Schempp, James I. 3681
Schenone, Francesca, ed. 548
Scherer, Barrymore Laurence. 4576, 4757
Scherer, Colette. 3114
Schiavi, Michael R. 3682
Schiel, Katherine West. 3013
Schiff, David. 4749
Schiffman, Jean. 2740, 3683
Schiller, Beatriz. 4713
Schiller, Beatriz, photo. 1089
Schirmer, Lothar. 843
Schlewitt, Carena. 2225
Schlosberg, Eve Harriett. 671
Schlueter, June. 2016
Schmidgall, Gary. 4838
Schmidt, Dagmar. 1657
Schmidt, Goran, ed. 1459
Schmidt, Kekke. 3161
Schmitz-Gielsdorf, Uwe. 4775
Schmoll, Linda Brigitte. 4061
Schneider, Katja. 930, 931, 1283
Schneider, Robert. 3684
Schneider, Wolfgang. 367, 537, 2155, 2389
Schnitzler, Arthur. 1408
Schoch, Richard W. 3014
Schoenberg, Arnold. 4533, 4604
Schoenfeld, Gerald. 425
Schor, Alison Linda. 808
Schraft, Robin John. 324
Schreiber, Loren. 325
Schreiber, Ulrich. 2017, 4702
Schubert, Lia. 1021
Schuller, Gabriella. 2131, 2321
Schulman, Peter. 1613
Schulman, Sarah. 3685
Schulz-Reimpell, Werner. 1810
Schulz, Genia. 3162
Schulze-Reimpell, Werner. 1658
Schumacher, Claude. 3115
Schumacher, Claude, ed. 2022, 2168, 2784, 3054, 3064, 3092, 3097, 3105, 3115, 3137, 3217, 3218, 3310, 3600, 3605, 3628, 4153, 4220
Schumacher, Ernst. 3063
Schvey, Henry I. 3552
Schwab, Norm. 276
Schwanitz, Dietrich. 1978
Schwartz, Beth Carrol. 3779
Schwarz, J. Robert. 4750
Schwarz, Kathryn. 3015
Schwerin von Krosigk, Barbara. 2226
Scofield, Martin. 3754
Scoll, Shelley. 341
Scott, Michael. 4536
Scott, Shelley. 4888
Scott, Virginia. 553
Sears, Djanet. 2826
Sears, Linda Roseanne. 672
Seay, Donald Walter. 133
Sebestyén, Rita. 2132
Secor, James Leo. 1364
Secrest, Meryle. 4399
Sediánszky, Nóra. 2133, 4638
Sedov, A. 4688, 4689
Sedov, Ja. 1077, 1252, 4463, 4690
Seib, Al, photo. 4179
Seita, Mario. 3116
Seitinger, Astrid. 4116
Šejkina, M. 3336
Sel'vinskaja, T. 216
Seleznev, V. 3337
Sellers-Young, Barbara. 809
Selling, Jan. 2018
Selmon, Michael Layne. 3493
Senici, Emanuele Giuseppe. 4812
Serazetdinov, B. 1712
Serôdio, Maria Helena. 3816
Serrallonga, Carme, transl. 1437
Server, Lee. 4025, 4026
Servos, Norbert. 932, 933, 1270, 1279, 1284, 1285
Sessi, Carla Castiglione. 2182
Šestakova, N. 2322
Sever, Boštjan, ed. 4875
Severin, Laura. 770
Sevilla-Gonzaga, Marylis. 4544, 4751
Sevilla-Gonzaga, Marylis, comp. 4445
Sfyris, Panagiotis. 2183, 3260
Shafer, Yvonne. 538, 1522, 1780, 2747, 4605
Shakespeare, William. 1419, 1420, 1421, 1422
Shantz, Valerie. 2827
Shapiro, Michael. 3016
Sharp, Allison Gappmayer. 3686
Shart, Raffy. 1435
Shattuck, Charles H. 810
Shaughnessy, Edward L. 2154, 3687
Shaughnessy, Robert. 2636
Shaw, George Bernard. 1478
Shawe-Taylor, Desmond. 1903
Shearer, Sybil. 1082
Sheehy, Henry. 3688
Sheen, J.E. 3017
Shelton, Lewis E. 2741
Shen, Grant. 1872
Shen, Virginia Shiang-Lan. 2846
Sherin, Edwin. 2742
Shevtsova, Maria. 1942, 1943, 2019
Shields, Shirlee Hurst. 811
Shimizu, Tetsuo. 4242
Shmeruk, Chone. 3307
Shteir, Rachel. 1713, 4400
Shull, Thomas Allen. 2743
Siberry, Michael. 2637
Šichman, S.Ja., ed. 1716
Sieben, Irene. 892, 1015, 1286, 1287
Siebenhaar, Klaus. 153
Siegal, Jessica. 3689
Siegal, Nina. 1781
Siegel, Marcia B. 1014
Sierz, Aleks. 3494
Silant'eva, I.I. 4691
Siljunas, V. Ju. 2362
Sills, Paul. 617
Siltala, Juha. 732
Silverstein, Marc. 2364, 3690
Simara, László, photo. 2067, 2092, 2095, 2110, 2117, 2123, 2149
Simmons, Pat. 326
Simon, John. 4606
Simons, Johan. 3280
Simonsen, Majbrit. 1271
Sims, Caitlin. 1191, 4092
Sinel'nikova, T.A. 1029
Singer, Mark. 3871
Singer, Stanford Paul. 4146
Singh, Yvonne Marie. 3691
Singman, Jeffrey L. 3018
Sinko, Grzegorz. 856
Sitar, Jelena. 4926
Sjöberg, Lars. 4701
Sjögren, Henrik. 2855
Skasa, Michael. 2020, 2021
Skloot, Robert. 3064, 3290
Škorpil, Jakub. 1884
Skura, Meredith. 3019
Slater, Thomas J. 3959
Slattery, Bryan. 864
Slights, Camille Wells. 3020
Slights, Jessica. 3021
Slingerland, Amy L. 1032, 1033, 1034, 1035, 3922
Ślusarska, Magdalena. 1691
Slusser, Dean. 402
Smallwood, Robert. 2638
Smallwood, Robert, ed. 2593, 2606, 2616, 2617, 2619, 2620, 2623, 2625, 2637, 2638, 2640, 2642, 2643
Smith, A.H. 3022
Smith, Alison Sealy. 2826
Smith, Armin. 4169
Smith, Bryan. 913
Smith, Cary. 4444
Smith, Ian. 3023
Smith, Iris. 852
Smith, Joseph Andrew. 3313
Smith, Marian Elizabeth. 1078
Smith, Matthew W. 35
Smith, Molly Easo. 3024
Smith, Patricia Juliana. 4813
Smith, Patrick J. 4559, 4752
Smith, Peter J. 3025
Smith, Sidonie. 1904
Smith, Susan Manell. 3395
Smoktunovskij, I.M. 2323
Smythe, Eva. 1746
Šnajder, Slobodan. 1415
Snape, Libby. 1332
Snow, Stephen Eddy. 4147
Söderberg, Olle. 369, 370, 1677
Sofer, Andrew. 3026
Sohl, Marty, photo. 1061
Sohn, Sonja. 3893
Sokol, B.J. 3027
Sokół, Lech. 3308
Sokolova, I. 2324
Sokur, G. 2325
Soldini, Elisabetta. 4503, 4504, 4514, 4515, 4516, 4517, 4518, 4519
Soldini, Elisabetta, comp. 4520, 4521
Solie, Ruth A. 4411
Solomin, Ju. 2326
Solomon, Alisa. 4282
Solov'eva, I. 1714
Solov'eva, I.N., ed. 2327
Solymosi Tari, Emőke. 4668
Sólyom, György. 4800
Somerset, Alan. 4195
Sommaiolo, Paolo. 3261, 4273
Sonntag-Kunst, Helga. 444

Sørensen, Lilo. 4449
Sörenson, Elisabeth. 525, 2390
Sörenson, Margareta. 1153, 1210, 1304, 1305, 4182
Sorge, Thomas. 2052
Sorgeloos, Herman, photo. 1260
Sorokin, V.F. 2194
Sorokina, I. 4463
Soum, Corinne. 4090
Spackman, Helen. 4244, 4261
Špalikov, Gennadij. 3975, 3976
Spångberg, Mårten. 1314
Speaight, George. 2639
Speirs, Jonathan. 278
Speisman, Barbara Waddell. 1510
Spencer, Jenny S., ed. 529, 535, 846, 870, 1815, 1925, 2351, 2797, 3212, 3572, 3582, 3629, 3635, 4878
Sperdakos, Paula. 1865
Spiegel, Jan Ellen. 908
Spier, Steven. 4133
Spindler, Fredrika. 1814, 1944
Spinneweber, Rémy, transl. 1505
Spiró, György. 16
Splawn, P. Jane. 3692
Spreng, Eberhard. 3117
Springhall, John. 4038
Squires, Richard. 673
Srampickal, Jacob. 541
Stachov, D. 1715
Ståhle, Anna Greta. 556, 889, 1244
Stähr, Susanne. 4316, 4607
Stahura, Mark. 4549
Staicer, Judy. 327
Stajewski, Marcin. 1688
Stammen, Silvia. 1659, 1660
Stancavage, Sharon. 328
Stanislavskij, Konstantin Sergejévič. 2327, 2328
Stanton, Stephen S. 3298
Stapper, Lion. 695
Starikova, L.M. 2329
Stasio, Marilyn. 474, 2744, 2745
Staub, August W. 4048
Stavbar, Vlasta. 593
Steadman, Ian. 3365
Stearns, David Patrick. 4522, 4560
Steen, Shannon. 3810
Stegassy, Ruth. 4170
Stehlíková, Eva. 1885
Stein, Charles. 4258
Stein, Jean. 3875
Steiner, George. 4577
Steinlauf, Michael Charles. 577
Stejnberg Gusman, D. 484
Stenberg, Douglas G. 4027
Stenberg, Roger, photo. 2391
Stensson, Ola. 4699
Stepanenko, E. 2330
Stepanian, Laurie Anne. 134
Stephan, Erika. 1661
Stephenson, Nan Louise. 135
Stephenson, Tracy. 4223
Stepnov, V. 2331
Sterling, Eric. 3693
Stern, T. 1905
Sterner, Mark Hamilton. 3495
Sternglantz, Ruth Esther. 3028
Stevens, Louise K. 136
Stevenson, David R. 137
Stevenson, Melanie. 1866
Still, James. 852
Stillmark, Alexander. 2022
Stites, Richard. 815
Stobernack, Michael. 12
Stöckemann, Patricia. 934, 1288
Stockman, Todd. 4148, 4149, 4907, 4908, 4909
Stoiber, Rainer M. 2023
Stoll, Anita K. 3396
Stolt, Bengt. 2392
Storožuk, A.G. 1080
Story, Rosalyn M. 4489
Stovall, Count. 1782
Strand, Ginger. 674
Strassburger, Alexandra, photo. 2084, 2108, 4667
Stratton, Richard. 3893
Straub, Kristina. 1906
Straznicky, Marta. 3065
Strehler, Giorgio. 2184
Strein, Jürgen. 1662
Streisand, Marianne. 4856
Strel'cova, E. 1827
Strenger, Elisabeth Maria. 3163
Strongman, Wayne. 4346
Stroud, Matthew D. 3397
Strutinskaja, E.I. 217
Stuart, Ian. 3834
Stuber, Andrea. 2134, 2135
Stuckert, Heike. 4266
Stucky, Nathan Paul. 3694
Stumm, Reinhardt. 1663, 1737
Stumpfe, Mario. 539, 2024
Subhra, Madžumdar. 1349, 1369
Suhr, Moon Ja Minn. 954
Šul'pin, A. 382
Sulcas, Roslyn. 991
Sullivan, Claudia Norene. 675
Sullivan, Esther Beth. 3212
Sullivan, Garrett A., Jr. 3029
Sullivan, Michael R. 3398
Sullivan, Sharon L. 853
Summers, Ellen Louise. 3030
Sun, William H. 2845
Sundberg, Björn. 3413
Sündermann, Anja. 4608
Sung, Hae-Kyung. 3213
Suric, E. 961
Sussman, Mark. 812
Sutcliffe, Tom. 4479, 4705, 4839
Sutinen, Virve. 1204
Švarc, E.L. 1451
Svečnikov, V. 4274
Svenstam, Åke. 225
Svetaeva, M.G., ed. 1716
Svetina, Ivo. 3360
Svetina, Ivo, ed., transl. 1470
Swartz, Mark. 426
Swearingen, Darryl Duane. 2746
Sweeney, Megan. 4862
Syčeva, L. 4692
Szabó, István. 364
Szabó, Péter, photo. 2082, 2136
Szabó, Viktória. 1044
Szalczer, Eszter. 2393
Szántó, Judit. 2136, 2137, 2138, 2139
Szántó, Judit, transl. 836, 842, 3066
Szász, Anna. 1115
Szebeni, Zsuzsa. 365, 383
Szebeni, Zsuzsa, comp. 698
Szegő, György. 447
Szegő, György, ed. 197
Szegő, György, et al. 448
Szegvári, Katalin. 4639
Székely, Gábor. 1672
Székely, György. 4911
Szendy, Peter. 4776
Szigethy, Gábor. 2140
Sziládi, János. 1672
Szilágyi, Lenke, photo. 2079
Szilagyi, Stephen. 3031
Szilvási, Zsuzsa. 450
Szoboszlai, Gábor, photo. 4644
Szokolay, Sándor. 4801
Szomory, György. 4299, 4640, 4641
Szpakowska, Małgorzata. 3309
Szűcs, Zoltán, photo. 2061, 2066, 2096, 2098, 2125
Szyber, Bogdan. 1301
Tabert, Nils. 3496
Tackels, Bruno. 1614
Taddei, Mirian Hunter. 3032
Taffon, Giorgio. 3262
Tait, Peta. 492, 1664
Tal'kova, O. Ju. 4368
Tanitch, Robert. 1783, 1784, 2394, 3835, 4066
Tanjuk, L., ed. 2279
Tanner, Martha Alison. 3033
Taras, John. 1079
Tarján, Tamás. 3314
Tarleton, Angela Brannon. 4323
Taszman, Maurice. 3118
Taub, Lora Elisabeth. 518
Tawast, Minna. 921
Taylor, Diana. 4259
Taylor, Dominick A. 1511
Taylor, Edward Wallace. 1564
Taylor, John Russel. 4372
Taylor, Jujuan Carolyn. 813
Taylor, Lib. 1945
Taylor, Merideth. 3527
Teevan, Colin. 3214
Teixidor, Jordi. 1468
Teixidor, Jordi, transl. 1432
Teljakovskij, V.A. 1716
Templeton, Alice. 4028
Templeton, Joan. 2747
Tennant, David. 2640
Tenney, John. 427
Tereščenko, V. 4163
Terneuil, Alexandre. 3119
Tersman, Ninna. 3414
Teschke, Holger. 745, 2641, 4609
Thaggert, Miriam. 4029
Theaterwerkstatt Pilkentafel. 1401
Theissen, Hermann. 1272
Thelestam, Sunniva. 167, 175, 1519
Thielemans, Johan. 2206
Thomas, Alan. 2828
Thomas, Helen. 1200
Thomas, Jacqueline. 3120
Thomas, Melody Ann. 1785
Thomas, Philip V. 1907
Thomas, Richard K. 329
Thomas, Sidney. 3034
Thomas, Veona. 1399
Thomason, Paul. 4610, 4753, 4754, 4755, 4765
Thomason, Phillip Brian. 457
Thöming, Anja-Rose. 4459
Thompson, Ann. 3497
Thompson, Eric C. 138
Thompson, Fred. 4883
Thompson, Garland Lee. 1786
Thomson, Helen. 2777, 2778
Thorell, Bernt. 226, 227
Thorne, Simon. 4260
Thoss, Michael M. 1946
Thresher, Tanya. 3299
Throne, Stephanie Susanne. 3399
Thuresson, Anders. 2395
Tian, Min. 1346
Tichy, Charles Allen. 676
Tichý, Zdeněk Aleš, ed. 1878, 1879
Tiedemann, Kathrin. 1385, 2025, 4234
Tiedtke, Marion. 3164
Tiffany, Grace. 3755
Timm, Mikael. 3300
Timofeev, P.T. 2332
Tinterri, Alessandro, ed. 752, 4227
Tipton, Alzada J. 3035
Titarenko, V. 2333
Titkova, N. 3338

Tjäder, Per Arne. 3165
Toben, Ingo. 2026
Tobin, Ronald W. 3695
Toiminen, Marjaana. 1273
Tóka, Ágnes. 2185
Tolchinsky, David E. 4030
Tompkins, Joanne. 3807
Tooks, Kim. 2748, 2749, 3696
Toomer, Jeanette. 1787
Topaz, Muriel. 1256
Tordai, Zádor. 2141
Torky, Karin. 2787
Törner, Oliver. 352
Törnqvist, Egil. 3697
Török, Tamara. 2142, 2186
Tóth, Hajnalka. 4921
Tóth, László, photo. 1112
Totland, Steven Bradley. 1788
Tracie, Rachel Elisabeth. 507
Tranberg, Sören. 4439, 4465, 4663, 4665, 4848, 4859
Traub, Valerie. 3756
Trautmann, Gretchen. 3400
Treadwell, James. 4837
Treadwell, Nina. 4814
Trebbi, Fernando. 3263
Trencsényi, Katalin. 1615
Triebold, Wilhelm. 168, 1665
Troiani, Elisa A. 3698
Troisi, Massimo. 3858
Trotter, Mary. 1404
Troughton, David. 2642
Trumbo, Dalton. 3891
Truppel, Mariann. 1219
Trušin, E. 1595
Tsehaye, Solomon. 3048
Tseng, Tin-Yu. 3166
Tucker, Edward L. 3699
Tucker, Sharon Gayle. 1512
Tuganov, R.U. 706
Tullio, Leslie A. 35
Turley, Hans. 1908
Turnbaugh, Douglas Blair. 3700
Turner, Beth. 2750
Turner, Henry S. 3036
Tuuling, Mari. 1600
Tyler, Kelsey Duane. 3701
Tyler, Mary Kathleen. 3037
Tyszka, Juliusz. 375, 438
Ueding, Cornelie. 4611
Uitman, Hans. 1122
Ukpokodu, I. Peter. 687
Ulchur Collazos, Leobardo Ivan. 2847
Ulrich, Judy A.P. 3702
Underdelinden, Sjaak. 564
Underiner, Tamara L. 560
Unruh, Delbert. 173
Upor, László. 677, 845, 2143
Upton, Carole-Anne. 3271
Urbán, Balázs. 2144, 2145
Urbán, Mária, transl. 892
Ušakov, S. 3339
Utz, James Edward, Jr. 565
Uvarova, E.D., ed. 583
Uyen, Michel. 695
V.F., Ščerbakova. 2291
Vadasi, Tibor. 1220, 1295
Vagapova, N. 1875
Vail, June. 1245
Vaïs, Michel. 688, 835, 1591, 1867, 3737, 3738, 3739, 3928
Vajda, M. Pál, photo. 4625
Valenti, Cristina, ed. 1602
Valentini, Valentina. 554
Valentini, Valentina, ed. 1670
Valette, Colette L. 678
Vallillo, Stephen M. 2751
Valukin, M.E. 1202
van Berlaer-Hellemans, Dina. 3180, 3555
Van Daele, Koen, ed. 384
Van den Dries, Luk. 3180, 3555
Van Der Merwe, Quintus. 3121
Van Dyke, Margaret. 2829
van Erven, Eugene. 535
Van Kerkhoven, Marianne. 3180, 3555
Van Meer, Deen, photo. 1121
van Moere, Didier. 4523, 4524, 4525
van Romondt, Alice C., ed. 3725
Vanden Heuvel, Michael John. 526
Vangeli, Nina. 1266
Vanni, Simona. 704
Varga, Judit. 2146
Varl, Breda. 4885
Varley, Julia. 952
Varma, Rahul. 1412, 1592
Várnai, Dóra. 950
Várszegi, Tibor. 924
Vasil'čikova, L. 1616
Vasil'ev, A. 4353
Vasil'ev, V. 1147
Vasil'eva, M. 1148
Vasina, E.N. 2791
Vasjuchin, V. 3859
Vaughan, Alden T. 3038
Vaughan, Stewart, transl. 1473
Vaughan, Virginia Mason. 1909
Vaze, Bageshree. 508
Vazsó, Vera. 951, 1045, 1116
Velarde, Olga Angelica. 3401
Veldhuis, Jenny J. 1053
Velemanová, Věra. 1518
Verdone, Mario. 452
Veréb, Simon, photo. 2086, 2121, 2126, 2135, 4359, 4362, 4622, 4631
Vereecke, Father Robert, S.J. 1192
Verma, Jatinder. 614
Veroli, Patricia. 1289
Verschuer, Leopold von. 3122
Versényi, Adam, transl. 1447
Versluys, Kristiaan, ed. 4007
Vertinskaja, M. 2334
Vervliet, Raymond. 3547
Vescovo, Marisa. 204
Veselovskij, S. 2335
Vesnik, E. 586, 2336
Vesterinen, Minna. 1008
Vevar, Rok. 594, 4873
Vevar, Štefan. 595
Vevar, Štefan, ed. 708
Vey, Shauna A. 139
Vianello, Daniele. 2187, 2188
Viazzi, Cesare. 4126
Vicente, Arie I. 3402
Vidal, Josep M., transl. 1433
Vigeant, Louise. 342, 1365, 2830, 2831, 4031
Vincent, Renée. 237
Vingoe, Mary. 1868
Vinogradova, T.I. 4311
Vinokur, V. 2337
Vinter, Marie, transl. 182
Viola, György. 1083
Visdei, Anca. 1436
Vislov, A. 2338
Vlachos, Helen. 1412
Vogel, Paula. 1789
Vogel, Viveka. 2396
Voglino, Barbara. 3703
Vogt, Matthias Theodor. 746
Voigt, Thomas. 4860
Volodarskaja, L. 3039
Volz, Sabrina Rose. 3167
Von Geldern, James R. 4113
Voros, Sharon D. 3403
Voss, Joan M. 814
Voss, Philip. 2643
Vowells, John J. 679
Voznesenskij, A., transl. 3649
Vranc, Danilo. 4914
Vries, Lyckle de. 208
Vukolov, N. 1154
Vul'f, V. 587
Vul'f, V., ed. 2243
Vuori, Suna. 1274, 1920, 4181
Vysockij, V.S. 164, 1452, 1453
Wagner, Gottfried. 4799
Wagner, Vit. 2832, 2833, 2834, 2835
Wahlin, Claes. 2397
Wainscott, Ronald. 2752
Waites, Aline. 27, 1747, 1748, 2644, 2645, 2646, 3498, 3780, 4284
Walczak, Barbara. 1060
Walen, Denise A. 680
Walker, John. 3168
Walker, Pierre A. 3704
Wall, Clare-Marie. 2647
Wallace, Lea. 4910
Wallace, Lillian Utermohlen. 681
Wallström, Catharina. 1734, 3415
Walser, Theresia. 2027
Walsh, Basil F. 4645
Walsh, Marcus. 3040
Walsh, Martin W. 4171
Walsh, Paul James. 3416
Walter, Péter, photo. 2134
Walters, Scott Edward. 3848
Walther, Ingeborg Christina. 3178
Walton, Glenn. 1869, 2836, 3705
Walton, Tony. 330
Walz, Ruth, photo. 1569
Wang, H.C. 3499
Wang, Hsiao-Mei. 4312
Wardle, Irving. 617
Warfield, Jean Mae. 4423
Wassenberg, Anya. 1593
Wasserstein, Wendy. 3589
Waszkiel, Marek, ed. 4895
Watermeier, Daniel J. 1790, 3706
Watson-Wright, Susan. 2753
Watson, Gray. 4230
Watson, Ian. 4084
Watson, John Clair. 3707
Watson, Keith. 1315
Watson, Robert N. 3041
Watson, William Van. 3264
Watt, Ian. 730
Wattenberg, Richard. 3708
Weathersby, William, Jr. 475, 476, 477, 478, 479
Weaver, Michael S. 3709
Weber, Brigitta. 4777
Weber, Manfred. 3730
Wedekind, Frank. 3169
Weeks, Stephen Hyer. 3500
Wegner, Pamela Sydney. 1791
Wehle, Philippa. 2189
Weidle, Roland. 1978
Weimann, Robert. 2053, 3042
Weimer, Christopher B. 3404
Weinstein, Arnold. 617
Weinstein, Katherine. 2769
Weiss, Alfred. 2653
Weiss, Rudolf. 3501
Weiss, Sarah. 4925
Weissengruber, Erik Paul. 3502
Welch, Patricia Marie. 2195
Welsh, Alexander. 3757
Wengrow, Arnold. 4501
Werner, Frank. 959
Werner, Jessica. 2754
Werry, Margaret. 3810
Werstine, Paul. 3043

West, Martha Ullman. 1333
West, William D. 4490
West, William N. 731
Westerlund, Lennart. 3960
Westfahl, Lynne Lundquist. 682
Westman, Nany. 883
Wetzel, Johannes. 1617
Whitaker, Rick. 1185, 1308
White, G. 771
White, Harry. 3215
White, Robert Allwyn. 683
Wholsen, Barbara J. 331
Wickham, Philip. 343, 509, 1870, 1871, 3967, 3990, 4118
Wieck, Thomas. 13, 2028, 3170
Wigman, Mary. 1290
Wikander, Matthew H. 3503, 3710
Wilcock, M.S. 1911
Wild, Christopher Joachim. 3171
Wilde, Oscar. 1479
Wildeman, Maartje. 957
Wilder, Gene. 3898
Wilheim, András. 4642
Wilkes, G.A. 3044
Wilkins, Darrell. 1084
Wilkins, Stephen. 4494
Willard, Penelope D. 3172
Wille, Frank. 4393
Wille, Franz. 11, 738, 743, 747, 1379, 1386, 1390, 1572, 1573, 1666, 2004, 2029, 2030, 2031, 2032, 2033, 2401, 2402, 2403, 2788, 3067, 3173, 3174, 3175, 3417, 4612
Willem, Linda M. 3978
Williams, Albert. 1792
Williams, Carolyn. 2755
Williams, David Alan. 1749
Williams, Huw. 2607
Williams, Ian. 1793
Williams, Philip Middleton. 2756
Williams, Saul. 3893
Williamson, Kim. 1565
Willingham, Camille Aljean. 3287
Willingham, Ralph. 3711
Willis, Margaret. 1193
Wilmeth, Don B. 710, 829
Wilmore, David. 1528
Wilson, Ann. 3504
Wilson, Karen Peterson. 140
Wing, Joylynn. 3505
Wing, Joylynn W.D. 3265
Winkelsesser, Karin. 183, 185, 192, 459, 4431
Winkelsesser, Karin, transl. 177
Winkler, Martin M. 4032
Winters, Jay. 276
Wippoo, Pim. 566
Wirsing, Sibylle. 2034
Wirthmann, Julianna. 4643
Wisenthal, J.L. 3506
Witchel, Leigh. 1334, 1335
Witham, Barry B. 428
Wittmann, Gabriele. 1338
Wixson, Christopher. 3507, 3712
Wolf, Matt. 3216, 4289, 4373
Wolf, Milton T., ed. 3508
Wolf, Richard B. 3045
Wolf, Stacy. 162, 783, 2757
Wolfe, Donald. 684
Wolitz, Seth. 3310
Wongchanta, Tipchan. 3713
Wood, Jacqueline E. 3714
Wood, Jane Philbin. 1060
Woods, Alan. 685
Woodyard, George. 2772
Worland, Rick. 4080
Worley, Robert Donald, Jr. 3405
Worman, Dee A. 2343
Worth, Katharine. 3509
Worthen, W.B. 1912, 3849
Wrange, Ann-Marie. 901, 902, 968, 1211, 1235, 1237, 1253, 1301, 1306
Wrange, Ann-Marie, transl. 1311
Wright, Nancy E. 4215
Wright, Stephen K. 3176, 3771
Wry, Joan. 2865
Wulff, Helena. 1117
Wuschek, Kay. 3731
Wutrich, Timothy Richard. 3315
Wynchank, Anny. 3938
Wynne, Peter. 4756
Wysiński, Kazimierz Andrzej. 1692
Wyszomirski, Margaret Jane. 141, 142, 143
Yan, Haiping, ed. 1414
Yankowitz, Susan. 617, 3589
Yanosky, Sabrina Klein. 3046
Yates, Thomas Alfred. 429
Yokobosky, Matthew. 4037
Yon, Jean-Claude. 4758, 4855
York, Julie. 3715
Yoshiko, Uéno. 1366
Young, David. 2837
Young, Henry. 886
Young, Jennifer S. 35
Young, Stuart. 3510
Zacharias, Gun. 903
Zacharov, I.V., ed. 584
Zagorc, Meta. 1023
Zaich, Katja B. 4155
Zajcev, M.S. 1717
Zajcev, S.N. 2339
Zakaryan, James Warren. 686
Zakrževskaja, N.I. 1080
Zala, Szilárd Zoltán. 2147, 2148, 4644
Zalán, Magda. 1061, 1194, 1195, 1241, 1336
Zampelli, Michael Angelo. 2190
Zanardini, Angelo. 4416
Zanella, Andrea. 452
Zapp, Peter. 2758
Zappe, László. 2149, 2150
Zarhina, Regina. 992, 1149
Zarhy-Levo, Yael. 3836
Zarubin, V.I. 4693
Zatlin, Phyllis. 2363
Ždanko, O. 1446
Zeininger, Axel, photo. 1063
Zelenak, Michael. 3185
Zemlinsky, Alexander. 4419, 4420, 4613
Zern, Leif. 1389, 2648, 3068
Zerull, Ludwig. 353
Zesch, Lindy. 3716
Žigarev, A. 4365
Žil'cov, S., ed. 1452
Zilliacus, Jutta. 1606
Zimic, Stanislav. 3406
Zimmerman, Mark. 2759
Zimmerman, Mary. 3589
Zingerman, B.I. ed. 2296
Zink, Geoff. 332
Zinman, Toby. 2760, 3717, 4401
Zinno, Sally. 144
Zinov'eva, A.G. 3850
Zlatescu, Andrei-Paul. 3291
Zlobina, A. 2340
Znamenák, István, photo. 2146
Zoldessy, Brian. 2761
Zorin, A. 3322
Zoščenko, V.V. 3340
Zsámbéki, Gábor. 1672
Zuba, Manya. 4720
Zubanova, L. 4130
Zubcova, Ja. 4131
Zuck, Barbara. 1062
Žučkov, V. 588, 4301
Žukova, I. 762
Zünder, Ralf. 14, 354, 748, 749
Zupan, Jože. 596
Zupančič, Mirko. 3047
Žurčeva, O.V. 3341
Zvezdova, V. 2341
Zvonchenko, Walter. 430
Zykina, L.G. 4302

FINDING LIST OF PERIODICAL TITLES WITH ACRONYMS

AATT News ... AATTN
Abel Value News ... Abel
Abhinaya (Calcutta) ... AbhC
Abhinaya (Delhi) ... AbhD
Abhnaya Samvad ... ASamvad
Acta Classica ... ACTA
Act: Theatre in New Zealand ... Act
Acteurs/Auteurs ... Acteurs
Action Théâtre ... ActT
Actualité de la Scénographie ... ActS
Actualités ... Actualites
AET Revista ... AETR
Afreshiya ... Afr
Africa Perspective ... AfricaP
African American Art ... AfAmArt
African American Review ... AfAmR
African Arts ... AfrA
African Theatre Review ... AfTR
Afro-Americans in New York Life and History ... AAinNYLH
After Dark ... AD
Aha! Hispanic Arts News ... AHA
Akademiceskietetrady ... AT
AKT: Aktuelles Theater ... AKT
Al Fikr ... Fikr
Al Funoun: The Arts ... Funoun
Al-Hayat At-T'aqafiyya ... AHAT
Al-Idaa Wa At-Talfaza ... AIWAT
Alföld ... Alfold
Alif ... Alif
Alive: The New Performance Magazine ... Alive
Almanacco della Canzone e del Cinema e della TV ... ACCTV
Almanach Sceny Polskiej ... Almanach
Altaj ... Altaj
Alternate Roots ... AltR
Alternatives Théâtrales ... AltT
Amaterska Scena ... AmS
Amateur Stage ... AmatS
Amateur Theatre Yearbook ... AmatT
American Drama ... AmerD
American Imago ... AImago
American Indian Culture & Research Journal ... AICRJ
American Literature ... AL
American Music ... AmerM
American Quarterly ... AQ
American Stage ... AStage
American Studies International ... ASInt
American Theatre ... AmTh
Amers Theatrical Times ... ATT
Amyri ... Amyri
An Gael ... AG
Andere Theater, Das ... DAT
Animations: Review of Puppets and Related Theatre ... Anim
Annuaire du Spectacle ... AdSpect
Annuaire du Spectacle de la Communauté Française de Belgique ... ASCFB
Annuaire International du Théâtre: SEE: Miedzynarodowny Rocznik Teatralny (Acro: MRT) ... AIT
Annuaire Théâtral, L' ... AnT
Annuario del Teatro Argentino ... ATArg
Annuario del Teatro Italiano ... AdTI
Annuario do Teatro Brasileiro ... ATB
Annuel de Théâtre ... Annuel
Another Standard ... AnSt
Antipodes ... Antipodes
Antithesis ... Antithesis
Apollo ... Apollo
Apuntes ... Apuntes
Arabesque ... AbqN
Araldo dello Spettacolo, L' ... Araldo
Architect & Builder ... A&B
Archivio del Teatro Italiano ... Archivio
Arcoscenico ... Arco
Ariel ... Ariel
Ariel: Review of International English Literature ... ArielR
Arkhitektura SSSR ... ArkSSSR
Arkkitehti: The Finnish Architectural Review ... Ark
Around the Globe ... AtG
Arrel ... Arrel
Ars-Uomo ... ArsU
Art and Artists (New York) ... A&AR
Art and Australia ... Art&A
Art and the Law ... A&L
Art Com: Contemporary Art Communication ... ACom
Art du Théâtre, L' ... AdT
Artist, The (Kent) ... A&A
Artlink ... ArtL
Art-Press (International) ... ArtP
Arte Nyt ... ArNy
Artists and Influences ... AInf
Arts Advocate ... ArtsAd
Arts Atlantic: Atlantic Canada's Journal of the Arts ... ArtsAtl
Arts Documentation Monthly ... ADoc
Arts du Spectacle en Belgique ... ASBelg
Arts Management Newsletter ... AMN
Arts Reporting Service, The ... ArtsRS
Arts Review ... AReview
As-Sabah ... ASabah
Asian Theatre Journal ... ATJ
ASSAPH: Section C. Studies in the Theatre ... ASSAPHc
ASTR Newsletter ... ASTRN
Atti dello Psicodramma ... AdP
Audiences Magazine ... Audiences
Aujourd'hui Tendances Art Culture ... ATAC
Australian Antique Collector ... AAC
Australian-Canadian Studies ... ACS
Australian Cultural History ... ACH
Australasian Drama Studies ... ADS
Australian Feminist Studies ... AFS
Australian Historical Studies ... AHS
Australian Journal of Chinese Affairs ... AJChA
Australian Journal of Communication ... AuJCom
Australian Journal of Cultural Studies ... AJCS
Australian Journal of French Studies ... AJFS
Australian Literary Studies ... ALS
Australian and New Zealand Studies in Canada ... ANZSC
Australian and New Zealand Theatre Record ... ANZTR
Australian Women's Book Review ... AWBR
Autor, Der ... Autor
Autores ... Autores
Autre Scène, L' ... AScene
Avant Scéne Théâtre, L' ... AST
Avant Scène Opéra, L' ... ASO
Avrora ... Avrora
Bahubacana ... Bahub
Balet ... Balet
Balkon ... Balkon
Ballet News ... BaNe
Ballet Review ... BR
Ballett International ... BI
Ballett Journal/Das Tanzarchiv ... BJDT
Balrangmanch ... Bal
Bamah: Educational Theatre Review ... Bamah
Bandwagon ... Band
Bauten der Kultur ... BK
Beckett Circle/Cercle de Beckett ... BCl
Bergens Theatermuseum Skrifter ... Bergens
Bericht ... Bericht
Berliner Theaterwissenschaft ... BT
Bernard Shaw Newsletter ... BSSJ
Bibliographic Guide to Theatre Arts ... BGTA
Biblioteca Nacional José Marti ... BNJMtd
Biblioteca Teatrale ... BiT
Biladi ... Biladi
Biuletyn Mlodego Teatru ... BMT
Black American Literature Forum ... BALF
Black Arts New York ... BANY
Black Collegian, The ... BlC
Black Masks ... BlackM
Black Perspective in Music ... BPM
BMI Music World ... BMI
Boletin Iberoamericano de Teatro para la Infancia y la Juventud ... BITIJ
Boletin Informativo del Instituto Nacional de Estudios de Teatro ... BIINET
Bomb ... Bomb

FINDING LIST OF PERIODICAL TITLES WITH ACRONYMS

Books in Canada	BooksC
Børneteateravisen	BTA
Botteghe della Fantasia, Le	BFant
Bouffonneries	Bouff
Brecht Jahrbuch	BrechtJ
Brecht Yearbook	BY
British Performing Arts Newsletter	BPAN
Britis Theatrelog	BTlog
Budapesti Negyed	BudN
Broadside	Brs
Buenos Aires Musical	BAMu
Bühne, Die	Buhne
Bühne Kursbuch Kultur	BKK
Bühne und Parkett	BPTV
Bühnen- und Musikrecht	BuM
Bühnengenossenschaft	BGs
Bühnentarifrecht	Buhnent
Bühnentechnische Rundschau	BtR
Builder N.S.	BNS
Bulletin	BulS
Bulletin	BulV
Bulletin ASSITEJ	BASSITEJ
Bulletin de la Société Paul Claudel	BSPC
Bulleti Magisch Plätze	BMP
Bulletin of the Comediantes	BCom
Bulletin of the School of Oriental & African Studies	BSOAS
Bulletin: Van het Belgisch Centrum ITI	BelgITI
Bundesverband Studentische Kulturarbeit	BSK
Burlington Magazine	BM
Cabra, La	CRT
Cahiers Césairiens	CahiersC
Cahiers CERT/CIRCE	CahiersCC
Cahiers de la Bibliothèque Gaston Baty	CBGB
Cahiers de la Maison Jean Vilar	CMJV
Cahiers de la NCT	CNCT
Cahiers du Rideau	CdRideau
Cahiers du Théâtre Populaire d'Amiens	CTPA
Cahiers Jean Cocteau	CJC
Cahiers Jean Giraudoux	CJG
Cahiers Renaud Barrault	CRB
Cahiers Théâtre Louvain	CTL
California Theatre Annual	CTA
Californian Shavian	CShav
Call Board	CB
Call Boy, The	CallB
Callahan's Irish Quarterly	CIQ
Callaloo: A Black South Journal of Arts and Letters	Callaloo
Callboard	Callboard
Calliope	Calliope
Cambridge Opera Journal	COJ
Canada on Stage	CS
Canadian Drama/Art Dramatique Canadien	CDr
Canadian Literature/Littérature Canadienne	CanL
Canadian Theatre Review (Toronto)	CTR
Canadian Theatre Checklist	CTCheck
Canadian Theatre Review Yearbook (Downsview)	CTRY
Caratula	Caratula
Carnet	Carnet
Časopis za zgodovino in narodopisje	CZN
Castelets	Castelets
Celcit	Celcit
Celjski zbornik	Celjz
Celovek	Cel
Central Opera Service Bulletin	COS
Ceskoslovenski Loutkar	CeskL
Čest'imeju	Cesti
Chhaya Nat	Chhaya
Children's Theatre Review	ChTR
Chinese Literature	ChinL
Chronico	Chronico
Cineschedario: Letture Drammatiche	CineLD
Circus Report	CircusR
Circuszeitung, Die	Cz
Cirque dans l'Univers, Le	CU
Città Aperta	CittaA
City Arts Monthly	CAM
City Limits	CityL
Classical and Modern Literature	CLM
Classical Journal, The	ClassJ
Claudel Studies	ClaudelS
Clipper Studies in the American Theater	Clip
CLSU Journal of the Arts	CLSUJ
Club	Club
Coleçao Teatro	ColecaoT
College English	CE
College Language Association Journal	CLAJ
Columbia-VLA Journal of Law & the Arts	ColJL&A
Comédie de l'Ouest	CO
Comédie-Française	CF
Comedy	Comedy
Communications from the International Brecht Society	ComIBS
Comparative Drama	CompD
Comparative Literature Studies	CLS
Confessio	Confes
Conjunto: Revista de Teatro Latinamericano	Cjo
Connoisseur	Con
Contact Quarterly	ContactQ
Contemporary French Civilization	CFT
Contenido	Contenido
Continuum	Contin
CORD Dance Research Annual	CORD
Corps écrit	CorpsE
Costume: The Journal of the Costume Society	Costume
Courrier Dramatique de l'Ouest	CDO
Courrier du Centre international d'études poétiques	CCIEP
Čovaškoe iskusstvo, Voprosy teorii istorii	CoviVt
Creative Drama	CreD
Crépuscule, Le	Crepuscl
Crisis	Crisis
Critical Arts	CrAr
Critical Digest	CritD
Critical Quarterly	CritQ
Critical Review	CritR
Critique	CritNY
Criticism	Criticism
CSA News: The Newsletter of the Costume Society of America	CSAN
Cuadernos El Publico	Cuaderno
Cue New York	CueNY
Cue, The	CueM
Cue International	Cue
Cultural Post	CuPo
Culture et Communication	CetC
Culture	Culture
Current Writing	CW
C'wan t'ong Xiju Yishu/Art of Traditional Opera	CTXY
Czech Theatre	CzechT
DABEI	Dabei
Dalnij Vostok: (Far East)	DalVostok
Dance and Dancers	D&D
Dance Australia	DA
Dance Chronicle	DnC
Dance in Canada/Danse au Canada	DC
Dance Magazine	Dm
Dance Research	DRs
Dance Research Journal	DRJ
Dance Theatre Journal	DTJ
Dancing Times	DTi
Danstidningen	Danst
David Mamet Review	DMR
Dekorativnoje Iskusstvo SSR	DekorIsk
Detskaja Literatura	DetLit
Deutsche Bühne, Die	DB
Deutsche Shakespeare Gesellschaft/Deutsche Shakespeare Gesellschaft West, Jahrbuch	DShG
Deutsche Zeitschrift für Philosophie	DZP
Deutsches Bühnenjahrbuch	DBj
Deutsches Institut für Puppenspiel Forschung und Lehre	DIPFL
De Vlaamse Gids	DVG
Devlet Tijatrolari (State Theatres)	Devlet
Dewan Budaya	Dewan
Diadja Vanja. Literaturnij al'manah	DVLa
Dialog: Miesiecznik Poswiecony Dramaturgii Wspolczesnej	DialogW
Dialog	DialogA
Dialog	DialogR
Dialogi	Dialogi
Dialogue: Canadian Philosophical Review	Dialogue
Dialogue (Tunisia)	DialogTu
Dioniso	Dioniso
Directors Notes	DirNotes
Diskurs	Diskurs
Diskurs	DRostock
Divadelni Noviny	DiN
Divadelni revue	DivR
Divadlo: (Theatre)	DTh
Dix-Huitième Siècle	DHS
Dix-Septième Siècle	DSS
Dockteatereko	Dockt
Documentation Théâtrale	DocTh
Documents del Centre Dramatic	DCD
Documents of the Slovenian Theatre and Film Museum	DSTFM
DOE	DOE
Dokumenti Slovenskega Gledaliskega Muzeja	DSGM
Don Saturio: Boletin Informativo de Teatro Gallego	DSat
Dong-Guk Dramatic Art	DongukDA
Drama and the School	DSchool
Drama and Theater	D&T
Drama and Theatre Newsletter	DTN
Drama Review, The	TDR
Drama Review	DrRev
Drama: Nordisk dramapedagogisk tidsskrift	DNDT
Drama: The Quarterly Theatre Review	Drama
Drama	DramaY
Dramat	Dramat
Dramatherapy: SEE: Journal of Dramatherapy (JDt)	Dtherapy
Dramatics	DMC
Dramatists Guild Quarterly	DGQ
Dramatists Sourcebook	DSo
dRAMATURg	dRAMATURg
Dramaturgi: Tedri Og Praksis	DTOP
Dramma	DrammaR
Dramma: Il Mensile dello Spettacolo	DrammaT
Drammaturgia	Drammaturgia
Dress	Dress
Družba	Druzba
Družba Narodov	DruzNar
Dvatisoč 2000:časnik za mišljenje, umetnost, kulturna	Dvat
Early American Literature	EAL
Early Drama, Art, and Music Review, The	EDAM
East Asian History	EAH
Ebony	Ebony
Echanges	Echanges
Echo Planety	EchoP
Economic Efficiency and the Performing Arts	EE&PA
Economic History Review	EHR
Economist Financial Report	Econ
Editorial Nuevo Grupo	ENG
Educational Theatre News	ETN
Eighteenth-Century Studies	ECS
Eire-Ireland	Eire
Ekran	Ekran

FINDING LIST OF PERIODICAL TITLES WITH ACRONYMS

Elet és Irodalom: irodalmi es politkai hetilap ..... ElI
Eletunk ..... Elet
Elizabethan Review ..... ERev
Elizabethan Theatre ..... ETh
Ellenfény ..... Ellenfény
Empirical Research in Theatre ..... ERT
Enact: monthly theatre magazine ..... Enact
Encore (Australia) ..... EncoreA
Encore (Georgia) ..... Encore
Engekikai: Theatre World ..... Egk
English Academy Review, The ..... EAR
Englis i Africa ..... EinA
English Language Notes ..... ELN
English Literary Renaissance Journal ..... ELR
English Studies ..... EnSt
English Studies in Africa ..... ESA
English Studies in Canada ..... ESC
Entertainment and Arts Manager ..... E&AM
Entré ..... Entre
Envers du Décor, L' ..... ED
Epic Theatre ..... EpicT
Equity Journal ..... EquityJ
Equity News ..... EN
Escena: Informativo Teatral ..... EIT
Escena ..... Escena
Escenica ..... Escenica
Espill, L' ..... Espill
Esprit Créateur, L' ..... ECR
Esprit ..... Esprit
Essays in Criticism ..... ECrit
Essays in Theatre ..... ET
Essays on Canadian Writing ..... ECW
Essence ..... Essence
Estafeta Literaria: La Revista ..... EstLit
Estrada i cirk ..... EiC
Estreno: Journal on the Contemporary Spanish Theater ..... Estreno
Estudis Escenics ..... EECIT
Etnografičeskoe obozrenie ..... EO
Etoile de la Foire ..... Etoile
Etudes Theatrales ..... Etudes
Eugene O'Neill Review ..... EOR
Európai utas ..... Europai
Europe: Revue Littéraire Mensuelle ..... Europe
Evento Teatrale ..... Evento
Exchange ..... Exchange
Ežegodnik MChAT ..... MChAT
Farsa, La ..... Farsa
Federal One ..... FO
Feminist Review ..... FemR
Feminist Studies ..... FemS
Fight Master, The ..... FMa
Figura ..... Figura
Figurentheater ..... Ftr
Film a Divadlo ..... FDi
Film, Szinház, Muzsika ..... FSM
Filologičeskije Nauki ..... FN
Filológiai Közlöny ..... FiloK
Finnish Theatre ..... FT
FIRT/SIBMAS Bulletin d'information ..... FIRTSIB
Flamboyant ..... Flamb
Fliegende Teppich, Der ..... fTep
Footnotes ..... Fnotes
Forrás ..... Forras
Forum Modernes Theater ..... FMT
France Théâtre ..... FranceT
Freedomways: A Quarterly Review of the Freedom Movement ..... Fds
Freilichtbühne, Die ..... FreilD
Fremantle Arts Review ..... FAR
French Forum ..... FrF
French Review, The ..... FR
French Studies ..... FS
Frontiers: A Journal of Women Studies ..... Front
Fundarte ..... Fundarte
Fundevogel ..... Fundevogel
Fundraising Management ..... FundM

Gambit ..... Gambit
Gap, The ..... Gap
Garcin: Libro de Cultura ..... Garcin
Gazette des Beaux Arts ..... GdBA
Gazette du Français ..... GdF
Gazette Officielle du Spectacle ..... GOS
Gazit ..... Gazit
George Spelvin's Theatre Book ..... GSTB
Georgia Review ..... GaR
German Life and Letters ..... GL&L
German Quarterly ..... GQ
German Studies Review ..... GerSR
Gestos: teoria y practica del teatro hispanico ..... Gestos
Gestus: A Quarterly Journal of Brechtian Studies ..... Gestus
Gewerkschaft Kunst, Medien, Freie Berufe .. KMFB
Gilbert and Sullivan Journal ..... GSJ
Giornale dello Spettacolo ..... GdS
Goethe Yearbook: Publication of the Goethe Society of North America ..... Goethe
Gosteri: Performance ..... Gosteri
Gosudarstvo i pravo ..... GiP
Grande République ..... GrandR
Graumann TZ ..... GrTZ
Grimm & Gripps, Jahrbuch für Kinder- und Jugendtheater ..... G&GJKJ
Grimm & Gripps. Beilage zum Kritischen kinder Medien Magazin ..... G&GBKM
Grupo Teatral Antifaz: Revista ..... GTAR
Guida dello Spettacolo ..... Guida
Guidateatro: Estera ..... GtE
Guidateatro: Italiana ..... GtI
Habitat Australia ..... HA
Hamlet Studies ..... HSt
Harlekijn ..... Harlekijn
Hecate: Women's Interdisciplinary Journal ..... Hecate
Helikon ..... Helik
Heresi Napló ..... HevN
Hermes: Zeitschrift für Klassische Philologie ..... Hermes
Higeki Kigeki: Tragedy and Comedy ..... HgK
High Performance ..... HP
Hispanic Arts ..... HispArts
Historical Journal of Film, Radio and Television ..... HJFRT
Historical Performance ..... HistP
Historical Studies ..... HisSt
History of Political Thought ..... HPT
History Workshop ..... HW
Horisont ..... Horis
Hungarian Journal of English and American Studies ..... HJEAS
Hungarian Quarterly ..... HQ
Hungarian Theatre/Hungarian Drama ..... HTHD
Hungarian Theatre News ..... HTN
Ibsen News & Comments ..... INC
Ibsenårboken/Ibsen Yearbook ..... IA
Il Castello di Elsinore ..... IlCast
Impressum ..... Impressum
Impuls ..... Impuls
In Sachen Spiel und Theatre ..... ISST
In the Arts: Search, Research, and Discovery ..... InArts
Independent Shavian ..... IndSh
Indonesia ..... Indonesia
Information du Spectacle, L' ..... IdS
Information on New Plays ..... Info
Inostrannaja Literatura ..... InoLit
Instituto Internacional del Teatro ..... IITBI
International Theatre Yearbook ..... ITY
Interscena/Acta Scenographica ..... IAS
Ireland of the Welcomes ..... IW
Irish Drama Selections ..... IDSelect
Irish Historical Studies ..... IHS
Irish Theatre Archive's Newsletter ..... ITAN

Irish University Review ..... IUR
Irodalomtörténet ..... IHoL
Irodalomtörténeti Közlemények ..... IK
Iskusstvo ..... Iskusstvo
Iskusstvo Kino ..... ISK
Iskusstvo v škole ..... Iskv
Island Magazine ..... IM
Istituto di Studi Pirandelliani e sul Teatro Contemporaneo ..... ISPTC
Jacobean Drama Studies ..... JDS
Jahrbuch der Deutsche Shakespeare-Gesellschaft ..... JDSh
Jahrbuch der Grillparzer-Gesellschaft ..... JGG
Jahrbuch der Städte mit Theater gastspielen ..... JahrST
Jahrbuch der Wiener Gesellschaft für Theaterforschung ..... JWGT
Jahrbuch für Opernforschung ..... Jahrfo
Jahrbuch Tanzforschung ..... JahrT
Javisko ..... Javisko
JEB Théâtre ..... JEBT
Jelenkor ..... Jelenkor
Jeu: Cahiers de Théâtre ..... JCT
Jeune Théâtre ..... JT
JITT ..... JITT
Journal de Chaillot ..... JdCh
Journal du Grenier de Toulouse ..... JGT
Journal du Théâtre Populaire Romand ..... JTPR
Journal du Théâtre de la Ville ..... JTV
Journal for Stage Directors and Choreographers ..... JSDC
Journal Freie Theater ..... JFT
Journal of Aesthetic Education ..... JAE
Journal of Aesthetics and Art Criticism, The ..... JAAC
Journal of African Studies ..... JAfS
Journal of American Culture ..... JAC
Journal of American Drama and Theatre, The ..... JADT
Journal of Arts Management, Law and Society ..... JAMLS
Journal of Arts Policy and Management ..... JAP&M
Journal of Asian Studies ..... JASt
Journal of Beckett Studies ..... JBeckS
Journal of Canadian Studies ..... JCNREC
Journal of Caribbean Studies ..... JCSt
Journal of Cross-Cultural Psychology ..... JCCP
Journal of Dramatherapy ..... JDt
Journal of Dramatic Theory and Criticism ..... JDTC
Journal of Film and Video ..... JFV
Journal of Irish Literature ..... JIL
Journal of Japanese Studies ..... JJS
Journal of Literary Studies: Tydskrif vir Literatuurwetenskap ..... JLS/TLW
Journal of Magic History ..... JMH
Journal of Midwest Modern Language Association ..... JMMLA
Journal of Musicology ..... JoM
Journal of New Zealand Literature ..... JNZL
Journal of Popular Culture ..... JPC
Journal of Research in Singing and Applied Vocal Pedagogy ..... JRSAVP
Journal of Social History ..... JSH
Journal of the Australian Universities Language & Literature Association ..... AULLA
Journal of the Eighteen Nineties ..... JENS
Journal of the Illuminating Engineering Society ..... JIES
Journal of the Royal Asiatic Society of Malaysia ..... JRASM
Journal of the Siam Society ..... JSS
Journal of the Warburg & Courtauld Institutes ..... JWCI
Journal of Voice ..... JOV
Juben: (Playtexts) ..... Juben
Jugoslovenske: Pozorišne Igre ..... JugoIgre
Junkanoo ..... Junkanoo

Kabuki ... Kabuki
Kaekseok ... Kaekseok
Kalakalpam ... Kalak
Kalliope:A Journal of Women's Art ... Kalliope
Kanava ... Kanava
Kassette: Almanach für Bühne, Podium und Manege ... KAPM
Kathakali ... Kathakali
Kazaliste ... Kazal
Keshet ... Keshet
King Pole Circus Magazine ... KingP
Kino ... Kino
Kleine Schriften ... KS
Kleine Schriften der Gesellschaft für Theatergeschichte ... KSGT
Klub i Chudožestvennaja Samodejetelnost ... Klub
Kommunist ... Kommunist
Kontinent ... Kon
Korea Journal ... KoJ
Korean Culture & Arts Bi-Monthly ... KCAB
Korean Drama ... KoreanD
Korean Studies Forum ... KSF
Korean Theatre Review ... KTR
Kortárs ... Kortars
Kraj smolenskij ... Krajs
Kritika ... Krit
Kronika ... KZphK
Kulis ... Kulis
Kultur-Journal ... KJ
Kultura és Közösség ... KesK
Kultura i Žizn (Culture and Life) ... KZ
Kulturno-Prosvetitelnaja Rabota ... KPR
Kultuurivihkot ... Kvihkot
Kunst Bulletin ... KB
Kurt Weill Newsletter ... KWN
La Trobe Library Journal ... LLJ
Labour History ... LabH
Laientheater ... Laien
Latin American Theatre Review ... LATR
Lettera Dall'Italia ... LettDI
Lettres Québécoises ... LetQu
Letture: Libro e spettacolo ... Letture
Leteraturnaja ucheba ... Letuch
Light ... Light
Lighting Design + Application ... LD&A
Lighting Dimensions ... LDim
Lik Cuvasija ... LikC
Lilith:a Feminist History Journal ... Lilith
Linzer Theaterzeitung ... LinzerT
Lipika ... Lipika
Literator: Journal of Comparative Literature and Linguistics ... Literator
Literatura ... Literatura
Literature & History ... L&H
Literature/Film Quarterly ... LFQ
Literature in North Queensland ... LiNQ
Literature in Performance ... LPer
Literaturnaja Gruzia ... LitGruzia
Literaturnojě Obozrenijě ... LO
Litva literaturnaja ... Litva
Live ... Live
Livres et Auteurs Québecois ... LAQ
Loisir ... Loisir
Lok Kala ... LokK
Lowdown ... Lowdown
Ludus ... Ludus
Loutkar ... Loutkar
Lutka ... Lutka
Magazine du TNB ... MdTNB
Magyar Iparművészet ... MagIp
Magyar Múzeum ... MagM
Maksla ... Maksla
Mala Biblioteka Baletowa ... MBB
Mamulengo ... Mamulengo
Manadens Premiärer och Information ... MPI
Manipulation ... Manip
Marges, El ... EIM
Marquee: The Journal of the Theatre Historical Society ... MarqJTHS
Marquee ... Marquee
Mask ... Mask
MASKA ... MASKA
Maske und Kothurn ... MuK
Maske ... Maske
Masque ... Masque
Masterstvo ... Mast
Material zum Theater ... MT
Matya Prasanga ... Matya
Meanjin ... Meanjin
Media, Culture and Society ... MC&S
Medieval and Renaissance Drama ... MRenD
Medieval and Renaissance Drama in England ... MRDE
Medieval English Theatre ... MET
Medieval Music-Drama News ... MMDN
Meister des Puppenspiels ... MeisterP
Meridian ... Meridian
Merker, Der ... Merker
Mestno gledališče Ljubljansko ... MGL
Miedzynarodowny Rocznik Teatralny ... MRT
Milliyet Sanat Dergisi ... MSD
Mim: Revija za glumu i glumište ... Mim
Mime Journal ... MimeJ
Mime News ... MimeN
Mimos ... Mimos
Minority Voices ... MV
Mitgliederzeitung ... Mit
Mitteilungen der Puppentheatersammlung .. MPSKD
Mitteilungen der Vereinigung ... MdVO
Mobile ... Mobile
Modern Austrian Literature ... MAL
Modern Drama ... MD
Modern International Drama ... MID
Modern Language Review ... MLR
Modern Philology ... MP
Moja Moskva ... MojM
Molodaja Gvardija ... MolGvar
Molodoi Kommunist ... MK
Monographs on Music, Dance and Theater in Asia ... MMDTA
Monsalvat ... Monsalvat
Monte Avilia ... MAvilia
Monthly Diary ... MoD
Monumenta Nipponica: Studies in Japanese Culture ... MN
Moskovskij Nabljudatel' ... MoskNab
Moskva ... Mosk
Mozgó Világ ... Mozgo
Mühely ... Muhely
Münchener Beiträge zur Theaterwissenschaft ... MBzT
Music & Letters ... MLet
Music Hall ... MHall
Musical Quarterly ... MuQ
Musicals Das Musicalmagazin ... MDM
Musical'naja Academija ... MA
Musik & Teater ... M&T
MusikDramatik ... MuD
Musik und Gesellschaft ... MusGes
Musik und Theater ... MuT
Muzsika ... Muzsika
Muzyka ... Muzyka
Muzykal'naja akademija ... MA
Muzykalnaja Žizn: (Musical Life) ... MuZizn
My ... My
Mykenae ... Mykenae
Nadie Journal ... NADIE
Näköpiiri ... Nk
Naš Sovremennik ... NasSovr
Nagyvilág ... Nvilag
Napjaink ... Napj
Narodna tvorchestvo ... NTE
National Center for the Performing Arts ... NCPA
Natrang ... Natrang
Natya Kala ... NKala
Natya Varta ... NVarta
Natya ... Natya
Nauka i Religija (Science and Religion) ... NiR
Nauka v Rossii ... NvR
Navi Prolog ... NP
Naytelmauutiset ... Nayt
Nederlands Theatre-en-Televisie Jaarboek ... NTTJ
New Theatre Review, The ... NTR
Neohelicon ... Neoh
Nestroyana ... Ns
Netherlands Centraal Bureau voor de Statistiek: Bezoek ... NCBSBV
Netherlands Centraal Bureau voor de Statistiek: Muziek en Theater ... NCBSMT
Neue Blätter des Theaters in Der Josefstadt ... NBT
neue Merker, Der ... neueM
Neue Musikzeitung ... NMZ
Neva ... Neva
New Contrasts ... NC
New England Theatre Journal ... NETJ
New Literatures Review ... NLR
New Observations ... NO
New Performance ... NewPerf
New Theatre Australia ... NTA
New Theatre Quarterly ... NTQ
New Theatre Review ... NTR
New York Onstage ... NYO
New York Theatre Critics Review ... NYTCR
New York Theatre Reviews ... NYTR
New Yorker, The ... NewY
NeWest Review ... NWR
News from the Finnish Theatre ... NFT
Newsletter of the ITI of the United States, Inc. ... NITI
Nihon-Unima ... NihonU
Nineteenth Century Music ... NCM
Nineteenth Century Theatre ... NCT
Nineteenth Century Theatre Research ... NCTR
Nōgaku-kenkyū ... NoK
Nōgaku Shiryo Shusei ... NoSS
Noh ... Noh
Nohgaku Times ... NTimes
Nordic Theatre Studies ... NTS
Notate ... NIMBZ
Notes on Contemporary Literature ... NConL
Nova revija ... Novr
Novaja Rossija ... NovRos
Novoe Vremija ... NV
Novyj Mir ... NovyjMir
Numero ... Numero
Nya Teatertidningen ... NT
Očag Semejnij Zurnal ... OSZ
O'Casey Annual ... OCA
Obliques ... Obliques
Off-Informationen ... OffI
Ogonek ... Ogonek
Oktiabr ... Oktiabr
Ollantay Theater Magazine ... Ollan
On-Stage Studies ... OSS
Ons Amsterdam ... OnsA
Opal ... Opal
Oper Heute ... OperH
Oper ... Oper
Oper und Konzert ... Opuk
Oper & Tanz ... Op&T
Opera Australia ... OperaA
Opera Canada ... OC
Opera Index ... OperaIn
Opéra International ... OI
Opera Journal ... OJ
Opera News ... OpN
Opera Quarterly ... OQ
Opera (London) ... Opera
Opera (Cape Town) ... OperaCT
Opera (Milan) ... OperaR
Operaélet/Operalife ... OperaL

FINDING LIST OF PERIODICAL TITLES WITH ACRONYMS

Opernglas, Das .... Opern
Opernwelt .... Opw
Opuscula .... Opuscula
Opus Osterreichische Puppenspiel-Journalette .... Opus
Organon .... Organon
Orpheus Clauspeter Koscielny .... Orpheus
Österreichische Dramatiker der Gegenwart .... ODG
Otchij kraj .... OtK
Otecestvennye arhivy .... Otecest
Otro i Knjiga .... Oik
Outrage .... Outrage
Overland .... Over
Overture .... OvA
Palócföld .... Pal
Pamiętnik Teatralny .... PaT
Pamir .... Pamir
Pantallas y Escenarios .... Pantallas
Pantuflas del Obispo .... PdO
Papers on Language & Literature .... PLL
Paraules al Vent .... PaV
Parergon .... Parergon
Parnass .... Parnass
Parnasso .... Parnasso
Passing Show (Australia) .... PasShowA
Passing Show: Newsletter of the Shubert Archive .... PasShow
Past and Present .... Pa&Pr
Performance Magazine, The .... PM
Performance-Management .... PerfM
Performance Handboo o th Performin Art i Ne-Zealand .... PerfNZ
Performance .... Pe
Performance Research .... PerfR
Performing Arts Annual .... PAA
Performing Arts in Canada .... PAC
Performing Arts Journal .... PerAJ
Performing Arts at the Library of Congress .. PALC
Performing Arts Magazine .... PArtsSF
Performing Arts Resources .... PAR
Performing Arts: The Music and Theatre Monthly .... PArts
Performing Arts Year Book of Australia .... PAYBA
Perlicko-Perlacko .... Perlicko
Perspektiva .... Perspek
Pesti Műsor .... PeM
Peterburgskij Teatral'nyj Žurnal .... PTZ
Peuples noirs, peuples africains .... Pnpa
Philippine Quarterly of Culture and Society .. PQCS
Philological Quarterly .... PQ
Philosophy and Literature .... P&L
Pinter Review .... PintR
Pipirijaina .... Pja
Plateaux .... Plateaux
Platform .... Pf
Play .... Play
Playbill .... Pb
Players Magazine .... PlayM
Playmarket News .... PmN
Plays and Players .... PlPl
Plays in Process .... PiP
Plays International .... PI
Plays .... Plays
PLUG .... PLUG
PMLA .... PMLA
Podium: Zeitschrift für Bühnenbildner und Theatertechnik .... PodiumB
Podiumkunsten .... Podium
Poppenspelbereichten .... Poppen
Post Script .... PS
Pozorište: Časopis za pozorišnu umjetnost (Novi Sad) .... PozL
Préface .... Preface
Présence Africaine .... PA
Présence Francophone .... PFr
Pratiques Théâtrales .... PrTh
Première .... Premiere
Premier Zeitshrif fü Oper Sprech- un Tanztheater .... PZOST
Premiéry ceskoslovenských divadel .... PCD
Premijera: List Narodnog Pozorista Sombor .... Premijera
Prešeren Theatre of Kranj .... PTKranj
Prešernovo gledališče .... Presg
Pretexts .... Pretexts
Primer Acto .... PrAc
Primerjalna Književnost .... Primk
Primorsko dramsko gledališče .... Primdg
prinzenstrasse .... prinz
Pro philosophia füzetek .... Propf
Profile .... Prof
Programa .... Programa
Program .... Program
Prolog: Revija za dramsku umjetnost .... Prolog
Prolog .... PrologTX
Prologue .... Prologue
Prompts .... Prompts
ProScen .... ProScen
ProScenium .... ProS
Proszenium .... Pz
Protestáns Szemle .... ProZ
Publico, El .... ElPu
Publiekstheaterkrant .... Ptk
Puppenspiel-Information .... PInfo
Puppenspiel und Puppenspieler .... Pusp
Puppet Master .... PupM
Puppetry Journal .... PuJ
Quaderni del Teatro Stabile di Torino .... QTST
Quaderni di Teatro .... QT
Quarta Parete .... Quarta
Queen's Quarterly .... QQ
Quellen zur Theatergeschichte .... QuellenT
Raduga .... Raduga
Rajatabla .... Raja
Rampelyset .... Rampel
Randa .... Randa
Rangarupa .... Rangarupa
Rangayan .... Rangayan
Rangbharati .... Rbharati
Rangyog .... Rangyog
Raritan .... Raritan
Rassegna dello Spettacolo .... RdS
Rassegna di Dritto Cinematografico, Teatrale e della Televisione .... RdD
Rassegna Melodrammatica .... RMelo
Recorder, The .... Recorder
Records of Early English Drama Newsletter .... REEDN
Red Letters .... RLtrs
Regionologia .... Region
Renaissance Drama .... RenD
Renaissance Quarterly .... RenQ
Renmin Xiju: People's Theatre .... Renmin
Repliikki .... Repliikki
Research in African Literature .... RAL
Researc i Dram Education .... RDE
Research Opportunities in Renaissance Drama .... RORD
Restoration and Eighteenth Century Theatre Research .... Restor
Review:Asian Studies Assoc. of Australia .... RevAS
Review of English Studies .... REVES
Review of Indonesian & Malaysian Affairs .... RevIM
Revista d'Art .... RdArt
Revista de Estudios de Teatro: Boletin .... REsT
Revue d'esthétique .... RE
Revue d'Histoire du Théâtre .... RHT
Revue de l'Art .... RdA
Revue de Littérature Comparée .... RLC
Revue Roumaine d'Histoire de l'Art .... RHSTMC
Revue .... Revue
Ridotto: Rassegna Mensile di Teatro .... RRMT
Rivista di Studi Pirandelliani .... RSP
Rivista Italiana di Drammaturgia .... RIDr
Roda Lyktan .... Roda
Rodina .... Rodina
Romance Quarterly .... RQ
Rossijskij Literaturovedčeskij Žurnal .... RLZ
Rossiskaja provincija .... Rossp
Rouge et Noir .... RN
Russkaja Literatura .... RLit
SAADYT Journal .... SAADYT
Sage: A Scholarly Journal on Black Women ... Sage
Sahne (The Stage) .... Sahne
SAITT Focus .... SAITT
Sanajans Cagdas .... SCagdas
Sanat Olayi (Art Event) .... SanatO
Sangeet Natak: Journal of the Performing Arts .... SNJPA
Scandinavica .... Scan
Scen och Salong .... ScenoS
Scena (Berlin) .... ScenaB
Scena (Milan) .... ScenaM
Scéna (Czech Republic) .... ScenaP
Scena (Warsaw) .... ScenaW
Scena IDI, La .... ScIDI
Scena: Časopis za pozorišnu umetnost .... Scena
Scenaria .... Scenaria
Scenario .... Scenario
Scenarium .... Scenarium
Scene Changes .... ScCh
Scene, Die .... Scene
Sceničeskaja Technika i Technologija .... STT
Scénografický Obzor .... SObzor
Scénografie .... Scenograf
Schauspielfuehrer .... Schaus
Schriften der Gesellschaft für Theatergeschichte .... SGT
Schriftenreihe, Gesellschaft für Unterhaltende Bühnenkunst e.V .... SGfUB
Schweizer Theaterjahrbuch .... SchwT
Schweizerische Gesellschaft für Theaterkultur Jahrbüche .... SGTJ
Schweizerische Gesellschaft für Theaterkultur Schriften .... SGTS
Scottish Opera News .... SON
Scottish Theater News .... STN
Screen .... Screen
Screen Actor .... SA
SCYPT Journal .... SCYPT
Sean O'Casey Review, The .... SORev
Secondary School Theater Journal .... SSTJ
Segismundo .... Segmundo
Sehir Tijatrolari (City Theatre) .... Sehir
SEL Studie i Englis Literature 1500-1900 .... SEL
Sel'skaj molodež .... Selmol
Sembianza .... Sembianza
Sentjakobsko gledališče .... Sentg
Serra d'Or .... SdO
Seventeenth-Century News .... SCN
Shahaab .... Shahaab
Shakespeare and Renaissance Association: Selected Papers .... ShRA
Shakespeare Bulletin .... ShB
Shakespeare in Southern Africa .... ShSA
Shakespeare Jahrbuch .... SJW
Shakespeare Newsletter .... ShN
Shakespeare on Film Newsletter .... SFN
Shakespeare Quarterly .... SQ
Shakespeare Studies (Nashville) .... ShakSN
Shakespeare Studies (New York) .... ShakS
Shakespeare Survey .... ShS
Shavian .... Shavian
Shaw: The Annual of Bernard Shaw Studies .... ShawR
Shilpakala .... Spa
Shingeki .... Sg
Show .... Show
Show Music .... ShowM
Sibmas-Rundbrief .... SR

Sight and Sound ... SiSo
Sightline: The Journal of Theatre Technology and Design ... Sin
Sightlines ... Sis
Silex ... Silex
Sinn und Form: Beiträge zur Literatur ... SuF
Sipario ... Sipario
Sirp ja Vasar ... SjV
Skripichnija Kluch ... SK
Skript ... Skript
Slavic & East European Arts ... SEEA
Slavistična revija ... Slavr
Slavjanovedenie ... Slav
Slovenské Divadlo ... SDi
Slovensko ljudsko gledakišče Celje ... Slovl
Slovensko mladinsko gledališče ... Slovm
Slovensko narodno gledališče—Drama ... SlovD
Slovensko narodno gledališče—Opera in balet ... SlovO
Smena ... Smena
Sobcota Chelovneta ... SobCh
Sobesednik ... Sobesednik
Sodobnost ... Sodob
Social Alternatives ... SocA
Social History ... SocH
Soglasije ... Sog
Sōgō geijutsu Toshite no nō ... SogogT
Somogy ... Somo
SourceMonthly: The Resource for Mimes, Clowns, Jugglers, and Puppeteers ... SMR
South African Journal of African Languages ... SAJAL
South African Theatre Journal ... SATJ
Southerly: A Review of Australian Literature ... SOUTHERLY
Southern Quarterly, The ... SoQ
Southern Review ... SouthR
Southern Sawdust ... SoSaw
Southern Theatre ... SoTh
Sovėckaja Estrada i Cirk ... SovEC
Sovėckaja Ethnografia ... SovEt
Sovėckaja Kultura ... SovKult
Sovėckaja Muzyka: (Soviet Music) ... SovMuzyka
Sovėckij Balet ... SovBal
Sovėckij Teat'r/Soviet Theatre ... SovT
Sovėckojė Slavjanovėdėnjė: (Soviet Slavonic Studies) ... SovSlav
Sovetskie Arkhivy ... SovAr
Sovetskij Teatr ... TR
Sovetskoe Gosudarstvo i Pravo ... SGIP
Soviet and East-European Drama, Theatre and Film ... SEEDTF
Soviet and East-European Performance ... SEEP
Sovremėnnaja Dramaturgija ... SovD
Speak ... Speak
Speaking of Mime ... SoM
Spectacles Magazine ... SM
Speech & Drama ... S&D
Spettacolo in Italia, Lo ... SpIt
Spettacolo Viaggiante ... SpViag
Spiel & Bühne ... S&B
Spiel und Theater ... SuT
Spielplan, Der ... Spl
Spielplan Journal ... SJ
Spirale: Art, letters, spectacles, sciences humaines ... Spirale
Staffrider ... Staff
Stage ... StageZ
Stage Directions ... SD
Stage of the Art ... StageA
Standpunte ... Standpunte
Sterijino Pozorje: Informativno Glasilo ... Sterijino
Stikord ... Stikord
STILB ... STILB
Stilet ... Stilet
Stolica ... Stol
Stratford-upon-Avon Studies ... SuAS
Strindbergiana ... Strind
Studenčeskij Meridian ... StudM
Studia i Materialy do Dziejow Teatru Polskiego ... StudiaP
Studies in American Drama, 1945-Present ... SAD
Studies in Philology ... StPh
Studies in Popular Culture ... SPC
Studies in Romanticism ... SiR
Studies in Theatre Production ... STP
Studies in Western Australian History ... StWAusH
Studii si Cercetari de Istoria Artel ... StudiiR
STYolainen ... STYol
Suffløren ... Suffloren
Suid-Afrikaan, Die ... SuidAfr
Svét a divadlo ... Svet
Swedish Theater/Théâtre Suédois ... SwTS
Szabolcs-Szatmári Beregi Szemle ... Szab
Szene Schweiz/Scène-Suisse/Scena Svizzera ... SSSS
Szene: Fachzeitschrift der DDR ... SzeneAT
Szene ... Szene
Szene Schweiz ... SzeneS
Szinház (Theatre) ... Sz
Szinháztechnikai Fórum ... SFo
Szinháztudományi Szemle ... SzSz
Tablas Nationa Counci o Performin Art' Journal ... Tablas
Tabs ... Tabs
Talent Management ... Talent
TamKang Review ... TkR
Tampereen Työväen Teatteri ... Tampereen
Táncművészet ... Tanc
Tanecni Listy ... Tanecni
Tanssin Tiedotuskeskus ... Tanssi
Tantsovo Izkustvo ... TantI
Tanz Affiche ... TanzA
Tanz und Gymnastik ... TanzG
Tanzdrama ... Tanzd
Tatarstan Republic ... Tatar
Tatr ... Tatr
TCG National Working Conference Proceedings ... TCGNWCP
TCI: Theatre Crafts International ... TCI
Teat'r žurnal dramaturgii i teatra ... TeatrM
Teatarski Glasnik ... TGlasnik
Teater Et ... TE
Teater Film & TV ... TF&TV
Teater i Danmark: Theatre in Denmark ... TeaterD
Teater Jaarboek voor Vlaanderen ... TJV
Teater, Musika, Kyno ... TMK
Teaterårsboken ... TArsb
Teaterforum (Sweden) ... Teaterf
Teaterforum (South Africa) ... TF
Teatern ... Teatern
Teatertidningen ... Tningen
Teatervetenskap ... Tv
Teatervidenskabelige Studier ... TSt
Teatoro ... Teatoro
Teatr Lalek ... TeatL
Teatr ... TeatrW
Teatralnaja Žizn ... TeatZ
Teatraluri Moambe ... TeatM
Teatras ... Teatras
Teatro Archivio ... TArch
Teatro Clásico: Boletin ... TCB
Teatro Contemporaneo ... TeatrC
Teatro del Siglo de Oro: Ediciones Criticas ... TSO
Teatro del Siglo de Oro: Estudios de Literatura ... TSOL
Teatro e Cinema ... TeC
Teatro e Storia ... TeatroS
Teatro en España ... TeatrE
Teatron ... TeatY
Teatron ... Teatron
TeatroSM ... TeatroSM
Teatrul ... Teatrul
Teatteri ... Teat
Teatterikorkeakoulun Tiedotuslehti ... TeatterT
Teatur ... TeaturS
Technical Brief ... TechB
Teleradioephir ... Telerad
Tenaz Talks Teatro ... TTT
Tennessee Williams Review ... TWNew
Text and Performance: Journal of the Comparative Drama Conference ... T&P
Text and Performance Quarterly ... TextPQ
Textual ... Textual
Textuel ... Textuel
Théâtre de l'Est Parisien ... TEP
Théâtre en Europe ... ThE
Théâtre Enfance et Jeunesse ... TEJ
Théâtre et Animation ... TAnim
Théâtre et université ... TU
Théâtre International ... TI
Théâtre National de Strasbourg: Actualité ... TNS
Théâtre Ouvert/Ecritures ... TOE
Théâtre Professionnel ... TProf
Théâtre ... Th
Théâtre Public ... ThPu
Theater Across America ... TAAm
Theater Computer Users Group Notes ... TCUG
Theater der Zeit ... TZ
Theater Heute ... THeute
Theater in Graz ... TGraz
Theater in Österreich ... TiO
Theater Magazine ... ThM
Theater Phönix ... ThP
Theater pur ... Thpur
Theater Rundschau ... TR
Theaterarbeit in der DDR ... TDDR
Theaterbuch ... Tbuch
Theatermaker Vakbla voo d Podiumkunst ... Tmaker
Theaterpaedagogische Bibliothek ... TpaedB
Theaterschrift ... Thsch
TheaterWeek ... TheaterW
Theaterwissenschaftlicher Informationsdienst ... TWI
Theaterwork ... Tk
Theaterzeitschrift ... Tzs
Theatre and Religion ... T&R
Theatre Annual ... TA
Theatre Australia ... TAus
Theatre Chicago ... TChicago
Theatre Communications ... TCom
Theatre Crafts ... ThCr
Theatre Design and Technology ... TD&T
Theatre History in Canada/Histoire du Théâtre ... THC
Theatre History Studies ... THSt
Theatre in Poland/Théâtre en Pologne ... TP
Theatre in the GDR ... TGDR
Theatre Insight ... TInsight
Theatre Ireland ... ThIr
Theatre Journal ... TJ
Theatre Movement Journal ... TMJ
Theatre News ... ThNe
Theatre Notebook ... TN
Theatre Notes ... TNotes
Theatre Papers ... ThPa
Theatre Quarterly ... TQ
Theatre Record ... LTR
Theatre Research in Canada/Recherches Theatrales au Canada ... TRC
Theatre Research International ... ThR
Theatre SA: Quarterly for South African Theater ... TSA
Theatre Scotland ... ThScot
Theatre Southwest ... ThSw
Theatre Studies ... TheatreS
Theatre Survey ... ThS
Theatre Three ... TheatreT
Theatre Times ... TT
Theatre Today ... ThToday
Theatre Topics ... TTop
Theatre Year ... ThYear

FINDING LIST OF PERIODICAL TITLES WITH ACRONYMS

Theatre: Ex .... TheatreEx
Theatre: News from the Finnish Theatre .... NFT
Theatrecraft .... TCraft
TheatreForum .... TheatreF
Theatrephile .... ThPh
Theatrika .... Tka
Theatro .... Theatro
Theatron .... Theatron
Theatron (Hungary) .... TheatronH
Theatrum: A Theatre Journal .... Theatrum
Themes in Drama .... TID
Theoria .... Theoria
Thespis .... Thespis
Tiyatro Araştirmalari Dergisi (Theatre Research Magazine) .... TAD
Tijatro .... Tijatro
Tijdschrift voor de Podium Kunst .... TvPK
Tijdschrift voor Theaterwetenschap .... TvT
Tiszatáj .... Tisz
Toneel Teatraal .... Toneel
Tournées de Spectacles .... Tournees
Tréteaux .... Treteaux
Traces .... Traces
Tramoya: Cuaderno de teatro .... Tramoya
Transforming Art .... TransA
Transition: Discourse on Architecture .... TDonA
Travail Théâtral .... TTh
Trujaman .... Trujaman
Tvorchestvo .... TVOR
Two Thousand .... Twot
Tydskrif vir Letterkunde .... TvL
Tydskrif vir Volkskunde en Volkstaal .... TvVV
Ufahamu: Journal of the African Activist Association .... Ufa
Új Auróra .... UjA
Új Forrás .... UjF
Új Írás .... UjIras
Ukrainskij Teat'r .... UTeatr
UNIMA France .... UNIMA
Unisa English Studies .... UES
Universidad de Murcia Catedra de Teatro Cuadernos .... UMurcia
Universitas Tarraconensis .... UTarra
University of Dar es Salaam .... UDSalaam
University of Toronto Quarterly .... UTQ
Unterhaltungskunst .... UZ
Upstart Crow, The .... UCrow
Ural .... Ural
Usbu Al-Masrah .... Usbu
USITT Newsletter .... USITT
Uusi-Laulu .... Uusi
V sovėckom teatrė .... VSov
Valóság .... Valo
Valiverho .... Valivero
Vantage Point: Issues in American Arts .... VantageP
Vasi Szemle .... Vasi
Vestnik MGU: Series 9-Filologia .... VMGUf
Victorian Historical Journal .... VHJ
Victorian Studies .... VS
Vigilia .... Vig
Világszinház .... Vilag
Voice: Newsletter for Chorus America .... VCA
Volga .... Volga
Voprosy filosofii .... VFil
Voprosy istorii KPSS .... VoprosyK
Voprosy Literatury .... VLit
Voprosy Teatra .... Voprosy
Vozroždenije .... Voz
Vstreča .... Vstreča
Vyakat .... Vyakat
Waiguo Xiju .... Waiguo
Washington International Arts .... WIAL
Weimarer Beiträge .... WB
Wer spielte was .... Wsw
West Coast Plays .... WCP
Westerly .... WEST
Western European Stages .... WES
Western Journal of Black Studies .... WJBS
White Tops .... WTops
Wiener Forschungen zur Theater und Medienwissenschaft .... WFTM
Wiener Gesellschaft für Theaterforschung Jahrbuch .... WGTJ
WIJ, Poppenspelers .... WijP
Women & Performance: A Journal of Feminist Theory .... WPerf
Women's Review .... WomenR
Women's Studies .... WS
Working Papers in Irish Studies .... WPIS
World Literature Today .... WLT
World of Opera .... WOpera
World Premieres Listing .... WPList
Writings on Dance .... WonD
Xiju Luncong: Selected Essays of Theatre .... XLunc
Xiju Xuexi: Theatre .... XXuexi
Xiju Yishu: Theatre Arts .... XYishu
Xiqu Yanjiu .... XYanj
Yeats Annual .... YA
Yorick: Revista e Teatro .... Yorick
Young Cinema & Theatre/Jeune Cinéma et Théâtre .... YCT
Youth Theatre Journal .... YTJ
Zahranicni Divadlo: (Theatre Abroad) .... ZDi
Zapad Rossii .... ZR
Zeitschrift für Anglistik und Amerikanistik .... ZAA
Zeitschrift für Kulturaustausch .... ZfK
Zeitschrift für Germanistik .... ZG

Zeitschrift für Anglistik und Amerikanistik .... ZAA
Zeitschrift für Kulturaustausch .... ZfK
Zeitschrift für Germanistik .... ZG

Zeitschrift für Slawistik .... ZS
Zene-Zene Tanc .... ZZT
Znamya .... Znamya
Zpravy DILIA .... Zpravy
Zreliščnyjė Iskusstva (Performing Arts) .... ZreIssk
Zvezda .... Zvezda

LIST OF PERIODICALS

The following list is an attempt to provide an updated and comprehensive listing of periodical literature, current and recent past, devoted to theatre and related subjects.

This Bibliography provides full coverage of materials published in periodicals marked "Full" and selected coverage of those marked "Scan".

We have not dropped periodicals that are no longer published for the sake of researchers for whom that information can be valuable. We also note and list title changes.

A&A ***The Artist. (Incorporates Art & Artists)***. Freq: 12; Lang: Eng; Subj: Related. ISSN: 0004-3877
▪The Artists' Publishing Company Ltd.; Caxton House, 63-65 High Street Tenderden, Kent TN30 6BD; UK.

A&B ***Architect & Builder***. Freq: 12; Began: 1951; Lang: Eng; Subj: Related. ISSN: 0003-8407
▪Laurie Wale (Pty) Ltd.; Box 4591; Cape Town; SOUTH AFRICA.

A&AR ***Art and Artists***. Formerly: *Art Workers News; Art Workers Newsletter*. Freq: 10; Began: 1982; Lang: Eng; Subj: Related. ISSN: 0740-5723
▪Foundation for the Community of Artists; 280 Broadway, Ste 412; New York, NY 10007; USA.

A&L ***Art and the Law***: Columbia Journal of Art and the Law. Freq: 4; Began: 1974; Ceased: 1985; Cov: Full; Lang: Eng; Subj: Related. ISSN: 0743-5266
▪Volunteer Lawyers for the Arts; 1500 Broadway; Ste. 711 New York, NY 10036; USA.

AAC ***Australian Antique Collector***. Freq: IRR; Began: 1966; Cov: Scan; Lang: Eng; Subj: Related.
▪Editor, Australian Antique Collector; P.O. Box 5487; West Chatswood 2067; AUSTRALIA.

AAinNYLH ***Afro-Americans in New York Life and History***. Freq: 2; Began: 1977; Lang: Eng; Subj: Related. ISSN: 0364-2437
▪Afro-American Historical Assoc. of the, Niagara Frontier; Box 63; Buffalo, NY 14207; USA.

AATTN ***AATT News***. Freq: 11; Began: 1976; Lang: Eng; Subj: Theatre.
▪Australian Assoc. for Theatre Tech.; 40 Wave Avenue Mountain; 3149 Waverly; AUSTRALIA.

Abel ***Abel Value News***. Formerly: *Abel: Panem et Circenses/Bread and Circuses*. Freq: 12; Began: 1969; Lang: Eng; Subj: Theatre. ISSN: 0001-3153
▪Abel News Agencies; 403 1st Ave.; Estherville, IA 51334-2223; USA.

AbhC ***Abhinaya***. Freq: 12; Lang: Ben; Subj: Theatre.
▪Dilipa Bandyopadhyaya; 121 Harish Mukherjee Road; Calcutta; INDIA.

AbhD ***Abhinaya***. Freq: 24; Lang: Hin; Subj: Theatre.
▪Yuvamanch; 4526 Amirchand Marg; Delhi; INDIA.

AbqN ***Arabesque***: A magazine of international dance. Freq: 6; Began: 1975; Cov: Scan; Lang: Eng; Subj: Related. ISSN: 0148-5865
▪Ibrahim Farrah Inc.; One Sherman Square, Suite 22F; New York, NY 10023; USA.

ACH ***Australian Cultural History***. Freq: 1; Began: 1982; Cov: Scan; Lang: Eng; Subj: Related. ISSN: 0728-8433
▪Faculty of Arts, Centre for Australian Studies; Deakin University; Geelong Victoria 3217; AUSTRALIA.

ACCTV ***Almanacco della Canzone e del Cinema e della TV***. Lang: Ita; Subj: Theatre.
▪Viale del Vignola 105; Rome; ITALY.

ACom ***Art Com***: Contemporary Art Communication. Formerly: *Mamelle Magazine: Art Contemporary*. Available only through electronic mail 415/332-4335. Freq: 4; Began: 1975; Lang: Eng; Subj: Related. ISSN: 0732-2852
▪Contemporary Arts Press; Box 3123; San Francisco, CA 94119; USA.

ACS ***Australian-Canadian Studies: an interdisciplinary social science review***. Freq: 1; Began: 1983; Cov: Scan; Lang: Eng; Subj: Related. ISSN: 0810-1906
▪Department of Sociology; LaTrobe University; Bundoora Victoria 3083; AUSTRALIA.

Act ***Act***: Theatre in New Zealand. Formerly: *Theatre*. Freq: 6; Began: 1976; Ceased: 1986; Lang: Eng; Subj: Theatre. ISSN: 0010-0106
▪Playmarket Inc.; Box 9767; Wellington; NEW ZEALAND.

ACTA ***Acta Classica (Proceedings of the Classical Association of South Africa)***. Freq: 1; Began: 1958; Cov: Scan; Lang: Eng.; Subj: Related. ISSN: 0065-1141
▪Classical Association of South Africa; P.O. Box 392; Pretoria 0001; SOUTH AFRICA.

Acteurs ***Acteurs/Auteurs***. Formerly: *Acteurs*. Freq: 10; Began: 1982; Lang: Fre; Subj: Theatre. ISSN: 0991-949X
▪Actes Sud, 18; 75006 rue de Savoie Paris; FRANCE.

ActS ***Actualité de Scénographie***. Freq: 6; Began: 1977; Lang: Fre; Subj: Theatre.
▪Assoc. Belgique des Scénographes et Techniciens de Théâtre; 58 rue Servan; 75011 Paris et l'editeur; FRANCE.

ActT ***Action Théâtre***. Lang: Fre; Subj: Theatre.
▪Action Culturelle de Sud-Est; 4 rue du Théâtre Français; 13001 Marseille; FRANCE.

Actualites ***Actualités***. Lang: Fre; Subj: Theatre.
▪Actualités Spectacles; 1 rue Marietta Martin; 75016 Paris; FRANCE.

AD ***After Dark***. Freq: 12; Began: 1968; Ceased: 1983; Lang: Eng; Subj: Theatre. ISSN: 0002-0702
▪Dance Magazine, Inc.; 175 Fifth Avenue; New York, NY 10010; USA.

ADoc ***Arts Documentation Monthly***. Freq: 10; Began: 1978; Ceased: 1989; Last Known Address; Lang: Eng; Subj: Theatre. ISSN: 0140-6965
▪The Arts Council of Great Britain Library, Information and Research Section; 105 Piccadilly; W1V OAU London; UK.

AdP ***Atti dello Psicodramma***. Freq: 1; Began: 1975; Lang: Ita; Subj: Related.
▪Astrolabio-Ubaldini, Via Lungara 3, 00165 Rome; ITALY.

ADS ***Australasian Drama Studies***. Freq: 2; Began: 1982; Cov: Full; Lang: Eng; Subj: Theatre. ISSN: 0810-4123
▪Australasia Drama Studies, English Dept., University of Queensland; Q 4072 St. Lucia; AUSTRALIA.

AdSpect ***Annuaire du Spectacle***. Freq: 1; Began: 1956; Lang: Fre; Subj: Theatre. ISSN: 0066-3026
▪Publications Mandel L'Edison; 43 bd. Vauban 78182 St. Quentin-en-Yvelines Cedex; FRANCE.

AdT *Art du Théâtre, L'*. Freq: 3; Began: 1985; Lang: Fre; Subj: Theatre.
■Théâtre National de Chaillot; 1 Place du Trocadéro; 75116 Paris; FRANCE.

AdTI *Annuario del Teatro Italiano*. Freq: 1; Began: 1934; Lang: Ita; Subj: Theatre.
■S.I.A.E. - I.D.I.; Viale della Letteratura 30; 00100 Rome; ITALY.

AETR *AET Revista*. Lang: Spa; Subj: Theatre.
■Associación de Estudiantes de Teatro; Viamonte 1443; Buenos Aires; ARGENTINA.

AfAmArt *African American Art*. Formerly: *Black American Quarterly*. Freq: 4; Began: 1984; Cov: Scan; Lang: Eng; Subj: Related. ISSN: 1045-0920
■Museum of African American Art; Santa Monica, CA; USA.

AfAmR *African-American Review*. Freq: 4; Lang: Eng; Subj: Related.
■Department of English; Indiana State University; Terre Haute, IN 47809; USA.

Afr *Afreshiya*. Began: 1945; Last Known Address; Lang: Eng; Subj: Theatre.
■42 Commercial Buildings; Shahrah-e-Quaid-e-Azam; Lahore; PAKISTAN.

AfrA *African Arts*. Freq: 4; Began: 1967; Ceased: 1987; Cov: Scan; Lang: Eng; Subj: Related. ISSN: 0001-9933
■African Studies Center, Univ. of California, Los Angeles; 405 Hilgard Avenue; Los Angeles, CA 90024; USA.

AfricaP *Africa Perspective*. Freq: 2; Began: 1976; Lang: Eng; Subj: Related. ISSN: 0145-5311
■Students' African Studies Society, Univ. of Witwatersrand; 1 Jan Smuts Ave; 2001 Johannesburg; SOUTH AFRICA.

AFS *Australian Feminist Studies*. Freq: 2; Began: 1991; Lang: Eng; Subj: Related. ISSN: 0816-4649
■Research Centre for Women's Studies; University of Adelaide; South Australia, 5005; AUSTRALIA.

AfTR *African Theatre Review*. Freq: IRR; Began: 1985; Lang: Eng; Subj: Theatre.
■Dept. of African Literature, Fac. of Letters & Social Science; University Yaoumde, PO Box 755; Yaounde; CAMEROON.

AG *An Gael*: Irish Traditional Culture Alive in America Today. Freq: 4; Began: 1975; Lang: Eng; Subj: Related.
■An Claidheamh Soluis, The Irish Arts Center; 553 W. 51st Street; New York, NY 10019; USA.

AHA *Aha! Hispanic Arts News*. Freq: 10; Began: 1976; Lang: Eng/Spa; Subj: Related. ISSN: 0732-1643
■Association of Hispanic Arts; 200 E. 87 St.; New York, NY 10028; USA.

AHAT *Al-Hayat At-T'aqafiyya*. Lang: Ara; Subj: Theatre.
■Ministère des Affaires Culturelles; La Kasbah; Tunis; TUNISIA.

AHS *Australian Historical Studies*. Formerly: *Historical Studies*. Freq: 2 Began: 1988; Cov: Scan; Lang: Eng; Subj: Related. ISSN: 0018-2559
■Dept. of History; University of Melbourne; Parkville, Victoria 3052; AUSTRALIA.

AICRJ *American Indian Culture & Research Journal*. Freq: 4; Lang: Eng; Subj: Related.
■American Indian Studies Center; 3220 Campbell Hall; UCLA Los Angeles, CA 90095-1548; USA.

AImago *American imago: Studies in Psychoanalysis and Culture.*. Freq: 4; Cov: Scan; Lang: Eng; Subj: Related. issn: 0065-860X
■John Hopkins Univ. Press;; 2715 North Charles St; Baltimore, MD 21218; USA.

AInf *Artists and Influences*. Freq: 1; Began: 1981; Cov: Scan; Lang: Eng; Subj: Related.
■Hatch-Billops Collection, Inc.; 691 Broadway; New York, NY; USA.

AIT *Annuaire International du Théâtre*: SEE: Miedzynarodowny Rocznik Teatralny (Acro: MRT). Freq: 1; Began: 1977; Lang: Fre/Eng; Subj: Theatre.
■Warsaw; POLAND.

AIWAT *Al-Idaa Wa At-Talfaza*. Lang: Ara; Subj: Theatre.
■R.T.T.; 71 Avenue de la Liberté; Tunis; TUNISIA.

AJCS *Australian Journal of Cultural Studies*. Freq: 3; Began: 1983; Ceased: 1987; Cov: Scan; Lang: Eng; Subj: Related. ISSN: 0810-9648
■School of English; Western Australian Institute of Technology; Bentley, Western Australia 6102; AUSTRALIA.

AJChA *Australian Journal of Chinese Affairs*. Freq: 2; Began: 1979; Cov: Scan; Lang: Eng. ISSN: 0156-7365
■Contemporary China Centre, Research School of Pacific Studies, Australia National University; GPO Box 4; Canberra, ACT 2601; AUSTRALIA.

AJFS *Australian Journal of French Studies*. Freq: 3; Began: 1964; Lang: Eng; Subj: Related. ISSN: 0004-9468
■Dept. of Modern Languages; Monash University; Wellington Road, Clayton, Victoria 3168; AUSTRALIA.

AKT *AKT*: Aktuelles Theater. Freq: 12; Began: 1969; Lang: Ger; Subj: Theatre.
■Frankfurter Bund für Volksbildung GmbH; Eschersheimer Landstrasse 2; 6000 Frankfurt/1, W; GERMANY.

AL *American Literature*. Freq: 4; Began: 1929; Lang: Eng; Subj: Related. ISSN: 0002-9831
■Duke Univ. Press, Box 6697; College Station; Durham, NC 27708; USA.

Alfold *Alföld*. Freq: 12; Began: 1954; Cov: Scan; Lang: Hun; Subj: Related. ISSN: 0401-3174
■Alföld Alapítvány, Csokonai Kft.; Piac u. 26/A. I; 4024 Debrecen; HUNGARY.

Alif *Alif*. Lang: Fre; Subj: Theatre.
■24 rue Gamel Abdel-Nasser; Tunis; TUNISIA.

Alive *Alive*: The New Performance Magazine. Freq: 24; Began: 1982; Lang: Eng; Subj: Theatre.
■New York, NY; USA.

Almanach *Almanach Sceny Polskiej*. Freq: 1; Began: 1961; Lang: Pol; Subj: Theatre. ISSN: 0065-6526
■Wydawnicta Artystyczne i Filmowe; Pulawska 61; 02 595 Warsaw; POLAND.

ALS *Australian Literary Studies*. Freq: 2; Began: 1963; Cov: Scan; Lang: Eng; Subj: Related. ISSN: 0004-9697
■Univ. of Queensland, Dept. of English; Box 88; St. Lucia; Queensland 4067; AUSTRALIA.

Altaj *Altaj*. Began: 1947; Cov: Scan; Lang: Rus; Subj: Related. ISSN: 0320-7447
■Krupskaja Street, Building 91A; Barnaul City; RUSSIA.

AltR *Alternate Roots*. Lang: Eng; Subj: Related.
■1083 Austin Ave., N.E.; Atlanta, GA 30307; USA.

AltT *Alternatives Théâtrales*. Freq: 4; Began: 1979; Cov: Scan; Lang: Fre; Subj: Theatre.
■13 rue des Poissonniers, bte 15-1000 Brussels; BELGIUM.

AmatS *Amateur Stage*. Freq: 12; Began: 1946; Lang: Eng; Subj: Theatre. ISSN: 0002-6867
■Platform Publications Ltd.; 83 George Street; London W1H 5PL; UK.

AmatT *Amateur Theatre Yearbook*. Freq: 1; Began: 1988; Lang: Eng; Subj: Theatre.
■Platform Publications Ltd.; 83 George Street; London W1H 5PL; UK.

AmerD *American Drama*. Freq: 2; Began: 1991; Cov: Full; Lang: Eng; Subj: Theatre. ISSN: 1061-0057
■American Drama Institute; Department of English; ML 69, University of Cincinnati Cincinnati, OH 45221-0069; USA.

AmerM *American Music*. Freq: 4; Began: 1983; Lang: Eng; Subj: Related. ISSN: 0734-4392
■University of Illinois Press; Box 5081, Station A; Champaign, IL 61820; USA.

AMN *Arts Management Newsletter*. Freq: 5; Began: 1962; Lang: Eng; Subj: Related. ISSN: 0004-4067
■Radius Group, Inc.; 408 W. 57th Street; New York, NY 10019; USA.

AmS *Amaterska Scena*: Ochotnicke divadlo. Freq: 12; Began: 1964; Lang: Cze; Subj: Theatre. ISSN: 0002-6786
■Panorama; Halkova 1; 120 72 Prague 2; CZECH REPUBLIC.

AmTh *American Theatre*. Formerly: *Theatre Communications*. Freq: 11; Began: 1984; Cov: Full; Lang: Eng; Subj: Theatre. ISSN: 0275-5971
■Theatre Communications Group; 355 Lexington Avenue; New York, NY 10017; USA.

Amyri *Amyri*. Freq: 4; Lang: Fin; Subj: Theatre.
■Suomen Nayttelijaliitto r.y.; Arkadiankatu 12 A 18; 00100 Helsinki 10/52; FINLAND.

Anim *Animations*: Review of Puppets and Related Theatre. Freq: 6; Began: 1977; Cov: Scan; Lang: Eng; Subj: Theatre. ISSN: 0140-7740
■Puppet Centre Trust, Battersea Arts Centre; Lavender Hill; London SW11 5TN; UK.

Annuel *Annuel de Théâtre*. Freq: 1; Lang: Fre; Subj: Theatre.
■Association Loi de 1901; 30, rue de la Belgique; 92190 Meudon; FRANCE.

AnSt ***Another Standard***. Freq: 6; Ceased: 1986; Cov: Scan; Lang: Eng; Subj: Related.
■PO Box 900; B70 6JP West Bromwich; UK.

AnT ***Annuaire Théâtral, L'***. Freq: 1; Lang: Fre; Subj: Theatre. ISSN: 0827-0198
■Societe d'histoire du theatre du Quebec; Montreal, PQ; CANADA.

Antipodes ***Antipodes***. Freq: 1; Began: 1987; Cov: Scan; Lang: Eng; Subj: Related. ISSN: 0893-5580
■American Association of Australian Literary Studies; 190 6th Avenue; Brooklyn, NY 11217; USA.

Antithesis ***Antithesis***. Freq: 3; Began: 1987; Cov: Full; Lang: Eng; Subj: Related. ISSN: 1030-3839
■English Department; University of Melbourne; Parkville Victoria 3052; AUSTRALIA.

ANZSC ***Australian and New Zealand Studies in Canada***. Freq: 2; Began: 1989; Cov: Scan; Lang: Eng; Subj: Related. ISSN: 0843-5049
■Dept. of English; University of Western Ontario London ON N6A 3K7 CANADA.

ANZTR ***Australian and New Zealand Theatre Record***. Freq: 12; Lang: Eng; Subj: Theatre. ISSN: 1032-0091
■Australian Theatre Studies Centre; University of New South Wales; Sydney NSW 2052; AUSTRALIA.

Apollo ***Apollo***: The international magazine of art and antiques. Freq: 12; Began: 1925; Lang: Eng; Subj: Related. ISSN: 0003-6536
■Apollo Magazine Ltd.; 45-46 Poland Street; London W1V 4AU; UK.

Apuntes ***Apuntes***. Freq: 2; Began: 1960; Lang: Spa; Subj: Theatre. ISSN: 0716-4440
■Universidad Católica de Chile, Escuela de Artes de la Comunicacion; Diagonal Oriente 3300, Casilla 114D; Santiago; CHILE.

AQ ***American Quarterly***. Freq: 24; Began: 1949; Lang: Eng; Subj: Related. ISSN: 0003-0678
■Univ. of Philadelphia; 307 College Hall; Philadelphia, PA 19104 6303; USA.

Araldo ***Araldo dello Spettacolo, L'***. Lang: Ita; Subj: Theatre.
■Via Aureliana 63; Rome; ITALY.

Archivio ***Archivio del Teatro Italiano***. Freq: IRR; Began: 1968; Lang: Ita; Subj: Theatre. ISSN: 0066-6661
■Edizioni Il Polifilo; Via Borgonuovo 2; 20121 Milan; ITALY.

Arco ***Arcoscenico***. Freq: 12; Began: 1945; Lang: Ita; Subj: Theatre.
■Sindacato nazionale autori drammatici; Via Ormisda 10; Rome; ITALY.

AReview ***Arts Review***. Freq: 4; Began: 1983; Ceased: 1988; Lang: Eng; Subj: Related.
■National Endowment for the Arts; 1100 Pennsylvania Avenue NW; Washington, DC 20506; USA.

Ariel ***Ariel***. Freq: 3; Began: 1986; Cov: Full; Lang: Ita; Subj: Theatre. ISSN: 0901-9901
■Instituto di Studi Pirandelliani; Bulzoni Editore; Via dei Liburni n. 14; 00185 Rome; ITALY.

ArielR ***Ariel:Review of International English Literature***; Began: 1970; Cov: Scan; Lang: Eng; Subj: Related.
■University of Calgary; CANADA.

Ark ***Arkkitehti***: The Finnish Architectural Review. Freq: 6; Began: 1903; Cov: Scan; Lang: Fin/ Eng; Subj: Related. ISSN: 0004-2129
■The Finnish Association of Architects; Yrjönkatu 11 A; 00120 Helsinki; FINLAND.

ArkSSSR ***Arkhitektura SSSR***. Freq: 6; Ceased: 1991; Cov: Scan; Lang: Rus; Subj: Related. ISSN: 0004-1939
■Schuseva Street 7; Room 60; 103001 Moscow; RUSSIA.

ArNy ***Arte Nyt***. Lang: Dut; Subj: Related.
■Hvidkildevej 64; 2400 Copenhagen NV; DENMARK.

Arrel ***Arrel***. Freq: 4; Cov: Scan; Lang: Spa; Subj: Theatre.
■Disputacio de Barcelona; Placa de Sant Juame 1; 08002 Barcelona; SPAIN.

ArsU ***Ars-Uomo***. Freq: 12; Began: 1975; Lang: Ita; Subj: Theatre.
■Bulzoni Editore; Via F. Cocco Ortu 120; 00139 Rome; ITALY.

Art&A ***Art and Australia***. Freq: 4; Began: 1963; Cov: Scan; Lang: Eng; Subj: Related. ISSN: 0004-301x;
■Fine Arts Press Pty Ltd; P.O. Box 480; Roseville, NSW 2069; AUSTRALIA.

ArtL ***Artlink***. Freq: 6; Began: 1981; Cov: Full; Lang: Eng; Subj: Theatre. ISSN: 0727-1239
■363 The Esplanade; Henley Beach S.A. 5022; AUSTRALIA.

ArtP ***Art-Press (International)***. Freq: 12; Began: 1976; Ceased: 1979; Cov: Scan; Lang: Fre; Subj: Related. ISSN: 0245-5676
■Paris; FRANCE.

ArtsAd ***Arts Advocate***. Freq: 3; Began: 1988; Lang: Eng Formerly: *In the Arts*; Subj: Theatre.
■Ohio State University College of the Arts; Office of Communications; 30 West 15th Ave. Columbus, OH 43210-1305; USA.

ArtsAtl ***Arts Atlantic***: Atlantic Canada's Journal of the Arts. Freq: 4; Began: 1977; Cov: Scan; Lang: Eng; Subj: Related. ISSN: 0704-7916
■Confederation Centre of the Arts; 145 Richmond St.; Charlottetown, PE C1A 9Z9; CANADA.

ArtsRS ***Arts Reporting Service, The***. Freq: 24; Began: 1970; Ceased: 1976; Lang: Eng; Subj: Theatre. ISSN: 0196-4186
■Charles Christopher Mark; PO Box 39008; Washington, DC 20016; USA.

ASabah ***As-Sabah***. Freq: Daily; Began: 1951; Lang: Ara; Subj: Theatre.
■Avenue Du 7 Novembre; P.O. Box 441 Tunis 1004; TUNISIA.

ASamvad ***Abhnaya Samvad***. Freq: 12; Lang: Hin; Subj: Theatre.
■20 Muktaram Babu Street; Calcutta; INDIA.

ASBelg ***Arts du Spectacle en Belgique***. Formerly: *Centre d'Etudes Theatrales, Louvain: Annuaire*. Freq: IRR; Began: 1968; Ceased: 1991; Lang: Fre; Subj: Theatre. ISSN: 0069-1860
■Université Catholique de Louvain, Centre d'Etudes Théâtrales; 1, place de l'Université; 1348 Louvain-la-Neuve; BELGIUM.

AScene ***Autre Scène, L'***. Lang: Fre; Subj: Theatre.
■Editions Albatros; 14 rue de l'Amérique; 75015 Paris; FRANCE.

ASCFB ***Annuaire du Spectacle de la Communauté Française de Belgique***. Freq: 1; Began: 1981; Lang: Fre; Subj: Theatre.
■Archives et Musée de la Littérature, ASBL; 4 Bd de l'Empereur; 1000 Brussels; BELGIUM.

ASInt ***American Studies International***. Freq: 4; Began: 1975; Ceased: 1983; Cov: Scan; Lang: Eng; Subj: Related. ISSN: 0003-1321
■American Studies Program, George Washington University; Washington, DC 20052; USA.

ASO ***Avant Scène Opéra, L'***. Freq: 6; Began 1976; Lang Fre Subj Theatre. ISSN: 0764-2873
■15 rue Tiquetonne; 75002 Paris; FRANCE.

ASSAPHc ***ASSAPH***: Section C. Studies in the Theatre. Freq: 1; Began: 1984; Cov: Full; Lang: Eng; Subj: Theatre. ISSN: 0334-5963
■Dept. of Theatre Arts, Tel Aviv University; 69978 Ramat Aviv Tel Aviv; ISRAEL.

AST ***Avant Scène Théâtre, L'***. Freq: 20; Began: 1949; Cov: Scan; Lang: Fre; Subj: Theatre. ISSN: 0045-1169
■Editions de l'Avant Scène; 6 rue Git-le-Coeur; 75006 Paris; FRANCE.

AStage ***American Stage***. Freq: 10; Began: 1979; Lang: Eng; Subj: Theatre.
■American Stage Publishing Company; 217 East 28th Street; New York, NY 10016; USA.

ASTRN ***ASTR Newsletter***. Freq: 2; Began: 1972; Cov: Scan; Lang: Eng; Subj: Theatre. ISSN: 0044-7927
■American Society for Theatre Research, C.W. Post College; Department of English; Brookvale, NY 11548; USA.

AT ***AkademiceskieTetrady***. Freq: 4; Began: 1996; Cov: Scan; Lang: Rus; Subj: Related.
■20 Ul. Povarskaja; Moscow 121069; RUSSIA.

ATAC ***Aujourd'hui Tendances Art Culture***. Formerly: *Partenaires*. Lang: Fre; Subj: Related.
■FRANCE.

ATArg ***Annuario del Teatro Argentino***. Freq: 1; Lang: Spa; Subj: Theatre.
■F.N.A.; Calle Alsina 673; Buenos Aires; ARGENTINA.

ATB ***Annuario do Teatro Brasileiro***. Freq: 1; Began: 1976; Lang: Por; Subj: Theatre.
■Ministerio da Educacao e Cultura; Service Nacional de Teatro; Rio de Janeiro; BRAZIL.

AtG ***Around the Globe***. Freq: 2; Began: 1996; Cov: Scan; Lang: Eng; Subj: Theatre. ISSN: 1366-2317
■Shakespeare's Globe; 1 Bear Gardens; Bankside London SE1 9ED; UK.

ATJ ***Asian Theatre Journal.*** Formerly: *Asian Theatre Reports.* Freq: 2; Began: 1984; Cov: Full; Lang: Eng; Subj: Theatre. ISSN: 0742-5457
▪Univ. of Hawaii Press; 2840 Kolowalu Street; Honolulu, HI 96822; USA.

ATT ***Amers Theatrical Times.*** Freq: 12; Began: 1976; Lang: Eng; Subj: Related.
▪William Amer (Pty) Ltd.; 15 Montgomery Avenue; NSW 2142 South Granville; AUSTRALIA.

Audiences ***Audiences Magazine.*** Freq: 12; Last Known Address; Lang: Fre; Subj: Theatre.
▪55 avenue Jean Jaurés; 75019 Paris; FRANCE.

AuJCom ***Australian Journal of Communication.*** Freq: 2; Began: 1982; Cov: Scan; Lang: Eng; Subj: Related. ISSN: 0810-6202
▪Queensland University of Technology; GPO Box 2434; Brisbane Qld 4001; AUSTRALIA.

AULLA ***Journal of the Australian Universities Language & Literature Association.*** Freq: 2; Began: 1953; Cov: Scan; Lang: Eng; Subj: Related. ISSN: 0001-2793
▪Australasian Universities Language & Literature Association; Monash University; Clayton, Victoria 3168; AUSTRALIA.

Autor ***Autor, Der.*** Freq: 2; Began: 1926; Cov: Scan; Lang: Ger; Subj: Related. ISSN: 0344-7197
▪Dramatiker-Union, Eckhard Schulz; Babelsberger Str. 43; D-10715 Berlin; GERMANY.

Autores ***Autores.*** Freq: 4; Lang: Por; Subj: Theatre.
▪Sociedade Portuguesa de Autores; Av. Duque de Loule, 31; 1098 Lisbon Codex; PORTUGAL.

Avrora ***Avrora.*** Freq: 12; Began: 1969; Cov: Scan; Lang: Rus; Subj: Related. ISSN: 0320-6858
▪4 Millionnaja Ul; St. Petersburg 191186; RUSSIA.

AWBR ***Australian Women's Book Review.*** Freq: 1; Began: 1988; Cov: Scan; Lang: Eng; Subj: Related. ISSB: 1033-9434
▪Carole Ferrier; Dept. of English, University of Queensland; Brisbane 4072; AUSTRALIA.

Bal ***Balrangmanch.*** Freq: 6; Lang: Hin; Subj: Theatre.
▪Post Box No. 37, G.P.O.; Lueknowy; 226001; INDIA.

Bahub ***Bahubacana.*** Began: 1978; Lang: Ben; Subj: Theatre.
▪Bahubacana Natyagoshthi; 11/2 Jaynag Road, Bakshi Bazar; Dhaka 1; BANGLADESH.

Balet ***Balet.*** Freq: 6; Cov: Scan; Began: 1992; Lang: Rus; Subj: Theatre. ISSN: 0207-4788
▪Tverskaja St.; Moscow 103050; RUSSIA.

BALF ***Black American Literature Forum.*** Formerly: *Negro American Literature.* Freq: 4; Began: 1967; Ceased: 1991; Cov: Scan; Lang: Eng; Subj: Related. ISSN: 0148-6179
▪Parsons Hall 237, Indiana State Univ.; Terre Haute, IN 47809; USA.

Balkon ***Balkon.*** Freq: 12; Began: 1993; Cov: Scan; Lang: Hun; Subj: Related. ISSN: 1216-8890
▪Enciklopédia Kiadó; Bartók Béla út 82; 1113 Budapest; HUNGARY.

Bamah ***Bamah:*** Educational Theatre Review. Freq: 4; Began: 1959; Cov: Full; Lang: Heb; Subj: Theatre. ISSN: 0045-138X
▪Bamah Association; PO Box 7098; 910 70 Jerusalem; ISRAEL.

BAMu ***Buenos Aires Musical.*** Freq: IRR; Began: 1946; Lang Spa; Subj: Theatre. ISSN: 0007-3113
▪Calle Alsina 912; Buenos Aires; ARGENTINA.

Band ***Bandwagon.*** Freq: 6; Began: 1939; Cov: Scan; Lang: Eng; Subj: Theatre. ISSN: 0005-4968
▪Circus Historical Society; 2515 Dorset Road; Columbus, OH 43221; USA.

BaNe ***Ballet News.*** Freq: 12; Began: 1979; Lang: Eng; Subj: Related. ISSN: 0191-2690
▪Metropolitan Opera Guild, Inc.; 1865 Broadway; New York, NY 10023; USA.

BANY ***Black Arts New York.*** Freq: 10; Cov: Scan; Lang: Eng; Subj: Related. ISSN: 1057-4239
▪215 West 125th St. Dr. Martin Luther King, Jr. Blvd; 4th Floor New York, NY 10027; USA.

BASSITEJ ***Bulletin ASSITEJ.*** Formerly: *Bulletin d'Information ASSITEJ.* Freq: 3; Began: 1966; Ceased: 1994; Lang: Fre/Eng/Rus; Subj: Theatre.
▪ASSITEJ; Celetna 17; 110 01 Prague 1; CZECH REPUBLIC.

BCl ***Beckett Circle/Cercle de Beckett.*** Freq: 2; Began: 1978; Lang: Eng/Fre; Subj: Theatre. ISSN: 0732-2224
▪Samuel Beckett Society; University of California at Los Angeles; Los Angeles, CA 90024; USA.

BCom ***Bulletin of the Comediantes.*** Freq: 2; Began: 1949; Lang: Eng/ Spa; Subj: Theatre. ISSN: 0007-5108
▪James A. Parr, Dept. of Spa. & Portuguese; University of California; Riverside, CA 92521; USA.

BelgITI ***Bulletin:*** Van het Belgisch Centrum ITI. Ceased; Lang: Fre; Subj: Theatre.
▪Belgisch Centrum van het ITI, c/o Mark Hermans; Rudolfstraat 33; B 2000 Antwerp; BELGIUM.

Bergens ***Bergens Theatermuseum Skrifter.*** Began: 1970; Lang: Nor; Subj: Theatre.
▪Bergens Theatermuseum, Kolstadgt 1; Box 2959 Toeyen; 6 Oslo; NORWAY.

Bericht ***Bericht.*** Lang: Ger; Subj: Theatre. ISSN: 0067-6047
▪UMLOsterreichischer Bundestheaterverband; Goethegasse 1; A 1010 Vienna; AUSTRIA.

BFant ***Botteghe della Fantasia, Le.*** Last Known Address; Began: 1979; Lang: Ita; Subj: Theatre.
▪Via S. Manlio 13; Milan; ITALY.

BGs ***Bühnengenossenschaft.*** Freq: 12; Began: 1949; Lang: Ger; Subj: Theatre. ISSN: 0007-3083
▪Bühnenschriften-Vertriebs-Gesellschaft; Pf. 13 02 70; D-20102 Hamburg; GERMANY.

BGTA ***Bibliographic Guide to Theatre Arts.*** Freq: 1; Lang: Eng; Subj: Theatre. ISSN: 0360-2788
▪G. K. Hall & Co.; 70 Lincoln Street; Boston, MA 02111; USA.

BI ***Ballett International/tanz aktuell:*** Aktuelle Monatszeitung für Ballett und Tanztheater. Formerly: *Ballett Info.* Freq: 12; Began: 1978; Lang: Ger; Subj: Related. ISSN: 0947-0484
▪Friedrich Berlin Verlagsges; mbH, Lützowplatz 7; D-10785 Berlin; GERMANY.

BIINET ***Boletin informativo del Instituto Nacional de Estudios de Teatro.*** Freq: 10; Began: 1978; Lang: Spa; Subj: Theatre.
▪1055 Avenida Cordoba; 1199 Buenos Aires; ARGENTINA.

Biladi ***Biladi.*** Lang: Ara; Subj: Theatre.
▪Parti Socialiste Desourien, Maison du Parti, BP 1033; Blvd. du 9 Avril, La Kasbah; Tunis; TUNISIA.

BiT ***Biblioteca Teatrale.*** Freq: 4; Began: 1986; Cov: Full; Lang: Ita; Subj: Theatre. ISSN: 0045-1959
▪Bulzoni Editore; 14 Via dei Liburni; 00185 Rome; ITALY.

BITIJ ***Boletin Iberoamericano de Teatro para la Infancia y la Juventud.*** Lang: Spa; Subj: Theatre.
▪Associación Española de Teatro para la Infancia y la Juventud; Claudio Coello 141; 6 Madrid; SPAIN.

BJDT ***Ballett-Journal/Das Tanzarchiv.*** Freq: 5; Began: 1953; Cov: Scan; Lang: Ger; Subject: Related. ISSN 0720-3896
▪Zeitung für Tanzpädagogik und Ballett-Theater; Ulrich Steiner Verlag; Obersteinbach 5 a D-51429 Bergisch Gladbach; GERMANY.

BK ***Bauten der Kultur.*** Freq: IRR; Began: 1976; Lang: Ger; Subj: Related. ISSN: 0323-5696
▪Institut für Kulturbauten; Clara-Zetkin-Strasse 105; 1080 Berlin; GERMANY.

BKK ***Bühne Kursbuch Kultur.*** Freq: 2; Cov: Scan; Lang: Ger; Subj: Related.
▪Orac Zeitschriftenverlag GmbH; Schönbrunner Str. 59-61; A-1010 Vienna; GERMANY.

BlackM ***Black Masks.*** Freq: 12; Began: 1984; Cov: Scan; Lang: Eng; Subj: Related.
▪P.O. Box 2; Bronx, NY 10471; USA.

BlC ***Black Collegian, The:*** The National Magazine of Black College Students. Formerly: *Expressions.* Freq: IRR; Began: 1970; Cov: Scan; Lang: Eng; Subj: Related. ISSN: 0192-3757
▪Black Collegiate Services, Inc.; 1240 South Broad Street; New Orleans, LA 70125; USA.

BM ***Burlington Magazine.*** Freq: 12; Began: 1903; Cov: Scan; Lang: Eng; Subj: Related. ISSN: 0007-6287
▪Burlington Magazine Publications; 6 Bloomsbury Square; London WC1A 2LP; UK.

BMI ***BMI Music World.*** Freq: 4 Began: 1964; Lang: Eng; Subj: Related.
▪New York, NY; USA.

BMP ***Bulletin Magische Plätze.*** Freq: 12; Cov: Scan; Lang: Ger; Subj: Related.
▪B. Kohler Verlag; Wydlerweg 17; CH-8047 Zurich; SWITZERLAND.

BMT ***Biuletyn Mlodego Teatru.*** Last Known Address; Began: 1978; Lang: Pol; Subj: Theatre.

■Gwido Zlatkes; Bednarska 24 m; 00 321 Warsaw; POLAND.

BNJMtd ***Biblioteca Nacional José Marti***: Informacion y Documentacion de la Cultura. Serie Teatro y Danza. Freq: 12; Lang: Spa; Subj: Theatre.
■Biblioteca Nacional José Marti, Dept. Info. y Doc. de Cultura; Plaza de la Revolución; Havana; CUBA.

BNS ***Builder N.S.*** Formerly: *Builder N.S.W.*. Freq: 12; Began: 1907; Cov: Scan; Lang: Eng; Subj: Related.
■Master Builders Asso. of New South Wales; Private Bag 9; Broadway; N.S.W. 2007; AUSTRALIA.Tel: 660-7188.

Bomb ***Bomb***. Freq: 4; Cov: Scan; Lang: Eng; Subj: Related.
■New Arts Publications; 594 Broadway, 10th Flr.; New York,, NY 10012; USA.

BooksC ***Books in Canada***. Freq: 9; Began: 1971; Cov: Scan; Lang: Eng/Fre; Subj: Related. ISSN: 0045-2564
■Canadian Review of Books, Ltd.; 130 Spadina Ave.; Suite 603 Toronto, ON M5V 2L4; CANADA.

Bouff ***Bouffonneries***. Began: 1980; Lang: Fre; Subj: Theatre. ISSN: 028-4455
■Domaine de Lestanière; 11000 Cazilhac; FRANCE.

BPAN ***British Performing Arts Newsletter***. Ceased: 1980; Lang: Eng; Subj: Related.
■London; UK.

BPM ***Black Perspective in Music***. Freq: 2; Began: 1973; Ceased: 1990; Cov: Scan; Lang: Eng; Subj: Related. ISSN: 0090-7790
■Foundation for Research in the Afro-American Creative Arts; P.O. Drawer One; Cambria Heights, NY 11411; USA.

BPTV ***Bühne und Parkett***: Theater Journal Volksbühnen-Spiegel. Formerly: *Volksbuhnen-Spiegel*. Freq: 3; Began: 1955; Lang: Ger; Subj: Theatre. ISSN: 0172-1321
■Verband der deutschen Volksbühne e.v.; Bismarckstrasse 17; 1000 Berlin 12; GERMANY.

BR ***Ballet Review***. Freq: 4; Began: 1965; Lang: Eng; Subj: Related. ISSN: 0522-0653
■Dance Research Foundation, Inc.; 46 Morton Street; New York, NY 10014; USA.

BrechtJ ***Brecht Jahrbuch***. Freq: 1; Began: 1971; Ceased: 1987; Lang: Ger/Eng/Fre; Subj: Theatre.
■Wayne State University; 5959 Woodward Ave.; Detroit, MI 48202; USA.

Brs ***Broadside***. Freq: 4; Began: 1940; Lang: Eng; Subj: Theatre. ISSN: 0068-2748
■Theatre Library Assoc.; 111 Amsterdam Avenue; New York, NY 10023; USA.

BSK ***Bundesverband Studentische Kulturarbeit***. Freq: 4; Cov: Scan; Lang: Ger; Subj: Related. ISBN: 3-927451-11-8
■BSK, Berliner Platz 31; D-53111 Bonn; GERMANY.

BSOAS ***Bulletin of the School of Oriental & African Studies***. Lang: Eng; Subj: Related. London; UK.

BSPC ***Bulletin de la Société Paul Claudel***. Freq: IRR; Lang: Fre; Subj: Related.13, rue du Pont Louis-Philippe; 75004 Paris; FRANCE.

BSSJ ***Bernard Shaw Newsletter***. Formerly: *Newsletter & Journal of the Shaw Society of London*. Freq: 1; Began: 1976; Lang: Eng; Subj: Related.
■Bernard Shaw Centre, High Orchard; 125 Markyate Road; EM8 2LB Dagenahm, Essex; UK.

BT ***Berliner Theaterwissenschaft***. Freq: 1; Began: 1995; Lang: Ger; Subj: Theatre. ISSN: 0948-7646
■Vistas Verlag Gmbh; Bismarckstr. 84; D-10627 Berlin; GERMANY.

BTA ***Børneteateravisen***. Freq: 4; Began: 1972; Lang: Dan; Subj: Theatre.
■Teatercentrum i Danmark; Frederiksborggade 20; 1360 Copenhagen; DENMARK.

BTlog ***British Theatrelog***. Freq: 4; Began: 1978; Ceased: 1980; Lang: Eng; Subj: Theatre. ISSN: 0141-9056
■Associate British Centre of the ITI; 15 Hanover Sq.; London WIR 9AJ; UK.

BtR ***Bühnentechnische Rundschau***: Zeitschrift für Theatertechnik, Bühnenbau und Bühnengestaltung. Freq: 6; Began: 1907; Cov: Scan; Lang: Ger/Eng/Fre; Subj: Theatre. ISSN: 0007-3091
■Erhard Friedrich Verlag; Postfach 10 01 50; D-30917 Seelze; SWITZERLAND.

BudN ***Budapesti Negyed***. Freq: 4; Began: 1993; Cov: Scan; Lang: Hun; Subj: Related. ISSN: 1217-5846
■Budapest Fovaros Leveltara; Katona Jozsef u. 24; 1137 Budapest; HUNGARY.

Buhne ***Bühne, Die***. Freq: 11; Began: 1958; Lang: Ger; Subj: Theatre. ISSN: 0007-3075
■Orac Zeitschriftenverlag GmbH; Schönbrunner Str. 59-61; A1010 Vienna; AUSTRIA.

Buhnent ***Bühnentarifrecht***. Freq: 4; Cov: Scan; Lang: Ger; Subj: Related. ISBN: 3-7685-2731-X
■R.v. Decker's Verlag; Hüthig GmbH, Pf. 102869; D-69018 Heidelberg; GERMANY.

BulS ***Bulletin***. Freq: 10; Cov: Scan; Lang: Ger/Fre; Subj: Related.
■Schweizerischer Dachverband der Fachkräfte des künstlerischen Tanzes SDT

BulS ***Bulletin***. Freq: 10; Cov: Scan; Lang: Ger/Fre; Subj: Related.
; Dufourstr. 45; CH-3005 Bern; SWITZERLAND.

BulV ***Bulletin***. Freq: 4; Began: 1974; Cov: Scan; Lang: Ger/Fre/Ita; Subj: Related.
■Vereinigun fü Künstler/innen Theate Veranstalter/innen; Schweiz (KTV); Pf. 3350 CH-2500 Biel 3; SWITZERLAND.

BuM ***Bühnen- und Musikrecht***. Cov: Scan; Lang: Ger; Subj: Related.
■Mykenae Verlag Rossberg KG; Ahastr. 9; D-64285 Darmstadt; GERMANY.

BY ***Brecht Yearbook***. Freq: 1; Lang: Eng; Subj: Theatre.
■German Department; 818 Van Hise Hall; University of Wisconsin Madison, WI 53706; USA.

CahiersC ***Cahiers Césairiens***. Freq: 2; Began: 1974; Lang: Eng/Fre; Subj: Theatre.
■Pennsylvania State University, Dept. of French; University Park, PA 16802; USA.

CahiersCC ***Cahiers CERT/CIRCE***. Lang: Fre; Subj: Theatre.
■Centre Etudes Recherches Théâtrale, Université de Bordeaux III; Esplanade des Antilles; 33405 Talence; FRANCE.

Callaloo ***Callaloo***: A Black South Journal of Arts and Letters. Freq: 3; Began: 1976; Cov: Scan; Lang: Eng; Subj: Related. ISSN: 0161-2492
■Department of English; 322 Bryan Hall; University of Virginia Charlottesville, VA 22903; USA.

CallB ***Call Boy, The***: Journal of the British Music Hall Society. Freq: 4; Began: 1963; Lang: Eng; Subj: Theatre.
■British Music Hall Society; 32 Hazelbourne Road; London SW12; UK.

Callboard ***Callboard***. Freq: 4; Began: 1951; Lang: Eng; Subj: Theatre. ISSN: 0045-4044
■1809 Barrington St., Ste. 901; Halifax, NS B3J 3K8; CANADA.

Calliope ***Calliope***. Freq: 12; Began: 1968; Lang: Eng; Subj: Theatre.
■Clowns of America Inc.; 1052 Foxwood Ln.; Baltimore, MD 21221; USA.

CAM ***City Arts Monthly***. Freq: 12; Lang: Eng; Subj: Related.
■640 Natoma St.; San Francisco, CA 94103; USA.

CanL ***Canadian Literature/Littérature Canadienne***: A Quarterly of Criticism and Review. Freq: 4; Began: 1959; Cov: Scan; Lang: Eng/Fre; Subj: Related. ISSN: 0008-4360
■University of British Columbia; 2029 West Mall; Vancouver, BC V6T 1Z2; CANADA.

Caratula ***Caratula***. Freq: 12; Last Known Address; Lang: Spa; Subj: Theatre.
■Sanchez Pacheco 83; 2 Madrid; SPAIN.

Carnet ***Carnet***. Cov: Scan; Began: 1994; Lang: Eng /Fre; Subj: Related. ISSN: 0929-936x
■Theater Institut Nederland; Herengracht 168-1016 BP Amsterdam; NETHERLANDS.

Castelets ***Castelets***. Lang: Fre; Subj: Theatre.
■Centre Provincial de la Marionnette de Namur; Rue des Brasseurs 109; 5000 Namur; BELGIUM.

CB ***Call Board***. Formerly: *Monthly Theatre Magazine of TCCBA*. Freq: IRR; Began: 1931; Lang: Eng; Subj: Theatre. ISSN: 0008-1701
■Theatre Bay Area; 657 Mission Street, Ste. 402; San Francisco, CA 94116; USA.

CBGB ***Cahiers de la Bibliothèque Gaston Baty***. Lang: Fre; Subj: Related.
■Paris; FRANCE.

CCIEP ***Courrier du Centre international d'études poétiques***. Freq: 4; Cov: Scan; Lang: Fre; Subj: Related.
■Archives et Musée de la Littérature; Boulevard de l'empereur, 4; 1000 Bruxelles; BELGIUM.

CDO ***Courrier Dramatique de l'Ouest***. Freq: 4; Began: 1973; Ceased; Lang: Fre; Subj: Theatre.
■Théâtre du Bout du Monde, Ctre Dramatique Natl de l'Ouest; 9B Avenue Janvier; 35100 Rennes; FRANCE.

CDr ***Canadian Drama/Art Dramatique Canadien***. Freq: 2; Began: 1975; Cov: Full; Lang: Eng/Fre; Subj: Theatre. ISSN: 0317-9044
■Dept. of English, University of Waterloo; Waterloo, ON N2L 3G1; CANADA.

CdRideau ***Cahiers du Rideau***. Freq: 3; Began: 1976; Ceased: Lang: Fre; Subj: Theatre.
■Rideau de Bruxelles; 23 rue Ravenstein; B 1000 Bruxelles; BELGIUM.

CE ***College English***. Freq: 8; Began: 1937; Lang: Eng; Subj: Related. ISSN: 0010-0994
■National Council of Teachers of English; 1111 Kenyon Road; Urbana, IL 61801; USA.

Cel ***Čelovek***. Lang: Rus; Subj: Related. ISSN: 0236-2007
■RUSSIA.

Celcit ***Celcit***. Lang: Spa; Subj: Theatre.
■Apartado 662; 105 Caracas; VENEZUELA.

Celjz ***Celjski zbornik***. Freq: 1; Began: 1958; Lang: Slo; Subj: Theatre. ISSN: 0576-9760
■Osrednja knji*07znica Celje; Muzejski trg 1; 3000 Celje; SLOVENIA.

CeskL ***Ceskoslovenski Loutkar***. SEE *Loutkar*. Began: 1951; Ceased: 1993; Lang: Cze; Subj: Theatre.
■Panorama; Mrstikova 23; 10 000 Prague 10; CZECH REPUBLIC.

Cesti ***Čest'imeju***. Freq: 12; Cov: Scan; Began: 1919; Lang: Rus; Subj: Related.
■D-7 Chorosevskoje šosse; 32-A, Building 3 Moscow 123007; RUSSIA.

CetC ***Culture et Communication***. Freq: 10; Lang: Fre; Subj: Theatre.
■Min. de la Culture et de la Documentation; 3 rue de Valois; 75001 Paris; FRANCE.

CF ***Comédie-Française***. Freq: 4; Began: 1971; Lang: Fre; Subj: Theatre. ISSN: 0759-125x
■1 Place Colette; 75001 Paris; FRANCE.

CFT ***Contemporary French Civilization***. Freq: 3; Began: 1976; Cov: Scan; Lang: Fre/Eng; Subj: Related. ISSN: 0147-9156
■Dept. of Modern Languages, Montana State University; Bozeman, MT 59717; USA.

Chhaya ***Chhaya Nat***. Freq: 4; Lang: Hin; Subj: Theatre.
■U.P. Sangeet Natak Akademi; Lucknow; INDIA.

ChinL ***Chinese Literature***. Freq: 4; Began: 1951; Lang: Eng; Subj: Related. ISSN: 0009-4617
■Bai Wan Zhuang; Beijing 100037; CHINA.

Chronico ***Chronico***. Lang: Gre; Subj: Theatre.
■ Horo'; Xenofontos 7; Athens; GREECE.

ChTR ***Children's Theatre Review***. Freq: 4; Began: 1952; Cov: Full; Ceased: 1985; Lang: Eng; Subj: Theatre. ISSN: 0009-4196
■c/o Milton W. Hamlin, Shoreline High School; 18560 1st Avenue N.E.; Seattle, WA 98155; USA.

CineLD ***Cineschedario***: Letture Drammatiche. Freq: 12; Began: 1964; Lang: Ita; Subj: Related. ISSN: 0024-1458
■Centro Salesiano dello Spettacolo; Via M. Ausiliatrice 32; Turin 10121; ITALY.

CIQ ***Callahan's Irish Quarterly***. Freq: 4; Ceased: 1983; Cov: Scan; Lang: Eng; Subj: Related.
■P.O. Box 5935; Berkeley, CA 94705; USA.

CircusR ***Circus Report***. Freq: IRR; Began: 1972; Lang: Eng; Subj: Theatre; ISSN: 0889-5996
■525 Oak St.; El Cerrito, CA 94530-3699; USA.

CittaA ***Città Aperta***. Freq: 1; Began: 1981; Lang: Ita; Subj: Theatre.
■Associazione Piccolo Teatro; Via Cesalpino 20; 52100 Arezzo; ITALY.

CityL ***City Limits***. Freq: 10; Began: 1976; Lang: Eng; Subj: Related. ISSN: 0199-0330
■City Limits, Assoc. of Neighborhood Housing Developers; 424 W. 23rd Street; New York, NY 10001; USA.

CJC ***Cahiers Jean Cocteau***. Freq: 1; Began: 1969; Lang: Fre; Subj: Theatre. ISSN: 0068-5178
■6 rue Bonaparte; 75006 Paris; FRANCE.

CJG ***Cahiers Jean Giraudoux***. Freq: 1; Began: 1972; Lang: Fre; Subj: Theatre.
■Association des Amis de Jean Giraudoux; Université F. Rabelais; 3 Rue du Tanneus 37000 TOURS; FRANCE.

Cjo ***Conjunto***: Revista de Teatro Latinamericano. Freq: 4; Began: 1964; Cov: Full; Lang: Spa; Subj: Theatre. ISSN: 0010-5937
■Departamento de Teatro Latino Americano, Casa de las Americas; Ediciones Cubanes, Obispo No. 527; Aptdo. 605, Havana; CUBA.

CLAJ ***College Language Association Journal***. Freq: 4; Began: 1957; Lang: Eng; Subj: Related. ISSN: 0007-8549
■College Language Assoc., c/o Cason Hill; Morehouse College; Atlanta, GA 30314; USA.

ClassJ ***Classical Journal, The***. Freq: 4; Lang: Eng; Subj: Theatre.
■Department of Classics; 146 New Cabell Hall; University of Virginia Charlottesville, VA 22903; USA.

ClaudelS ***Claudel Studies***. Freq: 2; Began: 1972; Lang: Eng; Subj: Related. ISSN: 0900-1237
■University of Dallas, Dept. of French; PO Box 464; Irving, TX 75060; USA.

Clip ***Clipper Studies in the American Theater***. Freq: IRR; Began: 1985; Lang: Eng; Subj: Theatre. ISSN: 0748-237X
■Borgo Press; Box 2845; San Bernardino, CA 92406; USA.

CLS ***Comparative Literature Studies***. Freq: 4; Cov: Scan; Lang: Eng; Subj: Related. ISSN: 0010-4132
■Pennsylvania State University Press; 820 University Drive; University Park, PA 16802; USA.

CLSUJ ***CLSU Journal of the Arts***. Freq: 1; Began: 1981; Lang: Eng/Phi; Subj: Theatre.
■Central Luzon State University, Publications House; Munoz; Nueva Ecija; PHILIPPINES.

Club ***Club***. Began: 1923; Cov: Scan; Freq: 12; Lang: Rus; Subj: Related.
■Stardca'luzzroje šosse, I; Moscow 117630; RUSSIA.

CMJV ***Cahiers de la Maison Jean Vilar***. Lang: Fre; Subj: Theatre.
■Avignon; FRANCE.

CML ***Classical and Modern Literature***. Freq: 4; Lang: Eng; Subj: Related ISSN: 0197-2227
■P.O. Box 629; Terre Haute, IN 47808-0629; USA.

CNCT ***Cahiers de la NCT***. Freq: 3; Began: 1965; Lang: Fre; Subj: Theatre. ISSN: 1188-1461
■Nouvelle Compagnie Théâtrale; 4353 rue Ste. Catherine est.; Montreal, PQ H1V 1Y2; CANADA.

CO ***Comédie de l'Ouest***. Lang: Fre; Subj: Theatre.
■Assoc. des Amis de la Comediede l'ouest; Centre Dramatique National; Rennes; FRANCE.

COJ ***Cambridge Opera Journal***.Began: 1989;Cov: Scan;Lang: Eng Subj: Related. ISSN: 0954-5867
■Cambridge University Press; The Edinburgh Building; Shaftesbury Road, Cambridge CB2 2RU; UK

ColecaoT ***Coleçao Teatro***. Freq: IRR; Began: 1974; Lang: Por; Subj: Theatre.
■Universidade Federal do Rio Grande do Sul; Porto Alegre; BRAZIL.

ColJL&A ***Columbia-VLA Journal of Law & the Arts***. Formerly: *Art & the Law*. Freq: 4; Began: 1985; Cov: Full; Lang: Eng; Subj: Related. ISSN: 0743-5226
■Columbia University School of Law &, Volunteer Lawyers for the Arts; 435 West 116 Street; New York, NY 10027; USA.

Comedy ***Comedy***. Freq: 4; Began: 1980; Lang: Eng; Subj: Theatre. ISSN: 0272-7404
■Trite Explanations Ltd.; Box 505, Canal Street Station; New York, NY 10013; USA.

ComIBS ***Communications from the International Brecht Society***: The Global Brecht. Freq: 2; Began: 1970; Lang: Eng/Ger; Subj: Theatre. ISSN: 0740-8943
■Foreign Languages; Maginnes Hall #9; Lehigh University Bethlehem, PA 18015; USA.

CompD ***Comparative Drama***. Freq: 4; Began: 1967; Cov: Full; Lang: Eng; Subj: Theatre. ISSN: 0010-4078
■Department of English, Western Michigan University; Kalamazoo, MI 49008-3899; USA.

Con ***Connoisseur***. Freq: 12; Began: 1901; Lang: Eng; Subj: Related. ISSN: 0010-6275
■Hearst Magazines, Connoisseur; 250 W. 55th St.; New York, NY 10019; USA.

Confes ***Confessio***. Freq: 4; Began: 1976; Cov: Scan; Lang: Hun; Subj: Related. ISSN: 0133-8889
■Református Zsinati Iroda Sajtóosztálya; Abonyi u. 21; 1146 Budapest; HUNGARY.

ContactQ ***Contact Quarterly***. Freq: 2; Began: 1975; Lang: Eng; Subj: Related. ISSN: 0198-9634
■Contact Collaborations Inc.; Box 603; Northampton, MA 01061; USA.

Contenido ***Contenido***. Lang: Spa; Subj: Theatre.
■Centro Venezolano del ITI; Apartado 51-456; 105 Caracas; VENEZUELA.

Contin ***Continuum***. Formerly: *Continuing Higher Education Association*. Freq: 3; Began: 1977 Lang: Eng;; Subj: Related.

■National University of Continuing Education Association; 1 Dupont Circle N.W., Ste. 615; Washington, DC 20036; USA.

CORD ***CORD Dance Research Annual.*** Lang: Eng; Subj: Related.
■CORD Editorial Board, NYU Dance and Dance Educ. Dept.; 35 W. 4th St., Room 675; New York, NY 10003; USA.

CorpsE ***Corps écrit.*** Freq: 4; Lang: Fre; Subj: Theatre.
■Presses Universitaires de France; 12, rue Jean de Beauvais; 75005 Paris; FRANCE.

COS ***Central Opera Service Bulletin.*** Freq: 4; Began: 1954; Lang: Eng; Subj: Theatre. ISSN: 0008-9508
■Metropolitan Opera Nat'l Council, Central Opera Service; Lincoln Center; New York, NY 10023; USA.

Costume ***Costume***: The Journal of the Costume Society. Freq: 1; Began: 1967; Cov: Scan; Lang: Eng; Subj: Related. ISSN: 0590-8876
■c/o Miss Anne Brogden; 3 Meadway Gate; London NW11 7LA; UK.

Covivt ***Čovaškoe iskusstvo, Voprosy teorri i istorii.*** Cov: Scan; Lang: Rus; Subj: Related. ISBN: 5-87677-003-5
■Moscow; RUSSIA.

CrAr ***Critical Arts.*** Freq: IRR; Began: 1980; Cov: Scan; Lang: Eng; Subj: Related.
■Critical Arts Study Group, c/o Dept. of Journalism & Media; Rhodes University; 6140 Grahamstown; SOUTH AFRICA.

CRB ***Cahiers Renaud Barrault.*** Freq: 4; Began: 1953; Lang: Fre; Subj: Theatre. ISSN: 0008-0470
■Editions Gallimard; S. Benmussa; 8 rue St. Placide; 75007 Paris; FRANCE.

CreD ***Creative Drama.*** Freq: 1; Began: 1949; Lang: Eng; Subj: Theatre. ISSN: 0011-0892
■Educational Drama Association, c/o Stacey Publications; 1 Hawthorndene Road; BR2 7DZ Kent; UK.

Crepuscl ***Crépuscule, Le.*** Ceased: 1979; Lang: Fre; Subj: Theatre.
■Théâtre Varia; rue du Sceptre; 78 à 1040 Bruxelles; BELGIUM.

Crisis ***Crisis.*** Freq: 6; Began: 1910; Lang: Eng; Subj: Related. ISSN: 0011-1422
■Crisis Publishing Co.; 186 Remsen St.; Brooklyn, NY 11201; USA.

CritD ***Critical Digest.*** Freq: 24; Began: 1948; Ceased: 1985; Lang: Eng; Subj: Theatre.
■225 West 34th Street, Room 918; New York, NY 10001; USA.

Criticism ***Criticism.*** Freq: 4; Lang: Eng; Subj: Related.
■Department of English; Wayne State University; Detroit, MI 42802; USA.

CritNY ***Critique.*** Freq: 4; Began: 1976; Lang: Eng; Subj: Theatre.
■417 Convent Avenue; New York, NY 10031; USA.

CritQ ***Critical Quarterly.*** Freq: 4; Began: 1959; Lang: Eng; Subj: Related. ISSN: 0011-1562
■Blackwell Publishers; 108 Cowley Road; Oxford OX4 1JF; UK.

CritRev ***Critical Review, The.*** Freq: IRR; Began: 1965; Lang: Eng; Subj: Related. ISSN: 0070-1548
■University of Melbourn; Department of English, Melbourne; AUSTRALIA.

CRT ***Cabra, La***: Revista de Teatro. Lang: Spa; Subj: Theatre.
■Mexico City; MEXICO.

CS ***Canada on Stage:The National Theatre Yearbook.*** Formerly: *Canada on Stage-:Canadien Theatre Review Yearbook.* Freq: 1; Began: 1975; Lang: Eng; Subj: Theatre. ISSN: 0380-9455
■PACT Communications Centre; 64 Charles St. E.; Toronto, ON M4Y ITI; CANADA.

CSAN ***CSA News: The Newsletter of the Costume Society of America.*** Formerly *Newsletter Quarterly and Dress.* Began: 1975; Lang: Eng; Subj: Related. ISSN: 0361-2112
■The Costume Society of America; 55 Edgewater Drive; P.O. Box 73 Earleville, MD 21919; USA.

CShav ***Californian Shavian.*** Freq: 6; Began: 1958; Ceased: 1966; Lang: Eng; Subj: Theatre. ISSN: 0008-154X
■Shaw Society of California; 1933 S. Broadway; Los Angeles, CA 90007; USA.

CTA ***California Theatre Annual.*** Ceased: 1986; Freq: 1; Lang: Eng; Subj: Theatre. ISSN: 0733-5806
■Performing Arts Network; 9025 Wilshire Blvd.; Beverly Hills, CA 90211; USA.

CTCheck ***Canadian Theatre Checklist.*** Formerly: *Checklist of Canadian Theatres.* Freq: 1; Began: 1979; Ceased: 1983; Lang: Eng; Subj: Theatre. ISSN: 0226-5125
■University of Toronto Press; 63A St. George Street; Toronto, ON M5S 1A6; CANADA.

CTL ***Cahiers Théâtre Louvain.*** Formerly *Cahiers Théâtre.* SEE *Etudes Théâtrales.* Freq: 4; Began: 1968; Ceased: 1991; Cov: Full; Lang: Fre; Subj: Theatre. ISSN: 0771-4653
■q. 1450 Fr. Ferme de Blocry, Place de l' Hocaille; B-1348 Louvain-La-Neuve; BELGIUM.

CTPA ***Cahiers du Théâtre Populaire d'Amiens.*** Began: 1984; Lang: Fre; Subj: Theatre.
■Amiens; FRANCE.

CTR ***Canadian Theatre Review.*** Freq: 4; Began: 1974; Cov: Full; Lang: Eng; Subj: Theatre. ISSN: 0315-0836
■Department of Drama; University of Guelph; Guelp, ON N1G 2WI; CANADA.

CTRY ***Canadian Theatre Review Yearbook.*** Freq: 1; Began: 1974; Ceased; Lang: Eng; Subj: Theatre. ISSN: 0380-9455
■Canadian Theatre Review Publications, York University;, P.O. Box 1280 1011 Sheppard Ave. Downsview, ON M3J 1P3; CANADA.

CTXY ***C'wan t'ong Xiju Yishu/Art of Traditional Opera.*** Freq: 4; Began: 1979; Lang: Chi; Subj: Theatre.
■Institute of Traditional Chinese Opera; Beijing; CHINA.

CU ***Cirque dans l'Univers, Le.*** Freq: 4; Began: 1950; Lang: Fre; Subj: Theatre. ISSN: 0009-7373
■lub du Cirque; 11, rue Ch-Silvestri; 94300 Vincennes; FRANCE.

Cuaderno ***Cuadernos El Publico.*** Freq: 10; Began: 1985; Ceased: 1989; Lang: Spa/Cat; Subj: Theatre. ISSN: 8602-3573
■Centro de Documentacion Teatral, Organismo Autonomo Teatros Ncnl; c/ Capitan Haya 44; 28020 Madrid; SPAIN.

Cue ***Cue International.*** Formerly: *Cue: Technical Theatre Review.* Freq: 6; Began: 1979; Ceased: 1987; Cov: Full; Lang: Eng; Subj: Theatre. ISSN: 0144-6088
■Twynam Publishing Ltd.; Kitemore;, Faningdon, Oxfordshire SN7 8HR; UK.

CueM ***Cue, The.*** Freq: 2; Began: 1928; Ceased; Cov: Scan; Lang: Eng; Subj: Theatre. ISSN: 0011-2666
■Theta Alpha Phi Fraternity, Dept. of Speech/Theatre; Montclair State College; Upper Montclair, NJ 07043; USA.

CueNY ***Cue New York.*** Freq: 26; Began: 1932; Ceased: 1978; Lang: Eng; Subj: Theatre. ISSN: 0011-2658
■North American Publishing Company; 545 Madison Avenue; New York, NY 10022; USA.

Culture ***Culture.*** Freq: 4; Lang: Fre; Subj: Theatre.
■Maison de la Culture de La Rochelle; 11 rue Chef-de-Ville; 17000 La Rochelle; FRANCE.

CuPo ***Cultural Post.*** Freq: IRR; Began: 1975; Ceased: 1983; Lang: Eng; Subj: Related.
■National Endowment for the Arts; 1100 Pennsylvania Avenue N.W.; Washington, DC 20506; USA.

CW ***Current Writing.*** Freq: 2; Began: 1989; Cov: Scan; Lang: Eng; Subj: Related. ISSN 1013-929X
■English Dept.; University of Natal; King George V Ave, Durban 4001; SOUTH AFRICA.

Cz ***Circuszeitung, Die (Circus-Parade).*** Freq: 12; Began: 1955; Lang: Ger; Subj: Theatre.
■Gesellschaft für Circusfreunde; Klosterhof 10; 2308 Preetz; GERMANY.

CzechT ***Czech Theatre.*** ***Formerly*** *Czech Theatre/Théâtre.* tchèque.. Freq: 1; Began: 1991; Cov: Full; Lang: Eng; Subj: Theatre. ISSN: 0862-9380
■Divadelní ústav, Celetná 17; 1100 Parague 1;; CZECH REPUBLIC.

CZN ***Časopis za zgodovino in narodopisje.*** Freq: 2; Began: 1904; Lang: Slo; Subj: Theatre. ISSN: 0590-5968
■Založba Obzorja d.d.; Partizanska 3-5; 2000 Maribor; SLOVENIA.

D&D ***Dance and Dancers.*** Freq: 12; Began: 1950; Lang: Eng; Subj: Related. ISSN: 0011-5983
■214 Panther House; 38 Mount Pleasant; London WCIX OAP; UK.

D&T ***Drama and Theater.*** Freq: 3; Began: 1968; Ceased: 1980; Lang: Eng; Subj: Theatre. Dept. of English, State University; Fredonia, NY 14063; USA.

DA ***Dance Australia.*** Freq: 4; Began: 1980; Cov: Scan; Lang: Eng; Subj: Related. ISSN: 0159-6330
■Dance Australia; GPO Box 606; Sydney, NSW 2001; AUSTRALIA.

LIST OF PERIODICALS

DABEI *Dabei*. Freq: 6; Cov: Scan; Lang: Ger; Subj: Related. Gewerkschaft Kunst, Medien, Freie Berufe; Maria-Theresienstr. 11; A-1090 Vienna; AUSTRIA.

DalVostok *Dalnij Vostok*: (Far East). Freq: 12; Began: 1933; Cov: Scan; Lang: Rus; Subj: Related. ISSN: 0130-3028
▪Kniznoe izdatel'stvo; Khabarovsk; RUSSIA.

Danst *Danstidningen*. Freq: 4; Began: 1991; Cov: Full; Lang: Swe; Subj: Related. ISSN: 1102-0814
▪Box 20 137; 104 60 Stockholm; SWEDEN.

DAT *Andere Theatre, Das*. Freq: 4; Began: 1990; Lang: Ger; Subj: Theatre. ISSN: 0936-0662
▪Union Internationale de la Marionette; Zentrum Brd e.V., Die Schaubude; Greifswalder Str. 81-84 D-10405 Berlin; GERMANY.

DB *Deutsche Bühne, Die*. Freq: 12; Began: 1909; Lang: Ger; Subj: Theatre. ISSN: 0011-975X
▪Erhard Friedrich Verlag; Postfach 10 01 50 D-30917 Seelze; GERMANY.

DBj *Deutsches Bühnenjahrbuch*. Freq: 1; Began: 1889; Lang: Ger; Subj: Theatre. ISSN: 0070-4431
▪Genossenschaft Deutscher Bühnen Angehöriger; Buhnenschriften-Vertriebs Gmbh; Pf. 13 02 70; D-20102 Hamburg; GERMANY.

DC *Dance in Canada/Danse au Canada*. Freq: 4; Began: 1973; Ceased; Lang: Eng/Fre; Subj: Theatre. ISSN: 0317-9737
▪Dance in Canada Association; 4700 Keele St.; Downsview, ON M3J 1P3; CANADA.

DCD *Documents del Centre Dramàtic*. Freq: 4; Ceased; Lang: Spa; Subj: Theatre. c/o Hospital, 51, 1er; Barcelona 08001; SPAIN.

DekorIsk *Dekorativnojė Iskusstvo SSR*. Freq: 12; Began: 1957; Cov: Scan; Lang: Rus; Subj: Related. ISSN: 0418-5153
▪Soveckij Chudožnik; Moscow; RUSSIA.

DetLit *Detskaja Literatura*. Freq: 12; Began: 1932; Cov: Scan; Lang: Rus; Subj: Related. ISSN: 0130-3104
▪Moscow; RUSSIA.

Devlet *Devlet Tijatrolari (State Theatres)*. Freq: 4; Lang: Tur; Subj: Theatre.Genel Mudurugu; Ankara; TURKEY.

Dewan *Dewan Budaya*. Freq: 12; Began: 1979; Lang: Mal; Subj: Theatre. ISSN: 0126-8473
▪Peti Surat 803; Kuala Lumpur; MALAYSIA.

DGQ *Dramatists Guild Quarterly*. Freq: 4; Began: 1964; Cov: Full; Lang: Eng; Subj: Theatre. ISSN: 0012-6004
▪The Dramatists Guild, Inc.; 234 W. 44th St.; New York, NY 10036; USA.

DHS *Dix-Huitième Siècle*. Freq: 1; Began: 1969; Lang: Fre; Subj: Related. ISSN: 0070-6760
▪Soc. Française d'Etude du 18e Siecle; 23 Quai de Grenelle; 75015 Paris; FRANCE.

DialogA *Dialog*. Freq: 10; Began: 1973; Lang: Ger; Subj: Theatre. ISSN: 0378-6935
▪Verlag Sauerländer; Laurenzenvorstadt 89; CH 5001 Aarau; SWITZERLAND.

Dialogi *Dialogi*. Freq: 12; Began: 1965; Lang: Slo; Subj: Theatre. ISSN: 0012-2068
▪Založba Aristej d.o.o.; Dialogi, Šentilj 119a; 2212 Šentij; SLOVENIA.

DialogR *Dialog*. Freq: 12; Lang: Rus; Subj: Theatre. ISSN: 0236-0942
▪Miusskaja Square, 6; 125267 Moscow; RUSSIA.

DialogTu *Dialogue*. Lang: Fre; Subj: Theatre. Parti Socialiste Desourien, Maison du Parti, BP 1033; Blvd. du 9 Avril, La Kasbah; Tunis; TUNISIA.

Dialogue *Dialogue*: Canadian Philosophical Review/Revue Canadienne de Philosophie. Freq: 4; Began: 1962; Lang: Eng; Subj: Related. ISSN: 0012-2173
▪Ste. 46, 1390 Sherbrooke St. West; H3G 1K2 Montreal, PQ; CANADA.

DialogW *Dialog*: Miesiecznik Poswiecony Dramaturgii Wspolczesnej. Freq: 12; Began: 1956; Cov: Full; Lang: Pol; Subj: Theatre. ISSN: 0012-2041
▪Teatr Współczesny, ul. Mokotowska 13; 00670 Warsaw; POLAND.

DiN *Divadelni Noviny*. Freq: 26; Began: 1992; Cov: Scan; Lang: Cze; Subj: Theatre. ISSN: 0012-4141
▪Svaz Ceskoslovenskych Divadelnich a Rozhlasovych Umelcu; Valdstejnske nam. 3; Prague 1; CZECH REPUBLIC.

Dioniso *Dioniso*. Freq: 1; Began: 1929; Lang: Ita/Eng/Fre/Spa; Subj: Theatre. Instituto Nazionale del Dramma Antico; Corso Matteoti 29; Siracusa; ITALY.

DIPFL *Deutsches Institut für Puppenspiel Forschung und Lehre*. Freq: IRR; Began: 1964; Last Known Address; Lang: Ger; Subj: Theatre. ISSN: 0070-4490
▪Deutsches Institut für Puppenspiel; Bergstrasse 115; 4630 Bochum; GERMANY.

DirNotes *Directors Notes*. Lang: Eng; Subj: Theatre. American Directors Institute; 248 W. 74th St., Suite 10; New York, NY 10023; USA.

Diskurs *Diskurs*. Freq: 4; Last Known Address; Lang: Ger; Subj: Theatre. Schauble Verlag; Waldgurtel 5; 506 Bensberg; GERMANY.

DivR *Divadelni revue*. Freq: 4; Began: 1990; Cov: Full; Lang: Cze; Subj: Theatre. ISSN: 0862-5409
▪Theatre Institute; Divadelni Ústav; 110 01 Prague 1 Celetna 17; CZECH REPUBLIC.

Dm *Dance Magazine*. Freq: 12; Began: 1926; Cov: Scan; Lang: Eng; Subj: Related. ISSN: 0011-6009
▪Dance Magazine, Inc.; 33 W. 60th St.; New York, NY 10023; USA.

DMC *Dramatics*. Freq: 9; Began: 1929; Lang: Eng; Subj: Theatre. ISSN: 0012-5989
▪Educational Theatre Association; 3368 Central Parkway; Cincinnati, OH 45225; USA.

DMR *David Mamet Review*. Cov: Scan; Lang: Eng ; Subj: Theatre. Box 455076; Las Vegas, NV 89154-5076; USA.

DnC *Dance Chronicle: Studies in Dance & the Related Arts*. Freq: 2; Began: 1978; Lang: Eng; Subj: Theatre. ISSN: 0147-2526
▪Marcel Dekker Journals; 270 Madison Avenue; New York, NY 10016; USA.

DNDT *Drama*: Nordisk dramapedagogisk tidsskrift. Freq: 4; Began: 1963; Lang: Nor/Swe/Dan; Subj: Theatre. ISSN: 0332-5296
▪Landslaget Drama i Skolen, Kongensgt. 4.; 0153 Oslo; NORWAY.

Dockt *Dockteatereko*. Freq: 4; Began: 1971; Lang: Swe; Subj: Theatre. ISSN: 0349-9944
▪Dockteaterforeningen; Sandavagen 10; 14032 Grodinge; SWEDEN.

DocTh *Documentation Théâtrale*. Began: 1974; Lang: Fre; Subj: Theatre. Centre d'Etudes Théâtrales, Université Paris X; 200 Avenue de la République; 92001 Nanterre Cedex; FRANCE.

DOE *DOE*. Formerly: *Speel*. Freq: 24; Began: 1951; Lang: Dut; Subj: Theatre. ISSN: 0038-7258
▪Stichting Ons Leekenspel'; Gudelalaan 2; Bussum; NETHERLANDS.

DongukDA *Dong-Guk Dramatic Art*. Freq: 1; Began: 1970; Cov: Full; Lang: Kor; Subj: Theatre. Department of Drama & Cinema, Dongguk University; Seoul; SOUTH KOREA.

Drama *Drama: The Quarterly Theatre Review*: Third Series. Formerly: *Drama*. Freq: 4; Began: 1919; Ceased: 1989; Cov: Scan; Lang: Eng; Subj: Theatre. ISSN: 0012-5946
▪Cranbourne Mansions; Cranbourne Street; London WC2H 7AG; UK.

Dramat *Dramat*. Freq: 4 Began: 1993; Cov: Full; Lang: Swe; Subj: Theatre. ISSN: 1104-2885
▪Kungliga Dramatiska Teatern; Nybrogatan2; P.O. Box 5037 S-102 41 Stockholm; SWEDEN.

DrammaR *Dramma*. Freq: 12; Began: 1925; Cov: Scan; Lang: Ita; Subj: Theatre. ISSN: 0012-6004
▪Romana Teatri s.r.l.; Via Torino 29; 00184 Rome; ITALY.

DrammaT *Dramma*: II Mensile dello Spettacolo. Freq: 12; Lang: Ita; Subj: Theatre. I.L.T.E.; Corso Bramante 20; Turin; ITALY.

dRAMATURg *dRAMATURg*. Freq: 2; Began: 1970; Cov: Scan; Lang: Ger; Subj: Theatre. ISSN: 1432-3966
▪Nachrichtenbrief; Dramaturgische Gesellschaft e.V.; Tempelherrenstr. 4 D-10961 Berlin; GERMANY.

Drammaturgia *Drammaturgia*. Freq: 2; Cov: Scan; Began: 1994; Lang: Ita; Subj: Theatre. ISSN: 1122-9365;
▪Salerno Editrice Via di Donna Olimpia; 20-Roma; ITALY.

DramaY *Drama*. Lang: Slo; Subj: Theatre. Erjavceva; Ljubljana; SLOVENIA.

Dress *Dress*. Freq: 1; Began: 1975; Lang: Eng; Subj: Related. ISSN: 0361-2112
▪Costume Society of America; 55 Edgewater Drive; P.O. Box 73 Earleville, MD 21919; USA.

DRJ *Dance Research Journal*. Freq: 2; Began: 1967; Lang: Eng; Subj: Related. ISSN: 0149-7677
▪Congress on Research in Dance, Department of Dance; State University of New York College at Brockport, Brockport, NY 14420-2939; USA.

DRostock *Diskurs*. Freq: 4; Began: 1973; Ceased: 1980; Lang: Ger; Subj: Theatre. Volkstheater Rostock; Patriotischer Weg 33; 25 Rostock; GERMANY.

DrRev *Drama Review*. Freq: 2; Began: 1970; Last Known Address; Lang: Kor; Subj: Theatre. Yonguk-pyongron-sa; 131-51 Nokbun-dong, Eunpyong-ku; 122 Seoul; SOUTH KOREA.

DRs *Dance Research*. Freq: 2; Lang: Eng; Subj: Related. c/o Dance Books Ltd.; 9 Cecil Court; London WC2N 4EZ; UK.

Druzba *Družba*. SEE *Rossijane*. Freq: 6; Began: 1977; Ceased: 1992; Cov: Scan; Lang: Rus/Bul; Subj: Related. ISSN: 0320-1031 ■Moscow-Sofija; RUSSIA.

DruzNar *Družba Narodov*. Freq: 12; Began: 1939; Cov: Scan; Lang: Rus; Subj: Related. ISSN: 0012-6756 ■Sovetskii pisatel; Izvestiia Sovetov narodnykh deputatov SSSR; Moscow; RUSSIA.

DSat *Don Saturio: Boletin Informativo de Teatro Gallego*. Last Known Address; Lang: Spa; Subj: Theatre. Coruna 70-30; Esda; SPAIN.

DSchool *Drama and the School*. Freq: 2; Began: 1948; Last Known Address; Lang: Eng; Subj: Theatre. Whitehall Productions; 63 Elizabeth Bay Road; NSW 2011 Elizabeth Bay; AUSTRALIA.

DSGM *Dokumenti Slovenskega Gledaliskega Muzeja*. Freq: 2; Began: 1964; Lang: Slo; Subj: Theatre. Slovenski Gledaliski in Filski muzej; Cankarjeva 11; Ljubljana; SLOVENIA.

DShG *Deutsche Shakespeare Gesellschaft/Deutsche Shakespeare Gesellschaft West, Jahrbuch*. Freq: 1; Began: 1993; Lang: Ger; Subj: Theatre. ISSN: 0945-5094 ■Ferdinand Kamp Verlag GmbH; Widumestr. 6-8; D-44787 Bochum; GERMANY.

DSo *Dramatists Sourcebook*. Formerly: *Information for Playwrights*. Freq: 1; Began: 1981; Cov: Scan; Lang: Eng; Subj: Theatre. ISSN: 0733-1606 ■Theatre Comm. Group, Inc; 355 Lexington Ave.; New York, NY 10017; USA.

DSS *Dix-Septième Siècle*. Freq: 4; Began: 1949; Last Known Address; Cov: Scan; Lang: Fre; Subj: Related. ISSN: 0012-4273 ■Commission des Publications, c/o Collège de France; 11 Place M. Berthelot; 75005 Paris; FRANCE.

DSTFM *Documents of the Slovenian Theatre and Film Museum*. Began: 1979; Cov: Scan; Lang: Slo; Subj: Theatre. Slovenian Theatre and Film Museum; Ljubljana; SLOVENIA.

DTh *Divadelní ústar*. Freq: 2; Cov: Full; Lang: Slo; Subj: Theatre. Celetná 17; 11001 Prague 1; CZECH REPUBLIC.

Dtherapy *Dramatherapy*: SEE: Journal of Dramatherapy (JDt). Lang: Eng; Subj: Theatre. The Old Mill, Tolpuddle; Dorchester; Dorset DT2 7EX; UK.

DTi *Dancing Times*. Freq: 12; Began: 1910; Lang: Eng; Subj: Theatre. ISSN: 0011-605X ■Dancing Times Ltd., Clerkenwell House; 45-47 Clerkenwell Green; London EC1R 0BE; UK.

DTJ *Dance Theatre Journal*. Freq: 4; Began: 1983; Cov: Scan; Lang: Eng; Subj: Theatre. ISSN: 02464-9160 ■Laban Centre for Movement & Dance, Laurie Grove; London, SE14 6NH; UK.

DTN *Drama and Theatre Newsletter*. Freq: 4; Began: 1975; Ceased: 1982; Lang: Eng; Subj: Theatre. British Theatre Institute; 30 Clareville Street; London SW7 5AW; UK.

DTOP *Dramaturgi: Tedri Og Praksis*. Lang: Dan; Subj: Theatre. Akademisk Forlag; St. Kannikestraede 8; 1169 Copenhagen; DENMARK.

Dvat *Dvatisoč 2000: časnik za mišljenje, umetnost, kulturna*. Began: 1969; Lang: Slo; Subj: Related. Društvo izdajateljev časnika 2000; Ljubljana; SLOVENIA.

DVG *De Vlaamse Gids.*.Freg: 6; Cov: Scan ; Lang: Flem;; Subj: Related. ISSN: 0042-7675 ■Antwerp;; BELGIUM.

DVLa *Diadja Vanja. Literaturnij al'manah*. Began: 1994; Lang: Rus; Subj: Related. ISSN: 0132-8204 ■Gertsen Street 50/5; Room 44; 121069 Moscow; RUSSIA.

DZP *Deutsche Zeitschrift für Philosophie*. Freq: 12; Began: 1953; Cov: Scan; Lang: Ger; Subj: Related. ISSN: 0012-1045 ■VEB Deutscher Verlag der Wissenschaften; Johannes-Dieckmann-Str. 10, Postfach 1216; 1080 Berlin; GERMANY.

E&AM *Entertainment and Arts Manager*. Formerly: *Entertainment and Arts Management*. Freq: 4; Began: 1973; Ceased: 1989; Cov: Scan; Lang: Eng; Subj: Theatre. ISSN: 0143-8980 ■Assoc. of Entertainment & Arts Mangement, T.G. Scott and Son Ltd.; 30-32 Southampton St., Covent Garden; London WC2E 7HR; UK.

EAH *East Asian History*: Formerly: *Papers on Far Eastern History*. Freq: 2; Began: 1991; Cov: Scan; Lang: Eng; Subj: Related. ISSN: 1036-6008 ■A.C.T.: Division of Pacific and Asian Histor; Research School of Pacific Studies; Australian National University, Canberra; AUSTRALIA.

EAL *Early American Literature*. Freq: 3; Cov: Scan; Lang: Eng; Subj: Related. ISSN: 0012-8163 ■University of North Carolina Press; Box 228; Chapel Hill,, North Carolina; USA.

EAR *English Academy Review, The*. Began: 1983; Cov: Scan; Lang: Eng; Subj: Related. English Academy of Southern Africa, Bollater House; 35 Melle St., Braamfontein; 2001 Johannesburg; SOUTH AFRICA.

Ebony *Ebony*. Freq: 12; Began: 1945; Cov: Scan; Lang: Eng; Subj: Related. ISSN: 0012-9011 ■Johnson Publishing Co., Inc.; 820 S. Michigan; Chicago, IL 60605; USA.

Echanges *Echanges*. Freq: 12; Lang: Fre; Subj: Theatre. Théâtre Romain-Rolland; rue Eugène Varlin; 94 Villejuif; FRANCE.

EchoP *Echo Planety*. Freq: 52; Began: 1988; Lang: Rus; Subj: Related. ISSN: 0234-1670 ■State Union Publishing; 103009; Tversko Boulevard 10-12 Moscow K-9; RUSSIA.

Econ *Economist Financial Report*. Freq: 48; Began: 1976; Cov: Scan; Lang: Eng; Subj: Related. ISSN: 0013-0613 ■Economist Newspaper Ltd.; 25 St. James St.; London SW1A 1HG; UK.

ECr *Esprit Créateur, L'*. Freq: 4; Began: 1961; Lang: Fre; Subj: Theatre. ISSN: 0014-0767 ■John D. Erickson; Box 222; Lawrence, KS 66044; USA.

ECrit *Essays in Criticism*. Freq: 4; Began: 1951; Lang: Eng; Subj: Related. ISSN: 0014-0856 ■6A Rawlinson Rd.; Oxford OX2 6UE; UK.

ECS *Eighteenth-Century Studies*. Freq: 4 Cov: Scan; Lang: Eng; Subj: Related. Johns Hopkins Univ. Press; 2715 North Charles St.; Baltimore, MD 21218; US.

ECW *Essays on Canadian Writing*. Freq: IRR; Began: 1974; Cov: Scan; Lang: Eng; Subj: Related. ISSN: 0313-0300 ■1980 Queen St. E.; Toronto, ON M4L 1J2; CANADA.

ED *Envers du Décor, L'*. Freq: 6; Began: 1973; Lang: Fre; Subj: Theatre. ISSN: 0319-8650 ■Théâtre du Nouveau Monde; 84 Ouest, Rue Ste-Catharine; Montreal, PQ H2X 1Z6; CANADA.

EDAM *The Early Drama, Art, and Music Review*. Formerly *EDAM Newsletter*. Freq: 2; Began: 1978; Cov: Scan; Lang: Eng; Subj: Theatre. ISSN: 0196-5816 ■Medieval Institute Publications; Western Michigan University; Kalamazoo, MI 49008; USA.

EE&PA *Economic Efficiency and the Performing Arts*. Lang: Eng; Subj: Theatre. Association for Cultural Economics, University of Akron; Akron, OH 44235; USA.

EECIT *Estudis Escenics*. Freq: 2; Began: 1979; Lang: Cat; Subj: Theatre. ISSN: 0212-3819 ■Inst. del Theatre de Barcelona, c/o Nou de la Rambla; 08001 Barcelona 3; SPAIN.

Egk *Engekikai*: Theatre World. Freq: 12; Began: 1940; Lang: Jap; Subj: Theatre. Engeki Shuppan-sha, Chiyoda-ku; 2-11 Kanda-Jinpo-cho; Tokyo 101; JAPAN.

EHR *Economic History Review*. Freq: 4; Began: 1927; Lang: Eng; Subj: Related. ISSN: 0013-0117 ■Blackwell Ltd.; 108 Cowley Rd; Oxford OX4 1JF; UK.

EiC *Estrada i cirk*. Freq: 12; Began: 1992; Cov: Scan; Lang: Rus; Subj: Theatre. ISSN: 0131-6769 ■Moscow; RUSSIA.

EinA *English in Africa*. Freq: 2; Began: 1974; Cov: Scan; Lang: Eng; Subj: Related. ISEA, Rhodes University; Grahamstown; 6140; SOUTH AFRICA.

Eire ***Eire-Ireland.*** Freq: 4; Began: 1966; Cov: Scan; Lang: Eng; Subj: Related. ISSN: 0013-2683
■Irish American Cultural Institute; 2115 Summit Avenue; College of St. Thomas Box 5026, St. Paul, MN 55105; USA.

EIT ***Escena***: Informativo Teatral. Freq: 4; Began: 1979; Lang: Spa; Subj: Theatre. Universidad de Costa Rica, Teatro Universitario, Apt. 92; San Pedro de Montes de Oca; San José; COSTA RICA

Ekran ***Ekran.*** Formerly *Sovetski Ekran.* Freq: 4; Began: 1992; Cov: Scan; Lang: Rus; Subj: Related. A-319 Ul. Chasovaja 5-6; Moscow 125319; RUSSIA.

Elet ***Életünk.*** Freq: 12; Began: 1963; Cov: Scan; Lang: Hun; Subj: Related. ISSN: 0133-4751
■Arany János Lap- és Könyvkiadó Kft.; Forgó u. 1; 9701 Szombathely; HUNGARY.

EII ***Elet és Irodalom***: irodalmi es politkai hetilap. Freq: 52; Began: 1957; Lang: Hun; Subj: Related. ISSN: 0424-8848
■Ft. Lapkiado Vallalat; Széchenyi rkp. 1; 1054 Budapest V; HUNGARY.

Ellenfény ***Ellenfény.*** Freq: 5; Began: 1996; Cov: Full; Lang: Hun; Subj: Dance & Theatre. ISSN: 1416-499x
■Ú-j Színházért Alapívány; Baross u. 45; 1088 Budapest; HUNGARY.

ElM ***Marges, El.*** Freq: 4; Cov: Scan; Lang: Cat; Subj: Related. ISSN: 0210-0452
■Curial Edicions Catalanes SA; carrer del Bruc 144; 08037 Barcelona; SPAIN.

ELN ***English Language Notes.*** Freq: 4; Cov: Scan; Lang: Eng; Subj: Related. ISSN: 0013-8282
■Department of English, Campus Box 226; University of Colorado at Boulder; Boulder, CO 80309-0226; USA.

ElPu ***Publico, El***: Periodico mensual de teatro. Freq: 12; Began: 1983; Cov: Scan; Lang: Spa; Subj: Theatre. ISSN: 0213-4926
■Centro de Documentación Teatral; c/ Capitán Haya, 44; 28020 Madrid; SPAIN.

ELR ***English Literary Renaissance Journal.*** Freq: 3; Began: 1971; Cov: Scan; Lang: Eng; Subj: Related. University of Massachusetts; Department of English; Amherst, MA 01003; USA.

EN ***Equity News.*** Freq: 12; Began: 1915; Cov: Scan; Lang: Eng; Subj: Theatre. ISSN: 0013-9890
■Actors Equity Association; 165 W. 46 St.; New York, NY 10036; USA.

Enact ***Enact***: monthly theatre magazine. Freq: 12; Began: 1967; Lang: Eng; Subj: Theatre. ISSN: 0013-6980
■Paul's Press, E44-11; Okhla Industrial Area, Phase II; 110020 New Delhi; INDIA.

Encore ***Encore.*** Lang: Eng; Subj: Theatre. Fort Valley State College; Fort Valley, GA 31030; USA.

EncoreA ***Encore.*** Freq: 12; Began: 1976; Lang: Eng; Subj: Theatre. PO Box 247; NSW 2154 Castle Hill; AUSTRALIA.

ENG ***Editorial Nuevo Grupo.*** Lang: Spa; Subj: Theatre. Avenida La Colina, Prolongación Los Manolos; La Florida; 105 Caracas; VENEZUELA.

EnSt ***English Studies.*** Freq: 6; Cov: Scan; Lang: Eng; Subj: Related. ISSN: 0013-838X
■Swets & Zeitlinger; P.O. Box 825; 2160 SZ Lisse; NETHERLANDS.

Entre ***Entré.*** Freq: 6; Began: 1974; Cov: Full; Lang: Swe; Subj: Theatre. ISSN: 0345-2581
■Svenska Riksteatern, Swedish National Theatre Centre; S-145 83; Norsborg; SWEDEN.

EO ***Etnograjicesko obozrenie.*** Freq: 6; Began: 1992; Cov: Scan; Lang: Rus; Subj: Related. ISSN: 0038-5050
■Ulica D. Uljanova 19; B 36 Moscow; RUSSIA.

EOR ***Eugene O'Neill Review.*** Freq: 3; Began: 1977; Cov: Full; Lang: Eng; Subj: Theatre. Formerly: *Eugene O'Neill Newsletter, The.* ISSN: 0733-0456
■Suffolk University, Department of English; Boston, MA 02114; USA.

EpicT ***Epic Theatre.*** Freq: 4; Lang: Ben; Subj: Theatre. 140/24 Netaji Subhashchandra Bose Road; Calcutta; INDIA.

EquityJ ***Equity Journal.*** Freq: 4; Began: 1931; Lang: Eng; Subj: Theatre. ISSN: 0141-3147
■British Actor's Equity Association; Guild House, Upper St. Martin's Lane; London WC2H 9EG; UK.

ERev ***Elizabethan Review.*** Freq: 2; Cov: Scan; Lang: Eng; Subj: Related. ISSN: 1066-7059
■8435 62nd Drive, #T41; Middle Village, NY 11379; USA.

ERT ***Empirical Research in Theatre.*** Freq: 1; Began: 1971; Ceased: 1984; Cov: Full; Lang: Eng; Subj: Theatre. ISSN: 0361-2767
■Center for Communications Research; Bowling Green State University; Bowling Green, OH 43403; USA.

ESA ***English Studies in Africa: A Journal of the Humanities.*** Freq: 2; Began: 1958; Cov: Scan; Lang: Eng; Subj: Related. ISSN: 0013-8398
■Witwatersrand Univ. Press; Jan Smuts Ave.; Johannesburg 2001; SOUTH AFRICA.

ESC ***English Studies in Canada.*** Freq: 4; Began: 1975; Cov: Scan; Lang: Eng; Subj: Related. Association of Canadian College and University Teachers of English; c/o Dept. of English; Carleton University Ottawa, ON K1S 5B6; CANADA.

Escena ***Escena.*** Lang: Spa; Subj: Theatre. Departamento de Publicaciones, Consejo Nacional de la Cultura; Calle Paris, Edificio Macanao 3er. Piso; 106 Caracas; VENEZUELA.

Escenica ***Escénica.*** Began: 1990; Lang: Spa; Subj: Theatre. Universidad Nacional Autónoma de México; Coordinación de Difusión Cultural; Centro Cultural Universitario Ciudad Universitaria, C.P. 04510; MEXICO.

Espill ***Espill, L'.*** Freq: 4; Lang: Cat; Subj: Related. Editorial 3 i 4, c/o Moratin 15; Porta 3; 46002 Valencia; SPAIN.

Esprit ***Esprit.*** Freq: 12; Began: 1932; Lang: Fre; Subj: Related. ISSN: 0014-0759
■19, rue Jacob; 75006 Paris; FRANCE.

Essence ***Essence.*** Freq: 12; Began: 1970; Lang: Eng; Subj: Related. ISSN: 0014-0880
■Essence Comm., Inc.; P.O. Box 53400 Boulder, CO 80322-3400; USA.

EstLit ***Estafeta Literaria***: La Revista Quincenal de Libros, Artes y Espetáculos. Freq: 24; Began: 1958; Lang: Spa; Subj: Theatre. ISSN: 0014-1186
■Avda. de José Antonio, 62; 13 Madrid; SPAIN.

Estreno ***Estreno***: Journal on the Contemporary Spanish Theater. Freq: 2; Began: 1975; Cov: Full; Lang: Eng/Spa; Subj: Theatre. ISSN: 0097-8663
■Penn State University; 350 N. Burrowes Bldg; University Park, PA 16802; USA.

ET ***Essays in Theatre.*** Freq: 2; Began: 1982; Cov: Full; Lang: Eng; Subj: Theatre. ISSN: 0821-4425
■University of Guelph, Department of Drama; Guelph, ON N1G 2W1; CANADA.

ETh ***Elizabethan Theatre.*** Began: 1968; Lang: Eng; Subj: Theatre. ISSN: 0071-0032
■Archon Books; 995 Sherman Avenue; Hamden, CT 06514; USA.

ETN ***Educational Theatre News.*** Freq: 6; Began: 1953; Lang: Eng; Subj: Theatre. ISSN: 0013-1997
■Southern California Education Theatre Association; 9811 Pounds Avenue; Whittier, CA 90603; USA.

Etoile ***Etoile de la Foire.*** Freq: 12; Began: 1945; Ceased: 1982; Lang: Fle/Fre; Subj: Theatre. ISSN: 0014-1895
■15 rue Vanderlinden; Brussels 3; BELGIUM.

Etudes ***Etudes Theatrales.*** Formerly *Arts du Spectacle en Belgique.* Freq: 2; Began: 1992; Lang: Fre; Subj: Theatre. ISSN: 0778-8738
■Centre d'études théâtrales; Université catholique de Louvain; place de l'Hocaille 5 1348 Louvain-la-Neuve; BELGIUM.

Europai ***Európai utas.*** Cov: Scan; Lang: Rus; Subj: Related. Moscow; RUSSIA.

Europe ***Europe***: Revue Littéraire Mensuelle. Freq: 8; Began: 1923; Cov: Scan; Lang: Fre; Subj: Related. ISSN: 0014-2751
■146, rue du Fg. Poisonnière; 75010 Paris; FRANCE.

Evento ***Evento Teatrale.*** Freq: 3; Began: 1975; Lang: Ita; Subj: Theatre. A.BE.TE.spa; Via Presentina 683; 00155 Rome; ITALY.

Exchange ***Exchange.*** Freq: 3; Began: 1975; Lang: Eng; Subj: Theatre. University of Missouri: Columbia, Dept. of Speech/Drama; 129 Fine Arts Centre; Columbia, MS 65211; USA.

FAR ***Fremantle Arts Review: monthly arts digest.*** Freq: 6; Began: 1986; Cov: Scan; Lang: Eng; Subj: Related. ISSN: 0816-6919
■Fremantle Arts Centre; P.O. Box 891; Fremantle 6160; AUSTRALIA.

Farsa ***Farsa, La.*** Freq: 20; Last Known Address; Lang: Spa; Subj: Theatre. Pza. de los Mostenses 11; 9 Madrid; SPAIN.

FDi *Film a Divadlo*. Freq: 26; Lang: Cze; Subj: Related. Theatre Intitute in Bratislava; Obzor, Ceskoslovenskej Armady 35; Bratislava 815 85; SLOVAKIA.

Fds *Freedomways*: A Quarterly Review of the Freedom Movement. Freq: 4; Began: 1961; Cov: Scan; Lang: Eng; Subj: Related. ISSN: 0016-061X
▪Freedomways Assoc., Inc.; 799 Broadway; New York, NY 10003 6849; USA.

FemR *Feminist Review*. Freq: 3; Began: 1979; Lang: Eng; Subj: Related. ISSN: 0141-7789
▪11 Carleton Gardens, Brecknock Rd.; London N19 5AQ; UK.

FemS *Feminist Studies*. Freq: 3; Lang: Eng; Subj: Related. c/o Women's Studies; 2101 Woods Hall; University of Maryland College Park, MD 20742; USA.

Figura *Figura. Zeitschrift für Theater und Spiel mit Figuren*. Formerly: *Puppenspiel und Puppenspieler*. Freq: 4; Began: 1993; Cov: Scan; Lang: Ger;; Subj: Related. ISSN: 1021-3244
▪Brigitta Weber; Pf. 501; CH-8401 Winterthur; GERMANY.

Fikr *Al Fikr*. Lang: Ara; Subj: Theatre. Rue Dar Eg-gild; Tunis; TUNISIA.

FiloK *Filológiai Közlöny*. Freq: 4; Began: 1955; Cov: Scan; Lang: Hun; Subj: Related. ISSN: 0015-1785
▪Akadémiai Kiadó; Amerikai út 96; 1145 Budapest V; HUNGARY.

FIRTSIB *FIRT/SIBMAS Bulletin d'information*. Freq: 4; Began: 1977; Lang: Fre/Eng; Subj: Theatre. Fédération Internationale pour la Recherche Théâtrale; c/o van Eeghenstraat 11311, 1071 EZ Amsterdam; NETHERLANDS.

Flam *Flamboyant. Schriften zum Theater*. Freq: 4; Began: 1995; Cov: Scan; Lang: Ger; Subj: Theatre. ISBN: 3-9804764-3-X
▪Studio 7, International Theatre Ensemble e.v.; Vitalisstr. 386; D-50933 Köln; GERMANY.

FMa *Fight Master, The*. Freq: 4; Cov: Scan; Lang: Eng; Subj: Theatre. Society of American Fight Directors; 1834 Camp Avenue; Rockford, IL 61103; USA.

FMT *Forum Modernes Theater*. Freq: 2; Began: 1986; Cov: Scan; Lang: Ger/Eng/Fre; Subj: Theatre. ISSN: 0930-5874
▪Gunter Narr Verlag; Pf. 2567 D-72015 Tübingen; GERMANY.

FN *Filologičeskije Nauki*. Freq: 6; Began: 1958; Cov: Scan; Lang: Rus; Subj: Related. ISSN: 0130-9730
▪Izdatelstvo Vysšaja Škola; Prospekt Marksa 18; 103009 Moscow K-9; RUSSIA.

Fnotes *Footnotes*. Freq: 1; Began: 1975; Lang: Eng; Subj: Theatre. Stagestep; Box 328; Philadelphia, PA 19105; USA.

FO *Federal One*. Freq: IRR; Began: 1975; Cov: Scan; Lang: Eng; Subj: Related. George Mason University; 4400 University Dr.; Fairfax, VA 22030; USA.

Forras *Forrás*. Freq: 12; Began: 1969; Cov: Scan; Lang: Hun; Subj: Related. ISSN: 0133-056X
▪Petőfi Lap- és Könyvkiadó Kft.; Május 1. tér 3; 6001 Kecskemét; HUNGARY.

FR *French Review, The*. Freq: 6; Began: 1927; Cov: Scan; Lang: Fre/Eng; Subj: Related. ISSN: 0016-111X
▪American Association of Teachers of French; 57 E. Armory Ave.; Champaign, IL 61820; USA.

FranceT *France Théâtre*. Freq: 24; Began: 1957; Lang: Fre; Subj: Theatre. ISSN: 0015-9433
▪Syndicat National des Agences; 16 Avenue l'Opéra.; 75001 Paris; FRANCE.

FreilD *Freilichtbühne, Die*. Freq: 2; Began: 1956; Cov: Scan; Lang: Ger; Subj: Related. Verband deutscher Freilichtbühnen e.V.; Gebrüder-Funke-Weg 3; D-59073 Hamm; GERMANY.

FrF *French Forum*. Freq: 3; Began: 1976; Lang: Fre/Eng; Subj: Related. ISSN: 0098-9355
▪French Forum Publishers, Inc.; Box 5108; Lexington, KY 40505; USA.

Front *Frontiers: A Journal of Women Studies*. Freq: 3; Lang: Eng; Subj: Related. Wilson 12; Washington State University; Pullman, WA 99164-4007; USA.

FS *French Studies*: A quarterly review. Freq: 4; Began: 1947; Cov: Scan; Lang: Eng; Subj: Related. ISSN: 0016-1128
▪Society for French Studies, c/o Dr. J.M. Lewis; Dept. of French; Queen's University Belfast BT7 1NN; NORTHERN IRELAND.

FSM *Film, Szinház, Muzsika*. Freq: 52; Began: 1957; Ceased: 1990; Cov: Scan; Lang: Hun; Subj: Theatre. ISSN: 0015-1416
▪Lapkiadó Vállalat; Erzsébet körút 9-11; 1073 Budapest VII; HUNGARY.

FT *Finnish Theatre*. Formerly *News From the Finnish Theatre*. Freq: 1 Began: 1995; Cov: Full; Lang: Fin/Eng; Subj: Theatre. ISSN 1238-6057
▪Finnish Theatre Information Centre; Meritullinkatu 33; 00170 Helsinki; FINLAND.

fTep *fliegende Teppich, Der. Zeitung für Kinderkultur und Kindertheater*. Freq: 5; Cov: Scan Lang: Ger; Subj: Theatre. Verein IchduwirAnimation und Mitspieltheater für Kinder; Hockegasse 40/27; A-1180 Vienna; AUSTRIA.

Ftr *Figurentheater*. Freq: IRR; Began: 1923; Ceased; Lang: Ger; Subj: Theatre. ISSN: 0430-3873
▪Deutsches Institut für Puppenspiel; Hattingerstr. 467; D-4630 Bochum; GERMANY.

Fundarte *Fundarte*. Lang: Spa; Subj: Theatre. Edificio Tajamar, P.H., Parque Central; Avenida Lecuna; 105 Caracas; VENEZUELA.

Fundevogel *Fundevogel. Kritisches Kinder-Medien-Magazin*. Freq: 4; Began: 1984; Cov: Scan; Lang: Ger; Subj: Related. ISSN: 0176-2753
▪dipa-Verlag, Nassauer Str. 1-3; D-60439 Frankfurt/M; GERMANY.

FundM *Fundraising Management*. Freq: 12; Began: 1972; Cov: Scan; Lang: Eng; Subj: Related. Hoke Communications Inc.; 224 7th Street; Garden City, NY 11530-5771 USA.

Funoun *Al Funoun*: The Arts. Freq: 12; Lang: Ara; Subj: Theatre. Ministry of Information, Dept. of Culture and Arts; PO Box 6140; Amman; JORDAN.

G&GBKM *Grimm & Grips. Beilage zum Kritischen Kinder-Medien Magazin-Fundevogel*. Freq: 4; Cov: Scan; Lang: Ger; Subj: Related. ISSN: 0176-2753
▪Assitej e.V. Bundesrepublik Deutschland; Schützenstr. 12; D-60311 Frankfurt/M; GERMANY.

G&GJKJ *Grimm & Grips. Jahrbuch für Kinder- und Jugendtheater*. Freq: 1; Began: 1987; Cov: Scan; Lang: Ger; Subj: Related. ISSN: 0933-4149
▪Assitej e.V. Sektion BRD; Schützenstr. 12; D-60311 Frankfurt/M; GERMANY.

Gambit *Gambit*. Freq: IRR; Began: 1963; Ceased: 1986; Cov: Scan; Lang: Eng; Subj: Theatre. ISSN: 0016-4283
▪John Calder, Ltd.; 9-15 Neal Street; London WC2H 9TU; UK.

Gap *Gap, The*. Lang: Eng; Subj: Related. Washington, DC; USA.

GaR *Georgia Review*. Freq: 4; Began: 1947; Lang: Eng; Subj: Related. ISSN: 0016-8386
▪University of Georgia; Athens, GA 30602; USA.

Garcin *Garcin: Libro de Cultura*. Freq: 12; Began: 1981; Lang: Spa; Subj: Related. Acali Editoria; Ituzaingo 1495; Montevideo; URUGUAY.

Gazit *Gazit*. Lang: Heb; Subj: Theatre. 8 Brook Street; Tel Aviv; ISRAEL.

GdBA *Gazette des Beaux Arts*. Freq: 12; Began: 1859; Lang: Fre; Subj: Related. ISSN: 0016-5530
▪Imprimerie Louis Jean, B.P. 87; Gap Cedex 05002; SWITZERLAND.

GdF *Gazette du Français*. Freq: 12; Began: 1983; Lang: Fre; Subj: Related. ISSN: 0759-1268
▪Paris; FRANCE.

GdS *Giornale dello Spettacolo*. Freq: 52; Lang: Ita; Subj: Theatre. ISSN: 0017-0232
▪Associazione Generale Italiana dello Spettacolo; Via di Villa Patrizi 10; 00161 Rome; ITALY.

GerSR *German Studies Review*. Freq: 3; Began: 1978; Cov: Scan; Lang: Ger; Subj: Related. ISSN: 0149-7952
▪German Studies Association, c/o Prof. Gerald R. Kleinfeld; Arizona State University; Tempe, AZ 85281; USA.

Gestos *Gestos*: teoria y práctica del teatro hispánico. Freq: 2; Began: 1986; Cov: Full; Lang:Eng /Spa; Subj: Theatre. ISBN: 0-9656914-1
▪University of California, Irvine, Department of Spanish and Portuguese; Irvine, CA 92697; USA.

Gestus *Gestus*: A Quarterly Journal of Brechtian Studies. Freq: 4; Began: 1985; Cov: Full; Lang: Eng/Ger/Fre/Ita/Spa; Subj: Theatre. ISSN: 0749-7644
▪Brecht Society of America; 59 S. New St.; Dover, DE 19901; USA.

GiP *Gosudarstvo i pravo*. Freq: 12; Began: 1992; Cov: Scan; Lang: Rus; Subj: Related. ISSN: 0132-0769 ▪Akad. Nauk S.S.S.R.; Inst. Gosudarstva i Prava; Izdatel'stvo Nauka; Podsosenskii Per., 21; Moscow K-62; RUSSIA.

GL&L *German Life and Letters*. Freq: 4; Began: 1936; Cov: Scan; Lang: Eng; Subj: Related. ISSN: 0016-8777 ▪Basil Blackwell Publisher, Ltd.; 108 Cowley Road; Oxford 0X4 1JF; UK.

Goethe *Goethe Yearbook: Publication of the Goethe Society of North America*. Freq: IRR; Lang: Eng /Ger; Subj: Related. Department of German; University of California; Irvine, CA 92717; USA.

GOS *Gazette Officielle du Spectacle*. Freq: 36; Began: 1969; Lang: Fre; Subj: Theatre. Office des Nouvelles Internationales; 12 rue de Miromesnil; 75008 Paris; FRANCE.

Gosteri *Gosteri*: Performance. Freq: 12; Lang: Tur; Subj: Theatre. Uluslararasi Sanat Gosterileri A.S.; Narlpbahce Sok. 15; Cagaloglu-Istanbul; TURKEY.

GQ *German Quarterly*. Freq: 4; Began: 1928; Last Known Address; Cov: Scan; Lang: Ger; Subj: Related. ISSN: 0016-8831 ▪American Assoc. of Teachers of German; 523 Building, Suite 201, Rt. 38; Cherry Hill, NJ 08034; USA.

GrandR *Grande République*. Formerly: *Pratiques Théâtrales*. Freq: 3; Began: 1978; Ceased: 1981; Lang: Fre; Subj: Theatre. ISSN: 0714-8178 ▪University of Québec; 200 Rue Sherbrooke Ouest; Montreal, PQ H2X 3P2; CANADA.

GrTZ *Graumann TZ*; Freq: 4; Cov: Scan; Lang: Ger; Subj: Related. GraumannEigenArt, Theaterverlag Wien-Hamburg; Wipplingerstr. 34; A-1001 Vienna; AUSTRIA.

GSJ *Gilbert and Sullivan Journal*. Freq: 3; Began: 1925; Ceased: 1986; Lang: Eng; Subj: Theatre. ISSN: 0016-9951 ▪Gilbert and Sullivan Society; 23 Burnside, Sawbridgeworth; Hertfordshire CM21 OEP; UK.

GSTB *George Spelvin's Theatre Book*. Freq: 3; Began: 1978; Lang: Eng; Subj: Theatre. ISSN: 0730-6431 ▪Proscenium Press; Box 361; Newark, NJ 19711; USA.

GTAR *Grupo Teatral Antifaz: Revista*. Freq: 12; Lang: Spa; Subj: Theatre. San Addres 146; 16 Barcelona; SPAIN.

GtE *Guidateatro: Estera*. Freq: 1; Began: 1967; Ceased; Lang: Ita; Subj: Theatre. Edizione Teatron; Via Fabiola 1; 00152 Rome; ITALY.

GtI *Guidateatro: Italiana*. Freq: 1; Began: 1967; Lang: Ita; Subj: Theatre.La guidateatro è venduta direttamente dall 'Théatron'; Via Fabiola 1; 00152 Rome; ITALY.

Guida *Guida dello Spettacolo*. Lang: Ita; Subj: Theatre. Via Palombini 6; Rome; ITALY.

HA *Habitat Australia*. Freq: 6; Began: 1973; Cov: Scan; Lang: Eng; Subj: Related. ISSN: 0310-2939 ▪Australian Conservation Foundation; 340 Gore St. Fitzroy; Melbourne, Victoria; AUSTRALIA.

Harlekijn *Harlekijn*. Freq: 4; Began: 1970; Ceased; Lang: Dut; Subj: Theatre. Kerkdijk 11; 3615 BA Westbroek; NETHERLANDS.

Hecate *Hecate: Women's Interdisciplinary Journal*. Freq: 2; Began: 1975; Cov: Scan; Lang: Eng; Subj: Related. ISSN: 0311-4198 ▪Hecate Press; English Dept., University of Queensland; P.O. Box 99 St. Lucia, Qld. 4067; AUSTRALIA.

Helik *Helikon*. Freq: 4; Began: 1955; Cov: Scan; Lang: Hun; Subj: Related. ISSN: 0017-999X ▪Argumentum Kiadó; Ménesi út 11-13 1118 Budapest; HUNGARY.

Hermes *Hermes: Zeitschrift für Klassische Philologie*. Freq: 4; Began: 1866; Lang: Eng/Ger/Fre/Ita; Subj: Related. ISSN: 0018-0777 ▪Franz Steiner Verlag Wiesbaden GmbH; Birkenwaldstr. 44; D-70191; Stuttgart; GERMANY.

Hev *Hevesi Napló*Freq: 4;Began: 1991;Lang: Hun; Subj: Related. ISSN: 1217-3746 ▪András Farkas; Vőrősmarty út 26 3300 Eger; HUNGARY.

HgK *Higeki Kigeki*: Tragedy and Comedy. Freq: 12; Began: 1948; Lang: Jap; Subj: Theatre. Hayakawa-Shobo, Chiyoda-ku; 2-2 Kanda-Tacho; 101 Tokyo; JAPAN.

HispArts *Hispanic Arts*. Freq: 5; Began: 1976; Last Known Address; Lang: Spa/Eng; Subj: Theatre. ISSN: 0732-1643 ▪Association of Hispanic Arts Inc.; 200 East 87th Street; New York, NY 10028; USA.

HisSt *Historical Studies*. Formerly: *Historical Studies: Australia and New Zealand*. SEE *Australian Historical Studies*. Freq: 2; Began: 1940; Ceased: 1988; Lang: Eng; Subj: Related. ISSN: 0018-2559 ▪University of Melbourne, Dept. of History; Parkville 3052; AUSTRALIA.

HistP *Historical Performance: Journal of Early Music America*. Freq: 2; Began: 1988; Lang: Eng; Subj: Related. ISSN: 0898-8587 ▪Early Music America; New York, NY; USA.

HJEAS *Hungarian Journal of English and American Studies*. Cov: Scan; Subj: Related. HUNGARY.

HJFTR *Historical Journal of Film, Radio and Television*. Freq: 2; Began: 1980; Lang: Eng; Subj: Related. ISSN: 0143-9685 ▪Carfax Pulbishing Co.; Box 25; Abingdon OX14 3UE; UK.

Horis *Horisont*. Freq: 6; Began: 1954; Lang: Swe; Subj: Related. ISSN: 0439-5530 ▪c/o Landsleapsförburden; Handelsesplanaden 23A; F 651 00 VASA; FINLAND.

HP *High Performance*. Freq: 4; Began: 1978; Lang: Eng; Subj: Related. ISSN: 0160-9769 ▪Astro Artz; 240 S. Broadway, 5th Floor; Los Angeles, CA 90012; USA.

HPT *History of Political Thought*. Freq: 4; Cov: Scan; Lang: Eng. Subj: Related.ISSN: 0143-781xImprint Academic;PO BOX 1;Thorverton, EX5 5YX;; UK.

HQ *Hungarian Quarterly*. Freq: 4; Began: 1959; Cov: Scan; Lang: Hun. Subj: Related.ISSN: 0028-5390MTI;Naphegy tér 8;1016 Budapest; HUNGARY.

HSt *Hamlet Studies*. Freq: 2; Began: 1978; Lang: Eng; Subj: Related. ISSN: 0256-2480 ▪Vikas Publishing House Ltd.; 5 Ansari Road; 110 002 New Delhi; INDIA.

HTHD *Hungarian Theatre/Hungarian Drama*. Freq: 1; Began: 1981; Cov: Scan; Ceased: 1988; Lang: Eng; Subj: Theatre. ISSN: 0230-1229 ▪Hungarian Theatre Institute; Krisztina körút. 57; 1016 Budapest; HUNGARY.

HTN *Hungarian Theatre News/ Ungarische Theaternachrichten*. Freq: 2; Began: 1985; Cov: Scan; Lang: Eng; Subj: Theatre. ISSN: 0237-3963 ▪Hungarian Centre of the International Theatre Institute; Krisztina krt. 57; 1016 Budapest; HUNGARY.

HW *History Workshop*. Freq: 2; Began: 1976; Lang: Eng; Subj: Related. ISSN: 0309-2984 ▪Oxford University Press; Pinkhill House; Southfield Road Eynsham, Oxford OX8 1JJ; UK.

IA *Ibsenårboken/Ibsen Yearbook*: Contemporary Approaches to Ibsen. Freq: 1; Began: 1952; Cov: Full; Lang: Nor/Eng; Subj: Theatre. ISSN: 0073-4365 ▪Universitetssorleget; Box 2959; 0608 Oslo 6; NORWAY.

IAS *Interscena/Acta Scenographica*. Freq: 2; Ceased: 1984; Lang: Eng/Fre/Ger; Subj: Theatre. Divadelni Ustav; Celetna 17; Prague 1; CZECH REPUBLIC.

IdS *Information du Spectacle, L'*. Freq: 11; Lang: Fre; Subj: Theatre. 7 rue du Helder; 75009 Paris; FRANCE.

IDSelect *Irish Drama Selections*. Freq: IRR; Began: 1982; Lang: Eng; Subj: Theatre. ISSN: 0260-7964 ▪Colin Smythe Ltd., Box 6; Gerrards Cross; Buckinghamshire SL9 8XA; UK.

IHoL *Irodalomtörténet*. Freq: 4; Began: 1912; Cov: Scan; Lang: Hun; Subj: Related. ISSN: 0324-4970 ▪Magyar Irodalomtörténeti Társaság; Piarista köz 1. I. 59; 1052 Budapest; HUNGARY.

IHS *Irish Historical Studies*. Freq: 2; Began: 1938; Lang: Eng; Subj: Related. ISSN: 0021-1214 ▪Irish Historical Society, Dept. of Modern Irish History; Arts-Commerce Bldg, University College; Dublin 4; IRELAND.

IITBI *Instituto Internacional del Teatro, Centro Espanol*: Boletin Informativo. Freq: 4; Last Known Address; Lang: Spa; Subj: Theatre. Paseo de Recoletos 18-60; 1 Madrid; SPAIN.

IK *Irodalomtörténeti Közlemények*. Freq: 6; Began: 1891; Cov: Scan; Lang: Hun; Subj: Related. ISSN: 0021-1486 ▪Balassi Kiadó; Ménesi út 11-13; 1118 Budapest; HUNGARY.

IlCast *Il Castello di Elsinore*. Freq: 3; Began: 1988; Cov: Scan; Lang: Ita; Subj: Related. ISSN: 0394-9389

■Rosenberg & Sellier; Via Andrea Doria, 14; 00192 Torino; ITALY.

IM ***Island Magazine*** Formerly: *Tasmanian Review;*. Freq: 4; Lang: Eng Cov: Scan;; Subj: Related. ISSN: 1035-3127 ■c/o Univ. of Tasmania; P.O. Box 207; Tasmania 7005; AUSTRALIA.

Impressum ***Impressum.*** Freq: 4; Lang: Ger; Subj: Related. Henschelverlag Kunst und Gesellschaft; Oranienburger Strasse 67/68; 1040 Berlin; GERMANY.

Impuls ***Impuls.*** Freq: 3; Cov: Scan; Lang: Ger; Subj: Related. Internationales Theaterinstitut; Schloss str. 48; D-12165 Berlin; GERMANY.

InArts ***In the Arts***: Search, Research, and Discovery. Began: 1978; Ceased: 1988; Lang: Eng; Subj: Related. Ohio State University, College of the Arts; Columbus, OH 43210; USA.

INC ***Ibsen News & Comments.*** Freq: 1; Began: 1980; Cov: Scan; Lang: Eng; Subj: Theatre. Ibsen Society in America, Mellon Programs, Dekalb Hall 3; Pratt Institute; Brooklyn, NY 11205; USA.

Indonesia ***Indonesia.*** Freq: 2; Began: 1966; Lang: Eng; Subj: Related. ISBN: 0-87727 ■Cornell University, Southeast Asia Program Publications; East Hill Plaza; Ithaca, NY 14850; USA.

IndSh ***Independent Shavian.*** Freq: 3; Began: 1962; Lang: Eng; Subj: Theatre. ISSN: 0019-3763 ■The Bernard Shaw Society; Box 1159, Madison Square Station; New York, NY 10159-1159; USA.

Info ***Information on New Plays.*** Freq: IRR; Lang: Eng; Subj: Theatre. ISSN: 0236-6959 ■Hungarian Information Service; Krisztina krt. 57; H-1016 Budapest; HUNGARY.

InoLit ***Inostrannaja Literatura***: (Foreign Literature). Freq: 12; Began: 1955; Cov: Scan; Lang: Rus; Subj: Related. ISSN: 0130-6545 ■Izvestija; Moscow; RUSSIA.

ISK ***Iskusstvo Kino.*** Freq: 12; Cov: Scan; Lang: Rus; Subj: Related. ISSN: 0130-6405 ■Moscow; RUSSIA.

Iskusstvo ***Iskusstvo.*** Freq: 12; Last Known Address; Began: 1918; Cov: Scan; Lang: Rus; Subj: Related. ISSN: 0130-2523 ■Tsvetnoi Bulvar 25; K 51 Moscow; RUSSIA.

Iskv ***Iskusstvo v škole.*** Began: 1927; Cov: Scan; Lang: Rus; Subj: Related. ISSN: 0869-4966 ■State Union Publishing; Kedrov Street 8; 117804 Moscow; RUSSIA.

ISPTC ***Istituto di Studi Pirandelliani e sul Teatro Contemporaneo.*** Freq: 1; Began: 1967; Lang: Ita; Subj: Theatre. ISSN: 0075-1480 ■Casa Editrice Felice le Monnier; Via Scipione Ammirato 100; 50136 Florence; ITALY.

ISST ***In Sachen Spiel und Theater.*** Formerly *Bunte Wagen.* Freq: 6; Began: 1949; Lang: Ger; Subj: Theatre. Höfling Verlag, Dr. V. Mayer; Str. 18-22; 6940 Weinheim; GERMANY.

ITAN ***Irish Theatre Archive's Newsletter.*** Freq: 2; Began: 1993; Lang: Eng; Subj: Theatre. Irish Theatre Archive, Archives Division; City Hall; Dublin 2; IRELAND.

ITY ***International Theatre Yearbook***: SEE: Miedzynarodowny Rocznik Teatralny (Acro: MRT). Lang: Pol; Subj: Theatre. Warsaw; POLAND.

IUR ***Irish University Review.*** Freq: 2; Began: 1970; Cov: Scan; Lang: Eng; Subj: Related. ISSN: 0021-1427 ■University College; Room K203; Arts Building; Dublin 4; IRELAND.

IW ***Ireland of the Welcomes.*** Freq: 6; Began: 1952; Cov: Scan; Lang: Eng; Subj: Related. ISSN: 0021-0943 ■Bord Failte - Irish Tourist Board; Baggot St. Bridge; Dublin 2; IRELAND.

JAAC ***Journal of Aesthetics and Art Criticism, The.*** Freq: 4; Began: 1941; Cov: Scan; Lang: Eng; Subj: Related. ISSN: 0021-8529 ■114 N. Murray St.; Madison, WI 53715; USA.

JAC ***Journal of American Culture.*** Freq: 4; Began: 1978; Cov: Scan; Lang: Eng; Subj: Related. ISSN: 0191-1813 ■American Culture Association, Bowling Green State University; Bowling Green, OH 43403; USA.

JADT ***Journal of American Drama and Theatre, The.*** Freq: 3; Began: 1989; Cov: Full; Lang: Eng; Subj: Theatre. ISSN: 1044-937X ■CASTA, Grad. School and Univ. Centre, City University of New York; 33 West 42nd Street; New York, NY 10036; USA.

JAE ***Journal of Aesthetic Education.*** Freq: 4; Cov: Scan; Lang: English; Subj: Related. ISSN: 0021-8510 ■University of Illinois Press; 1325 S. Oak St.; Champaig, IL 61820-6903; USA.

JAfS ***Journal of African Studies.*** Freq: 4; Began: 1974; Cov: Scan; Lang: Eng; Subj: Related. ISSN: 0095-4993 ■Heldref Publications; 4000 Albemarle St, N.W.; Wasington, DC 20016; USA.

JahrfO ***Jahrbuch für Opernforschung.*** Cov: Scan; Lang: Ger; Subj: Related. ISSN: 0724-8156 ■Verlag Peter Lang GmbH; Eschborner Landstr. 42; D-60489 Frankfurt; GERMANY.

JahrST ***Jahrbuch der Städte mit Theatergastspielen.*** Freg: 1; Began: 1990; Cov: Scan; Lang: Ger; Subj: Related. ISSN: 0938-7943 ■Interessengemeinschaft der Städte mit Theatergastpielen; Mykenae-Verlag, Ahastr. 9; D-64285 Darmstadt; GERMANY.

JahrT ***Jahrbuch Tanzforschung.*** Freq: 1; Cov: Scan; Lang: Ger; Subj: Related. ISSN: 0940-1008 ■Florian Noetzel Verlag; Valoisstr. 11; D-29382 Wilhelmshaven; GERMANY.

JAML ***Journal of Arts Management, Law and Society.*** Formerly *Journal of Arts Management and Law.* Freq: 4; Began: 1969; Cov: Scan; Lang: Eng; Subj: Related. ISSN: 1063-2921 ■Heldref Publications; 1319 Eighteenth Street, NW; Washington, DC 20036-1802; USA.

JAP&M ***Journal of Arts Policy and Management.*** Freq: 3; Began: 1984; Ceased: 1989; Cov: Full; Lang: Eng; Subj: Theatre. ISSN: 0265-0924 ■City University, Dept. of Arts Policy and Management; Level 12, Frobisher Crescent; Barbican, Silk Street; London EC2Y 8HB; UK.

JASt ***Journal of Asian Studies.*** Freq: 4; Began: 1941; Cov: Scan; Lang: Eng; Subj: Related. ISSN: 0021-9118 ■Association for Asian Studies, Inc., University of Michigan; One Lane Hall; Ann Arbor, MI 48109; USA.

Javisko ***Javisko.*** Freq: 12; Lang: Cze; Subj: Related. ISSN: 0323-2883 ■Vydavatel'stvo tosveta; Osloboditelov 21; 036-54 Martin; SLOVAKIA.

JBeckS ***Journal of Beckett Studies.*** Freq: 2; Began: 1976; Cov: Full; Lang: Eng; Subj: Theatre. ISSN: 0309-5207 ■John Calder Ltd.; 9-15 Neal Street; London WC2H 9TU; UK.

JCCP ***Journal of Cross-Cultural Psychology.*** Freq: 6; Cov: Scan; Lang: Eng; Subj: Related. ISSN: 0022-0221 ■SAGE Publications, Inc.; P.O. Box 5084; Thousand Oaks, CA 91359; USA.

JCNREC ***Journal of Canadian Studies/ Revue d'études canadiennes.*** Freq: 4; Began: 1966; Cov: Scan; Lang: Eng/Fre; Subj: Related. ISSN: 0021-9495 ■Trent University; Box 4800; Peterborough, ON K9J 7B8; CANADA.

JCSt ***Journal of Caribbean Studies.*** Freq: 2; Began: 1970; Lang: Eng/Fre/Spa; Subj: Related. ISSN: 0190-2008 ■Association of Caribbean Studies; Box 248231; Coral Gables, FL 33124; USA.

JCT ***Jeu***: Cahiers de Théâtre. Freq: 4; Began: 1976; Cov: Full; Lang: Fre; Subj: Theatre. ISSN: 0382-0335 ■Cahiers de Theatre Jeu Inc.; C.P. 1600 Succursale E.; Montreal, PQ H2T 3B1; CANADA.

JdCh ***Journal de Chaillot.*** Freq: 8; Began: 1974; Cov: Scan; Lang: Fre; Subj: Related. Théâtre National de Chaillot; Place du Tracadéro; 75116 Paris; FRANCE.

JDS ***Jacobean Drama Studies.*** Freq: IRR; Began: 1972; Ceased: 1987; Lang: Eng; Subj: Theatre. Universität Salzburg, Institut für Englische Sprach; Akademiestr. 24; A 5020 Salzburg; AUSTRIA.

JDSh ***Jahrbuch der Deutsche Shakespeare-Gesellschaft.*** SEE: *Deutsche Shakespeare Gesellschaft/Deutsche Shakespeare Gesellschaft West.* Cov: Scan; Lang: Ger; Subj: Theatre. Deutsche Shakespeare-Gesellschaft West; Rathaus; D 4630 Bochum; GERMANY.

JDt ***Journal of Dramatherapy.*** Formerly: *Dramatherapy.* Freq: 2; Began: 1977; Lang: Eng; Subj: Related. ISSN: 0263-0672 ■David Powley, British Association for Dramatherapy; PO Box 98; Kirkbymoorside YD6 6EX; UK.

JDTC ***Journal of Dramatic Theory and Criticism.*** Freq: 2; Began: 1986; Cov: Full; Lang: Eng; Subj: Theatre. ISSN: 0888-3203

■University of Kansas, Dept. of Theatre and Film; 356 Murphy Hall; Lawrence, KS 66045; USA.

JEBT ***JEB Théâtre***. Lang: Fre; Ceased: 1982; Subj: Theatre. Documentation Générale de la jeunesse, des Loisirs; Galerie Ravenstein 78; 1000 Brussels; BELGIUM.

Jelenkor ***Jelenkor***. Freq: 12; Began: 1958; Cov: Scan; Lang: Hun; Subj: Related. ISSN: 0447-6425
■Jelenkor Irodalmi és Müvészeti Kiadó; Széchenyi tér 17 7621 Pécs; HUNGARY.

JENS ***Journal of the Eighteen Nineties Society***. Freq: 1; Began: 1970; Lang: Eng; Subj: Related. ISSN: 0144-008X
■28 Carlingford Rd., Hampstead; London NW3 1RQ; UK.

JFT ***Journal Freie Theater***. Freq: 1; Cov: Scan; Lang: Ger; Subj: Related. Bundesverband Freier Theater e.V.; Mykenae-Verlag, Ahastr. 9; D-64285 Darmstadt; GERMANY.

JFV ***Journal of Film and Video***. Freq: 4; Cov: Scan; Lang: Eng; Subj: Related. ISSN: 0724-4671
■University Film and Video Association;; USA.

JGG ***Jahrbuch der Grillparzer-Gesellschaft***. Freq: IRR; Began: 1897; Cov: Scan; Lang: Ger; Subj: Related. ISBN: 3-273-00043-4
■Grillparzer-Gesellschaft; Gumpendorfer Strasse 15/1; A 1060 Vienna; AUSTRIA.

JGT ***Journal du Grenier de Toulouse***. Freq: 12; Lang: Fre; Subj: Theatre. Grenier de Toulouse; 3, rue de la Digue; 31300 Toulouse; FRANCE.

JIES ***Journal of the Illuminating Engineering Society***. Freq: 1; Lang: Eng; Subj: Related. ISSN: 0099-4480
■Illuminating Engineering Society of North America; 120 Wall Street, 17th Floor; New York, NY 10005-4001; USA.

JIL ***Journal of Irish Literature***. Freq: 3; Began: 1972; Ceased: 1994; Cov: Scan; Lang: Eng; Subj: Related. P.O. Box 361; Newark, DE 19711; USA.

JITT ***JITT***. Lang: Jap; Subj: Theatre. Japanese Institute for Theatre Technology; 4-437 Ikebukuro, Toshima-ku; Tokyo; JAPAN.

JJS ***Journal of Japanese Studies***. Freq: 2; Began: 1974; Lang: Eng; Subj: Related. ISSN: 0095-6848
■Society for Japanese Studies, University of Washington; Thomson Hall DR-05; Seattle, WA 98195; USA.

JLS/TLW ***Journal of Literary Studies/ Tydskrif vir Literatuurwetenskap***. Freq: 4; Began: 1985; Cov: Scan; Lang: Eng/Afr; Subj: Related. ISSN: 0256-4718
■South African Society for General Literary Studies; Department of Theory of Literature Unisa P.O. Box 392 Pretoria 0001; SOUTH AFRICA.

JMH ***Journal of Magic History***. Began: 1979; Lang: Eng; Subj: Related. ISSN: 0192-9917
■Toledo, OH; USA.

JMMLA ***Journal of the Midwest Modern Language Association***. Freq: 2; Began: 1959; Cov: Scan; Lang: Eng; Subj: Related. ISSN: 0742-5562
■302 English-Philosophy Building; University of Iowa; Iowa City, IA 52242; USA.

JNZL ***Journal of New Zealand Literature***. Lang: Eng; Subj: Related. Wellington; NEW ZEALAND.

JoM ***Journal of Musicology***. Freq: 4; Cov: Scan; Lang: Eng; Subj: Related. ISSN: 0277-9269
■University of California Press; 2120 Berkeley Way; Berkeley, CA 94720; USA.

JOV ***Journal of Voice***. Freq: 4; Began: 1987; Cov: Scan; Lang: Eng; Subj: Related. Raven Press Books, Ltd.; 1185 Avenue of the Americas; New York, NY 10036; USA.

JPC ***Journal of Popular Culture***. Freq: 4; Began: 1967; Cov: Scan; Lang: Eng; Subj: Related. ISSN: 0022-3840
■Popular Culture Association, Bowling Green State University; Bowling Green, OH 43403; USA.

JRASM ***Journal of the Royal Asiatic Society of Malaysia***. Freq: 2; Began: 1936; Lang: Eng; Subj: Related. Kuala Lumpur; MALAYSIA.

JRSAVP ***Journal of Research in Singing and Applied Vocal Pedagogy***. Freq: 2; Lang: Eng; Subj: Related. Texas Christian University; Department of Music; P.O. Box 32887 Fort Worth, TX 76129; USA.

JSDC ***Journal for Stage Directors and Choreographers***. Freq: 2; Began: 1996; Cov: Scan; Lang: Eng; Subj: Theatre. SDC Foundation; 1501 Broadway, Suite 1701; New York, NY 10036; USA.

JSH ***Journal of Social History***. Freq: 4; Began: 1967; Cov: Scan; Lang: Eng; Subj: Related. ISSN: 0022-4529
■Carnegie-Mellon University Press; Schenley Park; Pittsburgh, PA 15213; USA.

JSS ***Journal of the Siam Society***. Began: 1926; Lang: Eng/Tha/Fre/Ger; Subj: Related. 131 Soi Asoke; Sukhumvit 21 Road; Bangkok 10110; THAILAND.

JT ***Jeune Théâtre***. Began: 1970; Ceased: 1982; Lang: Fre; Subj: Theatre. ISSN: 0315-0402
■Assoc. Québecoise du, Jeune Théâtre; 952 rue Cherrier; Montreal, PQ H2L 1H7; CANADA.

JTPR ***Journal du Théâtre Populaire Romand***. Freq: 8; Began: 1962; Lang: Fre; Subj: Theatre. Case Postale 80; 2301 La Chaux-de-Fonds; SWITZERLAND.

JTV ***Journal du Théâtre de la Ville***. Freq: 4; Began: 1968; Lang: Fre; Subj: Theatre. Theatre de la Ville; 16 quai de Gesvres; Paris; FRANCE.

Juben ***Juben***: (Playtexts). Freq: 12; Began: 1952; Lang: Chi; Subj: Theatre. ISSN: 0578-0659
■Zhongguo Xiju Chubanshe, 52; Dongsi Ba (8), Tiao 100700 Beijing; CHINA.

JugoIgre ***Jugoslovenske***: Pozorišne Igre. Began: 1962; Lang: Ser; Subj: Theatre. Sterijino Pozorje; Zmaj Jovina 22; Novi Sad; SERBIA.

Junkanoo ***Junkanoo***. Freq: 12; Lang: Eng; Subj: Theatre. Junkanoo Publications; Box N 4923; Nassau; BAHAMAS.

JWCI ***Journal of the Warburg & Courtauld Institutes***. Freq: 1; Began: 1937; Cov: Scan; Lang: Eng; Subj: Related. Woburn Square; London WC1H OAB; UK.

JWGT ***Jahrbuch der Wiener Gesellschaft für Theaterforschung***. Freq: 1; Lang: Ger; Subj: Related. Vienna; AUSTRIA.

Kabuki ***Kabuki***. Lang: Jap Cov: Scan; Lang: Jap; Subj: Theatre. 4-12-15 Ginza; 104 Chuo-ku, Tokyo; JAPAN.

Kaekseok ***Kaekseok***. Freq: 12; Began: 1992; Cov: Scan; Lang: Kor; Subj: Related. 58-1 Chung Jung-No 1 Ga; Jung Ku; Seoul;SOUTH KOREA.

Kalak ***Kalakalpam***. Freq: 2; Began: 1966; Lang: Eng; Subj: Theatre. Karyalaya Matya Kala Institute; 30-A Paddapukur Road; 20 Calcutta; INDIA.

Kalliope ***Kalliope***. Freq: 3; Began: 1995 Lang: Eng; Subj: Theatre. 3939 Roosevelt Blvd.; Jacksonville, FL 32205; USA.

Kanava ***Kanava***. Formerly: *Aika*. Freq: 9; Began: 1932; Lang: Fin; Subj: Related. ISSN: 0355-0303
■Yhtyneet Kuvalehdet Oy; Hietalahdenranta 13; 00180 Helsinki 18; FINLAND.

KAPM ***Kassette***: Almanach für Bühne, Podium und Manege. Freq: 1; Lang: Ger; Subj: Theatre. Berlin; GERMANY.

Kathakali ***Kathakali***. Freq: 4; Began: 1969; Lang: Eng/Hin; Subj: Theatre. ISSN: 0022-9326
■International Centre for Kathakali; 1-84 Rajandra Nagar; New Delhi; INDIA.

Kazal ***Kazaliste***. Freq: 26; Began: 1965; Ceased; Lang: Yug; Subj: Theatre.
■Prolaz Radoslava Bacica 1; Osijek; CROATIA.

KB ***Kunst Bulletin***. Freq: 12; Cov: Scan; Subj: Related.
■Fr. Hallwag AG; Nording 4; 4001 Bern; SWITZERLAND.

KCAB ***Korean Culture & Arts Bi-Monthly***. Freq: 6; Cov: Scan; Began: 1974; Lang: Kor; Subj: Related.
■Hankug Munhwa Yeasul Jinhyeng Won; 1-130 Chongrogu Dongsun Dong; Seoul; SOUTH KOREA.

Keshet ***Keshet***. Last Known Address; Began: 1982; Lang: Heb; Subj: Theatre.
■9 Bialik Street; Tel Aviv; ISRAEL.

KesK ***Kultúra és Közösség***. Freq: 6; Began: 1974; Ceased: 1990; Cov: Scan; Lang: Hun; Subj: Related. ISSN: 0133-2597
■Arany János Lap- és Könyvkiadó Kft.; Corvin tér 8; 1011 Budapest; HUNGARY.

KingP ***King Pole Circus Magazine***. Freq: 4; Began: 1934; Cov: Scan; Lang: Eng; Subj: Theatre.
■Circus Fans' Assoc. of UK, c/o John Exton; 20 Foot Wood Crescent; Shawclough Rochdale, Lancaster OL12 6PB; UK.

Kino ***Kino***. Freq: 4; Cov: Scan; Lang: Eng; Subj: Theatre;
■Australian Theatre Historical Society; P.O. Box 447; Campbelltown New South Wales 2560; AUSTRALIA.

KJ *Kultur-Journal*. Freq: 4; Lang: Ger; Subj: Related.
▪Mykenae-Verlag; Ahastr. 9; D-64285 Darmstadt; GERMAN.

KJAZU *Kronika*: Zavod za povijest hrvatske knjizevnisti. Began: 1975; Lang: Cro; Subj: Theatre. ISSN: 0023-4929
▪kazalista i glazbe Hrvatske akademije znanosti i umjetnosti; Opaticka 18; 41.000 Zagreb; CROATIA.

Klub *Klub i Chudožestvennaja Samodejetelnost*. Freq: 26; Lang: Rus; Subj: Theatre.
▪Profizdat; Ulitza Korova 13; Moscow; RUSSIA.

KMFB *Gewerkschaft Kunst, Medien, Freie Berufe*. Freq: 11; Began: 1945; Lang: Ger; Subj: Theatre.
▪UMLOsterreichischer Gewerkschaftsbund, Gewrkshft. Kunst, Medien, Freie, Berufe; Maria-Theresienstrasse 11; A 1090 Vienna; AUSTRIA.

KoJ *Korea Journal*. Freq: 4; Began: 1961; Cov: Scan; Lang: Eng; Subj: Related. ISSN: 0023-3900
▪Korean National Commission for UNESCO; P.O. Box Central 64; Seoul; SOUTH KOREA.

Kommunist *Kommunist*. Began: 1924; Cov: Scan; Lang: Rus; Subj: Related. ISSN: 0131-1212
▪Svobodnaja mysl'; Moscow; RUSSIA.

Kont *Kontinent*. Freq: 4; Cov: Scan; Lang: Rus; Subj: Related. ISSN: 0934-6317
▪Čistoprudnij Boulevard, 8A; 101923 Moscow; RUSSIA.

KoreanD *Korean Drama*. Last Known Address; Lang: Kor; Subj: Theatre.
▪National Drama Association of Korea, Insadong, Jongno-gu; Fed. of Arts & Cult. Org. Building; 110 Seoul; SOUTH KOREA.

Kortars *Kortárs*. Freq: 12; Began: 1957; Cov: Scan; Lang: Hun; Subj: Related. ISSN: 0023-415X
▪Magyar Írószövetség; Bajza u. 18; 1062 Budapest; HUNGARY.

KPR *Kulturno-Prosvetitelnaja Rabota*. SEE *Vstreča*. Freq: 12; Ceased: 1990; Lang: Rus; Subj: Related.
▪Sovéckaja Rossija; Bersenevskaja Naberež-naja 22; Moscow; RUSSIA.

Krajs *Kraj smolenskij* Began: 1996; Cov: Scan; Subj: Related.
▪Dom Sovietov k. 163; Smolensk 214008; RUSSIA.

Krit *Kritika*. Freq: 12; Began: 1963; Cov: Full; Lang: Hun; Subj: Related. ISSN: 0324-7775
▪Népszabadság Rt; Bécsi út 122-124; 1034 Budapest; HUNGARY.

KS *Kleine Schriften*. Freq: 1; Began: 1992; Cov: Scan; Lang: Ger; Subj: Related. 3-925191-95-X
▪Gesellschaft für unterhaltende Bühnenkunst e.V.; Grupellellostr. 21; D-40210 Dusseldorf; GERMANY.

KSF *Korean Studies Forum*. Freq: 2; Began 1976; Last Known Address; Lang: Kor; Subj: Related. ISSN: 0147-6335
▪Korean-American Educ. Commission, Garden Towers; No. 1803, 98-78 Wooni-Dong, Chongro-Ku; Seoul 110; SOUTH KOREA.

KSGT *Kleine Schriften der Gesellschaft für Theatergeschichte*. Freq: 1; Cov: Scan; Lang: Ger; Subj: Theatre.
▪Gesellschaft für Theatergeschichte e.V.; Mecklenburgische Str. 56; D-14197 Berlin; GERMANY.

KTR *Korean Theatre Review*. Freq: 12; Lang: Kor; Cov: Scan; Subj: Theatre.
▪National Theatre Association of Korea; Yechong Bldg; 1-117 Dongsoon-dong; Chongno-ku Seoul 110; SOUTH KOREA.

Kulis *Kulis*. Freq: 12; Began: 1946; Lang: Arm; Subj: Theatre.
▪H. Ayvaz; PK 83; 10 A Cagaloglu Yokusu; TURKEY.

Kvihkot *Kultuurivihkot*. Freq: 8; Began: 1973; Last Known Address; Lang: Fin/Swe; Subj: Theatre.
▪Kultuurityontekijain Liitto; Korkeavuorenkatu 4 C 15; 00130 Helsinki; FINLAND.

KWN *Kurt Weill Newsletter*. Freq: 2; Began: 1983; Cov: Scan; Lang: Eng; Subj: Related. ISSN: 0899-6407
▪Weill Foundation for Music; 7 East 20th Street; New York, NY 10003-1106; USA.

KZ *Kultura i Žizn*. (Culture and Life). Freq: 12; Began: 1957; Cov: Scan; Lang: Rus/Eng/Ger/Fre/Spa; Subj: Related.ISSN: 0023-5199
▪Sovéckaja Rossija; Projézd Sapunova 13-15; Moscow K-12; RUSSIA.

L&H *Literature & History*. Freq: 2; Began: 1975; Cov: Scan; Lang: Eng; Subj: Related. ISSN: 0306-1973
▪Ohio State University, Dept. of English; 421 Denney Hall; 164 W. 17th Ave. OH 43210; USA.

LabH *Labour History*. Freq: 2; Began: 1963; Cov: Scan; Lang: Eng; Subj: Related. ISSN: 0023-6942
▪Economic History Department; HO4, University of Sydney; NSW 2006; AUSTRALIA.

Laien *Laientheater*. Freq: 12; Began: 1972; Lang: Ger; Subj: Theatre.
▪Schweizerischen Volkstheater; 30 Bern; SWITZERLAND.

LAQ *Livres et Auteurs Québecois*. Freq: 1; Began: 1969; Ceased; Lang: Fre; Subj: Related. ISSN: 0316-2621
▪Presses de l'Université Laval, Cité Universitaire; Québec, PQ G1K 7R4; CANADA.

LATR *Latin American Theatre Review*. Freq: 2; Began: 1967; Cov: Full; Lang: Eng/Spa/Por; Subj: Theatre. ISSN: 0023-8813
▪University of Kansas, Center of Latin American Studies; 107 Lippincott Hall; Lawrence, KS 66045; USA.

LD+A *Lighting Design + Application*. Freq: 12; Began: 1906; Cov: Scan; Lang: Eng; Subj: Theatre. ISSN: 0360-6325
▪Illuminating Engineering Society; 120 Wall Street; 17th Floor New York, NY 10005-4001; USA.

LDim *Lighting Dimensions*: For the Entertainment Lighting Industry. Freq: 6; Began: 1977; Cov: Scan; Lang: Eng; Subj: Theatre.
▪Lighting Dimensions Publishing; 1590 S. Coast Highway, Suite 8; Laguna, CA 92651; USA.

LetQu *Lettres Québécoises*. Freq: 4; Began: 1976; Lang: Fre; Subj: Related. ISSN: 0382-084X
▪Editions Jumonville; 1781 rue Saint-Hubert; Montreal, PQ, H2L 3Z1; CANADA.

LettDI *Lettera Dall'Italia:* Bollettino trimestrale realizzato dall'Istituto dell'Enciclopedia Italiana. Freq: 4; Began: 1985; Lang: Ita; Subj: Related. ISSN: 0393-64457
▪Piazza dell'Enciclopedia Italiana, 4; 00186 Rome; ITALY.

Letture *Letture*: Libro e spettacolo, mensile di studi e rassegne. Freq: 10; Began: 1946; Lang: Ita; Subj: Related. ISSN: 0024-144X
▪Edizioni Letture; Piazza San Fedele 4; 20121 Milan; ITALY.

Letuch *Leteraturnaja ucheba*. Freq: 6; Lang: Rus; Subj: Related. ISSN: 0203-5847
▪Novodmitrovskaja Street, 5A; 125015 Moscow; RUSSIA.

LFQ *Literature/Film Quarterly*. Freq: 4; Began: 1973; Cov: Scan; Lang: Eng; Subj: Related. ISSN: 0090-4260
▪Salisbury State University; Salisbury, MD 21801; USA.

Light *Light*. Freq: 24; Began: 1921; Lang: Eng; Subj: Theatre.
▪Ahmadiyya Building; Brandreth Road; Lahore; PAKISTAN.

LikC *Lik Čuvašija*; Freq: 6; Began: 1994; Cov: Scan; Lang: Rus; Subj: Related.
▪Dom Pečaty k. 613; 13 pr. I. Jakovleva; Cheboksary 428019; CHUVASHIA.

Lilith *Lilith: a Feminist History Journal*. Freq: 1; Began: 1984; Cov: Scan; Lang: Eng; Subj: Related; ISSN: 0813-8990
▪Lilith Collective; P.O. Box 154; Fitzroy, Victoria 3065; AUSTRALIA.

LiNQ *Literature in North Queensland*. Freq: 2; Began: 1971; Cov: Scan; Lang: Eng; Subj: Related.
▪Dept. of English; James Cook University of North Queensland; Townsville, 4811; AUSTRALIA.

LinzerT *Linzer Theaterzeitung*. Freq: 10; Began: 1955; Lang: Ger; Subj: Theatre. ISSN: 0024-4139
▪Landestheater Linz; Promenade 39; A 4010 Linz; AUSTRIA.

Lipika *Lipika*. Freq: 4; Began: 1972; Lang: Eng; Subj: Theatre.
▪F-20 Nizzamudin West; 10013 New Delhi; INDIA.

Literator *Literator: Journal of Comparative Literature and Linguistics*. Freq: 3; Began: 1980; Cov: Scan; Lang: Afr/Eng; Subj: Related; ISSN: 0258-2279
▪Bureau for Scholarly Journals; Private Bag X6001; Potchefstroom 2520; REPUBLIC OF SOUTH AFRICA.

Literatura *Literatura*. Freq: 4; Began: 1974; Lang: Hun; Subj: Related. ISSN: 0133-2368
▪Balassi Kiadó; Ménesi út 11-13; 1118 Budapest; HUNGARY.

LitGruzia *Literaturnaja Gruzija*. Freq: 12; Began: 1957; Cov: Scan; Lang: Rus; Subj: Related. ISSN: 0130-3600
▪Sojuz pisatelej Gruzii; Tbilisi, Georg. SSR; GEORGIA.

Litva *Litva literaturnaja*. Freq: 12; Cov: Scan; Lang: Rus; Subj: Related. ISSN: 0206-296X
■Labdaryu Street, 3; 232600 Viln'yus; LITHUANIA.

Live *Live*. Freq: 4; Lang: Eng; Subj: Related.
■New York, NY; USA.

LLJ *La Trobe Library Journal*. Freq: 2; Began: 1968; Cov: Scan; Lang: Eng; Subj: Related. ISSN: 0041-3151
■Friends of the State Library of Victoria; State Library of Victoria; Swanston Street; Melbourne, 3000; AUSTRALIA.

LO *Literaturnojė Obozrenijė*. Freq: 12; Began: 1973; Cov: Scan; Lang: Rus; Subj: Related. ISSN: 0321-2904
■Sojuz Pisatelej SSSR; 9/10 ul. Dobroliubova; 127254 Moscow I-254,; RUSSIA.

Loisir *Loisir*. Freq: 4; Began: 1962; Lang: Fre; Subj: Theatre.
■Comédie de Caen; 120 rue St. Pierre; 1400 Caen; FRANCE.

LokK *Lok Kala*. Freq: 2; Ceased: 1977; Lang: Hin; Subj: Theatre.
■Bhartiya Lok kala Mandal; Udaipur 313001 Rajasthan; INDIA.

Loutkar *Loutkar*. Formerly Ceskoslovensky loutkar. Freq: 12; Began: 1993; Cov: Scan; Lang: Cze; Subj: Related. ISSN: 0323-1178
■Nina Malikova, Divadelni ustav; Celetna 17; 110 01 Praha 1; CZECH REPUBLIC.

Lowdown *Lowdown*. Freq: 6; Began: 1979; Cov: Scan; Lang: Eng; Subj: Theatre.
■Youth Performing Arts Assoc.; 11 Jeffcott St.; Adelaide SA 5000; AUSTRALIA.

LPer *Literature in Performance*. SEE *Text and Performance Quarterly*. Freq: 2; Began: 1980; Ceased; Lang: Eng; Subj: Theatre. ISSN: 0734-0796
■Inter. Div.,Speech Comm. Assoc., Dept. of Speech Communication; U. of NC, 115 Bingham Hall; Chapel Hill, NC 27514; USA.

LTR *Theatre Record*. Freq: 26; Began: 1981; Cov: Full; Lang: Eng; Subj: Theatre. ISSN: 0261-5282
■4 Cross Deep Gardens; Twickenham TW1 4QU Middlesex; UK.

Ludus *Ludus*: List Udruženja Dramskih Umetnika Srbije. Freq: 6; Began: 1983; Lang: Ser; Subj: Theatre.
■Udruženja Dramskih Umetnika Srbije; Terazije 26; Belgrade; SERBIA.

Lutka *Lutka*: Revija za lutkovno kulturo. Freq: 3; Began: 1966; Cov: Scan; Lang: Slo; Subj: Theatre. ISSN: 0350-9303
■Zveza kulturnih organizacij Slovenije; Kidričeva 5; Ljubljana; SLOVENIA.

M&T *Musik & Teater*. SEE *Teater Et*. Freq: 6; Began: 1979; Ceased: 1989; Lang: Dan; Subj: Theatre.
■Bagsvard Horedgade 9914E; 2800 Bagsvard; DENMARK.

MA *Muzykal'naja akademija*. Freq: 6; Began: 1957; Cov: Scan; Lang: Rus; Subj: Related. ISSN: 0869-4516
■Gadovaja Triumfal'naja uliča; #14/12;, Moscow 103006; RUSSIA.

MagIp *Magyar Iparművészet*. Freq: 6; Began: 1994; Cov: Scan; Lang: Hun; Subj: Related. ISSN: 1217-839X
■Forka Tömegkommunikációs Kft.; Nádor u. 32; 1051 Budapest; HUNGARY.

MagM *Magyar Múzeum*. Formerly *Új Erdélyi Múzeum*. Freq: 4; Began: 1991; Lang: Hun; Subj: Related. ISSN: 0866-4625
■Akadémiai Kiadó és a Közép-Európai Múzeum; Alapítvány; Meredek u. 25 1124 Budapest; HUNGARY.

Maksla *Maksla*. Began: 1959; Lang: Lat; Subj: Related. ISSN: 0455-3772
■Riga; LATVIA.

MAL *Modern Austrian Literature*. Freq: 4; Began: 1961; Lang: Eng/Ger; Subj: Related. ISSN: 0026-7503
■Intl A. Schnitzler Research Assoc., c/o Donald G. Daviau, Ed.; Dept. of Lit. & Langs, Univ. of CA; Riverside, CA 92521; USA.

Mamulengo *Mamulengo*. Lang: Por; Subj: Theatre.
■Assoc. Brasileira de Teatro de Bonecos; Rua Barata Ribeiro; 60 C 01 Guanabara; BRAZIL.

Manip *Manipulation*. Last Known Address; Lang: Eng; Subj: Theatre.
■Mrs. Maeve Vella; 28 Macarthur Place; 3053 Carlton, Victoria; AUSTRALIA.

MarqJTHS *Marquee*: The Journal of the Theatre Historical Society. Freq: 4; Began: 1969; Cov: Full; Lang: Eng; Subj: Theatre. ISSN: 0025-3928
■624 Wynne Rd; Springfield, PA 19064; USA.

Marquee *Marquee*. Freq: 8; Began: 1976; Cov: Scan; Last Known Address; Lang: Eng; Subj: Related. ISSN: 0700-5008
■Marquee Communications Inc.; 277 Richmond St. W.; Toronto, ON M5V 1X1; CANADA.

Mask *Mask*. Freq: 6; Began: 1967; Lang: Eng; Subj: Theatre. ISSN: 0726-9072
■Simon Pryor, Executive Officer, VADIE; 117 Bouverie Street; 3053 Carlton; AUSTRALIA.

MASKA *MASKA*. Freq: 4; Began: 1991; Lang: Slo/Eng; Subj: Theatre. ISSN: 1318-0509
■Dunajska 22; 61000 Ljubljana; SLOVENIA.

Maske *Maske*. SEE *Maska*. Began: 1985; Ceased: 1991; Lang: Slo/Eng; Subj: Theatre. ISSN: 0352-7913
■Zveza kulturnih organizacij Slovenije; Ljubljana; SLOVENIA.

Masque *Masque*. Freq: 24; Began: 1967; Lang: Eng; Subj: Theatre. ISSN: 0025-469X
■Masque Publications; Box 3504; 2001 Sydney NSW; AUSTRALIA.

Mast *Masterstvo*. Freq: 6; Lang: Ukr; Subj: Theatre.
■Pouchkineskaia Street 5; Kiev; UKRAINE.

Matya *Matya Prasanga*. Freq: 12; Lang: Ben; Subj: Theatre.
■54/1 B Patuatola Lane; Emherst Street; Calcutta; INDIA.

MAvilia *Monte Avilia*. Freq: 12; Began: 1980; Lang: Spa; Subj: Theatre.
■Apartado 70-712; 107 Caracas; VENEZUELA.

MBB *Mala Biblioteka Baletowa*. Began: 1957; Ceased: 1981; Lang: Pol; Subj: Theatre.
■Polskie Wydawnictwo Muzyczne; Al. Krasińskiego 11a; 31-111 Kraków; POLAND.

MBzT *Münchener Beiträge zur Theaterwissenschaft*. Cov: Scan; Lang: Ger; Subj: Related. ISSN: 0343-7604
■J. Kitzinger oHG, Schellingstr. 25; D-80799 Munich; GERMANY.

MC&S *Media, Culture and Society*. Freq: 4; Began: 1979; Lang: Eng; Subj: Related. ISSN: 0163-4437
■Sage Publications; 6 Bonhill Street; London EC2A 4PU; UK.

MChAT *Eżėgodnik MChAT*. Freq: 1; Lang: Rus; Subj: Theatre.
■Association of Soviet Writers; Hertsen 49; Moscow; RUSSIA.

MD *Modern Drama*. Freq: 4; Began: 1958; Cov: Full; Lang: Eng; Subj: Theatre. ISSN: 0026-7694
■Univ. of Toronto Press; 5201 Dufferin Street; Downsview, ON M5T 2Z9; CANADA.

MDM *Musicals—Das Musicalmagazin*. Freq: 6; Began: 1986; Lang: Ger; Subj: Related. ISSN: 0931-8194
■Balanstr. 19; D-81669 Munich; GERMANY.

MdTNB *Magazine du TNB*. Lang: Fre; Subj: Theatre. ISSN: 1164-8600
■Theatre National De Bretagne; 1, rue St. Helier; 35008 Rennes Cedex BP 675; FRANCE.

MdVO *Mitteilungen der Vereinigung Österreichischer Bibliotheken*. Lang: Ger; Subj: Related.
■Vienna; AUSTRIA.

Meanjin *Meanjin*. Formerly: *Meanjin Quarterly* Freq: 3; Began: 1940; Cov: Scan; Lang: Eng; Subj: Related. ISSN: 0025-6293
■Meanjin Co. Ltd.; 211 Grattan Street; Parkville, Victoria 3052; AUSTRALIA.

MeisterP *Meister des Puppenspiels*. Freq: IRR; Began: 1959; Lang: Ger; Subj: Theatre. ISSN: 0076-6216
■Deutsches Institut für Puppenspiel; Hattingerstr. 467; 4630 Bochum; GERMANY.

Meridian *Meridian*. Began: 1982; Cov: Scan; Lang: Eng; Subj: Theatre. ISSN: 0728-5914
■Dept. of English, La Trobe University; Bundoora; Victoria 3083; AUSTRALIA.

Merker *Neue Merker, Der*.Oper in Wien und aller welt. Freq: 12; Lang: Ger; Subj: Theatre. ISSN: 1017-5202
■Dr. Sieglinde Pfabigan; Merker-Verein; Peitglasse 7/3/4 A 1210 Vienna; AUSTRIA.

MET *Medieval English Theatre*. Freq: 2; Began: 1979; Cov: Full; Lang: Eng; Subj: Theatre. ISSN: 0143-3784
■c/o M. Twycross, Dept. of English; University of Lancaster; Lancaster LA1 4YT; UK.

MGL *Mestno gledališče Ljubljansko*. Freq: IRR; Began: 1959; Lang: Slo; Subj: Theatre.
■Ljubljana Čopova 14; 61000; SLOVENIJA.

MHall *Music Hall*. Freq: 6; Began: 1978; Lang: Eng; Subj: Theatre.
■Tony Barker; 50 Reperton Road; London SW6; UK.

MID ***Modern International Drama***: Magazine for Contemporary International Drama in Translation. Freq: 2; Began: 1967; Cov: Full; Lang: Eng; Subj: Theatre. ISSN: 0026-7856
▪State University of NY; P.O. Box 6000; Binghamton, NY 13902-6000; USA.

Mim ***Mim: Revija za glumu i glumište***: Glasilo Udruženja dramskih umjetnika Hrvatske. Freq: 12; Began: 1984; Lang: Cro; Subj: Theatre.
▪Udruž. Dramskih Umjetnika Hravatske; Ilica 42; Zagreb; CROATIA.

MimeJ ***Mime Journal***. Freq: 1; Began: 1974; Cov: Full; Lang: Eng; Subj: Theatre. ISSN: 0145-787X
▪Pomona College Theater Department, Claremont Colleges; Claremont, CA 91711; USA.

MimeN ***Mime News***. Freq: 5; Began: 1983; Cov: Scan; Lang: Eng; Subj: Theatre. ISSN: 0892-4910
▪National Mime Association; Box 148277; Chicago, IL 60614; USA.

Mimos ***Mimos***. Freq: 3; Began: 1949; Cov: Scan; Lang: Ger; Subj: Theatre. ISSN: 0026-4385
▪Schweizerische Gesellschaft für Theaterkultur; Theaterkultur-Verlag; Pf. 1940 CH-4001 Basel; SWITZERLAND.

Mit ***Mitgliederzeitung***. Freq: 4; Cov: Scan; Lang: Ger; Subj: Related.
▪Gesellschaft für unterhaltende Bühnenkunst e.V.; Hertzbergstr. 21; D-12055 Berlin; GERMANY.

MK ***Molodoi Kommunist***. SEE *Perspektiva*. Freq: 12; Began: 1918; Ceased: 1990; Cov: Scan; Lang: Rus; Subj: Related. ISSN: 0131-2278
▪Izdatel'stvo Molodaya Gvardiya, U1.; Sushevskaya, 21; Moscow A-55; RUSSIA.

MLet ***Music & Letters***. Freq: 4; Began: 1920; Cov: Scan; Lang: Eng; Subj: Related. ISSN: 0027-4224
▪Oxford University Press; Walton Street; Oxford OX2 6DP; UK.

MLR ***Modern Language Review***. Freq: 4; Began: 1905; Cov: Scan; Lang: Eng; Subj: Related. ISSN: 0026-7937
▪King's College London; Strand; London WC2 R 2LS; UK.

MMDN ***Medieval Music-Drama News***. Freq: 2; Began: 1982; Ceased: 1991; Lang: Eng; Subj: Related. ISSN: 0731-0374
▪Kalamazoo, MI; USA.

MMDTA ***Monographs on Music, Dance and Theater in Asia***. Freq: 1; Began 1971; Last Known Address; Lang: Eng; Subj: Theatre.
▪The Asia Society, Performing Arts Program; 133 East 58th Street; New York, NY 10022; USA.

MN ***Monumenta Nipponica***: Studies in Japanese Culture. Freq: 4; Began: 1938; Cov: Scan; Lang: Eng; Subj: Related. ISSN: 0027-0741
▪Sophia University, 7-1 Kioi-cho; Chiyoda-ku; 102 Tokyo; JAPAN.

Mobile ***Mobile***. Freq: 12; Lang: Fre; Subj: Theatre.
▪Maison de la Culture d'Amiens; Place Léon Gontier; 80000 Amiens; FRANCE.

MoD ***Monthly Diary***. Lang: Eng; Subj: Theatre.
▪Sydney; AUSTRALIA.

MojM ***Moja Moskva***.Cov: Scan;Lang: Rus Subj: Related.
▪ul. Tverskaja, 13 Moscow 103032 RUSSIA

MolGvar ***Molodaja gvardija***. Freq: 12; Began: 1922; Cov: Scan; Lang: Rus; Subj: Related. ISSN: 0131-2257
▪ Moscow; RUSSIA.

Monsalvat ***Monsalvat***. Freq: 11; Began: 1973; Lang: Spa; Subj: Theatre.
▪Ediciones de Nuevo Arte; Plaza Gala Placidia 1; 6 Barcelona; SPAIN.

Mosk ***Moskva***. Freq: 12; Began: 1957; Cov: Scan; Lang: Rus; Subj: Related. ISSN: 0132-2382
▪Chudozestvennaja Literatura; 24 Rub. Sojuz pisatelej Rossiiskoi; Moscow; RUSSIA.

MoskNab ***Moskovskij Nabljudatel'***. Began: 1991; Cov: Scan; Lang: Rus; Subj: Related. ISSN: 0868-8524
▪Arbat, 35; 121835 Moscow; RUSSIA.

MoskZ ***Moskovskij Žurnal***. Cov: Scan; Lang: Rus; Subj: Related.
▪RUSSIA.

Mozgo ***Mozgó Világ***. Freq: 12; Began: 1971; Ceased; Cov: Scan; Lang: Hun; Subj: Related.
▪Münnich F. u. 26; 1051 Budapest V; HUNGARY.

MP ***Modern Philology***: Research in Medieval and Modern Literature. Freq: 4; Began: 1903; Cov: Scan; Lang: Eng; Subj: Related. ISSN: 0026-8232
▪University of Chicago Press; 5720 S. Woodlawn Avenue; Chicago, IL 60637; USA.

MPI ***Manadens Premiärer och Information***. Lang: Swe; Subj: Related.
▪Svenska Teaterunionen; Svenska ITI; Nybrokajen 13 S-111 48, Stockholm; SWEDEN.

MPSKD ***Mitteilungen der Puppentheatersammlung der Staatlichen Kunstsammlungen Dresde***. Freq: 32; Began: 1958; Lang: Ger; Subj: Theatre. ISSN: 0323-7567
▪Puppentheatersammlung; Hohenhaus; Barkengasse 6 01445 Radebeul; GERMANY.

MRenD ***Medieval and Renaissance Drama***. SEE *Medieval and Renaissance Drama in England*. Freq: IRR; Lang: Eng; Began: 1984; Ceased: 1996; Cov: Full; Subj: Theatre. ISSN: 0731-3403
▪AMS Press; 56 E. 13th Street; New York, NY 10003; USA.

MRDE ***Medieval and Renaissance Drama in England***. Freq: IRR; Began: 1996; Cov: Full; Subj: Theatre. ISSN: 08386-37035
▪Associated University Press; 56 East 13th St.; New York, NY 10003; USA.

MRT ***Miedzynarodowny Rocznik Teatralny***: Annuaire Intl. du Théâtre/Intl. Theatre Yearbook. Freq: 1; Began: 1977; Ceased: 1982; Lang: Pol/Fre/Eng; Subj: Theatre.
▪International Association of Theatre Critics; ul. Moliera 1; 00 076 Warsaw; POLAND.

MSD ***Milliyet Sanat Dergisi***. Freq: 26; Lang: Tur; Subj: Theatre.
▪Aydin Dogan; Nurosmaniye Cad. 65/67; Cagaloglu-Istanbul; TURKEY.

MT ***Material zum Theater***. Freq: 12; Began: 1970; Lang: Ger; Subj: Theatre.
▪Verband der Theaterschaffended der DDR; Hermann-Matern-Strasse 18; 1040 Berlin; GERMANY.

MuD ***MusikDramatik***. Freq: 4; Cov: Full; Lang: Swe; Subj: Theatre. ISSN: 0283-5754
▪Box 4038; 5102 61 Stockholm; SWEDEN.

Muhely ***Műhely***. Freq: 6; Began: 1978; Lang: Hun; Cov: Scan; Subj: Related. ISSN: 0138-922X
▪Hazánk Kft.; Árpád u. 32; 9021 Győr; HUNGARY.

MuK ***Maske und Kothurn***: Internationale Beiträge zur Theaterwissenschaft. Freq: 1; Began: 1955; Cov: Scan; Lang: Ger/Eng/Fre; Subj: Theatre. ISSN: 0175-1611
▪Universität Wien; Institut für Theaterwissenschaft; Böhlau Verlag Sachsenplatz 4-6 A-1201 Vienna; AUSTRIA.

MuQ ***Musical Quarterly***. Freq: 4; Began: 1915; Last Known Address; Lang: Eng; Subj: Related. ISSN: 0027-4631
▪GoodKind Indexes, Pub.; 866 Third Avenue; New York, NY 10022; USA.

MusGes ***Musik und Gesellschaft***. Freq: 12; Began: 1951; Cov: Scan; Lang: Ger; Subj: Related. ISSN: 0027-4755
▪Henschelverlag Kunst und Gesellschaft; Oranienburger Str. 67/68; 1040 Berlin; GERMANY.

MuT ***Musik und Theater***:Die Internationale Kulturzeitschrift. Freq: 10; Began: 1979; Cov: Scan; Lang: Ger; Subj: Theatre. ISSN: 0931-8194
▪Meuli & Masüger Media GmbH; Pf. 16 80 CH-8040 Zurich; SWITZERLAND.

MuZizn ***MuzykalnajaŽizn***: (Musical Life). Freq: 24; Began: 1957; Cov: Scan; Lang: Rus; Subj: Related. ISSN: 0131-2383
▪Moscow; RUSSIA.

Muzsika ***Muzsika***. Freq: 12; Began: 1958; Cov: Scan; Lang: Hun; Subj: Related. ISSN: 0027-5336
▪Pro Musica Alapítvány; Károly krt. 7; 1075 Budapest; HUNGARY.

Muzyka ***Muzyka:Bibliografičeskaja informacija***. Freq: 12; Began: 1974; Cov: Full; Lang: Rus; Subj: Related. ISSN: 0208-3086
▪Gos. Biblioteka SSSR im. Lenina; NIO Informkultura; Prospekt Kalinina 101000 Moscow; RUSSIA.

MV ***Minority Voices***: An Interdisciplinary Journal of Literature & Arts. Freq: 2; Began: 1977; Ceased: 1989; Lang: Eng; Subj: Theatre.
▪Paul Robeson Cultural Center, 114 Walnut Bldg.; Pennsylvania State Univ.; University Park, PA 16802; USA.

My ***My***. Freq: 12; Began: 1990; Cov: Scan; Lang: Rus; Subj: Related.
▪B-5 ab. 1; Moscow 107005; RUSSIA.

Mykenae ***Mykenae Theater-Korrespondenz***. Freq: 24; Began: 1951; Lang: Ger; Subj: Theatre.

▪Der aktuelle Theaternachrichtenund Feuilletondienst; Mykenae Verlag Rossberg KG; Ahastr. 9 D-64285 Darmstadt; GERMANY.

NADIE ***Nadie Journal.*** Formerly: *Drama in Education.* Freq: 2; Began: 1981; Cov: Scan; Lang: Eng; Subj: Related. ISSN: 0159-6659
▪National Assoc. for Drama in Education; P.O. Box 168; Carlton Victoria 3054; AUSTRALIA.

Napj ***Napjaink.*** Freq: 12; Began: 1962; Ceased: 1990; Cov: Scan; Lang: Hun; Subj: Related. ISSN: 0547-2075
▪Borsod Megyei Lapkiadó Vállalat; Korvin Ottó u. 1; 3530 Miskolc; HUNGARY.

NasSovr ***Naš sovremennik.*** Freq: 12; Began: 1933; Cov: Scan; Lang: Rus; Subj: Related. ISSN: 0027-8288
▪Souz pisatelej RF; Moscow; RUSSIA.

Natrang ***Natrang.*** Freq: 4; Lang: Hin; Subj: Theatre.
▪I-47 Jangoura Extension; New Delhi; INDIA.

Natya ***Natya.*** Freq: 4; Began: 1969; Last Known Address; Lang: Eng; Subj: Theatre. ISSN: 0028-1115
▪Bharatiya Natya Sangh; 34 New Central Market; New Delhi; INDIA.

Nayt ***Näytelmäuutiset (Drama News).*** Lang: Fin; Subj: Theatre.
▪Näytelmäkulma, Drama Corner; Meritullinkatu 33; 00170 Helsinki; FINLAND.

NBT ***Neue Blätter des Theaters in Der Josefstadt.*** Freq: 6; Began: 1953; Lang: Ger/Eng/Fre; Subj: Theatre. ISSN: 0028-3096
▪Theater in der Josefstadt, Direktion; Josefstaedterstrasse 26; A 1082 Vienna; AUSTRIA.

NC ***New Contrast.*** Freq: 4; Cov: Scan; Lang: Eng; Subj: Related. ISSN: 1017-5415
▪P.O. Box 3841; Cape Town, 8000; SOUTH AFRICA.

NCBSBV ***Netherlands Centraal Bureau Voor de Statistiek***: Bezoek aan Vermakelukheidsinstellingen. Freq: 1; Began: 1940; Ceased: 1963; Lang: Dut/Eng; Subj: Related. ISSN: 0077-6688
▪Centraal Bureau voor de Statistiek; Prinses Beatrixlaan 428; Voorburg; NETHERLANDS.

NCBSMT ***Centraal Bureau voor de Statistiek (Statistics Netherlands)***: Muziek en theater. Formerly: *Statistiek van het Gesubsidieerde Toneel.* Freq: 1; Began: 1977; Lang: Dut; Subj: Theatre. ISSN: 0168-3519
▪Statistics Netherlands; Postbox 428; 2270 AZ Voorburg; NETHERLANDS.

NCM ***Nineteenth Century Music.*** Freq: 3; Began: 1977; Coc: Scan; Lang: Eng; Subj: Related.
▪University of California Press; 2120 Berkeley Way; Berkeley, CA 94720; USA.

NConL ***Notes on Contemporary Literature.*** Freq: 4; Began: 1971; Lang: Eng; Subj: Related. ISSN: 0029-4047
▪English Department, West Georgia College; Carollton, GA 30118; USA.

NCPA ***National Center for the Performing Arts***: Quarterly Journal. Freq: 4; Began: 1972; Lang: Eng; Subj: Related.
▪Natl Ctr for the Performing Arts; Nariman Point; 400021 Bombay; INDIA.

NCT ***Nineteenth Century Theatre.*** Formerly: *Nineteenth Century Theatre Research.* Freq: 2; Began: 1987; Cov: Full; Lang: Eng; Subj: Theatre. ISSN: 0893-3766
▪University of Massachusetts; Department of English; Amherst, MA 01003; USA.

NCTR ***Nineteenth Century Theatre Research.*** Freq: 2; Began: 1973; Ceased: 1986; Cov: Full; Lang: Eng; Subj: Theatre. ISSN: 0316-5329
▪Department of English, University of Arizona; Tuscon, AZ 85721; USA.

Neoh ***Neohelicon/Acta Comparationis Litterarum Universarum.*** Freq: 2; Began: 1974; Cov: Scan; Lang: Eng /Ger /Fre; Subj: Related. ISSN: 0324-4652
▪Akadémiai Kiadó; Ménesi út 11-13; 1118 Budapest; HUNGARY.

NETJ ***New England Theatre Journal.*** Freq: 1; Lang: Eng; Subj: Theatre.
▪School of Fine and Performing Arts; Roger Williams College; 1 Old Ferry Road Bristol, RI 02809-2921; USA.

neueM ***neue Merker, Der.*** Freq: 12; Lang: Ger; Subj: Related. ISSN: 1017-5202
▪Dr. Sieglinde Pfabigan; Peitlgasse /III/4; A-1210 Vienna; AUSTRIA.

Neva ***Neva.*** Freq: 12; Began: 1955; Cov: Scan; Lang: Rus; Subj: Related. ISSN: 0130-741X
▪3 Nevskij Pr.; St. Petersburg 191186; RUSSIA.

NewPerf ***New Performance.*** Freq: 4; Began: 1977; Lang: Eng; Subj: Theatre. ISSN: 0277-514X
▪One 14th Street; San Francisco, CA 94103; USA.

NewY ***New Yorker, The.*** Freq: 50; Cov: Scan; Lang: Eng; Subj: Related. ISSN: 0028-792X
▪The New Yorker Magazine, Inc.; 20 West 43rd Street; New York; NY 10036; USA.

NFT ***Theatre***: News from the Finnish Theatre. Formerly: *News from the Finnish Theatre.* SEE *Finnish Theatre.* Freq: IRR; Began: 1958; Ceased: 1995; Cov: Scan; Lang: Eng/Fre; Subj: Theatre. ISSN: 0358-3627
▪Finnish Center of the ITI; Teatterikulma Meritullinkatu 33 00170 Helsinki; FINLAND.

NihonU ***Nihon-Unima.*** Lang: Jap; Subj: Theatre.
▪Taoko Kawajiri, Puppet Theatre PUK; 2-12 Yoyogi, Shibuya; 151 Tokyo; JAPAN.

NIMBZ ***Notate***: Informations-und-Mitteilungsblatt des Brecht-Zentrums der DDR. Lang: Ger; Subj: Theatre.
▪Brecht Zentrum der DDR; Chausseestrasse 125; 1040 Berlin; GERMANY.

NITI ***Newsletter of the International Theatre Institute of the U.S., Inc.*.** Freq: 4; Began: 1988; Lang: Eng; Subj: Theatre.
▪220 West 42nd Street; New York, NY 10036; USA.

NiR ***Nauka i Religija***: (Science and Religion). Freq: 12; Began: 1959; Cov: Scan; Lang: Rus; Subj: Related. ISSN: 0130-7045
▪Moscow; RUSSIA.

Nk ***Näköpiiri.*** Ceased: 1983; Lang: Fin; Subj: Theatre.
▪Osuuskunta Näköpiiri; Annakatu 13 B; 00120 Helsinki 12; FINLAND.

NKala ***Natya Kala.*** Freq: 12; Lang: Tel; Subj: Theatre.
▪Kala Bhawan; Saifabad; Hyderabad; INDIA.

NLR ***New Literatures Review.*** Freq: 2; Began: 1975; Cov: Scan; Lang: Eng; Subj: Related. ISSN: 0314-7495
▪English Department, University of Wollongong; P.O. Box 1144; Wollongong NSW 2500; AUSTRALIA.

NMZ ***Neue Musikzeitung.*** Freq: 6; Began: 1951; Cov: Scan; Lang: Ger; Subj: Related. ISSN: 0944-8136
▪Verlag Neue Musikzeitung GmbH; Pf. 100245; D-93047 Regensburg; GERMANY

NO ***New Observations.*** Freq: 10; Lang: Eng; Subj: Related.
▪144 Greene Street; New York, NY 10012; USA.

Noh ***Noh.*** Freq: 12; Lang: Jap; Subj: Theatre.
▪Ginza-Nohgakudo Building; 6-5-15 Ginza, Chuo-Ku; 104 Tokyo; JAPAN.

NoK ***Nōgaku-kenkyū.*** Freq: Irreg. Began: 1916; Lang: Jap; Subj: Related. ISSN: 0029-0874
▪Hosei University; JAPAN.

NoSS ***Nōgaku Shiryo Shusei.*** Freq: Irreg. Began: 1973Lang: Jap;Subj: Related.
▪Hosei University; JAPAN.

Novr ***Nova revija***:mesečnik za kulturo Freq: 12; Began: 1982 Cov: Scan; Lang: Slo; Subj: Theatre. ISSN: 0351-9805
▪ČZP Nova revija d.o.o.; Dalmatinova 1; 1001 Ljubljana; SLOVENIA.

NovRos ***Novaja Rossija.*** Freq: 4; Began: 1930; Lang: Rus; Subj: Related.
▪GSP, 8 Moskvina K-31; Moscow 103772; RUSSIA.

NovyjMir ***Novyj Mir.*** Freq: 12; Began: 1925; Cov: Scan; Lang: Rus; Subj: Related. ISSN: 0130-7673
▪Moscow; RUSSIA.

Ns ***Nestroyana***: Blätter der Internationalen Nestroy-Gesellschaft. Freq: 4; Began: 1979; Cov: Scan; Lang: Ger; Subj: Theatre.
▪Internationale Nestroy-Gesellschaft, Volkstheater; Neustiftgasse 1; A 1070 Vienna; AUSTRIA.

NT ***Nya Teatertidningen.*** SEE: *Teatertidningen.* Freq: 4; Began: 1977; Ceased: 1990; Cov: Full; Lang: Swe; Subj: Theatre. ISSN: 0348-0119
▪Box 20137 S10460 Stockholm; SWEDEN.

NTA ***New Theatre Australia.*** Freq: 6; Began: 1987; Ceased: 1989; Cov: Scan; Lang: Eng; Subj: Theatre. ISSN: 1030-441X
▪New Theatre Australia Publications; P.O. Box 242 Kings Cross, NSW, 2011; AUSTRALIA.

NTE ***Narodna tvorchestvo.*** Freq: 12; Began: 1925; Cov: Scan; Lang: Ukr; Subj: Related. ISSN: 0023-219x
▪Starokaluzhskoe shosse, I. 117630; Moscow; RUSSIA.

NTimes ***Nohgaku Times.*** Freq: 12; Began: 1953; Lang: Jap; Subj: Theatre.
▪Nohgaku Shorin Ltd.; 3-6 Kanda-Jinpo-cho, Chiyoda-ku; 101 Tokyo; JAPAN.

NTQ *New Theatre Quarterly*. Freq: 4; Began: 1985; Cov: Full; Lang: Eng; Subj: Theatre. ISSN: 0266-464X
▪Cambridge University Press, Edinburgh Bldg.; Shaftesbury Rd.; Cambridge CB2 2RU; UK.

NTR *New Theatre Review*. Freq: 3; Lang: Eng; Subj: Theatre.
▪Lincoln Center Theater; 150 West 65 Street; New York NY 10023; USA.

NTS *Nordic Theatre Studies*: Yearbook for Theatre Research in Scandinavia. Freq: 1; Began: 1988; Cov: Full; Lang: Eng; Subj: Theatre.
▪Munksgaard; Postbox 2148; 1016 Copenhagen K; DENMARK.

NTTJ *Nederlands Theatre-en-Televisie Jaarboek*. Freq: 1; Lang: Dut; Subj: Theatre.
▪Amsterdam; NETHERLANDS.

Numero *Numero*. Freq: 12; Lang: Spa; Subj: Related.
▪Apt. Post. 75570; El Marques; Caracas; VENEZUELA.

NV *Novoe Vremija*. Cov: Scan; Lang: Rus; Subj: Related. ISSN: 0137-0723
▪Moscow; RUSSIA.

NVarta *Natya Varta*. Freq: 12; Lang: Hin; Subj: Theatre.
▪Anakima; 4 Bishop Lefroy Road; Calcutta; INDIA.

Nvilag *Nagyvilág*. Freq: 12; Began: 1956; Cov: Scan; Lang: Hun; Subj: Related. ISSN: 0547-1613
▪Arany János Lap- és Könyvkiadó Kft.; Széchenyi u. 1 1054 Budapest; HUNGARY.

NvR *Nauka v Rossii*. Freq: 6; Began: 1961; Cov: Scan; Lang: Rus; Subj: Related.
▪Maranovskij Per., 26; 117810 Moscow GSP-1; RUSSIA.

NWR *NeWest Review*: A Journal of Culture and Current Events in the West. Freq: 6; Began: 1975; Cov: Scan; Lang: Eng; Subj: Theatre. ISSN: 0380-2917
▪NeWest Review Co-operative; Box 394, RPO University; Saskatoon, SK S7N 9Z9; CANADA.

NYO *New York Onstage*. Freq: 12; Lang: Eng; Subj: Theatre.
▪c/o Theatre Development Fund; 1501 Broadway; Room 2110 New York, NY 10036; USA.

NYTCR *New York Theatre Critics Review*. Freq: 30; Began: 1940; Ceased 1996; Cov: Full; Lang: Eng; Subj: Theatre. ISSN: 0028-7784
▪Critics Theatre Review; 52 Vanderbilt Avenue, 11th Floor; New York, NY 10017; USA.

NYTR *New York Theatre Reviews*. Began: 1977; Ceased: 1980; Lang: Eng; Subj: Theatre.
▪Ira J. Bilowit; 55 West 42nd Street; New York, NY 10036; USA.

Obliques *Obliques*. Freq: 4; Last Known Address; Began: 1972; Lang: Fre; Subj: Related.
▪Roger Borderie; BP1, Les Pilles; 26110 Lyons; FRANCE.

OC *Opera Canada*. Freq: 4; Began: 1960; Cov: Scan; Lang: Eng; Subj: Related. ISSN: 0030-3577
▪Foundation for Coast to Coast, Opera Publication; 366 Adelaide Street E., Suite 434; Toronto, ON M5A 3X9; CANADA.

OCA *O'Casey Annual*. Freq: 1; Began: 1982; Ceased; Cov: Scan; Lang: Eng; Subj: Theatre.
▪MacMillan Publishers Ltd.; Houndmills Basingstoke; Hampshire RG21 2XS; UK.

ODG *Österreichische Dramatiker der Gegenwart*. Lang: Ger; Subj: Theatre.
▪Inst. für Österreichische Dramaturgie; Singerstrasse 26; A 1010 Vienna; AUSTRIA.

OffI *OFF-Informationen. Bundesverband Freier Theater e.V.*. Freq: IRR; Began: 1984; Lang: Ger; Subj: Theatre.
▪Kooperative Freier Theater NRW; Güntherstr. 65; D-44143 Dortmund; GERMANY.

Ogonek *Ogonek*. Cov: Scan; Lang: Rus; Subj: Related.
▪RUSSIA.

OI *Opéra International*. Freq: 1; Began: 1963; Lang: Fre; Subj: Related.
▪10 Galerie Vero-Dodat; 75001 Paris; FRANCE.

Oik *Otrok in knjiga*: Revija za vprašanja mladinske književnosti in knjižne vzgoje. Freq: 2; Began: 1972; Cov: Scan; Lang: Slo; Subj: Theatre. ISSN: 0351-5141
▪Mariborska knjižnica; Rotovški trg 2; 2000 Maribo; SLOVENIA.

OJ *Opera Journal*. Freq: 4; Began: 1968; Cov: Scan; Lang: Eng; Subj: Theatre. ISSN: 0030-3585
▪National Opera Association, Inc., University of Mississippi; Division of Continuing Ed. and Extension; University, MS 38677; USA.

OK *Oper und Konzert*. Freq: 12; Began: 1963; Lang: Ger; Subj: Theatre. ISSN: 0030-3518
▪A. Hanuschik; Ungererstrasse 19/VI (Fuchsbau); 8000 Munich 40; GERMANY.

Oktiabr *Oktiabr*. Freq: 12; Began: 1924; Cov: Scan; Lang: Rus; Subj: Related. ISSN: 0132-0637
▪Pravda; Moscow; RUSSIA.

Ollan *Ollantay Theater Magazine*. Freq: 2; Began: 1993; Cov: Scan; Lang: Eng /Spa; Subj: Theatre. ISSN: 1065-805X
▪Ollantay Press; P.O. Box 449; Jackson Heights, NY 11372; USA.

OnsA *Ons Amsterdam*. Cov: Scan; Lang: Dut; Subj: Related. ISSN: 0166-1809
▪Weekbladpers; Amsterdam; NETHERLANDS.

Op&T *Oper & Tanz*. Freq: 6; Lang: Ger; Subj: Related.
▪Vereinigung Deutscher Opernchöre und Bühnentänzer e.V. in der DAG; Oper & Tanz GmbH, Georgstr. 2; D-50374 Erfstadt; GERMANY.

Opal *Opal*. Freq: 6; Began: 1962; Lang: Eng; Subj: Theatre. ISSN: 0030-3062
▪Ontario Puppetry Association; 171 Avondale Avenue; Willowdale, ON M2N 2V4; CANADA.

Oper *Oper*. Freq: 1; Began: 1966; Lang: Ger; Subj: Theatre.
▪Zurich; SWITZERLAND.

Opera *Opera*. Freq: 12; Began: 1950; Lang: Eng; Subj: Theatre. ISSN: 0030-3542
▪DSB, 2a Sopwith Crescent; Hurricane Way; Shotgate Wickford, Essex SS11 8YU; UK.

OperaA *Opera Australasia*. Freq: 12; Began: 1978; Lang: Eng; Subj: Theatre. ISSN: 1320-9299
▪PO Box R361; NSW 2000 Royal Exchange; AUSTRALIA.

OperaCT *Opera*. Freq: 4; Began: 1974; Ceased; Lang: Eng/Afr; Subj: Theatre.
▪Cape Performing Arts Board; POB 4107; 8000 Cape Town; SOUTH AFRICA.

OperaIn *Opera Index*. Freq: 1; Lang: Eng; Subj: Related. ISSN: 0030-3526
▪Seymour Press Ltd.; Windsor House; 1270 London Road London; SW16 4DH; UK.

OperaL *Operaélet/Operalife*. Freq: 5; Began: 1992; Cov: Full; Lang: Hun; Subj: Theatre. ISSN: 1215-6590
▪Budapesti Operabarát Alapítvány; Hajós u. 19; 1065 Budapest; HUNGARY.

OperaR *Opera*. Freq: 4; Began: 1965; Last Known Address; Lang: Ita/Eng/Fre/Ger/Spa; Subj: Theatre. ISSN: 0030-3542
▪Editoriale Fenarete; Via Beruto 7; Milan; ITALY.

OperH *Oper Heute*. Lang: Ger; Subj: Theatre.
▪Berlin; GERMANY.

Opern *Opernglas, Das*. Freq: 11; Began: 1980; Cov: Scan; Lang: Ger; Subj: Related. ISSN: 0935-6398
▪Opernglas Verlagsgesellschaft mbH; Lappenbergsallee 45; D-20257 Hamburg; GERMAN.

OpN *Opera News*. Freq: 17; Began: 1936; Cov: Full; Lang: Eng; Subj: Theatre. ISSN: 0030-3607
▪Metropolitan Opera Guild, Inc.; 70 Lincoln Center Plaza; New York, NY 10023; USA.

OpuK *Oper und Konzert*. Freq: 4 Began: 1963; Cov: Scan; Lang: Ger; Subj: Related. ISSN: 0030-3518
▪Ungererstr. 19; D-80802 Munich; GERMANY.

Opus. *Opus. Osterreichische Puppenspiel-Journalette*. Freq: 4; Lang: Ger; Subj: Related.
▪Österreichischer Puppenclub; Postfach; A-3130 Herzogenburg; GERMANY.

Opuscula *Opuscula*. Freq: 3; Began: 1976; Last Known Address; Lang: Dan; Subj: Theatre.
▪Det Teatervidenskabelige Institot; Fredericingade 18; 1310 Copenhagen; DENMARK.

Opw *Opernwelt*. Freq: 12; Began: 1959; Lang: Ger; Subj: Theatre. ISSN: 0030-3690
▪Friedrich Berlin Verlagsges; mbH, Lützowplatz 7; D-10785 Berlin; GERMANY.

OQ *Opera Quarterly*. Freq: 4; Began: 1983; Cov: Full; Lang: Eng; Subj: Theatre. ISSN: 0736-0053
▪University of North Carolina Press; Box 2288; Chapel Hill, NC 27514; USA.

Organon *Organon*. Freq: 1; Began: 1975; Lang: Fre; Subj: Theatre.
▪Ctre de Recherches Théâtrales, Univ. Lyon II; Ensemble Univ., Ave. de l'Universite; 69500 Bron; FRANCE.

Orpheus *Orpheus*. Freq: 12; Began: 1972; Lang: Ger; Subj: Related. ISSN: 0932-611

■Neue Gesellschaft für Musikinformation mbH; Livländische Str. 27; D-10715 Berlin; GERMANY.

OSS ***On-Stage Studies***. Formerly: *Colorado Shakespeare Festival Annual*. Freq: 1; Began: 1976; Cov: Scan; Lang: Eng; Subj: Theatre. ISSN: 0749-1549
■Colorado Shakespeare Festival, Campus Box 261; University of Colorado; Boulder, CO 80309 0261; USA.

OSZ ***Očag. Semejnij Zurnal***. Began: 1992; Cov: Scan; Lang: Rus; Subj: Related. ISSN: 0869-5091
■Ist Tverskaja-Tamskaja Street; Building 2, Section 1; Moscow 103006; RUSSIA.

Otecest ***Otečestvennije arhivy***. Freq: 6; Began: 1992; Cov: Scan; Lang: Rus; Subj: Related. ISSN: 0869-4427
■Glavnoe Arkhivnoe Upravlenie; 119817 B. Pirogovskaja 17; Moscow G-435; RUSSIA.

OtK ***Otcij kraj***. Freq: 4; Cov: Scan; Lang: Rus;; Subj: Related.
■1 ul Barrykadnaya; Volgograd;; RUSSIA.

Outrage ***Outrage***. Freq: 12; Began: 1983; Cov: Scan; Lang: Eng; Subj: Related.
■Gay Publications Co-operative; P.O. Box 21; Carlton South Victoria 3053; AUSTRALIA.

OvA ***Overture***. Freq: 12; Began: 1919; Cov: Scan; Lang: Eng; Subj: Theatre. ISSN: 0030-7556
■Los Angeles Musicians' Union, Local 47; 817 Vine Street; Los Angeles, CA 90038; USA.

Over ***Overland***. Freq: 3; Began: 1954; Cov: Scan; Lang: Eng; Subj: Related. ISSN: 0043-342X
■P.O. Box 14146; Melbourne Victoria 3000; AUSTRALIA.

P&L ***Philosophy and Literature***. Freq: 2; Began: 1976; Lang: Eng; Subj: Related. ISSN: 0190-0013
■Fine Arts; University of Canterbury; Christchurch; NEW ZEALAND.

PA ***Présence Africaine***. Freq: 4; Began: 1947; Lang: Fre/Eng; Subj: Related. ISSN: 0032-7638
■Nouvelle Société Presence Africaine; 25 bis rue des Ecoles; Paris 75005; FRANCE.

Pa&Pr ***Past and Present***: A Journal of Historical Studies. Freq: 4; Began: 1952; Lang: Eng; Subj: Related. ISSN: 0031-2746
■Oxford University Press; Pinkhill House; Southfield Road Eynsham; Oxford OX8 1JJ; UK.

PAA ***Performing Arts Annual***. SEE *Performing Arts at the Library of Congress*. Freq: 1; Began: 1986; Ceased: 1990; Cov: Full; Lang: Eng; Subj: Theatre. ISSN: 0887-8234
■Library of Congress, Performing Arts Library Resources; Dist. by G.O.P.; Washington, DC 20540; USA.

PAaLC ***Performing Arts at the Library of Congress***. Formerly *Performing Arts Annual*. Freq: IRR; Began: 1990; Cov: Full; Lang: Eng; Subj: Theatre. ISSN: 0887-8234
■Library of Congress, Performing Arts Library Resources; Dist. by G.O.P.; Washington, DC 20540; USA.

PAC ***Performing Arts in Canada***. SEE *Performing Arts & Entertainment in Canada*. Freq: 4; Began 1961; Ceased: 1991; Cov: Full; Lang: Eng; Subj: Theatre. ISSN: 0031-5230
■Performing Arts & Entertainment Magazine; 1100 Caledonia Road; Toronto, ON M6A 2W5; CANADA.

PAEC ***Performing Arts & Entertainment in Canada***. Freq: 4; Began: 1991; Cov: Full; Lang: Eng; Subj: Theatre. ISSN: 1185-3433
■Performing Arts & Entertainment Magazine; 1100 Caledonia Road; Toronto, ON M6A 2W5; CANADA.

Pal ***Palócföld***. Freq: 6; Began: 1967; Cov: Scan; Lang: Hun; Subj: Related. ISSN: 0555-8867
■Nógrád Megyei Művelődési Központ Rákóczi út 192; 310 Salgótarján; HUNGARY.

Pamir ***Pamir***. Freq: 12; Began: 1949; Cov: Scan; Lang: Rus; Subj: Related. ISSN: 0131-2650
■Dushanbe; TAJIKISTAN.

Pantallas ***Pantallas y Escenarios***. Freq: 5; Last Known Address; Lang: Spa; Subj: Theatre.
■Maria Lostal 24; 8 Zaragoza; SPAIN.

PAR ***Performing Arts Resources***. Freq: 1; Began: 1974; Cov: Scan; Lang: Eng; Subj: Theatre. ISSN: 0360-3814
■111 Amsterdam Avenue New York, NY 10023; USA.

Parergon ***Parergon***. Freq: 2; Began: 1971; Cov: Scan; Lang: Eng; Subj: Related. ISSN: 0313-6221
■Dept. of English; University of Sydney; NSW 2006; AUSTRALIA.

Parnass ***Parnass***: Die Österreichische Kunst- und Kulturzeitschrift. Freq: 6; Began: 1981; Cov: Scan; Lang: Ger; Subj: Theatre.
■C & E Grosser, Druckerei Verlag; Wiener Strasse 290; A 4020 Linz; AUSTRIA.

Parnasso ***Parnasso***. Freq: 8; Began: 1951; Lang: Fin; Subj: Theatre. ISSN: 0031-2320
■Yhtyneet Kuvalehdet Oy; Maistraatinportti 1; 00240 Helsinki; FINLAND.

PArts ***Performing Arts***: The Music and Theatre Monthly. Freq: 12; Began: 1967; Lang: Eng; Subj: Theatre. ISSN: 0031-5222
■Performing Arts Network; 3539 Motor Ave.; Los Angeles, CA 90034-4800; USA.

PArtsSF ***Performing Arts Magazine***: San Francisco Music & Theatre Monthly. Freq: 12; Began: 1967; Ceased: 1987; Lang: Eng; Subj: Theatre. ISSN: 0480-0257
■Theatre Publications, Inc.; 2999 Overland Ave., Ste. 201; Los Angeles, CA 90064; USA.

PasShowA ***Passing Show***. Freq: IRR; Began: 1981; Lang: Eng; Subj: Theatre. ISSN: 0706-1897
■Performing Arts Museum, Victorian Arts Centre; 1 City Rd; 3205 S. Melbourne, Victoria; AUSTRALIA.

PasShow ***Passing Show: Newsletter of the Shubert Archive***. Freq: 3; Began: 1983; Cov: Full; Lang: Eng; Subj: Theatre.
■Shubert Archive, Lyceum Theatre; 149 West 45th Street; New York, NY 10026; USA.

PaT ***Pamiętnik Teatralny***: Poswiecony historii i krytyce teatru. Freq: 4; Began: 1952; Cov: Full; Lang: Pol; Subj: Theatre. ISSN: 0031-0522
■Institute of the Polish Academy of Sciences; Dluga 26/28; 00950 Warsaw; POLAND.

PaV ***Paraules al Vent***. Freq: 12; Lang: Spa; Subj: Related.
■Associació de Joves 'Paraules al Vent'; Casal de Sant Jordi; Sant Jordi Desvalls; SPAIN.

PAYBA ***Performing Arts Year Book of Australia***. Freq: 1; Began: 1977; Lang: Eng; Subj: Theatre.
■Showcast Publications Ltd; Box 141; 2088 Spit Junction N.S.W; AUSTRALIA.

Pb ***Playbill***: A National Magazine of the Theatre. Freq: 12; Began: 1982; Lang: Eng; Subj: Theatre. ISSN: 0032-146X
■Playbill Incorporated; 52 Vanderbilt Avenue; 11th Floor New York, NY 10017-3893; USA.

PCD ***Premiéry československých divadel***. Freq: 12; Lang: Cze; Subj: Theatre.
■Divadelní ústav; Celetná 17; 110 01 Prague 1; CZECH REPUBLIC.

PdO ***Pantuflas del Obispo***. Began: 1966; Lang: Spa; Subj: Theatre.
■Semanario Sabado; Vargas 219; Quito; ECUADOR.

Pe ***Performance***. Freq: 6; Began: 1981; Cov: Scan; Lang: Eng; Subj: Related.
■Brevet Publishing Ltd.; 445 Brighton Road; South Croydon CR2 6EU; UK.

PeM ***Pesti Műsor***. Freq: 52; Began: 1957; Lang: Hun; Subj: Theatre.
■Garay u.5; 1076 Budapest VII; HUNGARY.

PerAJ ***Performing Arts Journal***. Freq: 3; Began: 1976; Cov: Full; Lang: Eng; Subj: Theatre. ISSN: 0735-8393
■Performing Arts Journal, Inc.; P.O. Box 260, Village Station; New York, NY 10014; USA.

PerfM ***Performance-Management***. Freq: 2; Cov: Scan; Lang: Eng; Subj: Theatre.
■Brooklyn College, Dept. of Theatre; Brooklyn, NY 11210; USA.

PerfNZ ***Performance: A Handbook of the Performing Arts in New Zealand***. Freq: 5; Began: 1980; Lang: Eng; Subj: Theatre. ISSN: 0112-0654
■Association of Community Theatres; P.O. 68-257; Newton, Aukland; NEW ZEALAND.

PerfR ***Performance Research***. Freq: 3; Began: 1996; Cov: Full; Lang: Eng; Subj: Theatre. ISSN: 1352-8165
■Center for Performance Research; Market Road; Canton Cardiff CF5 1QE; WALES.

Perlicko ***Perlicko-Perlacko***. Began: 1950; Last Known Address; Lang: Ger; Subj: Theatre.
■Dr. Hans R. Purschke; Postfach 550135; 6000 Frankfurt; GERMANY.

Perspek ***Perspektiva***. Freq: 12; Began: 1990; Cov: Scan; Lang: Rus; Subj: Related. ISSN: 0131-2278
■Izdatel'stvo Molodaya Gvardiya, Ul.; Sushevskaya, 21; Moscow A-55; RUSSIA.

Pf ***Platform***. Freq: 2; Began: 1979; Ceased: 1983; Cov: Scan; Lang: Eng; Subj: Theatre.

■Dept of Literature, University of Essex; Wivenhoe Park; Colchester; UK.

PFr ***Présence Francophone.*** Freq: 2; Began: 1970; Ceased: 1970; Cov: Scan; Lang: Fre; Subj: Related. ISSN: 0048-5195
■Université de Sherbrooke; Sherbrooke, PQ J1K 2R1; CANADA.

PI ***Plays International.*** Formerly: *Plays/Plays International.* Freq: 12; Began: 1985; Cov: Full; Lang: Eng; Subj: Theatre. ISSN: 0268-2028
■33a Lurline Gardens; London SW11 4DD; UK.

PInfo ***Puppenspiel-Information.*** Freq: 2; Began: 1967; Cov: Scan; Lang: Ger; Subj: Theatre. ISSN: 0720-7265
■Deutsche Puppentheater e.V.; Moorweg 1 D-21337 Lüneburg; GERMANY.

PintR ***Pinter Review.*** Began: 1987; Cov: Full; Lang: Eng; Subj: Theatre. ISSN: 0895-9706
■Harold Pinter Society; University of Tampa; Box 11F Tampa, FL 33606; USA.

PiP ***Plays in Process.*** Lang: Eng; Subj: Theatre. ISSN: 0736-0711
■Theatre Communications Group 355 Lexington Avenue; New York, NY 10017; USA.

Pja ***Pipirijaina.*** Freq: 6; Began: 1979; Lang: Spa; Subj: Theatre.
■c/o San Enrique 16; 20 Madrid; SPAIN.

Plateaux ***Plateaux.*** Formerly: *Bulletin de l'Union des Artistes.* Freq: 4; Began: 1925; Lang: Fre; Subj: Theatre.
■Syndicat Français des Artistes-Interprètes (SFA) 21 bis, rue Victor-Massé; 75009 Paris; FRANCE.

Play ***Play.*** Freq: 12; Began: 1974; Lang: Eng; Subj: Theatre. ISSN: 0311-4031
■Main Street; PO Box 67; 5245 Hahndorf; SOUTH AFRICA.

PlayM ***Players Magazine.*** Freq: 22; Began: 1924; Ceased: 1967; Lang: Eng; Subj: Theatre. ISSN: 0032-1486
■National Collegiate Players, Northern Illinois University; University Theatre; Dekalb, IL 60115; USA.

PlayN ***Playmarket News.*** Formerly: *Act: Theatre in New Zealand.* Freq: 2; Began: 1988; Lang: Eng; Subj: Theatre. ISSN: 0113-9703
■Level 2, 16 Cambridge Terrace; P.O. Box 9767, Te Aro; TeWhanganui-a-Tara Wellington, Aotearoa; NEW ZEALAND.

Plays ***Plays:*** (In 1985 became part of *Plays and Players*). Formerly: *Plays/Plays International.* Freq: 12; Began: 1983; Ceased: 1985; Cov: Scan; Lang: Eng; Subj: Theatre.
■Ocean Publications; 34 Buckingham Palace Road; London SW1; UK.

PLL ***PLL: Papers on Language & Literature;*** Freq: 4; Cov: Scan; Lang: Eng; Subj: Related. ISSN: 0031-1294
■Southern Illinois University at Edwardsville; Edwardsville, IL 62026-1434; USA.

PlPl ***Plays and Players.*** Freq: 12; Began: 1953; Cov: Full; Lang: Eng; Subj: Theatre. ISSN: 0032-1559
■Mineco Design Ltd.; 18 Friern Park London N12 9DA; UK.

PLUG ***PLUG:*** Maandelijks informatieblad van het Cultureel Jongeren Paspoort. Freq: 12; Began: 1967; Lang: Dut; Subj: Theatre. ISSN: 0032-1621
■Cultureel Jongeren Paspoort; Kleine Gartmanplts. 10; 1017 RR Amsterdam; NETHERLANDS.

PM ***Performance Magazine, The.*** Freq: 6; Began: 1979; Ceased: 1992; Cov: Scan; Lang: Eng; Subj: Theatre. ISSN: 0144-5901
■Performance Magazine Ltd.; P.O. Box 717; London SW5 9BS; UK.

PMLA ***PMLA:*** Publications of the Modern Language Assoc. of America. Freq: 6; Began: 1929; Last Known Address; Cov: Scan; Lang: Eng; Subj: Related. ISSN: 0030-8129
■Modern Language Assoc. of America; 62 5th Avenue; New York, NY 10011; USA.

Pnpa ***Peuples noirs, peuples africains.*** Freq: 4; Began: 1977; Lang: Fre; Subj: Related.
■82, avenue de la Porte-des-Champs; 76000 Rouen; FRANCE.

Podium ***Podiumkunsten.*** Freq: 1 Began: 1987; Lang: Dut; Subj: Theatre. ISSN: 0922-1409
■Centraal Bureau voor de Statistiek (Statistics Netherlands); Postbox 428; 2270 AZ Voorburg; NETHERLANDS.

PodiumB ***Podium:*** Zeitschrift für Bühnenbildner und Theatertechnik. Freq: 4; Lang: Ger; Subj: Theatre.
■Abteilung Berufsbildung; Munzstrasse 21; 1020 Berlin; GERMANY.

Poppen ***Poppenspelbereichten.*** Freq: 4; Lang: Dut; Subj: Theatre.
■Mechelen; BELGIUM.

Pozoriste ***Pozorište:*** Časopis za pozorišnu umjetnost. Freq: 6; Began: 1959; Lang: Cro; Subj: Theatre. ISSN: 0032-616X
■Narodno Pozorište; Matija Gupca 6; 75000 Tuzla; BOSNIA AND HERZEGOVINA.

PQ ***Philological Quarterly:*** Investigation of Classical & Modern Langs. and Lit. Freq: 4; Began: 1922; Cov: Scan; Lang: Eng; Subj: Related. ISSN: 0031-7977
■Editor, Philological Quarterly; University of Iowa; Iowa City, IA 52242; USA.

PQCS ***Philippine Quarterly of Culture and Society.*** Freq: 4; Began: 1973; Lang: Eng; Subj: Related. ISSN: 0115-0243
■San Carlos Publications; 6000 Cebu City; PHILIPPINES.

PrAc ***Primer Acto.*** Freq: 5; Began: 1957; Last Known Address; Lang: Spa; Subj: Theatre.
■Cervantes, 21-1 Oficina 3; 28014 Madrid; SPAIN.

Preface ***Préface.*** Freq: 12; Lang: Fre; Subj: Theatre.
■Centre National Nice-Côte d'Azur; Esplanade des Victoires; 06300 Nice; FRANCE.

Premiere ***Première.*** Lang: Ger/Fre; Subj: Related.
■Schweizerischer Bühnenverband; Pf. 9; CH-8126 Zumikon; GERMANY.

Premijera ***Premijera:*** List Narodnog Pozorista Sombor. Lang: Ser; Subj: Theatre.
■Koste Trifkovica 2; Sombor; SERBIA.

Presg ***Prešernovo gledališče.*** Cov: Scan; Lang: Slo; Subj: Related.
■Glavni trg 6; 6400 Kranj; SLOVENIA.

Pretexts ***Pretexts.*** Began: 1989; Cov: Scan; Lang: Eng; Subj: Related. ISSN: 1015-549X
■University of Cape Town; Private Bag Rondebosch 7700; SOUTH AFRICA.

Primdg ***Primorsko dramsko gledališče.*** Cov: Scan; Lang: Slo; Subj: Related.
■Bevkov trg 4; 65000 Nova Gorica; SLOVENIA.

Primk ***Primerjalna književnost.*** Freq: 2; Began: 1978; Cov: Scan; Lang: Slo; Subj: Related. ISSN: 0351-1189
■Slovensko društvo za primerjalno književnost; Aškerčeva 2; 1000 Ljubljana; SLOVENIA.

prinz ***prinzenstrasse. Hannoversche Hefte zur Theatergeschichte.*** Freq: 2/3; Began: 1994; Lang: Ger; Subj: Theatre. ISSN: 0949-4049
■Theatermuseum und -archiv Hannover; Prinzenstrasse 9 (im Schasupielhaus); D-30159 Hannover; GERMANY.

Prof ***Profile:*** The Newsletter of the New Zealand Assoc. of Theatre Technicians. Freq: 4; Lang: Eng; Subj: Related.
■Ponsonby, Auckland; NEW ZEALAND.

Program ***Program.*** Began: 1925; Ceased; Lang: Cze; Subj: Theatre.
■Zemske divadlo; Dvorakova 11; Brno; CZECH REPUBLIC.

Programa ***Programa.*** Began: 1978; Lang: Por; Subj: Theatre.
■Grupo de Teatro de Campolide; 43, 20 D. Cde. Antas; Lisbon; PORTUGAL.

Prolog ***Prolog:*** Revija za dramsku umjetnost. In 1986 became Novi Prolog. Freq: 2; Began: 1968; Lang: Cro; Subj: Theatre.
■Centar za kulturnu djelatnost; Mihanoviceva 28/1; 41000 Zagreb; CROATIA.

PrologTX ***Prolog.*** Freq: 4; Began: 1973; Lang: Eng; Subj: Theatre. ISSN: 0271-7743
■Theatre Sources Inc., c/o Michael Firth; 104 North St. Mary; Dallas, TX 75214; USA.

Prologue ***Prologue.*** Freq: 4; Began: 1944; Lang: Eng; Subj: Theatre. ISSN: 0033-1007
■Arena Theater; Tufts University; Medford, MA 02155; USA.

Prompts ***Prompts.*** SEE *Irish Theatre Archive's Newsletter.* Freq: IRR; Began: 1981; Ceased: 1992; Lang: Eng; Subj: Theatre.
■Irish Theatre Archive, Archives Division; City Hall; 2 Dublin; IRELAND.

Propf ***Pro philosophia füzetek.*** Cov: Scan; Lang: Hun; Subj: Related.
■HUNGARY.

ProS ***ProScenium.*** Freq: 4; Cov: Scan; Lang: Ger; Subj: Related.
■Schweizer Verband technischer Bühnenberufe; Aescherweg 20; CH-5725 Leutwil; GERMANY.

ProScen ***ProScen.*** Freq: 4; Began: 1986; Cov: Full; Lang: Swe; Subj: Theatre. ISSN: 0284-4346
■Svensk Teaterteknisk Förening, Section of OISTT; Mosebacke Torg 1 116 46 Stockholm; SWEDEN.

PrTh ***Pratiques Théâtrales***: In 1978 became Grande République. Freq: 3; Ceased: 1978; Lang: Fre; Subj: Theatre.
▪200 Ouest rue Sherbrooke; Montreal, PQ H2Y 3P2; CANADA.

PS ***Post Script***; Freq: 3; Began: 1981; Cov: Scan; Lang: Eng; Subj: Related. 0277-9897
▪Texas A & M University; Literature and Languages Dept; Commerce, TX 75429; USA.

Ptk ***Publiekstheaterkrant***. Freq: 5; Began: 1978; Lang: Dut; Subj: Theatre.
▪Publiekstheater; Marnixstraat 427; 1017 PK Amsterdam; NETHERLANDS.

PTKranj ***Prešeren Theatre of Kranj***. Began: 1945; Cov: Scan; Lang: Slo; Subj: Theatre.
▪Prešeren Theatre; Kranj; SLOVENIA.

PTZ ***Petersburgskij Teatral'nyj Žurnal***. Began: 1992; Cov: Scan; Lang: Rus; Subj: Related.
▪5 Pl. Iskusstv; kv. 56-a St. Petersburg 191011; RUSSIA.

PuJ ***Puppetry Journal***. Freq: 4; Began: 1949; Cov: Full; Lang: Eng; Subj: Theatre. ISSN: 0033-443X
▪Puppeteers of America; 8005 Swallow Dr.; Macedonia, OH 44056; USA.

PupM ***Puppet Master***. Freq: 4; Began: 1946; Lang: Eng; Subj: Theatre.
▪British Puppet and Model Theatre Guild, c/o Gordon Shapley (Hon. Sec.); 18 Maple Road, Yeading, Nr Hayes; Middlesex; UK.

Pusp ***Puppenspiel und Puppenspieler***. Freq: 2; Began: 1960; Lang: Ger/Fre; Subj: Theatre. ISSN: 0033-4405
▪Schweiz. Vereinigung Puppenspiel, c/o Gustav Gysin, Ed.; Roggenstr. 1; Riehen CH-4125; SWITZERLAND.

Pz ***Proszenium***. Lang: Ger; Subj: Theatre.
▪Zurich; SWITZERLAND.

PZOST ***Premiere. Zeitschrift für Oper, Sprech- und Tanztheater***. Freq: 4; Lang: Ger; Subj: Theatre. ISSN: 0933-5390
▪Andreas Berger; Berner Str. 2; D-38106 Braunschweig; GERMANY.

QQ ***Queen's Quarterly***. Freq: 4; Cov: Scan; Lang: Eng; Subj: Related.
▪Queen's University; Kingston, ON K7L 3N6; CANADA.

QT ***Quaderni di Teatro***: Rivista Trimestrale del Teatro Regionale Toscano. Freq: 4; Began: 1978; Ceased: 1987; Cov: Full; Lang: Ita; Subj: Theatre.
▪Casa Editrice Vallecchi; Viale Milton 7; 50129 Florence; ITALY.

QTST ***Quaderni del Teatro Stabile di Torino***. Freq: IRR; Lang: Ita; Subj: Theatre.
▪Teatro Stabile di Torino; Turin; ITALY.

Quarta ***Quarta Parete***. Freq: 4; Began: 1975; Ceased: 1983; Lang: Ita; Subj: Theatre.
▪Via Sant'Ottavio 15; Turin; ITALY.

QuellenT ***Quellen zur Theatergeschichte***. Freq: IRR; Began: 1981; Lang: Ger; Subj: Theatre. ISSN: 0259-0786
▪Verband der Wissenschaftlichen, Gesellschaften Oesterreichs; Lindengasse 37; A1070 Vienna; AUSTRIA.

Raduga ***Raduga***. Freq: 12; Began: 1986; Cov: Scan; Lang: Rus; Subj: Related. ISSN: 0131-8136
▪Izd-vo TSKKPE; Kiev; ESTONIA.

Raja ***Rajatabla***. Lang: Spa; Subj: Theatre.
▪Apartado 662; 105 Caracas; VENEZUELA.

RAL ***Research in African Literature***. Freq: 4; Began: 1970; Cov: Scan; Lang: Eng; Subj: Related. ISSN: 0034-5210
▪Indiana Univ. Press; 10th and Morton Sts.; Bloomington, IN 47405; USA.

Rampel ***Rampelyset***. Freq: 6; Began: 1948; Lang: Dan; Subj: Theatre.
▪Danske Amatør Teater Samvirke; Box 70; DK 6300 Grasten; DENMARK.

Randa ***Randa***. Freq: 2; Cov: Scan; Lang: Spa; Subj: Related. ISSN: 0210-5993
▪Editat per Curial Edicions Catalanes S.A.; carrer del Bruc 144; 08037 Barcelona; SPAIN.

Rangarupa ***Rangarupa***. Began: 1976; Last Known Address; Lang: Ben; Subj: Theatre.
▪Rangarup Natya Academy; 27/76 Central Rd.; Dhanmondi, Dacca; BANGLADESH.

Rangayan ***Rangayan***. Freq: 4; Lang: Hin; Subj: Theatre.
▪Bhartiya Lok kala Mandal; Udaipur 313001 Rajasthan; INDIA.

Rangyog ***Rangyog***. Freq: 4; Lang: Hin; Subj: Theatre.
▪Rajasthan Sangeet Natak Adademi; Paota; Jodhpur; INDIA.

Raritan ***Raritan***. Freq: 4; Began: 1981; Cov: Scan; Lang: Eng; Subj: Related. ISSN: 0275-1607
▪Rutgers University; 165 College Ave.; New Brunswick, NJ 08903; USA.

Rbharati ***Rangbharati***. Freq: 12; Lang: Hin; Subj: Theatre.
▪Bharatendu Rangmanch; Chowk;Lucknow; INDIA.

RdA ***Revue de l'Art***. Freq: 4; Began: 1968; Cov: Scan; Lang: Fre; Subj: Related. ISSN: 0035-1326
▪Editions du CNRS; Collège de France; 11, Place Marcelin-Berthelot 75005 Paris; FRANCE.

RdArt ***Revista d'Art***. Freq: 1; Lang: Spa; Subj: Related.
▪c/o Baldiri Reixac, Departament d'Historia de l'Art; Facultat de Geografia i Historia; 08028 Barcelona; SPAIN.

RdD ***Rassegna di Diritto Cinematografico, Teatrale e della Televisione***. Lang: Ita; Subj: Theatre.
▪Via Ennio Quirino Visconti 99; Rome; ITALY.

RDE ***Research in Drama Education***. Freq: 2; Began: 1996; Cov: Full; Lang: Eng; Subj: Theatre.
▪Carfax Publishing, Ltd.; P.O. Box 25; Abingdon, Oxfordshire OX14 2UE; UK.

RdS ***Rassegna dello Spettacolo***. Began: 1953; Lang: Ita; Subj: Theatre. ISSN: 0033-9474
▪Assoc. Gen. Italiana dello Spettacolo; Via di Villa Patrizi 10; 00161 Rome; ITALY.

RE ***Revue d'esthétique***. Freq 4; Lang: Fre; Subj: Theatre.
▪Privat et Cie; 14, rue des Arts; 31068 Toulouse CEDEX; FRANCE.

Recorder ***Recorder, The: A Journal of the American Irish Historical Society***. Freq: 2; Began: 1985; Cov: Scan; Lang: Eng; Subj: Related.
▪American Irish Historical Society; 991 Fifth Avenue; New York, NY 10028; USA.

REEDN ***Records of Early English Drama Newsletter***. Freq: 2; Began: 1976; Cov: Full; Lang: Eng; Subj: Theatre. ISSN: 0070-9283
▪University of Toronto, Erindale College, English Section; Mississauga, ON L5L 1C6; CANADA.

Region ***Regionologia***. Began: 1992; Cov: Scan; Lang: Rus; Subj: Related. ISSN: 0131-5706
▪Scientific Research Institute of Regionology;Proletarskaj Street 61;430000 Saransk-City RUSSIA

RenD ***Renaissance Drama***. Freq: 1; Began: 1964; Cov: Full; Lang: Eng; Subj: Theatre. ISSN: 0486-3739
▪Center for Renaissance Studies; Newberry Library; 60 West Walton St. Chicago, IL 60610; USA.

Renmin ***Renmin Xiju***: People's Theatre. Freq: 12; Began: 1950; Lang: Chi; Subj: Theatre.
▪52 Dongai Batiao; Beijing; CHINA.

RenQ ***Renaissance Quarterly***. Freq: 4; Began: 1967; Lang: Eng; Subj: Related. ISSN: 0034-4338
▪The Renaissance Society of America, Inc.; 24 West 12th Street; New York, NY 10011; USA.

Repliikki ***Repliikki***. Freq: 4; Began: 1970; Lang: Fin; Subj: Theatre.
▪Suomen Harrastajateatteriliitto; Minervankatu 1 C 21; 00100 Helsinki; FINLAND.

REsT ***Revista de Estudios de Teatro***: Boletin. Freq: 3; Began: 1964; Lang: Spa; Subj: Theatre. ISSN: 0034-8171
▪Instituto Nacional de Estudios de Teatro; Av. Córdoba 1199; Buenos Aires; ARGENTINA.

Restor ***Restoration and Eighteenth Century Theatre Research***. Freq: 2; Began: 1962; Cov: Full; Lang: Eng; Subj: Theatre. ISSN: 0034-5822
▪Loyola University of Chicago, Dept. of English; 6525 North Sheridan Road; Chicago, IL 60626; USA.

RevAS ***Review: Asian Studies Association of Australia***. Freq: 3; Began: 1975; Lang: Eng; Subj: Related. ISSN: 0314-7533
▪Robin Jeffrey, Dept. of Politics, La Trobe University; Bundoora; Victoria 3083; AUSTRALIA.

RevES ***Review of English Studies***. Freq: 4; Cov: Scan; Lang: Eng; Subj: Related. ISSN: 0034-6551
▪Oxford University Press; Oxford;; UK.

RevIM ***Review of Indonesian and Malaysian Affairs***. Freq: 2; Began: 1962; Cov: Scan; Lang: Eng; Subj: Related. ISSN: 0034-6594
▪Dept. of Indonesian & Malaysian Studies; University of Sydney; NSW 2006; AUSTRALIA.

Revue ***Revue***. Freq: 6; Lang: Fre; Subj: Theatre.

■Theatre de la Commune, BP 157; 2 rue Edouard Poisson; 93304 Aubervilliers; FRANCE.

RHSTMC ***Revue Roumaine d'Histoire de l'Art***: Série Théâtre, Musique, Cinéma. Freq: 4; Began: 1980; Lang: Fre; Subj: Related.
■Ed. Academiei Rep. Soc. Romania; Calea Victoriei 125; 79717 Bucharest; ROMANIA.

RHT ***Revue d'Histoire du Théâtre***. Freq: 4; Began: 1948; Cov: Full; Lang: Fre; Subj: Theatre. ISSN: 0035-2373
■Société d'Histoire du Théâtre; 98 Boulevard Kellermann; 75013 Paris; FRANCE.

RIDr ***Rivista Italiana di Drammaturgia***. Freq: 4; Began: 1976; Last Known Address; Lang: Ita; Subj: Theatre.
■Istituto del Dramma Italiano; Via Monte della Farina 42; Rome; ITALY.

RLC ***Revue de Littérature Comparée***. Freq: 4; Began: 1921; Cov: Scan; Lang: Fre/Eng; Subj: Related. ISSN: 0035-1466
■F. Didier Erudition; 6 rue de la Sorbonne; 75005 Paris; FRANCE.

RLit ***Russkaja Literatura: Istoriko-Literaturnyj Žurnal***: (Russian Literature: Historical Literary Journal). Freq: 4; Began: 1958; Cov: Scan; Lang: Rus; Subj: Related. ISSN: 0131-6095
■Inst. Russkoj Lit. Akademii Nauk SSSR, Puškinskij Dom; Nab. Makarova 4; 199164 St. Petersburg; RUSSIA.

RLtrs ***Red Letters***. Freq: 3; Began: 1976; Lang: Eng; Subj: Related. ISSN: 0308-6852
■A Journal of Cultural Politics; 6 Cynthia Street; London N1 9JF; UK.

RLZ ***Rossijskij Literaturovedčeskij Žurnal***. Began: 1992; Lang: Rus; Subj: Related.
■Krasikov Street 28/21; Union Ran, Literature Section; 117418 Moscow RUSSIA.

RMelo ***Rassegna Melodrammatica***. Last Known Address; Lang: Ita; Subj: Theatre.
■Corso di Porta Romana 80; Milan; ITALY.

RN ***Rouge et Noir***. Freq: 9; Began: 1968; Lang: Fre; Subj: Related.
■Maison de la Culture de Grenoble; BP 70-40; 38020 Grenoble; FRANCE.

Roda ***Roda Lyktan***. Freq: 1; Began: 1976; Ceased: 1980; Lang: Swe; Subj: Theatre. ISSN: 0040-0750
■Skanska Teatern; Osterg 31; 26134 Landskrona; SWEDEN.

Rodina ***Rodina***. Freq: 52; Began: 1989; Cov: Scan; Lang: Rus; Subj: Related. ISSN: 0235-7089
■Vozdvizenva Street, 4/7 Building; 103728 Moscow; RUSSIA.

Rossp ***Rossiskaja provincija***. Cov: Scan; Lang: Rus; Subj: Related. ISSN: 0869-8376
■Moscow.; RUSSIA.

RORD ***Research Opportunities in Renaissance Drama***. Freq: 1/2 yrs; Began: 1956; Cov: Full; Lang: Eng; Subj: Theatre. ISSN: 0098-647x
■Department of English; University of Kansas; Lawrence, KS 66045; USA.

RQ ***Romance Quarterly***. Freq: 4; Began: 1953; Cov: Scan; Lang: Eng; Subj: Related. ISSN: 0883-1157
■Heldref Publication; 1319 Eighteenth Street N.W.; Washington, DC 20036-1802;

RRMT ***Ridotto***: Rassegna Mensile di Teatro. Freq: 12; Began: 1951; Cov: Scan; Lang: Ita; Subj: Theatre. ISSN: 0035-5186
■Società Italiana Autori Drammatici; Via Po 10; 00198 Rome; ITALY.

RSP ***Rivista di Studi Pirandelliani***. Freq: 3; Began: 1978; Cov: Scan; Lang: Ita; Subj: Theatre.
■Centro Nazionale di Studi Pirandelliani; Agrigento; ITALY.

S&B ***Spiel & B*04uhne (Bund Deutscher Amateurtheater)***. Freq: 3; Cov: Scan; Lang: Ger; Subj: Theatre
■Steinheimer Str. 7/1; D-89518 Heidenheim; GERMANY.

S&D ***Speech & Drama***. Began: 1951; Cov: Scan; Lang: Eng; Subj: Related.
■Society of Teachers of Speech and Drama; 23 High Ash Avenue; Leeds LS17 8RS; UK.

SA ***Screen Actor***. Freq: 4; Cov: Scan; Lang: Eng; Subj: Related. ISSN: 0036-956X
■Screen Actors Guild; 7065 Hollywood Boulevard; Los Angeles, CA 90028-6065; USA.

SAADYT ***SAADYT Journal***. Formerly: *SAADYT Newsletter*. Began: 1979; Cov: Scan; Lang: Eng/Afr; Subj: Theatre.
■South African Assoc. for Drama and, Youth Theatre; Private Bag X41; Pretoria; SOUTH AFRICA.

SAD ***Studies in American Drama, 1945-Present***. Freq: 2; Began: 1986; Cov: Full; Lang: Eng; Subj: Theatre. ISSN: 0886-7097
■Ohio State University Press; 1070 Carmack Road; Columbus, OH 43210; USA.

Sage ***Sage***: A Scholarly Journal on Black Women. Freq: 2; Began: 1984; Lang: Eng; Subj: Related. ISSN: 0741-8369
■Sage Women's Educational Press, Inc.; Box 42741; Atlanta, GA 30311 0741; USA.

Sahne ***Sahne (The Stage)***. Freq: 12; Began: 1981; Lang: Tur; Subj: Theatre.
■Nes'e Altiner; Cagaloglu Yokusu 2; Istanbul; TURKEY.

SAITT ***SAITT Focus***. Freq: IRR; Last Known Address; Began: 1969; Lang: Eng/Afr; Subj: Theatre.
■S. African Inst. for Theatre Technology; Pretoria; SOUTH AFRICA.

SAJAL ***South African Journal of African Languages***. Freq: 4; Began: 1981; Lang: Eng & Afrikaans;; Subj: Related. ISSN: 0257-2117
■African Languages Asso. of Southern Africa; Bureau for Scientific Publications; Box 1758; Pretoria 0001; SOUTH AFRICA.

SanatO ***Sanat Olayi (Art Event)***. Freq: 12; Last Known Address; Lang: Tur; Subj: Theatre.
■Karacan Yayinlari; Basin Sarayi; Cagaloglu-Istanbul; TURKEY.

SATJ ***South African Theatre Journal***. Freq: 2; Began: 1987; Cov: Full; Lang: Eng;; Subj: Theatre.
■SATJ School of Dramatic Art; University of Witwatersrand; WITS 2050; SOUTH AFRICA.

SCagdas ***Sanajans Cagdas***. Freq: 12; Lang: Tur; Subj: Theatre.
■Istiklal Caddesi Botter Han; 475/479 Kat. 3; Istanbul; TURKEY.

Scan ***Scandinavica***. Freq: 2; Lang: Eng/Dan/Ger/Fre/Swe; Subj: Related.
■University of East Anglia; Norwich; NR4 7TJ; UK.

ScCh ***Scene Changes***. Freq: 9; Began: 1973; Ceased: 1981; Cov: Scan; Lang: Eng; Subj: Theatre. ISSN: 0381-8098
■Theatre Ontario; 8 York Street, 7th floor; Toronto, ON M5R 1J2; CANADA.

Scena ***Scena***:Časopis za pozorišnu umetnost. Freq: 6; Began: 1965; Lang: Ser; Subj: Theatre. ISSN: 0036-5734
■Sterijino Pozorje; Zmaj Jovina 22; 21000 Novi Sad; SERBIA.

ScenaB ***Scena***. Freq: 4; Began: 1962; Lang: Ger; Subj: Theatre. ISSN: 0036-5726
■Institut für Technologie Kultureller Einrichtung; Clara Zetkin-Str. 1205; 108 Berlin; GERMANY.

ScenaM ***Scena***. Freq: 12; Began: 1976; Lang: Ita; Subj: Theatre.
■Morrison Hotel; Via Modena 16; 20129 Milan; ITALY.

ScenaP ***Scena***. Freq: 26; Began: 1976; Ceased; Cov: Scan; Lang: Cze; Subj: Theatre. ISSN: 0139-5386
■Scena; Valdstejnske nam. 3; Prague 1; CZECH REPUBLIC.

Scenaria ***Scenaria***. Freq: 24; Began: 1977; Cov: Scan; Lang: Eng; Subj: Theatre. ISSN: 0256-002X
■Triad Publishers Ltd.; Box 72161, Parkview 2122; Johannesburg; SOUTH AFRICA.

Scenario ***Scenario***. Freq: 4; Cov: Scan; Lang: Eng; Subj: Related.
■3200 Tower Oaks Blvd.; Rockville, MD 20852; USA.

Scenarium ***Scenarium***. Freq: 10; Began: 1879; Lang: Dut; Subj: Theatre.
■De Walburg Pres; P. O. Box 222; 7200 AE Zutphen; NETHERLANDS.

ScenaW ***Scena***. Formerly: *Poradnik Teatrow, Lirnik Wioskowy*. Freq: 48; Began: 1908; Lang: Pol; Subj: Theatre.
■Wydawnictwo Prasa ZSL; ul. Reja 9; 02 053 Warsaw; POLAND.

Scene ***Scene, De***. Freq: 10; Began: 1959; Lang: Dut; Subj: Theatre.
■Theatercentrum; Jan van Rijswijcklaan 28; B 2000 Antwerpen; BELGIUM.

Scenograf ***Scénografie***. Freq: 4; Began: 1963; Lang: Cze; Subj: Theatre. ISSN: 0036-5815
■Divadelní ústav; Celetná 17; 110 01 Prague 1; CZECH REPUBLIC.

ScenoS ***Scen och Salong***. Freq: 12; Began: 1915; Ceased: 1990; Lang: Swe; Subj: Theatre. ISSN: 0036-5718
■Folkparkernas Centralorganisation; Svedenborgsgatan 1; S 116 48 Stockholm; SWEDEN.

Schaus ***Schauspielfuehrer***: Der Inhalt der wichtigsten Theaterstuecke aus aller Welt. Freq: IRR; Began: 1953; Lang: Ger; Subj: Theatre. ISSN: 0342-4553
■Anton Hiersemann Verlag, Rosenbergstr 113; 70193 Stuttgart 1; GERMANY.

SchwT ***Schweizer Theaterjahrbuch***. Freq: 1; Lang: Ger; Subj: Related.
■Gesellschaft für Theaterkultur; Theaterkultur-Verlag Postfach 1940, CH-4001 Basel; SWITZERLAND.

ScIDI ***Scena IDI, La.*** Freq: 4; Began: 1971; Lang: Ita; Subj: Theatre.
▪Bulzoni Editore; Via Liburni 14; 00185 Rome; ITALY.

SCN ***Seventeenth-Century News.*** Freq: 4; Lang: Eng; Subj: Theatre.
▪English Department; Blocker Building; Texas A & M University; College Station, TX 77843; USA.

Screen ***Screen.*** Freq: 24; Began: 1959; Lang: Eng; Subj: Related. ISSN: 0036-9543
▪Oxford University Press; Pinkhill House; Southfield Road Eynsham Oxford OX8 1JJ; UK.

SCYPT ***SCYPT Journal.*** Freq: 2; Began: 1977; Ceased: 1986; Cov: Scan; Lang: Eng; Subj: Theatre.
▪Standing Conf. on Young People's Theatre, c/o Cockpit Theatre; Gateforth Street; London NW8; UK.

SD ***Stage Directions.*** Cov: Scan; Lang: Eng; Subj: Theatre.
▪SMW Communications Inc.; 3101 Poplarwood Court; Suite 310; Raleigh, NC 27604-1010; USA.

SDi ***Slovenské Divadlo.*** Freq: 4; Began: 1952; Cov: Full; Lang: Slo; Subj: Theatre. ISSN: 0037-699X
▪Slovanian Acad. of Sciences; Klemensova 19; 814 30 Bratislava; SLOVAKIA.

SdO ***Serra d'Or.*** Freq: 12; Began: 1959; Cov: Scan; Lang: Spa; Subj: Related. ISSN: 0037-2501
▪Publicacions de l'Abadia de Montser, Ausias March 92-98; Apdo. 244; 13 Barcelona; SPAIN.

SEEA ***Slavic & East European Arts.*** Freq: 2; Began: 1982; Cov: Full; Lang: Eng; Subj: Related. ISSN: 0737-7002
▪State Univ. of NY, Stonybrook, Dept. of Germanic & Slavic Lang.; Slavic & East European Arts; Stonybrook, NY 11794; USA.

SEEDTF ***Soviet and East European Performance: Drama Theatre Film.*** Formerly: *Newsnotes on Soviet & East European Drama & Theatre.* SEE *Slavic and East European Performance.* Freq: 3; Began: 1981; Ceased: 1989; Cov: Scan; Lang: Eng; Subj: Theatre.
▪Inst. for Contemporary East European and Soviet Drama and Theatre; Graduate Ctre, CUNY, 33 West 42nd St., Room 1206A; New York, NY 10036; USA.

SEEP ***Slavic and East European Performance: Drama, Theatre, Film.*** Formerly: *Soviet and East-European Performance: Drama Theatre Film.* Freq: 3; Began: 1989; Cov: Scan; Lang: Eng; Subj: Theatre.
▪Inst. for Contemporary East European and Soviet Drama and Theatre; Graduate Ctre, CUNY, 33 West 42nd St., Room 1206A; New York, NY 10036; USA.

Segmundo ***Segismundo.*** Freq: 6; Began: 1965; Lang: Spa; Subj: Theatre.
▪Consejo Superior de Investigaciones Científicas; Vitruvio 8, Apartado 14.458; Madrid 6; SPAIN.

Sehir ***Sehir Tijatrolari (City Theatre).*** Freq: 12; Began: 1930; Lang: Tur; Subj: Theatre.
▪Sunusi Tekiner; Basin ve Halka Iliskiler Danismanligi; Harbiye-Istanbul; TURKEY.

SEL ***SEL: Studies in English Literature, 1500-1900.*** Freq: 4; Lang: Eng; Subj: Related.
▪Rice University; 6100 Main Street; Houston, TX 77005-1892; USA.

Selmol ***Sel'skaja molodež.*** Freq: 12; Began: 1925; Cov: Scan; Lang: Rus; Subj: Related. ISSN: 0203-3569
▪5a Novomitrovskaja ul.; Moscow 125015; RUSSIA.

Sembianza ***Sembianza.*** Freq: 6; Began: 1981; Last Known Address; Lang: Ita; Subj: Theatre.
▪Via Manzoni 14; 20121 Milan; ITALY.

Sentg ***Sentjakobsko gledališče.*** Cov: Scan; Lang: Slo; Subj: Related.
▪Mestni dom; 61000 Ljubljana; SLOVENIA.

SFN ***Shakespeare on Film Newsletter.*** SEE *Shakespeare Bulletin.* Freq: 2; Began: 1977; Ceased: 1993; Cov: Scan; Lang: Eng; Subj: Related. ISSN: 0739-6570
▪Dept. of English; Nassau Community College; Garden City, NY 11530; USA.

SFo ***Szinháztechnikai Fórum.*** Journal of the Section for Theatre Technology of the Hungarian Optical, Acoustic and Cinematographical Society of the Hungarian Centre of the OISTAT. Freq: 4; Began: 1974; Cov: Scan; Lang: Hun; Subj: Theatre. ISSN: 0139-1542
▪OPAKFI; Fő u. 68; 1027 Budapest; HUNGARY.

Sg ***Shingeki.*** Freq: 12; Began: 1954; Lang: Jap; Subj: Theatre.
▪Hakusui-sha, Chiyoda-ku; 3-24 Kanda-Ogawa-cho; 101 Tokyo; JAPAN.

SGfUB ***Schriftenreihe, Gesellschaft für Unterhaltende Bühnenkunst e.V..*** Freq: 1; Cov: Scan; Lang: Ger; Subj: Related.
▪Hertzbergstr. 21; D-12055 Berlin; GERMANY.

SGIP ***Sovetskoe Gosudarstvo i Pravo.*** SEE *Gosudarstvo i pravo.* Freq: 12; Began: 1927; Ceased: 1992; Cov: Scan; Lang: Rus; Subj: Related. ISSN: 0132-0769
▪Akad. Nauk S.S.S.R.; Inst. Gosudarstva i Prava; Izdatel'stvo Nauka; Podsosenskii Per., 21; Moscow K-62; RUSSIA.

SGT ***Schriften der Gesellschaft für Theatergeschichte.*** Lang: Ger; Subj: Theatre.
▪Berlin; GERMANY.

SGTJ ***Schweizerische Gesellschaft für Theaterkultur Jahrbücher.*** Freq: IRR; Began: 1928; Lang: Ger; Subj: Theatre.
▪Swiss Association for Theatre Research, c/o Louis Naef; Postfach 180; CH-6130 Willisau; SWITZERLAND.

SGTS ***Schweizerische Gesellschaft für Theaterkultur Schriften.*** Freq: IRR; Began: 1928; Ceased: 1982; Lang: Ger; Subj: Theatre.
▪Swiss Association for Theatre Research, c/o Louis Naef; Postfach 180; CH-6130 Willisau; SWITZERLAND.

Shahaab ***Shahaab.*** Last Known Address; Lang: Ara; Subj: Theatre.
▪Hayassat Building; Cooper Road; Rawlpindi; PAKISTAN.

ShakS ***Shakespeare Studies.*** Freq: 1; Lang: Eng; Subj: Theatre. ISSN: 1067-0823
▪Peter Lang Publishers; New York, NY; USA.

Shavian ***Shavian.*** Freq: 2; Began: 1946; Lang: Eng; Subj: Theatre. ISSN: 0037-3346
▪Shaw Society; 6 Stanstead Grove; London SE6 4UD; UK.

ShawR ***Shaw:*** The Annual of Bernard Shaw Studies. Formerly: *Shaw Review (ISSN: 0037-3354).* Freq: 1; Began: 1981; Cov: Scan; Lang: Eng; Subj: Theatre. ISSN: 0741-5842
▪Penn State Press; Barbara Building; University Park, PA 16802; USA.

ShB ***Shakespeare Bulletin:A Journal of Performance Criticism and Scholarship:***Incorporating *Shakespeare on Film Newsletter.* Freq: 4; Began: 1982; Lang: Eng; Subj: Theatre.
▪English Department; Lafayette College; Easton, PA 18042; USA.

ShN ***Shakespeare Newsletter.*** Freq: 4; Began: 1951; Lang: Eng; Subj: Theatre. ISSN: 0037-3214
▪Iona College; New Rochelle, NY 10801; USA.

Show ***Show.*** Last Known Address; Lang: Eng; Subj: Theatre.
▪9/2 Nazimabad; Karachi; PAKISTAN.

ShowM ***Show Music.*** Freq: 4; Began: 1981; Cov: Scan; Lang: Eng; Subj: Theatre.
▪P.O. Box 466; East Haddam, CT 06423-0466; USA.

ShRA ***Shakespeare and Renaissance Association: Selected Papers.*** Freq: 1; Lang: Eng; Subj: Related.
▪Department of English; 400 Hal Greer Blvd.; Marshall University Huntington, WV 25755-2646; USA.

ShS ***Shakespeare Survey.*** Freq: 1; Began: 1948; Cov: Full; Lang: Eng; Subj: Theatre. ISSN: 0080-9152
▪Cambridge University Press, The Edinburgh Building; Shaftesbury Road; Cambridge CB2 2RU; UK.

ShSA ***Shakespeare in Southern Africa.*** Freq: 1; Began: 1987; Cov: Full; Lang: Eng; Subj: Theatre.
▪ISEA; Rhodes University; Grahamstown 6140; SOUTH AFRICA.

Silex ***Silex.*** Last Known Address; Lang: Fre; Subj: Theatre.
▪BP 554 RP; 38013 Grenoble; FRANCE.

Sin ***Sightline:*** The Journal of Theatre Technology and Design. Freq: 2; Began: 1974; Ceased: 1993; Cov: Scan; Lang: Eng; Subj: Theatre. ISSN: 0265-9808
▪Assoc. of British Theatre Technicians; 4 Gt. Pulteney Street; London W1R 3DF; UK.

Sipario ***Sipario.*** Freq: 12; Began: 1946; Last Known Address; Lang: Ita; Subj: Theatre.
▪Sipario Editrice S.R.L.; Via Flaminia 167; 00196 Milan; ITALY.

SiR ***Studies in Romanticism.*** Freq: 4; Cov: Scan; Lang: Eng; Subj: Related. ISSN: 0039-3762
▪Boston U. Scholarly Publications; 985 Commonwealth Ave; Boston, MA 02215; USA.

Sis ***Sightlines.*** Freq: 4; Began: 1965; Cov: Scan; Lang: Eng; Subj: Related. ISSN: 0065-6311
▪USITT; 10 West 19th St., Ste. 5A; New York, NY 10011; USA.

SiSo ***Sight and Sound.*** Freq: 4; Began: 1932; Cov: Scan; Lang: Eng; Subj: Related. ISSN: 0037-4806
▪21 Stephen Street; London W1P 1PL; UK.

SJ ***Spielplan Journal***. Freq: 1; Cov: Scan; Lang: Ger; Subj: Related.
■Mykenae-Verlag, Ahastr. 9; D-64285 Darmstadt; GERMANY.

SjV ***Sirp ja Vasar***. Freq: 52; Began: 1940; Lang: Est; Subj: Theatre.
■Postkast 388, Pikk t. 40; 200 001 Talin; ESTONIA.

SJW ***Shakespeare Jahrbuch***. SEE: *Deutsche Shakespeare Gesellschaft/Deutsche Shakespeare Gesellschaft West, Jahrbuch.* Freq: 1; Began: 1865; Lang: Ger; Subj: Theatre. ISSN: 0080-9128
■Deutsche Shakespeare Gesellschaft; Kamp-Kontor, Ferdinand Kamp Verlag; Widumestr. 6-8 D-44787 Bochum; GERMANY.

SK ***Skripicnyj kluch***. Cov: Scan; Lang: Rus; Subj: Related.
■Lyniya, V.O 199053; St. Petersburg;; RUSSIA.

Skript ***Skript***. Freq: 10; Last Known Address; Lang: Dut; Subj: Theatre.
■N.C.A.; Postbus 64; 3600 AB Maarssen; NETHERLANDS.

Slav ***Slavjanovedenie***. Freq: 6; Began: 1992; Cov: Scan; Lang: Rus; Subj: Related. ISSN: 0132-1366
■Izdatel'stvo Nauka; Podsosenskii Per. 21; K 62 Moscow; RUSSIA.

Slavr ***Slavistična revija: časopis za jezikoslovje in literarne vede***. Freq: 4; Began: 1948; Cov: Scan; Lang: Slo; Subj: Related. ISSN: 0350-6894
■Slavistično društvo Slovenij; Aškerčeva 2; 1000 Ljubljana; SLOVENIA.

SlovD ***Slovensko narodno gledališče-Drama***. Cov: Scan; Lang: Slo; Subj: Related.
■Erjavčeva o.1; 61000 Ljubljana; SLOVENIA.

Slovl ***Slovensko ljudsko gledališče Celje***. Cov: Scan; Lang: Slo; Subj: Related.
■Gledališki trg 5; 63000 Celje; SLOVENIA.

Slovm ***Slovensko mladinsko gledališče***. Cov: Scan; Lang: Slo; Subj: Related.
■Vilharjeva o.11; 61000 Ljubljana; SLOVENIA.

SlovO ***Slovensko narodno gledališče-Opera in balet***. Cov: Scan; Lang: Slo; Subj: Related.
■Župančičeva 1; 61000 Ljubljana; SLOVENIA.

SM ***Spectacles Magazine***. Freq: 12; Lang: Fre; Subj: Theatre.
■42 Blvd. du Temple; 75011 Paris; FRANCE.

Smena ***Smena***. Freq: 12; Began: 1924; Cov: Scan; Lang: Rus; Subj: Related. ISSN: 0131-6658
■Pravda ; Moscow; RUSSIA.

SMR ***SourceMonthly***: The Resource for Mimes, Clowns, Jugglers, and Puppeteers. Freq: 12; Lang: Eng; Subj: Theatre.
■Mimesource Inc.; 125 Sherman Str.; Brooklyn, NY 11218; USA.

SNJPA ***Sangeet Natak***: Journal of the Performing Arts. Freq: 4; Began: 1965; Lang: Eng; Subj: Theatre. ISSN: 0036-4339
■Sangeet Natak Akademi, Rabindra Bhavan; Ferozeshah Rd.; 110001 New Delhi; INDIA.

SobCh ***Sobcota Chelovneta***. Lang: Geo; Subj: Theatre.
■Tbilisi; GEORGIA.

Sobesednik ***Sobesednik***. Freq: 12; Began: 1949; Cov: Scan; Lang: Rus; Subj: Related. ISSN: 0202-3180
■Moscow; RUSSIA.

SObzor ***Scénografický Obzor***. Freq: 6; Began: 1958; Ceased: 1973; Lang: Cze; Subj: Theatre.
■Vinohradska 2; Prague 1; CZECH REPUBLIC.

SocA ***Social Alternatives***. Freq: 4; Began: 1977; Cov: Scan; Lang: Eng; Subj: Related. ISSN: 0155-0306
■c/ Department of Government, University of Queensland; St. Lucia Qld 4067; AUSTRALIA.

SocH ***Social History***. Freq: 3; Began: 1976; Lang: Eng; Subj: Related. ISSN: 0307-1022
■Routledge Ltd.; 11 New Fetter Lane; London EC4P 4EE; UK.

Sodob ***Sodobnost***. Freq: 12; Began: 1953; Cov: Scan; Lang: Slo; Subj: Related. ISSN: 0038-0482
■DZS d.d. Mestni trg 26;; 1000 Ljubljana;; SLOVENIA.

Sog ***Soglasije***. Began: 1990; Cov: Scan; Lang: Rus; Subj: Related. ISSN: 0868-8710
■Bakhrušin Street, 28; 113054 Moscow; RUSSIA.

SogogT ***Sōgō geijutsu Toshite no nō***. Freq: Irreg; Began: 1994; Lang: Jap; ISSN: 1343-1331
■International Zeami Society, JAPAN.

SoM ***Speaking of Mime***. Freq: IRR; Began: 1976; Ceased; Lang: Eng; Subj: Theatre. ISSN: 0381-9035
■Canadian Mime Council; Niagara-on-the-Lake, ON L0S 1J0; CANADA.

Somo ***Somogy***. Formerly: *Somogyi Szemle.* Freq: 6; Began: 1970; Cov: Scan; Lang: Hun; Subj: Related. ISSN: 0133-0144
■Somogy Megyei Könyvtár; Május 1. u. 10 7400 Kaposvár; HUNGARY.

SON ***Scottish Opera News***. Freq: 12; Ceased: 1987; Lang: Eng; Subj: Theatre. ISSN: 0309-7323
■Scottish Opera Club; Elmbank Crescent; Glasgow G2 4PT; UK.

SoQ ***Southern Quarterly, The***: A Journal of the Arts in the South. Freq: 4; Began: 1962; Lang: Eng; Subj: Related. ISSN: 0038-4496
■PO Box 5078 Southern Station; Hattiesburg, MS 39406-5078; USA.

SORev ***Sean O'Casey Review, The***. Freq: 2; Began: 1974; Last Known Address; Lang: Eng; Subj: Theatre. ISSN: 0365-2245
■O'Casey Studies; PO Box 333; Holbrook, NY 11741; USA.

SoSaw ***Southern Sawdust***. Freq: 4; Began: 1954; Last Known Address; Lang: Eng; Subj: Theatre. ISSN: 0038-4542
■L. Wilson Poarch Jr.; 2965 Freeman Avenue; Sarasota, FL 33580; USA.

SoTh ***Southern Theatre***. Began: 1964; Cov: Scan; Lang: Eng; Subj: Theatre. ISSN: 0584-4738
■Southeastern Theatre Conference; University of Carolina; Box 9868 Greensboro, NC 27412-0868; USA.

SOUTHERLY ***Southerly: A Review of Australian Literature***. Freq: 4; Began: 1939; Cov: Scan; Lang: Eng; Subj: Related. ISSN: 0038-3732
■Dept. of English; Univ. of Sydney; Sydney N.S.W. 2006; AUSTRALIA.

SouthR ***Southern Review*** Freq: 3; Began: 1963; Cov: Scan; Lang: Eng; Subj: Related. ISSN: 0038-4526
■School of Humanities and Social Sciences, Monash University; Gippsland, Chuschill VIC 3842; AUSTRALIA.

SovAr ***Sovetskie Arkhivy***. SEE *Otecestvennye arhivy.* Freq: 6; Began: 1966; Ceased: 1992; Cov: Scan; Lang: Rus; Subj: Related. ISSN: 0038-5166
■Glavnoe Arkhivnoe Upravlenie; Pirogovskaya 17; Moscow G-435; RUSSIA.

SovBal ***Sovėtskij Balet***. SEE *Balet.* Cov: Scan; Ceased: 1992; Lang: Rus; Subj: Theatre.
■Moscow; RUSSIA.

SovD ***Sovremėnnaja Dramaturgija***. Freq: 4; Began: 1982; Cov: Scan; Lang: Rus; Subj: Theatre. ISSN: 6207-7698
■Moscow; RUSSIA.

SovEC ***Sovėtskaja Estrada i Cirk***. SEE *Estrada i cirk.* Freq: 12; Ceased: 1992; Cov: Scan; Lang: Rus; Subj: Theatre. ISSN: 0131-6769
■Moscow; RUSSIA.

SovEt ***Sovėtskaja Ethnografia***. SEE *Etnograjiceskoe obozrenie.* Freq: 6; Began: 1926; Ceased: 1992; Cov: Scan; Lang: Rus; Subj: Related. ISSN: 0038-5050
■Ulica D. Uljanova 19; B 36 Moscow; RUSSIA.

SovKult ***Sovėtskaja Kultura***. Cov: Scan; Lang: Rus; Subj: Related.
■Novoslobodskaja ul. 73; K 55 Moscow; RUSSIA.

SovMuzyka ***Sovėtskaja Muzyka***: (Soviet Music). SEE *Muzykal'naja akademija.* Freq: 12; Began: 1933; Ceased: 1992; Cov: Scan; Lang: Rus; Subj: Related. ISSN: 0131-6818
■Moscow; RUSSIA.

SovSlav ***Sovėtskojė Slavjanovėdėnjė***: (Soviet Slavonic Studies). SEE *Slavjanovedenie.* Freq: 6; Began: 1965; Ceased: 1992; Cov: Scan; Lang: Rus; Subj: Related. ISSN: 0132-1366
■Izdatel'stvo Nauka; Podsosenskii Per. 21; K 62 Moscow; RUSSIA.

SovT ***Sovėtskij Teat'r/Soviet Theatre***. Freq: 4; Began: 1976; Cov: Scan; Lang: Rus/Ger/Eng/Fre/Spa; Subj: Theatre.
■Copyright Agency of the USSR; 6a Bolshaya Bronnaya St.; K 104 Moscow 103670; RUSSIA.

Spa ***Shilpakala***. Lang: Ben; Subj: Related.
■Dacca; BANGLADESH.

SPC ***Studies in Popular Culture***. Freq: 2; Began: 1977; Lang: Eng; Subj: Related.
■Popular Culture Association in the South, Florida State Univ., English Dp.; Tallahassee, FL 32306; USA.

Speak ***Speak***. Began: 1977; Lang: Eng; Subj: Theatre.
■PO Box 126, Newlands; 7725 Cape Town; SOUTH AFRICA.

Spirale ***Spirale: Art, letters, spectacles, sciences humaines***. Freq: 12; Began: 1979; Last Known Address; Lang: Fre; Subj: Theatre. ISSN: 0225-9004
▪C.P. 98, Succ. E; Montreal, PQ; CANADA.

SpIt ***Spettacolo in Italia, Lo***. Freq: 1; Began: 1951; Lang: Ita; Subj: Theatre. ISSN: 0038-738X
▪S.I.A.E.; Viale della Letteratura 30; 00100 Rome; ITALY.

Spl ***Spielplan, Der***. Freq: 12; Began: 1954; Lang: Ger; Subj: Theatre. ISSN: 0038-7517
▪Die monatliche Theatervorschau, Hg. Löwendruck Bertram GmbH; Pf. 6202; D-38108 Braunschweig; GERMANY.

SpViag ***Spettacolo Viaggiante***. Began: 1948; Lang: Ita; Subj: Theatre.
▪Assoc. Naz. Eserc. Spet. Viaggianti; Via di Villa Patrizi 10; 00161 Rome; ITALY.

SQ ***Shakespeare Quarterly***. Freq: 4; Began: 1950; Cov: Full; Lang: Eng; Subj: Related. ISSN: 0037-3222
▪Folger Shakespeare Library; 201 E. Capitol St. S.E. Washington, DC 20003; USA.

SR ***SIBMAS-Rundbrief, Hg. Bundesverband der Bibliotheken und Museen für Darstellende Künste e.v.***. Freq: 2; Cov: Scan; Lang: Ger; Subj: Related.
▪c/o Dr. Winrich Meiszies, Theatermuseum Düsseldorf; Jägerhofstr. 1; D-40479 Düsseldorf; GERMANY.

SSSS ***Szene Schweiz/Scène Suisse/Scena Svizzera***. Freq: 1; Began: 1973; Lang: Ger/Fre/Ita; Subj: Theatre.
▪Swiss Association for Theatre Research; c/o Louis Naef; Postfach 180; CH-6130 Willisau; SWITZERLAND.

SSTJ ***Secondary School Theater Journal***. Freq: 3; Began: 1962; Last Known Address; Lang: Eng; Subj: Theatre.
▪ATHE; P.O. Box 15282; Evansville, IL 47716-0282; USA.

ST ***Sovetskij Teatr***. Freq: 3; Began: 1983; Cov: Scan; Lang: Rus; Subj: Theatre.
▪Vestnik; Moscow; RUSSIA.

Staff ***Staffrider***. Freq: 4; Began: 1982; Cov: Scan; Lang: Eng/Afr; Subj: Related.
▪Ravan Press Ltd.; Box 31134; 2017 Braamfontein; SOUTH AFRICA.

StageA ***Stage of the Art***. Freq: 4; Cov: Scan; Lang: Eng; Subj: Related. ISSN: 1046-5022
▪American Alliance for Theatre and Education; Tempe, AZ; USA.

StageZ ***Stage***. Freq: IRR; Began: 1956; Lang: Eng; Subj: Theatre.
▪Lusaka Theatre Club Ltd; Box 30615; Lusaka; ZAMBIA.

Standpunte ***Standpunte***. Freq: 6; Last Known Address; Began: 1945; Cov: Scan; Lang: Afr;; Subj: Related. ISSN: 0038-9730
▪Tafelberg Publishers; c/o J.C. Kannemeyer, Ed.; P.O. Box 91073; Auckland Park 2006;; SOUTH AFRICA.

Sterijino ***Sterijino Pozorje***: Informativno Glasilo. Freq: IRR; Began: 1982; Lang: Ser; Subj: Theatre.
▪Sterijino Pozorje; Zmaj Jovina 22; Novi Sad; SERBIA.

Stikord ***Stikord***. Freq: 4; Began: 1981; Ceased; Lang: Dan; Subj: Theatre. ISSN: 0107-6582
▪Foreningen Hidovre Teater; Hidovre Strandvej 70A; 2650 Hvidovre; DENMARK.

Stilet ***Stilet***. Freq: 2; Began: 1989; Cov: Scan; Lang: Afr/Eng; Subj: Related.
▪Serva-Uitgewers; P.O. Box 36721, Menlopark 0102; SOUTH AFRICA.

STILB ***STILB***. Freq: 5; Began: 1981; Last Known Address; Lang: Ita; Subj: Theatre.
▪Via della Fosse di Castello 6; 00193 Rome; ITALY.

Stol ***Stolica***. Freq: 52; Began 1990; Cov: Scan; Lang: Rus; Subj: Related. ISSN: 0868-698X
▪State Union Publishing; Petrovka Street, 16 Moscow 101425; RUSSIA.

STN ***Scottish Theater News***. Freq: 12; Began: 1981; Ceased: 1986; Cov: Scan; Lang: Eng; Subj: Theatre. ISSN: 0261-4057
▪Scottish Society of Playwrights; 346 Sauchiehall St.; Glasgow G2 3JD; UK.

STP ***Studies in Theatre Production***. Freq: 2; Cov: Full; Lang: Eng; Subj: Theatre. ISSN: 1357-5341
▪Department of Drama; University of Exeter; Thornlea, New North Road Exeter, Devon EX4 4JZ; UNITED KINGDOM.

StPh ***Studies in Philology***. Freq: 3; Began: 1906; Lang: Eng; Subj: Related. ISSN: 0039-3738
▪University of North Carolina Press; Box 2288; Chapel Hill, NC 27514; USA.

Strind ***Strindbergiana***: Meddelanden från Strindbergssällskapet. Formerly: *Meddelanden från Strindbergssällskapet*. Freq: 1; Began: 1985; Cov: Full; Lang: Swe; Subj: Theatre. ISSN: 0282-8006
▪Strindbergssällskapet, c/o C. R. Smedmark; Drottninggatan 85; 111 60 Stockholm; SWEDEN.

STT ***Sceničeskaja Technika i Technologija***. Freq: 6; Began: 1963; Cov: Full; Lang: Rus; Subj: Theatre. ISSN: 0131-9248
▪Serebriančeskij Per. 2/5; 109028 Moscow; RUSSIA.

StudiaP ***Studia i Materialy do Dziejow Teatru Polskiego***. Formerly: *Studia i Materialy z Dziejow Teatru Polskiego*. Freq: IRR; Began: 1957; Lang: Pol; Subj: Theatre. ISSN: 0208-404X
▪Polish Academy of Sciences; Rynek 9; Wroclaw; POLAND.

StudiiR ***Studii si Cercetari de Istoria Artel***: Seria Teatru-Muzica-Cinematografie. Freq: 1; Began: 1954; Lang: Rom; Subj: Theatre. ISSN: 0039-3991
▪Academia Rep. Soc. Romania; Calea Victoriei 125; 79717 Bucharest; ROMANIA.

StudM ***Studenčeskij Meridian***. Freq: 12; Began: 1924; Cov: Scan; Lang: Rus; Subj: Related. ISSN: 0321-3883
▪Moscow; RUSSIA.

StWAusH ***Studies in Western Australian History***. Freq: IRR; Began: 1977; Cov: Scan; Lang: Eng; Subj: Related. ISSN: 0314-7525
▪Department of History; University of Western Australia; Nedlands, WA 6009; AUSTRALIA.

STYol ***STYolainen***. Freq: 6; Began: 1975; Lang: Fin; Subj: Theatre.
▪Suomen Teatterityontekijain, Yhteisjarjesto; Maneesikatu 4c; 00170 Helsinki 17; FINLAND.

SuAS ***Stratford-upon-Avon Studies***. Freq: IRR; Began: 1961; Lang: Eng; Subj: Theatre.
▪Edward Arnold Ltd; 41 Bedford Square; London WC1B 3DQ; UK.

SuF ***Sinn und Form: Beiträge zur Literatur***. Freq: 6; Began: 1949; Lang: Ger; Subj: Related. ISSN: 0037-5756
▪Aufbau-Verlag Berlin; Französische Str. 32; 10117 Berlin; GERMANY.

Suffloren ***Suffløren***. Last Known Address; Lang: Dan; Subj: Theatre.
▪Medlemsblad for Dansk Dukketeaterforening; Vestergrade 3; 1456 Copenhagen; DENMARK.

SuidAfr ***Suid-Afrikaan, Die***. Began: 1985; Cov: Scan; Lang: Afr; Subj: Related.
▪Die Suid-Afrikaan; P.O. Box 7010; 7610 Dalsig Stellembosch; SOUTH AFRICA.

SuT ***Spiel und Theater. Zeitschrift f*04ur Amateur-, Jugend- und Schultheater***. Freq: 2; Cov: Scan; Lang: Ger; Subj: Theatre.
▪Oberschleissheim u.a., Deutscher Theaterverlag; Pf. 100261; D-69442 Weinheim; GERMANY.

Svet ***Svět a divadlo***. Began: 1990; Cov: Full; Lang: Cze; Subj: Theatre. ISSN: 0862-7258
▪Divadelní obec; Štefánikova 57; 150 43 Prague 5; CZECH REPUBLIC.

SwTS ***Swedish Theater/Théâtre Suédois***. Lang: Eng/Fre; Subj: Theatre.
▪Stockholm; SWEDEN.

Sz ***Szinház***: (Theatre). Freq: 12; Began: 1968; Cov: Full; Lang: Hun; Subj: Theatre. ISSN: 0039-8136
▪Színház Alapítvány; Báthory u. 10; 1054 Budapest; HUNGARY.

Szab ***Szabolcs-Szatmár-Beregi Szemle***. Freq: 4; Began: 1965; Cov: Scan; Lang: Hun; Subj: Related. ISSN: 1216-092x
▪Móricz Zsigmond Könyvtár; Szabadság tér 2; 4400 Nyíregyháza; HUNGARY.

Szene ***Szene***. Lang: Ger; Subj: Theatre.
▪UMLOsterreichischer Bundestheaterverband; Goethegasse 1; A 1010 Vienna; AUSTRIA.

SzeneAT ***Szene: Fachzeitschrift der DDR Amateur-theater, -kabarett, -puppenspiel und*** -ntomime. Freq: 4; Began: 1966; Last Known Address; Cov: Scan; Lang: Ger; Subj: Theatre. ISSN: 0039-811X
▪Zentralhaus für Kulturarbeit, Dittrichring 4; Postfach 1051; 7010 Leipzig; GERMANY.

SzeneS ***Szene Schweiz. Eine Dokumentation des Theaterlebens in der Schweiz***. Freq: 1; Cov: Scan; Lang: Ger; Subj: Theatre.
▪Hg. Schweizerische Gesellschaft für Theaterkultur; Theaterkultur-Verlag, Pf. 1940; CH-3001 Basel, Schanzenstr. 15; SWITZERLAND.

SzSz ***Szinháztudományi Szemle***. Freq: 1; Began: 1977; Cov: Full; Lang: Hun; Subj: Theatre. ISSN: 0133-9907
▪Országos Színháztörténeti Múzeum és Intézet; Krisztina körut 57; 1016 Budapest; HUNGARY.

T&P ***Text and Performance: Journal of the Comparative Drama Conference.*** Freq: 1; Lang: Eng; Subj: Theatre.
▪Department of Classics; 3-C Daver Hall; University of Florida Gainesville, FL 32611; USA.

T&R ***Theatre and Religion.*** Freq: IRR; Lang: Eng; Subj: Theatre.
▪Box 727; Goshen College; Goshen, IN 46526; USA.

TA ***Theatre Annual.*** Freq: 1; Began: 1942; Cov: Full; Lang: Eng; Subj: Theatre. ISSN: 0082-3821
▪Department of Theatre and Speech; College of William and Mary; Williamsburg, VA 23187; USA.

TAAm ***Theater Across America.*** Freq: 5; Began: 1975; Lang: Eng; Subj: Theatre.
▪Theatre Sources Inc.; 104 North St. Mary; Dallas, TX 75214; USA.

Tablas ***Tablas***: National Council of Performing Art's Journal. Freq: 4; Began: 1982; Lang: Spa; Subj: Theatre.
▪San Ignacio #166 e/Obispo y Obrapia; Habana Vieja. C.P. 10100; CUBA.

Tabs ***Tabs.*** Freq: 2; Began: 1937; Ceased: 1986; Cov: Scan; Lang: Eng; Subj: Theatre. ISSN: 0306-9389
▪Rank Strand Ltd., P.O. Box 51, Great West Road; Brentford; Middlesex TW8 9HR; UK.

TAD ***Tiyatro Araştirmalari Dergisi (Theatre Research Magazine).*** Freq: 1; Began: 1970; Lang: Tur/Eng/Fre; Subj: Theatre.
▪Tiyatro Bölümü, Ankara Universitesi; D.T.C. Fakültesi, Sihhiye; Ankara; TURKEY.

Talent ***Talent Management.*** Freq: 12; Began: 1981; Lang: Eng; Subj: Related.
▪T M Publishing; 1501 Broadway; New York, NY 10036; USA.

Tampereen ***TTT-Tampereen Työväen Teatteri.*** Lang: Fin; Subj: Theatre.
▪Hämeenpuisto 30-32; 33200 Tampere; FINLAND.

Tanc ***Táncművészet.*** Freq: 4; Began: 1976; Cov: Full; Lang: Hun;; Subj: Dance. ISSN: 0134-1421
▪Táncművészeti Alapítvány; Kerék u. 34; 1035 Budapest; HUNGARY.

Tanecni ***Tanecni Listy.*** Freq: 10; Began: 1963; Lang: Cze; Subj: Theatre. ISSN: 0039-937X
▪Panorama; Halkova 1; 120 72 Prague 2; CZECH REPUBLIC.

TAnim ***Théâtre et Animation.*** Freq: 4; Began: 1976; Lang: Fre; Subj: Theatre. ISSN: 0398-0049
▪Fédération National du Théâtre et d'Animation; 12 Chaussée d'Antin; 75441 Paris Cedex 09; FRANCE.

Tanssi ***Tanssin Tiedotuskeskus.*** Freq: 4; Began: 1981; Cov: Full; Lang: Fin; Subj: Theatre. ISSN: 0492-4401
▪Bulevardi 23-27; 00180 Helsinki; Finland.

TantI ***Tantsovo Izkustvo.*** Freq: 12; Began: 1954; Lang: Bul; Subj: Theatre.
▪Izdatelstvo Nauka i Izkustvo; 6 Rouski Blvd; Sofia; BULGARIA.

TanzA ***Tanz Affiche.*** Freq: 6; Cov: Scan; Lang: Ger; Subj: Related.
▪Publikation für Tanz und Kultur, Hg. Affiche; Verein zur Förderung von Information und Kommunikation in künstlerischen Belangen; Eggerthgasse 10/1; A-1060 Wien; AUSTRIA.

Tanzd ***Tanzdrama.*** Freq: 4; Began: 1987; Cov: Scan; Lang: Ger; Subj: Theatre. ISSN: 0932-8688
▪Erhard Friedrich Verlag; Postfach 100 150 D-30917 Seelze; GERMANY.

TanzG ***Tanz und Gymnastik.*** Freq: 4; Began: 1944; Last Known Address; Lang: Ger; Subj: Theatre.
▪Schweizerischer Berufsverband für Tanz und Gymnastik; Riedbergstrasse 1; 4059 Basel; SWITZERLAND.

TArch ***Teatro Archivio.*** Formerly: *Bolletino del Museo Biblioteca dell'attore.* Freq: IRR; Began: 1979; Cov: Full; Lang: Ita; Subj: Theatre.
▪Bulzoni Editore; Via dei Liburni n 14; 00185 Rome; ITALY.

TArsb ***Teaterdrsboken.*** Freq: 1; Began: 1982; Cov: Scan; Lang: Swe; Subj: Theatre.
▪Svenska Riksteatern; 145 83 Norsborg; SWEDEN.

Tatar ***Tatarstan Republic.*** Freq: 12; Began: 1920; Cov: Scan; Lang: Rus; Subj: Related. ISSN: 0130-2418
▪Decabristy Street, #2; 420066 Kazan' City; RUSSIA.

Tatr ***Tatr.*** Freq: 4; Began: 1985; Cov: Scan; Lang: Ger/Fre; Subj: Related.
▪Astej, Gessnerallee 13; CH-8001 Zurich; SWITZERLAND.

TAus ***Theatre Australia.*** Freq: 12; Began: 1976; Lang: Eng; Subj: Theatre.
▪Pellinor Pty Ltd. A.C.N.; 001 713 319, Level 2; 44 Bridge Street NSW 2000 Sydney; AUSTRALIA.

Tbuch ***Theaterbuch.*** Freq: 1; Lang: Ger; Subj: Theatre.
▪Munich; GERMANY.

TCB ***Teatro Clásico: Boletin.*** Freq: 1; Lang: Spa; Subj: Theatre.
▪Teatro Clásico de México; Apartado 61-077; MEXICO.

TCGNWCP ***TCG National Working Conference Proceedings.*** Freq: IRR; Began: 1976; Lang: Eng; Subj: Theatre.
▪Theatre Communications Group; 355 Lexington Ave; New York, NY 10017; USA.

TChicago ***Theatre Chicago.*** Freq: 12; Began: 1986; Last Known Address; Lang: Eng; Subj: Theatre.
▪22 W Monroe, Suite 801; 60603 Chicago, IL; USA.

TCI ***TCI: Theatre Crafts International.*** Formerly *Theatre Crafts.* Freq: 10; Began: 1995; Cov: Full; Lang: Eng; Subj: Theatre. ISSN: 1063-9497
▪Intertec Publishing Corp.; 32 West 18th Street; New York, NY 10011-4612; USA.

TCom ***Theatre Communications.*** Freq: 12; Began: 1979; Ceased: 1983; Lang: Eng; Subj: Theatre. ISSN: 0275-5971
▪Theatre Communications Group Inc; 355 Lexington Avenue; New York, NY 10017; USA.

TCraft ***Theatrecraft.*** Freq: 12; Began: 1964; Lang: Eng; Subj: Theatre.
▪Victorian Drama League, Fifth Floor; 17 Elizabeth Street; Melbourne 3000 Victoria; AUSTRALIA.

TCUG ***Theater Computer Users Group Notes.*** Began: 1978; Lang: Eng; Subj: Theatre.
▪Theatre Sources Inc.; 104 N Saint Mary; Dallas, TX 76214; USA.

TD&T ***Theatre Design and Technology.*** Freq: 4; Began: 1965; Cov: Full; Lang: Eng; Subj: Theatre. ISSN: 0040-5477
▪U.S. Institute for Theatre Technology; 966 East 1030 North; Orem, UT 84057; USA.

TDDR ***Theaterarbeit in der DDR.*** Freq: 3; Began: 1979; Lang: Ger; Subj: Theatre.
▪Verband der Theaterschaffended der DDR; Hermann-Matern-Strasse 18; 1040 Berlin; GERMANY.

TDonA ***Transition: Discourse on Architecture.*** Freq: 4; Began: 1979; Cov: Scan; Lang: Eng; Subj: Related. ISSN: 0157-7344
▪Faculty of Environmental Design and Construction; RMIT GPO Box 2476V Melbourne Victoria 3001; AUSTRALIA.

TDR ***Drama Review, The.*** Freq: 4; Began: 1955; Cov: Full; Lang: Eng; Subj: Theatre. ISSN: 0012-5962
▪Tisch School of the Arts; 721 Broadway, Room 626 New York, NY 10003; USA.

TE ***Teater Et.*** Freq: 5; Began: 1989; Cov: Full; Lang: Dan; Subj: Theatre.
▪Købmagergade 5, 3.; Postbox 191; 1006 København K; DENMARK.

Teat ***Teatteri.*** Freq: 8; Began: 1945; Cov: Full; Lang: Fin Subj: Theatre. ISSN: 0492-4401
▪Kustannus Oy Teatteri; Merítullinkatu 33; 00170 Helsinki; FINLAND.

TeaterD ***Teater i Danmark***: Theatre in Denmark. Freq: 1; Began: 1980; Ceased: 1987; Lang: Dan; Subj: Theatre. ISSN: 0106-7672
▪Teater i Danmark; Vesterbrogade 26, 3.; DK-1620 København V.; DENMARK.

Teaterf ***Teaterforum.*** Freq: 6; Began: 1968; Cov: Full; Lang: Swe; Subj: Theatre. ISSN: 0347-8890
▪Swedish Society for Amateur Theatres; Von Rosens väg 1 A; 737 40 Fagersta; SWEDEN.

Teatern ***Teatern.*** Freq: 4; Began: 1934; Lang: Swe; Subj: Theatre. ISSN: 0040-0750
▪Riksteatern; Svenska Riksteatern; S 145 83 Norsborg; SWEDEN.

TeatL ***Teatr Lalek.*** Lang: Pol; Subj: Theatre.
▪Warsaw; POLAND.

TeatM ***Teatraluri Moambe.*** Cov: Full; Lang: Geo; Subj: Theatre.
▪Tbilisi; GEORGIA.

Teatoro ***Teatoro.*** Freq: 12; Began: 1944; Lang: Jap; Subj: Theatre.
▪c/o Hagiwara Building, 2-3-1 Sarugaku-cho; Chiyoda-ku; 101 Tokyo; JAPAN.

Teatras ***Teatras.*** Lang: Lit; Subj: Theatre.
▪Vilnius; LITHUANIA.

TeatrC ***Teatro Contemporaneo.*** Freq: 3; Began: 1982; Last Known Address; Cov: Full; Lang: Ita; Subj: Theatre.
▪Via Trionfale 8406; 00135 Rome; ITALY.

TeatrE ***Teatro en España.*** Lang: Spa; Subj: Theatre.

▪Madrid; SPAIN.

TeatrM *Teat'r. žurnal dramaturgii i teatra.* Freq: 12; Began: 1937; Cov: Full; Lang: Rus; Subj: Theatre. ISSN: 0131-6805
▪Izdatel'stvo Iskusstvo; Ul. Gertsena 49; Moscow 49; RUSSIA.

Teatron *Teatron.* Began: 1962; Lang: Heb; Subj: Theatre.
▪Municipal Theatre; 20 Pevsner Street; Haifa; ISRAEL.

TeatroS *Teatro e Storia.* Began: 1986; Cov: Scan; Lang: Ita; Subj: Theatre. ISSN: 1120-9569
▪Centro per la Sperimentazione e la Ricerca Teatrale di Pontedera; Societa Editrice Il Mulino, Strada Maggiore 37 40125 Bologna; ITALY.

TeatroSM *TeatroSM.* Began: 1980; Lang: Spa; Subj: Theatre.
▪Teatro Municipal General San Martin; Ave. Corrientes 1530, 50 piso; 1042 Buenos Aires; ARGENTINA.

Teatrul *Teatrul.* Freq: 12; Began: 1956; Lang: Rom; Subj: Theatre. ISSN: 0040-0815
▪Consiliul Culturii si Educatiei Socialiste; Calea Victoriei 174; Bucharest; ROMANIA.

TeatrW *Teatr.* Freq: 12; Began: 1946; Cov: Scan; Lang: Pol; Subj: Theatre. ISSN: 0040-0769
▪Zarząd Glowny Związku Artystów Scen Polskich; ul. Jakubowska 14; 03-902 Warsaw; POLAND.

TeatterT *Teatterikorkeakoulun Tiedotuslehti.* Freq: 4; Began: 1984; Cov: Full; Lang: Fin; Subj: Theatre. ISSN: 0781-0164
▪Teatterikorkeakoulu; PL 148; 00511 Helsinki; FINLAND.

TeaturS *Teatur.* Freq: 12; Began: 1946; Cov: Full; Lang: Bul; Subj: Theatre. ISSN: 0204-6253
▪Komitet za Izkustvo i Kultura; 7 Levsky St.; 1000 Sofia; BULGARIA.

TeatY *Teatron*: Časopis za pozirišnu istoriju i teatrologiju. Freq: 4; Began: 1974; Cov: Scan; Lang: Ser; Subj: Theatre. ISSN: 0351-7500
▪Muzej Pozorišne umetnosti Srbije; Gospodar Jevremova 19; 11000 Belgrade; SERBIA.

TeatZ *Teatralnaja Žizn.* Freq: 24; Began: 1958; Cov: Scan; Lang: Rus; Subj: Theatre. ISSN: 0131-6915
▪Teatral'noe obschestvo, Theatrical Workers Union; Kiselni Typik dom 1 103031 Moscow; RUSSIA.

TeC *Teatro e Cinema.* Freq: 4; Began: 1968; Last Known Address; Lang: Ita; Subj: Theatre. ISSN: 0040-0807
▪Silva Editore; Viale Salita Salvatore 1; 28 16128 Genoa; ITALY.

TechB *Technical Brief.* Freq: 3; Began: 1982; Cov: Full; Lang: Eng; Subj: Theatre. ISSN: 1053-8860
▪TD&P Dept., Yale School of Drama; 222 York St.; New Haven, CT 06520; USA.

TEJ *Théâtre Enfance et Jeunesse.* Freq: 2; Began: 1963; Lang: Fre/Eng; Subj: Theatre. ISSN: 0049-3597
▪Assoc. du Théâtre pour l'Enfance, et la Jeunesse; 98 Blvd. Kellermann; 75013 Paris; FRANCE.

Telerad *Teleradioephir.* Formerly *Televidenie i Radioveščanie.* Began: 1952; Lang: Rus; Subj: Related. ISSN: 0869-1932
▪Pushkinskaja str. 23/8; 103009 Moscow; RUSSIA.

TEP *Théâtre de l'Est Parisien*: TEP Actualité. Lang: Fre; Subj: Theatre.
▪Paris; FRANCE.

TextPQ *Text and Performance Quarterly.* Formerly: *Literature in Performance.* Freq: 4; Began: 1980; Lang: Eng; Subj: Theatre. ISSN: 1046-2937
▪Speech Communication Association; 5774 Stevens; University of Maine; Orono, ME 04469-5774; USA.

Textual *Textual.* Lang: Spa; Subj: Theatre.
▪I.N.C.; Ancash; 390 Idma; PERU.

Textuel *Textuel.* Freq: 2; Lang: Fre;; Subj: Related.
▪Université de Paris VII; 2, place Jussieu; 75221 Paris CEDEX 05; FRANCE.

TF *Teaterforum.* Freq: 2; Began: 1980; Cov: Scan; Lang: Eng/Afr; Subj: Theatre.
▪University of Potchefstroom, Departement Spraakler en Drama; Potchefstroom; SOUTH AFRICA.

TF&TV *Teater Film & TV.* Freq: 8; Began: 1974; Lang: Dan; Subj: Theatre.
▪Faellesforbundet for Teater Film & TV; Ny Oestergade 12; DK 1101 Copenhagen; DENMARK.

TGDR *Theatre in the GDR.* Lang: Ger; Subj: Theatre.
▪Berlin; GERMANY.

TGlasnik *Teatarski Glasnik*: S. Spisanic na teatrite na Republika Makedonija. Freq: 2; Began: 1977; Lang: Slo; Subj: Theatre.
▪MKO, kej Dimitar Vlahov B.B.; 91000 Skopje; REPUBLIC OF MACEDONIA.

TGraz *Theater in Graz.* Freq: 4; Began: 1952; Lang: Ger; Subj: Theatre.
▪Vereinigte Bühnen Graz; Burggasse 16; A 8010 Graz; AUSTRIA.

Th *Théâtre.* Formerly: *Théâtre du Trident.* Lang: Fre; Subj: Theatre.
▪Théâtre du Trident, Edifice Palais Montcalm; 975 Place d'Youville; Quebec, PQ; CANADA.

THC *Theatre History in Canada/ Histoire du Théâtre.* Freq: 2; Began: 1980; Ceased; Cov: Full; Lang: Eng/Fre; Subj: Theatre. ISSN: 0226-5761
▪Graduate Centre for the Study of Drama, University of Toronto; 214 College Street; Toronto, ON M5T 2Z9; CANADA.

ThCr *Theatre Crafts.* SEE TCI. Freq: 9; Began: 1967; Ceased: 1995; Cov: Full; Lang: Eng; Subj: Theatre. ISSN: 0040-5469
▪Theatre Crafts Associates; 135 Fifth Avenue; New York, NY 10010; USA.

ThE *Théâtre en Europe.* Freq: 4; Began: 1984; Lang: Fre; Subj: Theatre.
▪Theatre de l'Europe, 1; Place Paul Claudel; 75006 Paris; FRANCE.

TheaterW *TheaterWeek.* Freq: 52; Began: 1987; Cov: Full; Lang: Eng; Subj: Theatre. ISSN: 0896-1956
▪That New Magazine; 28 West 25th St., 4th Floor; New York, NY 10010; USA.

TheatreEx *Theatre: Ex.* Freq: 3; Began: 1985; Lang: Eng; Subj: Theatre.
▪104 E. 4th Street; New York, NY 10003; USA.

TheatreF *TheatreForum.* Freq: 2; Began: 1991; Cov: Full; Lang: Eng; Subj: Theatre. ISSN: 1060-5320
▪Department of Theatre; University of California, San Diego; 9500 Gilman Dr La Jolla, CA 92093-0344; USA.

TheatreS *Theatre Studies.* Freq: 1; Began: 1954; Cov: Full; Lang: Eng; Subj: Theatre. ISSN: 0362-0964
▪Ohio State Univ., Lawrence and Lee, Theatre Research Institute; 1430 Lincoln Tower, 1800 Cannon Drive; Columbus, OH 43210 1230; USA.

TheatreT *Theatre Three.* Began: 1986; Ceased: 1991; Lang: Eng; Subj: Theatre.
▪Carnegie Mellon, Department of Drama; Pittsburgh, PA 15213; USA.

Theatro *Theatro.* Lang: Gre; Subj: Theatre.
▪Kosta Nitsos; Christou Lada 5-7; Athens; GREECE.

Theatron *Theatron*: Rivista quindicinale di cultura, documentazione ed informazione teatrale. Freq: 26; Began: 1961; Lang: Ita/Eng/Ger; Subj: Theatre. ISSN: 0040-5604
▪Quadrimestrale di Cultura, Documentazione e Informazione Teatrale del Centro; Via Fabiola 1; 00152 Rome; ITALY.

TheatronH *Theatron.* Freq: 26; Began: 1998; Lang: Hun; Subj: Theatre. ISSN: 1418-9441
▪Theatron; Társulás Veszarémi Egyetem; Sznháztudományi Tanszék. Wartha Vince u. 1,, 8200 VESZPRÉM;; HUNGARY.

Theatrum *Theatrum: A Theatre Journal.* Freq: 3; Began: 1985; Ceased: 1995; Cov: Full; Lang: Eng; Subj: Theatre. ISSN: 0838-5696
▪Theatrum; P.O. Box 688, Station C; Toronto, ON M6J 3S1; CANADA.

Theoria *Theoria*: A Journal of Studies in the Arts, Humanities and Social Studies. Freq: 2; Began: 1947; Cov: Scan; Lang: Eng; Subj: Related. ISSN: 0040-5817
▪University of Natal Press; Box 375; Pietermaritzburg; SOUTH AFRICA.

Thespis *Thespis.* Last Known Address; Lang: Gre; Subj: Theatre.
▪Greek Centre of the ITI; Anthinou Gazi 9; Athens; GREECE.

THeute *Theater Heute.* Freq: 12; Began: 1960; Cov: Full; Lang: Ger; Subj: Theatre. ISSN: 0040-5507
▪Friedrich Berlin Verlagsges; mbH, L*04utzowplatz 7; D-10785 Berlin; GERMANY.

ThIr *Theatre Ireland.* Freq: 3; Began: 1982; Ceased 1998; Cov: Full; Lang: Eng; Subj: Theatre. ISSN: 0263-6344
▪Theatre Ireland, Ltd; 29 Main St.; Castlerock Co. Derry BT51 4RA; NORTHERN IRELAND.

ThM *Theater Magazine.* Freq: 3; Began: 1968; Cov: Full; Lang: Eng; Subj: Theatre. ISSN: 0161-0775
▪Yale University, School of Theater; 222 York Street Yale Station; New Haven, CT 06520; USA.

ThNe ***Theatre News***. Freq: 6; Began: 1968; Ceased: 1985; Cov: Scan; Lang: Eng; Subj: Theatre. ISSN: 0563-4040
■American Theatre Association; 1010 Wisconsin Ave., NW, Suite 620; Washington, DC 20007; USA.

ThP ***Theater Phönix***:Zeitung für dramatische Kultur. Freq: 5; Lang: Ger; Subj: Theatre.
■Verein Theater Phönix; Wiener Str. 25; A-4020 Linz; AUSTRIA.

ThPa ***Theatre Papers***. Freq: IRR; Began: 1978; Ceased: 1985; Cov: Full; Lang: Eng; Subj: Theatre. ISSN: 0309-8036
■Documentation Unit, Dartington College of Arts; Totnes; Devon TQ9 6EJ; UK.

ThPh ***Theatrephile***. Freq: 4; Began: 1983; Ceased: 1985; Cov: Full; Lang: Eng; Subj: Theatre. ISSN: 0265-2609
■D. Cheshire & S. McCarthy Eds. & Publ.; 5 Dryden Street, Covent Garden; London WC2E 9NW; UK.

ThPu ***Théâtre Public***. Freq: 6; Began: 1974; Lang: Fre; Subj: Theatre. ISSN: 0335-2927
■Théâtre de Gennevilliers; 41, avenue des Gresillons; 92230 Gennevilliers; FRANCE.

Thpur ***Theater pur***. Freq: 10; Lang: Ger; Subj: Theatre. ISSN: 0949-1481
■Pocket Verlag; Alfredstr. 58; D-45130 Essen; GERMANY.

ThR ***Theatre Research International***. Freq: 3; Began: 1958; Cov: Full; Lang: Eng; Subj: Theatre. ISSN: 0307-8833
■Oxford University Press; Pinkhill House; Southfield Road, Eynsham, Oxford OX8 1JJ; UK.

ThS ***Theatre Survey: Journal of the American Society for Theatre Research***. Freq: 2; Began: 1960; Cov: Full; Lang: Eng; Subj: Theatre. ISSN: 0040-5574
■Gary Jay Williams, Dept Of Drama;; The Catholic University of America Washington,, DC 20064; USA.

Thsch ***Theaterschrift***. Began: 1992; Cov: Scan; Lang: Ger /Dut /Fre /Eng; Subj: Related.
■K*04unstlerhaus Bethanien; Marianneplatz 2; D-10997 Berlin; GERMANY.

ThScot ***Theatre Scotland***. Freq: 4; Cov: Scan; Lang: Eng; Subj: Theatre; ISSN: 0968-5499
■9a Annandale Street; Edinburgh EH7 4AW; UK.

THSt ***Theatre History Studies***. Freq: 1; Began: 1981; Cov: Full; Lang: Eng; Subj: Theatre. ISSN: 0733-2033
■Theatre Dept.; Central College; Pella, IA 50219; USA.

ThSw ***Theatre Southwest***. Freq: 3; Began: 1974; Cov: Full; Lang: Eng; Subj: Theatre.
■Oklahoma State University; 102 Seretean Center; Stillwater, OK 74078; USA.

ThToday ***Theatre Today***. Last Known Address; Lang: Eng; Subj: Theatre.
■Advanced Institute for Development, American Repertory Theatre; 245 West 52nd Street; New York, NY 10019; USA.

ThYear ***Theatre Year***. Freq: 1; Began: 1980; Ceased: 1983; Cov: Scan; Lang: Eng; Subj: Theatre. ISSN: 0261-2348
■In (Parenthesis) Ltd.; 21 Wellington Street; London WC2E 7DN; UK.

TI ***Théâtre International***. Freq: 4; Began: 1981; Ceased: 1984; Lang: Eng/Fre; Subj: Theatre.
■British Centre of the ITI; 31 Shelton Street; London WC2H 9HT; UK.

TID ***Themes in Drama***. Freq: 1; Began: 1979; Cov: Full; Lang: Eng; Subj: Theatre. ISSN: 0263-676X
■Cambridge Univ. Press; Edinburgh Bldg., Shaftesbury Road, Cambridge CB2 2RU; UK.

Tijatro ***Tijatro***. Freq: 12; Began: 1970; Lang: Tur; Subj: Theatre.
■PK 58; Besiktas-Istanbul; TURKEY.

TInsight ***Theatre Insight***: A Journal of Performance and Drama. Freq: 2; Began: 1988; Lang: Eng; Subj: Theatre.
■Department of Theatre and Dance, University of Texas at Austin; Austin, TX 78712-1168; USA.

TiO ***Theater in Österreich***. Freq: 1; Began: 1993; Cov: Scan; Lang: Ger; Subj: Theatre. ISBN: 3-901126-64-3
■Jahrbuch der Wiener Gesellschaft für Theaterforschung; Edition Praesens; Umlauftgasse 3 A-1170 Vienna; AUSTRIA.

Tisz ***Tiszatáj***. Freq: 12; Began: 1947; Cov: Scan; Lang: Hun; Subj: Related. ISSN: 0133-1167
■Tiszatáj Alapítvány Kuratóriuma; Rákóczi tér 1; 6741 Szeged; HUNGARY.

TJ ***Theatre Journal***. Formerly: *Educational Theatre Journal*. Freq: 4; Began: 1949; Cov: Full; Lang: Eng; Subj: Theatre. ISSN: 0192-2282
■Univ./College Theatre Assoc., The Johns Hopkins Univ. Press; 701 West 40th St. Suite 275; Baltimore, MD 21211; USA.

TJV ***Teater Jaarboek voor Vlaanderen***. Lang: Dut; Subj: Theatre.
■Antwerp; BELGIUM.

Tk ***Theaterwork***. Freq: 6; Began: 1980; Ceased: 1983; Cov: Full; Lang: Eng; Subj: Theatre. ISSN: 0735-1895
■Theaterwork; Box 8150; Sante Fe, NM 87504-8150; USA.

Tka ***Theatrika***. Freq: 52; Lang: Eng; Subj: Theatre.
■Athens; GREECE.

TkR ***TamKang Review***: Comparative Studies Between Chinese & Foreign Literature. Freq: 4; Began: 1970; Lang: Eng; Subj: Related. ISSN: 0049-2949
■Tamkang University, Grad. Inst. of West. Langs & Lit.; Tamsui; Taipei Hsien 251; TAIWAN.

Tmaker ***Theatermaker: Vakblad voor de Podiumkunst***. Freq: 10; Lang: Dut; Subj: Related. ISSN: 1385-7754;
■Stichting Vakblad voor de Podiumkunst; Herengracht 174; 1016 BR Amsterdam; NETHERLANDS.

TMJ ***Theatre Movement Journal***. Lang: Eng; Subj: Theatre.
■Ohio State University, Dept. of Theatre; 1849 Cannon Drive; Columbus, OH 43210; USA.

TMK ***Teater, Musika, Kyno***. Lang: Est; Subj: Theatre.
■Talin; ESTONIA.

TN ***Theatre Notebook***: Journal of the History and Technique of the British Theatre. Freq: 3; Began: 1946; Cov: Full; Lang: Eng; Subj: Theatre. ISSN: 0040-5523
■The Society for Theatre Research; c/o The Theatre Museum 1E Tavistock St.; London WC2E 7PA; UK.

Tningen ***Teatertidningen***. Formerly *Nya Teatertidningen*. Freq: 4; Began: 1990; Cov: Full; Lang: Swe; Subj: Theatre. ISSN: 0348-0119
■Box 20137; S10460; Stockholm; SWEDEN.

TNotes ***Theatre Notes***. SEE *Newsletter of the International Theatre Institute of The U.S., Inc.*. Freq: 10; Began: 1970; Ceased: 1984; Lang: Eng; Subj: Theatre.
■US Centre of the ITI; 1860 Broadway, Suite 1510; New York, NY 10023; USA.

TNS ***Théâtre National de Strasbourg***: Actualité. Lang: Fre; Subj: Theatre.
■Théâtre National de Strasbourg; 1, rue André Malraux-BP 184/R5 67005 Strasbourg; FRANCE.

TOE ***Théâtre Ouvert/Ecritures***. Freq: 4; Last Known Address; Began: 1978; Lang: Fre; Subj: Theatre. ISSN: 0181-5393
■21 rue Cassette; 75006 Paris; FRANCE.

Toneel ***Toneel Teatraal***. Formerly: *Mickery Mouth and Toneel Teatraal*. Freq: 10; Began: 1879; Cov: Full; Lang: Dut; Subj: Theatre. ISSN: 0040-9170
■Nederlands Theaterinstituut; Herengracht 166-168; 1016 BP Amsterdam; NETHERLANDS.

Tournees ***Tournées de Spectacles***. Freq: 12; Began: 1975; Ceased; Cov: Scan; Lang: Fre; Subj: Theatre. ISSN: 0317-5979
■Conseil des Arts du Canada; Office des Tournées; Ottawa, ON; CANADA.

TP ***Theatre in Poland/Théâtre en Pologne***. Freq: 6; Began: 1958; Cov: Full; Lang: Eng/Fre; Subj: Theatre. ISSN: 0040-5493
■ITI, Polish Center; pl. Piłsudskiego 9; 00-078 Warsaw; POLAND.

TpaedB ***Theaterpaedagogische Bibliothek***. Freq: IRR; Began: 1983; Lang: Ger; Subj: Theatre.
■Heinrichshofen Buecher; Valoisstrasse 11; 2940 Wilhelmshaven; GERMANY.

TProf ***Théâtre Professionnel***. Lang: Fre; Subj: Theatre.
■14 rue de la Promenade; Asnieres; FRANCE.

TQ ***Theatre Quarterly***: Since 1985 published as New Theatre Quarterly (NTQ). Freq: 4; Began: 1971; Ceased: 1981; Lang: Eng; Subj: Theatre. ISSN: 0049-3600
■TQ Publications, Ltd.; 44 Earlham Street; WC2 9LA London; UK.

TR ***Theater Rundschau***. Freq: 12; Began: 1955; Lang: Ger; Subj: Theatre. ISSN: 0040-5442
■Bonner Talweg 10; D-53113 Bonn; GERMANY.

Traces ***Traces***. Freq: 6; Lang: Fre; Subj: Theatre.
■Comédie de Rennes; Théâtre de la Parcheminerie; 35100 Rennes; FRANCE.

Tramoya *Tramoya*: Cuaderno de teatro. Freq: 4; Began: 1975; Lang: Spa; Subj: Theatre.
▪Universidad Veracruzana; Zona Universitaria; Lomas del Estadio Jalapa; MEXICO.

TransA *Transforming: Art: the arts and self-knowledge*. Freq: 2; Began: 1986; Cov: Scan; Lang; Eng; Subj; Related. ISSN: 0817-2080
▪Transforming Art; P.O. Box C168; Sydney, NSW 2000; AUSTRALIA.

TRC *Theatre Research in Canada/ Recherches Theatrales au Canada*. Formerly: *Theatre History in Canada*. Freq: 2; Began: 1991; Cov: FULL; Lang: Eng/Fre; Subj: Theatre.
▪Graduate Center for Study of Drama; University of Toronto; Toronto, ON M5T 2Z9; CANADA.

Treteaux *Tréteaux*. Freq: 2; Lang: Eng; Subj: Theatre. ISSN: 0161-4479
▪University of Maine at Orono Press; University of Maine; Farmington, ME 04938; USA.

Trujaman *Trujaman*. Last Known Address; Lang: Spa; Subj: Theatre.
▪Casilla de Correos 3234; Buenos Aires; ARGENTINA.

TSA *Theatre SA*: Quarterly for South African Theater. Freq: 4; Began: 1968; Lang: Eng; Subj: Theatre.
▪PO Box 2153; Cape Town; SOUTH AFRICA.

TSO *Teatro del Siglo de Oro: Ediciones Criticas*. Freq: 2; Began: 1982; Lang: Eng/ Spa/Fre; Subj: Theatre. ISSN: 7188-4400
▪Edition Reichenberger; Pfannkuchstr. 4; D 3500 Kassel; GERMANY.

TSOL *Teatro del Siglo de Oro: Estudios de Literatura*. Freq: IRR; Began: 1984; Lang: Spa/Eng; Subj: Theatre. ISSN: 7200-9300
▪Edition Reichenberger; Pfannkuchstr. 4; D 3500 Kassel; GERMANY.

TSt *Teatervidenskabelige Studier*. Freq: 1; Began: 1974; Lang: Dan; Subj: Theatre.
▪Akademisk Forlag; St. Kannikestraede 8; 1169 Copenhagen; DENMARK.

TT *Theatre Times*. Formerly: *OOBA Newsletter (OOBA Guidebook to Theatre)*. Freq: 6; Began: 1982; Cov: Scan; Lang: Eng; Subj: Theatre. ISSN: 0732-300X
▪Alliance of Resident Theatres; 131 Varick Street, Suite 904; New York, NY 10013-1410; USA.

TTh *Travail Théâtral*. Freq: 4; Began: 1970; Lang: Fre; Subj: Theatre. ISSN: 0049-4534
▪Editions l'Age d'Homme-la Cite; Case Postale 263; 1000 Lausanne 9; SWITZERLAND.

TTop *Theatre Topics*. Freq: 2; Began: 1991; Cov: Full; Lang: Eng; Subj: Theatre. ISSN: 1054-8378
▪Johns Hopkins University Press; 2715 North Charles Street; Baltimore, MD 21218-4319; USA.

TTT *Tenaz Talks Teatro*. Freq: 4; Began: 1977; Last Known Address; Lang: Eng/ Spa; Subj: Theatre.
▪University of California-La Jolla, Chicano Studies Program, D-009; La Jolla, CA 92093; USA.

TU *Théâtre et université*. Lang: Fre; Subj: Theatre.
▪Centre Universitaire International, Form. & Recherche Dramatique; Nancy; FRANCE.

Tv *Teatervetenskap*. Freq: 2; Began: 1968; Lang: Swe/Eng; Subj: Theatre.
▪Inst. för Teater & Filmvetenskap; Box 27026; S 102 Stockholm 27; SWEDEN.

TvL *Tydskri vi Letterkunde*. Freq: 4; Began: 1963; Cov: Scan; Lang: Eng & Afrikaans; Subj: Related. ISSN: 0041-476X
▪Elize Botha; Posbus 1758; Pretoria;; SOUTH AFRICA.

TVOR *Tvorchestvo*. Freq: 12; Began: 1957; Cov: Scan; Lang: Rus; Subj: Related. ISSN: 0131-6877
▪Izdatel'stvo Sovetskii Khudozhnik; Ul. Chernyakhovskogo; 4A; Moscow; RUSSIA.

TvT *Tijdschrift voor Theaterwetenschap*. Freq: 4; Lang: Dut; Subj: Theatre.
▪Instituut voor Wetenschap, Nw.; Doelenstraat 16; 1012 CP Amsterdam; NETHERLANDS.

TvVV *Tydskrif vir Volkskunde en Volkstaal*. Freq: 3; Began: 1944; Cov: Scan; Lang: Eng. & Afrikaans; Subj: Related. ISSN: 0049-4933
▪Genootskap vir Afrikaanse Volkskunde; Box 4585; Johannesburg 2000; SOUTH AFRICA.

TWI *Theaterwissenschaftlicher Informationsdienst*. Lang: Ger; Subj: Theatre.
▪Theaterhochschule Hans Otto'; Sec. für Theaterwissenschaftliche Dok.; Leipzig; GERMANY.

TWNew *Tennessee Williams Review*. Formerly: *Tennessee Williams Newsletter*. Freq: 2; Began: 1980; Ceased: 1983; Lang: Eng; Subj: Theatre. ISSN: 0276-993X
▪Northeastern University, Division of the Arts; 360 Huntington Ave. Boston, MA 02115; USA.

TwoT *Two Thousand (2000)*. Freq: 4; Began: 1969; Cov: Scan; Lang: Slo; Subj: Related. ISSN: 0350-8935
▪Journal for Thought, Art, Cultural and Religious Issues; Association 2000 Ljubljana; SLOVENIA.

TZ *Theater der Zeit*. Freq: 6; Began: 1946; Cov: Full; Lang: Ger; Subj: Theatre. ISSN: 0040-5418
▪Interessengemeinschaft Theater der Zeit e.V., Podewil; Klosterstr. 68/70; D-10179 Berlin; GERMANY.

Tzs *Theaterzeitschrift*: Beiträge zu Theater, Medien, Kulturpolitik. Lang: Ger; Subj: Theatre. ISSN: 0723-1172
▪Verein zur Erforschung theatraler Verkehrsformen; Tzs-Wochenschau Verlag; Adolf-Damaschke Str. 103-105 6231 Schawlbach; GERMANY.

UCrow *Upstart Crow, The*. Freq: 1; Began: 1978; Last Known Address; Lang: Eng; Subj: Theatre.
▪P.O. Box 740; Martin, TN 38237; USA.

UDSalaam *University of Dar es Salaam: Theatre Arts Department*: Annual Report. Freq: 1; Lang: Eng; Subj: Theatre.
▪University of Dar es Salaam, Theatre Arts Department; Box 35091; Dar es Salaam; TANZANIA.

UES *Unisa English Studies: Journal of the Department of English*. Freq: 2; Began: 1963; Cov: Scan; Lang: Eng & Afr; Subj: Related. ISSN: 0041-5359
▪S.G. Kossick, Ed.; Dept. of English; Univ. of South Africa; P.O. Box 392; 0001 Pretoria; SOUTH AFRICA.

Ufa *Ufahamu*: Journal of the African Activist Association. Freq: 3; Began: 1970; Cov: Scan; Lang: Eng; Subj: Related. ISSN: 0041-5715
▪James S. Coleman African Studies Center; University of California; Los Angeles, CA 90024-1130; USA.

UjA *Új Auróra*. Freq: 3; Began: 1972; Ceased: 1989; Cov: Scan; Lang: Hun; Subj: Related. ISSN: 0133-2295
▪Békéscsabai Városi Tanács; István király tér 9; 5600 Békéscsaba; HUNGARY.

UjF *Új Forrás*. Freq: 10; Began: 1968; Cov: Scan; Lang: Hun; Subj: Related. ISSN: 0133-5332
▪Komárom-Esztergom Megye Önkormányzata; Március 15. út 2 2800 Tatabánya; HUNGARY.

UjIras *Új Irás*. Freq: 12; Began: 1961; Ceased; Cov: Scan; Lang: Hun; Subj: Related. ISSN: 0041-5952
▪Lapkiadó Vállalat; Erzsébet körut 9-11; 1073 Budapest; HUNGARY.

UMurcia *Universidad de Murcia Catedra de Teatro Cuadernos*. Freq: IRR; Began: 1978; Lang: Spa; Subj: Theatre.
▪Universidad de Murcia, Secretariado de Publicaciones y Intercambio Cientifico; Santo Cristo 1; 30001 Murcia; SPAIN.

UNIMA *UNIMA France*. Freq: 4; Began: 1962; Lang: Fre; Subj: Theatre.
▪Union Internationale de la Marionette, Section Française; 7 Rue du Helder; 75009 Paris; FRANCE.

Ural *Ural*. Cov: Scan; Lang: Rus; Subj: Related. ISSN: 130-5409
▪RUSSIA.

Usbu *Usbu Al-Masrah*. Lang: Ara; Subj: Theatre.
▪Ministère des Affaires Culturelles; La Kasbah; Tunis; TUNISIA.

USITT *USITT Newsletter*. Freq: 4; Began: 1965; Cov: Scan; Lang: Eng; Subj: Theatre. ISSN: 0565-6311
▪US Inst. for Theatre Technology; 10 West 19th Street; Ste. 5A New York, NY 10011; USA.

UTarra *Universitas Tarraconensis*. Freq: 1; Cov: Scan; Lang: Spa; Subj: Related.
▪División de Filologia; Placa Imperial Tarraco, 1; 43005 Tarragona; SPAIN.

UTeatr *Ukrainskij Teat'r*. Lang: Ukr; Subj: Related.
▪Kiev; UKRAINE.

UTQ *University of Toronto Quarterly*. Freq: 4; Cov: Scan; Lang: Eng; Subj: Related. ISSN: 0042-0247
▪University of Toronto Press; 10 St. Mary Street; Toronto, ON M4Y 2W8; CANADA.

Uusi *Uusi-Laulu*. Lang: Fin; Subj: Theatre.
▪Uusi-Laulu-yhdistys; Eerikinkatu 14 A 9; 00100 Helsinki 10; FINLAND.

UZ *Unterhaltungskunst*: Zeitschrift für Bühne, Podium und Manege. Freq: 12; Began: 1969; Lang: Ger; Subj: Related. ISSN: 0042-0565

▪Henschelverlag Kunst und, Gesellschaft; Oranienburger Strasse 67/68; 104 Berlin; GERMANY.

Valivero ***Valiverho***. Freq: 3; Lang: Fin; Subj: Theatre.
▪Helsinki; FINLAND.

Valo ***Valóság***. Freq: 12; Began: 1964; Ceased; Cov: Scan; Lang: Hun; Subj: Related.
▪Kirlapkiado; Lenin krt. 5; 1073 Budapest VII; HUNGARY.

VantageP ***Vantage Point***: Issues in American Arts. Formerly: *American Arts*. Freq: 6; Began: 1984; Lang: Eng; Subj: Related. ISSN: 0194-1305
▪American Council for the Arts; 1285 Ave. of the Americas, 3rd Floor; New York, NY 10019; USA.

VCA ***Voice***: Newsletter for Chorus America. Freq: 4; Cov: Scan; Lang: Eng; Subj: Related.
▪Association of Professional Vocal Ensembles; 2111 Sansom Street Philadelphia, PA 19103; USA.

VFil ***Voprosy filosofii***. Freq: 12; Began: 1947; Lang: Eng/Rus;; Subj: Related. ISSN: 0042-8744
▪Akademiya Nauk S.S.S.R., Institut Filosofii; Izdatel'stvo Pravda, Ul. Pravdy, 24; Moscow 125047; RUSSIA.

VHJ ***Victorian Historical Journal***. Formerly: *Journal of the Royal Historical Society*. Freq: 4; Began: 1987; Lang: Eng; Subj: Related. ISSN: 1030-7710
▪Royal Historical Society of Victoria; Royal Mint; 280 William Street Melbourne Victoria 3000; AUSTRALIA.

Vig ***Vigilia***. Freq: 12; Began: 1935; Cov: Scan; Lang: Hun; Subj: Related. ISSN: 0042-6024
▪Vigilia Kiadóhivatala; Kossuth Lajos u. 1 1053 Budapest; HUNGARY.

Vilag ***Világszinház***. Formerly: *Dramaturgical News 1965-1982*. Freq: 4; Began: 1982; Cov: Scan; Lang: Hun; Subj: Theatre. ISSN: 0231-4541
▪Országos Színháztörténeti Múzeum és Intézet; Krisztina körút 57; 1016 Budapest I; HUNGARY.

VLit ***Voprosy literatury***. Freq: 6; Began: 1957; Cov: Scan; Lang: Rus; Subj: Related. ISSN: 0042-8705
▪Sojuz Pisatelej SSSR, Inst. Mirovoj Literatury; Bolšoj Gnezdnikovskij per 10; 103009 Moscow; RUSSIA.

VMGUf ***Vestnik Moskovskogo universiteta***. Freq: 6; Began: 1946; Cov: Scan; Lang: Rus; Subj: Related. ISSN: 0201-7385
▪Moscow State University; Ul. Gercena 5/7; 103009 Moscow; RUSSIA.

Volga ***Volga***. Began: 1966; Cov: Scan; Lang: Rus; Subj: Related. ISSN: 0321-0677
▪Naberežnaja Kosmonautov Street, 3; 410002 Saratov City; RUSSIA.

Voprosy ***Voprosy teatra***. Freq: 1; Began: 1965; Lang: Rus; Subj: Theatre. ISSN: 0201-7482
▪Teatral'noe Obshchestvo, Theatre Workers Union; Kiselni Typik doml 103031; Moscow; RUSSIA.

VoprosyK ***Voprosy istorii KPSS***: SEE Kentavr. Freq: 12; Ceased: 1991; Lang: Rus; Subj: Related. ISSN: 0320-8907
▪Vil'gel'ma Pika Street; 129256 Moscow; RUSSIA.

Vos ***Vosroždenije***. Began: 1994; Cov: Scan; Lang: Rus; Subj: Related. ISSN: 0869-7930
▪Oleg Koševoj Street, 34 a; 367025 Makhačkala City; RUSSIA.

VS ***Victorian Studies***:An Interdisciplinary Journal of Social, Political and Cultural Studies. Freq: 4; Began: 1957; Cov: Scan; Lang: Eng; Subj: Related. ISSN: 0042-5222
▪Program for Victorian Studies, Indiana University; Ballantine Hall; Bloomington, IN 47405; USA.

VSov ***V sovèckom teatrè***. SEE *Sovetskij Teatr*. Freq: 3; Began: 1978; Ceased: 1982; Cov: Scan; Lang: Rus; Subj: Theatre.
▪Moscow; RUSSIA.

Vstreča ***Vstreča***. Freq: 12; Began: 1940; Lang: Rus; Subj: Related.
▪Sovèckaja Rossija; 3 Krapirenskij per. #2; Moscow 103051; RUSSIA.

Vyakat ***Vyakat***. Freq: 4; Lang: Eng; Subj: Theatre.
▪A-28 Nizamuddin West; New Delhi; INDIA.

Waiguo ***Waiguo Xiju***. Freq: 4; Began: 1962; Lang: Chi; Subj: Theatre.
▪52 Dongai Ba tiao; Beijing; CHINA.

WB ***Weimarer Beiträge***: Zeitschrift für Literaturwissenschaft, Aesthetik und Kultur Wisssenschafn. Freq: 4; Began: 1955; Lang: Ger; Subj: Related. ISSN: 0043-2199
▪Passagen Verlag, Walfischgasse 15/14; A-1010 Wien; AUSTRIA.

WCP ***West Coast Plays***. Freq: 2; Began: 1977; Ceased: 1988; Lang: Eng; Subj: Theatre. ISSN: 0147-4502
▪California Theatre Council; 135 N. Grand Ave.; Los Angeles, CA 90014; USA.

WES ***Western European Stages***. Freq: 2; Began: 1989; Cov: Full; Lang: Eng; Subj: Theatre.
▪Center for Advanced Study in Theatre Arts; CUNY Graduate School; 33 West 42nd Street New York, NY 10036; USA.

WEST ***Westerly***. Freq: 4; Began: 1956; Cov: Scan;; Subj: Related. ISSN: 0043-342x
▪University of Western Australia; Nedlands, WA 6009; AUSTRALIA.

WFTM ***Wiener Forschungen zur Theater und Medienwissenschaft***. Freq: IRR; Began: 1972; Lang: Ger; Subj: Theatre.
▪Universitäts-Verlagsbuchhandlung Gmb; Servitengasse 5; A1092 Vienna; AUSTRIA.

WGTJ ***Wiener Gesellschaft für Theaterforschung Jahrbuch***. Freq: IRR; Began: 1944; Ceased: 1986; Lang: Ger; Subj: Theatre.
▪Verband der Wissenshaftlichen, Gesellschaften Oesterreichs; Lindengasse 37; A1070 Vienna; AUSTRIA.

WIAL ***Washington International Arts Letter***. Freq: 10; Began: 1962; Last Known Address; Lang: Eng; Subj: Related. ISSN: 0043-0609
▪Box 9005; Washington, DC 20003; USA.

WijP ***WIJ Poppenspelers***. Began: 1955; Lang: Dut; Subj: Theatre.
▪Wij Poppenspelers; Warmoesstraat 11 NL 2011 HN Haarlem; NETHERLANDS.

WJBS ***Western Journal of Black Studies***. Freq: 4; Began: 1977; Cov: Scan; Lang: Eng; Subj: Related. ISSN: 0197-4327
▪Washington State Univ. Press; Pullman, WA 99164 5910; USA.

WLT ***World Literature Today***: a literary quarterly of the University of Oklahoma. Formerly: *Books Abroad*. Freq: 4; Began: 1927; Lang: Eng; Subj: Related. ISSN: 0196-3570
▪University of Oklahoma; 110 Monnet Hall; Norman, OK 73019; USA.

WomenR ***Women's Review***. Freq: 12; Began: 1985; Ceased: 1986; Cov: Scan; Lang: Eng; Subj: Related. ISSN: 0267-5080
▪1-4 Christina St.; London EC2A 4PA; UK.

WonD ***Writings on Dance***. Began: 1987; Cov: Scan; Lang: Eng; Subj: Related. ISSN: 0817-3710
▪Elizabeth Dempster and Sally Gardner; P.O. Box 1172; Collingwood Victoria 3066; AUSTRALIA;.

WOpera ***World of Opera***. Freq: 6; Lang: Eng; Subj: Theatre. ISSN: 0160-8673
▪Marcel Dekker Inc.; 270 Madison Avenue; New York, NY 10016; USA.

WPerf ***Women & Performance***: A Journal of Feminist Theory. Freq: 2; Began: 1983; Cov: Full; Lang: Eng; Subj: Theatre. ISSN: 0740-770X
▪NYU Tisch School of the Arts, Women and Performance Project; 721 Broadway, 6th Floor; New York, NY 10003; USA.

WPIS ***Working Papers in Irish Studies***. Lang: Eng; Subj: Related.
▪Northeastern University; 236 Huntington Avenue; Boston, MA 02115; USA.

WPList ***World Premieres Listing***. Began: 1981; Lang: Eng; Subj: Theatre.
▪Hungarian Centre of the ITI; Hevesi Sandor Ter. 2; 1077 Budapest VII; HUNGARY.

WS ***Women's Studies***. Freq: 4; Lang: Eng; Subj: Theatre.
▪Department of English; McManus Hall; The Claremont Graduate School Claremont, CA 91711; USA.

Wsw ***Wer spielte was? Werkstatistik Deutschland Österreich Schweiz***. Freq: 1; Lang: Ger; Subj: Related. ISSN: 0941-5823
▪Mykenae Verlag Rossberg KG; Ahastr. 9; D-64285 Darmstadt; GERMANY.

WTops ***White Tops***. Freq: 6; Began: 1927; Lang: Eng; Subj: Theatre. ISSN: 0043-499X
▪Circus Fans Assoc. of America; Rt. 1, Box 6735; White Stone, VA 22578; USA.

XLunc ***Xiju Luncong***: Selected Essays of Theatre. Freq: 4; Began: 1957; Lang: Chi; Subj: Theatre.
▪52 Dongai Ba tiao; Beijing; CHINA.

XXuexi ***Xiju Xuexi***: Theatre. Freq: 4; Began: 1957; Lang: Chi; Subj: Theatre.
▪Central Institute for Modern Theatre; Jiaonan Qitiao; Beijing; CHINA.

XYanj ***Xiqu Yanjiu***. Freq: 4; Began: 1980; Cov: Full; Lang: Chi; Subj: Theatre.

▪Cultural and Artistic Publishing; 17 Qianhai Xijie; Beijing; CHINA.

XYishu ***Xiju Yishu***: Theatre Arts. Freq: 4; Began: 1978; Cov: Full; Lang: Chi; Subj: Theatre. ISSN: 0257-943X
▪Shanghai Theatre Academy; 630 Huashan Lu Road; 200040 Shanghai; CHINA.

YA ***Yeats Annual;***. Freq: 14; Cov: Scan; Lang: Eng; Subj: Related.
▪MacMillan Press Ltd.; Houndmills, Basingstoke; Hampshire RG21 6XS; ENGLAND.

YCT ***Young Cinema & Theatre/Jeune Cinéma et Théâtre***: Cultural Magazine of the IUS. Freq: 4; Began: 1964; Lang: Eng/Fre/Spa; Subj: Theatre.
▪International Union of Students; 17th November Street; 110 01 Prague 1; CZECH REPUBLIC.

Yorick ***Yorick***: Revista de Teatro. Lang: Spa; Subj: Theatre.
▪Via Layetana 30; 3 Barcelona; SPAIN.

YTJ ***Youth Theatre Journal***. Freq: 4; Began: 1986; Cov: Full; Lang: Eng; Formerly: *Children's Theatre Review;* Subj: Theatre. ISSN: 0892-9092
▪American Alliance for Theatre and Education;, Theatre Department; Arizona State University; Tempe, AZ 85287-3411; USA.

ZAA ***Zeitschrift für Anglistik und Amerikanistik***. Freq: 4; Began: 1953; Lang: Ger/Eng; Subj: Related. ISSN: 0044-2305
▪Verlag Enzyklopädie; Gerichtsweg 26; 7010 Leipzig; GERMANY.

ZDi ***Zahranicni Divadlo***: (Theatre Abroad). Lang: Cze; Subj: Theatre.
▪Prague; CZECH REPUBLIC.

ZfK ***Zeitschrift für Kulturaustausch***. Freq: 4; Lang: Ger; Subj: Theatre. ISSN: 0044-2976
▪Horst Erdmann Verlag für, Internationalen-Kulturaustausch; Hartmeyerstrasse 117; 7400 Tübingen 1; GERMANY.

ZG ***Zeitschrift für Germanistik***. Freq: 6; Began: 1980; Last Known Address; Lang: Ger; Subj: Related. ISSN: 0323-7982
▪Verlag Enzyklopädie; Gerichtsweg 26; 7010 Leipzig; GERMANY.

Znamia ***Znamja***. Freq: 12; Began: 1931; Lang: Rus; Subj: Related. ISSN: 0130-1616
▪Soyuz Pisatelei; Moscow; RUSSIA.

Zpravy ***Zprávy DILIA***. Freq: 3; Lang: Cze/Eng; Subj: Theatre.
▪Dilia; Polská 1; Prague 2 Vinohrady; CZECH REPUBLIC.

ZR ***Zapad Rossii***. Cov: Scan; Lang: Rus; Subj: Related. ISSN: 0132-8166
▪Soviet Prospect Street, 21; 236000 Kalingrad City; RUSSIA.

ZreIssk ***Zreliščnye iskusstva*** (Performing Arts). Freq: 12; Began: 1983; Cov: Full; Lang: Rus; Subj: Theatre. ISSN: 0207-9739
▪Gos. Biblioteka SSSR im. Lenina, NIO Informkul'tura; Prospekt Kalinina 3; 101000 Moscow; RUSSIA.

ZS ***Zeitschrift für Slawistik***. Freq: 4; Began: 1956; Lang: Ger/Eng; Subj: Related. ISSN: 0044-3506
▪Akademie Verlag; Mühlenstr. 33-34; D-13187 Berlin; GERMANY.

Zvezda ***Zvezda***. Freq: 12; Began: 1924; Cov: Scan; Lang: Rus; Subj: Related. ISSN: 0321-1878
▪Iztadel. Chudožestvennaja Literatura; Mochovaja 20; 192028 St. Petersburg; RUSSIA.

ZZT ***Zene-Zene Tánc***. Freq: 2; Began: 1994; Cov: Scan; Lang: Hun; Subj: Related. ISSN: 1218-6678
▪Zene-Zene Tánc Alapítvány; Vőrősmarty téri; 1051 Budapest; HUNGARY.

Photocomposition and printing services for this volume
of the *International Bibliography of Theatre* were
provided by Volt Information Sciences Inc.,

Cover Design by Irving M. Brown